THE

Norton Anthology

OF

Short Fiction

FOURTH EDITION

THE Norton Anthology OF Short Fiction

FOURTH EDITION

R. V. Cassill
Brown University

W · W · NORTON & COMPANY
New York · London

Printed in the United States of America.

ISBN 0-393-95933-3

W. W. Norton & Company, Inc., 500 Fifth Avenue, New York, N.Y. 10110
W. W. Norton & Company Ltd., 10 Coptic Street, London WC1A 1PU

6 7 8 9 0

Contents

Chronological Table of Contents

The date given for each story is that of first book publication; if, however, the story was published significantly earlier in a journal or magazine, the date of first periodical publication is given instead. (In the anthology itself, when an author is represented by more than one story, his or her stories are ordered chronologically, unless the author's own preferred order is well established—as in the case of Katherine Anne Porter.)

Preface

The first principle for composing the ideal fiction anthology is self-evident: Fill it with stories that discriminating readers have liked most. "Nothing, of course, will ever take the place of the good old fashion of 'liking' a work of art or not liking it," said Henry James. He called this the "primitive" and the "ultimate" test—stressing at the same time the necessity of other critical tactics and measures to be employed along the way. As usual, James was right.

It can be taken for granted that the anthologist likes the stories he has included, but that is not quite enough. Teaching is a collective enterprise. So, in assembling the contents of this book I leaned very heavily on the advice, opinion, and preferences that my publishers had assembled from correspondence with teachers of fiction at colleges and universities across the country. In a real sense, then, the table of contents represents a collaborative effort. This is a collection that has met James's fundamental test of being liked by many experienced and devoted readers.

An anthology designed as a teaching instrument must also, however, entice and guide those who are just learning to like what has long been delighting others. It must provide the calculated variety which permits the teacher to lead the way with the least encumbrance and the largest resources to draw on. While this text makes no pretense of displaying "the history of the short story" in a systematic way, the selections were made with a view to supporting those historical interpretations which classroom teachers might elect to develop from it. The chronological table of contents provides the groundwork for such an approach.

Discreet footnoting was designed to make each piece accessible to the contemporary student reader. Questions appended to the stories will help students reflect on stylistic and topical features and may also outline the shape of class discussions or themes. Many questions are phrased to increase students' awareness of the technical options available to the storyteller, since in assembling the collection I chose works that will demonstrate the spectrum of contemporary techniques and show, in the work of earlier times, that technical variations are in themselves part of the meaning of fiction.

The amplitude of the text has permitted the inclusion of more than one story by several important writers. Where this is the case, care was taken to suggest the range as well as the particular voice and manner of the author. Partial lists of each author's books point the way to wider reading.

The Glossary is a handy compilation of those critical terms most useful in a disciplined classroom discussion of fiction. And, since talking constructively about stories is so crucial a part of the experience that begins with reading them, I have shaped an introductory part of the book as an initiation to that rewarding practice. The short selections in "Talking about Fiction" are the gleanings of a lifetime in which I sought—and tested in the classroom—examples that would show with maximum brevity, clarity, and force the truly fundamental characteristics of the storyteller's art.

A glance at the table of contents will show you that many things in this book have been frequently anthologized. Some have never appeared before in anthologies. In the old as in the new, the freshness and vitality of the collection as a whole was the governing consideration. The goal was to put together a very large group of stories that would, in detail and overall design, express both the living tradition of short fiction and the culture of which it is a part.

For their generous and invaluable help in the movement toward that goal I want to thank M. H. Abrams, Cornell University; Donald K. Adams, Occidental College; Martha Y. Battle, University of Tennessee at Martin; Steven D. Blume, Marietta College; E. C. Bufkin, University of Georgia; Pat M. Carr, University of Texas at El Paso; Thomas Cooley, Ohio State University; Richard C. Day, Humboldt State University; James E. Evans, University of North Carolina at Greensboro; Suzanne Ferguson, Ohio State University; H. Ramsey Fowler, Memphis State University; John R. Griffin, Southern Colorado State College; Cyril Gulassa, De Anza College; Carolyn Heilbrun, Columbia University; Mary Hesky, Goucher College; Michael Hoffman, University of California at Davis; Irene Honeycutt, Central Piedmont Community College; William L. Howarth, Princeton University; Michael Joyce, Jackson (Michigan) Community College; Sylvan M. Karchmer, University of Houston; Anne Thompson Lee, Bates College; Frank Lentricchia, University of California at Irvine; Michael McKeon, Boston University; Rose Moss, Wellesley College; Raymond M. Olderman, University of Wisconsin; Guy Owen, North Carolina State University at Raleigh; James K. Robinson, University of Cincinnati; Robert Storey, University of Pennsylvania; Walter Waring, Kalamazoo College; Shirley Yarnall, The American University; James L. Yoch, University of Oklahoma. My assistant Wayne Eason deserves special thanks for his help in preparing the manuscript.

R. V. CASSILL

Preface to the Fourth Edition

In a wisely witty poem Marianne Moore says that the truly vital elements of poetry are important because they are "useful." That adjective may startle us, because we are not perhaps accustomed to thinking of poetry as utilitarian. Is it useful for planting and harvesting, for opening cans, for nailing up a wall? Of course it is not. Its powers are disposed elsewhere. Its use is in nourishing spirit and mind, in fretting and soothing the yearnings of our deepest nature.

And the same must be said of short fiction. It is not merely useful as an introduction to literary studies, though, to be sure, it has proved an excellent resource for the development of capacities for critical reading in a host of curricula. It is comfortable and manageable for classroom use as the other forms may not be. Some elements of literary structure can best be perceived and compared where the bulk is slight and the language apt to be familiar to the great majority of students. But beyond such conveniences, short fiction is useful in the large, high sense that Moore summons us to recognize. It is as limitless as any other mode of literary expression. The insights are as keen, the play of invention as nimble, and the revelations as profound as the imagination can compass. It abides on the same plateau as poetry, drama, or the novel.

These comments could as well have prefaced any of the three editions of the anthology that preceded this one. The importance of short fiction has long been admitted, as its popularity inside and outside the academic fold has steadily expanded. There are major constancies spanning the decades, though the short forms have been diversified and enriched by ever more numerous talents as the generations have succeeded one another.

It is not within the scope (or intent) of this anthology to keep abreast of all the experimental movements and extraordinary individual accomplishments that have quietly or noisily laid their claims on the reading public, but I have sedulously tried to make some room for what is very new, as I have (sometimes regretfully) dropped stories that seem no longer to strike the response that they did once. As best I could I have kept track of what has bloomed and what has faded, with the help of numerous associates actively engaged in classroom use of this book, and with writers and editors who have been busy on this fertile ground. If I cannot by name single out all who have helped with my choices in these most recent years, I wish at least to express my gratitude to one and all of them.

Talking about Fiction

Discussion and analysis follow naturally from the imaginative responses we make while we are reading. There need be no deliberate decision to "take the story apart." The illusionistic aspect of fiction begins to come apart almost at the instant it is experienced, fading passage by passage behind us as our reading moves from the beginning toward the end. When the spell cast by the whole is dissolving in our memory into its component parts, we are in a favorable position to sort them out and ask what each part did to direct our imagination along lines imagined by the person who wrote the story for us.

Readers with some degree of critical experience have the habit of noting aspects of plot, character, tone, theme, imagery, point of view, and numerous other variations of literary form as they sum up and discuss their reading experience. But before we begin to examine any of these aspects in isolation, we can here consider some truly basic features characteristic of fiction in general. We can do that conveniently with the pieces in this section because they are all brief enough to permit an easy reference from text to commentary. They include a poem, three excerpts from stories printed in full farther along in the book, and four selections that are essentially complete short stories. For all their brevity these four display the unity and completeness you will find in the rest of the stories included in this anthology.

Character and Setting

Nothing is more fundamental to creating a story than establishing a spatial, temporal environment and peopling it with actors. Here is an example by a modern master.

Ernest Hemingway

story from **In Our Time**[1]

Nick sat against the wall of the church where they had dragged him to be clear of machine-gun fire in the street. Both legs stuck out awkwardly. He had been hit in the spine. His face was sweaty and dirty. The sun shone on his face. The day was very hot. Rinaldi, big backed, his equipment sprawling, lay face downward against the wall. Nick looked straight ahead brilliantly. The pink wall of the house opposite had fallen out from the roof, and an iron bedstead hung twisted toward the street. Two Austrian dead lay in the rubble in the shade of the house. Up the street were other dead. Things were getting forward in the town. It was going well. Stretcher bearers would be along any time now. Nick turned his head carefully and looked at Rinaldi. "Senta Rinaldi. Senta.[2] You and me we've made a separate peace." Rinaldi lay still in the sun breathing with difficulty. "Not patriots." Nick turned his head carefully away smiling sweatily. Rinaldi was a disappointing audience.

The first sentence specifies a battle setting (by mention of the machine-gun fire in the street) and the particular spot, the foot of a church wall, where Nick is seated. His name, the bare beginning of characterization, is given, and we quickly learn that he has been wounded.

The ruined house across the street is a consistent and specially meaningful part of the setting. Nick is looking at it "brilliantly"—seeing it, that is, with the sharpened, almost desperate awareness that accompanies his injury. The dead bodies of Austrian soldiers mean (to Nick, who is obliged by his role to see them as enemies) that the battle is "going well." The split between his personal concern and his merely military recognition of things is signaled by his next thought: Since the battle is going well for his side, stretcher bearers will soon come to pick him up. This consoling thought leads directly to one more consoling yet: For him the war is over. With an effort at cheerfulness, Nick puts his realization into words, saying, ". . . we've made a separate peace."

His wounded comrade Rinaldi does not answer. Perhaps he can't. His silence suggests that Nick's joy at the prospect of getting

1. Chapter VI of the pamphlet *in our time*, published in a limited edition in January, 1924; each of its chapters was virtually a miniature short story in the mode Hemingway was then perfecting. In the following year these nonconsecutive chapters were printed in alternation with longer stories in an expanded volume called *In Our Time*. 2. "Listen."

out of the war is a limited and probably temporary response to the bad thing that has happened to him. Such a suggestion gives a bleak coloration to the inferences we can make about Nick's future, though the story stops short of any explicit prediction.

Action, Plot, and Complication

Much of what we understand and feel about people comes from watching them act in relation to others and to the entanglements they create as the action proceeds. The following story by a medieval writer depends almost exclusively on elements of action in developing the complications which give meaning to its plot.

Giraldis Cambrensis

Revenge

. . . The lord of Chateau-roux in France maintained in the castle a man whose eyes he had formerly put out, but who, by long habit, recollected the ways of the castle, and the steps leading to the towers. Seizing an opportunity of revenge, and meditating the destruction of the youth, he fastened the inward doors of the castle, and took the only son and heir of the governor of the castle to the summit of a high tower, from whence he was seen with the utmost concern by the people beneath. The father of the boy hastened thither, and, struck with terror, attempted by every possible means to procure the ransom of his son, but received for answer, that this could not be effected, but by the same mutilation of those lower parts, which he had likewise inflicted on him. The father, having in vain entreated mercy, at length assented, and caused a violent blow to be struck on his body; and the people around him cried out lamentably, as if he had suffered mutilation. The blind man asked him where he felt the greatest pain? When he replied in his reins,[3] he declared it was false and prepared to precipitate the boy. A second blow was given, and the lord of the castle asserting that the greatest pain was at his heart, the blind man expressing his disbelief, again carried the boy to the summit of the tower. The third time, however, the father, to save his son, really mutilated himself; and when he exclaimed that the greatest pain was in his teeth; "It is true," said he, "as a man who has had experience should be believed, and thou

3. Kidneys.

hast in part revenged my injuries. I shall meet death with more satisfaction, and thou shalt neither beget any other son, nor receive comfort from this." Then, precipitating himself and the boy from the summit of the tower, their limbs were broken, and both instantly expired. The knight ordered a monastery built on the spot for the soul of the boy, which is still extant, and called De Doloribus. . . .[4]

The revenger's wish to pay back the man who has blinded and castrated him provides the initial motivation from which the fictional plot spins forward. The sequence of following events, complicating the plot, represents an accelerating contest of will and cunning between the chief antagonists. The three blows to which the father submits are graduated tests of his affection for his son and of his confidence in his ability to outwit his opponent. Since affection, confidence, and cleverness are attributes of character, we see thus how progress in the action reveals character.

The blind man's response to the blows is motivated by his interpretation (correct in each case) of what has really happened. Note that in the case of the first two blows a part of what has happened is a further attempt to victimize him, by deceit. At each test the father's confidence diminishes, and he is motivated by this progressive diminishing of confidence, as well as by growing anxiety for his son, to submit to castration. Probably it is his mushrooming panic that prevents his considering what may happen after he has yielded to the demand.

The straightforward movement of the plot toward the anticipated end shifts when the revenger declares himself only partially satisfied by the father's castration. The suicide and murder of the boy held hostage carry the action to the point of fully measuring the degree of fury that began it.

We should note that in this story the characterization—aside from that accomplished by the action itself—is kept to a stark minimum. Nevertheless it may stimulate our imagination to speculate on the variables of sensation and emotion that are usually included in fictional characterization. The momentum of excitement generated by the force of the action carries us into wondering what the boy may have seen as he looked down from the tower where he was held captive. What did he remember as he heard his father bargain for his life? What did he want his father to do? Perhaps we are even impelled to imagine answers for such questions; a good story incites

4. Place of Sorrow.

the reader's imagination to go a bit beyond what is actually and literally told.

Point of View

We are moved to make judgments about characters by their actions in a story, by what they choose to do and what is done to them. Our response is enhanced and given particular coloration by the attitude, personal vision, and interpretations with which the characters respond as the events of the story unfold. This individualized response is called point of view. *It is an element in stories told in the third person as well as in the first, though the degree to which an author exploits it may vary over wide ranges.*

Alice Walker

from **Everyday Use**

Sometimes I dream a dream in which Dee and I are suddenly brought together on a TV program. . . . Out of a dark and soft-seated limousine I am ushered into a bright room filled with many people. There I meet a smiling, gray, sporty man like Johnny Carson who shakes my hand and tells me what a fine girl I have. Then we are on the stage and Dee is embracing me with tears in her eyes. She pins on my dress a large orchid, even though she has told me once she thinks orchids are tacky flowers.

In real life I am a large, big-boned woman with rough, man-working hands. . . . I can kill and clean a hog as mercilessly as a man. My fat keeps me hot in zero weather. I can work outside all day, breaking ice to get water for washing. I can eat pork liver cooked over an open fire minutes after it comes steaming from the hog. . . .

This woman is intentionally portraying herself without any attempt to falsify the harsh demands of her life, her daydreams, or her appearance. But her candor and the touch of self-mockery in her dream of appearing on TV are testimony to a certain kind of self-confident pride. She knows who she is, after all, and speaks as someone who knows how to make the best of her strength and her shortcomings.

Her narrative voice will remain a stabilizing force throughout the story, guiding the reader's discriminations between the claims made by different life-styles as they conflict and compete. Thus the point of view contributes a necessary trust to the outcome, in which certain strident claims are vanquished.

But it is not only in stories told in the first person that we look at the objective world through the eyes of a character.

Flannery O'Connor

from Everything That Rises Must Converge

His mother continued to gaze at him but she did not take advantage of his momentary discomfort. Her eyes retained their battered look. Her face seemed to be unnaturally red, as if her blood pressure had risen. Julian allowed no glimmer of sympathy to show on his face. Having got the advantage he wanted desperately to keep it and carry it through. He would have liked to teach her a lesson that would last a while, but there seemed no way to continue the point. The Negro refused to come out from behind his paper.

This passage begins with a statement that is essentially objective. It could have been made by a neutral reporter without any special insight or interest in Julian. But then we are moved briskly to where Julian's special and prejudiced point of view prevails. When we come to the word seemed *in the third sentence, we know that his mother's face seems particularly red because of his intimacy with her and his inverted concern with her blood pressure. We move then beyond his notation of her symptoms into the hostile wish that is motivating his behavior in the bus. Now we are fully in his point of view, seeing things as he does and beholding the malevolence that shapes his vision. "He would have liked to teach her a lesson that would last a while. . . ." This glimpse into his mind underlines his complicity with the deadly forces gathering to finish the woman off.*

Some stories told in the third person may shift the point of view from that of one character to another's, and in some it is hard to say with certainty that the author has adopted the point of view of any of *the characters, for some styles and types of diction will indicate that we are reading of matters that could only be known by the writer. There is a great range of possibilities in the distance that can be set between the creator and the imagined creatures populating the printed page. For the reader it is always well to assume that something in the nature of the material has influenced the writer's choice to move in close or keep an Olympian distance. The closer he or she wants to be to the characters in their travails, the more the writer will immerse himself or herself in the point of view of this person or that in the story.*

In the story from which the following excerpt is taken, Freeman mostly chooses to show what is happening from the point of view of her main female character. But just for a little she lapses, intruding with summary and evaluative comment on certain developments. This "author intrusion" (see Glossary) is generally shunned because it dilutes the concreteness and sensuousness of the action being rendered.

Mary E. Wilkins Freeman

from **A New England Nun**

. . . Louisa's father and brother had died, and she was all alone in the world. But greatest happening of all—a subtle happening which both were too simple to understand—Louisa's feet had turned into a path, smooth maybe under a calm, serene sky, but so straight and unswerving that it could only meet a check at her grave, and so narrow that there was no room for any one at her side.

You will find when you read the whole story that such judgmental authorial comment is by no means typical of most of the narrative manner. But in this quoted passage we are unmistakably being told things Louisa could not know about herself, and a projection into the future is made. For the moment the author is speaking directly to the reader—and perhaps unnecessarily lapsing from the disciplined point of view she chose. But if we were to call this a fault, we would certainly concede that it is a very minor one, which might readily be excused by citing the nature of the material. After all, the narrative covers a period of many years, and compression of some parts is absolutely required. I have cited it here not to criticize it but only to illustrate another of the choices available to the fiction writer.

Indirection

The revelations of fiction are not usually made by direct statement. The "bottom line" is not spelled out in a positive or unambiguous summation. Rather the tactic of the fictional art is to guide, direct, and entice the imagination of the reader to a point where intuition blends with a comprehension of detail to engender a sympathetic understanding still shaded by mysteries of a moral or psychological sort.

Barbara L. Greenberg

Important Things

For years the children whimpered and tugged. "Tell us, tell us."

You promised to tell the children some other time, later, when they were old enough.

Now the children stand eye to eye with you and show you their teeth. "Tell us."

"Tell you what?" you ask, ingenuous.

"Tell us The Important Things."

You tell the children there are six continents and five oceans, or vice versa.

You tell your children the little you know about sex. Your children tell you there are better words for what you choose to call The Married Embrace.

You tell your children to be true to themselves. They say they are true to themselves. You tell them they're lying, you always know when they're lying. They tell you you're crazy. You tell them to mind their manners. They think you mean it as a joke; they laugh.

There are tears in your eyes. You tell the children the dawn will follow the dark, the tide will come in, the grass will be renewed, every dog will have its day. You tell them the story of The Littlest Soldier whose right arm, which he sacrificed while fighting for a noble cause, grew back again.

You say that if there were no Evil we wouldn't have the satisfaction of choosing The Good. And if there were no pain, you say, we'd never know our greatest joy, relief from pain.

You offer to bake a cake for the children, a fudge cake with chocolate frosting, their favorite.

"Tell us," say the children.

You say to your children, "I am going to die."

"When?"

"Someday."

"Oh."

You tell your children that they, too, are going to die. They already knew it.

You can't think of anything else to tell the children. You say you're sorry. You *are* sorry. But the children have had enough of your excuses.

"A promise is a promise," say the children.

They'll give you one more chance to tell them of your own accord. If you don't, they'll have to resort to torture.

This little story is a teaser, crafted not only to keep the children (and the narrator) baffled about what "important things" are, but to lure us into our own creative speculation about the great secrets of existence. By a process of elimination, those things we would readily think of as important are dismissed as unsatisfactory. The fundamentals of common knowledge are denied their fundamental status. The challenge to name what is truly important slips by the narrator and is slyly posed to us. Once the attempt at direct answers is used up, the story has put it up to us to scrape our souls for what we have to declare.

In some sense most of the stories we will encounter in this book bring us to the same pass, for even in those where the author has come down hard with a positive declaration about what is important, there will be a nimbus or shadowy fringe in which conviction and full comprehension can only be established by our emotional insight and a seizure of implications that are not spelled out in the text. Most stories—much larger than this one in bulk—stir up questions of right and wrong, of what is worth living for and dying for. Truly these are "important things," and authors work with all their skill to guide us to a point where the inexpressible can be sensed. It is the best tactic of fiction to move circuitously to the point of revelation. Then those readers who have followed the path of indirections complete the reading transaction by going somewhat farther than they have been led, by drawing from themselves the impassioned judgment that will make the story whole.

The Part and the Whole

In our reading of fiction (or any literary form, for that matter) we will often pause to consider the relation between some single word and the overall meaning of the situation and action, between a significant part and the significance of the whole, as in this poem:

William Stafford

Traveling through the Dark

Traveling through the dark I found a deer
dead on the edge of the Wilson River road.
It is usually best to roll them into the canyon:
that road is narrow; to swerve might make more dead.

By glow of the tail-light I stumbled back of the car
and stood by the heap, a doe, a recent killing;
she had stiffened already, almost cold.
I dragged her off; she was large in the belly.

My fingers touching her side brought me the reason—
her side was warm; her fawn lay there waiting,
alive, still, never to be born.
Beside that mountain road I hesitated.

The car aimed ahead its lowered parking lights;
under the hood purred the steady engine.
I stood in the glare of the warm exhaust turning red;
around our group I could hear the wilderness listen.

I thought hard for us all—my only swerving—,
then pushed her over the edge into the river.

Like many other poems, this one tells a story, and our immediate concern with it is to demonstrate how one part—the verb to swerve*—expands the meaning of the episode, opening dimensions of thought that may be inherent in the action but might elude a casual observer of what is being done.*

There is probably no way the narrator can save the life of the unborn fawn trapped in the dead body of its mother. Yet the very hopelessness of the fawn's plight calls to him to take sides with it against the threat of extinction. So he faces a dilemma. If he does not kill the fawn by pushing the deer into the river, he will have failed in his duty to other people who will be using the road, and he may be to blame for any accident that might ensue if a car either struck the deer's body or swerved to avoid it.

In the ultimate decision to push the entrapped fawn to its doom we see the pattern of all anguishing predicaments in which people who yearn to do good must commit what they believe to be the lesser evil. No wonder the narrator hesitates.

Now, consider how the verb to swerve *(and its other form,* swerving*) intensifies and expands the meaning of that hesitation. In the fourth line* to swerve *is firmly associated with danger of death. That association is recalled to our minds when the narrator, who has paused to think before acting, calls his thought "my only swerving." The dispute in his mind between natural impulse and social duty and the wish for time to seek some gentler alternative is thus equated with a dangerous human weakness. Still, because the double meaning given to swerving permits a double vision, we see that the weakness is, simultaneously, a noble and human response, worth the practical risk it entails.*

Are the processes of thought that expose us to contradictory motivations a weakness, a costly form of nobility, or a mysterious combination of both? That is the multidimensional quandary we are brought to confront by the wordplay in this poem. The story situation applies great pressure on a single word, and, just as great pressure applied to carbon produces a diamond, pressure of meaning converging on a single word produces something that will refract special lights back through the whole substance of the story.

When you come to read Herman Melville's Bartleby the Scrivener, *you will note how that massive story puts the same sort of presure on the single word* prefer. *Other stories that do not depend so much on wordplay will force a reciprocal action between the whole and some detail of gesture, a bit of unintentionally revealing dialogue or fragmentary glimpse of a passion ordinarily hidden behind a civilized exterior.*

In some sense, of course, every word and every detail in a story is crucial to the development of meaning in the larger movements of plot or character development. But those special parts that echo, qualify, or expand the larger concept are those to which we direct our closest scrutiny.

Coherence

In well-made fiction one thing follows from another, and the connected parts all work together to deliver the effect and meaning. Let's examine the cooperative interconnections of parts in the following.

Wright Morris

story from **God's Country and My People**[5]

My feet were not big. My knee pants were always below my knees. I preferred to ride a man's bike side-saddle, the sprocket wearing a grease spot on one shin, and my father often wondered what was on my mind. He spoke to Mrs. Healy, in the eighth grade, about it, and she referred him to *Tom Sawyer*. In case I might be too smart for *Tom Sawyer*, she gave him three books by Ralph Henry Barbour.[6] My father read them late at night, in the bathroom, or in the egg-candling[7] room of his produce business, using the light that came through the holes of the candler. If he could believe what he read, all I had on my mind was good clean fun. All I wanted to do was pitch the winning game and win the cross-country run. That seemed a long way to run, but my father believed that I could. Later he hoped to send me to an Eastern school where I would live in a room hung with college pennants, and spend Christmas with my roommate whose younger sister was home from her boarding school. Playing run-sheep-run[8] at night with Lillian Eichler, we stood holding hands in Mrs. Seidel's coal bin, where my breathing was noisy but I had no idea what was on my mind.

The first two sentences and the first principal clause of the third explain the situation. They define the boy's adolescent foibles, which—as indicated in the second clause of the third sentence—cause the father concern. For the narrator to state here that his father "often wondered" is to expand the time range and the sophistication of the voice recounting the events. The words signal that the narrator is looking back—probably from adulthood—to contemplate a problem that endured through a phase of his youth.

Now the fourth sentence adds a particular, concrete action, performed at a specific point in time, which follows coherently from

5. Morris's book consists of photographs by the author with prose vignettes or stories on unnumbered facing pages. 6. American author of juvenile inspirational fiction. 7. A method of checking eggs for edibility by holding them against a lighted hole in a dark-walled box. 8. Variant of hide-and-seek.

the habitual action recounted in the third sentence. In a story on a larger scale such transition from habitual to specific would ordinarily be accomplished by passing over from narration to a scene. (We might guess that the scene between the father and Mrs. Healy would open with words on the order of: One day my exasperated father went for help to my eighth grade teacher. "My kid's floundering," he told her. . . . *)*

Next, characterization of Mrs. Healy is provided by her naive, schoolmarm faith that books will fix whatever is wrong. She is further characterized (and derided in the tone of fond irony that pervades the whole) by her topsy-turvy notion that books by Ralph Henry Barbour are more sophisticated than Tom Sawyer. *The author thus satirizes not only Mrs. Healy but the quaint provincialism of the milieu in which the action is taking place.*

The sixth sentence smoothly continues the line of action and fills in some information about family circumstances that was postponed from the expository opening. That the books are read by night "in the bathroom" must mean that the father and his motherless son live in a single room with adjacent bath. Their poverty and the father's commitment to his son's welfare are indicated by the father's use of light from the egg candler to read by. Frugality and aspiration are seen pathetically blended in the father's nature.

As we register this pathos we come to a shift in the direction of the plot action. Intending to come closer to his son by reading the prescribed books, the father is misled into a dream of glory that can only widen the distance between them. Paternal altruism detours into self-indulgent sentimentality. The specific ingredients of the father's reading, given in the eighth and tenth sentences, not only play up the ironic tone of the whole—they retroactively satirize Mrs. Healy and parody the national dream of what we call "upward mobility."

Finally, the increasing likelihood that the father's efforts will backfire is confirmed by the eleventh sentence. When the focus of narration shifts to the son, we see he is very far off the track of his father's daydreams.

It might appear that in a story so brief no space could be found to individualize Lillian Eichler. A multitude of teen-age girls have played run-sheep-run at night in Midwestern towns. Yet the single verb stood *sets her apart from the nameless multitude. It is not every girl who could be hypnotized (or self-hypnotized) into patience while she waits for the mixed-up boy to discover what truly is on his mind at this opportune moment.*

From a minimal cast of characters the author has made a maximum statement about human relations by (1) choosing characters whose differences provide meaningful contrast and (2) relying on dramatic progression to show off facets of each character in successive phases of the action. The end of the story was implicit in its beginning. The significant relation between setting and characters is exposed as they interact within a small but dense design. Details that further the plot serve, at the same time, to establish and modulate the tone. The last three words repeat (with ironic variation) something said before—and tie the last knot on an elegantly neat package.

THE *Norton Anthology* OF *Short Fiction*

FOURTH EDITION

Sherwood Anderson

Anderson (1876–1941) was born in Camden, Ohio, the son of a roving, likable, improvident, and talkative man, who often appears under one name or another in Anderson's works. After some intermittent schooling, Anderson enlisted in the Army for service in Cuba during the Spanish-American War. A few years later—in the spirit of rebellion against industrial and commercial civilization which was to color his writing thereafter—he walked out of his job as manager of an Ohio paint factory. Going to Chicago, then in the ferment of a literary renaissance, he made friends with writers and began to publish his own poetry and fiction. With the appearance in 1919 of Winesburg, Ohio *he became famous. As in the collections that followed, the stories of this book show life and desire frustrated by the provincialism of the Midwest. Characteristic of his work is a tone of melancholy reminiscence in which he projects remembered realities on the screen of a philosophic imagination. His autobiography,* A Story-Teller's Story *(1924), is partly fictional, as most of his fiction is partly autobiographical. His novels include* Windy McPherson's Son *(1916),* Poor White *(1920),* Many Marriages *(1923), and* Dark Laughter *(1925). His later collections of stories are* The Triumph of the Egg *(1921),* Horses and Men *(1923), and* Death in the Woods and Other Stories *(1933).*

I Want to Know Why

We got up at four in the morning, that first day in the East. On the evening before, we had climbed off a freight train at the edge of town and with the true instinct of Kentucky boys had found our way across town and to the race track and the stables at once. Then we knew we were all right. Hanley Turner right away found a nigger we knew. It was Bildad Johnson, who in the winter works at Ed Becker's livery barn in our home town, Beckersville. Bildad is a good cook as almost all our niggers are and of course he, like everyone in our part of Kentucky who is anyone at all, likes the horses. In the spring Bildad begins to scratch around. A nigger from our country can flatter and wheedle anyone into letting him do most anything he wants. Bildad wheedles the stable men and the trainers from the horse farms in our country around Lexington. The trainers come into town in the evening to stand around and talk and maybe get into a poker game. Bildad gets in with them. He is always doing little favors and telling about things to eat, chicken browned in a pan, and how is the best way to cook sweet potatoes and corn bread. It makes your mouth water to hear him.

When the racing season comes on and the horses go to the races and there is all the talk on the streets in the evenings about the new colts, and everyone says when they are going over to Lexington or to the spring meeting at Churchill Downs or to Latonia,[1] and the horsemen that have been down to New Orleans or maybe at the winter meeting[2] at Havana in Cuba come home to spend a week before they start out again, at such a time when everything talked about in Beckersville is just horses and nothing else and the outfits start out and horse racing is in every breath of air you breathe, Bildad shows up with a job as cook for some outfit. Often when I think about it, his always going all season to the races and working in the livery barn in the winter where horses are and where men like to come and talk about horses, I wish I was a nigger. It's a foolish thing to say, but that's the way I am about being around horses, just crazy. I can't help it.

Well, I must tell you about what we did and let you in on what I'm talking about. Four of us boys from Beckersville, all whites and sons of men who live in Beckersville regular, made up our minds we were going to the races, not just to Lexington or Louisville, I don't mean, but to the big Eastern track we were always hearing our Beckersville men talk about, to Saratoga.[3] We were all pretty young then. I was just turned fifteen and I was the oldest of the four. It was my scheme. I admit that, and I talked the others into trying it. There was Hanley Turner and Henry Rieback and Tom Tumberton and myself. I had thirty-seven dollars I had earned during the winter working nights and Saturdays in Enoch Myer's grocery. Henry Rieback had eleven dollars and the others, Hanley and Tom, had only a dollar or two each. We fixed it all up and laid low until the Kentucky spring meetings were over and some of our men, the sportiest ones, the ones we envied the most, had cut out. Then we cut out too.

I won't tell you the trouble we had beating our way on freights and all. We went through Cleveland and Buffalo and other cities and saw Niagara Falls. We bought things there, souvenirs and spoons and cards and shells with pictures of the falls on them for our sisters and mothers, but thought we had better not send any of the things home. We didn't want to put the folks on our trail and maybe be nabbed.

We got into Saratoga as I said at night and went to the track.

1. Race track in Covington, Kentucky. Churchill Downs is the famous track in Louisville, Kentucky, where the Kentucky Derby is run every year. 2. I.e., the entire number of horse races for the season. 3. Famous resort town and site of race track in upstate New York.

Bildad fed us up. He showed us a place to sleep in hay over a shed and promised to keep still. Niggers are all right about things like that. They won't squeal on you. Often a white man you might meet, when you had run away from home like that, might appear to be all right and give you a quarter or a half dollar or something, and then go right and give you away. White men will do that, but not a nigger. You can trust them. They are squarer with kids. I don't know why.

At the Saratoga meeting that year there were a lot of men from home. Dave Williams and Arthur Mulford and Jerry Myers and others. Then there was a lot from Louisville and Lexington Henry Rieback knew but I didn't. They were professional gamblers and Henry Rieback's father is one too. He is what is called a sheet writer and goes away most of the year to tracks. In the winter when he is home in Beckersville he don't stay there much but goes away to cities and deals faro.[4] He is a nice man and generous, is always sending Henry presents, a bicycle and a gold watch and a boy scout suit of clothes and things like that.

My own father is a lawyer. He's all right, but don't make much money and can't buy me things, and anyway I'm getting so old now I don't expect it. He never said nothing to me against Henry, but Hanley Turner and Tom Tumberton's fathers did. They said to their boys that money so come by is no good and they didn't want their boys brought up to hear gamblers' talk and be thinking about such things and maybe embrace them.

That's all right and I guess the men know what they are talking about, but I don't see what it's got to do with Henry or with horses either. That's what I'm writing this story about. I'm puzzled. I'm getting to be a man and want to think straight and be O. K., and there's something I saw at the race meeting at the Eastern track I can't figure out.

I can't help it, I'm crazy about thoroughbred horses, I've always been that way. When I was ten years old and saw I was growing to be big and couldn't be a rider I was so sorry I nearly died. Harry Hellinfinger in Beckersville, whose father is Postmaster, is grown up and too lazy to work, but likes to stand around in the street and get up jokes on boys like sending them to a hardware store for a gimlet to bore square holes and other jokes like that. He played one on me. He told me that if I would eat a half a cigar I would be stunted and not grow any more and maybe could be a rider. I did it. When father wasn't looking I took a cigar out of his pocket and gagged it down some way. It made me awful sick and the doctor had to be sent for, and then it did no good. I kept right on growing. It was a joke. When I told what

4. A card game, favorite of gamblers. A sheet writer is a bookmaker.

I had done and why, most fathers would have whipped me, but mine didn't.

Well, I didn't get stunted and didn't die. It serves Harry Hellinfinger right. Then I made up my mind I would like to be a stableboy, but had to give that up too. Mostly niggers do that work and I knew father wouldn't let me go into it. No use to ask him.

If you've never been crazy about thoroughbreds, it's because you've never been around where they are much and don't know any better. They're beautiful. There isn't anything so lovely and clean and full of spunk and honest and everything as some race horses. On the big horse farms that are all around our town Beckersville there are tracks, and the horses run in the early morning. More than a thousand times I've got out of bed before daylight and walked two or three miles to the tracks. Mother wouldn't of let me go, but father always says, "Let him alone." So I got some bread out of the breadbox and some butter and jam, gobbled it and lit out.

At the tracks you sit on the fence with men, whites and niggers, and they chew tobacco and talk, and then the colts are brought out. It's early and the grass is covered with shiny dew and in another field a man is plowing and they are frying things in a shed where the track niggers sleep, and you know how a nigger can giggle and laugh and say things that make you laugh. A white man can't do it and some niggers can't, but a track nigger can every time.

And so the colts are brought out and some are just galloped by stableboys, but almost every morning on a big track owned by a rich man who lives maybe in New York, there are always, nearly every morning, a few colts and some of the old race horses and geldings and mares that are cut loose.

It brings a lump up into my throat when a horse runs. I don't mean all horses, but some. I can pick them nearly every time. It's in my blood like in the blood of race track niggers and trainers. Even when they just go slop-jogging along with a little nigger on their backs, I can tell a winner. If my throat hurts and it's hard for me to swallow, that's him. He'll run like Sam Hill[5] when you let him out. If he don't win every time it'll be a wonder and because they've got him in a pocket behind another or he was pulled or got off bad at the post or something. If I wanted to be a gambler like Henry Rieback's father I could get rich. I know I could and Henry says so too. All I would have to do is to wait till that hurt comes when I see a horse and then bet every cent. That's what I would do if I wanted to be a gambler, but I don't.

When you're at the tracks in the morning—not the race tracks

5. Euphemism for Hell.

but the training tracks around Beckersville—you don't see a horse, the kind I've been talking about, very often, but it's nice anyway. Any thoroughbred, that is sired right and out of a good mare and trained by a man that knows how, can run. If he couldn't, what would he be there for and not pulling a plow?

Well, out of the stables they come and the boys are on their backs and it's lovely to be there. You hunch down on top of the fence and itch inside you. Over in the sheds the niggers giggle and sing. Bacon is being fried and coffee made. Everything smells lovely. Nothing smells better than coffee and manure and horses and niggers and bacon frying and pipes being smoked out of doors on a morning like that. It just gets you, that's what it does.

But about Saratoga. We was there six days and not a soul from home seen us and everything came off just as we wanted it to, fine weather and horses and races and all. We beat our way home and Bildad gave us a basket with fried chicken and bread and other eatables in, and I had eighteen dollars when we got back to Beckersville. Mother jawed and cried, but Pop didn't say much. I told everything we done, except one thing. I did and saw that alone. That's what I'm writing about. It got me upset. I think about it at night. Here it is.

At Saratoga we laid up nights in the hay in the shed Bildad had showed us and ate with the niggers early and at night when the race people had all gone away. The men from home stayed mostly in the grandstand and betting field and didn't come out around the places where the horses are kept except to the paddocks just before a race when the horses are saddled. At Saratoga they don't have paddocks under an open shed as at Lexington and Churchill Downs and other tracks down in our country, but saddle the horses right out in an open place under trees on a lawn as smooth and nice as Banker Bohon's front yard here in Beckersville. It's lovely. The horses are sweaty and nervous and shine and the men come out and smoke cigars and look at them and the trainers are there and the owners, and your heart thumps so you can hardly breathe.

Then the bugle blows for post and the boys that ride come running out with their silk clothes on and you run to get a place by the fence with the niggers.

I always am wanting to be a trainer or owner, and at the risk of being seen and caught and sent home I went to the paddocks before every race. The other boys didn't, but I did.

We got to Saratoga on a Friday, and on Wednesday the next week the big Mullford Handicap was to be run. Middlestride was in it and Sunstreak. The weather was fine and the track fast. I couldn't sleep the night before.

What had happened was that both these horses are the kind it makes my throat hurt to see. Middlestride is long and looks awkward and is a gelding. He belongs to Joe Thompson, a little owner from home who only has half a dozen horses. The Mullford Handicap is for a mile and Middlestride can't untrack fast. He goes away slow and is always 'way back at the half, then he begins to run and if the race is a mile and a quarter he'll just eat up everything and get there.

Sunstreak is different. He is a stallion and nervous and belongs on the biggest farm we've got in our country, the Van Riddle place that belongs to Mr. Van Riddle of New York. Sunstreak is like a girl you think about sometimes but never see. He is hard all over and lovely too. When you look at his head you want to kiss him. He is trained by Jerry Tillford who knows me and has been good to me lots of times, lets me walk into a horse's stall to look at him close and other things. There isn't anything as sweet as that horse. He stands at the post quiet and not letting on, but he is just burning up inside. Then when the barrier goes up he is off like his name, Sunstreak. It makes you ache to see him. It hurts you. He just lays down and runs like a bird dog. There can't anything I ever see run like him except Middlestride when he gets untracked and stretches himself.

Gee! I ached to see that race and those two horses run, ached and dreaded it too. I didn't want to see either of our horses beaten. We had never sent a pair like that to the races before. Old men in Beckersville said so and the niggers said so. It was a fact.

Before the race, I went over to the paddocks to see. I looked a last look at Middlestride, who isn't such a much standing in a paddock that way, then I went to see Sunstreak.

It was his day. I knew when I see him. I forgot all about being seen myself and walked right up. All the men from Beckersville were there and no one noticed me except Jerry Tillford. He saw me and something happened. I'll tell you about that.

I was standing looking at that horse and aching. In some way, I can't tell how, I knew just how Sunstreak felt inside. He was quiet and letting the niggers rub his legs and Mr. Van Riddle himself put the saddle on, but he was just a raging torrent inside. He was like the water in the river at Niagara Falls just before it goes plunk down. That horse wasn't thinking about running. He don't have to think about that. He was just thinking about holding himself back till the time for the running came. I knew that. I could just in a way see right inside him. He was going to do some awful running and I knew it. He wasn't bragging or letting on much or prancing or making a fuss, but just waiting. I knew it and Jerry Tillford his trainer knew. I looked up, and then that man and I looked into each other's eyes. Something happened to me. I guess I loved the man as much as I did the horse because he knew what I knew. Seemed to me there wasn't anything in the world but that man and the horse and me. I cried and Jerry Tillford had a shine in his eyes. Then I came away to the fence to wait for the race. The horse was better than me, more steadier and, now I know, better than Jerry. He was the quietest and he had to do the running.

Sunstreak ran first of course and he busted the world's record for a mile. I've seen that if I never see anything more. Everything came out just as I expected. Middlestride got left at the post and was 'way back and closed up to be second, just as I knew he would. He'll get a world's record too some day. They can't skin the Beckersville country on horses.

I watched the race calm because I knew what would happen. I was sure. Hanley Turner and Henry Rieback and Tom Tumberton were all more excited than me.

A funny thing that happened to me. I was thinking about Jerry Tillford the trainer and how happy he was all through the race. I liked him that afternoon even more than I ever liked my own father. I almost forgot the horses thinking that way about him. It was because of what I had seen in his eyes as he stood in the paddocks beside Sunstreak before the race started. I knew he had been watching and working with Sunstreak since the horse was a baby colt, had taught him to run and be patient and when to let himself out and not to quit, never. I knew that for him it was like a mother seeing her child do something brave or wonderful. It was the first time I ever felt for a man like that.

After the race that night I cut out from Tom and Hanley and Henry. I wanted to be by myself and I wanted to be near Jerry Tillford if I could work it. Here is what happened.

The track in Saratoga is near the edge of town. It is all polished up and trees around, the everygreen kind, and grass and everything painted and nice. If you go past the track you get to a hard road made of asphalt for automobiles, and if you go along this for a few miles there is a road turns off to a little rummy-looking farmhouse set in a yard.

That night after the race I went along that road because I had seen Jerry and some other men go that way in an automobile. I didn't expect to find them. I walked for a ways and then sat down by a fence to think. It was the direction they went in. I wanted to be as near Jerry as I could. I felt close to him. Pretty soon I went up the side road—I don't know why—and came to the rummy farmhouse. I was just lonesome to see Jerry, like wanting to see your father at night when you are a young kid. Just then an automobile came along and turned in. Jerry was in it and Henry Rieback's father, and Arthur Bedford from home, and Dave Williams and two other men I didn't know. They got out of the car and went into the house, all but Henry Rieback's father who quarreled with them and said he wouldn't go. It was only about nine o'clock, but they were all drunk and the rummy-looking farmhouse was a place for bad women to stay in. That's what it was. I crept up along a fence and looked through a window and saw.

It's what give me the fantods.[6] I can't make it out. The women in the house were all ugly mean-looking women, not nice to look at or be near. They were homely too, except one who was tall and looked a little like the gelding Middlestride, but not clean like him, but with a hard ugly mouth. She had red hair. I saw everything plain. I got up by an old rosebush by an open window and looked. The women had on loose dresses and sat around in chairs. The men came in and some sat on the women's laps. The place smelled rotten and there was rotten talk, the kind a kid hears around a livery stable in a town like Beckersville in the winter but don't ever expect to hear talked when there are women around. It was rotten. A nigger wouldn't go into such a place.

I looked at Jerry Tillford. I've told you how I had been feeling about him on account of his knowing what was going on inside of Sunstreak in the minute before he went to the post for the race in which he made a world's record.

Jerry bragged in that bad woman house as I knew Sunstreak wouldn't never have bragged. He said that he made that horse, that it was him that won the race and made the record. He lied and bragged like a fool. I never heard such silly talk.

And then, what do you suppose he did! He looked at the woman in there, the one that was lean and hard-mouthed and looked a little like the gelding Middlestride but not clean like him, and his eyes began to shine just as they did when he looked at me and at Sunstreak in the paddocks at the track in the afternoon. I stood there by the window—gee!—but I wished I hadn't gone away from the tracks, but had stayed with the boys and the niggers and the horses. The tall rotten-looking woman was between us just as Sunstreak was in the paddocks in the afternoon.

Then, all of a sudden, I began to hate that man. I wanted to scream and rush in the room and kill him. I never had such a feeling before. I was so mad clean through that I cried and my fists were doubled up so my fingernails cut my hands.

And Jerry's eyes kept shining and he waved back and forth, and then he went and kissed that woman and I crept away and went back to the tracks and to bed and didn't sleep hardly any, and then next day I got the other kids to start home with me and never told them anything I seen.

I been thinking about it ever since. I can't make it out. Spring has come again and I'm nearly sixteen and go to the tracks mornings same as always, and I see Sunstreak and Middlestride and a new colt

6. Slang for being very shaken and upset.

named Strident I'll bet will lay them all out, but no one thinks so but me and two or three niggers.

But things are different. At the tracks the air don't taste as good or smell as good. It's because a man like Jerry Tillford, who knows what he does, could see a horse like Sunstreak run, and kiss a woman like that the same day. I can't make it out. Darn him, what did he want to do like that for? I kept thinking about it and it spoils looking at horses and smelling things and hearing niggers laugh and everything. Sometimes I'm so mad about it I want to fight someone. It gives me the fantods. What did he do it for? I want to know why.

---

1. What kinship with nature does the boy feel and how is this expressed by the choice of details and language in the story?
2. Why is the boy's discovery about Tillford so acute at his age?
3. What does the boy want his own life to be like? Does he lose faith that it can be as he wants it?
4. What elements in his own nature does the boy see embodied in the horse Sunstreak? Does Jerry Tillford possess the same characteristics?
5. Has Tillford betrayed the boy's trust? Or taught him a good and useful lesson? Discuss Tillford's role as teacher.

Margaret Atwood

Atwood (1939–) was born in Ottawa, Ontario, the daughter of an entomologist. After her education at the University of Toronto, Radcliffe, and Harvard, she held various jobs as cashier, waitress, market-research writer, and writer of film scripts. She has won numerous prizes for her poetry as well as her fiction. Her novels include The Edible Woman *(1969),* Surfacing *(1972),* Lady Oracle *(1976),* Life before Man *(1979),* Bodily Harm *(1982),* The Handmaid's Tale *(1985), and* Cat's Eye *(1988). Many of her stories have been collected in* Dancing Girls and Other Stories *(1978),* Murder in the Dark *(1983), and* Bluebeard's Egg *(1983).*

Rape Fantasies

The way they're going on about it in the magazines you'd think it was just invented, and not only that but it's something terrific, like a vaccine for cancer. They put it in capital letters on the front cover, and inside they have these questionnaires like the ones they used to have about whether you were a good enough wife or an endomorph or an ectomorph,[1] remember that? with the scoring upside down on page 73, and then these numbered do-it-yourself dealies, you know? RAPE, TEN THINGS TO DO ABOUT IT, like it was ten new hairdos or something. I mean, what's so new about it?

So at work they all have to talk about it because no matter what magazine you open, there it is, staring you right between the eyes, and they're beginning to have it on the television, too. Personally I'd prefer a June Allyson movie[2] anytime but they don't make them any more and they don't even have them that much on the Late Show. For instance, day before yesterday, that would be Wednesday, thank god it's Friday as they say, we were sitting around in the women's lunch room—the *lunch* room, I mean you'd think you could get some peace and quiet in there—and Chrissy closes up the magazine she's been reading and says, "How about it, girls, do you have rape fantasies?"

The four of us were having our game of bridge the way we always do, and I had a bare twelve points counting the singleton with not that

1. Popularized terms for types of body structure.
2. Sentimentalized love story.

much of a bid in anything. So I said one club, hoping Sondra would remember about the one club convention, because the time before when I used that she thought I really meant clubs and she bid us up to three, and all I had was four little ones with nothing higher than a six, and we went down two and on top of that we were vulnerable. She is not the world's best bridge player. I mean, neither am I but there's a limit.

Darlene passed but the damage was done, Sondra's head went round like it was on ball bearings and she said, "*What* fantasies?"

"Rape fantasies," Chrissy said. She's a receptionist and she looks like one; she's pretty but cool as a cucumber, like she's been painted all over with nail polish, if you know what I mean. Varnished. "It says here all women have rape fantasies."

"For Chrissake, I'm eating an egg sandwich," I said, "and I bid one club and Darlene passed."

"You mean, like some guy jumping you in an alley or something," Sondra said. She was eating her lunch, we all eat our lunches during the game, and she bit into a piece of that celery she always brings and started to chew away on it with this thoughtful expression in her eyes and I knew we might as well pack it in as far as the game was concerned.

"Yeah, sort of like that," Chrissy said. She was blushing a little, you could see it even under her makeup.

"I don't think you should go out alone at night," Darlene said, "you put yourself in a position," and I may have been mistaken but she was looking at me. She's the oldest, she's forty-one though you wouldn't know it and neither does she, but I looked it up in the employees' file. I like to guess a person's age and then look it up to see if I'm right. I let myself have an extra pack of cigarettes if I am, though I'm trying to cut down. I figure it's harmless as long as you don't tell. I mean, not everyone has access to that file, it's more or less confidential. But it's all right if I tell you, I don't expect you'll ever meet her, though you never know, it's a small world. Anyway.

"For *heaven's* sake, it's only *Toronto*," Greta said. She worked in Detroit for three years and she never lets you forget it, it's like she thinks she's a war hero or something, we should all admire her just for the fact that she's still walking this earth, though she was really living in Windsor the whole time, she just worked in Detroit. Which for me doesn't really count. It's where you sleep, right?

"Well, do you?" Chrissy said. She was obviously trying to tell us about hers but she wasn't about to go first, she's cautious, that one.

"I certainly don't," Darlene said, and she wrinkled up her nose, like this, and I had to laugh. "I think it's disgusting." She's divorced, I read that in the file too, she never talks about it. It must've been years ago anyway. She got up and went over to the coffee machine and turned her back on us as though she wasn't going to have anything more to do with it.

"Well," Greta said. I could see it was going to be between her and Chrissy. They're both blondes, I don't mean that in a bitchy way but they do try to outdress each other. Greta would like to get out of Filing, she'd like to be a receptionist too so she could meet more people. You don't meet much of anyone in Filing except other people in Filing. Me, I don't mind it so much, I have outside interests.

"Well," Greta said, "I sometimes think about, you know my apartment? It's got this little balcony, I like to sit out there in the summer and I have a few plants out there. I never bother that much about locking the door to the balcony, it's one of those sliding glass ones, I'm on the eighteenth floor for heaven's sake, I've got a good view of the lake and the CN Tower and all. But I'm sitting around one night in my housecoat, watching TV with my shoes off, you know how you do, and I see this guy's feet, coming down past the window, and the next thing you know he's standing on the balcony, he's let himself down by a rope with a hook on the end of it from the floor above, that's the nineteenth, and before I can even get up off the chesterfield he's inside the apartment. He's all dressed in black with black gloves on"—I knew right away what show she got the black gloves off because I saw the same one—"and then he, well, you know."

"You know what?" Chrissy said, but Greta said, "And afterwards he tells me that he goes all over the outside of the apartment building like that, from one floor to another, with his rope and his hook . . . and then he goes out to the balcony and tosses his rope, and he climbs up it and disappears."

"Just like Tarzan," I said, but nobody laughed.

"Is that all?" Chrissy said. "Don't you ever think about, well, I think about being in the bathtub, with no clothes on . . ."

"So who takes a bath in their clothes?" I said, you have to admit it's stupid when you come to think of it, but she just went on, ". . . with lots of bubbles, what I use is Vitabath, it's more expensive but it's so relaxing, and my hair pinned up, and the door opens and this fellow's standing there. . . ."

"How'd he get in?" Greta said.

"Oh, I don't know, through a window or something. Well, I can't very well get out of the bathtub, the bathroom's too small and besides he's blocking the doorway, so I just *lie* there, and he starts to very slowly take his own clothes off, and then he gets into the bathtub with me."

"Don't you scream or anything?" said Darlene. She'd come back with her cup of coffee, she was getting really interested. "I'd scream like bloody murder."

"Who'd hear me?" Chrissy said. "Besides, all the articles say it's better not to resist, that way you don't get hurt."

"Anyway you might get bubbles up your nose," I said, "from the deep breathing," and I swear all four of them looked at me like I was in bad taste, like I'd insulted the Virgin Mary or something. I mean, I don't see what's wrong with a little joke now and then. Life's too short, right?

"Listen," I said, "those aren't *rape* fantasies. I mean, you aren't getting *raped,* it's just some guy you haven't met formally who happens to be more attractive than Derek Cummins"—he's the Assistant Manager, he wears elevator shoes or at any rate they have these thick soles and he has this funny way of talking, we call him Derek Duck—"and you have a good time. Rape is when they've got a knife or something and you don't want to."

"So what about you, Estelle," Chrissy said, she was miffed because I laughed at her fantasy, she thought I was putting her down. Sondra was miffed too, by this time she'd finished her celery and she wanted to tell about hers, but she hadn't got in fast enough.

"All right, let me tell you one," I said. "I'm walking down this dark street at night and this fellow comes up and grabs my arm. Now it so happens that I have a plastic lemon in my purse, you know how it always says you should carry a plastic lemon in your purse? I don't really do it, I tried it once but the darn thing leaked all over my chequebook, but in this fantasy I have one, and I say to him, "You're intending to rape me, right?" and he nods, so I open my purse to get the plastic lemon, and I can't find it! My purse is full of all this junk, Kleenex and cigarettes and my change purse and my lipstick and my driver's licence, you know the kind of stuff; so I ask him to hold out his hands, like this, and I pile all this junk into them and down at the bottom there's the plastic lemon, and I can't get the top off. So I hand it to him and he's very obliging, he twists the top off and hands it back to me, and I squirt him in the eye."

I hope you don't think that's too vicious. Come to think of it, it is a bit mean, especially when he was so polite and all.

"*That's* your rape fantasy?" Chrissy says. "I don't believe it."

"She's a card," Darlene says, she and I are the ones that've been here the longest and she never will forget the time I got drunk at the office party and insisted I was going to dance under the table instead of on top of it, I did a sort of Cossack number[3] but then I hit my head

3. Russian folk dance called the *kazatzka*.

on the bottom of the table—actually it was a desk—when I went to get up, and I knocked myself out cold. She's decided that's the mark of an original mind and she tells everyone new about it and I'm not sure that's fair. Though I did do it.

"I'm being totally honest," I say. I always am and they know it. There's no point in being anything else, is the way I look at it, and sooner or later the truth will out so you might as well not waste the time, right? "You should hear the one about the Easy-Off Oven Cleaner."

But that was the end of the lunch hour, with one bridge game shot to hell, and the next day we spent most of the time arguing over whether to start a new game or play out the hands we had left over from the day before, so Sondra never did get a chance to tell about her rape fantasy.

It started me thinking though, about my own rape fantasies. Maybe I'm abnormal or something, I mean I have fantasies about handsome strangers coming in through the window too, like Mr. Clean,[4] I wish one would, please god somebody without flat feet and big sweat marks on his shirt, and over five feet five, believe me being tall is a handicap though it's getting better, tall guys are starting to like someone whose nose reaches higher than their belly button. But if you're being totally honest you can't count those as rape fantasies. In a real rape fantasy, what you should feel is this anxiety, like when you think about your apartment building catching on fire and whether you should use the elevator or the stairs or maybe just stick your head under a wet towel, and you try to remember everything you've read about what to do but you can't decide.

For instance, I'm walking along this dark street at night and this short, ugly fellow comes up and grabs my arm, and not only is he ugly, you know, with a sort of puffy nothing face, like those fellows you have to talk to in the bank when your account's overdrawn—of course I don't mean they're all like that—but he's absolutely covered in pimples. So he gets me pinned against the wall, he's short but he's heavy, and he starts to undo himself and the zipper gets stuck. I mean, one of the most significant moments in a girl's life, it's almost like getting married or having a baby or something, and he sticks the zipper.

So I say, kind of disgusted, "Oh for Chrissake," and he starts to cry. He tells me he's never been able to get anything right in his entire life, and this is the last straw, he's going to go jump off a bridge.

"Look," I say, I feel so sorry for him, in my rape fantasies I always end up feeling sorry for the guy, I mean there has to be something *wrong* with them, if it was Clint Eastwood it'd be different but worse luck it never is. I was the kind of little girl who buried dead robins,

4. Character featured in detergent ads.

know what I mean? It used to drive my mother nuts, she didn't like me touching them, because of the germs I guess. So I say, "Listen, I know how you feel. You really should do something about those pimples, if you got rid of them you'd be quite good looking, honest; then you wouldn't have to go around doing stuff like this. I had them myself once," I say, to comfort him, but in fact I did, and it ends up I give him the name of my old dermatologist, the one I had in high school, that was back in Leamington, except I used to go to St. Catharine's for the dermatologist. I'm telling you, I was really lonely when I first came here; I thought it was going to be such a big adventure and all, but it's a lot harder to meet people in a city. But I guess it's different for a guy.

Or I'm lying in bed with this terrible cold, my face is all swollen up, my eyes are red and my nose is dripping like a leaky tap, and this fellow comes in through the window and *he* has a terrible cold too, it's a new kind of flu that's been going around. So he says, "I'b goig do rabe you"—I hope you don't mind me holding my nose like this but that's the way I imagine it—and he lets out this terrific sneeze, which slows him down a bit, also I'm no object of beauty myself, you'd have to be some kind of pervert to want to rape someone with a cold like mine, it'd be like raping a bottle of LePage's mucilage the way my nose is running. He's looking wildly around the room, and I realize it's because he doesn't have a piece of Kleenex! "Id's ride here," I say, and I pass him the Kleenex, god knows why he even bothered to get out of bed, you'd think if you were going to go around climbing in windows you'd wait till you were healthier, right? I mean, that takes a certain amount of energy. So I ask him why doesn't he let me fix him a NeoCitran[5] and scotch, that's what I always take, you still have the cold but you don't feel it, so I do and we end up watching the Late Show together. I mean, they aren't all sex maniacs, the rest of the time they must lead a normal life. I figure they enjoy watching the Late Show just like anybody else.

I do have a scarier one though . . . where the fellow says he's hearing angel voices that're telling him he's got to kill me, you know, you read about things like that all the time in the papers. In this one I'm not in the apartment where I live now, I'm back in my mother's house in Leamington and the fellow's been hiding in the cellar, he grabs my arm when I go downstairs to get a jar of jam and he's got hold of the axe too, out of the garage, that one is really scary. I mean, what do you say to a nut like that?

So I start to shake but after a minute I get control of myself and I say, is he sure the angel voices have got the right person, because I hear the same angel voices and they've been telling me for some time

5. Patented cold medicine.

that I'm going to give birth to the reincarnation of St. Anne who in turn has the Virgin Mary and right after that comes Jesus Christ and the end of the world, and he wouldn't want to interfere with that, would he? So he gets confused and listens some more, and then he asks for a sign and I show him my vaccination mark, you can see it's sort of an odd-shaped one, it got infected because I scratched the top off, and that does it, he apologizes and climbs out the coal chute again, which is how he got in in the first place, and I say to myself there's some advantage in having been brought up a Catholic even though I haven't been to church since they changed the service into English, it just isn't the same, you might as well be a Protestant. I must write to Mother and tell her to nail up that coal chute, it always has bothered me. Funny, I couldn't tell you at all what this man looks like but I know exactly what kind of shoes he's wearing, because that's the last I see of him, his shoes going up the coal chute, and they're the old-fashioned kind that lace up the ankles, even though he's a young fellow. That's strange, isn't it?

Let me tell you though I really sweat until I see him safely out of there and I go upstairs right away and make myself a cup of tea. I don't think about that one much. My mother always said you shouldn't dwell on unpleasant things and I generally agree with that, I mean, dwelling on them doesn't make them go away. Though not dwelling on them doesn't make them go away either, when you come to think of it.

Sometimes I have these short ones where the fellow grabs my arm but I'm really a Kung-Fu expert, can you believe it, in real life I'm sure it would just be a conk on the head and that's that, like getting your tonsils out, you'd wake up and it would be all over except for the sore places, and you'd be lucky if your neck wasn't broken or something, I could never even hit the volleyball in gym and a volleyball is fairly large, you know?—and I just go *zap* with my fingers into his eyes and that's it, he falls over, or I flip him against a wall or something. But I could never really stick my fingers in anyone's eyes, could you? It would feel like hot jello and I don't even like cold jello, just thinking about it gives me the creeps. I feel a bit guilty about that one, I mean how would you like walking around knowing someone's been blinded for life because of you?

But maybe it's different for a guy.

The most touching one I have is when the fellow grabs my arm and I say, sad and kind of dignified, "You'd be raping a corpse." That pulls him up short and I explain that I've just found out I have leukaemia and the doctors have only given me a few months to live. That's why I'm out pacing the streets alone at night, I need to think, you know, come to terms with myself. I don't really have leukaemia but in the fantasy I do, I guess I chose that particular disease because a girl in my grade four class died of it, the whole class sent her flowers when she was in the hospital. I didn't understand then that she was going to die and I wanted to have leukaemia too so I could get flowers. Kids are funny, aren't they? Well, it turns out that he has leukaemia himself, and *he* only has a few months to live, that's why he's going around raping people, he's very bitter because he's so young and his life is being taken from him before he's really lived it. So we walk along gently under the street lights, it's spring and sort of misty, and we end up going for coffee, we're happy we've found the only other person in the world who can understand what we're going through, it's almost like fate, and after a while we just sort of look at each other and our hands touch, and he comes back with me and moves into my apartment and we spend our last months together before we die, we just sort of don't wake up in the morning, though I've never decided which one of us gets to die first. If it's him I have to go on and fantasize about the funeral, if it's me I don't have to worry about that, so it just about depends on how tired I am at the time. You may not believe this but sometimes I even start crying. I cry at the ends of movies, even the ones that aren't all that sad, so I guess it's the same thing. My mother's like that too.

The funny thing about these fantasies is that the man is always someone I don't know, and the statistics in the magazines, well, most of them anyway, they say it's often someone you do know, at least a little bit, like your boss or something—I mean, it wouldn't be *my* boss, he's over sixty and I'm sure he couldn't rape his way out of a paper bag, poor old thing, but it might be someone like Derek Duck, in his elevator shoes, perish the thought—or someone you just met, who invites you up for a drink, it's getting so you can hardly be sociable any more, and how are you supposed to meet people if you can't trust them even that basic amount? You can't spend your whole life in the Filing Department or cooped up in your own apartment with all the doors and windows locked and the shades down. I'm not what you would call a drinker but I like to go out now and then for a drink or two in a nice place, even if I am by myself, I'm with Women's Lib on that even though I can't agree with a lot of the other things they say. Like here for instance, the waiters all know me and if anyone, you know, bothers me . . . I don't know why I'm telling you all this, except I think it helps you get to know a person, especially at first, hearing some of the things they think about. At work they call me the office worry wart, but it isn't so much like worrying, it's more like figuring out what you should do in an emergency, like I said before.

Anyway, another thing about it is that there's a lot of conversation, in fact I spend most of my time, in the fantasy that is, wondering what I'm going to say and what he's going to say, I think it would be better if you could get a conversation going. Like, how could a fellow do that to a person he's just had a long conversation with, once you let them know you're human, you have a life too, I don't see how they could go ahead with it, right? I mean, I know it happens but I just don't understand it, that's the part I really don't understand.

---

1. What is the tone of this story and how is it related to characterization? To the general subject announced by the title?
2. How does the story satirize the popularization of rape as a subject for contemporary journalism? (Consider the story as a whole, not just the opening paragraph.)
3. Are the characters credible as types? As individuals? Are they rounded or flat? *(See Glossary of Critical Terms.)*
4. Whom do you imagine as the person listening to the narrator? What is the occasion for the narrator to tell such a story?

Isaac Babel

Babel (1894–1939?) was born in Odessa, Russia, and spent much of his boyhood there in a part of the city steeped in poverty and crime. As a schoolboy of fifteen—while still frequenting the harbor district, drinking and mingling with rough and vicious characters—he began to write stories in French, imitating the manner of the French writer Guy de Maupassant. Some of Babel's earliest efforts in his own language appeared in a magazine edited by the writer Maxim Gorky, who encouraged him to continue his interest in social misfits and in the life of the poor. From 1917 to 1924 Babel was a soldier on the Rumanian front, riding with a Communist cavalry army during the upheavals of Russia's civil war and revolution. Many of his stories are first-hand accounts of incidents he witnessed as a soldier, the vigor and pace of his reportage reflecting the shock of military and social change in Eastern Europe during this period. His literary career began in earnest with the publication of Odessa Tales *(1924), followed by more short stories in* Red Cavalry *(1926). Sometime in the 1930's he fell out of favor with the Stalinist regime and disappeared from public view. It is probable that he died in a prison camp before 1940.*

My First Goose

Savitsky, Commander of the VI Division, rose when he saw me, and I wondered at the beauty of his giant's body. He rose, the purple of his riding breeches and the crimson of his little tilted cap and the decorations stuck on his chest cleaving the hut as a standard cleaves the sky. A smell of scent and the sickly sweet freshness of soap emanated from him. His long legs were like girls sheathed to the neck in shining riding boots.

He smiled at me, struck his riding whip on the table, and drew toward him an order that the Chief of Staff had just finished dictating. It was an order for Ivan Chesnokov to advance on Chugunov-Dobryvodka with the regiment entrusted to him, to make contact with the enemy and destroy the same.

"For which destruction," the Commander began to write, smearing the whole sheet, "I make this same Chesnokov entirely responsible, up to and including the supreme penalty, and will if necessary strike him down on the spot; which you, Chesnokov, who have been working with me at the front for some months now, cannot doubt."

The Commander signed the order with a flourish, tossed it to his orderlies and turned upon me gray eyes that danced with merriment.

I handed him a paper with my appointment to the Staff of the Division.

"Put it down in the Order of the Day," said the Commander. "Put him down for every satisfaction save the front one. Can you read and write?"

"Yes, I can read and write," I replied, envying the flower and iron of that youthfulness. "I graduated in law from St. Petersburg University."

"Oh, are you one of those grinds?" he laughed. "Specs on your nose, too! What a nasty little object! They've sent you along without making any enquiries; and this is a hot place for specs. Think you'll get on with us?"

"I'll get on all right," I answered, and went off to the village with the quartermaster to find a billet for the night.

The quartermaster carried my trunk on his shoulder. Before us stretched the village street. The dying sun, round and yellow as a pumpkin, was giving up its roseate ghost to the skies.

We went up to a hut painted over with garlands. The quartermaster stopped, and said suddenly, with a guilty smile:

"Nuisance with specs. Can't do anything to stop it, either. Not a life for the brainy type here. But you go and mess up a lady, and a good lady too, and you'll have the boys patting you on the back."

He hesitated, my little trunk on his shoulder; then he came quite close to me, only to dart away again despairingly and run to the nearest yard. Cossacks were sitting there, shaving one another.

"Here, you soldiers," said the quartermaster, setting my little trunk down on the ground. "Comrade Savitsky's orders are that you're to take this chap in your billets, so no nonsense about it, because the chap's been through a lot in the learning line."

The quartermaster, purple in the face, left us without looking back. I raised my hand to my cap and saluted the Cossacks. A lad with long straight flaxen hair and the handsome face of the Ryazan Cossacks went over to my little trunk and tossed it out at the gate. Then he turned his back on me and with remarkable skill emitted a series of shameful noises.

"To your guns—number double-zero!" an older Cossack shouted at him, and burst out laughing. "Running fire!"

His guileless art exhausted, the lad made off. Then, crawling over the ground, I began to gather together the manuscript and tattered garments that had fallen out of the trunk. I gathered them up and carried them to the other end of the yard. Near the hut, on a brick stove, stood a cauldron in which pork was cooking. The steam that rose from it was like the far-off smoke of home in the village, and it mingled hunger with desperate loneliness in my head. Then I covered my little broken trunk with hay, turning it into a pillow, and lay down on the ground to read in *Pravda* Lenin's speech at the Second Congress of the Comintern. The sun fell upon me from behind the toothed hillocks, the Cossacks trod on my feet, the lad made fun of me untiringly, the beloved lines came toward me along a thorny path and could not reach me. Then I put aside the paper and went out to the landlady, who was spinning on the porch.

"Landlady," I said, "I've got to eat."

The old woman raised to me the diffused whites of her purblind eyes and lowered them again.

"Comrade," she said, after a pause, "what with all this going on, I want to go and hang myself."

"Christ!" I muttered, and pushed the old woman in the chest with my fist. "You don't suppose I'm going to go into explanations with you, do you?"

And turning around I saw somebody's sword lying within reach. A severe-looking goose was waddling about the yard, inoffensively preening its feathers, I overtook it and pressed it to the ground. Its head cracked beneath my boot, cracked and emptied itself. The white neck lay stretched out in the dung, the wings twitched.

"Christ!" I said, digging into the goose with my sword. "Go and cook it for me, landlady."

Her blind eyes and glasses glistening, the old woman picked up the slaughtered bird, wrapped it in her apron, and started to bear it off toward the kitchen.

"Comrade," she said to me, after a while, "I want to go and hang myself." And she closed the door behind her.

The Cossacks in the yard were already sitting around their cauldron. They sat motionless, stiff as heathen priests at a sacrifice, and had not looked at the goose.

"The lad's all right," one of them said, winking and scooping up the cabbage soup with his spoon.

The Cossacks commenced their supper with all the elegance and restraint of peasants who respect one another. And I wiped the sword with sand, went out at the gate, and came in again, depressed. Already the moon hung above the yard like a cheap earring.

"Hey, you," suddenly said Surovkov, an older Cossack. "Sit down and feed with us till your goose is done."

He produced a spare spoon from his boot and handed it to me. We supped up the cabbage soup they had made, and ate the pork.

"What's in the newspaper?" asked the flaxen-haired lad, making room for me.

"Lenin writes in the paper," I said, pulling out *Pravda*. "Lenin writes that there's a shortage of everything."

And loudly, like a triumphant man hard of hearing, I read Lenin's speech out to the Cossacks.

Evening wrapped about me the quickening moisture of its twilight sheets; evening laid a mother's hand upon my burning forehead. I read on and rejoiced, spying out exultingly the secret curve of Lenin's straight line.

"Truth tickles everyone's nostrils," said Surovkov, when I had come to the end. "The question is, how's it to be pulled from the heap. But he goes and strikes at it straight off like a hen pecking at a grain!"

This remark about Lenin was made by Surovkov, platoon commander of the Staff Squadron; after which we lay down to sleep in the hayloft. We slept, all six of us, beneath a wooden roof that let in the stars, warming one another, our legs intermingled. I dreamed: and in my dreams saw women. But my heart, stained with bloodshed, grated and brimmed over.

---

1. What enables the narrator to accept the brutality of his initiation into army life?
2. Does he have resources that will permit him to hold his own with his rougher comrades?
3. Is the killing of the goose what he is thinking of when he thinks of "bloodshed" at the end of the story?
4. Does the brevity of the story leave important things unaccounted for? What?

James Baldwin

Baldwin (1924–1987) was born in New York City. Son of a revivalist minister and himself active in the ministry for three years, he has drawn upon and refined the passionate eloquence of religious oratory as one ingredient of his style. He began his literary career while living in Paris, during a time when he had to support himself by a variety of odd jobs to supplement his income from writing. Recognition of his talents as a novelist and short story writer was paralleled by the attention paid to him as an essayist who illumined the American racial dilemma. He has directed our conscience to the inequities that blight our country. Much of his work has aimed at unraveling the repressive myths of white society and at healing the disastrous estrangement he finds in the lives of black people in America. His novels include: Go Tell It on the Mountain *(1953),* Giovanni's Room *(1957),* Another Country *(1962),* Tell Me How Long the Train's Been Gone *(1968),* If Beale Street Could Talk *(1974), and* Just Above My Head *(1979). His books of essays are:* Notes of a Native Son *(1955),* Nobody Knows My Name *(1961),* The Fire Next Time *(1963), and* No Name in the Street *(1972). His short stories are collected in* Going to Meet the Man *(1965).*

Sonny's Blues

I read about it in the paper, in the subway, on my way to work. I read it, and I couldn't believe it, and I read it again. Then perhaps I just stared at it, at the newsprint spelling out his name, spelling out the story. I stared at it in the swinging lights of the subway car, and in the faces and bodies of the people, and in my own face, trapped in the darkness which roared outside.

It was not to be believed and I kept telling myself that, as I walked from the subway station to the high school. And at the same time I couldn't doubt it. I was scared, scared for Sonny. He became real to me again. A great block of ice got settled in my belly and kept melting there slowly all day long, while I taught my classes algebra. It was a special kind of ice. It kept melting, sending trickles of ice water all up and down my veins, but it never got less. Sometimes it hardened and seemed to expand until I felt my guts were going to come spilling out or that I was going to choke or scream. This would always be at a moment when I was remembering some specific thing Sonny had once said or done.

When he was about as old as the boys in my classes his face had been bright and open, there was a lot of copper in it; and he'd had wonderfully direct brown eyes, and great gentleness and privacy. I wondered what he looked like now. He had been picked up, the evening before, in a raid on an apartment downtown, for peddling and using heroin.

I couldn't believe it: but what I mean by that is that I couldn't find any room for it anywhere inside me. I had kept it outside me for a long time. I hadn't wanted to know. I had had suspicions, but I didn't name them, I kept putting them away. I told myself that Sonny was wild, but he wasn't crazy. And he'd always been a good boy, he hadn't ever turned hard or evil or disrespectful, the way kids can, so quick, so quick, especially in Harlem. I didn't want to believe that I'd ever see my brother going down, coming to nothing, all that light in his face gone out, in the condition I'd already seen so many others. Yet it had happened and here I was, talking about algebra to a lot of boys who might, every one of them for all I knew, be popping off needles every time they went to the head.[1] Maybe it did more for them than algebra could.

I was sure that the first time Sonny had ever had horse,[2] he couldn't have been much older than these boys were now. These boys, now, were living as we'd been living then, they were growing up with a rush and their heads bumped abruptly against the low ceiling of their actual possibilities. They were filled with rage. All they really knew were two darknesses, the darkness of their lives, which was now closing in on them, and the darkness of the movies, which had blinded them to that other darkness, and in which they now, vindictively, dreamed, at once more together than they were at any other time, and more alone.

When the last bell rang, the last class ended, I let out my breath. It seemed I'd been holding it for all that time. My clothes were wet—I may have looked as though I'd been sitting in a steam bath, all dressed up, all afternoon. I sat alone in the classroom a long time. I listened to the boys outside, downstairs, shouting and cursing and laughing. Their laughter struck me for perhaps the first time. It was not the joyous laughter which—God knows why—one associates with children. It was mocking and insular, its intent was to denigrate. It was disenchanted, and in this, also, lay the authority of their curses. Perhaps I was listening to them because I was thinking about my brother and in them I heard my brother. And myself.

One boy was whistling a tune, at once very complicated and very

1. Toilet. 2. Heroin.

simple, it seemed to be pouring out of him as though he were a bird, and it sounded very cool and moving through all that harsh, bright air, only just holding its own through all those other sounds.

I stood up and walked over to the window and looked down into the courtyard. It was the beginning of the spring and the sap was rising in the boys. A teacher passed through them every now and again, quickly, as though he or she couldn't wait to get out of that courtyard, to get those boys out of their sight and off their minds. I started collecting my stuff. I thought I'd better get home and talk to Isabel.

The courtyard was almost deserted by the time I got downstairs. I saw this boy standing in the shadow of a doorway, looking just like Sonny. I almost called his name. Then I saw that it wasn't Sonny, but somebody we used to know, a boy from around our block. He'd been Sonny's friend. He'd never been mine, having been too young for me, and, anyway, I'd never liked him. And now, even though he was a grown-up man, he still hung around that block, still spent hours on the street corners, was always high and raggy. I used to run into him from time to time and he'd often work around to asking me for a quarter or fifty cents. He always had some real good excuse, too, and I always gave it to him. I don't know why.

But now, abruptly, I hated him. I couldn't stand the way he looked at me, partly like a dog, partly like a cunning child. I wanted to ask him what the hell he was doing in the school courtyard.

He sort of shuffled over to me, and he said, "I see you got the papers. So you already know about it."

"You mean about Sonny? Yes, I already know about it. How come they didn't get you?"

He grinned. It made him repulsive and it also brought to mind what he'd looked like as a kid. "I wasn't there. I stay away from them people."

"Good for you." I offered him a cigarette and I watched him through the smoke. "You come all the way down here just to tell me about Sonny?"

"That's right." He was sort of shaking his head and his eyes looked strange, as though they were about to cross. The bright sun deadened his damp dark brown skin and it made his eyes look yellow and showed up the dirt in his kinked hair. He smelled funky.[3] I moved a little away from him and I said, "Well, thanks. But I already know about it and I got to get home."

"I'll walk you a little ways," he said. We started walking. There were a couple of kids still loitering in the courtyard and one of them said goodnight to me and looked strangely at the boy beside me.

3. Unwashed.

"What're you going to do?" he asked me. "I mean, about Sonny?"

"Look. I haven't seen Sonny for over a year, I'm not sure I'm going to do anything. Anyway, what the hell *can* I do?"

"That's right," he said quickly, "ain't nothing you can do. Can't much help old Sonny no more, I guess."

It was what I was thinking and so it seemed to me he had no right to say it.

"I'm surprised at Sonny, though," he went on—he had a funny way of talking, he looked straight ahead as though he were talking to himself—"I thought Sonny was a smart boy, I thought he was too smart to get hung."

"I guess he thought so too," I said sharply, "and that's how he got hung. And how about you? You're pretty goddamn smart, I bet."

Then he looked directly at me, just for a minute. "I ain't smart," he said. "If I was smart, I'd have reached for a pistol a long time ago."

"Look. Don't tell *me* your sad story, if it was up to me, I'd give you one." Then I felt guilty—guilty, probably, for never having supposed that the poor bastard *had* a story of his own, much less a sad one, and I asked, quickly, "What's going to happen to him now?"

He didn't answer this. He was off by himself some place.

"Funny thing," he said, and from his tone we might have been discussing the quickest way to get to Brooklyn, "when I saw the papers this morning, the first thing I asked myself was if I had anything to do with it. I felt sort of responsible."

I began to listen more carefully. The subway station was on the corner, just before us, and I stopped. He stopped, too. We were in front of a bar and he ducked slightly, peering in, but whoever he was looking for didn't seem to be there. The juke box was blasting away with something black and bouncy and I half watched the barmaid as she danced her way from the juke box to her place behind the bar. And I watched her face as she laughingly responded to something someone said to her, still keeping time to the music. When she smiled one saw the little girl, one sensed the doomed, still-struggling woman beneath the battered face of the semi-whore.

"I never *give* Sonny nothing," the boy said finally, "but a long time ago I come to school high and Sonny asked me how it felt." He paused, I couldn't bear to watch him, I watched the barmaid, and I listened to the music which seemed to be causing the pavement to shake. "I told him it felt great." The music stopped, the barmaid paused and watched the juke box until the music began again. "It did."

All this was carrying me some place I didn't want to go. I certainly didn't want to know how it felt. It filled everything, the people, the houses, the music, the dark, quicksilver barmaid, with menace; and this menace was their reality.

"What's going to happen to him now?" I asked again.

"They'll send him away some place and they'll try to cure him." He shook his head. "Maybe he'll even think he's kicked the habit. Then they'll let him loose"—he gestured, throwing his cigarette into the gutter. "That's all."

"What do you mean, that's *all?*"

But I knew what he meant.

"I *mean,* that's *all.*" He turned his head and looked at me, pulling down the corners of his mouth. "Don't you know what I mean?" he asked, softly.

"How the hell *would* I know what you mean?" I almost whispered it, I don't know why.

"That's right," he said to the air, "how would *he* know what I mean?" He turned toward me again, patient and calm, and yet I somehow felt him shaking, shaking as though he were going to fall apart. I felt that ice in my guts again, the dread I'd felt all afternoon; and again I watched the barmaid, moving about the bar, washing glasses, and singing. "Listen. They'll let him out and then it'll just start all over again. That's what I mean."

"You mean—they'll let him out. And then he'll just start working his way back in again. You mean he'll never kick the habit. Is that what you mean?"

"That's right," he said, cheerfully. "*You* see what I mean."

"Tell me," I said at last, "why does he want to die? He must want to die, he's killing himself, why does he want to die?"

He looked at me in surprise. He licked his lips. "He don't want to die. He wants to live. Don't nobody want to die, ever."

Then I wanted to ask him—too many things. He could not have answered, or if he had, I could not have borne the answers. I started walking. "Well, I guess it's none of my business."

"It's going to be rough on old Sonny," he said. We reached the subway station. "This is your station?" he asked. I nodded. I took one step down. "Damn!" he said, suddenly. I looked up at him. He grinned again. "Damn it if I didn't leave all my money home. You ain't got a dollar on you, have you? Just for a couple of days, is all."

All at once something inside gave and threatened to come pouring out of me. I didn't hate him any more. I felt that in another moment I'd start crying like a child.

"Sure," I said. "Don't sweat." I looked in my wallet and didn't have a dollar, I only had a five. "Here," I said. "That hold you?"

He didn't look at it—he didn't want to look at it. A terrible, closed look came over his face, as though he were keeping the number on the bill a secret from him and me. "Thanks," he said, and now he was dying to see me go. "Don't worry about Sonny. Maybe I'll write him or something."

"Sure," I said. "You do that. So long."

"Be seeing you," he said. I went on down the steps.

And I didn't write Sonny or send him anything for a long time. When I finally did, it was just after my little girl died, and he wrote me back a letter which made me feel like a bastard.

Here's what he said:

Dear brother,

You don't know how much I needed to hear from you. I wanted to write you many a time but I dug how much I must have hurt you and so I didn't write. But now I feel like a man who's been trying to climb up out of some deep, real deep and funky hole and just saw the sun up there, outside. I got to get outside.

I can't tell you much about how I got here. I mean I don't know how to tell you. I guess I was afraid of something or I was trying to escape from something and you know I have never been very strong in the head (smile). I'm glad Mama and Daddy are dead and can't see what's happened to their son and I swear if I'd known what I was doing I would never have hurt you so, you and a lot of other fine people who were nice to me and who believed in me.

I don't want you to think it had anything to do with me being a musician. It's more than that. Or maybe less than that. I can't get anything straight in my head down here and I try not to think about what's going to happen to me when I get outside again. Sometime I think I'm going to flip and *never* get outside and sometime I think I'll come straight back. I tell you one thing, though, I'd rather blow my brains out than go through this again. But that's what they all say, so they tell me. If I tell you when I'm coming to New York and if you could meet me, I sure would appreciate it. Give my love to Isabel and the kids and I was sure sorry to hear about little Gracie. I wish I could be like Mama and say the Lord's will be done, but I don't know it seems to me that trouble is the one thing that never does get stopped and I don't know what good it does to blame it on the Lord. But maybe it does some good if you believe it.

Your brother,
Sonny

Then I kept in constant touch with him and I sent him whatever I could and I went to meet him when he came back to New York. When I saw him many things I thought I had forgotten came flooding back to me. This was because I had begun, finally, to wonder about

Sonny, about the life that Sonny lived inside. This life, whatever it was, had made him older and thinner and it had deepened the distant stillness in which he had always moved. He looked very unlike my baby brother. Yet, when he smiled, when we shook hands, the baby brother I'd never known looked out from the depths of his private life, like an animal waiting to be coaxed into the light.

"How you been keeping?" he asked me.

"All right. And you?"

"Just fine." He was smiling all over his face. "It's good to see you again."

"It's good to see you."

The seven years' difference in our ages lay between us like a chasm: I wondered if these years would ever operate between us as a bridge. I was remembering, and it made it hard to catch my breath, that I had been there when he was born; and I had heard the first words he had ever spoken. When he started to walk, he walked from our mother straight to me. I caught him just before he fell when he took the first steps he ever took in this world.

"How's Isabel?"

"Just fine. She's dying to see you."

"And the boys?"

"They're fine, too. They're anxious to see their uncle."

"Oh, come on. You know they don't remember me."

"Are you kidding? Of course they remember you."

He grinned again. We got into a taxi. We had a lot to say to each other, far too much to know how to begin.

As the taxi began to move, I asked, "You still want to go to India?"

He laughed. "You still remember that. Hell, no. This place is Indian enough for me."

"It used to belong to them," I said.

And he laughed again. "They damn sure knew what they were doing when they got rid of it."

Years ago, when he was around fourteen, he'd been all hipped on the idea of going to India. He read books about people sitting on rocks, naked, in all kinds of weather, but mostly bad, naturally, and walking barefoot through hot coals and arriving at wisdom. I used to say that it sounded to me as though they were getting away from wisdom as fast as they could. I think he sort of looked down on me for that.

"Do you mind," he asked, "if we have the driver drive alongside the park? On the west side—I haven't seen the city in so long."

"Of course not," I said. I was afraid that I might sound as though I were humoring him, but I hoped he wouldn't take it that way.

So we drove along, between the green of the park and the stony, lifeless elegance of hotels and apartment buildings, toward the vivid, killing streets of our childhood. These streets hadn't changed, though housing projects jutted up out of them now like rocks in the middle of a boiling sea. Most of the houses in which we had grown up had vanished, as had the stores from which we had stolen, the basements in which we had first tried sex, the rooftops from which we had hurled tin cans and bricks. But houses exactly like the houses of our past yet dominated the landscape, boys exactly like the boys we once had been found themselves smothering in these houses, came down into the streets for light and air and found themselves encircled by disaster. Some escaped the trap, most didn't. Those who got out always left something of themselves behind, as some animals amputate a leg and leave it in the trap. It might be said, perhaps, that I had escaped, after all, I was a school teacher; or that Sonny had, he hadn't lived in Harlem for years. Yet, as the cab moved uptown through streets which seemed, with a rush, to darken with dark people, and as I covertly studied Sonny's face, it came to me that what we both were seeking through our separate cab windows was that part of ourselves which had been left behind. It's always at the hour of trouble and confrontation that the missing member aches.

We hit 110th Street and started rolling up Lenox Avenue. And I'd known this avenue all my life, but it seemed to me again, as it had seemed on the day I'd first heard about Sonny's trouble, filled with a hidden menace which was its very breath of life.

"We almost there," said Sonny.

"Almost." We were both too nervous to say anything more.

We live in a housing project. It hasn't been up long. A few days after it was up it seemed uninhabitably new, now, of course, it's already rundown. It looks like a parody of the good, clean, faceless life—God knows the people who live in it do their best to make it a parody. The beat-looking grass lying around isn't enough to make their lives green, the hedges will never hold out the streets, and they know it. The big windows fool no one, they aren't big enough to make space out of no space. They don't bother with the windows, they watch the TV screen instead. The playground is most popular with the children who don't play at jacks, or skip rope, or roller skate, or swing, and they can be found in it after dark. We moved in partly because it's not too far from where I teach, and partly for the kids; but it's really just like the houses in which Sonny and I grew up. The same things happen, they'll have the same things to remember. The moment Sonny and I started into the house I had the feeling that I was simply bringing him back into the danger he had almost died trying to escape.

Sonny has never been talkative. So I don't know why I was sure he'd be dying to talk to me when supper was over the first night.

Everything went fine, the oldest boy remembered him, and the youngest boy liked him, and Sonny had remembered to bring something for each of them; and Isabel, who is really much nicer than I am, more open and giving, had gone to a lot of trouble about dinner and was genuinely glad to see him. And she's always been able to tease Sonny in a way that I haven't. It was nice to see her face so vivid again and to hear her laugh and watch her make Sonny laugh. She wasn't, or, anyway, she didn't seem to be, at all uneasy or embarrassed. She chatted as though there were no subject which had to be avoided and she got Sonny past his first, faint stiffness. And thank God she was there, for I was filled with that icy dread again. Everything I did seemed awkward to me, and everything I said sounded freighted with hidden meaning. I was trying to remember everything I'd heard about dope addiction and I couldn't help watching Sonny for signs. I wasn't doing it out of malice. I was trying to find out something about my brother. I was dying to hear him tell me he was safe.

"Safe!" my father grunted, whenever Mama suggested trying to move to a neighborhood which might be safer for children. "Safe, hell! Ain't no place safe for kids, nor nobody."

He always went on like this, but he wasn't, ever, really as bad as he sounded, not even on weekends, when he got drunk. As a matter of fact, he was always on the lookout for "something a little better," but he died before he found it. He died suddenly, during a drunken weekend in the middle of the war, when Sonny was fifteen. He and Sonny hadn't ever got on too well. And this was partly because Sonny was the apple of his father's eye. It was because he loved Sonny so much and was frightened for him, that he was always fighting with him. It doesn't do any good to fight with Sonny. Sonny just moves back, inside himself, where he can't be reached. But the principal reason that they never hit it off is that they were so much alike. Daddy was big and rough and loud-talking, just the opposite of Sonny, but they both had—that same privacy.

Mama tried to tell me something about this, just after Daddy died. I was home on leave from the army.

This was the last time I ever saw my mother alive. Just the same, this picture gets all mixed up in my mind with pictures I had of her when she was younger. The way I always see her is the way she used to be on a Sunday afternoon, say, when the old folks were talking after the big Sunday dinner. I always see her wearing pale blue. She'd be sitting on the sofa. And my father would be sitting in the easy chair, not far from her. And the living room would be full of church folks and relatives. There they sit, in chairs all around the living room, and the night is creeping up outside, but nobody knows it yet. You can see the darkness growing against the windowpanes and you hear the street noises every now and again, or maybe the jangling beat of a tambourine from one of the churches close by, but it's real quiet in the room. For a moment nobody's talking, but every face looks darkening, like the sky outside. And my mother rocks a little from the waist, and my father's eyes are closed. Everyone is looking at something a child can't see. For a minute they've forgotten the children. Maybe a kid is lying on the rug, half asleep. Maybe somebody's got a kid in his lap and is absent-mindedly stroking the kid's head. Maybe there's a kid, quiet and big-eyed, curled up in a big chair in the corner. The silence, the darkness coming, and the darkness in the faces frighten the child obscurely. He hopes that the hand which strokes his forehead will never stop—will never die. He hopes that there will never come a time when the old folks won't be sitting around the living room, talking about where they've come from, and what they've seen, and what's happened to them and their kinfolk.

But something deep and watchful in the child knows that this is bound to end, is already ending. In a moment someone will get up and turn on the light. Then the old folks will remember the children and they won't talk any more that day. And when light fills the room, the child is filled with darkness. He knows that every time this happens he's moved just a little closer to that darkness outside. The darkness outside is what the old folks have been talking about. It's what they've come from. It's what they endure. The child knows that they won't talk any more because if he knows too much about what's happened to *them*, he'll know too much too soon, about what's going to happen to *him*.

The last time I talked to my mother, I remember I was restless. I wanted to get out and see Isabel. We weren't married then and we had a lot to straighten out between us.

There Mama sat, in black, by the window. She was humming an old church song, *Lord, you brought me from a long ways off*. Sonny was out somewhere. Mama kept watching the streets.

"I don't know," she said, "if I'll ever see you again, after you go off from here. But I hope you'll remember the things I tried to teach you."

"Don't talk like that," I said, and smiled. "You'll be here a long time yet."

She smiled, too, but she said nothing. She was quiet for a long time. And I said, "Mama, don't you worry about nothing. I'll be writing all the time, and you be getting the checks. . . ."

"I want to talk to you about your brother," she said, suddenly. "If anything happens to me he ain't going to have nobody to look out for him."

"Mama," I said, "ain't nothing going to happen to you *or* Sonny. Sonny's all right. He's a good boy and he's got good sense."

"It ain't a question of his being a good boy," Mama said, "nor of his having good sense. It ain't only the bad ones, nor yet the dumb ones that gets sucked under." She stopped, looking at me. "Your Daddy once had a brother," she said, and she smiled in a way that made me feel she was in pain. "You didn't never know that, did you?"

"No," I said, "I never knew that," and I watched her face.

"Oh, yes," she said, "your Daddy had a brother." She looked out of the window again. "I know you never saw your Daddy cry. But *I* did—many a time, through all these years."

I asked her, "What happened to his brother? How come nobody's ever talked about him?"

This was the first time I ever saw my mother look old.

"His brother got killed," she said, "when he was just a little younger than you are now. I knew him. He was a fine boy. He was maybe a little full of the devil, but he didn't mean nobody no harm."

Then she stopped and the room was silent, exactly as it had sometimes been on those Sunday afternoons. Mama kept looking out into the streets.

"He used to have a job in the mill," she said, "and, like all young folks, he just liked to perform on Saturday nights. Saturday nights, him and your father would drift around to different places, go to dances and things like that, or just sit around with people they knew, and your father's brother would sing, he had a fine voice, and play along with himself on his guitar. Well, this particular Saturday night, him and your father was coming home from some place, and they were both a little drunk and there was a moon that night, it was bright like day. Your father's brother was feeling kind of good, and he was whistling to himself, and he had his guitar slung over his shoulder. They was coming down a hill and beneath them was a road that turned off from the highway. Well, your father's brother, being always kind of frisky, decided to run down this hill, and he did, with that guitar banging and clanging behind him, and he ran across the road, and he was making water behind a tree. And your father was sort of amused at him and he was still coming down the hill, kind of slow. Then he heard a car motor and that same minute his brother stepped from behind the tree, into the road, in the moonlight. And he started to cross the road. And your father started to run down the hill, he says he don't know why. This car was full of white men. They was all drunk, and when they seen your father's brother they let out a great whoop and holler and they aimed the car straight at him. They was having fun, they just wanted to scare him, the way they do sometimes, you know. But they was drunk. And I guess the boy, being drunk, too, and scared, kind of lost his head. By the time he jumped it was too late. Your father says he heard his brother scream when the car rolled over him, and he heard the wood of that guitar when it give, and he heard them strings go flying, and he heard them white men shouting, and the car kept on a-going and it ain't stopped till this day. And, time your father got down the hill, his brother weren't nothing but blood and pulp."

Tears were gleaming on my mother's face. There wasn't anything I could say.

"He never mentioned it," she said, "because I never let him mention it before you children. Your Daddy was like a crazy man that night and for many a night thereafter. He says he never in his life seen anything as dark as that road after the lights of that car had gone away. Weren't nothing, weren't nobody on that road, just your Daddy and his brother and that busted guitar. Oh, yes. Your Daddy never did really get right again. Till the day he died he weren't sure but that every white man he saw was the man that killed his brother."

She stopped and took out her handkerchief and dried her eyes and looked at me.

"I ain't telling you all this," she said, "to make you scared or bitter or to make you hate nobody. I'm telling you this because you got a brother. And the world ain't changed."

I guess I didn't want to believe this. I guess she saw this in my face. She turned away from me, toward the window again, searching those streets.

"But I praise my Redeemer," she said at last, "that He called your Daddy home before me. I ain't saying it to throw no flowers at myself, but, I declare, it keeps me from feeling too cast down to know I helped your father get safely through this world. Your father always acted like he was the roughest, strongest man on earth. And everybody took him to be like that. But if he hadn't had me there—to see his tears!"

She was crying again. Still, I couldn't move. I said, "Lord, Lord, Mama, I didn't know it was like that."

"Oh, honey," she said, "there's a lot that you don't know. But you are going to find out." She stood up from the window and came over to me. "You got to hold on to your brother," she said, "and don't let him fall, no matter what it looks like is happening to him and no matter how evil you gets with him. You going to be evil with him many a time. But don't you forget what I told you, you hear?"

"I won't forget," I said. "Don't you worry, I won't forget. I won't let nothing happen to Sonny."

My mother smiled as though she was amused at something she saw in my face. Then, "You may not be able to stop nothing from happening. But you got to let him know you's *there*."

Two days later I was married, and then I was gone. And I had a lot of things on my mind and I pretty well forgot my promise to Mama until I got shipped home on a special furlough for her funeral.

And, after the funeral, with just Sonny and me alone in the empty kitchen, I tried to find out something about him.

"What do you want to do?" I asked him.

"I'm going to be a musician," he said.

For he had graduated, in the time I had been away, from dancing to the juke box to finding out who was playing what, and what they were doing with it, and he had bought himself a set of drums.

"You mean, you want to be a drummer?" I somehow had the feeling that being a drummer might be all right for other people but not for my brother Sonny.

"I don't think," he said, looking at me very gravely, "that I'll ever be a good drummer. But I think I can play a piano."

I frowned. I'd never played the role of the oldest brother quite so seriously before, had scarcely ever, in fact, *asked* Sonny a damn thing. I sensed myself in the presence of something I didn't really know how to handle, didn't understand. So I made my frown a little deeper as I asked: "What kind of musician do you want to be?"

He grinned. "How many kinds do you think there are?"

"Be *serious*," I said.

He laughed, throwing his head back, and then looked at me. "I *am* serious."

"Well, then, for Christ's sake, stop kidding around and answer a serious question. I mean, do you want to be a concert pianist, you want to play classical music and all that, or—or what?" Long before I finished he was laughing again. "For Christ's *sake*, Sonny!"

He sobered, but with difficulty. "I'm sorry. But you sound so—*scared!*" and he was off again.

"Well, you may think it's funny now, baby, but it's not going to be so funny when you have to make your living at it, let me tell you *that*." I was furious because I knew he was laughing at me and I didn't know why.

"No," he said, very sober now, and afraid, perhaps, that he'd hurt me, "I don't want to be a classical pianist. That isn't what interests me. I mean"—he paused, looking hard at me, as though his eyes would help me to understand, and then gestured helplessly, as though perhaps his hand would help—"I mean, I'll have a lot of studying to do, and I'll have to study *everything*, but, I mean, I want to play *with*—jazz musicians." He stopped. "I want to play jazz," he said.

Well, the word had never before sounded as heavy, as real, as it sounded that afternoon in Sonny's mouth. I just looked at him and I was probably frowning a real frown by this time. I simply couldn't see why on earth he'd want to spend his time hanging around nightclubs, clowning around on bandstands, while people pushed each other around a dance floor. It seemed—beneath him, somehow. I had never thought about it before, had never been forced to, but I suppose I had always put jazz musicians in a class with what Daddy called "good-time people."

"Are you *serious?*"

"Hell, *yes*, I'm serious."

He looked more helpless than ever, and annoyed, and deeply hurt.

I suggested, helpfully: "You mean—like Louis Armstrong?"

His face closed as though I'd struck him. "No. I'm not talking about none of that old-time, down home crap."

"Well, look, Sonny, I'm sorry, don't get mad. I just don't altogether get it, that's all. Name somebody—you know, a jazz musician you admire."

"Bird."

"Who?"

"Bird! Charlie Parker![4] Don't they teach you nothing in the goddamn army?"

I lit a cigarette. I was surprised and then a little amused to discover that I was trembling. "I've been out of touch," I said. "You'll have to be patient with me. Now. Who's this Parker character?"

"He's just one of the greatest jazz musicians alive," said Sonny, sullenly, his hands in his pockets, his back to me. "Maybe *the* greatest," he added, bitterly, "that's probably why *you* never heard of him."

"All right," I said, "I'm ignorant. I'm sorry. I'll go out and buy all the cat's records right away, all right?"

"It don't," said Sonny, with dignity, "make any difference to me. I don't care what you listen to. Don't do me no favors."

I was beginning to realize that I'd never seen him so upset before. With another part of my mind I was thinking that this would probably turn out to be one of those things kids go through and that I shouldn't make it seem important by pushing it too hard. Still, I didn't think it would do any harm to ask: "Doesn't all this take a lot of time? Can you make a living at it?"

He turned back to me and half leaned, half sat, on the kitchen table. "Everything takes time," he said, "and—well, yes, sure, I can make a living at it. But what I don't seem to be able to make you understand is that it's the only thing I want to do."

"Well, Sonny," I said gently, "you know people can't always do exactly what they *want* to do—"

4. Charlie "Bird" Parker (1920–1955), musician for whom Birdland ballroom in New York was named. A founder of the new jazz that began to flourish in the 1940's.

"*No,* I don't know that," said Sonny, surprising me. "I think people *ought* to do what they want to do, what else are they alive for?"

"You getting to be a big boy," I said desperately, "it's time you started thinking about your future."

"I'm thinking about my future," said Sonny, grimly. "I think about it all the time."

I gave up. I decided, if he didn't change his mind, that we could always talk about it later. "In the meantime," I said, "you got to finish school." We had already decided that he'd have to move in with Isabel and her folks. I knew this wasn't the ideal arrangement because Isabel's folks are inclined to be dicty[5] and they hadn't especially wanted Isabel to marry me. But I didn't know what else to do. "And we have to get you fixed up at Isabel's."

There was a long silence. He moved from the kitchen table to the window. "That's a terrible idea. You know it yourself."

"Do you have a *better* idea?"

He just walked up and down the kitchen for a minute. He was as tall as I was. He had started to shave. I suddenly had the feeling that I didn't know him at all.

He stopped at the kitchen table and picked up my cigarettes. Looking at me with a kind of mocking, amused defiance, he put one between his lips. "You mind?"

"You smoking already?"

He lit the cigarette and nodded, watching me through the smoke. "I just wanted to see if I'd have the courage to smoke in front of you." He grinned and blew a great cloud of smoke to the ceiling. "It was easy." He looked at my face. "Come on, now. I bet you was smoking at my age, tell the truth."

I didn't say anything but the truth was on my face, and he laughed. But now there was something very strained in his laugh. "Sure. And I bet that ain't all you was doing."

He was frightening me a little. "Cut the crap," I said. "We already decided that you was going to go and live at Isabel's. Now what's got into you all of a sudden?"

"*You* decided it," he pointed out. "*I* didn't decide nothing." He stopped in front of me, leaning against the stove, arms loosely folded. "Look, brother. I don't want to stay in Harlem no more, I really don't." He was very earnest. He looked at me, then over toward the kitchen window. There was something in his eyes I'd never seen before, some thoughtfulness, some worry all his own. He rubbed the muscle of one arm. "It's time I was getting out of here."

"Where do you want to *go,* Sonny?"

5. Dictatorial, overbearing.

to join the army. Or the navy, I don't care. If I say I'm ., they'll believe me."

en I got mad. It was because I was so scared. "You must be You goddamn fool, what the hell do you want to go and join the y for?"

"I just told you. To get out of Harlem."

"Sonny, you haven't even finished *school*. And if you really want to be a musician, how do you expect to study if you're in the *army?*"

He looked at me, trapped, and in anguish. "There's ways. I might be able to work out some kind of deal. Anyway, I'll have the G.I. Bill when I come out."

"*If* you come out." We stared at each other. "Sonny, please. Be reasonable. I know the setup is far from perfect. But we got to do the best we can."

"I ain't learning nothing in school," he said. "Even when I go." He turned away from me and opened the window and threw his cigarette out into the narrow alley. I watched his back. "At least, I ain't learning nothing you'd want me to learn." He slammed the window so hard I thought the glass would fly out, and turned back to me. "And I'm sick of the stink of these garbage cans!"

"Sonny," I said, "I know how you feel. But if you don't finish school now, you're going to be sorry later that you didn't." I grabbed him by the shoulders. "And you only got another year. It ain't so bad. And I'll come back and I swear I'll help you do *whatever* you want to do. Just try to put up with it till I come back. Will you please do that? For me?"

He didn't answer and he wouldn't look at me.

"Sonny. You hear me?"

He pulled away. "I hear you. But you never hear anything *I* say."

I didn't know what to say to that. He looked out of the window and then back at me. "OK," he said, and sighed. "I'll try."

Then I said, trying to cheer him up a little, "They got a piano at Isabel's. You can practice on it."

And as a matter of fact, it did cheer him up for a minute. "That's right," he said to himself. "I forgot that." His face relaxed a little. But the worry, the thoughtfulness, played on it still, the way shadows play on a face which is staring into the fire.

But I thought I'd never hear the end of that piano. At first, Isabel would write me, saying how nice it was that Sonny was so serious about his music and how, as soon as he came in from school, or wherever he had been when he was supposed to be at school, he went straight to that piano and stayed there until suppertime. And, after supper, he went back to that piano and stayed there until everybody went to bed.

He was at the piano all day Saturday and all day Sunday. Then he bought a record player and started playing records. He'd play one record over and over again, all day long sometimes, and he'd improvise along with it on the piano. Or he'd play one section of the record, one chord, one change, one progression, then he'd do it on the piano. Then back to the record. Then back to the piano.

Well, I really don't know how they stood it. Isabel finally confessed that it wasn't like living with a person at all, it was like living with sound. And the sound didn't make any sense to her, didn't make any sense to any of them—naturally. They began, in a way, to be afflicted by this presence that was living in their home. It was as though Sonny were some sort of god, or monster. He moved in an atmosphere which wasn't like theirs at all. They fed him and he ate, he washed himself, he walked in and out of their door; he certainly wasn't nasty or unpleasant or rude, Sonny isn't any of those things; but it was as though he were all wrapped up in some cloud, some fire, some vision all his own; and there wasn't any way to reach him.

At the same time, he wasn't really a man yet, he was still a child, and they had to watch out for him in all kinds of ways. They certainly couldn't throw him out. Neither did they dare to make a great scene about that piano because even they dimly sensed, as I sensed, from so many thousands of miles away, that Sonny was at that piano playing for his life.

But he hadn't been going to school. One day a letter came from the school board and Isabel's mother got it—there had, apparently, been other letters but Sonny had torn them up. This day, when Sonny came in, Isabel's mother showed him the letter and asked where he'd been spending his time. And she finally got it out of him that he'd been down in Greenwich Village, with musicians and other characters, in a white girl's apartment. And this scared her and she started to scream at him and what came up, once she began—though she denies it to this day—was what sacrifices they were making to give Sonny a decent home and how little he appreciated it.

Sonny didn't play the piano that day. By evening, Isabel's mother had calmed down but then there was the old man to deal with, and Isabel herself. Isabel says she did her best to be calm but she broke down and started crying. She says she just watched Sonny's face. She could tell, by watching him, what was happening with him. And what was happening was that they penetrated his cloud, they had reached him. Even if their fingers had been a thousand times more gentle than human fingers ever are, he could hardly help feeling that they had stripped him naked and were spitting on that nakedness. For he also had to see that his presence, that music, which was life or death to him, had been torture for them and that they had endured it, not at all for his sake, but only for mine. And Sonny couldn't take that. He can take it a little better today than he could then but he's still not very good at it and, frankly, I don't know anybody who is.

The silence of the next few days must have been louder than the sound of all the music ever played since time began. One morning, before she went to work, Isabel was in his room for something and she suddenly realized that all of his records were gone. And she knew for certain that he was gone. And he was. He went as far as the navy would carry him. He finally sent me a postcard from some place in Greece and that was the first I knew that Sonny was still alive. I didn't see him any more until we were both back in New York and the war had long been over.

He was a man by then, of course, but I wasn't willing to see it. He came by the house from time to time, but we fought almost every time we met. I didn't like the way he carried himself, loose and dream-like all the time, and I didn't like his friends, and his music seemed to be merely an excuse for the life he led. It sounded just that weird and disordered.

Then we had a fight, a pretty awful fight, and I didn't see him for months. By and by I looked him up, where he was living, in a furnished room in the Village, and I tried to make it up. But there were lots of other people in the room and Sonny just lay on his bed, and he wouldn't come downstairs with me, and he treated these other people as though they were his family and I weren't. So I got mad and then he got mad, and then I told him that he might just as well be dead as live the way he was living. Then he stood up and he told me not to worry about him any more in life, that he *was* dead as far as I was concerned. Then he pushed me to the door and the other people looked on as though nothing were happening, and he slammed the door behind me. I stood in the hallway, staring at the door. I heard somebody laugh in the room and then the tears came to my eyes. I started down the steps, whistling to keep from crying, I kept whistling to myself, *You going to need me, baby, one of these cold, rainy days.*

I read about Sonny's trouble in the spring. Little Grace died in the fall. She was a beautiful little girl. But she only lived a little over two years. She died of polio and she suffered. She had a slight fever for a couple of days, but it didn't seem like anything and we just kept her in bed. And we would certainly have called the doctor, but the fever dropped, she seemed to be all right. So we thought it had just been a cold. Then, one day, she was up, playing, Isabel was in the kitchen fixing lunch for the two boys when they'd come in from school, and she heard Grace fall down in the living room. When you have a lot of children you don't always start running when one of them falls, unless they start screaming or something. And, this time, Gracie was quiet.

Yet, Isabel says that when she heard that *thump* and then that silence, something happened to her to make her afraid. And she ran to the living room and there was little Grace on the floor, all twisted up, and the reason she hadn't screamed was that she couldn't get her breath. And when she did scream, it was the worst sound, Isabel says, that she'd ever heard in all her life, and she still hears it sometimes in her dreams. Isabel will sometimes wake me up with a low, moaning, strangling sound and I have to be quick to awaken her and hold her to me and where Isabel is weeping against me seems a mortal wound.

I think I may have written Sonny the very day that little Grace was buried. I was sitting in the living room in the dark, by myself, and I suddenly thought of Sonny. My trouble made his real.

One Saturday afternoon, when Sonny had been living with us, or anyway, been in our house, for nearly two weeks, I found myself wandering aimlessly about the living room, drinking from a can of beer, and trying to work up courage to search Sonny's room. He was out, he was usually out whenever I was home, and Isabel had taken the children to see their grandparents. Suddenly I was standing still in front of the living room window, watching Seventh Avenue. The idea of searching Sonny's room made me still. I scarcely dared to admit to myself what I'd be searching for. I didn't know what I'd do if I found it. Or if I didn't.

On the sidewalk across from me, near the entrance to a barbecue joint, some people were holding an old-fashioned revival meeting. The barbecue cook, wearing a dirty white apron, his conked[6] hair reddish and metallic in the pale sun, and a cigarette between his lips, stood in the doorway, watching them. Kids and older people paused in their errands and stood there, along with some older men and a couple of very tough-looking women who watched everything that happened on the avenue, as though they owned it, or were maybe owned by it. Well, they were watching this, too. The revival was being carried on by three sisters in black, and a brother. All they had were their voices and their Bibles and a tambourine. The brother was testifying[7] and while he testified two of the sisters stood together, seeming to say, amen, and the third sister walked around with the tambourine outstretched and a couple of people dropped coins into it. Then the brother's testimony ended and the sister who had been taking up the collection dumped the coins into her palm and transferred them to the pocket of her long black robe. Then she raised both hands, striking the tambourine against the air, and then against one hand, and she started to sing. And the two other sisters and the brother joined in.

It was strange, suddenly, to watch, though I had been seeing

6. Straightened and greased. 7. Proclaiming his religious belief.

these meetings all my life. So, of course, had everybody else down there. Yet, they paused and watched and listened and I stood still at the window. " *'Tis the old ship of Zion,*" they sang, and the sister with the tambourine kept a steady, jangling beat, "*it has rescued many a thousand!*" Not a soul under the sound of their voices was hearing this song for the first time, not one of them had been rescued. Nor had they seen much in the way of rescue work being done around them. Neither did they especially believe in the holiness of the three sisters and the brother, they knew too much about them, knew where they lived, and how. The woman with the tambourine, whose voice dominated the air, whose face was bright with joy, was divided by very little from the woman who stood watching her, a cigarette between her heavy, chapped lips, her hair a cuckoo's nest, her face scarred and swollen from many beatings, and her black eyes glittering like coal. Perhaps they both knew this, which was why, when, as rarely, they addressed each other, they addressed each other as Sister. As the singing filled the air the watching, listening faces underwent a change, the eyes focusing on something within; the music seemed to soothe a poison out of them; and time seemed, nearly, to fall away from the sullen, belligerent, battered faces, as though they were fleeing back to their first condition, while dreaming of their last. The barbecue cook half shook his head and smiled, and dropped his cigarette and disappeared into his joint. A man fumbled in his pockets for change and stood holding it in his hand impatiently, as though he had just remembered a pressing appointment further up the avenue. He looked furious. Then I saw Sonny, standing on the edge of the crowd. He was carrying a wide, flat notebook with a green cover, and it made him look, from where I was standing, almost like a schoolboy. The coppery sun brought out the copper in his skin, he was very faintly smiling, standing very still. Then the singing stopped, the tambourine turned into a collection plate again. The furious man dropped in his coins and vanished, so did a couple of the women, and Sonny dropped some change in the plate, looking directly at the woman with a little smile. He started across the avenue, toward the house. He has a slow, loping walk, something like the way Harlem hipsters walk, only he's imposed on this his own half-beat. I had never really noticed it before.

I stayed at the window, both relieved and apprehensive. As Sonny disappeared from my sight, they began singing again. And they were still singing when his key turned in the lock.

"Hey," he said.

"Hey, yourself. You want some beer?"

"No. Well, maybe." But he came up to the window and stood beside me, looking out. "What a warm voice," he said.

They were singing *If I could only hear my mother pray again!*

"Yes," I said, "and she can sure beat that tambourine."

"But what a terrible song," he said, and laughed. He dropped his notebook on the sofa and disappeared into the kitchen. "Where's Isabel and the kids?"

"I think they want to see their grandparents. You hungry?"

"No." He came back into the living room with his can of beer. "You want to come some place with me tonight?"

I sensed, I don't know how, that I couldn't possibly say no. "Sure. Where?"

He sat down on the sofa and picked up his notebook and started leafing through it. "I'm going to sit in with some fellows in a joint in the Village."

"You mean, you're going to play, tonight?"

"That's right." He took a swallow of his beer and moved back to the window. He gave me a sidelong look. "If you can stand it."

"I'll try," I said.

He smiled to himself and we both watched as the meeting across the way broke up. The three sisters and the brother, heads bowed, were singing *God be with you till we meet again.* The faces around them were very quiet. Then the song ended. The small crowd dispersed. We watched the three women and the lone man walk slowly up the avenue.

"When she was singing before," said Sonny, abruptly, "her voice reminded me for a minute of what heroin feels like sometimes—when it's in your veins. It makes you feel sort of warm and cool at the same time. And distant. And—and sure." He sipped his beer, very deliberately not looking at me. I watched his face. "It makes you feel—in control. Sometimes you've got to have that feeling."

"Do you?" I sat down slowly in the easy chair.

"Sometimes." He went to the sofa and picked up his notebook again. "Some people do."

"In order," I asked, "to play?" And my voice was very ugly, full of contempt and anger.

"Well"—he looked at me with great, troubled eyes, as though, in fact, he hoped his eyes would tell me things he could never otherwise say—"they *think* so. And *if* they think so—!"

"And what do *you* think?" I asked.

He sat on the sofa and put his can of beer on the floor. "I don't know," he said, and I couldn't be sure if he were answering my question or pursuing his thoughts. His face didn't tell me. "It's not so much to *play.* It's to *stand* it, to be able to make it at all. On any level." He frowned and smiled: "In order to keep from shaking to pieces."

"But these friends of yours," I said, "they seem to shake themselves to pieces pretty goddamn fast."

"Maybe." He played with the notebook. And something told me that I should curb my tongue, that Sonny was doing his best to talk, that I should listen. "But of course you only know the ones that've gone to pieces. Some don't—or at least they haven't *yet* and that's just about all *any* of us can say." He paused. "And then there are some who just live, really, in hell, and they know it and they see what's happening and they go right on. I don't know." He sighed, dropped the notebook, folded his arms. "Some guys, you can tell from the way they play, they on something *all* the time. And you can see that, well, it makes something real for them. But of course," he picked up his beer from the floor and sipped it and put the can down again, "they *want* to, too, you've got to see that. Even some of them that say they don't—*some*, not all."

"And what about you?" I asked—I couldn't help it. "What about you? Do *you* want to?"

He stood up and walked to the window and I remained silent for a long time. Then he sighed. "Me," he said. Then: "While I was downstairs before, on my way here, listening to that woman sing, it struck me all of a sudden how much suffering she must have had to go through—to sing like that. It's *repulsive* to think you have to suffer that much."

I said: "But there's no way not to suffer—is there, Sonny?"

"I believe not," he said and smiled, "but that's never stopped anyone from trying." He looked at me. "Has it?" I realized, with this mocking look, that there stood between us, forever, beyond the power of time or forgiveness, the fact that I had held silence—so long!—when he had needed human speech to help him. He turned back to the window. "No, there's no way not to suffer. But you try all kinds of ways to keep from drowning in it, to keep on top of it, and to make it seem—well, like *you*. Like you did something, all right, and now you're suffering for it. You know?" I said nothing. "Well you know," he said, impatiently, "why *do* people suffer? Maybe it's better to do something to give it a reason, *any* reason."

"But we just agreed," I said, "that there's no way not to suffer. Isn't it better, then, just to—take it?"

"But nobody just takes it," Sonny cried, "that's what I'm telling you! *Everybody* tries not to. You're just hung up on the *way* some people try—it's not *your* way!"

The hair on my face began to itch, my face felt wet. "That's not true," I said, "that's not true. I don't give a damn what other people do, I don't even care how they suffer. I just care how *you* suffer." And he looked at me. "Please believe me," I said, "I don't want to see you—die—trying not to suffer."

"I won't," he said flatly, "die trying not to suffer. At least, not any faster than anybody else."

"But there's no need," I said, trying to laugh, "is there? in killing yourself."

I wanted to say more, but I couldn't. I wanted to talk about will power and how life could be—well, beautiful. I wanted to say that it was all within; but was it? or, rather, wasn't that exactly the trouble? And I wanted to promise that I would never fail him again. But it would all have sounded—empty words and lies.

So I made the promise to myself and prayed that I would keep it.

"It's terrible sometimes, inside," he said, "that's what's the trouble. You walk these streets, black and funky and cold, and there's not really a living ass to talk to, and there's nothing shaking, and there's no way of getting it out—that storm inside. You can't talk it and you can't make love with it, and when you finally try to get with it and play it, you realize *nobody's* listening. So *you've* got to listen. You got to find a way to listen."

And then he walked away from the window and sat on the sofa again, as though all the wind had suddenly been knocked out of him. "Sometimes you'll do *anything* to play, even cut your mother's throat." He laughed and looked at me. "Or your brother's." Then he sobered. "Or your own." Then: "Don't worry. I'm all right now and I think I'll *be* all right. But I can't forget—where I've been. I don't mean just the physical place I've been, I mean where I've *been.* And *what* I've been."

"What have you been, Sonny?" I asked.

He smiled—but sat sideways on the sofa, his elbow resting on the back, his fingers playing with his mouth and chin, not looking at me. "I've been something I didn't recognize, didn't know I could be. Didn't know anybody could be." He stopped, looking inward, looking helplessly young, looking old. "I'm not talking about it now because I feel *guilty* or anything like that—maybe it would be better if I did, I don't know. Anyway, I can't really talk about it. Not to you, not to anybody," and now he turned and faced me. "Sometimes, you know, and it was actually when I was most *out* of the world, I felt that I was in it, that I was *with* it, really, and I could play or I didn't really have to *play,* it just came out of me, it was there. And I don't know how I played, thinking about it now, but I know I did awful things, those times, sometimes, to people. Or it wasn't that I *did* anything to them—it was that they weren't real." He picked up the beer can; it was empty; he rolled it between his palms: "And other times—well, I needed a fix, I needed to find a place to lean, I needed to clear a space to *listen*—and I couldn't find it, and I—went crazy, I did terrible things to *me,* I was terrible *for* me." He began pressing the beer can between his hands, I watched the metal begin to give. It glittered, as he played with it like a knife, and I was afraid he would cut himself, but I said nothing. "Oh well. I can never tell you. I was all by myself at the bottom of something, stinking and sweating and crying and shaking, and I smelled it, you know? *my* stink, and I thought I'd die if I couldn't get away from it and yet, all the same, I knew that everything I was doing was just locking me in with it. And I didn't know," he paused, still flattening the beer can, "I didn't know, I still *don't* know, something kept telling me that maybe it was good to smell your own stink, but I didn't think that *that* was what I'd been trying to do—and—who can stand it?" and he abruptly dropped the ruined beer can, looking at me with a small, still smile, and then rose, walking to the window as though it were the lodestone rock. I watched his face, he watched the avenue. "I couldn't tell you when Mama died—but the reason I wanted to leave Harlem so bad was to get away from drugs. And then, when I ran away, that's what I was running from—really. When I came back, nothing had changed, *I* hadn't changed, I was just—older." And he stopped, drumming with his fingers on the windowpane. The sun had vanished, soon darkness would fall. I watched his face. "It can come again," he said, almost as though speaking to himself. Then he turned to me. "It can come again," he repeated. "I just want you to know that."

"All right," I said, at last. "So it can come again. All right."

He smiled, but the smile was sorrowful. "I had to try to tell you," he said.

"Yes," I said. "I understand that."

"You're my brother," he said, looking straight at me, and not smiling at all.

"Yes," I repeated, "yes. I understand that."

He turned back to the window, looking out. "All that hatred down there," he said, "all that hatred and misery and love. It's a wonder it doesn't blow the avenue apart."

We went to the only nightclub on a short, dark street, downtown. We squeezed through the narrow, chattering, jampacked bar to the entrance of the big room, where the bandstand was. And we stood there for a moment, for the lights were very dim in this room and we couldn't see. Then, "Hello, boy," said the voice and an enormous black man, much older than Sonny or myself, erupted out of all that atmospheric lighting and put an arm around Sonny's shoulder. "I been sitting right here," he said, "waiting for you."

He had a big voice, too, and heads in the darkness turned toward us.

Sonny grinned and pulled a little away, and said, "Creole, this is my brother. I told you about him."

Creole shook my hand. "I'm glad to meet you, son," he said, and it was clear that he was glad to meet me *there*, for Sonny's sake. And he smiled, "You got a real musician in *your* family," and he took his arm from Sonny's shoulder and slapped him, lightly, affectionately, with the back of his hand.

"Well. Now I've heard it all," said a voice behind us. This was another musician, and a friend of Sonny's, a coal-black, cheerful-looking man, built close to the ground. He immediately began confiding to me, at the top of his lungs, the most terrible things about Sonny, his teeth gleaming like a lighthouse and his laugh coming up out of him like the beginning of an earthquake. And it turned out that everyone at the bar knew Sonny, or almost everyone; some were musicians, working there, or nearby, or not working, some were simply hangers-on, and some were there to hear Sonny play. I was introduced to all of them and they were all very polite to me. Yet, it was clear that, for them, I was only Sonny's brother. Here, I was in Sonny's world. Or, rather: his kingdom. Here, it was not even a question that his veins bore royal blood.

They were going to play soon and Creole installed me, by myself, at a table in a dark corner. Then I watched them, Creole, and the little black man, and Sonny, and the others, while they horsed around, standing just below the bandstand. The light from the bandstand spilled just a little short of them and, watching them laughing and gesturing and moving about, I had the feeling that they, nevertheless, were being most careful not to step into that circle of light too suddenly; that if they moved into the light too suddenly, without thinking, they would perish in flame. Then, while I watched, one of them, the small black man, moved into the light and crossed the bandstand and started fooling around with his drums. Then—being funny and being, also, extremely ceremonious—Creole took Sonny by the arm and led him to the piano. A woman's voice called Sonny's name and a few hands started clapping. And Sonny, also being funny and being ceremonious, and so touched, I think, that he could have cried, but neither hiding it nor showing it, riding it like a man, grinned, and put both hands to his heart and bowed from the waist.

Creole then went to the bass fiddle and a lean, very bright-skinned brown man jumped up on the bandstand and picked up his horn. So there they were, and the atmosphere on the bandstand and in the room began to change and tighten. Someone stepped up to the microphone and announced them. Then there were all kinds of murmurs. Some people at the bar shushed others. The waitress ran around, frantically getting in the last orders, guys and chicks got closer to each other, and the lights on the bandstand, on the quartet, turned to a kind of indigo. Then they all looked different there. Creole looked about him for the last time, as though he were making certain that all his chickens were in the coop, and then he—jumped and struck the fiddle. And there they were.

All I know about music is that not many people ever really hear it. And even then, on the rare occasions when something opens within, and the music enters, what we mainly hear, or hear corroborated, are personal, private, vanishing evocations. But the man who creates the music is hearing something else, is dealing with the roar rising from the void and imposing order on it as it hits the air. What is evoked in him, then, is of another order, more terrible because it has no words, and triumphant, too, for that same reason. And his triumph, when he triumphs, is ours. I just watched Sonny's face. His face was troubled, he was working hard, but he wasn't with it. And I had the feeling that, in a way, everyone on the bandstand was waiting for him, both waiting for him and pushing him along. But as I began to watch Creole, I realized that it was Creole who held them all back. He had them on a short rein. Up there, keeping the beat with his whole body, wailing on the fiddle, with his eyes half closed, he was listening to everything, but he was listening to Sonny. He was having a dialogue with Sonny. He wanted Sonny to leave the shoreline and strike out for the deep water. He was Sonny's witness that deep water and drowning were not the same thing—he had been there, and he knew. And he wanted Sonny to know. He was waiting for Sonny to do the things on the keys which would let Creole know that Sonny was in the water.

And, while Creole listened, Sonny moved, deep within, exactly like someone in torment. I had never before thought of how awful the relationship must be between the musician and his instrument. He has to fill it, this instrument, with the breath of life, his own. He has to make it do what he wants it to do. And a piano is just a piano. It's made out of so much wood and wires and little hammers and big ones, and ivory. While there's only so much you can do with it, the only way to find this out is to try; to try and make it do everything.

And Sonny hadn't been near a piano for over a year. And he wasn't on much better terms with his life, not the life that stretched before him now. He and the piano stammered, started one way, got scared, stopped; started another way, panicked, marked time, started again; then seemed to have found a direction, panicked again, got stuck. And the face I saw on Sonny I'd never seen before. Everything had been burned out of it, and, at the same time, things usually hidden were being burned in, by the fire and fury of the battle which was occurring in him up there.

Yet, watching Creole's face as they neared the end of the first set, I had the feeling that something had happened, something I hadn't heard. Then they finished, there was scattered applause, and then, without an instant's warning, Creole started into something else, it was almost sardonic, it was *Am I Blue*. And, as though he commanded, Sonny began to play. Something began to happen. And Creole let out the reins. The dry, low, black man said something awful on the drums, Creole answered, and the drums talked back. Then the horn insisted, sweet and high, slightly detached perhaps, and Creole listened, commenting now and then, dry, and driving, beautiful and calm and old. Then they all came together again, and Sonny was part of the family again. I could tell this from his face. He seemed to have found, right there beneath his fingers, a damn brand-new piano. It seemed that he couldn't get over it. Then, for a while, just being happy with Sonny, they seemed to be agreeing with him that brand-new pianos certainly were a gas.

Then Creole stepped forward to remind them that what they were playing was the blues. He hit something in all of them, he hit something in me, myself, and the music tightened and deepened, apprehension began to beat the air. Creole began to tell us what the blues were all about. They were not about anything very new. He and his boys up there were keeping it new, at the risk of ruin, destruction, madness, and death, in order to find new ways to make us listen. For, while the tale of how we suffer, and how we are delighted, and how we may triumph is never new, it always must be heard. There isn't any other tale to tell, it's the only light we've got in all this darkness.

And this tale, according to that face, that body, those strong hands on those strings, has another aspect in every country, and a new depth in every generation. Listen, Creole seemed to be saying, listen. Now these are Sonny's blues. He made the little black man on the drums know it, and the bright, brown man on the horn. Creole wasn't trying any longer to get Sonny in the water. He was wishing him Godspeed. Then he stepped back, very slowly, filling the air with the immense suggestion that Sonny speak for himself.

Then they all gathered around Sonny and Sonny played. Every now and again one of them seemed to say, amen. Sonny's fingers filled the air with life, his life. But that life contained so many others. And Sonny went all the way back, he really began with the spare, flat statement of the opening phrase of the song. Then he began to make it his. It was very beautiful because it wasn't hurried and it was no longer a lament. I seemed to hear with what burning he had made it his, and what burning we had yet to make it ours, how we could cease lamenting. Freedom lurked around us and I understood, at last, that he could help us to be free if we would listen, that he would never be free until we did. Yet, there was no battle in his face now, I heard what he had gone through, and would continue to go through until he came to rest in earth. He had made it his: that long line, of which we knew only Mama and Daddy. And he was giving it back, as everything must be given back, so that, passing through death, it can live forever. I saw my mother's face again, and felt, for the first time, how the stones of the road she had walked on must have bruised her feet. I saw the moonlit road where my father's brother died. And it brought something else back to me, and carried me past it, I saw my little girl again and felt Isabel's tears again, and I felt my own tears begin to rise. And I was yet aware that this was only a moment, that the world waited outside, as hungry as a tiger, and that trouble stretched above us, longer than the sky.

Then it was over. Creole and Sonny let out their breath, both soaking wet, and grinning. There was a lot of applause and some of it was real. In the dark, the girl came by and I asked her to take drinks to the bandstand. There was a long pause, while they talked up there in the indigo light and after awhile I saw the girl put a Scotch and milk on top of the piano for Sonny. He didn't seem to notice it, but just before they started playing again, he sipped from it and looked toward me, and nodded. Then he put it back on top of the piano. For me, then, as they began to play again, it glowed and shook above my brother's head like the very cup of trembling.[8]

---

1. What views of life and its meaning are in conflict in this story? Does one appear to triumph over the other?
2. What does the "privacy" of Sonny's character come from and what are its results?
3. What relationship does the author see between art and religion?
4. What does the narrator reveal when he says, "My trouble made his real"? What does the story say about living a "safe" life?
5. What does the mother contribute to the older brother's knowledge of Sonny? What does she mean when she says, "Let him know you's *there*"?
6. Interpret this passage and relate it to the theme of the story: "For, while the tale of how we suffer and how we are delighted and how we may triumph is never new, it always must be heard."

8. Isaiah 51:22. ". . . I have taken out of thine hand the cup of trembling . . . thou shalt no more drink it again . . ."

Honoré de Balzac

Balzac (1799–1850) was born in Tours, France, and moved with his family to Paris in 1814. After three years as a lawyer's clerk he turned his prodigious energy toward printing, manufacturing type, and publishing. He also set out to gain a fortune by writing. His first novels were influenced by Sir Walter Scott and other popular romantic authors, but in about 1830 Balzac shifted to a more realistic vein, beginning the vast cycle of novels which is called collectively The Human Comedy. *This group of interrelated stories was to be a social history of his times, covering the activities and characteristics of every social level and all occupations. But his scrutiny of the manners and morals of his countrymen was mingled in some of his later fiction with excursions into fantasy and mysticism. A romantic strain persisted and found its outlet in such tales as the one here selected. In his private life, as well, there was a mixture of the hardworking professional writer with the orgiastic seeker of pleasure in all quarters of Parisian life. After weeks or months of exhausting labor on a novel he would frequently relax with a bout of dissipation, and he burned himself out with indulgences as ferocious as his creative concentrations. Among his most famous novels are:* Old Goriot *(1835),* Cousin Bette *(1846), and* Louis Lambert *(1832).*

A Passion in the Desert[1]

The whole show is dreadful," she cried, coming out of the menagerie of M. Martin. She had just been looking at that daring speculator "working with his hyena,"—to speak in the style of the programme.

"By what means," she continued, "can he have tamed these animals to such a point as to be certain of their affection for——"

"What seems to you a problem," said I, interrupting, "is really quite natural."

"Oh!" she cried, letting an incredulous smile wander over her lips.

"You think that beasts are wholly without passions?" I asked her. "Quite the reverse; we can communicate to them all the vices arising in our own state of civilization."

She looked at me with an air of astonishment.

1. From a translation by J. Alfred Burgan and Peter P. Breen.

"But," I continued, "the first time I saw M. Martin, I admit, like you, I did give vent to an exclamation of surprise. I found myself next to an old soldier with the right leg amputated, who had come in with me. His face had struck me. He had one of those heroic heads, stamped with the seal of warfare, and on which the battles of Napoleon[2] are written. Besides, he had that frank, good-humored expression which always impresses me favorably. He was without doubt one of those troopers who are surprised at nothing, who find matter for laughter in the contortions of a dying comrade, who bury or plunder him quite light-heartedly, who stand intrepidly in the way of bullets;—in fact, one of those men who waste no time in deliberation, and would not hesitate to make friends with the devil himself. After looking very attentively at the proprietor of the menagerie getting out of his box, my companion pursed up his lips with an air of mockery and contempt, with that peculiar and expressive twist which superior people assume to show they are not taken in. Then, when I was expatiating on the courage of M. Martin, he smiled, shook his head knowingly, and said, 'Well known.' "

" 'How "well known"?' I said. 'If you would only explain me the mystery, I should be vastly obliged.'

"After a few minutes, during which we made acquaintance, we went to dine at the first *restaurateur's* whose shop caught our eye. At dessert a bottle of champagne completely refreshed and brightened up the memories of this odd old soldier. He told me his story, and I saw that he was right when he exclaimed, 'Well known.' "

When she got home, she teased me to that extent, was so charming, and made so many promises, that I consented to communicate to her the confidences of the old soldier. Next day she received the following episode of an epic which one might call "The French in Egypt."

During the expedition in Upper Egypt under General Desaix, a Provençal[3] soldier fell into the hands of the Maugrabins, and was taken by these Arabs into the deserts beyond the falls of the Nile.

In order to place a sufficient distance between themselves and the French army, the Maugrabins made forced marches, and only halted when night was upon them. They camped round a well overshadowed by palm trees under which they had previously concealed a store of provisions. Not surmising that the notion of flight would occur to their prisoner, they contented themselves with binding his hands, and after eating a few dates, and giving provender to their horses, went to sleep.

When the brave Provençal saw that his enemies were no longer

2. As general of the French Revolutionary armies and later as Emperor, Napoleon Bonaparte (1769–1821) fought in many parts of Europe and led an expedition into Egypt. Those of his soldiers who fought in all of his campaigns were looked on as a breed apart from other men. 3. Provence is a southern province of France.

watching him, he made use of his teeth to steal a scimitar, fixed the blade between his knees, and cut the cords which prevented him using his hands; in a moment he was free. He at once seized a rifle and a dagger, then taking the precaution to provide himself with a sack of dried dates, oats, and powder and shot, and to fasten a scimitar to his waist, he leaped on to a horse, and spurred on vigorously in the direction where he thought to find the French army. So impatient was he to see a bivouac again that he pressed on the already tired courser at such speed, that its flanks were lacerated with his spurs, and at last the poor animal died, leaving the Frenchman alone in the desert. After walking some time in the sand with all the courage of an escaped convict, the soldier was obliged to stop, as the day had already ended. In spite of the beauty of an Oriental sky at night, he felt he had not strength enough to go on. Fortunately he had been able to find a small hill, on the summit of which a few palm trees shot up into the air; it was their verdure seen from afar which had brought hope and consolation to his heart. His fatigue was so great that he lay down upon a rock of granite, capriciously cut out like a camp-bed; there he fell asleep without taking any precaution to defend himself while he slept. He had made the sacrifice of his life. His last thought was one of regret. He repented having left the Maugrabins, whose nomadic life seemed to smile upon him now that he was far from them and without help. He was awakened by the sun, whose pitiless rays fell with all their force on the granite and produced an intolerable heat—for he had had the stupidity to place himself inversely to the shadow thrown by the verdant majestic heads of the palm trees. He looked at the solitary trees and shuddered—they reminded him of the graceful shafts crowned with foliage which characterize the Saracen columns in the cathedral of Arles.[4]

But when, after counting the palm trees, he cast his eyes around him, the most horrible despair was infused into his soul. Before him stretched an ocean without limit. The dark sand of the desert spread further than eye could reach in every direction, and glittered like steel struck with bright light. It might have been a sea of looking-glass, or lakes melted together in a mirror. A fiery vapor carried up in surging waves made a perpetual whirlwind over the quivering land. The sky was lit with an Oriental splendor of insupportable purity, leaving naught for the imagination to desire. Heaven and earth were on fire.

The silence was awful in its wild and terrible majesty. Infinity, immensity, closed in upon the soul from every side. Not a cloud in the sky, not a breath in the air, not a flaw on the bosom of the sand, ever moving in diminutive waves; the horizon ended as at sea on a clear day, with one line of light, definite as the cut of a sword.

4. A city in Provence; Saracen architecture is brilliantly colored and heavily decorated, sometimes with patterns derived from foliage.

The Provençal threw his arms round the trunk of one of the palm trees, as though it were the body of a friend, and then, in the shelter of the thin, straight shadow that the palm cast upon the granite, he wept. Then sitting down he remained as he was, contemplating with profound sadness the implacable scene, which was all he had to look upon. He cried aloud, to measure the solitude. His voice, lost in the hollows of the hill, sounded faintly, and aroused no echo—the echo was in his own heart. The Provençal was twenty-two years old:—he loaded his carbine.

"There'll be time enough," he said to himself, laying on the ground the weapon which alone could bring him deliverance.

Viewing alternately the dark expanse of the desert and the blue expanse of the sky, the soldier dreamed of France—he smelled with delight the gutters of Paris—he remembered the towns through which he had passed, the faces of his comrades, the most minute details of his life. His Southern fancy soon showed him the stones of his beloved Provence, in the play of the heat which undulated above the wide expanse of the desert. Realizing the danger of this cruel mirage, he went down the opposite side of the hill to that by which he had come up the day before. The remains of a rug showed that this place of refuge had at one time been inhabited; at a short distance he saw some palm trees full of dates. Then the instinct which binds us to life awoke again in his heart. He hoped to live long enough to await the passing of some Maugrabins, or perhaps he might hear the sound of cannon; for at this time Bonaparte was traversing Egypt.

This thought gave him new life. The palm tree seemed to bend with the weight of the ripe fruit. He shook some of it down. When he tasted this unhoped-for manna, he felt sure that the palms had been cultivated by a former inhabitant—the savory, fresh meat of the dates were proof of the care of his predecessor. He passed suddenly from dark despair to an almost insane joy. He went up again to the top of the hill, and spent the rest of the day in cutting down one of the sterile palm trees, which the night before had served him for shelter. A vague memory made him think of the animals of the desert; and in case they might come to drink at the spring, visible from the base of the rocks but lost further down, he resolved to guard himself from their visits by placing a barrier at the entrance of his hermitage.

In spite of his diligence, and the strength which the fear of being devoured asleep gave him, he was unable to cut the palm in pieces, though he succeeded in cutting it down. At eventide the king of the desert fell; the sound of its fall resounded far and wide, like a sigh in the solitude; the soldier shuddered as though he had heard some voice predicting woe.

But like an heir who does not long bewail a deceased relative, he tore off from this beautiful tree the tall broad green leaves which are its poetic adornment, and used them to mend the mat on which he was to sleep.

Fatigued by the heat and his work, he fell asleep under the red curtains of his wet cave.

In the middle of the night his sleep was troubled by an extraordinary noise; he sat up, and the deep silence around allowed him to distinguish the alternative accents of a respiration whose savage energy could not belong to a human creature.

A profound terror, increased still further by the darkness, the silence, and his waking images, froze his heart within him. He almost felt his hair stand on end, when by straining his eyes to their utmost he perceived through the shadow two faint yellow lights. At first he attributed these lights to the reflection of his own pupils, but soon the vivid brilliance of the night aided him gradually to distinguish the objects around him in the cave, and he beheld a huge animal lying but two steps from him. Was it a lion, a tiger, or a crocodile?

The Provençal was not sufficiently educated to know under what species his enemy ought to be classed; but his fright was all the greater, as his ignorance led him to imagine all terrors at once; he endured a cruel torture, noting every variation of the breathing close to him without daring to make the slightest movement. An odor, pungent like that of a fox, but more penetrating, more profound,—so to speak,—filled the cave, and when the Provençal became sensible of this, his terror reached its height, for he could no longer doubt the proximity of a terrible companion, whose royal dwelling served him for a shelter.

Presently the reflection of the moon descending on the horizon lit up the den, rendering gradually visible and resplendent the spotted skin of a panther.

This lion of Egypt slept, curled up like a big dog, the peaceful possessor of a sumptuous niche at the gate of an *hôtel;*[5] its eyes opened for a moment and closed again; its face was turned towards the man. A thousand confused thoughts passed through the Frenchman's mind; first he thought of killing it with a bullet from his gun, but he saw there was not enough distance between them for him to take proper aim—the shot would miss the mark. And if it were to wake!—the thought made his limbs rigid. He listened to his own heart beating in the midst of the silence, and cursed the too violent pulsations which the flow of blood brought on, fearing to disturb that sleep which allowed him time to think of some means of escape.

Twice he placed his hand on his scimitar, intending to cut off the head of his enemy; but the difficulty of cutting the stiff short hair com-

5. A mansion.

pelled him to abandon this daring project. To miss would be to die for *certain,* he thought; he preferred the chances of fair fight, and made up his mind to wait till morning; the morning did not leave him long to wait.

He could now examine the panther at ease; its muzzle was smeared with blood.

"She's had a good dinner," he thought, without troubling himself as to whether her feast might have been on human flesh. "She won't be hungry when she gets up."

It was a female. The fur on her belly and flanks was glistening white; many small marks like velvet formed beautiful bracelets round her feet; her sinuous tail was also white, ending with black rings; the overpart of her dress, yellow like burnished gold, very lissome and soft, had the characteristic blotches in the form of rosettes, which distinguish the panther from every other feline species.

This tranquil and formidable hostess snored in an attitude as graceful as that of a cat lying on a cushion. Her bloodstained paws, nervous and well armed, were stretched out before her face, which rested upon them, and from which radiated her straight slender whiskers, like threads of silver.

If she had been like that in a cage, the Provençal would doubtless have admired the grace of the animal, and the vigorous contrasts of vivid color which gave her robe an imperial splendor; but just then his sight was troubled by her sinister appearance.

The presence of the panther, even asleep, could not fail to produce the effect which the magnetic eyes of the serpent are said to have on the nightingale.

For a moment the courage of the soldier began to fail before this danger, though no doubt it would have risen at the mouth of a cannon charged with shell. Nevertheless, a bold thought brought daylight to his soul and sealed up the source of the cold sweat which sprang forth on his brow. Like men driven to bay, who defy death and offer their body to the smiter, so he, seeing in this merely a tragic episode, resolved to play his part with honor to the last.

"The day before yesterday the Arabs would have killed me, perhaps," he said; so considering himself as good as dead already, he waited bravely, with excited curiosity, the awakening of his enemy.

When the sun appeared, the panther suddenly opened her eyes; then she put out her paws with energy, as if to stretch them and get rid of cramp. At last she yawned, showing the formidable apparatus of her teeth and pointed tongue, rough as a file.

"A regular *petite maîtresse*,"[6] thought the Frenchman, seeing her

6. Little lady.

roll herself about so softly and coquettishly. She licked off the blood which stained her paws and muzzle, and scratched her head with reiterated gestures full of prettiness. "All right, make a little toilet,"[7] the Frenchman said to himself, beginning to recover his gaiety with his courage; "we'll say good-morning to each other presently;" and he seized the small, short dagger which he had taken from the Maugrabins.

At this moment the panther turned her head towards the man and looked at him fixedly without moving. The rigidity of her metallic eyes and their insupportable lustre made him shudder, especially when the animal walked towards him. But he looked at her caressingly, staring into her eyes in order to magnetize her, and let her come quite close to him; then with a movement both gentle and amorous, as though he were caressing the most beautiful of women, he passed his hand over her whole body, from the head to the tail, scratching the flexible vertebræ which divided the panther's yellow back. The animal waved her tail voluptuously, and her eyes grew gentle; and when for the third time the Frenchman accomplished this interesting flattery, she gave forth one of those purrings by which cats express their pleasure; but this murmur issued from a throat so powerful and so deep, that it resounded through the cave like the vast vibrations of an organ in a church. The man, understanding the importance of his caresses, redoubled them in such a way as to surprise and stupefy his imperious courtesan. When he felt sure of having extinguished the ferocity of his capricious companion, whose hunger had so fortunately been satisfied the day before, he got up to go out of the cave; the panther let him go out, but when he had reached the summit of the hill she sprang with the lightness of a sparrow hopping from twig to twig, and rubbed herself against his legs, putting up her back after the manner of all the race of cats. Then regarding her guest with eyes whose glare had softened a little, she gave vent to that wild cry which naturalists compare to the grating of a saw.

"She is exacting," said the Frenchman, smiling.

He was bold enough to play with her ears; he caressed her belly and scratched her head as hard as he could. When he saw he was successful he tickled her skull with the point of his dagger, watching for the moment to kill her, but the hardness of her bones made him tremble for his success.

The sultana of the desert showed herself gracious to her slave; she lifted her head, stretched out her neck, and manifested her delight by the tranquillity of her attitude. It suddenly occurred to the soldier that to kill this savage princess with one blow he must poniard her in the throat.

7. I.e., clean and freshen up.

He raised the blade, when the panther, satisfied, no doubt, laid herself gracefully at his feet, and cast up at him glances in which, in spite of their natural fierceness, was mingled confusedly a kind of good-will. The poor Provençal ate his dates, leaning against one of the palm trees, and casting his eyes alternately on the desert in quest of some liberator and on his terrible companion to watch her uncertain clemency.

The panther looked at the place where the date stones fell, and every time that he threw one down her eyes expressed an incredible mistrust.

She examined the man with an almost commercial prudence. However, this examination was favorable to him, for when he had finished his meagre meal she licked his boots with her powerful rough tongue, brushing off with marvelous skill the dust gathered in the creases.

"Ah, but when she's really hungry!" thought the Frenchman. In spite of the shudder this thought caused him, the soldier began to measure curiously the proportions of the panther, certainly one of the most splendid specimens of its race. She was three feet high and four feet long without counting her tail; this powerful weapon, rounded like a cudgel, was nearly three feet long. The head, large as that of a lioness, was distinguished by a rare expression of refinement. The cold cruelty of a tiger was dominant, it was true, but there was also a vague resemblance to the face of a sensual woman. Indeed, the face of this solitary queen had something of the gaiety of a drunken Nero: she had satiated herself with blood, and she wanted to play.

The soldier tried if he might walk up and down, and the panther left him free, contenting herself with following him with her eyes, less like a faithful dog than a big Angora cat, observing everything, and every movement of her master.

When he looked round, he saw, by the spring, the remains of his horse; the panther had dragged the carcass all that way; about two-thirds of it had been devoured already. The sight reassured him.

It was easy to explain the panther's absence, and the respect she had had for him while he slept. The first piece of good luck emboldened him to tempt the future, and he conceived the wild hope of continuing on good terms with the panther during the entire day, neglecting no means of taming her and remaining in her good graces.

He returned to her, and had the unspeakable joy of seeing her wag her tail with an almost imperceptible movement at his approach. He sat down, then, without fear, by her side, and they began to play together; he took her paws and muzzle, pulled her ears, rolled her over on her back, stroked her warm, delicate flanks. She let him do whatever he liked, and when he began to stroke the hair on her feet she drew her claws in carefully.

The man, keeping the dagger in one hand, thought to plunge it into the belly of the too confiding panther, but he was afraid that he would be immediately strangled in her last convulsive struggle; besides, he felt in his heart a sort of remorse which bade him respect a creature that had done him no harm. He seemed to have found a friend, in a boundless desert; half unconsciously he thought of his first sweetheart, whom he had nicknamed "Mignonne"[8] by way of contrast, because she was so atrociously jealous that all the time of their love he was in fear of the knife with which she had always threatened him.

This memory of his early days suggested to him the idea of making the young panther answer to this name, now that he began to admire with less terror her swiftness, suppleness, and softness. Towards the end of the day he had familiarized himself with his perilous position; he now almost liked the painfulness of it. At last his companion had got into the habit of looking up at him whenever he cried in a falsetto voice, "Mignonne."

At the setting of the sun Mignonne gave, several times running, a profound melancholy cry. "She's been well brought up," said the light-hearted soldier; "she says her prayers." But this mental joke only occurred to him when he noticed what a pacific attitude his companion remained in. "Come, *ma petite blonde*,[9] I'll let you go to bed first," he said to her, counting on the activity of his own legs to run away as quickly as possible, directly she was asleep, and seek another shelter for the night.

The soldier awaited with impatience the hour of his flight, and when it had arrived he walked vigorously in the direction of the Nile; but hardly had he made a quarter of a league in the sand when he heard the panther bounding after him, crying with that saw-like cry, more dreadful even than the sound of her leaping.

"Ah!" he said, "then she's taken a fancy to me; she has never met any one before, and it is really quite flattering to have her first love." That instant the man fell into one of those movable quicksands so terrible to travelers and from which it is impossible to save oneself. Feeling himself caught he gave a shriek of alarm; the panther seized him with her teeth by the collar, and, springing vigorously backwards, drew him as if by magic out of the whirling sand.

"Ah, Mignonne!" cried the soldier, caressing her enthusiastically, "we're bound together for life and death—but no jokes, mind!" and he retraced his steps.

From that time the desert seemed inhabited. It contained a being to whom the man could talk, and whose ferocity was rendered gentle by him, though he could not explain to himself the reason for their

8. Literally, "Darling." 9. "My little blonde."

strange friendship. Great as was the soldier's desire to stay up on guard, he slept.

On awakening he could not find Mignonne; he mounted the hill, and in the distance saw her springing towards him after the habit of these animals, who cannot run on account of the extreme flexibility of the vertebral column. Mignonne arrived, her jaws covered with blood; she received the wonted caress of her companion, showing with much purring how happy it made her. Her eyes, full of languor, turned still more gently than the day before towards the Provençal, who talked to her as one would to a tame animal.

"Ah! mademoiselle, you are a nice girl, aren't you? Just look at that! so we like to be made much of, don't we? Aren't you ashamed of yourself? So you have been eating some Arab or other, have you? That doesn't matter. They're animals just the same as you are; but don't you take to eating Frenchmen, or I shan't like you any longer."

She played like a dog with its master, letting herself be rolled over, knocked about, and stroked, alternately; sometimes she herself would provoke the soldier, putting up her paw with a soliciting gesture.

Some days passed in this manner. This companionship permitted the Provençal to appreciate the sublime beauty of the desert; now that he had a living thing to think about, alternations of fear and quiet, and plenty to eat, his mind became filled with contrasts and his life began to be diversified.

Solitude revealed to him all her secrets, and enveloped him in her delights. He discovered in the rising and setting of the sun sights unknown to the world. He knew what it was to tremble when he heard over his head the hiss of a bird's wings, so rarely did they pass, or when he saw the clouds, changing and many colored travelers, melt one into another. He studied in the night-time the effect of the moon upon the ocean of sand, where the simoom[1] made waves swift of movement and rapid in their change. He lived the life of the Eastern day, marveling at its wonderful pomp; then, after having reveled in the sight of a hurricane over the plain where the whirling sands made red, dry mists and death-bearing clouds, he would welcome the night with joy, and then fell the healthful freshness of the stars, and he listened to imaginary music in the skies. Then solitude taught him to unroll the treasures of dreams. He passed whole hours in remembering mere nothings, and comparing his present life with his past.

At last he grew passionately fond of the panther; for some sort of affection was a necessity.

1. A hot, dry desert wind.

Whether it was that his will powerfully projected had modified the character of his companion, or whether, because she found abundant food in her predatory excursions in the deserts, she respected the man's life, he began to fear for it no longer, seeing her so well tamed.

He devoted the greater part of his time to sleep, but he was obliged to watch like a spider in its web that the moment of his deliverance might not escape him, if any one should pass the line marked by the horizon. He had sacrificed his shirt to make a flag with, which he hung at the top of a palm tree, whose foliage he had torn off. Taught by necessity, he found the means of keeping it spread out, by fastening it with little sticks; for the wind might not be blowing at the moment when the passing traveler was looking through the desert.

It was during the long hours, when he had abandoned hope, that he amused himself with the panther. He had come to learn the different inflections of her voice, the expressions of her eyes; he had studied the capricious patterns of all the rosettes which marked the gold of her robe. Mignonne was not angry even when he took hold of the tuft at the end of her tail to count the rings, those graceful ornaments which glittered in the sun like jewelry. It gave him pleasure to contemplate the supple, fine outlines of her form, the whiteness of her belly, the graceful pose of her head. But it was especially when she was playing that he felt most pleasure in looking at her; the agility and youthful lightness of her movements were a continual surprise to him; he wondered at the supple way which she jumped and climbed, washed herself and arranged her fur, crouched down and prepared to spring. However rapid her spring might be, however slippery the stone she was on, she would always stop short at the word "Mignonne."

One day, in a bright mid-day sun, an enormous bird coursed through the air. The man left his panther to look at his new guest; but after waiting a moment the deserted sultana growled deeply.

"My goodness! I do believe she's jealous," he cried, seeing her eyes become hard again; "the soul of Virginie has passed into her body, that's certain."

The eagle disappeared into the air, whilst the soldier admired the curved contour of the panther.

But there was such youth and grace in her form! she was beautiful as a woman! the blond fur of her robe mingled well with the delicate tints of faint white which marked her flanks.

The profuse light cast down by the sun made this living gold, these russet markings, to burn in a way to give them an indefinable attraction.

The man and the panther looked at one another with a look full of meaning; the coquette quivered when she felt her friend stroke her head; her eyes flashed like lightning—then she shut them tightly.

"She has a soul," he said, looking at the stillness of this queen of the sands, golden like them, white like them, solitary and burning like them.

"Well," she said, "I have read your plea in favor of beasts; but how did two so well adapted to understand each other end?"

"Ah, well! You see, they ended as all great passions do end—by a misunderstanding. From some reason *one* suspects the other of treason; they don't come to an explanation through pride, and quarrel and part from sheer obstinacy."

"Yet sometimes at the best moments a single word or a look is enough—but anyhow go on with your story."

"It's horribly difficult, but you will understand, after what the old villain told me over his champagne. He said—'I don't know if I hurt her, but she turned round, as if enraged, and with her sharp teeth caught hold of my leg—gently, I dare say; but I, thinking she would devour me, plunged my dagger into her throat. She rolled over, giving a cry that froze my heart; and I saw her dying, still looking at me without anger. I would have given all the world—my cross even, which I had not got then—to have brought her to life again. It was as though I had murdered a real person; and the soldiers who had seen my flag, and were come to my assistance, found me in tears.

" 'Well, sir,' he said, after a moment of silence, 'since then I have been in war in Germany, in Spain, in Russia, in France; I've certainly carried my carcass about a good deal, but never have I seen anything like the desert. Ah! yes, it is very beautiful!'

" 'What did you feel there?' I asked him.

" 'Oh! that can't be described, young man! Besides, I am not always regretting my palm trees and my panther. I should have to be very melancholy for that. In the desert, you see, there is anything, and nothing.'

" 'Yes, but explain—'

" 'Well,' he said, with an impatient gesture, 'it is God without mankind.' "

---

1. The main events of the story are reported by a stranger encountered in a menagerie (though they are narrated in the third person). Are they more or less credible than if Balzac had narrated them on his own authority? Are they credible at all?
2. Interpret the story as an allegory of human love.
3. Is it sheer coincidence that the soldier is rescued just after he has killed his beloved panther?

4. What effect is obtained by making the love object both beautiful and frightening?
5. What is the meaning of the soldier's last line?
6. Compare the qualities of this story with those of modern fantasy and science fiction.

Ann Beattie

Beattie (1947–) was born in Washington, D.C. She attended American University and the University of Connecticut. Subsequently she taught at Harvard and the University of Virginia. She has received a Guggenheim Fellowship and has built a broad reputation for the many stories she has published in The New Yorker. *These stories have made her the spokesperson for the generation of the sixties as they adapt to or are baffled and worn down by the oncoming years. She writes of those who took the sixties to be a Golden Age and cannot free themselves from the enchantment laid on them in their youth. Her books of short stories include* Distortions *(1976),* Secrets and Surprises *(1979),* The Burning House *(1982), and* Where You'll Find Me *(1986). Her novels are* Chilly Scenes of Winter *(1976),* Falling in Place *(1980),* Love Always *(1985), and* Picturing Will *(1990).*

Janus[1]

The bowl was perfect. Perhaps it was not what you'd select if you faced a shelf of bowls, and not the sort of thing that would inevitably attract a lot of attention at a crafts fair, yet it had real presence. It was as predictably admired as a mutt who has no reason to suspect he might be funny. Just such a dog, in fact, was often brought out (and in) along with the bowl.

Andrea was a real estate agent, and when she thought that some prospective buyers might be dog lovers, she would drop off her dog at the same time she placed the bowl in the house that was up for sale. She would put a dish of water in the kitchen for Mondo, take his squeaking plastic frog out of her purse and drop it on the floor. He would pounce delightedly, just as he did every day at home, batting around his favorite toy. The bowl usually sat on a coffee table, though recently she had displayed it on top of a pine blanket chest and on a lacquered table. It was once placed on a cherry table beneath a Bonnard[2] still life, where it held its own.

Everyone who has purchased a house or who has wanted to sell a house must be familiar with some of the tricks used to convince a

1. Roman god with two faces. 2. Pierre Bonnard (1867–1947), French painter.

buyer that the house is quite special: a fire in the fireplace in early evening; jonquils in a pitcher on the kitchen counter, where no one ordinarily has space to put flowers; perhaps the slight aroma of spring, made by a single drop of scent vaporizing from a lamp bulb.

The wonderful thing about the bowl, Andrea thought, was that it was both subtle and noticeable—a paradox of a bowl. Its glaze was the color of cream and seemed to glow no matter what light it was placed in. There were a few bits of color in it—tiny geometric flashes—and some of these were tinged with flecks of silver. They were as mysterious as cells seen under a microscope; it was difficult not to study them, because they shimmered, flashing for a split second, and then resumed their shape. Something about the colors and their random placement suggested motion. People who liked country furniture always commented on the bowl, but then it turned out that people who felt comfortable with Biedermeier[3] loved it just as much. But the bowl was not at all ostentatious, or even so noticeable that anyone would suspect that it had been put in place deliberately. They might notice the height of the ceiling on first entering a room, and only when their eye moved down from that, or away from the refraction of sunlight on a pale wall, would they see the bowl. Then they would go immediately to it and comment. Yet they always faltered when they tried to say something. Perhaps it was because they were in the house for a serious reason, not to notice some object.

Once, Andrea got a call from a woman who had not put in an offer on a house she had shown her. That bowl, she said—would it be possible to find out where the owners had bought that beautiful bowl? Andrea pretended that she did not know what the woman was referring to. A bowl, somewhere in the house? Oh, on a table under the window. Yes, she would ask, of course. She let a couple of days pass, then called back to say that the bowl had been a present and the people did not know where it had been purchased.

When the bowl was not being taken from house to house, it sat on Andrea's coffee table at home. She didn't keep it carefully wrapped (although she transported it that way, in a box); she kept it on the table, because she liked to see it. It was large enough so that it didn't seem fragile, or particularly vulnerable if anyone sideswiped the table or Mondo blundered into it at play. She had asked her husband to please not drop his house key in it. It was meant to be empty.

When her husband first noticed the bowl, he had peered into it and smiled briefly. He always urged her to buy things she liked. In recent years, both of them had acquired many things to make up for all the lean years when they were graduate students, but now that they

3. A style of furnishing common in German-speaking areas in the early nineteenth century.

had been comfortable for quite a while, the pleasure of new possessions dwindled. Her husband had pronounced the bowl "pretty," and he had turned away without picking it up to examine it. He had no more interest in the bowl than she had in his new Leica.[4]

She was sure that the bowl brought her luck. Bids were often put in on houses where she had displayed the bowl. Sometimes the owners, who were always asked to be away or to step outside when the house was being shown, didn't even know that the bowl had been in their house. Once—she could not imagine how—she left it behind, and then she was so afraid that something might have happened to it that she rushed back to the house and sighed with relief when the woman owner opened the door. The bowl, Andrea explained—she had purchased a bowl and set it on the chest for safekeeping while she toured the house with the prospective buyers, and she . . . She felt like rushing past the frowning woman and seizing her bowl. The owner stepped aside, and it was only when Andrea ran to the chest that the lady glanced at her a little strangely. In the few seconds before Andrea picked up the bowl, she realized that the owner must have just seen that it had been perfectly placed, that the sunlight struck the bluer part of it. Her pitcher had been moved to the far side of the chest, and the bowl predominated. All the way home, Andrea wondered how she could have left the bowl behind. It was like leaving a friend at an outing—just walking off. Sometimes there were stories in the paper about families forgetting a child somewhere and driving to the next city. Andrea had only gone a mile down the road before she remembered.

In time, she dreamed of the bowl. Twice, in a waking dream—early in the morning, between sleep and a last nap before rising—she had a clear vision of it. It came into sharp focus and startled her for a moment—the same bowl she looked at every day.

She had a very profitable year selling real estate. Word spread, and she had more clients than she felt comfortable with. She had the foolish thought that if only the bowl were an animate object she could thank it. There were times when she wanted to talk to her husband about the bowl. He was a stockbroker, and sometimes told people that he was fortunate to be married to a woman who had such a fine aesthetic sense and yet could also function in the real world. They were a lot alike, really—they had agreed on that. They were both quiet people—reflective, slow to make value judgments, but almost intractable once they had come to a conclusion. They both liked details, but while ironies attracted her, he was more impatient and dismissive when matters became many sided or unclear. But they both knew this; it was

4. An expensive camera.

the kind of thing they could talk about when they were alone in the car together, coming home from a party or after a weekend with friends. But she never talked to him about the bowl. When they were at dinner, exchanging their news of the day, or while they lay in bed at night listening to the stereo and murmuring sleepy disconnections, she was often tempted to come right out and say that she thought that the bowl in the living room, the cream-colored bowl, was responsible for her success. But she didn't say it. She couldn't begin to explain it. Sometimes in the morning, she would look at him and feel guilty that she had such a constant secret.

Could it be that she had some deeper connection with the bowl—a relationship of some kind? She corrected her thinking: how could she imagine such a thing, when she was a human being and it was a bowl? It was ridiculous. Just think of how people lived together and loved each other . . . But was that always so clear, always a relationship? She was confused by these thoughts, but they remained in her mind. There was something within her now, something real, that she never talked about.

The bowl was a mystery, even to her. It was frustrating, because her involvement with the bowl contained a steady sense of unrequited good fortune; it would have been easier to respond if some sort of demand were made in return. But that only happened in fairy tales. The bowl was just a bowl. She did not believe that for one second. What she believed was that it was something she loved.

In the past, she had sometimes talked to her husband about a new property she was about to buy or sell—confiding some clever strategy she had devised to persuade owners who seemed ready to sell. Now she stopped doing that, for all her strategies involved the bowl. She became more deliberate with the bowl, and more possessive. She put it in houses only when no one was there, and removed it when she left the house. Instead of just moving a pitcher or a dish, she would remove all the other objects from a table. She had to force herself to handle them carefully, because she didn't really care about them. She just wanted them out of sight.

She wondered how the situation would end. As with a lover, there was no exact scenario of how matters would come to a close. Anxiety became the operative force. It would be irrelevant if the lover rushed into someone else's arms, or wrote her a note and departed to another city. The horror was the possibility of the disappearance. That was what mattered.

She would get up at night and look at the bowl. It never occurred to her that she might break it. She washed and dried it without anxiety, and she moved it often, from coffee table to mahogany corner table or wherever, without fearing an accident. It was clear that she would not be the one who would do anything to the bowl. The bowl was only handled by her, set safely on one surface or another; it was not very likely that anyone would break it. A bowl was a poor conductor of electricity: it would not be hit by lightning. Yet the idea of damage persisted. She did not think beyond that—to what her life would be without the bowl. She only continued to fear that some accident would happen. Why not, in a world where people set plants where they did not belong, so that visitors touring a house would be fooled into thinking that dark corners got sunlight—a world full of tricks?

She had first seen the bowl several years earlier, at a crafts fair she had visited half in secret, with her lover. He had urged her to buy the bowl. She didn't *need* any more things, she told him. But she had been drawn to the bowl, and they had lingered near it. Then she went on to the next booth, and he came up behind her, tapping the rim against her shoulder as she ran her fingers over a wood carving. "You're still insisting that I buy that?" she said. "No," he said. "I bought it for you." He had bought her other things before this—things she liked more, at first—the child's ebony-and-turquoise ring that fitted her little finger; the wooden box, long and thin, beautifully dovetailed, that she used to hold paper clips; the soft gray sweater with a pouch pocket. It was his idea that when he could not be there to hold her hand she could hold her own—clasp her hands inside the lone pocket that stretched across the front. But in time she became more attached to the bowl than to any of his other presents. She tried to talk herself out of it. She owned other things that were more striking or valuable. It wasn't an object whose beauty jumped out at you; a lot of people must have passed it by before the two of them saw it that day.

Her lover had said that she was always too slow to know what she really loved. Why continue with her life the way it was? Why be two-faced, he asked her. He had made the first move toward her. When she would not decide in his favor, would not change her life and come to him, he asked her what made her think she could have it both ways. And then he made the last move and left. It was a decision meant to break her will, to shatter her intransigent ideas about honoring previous commitments.

Time passed. Alone in the living room at night, she often looked at the bowl sitting on the table, still and safe, unilluminated. In its way, it was perfect: the world cut in half, deep and smoothly empty. Near the rim, even in dim light, the eye moved toward one small flash of blue, a vanishing point on the horizon.

---

1. How do you account for the affinity between Andrea and the bowl? Is the base of this relationship supernatural, psychological, or aesthetic?

2. Is it important that the bowl was a gift from a lover who, in effect, cast her off?
3. How does the bowl, and her feelings for it, fit into Andrea's marriage?
4. Is the emptiness of the bowl a significant quality in its symbolic communication to Andrea . . . and to the reader?

Saul Bellow

Bellow (1915–) was born in Lachine, Quebec. He was educated at the University of Chicago, Northwestern University, and the University of Wisconsin, where he gradually drifted from studies in anthropology into a determination to write fiction. His first two novels, Dangling Man *(1944) and* The Victim *(1945), were tightly controlled in language and conception, but with* The Adventures of Augie March *(1953) Bellow burst into the flamboyant celebration of the potentials of the individual that has characterized his subsequent work. He has lived in Chicago for most of his later life, teaching and writing there, and this mid-American location seems to be reflected by the spirit and subject matter of his fiction, with its discoveries of eccentrics who wrestle with the quandaries of the individual destiny in a variety of American settings. Bellow has won numerous prizes and honors, among them the National Book Awards of 1954, 1965, and 1971. He was given the Nobel Prize in 1976. His novels include* Henderson the Rain King *(1959),* Herzog *(1964),* Mr. Sammler's Planet *(1970),* Humboldt's Gift *(1975),* The Dean's December *(1982), and* More Die of Heartbreak *(1987). Some of his stories are collected in* Seize the Day *(1956),* Mosby's Memoirs and Other Stories *(1968), and* Him with His Foot in His Mouth and Other Stories *(1984). His novella* A Theft *was published in 1989.*

Leaving the Yellow House

The neighbors—there were in all six white people who lived at Sego Desert Lake—told one another that old Hattie could no longer make it alone. The desert life, even with a forced-air furnace in the house and butane gas brought from town in a truck, was still too difficult for her. There were women even older than Hattie in the county. Twenty miles away was Amy Walters, the gold miner's widow. But she was a hardier old girl. Every day of the year she took a bath in the icy lake. And Amy was crazy about money and knew how to manage it, as Hattie did not. Hattie was not exactly a drunkard, but she hit the bottle pretty hard, and now she was in trouble and there was a limit to the help she could expect from even the best of neighbors.

They were fond of her, though. You couldn't help being fond of Hattie. She was big and cheerful, puffy, comic, boastful, with a big round back and stiff, rather long legs. Before the century began she had graduated from finishing school and studied the organ in Paris. But now she didn't know a note from a skillet. She had tantrums when she played canasta. And all that remained of her fine fair hair was frizzled along her forehead in small gray curls. Her forehead was not much wrinkled, but the skin was bluish, the color of skim milk. She walked with long strides in spite of the heaviness of her hips, pushing on, roundbacked, with her shoulders and showing the flat rubber bottoms of her shoes.

Once a week, in the same cheerful, plugging but absent way, she took off her short skirt and the dirty aviator's jacket with the wool collar and put on a girdle, a dress, and high-heeled shoes. When she stood on these heels her fat old body trembled. She wore a big brown Rembrandt-like tam with a ten-cent-store brooch, eye-like, carefully centered. She drew a straight line with lipstick on her mouth, leaving part of the upper lip pale. At the wheel of her old turret-shaped car, she drove, seemingly methodical but speeding dangerously, across forty miles of mountainous desert to buy frozen meat pies and whisky. She went to the Laundromat and the hairdresser, and then had lunch with two martinis at the Arlington. Afterward she would often visit Marian Nabot's Silvermine Hotel at Miller Street near skid row and pass the rest of the day gossiping and drinking with her cronies, old divorcees like herself who had settled in the West. Hattie never gambled anymore and she didn't care for the movies. And at five o'clock she drove back at the same speed, calmly, partly blinded by the smoke of her cigarette. The fixed cigarette gave her a watering eye.

The Rolfes and the Paces were her only white neighbors at Sego Desert Lake. There was Sam Jervis too, but he was only an old gandywalker[1] who did odd jobs in her garden, and she did not count him. Nor did she count among her neighbors Darly, the dudes' cowboy who worked for the Paces, nor Swede, the telegrapher. Pace had a guest ranch, and Rolfe and his wife were rich and had retired. Thus there were three good houses at the lake, Hattie's yellow house, Paces's, and the Rolfes'. All the rest of the population—Sam, Swede, Watchtah the section foreman, and the Mexicans and Indians and Negroes—lived in shacks and boxcars. There were very few trees, cottonwoods and box elders. Everything else, down to the shores, was sagebrush and juniper. The lake was what remained of an old sea that had covered the volcanic mountains. To the north there were some tungsten mines; to the south, fifteen miles, was an Indian village—shacks built of plywood or railroad ties.

In this barren place Hattie had lived for more than twenty years.

1. Railroad employee who walks the tracks to inspect them and make minor repairs.

Her first summer was spent not in a house but in an Indian wickiup on the shore. She used to say that she had watched the stars from this almost roofless shelter. After her divorce she took up with a cowboy named Wicks. Neither of them had any money—it was the Depression—and they had lived on the range, trapping coyotes for a living. Once a month they would come into town and rent a room and go on a bender. Hattie told this sadly, but also gloatingly, and with many trimmings. A thing no sooner happened to her than it was transformed into something else. "We were caught in a storm," she said, "and we rode hard, down to the lake and knocked on the door of the yellow house"—now her house. "Alice Parmenter took us in and let us sleep on the floor." What had actually happened was that the wind was blowing—there had been no storm—and they were not far from the house anyway; and Alice Parmenter, who knew that Hattie and Wicks were not married, offered them separate beds; but Hattie, swaggering, had said in a loud voice, "Why get two sets of sheets dirty?" And her and her cowboy had slept in Alice's bed while Alice had taken the sofa.

Then Wicks went away. There was never anybody like him in the sack; he was brought up in a whorehouse and the girls had taught him everything, said Hattie. She didn't really understand what she was saying but believed that she was being Western. More than anything else she wanted to be thought of as a rough, experienced woman of the West. Still, she was a lady, too. She had good silver and good china and engraved stationery, but she kept canned beans and A-1 sauce and tuna fish and bottles of catsup and fruit salad on the library shelves of her living room. On her night table was the Bible her pious brother Angus—the other brother was a heller—had given her; but behind the little door of the commode was a bottle of bourbon. When she awoke in the night she tippled herself back to sleep. In the glove compartment of her old car she kept little sample bottles for emergencies on the road. Old Darly found them after her accident.

The accident did not happen far out in the desert as she had always feared, but very near home. She had had a few martinis with the Rolfes one evening, and as she was driving home over the railroad crossing she lost control of the car and veered off the crossing onto the tracks. The explanation she gave was that she had sneezed, and the sneeze had blinded her and made her twist the wheel. The motor was killed and all four wheels of the car sat smack on the rails. Hattie crept down from the door, high off the roadbed. A great fear took hold of her—for the car, for the future, and not only for the future but spreading back into the past—and she began to hurry on stiff legs through the sagebrush to Pace's ranch.

Now the Paces were away on a hunting trip and had left Darly in charge; he was tending bar in the old cabin that went back to the days of the pony express, when Hattie burst in. There were two customers, a tungsten miner and his girl.

"Darly, I'm in trouble. Help me. I've had an accident," said Hattie.

How the face of a man will alter when a woman had bad news to tell him! It happened now to lean old Darly; his eyes went flat and looked unwilling, his jaw moved in and out, his wrinkled cheeks began to flush, and he said, "What's the matter—what's happened to you now?"

"I'm stuck on the tracks. I sneezed. I lost control of the car. Tow me off, Darly. With the pickup. Before the train comes."

Darly threw down his towel and stamped his high-heeled boots. "Now what have you gone and done?" he said. "I told you to stay home after dark."

"Where's Pace? Ring the fire bell and fetch Pace."

"There's nobody on the property except me," said the lean old man. "And I'm not supposed to close the bar and you know it as well as I do."

"Please, Darly. I can't leave my car on the tracks."

"Too bad!" he said. Nevertheless he moved from behind the bar. "How did you say it happened?"

"I told you, I sneezed," said Hattie.

Everyone, as she later told it, was as drunk as sixteen thousand dollars: Darly, the miner, and the miner's girl.

Darly was limping as he locked the door of the bar. A year before, a kick from one of Pace's mares had broken his ribs as he was loading her into the trailer, and he hadn't recovered from it. He was too old. But he dissembled the pain. The high-heeled narrow boots helped, and his painful bending looked like the ordinary stooping posture of a cowboy. However, Darly was not a genuine cowboy, like Pace who had grown up in the saddle. He was a latecomer from the East and until the age of forty had never been on horseback. In this respect he and Hattie were alike. They were not genuine Westerners.

Hattie hurried after him through the ranch yard.

"Damn you!" he said to her. "I got thirty bucks out of that sucker and I would have skinned him out of his whole pay check if you minded your business. Pace is going to be sore as hell."

"You've got to help me. We're neighbors," said Hattie.

"You're not fit to be living out here. You can't do it any more. Besides, you're swacked all the time."

Hattie couldn't afford to talk back. The thought of her car on the tracks made her frantic. If a freight came now and smashed it, her life at Sego Desert Lake would be finished. And where would she go then? She was not fit to live in this place. She had never made the grade at all, only seemed to have made it. And Darly—why did he say such hurtful things to her? Because he himself was sixty-eight years old, and he had no other place to go, either; he took bad treatment from Pace besides. Darly stayed because his only alternative was to go to the soldiers' home. Moreover, the dude women would still crawl into his sack. They wanted a cowboy and they thought he was one. Why, he couldn't even raise himself out of his bunk in the morning. And where else would he get women? "After the dude season," she wanted to say to him, "you always have to go to the Veterans' Hospital to get fixed up again." But she didn't dare offend him now.

The moon was due to rise. It appeared as they drove over the ungraded dirt road toward the crossing where Hattie's turret-shaped car was sitting on the rails. Driving very fast, Darly wheeled the pickup around, spraying dirt on the miner and his girl, who had followed in their car.

"You get behind the wheel and steer," Darly told Hattie.

She climbed into the seat. Waiting at the wheel, she lifted up her face and said, "Please God, I didn't bend the axle or crack the oil pan."

When Darly crawled under the bumper of Hattie's car the pain in his ribs suddenly cut off his breath, so instead of doubling the tow chain he fastened it at full length. He rose and trotted back to the truck on the tight boots. Motion seemed the only remedy for the pain; not even booze did the trick any more. He put the pickup into towing gear and began to pull. One side of Hattie's car dropped into the roadbed with a heave of springs. She sat with a stormy, frightened, conscience-stricken face, racing the motor until she flooded it.

The tungsten miner yelled, "Your chain's too long."

Hattie was raised high in the air by the pitch of the wheels. She had to roll down the window to let herself out because the door handle had been jammed from inside for years. Hattie struggled out on the uplifted side crying, "I better call the Swede. I better have him signal. There's a train due."

"Go on, then," said Darly. "You're no good here."

"Darly, be careful with my car. Be careful."

The ancient sea bed at this place was flat and low, and the lights of her car and of the truck and of the tungsten miner's Chevrolet were bright and big at twenty miles. Hattie was too frightened to think of this. All she could think was that she was a procrastinating old woman, she had lived by delays; she had meant to stop drinking, she had put off the time, and now she had smashed her car—a terrible end, a terrible judgment on her. She got to the ground and, drawing up her skirt, she started to get over the tow chain. To prove that the chain didn't have to be shortened, and to get the whole thing over with,

Darly threw the pickup forward again. The chain jerked up and struck Hattie in the knee and she fell forward and broke her arm.

She cried, "Darly, Darly, I'm hurt. I fell."

"The old lady tripped on the chain," said the miner. "Back up here and I'll double it for you. You're getting nowheres."

Drunkenly the miner lay down on his back in the dark, soft red cinders of the roadbed. Darly had backed up to slacken the chain.

Darly hurt the miner, too. He tore some skin from his fingers by racing ahead before the chain was secure. Without complaining, the miner wrapped his hand in his shirttail saying, "She'll do it now." The old car came down from the tracks and stood on the shoulder of the road.

"There's your goddamn car," said Darly to Hattie.

"Is it all right?" she said. Her left side was covered with dirt, but she managed to pick herself up and stand, roundbacked and heavy, on her stiff legs. "I'm hurt, Darly." She tried to convince him of it.

"Hell if you are," he said. He believed she was putting on an act to escape blame. The pain in his ribs made him especially impatient with her. "Christ, if you can't look after yourself any more you've got no business out here."

"You're old yourself," she said. "Look what you did to me. You can't hold your liquor."

This offended him greatly. He said, "I'll take you to the Rolfes. They let you booze it up in the first place, so let them worry about you. I'm tired of your bunk, Hattie."

He raced uphill. Chains, spade, and crowbar clashed on the sides of the pickup. She was frightened and held her arm and cried. Rolfe's dogs jumped at her to lick her when she went through the gate. She shrank from them crying, "Down, down."

"Darly," she cried in the darkness, "take care of my car. Don't leave it standing there on the road. Darly, take care of it, please."

But Darly in his ten-gallon hat, his chin-bent face wrinkled, small and angry, a furious pain in his ribs, tore away at high speed.

"Oh, God, what will I do," she said.

The Rolfes were having a last drink before dinner, sitting at their fire of pitchy railroad ties, when Hattie opened the door. Her knee was bleeding, her eyes were tiny with shock, her face gray with dust.

"I'm hurt," she said desperately. "I had an accident. I sneezed and lost control of the wheel. Jerry, look after the car. It's on the road."

They bandaged her knee and took her home and put her to bed. Helen Rolfe wrapped a heating pad around her arm.

"I can't have the pad," Hattie complained. "The switch goes on and off, and every time it does it starts my generator and uses up the gas."

"Ah, now, Hattie," Rolfe said, "this is not the time to be stingy. We'll take you to town in the morning and have you looked over. Helen will phone Dr. Stroud."

Hattie wanted to say, "Stingy! Why you're the stingy ones. I just haven't got anything. You and Helen are ready to hit each other over two bits in canasta." But the Rolfes were good to her; they were her only real friends here. Darly would have let her lie in the yard all night, and Pace would have sold her to the bone man. He'd give her to the knacker[2] for a buck.

So she didn't talk back to the Rolfes, but as soon as they left the yellow house and walked through the super-clear moonlight under the great skirt of box-elder shadows to their new station wagon, Hattie turned off the switch, and the heavy swirling and battering of the generator stopped. Presently she became aware of real pain, deeper pain, in her arm, and she sat rigid, warming the injured place with her hand. It seemed to her that she could feel the bone sticking out. Before leaving, Helen Rolfe had thrown over her a comforter that had belonged to Hattie's dead friend India, from whom she had inherited the small house and everything in it. Had the comforter lain on India's bed the night she died? Hattie tried to remember, but her thoughts were mixed up. She was fairly sure the deathbed pillow was in the loft, and she believed she had put the death bedding in a trunk. Then how had this comforter got out? She couldn't do anything about it now but draw it away from contact with her skin. It kept her legs warm. This she accepted, but she didn't want it any nearer.

More and more Hattie saw her own life as though, from birth to the present, every moment had been filmed. Her fancy was that when she died she would see the film shown. Then she would know how she had appeared from the back, watering the plants, in the bathroom, asleep, playing the organ, embracing—everything, even tonight, in pain, almost the last pain, perhaps, for she couldn't take much more. How many twists and angles had life to show her yet? There couldn't be much film left. To lie awake and think such thoughts was the worst thing in the world. Better death than insomnia. Hattie not only loved sleep, she believed in it.

The first attempt to set the bone was not successful. "Look what they've done to me," said Hattie and showed visitors the discolored breast. After the second operation her mind wandered. The sides of her bed had to be raised, for in her delirium she roamed the wards. She cursed at the nurses when they shut her in. "You can't make people prisoners in a democracy without a trial, you bitches." She had

2. Someone who buys decrepit domestic animals and butchers them for food or fertilizer.

learned from Wicks how to swear. "*He* was profane," she used to say. "I picked it up unconsciously."

For several weeks her mind was not clear. Asleep, her face was lifeless; her cheeks were puffed out and her mouth, no longer wide and grinning, was drawn round and small. Helen sighed when she saw her.

"Shall we get in touch with her family?" Helen asked the doctor. His skin was white and thick. He had chestnut hair, abundant but very dry. He sometimes explained to his patients, "I had a tropical disease during the war."

He asked, "Is there a family?"

"Old brothers. Cousins' children," said Helen. She tried to think who would be called to her own bedside (she was old enough for that). Rolfe would see that she was cared for. He would hire private nurses. Hattie could not afford that. She had already gone beyond her means. A trust company in Philadelphia paid her eighty dollars a month. She had a small savings account.

"I suppose it'll be up to us to get her out of hock," said Rolfe. "Unless the brother down in Mexico comes across. We may have to phone one of those old guys."

In the end, no relations had to be called. Hattie began to recover. At last she could recognize visitors, though her mind was still in disorder. Much that had happened she couldn't recall.

"How many quarts of blood did they have to give me?" she kept asking. "I seem to remember five, six, eight different transfusions. Daylight, electric light . . ." She tried to smile, but she couldn't make a pleasant face as yet. "How am I going to pay?" she said. "At twenty-five bucks a quart. My little bit of money is just about wiped out."

Blood became her constant topic, her preoccupation. She told everyone who came to see her, "—have to replace all that blood. They poured gallons into me. Gallons. I hope it was all good." And, though very weak, she began to grin and laugh again. There was more hissing in her laughter than formerly; the illness had affected her chest.

"No cigarettes, no booze," the doctor told Helen.

"Doctor," Helen asked him, "do you expect her to change?"

"All the same, I am obliged to say it."

"Life sober may not be much of a temptation to her," said Helen.

Her husband laughed. When Rolfe's laughter was intense it blinded one of his eyes. His short Irish face turned red; on the bridge of his small, sharp nose the skin whitened. "Hattie's like me," he said. "She'll be in business till she's cleaned out. And if Sego Lake turned to whisky she'd use her last strength to knock her old yellow house down to build a raft of it. She'd float away on whisky. So why talk temperance?"

Hattie recognized the similarity between them. When he came to see her she said, "Jerry, you're the only one I can really talk to about my troubles. What am I going to do for money? I have Hotchkiss Insurance. I paid eight dollars a month."

"That won't do you much good, Hat. No Blue Cross?"

"I let it drop ten years ago. Maybe I could sell some of my valuables."

"What valuables have you got?" he said. His eye began to droop with laughter.

"Why," she said defiantly, "there's plenty. First there's the beautiful, precious Persian rug that India left me."

"Coals from the fireplace have been burning it for years, Hat!"

"The rug is in *perfect* condition," she said with an angry sway of the shoulders. "As beautiful object like that never loses its value. And the oak table from the Spanish monastery is three hundred years old."

"With luck you could get twenty bucks for it. It would cost fifty to haul it out of here. It's the house you ought to sell."

"The house?" she said. Yes, that had been in her mind. "I'd have to get twenty thousand for it."

"Eight is a fair price."

"Fifteen. . . ." She was offended, and her voice recovered its strength. "India put eight into it in two years. And don't forget that Sego Lake is one of the most beautiful places in the world."

"But where is it? Five hundred and some miles to San Francisco and two hundred to Salt Lake City. Who wants to live way out here but a few eccentrics like you and India? And me?"

"There are things you can't put a price tag on. Beautiful things."

"Oh, bull, Hattie! You don't know squat about beautiful things. Any more than I do. I live here because it figures for me, and you because India left you the house. And just in the nick of time, too. Without it you wouldn't have had a pot of your own."

His words offended Hattie; more than that, they frightened her. She was silent and then grew thoughtful, for she was fond of Jerry Rolfe and he of her. He had good sense and moreover he only expressed her own thoughts. He spoke no more than the truth about India's death and the house. But she told herself, He doesn't know everything. You'd have to pay a San Francisco architect ten thousand just to *think* of such a house. Before he drew a line.

"Jerry," the old woman said, "what am I going to do about replacing the blood in the blood bank?"

"Do you want a quart from me, Hat?" His eye began to fall shut.

"You won't do. You had that tumor, two years ago. I think Darly ought to give some."

"The old man?" Rolfe laughed at her. "You want to kill him?"

"Why!" said Hattie with anger, lifting up her massive face. Fever and perspiration had frayed the fringe of curls; at the back of the head the hair had knotted and matted so that it had to be shaved. "Darly almost killed me. It's his fault that I'm in this condition. He must have *some* blood in him. He runs after all the chicks—all of them—young and old."

"Come, you were drunk, too," said Rolfe.

"I've driven drunk for forty years. It was the sneeze. Oh, Jerry, I feel wrung out," said Hattie, haggard, sitting forward in bed. But her face was cleft by her nonsensically happy grin. She was not one to be miserable for long; she had the expression of a perennial survivor.

Every other day she went to the therapist. The young woman worked her arm for her; it was a pleasure and a comfort to Hattie, who would have been glad to leave the whole cure to her. However, she was given other exercises to do, and these were not so easy. They rigged a pulley for her and Hattie had to hold both ends of a rope and saw it back and forth through the scraping little wheel. She bent heavily from the hips and coughed over her cigarette. But the most important exercise of all she shirked. This required her to put the flat of her hand to the wall at the level of her hips and, by working her finger tips slowly, to make the hand ascend to the height of her shoulders. That was painful; she often forgot to do it, although the doctor warned her, "Hattie, you don't want adhesions,[3] do you?"

A light of despair crossed Hattie's eyes. Then she said, "Oh, Dr. Stroud, buy my house from me."

"I'm a bachelor. What would I do with a house?"

"I know just the girl for you—my cousin's daughter. Perfectly charming and very brainy. Just about got her Ph.D."

"You must get quite a few proposals yourself," said the doctor.

"From crazy desert rats. They chase me. But," she said, "after I pay my bills I'll be in pretty punk shape. If at least I could replace that blood in the blood bank I'd feel easier."

"If you don't do as the therapist tells you, Hattie, you'll need another operation. Do you know what adhesions are?"

She knew. But Hattie thought, *How long must I go on taking care of myself?* It made her angry to hear him speak of another operation. She had a moment of panic, but she covered it up. With him, this young man whose skin was already as thick as buttermilk and whose chestnut hair was as dry as death, she always assumed the part of a child. In a small voice she said, "Yes, doctor." But her heart was in a fury.

3. Consequences of an operation or injury in which body tissues in healing become attached to the wrong muscles or organs.

Night and day, however, she repeated, "I was in the Valley of the Shadow.[4] But I'm alive." She was weak, she was old, she couldn't follow a train of thought very easily, she felt faint in the head. But she was still here; here was her body, it filled space, a great body. And though she had worries and perplexities, and once in a while her arm felt as though it was about to give her the last stab of all; and though her hair was scrappy and old, like onion roots, and scattered like nothing under the comb, yet she sat and amused herself with visitors; her great grin split her face; her heart warmed with every kind word.

And she thought, People will help me out. It never did me any good to worry. At the last minute something turned up, when I wasn't looking for it. Marian loves me. Helen and Jerry love me. Half Pint loves me. They would never let me go to the ground. And I love them. If it were the other way around, I'd never let them go down.

Above the horizon, in a baggy vastness which Hattie by herself occasionally visited, the features of India, her *shade,* sometimes rose. India was indignant and scolding. Not mean. Not really mean. Few people had ever been really mean to Hattie. But India was annoyed with her. "The garden is going to hell, Hattie," she said. "Those lilac bushes are all shriveled."

"But what can I do? The hose is rotten. It broke. It won't reach."

"Then dig a trench," said the phantom of India. "Have old Sam dig a trench. But save the bushes."

Am I thy servant still? said Hattie to herself. *No,* she thought, *let the dead bury their dead.*[5]

But she didn't defy India now any more than she had done when they lived together. Hattie was supposed to keep India off the bottle, but often both of them began to get drunk after breakfast. They forgot to dress, and in their slips the two of them wandered drunkenly around the house and blundered into each other, and they were in despair at having been so weak. Late in the afternoon they would be sitting in the living room, waiting for the sun to set. It shrank, burning itself out on the crumbling edges of the mountains. When the sun passed, the fury of the daylight ended and the mountain surfaces were more blue, broken, like cliffs of coal. They no longer suggested faces. The east began to look simple, and the lake less inhuman and haughty. At last India would say, "Hattie—it's time for the lights." And Hattie would pull the switch chains of the lamps, several of them, to give the generator a good shove. She would turn on some of the wobbling eighteenth-century-style lamps whose shades stood out from their slender bodies like dragonflies' wings. The little engine in the shed would shuf-

4. Psalms 23:4: "Yea, though I walk through the valley of the shadow of death, I will fear no evil. . . ."
5. Luke 9:60 "Jesus said unto him, Let the dead bury their dead; but go thou and preach the kingdom of God."

fle, then spit, then charge and bang, and the first weak light would rise unevenly in the bulbs.

"Hettie!" cried India. After she drank she was penitent, but her penitence too was a hardship to Hattie, and the worse her temper the more British her accent became. *"Where the hell ah you Hettie!"* After India's death Hattie found some poems she had written in which she, Hattie, was affectionately and even touchingly mentioned. That was a good thing—Literature. Education. Breeding. But Hattie's interest in ideas was very small, whereas India had been all over the world. India was used to brilliant society. India wanted her to discuss Eastern religion, Bergson and Proust,[6] and Hattie had no head for this, and so India blamed her drinking on Hattie. "I can't talk to you," she would say. "You don't understand religion or culture. And I'm here because I'm not fit to be anywhere else. I can't live in New York any more. It's too dangerous for a woman my age to be drunk in the street at night."

And Hattie, talking to her Western friends about India, would say, "She is a lady" (implying that they made a pair). "She is a creative person" (this was why they found each other so congenial). "But helpless? Completely. Why she can't even get her own girdle on."

"Hettie! Come here. Het-tie! Do you know what sloth is?"

Undressed, India sat on her bed and with the cigarette in her drunken, wrinkled, ringed hand she burned holes in the blankets. On Hattie's pride she left many small scars, too. She treated her like a servant.

Weeping, India begged her afterward to forgive her. *"Hattie, please don't condemn me in your heart. Forgive me, dear, I know I am bad. But I hurt myself more in my evil than I hurt you."*

Hattie would keep a stiff bearing. She would lift up her face with its incurved nose and puffy eyes and say, "I am a Christian person. I never bear a grudge." And by repeating this she actually brought herself to forgive India.

But of course Hattie had no husband, no child, no skill, no savings. And what she would have done if India had not died and left her the yellow house nobody knows.

Jerry Rolfe said privately to Marian, "Hattie can't do anything for herself. If I hadn't been around during the forty-four blizzard she and India both would have starved. She's always been careless and lazy and now she can't even chase a cow out of the yard. She's too feeble. The thing for her to do is to go East to her damn brother. Hattie would have ended at the poor farm if it hadn't been for India. But besides the damn house India should have left her some dough. She didn't use her goddamn head."

6. Henri Bergson (1859–1941), French philosopher; Marcel Proust (1871–1922), French novelist.

When Hattie returned to the lake she stayed with the Rolfes. "Well, old shellback," said Jerry, "there's a little more life in you now."

Indeed, with joyous eyes, the cigarette in her mouth and her hair newly frizzed and overhanging her forehead, she seemed to have triumphed again. She was pale, but she grinned, she chuckled, and she held a bourbon old-fashioned with a cherry and a slice of orange in it. She was on rations; the Rolfes allowed her two a day. Her back, Helen noted, was more bent than before. Her knees went outward a little weakly; her feet, however, came close together at the ankles.

"Oh, Helen dear and Jerry dear, I am so thankful, so glad to be back at the lake. I can look after my place again, and I'm here to see the spring. It's more gorgeous than ever."

Heavy rains had fallen while Hattie was away. The sego lilies, which bloomed only after a wet winter, came up from the loose dust, especially around the marl[7] pit; but even on the burnt granite they seemed to grow. Desert peach was beginning to appear, and in Hattie's yard the rosebushes were filling out. The roses were yellow and abundant, and the odor they gave off was like that of damp tea leaves.

"Before it gets hot enough for the rattlesnakes," said Hattie to Helen, "we ought to drive up to Marky's ranch and gather watercress."

Hattie was going to attend to lots of things, but the heat came early that year and, as there was no television to keep her awake, she slept most of the day. She was now able to dress herself, though there was little more that she could do. Sam Jervis rigged the pulley for her on the porch and she remembered once in a while to use it. Mornings when she had her strength she rambled over to her own house, examining things, being important and giving orders to Sam Jervis and Wanda Gingham. At ninety, Wanda, a Shoshone,[8] was still an excellent seamstress and housecleaner.

Hattie looked over the car, which was parked under a cottonwood tree. She tested the engine. Yes, the old pot would still go. Proudly, happily, she listened to the noise of tappets; the dry old pipe shook as the smoke went out at the rear. She tried to work the shift, turn the wheel. That, as yet, she couldn't do. But it would come soon, she was confident.

At the back of the house the soil had caved in a little over the cesspool and a few of the old railroad ties over the top had rotted. Otherwise things were in good shape. Sam had looked after the garden. He had fixed a new catch for the gate after Pace's horses—maybe because he could never afford to keep them in hay—had broken in and Sam found them grazing and drove them out. Luckily, they hadn't damaged many of her plants. Hattie felt a moment of wild rage against

7. An earth deposit of sand, silt, or clay. 8. A tribe of Indians indigenous to the West.

Pace. He had brought the horses into her garden for a free feed, she was sure. But her anger didn't last long. It was reabsorbed into the feeling of golden pleasure that enveloped her. She had little strength, but all that she had was a pleasure to her. So she forgave even Pace, who would have liked to do her out of the house, who had always used her, embarrassed her, cheated her at cards, swindled her. All that he did he did for the sake of his quarter horses. He was a fool about horses. They were ruining him. Racing horses was a millionaire's amusement.

She saw his animals in the distance, feeding. Unsaddled, the mares appeared undressed; they reminded her of naked women walking with their glossy flanks in the sego lilies which curled on the ground. The flowers were yellowish, like winter wool, but fragrant; the mares, naked and gentle, walked through them. Their strolling, their perfect beauty, the sound of their hoofs on stone touched a deep place in Hattie's nature. Her love for horses, birds, and dogs was well known. Dogs led the list. And now a piece cut from a green blanket reminded Hattie of her dog Richie. The blanket was one he had torn, and she had cut it into strips and placed them under the doors to keep out the drafts. In the house she found more traces of him: hair he had shed on the furniture. Hattie was going to borrow Helen's vacuum cleaner, but there wasn't really enough current to make it pull as it should. On the doorknob of India's room hung the dog collar.

Hattie had decided that she would have herself moved into India's bed when it was time to die. Why should there be two deathbeds? A perilous look came into her eyes, her lips were pressed together forbiddingly. I *follow,* she said, speaking to India with an inner voice, *so never mind.* Presently—before long—she would have to leave the yellow house in her turn. And as she went into the parlor, thinking of the will, she sighed. Pretty soon she would have to attend to it. India's lawyer, Claiborne, helped her with such things. She had phoned him in town, while she was staying with Marian, and talked matters over with him. He had promised to try to sell the house for her. Fifteen thousand was her bottom price, she said. If he couldn't find a buyer, perhaps he could find a tenant. Two hundred dollars a month was the rental she set. Rolfe laughed. Hattie turned toward him one of those proud, dulled looks she always took on when he angered her. Haughtily she said, "For summer on Sego Lake? That's reasonable."

"You're competing with Pace's ranch."

"Why, the food is stinking down there. And he cheats the dudes," said Hattie. "He really cheats them at cards. You'll never catch me playing blackjack with him again."

And what would she do, thought Hattie, if Claiborne could neither rent nor sell the house? This question she shook off as regularly as it returned. *I don't have to be a burden on anybody,* thought Hattie.

It's looked bad many a time before, but when push came to shove, I made it. Somehow I got by. But she argued with herself: *How many times? How long, O God—an old thing, feeble, no use to anyone?* Who said she had any right to own property?

She was sitting on her sofa, which was very old—India's sofa—eight feet long, kidney-shaped, puffy, and bald. An underlying pink shone through the green; the upholstered tufts were like the pads of dogs' paws; between them rose bunches of hair. Here Hattie slouched, resting, with knees wide apart and a cigarette in her mouth, eyes half-shut but farseeing. The mountains seemed not fifteen miles but fifteen hundred feet away, the lake a blue band; the tealike odor of the roses, though they were still unopened, was already in the air, for Sam was watering them in the heat. Gratefully Hattie yelled, "Sam!"

Sam was very old, and all shanks. His feet looked big. His old railroad jacket was made tight across the back by his stoop. A crooked finger with its great broad nail over the mouth of the hose made the water spray and sparkle. Happy to see Hattie, he turned his long jaw, empty of teeth, and his long blue eyes, which seemed to bend back to penetrate into his temples (it was his face that turned, not his body), and he said, "Oh, there, Hattie. You've made it home today? Welcome, Hattie."

"Have a beer, Sam. Come around the kitchen door and I'll give you a beer."

She never had Sam in the house, owing to his skin disease. There were raw patches on his chin and behind his ears. Hattie feared infection from his touch, having decided that he had impetigo. She gave him the beer can, never a glass, and she put on gloves before she used the garden tools. Since he would take no money from her—Wanda Gingham charged a dollar a day—she got Marian to find old clothes for him in town and she left food for him at the door of the damp-wood-smelling boxcar where he lived.

"How's the old wing, Hat?" he said.

"It's coming. I'll be driving the car again before you know it," she told him. "By the first of May I'll be driving again." Every week she moved the date forward. "By Decoration Day I expect to be on my own again," she said.

In mid-June, however, she was still unable to drive. Helen Rolfe said to her, "Hattie, Jerry and I are due in Seattle the first week of July."

"Why, you never told me that," said Hattie.

"You don't mean to tell me this is the first you heard of it," said Helen. "You've known about it from the first—since Christmas."

It wasn't easy for Hattie to meet her eyes. She presently put her head down. Her face became very dry, especially the lips. "Well, don't you worry about me. I'll be all right here," she said.

"Who's going to look after you?" said Jerry. He evaded nothing himself and tolerated no evasion in others. Except that, as Hattie knew, he made every possible allowance for her. But who would help her? She couldn't count on her friend Half Pint, she couldn't really count on Marian either. She had had only the Rolfes to turn to. Helen, trying to be steady, gazed at her and made sad, involuntary movements with her head, sometimes nodding, sometimes seeming as if she disagreed. Hattie, with her inner voice, swore at her: *Bitch-eyes. I can't make it the way she does because I'm old. Is that fair?* And yet she admired Helen's eyes. Even the skin about them, slightly wrinkled, heavy underneath, was touching, beautiful. There was a heaviness in her bust that went, as if by attachment, with the heaviness of her eyes. Her head, her hands and feet should have taken a more slender body. Helen, said Hattie, was the nearest thing she had on earth to a sister. But there was no reason to go to Seattle—no genuine business. Why the hell Seattle? It was only idleness, only a holiday. The only reason was Hattie herself; this was their way of telling her that there was a limit to what she could expect them to do for her. Helen's nervous head wavered, but her thoughts were steady. She knew what was passing through Hattie's mind. Like Hattie, she was an idle woman. Why was her right to idleness better?

Because of money? thought Hattie. Because of age? Because she has a husband? Because she had a daughter in Swarthmore College? But an interesting thing occurred to her. Helen disliked being idle, whereas Hattie herself had never made any bones about it: an idle life was all she was good for. But for her it had been uphill all the way, because when Waggoner divorced her she didn't have a cent. She even had to support Wicks for seven or eight years. Except with horses, Wicks had no sense. And then she had had to take tons of dirt from India. *I am the one,* Hattie asserted to herself. *I would know what to do with Helen's advantages. She only suffers from them. And if she wants to stop being an idle woman why can't she start with me, her neighbor?* Hattie's skin, for all its puffiness, burned with anger. She said to Rolfe and Helen, "Don't worry. I'll make out. But if I have to leave the lake you'll be ten times more lonely than before. Now I'm going back to my house."

She lifted up her broad old face, and her lips were childlike with suffering. She would never take back what she had said.

But the trouble was no ordinary trouble. Hattie was herself aware that she rambled, forgot names, and answered when no one spoke.

"We can't just take charge of her," Rolfe said. "What's more, she ought to be near a doctor. She keeps her shotgun loaded so she can fire it if anything happens to her in the house. But who knows what she'll shoot? I don't believe it was Jacamares who killed that Doberman of hers."

Rolfe drove into the yard the day after she moved back to the yellow house and said, "I'm going into town. I can bring you some chow if you like."

She couldn't afford to refuse his offer, angry though she was, and she said, "Yes, bring me some stuff from the Mountain Street Market. Charge it." She had only some frozen shrimp and a few cans of beer in the icebox. When Rolfe had gone she put out the package of shrimp to thaw.

People really used to stick by one another in the West. Hattie now saw herself as one of the pioneers. The modern breed had come later. After all, she had lived on the range like an old-timer. Wicks had had to shoot their Christmas dinner and she had cooked it—venison. He killed it on the reservation, and if the Indians had caught them, there would have been hell to pay.

The weather was hot, the clouds were heavy and calm in a large sky. The horizon was so huge that in it the lake must have seemed like a saucer of milk. *Some milk!* Hattie thought. Two thousand feet down in the middle, so deep no corpse could ever be recovered. A body, they said, went around with the currents. And there were rocks like eyeteeth, and hot springs, and colorless fish at the bottom which were never caught. Now that the white pelicans were nesting they patrolled the rocks for snakes and other egg thieves. They were so big and flew so slow you might imagine they were angels. Hattie no longer visited the lake shore; the walk exhausted her. She saved her strength to go to Pace's bar in the afternoon.

She took off her shoes and stockings and walked on bare feet from one end of her house to the other. On the land side she saw Wanda Gingham sitting near the tracks while her great-grandson played in the soft red gravel. Wanda wore a large purple shawl and her black head was bare. All about her was—was nothing, Hattie thought; for she had taken a drink, breaking her rule. Nothing but mountains, thrust out like men's bodies; the sagebrush was the hair on their chests.

The warm wind blew dust from the marl pit. This white powder made her sky less blue. On the water side were the pelicans, pure as spirits, slow as angels, blessing the air as they flew with great wings.

Should she or should she not have Sam do something about the vine on the chimney? Sparrows nested in it, and she was glad of that. But all summer long the king snakes were after them and she was afraid to walk in the garden. When the sparrows scratched the ground for seed they took a funny bound; they held their legs stiff and flung back the dust with both feet. Hattie sat down at her old Spanish monastery table, watching them in the cloudy warmth of the day, clasping her hands, chuckling and sad. The bushes were crowded with yellow roses, half of them now rotted. The lizards scrambled from shadow to shadow. The water was smooth as air, gaudy as silk. The mountains succumbed, falling asleep in the heat. Drowsy, Hattie lay down on her sofa. Its pads were like dogs' paws. She gave in to sleep and when she woke it was midnight; she did not want to alarm the Rolfes by putting on her lights so took advantage of the moon to eat a few thawed shrimps and go to the bathroom. She undressed and lifted herself into bed and lay there feeling her sore arm. Now she knew how much she missed her dog. The whole matter of the dog weighed heavily on her soul. She came close to tears, thinking about him, and she went to sleep oppressed by her secret.

I suppose I had better try to pull myself together a little, thought Hattie nervously in the morning. *I can't just sleep my way through.* She knew what her difficulty was. Before any serious question her mind gave way. It scattered or diffused. She said to herself, *I can see bright, but I feel dim. I guess I'm not so lively any more. Maybe I'm becoming a little touched in the head, as Mother was.* But she was not so old as her mother was when she did those strange things. At eighty-five, her mother had to be kept from going naked in the street. *I'm not as bad as that yet. Thank God! Yes, I walked into the men's wards, but that was when I had a fever, and my nightie was on.*

She drank a cup of Nescafé and it strengthened her determination to do something for herself. In all the world she had only her brother Angus to go to. Her brother Will had led a rough life; he was an old heller, and now he drove everyone away. He was too crabby, thought Hattie. Besides he was angry because she had lived so long with Wicks. Angus would forgive her. But then he and his wife were not her kind. With them she couldn't drink, she couldn't smoke, she had to make herself small-mouthed, and she would have to wait while they read a chapter of the Bible before breakfast. Hattie could not bear to sit at table waiting for meals. Besides, she had a house of her own at last. Why should she have to leave it? She had never owned a thing before. And now she was not allowed to enjoy her yellow house. *But I'll keep it,* she said to herself rebelliously. *I swear to God I'll keep it. Why, I barely just got it. I haven't had time.* And she went out on the porch to work the pulley and do something about the adhesions in her arm. She was sure now that they were there. *And what will I do?* she cried to herself. *What will I do? Why did I ever go to Rolfe's that night—and why did I lose control on the crossing?* She couldn't say, now, "I sneezed." She couldn't even remember what had happened, except that she saw the boulders and the twisting blue rails and Darly.

It was Darly's fault. He was sick and old himself. *He* couldn't make it. He envied her the house, and her woman's peaceful life. Since she returned from the hospital he hadn't even come to visit her. He only said, "Hell, I'm sorry for her, but it was her fault." What hurt him most was that she had said he couldn't hold his liquor.

Fierceness, swearing to God did no good. She was still the same procrastinating old woman. She had a letter to answer from Hitchkiss Insurance and it drifted out of sight. She was going to phone Claiborne the lawyer, but it slipped her mind. One morning she announced to Helen that she believed she would apply to an institution in Los Angeles that took over the property of old people and managed it for them. They gave you an apartment right on the ocean, and your meals and medical care. You had to sign over half of your estate. "It's fair enough," said Hattie. "They take a gamble. I may live to be a hundred."

"I wouldn't be surprised," said Helen.

However, Hattie never got around to sending to Los Angeles for the brochure. But Jerry Rolfe took it on himself to write a letter to her brother Angus about her condition. And he drove over also to have a talk with Amy Walters, the gold miner's widow at Fort Walters—as the ancient woman called it. The Fort was an old tarpaper building over the mine. The shaft made a cesspool unnecessary. Since the death of her second husband no one had dug for gold. On a heap of stones near the road a crimson sign FORT WALTERS was placed. Behind it was a flagpole. The American flag was raised every day.

Amy was working in the garden in one of dead Bill's shirts. Bill had brought water down from the mountains for her in a homemade aqueduct so she could raise her own peaches and vegetables.

"Amy," Rolfe said, "Hattie's back from the hospital and living all alone. You have no folks and neither has she. Not to beat around the bush about it, why don't you live together?"

Amy's face had great delicacy. Her winter baths in the lake, her vegetable soups, the waltzes she played for herself alone on the grand piano that stood beside her wood stove, the murder stories she read till darkness obliged her to close the book—this life of hers had made her remote. She looked delicate, yet there was no way to affect her composure, she couldn't be touched. It was very strange.

"Hattie and me have different habits, Jerry," said Amy. "And Hattie wouldn't like my company. I can't drink with her. I'm a teetotaller."

"That's true," said Rolfe, recalling that Hattie referred to Amy as if she were a ghost. He couldn't speak to Amy of the solitary death in store for her. There was not a cloud in the arid sky today, and there was no shadow of death on Amy. She was tranquil, she seemed to be supplied with a sort of pure fluid that would feed her life slowly for years to come.

He said, "All kinds of things could happen to a woman like Hattie in that yellow house, and nobody would know."

"That's a fact. She doesn't know how to take care of herself."

"She can't. Her arm hasn't healed."

Amy didn't say that she was sorry to hear it. In the place of those words came a silence which might have meant that. Then she said, "I might go over there a few hours a day, but she would have to pay me."

"Now, Amy, you must know as well as I do that Hattie has no money—not much more than her pension. Just the house."

At once Amy said, no pause coming between his words and hers, "I would take care of her if she'd agree to leave the house to me."

"Leave it in your hands, you mean?" said Rolfe. "To manage?"

"In her will. To belong to me."

"Why, Amy, what would you do with Hattie's house?" he said.

"It would be my property, that's all. I'd have it."

"Maybe you would leave Fort Walters to her in your will," he said.

"Oh, no," she said. "Why should I? I'm not asking Hattie for her help. I don't need it. Hattie is a city woman."

Rolfe could not carry this proposal back to Hattie. He was too wise ever to mention her will to her.

But Pace was not so careful of her feelings. By mid-June Hattie had begun to visit his bar regularly. She had so many things to think about she couldn't stay home. When Pace came in from the yard one day—he had been packing the wheels of his horse-trailer and was wiping grease from his fingers—he said with his usual bluntness, "How would you like it if I paid you fifty bucks a month for the rest of your life, Hat?"

Hattie was holding her second old-fashioned of the day. At the bar she made it appear that she observed the limit; but she had started drinking at home. One before lunch, one during, one after lunch. She began to grin, expecting Pace to make one of his jokes. But he was wearing his scoop-shaped Western hat as level as a Quaker, and he had drawn down his chin, a sign that he was not fooling. She said, "That would be nice, but what's the catch?"

"No catch," he said. "This is what we'd do. I'd give you five hundred dollars cash, and fifty bucks a month for life, and you let me sleep some dudes in the yellow house, and you'd leave the house to me in your will."

"What kind of a deal is that?" said Hattie, her look changing. "I thought we were friends."

"It's the best deal you'll ever get," he said.

The weather was sultry, but Hattie till now had thought that it was nice. She had been dreamy but comfortable, about to begin to enjoy the cool of the day; but now she felt that such cruelty and injustice had been waiting to attack her, that it would have been better to die in the hospital than be so disillusioned.

She cried, "Everybody wants to push me out. You're a cheater, Pace. God! I know you. Pick on somebody else. Why do you have to pick on me? Just because I happen to be around?"

"Why, no, Hattie," he said, trying now to be careful. "It was just a business offer."

"Why don't you give me some blood for the bank if you're such a friend of mine?"

"Well, Hattie, you drink too much and you oughtn't to have been driving anyway."

"I sneezed, and you know it. The whole thing happened because I sneezed. Everybody knows that. I wouldn't sell you my house. I'd give it away to the lepers first. You'd let me go away and never send me a cent. You never pay anybody. You can't even buy wholesale in town any more because nobody trusts you. I'm stuck, that's all, just stuck. I keep on saying that this is my only home in all the world, this is where my friends are, and the weather is always perfect and the lake is beautiful. But I wish the whole damn empty old place were in Hell. It's not human and neither are you. But I'll be here the day the sheriff takes away your horses—you never mind! I'll be clapping and applauding!"

He told her then that she was drunk again, and so she was, but she was more than that, and though her head was spinning she decided to go back to the house at once and take care of some things she had been putting off. This very day she was going to write to the lawyer, Claiborne, and make sure that Pace never got her property. She wouldn't put it past him to swear in court that India had promised him the yellow house.

She sat at the table with pen and paper, trying to think how to put it.

"I want this on record," she wrote, "I could kick myself in the head when I think of how he's led me on. I have been his patsy ten thousand times. As when that drunk crashed his Cub plane on the lake shore. At the coroner's jury he let me take the whole blame. He said he had instructed me when I was working for him never to take in any drunks. And this flier was drunk. He had nothing on but a T shirt and Bermuda shorts and he was flying from Sacramento to Salt Lake City. At the inquest Pace said I had disobeyed his instructions. The same was true when the cook went haywire. She was a tramp. He never hires decent help. He cheated her on the bar bill and blamed me and she went after me with a meat cleaver. She disliked me because I criticized her for drinking at the bar in her one-piece white bathing suit with the dude guests. But he turned her loose on me. He hints that he did certain services for India. She would never have let him touch one single finger. He was too common for her. It can never be said about India that she was not a lady in every way. He thinks he is the greatest sack-artist in the world. He only loves horses, as a fact. He has no claims at all, oral or written, on this yellow house. I want you to have this over my signature. He was cruel to Pickle-Tits who was his first wife, and he's no better to the charming woman who is his present one. I don't know why she takes it. It must be despair." Hattie said to herself, *I don't suppose I'd better send that.*

She was still angry. Her heart was knocking within; the deep pulses, as after a hot bath, beat at the back of her thighs. The air outside was dotted with transparent particles. The mountains were as red as furnace clinkers. The iris leaves were fan sticks—they stuck out like Jiggs's hair.

She always ended by looking out of the window at the desert and lake. *They drew you from yourself. But after they had drawn you, what did they do with you? It was too late to find out. I'll never know. I wasn't meant to. I'm not the type,* Hattie reflected. *Maybe something too cruel for women, young or old.*

So she stood up and, rising, she had the sensation that she had gradually become a container for herself. You get old, your heart, your liver, your lungs seem to expand in size, and the walls of the body give way outward, swelling, she thought, and you take the shape of an old jug, wider and wider toward the top. You swell up with tears and fat. She no longer even smelled to herself like a woman. Her face with its much-slept-upon skin was only faintly like her own—like a cloud that has changed. It was a face. It became a ball of yarn. It had drifted open. It had scattered.

I was never one single thing anyway, she thought. *Never my own. I was only loaned to myself.*

But the thing wasn't over yet. And in fact she didn't know for certain that it was ever going to be over. You only had other people's word for it that death was such-and-such. How do I know? she asked herself challengingly. Her anger had sobered her for a little while. Now she was again drunk. . . . *It was strange. It is strange. It may continue being strange.* She further thought, *I used to wish for death more than I do now. Because I didn't have anything at all. I changed when I got a roof of my own over me. And now? Do I have to go? I thought Marian loved me, but she already has a sister. And I thought Helen and Jerry would never desert me, but they've beat it. And now Pace has insulted me. They think I'm not going to make it.*

She went to the cupboard—she kept the bourbon bottle there; she drank less if each time she had to rise and open the cupboard door. And, as if she were being watched, she poured a drink and swallowed it.

The notion that in the emptiness someone saw her was connected with the other notion that she was being filmed from birth to death. That this was done for everyone. And afterward you could view your life. A hereafter movie.

Hattie wanted to see some of it now, and she sat down on the dogs'-paw cushions of her sofa and, with her knees far apart and a smile of yearning and of fright, she bent her round back, burned a cigarette at the corner of her mouth and saw—the Church of Saint Sulpice in Paris where her organ teacher used to bring her. It looked like country walls of stone, but rising high and leaning outward were towers. She was very young. She knew music. How she could ever have been so clever was beyond her. But she did know it. She could read all those notes. The sky was gray. After this she saw some entertaining things she liked to tell people about. She was a young wife. She was in Aix-les-Bains with her mother-in-law, and they played bridge in a mud bath with a British general and his aide. There were artificial waves in the swimming pool. She lost her bathing suit because it was a size too big. How did she get out? Ah, you got out of everything.

She saw her husband, James John Waggoner IV. They were snowbound together in New Hampshire. "Jimmy, Jimmy, how can you fling a wife away?" she asked him. "Have you forgotten love? Did I drink too much—did I bore you?" He had married again and had two children. He had gotten tired of her. And though he was a vain man with nothing to be vain about—no looks, not too much intelligence, nothing but an old Philadelphia family—she had loved him. She too had been a snob about her Philadelphia connections. Give up the name of Waggoner? How could she? For this reason she had never married Wicks. "How dare you," she had said to Wicks, "come without a shave in a dirty shirt and muck on you, come and ask me to marry! If you want to propose, go and clean up first." But his dirt was only a pretext.

Trade Waggoner for Wicks? she asked herself again with a swing of her shoulders. She wouldn't think of it. Wicks was an excellent man. But he was a cowboy. Socially nothing. He couldn't even read. But she saw this on her film. They were in Athens Canyon, in a cratelike house, and she was reading aloud to him from *The Count of Monte Cristo.*[9]

9. A romantic novel (1844) by the French novelist Alexandre Dumas.

He wouldn't let her stop. While walking to stretch her legs, she read, and he followed her about to catch each word. After all, he was very dear to her. Such a man! Now she saw him jump from his horse. They were living on the range, trapping coyotes. It was just the second gray of evening, cloudy, moments after the sun had gone down. There was an animal in the trap, and he went toward it to kill it. He wouldn't waste a bullet on the creatures but killed them with a kick, with his boot. And then Hattie saw that this coyote was all white—snarling teeth, white scruff. "Wicks, he's white! White as a polar bear. You're not going to kill him, are you?" The animal flattened to the ground. He snarled and cried. He couldn't pull away because of the heavy trap. And Wicks killed him. What else could he have done? The white beast lay dead. The dust of Wicks's boots hardly showed on its head and jaws. Blood ran from the muzzle.

And now came something on Hattie's film she tried to shun. It was she herself who had killed her dog, Richie. Just as Rolfe and Pace had warned her, he was vicious, his brain was turned. She, because she was on the side of all dumb creatures, defended him when he bit the trashy woman Jacamares was living with. Perhaps if she had had Richie from a puppy he wouldn't have turned on her. When she got him he was already a year and a half old and she couldn't break him of his habits. But she thought that only she understood him. And Rolfe had warned her, "You'll be sued, do you know that? The dog will take out after somebody smarter than that Jacamares's woman, and you'll be in for it."

Hattie saw herself as she swayed her shoulders and said, "Nonsense."

But what fear she had felt when the dog went for her on the porch. Suddenly she could see, by his skull, by his eyes that he was evil. She screamed at him, "Richie!" And what had she done to him? He had lain under the gas range all day growling and wouldn't come out. She tried to urge him out with the broom, and he snatched it in his teeth. She pulled him out, and he left the stick and tore at her. Now, as the spectator of this, her eyes opened, beyond the pregnant curtain and the air-wave of marl dust, summer's snow, drifting over the water. "Oh, my God! Richie!" Her thigh was snatched by his jaws. His teeth went through her skirt. She felt she would fall. Would she go down? Then the dog would rush at her throat—then black night, bad-odored mouth, the blood pouring from her neck, from torn veins. Her heart shriveled as the teeth went into her thigh, and she couldn't delay another second but took her kindling hatchet from the nail, strengthened her grip on the smooth wood, and hit the dog. She saw the blow. She saw him die at once. And then in fear and shame she hid the body. And at night she buried him in the yard. Next day she accused Jacamares. On him she laid the blame for the disappearance of her dog.

She stood up; she spoke to herself in silence, as was her habit. *God, what shall I do? I have taken life. I have lied. I have borne false witness. I have stalled. And now what shall I do? Nobody will help me.*

And suddenly she made up her mind that she should go and do what she had been putting off for weeks, namely, test herself with the car, and she slipped on her shoes and went outside. Lizards ran before her in the thirsty dust. She opened the hot, broad door of the car. She lifted her lame hand onto the wheel. Her right hand she reached far to the left and turned the wheel with all her might. Then she started the motor and tried to drive out of the yard. But she could not release the emergency brake with its rasplike rod. She reached with her good hand, the right, under the steering wheel and pressed her bosom on it and strained. No, she could not shift the gears and steer. She couldn't even reach down to the hand brake. The sweat broke out on her skin. Her efforts were too much. She was deeply wounded by the pain in her arm. The door of the car fell open again and she turned from the wheel and with her stiff legs hanging from the door she wept. What could she do now? And when she had wept over the ruin of her life she got out of the old car and went back to the house. She took the bourbon from the cupboard and picked up the ink bottle and a pad of paper and sat down to write her will.

"My Will," she wrote, and sobbed to herself.

Since the death of India she had numberless times asked the question, To Whom? Who will get this when I die? She had unconsciously put people to the test to find out whether they were worthy. It made her more severe than before.

Now she wrote, "I Harriet Simmons Waggoner, being of sound mind and not knowing what may be in store for me at the age of seventy-two (born 1885), living alone at Sego Desert Lake, instruct my lawyer, Harold Claiborne, Paiute County Court Building, to draw my last will and testament upon the following terms."

She sat perfectly still now to hear from within who would be the lucky one, who would inherit the yellow house. For which she had waited. Yes, waited for India's death, choking on her bread because she was a rich woman's servant and whipping girl. But who had done for her, Hattie, what she had done for India? And who, apart from India, had ever held out a hand to her? Kindness, yes. Here and there people had been kind. But the word in her head was not kindness, it was succor. And who had given her that? *Succor?* Only India. If at least, next best after succor, someone had given her a shake and said, "Stop stalling. Don't be such a slow, old, procrastinating sit-stiller."

Again, it was only India who had done her good. She had offered her succor. "Het-tie!" said that drunken mask. "Do you know what sloth is? Demn you! poky old demned thing!"

But I was waiting, Hattie realized. *I was waiting, thinking, "Youth is terrible, frightening. I will wait it out. And men? Men are cruel and strong. They want things I haven't got to give." There were no kids in me,* thought Hattie. *Not that I wouldn't have loved them, but such my nature was. And who can blame me for having it? My nature?*

She drank from an old-fashioned glass. There was no orange in it, no ice, no bitters or sugar, only the stinging, clear bourbon.

So then, she continued, looking at the dry sun-stamped dust and the last freckled flowers of red wild peach, *to live with Angus and his wife? And to have to hear a chapter from the Bible before breakfast? Once more in the house—not of a stranger, perhaps, but not far from it either?* In other houses, in someone else's house, to wait for mealtimes was her lifelong punishment. She always felt it in the throat and stomach. And so she would again, and to the very end. However, she must think of someone to leave the house to.

And first of all she wanted to do right by her family. None of them had ever dreamed that she, Hattie, would ever have something to bequeath. Until a few years ago it had certainly looked as if she would die a pauper. So now she could keep her head up with the proudest of them. And, as this occurred to her, she actually lifted up her face with its broad nose and victorious eyes; if her hair had become shabby as onion roots, if, at the back, her head was round and bald as a newel post, what did that matter? Her heart experienced a childish glory, not yet tired of it after seventy-two years. She, too, had amounted to something. *I'll do some good by going,* she thought. *Now I believe I should leave it to, to . . .* She returned to the old point of struggle. She had decided many times and many times changed her mind. She tried to think, *Who would get the most out of this yellow house?* It was a tearing thing to go through. If it had not been the house but, instead, some brittle thing she could hold in her hand, then her last action would be to throw and smash it, and so the thing and she herself would be demolished together. But it was vain to think such thoughts. To whom should she leave it? Her brothers? Not they. Nephews? One was a submarine commander. The other was a bachelor in the State Department. Then began the roll call of cousins. Merton? He owned an estate in Connecticut. Anna? She had a face like a hot-water bottle. That left Joyce, the orphaned daughter of her cousin Wilfred. Joyce was the most likely heiress. Hattie had already written to her and had her out to the lake at Thanksgiving, two years ago. But this Joyce was another odd one; over thirty, good, yes, but placid, running to fat, a scholar—ten years in Eugene, Oregon, working for her degree. In

Hattie's opinion this was only another form of sloth. Nevertheless, Joyce yet hoped to marry. Whom? Not Dr. Stroud. He wouldn't. And still Joyce had vague hope. Hattie knew how that could be. At least have a man she could argue with.

She was now more drunk than at any time since her accident. Again she filled her glass. *Have ye eyes and see not?*[1] *Sleepers awake!*

Knees wide apart she sat in the twilight, thinking. Marian? Marian didn't need another house. Half Pint? She wouldn't know what to do with it. Brother Louis came up for consideration next. He was an old actor who had a church for the Indians at Athens Canyon. Hollywood stars of the silent days sent him their negligees; he altered them and wore them in the pulpit. The Indians loved his show. But when Billy Shawah blew his brains out after his two-week bender, they still tore his shack down and turned the boards inside out to get rid of his ghost. They had their old religion. No, not Brother Louis. He'd show movies in the yellow house to the tribe or make a nursery out of it for the Indian brats.

And now she began to consider Wicks. When last heard from he was south of Bishop, California, a handy man in a saloon off toward Death Valley. It wasn't she who heard from him but Pace. Herself, she hadn't actually seen Wicks since—how low she had sunk then!—she had kept the hamburger stand on Route 158. The little lunchroom had supported them both. Wicks hung around on the end stool, rolling cigarettes (she saw it on the film). Then there was a quarrel. Things had been going from bad to worse. He'd begun to grouse now about this and now about that. He beefed about the food, at last. She saw and heard him. "Hat," he said, "I'm good and tired of hamburger." "Well, what do you think I eat?" she said with that round, defiant movement of her shoulders which she herself recognized as characteristic (*me all over,* she thought). But he opened the cash register and took out thirty cents and crossed the street to the butcher's and brought back a steak. He threw it on the griddle. "Fry it," he said. She did, and watched him eat.

And when he was through she could bear her rage no longer. "Now," she said, "you've had your meat. Get out. Never come back." She kept a pistol under the counter. She picked it up, cocked it, pointed it at his heart. "If you ever come in that door again, I'll kill you," she said.

She saw it all. *I couldn't bear to fall so low,* she thought, *to be slave to a shiftless cowboy.*

Wicks said, "Don't do that, Hat. Guess I went too far. You're right."

1. Psalms 115:5: ". . . eyes have they, but they see not."

"You'll never have a chance to make it up," she cried. "Get out!"

On that cry he disappeared, and since then she had never seen him.

"Wicks, dear," she said. "Please! I'm sorry. Don't condemn me in your heart. Forgive me. I hurt myself in my evil. I always had a thick idiot head. I was born with a thick head."

Again she wept, for Wicks. She was too proud. A snob. Now they might have lived together in this house, old friends, simple and plain.

She thought, *He really was my good friend.*

But what would Wicks do with a house like this, alone, if he was alive and survived her? He was too wiry for soft beds or easy chairs.

And she was the one who had said stiffly to India, "I'm a Christian person. I do not bear a grudge."

Ah yes, she said to herself. *I have caught myself out too often. How long can this go on?* And she began to think, or try to think, of Joyce, her cousin's daughter. Joyce was like herself, a woman alone, getting on in years, clumsy. Probably never been laid. Too bad. She would have given much, now, to succor Joyce.

But it seemed to her now that that too, the succor, had been a story. First you heard the pure story. Then you heard the impure story. Both stories. She had paid out years, now to one shadow, now to another shadow.

Joyce would come here to the house. She had a little income and could manage. She would live as Hattie had lived, alone. Here she would rot, start to drink, maybe, and day after day read, day after day sleep. See how beautiful it was here? I burned you out. How empty! It turned you into ash.

How can I doom a younger person to the same life? asked Hattie. It's for somebody like me. When I was younger it wasn't right. But now it is, exactly. Only I fit in here. It was made for my old age, to spend my last years peacefully. If I hadn't let Jerry make me drunk that night—if I hadn't sneezed! Because of this arm, I'll have to live with Angus. My heart will break there away from my only home.

She was now very drunk, and she said to herself, *Take what God brings. He gives no gifts unmixed. He makes loans.*

She resumed her letter of instructions to lawyer Claiborne: "Upon the following terms," she wrote a second time. "Because I have suffered much. Because I only lately received what I have to give away, I can't bear it." The drunken blood was soaring to her head. But her hand was clear enough. She wrote, "It is too soon! Too soon! Because I do not find it in my heart to care for anyone as I would wish. Being cast off and lonely, and doing no harm where I am. Why should it be? This breaks my heart. In addition to everything else, why must I worry about this, which I must leave? I am tormented out of my mind. Even though by my own fault I have put myself into this position. And I am not ready to give up on this. No, not yet. And so I'll tell you what, I leave this property, land, house, garden, and water rights, to Hattie Simmons Waggoner. Me! I realize this is bad and wrong. Not possible. Yet it is the only thing I really wish to do, so may God have mercy on my soul."

How could that happen? She studied what she had written and finally she acknowledged that she was drunk. "I'm drunk," she said, "and don't know what I'm doing. I'll die, and end. Like India. Dead as that lilac bush."

Then she thought that there was a beginning, and a middle. She shrank from the last term. She began once more—a beginning. After that, there was the early middle, then middle middle, late middle middle, quite late middle. In fact the middle is all I know. The rest is just a rumor.

Only tonight I can't give the house away. I'm drunk and so I need it. And tomorrow, she promised herself, I'll think again. I'll work it out, for sure.

---

1. Discuss the importance of the setting in its relation to Hattie's problems and whatever solution she finds for them.
2. What does the story say about the resources of a human being faced with extinction? About dying with dignity?
3. What does Hattie's pride have to do with the outcome of the action?
4. How do the attitudes and actions of the minor characters contribute to our understanding Hattie?
5. How is the point of view related to the development of the theme? To what extent has the author used his main character as a witness testifying to the world around her?

Ambrose Bierce

Bierce (1842–1913?) was born on a religious campground at Western Reserve, Ohio. The poverty of his family required him early in life to work for a newspaper in a menial capacity before his enlistment with the Indiana Infantry for duty in the Civil War. He rose through the military ranks to become a staff officer and was twice wounded. The horrors of war shaped his attitudes with an enduring pessimism, and his war stories are among the first to treat the subject with detailed realism. In San Francisco after the war he began his literary career by working, along with Mark Twain and Bret Harte, as a journalist. He spent the years between 1872 and 1876 in London, where his boisterous Western mannerisms and savage wit made him a celebrity, first earning him the nickname "Bitter Bierce." Poor health forced him to return in 1876 to his journalistic career in California. In 1891 he published Tales of Soldiers and Civilians, *followed two years later by another volume of short stories,* Can Such Things Be? *The death of his two sons in 1889 and 1901, along with his divorce in 1891, intensified his prevailing pessimism and resulted at length in his disappearance into Mexico, where he is believed to have died in 1913. His sardonic wit can be sampled in* The Devil's Dictionary *(1911). Twelve volumes of his* Collected Works *(prose and poetry) were published in 1909–12.*

An Occurrence at Owl Creek Bridge

I

A man stood upon a railroad bridge in Northern Alabama, looking down into the swift waters twenty feet below. The man's hands were behind his back, the wrists bound with a cord. A rope loosely encircled his neck. It was attached to a stout cross-timber above his head, and the slack fell to the level of his knees. Some loose boards laid upon the sleepers supporting the metals of the railway supplied a footing for him and his executioners—two private soldiers of the Federal army, directed by a sergeant, who in civil life may have been a deputy sheriff. At a short remove upon the same temporary platform was an officer in the uniform of his rank, armed. He was a captain. A sentinel at each end of the bridge stood with his rifle in the position known as "support," that is to say, vertical in front of the left shoulder, the hammer resting on the forearm thrown straight across the chest—

a formal and unnatural position, enforcing an erect carriage of the body. It did not appear to be the duty of these two men to know what was occurring at the centre of the bridge; they merely blockaded the two ends of the foot plank which traversed it.

Beyond one of the sentinels nobody was in sight; the railroad ran straight away into a forest for a hundred yards, then, curving, was lost to view. Doubtless there was an outpost further along. The other bank of the stream was open ground—a gentle acclivity crowned with a stockade of vertical tree trunks, loop-holed for rifles, with a single embrasure through which protruded the muzzle of a brass cannon commanding the bridge. Midway of the slope between bridge and fort were the spectators—a single company of infantry in line, at "parade rest," the butts of the rifles on the ground, the barrels inclining slightly backward against the right shoulder, the hands crossed upon the stock. A lieutenant stood at the right of the line, the point of his sword upon the ground, his left hand resting upon his right. Excepting the group of four at the centre of the bridge not a man moved. The company faced the bridge, staring stonily, motionless. The sentinels, facing the banks of the stream, might have been statues to adorn the bridge. The captain stood with folded arms, silent, observing the work of his subordinates but making no sign. Death is a dignitary who, when he comes announced, is to be received with formal manifestations of respect, even by those most familiar with him. In the code of military etiquette silence and fixity are forms of deference.

The man who was engaged in being hanged was apparently about thirty-five years of age. He was a civilian, if one might judge from his dress, which was that of a planter. His features were good—a straight nose, firm mouth, broad forehead, from which his long, dark hair was combed straight back, falling behind his ears to the collar of his well-fitting frock coat. He wore a moustache and pointed beard, but no whiskers; his eyes were large and dark grey and had a kindly expression which one would hardly have expected in one whose neck was in the hemp. Evidently this was no vulgar assassin. The liberal military code makes provision for hanging many kinds of people, and gentlemen are not excluded.

The preparations being complete, the two private soldiers stepped aside and each drew away the plank upon which he had been standing. The sergeant turned to the captain, saluted and placed himself immediately behind that officer, who in turn moved apart one pace. These movements left the condemned man and the sergeant standing on the two ends of the same plank, which spanned three of the cross-ties of the bridge. The end upon which the civilian stood almost, but not quite, reached a fourth. This plank had been held in place by the weight of the captain; it was now held by that of the sergeant. At a signal from the former, the latter would step aside, the plank would tilt and the condemned man go down between two ties. The arrangement commended itself to his judgment as simple and effective. His face had not been covered nor his eyes bandaged. He looked a moment at his "unsteadfast footing," then let his gaze wander to the swirling water of the stream racing madly beneath his feet. A piece of dancing driftwood caught his attention and his eyes followed it down the current. How slowly it appeared to move! What a sluggish stream!

He closed his eyes in order to fix his last thoughts upon his wife and children. The water, touched to gold by the early sun, the brooding mists under the banks at some distance down the stream, the fort, the soldiers, the piece of drift—all had distracted him. And now he became conscious of a new disturbance. Striking through the thought of his dear ones was a sound which he could neither ignore nor understand, a sharp, distinct, metallic percussion like the stroke of a blacksmith's hammer upon the anvil; it had the same ringing quality. He wondered what it was, and whether immeasurably distant or near by—it seemed both. Its recurrence was regular, but as slow as the tolling of a death knell. He awaited each stroke with impatience and—he knew not why—apprehension. The intervals of silence grew progressively longer, the delays became maddening. With their greater infrequency the sounds increased in strength and sharpness. They hurt his ear like the thrust of a knife; he feared he would shriek. What he heard was the ticking of his watch.

He unclosed his eyes and saw again the water below him. "If I could free my hands," he thought, "I might throw off the noose and spring into the stream. By diving I could evade the bullets, and, swimming vigorously, reach the bank, take to the woods, and get away home. My home, thank God, is as yet outside their lines; my wife and little ones are still beyond the invader's farthest advance."

As these thoughts, which have here to be set down in words, were flashed into the doomed man's brain rather than evolved from it, the captain nodded to the sergeant. The sergeant stepped aside.

II

Peyton Farquhar was a well-to-do planter, of an old and highly-respected Alabama family. Being a slave owner, and, like other slave owners, a politician, he was naturally an original secessionist and ardently devoted to the Southern cause. Circumstances of an imperious nature which it is unnecessary to relate here, had prevented him from taking service with the gallant army which had fought the disastrous campaigns ending with the fall of Corinth,[1] and he chafed under the inglorious restraint, longing for the release of his energies, the larger life of the soldier, the opportunity for distinction. That opportunity, he felt, would come, as it comes to all in war time. Meanwhile he did what he could. No service was too humble for him to perform in aid of the South, no adventure too perilous for him to undertake if consistent with the character of a civilian who was at heart a soldier, and who in good faith and without too much qualification assented to at least a part of the frankly villainous dictum that all is fair in love and war.

One evening while Farquhar and his wife were sitting on a rustic bench near the entrance to his grounds, a grey-clad soldier rode up to the gate and asked for a drink of water. Mrs. Farquhar was only too happy to serve him with her own white hands. While she was gone to fetch the water, her husband approached the dusty horseman and inquired eagerly for news from the front.

"The Yanks are repairing the railroads," said the man, "and are getting ready for another advance. They have reached the Owl Creek bridge, put it in order, and built a stockade on the other bank. The commandant has issued an order, which is posted everywhere, declaring that any civilian caught interfering with the railroad, its bridges, tunnels, or trains, will be summarily hanged. I saw the order."

"How far is it to the Owl Creek bridge?" Farquhar asked.

"About thirty miles."

"Is there no force on this side the creek?"

"Only a picket post half a mile out, on the railroad, and a single sentinel at this end of the bridge."

"Suppose a man—a civilian and student of hanging—should elude the picket post and perhaps get the better of the sentinel," said Farquhar, smiling, "what could he accomplish?"

The soldier reflected. "I was there a month ago," he replied. "I observed that the flood of last winter had lodged a great quantity of driftwood against the wooden pier at this end of the bridge. It is now dry and would burn like tow."

The lady had now brought the water, which the soldier drank. He thanked her ceremoniously, bowed to her husband, and rode away. An hour later, after nightfall, he repassed the plantation, going northward in the direction from which he had come. He was a Federal scout.

III

As Peyton Farquhar fell straight downward through the bridge, he lost consciousness and was as one already dead. From this state he was

1. Corinth, Mississippi. The main battle for Corinth occurred in 1862 when the Confederates tried to retake the town and were decisively beaten.

awakened—ages later, it seemed to him—by the pain of a sharp pressure upon his throat, followed by a sense of suffocation. Keen, poignant agonies seemed to shoot from his neck downward through every fibre of his body and limbs. These pains appeared to flash along well-defined lines of ramification, and to beat with an inconceivably rapid periodicity. They seemed like streams of pulsating fire heating him to an intolerable temperature. As to his head, he was conscious of nothing but a feeling of fullness—of congestion. These sensations were unaccompanied by thought. The intellectual part of his nature was already effaced; he had power only to feel, and feeling was torment. He was conscious of motion. Encompassed in a luminous cloud, of which he was now merely the fiery heart, without material substance, he swung through unthinkable arcs of oscillation, like a vast pendulum. Then all at once, with terrible suddenness, the light about him shot upward with the noise of a loud plash; a frightful roaring was in his ears, and all was cold and dark. The power of thought was restored; he knew that the rope had broken and he had fallen into the stream. There was no additional strangulation; the noose about his neck was already suffocating him, and kept the water from his lungs. To die of hanging at the bottom of a river!—the idea seemed to him ludicrous. He opened his eyes in the blackness and saw above him a gleam of light, but how distant, how inaccessible! He was still sinking, for the light became fainter and fainter until it was a mere glimmer. Then it began to grow and brighten, and he knew that he was rising toward the surface—knew it with reluctance, for he was now very comfortable. "To be hanged and drowned," he thought, "that is not so bad; but I do not wish to be shot. No; I will not be shot; that is not fair."

He was not conscious of an effort, but a sharp pain in his wrist apprised him that he was trying to free his hands. He gave the struggle his attention, as an idler might observe the feat of a juggler, without interest in the outcome. What splendid effort!—what magnificent, what superhuman strength! Ah, that was a fine endeavour! Bravo! The cord fell away; his arms parted and floated upward, the hands dimly seen on each side in the growing light. He watched them with a new interest as first one and then the other pounced upon the noose at his neck. They tore it away and thrust it fiercely aside, its undulations resembling those of a water-snake. "Put it back, put it back!" He thought he shouted these words to his hands, for the undoing of the noose had been succeeded by the direst pang which he had yet experienced. His neck ached horribly; his brain was on fire; his heart, which had been fluttering faintly, gave a great leap, trying to force itself out at his mouth. His whole body was racked and wrenched with an insupportable anguish! But his disobedient hands gave no heed to the command. They beat the water vigorously with quick, downward strokes, forcing him to the surface. He felt his head emerge; his eyes were blinded by the sunlight; his chest expanded convulsively, and with a supreme and crowning agony his lungs engulfed a great draught of air, which instantly he expelled in a shriek!

He was now in full possession of his physical senses. They were, indeed, preternaturally keen and alert. Something in the awful disturbance of his organic system had so exalted and refined them that they made record of things never before perceived. He felt the ripples upon his face and heard their separate sounds as they struck. He looked at the forest on the bank of the stream, saw the individual trees, the leaves and the veining of each leaf—the very insects upon them, the locusts, the brilliant-bodied flies, the grey spiders stretching their webs from twig to twig. He noted the prismatic colors in all the dewdrops upon a million blades of grass. The humming of the gnats that danced above the eddies of the stream, the beating of the dragon flies' wings, the strokes of the water spiders' legs, like oars which had lifted their boat—all these made audible music. A fish slid along beneath his eyes and he heard the rush of its body parting the water.

He had come to the surface facing down the stream; in a moment the visible world seemed to wheel slowly round, himself the pivotal point, and he saw the bridge, the fort, the soldiers upon the bridge, the captain, the sergeant, the two privates, his executioners. They were in silhouette against the blue sky. They shouted and gesticulated, pointing at him; the captain had drawn his pistol, but did not fire; the others were unarmed. Their movements were grotesque and horrible, their forms gigantic.

Suddenly he heard a sharp report and something struck the water smartly within a few inches of his head, spattering his face with spray. He heard a second report, and saw one of the sentinels with his rifle at his shoulder, a light cloud of blue smoke rising from the muzzle. The man in the water saw the eye of the man on the bridge gazing into his own through the sights of the rifle. He observed that it was a grey eye, and remembered having read that grey eyes were keenest and that all famous marksmen had them. Nevertheless, this one had missed.

A counter swirl had caught Farquhar and turned him half round; he was again looking into the forest on the bank opposite the fort. The sound of a clear, high voice in a monotonous singsong now rang out behind him and came across the water with a distinctness that pierced and subdued all other sounds, even the beating of the ripples in his ears. Although no soldier, he had frequented camps enough to know the dread significance of that deliberate, drawling, aspirated chant; the lieutenant on shore was taking a part in the morning's work. How coldly and pitilessly—with what an even, calm intonation, presaging and enforcing tranquillity in the men—with what accurately-measured intervals fell those cruel words:

"Attention, company. . . . Shoulder arms. . . . Ready. . . . Aim . . . Fire."

Farquhar dived—dived as deeply as he could. The water roared in his ears like the voice of Niagara, yet he heard the dulled thunder of the volley, and rising again toward the surface, met shining bits of metal, singularly flattened, oscillating slowly downward. Some of them touched him on the face and hands, then fell away, continuing their descent. One lodged between his collar and neck; it was uncomfortably warm, and he snatched it out.

As he rose to the surface, gasping for breath, he saw that he had been a long time under water; he was perceptibly farther down stream—nearer to safety. The soldiers had almost finished reloading; the metal ramrods flashed all at once in the sunshine as they were drawn from the barrels, turned in the air, and thrust into their sockets. The two sentinels fired again, independently and ineffectually.

The hunted man saw all this over his shoulder; he was now swimming vigorously with the current. His brain was as energetic as his arms and legs; he thought with the rapidity of lightning.

"The officer," he reasoned, "will not make that martinet's error a second time. It is as easy to dodge a volley as a single shot. He has probably already given the command to fire at will. God help me, I cannot dodge them all!"

An appalling plash within two yards of him, followed by a loud rushing sound, *diminuendo*,[2] which seemed to travel back through the air to the fort and died in an explosion which stirred the very river to its deeps! A rising sheet of water, which curved over him, fell down upon him, blinded him, strangled him! The cannon had taken a hand in the game. As he shook his head free from the commotion of the smitten water, he heard the deflected shot humming through the air ahead, and in an instant it was cracking and smashing the branches in the forest beyond.

"They will not do that again," he thought; "the next time they will use a charge of grape.[3] I must keep my eye upon the gun; the smoke will apprise me—the report arrives too late; it lags behind the missile. It is a good gun."

Suddenly he felt himself whirled round and round—spinning like a top. The water, the banks, the forest, the now distant bridge, fort and men—all were commingled and blurred. Objects were represented by their colors only; circular horizontal streaks of color—that

2. Diminishing. 3. Grapeshot, a cluster of small pellets fired from a cannon.

was all he saw. He had been caught in a vortex and was being whirled on with a velocity of advance and gyration which made him giddy and sick. In a few moments he was flung upon the gravel at the foot of the left bank of the stream—the southern bank—and behind a projecting point which concealed him from his enemies. The sudden arrest of his motion, the abrasion of one of his hands on the gravel, restored him and he wept with delight. He dug his fingers into the sand, threw it over himself in handfuls and audibly blessed it. It looked like gold, like diamonds, rubies, emeralds; he could think of nothing beautiful which it did not resemble. The trees upon the bank were giant garden plants; he noted a definite order in their arrangement, inhaled the fragrance of their blooms. A strange, roseate light shone through the spaces among their trunks, and the wind made in their branches the music of æolian harps. He had no wish to perfect his escape, was content to remain in that enchanting spot until retaken.

A whizz and rattle of grapeshot among the branches high above his head roused him from his dream. The baffled cannoneer had fired him a random farewell. He sprang to his feet, rushed up the sloping bank, and plunged into the forest.

All that day he travelled, laying his course by the rounding sun. The forest seemed interminable; nowhere did he discover a break in it, not even a woodman's road. He had not known that he lived in so wild a region. There was something uncanny in the revelation.

By nightfall he was fatigued, footsore, famishing. The thought of his wife and children urged him on. At last he found a road which led him in what he knew to be the right direction. It was as wide and straight as a city street, yet it seemed untravelled. No fields bordered it, no dwelling anywhere. Not so much as the barking of a dog suggested human habitation. The black bodies of the great trees formed a straight wall on both sides, terminating on the horizon in a point, like a diagram in a lesson in perspective. Overhead, as he looked up through this rift in the wood, shone great golden stars looking unfamiliar and grouped in strange constellations. He was sure they were arranged in some order which had a secret and malign significance. The wood on either side was full of singular noises, among which—once, twice, and again—he distinctly heard whispers in an unknown tongue.

His neck was in pain, and, lifting his hand to it, he found it horribly swollen. He knew that it had a circle of black where the rope had bruised it. His eyes felt congested; he could no longer close them. His tongue was swollen with thirst; he relieved its fever by thrusting it forward from between his teeth into the cool air. How softly the turf had carpeted the untravelled avenue! He could no longer feel the roadway beneath his feet!

Doubtless, despite his suffering, he fell asleep while walking, for now he sees another scene—perhaps he has merely recovered from a delirium. He stands at the gate of his own home. All is as he left it, and all bright and beautiful in the morning sunshine. He must have travelled the entire night. As he pushes open the gate and passes up the wide white walk, he sees a flutter of female garments; his wife, looking fresh and cool and sweet, steps down from the verandah to meet him. At the bottom of the steps she stands waiting, with a smile of ineffable joy, an attitude of matchless grace and dignity. Ah, how beautiful she is! He springs forward with extended arms. As he is about to clasp her, he feels a stunning blow upon the back of the neck; a blinding white light blazes all about him, with a sound like the shock of a cannon—then all is darkness and silence!

Peyton Farquhar was dead; his body, with a broken neck, swung gently from side to side beneath the timbers of the Owl Creek bridge.

---

1. If the story is not, in your view, intended as realism, what purpose is served by the realistic details and descriptions?
2. Why does the disguised Federal scout suggest to Farquhar that he should burn the bridge?
3. Account for Farquhar's intense sensitivity to his surroundings after his "escape."
4. At what point in the story do you get the first hint that the escape is an hallucination? At what point are you sure?
5. Account for the departures from Farquhar's point of view.

Jorge Luis Borges

Borges (1899–1986) was born in Buenos Aires, Argentina, the descendant of middle class intellectuals. After his education in Geneva and some years in Europe, where he associated with avant garde *literary groups, he returned to Buenos Aires in 1921 and became the leader of a South American literary movement based on Surrealism and Imagism. In the early phases of his career, he wrote poetry for the most part, turning to prose as his varied intellectual interests came together to suggest new forms. A vastly erudite man, who directed the National Library until the dictator Peron removed him for political reasons, Borges built a "literature about literature"; his typically brief essays and short narratives are miniature encyclopedias of literary history, mingling gravity with absurdity in a constant exposure of the complexities of human awareness. Though he was blind and a partial invalid in his later years, he lectured and taught in the United States. His books available in English include* Labyrinths *(1962),* Ficciones *(1962),* Dreamtigers *(1964),* The Book of Imaginary Beings *(1969),* The Aleph and Other Stories *(1970),* Dr. Brodie's Report *(1972), and* The Book of Sand *(1979).*

Pierre Menard, Author of the *Quixote*[1]

The *visible*[2] work left by this novelist is easily and briefly enumerated. Impardonable therefore, are the omissions and additions perpetrated by Madame Henri Bachelier in a fallacious catalogue which a certain daily, whose *Protestant* tendency is no secret, has had the inconsideration to inflict upon its deplorable readers—though these be few and Calvinist, if not Masonic and circumcised.[3] The true friends of Menard have viewed this catalogue with alarm and even with a certain melancholy. One might say that only yesterday we gathered before his final monument, amidst the lugubrious cypresses, and already Error

1. Translated by James E. Irby. This story parodies a scholarly study. It comes complete with footnotes of its own, and these footnotes must be considered an integral part of the parody. So—to avoid confusion—Borges' footnotes are marked with an asterisk and printed above a ruled line at the bottom of each page. The editor's footnotes are printed below the line. The editor's footnotes are necessarily numerous because Borges' method is to mix an abundance of scholarly allusions to real personalities and literary works with names of fictitious authors and their fictitious works. 2. I.e., that which actually exists on paper. 3. I.e., those who are prejudiced by their Protestant, Free Thinking, of Jewish biases.

tries to tarnish his Memory . . . Decidedly, a brief rectification is unavoidable.

I am aware that it is quite easy to challenge my slight authority. I hope, however, that I shall not be prohibited from mentioning two eminent testimonies. The Baroness de Bacourt (at whose unforgettable *vendredis*[4] I had the honor of meeting the lamented poet) has seen fit to approve the pages which follow. The Countess de Bagnoregio,[5] one of the most delicate spirits of the Principality of Monaco (and now of Pittsburgh, Pennsylvania, following her recent marriage to the international philanthropist Simon Kautzsch, who has been so inconsiderately slandered, alas! by the victims of his disinterested maneuvers) has sacrificed "to veracity and to death" (such were her words) the stately reserve which is her distinction, and, in an open letter published in the magazine *Luxe*,[6] concedes me her approval as well. These authorizations, I think, are not entirely insufficient.

I have said that Menard's visible work can be easily enumerated. Having examined with care his personal files, I find that they contain the following items:

a) A Symbolist sonnet[7] which appeared twice (with variants) in the review *La conque* (Issues of March and October 1899).

b) A monograph on the possibility of constructing a poetic vocabulary of concepts which would not be synonyms or periphrases of those which make up our everyday language, "but rather ideal objects created according to convention and essentially designed to satisfy poetic needs" (Nîmes,[8] 1901).

c) A monograph on "certain connections or affinities" between the thought of Descartes, Leibniz and John Wilkins[9] (Nîmes, 1903).

d) A monograph on Leibniz's *Characteristica universalis*[1] (Nîmes, 1904).

e) A technical article on the possibility of improving the game of chess, eliminating one of the rook's pawns. Menard proposes, recommends, discusses and finally rejects this innovation.

f) A monograph on Raymond Lully's *Ars magna generalis*[2] (Nîmes, 1906).

4. Regular Friday meetings devoted to a discussion of the arts. 5. Evidently a fictitious patroness of the arts. 6. *Luxury*. 7. In the second half of the nineteenth century there arose in France what has come to be known as the Symbolist Movement. The Symbolists sought to express or suggest ideas and emotions by means of symbols, as by the mention or introduction of things or the use of words and word sounds to convey a meaning, often with mystical or vague effects. *La conque: seashell*. 8. A city in southern France. 9. Bishop of Chester (1614–1672); René Descartes (1596–1650), French philosopher and mathematician; Gottfried Wilhelm Leibniz (1646–1716), German philosopher, mathematician, and theologian. 1. *Universal Characteristics*, written in 1679. 2. *The Great Art of the General*, Raymond Lully (c. 1232–1315).

g) A translation, with prologue and notes, of Ruy López de Segura's *Libro de la invención liberal y arte del juego del axedrez*[3] (Paris, 1907).

h) The work sheets of a monograph on George Boole's[4] symbolic logic.

i) An examination of the essential metric laws of French prose, illustrated with examples taken from Saint-Simon (*Revue des langues romanes*, Montpellier, October 1909).[5]

j) A reply to Luc Durtain[6] (who had denied the existence of such laws), illustrated with examples from Luc Durtain (*Revue des langues romanes*, Montpellier, December 1909).

k) A manuscript translation of the *Aguja de navegar cultos* of Quevedo, entitled *La boussole des précieux*.[7]

l) A preface to the Catalogue of an exposition of lithographs by Carolus Hourcade[8] (Nîmes, 1914).

m) The work *Les problèmes d'un problème*[9] (Paris, 1917) which discusses, in chronological order, the different solutions given to the illustrous problem of Achilles and the tortoise.[1] Two editions of this book have appeared so far; the second bears as an epigraph Leibniz's recommendation "*Ne craignez point, monsieur, la tortue*"[2] and revises the chapters dedicated to Russell[3] and Descartes.

n) A determined analysis of the "syntactical customs" of Toulet (N. R. F.,[4] March 1921). Menard—I recall—declared that censure and praise are sentimental operations which have nothing to do with literary criticism.

o) A transposition into alexandrines of Paul Valéry's *Le cimetière marin*[5] (N. R. F., January 1928).

p) An invective against Paul Valéry, in the *Papers for the Suppression of Reality* of Jacques Reboul.[6] (This invective, we might say parenthetically, is the exact opposite of his true opinion of Valéry. The latter understood it as such and their old friendship was not endangered.)

3. *The Book of Liberal Invention and the Game of Chess* published in 1561. 4. English mathematician, metaphysician, and author (1815–1864). 5. *Review of Romance Languages* published in Montpellier, France. No article on the Duc de Saint-Simon (1675–1755) appears in the issue cited. 6. *Luc Durtain* (b. 1881) does not appear in the issue cited. 7. Both titles mean *Guide to* (or *Compass for*) *the Euphuists* (or *Aesthetes*), by Vasco Mousinho Quevedo, Portuguese poet (d. 1628). 8. Carolus Hourcade is unidentified, probably fictitious. 9. *Problems of a problem.* 1. The Eleatic school of philosophers, including most probably Zeno and Parmenides, flourished in Greece in the fifth century B.C. It held that being is the only reality and that plurality, change, and motion are illusory. Among Zeno's arguments against motion, for example, are these paradoxes: motion cannot begin because a body in motion cannot arrive at another place until it has passed through an unlimited number of places intermediate; Achilles cannot overtake a tortoise, because as often as he reaches the place occupied by the tortoise at some previous moment the tortoise has already left it; a flying arrow is at rest, for it is at every moment in only one place. 2. "Don't fear, sir, the tortoise." 3. Bertrand Russell (1872–1970), English philosopher and mathematician. 4. *New French Review (La Nouvelle revue française);* Pierre-Jean Toulet (1867–1920), French poet. 5. Paul Valéry (1871–1945), French poet. "The Graveyard by the Sea." 6. Jacques Reboul is unidentified, probably fictitious.

q) A "definition" of the Countess de Bagnoregio, in the "victorious volume"—the locution is Gabriele d'Annunzio's,[7] another of its collaborators—published annually by this lady to rectify the inevitable falsifications of journalists and to present "to the world and to Italy" an authentic image of her person, so often exposed (by very reason of her beauty and her activities) to erroneous or hasty interpretations.

r) A cycle of admirable sonnets for the Baroness de Bacourt (1934).

s) A manuscript list of verses which owe their efficacy to their punctuation.*

This, then, is the *visible* work of Menard, in chronological order (with no omission other than a few vague sonnets of circumstance written for the hospitable, or avid, album of Madame Henri Bachelier). I turn now to his other work: the subterranean, the interminably heroic, the peerless. And—such are the capacities of man!—the unfinished. This work, perhaps the most significant of our time, consists of the ninth and thirty-eighth chapters of the first part of *Don Quixote*[8] and a fragment of chapter twenty-two. I know such an affirmation seems an absurdity; to justify this "absurdity" is the primordial object of this note.†

Two texts of unequal value inspired this undertaking. One is that philological fragment by Novalis[9]—the one numbered 2005 in the Dresden edition—which outlines the theme of a *total* identification with a given author. The other is one of those parasitic books which situate Christ on a boulevard, Hamlet on La Cannebière[1] or Don Quixote on Wall Street. Like all men of good taste, Menard abhorred these useless carnivals, fit only—as he would say—to produce the plebeian pleasure of anachronism or (what is worse) to enthrall us with the elementary idea that all epochs are the same or are different. More interesting, though contradictory and superficial of execution, seemed to him the famous plan of Daudet: to conjoin the Ingenious Gentleman and his squire in *one* figure, which was Tartarin[2] . . . Those who have

*Madame Henri Bachelier also lists a literal translation of Quevedo's literal translation of the *Introduction à la vie dévote* of St. Francis of Sales [*Introduction to the Devout Life* of St. Francis of Sales (1567–1622) Bishop and prince of Geneva]. There are no traces of such a work in Menard's library. It must have been a jest of our friend, misunderstood by the lady. †I also had the secondary intention of sketching a personal portrait of Pierre Menard. But how could I dare to compete with the golden pages which, I am told, the Baroness de Bacourt is preparing or with the delicate and punctual pencil of Carolus Hourcade?

7. Gabriele d'Annunzio (1863–1938), Italian poet, novelist, and dramatist. 8. Famous novel by Miguel de Cervantes (1547–1616). 9. Friedrich von (Hardenberg) Novalis (1772–1801), German poet and philosopher. 1. Street in Paris, an incongruous or absurd setting for Hamlet. 2. Chief character in *Tartarin de Tarascon* (1872) and *Tartarin sur les Alpes* (1885), novels by French writer Alphonse Daudet (1840–1897). The "Ingenious Gentleman and his squire" is a reference to Don Quixote and Sancho Panza in Cervantes' *Don Quixote*. Tartarin is, in Daudet's treatment, alternately practical—like Sancho Panza—and recklessly idealistic—like Don Quixote.

insinuated that Menard dedicated his life to writing a contemporary *Quixote* calumniate his illustrious memory.

He did not want to compose another *Quixote*—which is easy—but *the Quixote itself*. Needless to say, he never contemplated a mechanical transcription of the original; he did not propose to copy it. His admirable intention was to produce a few pages which would coincide—word for word and line for line—with those of Miguel de Cervantes.

"My intent is no more than astonishing," he wrote me the 30th of September, 1934, from Bayonne. "The final term in a theological or metaphysical demonstration—the objective world, God, causality, the forms of the universe—is no less previous and common than my famed novel. The only difference is that the philosophers publish the intermediary stages of their labor in pleasant volumes and I have resolved to do away with those stages." In truth, not one worksheet remains to bear witness to his years of effort.

The first method he conceived was relatively simple. Know Spanish well, recover the Catholic faith, fight against the Moors or the Turk, forget the history of Europe between the years 1602 and 1918, *be* Miguel de Cervantes, Pierre Menard studied this procedure (I know he attained a fairly accurate command of seventeenth-century Spanish) but discarded it as too easy. Rather as impossible! my reader will say. Granted, but the undertaking was impossible from the very beginning and of all the impossible ways of carrying it out, this was the least interesting. To be, in the twentieth century, a popular novelist of the seventeenth seemed to him a diminution. To be, in some way, Cervantes and reach the *Quixote* seemed less arduous to him—and, consequently, less interesting—than to go on being Pierre Menard and reach the *Quixote* through the experiences of Pierre Menard. (This conviction, we might say in passing, made him omit the autobiographical prologue to the second part of *Don Quixote*. To include that prologue would have been to create another character—Cervantes—but it would also have meant presenting the *Quixote* in terms of that character and not of Menard. The latter, naturally, declined that facility.) "My undertaking is not difficult, essentially," I read in another part of his letter. "I should only have to be immortal to carry it out." Shall I confess that I often imagine he did finish it and that I read the *Quixote*—all of it—as if Menard had conceived it? Some nights past, while leafing through chapter XXVI—never essayed by him—I recognized our friend's style and something of his voice in this exceptional phrase: "the river nymphs and the dolorous and humid Echo."[3] This happy

3. In Greek mythology Hera (Juno), the wife and sister of Zeus, condemned the nymph Echo to never use her tongue again except to repeat what was said to her.

conjunction of a spiritual and a physical adjective brought to my mind a verse by Shakespeare which we discussed one afternoon:

> Where a malignant and a turbaned Turk . . .[4]

But why precisely the *Quixote?* our reader will ask. Such a preference, in a Spaniard, would not have been inexplicable; but it is, no doubt, in a Symbolist from Nîmes, essentially a devoté of Poe, who engendered Baudelaire, who engendered Mallarmé, who engendered Valéry, who engendered Edmond Teste.[5] The aforementioned letter illuminates this point. "The *Quixote,*" clarifies Menard, "interests me deeply, but it does not seem—how shall I say it?—inevitable. I cannot imagine the universe without Edgar Allan Poe's exclamation:

> Ah, bear in mind this garden was enchanted![6]

or without the *Bateau ivre* or the *Ancient Mariner,*[7] but I am quite capable of imagining it without the *Quixote.* (I speak, naturally, of my personal capacity and not of those works' historical resonance.) The *Quixote* is a contingent book; the *Quixote* is unnecessary. I can premeditate writing it, I can write it, without falling into a tautology, When I was ten or twelve years old, I read it, perhaps in its entirety. Later, I have reread closely certain chapters, those which I shall not attempt for the time being. I have also gone through the interludes, the plays, the *Galatea,* the exemplary novels, the undoubtedly laborious tribulations of Persiles and Segismunda and the *Viaje del Parnaso*[8] . . . My general recollection of the *Quixote,* simplified by forgetfulness and indifference, can well equal the imprecise and prior image of a book not yet written. Once that image (which no one can legitimately deny me) is postulated, it is certain that my problem is a good bit more difficult than Cervantes' was. My obliging predecessor did not refuse the collaboration of chance: he composed his immortal work somewhat *à la diable,*[9] carried along by the inertias of language and invention. I have taken on the mysterious duty of reconstructing literally his spon-

4. *Othello* V.ii. 5. A fictional character in *Monsieur Teste,* a novel by Paul Valéry (1871–1945), French writer and philosopher. Edgar Allan Poe (1809–1849) was an American poet and short story writer; Charles Baudelaire (1821–1867) was a French poet, as was Stéphane Mallarmé (1842–1898). The names in this sequence are said to engender their successors in the sense that they influenced them and, by their work, provided points for new departures. That the sequence ends with a fictional personage, Monsieur Teste, suggests that both Borges and Pierre Menard—his fictional creation—have been "engendered" by the same ancestors. 6. From one of Poe's two poems entitled *To Helen.* This, the lesser known one, is dedicated to Mrs. Sarah Helen Whitman. 7. *The Rime of the Ancient Mariner* by the English poet Samuel Taylor Coleridge (1772–1834); *Bateau ivre* is "The Drunken Boat" by Arthur Rimbaud (1854–1891), a Belgian poet. Both poems and both poets are important forerunners of the literary mode that Menard practices. 8. *Voyage to Parnassus; Galatea* is a poem of Cervantes, first published in 1914. Other allusions in the line are to Cervantes' works. 9. Like the devil; i.e., with inspired haste.

taneous work. My solitary game is governed by two polar laws. The first permits me to essay variations of a formal or psychological type; the second obliges me to sacrifice these variations to the "original" text and reason out this annihilation in an irrefutable manner . . . To these artificial hindrances, another—of a congenital kind—must be added. To compose the *Quixote* at the beginning of the seventeenth century was a reasonable undertaking, necessary and perhaps even unavoidable; at the beginning of the twentieth, it is almost impossible. It is not in vain that three hundred years have gone by, filled with exceedingly complex events. Amongst them, to mention only one, is the *Quixote* itself."

In spite of these three obstacles, Menard's fragmentary *Quixote* is more subtle than Cervantes'. The latter, in a clumsy fashion, opposes to the fictions of chivalry the tawdry provincial reality of his country; Menard selects as his "reality" the land of Carmen during the century of Lepanto and Lope de Vega.[1] What a series of *espagnolades* that selection would have suggested to Maurice Barrès or Dr. Rodríguez Larreta![2] Menard eludes them with complete naturalness. In his work there are no gypsy flourishes or conquistadors or mystics or Philip the Seconds or *autos da fé*.[3] He neglects or eliminates local color. This disdain points to a new conception of the historical novel. This disdain condemns *Salammbô*,[4] with no possibility of appeal.

It is no less astounding to consider isolated chapters. For example, let us examine Chapter XXXVIII of the first part, "which treats of the curious discourse of Don Quixote on arms and letters." It is well known that Don Quixote (like Quevedo in an analogous and later passage in *La hora de todos*[5]) decided the debate against letters and in favor of arms. Cervantes was a former soldier: his verdict is understandable. But that Pierre Menard's Don Quixote—a contemporary of *La trahison des clercs*[6] and Bertrand Russell—should fall prey to such nebulous sophistries! Madame Bachelier has seen here an admirable and typical subordination on the part of the author to the hero's psychology; others (not at all perspicaciously), a *transcription* of the *Quixote*;

1. Carmen is the Gypsy heroine of a novel by Prosper Merimée (1803–1870), French writer. The novel was made into an immensely popular opera by the composer Georges Bizet (1838–1875). The Battle of Lepanto, in which a largely Spanish fleet destroyed the Turkish naval power, was fought in 1571, and Lope de Vega, Spanish poet, lived from 1562 to 1635—thus both references are to the century in which Cervantes lived. 2. Barrès was a French novelist (1862–1923); Larreta is unidentified and possibly fictitious. *Espagnolades* is a French term for a literary work heavily saturated with the local color of Spain. 3. Philip the Second was a Spanish king (1527–1598), sponsor of the Spanish Inquisition and leader of the Counter Reformation, a movement in opposition to the Protestant Reformation. *Autos da fe* were executions by fire of heretics condemned by the Inquisition. 4. A colorful and detailed historical novel by French writer Gustave Flaubert (1821–1880). 5. *La hora de todos y la fortuna con seso*, literally *Everyone's Hour (or Time) and the Wit of Fortune*, roughly equivalent to "every dog has his day by the irony of Fortune." 6. *The Treason of the Intellectuals*, by Julien Benda (1867–1956), French essayist who in this book attacks European intellectuals for allowing their talents to be exploited for nationalist political ends.

the Baroness de Bacourt, the influence of Nietzsche.[7] To this third interpretation (which I judge to be irrefutable) I am not sure I dare to add a fourth, which concords very well with the almost divine modesty of Pierre Menard: his resigned or ironical habit of propagating ideas which were the strict reverse of those he preferred. (Let us recall once more his diatribe against Paul Valéry in Jacques Reboul's ephemeral Surrealist sheet.) Cervantes' text and Menard's are verbally identical, but the second is almost infinitely richer. (More ambiguous, his detractors will say, but ambiguity is richness.)

It is a revelation to compare Menard's *Don Quixote* with Cervantes'. The latter, for example, wrote (part one, chapter nine):

> . . . truth, whose mother is history, rival of time, depository of deeds, witness of the past, exemplar and adviser to the present, and the future's counselor.

Written in the seventeenth century, written by the "lay genius" Cervantes, this enumeration is a mere rhetorical praise of history. Menard, on the other hand, writes:

> . . . truth, whose mother is history, rival of time, depository of deeds, witness of the past, exemplar and adviser to the present, and the future's counselor.

History, the *mother* of truth: the idea is astounding. Menard, a contemporary of William James,[8] does not define history as an inquiry into reality but as its origin. Historical truth, for him, is not what has happened; it is what we judge to have happened. The final phrases—*exemplar and adviser to the present, and the future's counselor*—are brazenly pragmatic.

The contrast in style is also vivid. The archaic style of Menard—quite foreign, after all—suffers from a certain affectation. Not so that of his forerunner, who handles with ease the current Spanish of his time.

There is no exercise of the intellect which is not, in the final analysis, useless. A philosophical doctrine begins as a plausible description of the universe; with the passage of the years it becomes a mere chapter—if not a paragraph or a name—in the history of philosophy. In literature, this eventual caducity is even more notorious. The *Quixote*—-Menard told me—was, above all, an entertaining book; now it is the occasion for patriotic toasts, grammatical insolence and obscene

7. Friedrich Nietzsche (1844–1900), German philosopher. The allusion is probably to his idea of "Eternal Recurrence"—a belief that everything that happens will happen again and again within the frame of eternity, as Menard's *Quixote* recurs after that of Cervantes. 8. American pragmatist philosopher (1842–1910).

de luxe editions. Fame is a form of incomprehension, perhaps the worst.

There is nothing new in these nihilistic verifications; what is singular is the determination Menard derived from them. He decided to anticipate the vanity awaiting all man's efforts; he set himself to an undertaking which was exceedingly complex and, from the very beginning, futile. He dedicated his scruples and his sleepless nights to repeating an already extant book in an alien tongue. He multiplied draft upon draft, revised tenaciously and tore up thousands of manuscript pages.* He did not let anyone examine these drafts and took care they should not survive him. In vain have I tried to reconstruct them.

I have reflected that it is permissible to see in this "final" *Quixote* a kind of palimpsest,[9] through which the traces—tenuous but not indecipherable—of our friend's "previous" writing should be translucently visible. Unfortunately, only a second Pierre Menard, inverting the other's work, would be able to exhume and revive those lost Troys[1] . . .

"Thinking, analyzing, inventing (he also wrote me) are not anomalous acts; they are the normal respiration of the intelligence. To glorify the occasional performance of that function, to hoard ancient and alien thoughts, to recall with incredulous stupor that the *doctor universalis*[2] thought, is to confess our laziness or our barbarity. Every man should be capable of all ideas and I understand that in the future this will be the case."

Menard (perhaps without wanting to) has enriched, by means of a new technique, the halting and rudimentary art of reading: this new technique is that of the deliberate anachronism and the erroneous attribution. This technique, whose applications are infinite, prompts us to go through the *Odyssey* as if it were posterior to the *Aeneid*[3] and the book *Le jardin du Centaure*[4] of Madame Henri Bachelier as if it were by Madame Henri Bachelier. This technique fills the most placid works with adventure. To attribute the *Imitatio Christi* to Louis Fer-

*I remember his quadricular notebooks, his black crossed-out passages, his peculiar typographical symbols and his insect-like handwriting. In the afternoons he liked to go out for a walk around the outskirts of Nîmes; he would take a notebook with him and make a merry bonfire.

---

9. A parchment document from which writing has been partially erased to make room for another text. Frequently fragments of the original text are inadvertently combined with the new additions. 1. Troy, which was destroyed by the Greeks in the Trojan War, has become a conventional symbol of lost cultures. 2. The universal doctor or savant; a term sometimes applied to the philosophers Aristotle and Thomas Aquinas. 3. Homer's epic poem *The Odyssey* dates from the seventh or eighth century B.C., while Virgil's *Aeneid* was written in the first century B.C. Borges is playing with anachronism. 4. *The Centaur's Garden*, obviously a fictitious work by a fictitious author.

dinand Céline or to James Joyce,[5] is this not a sufficient renovation of its tenuous spiritual indications?

For Silvina Ocampo

---

1. Is Menard's self-appointed task of rewriting *Don Quixote* an absurdity or a meaningful literary undertaking?
2. To what extent does the personality of the narrator color the story? What does his enthusiasm for Menard's "impossible" undertaking tell us about his own values and literary aims?
3. To what extent is the story a satire on scholarly methods?
4. What does the story say about the value of tangible evidence of productivity in an intellectual enterprise?
5. Is Menard's work a hoax? Is Borges' story about it a hoax? Is the fabrication of a hoax a legitimate, entertaining, and enlightening form of literary activity?

5. *Imitatio Christi* was written by Thomas à Kempis (1380–1471), while Louis Ferdinand Céline (pen name for Ferdinand Destouches) (1894–1961) and James Joyce (1882–1941) are 20th-century writers. More anachronism.

Kay Boyle

Boyle (1903–) was born in St. Paul, Minnesota, and from childhood on has been a dedicated and prolific writer. She went to Europe with her first husband when she was nineteen, living in England, France, and Austria during many years in which her delicate health was threatened by tuberculosis. In 1941 she fled from France and has lived in the U.S. since then. From time to time she has worked as a magazine editor, has contributed nonfiction to many leading periodicals, and has taught writing classes at the New School for Social Research in New York and San Francisco State University. Through the shifting pageantry of her fictional subject matter the need for love has emerged as a persisting theme. Her novels include My Next Bride *(1934),* Monday Night *(1938), and* The Seagull on the Step *(1955). Her short stories appear in* The White Horses of Vienna *(1936),* Thirty Stories *(1946),* Nothing Ever Breaks Except the Heart *(1966), and* Life Being the Best & Other Stories *(1988). Some of her poetry is collected in* Testament for My Students *(1970).*

Art Colony

Paris has a grief of its own on some nights in December. If you walked the streets all night with it, you could not make it sleep. A drenching blast of snow worn thin swings down the steps of the Métro.[1] It combs your hair out long on your face, and dries its tears with your hands.

Such a piece of its violence blew in through the door with the young woman. She came in from the street and turned the lock, and stood breathing deep and looking awhile before her. There was a yellow bulb left burning beyond in the kitchen, as good as a lemon squeezed out and the sallow drops of it falling. *Hush, hush,* said the wily step of the snow outside pacing the long bare windows of the room.

The house was cold, and down the length of the table stood the dishes and disorder left over from supper. The warmest things in the place were the mouse and her young scampering off from the rinds of

1. Subway.

cheese left there by the dozen people who had eaten. The shy little beasts went scattering and whistling away when Shiloh threw her cap down and walked across the room. Three woodcuts, as wide as posters, waved from the walls in the sharp draughts of air that came and went like the lifting of a fan: one of a man spading in a rich field, another of a muscular archer setting an arrow to his bow, and another of a strong man sowing handfuls of golden grain. The wooden seats that stood against the walls were covered with soiled, woolly hides.

The range stood black and burdened in the corner, piled up with the day's dishes and wigged with long, thick curls of shining grease. "Blessèd is the artisan," said the poster in block letters pinned above it on the plaster, "for his is the joy of creation." The sink was clogged with strips of salad and match butts, and Shiloh gathered up the small bouquet of refuse in her fingers. She turned on the water and, as the pan filled, she stared mindlessly ahead at the photograph that hung over the spigot. Whenever Shiloh turned on the water at night to heat it for the dishes, there stood the photograph before her of a strong, beautiful woman in a tunic, with her arms stretched out from the picture. Under her was printed: "I would teach the whole world to dance!"

Shiloh waited there at night in the cold with the stalk of fresh water falling between them, looking a long while at the face of the strong, dead woman. She had not known her alive, but the long, humorous upper lip and the shapely arms were like Sorrel's. She stood quiet, with her wet coat still buttoned over, and looked at the face of Sorrel's dead sister, and the water brimmed up to the edge of the pan and rippled over. I used to believe in it, she thought: in Sorrel, in the old Roman, an old man with great white ropes of hair, standing clean and tall, like his sister, on his bare sandaled feet.

I used to believe in it, she thought as she set a match to the gas. Everything all about lay deep and foul in its own dirt. Whenever he spoke, I believed in the action of poetry, and in the door standing wide for anybody at all who might be wanting shelter. But if ever she said: "There are some nights in December or some other times when I can't come back to it," he would roll himself up in his toga and cry to himself for weeks.

She went upstairs, two at a time, but softly. The rooms above were dark, but from the light on the landing she could see there was a woman sitting still on the floor. She was sitting near to the bench where the child must be sleeping. Her head was bowed, as though in sleep, and a part ran up the middle. She had drawn the woven rug around her for warmth, for there were no fires to bring comfort to the night.

Shiloh stepped into the dark, chill room, silently around the woman. Strangers, disciples of Sorrel's, often came and went, but this one she had never seen before. She could see the child's face shining on the black, woolly hide that lay beneath its head, and stooped to touch the child's cheek with her fingers. Suddenly the woman near the open door raised up her fallen head and swung her face around.

"Who's there?" she said sharply. Shiloh could see her stiffen and rear against the light.

"What are *you* doing, sitting there?" said Shiloh indolently out of the darkness. She felt the child's hands bloodless as snow on the shaggy cover. In the dark she took off her coat and laid it over the shape that was sleeping there.

"I'm here all right," said the woman sharply. "I'm here, but I'll get out pretty God damn quick."

She spoke with an accent, but scarcely, and Shiloh could see against the light the fierce, wild angles of her face. Her evil neck reached out of her clothes, and her viperous tongue turned sharp on Shiloh. "What do you have to be touching that baby for?" she said. "It was me who got it to sleep, it wasn't you."

Shiloh sat down on the floor close to the bench and lit a cigarette in the darkness. She opened her mouth in the cold and breathed the warm smoke over the child's fingers in her palm. The stale weather in the room went icily up and down her spine, and the woman rolled up in the rug on the other side sat shaking.

"You ain't got no reason to come and set in waking it," said the woman. "None of you have no care for it," she said bitterly. "It didn't have no supper before I come along. All of you coming in at any hour it pleases you. They was all dressed up going out to the moving pictures when I come along."

"Where are you from?" said Shiloh out of the darkness. So many came and went on again that it was of no interest any more.

"I came up third[2] from Marseilles," said the woman's sour voice. "I walked that way from the *gare* because I didn't have as much as the Métro fare."

"That's one way of getting warm," said Shiloh languidly. She felt the south wind of her own breath blowing on the child's white hands.

"You don't know nothing I been through with!" the woman shouted out in grief. She drew herself into the rug and sat dark and mourning by the door. "You come and go in your sheets and your shawls and live the way you please!"

"Why did you come here to Sorrel?" said Shiloh in a little while.

"Hell," said the woman, "I knew the old guy in Germany." She threw up her sharp, thin head in anger. The thought of something else had stirred her scalding bile. "To hell with him and his tribe," she said,

2. In a third-class railway coach. *Gare:* railway station.

"if they wasn't in hell already! This place is as like it as anything I ever seen. I tell you, I'm Russian and I beat it through the revolution, but I never hope to see worse than this place," she said.

Her hands came out like scrawny men against the light, and scratched their hollow spines aloud with her nails.

"That baby there!" she cried out suddenly in fury. "Why don't they put talcum powder on it like they do on other babies? That's what I asked them. Little thing not more than two years old. I come to the door and they had their glad rags on, dressed up like a lot of Arabs setting off to the moving pictures. Here's your part in the colony, says Sorrel, set where you are and look to the house. As if I was to wash up their filth after them. I ain't had no supper. I found the baby crying. It's got a bottom sore like a chimpanzee."

Shiloh sat smoking with the child's fingers against her mouth. A shadow of warmth was stealing now across its flesh.

"Young ones like you," said the Russian woman with venom, "got no ideas in your head but your own lookout! I've known a lot of your sort," she said, "all I want to know. To hell with the old ones, you say. You got no kick coming."

"What were you doing in Marseilles?" said Shiloh after a little.

"Hell," said the woman, "I got stranded."

They sat quiet in the dark, icy room, harking to the child's breath coming and going.

"I ain't used to anything like this," the woman said. "I was ten years with the Baroness von Hoffen," she said, and her bitter voice had turned to sorrow. "We been living all the time on Riverside Drive, and on the Champs Élysées, and on the Riviera. She's an American, always spending her money on Sorrel's bum rugs and scarves and things."

Her voice went small and grim in her throat as the thoughts came to her.

"She believes in the artists, eh! She ought to get a night sleeping on the floor! She fell for the artistic life and bought sandals and tunics off him and went around half-naked too. She ain't got no use for the Baron except his money. She shipped me," said the Russian woman in sorrow. "She give me the gate because she thought it was me had give her away. I don't know how she's making out without me," she said after a moment. "She can't do her own hair for a nickel, and it was always me made every stitch for her, copying after models."

"Did you ever know Sorrel's sister?" Shiloh said.

"Whenever we went to the grand hotels," said the Russian woman, "she used to come along. She cried in the Ritz in London at the table because they didn't have no silver plate for her to eat her asparagus from. There was nothing alike between the two," she said. "The sister was always at the brother. You ain't the only one to know them," the Russian woman said.

"I didn't know his sister," said Shiloh. She lit another cigarette and sat back with her legs stretched out in the dark.

"She taught the Baroness to dance," said the Russian woman with her voice turned proud. "They used to dance on the Dutch beaches, jumping up and down. But the Baroness couldn't run so fast, and she'd get left behind her. Hell, the sister'd come into the room in Germany when Sorrel had the colony. Set down a bottle of whisky and a beefsteak thicker than your arm, and say hell, Sorrel, to hell with your vegetation! Give these poor guys a meal for a change! He'd stand there and cry, her brother, and then she'd start in crying with him and smoothing him down. But she'd have some one cook her the beefsteak just the same. A good thick one," said the Russian woman eagerly, "running with juice and cooked up with French frieds. I knew how she liked them. It was me that made them right for her sometimes. She loved hollandaise sauce like money, and she'd eat it with a spoon. She used to like to start off with artichokes," said the Russian woman, "and them big American olives—"

"Listen, *ma vieille*," said Shiloh. "I'll go down and cook us something for supper. It's ten o'clock at night, but that's not such a bad hour."

The Russian woman looked suddenly toward Shiloh.

"Ain't you had nothing to eat neither?" she said.

Shiloh slipped her hand away, softly, slowly, from the embrace of the child's warm fingers.

"I cook something for myself every night after I get home," she said. She saw the Russian woman's head lifted curiously to watch her step across the room to the lighted door. In the kitchen the water was boiling on the gas.

In a little while the woman came down the stairs with the rug folded over her shoulders. She moved cautiously down, without sound, like a specter in the hall. She was yellow as saffron in the face and her thin hair hung from her starving skull. There was naught but a bone or two of her body left under the hanging clothes.

The woman followed her wherever she went, swaying, like a woman drunk with weariness and sorrow. She helped Shiloh stack the thick, foul dishes and bear them in to the sink.

"Sit down there and warm yourself at the gas," said Shiloh. Whatever she did, the Russian woman stood by looking curiously at her face. The pile of dishes slid down and settled in the soapy water, and Shiloh turned to break the eggs into the pan.

"What is it you have to do all day?" said the woman shyly in a moment.

"Oh, I sell Sorrel's things at the shop," said Shiloh. "That's what gets me home so late."

"Hell," said the Russian woman, "you got a pretty face. Ain't there nothing better you can do?"

Shiloh sliced the few remaining cold potatoes in and watched them browning sweetly in the butter. The other woman stood up from the chair, and her face hung, avid and thirsting, above the steaming pan.

"The Baroness," said the Russian woman softly, "she used to like nothing better than a roasted chicken. When Sorrel's sister would come in, they'd finish one between them in no time at all."

Shiloh slid the eggs off onto a plate, and they carried their supper in, side by side, to the big, bare room. All around in the bleakness could Sorrel's craft be seen: his woodcuts, his tapestries, his handmade rugs standing upright, like dead men, in the corners.

"My God," said the Russian woman, beginning to eat, "I'll get out of here in a hurry! The Baroness'll send me the fare. I know how she is. She kicked me out, but that ain't all there is to it. She thought it was me told the Baron about her and Sorrel, but I never gave her away." They sat close together in the cold room, with the food beginning to warm their bodies. "In ten years," said the Russian woman with sorrow, "I never gave them away."

They took the dry cheese apart between them and laid the parings as well, flat on their bread, and chewed side by side.

"When I joined," said Shiloh slowly as she ate, "we were going to work the hand press." She looked around the room at the disorder, and grinned at the Russian woman. "We were going to print poetry, and revive the dramy," she said. "But nothing ever came of it. Sorrel got some money and bought a new car instead."

"What's keeping you from clearing out?" said the Russian woman. Shiloh wiped her plate clean leisurely with a crust of bread, and then she shrugged her shoulders.

"One thing and another," she said.

"My God," said the Russian woman, "I'll write to the Baroness tomorrow. She won't get anyone to be like I was with the children. Sorrel used to give her hell," she said bitterly, "about mother-loving your own."

"Yes," said Shiloh. She felt the woman fixed small and terrible in grief beside her.

After a little while the Russian woman said: "Don't the mother of that baby upstairs ever come here and see it?"

"Yes," said Shiloh slowly, "she comes sometimes."

"Ain't she got no money or what?" said the Russian woman.

"No," said Shiloh. She saw her own hand playing slowly with the crumbs left on the table. "She hasn't any money," said Shiloh, "and its father's dead."

---

1. Discuss the importance of the setting, including the weather.
2. What are the disparities between the reality of the colony and its pretenses? How does the personality of Sorrel seem to account for such disparity?
3. What standards of morality and practicality does the Russian woman speak for?
4. Is Shiloh the mother of the sleeping child? How much evidence can you point to for your view? Is it an effective tactic in the story to leave this question uncertain?

Ray Bradbury

Bradbury (1920–) was born in Waukegan, Illinois. After attending high school in Los Angeles, he joined a little theater group there and by 1941 had begun to publish the stories that would make him one of the stars among science fiction writers. His concern about the multitude of threats to the imagination in the modern world has led him occasionally to the social criticism that particularly distinguishes his novel Fahrenheit 451 *(1953) and to serious expositions of the threat inherent in expansionist technology. His other novels include* Something Wicked This Way Comes *(1962) and* The Halloween Tree *(1972). He has written plays and screenplays—including the one for* Moby Dick *(1954). Among his numerous books of short stories are:* The Martian Chronicles *(1950),* The Golden Apples of the Sun *(1953),* Dandelion Wine *(1957),* I Sing the Body Electric! *(1969), and* The Stories of Ray Bradbury *(1980). He has also published a book of poetry:* When Elephants Last in the Dooryard Bloomed *(1972).*

The Veldt

George, I wish you'd look at the nursery."

"What's wrong with it?"

"I don't know."

"Well, then."

"I just want you to look at it, is all, or call a psychologist in to look at it."

"What would a psychologist want with a nursery?"

"You know very well what he'd want." His wife paused in the middle of the kitchen and watched the stove busy humming to itself, making supper for four.

"It's just that the nursery is different now than it was."

"All right, let's have a look."

They walked down the hall of their soundproofed, Happylife Home, which had cost them thirty thousand dollars installed, this house which clothed and fed and rocked them to sleep and played and sang and was good to them. Their approach sensitized a switch somewhere and the nursery light flicked on when they came within ten feet of it.

Similarly, behind them, in the halls, lights went on and off as they left them behind, with a soft automaticity.

"Well," said George Hadley.

They stood on the thatched floor of the nursery. It was forty feet across by forty feet long and thirty feet high; it had cost half again as much as the rest of the house. "But nothing's too good for our children," George had said.

The nursery was silent. It was empty as a jungle glade at hot high noon. The walls were blank and two dimensional. Now, as George and Lydia Hadley stood in the center of the room, the walls began to purr and recede into crystalline distance, it seemed, and presently an African veldt appeared, in three dimensions; on all sides, in colors reproduced to the final pebble and bit of straw. The ceiling above them became a deep sky with a hot yellow sun.

George Hadley felt the perspiration start on his brow.

"Let's get out of the sun," he said. "This is a little too real. But I don't see anything wrong."

"Wait a moment, you'll see," said his wife.

Now the hidden odorophonics were beginning to blow a wind of odor at the two people in the middle of the baked veldtland. The hot straw smell of lion grass, the cool green smell of the hidden water hole, the great rusty smell of animals, the smell of dust like a red paprika in the hot air. And now the sounds: the thump of distant antelope feet on grassy sod, the papery rustling of vultures. A shadow passed through the sky. The shadow flickered on George Hadley's upturned, sweating face.

"Filthy creatures," he heard his wife say.

"The vultures."

"You see, there are the lions, far over, that way. Now they're on their way to the water hole. They've just been eating," said Lydia. "I don't know what."

"Some animal." Georger Hadley put his hand up to shield off the burning light from his squinted eyes. "A zebra or a baby giraffe, maybe."

"Are you sure?" His wife sounded peculiarly tense.

"No, it's a little late to be sure," he said, amused. "Nothing over there I can see but cleaned bone, and the vultures dropping for what's left."

"Did you hear that scream?" she asked.

"No."

"About a minute ago?"

"Sorry, no."

The lions were coming. And again George Hadley was filled with admiration for the mechanical genius who had conceived this room. A miracle of efficiency selling for an absurdly low price. Every home should have one. Oh, occasionally they frightened you with their clinical accuracy, they startled you, gave you a twinge, but most of the time what fun for everyone, not only your own son and daughter, but for yourself when you felt like a quick jaunt to a foreign land, a quick change of scenery. Well, here it was!

And here were the lions now, fifteen feet away, so real, so feverishly and startlingly real that you could feel the prickling fur on your hand, and your mouth was stuffed with the dusty upholstery smell of their heated pelts, and the yellow of them was in your eyes like the yellow of an exquisite French tapestry, the yellows of lions and summer grass, and the sound of the matted lion lungs exhaling on the silent noontide, and the smell of meat from the panting, dripping mouths.

The lions stood looking at George and Lydia Hadley with terrible green-yellow eyes.

"Watch out!" screamed Lydia.

The lions came running at them.

Lydia bolted and ran. Instinctively, George sprang after her. Outside, in the hall, with the door slammed, he was laughing and she was crying, and they both stood appalled at the other's reaction.

"George!"

"Lydia! Oh, my dear poor sweet Lydia!"

"They almost got us!"

"Walls, Lydia, remember; crystal walls, that's all they are. Oh, they look real, I must admit—Africa in your parlor—but it's all dimensional superreactionary, supersensitive color film and mental tape film behind glass screens. It's all odorophonics and sonics, Lydia. Here's my handkerchief."

"I'm afraid." She came to him and put her body against him and cried steadily. "Did you see? Did you *feel?* It's too real."

"Now, Lydia . . ."

"You've got to tell Wendy and Peter not to read any more on Africa."

"Of course—of course." He patted her.

"Promise?"

"Sure."

"And lock the nursery for a few days until I get my nerves settled."

"You know how difficult Peter is about that. When I punished him a month ago by locking the nursery for even a few hours—the tantrum he threw! And Wendy too. They *live* for the nursery."

"It's got to be locked, that's all there is to it."

"All right." Reluctantly he locked the huge door. "You've been working too hard. You need a rest."

"I don't know—I don't know," she said, blowing her nose, sitting down in a chair that immediately began to rock and comfort her. "Maybe I don't have enough to do. Maybe I have time to think too much. Why don't we shut the whole house off for a few days and take a vacation?"

"You mean you want to fry my eggs for me?"

"Yes." She nodded.

"And darn my socks?"

"Yes." A frantic, watery-eyed nodding.

"And sweep the house?"

"Yes, yes—oh, yes!"

"But I thought that's why we bought this house, so we wouldn't have to do anything?"

"That's just it. I feel like I don't belong here. The house is wife and mother now and nursemaid. Can I compete with an African veldt? Can I give a bath and scrub the children as efficiently or quickly as the automatic scrub bath can? I can not. And it isn't just me. It's you. You've been awfully nervous lately."

"I suppose I have been smoking too much."

"You look as if you didn't know what to do with yourself in this house, either. You smoke a little more every morning and drink a little more every afternoon and need a little more sedative every night. You're beginning to feel unnecessary too."

"Am I?" He paused and tried to feel into himself to see what was really there.

"Oh, George!" She looked beyond him, at the nursery door. "Those lions can't get out of there, can they?"

He looked at the door and saw it tremble as if something had jumped against it from the other side.

"Of course not," he said.

At dinner they ate alone, for Wendy and Peter were at a special plastic carnival across town and had televised home to say they'd be late, to go ahead eating. So George Hadley, bemused, sat watching the dining-room table produce warm dishes of food from its mechanical interior.

"We forgot the ketchup," he said.

"Sorry," said a small voice within the table, and ketchup appeared.

As for the nursery, thought George Hadley, it won't hurt for the children to be locked out of it awhile. Too much of anything isn't good for anyone. And it was clearly indicated that the children had been spending a little too much time on Africa. That sun. He could feel it on his neck, still, like a hot paw. And the lions. And the smell of blood. Remarkable how the nursery caught the telepathic emanations of the children's minds and created life to fill their every desire. The children thought lions, and there were lions. The children thought zebras, and there were zebras. Sun—sun. Giraffes—giraffes. Death and death.

That last. He chewed tastelessly on the meat that the table had cut for him. Death thoughts. They were awfully young, Wendy and Peter, for death thoughts. Or, no, you were never too young, really. Long before you knew what death was you were wishing it on someone else. When you were two years old you were shooting people with cap pistols.

But this—the long, hot African veldt—the awful death in the jaws of a lion. And repeated again and again.

"Where are you going?"

He didn't answer Lydia. Preoccupied, he let the lights glow softly on ahead of him, extinguished behind him as he padded to the nursery door. He listened against it. Far away, a lion roared.

He unlocked the door and opened it. Just before he stepped inside, he heard a faraway scream. And then another roar from the lions, which subsided quickly.

He stepped into Africa. How many times in the last year had he opened this door and found Wonderland, Alice, the Mock Turtle, or Aladdin and his Magical Lamp, or Jack Pumpkinhead of Oz, or Dr. Doolittle, or the cow jumping over a very real-appearing moon[1]—all the delightful contraptions of a make-believe world. How often had he seen Pegasus[2] flying in the sky ceiling, or seen fountains of red fireworks, or heard angel voices singing. But now, this yellow hot Africa, this bake oven with murder in the heat. Perhaps Lydia was right. Perhaps they needed a little vacation from the fantasy which was growing a bit too real for ten-year-old children. It was all right to exercise one's mind with gymnastic fantasies, but when the lively child mind settled on *one* pattern . . . ? It seemed that, at a distance, for the past month, he had heard lions roaring, and smelled their strong odor seeping as far away as his study door. But, being busy, he had paid it no attention.

George Hadley stood on the African grassland alone. The lions looked up from their feeding, watching him. The only flaw to the illusion was the open door through which he could see his wife, far down the dark hall, like a framed picture, eating her dinner abstractedly.

"Go away," he said to the lions.

They did not go.

He knew the principle of the room exactly. You sent out your thoughts. Whatever you thought would appear.

"Let's have Aladdin and his lamp," he snapped.

The veldtland remained; the lions remained.

1. Characters from famous children's stories and nursery rhymes. 2. In Greek mythology, the flying horse.

"Come on, room! I demand Aladdin!" he said.

Nothing happened. The lions mumbled in their baked pelts.

"Aladdin!"

He went back to dinner. "The fool room's out of order," he said. "It won't respond."

"Or——"

"Or what?"

"Or it *can't* respond," said Lydia, "because the children have thought about Africa and lions and killing so many days that the room's in a rut."

"Could be."

"Or Peter's set it to remain that way."

"*Set* it?"

"He may have got into the machinery and fixed something."

"Peter doesn't know machinery."

"He's a wise one for ten. That I.Q. of his——"

"Nevertheless——"

"Hello, Mom. Hello, Dad."

The Hadleys turned. Wendy and Peter were coming in the front door, cheeks like peppermint candy, eyes like bright blue agate marbles, a smell of ozone on their jumpers from their trip in the helicopter.

"You're just in time for supper," said both parents.

"We're full of strawberry ice cream and hot dogs," said the children, holding hands. "But we'll sit and watch."

"Yes, come tell us about the nursery," said George Hadley.

The brother and sister blinked at him and then at each other. "Nursery?"

"All about Africa and everything," said the father with false joviality.

"I don't understand," said Peter.

"Your mother and I were just traveling through Africa with rod and reel; Tom Swift and his Electric Lion,"[3] said George Hadley.

"There's no Africa in the nursery," said Peter simply.

"Oh, come now, Peter. We know better."

"I don't remember any Africa," said Peter to Wendy. "Do you?"

"No."

"Run see and come tell."

She obeyed.

"Wendy, come back here!" said George Hadley, but she was gone.

3. Tom Swift is the hero of a series of adventure novels for boys by Victor Appleton (pseudonym).

The house lights followed her like a flock of fireflies. Too late, he realized he had forgotten to lock the nursery door after his last inspection.

"Wendy'll look and come tell us," said Peter.

"She doesn't have to tell *me*. I've seen it."

"I'm sure you're mistaken, Father."

"I'm not, Peter. Come along now."

But Wendy was back. "It's not Africa," she said breathlessly.

"We'll see about this," said George Hadley, and they all walked down the hall together and opened the nursery door.

There was a green, lovely forest, a lovely river, a purple mountain, high voices singing, and Rima,[4] lovely and mysterious, lurking in the trees with colorful flights of butterflies, like animated bouquets, lingering on her long hair. The African veldtland was gone. The lions were gone. Only Rima was here now, singing a song so beautiful that it brought tears to your eyes.

George Hadley looked in at the changed scene. "Go to bed," he said to the children.

They opened their mouths.

"You heard me," he said.

They went off to the air closet, where a wind sucked them like brown leaves up the flue to their slumber rooms.

George Hadley walked through the singing glade and picked up something that lay in the corner near where the lions had been. He walked slowly back to his wife.

"What is that?" she asked.

"An old wallet of mine," he said.

He showed it to her. The smell of hot grass was on it and the smell of a lion. There were drops of saliva on it, it had been chewed, and there were blood smears on both sides.

He closed the nursery door and locked it, tight.

In the middle of the night he was still awake and he knew his wife was awake. "Do you think Wendy changed it?" she said at last, in the dark room.

"Of course."

"Made it from a veldt into a forest and put Rima there instead of lions?"

"Yes."

"Why?"

"I don't know. But it's staying locked until I find out."

"How did your wallet get there?"

"I don't know anything," he said, "except that I'm beginning to

4. Heroine in *Green Mansions* by W. H. Hudson (1841–1922).

be sorry we bought that room for the children. If children are neurotic at all, a room like that——"

"It's supposed to help them work off their neuroses in a healthful way."

"I'm starting to wonder." He stared at the ceiling.

"We've given the children everything they ever wanted. Is this our reward—secrecy, disobedience?"

"Who was it said, 'Children are carpets, they should be stepped on occasionally'? We've never lifted a hand. They're insufferable—let's admit it. They come and go when they like; they treat us as if *we* were offspring. They're spoiled and we're spoiled."

"They've been acting funny ever since you forbade them to take the rocket to New York a few months ago."

"They're not old enough to do that alone, I explained."

"Nevertheless, I've noticed they've been decidedly cool toward us since."

"I think I'll have David McClean come tomorrow morning to have a look at Africa."

"But it's not Africa now, it's Green Mansions country and Rima."

"I have a feeling it'll be Africa again before then."

A moment later they heard the screams.

Two screams. Two people screaming from downstairs. And then a roar of lions.

"Wendy and Peter aren't in their rooms," said his wife.

He lay in his bed with his beating heart. "No," he said. "They've broken into the nursery."

"Those screams—they sound familiar."

"Do they?"

"Yes, awfully."

And although their beds tried very hard, the two adults couldn't be rocked to sleep for another hour. A smell of cats was in the night air.

"Father?" said Peter.

"Yes."

Peter looked at his shoes. He never looked at his father any more, nor at his mother. "You aren't going to lock up the nursery for good, are you?"

"That all depends."

"On what?" snapped Peter.

"On you and your sister. If you intersperse this Africa with a little variety—oh, Sweden perhaps, or Denmark or China——"

"I thought we were free to play as we wished."

"You are, within reasonable bounds."

"What's wrong with Africa, Father?"

"Oh, so now you admit you have been conjuring up Africa, do you?"

"I wouldn't want the nursery locked up," said Peter coldly. "Ever."

"Matter of fact, we're thinking of turning the whole house off for about a month. Live sort of a carefree one-for-all existence."

"That sounds dreadful! Would I have to tie my own shoes instead of letting the shoe tier do it? And brush my own teeth and comb my hair and give myself a bath?"

"It would be fun for a change, don't you think?"

"No, it would be horrid. I didn't like it when you took out the picture painter last month."

"That's because I wanted you to learn to paint all by yourself, son."

"I don't want to do anything but look and listen and smell; what else *is* there to do?"

"All right, go play in Africa."

"Will you shut off the house sometime soon?"

"We're considering it."

"I don't think you'd better consider it any more, Father."

"I won't have any threats from my son!"

"Very well." And Peter strolled off to the nursery.

"Am I on time?" said David McClean.

"Breakfast?" asked George Hadley.

"Thanks, had some. What's the trouble?"

"David, you're a psychologist."

"I should hope so."

"Well, then, have a look at our nursery. You saw it a year ago when you dropped by; did you notice anything peculiar about it then?"

"Can't say I did; the usual violences, a tendency toward a slight paranoia here or there, usual in children because they feel persecuted by parents constantly, but, oh, really nothing."

They walked down the hall. "I locked the nursery up," explained the father, "and the children broke back into it during the night. I let them stay so they could form the patterns for you to see."

There was a terrible screaming from the nursery.

"There it is," said George Hadley. "See what you make of it."

They walked in on the children without rapping.

The screams had faded. The lions were feeding.

"Run outside a moment, children," said George Hadley. "No, don't change the mental combination. Leave the walls as they are. Get!"

With the children gone, the two men stood studying the lions clustered at a distance, eating with great relish whatever it was they had caught.

"I wish I knew what it was," said George Hadley. "Sometimes I can almost see. Do you think if I brought high-powered binoculars here and——"

David McClean laughed dryly. "Hardly." He turned to study all four walls. "How long has this been going on?"

"A little over a month."

"It certainly doesn't *feel* good."

"I want facts, not feelings."

"My dear George, a psychologist never saw a fact in his life. He only hears about feelings; vague things. This doesn't feel good, I tell you. Trust my hunches and my instincts. I have a nose for something bad. This is very bad. My advice to you is to have the whole damn room torn down and your children brought to me every day during the next year for treatment."

"Is it that bad?"

"I'm afraid so. One of the original uses of these nurseries was so that we could study the patterns left on the walls by the child's mind, study at our leisure, and help the child. In this case, however, the room has become a channel toward—destructive thoughts, instead of a release away from them."

"Didn't you sense this before?"

"I sensed only that you had spoiled your children more than most. And now you're letting them down in some way. What way?"

"I wouldn't let them go to New York."

"What else?"

"I've taken a few machines from the house and threatened them, a month ago, with closing up the nursery unless they did their homework. I did close it for a few days to show I meant business."

"Ah, ha!"

"Does that mean anything?"

"Everything. Where before they had a Santa Claus now they have a Scrooge. Children prefer Santas. You've let this room and this house replace you and your wife in your children's affections. This room is their mother and father, far more important in their lives than their real parents. And now you come along and want to shut it off. No wonder there's hatred here. You can feel it coming out of the sky. Feel that sun. George, you'll have to change your life. Like too many others, you've built it around creature comforts. Why, you'd starve tomorrow if something went wrong in your kitchen. You wouldn't know how to tap an egg. Nevertheless, turn everything off. Start new. It'll take time. But we'll make good children out of bad in a year, wait and see."

"But won't the shock be too much for the children, shutting the room up abruptly, for good?"

"I don't want them going any deeper into this, that's all."

The lions were finished with their red feast.

The lions were standing on the edge of the clearing watching the two men.

"Now *I'm* feeling persecuted," said McClean. "Let's get out of here. I never have cared for these damned rooms. Make me nervous."

"The lions look real, don't they?" said George Hadley. "I don't suppose there's any way——"

"What?"

"—that they could *become* real?"

"Not that I know."

"Some flaw in the machinery, a tampering or someting?"

"No."

They went to the door.

"I don't imagine the room will like being turned off," said the father.

"Nothing ever likes to die—even a room."

"I wonder if it hates me for wanting to switch it off?"

"Paranoia is thick around here today," said David McClean. "You can follow it like a spoor. Hello." He bent and picked up a bloody scarf. "This yours?"

"No." George Hadley's face was rigid. "It belongs to Lydia."

They went to the fuse box together and threw the switch that killed the nursery.

The two children were in hysterics. They screamed and pranced and threw things. They yelled and sobbed and swore and jumped at the furniture.

"You can't do that to the nursery, you can't!"

"Now, children."

The children flung themselves onto a couch, weeping.

"George," said Lydia Hadley, "turn on the nursery, just for a few moments. You can't be so abrupt."

"No."

"You can't be so cruel."

"Lydia, it's off, and it stays off. And the whole damn house dies as of here and now. The more I see of the mess we've put ourselves in, the more it sickens me. We've been contemplating our mechanical, electronic navels for too long. My God, how we need a breath of honest air!"

And he marched about the house turning off the voice clocks, the stoves, the heaters, the shoe shiners, the shoe lacers, the body scrubbers and swabbers and massagers, and every other machine he could put his hand to.

The house was full of dead bodies, it seemed. It felt like a mechanical cemetery. So silent. None of the humming hidden energy of machines waiting to function at the tap of a button.

"Don't let them do it!" wailed Peter at the ceiling, as if he was talking to the house, the nursery. "Don't let Father kill everything." He turned to his father. "Oh, I hate you!"

"Insults won't get you anywhere."

"I wish you were dead!"

"We were, for a long while. Now we're going to really start living. Instead of being handled and massaged, we're going to *live*."

Wendy was still crying and Peter joined her again. "Just a moment, just one moment, just another moment of nursery," they wailed.

"Oh, George," said the wife, "it can't hurt."

"All right—all right, if they'll only just shut up. One minute, mind you, and then off forever."

"Daddy, Daddy, Daddy!" sang the children, smiling with wet faces.

"And then we're going on a vacation. David McClean is coming back in half an hour to help us move out and get to the airport. I'm going to dress. You turn the nursery on for a minute, Lydia, just a minute, mind you."

And the three of them went babbling off while he let himself be vacuumed upstairs through the air flue and set about dressing himself. A minute later Lydia appeared.

"I'll be glad when we get away," she sighed.

"Did you leave them in the nursery?"

"I wanted to dress too. Oh, that horrid Africa. What can they see in it?"

"Well, in five minutes we'll be on our way to Iowa. Lord, how did we ever get in this house? What prompted us to buy a nightmare?"

"Pride, money, foolishness."

"I think we'd better get downstairs before those kids get engrossed with those damned beasts again."

Just then they heard the children calling, "Daddy, Mommy, come quick—quick!"

They went downstairs in the air flue and ran down the hall. The children were nowhere in sight. "Wendy? Peter!"

They ran into the nursery. The veldtland was empty save for the lions waiting, looking at them. "Peter, Wendy?"

The door slammed.

"Wendy, Peter!"

George Hadley and his wife whirled and ran back to the door.

"Open the door!" cried George Hadley, trying the knob. "Why, they've locked it from the outside! Peter!" He beat at the door. "Open up!"

He heard Peter's voice outside, against the door.

"Don't let them switch off the nursery and the house," he was saying.

Mr. and Mrs. George Hadley beat at the door. "Now, don't be ridiculous, children. It's time to go. Mr. McClean'll be here in a minute and . . ."

And then they heard the sounds.

The lions on three sides of them, in the yellow veldt grass, padding through the dry straw, rumbling and roaring in their throats.

The lions.

Mr. Hadley looked at his wife and they turned and looked back at the beasts edging slowly forward, crouching, tails stiff.

Mr. and Mrs. Hadley screamed.

And suddenly they realized why those other screams had sounded familiar.

"Well, here I am," said David McClean in the nursery doorway. "Oh, hello." He stared at the two children seated in the center of the open glade eating a little picnic lunch. Beyond them was the water hole and the yellow veldtland; above was the hot sun. He began to perspire. "Where are your father and mother?"

The children looked up and smiled. "Oh, they'll be here directly."

"Good, we must get going." At a distance Mr. McClean saw the lions fighting and clawing and then quieting down to feed in silence under the shady trees.

He squinted at the lions with his hand up to his eyes.

Now the lions were done feeding. They moved to the water hole to drink.

A shadow flickered over Mr. McClean's hot face. Many shadows flickered. The vultures were dropping down the blazing sky.

"A cup of tea?" asked Wendy in the silence.

---

1. In what ways are the Hadleys a typical American family?
2. What is the significance of the change of program in the nursery, from innocent fairy tales to the appearance of the lions?
3. Why does the psychologist recommend tearing down the nursery? Does his appearance in the story have any bearing on the theme of the story?
4. What explains the hatred the children feel for their parents?
5. Can the story be considered humorous, since it is constructed of superficial horror and underlying pessimism about parents and children?

Morley Callaghan

Callaghan (1903-1990) was born in Toronto, Ontario. While still a student at the University of Toronto he began writing for the Toronto Daily Star, *a paper for which Ernest Hemingway also worked, and through Hemingway's assistance some of his first short stories were published in little magazines in Paris. After graduating from law school in 1928 Callaghan went to Paris for a year and subsequently wrote about his friendship there with Hemingway and Fitzgerald in* That Summer in Paris *(1963). Among his awards are the Governor General's Award for fiction in 1952 and the Royal Bank of Canada award of 1970. His novels include* Strange Fugitive *(1928),* It's Never Over *(1930),* They Shall Inherit the Earth *(1935), and* A Passion in Rome *(1961). His short stories are collected in* Native Argosy *(1929),* No Man's Meat *(1931),* Now That April's Here and Other Stories *(1936), and* Morley Callaghan's Stories *(1959).*

Now That April's Here[1]

As soon as they got the money they bought two large black hats and left America to live permanently in Paris. They were bored in their native city in the Middle West and convinced that the American continent had nothing to offer them. Charles Milford, who was four years older than Johnny Hill, had a large round head that ought to have belonged to a Presbyterian minister. Johnny had a rather chinless faun's head. When they walked down the street the heads together seemed more interesting. They came to Paris in the late autumn.

They got on very quickly in Montparnasse.[2] In the afternoons they wandered around the streets, looking in art gallery windows at the prints of the delicate clever unsubstantial line work of Foujita.[3] Pressing his nose against the window Johnny said, "Quite a sound technique, don't you think, Charles?"

"Oh sound, quite sound."

They never went to the Louvre or the museum in the Luxembourg Gardens, thinking it would be in the fashion of tourists, when

1. Modified quote from "Home-Thoughts from Abroad" by Robert Browning (1812–1889), English poet. 2. A quarter in Paris noted during the twenties as a gathering place for expatriates and artists. 3. Japanese painter working in France (1886–1968).

they intended really to settle in Paris. In the evenings they sat together at a table on the terrace of the café, and clients, noticing them, began thinking of them as "the two boys." One night, Fanny Lee, a blonde, fat American girl who had been an entertainer at Zelli's until she lost her shape, but not her hilarity, stepped over to the boys' table and yelled, "Oh, gee, look what I've found." They were discovered. Fanny, liking them for their quiet, well-mannered behavior, insisted on introducing them to everybody at the bar. They bowed together at the same angle, smiling so cheerfully, so obviously willing to be obliging, that Fanny was anxious to have them follow her from one bar to another, hoping they would pay for her drinks.

They felt much better after the evening with Fanny. Johnny, the younger one, who had a small income of $100 a month, was supporting Charles, who, he was sure, would one day become a famous writer. Johnny did take his own talent very seriously; he had been writing his memoirs of their adventures since they were fifteen, after reading George Moore's[4] *Confessions of a Young Man*. George Moore's book had been mainly responsible for their visit to Paris. Johnny's memoirs, written in a snobbishly aristocratic manner, had been brought up to the present and now he was waiting for something to happen to them. They were much happier the day they got a cheaper room on Boulevard Arago near the tennis court.

They were happy at cafés in the evenings but liked best being at home together in their own studio, five minutes away from the cafés. They lay awake in bed together a long time talking about everything that happened during the day, consoling each other by saying the weather would be finer later on and anyway they could always look forward to the spring days next April. Fanny Lee, who really liked them, was extraordinarily friendly and only cost them nine or ten drinks an evening. They lay awake in bed talking about her, sometimes laughing so hard the bed springs squeaked. Charles, his large round head buried in the pillow, snickered gleefully listening to Johnny making fun of Fanny Lee.

Soon they knew everybody in the Quarter, though no one knew either of them very intimately. People sitting at the café in the evening when the lights were on, saw them crossing the road together under the street lamp, their bodies leaning forward at the same angle, and walking on tiptoe. No one knew where they were going. Really they weren't going anywhere in particular. They had been sitting at the café, nibbling pieces of sugar they had dipped in coffee, till Johnny said, "We're being seen here too much, don't you think, Charles?" And Charles said, "I think we ought to be seen at all the bars. We

4. Irish novelist, critic, and dramatist (1852–1933).

ought to go more often to the new bar." So they had paid for their coffee and walked over to a side-street bar paneled in the old English style, with a good-natured English bartender, and sat together at a table listening to the careless talk of five customers at the bar, occasionally snickering out loud when a sentence overheard seemed incredibly funny. Stan Mason, an ingenuous heavy drinker, who had cultivated a very worldly feeling sitting at the same bars every night, explaining the depth of his sophistication to the same people, saw the boys holding their heads together and yelled, "What are you two little goats snickering at?" The boys stood up, bowing to him so politely and seriously he was ashamed of himself and asked them to have a drink with him. The rest of the evening they laughed so charmingly at his jokes he was fully convinced they were the brightest youngsters who had come to the Quarter in years. He asked the boys if they liked Paris, and smiling at each other and raising their glasses together they said that architecturally it was a great improvement over America. They had never been in New York or any other large American city but had no use for American buildings. There was no purpose in arguing directly with them. Charles would simply have raised his eyebrows and glanced slyly at Johnny, who would have snickered with his fingers over his mouth. Mason, who was irritated, and anxious to make an explanation, began talking slowly about the early block-like houses of the Taos Indians[5] and the geometrical block style of the New York skyscrapers. For ten minutes he talked steadily about the Indians and a development of the American spirit. The boys listened politely, never moving their heads at all. Watching them, while he talked, Mason began to feel uncomfortable. He began to feel that anything he had to say was utterly unimportant because the two boys were listening to him so politely. But he finished strongly and said, "What do you think?"

"Do you really believe all that's important?" Charles said.

"I don't know, maybe it's not."

"Well, as long as you don't think it important," Johnny said.

At home the boys sat on the edge of the bed talking about Stan Mason and snickered so long they were up half the night.

They had their first minor disagreement in the Quarter one evening in November with Milton Simpson, a prosperous, bright and effeminate young American business man who was living in Paris because he felt vaguely that the best approach to life was through all the arts together. He was secretly trying to write, paint, and compose pieces for the piano. The boys were at a small bar with a floor for dancing and an American jazz artist at the piano, and Simpson and his wife came

5. A tribe native to New Mexico.

in. Passing, Simpson brushed against Charles, who, without any provocation at all, suddenly pushed him away. Simpson pushed too and they stood there pushing each other. Simpson began waving his arms in circles, and the man at the piano threw his arms around Charles, dragging him away. Neither one of them could have hurt each other seriously and everybody in the room was laughing at them. Finally Simpson sat down and Charles, standing alone, began to tremble so much he had to put his head down on the table and cry. His shoulders were moving jerkily. Then everybody in the room was sorry for Charles. Johnny, putting his arm around him, led him outside. Simpson, whose thin straight lips were moving nervously, was so impressed by Charles's tears, that he and his wife followed them outside and over to the corner café where they insisted on sitting down with them at one of the brown oblong tables inside. Simpson bought the boys a brandy and his wife, who was interested in the new psychology, began to talk eagerly with Charles, evidently expecting some kind of an emotional revelation. The boys finished their brandies and Simpson quickly ordered another for them. For an hour the boys drank brandies and listened patiently and seriously to Simpson, who was talking ecstatically because he thought they were sensitive, sympathetic boys. They only smiled at him when he excitedly called them "sensitive organisms." Charles, listening wide-eyed, was nervously scratching his cheek with the nail of his right forefinger till the flesh was torn and raw.

Afterwards, undressing slowly at home, Johnny said, "Simpson is such a bore, don't you think so, Charles?"

"I know, but the brandies were very good." They never mentioned the fight at the bar.

"It was so funny when you looked at him with that blue-eyed Danish stare of yours," Johnny said, chuckling.

"People think I expect them to do tricks like little animals when I look at them like that," Charles explained.

Naked, they sat on the edge of the bed, laughing at Simpson's eagerness to buy them brandies, and they made so many witty sallies they tired themselves out and fell asleep.

For two weeks they weren't seen around the cafés. Charles was writing another book and Johnny was typing it for him. It was a literary two weeks for both of them. They talked about all the modern authors and Johnny suggested that not one of them since Henry James had half Charles's perception or subtle delicacy. Actually Charles did write creditably enough and everything he did had three or four good paragraphs in it. The winter was coming on and when this literary work was finished they wanted to go south.

No one ever knew how they got the money to go to the Riviera for the winter. No one knew how they were able to drink so much when they had only Johnny's hundred dollars a month. At Nice,[6] where Stan Mason was living, they were very cheerful and Mason, admiring their optimism because he thought they had no money, let them have a room in his apartment. They lived with him till the evening he put his ear against the thin wall and heard them snickering, sitting on the edge of the bed. They were talking about him and having a good laugh. Stan Mason was hurt because he had thought them bright boys and really liked them. He merely suggested next morning that they would have to move since he needed the room.

The boys were mainly happy in Nice because they were looking forward to returning to Paris in April. The leaves would be on all the trees and people would be sitting outside on the terraces at the cafés. Everybody they met in Nice told them how beautiful it was in Paris in the early spring, so they counted upon having the happiest time they had ever had together. When they did leave Nice they owed many thousand francs for a hotel bill, payment of which they had avoided by tossing their bags out of the window at two o'clock in the morning. They even had a little extra money at the time, almost twenty dollars they had received from an elderly English gentleman, who had suggested, after talking to them all one morning, he would pay well to see the boys make a "tableau"[7] for him. The old fellow was enthusiastic about the "tableau" and the boys had something to amuse them for almost two weeks.

They returned to Paris the first week in April. Now that April was here they had expected to have so much fun, but the weather was disagreeable and cold. This year the leaves were hardly on the trees and there was always rain in the dull skies. They assured each other that the dull days could not last because it was April and Paris was the loveliest city in the world in the early spring.

Johnny's father had been writing many irritable letters from England, where he was for a few months, and the boys decided it was an opportune time for Johnny to go and see him for a week. When he returned they would be together for the good days at the end of the month.

People were not very interested in Charles while Johnny was away. They liked him better when he was with Johnny. All week he walked around on tiptoe or sat alone at a corner table in the café. The two boys together seemed well mannered and bright, but Charles, alone, looked rather insignificant. Without thinking much about it he knew the feeling people had for him and avoided company, waiting impatiently for the days to pass, worrying about Johnny. He said to

6. The major city on the French Riviera, a stretch of the Mediterranean coast noted for its resorts. 7. Presumably a homosexual exhibition.

Stan Mason late one night, "I hope Johnny has enough sense not to pick up with a girl over in England."

"Why worry? Do it yourself now."

"Oh I do, too, only I don't take them as seriously as Johnny does. Not that I mind Johnny having a girl," he said, "only I don't want him to have a complicated affair with one."

The night Johnny returned to Paris they went around to all the bars and people, smiling, said, "There go the two boys." They were happy, nervously happy, and Charles was scratching his cheek with his nail. Later on they wanted to be entirely alone and left the café district and the crowds to walk down the narrow side streets to the Seine while Johnny, chuckling, related the disagreeable circumstances of his visit to his father. His father had contended that he was a wastrel who ought to be earning his own living, and Johnny had jeeringly pointed out that the old man had inherited his money without having to work for it. They were angry with each other, and the father had slapped Johnny, who retaliated by poking him in the jaw. That was the most amusing part of the story the boys talked about, walking along the left bank of the Seine opposite the Louvre. Casually Johnny told about a few affairs he had had with cheap women in London, and Charles understood that these affairs had not touched him at all. It was a warm clean evening, the beginning of the real spring days in April, and the boys were happy walking by the river in the moonlight, the polished water surface reflecting the red and white lights on the bridges.

Near the end of the month Constance Foy, whom the boys had known at Nice, came to Paris, and they asked her to live with them. She was a simple-minded fat-faced girl with a boy's body and short hair dyed red, who had hardly a franc left and was eager to live with anybody who would keep her. For a week the three of them were happy in the big studio. The boys were proud of their girl and took her around to all the bars, buying drinks for her, actually managing to do it on the hundred dollars a month. In the nighttime they were impartial and fair about Constance, who appeared to have all her enthusiasm for the one who, at the moment, was making love to her. But she said to Stan Mason one evening. "I don't know whether or not I ought to be there messing up that relationship."

"Aren't the three of you having a good time?"

"Good enough, but funny things are happening."

The boys were satisfied till Charles began to feel that Johnny was making love to Constance too seriously. It was disappointing, for he had never objected to having her in the studio, and now Johnny was so obvious in his appreciation of her. Charles, having this feeling, was now unable to touch her at all, and resented Johnny's unabated eagerness for her. It was all the same to Constance.

Before the end of the month the two boys were hardly speaking to each other, though always together at the cafés in the evening. It was too bad, for the days were bright and clear, the best of the April weather, and Paris was gay and lively. The boys were sad and hurt and sorry but determined to be fair with each other. The evening they were at the English bar, sitting at one of the table beer barrels, Charles had a hard time preventing himself crying. He was very much in love with Johnny and felt him slipping away. Johnny, his fingers over his mouth, sometimes shook his head but didn't know what to say.

Finally they left the bar to walk home. They were going down the short, quiet street leading to the Boulevard.

"What are you going to do about Constance?" Charles said.

"If it's all the same to you I'll have her to myself."

"But what are you going to do with her?"

"I don't know."

"You'd let a little tart like that smash things," Charles said, shaking his hand at Johnny.

"Don't you dare call her a tart."

"Please, Johnny, don't strike at me."

But Johnny who was nearly crying with rage swung his palm at Charles, hitting him across the face. Stan Mason had just turned the corner at the Boulevard, coming up to the bar to have a drink, and saw the two of them standing there.

"What's wrong?" he said.

"I begged him, I implored him not to hit me," Charles said.

"Oh, I hit him, I hit him, I hit him, what'll I do?" Johnny said, tears running down his cheeks.

They stood there crying and shaking their heads, but would not go home together. Finally Charles consented to go with Stan to his hotel and Johnny went home to Constance.

Charles stayed with Mason all week. He would not eat at all and didn't care what he was drinking. The night Mason told him Johnny was going back to America, taking Constance with him, he shook his head helplessly and said, "How could he hit me, how could he hit me, and he knew I loved him so much."

"But what are you going to do?"

"I don't know."

"How are you going to live?"

"I'll make enough to have a drink occasionally."

At the time, he was having a glass of Scotch, his arm trembling so weakly he could hardly lift the glass.

The day Johnny left Paris it rained and it was cold again, sitting at the café in the evening. There had been only one really good week in April. The boys always used to sit at the cafés without their hats on, their hair brushed nicely. This evening Charles had to go home and get his overcoat and the big black hat he had bought in America. Sitting alone at his table in the cool evening, his overcoat wrapped around him, and the black hat on, he did not look the same at all. It was the first time he had worn the hat in France.

---

1. How important is the setting in the progress and outcome of the action? In developing the general tone of the story?
2. What attempts, if any, has the author made to generate sympathy for the two major characters?
3. How credible is their sexual ambivalence? How is it related to motives for specific parts of the action?
4. What influences do the minor characters have on the developing course of the relationship?
5. How do you interpret the boys' tendency to "snicker" at a variety of people or circumstances they encounter?

Italo Calvino

Calvino (1923–1985) was born in Santiago de Las Vegas, Cuba, but grew up and was educated in Italy. It was in Italy that he did the bulk of his writing and was active as an editor and lecturer. Though his work is kin to science fiction, it really consists of fairy tales concocted around scientific premises, and it finds its closest parallels in the imaginative creations of Jorge Luis Borges and Gabriel García Márquez. His titles include Path to the Nest of Spiders *(1956),* Adam, One Afternoon and Other Stories *(1957),* The Non-existent Knight and the Cloven Viscount *(1962), and* Cosmicomics *(1965).*

The Distance of the Moon[1]

At one time, according to Sir George H. Darwin, the Moon was very close to the Earth. Then the tides gradually pushed her far away: the tides that the Moon herself causes in the Earth's waters, where the Earth slowly loses energy.

How well I know!—*old Qfwfq cried,*—the rest of you can't remember, but I can. We had her on top of us all the time, that enormous Moon: when she was full—nights as bright as day, but with a butter-colored light—it looked as if she were going to crush us; when she was new, she rolled around the sky like a black umbrella blown by the wind; and when she was waxing, she came forward with her horns so low she seemed about to stick into the peak of a promontory and get caught there. But the whole business of the Moon's phases worked in a different way then: because the distances from the Sun were different, and the orbits, and the angle of something or other, I forget what; as for eclipses, with Earth and Moon stuck together the way they were, why, we had eclipses every minute: naturally, those two big monsters managed to put each other in the shade constantly, first one, then the other.

Orbit? Oh, elliptical, of course: for a while it would huddle against us and then it would take flight for a while. The tides, when the Moon swung closer, rose so high nobody could hold them back. There were nights when the Moon was full and very, very low, and the tide was so high that the Moon missed a ducking in the sea by a hair's-breadth;

1. Translated by William Weaver.

well, let's say a few yards anyway. Climb up on the Moon? Of course we did. All you had to do was row out to it in a boat and, when you were underneath, prop a ladder against her and scramble up.

The spot where the Moon was lowest, as she went by, was off the Zinc Cliffs. We used to go out with those little rowboats they had in those days, round and flat, made of cork. They held quite a few of us: me, Captain Vhd Vhd, his wife, my deaf cousin, and sometimes little Xlthlx—she was twelve or so at that time. On those nights the water was very calm, so silvery it looked like mercury, and the fish in it, violet-colored, unable to resist the Moon's attraction, rose to the surface, all of them, and so did the octopuses and the saffron medusas. There was always a flight of tiny creatures—little crabs, squid, and even some weeds, light and filmy, and coral plants—that broke from the sea and ended up on the Moon, hanging down from that lime-white ceiling, or else they stayed in midair, a phosphorescent swarm we had to drive off, waving banana leaves at them.

This is how we did the job: in the boat we had a ladder: one of us held it, another climbed to the top, and a third, at the oars, rowed until we were right under the Moon; that's why there had to be so many of us (I only mentioned the main ones). The man at the top of the ladder, as the boat approached the Moon, would become scared and start shouting: "Stop! Stop! I'm going to bang my head!" That was the impression you had, seeing her on top of you, immense, and all rough with sharp spikes and jagged, saw-tooth edges. It may be different now, but then the Moon, or rather the bottom, the underbelly of the Moon, the part that passed closest to the Earth and almost scraped it, was covered with a crust of sharp scales. It had come to resemble the belly of a fish, and the smell too, as I recall, if not downright fishy, was faintly similar, like smoked salmon.

In reality, from the top of the ladder, standing erect on the last rung, you could just touch the Moon if you held your arms up. We had taken the measurements carefully (we didn't yet suspect that she was moving away from us); the only thing you had to be very careful about was where you put your hands. I always chose a scale that seemed fast (we climbed up in groups of five or six at a time), then I would cling first with one hand, then with both, and immediately I would feel ladder and boat drifting away from below me, and the motion of the Moon would tear me from the Earth's attraction. Yes, the Moon was so strong that she pulled you up; you realized this the moment you passed from one to the other: you had to swing up abruptly, with a kind of somersault, grabbing the scales, throwing your legs over your head, until your feet were on the Moon's surface. Seen from the Earth, you looked as if you were hanging there with your head down, but for you, it was the normal position, and the only odd thing was that when you raised your eyes you saw the sea above you, glistening, with the boat and the others upside down, hanging like a bunch of grapes from the vine.

My cousin, the Deaf One, showed a special talent for making those leaps. His clumsy hands, as soon as they touched the lunar surface (he was always the first to jump up from the ladder), suddenly became deft and sensitive. They found immediately the spot where he could hoist himself up; in fact just the pressure of his palms seemed enough to make him stick to the satellite's crust. Once I even thought I saw the Moon come toward him, as he held out his hands.

He was just as dextrous in coming back down to Earth, an operation still more difficult. For us, it consisted in jumping, as high as we could, our arms upraised (seen from the Moon, that is, because seen from the Earth it looked more like a dive, or like swimming downwards, arms at our sides), like jumping up from the Earth in other words, only now we were without the ladder, because there was nothing to prop it against on the Moon. But instead of jumping with his arms out, my cousin bent toward the Moon's surface, his head down as if for a somersault, then made a leap, pushing with his hands. From the boat we watched him, erect in the air as if he were supporting the Moon's enormous ball and were tossing it, striking it with his palms; then, when his legs came within reach, we managed to grab his ankles and pull him down on board.

Now, you will ask me what in the world we went up on the Moon for; I'll explain it to you. We went to collect the milk, with a big spoon and a bucket. Moon-milk was very thick, like a kind of cream cheese. It formed in the crevices between one scale and the next, through the fermentation of various bodies and substances of terrestrial origin which had flown up from the prairies and forests and lakes, as the Moon sailed over them. It was composed chiefly of vegetal juices, tadpoles, bitumen, lentils, honey, starch crystals, sturgeon eggs, molds, pollens, gelatinous matter, worms, resins, pepper, mineral salts, combustion residue. You had only to dip the spoon under the scales that covered the Moon's scabby terrain, and you brought it out filled with that precious muck. Not in the pure state, obviously; there was a lot of refuse. In the fermentation (which took place as the Moon passed over the expanses of hot air above the deserts) not all the bodies melted; some remained stuck in it: fingernails and cartilage, bolts, sea horses, nuts and peduncles, shards of crockery, fishhooks, at times even a comb. So this paste, after it was collected, had to be refined, filtered. But that wasn't the difficulty: the hard part was transporting it down to the Earth. This is how we did it: we hurled each spoonful into the air with both hands, using the spoon as a catapult. The cheese flew, and if we had thrown it hard enough, it stuck to the ceiling, I mean the surface of the sea. Once there, it floated, and it was easy enough to pull it into the boat. In this operation, too, my deaf cousin displayed a special gift; he had strength and a good aim; with a single, sharp throw, he could send the cheese straight into a bucket we held up to him from the boat. As for me, I occasionally misfired; the contents of the spoon would fail to overcome the Moon's attraction and they would fall back into my eye.

I still haven't told you everything, about the things my cousin was good at. That job of extracting lunar milk from the Moon's scales was child's play to him: instead of the spoon, at times he had only to thrust his bare hand under the scales, or even one finger. He didn't proceed in any orderly way, but went to isolated places, jumping from one to the other, as if he were playing tricks on the Moon, surprising her, or perhaps tickling her. And wherever he put his hand, the milk spurted out as if from a nanny goat's teats. So the rest of us had only to follow him and collect with our spoons the substance that he was pressing out, first here, then there, but always as if by chance, since the Deaf One's movements seemed to have no clear, practical sense. There were places, for example, that he touched merely for the fun of touching them: gaps between two scales, naked and tender folds of lunar flesh. At times my cousin pressed not only his fingers but—in a carefully gauged leap—his big toe (he climbed onto the Moon barefoot) and this seemed to be the height of amusement for him, if we could judge by the chirping sounds that came from his throat as he went on leaping.

The soil of the Moon was not uniformly scaly, but revealed irregular bare patches of pale, slippery clay. These soft areas inspired the Deaf One to turn somersaults or to fly almost like a bird, as if he wanted to impress his whole body into the Moon's pulp. As he ventured farther in this way, we lost sight of him at one point. On the Moon there were vast areas we had never had any reason or curiosity to explore, and that was where my cousin vanished; I had suspected that all those somersaults and nudges he indulged in before our eyes were only a preparation, a prelude to something secret meant to take place in the hidden zones.

We fell into a special mood on those nights off the Zinc Cliffs: gay, but with a touch of suspense, as if inside our skulls, instead of the brain, we felt a fish, floating, attracted by the Moon. And so we navigated, playing and singing. The Captain's wife played the harp; she had very long arms, silvery as eels on those nights, and armpits as dark and mysterious as sea urchins; and the sound of the harp was sweet and piercing, so sweet and piercing it was almost unbearable, and we were forced to let out long cries, not so much to accompany the music as to protect our hearing from it.

Transparent medusas rose to the sea's surface, throbbed there a moment, then flew off, swaying toward the Moon. Little Xlthlx amused herself by catching them in midair, though it wasn't easy. Once, as she stretched her little arms out to catch one, she jumped up slightly and was also set free. Thin as she was, she was an ounce or two short of the weight necessary for the Earth's gravity to overcome the Moon's attraction and bring her back: so she flew up among the medusas, suspended over the sea. She took fright, cried, then laughed and started playing, catching shellfish and minnows as they flew, sticking some into her mouth and chewing them. We rowed hard, to keep up with the child: the Moon ran off in her ellipse, dragging that swarm of marine fauna through the sky, and a train of long, entwined seaweeds, and Xlthlx hanging there in the midst. Her two wispy braids seemed to be flying on their own, outstretched toward the Moon; but all the while she kept wriggling and kicking at the air, as if she wanted to fight that influence, and her socks—she had lost her shoes in the flight—slipped off her feet and swayed, attracted by the Earth's force. On the ladder, we tried to grab them.

The idea of eating the little animals in the air had been a good one; the more weight Xlthlx gained, the more she sank toward the Earth; in fact, since among those hovering bodies hers was the largest, mollusks and seaweeds and plankton began to gravitate about her, and soon the child was covered with siliceous little shells, chitinous carapaces, and fibers of sea plants. And the farther she vanished into that tangle, the more she was freed of the Moon's influence, until she grazed the surface of the water and sank into the sea.

We rowed quickly, to pull her out and save her: her body had remained magnetized, and we had to work hard to scrape off all the things encrusted on her. Tender corals were wound about her head, and every time we ran the comb through her hair there was a shower of crayfish and sardines; her eyes were sealed shut by limpets clinging to the lids with their suckers; squids' tentacles were coiled around her arms and her neck; and her little dress now seemed woven only of weeds and sponges. We got the worst of it off her, but for weeks afterwards she went on pulling out fins and shells, and her skin, dotted with little diatoms, remained affected forever, looking—to someone who didn't observe her carefully—as if it were faintly dusted with freckles.

This should give you an idea of how the influences of Earth and Moon, practically equal, fought over the space between them. I'll tell you something else: a body that descended to the Earth from the satellite was still charged for a while with lunar force and rejected the attraction of our world. Even I, big and heavy as I was: every time I had been up there, I took a while to get used to the Earth's up and its down, and the others would have to grab my arms and hold me, clinging in a bunch in the swaying boat while I still had my head hanging and my legs stretching up toward the sky.

"Hold on! Hold on to us!" they shouted at me, and in all that groping, sometimes I ended up by seizing one of Mrs. Vhd Vhd's breasts, which were round and firm, and the contact was good and secure and had an attraction as strong as the Moon's or even stronger, especially if I managed, as I plunged down, to put my other arm around her hips, and with this I passed back into our world and fell with a thud into the bottom of the boat, where Captain Vhd Vhd brought me around, throwing a bucket of water in my face.

This is how the story of my love for the Captain's wife began, and my suffering. Because it didn't take me long to realize whom the lady kept looking at insistently: when my cousin's hands clasped the satellite, I watched Mrs. Vhd Vhd, and in her eyes I could read the thoughts that the deaf man's familiarity with the Moon were arousing in her; and when he disappeared in his mysterious lunar explorations, I saw her become restless, as if on pins and needles, and then it was all clear to me, how Mrs. Vhd Vhd was becoming jealous of the Moon and I was jealous of my cousin. Her eyes were made of diamonds, Mrs. Vhd Vhd's; they flared when she looked at the Moon, almost challengingly, as if she were saying: "You shan't have him!" And I felt like an outsider.

The one who least understood all of this was my deaf cousin. When we helped him down, pulling him—as I explained to you—by his legs, Mrs. Vhd Vhd lost all her self-control, doing everything she could to take his weight against her own body, folding her long silvery arms around him; I felt a pang in my heart (the times I clung to her, her body was soft and kind, but not thrust forward, the way it was with my cousin), while he was indifferent, still lost in his lunar bliss.

I looked at the Captain, wondering if he also noticed his wife's behavior; but there was never a trace of any expression on that face of his, eaten by brine, marked with tarry wrinkles. Since the Deaf One was always the last to break away from the Moon, his return was the signal for the boats to move off. Then, with an unusually polite gesture, Vhd Vhd picked up the harp from the bottom of the boat and handed it to his wife. She was obliged to take it and play a few notes. Nothing could separate her more from the Deaf One than the sound of the harp. I took to singing in a low voice that sad song that goes: "Every shiny fish is floating, floating; and every dark fish is at the bottom, at the bottom of the sea . . ." and all the others, except my cousin, echoed my words.

Every month, once the satellite had moved on, the Deaf One returned to his solitary detachment from the things of the world; only the approach of the full Moon aroused him again. That time I had arranged things so it wasn't my turn to go up, I could stay in the boat with the Captain's wife. But then, as soon as my cousin had climbed the ladder, Mrs. Vhd Vhd said: "This time I want to go up there, too!"

This had never happened before; the Captain's wife had never gone up on the Moon. But Vhd Vhd made no objection, in fact he almost pushed her up the ladder bodily, exclaiming: "Go ahead then!," and we all started helping her, and I held her from behind, felt her round and soft on my arms, and to hold her up I began to press my face and the palms of my hands against her, and when I felt her rising into the Moon's sphere I was heartsick at that lost contact, so I started to rush after her, saying: "I'm going to go up for a while, too, to help out!"

I was held back as if in a vise. "You stay here; you have work to do later," the Captain commanded, without raising his voice.

At that moment each one's intentions were already clear. And yet I couldn't figure things out; even now I'm not sure I've interpreted it all correctly. Certainly the Captain's wife had for a long time been cherishing the desire to go off privately with my cousin up there (or at least to prevent him from going off alone with the Moon), but probably she had a still more ambitious plan, one that would have to be carried out in agreement with the Deaf One: she wanted the two of them to hide up there together and stay on the Moon for a month. But perhaps my cousin, deaf as he was, hadn't understood anything of what she had tried to explain to him, or perhaps he hadn't even realized that he was the object of the lady's desires. And the Captain? He wanted nothing better than to be rid of his wife; in fact, as soon as she was confined up there, we saw him give free rein to his inclinations and plunge into vice, and then we understood why he had done nothing to hold her back. But had he known from the beginning that the Moon's orbit was widening?

None of us could have suspected it. The Deaf One perhaps, but only he: in the shadowy way he knew things, he may have had a presentiment that he would be forced to bid the Moon farewell that night. This is why he hid in his secret places and reappeared only when it was time to come back down on board. It was no use for the Captain's wife to try to follow him: we saw her cross the scaly zone various times, length and breadth, then suddenly she stopped, looking at us in the boat, as if about to ask us whether we had seen him.

Surely there was something strange about that night. The sea's surface, instead of being taut as it was during the full Moon, or even arched a bit toward the sky, now seemed limp, sagging, as if the lunar magnet no longer exercised its full power. And the light, too, wasn't the same as the light of other full Moons; the night's shadows seemed somehow to have thickened. Our friends up there must have realized what was happening; in fact, they looked up at us with frightened eyes. And from their mouths and ours, at the same moment, came a cry: "The Moon's going away!"

The cry hadn't died out when my cousin appeared on the Moon, running. He didn't seem frightened, or even amazed: he placed his hands on the terrain, flinging himself into his usual somersault, but this time after he had hurled himself into the air he remained suspended, as little Xlthlx had. He hovered a moment between Moon and Earth, upside down, then laboriously moving his arms, like someone swimming against a current, he headed with unusual slowness toward our planet.

From the Moon the other sailors hastened to follow his example. Nobody gave a thought to getting the Moon-milk that had been collected into the boats, nor did the Captain scold them for this. They had already waited too long, the distance was difficult to cross by now; when they tried to imitate my cousin's leap or his swimming, they remained there groping, suspended in midair. "Cling together! Idiots! Cling together!" the Captain yelled. At this command, the sailors tried to form a group, a mass, to push all together until they reached the zone of the Earth's attraction: all of a sudden a cascade of bodies plunged into the sea with a loud splash.

The boats were now rowing to pick them up. "Wait! The Captain's wife is missing!" I shouted. The Captain's wife had also tried to jump, but she was still floating only a few yards from the Moon, slowly moving her long, silvery arms in the air. I climbed up the ladder, and in a vain attempt to give her something to grasp I held the harp out toward her. "I can't reach her! We have to go after her!" and I started to jump up, brandishing the harp. Above me the enormous lunar disk no longer seemed the same as before: it had become much smaller, it kept contracting, as if my gaze were driving it away, and the emptied sky gaped like an abyss where, at the bottom, the stars had begun multiplying, and the night poured a river of emptiness over me, drowned me in dizziness and alarm.

"I'm afraid," I thought. "I'm too afraid to jump. I'm a coward!" and at that moment I jumped. I swam furiously through the sky, and held the harp out to her, and instead of coming toward me she rolled over and over, showing me first her impassive face and then her backside.

"Hold tight to me!" I shouted, and I was already overtaking her, entwining my limbs with hers. "If we cling together we can go down!" and I was concentrating all my strength on uniting myself more closely with her, and I concentrated my sensations as I enjoyed the fullness of that embrace. I was so absorbed I didn't realize at first that I was, indeed, tearing her from her weightless condition, but was making her fall back on the Moon. Didn't I realize it? Or had that been my intention from the very beginning? Before I could think properly, a cry was already bursting from my throat. "I'll be the one to stay with you for a month!" Or rather, "On you!" I shouted, in my excitement: "On you for a month!" and at that moment our embrace was broken by our fall to the Moon's surface, where we rolled away from each other among those cold scales.

I raised my eyes as I did every time I touched the Moon's crust, sure that I would see above me the native sea like an endless ceiling, and I saw it, yes, I saw it this time, too, but much higher, and much more narrow, bound by its borders of coasts and cliffs and promontories, and how small the boats seemed, and how unfamiliar my friends' faces and how weak their cries! A sound reached me from nearby: Mrs. Vhd Vhd had discovered her harp and was caressing it, sketching out a chord as sad as weeping.

A long month began. The Moon turned slowly around the Earth. On the suspended globe we no longer saw our familiar shore, but the passage of oceans as deep as abysses and deserts of glowing lapilli, and continents of ice, and forests writhing with reptiles, and the rocky walls of mountain chains gashed by swift rivers, and swampy cities, and stone graveyards, and empires of clay and mud. The distance spread a uniform color over everything: the alien perspectives made every image alien; herds of elephants and swarms of locusts ran over the plains, so evenly vast and dense and thickly grown that there was no difference among them.

I should have been happy: as I had dreamed, I was alone with her, that intimacy with the Moon I had so often envied my cousin and with Mrs. Vhd Vhd was now my exclusive prerogative, a month of days and lunar nights stretched uninterrupted before us, the crust of the satellite nourished us with its milk, whose tart flavor was familiar to us, we raised our eyes up, up to the world where we had been born, finally traversed in all its various expanse, explored landscapes no Earth-being had ever seen, or else we contemplated the stars beyond the Moon, big as pieces of fruit, made of light, ripened on the curved branches of the sky, and everything exceeded my most luminous hopes, and yet, and yet, it was, instead, exile.

I thought only of the Earth. It was the Earth that caused each of us to be that someone he was rather than someone else; up there, wrested from the Earth, it was as if I were no longer that I, nor she that She, for me. I was eager to return to the Earth, and I trembled at the fear of having lost it. The fulfillment of my dream of love had lasted only that instant when we had been united, spinning between Earth and Moon; torn from its earthly soil, my love now knew only the heart-rending nostalgia for what it lacked: a where, a surrounding, a before, an after.

This is what I was feeling. But she? As I asked myself, I was torn by my fears. Because if she also thought only of the Earth, this could be a good sign, a sign that she had finally come to understand me, but it could also mean that everything had been useless, that her longings were directed still and only toward my deaf cousin. Instead, she felt nothing. She never raised her eyes to the old planet, she went off, pale, among those wastelands, mumbling dirges and stroking her harp, as if completely identified with her temporary (as I thought) lunar state. Did this mean I had won out over my rival? No; I had lost: a hopeless defeat. Because she had finally realized that my cousin loved only the Moon, and the only thing she wanted now was to become the Moon, to be assimilated into the object of that extrahuman love.

When the Moon had completed its circling of the planet, there we were again over the Zinc Cliffs. I recognized them with dismay: not even in my darkest previsions had I thought the distance would have made them so tiny. In that mud puddle of the sea, my friends had set forth again, without the now useless ladders; but from the boats rose a kind of forest of long poles; everybody was brandishing one, with a harpoon or a grappling hook at the end, perhaps in the hope of scraping off a last bit of Moon-milk or of lending some kind of help to us wretches up there. But it was soon clear that no pole was long enough to reach the Moon; and they dropped back, ridiculously short, humbled, floating on the sea; and in that confusion some of the boats were thrown off balance and overturned. But just then, from another vessel a longer pole, which till then they had dragged along on the water's surface, began to rise: it must have been made of bamboo, of many, many bamboo poles stuck one into the other, and to raise it they had to go slowly because—thin as it was—if they let it sway too much it might break. Therefore, they had to use it with great strength and skill, so that the wholly vertical weight wouldn't rock the boat.

Suddenly it was clear that the tip of that pole would touch the Moon, and we saw it graze, then press against the scaly terrain, rest there a moment, give a kind of little push, or rather a strong push that made it bounce off again, then come back and strike that same spot as if on the rebound, then move away once more. And I recognized, we both—the Captain's wife and I—recognized my cousin: it couldn't have been anyone else, he was playing his last game with the Moon, one of his tricks, with the Moon on the tip of his pole as if he were juggling with her. And we realized that his virtuosity had no purpose, aimed at no practical result, indeed you would have said he was driving the Moon away, that he was helping her departure, that he wanted to show her to her more distant orbit. And this, too, was just like him: he was unable to conceive desires that went against the Moon's nature, the Moon's course and destiny, and if the Moon now tended to go away from him, then he would take delight in this separation just as, till now, he had delighted in the Moon's nearness.

What could Mrs. Vhd Vhd do, in the face of this? It was only at this moment that she proved her passion for the deaf man hadn't been a frivolous whim but an irrevocable vow. If what my cousin now loved was the distant Moon, then she too would remain distant, on the Moon. I sensed this, seeing that she didn't take a step toward the bamboo pole, but simply turned her harp toward the Earth, high in the sky, and plucked the strings. I say I saw her, but to tell the truth I only caught a glimpse of her out of the corner of my eye, because the minute the pole had touched the lunar crust, I had sprung and grasped it, and now, fast as a snake, I was climbing up the bamboo knots, pushing myself along with jerks of my arms and knees, light in the rarefied space, driven by a natural power that ordered me to return to the Earth, oblivious of the motive that had brought me here, or perhaps more aware of it than ever and of its unfortunate outcome; and already my climb up the swaying pole had reached the point where I no longer had to make any effort but could just allow myself to slide, head-first, attracted by the Earth, until in my haste the pole broke into a thousand pieces and I fell into the sea, among the boats.

My return was sweet, my home refound, but my thoughts were filled only with grief at having lost her, and my eyes gazed at the Moon, forever beyond my reach, as I sought her. And I saw her. She was there where I had left her, lying on a beach directly over our heads, and she said nothing. She was the color of the Moon; she held the harp at her side and moved one hand now and then in slow arpeggios. I could distinguish the shape of her bosom, her arms, her thighs, just as I remember them now, just as now, when the Moon has become that flat, remote circle, I still look for her as soon as the first sliver appears in the sky, and the more it waxes, the more clearly I imagine I can see her, her or something of her, but only her, in a hundred, a thousand different vistas, she who makes the Moon the Moon and, whenever she is full, sets the dogs to howling all night long, and me with them.

---

1. Since this is a pure fantasy, on what fictional elements does its success depend?
2. What do you conjecture as the reason for the deaf cousin's indifference to Mrs. Vhd Vhd?

3. Are the physical details of the ascent to the moon in any way consistent with the physical world we know? Which details?
4. How does the story draw from other fantasies and folklore about the moon?
5. Discuss the effect of having the story told in the first person. What sense do you get of the personality of the narrator?

Raymond Carver

Carver (1939–1988) was born in Clatskanie, Oregon, and attended Humboldt State University in California before going on to graduate work at the University of Iowa. For several years he taught writing at Syracuse University. In the late seventies his poetry and fiction marked him as one of the more noteworthy talents of his generation, and his reputation continues to soar. His stories are collected in Will You Please Be Quiet, Please? *(1978),* What We Talk about When We Talk about Love *(1981),* Cathedral *(1983), and* Where I'm Calling From: New and Selected Stories *(1988).*

Where I'm Calling From

We are on the front porch at Frank Martin's drying-out facility. Like the rest of us at Frank Martin's, J.P. is first and foremost a drunk. But he's also a chimney sweep. It's his first time here, and he's scared. I've been here once before. What's to say? I'm back. J.P.'s real name is Joe Penny, but he says I should call him J.P. He's about thirty years old. Younger than I am. Not much younger, but a little. He's telling me how he decided to go into his line of work, and he wants to use his hands when he talks. But his hands tremble. I mean, they won't keep still. "This has never happened to me before," he says. He means the trembling. I tell him I sympathize. I tell him the shakes will idle down. And they will. But it takes time.

We've only been in here a couple of days. We're not out of the woods yet. J.P. has these shakes, and every so often a nerve—maybe it isn't a nerve, but it's something—begins to jerk in my shoulder. Sometimes it's at the side of my neck. When this happens my mouth dries up. It's an effort just to swallow then. I know something's about to happen and I want to head it off. I want to hide from it, that's what I want to do. Just close my eyes and let it pass by, let it take the next man. J.P. can wait a minute.

I saw a seizure yesterday morning. A guy they call Tiny. A big fat guy, an electrician from Santa Rosa. They said he'd been in here for nearly two weeks and that he was over the hump. He was going home in a day or two and would spend New Year's Eve with his wife in front of the TV. On New Year's Eve, Tiny planned to drink hot chocolate and eat cookies. Yesterday morning he seemed just fine when he came down for breakfast. He was letting out with quacking noises, showing some guy how he called ducks right down onto his head. "Blam. Blam," said Tiny, picking off a couple. Tiny's hair was damp and was slicked back along the sides of his head. He'd just come out of the shower. He'd also nicked himself on the chin with his razor. But so what? Just about everybody at Frank Martin's has nicks on his face. It's something that happens. Tiny edged in at the head of the table and began telling about something that had happened on one of his drinking bouts. People at the table laughed and shook their heads as they shovelled up their eggs. Tiny would say something, grin, then look around the table for a sign of recognition. We'd all done things just as bad and crazy, so, sure, that's why we laughed. Tiny had scrambled eggs on his plate, and some biscuits and honey. I was at the table but I wasn't hungry. I had some coffee in front of me. Suddenly Tiny wasn't there anymore. He'd gone over in his chair with a big clatter. He was on his back on the floor with his eyes closed, his heels drumming the linoleum. People hollered for Frank Martin. But he was right there. A couple of guys got down on the floor beside Tiny. One of the guys put his fingers inside Tiny's mouth and tried to hold his tongue. Frank Martin yelled, "Everybody stand back!" Then I noticed that the bunch of us were leaning over Tiny, just looking at him, not able to take our eyes off him. "Give him air!" Frank Martin said. Then he ran into the office and called the ambulance.

Tiny is on board again today. Talk about bouncing back. This morning Frank Martin drove the station wagon to the hospital to get him. Tiny got back too late for his eggs, but he took some coffee into the dining room and sat down at the table anyway. Somebody in the kitchen made toast for him, but Tiny didn't eat it. He just sat with his coffee and looked into his cup. Every now and then he moved his cup back and forth in front of him.

I'd like to ask him if he had any signal just before it happened. I'd like to know if he felt his ticker skip a beat, or else begin to race. Did his eyelid twitch? But I'm not about to say anything. He doesn't look like he's hot to talk about it anyway. But what happened to Tiny is something I won't ever forget. Old Tiny flat on the floor, kicking his heels. So every time this little flitter starts up anywhere, I draw some breath and wait to find myself on my back, looking up, somebody's fingers in my mouth.

In his chair on the front porch, J.P. keeps his hands in his lap. I smoke cigarettes and use an old coal bucket for an ashtray. I listen to J.P. ramble on. It's eleven o'clock in the morning—an hour and a half until lunch. Neither one of us is hungry. But just the same we look forward to going inside and sitting down at the table. Maybe we'll get hungry.

What's J.P. talking about, anyway? He's saying how when he was twelve years old he fell into a well in the vicinity of the farm he grew up on. It was a dry well, lucky for him. "Or unlucky," he says, looking around him and shaking his head. He says how late that afternoon, after he'd been located, his dad hauled him out with a rope. J.P. had wet his pants down there. He'd suffered all kinds of terror in that well, hollering for help, waiting, and then hollering some more. He hollered himself hoarse before it was over. But he told me that being at the bottom of that well had made a lasting impression. He'd sat there and looked up at the well mouth. Way up at the top he could see a circle of blue sky. Every once in a while a white cloud passed over. A flock of birds flew across, and it seemed to J.P. their wingbeats set up this odd commotion. He heard other things. He heard tiny rustlings above him in the well, which made him wonder if things might fall down into his hair. He was thinking of insects. He heard wind blow over the well mouth, and that sound made an impression on him, too. In short, everything about his life was different for him at the bottom of that well. But nothing fell on him and nothing closed off that little circle of blue. Then his dad came along with the rope, and it wasn't long before J.P. was back in the world he'd always lived in.

"Keep talking, J.P. Then what?" I say.

When he was eighteen or nineteen years old and out of high school and had nothing whatsoever he wanted to do with his life, he went across town one afternoon to visit a friend. This friend lived in a house with a fireplace. J.P. and his friend sat around drinking beer and batting the breeze. They played some records. Then the doorbell rings. The friend goes to the door. This young woman chimney sweep is there with her cleaning things. She's wearing a top hat, the sight of which knocked J.P. for a loop. She tells J.P.'s friend that she has an appointment to clean the fireplace. The friend lets her in and bows. The young woman doesn't pay him any mind. She spreads a blanket on the hearth and lays out her gear. She's wearing these black pants, black shirt, black shoes and socks. Of course by now she's taken her hat off. J.P. says it nearly drove him nuts to look at her. She does the work, she cleans the chimney, while J.P. and his friend play records and drink beer. But they watch her and they watch what she does. Now and then J.P. and his friend look at each other and grin, or else they wink. They raise their eyebrows when the upper half of the young woman disappears into the chimney. She was all-right-looking, too, J.P. said. She was about his age.

When she'd finished her work, she rolled her things up in the blanket. From J.P.'s friend she took a check that had been made out to her by his parents. And then she asks the friend if he wants to kiss her. "It's supposed to bring good luck," she says. That does it for J.P. The friend rolls his eyes. He clowns some more. Then, probably blushing, he kisses her on the cheek. At this minute J.P. made his mind up about something. He put his beer down. He got up from the sofa. He went over to the young woman as she was starting to go out the door.

"Me, too?" J.P. said to her. She swept her eyes over him. J.P. says he could feel his heart knocking. The young woman's name, it turns out, was Roxy.

"Sure," Roxy says. "Why not? I've got some extra kisses." And she kisses him a good one right on the lips and then turned to go.

Like that, quick as a wink, J.P. followed her onto the porch. He held the porch screen door for her. He went down the steps with her and out to the drive, where she'd parked her panel truck. It was something that was out of his hands. Nothing else in the world counted for anything. He knew he'd met somebody who could set his legs atremble. He could feel her kiss still burning on his lips, etc. At that minute J.P. couldn't begin to sort anything out. He was filled with sensations that were carrying him every which way.

He opened the rear door of the panel truck for her. He helped her store her things inside. "Thanks," she told him. Then he blurted it out—that he'd like to see her again. Would she go to a movie with him sometime? He'd realized, too, what he wanted to do with his life. He wanted to do what she did. He wanted to be a chimney sweep. But he didn't tell her that then.

J.P. says she put her hands on her hips and looked him over. Then she found a business card in the front seat of her truck. She gave it to him. She said, "Call this number after ten o'clock tonight. The answering machine will be turned off then. We can talk. I have to go now." She put the top hat on and then took it off. She looked at J.P. once more. She must have liked what she saw, because this time she grinned. He told her there was a smudge near her mouth. Then she got into her truck, tooted the horn, and drove away.

"Then what?" I say. "Don't stop now, J.P." I was interested. But I would have listened if he'd been going on about how one day he'd decided to start pitching horseshoes.

It rained last night. The clouds are banked up against the hills across the valley. J.P. clears his throat and looks at the hills and the clouds. He pulls his chin. Then he goes on with what he was saying.

Roxy starts going out with him on dates. And little by little he talks her into letting him go along on jobs with her. But Roxy's in business with her father and brother and they've got just the right amount of work. They don't need anybody else. Besides, who was this guy J.P.? J.P. what? Watch out, they warned her.

So she and J.P. saw some movies together. They went to a few dances. But mainly the courtship revolved around their cleaning chimneys together. Before you know it, J.P. says, they're talking about tying the knot. And after a while they do it, they get married. J.P.'s new father-in-law takes him in as a full partner. In a year or so, Roxy had a kid. She's quit being a chimney sweep. At any rate, she's quit doing the work. Pretty soon she has another kid. J.P.'s in his mid-twenties by now. He's buying a house. He says he was happy with his life. "I was happy with the way things were going," he says. "I had everything I wanted. I had a wife and kids I loved, and I was doing what I wanted to do with my life." But for some reason—who knows why we do what we do?—his drinking picks up. For a long time he drinks beer and beer only. Any kind of beer—it didn't matter. He says he could drink beer twenty-four hours a day. He'd drink beer at night while he watched TV. Sure, once in a while he drank hard stuff. But that was only if they went out on the town, which was not often, or else when they had company over. Then a time comes, he doesn't know why, when he makes the switch from beer to gin and tonic. And he'd have more gin and tonic after dinner, sitting in front of the TV. There was always a glass of gin and tonic in his hand. He says he actually liked the taste of it. He began stopping off after work for drinks before he went home to have more drinks. Then he began missing some dinners. He just wouldn't show up. Or else he'd show up but he wouldn't want anything to eat. He'd filled up on snacks at the bar. Sometimes he'd walk in the door and for no good reason throw his lunch pail across the living room. When Roxy yelled at him, he'd turn around and go out again. He moved his drinking time up to early afternoon, while he was still supposed to be working. He tells me that he was starting off the morning with a couple of drinks. He'd have a belt of the stuff before he brushed his teeth. Then he'd have his coffee. He'd go to work with a thermos bottle of vodka in his lunch pail.

J.P. quits talking. He just clams up. What's going on? I'm listening. It's helping me relax, for one thing. It's taking me away from my own situation. After a minute, I say, "What the hell? Go on, J.P." He's pulling his chin. But pretty soon he starts talking again.

J.P. and Roxy are having some real fights now. I mean *fights*. J.P. says that one time she hit him in the face with her fist and broke his nose. "Look at this," he says. "Right here." He shows me a line across the bridge of his nose. "That's a broken nose." He returned the favor. He dislocated her shoulder for her on that occasion. Another time he split her lip. They beat on each other in front of the kids. Things got out of hand. But he kept on drinking. He couldn't stop. And nothing could make him stop. Not even with Roxy's dad and her brother threatening to beat hell out of him. They told Roxy she should take the kids and clear out. But Roxy said it was her problem. She got herself into it, and she'd solve it.

Now J.P. gets real quiet again. He hunches his shoulders and pulls down in his chair. He watches a car driving down the road between this place and the hills.

I say, "I want to hear the rest of this, J.P. You better keep talking."

"I just don't know," he says. He shrugs.

"It's all right," I say. And I mean it's O.K. for him to tell it. "Go on, J.P."

One way she tried to solve things, J.P. says, was by finding a boyfriend. J.P. would like to know how she found the time with the house and kids.

I looked at him and I'm surprised. He's a grown man. "If you want to do that," I say, "you find the time. You make the time."

J.P. shakes his head. "I guess so," he says.

Anyway, he found out about it—about Roxy's boyfriend—and he went wild. He manages to get Roxy's wedding ring off her finger. And when he does he cuts it into several pieces with a pair of wire cutters. Good solid fun. They'd already gone a couple of rounds on this occasion. On his way to work the next morning he gets arrested on a drunk-driving charge. He loses his driver's license. He can't drive the truck to work anymore. Just as well, he says. He'd already fallen off a roof the week before and broken his thumb. It was just a matter of time until he broke his God-damned neck, he says.

He was here at Frank Martin's to dry out and to figure how to get his life back on track. But he wasn't here against his will, any more than I was. We weren't locked up. We could leave anytime we wanted. But a minimum stay of a week was recommended, and two weeks or a month was, as they put it, "strongly advised."

As I said, this is my second time at Frank Martin's. When I was trying to sign a check to pay in advance for a week's stay, Frank Martin said, "The holidays are always a bad time. Maybe you should think of sticking around a little longer this time? Think in terms of a couple of weeks. Can you do a couple of weeks? Think about it, anyway. You don't have to decide anything right now," he said. He held his thumb on the check and I signed my name. Then I walked my girlfriend to the front door and said goodbye. "Goodbye," she said, and she lurched into the doorjamb and then onto the porch. It's late afternoon. It's raining. I go from the door to the window. I move the curtain and watch her drive away. She's in my car. She's drunk. But I'm drunk, too, and there's nothing I can do. I make it to a big old chair that's close to the radiator, and I sit down. Some guys look up from their TV. Then slowly they shift back to what they were watching. I just sit there.

Now and then I look up at something that's happening on the screen.

Later that afternoon the front door banged open and J.P. was brought in between these two big guys—his father-in-law and brother-in-law, I find out afterward. They steered J.P. across the room. The old guy signed him in and gave Frank Martin a check. Then these two guys helped J.P. upstairs. I guess they put him to bed. Pretty soon the old guy and the other guy came downstairs and headed for the front door. They couldn't seem to get out of the place fast enough. It was as if they couldn't wait to wash their hands of all this. I didn't blame them. Hell, no. I don't know how I'd act if I was in their shoes.

A day and half later J.P. and I meet up on the front porch. We shake hands and comment on the weather. J.P. has a case of the shakes. We sit down and prop our feet on the railing. We lean back in our chairs as if we're just out there taking our ease, as if we might be getting ready to talk about our bird dogs. That's when J.P. gets going with his story.

It's cold out, but not too cold. It's a little overcast. At one point Frank Martin comes outside to finish his cigar. He has on a sweater buttoned up to his Adam's apple. Frank Martin is short and heavyset. He has curly gray hair and a small head. His head is out of proportion with the rest of his body. Frank Martin puts the cigar in his mouth and stands with his arms crossed over his chest. He works that cigar in his mouth and looks across the valley. He stands there like a prizefighter, like somebody who knows the score.

J.P. gets real quiet again. I mean, he's hardly breathing. I toss my cigarette into the coal bucket and look hard at J.P., who scoots farther down in his chair. J.P. pulls up his collar. What the hell's going on, I wonder. Frank Martin uncrosses his arms and takes a puff on the cigar. He lets the smoke carry out of his mouth. Then he raises his chin toward the hills and says, "Jack London[1] used to have a big place on the other side of this valley. Right over there behind that green hill you're looking at. But alcohol killed him. Let that be a lesson. He was a better man than any of us. But he couldn't handle the stuff, either." He looks at what's left of his cigar. It's gone out. He tosses it into the bucket. "You guys want to read something while you're here, read that book of his *The Call of the Wild.* You know the one I'm talking about? We have it inside, if you want to read something. It's about this animal that's half dog and half wolf. They don't write books like that anymore. But we could have helped Jack London, if we'd been here in those days. And if he'd let us. If he'd asked for our help. Hear me? Like we can help you. *If. If* you ask for it and *if* you listen. End of sermon. But

1. U.S. novelist and short-story writer (1876–1916).

don't forget. If," he says again. Then he hitches his pants and tugs his sweater down. "I'm going inside," he says. "See you at lunch."

"I feel like a bug when he's around," J.P. says. "He makes me feel like a bug. Something you could step on." J.P. shakes his head. Then he says, "Jack London. What a name! I wish I had me a name like that. Instead of the name I got."

Frank Martin talked about that "if" the first time I was here. My wife brought me up here that time. That's when we were still living together, trying to make things work out. She brought me here and she stayed around for an hour or two, talking to Frank Martin in private. Then she left. The next morning Frank Martin got me aside and said, "We can help you. If you want help and want to listen to what we say." But I didn't know if they could help me or not. Part of me wanted help. But there was another part. All said, it was a very big if.

This time around, six months after my first stay, it was my girlfriend who drove me here. She was driving my car. She drove us through a rainstorm. We drank champagne all the way. We were both drunk when she pulled up in the drive. She intended to drop me off, turn around, and drive home again. She had things to do. One thing she had to do was to go to work the next day. She was a secretary. She had an O.K. job with this electronic-parts firm. She also had this mouthy teen-age son. I wanted her to get a motel room in town, spend the night, and then drive home. I don't know if she got the room or not. I haven't heard from her since she led me up the front steps the other day and walked me into Frank Martin's office and said, "Guess who's here."

But I wasn't mad at her. In the first place she didn't have any idea what she was letting herself in for when she said I could stay with her after my wife asked me to leave. I felt sorry for her. The reason I felt sorry for her was on the day before Christmas her Pap smear[2] came back from the lab, and the news was not cheery. She'd have to go back to the doctor, and real soon. That kind of news was reason enough for both of us to start drinking. So what we did was get ourselves good and drunk. And on Christmas Day we were still drunk. We had to go out to a restaurant to eat, because she didn't feel anything like cooking. The two of us and her mouthy teen-age son opened some presents, and then we went to this steak house near her apartment. I wasn't hungry. I had some soup and a hot roll. I drank a bottle of wine with the soup. She drank some wine, too. Then we started in on Bloody Marys. For the next couple of days I didn't eat anything except cashew nuts. But I drank a lot of bourbon. On the morning of the twenty-

2. A test for cancer of the uterus.

eighth I said to her, "Sugar, I think I'd better pack up. I better go back to Frank Martin's. I need to try that place on again. Hey, how about you driving me?"

She tried to explain to her son that she was going to be gone that afternoon and evening, and he'd have to get his own dinner. But right as we were going out the door this God-damned kid screamed at us. He screamed, "You call this love? The hell with you both! I hope you never come back. I hope you kill yourselves!" Imagine this kid!

Before we left town I had her stop at the liquor store, where I bought us three bottles of champagne. Quality stuff—Piper. We stopped someplace else for plastic glasses. Then we picked up a bucket of fried chicken. We set out for Frank Martin's in this rainstorm, drinking champagne and listening to music on the radio. She drove. I looked after the radio and poured champagne. We tried to make a little party out of it. But we were sad, too. There was that fried chicken, but we didn't eat any of it.

I guess she got home O.K. I think I would have heard something if she hadn't made it back. But she hasn't called me, and I haven't called her. Maybe she's had some news about herself by now. Then again, maybe she hasn't heard anything. Maybe it was all a mistake. Maybe it was somebody else's test. But she has my car, and I have things at her house. I know we'll be seeing each other again.

They clang an old farm bell here to signal mealtime. J.P. and I get out of our chairs slowly, like old geezers, and we go inside. It's starting to get too cold on the porch anyway. We can see our breath drifting out from us as we talk.

New Year's Eve morning I try to call my wife. There's no answer. It's O.K. But even if it wasn't O.K., what am I supposed to do? The last time we talked on the phone, a couple of weeks ago, we screamed at each other. I hung a few names on her. "Wet brain!" she said, and put the phone back where it belonged.

But I wanted to talk to her now. Something had to be done about my stuff. I still had things at her house, too.

One of the guys here is a guy who travels. He goes to Europe and the Middle East. That's what he says, anyway. Business, he says. He also says he has his drinking under control and doesn't have any idea why he's here at Frank Martin's. But he doesn't remember getting here. He laughs about it, about his not remembering. "Anyone can have a blackout," he says. "That doesn't prove a thing." He's not a drunk—he tells us this and we listen. "That's a serious charge to make," he says. "That kind of talk can ruin a good man's prospects." He further says that if he'd only stick to whiskey and water, no ice, he'd never get "intoxicated"—his word—and have these blackouts. It's the ice they put into your drink that does it. "Who do you know in Egypt?" he asks me. "I can use a few names over there."

For New Year's Eve dinner Frank Martin serves steak and baked potato. A green salad. My appetite's coming back. I eat the salad. I clean up everything on my plate and I could eat more. I look over at Tiny's plate. Hell, he's hardly touched anything. His steak is just sitting there getting cold. Tiny is not the same old Tiny. The poor bastard had planned to be at home tonight. He'd planned to be in his robe and slippers in front of the TV, holding hands with his wife. Now he's afraid to leave. I can understand. One seizure means you're a candidate for another. Tiny hasn't told any more nutty stories on himself since it happened. He's stayed quiet and kept to himself. Pretty soon I ask him if I can have his steak, and he pushes his plate over to me.

They let us keep the TV on until the New Year has been rung in at Times Square. Some of us are still up, sitting around the TV, watching the crowds on the screen, when Frank Martin comes in to show us his cake. He brings it around and shows it to each of us. I know he didn't make it. It's a God-damned bakery cake. But still it's a cake. It's a big white cake. Across the top of the cake there's writing in pink letters. The writing says "Happy New Year—1 Day At A Time."

"I don't want any stupid cake," says the guy who goes to Europe and the Middle East. "Where's the champagne?" he says, and laughs.

We all go into the dining room. Frank Martin cuts the cake. I sit next to J.P. J.P. eats two pieces and drinks a Coke. I eat a piece and wrap another piece in a napkin, thinking of later.

J.P. lights a cigarette—his hands are steady now—and he tells me his wife is coming to visit him in the morning. The first day of the New Year.

"That's great," I say. I nod. I lick the frosting off my finger. "That's good news, J.P."

"I'll introduce you," he says.

"I look forward to it," I say.

We say good night. We say Happy New Year. Sleep well. I use a napkin on my fingers. We shake hands.

I go to the pay phone once more, put in a dime, and call my wife collect. But nobody answers this time, either. I think about calling my girlfriend, and I'm dialing her number when I realize I don't want to talk to her. She's probably at home watching the same thing on TV that I've been watching. But maybe she isn't. Maybe she's out. Why shouldn't she be? Anyway, I don't want to talk to her. I hope she's O.K. But if she has something wrong with her I don't want to know about it. Not now. In any case, I won't talk to her tonight.

After breakfast J.P. and I take coffee out to the porch, where we plan to wait for his wife. The sky is clear, but it's cold enough so we're wearing our sweaters and jackets.

"She asked me if she should bring the kids," J.P. says. "I told her she should keep the kids at home. Can you imagine? My God, I don't want my kids up here."

We use the coal bucket for an ashtray. We look across the valley where Jack London used to live. We're drinking more coffee, when this car turns off the road and comes down the drive.

"That's her!" J.P. says. He puts his cup next to his chair. He gets up and goes down the steps to the drive.

I see this woman stop the car and set the brake. I see J.P. open the car door. I watch her get out, and I see them embrace. They hug each other. I look away. Then I look back. J.P. takes the woman's arm and they come up the stairs. This woman has crawled into chimneys. This woman broke a man's nose once. She has had two kids, and much trouble, but she loves this man who has her by the arm. I get up from the chair.

"This is my friend," J.P. says to his wife. "Hey, this is Roxy."

Roxy takes my hand. She's a tall, good-looking woman in a blue knit cap. She has on a coat, a heavy white sweater, and dark slacks. I recall what J.P. told me about the boyfriend and the wire cutters—all that—and I glance at her hands. Right. I don't see any wedding ring. That's in pieces somewhere. Her hands are broad and the fingers have these big knuckles. This is a woman who can make fists if she has to.

"I've heard about you," I say. "J.P. told me how you got acquainted. Something about a chimney, J.P. said."

"Yes, a chimney," she says. Her eyes move away from my face, then return. She nods. She's anxious to be alone with J.P., which I can understand. "There's probably a lot else he didn't tell you," she says. "I bet he didn't tell you everything," she says, and laughs. Then—she can't wait any longer—she slips her arm around J.P.'s waist and kisses him on the cheek. They start to move toward the door. "Nice meeting you," she says over her shoulder. "Hey, did he tell you he's the best sweep in the business?" She lets her hand down from J.P.'s waist onto his hip.

"Come on now, Roxy," J.P. says. He has his hand on the door knob.

"He told me he learned everything he knew from you," I say.

"Well, that much is sure true," she says. She laughs again. But it's as if she's thinking about something else. J.P. turns the doorknob. Roxy lays her hand over his hand. "Joe, can't we go into town for lunch? Can't I take you someplace for lunch?"

J.P. clears his throat. He says, "It hasn't been a week yet." He takes his hand off the doorknob and brings his fingers to his chin. "I think they'd like it, you know, if I didn't leave the place for a little while yet. We can have some coffee inside," he says.

"That's fine," she says. Her eyes light on me once more. "I'm glad Joe's made a friend here. Nice to meet you," she says again.

They start to go inside. I know it's a foolish thing to do, but I do it anyway. "Roxy," I say. And they stop in the doorway and look at me. "I need some luck," I say. "No kidding. I could do with a kiss myself."

J.P. looks down. He's still holding the doorknob, even though the door is open. He turns the doorknob back and forth. He's embarrassed. I'm embarrassed, too. But I keep looking at her. Roxy doesn't know what to make of it. She grins. "I'm not a sweep anymore," she says. "Not for years. Didn't Joe tell you? What the hell. Sure, I'll kiss you. Sure. For luck."

She moves over, she takes me by the shoulders—I'm a big man—and she plants this kiss on my lips. "How's that?" she says.

"That's fine," I say.

"Nothing to it," she says. She's still holding me by the shoulders. She's looking me right in the eyes. "Good luck," she says, and then she let go of me.

"See you later, pal," J.P. says. He opens the door all the way, and they go inside.

I sit down on the front steps and light a cigarette. I watch what my hand does, then I blow out the match. I've got a case of the shakes. I started out with them this morning. This morning I wanted something to drink. It's depressing, and I didn't say anything about it to J.P. I try to put my mind on something else and for once it works.

I'm thinking about chimney sweeps—all that stuff I heard from J.P.—when for some reason I start to think about the house my wife and I lived in just after we were married. That house didn't have a chimney—hell, no—so I don't know what makes me remember it now. But I remember the house and how we'd only been in there a few weeks when I heard a noise outside one morning and woke up. It was Sunday morning and so early it was still dark in the bedroom. But there was this pale light coming in from the bedroom windows. I listened. I could hear something scrape against the side of the house. I jumped out of bed and went to the window.

"My God!" my wife says, sitting up in bed and shaking the hair away from her face. Then she starts to laugh. "It's Mr. Venturini," she says. "The landlord. I forgot to tell you. He said he was coming to paint the house today. Early. Before it gets too hot. I forgot all about it," she says, and laughs some more. "Come on back to bed, honey. It's just the landlord."

"In a minute," I say.

I push the curtain away from the window. Outside, this old guy in white coveralls is standing next to his ladder. The sun is just starting to break above the mountains. The old guy and I look each other over. It's the landlord, all right—this old guy in coveralls. But his coveralls are too big for him. He needs a shave, too. And he's wearing this baseball cap to cover his bald head. God damn it, I think, if he isn't a weird old hombre, then I've never seen one. And at that minute a wave of happiness comes over me that I'm not him—that I'm me and that I'm inside this bedroom with my wife. He jerks his thumb toward the sun. He pretends to wipe his forehead. He's letting me know he doesn't have all that much time. The old duffer breaks into a grin. It's then I realize I'm naked. I look down at myself. I look at him again and shrug. I'm smiling. What'd he expect?

My wife laughs. "Come *on,*" she says. "Get back in this bed. Right now. This minute. Come on back to bed."

I let go of the curtain. But I keep standing there at the window. I can see the landlord nod to himself as if to say, "Go on, sonny, go back to bed. I understand," as if he'd heard my wife calling me. He tugs the bill of his cap. Then he sets about his business. He picks up his bucket. He starts climbing the ladder.

I lean back into the step behind me now and cross one leg over the other. Maybe later this afternoon I'll try calling my wife again. And then I'll call to see what's happening with my girlfriend. But I don't want to get her mouthy son on the line. If I do call, I hope he'll be out somewhere doing whatever he does when he's not hanging around the house. I try to remember if I ever read any Jack London books. I can't remember. But there was a story of his I read in high school. "To Build a Fire" it was called. This guy in the Yukon is freezing. Imagine it—he's actually going to freeze to death if he can't get a fire going. With a fire he can dry his socks and clothing and warm himself. He gets his fire going, but then something happens to it. A branchful of snow drops on it. It goes out. Meanwhile, the temperature is falling. Night is coming on.

I bring some change out of my pocket. I'll try my wife first. If she answers, I'll wish her a Happy New Year. But that's it. I won't bring up business. I won't raise my voice. Not even if she starts something. She'll ask me where I'm calling from, and I'll have to tell her. I won't say anything about New Year's resolutions. There's no way to make a joke out of this. After I talk to her, I'll call my girlfriend. Maybe I'll call her first. I'll just have to hope I don't get her son on the line. "Hello, sugar," I'll say when she answers. "It's me."

1. What is emphasized and what is subordinated by use of a first person narrator in a story that might have been reduced to a clinical and sociological record?
2. Discuss the ironic double meaning of the title. What does it refer to besides Frank Martin's treatment center?
3. Is the narrator so far gone in his own troubles that he is literally unable to sympathize with the woes of others? Or is he transfigured into a witness for everyone sunk in the lower depths?
4. Discuss the relation of oral activities (like eating, kissing, drinking, talking) with the alcoholism that afflicts most of the characters.
5. Is this story strikingly contemporary? Or could it have come from any historical epoch you can imagine?

R. V. Cassill

Cassill (1919–) was born in Cedar Falls, Iowa. As a young man he studied art with the intention of becoming a painter, but after Army service in the South Pacific during World War II, he began to write and publish fiction. As a teacher of writing at the University of Iowa, Purdue, Columbia, Harvard, and Brown, he numbers many novelists and short story writers among his former students. His themes range from the little wars of childhood to the clashes of political ideologies, and several of his works deal with the role of the artist in our times. His novels include Clem Anderson *(1961),* The President *(1964),* The Goss Women *(1974),* Hoyt's Child *(1976),* Labors of Love *(1980), and* After Goliath *(1985). Several of his stories have been collected in* The Father *(1965) and* The Happy Marriage *(1967). His* Collected Stories *appeared in 1989.*

The Father

This began many years ago. Since its origin was from an accident and since many of the consequences would never be duplicated, it may stand as a unique little history without much relation to the fated march of public events of the destinies of most people.

It began on a March morning when Cory Johnson was shelling corn in the crib on his farm. He had a rattletrap old sheller that he was rather proud of. Some of its parts—the gears and the rust-pitted flywheel bored for a hand crank—had come from a machine in use on this farm for longer than Cory had lived. But he had rebuilt the frame and replaced the shelling spikes inside. He had rigged an electric motor and a system of belts to run the apparatus after the REA[1] brought the wires out on this mail route west of Boda.

The sheller worked well enough. When there was no load of corn hitting the spikes, the rising and falling hum of the motor and the sibilance of the belts on the pulley faces were reasonably quiet. Of course, when corn was actually being shelled, a deafening racket filled this solid-walled room in the corner of the slatted crib.

1. Rural Electrification Administration—a Federal agency set up in the Thirties to bring electricity to all areas of the country.

Cory thought he was alone on the farm at this hour. His wife had taken all three children with her in the Model A.[2] The two older boys were in school and would not come home until late afternoon. His wife hoped to drive into Boda to see her parents if the roads had not thawed too badly. She meant to take Bobbie, the youngest boy, along with her. Probably those two would not be back much before noon.

Cory liked being alone on his place. The job he had laid out for himself this morning was not pressing. At midmorning he would go to the house for coffee and cold pancakes with jelly. While he ate the snack he meant to listen to a science program broadcast daily from the station of the state university. He liked science. In his rural isolation he believed—then, early in the Thirties, almost a full century after it began to dominate the life of the western world—that science was "the coming thing."

As he fell into the rhythm of it, he was enjoying his work as much as he ever had. The warming day, which would probably take the bottom out of the gravel roads between here and town before it was through, permitted him to take off his sheepskin coat. He was warm enough in a sweater as long as he kept busy, and for a good hour he worked without pause, bringing tin bushels full of corn from a pile in the slatted corncrib and feeding it into the machine.

While the ears ran down the trough to the hopper, Cory sometimes watched the throat of the outlet where the shelled grains poured into gunnysacks. Mostly the grains flowed out in a brisk, placid stream, but now and then above the main flow some single grains would leap like fast, yellow sparks from a grinding wheel. There was of course nothing extraordinary in the maverick behavior of these grains. They were the ones that had caught somehow between the cobs and the whirling spikes just long enough for elastic and centrifugal forces to build up, then hurl them like bullets ricocheting out the metal chute that filled the sacks. Still, their unpredictable flight suggested mysteries beyond the fringe of his experience. He had read in *Popular Science Monthly* where some Jap had invented a centrifugal machine gun. It pleased him mildly to think he was watching the principle of the gun being demonstrated by the apparatus he had put together. In another issue of the same magazine he had seen a photograph of electrons leaping through the dark of an experimental chamber, and though these pictures had showed no more than the scratch of a white line across a black rectangle, it pleased him to believe that electrons *really* looked like these hard-flung, zinging grains of corn.

Once that morning when Cory went out into the main storage bins of the crib to fill his bushels, he heard the electric motor change

2. Ford automobile that replaced the simpler Model T of the 1920s.

pitch. Its normal whine became a level, unpleasant hum. The slap and hiss of the driving belts had stopped. The motor was no longer turning over, and he had better shut down the current quickly before the armature burned out.

As he skipped for the door, the motor began to run again. A belt whistled on an immobilized pulley.

He saw his four-year-old son Bobbie standing beside the fly wheel with his gloved hand raised to the gear reduction. The boy's face was turned back over his sheepskin collar, and he was grinning the not quite honest grin he often showed when caught doing something destructive and forbidden—he grinned as if trying to minimize his offense.

Cory thought the boy had pushed a cob into the gears, experimentally, and thus had stopped the whole complex of machinery cold.

Then with a hawking scream that scalded his throat and the inside of his nose with bile, Cory called his wife's name. The boy's hand was in the gears. Down the fringed and starred cuff of his glove, blood was oozing briskly onto his sleeve and down the sleeve to the hem of his coat.

Cory had turned the power off and knelt with the boy in his arms by the time his wife ran from the car she had just parked.

As pain returned to the shocked nerves of the hand, the boy's grin merely enlarged until his mouth stood in a ridged O like the corolla of a white flower. He was now shrieking incessantly in fear and pain. He danced in his father's arms and jerked and jerked to free his hand. Urine bubbled through his overalls and mixed with the blood under his boots.

"Daddy'll get you out," Belle Johnson shouted in the boy's face.

"Daddy, Daddy, Daddy, Daddy," she moaned to Cory, depending like the child on his act to save them.

"Hold'm," Cory said. He vaulted the machine and knocked the belt from the drive shaft, vaulted back and set his shoulder to a spoke of the flywheel. When the gears moved, the boy shrieked louder and fainted.

"I'll take the sonofabitch apart," Cory said. He looked under the motor table for his toolbox. He remembered having put it in the trunk of the car. He was not sure whether he had left it there or had taken it out later in the barn.

"Daddy, he's swallowing his tongue," Belle said.

Cory put a finger and thumb in the boy's mouth. It was like putting them into an electric socket with the current on. The strength of the curling tongue seemed greater than any he could force into his own hand.

It took him five seconds to secure the tongue and press his wife's nails into it. He believed it had taken two or three minutes.

Sweat was blinding him. He thought the boy might die if he did not hurry, but he caught himself staring with revulsion at the machine, taking time to blame himself not only for the failure to enclose the gears in a safety box, but for making anything so ugly and rough—for presuming to do something that only factory technicians working for pay could do right.

He fished out his jackknife and cut away the blood-sopped glove from the jammed hand. He thought it was possible that the jersey might have cushioned the bones at least. What he saw looked like boiled and shredded chicken in which a bad cook had left bits of gristle and bone.

"Daddy, his mouth is turning blue," Belle said.

"All right. Hold onto him. Hold him tight," Cory said.

He took a dark-bladed hatchet from its hanging place on the wall. There was not much room for it between the gears and the bottom of the hopper. With a three-inch blow he clipped the hand just above the wristbone.

"Get a tourniquet on him. I'll get the car," he told his wife.

The doctor in Boda, young Doctor Grant, said that Cory had done a pretty good job of amputation, all things considered.

"Bobbie probably never even felt what you did," Doctor Grant said, with his clean, pink-nailed fingers resting on Cory's sleeve. "There was quite a little shock. Naturally. But if his hand was so badly mangled you couldn't get it free, you can be sure that's where the shock came from. Say, it didn't take you long to get him in here to me," he said with an encouraging gleam of admiration in his eyes.

"No," Cory said. "I just didn't pay any attention to the mudholes. I came through the bad stretch the other side of the bridge doing about sixty-five, I guess."

The doctor laughed quite loudly. "I'll bet you jumped that Model A right over the bad spots."

Now that he knew his boy was going to be all right—which at the moment meant that he was going to live—Cory felt an unaccountable but decent pride in his behavior after the accident. By God, he had held back nothing. He had ripped the guts out of his Model A, coming in from the farm in just seventeen minutes. By God, he had seen the mail carrier—the mail carrier, mind you—out beside his car studying the mire of gravel and standing water in the low spot beyond the creek and probably deciding it had thawed too bad for him to get the mail through. Now Cory could remind himself—what he wouldn't bend the doctor's ear with—that Belle had shouted from the back seat to go around the longer way by Hopewell Church when he took it on his own shoulders to give this way a try. He hated to think what might have happened if he had stuck the car in deep there, a mile and a quarter from town. And for a minute or two it had been touch-and-go with the mud geysering over his windshield and the car skidding always to the left against his pull on the steering wheel. He had seen the face of the mail carrier through a muddy window, puckered in disbelief, almost in awe, as he watched the Model A churn past him.

The car was still fishtailing uncontrollably when Cory took her up the bridge approach. The whipping rear end grazed half the girders of the span before he got her straightened. The rear bumper was gone and somewhere along the line he'd overtaxed the transmission so he couldn't get her shifted down from high when he had to wait for a truck to cross at the Boda stop sign. He killed the motor then and ran three blocks to the doctor's office with the boy in his arms and Belle unable to keep up with him. And made it in time.

In time. In time. In time. The thought quieted the thudding of his heart.

"I don't think there's enough loss of blood to worry us," Doctor Grant said. "The tourniquet worked very nicely." Doctor Grant was only concerned—just a little—about the effects of shock, he said. He wanted to drive the boy over to the hospital in the county seat as soon as he had seen two more patients. He wanted to make sure Bobbie had his strength built up "before I finish the job for you," as he put it to Cory, with a wink of complicity. The Johnsons could ride along in the doctor's car. Belle could hold the little fellow in her lap, and everything would be arranged so one of them could stay all night with him in the hospital.

In the meantime, while his parents waited, the boy was sleeping in one of the doctor's examination rooms. He had been given morphine. Everything seemed to be under control. The orderly flow of circumstance had resumed again.

Cory opened a magazine, there in the doctor's waiting room—not so much because he thought he could read anything just now as because he wanted some shield behind which to hide until he came to terms with himself. Most importantly, he had to choke down the boisterous, excessive pride that had come on the rebound of his relief. He kept wanting to grin when he thought of the mail carrier's face. But if he couldn't help grinning, no one ought to see him do it. Then, too, he might want to pray out some of his thanksgiving that the roads hadn't been too bad, that Doctor Grant knew his business, and so on. Cory was still religious in crisis, though in normal times he lived by the opinion that "a lot of people went too far" with the religious business.

"Cory?"

He heard Belle's whisper like something whispering to him out of the past—like his mother come to wake him for a fine day in summer after vacation from school had begun and he could enjoy himself helping *his* daddy around the farm.

He looked up from the magazine. Belle's face was so pale he was frightened for her. Her blue eyes looked black against her ghostly skin.

"Daddy," she said, "don't feel too bad. You had to do it."

Of course it would have occurred to him sooner or later, without any prompting from Belle, that he and he alone was guilty for the loss of Bobbie's hand.

Since Cory would rather—if wishes had anything to do with the matter—have given his own hand, the way the guilt came to present itself was especially hard for him to master.

The point wasn't his negligence. As his father-in-law said, "There's a great many dangerous things around a farm, Cory. There always will be for kids."

"I know it," Cory said. "There's got to be machinery and animals and the pony that Joe and Gordon ride. You take the windmill tower for an example. I've caught Joe and Gordon up there I don't know how many times. They might any time fall and break their necks. Or the fan's going and they stick their heads up through the platform. Pfffttt!"

The older man extended the rhythm of agreement. "That's a fact, and you know Belle, when she was little, one time I nearly toppled a horse tank I was loading right onto her." He shuddered even now.

"Ah, but Dad, you held it," Belle recalled.

"I did," her father said. "And I paddled you for it when I saw you were safe. And I always remembered what a scare I had. But the point is that accidents just happen, Cory. After all, that's what the word *accident* means."

"Yeah, it does," Cory said.

The conversation was one of a great many that took place in the spring and summer after Bobbie lost his hand. They amounted to a kind of informal funeral, commemorating and at the same time draining away the immediate emotions of loss. It appeared, even to Cory, that it did him good to speak of the accident. He found no difficulty in saying man to man, man to wife, father to children—even to Bobbie—that an accident was something that just happened. Cory knew as well as any man that this was so.

Though he said many times that he could shoot himself for not having put a safety box around those gears on the sheller, this negligence was not the point that proved most crucial, either.

"You should have done that," his father-in-law said once when Cory lamented the absence of such a guard. "Well, we go on and try to make up for our past mistakes, and it does seem kind of sad to lock the door after the horse is gone, but that's what we do. I notice you took some rungs out of the ladder up the windmill."

"And Gordon climbed it the other night anyway," Belle said. "Shinnied right up the frame and had to yell for Cory to come and get him off."

They laughed and Cory laughed with them. Yes. Just to go on living he had to accept the likelihood of accidents, particularly where boys were involved, and he could do that.

But it wasn't the accidental part of Bobbie's misfortune that settled permanently into Cory's mind, freezing it to a pattern of distress. What he could never face—could never understand—was that he was guilty in taking that hatchet down from its hanging place on the wall and cutting off his son's hand.

"You had to do it," Belle said. She was willing to repeat this assurance wherever she thought it would help.

It never helped. Cory knew he'd had to do it. But necessity was no excuse at all for the guilt that rode him. The more he rehearsed his motives, the less important they seemed in comparison with the immortal act. If it was only bad luck that had put him in a situation where he had no choice, still, that luck was *his*. The guilt seemed to reside in that simple fact.

"It's like if I'd been someone else, not any part of this awful thing would have happened," he said to Belle.

Now that her emotions had resumed their normal level, she was almost as much amused as concerned at this odd way of putting it. She probably thought he was fishing for sympathy, and though she didn't mind sympathizing with him all he wanted, she didn't know how to offer the right response to his fancy. She said, "Sure. Sure. If you were someone else you wouldn't have this farm. You wouldn't have your nice kids. You wouldn't be stuck with me. Well, that's all a pipe dream, old man. You're stuck with all of us, and we'll get along. You know we will. Bobbie's a brave little guy. We might just thank God he was always left-handed."

"I know we'll get along," Cory said.

"You shouldn't punish yourself this way, because there's nothing to punish yourself for."

"I know that too."

"Then don't get depressed like this."

He had not spoken from depression, but from guilt. He knew well enough what depression was. He was depressed in those years of the Thirties when the drought took most of his corn crop two years in succession; when he let himself be cheated in buying a secondhand car that turned out to have a cracked block; when he had trouble with his gallstones and had to cripple around all one winter; when his oldest boy, Joe, had trouble with his high-school studies and went off to join the Navy; when Belle's father, a man who'd been so good to Cory and his family and so dear to Bobbie, died of cancer; when the war came and Joe was out there at Pearl Harbor, where the Japs dropped on them with their newfangled weapons, and so many didn't have a chance on the anchored ships.

Year by year there were things to depress him. Big things and little things. And through the same years there'd been good times and times of satisfaction when he *wasn't* depressed. Take the summer he'd put the family in the car and driven them out to Yellowstone Park. That trip was a pure satisfaction. He couldn't remember a thing wrong with it.

Easily he remembered the good winters when he and Gordon were teaching Bobbie to hunt with them. They would load the dogs in the back seat of the car and drive over to the creek bottom to look for rabbits, quail, or pheasants. Cory had his pump gun. Gordon and Bobbie "shared" the single-shot .410 that had been bought for Joe when he turned twelve. Off they'd mush through the snow and broken cornstalks, trying to keep up with the badly trained dogs, joking and trading insults like three men—or three boys, it didn't matter which. Once, Cory'd knocked down three cock pheasants from a rising covey. Bobbie clapped his mitten to the side of his head and howled in admiration and disbelief. "Purty good, for an old man," he yelled over the snow. "Purty good."

"Even if you did get more than the limit," Gordon put in. "You going to tell the game warden I shot one of them?"

What he'd seen in the boys' eyes that afternoon was unmistakable and worth treasuring—just standing there in the snow with the dead birds around them, the boys being proud of their old man. It was like the male satisfaction he'd felt the day he took Bobbie in through the mud to the doctor's. In time. Only now the boys were here to share and mirror back the lonely pride of his manhood.

There had also been the good times—not to mention *all* the blessings of the years—when Joe came home on boot leave; when prices picked up in thirty-nine and the same year Belle had another boy, Cory, Jr.; and when they got the first letter from Joe after Pearl Harbor saying he was all right.

The good things and the bad things of an ordinary farmer's life had happened to him. He had responded to them like an ordinary man, with satisfaction or depression.

But the guilt he endured was something else. It seemed to have a life of its own, to be almost a distinct life he lived when his ordinary life gave him the opportunity.

Weeks, months, years went by in which he forgot that he was guilty. During those periods he got quite used to Bobbie's disfigurement, as if it were a condition that had always existed, one intended by nature.

Fortunately, Bobbie wasn't the boy to feed on sympathy. He managed. As far as his parents could tell, he was a happier boy than Joe had been.

Cory watched without sentimentality as his maimed son grew up. But when the awareness of his guilt came back in one of its cyclic manifestations, he found that it had not diminished with time. After ten years it was as keen and lively as it had been that morning in Doctor Grant's office when Belle had unintentionally announced it to him.

An assortment of events served, through the years, to recall it, the way symptoms in the throat announce the approach of a general systemic infection.

For example, there was Bobbie's fight in the school yard when he was in the second grade.

Cory saw most of the mix-up. Driving homeward from an errand in Boda, he and Gordon stopped to pick up Bobbie from his play after school. From where the car was parked, they could see some boys darting back and forth beyond the schoolhouse, dodging, turning, skidding in the grass, swinging at each other in what seemed to be a game of tag. Then Glen Horstman chased Bobbie down into the corner by the well. Bobbie backed into the hedge separating the school yard from a cornfield. He sparred away the jabs and pokes the bigger boy aimed at him. It looked as if both boys were laughing breathlessly, having a lot of fun.

They saw Glen Horstman feint a kick and follow the feint with a blow of his fist that started Bobbie's nose bleeding. Bobbie signaled that he'd had enough: *Lay off. I surrender*.

Glen kept punching. He had knocked Bobbie to the ground and was sitting on him when Gordon leaped the ditch and went running to the rescue.

Laggardly, Cory followed. He was only a few steps from the car when he saw Gordon chase Glen into the schoolhouse.

"Gordon!" he commanded.

Gordon stopped on the wooden stairs by the door and turned. His face was quizzical and angry. "Why, I'll just knock *him* around a little bit," he said.

"No, you won't," Cory told him. "You and Bobbie come on and get in the car now. Bobbie'd better wash his face at the pump."

"But he's bigger than Bobbie," Gordon said. He blushed because he did not want to mention that Bobbie lacked one hand to use in self-defense.

"Get in the car!" Cory shouted.

All the way home from the schoolhouse, Gordon sat in incredulous, wounded silence. Bobbie, though, was talkative enough. He wasn't in any pain from his beating. He wasn't really mad at Glen Horstman. Now that it was over, the fight seemed to him a pure entertainment.

But that, as Gordon's silence implied, was not all that must be taken into account. On almost any other day he would have been there at school to protect his brother. At least, without his father's inexplicable attitude to reckon with, he would have known what he ought to do tomorrow.

After supper, Gordon went to his mother about what had happened. She, in turn, spoke furiously to Cory as soon as the boys were in bed.

"I think I'd just better get on the telephone and find out from his teacher if this has ever happened before—the kids picking on Bobbie. I won't have it. Just because he's crippled—"

"Aw, Belle, that wasn't why Glen done it. They was playing and he got carried away."

"Playing? Gordon said he hit Bobbie with his fist. He was sitting on him, pounding his head, and you didn't . . ." She didn't say what Cory should have done that he had omitted, but she shook her head bitterly. The more she thought, the more worked up she got.

"Well, you go ahead and call the teacher if you want to put your nose in it," Cory growled.

"I *will* put my nose in it," she said, "and you'd better go over to the Horstmans' place and have a little talk with Glen's dad, because I don't intend to have this kind of thing going on, whatever you intend."

"But Bobbie wouldn't want—"

"You can drive me over and sit in the car while I go in and have it out with them," she raged. "You can sit in the car if you're scared to tell Ralph Horstman we want this stopped."

The Horstman farm was less than a two-mile drive. Through the spring night and the murmur of a rainy wind, Cory drove slowly, telling himself that of course Belle was right. He sighed heavily and thought he'd want his friends who lived around him to come and tell him about it if one of his boys had done a wrong. But he seldom felt so uneasy about anything as he did walking in under the elms of the Horstman yard and knocking at the screen door of the back porch.

"He what? Glen done *what?*" Ralph Horstman bellowed. He grabbed Cory's shoulder and dragged him in from the back porch to the kitchen. "When'd he do that? This afternoon?" Horstman's throat began to swell rhythmically. He seemed to be growing taller and broader. "Mama, give Cory a cup of coffee or—some *beer!*" he shouted to his wife. Then he fled the kitchen, pounding up the stairway from the living room like a plow horse frenzied in a burning building.

Cory and Mrs. Horstman heard the thump of a body dumped from its bed onto the floor and then a long, sleepy, uninterrupted wail, accompanied irregularly by the sound of slaps. In a minute Mrs. Horstman ran upstairs, too.

More slaps then. A more complicated sound of struggle began as the woman tried to mediate. Again and again, like the boom of outraged justice itself, Ralph Horstman's voice shouted, "He hit li'l Bobbie!"

After the condemnation, the smack of a hand on a rump, and then the woman's plea, seeming only to convince her husband that she had not understood the enormity of the offense. "But he hit li'l Bobbie!"

Downstairs Cory listened in what he could no longer doubt was envy. He knew well enough what he had no wish and no way of explaining to Gordon or Belle—that when he had seen Glen Horstman's fist bring blood from Bobbie's nose, he had felt a merciless identification with the aggressor. He had been unmanned by the recognition.

He had not wanted Bobbie hurt. No! He had never wanted Bobbie hurt, but he had seen his own act reenacted and known himself as powerless to prevent the pain as before.

But Glen Horstman, because he was a little boy, could be punished for what was, after all, a small offense. Cory, for his immeasurably greater offense, could expect no such squaring of accounts.

Afterward, each time his guilt flared in his face, he had to endure it in the same way until, mysteriously, it faded in his mind again—not dead, not even eroded by the remorse he had paid for it, merely waiting to be wakened again and endured again like an operation submitted to without anesthetic because, though he was guilty, no one owed him punishment.

He was punished. In the last year of the war, Gordon had just been drafted and sent to Fort Bragg when Joe was killed near Okinawa. By that time Joe was a seaman first class serving on a destroyer escort.

The DE was on picket duty about seventy miles east of Buckner Bay[3] when it was attacked by a George fighter. The attack occurred near sundown. A broad highway of gold and choppy crimson opened away from the little ship toward the west. The fighter came down this road like an erratic spark of gallantry and panic, hurled without conscious aim. The big ring sights on Joe's 20-mm cannon must have circumscribed the sun itself as he swung it over to defend the ship. The fighter struck just abaft and below the bridge. The ship lived for several hours more, time enough for the survivors to be transferred to a destroyer. None of Joe's shipmates saw him or his body after the attack.

When the news came to the Johnson farm, Cory wept like any father bereft. And his tears were partly tears of relief, for it seemed to him in the first debility of sorrow that this extravagant punishment might, at last, pay off his guilt. It was not even in his heart to protest that the payment was too great, though he saw no equivalence between the hand he had taken from one child and the life he must now yield helplessly back to darkness. If he was quits, he must be satisfied.

But when his grief diminished and his strength returned, Cory saw that whatever had happened to Joe had nothing to do with his old guilt, which was neither increased nor minimized by Joe's death. What little religion Cory had kept through the years melted with this discovery. Religion seemed foolish to him now, a windy pretense at linking things that had no real connection. The issue was between himself and a chaos to which only a fool would pray.

He had nothing with which to replace religion. His irregular and shallow enthusiasm for science had long since vanished of its own inanity. Besides, though science had once seemed to him "the coming thing," he had never been notified that science might pretend to explain what he thirsted terribly to know. It had been fun to read about the novelties science discovered. He had got bored. That was all.

In his whole life, as he could look back at it now, only one condition had given meaning to his work and the depressions or satisfactions that went with it. That condition was his fatherhood. Even if he had fathered his boys more or less accidentally, in lust, in lukewarm fondness for his wife, his fatherhood had come to be more than the sum of days and of forgotten wishes. Before anything else, he was a father—and it was against this definition of himself that he had been forced to strike that day in the corncrib.

Belle died in 1950. Cory wept for her, too; envied her, too, for he suspected she must have carried through life some secret, like his,

3. The American name for the Okinawa bay, honoring General Simon Bolivar Buckner, Jr. (1886–1945), killed during the battle of Okinawa. *George fighter:* U.S. code name for a late model of Japanese aircraft.

of undiminishable guilt for rebellion against the self that time and accident had given her. But now she was free of it.

They said Cory's mind began to fail him after Belle's death.

His mind was working better than ever—and he understood that was what his family and Doctor Grant *meant,* though they had to express themselves by an exact inversion of the truth.

If they had said he was troublesome and a bit frightening to live with, he could have agreed straightforwardly. But they needed more than that. Like most people, they needed a shallow burrow of "reasons" and "explanations" because they dared not deal with a sheer, objective fact. He could no longer live on their sort of explanations, but he sympathized with them. So he said, Yes, he reckoned his mind was going back on him. He didn't want to be a trouble to them, and if he couldn't straighten up by himself, he would certainly do what Doctor Grant recommended. He would go to the asylum "for a while." In the meantime, while they gave him a chance, he wanted to carry on his share of the work on the farm.

In this period there were five of the family living together there. Cory, Bobbie and his wife Lucy, and their little boy Ed (after Lucy's father), and Cory, Jr. Between them, Bobbie and Cory, Jr., could just about take care of the farm work. Bobbie had been to Ag school at the state university and he was a fine manager, very good with bookwork and planning ahead about the crops and machinery and soil, and figuring how they could afford the new things they needed. Farm work was more and more a matter of business brains these days, and he was sure that Bobbie was all right in that department.

Bobbie had got himself a new device to use for a right hand, too, now that they could afford it. There had been so much more money coming in during and after the war! Now you take Joe, Cory would tell himself, we just couldn't have afforded to send him to the university, Mother and I, back when he might have wanted to go. Then, quicker than anyone else could have reminded him that Joe was not a great one for study or using his brain, Cory would throw in that very qualification and go on: Yes, but things are getting so well-organized that they can take a boy who's not so bright to begin with and kind of guide him over the hurdles and give him remedial work and guide him into the right niche and he does all right! This was the way Cory's mind went on and on in an endless series of examinations and connections. His mind was far from failing. It dealt with more all the time, and insofar as the mind alone was concerned, it was dealing more effectively. The sickness was elsewhere.

What Bobbie had was too grand and clever to be called a hook, though he good-humoredly called it that on weekdays. On Sundays, for fun, he called it a prosthesis. It was really three hooks and a bar, all with a bright chromium finish that twinkled wonderfully in the May morning sun when the young man swung himself up onto the tractor seat and headed out to the fields, while Lucy held little Ed and waved to him from the back door.

It was so strange, sometimes, to Cory to see that shiny batch of levered claws on the baby's back when Bobbie was holding him—as at the homecoming picnic in Boda when there was a crowd and the Johnsons drove in to see all their old friends come back to this hick town. Gordon was with them, too, on that occasion, visiting a week from his job in Seattle, where he'd remained with an opportunity after the service.

That *thing* on the baby's back would look just as firm and tender as a human hand. Odd how Bobbie could use it to caress with sometimes, as if it were alive, though of course it had no sense of touch. It could express feeling though it had none. The only time the baby minded being touched with it was in cold weather. But Cory's thoughts were often busy on conjectures as to whether the baby *ought* to mind being touched by the lifeless thing. No end to considerations involved there.

With his prosthesis Bobbie could manage nearly any chore on the farm. No doubt if worst came to worst, everything could be handled without hired help if Cory went away. But Cory had made his place, now that the boys were taking over so much, by doing the dirty and menial jobs that their machinery still left undone. True, they had a milker, and even Cory, Jr., could handle the milking of their twelve cows without complaining he had been put upon. Someone still had to shovel up after the stock. The boys rented a corn picker from the elevator in Boda for the corn shucking. Someone had to drive the tractor into town through a November rain to get the picker and see that it got back on schedule. Cory always did jobs like that.

Doctor Grant didn't like it much that Cory should make himself into a nigger—that was his word—for the boys. As he saw it, this was another symptom of Cory's mental deterioration. But the doctor's opinion on this account was only one way of looking at it, and Cory was very well aware of this.

He realized that quite aside from any help he gave with the work or any hardship he imposed on Lucy by giving her another mouth to cook for, he *worried* his family.

He was sorry for this, but deliberately he went ahead with his alarming and aberrant courses. In the winter of 1952 he spent part of every day in the corncrib, where he was reconstructing the corn sheller that used to stand in the corner room. He scoured the neighborhood and the junk piles around Boda for old parts. He rebuilt the wooden frame where the electric motor had sat. He drilled bolt holes in the concrete floor he and Gordon had poured back in wartime when they junked the old sheller. He begged some secondhand lumber from people who had moved onto the Horstman farm, not wanting to spend any more good money than he had to on his "foolishness."

It took Bobbie less than a week to figure out what his father was doing—a little longer to decide to intervene. Then one morning he made a point of sauntering down to the crib and entering the room where his father was hammering and sweating.

"What you up to?" Bobbie said. "I thought since I didn't have much to do this morning, maybe I could . . ."

The brightness and pretense—from both sides—faded quickly enough. A reckless pity shone from Bobbie's face. He wet his lips.

"Dad, you're making that sheller again, isn't that it?"

"Well, Bobbie, yeah, I thought I'd run her up again and see if maybe I could improve the design. Like you say, there's not too awful much work to be done these days, though maybe I ought to be down at the barn having a look at that loader Cory broke last summer." He started to leave the room.

Bobbie stopped him. "I didn't mean that, Dad. You don't have to work every minute. But—but, it seems kind of useless for you to be making a sheller."

"Yeah, it does."

"Then—"

"It kind of—"

"Dad, Lucy and I've been talking and want you to, well, go out to Seattle and see Gordon awhile. You keep saying it would cost too much, and Seattle's a big place if you don't want to stay with Gordon. Look, I'm going to come right out with it. Lucy and I don't feel right for having called Doctor Grant in on you. Doctors don't know everything. But a family is different, and I know that Gordon would want you to come."

"—kind of helps me think things out," Cory said mildly, touching the homely machine he was building. "I'm not a hand like you are to put things down on paper or in words, either, and if I can build something to see, that helps with my brain work."

Bobbie gritted his teeth. "But you're thinking about things you ought to leave alone," he said. He held up his claw, glittering and lightly sweating in the cold room. "You're brooding about *this* again. For my sake, leave it alone. You think all my life I've blamed you somehow and I haven't. Can't you believe me when I say it? You *saved* my life and everyone knows that."

"I don't know," Cory said. "Maybe there was some other way to do it."

"*Was!*" The horror of that exploded syllable stood with them like the angel of death. What had been in time was not, any longer, in time. The past was unalterable, and yet they could not shake from their minds the illusion of free choice.

"I've had a good life," Bobbie said—as if that bore on the enigma that Cory wrestled. He might have had *another* life if his father had been the man to find another means of saving him. "What more could I want? I've been happy," Bobbie said.

"I know, son," Cory answered. "What I'll do, I'll get the pickup this afternoon and carry this junk down in the east forty and dump it. Guess I'd better save the lumber and use it for kindling."

Bobbie snarled in his frustration. "You don't have to do *that,* Dad. You don't have to do anything I tell you or anything for my sake. That's the point. Don't you get it?"

"Sure I see what you mean," Cory said. "I wasn't thinking about how you—and Lucy, I suppose—would feel about this contraption. Now let's just walk up to the house for some coffee and I'll tell Lucy I'm sorry I started it."

Bobbie said, "Maybe you'd better not mention it to her."

"All right," Cory said. "Whatever you think is best."

The next morning he was working on the sheller again. He had got to the point of installing the gears and covering them with a steel safety box.

Probably his queer behavior and his family's concern with it had been going on longer than he realized. Because they cared for him they would have taken what pains they could not to let him notice their precautions. Noting their few failures to be discreet was like seeing an advance guard of rats begin to invade the farm. Experience had convinced him that if you saw only the signs of depredation, that meant there were ten rats around your buildings. If you saw one rat, that meant a hundred. If you saw two together, a thousand, probably.

Now, to all his other considerations, he added the task of measuring the impressions he made each day on Lucy, Bobbie, and Cory, Jr. Like a stock-market gambler he read the daily quotations of his stock with them. Better this afternoon. Low and worried this week. Cautious. Desperate. Better. Better. The same.

They could not bring themselves to wound him by flat and final decisions in his behalf. If Bobbie had really insisted, Cory would have packed and gone to Seattle. Probably he would never have come back from that city.

At the same time, he realized that he confused their impressions by the very act of measuring them. And if their sanity wavered to the magnetism of his craziness—as he saw it did—then how could he trust them for reliable guidance, even in what he ought to do?

He understood, sometime during 1953, that they had been cautioned by Doctor Grant—or another authority they might have consulted at Grant's recommendation—to be on the lookout for a suicide attempt. He knew this first by subtle signs, as he would have known about a family of rats in the corncrib before he saw the first darting black shape and prepared for a campaign of poison and traps. The subtle signs were followed by a blunder so loving and crude it made him weep.

One morning he found that his straight razor had disappeared from the cabinet in the bathroom and had been replaced with an electric shaver. The exchange had been made just one week before Christmas, and he knew the electric gadget had been bought as a present for him. In their anxiety they had been unable to wait.

He picked up the shaver without hesitation. He accepted whatever Lucy and Bobbie (or was it Lucy alone, weaker in her fear, who had made the switch?) thought had to be done. He put the plug into an outlet and set the humming head to his cheek. He saw his cowed eyes under the windburnt sag of lids. It seemed to him his courage was not adequate to his pity.

"Father," he said, as he used to pray in the time he had not taken religion seriously enough to reject it. "Father." He heard no distinct syllables, but a shapeless groan.

The futility of their gesture seemed unendurable. They had taken his razor—didn't these children know that, on a farm, as Belle's Dad had put it, the means to harm were never lacking? He supposed they had hidden away the shells for his pump gun, too, though he had not bothered to check for some time. Odds and ends of rope had probably been gathered from the barn and outbuildings (by Bobbie, careful not to let on to Cory, Jr., why he was being so neat these days). They probably timed his comings and goings, not to permit him to be too long alone. And what good would all that do if he could claim the right to kill himself?

To put their minds at ease he wanted to go to them now and tell them how he had once determined to do away with himself and why that was all past. The occasion had come soon after Joe's death. The absence of the coffin from the funeral services had served as a reminder of the absence of justice due from the empty heavens. That had been more than eight years ago. No one had worried then about gathering up ropes from the sheds, garage, or barn.

He had put a rope around his neck one morning before anyone else was out of bed, standing by the square opening in the floor of the haymow. There was enough light at that hour to show the churchlike vaulting of rafters in the empty mow. Nothing had ever tempted him more seductively than the black square in front of his toes.

But he had taken the rope off with the slow deliberation of a judge—not for a moment assuming that he was granting himself reprieve, but that in all solemnity he was refusing it. Self-execution was inappropriate to his guilt.

Well—of course he must not go to the children and tell them what he remembered of that morning. He was poor with words; he was more likely to scare them than to appease them. They weren't prepared to understand that what he had sentenced himself to that morning in the barn was *to think*. Under that sentence, he was obliged to respect all the problems raised whenever he was rash enough to solve one of them.

He had to think, though it was not easy for him. It was not easy to rid the farm of a pestilence of rats, either, but, again and again through his years on this place, he had set himself the task of poisoning and trapping creatures who had over him the advantages of number, secrecy, and natures that recognized no obligation except to exist. He supposed there had never been a day when the farm was free of rats. Yet, by unwavering persistence he had thinned the rat population again and again to the point at which it was tolerable.

It wasn't easy for him to get ahead of the problem he now presented to his anxious children, but he set himself to find how to make it easier for them.

Through that spring and much of the following summer he appeared to be succeeding. The cycles of compulsive thought that had made him careless of his behavior since Belle's death sped faster—of necessity—as they seemed to settle down into the tranquillity of age. Once upon a time he would have refused to believe himself capable of the nimble calculations that now became a commonplace.

He gave up working on the sheller in the corncrib—because he had now got the whole material apparatus in his mind, from the grain of old wood to the bolts that fastened the electric motor to its bench, the pulleys and flywheel and their weight, strength, appearance, sound, and speed—all of this so completely transposed into an image that he could set the machine going in his imagination whenever he wanted. While he helped his youngest son with homework, or went over the accounts with Bobbie, or listened attentively to Lucy's frets about her new pregnancy, another part of his mind could repeat the crucial morning of his life.

So his family thought him better. They said he was "more himself" than he had been for years. They noticed how he gave up a share of the meanest work to each of his boys. Sometimes now he talked voluntarily of going to visit Gordon.

They were glad, again, to invert the truth. He saw that this second inversion did not cancel out the first—when they had believed him mad—but only made it incalculably more difficult to encompass, as if an already insoluble labyrinth should suddenly open out into its duplicate.

World without end, the world of thought that seemed bent on returning to some safe, lost starting point; but the prospect of its difficulty neither cheered nor daunted him. While he had strength of mind, he would go on as best he could, pretending that he was a juggler, an explorer, an acrobat, though he was only a big-footed farmer. At least he had learned to pace himself in his pursuit of multiplying complications. He had learned not to try too much at once. He was glad to think this adjusted pace—whether it meant success or failure to him—comforted his family.

One night in late summer he reached the end of thought. He had not foreseen (as a man with greater original gifts might have) that there could be an end of it. But there it was, confronting him. What had been a constantly accelerating series of wheels within wheels, wheels begetting wheels, a spinning and a spiraling that multiplied and exploded toward the ultimate horizons—all that was frozen in an instant into what seemed to him an immense sphere of light, motionless, achieved.

On the night it happened he was alone on the farm except for his grandson, who was sleeping upstairs. At suppertime Lucy had said with unusual petulance that she probably wouldn't get to go anywhere again for months or see any of their friends. The new baby was due soon. She would be tied down permanently after its arrival, so why didn't Bobbie take her anyplace any more?

Since he had been working hard in the hayfield all day, Bobbie might have snapped back at her. But Cory smoothed things over. He suggested that they drive through Boda to the county seat and find a place to dance or go to a movie. He was kind of tired himself, but would be glad to bathe Ed and read him a story and let him watch TV awhile before he went to bed.

Then Cory, Jr., had popped up and said he wanted to go along, too, and again there had been the threat of friction that Cory had to deflate judiciously. Why didn't young Cory ride just as far as Boda, he suggested, and drop off there to see some of his buddies? He could stay all night with Mickey Carnahan if he wanted, as a reward for working so well all day.

Cory had eased them away smoothly. The three young people left the farm after supper in a jolly mood. Young Ed had turned out to be no trouble at all. He nodded in front of the TV and went to bed early.

It was still not altogether dark when Cory took his cigar onto the screen porch to sit on the glider and do some thinking. On quiet evenings, left alone, he felt able to catch up on the arrears in his thought.

The night was faintly oppressive, though mild. He could hear the tree frogs dinning in the yard and the chug of the pump down by the barn. He heard the intermittent traffic of his neighbors going in late to Boda or the county seat, most of them traveling the new blacktop.

He thought about the highway and his neighbors and the way things had changed and the way things had been before. He thought, without emotion, of the difference between the blacktop and the muddy gravel he had charged through the day he cut off Bobbie's hand. Then he thought of the real sheller that had caused the accident and of the imaginary sheller that had duplicated it in his mind. And presently he was sure as could be that the sheller he imagined was run by the same principles that had run the sheller made of wood and steel. His creation and he were indistinguishable.

With that realization he reached the end of thought, knowing neither good nor evil but only guilt. The tree frogs, perhaps, continued their monotonous, hysterical song in the dark leaves around him. There may have been a continuing traffic on the roads and the sound of the pump's piston beating back and forth in its imprisoning cylinder. He did not hear them. Whatever existed was silent and motionless. Eternal. As it had been and as it would be when time ended.

In that silence he rose from the soft glider and let himself out the screen door onto the grass of the yard. He walked, without needing a light, to the shed by the back gate. The motion of his body was fluent and easy, but he felt nothing. It seemed to him that he was constituted of the same material as Bobbie's well-wrought hook and had been able, like it, to express love without the ability of knowing it. (The proposition was the same if exactly reversed: to know love without the ability to express it.) The only passion remaining was for a justice that would bring a man in phase with the total equilibrium of the night.

From the shed he took a short ax and went upstairs to his grandson's bedroom. He came down a little later without it.

He sat in the glider and relit his cigar. After a while he found himself straining to hear the tree frogs. To hear anything. Because he was not dead he had to break the motionless, soundless sphere of the thoughtless universe. He needed a noise to start him thinking again.

It was peaceful enough not to think—just to suck on the sweet cigar and let it all go up in a gentle exhalation. But he had to resume, if he could, the pain of thought so he could review what he had done in that silence when the sound of machinery stopped.

He had to plan the right way to present his act, or all those folks who relied on explanations would refuse to believe him sane. If they did not believe him sane, they would not punish him for this repetition of his guilt, and if he could not trick those who ought to love him into responsibility for a just punishment, then there was no hope for him in all this vast gleam of silence.

---

1. If the guilt of Cory Johnson is not legal guilt, how is it to be characterized?
2. Is Cory's "thinking" deformed by his lack of formal education? What might he have got from formal education that would have given a different direction to his thought?
3. Why are the minor characters unable to reach Cory and persuade him to accept what has happened?
4. What is the meaning of the episode in which Bobbie is beaten in a schoolyard fight?
5. What does the story say about justice and the human hunger for it?

Willa Cather

Cather (1873–1947) was born of Anglo-Irish parents in Back Creek Valley, Virginia. At ten she moved with her family to Red Cloud, Nebraska, where she grew up, exploring the prairies on horseback and making friends with the immigrant farmers of the area. While she worked her way through the University of Nebraska, she acquired an enduring passion for music and determined to devote her energies to writing. From 1896 to 1905 she worked for a newspaper in Pittsburgh and later held editorial positions in New York, but her poetry and fiction looked to the Midwest and Southwest for their subject matters and to the depths of the American past for their values. She never married. The last part of her life was spent in New York, with occasional European travels that never swayed her from nostalgia or the conservatism of her views. Once she declared that the world had "broken apart" about 1922; unmistakably she preferred the manners, styles, and virtues that prevailed before that date. Among her novels are My Antonia *(1918),* A Lost Lady *(1923),* The Professor's House *(1925), and* Death Comes for the Archbishop *(1927).* Not under Forty *(1936) contains many of her essays. Her collections of short stories are* Youth and the Bright Medusa *(1920),* Obscure Destinies *(1932), and* The Old Beauty and Others *(1948).*

Paul's Case

A *Study in Temperament*

It was Paul's afternoon to appear before the faculty of the Pittsburgh High School to account for his various misdemeanors. He had been suspended a week ago, and his father had called at the Principal's office and confessed his perplexity about his son. Paul entered the faculty room suave and smiling. His clothes were a trifle outgrown, and the tan velvet on the collar of his open overcoat was frayed and worn; but for all that there was something of the dandy about him, and he wore an opal pin in his neatly knotted black four-in-hand,[1] and a red carnation in his buttonhole. This latter adornment the faculty somehow felt was not properly significant of the contrite spirit befitting a boy under the ban of suspension.

Paul was tall for his age and very thin, with high, cramped shoul-

1. The long necktie we are now familiar with.

ders and a narrow chest. His eyes were remarkable for a certain hysterical brilliancy, and he continually used them in a conscious, theatrical sort of way, peculiarly offensive in a boy. The pupils were abnormally large, as though he were addicted to belladonna, but there was a glassy glitter about them which that drug does not produce.

When questioned by the Principal as to why he was there Paul stated, politely enough, that he wanted to come back to school. This was a lie, but Paul was quite accustomed to lying; found it, indeed, indispensable for overcoming friction. His teachers were asked to state their respective charges against him, which they did with such a rancor and aggrievedness as evinced that this was not a usual case. Disorder and impertinence were among the offenses named, yet each of his instructors felt that it was scarcely possible to put into words the real cause of the trouble, which lay in a sort of hysterically defiant manner of the boy's; in the contempt which they all knew he felt for them, and which he seemingly made not the least effort to conceal. Once, when he had been making a synopsis of a paragraph at the blackboard, his English teacher had stepped to his side and attempted to guide his hand. Paul had started back with a shudder and thrust his hands violently behind him. The astonished woman could scarcely have been more hurt and embarrassed had he struck at her. The insult was so involuntary and definitely personal as to be unforgettable. In one way and another he had made all his teachers, men and women alike, conscious of the same feeling of physical aversion. In one class he habitually sat with his hand shading his eyes; in another he always looked out of the window during the recitation; in another he made a running commentary on the lecture, with humorous intention.

His teachers felt this afternoon that his whole attitude was symbolized by his shrug and his flippantly red carnation flower, and they fell upon him without mercy, his English teacher leading the pack. He stood through it smiling, his pale lips parted over his white teeth. (His lips were continually twitching, and he had a habit of raising his eyebrows that was contemptuous and irritating to the last degree.) Older boys than Paul had broken down and shed tears under that baptism of fire, but his set smile did not once desert him, and his only sign of discomfort was the nervous trembling of the fingers that toyed with the buttons of his overcoat, and an occasional jerking of the other hand that held his hat. Paul was always smiling, always glancing about him, seeming to feel that people might be watching him and trying to detect something. This conscious expression, since it was as far as possible from boyish mirthfulness, was usually attributed to insolence or "smartness."

As the inquisition proceeded one of his instructors repeated an impertinent remark of the boy's, and the Principal asked him whether he thought that a courteous speech to have made a woman. Paul shrugged his shoulders slightly and his eyebrows twitched.

"I don't know," he replied. "I didn't mean to be polite or impolite, either. I guess it's a sort of way I have of saying things regardless."

The Principal, who was a sympathetic man, asked him whether he didn't think that a way it would be well to get rid of. Paul grinned and said he guessed so. When he was told that he could go he bowed gracefully and went out. His bow was but a repetition of the scandalous red carnation.

His teachers were in despair, and his drawing master voiced the feeling of them all when he declared there was something about the boy which none of them understood. He added: "I don't really believe that smile of his comes altogether from insolence; there's something sort of haunted about it. The boy is not strong, for one thing. I happen to know that he was born in Colorado, only a few months before his mother died out there of a long illness. There is something wrong about the fellow."

The drawing master had come to realize that, in looking at Paul, one saw only his white teeth and the forced animation of his eyes. One warm afternoon the boy had gone to sleep at his drawing board, and his master had noted with amazement what a white, blue-veined face it was; drawn and wrinkled like an old man's about the eyes, the lips twitching even in his sleep, and stiff with a nervous tension that drew them back from his teeth.

His teachers left the building dissatisfied and unhappy; humiliated to have felt so vindictive toward a mere boy, to have uttered this feeling in cutting terms, and to have set each other on, as it were, in the gruesome game of intemperate reproach. Some of them remembered having seen a miserable street cat set at bay by a ring of tormentors.

As for Paul, he ran down the hill whistling the "Soldiers' Chorus" from *Faust*,[2] looking wildly behind him now and then to see whether some of his teachers were not there to writhe under his lightheartedness. As it was now late in the afternoon and Paul was on duty that evening as usher at Carnegie Hall,[3] he decided that he would not go home to supper. When he reached the concert hall the doors were not yet open and, as it was chilly outside, he decided to go up into the picture gallery—always deserted at this hour—where there were some of Raffelli's[4] gay studies of Paris streets and an airy blue Venetian scene or two that always exhilarated him. He was delighted to find no one in the gallery but the old guard, who sat in one corner, a newspaper on

2. Opera by Charles Gounod (1818–1893). 3. Named for Andrew Carnegie (1835–1919), famous industrialist and philanthropist. 4. Jean-François Raffaelli (1850–1924), French painter, sculptor, and etcher.

his knee, a black patch over one eye and the other closed. Paul possessed himself of the place and walked confidently up and down, whistling under his breath. After a while he sat down before a blue Rico[5] and lost himself. When he bethought him to look at his watch, it was after seven o'clock, and he rose with a start and ran downstairs, making a face at Augustus, peering out from the cast room, and an evil gesture at the Venus de Milo[6] as he passed her on the stairway.

When Paul reached the ushers' dressing room half a dozen boys were there already, and he began excitedly to tumble into his uniform. It was one of the few that at all approached fitting, and Paul thought it very becoming—though he knew that the tight, straight coat accentuated his narrow chest, about which he was exceedingly sensitive. He was always considerably excited while he dressed, twanging all over to the tuning of the strings and the preliminary flourishes of the horns in the music room; but tonight he seemed quite beside himself, and he teased and plagued the boys until, telling him that he was crazy, they put him down on the floor and sat on him.

Somewhat calmed by his suppression, Paul dashed out to the front of the house to seat the early comers. He was a model usher; gracious and smiling he ran up and down the aisles; nothing was too much trouble for him; he carried messages and brought programs as though it were his greatest pleasure in life, and all the people in his section thought him a charming boy, feeling that he remembered and admired them. As the house filled, he grew more and more vivacious and animated, and the color came to his cheeks and lips. It was very much as though this were a great reception and Paul were the host. Just as the musicians came out to take their places, his English teacher arrived with checks for the seats which a prominent manufacturer had taken for the season. She betrayed some embarrassment when she handed Paul the tickets, and a hauteur which subsequently made her feel very foolish. Paul was startled for a moment, and had the feeling of wanting to put her out; what business had she here among all these fine people and gay colors? He looked her over and decided that she was not appropriately dressed and must be a fool to sit downstairs in such togs. The tickets had probably been sent her out of kindness, he reflected as he put down a seat for her, and she had about as much right to sit there as he had.

When the symphony began Paul sank into one of the rear seats with a long sigh of relief, and lost himself, as he had done before the Rico. It was not that symphonies, as such, meant anything in particular to Paul, but the first sigh of the instruments seemed to free some hilar-

5. Andreas Rico (1500–1550), Cretan-Italian painter. 6. A famous Greek statue; the original is in the Louvre, Paris. Augustus (63 B.C.–14 A.D.) was the first Roman emperor.

ious and potent spirit within him; something that struggled there like the genie in the bottle found by the Arab fisherman.[7] He felt a sudden zest of life; the lights danced before his eyes and the concert hall blazed into unimaginable splendor. When the soprano soloist came on Paul forgot even the nastiness of his teacher's being there and gave himself up to the peculiar stimulus such personages always had for him. The soloist chanced to be a German woman, by no means in her first youth, and the mother of many children; but she wore an elaborate gown and tiara, and above all she had that indefinable air of achievement, that worldshine upon her, which, in Paul's eyes, made her a veritable queen of Romance.

After a concert was over Paul was always irritable and wretched until he got to sleep, and tonight he was even more than usually restless. He had the feeling of not being able to let down, of its being impossible to give up this delicious excitement which was the only thing that could be called living at all. During the last number he withdrew and, after hastily changing his clothes in the dressing room, slipped out to the side door where the soprano's carriage stood. Here he began pacing rapidly up and down the walk, waiting to see her come out.

Over yonder, the Schenley, in its vacant stretch, loomed big and square through the fine rain, the windows of its twelve stories glowing like those of a lighted cardboard house under a Christmas tree. All the actors and singers of the better class stayed there when they were in the city, and a number of the big manufacturers of the place lived there in the winter. Paul had often hung about the hotel, watching the people go in and out, longing to enter and leave schoolmasters and dull care behind him forever.

At last the singer came out, accompanied by the conductor, who helped her into her carriage and closed the door with a cordial *auf wiedersehen*[8] which set Paul to wondering whether she were not an old sweetheart of his. Paul followed the carriage over to the hotel, walking so rapidly as not to be far from the entrance when the singer alighted, and disappeared behind the swinging glass doors that were opened by a Negro in a tall hat and a long coat. In the moment that the door was ajar it seemed to Paul that he, too, entered. He seemed to feel himself go after her up the steps, into the warm, lighted building, into an exotic, tropical world of shiny, glistening surfaces and basking ease. He reflected upon the mysterious dishes that were brought into the dining room, the green bottles in buckets of ice, as he had seen

7. In one of the tales of the *Arabian Nights* (also called *Thousand and One Nights*), the fisherman Ali Baba finds a genie imprisoned in a bottle who is able to perform miracles. 8. Good-by.

them in the supper party pictures of the *Sunday World* supplement. A quick gust of wind brought the rain down with sudden vehemence, and Paul was startled to find that he was still outside in the slush of the gravel driveway; that his boots were letting in the water and his scanty overcoat was clinging wet about him; that the lights in front of the concert hall were out and that the rain was driving in sheets between him and the orange glow of the windows above him. There it was, what he wanted—tangibly before him, like the fairy world of a Christmas pantomime—but mocking spirits stood guard at the doors, and, as the rain beat in his face, Paul wondered whether he were destined always to shiver in the black night outside, looking up at it.

He turned and walked reluctantly toward the car[9] tracks. The end had to come sometime; his father in his nightclothes at the top of the stairs, explanations that did not explain, hastily improvised fictions that were forever tripping him up, his upstairs room and its horrible yellow wallpaper, the creaking bureau with the greasy plush collarbox, and over his painted wooden bed the pictures of George Washington and John Calvin,[1] and the framed motto, "Feed my Lambs," which had been worked in red worsted by his mother.

Half an hour later Paul alighted from his car and went slowly down one of the side streets off the main thoroughfare. It was a highly respectable street, where all the houses were exactly alike, and where businessmen of moderate means begot and reared large families of children, all of whom went to Sabbath school and learned the shorter catechism, and were interested in arithmetic; all of whom were as exactly alike as their homes, and of a piece with the monotony in which they lived. Paul never went up Cordelia Street without a shudder of loathing. His home was next to the house of the Cumberland[2] minister. He approached it tonight with the nerveless sense of defeat, the hopeless feeling of sinking back forever into ugliness and commonness that he had always had when he came home. The moment he turned into Cordelia Street he felt the waters close above his head. After each of these orgies of living he experienced all the physical depression which follows a debauch; the loathing of respectable beds, of common food, of a house penetrated by kitchen odors; a shuddering repulsion for the flavorless, colorless mass of everyday existence; a morbid desire for cool things and soft lights and fresh flowers.

The nearer he approached the house, the more absolutely unequal Paul felt to the sight of it all: his ugly sleeping chamber; the cold bathroom with the grimy zinc tub, the cracked mirror, the dripping spigots; his father, at the top of the stairs, his hairy legs sticking out from his

9. I.e., streetcar. 1. John Calvin (1509–1564), French Protestant reformer who lived in Geneva.
2. A division of the Presbyterian Church in the United States.

nightshirt, his feet thrust into carpet slippers. He was so much later than usual that there would certainly be inquiries and reproaches. Paul stopped short before the door. He felt that he could not be accosted by his father tonight; that he could not toss again on that miserable bed. He would not go in. He would tell his father that he had no carfare and it was raining so hard he had gone home with one of the boys and stayed all night.

Meanwhile, he was wet and cold. He went around to the back of the house and tried one of the basement windows, found it open, raised it cautiously, and scrambled down the cellar wall to the floor. There he stood, holding his breath, terrified by the noise he had made, but the floor above him was silent, and there was no creak on the stairs. He found a soapbox, and carried it over to the soft ring of light that streamed from the furnace door, and sat down. He was horribly afraid of rats, so he did not try to sleep, but sat looking distrustfully at the dark, still terrified lest he might have awakened his father. In such reactions, after one of the experiences which made days and nights out of the dreary blanks of the calendar, when his senses were deadened, Paul's head was always singularly clear. Suppose his father had heard him getting in at the window and had come down and shot him for a burglar? Then, again, suppose his father had come down, pistol in hand, and he had cried out in time to save himself, and his father had been horrified to think how nearly he had killed him? Then, again, suppose a day should come when his father would remember that night, and wish there had been no warning cry to stay his hand? With this last supposition Paul entertained himself until daybreak.

The following Sunday was fine; the sodden November chill was broken by the last flash of autumnal summer. In the morning Paul had to go to church and Sabbath school, as always. On seasonable Sunday afternoons the burghers of Cordelia Street always sat out on their front stoops and talked to their neighbors on the next stoop, or called to those across the street in neighborly fashion. The men usually sat on gay cushions placed upon the steps that led down to the sidewalk, while the women, in their Sunday "waists,"[3] sat in rockers on the cramped porches, pretending to be greatly at their ease. The children played in the streets; there were so many of them that the place resembled the recreation grounds of a kindergarten. The men on the steps—all in their shirt sleeves their vests unbuttoned—sat with their legs well apart, their stomachs comfortably protruding, and talked of the prices of things, or told anecdotes of the sagacity of their various chiefs and overlords. They occasionally looked over the multitude of squabbling children, listened affectionately to their high-pitched, nasal voices,

3. Bodices or blouses.

smiling to see their own proclivities reproduced in their offspring, and interspersed their legends of the iron kings[4] with remarks about their sons' progress at school, their grades in arithmetic, and the amounts they had saved in their toy banks.

On this last Sunday of November Paul sat all the afternoon on the lowest step of his stoop, staring into the street, while his sisters, in their rockers, were talking to the minister's daughters next door about how many shirtwaists they had made in the last week, and how many waffles someone had eaten at the last church supper. When the weather was warm, and his father was in a particularly jovial frame of mind, the girls made lemonade, which was always brought out in a red-glass pitcher, ornamented with forget-me-nots in blue enamel. This the girls thought very fine, and the neighbors always joked about the suspicious color of the pitcher.

Today Paul's father sat on the top step, talking to a young man who shifted a restless baby from knee to knee. He happened to be the young man who was daily held up to Paul as a model, and after whom it was his father's dearest hope that he would pattern. This young man was of a ruddy complexion, with a compressed, red mouth, and faded, nearsighted eyes, over which he wore thick spectacles, with gold bows that curved about his ears. He was clerk to one of the magnates of a great steel corporation, and was looked upon in Cordelia Street as a young man with a future. There was a story that, some five years ago—he was now barely twenty-six—he had been a trifle dissipated, but in order to curb his appetites and save the loss of time and strength that a sowing of wild oats might have entailed, he had taken his chief's advice, oft reiterated to his employees, and at twenty-one had married the first woman whom he could persuade to share his fortunes. She happened to be an angular schoolmistress, much older than he, who also wore thick glasses, and who had now borne him four children, all nearsighted, like herself.

The young man was relating how his chief, now cruising in the Mediterranean, kept in touch with all the details of the business, arranging his office hours on his yacht just as though he were at home, and "knocking off work enough to keep two stenographers busy." His father told, in turn, the plan his corporation was considering, of putting in an electric railway plant in Cairo. Paul snapped his teeth; he had an awful apprehension that they might spoil it all before he got there. Yet he rather liked to hear these legends of the iron kings that were told and retold on Sundays and holidays; these stories of palaces in Venice, yachts on the Mediterranean, and high play at Monte Carlo appealed to his fancy, and he was interested in the triumphs of these cash boys

4. Tycoons of the iron and steel industry.

who had become famous, though he had no mind for the cash-boy stage.

After supper was over and he had helped to dry the dishes, Paul nervously asked his father whether he could go to George's to get some help in his geometry, and still more nervously asked for carfare. This latter request he had to repeat, as his father, on principle, did not like to hear requests for money, whether much or little. He asked Paul whether he could not go to some boy who lived nearer, and told him that he ought not to leave his schoolwork until Sunday; but he gave him the dime. He was not a poor man, but he had a worthy ambition to come up in the world. His only reason for allowing Paul to usher was that he thought a boy ought to be earning a little.

Paul bounded upstairs, scrubbed the greasy odor of the dishwater from his hands with the ill-smelling soap he hated, and then shook over his fingers a few drops of violet water from the bottle he kept hidden in his drawer. He left the house with his geometry conspicuously under his arm, and the moment he got out of Cordelia Street and boarded a downtown car, he shook off the lethargy of two deadening days and began to live again.

The leading juvenile[5] of the permanent stock company which played at one of the downtown theaters was an acquaintance of Paul's, and the boy had been invited to drop in at the Sunday-night rehearsals whenever he could. For more than a year Paul had spent every available moment loitering about Charley Edwards's dressing room. He had won a place among Edwards's following not only because the young actor, who could not afford to employ a dresser, often found him useful, but because he recognized in Paul something akin to what churchmen term "vocation."

It was at the theater and at Carnegie Hall that Paul really lived; the rest was but a sleep and a forgetting. This was Paul's fairy tale, and it had for him all the allurement of a secret love. The moment he inhaled the gassy, painty, dusty odor behind the scenes, he breathed like a prisoner set free, and felt within him the possibility of doing or saying splendid, brilliant, poetic things. The moment the cracked orchestra beat out the overture from *Martha*, or jerked at the serenade from *Rigoletto*,[6] all stupid and ugly things slid from him, and his senses were deliciously, yet delicately fired.

Perhaps it was because, in Paul's world, the natural nearly always wore the guise of ugliness, that a certain element of artificiality seemed to him necessary in beauty. Perhaps it was because his experience of life elsewhere was so full of Sabbath-school picnics, petty economies,

5. Youthful male actor. 6. Operas by Friedrich von Flotow (1812–1883) and Giuseppe Verdi (1813–1901).

wholesome advice as to how to succeed in life, and the inescapable odors of cooking, that he found this existence so alluring, these smartly clad men and women so attractive, that he was so moved by these starry apple orchards that bloomed perennially under the limelight.

It would be difficult to put it strongly enough how convincingly the stage entrance of that theater was for Paul the actual portal of Romance. Certainly none of the company ever suspected it, least of all Charley Edwards. It was very like the old stories that used to float about London of fabulously rich Jews, who had subterranean halls there, with palms, and fountains, and soft lamps and richly appareled women who never saw the disenchanting light of London day. So, in the midst of that smoke-palled city, enamored of figures and grimy toil, Paul had his secret temple, his wishing carpet, his bit of blue-and-white Mediterranean shore bathed in perpetual sunshine.

Several of Paul's teachers had a theory that his imagination had been perverted by garish fiction but the truth was that he scarcely ever read at all. The books at home were not such as would either tempt or corrupt a youthful mind, and as for reading the novels that some of his friends urged upon him—well, he got what he wanted much more quickly from music; any sort of music, from an orchestra to a barrel organ. He needed only the spark, the indescribable thrill that made his imagination master of his senses, and he could make plots and pictures enough of his own. It was equally true that he was not stage-struck—not, at any rate, in the usual acceptation of that expression. He had no desire to become an actor, any more than he had to become a musician. He felt no necessity to do any of these things; what he wanted was to see, to be in the atmosphere, float on the wave of it, to be carried out, blue league after blue league, away from everything.

After a night behind the scenes Paul found the schoolroom more than ever repulsive; the bare floors and naked walls; the prosy men who never wore frock coats, or violets in their bottonholes; the women with their dull gowns, shrill voices, and pitiful seriousness about prepositions that govern the dative. He could not bear to have the other pupils think, for a moment, that he took these people seriously; he must convey to them that he considered it all trivial, and was there only by way of a jest, anyway. He had autographed pictures of all the members of the stock company which he showed his classmates, telling them the most incredible stories of his familiarity with these people, of his acquaintance with the soloists who came to Carnegie Hall, his suppers with them and the flowers he sent them. When these stories lost their effect, and his audience grew listless, he became desperate and would bid all the boys good-by, announcing that he was going to travel for a while; going to Naples, to Venice, to Egypt. Then, next

Monday, he would slip back, conscious and nervously smiling; his sister was ill, and he should have to defer his voyage until spring.

Matters went steadily worse with Paul at school. In the itch to let his instructors know how heartily he despised them and their homilies, and how thoroughly he was appreciated elsewhere, he mentioned once or twice that he had no time to fool with theorems; adding—with a twitch of the eyebrows and a touch of that nervous bravado which so perplexed them—that he was helping the people down at the stock company; they were old friends of his.

The upshot of the matter was that the Principal went to Paul's father, and Paul was taken out of school and put to work. The manager at Carnegie Hall was told to get another usher in his stead; the doorkeeper at the theater was warned not to admit him to the house; and Charley Edwards remorsefully promised the boy's father not to see him again.

The members of the stock company were vastly amused when some of Paul's stories reached them—especially the women. They were hard-working women, most of them supporting indigent husbands or brothers, and they laughed rather bitterly at having stirred the boy to such fervid and florid inventions. They agreed with the faculty and with his father that Paul's was a bad case.

The eastbound train was plowing through a January snowstorm; the dull dawn was beginning to show gray when the engine whistled a mile out of Newark.[7] Paul started up from the seat where he had lain curled in uneasy slumber, rubbed the breath-misted window glass with his hand, and peered out. The snow was whirling in curling eddies above the white bottom lands, and the drifts lay already deep in the fields and along the fences, while here and there the long dead grass and dried weed stalks protruded black above it. Lights shone from the scattered houses, and a gang of laborers who stood beside the track waved their lanterns.

Paul had slept very little, and he felt grimy and uncomfortable. He had made the all-night journey in a day coach, partly because he was ashamed, dressed as he was, to go into a Pullman, and partly because he was afraid of being seen there by some Pittsburgh businessman, who might have noticed him in Denny & Carson's office. When the whistle awoke him, he clutched quickly at his breast pocket, glancing about him with an uncertain smile. But the little, clay-bespattered Italians were still sleeping, the slatternly women across the aisle were in open-mouthed oblivion, and even the crumby, crying babies were for

7. City in New Jersey just outside of New York City.

the nonce stilled. Paul settled back to struggle with his impatience as best he could.

When he arrived at the Jersey City station he hurried through his breakfast, manifestly ill at ease and keeping a sharp eye about him. After he reached the Twenty-third Street station,[8] he consulted a cabman and had himself driven to a men's-furnishings establishment that was just opening for the day. He spent upward of two hours, buying with endless reconsidering and great care. His new street suit he put on in the fitting room; the frock coat and dress clothes he had bundled into the cab with his linen. Then he drove to a hatter's and a shoe house. His next errand was at Tiffany's, where he selected his silver[9] and a new scarf pin. He would not wait to have his silver marked, he said. Lastly, he stopped at a trunk shop on Broadway and had his purchases packed into various traveling bags.

It was a little after one o'clock when he drove up to the Waldorf,[1] and after settling with the cabman, went into the office. He registered from Washington; said his mother and father had been abroad, and that he had come down to await the arrival of their steamer. He told his story plausibly and had no trouble, since he volunteered to pay for them in advance, in engaging his rooms; a sleeping room, sitting room, and bath.

Not once, but a hundred times, Paul had planned this entry into New York. He had gone over every detail of it with Charley Edwards, and in his scrapbook at home there were pages of description about New York hotels, cut from the Sunday papers. When he was shown to his sitting room on the eighth floor he saw at a glance that everything was as it should be; there was but one detail in his mental picture that the place did not realize, so he rang for the bellboy and sent him down for flowers. He moved about nervously until the boy returned, putting away his new linen and fingering it delightedly as he did so. When the flowers came he put them hastily into water, and then tumbled into a hot bath. Presently he came out of his white bathroom, resplendent in his new silk underwear, and playing with the tassels of his red robe. The snow was whirling so fiercely outside his windows that he could scarcely see across the street, but within the air was deliciously soft and fragrant. He put the violets and jonquils on the taboret beside the couch, and threw himself down, with a long sigh, covering himself with a Roman blanket. He was thoroughly tired; he had been in such haste, he had stood up to such a strain, covered so much ground in the last twenty-four hours, that he wanted to think how it had all come about.

8. Railway terminal in Manhattan. 9. Comb and brush set. Paul did not want to have it monogrammed ("marked"). Tiffany's is a fashionable jewelry store in Manhattan. 1. Fashionable hotel in Manhattan.

Lulled by the sound of the wind, the warm air, and the cool fragrance of the flowers, he sank into deep, drowsy retrospection.

It had been wonderfully simple; when they had shut him out of the theater and concert hall, when they had taken away his bone, the whole thing was virtually determined. The rest was a mere matter of opportunity. The only thing that at all surprised him was his own courage—for he realized well enough that he had always been tormented by fear, a sort of apprehensive dread that, of late years, as the meshes of the lies he had told closed about him, had been pulling the muscles of his body tighter and tighter. Until now he could not remember the time when he had not been dreading something. Even when he was a little boy it was always there—behind him, or before, or on either side. There had always been the shadowed corner, the dark place into which he dared not look, but from which something seemed always to be watching him—and Paul had done things that were not pretty to watch, he knew.

But now he had a curious sense of relief, as though he had at last thrown down the gauntlet to the thing in the corner.

Yet it was but a day since he had been sulking in the traces; but yesterday afternoon that he had been sent to the bank with Denny & Carson's deposit, as usual—but this time he was instructed to leave the book to be balanced. There was above two thousand dollars in checks, and nearly a thousand in the bank notes which he had taken from the book and quietly transferred to his pocket. At the bank he had made out a new deposit slip. His nerves had been steady enough to permit of his returning to the office, where he had finished his work and asked for a full day's holiday tomorrow, Saturday, giving a perfectly reasonable pretext. The bankbook, he knew, would not be returned before Monday or Tuesday, and his father would be out of town for the next week. From the time he slipped the bank notes into his pocket until he boarded the night train for New York, he had not known a moment's hesitation. It was not the first time Paul had steered through treacherous waters.

How astonishingly easy it had all been; here he was, the thing done; and this time there would be no awakening, no figure at the top of the stairs. He watched the snowflakes whirling by his window until he fell asleep.

When he awoke, it was three o'clock in the afternoon. He bounded up with a start; half of one of his precious days gone already! He spent more than an hour in dressing, watching every stage of his toilet carefully in the mirror. Everything was quite perfect; he was exactly the kind of boy he had always wanted to be.

When he went downstairs Paul took a carriage and drove up Fifth

Avenue toward the Park.[2] The snow had somewhat abated; carriages and tradesmen's wagons were hurrying soundlessly to and fro in the winter twilight; boys in woolen mufflers were shoveling off the doorsteps; the avenue stages[3] made fine spots of color against the white street. Here and there on the corners were stands, with whole flower gardens blooming under glass cases, against the sides of which the snowflakes stuck and melted; violets, roses, carnations, lilies of the valley—somehow vastly more lovely and alluring that they blossomed thus unnaturally in the snow. The Park itself was a wonderful stage winterpiece.

When he returned, the pause of the twilight had ceased and the tune of the streets had changed. The snow was falling faster, lights streamed from the hotels that reared their dozen stories fearlessly up into the storm, defying the raging Atlantic winds. A long, black stream of carriages poured down the avenue, intersected here and there by other streams, tending horizontally. There were a score of cabs about the entrance of this hotel, and his driver had to wait. Boys in livery were running in and out of the awning stretched across the sidewalk, up and down the red velvet carpet laid from the door to the street. Above, about, within it all was the rumble and roar, the hurry and toss of thousands of human beings as hot for pleasure as himself, and on every side of him towered the glaring affirmation of the omnipotence of wealth.

The boy set his teeth and drew his shoulders together in a spasm of realization; the plot of all dramas, the text of all romances, the nerve-stuff of all sensations was whirling about him like the snowflakes. He burnt like a faggot in a tempest.

When Paul went down to dinner the music of the orchestra came floating up the elevator shaft to greet him. His head whirled as he stepped into the thronged corridor, and he sank back into one of the chairs against the wall to get his breath. The lights, the chatter, the perfumes, the bewildering medley of color—he had, for a moment, the feeling of not being able to stand it. But only for a moment; these were his own people, he told himself. He went slowly about the corridors, through the writing rooms, smoking rooms, reception rooms, as though he were exploring the chambers of an enchanted palace, built and peopled for him alone.

When he reached the dining room he sat down at a table near a window. The flowers, the white linen, the many-colored wineglasses, the gay toilettes of the women, the low popping of corks, the undulating repetitions of the *Blue Danube*[4] from the orchestra, all flooded

2. Central Park is the principal park in Manhattan. 3. Window displays. 4. Waltz by Johann Strauss (1825–1899), Austrian composer.

Paul's dream with bewildering radiance. When the roseate tinge of his champagne was added—that cold, precious, bubbling stuff that creamed and foamed in his glass—Paul wondered that there were honest men in the world at all. This was what all the world was fighting for, he reflected; this was what all the struggle was about. He doubted the reality of his past. Had he ever known a place called Cordelia Street, a place where fagged-looking businessmen got on the early car; mere rivets in a machine they seemed to Paul,—sickening men, with combings of children's hair always hanging to their coats, and the smell of cooking in their clothes. Cordelia Street—Ah, that belonged to another time and country; had he not always been thus, had he not sat here night after night, from as far back as he could remember, looking pensively over just such shimmering textures and slowly twirling the stem of a glass like this one between his thumb and middle finger? He rather thought he had.

He was not the least abashed or lonely. He had no especial desire to meet or to know any of these people; all he demanded was the right to look on and conjecture, to watch the pageant. The mere stage properties were all he contended for. Nor was he lonely later in the evening, in his lodge at the Metropolitan.[5] He was now entirely rid of his nervous misgivings, of his forced aggressiveness, of the imperative desire to show himself different from his surroundings. He felt now that his surroundings explained him. Nobody questioned the purple,[6] he had only to wear it passively. He had only to glance down at his attire to reassure himself that here it would be impossible for anyone to humiliate him.

He found it hard to leave his beautiful sitting room to go to bed that night, and sat long watching the raging storm from his turret window. When he went to sleep it was with the lights turned on in his bedroom; partly because of his old timidity, and partly so that, if he should wake in the night, there would be no wretched moment of doubt, no horrible suspicion of yellow wallpaper, or of Washington and Calvin above his bed.

Sunday morning the city was practically snowbound. Paul breakfasted late, and in the afternoon he fell in with a wild San Francisco boy, a freshman at Yale, who said he had run down for a "little flyer" over Sunday. The young man offered to show Paul the night side of the town, and the two boys went out together after dinner, not returning to the hotel until seven o'clock the next morning. They had started out in the confiding warmth of a champagne friendship, but their parting in the elevator was singularly cool. The freshman pulled himself together to make his train, and Paul went to bed. He awoke at two

5. His box at the Metropolitan Opera House. 6. I.e., his assumption of a royal robe.

o'clock in the afternoon, very thirsty and dizzy, and rang for ice-water, coffee, and the Pittsburgh papers.

On the part of the hotel management, Paul excited no suspicion. There was this to be said for him, that he wore his spoils with dignity and in no way made himself conspicuous. Even under the glow of his wine he was never boisterous, though he found the stuff like a magician's wand for wonder-building. His chief greediness lay in his ears and eyes, and his excesses were not offensive ones. His dearest pleasures were the gray winter twilights in his sitting room; his quiet enjoyment of his flowers, his clothes, his wide divan, his cigarette, and his sense of power. He could not remember a time when he had felt so at peace with himself. The mere release from the necessity of petty lying, lying every day and every day, restored his self-respect. He had never lied for pleasure, even at school; but to be noticed and admired, to assert his difference from other Cordelia Street boys; and he felt a good deal more manly, more honest, even, now that he had no need for boastful pretensions, now that he could, as his actor friends used to say, "dress the part." It was characteristic that remorse did not occur to him. His golden days went by without a shadow, and he made each as perfect as he could.

On the eighth day after his arrival in New York he found the whole affair exploited in the Pittsburgh papers, exploited with a wealth of detail which indicated that local news of a sensational nature was at a low ebb. The firm of Denny & Carson announced that the boy's father had refunded the full amount of the theft and that they had no intention of prosecuting. The Cumberland minister had been interviewed, and expressed his hope of yet reclaiming the motherless lad, and his Sabbath-school teacher declared that she would spare no effort to that end. The rumor had reached Pittsburgh that the boy had been seen in a New York hotel, and his father had gone East to find him and bring him home.

Paul had just come in to dress for dinner; he sank into a chair, weak to the knees, and clasped his head in his hands. It was to be worse than jail, even; the tepid waters of Cordelia Street were to close over him finally and forever. The gray monotony stretched before him in hopeless, unrelieved years; Sabbath school, Young People's Meeting, the yellow-papered room, the damp dish-towels; it all rushed back upon him with a sickening vividness. He had the old feeling that the orchestra had suddenly stopped, the sinking sensation that the play was over. The sweat broke out on his face, and he sprang to his feet, looked about him with his white, conscious smile, and winked at himself in the mirror. With something of the old childish belief in miracles with which he had so often gone to class, all his lessons unlearned, Paul dressed and dashed whistling down the corridor to the elevator.

He had no sooner entered the dining room and caught the measure of the music than his remembrance was lightened by his old elastic power of claiming the moment, mounting with it, and finding it all-sufficient. The glare and glitter about him, the mere scenic accessories had again, and for the last time, their old potency. He would show himself that he was game, he would finish the thing splendidly. He doubted, more than ever, the existence of Cordelia Street, and for the first time he drank his wine recklessly. Was he not, after all, one of those fortunate beings born to the purple, was he not still himself and in his own place? He drummed a nervous accompaniment to the Pagliacci[7] music and looked about him, telling himself over and over that it had paid.

He reflected drowsily, to the swell of the music and the chill sweetness of his wine, that he might have done it more wisely. He might have caught an outbound steamer and been well out of their clutches before now. But the other side of the world had seemed too far away and too uncertain then; he could not have waited for it; his need had been too sharp. If he had to choose over again, he would do the same thing tomorrow. He looked affectionately about the dining room, now gilded with a soft mist. Ah, it had paid indeed!

Paul was awakened next morning by a painful throbbing in his head and feet. He had thrown himself across the bed without undressing, and had slept with his shoes on. His limbs and hands were lead heavy, and his tongue and throat were parched and burnt. There came upon him one of those fateful attacks of clearheadedness that never occurred except when he was physically exhausted and his nerves hung loose. He lay still, closed his eyes, and let the tide of things wash over him.

His father was in New York; "stopping at some joint or other," he told himself. The memory of successive summers on the front stoop fell upon him like a weight of black water. He had not a hundred dollars left; and he knew now, more than ever, that money was everything, the wall that stood between all he loathed and all he wanted. The thing was winding itself up; he had thought of that on his first glorious day in New York, and had even provided a way to snap the thread. It lay on his dressing table now; he had got it out last night when he came blindly up from dinner, but the shiny metal hurt his eyes, and he disliked the looks of it.

He rose and moved about with a painful effort, succumbing now and again to attacks of nausea. It was the old depression exaggerated; all the world had become Cordelia Street. Yet somehow he was not afraid of anything, was absolutely calm; perhaps because he had looked

7. Opera by Ruggiero Leoncavallo (1858–1919).

into the dark corner at last and knew. It was bad enough, what he saw there, but somehow not so bad as his long fear of it had been. He saw everything clearly now. He had a feeling that he had made the best of it, that he had lived the sort of life he was meant to live, and for half an hour he sat staring at the revolver. But he told himself that was not the way, so he went downstairs and took a cab to the ferry.

When Paul arrived in Newark he got off the train and took another cab, directing the driver to follow the Pennsylvania tracks out of the town. The snow lay heavy on the roadways and had drifted deep in the open fields. Only here and there the dead grass or dried weed stalks projected, singularly black, above it. Once well into the country, Paul dismissed the carriage and walked, floundering along the tracks, his mind a medley of irrelevant things. He seemed to hold in his brain an actual picture of everything he had seen that morning. He remembered every feature of both his drivers, of the toothless old woman from whom he had bought the red flowers in his coat, the agent from whom he had got his ticket, and all of his fellow passengers on the ferry. His mind, unable to cope with vital matters near at hand, worked feverishly and deftly at sorting and grouping these images. They made for him a part of the ugliness of the world, of the ache in his head, and the bitter burning on his tongue. He stooped and put a handful of snow into his mouth as he walked, but that, too, seemed hot. When he reached a little hillside, where the tracks ran through a cut some twenty feet below him, he stopped and sat down.

The carnations in his coat were drooping with the cold, he noticed, their red glory all over. It occurred to him that all the flowers he had seen in the glass cases that first night must have gone the same way, long before this. It was only one splendid breath they had, in spite of their brave mockery at the winter outside the glass; and it was a losing game in the end, it seemed, this revolt against the homilies by which the world is run. Paul took one of the blossoms carefully from his coat and scooped a little hole in the snow, where he covered it up. Then he dozed awhile, from his weak condition, seemingly insensible to the cold.

The sound of an approaching train awoke him, and he started to his feet, remembering only his resolution, and afraid lest he should be too late. He stood watching the approaching locomotive, his teeth chattering, his lips drawn away from them in a frightened smile; once or twice he glanced nervously sidewise, as though he were being watched. When the right moment came, he jumped. As he fell, the folly of his haste occurred to him with merciless clearness, the vastness of what he had left undone. There flashed through his brain, clearer than ever before, the blue of Adriatic water, the yellow of Algerian sands.

He felt something strike his chest, and that his body was being thrown swiftly through the air, on and on, immeasurably far and fast, while his limbs were gently relaxed. Then, because the picturemaking mechanism was crushed, the disturbing visions flashed into black, and Paul dropped back into the immense design of things.

---

1. If you feel that Paul has been unjustly treated by parents, teachers, or society at large, explain the injustice.
2. If, on the other hand, you feel he suffers from a defect of character, define it.
3. What is the connection between Paul's fascination with the theater and his crime?
4. Why is his father's repayment of the stolen money "worse than jail"?
5. Does Paul repent at the moment of his death? If you think he does not, how do you interpret the end?

John Cheever

Cheever (1912–1982) was born in Quincy, Massachusetts. His formal education ended when he was expelled from Thayer Academy at the age of seventeen—a circumstance that gave him subject matter for his first publication. Thereafter he devoted himself completely to writing, except for brief interludes of teaching at Barnard and the University of Iowa. He wrote television scripts and four novels, but his fame rests on the large number of short stories, many appearing in The New Yorker, *that he published in a steady stream beginning in the 1940's. Built around a strong moral core and tinged with melancholy nostalgia for the past, these stories form a running commentary on the tensions, manners, and crippled aspirations of urban and suburban life. Many of his stories have been collected in* The Enormous Radio and Other Stories *(1953),* The Housebreaker of Shady Hill and Other Stories *(1958),* The Brigadier and the Golf Widow *(1964), and* The World of Apples *(1973). His novels are* The Wapshot Chronicle *(1957),* The Wapshot Scandal *(1964),* Bullet Park *(1969), and* Falconer *(1977).* The Stories of John Cheever *(1978) won the Pulitzer Prize.*

The Enormous Radio

Jim and Irene Westcott were the kind of people who seem to strike that satisfactory average of income, endeavor, and respectability that is reached by the statistical reports in college alumni bulletins. They were the parents of two young children, they had been married nine years, they lived on the twelfth floor of an apartment house near Sutton Place,[1] they went to the theatre on an average of 10.3 times a year, and they hoped someday to live in Westchester.[2] Irene Westcott was a pleasant, rather plain girl with soft brown hair and a wide, fine forehead upon which nothing at all had been written, and in the cold weather she wore a coat of fitch skins dyed to resemble mink. You could not say that Jim Westcott looked younger than he was, but you could at least say of him that he seemed to feel younger. He wore his graying hair cut very short, he dressed in the kind of clothes his class had worn

1. Fashionable area on New York City's East Side.

2. Affluent suburban county outside New York City.

at Andover,[3] and his manner was earnest, vehement, and intentionally naïve. The Westcotts differed from their friends, their classmates, and their neighbors only in an interest they shared in serious music. They went to a great many concerts—although they seldom mentioned this to anyone—and they spent a good deal of time listening to music on the radio.

Their radio was an old instrument, sensitive, unpredictable, and beyond repair. Neither of them understood the mechanics of radio—or of any of the other appliances that surrounded them—and when the instrument faltered, Jim would strike the side of the cabinet with his hand. This sometimes helped. One Sunday afternoon, in the middle of a Schubert[4] quartet, the music faded away altogether. Jim struck the cabinet repeatedly, but there was no response; the Schubert was lost to them forever. He promised to buy Irene a new radio, and on Monday when he came home from work he told her that he had got one. He refused to describe it, and said it would be a surprise for her when it came.

The radio was delivered at the kitchen door the following afternoon, and with the assistance of her maid and the handyman Irene uncrated it and brought it into the living room. She was struck at once with the physical ugliness of the large gumwood cabinet. Irene was proud of her living room, she had chosen its furnishings and colors as carefully as she chose her clothes, and now it seemed to her that the new radio stood among her intimate possessions like an aggressive intruder. She was confounded by the number of dials and switches on the instrument panel, and she studied them thoroughly before she put the plug into a wall socket and turned the radio on. The dials flooded with a malevolent green light, and in the distance she heard the music of a piano quintet. The quintet was in the distance for only an instant; it bore down upon her with a speed greater than light and filled the apartment with the noise of music amplified so mightily that it knocked a china ornament from a table to the floor. She rushed to the instrument and reduced the volume. The violent forces that were snared in the ugly gumwood cabinet made her uneasy. Her children came home from school then, and she took them to the Park. It was not until later in the afternoon that she was able to return to the radio.

The maid had given the children their suppers and was supervising their baths when Irene turned on the radio, reduced the volume, and sat down to listen to a Mozart[5] quintet that she knew and enjoyed. The music came through clearly. The new instrument had a much purer tone, she thought, than the old one. She decided that tone was most important and that she could conceal the cabinet behind a sofa. But as

3. Elite boarding school. 4. Franz Peter Schubert (1797–1828), Austrian composer. 5. Wolfgang Amadeus Mozart (1756–1791), Austrian composer.

soon as she had made her peace with the radio, the interference began. A crackling sound like the noise of a burning powder fuse began to accompany the singing of the strings. Beyond the music, there was a rustling that reminded Irene unpleasantly of the sea, and as the quintet progressed, these noises were joined by many others. She tried all the dials and switches but nothing dimmed the interference, and she sat down, disappointed and bewildered, and tried to trace the flight of the melody. The elevator shaft in her building ran beside the living-room wall, and it was the noise of the elevator that gave her a clue to the character of the static. The rattling of the elevator cables and the opening and closing of the elevator doors were reproduced in her loudspeaker, and, realizing that the radio was sensitive to electrical currents of all sorts, she began to discern through the Mozart the ringing of telephone bells, the dialing of phones, and the lamentation of a vacuum cleaner. By listening more carefully, she was able to distinguish doorbells, elevator bells, electric razors, and Waring mixers, whose sounds had been picked up from the apartments that surrounded hers and transmitted through her loudspeaker. The powerful and ugly instrument, with its mistaken sensitivity to discord, was more than she could hope to master, so she turned the thing off and went into the nursery to see her children.

When Jim Westcott came home that night, he went to the radio confidently and worked the controls. He had the same sort of experience Irene had had. A man was speaking on the station Jim had chosen, and his voice swung instantly from the distance into a force so powerful that it shook the apartment. Jim turned the volume control and reduced the voice. Then, a minute or two later, the interference began. The ringing of telephones and doorbells set in, joined by the rasp of the elevator doors and the whir of cooking appliances. The character of the noise had changed since Irene had tried the radio earlier; the last of the electric razors was being unplugged, the vacuum cleaners had all been returned to their closets, and the static reflected that change in pace that overtakes the city after the sun goes down. He fiddled with the knobs but couldn't get rid of the noises, so he turned the radio off and told Irene that in the morning he'd call the people who had sold it to him and give them hell.

The following afternoon, when Irene returned to the apartment from a luncheon date, the maid told her that a man had come and fixed the radio. Irene went into the living room before she took off her hat or her furs and tried the instrument. From the loudspeaker came a recording of the "Missouri Waltz."[6] It reminded her of the thin, scratchy

6. Popular tune of 1916 by J. R. Shannon and Frederick Knight Logan. It was made popular again in the 1940's by President Harry Truman.

music from an old-fashioned phonograph that she sometimes heard across the lake where she spent her summers. She waited until the waltz had finished, expecting an explanation of the recording, but there was none. The music was followed by silence, and then the plaintive and scratchy record was repeated. She turned the dial and got a satisfactory burst of Caucasian music—the thump of bare feet in the dust and the rattle of coin jewelry—but in the background she could hear the ringing of bells and a confusion of voices. Her children came home from school then, and she turned off the radio and went to the nursery.

When Jim came home that night, he was tired, and he took a bath and changed his clothes. Then he joined Irene in the living room. He had just turned on the radio when the maid announced dinner, so he left it on, and he and Irene went to the table.

Jim was too tired to make even pretense of sociability, and there was nothing about the dinner to hold Irene's interest, so her attention wandered from the food to the deposits of silver polish on the candlesticks and from there to the music in the other room. She listened for a few minutes to a Chopin[7] prelude and then was surprised to hear a man's voice break in. "For Christ's sake, Kathy," he said, "do you always have to play the piano when I get home?" The music stopped abruptly. "It's the only chance I have," a woman said. "I'm at the office all day." "So am I," the man said. He added something obscene about an upright piano, and slammed a door. The passionate and melancholy music began again.

"Did you hear that?" Irene asked.

"What?" Jim was eating his dessert.

"The radio. A man said something while the music was still going on—something dirty."

"It's probably a play."

"I don't think it *is* a play," Irene said.

They left the table and took their coffee into the living room. Irene asked Jim to try another station. He turned the knob. "Have you seen my garters?" a man asked. "Button me up," a woman said. "Have you seen my garters?" the man said again. "Just button me up and I'll find your garters," the woman said. Jim shifted to another station. "I wish you wouldn't leave apple cores in the ashtrays," a man said. "I hate the smell."

"This is strange," Jim said.

"Isn't it?" Irene said.

Jim turned the knob again. " 'On the coast of Coromandel where the early pumpkins blow,' " a woman with a pronounced English accent

7. Frédéric François Chopin (1810–1849), Polish-French composer and pianist.

said, " 'in the middle of the woods lived the Yonghy-Bonghy-Bò. Two old chairs, and half a candle, one old jug without a handle . . .' "[8]

"My God!" Irene cried. "That's the Sweeneys' nurse."

" 'These were all his worldly goods,' " the British voice continued.

"Turn that thing off," Irene said. "Maybe they can hear *us*." Jim switched the radio off. "That was Miss Armstrong, the Sweeneys' nurse," Irene said. "She must be reading to the little girl. They live in 17-B. I've talked with Miss Armstrong in the Park. I know her voice very well. We must be getting other people's apartments."

"That's impossible," Jim said.

"Well, that was the Sweeneys' nurse," Irene said hotly. "I know her voice. I know it very well. I'm wondering if they can hear us."

Jim turned the switch. First from a distance and then nearer, nearer, as if borne on the wind, came the pure accents of the Sweeneys' nurse again: " '*Lady Jingly! Lady Jingly!*' " she said, " '*sitting where the pumpkins blow, will you come and be my wife?* said the Yonghy-Bonghy-Bò . . .' "

Jim went over to the radio and said "Hello" loudly into the speaker.

" '*I am tired of living singly,*' the nurse went on, " '*on this coast so wild and shingly, I'm a-weary of my life; if you'll come and be my wife, quite serene would be my life . . .*' "

"I guess she can't hear us," Irene said. "Try something else."

Jim turned to another station, and the living room was filled with the uproar of a cocktail party that had overshot its mark. Someone was playing the piano and singing the "Whiffenpoof Song,"[9] and the voices that surrounded the piano were vehement and happy. "Eat some more sandwiches," a woman shrieked. There were screams of laughter and a dish of some sort crashed to the floor.

"Those must be the Fullers, in 11-E," Irene said. "I knew they were giving a party this afternoon. I saw her in the liquor store. Isn't this too divine? Try something else. See if you can get those people in 18-C."

The Westcotts overheard that evening a monologue on salmon fishing in Canada, a bridge game, running comments on home movies of what had apparently been a fortnight at Sea Island, and a bitter family quarrel about an overdraft at the bank. They turned off their radio at midnight and went to bed, weak with laughter. Sometime in the night, their son began to call for a glass of water and Irene got one and took it to his room. It was very early. All the lights in the neighborhood were extinguished, and from the boy's window she could see

8. From "The Courtship of the Yonghy-Bonghy-Bò" by Edward Lear (1812–1888), English nonsense poet. 9. Famous Yale drinking song.

the empty street. She went into the living room and tried the radio. There was some faint coughing, a moan, and then a man spoke. "Are you all right, darling?" he asked. "Yes," a woman said wearily. "Yes, I'm all right, I guess," and then she added with great feeling, "But, you know, Charlie, I don't feel like myself any more. Sometimes there are about fifteen or twenty minutes in the week when I feel like myself. I don't like to go to another doctor, because the doctor's bills are so awful already, but I just don't feel like myself, Charlie. I just never feel like myself." They were not young, Irene thought. She guessed from the timbre of their voices that they were middle-aged. The restrained melancholy of the dialogue and the draft from the bedroom window made her shiver, and she went back to bed.

The following morning, Irene cooked breakfast for the family—the maid didn't come up from her room in the basement until ten—braided her daughter's hair, and waited at the door until her children and her husband had been carried away in the elevator. Then she went into the living room and tried the radio. "I don't want to go to school," a child screamed. "I hate school. I won't go to school. I hate school." "You will go to school," an enraged woman said. "We paid eight hundred dollars to get you into that school and you'll go if it kills you." The next number on the dial produced the worn record of the "Missouri Waltz." Irene shifted the control and invaded the privacy of several breakfast tables. She overheard demonstrations of indigestion, carnal love, abysmal vanity, faith, and despair. Irene's life was nearly as simple and sheltered as it appeared to be, and the forthright and sometimes brutal language that came from the loudspeaker that morning astonished and troubled her. She continued to listen until her maid came in. Then she turned off the radio quickly, since this insight, she realized, was a furtive one.

Irene had a luncheon date with a friend that day, and she left her apartment at a little after twelve. There were a number of women in the elevator when it stopped at her floor. She stared at their handsome and impassive faces, their furs, and the cloth flowers in their hats. Which one of them had been to Sea Island? she wondered. Which one had overdrawn her bank account. The elevator stopped at the tenth floor and a woman with a pair of Skye terriers joined them. Her hair was rigged high on her head and she wore a mink cape. She was humming the "Missouri Waltz."

Irene had two Martinis at lunch, and she looked searchingly at her friend and wondered what her secrets were. They had intended to go shopping after lunch, but Irene excused herself and went home. She told the maid that she was not to be disturbed; then she went into the living room, closed the doors, and switched on the radio. She heard, in the course of the afternoon, the halting conversation of a woman entertaining her aunt, the hysterical conclusion of a luncheon party, and a hostess briefing her maid about some cocktail guests. "Don't give the best Scotch to anyone who hasn't white hair," the hostess said. "See if you can get rid of that liver paste before you pass those hot things, and could you lend me five dollars? I want to tip the elevator man."

As the afternoon waned, the conversations increased in intensity. From where Irene sat, she could see the open sky above the East River. There were hundreds of clouds in the sky, as though the south wind had broken the winter into pieces and were blowing it north, and on her radio she could hear the arrival of cocktail guests and the return of children and businessmen from their schools and offices. "I found a good-sized diamond on the bathroom floor this morning," a woman said. "It must have fallen out of that bracelet Mrs. Dunston was wearing last night." "We'll sell it," a man said. "Take it down to the jeweler on Madison Avenue and sell it. Mrs. Dunston won't know the difference, and we could use a couple of hundred bucks . . ." " 'Oranges and lemons, say the bells of St. Clement's,' " the Sweeneys' nurse sang. " 'Halfpence and farthings, say the bells of St. Martin's. When will you pay me? say the bells at old Bailey . . .' "[1] "It's not a hat," a woman cried, and at her back roared a cocktail party. "It's not a hat, it's a love affair. That's what Walter Florell said. He said it's not a hat, it's a love affair," and then, in a lower voice, the same woman added, "Talk to somebody, for Christ's sake, honey, talk to somebody. If she catches you standing here not talking to anybody, she'll take us off her invitation list, and I love these parties."

The Westcotts were going out for dinner that night, and when Jim came home, Irene was dressing. She seemed sad and vague, and he brought her a drink. They were dining with friends in the neighborhood, and they walked to where they were going. The sky was broad and filled with light. It was one of those splendid spring evenings that excite memory and desire, and the air that touched their hands and faces felt very soft. A Salvation Army band was on the corner playing "Jesus Is Sweeter." Irene drew on her husband's arm and held him there for a minute, to hear the music. "They're really such nice people, aren't they?" she said. "They have such nice faces. Actually, they're so much nicer than a lot of the people we know." She took a bill from her purse and walked over and dropped it into the tambourine. There was in her face, when she returned to her hsuband, a look of radiant melancholy that he was not familiar with. And her conduct at the dinner party that night seemed strange to him, too. She interrupted her host-

1. British folk song.

ess rudely and stared at the people across the table from her with an intensity for which she would have punished her children.

It was still mild when they walked home from the party, and Irene looked up at the spring stars. " 'How far that little candle throws its beams,' " she exclaimed. " 'So shines a good deed in a naughty world.' "[2] She waited that night until Jim had fallen asleep, and then went into the living room and turned on the radio.

Jim came home at about six the next night. Emma, the maid, let him in, and he had taken off his hat and was taking off his coat when Irene ran into the hall. Her face was shining with tears and her hair was disordered. "Go up to 16-C, Jim!" she screamed. "Don't take off your coat. Go up to 16-C. Mr. Osborn's beating his wife. They've been quarreling since four o'clock, and now he's hitting her. Go up there and stop him."

From the radio in the living room, Jim heards screams, obscenities, and thuds. "You know you don't have to listen to this sort of thing," he said. He strode into the living room and turned the switch. "It's indecent," he said. "It's like looking in windows. You know you don't have to listen to this sort of thing. You can turn it off."

"Oh, it's so horrible, it's so dreadful," Irene was sobbing. "I've been listening all day, and it's so depressing."

"Well, if it's so depressing, why do you listen to it? I bought this damned radio to give you some pleasure," he said. "I paid a great deal of money for it. I thought it might make you happy. I wanted to make you happy."

"Don't, don't, don't, don't quarrel with me," she moaned, and laid her head on his shoulder. "All the others have been quarreling all day. Everybody's been quarreling. They're all worried about money. Mrs. Hutchinson's mother is dying of cancer in Florida and they don't have enough money to send her to the Mayo Clinic.[3] At least, Mr. Hutchinson says they don't have enough money. And some woman in this building is having an affair with the handyman—with that hideous handyman. It's too disgusting. And Mrs. Melville has heart trouble, and Mr. Hendricks is going to lose his job in April and Mrs. Hendricks is horrid about the whole thing and that girl who plays the 'Missouri Waltz' is a whore, a common whore, and the elevator man has tuberculosis and Mr. Osborn has been beating Mrs. Osborn." She wailed, she trembled with grief and checked the stream of tears down her face with the heel of her palm.

"Well, why do you have to listen?" Jim asked again. "Why do you have to listen to this stuff if it makes you so miserable?"

2. Shakespeare's *Merchant of Venice*, V. i. 3. Internationally famous hospital and diagnostic center in Rochester, Minnesota.

"Oh, don't, don't, don't," she cried. "Life is too terrible, too sordid and awful. But we've never been like that, have we, darling? Have we? I mean, we've always been good and decent and loving to one another, haven't we? And we have two children, two beautiful children. Our lives aren't sordid, are they, darling? Are they?" She flung her arms around his neck and drew his face down to hers. "We're happy, aren't we, darling? We are happy, aren't we?"

"Of course we're happy," he said tiredly. He began to surrender his resentment. "Of course we're happy. I'll have that damned radio fixed or taken away tomorrow." He stroked her soft hair. "My poor girl," he said.

"You love me, don't you? she asked. "And we're not hypercritical or worried about money or dishonest, are we?"

"No, darling," he said.

A man came in the morning and fixed the radio. Irene turned it on cautiously and was happy to hear a California-wine commercial and a recording of Beethoven's Ninth Symphony, including Schiller's "Ode to Joy." She kept the radio on all day and nothing untoward came from the speaker.

A Spanish suite was being played when Jim came home. "Is everything all right?" he asked. His face was pale, she thought. They had some cocktails and went in to dinner to the "Anvil Chorus" from *Il Trovatore*. This was followed by Debussy's "La Mer."[4]

"I paid the bill for the radio today," Jim said. "It cost four hundred dollars. I hope you'll get some enjoyment out of it."

"Oh, I'm sure I will," Irene said.

"Four hundred dollars is a good deal more than I can afford," he went on. "I wanted to get something that you'd enjoy. It's the last extravagance we'll be able to indulge in this year. I see that you haven't paid your clothing bills yet. I saw them on your dressing table." He looked directly at her. "Why did you tell me you'd paid them? Why did you lie to me?"

"I just didn't want you to worry, Jim," she said. She drank some water. "I'll be able to pay my bills out of this month's allowance. There were the slipcovers last month, and that party."

"You've got to learn to handle the money I give you a little more intelligently, Irene," he said. "You've got to understand that we don't have as much money this year as we had last. I had a very sobering talk with Mitchell today. No one is buying anything. We're spending all our time promoting new issues, and you know how long that takes. I'm not getting any younger, you know. I'm thirty-seven. My hair will

4. Ludwig van Beethoven (1770–1827), German composer; Johann Christoph Friedrich von Schiller (1759–1805), German poet and dramatist; *Il Trovatore*, opera by Giuseppe Verdi (1813–1901), Italian composer; Claude Achille Debussy (1862–1918), French composer.

be gray next year. I haven't done as well as I'd hoped to do. And I don't suppose things will get any better."

"Yes, dear," she said.

"We've got to start cutting down," Jim said. "We've got to think of the children. To be perfectly frank with you, I worry about money a great deal. I'm not at all sure of the future. No one is. If anything should happen to me, there's the insurance, but that wouldn't go very far today. I've worked awfully hard to give you and the children a comfortable life," he said bitterly. "I don't like to see all my energies, all of my youth, wasted in fur coats and radios and slipcovers and—"

"Please, Jim," she said. "Please. They'll hear us."

"*Who'll hear us?* Emma can't hear us."

"The radio."

"Oh, I'm sick!" he shouted. "I'm sick to death of your apprehensiveness. The radio can't hear us. Nobody can hear us. And what if they can hear us? Who cares?"

Irene got up from the table and went into the living room. Jim went to the door and shouted at her from there. "Why are you so Christly all of a sudden? What's turned you overnight into a convent girl? You stole your mother's jewelry before they probated her will. You never gave your sister a cent of that money that was intended for her—not even when she needed it. You made Grace Howland's life miserable, and where was all your piety and your virtue when you went to that abortionist? I'll never forget how cool you were. You packed your bag and went off to have that child murdered as if you were going to Nassau. If you'd had any reasons, if you'd had any good reasons—"

Irene stood for a minute before the hideous cabinet, disgraced and sickened, but she held her hand on the switch before she extinguished the music and the voices, hoping that the instrument might speak to her kindly, that she might hear the Sweeneys' nurse. Jim continued to shout at her from the door. The voice on the radio was suave and noncommital. "An early-morning railroad disaster in Tokyo," the loudspeaker said, "killed twenty-nine people. A fire in a Catholic hospital near Buffalo for the care of blind children was extinguished early this morning by nuns. The temperature is forty-seven. The humidity is eighty-nine."

---

1. What, if anything, significantly distinguishes the Westcotts from the other tenants of their building? From other young couples of their time and social position?
2. Is there anything in the story besides the radio itself that could be labeled an element of fantasy?
3. Is most of the information brought by the radio about the Westcotts' neigh-

bors shocking or sordid? What exceptions can you note? What do all the exposures of private lives add up to?
4. Does possession of the radio give the Westcotts any advantage over their neighbors? Disadvantage? Explain.
5. Socrates said that the "unexamined life is not worth living." Does the outcome of this story support or contradict his view?

The Five-Forty-Eight

When Blake stepped out of the elevator, he saw her. A few people, mostly men waiting for girls, stood in the lobby watching the elevator doors. She was among them. As he saw her, her face took on a look of such loathing and purpose that he realized she had been waiting for him. He did not approach her. She had no legitimate business with him. They had nothing to say. He turned and walked toward the glass doors at the end of the lobby, feeling that faint guilt and bewilderment we experience when we bypass some old friend or classmate who seems threadbare, or sick, or miserable in some other way. It was five-eighteen by the clock in the Western Union office. He could catch the express. As he waited his turn at the revolving doors, he saw that it was still raining. It had been raining all day, and he noticed now how much louder the rain made the noises of the street. Outside, he started walking briskly east toward Madison Avenue. Traffic was tied up, and horns were blowing urgently on a crosstown street in the distance. The sidewalk was crowded. He wondered what she had hoped to gain by a glimpse of him coming out of the office building at the end of the day. Then he wondered if she was following him.

Walking in the city, we seldom turn and look back. The habit restrained Blake. He listened for a minute—foolishly—as he walked, as if he could distinguish her footsteps from the worlds of sound in the city at the end of a rainy day. Then he noticed, ahead of him on the other side of the street, a break in the wall of buildings. Something had been torn down; something was being put up, but the steel structure had only just risen above the sidewalk fence and daylight poured through the gap. Blake stopped opposite here and looked into a store window. It was a decorator's or an auctioneer's. The window was arranged like a room in which people live and entertain their friends. There were cups on the coffee table, magazines to read, and flowers in the vases, but the flowers were dead and the cups were empty and the guests had not come. In the plate glass, Blake saw a clear reflection of himself and the crowds that were passing, like shadows, at his back.

Then he saw her image—so close to him that it shocked him. She was standing only a foot or two behind him. He could have turned then and asked her what she wanted, but instead of recognizing her, he shied away abruptly from the reflection of her contorted face and went along the street. She might be meaning to do him harm—she might be meaning to kill him.

The suddenness with which he moved when he saw the reflection of her face tipped the water out of his hat brim in such a way that some of it ran down his neck. It felt unpleasantly like the sweat of fear. Then the cold water falling into his face and onto his bare hands, the rancid smell of the wet gutters and paving, the knowledge that his feet were beginning to get wet and that he might catch cold—all the common discomforts of walking in the rain—seemed to heighten the menace of his pursuer and to give him a morbid consciousness of his own physicalness and of the ease with which he could be hurt. He could see ahead of him the corner of Madison Avenue, where the lights were brighter. He felt that if he could get to Madison Avenue he would be all right. At the corner, there was a bakery shop with two entrances, and he went in by the door on the crosstown street, bought a coffee ring, like any other commuter, and went out the Madison Avenue door. As he started down Madison Avenue, he saw her waiting for him by a hut where newspapers were sold.

She was not clever. She would be easy to shake. He could get into a taxi by one door and leave by the other. He could speak to a policeman. He could run—although he was afraid that if he did run, it might precipitate the violence he now felt sure she had planned. He was approaching a part of the city that he knew well and where the maze of street-level and underground passages, elevator banks, and crowded lobbies made it easy for a man to lose a pursuer. The thought of this, and a whiff of sugary warmth from the coffee ring, cheered him. It was absurd to imagine being harmed on a crowded street. She was foolish, misled, lonely perhaps—that was all it could amount to. He was an insignificant man, and there was no point in anyone's following him from his office to the station. He knew no secrets of any consequence. The reports in his briefcase had no bearing on war, peace, the dope traffic, the hydrogen bomb, or any of the other international skulduggeries that he associated with pursuers, men in trench coats, and wet sidewalks. Then he saw ahead of him the door of a men's bar. Oh, it was so simple!

He ordered a Gibson and shouldered his way in between two other men at the bar, so that if she should be watching from the window she would lose sight of him. The place was crowded with commuters putting down a drink before the ride home. They had brought in on their clothes—on their shoes and umbrellas—the rancid smell of the wet dusk outside, but Blake began to relax as soon as he tasted his Gibson and looked around at the common, mostly not-young faces that surrounded him and that were worried, if they were worried at all, about tax rates and who would be put in charge of merchandising. He tried to remember her name—Miss Dent, Miss Bent, Miss Lent—and he was surprised to find that he could not remember it, although he was proud of the retentiveness and reach of his memory and it had only been six months ago.

Personnel had sent her up one afternoon—he was looking for a secretary. He saw a dark woman—in her twenties, perhaps—who was slender and shy. Her dress was simple, her figure was not much, one of her stockings was crooked, but her voice was soft and he had been willing to try her out. After she had been working for him a few days, she told him that she had been in the hospital for eight months and that it had been hard after this for her to find work, and she wanted to thank him for giving her a chance. Her hair was dark, her eyes were dark; she left with him a pleasant impression of darkness. As he got to know her better, he felt that she was oversensitive and, as a consequence, lonely. Once, when she was speaking to him of what she imagined his life to be—full of friendships, money, and a large and loving family—he had thought he recognized a peculiar feeling of deprivation. She seemed to imagine the lives of the rest of the world to be more brilliant than they were. Once, she had put a rose on his desk, and he had dropped it into the wastebasket. "I don't like roses," he told her.

She had been competent, punctual, and a good typist, and he had found only one thing in her that he could object to—her handwriting. He could not associate the crudeness of her handwriting with her appearance. He would have expected her to write a rounded backhand, and in her writing there were intermittent traces of this, mixed with clumsy printing. Her writing gave him the feeling that she had been the victim of some inner—some emotional—conflict that had in its violence broken the continuity of the lines she was able to make on paper. When she had been working for him three weeks—no longer—they stayed late one night and he offered, after work, to buy her a drink. "If you really want a drink," she said, "I have some whiskey at my place."

She lived in a room that seemed to him like a closet. There were suit boxes and hatboxes piled in a corner, and although the room seemed hardly big enough to hold the bed, the dresser, and the chair he sat in, there was an upright piano against one wall, with a book of Beethoven sonatas on the rack. She gave him a drink and said that she was going to put on something more comfortable. He urged her to; that was, after all, what he had come for. If he had any qualms, they would have been practical. Her diffidence, the feeling of deprivation in her point of view, promised to protect him from any consequences. Most of the many women he had known had been picked for their lack of self-esteem.

When he put on his clothes again, an hour or so later, she was weeping. He felt too contented and warm and sleepy to worry much about her tears. As he was dressing, he noticed on the dresser a note she had written to a cleaning woman. The only light came from the bathroom—the door was ajar—and in this half light the hideously scrawled letters again seemed entirely wrong for her, and as if they must be the handwriting of some other and very gross woman. The next day, he did what he felt was the only sensible thing. When she was out for lunch, he called personnel and asked them to fire her. Then he took the afternoon off. A few days later, she came to the office, asking to see him. He told the switchboard girl not to let her in. He had not seen her again until this evening.

Blake drank a second Gibson and saw by the clock that he had missed the express. He would get the local—the five-forty-eight. When he left the bar the sky was still light; it was still raining. He looked carefully up and down the street and saw that the poor woman had gone. Once or twice, he looked over his shoulder, walking to the station, but he seemed to be safe. He was still not quite himself, he realized, because he had left his coffee ring at the bar, and he was not a man who forgot things. This lapse of memory pained him.

He bought a paper. The local was only half full when he boarded it, and he got a seat on the river side and took off his raincoat. He was a slender man with brown hair—undistinguished in every way, unless you could have divined in his pallor or his gray eyes his unpleasant tastes. He dressed—like the rest of us—as if he admitted the existence of sumptuary laws. His raincoat was the pale buff color of a mushroom. His hat was dark brown; so was his suit. Except for the few bright threads in his necktie, there was a scrupulous lack of color in his clothing that seemed protective.

He looked around the car for neighbors. Mrs. Compton was several seats in front of him, to the right. She smiled, but her smile was fleeting. It died swiftly and horribly. Mr. Watkins was directly in front of Blake. Mr. Watkins needed a haircut, and he had broken the sumptuary laws; he was wearing a corduroy jacket. He and Blake had quarreled, so they did not speak.

The swift death of Mrs. Compton's smile did not affect Blake at all. The Comptons lived in the house next to the Blakes, and Mrs. Compton had never understood the importance of minding her own business. Louise Blake took her troubles to Mrs. Compton, Blake knew, and instead of discouraging her crying jags, Mrs. Compton had come to imagine herself a sort of confessor and had developed a lively curiosity about the Blakes' intimate affairs. She had probably been given an account of their most recent quarrel. Blake had come home one night, overworked and tired, and had found that Louise had done nothing about getting supper. He had gone into the kitchen, followed by Louise, and had pointed out to her that the date was the fifth. He had drawn a circle around the date on the kitchen calendar. "One week is the twelfth," he had said. "Two weeks will be the nineteenth." He drew a circle around the nineteenth. "I'm not going to speak to you for two weeks," he had said. "That will be the nineteenth." She had wept, she had protested, but it had been eight or ten years since she had been able to touch him with her entreaties. Louise had got old. Now the lines in her face were ineradicable, and when she clapped her glasses onto her nose to read the evening paper, she looked to him like an unpleasant stranger. The physical charms that had been her only attraction were gone. It had been nine years since Blake had built a bookshelf in the doorway that connected their rooms and had fitted into the bookshelf wooden doors that could be locked, since he did not want the children to see his books. But their prolonged estrangement didn't seem remarkable to Blake. He had quarreled with his wife, but so did every other man born of woman. It was human nature. In any place where you can hear their voices—a hotel courtyard, an air shaft, a street on a summer evening—you will hear harsh words.

The hard feeling between Blake and Mr. Watkins also had to do with Blake's family, but it was not as serious or as troublesome as what lay behind Mrs. Compton's fleeting smile. The Watkinses rented. Mr. Watkins broke the sumptuary laws day after day—he once went to the eight-fourteen in a pair of sandals—and he made his living as a commercial artist. Blake's oldest son—Charlie was fourteen—had made friends with the Watkins boy. He had spent a lot of time in the sloppy rented house where the Watkinses lived. The friendship had affected his manners and his neatness. Then he had begun to take some meals with the Watkinses, and to spend Saturday nights there. When he had moved most of his possessions over to the Watkinses' and had begun to spend more than half his nights there, Blake had been forced to act. He had spoken not to Charlie but to Mr. Watkins, and had, of necessity, said a number of things that must have sounded critical. Mr. Watkins' long and dirty hair and his corduroy jacket reassured Blake that he had been in the right.

But Mrs. Compton's dying smile and Mr. Watkins' dirty hair did not lessen the pleasure Blake took in setting himself in an uncomfortable seat on the five-forty-eight deep underground. The coach was old and smelled oddly like a bomb shelter in which whole families had spent the night. The light that spread from the ceiling down onto their heads and shoulders was dim. The filth on the window glass was streaked with rain from some other journey, and clouds of rank pipe and cigarette smoke had begun to rise from behind each newspaper, but it was a scene that meant to Blake that he was on a safe path, and after his brush with danger he even felt a little warmth toward Mrs. Compton and Mr. Watkins.

The train traveled up from underground into the weak daylight, and the slums and the city reminded Blake vaguely of the woman who had followed him. To avoid speculation or remorse about her, he turned his attention to the evening paper. Out of the corner of his eye he could see the landscape. It was industrial and, at that hour, sad. There were machine sheds and warehouses, and above these he saw a break in the clouds—a piece of yellow light. "Mr. Blake," someone said. He looked up. It was she. She was standing there holding one hand on the back of the seat to steady herself in the swaying coach. He remembered her name then—Miss Dent. "Hello, Miss Dent," he said.

"Do you mind if I sit here?"

"I guess not."

"Thank you. It's very kind of you. I don't like to inconvenience you like this. I don't want to . . . ." He had been frightened when he looked up and saw her, but her timid voice rapidly reassured him. He shifted his hams—that futile and reflexive gesture of hospitality—and she sat down. She sighed. He smelled her wet clothing. She wore a formless black hat with a cheap crest stitched onto it. Her coat was thin cloth, he saw, and she wore gloves and carried a large pocketbook.

"Are you living out in this direction now, Miss Dent?"

"No."

She opened her purse and reached for her handkerchief. She had begun to cry. He turned his head to see if anyone in the car was looking, but no one was. He had sat beside a thousand passengers on the evening train. He had noticed their clothes, the holes in their gloves; and if they fell asleep and mumbled he had wondered what their worries were. He had classified almost all of them briefly before he buried his nose in the paper. He had marked them as rich, poor, brilliant or dull, neighbors or strangers, but no one of the thousand had ever wept. When she opened her purse, he remembered her perfume. It had clung to his skin the night he went to her place for a drink.

"I've been very sick," she said. "This is the first time I've been out of bed in two weeks. I've been terribly sick."

"I'm sorry that you've been sick, Miss Dent," he said in a voice loud enough to be heard by Mr. Watkins and Mrs. Compton. "Where are you working now?"

"What?"

"Where are you working now?"

"Oh, don't make me laugh," she said softly.

"I don't understand."

"You poisoned their minds."

He straightened his neck and braced his shoulders. These wrenching movements expressed a brief—and hopeless—longing to be in some other place. She meant trouble. He took a breath. He looked with deep feeling at the half-filled, half-lighted coach to affirm his sense of actuality, of a world in which there was not very much bad trouble after all. He was conscious of her heavy breathing and the smell of her rain-soaked coat. The train stopped. A nun and a man in overalls got off. When it started again, Blake put on his hat and reached for his raincoat.

"Where are you going?" she said.

"I'm going to the next car."

"Oh, no," she said. "No, no, no." She put her white face so close to his ear that he could feel her warm breath on his cheek. "Don't do that," she whispered. "Don't try and escape me. I have a pistol and I'll have to kill you and I don't want to. All I want to do is to talk with you. Don't move or I'll kill you. Don't, don't, don't!"

Blake sat back abruptly in his seat. If he had wanted to stand and shout for help, he would not have been able to. His tongue had swelled to twice its size, and when he tried to move it, it stuck horribly to the roof of his mouth. His legs were limp. All he could think of to do then was to wait for his heart to stop its hysterical beating, so that he could judge the extent of his danger. She was sitting a little sidewise, and in her pocketbook was the pistol, aimed at his belly.

"You understand me now, don't you?" she said. "You understand that I'm serious?" He tried to speak but he was still mute. He nodded his head. "Now we'll sit quietly for a little while," she said. "I got so excited that my thoughts are all confused. We'll sit quietly for a little while, until I can get my thoughts in order again."

Help would come, Blake thought. It was only a question of minutes. Someone, noticing the look on his face or her peculiar posture, would stop and interfere, and it would all be over. All he had to do was to wait until someone noticed his predicament. Out of the window he saw the river and the sky. The rain clouds were rolling down like a shutter, and while he watched, a streak of orange light on the horizon became brilliant. Its brilliance spread—he could see it move—across the waves until it raked the banks of the river with a dim firelight. Then it was put out. Help would come in a minute, he thought. Help would come before they stopped again; but the train stopped, there were some comings and goings, and Blake still lived on, at the mercy of the woman beside him. The possibility that help might not come was one that he could not face. The possibility that his predicament was not noticeable, that Mrs. Compton would guess that he was taking a poor relation out to dinner at Shady Hill, was something he would think about later. Then the saliva came back into his mouth and he was able to speak.

"Miss Dent?"

"Yes."

"What do you want?"

"I want to talk to you."

"You can come to my office."

"Oh, no. I went there every day for two weeks."

"You could make an appointment."

"No," she said. "I think we can talk here. I wrote you a letter but I've been too sick to go out and mail it. I've put down all my thoughts. I like to travel. I like trains. One of my troubles has always been that I could never afford to travel. I suppose you see this scenery every night and don't notice it any more, but it's nice for someone who's been in bed a long time. They say that He's not in the river and the hills but I think He is. 'Where shall wisdom be found?' it says. 'Where is the place of understanding? The depth saith it is not in me; the sea saith it is not with me. Destruction and death say we have heard the force with our ears.'[1]

"Oh, I know what you're thinking," she said. "You're thinking that I'm crazy, and I have been very sick again but I'm going to be better. It's going to make me better to talk with you. I was in the hospital all the time before I came to work for you but they never tried to cure me, they only wanted to take away my self-respect. I haven't had any work now for three months. Even if I did have to kill you, they wouldn't be able to do anything to me except put me back in the hospital, so you see I'm not afraid. But let's sit quietly for a little while longer. I have to be calm."

The train continued its halting progress up the bank of the river, and Blake tried to force himself to make some plans for escape, but the immediate threat to his life made this difficult, and instead of planning sensibly, he thought of the many ways in which he could have avoided her in the first place. As soon as he had felt these regrets, he realized their futility. It was like regretting his lack of suspicion when she first mentioned her months in the hospital. It was like regretting his failure to have been warned by her shyness, her diffidence, and the handwriting that looked like the marks of a claw. There was no way of rectifying his mistakes, and he felt—for perhaps the first time in his mature life—the full force of regret. Out of the window, he saw some men

1. A slight misquotation of Job 28:12, 14, 22.

fishing on the nearly dark river, and then a ramshackle boat club that seemed to have been nailed together out of scraps of wood that had been washed up on the shore.

Mr. Watkins had fallen asleep. He was snoring. Mrs. Compton read her paper. The train creaked, slowed, and halted infirmly at another station. Blake could see the southbound platform, where a few passengers were waiting to go into the city. There was a workman with a lunch pail, a dressed-up woman, and a woman with a suitcase. They stood apart from one another. Some advertisements were posted on the wall behind them. There was a picture of a couple drinking a toast in wine, a picture of a Cat's Paw rubber heel, and a picture of a Hawaiian dancer. Their cheerful intent seemed to go no farther than the puddles of water on the platform and to expire there. The platform and the people on it looked lonely. The train drew away from the station into the scattered lights of a slum and then into the darkness of the country and the river.

"I want you to read my letter before we get to Shady Hill," she said. "It's on the seat. Pick it up. I would have mailed it to you, but I've been too sick to go out. I haven't gone out for two weeks. I haven't had any work for three months. I haven't spoken to anybody but the landlady. Please read my letter."

He picked up the letter from the seat where she had put it. The cheap paper felt abhorrent and filthy to his fingers. It was folded and refolded. "Dear Husband," she had written, in that crazy, wandering hand, "they say that human love leads us to divine love, but is this true? I dream about you every night. I have such terrible desires. I have always had a gift for dreams. I dreamed on Tuesday of a volcano erupting with blood. When I was in the hospital they said they wanted to cure me but they only wanted to take away my self-respect. They only wanted me to dream about sewing and basketwork but I protected my gift for dreams. I'm clairvoyant. I can tell when the telephone is going to ring. I've never had a true friend in my whole life. . . ."

The train stopped again. There was another platform, another picture of the couple drinking a toast, the rubber heel, and the Hawaiian dancer. Suddenly she pressed her face close to Blake's again and whispered in his ear. "I know what you're thinking. I can see it in your face. You're thinking you can get away from me in Shady Hill, aren't you? Oh, I've been planning this for weeks. It's all I've had to think about. I won't harm you if you'll let me talk. I've been thinking about devils. I mean, if there are devils in the world, if there are people in the world who represent evil, is it our duty to exterminate them? I know that you always prey on weak people. I can tell. Oh, sometimes I think I ought to kill you. Sometimes I think you're the only obstacle between me and my happiness. Sometimes . . ."

She touched Blake with the pistol. He felt the muzzle against his belly. The bullet, at that distance, would make a small hole where it entered, but it would rip out of his back a place as big as a soccer ball. He remembered the unburied dead he had seen in the war. The memory came in a rush; entrails, eyes, shattered bone, ordure, and other filth.

"All I've ever wanted in life is a little love," she said. She lightened the pressure of the gun. Mr. Watkins still slept. Mrs. Compton was sitting calmly with her hands folded in her lap. The coach rocked gently, and the coats and mushroom-colored raincoats that hung between the windows swayed a little as the car moved. Blake's elbow was on the window sill and his left shoe was on the guard above the steampipe. The car smelled like some dismal classroom. The passengers seemed asleep and apart, and Blake felt that he might never escape the smell of heat and wet clothing and the dimness of the light. He tried to summon the calculated self-deceptions with which he sometimes cheered himself, but he was left without any energy for hope of self-deception.

The conductor put his head in the door and said, "Shady Hill, next, Shady Hill."

"Now," she said. "Now you get out ahead of me."

Mr. Watkins waked suddenly, put on his coat and hat, and smiled at Mrs. Compton, who was gathering her parcels to her in a series of maternal gestures. They went to the door. Blake joined them, but neither of them spoke to him or seemed to notice the woman at his back. The conductor threw open the door, and Blake saw on the platform of the next car a few other neighbors who had missed the express, waiting patiently and tiredly in the wan light for their trip to end. He raised his head to see through the open door the abandoned mansion out of town, a NO TRESPASSING sign nailed to a tree, and then the oil tanks. The concrete abutments of the bridge passed, so close to the open door that he could have touched them. Then he saw the first of the lampposts on the northbound platform, the sign SHADY HILL in black and gold, and the little lawn and flower bed kept up by the Improvement Association, and then the cab stand and a corner of the old-fashioned depot. It was raining again; it was pouring. He could hear the splash of water and see the lights reflected in puddles and in the shining pavement, and the idle sound of splashing and dripping formed in his mind a conception of shelter, so light and strange that it seemed to belong to a time of his life that he could not remember.

He went down the steps with her at his back. A dozen or so cars were waiting by the station with their motors running. A few people got off from each of the other coaches; he recognized most of them, but none of them offered to give him a ride. They walked separately or in pairs—purposefully out of the rain to the shelter of the platform, where the car horns called to them. It was time to go home, time for a drink, time for love, time for supper, and he could see the lights on the hill—lights by which children were being bathed, meat cooked, dishes washed—shining in the rain. One by one, the cars picked up the heads of families, until there were only four left. Two of the stranded passengers drove off in the only taxi the village had. "I'm sorry, darling," a woman said tenderly to her husband when she drove up a few minutes later. "All our clocks are slow." The last man looked at his watch, looked at the rain, and then walked off into it, and Blake saw him go as if they had some reason to say goodbye—not as we say goodbye to friends after a party but as we say goodbye when we are faced with an inexorable and unwanted parting of the spirit and the heart. The man's footsteps sounded as he crossed the parking lot to the sidewalk, and then they were lost. In the station, a telephone began to ring. The ringing was loud, evenly spaced, and unanswered. Someone wanted to know about the next train to Albany, but Mr. Flanagan, the stationmaster, had gone home an hour ago. He had turned on all his lights before he went away. They burned in the empty waiting room. They burned, tin-shaded, at intervals up and down the platform and with the peculiar sadness of dim and purposeless lights. They lighted the Hawaiian dancer, the couple drinking a toast, the rubber heel.

"I've never been here before," she said. "I thought it would look different. I didn't think it would look so shabby. Let's get out of the light. Go over there."

His legs felt sore. All his strength was gone. "Go on," she said.

North of the station there were a freight house and a coalyard and an inlet where the butcher and the baker and the man who ran the service station moored the dinghies, from which they fished on Sundays, sunk now to the gunwales with the rain. As he walked toward the freight house, he saw a movement on the ground and heard a scraping sound, and then he saw a rat take its head out of a paper bag and regard him. The rat seized the bag in its teeth and dragged it into a culvert.

"Stop," she said. "Turn around. Oh, I ought to feel sorry for you. Look at your poor face. But you don't know what I've been through. I'm afraid to go out in the daylight. I'm afraid the blue sky will fall down on me. I'm like poor Chicken-Licken. I only feel like myself when it begins to get dark. But still and all I'm better than you. I still have good dreams sometimes. I dream about picnics and heaven and the brotherhood of man, and about castles in the moonlight and a river with willow trees all along the edge of it and foreign cities, and after all I know more about love than you."

He heard from off the dark river the drone of an outboard motor, a sound that drew slowly behind it across the dark water such a burden of clear, sweet memories of gone summers and gone pleasures that it made his flesh crawl, and he thought of dark in the mountains and the children singing. "They never wanted to cure me," she said. "They . . ." The noise of train coming down from the north drowned out her voice, but she went on talking. The noise filled his ears, and the windows where people ate, drank, slept, and read flew past. When the train had passed beyond the bridge, the noise grew distant, and he heard her screaming at him, "*Kneel down!* Kneel down! Do what I say. *Kneel down!*"

He got to his knees. He bent his head. "There," she said. "You see, if you do what I say, I won't harm you, because I really don't want to harm you, I want to help you, but when I see your face it sometimes seems to me that I can't help you. Sometimes it seems to me that if I were good and loving and sane—oh, much better than I am—sometimes it seems to me that if I were all these things and young and beautiful, too, and if I called to show you the right way, you wouldn't heed me. Oh, I'm better than you, I'm better than you, and I shouldn't waste my time or spoil my life like this. Put your face in the dirt. *Put your face in the dirt!* Do what I say. Put your face in the dirt."

He fell forward in the filth. The coal skinned his face. He stretched out on the ground, weeping. "Now I feel better," she said. "Now I can wash my hands of you, I can wash my hands of all this, because you see there is some kindness, some saneness in me that I can find and use. I can wash my hands." Then he heard her footsteps go away from him, over the rubble. He heard the clearer and more distant sound they made on the hard surface of the platform. He heard them diminish. He raised his head. He saw her climb the stairs of the wooden footbridge and cross it and go down to the other platform, where her figure in the dim light looked small, common, and harmless. He raised himself out of the dust—warily at first, until he saw by her attitude, her looks, that she had forgotten him; that she had completed what she had wanted to do, and that he was safe. He got to his feet and picked up his hat from the ground where it had fallen and walked home.

---

1. How has the author contrived an air of menace from the commonplace street scene of the beginning?
2. Is Miss Dent's handwriting any evidence of a disordered personality?
3. Does her disorder permit her superior insights into right and wrong and the requirements of justice in human relationships?
4. What are the shortcomings in Blake's behavior for which he deserves punishment (or correction)? Would he recognize these without her threats?
5. Miss Dent says he "prey[s] on weak people." Is this because Blake himself is weak? Is he something worse than weak? Is he, in her words, a devil, someone who "represent[s] evil"?

Anton Chekhov

Chekhov (1860–1904) was born in Taganrog, Russia, the son of a despotic, dishonest, and rough-grained father—who was nevertheless eager to impart to his children his love for music and art. Trained as a physician at Moscow University, Chekhov practiced medicine only intermittently, although he credited his scientific training with conditioning him to be a realistic observer of society and individual behavior. While still a medical student he began to write short pieces for humorous magazines; the popularity of these sketches roused his determination to become a serious artist. In 1890 he visited the Russian penal island of Sakhalin and without fanfare or special pleading wrote a moving account of convict life as he saw it there. He was at the height of his literary powers and his fame in 1901 when he married a young actress, but the state of his health by then was disastrous. In the short time remaining to him he was confined mostly to the house he had built from his literary earnings at Yalta in southern Russia, infrequently able to accompany his wife to Moscow to watch her performances in his plays. Those plays—among them The Seagull *(1896),* Uncle Vanya *(1899),* The Three Sisters *(1901), and* The Cherry Orchard *(1904)—established him as one of the great dramatists of modern times, while his hundreds of short stories and novellas have immensely influenced the art of fiction since his death. In tribute to the humanity and responsibility of his work, Leo Tolstoy called him "an artist of life."*

The Lady with the Dog

I

People were telling one another that a newcomer had been seen on the promenade—a lady with a dog. Dmitry Dmitrich Gurov had been a fortnight in Yalta,[1] and was accustomed to its ways, and he, too, had begun to take an interest in fresh arrivals. From his seat in Vernet's outdoor café, he caught sight of a young woman in a toque, passing along the promenade; she was fair and not very tall; after her trotted a white Pomeranian.

Later he encountered her in the municipal park and in the square several times a day. She was always alone, wearing the same toque,

1. Russian city on the Black Sea; a resort for southern vacations.

and the Pomeranian always trotted at her side. Nobody knew who she was, and people referred to her simply as "the lady with the dog."

"If she's here without her husband, and without any friends," thought Gurov, "it wouldn't be a bad idea to make her acquaintance."

He was not yet forty but had a twelve-year-old daughter and two sons in high school. He had been talked into marrying in his third year at college, and his wife now looked nearly twice as old as he did. She was a tall woman with dark eyebrows, erect, dignified, imposing, and, as she said of herself, a "thinker." She was a great reader, omitted the "hard sign"[2] at the end of words in her letters, and called her husband "Dimitry" instead of Dmitry; and though he secretly considered her shallow, narrow-minded, and dowdy, he stood in awe of her, and disliked being at home. He had first begun deceiving her long ago and he was now constantly unfaithful to her, and this was no doubt why he spoke slightingly of women, to whom he referred as *the lower race.*

He considered that the ample lessons he had received from bitter experience entitled him to call them whatever he liked, but without this "lower race" he could not have existed a single day. He was bored and ill-at-ease in the company of men, with whom he was always cold and reserved, but felt quite at home among women, and knew exactly what to say to them, and how to behave; he could even be silent in their company without feeling the slightest awkwardness. There was an elusive charm in his appearance and disposition which attracted women and caught their sympathies. He knew this and was himself attracted to them by some invisible force.

Repeated and bitter experience had taught him that every fresh intimacy, while at first introducing such pleasant variety into everyday life, and offering itself as a charming, light adventure, inevitably developed, among decent people (especially in Moscow, where they are so irresolute and slow to move), into a problem of excessive complication leading to an intolerably irksome situation. But every time he encountered an attractive woman he forgot all about this experience, the desire for life surged up in him, and everything suddenly seemed simple and amusing.

One evening, then, while he was dining at the restaurant in the park, the lady in the toque came strolling up and took a seat at a neighboring table. Her expression, gait, dress, coiffure, all told him that she was from the upper classes, that she was married, that she was in Yalta for the first time, alone and bored. . . . The accounts of the laxity of morals among visitors to Yalta are greatly exaggerated, and he paid no heed to them, knowing that for the most part they were invented by

2. Certain progressive intellectuals omitted the hard sign after consonants in writing, anticipating the later reform in the Russian alphabet. Here used rather as emancipated affectation.

people who would gladly have transgressed themselves, had they known how to set about it. But when the lady sat down at a neighboring table a few yards away from him, these stories of easy conquests, of excursions to the mountains, came back to him, and the seductive idea of a brisk transitory liaison, an affair with a woman whose very name he did not know, suddenly took possession of his mind.

He snapped his fingers at the Pomeranian and, when it trotted up to him, shook his forefinger at it. The Pomeranian growled. Gurov shook his finger again.

The lady glanced at him and instantly lowered her eyes.

"He doesn't bite," she said, and blushed.

"May I give him a bone?" he asked, and on her nod of consent added in friendly tones: "Have you been long in Yalta?"

"About five days."

"And I am dragging out my second week here."

Neither spoke for a few minutes.

"The days pass quickly, and yet one is so bored here," she said, not looking at him.

"It's the thing to say it's boring here. People never complain of boredom in godforsaken holes like Belyev or Zhizdra,[3] but when they get here it's: 'Oh, the dullness! Oh, the dust!' You'd think they'd come from Granada[4] to say the least."

She laughed. Then they both went on eating in silence, like complete strangers. But after dinner they left the restaurant together, and embarked upon the light, jesting talk of people free and contented, for whom it is all the same where they go, or what they talk about. They strolled along, remarking on the strange light over the sea. The water was a warm, tender purple, the moonlight lay on its surface in a golden strip. They said how close it was, after the hot day. Gurov told her he was from Moscow, had a degree in literature but worked in a bank; that he had at one time trained himself to sing in a private opera company, but had given up the idea; that he owned two houses in Moscow. . . . And from her he learned that she had grown up in Petersburg, but had gotten married in the town of S., where she had been living two years, that she would stay another month in Yalta, and that perhaps her husband, who also needed a rest, would join her. She was quite unable to explain whether her husband was a member of the province council, or on the board of the *zemstvo*,[5] and was greatly amused at herself for this. Further, Gurov learned that her name was Anna Sergeyevna.

3. Dull, provincial Russian cities. 4. City in southern Spain, legendary for its charm. 5. A county council.

Back in his own room he thought about her, and felt sure he would meet her the next day. It was inevitable. As he went to bed he reminded himself that only a very short time ago she had been a schoolgirl, like his own daughter, learning her lessons, he remembered how much there was of shyness and constraint in her laughter, in her way of conversing with a stranger—it was probably the first time in her life that she found herself alone, and in a situation in which men could follow her and watch her, and speak to her, all the time with a secret aim she could not fail to divine. He recalled her slender, delicate neck, her fine gray eyes.

"And yet there's something pathetic about her," he thought to himself as he fell asleep.

II

A week had passed since the beginning of their acquaintance. It was a holiday. Indoors it was stuffy, but the dust rose in clouds out of doors, and people's hats blew off. It was a parching day and Gurov kept going to the outdoor café for fruit drinks and ices to offer Anna Sergeyevna. The heat was overpowering.

In the evening, when the wind had dropped, they walked to the pier to see the steamer come in. There were a great many people strolling about the landing-place; some, bunches of flowers in their hands, were meeting friends. Two peculiarities of the smart Yalta crowd stood out distinctly—the elderly ladies all tried to dress very youthfully, and there seemed to be an inordinate number of generals about.

Owing to the roughness of the sea the steamer arrived late, after the sun had gone down, and it had to maneuver for some time before it could get alongside the pier. Anna Sergeyevna scanned the steamer and passengers through her lorgnette, as if looking for someone she knew, and when she turned to Gurov her eyes were glistening. She talked a great deal, firing off abrupt questions and forgetting immediately what it was she had wanted to know. Then she lost her lorgnette in the crush.

The smart crowd began dispersing, features could no longer be made out, the wind had quite dropped, and Gurov and Anna Sergeyevna stood there as if waiting for someone else to come off the steamer. Anna Sergeyevna had fallen silent, every now and then smelling her flowers, but not looking at Gurov.

"It's turning out a fine evening," he said. "What shall we do? We might go for a drive."

She made no reply.

He looked steadily at her and suddenly took her in his arms and kissed her lips, and the fragrance and dampness of the flowers closed round him, but the next moment he looked behind him in alarm—had anyone seen them?

"Let's go to your room," he murmured.

And they walked off together, very quickly.

Her room was stuffy and smelt of some scent she had bought in the Japanese shop. Gurov looked at her, thinking to himself: "How full of strange encounters life is!" He could remember carefree, good-natured women who were exhilarated by love-making and grateful to him for the happiness he gave them, however short-lived; and there had been others—his wife among them—whose caresses were insincere, affected, hysterical, mixed up with a great deal of quite unnecessary talk, and whose expression seemed to say that all this was not just love-making or passion, but something much more significant; then there had been two or three beautiful, cold women, over whose features flitted a predatory expression, betraying a determination to wring from life more than it could give, women no longer in their first youth, capricious, irrational, despotic, brainless, and when Gurov had cooled to these, their beauty aroused in him nothing but repulsion, and the lace trimming on their underclothes reminded him of fish-scales.

But here the timidity and awkwardness of youth and inexperience were still apparent; and there was a feeling of embarrassment in the atmosphere, as if someone had just knocked at the door. Anna Sergeyevna, "the lady with the dog," seemed to regard the affair as something very special, very serious, as if she had become a fallen woman, an attitude he found odd and disconcerting. Her features lengthened and drooped, and her long hair hung mournfully on either side of her face. She assumed a pose of dismal meditation, like a repentant sinner in some classical painting.

"It isn't right," she said. "You will never respect me anymore."

On the table was a watermelon. Gurov cut himself a slice from it and began slowly eating it. At least half an hour passed in silence.

Anna Sergeyevna was very touching, revealing the purity of a decent, naïve woman who had seen very little of life. The solitary candle burning on the table scarcely lit up her face, but it was obvious that her heart was heavy.

"Why should I stop respecting you?" asked Gurov. "You don't know what you're saying."

"May God forgive me!" she exclaimed, and her eyes filled with tears. "It's terrible."

"No need to seek to justify yourself."

"How can I justify myself? I'm a wicked, fallen woman, I despise myself and have not the least thought of self-justification. It isn't my husband I have deceived, it's myself. And not only now, I have been deceiving myself for ever so long. My husband is no doubt an honest, worthy man, but he's a flunky. I don't know what it is he does at his office, but I know he's a flunky. I was only twenty when I married him, and I was devoured by curiosity, I wanted something higher. I told myself that there must be a different kind of life I wanted to live, to live. . . . I was burning with curiosity . . . you'll never understand that, but I swear to God I could no longer control myself, nothing could hold me back, I told my husband I was ill, and I came here. . . . And I started going about like one possessed, like a madwoman . . . and now I have become an ordinary, worthless woman, and everyone has a right to despise me."

Gurov listened to her, bored to death. The naïve accents, the remorse, all was so unexpected, so out of place. But for the tears in her eyes, she might have been jesting or play-acting.

"I don't understand," he said gently. "What is it you want?"

She hid her face against his breast and pressed closer to him.

"Do believe me, I implore you to believe me," she said. "I love all that is honest and pure in life, vice is revolting to me, I don't know what I'm doing. The common people say they are snared by the Devil. And now I can say that I have been snared by the Devil, too."

"Come, come," he murmured.

He gazed into her fixed, terrified eyes, kissed her, and soothed her with gentle affectionate words, and gradually she calmed down and regained her cheerfulness. Soon they were laughing together again.

When, a little later, they went out, there was not a soul on the promenade, the town and its cypresses looked dead, but the sea was still roaring as it dashed against the beach. A solitary fishing-boat tossed on the waves, its lamp blinking sleepily.

They found a carriage and drove to Oreanda.

"I discovered your name in the hall, just now," said Gurov, "written up on the board. Von Diederitz. Is your husband a German?"

"No. His grandfather was, I think, but he belongs to the Orthodox Church himself."

When they got out of the carriage at Oreanda they sat down on a bench not far from the church, and looked down at the sea, without talking. Yalta could be dimly discerned through the morning mist, and white clouds rested motionless on the summits of the mountains. Not a leaf stirred, the grasshoppers chirruped, and the monotonous hollow roar of the sea came up to them, speaking of peace, of the eternal sleep lying in wait for us all. The sea had roared like this long before there was any Yalta or Oreanda, it was roaring now, and it would go on roaring, just as indifferently and hollowly, when we had passed away. And it may be that in this continuity, this utter indifference to the life and death of each of us lies hidden the pledge of our eternal salvation, of the continuous movement of life on earth, of the continuous movement toward perfection.

Side by side with a young woman, who looked so exquisite in the early light, soothed and enchanted by the sight of all this magical beauty—sea, mountains, clouds and the vast expanse of the sky—Gurov told himself that, when you came to think of it, everything in the world is beautiful really, everything but our own thoughts and actions, when we lose sight of the higher aims of life, and of our dignity as human beings.

Someone approached them—a watchman, probably—looked at them and went away. And there was something mysterious and beautiful even in this. The steamer from Feodosia could be seen coming towards the pier, lit up by the dawn, its lamps out.

"There's dew on the grass," said Anna Sergeyevna, breaking the silence.

"Yes. Time to go home."

They went back to the town.

After this they met every day at noon on the promenade, lunching and dining together, going for walks, and admiring the sea. She complained of sleeplessness, of palpitations, asked the same questions over and over again, alternately surrendering to jealousy and the fear that he did not really respect her. And often, when there was nobody in sight in the square or the park, he would draw her to him and kiss her passionately. The utter idleness, these kisses in broad daylight, accompanied by furtive glances and the fear of discovery, the heat, the smell of the sea, and the idle, smart, well-fed people continually crossing their field of vision, seemed to have given him a new lease on life. He told Anna Sergeyevna she was beautiful and seductive, made love to her with impetuous passion, and never left her side, while she was always pensive, always trying to force from him the admission that he did not respect her, that he did not love her a bit, and considered her just an ordinary woman. Almost every night they drove out of town, to Oreanda, the waterfall, or some other beauty-spot. And these excursions were invariably a success, each contributing fresh impressions of majestic beauty.

All this time they kept expecting her husband to arrive. But a letter came in which he told his wife that he was having trouble with his eyes, and implored her to come home as soon as possible. Anna Sergeyevna made hasty preparations for leaving.

"It's a good thing I'm going," she said to Gurov. "It's the intervention of fate."

She left Yalta in a carriage, and he went with her as far as the railway station. The drive took nearly a whole day. When she got into the express train, after the second bell had been rung, she said:

"Let me have one more look at you. . . . One last look. That's right."

She did not weep, but was mournful, and seemed ill, the muscles of her cheeks twitching.

"I shall think of you . . . I shall think of you all the time," she said. "God bless you! Think kindly of me. We are parting forever, it must be so, because we ought never to have met. Good-bye—God bless you."

The train steamed rapidly out of the station, its lights soon disappearing, and a minute later even the sound it made was silenced, as if everything were conspiring to bring this sweet oblivion, this madness, to an end as quickly as possible. And Gurov, standing alone on the platform and gazing into the dark distance, listened to the shrilling of the grasshoppers and the humming of the telegraph wires, with a feeling that he had only just awakened. And he told himself that this had been just one more of the many adventures in his life, and that it, too, was over, leaving nothing but a memory. . . . He was moved and sad, and felt a slight remorse. After all, this young woman whom he would never again see had not been really happy with him. He had been friendly and affectionate with her, but in his whole behaviour, in the tones of his voice, in his very caresses, there had been a shade of irony, the insulting indulgence of the fortunate male, who was, moreover, almost twice her age. She had insisted in calling him good, remarkable, high-minded. Evidently he had appeared to her different from his real self, in a word he had involuntarily deceived her. . . .

There was an autumnal feeling in the air, and the evening was chilly.

"It's time for me to be going north, too," thought Gurov, as he walked away from the platform. "High time!"

III

When he got back to Moscow it was beginning to look like winter; the stoves were heated every day, and it was still dark when the children got up to go to school and drank their tea, so that the nurse had to light the lamp for a short time. Frost had set in. When the first snow falls, and one goes for one's first sleigh-ride, it is pleasant to see the white ground, the white roofs; one breathes freely and lightly, and remembers the days of one's youth. The ancient lime-trees and birches, white with hoarfrost, have a good-natured look, they are closer to the heart than cypresses and palms, and beneath their branches one is no longer haunted by the memory of mountains and the sea.

Gurov had always lived in Moscow, and he returned to Moscow on a fine frosty day, and when he put on his fur-lined overcoat and thick gloves, and sauntered down Petrovka Street, and when, on Saturday evening, he heard the church bells ringing, his recent journey and the places he had visited lost their charm for him. He became gradually immersed in Moscow life, reading with avidity three newspapers a day, while declaring he never read Moscow newspapers on principle. Once more he was caught up in a whirl of restaurants, clubs, banquets, and celebrations, once more glowed with the flattering consciousness that well-known lawyers and actors came to his house, that he played cards in the Medical Club opposite a professor. He could once again eat a whole serving of Moscow Fish Stew served in a pan.

He had believed that in a month's time Anna Sergeyevna would be nothing but a vague memory, and that hereafter, with her wistful smile, she would only occasionally appear to him in dreams, like others before her. But the month was now well over and winter was in full swing, and all was as clear in his memory as if he had parted with Anna Sergeyevna only the day before. And his recollections grew ever more insistent. When the voices of his children at their lessons reached him in his study through the evening stillness, when he heard a song, or the sounds of a music-box in a restaurant, when the wind howled in the chimney, it all came back to him: early morning on the pier, the misty mountains, the steamer from Feodosia, the kisses. He would pace up and down his room for a long time, smiling at his memories, and then memory turned into dreaming, and what had happened mingled in his imagination with what was going to happen. Anna Sergeyevna did not come to him in his dreams, she accompanied him everywhere, like his shadow, following him everywhere he went. When he closed his eyes, she seemed to stand before him in the flesh, still lovelier, younger, tenderer than she had really been, and looking back, he saw himself, too, as better than he had been in Yalta. In the evenings she looked out at him from the bookshelves, the fireplace, the corner, he could hear her breathing, the sweet rustle of her skirts. In the streets he followed women with his eyes, to see if there were any like her. . . .

He began to feel an overwhelming desire to share his memories with someone. But he could not speak of his love at home, and outside his home who was there for him to confide in? Not the tenants living in his house, and certainly not his colleagues at the bank. And what was there to tell? Was it love that he had felt? Had there been anything exquisite, poetic, anything instructive or even amusing about his relations with Anna Sergeyevna? He had to content himself with uttering vague generalizations about love and women, and nobody guessed what he meant, though his wife's dark eyebrows twitched as she said:

"The role of a coxcomb doesn't suit you a bit, Dimitry."

One evening, leaving the Medical Club with one of his card-partners, a government official, he could not refrain from remarking:

"If you only knew what a charming woman I met in Yalta!"

The official got into his sleigh, and just before driving off, turned and called out:

"Dmitry Dmitrich!"

"Yes?"

"You were quite right, you know—the sturgeon was just a *leetle* off."

These words, in themselves so commonplace, for some reason infuriated Gurov, seemed to him humiliating, gross. What savage manners, what people! What wasted evenings, what tedious, empty days! Frantic card-playing, gluttony, drunkenness, perpetual talk always about the same thing. The greater part of one's time and energy went on business that was no use to anyone, and on discussing the same thing over and over again, and there was nothing to show for it all but a stunted wingless existence and a round of trivialities, and there was nowhere to escape to, you might as well be in a madhouse or a convict settlement.

Gurov lay awake all night, raging, and went about the whole of the next day with a headache. He slept badly on the succeeding nights, too, sitting up in bed, thinking, or pacing the floor of his room. He was sick of his children, sick of the bank, felt not the slightest desire to go anywhere or talk about anything.

When the Christmas holidays came, he packed his things, telling his wife he had to go to Petersburg in the interests of a certain young man, and set off for the town of S. To what end? He hardly knew himself. He only knew that he must see Anna Sergeyevna, must speak to her, arrange a meeting, if possible.

He arrived at S. in the morning and engaged the best suite in the hotel, which had a carpet of gray military frieze, and a dusty ink-pot on the table, surmounted by a headless rider, holding his hat in his raised hand. The hall porter told him what he wanted to know: von Diederitz had a house of his own in Staro-Goncharnaya Street. It wasn't far from the hotel, he lived on a grand scale, luxuriously, kept carriage-horses, the whole town knew him. The hall porter pronounced the name "Drideritz."

Gurov strolled over to Staro-Goncharnaya Street and discovered the house. In front of it was a long gray fence with inverted nails hammered into the tops of the palings.

"A fence like that is enough to make anyone want to run away," thought Gurov, looking at the windows of the house and the fence.

He reasoned that since it was a holiday, Anna's husband would probably be at home. In any case it would be tactless to embarrass her by calling at the house. And a note might fall into the hands of the husband, and bring about catastrophe. The best thing would be to wait about on the chance of seeing her. And he walked up and down the street, hovering in the vicinity of the fence, watching for his chance. A beggar entered the gate, only to be attacked by dogs, then, an hour later, the faint, vague sounds of a piano reached his ears. That would be Anna Sergeyevna playing. Suddenly the front door opened and an old woman came out, followed by a familiar white Pomeranian. Gurov tried to call to it, but his heart beat violently, and in his agitation he could not remember its name.

He walked on, hating the gray fence more and more, and now ready to tell himself irately that Anna Sergeyevna had forgotten him, had already, perhaps, found distraction in another—what could be more natural in a young woman who had to look at this accursed fence from morning to night? He went back to his hotel and sat on the sofa in his suite for some time, not knowing what to do, then he ordered dinner, and after dinner, had a long sleep.

"What a foolish, restless business," he thought, waking up and looking towards the dark windowpanes. It was evening by now. "Well, I've had my sleep out. And what am I to do in the night?"

He sat up in bed, covered by the cheap gray quilt, which reminded him of a hospital blanket, and in his vexation he fell to taunting himself.

"You and your lady with a dog . . . there's adventure for you! See what you get for your pains."

On his arrival at the station that morning he had noticed a poster announcing in enormous letters the first performance at the local theatre of *The Geisha*.[6] Remembering this, he got up and made for the theatre.

"It's highly probable that she goes to first nights," he told himself.

The theatre was full. It was a typical provincial theatre, with a mist collecting over the chandeliers, and the crowd in the gallery fidgeting noisily. In the first row of the stalls the local dandies stood waiting for the curtain to go up, their hands clasped behind them. There, in the front seat of the governor's box, sat the governor's daughter, wearing a boa, the governor himself hiding modestly behind the drapes, so that only his hands were visible. The curtain stirred, the orchestra took a long time tuning up their instruments. Gurov's eyes roamed eagerly over the audience as they filed in and occupied their seats.

Anna Sergeyevna came in, too. She seated herself in the third row of the stalls, and when Gurov's glance fell on her, his heart seemed to stop, and he knew in a flash that the whole world contained no one nearer or dearer to him, no one more important to his happiness. This

6. An operetta (1897) by the English composer Sidney Jones.

little woman, lost in the provincial crowd, in no way remarkable, holding a silly lorgnette in her hand, now filled his whole life, was his grief, his joy, all that he desired. Lulled by the sounds coming from the wretched orchestra, with its feeble, amateurish violinists, he thought how beautiful she was . . . thought and dreamed. . . .

Anna Sergeyevna was accompanied by a tall, round-shouldered young man with small whiskers, who nodded at every step before taking the seat beside her and seemed to be continually bowing to someone. This must be her husband, whom, in a fit of bitterness, at Yalta, she had called a "flunky." And there really was something of a lackey's servility in his lanky figure, his side-whiskers, and the little bald spot on the top of his head. And he smiled sweetly, and the badge of some scientific society gleaming in his buttonhole was like the number on a footman's livery.

The husband went out to smoke in the first interval, and she was left alone in her seat. Gurov, who had taken a seat in the stalls, went up to her and said in a trembling voice, with a forced smile: "How d'you do?"

She glanced up at him and turned pale, then looked at him again in alarm, unable to believe her eyes, squeezing her fan and lorgnette in one hand, evidently struggling to overcome a feeling of faintness. Neither of them said a word. She sat there, and he stood beside her, disconcerted by her embarrassment, and not daring to sit down. The violins and flutes sang out as they were tuned, and there was a tense sensation in the atmosphere, as if they were being watched from all the boxes. At last she got up and moved rapidly towards one of the exits. He followed her and they wandered aimlessly along corridors, up and down stairs; figures flashed by in the uniforms of legal officials, high-school teachers and civil servants, all wearing badges; ladies, coats hanging from pegs flashed by; there was a sharp draft, bringing with it an odor of cigarette butts. And Gurov, whose heart was beating violently, thought:

"What on earth are all these people, this orchestra for? . . ."

The next minute he suddenly remembered how, after seeing Anna Sergeyevna off that evening at the station, he had told himself that all was over, and they would never meet again. And how far away the end seemed to be now!

She stopped on a dark narrow staircase over which was a notice bearing the inscription "To the upper circle."

"How you frightened me!" she said, breathing heavily, still pale and half-stunned. "Oh, how you frightened me! I'm almost dead! Why did you come? Oh, why?"

"But, Anna," he said, in low, hasty tones. "But, Anna. . . . Try to understand . . . do try. . . ."

She cast him a glance of fear, entreaty, love, and then gazed at him steadily, as if to fix his features firmly in her memory.

"I've been so unhappy," she continued, taking no notice of his words. "I could think of nothing but you the whole time, I lived on the thoughts of you. I tried to forget—why, oh, why did you come?"

On the landing above them were two schoolboys, smoking and looking down, but Gurov did not care, and, drawing Anna Sergeyevna towards him, began kissing her face, her lips, her hands.

"What are you doing, oh, what are you doing?" she said in horror, drawing back. "We have both gone mad. Go away this very night, this moment. . . . By all that is sacred, I implore you. . . . Somebody is coming."

Someone was ascending the stairs.

"You must go away," went on Anna Sergeyevna in a whisper. "D'you hear me, Dmitry Dmitrich? I'll come to you in Moscow. I have never been happy, I am unhappy now, and I shall never be happy—never! Do not make me suffer still more! I will come to you in Moscow, I swear it! And now we must part! My dear one, my kind one, my darling, we must part."

She pressed his hand and hurried down the stairs, looking back at him continually, and her eyes showed that she was in truth unhappy. Gurov stood where he was for a short time, listening, and when all was quiet, went to look for his coat, and left the theatre.

IV

And Anna Sergeyevna began going to Moscow to see him. Every two or three months she left the town of S., telling her husband that she was going to consult a specialist on female diseases, and her husband believed her and did not believe her. In Moscow she always stayed at the Slavyanski Bazaar, sending a man in a red cap to Gurov the moment she arrived. Gurov went to her, and no one in Moscow knew anything about it.

One winter morning he went to see her as usual (the messenger had been to him the evening before, but had not found him at home). His daughter was with him, for her school was on the way and he thought he might as well see her to it.

"It is forty degrees," said Gurov to his daughter, "and yet it is snowing. You see it is only above freezing close to the ground, the temperature in the upper layers of the atmosphere is quite different."

"Why doesn't it ever thunder in winter, Papa?"

He explained this, too. As he was speaking, he kept reminding himself that he was going to a rendezvous and that not a living soul knew about it, or, probably, ever would. He led a double life—one in

71

public, in the sight of all whom it concerned, full of conventional truth and conventional deception, exactly like the lives of his friends and acquaintances, and another which flowed in secret. And, owing to some strange, possibly quite accidental chain of circumstances, everything that was important, interesting, essential, everything about which he was sincere and never deceived himself, everything that composed the kernel of his life, went on in secret, while everything that was false in him, everything that composed the husk in which he hid himself and the truth which was in him—his work at the bank, discussions at the club, his "lower race," his attendance at anniversary celebrations with his wife—was on the surface. He began to judge others by himself, no longer believing what he saw, and always assuming that the real, the only interesting life of every individual goes on as under cover of night, secretly. Every individual existence revolves around mystery, and perhaps that is the chief reason that all cultivated individuals insisted so strongly on the respect due to personal secrets.

After leaving his daughter at the door of her school Gurov set off for the Slavyanski Bazaar. Taking off his overcoat in the lobby, he went upstairs and knocked softly on the door. Anna Sergeyevna, wearing the gray dress he liked most, exhausted by her journey and by suspense, had been expecting him since the evening before. She was pale and looked at him without smiling, but was in his arms almost before he was fairly in the room. Their kiss was lingering, prolonged, as if they had not met for years.

"Well, how are you?" he asked. "Anything new?"

"Wait, I'll tell you in a minute. . . . . I can't. . . ."

She could not speak, because she was crying. Turning away, she held her handkerchief to her eyes.

"I'll wait till she's had her cry out," he thought, and sank into a chair.

He rang for tea, and a little later, while he was drinking it, she was still standing there, her face to the window. She wept from emotion, from her bitter consciousness of the sadness of their life; they could only see one another in secret, hiding from people, as if they were thieves. Was not their life a broken one?

"Don't cry," he said.

It was quite obvious to him that this love of theirs would not soon come to an end, and that no one could say when this end would be. Anna Sergeyevna loved him ever more fondly, worshipped him, and there would have been no point in telling her that one day it must end. Indeed, she would not have believed him.

He moved over and took her by the shoulders, intending to caress her, to make a joke, but suddenly he caught sight of himself in the looking-glass.

His hair was already beginning to turn gray. It struck him as strange that he should have aged so much in the last few years, have lost so much of his looks. The shoulders on which his hands lay were warm and quivering. He felt a pity for this life, still so warm and exquisite, but probably soon to fade and droop like his own. Why did she love him so? Women had always believed him different from what he really was, had loved in him not himself but the man their imagination pictured him, a man they had sought for eagerly all their lives. And afterwards when they discovered their mistake, they went on loving him just the same. And not one of them had ever been happy with him. Time had passed, he had met one woman after another, become intimate with each, parted with each, but had never loved. There had been all sorts of things between them, but never love.

And only now, when he was gray-haired, had he fallen in love properly, thoroughly, for the first time in his life.

He and Anna Sergeyevna loved one another as people who are very close and intimate, as husband and wife, as dear friends love one another. It seemd to them that fate had intended them for one another, and they could not understand why she should have a husband, and he a wife. They were like two migrating birds, the male and the female, who had been caught and put into separate cages. They forgave one another all that they were ashamed of in the past and in the present, and felt that this love of theirs had changed them both.

Formerly, in moments of melancholy, he had consoled himself by the first argument that came into his head, but now arguments were nothing to him, he felt profound pity, desired to be sincere, tender.

"Stop crying, my dearest," he said. "You've had your cry, now stop. . . . Now let us have a talk, let us try and think what we are to do."

Then they discussed their situation for a long time, trying to think how they could get rid of the necessity for hiding, deception, living in different towns, being so long without meeting. How were they to shake off these intolerable fetters?

"How? How?" he repeated, clutching his head. "How?"

And it seemed to them that they were within an inch of arriving at a decision, and that then a new, beautiful life would begin. And they both realized that the end was still far, far away, and that the hardest, the most complicated part was only just beginning.

---

1. What has the resort atmosphere of Yalta to do with the way Gurov and Anna become lovers? Does it help mislead Gurov about what is really happening to him?
2. What is the importance of Anna's "awkwardness" and pathetic simplicity in

shaping Gurov's feelings? Of the "insulting indulgence" and "irony" in his treatment of her?

3. Does the story suggest that a person's public life and the attitudes formed by it can never be reconciled with the personal life? Consider the antithesis stated in the last paragraph in shaping your answer.
4. What does the story say about Time (or timing) in its relation to human affairs?
5. What is the point of view and how does it help bring out the essence of the situation described?
6. How are the three different settings of the story related to the developing action?

A Visit to Friends[1]

The morning mail brought this note:

> Dear Misha! Kuzminki, July 7
>
> You have completely forgotten us, come to see us, we want to have a glimpse of you. Both of us entreat you on our knees, come today, show us your fair countenance. We are waiting for you impatiently.
>
> Ta and Va

The letter was from Tatyana Alexeyevna Loseva, whom they had called Ta for short a dozen years previously, when Podgorin was staying at Kuzminki. But who was Va? Oh, yes, it was Varya, or Varvara Pavlovna, a friend of Tatyana's. Podgorin recalled the long talks, the gay laughter, the flirtations, the evenings walks, and the flower garden of girls and young women who were then staying at Kuzminki, and he also recalled the plain, animated, intelligent face and the freckles that went so well with Varya's dark-red hair. Since then she had graduated from medical school, taken a position as a doctor in a factory somewhere near Tula, and now was apparently visiting Kuzminki.

"Dear Va!" thought Podgorin, giving himself up to reminiscences. "How nice she is!"

Tatyana, Varya and he were almost of the same age. But at the time he had been only a student, and they marriageable girls. He had been considered a mere boy. And now, although he was already an established lawyer and his hair was beginning to turn gray, they still

1. Translated by Avrahm Yarmolinsky.

called him Misha, thought of him as a young man and declared that he had not lived.

He loved them dearly, but it would seem rather as memories than in actuality. The present was scarcely real to him, was incomprehensible and alien. Alien also was this short, playful letter. Much time and effort must have gone to composing it, and as Tatyana was writing it, her husband, Sergey Sergeich, must have been standing behind her. The Kuzminki estate had become Tatyana's property six years ago when she was married, but this Sergey Sergeich had already succeeded in ruining it, and now every time payment to the bank or on a mortgage fell due, they turned to Podgorin, as a lawyer, for advice. Besides, they had already tried to borrow from him twice. Apparently, now too they wanted money or advice from him.

He was no longer drawn to Kuzminki, as he used to be. There was something melancholy about the place. The laughter, the clamor, the bright carefree faces, trysts on still moonlit nights—all that was gone, above all, youth was gone; and, furthermore, all this was probably fascinating only in retrospect. . . . In addition to Ta and Va, there had then been Na, Tatyana's sister Nadezhda. Half in jest, half in earnest they had called her his fiancée. She had grown up before his eyes, everyone thought that he would marry her, and indeed at one time he had been in love with her and was ready to propose to her. Yet she was already in her twenty-fourth year, and he hadn't proposed to her.

"Strange, how it all turned out," he reflected, rereading the note with embarrassment. "But I can't *not go,* they'll be offended. . . ."

The fact that he hadn't been to see the Losevs for a long time lay like a weight on his conscience. And after he had paced the room for a while and turned the matter over in his mind, he overcame his reluctance and decided to go to Kuzminki for a stay of two or three days, and then be free from any sense of obligation at least until the following summer. And as he was getting ready to drive to the Brest Station after breakfast he told the servants that he would return in three days.

There was a two hours' train ride from Moscow to Kuzminki and a twenty minutes' drive from the station to the estate. When one got off the train, Tatyana's forest came into view, as well as three summer cottages, which Losev had started building but had not completed—during the first years of his marriage he had had all kinds of schemes. He was ruined by these summer cottages and other money-making enterprises, and by frequent trips to Moscow, where he lunched at the Slavyansky Bazaar, dined at the Hermitage and at the close of the day wound up on Malaya Bronnaya Street[2] or at the Gypsy place known as The Slaughterhouse (he called this "getting shaken up"). Podgorin himself

2. Site of houses of prostitution.

drank, sometimes rather heavily, took up with all kinds of women, but indolently, coldly, without enjoyment, and he was disgusted when in his presence others gave themselves over to that sort of thing passionately; he did not understand men who were more at ease at The Slaughterhouse than at home, in the company of decent women, and he disliked such men. It seemed to him that all kinds of dirt clung to them like burrs. He disliked Losev and considered him a dull fellow, lazy and without ability, and more than once he felt a sense of distaste for his company . . .

Sergey Sergeich and Nadezhda were waiting for him just beyond the forest.

"My dear fellow, why have you been completely neglecting us?" asked Sergey Sergeich, kissing him three times and putting both arms around his waist. "You don't love us any more, old man."

He had massive features, a fleshy nose, a rather thin blond beard, and he combed his hair to one side, like a merchant, to give himself a simple, typically Russian appearance. He had a way of breathing in the face of the person he was speaking to, and when he was silent he breathed heavily, through his nose. His obesity and his habit of overeating made it hard for him to fill his lungs, and in consequence he kept thrusting out his chest, which gave him an air of haughtiness. Beside him, Nadezhda, his sister-in-law, seemed ethereal. She was a pale, slim blonde with kindly eyes that seemed to caress you. Whether she was beautiful or not Podgorin could not tell, for he had known her since childhood and he took her for granted. She wore a white dress, open at the neck, and the sight of her long, white, naked throat was strange to him and affected him disagreeably.

"Sister and I have been waiting for you since morning," she said. "Varya is with us, and she has been waiting for you, too."

She took his arm, laughed abruptly without any reason, and gave a light, joyous cry, as though suddenly struck by some pleasant thought. The field of flowering rye, motionless in the still air, the forest lit by the sun, were beautiful, and it seemed as though Nadezhda had noticed it just now, as she walked beside Podgorin.

"I can stay three days," he said. "Forgive me, I couldn't get away from Moscow any sooner."

"It's wrong, wrong, you've completely neglected us," said Sergey Sergeich, in good-natured reproach. "*Jamais de ma vie!*"[3] he said suddenly and snapped his fingers.

He had a way of astonishing the person to whom he was speaking by an exclamation that had no bearing whatever on the talk, at the same time snapping his fingers. And he was always aping someone. If

3. "Never in my life."

he rolled his eyes, or nonchalantly tossed back his hair, or turned bathetic, it meant that the previous evening he had been to the theatre or had attended a banquet with speeches. He was now walking mincingly like a victim of gout without bending his knees—apparently imitating someone.

"You know, Tanya didn't think that you would come," said Nadezhda. "But I had a premonition that you would, and so did Varya; for some reason I knew that you would come on this train."

"*Jamais de ma vie!*" repeated Sergey Sergeich.

The ladies were waiting on the terrace in the garden. Ten years back Podgorin, then a needy student, had tutored Nadezhda in mathematics and history for room and board. He had also given Latin lessons to Varya, a medical student. As for Tanya, at the time already a grown girl and a beauty, she had thought of nothing but love, and had wanted only love and happiness, passionately wanted and hoped for a husband, of whom she dreamed day and night. And now when she was over thirty and just as beautiful as ever, in a loose tea gown, with her full, white arms, she had thoughts for nothing but her husband and her two little girls. She wore an expression which seemed to say that although there she was talking and smiling so casually, she was nevertheless on guard, she stood prepared to defend her love and her right to this love, and at a moment's notice she was ready to pounce on an enemy who wanted to take away her husband and her children. She loved devotedly and she believed that she was loved in the same way, but jealousy and fear for her children constantly tormented her and interfered with her happiness.

After a clamorous reunion on the terrace, everyone went off to Tatyana's room, with the exception of Sergey Sergeich.

The lowered blinds kept out the sun and created a twilight in the room, so that all the roses in a large bouquet seemed to be of the same color. They made Podgorin sit down in an old armchair at the window. Nadezhda sat on a low stool at his feet. He knew that in addition to friendly reproaches, jokes, laughter, which so keenly reminded him of the past, there would also be an unpleasant conversation on the subject of promissory notes and mortgages—that was unavoidable—and it occurred to him that it would be best to have the business talk at once, without delay, to put it behind them and then go out into the open, to the garden. . . .

"Shouldn't we first talk about business?" he said. "What's new at Kuzminki? There's nothing rotten in the state of Denmark?"

"Things are out of joint at Kuzminki," replied Tatyana, sighing sadly. "Oh, the situation there is bad, so bad that I don't think it could be worse," she said, agitatedly pacing the room. "The estate is to be sold, August 7th is the date of the auction; the announcement has already been published, and buyers have started coming here, they walk through the house, they stare . . . Anyone has the right to come into my room now, and look. Perhaps according to law this is as it should be, but it humiliates me, it offends me deeply. We have no money and there is no one we can borrow from. It's simply terrible, terrible! I swear to you by all that's holy," she continued, halting in the middle of the room, her voice breaking and her eyes filling with tears, "I swear to you by the happiness of my children, I cannot live without Kuzminki! I was born here, it's my home, and if it's taken from me, I shan't be able to go on, I shall die of despair."

"It seems to me you are taking too black a view of the matter," said Podgorin. "Things will arrange themselves. Your husband will find a position, you will adjust yourself to a new setting and live a new life."

"How can you say such a thing?" cried Tatyana. As she spoke, she looked very beautiful and strong, and her readiness to pounce instantly on the enemy who would take her husband, her children, her home away from her was very evident in her face and in her whole bearing. "A new life, indeed! Sergey is busy trying to make connections, he has been promised the post of tax collector somewhere in the province of Ufa or Perm. I am prepared to go anywhere, even to Siberia, I am ready to live there ten years, twenty, but I must know that sooner or later I'll return to Kuzminki. Without Kuzminki I cannot live. I can't and I don't want to. I don't want to!" she cried, and stamped her foot.

"You are a lawyer, Misha," said Varya, "you know how to turn a trick, and it's your business to advise us what to do."

There was only one piece of sensible advice that he could offer: "Nothing can be done," but Podgorin did not have the heart to blurt it out, and he mumbled hesitantly:

"I'll have to give the matter some thought. . . . I'll think it over."

There were two men in him. As a lawyer he occasionally had to deal with pretty ugly affairs. At court and with clients he behaved haughtily and spoke his mind bluntly. With casual acquaintances he could be rather cutting. But with intimates or friends of long standing he was exceedingly delicate, shy and sensitive, and could not speak harshly. A tear, a sidelong glance, a lie, or even an unseemly gesture was sufficient to make him flinch and lose his self-possession. Nadezhda was still sitting at his feet, and her bare throat offended him. This was a source of distress, so that he even thought of going home. The previous year he had happened to run into Sergey Sergeich in the flat of a certain lady on Bronnaya Street, and now he felt embarrassed in Tatyana's presence, as if he himself had been party to her husband's infidelity. And this conversation about the estate placed him in a very awkward position. He was used to having all thorny and unpleasant questions settled by judges or jurymen, or simply by some statute. But when a matter was put up to him personally for decision, he was lost.

"Misha, you're our friend, we all love you as one of our own," continued Tatyana, "and I'll be frank with you; you are our only hope. For God's sake, tell us what to do. Maybe an appeal is possible? Perhaps it isn't too late to put the estate in Nadya's name, or Varya's? What shall we do?"

"Come to our rescue, Misha, do," said Varya, lighting up. "You were always so clever. You haven't really lived, you've had no experience, but you've a good head on your shoulders. You'll help Tanya, you know you will.

"I must think it over. . . . Maybe, I'll come up with some scheme."

They all went out for a walk in the garden, and then they wandered off into the fields. Sergey Sergeich went along. He took Podgorin by the arm and tried to walk ahead of the rest, apparently intending to broach the subject of his financial straits. To walk beside him and talk to him was torment. Now and then he would kiss his guest, always three times, put his arms around his waist, breathe in his face, and it seemed as though he were covered with a sweet glue and would actually stick to his companion. And that expression of his eyes, which showed that he wanted something from Podgorin, that he was going to ask him for something, had a painful effect, as if he were aiming a gun at his guest.

The sun set, it was getting dark. Here and there along the railway line lights appeared, green, red. . . . Varya halted, and looking at the signals, recited:

"There is a straight and shining road,
With rails and posts, a bridge afar,
On either side lie Russian bones,
Oh, what huge heaps of them there are! . . .

How does it go on? Oh good Lord, I can't remember any of it!

We labored in the heat, the cold,
Our heads were bowed, our backs were bent . . ."

She recited with deep feeling, in a magnificent chest-voice. Her face grew flushed and tears came into her eyes. It was the old Varya, Varya the student, and as he listened to her Podgorin thought of the past and recalled that as a student himself he had known many fine poems by heart and had liked to recite them.

"And even now his back is bent,
His silence stolid as before . . ."

Varya could not remember any more. She fell silent and smiled uncertainly and faintly, and the green and red signals had a melancholy look.

"Oh, I've forgotten it!"

But Podgorin recalled the way it went on—somehow the lines had remained in his memory from his student days, and he recited quietly, under his breath:

"The Russian folk have borne enough,
This road-building—a fearful load—
They've borne and more will they endure,
And build themselves a glorious road.
The pity is . . ."

" 'The pity is,' " Varya broke in, having remembered:

"The pity is that neither you nor I
Will be alive to greet that glorious time."

She laughed and slapped him on the back.

They returned to the house and sat down to supper. Aping someone, Sergey Sergeich carelessly stuck a corner of his napkin into his collar.

"Let's have a drink," he said, pouring some vodka for himself and Podgorin. "In our student days we knew how to drink, how to make a speech, how to work seriously. I drink your health, friend, and you drink the health of an old fool of an idealist and wish him this: that he die an idealist."

All during supper Tatyana kept looking tenderly at her husband, fretting lest he eat or drink something that might disagree with him. It seemed to her that he was weary, that he was spoiled by women—she liked this in him, but at the same time she suffered from jealousy. Varya and Nadya, too, were tender with him and looked at him anxiously, as though afraid that he would suddenly get up and leave them. When he wanted to pour himself a second glass of vodka, Varya made an angry face and said:

"You're poisoning yourself, Sergey Sergeich. You're a nervous, impressionable sort, and you can easily become an alcoholic. Tanya, tell them to remove the vodka."

Sergey Sergeich was generally very successful with women. They loved his stature, his build, his massive features, his idleness, his misfortunes. They said that he was very kind and therefore a spendthrift, an idealist and therefore impractical, that he was honest, pure of heart, that he could not adjust himself to people and circumstances, and so owned nothing and could find no definite occupation. They believed him implicitly, adored him, and so spoiled him by their admiration that he himself became convinced that he was idealistic, impractical, honest, pure of heart, and that he was superior to these women and that they should look up to him.

"Why don't you say a word of praise about my little girls?" asked Tatyana, feasting her eyes on her two little daughters and piling high with rice the plates of these healthy-looking, well-nourished children, who made one think of dinner rolls. "Just look at them! They say that all mothers dote on their children, but I assure you I'm unbiased, my little girls are extraordinary. Particularly the elder."

Podgorin smiled at her and at the little girls, but he found it odd that this young, healthy, rather intelligent woman—a big complex organism—should spend all her energy, all her vital forces on such a simple, petty job as the building of this nest, that in any case was complete.

"Perhaps that's as it should be," he reflected, "but it's dull and stupid."

"Before the clumsy churl could gasp,
Old Bruin had him in his grasp,"

said Sergey Sergeich, and snapped his fingers.

Supper was over. Tatyana and Varya made Podgorin sit down on a divan in the drawing room and again started talking to him about business matters.

"You must rescue Sergey Sergeich," said Varya. "It is your moral duty. He has his weaknesses, he's not thrifty, he doesn't plan for a rainy day, but that's because he is kind and generous. He has the soul of a child. Present him with a million, and in a month there'll be nothing left of it, he will have given it all away."

"It's true, it's true," said Tatyana, and tears streamed down her cheeks. "He has made me suffer very much, but I must admit, he's a wonderful human being."

And neither of them, Tatyana or Varya, could refrain from the little cruelty of saying to Podgorin reproachfully:

"Your generation, Misha, is different!"

"What has my generation to do with it!" thought Podgorin. "Losev isn't more than half a dozen years older than I. . . ."

"Life is not easy," said Varya, and sighed. "You are always threatened by a loss. They want to take your property away, or someone close to you falls ill and you fear for his life—and so on, day after day. But what's to be done, my dears? One must submit to the higher Will without a murmur, one must remember that in this world nothing is accidental, everything has its purpose, no matter how remote. You haven't really lived, Misha, and you haven't suffered much, and you will laugh at me; laugh, but I will say this, nevertheless: during the period when I was most anxious, I had several experiences of clairvoyance, and the result has been a spiritual revolution within me, and now I know that nothing is accidental, and that everything that happens to us is necessary."

How different she was, this Varya, already gray-haired, corseted, wearing a fashionable dress with puffed sleeves, rolling a cigarette in long, thin fingers, that trembled for some reason, this Varya, easily falling prey to mysticism, speaking in such a weak, monotonous voice, how different she was from Varya, the medical student, the gay, noisy, bold red-head. . . .

"What has time done to them?" Podgorin wondered, listening to her with boredom.

"Sing us something, Va," he said, to put an end to the talk about clairvoyance. "You used to sing beautifully."

"Oh, Misha, That's all past and gone.

"Or recite something by Nekrasov."[4]

"I don't remember any of it. It was just an accident that I recalled those lines earlier in the evening."

In spite of the corset and the fashionable sleeves, it was plain that she was far from prosperous and that she lived meagerly at the factory beyond Tula. It was noticeable, too, that she was overworked. Heavy, monotonous work and the constant concern with other people's affairs, her fretting about other people had been a strain on her, and had aged her prematurely, and Podgorin, looking now at her sad face, already faded, thought that not Kuzminki, not Sergey Sergeich, but she herself who was so concerned about them, was in need of help.

Higher education and the fact that she was a physician did not seem to have affected the woman in her. Like Tatyana, she took pleasure in weddings, births, baptisms, lengthy conversations about children, she liked terrifying novels with happy endings; when she took up a newspaper it was to read only about fires, floods and public ceremonies. She was dying to have Podgorin propose to Nadezhda, and were it to happen, she would burst into tears.

He did not know whether it was by chance or whether Varya had arranged it, but he found himself alone with Nadezhda. The mere sus-

4. Nikolai Nekrasov (1821–1877), Russian poet famous for his portrayal of peasant life.

picion that he was being watched and that something was wanted of him constrained and embarrassed him, and sitting beside Nadezhda, he felt as though the two of them had been placed in a cage.

"Let us go down to the garden," she said.

They went off to the garden: he, disgruntled, vexed, not knowing what to talk to her about, she—joyous, proud of having him at her side, obviously happy that he would stay there another three days, and perhaps full of sweet reveries and hopes. He did not know if she was in love with him, but he was aware that she had long since grown used to him and was attached to him, that she still saw her tutor in him, and that she was just the way Tatyana used to be, that is, she thought of nothing but love, of how to get married as soon as possible, to have a husband, children, a nook of her own. She had preserved that feeling about friendship which is so intense in children, and it was possible that she merely respected Podgorin and was fond of him as of a friend, that she was in love not with him, but with her dreams of a husband and children.

"It's getting dark," said he.

"Yes. The moon rises late now."

They kept strolling along one alley, near the house. Podgorin was loath to go far into the garden: it was dark there, he would have to take her by the arm, be very close to her. Shadows were moving on the terrace, and it seemed to him that Tatyana and Varya were watching them.

"I must ask your advice," said Nadezhda, halting. "If Kuzminki is sold, then Sergey Sergeich will take a position, and our life will be completely changed. I'm not going to stay with sister, we shall separate, because I don't want to be a burden on the family. One must work. I'll find some employment in Moscow, I'll earn money and be able to help sister and her husband. You'll advise me, won't you?"

Knowing nothing at all about it, she was now animated by the idea of working and of independence, she was making plans for the future—this was written on her face, and the prospect of working and helping others seemed to her beautiful, poetical. He saw her pallid face and dark eyebrows at close range and recalled what an intelligent, keen, capable pupil she had been, and how pleasant it had been to tutor her. And it might well be that now she was not simply a young lady who wanted a husband, but a high-minded girl, of extraordinary kindness, with a gentle, pliable soul, which could be molded into any shape, like wax, a girl who, given proper surroundings, could grow into an admirable woman.

"Why not marry her, really?" thought Podgorin, but was immediately frightened by the thought and began walking in the direction of the house.

When they entered the drawing room, they found Tatyana sitting at the piano, and her playing vividly brought back the past, when in this very drawing room there was playing, singing and dancing late into the night, with the windows open, and the birds in the garden and on the river singing, too. Podgorin brightened, grew playful, danced with Nadezhda and with Varya, and afterwards he sang. A corn on his foot annoyed him, so he asked if he might wear Sergey Sergeich's slippers, and, strange to say, in slippers he felt like one of the family, a relative ("like a brother-in-law" flashed through his mind) and he grew even gayer. This made all of them come to life, they brightened, were rejuvenated, as it were; hope shone in everyone's face: Kuzminki was saved! It was a simple matter: all that was needed was to think up something, dig up a law, or if Podgorin were to marry Nadya . . . And, obviously, the affair was under way. Nadya, pink-cheeked, happy, her eyes shining with tears in the expectation of something extraordinary, circled in the dance, her white dress billowing and showing glimpses of her slim, pretty legs in their flesh-tinted stockings. Varya, thoroughly contented, took Podgorin by the arm and said to him under her breath with a significant expression:

"Misha, don't run away from your happiness. Take it while it offers itself to you freely, later you will be running after it, but you won't overtake it."

Podgorin wanted to promise, to be encouraging, and he himself believed that Kuzminki was saved, and that it could all be arranged very simply.

"And thou shalt be queen of the world," he broke into song, striking a pose, but suddenly remembering that he could do nothing for these people, nothing at all, he fell silent like one stricken with guilt.

And there he sat in a corner, mute, cross-legged, with his feet in another man's slippers.

At the sight of him, the others understood that nothing could be done, and fell silent, too. The piano was closed. Everyone noticed that it was late, time to go to bed, and Tatyana put out the big lamp in the drawing room.

A bed was made up for Podgorin in the same wing in which he used to live years back. Sergey Sergeich went to see him settled, holding the candle high above his head, although the moon had risen and it was light. They walked between lilac bushes, and the gravel of the path crunched under their feet.

> "Before the clumsy churl could gasp,
> Old Bruin had him in his grasp,"

said Sergey Sergeich.

It seemed to Podgorin as if he had heard these lines a thousand times. He was fed up with them. When they reached the wing, Sergey Sergeich produced a bottle and two glasses from the pocket of his ample jacket and put them on the table.

"It's cognac," he said. "Number zero-zero. Varya's in the house, you can't drink in her presence, she'll start squawking about alcoholism, but here we're free. It's excellent cognac."

They sat down. The cognac was indeed excellent.

"This time we must finish the bottle," continued Sergey Sergeich, biting into a lemon. "I haven't forgotten my student days, sometimes I like to let myself go. One has to."

But there was that look in his eyes that said he needed something from Podgorin and was about to ask for something.

"Let's drink, old chap," he continued, sighing, "life is getting too hard for me. My kind is finished, for good. Idealism is out of fashion. The ruble is king nowadays, and you have to kneel down and worship it if you don't want to be kicked out, left nowhere. I can't do it. It's disgusting!"

"When is the auction?" asked Podgorin, to change the subject.

"The seventh of August. But I have no hope of being able to save Kuzminki, my dear friend. The arrears are enormous, and the estate brings in nothing, there are only losses every year. The game isn't worth the candle. . . . Of course, Tanya is cut up, it's her patrimony, but as for me, to be frank, I'm rather glad. I don't care for the country. Give me the big, bustling city, with its struggle—then I'm in my element!"

He kept on talking, but he didn't say what he wanted to say, and he watched Podgorin intently, as though looking for an opportune moment. And suddenly Podgorin felt the man's eyes peering closely into his and the man's breath on his face.

"My dear fellow, save me!" Sergey Sergeich brought out, breathing heavily. "Give me two hundred rubles! I implore you!"

Podgorin wanted to say that he was short of funds, and it flashed through his mind that it would be better to give the two hundred rubles to some poor devil or even lose them at cards, but he became terribly embarrassed, and feeling himself trapped in this little room with the one candle, and wishing to rid himself as soon as possible of this breath on his face, these soft, sticky arms which clasped his waist and already seemed glued to him, he began to rummage hastily in his pockets for his wallet.

"Here . . ." he mumbled, taking out a hundred rubles. "The rest later. I don't have any more on me. As you see, I can't refuse," he went on with irritation, beginning to get angry. "I have an insufferably flabby character. Only, please, consider this a loan. I'm hard up myself."

"Thank you! Thank you, old chap!"

"And please, stop imagining that you're an idealist. You are as much of an idealist as I am a turkey. You are just an unthinking loafer and nothing else."

"You're angry, my dear fellow," he said, "but if you knew what I'm going through! I'm having a hellish time. My dear fellow, I swear to you—it's not myself I'm sorry for, not a bit of it! I'm only sorry for my wife and the children. If it weren't for my wife and the children, I'd have committed suicide long ago."

And suddenly his head and shoulders began to shake, and he burst into sobs.

"That's all that was wanting," said Podgorin, dreadfully vexed, pacing the room in agitation. "Well, what am I to do with a man who has behaved like a rascal and then starts to sob? Your tears disarm me, I can't say anything to you. You sob, therefore you are right."

"I behaved like a rascal?" asked Sergey Sergeich, getting up, and looking at Podgorin in amazement. "My dear fellow, how can you say such a thing? I behaved like a rascal? Oh, how little you know me! How little you understand me!"

"Very well, I don't understand you, only please stop blubbering. It's disgusting."

"Oh, how little you know me!" Losev repeated, quite sincerely. "How little you know me!"

"Look at yourself in the mirror," Podgorin continued, "you're no longer young, soon you will be an old man, it's high time for you to come to your senses, to realize who you are and what you are. All your life you've done nothing, all your life—this idle, puerile chatter, these airs, these affectations—aren't you fed up with all this, aren't you sick of it all? It's painful to be with you! And so dreadfully boring!"

With this, Podgorin left the room, banging the door. Almost for the first time in his life he had been completely sincere and had said what he wanted to say.

A little later he was sorry that he had been so harsh. What good was it to speak seriously to or argue with a man who lied constantly, ate a lot, drank a lot, spent a lot of money belonging to other people and at the same time was convinced that he was an idealist and a martyr? You were dealing with stupidity or with inveterate bad habits, which are as firmly lodged in the organism as an incurable disease. At any rate, indignation and severe reproaches were useless. It would have been better to laugh at it all; one good gibe could do more than ten sermons!

"Still better, pay no attention," thought Podgorin, "and, above all, don't lend him money."

A little later, Sergey Sergeich and his hundred rubles were far from his thoughts. There was something pensive about the night, which was still and brilliant. When Podgorin looked at the sky on moonlit nights, it seemed to him that only he and the moon were awake, while everything else was either asleep or drowsing; he didn't think of people or of money, and gradually a quiet, peaceful mood possessed him; he felt alone in the world, and in the nocturnal silence the sound of his own footsteps seemed melancholy to him.

The garden was enclosed by a white stone wall. In the right corner of the side facing the fields there was a tower, built a long time back, in the days of serfdom. The lower part of the tower was of stone, the upper was built of wood, and had a balcony; from the conical roof rose a tall spire topped by a black weathervane. Below there were two doors, so that one could either pass from the garden into the fields or reach the balcony by a stairway that creaked underfoot. Under the stairs old broken armchairs were lying about; the moonlight, coming through the door, made them gleam, so that with their crooked legs sticking up they seemed to have come to life in the night and to be lying in wait for someone there in the stillness.

Podgorin walked up the stairs and sat down on the balcony. Just beyond the wall there was a ditch with an embankment marking the boundary of the property. Farther off, were the broad fields, flooded with moonlight. Podgorin knew that there was a forest straight ahead, about two miles from the house, and it seemed to him that he saw a dark stripe in the distance. Quails and corn crakes were calling, and from time to time the voice of the cuckoo, which was also still wakeful, came from the direction of the woods.

There was the sound of footsteps. Someone was walking in the garden, approaching the tower.

A dog barked.

"Beetle!" a woman's voice called gently. "Beetle, come back!"

One could hear below someone entering the tower, and after a moment a black dog, an old friend of Podgorin's, appeared on the embankment. It stood still and, looking up to where Podgorin was sitting, wagged its tail in a friendly fashion. A little later a white figure rose like a shadow from the black ditch and also stood still on the embankment. It was Nadezhda.

"What do you see up there?" she asked the dog, as she too looked up.

She did not see Podgorin, but apparently felt his presence: she was smiling, and her pale face, lighted by the moon, seemed happy.

The black shadow of the tower that stretched far out over the field, the motionless white figure and the pale face smiling happily, the black dog, the shadows cast by the two—it was all like a dream.

"There is someone there . . ." said Nadezhda softly.

She stood and waited, hoping that he would either come down or call her to him, and that he would finally propose to her, and they would be happy in this still, beautiful night. White, pale, slim, very lovely in the moonlight, she was longing for caresses. Her continual dreams of happiness and love had wearied her, she could no longer hide her feelings, and her whole posture, the brilliance of her eyes, her fixed, blissful smile, betrayed her sweet thoughts. As for him, he was ill at ease, he shrank together, he froze, not knowing whether to say something so as to turn it all into a joke, or to remain silent, and he was vexed, and could only reflect that here in the country, on a moonlit night, with a beautiful, enamored, dreamy girl so near, his emotions were as little involved as on Malaya Bronskaya Street—clearly this fine poetry meant no more to him than that crude prose. All this was dead: trysts on moonlit nights, slimwaisted figures in white, mysterious shadows, towers and country houses, and "types" like Sergey Sergeich, and like himself, Podgorin, with his chilly boredom, constant vexation, his inability to adjust himself to real life, inability to take from it what it had to offer, and with an aching, wearying thirst for what was not and could not be on earth. And now, sitting here in this tower, he would have preferred a good display of fireworks or a procession in the moonlight, or to have Varya recite Nekrasov's "Railroad" again, or some other woman, who, standing there on the embankment where Nadezhda was standing, would speak of something absorbing, novel, having no relation to love or happiness, or if she did speak of love, it would be a call to a new kind of life, exalted and yet reasonable, a life on the threshold of which we live and of which we sometimes have a premonition. . . .

"No one there," said Nadezhda.

And, after waiting another moment, she walked off slowly with lowered head in the direction of the woods. The dog ran in front of her. For quite a long while Podgorin could see a white spot moving in the distance.

"Strange, how it all turned out," he kept repeating to himself, as he went back to his room.

He could not picture what he would talk about to Sergey Sergeich, to Tatyana, the next day, and the day after that, how he would behave toward Nadezhda—and in anticipation he felt embarrassment, fear and boredom. How was he going to fill the interminable three days that he had promised to stay on? He recalled the talk about clairvoyance, Sergey Sergeich's phrase:

"Before the clumsy churl could gasp,
Old Bruin had him in his grasp."

He recalled that the next day, to please Tatyana, he would have to smile at her plump, well-fed little girls—and he decided to leave.

At half past five Sergey Sergeich, wearing a Bokharan dressing-gown and a fez with a tassel, appeared on the terrace of the big house. Without losing a moment's time, Podgorin went up to him and began his farewells.

"I have to be in Moscow at ten," he said, without looking at his host. "I had completely forgotten that they would be waiting for me at the notary public's. Please, don't detain me. When the family is up, give them my apologies, I am terribly sorry . . ."

He did not hear what Sergey Sergeich was saying to him, and hurried off, and kept looking back at the windows of the big house, afraid that the ladies would wake up and try to detain him. He was ashamed of his nervousness. He felt that this was his last visit to Kuzminki, that he would not come there again. Several times, as he was driving off, he looked back at the wing in which he had spent so many happy days, but his heart was unmoved and he did not grow melancholy.

When he reached home, the first thing he noticed on his table was the note he had received the previous day. "Dear Misha," he read, "you have completely forgotten us, come as soon as possible. . . ." And for some reason he recalled how Nadezhda had circled in the dance, how her dress billowed, showing her legs in the flesh tinted stockings.

Ten minutes later he was at his desk, working, and without a thought of Kuzminki.

---

1. Who has changed more, Podgorin or his friends, during the time they have not seen each other?
2. Can you find a consistent line of motivation for Podgorin? What are the main ingredients of his present character and how are these decisive? How important is his feeling for Sergey Losev in determining the outcome?
3. Why doesn't Podgorin speak to Nadezhda when she is standing under the balcony of the tower? What is the full meaning of her declaration " 'No one there' "?
4. Account for the repetitions of the doggerel verse about "Old Bruin." Is it related to theme or action?

Dushechka[1]

Olenka Plemynikova, daughter of a retired college assessor, was sitting on the steps in the yard, dreaming. It was hot; the flies would not let one alone, and it was pleasant to think that evening was coming. Dark rainy clouds were moving over from the east, and every now and then a little rain fell.

In the middle of the yard stood Kukin—lessee and manager of the "Tivoli" pleasure-garden, who had his lodging in the little cottage in the yard. He was looking up at the sky.

"Again!" said he, in despair. "It's raining again! It rains every day; every day it rains, as if on purpose. You can't get away from it. It's ruin. Heavy losses every day!"

He wrung his hands and went on, turning to Olenka: "There you are, Olga Semenovna, that's our life. I could try! You work, and strive, and worry! you can't sleep thinking how things could be improved; and then what? On the one hand, the public, uncultured and illiterate. I give them the very best operetta, fairies, splendid artists; but do they really want it? Do they understand anything about it? They'd like a rowdy show. They want rubbish! On the other hand, just look at the weather! Almost every evening it rains. From the tenth of May, when we opened, right on through the whole of May and June—it's just dreadful. The public doesn't come, so how can I pay the rent? And the artists?"

Next day, as evening was coming on, the sky was again overcast, and Kukin said with a hysterical guffaw:

"Well, what if it does rain! Let it! Let it wash all the garden away and me with it! There's no happiness for me in this world or the next. Let the artists bring me to court! What does it matter? Let them send me to Siberia—or the scaffold! Ha, ha, ha!"

And the next day, just the same.

Olenka listened to Kukin in silence. She took him seriously, and sometimes the tears came into her eyes. In the end the misfortunes of Kukin moved her to pity, and she fell in love with him.

He was of squat stature, short and sallow; his hair was combed back from his temples; he had a thin tenor voice and twisted his mouth as he spoke; despair was always written on his face, but all the same he aroused in her a deep and genuine emotion. She had always been in love with somebody or other, and could not exist otherwise. Formerly she had loved her father, who was now an invalid and sat all the

1. Translated by Rosa Graham. Sometimes published under the title "The Darling."

time in an armchair in a darkened room, breathing with difficulty; then she had loved her aunt, who sometimes, perhaps once in two years, came to visit them from Briansk; and before that, when she was still a young schoolgirl, she had been in love with the French master. She was a gentle, good-natured, sympathetic girl, with a sweet engaging manner, and healthy-looking. She had plump rosy cheeks, a soft white neck with a little dark mole upon it, and her smile, whenever she heard anything pleasant, was naïve and friendly. When men observed her they commonly said to themselves, "Yes, not at all bad . . ." and they would smile also. As for other women, they went into raptures over her and, unable to restrain themselves, would snatch up her hand in theirs and exclaim in a burst of pleasure:

"Dushechka!"[2]

The house in which she had lived ever since she was born, and which she had now inherited, was on the outskirts of the town, in the Gipsy Suburb, not far from the "Tivoli" pleasure-garden. In the evenings and at night she could hear the orchestra playing and the bursting of the rockets as they fell. It seemed to her that this Kukin was at war with his destiny and was rushing to the final assault of his chief enemy—an indifferent public; her heart was sweetly anxious for him; she liked to lie awake all night so that towards morning when he returned home she could tap lightly on her bedroom window-pane, and, pulling aside the curtains, show him just her face and one shoulder and smile tenderly at him. . . .

He proposed to her, and they were married. And when he saw the curves of her neck and of her full healthy shoulders he clasped his hands as in prayer and exclaimed:

"Dushechka!"

He was happy, but as the wedding day and the whole evening after it had been rainy, a despairing expression had become fixed on his face and did not wear off.

They lived happily together after their marriage. She kept the accounts, saw that everything was in order in the garden; she tabulated the expenses, and paid the wages, and her rosy cheeks and gentle naïve smile looked like a sunbeam gleaming from the little office-window, in the wings of the open theatre, or in the restaurant. And very soon she began to say to her acquaintances that the most remarkable, the most necessary and important thing on earth was the theatre, and that one could only get real pleasure and become cultured and human by means of the theatre.

"But do you think the public understands that?" she would say. "No; they want a show. Yesterday we had 'Faust Reversed,' and the

2. An expression of endearment and delight.

stalls were almost empty; but if Vanitchka and I were to put on any kind of rubbish, would you believe it, the theatre would be crowded out. We're giving 'Orpheus in Hell'[3] to-morrow—come and see it."

And she would repeat everything Kukin said about the theatre and about the actors. Like him, she despised the public for its indifference toward Art and for its lack of culture; she interfered in the rehearsals, corrected the actors, looked after the behaviour of the musicians, and when the local newspaper commented unfavourably on their productions she would weep and afterwards go to the editor to obtain an explanation.

The actors loved her and called her "Vanitchka and I" and "Dushechka." She was sorry for their poverty and made them little loans now and then, and when, as sometimes happened, the actors told her a false story or did not pay her back, she would have a little cry on the quiet but made no complaint to her husband about it.

They had a good winter—they leased the town theatre for the whole season and sub-let it for short periods to Ukrainian singers, a conjuror, the local amateurs, and others. Olenka put on flesh and just radiated happiness, but Kukin grew thinner and more yellow, complaining of dreadful losses, though as a matter of fact business remained pretty good all the time. He coughed at nights, and she gave him lime-tea and raspberry syrup, rubbed him with eau-de-Cologne, and wrapped her own soft shawls about him.

"What a splendid man I've got!" said she, smoothing his hair with her hand, and she was absolutely sincere. "What a fine man I've got!"

He went to Moscow in Lent, to get together a new company, and while he was away she could not sleep, but sat at the window at night and looked at the stars. She compared herself with the hens who, when they are shut up in their coop without a cock, cannot sleep at all at nights and remain in a state of constant flutter. Kukin was held up in Moscow, but wrote that he would return in Holy Week. In his letters he gave various orders regarding the "Tivoli." But on the Monday before Easter, late in the evening, there was a sinister knocking at the outside gate. Someone was beating upon it as upon a barrel—boom, boom, boom. The sleepy cook jumped out of bed and splashed through the puddles of the yard in her bare feet to find out who it was.

"For goodness' sake, open!" cried someone in a deep bass voice. "There's a telegram."

Olenka had received telegrams from her husband at various times, but she took this one with trembling hands, and for some reason or other went white as chalk. She unsealed it, and read the following words:

3. Comic operetta by Jacques Offenbach (1819–1880).

"Ivan Petrovitch died suddenly this morning. Sutchala. Awaiting instructions for funeral Tuesday."

The word funeral was mis-spelt, and the telegram contained the incomprehensible word *sutchala;* it was signed by the stage-manager.

"My darling!" sobbed Olenka. "My darling Vanitchka, my loved one! Why did we ever meet? Why did I know you and love you? For whom have you abandoned your poor, poor, unhappy Olenka?"

Kukin was buried on the Tuesday, in Moscow, in the Vagankof cemetery; Olenka came home again on the Wednesday, and as soon as she got indoors she threw herself on the bed and sobbed so loudly that all the people in the street and in the neighbouring houses could hear her.

"Dushechka!" said the neighbours, crossing themselves. "Dushechka! Olga Semenovna 'll die of grief!"

Three months later, Olenka was coming home from church one day, grief-stricken and in deep mourning. One of her neighbours, also returning from church, walked along with her—Vassily Andreitch Pustovalof, managing director of the merchant Babakaief's timber warehouse. He wore a straw hat and a white waistcoat with a gold chain, and he looked more like a landowner than a trader.

"There's a certain fitness in things, Olga Semenovna," said he, sombrely, with sympathy in his voice. "If one of our near ones dies, it means that it is God's will, and in that case we ought to recognise it and bear it with humility."

He accompanied Olenka to her little gate, said good-bye, and went on. And during the whole day she could hear his sombre voice, and directly she closed her eyes at night in fancy she saw again his dark beard. She was much attracted to him. And evidently she also made an impression on him, for soon after, a slight acquaintance of hers, a middle-aged woman, came to drink coffee with her, and Olenka had no sooner sat herself down at the table than she began to talk of Pustovalof, saying what a good reliable man he was and how any woman would be pleased to marry him. Three days later Pustovalof himself visited her; he only stayed about ten minutes and said little, but Olenka was in love with him, so much in love that all that night she could not sleep and was burning as if with fever. Next morning she sent a message to the middle-aged lady. An engagement soon followed, and then the wedding.

Pustovalof and Olenka lived happily together after their marriage. He generally sat in the timber warehouse up till dinner-time; then he went out on business and Olenka took his place, sitting in the office till evening, writing up accounts and sending out the goods.

"Nowadays timber gets twenty percent dearer every year," she would say to her customers and friends. "We used to get wood from the forests near by, but now Vassitchka has to go every year to the forests in Mogilyovsky Government. And the cost of freight!" said she, covering her face with her hands in horror. "The cost of freight!"

It seemed to her that she had traded in timber for long long years, that timber was the most important and necessary thing in life, and that there was something familiar and touching in the sound of words like beam, joist, planks, props, deal, laths, beadings, match-board.

She used to dream at night of wood, and saw mountains of planks and boards, endless fences, stretching like forests far beyond the town. Once she dreamed that a whole regiment of twelve-yard poles was advancing to assault the timber-yard; there was a terrific collision and collapse, boards and beams rolling down with the dull sonorous sound of dry wood. The yard-timber fell and then stood up again and ranged itself in piles. Olenka cried out in her sleep, waking Pustovalof, who said tenderly:

"What's the matter, Olenka dear? Cross yourself!"

Whatever were her husband's thoughts, hers were the same. If he felt that it was hot in the room, so did she, and if he remarked that business was becoming rather quiet, the same thing had occurred to her. Her husband took little pleasure in outside amusements; he just sat indoors on holidays, and so did she.

"You're always either at home or in the office," said her acquaintances. "If I were you, Dushechka, I'd go to the theatre or the circus sometimes!"

"Vassitchka and I never go to the theatres," said she, unmoved. "We are working people. We haven't time for nonsense. What is there in all these theatres?"

The pair went to church on Saturday evenings regularly, and to early mass on Sundays and Saints' days, and they returned from church side by side. There was a sweet expression on their faces, and a sort of pleasant odour about them; her silk dress rustled agreeably as she walked along. When they got home they would have tea, sweet rolls, and saucer-fulls of various jams, and later, munched hot meat-pies together. Their beetroot soup smelt good each day at noon; you could smell it in the street and in the yard; yes, and there was roast mutton there, or duck, though it would be fish on fast-days; no one passed their door without suddenly feeling hungry. A samovar was always in the office, always on the boil, and they could offer tea and buttered bubliks to the customers. Once a week this happy couple went to the public bath, and might be seen returning thence together, both their faces red with steam.

"Yes, it's all right. We live well, glory be to God," said Olenka to her friends. "God grant everyone such a life as He has given to Vassitchka and me."

When Pustovalof went off to Mogilyof to buy timber, Olenka was terribly miserable; she wept, she could not sleep at night. Sometimes she would receive visits from the regimental veterinary surgeon, Smirnin, a young fellow who was lodging in the wing of the house. He told her stories, or played cards with her, and that distracted her a little. She was much interested in the stories he told of his private family life; he was a married man and had a son, but had separated from his wife because she had been unfaithful to him, and now he hated her. He sent her forty rubles a month for the upkeep of the child. And when Olenka heard this sad story she sighed and shook her head and was sorry for him.

"Well, God bless you!" she would say, as she showed him down the stairs, candle in hand. "Thank you for coming to cheer me; God keep you, and may the Queen of Heaven . . ."

She spoke slowly and thoughtfully, imitating her husband. The surgeon had got to the outside door, and she called to him once more: "Vladimir Platonitch, d'you know, I think it would be better if you made it up with your wife. I would forgive her, if it were only for the child's sake! You may be sure the little lad understands everything."

And when Pustovalof returned, she told him in a half-whisper about the veterinary surgeon and his unhappy married life, and they both sighed and shook their heads and spoke of the little boy, who no doubt fretted for his father. And afterwards, by some strange association of ideas, they both stood before the ikons and, bowing down to the ground, prayed that God would send them children.

And so the Pustovalofs spent the first six years of their married life, quietly and humbly, in love and complete harmony. But one winter day, Vassily Andreitch, after drinking tea in the office and getting heated, went off without his hat to despatch some timber. He took cold and was laid up. They had the best doctors for him, but the illness took a fatal course; after six months' illness, he died. And Olenka once more was a widow.

"For whom have you abandoned me, my darling?" sobbed she, at her husband's funeral. "How can I live now without you, in grief and bitterness? Good people, pity me, the complete orphan!"

She wore black; she wore a widow's veil, and renounced hats and gloves for ever. She rarely left the house, only going out to church or to her husband's grave, and lived the life of a nun. Only after six months did she put her veil aside, and open the shutters of her windows. Sometimes she could be seen in the mornings, going to the bazaar with her cook to buy provisions, but no one knew how she was living at that time, or what was happening in her home; they could only guess. For instance, people guessed something because upon occasion they had seen her in her garden drinking tea with the veterinary surgeon while he read a newspaper aloud to her; and one day, meeting a lady whom she knew at the post-office, Olenka had said to her:

"There's no proper veterinary supervision in our town—that's why there's so much illness. One hears often that people get ill from drinking milk, and they get infection from horses and cows. Really we ought to look after the health of our domestic animals as much as after our own."

She repeated the ideas of the veterinary surgeon, and came to have just the same opinions as he had. It was clear that she could not live one year without becoming attached to somebody, and that she had found her new happiness in the wing of her own house. Another person might have been censured for this, but no one could think badly of Olenka, and her life was quite clear to everybody. Neither she nor the veterinary surgeon told anyone of the change in their relationship, and they tried to hide it, but they were not successful because Olenka could never keep a secret. When he received guests, Olenka, while pouring out tea or serving supper, would begin talking about foot-and-mouth disease, the so-called pearly disease, and of the municipal slaughter-houses. On these occasions Smirnin would get dreadfully embarrassed, and after the guests had gone he would seize her hand and hiss out angrily:

"Didn't I ask you to keep quiet about things you don't understand? When we veterinary surgeons talk among ourselves, please don't interfere. It really becomes annoying!"

And she would look at him in wonder and alarm, and ask:

"But, Voloditchka, what was there for me to talk about?"

And she would tearfully embrace him, and beg him not to be angry, and both would be happy again.

But this happiness, however, did not last long. The veterinary surgeon went off with his regiment—went off for ever, it seemed, for the regiment had been transferred to some place very distant, almost to Siberia. And Olenka was left alone.

And now she really was quite alone. Her father had died long ago, and his armchair, with one leg missing, reposed in the dust in the attic. Olenka grew thinner and less good-looking, and when her acquaintances met her in the street they no longer looked on her as they used to do, with a smile; it was evident that her best years had passed, and that now a kind of new life was beginning for her, an unfamiliar life concerning which it were best not to think. In the evenings Olenka sat on the steps, and she could hear the orchestra of the "Tivoli" and the bursting of the rockets there, but they did not arouse in her mind any thought at all.

She gazed with indifference on her empty yard—she thought of nothing and wished for nothing—and when, later, night came on, she went to sleep and saw in her dreams the same empty yard. She ate and drank as if against her will.

And, worst of all, she had no opinions of any kind. She saw the things around her and she understood all that was going on, but she couldn't form an opinion about anything, and she didn't know what to talk about. And how dreadful it is not to have any opinions! You see, for instance, that a bottle is standing there, or that it rains, or that a peasant is going by in his cart, but what the bottle is there for, or the rain, or the peasant, and what they all mean, you can't say, and if anyone were to give you a thousand rubles, you couldn't say. In Kukin's time, or Pustovalof's, and later, with the veterinary surgeon, Olga could explain everything and give her opinion on anything you like; but now, in her thought and in her heart, there was just the same emptiness as in her yard. And it was as dreary and as bitter as the taste of wormwood in the mouth.

The town was spreading itself by degrees in all directions. The Gipsy Suburb was now called a street, and where the "Tivoli" and the timber warehouse had been, houses had been built, and there was a row of little streets. How quickly time flies! Olenka's house grew shabby in appearance, the roof rusted, the shed caved in, and the whole yard was overgrown with burdock and nettle. Olenka herself had become older and plainer. In summer she sat, as of old, on the steps of her house, and her soul was empty and dreary. In winter she sat at the window and looked out at the snow. When a gleam of spring sunshine came in at the window, or when she heard the chiming of the cathedral bells on the wind, she would have a sudden stab of recollection; her heart would ache sweetly, and her eyes would fill with abundant tears; but then that would be only for a moment, and once more, emptiness and the unanswerable question, "What is life for?" Breeska, her black cat, would rub itself against her and purr gently, but cat's caresses could not touch Olenka. She didn't want them. She wanted such a love as would satisfy her whole being, her whole soul and mind, would give her ideas, direction in life, and would warm up her aging heart. She would push the cat off her skirt and say sadly:

"Run along . . . I've nothing for you."

And so day after day, year after year, and no joy, and no opinions whatsoever. Whatever the cook Mavra said was all right for her.

But one hot July day, towards evening, when the cows were all being driven home down the street, and the whole yard was in dust, someone suddenly knocked. Olenka herself went to open the door, and when she saw who it was she nearly fainted. There on the threshold stood Smirnin, now a grey-headed man in civilian clothes. Suddenly the past flooded back to her consciousness, and she could not restrain herself; she rested her head on his breast and wept. She did not say one word, and was so agitated that she did not even observe how they went inside the house and sat down to take tea.

"Darling!" murmured she, trembling with joy. "Vladimir Platonitch! Where on earth have you come from?"

"I want to come and live here for always," he told her. "I've retired from the army, and I want to try and get a little happiness in freedom, and live a settled life. What's more, it's time for my boy to go to the high school. He's growing up! And, you know, I've made it up with my wife."

"And where is she?" asked Olenka.

"She's living in a hotel with the boy, and I'm just looking for lodgings."

"Good Lord! Dear man, come and take my house. Isn't that better than lodgings? And, Lord knows, I shouldn't want any rent," said Olenka, in excitement, and she began to weep again. "You live here, and I will take the lodging in the wing. O Lord, what a pleasure it is!"

And the very next day the roof was painted and the walls whitewashed, and Olenka walked about the yard with her hands on her hips, and gave her orders. Her old radiant smile had come back, and she was as fresh and vivacious as if she had just awakened from a long sleep. The veterinary surgeon's wife arrived. She was lean and ugly, wore her hair short, and her face wore a petted, difficult expression. With her came the boy. Sasha was small for his years—he was not yet ten—but he was chubby; he had bright blue eyes and dimpled cheeks. Directly he came into the yard he ran after the cat, and at once you could hear his gay, joyful laughter.

"Auntie, is this your cat?" asked he of Olenka. "When she has kittens, please give us one. Mother's dreadfully afraid of mice."

Olenka talked to him and gave him tea, and her heart felt suddenly warm and sweetly happy, as if this little boy were her own child. And when in the evening he sat at the table and went over his lessons, she looked at him with tenderness and sympathy, whispering:

"My darling, my handsome one, my little child; what a clever boy you are, and what a nice white skin you have."

"An island . . ." he was reading, "is a piece of land, entirely surrounded by water."

"An island is a piece of land . . ." she repeated after him, and this was the first opinion which she had expressed with conviction after so many years of silence and emptiness of mind.

And now she had her own opinions, and after supper she told the parents how difficult it is for children nowadays in the high school, but that a high school education is better than the ordinary school, because from the high school the way stands clear if you want to be a doctor, or if you want to be an engineer.

Sasha started going to school. His mother went off to Kharkov to visit her sister, and did not come back; his father went out every day to inspect cattle, and sometimes he was away for three days at a time, and it seemed to Olenka as if Sasha were quite forsaken—he was all alone in the house, and she thought he might die of hunger, so she brought him over to her own wing and put a little room in order for him.

Six months passed, and Sasha was still living with Olenka in the wing. Every morning she would go into his room; he slept soundly, with his hand under his cheek, breathing gently. She felt sorry to awaken him.

"Sashenka," she would say, sorrowfully. "Get up, dearie! Time to go to school!"

He would get up and dress and say his prayers, and then sit down to drink tea—he would drink up three glasses of tea and eat two large bubliks and half a French roll and butter. Generally he was but half awake, and not in a very good humour.

"Sashenka, you didn't learn your fable very well," Olenka would say, and look at him as if he were setting out on a long journey. "What a trouble I have with you! You're getting older, darling, and you must learn. Do what your teacher tells you!"

"Oh, stop it, please!" Sasha would say.

Then he would go along the street to the school—such a little boy, but wearing a big cap and a satchel on his back. Olenka would tiptoe after him.

"Sashenka-a!" she would cry.

He would look round, and she would slip into his hand a date or a caramel. When he turned into the side street where the school stood, he would become self-conscious because of this tall stout woman behind him, and he would look round and say:

"Now, Auntie, you go home. I can go along by myself now."

She would stand still and watch him, unmoving, until he was hidden in the school entrance. Oh, how she loved him! None of her previous attachments had been so deep as this; never had her soul submitted so absolutely, so disinterestedly, and with such joyful abandon, as at this time when her maternal feeling developed in her. She would have been ready to give her whole life and all her happiness for the sake of this other person's child, with the dimpled cheeks and the cap, yes, with joyful tears. Why would she have done that? And who knows—just why?

When she had seen Sasha off to school she would return home with soft steps, most happy, contented and loving. Her face had grown younger in these six months; it smiled, it radiated. People who met her took pleasure from her appearance.

"Good-day, Dushechka Olga Semenovna," they would say. "How are you getting on, Dushechka?"

When she went out to shop, she would gossip with the stall-keepers. "It's getting quite difficult for a boy in the high school now," she would say. "It's no joke to have to learn a fable by heart—and that's what they set for home-work in the first class yesterday, and a Latin translation, and a problem . . . that's a lot for a little boy, isn't it?"

She began to discuss the teachers, the lessons, the school-books, and said about them just what Sasha said.

Olenka and Sasha had dinner together at three in the afternoon, and in the evenings they worked together on the home-work, and grieved over the difficulties. When at last she tucked him into bed, she would make the sign of the cross over him many times and whisper her prayers. Then she would lie down to sleep herself, and dream of that distant and misty future when Sasha, having passed through the University, would become a doctor or an engineer, would have his own large house, his horse and carriage, would marry and have children. . . . With gentle tears trickling down her cheeks from her shut eyes, she would slumber on, still thinking of the same thing, while the black cat lying curled up against her side purred steadily:

"Mur . . . mur . . . mur."

One night Olenka was awakened by a sudden knocking at the outside door and could hardly breathe for terror, her heart beat so powerfully. Half a minute passed, and the knocking was repeated.

"It's a telegram from Kharkov," she thought, beginning to tremble all over. "The mother wants Sasha to be sent to her at Kharkov . . . Lord help me!"

She was in despair, and went cold all over, feeling that she was the most unfortunate being in the whole world. But another minute passed, and she heard voices: it was only the veterinary surgeon returning from the club.

"Well, glory be to God!"

The burden was gradually lifted from her heart. Once more she was at ease. She stretched herself on her bed and thought of Sasha, who was fast asleep in the adjoining room but kept calling out in a dream:

"I'll—I'll give it you! You go away! Don't tug!"

1. What is the theme of the story? Does the presentation of the theme seem more important in this story than the rendition of individual characters or social manners?
2. Why is it so important for Olenka to have "opinions"? Are they of any value in themselves? Do they stand for something else the author chooses not to name?
3. What is the attitude of the community toward Olenka? Does she care?
4. Does Olenka settle for less and less as she moves through a series of relations with men? How does her progress affect the tone and theme of the story?
5. What is the author's attitude toward his main character?

Kate Chopin

Chopin (1851–1904) was born in St. Louis. On a visit to New Orleans she met her husband-to-be and returned there to live with him when she married at twenty. After her husband's early death she went back to St. Louis and began to write, largely drawing on the experiences of her years in the Deep South. She contributed to many of the popular periodicals of her time, but her writing career came to an end with the publication of her novel The Awakening *(1899), which was sharply condemned for its frank representation of adultery and mixed marriage. This book has subsequently been praised for its sensitive portrayal of a woman in quest of her individuality. Several of her stories were collected in* Bayou Folk *(1894).*

The Story of an Hour

Knowing that Mrs. Mallard was afflicted with a heart trouble, great care was taken to break to her as gently as possible the news of her husband's death.

It was her sister Josephine who told her, in broken sentences; veiled hints that revealed in half concealing. Her husband's friend Richards was there, too, near her. It was he who had been in the newspaper office when intelligence of the railroad disaster was received, with Brently Mallard's name leading the list of "killed." He had only taken the time to assure himself of its truth by a second telegram, and had hastened to forestall any less careful, less tender friend in bearing the sad message.

She did not hear the story as many women have heard the same, with a paralyzed inability to accept its significance. She wept at once, with sudden, wild abandonment, in her sister's arms. When the storm of grief had spent itself she went away to her room alone. She would have no one follow her.

There stood, facing the open window, a comfortable, roomy arm-chair. Into this she sank, pressed down by a physical exhaustion that haunted her body and seemed to reach into her soul.

She could see in the open square before her house the tops of trees that were all aquiver with the new spring life. The delicious breath of rain was in the air. In the street below a peddler was crying his wares. The notes of a distant song which some one was singing reached her faintly, and countless sparrows were twittering in the eaves.

There were patches of blue sky showing here and there through the clouds that had met and piled one above the other in the west facing her window.

She sat with her head thrown back upon the cushion of the chair, quite motionless, except when a sob came up into her throat and shook her, as a child who has cried itself to sleep continues to sob in its dreams.

She was young, with a fair, calm face, whose lines bespoke repression and even a certain strength. But now there was a dull stare in her eyes, whose gaze was fixed away off yonder on one of those patches of blue sky. It was not a glance of reflection, but rather indicated a suspension of intelligent thought.

There was something coming to her and she was waiting for it, fearfully. What was it? She did not know; it was too subtle and elusive to name. But she felt it, creeping out of the sky, reaching toward her through the sounds, the scents, the color that filled the air.

Now her bosom rose and fell tumultuously. She was beginning to recognize this thing that was approaching to possess her, and she was striving to beat it back with her will—as powerless as her two white slender hands would have been.

When she abandoned herself a little whispered word escaped her slightly parted lips. She said it over and over under her breath: "free, free, free!" The vacant stare and the look of terror that had followed it went from her eyes. They stayed keen and bright. Her pulses beat fast, and the coursing blood warmed and relaxed every inch of her body.

She did not stop to ask if it were or were not a monstrous joy that held her. A clear and exalted perception enabled her to dismiss the suggestion as trivial.

She knew that she would weep again when she saw the kind, tender hands folded in death; the face that had never looked save with love upon her, fixed and gray and dead. But she saw beyond that bitter moment a long procession of years to come that would belong to her absolutely. And she opened and spread her arms out to them in welcome.

There would be no one to live for her during those coming years; she would live for herself. There would be no powerful will bending hers in that blind persistence with which men and women believe they have a right to impose a private will upon a fellow-creature. A kind intention or a cruel intention made the act seem no less a crime as she looked upon it in that brief moment of illumination.

And yet she had loved him—sometimes. Often she had not. What did it matter! What could love, the unsolved mystery, count for in face of this possession of self-assertion which she suddenly recognized as the strongest impulse of her being!

"Free! Body and soul free!" she kept whispering.

Josephine was kneeling before the closed door with her lips to the keyhold, imploring for admission. "Louise, open the door! I beg; open the door—you will make yourself ill. What are you doing, Louise? For heaven's sake open the door."

"Go away. I am not making myself ill." No; she was drinking in a very elixir of life through that open window.

Her fancy was running riot along those days ahead of her. Spring days, and summer days, and all sorts of days that would be her own. She breathed a quick prayer that life might be long. It was only yesterday she had thought with a shudder that life might be long.

She arose at length and opened the door to her sister's importunities. There was a feverish triumph in her eyes, and she carried herself unwittingly like a goddess of Victory. She clasped her sister's waist, and together they descended the stairs. Richards stood waiting for them at the bottom.

Some one was opening the front door with a latchkey. It was Brently Mallard who entered, a little travel-stained, composedly carrying his grip-sack and umbrella. He had been far from the scene of accident, and did not even know there had been one. He stood amazed at Josephine's piercing cry; at Richards' quick motion to screen him from the view of his wife.

But Richards was too late.

When the doctors came they said she had died of heart disease—of joy that kills.

---

1. Is Louise Mallard glad to be free of her actual marriage—or of any marriage whatsoever, or of any relationship that might curb her personal will?
2. Does the freedom she anticipates have any particular form or content? Is it positive or negative?
3. Is there such a medical diagnosis as the "joy that kills"?
4. Discuss the theme expressed by the story.

Arthur C. Clarke

Clarke (1917–   ) was born in Minehead, England. Early interested in science, he constructed his first telescope at the age of thirteen. He was a radar specialist with the Royal Air Force during World War II. He originated the proposal for use of satellites in communication, his career as an astronomer has led to his becoming a Fellow of the Royal Astronomical Society, and he has explored the Great Barrier Reef of Australia. He is prominent among the writers who have used science fiction as a vehicle for philosophic ideas, while his numerous nonfictional publications, including Interplanetary Flight *(1950),* The Reefs of Taprobane *(1957),* The Making of a Moon (1957), *and* View from Serendip *(1978), have introduced contemporary readers to scientific marvels now unfolding. His novels include* The Sands of Mars *(1951),* Childhood's End *(1953),* Earthlight *(1955),* A Fall of Moondust *(1961),* Imperial Earth *(1976), and* The Fountains of Paradise *(1979). He has published well over a hundred short stories, many of which are collected in* The Other Side of the Sky *(1958),* The Nine Billion Names of God *(1967), and* The Wind from the Sun *(1972). He is the author of the screenplay of Stanley Kubrick's film* 2001: A Space Odyssey.

The Star

It is three thousand light-years to the Vatican. Once, I believed that space could have no power over faith, just as I believed that the heavens declared the glory of God's handiwork. Now I have seen that handiwork, and my faith is sorely troubled. I stare at the crucifix that hangs on the cabin wall above the Mark VI Computer, and for the first time in my life I wonder if it is no more than an empty symbol.

I have told no one yet, but the truth cannot be concealed. The facts are there for all to read, recorded on the countless miles of magnetic tape and the thousands of photographs we are carrying back to Earth. Other scientists can interpret them as easily as I can, and I am not one who would condone that tampering with the truth which often gave my order a bad name in the olden days.

The crew are already sufficiently depressed: I wonder how they will take this ultimate irony. Few of them have any religious faith, yet they will not relish using this final weapon in their campaign against me—that private, good-natured, but fundamentally serious, war which lasted all the way from Earth. It amused them to have a Jesuit[1] as chief astrophysicist: Dr. Chandler, for instance, could never get over it (why are medical men such notorious atheists?). Sometimes he would meet me on the observation deck, where the lights are always low so that the stars shine with undiminished glory. He would come up to me in the gloom and stand staring out of the great oval port, while the heavens crawled slowly around us as the ship turned end over end with the residual spin we had never bothered to correct.

"Well, Father," he would say at last, "it goes on forever and forever, and perhaps *Something* made it. But how you can believe that *Something* has a special interest in us and our miserable little world—that just beats me." Then the argument would start, while the stars and nebulae would swing around us in silent, endless arcs beyond the flawlessly clear plastic of the observation port.

It was, I think, the apparent incongruity of my position that caused most amusement to the crew. In vain I would point to my three papers in the *Astrophysical Journal*, my five in the *Monthly Notices of the Royal Astronomical Society*. I would remind them that my order has long been famous for its scientific works. We may be few now, but ever since the eighteenth century we have made contributions to astronomy and geophysics out of all proportion to our numbers. Will my report on the Phoenix Nebula end our thousand years of history? It will end, I fear, much more than that.

I do not know who gave the nebula its name, which seems to me a very bad one. If it contains a prophecy, it is one that cannot be verified for several billion years. Even the word nebula is misleading: this is a far smaller object than those stupendous clouds of mist—the stuff of unborn stars—that are scattered throughout the length of the Milky Way. On the cosmic scale, indeed, the Phoenix Nebula is a tiny thing—a tenuous shell of gas surrounding a single star.

Or what is left of a star . . .

The Rubens engraving of Loyola[2] seems to mock me as it hangs there above the spectrophotometer tracings. What would *you*, Father, have made of this knowledge that has come into my keeping, so far from the little world that was all the universe you knew? Would your faith have risen to the challenge, as mine has failed to do?

You gaze into the distance, Father, but I have traveled a distance beyond any that you could have imagined when you founded our order a thousand years ago. No other survey ship has been so far from Earth: we are at the very frontiers of the explored universe. We set out to reach the Phoenix Nebula, we succeeded, and we are homeward bound

1. Member of the Society of Jesus, Catholic order founded in 1534, devoted to missionary and educational works. 2. Ignatius Loyola (1491–1556), founder of the Society of Jesus; portrayed by Peter Paul Rubens, Flemish artist (1577–1640).

with our burden of knowledge. I wish I could lift that burden from my shoulders, but I call to you in vain across the centuries and the light-years that lie between us.

On the book you are holding the words are plain to read. AD MAIOREM DEI GLORIAM,[3] the message runs, but it is a message I can no longer believe. Would you still believe it, if you could see what we have found?

We knew, of course, what the Phoenix Nebula was. Every year, in our galaxy alone, more than a hundred stars explode, blazing for a few hours or days with thousands of times their normal brilliance before they sink back into death and obscurity. Such are the ordinary novae—the commonplace disasters of the universe. I have recorded the spectrograms and light curves of dozens since I started working at the Lunar Observatory.

But three or four times in every thousand years occurs something beside which even a nova pales into total insignificance.

When a star becomes a supernova, it may for a little while outshine all the massed suns of the galaxy. The Chinese astronomers watched this happen in A.D. 1054, not knowing what it was they saw. Five centuries later, in 1572, a supernova blazed in Cassiopeia so brilliantly that it was visible in the daylight sky. There have been three more in the thousand years that have passed since then.

Our mission was to visit the remnants of such a catastrophe, to reconstruct the events that led up to it, and, if possible, to learn its cause. We came slowly in through the concentric shells of gas that had been blasted out six thousand years before, yet were expanding still. They were immensely hot, radiating even now with a fierce violet light, but were far too tenuous to do us any damage. When the star had exploded, its outer layers had been driven upward with such speed that they had escaped completely from its gravitational field. Now they formed a hollow shell large enough to engulf a thousand solar systems, and at its center burned the tiny, fantastic object which the star had now become—a White Dwarf, smaller than the Earth, yet weighing a million times as much.

The glowing gas shells were all around us, banishing the normal night of interstellar space. We were flying into the center of a cosmic bomb that had detonated millennia ago and whose incandescent fragments were still hurtling apart. The immense scale of the explosion, and the fact that the debris already covered a volume of space many billions of miles across, robbed the scene of any visible movement. It would take decades before the unaided eye could detect any motion in

3. For the greater glory of God.

these tortured wisps and eddies of gas, yet the sense of turbulent expansion was overwhelming.

We had checked our primary drive hours before, and were drifting slowly toward the fierce little star ahead. Once it had been a sun like our own, but it had squandered in a few hours the energy that should have kept it shining for a million years. Now it was a shrunken miser, hoarding its resources as if trying to make amends for its prodigal youth.

No one seriously expected to find planets. If there had been any before the explosion, they would have been boiled into puffs of vapor, and their substance lost in the greater wreckage of the star itself. But we made the automatic search, as we always do when approaching an unknown sun, and presently we found a single small world circling the star at an immense distance. It must have been the Pluto of this vanished solar system, orbiting on the frontiers of the night. Too far from the central sun ever to have known life, its remoteness had saved it from the fate of all its lost companions.

The passing fires had seared its rocks and burned away the mantle of frozen gas that must have covered it in the days before the disaster. We landed, and we found the Vault.

Its builders had made sure that we would. The monolithic marker that stood above the entrance was now a fused stump, but even the first long-range photographs told us that here was the work of intelligence. A little later we detected the continent-wide pattern of radioactivity that had been buried in the rock. Even if the pylon above the Vault had been destroyed, this would have remained, an immovable and all but eternal beacon calling to the stars. Our ship fell toward this gigantic bull's-eye like an arrow into its target.

The pylon must have been a mile high when it was built, but now it looked like a candle that had melted down into a puddle of wax. It took us a week to drill through the fused rock, since we did not have the proper tools for a task like this. We were astronomers, not archaeologists, but we could improvise. Our original purpose was forgotten: this lonely monument, reared with such labor at the greatest possible distance from the doomed sun, could have only one meaning. A civilization that knew it was about to die had made its last bid for immortality.

It will take us generations to examine all the treasures that were placed in the Vault. They had plenty of time to prepare, for their sun must have given its first warnings many years before the final detonation. Everything that they wished to preserve, all the fruit of their genius, they brought here to this distant world in the days before the end, hoping that some other race would find it and that they would not be utterly forgotten. Would we have done as well, or would we have been too lost in our own misery to give thought to a future we could never see or share?

If only they had had a little more time! They could travel freely enough between the planets of their own sun, but they had not yet learned to cross the interstellar gulfs, and the nearest solar system was a hundred light-years away. Yet even had they possessed the secret of the Transfinite Drive, no more than a few millions could have been saved. Perhaps it was better thus.

Even if they had not been so disturbingly human as their sculpture shows, we could not have helped admiring them and grieving for their fate. They left thousands of visual records and the machines for projecting them, together with elaborate pictorial instructions from which it will not be difficult to learn their written language. We have examined many of these records, and brought to life for the first time in six thousand years the warmth and beauty of a civilization that in many ways must have been superior to our own. Perhaps they only showed us the best, and one can hardly blame them. But their worlds were very lovely, and their cities were built with a grace that matches anything of man's. We have watched them at work and play, and listened to their musical speech sounding across the centuries. One scene is still before my eyes—a group of children on a beach of strange blue sand, playing in the waves as children play on Earth. Curious whiplike trees line the shore, and some very large animal is wading in the shadows yet attracting no attention at all.

And sinking into the sea, still warm and friendly and lifegiving, is the sun that will soon turn traitor and obliterate all this innocent happiness.

Perhaps if we had not been so far from home and so vulnerable to loneliness, we would not have been so deeply moved. Many of us had seen the ruins of ancient civilizations on other worlds, but they had never affected us so profoundly. This tragedy was unique. It is one thing for a race to fail and die, as nations and cultures have done on Earth. But to be destroyed so completely in the full flower of its achievement, leaving no survivors—how could that be reconciled with the mercy of God?

My colleagues have asked me that, and I have given what answers I can. Perhaps you could have done better, Father Loyola, but I have found nothing in the *Exercitia Spiritualia*[4] that helps me here. They were not an evil people: I do not know what gods they worshiped, if indeed they worshiped any. But I have looked back at them across the centuries, and have watched while the loveliness they used their last

4. *Spiritual Exercises*, book written by Loyola for the guidance of Jesuits.

strength to preserve was brought forth again into the light of their shrunken sun. They could have taught us much: why were they destroyed?

I know the answers that my colleagues will give when they get back to Earth. They will say that the universe has no purpose and no plan, that since a hundred suns exploded every year in our galaxy, at this very moment some race is dying in the depths of space. Whether that race has done good or evil during its lifetime will make no difference in the end: there is no divine justice, for there is no God.

Yet, of course, what we have seen proves nothing of the sort. Anyone who argues thus is being swayed by emotion, not logic. God has no need to justify His actions to man. He who built the universe can destroy it when He chooses. It is arrogance—it is perilously near blasphemy—for us to say what He may or may not do.

This I could have accepted, hard though it is to look upon whole worlds and peoples thrown into the furnace. But there comes a point when even the deepest faith must falter, and now, as I look at the calculations lying before me, I know I have reached that point at last.

We could not tell, before we reached the nebula, how long ago the explosion took place. Now, from the astronomical evidence and the record in the rocks of that one surviving planet, I have been able to date it very exactly. I know in what year the light of this colossal conflagration reached our Earth. I know how brilliantly the supernova whose corpse now dwindles behind our speeding ship once shone in terrestrial skies. I know how it must have blazed low in the east before sunrise, like a beacon in that oriental dawn.

There can be no reasonable doubt: the ancient mystery is solved at last. Yet, oh God, there were so many stars you could have used. What was the need to give these people to the fire, that the symbol of their passing might shine above Bethlehem?

---

1. How important is the individual character of the narrator as distinct from his formal beliefs? Why is the discovery of the dead civilization more painful for him than for the other scientists on the voyage?
2. Has anything at all been proved about the nature of God by the discovery of the dead planet? What inferences might be drawn about God's motives in choosing an inhabited part of the universe to destroy in announcing to men the birth of Christ?
3. Why did the race that knew itself doomed use its last strength to preserve "loveliness"?
4. Is the central issue of the story the *mercy* of God? If the narrator has wholly rejected his faith, is this rejection the result of a moral or an intellectual decision?
5. How is this story relevant to your own religious views and values?

Samuel Clemens (Mark Twain)

Clemens (Mark Twain) (1835–1910) was born in Florida, Missouri. When he was four, his family took him to the town of Hannibal in the same state, where he experienced some of the adventures described in his novels The Adventures of Tom Sawyer *(1876) and* Adventures of Huckleberry Finn *(1884). In his twenties he was an apprentice pilot on a Mississippi River steamer, and in "learning the river" he discovered that his true teacher would be the American land itself, with its western reaches just then opening to the surge of farmers, hunters, traders, and gold-seekers. He went to California and with his readings and journalism won literary success in the mining camps up-river from San Francisco before the East caught on to his vivid and earthy style or the significance of his subject matter. In San Francisco he began his career as a lecturer—so successfully that in years to come he delighted audiences around the world with his platform manner and the astounding turns of his wit. By the late 1860's, when he went to travel in Europe and the Holy Land, he was looked on by his countrymen as their natural emissary to the Old World, and his report on these travels in* Innocents Abroad *(1869) gave a new definition to the uniqueness of the American way of looking at things. After two decades of prosperity and popularity he lost his fortune in bad investments, but after 1895 his unceasing work as writer and lecturer enabled him to recoup his losses and build a mansion (now a museum) at Redding, Connecticut, where he died at the height of his fame. The darker, pessimistic side of his outlook was hardly stressed or noted before the publication in 1916 of his novel* The Mysterious Stranger. *Best known among his other works are* Roughing It *(1872),* Life on the Mississippi *(1883), and* A Connecticut Yankee in King Arthur's Court *(1889).*

The Notorious Jumping Frog of Calaveras County

In compliance with the request of a friend of mine, who wrote me from the East, I called on good-natured, garrulous old Simon Wheeler, and inquired about my friend's friend, Leonidas W. Smiley, as requested to do, and I hereunto append the result. I have a lurking suspicion that *Leonidas* W. Smiley is a myth; that my friend never knew such a personage; and that he only conjectured that if I asked old Wheeler about him, it would remind him of his infamous *Jim* Smiley, and he would go to work and bore me to death with some exasperating reminiscence of him as long and as tedious as it should be useless to me. If that was the design, it succeeded.

I found Simon Wheeler dozing comfortably by the bar-room stove of the dilapidated tavern in the decayed mining camp of Angel's, and I noticed that he was fat and bald-headed, and had an expression of winning gentleness and simplicity upon his tranquil countenance. He roused up, and gave me good-day. I told him that a friend of mine had commissioned me to make some inquiries about a cherished companion of his boyhood named *Leonidas* W. Smiley—*Rev. Leonidas* W. Smiley, a young minister of the Gospel, who he had heard was at one time a resident of Angel's Camp. I added that if Mr. Wheeler could tell me anything about this Rev. Leonidas W. Smiley, I would feel under many obligations to him.

Simon Wheeler backed me into a corner and blockaded me there with his chair, and then sat down and reeled off the monotonous narrative which follows this paragraph. He never smiled, he never frowned, he never changed his voice from the gentle-flowing key to which he tuned his initial sentence, he never betrayed the slightest suspicion of enthusiasm; but all through the interminable narrative there ran a vein of impressive earnestness and sincerity, which showed me plainly that, so far from his imagining that there was anything ridiculous or funny about his story, he regarded it as a really important matter, and admired its two heroes as men of transcendent genius in *finesse*.[1] I let him go on in his own way, and never interrupted him once.

"Rev. Leonidas W. H'm, Reverend Le—well, there was a feller here once by the name of *Jim* Smiley, in the winter of '49—or maybe it was the spring of '50—I don't recollect exactly, somehow, though what makes me think it was one or the other is because I remember the big flume[2] warn't finished when he first came to the camp; but anyway, he was the curiousest man about always betting on anything that turned up you ever see, if he could get anybody to bet on the other side; and if he couldn't he'd change sides. Any way that suited the other man would suit *him*—any way just so's he got a bet, *he* was satisfied. But still he was lucky, uncommon lucky; he most always come out winner. He was always ready and laying for a chance; there couldn't be no solit'ry thing mentioned but that feller'd offer to bet on it, and take ary side you please, as I was just telling you. If there was a horse-race, you'd find him flush or you'd find him busted at the end of it; if there was a dog-fight, he'd bet on it; if there was a cat-fight, he'd bet on it; if there was a chicken-fight, he'd bet on it; why, if there was two

1. Subtle, discriminating skill. 2. Artificial channel to carry water to gold diggings.

birds setting on a fence, he would bet you which one would fly first; or if there was a camp-meeting,[3] he would be there reg'lar to bet on Parson Walker, which he judged to be the best exhorter about here, and so he was too, and a good man. If he even see a straddle-bug start to go anywheres, he would bet you how long it would take him to get to—to wherever he was going to, and if you took him up, he would foller that straddle-bug to Mexico but what he would find out where he was bound for and how long he was on the road. Lots of the boys here has seen that Smiley, and can tell you about him. Why, it never made no difference to *him*—he'd bet on *any* thing—the dangdest feller. Parson Walker's wife laid very sick once, for a good while, and it seemed as if they warn't going to save her; but one morning he come in, and Smiley up and asked him how she was, and he said she was considerable better—thank the Lord for his inf'nite mercy—and coming on so smart that with the blessing of Prov'dence she'd get well yet; and Smiley, before he thought, says, 'Well, I'll resk two-and-a-half she don't anyway.'

"Thish-yer Smiley had a mare—the boys called her the fifteen-minute nag, but that was only in fun, you know, because of course she was faster than that—and he used to win money on that horse, for all she was so slow and always had the asthma, or the distemper, or the consumption, or something of that kind. They used to give her two or three hundred yards' start, and then pass her under way; but always at the fag end of the race she'd get excited and desperate like, and come cavorting and straddling up, and scattering her legs around limber, sometimes in the air, and sometimes out to one side among the fences, and kicking up m-o-r-e dust and raising m-o-r-e racket with her coughing and sneezing and blowing her nose—and *always* fetch up at the stand just about a neck ahead, as near as you could cipher it down.

"And he had a little small bull-pup, that to look at him you'd think he warn't worth a cent but to set around and look ornery and lay for a chance to steal something. But as soon as money was up on him he was a different dog; his under-jaw'd begin to stick out like the fo'castle of a steamboat, and his teeth would uncover and shine like the furnaces. And a dog might tackle him and bully-rag him, and bite him, and throw him over his shoulder two or three times, and Andrew Jackson[4]—which was the name of the pup—Andrew Jackson would never let on but what *he* was satisfied, and hadn't expected nothing else—and the bets being doubled and doubled on the other side all the time, till the money was all up; and then all of a sudden he would grab that other dog jest by the j'int of his hind leg and freeze to it—

3. Outdoor religious meeting. 4. Andrew Jackson (1767–1845) was the seventh president of the United States. Jackson was famous in legend for his iron will.

not chaw, you understand, but only just grip and hang on till they throwed up the sponge, if it was a year. Smiley always come out winner on that pup, till he harnessed a dog once that didn't have no hind legs, because they'd been sawed off in a circular saw, and when the thing had gone along far enough, and the money was all up, and he come to make a snatch for his pet holt, he see in a minute how he'd been imposed on, and how the other dog had him in the door, so to speak, and he 'peared surprised, and then he looked sorter discouraged-like, and didn't try no more to win the fight, and so he got shucked out bad. He give Smiley a look, as much as to say his heart was broke, and it was *his* fault, for putting up a dog that hadn't no hind legs for him to take holt of, which was his main dependence in a fight, and then he limped off a piece and laid down and died. It was a good pup, was that Andrew Jackson, and would have made a name for hisself if he'd lived, for the stuff was in him and he had genius—I know it, because he hadn't no opportunities to speak of, and it don't stand to reason that a dog could make such a fight as he could under them circumstances if he hadn't no talent. It always makes me feel sorry when I think of that last fight of his'n, and the way it turned out.

"Well, thish-yer Smiley had rat-tarriers, and chicken cocks, and tom-cats and all them kind of things, till you couldn't rest, and you couldn't fetch nothing for him to bet on but he'd match you. He ketched a frog one day, and took him home, and said he cal'lated to educate him; and so he never done nothing for three months but set in his back yard and learn that frog to jump. And you bet you he *did* learn him, too. He'd give him a little punch behind, and the next minute you'd see that frog whirling in the air like a doughnut—see him turn one summerset, or maybe a couple, if he got a good start, and come down flat-footed and all right, like a cat. He got him up so in the matter of ketching flies, and kep' him in practice so constant, that he'd nail a fly every time as fur as he could see him. Smiley said all a frog wanted was education, and he could do 'most anything—and I believe him. Why, I've seen him set Dan'l Webster[5] down here on this floor—Dan'l Webster was the name of the frog—and sing out, 'Flies, Dan'l, flies!' and quicker'n you could wink he'd spring straight up and snake a fly off'n the counter there, and flop down on the floor ag'in as solid as a gob of mud, and fall to scratching the side of his head with his hind foot as indifferent as if he hadn't no idea he'd been doin' any more'n any frog might do. You never see a frog so modest and straightfor'ard as he was, for all he was so gifted. And when it come to fair and square jumping on a dead level, he could get over more ground at one strad-

5. The frog is named for Daniel Webster, distinguished American statesman and orator (1782–1852).

dle than any animal of his breed you ever see. Jumping on a dead level was his strong suit, you understand; and when it come to that, Smiley would ante up money on him as long as he had a red.[6] Smiley was monstrous proud of his frog, and well he might be, for fellers that had traveled and been everywheres, all said he laid over any frog that ever *they* see.

"Well, Smiley kep' the beast in a little lattice box, and he used to fetch him down-town sometimes and lay for a bet. One day a feller—a stranger in the camp, he was—come acrost him with his box, and says:

" 'What might it be that you've got in the box?'

"And Smiley says, sorter indifferent-like, 'It might be a parrot, or it might be a canary, maybe, but it ain't—it's only just a frog.'

"And the feller took it, and looked at it careful, and turned it round this way and that, and says, 'H'm—so 'tis. Well, what's *he* good for?'

" 'Well,' Smiley says, easy and careless, 'he's good enough for *one* thing, I should judge—he can outjump any frog in Calaveras County.'

"The feller took the box again, and took another long, particular look, and give it back to Smiley, and says, very deliberate, 'Well,' he says, 'I don't see no p'ints about that frog that's any better'n any other frog.'

" 'Maybe you don't,' Smiley says. 'Maybe you understand frogs and maybe you don't understand 'em; maybe you've had experience, and maybe you ain't only a amature, as it were. Anyways, I've got *my* opinion, and I'll resk forty dollars that he can outjump any frog in Calaveras County.'

"And the feller studied a minute, and then says, kinder sadlike 'Well, I'm only a stranger here, and I ain't got no frog; but if I had a frog, I'd bet you.'

"And then Smiley says, 'That's all right—that's all right—if you'll hold my box a minute, I'll go and get you a frog.' And so the feller took the box, and put up his forty dollars along with Smiley's, and set down to wait.

"So he set there a good while thinking and thinking to himself, and then he got the frog out and prized his mouth open and took a teaspoon and filled him full of quail shot—filled him pretty near up to his chin—and set him on the floor. Smiley he went to the swamp and slopped around in the mud for a long time, and finally he ketched a frog, and fetched him in, and give him to this feller, and says:

" 'Now, if you're ready, set him alongside of Dan'l, with his fore paws just even with Dan'l's, and I'll give the word.' Then he says,

6. A red cent; i.e., any money whatsoever.

'One—two—three—*git!*' and him and the feller touched up the frogs from behind, and the new frog hopped off lively, but Dan'l give a heave, and hysted up his shoulders—so—like a Frenchman, but it warn't no use—he couldn't budge; he was planted as solid as a church, and he couldn't no more stir than if he was anchored out. Smiley was a good deal surprised, and he was disgusted too, but he didn't have no idea what the matter was, of course.

"The feller took the money and started away; and when he was going out at the door, he sorter jerked his thumb over his shoulder—so—at Dan'l, and says again, very deliberate, 'Well,' he says, '*I* don't see no p'ints about that frog that's any better'n any other frog.'

"Smiley he stood scratching his head and looking down at Dan'l a long time, and at last he says, 'I do wonder what in the nation that frog throw'd off for—I wonder if there ain't something the matter with him—he 'pears to look mighty baggy, somehow.' And he ketched Dan'l by the nap of the neck, and hefted him, and says, 'Why blame my cats if he don't weigh five pound! " and turned him upside down and he belched out a double handful of shot. And then he see how it was, and he was the maddest man—he set the frog down and took out after that feller, but he never ketched him. And—"

[Here Simon Wheeler heard his name called from the front yard, and got up to see what was wanted.] And turning to me as he moved away, he said: "Just set where you are, stranger, and rest easy—I ain't going to be gone a second."

But, by your leave, I did not think that a continuation of the history of the enterprising vagabond *Jim* Smiley would be likely to afford me much information concerning the Rev. *Leonidas* W. Smiley, and so I started away.

At the door I met the sociable Wheeler returning, and he buttonholed me and recommenced:

"Well, thish-yer Smiley had a yaller one-eyed cow that didn't have no tail, only just a short stump like a bannanner, and—"

However, lacking both time and inclination, I did not wait to hear about the afflicted cow, but took my leave.

---

1. What are the differences in character and cultural background between the first narrator and Simon Wheeler?
2. Discuss the relationship between the episode of the frog-jumping contest and Simon Wheeler's prologue to it. Which is more important—prologue or episode?
3. Select and list some examples of the peculiarities in Wheeler's language. List some of his figurative expressions.
4. What is accomplished by giving a touch of human personality to the frog Dan'l Webster?

5. What does the story say about the extent of human gullibility?
6. How do various elements of the story contribute to its tone? Do they all work harmoniously, or is there contradiction between one element and another?

Colette

Colette (Sidonie-Gabrielle Colette) (1873–1954) was born in a provincial village in France. From her girlhood on, her mother was her closest intellectual and emotional companion, though Colette strayed far from home in the accomplishment of her career. Moving to Paris, she married a raffish and enterprising writer, who collaborated with her on her first novels, which were spiced-up memories of her days in school. After her divorce from this man, Colette worked as an entertainer in music halls. This experience also provided her with material for her writing. She was married and divorced again, and again married, finally to a devoted husband who was lavish in caring for her and in promoting her career. Through all the years of personal tribulation, her books poured forth in a steady stream—books not concerned with the philosophical quandaries of the time but with sensuous pleasures, people, and typically French environments.

Colette's fame grew evenly and steadily over the years. She published more than fifty novels and a greater number of short stories and reminiscences. Readers found in her work compellingly sensitive observations of women and the qualities they bring to their relations with men. She was the first woman to be elected president of the Goncourt Academy and the second to be made an officer of the Legion of Honor.

Among her best-known novels are The Vagrant *(1910),* Chéri *(1920),* The Ripening Seed *(1923),* The Last of Chéri *(1926), and* Gigi *(1944). The bulk of her short fiction is available in* The Collected Stories of Colette *(1983).*

The Hidden Woman[1]

He had been looking at the swirl of masks in front of him for a long time, suffering vaguely from the intermingling of their colors and the synchronized sound of two orchestras too close together. His cowl pressed his temples; a nervous headache was building between his eyes. But he savored, without impatience, a mixture of malaise and pleasure which allowed the hours to fly by unnoticed. He had wandered down all the corridors of the Opéra,[2] had drunk in the silvery dust of the dance floor, recognized bored friends, and wrapped around

1. Translated by Matthew Ward. 2. The opera house in Paris.

his neck the indifferent arms of a very fat girl humorously disguised as a sylph. Though embarrassed by his long domino, tripping over it like a man in skirts, the cowled doctor did not dare take off either the domino or the hood, because of his schoolboy lie.

"I'll be spending tomorrow night in Nogent," he had told his wife the evening before. "They just telephoned and I'm afraid that my patient, you know, that poor old lady . . . Can you imagine? And I was looking forward to this ball like a kid. It's ridiculous, isn't it, a man my age who's never been to the Opéra Ball?"

"Very, darling, very ridiculous! If I had known I might never have married you . . ."

She laughed, and he admired her narrow face, pink, matte, and long, like a thin sugared almond.

"But . . . don't you want to go to the Green and Purple Ball? You know you can go without me if you want, darling."

She trembled with one of those long shivers of disgust which made her hair, her delicate hands, and her chest in her white dress shudder at the sight of a slug or some filthy passer-by.

"Oh, no! Can you see me in a crowd, all those hands . . . What can I do? It's not that I'm a prude, it's . . . it makes my skin crawl. There's nothing I can do about it."

Leaning against the balustrade of the loggia, above the main staircase, he thought about this trembling hind, as he contemplated, directly in front of him, on the bare back of a sultana, the grasp of two enormous square hands with black nails. Bursting out of the braid-trimmed sleeves of a Venetian lord, they sank into the white female flesh as if it were dough. Because he was thinking about her, it gave him quite a start to hear, next to him, a little "ahem," a little cough typical of his wife. He turned around and saw someone in a long and impenetrable disguise, sitting sidesaddle on the balustrade, Pierrot by the looks of the huge-sleeved tunic, the loose-fitting pantaloons, the skullcap, the plaster-like whiteness coating the little bit of skin visible above the half-mask bearded with lace. The fabric of the costume and skullcap, woven of dark violet and silver, glistened like the conger eel fished for by night with iron hooks, in boats with resin lanterns. Overcome with surprise, he waited to hear the little "ahem," which did not come again. The Pierrot-Eel, seated, casual, tapped the marble balusters with a dangling heel, revealing only its two satin slippers and a black-gloved hand bent back against one hip. The two oblique slits in the mask, carefully covered over with a tulle mesh, allowed only a smothered fire of indeterminate color to pass through.

He almost called out, "Irene!" but held back, remembering his own lie. Not good at playacting, he also decided against disguising his voice. The Pierrot scratched its thigh, with a free and uninhibited gesture, and the anxious husband sighed in relief.

"Ah! It's not her."

But out of a pocket the Pierrot pulled a flat gold box, opened it to take out a lipstick, and the anxious husband recognized an antique snuffbox, fitted with a mirror inside, the last birthday present . . . He put his left hand on the pain in his chest with so brusque and so involuntarily theatrical a motion that the Pierrot-Eel noticed him.

"Is that a declaration, Purple Domino?"

He did not answer, half choked with surprise, anticipating, as in a bad dream, and listened for a long moment to the thinly disguised voice—the voice of his wife. The Eel, sitting there cavalierly, its head tilted like a bird's, looked at him; she shrugged her shoulders, hopped down, and walked away. Her movement freed the distraught husband, who, restored to an active and normal jealousy, started to think clearly again, and calmly rose to follow his wife.

"She's here for someone, with someone. In less than an hour I'll know everything."

A hundred other purple or green cowls guaranteed that he would be neither noticed nor recognized. Irene walked ahead of him nonchalantly. He was amazed to see her roll her hips softly and drag her feet a little as if she were wearing Turkish slippers. A Byzantine, in embroidered emerald green and gold, grabbed her as she passed, and she bent back, grown thinner in his arms, as if his grasp were going to cut her in half. Her husband ran a few steps forward and reached the couple as Irene cried out flatteringly, "You big brute, you!"

She walked away, with the same relaxed and calm step, stopping often, musing at the open doors of the boxes, almost never turning around. She hesitated at the bottom of a staircase, turned aside, came back toward the entrance to the orchestra stalls, slid into a noisy, dense group with slippery skillfulness, the exact movement of a knife blade sliding into its sheath. Ten arms imprisoned her, an almost naked wrestler roughly pinned her up against the edge of the boxes on the main floor and held her there. She yielded under the weight of the naked man, threw back her head with a laugh that was drowned out by other laughter, and the man in the purple cowl saw her teeth flash beneath the mask's lacy beard. Then she slipped away again with ease and sat down on the steps which led to the dance floor. Her husband, standing two steps behind, watched her. She readjusted her mask, and her crumpled tunic, and tightened the roll of her headband. She seemed calm, as though alone, and walked away again after a few minutes' rest. She went down the steps, put her arms on the shoulders of a warrior who invited her, without speaking, to dance, and she danced, clinging to him.

"That's him," the husband said to himself.

But she did not say a word to the dancer, clad in iron and moist skin, and left him quietly, when the dance ended. She went off to have a glass of champagne at the buffet, and then a second glass, paid, and then watched, motionless and curious, as two men began scuffling, surrounded by screaming women. Then she amused herself by placing her little satanic hands, all black, on the white throat of a Dutch girl with golden hair, who cried out nervously. At last the anxious man who was following her saw her stop as she bumped up against a young man collapsed on a banquette, out of breath, fanning himself with his mask. She leaned over, disdainfully took his handsome face, rugged and fresh, by the chin, and kissed the panting, half-open mouth . . .

But her husband, instead of rushing forward and tearing the two joined mouths away from each other, disappeared into the crowd. Dismayed, he no longer feared, he no longer hoped for betrayal. He was sure now that Irene did not know the adolescent, drunk with dancing, whom she was kissing, or the Hercules. He was sure that she was not waiting or looking for anyone, that the lips she held beneath her own like a crushed grape, she would abandon, leave again the next minute, then wander about again, gather up some other passer-by, forget him, until she felt tired and it was time to go back home, tasting only the monstrous pleasure of being alone, free, honest, in her native brutality, of being the one who is unknown, forever solitary and without shame, whom a little mask and a hermetic costume had restored to her irremediable solitude and her immodest innocence.

---

1. Is the husband's jealousy transformed into something else by what he sees of his wife's behavior?
2. Is Irene's "immodest innocence" easier for the husband to deal with than infidelity?
3. Does the licentious atmosphere of the ball present a challenge the husband cannot deal with?
4. Does the story show an insurmountable estrangement between the pair?

Joseph Conrad

Conrad (1857–1924) (christened Jozef Teodor Konrad Nalecz Korzeniowski) was born in the Polish Ukraine to a family of landed gentry. In 1863 his hot-headed father was exiled for revolutionary activities to an area northeast of Moscow. He took his family with him to this inhospitable region, where the climate proved too much for both parents. The orphaned Conrad at seventeen persuaded his guardian uncle to let him join the French merchant navy, and for about twenty years he sailed to many exotic places, surviving shipwrecks and (probably) an attempted suicide, running guns at intervals in his more respectable occupations and rising, finally, to the rank of master (captain) in the British merchant fleet. He began to write before he gave up his seagoing career, and some of his early work led to his friendship with such literary figures as Henry James, Stephen Crane, and Ford Madox Ford. With their encouragement he not only devoted himself full time to fiction but developed the style and form of narration that are so much his own. (One of the marvels is that so fine a stylist should have written in English when Polish was his native tongue and French his "second language.") Though he was respected from the beginning of his writing career and critically acclaimed after the publication of The Nigger of the "Narcissus" *(1897), he had small popular success before his novel* Chance *was brought out in 1914. In his later years, after World War I, he was one of the most venerated of English novelists. He was working on a novel of Napoleon's escape from Elba when he died. His novels include* Lord Jim *(1900),* Nostromo *(1904),* Under Western Eyes *(1910), and* Victory *(1915). Three works of medium length were published in* Youth *(1902).*

Heart of Darkness

I

The *Nellie*, a cruising yawl, swung to her anchor without a flutter of the sails, and was at rest. The flood had made, the wind was nearly calm, and being bound down the river, the only thing for it was to come to and wait for the turn of the tide.

The sea-reach[1] of the Thames stretched before us like the beginning of an interminable waterway. In the offing[2] the sea and the sky

1. Tidal part of the river as it broadens toward the sea. 2. Part of the sea visible from the river's mouth.

were welded together without a joint, and in the luminous space the tanned sails of the barges drifting up with the tide seemed to stand still in red clusters of canvas sharply peaked, with gleams of varnished sprits. A haze rested on the low shores that ran out to sea in vanishing flatness. The air was dark above Gravesend,[3] and farther back still seemed condensed into a mournful gloom, brooding motionless over the biggest, and the greatest, town on earth.

The Director of Companies was our captain and our host. We four affectionately watched his back as he stood in the bows looking to seaward. On the whole river there was nothing that looked half so nautical. He resembled a pilot, which to a seaman is trustworthiness personified. It was difficult to realize his work was not out there in the luminous estuary, but behind him, within the brooding gloom.

Between us there was, as I have already said somewhere, the bond of the sea. Besides holding our hearts together through long periods of separation, it had the effect of making us tolerant of each other's yarns—and even convictions. The Lawyer—the best of old fellows—had, because of his many years and many virtues, the only cushion on deck, and was lying on the only rug. The accountant had brought out already a box of dominoes, and was toying architecturally with the bones. Marlow sat cross-legged right aft, leaning against the mizzen-mast. He had sunken cheeks, a yellow complexion, a straight back, and ascetic aspect, and, with his arms dropped, the palms of hands outwards, resembled an idol. The director, satisfied the anchor had good hold, made his way aft and sat down amongst us. We exchanged a few words lazily. Afterwards there was silence on board the yacht. For some reason or other we did not begin that game of dominoes. We felt meditative, and fit for nothing but placid staring. The day was ending in a serenity of still and exquisite brilliance. The water shone pacifically; the sky, without a speck, was a benign immensity of unstained light; the very mist on the Essex marshes[4] was like a gauzy and radiant fabric, hung from the wooded rises inland, and draping the low shores in diaphanous folds. Only the gloom to the west, brooding over the upper reaches, became more somber every minute, as if angered by the approach of the sun.

And at last, in its curved and imperceptible fall, the sun sank low, and from glowing white changed to a dull red without rays and without heat, as if about to go out suddenly, stricken to death by the touch of that gloom brooding over a crowd of men.

Forthwith a change came over the waters, and the serenity became less brilliant but more profound. The old river in its broad reach rested unruffled at the decline of day, after ages of good service done to the

3. City on the Thames 26 miles east of London. 4. On the north bank of the Thames.

race that peopled its banks, spread out in the tranquil dignity of a waterway leading to the uttermost ends of the earth. We looked at the venerable stream not in the vivid flush of a short day that comes and departs forever, but in the august light of abiding memories. And indeed nothing is easier for a man who has, as the phrase goes, "followed the sea" with reverence and affection, than to evoke the great spirit of the past upon the lower reaches of the Thames. The tidal current runs to and fro in its unceasing service, crowded with memories of men and ships it had borne to the rest of home or to the battles of the sea. It had known and served all the men of whom the nation is proud, from Sir Francis Drake to Sir John Franklin,[5] knights all, titled and untitled—the great knights-errant of the sea. It had borne all the ships whose names are like jewels flashing in the night of time, from the *Golden Hind* returning with her round flanks full of treasure, to be visited by the Queen's Highness and thus pass out of the gigantic tale, to the *Erebus* and *Terror*, bound on other conquests—and that never returned. It had known the ships and the men. They had sailed from Deptford, from Greenwich, from Erith—the adventurers and the settlers; kings' ships and the ships of men on 'Change; captains, admirals, the dark "interlopers" of the Eastern trade, and the commissioned "Generals" of East India fleets.[6] Hunters for gold or pursuers of fame, they all had gone out on that stream, bearing the sword, and often the torch, messengers of the might within the land, bearers of a spark from the sacred fire. What greatness had not floated on the ebb of that river into the mystery of an unknown earth! . . . The dreams of men, the seed of commonwealths, the germs of empires.

The sun set; the dusk fell on the stream, and lights began to appear along the shore. The Chapman lighthouse, a three-legged thing erect on a mud-flat, shone strongly. Lights of ships moved in the fairway—a great stir of lights going up and going down. And farther west on the upper reaches the place of the monstrous town was still marked ominously on the sky, a brooding gloom in sunshine, a lurid glare under the stars.

"And this also," said Marlow suddenly, "has been one of the dark places on the earth."

He was the only man of us who still "followed the sea." The worst that could be said of him was that he did not represent his class. He was a seaman, but he was a wanderer, too, while most seamen lead, if one may so express it, a sedentary life. Their minds are of the stay-at-

5. Drake (1540–1596) sailed around the world (1577–1580) and defeated the Spanish Armada. Franklin (1786–1847), was an arctic explorer who commanded an expedition including the ships *Erebus* and *Terror*, lost in a search for the Northwest Passage. 6. Deptford, Greenwich, and Erith are seaports on the Thames. The 'Change is the financial district of London. "Interlopers" were unauthorized competitors of the East India Company, chartered by the British Crown and in the reign of Charles II given the right to maintain troops in India and thus to appoint "generals."

home order, and their home is always with them—the ship; and so is their country—the sea. One ship is very much like another, and the sea is always the same. In the immutability of their surroundings the foreign shores, the foreign faces, the changing immensity of life, glide past, veiled not by a sense of mystery but by a slightly disdainful ignorance; for there is nothing mysterious to a seaman unless it be the sea itself, which is the mistress of his existence and as inscrutable as Destiny. For the rest, after his hours of work, a casual stroll or a casual spree on shore suffices to unfold for him the secret of a whole continent, and generally he finds the secret not worth knowing. The yarns of seamen have a direct simplicity, the whole meaning of which lies within the shell of a cracked nut. But Marlow was not typical (if his propensity to spin yarns be excepted), and to him the meaning of an episode was not inside like a kernel but outside, enveloping the tale which brought it out only as a glow brings out a haze, in the likeness of one of these misty halos that sometimes are made visible by the spectral illumination of moonshine.

His remark did not seem at all surprising. It was just like Marlow. It was accepted in silence. No one took the trouble to grunt even; and presently he said, very slow—

"I was thinking of very old times, when the Romans first came here, nineteen hundred years ago—the other day. . . . Light came out of this river since—you say Knights? Yes; but it is like a running blaze on a plain, like a flash of lightning in the clouds. We live in the flicker—may it last as long as the old earth keeps rolling! But darkness was here yesterday. Imagine the feelings of a commander of a fine—what d'ye call 'em?—trireme[7] in the Mediterranean, ordered suddenly to the north; run overland across the Gauls[8] in a hurry; put in charge of one of these craft the legionaries—a wonderful lot of handy men they must have been, too—used to build, apparently by the hundred, in a month or two, if we may believe what we read. Imagine him here—the very end of the world, a sea the color of lead, a sky the color of smoke, a kind of ship about as rigid as a concertina—and going up this river with stores, or orders, or what you like. Sand-banks, marshes, forests, savages,—precious little to eat fit for a civilized man, nothing but Thames water to drink. No Falernian wine[9] here, no going ashore. Here and there a military camp lost in a wilderness, like a needle in a bundle of hay—cold, fog, tempests, disease, exile, and death,—death skulking in the air, in the water, in the bush. They must have been dying like flies here. Oh yes—he did it. Did it very well, too, no doubt, and without thinking much about it either, except afterwards to brag of

7. Roman galley propelled by three banks of oars. 8. Inhabitants of France in Roman times. 9. Legendary Roman wine.

what he had gone through in his time, perhaps. They were men enough to face the darkness. And perhaps he was cheered by keeping his eye on a chance of promotion to the fleet at Ravenna[1] by and by, if he had good friends in Rome and survived the awful climate. Or think of a decent young citizen in a toga—perhaps too much dice, you know—coming out here in the train of some prefect,[2] or taxgatherer, or trader even, to mend his fortunes. Land in a swamp, march through the woods, and in some inland post feel the savagery, the utter savagery, had closed round him,—all that mysterious life of the wilderness that stirs in the forest, in the jungles, in the hearts of wild men. There's no initiation either into such mysteries. He has to live in the midst of the incomprehensible, which is also detestable. And it has a fascination, too, that goes to work upon him. The fascination of the abomination—you know, imagine the growing regrets, the longing to escape, the powerless disgust, the surrender, the hate."

He paused.

"Mind," he began again, lifting one arm from the elbow, the palm of the hand outwards, so that, with his legs folded before him, he had the pose of a Buddha preaching in European clothes and without a lotus-flower—"Mind, none of us would feel exactly like this. What saves us is efficiency—the devotion to efficiency. But these chaps were not much account, really. They were no colonists; their administration was merely a squeeze, and nothing more, I suspect. They were conquerors, and for that you want only brute force—nothing to boast of, when you have it, since your strength is just an accident arising from the weakness of others. They grabbed what they could get for the sake of what was to be got. It was just robbery with violence, aggravated murder on a great scale, and men going at it blind—as is very proper for those who tackle a darkness. The conquest of the earth, which mostly means the taking it away from those who have a different complexion or slightly flatter noses than ourselves, is not a pretty thing when you look into it too much. What redeems it is the idea only. An idea at the back of it; not a sentimental pretense but an idea; and an unselfish belief in the idea—something you can set up, and bow down before, and offer a sacrifice to. . . ."

He broke off. Flames glided in the river, small green flames, red flames, white flames, pursuing, overtaking, joining, crossing each other—then separating slowly or hastily. The traffic of the great city went on in the deepening night upon the sleepless river. We looked on, waiting patiently—there was nothing else to do till the end of the flood; but it was only after a long silence, when he said, in a hesitating voice, "I suppose you fellows remember I did once turn fresh-water sailor for a

1. Base on the Adriatic in northern Italy—a comfortable assignment. 2. High official.

bit," that we knew we were fated, before the ebb began to run, to hear one of Marlow's inconclusive experiences.

"I don't want to bother you much with what happened to me personally," he began, showing in this remark the weakness of many tellers of tales who seem so often unaware of what their audience would best like to hear; "yet to understand the effect of it on me you ought to know how I got out there, what I saw, how I went up that river to the place where I first met the poor chap. It was the farthest point of navigation and the culminating point of my experience. It seemed somehow to throw a kind of light on everything about me—and into my thoughts. It was somber enough, too—and pitiful—not extraordinary in any way—not very clear either. No, not very clear. And yet it seemed to throw a kind of light.

"I had then, as you remember, just returned to London after a lot of Indian Ocean, Pacific, China Seas—a regular dose of the East—six years or so, and I was loafing about, hindering you fellows in your work and invading your homes, just as though I had got a heavenly mission to civilize you. It was very fine for a time, but after a bit I did get tired of resting. Then I began to look for a ship—I should think the hardest work on earth. But the ships wouldn't even look at me. And I got tired of that game too.

"Now when I was a little chap I had a passion for maps. I would look for hours at South America, or Africa, or Australia, and lose myself in all the glories of exploration. At that time there were many blank spaces on the earth, and when I saw one that looked particularly inviting on a map (but they all look that) I would put my finger on it and say, When I grow up I will go there. The North Pole was one of these places, I remember. Well, I haven't been there yet, and shall not try now. The glamour's off. Other places were scattered about the Equator, and in every sort of latitude all over the two hemispheres. I have been in some of them, and . . . well, we won't talk about that. But there was one[3] yet—the biggest, the most blank, so to speak—that I had a hankering after.

"True, by this time it was not a blank space any more. It had got filled since my childhood with rivers and lakes and names. It had ceased to be a blank space of delightful mystery—a white patch for a boy to dream gloriously over. It had become a place of darkness. But there was in it one river especially, a mighty big river, that you could see on the map, resembling an immense snake uncoiled, with its head in the sea, its body at rest curving afar over a vast country, and its tail lost in the depths of the land. And as I looked at the map of it in a shop-

3. Congo Free State (now Zaire). At the time of the story it was a colony owned personally, in effect, by Leopold II, King of Belgium; it consisted of the Congo River basin and some adjacent territories.

window, it fascinated me as a snake would a bird—a silly little bird. Then I remembered there was a big concern, a Company for trade on that river. Dash it all! I thought to myself, they can't trade without using some kind of craft on that lot of fresh water—steamboats! Why shouldn't I try to get charge of one? I went on along Fleet Street, but could not shake off the idea. The snake had charmed me.

"You understand it was a Continental concern, that Trading society; but I have a lot of relations living on the Continent, because it's cheap and not so nasty as it looks, they say.

"I am sorry to own I began to worry them. This was already a fresh departure for me. I was not used to getting things that way, you know. I always went my own road and on my own legs where I had a mind to go. I wouldn't have believed it of myself; but, then—you see—I felt somehow I must get there by hook or by crook. So I worried them. The men said, 'My dear fellow,' and did nothing. Then—would you believe it?—I tried the women. I, Charlie Marlow, set the women to work—to get a job. Heavens! Well, you see, the notion drove me. I had an aunt, a dear enthusiastic soul. She wrote: 'It will be delightful. I am ready to do anything, anything for you. It is a glorious idea. I know the wife of a very high personage in the Administration, and also a man who has lots of influence with,' etc. etc. She was determined to make no end of fuss to get me appointed skipper of a river steamboat, if such was my fancy.

"I got my appointment—of course; and I got it very quick. It appears the Company had received news that one of their captains had been killed in a scuffle with the natives. This was my chance, and it made me the more anxious to go. It was only months and months afterwards, when I made the attempt to recover what was left of the body, that I heard the original quarrel arose from a misunderstanding about some hens. Yes, two black hens. Fresleven—that was the fellow's name, a Dane—thought himself wronged somehow in the bargain, so he went ashore and started to hammer the chief of the village with a stick. Oh, it didn't surprise me in the least to hear this, and at the same time to be told that Fresleven was the gentlest, quietest creature that ever walked on two legs. No doubt he was; but he had been a couple of years already out there engaged in the noble cause, you know, and he probably felt the need at last of asserting his self-respect in some way. Therefore he whacked the old nigger mercilessly, while a big crowd of his people watched him, thunderstruck, till some man—I was told the chief's son—in desperation at hearing the old chap yell, made a tentative jab with a spear at the white man—and of course it went quite easy between the shoulder blades. Then the whole population cleared into the forest, expecting all kinds of calamities to happen, while, on the other hand, the steamer Fresleven commanded left also in a bad panic, in charge of the engineer, I believe. Afterwards nobody seemed to trouble much about Fresleven's remains, till I got out and stepped into his shoes. I couldn't let it rest, though; but when an opportunity offered at last to meet my predecessor, the grass growing through his ribs was tall enough to hide his bones. They were all there. The supernatural being had not been touched after he fell. And the village was deserted, the huts gaped black, rotting, all askew within the fallen enclosures. A calamity had come to it, sure enough. The people had vanished. Mad terror had scattered them, men, women, and children, through the bush, and they had never returned. What became of the hens I don't know either. I should think the cause of progress got them, anyhow. However, through this glorious affair I got my appointment, before I had fairly begun to hope for it.

"I flew around like mad to get ready, and before forty-eight hours I was crossing the Channel to show myself to my employers, and sign the contract. In a very few hours I arrived in a city[4] that always makes me think of a whited sepulcher. Prejudice no doubt. I had no difficulty in finding the Company's offices. It was the biggest thing in the town, and everybody I met was full of it. They were going to run an oversea empire, and make no end of coin by trade.

"A narrow and deserted street in deep shadow, high houses, innumerable windows with venetian blinds, a dead silence, grass sprouting between the stones, imposing carriage archways right and left, immense double doors standing ponderously ajar. I slipped through one of these cracks, went up a swept and ungarnished staircase, as arid as a desert, and opened the first door I came to. Two women, one fat and the other slim, sat on straw-bottomed chairs, knitting black wool. The slim one got up and walked straight at me—still knitting with downcast eyes—and only just as I began to think of getting out of her way, as you would for a somnambulist, stood still, and looked up. Her dress was as plain as an umbrella-cover, and she turned round without a word and preceded me into a waiting-room. I gave my name, and looked about. Deal table in the middle, plain chairs all around the walls, on one end a large shining map, marked with all the colors of a rainbow. There was a vast amount of red—good to see at any time, because one knows that some real work is done in there, a deuce of a lot of blue, a little green, smears of orange, and, on the East Coast, a purple patch, to show where the jolly pioneers of progress drink the jolly lager-beer.[5] However, I wasn't going into any of these. I was going into the yellow. Dead in the center. And the river was there—fascinating—deadly—like a snake. Ough! A door opened, a white-haired

4. Brussels, Belgium. 5. The red areas on the map were British colonies, blue French, green Italian, orange Portuguese, and the "purple patch" was German East Africa.

secretarial head, but wearing a compassionate expression, appeared, and a skinny forefinger beckoned me into the sanctuary. Its light was dim, and a heavy writing-desk squatted in the middle. From behind that structure came out an impression of pale plumpness in a frock-coat. The great man himself. He was five feet six, I should judge, and had his grip on the handle-end of ever so many millions. He shook hands, I fancy, murmured vaguely, was satisfied with my French. *Bon voyage.*[6]

"In about forty-five seconds I found myself again in the waiting-room with the compassionate secretary, who, full of desolation and sympathy, made me sign some document. I believe I undertook amongst other things not to disclose any trade secrets. Well, I am not going to.

"I began to feel slightly uneasy. You know I am not used to such ceremonies, and there was something ominous in the atmosphere. It was just as though I had been let into some conspiracy—I don't know—something not quite right; and I was glad to get out. In the outer room the two women knitted black wool feverishly. People were arriving, and the younger one was walking back and forth introducing them. The old one sat on her chair. Her flat cloth slippers were propped up on a footwarmer, and a cat reposed on her lap. She wore a starched white affair on her head, had a wart on one cheek, and silver-rimmed spectacles hung on the tip of her nose. She glanced at me above the glasses. The swift and indifferent placidity of that look troubled me. Two youths with foolish and cheery countenances were being piloted over, and she threw at them the same quick glance of unconcerned wisdom. She seemed to know all about them and about me, too. An eerie feeling came over me. She seemed uncanny and fateful. Often far away there I thought of these two, guarding the door of Darkness, knitting black wool as for a warm pall, one introducing, introducing continuously to the unknown, the other scrutinizing the cheery and foolish faces with unconcerned old eyes. *Ave!* Old knitter of black wool. *Morituri te salutant.*[7] Not many of those she looked at ever saw her again—not half, by a long way.

"There was yet a visit to the doctor. 'A simple formality,' assured me the secretary, with an air of taking an immense part in all my sorrows. Accordingly a young chap wearing his hat over the left eyebrow, some clerk I suppose—there must have been clerks in the business, though the house was as still as a house in a city of the dead—came from somewhere upstairs, and led me forth. He was shabby and careless, with inkstains on the sleeves of his jacket, and his cravat was large and billowy, under a chin shaped like the toe of an old boot. It was a little too early for the doctor, so I proposed a drink, and thereupon he

6. "Have a good trip." 7. "Hail . . . they who are about to die salute you."

developed a vein of joviality. As we sat over our vermouths he glorified the Company's business, and by and by I expressed casually my surprise at him not going out there. He became very cool and collected all at once. 'I am not such a fool as I look, quoth Plato to his disciples,' he said sententiously, emptied his glass with great resolution, and we rose.

"The old doctor felt my pulse, evidently thinking of something else the while. 'Good, good for there,' he mumbled, and then with a certain eagerness asked me whether I would let him measure my head. Rather surprised, I said Yes, when he produced a thing like calipers and got the dimensions back and front and every way, taking notes carefully.[8] He was an unshaven little man in a threadbare coat like a gaberdine, with his feet in slippers, and I thought him a harmless fool. 'I always ask leave, in the interests of science, to measure the crania of those going out there,' he said. 'And when they come back, too?' I asked. 'Oh, I never see them,' he remarked; 'and, moreover, the changes take place inside, you know.' He smiled, as if at some quiet joke. 'So you are going out there. Famous. Interesting too.' He gave me a searching glance, and made another note. 'Ever any madness in your family?' he asked, in a matter-of-fact tone. I felt very annoyed. 'Is that question in the interests of science, too?' 'It would be,' he said, without taking notice of my irritation, 'interesting for science to watch the mental changes of individuals, on the spot, but . . .' 'Are you an alienist?'[9] I interrupted. 'Every doctor should be—a little,' answered that original, imperturbably. 'I have a little theory which you Messieurs who go out there must help me to prove. This is my share in the advantages my country shall reap from the possession of such a magnificent dependency. The mere wealth I leave to others. Pardon my questions, but you are the first Englishman coming under my observation . . .' I hastened to assure him I was not in the least typical. 'If I were,' said I, 'I wouldn't be talking like this with you.' 'What you say is rather profound, and probably erroneous,' he said, with a laugh. 'Avoid irritation more than exposure to the sun. Adieu. How do you English say, eh? Good-by. Ah! Good-by. Adieu. In the tropics one must before everything keep calm.' . . . He lifted a warning forefinger. . . . '*Du calme, du calme. Adieu.*'[1]

"One thing more remained to do—say good-by to my excellent aunt. I found her triumphant. I had a cup of tea—the last decent cup of tea for many days—and in a room that most soothingly looked just as you would expect a lady's drawing-room to look, we had a long quiet chat by the fireside. In the course of these confidences it became quite

8. Phrenology, the study of skull conformation as an index of mind and personality, was a more or less respectable part of 19th-century medical study. 9. Doctor who treats mental disease. 1. "Keep calm, keep calm. Goodbye."

plain to me I had been represented to the wife of the high dignitary, and goodness knows to how many more people besides, as an exceptional and gifted creature—a piece of good fortune for the Company—a man you don't get hold of every day. Good heavens! and I was going to take charge of a two-penny-half-penny river-steamboat with a penny whistle attached! It appeared, however, I was also one of the Workers, with a capital—you know. Something like an emissary of light, something like a lower sort of apostle. There had been a lot of such rot let loose in print and talk just about that time, and the excellent woman, living right in the rush of all that humbug, got carried off her feet. She talked about 'weaning those ignorant millions from their horrid ways,' till, upon my word, she made me quite uncomfortable. I ventured to hint that the Company was run for profit.

" 'You forget, dear Charlie, that the laborer is worthy of his hire,'[2] she said, brightly. It's queer how out of touch with truth women are. They live in a world of their own, and there has never been anything like it, and never can be. It is too beautiful altogether, and if they were to set it up it would go to pieces before the first sunset. Some confounded fact we men have been living contentedly with ever since the day of creation would start up and knock the whole thing over.

"After this I got embraced, told to wear flannel, be sure to write often, and so on—and I left. In the street—I don't know why—a queer feeling came to me that I was an impostor. Odd thing that I, who used to clear out for any part of the world at twenty-four hours' notice, with less thought than most men give to the crossing of a street, had a moment—I won't say of hesitation, but of startled pause, before this commonplace affair. The best way I can explain it to you is by saying that, for a second or two, I felt as though, instead of going to the center of a continent, I were about to set off for the center of the earth.

"I left in a French steamer, and she called in every blamed port they have out there,[3] for, as far as I could see, the sole purpose of landing soldiers and custom-house officers. I watched the coast. Watching a coast as it slips by the ship is like thinking about an enigma. There it is before you—smiling, frowning, inviting, grand, mean, insipid, or savage, and always mute with an air of whispering, Come and find out. This one was almost featureless, as if still in the making, with an aspect of monotonous grimness. The edge of a colossal jungle, so dark-green as to be almost black, fringed with white surf, ran straight, like a ruled line, far, far away along a blue sea whose glitter was blurred by a creeping mist. The sun was fierce, the land seemed to glisten and drip with steam. Here and there grayish-whitish specks showed up clustered

2. Words of Christ (Luke 10:7). 3. French colonies stretched down most of the West African Coast to the mouth of the Congo, with major ports at Casablanca and Dakar.

inside the white surf, with a flag flying above them perhaps. Settlements some centuries old, and still no bigger than pinheads on the untouched expanse of their background. We pounded along, stopped, landed soldiers; went on, landed custom-house clerks to levy toll in what looked like a God-forsaken wilderness, with a tin shed and a flagpole lost in it; landed more soldiers—to take care of the custom-house clerks, presumably. Some, I heard, got drowned in the surf; but whether they did or not, nobody seemed particularly to care. They were just flung out there, and on we went. Every day the coast looked the same, as though we had not moved; but we passed various places—trading places—with names like Gran' Bassam, Little Popo; names that seemed to belong to some sordid farce acted in front of a sinister backcloth. The idleness of a passenger, my isolation amongst all these men with whom I had no point of contact, the oily and languid sea, the uniform somberness of the coast, seemed to keep me away from the truth of things, within the toil of a mournful and senseless delusion. The voice of the surf heard now and then was a positive pleasure, like the speech of a brother. It was something natural, that had its reason, that had a meaning. Now and then a boat from the shore gave one a momentary contact with reality. It was paddled by black fellows. You could see from afar the white of their eyeballs glistening. They shouted, sang; their bodies streamed with perspiration; they had faces like grotesque masks—these chaps; but they had bone, muscle, a wild vitality, an intense energy of movement, that was as natural and true as the surf along their coast. They wanted no excuse for being there. They were a great comfort to look at. For a time I would feel I belonged still to a world of straightforward facts, but the feeling would not last long. Something would turn up to scare it away. Once, I remember, we came upon a man-of-war anchored off the coast. There wasn't even a shed there, and she was shelling the bush. It appears the French had one of their wars going on thereabouts. Her ensign[4] dropped limp like a rag; the muzzles of the long six-inch guns stuck out all over the low hull; the greasy, slimy swell swung her up lazily and let her down, swaying her thin masts. In the empty immensity of earth, sky, and water, there she was, incomprehensible, firing into a continent. Pop, would go one of the six-inch guns; a small flame would dart and vanish, a little white smoke would disappear, a tiny projectile would give a feeble screech—and nothing happened. Nothing could happen. There was a touch of insanity in the proceeding, a sense of lugubrious drollery in the sight; and it was not dissipated by somebody on board assuring me earnestly there was a camp of natives—he called them enemies!—hidden out of sight somewhere.

4. Flag.

"We gave her her letters (I heard the men in that lonely ship were dying of fever at the rate of three a day) and went on. We called at some more places with farcical names, where the merry dance of death and trade goes on in a still and earthy atmosphere as of an overheated catacomb; all along the formless coast bordered by dangerous surf, as if Nature herself had tried to ward off intruders; in and out of rivers, streams of death in life, whose banks were rotting into mud, whose waters, thickened into slime, invaded the contorted mangroves, that seemed to writhe at us in the extremity of an impotent despair. Nowhere did we stop long enough to get a particularized impression, but the general sense of vague and oppressive wonder grew upon me. It was like a weary pilgrimage amongst hints for nightmares.

"It was upward of thirty days before I saw the mouth of the big river. We anchored off the seat of the government.[5] But my work would not begin till some two hundred miles farther on. So as soon as I could I made a start for a place thirty miles higher up.

"I had my passage on a little sea-going steamer. Her captain was a Swede, and knowing me for a seaman, invited me on the bridge. He was a young man, lean, fair, and morose, with lanky hair and a shuffling gait. As we left the miserable little wharf, he tossed his head contemptuously at the shore. 'Been living there?' he asked. I said, 'Yes.' 'Fine lot these government chaps—are they not?' he went on, speaking English with great precision and considerable bitterness. 'It is funny what some people will do for a few francs a month. I wonder what becomes of that kind when it goes up-country?' I said to him I expected to see that soon. 'So-o-o!' he exclaimed. He shuffled athwart, keeping one eye ahead vigilantly. 'Don't be too sure,' he continued. 'The other day I took up a man who hanged himself on the road. He was a Swede, too.' 'Hanged himself! Why, in God's name?' I cried. He kept on looking out watchfully. 'Who knows? The sun was too much for him, or the country perhaps.'

"At last we opened a reach.[6] A rocky cliff appeared, mounds of turned-up earth by the shore, houses on a hill, others with iron roofs, amongst a waste of excavations, or hanging to the declivity.[7] A continuous noise of the rapids above hovered over this scene of inhabited devastation. A lot of people, mostly black and naked, moved about like ants. A jetty projected into the river. A blinding sunlight drowned all this at times in a sudden recrudescence of glare. 'There's your Company's station,' said the Swede, pointing to three wooden barrack-like structures on the rocky slope. 'I will send your things up. Four boxes did you say? So. Farewell.'

5. Boma, in the mouth of Congo River. 6. I.e., came to a clear stretch of the river. 7. Town of Matadi.

"I came upon a boiler wallowing in the grass, then found a path leading up the hill. It turned aside for the boulders, and also for an undersized railway-truck lying there on its back with its wheels in the air. One was off. The thing looked as dead as the carcass of some animal. I came upon more pieces of decaying machinery, a stack of rusty nails. To the left a clump of trees made a shady spot, where dark things seemed to stir feebly. I blinked, the path was steep. A horn tooted to the right, and I saw the black people run. A heavy and dull detonation shook the ground, a puff of smoke came out of the cliff, and that was all. No change appeared on the face of the rock. They were building a railway. The cliff was not in the way or anything; but this objectless blasting was all the work going on.

"A slight clinking behind me made me turn my head. Six black men advanced in a file, toiling up the path. They walked erect and slow, balancing small baskets full of earth on their heads, and the clink kept time with their footsteps. Black rags were wound round their loins, and the short ends behind waggled to and fro like tails. I could see every rib, the joints of their limbs were like knots in a rope; each had an iron collar on his neck, and all were connected together with a chain whose bights[8] swung between them, rhythmically clinking. Another report from the cliff made me think suddenly of that ship of war I had seen firing into a continent. It was the same kind of ominous voice; but these men could by no stretch of imagination be called enemies. They were called criminals, and the outraged law, like the bursting shells, had come to them, an insoluble mystery from the sea. All their meager breasts panted together, the violently dilated nostrils quivered, the eyes stared stonily up-hill. They passed me within six inches, without a glance, with that complete, deathlike indifference of unhappy savages. Behind this raw matter one of the reclaimed, the product of the new forces at work, strolled despondently, carrying a rifle by its middle. He had a uniform jacket with one button off, and seeing a white man on the path, hoisted his weapon to his shoulder with alacrity. This was simple prudence, white men being so much alike at a distance that he could not tell who I might be. He was speeddily reassured, and with a large, white, rascally grin, and a glance at his charge, seemed to take me into partnership in his exalted trust. After all, I also was a part of the great cause of these high and just proceedings.

"Instead of going up, I turned and descended to the left. My idea was to let that chain-gang get out of sight before I climbed the hill. You know I am not particularly tender; I've had to strike and to fend off. I've had to resist and to attack sometimes—that's only one way of

8. Loops.

resisting—without counting the exact cost, according to the demands of such sort of life as I had blundered into. I've seen the devil of violence, and the devil of greed, and the devil of hot desire; but, by all the stars! these were strong, lusty, red-eyed devils, that swayed and drove men—men, I tell you. But as I stood on this hillside, I foresaw that in the blinding sunshine of that land I would become acquainted with a flabby, pretending, weak-eyed devil of a rapacious and pitiless folly. How insidious he could be, too, I was only to find out several months later and a thousand miles farther. For a moment I stood appalled, as though by a warning. Finally I descended the hill, obliquely, towards the trees I had seen.

"I avoided a vast artificial hole somebody had been digging on the slope, the purpose of which I found it impossible to divine. It wasn't a quarry or a sandpit, anyhow. It was just a hole. It might have been connected with the philanthropic desire of giving the criminals something to do. I don't know. Then I nearly fell into a very narrow ravine, almost no more than a scar in the hillside. I discovered that a lot of imported drainage-pipes for the settlement had been tumbled in there. There wasn't one that was not broken. It was a wanton smash-up. At last I got under the trees. My purpose was to stroll into the shade for a moment; but no sooner within than it seemed to me I had stepped into the gloomy circle of some Inferno. The rapids were near, and an uninterrupted, uniform, headlong, rushing noise filled the mournful stillness of the grove, where not a breath stirred, not a leaf moved, with a mysterious sound—as though the tearing pace of the launched earth had suddenly become audible.

"Black shapes crouched, lay, sat between the trees, leaning against the trunks, clinging to the earth, half coming out, half effaced within the dim light, in all the attitudes of pain, abandonment, and despair. Another mine[9] on the cliff went off, followed by a slight shudder of the soil under my feet. The work was going on. The work! And this was the place where some of the helpers had withdrawn to die.

"They were dying slowly—it was very clear. They were not enemies, they were not criminals, they were nothing earthly now,—nothing but black shadows of disease and starvation, lying confusedly in the greenish gloom. Brought from all the recesses of the coast in all the legality of time contracts, lost in uncongenial surroundings, fed on unfamiliar food, they sickened, became inefficient, and were then allowed to crawl away and rest. These moribund shapes were free as air—and nearly as thin. I began to distinguish the gleam of the eyes under the trees. Then, glancing down, I saw a face near my hand. The black bones reclined at full length with one shoulder against the tree,

9. Explosive charge.

and slowly the eyelids rose and the sunken eyes looked up at me, enormous and vacant, a kind of blind, white flicker in the depths of the orbs, which died out slowly. The man seemed young—almost a boy—but you know with them it's hard to tell. I found nothing else to do but to offer him one of my good Swede's ship's biscuits I had in my pocket. The fingers closed slowly on it and held—there was no other movement and no other glance. He had tied a bit of white worsted round his neck—Why? Where did he get it? Was it a badge—an ornament—a charm—a propitiatory act? Was there any idea at all connected with it? It looked startling round his black neck, this bit of white thread from beyond the seas.

"Near the same tree two more bundles of acute angles sat with their legs drawn up. One, with his chin propped on his knees, stared at nothing, in an intolerable and appalling manner: his brother phantom rested its forehead, as if overcome with a great weariness; and all about others were scattered in every pose of contorted collapse, as in some picture of a massacre or a pestilence. While I stood horror-struck, one of these creatures rose to his hands and knees, and went off on all-fours towards the river to drink. He lapped out of his hand, then sat up in the sunlight, crossing his shins in front of him, and after a time let his woolly head fall on his breastbone.

"I didn't want any more loitering in the shade, and I made haste towards the station. When near the buildings I met a white man, in such an unexpected elegance of get-up that in the first moment I took him for a sort of vision. I saw a high starched collar, white cuffs, a light alpaca jacket, snowy trousers, a clear necktie, and varnished boots. No hat. Hair parted, brushed, oiled, under a green-lined parasol held in a big white hand. He was amazing, and had a penholder behind his ear.

"I shook hands with this miracle, and I learned he was the Company's chief accountant, and that all the bookkeeping was done at this station. He had come out for a moment, he said, 'to get a breath of fresh air.' The expression sounded wonderfully odd, with its suggestion of sedentary desk-life. I wouldn't have mentioned the fellow to you at all, only it was from his lips that I first heard the name of the man who is so indissolubly connected with the memories of that time. Moreover, I respected the fellow. Yes; I respected his collars, his vast cuffs, his brushed hair. His appearance was certainly that of a hairdresser's dummy; but in the great demoralization of the land he kept up his appearance. That's backbone. His starched collars and got-up shirt-fronts were achievements of character. He had been out nearly three years; and, later, I could not help asking him how he managed to sport such linen. He had just the faintest blush, and said modestly, 'I've been teaching one of the native women about the station. It was difficult. She had a distaste for the work.' Thus this man had verily accomplished something. And he was devoted to his books, which were in apple-pie order.

"Everything else in the station was in a muddle,—heads, things, buildings. Strings of dusty niggers with splay feet arrived and departed; a stream of manufactured goods, rubbishy cottons, beads, and brass-wire set into the depths of darkness, and in return came a precious trickle of ivory.

"I had to wait in the station for ten days—an eternity. I lived in a hut in the yard, but to be out of the chaos I would sometimes get into the accountant's office. It was built of horizontal planks, and so badly put together that, as he bent over his high desk, he was barred from neck to heels with narrow strips of sunlight. There was no need to open the big shutter to see. It was hot there, too; big flies buzzed fiendishly, and did not sting, but stabbed. I sat generally on the floor, while, of faultless appearance (and even slightly scented), perching on a high stool, he wrote, he wrote. Sometimes he stood up for exercise. When a trucklebed with a sick man (some invalid agent from up-country) was put in there, he exhibited a gentle annoyance. 'The groans of this sick person,' he said, 'distract my attention. And without that it is extremely difficult to guard against clerical errors in this climate.'

"One day he remarked, without lifting his head, 'In the interior you will no doubt meet Mr. Kurtz.' On my asking who Mr. Kurtz was, he said he was a first-class agent; and seeing my disappointment at this information, he added slowly, laying down his pen, 'He is a very remarkable person.' Further questions elicited from him that Mr. Kurtz was at present in charge of a trading post, a very important one, in the true ivory-country, at 'the very bottom of there. Sends in as much ivory[1] as all the others put together. . . .' He began to write again. The sick man was too ill to groan. The flies buzzed in a great peace.

"Suddenly there was a growing murmur of voices and a great tramping of feet. A caravan had come in. A violent babble of uncouth sounds burst out on the other side of the planks. All the carriers were speaking together, and in the midst of the uproar the lamentable voice of the chief agent was heard 'giving it up' tearfully for the twentieth time that day. . . . He rose slowly. 'What a frightful row,' he said. He crossed the room gently to look at the sick man, and returning, said to me, 'He does not hear.' 'What! Dead?' I asked, startled. 'No, not yet,' he answered, with great composure. Then, alluding with a toss of the head to the tumult in the station-yard, 'When one has got to make correct entries, one comes to hate those savages—hate them to the death.' He remained thoughtful for a moment. 'When you see Mr.

1. Ivory and rubber were the main commercial resources traded from the Congo Free State. Ivory was used for billiard balls, piano keys, and carved art objects.

Kurtz,' he went on, 'tell him for me that everything here'—he glanced at the desk—'is very satisfactory. I don't like to write to him—with those messengers of ours you never know who may get hold of your letter—at that Central Station.' He stared at me for a moment with his mild, bulging eyes. 'Oh, he will go far, very far,' he began again. 'He will be a somebody in the Administration before long. They, above—the Council in Europe, you know—mean him to be.'

"He turned to his work. The noise outside had ceased, and presently in going out I stopped at the door. In the steady buzz of flies the homeward-bound agent was lying flushed and insensible; the other, bent over his books, was making correct entries of perfectly correct transactions; and fifty feet below the doorstep I could see the still treetops of the grove of death.

"Next day I left that station at last, with a caravan of sixty men, for a two-hundred-mile tramp.

"No use telling you much about that. Paths, paths, everywhere; a stamped-in network of paths spreading over the empty land, through long grass, through burnt grass, through thickets, down and up chilly ravines, up and down stony hills ablaze with heat; and a solitude, a solitude, nobody, not a hut. The population had cleared out a long time ago. Well, if a lot of mysterious niggers armed with all kinds of fearful weapons suddenly took to traveling on the road between Deal and Gravesend,[2] catching the yokels right and left to carry heavy loads for them, I fancy every farm and cottage thereabouts would get empty very soon. Only here the dwellings were gone, too. Still I passed through several abandoned villages. There's something pathetically childish in the ruins of grass walls. Day after day, with the stamp and shuffle of sixty pair of bare feet behind me, each pair under a sixty-pound load. Camp, cook, sleep, strike camp, march. Now and then a carrier dead in harness, at rest in the long grass near the path, with an empty water-gourd and his long staff lying by his side. A great silence around and above. Perhaps on some quiet night the tremor of far-off drums, sinking, swelling, a tremor vast, faint; a sound weird, appealing, suggestive, and wild—and perhaps with as profound a meaning as the sound of bells in a Christian country. Once a white man in an unbuttoned uniform, camping on the path with an armed escort of lank Zanzibaris,[3] very hospitable and festive—not to say drunk. Was looking after the upkeep of the road, he declared. Can't say I saw any road or any upkeep, unless the body of a middle-aged Negro, with a bullet-hole in the forehead, upon which I absolutely stumbled three miles farther on, may be considered as a permanent improvement. I had a white companion, too, not a bad chap, but rather too fleshy and with the exasperating

2. English coastal cities. 3. Mercenary soldiers from Zanzibar, an island off the east coast of Africa.

habit of fainting on the hot hillsides, miles away from the least bit of shade and water. Annoying, you know, to hold your own coat like a parasol over a man's head while he is coming-to. I couldn't help asking him once what he meant by coming there at all. 'To make money, of course. What do you think?' he said, scornfully. Then he got fever, and had to be carried in a hammock slung under a pole. As he weighed sixteen stone[4] I had no end of rows with the carriers. They jibbed, ran away, sneaked off with their loads in the night—quite a mutiny. So, one evening, I made a speech in English with gestures, not one of which was lost to the sixty pairs of eyes before me, and the next morning I started the hammock off in front all right. An hour afterwards I came upon the whole concern wrecked in a bush—man, hammock, groans, blankets, horrors. The heavy pole had skinned his poor nose. He was very anxious for me to kill somebody, but there wasn't the shadow of a carrier near. I remembered the old doctor—'It would be interesting for science to watch the mental changes of individuals, on the spot.' I felt I was becoming scientifically interesting. However, all that is to no purpose. On the fifteenth day I came in sight of the big river again, and hobbled into the Central Station. It was on a backwater surrounded by scrub and forest, with a pretty border of smelly mud on one side, and on the three others enclosed by a crazy fence of rushes. A neglected gap was all the gate it had, and the first glance at the place was enough to let you see the flabby devil was running that show. White men with long staves in their hands appeared languidly from amongst the buildings, strolling up to take a look at me, and then retired out of sight somewhere. One of them, a stout, excitable chap with black mustaches, informed me with great volubility and many digressions, as soon as I told him who I was, that my steamer was at the bottom of the river. I was thunderstruck. What, how, why? Oh, it was 'all right.' The 'manager himself' was there. All quite correct. 'Everybody had behaved splendidly! splendidly!'—'you must,' he said in agitation, 'go and see the general manager at once. He is waiting!'

"I did not see the real significance of that wreck at once. I fancy I see it now, but I am not sure—not at all. Certainly the affair was too stupid—when I think of it—to be altogether natural. Still . . . . But at the moment it presented itself simply as a confounded nuisance. The steamer was sunk. They had started two days before in a sudden hurry up the river with the manager on board, in charge of some volunteer skipper, and before they had been out three hours they tore the bottom out of her on stones, and she sank near the south bank. I asked myself what I was to do there, now my boat was lost. As a matter of fact, I had plenty to do in fishing my command out of the river. I had

4. British unit of weight equaling 14 pounds—hence 224 pounds.

to set about it the very next day. That, and the repairs when I brought the pieces to the station, took some months.

"My first interview with the manager was curious. He did not ask me to sit down after my twenty-mile walk that morning. He was commonplace in complexion, in feature, in manners, and in voice. He was of middle size and of ordinary build. His eyes, of the usual blue, were perhaps remarkably cold, and he certainly could make his glance fall on one as trenchant and heavy as an ax. But even at these times the rest of his person seemed to disclaim the intention. Otherwise there was only an indefinable, faint expression of his lips, something stealthy—a smile—not a smile—I remember it, but I can't explain. It was unconscious, this smile was, though just after he had said something it got intensified for an instant. It came at the end of his speeches like a seal applied on the words to make the meaning of the commonest phrase appear absolutely inscrutable. He was a common trader, from his youth up employed in these parts—nothing more. He was obeyed, yet he inspired neither love nor fear, nor even respect. He inspired uneasiness. That was it! Uneasiness. Not a definite mistrust—just uneasiness—nothing more. You have no idea how effective such a . . . a . . . faculty can be. He had no genius for organizing, for initiative, or for order even. That was evident in such things as the deplorable state of the station. He had no learning, and no intelligence. His position had come to him—why? Perhaps because he was never ill. . . . He had served three terms of three years out there. . . . Because triumphant health in the general rout of constitutions is a kind of power in itself. When he went home on leave he rioted on a large scale—pompously. Jack ashore[5]—with a difference—in externals only. This one could gather from his casual talk. He originated nothing, he could keep the routine going—that's all. But he was great. He was great by this little thing that it was impossible to tell what could control such a man. He never gave that secret away. Perhaps there was nothing within him. Such a suspicion made one pause—for out there there were no external checks. Once when various tropical diseases had laid low almost every 'agent' in the station, he was heard to say, 'Men who come out here should have no entrails.' He sealed the utterance with that smile of his, as though it had been a door opening into a darkness he had in his keeping. You fancied you had seen things—but the seal was on. When annoyed at meal-times by the constant quarrels of the white men about precedence, he ordered an immense round table to be made, for which a special house had to be built. This was the station's messroom. Where he sat was the first place—the rest were nowhere. One felt this to be his unalterable conviction. He was neither civil nor uncivil. He was

5. I.e., like a sailor on shore leave.

quiet. He allowed his 'boy'—an overfed young Negro from the coast—to treat the white men, under his very eyes, with provoking insolence.

"He began to speak as soon as he saw me. I had been very long on the road. He could not wait. Had to start without me. The upriver stations had to be relieved. There had been so many delays already that he did not know who was dead and who was alive, and how they got on—and so on, and so on. He paid no attention to my explanations, and, playing with a stick of sealing-wax, repeated several times that the situation was 'very grave, very grave.' There were rumors that a very important station was in jeopardy, and its chief, Mr. Kurtz, was ill. Hoped it was not true. Mr. Kurtz was . . . I felt weary and irritable. Hang Kurtz, I thought. I interrupted him by saying I had heard of Mr. Kurtz on the coast. 'Ah! So they talk of him down there,' he murmured to himself. Then he began again, assuring me Mr. Kurtz was the best agent he had, an exceptional man, of the greatest importance to the Company; therefore I could understand his anxiety. He was, he said, 'very, very uneasy.' Certainly he fidgeted on his chair a good deal, exclaimed, 'Ah, Mr. Kurtz!' broke the stick of sealing-wax and seemed dumfounded by the accident. Next thing he wanted to know 'how long it would take to . . .' I interrupted him again. Being hungry, you know, and kept on my feet too, I was getting savage. 'How can I tell?' I said, 'I haven't even seen the wreck yet—some months, no doubt.' All this talk seemed to me so futile. 'Some months,' he said. 'Well, let us say three months before we can make a start. Yes. That ought to do the affair.' I flung out of his hut (he lived all alone in a clay hut with a sort of veranda) muttering to myself my opinion of him. He was a chattering idiot. Afterwards I took it back when it was borne in upon me startlingly with what extreme nicety he had estimated the time requisite for the 'affair.'

"I went to work the next day, turning, so to speak, my back on that station. In that way only it seemed to me I could keep my hold on the redeeming facts of life. Still, one must look about sometimes; and then I saw this station, these men strolling aimlessly about in the sunshine of the yard. I asked myself sometimes what it all meant. They wandered here and there with their absurd long staves in their hands, like a lot of faithless pilgrims bewitched inside a rotten fence. The word 'ivory' rang in the air, was whispered, was sighed. You would think they were praying to it. A taint of imbecile rapacity blew through it all, like a whiff from some corpse. By Jove! I've never seen anything so unreal in my life. And outside, the silent wilderness surrounding this cleared speck on the earth struck me as something great and invincible, like evil or truth, waiting patiently for the passing away of this fantastic invasion.

"Oh, these months! Well, never mind. Various things happened.

One evening a grass shed full of calico, cotton prints, beads, and I don't know what else, burst into a blaze so suddenly that you would have thought the earth had opened to let an avenging fire consume all that trash. I was smoking my pipe quietly by my dismantled steamer, and saw them all cutting capers in the light, with their arms lifted high, when the stout man with mustaches came tearing down to the river, a tin pail in his hand, assured me that everybody was 'behaving splendidly, splendidly,' dipped about a quart of water and tore back again. I noticed there was a hole in the bottom of his pail.

"I strolled up. There was no hurry. You see the thing had gone off like a box of matches. It had been hopeless from the very first. The flame had leaped high, driven everybody back, lighted up everything—and collapsed. The shed was already a heap of embers glowing fiercely. A nigger was being beaten near by. They said he had caused the fire in some way; be that as it may, he was screeching most horribly. I saw him, later, for several days, sitting in a bit of shade looking very sick and trying to recover himself: afterwards he arose and went out—and the wilderness without a sound took him into its bosom again. As I approached the glow from the dark I found myself at the back of two men, talking. I heard the name of Kurtz pronounced, then the words, 'take advantage of this unfortunate accident.' One of the men was the manager. I wished him a good evening. 'Did you ever see anything like it—eh? it is incredible,' he said, and walked off. The other man remained. He was a first-class agent, young, gentlemanly, a bit reserved, with a forked little beard and a hooked nose. He was standoffish with the other agents, and they on their side said he was the manager's spy among them. As to me, I had hardly ever spoken to him before. We got into talk, and by and by we strolled away from the hissing ruins. Then he asked me to his room, which was in the main building of the station. He struck a match, and I perceived that this young aristocrat had not only a silver-mounted dressing-case but also a whole candle all to himself. Just at that time the manager was the only man supposed to have any right to candles. Native mats covered the clay walls; a collection of spears, assegais,[6] shields, knives was hung up in trophies. The business intrusted to this fellow was the making of bricks—so I had been informed; but there wasn't a fragment of a brick anywhere in the station, and he had been there more than a year—waiting. It seems he could not make bricks without something, I don't know what—straw, maybe. Anyways, it could not be found there, and as it was not likely to be sent from Europe, it did not appear clear to me what he was waiting for. An act of special creation perhaps. However, they were all waiting—all the sixteen or twenty pilgrims of them—

6. Slender South African throwing spears.

for something; and upon my word it did not seem an uncongenial occupation, from the way they took it, though the only thing that ever came to them was disease—as far as I could see. They beguiled the time by backbiting and intriguing against each other in a foolish kind of way. There was an air of plotting about that station, but nothing came of it, of course. It was as unreal as everything else—as the philanthropic pretense of the whole concern, as their talk, as their government, as their show of work. The only real feeling was a desire to get appointed to a trading-post where ivory was to be had, so that they could earn percentages. They intrigued and slandered and hated each other only on that account,—but as to effectually lifting a little finger—oh, no. By heavens! there is something after all in the world allowing one man to steal a horse while another must not look at the halter. Steal a horse straight out. Very well. He has done it. Perhaps he can ride. But there is a way of looking at a halter that would provoke the most charitable of saints into a kick.

"I had no idea why he wanted to be sociable, but as we chatted in there it suddenly occurred to me the fellow was trying to get at something—in fact, pumping me. He alluded constantly to Europe, to the people I was supposed to know there—putting leading questions as to my acquaintances in the sepulchral city, and so on. His little eyes glittered like mica discs—with curiosity—though he tried to keep up a bit of superciliousness. At first I was astonished, but very soon I became awfully curious to see what he would find out from me. I couldn't possibly imagine what I had in me to make it worth his while. It was very pretty to see how he baffled himself, for in truth my body was full only of chills, and my head had nothing in it but that wretched steamboat business. It was evident he took me for a perfectly shameless prevaricator. At last he got angry, and, to conceal a movement of furious annoyance, he yawned. I rose. Then I noticed a small sketch in oils, on a panel, representing a woman, draped and blindfolded, carrying a lighted torch. The background was somber—almost black. The movement of the woman was stately, and the effect of the torchlight on the face was sinister.

"It arrested me, and he stood by civilly, holding an empty half-pint champagne bottle (medical comforts) with the candle stuck in it. To my question he said Mr. Kurtz had painted this—in this very station more than a year ago—while waiting for means to go to his trading-post. 'Tell me, pray,' said I, 'who is this Mr. Kurtz?'

" 'The chief of the Inner Station,' he answered in a short tone, looking away. 'Much obliged,' I said, laughing. 'And you are the brick-maker of the Central Station. Everyone knows that.' He was silent for a while. 'He is a prodigy,' he said at last. 'He is an emissary of pity, and science, and progress, and devil knows what else. We want,' he began to declaim suddenly, 'for the guidance of the cause intrusted to us by Europe, so to speak, higher intelligence, wide sympathies, a singleness of purpose.' 'Who says that?' I asked. 'Lots of them,' he replied. 'Some even write that; and so *he* comes here, a special being, as you ought to know.' 'Why ought I to know?' I interrupted, really surprised. He paid no attention. 'Yes. Today he is chief of the best station, next year he will be assistant-manager, two years more and . . . but I daresay you know what he will be in two years' time. You are of the new gang—the gang of virtue. The same people who sent him specially also recommended you. Oh, don't say no. I've my own eyes to trust.' Light dawned upon me. My dear aunt's influential acquaintances were producing an unexpected effect upon that young man. I nearly burst into a laugh. 'Do you read the Company's confidential correspondence?' I asked. He hadn't a word to say. It was great fun. 'When Mr. Kurtz,' I continued, severely, 'is General Manager, you won't have the opportunity.'

"He blew the candle out suddenly, and we went outside. The moon had risen. Black figures strolled about listlessly, pouring water on the glow, whence proceeded a sound of hissing; steam ascended in the moonlight, the beaten nigger groaned somewhere. 'What a row the brute makes!' said the indefatigable man with the mustaches, appearing near us. 'Serves him right. Transgression—punishment—bang! Pitiless, pitiless. That's the only way. This will prevent all conflagrations for the future. I was just telling the manager. . . .' He noticed my companion, and became crestfallen all at once. 'Not in bed yet,' he said, with a kind of servile heartiness; 'it's so natural. Ha! Danger—agitation.' He vanished. I went on to the river-side, and the other followed me. I heard a scathing murmur at my ear, 'Heap of muffs[7]—go to.' The pilgrims could be seen in knots gesticulating, discussing. Several had still their staves in their hands. I verily believe they took these sticks to bed with them. Beyond the fence the forest stood up spectrally in the moonlight, and through the dim stir, through the faint sounds of that lamentable courtyard, the silence of the land went home to one's very heart—its mystery, its greatness, the amazing reality of its concealed life. The hurt nigger moaned feebly somewhere near by, and then fetched a deep sigh that made me mend my pace away from there. I felt a hand introducing itself under my arm. 'My dear sir,' said the fellow, 'I don't want to be misunderstood, and especially by you, who will see Mr. Kurtz long before I can have that pleasure. I wouldn't like him to get a false idea of my disposition. . . .'

"I let him run on, this papier-mâché Mephistopheles,[8] and it seemed to me that if I tried I could poke my forefinger through him,

7. Gang of bunglers. 8. I.e., devil made of pasteboard.

and would find nothing inside but a little loose dirt, maybe. He, don't you see, had been planning to be assistant-manager by and by under the present man, and I could see that the coming of that Kurtz had upset them both not a little. He talked precipitately, and I did not try to stop him. I had my shoulders against the wreck of my steamer, hauled up on the slope like a carcass of some big river animal. The smell of mud, of primeval mud, by Jove! was in my nostrils, the high stillness of primeval forest was before my eyes; there were shiny patches on the black creek. The moon had spread over everything a thin layer of silver—over the rank grass, over the mud, upon the wall of matted vegetation standing higher than the wall of a temple, over the great river I could see through a somber gap glittering, glittering, as it flowed broadly by without a murmur. All this was great, expectant, mute, while the man jabbered about himself. I wondered whether the stillness on the face of the immensity looking at us two were meant as an appeal or as a menace. What were we who had strayed in here? Could we handle that dumb thing, or would it handle us? I felt how big, how confoundedly big, was that thing that couldn't talk, and perhaps was deaf as well. What was in there? I could see a little ivory coming out from there, and I had heard Mr. Kurtz was in there. I had heard enough about it, too—God knows! Yet somehow it didn't bring any image with it—no more than if I had been told an angel or a fiend was in there. I believed it in the same way one of you might believe there are inhabitants in the planet Mars. I knew once a Scotch sailmaker who was certain, dead sure, there were people in Mars. If you asked him for some idea how they looked and behaved, he would get shy and mutter something about 'walking on all-fours.' If you as much as smiled, he would—though a man of sixty—offer to fight you. I would not have gone so far as to fight for Kurtz, but I went for him near enough to a lie. You know I hate, detest, and can't bear a lie, not because I am straighter than the rest of us, but simply because it appalls me. There is a taint of death, a flavor of mortality in lies—which is exactly what I hate and detest in the world—what I want to forget. It makes me miserable and sick, like biting something rotten would do. Temperament, I suppose. Well, I went near enough to it by letting the young fool there believe anything he liked to imagine as to my influence in Europe. I became in an instant as much of a pretence as the rest of the bewitched pilgrims. This simply because I had a notion it somehow would be of help to that Kurtz whom at the time I did not see—you understand. He was just a word for me. I did not see the man in the name any more than you do. Do you see him? Do you see the story? Do you see anything? It seems to me I am trying to tell you a dream—making a vain attempt, because no relation of a dream can convey the dream-sensation, that commingling of absurdity, surprise, and bewilderment in a tremor of struggling revolt, that notion of being captured by the incredible which is of the very essence of dreams. . . ."

He was silent for a while.

". . . No, it is impossible; it is impossible to convey the life-sensation of any given epoch of one's existence—that which makes its truth, its meaning—its subtle and penetrating essence. It is impossible. We live, as we dream—alone. . . ."

He paused again as if reflecting, then added—

"Of course in this you fellows see more than I could then. You see me, whom you know. . . ."

It had become so pitch dark that we listeners could hardly see one another. For a long time already he, sitting apart, had been no more to us than a voice. There was not a word from anybody. The others might have been asleep, but I was awake. I listened, I listened on the watch for the sentence, for the word, that would give me the clew to the faint uneasiness inspired by this narrative that seemed to shape itself without human lips in the heavy night-air of the river.

". . . Yes—I let him run on," Marlow began again, "and think what he pleased about the powers that were behind me. I did! And there was nothing behind me! There was nothing but that wretched, old, mangled steamboat I was leaning against, while he talked fluently about 'the necessity for every man to get on.' 'And when one comes out here, you conceive, it is not to gaze at the moon.' Mr. Kurtz was a 'universal genius,' but even a genius would find it easier to work with 'adequate tools—intelligent men.' He did not make bricks—why, there was a physical impossibility in the way—as I was well aware; and if he did secretarial work for the manager, it was because 'no sensible man rejects wantonly the confidence of his superiors.' Did I see it? I saw it. What more did I want? What I really wanted was rivets, by heaven! Rivets. To get on with the work—to stop the hole. Rivets I wanted. There were cases of them down at the coast—cases—piled up—burst—split! You kicked a loose rivet at every second step in that station yard on the hillside. Rivets had rolled into the grove of death. You could fill your pockets with rivets for the trouble of stooping down—and there wasn't one rivet to be found where it was wanted. We had plates that would do, but nothing to fasten them with. And every week the messenger, a lone Negro, letter-bag on shoulder and staff in hand, left our station for the coast. And several times a week a coast caravan came in with trade goods—ghastly glazed calico that made you shudder only to look at it; glass beads, valued about a penny a quart, confounded spotted cotton handkerchiefs. And no rivets. Three carriers could have brought all that was wanted to set that steamboat afloat.

"He was becoming confidential now, but I fancy my unresponsive attitude must have exasperated him at last, for he judged it necessary to inform me he feared neither God nor devil, let alone any mere man. I said I could see that very well, but what I wanted was a certain quantity of rivets—and rivets were what really Mr. Kurtz wanted, if he had only known it. Now letters went to the coast every week. . . . 'My dear sir,' he cried, 'I write from dictation.' I demanded rivets. There was a way—for an intelligent man. He changed his manner; became very cold, and suddenly began to talk about a hippopotamus; wondered whether sleeping on board the steamer (I stuck to my salvage night and day) I wasn't disturbed. There was an old hippo that had the bad habit of getting out on the bank and roaming at night over the station grounds. The pilgrims used to turn out in a body and empty every rifle they could lay hands on at him. Some even had sat up o' nights for him. All his energy was wasted, though. 'That animal has a charmed life,' he said; 'but you can say this only of brutes in this country. No man—you apprehend me?—no man here bears a charmed life.' He stood there for a moment in the moonlight with his delicate hooked nose set a little askew, and his mica eyes glittering without a wink, then, with a curt good night, he strode off. I could see he was disturbed and considerably puzzled, which made me feel more hopeful than I had been for days. It was a great comfort to turn from that chap to my influential friend, the battered, twisted, ruined, tin-pot steamboat. I clambered on board. She rang under my feet like an empty Huntley & Palmer biscuit-tin kicked along a gutter; she was nothing so solid in make, and rather less pretty in shape, but I had expended enough hard work on her to make me love her. No influential friend would have served me better. She had given me a chance to come out a bit—to find out what I could do. No, I don't like work. I had rather laze about and think of all the fine things that can be done. I don't like work—no man does—but I like what is in the work,—the chance to find yourself. Your own reality—for yourself, not for others—what no other man can ever know. They can only see the mere show, and never can tell what it really means.

"I was not surprised to see somebody sitting aft, on the deck, with his legs dangling over the mud. You see I rather chummed with the few mechanics there were in that station, whom the other pilgrims naturally despised—on account of their imperfect manners, I suppose. This was the foreman—a boiler-maker by trade—a good worker. He was a lank, bony, yellow-faced man, with big intense eyes. His aspect was worried, and his head was as bald as the palm of my hand; but his hair in falling seemed to have stuck to his chin, and had prospered in the new locality, for his beard hung down to his waist. He was a widower with six young children (he had left them in charge of a sister of his to come out there), and the passion of his life was pigeon-flying. He was an enthusiast and a connoisseur. He would rave about pigeons.

After work hours he used sometimes to come over from his hut for a talk about his children and his pigeons; at work, when he had to crawl in the mud under the bottom of the steamboat, he would tie up that beard of his in a kind of white serviette[9] he brought for the purpose. It had loops to go over his ears. In the evening he could be seen squatted on the bank rinsing that wrapper in the creek with great care, then spreading it solemnly on a bush to dry.

"I slapped him on the back and shouted, 'We shall have rivets!' He scrambled to his feet exclaiming, 'No! Rivets!' as though he couldn't believe his ears. Then in a low voice, 'You . . . eh?' I don't know why we behaved like lunatics. I put my finger to the side of my nose and nodded mysteriously. 'Good for you!' he cried, snapped his fingers above his head, lifting one foot. I tried a jig. We capered on the iron deck. A frightful clatter came out of that hulk, and the virgin forest on the other bank of the creek sent it back in a thundering roll upon the sleeping station. It must have made some of the pilgrims sit up in their hovels. A dark figure obscured the lighted doorway of the manager's hut, vanished, then, a second or so after, the doorway itself vanished, too. We stopped, and the silence driven away by the stamping of our feet flowed back again from the recesses of the land. The great wall of vegetation, an exuberant and entangled mass of trunks, branches, leaves, boughs, festoons, motionless in the moonlight, was like a rioting invasion of soundless life, a rolling wave of plants, piled up, crested, ready to topple over the creek, to sweep every little man of us out of his little existence. And it moved not. A deadened burst of mighty splashes and snorts reached us from afar as though an ichthyosaurus[1] had been taking a bath of glitter in the great river. 'After all,' said the boilermaker in a reasonable tone, 'why shouldn't we get the rivets?' Why not, indeed! I did not know of any reason why we shouldn't. 'They'll come in three weeks,' I said, confidently.

"But they didn't. Instead of rivets there came an invasion, an infliction, a visitation. It came in sections during the next three weeks, each section headed by a donkey carrying a white man in new clothes and tan shoes, bowing from that elevation right and left to the impressed pilgrims. A quarrelsome band of footsore sulky niggers trod on the heels of the donkeys; a lot of tents, campstools, tin boxes, white cases, brown bales would be shot down in the courtyard, and the air of mystery would deepen a little over the muddle of the station. Five such installments came, with their absurd air of disorderly flight with the loot of innumerable outfit shops and provision stores, that, one would think, they were lugging, after a raid, into the wilderness for equitable

9. Napkin. 1. Prehistoric marine reptile.

division. It was an extricable mess of things decent in themselves but that human folly made look like the spoils of thieving.

"This devoted band called itself the Eldorado Exploring Expedition, and I believe they were sworn to secrecy. Their talk, however, was the talk of sordid buccaneers: it was reckless without hardihood, greedy without audacity, and cruel without courage; there was not an atom of foresight or of serious intention in the whole batch of them, and they did not seem aware these things are wanted for the work of the world. To tear treasure out of the bowels of the land was their desire, with no more moral purpose at the back of it than there is in burglars breaking into a safe. Who paid the expenses of the noble enterprise I don't know; but the uncle of our manager was leader of that lot.

"In exterior he resembled a butcher in a poor neighborhood, and his eyes had a look of sleepy cunning. He carried his fat paunch with ostentation on his short legs, and during the time his gang infested the station spoke to no one but his nephew. You could see these two roaming about all day long with their heads close together in an everlasting confab.

"I had given up worrying myself about the rivets. One's capacity for that kind of folly is more limited than you would suppose. I said Hang!—and let things slide. I had plenty of time for meditation, and now and then I would give some thought to Kurtz. I wasn't very interested in him. No. Still, I was curious to see whether this man, who had come out equipped with moral ideas of some sort, would climb to the top after all and how he would set about his work when there."

II

"One evening as I was lying flat on the deck of my steamboat, I heard voices approaching—and there were the nephew and the uncle strolling along the bank. I laid my head on my arm again, and had nearly lost myself in a doze, when somebody said in my ear, as it were: 'I am as harmless as a little child, but I don't like to be dictated to. Am I the manager—or am I not? I was ordered to send him there. It's incredible.' . . . I became aware that the two were standing on the shore alongside the forepart of the steamboat, just below my head. I did not move; it did not occur to me to move: I was sleepy. 'It *is* unpleasant,' grunted the uncle. 'He has asked the Administration to be sent there,' said the other, 'with the idea of showing what he could do; and I was instructed accordingly. Look at the influence that man must have. Is it not frightful?' They both agreed it was frightful, then made several bizarre remarks: 'Make rain and fine weather—one man—the Council—by the nose'—bits of absurd sentences that got the better of my drowsiness, so that I had pretty near the whole of my wits about me when the uncle said, 'The climate may do away with this difficulty for you. Is he alone there?' 'Yes,' answered the manager; 'he sent his assistant down the river with a note to me in these terms: "Clear this poor devil out of the country, and don't bother sending more of that sort. I had rather be alone than have the kind of men you can dispose of with me." It was more than a year ago. Can you imagine such impudence?' 'Anything since then?' asked the other, hoarsely. 'Ivory,' jerked the nephew; 'lots of it—prime sort—lots—most annoying, from him.' 'And with that?' questioned the heavy rumble. 'Invoice,' was the reply fired out, so to speak. Then silence. They had been talking about Kurtz.

"I was broad awake by this time, but, lying perfectly at ease, remained still, having no inducement to change my position. 'How did that ivory come all this way?' growled the elder man, who seemed very vexed. The other explained that it had come with a fleet of canoes in charge of an English half-caste clerk Kurtz had with him; that Kurtz had apparently intended to return himself, the station being by that time bare of goods and stores, but after coming three hundred miles, had suddenly decided to go back, which he started to do alone in a small dugout with four paddlers, leaving the half-caste to continue down the river with the ivory. The two fellows there seemed astounded at anybody attempting such a thing. They were at a loss for an adequate motive. As to me, I seemed to see Kurtz for the first time. It was a distinct glimpse: the dugout, four paddling savages, and the lone white man turning his back suddenly on the headquarters, on relief, on thoughts of home—perhaps; setting his face towards the depths of the wilderness, towards his empty and desolate station. I did not know the motive. Perhaps he was just simply a fine fellow who stuck to his work for its own sake. His name, you understand, had not been pronounced once. He was 'that man.' The half-caste, who, as far as I could see, had conducted a difficult trip with great prudence and pluck, was invariably alluded to as 'that scoundrel.' The 'scoundrel' had reported that the 'man' had been very ill—had recovered imperfectly. . . . The two below me moved away then a few paces, and strolled back and forth at some little distance. I heard: 'Military post—doctor—two hundred miles—quite alone now—unavoidable delays—nine months—no news—strange rumors.' They approached again, just as the manager was saying, 'No one, as far as I know, unless a species of wandering trader—a pestilential fellow, snapping ivory from the natives.' Who was it they were talking about now? I gathered in snatches that this was some man supposed to be in Kurtz's district, and of whom the manager did not approve. 'We will not be free from unfair competition till one of these fellows is hanged for an example,' he said. 'Certainly,' grunted the other; 'get him hanged! Why not? Anything—anything can be done in this country. That's what I say; nobody here, you understand, *here*, can endanger your position. And why? You stand the climate—you outlast them all. The danger is in Europe; but there before I left I took care to—' They moved off and whispered, then their voices rose again. 'The extraordinary series of delays is not my fault. I did my best.' The fat man sighed. 'Very sad.' 'And the pestiferous absurdity of his talk,' continued the other; 'he bothered me enough when he was here. "Each station should be like a beacon on the road towards better things, a center for trade, of course, but also for humanizing, improving, instructing." Conceive you—that ass! And he wants to be manager! No, it's—' Here he got choked by excessive indignation, and I lifted my head the least bit. I was surprised to see how near they were—right under me. I could have spat upon their hats. They were looking on the ground, absorbed in thought. The manager was switching his leg with a slender twig: his sagacious relative lifted his head. 'You have been well since you came out this time?' he asked. The other gave a start. 'Who? I? Oh! Like a charm—like a charm. But the rest—oh, my goodness! All sick. They die so quick, too, that I haven't the time to send them out of the country—it's incredible!' 'H'm. Just so,' grunted the uncle. 'Ah! my boy, trust to this—I say, trust to this.' I saw him extend his short flipper of an arm for a gesture that took in the forest, the creek, the mud, the river,—seemed to beckon with a dishonoring flourish before the sunlit face of the land a treacherous appeal to the lurking death, to the hidden evil, to the profound darkness of its heart. It was so startling that I leaped to my feet and looked back at the edge of the forest, as though I had expected an answer of some sort to that black display of confidence. You know the foolish notions that come to one sometimes. The high stillness confronted these two figures with its ominous patience, waiting for the passing away of a fantastic invasion.

"They swore aloud together—out of sheer fright, I believe—then pretending not to know anything of my existence, turned back to the station. The sun was low; and leaning forward side by side, they seemed to be tugging painfully uphill their two ridiculous shadows of unequal length, that trailed behind them slowly over the tall grass without bending a single blade.

"In a few days the Eldorado Expedition went into the patient wilderness, that closed upon it as the sea closes over a diver. Long afterwards the news came that all the donkeys were dead. I know nothing as to the fate of the less valuable animals. They, no doubt, like the rest of us, found what they deserved. I did not inquire. I was then rather excited at the prospect of meeting Kurtz very soon. When I say very soon I mean it comparatively. It was just two months from the day we left the creek when we came to the bank below Kurtz's station.

"Going up that river was like traveling back to the earliest beginnings of the world, when vegetation rioted on the earth and the big trees were kings. An empty stream, a great silence, an impenetrable forest. The air was warm, thick, heavy, sluggish. There was no joy in the brilliance of sunshine. The long stretches of the waterway ran on, deserted, into the gloom of overshadowed distances. On silvery sandbanks hippos and alligators sunned themselves side by side. The broadening waters flowed through a mob of wooded islands; you lost your way on that river as you would in a desert, and butted all day long against shoals, trying to find the channel, till you thought yourself bewitched and cut off forever from everything you had known once—somewhere—far away—in another existence perhaps. There were moments when one's past came back to one, as it will sometimes when you have not a moment to spare to yourself; but it came in the shape of an unrestful and noisy dream, remembered with wonder amongst the overwhelming realities of this strange world of plants, and water, and silence. And this stillness of life did not in the least resemble a peace. It was the stillness of an implacable force brooding over an inscrutable intention. It looked at you with a vengeful aspect. I got used to it afterwards; I did not see it any more; I had no time. I had to keep guessing at the channel; I had to discern, mostly by inspiration, the signs of hidden banks; I watched for sunken stones; I was learning to clap my teeth smartly before my heart flew out, when I shaved by a fluke some infernal sly old snag that would have ripped the life out of the tin-pot steamboat and drowned all the pilgrims; I had to keep a lookout for the signs of dead wood we could cut up in the night for next day's steaming. When you have to attend to things of that sort, to the mere incidents of the surface, the reality—the reality, I tell you—fades. The inner truth is hidden—luckily, luckily. But I felt it all the same; I felt often its mysterious stillness watching me at my monkey tricks, just as it watches you fellows performing on your respective tight-ropes for—what is it? half-a-crown a tumble—"

"Try to be civil, Marlow," growled a voice, and I knew there was at least one listener awake besides myself.

"I beg your pardon. I forgot the heartache which makes up the rest of the price. And indeed what does the price matter, if the trick be well done? You do your tricks very well. And I didn't do badly either, since I managed not to sink that steamboat on my first trip. It's a wonder to me yet. Imagine a blindfolded man set to drive a van over a bad road. I sweated and shivered over that business considerably, I can tell you. After all, for a seaman, to scrape the bottom of the thing that's supposed to float all the time under his care is the unpardonable sin. No one may know of it, but you never forget the thump—eh? A blow on the very heart. You remember it, you dream of it, you wake up at night and think of it—years after—and go hot and cold all over. I don't pretend to say that steamboat floated all the time. More than once she had to wade for a bit, with twenty cannibals splashing around and pushing. We had enlisted some of these chaps on the way for a crew. Fine fellows—cannibals—in their place. They were men one could work with, and I am grateful to them. And, after all, they did not eat each other before my face: they had brought along a provision of hippo-meat which went rotten, and made the mystery of the wilderness stink in my nostrils. Phoo! I can sniff it now. I had the manager on board and three or four pilgrims with their staves—all complete. Sometimes we came upon a station close by the bank, clinging to the skirts of the unknown, and the white men rushing out of a tumble-down hovel, with great gestures of joy and surprise and welcome, seemed very strange—had the appearance of being held there captive by a spell. The word ivory would ring in the air for a while—and on we went again into the silence, along empty reaches, round the still bends, between the high walls of our winding way, reverberating in hollow claps the ponderous beat of the stern-wheel. Trees, trees, millions of trees, massive, immense, running up high; and at their foot, hugging the bank against the stream, crept the little begrimed steamboat, like a sluggish beetle crawling on the floor of a lofty portico. It made you feel very small, very lost, and yet it was not altogether depressing, that feeling. After all, if you were small, the grimy beetle crawled on—which was just what you wanted it to do. Where the pilgrims imagined it crawled to I don't know. To some place where they expected to get something, I bet! For me it crawled towards Kurtz—exclusively; but when the steam-pipes started leaking we crawled very slow. The reaches opened before us and closed behind, as if the forest had stepped leisurely across the water to bar the way for our return. We penetrated deeper and deeper into the heart of darkness. It was very quiet there. At night sometimes the roll of drums behind the curtain of trees would run up the river and remain sustained faintly, as if hovering in the air high over our heads, till the first break of day. Whether it meant war, peace, or prayer we could not tell. The dawns were heralded by the descent of a chill stillness; the woodcutters slept, their fires burned low; the snapping of a twig would make you start. We were wanderers on a prehistoric earth, on an earth that wore the aspect of an unknown planet. We could have fancied ourselves the first men taking possession of an accursed inheritance, to be subdued at the cost of profound anguish and of excessive toil. But suddenly, as we struggled round a bend, there would be a glimpse of rush walls, of peaked grass-roofs, a burst of yells, a whirl of black limbs, a mass of hands clapping, of feet stamping, of bodies swaying, of eyes rolling, under the droop of heavy and motionless foliage. The steamer toiled along slowly on the edge of a black and incomprehensible frenzy. The prehistoric man was cursing us, praying to us, welcoming us—who could tell? We were cut off from the comprehension of our surroundings; we glided past like phantoms, wondering and secretly appalled, as sane men would be before an enthusiastic outbreak in a madhouse. We could not understand because we were too far and could not remember, because we were traveling in the night of first ages, of those ages that are gone, leaving hardly a sign—and no memories.

"The earth seemed unearthly. We are accustomed to look upon the shackled form of a conquered monster, but there—there you could look at a thing monstrous and free. It was unearthly, and the men were—No, they were not inhuman. Well, you know, that was the worst of it—this suspicion of their not being inhuman. It would come slowly to one. They howled and leaped, and spun, and made horrid faces; but what thrilled you was just the thought of their humanity—like yours—the thought of your remote kinship with this wild and passionate uproar. Ugly. Yes, it was ugly enough; but if you were man enough you would admit to yourself that there was in you just the faintest trace of a response to the terrible frankness of that noise, a dim suspicion of there being a meaning in it which you—you so remote from the night of first ages—could comprehend. And why not? The mind of man is capable of anything—because everything is in it, all the past as well as all the future. What was there after all? Joy, fear, sorrow, devotion, valor, rage—who can tell?—but truth—truth stripped of its cloak of time. Let the fool gape and shudder—the man knows, and can look on without a wink. But he must at least be as much of a man as these on the shore. He must meet that truth with his own true stuff—with his own inborn strength. Principles won't do. Acquisitions, clothes, pretty rags—rags that would fly off at the first good shake. No; you want a deliberate belief. An appeal to me in this fiendish row—is there? Very well; I hear; I admit, but I have a voice too, and for good or evil mine is the speech that cannot be silenced. Of course, a fool, what with sheer fright and fine sentiments, is always safe. Who's that grunting? You wonder I didn't go ashore for a howl and a dance? Well, no—I didn't. Fine sentiments, you say? Fine sentiments, be hanged! I had no time. I had to mess about with white-lead and strips of woolen blanket helping to put bandages on those leaky steam-pipes—I tell you. I had to watch the steering, and circumvent those snags, and get the tin-pot along by hook or by crook. There was surface-truth enough in these things to save a wiser man. And between whiles I had to look after the savage who was fireman. He was an improved specimen; he could fire up a vertical boiler.[2] He was there below me, and, upon my word, to look at him was as edifying as seeing a dog in a parody of breeches and a feather hat, walking on his hindlegs. A few months of training had done for that really fine chap. He squinted at the steam-gauge and at the water-gauge with an evident effort of intrepidity—and he had filed teeth, too, the poor devil, and the wool of his pate shaved into queer patterns, and three ornamental scars on each of his cheeks. He ought to have been clapping his hands and stamping his feet on the bank, instead of which he was hard at work, a thrall to strange witchcraft, full of improving knowledge. He was useful because he had been instructed; and what he knew was this—that should the water in that transparent thing disappear, the evil spirit inside the boiler would get angry through the greatness of his thirst, and take a terrible vengeance. So he sweated and fired up and watched the glass fearfully (with an impromptu charm, made of rags, tied to his arm, and a piece of polished bone, as big as a watch, stuck flatways through his lower lip), while the wooden banks slipped past us slowly, the short noise was left behind, the interminable miles of silence—and we crept on, towards Kurtz. But the snags were thick, the water was treacherous and shallow, the boiler seemed indeed to have a sulky devil in it, and thus neither that fireman nor I had any time to peer into our creepy thoughts.

"Some fifty miles below the Inner Station we came upon a hut of reeds, an inclined and melancholy pole, with the unrecognizable tatters of what had been a flag of some sort flying from it, and a neatly stacked woodpile. This was unexpected. We came to the bank, and on the stack of firewood found a flat piece of board with some faded pencil-writing on it. When deciphered it said: 'Wood for you. Hurry up. Approach cautiously.' There was a signature, but it was illegible—not Kurtz—a much longer word. 'Hurry up.' Where? Up the river? 'Approach cautiously.' We had not done so. But the warning could not have been meant for the place where it could be only found after approach. Something was wrong above. But what—and how much? That was the question. We commented adversely upon the imbecility of that telegraphic style. The bush around said nothing, and would not let us look very far, either. A torn curtain of red twill hung in the doorway of the hut, and flapped sadly in our faces. The dwelling was dismantled; but we could see a white man had lived there not very long ago. There remained a rude table—a plank on two posts; a heap of rubbish reposed in a dark corner, and by the door I picked up a book. It had lost its covers, and the pages had been thumbed into a state of extremely dirty softness; but the back had been lovingly stitched afresh with white cotton thread, which looked clean yet. It was an

2. Simple, easily fired boiler, typical of the primitive machinery on Marlow's "tin-pot" boat.

extraordinary find. Its title was, *An Inquiry into some Points of Seamanship*, by a man Towser, Towson—some such name—Master in his Majesty's Navy. The matter looked dreary reading enough, with illustrative diagrams and repulsive tables of figures, and the copy was sixty years old. I handled this amazing antiquity with the greatest possible tenderness, lest it should dissolve in my hands. Within, Towson or Towser was inquiring earnestly into the breaking strain of ships' chains and tackle, and other such matters. Not a very enthralling book; but at the first glance you could see there a singleness of intention, an honest concern for the right way of going to work, which made these humble pages, thought out so many years ago, luminous with another than a professional light. The simple old sailor, with his talk of chains and purchases,[3] made me forget the jungle and the pilgrims in a delicious sensation of having come upon something unmistakably real. Such a book being there was wonderful enough; but still more astounding were the notes penciled in the margin, and plainly referring to the text. I couldn't believe my eyes! They were in cipher! Yes, it looked like cipher. Fancy a man lugging with him a book of that description into this nowhere and studying it—and making notes—in cipher at that! It was an extravagant mystery.

"I had been dimly aware for some time of a worrying noise, and when I lifted my eyes I saw the woodpile was gone, and the manager, aided by all the pilgrims, was shouting at me from the river-side. I slipped the book into my pocket. I assure you to leave off reading was like tearing myself away from the shelter of an old and solid friendship.

"I started the lame engine ahead. 'It must be this miserable trader—this intruder,' exclaimed the manager, looking back malevolently at the place we had left. 'He must be English,' I said. 'It will not save him from getting into trouble if he is not careful,' muttered the manager darkly. I observed with assumed innocence that no man was safe from trouble in this world.

"The current was more rapid now, the steamer seemed at her last gasp, the stern-wheel flopped languidly, and I caught myself listening on tiptoe for the next beat of the float,[4] for in sober truth I expected the wretched thing to give up every moment. It was like watching the last flickers of a life. But still we crawled. Sometimes I would pick out a tree a little way ahead to measure our progress towards Kurtz by, but I lost it invariably before we got abreast. To keep the eyes so long on one thing was too much for human patience. The manager displayed a beautiful resignation. I fretted and fumed and took to arguing with myself whether or no I would talk openly with Kurtz; but before I could come to any conclusion it occurred to me that my speech

3. Leverages 4. A blade of the multibladed paddle wheel.

or my silence, indeed any action of mine, would be a mere futility. What did it matter what anyone knew or ignored? What did it matter who was manager? One gets sometimes such a flash of insight. The essentials of this affair lay deep under the surface, beyond my reach, and beyond my power of meddling.

"Towards the evening of the second day we judged ourselves about eight miles from Kurtz's station. I wanted to push on; but the manager looked grave, and told me the navigation up there was so dangerous that it would be advisable, the sun being very low already, to wait where we were till next morning. Moreover, he pointed out that if the warning to approach cautiously were to be followed, we must approach in daylight—not at dusk, or in the dark. This was sensible enough. Eight miles meant nearly three hours' steaming for us, and I could also see suspicious ripples at the upper end of the reach. Nevertheless, I was annoyed beyond expression at the delay, and most unreasonably, too, since one night more could not matter much after so many months. As we had plenty of wood, and caution was the word, I brought up in the middle of the stream. The reach was narrow, straight, with high sides like a railway cutting. The dusk came gliding into it long before the sun had set. The current ran smooth and swift, but a dumb immobility sat on the banks. The living trees, lashed together by the creepers and every living bush of the undergrowth, might have been changed into stone, even to the slenderest twig, to the lightest leaf. It was not sleep—it seemed unnatural, like a state of trance. Not the faintest sound of any kind could be heard. You looked on amazed, and began to suspect yourself of being deaf—then the night came suddenly, and struck you blind as well. About three in the morning some large fish leaped, and the loud splash made me jump as though a gun had been fired. When the sun rose there was a white fog, very warm and clammy, and more blinding than the night. It did not shift or drive; it was just there, standing all around you like something solid. At eight or nine, perhaps, it lifted as a shutter lifts. We had a glimpse of the towering multitude of trees, of the immense matted jungle, with the blazing little ball of the sun hanging over it—all perfectly still—and then the white shutter came down again, smoothly, as if sliding in greased grooves. I ordered the chain, which we had begun to heave in, to be paid out again. Before it stopped running with a muffled rattle, a cry, a very loud cry, as of infinite desolation, soared slowly in the opaque air. It ceased. A complaining clamor, modulated in savage discords, filled our ears. The sheer unexpectedness of it made my hair stir under my cap. I don't know how it struck the others: to me it seemed as though the mist itself had screamed, so suddenly, and apparently from all sides at once, did this tumultuous and mournful uproar arise. It culminated in a hurried outbreak of almost intolerably excessive shrieking, which stopped short, leaving us stiffened in a variety of silly attitudes, and obstinately listening to the nearly as appalling and excessive silence. 'Good God! What is the meaning—' stammered at my elbow one of the pilgrims,—a little fat man, with sandy hair and red whiskers, who wore side-spring boots, and pink pajamas tucked into his socks. Two others remained open-mouthed a whole minute, then dashed into the little cabin, to rush out incontinently and stand darting scared glances, with Winchesters[5] at 'ready' in their hands. What we could see was just the steamer we were on, her outlines blurred as though she had been on the point of dissolving, and a misty strip of water, perhaps two feet broad, around her—and that was all. The rest of the world was nowhere, as far as our eyes and ears were concerned. Just nowhere. Gone, disappeared; swept off without leaving a whisper or a shadow behind.

"I went forward, and ordered the chain to be hauled in short, so as to be ready to trip the anchor and move the steamboat at once if necessary. 'Will they attack?' whispered an awed voice. 'We will be all butchered in this fog,' murmured another. The faces twitched with the strain, the hands trembling slightly, the eyes forgot to wink. It was very curious to see the contrast of expressions of the white men and of the black fellows of our crew, who were as much strangers to that part of the river as we, though their homes were only eight hundred miles away. The whites, of course, greatly discomposed, had besides a curious look of being painfully shocked by such an outrageous row. The others had an alert, naturally interested expression; but their faces were essentially quiet, even those of the one or two who grinned as they hauled at the chain. Several exchanged short, grunting phrases, which seemed to settle the matter to their satisfaction. Their headman, a young, broad-chested black, severely draped in dark-blue fringed cloths, with fierce nostrils and his hair all done up artfully in oily ringlets, stood near me. 'Aha!' I said, just for good fellowship's sake. 'Catch 'em,' he snapped, with a bloodshot widening of his eyes and a flash of sharp teeth—'catch 'im. Give 'im to us.' 'To you, eh?' I asked; 'what would you do with them?' 'Eat 'em!' he said, curtly, and, leaning his elbow on the rail, looked out into the fog in a dignified and profoundly pensive attitude. I would no doubt have been properly horrified, had it not occurred to me that he and his chaps must be very hungry: that they must have been growing increasingly hungry for at least this month past. They had been engaged for six months (I don't think a single one of them had any clear idea of time, as we at the end of countless ages have. They still belonged to the beginnings of time—had no inherited experience to teach them as it were), and of course, as long as there

5. American repeating rifles.

was a piece of paper written over in accordance with some farcical law or other made down the river, it didn't enter anybody's head to trouble how they would live. Certainly they had brought with them some rotten hippo-meat, which couldn't have lasted very long, anyway, even if the pilgrims hadn't, in the midst of a shocking hullabaloo, thrown a considerable quantity of it overboard. It looked like a high-handed proceeding; but it was really a case of legitimate self-defense. You can't breathe dead hippo waking, sleeping, and eating, and at the same time keep your precarious grip on existence. Besides that, they had given them every week three pieces of brass wire, each about nine inches long; and the theory was they were to buy their provisions with that currency in riverside villages. You can see how *that* worked. There were either no villages, or the people were hostile, or the director, who like the rest of us fed out of tins, with an occasional old he-goat thrown in, didn't want to stop the steamer for some more or less recondite reason. So, unless they swallowed the wire itself, or made loops of it to snare the fishes with, I don't see what good their extravagant salary could be to them. I must say it was paid with a regularity worthy of a large and honorable trading company. For the rest, the only thing to eat—though it didn't look eatable in the least—I saw in their possession was a few lumps of some stuff like half-cooked dough, of a dirty lavender color, they kept wrapped in leaves, and now and then swallowed a piece of, but so small that it seemed done more for the looks of the thing than for any serious purpose of sustenance. Why in the name of all the gnawing devils of hunger they didn't go for us—they were thirty to five—and have a good tuck-in[6] for once, amazes me now when I think of it. They were big powerful men, with not much capacity to weigh the consequences, with courage, with strength, even yet, though their skins were no longer glossy and their muscles no longer hard. And I saw that something restraining, one of those human secrets that baffle probability, had come into play there. I looked at them with a swift quickening of interest—not because it occurred to me I might be eaten by them before very long, though I own to you that just then I perceived—in a new light, as it were—how unwholesome the pilgrims looked, and I hoped, yes, I positively hoped, that my aspect was not so—what shall I say?—so—unappetizing: a touch of fantastic vanity which fitted well with the dream-sensation that pervaded all my days at that time. Perhaps I had a little fever, too. One can't live with one's finger everlastingly on one's pulse. I had often 'a little fever,' or a little touch of other things—the playful paw-strokes of the wilderness, the preliminary trifling before the more serious onslaught which came in due course. Yes; I looked at them as you would on any human being,

6. British slang for "a good meal."

with a curiosity of their impulses, motives, capacities, weaknesses, when brought to the test of an inexorable physical necessity. Restraint! What possible restraint? Was it superstition, disgust, patience, fear—or some kind of primitive honor? No fear can stand up to hunger, no patience can wear it out, disgust simply does not exist where hunger is; and as to superstition, beliefs, and what you may call principles, they are less than chaff in a breeze. Don't you know the devilry of lingering starvation, its exasperating torment, its black thoughts, its somber and brooding ferocity? Well, I do. It takes a man all his inborn strength to fight hunger properly. It's really easier to face bereavement, dishonor, and the perdition of one's soul—than this kind of prolonged hunger. Sad, but true. And these chaps, too, had no earthly reason for any kind of scruple. Restraint! I would just as soon have expected restraint from a hyena prowling amongst the corpses of a battlefield. But there was the fact facing me—the fact dazzling, to be seen, like the foam on the depths of the sea, like a ripple on an unfathomable enigma, a mystery greater—when I thought of it—than the curious, inexplicable note of desperate grief in this savage clamor that had swept by us on the river-bank, behind the blind whiteness of the fog.

"Two pilgrims were quarreling in hurried whispers as to which bank. 'Left.' 'No, no; how can you? Right, right, of course.' 'It is very serious,' said the manager's voice behind me; 'I would be desolated if anything should happen to Mr. Kurtz before we came up.' I looked at him, and had not the slightest doubt he was sincere. He was just the kind of man who would wish to preserve appearances. That was his restraint. But when he muttered something about going on at once, I did not even take the trouble to answer him. I knew, and he knew, that it was impossible. Were we to let go our hold of the bottom, we would be absolutely in the air—in space. We wouldn't be able to tell where we were going to—whether up or down stream, or across—till we fetched against one bank or the other,—and then we wouldn't know at first which it was. Of course I made no move. I had no mind for a smash-up. You couldn't imagine a more deadly place for a shipwreck. Whether drowned at once or not, we were sure to perish speedily in one way or another. 'I authorize you to take all the risks,' he said, after a short silence. 'I refuse to take any,' I said, shortly; which was just the answer he expected, though its tone might have surprised him. 'Well, I must defer to your judgment. You are captain,' he said, with marked civility. I turned my shoulder to him in sign of my appreciation, and looked into the fog. How long would it last? It was the most hopeless lookout. The approach to this Kurtz grubbing for ivory in the wretched bush was beset by as many dangers as though he had been an enchanted princess sleeping in a fabulous castle. 'Will they attack, do you think?' asked the manager, in a confidential tone.

"I did not think they would attack, for several obvious reasons. The thick fog was one. If they left the bank in their canoes they would get lost in it, as we would be if we attempted to move. Still, I had also judged the jungle of both banks quite impenetrable—and yet eyes were in it, eyes that had seen us. The river-side bushes were certainly very thick; but the undergrowth behind was evidently penetrable. However, during the short lift I had seen no canoes anywhere in the reach—certainly not abreast of the steamer. But what made the idea of attack inconceivable to me was the nature of the noise—of the cries we had heard. They had not the fierce character boding immediate hostile intention. Unexpected, wild, and violent as they had been, they had given me an irresistible impression of sorrow. The glimpse of the steamboat had for some reason filled those savages with unrestrained grief. The danger, if any, I expounded, was from our proximity to a great human passion let loose. Even extreme grief may ultimately vent itself in violence—but more generally takes the form of apathy. . . .

"You should have seen the pilgrims stare! They had no heart to grin, or even to revile me: but I believe they thought me gone mad—with fright, maybe. I delivered a regular lecture. My dear boys, it was no good bothering. Keep a look-out? Well, you may guess I watched the fog for the signs of lifting as a cat watches a mouse; but for anything else our eyes were of no more use to us than if we had been buried miles deep in a heap of cotton-wool. It felt like it, too—choking, warm, stifling. Besides, all I said, though it sounded extravagant, was absolutely true to fact. What we afterwards alluded to as an attack was really an attempt at repulse. The action was very far from being aggressive—it was not even defensive, in the usual sense: it was undertaken under the stress of desperation, and in its essence was purely protective.

"It developed itself, I should say, two hours after the fog lifted, and its commencement was at a spot, roughly speaking, about a mile and a half below Kurtz's station. We had just floundered and flopped round a bend, when I saw an islet, a mere grassy hummock of bright green, in the middle of the stream. It was the only thing of the kind; but as we opened the reach more, I perceived it was the head of a long sandbank, or rather of a chain of shallow patches stretching down the middle of the river. They were discolored, just awash, and the whole lot was seen just under the water, exactly as a man's backbone is seen running down the middle of his back under the skin. Now, as far as I did see, I could go to the right or to the left of this. I didn't know either channel, of course. The banks looked pretty well alike, the depth appeared the same; but as I had been informed the station was on the west side, I naturally headed for the western passage.

"No sooner had we fairly entered it than I became aware it was much narrower than I had supposed. To the left of us there was the long uninterrupted shoal, and to the right a high, steep bank heavily overgrown with bushes. Above the bush the trees stood in serried ranks. The twigs overhung the current thickly, and from distance to distance a large limb of some tree projected rigidly over the stream. It was then well on in the afternoon, the face of the forest was gloomy, and a broad strip of shadow had already fallen on the water. In this shadow we steamed up—very slowly, as you may imagine. I sheered her well inshore—the water being deepest near the bank, as the sounding-pole informed me.

"One of my hungry and forbearing friends was sounding[7] in the bows just below me. This steamboat was exactly like a decked scow. On the deck, there were two little teak-wood houses, with doors and windows. The boiler was in the fore-end, and the machinery right astern. Over the whole there was a light roof, supported on stanchions. The funnel projected through that roof, and in front of the funnel a small cabin built of light planks served for a pilot-house. It contained a couch, two campstools, a loaded Martini-Henry[8] leaning in one corner, a tiny table, and the steering-wheel. It had a wide door in front and a broad shutter at each side. All these were always thrown open, of course. I spent my days perched up there on the extreme fore-end of that roof, before the door. At night I slept, or tried to, on the couch. An athletic black belonging to some coast tribe, and educated by my poor predecessor, was the helmsman. He sported a pair of brass earrings, wore a blue cloth wrapper from the waist to the ankles, and thought all the world of himself. He was the most unstable kind of fool I had ever seen. He steered with no end of a swagger while you were by; but if he lost sight of you, he became instantly the prey of an abject funk, and would let that cripple of a steamboat get the upper hand of him in a minute.

"I was looking down at the sounding-pole, and feeling much annoyed to see at each try a little more of it stick out of that river, when I saw my poleman give up the business suddenly, and stretch himself flat on the deck, without even taking the trouble to haul his pole in. He kept hold on it though, and it trailed in the water. At the same time the fireman, whom I could also see below me, sat down abruptly before his furnace and ducked his head. I was amazed. Then I had to look at the river mighty quick, because there was a snag in the fairway. Sticks, little sticks, were flying about—thick: they were whizzing before my nose, dropping below me, striking behind me against my pilot-house. All this time the river, the shore, the woods, were very quiet—perfectly quiet. I could only hear the heavy splashing thump

7. Measuring water depth with a sounding line. 8. Heavy military rifle.

of the stern-wheel and the patter of these things. We cleared the snag clumsily. Arrows, by Jove! We were being shot at! I stepped in quickly to close the shutter on the land-side. That fool-helmsman, his hands on the spokes, was lifting his knees high, stamping his feet, champing his mouth, like a reined-in horse. Confound him! And we were staggering within ten feet of the bank. I had to lean right out to swing the heavy shutter, and I saw a face amongst the leaves on the level with my own, looking at me very fierce and steady; and then suddenly, as though a veil had been removed from my eyes, I made out, deep in the tangled gloom, naked breasts, arms, legs, glaring eyes,—the bush was swarming with human limbs in movement, glistening, of bronze color. The twigs shook, swayed, and rustled, the arrows flew out of them, and then the shutter came to. 'Steer her straight,' I said to the helmsman. He held his head rigid, face forward; but his eyes rolled, he kept on lifting and setting down his feet gently, his mouth foamed a little. 'Keep quiet!' I said in a fury. I might just as well have ordered a tree not to sway in the wind. I darted out. Below me there was a great scuffle of feet on the iron deck; confused exclamations; a voice screamed, 'Can you turn back?' I caught sight of a V-shaped ripple on the water ahead. What? Another snag! A fusillade burst out under my feet. The pilgrims had opened with their Winchesters, and were simply squirting lead into that bush. A deuce of a lot of smoke came up and drove slowly forward. I swore at it. Now I couldn't see the ripple or the snag either. I stood in the doorway, peering, and the arrows came in swarms. They might have been poisoned, but they looked as though they wouldn't kill a cat. The bush began to howl. Our woodcutters raised a warlike whoop; the report of a rifle just at my back deafened me. I glanced over my shoulder, and the pilot-house was yet full of noise and smoke when I made a dash at the wheel. The fool-nigger had dropped everything to throw the shutter open and let off[9] that Martini-Henry. He stood before the wide opening, glaring, and I yelled at him to come back, while I straightened the sudden twist out of that steamboat. There was no room to turn even if I had wanted to, the snag was somewhere very near ahead in that confounded smoke, there was no time to lose, so I just crowded her into the bank—right into the bank, where I knew the water was deep.

"We tore slowly along the overhanging bushes in a whirl of broken twigs and flying leaves. The fusillade below stopped short, as I had foreseen it would when the squirts got empty. I threw my head back to a glinting whizz that traversed the pilot-house, in at one shutter-hole and out at the other. Looking past that mad helmsman, who was shaking the empty rifle and yelling at the shore, I saw vague forms of

9. Fire.

men running bent double, leaping, gliding, distinct, incomplete, evanescent. Something big appeared in the air before the shutter, the rifle went overboard, and the man stepped back swiftly, looked at me over his shoulder in an extraordinary, profound, familiar manner, and fell upon my feet. The side of his head hit the wheel twice, and the end of what appeared a long cane clattered round and knocked over a little campstool. It looked as though after wrenching that thing from somebody ashore he had lost his balance in the effort. The thin smoke had blown away, we were clear of the snag, and looking ahead I could see that in another hundred yards or so I would be free to sheer off, away from the bank; but my feet felt so very warm and wet that I had to look down. The man had rolled on his back and stared straight up at me; both his hands clutched that cane. It was the shaft of a spear that, either thrown or lunged through the opening, had caught him in the side just below the ribs; the blade had gone in out of sight, after making a frightful gash; my shoes were full; a pool of blood lay very still, gleaming dark-red under the wheel; his eyes shone with an amazing luster. The fusillade burst out again. He looked at me anxiously, gripping the spear like something precious, with an air of being afraid I would try to take it away from him. I had to make an effort to free my eyes from his gaze and attend to steering. With one hand I felt above my head for the line of the steam-whistle, and jerked out screech after screech hurriedly. The tumult of angry and warlike yells was checked instantly, and then from the depths of the woods went out such a tremulous and prolonged wail of mournful fear and utter despair as may be imagined to follow the flight of the last hope from the earth. There was a great commotion in the bush; the shower of arrows stopped, a few dropping shots rang out sharply—then silence, in which the languid beat of the stern-wheel came plainly to my ears. I put the helm hard a-starboard at the moment when the pilgrim in pink pajamas, very hot and agitated, appeared in the doorway. 'The manager sends me—' he began in an official tone, and stopped short. 'Good God!' he said, glaring at the wounded man.

"We two whites stood over him, and his lustrous and inquiring glance enveloped us both. I declare it looked as though he would presently put to us some question in an understandable language; but he died without uttering a sound, without moving a limb, without twitching a muscle. Only in the very last moment, as though in response to some sign we could not see, to some whisper we could not hear, he frowned heavily, and that frown gave to his black death-mask an inconceivably somber, brooding, and menacing expression. The luster of inquiring glance faded swiftly into vacant glassiness. 'Can you steer?' I asked the agent eagerly. He looked very dubious; but I made a grab at his arm, and he understood at once I meant him to steer whether or no. To tell you the truth, I was morbidly anxious to change my shoes and socks. 'He is dead,' murmured the fellow, immensely impressed. 'No doubt about it,' said I tugging like mad at the shoe-laces. 'And by the way, I suppose Mr. Kurtz is dead as well by this time.'

"For the moment that was the dominant thought. There was a sense of extreme disappointment, as though I had found out I had been striving after something altogether without a substance. I couldn't have been more disgusted if I had traveled all this way for the sole purpose of talking with Mr. Kurtz. Talking with . . . I flung one shoe overboard, and became aware that that was exactly what I had been looking forward to—a talk with Kurtz. I made the strange discovery that I had never imagined him as doing, you know, but as discoursing. I didn't say to myself, 'Now I will never see him,' or 'Now I will never shake him by the hand,' but, 'Now I will never hear him.' The man presented himself as a voice. Not of course that I did not connect him with some sort of action. Hadn't I been told in all the tones of jealousy and admiration that he had collected, bartered, swindled, or stolen more ivory than all the other agents together? That was not the point. The point was in his being a gifted creature, and that of all his gifts the one that stood out preeminently, that carried with it a sense of real presence, was his ability to talk, his words—the gift of expression, the bewildering, the illuminating, the most exalted and the most contemptible, the pulsating stream of light, or the deceitful flow from the heart of an impenetrable darkness.

"The other shoe went flying unto the devil-god of that river. I thought, by Jove! it's all over. We are too late; he has vanished—the gift has vanished, by means of some spear, arrow, or club. I will never hear that chap speak after all,—and my sorrow had a startling extravagance of emotion, even such as I had noticed in the howling sorrow of these savages in the bush. I couldn't have felt more lonely desolation somehow, had I been robbed of a belief or had missed my destiny in life. . . . Why do you sigh in this beastly way, somebody? Absurd? Well, absurd. Good Lord! mustn't a man ever—Here, give me some tobacco." . . .

There was a pause of profound stillness, then a match flared, and Marlow's lean face appeared, worn, hollow, with downward folds and drooped eyelids, with an aspect of concentrated attention; and as he took vigorous draws at his pipe, it seemed to retreat and advance out of the night in the regular flicker of the tiny flame. The match went out.

"Absurd!" he cried. "This is the worst of trying to tell . . . . Here you all are, each moored with two good addresses, like a hulk with two anchors, a butcher round one corner, a policeman round another, excellent appetites, and temperature normal—you hear—normal from year's end to year's end. And you say, Absurd! Absurd be—exploded! Absurd! My dear boys, what can you expect from a man who out of sheer nervousness had just flung overboard a pair of new shoes? Now I think of it, it is amazing I did not shed tears. I am, upon the whole, proud of my fortitude. I was cut to the quick at the idea of having lost the inestimable privilege of listening to the gifted Kurtz. Of course I was wrong. The privilege was waiting for me. Oh yes, I heard more than enough. And I was right, too. A voice. He was very little more than a voice. And I heard—him—it—this voice—other voices—all of them were so little more than voices—and the memory of that time itself lingers around me, impalpable, like a dying vibration of one immense jabber, silly, atrocious, sordid, savage, or simply mean, without any kind of sense. Voices, voices—even the girl herself—now—"

He was silent for a long time.

"I laid the ghost of his gifts at last with a lie," he began, suddenly. "Girl! What? Did I mention a girl? Oh, she is out of it—completely. They—the women I mean—are out of it—should be out of it. We must help them to stay in that beautiful world of their own, lest ours gets worse. Oh, she had to be out of it. You should have heard the disinterred body of Mr. Kurtz saying, 'My Intended.' You would have perceived directly then how completely she was out of it. And the lofty frontal bone of Mr. Kurtz! They say the hair goes on growing sometimes, but this—ah—specimen, was impressively bald. The wilderness had patted him on the head, and, behold, it was like a ball—an ivory ball; it had caressed him, and—lo!—he had withered; it had taken him, loved him, embraced him, got into his veins, consumed his flesh, and sealed his soul to its own by the inconceivable ceremonies of some devilish initiation. He was its spoiled and pampered favorite. Ivory? I should think so. Heaps of it, stacks of it. The old mud shanty was bursting with it. You would think here was not a single tusk left either above or below the ground in the whole country. 'Mostly fossil,' the manager had remarked, disparagingly. It was no more fossil than I am; but they call it fossil when it is dug up. It appears these niggers do bury the tusks sometimes—but evidently they couldn't bury this parcel deep enough to save the gifted Mr. Kurtz from his fate. We filled the steamboat with it, and had to pile a lot on the deck. Thus he could see and enjoy as long as he could see, because the appreciation of this favor had remained with him to the last. You should have heard him say, 'My ivory.' Oh yes, I heard him. 'My Intended, my ivory, my station, my river, my—' everything belonged to him. It made me hold my breath in expectation of hearing the wilderness burst into a prodigious peal of laughter that would shake the fixed stars in their places. Everything belonged to him—but that was a trifle. The thing was to know what he belonged to, how many powers of darkness claimed him for their own. That was the reflection that made you creepy all over. It was impossible—it was not good for one either—trying to imagine. He had taken a high seat amongst the devils of the land—I mean literally. You can't understand. How could you?—with solid pavement under your feet, surrounded by kind neighbors ready to cheer you or to fall on you, stepping delicately between the butcher and the policeman, in the holy terror of scandal and gallows and lunatic asylums—how can you imagine what particular region of the first ages a man's untrammeled feet may take him into by the way of solitude—utter solitude without a policeman—by the way of silence—utter silence, where no warning voice of a kind neighbor can be heard whispering of public opinion? These little things make all the great difference. When they are gone you must fall back upon your own innate strength, upon your own capacity for faithfulness. Of course you may be too much of a fool to go wrong—too dull even to know you are being assaulted by the powers of darkness. I take it, no fool ever made a bargain for his soul with the devil: the fool is too much of a fool, or the devil too much of a devil—I don't know which. Or you may be such a thunderingly exalted creature as to be altogether deaf and blind to anything but heavenly sights and sounds. Then the earth for you is only a standing place—and whether to be like this is your loss or your gain I won't pretend to say. But most of us are neither one nor the other. The earth for us is a place to live in, where we must put up with sights, with sounds, with smells, too, by Jove!—breathe dead hippo, so to speak, and not be contaminated. And there, don't you see? your strength comes in, the faith in your ability for the digging of unostentatious holes to bury the stuff in—your power of devotion, not to yourself, but to an obscure, back-breaking business. And that's difficult enough. Mind, I am not trying to excuse or even explain—I am trying to account to myself for—for—Mr. Kurtz—for the shade of Mr. Kurtz. This initiated wraith from the back of Nowhere honored me with its amazing confidence before it vanished altogether. This was because it could speak English to me. The original Kurtz had been educated partly in England, and—as he was good enough to say himself—his sympathies were in the right place. His mother was half-English, his father was half-French. All Europe contributed to the making of Kurtz; and by and by I learned that, most appropriately, the International Society for the Suppression of Savage Customs had intrusted him with the making of a report, for its future guidance. And he had written it, too. I've seen it. I've read it. It was eloquent, vibrating with eloquence, but too high-strung, I think. Seventeen pages of close writing he had found time for! But this must have been before his—let us say—nerves, went wrong, and caused him to preside at certain midnight dances ending with unspeakable rites, which—as far as I reluctantly gathered from what I heard at various times—were offered up to him—do you understand?—to Mr. Kurtz himself. But it was a beautiful piece of writing. The opening paragraph, however, in the light of later information, strikes me now as ominous. He began with the argument that we whites, from the point of development we had arrived at, 'must necessarily appear to them [savages] in the nature of supernatural beings—we approach them with the might as of a deity,' and so on, and so on. 'By the simple exercise of our will we can exert a power for good practically unbounded,' etc., etc. From that point he soared and took me with him. The peroration was magnificent, though difficult to remember, you know. It gave me the notion of an exotic Immensity ruled by an august Benevolence. It made me tingle with enthusiasm. This was the unbounded power of eloquence—of words—of burning noble words. There were no practical hints to interrupt the magic current of phrases, unless a kind of note at the foot of the last page, scrawled evidently much later, in an unsteady hand, may be regarded as the exposition of a method. It was very simple, and at the end of that moving appeal to every altruistic sentiment it blazed at you, luminous and terrifying, like a flash of lightning in a serene sky: 'Exterminate all the brutes!' The curious part was that he had apparently forgotten all about that valuable postscriptum, because, later on, when he in a sense came to himself, he repeatedly entreated me to take good care of 'my pamphlet' (he called it), as it was sure to have in the future a good influence upon his career. I had full information about all these things, and, besides, as it turned out, I was to have the care of his memory. I've done enough for it to give me the indisputable right to lay it, if I choose, for an everlasting rest in the dust-bin of progress, amongst all the sweepings and, figuratively speaking, all the dead cats of civilization. But then, you see, I can't choose. He won't be forgotten. Whatever he was, he was not common. He had the power to charm or frighten rudimentary souls into an aggravated witch-dance in his honor; he could also fill the small souls of the pilgrims with bitter misgivings: he had one devoted friend at least, and he had conquered one soul in the world that was neither rudimentary nor tainted with self-seeking. No; I can't forget him, though I am not prepared to affirm the fellow was exactly worth the life we lost in getting to him. I missed my late helmsman awfully,—I missed him even while his body was still lying in the pilot-house. Perhaps you will think it passing strange this regret for a savage who was no more account than a grain of sand in a black Sahara. Well, don't you see, he had done something, he had steered; for months I had him at my back—a help—an instrument. It was a kind of partnership. He steered for me—I had to look after him, I worried about his deficiencies, and thus a subtle bond had been created, of which I only became aware when it was suddenly broken. And the intimate profundity of that look he gave me when he received his hurt remains to this day in my memory—like a claim of distant kinship affirmed in a supreme moment.

"Poor fool! If he had only left that shutter alone. He had no restraint, no restraint—just like Kurtz—a tree swayed by the wind. As soon as I had put on a dry pair of slippers, I dragged him out, after first jerking the spear out of his side, which operation I confess I performed with my eyes shut tight. His heels leaped together over the little doorstep; his shoulders were pressed to my breast; I hugged him from behind desperately. Oh! he was heavy, heavy; heavier than any man on earth, I should imagine. Then without more ado I tipped him overboard. The current snatched him as though he had been a wisp of grass, and I saw the body roll over twice before I lost sight of it forever. All the pilgrims and the manager were then congregated on the awning-deck about the pilot-house, chattering at each other like a flock of excited magpies, and there was a scandalized murmur at my heartless promptitude. What they wanted to keep that body hanging about for I can't guess. Embalm it, maybe. But I had also heard another, and a very ominous, murmur on the deck below. My friends the wood-cutters were likewise scandalized, and with a better show of reason—though I admit that the reason itself was quite inadmissible. Oh, quite! I had made up my mind that if my late helmsman was to be eaten, the fishes alone should have him. He had been a very second-rate helmsman while alive, but now he was dead he might have become a first-class temptation, and possibly cause some startling trouble. Besides, I was anxious to take the wheel, the man in pink pajamas showing himself a hopeless duffer at the business.

"This I did directly the simple funeral was over. We were going half-speed, keeping right in the middle of the stream, and I listened to the talk about me. They had given up Kurtz, they had given up the station; Kurtz was dead, and the station had been burnt—and so on—and so on. The red-haired pilgrim was beside himself with the thought that at least this poor Kurtz had been properly avenged. 'Say! We must have made a glorious slaughter of them in the bush. Eh? What do you think? Say?' He positively danced, the bloodthirsty little gingery beggar.[1] And he had nearly fainted when he saw the wounded man! I could not help saying, 'You made a glorious lot of smoke, anyhow.' I had seen, from the way the tops of the bushes rustled and flew, that almost all the shots had gone too high. You can't hit anything unless you take aim and fire from the shoulder; but these chaps fired from the hip with their eyes shut. The retreat, I maintained—and I was right—was caused by the screeching of the steam-whistle. Upon this they forgot Kurtz, and began to howl at me with indignant protests.

1. British slang for "red-headed rascal."

"The manager stood by the wheel murmuring confidentially about the necessity of getting well away down the river before dark at all events, when I saw in the distance a clearing on the river-side and the outlines of some sort of building. 'What's this?' I asked. He clapped his hands in wonder. 'The station!' he cried. I edged in at once, still going half-speed.

"Through my glasses I saw the slope of a hill interspersed with rare trees and perfectly free from undergrowth. A long decaying building on the summit was half buried in the high grass; the large holes in the peaked roof gaped black from afar; the jungle and the woods made a background. There was no enclosure or fence of any kind; but there had been one apparently, for near the house half-a-dozen slim posts remained in a row, roughly trimmed, and with their upper ends ornamented with round carved balls. The rails, or whatever there had been between, had disappeared. Of course the forest surrounded all that. The river-bank was clear, and on the water-side I saw a white man under a hat like a cart-wheel beckoning persistently with his whole arm. Examining the edge of the forest above and below, I was almost certain I could see movements—human forms gliding here and there. I steamed past prudently, then stopped the engines and let her drift down. The man on the shore began to shout, urging us to land. 'We have been attacked,' screamed the manager. 'I know—I know. It's all right,' yelled back the other, as cheerful as you please. 'Come along. It's all right. I am glad.'

"His aspect reminded me of something I had seen—something funny I had seen somewhere. As I maneuvered to get alongside, I was asking myself, 'What does this fellow look like?' Suddenly I got it. He looked like a harlequin. His clothes had been made of some stuff that was brown holland probably, but it was covered with patches all over, with bright patches, blue, red, and yellow,—patches on the back, patches on the front, patches on elbows, on knees; colored binding around his jacket, scarlet edging at the bottom of his trousers; and the sunshine made him look extremely gay and wonderfully neat withal, because you could see how beautifully all this patching had been done. A beardless, boyish face, very fair, no features to speak of, nose peeling, little blue eyes, smiles and frowns chasing each other over that open countenance like sunshine and shadow on a windswept plain. 'Look out, captain!' he cried; 'there's a snag lodged in here last night.' What! Another snag? I confess I swore shamefully. I had nearly holed my cripple, to finish off that charming trip. The harlequin on the bank turned his little pug-nose up to me. 'You English?' he asked, all smiles. 'Are you?' I shouted from the wheel. The smiles vanished, and he shook his head as if sorry for my disappointment. Then he brightened up. 'Never mind!' he cried, encouragingly. 'Are we in time?' I asked.

'He is up there,' he replied, with a toss of the head up the hill, and becoming gloomy all of a sudden. His face was like the autumn sky, overcast one moment and bright the next.

"When the manager, escorted by the pilgrims, all of them armed to the teeth, had gone to the house this chap came on board. 'I say, I don't like this. These natives are in the bush,' I said. He assured me earnestly it was all right. 'They are simple people,' he added; 'well, I am glad you came. It took me all my time to keep them off.' 'But you said it was all right,' I cried. 'Oh, they meant no harm,' he said; and as I stared he corrected himself, 'Not exactly.' Then vivaciously, 'My faith, your pilot-house wants a clean-up!' In the next breath he advised me to keep enough steam on the boiler to blow the whistle in case of any trouble. 'One good screech will do more for you than all your rifles. They are simple people,' he repeated. He rattled away at such a rate he quite overwhelmed me. He seemed to be trying to make up for lots of silence, and actually hinted, laughing, that such was the case. 'Don't you talk with Mr. Kurtz?' I said. 'You don't talk with that man—you listen to him,' he exclaimed with severe exaltation. 'But now—' He waved his arm, and in the twinkling of an eye was in the uttermost depths of despondency. In a moment he came up again with a jump, possessed himself of both my hands, shook them continuously, while he gabbled: 'Brother sailor . . . honor . . . pleasure . . . delight . . . introduce myself . . . Russian . . . son of an arch-priest . . . Government of Tambov. . . . What? Tobacco! English tobacco; the excellent English tobacco! Now, that's brotherly. Smoke? Where's a sailor that does not smoke?'

"The pipe soothed him, and gradually I made out he had run away from school, had gone to sea in a Russian ship; ran away again; served some time in English ships; was now reconciled with the arch-priest. He made a point of that. 'But when one is young one must see things, gather experience, ideas; enlarge the mind.' 'Here!' I interrupted. 'You can never tell! Here I met Mr. Kurtz,' he said, youthfully solemn and reproachful. I held my tongue after that. It appears he had persuaded a Dutch trading-house on the coast to fit him out with stores and goods, and had started for the interior with a light heart, and no more idea of what would happen to him than a baby. He had been wandering about that river for nearly two years alone, cut off from everybody and everything. 'I am not so young as I look. I am twenty-five,' he said. 'At first old Van Shuyten would tell me to go to the devil,' he narrated with keen enjoyment; 'but I stuck to him, and talked and talked, till at last he got afraid I would talk the hind-leg off his favorite dog, so he gave me some cheap things and a few guns, and told me he hoped he would never see my face again. Good old Dutchman, Van Shuyten. I've sent him one small lot of ivory a year ago, so that he can't call me a little thief when I get back. I hope he got it. And for the rest I don't care. I had some wood stacked for you. That was my old house. Did you see?'

"I gave him Towson's book. He made as though he would kiss me, but restrained himself. 'The only book I had left, and I thought I had lost it,' he said, looking at it ecstatically. 'So many accidents happen to a man going about alone, you know. Canoes get upset sometimes—and sometimes you've got to clear out so quick when the people get angry.' He thumbed the pages. 'You made notes in Russian?' I asked. He nodded. 'I thought they were written in cipher,' I said. He laughed, then became serious. 'I had lots of trouble to keep these people off,' he said. 'Did they want to kill you?' I asked. 'Oh no!' he cried, and checked himself. 'Why did they attack us?' I pursued. He hesitated, then said shamefacedly, 'They don't want him to go.' 'Don't they?' I said curiously. He nodded a nod full of mystery and wisdom. 'I tell you,' he cried, 'this man has enlarged my mind.' He opened his arms wide, staring at me with his little blue eyes that were perfectly round."

III

"I looked at him, lost in astonishment. There he was before me, in motley, as though he had absconded from a troupe of mimes, enthusiastic, fabulous. His very existence was improbable, inexplicable, and altogether bewildering. He was an insoluble problem. It was inconceivable how he had existed, how he had succeeded in getting so far, how he had managed to remain—why he did not instantly disappear. 'I went a little farther,' he said, 'then still a little farther—till I had gone so far that I don't know how I'll ever get back. Never mind. Plenty time. I can manage. You take Kurtz away quick—quick—I tell you.' The glamour of youth enveloped his parti-colored rags, his destitution, his loneliness, the essential desolation of his futile wanderings. For months—for years—his life hadn't been worth a day's purchase; and there he was gallantly, thoughtlessly alive, to all appearance indestructible solely by the virtue of his few years and of his unreflecting audacity. I was seduced into something like admiration—like envy. Glamour urged him on, glamour kept him unscathed. He surely wanted nothing from the wilderness but space to breathe in and to push on through. His need was to exist, and to move onwards at the greatest possible risk, and with a maximum of privation. If the absolutely pure, uncalculating, unpractical spirit of adventure had ever ruled a human being, it ruled this be-patched youth. I almost envied him the possession of this modest and clear flame. It seemed to have consumed all thought of self so completely, that even while he was talking to you, you forgot that it was he—the man before your eyes—who had gone through these things. I did not envy him his devotion to Kurtz, though. He had not meditated over it. It came to him and he accepted it with a sort of eager fatalism. I must say that to me it appeared about the most dangerous thing in every way he had come upon so far.

"They had come together unavoidably, like two ships becalmed near each other, and lay rubbing sides at last. I suppose Kurtz wanted an audience, because on a certain occasion, when encamped in the forest, they had talked all night, or more probably Kurtz had talked. 'We talked of everything,' he said, quite transported at the recollection. 'I forgot there was such a thing as sleep. The night did not seem to last an hour. Everything! Everything! . . . Of love, too.' 'Ah, he talked to you of love!' I said, much amused. 'It isn't what you think,' he cried, almost passionately. 'It was in general. He made me see things—things.'

"He threw his arms up. We were on deck at the time, and the headman of my wood-cutters, lounging near by, turned upon him his heavy and glittering eyes. I looked around, and I don't know why, but I assure you that never, never before, did this land, this river, this jungle, the very arch of this blazing sky, appear to me so hopeless and so dark, so impenetrable to human thought, so pitiless to human weakness. 'And, ever since, you have been with him, of course?' I said.

"On the contrary. It appears their intercourse had been very much broken by various causes. He had, as he informed me proudly, managed to nurse Kurtz through two illnesses (he alluded to it as you would to some risky feat), but as a rule Kurtz wandered alone far in the depths of the forest. 'Very often coming to this station, I had to wait days and days before he would turn up,' he said. 'Ah, it was worth waiting for!—sometimes.' 'What was he doing? exploring or what?' I asked. 'Oh, yes, of course'; he had discovered lots of villages, a lake, too—he did not know exactly in what direction; it was dangerous to inquire too much—but mostly his expeditions had been for ivory. 'But he had no goods to trade with by that time,' I objected. 'There's a good lot of cartridges left even yet,' he answered, looking away. 'To speak plainly, he raided the country,' I said. He nodded. 'Not alone, surely!' He muttered something about the villages round that lake. 'Kurtz got the tribe to follow him, did he?' I suggested. He fidgeted a little. 'They adored him,' he said. The tone of these words was so extraordinary that I looked at him searchingly. It was curious to see his mingled eagerness and reluctance to speak of Kurtz. The man filled his life, occupied his thoughts, swayed his emotions. 'What can you expect?' he burst out; 'he came to them with thunder and lightning, you know—and they had never seen anything like it—and very terrible. He could be very terrible. You can't judge Mr. Kurtz as you would an ordinary man. No, no, no! Now—just to give you an idea—I don't mind telling you, he wanted to shoot me, too, one day—but I don't judge him.' 'Shoot you!' I cried. 'What for?' 'Well, I had a small lot of ivory the chief of that village near my house gave me. You see I used to shoot game for them. Well, he wanted it, and wouldn't hear reason. He declared he would shoot me unless I gave him the ivory and then cleared out of the country, because he could do so, and had a fancy for it, and there was nothing on earth to prevent him killing whom he jolly well pleased. And it was true, too. I gave him the ivory. What did I care! But I didn't clear out. No, no. I couldn't leave him. I had to be careful, of course, till we got friendly again for a time. He had his second illness then. Afterwards I had to keep out of the way; but I didn't mind. He was living for the most part in those villages on the lake. When he came down to the river, sometimes he would take to me, and sometimes it was better for me to be careful. This man suffered too much. He hated all this, and somehow he couldn't get away. When I had a chance I begged him to try and leave while there was time; I offered to go back with him. And he would say yes, and then he would remain; go off on another ivory hunt; disappear for weeks; forget himself amongst these people—forget himself—you know.' 'Why! he's mad,' I said. He protested indignantly. Mr. Kurtz couldn't be mad. If I had heard him talk, only two days ago, I wouldn't dare hint at such a thing. . . . I had taken up my binoculars while we talked, and was looking at the shore, sweeping the limit of the forest at each side and at the back of the house. The consciousness of there being people in that bush, so silent, so quiet—as silent and quiet as the ruined house on the hill—made me uneasy. There was no sign on the face of nature of this amazing tale that was not so much told as suggested to me in desolate exclamations, completed by shrugs, in interrupted phrases, in hints ending in deep sighs. The woods were unmoved, like a mask—heavy, like the closed door of a prison—they looked with their air of hidden knowledge, of patient expectation, of unapproachable silence. The Russian was explaining to me that it was only lately that Mr. Kurtz had come down to the river, bringing along with him all the fighting men of that lake tribe. He had been absent for several months—getting himself adored, I suppose—and had come down unexpectedly, with the intention to all appearance of making a raid either across the river or down stream. Evidently the appetite for more ivory had got the better of the—what shall I say?—less material aspirations. However he had got much worse suddenly. 'I heard he was lying helpless, and so I came up—took my chance,' said the Russian. 'Oh, he is bad, very bad.' I directed my glass to the house. There were no signs of life, but there was the ruined roof, the long mud wall peeping above the grass, with three little square window-holes, no two of the same size; all this brought within reach of my hand, as it were. And then I made a brusque movement, and one of the remaining posts of that vanished fence leaped up in the field of my glass. You remember I told you I had been struck at the distance by certain attempts at ornamentation, rather remarkable in the ruinous aspect of the place. Now I had suddenly a nearer view, and its first result was to make me throw my head back as if before a blow. Then I went carefully from post to post with my glass, and I saw my mistake. These round knobs were not ornamental but symbolic; they were expressive and puzzling, striking and disturbing—food for thought and also for vultures if there had been any looking down from the sky; but at all events for such ants as were industrious enough to ascend the pole. They would have been even more impressive, those heads on the stakes, if their faces had not been turned to the house. Only one, the first I had made out, was facing my way. I was not so shocked as you may think. The start back I had given was really nothing but a movement of surprise. I had expected to see a knob of wood there, you know. I returned deliberately to the first I had seen—and there it was, black, dried, sunken, with closed eyelids,—a head that seemed to sleep at the top of that pole, and with the shrunken dry lips showing a narrow white line of the teeth, was smiling, too, smiling continuously at some endless and jocose dream of that eternal slumber.

"I am not disclosing any trade secrets. In fact, the manager said afterwards that Mr. Kurtz's methods had ruined the district. I have no opinion on that point, but I want you clearly to understand that there was nothing exactly profitable in these heads being there. They only showed that Mr. Kurtz lacked restraint in the gratification of his various lusts, that there was something wanting in him—some small matter which, when the pressing need arose, could not be found under his magnificent eloquence. Whether he knew of this deficiency himself I can't say. I think the knowledge came to him at last—only at the very last. But the wilderness had found him out early, and had taken on him a terrible vengeance for the fantastic invasion. I think it had whispered to him things about himself which he did not know, things of which he had no conception till he took counsel with this great solitude—and the whisper had proved irresistibly fascinating. It echoed loudly within him because he was hollow at the core. . . . I put down the glass, and the head that had appeared near enough to be spoken to seemed at once to have leaped away from me into inaccessible distance.

"The admirer of Mr. Kurtz was a bit crestfallen. In a hurried indistinct voice he began to assure me he had not dared to take these—say, symbols—down. He was not afraid of the natives; they would not stir till Mr. Kurtz gave the word. His ascendancy was extraordinary. The camps of these people surrounded the place, and the chiefs came every day to see him. They would crawl. . . . 'I don't want to know anything of the ceremonies used when approaching Mr. Kurtz,' I shouted. Curious, this feeling that came over me that such details would be more intolerable than those heads drying on the stakes under Mr. Kurtz's windows. After all, that was only a savage sight, while I seemed at one bound to have been transported into some lightless region of subtle horrors, where pure, uncomplicated savagery was a positive relief, being something that had a right to exist—obviously—in the sunshine. The young man looked at me with surprise. I suppose it did not occur to him that Mr. Kurtz was no idol of mine. He forgot I hadn't heard any of these splendid monologues on, what was it? on love, justice, conduct of life—or what not. If it had come to crawling before Mr. Kurtz, he crawled as much as the veriest savage of them all. I had no idea of the conditions, he said: these heads were the heads of rebels. I shocked him excessively by laughing. Rebels! What would be the next definition I was to hear? There had been enemies, criminals, workers—and these were rebels. Those rebellious heads looked very subdued to me on their sticks. 'You don't know how such a life tries a man like Kurtz,' cried Kurtz's last disciple. 'Well, and you?' I said. 'I! I! I am a simple man. I have no great thoughts. I want nothing from anybody. How can you compare me to . . . ?' His feelings were too much for speech, and suddenly he broke down. 'I don't understand,' he groaned. 'I've been doing my best to keep him alive, and that's enough. I had no hand in all this. I have no abilities. There hasn't been a drop of medicine or a mouthful of invalid food for months here. He was shamefully abandoned. A man like this, with such ideas. Shamefully! Shamefully! I—I—haven't slept for the last ten nights. . . .'

"His voice lost itself in the calm of the evening. The long shadows of the forest had slipped downhill while we talked, had gone far beyond the ruined hovel, beyond the symbolic row of stakes. All this was in the gloom, while we down there were yet in the sunshine, and the stretch of the river abreast of the clearing glittered in a still and dazzling splendor, with a murky and overshadowed bend above and below. Not a living soul was seen on the shore. The bushes did not rustle.

"Suddenly round the corner of the house a group of men appeared, as though they had come up from the ground. They waded waist-deep in the grass, in a compact body, bearing an improvised stretcher in their midst. Instantly, in the emptiness of the landscape, a cry arose whose shrillness pierced the still air like a sharp arrow flying straight to the very heart of the land; and, as if by enchantment, streams of human beings—of naked human beings—with spears in their hands, with bows, with shields, with wild glances and savage movements, were poured into the clearing by the dark-faced and pensive forest. The bushes shook, the grass swayed for a time, and then everything stood still in attentive immobility.

" 'Now, if he does not say the right thing to them we are all done for,' said the Russian at my elbow. The knot of men with the stretcher had stopped, too, halfway to the steamer, as if petrified. I saw the man on the stretcher sit up, lank and with an uplifted arm, above the shoulders of the bearers. 'Let us hope that the man who can talk so well of love in general will find some particular reason to spare us this time,' I said. I resented bitterly the absurd danger of our situation, as if to be at the mercy of that atrocious phantom had been a dishonoring necessity. I could not hear a sound, but through my glasses I saw the thin arm extended commandingly, the lower jaw moving, the eyes of that apparition shining darkly far in its bony head that nodded with grotesque jerks. Kurtz—Kurtz—that means short in German—don't it? Well, the name was as true as everything else in his life—and death. He looked at least seven feet long. His covering had fallen off, and his body emerged from it pitiful and appalling as from a winding-sheet. I could see the cage of his ribs all astir, the bones of his arm waving. It was as though an animated image of death carved out of old ivory had been shaking its hand with menaces at a motionless crowd of men made of dark and glittering bronze. I saw him open his mouth wide—it gave him a weirdly voracious aspect, as though he had wanted to swallow all the air, all the earth, all the men before him. A deep voice reached me faintly. He must have been shouting. He fell back suddenly. The stretcher shook as the bearers staggered forward again, and almost at the same time I noticed that the crowd of savages was vanishing without any perceptible movement of retreat, as if the forest that had ejected these beings so suddenly had drawn them in again as the breath is drawn in a long aspiration.

"Some of the pilgrims behind the stretcher carried his arms—two shotguns, a heavy rifle, and a light revolver-carbine[2]—the thunderbolts of that pitiful Jupiter. The manager bent over him murmuring as he walked beside his head. They laid him down in one of the little cabins—just a room for a bedplace and a campstool or two, you know. We had brought his belated correspondence, and a lot of torn envelopes and open letters littered his bed. His hand roamed feebly amongst these papers. I was struck by the fire in his eyes and the composed languor of his expression. It was not so much the exhaustion of disease. He did not seem in pain. This shadow looked satiated and calm, as though for the moment it had had its fill of all the emotions.

"He rustled one of the letters, and looking straight in my face said, 'I am glad.' Somebody had been writing to him about me. These special recommendations were turning up again. The volume of tone he emitted without effort, almost without the trouble of moving his lips, amazed me. A voice! a voice! It was grave, profound, vibrating,

2. Short-barreled, lightweight rifle with revolving, chambered cylinder.

while the man did not seem capable of a whisper. However, he had enough strength in him—factitious no doubt—to very nearly make an end of us, as you shall hear directly.

"The manager appeared silently in the doorway; I stepped out at once and he drew the curtain after me. The Russian, eyed curiously by the pilgrims, was staring at the shore. I followed the direction of his glance.

"Dark human shapes could be made out in the distance, flitting indistinctly against the gloomy border of the forest, and near the river two bronze figures, leaning on tall spears, stood in the sunlight under fantastic headdresses of spotted skins, war-like and still in statuesque repose. And from right to left along the lighted shore moved a wild and gorgeous apparition of a woman.

"She walked with measured steps, draped in striped and fringed cloths, treading the earth proudly, with a slight jingle and flash of barbarous ornaments. She carried her head high; her hair was done in the shape of a helmet; she had brass leggings to the knee, brass wire gauntlets to the elbow, a crimson spot on her tawny cheek, innumerable necklaces of glass beads on her neck; bizarre things, charms, gifts of witch-men, that hung about her, glittered and trembled at every step. She must have had the value of several elephant tusks upon her. She was savage and superb, wild-eyed and magnificent; there was something ominous and stately in her deliberate progress. And in the hush that had fallen suddenly upon the whole sorrowful land, the immense wilderness, the colossal body of the fecund and mysterious life seemed to look at her, pensive, as though it had been looking at the image of its own tenebrous and passionate soul.

"She came abreast of the steamer, stood still, and faced us. Her long shadow fell to the water's edge. Her face had a tragic and fierce aspect of wild sorrow and of dumb pain mingled with the fear of some struggling, half-shaped resolve. She stood looking at us without a stir, and like the wilderness itself, with an air of brooding over an inscrutable purpose. A whole minute passed, and then she made a step forward. There was a low jingle, a glint of yellow metal, a sway of fringed draperies, and she stopped as if her heart had failed her. The young fellow by my side growled. The pilgrims murmured at my back. She looked at us all as if her life had depended upon the unswerving steadiness of her glance. Suddenly she opened her bared arms and threw them up rigid above her head, as though in an uncontrollable desire to touch the sky, and at the same time the swift shadows darted out on the earth, swept around on the river, gathering the steamer into a shadowy embrace. A formidable silence hung over the scene.

"She turned away slowly, walked on, following the bank, and passed into the bushes to the left. Once only her eyes gleamed back at us in the dusk of the thickets before she disappeared.

" 'If she had offered to come aboard I really think I would have tried to shoot her,' said the man of patches, nervously. 'I have been risking my life every day for the last fortnight to keep her out of the house. She got in one day and kicked up a row about those miserable rags I picked up in the storeroom to mend my clothes with. I wasn't decent. At least it must have been that, for she talked like a fury to Kurtz for an hour, pointing at me now and then. I don't understand the dialect of this tribe. Luckily for me, I fancy Kurtz felt too ill that day to care, or there would have been mischief. I don't understand. . . . No—it's too much for me. Ah, well, it's all over now.'

"At this moment I heard Kurtz's deep voice behind the curtain: 'Save me!—save the ivory, you mean. Don't tell me. Save *me!* Why, I've had to save you. You are interrupting my plans now. Sick! Sick! Not so sick as you would like to believe. Never mind. I'll carry my ideas out yet—I will return. I'll show you what can be done. You with your little peddling notions—you are interfering with me. I will return. I . . .'

"The manager came out. He did me the honor to take me under the arm and lead me aside. 'He is very low, very low,' he said. He considered it necessary to sigh, but neglected to be consistently sorrowful. 'We have done all we could for him—haven't we? But there is no disguising the fact, Mr. Kurtz has done more harm than good to the Company. He did not see the time was not ripe for vigorous action. Cautiously, cautiously—that's my principle. We must be cautious yet. The district is closed to us for a time. Deplorable! Upon the whole, the trade will suffer. I don't deny there is a remarkable quantity of ivory—mostly fossil. We must save it, at all events—but look how precarious the position is—and why? Because the method is unsound.' 'Do you,' said I, looking at the shore, 'call it "unsound method"?' 'Without doubt,' he exclaimed hotly. 'Don't you?' . . . 'No method at all,' I murmured after a while. 'Exactly,' he exulted. 'I anticipated this. Shows a complete want of judgment. It is my duty to point it out in the proper quarter.' 'Oh,' said I, 'that fellow—what's his name?—the brick-maker, will make a readable report for you.' He appeared confounded for a moment. It seemed to me I had never breathed an atmosphere so vile, and I turned mentally to Kurtz for relief—positively for relief. 'Nevertheless I think Mr. Kurtz is a remarkable man,' I said with emphasis. He started, dropped on me a cold heavy glance, said very quietly, 'he *was*,' and turned his back on me. My hour of favor was over; I found myself lumped along with Kurtz as a partisan of methods for which the time was not ripe: I was unsound! Ah! but it was something to have at least a choice of nightmares.

"I had turned to the wilderness really, not to Mr. Kurtz, who, I was ready to admit, was as good as buried. And for a moment it seemed to me as if I also were buried in a vast grave full of unspeakable secrets. I felt an intolerable weight oppressing my breast, the smell of the damp earth, the unseen presence of victorious corruption, the darkness of an impenetrable night. . . . The Russian tapped me on the shoulder. I heard him mumbling and stammering something about 'brother seaman—couldn't conceal—knowledge of matters that would affect Mr. Kurtz's reputation.' I waited. For him evidently Mr. Kurtz was not in his grave; I suspect that for him Mr. Kurtz was one of the immortals. 'Well!' said I at last, 'speak out. As it happens, I am Mr. Kurtz's friend—in a way.'

"He stated with a good deal of formality that had we not been 'of the same profession,' he would have kept the matter to himself without regard to consequences. 'He suspected there was an active ill will towards him on the part of these white men that—' 'You are right,' I said, remembering a certain conversation I had overheard. 'The manager thinks you ought to be hanged.' He showed a concern at this intelligence which amused me at first. 'I had better get out of the way quietly,' he said, earnestly. 'I can do no more for Kurtz now, and they would soon find some excuse. What's to stop them? There's a military post three hundred miles from here.' 'Well, upon my word,' said I, 'perhaps you had better go if you have any friends amongst the savages near by.' 'Plenty,' he said. 'They are simple people—and I want nothing, you know.' He stood biting his lip, then: 'I don't want any harm to happen to these whites here, but of course I was thinking of Mr. Kurtz's reputation—but you are a brother seaman and—' 'All right,' said I, after a time. 'Mr. Kurtz's reputation is safe with me.' I did not know how truly I spoke.

"He informed me, lowering his voice, that it was Kurtz who had ordered the attack to be made on the steamer. 'He hated sometimes the idea of being taken away—and then again . . . But I don't understand these matters. I am a simple man. He thought it would scare you away—that you would give it up, thinking him dead. I could not stop him. Oh, I had an awful time of it this last month.' 'Very well,' I said. 'He is all right now.' 'Ye-e-es,' he muttered, not very convinced apparently. 'Thanks,' said I; 'I shall keep my eyes open.' 'But quiet—eh?' he urged, anxiously. 'It would be awful for his reputation if anybody here—' I promised a complete discretion with great gravity. 'I have a canoe and three black fellows waiting not very far. I am off. Could you give me a few Martini-Henry cartridges?' I could, and did, with proper secrecy. He helped himself, with a wink at me, to a handful of my tobacco. 'Between sailors—you know—good English tobacco.' At the door of the pilot-house he turned round—'I say, haven't you a pair of shoes you could spare?' He raised one leg. 'Look.' The soles were tied with knotted strings sandal-wise under his bare feet. I rooted out an old pair, at which he looked with admiration before tucking them under his left arm. One of his pockets (bright red) was bulging with cartridges, from the other (dark blue) peeped 'Towson's Inquiry,' etc., etc. He seemed to think himself excellently well equipped for a renewed encounter with the wilderness. 'Ah! I'll never, never meet such a man again. You ought to have heard him recite poetry—his own, too, it was, he told me. Poetry!' He rolled his eyes at the recollection of these delights. 'Oh, he enlarged my mind!' 'Good-by,' said I. He shook hands and vanished in the night. Sometimes I ask myself whether I had ever really seen him—whether it was possible to meet such a phenomenon! . . . .

"When I woke up shortly after midnight his warning came to my mind with its hint of danger that seemed, in the starred darkness, real enough to make me get up for the purpose of having a look round. On the hill a big fire burned, illuminating fitfully a crooked corner of the station-house. One of the agents with a picket of a few of our blacks, armed for the purpose, was keeping guard over the ivory; but deep within the forest, red gleams that wavered, that seemed to sink and rise from the ground amongst confused columnar shapes of intense blackness, showed the exact position of the camp where Mr. Kurtz's adorers were keeping their uneasy vigil. The monotonous beating of a big drum filled the air with muffled shocks and a lingering vibration. A steady droning sound of many men chanting each to himself some weird incantation came out from the black, flat wall of the woods as the humming of bees comes out of a hive, and had a strange narcotic effect upon my half-awake senses. I believe I dozed off leaning over the rail, till an abrupt burst of yells, an overwhelming outbreak of a pent-up and mysterious frenzy, woke me up in a bewildered wonder. It was cut short all at once, and the low droning went on with an effect of audible and soothing silence. I glanced casually into the little cabin. A light was burning within, but Mr. Kurtz was not there.

"I think I would have raised an outcry if I had believed my eyes. But I didn't believe them at first—the thing seemed so impossible. The fact is I was completely unnerved by a sheer blank fright, pure abstract terror, unconnected with any distinct shape of physical danger. What made this emotion so overpowering was—how shall I define it?—the moral shock I received, as if something altogether monstrous, intolerable to thought and odious to the soul, had been thrust upon me unexpectedly. This lasted of course the merest fraction of a second, and then the usual sense of commonplace, deadly danger, the possibility of a sudden onslaught and massacre, or something of the kind, which I saw impending, was positively welcome and composing. It pacified me, in fact, so much, that I did not raise an alarm.

"There was an agent buttoned up inside an ulster and sleeping on a chair on deck within three feet of me. The yells had not awakened him; he snored very slightly; I left him to his slumbers and leaped ashore. I did not betray Mr. Kurtz—it was ordered I should never betray him—it was written I should be loyal to the nightmare of my choice. I was anxious to deal with this shadow by myself alone,—and to this day I don't know why I was so jealous of sharing with anyone the peculiar blackness of that experience.

"As soon as I got on the bank I saw a trail—a broad trail through the grass. I remember the exultation with which I said to myself, 'He can't walk—he is crawling on all-fours—I've got him.' The grass was wet with dew. I strode rapidly with clenched fists. I fancy I had some vague notion of falling upon him and giving him a drubbing. I don't know. I had some imbecile thoughts. The knitting old woman with the cat obtruded herself upon my memory as a most improper person to be sitting at the other end of such an affair. I saw a row of pilgrims squirting lead in the air out of Winchesters held to the hip. I thought I would never get back to the steamer, and imagined myself living alone and unarmed in the woods to an advanced age. Such silly things—you know. And I remember I confounded the beat of the drum with the beating of my heart, and was pleased at its calm regularity.

"I kept to the track though—then stopped to listen. The night was very clear; a dark blue space, sparkling with dew and starlight, in which black things stood very still. I thought I could see a kind of motion ahead of me. I was strangely cocksure of everything that night. I actually left the track and ran in a wide semicircle (I verily believe chuckling to myself) so as to get in front of that stir, of that motion I had seen—if indeed I had seen anything. I was circumventing Kurtz as though it had been a boyish game.

"I came upon him, and, if he had not heard me coming, I would have fallen over him too, but he got up in time. He rose, unsteady, long, pale, indistinct, like a vapor exhaled by the earth, and swayed slightly, misty and silent before me; while at my back the fires loomed between the trees, and the murmur of many voices issued from the forest. I had cut him off cleverly; but when actually confronting him I seemed to come to my senses, I saw the danger in its right proportion. It was by no means over yet. Suppose he began to shout? Though he could hardly stand, there was still plenty of vigor in his voice. 'Go away—hide yourself,' he said, in that profound tone. It was very awful. I glanced back. We were within thirty yards from the nearest fire. A black figure stood up, strode on long black legs, waving long black arms, across the glow. It had horns—antelope horns, I think—on its head. Some sorcerer, some witchman, no doubt: it looked fiend-like enough. 'Do you know what you are doing?' I whispered. 'Perfectly,' he answered, raising his voice for that single word: it sounded to me far off and yet loud, like a hail through a speaking-trumpet. If he makes a row we are lost, I thought to myself. This clearly was not a case for fisticuffs, even apart from the very natural aversion I had to beat that Shadow—this wandering and tormented thing. 'You will be lost,' I said—'utterly lost.' One gets sometimes such a flash of inspiration, you know. I did say the right thing, though indeed he could not have been more irretrievably lost than he was at this very moment, when the foundations of our intimacy were being laid—to endure—to endure—even to the end—even beyond.

" 'I had immense plans,' he muttered irresolutely. 'Yes,' said I; 'but if you try to shout I'll smash your head with—' There was not a stick or a stone near. 'I will throttle you for good,' I corrected myself. 'I was on the threshold of great things,' he pleaded, in a voice of longing, with a wistfulness of tone that made my blood run cold. 'And now for this stupid scoundrel—' 'Your success in Europe is assured in any case,' I affirmed, steadily. I did not want to have the throttling of him, you understand—and indeed it would have been very little use for any practical purpose. I tried to break the spell—the heavy, mute spell of the wilderness—that seemed to draw him to its pitiless breast by the awakening of forgotten and brutal instincts, by the memory of gratified and monstrous passions. This alone, I was convinced, had driven him out to the edge of the forest, to the bush, towards the gleam of fires, the throb of drums, the drone of weird incantations; this alone had beguiled his unlawful soul beyond the bounds of permitted aspirations. And, don't you see, the terror of the position was not in being knocked on the head—though I had a very lively sense of that danger, too—but in this, that I had to deal with a being to whom I could not appeal in the name of anything high or low. I had, even like the niggers, to invoke him—himself—his own exalted and incredible degradation. There was nothing either above or below him, and I knew it. He had kicked himself loose of the earth. Confound the man! he had kicked the very earth to pieces. He was alone, and I before him did not know whether I stood on the ground or floated in the air. I've been telling you what we said—repeating the phrases we pronounced—but what's the good? They were common everyday words—the familiar, vague sounds exchanged on every waking day of life. But what of that? They had behind them, to my mind, the terrific suggestiveness of words heard in dreams, of phrases spoken in nightmares. Soul! If anybody had ever struggled with a soul, I am the man. And I wasn't arguing with a lunatic either. Believe me or not, his intelligence was perfectly clear—concentrated, it is true, upon himself with horrible intensity, yet clear; and therein was my only chance—barring, of course, the killing him there and then, which wasn't so good, on account of unavoidable noise. But his soul was mad. Being alone in the wilderness, it had looked within itself, and, by heavens! I tell you, it had gone mad. I had—for my sins, I suppose—to go through the ordeal of looking into it myself. No eloquence could have been so withering to one's belief in mankind as his final burst of sincerity. He struggled with himself, too. I saw it,—I heard it. I saw the inconceivable mystery of a soul that knew no restraint, no faith, and no fear, yet struggling blindly with itself. I kept my head pretty well; but when I had him at last stretched on the couch, I wiped my forehead, while my legs shook under me as though I had carried half a ton on my back down that hill. And yet I had only supported him, his bony arm clasped round my neck—and he was not much heavier than a child.

"When next day we left at noon, the crowd, of whose presence behind the curtain of trees I had been acutely conscious all the time, flowed out of the woods again, filled the clearing, covered the slope with a mass of naked, breathing, quivering, bronze bodies. I steamed up a bit, then swung downstream, and two thousand eyes followed the evolutions of the splashing, thumping, fierce river-demon beating the water with its terrible tail and breathing black smoke into the air. In front of the first rank, along the river, three men, plastered with bright red earth from head to foot, strutted to and fro restlessly. When we came abreast again, they faced the river, stamped their feet, nodded their horned heads, swayed their scarlet bodies; they shook towards the fierce river-demon a bunch of black feathers, a mangy skin with a pendent tail—something that looked like a dried gourd; they shouted periodically together strings of amazing words that resembled no sounds of human language; and the deep murmurs of the crowd, interrupted suddenly, were like the responses of some satanic litany.

"We had carried Kurtz into the pilot-house: there was more air there. Lying on the couch, he stared through the open shutter. There was an eddy in the mass of human bodies, and the woman with helmeted head and tawny cheeks rushed out to the very brink of the stream. She put out her hands, shouted something, and all that wild mob took up the shout in a roaring chorus of articulated, rapid, breathless utterance.

" 'Do you understand this?' I asked.

"He kept on looking out past me with fiery, longing eyes, with a mingled expression of wistfulness and hate. He made no answer, but I saw a smile, a smile of indefinable meaning, appear on his colorless lips that a moment after twitched convulsively. 'Do I not?' he said slowly, gasping, as if the words had been torn out of him by a supernatural power.

"I pulled the string of the whistle, and I did this because I saw the pilgrims on deck getting out their rifles with an air of anticipating a jolly lark. At the sudden screech there was a movement of abject terror through that wedged mass of bodies. 'Don't! don't you frighten them away,' cried someone on deck disconsolately. I pulled the string time after time. They broke and ran, they leaped, they crouched, they swerved, they dodged the flying terror of the sound. The three red chaps had fallen flat, face down on the shore, as though they had been shot dead. Only the barbarous and superb woman did not so much as flinch, and stretched tragically her bare arms after us over the somber and glittering river.

"And then that imbecile crowd down on the deck started their little fun, and I could see nothing more for smoke.

"The brown current ran swiftly out of the heart of darkness, bearing us down towards the sea with twice the speed of our upward progress; and Kurtz's life was running swiftly, too, ebbing, ebbing out of his heart into the sea of inexorable time. The manager was very placid, he had no vital anxieties now, he took us both in with a comprehensive and satisfied glance: the 'affair' had come off as well as could be wished. I saw the time approaching when I would be left alone of the party of 'unsound method.' The pilgrims looked upon me with disfavor. I was, so to speak, numbered with the dead. It is strange how I accepted this unforeseen partnership, this choice of nightmares forced upon me in the tenebrous land invaded by these mean and greedy phantoms.

"Kurtz discoursed. A voice! a voice! It rang deep to the very last. It survived his strength to hide in the magnificent folds of eloquence the barren darkness of his heart. Oh, he struggled! he struggled! The wastes of his weary brain were haunted by shadowy images now—images of wealth and fame revolving obsequiously round his unextinguishable gift of noble and lofty expression. My Intended, my station, my career, my ideas—these were the subjects for the occasional utterances of elevated sentiments. The shade of the original Kurtz frequented the bedside of the hollow sham, whose fate it was to be buried presently in the mold of primeval earth. But both the diabolic love and the unearthly hate of the mysteries it had penetrated fought for the possession of that soul satiated with primitive emotions, avid of lying fame, of sham distinction, of all the appearances of success and power.

"Sometimes he was contemptibly childish. He desired to have kings meet him at railway stations on his return from some ghastly Nowhere, where he intended to accomplish great things. 'You show them you have in you something that is really profitable, and then there will be no limits to the recognition of your ability,' he would say. 'Of course you must take care of the motives—right motives—always.' The long reaches that were like one and the same reach, monotonous bends that were exactly alike, slipped past the steamer with their multitude of secular[3] trees looking patiently after this grimy fragment of another world, the forerunner of change, of conquest, of trade, of massacres, of blessings. I looked ahead—piloting. 'Close the shutter,' said Kurtz suddenly one day; 'I can't bear to look at this.' I did so. There was a silence. 'Oh, but I will wring your heart yet!' he cried at the invisible wilderness.

"We broke down—as I had expected—and had to lie up for repairs at the head of an island. This delay was the first thing that shook Kurtz's confidence. One morning he gave me a packet of papers and a photograph—the lot tied together with a shoestring. 'Keep this for me,' he said. 'This noxious fool' (meaning the manager) 'is capable of prying into my boxes when I am not looking.' In the afternoon I saw him. He was lying on his back with closed eyes, and I withdrew quietly, but I heard him mutter, 'Live rightly, die, die. . . .' I listened. There was nothing more. Was he rehearsing some speech in his sleep, or was it a fragment of a phrase from some newspaper article? He had been writing for the papers and meant to do so again, 'for the furthering of my ideas. It's a duty.'

"His was an impenetrable darkness. I looked at him as you peer down at a man who is lying at the bottom of a precipice where the sun never shines. But I had not much time to give him, because I was helping the engine-driver to take to pieces the leaky cylinders, to straighten a bent connecting-rod, and in other such matters. I lived in an infernal mess of rust, filings, nuts, bolts, spanners, hammers, ratchet-drills—things I abominate, because I don't get on with them. I tended the little forge we fortunately had aboard; I toiled wearily in a wretched scrap-heap—unless I had the shakes too bad to stand.

"One evening coming in with a candle I was startled to hear him say a little tremulously, 'I am lying here in the dark waiting for death.' The light was within a foot of his eyes. I forced myself to murmur, 'Oh, nonsense!' and stood over him as if transfixed.

"Anything approaching the change that came over his features I have never seen before, and hope never to see again. Oh, I wasn't touched. I was fascinated. It was as though a veil had been rent. I saw on that ivory face the expression of somber pride, of ruthless power, of craven terror—of an intense and hopeless despair. Did he live his life again in every detail of desire, temptation, and surrender during that

3. Centuries-old.

supreme moment of complete knowledge? He cried in a whisper at some image, at some vision—he cried out twice, a cry that was no more than a breath—

" 'The horror! The horror!'

"I blew the candle out and left the cabin. The pilgrims were dining in the mess-room, and I took my place opposite the manager, who lifted his eyes to give me a questioning glance, which I successfully ignored. He leaned back, serene, with that peculiar smile of his sealing the unexpressed depths of his meanness. A continuous shower of small flies streamed upon the lamp, upon the cloth, upon our hands and faces. Suddenly the manager's boy put his insolent black head in the doorway, and said in a tone of scathing contempt—

" 'Mistah Kurtz—he dead.'

"All the pilgrims rushed out to see. I remained, and went on with my dinner. I believe I was considered brutally callous. However, I did not eat much. There was a lamp in there—light, don't you know—and outside it was so beastly, beastly dark. I went no more near the remarkable man who had pronounced a judgment upon the adventures of his soul on this earth. The voice was gone. What else had been there? But I am of course aware that next day the pilgrims buried something in a muddy hole.

"And then they very nearly buried me.

"However, as you see, I did not go to join Kurtz there and then. I did not. I remained to dream the nightmare out to the end, and to show my loyalty to Kurtz once more. Destiny. My destiny! Droll thing life is—that mysterious arrangement of merciless logic for a futile purpose. The most you can hope from it is some knowledge of yourself—that comes too late—a crop of unextinguishable regrets. I have wrestled with death. It is the most unexciting contest you can imagine. It takes place in an impalpable grayness, with nothing underfoot, with nothing around, without spectators, without clamor, without glory, without the great desire of victory, without the great fear of defeat, in a sickly atmosphere of tepid skepticism, without much belief in your own right, and still less in that of your adversary. If such is the form of ultimate wisdom, then life is a greater riddle than some of us think it to be. I was within a hair's breadth of the last opportunity for pronouncement, and I found with humiliation that probably I would have nothing to say. This is the reason why I affirm that Kurtz was a remarkable man. He had something to say. He said it. Since I had peeped over the edge myself, I understand better the meaning of his stare, that could not see the flame of the candle, but was wide enough to embrace the whole universe, piercing enough to penetrate all the hearts that beat in the darkness. He had summed up—he had judged. 'The horror!' He was a remarkable man. After all, this was the expression of some sort of belief; it had candor, it had conviction, it had a vibrating note of revolt in its whisper, it had the appalling face of a glimpsed truth—the strange commingling of desire and hate. And it is not my own extremity I remember best—a vision of grayness without form filled with physical pain, and a careless contempt for the evanescence of all things—even of this pain itself. No! It is his extremity that I seem to have lived through. True, he had made that last stride, he had stepped over the edge, while I had been permitted to draw back my hesitating foot. And perhaps in this is the whole difference; perhaps all the wisdom, and all truth, and all sincerity, are just compressed into that inappreciable moment of time in which we step over the threshold of the invisible. Perhaps! I like to think my summing-up would not have been a word of careless contempt. Better his cry—much better. It was an affirmation, a moral victory paid for by innumerable defeats, by abominable terrors, by abominable satisfactions. But it was a victory! That is why I have remained loyal to Kurtz to the last, and even beyond, when a long time after I heard once more, not his own voice, but the echo of his magnificent eloquence thrown to me from a soul as translucently pure as a cliff of crystal.

"No, they did not bury me, though there is a period of time which I remember mistily, with a shuddering wonder, like a passage through some inconceivable world that had no hope in it and no desire. I found myself back in the sepulchral city resenting the sight of people hurrying through the streets to filch a little money from each other, to devour their infamous cookery, to gulp their unwholesome beer, to dream their insignificant and silly dreams. They trespassed upon my thoughts. They were intruders whose knowledge of life was to me an irritating pretense, because I felt so sure they could not possibly know the things I knew. Their bearing, which was simply the bearing of commonplace individuals going about their business in the assurance of perfect safety, was offensive to me like the outrageous flauntings of folly in the face of a danger it is unable to comprehend. I had no particular desire to enlighten them, but I had some difficulty in restraining myself from laughing in their faces, so full of stupid importance. I daresay I was not very well at that time. I tottered about the streets—there were various affairs to settle—grinning bitterly at perfectly respectable persons. I admit my behavior was inexcusable, but then my temperature was seldom normal in these days. My dear aunt's endeavors to 'nurse up my strength' seemed altogether beside the mark. It was not my strength that wanted nursing, it was my imagination that wanted soothing. I kept the bundle of papers given me by Kurtz, not knowing exactly what to do with it. His mother had died lately, watched over, as I was told, by his Intended. A clean-shaven man, with an official manner and wearing gold-rimmed spectacles, called on me one day and made inquiries, at first circuitous, afterwards suavely pressing, about what he was pleased to denominate certain 'documents.' I was not surprised, because I had had two rows with the manager on the subject out there. I had refused to give up the smallest scrap out of that package, and I took the same attitude with the spectacled man. He became darkly menacing at last, and with much heat argued that the Company had the right to every bit of information about its 'territories.' And said he, 'Mr. Kurtz's knowledge of unexplored regions must have been necessarily extensive and peculiar—owing to his great abilities and to the deplorable circumstances in which he had been placed: therefore—' I assured him Mr. Kurtz's knowledge, however extensive, did not bear upon the problems of commerce or administration. He invoked then the name of science. 'It would be an incalculable loss if,' etc., etc. I offered him the report on the 'Suppression of Savage Customs,' with the postscriptum torn off. He took it up eagerly, but ended by sniffing at it with an air of contempt. 'This is not what we had a right to expect,' he remarked. 'Expect nothing else,' I said. 'There are only private letters.' He withdrew upon some threat of legal proceedings, and I saw him no more; but another fellow, calling himself Kurtz's cousin, appeared two days later, and was anxious to hear all the details about his dear relative's last moments. Incidentally he gave me to understand that Kurtz had been essentially a great musician. 'There was the making of an immense success,' said the man, who was an organist, I believe, with lank gray hair flowing over a greasy coat-collar. I had no reason to doubt his statement; and to this day I am unable to say what was Kurtz's profession, whether he ever had any—which was the greatest of his talents. I had taken him for a painter who wrote for the papers, or else for a journalist who could paint—but even the cousin (who took snuff during the interview) could not tell me what he had been—exactly. He was a universal genius—on that point I agreed with the old chap, who thereupon blew his nose noisily into a large cotton handkerchief and withdrew in senile agitation, bearing off some family letters and memoranda without importance. Ultimately a journalist anxious to know something of the fate of his 'dear colleague' turned up. This visitor informed me Kurtz's proper sphere ought to have been politics 'on the popular side.' He had furry straight eyebrows, bristly hair cropped short, an eye-glass on a broad ribbon, and, becoming expansive, confessed his opinion that Kurtz really couldn't write a bit—'But heavens! how that man could talk. He electrified large meetings. He had faith—don't you see?—he had the faith. He could get himself to believe anything—anything. He would have been a splendid leader of an extreme party.' 'What party?' I asked. 'Any party,' answered the other. 'He was an—an—extremist.' Did I not think so? I assented. Did I know, he asked, with a sudden flash of curiosity, 'what it was that had induced him to go out there?' 'Yes,' said I, and forthwith handed him the famous Report for publication, if he thought fit. He glanced through it hurriedly, mumbling all the time, judged 'it would do,' and took himself off with this plunder.

"Thus I was left at last with a slim packet of letters and the girl's portrait. She struck me as beautiful—I mean she had a beautiful expression. I know that the sunlight can be made to lie, too, yet one felt that no manipulation of light and pose could have conveyed the delicate shade of truthfulness upon those features. She seemed ready to listen without mental reservation, without suspicion, without a thought for herself. I concluded I would go and give her back her portrait and those letters myself. Curiosity? Yes; and also some other feeling perhaps. All that had been Kurtz's had passed out of my hands: his soul, his body, his station, his plans, his ivory, his career. There remained only this memory and his Intended—and I wanted to give that up, too, to the past, in a way—to surrender personally all that remained of him with me to that oblivion which is the last word of our common fate. I don't defend myself. I had no clear perception of what it was I really wanted. Perhaps it was an impulse of unconscious loyalty, or the fulfillment of one of those ironic necessities, that lurk in the facts of human existence. I don't know. I can't tell. But I went.

"I thought his memory was like the other memories of the dead that accumulate in every man's life—a vague impress on the brain of shadows that had fallen on it in their swift and final passage; but before the high and ponderous door, between the tall houses of a street as still and decorous as a well-kept alley in a cemetery, I had a vision of him on the stretcher, opening his mouth voraciously, as if to devour all the earth with all its mankind. He lived then before me; he lived as much as he had ever lived—a shadow insatiable of splendid appearances, of frightful realities; a shadow darker than the shadow of the night, and draped nobly in the folds of a gorgeous eloquence. The vision seemed to enter the house with me—the stretcher, the phantom-bearers, the wild crowd of obedient worshipers, the gloom of the forests, the glitter of the reach between the murky bends, the beat of the drum, regular and muffled like the beating of a heart—the heart of a conquering darkness. It was a moment of triumph for the wilderness, an invading and vengeful rush which, it seemed to me, I would have to keep back alone for the salvation of another soul. And the memory of what I had heard him say afar there, with the horned shapes stirring at my back, in the glow of fires, within the patient woods, those broken phrases came back to me, were heard again in their ominous and terrifying simplicity. I remembered his abject pleading, his abject threats, the colossal scale of his vile desires, the meanness, the torment, the tempestuous anguish of his soul. And later on I seem to see his collected languid manner, when he said one day, 'This lot of ivory now is really mine. The Company did not pay for it. I collected it myself at a very great personal risk. I am afraid they will try to claim it as theirs though. H'm. It is a difficult case. What do you think I ought to do—resist? Eh? I want no more than justice.' . . . He wanted no more than justice—no more than justice. I rang the bell before a mahogany door on the first floor, and while I waited he seemed to stare at me out of the glossy panel—stare with that wide and immense stare embracing, condemning, loathing all the universe. I seemed to hear the whispered cry, 'The horror! The horror!'

"The dusk was falling. I had to wait in a lofty drawing-room with three long windows from floor to ceiling that were like three luminous and bedraped columns. The bent gilt legs and backs of the furniture shone in indistinct curves. The tall marble fireplace had a cold and monumental whiteness. A grand piano stood massively in a corner; with dark gleams on the flat surfaces like a somber and polished sarcophagus. A high door opened—closed. I rose.

"She came forward, all in black, with a pale head, floating towards me in the dusk. She was in mourning. It was more than a year since his death, more than a year since the news came; she seemed as though she would remember and mourn forever. She took both my hands in hers and murmured, 'I had heard you were coming.' I noticed she was not very young—I mean not girlish. She had a mature capacity for fidelity, for belief, for suffering. The room seemed to have grown darker, as if all the sad light of the cloudy evening had taken refuge on her forehead. This fair hair, this pale visage, this pure brow, seemed surrounded by an ashy halo from which the dark eyes looked out at me. Their glance was guileless, profound, confident, and trustful. She carried her sorrowful head as though she were proud of that sorrow, as though she would say, I—I alone know how to mourn him as he deserves. But while we were still shaking hands, such a look of awful desolation came upon her face that I perceived she was one of those creatures that are not the playthings of Time. For her he had died only yesterday. And, by Jove! the impression was so powerful that for me, too, he seemed to have died only yesterday—nay, this very minute. I saw her and him in the same instant of time—his death and her sorrow—I saw her sorrow in the very moment of his death. Do you understand? I saw them together—I heard them together. She had said, with a deep catch of the breath, 'I have survived' while my strained ears seemed to hear distinctly, mingled with her tone of despairing regret, the summing up whisper of his eternal condemnation. I asked myself what I was doing there, with a sensation of panic in my heart as though I had blundered into a place of cruel and absurd mysteries not fit for a human being to behold. She motioned me to a chair. We sat down. I laid the packet gently on the little table, and she put her hand over it. . . . 'You knew him well,' she murmured, after a moment of mourning silence.

" 'Intimacy grows quickly out there,' I said. 'I knew him as well as it is possible for one man to know another.'

" 'And you admired him,' she said. 'It was impossible to know him and not to admire him. Was it?'

" 'He was a remarkable man,' I said, unsteadily. Then before the appealing fixity of her gaze, that seemed to watch for more words on my lips, I went on, 'It was impossible not to—'

" 'Love him,' she finished eagerly, silencing me into an appalled dumbness. 'How true! how true! But when you think that no one knew him so well as I! I had all his noble confidence. I knew him best.'

" 'You knew him best,' I repeated. And perhaps she did. But with every word spoken the room was growing darker, and only her forehead, smooth and white, remained illumined by the unextinguishable light of belief and love.

" 'You were his friend,' she went on. 'His friend,' she repeated, a little louder. 'You must have been, if he had given you this, and sent you to me. I feel I can speak to you—and oh! I must speak. I want you—you have heard his last words—to know I have been worthy of him. . . . It is not pride. . . . Yes! I am proud to know I understood him better than anyone on earth—he told me so himself. And since his mother died I have had no one—no one—to—to—'

"I listened. The darkness deepened. I was not even sure whether he had given me the right bundle. I rather suspect he wanted me to take care of another batch of his papers which, after his death, I saw the manager examining under the lamp. And the girl talked, easing her pain in the certitude of my sympathy; she talked as thirsty men drink. I had heard that her engagement with Kurtz had been disapproved by her people. He wasn't rich enough or something. And indeed I don't know whether he had not been a pauper all his life. He had given me some reason to infer that it was his impatience of comparative poverty that drove him out there.

" '. . . Who was not his friend who had heard him speak once?' she was saying. 'He drew men towards him by what was best in them.' She looked at me with intensity. 'It is the gift of the great,' she went on, and the sound of her low voice seemed to have the accompaniment of all the other sounds, full of mystery, desolation, and sorrow, I had ever heard—the ripple of the river, the soughing of the trees swayed by the wind, the murmurs of the crowds, the faint ring of incomprehensible words cried from afar, the whisper of a voice speaking from beyond the threshold of an eternal darkness. 'But you have heard him! You know!' she cried.

" 'Yes, I know,' I said with something like despair in my heart, but bowing my head before the faith that was in her, before that great and saving illusion that shone with an unearthly glow in the darkness, in the triumphant darkness from which I could not have defended her—from which I could not even defend myself.

" 'What a loss to me—to us!'—she corrected herself with beautiful generosity; then added in a murmur, 'To the world.' By the last gleams of twilight I could see the glitter of her eyes, full of tears—of tears that would not fall.

" 'I have been very happy—very fortunate—very proud,' she went on. 'Too fortunate. Too happy for a little while. And now I am unhappy for—for life.'

"She stood up; her fair hair seemed to catch all the remaining light in a glimmer of gold. I rose, too.

" 'And of all this,' she went on, mournfully, 'of all his promise, and of all his greatness, of his generous mind, of his noble heart, nothing remains—nothing but a memory. You and I—'

" 'We shall always remember him,' I said, hastily.

" 'No!' she cried. 'It is impossible that all this should be lost—that such a life should be sacrificed to leave nothing—but sorrow. You know what vast plans he had. I knew of them, too—I could not perhaps understand—but others knew of them. Something must remain. His words, at least, have not died.'

" 'His words will remain,' I said.

" 'And his example,' she whispered to herself. 'Men looked up to him—his goodness shone in every act. His example—'

" 'True,' I said; 'his example too. Yes, his example. I forgot that.'

" 'But I do not. I cannot—I cannot believe—not yet. I cannot believe that I shall never see him again, that nobody will see him again, never, never, never.'

"She put out her arms as if after a retreating figure, stretching them black and with clasped pale hands across the fading and narrow sheen of the window. Never see him! I saw him clearly enough then. I shall see this eloquent phantom as long as I live, and I shall see her, too, a tragic and familiar Shade, resembling in this gesture another one, tragic also, and bedecked with powerless charms, stretching bare brown arms over the glitter of the infernal stream, the stream of darkness. She said suddenly very low, 'He died as he lived.'

" 'His end,' said I, with dull anger stirring in me, 'was in every way worthy of his life.'

" 'And I was not with him,' she murmured. My anger subsided before a feeling of infinite pity.

" 'Everything that could be done—' I mumbled.

" 'Ah, but I believed in him more than anyone on earth—more than his own mother, more than—himself. He needed me! Me! I would have treasured every sigh, every word, every sign, every glance.'

"I felt like a chill grip on my chest. 'Don't,' I said, in a muffled voice.

" 'Forgive me. I—I—have mourned so long in silence—in silence. . . . You were with him—to the last? I think of his loneliness. Nobody near to understand him as I would have understood. Perhaps no one to hear. . . .'

" 'To the very end,' I said shakily. 'I heard his very last words. . . .' I stopped in a fright.

" 'Repeat them,' she murmured in a heart-broken tone. 'I want—I want—something—something—to—live with.'

"I was on the point of crying at her, 'Don't you hear them?' The dusk was repeating them in a persistent whisper all around us, in a whisper that seemed to swell menacingly like the first whisper of a rising wind. 'The horror! The horror!'

" 'His last word—to live with,' she insisted. 'Don't you understand I loved him—I loved him—I loved him!'

"I pulled myself together and spoke slowly.

" 'The last word he pronounced was—your name.'

"I heard a light sigh and then my heart stood still, stopped dead short by an exulting and terrible cry, by the cry of inconceivable triumph and of unspeakable pain. 'I knew it—I was sure!' . . . She knew. She was sure. I heard her weeping, she had hidden her face in her hands. It seemed to me that the house would collapse before I could escape, that the heavens would fall upon my head. But nothing happened. The heavens do not fall for such a trifle. Would they have fallen, I wonder, if I had rendered Kurtz that justice which was his due? Hadn't he said he wanted only justice? But I couldn't. I could not tell her. It would have been too dark—too dark altogether. . . ."

Marlow ceased, and sat apart, indistinct and silent, in the pose of a meditating Buddha. Nobody moved for a time. "We have lost the first of the ebb," said the Director, suddenly. I raised my head. The offing was barred by a black bank of clouds, and the tranquil waterway leading to the uttermost ends of the earth flowed somber under an overcast sky—seemed to lead into the heart of an immense darkness.

---

1. Interpret the first narrator's statement that "to [Marlow] the meaning of an episode was not inside like a kernel but outside, enveloping the tale which brought it out only as a glow brings out a haze." How does this apply to Marlow's report of the episodes that make up the novella?
2. What is the relation of the present setting (the deck of the yacht anchored in the Thames) to what Marlow has to say about Africa?

3. What is Marlow's attitude toward the people in Brussels who hire him and send him to Africa? Toward the things he witnesses on his sea voyage?
4. Why is Marlow appalled by what he sees on his arrival in Africa? What does he mean when he speaks of seeing "devils"? Of "seeing" Kurtz—when in fact he has not yet laid eyes on him? What special sense is given to the term "seeing" throughout the novella?
5. Marlow says he does not "at first" grasp the significance of the wreck of the steamboat. What significance does he later find in this circumstance?
6. What is the relation of the young Russian to Kurtz? What ironies lie in the young man's opinion of Kurtz? Is Marlow aware of these ironies or does he merely report what the young man says?
7. Of what significance is the "barbarous and superb" black woman, Kurtz's consort? By what contrasts and similarities is she related to Kurtz's "Intended"?
8. What does Marlow mean when he calls Kurtz "hollow"?
9. Why does Kurtz try to escape from the ship that has rescued him?
10. How is Kurtz's report on "The Suppression of Savage Customs" related to the meaning of the whole novella and to the tone that emerges from Marlow's sarcasm?
11. What is said about colonialism? Are these comments essential to the theme?
12. What elements of optimism and pessimism mingle in the conclusion? To what does Kurtz's pronouncement "The horror! The horror!" apply?
13. What is Marlow's ultimate judgment of Kurtz? What factors in his knowledge of Kurtz are most important in the formation of this judgment?

Robert Coover

Coover (1932–) was born in Charles City, Iowa. He got his education at Southern Illinois University, Indiana University, and the University of Chicago, with intervening service as an officer in the Navy. An author of plays as well as a writer of fiction, he has fused stylistic innovations with an exposure of new forms of consciousness emerging from our technological civilization. Some of his shorter work is based on the structure of fairy tales scrambled and recomposed by the television medium. Absurdity as a metaphysical principle combines with absurdity as a device for entertainment. His novels are The Origin of the Brunists *(1966).* The Universal Baseball Association, Inc., J. Henry Waugh, Prop. *(1968),* The Public Burning *(1977), and* Gerald's Party *(1987). Several of his best stories are collected in* Pricksongs & Descants *(1969). His novella* A Political Fable *was published in 1980.*

The Babysitter

She arrives at 7:40, ten minutes late, but the children, Jimmy and Bitsy, are still eating supper, and their parents are not ready to go yet. From other rooms come the sounds of a baby screaming, water running, a television musical (no words: probably a dance number—patterns of gliding figures come to mind). Mrs. Tucker sweeps into the kitchen, fussing with her hair, and snatches a baby bottle full of milk out of a pan of warm water, rushes out again. "Harry!" she calls. "The babysitter's here already!"

• • •

That's My Desire? I'll Be Around?[1] He smiles toothily, beckons faintly with his head, rubs his fast balding pate. Bewitched, maybe? Or, What's the Reason? He pulls on his shorts, gives his hips a slap. The baby goes silent in mid-scream. Isn't this the one who used their tub last time? Who's Sorry Now, that's it.

• • •

Jack is wandering around town, not knowing what to do. His girlfriend is babysitting at the Tuckers', and later, when she's got the kids in bed, maybe he'll drop over there. Sometimes he watches TV with her when

1. Titles of popular songs, as are *What's the Reason* and *Who's Sorry Now,* below.

she's babysitting, it's about the only chance he gets to make out a little since he doesn't own wheels, but they have to be careful because most people don't like their sitters to have boyfriends over. Just kissing her makes her nervous. She won't close her eyes because she has to be watching the door all the time. Married people really have it good, he thinks.

• • •

"Hi," the babysitter says to the children, and puts her books on top of the refrigerator. "What's for supper?" The little girl, Bitsy, only stares at her obliquely. She joins them at the end of the kitchen table. "I don't have to go to bed until nine," the boy announces flatly, and stuffs his mouth full of potato chips. The babysitter catches a glimpse of Mr. Tucker hurrying out of the bathroom in his underwear.

• • •

Her tummy. Under her arms. And her feet. Those are the best places. She'll spank him, she says sometimes. Let her.

• • •

That sweet odor that girls have. The softness of her blouse. He catches a glimpse of the gentle shadows amid her thighs, as she curls her legs up under her. He stares hard at her. He has a lot of meaning packed into that stare, but she's not even looking. She's popping her gum and watching television. She's sitting right there, inches away, soft, fragrant, and ready: but what's his next move? He notices his buddy Mark in the drugstore, playing the pinball machine, and joins him. "Hey, this mama's cold, Jack baby! She needs your touch!"

• • •

Mrs. Tucker appears at the kitchen doorway, holding a rolled-up diaper. "Now, don't just eat potato chips, Jimmy! See that he eats his hamburger, dear." She hurried away to the bathroom. The boy glares sullenly at the babysitter, silently daring her to carry out the order. "How about a little of that good hamburger now, Jimmy?" she says perfunctorily. He lets half of it drop to the floor. The baby is silent and a man is singing a love song on the TV. The children crunch chips.

• • •

He loves her. She loves him. They whirl airily, stirring a light breeze, through a magical landscape of rose and emerald and deep blue. Her light brown hair coils and wisps softly in the breeze, and the soft folds of her white gown tug at her body and then float away. He smiles in a pulsing crescendo of sincerity and song.

• • •

"You mean she's alone?" Mark asks. "Well, there's two or three kids," Jack says. He slides the coin in. There's a rumble of steel balls tumbling, lining up. He pushes a plunger with his thumb, and one ball pops up in place, hard and glittering with promise. His stare? to say he loves her. That he cares for her and would protect her, would shield her, if need be, with his own body. Grinning, he bends over the ball to take careful aim: he and Mark have studied this machine and have it figured out, but still it's not that easy to beat.

• • •

On the drive to the party, his mind is partly on the girl, partly on his own high-school days, long past. Sitting at the end of the kitchen table there with his children, she had seemed to be self-consciously arching her back, jutting her pert breasts, twitching her thighs: and for whom if not for him? So she'd seen him coming out of there, after all. He smiles. Yet what could he ever do about it? Those good times are gone, old man. He glances over at his wife, who, readjusting a garter, asks: "What do you think of our babysitter?"

• • •

He loves her. She loves him. And then the babies come. And dirty diapers and one goddamn meal after another. Dishes. Noise. Clutter. And fat. Not just tight, her girdle actually hurts. Somewhere recently she's read about women getting heart attacks or cancer or something from too-tight girdles. Dolly pulls the car door shut with a grunt, strangely irritated, not knowing why. Party mood. Why is her husband humming, "Who's Sorry Now?" Pulling out of the drive, she glances back at the lighted kitchen window. "What do you think of our babysitter?" she asks. While her husband stumbles all over himself trying to answer, she pulls a stocking tight, biting deeper with the garters.

• • •

"Stop it!" she laughs. Bitsy is pulling on her skirt and he is tickling her in the ribs. "Jimmy! Don't!" But she is laughing too much to stop him. He leaps on her, wrapping his legs around her waist, and they all fall to the carpet in front of the TV, where just now a man in a tuxedo and a little girl in a flouncy white dress are doing a tapdance together. The babysitter's blouse is pulling out of her skirt, showing a patch of bare tummy: the target. "I'll spank!"

• • •

Jack pushes the plunger, thrusting up a steel ball, and bends studiously over the machine. "You getting any off her?" Mark asks, and clears his throat, flicks ash from his cigarette. "Well, not exactly, not yet," Jack says, grinning awkwardly, but trying to suggest more than he admits to, and fires. He heaves his weight gently against the machine as the ball bounds off a rubber bumper. He can feel her warming up under his hands, the flippers suddenly coming alive, delicate rapid-fire patterns emerging in the flashing of the lights. 1000 WHEN LIT: *now!* "Got my hand on it, that's about all." Mark glances up from the machine, cigarette dangling from his lip. "Maybe you need some help," he suggests with a wry one-sided grin. "Like maybe together, man, we could do it."

• • •

She likes the big tub. She uses the Tuckers' bath salts, and loves to sink into the hot fragrant suds. She can stretch out, submerged, up to her chin. It gives her a good sleepy tingly feeling.

• • •

"What do you think of our babysitter?" Dolly asks, adjusting a garter. "Oh, I hardly noticed," he says, "Cute girl. She seems to get along fine with the kids. Why?" "I don't know." His wife tugs her skirt down, glances at a lighted window they are passing, adding: "I'm not sure I trust her completely, that's all. With the baby, I mean. She seems a little careless. And the other time, I'm almost sure she had a boyfriend over." He grins, claps one hand on his wife's broad gartered thigh. "What's wrong with that?" he asks. Still in anklets, too. Bare thighs, no girdles, nothing up there but a flimsy pair of panties and soft adolescent flesh. He's flooded with vague remembrances of football rallies and movie balconies.

• • •

How tiny and rubbery it is! she thinks, soaping between the boy's legs, giving him his bath. Just a funny jiggly little thing that looks like it shouldn't even be there at all. Is that what all the songs are about?

• • •

Jack watches Mark lunge and twist against the machine. Got her running now, racked them up. He's not too excited about the idea of Mark fooling around with his girlfriend, but Mark's a cooler operator than he is, and maybe, doing it together this once, he'd get over his own timidity. And if she didn't like it, there were other girls around. If Mark went too far, he could cut him off too. He feels his shoulders tense: enough's enough, man . . . but sees the flesh, too. "Maybe I'll call her later," he says.

• • •

"Hey, Harry! Dolly! Glad you could make it!" "I hope we're not late." "No, no, you're one of the first, come on in! By golly, Dolly, you're looking younger every day! How do you do it? Give my wife your secret, will you?" He pats her on her girdled bottom behind Mr. Tucker's back, leads them in for drinks.

• • •

8:00. The babysitter runs water in the tub, combs her hair in front of the bathroom mirror. There's a western on television, so she lets Jimmy watch it while she gives Bitsy her bath. But Bitsy doesn't want a bath. She's angry and crying because she has to be first. The babysitter tells her if she'll take her bath quickly, she'll let her watch television while

Jimmy takes his bath, but it does no good. The little girl fights to get out of the bathroom, and the babysitter has to squat with her back against the door and forcibly undress the child. There are better places to babysit. Both children mind badly, and then, sooner or later, the baby is sure to wake up for a diaper change and more bottle. The Tuckers do have a good color TV, though, and she hopes things will be settled down enough to catch the 8:30 program. She thrusts the child into the tub, but she's still screaming and thrashing around. "Stop it now, Bitsy, or you'll wake the baby!" "I have to go potty!" the child wails, switching tactics. The babysitter sighs, lifts the girl out of the tub and onto the toilet, getting her skirt and blouse all wet in the process. She glances at herself in the mirror. Before she knows it, the girl is off the seat and out of the bathroom. "Bitsy! Come back here!"

• • •

"Okay, that's enough!" Her skirt is ripped and she's flushed and crying. "Who says?" "I do, man!" The bastard goes for her, but she tackles him. They roll and tumble. Tables tip, lights topple, the TV crashes to the floor. He slams a hard right to the guy's gut, clips his chin with a rolling left.

• • •

"We hope it's a girl." That's hardly surprising, since they already have four boys. Dolly congratulates the woman like everybody else, but she doesn't envy her, not a bit. That's all she needs about now. She stares across the room at Harry, who is slapping backs and getting loud, as usual. He's spreading out through the middle, so why the hell does he have to complain about her all the time? "Dolly, you're looking younger every day!" was the nice greeting she got tonight. "What's your secret?" And Harry: "It's all those calories. She's getting back her baby fat." "Haw haw! Harry, have a heart!"

• • •

"Get her feet" he hollers at Bitsy, his fingers in her ribs, running over her naked tummy, tangling in the underbrush of straps and strange clothing. "Get her shoes off!" He holds her pinned by pressing his head against her soft chest. "No! No, Jimmy! Bitsy, stop!" But though she kicks and twists and rolls around, she doesn't get up, she can't get up, she's laughing too hard, and the shoes come off, and he grabs a stockinged foot and scratches the sole ruthlessly, and she raises up her legs, trying to pitch him off, she's wild, boy, but he hangs on, and she's laughing, and on the screen there's a rattle of hooves, and he and Bitsy are rolling around and around on the floor in a crazy rodeo of long bucking legs.

• • •

He slips the coin in. There's a metallic fall and a sharp click as the dial tone begins. "I hope the Tuckers have gone," he says. "Don't worry, they're at our place," Mark says. "They're always the first ones to come and the last ones to go home. My old man's always bitching about them." Jack laughs nervously and dials the number. "Tell her we're coming over to protect her from getting raped," Mark suggests, and lights a cigarette. Jack grins, leaning casually against the door jamb of the phonebooth, chewing gum, one hand in his pocket. He's really pretty uneasy, though. He has the feeling he's somehow messing up a good thing.

• • •

Bitsy runs naked into the livingroom, keeping a hassock between herself and the babysitter. "Bitsy . . . !" the babysitter threatens. Artificial reds and greens and purples flicker over the child's wet body, as hooves clatter, guns crackle, and stagecoach wheels thunder over rutted terrain. "Get outa the way, Bitsy!" the boy complains. "I can't see!" Bitsy streaks past and the babysitter chases, cornering the girl in the back bedroom. Bitsy throws something that hits her softly in the face: a pair of men's undershorts. She grabs the girl scampering by, carries her struggling to the bathroom, and with a smart crack on her glistening bottom, pops her back into the tub. In spite, Bitsy peepees in the bathwater.

• • •

Mr. Tucker stirs a little water into his bourbon and kids with his host and another man, just arrived, about their golf games. They set up a match for the weekend, a threesome looking for a fourth. Holding his drink in his right hand, Mr. Tucker swings his left through the motion of a tee-shot. "You'll have to give me a stroke a hole," he says. "I'll give you a stroke!" says his host: "Bend over!" Laughing, the other man asks: "Where's your boy Mark tonight?" "I don't know," replies the host, gathering up a trayful of drinks. Then he adds in a low growl: "Out chasing tail probably." They chuckle loosely at that, then shrug in commiseration and return to the livingroom to join their women.

• • •

Shades pulled. Door locked. Watching the TV. Under a blanket maybe. Yes, that's right, under a blanket. Her eyes close when he kisses her. Her breasts, under both their hands, are soft and yielding.

• • •

A hard blow to the belly. The face. The dark beardy one staggers, the lean-jawed sheriff moves in, but gets a spurred boot in his face. The dark one hurls himself forward, drives his shoulder into the sheriff's hard midriff, her own tummy tightens, withstands, as the sheriff smashes the dark man's nose, slams him up against a wall, slugs him again! and again! The dark man grunts rhythmically, backs off, then plunges suicidally forward—her own knees draw up protectively—the sheriff staggers! caught low! but instead of following through, the other man steps back—a pistol! the dark one has a pistol! the sheriff draws! shoots from the hip! explosions! she clutches her hands between her thighs—no! the sheriff spins! wounded! the dark man hesitates, aims, her legs stiffen toward the set, the sheriff rolls desperately in the straw, fires: dead! the dark man is dead! groans, crumples, his pistol drooping in his collapsing hand, dropping, he drops. The sheriff, spent, nicked, watches weakly from the floor where he lies. Oh, to be whole! to be good and strong and right! to embrace and be embraced by harmony and wholeness! The sheriff, drawing himself painfully up on one elbow, rubs his bruised mouth with the back of his other hand.

• • •

"Well, we just sorta thought we'd drop over," he says, and winks broadly at Mark. "Who's we?" "Oh, me and Mark here." "Tell her, good thing like her, gotta pass it around," whispers Mark, dragging on his smoke, then flicking the butt over under the pinball machine. "What's that?" she asks. "Oh, Mark and I were just saying, like two's company, three's an orgy," Jack says, and winks again. She giggles. "Oh Jack!" Behind her, he can hear shouts and gunfire. "Well, okay, for just a little while, if you'll both be good." Way to go, man.

• • •

Probably some damn kid over there right now. Wrestling around on the couch in front of his TV. Maybe he should drop back to the house. Just to check. None of that stuff, she was there to do a job! Park the car a couple doors down, slip in the front door before she knows it. He sees the disarray of clothing, the young thighs exposed to the flickering television light, hears his baby crying. "Hey, what's going on here! Get outa here, son, before I call the police!" Of course, they haven't really been doing anything. They probably don't even know how. He stares benignly down upon the girl, her skirt rumpled loosely around her thighs. Flushed, frightened, yet excited, she stares back at him. He smiles. His finger touches a knee, approaches the hem. Another couple arrives. Filling up here with people. He wouldn't be missed. Just slip out, stop back casually to pick up something or other he forgot, never mind what. He remembers that the other time they had this babysitter, she took a bath in their house. She had a date afterwards, and she'd come from cheerleading practice or something. Aspirin maybe. Just drop quietly and casually into the bathroom to pick up some aspirin. "Oh, excuse me, dear! I only . . . !" She gazes back at him, astonished, yet strangely moved. Her soft wet breasts rise and fall in the water, and her tummy looks pale and ripply. He recalls that her pubic hairs, left in the tub, were brown. Light brown.

• • •

She's no more than stepped into the tub for a quick bath, when Jimmy announces from outside the door that he has to go to the bathroom.

She sighs: just an excuse, she knows. "You'll have to wait." The little nuisance. "I can't wait." "Okay, then come ahead, but I'm taking a bath." She supposes that will stop him, but it doesn't. In he comes. She slides down into the suds until she's eye-level with the edge of the tub. He hesitates. "Go ahead, if you have to," she says, a little awkwardly, "but I'm not getting out." Don't look," he says. She: "I will if I want to."

• • •

She's crying. Mark is rubbing his jaw where he's just slugged him. A lamp lies shattered. "Enough's enough. Mark! Now get outa here!" Her skirt is ripped to the waist, her bare hip bruised. Her panties lie on the floor like a broken balloon. Later, he'll wash her wounds, help her dress, he'll take care of her. Pity washes through him, giving him a sudden hard-on. Mark laughs at it, pointing. Jack crouches, waiting, ready for anything.

• • •

Laughing, they roll and tumble. Their little hands are all over her, digging and pinching. She struggles to her hands and knees, but Bitsy leaps astride her neck, bowing her head to the carpet. "Spank her, Jimmy!" His swats sting: is her skirt up? The phone rings. "The cavalry to the rescue!" she laughs, and throws them off to go answer.

• • •

Kissing Mark, her eyes closed, her hips nudge toward Jack. He stares at the TV screen, unsure of himself, one hand slipping cautiously under her skirt. Her hand touches his arm as though to resist, then brushes on by to rub his leg. This blanket they're under was a good idea. "Hi! This is Jack!"

• • •

Bitsy's out and the water's running. "Come on, Jimmy, your turn!" Last time, he told her he took his own baths, but she came in anyway. "I'm not gonna take a bath," he announces, eyes glued on the set. He readies for the struggle. "But I've already run your water. Come on, Jimmy, please!" He shakes his head. She can't make him, he's sure he's as strong as she is. She sighs. "Well, it's up to you. I'll use the water myself then," she says. He waits until he's pretty sure she's not going to change her mind, then sneaks in and peeks through the keyhole in the bathroom door: just in time to see her big bottom as she bends over to stir in the bubblebath. Then she disappears. Trying to see as far down as the keyhole will allow, he bumps his head on the knob. "Jimmy, is that you?" "I—I have to go to the bathroom!" he stammers.

• • •

Not actually in the tub, just getting in. One foot on the mat, the other in the water. Bent over slightly, buttocks flexed, teats swaying, holding on to the edge of the tub. "Oh, excuse me! I only wanted. . . .!" He passes over her astonishment, the awkward excuses, moves quickly to the part where he reaches out to— "What on earth are you doing, Harry?" his wife asks, staring at his hand. His host, passing, laughs. "He's practicing his swing for Sunday, Dolly, but it's not going to do him a damn bit of good!" Mr. Tucker laughs, sweeps his right hand on through the air as though lifting a seven-iron shot onto the green. He makes a *dok!* sound with his tongue. "In there!"

• • •

"No, Jack, I don't think you'd better." "Well, we just called, we just, uh, thought we'd, you know, stop by for a minute, watch television for thirty minutes, or, or something." "Who's we?" "Well, Mark's here, I'm with him, and he said he'd like to, you know, like if it's all right, just—" "Well, it's *not* all right. The Tuckers said no." "Yeah, but if we only—" "And they seemed awfully suspicious about last time." "Why? We didn't—I mean, I just thought—" "No, Jack, and that's period." She hangs up. She returns to the TV, but the commercial is on. Anyway, she's missed most of the show. She decides maybe she'll take a quick bath. Jack might come by anyway, it'd make her mad, that'd be the end as far as he was concerned, but if he should, she doesn't want to be all sweaty. And besides, she likes the big tub the Tuckers have.

• • •

He is self-conscious and stands with his back to her, his little neck flushed. It takes him forever to get started, and when it finally does come, it's just a tiny trickle. "See, it was just an excuse," she scolds, but she's giggling inwardly at the boy's embarrassment. "You're just a nuisance, Jimmy." At the door, his hand on the knob, he hesitates, staring timidly down on his shoes. "Jimmy?" She peeks at him over the edge of the tub, trying to keep a straight face, as he sneaks a nervous glance back over his shoulder. "As long as you bothered me," she says, "you might as well soap my back."

• • •

"The aspirin . . ." They embrace. She huddles in his arms like a child. Lovingly, paternally, knowledgeably, he wraps her nakedness. How compact, how tight and small her body is! Kissing her ear, he stares down past her rump at the still clear water. "I'll join you," he whispers hoarsely.

• • •

She picks up the shorts Bitsy threw at her. Men's underwear. She holds them in front of her, looks at herself in the bedroom mirror. About twenty sizes too big for her, of course. She runs her hand inside the opening in front, pulls out her thumb. How funny it must feel!

• • •

"Well, man, I say we just go rape her," Mark says flatly, and swings his weight against the pinball machine. "Uff! Ahh! Get in there, you mother! Look at that! Hah! Man, I'm gonna turn this baby over!" Jack is embarrassed about the phone conversation. Mark just snorted in disgust when he hung up. He cracks down hard on his gum, angry that he's such a chicken. "Well, I'm game if you are," he says coldly.

• • •

8:30 "Okay, come on, Jimmy, it's time." He ignores her. The western gives way to a spy show. Bitsy, in pajamas, pads into the livingroom. "No, Bitsy, it's time to go to bed." "You said I could watch!" the girl whines, and starts to throw another tantrum. "But you were too slow and it's late. Jimmy, you get in that bathroom, and right now!" Jimmy stares sullenly at the set, unmoving. The babysitter tries to catch the opening scene of the television program so she can follow it later, since Jimmy gives himself his own baths. When the commercial interrupts, she turns off the sound, stands in front of the screen. "Okay, into the tub, Jimmy Tucker, or I'll take you in there and give you your bath myself!" "Just try it," he says, "and see what happens."

• • •

They stand outside, in the dark, crouched in the bushes, peeking in. She's on the floor, playing with the kids. Too early. They seem to be tickling her. She gets to her hands and knees, but the little girl leaps on her head, pressing her face to the floor. There's an obvious target, and the little boy proceeds to beat on it. "Hey, look at that kid go!" whispers Mark, laughing and snapping his fingers softly. Jack feels uneasy out here. Too many neighbors, too many cars going by, too many people in the world. That little boy in there is one up on him, though: he's never thought about tickling her as a starter.

• • •

His little hand, clutching the bar of soap, lathers shyly a narrow space between her shoulderblades. She is doubled forward against her knees, buried in rich suds, peeking at him over the edge of her shoulder. The soap slithers out of his grip and plunks into the water. "I . . . I dropped the soap," he whispers. She: "Find it."

• • •

"I dream of Jeannie with the light brown pubic hair!"[2] "Harry! Stop that! You're drunk!" But they're laughing, they're all laughing, damn! he's feeling pretty goddamn good at that, and now he just knows he needs that aspirin. Watching her there, her thighs spread for him, on the couch, in the tub, hell, on the kitchen table for that matter, he tees off on Number Nine, and —*whap!*—swats his host's wife on the

2. Parody of actual song title, *I Dream of Jeannie with the Light Brown Hair.*

bottom. "Hole in one!" he shouts. "Harry!" Why can't his goddamn wife Dolly ever get happy-drunk instead of sour-drunk all the time? "Gonna be tough Sunday, old buddy!" "You're pretty tough right now, Harry," says his host.

• • •

The babysitter lunges forward, grabs the boy by the arms and hauls him off the couch, pulling two cushions with him, and drags him toward the bathroom. He lashes out, knocking over an endtable full of magazines and ashtrays. "You leave my brother alone!" Bitsy cries and grabs the sitter around the waist. Jimmy jumps on her and down they all go. On the silent screen, there's a fade-in to a dark passageway in an old apartment building in some foreign country. She kicks out and somebody falls between her legs. Somebody else is sitting on her face. "Jimmy! Stop that!" the babysitter laughs, her voice muffled.

• • •

She's watching television. All alone. It seems like a good time to go in. Just remember: really, no matter what she says, she wants it. They're standing in the bushes, trying to get up the nerve. "We'll tell her to be good," Mark whispers, "and if she's not good, we'll spank her." Jack giggles softly, but his knees are weak. She stands. They freeze. She looks right at them. "She can't see us." Mark whispers tensely. "Is she coming out?" "No," says Mark, "she's going into—that must be the bathroom!" Jack takes a deep breath, his heart pounding. "Hey, is there a window back there?" Mark asks.

• • •

The phone rings. She leaves the tub, wrapped in a towel. Bitsy gives a tug on the towel. "Hey, Jimmy, get the towel!" she squeals. "Now stop that, Bitsy!" the babysitter hisses, but too late: with one hand on the phone, the other isn't enough to hang on to the towel. Her sudden nakedness awes them and it takes them a moment to remember about tickling her. By then, she's in the towel again. "I hope you got a good look," she says angrily. She feels chilled and oddly a little frightened. "Hello?" No answer. She glances at the window—is somebody out there? Something, she saw something, and a rustling—footsteps?

• • •

"Okay, I don't care, Jimmy, don't take a bath," she says irritably. Her blouse is pulled out and wrinkled, her hair is all mussed, and she feels sweaty. There's about a million things she'd rather be doing than babysitting with these two. Three: at least the baby's sleeping. She knocks on the overturned endtable for luck, rights it, replaces the magazines and ashtrays. The one thing that really makes her sick is a dirty diaper. "Just go on to bed." "I don't have to go to bed until nine," he reminds her. Really, she couldn't care less. She turns up the volume on the TV, settles down on the couch, poking her blouse back into her skirt, pushing her hair out of her eyes. Jimmy and Bitsy watch from the floor. Maybe, once they're in bed, she'll take a quick bath. She wishes Jack would come by. The man, no doubt the spy, is following a woman, but she doesn't know why. The woman passes another man. Something seems to happen, but it's not clear what. She's probably already missed too much. The phone rings.

• • •

Mark is kissing her. Jack is under the blanket, easing her panties down over her squirming hips. Her hand is in his pants, pulling it out, pulling it toward her, pulling it hard. She knew just where it was! Mark is stripping, too. God, it's really happening! he thinks with a kind of pious joy, and notices the open door. "Hey!" What's going on here?"

• • •

He soaps her back, smooth and slippery under his hand. She is doubled over, against her knees, between his legs. Her light brown hair, reaching to her gleaming shoulders, is wet at the edges. The soap slips, falls between his legs. He fishes for it, finds it, slips it behind him. "Help me find it," he whispers in her ear. "Sure Harry," says his host, going around behind him. "What'd you lose?"

• • •

Soon be nine, time to pack the kids off to bed. She clears the table, dumps paper plates and leftover hamburgers into the garbage, puts glasses and silverware into the sink, and the mayonnaise, mustard, and ketchup in the refrigerator. Neither child has eaten much supper finally, mostly potato chips and ice cream, but it's really not her problem. She glances at the books on the refrigerator. Not much chance she'll get to them, she's already pretty worn out. Maybe she'd feel better if she had a quick bath. She runs water into the tub, tosses in bubblebath salts, undresses. Before pushing down her panties, she stares for a moment at the smooth silken panel across her tummy, fingers the place where the opening would be if there were one. Then she steps quickly out of them, feeling somehow ashamed, unhooks her brassiere. She weighs her breasts in the palms of her hands, watching herself in the bathroom mirror, where, in the open window behind her, she sees a face. She screams.

• • •

She screams: "Jimmy! Give me that!" "What's the matter?" asks Jack on the other end. "Jimmy! Give me my towel! Right now!" "Hello? Hey, are you still there?" "I'm sorry, Jack," she says, panting. "You caught me in the tub. I'm just wrapped in a towel and these silly kids grabbed it away!" "Gee, I wish I'd been there!" "Jack—!" "To protect you, I mean." "Oh, sure," she says, giggling. "Well, what do you think, can I come over and watch TV with you?" "Well, not right this minute," she says. He laughs lightly. He feels very cool. "Jack?" "Yeah?" "Jack, I . . . I think there's somebody outside the window!"

• • •

She carries him, fighting all the way, to the tub, Bitsy pummeling her in the back and kicking her ankles. She can't hang on to him and undress him at the same time. "I'll throw you in, clothes and all, Jimmy Tucker!" she gasps. "You better not!" he cries. She sits on the toilet seat, locks her legs around him, whips his shirt up over his head before he knows what's happening. The pants are easier. Like all little boys his age, he has almost no hips at all. He hangs on desperately to his underpants, but when she succeeds in snapping these down out of his grip, too, he gives up, starts to bawl, and beats her wildly in the face with his fists. She ducks her head, laughing hysterically, oddly entranced by the spectacle of that pale little thing down there, bobbing and bouncing rubberlike about the boy's helpless fury and anguish.

• • •

"Aspirin? Whaddaya want aspirin for, Harry? I'm sure they got aspirin here, if you—" "Did I say aspirin? I meant uh, my glasses. And, you know, I thought, well, I'd sorta check to see if everything was okay at home." Why the hell is it his mouth feels like it's got about six sets of teeth packed in there, and a tongue the size of that liverwurst his host's wife is passing around? "Whaddaya want your glasses for, Harry? I don't understand you at all?" "Aw, well, honey, I was feeling kind of dizzy or something, and I thought—" "Dizzy is right. If you want to check on the kids, why don't you just call on the phone?"

• • •

They can tell she's naked and about to get into the tub, but the bathroom window is frosted glass, and they can't see anything clearly. "I got an idea," Mark whispers. "One of us goes and calls her on the phone, and the other watches when she comes out." "Okay, but who calls?" "Both of us, we'll do it twice. Or more."

• • •

Down forbidden alleys. Into secret passageways. Unlocking the world's terrible secrets. Sudden shocks: a trapdoor! a fall! or the stunning report of a rifle shot, the *whaaii-ii-ing!* of the bullet biting concrete by your ear! Careful! Then edge forward once more, avoiding the light, inch at a time, now a quick dash for an open doorway—*look out!* there's a knife! a struggle! no! the long blade glistens! jerks! thrusts! *stabbed!* No, no, it missed! The assailant's down, yes! the spy's on top, pinning him, a terrific thrashing about, the spy rips off the assailant's mask: *a woman!*

• • •

Fumbling behind her, she finds it, wraps her hands around it, tugs. "Oh!" she gasps, pulling her hand back quickly, her ears turning crimson. "I . . . I thought it was the soap!" He squeezes her close between his thighs, pulls her back toward him, one hand sliding down her tummy between her legs. I Dream of Jeannie— "I have to go to the bathroom!" says someone outside the door.

• • •

She's combing her hair in the bathroom when the phone rings. She hurries to answer it before it wakes the baby. "Hello, Tuckers." There's no answer. "Hello?" A soft click. Strange. She feels suddenly alone in the big house, and goes in to watch TV with the children.

• • •

"Stop it!" she screams, "Please stop!" She's on her hands and knees, trying to get up, but they're too strong for her. Mark holds her head down. "Now, baby, we're gonna teach you how to be a nice girl," he says coldly, and nods at Jack. When she's doubled over like that, her skirt rides up her thighs to the leg bands of her panties. "C'mon, man, go! This baby's cold! She needs your touch!"

• • •

Parks the car a couple blocks away. Slips up to the house, glances in his window. Just like he's expected. Her blouse is off and the kid's shirt is unbuttoned. He watches, while slowly, clumsily, childishly, they fumble with each other's clothes. My God, it takes them forever. "Some party!" "You said it!" When they're more or less naked, he walks in. "Hey! What's going on here?" They go white as bleu cheese. Haw haw! "What's the little thing you got sticking out there, boy?" "Harry, behave yourself!" No, he doesn't let the kid get dressed, he sends him home bareassed. "Bareassed!" He drinks to that. "Promises, promises," says his host's wife. "I'll mail you your clothes, son!" He gazes down on the naked little girl on his couch. "Looks like you and me, we got a little secret to keep, honey," he says coolly. "Less you wanna go home the same way your boyfriend did!" He chuckles at his easy wit, leans down over her, and unbuckles his belt. "Might as well make it two secrets, right?" "What in God's name are you talking about, Harry?" He staggers out of there, drink in hand, and goes to look for his car.

• • •

"Hey! What's going on here?" They huddle half-naked under the blanket, caught utterly unawares. On television: the clickety-click of frightened running feet on foreign pavements. Jack is fumbling for his shorts, tangled somehow around his ankles. The blanket is snatched away. "On your feet there!" Mr. Tucker, Mrs. Tucker, and Mark's mom and dad, the police, the neighbors, everybody comes crowding in. Hopelessly, he has a terrific erection. So hard it hurts. Everybody stares down at it.

• • •

Bitsy's sleeping on the floor. The babysitter is taking a bath. For more than an hour now, he'd had to use the bathroom. He doesn't know how much longer he can wait. Finally, he goes to knock on the bathroom door. "I have to use the bathroom." "Well, come ahead, if you have to." "Not while you're in there." She sighs loudly. "Okay, okay, just a minute," she says, "but you're a real nuisance, Jimmy!" He's holding on, pinching it as tight as he can. *"Hurry!"* He holds his breath, squeezing shut his eyes. No. Too late. At last, she opens the door. "Jimmy!" "I *told* you to hurry!" he sobs. She drags him into the bathroom and pulls his pants down.

• • •

He arrives just in time to see her emerge from the bathroom, wrapped in a towel, to answer the phone. His two kids sneak up behind her and pull the towel away. She's trying to hang onto the phone and get the towel back at the same time. It's quite a picture. She's got a sweet ass. Standing there in the bushes, pawing himself with one hand, he lifts his glass with the other and toasts her sweet ass, which his son now swats. Haw haw, maybe that boy's gonna shape up, after all.

• • •

They're in the bushes, arguing about their next move, when she comes out of the bathroom, wrapped in a towel. They can hear the baby crying. Then it stops. They see her running, naked, back to the bathroom like she's scared or something. "I'm going in after her, man, whether you're with me or not!" Mark whispers, and he starts out of the bushes. But just then, a light comes sweeping up through the yard, as a car swings in the drive. They hit the dirt, hearts pounding. "Is it the cops?" "I don't know!" "Do you think they saw us?" "Sshh!" A man comes staggering up the walk from the drive, a drink in his hand, stumbles on in the kitchen door and then straight into the bathroom. "It's Mr. Tucker!" Mark whispers. A scream. "Let's get outa here, man!"

• • •

9:00. Having missed most of the spy show anyway and having little else to do, the babysitter has washed the dishes and cleaned the kitchen up a little. The books on the refrigerator remind her of her better intentions, but she decides that first she'll see what's next on TV. In the livingroom, she finds little Bitsy sound asleep on the floor. She lifts her gently, carries her into her bed, and tucks her in. "Okay, Jimmy, it's nine o'clock, I've let you stay up, now be a good boy." Sullenly, his sleepy eyes glued still to the set, the boy backs out of the room toward his bedroom. A drama comes on. She switches channels. A ballgame and a murder mystery. She switches back to the drama. It's a love story of some kind. A man married to an aging invalid wife, but in love with a younger girl. "Use the bathroom and brush your teeth before going to bed, Jimmy!" she calls, but as quickly regrets it, for she hears the baby stir in its crib.

• • •

Two of them are talking about mothers they've salted away in rest homes. Oh boy, that's just wonderful, this is one helluva party. She leaves them to use the john, takes advantage of the retreat to ease her girdle down awhile, get a few good deep breaths. She has this picture of her three kids carting her off to a rest home. In a wheelbarrow. That sure is something to look forward to, all right. When she pulls her girdle back up, she can't seem to squeeze into it. The host looks in. "Hey, Dolly, are you all right?" "Yeah, I just can't get into my damn girdle, that's all." "Here, let me help."

• • •

She pulls them on, over her own, standing in front of the bedroom mirror, holding her skirt bundled up around the waist. About twenty sizes too big for her, of course. She pulls them tight from behind, runs her hand inside the opening in front, pulls out her thumb. "And what a good boy am I!" She giggles: how funny it must feel! Then, in the mirror, she sees him: in the doorway behind her, sullenly watching. "Jimmy! You're supposed to be in bed!" "Those are my daddy's!" the boy says. "I'm gonna tell!"

• • •

"Jimmy!" she drags him into the bathroom and pulls his pants down. "Even your shoes are wet! Get them off!" She soaps up a warm washcloth she's had with her in the bathtub, scrubs him from the waist down with it. Bitsy stands in the doorway, staring. "Get out! Get out!" the boy screams at his sister. "'Go back to bed, Bitsy. It's just an accident." "Get out!" The baby wakes and starts to howl.

• • •

The young lover feels sorry for her rival, the invalid wife; she believes the man has a duty toward the poor woman and insists she is willing to wait. But the man argues that he also has a duty toward himself: his life, too, is short, and he could not love his wife now even were she well. He embraces the young girl feverishly; she twists away in anguish. The door opens. They stand there grinning, looking devilish, but pretty silly at the same time. "Jack! I thought I told you not to come!" She's angry, but she's also glad in a way: she was beginning to feel a little too alone in the big house, with the children all sleeping. She should have taken that bath, after all. "We just came by to see if you were being a good girl," Jack says and blushes. The boys glance at each other nervously.

• • •

She's just sunk down into the tubful of warm fragrant suds, ready for a nice long soaking, when the phone rings. Wrapping a towel around her, she goes to answer: no one there. But now the baby's awake and bawling. She wonders if that's Jack bothering her all the time. If it is, brother, that's the end. Maybe it's the end anyway. She tries to calm the baby with the half-empty bottle, not wanting to change it until she's finished her bath. The bathroom's where the diapers go dirty, and they make it stink to high heaven. "Shush, shush!" she whispers, rocking the crib. The towel slips away, leaving an airy empty tingle up and down her backside. Even before she stoops for the towel, even before she turns around, she knows there's somebody behind her.

• • •

"We just came by to see if you were being a good girl," Jack says, grinning down at her. She's flushed and silent, her mouth half open. "Lean over," says Mark amiably. "We'll soap your back, as long as we're here." But she just huddles there, down in the suds, staring up at them with big eyes.

• • •

"Hey! What's going on here?" It's Mr. Tucker, stumbling through the door with a drink in his hand. She looks up from the TV. "What's the matter, Mr. Tucker?" "Oh, uh, I'm sorry, I got lost—no, I mean, I had to get some aspirin. Excuse me!" And he rushes past her into the bathroom, caroming off the livingroom door jamb on the way. The baby awakes.

• • •

"Okay, get off her, Mr. Tucker!" "Jack!" she cries, "what are *you* doing here?" He stares hard at them a moment: so that's where it goes. Then, as Mr. Tucker swings heavily off, he leans into the bastard with a hard right to the belly. Next thing he knows, though, he's got a face full of an old man's fist. He's not sure, as the lights go out, if that's his girlfriend screaming or the baby . . .

• • •

Her host pushes down on her fat fanny and tugs with all his might on her girdle, while she bawls on his shoulder: "I don't *wanna* go to a rest home!" "Now, now take it easy, Dolly, nobody's gonna make you—" "Ouch! Hey, you're hurting!" "You should buy a bigger girdle, Dolly." "You're telling me?" Some other guy pokes his head in. "Whatsa-matter? Dolly fall in?" "No, she fell out. Give me a hand."

• • •

By the time she's chased Jack and Mark out of there, she's lost track of the program she's been watching on television. There's another woman in the story now for some reason. That guy lives a very complicated life. Impatiently, she switches channels. She hates ballgames, so she settles for the murder mystery. She switches just in time, too: there's a dead man sprawled out on the floor of what looks like an office or a study or something. A heavyset detective gazes up from his crouch over the body: "He's been strangled." Maybe she'll take that bath, after all.

• • •

She drags him into the bathroom and pulls his pants down. She soaps up a warm washcloth she's had in the tub with her, but just as she reaches between his legs, it starts to spurt, spraying her arms and hands. "Oh, Jimmy! I thought you were done!" she cries, pulling him toward the toilet and aiming it into the bowl. How moist and rubbery it is! And you can turn it every which way. How funny it must feel!

• • •

"Stop it!" she screams. "Please stop!" She's on her hands and knees and Jack is holding her head down. "Now we're gonna teach you how to be a nice girl," Mark says and lifts her skirt. "Well, I'll be damned!" "What's the matter?" asks Jack, his heart pounding. "Look at this big pair of men's underpants she's got on!" "Those are my daddy's!" says Jimmy, watching them from the doorway. "I'm gonna tell!"

• • •

People are shooting at each other in the murder mystery, but she's so mixed up, she doesn't know which ones are the good guys. She switches back to the love story. Something seems to have happened, because now the man is kissing his invalid wife tenderly. Maybe she's finally dying. The baby wakes, begins to scream. Let it. She turns up the volume on the TV.

• • •

Leaning down over her, unbuckling his belt. It's all happening just like he's known it would. Beautiful! The kid is gone, though his pants, poor lad, remain. "Looks like you and me, we got a secret to keep, child!" But he's cramped on the couch and everything is too slippery and small. "Lift your legs up, honey. Put them around my back." But instead, she screams. He rolls off, crashing to the floor. There they all come, through the front door. On television, somebody is saying: "Am I a burden to you, darling?" "Dolly! My God! Dolly, I can explain . . . !"

• • •

The game of the night is Get Dolly Tucker Back in Her Girdle Again. They've got her down on her belly in the livingroom and the whole damn crowd is working on her. Several of them are stretching the girdle, while others try to jam the fat inside. "I think we made a couple inches on this side! Roll her over!" Harry?

• • •

She's just stepped into the tub, when the phone rings, waking the baby. She sinks down in the suds, trying not to hear. But that baby doesn't cry, it screams. Angrily, she wraps a towel around herself, stamps peevishly into the baby's room, just letting the phone jangle. She tosses the baby down on its back, unpins its diapers hastily, and gets yellowish baby stool all over her hands. Her towel drops away. She turns to find Jimmy staring at her like a little idiot. She slaps him in the face with her dirty hand, while the baby screams, the phone rings, and nagging voices argue on the TV. There are better things she might be doing.

• • •

What's happening? Now there's a young guy in it. Is he after the young girl or the old invalid? To tell the truth, it looks like he's after the same man the women are. In disgust, she switches channels. "The strangler again," growls the fat detective, hands on hips, staring down at the body of a half-naked girl. She's considering either switching back to the love story or taking a quick bath, when a hand suddenly clutches her mouth.

• • •

"You're both chicken," she says, staring up at them. "But what if Mr. Tucker comes home?" Mark asks nervously.

• • •

How did he get here? He's standing pissing in his own goddamn bathroom, his wife is still back at the party, the three of them are, like good kids, sitting in there in the livingroom watching TV. One of them is his host's boy Mark. "It's a good murder mystery, Mr. Tucker," Mark said, when he came staggering in on them a minute ago. "Sit still!" he shouted, "I am just home for a moment!" Then whump thump on into the bathroom. Long hike for a wee-wee, Mister. But something keeps bothering him. Then it hits him: the girl's panties hanging like a broken balloon from the rabbit-ear antennae on the TV! He barges back in there, giving his shoulder a helluva crack on the livingroom door jamb on the way—but they're not hanging there any more. Maybe he's only imagined it. "Hey, Mr. Tucker," Mark says flatly. "Your fly's open."

• • •

The baby's dirty. Stinks to high heaven. She hurries back to the livingroom, hearing sirens and gunshots. The detective is crouched outside a house, peering in. Already, she's completely lost. The baby screams at the top of its lungs. She turns up the volume. But it's all confused. She hurries back in there, claps an angry hand to the baby's mouth. "Shut up!" she cries. She throws the baby down on its back, starts to unpin the diaper, as the baby tunes up again. The phone rings. She answers it, one eye on the TV. "*What?*" The baby cries so hard it starts to choke. Let it. "I said, hi, this is Jack!" Then it hits her: oh no! the diaper pin!

• • •

"The aspirin . . ." But she's already in the tub. Way down in the tub. Staring at him through the water. Her tummy looks pale and ripply. He hears sirens, people on the porch.

• • •

Jimmy gets up to go to the bathroom and gets his face slapped and smeared with baby poop. Then she hauls him off to the bathroom, yanks off his pajamas, and throws him into the tub. That's okay, but next she gets naked and acts like she's gonna get in the tub, too. The baby's screaming and the phone's ringing like crazy and in walks his dad. Saved! he thinks, but, no, his dad grabs him right back out of the tub and whales the dickens out of him, no questions asked, while she watches, then sends him—*whack!*—back to bed. So he's lying there, wet and dirty and naked and sore, and he still has to go to the bathroom, and outside his window he hears two older guys talking. "Listen, you know where to do it if we get her pinned?" "No! Don't you?"

• • •

"Yo ho heave ho! *Ugh!*" Dolly's on her back and they're working on the belly side. Somebody got the great idea of buttering her down first. Not to lose the ground they've gained, they've shot it inside with a basting syringe. But now suddenly there's this big tug-of-war under way between those who want to stuff her in and those who want to let her out. Something rips, but she feels better. The odor of hot butter makes her think of movie theaters and popcorn. "Hey, has anybody seen Harry?" she asks. "Where's Harry?"

• • •

Somebody's getting chased. She switches back to the love story, and now the man's back kissing the young lover again. What's going on? She gives it up, decides to take a quick bath. She's just stepping into the tub, one foot in, one foot out, when Mr. Tucker walks in. "Oh, excuse me! I only wanted some aspirin . . ." She grabs for a towel, but he yanks it away. "Now, that's not how it's supposed to happen, child," he scolds. "Please! Mr. Tucker . . . !" He embraces her savagely, his calloused old hands clutching roughly at her backside. "Mr. Tucker!" she cries, squirming. "Your wife called—!" He's pushing something between her legs, hurting her. She slips, they both slip—something cold and hard slams her in the back, cracks her skull, she seems to be sinking into a sea . . .

• • •

They've got her over the hassock, skirt up and pants down. "Give her a little lesson there, Jack baby!" The television lights flicker and flash over her glossy flesh, 1000 WHEN LIT. Whack! Slap! Bumper to bumper! He leans into her, feeling her come alive.

• • •

The phone rings, waking the baby. "Jack, is that you? Now, you listen to me—" "No, dear, this is Mrs. Tucker. Isn't the TV awfully loud?" "Oh, I'm sorry, Mrs. Tucker! I've been getting—" "I tried to call you before, but I couldn't hang on. To the phone, I mean. I'm sorry, dear."

"Just a minute, Mrs. Tucker, the baby's—" "Honey, listen! Is Harry there? Is Mr. Tucker there, dear?"

• • •

"Stop it!" she screams and claps a hand over the baby's mouth. "Stop it! Stop it! *Stop it!*" Her other hand is full of baby stool and she's afraid she's going to be sick. The phone rings. "No!" she cries. She's hanging on to the baby, leaning woozily away, listening to the phone ring. "Okay, okay," she sighs, getting ahold of herself. But when she lets go of the baby, it isn't screaming any more. She shakes it. Oh no . . .

• • •

"Hello?" No answer. Strange. She hangs up and, wrapped only in a towel, stares out the window at the cold face staring in—she screams!

• • •

She screams, scaring the hell out of him. He leaps out of the tub, glances up at the window she's gaping at just in time to see two faces duck away, then slips on the bathroom tiles, and crashes to his ass, whacking his head on the sink on the way down. She stares down at him, trembling, a towel over her narrow shoulders. "Mr. Tucker! Mr. Tucker, are you all right . . . ?" Who's Sorry Now? Yessir, who's back is breaking with each . . . He stares up at the little tufted locus of all his woes, and passes out, dreaming of Jeannie . . .

• • •

The phone rings. "Dolly! It's for you!" "Hello?" "Hello, Mrs. Tucker?" "Yes, speaking." "Mrs. Tucker, this is the police calling . . ."

• • •

It's cramped and awkward and slippery, but he's pretty sure he got it in her, once anyway. When he gets the suds out of his eyes, he sees her staring up at them. Through the water. "Hey, Mark! Let her up!"

• • •

Down in the suds. Feeling sleepy. The phone rings, startling her. Wrapped in a towel, she goes to answer. "No, he's not here, Mrs. Tucker." Strange. Married people act pretty funny sometimes. The baby is awake and screaming. Dirty, a real mess. Oh boy, there's a lot of things she'd rather be doing than babysitting in this madhouse. She decides to wash the baby off in her own bathwater. She removes her towel, unplugs the tub, lowers the water level so the baby can sit. Glancing back over her shoulder, she sees Jimmy staring at her. "Go back to bed, Jimmy." "I have to go to the bathroom." "Good grief, Jimmy! It looks like you already have!" The phone rings. She doesn't bother with the towel—what can Jimmy see he hasn't already seen?—and goes to answer. "No, Jack, and that's final." Sirens, on the TV, as the police move in. But wasn't that the channel with the love story? Ambulance maybe. Get this over with so she can at least catch the news. "Get those wet pajamas off, Jimmy, and I'll find clean ones.

Maybe you better get in the tub, too." "I think something's wrong with the baby," he says. "It's down in the water and it's not swimming or anything."

• • •

She's staring up at them from the rug. They slap her. Nothing happens. "You just tilted her, man!" Mark says softly. "We gotta get outa here!" Two little kids are standing wideeyed in the doorway. Mark looks hard at Jack. "No, Mark, they're just little kids . . . !" "We gotta, man, or we're dead."

• • •

"Dolly! My God! Dolly, I can explain!" She glowers down at them, her ripped girdle around her ankles. "What the four of you are doing in the bathtub with *my* babysitter?" she says sourly. "I can hardly wait!"

• • •

Police sirens wail, lights flash. "I heard the scream!" somebody shouts. "There were two boys!" "I saw a man!" "She was running with the baby!" "My God!" somebody screams, "they're *all* dead!" Crowds come running. Spotlights probe the bushes.

• • •

"Harry, where the hell you been?" his wife whines, glaring blearily up at him from the carpet. "I can explain," he says. "Hey, whatsamatter, Harry?" his host asks, smeared with butter for some goddamn reason. "You look like you just seen a ghost!" Where did he leave his drink? Everybody's laughing, everybody except Dolly, whose cheeks are streaked with tears. "Hey, Harry, you won't let them take me to a rest home, will you, Harry?"

• • •

10:00. The dishes done, children to bed, her books read, she watches the news on television. Sleepy. The man's voice is gentle, soothing. She dozes—awakes with a start: a babysitter? Did the announcer say something about a babysitter?

• • •

"Just want to catch the weather," the host says, switching on the TV. Most of the guests are leaving, but the Tuckers stay to watch the news. As it comes on, the announcer is saying something about a babysitter. The host switches channels. "They got a better weatherman on four," he explains. "Wait!" says Mrs. Tucker. "There was something about a babysitter . . . !" The host switches back. "Details have not yet been released by the police," the announcer says. "Harry, maybe we'd better go . . ."

• • •

They stroll casually out of the drugstore, run into a buddy of theirs. "Hey! Did you hear about the babysitter?" the guy asks. Mark grunts, glances at Jack. "Got a smoke?" he asks the guy.

• • •

"I think I hear the baby screaming!" Mrs. Tucker cries, running across the lawn from the drive.

• • •

She wakes, startled, to find Mr. Tucker hovering over her. "I must have dozed off!" she exclaims. "Did you hear the news about the babysitter?" Mr. Tucker asks. "Part of it," she says, rising. "Too bad, wasn't it?" Mr. Tucker is watching the report of the ball scores and golf tournaments. "I'll drive you home in just a minute, dear," he says. "Why, how nice!" Mrs. Tucker exclaims from the kitchen. "The dishes are all done!"

• • •

"What can I say, Dolly?" the host says with a sigh, twisting the buttered strands of her ripped girdle between his fingers. "Your children are murdered, your husband gone, a corpse in your bathtub, and your house is wrecked. I'm sorry. But what can I say?" On the TV, the news is over, and they're selling aspirin. "Hell, *I* don't know," she says. "Let's see what's on the late late movie."

---

1. What comment does the story make about the way we live now? About such features of American life as babysitting, cocktail parties, and pinball machines?
2. Cite some instances in which fact blurs into fantasy. How do these blurrings comment on the social patterns in which the characters exist and act?
3. Why is the story separated into multiple points of view? Do these shifts from paragraph to paragraph help to keep the characters and the strands of action relatively distinct?
4. How are the images on the television screen related to the actions of the real characters?
5. The characters can be categorized in three distinct age levels: adults, adolescents, and children. Is there more consistency and rationality at one level than at the others?
6. Is it easier to keep the characters and situation straight at the beginning or at the end? How does the relative confusion or clarity relate to the meaning of the story as a whole?

Stephen Crane

Crane (1871–1900) was born in Newark, New Jersey, the son of a Methodist minister. After schooling at Lafayette College and Syracuse University, he worked in New York as a freelance journalist. In 1893 he published at his own expense Maggie: A Girl of the Streets, *a pioneering work of sociological realism. Two years later he brought out his famous short novel about the Civil War,* The Red Badge of Courage, *which in theme and technique foreshadows the war novels of the twentieth century. His short stories and experimental poetry also anticipate the ironic realism of the decades ahead. In his brief and energetic life he published fourteen books while acting out, in his personal adventures, the legend of the writer as soldier of fortune. On his way to Cuba for the first time he picked up a mistress at the Hotel de Dream in Jacksonville, Florida—a woman who accompanied him when he went on to Greece as a war correspondent. Malicious gossip about his private life subsequently drove him from America to England, where he settled in 1897 and made friends with leading English writers. In his travels he had accumulated a malignant tangle of debts. He was trying to free himself of them by writing when tuberculosis killed him, his promise only partially fulfilled. His short stories were collected in* The Open Boat and Other Tales of Adventure *(1898),* The Monster and Other Stories *(1899), and* Wounds in the Rain *(1900). His complete works in prose and verse were published in 1925–26.*

The Open Boat

A *Tale Intended to Be after the Fact:*[1] *Being the Experience of Four Men from the Sunk Steamer* COMMODORE

I

None of them knew the color of the sky. Their eyes glanced level and were fastened upon the waves that swept toward them. These waves were of the hue of slate, save for the tops, which were of foaming white, and all of the men knew the colors of the sea. The horizon narrowed and widened, and dipped and rose, and at all times its edge was jagged with waves that seemed thrust up in points like rocks.

1. Crane underwent the adventure that is here recreated in fiction. He also wrote a journalistic account of it, published in the New York *Press*, January 7, 1897.

Many a man ought to have a bathtub larger than the boat which here rode upon the sea. These waves were most wrongfully and barbarously abrupt and tall, and each froth-top was a problem in small-boat navigation.

The cook squatted in the bottom, and looked with both eyes at the six inches of gunwale which separated him from the ocean. His sleeves were rolled over his fat forearms, and the two flaps of his unbuttoned vest dangled as he bent to bail out the boat. Often he said, "Gawd! that was a narrow clip." As he remarked it he invariably gazed eastward over the broken sea.

The oiler, steering with one of the two oars in the boat, sometimes raised himself suddenly to keep clear of water that swirled in over the stern. It was a thin little oar, and it seemed often ready to snap.

The correspondent, pulling at the other oar, watched the waves and wondered why he was there.

The injured captain, lying in the bow, was at this time buried in that profound dejection and indifference which comes, temporarily at least, to even the bravest and most enduring when, willy-nilly, the firm fails, the army loses, the ship goes down. The mind of the master of a vessel is rooted deep in the timbers of her, though he command for a day or a decade; and this captain had on him the stern impression of a scene in the grays of dawn of seven turned faces, and later a stump of a topmast with a white ball on it, that slashed to and fro at the waves, went low and lower, and down. Thereafter there was something strange in his voice. Although steady, it was deep with mourning, and of a quality beyond oration or tears.

"Keep'er a little more south, Billie," said he.

"A little more south, sir," said the oiler in the stern.

A seat in his boat was not unlike a seat upon a bucking broncho, and by the same token a broncho is not much smaller. The craft pranced and reared and plunged like an animal. As each wave came, and she rose for it, she seemed like a horse making at a fence outrageously high. The manner of her scramble over these walls of water is a mystic thing, and, moreover, at the top of them were ordinarily these problems in white water, the foam racing down from the summit of each wave requiring a new leap, and a leap from the air. Then, after scornfully bumping a crest, she would slide and race and splash down a long incline, and arrive bobbing and nodding in front of the next menace.

A singular disadvantage of the sea lies in the fact that after successfully surmounting one wave you discover that there is another behind it just as important and just as nervously anxious to do something effective in the way of swamping boats. In a ten-foot dinghy one can get an idea of the resources of the sea in the line of waves that is not probable to the average experience, which is never at sea in a dinghy. As each slaty wall of water approached, it shut all else from the view of the men in the boat, and it was not difficult to imagine that this particular wave was the final outburst of the ocean, the last effort of the grim water. There was a terrible grace in the move of the waves, and they came in silence, save for the snarling of the crests.

In the wan light the faces of the men must have been gray. Their eyes must have glinted in strange ways as they gazed steadily astern. Viewed from a balcony, the whole thing would, doubtless, have been weirdly picturesque. But the men in the boat had no time to see it, and if they had had leisure, there were other things to occupy their minds. The sun swung steadily up the sky, and they knew it was broad day because the color of the sea changed from slate to emerald-green streaked with amber lights, and the foam was like tumbling snow. The process of the breaking day was unknown to them. They were aware only of this effect upon the color of the waves that rolled toward them.

In disjointed sentences the cook and the correspondent argued as to the difference between a life-saving station and a house of refuge. The cook had said: "There's a house of refuge just north of the Mosquito Inlet Light, and as soon as they see us they'll come off in their boat and pick us up."

"As soon as who see us?" said the correspondent.

"The crew," said the cook.

"Houses of refuge don't have crews," said the correspondent. "As I understand them, they are only places where clothes and grub are stored for the benefit of shipwrecked people. They don't carry crews."

"Oh, yes, they do," said the cook.

"No, they don't," said the correspondent.

"Well, we're not there yet, anyhow," said the oiler, in the stern.

"Well," said the cook, "perhaps it's not a house of refuge that I'm thinking of as being near Mosquito Inlet Light; perhaps it's a life-saving station."

"We're not there yet," said the oiler in the stern.

II

As the boat bounced from the top of each wave the wind tore through the hair of the hatless men, and as the craft plopped her stern down again the spray slashed past them. The crest of each of these waves was a hill, from the top of which the men surveyed for a moment a broad tumultuous expanse, shining and wind-riven. It was probably splendid, it was probably glorious, this play of the free sea, wild with lights of emerald and white and amber.

"Bully good thing it's an on-shore wind," said the cook. "If not, where would we be? Wouldn't have a show."

"That's right," said the correspondent.

The busy oiler nodded his assent.

Then the captain, in the bow, chuckled in a way that expressed humor, contempt, tragedy, all in one. "Do you think we've got much of a show now, boys?" said he.

Whereupon the three were silent, save for a trifle of hemming and hawing. To express any particular optimism at this time they felt to be childish and stupid, but they all doubtless possessed this sense of the situation in their minds. A young man thinks doggedly at such times. On the other hand, the ethics of their condition was decidedly against any open suggestion of hopelessness. So they were silent.

"Oh, well," said the captain, soothing his children, "we'll get ashore all right."

But there was that in his tone which made them think; so the oiler quoth, "Yes! if this wind holds."

The cook was bailing. "Yes! if we don't catch hell in the surf."

Canton-flannel[2] gulls flew near and far. Sometimes they sat down on the sea, near patches of brown seaweed that rolled over the waves with a movement like carpets on a line in a gale. The birds sat comfortably in groups, and they were envied by some in the dinghy, for the wrath of the sea was no more to them than it was to a covey of prairie chickens a thousand miles inland. Often they came very close and stared at the men with black bead-like eyes. At these times they were uncanny and sinister in their unblinking scrutiny, and the men hooted angrily at them, telling them to be gone. One came, and evidently decided to alight on the top of the captain's head. The bird flew parallel to the boat and did not circle, but made short sidelong jumps in the air in chicken fashion. His black eyes were wistfully fixed upon the captain's head. "Ugly brute," said the oiler to the bird. "You look as if you were made with a jackknife." The cook and the correspondent swore darkly at the creature. The captain naturally wished to knock it away with the end of the heavy painter, but he did not dare do it, because anything resembling an emphatic gesture would have capsized this freighted boat; and so, with his open hand, the captain gently and carefully waved the gull away. After it had been discouraged from the pursuit the captain breathed easier on account of his hair, and others breathed easier because the bird struck their minds at this time as being somehow gruesome and ominous.

In the meantime the oiler and the correspondent rowed; and also they rowed. They sat together in the same seat, and each rowed an

2. Actually a plain-weave cotton fabric.

oar. Then the oiler took both oars; then the correspondent took both oars, then the oiler; then the correspondent. They rowed and they rowed. The very ticklish part of the business was when the time came for the reclining one in the stern to take his turn at the oars. By the very last star of truth, it is easier to steal eggs from under a hen than it was to change seats in the dinghy. First the man in the stern slid his hand along the thwart and moved with care, as if he were of Sèvres.[3] Then the man in the rowing-seat slid his hand along the other thwart. It was all done with the most extraordinary care. As the two sidled past each other, the whole party kept watchful eyes on the coming wave, and the captain cried: "Look out, now! Steady, there!"

The brown mats of seaweed that appeared from time to time were like islands, bits of earth. They were travelling, apparently, neither one way nor the other. They were, to all intents, stationary. They informed the men in the boat that it was making progress slowly toward the land.

The captain, rearing cautiously in the bow after the dinghy soared on a great swell, said that he had seen the lighthouse at Mosquito Inlet. Presently the cook remarked that he had seen it. The correspondent was at the oars then, and for some reason he too wished to look at the lighthouse; but his back was toward the far shore, and the waves were important, and for some time he could not seize an opportunity to turn his head. But at last there came a wave more gentle than the others, and when at the crest of it he swiftly scoured the western horizon.

"See it?" said the captain.

"No," said the correspondent, slowly; "I didn't see anything."

"Look again," said the captain. He pointed. "It's exactly in that direction."

At the top of another wave the correspondent did as he was bid, and this time his eyes chanced on a small, still thing on the edge of the swaying horizon. It was precisely like the point of a pin. It took an anxious eye to find a lighthouse so tiny.

"Think we'll make it, Captain?"

"If this wind holds and the boat don't swamp, we can't do much else," said the captain.

The little boat, lifted by each towering sea and splashed viciously by the crests, made progress that in the absence of seaweed was not apparent to those in her. She seemed just a wee thing wallowing, miraculously top up, at the mercy of five oceans. Occasionally a great spread of water, like white flames, swarmed into her.

"Bail her, cook," said the captain, serenely.

"All right, Captain," said the cheerful cook.

3. A type of fine china.

III

It would be difficult to describe the subtle brotherhood of men that was here established on the seas. No one said that it was so. No one mentioned it. But it dwelt in the boat, and each man felt it warm him. They were a captain, an oiler, a cook, and a correspondent, and they were friends—friends in a more curiously iron-bound degree than may be common. The hurt captain, lying against the water jar in the bow, spoke always in a low voice and calmly; but he could never command a more ready and swiftly obedient crew than the motley three of the dinghy. It was more than a mere recognition of what was best for the common safety. There was surely in it a quality that was personal and heart-felt. And after this devotion to the commander of the boat, there was this comradeship, that the correspondent, for instance, who had been taught to be cynical of men, knew even at the time was the best experience of his life. But no one said that it was so. No one mentioned it.

"I wish we had a sail," remarked the captain. "We might try my overcoat on the end of an oar, and give you two boys a chance to rest." So the cook and the correspondent held the mast and spread wide the overcoat; the oiler steered; and the little boat made good way with her new rig. Sometimes the oiler had to scull sharply to keep a sea from breaking into the boat, but otherwise sailing was a success.

Meanwhile the lighthouse had been growing slowly larger. It had now almost assumed color, and appeared like a little gray shadow on the sky. The man at the oars could not be prevented from turning his head rather often to try for a glimpse of this little gray shadow.

At last, from the top of each wave, the men in the tossing boat could see land. Even as the lighthouse was an upright shadow on the sky, this land seemed but a long black shadow on the sea. It certainly was thinner than paper. "We must be about opposite New Smyrna,"[4] said the cook, who had coasted this shore often in schooners. "Captain, by the way, I believe they abandoned that life-saving station there about a year ago."

"Did they?" said the captain.

The wind slowly died away. The cook and the correspondent were not now obliged to slave in order to hold high the oar. But the waves continued their old impetuous swooping at the dinghy, and the little craft, no longer underway, struggled woundily over them. The oiler or the correspondent took the oars again.

Shipwrecks are *apropos* of nothing. If men could only train for them and have them occur when the men had reached pink condition,

4. Town on the Florida coast.

there would be less drowning at sea. Of the four in the dinghy none had slept any time worth mentioning for two days and two nights previous to embarking in the dinghy, and in the excitement of clambering about the deck of a foundering ship they had also forgotten to eat heartily.

For these reasons, and for others, neither the oiler nor the correspondent was fond of rowing at this time. The correspondent wondered ingenuously how in the name of all that was sane could there be people who thought it amusing to row a boat. It was not an amusement; it was a diabolical punishment, and even a genius of mental aberrations could never conclude that it was anything but a horror to the muscles and a crime against the back. He mentioned to the boat in general how the amusement of rowing struck him, and the weary-faced oiler smiled in full sympathy. Previously to the foundering, by the way, the oiler had worked a double watch in the engine-room of the ship.

"Take her easy, now, boys," said the captain. "Don't spend yourselves. If we have to run a surf you'll need all your strength, because we'll sure have to swim for it. Take your time."

Slowly the land arose from the sea. From a black line it became a line of black and a line of white—trees and sand. Finally the captain said that he could make out a house on the shore. "That's the house of refuge, sure," said the cook. "They'll see us before long, and come out after us."

The distant lighthouse reared high. "The keeper ought to be able to make us out now, if he's looking through a glass," said the captain. "He'll notify the life-saving people."

"None of those other boats could have got ashore to give word of the wreck," said the oiler, in a low voice, "else the life-boat would be out hunting us."

Slowly and beautifully the land loomed out of the sea. The wind came again. It had veered from the northeast to the southeast. Finally a new sound struck the ears of the men in the boat. It was the low thunder of the surf on the shore. "We'll never be able to make the lighthouse now," said the captain. "Swing her head a little more north, Billie."

"A little more north, sir," said the oiler.

Whereupon the little boat turned her nose once more down the wind, and all but the oarsman watched the shore grow. Under the influence of this expansion doubt and direful apprehension were leaving the minds of the men. The management of the boat was still most absorbing, but it could not prevent a quiet cheerfulness. In an hour, perhaps, they would be ashore.

Their backbones had become thoroughly used to balancing in the boat, and they now rode this wild colt of a dinghy like circus men. The correspondent thought that he had been drenched to the skin, but happening to feel in the top pocket of his coat, he found therein eight cigars. Four of them were soaked with sea-water; four were perfectly scatheless. After a search, somebody produced three dry matches; and thereupon the four waifs rode impudently in their little boat and, with an assurance of an impending rescue shining in their eyes, puffed at the big cigars, and judged well and ill of all men. Everybody took a drink of water.

IV

"Cook," remarked the captain, "there don't seem to be any signs of life about your house of refuge."

"No," replied the cook. "Funny they don't see us!"

A broad stretch of lowly coast lay before the eyes of the men. It was of low dunes topped with dark vegetation. The roar of the surf was plain, and sometimes they could see the white lip of a wave as it spun up the beach. A tiny house was blocked out black upon the sky. Southward, the slim lighthouse lifted its little gray length.

Tide, wind, and waves were swinging the dinghy northward. "Funny they don't see us," said the men.

The surf's roar was here dulled, but its tone was nevertheless thunderous and mighty. As the boat swam over the great rollers the men sat listening to this roar. "We'll swamp sure," said everybody.

It is fair to say here that there was not a life-saving station within twenty miles in either direction; but the men did not know this fact, and in consequence they made dark and opprobrious remarks concerning the eyesight of the nation's life-savers. Four scowling men sat in the dinghy and surpassed records in the invention of epithets.

"Funny they don't see us."

The light-heartedness of a former time had completely faded. To their sharpened minds it was easy to conjure pictures of all kinds of incompetency and blindness and, indeed, cowardice. There was the shore of the populous land, and it was bitter and bitter to them that from it came no sign.

"Well," said the captain, ultimately, "I suppose we'll have to make a try for ourselves. If we stay out here too long, we'll none of us have strength left to swim after the boat swamps."

And so the oiler, who was at the oars, turned the boat straight for the shore. There was a sudden tightening of muscles. There was some thinking.

"If we don't all get ashore," said the captain—"if we don't all get ashore, I suppose you fellows know where to send news of my finish?"

They then briefly exchanged some addresses and admonitions.

As for the reflections of the men, there was a great deal of rage in them. Perchance they might be formulated thus: "If I am going to be drowned—if I am going to be drowned—if I am going to be drowned, why, in the name of the seven mad gods who rule the sea, was I allowed to come thus far and contemplate sand and trees? Was I brought here merely to have my nose dragged away as I was about to nibble the sacred cheese of life? It is preposterous. If this old ninny-woman, Fate, cannot do better than this, she should be deprived of the management of men's fortunes. She is an old hen who knows not her intention. If she has decided to drown me, why did she not do it in the beginning and save me all this trouble? The whole affair is absurd. . . . But no; she cannot mean to drown me. She dare not drown me. She cannot drown me. Not after all this work." Afterward the man might have had an impulse to shake his fist at the clouds. "Just you drown me, now, and then hear what I call you!"

The billows that came at this time were more formidable. They seemed always just about to break and roll over the little boat in a turmoil of foam. There was a preparatory and long growl in the speech of them. No mind unused to the sea would have concluded that the dinghy could ascend these sheer heights in time. The shore was still afar. The oiler was a wily surfman. "Boys," he said, swiftly, "she won't live three minutes more, and we're too far out to swim. Shall I take her to sea again, Captain?"

"Yes; go ahead!" said the captain.

This oiler, by a series of quick miracles and fast and steady oarsmanship, turned the boat in the middle of the surf and took her safely to sea again.

There was a considerable silence as the boat bumped over the furrowed sea to deeper water. Then somebody in gloom spoke: "Well, anyhow, they must have seen us from the shore by now."

The gulls went in slanting flight up the wind toward the gray, desolate east. A squall, marked by dingy clouds and clouds brick-red, like smoke from a burning building, appeared from the southeast.

"What do you think of those life-saving people? Ain't they peaches?"

"Funny they haven't seen us."

"Maybe they think we're out here for sport! Maybe they think we're fishin'. Maybe they think we're damned fools."

It was a long afternoon. A changed tide tried to force them southward, but wind and wave said northward. Far ahead, where coast-line, sea, and sky formed their mighty angle, there were little dots which seemed to indicate a city on the shore.

"St. Augustine?"

The captain shook his head. "Too near Mosquito Inlet."

And the oiler rowed, and then the correspondent rowed; then the oiler rowed. It was a weary business. The human back can become the seat of more aches and pains than are registered in books for the composite anatomy of a regiment. It is a limited area, but it can become the theatre of innumerable muscular conflicts, tangles, wrenches, knots, and other comforts.

"Did you ever like to row, Billie?" asked the correspondent.

"No," said the oiler; "hang it!"

When one exchanged the rowing-seat for a place in the bottom of the boat, he suffered a bodily depression that caused him to be careless of everything save an obligation to wiggle one finger. There was cold sea-water swashing to and fro in the boat, and he lay in it. His head, pillowed on a thwart, was within an inch of the swirl of a wave-crest, and sometimes a particularly obstreperous sea came inboard and drenched him once more. But these matters did not annoy him. It is almost certain that if the boat had capsized he would have tumbled comfortably out upon the ocean as if he felt sure that it was a great soft mattress.

"Look! There's a man on the shore!"

"Where?"

"There? See 'im? See 'im?"

"Yes, sure! He's walking along."

"Now he's stopped. Look! He's facing us!"

"He's waving at us!"

"So he is! By thunder!"

"Ah, now we're all right! Now we're all right! There'll be a boat out here for us in half an hour."

"He's going on. He's running. He's going up to that house there."

The remote beach seemed lower than the sea, and it required a searching glance to discern the little black figure. The captain saw a floating stick, and they rowed to it. A bath towel was by some weird chance in the boat, and, tying this on the stick, the captain waved it. The oarsman did not dare turn his head, so he was obliged to ask questions.

"What's he doing now?"

"He's standing still again. He's looking, I think. . . . There he goes again—toward the house. . . . Now he's stopped again."

"Is he waving at us?"

"No, not now; he was, though."

"Look! There comes another man!"

"He's running."

"Look at him go, would you!"

"Why, he's on a bicycle. Now he's met the other man. They're both waving at us. Look!"

"There comes something up the beach."

"What the devil is that thing?"

"Why, it looks like a boat."

"Why, certainly, it's a boat."

"No; it's on wheels."

"Yes, so it is. Well, that must be the life-boat. They drag them along shore on a wagon."

"That's the life-boat, sure."

"No, by God, it's—it's an omnibus."

"I tell you it's a life-boat."

"It is not! It's an omnibus. I can see it plain. See? One of these big hotel omnibuses."

"By thunder, you're right. It's an omnibus, sure as fate. What do you suppose they are doing with an omnibus? Maybe they are going around collecting the life-crew, hey?"

"That's it, likely. Look! There's a fellow waving a little black flag. He's standing on the steps of the omnibus. There come those other two fellows. Now they're all talking together. Look at the fellow with the flag. Maybe he ain't waving it!"

"That ain't a flag, is it? That's his coat. Why, certainly, that's his coat."

"So it is; it's his coat. He's taken it off and is waving it around his head. But would you look at him swing it!"

"Oh, say, there isn't any life-saving station there. That's just a winter-resort hotel omnibus that has brought over some of the boarders to see us drown."

"What's that idiot with the coat mean? What's he signaling, anyhow?"

"It looks as if he were trying to tell us to go north. There must be a life-saving station up there."

"No; he thinks we're fishing. Just giving us a merry hand. See? Ah, there, Willie!"

"Well, I wish I could make something out of those signals. What do you suppose he means?"

"He don't mean anything; he's just playing."

"Well, if he'd just signal us to try the surf again, or to go to sea and wait, or go north, or go south, or go to hell, there would be some reason in it. But look at him! He just stands there and keeps his coat revolving like a wheel. The ass!"

"There come more people."

"Now there's quite a mob. Look! Isn't that a boat?"

"Where? Oh, I see where you mean. No, that's no boat."

"That fellow is still waving his coat."

"He must think we like to see him do that. Why don't he quit it? It don't mean anything."

"I don't know. I think he is trying to make us go north. It must be that there's a life-saving station there somewhere."

"Say, he ain't tired yet. Look at 'im wave!"

"Wonder how long he can keep that up. He's been revolving his coat ever since he caught sight of us. He's an idiot. Why aren't they getting men to bring a boat out? A fishing boat—one of those big yawls—could come out here all right. Why don't he do something?"

"Oh, it's all right now."

"They'll have a boat out here for us in less than no time, now that they've seen us."

A faint yellow tone came into the sky over the low land. The shadows on the sea slowly deepened. The wind bore coldness with it, and the men began to shiver.

"Holy smoke!" said one, allowing his voice to express his impious mood, "if we keep on monkeying out here! If we've got to flounder out here all night!"

"Oh, we'll never have to stay here all night! Don't you worry. They've seen us now, and it won't be long before they'll come chasing out after us."

The shore grew dusky. The man waving a coat blended gradually into this gloom, and it swallowed in the same manner the omnibus and the group of people. The spray, when it dashed uproariously over the side, made the voyagers shrink and swear like men who were being branded.

"I'd like to catch the chump who waved the coat. I feel like socking him one, just for luck."

"Why? What did he do?"

"Oh, nothing, but then he seemed so damned cheerful."

In the meantime the oiler rowed, and then the correspondent rowed, and then the oiler rowed. Gray-faced and bowed forward, they mechanically, turn by turn, plied the leaden oars. The form of the lighthouse had vanished from the southern horizon, but finally a pale star appeared, just lifting from the sea. The streaked saffron in the west passed before the all-merging darkness, and the sea to the east was black. The land had vanished, and was expressed only by the low and drear thunder of the surf.

"If I am going to be drowned—if I am going to be drowned—if I am going to be drowned, why, in the name of the seven mad gods who rule the sea, was I allowed to come thus far and contemplate sand and trees? Was I brought here merely to have my nose dragged away as I was about to nibble the sacred cheese of life?"

The patient captain, drooped over the water-jar, was sometimes obliged to speak to the oarsman.

"Keep her head up! Keep her head up!"

"Keep her head up, sir." The voices were weary and low.

This was surely a quiet evening. All save the oarsman lay heavily and listlessly in the boat's bottom. As for him, his eyes were just capable of noting the tall black waves that swept forward in a most sinister silence, save for an occasional subdued growl of a crest.

The cook's head was on a thwart, and he looked without interest at the water under his nose. He was deep in other scenes. Finally he spoke. "Billie," he murmured, dreamfully, "what kind of pie do you like best?"

V

"Pie!" said the oiler and the correspondent, agitatedly. "Don't talk about those things, blast you!"

"Well," said the cook, "I was just thinking about ham sandwiches, and——"

A night on the sea in an open boat is a long night. As darkness settled finally, the shine of the light, lifting from the sea in the south, changed to full gold. On the northern horizon a new light appeared, a small bluish gleam on the edge of the waters. These two lights were the furniture of the world. Otherwise there was nothing but waves.

Two men huddled in the stern, and distances were so magnificent in the dinghy that the rower was enabled to keep his feet partly warm by thrusting them under his companions. Their legs indeed extended far under the rowing-seat until they touched the feet of the captain forward. Sometimes, despite the efforts of the tired oarsman, a wave came piling into the boat, an icy wave of the night, and the chilling water soaked them anew. They would twist their bodies for a moment and groan, and sleep the dead sleep once more, while the water in the boat gurgled about them as the craft rocked.

The plan of the oiler and the correspondent was for one to row until he lost the ability, and then arouse the other from his sea-water couch in the bottom of the boat.

The oiler plied the oars until his head drooped forward and the overpowering sleep blinded him; and he rowed yet afterward. Then he touched a man in the bottom of the boat, and called his name. "Will you spell me for a little while?" he said meekly.

"Sure, Billie," said the correspondent, awaking and dragging himself to a sitting position. They exchanged places carefully, and the oiler, cuddling down in the sea-water at the cook's side, seemed to go to sleep instantly.

The particular violence of the sea had ceased. The waves came without snarling. The obligation of the man at the oars was to keep the boat headed so that the tilt of the rollers would not capsize her, and to preserve her from filling when the crests rushed past. The black waves were silent and hard to be seen in the darkness. Often one was almost upon the boat before the oarsman was aware.

In a low voice the correspondent addressed the captain. He was not sure that the captain was awake, although this iron man seemed to be always awake. "Captain, shall I keep her making for that light north, sir?"

The same steady voice answered him. "Yes. Keep it about two points off the port bow."

The cook had tied a life-belt around himself in order to get even the warmth which this clumsy cork contrivance could donate, and he seemed almost stove-like when a rower, whose teeth invariably chattered wildly as soon as he ceased his labor, dropped down to sleep.

The correspondent, as he rowed, looked down at the two men sleeping underfoot. The cook's arm was around the oiler's shoulders, and, with their fragmentary clothing and haggard faces, they were the babes of the sea—a grotesque rendering of the old babes in the wood.

Later he must have grown stupid at his work, for suddenly there was a growling of water, and a crest came with a roar and a swash into the boat, and it was a wonder that it did not set the cook afloat in his life-belt. The cook continued to sleep, but the oiler sat up, blinking his eyes and shaking with the new cold.

"Oh, I'm awful sorry, Billie," said the correspondent, contritely.

"That's all right, old boy," said the oiler, and lay down again and was asleep.

Presently it seemed that even the captain dozed, and the correspondent thought that he was the one man afloat on all the ocean. The wind had a voice as it came over the waves, and it was sadder than the end.

There was a long, loud swishing astern of the boat, and a gleaming trail of phosphorescence, like blue flame, was furrowed on the black waters. It might have been made by a monstrous knife.

Then there came a stillness, while the correspondent breathed with open mouth and looked at the sea.

Suddenly there was another swish and another long flash of bluish light, and this time it was alongside the boat, and might almost have been reached with an oar. The correspondent saw an enormous fin speed like a shadow through the water, hurling the crystalline spray and leaving the long glowing trail.

The correspondent looked over his shoulder at the captain. His face was hidden, and he seemed to be asleep. He looked at the babes of the sea. They certainly were asleep. So, being bereft of sympathy, he leaned a little way to one side and swore softly into the sea.

But the thing did not then leave the vicinity of the boat. Ahead or astern, on one side or the other, at intervals long or short, fled the long sparkling streak, and there was to be heard the *whirroo* of the dark fin. The speed and power of the thing was greatly to be admired. It cut the water like a gigantic and keen projectile.

The presence of this biding thing did not affect the man with the same horror that it would if he had been a picnicker. He simply looked at the sea dully and swore in an undertone.

Nevertheless, it is true that he did not wish to be alone with the thing. He wished one of his companions to awake by chance and keep him company with it. But the captain hung motionless over the water-jar and the oiler and the cook in the bottom of the boat were plunged in slumber.

VI

"If I am going to be drowned—if I am going to be drowned—if I am going to be drowned, why, in the name of the seven mad gods who rule the sea, was I allowed to come thus far and contemplate sand and trees?"

During this dismal night, it may be remarked that a man would conclude that it was really the intention of the seven mad gods to drown him, despite the abominable injustice of it. For it was certainly an abominable injustice to drown a man who had worked so hard, so hard. The man felt it would be a crime most unnatural. Other people had drowned at sea since galleys swarmed with painted sails, but still——

When it occurs to a man that nature does not regard him as important, and that she feels she would not maim the universe by disposing of him, he at first wishes to throw bricks at the temple, and he hates deeply the fact that there are no bricks and no temples. Any visible expression of nature would surely be pelleted with his jeers.

Then, if there be no tangible thing to hoot, he feels, perhaps, the desire to confront a personification and indulge in pleas, bowed to one knee, and with hands supplicant, saying, "Yes, but I love myself."

A high cold star on a winter's night is the word he feels that she says to him. Thereafter he knows the pathos of his situation.

The men in the dinghy had not discussed these matters, but each had, no doubt, reflected upon them in silence and according to his mind. There was seldom any expression upon their faces save the general one of complete weariness. Speech was devoted to the business of the boat.

To chime the notes of his emotions, a verse mysteriously entered the correspondent's head. He had even forgotten that he had forgotten this verse, but it suddenly was in his mind.

> A soldier of the Legion lay dying in Algiers;
> There was lack of woman's nursing,
> there was dearth of woman's tears;
> But a comrade stood beside him,
> and he took the comrade's hand,
> And he said, "I never more shall see
> my own, my native land."[5]

In his childhood the correspondent had been made acquainted with the fact that a soldier of the Legion lay dying in Algiers, but he had never regarded it as important. Myriads of his schoolfellows had informed him of the soldier's plight, but the dinning had naturally ended by making him perfectly indifferent. He had never considered it his affair that a soldier of the Legion lay dying in Algiers, nor had it appeared to him as a matter for sorrow. It was less to him than the breaking of a pencil's point.

Now, however, it quaintly came to him as a human, living thing. It was no longer merely a picture of a few throes in the breast of a poet, meanwhile drinking tea and warming his feet at the grate; it was an actuality—stern, mournful, and fine.

The correspondent plainly saw the soldier. He lay on the sand with his feet out straight and still. While his pale left hand was upon his chest in an attempt to thwart the going of his life, the blood came between his fingers. In the far Algerian distance, a city of low square forms was set against a sky that was faint with the last sunset hues. The correspondent, plying the oars and dreaming of the slow and slower movements of the lips of the soldier, was moved by a profound and perfectly impersonal comprehension. He was sorry for the soldier of the Legion who lay dying in Algiers.

The thing which had followed the boat and waited had evidently grown bored at the delay. There was no longer to be heard the slash of the cutwater, and there was no longer the flame of the long trail. The light in the north still glimmered, but it was apparently no nearer to the boat. Sometimes the boom of the surf rang in the correspondent's ears, and he turned the craft seaward then and rowed harder. Southward, some one had evidently built a watch-fire on the beach. It was

5. From *Bingen on the Rhine*, a sentimental poem by Caroline Norton (1808–1877).

too low and too far to be seen, but it made a shimmering, roseate reflection upon the bluff in back of it, and this could be discerned from the boat. The wind came stronger, and sometimes a wave suddenly raged out like a mountain-cat, and there was to be seen the sheen and sparkle of a broken crest.

The captain, in the bow, moved on his water-jar and sat erect. "Pretty long night," he observed to the correspondent. He looked at the shore. "Those life-saving people take their time."

"Did you see that shark playing around?"

"Yes, I saw him. He was a big fellow, all right."

"Wish I had known you were awake."

Later the correspondent spoke into the bottom of the boat. "Billie!" There was a slow and gradual disentanglement. "Billie, will you spell me?"

"Sure," said the oiler.

As soon as the correspondent touched the cold, comfortable sea-water in the bottom of the boat and had huddled close to the cook's life-belt he was deep in sleep, despite the fact that his teeth played all the popular airs. This sleep was so good to him that it was but a moment before he heard a voice call his name in a tone that demonstrated the last stages of exhaustion. "Will you spell me?"

"Sure, Billie."

The light in the north had mysteriously vanished, but the correspondent took his course from the wide-awake captain.

Later in the night they took the boat farther out to sea, and the captain directed the cook to take one oar at the stern and keep the boat facing the seas. He was to call out if he should hear the thunder of the surf. This plan enabled the oiler and the correspondent to get respite together. "We'll give those boys a chance to get into shape again," said the captain. They curled down and, after a few preliminary chatterings and trembles, slept once more the dead sleep. Neither knew they had bequeathed to the cook the company of another shark, or perhaps the same shark.

As the boat caroused on the waves, spray occasionally bumped over the side and gave them a fresh soaking, but this had no power to break their repose. The ominous slash of the wind and the water affected them as it would have affected mummies.

"Boys," said the cook, with the notes of every reluctance in his voice, "she's drifted in pretty close. I guess one of you had better take her to sea again." The correspondent, aroused, heard the crash of the toppled crests.

As he was rowing, the captain gave him some whiskey-and-water, and this steadied the chills out of him. "If I ever get ashore and anybody shows me even a photograph of an oar——"

At last there was a short conversation.

"Billie! . . . Billie, will you spell me?"

"Sure," said the oiler.

VII

When the correspondent again opened his eyes, the sea and the sky were each of the gray hue of the dawning. Later, carmine and gold was painted upon the waters. The morning appeared finally, in its splendor, with a sky of pure blue, and the sunlight flamed on the tips of the waves.

On the distant dunes were set many little black cottages, and a tall white windmill reared above them. No man, nor dog, nor bicycle appeared on the beach. The cottages might have formed a deserted village.

The voyagers scanned the shore. A conference was held in the boat. "Well," said the captain, "if no help is coming, we might better try a run through the surf right away. If we stay out here much longer we will be too weak to do anything for ourselves at all." The others silently acquiesced in this reasoning. The boat was headed for the beach. The correspondent wondered if none ever ascended the tall wind-tower, and if then they never looked seaward. This tower was a giant, standing with its back to the plight of the ants. It represented in a degree, to the correspondent, the serenity of nature amid the struggles of the individual—nature in the wind, and nature in the vision of men. She did not seem cruel to him then, nor beneficent, nor treacherous, nor wise. But she was indifferent, flatly indifferent. It is, perhaps, plausible that a man in this situation, impressed with the unconcern of the universe, should see the innumerable flaws of his life, and have them taste wickedly in his mind, and wish for another chance. A distinction between right and wrong seems absurdly clear to him, then, in this new ignorance of the grave-edge, and he understands that if he were given another opportunity he would mend his conduct and his words, and be better and brighter during an introduction or at a tea.

"Now, boys," said the captain, "she is going to swamp sure. All we can do is to work her in as far as possible, and then when she swamps, pile out and scramble for the beach. Keep cool now, and don't jump until she swamps sure."

The oiler took the oars. Over his shoulders he scanned the surf. "Captain," he said, "I think I'd better bring her about and keep her head-on to the seas and back her in."

"All right, Billie," said the captain. "Back her in." The oiler swung the boat then, and, seated in the stern, the cook and the correspondent were obliged to look over their shoulders to contemplate the lonely and indifferent shore.

The monstrous inshore rollers heaved the boat high until the men were again enabled to see the white sheets of water scudding up the slanted beach. "We won't get in very close," said the captain. Each time a man could wrest his attention from the rollers, he turned his glance toward the shore, and in the expression of the eyes during this contemplation there was a singular quality. The correspondent, observing the others, knew that they were not afraid, but the full meaning of their glances was shrouded.

As for himself, he was too tired to grapple fundamentally with the fact. He tried to coerce his mind into thinking of it, but the mind was dominated at this time by the muscles, and the muscles said they did not care. It merely occurred to him that if he should drown it would be a shame.

There were no hurried words, no pallor, no plain agitation. The men simply looked at the shore. "Now, remember to get well clear of the boat when you jump," said the captain.

Seaward the crest of a roller suddenly fell with a thunderous crash, and the long white comber came roaring down upon the boat.

"Steady now," said the captain. The men were silent. They turned their eyes from the shore to the comber and waited. The boat slid up the incline, leaped at the furious top, bounced over it, and swung down the long back of the wave. Some water had been shipped, and the cook bailed it out.

But the next crest crashed also. The tumbling, boiling flood of white water caught the boat and whirled it almost perpendicular. Water swarmed in from all sides. The correspondent had his hands on the gunwale at this time, and when the water entered at that place he swiftly withdrew his fingers, as if he objected to wetting them.

The little boat, drunken with this weight of water, reeled and snuggled deeper into the sea.

"Bail her out, cook! Bail her out!" said the captain.

"All right, Captain," said the cook.

"Now, boys, the next one will do for us sure," said the oiler. "Mind to jump clear of the boat."

The third wave moved forward, huge, furious, implacable. It fairly swallowed the dinghy, and almost simultaneously the men tumbled into the sea. A piece of life-belt had lain in the bottom of the boat, and as the correspondent went overboard he held this to his chest with his left hand.

The January water was icy, and reflected immediately that it was colder than he had expected to find it off the coast of Florida. This appeared to his dazed mind as a fact important enough to be noted at the time. The coldness of the water was sad; it was tragic. This fact was somehow mixed and confused with his opinion of his own situation, so that it seemed almost a proper reason for tears. The water was cold.

When he came to the surface he was conscious of little but the noisy water. Afterward he saw his companions in the sea. The oiler was ahead in the race. He was swimming strongly and rapidly. Off to the correspondent's left, the cook's great white and corked back bulged out of the water, and in the rear the captain was hanging with his one good hand to the keel of the overturned dinghy.

There is a certain immovable quality to a shore, and the correspondent wondered at it amid the confusion of the sea.

It seemed also very attractive; but the correspondent knew that it was a long journey, and he paddled leisurely. The piece of life-preserver lay under him, and sometimes he whirled down the incline of a wave as if he were on a hand-sled.

But finally he arrived at a place in the sea where travel was beset with difficulty. He did not pause swimming to inquire what manner of current had caught him, but there his progress ceased. The shore was set before him like a bit of scenery on a stage, and he looked at it and understood with his eyes each detail of it.

As the cook passed, much farther to the left, the captain was calling to him, "Turn over on your back, cook! Turn over on your back and use the oar."

"All right, sir." The cook turned on his back, and, paddling with an oar, went ahead as if he were a canoe.

Presently the boat also passed to the left of the correspondent, with the captain clinging with one hand to the keel. He would have appeared like a man raising himself to look over a board fence if it were not for the extraordinary gymnastics of the boat. The correspondent marvelled that the captain could still hold to it.

They passed on nearer to shore—the oiler, the cook, the captain—and following them went the water-jar, bouncing gaily over the seas.

The correspondent remained in the grip of this strange new enemy, a current. The shore, with its white slope of sand and its green bluff topped with little silent cottages, was spread like a picture before him. It was very near to him then, but he was impressed as one who, in a gallery, looks at a scene from Brittany or Algiers.

He thought: "I am going to drown? Can it be possible? Can it be possible? Can it be possible?" Perhaps an individual must consider his own death to be the final phenomenon of nature.

But later a wave perhaps whirled him out of this small deadly current, for he found suddenly that he could again make progress toward the shore. Later still he was aware that the captain, clinging with one hand to the keel of the dinghy, had his face turned away from the shore and toward him, and was calling his name. "Come to the boat! Come to the boat!"

In his struggle to reach the captain and the boat, he reflected that when one gets properly wearied drowning must really be a comfortable arrangement—a cessation of hostilities accompanied by a large degree of relief; and he was glad of it, for the main thing in his mind for some moments had been horror of the temporary agony; he did not wish to be hurt.

Presently he saw a man running along the shore. He was undressing with most remarkable speed. Coat, trousers, shirt, everything flew magically off him.

"Come to the boat!" called the captain.

"All right, Captain." As the correspondent paddled, he saw the captain let himself down to bottom and leave the boat. Then the correspondent performed his one little marvel of the voyage. A large wave caught him and flung him with ease and supreme speed completely over the boat and far beyond it. It struck him even then as an event in gymnastics and a true miracle of the sea. An overturned boat in the surf is not a plaything to a swimming man.

The correspondent arrived in water that reached only to his waist, but his condition did not enable him to stand for more than a moment. Each wave knocked him into a heap, and the undertow pulled at him.

Then he saw the man who had been running and undressing, and undressing and running, come bounding into the water. He dragged ashore the cook, and then waded toward the captain; but the captain waved him away and sent him to the correspondent. He was naked—naked as a tree in winter; but a halo was about his head, and he shone like a saint. He gave a strong pull, and a long drag, and a bully heave at the correspondent's hand. The correspondent, schooled in the minor formulae, said, "Thanks, old man." But suddenly the man cried, "What's that?" He pointed a swift finger. The correspondent said, "Go."

In the shallows, face downward, lay the oiler. His forehead touched sand that was periodically, between each wave, clear of the sea.

The correspondent did not know all that transpired afterward. When he achieved safe ground he fell, striking the sand with each particular part of his body. It was as if he had dropped from a roof, but the thud was grateful to him.

It seems that instantly the beach was populated with men with blankets, clothes, and flasks, and women with coffee-pots and all the remedies sacred to their minds. The welcome of the land to the men from the sea was warm and generous; but a still and dripping shape was carried slowly up the beach, and the land's welcome for it could only be the different and sinister hospitality of the grave.

When it came night, the white waves paced to and fro in the moonlight, and the wind brought the sound of the great sea's voice to the men on the shore, and they felt that they could then be interpreters.

---

1. What is the major conflict of this story? What minor conflicts accompany it?
2. Why does the indifference of nature to the fate of the men seem worse than hostility?
3. How do the men in the boat feel about each other? How is this revealed?
4. What is the meaning of the correspondent's remembrance of a sentimental verse about "a soldier of the Legion"?
5. Interpret the tone and meaning of the expression "nibble the sacred cheese of life."
6. Pick out examples and discuss the use of figurative language. Are statements made in such language consistent with the meaning of the events described?

The Blue Hotel

I

The Palace Hotel at Fort Romper was painted a light blue, a shade that is on the legs of a kind of heron, causing the bird to declare its position against any background. The Palace Hotel, then, was always screaming and howling in a way that made the dazzling winter landscape of Nebraska seem only a gray swampish hush. It stood alone on the prairie, and when the snow was falling the town two hundred yards away was not visible. But when the traveler alighted at the railway station he was obliged to pass the Palace Hotel before he could come upon the company of low clapboard houses which composed Fort Romper, and it was not to be thought that any traveler could pass the Palace Hotel without looking at it. Pat Scully, the proprietor, had proved himself a master of strategy when he chose his paints. It is true that on clear days, when the great transcontinental express, long lines of swaying Pullmans, swept through Fort Romper, passengers were overcome at the sight, and the cult that knows the brown-reds and the subdivisions of the dark greens of the East expressed shame, pity, horror, in a laugh. But to the citizens of this prairie town and to the people who would naturally stop there, Pat Scully had performed a feat. With this opulence and splendor, these creeds, classes, egotisms, that streamed through Romper on the rails day after day, they had no color in common.

As if the display delights of such a blue hotel were not sufficiently enticing, it was Scully's habit to go every morning and evening to meet the leisurely trains that stopped at Romper and work his seductions upon any man that he might see wavering, gripsack in hand.

One morning, when a snow-crusted engine dragged its long string of freight cars and its one passenger coach to the station, Scully performed the marvel of catching three men. One was a shaky and quick-eyed Swede, with a great shining cheap valise; one was a tall bronzed cowboy, who was on his way to a ranch near the Dakota line; one was a little silent man from the East, who didn't look it, and didn't announce it. Scully practically made them prisoners. He was so nimble and merry and kindly that each probably felt it would be the height of brutality to try to escape. They trudged off over the creaking board sidewalks in the wake of the eager little Irishman. He wore a heavy fur cap squeezed tightly down on his head. It caused his two red ears to stick out stiffly, as if they were made of tin.

At last, Scully, elaborately, with boisterous hospitality, conducted them through the portals of the blue hotel. The room which they entered was small. It seemed to be merely a proper temple for an enormous stove, which, in the center, was humming with godlike violence. At various points on its surface the iron had become luminous and glowed yellow from the heat. Beside the stove Scully's son Johnnie was playing High-Five with an old farmer who had whiskers both gray and sandy. They were quarrelling. Frequently the old farmer turned his face toward a box of sawdust—colored brown from tobacco juice—that was behind the stove, and spat with an air of great impatience and irritation. With a loud flourish of words Scully destroyed the game of cards, and bustled his son upstairs with part of the baggage of the new guests. He himself conducted them to three basins of the coldest water in the world. The cowboy and the Easterner burnished themselves fiery red with this water, until it seemed to be some kind of metal polish. The Swede, however, merely dipped his fingers gingerly and with trepidation. It was notable that throughout this series of small ceremonies the three travelers were made to feel that Scully was very benevolent. He was conferring great favors upon them. He handed the towel from one to another with an air of philanthropic impulse.

Afterward they went to the first room, and sitting about the stove, listened to Scully's officious clamor at his daughters, who were preparing the midday meal. They reflected in the silence of experienced men who tread carefully amid new people. Nevertheless, the old farmer, stationary, invincible in his chair near the warmest part of the stove, turned his face from the sawdust-box frequently and addressed a glowing commonplace to the strangers. Usually he was answered in short but adequate sentences by either the cowboy or the Easterner. The

Swede said nothing. He seemed to be occupied in making furtive estimates of each man in the room. One might have thought that he had the sense of silly suspicion which comes to guilt. He resembled a badly frightened man.

Later, at dinner, he spoke a little, addressing his conversation entirely to Scully. He volunteered that he had come from New York, where for ten years he had worked as a tailor. These facts seemed to strike Scully as fascinating, and afterward he volunteered that he had lived at Romper for fourteen years. The Swede asked about the crops and the price of labor. He seemed barely to listen to Scully's extended replies. His eyes continued to rove from man to man.

Finally, with a laugh and a wink, he said that some of these Western communities were very dangerous; and after his statement he straightened his legs under the table, tilted his head, and laughed again, loudly. It was plain that the demonstration had no meaning to the others. They looked at him wondering and in silence.

II

As the men trooped heavily back into the front room, the two little windows presented views of a turmoiling sea of snow. The huge arms of the wind were making attempts—mighty, circular, futile—to embrace the flakes as they sped. A gate-post like a still man with a blanched face stood aghast amid this profligate fury. In a hearty voice Scully announced the presence of a blizzard. The guests of the blue hotel, lighting their pipes, assented with grunts of lazy masculine contentment. No island of the sea could be exempt in the degree of this little room with its humming stove. Johnnie, son of Scully, in a tone which defined his opinion of his ability as a card-player, challenged the old farmer of both gray and sandy whiskers to a game of High-Five. The farmer agreed with a contemptuous and bitter scoff. They sat close to the stove, and squared their knees under a wide board. The cowboy and the Easterner watched the game with interest. The Swede remained near the window, aloof, but with a countenance that showed signs of an inexplicable excitement.

The play of Johnnie and the gray-beard was suddenly ended by another quarrel. The old man arose while casting a look of heated scorn at his adversary. He slowly buttoned his coat, and then stalked with fabulous dignity from the room. In the discreet silence of all the other men the Swede laughed. His laughter rang somehow childish. Men by this time had begun to look at him askance, as if they wished to inquire what ailed him.

A new game was formed jocosely. The cowboy volunteered to become the partner of Johnnie, and they all then turned to ask the

Swede to throw in his lot with the little Easterner. He asked some questions about the game, and, learning that it wore many names, and that he had played it when it was under an alias, he accepted the invitation. He strode toward the men nervously, as if he expected to be assaulted. Finally, seated, he gazed from face to face and laughed shrilly. This laugh was so strange that the Easterner looked up quickly, the cowboy sat intent and with his mouth open, and Johnnie paused, holding the cards with still fingers.

Afterward there was a short silence. Then Johnnie said, "Well, let's get at it. Come on now!" They pulled their chairs forward until their knees were bunched under the board. They began to play, and their interest in the game caused the others to forget the manner of the Swede.

The cowboy was a board-whacker. Each time that he held superior cards he whanged them, one by one, with exceeding force, down upon the improvised table, and took the tricks with a glowing air of prowess and pride that sent thrills of indignation into the hearts of his opponents. A game with a board-whacker in it is sure to become intense. The countenances of the Easterner and the Swede were miserable whenever the cowboy thundered down his aces and kings, while Johnnie, his eyes gleaming with joy, chuckled and chuckled.

Because of the absorbing play none considered the strange ways of the Swede. They paid strict heed to the game. Finally, during a lull caused by a new deal, the Swede suddenly addressed Johnnie: "I suppose there have been a good many men killed in this room." The jaws of the others dropped and they looked at him.

"What in hell are you talking about?" asked Johnnie.

The Swede laughed again his blatant laugh, full of a kind of false courage and defiance. "Oh, you know what I mean all right," he answered.

"I'm a liar if I do!" Johnnie protested. The card was halted, and the men stared at the Swede. Johnnie evidently felt that as the son of the proprietor he should make a direct inquiry. "Now, what might you be drivin' at, mister?" he asked. The Swede winked at him. It was a wink full of cunning. His fingers shook on the edge of the board. "Oh, maybe you think I have been to nowheres. Maybe you think I'm a tenderfoot?"

"I don't know nothin' about you," answered Johnnie, "and I don't give a damn where you've been. All I got to say is that I don't know what you're driving at. There hain't never been nobody killed in this room."

The cowboy, who had been steadily gazing at the Swede, then spoke: "What's wrong with you, mister?"

Apparently it seemed to the Swede that he was formidably menaced. He shivered and turned white near the corners of his mouth. He sent an appealing glance in the direction of the little Easterner. During these moments he did not forget to wear his air of advanced pot-valor. "They say they don't know what I mean," he remarked mockingly to the Easterner.

The latter answered after prolonged and cautious reflection. "I don't understand you," he said, impassively.

The Swede made a movement then which announced that he thought he had encountered treachery from the only quarter where he had expected sympathy, if not help. "Oh, I see you are all against me. I see—"

The cowboy was in a state of deep stupefaction. "Say," he cried, as he tumbled the deck violently down upon the board, "say, what are you gittin' at, hey?"

The Swede sprang up with the celerity of a man escaping from a snake on the floor. "I don't want to fight!" he shouted. "I don't want to fight!"

The cowboy stretched his long legs indolently and deliberately. His hands were in his pockets. He spat into the sawdust box. "Well, who the hell thought you did?" he inquired.

The Swede backed rapidly toward a corner of the room. His hands were out protectingly in front of his chest, but he was making an obvious struggle to control his fright. "Gentlemen," he quavered, "I suppose I am going to be killed before I can leave this house! I suppose I am going to be killed before I can leave this house!" In his eyes was the dying-swan look. Through the windows could be seen the snow turning blue in the shadow of dusk. The wind tore at the house, and some loose thing beat regularly against the clapboards like a spirit tapping.

A door opened, and Scully himself entered. He paused in surprise as he noted the tragic attitude of the Swede. Then he said, "What's the matter here?"

The Swede answered him swiftly and eagerly: "These men are going to kill me."

"Kill you!" ejaculated Scully. "Kill you! What are you talkin'?"

The Swede made the gesture of a martyr.

Scully wheeled sternly upon his son. "What is this, Johnnie?"

The lad had grown sullen. "Damned if I know," he answered. "I can't make no sense to it." He began to shuffle the cards, fluttering them together with an angry snap. "He says a good many men have been killed in this room, or something like that. And he says he's goin' to be killed here too. I don't know what ails him. He's crazy, I shouldn't wonder."

Scully then looked for explanation to the cowboy, but the cowboy simply shrugged his shoulders.

"Kill you?" said Scully again to the Swede. "Kill you? Man, you're off your nut."

"Oh, I know," burst out the Swede. "I know what will happen. Yes, I'm crazy—yes. Yes, of course, I'm crazy—yes. But I know one thing—" There was a sort of sweat of misery and terror upon his face. "I know I won't get out of here alive."

The cowboy drew a deep breath, as if his mind was passing into the last stages of dissolution. "Well, I'm doggoned," he whispered to himself.

Scully wheeled suddenly and faced his son. "You've been troublin' this man!"

Johnnie's voice was loud with its burden of grievance. "Why, good Gawd, I ain't done nothin' to 'im."

The Swede broke in. "Gentlemen, do not disturb yourselves. I will leave this house. I will go away, because"—he accused them dramatically with his glance—"because I do not want to be killed."

Scully was furious with his son. "Will you tell me what is the matter, you young divil? What's the matter, anyhow? Speak out!"

"Blame it!" cried Johnnie in despair, "don't I tell you I don't know? He—he says we want to kill him, and that's all I know. I can't tell what ails him."

The Swede continued to repeat: "Never mind, Mr. Scully; never mind. I will leave this house. I will go away, because I do not wish to be killed. Yes, of course, I am crazy—yes. But I know one thing! I will go away. I will leave this house. Never mind, Mr. Scully; never mind. I will go away."

"You will not go 'way," said Scully. "You will not go 'way until I hear the reason of this business. If anybody has troubled you I will take care of him. This is my house. You are under my roof, and I will not allow any peaceable man to be troubled here." He cast a terrible eye upon Johnnie, the cowboy, and the Easterner.

"Never mind, Mr. Scully, never mind. I will go away. I do not wish to be killed." The Swede moved toward the door which opened upon the stairs. It was evidently his intention to go at once for his baggage.

"No, no," shouted Scully peremptorily; but the white-faced man slid by him and disappeared. "Now," said Scully severely, "what does this mane?"

Johnnie and the cowboy cried together: "Why, we didn't do nothin' to 'im!"

Scully's eyes were cold. "No," he said, "you didn't?"

Johnnie swore a deep oath. "Why, this is the wildest loon I ever see. We didn't do nothin' at all. We were jest sittin' here playin' cards, and he—"

The father suddenly spoke to the Easterner. "Mr. Blanc," he asked, "what has these boys been doin'?"

The Easterner reflected again. "I didn't see anything wrong at all," he said at last, slowly.

Scully began to howl. "But what does it mane?" He stared ferociously at his son. "I have a mind to lather you for this, my boy."

Johnnie was frantic. "Well, what have I done?" he bawled at his father.

III

"I think you are tongue-tied," said Scully finally to his son, the cowboy, and the Easterner; and at the end of this scornful sentence he left the room.

Upstairs the Swede was swiftly fastening the straps of his great valise. Once his back happened to be half turned toward the door, and, hearing a noise there, he wheeled and sprang up, uttering a loud cry. Scully's wrinkled visage showed grimly in the light of the small lamp he carried. This yellow effulgence, streaming upward, colored only his prominent features, and left his eyes, for instance, in mysterious shadow. He resembled a murderer.

"Man! man!" he exclaimed, "have you gone daffy?"

"Oh, no! Oh, no!" rejoined the other. "There are people in this world who know pretty nearly as much as you do—understand?"

For a moment they stood gazing at each other. Upon the Swede's deathly pale cheeks were two spots brightly crimson and sharply edged, as if they had been carefully painted. Scully placed the light on the table and sat himself on the edge of the bed. He spoke ruminatively. "By cracky, I never heard of such a thing in my life. It's a complete muddle. I can't, for the soul of me, think how you ever got this idea into your head." Presently he lifted his eyes and asked: "And did you sure think they were going to kill you?"

The Swede scanned the old man as if he wished to see into his mind. "I did," he said at last. He obviously suspected that this answer might precipitate an outbreak. As he pulled on a strap his whole arm shook, the elbow wavering like a bit of paper.

Scully banged his hand impressively on the footboard of the bed. "Why, man, we're goin' to have a line of ilictric street-cars in this town next spring."

" 'A line of electric street-cars,' " repeated the Swede, stupidly.

"And," said Scully, "there's a new railroad goin' to be built down from Broken Arm to here. Not to mintion the four churches and the smashin' big brick schoolhouse. Then there's the big factory, too. Why, in two years Romper'll be a met-tro-*pol*-is."

Having finished the preparation of his baggage, the Swede

straightened himself. "Mr. Scully," he said, with sudden hardihood, "how much do I owe you?"

"You don't owe me anythin'," said the old man, angrily.

"Yes, I do," retorted the Swede. He took seventy-five cents from his pocket and tendered it to Scully; but the latter snapped his fingers in disdainful refusal. However, it happened that they both stood gazing in a strange fashion at three silver pieces on the Swede's open palm.

"I'll not take your money," said Scully at last. "Not after what's been goin' on here." Then a plan seemed to strike him. "Here," he cried, picking up his lamp and moving toward the door. "Here! Come with me a minute."

"No," said the Swede, in overwhelming alarm.

"Yes," urged the old man. "Come on! I want you to come and see a picter—just across the hall—in my room."

The Swede must have concluded that his hour was come. His jaw dropped and his teeth showed like a dead man's. He ultimately followed Scully across the corridor, but he had the step of one hung in chains.

Scully flashed the light high on the wall of his own chamber. There was revealed a ridiculous photograph of a little girl. She was leaning against a balustrade of gorgeous decoration, and the formidable bang to her hair was prominent. The figure was as graceful as an upright sled-stake, and, withal, it was the hue of lead. "There," said Scully tenderly, "that's the picter of my little girl that died. Her name was Carrie. She had the purtiest hair you ever saw! I was that fond of her, she—"

Turning then, he saw that the Swede was not contemplating the picture at all, but, instead, was keeping keen watch on the gloom in the rear.

"Look, man!" cried Scully, heartily. "That's the picter of my little gal that died. Her name was Carrie. And then here's the picter of my oldest boy, Michael. He's a lawyer in Lincoln, an' doin' well. I gave that boy a grand eddication, and I'm glad for it now. He's a fine boy. Look at 'im now. Ain't he bold as blazes, him there in Lincoln, an honored an' respicted gintleman! An honored and respected gintleman," concluded Scully with a flourish. And, so saying, he smote the Swede jovially on the back.

The Swede faintly smiled.

"Now," said the old man, "there's only one more thing." He dropped suddenly to the floor and thrust his head beneath the bed. The Swede could hear his muffled voice. "I'd keep it under me piller if it wasn't for that boy Johnnie. Then there's the old woman—Where is it now? I never put it twice in the same place. Ah, now come out with you!"

Presently he backed clumsily from under the bed, dragging with him an old coat rolled into a bundle. "I've fetched him," he muttered. Kneeling on the floor, he unrolled the coat and extracted from its heart a large yellow-brown whiskey-bottle.

His first manoeuver was to hold the bottle up to the light. Reassured, apparently, that nobody had been tampering with it, he thrust it with a generous movement toward the Swede.

The weak-kneed Swede was about to eagerly clutch this element of strength, but he suddenly jerked his hand away and cast a look of horror upon Scully.

"Drink," said the old man affectionately. He had risen to his feet, and now stood facing the Swede.

There was a silence. Then again Scully said: "Drink!"

The Swede laughed wildly. He grabbed the bottle, put it to his mouth; and as his lips curled absurdly around the opening and his throat worked, he kept his glance, burning with hatred, upon the old man's face.

IV

After the departure of Scully the three men, with the cardboard still upon their knees, preserved for a long time an astounded silence. Then Johnnie said: "That's the doddangedest Swede I ever see."

"He ain't no Swede," said the cowboy, scornfully.

"Well, what is he then?" cried Johnnie. "What is he then?"

"It's my opinion," replied the cowboy deliberately, "he's some kind of a Dutchman." It was a venerable custom of the country to entitle as Swedes all light-haired men who spoke with a heavy tongue. In consequence the idea of the cowboy was not without its daring. "Yes, sir," he repeated. "It's my opinion this feller is some kind of a Dutchman."

"Well, he says he's a Swede, anyhow," muttered Johnnie, sulkily. He turned to the Easterner: "What do you think, Mr. Blanc?"

"Oh, I don't know," replied the Easterner.

"Well, what do you think makes him act that way?" asked the cowboy.

"Why, he's frightened." The Easterner knocked his pipe against a rim of the stove. "He's clear frightened out of his boots."

"What at?" cried Johnnie and the cowboy together.

The Easterner reflected over his answer.

"What at?" cried the others again.

"Oh, I don't know, but it seems to me this man has been reading dime novels, and he thinks he's right out in the middle of it—the shootin' and stabbin' and all."

"But," said the cowboy, deeply scandalized, "this ain't Wyoming, ner none of them places. This is Nebrasker."

"Yes," added Johnnie, "an' why don't he wait till he gits *out West?*"

The travelled Easterner laughed. "It isn't different there even—not in these days. But he thinks he's right in the middle of hell."

Johnnie and the cowboy mused long.

"It's awful funny," remarked Johnnie at last.

"Yes," said the cowboy. "This is a queer game. I hope we don't git snowed in, because then we'd have to stand this here man bein' around with us all the time. That wouldn't be no good."

"I wish pop would throw him out," said Johnnie.

Presently they heard a loud stamping on the stairs, accompanied by ringing jokes in the voice of old Scully, and laughter, evidently from the Swede. The men around the stove stared vacantly at each other. "Gosh!" said the cowboy. The door flew open, and old Scully, flushed and anecdotal, came into the room. He was jabbering at the Swede, who followed him, laughing bravely. It was the entry of two roisterers from a banquet ball.

"Come now," said Scully sharply to the three seated men, "move up and give us a chance at the stove." The cowboy and the Easterner obediently sidled their chairs to make room for the newcomers. Johnnie, however, simply arranged himself in a more indolent attitude, and then remained motionless.

"Come! Git over, there," said Scully.

"Plenty of room on the other side of the stove," said Johnnie.

"Do you think we want to sit in the draught?" roared the father.

But the Swede here interposed with a grandeur of confidence. "No, no. Let the boy sit where he likes," he cried in a bullying voice to the father.

"All right! All right!" said Scully, deferentially. The cowboy and the Easterner exchanged glances of wonder.

The five chairs were formed in a crescent about one side of the stove. The Swede began to talk; he talked arrogantly, profanely, angrily. Johnnie, the cowboy, and the Easterner maintained a morose silence, while old Scully appeared to be receptive and eager, breaking in constantly with sympathetic ejaculations.

Finally the Swede announced that he was thirsty. He moved in his chair, and said that he would go for a drink of water.

"I'll git it for you," cried Scully at once.

"No," said the Swede, contemptuously. "I'll get it for myself." He arose and stalked with the air of an owner off into the executive parts of the hotel.

As soon as the Swede was out of hearing Scully sprang to his feet and whispered intensely to the others: "Up-stairs he thought I was tryin' to poison 'im."

"Say," said Johnnie, "this makes me sick. Why don't you throw 'im out in the snow?"

"Why, he's all right now," declared Scully. "It was only that he was from the East, and he thought this was a tough place. That's all. He's all right now."

The cowboy looked with admiration upon the Easterner. "You were straight," he said. "You were on to that there Dutchman."

"Well," said Johnnie to his father, "he may be all right now, but I don't see it. Other time he was scared, but now he's too fresh."

Scully's speech was always a combination of Irish brogue and idiom, Western twang and idiom, and scraps of curiously formal diction taken from the story-books and newspapers. He now hurled a strange mass of language at the head of his son. "What do I keep? What do I keep? What do I keep?" he demanded, in a voice of thunder. He slapped his knee impressively, to indicate that he himself was going to make reply, and that all should heed. "I keep a hotel," he shouted. "A hotel, do you mind? A guest under my roof has sacred privileges. He is to be intimidated by none. Not one word shall he hear that would prijudice him in favor of goin' away. I'll not have it. There's no place in this here town where they can say they iver took in a guest of mine because he was afraid to stay here." He wheeled suddenly upon the cowboy and the Easterner. "Am I right?"

"Yes, Mr. Scully," said the cowboy, "I think you're right."

"Yes, Mr. Scully," said the Easterner, "I think you're right."

V

At six-o'clock supper, the Swede fizzed like a fire-wheel. He sometimes seemed on the point of bursting into riotous song, and in all his madness he was encouraged by old Scully. The Easterner was encased in reserve; the cowboy sat in wide-mouthed amazement, forgetting to eat, while Johnnie wrathily demolished great plates of food. The daughters of the house, when they were obliged to replenish the biscuits, approached as warily as Indians, and, having succeeded in their purposes, fled with ill-concealed trepidation. The Swede domineered the whole feast, and he gave it the appearance of a cruel bacchanal. He seemed to have grown suddenly taller; he gazed, brutally disdainful, into every face. His voice rang through the room. Once when he jabbed out harpoon-fashion with his fork to pinion a biscuit, the weapon nearly impaled the hand of the Easterner, which had been stretched quietly out for the same biscuit.

After supper, as the men filed toward the other room, the Swede smote Scully ruthlessly on the shoulder. "Well, old boy, that was a good, square meal." Johnnie looked hopefully at his father; he knew that shoulder was tender from an old fall; and, indeed, it appeared for a moment as if Scully was going to flame out over the matter, but in the end he smiled a sickly smile and remained silent. The others understood from his manner that he was admitting his responsibility for the Swede's new view-point.

Johnnie, however, addressed his parent in an aside. "Why don't you license somebody to kick you downstairs?" Scully scowled darkly by way of reply.

When they were gathered about the stove, the Swede insisted on another game of High-Five. Scully gently deprecated the plan at first, but the Swede turned a wolfish glare upon him. The old man subsided, and the Swede canvassed the others. In his tone there was always a great threat. The cowboy and the Easterner both remarked indifferently that they would play. Scully said that he would presently have to go to meet the 6.58 train, and so the Swede turned menacingly upon Johnnie. For a moment their glances crossed like blades, and then Johnnie smiled and said, "Yes, I'll play."

They formed a square, with the little board on their knees. The Easterner and the Swede were again partners. As the play went on, it was noticeable that the cowboy was not board-whacking as usual. Meanwhile, Scully, near the lamp, had put on his spectacles and, with an appearance curiously like an old priest, was reading a newspaper. In time he went out to meet the 6.58 train, and, despite his precautions, a gust of polar wind whirled into the room as he opened the door. Besides scattering the cards, it chilled the players to the marrow. The Swede cursed frightfully. When Scully returned, his entrance disturbed a cozy and friendly scene. The Swede again cursed. But presently they were once more intent, their heads bent forward and their hands moving swiftly. The Swede had adopted the fashion of board-whacking.

Scully took up his paper and for a long time remained immersed in matters which were extraordinarily remote from him. The lamp burned badly, and once he stopped to adjust the wick. The newspaper, as he turned from page to page, rustled with a slow and comfortable sound. Then suddenly he heard three terrible words: "You are cheatin'!"

Such scenes often prove that there can be little of dramatic import in environment. Any room can present a tragic front; any room can be comic. This little den was now hideous as a torture-chamber. The new faces of the men themselves had changed it upon the instant. The Swede held a huge fist in front of Johnnie's face, while the latter looked steadily over it into the blazing orbs of his accuser. The Easterner had grown pallid; the cowboy's jaw had dropped in that expression of bovine amazement which was one of his important mannerisms. After the three words, the first sound in the room was made by Scully's paper as it floated forgotten to his feet. His spectacles had also fallen from his nose, but by a clutch he had saved them in air. His hand, grasping the spectacles, now remained poised awkwardly and near his shoulder. He stared at the card-players.

Probably the silence was while a second elapsed. Then, if the floor had been suddenly twitched out from under the men they could not have moved quicker. The five had projected themselves headlong toward a common point. It happened that Johnnie, in rising to hurl himself upon the Swede, had stumbled slightly because of his curiously instinctive care for the cards and the board. The loss of the moment allowed time for the arrival of Scully, and also allowed the cowboy time to give the Swede a great push which sent him staggering back. The men found tongue together, and hoarse shouts of rage, appeal, or fear burst from every throat. The cowboy pushed and jostled feverishly at the Swede, and the Easterner and Scully clung wildly to Johnnie; but through the smoky air, above the swaying bodies of the peace-compellers, the eyes of the two warriors ever sought each other in glances of challenge that were at once hot and steely.

Of course the board had been overturned, and now the whole company of cards was scattered over the floor, where the boots of the men trampled the fat and painted kings and queens as they gazed with their silly eyes at the war that was waging above them.

Scully's voice was dominating the yells. "Stop now! Stop, I say! Stop, now—"

Johnnie, as he struggled to burst through the rank formed by Scully and the Easterner, was crying, "Well, he says I cheated! He says I cheated! I won't allow no man to say I cheated! If he says I cheated, he's a——!"

The cowboy was telling the Swede, "Quit, now! Quit, d'ye hear—"

The screams of the Swede never ceased: "He did cheat! I saw him! I saw him—"

As for the Easterner, he was importuning in a voice that was not heeded: "Wait a moment, can't you? Oh, wait a moment. What's the good of a fight over a game of cards? Wait a moment—"

In this tumult no complete sentences were clear. "Cheat"—"Quit"—"He says"—these fragments pierced the uproar and rang out sharply. It was remarkable that, whereas Scully undoubtedly made the most noise, he was the least heard of any of the riotous band.

Then suddenly there was a great cessation. It was as if each man had paused for breath; and although the room was still lighted with the anger of men, it could be seen that there was no danger of immediate conflict, and at once Johnnie, shouldering his way forward, almost succeeded in confronting the Swede. "What did you say I cheated for? What did you say I cheated for? I don't cheat, and I won't let no man say I do!"

The Swede said, "I saw you! I saw you!"

"Well," cried Johnnie, "I'll fight any man what says I cheat!"

"No, you won't," said the cowboy. "Not here."

"Ah, be still, can't you?" said Scully, coming between them.

The quiet was sufficient to allow the Easterner's voice to be heard. He was repeating, "Oh, wait a moment, can't you? What's the good of a fight over a game of cards? Wait a moment!"

Johnnie, his red face appearing above his father's shoulder, hailed the Swede again. "Did you say I cheated?"

The Swede showed his teeth. "Yes."

"Then," said Johnnie, "we must fight."

"Yes, fight," roared the Swede. He was like a demoniac. "Yes, fight! I'll show you what kind of a man I am! I'll show you who you want to fight! Maybe you think I can't fight! Maybe you think I can't! I'll show you, you skin, you card-sharp! Yes, you cheated! You cheated! You cheated!"

"Well, let's go at it, then, mister," said Johnnie, coolly.

The cowboy's brow was beaded with sweat from his efforts in intercepting all sorts of raids. He turned in despair to Scully. "What are you goin' to do now?"

A change had come over the Celtic visage of the old man. He now seemed all eagerness; his eyes glowed.

"We'll let them fight," he answered stalwartly. "I can't put up with it any longer. I've stood this damned Swede till I'm sick. We'll let them fight."

VI

The men prepared to go out-of-doors. The Easterner was so nervous that he had great difficulty in getting his arms into the sleeves of his new leather coat. As the cowboy drew his fur cap down over his ears his hands trembled. In fact, Johnnie and old Scully were the only ones who displayed no agitation. These preliminaries were conducted without words.

Scully threw open the door. "Well, come on," he said. Instantly a terrific wind caused the flame of the lamp to struggle at its wick, while a puff of black smoke sprang from the chimney-top. The stove was in mid-current of the blast, and its voice swelled to equal the roar of the storm. Some of the scarred and bedabbled cards were caught up from the floor and dashed helplessly against the further wall. The men lowered their heads and plunged into the tempest as into a sea.

No snow was falling, but great whirls and clouds of flakes, swept up from the ground by the frantic winds, were streaming southward with the speed of bullets. The covered land was blue with the sheen of an unearthly satin, and there was no other hue save where, at the low, black railway station—which seemed incredibly distant—one light gleamed like a tiny jewel. As the men floundered into a thigh-deep drift, it was known that the Swede was bawling out something. Scully went to him, put a hand on his shoulder, and projected an ear. "What's that you say?" he shouted.

"I say," bawled the Swede again, "I won't stand much show against this gang. I know you'll all pitch on me."

Scully smote him reproachfully on the arm. "Tut, man!" he yelled. The wind tore the words from Scully's lips and scattered them far a-lee.

"You are all a gang of—" boomed the Swede, but the storm also seized the remainder of this sentence.

Immediately turning their backs upon the wind, the men had swung around a corner to the sheltered side of the hotel. It was the function of the little house to preserve here, amid this great devastation of snow, an irregular V-shape of heavily encrusted grass, which crackled beneath the feet. One could imagine the great drifts piled against the windward side. When the party reached the comparative peace of this spot it was found that the Swede was still bellowing.

"Oh, I know what kind of a thing this is! I know you'll all pitch on me. I can't lick you all!"

Scully turned upon him panther-fashion. "You'll not have to whip all of us. You'll have to whip my son Johnnie. An' the man what troubles you durin' that time will have me to dale with."

The arrangements were swiftly made. The two men faced each other, obedient to the harsh commands of Scully, whose face, in the subtly luminous gloom, could be seen set in the austere impersonal lines that are pictured on the countenances of the Roman veterans. The Easterner's teeth were chattering, and he was hopping up and down like a mechanical toy. The cowboy stood rocklike.

The contestants had not stripped off any clothing. Each was in his ordinary attire. Their fists were up, and they eyed each other in a calm that had the elements of leonine cruelty in it.

During this pause, the Easterner's mind, like a film, took lasting impressions of three men—the iron-nerved master of the ceremony; the Swede, pale, motionless, terrible; and Johnnie, serene yet ferocious, brutish yet heroic. The entire prelude had in it a tragedy greater than the tragedy of action, and this aspect was accentuated by the long, mellow cry of the blizzard, as it sped the tumbling and wailing flakes into the black abyss of the south.

"Now!" said Scully.

The two combatants leaped forward and crashed together like bullocks. There was heard the cushioned sound of blows, and of a curse squeezing out from between the tight teeth of one.

As for the spectators, the Easterner's pent-up breath exploded from him with a pop of relief, absolute relief from the tension of the preliminaries. The cowboy bounded into the air with a yowl. Scully was immovable as from supreme amazement and fear at the fury of the fight which he himself had permitted and arranged.

For a time the encounter in the darkness was such a perplexity of flying arms that it presented no more detail than would a swiftly revolving wheel. Occasionally a face, as if illumined by a flash of light, would shine out, ghastly and marked with pink spots. A moment later, the men might have been known as shadows, if it were not for the involuntary utterance of oaths that came from them in whispers.

Suddenly a holocaust of warlike desire caught the cowboy, and he bolted forward with the speed of a broncho. "Go it, Johnnie! Go it! Kill him! Kill him!"

Scully confronted him. "Kape back," he said; and by his glance the cowboy could tell that this man was Johnnie's father.

To the Easterner there was a monotony of unchangeable fighting that was an abomination. This confused mingling was eternal to his sense, which was concentrated in a longing for the end, the priceless end. Once the fighters lurched near him, and as he scrambled hastily backward he heard them breathe like men on the rack.

"Kill him, Johnnie! Kill him! Kill him! Kill him!" The cowboy's face was contorted like one of those agony masks in museums.

"Keep still," said Scully, icily.

Then there was a sudden loud grunt, incomplete, cut short, and Johnnie's body swung away from the Swede and fell with sickening heaviness to the grass. The cowboy was barely in time to prevent the mad Swede from flinging himself upon his prone adversary. "No, you don't," said the cowboy, interposing an arm. "Wait a second."

Scully was at his son's side. "Johnnie! Johnnie, me boy!" His voice had a quality of melancholy tenderness. "Johnnie! Can you go on with it?" He looked anxiously down into the bloody, pulpy face of his son.

There was a moment of silence, and then Johnnie answered in his ordinary voice, "Yes, I—it—yes."

Assisted by his father he struggled to his feet. "Wait a bit now till you git your wind," said the old man.

A few paces away the cowboy was lecturing the Swede. "No, you don't! Wait a second!"

The Easterner was plucking at Scully's sleeve. "Oh, this is enough," he pleaded. "This is enough! Let it go as it stands. This is enough!"

"Bill," said Scully, "git out of the road." The cowboy stepped aside. "Now." The combatants were actuated by a new caution as they advanced toward collision. They glared at each other, and then the Swede aimed a lightning blow that carried with it his entire weight. Johnnie was evidently half stupid from weakness, but he miraculously dodged, and his fist sent the overbalanced Swede sprawling.

The cowboy, Scully, and the Easterner burst into a cheer that was like a chorus of triumphant soldiery, but before its conclusion the Swede had scuffled agilely to his feet and come in berserk abandon at his foe. There was another perplexity of flying arms, and Johnnie's body again swung away and fell, even as a bundle might fall from a roof. The Swede instantly staggered to a little wind-waved tree and leaned upon it, breathing like an engine, while his savage and flame-lit eyes roamed from face to face as the men bent over Johnnie. There was a splendor of isolation in his situation at this time which the Easterner felt once when, lifting his eyes from the man on the ground, he beheld that mysterious and lonely figure, waiting.

"Are you any good yet, Johnnie?" asked Scully in a broken voice.

The son gasped and opened his eyes languidly. After a moment he answered, "No—I ain't—any good—any—more." Then, from shame and bodily ill, he began to weep, the tears furrowing down through the blood-stains on his face. "He was too—too—too heavy for me."

Scully straightened and addressed the waiting figure. "Stranger," he said, evenly, "it's all up with our side." Then his voice changed into that vibrant huskiness which is commonly the tone of the most simple and deadly announcements. "Johnnie is whipped."

Without replying, the victor moved off on the route to the front door of the hotel.

The cowboy was formulating new and unspellable blasphemies. The Easterner was startled to find that they were out in a wind that seemed to come direct from the shadowed arctic floes. He heard again the wail of the snow as it was flung to its grave in the south. He knew now that all this time the cold had been sinking into him deeper and deeper, and he wondered that he had not perished. He felt indifferent to the condition of the vanquished man.

"Johnnie, can you walk?" asked Scully.

"Did I hurt—hurt him any?" asked the son.

"Can you walk, boy? Can you walk?"

Johnnie's voice was suddenly strong. There was a robust impatience in it. "I asked you whether I hurt him any!"

"Yes, yes, Johnnie," answered the cowboy, consolingly; "he's hurt a good deal."

They raised him from the ground, and as soon as he was on his feet he went tottering off, rebuffing all attempts at assistance. When the party rounded the corner they were fairly blinded by the pelting of the snow. It burned their faces like fire. The cowboy carried Johnnie through the drift to the door. As they entered, some cards again rose from the floor and beat against the wall.

The Easterner rushed to the stove. He was so profoundly chilled that he almost dared to embrace the glowing iron. The Swede was not in the room. Johnnie sank into a chair and, folding his arms on his knees, buried his face in them. Scully, warming one foot and then the other at a rim of the stove, muttered to himself with Celtic mournfulness. The cowboy had removed his fur cap, and with a dazed and rueful air he was running one hand through his tousled locks. From overhead they could hear the creaking of boards, as the Swede tramped here and there in his room.

The sad quiet was broken by the sudden flinging open of a door that led toward the kitchen. It was instantly followed by an inrush of women. They precipitated themselves upon Johnnie amid a chorus of lamentation. Before they carried their prey off to the kitchen, there to be bathed and harangued with that mixture of sympathy and abuse which is a feat of their sex, the mother straightened herself and fixed old Scully with an eye of stern reproach. "Shame be upon you, Patrick Scully!" she cried. "Your own son, too. Shame be upon you!"

"There, now! Be quiet, now!" said the old man, weakly.

"Shame be upon you, Patrick Scully!" The girls, rallying to this slogan, sniffed disdainfully in the direction of those trembling accomplices, the cowboy and the Easterner. Presently they bore Johnnie away, and left the three men to dismal reflection.

VII

"I'd like to fight this here Dutchman myself," said the cowboy, breaking a long silence.

Scully wagged his head sadly. "No, that wouldn't do. It wouldn't be right. It wouldn't be right."

"Well, why wouldn't it?" argued the cowboy. "I don't see no harm in it."

"No," answered Scully, with mournful heroism. "It wouldn't be right. It was Johnnie's fight, and now we mustn't whip the man just because he whipped Johnnie."

"Yes, that's true enough," said the cowboy; "but—he better not get fresh with me, because I couldn't stand no more of it."

"You'll not say a word to him," commanded Scully, and even then they heard the tread of the Swede on the stairs. His entrance was made theatric. He swept the door back with a bang and swaggered to the middle of the room. No one looked at him. "Well," he cried, insolently, at Scully, "I s'pose you'll tell me now how much I owe you?"

The old man remained stolid. "You don't owe me nothin'."

"Huh!" said the Swede, "huh! Don't owe 'im nothin'."

The cowboy addressed the Swede. "Stranger, I don't see how you come to be so gay around here."

Old Scully was instantly alert. "Stop!" he shouted, holding his hand forth, fingers upward. "Bill, you shut up!"

The cowboy spat carelessly into the sawdust-box. "I didn't say a word, did I?" he asked.

"Mr. Scully," called the Swede, "how much do I owe you?" It was seen that he was attired for departure, and that he had his valise in his hand.

"You don't owe me nothin'," repeated Scully in his same imperturbable way.

"Huh!" said the Swede. "I guess you're right. I guess if it was any way at all, you'd owe me somethin'. That's what I guess." He turned to the cowboy. " 'Kill him! Kill him! Kill him!' " he mimicked, and then guffawed victoriously. " 'Kill him!' " He was convulsed with ironical humor.

But he might have been jeering the dead. The three men were immovable and silent, staring with glassy eyes at the stove.

The Swede opened the door and passed into the storm, one derisive glance backward at the still group.

As soon as the door was closed, Scully and the cowboy leaped to their feet and began to curse. They trampled to and fro, waving their arms and smashing into the air with their fists. "Oh, but that was a hard minute!" wailed Scully. "That was a hard minute! Him there leerin' and scoffin'! One bang at his nose was worth forty dollars to me that minute! How did you stand it, Bill?"

"How did I stand it?" cried the cowboy in a quivering voice. "How did I stand it? Oh!"

The old man burst into sudden brogue. "I'd loike to take that Swade," he wailed, "and hould 'im down on a shtone flure and bate 'im to a jelly wid a shtick!"

The cowboy groaned in sympathy. "I'd like to git him by the neck and ha-ammer him"—he brought his hand down on a chair with a noise like a pistol-shot—"hammer that there Dutchman until he couldn't tell himself from a dead coyote!"

"I'd bate 'im until he—"

"I'd show *him* some things—"

And then together they raised a yearning, fanatic cry— "Oh-o-oh! if we only could—"

"Yes!"

"Yes!"

"And then I'd—"

"O-o-oh!"

VIII

The Swede, tightly gripping his valise, tacked across the face of the storm as if he carried sails. He was following a line of little naked, gasping trees which, he knew, must mark the way of the road. His face, fresh from the pounding of Johnnie's fists, felt more pleasure than pain in the wind and the driving snow. A number of square shapes loomed upon him finally, and he knew them as the houses of the main body of the town. He found a street and made travel along it, leaning heavily upon the wind whenever, at a corner, a terrific blast caught him.

He might have been in a deserted village. We picture the world as thick with conquering and elate humanity, but here, with the bugles of the tempest pealing, it was hard to imagine a peopled earth. One viewed the existence of man then as a marvel, and conceded a glamor of wonder to these lice which were caused to cling to a whirling, fire-smitten, ice-locked, disease-stricken, space-lost bulb. The conceit of man was explained by this storm to be the very engine of life. One was a coxcomb not to die in it. However, the Swede found a saloon.

In front of it an indomitable red light was burning, and the snow-flakes were made blood-color as they flew through the circumscribed territory of the lamp's shining. The Swede pushed open the door of the saloon and entered. A sanded expanse was before him, and at the end of it four men sat about a table drinking. Down one side of the room extended a radiant bar, and its guardian was leaning upon his elbows listening to the talk of the men at the table. The Swede dropped his valise upon the floor and, smiling fraternally upon the barkeeper, said, "Gimme some whiskey, will you?" The man placed a bottle, a whiskey-glass, and a glass of ice-thick water upon the bar. The Swede poured himself an abnormal portion of whiskey and drank it in three gulps. "Pretty bad night," remarked the bartender, indifferently. He was making the pretension of blindness which is usually a distinction of his class; but it could have been seen that he was furtively studying the half-erased bloodstains on the face of the Swede. "Bad night," he said again.

"Oh, it's good enough for me," replied the Swede, hardily, as he poured himself more whiskey. The barkeeper took his coin and maneuvered it through its reception by the highly nickelled cash-machine. A bell rang; a card labeled "20 cts." had appeared.

"No," continued the Swede, "this isn't too bad weather. It's good enough for me."

"So?" murmured the barkeeper, languidly.

The copious drams made the Swede's eyes swim, and he breathed a trifle heavier. "Yes, I like this weather. I like it. It suits me." It was apparently his design to impart a deep significance to these words.

"So?" murmured the bartender again. He turned to gaze dreamily at the scroll-like birds and bird-like scrolls which had been drawn with soap upon the mirrors in back of the bar.

"Well, I guess I'll take another drink," said the Swede, presently. "Have something?"

"No, thanks; I'm not drinkin'," answered the bartender. Afterward he asked, "How did you hurt your face?"

The Swede immediately began to boast loudly. "Why, in a fight. I thumped the soul out of a man down here at Scully's hotel."

The interest of the four men at the table was at last aroused.

"Who was it?" said one.

"Johnnie Scully," blustered the Swede. "Son of the man what runs it. He will be pretty near dead for some weeks, I can tell you. I made a nice thing of him, I did. He couldn't get up. They carried him in the house. Have a drink?"

Instantly the men in some subtle way encased themselves in reserve. "No, thanks," said one. The group was of curious formation. Two were prominent local business men; one was the district attorney; and one was a professional gambler of the kind known as "square."[1] But a scrutiny of the group would not have enabled an observer to pick the gambler from the men of more reputable pursuits. He was, in fact, a man so delicate in manner, when among people of fair class, and so judicious in his choice of victims, that in the strictly masculine part of the town's life he had come to be explicitly trusted and admired. People called him a thoroughbred. The fear and contempt with which his craft was regarded were undoubtedly the reason why his quiet dignity shone conspicuous above the quiet dignity of men who might be merely hatters, billiard-markers, or grocery clerks. Beyond an occasional unwary traveller who came by rail, this gambler was supposed to prey solely upon reckless and senile farmers, who, when flush with good crops, drove into town in all the pride and confidence of an absolutely invulnerable stupidity. Hearing at times in circuitous fashion of the despoilment of such a farmer, the important men of Romper invariably

1. Honest.

laughed in contempt of the victim, and if they thought of the wolf at all, it was a kind of pride at the knowledge that he would never dare think of attacking their wisdom and courage. Besides, it was popular that this gambler had a real wife and two real children in a neat cottage in a suburb, where he led an exemplary home life; and when any one even suggested a discrepancy in his character, the crowd immediately vociferated descriptions of this virtuous family circle. Then men who led exemplary home lives, and men who did not lead exemplary home lives, all subsided in a bunch, remarking that there was nothing more to be said.

However, when a restriction was placed upon him—as, for instance, when a strong clique of members of the new Pollywog Club refused to permit him, even as a spectator, to appear in the rooms of the organization—the candor and gentleness with which he accepted the judgment disarmed many of his foes and made his friends more desperately partisan. He invariably distinguished between himself and a respectable Romper man so quickly and frankly that his manner actually appeared to be a continual broadcast compliment.

And one must not forget to declare the fundamental fact of his entire position in Romper. It is irrefutable that in all affairs outside his business, in all matters that occur eternally and commonly between man and man, this thieving card-player was so generous, so just, so moral, that, in a contest, he could have put to flight the consciences of nine tenths of the citizens of Romper.

And so it happened that he was seated in this saloon with the two prominent local merchants and the district attorney.

The Swede continued to drink raw whiskey, meanwhile babbling at the barkeeper and trying to induce him to indulge in potations. "Come on. Have a drink. Come on. What—no? Well, have a little one, then. By gawd, I've whipped a man tonight, and I want to celebrate. I whipped him good, too. Gentlemen," the Swede cried to the men at the table, "have a drink?"

"Ssh!" said the barkeeper.

The group at the table, although furtively attentive, had been pretending to be deep in talk, but now a man lifted his eyes toward the Swede and said, shortly, "Thanks. We don't want any more."

At this reply the Swede ruffled out his chest like a rooster. "Well," he exploded, "it seems I can't get anybody to drink with me in this town. Seems so, don't it? Well!"

"Ssh!" said the barkeeper.

"Say," snarled the Swede, "don't you try to shut me up. I won't have it. I'm a gentleman, and I want people to drink with me. And I want 'em to drink with me now. *Now*—do you understand?" He rapped the bar with his knuckles.

Years of experience had calloused the bartender. He merely grew sulky. "I hear you," he answered.

"Well," cried the Swede, "listen hard then. See those men over there? Well, they're going to drink with me, and don't you forget it. Now you watch."

"Hi!" yelled the barkeeper, "this won't do!"

"Why won't it?" demanded the Swede. He stalked over to the table, and by chance laid his hand upon the shoulder of the gambler. "How about this?" he asked wrathfully. "I asked you to drink with me."

The gambler simply twisted his head and spoke over his shoulder. "My friend, I don't know you."

"Oh, hell!" answered the Swede, "come and have a drink."

"Now, my boy," advised the gambler, kindly, "take your hand off my shoulder and go 'way and mind your own business." He was a little, slim man, and it seemed strange to hear him use this tone of heroic patronage to the burly Swede. The other men at the table said nothing.

"What! You won't drink with me, you little dude? I'll make you, then! I'll make you!" The Swede had grasped the gambler frenziedly at the throat, and was dragging him from his chair. The other men sprang up. The barkeeper dashed around the corner of his bar. There was a great tumult, and then was seen a long blade in the hand of the gambler. It shot forward, and a human body, this citadel of virtue, wisdom, power, was pierced as easily as if it had been a melon. The Swede fell with a cry of supreme astonishment.

The prominent merchants and the district attorney must have at once tumbled out of the place backward. The bartender found himself hanging limply to the arm of a chair and gazing into the eyes of a murderer.

"Henry," said the latter, as he wiped his knife on one of the towels that hung beneath the bar rail, "you tell 'em where to find me. I'll be home, waiting for 'em." Then he vanished. A moment afterward the barkeeper was in the street dinning through the storm for help and, moreover, companionship.

The corpse of the Swede, alone in the saloon, had its eye fixed upon a dreadful legend that dwelt atop of the cash-machine: "This registers the amount of your purchase."

IX

Months later, the cowboy was frying pork over the stove of a little ranch near the Dakota line, when there was a quick thud of hoofs outside, and presently the Easterner entered with the letters and the papers.

"Well," said the Easterner at once, "the chap that killed the Swede has got three years? Wasn't much, was it?"

"He has? Three years?" The cowboy poised his pan of pork, while he ruminated upon the news. "Three years. That ain't much."

"No. It was a light sentence," replied the Easterner as he unbuckled his spurs. "Seems there was a good deal of sympathy for him in Romper."

"If the bartender had been any good," observed the cowboy, thoughtfully, "he would have gone in and cracked that there Dutchman on the head with a bottle in the beginnin' of it and stopped all this here murderin'."

"Yes, a thousand things might have happened," said the Easterner, tartly.

The cowboy returned his pan of pork to the fire, but his philosophy continued. "It's funny, ain't it? If he hadn't said Johnnie was cheatin' he'd be alive this minute. He was an awful fool. Game played for fun, too. Not for money. I believe he was crazy."

"I feel sorry for that gambler," said the Easterner.

"Oh, so do I," said the cowboy. "He don't deserve none of it for killin' who he did."

"The Swede might not have been killed if everything had been square."

"Might not have been killed?" exclaimed the cowboy. "Everythin' square? Why, when he said that Johnnie was cheatin' and acted like such a jackass? And then in the saloon he fairly walked up to git hurt?" With these arguments the cowboy browbeat the Easterner and reduced him to rage.

"You're a fool!" cried the Easterner, viciously. "You're a bigger jackass than the Swede by a million majority. Now let me tell you one thing. Let me tell you something. Listen! Johnnie *was* cheating!"

" 'Johnnie,' " said the cowboy, blankly. There was a minute of silence, and then he said, robustly, "Why, no. The game was only for fun."

"Fun or not," said the Easterner, "Johnnie was cheating. I saw him. I know it. I saw him. And I refused to stand up and be a man. I let the Swede fight it out alone. And you—you were simply puffing around the place and wanting to fight. And then old Scully himself! We are all in it! This poor gambler isn't even a noun. He is kind of an adverb. Every sin is the result of a collaboration. We, five of us, have collaborated in the murder of this Swede. Usually there are from a dozen to forty women really involved in every murder, but in this case it seems to be only five men—you, I, Johnnie, old Scully; and that fool of an unfortunate gambler came merely as a culmination, the apex of a human movement, and gets all the punishment."

The cowboy, injured and rebellious, cried out blindly into this fog of mysterious theory: "Well, I didn't do anythin', did I?"

1. What ironies lie in the fact that the action takes place in Nebraska? Consider that everyone associates violence and danger with "The West." Is Nebraska somehow transformed into "The West"?
2. Is Scully acting from good motives in trying to keep peace in his hotel? Does the purity or impurity of his motives have anything to do with the outcome of the action?
3. Is Johnnie a victim or an aggressor? What does the story as a whole say about innocence and guilt?
4. How much faith can we have in the interpretation of the case given by the Easterner in the last section of the story? Is this just one man's opinion or is it a wise summary of all that has happened?
5. At one point the author tells us that the Swede's body is a "citadel of virtue, wisdom, power." Does this appear to be true when you take into account the man's behavior? If you see a discrepancy, account for it.

Isak Dinesen

Dinesen (pseudonym for Baroness Karen Blixen) (1885–1962) was born near Elsinore, Denmark, the descendant of an old and cultivated Danish family. She married a cousin and in 1914 went with him to British East Africa, where she remained for seventeen busy years acting as counselor, judge, teacher, and doctor for natives and settlers alike. The color and detail of her experience there flavors the reminiscences in Out of Africa *(1937). Several years after her divorce she returned to Denmark and began to write—in English—the spellbinding stories that made her world-famous in the 1930's. Her first collection was* Seven Gothic Tales *(1934), an immensely popular book that was a Book-of-the-Month Club selection, as was her* Winter's Tales *(1942). No literary or ideological formula fits her fiction, which seems to spring from a pure impulse to fascinate the reader by a tour among marvels and enchantments. While she was living under the Nazi occupation of Denmark during World War II, she wrote, using the name of Pierre Andrézel, a novel, published in 1946 as* The Angelic Avengers. *Later publications are* Last Tales *(1957) and* Anecdotes of Destiny *(1958).*

Sorrow-Acre

The low, undulating Danish landscape was silent and serene, mysteriously wide-awake in the hour before sunrise. There was not a cloud in the pale sky, not a shadow along the dim, pearly fields, hills and woods. The mist was lifting from the valleys and hollows, the air was cool, the grass and the foliage dripping wet with morning-dew. Unwatched by the eyes of man, and undisturbed by his activity, the country breathed a timeless life, to which language was inadequate.

All the same, a human race had lived on this land for a thousand years, had been formed by its soil and weather, and had marked it with its thoughts, so that now no one could tell where the existence of the one ceased and the other began. The thin grey line of a road, winding across the plain and up and down hills, was the fixed materialisation of human longing, and of the human notion that it is better to be in one place than another.

A child of the country would read this open landscape like a book. The irregular mosaic of meadows and cornlands was a picture, in timid green and yellow, of the people's struggle for its daily bread; the centuries had taught it to plough and sow in this way. On a distant hill the immovable wings of a windmill, in a small blue cross against the sky, delineated a later stage in the career of bread. The blurred outline of thatched roofs—a low, brown growth of the earth—where the huts of the village thronged together, told the history, from his cradle to his grave, of the peasant, the creature nearest to the soil and dependent on it, prospering in a fertile year and dying in years of drought and pests.

A little higher up, with the faint horizontal line of the white cemetery wall round it, and the vertical contour of tall poplars by its side, the red-tiled church bore witness, as far as the eye reached, that this was a Christian country. The child of the land knew it as a strange house, inhabited only for a few hours every seventh day, but with a strong, clear voice in it to give out the joys and sorrows of the land: a plain, square embodiment of the nation's trust in the justice and mercy of heaven. But where, amongst cupular woods and groves, the lordly, pyramidal silhouette of the cut lime avenues rose in the air, there a big country house lay.

The child of the land would read much within these elegant, geometrical ciphers on the hazy blue. They spoke of power, the lime trees paraded round a stronghold. Up here was decided the destiny of the surrounding land and of the men and beasts upon it, and the peasant lifted his eyes to the green pyramids with awe. They spoke of dignity, decorum and taste. Danish soil grew no finer flower than the mansion to which the long avenue led. In its lofty rooms life and death bore themselves with stately grace. The country house did not gaze upward, like the church, nor down to the ground like the huts; it had a wider earthly horizon than they, and was related to much noble architecture all over Europe. Foreign artisans had been called in to panel and stucco it, and its own inhabitants travelled and brought back ideas, fashions and things of beauty. Paintings, tapestries, silver and glass from distant countries had been made to feel at home here, and now formed part of Danish country life.

The big house stood as firmly rooted in the soil of Denmark as the peasants' huts, and was as faithfully allied to her four winds and her changing seasons, to her animal life, trees and flowers. Only its interests lay in a higher plane. Within the domain of the lime trees it was no longer cows, goats, and pigs on which the minds and the talk ran, but horses and dogs. The wild fauna, the game of the land, that the peasant shook his fist at, when he saw it on his young green rye or in his ripening wheat field, to the residents of the country houses were the main pursuit and the joy of existence.

The writing in the sky solemnly proclaimed continuance, a worldly immortality. The great country houses had held their ground through many generations. The families who lived in them revered the past as they honoured themselves, for the history of Denmark was their own history.

A Rosenkrantz had sat at Rosenholm, a Juel at Hverringe, a Skeel at Gammel-Estrup as long as people remembered. They had seen kings and schools of style succeed one another and, proudly and humbly, had made over their personal existence to that of their land, so that amongst their equals and with the peasants they passed by its name: Rosenholm, Hverringe, Gammel-Estrup. To the King and the country, to his family and to the individual lord of the manor himself it was a matter of minor consequence which particular Rosenkrantz, Juel or Skeel, out of a long row of fathers and sons, at the moment in his person incarnated the fields and woods, the peasants, cattle and game of the estate. Many duties rested on the shoulders of the big landowners—towards God in heaven, towards the King, his neighbour and himself—and they were all harmoniously consolidated into the idea of his duties towards his land. Highest amongst these ranked his obligation to uphold the sacred continuance, and to produce a new Rosenkrantz, Juel or Skeel for the service of Rosenholm, Hverringe and Gammel-Estrup.

Female grace was prized in the manors. Together with good hunting and fine wine it was the flower and emblem of the higher existence led there, and in many ways the families prided themselves more on their daughters than on their sons.

The ladies who promenaded in the lime avenues, or drove through them in heavy coaches with four horses, carried the future of the name in their laps and were, like dignified and debonair caryatides,[1] holding up the houses. They were themselves conscious of their value, kept up their price, and moved in a sphere of pretty worship and self-worship. They might even be thought to add to it, on their own, a graceful, arch, paradoxical haughtiness. For how free were they, how powerful! Their lords might rule the country, and allow themselves many liberties, but when it came to that supreme matter of legitimacy which was the vital principle of their world, the centre of gravity lay with them.

The lime trees were in bloom. But in the early morning only a faint fragrance drifted through the garden, an airy message, an aromatic echo of the dreams during the short summer night.

In a long avenue that led from the house all the way to the end of the garden, where, from a small white pavilion in the classic style, there was a great view over the fields, a young man walked. He was

1. Carvings of draped female figures supporting upper sections of walls in Greek architecture.

plainly dressed in brown, with pretty linen and lace, bare-headed, with his hair tied by a ribbon. He was dark, a strong and sturdy figure with fine eyes and hands; he limped a little on one leg.

The big house at the top of the avenue, the garden and the fields had been his childhood's paradise. But he had travelled and lived out of Denmark, in Rome and Paris, and he was at present appointed to the Danish Legation to the Court of King George,[2] the brother of the late, unfortunate young Danish Queen. He had not seen his ancestral home for nine years. It made him laugh to find, now, everything so much smaller than he remembered it, and at the same time he was strangely moved by meeting it again. Dead people came towards him and smiled at him; a small boy in a ruff ran past him with his hoop and kite, in passing gave him a clear glance and laughingly asked: "Do you mean to tell me that you are I?" He tried to catch him in the flight, and to answer him: "Yes, I assure you that I am you," but the light figure did not wait for a reply.

The young man, whose name was Adam, stood in a particular relation to the house and the land. For six months he had been heir to it all; nominally he was so even at this moment. It was this circumstance which had brought him from England, and on which his mind was dwelling, as he walked along slowly.

The old lord up at the manor, his father's brother, had had much misfortune in his domestic life. His wife had died young, and two of his children in infancy. The one son then left to him, his cousin's playmate, was a sickly and morose boy. For ten years the father travelled with him from one watering place to another, in Germany and Italy, hardly ever in other company than that of his silent, dying child, sheltering the faint flame of life with both hands, until such time as it could be passed over to a new bearer of the name. At the same time another misfortune had struck him: he fell into disfavour at Court, where till now he had held a fine position. He was about to rehabilitate his family's prestige through the marriage which he had arranged for his son, when before it could take place the bridegroom died, not yet twenty years old.

Adam learned of his cousin's death, and his own changed fortune, in England, through his ambitious and triumphant mother. He sat with her letter in his hand and did not know what to think about it.

If this, he reflected, had happened to him while he was still a boy, in Denmark, it would have meant all the world to him. It would be so now with his friends and schoolfellows, if they were in his place, and they would, at this moment, be congratulating or envying him.

2. Apparently a reference to George II of England. George was the father, not the brother, of Louisa, Queen of Denmark (1724–1751).

But he was neither covetous nor vain by nature; he had faith in his own talents and had been content to know that his success in life depended on his personal ability. His slight infirmity had always set him a little apart from other boys; it had, perhaps, given him a keener sensibility of many things in life, and he did not, now, deem it quite right that the head of the family should limp on one leg. He did not even see his prospects in the same light as his people at home. In England he had met with greater wealth and magnificence than they dreamed of; he had been in love with, and made happy by, an English lady of such rank and fortune that to her, he felt, the finest estate of Denmark would look but like a child's toy farm.

And in England, too, he had come in touch with the great new ideas of the age: of nature, of the right and freedom of man, of justice and beauty. The universe, through them, had become infinitely wider to him; he wanted to find out still more about it and was planning to travel to America, to the new world. For a moment he felt trapped and imprisoned, as if the dead people of his name, from the family vault at home, were stretching out their parched arms for him.

But at the same time he began to dream at night of the old house and garden. He had walked in these avenues in dream, and had smelled the scent of the flowering limes. When at Ranelagh an old gypsy woman looked at his hand and told him that a son of his was to sit in the seat of his father, he felt a sudden, deep satisfaction, queer in a young man who till now had never given his sons a thought.

Then, six months later, his mother again wrote to tell him that his uncle had himself married the girl intended for his dead son. The head of the family was still in his best age, not over sixty, and although Adam remembered him as a small, slight man, he was a vigorous person; it was likely that his young wife would bear him sons.

Adam's mother in her disappointment lay the blame on him. If he had returned to Denmark, she told him, his uncle might have come to look upon him as a son, and would not have married; nay, he might have handed the bride over to him. Adam knew better. The family estate, differing from the neighbouring properties, had gone down from father to son ever since a man of their name first sat there. The tradition of direct succession was the pride of the clan and a sacred dogma to his uncle; he would surely call for a son of his own flesh and bone.

But at the news the young man was seized by a strange, deep, aching remorse towards his old home in Denmark. It was as if he had been making light of a friendly and generous gesture, and disloyal to someone unfailingly loyal to him. It would be but just, he thought, if from now the place should disown and forget him. Nostalgia, which before he had never known, caught hold of him; for the first time he walked in the streets and parks of London as a stranger.

He wrote to his uncle and asked if he might come and stay with him, begged leave from the Legation and took ship for Denmark. He had come to the house to make his peace with it; he had slept little in the night, and was up so early and walking in the garden, to explain himself, and to be forgiven.

While he walked, the still garden slowly took up its day's work. A big snail, of the kind that his grandfather had brought back from France, and which he remembered eating in the house as a child, was already, with dignity, dragging a silver train down the avenue. The birds began to sing; in an old tree under which he stopped a number of them were worrying an owl; the rule of the night was over.

He stood at the end of the avenue and saw the sky lightening. An ecstatic clarity filled the world; in half an hour the sun would rise. A rye field here ran along the garden; two roe-deer were moving in it and looked roseate in the dawn. He gazed out over the fields, where as a small boy he had ridden his pony, and towards the wood where he had killed his first stag. He remembered the old servants who had taught him; some of them were now in their graves.

The ties which bound him to this place, he reflected, were of a mystic nature. He might never again come back to it, and it would make no difference. As long as a man of his own blood and name should sit in the house, hunt in the fields and be obeyed by the people in the huts, wherever he travelled on earth, in England or amongst the red Indians of America, he himself would still be safe, would still have a home, and would carry weight in the world.

His eyes rested on the church. In old days, before the time of Martin Luther,[3] younger sons of great families, he knew, had entered the Church of Rome, and had given up individual wealth and happiness to serve the greater ideals. They, too, had bestowed honour upon their homes and were remembered in its registers. In the solitude of the morning half in jest he let his mind run as it listed; it seemed to him that he might speak to the land as to a person, as to the mother of his race. "Is it only my body that you want," he asked her, "while you reject my imagination, energy and emotions? If the world might be brought to acknowledge that the virtue of our name does not belong to the past only, will it give you no satisfaction?" The landscape was so still that he could not tell whether it answered him yes or no.

After a while he walked on, and came to the new French rose garden laid out for the young mistress of the house. In England he had acquired a freer taste in gardening, and he wondered if he could liberate these blushing captives, and make them thrive outside their cut hedges. Perhaps, he meditated, the elegantly conventional garden would

3. Leader of the Protestant break from the Roman Catholic Church (1483–1546).

be a floral portrait of his young aunt from Court, whom he had not yet seen.

As once more he came to the pavilion at the end of the avenue his eyes were caught by a bouquet of delicate colours which could not possibly belong to the Danish summer morning. It was in fact his uncle himself, powdered and silk-stockinged, but still in a brocade dressing-gown, and obviously sunk in deep thought. "And what business, or what meditations," Adam asked himself, "drags a connoisseur of the beautiful, but three months married to a wife of seventeen, from his bed into his garden before sunrise?" He walked up to the small, slim, straight figure.

His uncle on his side showed no surprise at seeing him, but then he rarely seemed surprised at anything. He greeted him, with a compliment on his matunality,[4] as kindly as he had done on his arrival last evening. After a moment he looked to the sky, and solemnly proclaimed: "It will be a hot day." Adam, as a child, had often been impressed by the grand, ceremonial manner in which the old lord would state the common happenings of existence; it looked as if nothing had changed here, but all was what it used to be.

The uncle offered the nephew a pinch of snuff. "No, thank you, Uncle," said Adam, "it would ruin my nose to the scent of your garden, which is as fresh as the Garden of Eden, newly created." "From every tree of which," said his uncle, smiling, "thou, my Adam, mayest freely eat." They slowly walked up the avenue together.

The hidden sun was now already gilding the top of the tallest trees. Adam talked of the beauties of nature, and of the greatness of Nordic scenery, less marked by the hand of man than that of Italy. His uncle took the praise of the landscape as a personal compliment, and congratulated him because he had not, in likeness to many young travellers in foreign countries, learned to despise his native land. No, said Adam, he had lately in England longed for the fields and woods of his Danish home. And he had there become acquainted with a new piece of Danish poetry which had enchanted him more than any English or French work. He named the author, Johannes Ewald,[5] and quoted a few of the mighty, turbulent verses.

"And I have wondered, while I read," he went on after a pause, still moved by the lines he himself had declaimed, "that we have not till now understood how much our Nordic mythology in moral greatness surpasses that of Greece and Rome. If it had not been for the physical beauty of the ancient gods, which has come down to us in marble, no modern mind could hold them worthy of worship. They were mean, capricious and treacherous. The gods of our Danish fore-

4. Morning appearance. 5. Denmark's greatest lyric poet (1743–1781).

fathers are as much more divine than they as the Druid is nobler than the Augur.[6] For the fair gods of Asgaard[7] did possess the sublime human virtues; they were righteous, trustworthy, benevolent and even, within a barbaric age, chivalrous." His uncle here for the first time appeared to take any real interest in the conversation. He stopped, his majestic nose a little in the air. "Ah, it was easier to them," he said.

"What do you mean, Uncle?" Adam asked. "It was a great deal easier," said his uncle, "to the northern gods than to those of Greece to be, as you will have it, righteous and benevolent. To my mind it even reveals a weakness in the souls of our ancient Danes that they should consent to adore such divinities." "My dear uncle," said Adam, smiling, "I have always felt that you would be familiar with the modes of Olympus. Now please let me share your insight, and tell me why virtue should come easier to our Danish gods than to those of milder climates." "They were not as powerful," said his uncle.

"And does power," Adam again asked, "stand in the way of virtue?" "Nay," said his uncle gravely. "Nay, power is in itself the supreme virtue. But the gods of which you speak were never all-powerful. They had, at all times, by their side those darker powers which they named the Jotuns,[8] and who worked the suffering, the disasters, the ruin of our world. They might safely give themselves up to temperance and kindness. The omnipotent gods," he went on, "have no such facilitation. With their omnipotence they take over the woe of the universe."

They had walked up the avenue till they were in view of the house. The old lord stopped and ran his eyes over it. The stately building was the same as ever; behind the two tall front windows, Adam knew, was now his young aunt's room. His uncle turned and walked back.

"Chivalry," he said, "chivalry, of which you were speaking, is not a virtue of the omnipotent. It must needs imply mighty rival powers for the knight to defy. With a dragon inferior to him in strength, what figure will St. George[9] cut? The knight who finds no superior forces ready to hand must invent them, and combat wind-mills; his knighthood itself stipulates dangers, vileness, darkness on all sides of him. Nay, believe me, my nephew, in spite of his moral worth, your chivalrous Odin of Asgaard as a Regent must take rank below that of Jove[1] who avowed his sovereignty, and accepted the world which he ruled. But you are young," he added, "and the experience of the aged to you will sound pedantic."

6. I.e., as an ancient Celtic wizard-priest is nobler than an ancient Roman soothsayer. 7. In Teutonic mythology, the celestial dwelling place. 8. Race of giants. 9. In religious allegory the slayer of the dragon; patron saint of England, Aragon, and Portugal. 1. The chief of Roman gods, as Odin is chief of Norse gods.

He stood immovable for a moment and then with deep gravity proclaimed: "The sun is up."

The sun did indeed rise above the horizon. The wide landscape was suddenly animated by its splendour, and the dewy grass shone in a thousand gleams.

"I have listened to you, Uncle," said Adam, "with great interest. But while we have talked you yourself have seemed to me preoccupied; your eyes have rested on the field outside the garden, as if something of great moment, a matter of life and death, was going on there. Now that the sun is up, I see the mowers in the rye and hear them whetting their sickles. It is, I remember you telling me, the first day of the harvest. That is a great day to a landowner and enough to take his mind away from the gods. It is very fine weather, and I wish you a full barn."

The elder man stood still, his hands on his walking-stick. "There is indeed," he said at last, "something going on in that field, a matter of life and death. Come, let us sit down here, and I will tell you the whole story." They sat down on the seat that ran all along the pavilion, and while he spoke the old lord of the land did not take his eyes off the rye field.

"A week ago, on Thursday night," he said, "someone set fire to my barn at Rødmosegaard—you know the place, close to the moor—and burned it all down. For two or three days we could not lay hands on the offender. Then on Monday morning the keeper at Rødmose, with the wheelwright over there, came up to the house; they dragged with them a boy, Goske Piil, a widow's son, and they made their Bible oath that he had done it; they had themselves seen him sneaking round the barn by nightfall on Thursday. Goske had no good name on the farm; the keeper bore him a grudge upon an old matter of poaching, and the wheelwright did not like him either, for he did, I believe, suspect him with his young wife. The boy, when I talked to him, swore to his innocence, but he could not hold his own against the two old men. So I had him locked up, and meant to send him in to our judge of the district, with a letter.

"The judge is a fool, and would naturally do nothing but what he thought I wished him to do. He might have the boy sent to the convict prison for arson, or put amongst the soldiers as a bad character and a poacher. Or again, if he thought that that was what I wanted, he could let him off.

"I was out riding in the fields, looking at the corn that was soon ripe to be mowed, when a woman, the widow, Goske's mother, was brought up before me, and begged to speak to me. Anne-Marie is her name. You will remember her; she lives in the small house east of the village. She has not got a good name in the place either.

They tell as a girl she had a child and did away with it.

"From five days' weeping her voice was so cracked that it was difficult for me to understand what she said. Her son, she told me at last, had indeed been over at Rødmose on Thursday, but for no ill purpose; he had gone to see someone. He was her only son, she called the Lord God to witness on his innocence, and she wrung her hands to me that I should save the boy for her.

"We were in the rye field that you and I are looking at now. That gave me an idea. I said to the widow: 'If in one day, between sunrise and sunset, with your own hands you can mow this field, and it be well done, I will let the case drop and you shall keep your son. But if you cannot do it, he must go, and it is not likely that you will then ever see him again.'

"She stood up then and gazed over the field. She kissed my riding boot in gratitude for the favour shown to her.

The old lord here made a pause, and Adam said: "Her son meant much to her?" "He is her only child," said his uncle. "He means to her her daily bread and support in old age. It may be said that she holds him as dear as her own life. As," he added, "within a higher order of life, a son to his father means the name and the race, and he holds him as dear as life everlasting. Yes, her son means much to her. For the mowing of that field is a day's work to three men, or three days' work to one man. Today, as the sun rose, she set to her task. And down there, by the end of the field, you will see her now, in a blue headcloth, with the man I have set to follow her and to ascertain that she does the work unassisted, and with two or three friends by her, who are comforting her."

Adam looked down, and did indeed see a woman in a blue headcloth, and a few other figures in the corn.

They sat for a while in silence. "Do you yourself," Adam then said, "believe the boy to be innocent?" "I cannot tell," said his uncle. "There is no proof. The word of the keeper and the wheelwright stand against the boy's word. If indeed I did believe the one thing or the other, it would be merely a matter of chance, or maybe of sympathy. The boy," he said after a moment, "was my son's playmate, the only other child that I ever knew him to like or to get on with." "Do you," Adam again asked, "hold it possible to her to fulfill your condition?" "Nay, I cannot tell," said the old lord. "To an ordinary person it would not be possible. No ordinary person would ever have taken it on at all. I chose it so. We are not quibbling with the law, Anne-Marie and I."

Adam for a few minutes followed the movement of the small group in the rye. "Will you walk back?" he asked. "No," said his uncle, "I think that I shall stay here till I have seen the end of the thing." "Until sunset?" Adam asked with surprise. "Yes," said the old lord. Adam said: "It will be a long day." "Yes," said his uncle, "a long day. But," he added, as Adam rose to walk away, "if, as you said, you have got that tragedy of which you spoke in your pocket, be as kind as to leave it here, to keep me company." Adam handed him the book.

In the avenue he met two footmen who carried the old lord's morning chocolate down to the pavilion on large silver trays.

As now the sun rose in the sky, and the day grew hot, the lime trees gave forth their exuberance of scent, and the garden was filled with unsurpassed, unbelievable sweetness. Towards the still hour of midday the long avenue reverberated like a soundboard with a low, incessant murmur: the humming of a million bees that clung to the pendulous, thronging clusters of blossoms and were drunk with bliss.

In all the short lifetime of Danish summer there is no richer or more luscious moment than that week wherein the lime trees flower. The heavenly scent goes to the head and to the heart; it seems to unite the fields of Denmark with those of Elysium;[2] it contains both hay, honey and holy incense, and is half fairy-land and half apothecary's locker. The avenue was changed into a mystic edifice, a dryad's cathedral, outward from summit to base lavishly adorned, set with multitudinous ornaments, and golden in the sun. But behind the walls the vaults were benignly cool and sombre, like ambrosial sanctuaries in a dazzling and burning world, and in here the ground was still moist.

Up in the house, behind the silk curtains of the two front windows, the young mistress of the estate from the wide bed stuck her feet into two little high-heeled slippers. Her lace-trimmed nightgown had slid up above her knee and down from the shoulder; her hair, done up in curling-pins for the night, was still frosty with the powder of yesterday, her round face flushed with sleep. She stepped out to the middle of the floor and stood there, looking extremely grave and thoughtful, yet she did not think at all. But through her head a long procession of pictures marched, and she was unconsciously endeavouring to put them in order, as the pictures of her existence had used to be.

She had grown up at Court; it was her world, and there was probably not in the whole country a small creature more exquisitely and innocently drilled to the stately measure of a palace. By favour of the old Dowager Queen she bore her name and that of the King's sister, the Queen of Sweden: Sophie Magdalena. It was with a view to these things that her husband, when he wished to restore his status in high places, had chosen her as a bride, first for his son and then for himself. But her own father, who held an Office in the Royal Household and belonged to the new Court aristocracy, in his day had done

2. In classic mythology, the abode of the good after death.

the same thing the other way round, and had married a country lady, to get a foothold within the old nobility of Denmark. The little girl had her mother's blood in her veins. The country to her had been an immense surprise and delight.

To get into her castle-court she must drive through the farm yard, through the heavy stone gateway in the barn itself, wherein the rolling of her coach for a few seconds re-echoed like thunder. She must drive past the stables and the timber-mare,[3] from which sometimes a miscreant would follow her with sad eyes, and might here startle a long string of squalling geese, or pass the heavy, scowling bull, led on by a ring in his nose and kneading the earth in dumb fury. At first this had been to her, every time, a slight shock and a jest. But after a while all these creatures and things, which belonged to her, seemed to become part of herself. Her mothers, the old Danish country ladies, were robust persons, undismayed by any kind of weather; now she herself had walked in the rain and had laughed and glowed in it like a green tree.

She had taken her great new home in possession at a time when all the world was unfolding, mating and propagating. Flowers, which she had known only in bouquets and festoons, sprung from the earth round her; birds sang in all the trees. The new-born lambs seemed to her daintier than her dolls had been. From her husband's Hanoverian[4] stud, foals were brought to her to give names; she stood and watched as they poked their soft noses into their mothers' bellies to drink. Of this strange process she had till now only vaguely heard. She had happened to witness, from a path in the park, the rearing and screeching stallion on the mare. All this luxuriance, lust and fecundity was displayed before her eyes, as for her pleasure.

And for her own part, in the midst of it, she was given an old husband who treated her with punctilious respect because she was to bear him a son. Such was the compact; she had known of it from the beginning. Her husband, she found, was doing his best to fulfill his part of it, and she herself was loyal by nature and strictly brought up. She would not shirk her obligation. Only she was vaguely aware of a discord or an incompatibility within her majestic existence, which prevented her from being as happy as she had expected to be.

After a time her chagrin took a strange form: as the consciousness of an absence. Someone ought to have been with her who was not. She had no experience in analysing her feelings; there had not been time for that at Court. Now, as she was more often left to herself, she vaguely probed her own mind. She tried to set her father in that void place, her sisters, her music master, an Italian singer whom she had admired;

3. A crude wooden horse on which soldiers—or sometimes servants—were tied for punishment. 4. Hanover, in north-central Germany, was one of the states of the Holy Roman Empire.

but none of them would fill it for her. At times she felt lighter at heart, and believed the misfortune to have left her. And then again it would happen, if she were alone, or in her husband's company, and even within his embrace, that everything round her would cry out: Where? Where? so that she let her wild eyes run about the room in search for the being who should have been there, and who had not come.

When, six months ago, she was informed that her first young bridegroom had died and that she was to marry his father in his place, she had not been sorry. Her youthful suitor, the one time she had seen him, had appeared to her infantile and insipid; the father would make a statelier consort. Now she had sometimes thought of the dead boy, and wondered whether with him life would have been more joyful. But she soon again dismissed the picture, and that was the sad youth's last recall to the stage of this world.

Upon one wall of her room there hung a long mirror. As she gazed into it new images came along. The day before, driving with her husband, she had seen, at a distance, a party of village girls bathing in the river, and the sun shining on them. All her life she had moved amongst naked marble deities, but it had till now never occurred to her that the people she knew should themselves be naked under their bodices and trains, waistcoats and satin breeches, that indeed she herself felt naked within her clothes. Now, in front of the looking-glass, she tardily untied the ribbons of her nightgown, and let it drop to the floor.

The room was dim behind the drawn curtains. In the mirror her body was silvery like a white rose; only her cheeks and mouth, and the tips of her fingers and breasts had a faint carmine. Her slender torso was formed by the whalebones that had clasped it tightly from her childhood; above the slim, dimpled knee a gentle narrowness marked the place of the garter. Her limbs were rounded as if, at whatever place they might be cut through with a sharp knife, a perfectly circular transverse incision would be obtained. The side and belly were so smooth that her own gaze slipped and glided, and grasped for a hold. She was not altogether like a statue, she found, and lifted her arms above her head. She turned to get a view of her back, the curves below the waistline were still blushing from the pressure of the bed. She called to mind a few tales about nymphs and goddesses, but they all seemed a long way off, so her mind returned to the peasant girls in the river. They were, for a few minutes, idealized into playmates, or sisters even, since they belonged to her as did the meadow and the blue river itself. And within the next moment the sense of forlornness once more came upon her, a *horror vaccui*[5] like a physical pain. Surely, surely someone

5. Abhorrence of emptiness.

should have been with her now, her other self, like the image in the glass, but nearer, stronger, alive. There was no one, the universe was empty round her.

A sudden, keen itching under her knee took her out of her reveries, and awoke in her the hunting instincts of her breed. She wetted a finger on her tongue, slowly brought it down and quickly slapped it to the spot. She felt the diminutive, sharp body of the insect against the silky skin, pressed the thumb to it, and triumphantly lifted up the small prisoner between her fingertips. She stood quite still, as if meditating upon the fact that a flea was the only creature risking its life for her smoothness and sweet blood.

Her maid opened the door and came in, loaded with the attire of the day—shift, stays, hoop and petticoats. She remembered that she had a guest in the house, the new nephew arrived from England. Her husband had instructed her to be kind to their young kinsman, disinherited, so to say, by her presence in the house. They would ride out on the land together.

In the afternoon the sky was no longer blue as in the morning. Large clouds slowly towered up on it, and the great vault itself was colourless, as if diffused into vapours round the white-hot sun in zenith. A low thunder ran along the western horizon; once or twice the dust of the roads rose in tall spirals. But the fields, the hills and the woods were as still as a painted landscape.

Adam walked down the avenue to the pavilion, and found his uncle there, fully dressed, his hands upon his walking-stick and his eyes on the rye field. The book that Adam had given him lay by his side. The field now seemed alive with people. Small groups stood here and there in it, and a long row of men and women were slowly advancing towards the garden in the line of the swath.

The old lord nodded to his nephew, but did not speak or change his position. Adam stood by him as still as himself.

The day to him had been strangely disquieting. At the meeting again with old places the sweet melodies of the past had filled his senses and his mind, and had mingled with new, bewitching tunes of the present. He was back in Denmark, no longer a child but a youth, with a keener sense of the beautiful, with tales of other countries to tell, and still a true son of his own land and enchanted by its loveliness as he had never been before.

But through all these harmonies the tragic and cruel tale which the old lord had told him in the morning, and the sad contest which he knew to be going on so near by, in the corn field, had re-echoed, like the recurrent, hollow throbbing of a muffled drum, a redoubtable sound. It came back time after time, so that he had felt himself to change colour and to answer absently. It brought with it a deeper sense of pity with all that lived than he had ever known. When he had been riding with his young aunt, and their road ran along the scene of the drama, he had taken care to ride between her and the field, so that she should not see what was going on there, or question him about it. He had chosen the way home through the deep, green wood for the same reason.

More dominantly even than the figure of the woman struggling with her sickle for her son's life, the old man's figure, as he had seen it at sunrise, kept him company through the day. He came to ponder on the part which that lonely, determinate form had played in his own life. From the time when his father died, it had impersonated to the boy law and order, wisdom of life and kind guardianship. What was he to do, he thought, if after eighteen years these filial feelings must change, and his second father's figure take on to him a horrible aspect, as a symbol of the tyranny and oppression of the world? What was he to do if ever the two should come to stand in opposition to each other as adversaries?

At the same time an unaccountable, a sinister alarm and dread on behalf of the old man himself took hold of him. For surely here the Goddess Nemesis[6] could not be far away. This man had ruled the world round him for a longer period than Adam's own lifetime and had never been gainsaid by anyone. During the years when he had wandered through Europe with a sick boy of his own blood as his sole companion he had learned to set himself apart from his surroundings, and to close himself up to all outer life. and he had become insusceptible to the ideas and feelings of other human beings. Strange fancies might there have run in his mind, so that in the end he had seen himself as the only person really existing, and the world as a poor and vain shadow-play, which had no substance to it.

Now, in senile wilfullness, he would take in his hand the life of those simpler and weaker than himself, of a woman, using it to his own ends, and he feared of no retributive justice. Did he not know, the young man thought, that there were powers in the world, different from and more formidable than the short-lived might of a despot?

With the sultry heat of the day this foreboding of impending disaster grew upon him, until he felt ruin threatening not the old lord only, but the house, the name and himself with him. It seemed to him that he must cry out a warning to the man he had loved, before it was too late.

But as now he was once more in his uncle's company, the green calm of the garden was so deep that he did not find his voice to cry out. Instead a little French air which his aunt had sung to him up in

6. Greek goddess of retribution.

the house kept running in his mind.—"*C'est un trop doux effort . . .*"[7] He had good knowledge of music; he had heard the air before, in Paris, but not so sweetly sung.

After a time he asked: "Will the woman fulfill her bargain?" His uncle unfolded his hands. "It is an extraordinary thing," he said animatedly, "that it looks as if she might fulfill it. If you count the hours from sunrise till now, and from now till sunset, you will find the time left her to be half of that already gone. And see! She has now mowed two-thirds of the field. But then we will naturally have to reckon with her strength declining as she works on. All in all, it is an idle pursuit in you or me to bet on the issue of the matter; we must wait and see. Sit down, and keep me company in my watch." In two minds Adam sat down.

"And here," said his uncle, and took up the book from the seat, "is your book, which has passed the time finely. It is great poetry, ambrosia to the ear and the heart. And it has, with our discourse on divinity this morning, given me stuff for thought. I have been reflecting upon the law of retributive justice." He took a pinch of snuff, and went on. "A new age," he said, "has made to itself a god in its own image, an emotional god. And now you are already writing a tragedy on your god."

Adam had no wish to begin a debate on poetry with his uncle, but he also somehow dreaded a silence, and said: "It may be, then, that we hold tragedy to be, in the scheme of life, a noble, a divine phenomenon."

"Aye," said his uncle solemnly, "a noble phenomenon, the noblest on earth. But of the earth only, and never divine. Tragedy is the privilege of man, his highest privilege. The God of the Christian Church Himself, when He wished to experience tragedy, had to assume human form. And even at that," he added thoughtfully, "the tragedy was not wholly valid, as it would have become had the hero of it been, in very truth, a man. The divinity of Christ conveyed to it a divine note, the moment of comedy. The real tragic part, by the nature of things, fell to the executors, not to the victim. Nay, my nephew, we should not adulterate the pure elements of the cosmos. Tragedy should remain the right of human beings, subject, in their conditions or in their own nature, to the dire law of necessity. To them it is salvation and beatification. But the gods, whom we must believe to be unacquainted with and incomprehensive of necessity, can have no knowledge of the tragic. When they are brought face to face with it they will, according to my experience, have the good taste and decorum to keep still, and not interfere.

7. "It is too sweet an effort . . ."

"No," he said after a pause, "the true art of the gods is the comic. The comic is a condescension of the divine to the world of man; it is the sublime vision, which cannot be studied, but must ever be celestially granted. In the comic the gods see their own being reflected as in a mirror, and while the tragic poet is bound by strict laws, they will allow the comic artist a freedom as unlimited as their own. They do not even withhold their own existence from his sports. Jove may favour Lucianos of Samosata.[8] As long as your mockery is in true godly taste you may mock at the gods and still remain a sound devotee. But in pitying, or condoling with your god, you deny and annihilate him, and such is the most horrible of atheisms.

"And here on earth, too," he went on, "we, who stand in lieu of the gods and have emancipated ourselves from the tyranny of necessity, should leave to our vassals their monopoly of tragedy, and for ourselves accept the comic with grace. Only a boorish and cruel master—a parvenu, in fact—will make a jest of his servants' necessity, or force the comic upon them. Only a timid and pedantic ruler, a *petit-maître*,[9] will fear the ludicrous on his own behalf. Indeed," he finished his long speech, "the very same fatality, which, in striking the burgher or peasant, will become tragedy, with the aristocrat is exalted to the comic. By the grace and wit of our acceptance hereof our aristocracy is known."

Adam could not help smiling a little as he heard the apotheosis of the comic on the lips of the erect, ceremonious prophet. In this ironic smile he was, for the first time, estranging himself from the head of his house.

A shadow fell across the landscape. A cloud had crept over the sun; the country changed colour beneath it, faded and bleached, and even all sounds for a minute seemed to die out of it.

"Ah, now," said the old lord, "if it is going to rain, and the rye gets wet, Anne-Marie will not be able to finish in time. And who comes there?" he added, and turned his head a little.

Preceded by a lackey a man in riding boots and a striped waistcoat with silver buttons, and with his hat in his hand, came down the avenue. He bowed deeply, first to the old lord and then to Adam.

"My bailiff," said the old lord. "Good afternoon, Bailiff. What news have you to bring?" The bailiff made a sad gesture. "Poor news only, my lord," he said. "And how poor news?" asked his master. "There is," said the bailiff with weight, "not a soul at work on the land, and not a sickle going except that of Anne-Marie in this rye field. The mowing has stopped; they are all at her heels. It is a poor day for a first day

8. Greek satirist (A.D. 120–180). Jove would tolerate his satire because of its excellence.
9. Minor master.

of the harvest." "Yes, I see," said the old lord. The bailiff went on. "I have spoken kindly to them," he said, "and I have sworn at them; it is all one. They might as well all be deaf."

"Good bailiff," said the old lord, "leave them in peace; let them do as they like. This day may, all the same, do them more good than many others. Where is Goske, the boy, Anne-Marie's son?" "We have set him in the small room by the barn," said the bailiff. "Nay, let him be brought down," said the old lord; "let him see his mother at work. But what do you say—will she get the field mowed in time?" "If you ask me, my lord," said the bailiff, "I believe that she will. Who would have thought so? She is only a small woman. It is as hot a day today as, well, as I do ever remember. I myself, you yourself, my lord, could not have done what Anne-Marie has done today." "Nay, nay, we could not, Bailiff," said the old lord.

The bailiff pulled out a red handkerchief and wiped his brow, somewhat calmed by venting his wrath. "If," he remarked with bitterness, "they would all work as the widow works now, we would make a profit on the land." "Yes," said the old lord, and fell into thought, as if calculating the profit it might make. "Still," he said, "as to the question of profit and loss, that is more intricate than it looks. I will tell you something that you may not know: The most famous tissue ever woven was ravelled out again every night.[1] But come," he added, "she is close by now. We will go and have a look at her work ourselves." With these words he rose and set his hat on.

The cloud had drawn away again; the rays of the sun once more burned the wide landscape, and as the small party walked out from under the shade of the trees the dead-still heat was heavy as lead; the sweat sprang out on their faces and their eyelids smarted. On the narrow path they had to go one by one, the old lord stepping along first, all black, and the footman, in his bright livery, bringing up the rear.

The field was indeed filled with people like a marketplace; there were probably a hundred or more men and women in it. To Adam the scene recalled pictures from his Bible: the meeting between Esau and Jacob in Edom, or Boas' reapers in his barley field near Bethlehem.[2] Some were standing by the side of the field, others pressed in small groups close to the mowing woman, and a few followed in her wake, binding up sheaves where she had cut the corn, as if thereby they thought to help her, or as if by all means they meant to have part in her work. A younger woman with a pail on her head kept close to her side, and with her a number of half-grown children. One of these first caught sight of the lord of the estate and his suite, and pointed to him.

1. An allusion to Penelope's weaving, which she unraveled every night to delay suitors while her husband Odysseus was away (Homer's *Odyssey*). 2. References to Genesis 32 and Ruth 2.

The binders let their sheaves drop, and as the old man stood still many of the onlookers drew close round him.

The woman on whom till now the eyes of the whole field had rested—a small figure on the large stage—was advancing slowly and unevenly, bent double as if she were walking on her knees, and stumbling as she walked. His blue head-cloth had slipped back from her head; the grey hair was plastered to the skull with sweat, dusty and stuck with straw. She was obviously totally unaware of the multitude round her; neither did she now once turn her head or her gaze towards the new arrivals.

Absorbed in her work she again and again stretched out her left hand to grasp a handful of corn, and her right hand with the sickle in it to cut it off close to the soil, in wavering, groping pulls, like a tired swimmer's strokes. Her course took her so close to the feet of the old lord that his shadow fell on her. Just then she staggered and swayed sideways, and the woman who followed her lifted the pail from her head and held it to her lips. Anne-Marie drank without leaving her hold on her sickle, and the water ran from the corners of her mouth. A boy, close to her, quickly bent one knee, seized her hands in his own and, steadying and guiding them, cut off a gripe of rye. "No, no," said the old lord, "you must not do that, boy. Leave Anne-Marie in peace to her work." At the sound of his voice the woman, falteringly, lifted her face in his direction.

The bony and tanned face was streaked with sweat and dust; the eyes were dimmed. But there was not in its expression the slightest trace of fear or pain. Indeed amongst all the grave and concerned faces of the field hers was the only one perfectly calm, peaceful and mild. The mouth was drawn together in a thin line, a prim, keen, patient little smile, such as will be seen in the face of an old woman at her spinning-wheel or her knitting, eager on her work, and happy in it. And as the younger woman lifted back the pail, she immediately again fell to her mowing, with an ardent, tender craving, like that of a mother who lays a baby to the nipple. Like an insect that bustles along in high grass, or like a small vessel in a heavy sea, she butted her way on, her quiet face once more bent upon her task.

The whole throng of onlookers, and with them the small group from the pavilion, advanced as she advanced, slowly and as if drawn by a string. The bailiff, who felt the intense silence of the field heavy on him, said to the old lord: "The rye will yield better this year than last," and got no reply. He repeated his remark to Adam, and at last to the footman, who felt himself above a discussion on agriculture, and only cleared his throat in answer. In a while the bailiff again broke the silence. "There is the boy," he said and pointed with his thumb. "They have brought him down." At that moment the woman fell forward on her face and was lifted up by those nearest to her.

Adam suddenly stopped on the path, and covered his eyes with his hand. The old lord without turning asked him if he felt incommoded by the heat. "No," said Adam, "but stay. Let me speak to you." His uncle stopped, with his hand on the stick and looking ahead, as if regretful of being held back.

"In the name of God," cried the young man in French, "force not this woman to continue." There was a short pause. "But I force her not, my friend," said his uncle in the same language. "She is free to finish at any moment." "At the cost of her child only," again cried Adam. "Do you not see that she is dying? You know not what you are doing, or what it may bring upon you."

The old lord, perplexed by this unexpected animadversion, after a second turned all round, and his pale, clear eyes sought his nephew's face with stately surprise. His long, waxen face, with two symmetrical curls at the sides, had something of the mien of an idealized and ennobled old sheep or ram. He made sign to the bailiff to go on. The footman also withdrew a little, and the uncle and nephew were, so to say, alone on the path. For a minute neither of them spoke.

"In this very place where we now stand," said the old lord, then, with hauteur, "I gave Anne-Marie my word."

"My uncle!" said Adam. "A life is a greater thing even than a word. Recall that word, I beseech you, which was given in caprice, as a whim. I am praying you more for your sake than for my own, yet I shall be grateful to you all my life if you will grant me my prayer."

"You will have learned in school," said his uncle, "that in the beginning was the word.[3] It may have been pronounced in caprice, as a whim, the Scripture tells me nothing about it. It is still the principle of our world, its law of gravitation. My own humble word has been the principle of the land on which we stand, for an age of man. My father's word was the same, before my day."

"You are mistaken," cried Adam. "The word is creative—it is imagination, daring and passion. By it the world was made. How much greater are these powers which bring into being than any restricting or controlling law! You wish the land on which we look to produce and propagate; you should not banish from it the forces which cause, and which keep up life, nor turn it into a desert by dominance of law. And when you look at the people, simpler than we and nearer to the heart of nature, who do not analyse their feelings, whose life is one with the life of the earth, do they not inspire in you a tenderness, respect, reverence even? This woman is ready to die for her son; will it ever happen to you or me that a woman willingly gives up her life for us?

3. John 1:1.

And if it did indeed come to pass, should we make so light of it as not to give up a dogma in return?"

"You are young," said the old lord. "A new age will undoubtedly applaud you. I am old-fashioned, I have been quoting to you texts a thousand years old. We do not, perhaps, quite understand one another. But with my own people I am, I believe, in good understanding. Anne-Marie might well feel that I am making light of her exploit, if now, at the eleventh hour, I did nullify it by a second word. I myself should feel so in her place. Yes, my nephew, it is possible, did I grant you your prayer and pronounce such an amnesty, that I should find it void against her faithfulness, and that we would still see her at her work, unable to give it up, as a shuttle in the rye field, until she had it all mowed. But she would then be a shocking, a horrible sight, a figure of unseemly fun, like a small planet running wild in the sky, when the law of gravitation had been done away with."

"And if she dies at her task," Adam exclaimed, "her death, and its consequences will come upon your head."

The old lord took off his hat and gently ran his hand over his powdered head. "Upon my head?" he said. "I have kept up my head in many weathers. Even," he added proudly, "against the cold wind from high places. In what shape will it come upon my head, my nephew?" "I cannot tell," cried Adam in despair. "I have spoken to warn you. God only knows." "Amen," said the old lord with a little delicate smile. "Come, we will walk on." Adam drew in his breath deeply.

"No," he said in Danish. "I cannot come with you. This field is yours; things will happen here as you decide. But I myself must go away. I beg you to let me have, this evening, a coach as far as town. For I could not sleep another night under your roof, which I have honoured beyond any on earth." So many conflicting feelings at his own speech thronged in his breast that it would have been impossible for him to give them words.

The old lord, who had already begun to walk on, stood still, and with him the lackey. He did not speak for a minute, as if to give Adam time to collect his mind. But the young man's mind was in uproar and would not be collected.

"Must we," the old man asked, in Danish, "take leave here, in the rye field? I have held you dear, next to my own son. I have followed your career in life from year to year, and have been proud of you. I was happy when you wrote to say that you were coming back. If now you will go away, I wish you well." He shifted his walking-stick from the right hand to the left and gravely looked his nephew in the face.

Adam did not meet his eyes. He was gazing out over the landscape. In the late mellow afternoon it was resuming its colours, like a painting brought into proper light; in the meadows the little black stacks of peat stood gravely distinct upon the green sward. On this same morning he had greeted it all, like a child running laughingly to its mother's bosom; now already he must tear himself from it, in discordance, and forever. And at the moment of parting it seemed infinitely dearer than any time before, so much beautified and solemnized by the coming separation that it looked like the place in a dream, a landscape out of paradise, and he wondered if it was really the same. But, yes—there before him was, once more, the hunting-ground of long ago. And there was the road on which he had ridden today.

"But tell me where you mean to go from here," said the old lord slowly. "I myself have travelled a good deal in my days. I know the word of leaving, the wish to go away. But I have learned by experience that, in reality, the word has a meaning only to the place and the people which one leaves. When you have left my house—although it will see you go with sadness—as far as it is concerned the matter is finished and done with. But to the person who goes away it is a different thing, and not so simple. At the moment that he leaves one place he will be already, by the laws of life, on his way to another, upon this earth. Let me know, then, for the sake of our old acquaintance, to which place you are going when you leave here. To England?"

"No," said Adam. He felt in his heart that he could never again go back to England or to his easy and carefree life there. It was not far enough away; deeper waters than the North Sea must now be laid between him and Denmark. "No, not to England," he said. "I shall go to America, to the new world." For a moment he shut his eyes, trying to form to himself a picture of existence in America, with the grey Atlantic Ocean between him and these fields and woods.

"To America?" said his uncle and drew up his eyebrows. "Yes, I have heard of America. They have got freedom there, a big waterfall, savage red men. They shoot turkeys, I have read, as we shoot partridges. Well, if it be your wish, go to America, Adam, and be happy in the new world."

He stood for some time, sunk in thought, as if he had already sent off the young man to America, and had done with him. When at last he spoke, his words had the character of a monologue, enunciated by the person who watches things come and go, and himself stays on.

"Take service, there," he said, "with the power which will give you an easier bargain than this: That with your own life you may buy the life of your son."

Adam had not listened to his uncle's remarks about America, but the conclusive, solemn words caught his ear. He looked up. As if for the first time in his life, he saw the old man's figure as a whole, and conceived how small it was, so much smaller than himself, pale, a thin black anchorite upon his own land. A thought ran through his head: "How terrible to be old!" The abhorrence of the tyrant, and the sinister dread on his behalf, which had followed him all day, seemed to die out of him, and his pity with all creation to extend even to the sombre form before him.

His whole being had cried out for harmony. Now, with the possibility of forgiving, of a reconciliation, a sense of relief went through him; confusedly he bethought himself of Anne-Marie drinking the water held to her lips. He took off his hat, as his uncle had done a moment ago, so that to a beholder at a distance it would seem that the two dark-clad gentlemen on the path were repeatedly and respectfully saluting one another, and brushed the hair from his forehead. Once more the tune of the garden-room rang in his mind:

> "*Mourir pour ce qu'on aime*
> *C'est un trop doux effort . . .*"[4]

He stood for a long time immobile and dumb. He broke off a few ears of rye, kept them in his hand and looked at them.

He saw the ways of life, he thought, as a twined and tangled design, complicated and mazy; it was not given him or any mortal to command or control it. Life and death, happiness and woe, the past and present, were interlaced within the pattern. Yet to the initiated it might be read as easily as our ciphers—which to the savage must seem confused and incomprehensible—will be read by the schoolboy. And out of the contrasting elements concord rose. All that lived must suffer; the old man, whom he had judged hardly, had suffered, as he had watched his son die, and had dreaded the obliteration of his being. He himself would come to know ache, tears and remorse, and, even through these, the fullness of life. So might now, to the woman in the rye field, her ordeal be a triumphant procession. For to die for the one you loved was an effort too sweet for words.

As now he thought of it, he knew that all his life he had sought the unity of things, the secret which connects the phenomena of existence. It was this strife, this dim presage, which had sometimes made him stand still and inert in the midst of the games of his playfellows, or which had, at other moments—on moonlight nights, or in his little boat on the sea—lifted the boy to ecstatic happiness. Where other young people, in their pleasures or their amours, had searched for contrast and variety, he himself had yearned only to comprehend in full the oneness of the world. If things had come differently to him, if

4. "To die for one you love/Is too sweet an effort . . ."

his young cousin had not died, and the events that followed his death had not brought him to Denmark, his search for understanding and harmony might have taken him to America, and he might have found them there, in the virgin forests of a new world. Now they have been disclosed to him today, in the place where he had played as a child. As the song is one with the voice that sings it, as the road is one with the goal, as lovers are made one in their embrace, so is man one with his destiny, and he shall love it as himself.[5]

He looked up again, towards the horizon. If he wished to, he felt, he might find out what it was that had brought to him, here, the sudden conception of the unity of the universe. When this same morning he had philosophized, lightly and for his own sake, on his feeling of belonging to this land and soil, it had been the beginning of it. But since then it had grown; it had become a mightier thing, a revelation to his soul. Some time he would look into it, for the law of cause and effect was a wonderful and fascinating study. But not now. This hour was consecrated to greater emotions, to a surrender to fate and to the will of life.

"No," he said at last. "If you wish it I shall not go. I shall stay here."

At that moment a long, loud roll of thunder broke the stillness of the afternoon. It re-echoed for a while amongst the low hills, and it reverberated within the young man's breast as powerfully as if he had been seized and shaken by hands. The landscape had spoken. He remembered that twelve hours ago he had put a question to it, half in jest, and not knowing what he did. Here it gave him its answer.

What it contained he did not know; neither did he inquire. In his promise to his uncle he had given himself over to the mightier powers of the world. Now what must come must come.

"I thank you," said the old lord, and made a little stiff gesture with his hand. "I am happy to hear you say so. We should not let the difference in our ages, or of our views, separate us. In our family we have been wont to keep peace and faith with one another. You have made my heart lighter."

Something within his uncle's speech faintly recalled to Adam the misgivings of the afternoon. He rejected them; he would not let them trouble the new, sweet felicity which his resolution to stay had brought him.

"I shall go on now," said the old lord. "But there is no need for you to follow me. I will tell you tomorrow how the matter has ended."

5. Here Dinesen paraphrases a Roman motto revived by Friedrich Nietzsche (1844–1900), German philosopher—"Love your fate."

"No," said Adam, "I shall come back by sunset, to see the end of it myself."

All the same he did not come back. He kept the hour in his mind, and all through the evening the consciousness of the drama, and the profound concern and compassion with which, in his thoughts, he followed it, gave to his speech, glance and movements a grave and pathetic substance. But he felt that he was, in the rooms of the manor, and even by the harpsichord on which he accompanied his aunt to her air from *Alceste*,[6] as much in the centre of things as if he had stood in the rye field itself, and as near to those human beings whose fate was now decided there. Anne-Marie and he were both in the hands of destiny, and destiny would, by different ways, bring each to the designated end.

Later on he remembered what he had thought that evening.

But the old lord stayed on. Late in the afternoon he even had an idea; he called down his valet to the pavilion and made him shift his clothes on him and dress him up in a brocaded suit that he had worn at Court. He let a lace-trimmed shirt be drawn over his head and stuck out his slim legs to have them put into thin silk stockings and buckled shoes. In this majestic attire he dined alone, of a frugal meal, but took a bottle of Rhenish wine with it, to keep up his strength. He sat on for a while, a little sunk in his seat; then, as the sun neared the earth, he straightened himself, and took the way down to the field.

The shadows were now lengthening, azure blue along all the eastern slopes. The lonely trees in the corn marked their site by narrow blue pools running out from their feet, and as the old man walked a thin, immensely elongated reflection stirred behind him on the path. Once he stood still; he thought he heard a lark singing over his head, a spring-like sound; his tired head held no clear perception of the season; he seemed to be walking, and standing, in a kind of eternity.

The people in the field were no longer silent, as they had been in the afternoon. Many of them talked loudly among themselves, and a little farther away a woman was weeping.

When the bailiff saw his master, he came up to him. He told him, in great agitation, that the widow would, in all likelihood, finish the mowing of the field within a quarter of an hour.

"Are the keeper and the wheelwright here?" the old lord asked him. "They have been here," said the bailiff, "and have gone away, five times. Each time they have said that they would not come back. But they have come back again, all the same, and they are here now."

6. Opera by Christoph Willibald Gluck, Austrian composer (1714–1787). From the Greek myth of Alcestis, who died in her husband's place and was rescued from Hades by Hercules.

"And where is the boy?" the old lord asked again. "He is with her," said the bailiff. "I have given him leave to follow her. He has walked close to his mother all the afternoon, and you will see him now by her side, down there."

Anne-Marie was now working her way up towards them more evenly than before, but with extreme slowness, as if at any moment she might come to a standstill. This excessive tardiness, the old lord reflected, if it had been purposely performed, would have been an inimitable, dignified exhibition of skilled art; one might fancy the Emperor of China advancing in like manner on a divine procession or rite. He shaded his eyes with his hand, for the sun was now just beyond the horizon, and its last rays made light, wild, many-coloured specks dance before his sight. With such splendour did the sunset emblazon the earth and the air that the landscape was turned into a melting-pot of glorious metals. The meadows and the grasslands became pure gold; the barley field near by, with its long ears, was a live lake of shining silver.

There was only a small patch of straw standing in the rye field, when the woman, alarmed by the change in the light, turned her head a little to get a look at the sun. The while she did not stop her work, but grasped one handful of corn and cut it off, then another, and another. A great stir, and a sound like a manifold, deep sigh, ran through the crowd. The field was now mowed from one end to the other. Only the mower herself did not realize the fact; she stretched out her hand anew, and when she found nothing in it, she seemed puzzled or disappointed. Then she let her arms drop, and slowly sank to her knees.

Many of the women burst out weeping, and the swarm drew close round her, leaving only a small open space at the side where the old lord stood. Their sudden nearness frightened Anne-Marie; she made a slight, uneasy movement, as if terrified that they should put their hands on her.

The boy, who had kept by her all day, now fell on his knees beside her. Even he dared not touch her, but held one arm low behind her back and the other before her, level with her collar-bone, to catch hold of her if she should fall, and all the time he cried aloud. At that moment the sun went down.

The old lord stepped forward and solemnly took off his hat. The crowd became silent, waiting for him to speak. But for a minute or two he said nothing. Then he addressed her, very slowly.

"Your son is free, Anne-Marie," he said. He again waited a little, and added: "You have done a good day's work, which will long be remembered."

Anne-Marie raised her gaze only as high as his knees, and he understood that she had not heard what he said. He turned to the boy.

"You tell your mother, Goske," he said, gently, "what I have told her."

The boy had been sobbing wildly, in raucous, broken moans. It took him some time to collect and control himself. But when at last he spoke, straight into his mother's face, his voice was low, a little impatient, as if he were conveying an everyday message to her. "I am free, Mother," he said. "You have done a good day's work that will long be remembered."

At the sound of his voice she lifted her face to him. A faint, bland shadow of surprise ran over it, but still she gave no sign of having heard what he said, so that the people round them began to wonder if the exhaustion had turned her deaf. But after a moment she slowly and waveringly raised her hand, fumbling in the air as she aimed at his face, and with her fingers touched his cheek. The cheek was wet with tears, so that at the contact her fingertips lightly stuck to it, and she seemed unable to overcome the infinitely slight resistance, or to withdraw her hand. For a minute the two looked each other in the face. Then, softly and lingeringly, like a sheaf of corn that falls to the ground, she sank forward onto the boy's shoulder, and he closed his arms round her.

He held her thus, pressed against him, his own face buried in her hair and head-cloth, for such a long time that those nearest to them, frightened because her body looked so small in his embrace, drew closer, bent down and loosened his grip. The boy let them do so without a word or a movement. But the woman who held Anne-Marie, in her arms to lift her up, turned her face to the old lord. "She is dead," she said.

The people who had followed Anne-Marie all through the day kept standing and stirring in the field for many hours, as long as the evening light lasted, and longer. Long after some of them had made a stretcher from branches of the trees and had carried away the dead woman, others wandered on, up and down the stubble, imitating and measuring her course from one end of the rye field to the other, and binding up the last sheaves, where she had finished her mowing.

The old lord stayed with them for a long time, stepping along a little, and again standing still.

In the place where the woman had died the old lord later on had a stone set up, with a sickle engraved in it. The peasants on the land then named the rye field "Sorrow-Acre." By this name it was known a long time after the story of the woman and her son had itself been forgotten.

---

1. What is the importance of the physical setting? Of the traditions of the landowners? Of the descriptions of the young wife and her role?

2. Give a full summary of the old lord's ideas of law, power, and justice. In what ways are Adam's ideas opposed to these? Does Anne-Marie oppose or accept them?
3. What does the old lord mean when he says that Anne-Marie is not an ordinary person? Why is her accomplishment believable?
4. How does the story comment on democracy and aristocracy? Does the author seem to take sides?
5. Why does Adam give up his plan of going to America?
6. Discuss the story as a representation of conflicting ideas of justice. As an allegory based on Christian theology.
7. How do the values set forth by the story fit with your own sense of right and justice?

Ralph Ellison

Ellison (1914–) was born in Oklahoma City and educated at Tuskegee Institute. Though his publications have been few, his novel Invisible Man *(1952) is one of the most discussed and praised books published in America since World War II. While it announces no program for the liberation of blacks, it presents in an almost definitive way the moral, political, and psychological considerations involved in the enduring struggle. In his other writings, including the essays published in* Shadow and Act *(1964), Ellison has continued his exploration of the problem of identity within the context of black culture. He has brought to a culmination the double consciousness of blacks who also know themselves to be American.*

King of the Bingo Game

The woman in front of him was eating roasted peanuts that smelled so good that he could barely contain his hunger. He could not even sleep and wished they'd hurry and begin the bingo game. There, on his right, two fellows were drinking wine out of a bottle wrapped in a paper bag, and he could hear soft gurgling in the dark. His stomach gave a low, gnawing growl. "If this was down South," he thought, "all I'd have to do is lean over and say, 'Lady, gimme a few of those peanuts, please ma'am,' and she'd pass me the bag and never think nothing of it." Or he could ask the fellows for a drink in the same way. Folks down South stuck together that way; they didn't even have to know you. But up here it was different. Ask somebody for something, and they'd think you were crazy. Well, I ain't crazy. I'm just broke, 'cause I got no birth certificate to get a job, and Laura 'bout to die 'cause we got no money for a doctor. But I ain't crazy. And yet a pinpoint of doubt was focused in his mind as he glanced toward the screen and saw the hero stealthily entering a dark room and sending the beam of a flashlight along a wall of bookcases. This is where he finds the trapdoor, he remembered. The man would pass abruptly through the wall and find the girl tied to a bed, her legs and arms spread wide, and her clothing torn to rags. He laughed softly to himself. He had seen the picture three times, and this was one of the best scenes.

On his right the fellow whispered wide-eyed to his companion, "Man, look ayonder!"

"Damn!"

"Wouldn't I like to have her tied up like that . . ."

"Hey! That fool's letting her loose!"

"Aw, man, he loves her."

"Love or no love!"

The man moved impatiently beside him, and he tried to involve himself in the scene. But Laura was on his mind. Tiring quickly of watching the picture he looked back to where the white beam filtered from the projection room above the balcony. It started small and grew large, specks of dust dancing in its whiteness as it reached the screen. It was strange how the beam always landed right on the screen and didn't mess up and fall somewhere else. But they had it all fixed. Everything was fixed. Now suppose when they showed that girl with her dress torn the girl started taking off the rest of her clothes, and when the guy came in he didn't untie her but kept her there and went to taking off his own clothes? *That* would be something to see. If a picture got out of hand like that those guys up there would go nuts. Yeah, and there'd be so many folks in here you couldn't find a seat for nine months! A strange sensation played over his skin. He shuddered. Yesterday he'd seen a bedbug on a woman's neck as they walked out into the bright street. But exploring his thigh through a hole in his pocket he found only goose pimples and old scars.

The bottle gurgled again. He closed his eyes. Now a dreamy music was accompanying the film and train whistles were sounding in the distance, and he was a boy again walking along a railroad trestle down South, and seeing the train coming, and running back as fast as he could go, and hearing the whistle blowing, and getting off the trestle to solid ground just in time, with the earth trembling beneath his feet, and feeling relieved as he ran down the cinder-strewn embankment onto the highway, and looking back and seeing with terror that the train had left the track and was following him right down the middle of the street, and all the white people laughing as he ran screaming . . .

"Wake up there, buddy! What the hell do you mean hollering like that? Can't you see we trying to enjoy this here picture?"

He stared at the man with gratitude.

"I'm sorry, old man," he said. "I musta been dreaming."

"Well, here, have a drink. And don't be making no noise like that, damn!"

His hands trembled as he tilted his head. It was not wine, but whiskey. Cold rye whiskey. He took a deep swoller, decided it was better not to take another, and handed the bottle back to its owner.

"Thanks, old man," he said.

Now he felt the cold whiskey breaking a warm path straight through the middle of him, growing hotter and sharper as it moved. He had not eaten all day, and it made him light-headed. The smell of the peanuts stabbed him like a knife, and he got up and found a seat in the middle aisle. But no sooner did he sit than he saw a row of intense-faced young girls, and got up again, thinking, "You chicks musta been Lindy-hopping[1] somewhere." He found a seat several rows ahead as the lights came on, and he saw the screen disappear behind a heavy red and gold curtain; then the curtain rising, and the man with the microphone and a uniformed attendant coming on the stage.

He felt for his bingo cards, smiling. The guy at the door wouldn't like it if he knew about his having *five* cards. Well, not everyone played the bingo game; and even with five cards he didn't have much of a chance. For Laura, though, he had to have faith. He studied the cards, each with its different numerals, punching the free center hole in each and spreading them neatly across his lap; and when the lights faded he sat slouched in his seat so that he could look from his cards to the bingo wheel with but a quick shifting of his eyes.

Ahead, at the end of the darkness, the man with the microphone was pressing a button attached to a long cord and spinning the bingo wheel and calling out the number each time the wheel came to rest. And each time the voice rang out his finger raced over the cards for the number. With five cards he had to move fast. He became nervous; there were too many cards, and the man went too fast with his grating voice. Perhaps he should just select one and throw the others away. But he was afraid. He became warm. Wonder how much Laura's doctor would cost? Damn that, watch the cards! And with despair he heard the man call three in a row which he missed on all five cards. This way he'd never win . . .

When he saw the row of holes punched across the third card, he sat paralyzed and heard the man call three more numbers before he stumbled forward, screaming,

"Bingo! Bingo!"

"Let that fool up there," someone called.

"Get up there, man!"

He stumbled down the aisle and up the steps to the stage into a light so sharp and bright that for a moment it blinded him, and he felt that he had moved into the spell of some strange, mysterious power. Yet it was as familiar as the sun, and he knew it was the perfectly familiar bingo.

The man with the microphone was saying something to the audience as he held out his card. A cold light flashed from the man's finger

1. Dancing.

as the card left his hand. His knees trembled. The man stepped closer, checking the card against the numbers chalked on the board. Suppose he had made a mistake? The pomade on the man's hair made him feel faint, and he backed away. But the man was checking the card over the microphone now, and he had to stay. He stood tense, listening.

"Under the O, forty-four," the man chanted. 'Under the I, seven. Under the G, three. Under the B, ninety-six. Under the N, thirteen!"

His breath came easier as the man smiled at the audience.

"Yes sir, ladies and gentlemen, he's one of the chosen people!"

The audience rippled with laughter and applause.

"Step right up to the front of the stage."

He moved slowly forward, wishing that the light was not so bright.

"To win tonight's jackpot of $36.90 the wheel must stop between the double zero, understand?"

He nodded, knowing the ritual from the many days and nights he had watched the winners march across the stage to press the button that controlled the spinning wheel and receive the prizes. And now he followed the instructions as though he'd crossed the slippery stage a million prize-winning times.

The man was making some kind of joke, and he nodded vacantly. So tense had he become that he felt a sudden desire to cry and shook it away. He felt vaguely that his whole life was determined by the bingo wheel; not only that which would happen now that he was at last before it, but all that had gone before, since his birth, and his mother's birth and the birth of his father. It had always been there, even though he had not been aware of it, handing out the unlucky cards and numbers of his days. The feeling persisted, and he started quickly away. I better get down from here before I make a fool of myself, he thought.

"Here, boy," the man called. "You haven't started yet."

Someone laughed as he went hesitantly back.

"Are you all reet?"

He grinned at the man's jive talk, but no words would come, and he knew it was not a convincing grin. For suddenly he knew that he stood on the slippery brink of some terrible embarrassment.

"Where are you from, boy?" the man asked.

"Down South."

"He's from down South, ladies and gentlemen," the man said. "Where from? Speak right into the mike."

"Rocky Mont," he said. "Rock' Mont, North Car'lina."

"So you decided to come down off that mountain to the U.S.," the man laughed. He felt that the man was making a fool of him, but then something cold was placed in his hand, and the lights were no longer behind him.

Standing before the wheel he felt alone, but that was somehow right, and he remembered his plan. He would give the wheel a short quick twirl. Just a touch of the button. He had watched it many times, and always it came close to double zero when it was short and quick. He steeled himself; the fear had left, and he felt a profound sense of promise, as though he were about to be repaid for all the things he'd suffered all his life. Trembling, he pressed the button. There was a whirl of lights, and in a second he realized with finality that though he wanted to, he could not stop. It was as though he held a high-powered line in his naked hand. His nerves tightened. As the wheel increased its speed it seemed to draw him more and more into its power, as though it held his fate; and with it came a deep need to submit, to whirl, to lose himself in its swirl of color. He could not stop it now. So let it be.

The button rested snugly in his palm where the man had placed it. And now he became aware of the man beside him, advising him through the microphone, while behind the shadowy audience hummed with noisy voices. He shifted his feet. There was still that feeling of helplessness within him, making part of him desire to turn back, even now that the jackpot was right in his hand. He squeezed the button until his fist ached. Then, like the sudden shriek of a subway whistle, a doubt tore through his head. Suppose he did not spin the wheel long enough? What could he do, and how could he tell? And then he knew, even as he wondered, that as long as he pressed the button, he could control the jackpot. He and only he could determine whether or not it was to be his. Not even the man with the microphone could do anything about it now. He felt drunk. Then, as though he had come down from a high hill into a valley of people, he heard the audience yelling.

"Come down from there, you jerk!"

"Let somebody else have a chance . . ."

"Ole Jack thinks he done found the end of the rainbow . . ."

The last voice was not unfriendly, and he turned and smiled dreamily into the yelling mouths. Then he turned his back squarely on them.

"Don't take too long, boy," a voice said.

He nodded. They were yelling behind him. Those folks did not understand what had happened to him. They had been playing the bingo game day in and night out for years, trying to win rent money or hamburger change. But not one of those wise guys had discovered this wonderful thing. He watched the wheel whirling past the numbers and experienced a burst of exaltation: This is God! This is the really truly God! He said it aloud, "This is God!"

He said it with such absolute conviction that he feared he would fall fainting into the footlights. But the crowd yelled so loud that they could not hear. These fools, he thought. I'm here trying to tell them the most wonderful secret in the world, and they're yelling like they gone crazy. A hand fell upon his shoulder.

"You'll have to make a choice now, boy. You've taken too long."

He brushed the hand violently away.

"Leave me alone, man. I know what I'm doing!"

The man looked surprised and held on to the microphone for support. And because he did not wish to hurt the man's feelings he smiled, realizing with a sudden pang that there was no way of explaining to the man just why he had to stand there pressing the button forever.

"Come here," he called tiredly.

The man approached, rolling the heavy microphone across the stage.

"Anybody can play this bingo game, right?" he said.

"Sure, but . . ."

He smiled, feeling inclined to be patient with this slick looking white man with his blue shirt and his sharp gabardine suit.

"That's what I thought," he said. "Anybody can win the jackpot as long as they get the lucky number, right?"

"That's the rule, but after all . . ."

"That's what I thought," he said. "And the big prize goes to the man who knows how to win it?"

The man nodded speechlessly.

"Well then, go on over there and watch me win like I want to. I ain't going to hurt nobody," he said, "and I'll show you how to win. I mean to show the whole world how it's got to be done."

And because he understood, he smiled again to let the man know that he held nothing against him for being white and impatient. Then he refused to see the man any longer and stood pressing the button, the voices of the crowd reaching him like sounds in distant streets. Let them yell. All the Negroes down there were just ashamed because he was black like them. He smiled inwardly, knowing how it was. Most of the time he was ashamed of what Negroes did himself. Well, let them be ashamed for something this time. Like him. He was like a long thin black wire that was being stretched and wound upon the bingo wheel; wound until he wanted to scream; wound, but this time himself controlling the winding and the sadness and the shame, and because he did, Laura would be all right. Suddenly the lights flickered. He staggered backwards. Had something gone wrong? All this noise. Didn't they know that although he controlled the wheel, it also controlled him, and unless he pressed the button forever and forever and ever it would stop, leaving him high and dry, dry and high on this hard high slippery hill and Laura dead? There was only one chance; he had to do whatever the wheel demanded. And gripping the button in despair, he discovered with surprise that it imparted a nervous energy. His spine tingled. He felt a certain power.

Now he faced the raging crowd with defiance, its screams penetrating his eardrums like trumpets shrieking from a juke-box. The vague faces glowing in the bingo lights gave him a sense of himself that he had never known before. He was running the show, by God! They had to react to him, for he was their luck. This is *me*, he thought. Let the bastards yell. Then someone was laughing inside him, and he realized that somehow he had forgotten his own name. It was a sad, lost feeling to lose your name, and a crazy thing to do. That name had been given him by the white man who had owned his grandfather a long lost time ago down South. But maybe those wise guys knew his name.

"Who am I?" he screamed.

"Hurry up and bingo, you jerk!"

They didn't know either, he thought sadly. They didn't even know their own names, they were all poor nameless bastards. Well, he didn't need that old name; he was reborn. For as long as he pressed the button he was The-man-who-pressed-the-button-who-held-the-prize-who-was-the-King-of-Bingo. That was the way it was, and he'd have to press the button even if nobody understood, even though Laura did not understand.

"Live!" he shouted.

The audience quieted like the dying of a huge fan.

"Live, Laura, baby. I got holt of it now, sugar. Live!"

He screamed it, tears streaming down his face. "I got nobody but YOU!"

The screams tore from his very guts. He felt as though the rush of blood to his head would burst out in baseball seams of small red droplets, like a head beaten by police clubs. Bending over he saw a trickle of blood splashing the toe of his shoe. With his free hand he searched his head. It was his nose. God, suppose something has gone wrong? He felt that the whole audience had somehow entered him and was stamping its feet in his stomach and he was unable to throw them out. They wanted the prize, that was it. They wanted the secret for themselves. But they'd never get it; he would keep the bingo wheel whirling forever, and Laura would be safe in the wheel. But would she? It had to be, because if she were not safe the wheel would cease to turn; it could not go on. He had to get away, *vomit* all, and his mind formed an image of himself running with Laura in his arms down the tracks of the subway just ahead of an A train, running desperately *vomit* with people screaming for him to come out but knowing no way of leaving the tracks because to stop would bring the train crushing down upon him and to attempt to leave across the other tracks would mean to run into a hot third rail as high as his waist which threw blue sparks that blinded his eyes until he could hardly see.

He heard singing and the audience was clapping its hands.

Shoot the liquor to him, Jim boy!
Clap-clap-clap
Well a-calla the cop
He's blowing his top!
Shoot the liquor to him, Jim, boy!

Bitter anger grew within him at the singing. They think I'm crazy. Well let 'em laugh. I'll do what I got to do.

He was standing in an attitude of intense listening when he saw that they were watching something on the stage behind him. He felt weak. But when he turned he saw no one. If only his thumb did not ache so. Now they were applauding. And for a moment he thought that the wheel had stopped. But that was impossible, his thumb still pressed the button. Then he saw them. Two men in uniform beckoned from the end of the stage. They were coming toward him, walking in step, slowly, like a tap-dance team returning for a third encore. But their shoulders shot forward, and he backed away, looking wildly about. There was nothing to fight them with. He had only the long black cord which led to a plug somewhere back stage, and he couldn't use that because it operated the bingo wheel. He backed slowly, fixing the men with his eyes as his lips stretched over his teeth in a tight, fixed grin; moved toward the end of the stage and realizing that he couldn't go much further, for suddenly the cord became taut and he couldn't afford to break the cord. But he had to do something. The audience was howling. Suddenly he stopped dead, seeing the men halt, their legs lifted as in an interrupted step of a slow-motion dance. There was nothing to do but run in the other direction and he dashed forward, slipping and sliding. The men fell back, surprised. He struck out violently going past.

"Grab him!"

He ran, but all too quickly the cord tightened, resistingly, and he turned and ran back again. This time he slipped them, and discovered by running in a circle before the wheel he could keep the cord from tightening. But this way he had to flail his arms to keep the men away. Why couldn't they leave a man alone? He ran, circling.

"Ring down the curtain," someone yelled. But they couldn't do that. If they did the wheel flashing from the projection room would be cut off. But they had him before he could tell them so, trying to pry open his fist, and he was wrestling and trying to bring his knees into the fight and holding on to the button, for it was his life. And now he was down, seeing a foot coming down, crushing his wrist cruelly, down, as he saw the wheel whirling serenely above.

"I can't give it up," he screamed. Then quietly, in a confidential tone, "Boys, I really can't give it up."

It landed hard against his head. And in the blank moment they had it away from him, completely now. He fought them trying to pull him up from the stage as he watched the wheel spin slowly to a stop. Without surprise he saw it rest at double-zero.

"You see," he pointed bitterly.

"Sure, boy, sure, it's O.K.," one of the men said smiling.

And seeing the man bow his head to someone he could not see, he felt very, very happy; he would receive what all the winners received.

But as he warmed in the justice of the man's tight smile he did not see the man's slow wink, nor see the bow-legged man behind him step clear of the swiftly descending curtain and set himself for a blow. He only felt the dull pain exploding in his skull, and he knew even as it slipped out of him that his luck had run out on the stage.

---

1. How does the actual physical setting provide the symbols used in constructing the theme? How do the actual needs of the main character prepare him for what he feels when he is holding down the button and making the wheel run?
2. Is his sense of power hallucination or insight?
3. What is the significance of his forgetting his own name?
4. Interpret, by paraphrasing, the symbolic significance of the wheel.
5. What is the significance of the end of the story? Of the fact that the wheel comes to rest on the double-zero?

Louise Erdrich

Erdrich (1954–) was born in Little Falls, Minnesota, of German-American and Chippewa descent. She grew up in Wahpeton, North Dakota, and graduated from Dartmouth College. Her thriving literary career has included the publication of a book of poems, Jacklight *(1984), and the novels* Love Medicine *(1984),* The Beet Queen *(1986), and* Tracks *(1988). She has received ample recognition for the quality of her work, including a fellowship from the National Endowment for the Arts and a Guggenheim Fellowship.* Love Medicine *was the winner of the National Book Critics Circle Award for fiction.*

Matchimanito

We started dying before the snow, and, like the snow, we continued to fall. We were surprised that so many of us were left to die. For those who survived the spotted sickness from the south and our long fight west to Dakota land, where we signed the treaty, and then a wind from the east, bringing exile in a storm of government papers, what descended from the north in 1914 seemed terrible, and unjust.

By then we thought disaster must surely have spent its force, that disease must have claimed all of the Anishinabe that the earth could hold and bury.

But along with the first bitter punishments of early winter a new sickness swept down. The consumption, it was called by young Father Damien, who came in that year to replace the priest who had succumbed to the same devastation as his flock. This disease was different from the pox and fever, for it came on slowly. The outcome, however, was just as certain. Whole families of Anishinabe lay ill and helpless in its breath. On the reservation, where we were forced close together, the clans dwindled. Our tribe unraveled like a coarse rope, frayed at either end as the old and new among us were taken. My own family was wiped out one by one. I was the only Nanapush who lived. And after, although I had seen no more than fifty winters, I was considered an old man.

I guided the last buffalo hunt. I saw the last bear shot. I trapped the last beaver with a pelt of more than two years' growth. I spoke aloud the words of the government treaty and refused to sign the settlement papers that would take away our woods and lake. I axed the last birch that was older than I, and I saved the last of the Pillager family.

Fleur.

We found her on a cold afternoon in late winter, out in her family's cabin near Matchimanito Lake, where my companion, Edgar Pukwan, of the tribal police, was afraid to go. The water there was surrounded by the highest oaks, by woods inhabited by ghosts and roamed by Pillagers, who knew the secret ways to cure or kill, until their art deserted them. Dragging our sled into the clearing, we saw two things: the smokeless tin chimney spout jutting from the roof, and the empty hole in the door where the string was drawn inside. Pukwan did not want to enter, fearing that the unburied Pillager spirits might seize him by the throat and turn him windigo. So I was the one who broke the thin-scraped hide that made a window. I was the one who lowered himself into the stinking silence, onto the floor. I was also the one to find the old man and woman, the little brother and two sisters, stone cold and wrapped in gray horse blankets, their faces turned to the west.

Afraid as I was, stilled by their quiet forms, I touched each bundle in the gloom of the cabin, and wished each spirit a good journey on the three-day road, the old-time road, so well trampled by our people this deadly season. Then something in the corner knocked. I flung the door wide. It was the eldest daughter, Fleur, so feverish that she'd thrown off her covers. She huddled against the cold wood range, staring and shaking. She was wild as a filthy wolf, a big bony girl whose sudden bursts of strength and snarling cries terrified the listening Pukwan. I was the one who struggled to lash her to the sacks of supplies and to the boards of the sled. I wrapped blankets over her and tied them down as well.

Pukwan kept us back, convinced that he should carry out the agency's instructions to the letter: he carefully nailed up the official quarantine sign, and then, without removing the bodies, he tried to burn down the house. But though he threw kerosene repeatedly against the logs and even started a blaze with birch bark and chips of wood, the flames narrowed and shrank, went out in puffs of smoke. Pukwan cursed and looked desperate, caught between his official duties and his fear of Pillagers. The fear won out. He finally dropped the tinders and helped me drag Fleur along the trail.

And so we left five dead at Matchimanito, frozen behind their cabin door.

Some say that Pukwan and I should have done right and buried the Pillagers first thing. They say the unrest and curse of trouble that struck our people in the years that followed was the doing of dissatisfied spirits. I know what's fact, and have never been afraid of talking. Our trouble came from the living, from liquor and the dollar bill. We stumbled toward the government bait, never looking down, never noticing how the land was snatched from under us at every step.

When Edgar Pukwan's turn came to draw the sled, he took off like devils chased him, bounced Fleur over potholes as if she were a log, and tipped her twice into the snow. I followed the sled, encouraged Fleur with songs, cried at Pukwan to watch for hidden branches and deceptive drops, and finally got her to my cabin, a small, tightly tamped box overlooking the crossroads.

"Help me," I cried, cutting at the ropes, not even bothering with knots. Fleur closed her eyes, panted, and tossed her head from side to side. Her chest rattled as she strained for air; she grabbed me around the neck. Still weak from my own bout with the sickness, I staggered, fell, lurched into my cabin, wrestling the strong girl inside with me. I had no wind left over to curse Pukwan, who watched but refused to touch her, turned away, and vanished with the whole sled of supplies. I was neither surprised nor caused enduring sorrow later when Pukwan's son, also named Edgar and also of the tribal police, told me that his father came home, crawled into bed, and took no food from that moment until his last breath passed.

As for Fleur, each day she improved in small changes. First her gaze focused, and the next night her skin was cool and damp. She was clearheaded, and after a week she remembered what had befallen her family, how they had taken sick so suddenly, gone under. With her memory mine came back, only too sharply. I was not prepared to think of the people I had lost, or to speak of them, although we did, carefully, without letting their names loose in the wind that would reach their ears.

We feared that they would hear us and never rest, come back out of pity for the loneliness we felt. They would sit in the snow outside the door, waiting until from longing we joined them. We would all be together on the journey then, our destination the village at the end of the road, where people gamble day and night but never lose their money, eat but never fill their stomachs, drink but never leave their minds.

The snow receded enough for us to dig the ground with picks. As a tribal policeman, Pukwan's son was forced by regulation to help bury the dead. So again we took the dark road to Matchimanito, the son leading rather than the father. We spent the day chipping at the earth until we had a hole long and deep enough to lay the Pillagers shoulder to shoulder. We covered them and built five small board houses. I scratched out their clan markers, four crosshatched bears and a marten; then Pukwan Junior shouldered the government's tools and took off down the path. I settled myself near the graves.

I asked those Pillagers, as I had asked my own children and wives, to leave us now and never come back. I offered tobacco, smoked a pipe of red willow for the old man. I told them not to pester their daughter just because she had survived, or to blame me for finding them, or Pukwan Junior for leaving too soon. I told them that I was sorry, but they must abandon us. I insisted. But the Pillagers were as stubborn as the Nanapush clan and would not leave my thoughts. I think they followed me home. All the way down the trail, just beyond the edges of my sight, they flickered, thin as needles, shadows piercing shadows.

The sun had set by the time I got back, but Fleur was awake, sitting in the dark as if she knew. She never moved to build up the fire, never asked where I had been. I never told her about it either, and as the days passed we spoke rarely, always with roundabout caution. We felt the spirits of the dead so near that at length we just stopped talking.

This made it worse.

Their names grew within us, swelled to the brink of our lips, forced our eyes open in the middle of the night. We were filled with the water of the drowned, cold and black—airless water that lapped against the seal of our tongues or leaked slowly from the corners of our eyes. Within us, like ice shards, their names bobbed and shifted. Then the slivers of ice began to collect and cover us. We became so heavy, weighted down with the lead-gray frost, that we could not move. Our hands lay on the table like cloudy blocks. The blood within us grew thick. We needed no food. And little warmth. Days passed, weeks, and we didn't leave the cabin for fear we'd crack our cold and fragile bodies. We had gone half windigo. I learned later that this was common, that many of our people died in this manner, of the invisible sickness. Some could not swallow another bite of food because the names of their dead thickened on their tongues. Some let their blood stop, took the road west after all.

One day the new priest—just a boy, really—opened our door. A dazzling and painful light flooded through and surrounded Fleur and me. Numb, stupid as bears in a winter den, we blinked at the priest's slight silhouette. Our lips were parched, stuck together. We could hardly utter a greeting, but we were saved by one thought: a guest must eat. Fleur gave Father Damien her chair and put wood on the gray coals. She found flour for gaulette. I went to fetch snow to boil for tea water, but to my amazement the ground was bare. I was so surprised that I bent over and touched the soft, wet earth.

My voice rasped at first when I tried to speak, but then, oiled by strong tea, lard, and bread, I was off and talking. You could not stop me with a sledgehammer, once I started. Father Damien looked astonished, and then wary, as I began to creak and roll. I gathered speed. I talked both languages in streams that ran alongside each other, over every rock, around every obstacle. The sound of my voice convinced me I was alive. I kept Father Damien listening all night, his green eyes round, his thin face straining to understand, his odd brown hair in curls and clipped knots. Occasionally he took in air, as if to add observations of his own, but I pushed him under with my words.

I don't know when Fleur slipped out.

She was too young and had no stories or depth of life to rely upon. All she had was raw power, and the names of the dead that filled her. I can speak them now. They have no more interest in any of us. Old Pillager. Ogimaakwe, Boss Woman, his wife. Asasaweminikwesens, Chokecherry Girl. Bineshii, Small Bird, also known as Josette. And the last, the boy Ombaashi, He Is Lifted by Wind.

They are gone, but sometimes I don't know where they are anymore—this place of reservation surveys or the other place, boundless, where the dead sit talking, see too much, and regard the living as fools.

And we were. Starvation makes fools of anyone. In the past some had sold their allotment land for a hundred pound weight of flour. Others, who were desperate to hold on, now urged that we get together and buy back our land, or at least pay a tax and refuse the settlement money that would sweep the marks of our boundaries off the map like a pattern of straws. Many were determined not to allow the hired surveyors, or even our own people, to enter the deepest bush.

But that spring outsiders went in as before, permitted by the agent, a short round man with hair blond as chaff. The purpose of these people was to measure the lake. Only now they walked upon the fresh graves of Pillagers, crossed death roads to plot out the deepest water where the lake monster, Misshepeshu, hid and waited.

"Stay here with me," I said to Fleur when she came to visit.

She refused.

"The land will go," I told her. "The land will be sold and measured."

But she tossed back her hair and walked off, down the path, with nothing to eat till thaw but a bag of my onions and a sack of oats.

Who knows what happened? She returned to Matchimanito and stayed there alone in the cabin that even fire did not want. A young girl had never done such a thing before. I heard that in those months she was asked for fee money for the land. The agent went out there and got lost, spent a whole night following the moving lights and lamps of people who would not answer him but talked and laughed among themselves. They let him go, at dawn, only because he was so stupid. Yet he went out there to ask Fleur for money again, and the next thing we heard he was living in the woods and eating roots, gambling with ghosts.

Some had ideas. You know how old chickens scratch and gabble. That's how the tales started, all the gossip, the wondering, all the things people said without knowing and then believed, since they heard it with their own ears, from their own lips, each word.

I am not one to take notice of the talk of those who fatten in the shade of the new agent's storehouse. But I watched the old agent, the one who was never found, take the rutted turnoff to Matchimanito. He was replaced by a darker man who spoke long and hard with many of our own about a money settlement. But nothing changed my mind. I've seen too much go by—unturned grass below my feet, and overhead the great white cranes flung south forever.

I am a holdout, like the Pillagers, and I told the agent, in good English, what I thought of his treaty paper. I could have written my name, and much more too, in script. I had a Jesuit education in the halls of Saint John before I ran back to the woods and forgot all my prayers.

Since I had saved Fleur from the sickness, I was entangled with her. Not that I knew it at first. Only when I look back do I see a pattern. I was the vine of a wild grape that twined the timbers and drew them close. I was a branch that lived long enough to touch the next tree over, which was Pillagers. The story, like all stories, is never visible while it is happening. Only after, when an old man sits dreaming and talking in his chair, does the design spring clear.

There was so much I saw, and never knew.

When Fleur came down onto the reservation, walking right through town, no one guessed what she hid in that green rag of a dress. I do remember that it was too small, split down the back and strained across the front. That's what I noticed when I greeted her. Not whether she had money in the dress, or a child.

Other people speculated.

They added up the money she used now to buy supplies and how the agent disappeared from his post, and came out betting she would have a baby. He could have paid cash to Fleur and then run off in shame. She could even have stolen cash from him, cursed him dead, and hidden his remains. Everybody would have known, they thought, in nine months or less, if young Eli Kashpaw hadn't gone out and muddied the waters.

This Eli never cared to figure out business, politics, or church. He never applied for a chunk of land or registered himself. Eli hid from authorities, never saw the inside of a classroom, and although his mother, Margaret, got baptized in the church and tried to collar him for Mass, the best he could do was sit outside the big pine door and whittle pegs. For money Eli chopped wood, pitched hay, harvested potatoes or cranberry bark. He wanted to be a hunter, though, like me, and he had asked to partner that winter before the sickness.

I think like animals, have perfect understanding for where they hide. I can track a deer back through time and brush and cleared field to the place where it was born. Only one thing is wrong with teaching these things, however. I showed Eli how to hunt and trap from such an early age that he lived too much in the company of trees and wind. At fifteen he was uncomfortable around human beings. Especially women. So I had to help him out some.

I'm a Nanapush, remember. That's as good as saying I knew what interested Eli Kashpaw. He wanted something other than what I could teach him about the woods. He was no longer curious only about where a mink will fish or burrow, or when pike will lie low or bite. He wanted to hear how, in the days before the priest's ban and the sickness, I had satisfied three wives.

"Nanapush," Eli said, appearing at my door one day, "I have to ask you something."

"Come on in here, then," I said. "I won't bite you like the little girls do."

He was steadier, more serious, than he was the winter we went out together on the trapline. I was going to wonder what the different thing about him was when he said, "Fleur Pillager."

"She's no little girl," I answered, motioning toward the table. He told me his story.

It began when Eli got himself good and lost up near Matchimanito. He was hunting a doe in a light rain, having no luck until he rounded a slough and shot badly, which wasn't unusual. She was wounded to death but not crippled. She might walk all day, which shamed him, so he dabbed a bit of her blood on the barrel of his gun, the charm I taught him, and he followed her trail.

He had a time of it. She sawed through the woods, took the worst way, moved into heavy brush like a ghost. For hours Eli blazed his passage with snapped branches and clumps of leaves, scuffed the ground, or left a bootprint. But the trail and the day wore on, and for some reason that he did not understand, he gave up and quit leaving sign.

"That was when you should have turned back," I told him. "You should have known. It's no accident people don't like to go there. Those trees are too big, thick, and twisted at the top like bent arms. In the wind their limbs cast, creak against each other, snap. The leaves speak a cold language that overfills your brain. You want to lie down. You want never to get up. You hunger. You rake black chokecherries off their stems and stuff them down, and then you shit like a bird. Your blood thins. You're too close to where the Lake Man lives. And you're too close to where I buried the Pillagers during the long sickness that claimed them like it claimed the Nanapush clan."

I said this to Eli Kashpaw: "I understand Fleur. I am alone in this. I know that was no ordinary doe drawing you out there."

But the doe was real enough, he told me, and it was gut-shot and weakening. The blood dropped fresher, darker, until he thought he heard her just ahead and bent to the ground, desperate to see in the falling dusk, and looked ahead to catch a glimpse, and instead saw the glow of fire. He started toward it, then stopped just outside the circle of light. The deer hung, already split, turning back and forth on a rope. When he saw the woman, gutting with long quick movements, her arms bloody and bare, he stepped into the clearing.

"That's mine," he said.

I hid my face, shook my head.

"You should have turned back," I told him. "Stupid! You should have left it."

But he was stubborn, a vein of Kashpaw that held out for what it had coming. He couldn't have taken the carcass home anyway, couldn't have lugged it back, even if he had known his direction. Yet he stood his ground with the woman and said he'd tracked that deer too far to let it go. She did not respond. "Or maybe half," he thought, studying her back, uncomfortable. Even so, that was as generous as he could get.

She kept working. Never noticed him. He was so ignorant that he reached out and tapped her on the shoulder. She never even twitched. He walked around her, watched the knife cut, trespassed into her line of vision.

At last she saw him, he said, but then scorned him as though he were nothing.

"Little fly"—she straightened her back, the knife loose and casual in her hand—"quit buzzing."

Eli said she looked so wild her beauty didn't throw him, and I leaned closer, worried as he said this, worried as he reported how her hair was clumped with dirt, her face thin as a bony bitch's, her dress a rag that hung, and no curve to her except her breasts.

He noticed some things.

"No curve?" I said, thinking of the rumors.

He shook his head, impatient to continue his story. He felt sorry for her, he said. I told him the last man who was interested in Fleur Pillager had vanished, never to be found. She made us all uneasy, out there so alone. I was a friend to the Pillagers before they died off, I said, and I was safe from Fleur because the two of us had mourned the dead together. She was almost a relative. But that wasn't the case with him.

Eli looked at me with an unbelieving frown. Then he said he didn't see where she was so dangerous. After a while he had recognized her manner as exhaustion more than anger. She made no protest when he took out his own knife and helped her work. Halfway through the job she allowed him to finish, and then Eli hoisted most of the meat into the tree. He took the choice parts into the cabin. She let him in, hardly noticed him, and he helped her start the small range and even took it on himself to melt lard. She ate the whole heart, fell on it like a starved animal, and then her eyes shut.

From the way he described her actions, I was sure she was pregnant. I'm familiar with the signs, and I can talk about this since I'm an old man, far past anything a woman can do to weaken me. I was more certain still when Eli said that he took her in his arms, helped her to a pile of blankets on a willow bed. And then—hard to believe, even though it was, for the first time, the right thing to do—Eli rolled up in a coat on the other side of the cabin floor and lay there all night, and slept alone.

"So," I said, "why have you come to me now? You got away, you survived, she even let you find your way home. You learned your lesson and none the worse."

"I want her," Eli said.

I could not believe that I heard right, but we were sitting by the stove, face to face, so there was no doubt. I rose and turned away. Maybe I was less than generous, having lost my own girls. Maybe I wanted to keep Fleur as my daughter, who would visit me, joke with me, beat me at cards. But I believe it was only for Eli's own good that I was harsh.

"Forget that thing so heavy in our pocket," I said, "or put it somewhere else. Go town way and find yourself a tamer woman."

He brooded at my tabletop and then spoke. "I want know-how, not warnings, not my mother's caution."

"You don't want instruction!" I was pushed too far. "Love medicine is what you're after. A Nanapush never needed any, but Old Lady Aintapi or the Pillagers, they sell it. Go ask Moses for a medicine and pay your price."

"I don't want anything that can wear off," the boy said. He was determined. Maybe his new, steady coolness was the thing that turned my mind, the quiet of him. He was different, sitting there so still. It struck me that he had come into his growth, and who was I to hold him back from going to a Pillager, since someone had to, since the whole tribe had got to thinking that she couldn't be left alone out there, a girl ready to go wild, a woman whose family would not leave her, even dead, but stayed close to her, whispered, passed on their power. People said that she had to be harnessed. Maybe, I thought, Eli was the young man to do it, even though he couldn't rub two words together and get a spark.

So I gave in. I told him what he wanted to know. He asked me the old-time way to make a woman love him, and I went into detail so that he would make no disgraceful error. I told him about the first woman who had given herself to me. Sanawashonekek, her name was, The Lying-Down Grass, for the place where a deer has spent the night. I described the finicky taste of Omiimii, The Dove, and the trials I'd gone through to keep my second wife pleasured. Zezikaaikwe, The Unexpected, was a woman whose name was the exact prediction of her desires. I gave him a few things from the French trunk my third wife left—a white woman's fan, bead leggings, a little girl's soft doll made of fawn skin.

When Eli Kashpaw stroked their beauty and asked where these things had come from, I remembered the old days, opened my mouth.

Talk is an old man's last vice.

I wore out the boy's ears, but that is not my fault. I shouldn't have been caused to live so long, been shown so much of death, had to squeeze so many stories into the corners of my brain. They're all attached, and once I start, the telling doesn't end, because they're hooked from one side to the other, mouth to tail.

During the year of sickness, when I was the last one left, I saved myself by starting a story. One night I was ready to bring to the other side the fawn-skin doll I now gave Eli. My wife had sewn it together after our daughter died, and I held it in my hands when I fainted, lost breath so that I could hardly keep moving my lips. But I did continue and recovered. I got well by talking. Death could not get a word in edgewise, grew discouraged, and traveled on.

Eli returned to Fleur, and stopped badgering me, which I took as a sign she liked the fan, the bead leggings, and maybe the rest of Eli, the part where he was on his own. The thing I've found about women is that you must use every instinct to confuse.

"Look here," I told Eli, before he went out my door. "It's like you're a log in a stream. Along comes this bear. She jumps on. Don't let her dig in her claws."

So keeping Fleur off balance was what I presumed Eli was doing. But, as I learned in time, he was further along than that, way off and running beyond the reach of anything I said.

His mother was the one who gave me the news.

Margaret Kashpaw was a woman who had sunk her claws in the log and peeled it to a toothpick, and she wasn't going to let any man forget it. Especially me, her dead husband's partner in some youthful pursuits.

"Aneesh," she said, slamming my door shut. Margaret never knocked, because with warning you might get your breath, or escape. She was headlong, bossy, scared of nobody, and full of vinegar. She was a little woman, but so blinded by irritation that she'd take on anyone. She was thin on the top and plump as a turnip below, with a face like a round molasses cake. On each side of it gray plaits hung. With age her part had widened down the middle so that it looked as though the braids were slipping off her head. Her eyes were harsh, bright, and her tongue was honed keen. She sat right down.

"Would you care to know what you have my son doing?"

I mumbled, kept reading by the window, tucked my spectacles from Father Damien more comfortably around my ears. My newspaper came from Grand Forks once a week, and I wasn't about to let Margaret spoil my pleasure or get past my hiding place.

"*Sah!*" She swiped at the sheets with her hand, grazed the print, but never quite dared to flip it aside. This was not for any fear of me, however. She didn't want the tracks rubbing off on her skin. She never learned to read, and the mystery troubled her.

I took advantage of that, snapped the paper in front of my face and sat for a moment. But she won, of course, because she knew I'd get curious. I felt her eyes glittering beyond the paper, and when I put the pages down, she continued.

"Who learned my Eli to make love standing up? Who learned him to have a woman against a tree in clear daylight? Who learned him to . . ."

"Wait," I said. "How'd you get to know this?"

She shrugged it off, and said in a smaller voice, "Boy Lazarre."

And I, who knew that the dirty Lazarres don't spy for nothing, just smiled.

"How much did you pay the fat-bellied dog?"

"The Lazarres are like animals in their season! No sense of shame!" But the wind was out of her. "Against the wall of the cabin," she said. "Down beside it. In grass and up in trees. Who'd he learn that from?"

"Maybe my late partner Kashpaw."

She puffed her cheeks out, fumed. "Not from him!"

"Not that you knew." I put my spectacles carefully upon the windowsill. Her hand could snake out quickly.

She hissed. The words flew like razor grass between her teeth. "Old man," she said with scorn. "Two wrinkled berries and a twig."

"A twig can grow," I offered.

"But only in the spring."

Then she was gone, out the door, leaving my tongue tingling for the last word, and still ignorant of the full effect of my advice. I didn't wonder until later if it didn't go both ways, though—if Fleur had wound her private hairs around the buttons of Eli's shirt, if she had stirred smoky powders or crushed snakeroot into his tea. Perhaps she had bitten his nails in sleep and swallowed the ends, snipped threads from his clothing and made a doll of them to wear between her legs. For they got bolder, until the whole reservation gossiped.

Then one day the big, unsteady Lazarre, an Indian on whose birth certificate was recorded simply "Boy," returned from the woods talking backwards, garbled, mixing his words. At first people thought the sights of passion had cleft his mind. Then they figured otherwise, imagined that Fleur had caught Lazarre watching and tied him up, cut his tongue out, and sewn it in reversed.

The same day I heard this, Margaret burst into my house a second time.

"Take me out to their place, you four-eyes," she said. "And be ready with the boat tomorrow, sunup!"

She stamped through the door and vanished, leaving me with hardly time enough to patch the seams and holes of the old-time boat I kept, dragged up in a brush shelter on the quieter inlet, the south end of the lake. I took some boiled pine gum to the seams that afternoon, and did my best. I was drawn to the situation, curious myself, and though I didn't want to spy either on the girl whose life I'd saved or on the boy I'd advised on courting, I was down by the water with the paddles at dawn.

The light was chill and green, the waves on the lake were small, confused ripples, and no steady wind had gathered. The water could be deceptive, set snares for the careless young or for withered-up and eager fools like ourselves. I put my hand in the current.

"Margaret," I said, "the lake's too cold. I never could swim, either, not that well."

But Margaret had set her mind, and made her peace, too.

"If he wants me"—she was talking about the lake spirit but, out of caution, using no names—"I'll give him good as I get."

"Oh," I said, "has it been that long, Margaret?"

Her eyes lit and I wished I had kept my mouth shut. But she only commented, later, after we had launched, "Not so long that I would consider the dregs."

I handed her the lard can I kept my bait in. "You better take this, Margaret. You better bail."

So at least on that long trip across I had the satisfaction of seeing her bend to the dipping and pouring with a sour but desperate will.

We rode low. The water covered our ankles by the time we beached on shore, but Margaret was forced to shut her mouth in a firm line. The whole idea had been hers. She was so relieved to stand finally upon solid ground that she helped me haul the boat and wedge it in a pile of mangled roots. She wrung her skirt and sat beside me, panting. She shared some dried meat from the pocket of her dress, tore at it like a young snapping turtle. How I envied her sharp, strong teeth.

"Go on, eat," she said, "or I'll take an insult."

I put the jerky into my mouth.

"That's right," she sneered. "Suck long enough and it will soften."

I had no choice. I could think of no other way to get any of it down.

"Go now," I said, after a while. "I was thinking. I had this old barren she-dog once. She'd back up to anything. But the only satisfaction she could get was from watching the young."

Margaret jumped to her feet, skirts flapping. I had said too much. Her claws gave my ears too fast, furious jerks that set me whirling, sickening me so that I couldn't balance or even keep track of time. She took herself up the bank and into the Pillager woods, but I don't know when she went there or how long she stayed, and I had barely set myself to rights before she returned.

By then the sky had gone dead gray, the waves rolled white and fitful. Margaret took tobacco from a pouch in her pocket, threw it on the water, and said a few distracted, imploring words. We jumped into the boat, which leaked worse than ever, and pushed off. The wind blew harsh, in heavy circular gusts, and I was hard put. I never saw the bailing can move so fast, before or since. The old woman made it flash and dip, and hardly even broke the rhythm when, halfway across, she reached into her pocket again and this time dumped the whole pouch into the pounding waves. From then on she alternated between working her arms and addressing different Manitous along with the Blessed Virgin and Her heart, the sacred bloody lump that the blue-robed woman held in the awful picture Margaret kept nailed to her wall. We made it back by the time rain poured down, and hoisted ourselves over the edge of the boat. When we got back to my house, after she'd swallowed some warm broth and her clothes had begun to steam dry upon her, Margaret told me what she had seen with her own eyes.

Fleur Pillager was pregnant, going to have a child in spring. At least that's what Margaret had decided with her measuring gaze. I stirred the fire with my walking stick. Maybe I had a shiver, a feeling, a worry. I was close as a relative, closer perhaps. Maybe I knew already that when spring did come, the ice milky, porous, and broken, Margaret and I were the ones who would have to save Fleur a second time.

Margaret, however, had no such premonition. The child would turn out fork-footed, she predicted, with straw for hair, yellow as the agent's. Its eyes would glow blue, its skin shine white. As she sipped from her cup, Margaret's memory of the agent made a monster, and she savored the variations the child might reveal: red, flapping ears, a strange birthmark, chicken lips, an extra finger, by which the taint of its conception would be certain and people convinced, at last, that it did not belong to her son.

The morning we got word, the water had just opened for a boat, if you dared to travel that way so early in spring. Fleur was in trouble with her baby. That's all I heard, as the women kept the particulars to themselves. Out of desperation Eli had run to Margaret on the way to the midwife's. He wanted us to take the shortcut and stay with Fleur until he brought back the woman whose hands held the wisdom, who wore the dried caul of a rabbit in a little belt around her waist.

Margaret was puffed up, full of satisfaction, until she saw the boat, leaking even more than usual after another winter of neglect. On the ride, bailing for her life, Margaret raged at me between her prayers and muttered strict assurances that her reasons for helping in this matter were not ties of kinship. Her presence did not count as acknowledgment, she said. It was her duty to see the evidence, whatever that turned out to be—the hair gold as straw, the blazing eyes.

But the child had none of those markings.

She was born on the day we shot the last bear, drunk, on the reservation. The midwife was the one who shot it, and the bear was drunk, not her. That she-bear had broken into the trader's wine I had brought across the lake beneath my jacket and then stowed in a rotten stump off in the woods behind the house. She bit the cork and emptied the white clay jug. Then she lost her mind and stumbled into the beaten grass of Fleur's yard.

By then we were a day in the waiting. In all that time we heard not a sound from Fleur's cabin, just crushing silence, like the inside of a drum before the stick drops. Eli and I slumped against the woodpile. We made a fire, swaddled ourselves in blankets. My stomach creaked with the lack of food, for Eli was starving himself from worry and I hated to eat in front of him. His eyes were rimmed with blood as he moaned and talked and prayed beneath the burden, which grew heavier.

On the second day we leaned to the fire, strained for the sound of the cry a baby makes. Our ears picked up everything in the woods, the rustle of birds, the crack of dead spring leaves and twigs. Our hearing had by then grown so keen that we heard the muffled sounds the women made inside the house. Now we heard other activity, which gave us hope. The stove lid clanked, pans rang together. Margaret came to the door and we heard the tear of water splashing on the ground. Eli moved then, fetched more. But not until the afternoon of that second day did the stillness finally break, and then the Manitous all through the woods seemed to speak through Fleur, loose, arguing. I recognized them. Turtle's quavering scratch, Eagle's high shriek, Loon's crazy bitterness, Otter, the howl of Wolf, Bear's low rasp.

Perhaps the bear heard Fleur calling, and answered.

I was alone when it happened, because Eli had broken when the silence shattered, slashed his arm with his hunting knife, and run out of the clearing, straight north. I sat quietly after he was gone, and sampled the food that he had refused. I drew close to the fire, settled my back against the split logs, and was just about to have a second helping when the drunk bear rambled past. She sniffed the ground, rolled over in an odor that pleased her, drew up and sat, addled, on her haunches like a dog. I jumped straight onto the top of the woodpile—I don't know how, since my limbs were so stiff from the wet cold. I crouched, yelled at the house, screamed for the gun, but only attracted the bear. She dragged herself over, gave a drawn-out whine, a cough, and fixed me with a long patient stare.

Margaret flung the door open. "Shoot it, you old fool," she hollered. But I was empty-handed. Margaret was irritated with this trifle, put out that I had not obeyed her, anxious to get rid of the nuisance and go back to Fleur. She marched straight toward us. Her face was pinched with exhaustion, her pace furious. Her arms moved like pistons, and she came so fast that she and the bear were face to face before she realized that she had nothing with which to attack. She was sensible, Margaret Kashpaw, and turned straight around. Fleur kept her gun above the flour cupboard in a rack of antlers. The bear followed, heeling Margaret like a puppy, and at the door to the house, when Margaret turned, arms spread to bar the way, it swatted her aside with one sharp, dreamy blow. Then it ambled in and reared on its hind legs.

I am a man, so I don't know exactly what happened when the bear came into the birth house, but they talk among themselves, the women, and sometimes they forget I'm listening. So I know that when Fleur saw the bear in the house she was filled with such fear and power that she raised herself on the mound of blankets and gave birth. Then the midwife took down the gun and shot point-blank, filling the bear's heart. She says so, anyway. But Margaret says that the lead only gave the bear strength, and I'll support that. For I heard the gun go off and then saw the creature whirl and roar from the house. It barreled past me, crashed through the brush into the woods, and was not seen after. It left no trail, either, so it could have been a spirit bear. I don't know. I was still on the woodpile.

I took the precaution of finishing my meal there. From what I overheard later, they were sure Fleur was dead, she was so cold and still after giving birth. But then the baby cried. That I heard with my own ears. At that sound, they say, Fleur opened her eyes and breathed. That was when the women went to work and saved her, packed moss between her legs, wrapped her in blankets heated with stones, kneaded Fleur's stomach and forced her to drink cup after cup of boiled raspberry leaf, until at last Fleur groaned, drew the baby against her breast, and lived.

---

1. What are the chief elements of conflict in this story? Are the conflicts resolved happily?
2. Can you account for Fleur's unusual ability to endure? Does it partake of the supernatural?
3. The story pictures a people facing extinction. What do they require for survival?
4. What accounts for the degree of equanimity the narrator has achieved?
5. What is the tone of the story, and how is it achieved?

William Faulkner

Faulkner (1897–1962) was born in New Albany, Mississippi. His family had included wealthy and powerful people ruined by the Civil War. His great-grandfather was a popular novelist, and this ancestor serves, like other family members, as a model from whom Faulkner drew traits used in composing the characters in his fiction. He attended the University of Mississippi in Oxford before and after his service in the Royal Canadian Air Force in World War I. Thereafter he lived in Oxford most of his life, though he spent much time in Hollywood as a screenwriter and it was in New Orleans that his literary career began. There he met Sherwood Anderson, who encouraged him to turn from poetry to fiction and helped him get his first novel published. The work which won Faulkner a Nobel Prize in 1950 is often a depiction of life in his fictional Yoknapatawpha County, an imaginative reconstruction of the area adjacent to Oxford. Faulkner was a passionately devoted hunter and his love of the disappearing wilderness is expressed in many of his tales. He sought out the honor and courage of people balked by circumstance and the sum of his writing testifies to his faith that these virtues will prevail through the corruptions of modern life. His major novels were mostly the product of a prodigious decade of creative effort. They include The Sound and the Fury *(1929),* As I Lay Dying *(1930),* Sanctuary *(1931),* Light in August *(1932),* Absalom, Absalom! *(1936),* Wild Palms (1939), *and* The Hamlet *(1940). His books of short stories include* These Thirteen *(1931),* Go Down, Moses *(1942), and the* Collected Stories of William Faulkner *(1950).*

A Rose for Emily

I

When Miss Emily Grierson died, our whole town went to her funeral: the men through a sort of respectful affection for a fallen monument, the women mostly out of curiosity to see the inside of her house, which no one save an old manservant—a combined gardener and cook—had seen in at least ten years.

It was a big, squarish frame house that had once been white, decorated with cupolas and spires and scrolled balconies in the heavily lightsome style of the seventies, set on what had once been our most select street. But garages and cotton gins had encroached and obliterated even the august names of that neighborhood; only Miss Emily's house was left, lifting its stubborn and coquettish decay above the cotton wagons and the gasoline pumps—an eyesore among eyesores. And now Miss Emily had gone to join the representatives of those august names where they lay in the cedar-bemused cemetery among the ranked and anonymous graves of Union and Confederate soldiers who fell at the battle of Jefferson.

Alive, Miss Emily had been a tradition, a duty, and a care; a sort of hereditary obligation upon the town, dating from that day in 1894 when Colonel Sartoris,[1] the mayor—he who fathered the edict that no Negro woman should appear on the streets without an apron—remitted her taxes, the dispensation dating from the death of her father on into perpetuity. Not that Miss Emily would have accepted charity. Colonel Sartoris invented an involved tale to the effect that Miss Emily's father had loaned money to the town, which the town, as a matter of business, preferred this way of repaying. Only a man of Colonel Sartoris' generation and thought could have invented it, and only a woman could have believed it.

When the next generation, with its more modern ideas, became mayors and aldermen, this arrangement created some little dissatisfaction. On the first of the year they mailed her a tax notice. February came, and there was no reply. They wrote her a formal letter, asking her to call at the sheriff's office at her convenience. A week later the mayor wrote her himself, offering to call or to send his car for her, and received in reply a note on paper of an archaic shape, in a thin, flowing calligraphy in faded ink, to the effect that she no longer went out at all. The tax notice was also enclosed, without comment.

They called a special meeting of the Board of Aldermen. A deputation waited upon her, knocked at the door through which no visitor had passed since she ceased giving china-painting lessons eight or ten years earlier. They were admitted by the old Negro into a dim hall from which a stairway mounted into still more shadow. It smelled of dust and disuse—a close, dank smell. The Negro led them into the parlor. It was furnished in heavy, leather-covered furniture. When the Negro opened the blinds of one window, a faint dust rose sluggishly about their thighs, spinning with slow motes in the single sun-ray. On a tarnished gilt easel before the fireplace stood a crayon portrait of Miss Emily's father.

They rose when she entered—a small, fat woman in black, with a thin gold chain descending to her waist and vanishing into her belt, leaning on an ebony cane with a tarnished gold head. Her skeleton was small and spare; perhaps that was why what would have been merely

1. A major figure among Faulkner's fictional inhabitants of Yoknapatawpha County.

plumpness in another was obesity in her. She looked bloated, like a body long submerged in motionless water, and of that pallid hue. Her eyes, lost in the fatty ridges of her face, looked like two small pieces of coal pressed into a lump of dough as they moved from one face to another while the visitors stated their errand.

She did not ask them to sit. She just stood in the door and listened quietly until the spokesman came to a stumbling halt. Then they could hear the invisible watch ticking at the end of the gold chain.

Her voice was dry and cold. "I have no taxes in Jefferson. Colonel Sartoris explained it to me. Perhaps one of you can gain access to the city records and satisfy yourselves."

"But we have. We are the city authorities, Miss Emily. Didn't you get a notice from the sheriff, signed by him?"

"I received a paper, yes," Miss Emily said. "Perhaps he considers himself the sheriff. . . . I have no taxes in Jefferson."

"But there is nothing on the books to show that, you see. We must go by the—"

"See Colonel Sartoris. I have no taxes in Jefferson."

"But, Miss Emily—"

"See Colonel Sartoris." (Colonel Sartoris had been dead almost ten years.) "I have no taxes in Jefferson. Tobe!" The Negro appeared. "Show these gentlemen out."

II

So she vanquished them, horse and foot, just as she had vanquished their fathers thirty years before about the smell. That was two years after her father's death and a short time after her sweetheart—the one we believed would marry her—had deserted her. After her father's death she went out very little; after her sweetheart went away, people hardly saw her at all. A few of the ladies had the temerity to call, but were not received, and the only sign of life about the place was the Negro man—a young man then—going in and out with a market basket.

"Just as if a man—any man—could keep a kitchen properly," the ladies said; so they were not surprised when the smell developed. It was another link between the gross, teeming world and the high and mighty Griersons.

A neighbor, a woman, complained to the mayor, Judge Stevens, eighty years old.

"But what will you have me do about it, madam?" he said.

"Why, send her word to stop it," the woman said. "Isn't there a law?"

"I'm sure that won't be necessary," Judge Stevens said. "It's probably just a snake or a rat that nigger of hers killed in the yard. I'll speak to him about it."

The next day he received two more complaints, one from a man who came in diffident deprecation. "We really must do something about it, Judge. I'd be the last one in the world to bother Miss Emily, but we've got to do something." That night the Board of Aldermen met—three gray-beards and one younger man, a member of the rising generation.

"It's simple enough," he said. "Send her word to have her place cleaned up. Give her a certain time to do it in, and if she don't . . ."

"Dammit, sir," Judge Stevens said, "will you accuse a lady to her face of smelling bad?"

So the next night, after midnight, four men crossed Miss Emily's lawn and slunk about the house like burglars, sniffing along the base of the brickwork and at the cellar openings while one of them performed a regular sowing motion with his hand out of a sack slung from his shoulder. They broke open the cellar door and sprinkled lime there, and in all the outbuildings. As they recrossed the lawn, a window that had been dark was lighted and Miss Emily sat in it, the light behind her, and her upright torso motionless as that of an idol. They crept quietly across the lawn and into the shadow of the locusts that lined the street. After a week or two the smell went away.

That was when people had begun to feel really sorry for her. People in our town, remembering how old lady Wyatt, her great-aunt, had gone completely crazy at last, believed that the Griersons held themselves a little too high for what they really were. None of the young men were quite good enough for Miss Emily and such. We had long thought of them as a tableau; Miss Emily a slender figure in white in the background, her father a spraddled silhouette in the foreground, his back to her and clutching a horsewhip,[2] the two of them framed by the back-flung front door. So when she got to be thirty and was still single, we were not pleased exactly, but vindicated; even with insanity in the family she wouldn't have turned down all of her chances if they had really materialized.

When her father died, it got about that the house was all that was left to her; and in a way, people were glad. At last they could pity Miss Emily. Being left alone, and a pauper, she had become humanized. Now she too would know the old thrill and the old despair of a penny more or less.

The day after his death all the ladies prepared to call at the house and offer condolence and aid, as is our custom. Miss Emily met them

2. The horsewhip was the legendary weapon used by American fathers to protect their daughters from unwelcome suitors.

at the door, dressed as usual and with no trace of grief on her face. She told them that her father was not dead. She did that for three days, with the ministers calling on her, and the doctors, trying to persuade her to let them dispose of the body. Just as they were about to resort to law and force, she broke down, and they buried her father quickly.

We did not say she was crazy then. We believed she had to do that. We remembered all the young men her father had driven away, and we knew that with nothing left, she would have to cling to that which had robbed her, as people will.

III

She was sick for a long time. When we saw her again, her hair was cut short, making her look like a girl, with a vague resemblance to those angels in colored church windows—sort of tragic and serene.

The town had just let the contracts for paving the sidewalks, and in the summer after her father's death they began to work. The construction company came with niggers and mules and machinery, and a foreman named Homer Barron, a Yankee—a big, dark, ready man, with a big voice and eyes lighter than his face. The little boys would follow in groups to hear him cuss the niggers, and the niggers singing in time to the rise and fall of picks. Pretty soon he knew everybody in town. Whenever you heard a lot of laughing anywhere about the square, Homer Barron would be in the center of the group. Presently we began to see him and Miss Emily on Sunday afternoons driving in the yellow-wheeled buggy and the matched team of bays from the livery stable.

At first we were glad that Miss Emily would have an interest, because the ladies all said, "Of course a Grierson would not think seriously of a Northerner, a day laborer." But there were still others, older people, who said that even grief could not cause a real lady to forget *noblesse oblige*[3]—without calling it *noblesse oblige*. They just said, "Poor Emily. Her kinsfolk should come to her." She had some kin in Alabama; but years ago her father had fallen out with them over the estate of old lady Wyatt, the crazy woman, and there was no communication between the two families. They had not even been represented at the funeral.

And as soon as the old people said, "Poor Emily," the whispering began. "Do you suppose it's really so?" they said to one another. "Of course it is. What else could . . . " This behind their hands; rustling of craned silk and satin behind jalousies closed upon the sun of Sunday afternoon as the thin, swift clop-clop-clop of the matched team passed: "Poor Emily."

3. The obligations of the upper class.

She carried her head high enough—even when we believed that she was fallen. It was as if she demanded more than ever the recognition of her dignity as the last Grierson; as if it had wanted that touch of earthiness to reaffirm her imperviousness. Like when she bought the rat poison, the arsenic. That was over a year after they had begun to say "Poor Emily," and while the two female cousins were visiting her.

"I want some poison," she said to the druggist. She was over thirty then, still a slight woman, though thinner than usual, with cold, haughty black eyes in a face the flesh of which was strained across the temples and about the eyesockets as you imagine a lighthouse-keeper's face ought to look. "I want some poison," she said.

"Yes, Miss Emily. What kind? For rats and such? I'd recom—"

"I want the best you have. I don't care what kind."

The druggist named several. "They'll kill anything up to an elephant. But what you want is—"

"Arsenic," Miss Emily said. "Is that a good one?"

"Is . . . arsenic? Yes ma'am. But what you want—"

"I want arsenic."

The druggist looked down at her. She looked back at him, erect, her face like a strained flag. "Why, of course," the druggist said. "If that's what you want. But the law requires you to tell what you are going to use it for."

Miss Emily just stared at him, her head tilted back in order to look him eye for eye, until he looked away and went and got the arsenic and wrapped it up. The Negro delivery boy brought her the package; the druggist didn't come back. When she opened the package at home there was written on the box, under the skull and bones: "For rats."

IV

So the next day we all said, "She will kill herself"; and we said it would be the best thing. When she had first begun to be seen with Homer Barron, we had said, "She will marry him." Then we said, "She will persuade him yet," because Homer himself had remarked—he liked men, and it was known that he drank with the younger men in the Elk's Club—that he was not a marrying man. Later we said, "Poor Emily," behind the jalousies as they passed on Sunday afternoon in the glittering buggy, Miss Emily with her head high and Homer Barron with his hat cocked and a cigar in his teeth, reins and whip in a yellow glove.

Then some of the ladies began to say that it was a disgrace to the town and a bad example to the young people. The men did not want to interfere, but at last the ladies forced the Baptist minister—Miss Emily's people were Episcopal—to call upon her. He would never divulge what happened during that interview, but he refused to go back again. The next Sunday they again drove about the streets, and the following day the minister's wife wrote to Miss Emily's relations in Alabama.

So she had blood-kin under her roof again and we sat back to watch developments. At first nothing happened. Then we were sure that they were to be married. We learned that Miss Emily had been to the jeweler's and ordered a man's toilet set in silver, with the letters H. B. on each piece. Two days later we learned that she had bought a complete outfit of men's clothing, including a nightshirt, and we said, "They are married." We were really glad. We were glad because the two female cousins were even more Grierson than Miss Emily had ever been.

So we were not surprised when Homer Barron—the streets had been finished some time since—was gone. We were a little disappointed that there was not a public blowing-off, but we believed that he had gone on to prepare for Miss Emily's coming, or to give her a chance to get rid of the cousins. (By that time it was a cabal, and we were all Miss Emily's allies to help circumvent the cousins.) Sure enough, after another week they departed. And, as we had expected all along, within three days Homer Barron was back in town. A neighbor saw the Negro man admit him at the kitchen door at dusk one evening.

And that was the last we saw of Homer Barron. And of Miss Emily for some time. The Negro man went in and out with the market basket, but the front door remained closed. Now and then we would see her at a window for a moment, as the men did that night when they sprinkled the lime, but for almost six months she did not appear on the streets. Then we knew that this was to be expected too; as if that quality of her father which had thwarted her woman's life so many times had been too virulent and too furious to die.

When we next saw Miss Emily, she had grown fat and her hair was turning gray. During the next few years it grew grayer and grayer until it attained an even pepper-and-salt iron-gray, when it ceased turning. Up to the day of her death at seventy-four it was still that vigorous iron-gray, like the hair of an active man.

From that time on her front door remained closed, save for a period of six or seven years, when she was about forty, during which she gave lessons in china-painting. She fitted up a studio in one of the downstairs rooms, where the daughters and grand-daughters of Colonel Sartoris' contemporaries were sent to her with the same regularity and in the same spirit that they were sent on Sundays with a twenty-five cent piece for the collection plate. Meanwhile her taxes had been remitted.

Then the newer generation became the backbone and the spirit of the town, and the painting pupils grew up and fell away and did not send their children to her with boxes of color and tedious brushes and pictures cut from the ladies' magazines. The front door closed upon the last one and remained closed for good. When the town got free postal delivery Miss Emily alone refused to let them fasten the metal numbers above her door and attach a mailbox to it. She would not listen to them.

Daily, monthly, yearly we watched the Negro grow grayer and more stooped, going in and out with the market basket. Each December we sent her a tax notice, which would be returned by the post office a week later, unclaimed. Now and then we would see her in one of the downstairs windows—she had evidently shut up the top floor of the house—like the carven torso of an idol in a niche, looking or not looking at us, we could never tell which. Thus she passed from generation to generation—dear, inescapable, impervious, tranquil, and perverse.

And so she died. Fell ill in the house filled with dust and shadows, with only a doddering Negro man to wait on her. We did not even know she was sick; we had long since given up trying to get any information from the Negro. He talked to no one, probably not even to her, for his voice had grown harsh and rusty, as if from disuse.

She died in one of the downstairs rooms, in a heavy walnut bed with a curtain, her gray head propped on a pillow yellow and moldy with age and lack of sunlight.

V

The Negro met the first of the ladies at the front door and let them in, with their hushed, sibilant voices and their quick, curious glances, and then he disappeared. He walked right through the house and out the back and was not seen again.

The two female cousins came at once. They held the funeral on the second day, with the town coming to look at Miss Emily beneath a mass of bought flowers, with the crayon face of her father musing profoundly above the bier and the ladies sibilant and macabre; and the very old men—some in their brushed Confederate uniforms—on the porch and the lawn, talking of Miss Emily as if she had been a contemporary of theirs, believing that they had danced with her and courted her perhaps, confusing time with its mathematical progression, as the old do, to whom all the past is not a diminishing road, but, instead, a huge meadow which no winter ever quite touches, divided from them now by the narrow bottleneck of the most recent decade of years.

Already we knew that there was one room in that region above stairs which no one had seen in forty years, and which would have to be forced. They waited until Miss Emily was decently in the ground before they opened it.

The violence of breaking down the door seemed to fill this room with pervading dust. A thin, acrid pall as of the tomb seemed to lie everywhere upon this room decked and furnished as for a bridal: upon the valance curtains of faded rose color, upon the rose-shaded lights, upon the dressing table, upon the delicate array of crystal and the man's toilet things backed with tarnished silver, silver so tarnished that the monogram was obscured. Among them lay a collar and tie, as if they had just been removed, which, lifted, left upon the surface a pale crescent in the dust. Upon a chair hung the suit, carefully folded; beneath it the two mute shoes and the discarded socks.

The man himself lay in the bed.

For a long while we just stood there, looking down at the profound and fleshless grin. The body had apparently once lain in the attitude of an embrace, but now the long sleep that outlasts love, that conquers even the grimace of love, had cuckolded him. What was left of him, rotted beneath what was left of the nightshirt, had become inextricable from the bed in which he lay; and upon him and upon the pillow beside him lay that even coating of the patient and biding dust.

Then we noticed that in the second pillow was the indentation of a head. One of us lifted something from it, and leaning forward, that faint and invisible dust dry and acrid in the nostrils, we saw a long strand of iron-gray hair.

---

1. Account for the use of the pronoun "we" by the narrator.
2. How is Faulkner's handling of chronology expressive of the nature of memory?
3. What does Emily represent to her town and her region? What attitudes toward social classes figure in the action and how do these change?
4. What is the relation between comic elements and the melancholy or shocking ingredients of the story?
5. What does Homer Barron represent? How important is it that he is a Yankee?
6. What motives can you attribute to Emily for her killing of Homer Barron? How are these motives related to the theme?

Barn Burning

The store in which the Justice of the Peace's court was sitting smelled of cheese. The boy, crouched on his nail keg at the back of the crowded room, knew he smelled cheese, and more: from where he sat he could see the ranked shelves close-packed with the solid, squat, dynamic shapes of tin cans whose labels his stomach read, not from the lettering which meant nothing to his mind but from the scarlet devils and the silver curve of fish—this, the cheese which he knew he smelled and the hermetic meat[1] which his intestines believed he smelled coming in intermittent gusts momentary and brief between the other constant one, the smell and sense just a little of fear because mostly of despair and grief, the old fierce pull of blood. He could not see the table where the Justice sat and before which his father and his father's enemy *(our enemy* he thought in that despair; *ourn! mine and hisn both! He's my father!)* stood, but he could hear them, the two of them that is, because his father had said no word yet:

"But what proof have you, Mr. Harris?"

"I told you. The hog got into my corn. I caught it up and sent it back to him. He had no fence that would hold it. I told him so, warned him. The next time I put the hog in my pen. When he came to get it I gave him enough wire to patch up his pen. The next time I put the hog up and kept it. I rode down to his house and saw the wire I gave him still rolled on to the spool in his yard. I told him he could have the hog when he paid me a dollar pound fee. That evening a nigger came with the dollar and got the hog. He was a strange nigger. He said, 'He say to tell you wood and hay kin burn.' I said, 'What?' 'That whut he say to tell you,' the nigger said. 'Wood and hay kin burn.' That night my barn burned. I got the stock out but I lost the barn."

"Where is the nigger? Have you got him?"

"He was a strange nigger, I tell you. I don't know what became of him."

"But that's not proof. Don't you see that's not proof?"

"Get that boy up here. He knows." For a moment the boy thought too that the man meant his older brother until Harris said, "Not him. The little one. The boy," and, crouching, small for his age, small and wiry like his father, in patched and faded jeans even too small for him, with straight, uncombed, brown hair and eyes gray and wild as storm scud, he saw the men between himself and the table part and become

1. Canned meat.

a lane of grim faces, at the end of which he saw the Justice, a shabby, collarless, graying man in spectacles, beckoning him. He felt no floor under his bare feet; he seemed to walk beneath the palpable weight of the grim turning faces. His father, stiff in his black Sunday coat donned not for the trial but for the moving, did not even look at him. *He aims for me to lie,* he thought, again with that frantic grief and despair. *And I will have to do hit.*

"What's your name, boy?" the Justice said.

"Colonel Sartoris Snopes,"[2] the boy whispered.

"Hey?" the Justice said. "Talk louder. Colonel Sartoris? I reckon anybody named for Colonel Sartoris in this country can't help but tell the truth, can they?" The boy said nothing. *Enemy! Enemy!* he thought; for a moment he could not even see, could not see that the Justice's face was kindly nor discern that his voice was troubled when he spoke to the man named Harris: "Do you want me to question this boy?" But he could hear, and during those subsequent long seconds while there was absolutely no sound in the crowded little room save that of quiet and intent breathing it was as if he had swung outward at the end of a grape vine, over a ravine, and at the top of the swing had been caught in a prolonged instant of mesmerized gravity, weightless in time.

"No!" Harris said violently, explosively. "Damnation! Send him out of here!" Now time, the fluid world, rushed beneath him again, the voices coming to him again through the smell of cheese and sealed meat, the fear and despair and the old grief of blood:

"This case is closed. I can't find against you, Snopes, but I can give you advice. Leave this country and don't come back to it."

His father spoke for the first time, his voice cold and harsh, level, without emphasis: "I aim to. I don't figure to stay in a country among people who . . ." he said something unprintable and vile, addressed to no one.

"That'll do," the Justice said. "Take your wagon and get out of this country before dark. Case dismissed."

His father turned, and he followed the stiff black coat, the wiry figure walking a little stiffly from where a Confederate provost's man's[3] musket ball had taken him in the heel on a stolen horse thirty years ago, followed the two backs now, since his older brother had appeared from somewhere in the crowd, no taller than the father but thicker, chewing tobacco steadily, between the two lines of grim-faced men and out of the store and across the worn gallery and down the sagging steps and among the dogs and half-grown boys in the mild May dust, where as he passed a voice hissed:

2. The Snopes family figures in many Faulkner stories and novels; Colonel Sartoris is a major personage among Faulkner's fictional inhabitants of Yoknapatawpha County. 3. Military policeman's.

"Barn burner!"

Again he could not see, whirling; there was a face in a red haze, moonlike, bigger than the full moon, the owner of it half again his size, he leaping in the red haze toward the face, feeling no blow, feeling no shock when his head struck the earth, scrabbling up and leaping again, feeling no blow this time either and tasting no blood, scrabbling up to see the other boy in full flight and himself already leaping into pursuit as his father's hand jerked him back, the harsh, cold voice speaking above him: "Go get in the wagon."

It stood in a grove of locusts and mulberries across the road. His two hulking sisters in their Sunday dresses and his mother and her sister in calico and sunbonnets were already in it, sitting on and among the sorry residue of the dozen and more movings which even the boy could remember—the battered stove, the broken beds and chairs, the clock inlaid with mother-of-pearl, which would not run, stopped at some fourteen minutes past two o'clock of a dead and forgotten day and time, which had been his mother's dowry. She was crying, though when she saw him she drew her sleeve across her face and began to descend from the wagon. "Get back," the father said.

"He's hurt. I got to get some water and wash his . . ."

"Get back in the wagon," his father said. He got in too, over the tail-gate. His father mounted to the seat where the older brother already sat and struck the gaunt mules two savage blows with the peeled willow, but without heat. It was not even sadistic; it was exactly that same quality which in later years would cause his descendants to overrun the engine before putting a motor car into motion, striking and reining back in the same movement. The wagon went on, the store with its quiet crowd of grimly watching men dropped behind; a curve in the road hid it. *Forever* he thought. *Maybe he's done satisfied now, now that he has* . . . stopping himself, not to say it aloud even to himself. His mother's hand touched his shoulder.

"Does hit hurt?" she said.

"Naw," he said. "Hit don't hurt. Lemme be."

"Can't you wipe some of the blood off before hit dries?"

"I'll wash to-night," he said. "Lemme be, I tell you."

The wagon went on. He did not know where they were going. None of them ever did or ever asked, because it was always somewhere, always a house of sorts waiting for them a day or two days or even three days away. Likely his father had already arranged to make a crop on another farm before he . . . Again he had to stop himself. He (the father) always did. There was something about his wolf-like independence and even courage when the advantage was at least neutral which impressed strangers, as if they got from his latent ravening ferocity not so much a sense of dependability as a feeling that his ferocious conviction in the rightness of his own actions would be of advantage to all whose interest lay with his.

That night they camped, in a grove of oaks and beeches where a spring ran. The nights were still cool and they had a fire against it, of a rail lifted from a nearby fence and cut into lengths—a small fire, neat, niggard almost, a shrewd fire; such fires were his father's habit and custom always, even in freezing weather. Older, the boy might have remarked this and wondered why not a big one; why should not a man who had not only seen the waste and extravagance of war, but who had in his blood an inherent voracious prodigality with material not his own, have burned everything in sight? Then he might have gone a step farther and thought that that was the reason: that niggard blaze was the living fruit of nights passed during those four years in the woods hiding from all men, blue or gray, with his strings of horses (captured horses, he called them). And older still, he might have divined the true reason: that the element of fire spoke to some deep mainspring of his father's being, as the element of steel or of powder spoke to other men, as the one weapon for the preservation of integrity, else breath were not worth the breathing, and hence to be regarded with respect and used with discretion.

But he did not think this now and he had seen those same niggard blazes all his life. He merely ate his supper beside it and was already half asleep over his iron plate when his father called him, and once more he followed the stiff back, the stiff and ruthless limp, up the slope and on to the starlit road where, turning, he could see his father against the stars but without face or depth—a shape black, flat, and bloodless as though cut from tin in the iron folds of the frockcoat which had not been made for him, the voice harsh like tin and without heat like tin:

"You were fixing to tell them. You would have told him." He didn't answer. His father struck him with the flat of his hand on the side of the head, hard but without heat, exactly as he had struck the two mules at the store, exactly as he would strike either of them with any stick in order to kill a horse fly, his voice still without heat or anger: "You're getting to be a man. You got to learn. You got to learn to stick to your own blood or you ain't going to have any blood to stick to you. Do you think either of them, any man there this morning, would? Don't you know all they wanted was a chance to get at me because they knew I had them beat? Eh?" Later, twenty years later, he was to tell himself, "If I had said they wanted only truth, justice, he would have hit me again." But now he said nothing. He was not crying. He just stood there. "Answer me," his father said.

"Yes," he whispered. His father turned.

"Get on to bed. We'll be there tomorrow."

Tomorrow they were there. In the early afternoon the wagon stopped before a paintless two-room house identical almost with the dozen others it had stopped before even in the boy's ten years, and again, as on the other dozen occasions, his mother and aunt got down and began to unload the wagon, although his two sisters and his father and brother had not moved.

"Likely hit ain't fitten for hawgs," one of the sisters said.

"Nevertheless, fit it will and you'll hog it and like it," his father said. "Get out of them chairs and help your Ma unload."

The two sisters got down, big, bovine, in a flutter of cheap ribbons; one of them drew from the jumbled wagon bed a battered lantern, the other a worn broom. His father handed the reins to the older son and began to climb stiffly over the wheel. "When they get unloaded, take the team to the barn and feed them." Then he said, and at first the boy thought he was still speaking to his brother: "Come with me."

"Me?" he said.

"Yes," his father said. "You."

"Abner," his mother said. His father paused and looked back—the harsh level stare beneath the shaggy, graying, irascible brows.

"I reckon I'll have a word with the man that aims to begin tomorrow owning me body and soul for the next eight months."

They went back up the road. A week ago—or before last night, that is—he would have asked where they were going, but not now. His father had struck him before last night but never before had he paused afterward to explain why; it was as if the blow and the following calm, outrageous voice still rang, repercussed, divulging nothing to him save the terrible handicap of being young, the light weight of his few years, just heavy enough to prevent his soaring free of the world as it seemed to be ordered but not heavy enough to keep him footed solid in it, to resist it and try to change the course of its events.

Presently he could see the grove of oaks and cedars and the other flowering trees and shrubs, where the house would be, though not the house yet. They walked beside a fence massed with honeysuckle and Cherokee roses and came to a gate swinging open between two brick pillars, and now, beyond a sweep of drive, he saw the house for the first time and at that instant he forgot his father and the terror and despair both, and even when he remembered his father again (who had not stopped) the terror and despair did not return. Because, for all the twelve movings, they had sojourned until now in a poor country, a land of small farms and fields and houses, and he had never seen a house like this before. *Hit's big as a courthouse* he thought quietly, with a surge of peace and joy whose reason he could not have thought into words, being too young for that: *They are safe from him. People whose lives are a part of this peace and dignity are beyond his touch, he no more to them than a buzzing wasp: capable of stinging for a little moment but that's all; the spell of this peace and dignity rendering even the barns and stable and cribs which belong to it impervious to the puny flames he might contrive* . . . this, the peace and joy, ebbing for an instant as he looked again at the stiff black back, the stiff and implacable limp of the figure which was not dwarfed by the house, for the reason that it had never looked big anywhere and which now, against the serene columned backdrop, had more than ever that impervious quality of something cut ruthlessly from tin, depthless, as though, sidewise to the sun, it would cast no shadow. Watching him, the boy remarked the absolutely undeviating course which his father held and saw the stiff foot come squarely down in a pile of fresh droppings where a horse had stood in the drive and which his father could have avoided by a simple change of stride. But it ebbed only for a moment, though he could not have thought this into words either, walking on in the spell of the house, which he could even want but without envy, without sorrow, certainly never with that ravening and jealous rage which unknown to him walked in the ironlike black coat before him: *Maybe he will feel it too. Maybe it will even change him now from what maybe he couldn't help but be.*

They crossed the portico. Now he could hear his father's stiff foot as it came down on the boards with clocklike finality, a sound out of all proportion to the displacement of the body it bore and which was not dwarfed either by the white door before it, as though it had attained to a sort of vicious and ravening minimum not to be dwarfed by anything—the flat, wide, black hat, the formal coat of broadcloth which had once been black but which had now that friction-glazed greenish cast of the bodies of old house flies, the lifted sleeve which was too large, the lifted hand like a curled claw. The door opened so promptly that the boy knew the Negro must have been watching them all the time, an old man with neat grizzled hair, in a linen jacket, who stood barring the door with his body, saying, "Wipe yo foots, white man, fo you come in here. Major ain't home nohow."

"Get out of my way, nigger," his father said, without heat too, flinging the door back and the Negro also and entering, his hat still on his head. And now the boy saw the prints of the stiff foot on the doorjamb and saw them appear on the pale rug behind the machinelike deliberation of the foot which seemed to bear (or transmit) twice the weight which the body compassed. The Negro was shouting "Miss Lula! Miss Lula!" somewhere behind them, then the boy, deluged as though by a warm wave by a suave turn of carpeted stair and a pendant glitter of chandeliers and a mute gleam of gold frames, heard the swift feet and saw her too, a lady—perhaps he had never seen her like before either—in a gray, smooth gown with lace at the throat and an apron tied at the waist and the sleeves turned back, wiping cake or biscuit dough from her hands with a towel as she came up the hall, looking not at his father at all but at the tracks on the blond rug with an expression of incredulous amazement.

"I tried," the Negro cried. "I tole him to . . ."

"Will you please go away?" she said in a shaking voice. "Major de Spain is not at home. Will you please go away?"

His father had not spoken again. He did not speak again. He did not even look at her. He just stood stiff in the center of the rug, in his hat, the shaggy iron-gray brows twitching slightly above the pebble-colored eyes as he appeared to examine the house with brief deliberation. Then with the same deliberation he turned; the boy watched him pivot on the good leg and saw the stiff foot drag round the arc of the turning, leaving a final long and fading smear. His father never looked at it, he never once looked down at the rug. The Negro held the door. It closed behind them, upon the hysteric and indistinguishable woman-wail. His father stopped at the top of the steps and scraped his boot clean on the edge of it. At the gate he stopped again. He stood for a moment, planted stiffly on the stiff foot, looking back at the house. "Pretty and white, ain't it?" he said. "That's sweat. Nigger sweat. Maybe it ain't white enough yet to suit him. Maybe he wants to mix some white sweat with it."

Two hours later the boy was chopping wood behind the house within which his mother and aunt and the two sisters (the mother and aunt, not the two girls, he knew that; even at this distance and muffled by walls the flat loud voices of the two girls emanated an incorrigible idle inertia) were setting up the stove to prepare a meal, when he heard the hooves and saw the linen-clad man on a fine sorrel mare, whom he recognized even before he saw the rolled rug in front of the Negro youth following on a fat bay carriage horse—a suffused, angry face vanishing, still at full gallop, beyond the corner of the house where his father and brother were sitting in the two tilted chairs; and a moment later, almost before he could have put the axe down, he heard the hooves again and watched the sorrel mare go back out of the yard, already galloping again. Then his father began to shout one of the sisters' names, who presently emerged backward from the kitchen door dragging the rolled rug along the ground by one end while the other sister walked behind it.

"If you ain't going to tote, go on and set up the wash pot," the first said.

"You, Sarty!" the second shouted. "Set up the wash pot!" His father appeared at the door, framed against that shabbiness, as he had been against that other bland perfection, impervious to either, the mother's anxious face at his shoulder.

"Go on," the father said. "Pick it up." The two sisters stooped, broad, lethargic; stooping, they presented an incredible expanse of pale cloth and a flutter of tawdry ribbons.

"If I thought enough of a rug to have to git hit all the way from France I wouldn't keep hit where folks coming in would have to tromp on hit," the first said. They raised the rug.

"Abner," the mother said. "Let me do it."

"You go back and git dinner," his father said. "I'll tend to this."

From the woodpile through the rest of the afternoon the boy watched them, the rug spread flat in the dust beside the bubbling wash-pot, the two sisters stooping over it with that profound and lethargic reluctance, while the father stood over them in turn, implacable and grim, driving them though never raising his voice again. He could smell the harsh homemade lye[4] they were using; he saw his mother come to the door once and look toward them with an expression not anxious now but very like despair; he saw his father turn, and he fell to with the axe and saw from the corner of his eye his father raise from the ground a flattish fragment of field stone and examine it and return to the pot, and this time his mother actually spoke: "Abner. Abner. Please don't. Please, Abner."

Then he was done too. It was dusk; the whippoorwills had already begun. He could smell coffee from the room where they would presently eat the cold food remaining from the mid-afternoon meal, though when he entered the house he realized they were having coffee again probably because there was a fire on the hearth, before which the rug now lay spread over the backs of the two chairs. The tracks of his father's foot were gone. Where they had been were now long, water-cloudy scoriations resembling the sporadic course of a Lilliputian mowing machine.

It still hung there while they ate the cold food and then went to bed, scattered without order or claim up and down the two rooms, his mother in one bed, where his father would later lie, the older brother in the other, himself, the aunt, and the two sisters on pallets on the floor. But his father was not in bed yet. The last thing the boy remembered was the depthless, harsh silhouette of the hat and coat bending over the rug and it seemed to him that he had not even closed his eyes when the silhouette was standing over him, the fire almost dead behind it, the stiff foot prodding him awake. "Catch up the mule," his father said.

When he returned with the mule his father was standing in the black door, the rolled rug over his shoulder. "Ain't you going to ride?" he said.

4. A caustic, unsuitable for cleaning fine fabrics.

"No. Give me your foot."

He bent his knee into his father's hand, the wiry, surprising power flowed smoothly, rising, he rising with it, on to the mule's bare back (they had owned a saddle once; the boy could remember it though not when or where) and with the same effortlessness his father swung the rug up in front of him. Now in the starlight they retraced the afternoon's path, up the dusty road rife with honeysuckle, through the gate and up the black tunnel of the drive to the lightless house, where he sat on the mule and felt the rough warp of the rug drag across his thighs and vanish.

"Don't you want me to help?" he whispered. His father did not answer and now he heard again that stiff foot striking the hollow portico with that wooden and clocklike deliberation, that outrageous overstatement of the weight it carried. The rug, hunched, not flung (the boy could tell that even in the darkness) from his father's shoulder struck the angle of wall and floor with a sound unbelievably loud, thunderous, then the foot again, unhurried and enormous; a light came on in the house and the boy sat, tense, breathing steadily and quietly and just a little fast, though the foot itself did not increase its beat at all, descending the steps now; now the boy could see him.

"Don't you want to ride now?" he whispered. "We kin both ride now," the light within the house altering now, flaring up and sinking. *He's coming down the stairs now*, he thought. He had already ridden the mule up beside the horse block; presently his father was up behind him and he doubled the reins over and slashed the mule across the neck, but before the animal could begin to trot the hard, thin arm came round him, the hard, knotted hand jerking the mule back to a walk.

In the first red rays of the sun they were in the lot, putting plow gear on the mules. This time the sorrel mare was in the lot before he heard it at all, the rider collarless and even bareheaded, trembling, speaking in a shaking voice as the woman in the house had done, his father merely looking up once before stooping again to the hame he was buckling, so that the man on the mare spoke to his stooping back:

"You must realize you have ruined that rug. Wasn't there anybody here, any of your women . . ." he ceased, shaking, the boy watching him, the older brother leaning now in the stable door, chewing, blinking slowly and steadily at nothing apparently. "It cost a hundred dollars. But you never had a hundred dollars. You never will. So I'm going to charge you twenty bushels of corn against your crop. I'll add it in your contract and when you come to the commissary you can sign it. That won't keep Mrs. de Spain quiet but maybe it will teach you to wipe your feet off before you enter her house again."

Then he was gone. The boy looked at his father, who still had not spoken or even looked up again, who was now adjusting the loggerhead in the hame.

"Pap," he said. His father looked at him—the inscrutable face, the shaggy brows beneath which the gray eyes glinted coldly. Suddenly the boy went toward him, fast, stopping as suddenly. "You done the best you could!" he cried. "If he wanted hit done different why didn't he wait and tell you how? He won't git no twenty bushels! He won't git none! We'll gether hit and hide hit! I kin watch . . ."

"Did you put the cutter back in that straight stock like I told you?"

"No, sir," he said.

"Then go do it."

That was Wednesday. During the rest of that week he worked steadily, at what was within his scope and some which was beyond it, with an industry that did not need to be driven nor even commanded twice; he had this from his mother, with the difference that some at least of what he did he liked to do, such as splitting wood with the half-size axe which his mother and aunt had earned, or saved money somehow, to present him with at Christmas. In company with the two older women (and on one afternoon, even one of the sisters), he built pens for the shoat and the cow which were a part of his father's contract with the landlord, and one afternoon, his father being absent, gone somewhere on one of the mules, he went to the field.

They were running a middle buster now, his brother holding the plow straight while he handled the reins, and walking beside the straining mule, the rich black soil shearing cool and damp against his bare ankles, he thought *Maybe this is the end of it. Maybe even that twenty bushels that seems hard to have to pay for just a rug will be a cheap price for him to stop forever and always from being what he used to be;* thinking, dreaming now, so that his brother had to speak sharply to him to mind the mule: *Maybe he even won't collect the twenty bushels. Maybe it will all add up and balance and vanish—corn, rug, fire; the terror and grief, the being pulled two ways like between two teams of horses—gone, done with for ever and ever.*

Then it was Saturday; he looked up from beneath the mule he was harnessing and saw his father in the black coat and hat. "Not that," his father said. "The wagon gear." And then, two hours later, sitting in the wagon bed behind his father and brother on the seat, the wagon accomplished a final curve, and he saw the weathered paintless store with its tattered tobacco- and patent-medicine posters and the tethered wagons and saddle animals below the gallery. He mounted the gnawed steps behind his father and brother, and there again was the lane of quiet, watching faces for the three of them to walk through. He saw the man in spectacles sitting at the plank table and he did not need to be told this was a Justice of the Peace; he sent one glare of fierce, exultant, partisan defiance at the man in collar and cravat now, whom he had seen but twice before in his life, and that on a galloping horse, who now wore on his face an expression not of rage but of amazed unbelief which the boy could not have known was at the incredible circumstance of being sued by one of his own tenants, and came and stood against his father and cried at the Justice: "He ain't done it! He ain't burnt . . ."

"Go back to the wagon," his father said.

"Burnt?" the Justice said. "Do I understand this rug was burned too?"

"Does anybody here claim it was?" his father said. "Go back to the wagon." But he did not, he merely retreated to the rear of the room, crowded as that other had been, but not to sit down this time, instead, to stand pressing among the motionless bodies, listening to the voices:

"And you claim twenty bushels of corn is too high for the damage you did to the rug?"

"He brought the rug to me and said he wanted the tracks washed out of it. I washed the tracks out and took the rug back to him."

"But you didn't carry the rug back to him in the same condition it was in before you made the tracks on it."

His father did not answer, and now for perhaps half a minute there was no sound at all save that of breathing, the faint, steady suspiration of complete and intent listening.

"You decline to answer that, Mr. Snopes?" Again his father did not answer. "I'm going to find against you, Mr. Snopes. I'm going to find that you were responsible for the injury to Major de Spain's rug and hold you liable for it. But twenty bushels of corn seems a little high for a man in your circumstances to have to pay. Major de Spain claims it cost a hundred dollars. October corn will be worth about fifty cents. I figure that if Major de Spain can stand a ninety-five dollar loss on something he paid cash for, you can stand a five-dollar loss you haven't earned yet. I hold you in damages to Major de Spain to the amount of ten bushels of corn over and above your contract with him, to be paid to him out of your crop at gathering time. Court adjourned."

It had taken no time hardly, the morning was but half begun. He thought they would return home and perhaps back to the field, since they were late, far behind all other farmers. But instead his father passed on behind the wagon, merely indicating with his hand for the older brother to follow with it, and crossed the road toward the blacksmith shop opposite, pressing on after his father, overtaking him, speaking, whispering up at the harsh, calm face beneath the weathered hat: "He won't git no ten bushels neither. He won't git one. We'll . . ."

until his father glanced for an instant down at him, the face absolutely calm, the grizzled eyebrows tangled above the cold eyes, the voice almost pleasant, almost gentle:

"You think so? Well, we'll wait till October anyway."

The matter of the wagon—the setting of a spoke or two and the tightening of the tires—did not take long either, the business of the tires accomplished by driving the wagon into the spring branch behind the shop and letting it stand there, the mules nuzzling into the water from time to time, and the boy on the seat with the idle reins, looking up the slope and through the sooty tunnel of the shed where the slow hammer rang and where his father sat on an upended cypress bolt, easily, either talking or listening, still sitting there when the boy brought the dripping wagon up out of the branch and halted it before the door.

"Take them on to the shade and hitch," his father said. He did so and returned. His father and the smith and a third man squatting on his heels inside the door were talking, about crops and animals; the boy, squatting too in the ammoniac dust and hoof-parings and scales of rust, heard his father tell a long and unhurried story out of the time before the birth of the older brother even when he had been a professional horsetrader. And then his father came up beside him where he stood before a tattered last year's circus poster on the other side of the store, gazing rapt and quiet at the scarlet horses, the incredible poisings and convolutions of tulle and tights and the painted leers of comedians, and said, "It's time to eat."

But not at home. Squatting beside his brother against the front wall, he watched his father emerge from the store and produce from a paper sack a segment of cheese and divide it carefully and deliberately into three with his pocket knife and produce crackers from the same sack. They all three squatted on the gallery and ate, slowly, without talking; then in the store again, they drank from a tin dipper tepid water smelling of the cedar bucket and of living beech trees. And still they did not go home. It was a horse lot this time, a tall rail fence upon and along which men stood and sat and out of which one by one horses were led, to be walked and trotted and then cantered back and forth along the road while the slow swapping and buying went on and the sun began to slant westward, they—the three of them—watching and listening, the older brother with his muddy eyes and his steady, inevitable tobacco, the father commenting now and then on certain of the animals, to no one in particular.

It was after sundown when they reached home. They ate supper by lamplight, then, sitting on the doorstep, the boy watched the night fully accomplish, listening to the whippoorwills and the frogs, when he heard his mother's voice: "Abner! No! No! Oh, God. Oh, God. Abner!" and he rose, whirled, and saw the altered light through the door where a candle stub now burned in a bottle neck on the table and his father, still in the hat and coat, at once formal and burlesque as though dressed carefully for some shabby and ceremonial violence, emptying the reservoir of the lamp back into the five-gallon kerosene can from which it had been filled, while the mother tugged at his arm until he shifted the lamp to the other hand and flung her back, not savagely or viciously, just hard, into the wall, her hands flung out against the wall for balance, her mouth open and in her face the same quality of hopeless despair as had been in her voice. Then his father saw him standing in the door.

"Go to the barn and get that can of oil we were oiling the wagon with," he said. The boy did not move. Then he could speak.

"What . . ." he cried. "What are you . . ."

"Go get that oil," his father said. "Go."

Then he was moving, running, outside the house, toward the stable: this the old habit, the old blood which he had not been permitted to choose for himself, which had been bequeathed him willy nilly and which had run for so long (and who knew where, battening on what of outrage and savagery and lust) before it came to him. *I could keep on,* he thought. *I could run on and on and never look back, never need to see his face again. Only I can't. I can't,* the rusted can in his hand now, the liquid sploshing in it as he ran back to the house and into it, into the sound of his mother's weeping in the next room, and handed the can to his father.

"Ain't you going to even send a nigger?" he cried. "At least you sent a nigger before!"

This time his father didn't strike him. The hand came even faster than the blow had, the same hand which had set the can on the table with almost excruciating care flashing from the can toward him too quick for him to follow it, gripping him by the back of his shirt and on to tiptoe before he had seen it quit the can, the face stooping at him in breathless and frozen ferocity, the cold, dead voice speaking over him to the older brother, who leaned against the table, chewing with that steady, curious, sidewise motion of cows:

"Empty the can into the big one and go on. I'll catch up with you."

"Better tie him up to the bedpost," the brother said.

"Do like I told you," the father said. Then the boy was moving, his bunched shirt and the hard, bony hand between his shoulder-blades, his toes just touching the floor, across the room and into the other one, past the sisters sitting with spread heavy thighs in the two chairs over the cold hearth, and to where his mother and aunt sat side by side on the bed, the aunt's arms about his mother's shoulders.

"Hold him," the father said. The aunt made a startled movement. "Not you," the father said. "Lennie. Take hold of him. I want to see you do it." His mother took him by the wrist. "You'll hold him better than that. If he gets loose don't you know what he is going to do? He will go up yonder." He jerked his head toward the road. "Maybe I'd better tie him."

"I'll hold him," his mother whispered.

"See you do then." Then his father was gone, the stiff foot heavy and measured upon the boards, ceasing at last.

Then he began to struggle. His mother caught him in both arms, he jerking and wrenching at them. He would be stronger in the end, he knew that. But he had no time to wait for it. "Lemme go!" he cried. "I don't want to have to hit you!"

"Let him go!" the aunt said. "If he don't go, before God, I am going up there myself!"

"Don't you see I can't?" his mother cried. "Sarty! Sarty! No! No! Help me, Lizzie!"

Then he was free. His aunt grasped at him but it was too late. He whirled, running, his mother stumbled forward on to her knees behind him, crying to the nearer sister: "Catch him, Net! Catch him!" But that was too late too, the sister (the sisters were twins, born at the same time, yet either of them now gave the impression of being, encompassing as much living meat and volume and weight as any other two of the family) not yet having begun to rise from the chair, her head, face, alone merely turned, presenting to him in the flying instant an astonishing expanse of young female features untroubled by any surprise even, wearing only an expression of bovine interest. Then he was out of the room, out of the house, in the mild dust of the starlit road and the heavy rifeness of honeysuckle, the pale ribbon unspooling with terrific slowness under his running feet, reaching the gate at last and turning in, running, his heart and lungs drumming, on up the drive toward the lighted house, the lighted door. He did not knock, he burst in, sobbing for breath, incapable for the moment of speech; he saw the astonished face of the Negro in the linen jacket without knowing when the Negro had appeared.

"De Spain!" he cried, panted. "Where's . . ." then he saw the white man too emerging from a white door down the hall. "Barn!" he cried. "Barn!"

"What?" the white man said. "Barn?"

"Yes!" the boy cried. "Barn!"

"Catch him!" the white man shouted.

But it was too late this time too. The Negro grasped his shirt, but the entire sleeve, rotten with washing, carried away, and he was out that door too and in the drive again, and had actually never ceased to run even while he was screaming into the white man's face.

Behind him the white man was shouting, "My horse! Fetch my horse!" and he thought for an instant of cutting across the park and climbing the fence into the road, but he did not know the park nor how high the vine-massed fence might be and he dared not risk it. So he ran on down the drive, blood and breath roaring; presently he was in the road again though he could not see it. He could not hear either: the galloping mare was almost upon him before he heard her, and even then he held his course, as if the very urgency of his wild grief and need must in a moment more find his wings, waiting until the ultimate instant to hurl himself aside and into the weed-choked roadside ditch as the horse thundered past and on, for an instant in furious silhouette against the stars, the tranquil early summer night sky which, even before the shape of the horse and rider vanished, stained abruptly and violently upward: a long, swirling roar incredible and soundless, blotting the stars, and he springing up and into the road again, running again, knowing it was too late yet still running even after he heard the shot and, an instant later, two shots, pausing now without knowing he had ceased to run, crying "Pap! Pap!", running again before he knew he had begun to run, stumbling, tripping over something and scrabbling up again without ceasing to run, looking backward over his shoulder at the glare as he got up, running on among the invisible trees, panting, sobbing, "Father! Father!"

At midnight he was sitting on the crest of a hill. He did not know it was midnight and he did not know how far he had come. But there was no glare behind him now and he sat now, his back toward what he had called home for four days anyhow, his face toward the dark woods which he would enter when breath was strong again, small, shaking steadily in the chill darkness, hugging himself into the remainder of his thin, rotten shirt, the grief and despair now no longer terror and fear but just grief and despair. *Father. My father,* he thought. "He was brave!" he cried suddenly, aloud but not loud, no more than a whisper: "He was! He was in the war! He was in Colonel Sartoris' cav'ry!" not knowing that his father had gone to that war a private in the fine old European sense, wearing no uniform, admitting the authority of and giving fidelity to no man or army or flag, going to war as Malbrouck[5] himself did: for booty—it meant nothing and less than nothing to him if it were enemy booty or his own.

The slow constellations wheeled on. It would be dawn and then sun-up after a while and he would be hungry. But that would be tomorrow and now he was only cold, and walking would cure that. His breathing was easier now and he decided to get up and go on, and then

5. The reference is to the chief character in a popular and pervasive 18th-century nursery ditty about a legendary warrior. Originally this warrior figure may have derived from the character and exploits of John Churchill, duke of Marlborough (1650–1722).

he found that he had been asleep because he knew it was almost dawn, the night almost over. He could tell that from the whippoorwills. They were everywhere now among the dark trees below him, constant and inflectioned and ceaseless, so that, as the instant for giving over to the day birds drew nearer and nearer, there was no interval at all between them. He got up. He was a little stiff, but walking would cure that too as it would the cold, and soon there would be the sun. He went on down the hill, toward the dark woods within which the liquid silver voices of the birds called unceasing—the rapid and urgent beating of the urgent and quiring heart of the late spring night. He did not look back.

---

1. By what values does the boy's father live? Does the boy renounce all of them in the end? Is there a sense in which the boy is being true to his father by betraying him?
2. How is the principal conflict related to the "peace and joy" the boy feels at the sight of Major de Spain's house?
3. How is the language related to the point of view? Is it always appropriate to the experience being related or undergone by the point of view character?
4. Discuss concepts of justice that emerge from the story. What does the story say about the evolution of justice from its primitive to its more civilized forms?
5. How do the shifts of scene and setting serve to express the meaning of the unfolding action?
6. Is the tone essentially optimistic or pessimistic?

The Bear

I

There was a man and a dog too this time. Two beasts, counting Old Ben, the bear, and two men, counting Boon Hogganbeck, in whom some of the same blood ran which ran in Sam Fathers, even though Boon's was a plebeian strain of it and only Sam and Old Ben and the mongrel Lion were taintless and incorruptible.

Isaac McCaslin was sixteen. For six years now he had been a man's hunter. For six years now he had heard the best of all talking. It was of the wilderness, the big woods, bigger and older than any recorded document—of white man fatuous enough to believe he had bought any fragment of it, of Indian ruthless enough to pretend that any fragment of it had been his to convey; bigger than Major de Spain and the scrap he pretended to, knowing better; older than old Thomas Sutpen of whom Major de Spain had had it and who knew better; older even than old Ikkemoutubbe, the Chickasaw chief, of whom old Sutpen had had it and who knew better in his turn. It was of the men, not white nor black nor red, but men, hunters, with the will and hardihood to endure and the humility and skill to survive, and the dogs and the bear and deer juxtaposed and reliefed against it, ordered and compelled by and within the wilderness in the ancient and unremitting contest according to the ancient and immitigable rules which voided all regrets and brooked no quarter;—the best game of all, the best of all breathing and forever the best of all listening, the voices quiet and weighty and deliberate for retrospection and recollection and exactitude among the concrete trophies—the racked guns and the heads and skins—in the libraries of town houses or the offices of plantation houses or (and best of all) in the camps themselves where the intact and still-warm meat yet hung, the men who had slain it sitting before the burning logs on hearths, when there were houses and hearths, or about the smoky blazing of piled wood in front of stretched tarpaulins when there were not. There was always a bottle present, so that it would seem to him that those fine fierce instants of heart and brain and courage and wiliness and speed were concentrated and distilled into that brown liquor which not women, not boys and children, but only hunters drank, drinking not of the blood they spilled but some condensation of the wild immortal spirit, drinking it moderately, humbly even, not with the pagan's base and baseless hope of acquiring thereby the virtues of cunning and strength and speed but in salute to them. Thus it seemed to him on this December morning not only natural but actually fitting that this should have begun with whiskey.

He realized later that it had begun long before that. It had already begun on that day when he first wrote his age in two ciphers and his cousin McCaslin[1] brought him for the first time to the camp, the big woods, to earn for himself from the wilderness the name and state of hunter provided he in his turn were humble and enduring enough. He had already inherited then, without ever having seen it, the big old bear with one trap-ruined foot that in an area almost a hundred miles square had earned for himself a name, a definite designation like a living man:—the long legend of corncribs broken down and rifled, of shoats and grown pigs and even calves carried bodily into the woods and devoured, and traps and deadfalls overthrown and dogs mangled and slain, and shotgun and even rifle shots delivered at point-blank range yet with no more effect than so many peas blown through a tube by a child—a corridor of wreckage and destruction beginning back before

1. Carothers McCaslin Edmonds, called "Cass" later in the story.

the boy was born, through which sped, not fast but rather with the ruthless and irresistible deliberation of a locomotive, the shaggy tremendous shape. It ran in his knowledge before he ever saw it. It loomed and towered in his dreams before he even saw the unaxed woods where it left its crooked print, shaggy, tremendous, red-eyed, not malevolent but just big, too big for the dogs which tried to bay it, for the horses which tried to ride it down, for the men and the bullets they fired into it; too big for the very country which was its constricting scope. It was as if the boy had already divined what his senses and intellect had not encompassed yet: that doomed wilderness whose edges were being constantly and punily gnawed at by men with plows and axes who feared it because it was wilderness, men myriad and nameless even to one another in the land where the old bear had earned a name, and through which ran not even a mortal beast but an anachronism indomitable and invincible out of an old, dead time, a phantom, epitome and apotheosis of the old, wild life which the little puny humans swarmed and hacked at in a fury of abhorrence and fear, like pygmies about the ankles of a drowsing elephant;—the old bear, solitary, indomitable, and alone; widowered, childless, and absolved of mortality—old Priam[2] reft of his old wife and outlived all his sons.

Still a child, with three years, then two years, then one year yet before he too could make one of them, each November he would watch the wagon containing the dogs and the bedding and food and guns and his cousin McCaslin and Tennie's Jim and Sam Fathers too, until Sam moved to the camp to live, depart for the Big Bottom, the big woods. To him, they were going not to hunt bear and deer but to keep yearly rendezvous with the bear which they did not even intend to kill. Two weeks later they would return, with no trophy, no skin. He had not expected it. He had not even feared that it might be in the wagon this time with the other skins and heads. He did not even tell himself that in three years or two years or one year more he would be present and that it might even be his gun. He believed that only after he had served his apprenticeship in the woods which would prove him worthy to be a hunter, would he even be permitted to distinguish the crooked print, and that even then for two November weeks he would merely make another minor one, along with his cousin and Major de Spain and General Compson and Walter Ewell and Boon and the dogs which feared to bay it, and the shotguns and rifles which failed even to bleed it, in the yearly pageant-rite of the old bear's furious immortality.

His day came at last. In the surrey with his cousin and Major de Spain and General Compson he saw the wilderness through a slow drizzle of November rain just above the ice point, as it seemed to him

2. King of Troy at the time it was conquered by the Greeks.

later he always saw it or at least always remembered it—the tall and endless wall of dense November woods under the dissolving afternoon and the year's death, sombre, impenetrable (he could not even discern yet how, at what point they could possibly hope to enter it even though he knew that Sam Fathers was waiting there with the wagon), the surrey moving through the skeleton stalks of cotton and corn in the last of open country, the last trace of man's puny gnawing at the immemorial flank, until, dwarfed by that perspective into an almost ridiculous diminishment, the surrey itself seemed to have ceased to move (this too to be completed later, years later, after he had grown to a man and had seen the sea) as a solitary small boat hangs in lonely immobility, merely tossing up and down, in the infinite waste of the ocean, while the water and then the apparently impenetrable land which it nears without appreciable progress, swings slowly and opens the widening inlet which is the anchorage. He entered it. Sam was waiting, wrapped in a quilt on the wagon seat behind the patient and steaming mules. He entered his novitiate to the true wilderness with Sam beside him as he had begun his apprenticeship in miniature to manhood after the rabbits and such with Sam beside him, the two of them wrapped in the damp, warm, Negro-rank quilt, while the wilderness closed behind his entrance as it had opened momentarily to accept him, opening before his advancement as it closed behind his progress, no fixed path the wagon followed but a channel nonexistent ten yards ahead of it and ceasing to exist ten yards after it had passed, the wagon progressing not by its own volition but by attrition of their intact yet fluid circumambience, drowsing, earless, almost lightless.

It seemed to him that at the age of ten he was witnessing his own birth. It was not even strange to him. He had experienced it all before, and not merely in dreams. He saw the camp—a paintless six-room bungalow set on piles above the spring high-water—and he knew already how it was going to look. He helped in the rapid orderly disorder of their establishment in it, and even his motions were familiar to him, foreknown. Then for two weeks he ate the coarse, rapid food—the shapeless sour bread, the wild strange meat, venison and bear and turkey and coon which he had never tasted before—which men ate, cooked by men who were hunters first and cooks afterward; he slept in harsh sheetless blankets as hunters slept. Each morning the gray of dawn found him and Sam Fathers on the stand, the crossing, which had been allotted him. It was the poorest one, the most barren. He had expected that; he had not dared yet to hope even to himself that he would even hear the running dogs this first time. But he did hear them. It was on the third morning—a murmur, sourceless, almost indistinguishable, yet he knew what it was although he had never before heard that many dogs running at once, the murmur swelling into separate and distinct voices until he could call the five dogs which his cousin owned from among the others. "Now," Sam said, "slant your gun up a little and draw back the hammers and then stand still."

But it was not for him, not yet. The humility was there; he had learned that. And he could learn the patience. He was only ten, only one week. The instant had passed. It seemed to him that he could actually see the deer, the buck, smoke-colored, elongated with speed, vanished, the woods, the gray solitude still ringing even when the voices of the dogs had died away; from far away across the sombre woods and the gray half-liquid morning there came two shots. "Now let your hammers down," Sam said.

He did so. "You knew it too," he said.

"Yes," Sam said. "I want you to learn how to do when you didn't shoot. It's after the chance for the bear or the deer has done already come and gone that men and dogs get killed."

"Anyway, it wasn't him," the boy said. "It wasn't even a bear. It was just a deer."

"Yes," Sam said, "it was just a deer."

Then one morning, it was in the second week, he heard the dogs again. This time before Sam even spoke he readied the too-long, too-heavy, man-size gun as Sam had taught him, even though this time he knew the dogs and the deer were coming less close than ever, hardly within hearing even. They didn't sound like any running dogs he had ever heard before even. Then he found that Sam, who had taught him first of all to cock the gun and take position where he could see best in all directions and then never to move again, had himself moved up beside him. "There," he said. "Listen." The boy listened, to no ringing chorus strong and fast on a free scent but, a moiling yapping an octave too high and with something more than indecision and even abjectness in it which he could not yet recognize, reluctant, not even moving very fast, taking a long time to pass out of hearing, leaving even then in the air that echo of thin and almost human hysteria, abject, almost humanly grieving, with this time nothing ahead of it, no sense of a fleeing unseen smoke-colored shape. He could hear Sam breathing at his shoulder. He saw the arched curve of the old man's inhaling nostrils.

"It's Old Ben!" he cried, whispering.

Sam didn't move save for the slow gradual turning of his head as the voices faded on and the faint steady rapid arch and collapse of his nostrils. "Hah," he said. "Not even running. Walking."

"But up here!" the boy cried. "Way up here!"

"He do it every year," Sam said. "Once. Ash and Boon say he comes up here to run the other little bears away. Tell them to get to hell out of here and stay out until the hunters are gone. Maybe." The boy no longer heard anything at all, yet still Sam's head continued to turn gradually and steadily until the back of it was toward him. Then it turned back and looked down at him—the same face, grave, familiar, expressionless until it smiled, the same old man's eyes from which as he watched there faded slowly a quality darkly and fiercely lambent, passionate and proud. "He don't care no more for bears than he does for dogs or men neither. He come to see who's here, who's new in camp this year, whether he can shoot or not. Whether we got the dog yet that can bay and hold him until a man gets there with a gun. Because he's the head bear. He's the man." It faded, was gone; again they were the eyes as he had known them all his life. "He'll let them follow him to the river. Then he'll send them home. We might as well go too; see how they look when they get back to camp."

The dogs were there first, ten of them huddled back under the kitchen, himself and Sam squatting to peer back into the obscurity where they crouched, quiet, the eyes rolling and luminous, vanishing, and no sound, only that effluvium which the boy could not quite place yet, of something more than dog, stronger than dog and not just animal, just beast even. Because there had been nothing in front of the abject and painful yapping except the solitude, the wilderness, so that when the eleventh hound got back about midafternoon and he and Tennie's Jim held the passive and still trembling bitch while Sam daubed her tattered ear and raked shoulder with turpentine and axle-grease, it was still no living creature but only the wilderness which, leaning for a moment, had patted lightly once her temerity. "Just like a man," Sam said. "Just like folks. Put off as long as she could having to be brave, knowing all the time that sooner or later she would have to be brave once so she could keep on calling herself a dog, and knowing beforehand what was going to happen when she done it."

He did not know just when Sam left. He only knew that he was gone. For the next three mornings he rose and ate breakfast and Sam was not waiting for him. He went to his stand alone; he found it without help now and stood on it as Sam had taught him. On the third morning he heard the dogs again, running strong and free on a true scent again, and he readied the gun as he had learned to do and heard the hunt sweep past on since he was not ready yet, had not deserved other yet in just one short period of two weeks as compared to all the long life which he had already dedicated to the wilderness with patience and humility; he heard the shot again, one shot, the single clapping report of Walter Ewell's rifle. By now he could not only find his stand and then return to camp without guidance, by using the compass his cousin had given him he reached Walter, waiting beside the buck and the moiling of dogs over the cast entrails, before any of the other except

Major de Spain and Tennie's Jim on the horses, even before Uncle Ash arrived with the one-eyed wagon-mule which did not mind the smell of blood or even, so they said, of bear.

It was not Uncle Ash on the mule. It was Sam, returned. And Sam was waiting when he finished his dinner and, himself on the one-eyed mule and Sam on the other one of the wagon team, they rode for more than three hours through the rapid shortening sunless afternoon, following no path, no trail even that he could discern, into a section of country he had never seen before. Then he understood why Sam had made him ride the one-eyed mule which would not spook at the smell of blood, of wild animals. The other one, the sound one, stopped short and tried to whirl and bolt even as Sam got down, jerking and wrenching at the rein while Sam held it, coaxing it forward with his voice since he did not dare risk hitching it, drawing it forward while the boy dismounted from the marred one which would stand. Then, standing beside Sam in the thick great gloom of ancient woods and the winter's dying afternoon, he looked quietly down at the rotted log scored and gutted with clawmarks and, in the wet earth beside it, the print of the enormous warped two-toed foot. Now he knew what he had heard in the hounds' voices in the woods that morning and what he had smelled when he peered under the kitchen where they huddled. It was in him too, a little different because they were brute beasts and he was not, but only a little different—an eagerness, passive; an abjectness, a sense of his own fragility and impotence against the timeless woods, yet without doubt or dread; a flavor like brass in the sudden run of saliva in his mouth, a hard sharp constriction either in his brain or his stomach, he could not tell which and it did not matter; he knew only that for the first time he realized that the bear which had run in his listening and loomed in his dreams since before he could remember and which therefore must have existed in the listening and the dreams of his cousin and Major de Spain and even old General Compson before they began to remember in their turn, was a mortal animal and that they had departed for the camp each November with no actual intention of slaying it, not because it could not be slain but because so far they had no actual hope of being able to. "It will be tomorrow," he said.

"You mean we will try tomorrow," Sam said. "We ain't got the dog yet."

"We've got eleven," he said. "They ran him Monday."

"And you heard them," Sam said. "Saw them too. We ain't got the dog yet. It won't take but one. But he ain't there. Maybe he ain't nowhere. The only other way will be for him to run by accident over somebody that had a gun and knowed how to shoot it."

"That wouldn't be me," the boy said. "It would be Walter or Major or——"

"It might," Sam said. "You watch close tomorrow. Because he's smart. That's how come he has lived this long. If he gets hemmed up and has got to pick out somebody to run over, he will pick out you."

"How?" he said. "How will he know. . . . " He ceased. "You mean he already knows me, that I ain't never been to the big bottom before, ain't had time to find out yet whether I . . ." He ceased again, staring at Sam; he said humbly, not even amazed: "It was me he was watching. I don't reckon he did need to come but once."

"You watch tomorrow," Sam said. "I reckon we better start back. It'll be long after dark now before we get to camp."

The next morning they started three hours earlier than they had ever done. Even Uncle Ash went, the cook, who called himself by profession a camp cook and who did little else save cook for Major de Spain's hunting and camping parties, yet who had been marked by the wilderness from simple juxtaposition to it until he responded as they all did, even the boy who until two weeks ago had never even seen the wilderness, to a hound's ripped ear and shoulder and the print of a crooked foot in a patch of wet earth. They rode. It was too far to walk: the boy and Sam and Uncle Ash in the wagon with the dogs, his cousin and Major de Spain and General Compson and Boon and Walter and Tennie's Jim riding double on the horses; again the first gray light found him, as on that first morning two weeks ago, on the stand where Sam had placed and left him. With the gun which was too big for him, the breech-loader which did not even belong to him but to Major de Spain and which he had fired only once, at a stump on the first day to learn the recoil and how to reload it with the paper shells, he stood against a big gum tree beside a little bayou whose black still water crept without motion out of a cane-break, across a small clearing and into the cane again, where, invisible, a bird, the big woodpecker called Lord-to-God by Negroes, clattered at a dead trunk. It was a stand like any other stand, dissimilar only in incidentals to the one where he had stood each morning for two weeks; a territory new to him yet no less familiar than that other one which after two weeks he had come to believe he knew a little—the same solitude, the same loneliness through which frail and timorous man had merely passed without altering it, leaving no mark nor scar, which looked exactly as it must have looked when the first ancestor of Sam Fathers' Chickasaw predecessors crept into it and looked about him, club or stone axe or bone arrow drawn and ready, different only because, squatting at the edge of the kitchen, he had smelled the dogs huddled and cringing beneath it and saw the raked ear and side of the bitch that, as Sam had said, had to be brave once in order to keep on calling herself a dog and saw yesterday in the earth beside the gutted log the print of the living foot. He heard no dogs at all. He never did certainly hear them. He only heard the drumming of the woodpecker stop short off, and knew that the bear was looking at him. He never saw it. He did not know whether it was facing him from the cane or behind him. He did not move, holding the useless gun which he knew now he would never fire at it, now or ever, tasting in his saliva that taint of brass which he had smelled in the huddled dogs when he peered under the kitchen.

Then it was gone. As abruptly as it had stopped, the woodpecker's dry hammering set up again, and after a while he believed he even heard the dogs—a murmur, scarce a sound even, which he had probably been hearing for a time, perhaps a minute or two, before he remarked it, drifting into hearing and then out again, dying away. They came nowhere near him. If it was dogs he heard, he could not have sworn to it; if it was a bear they ran, it was another bear. It was Sam himself who emerged from the cane and crossed the bayou, the injured bitch following at heel as a bird dog is taught to walk. She came and crouched against his leg, trembling. "I didn't see him," he said. "I didn't, Sam."

"I know it," Sam said. "He done the looking. You didn't hear him neither, did you?"

"No," the boy said. "I——"

"He's smart," Sam said. "Too smart." Again the boy saw in his eyes that quality of dark and brooding lambence as Sam looked down at the bitch trembling faintly and steadily against the boy's leg. From her raked shoulder a few drops of fresh blood clung like bright berries. "Too big. We ain't got the dog yet. But maybe some day."

Because there would be a next time, after and after. He was only ten. It seemed to him that he could see them, the two of them, shadowy in the limbo from which time emerged and became time: the old bear absolved of mortality and himself who shared a little of it. Because he recognized now what he had smelled in the huddled dogs and tasted in his own saliva, recognized fear as a boy, a youth, recognizes the existence of love and passion and experience which in his heritage but not yet his patrimony, from entering by chance the presence or perhaps even merely the bedroom of a woman who has loved and been loved by many men. *So I will have to see him,* he thought, without dread or even hope. *I will have to look at him.* So it was in June of the next summer. They were at the camp again, celebrating Major de Spain's and General Compson's birthdays. Although the one had been born in September and the other in the depth of winter and almost thirty years earlier, each June the two of them and McCaslin and Boon and Walter Ewell (and the boy too from now on) spent two weeks at the camp, fishing and shooting squirrels and turkey and running coons and wildcats with the dogs at night. That is, Boon and the Negroes (and the boy too now) fished and shot squirrels and ran the coons and cats, because the proven hunters, not only Major de Spain and old General Compson (who spent those two weeks sitting in a rocking chair before a tremendous iron pot of Brunswick stew, stirring and tasting, with Uncle Ash to quarrel with about how he was making it and Tennie's Jim to pour whiskey into the tin dipper from which he drank it), but even McCaslin and Walter Ewell who were still young enough, scorned such, other than shooting the wild gobblers with pistols for wagers or to test their marksmanship.

That is, his cousin McCaslin and the others thought he was hunting squirrels. Until the third evening he believed that Sam Fathers thought so too. Each morning he would leave the camp right after breakfast. He had his own gun now, a new breech-loader, a Christmas gift; he would own and shoot it for almost seventy years, through two new pairs of barrels and locks and one new stock, until all that remained of the original gun was the silver-inlaid trigger-guard with his and McCaslin's engraved names and the date in 1878. He found the tree beside the little bayou where he had stood that morning. Using the compass he ranged from that point; he was teaching himself to be better than a fair woodsman without even knowing he was doing it. On the third day he even found the gutted log where he had first seen the print. It was almost completely crumbled now, healing with unbelievable speed, a passionate and almost visible relinquishment, back into the earth from which the tree had grown. He ranged the summer woods now, green with gloom, if anything actually dimmer than they had been in November's gray dissolution, where even at noon the sun fell only in windless dappling upon the earth which never completely dried and which crawled with snakes—moccasins and watersnakes and rattlers, themselves the color of the dappled gloom so that he would not always see them until they moved; returning to camp later and later and later, first day, second day, passing in the twilight of the third evening the little log pen enclosing the log barn where Sam was putting up the stock for the night. "You ain't looked right yet," Sam said.

He stopped. For a moment he didn't answer. Then he said peacefully, in a peaceful rushing burst, as when a boy's miniature dam in a little brook gives way: "All right. Yes. But how? I went to the bayou. I even found that log again. I——"

"I reckon that was all right. Likely he's been watching you. You never saw his foot?"

"I . . ." the boy said, "I didn't . . . I never thought . . ."

"It's the gun," Sam said. He stood beside the fence, motionless, the old man, son of a Negro slave and a Chickasaw chief, in the battered and faded overalls and the frayed five-cent straw hat which had been the badge of the Negro's slavery and was now the regalia of his freedom. The camp—the clearing, the house, the barn and its tiny lot with which Major de Spain in his turn had scratched punily and evanescently at the wilderness—faded in the dusk, back into the immemorial darkness of the woods. *The gun*, the boy thought. *The gun*. "You will have to choose," Sam said.

He left the next morning before light, without breakfast, long before Uncle Ash would wake in his quilts on the kitchen floor and start the fire. He had only the compass and a stick for the snakes. He could go almost a mile before he would need to see the compass. He sat on a log, the invisible compass in his hand, while the secret night-sounds which had ceased at his movements, scurried again and then fell still for good and the owls ceased and gave over to the waking day birds and there was light in the gray wet woods and he could see the compass. He went fast yet still quietly, becoming steadily better and better as a woodsman without yet having time to realize it; he jumped a doe and a fawn, walked them out of the bed, close enough to see them—the crash of undergrowth, the white scut, the fawn scudding along behind her, faster than he had known it could have run. He was hunting right, upwind, as Sam had taught him, but that didn't matter now. He had left the gun; by his own will and relinquishment he had accepted not a gambit, not a choice, but a condition in which not only the bear's heretofore inviolable anonymity but all the ancient rules and balances of hunter and hunted had been abrogated. He would not even be afraid, not even in the moment when the fear would take him completely: blood, skin, bowels, bones, memory from the long time before it even became his memory—all save that thin clear quenchless lucidity which alone differed him from this bear and from all the other bears and bucks he would follow during almost seventy years, to which Sam had said: "Be scared. You can't help that. But don't be afraid. Ain't nothing in the woods going to hurt you if you don't corner it or it don't smell that you are afraid. A bear or a deer has got to be scared of a coward the same as a brave man has got to be."

By noon he was far beyond the crossing on the little bayou, farther into the new and alien country than he had ever been, traveling now not only by the compass but by the old, heavy, biscuit-thick silver watch which had been his father's. He had left the camp nine hours ago; nine hours from now, dark would already have been an hour old. He stopped, for the first time since he had risen from the log when he could see the compass face at last, and looked about, mopping his sweating face on his sleeve. He had already relinquished, of his will, because of his need, in humility and peace and without regret, yet apparently that had not been enough, the leaving of the gun was not enough. He stood for a moment—a child, alien and lost in the green and soaring gloom of the markless wilderness. Then he relinquished completely to it. It was the watch and the compass. He was still tainted. He removed the linked chain of the one and the looped thong of the other from his overalls and hung them on a bush and leaned the stick beside them and entered it.

When he realized he was lost, he did as Sam had coached and drilled him: made a cast to cross his backtrack. He had not been going very fast for the last two or three hours, and he had gone even less fast since he left the compass and watch on the bush. So he went slower still now, since the tree could not be very far; in fact, he found it before he really expected to and turned and went to it. But there was no bush beneath it, no compass nor watch, so he did next as Sam had coached and drilled him: made this next circle in the opposite direction and much larger, so that the pattern of the two of them would bisect his track somewhere, but crossing no trace nor mark anywhere of his feet or any feet, and now he was going faster though still not panicked, his heart beating a little more rapidly but strong and steady enough, and this time it was not even the tree because there was a down log beside it which he had never seen before and beyond the log a little swamp, a seepage of moisture somewhere between earth and water, and he did what Sam had coached and drilled him as the next and the last, seeing as he sat down on the log the crooked print, the warped indentation in the wet ground which while he looked at it continued to fill with water until it was level full and the water began to overflow and the sides of the print began to dissolve away. Even as he looked up he saw the next one, and moving, the one beyond it; moving, not hurrying, running, but merely keeping pace with them as they appeared before him as though they were being shaped out of thin air just one constant pace short of where he would lose them forever and be lost forever himself, tireless, eager, without doubt or dread, panting a little above the strong rapid little hammer of his heart, emerging suddenly into a little glade, and the wilderness coalesced. It rushed, soundless, and solidified—the tree, the bush, the compass and the watch glinting where a ray of sunlight touched them. Then he saw the bear. It did not emerge, appear: it was just there, immobile, fixed in the green and windless noon's hot dappling, not as big as he had dreamed it but as big as he had expected, bigger, dimensionless against the dappled obscurity, looking at him. Then it moved. It crossed the glade without haste, walking for an instant into the sun's full glare and out of it, and stopped again and looked back at him across one shoulder. Then it was gone. It didn't walk into the woods. It faded, sank back into the wilderness without motion as he had watched a fish, a huge old bass, sink back into the dark depths of its pool and vanish without even any movement of its fins.

II

So he should have hated and feared Lion. He was thirteen then. He had killed his buck and Sam Fathers had marked his face with the hot blood,[3] and in the next November he killed a bear. But before that accolade he had become as competent in the woods as many grown men with the same experience. By now he was a better woodsman than most grown men with more. There was no territory within twenty-five miles of the camp that he did not know—bayou, ridge, landmark trees and path; he could have led anyone direct to any spot in it and brought him back. He knew game trails that even Sam Fathers had never seen; in the third fall he found a buck's bedding-place by himself and unbeknown to his cousin he borrowed Walter Ewell's rifle and lay in wait for the buck at dawn and killed it when it walked back to the bed as Sam had told him how the old Chickasaw fathers did.

By now he knew the old bear's footprint better than he did his own, and not only the crooked one. He could see any one of the three sound prints and distinguished it at once from any other, and not only because of its size. There were other bears within that fifty miles which left tracks almost as large, or at least so near that the one would have appeared larger only by juxtaposition. It was more than that. If Sam Fathers had been his mentor and the backyard rabbits and squirrels his kindergarten, then the wilderness the old bear ran was his college and the old male bear itself, so long unwifed and childless as to have become its own ungendered progenitor, was his alma mater.

He could find the crooked print now whenever he wished, ten miles or five miles or sometimes closer than that, to the camp. Twice while on stand during the next three years he heard the dogs strike its trail and once even jump it by chance, the voices high, abject, almost human in their hysteria. Once, still-hunting with Walter Ewell's rifle, he saw it cross a long corridor of down timber where a tornado had passed. It rushed through rather than across the tangle of trunks and branches as a locomotive would, faster than he had ever believed it could have moved, almost as fast as a deer even because the deer would have spent most of that distance in the air; he realized then why it would take a dog not only of abnormal courage but size and speed too ever to bring it to bay. He had a little dog at home, a mongrel, of the sort called fyce by Negroes, a ratter, itself not much bigger than a rat and possessing that sort of courage which had long since stopped being bravery and had become foolhardiness. He brought it with him one June and, timing them as if they were meeting an appointment with another human being, himself carrying the fyce with a sack over its

3. Traditional ceremony of initiation, performed when a boy kills his first big game.

head and Sam Fathers with a brace of the hounds on a rope leash, they lay downwind of the trail and actually ambushed the bear. They were so close that it turned at bay although he realized later this might have been from surprise and amazement at the shrill and frantic uproar of the fyce. It turned at bay against the trunk of a big cypress, on its hind feet; it seemed to the boy that it would never stop rising, taller and taller, and even the two hounds seemed to have taken a kind of desperate and despairing courage from the fyce. Then he realized that the fyce was actually not going to stop. He flung the gun down and ran. When he overtook and grasped the shrill, frantically pinwheeling little dog, it seemed to him that he was directly under the bear. He could smell it, strong and hot and rank. Sprawling, he looked up where it loomed and towered over him like a thunderclap. It was quite familiar, until he remembered: this was the way he had used to dream about it.

Then it was gone. He didn't see it go. He knelt, holding the frantic fyce with both hands, hearing the abased wailing of the two hounds drawing further and further away, until Sam came up, carrying the gun. He laid it quietly down beside the boy and stood looking down at him. "You've done seed him twice now, with a gun in your hands," he said. "This time you couldn't have missed him."

The boy rose. He still held the fyce. Even in his arms it continued to yap frantically, surging and straining toward the fading sound of the hounds like a collection of live-wire springs. The boy was panting a little. "Neither could you," he said. "You had the gun. Why didn't you shoot him?"

Sam didn't seem to have heard. He put out his hand and touched the little dog in the boy's arms which still yapped and strained even though the two hounds were out of hearing now. "He's done gone," Sam said. "You can slack off and rest now, until next time." He stroked the little dog until it began to grow quiet under his hand. "You's almost the one we wants," he said. "You just ain't big enough. We ain't got that one yet. He will need to be just a little bigger than smart, and a little braver than either." He withdrew his hand from the fyce's head and stood looking into the woods where the bear and the hounds had vanished. "Somebody is going to, some day."

"I know it," the boy said. "That's why it must be one of us. So it won't be until the last day. When even he don't want it to last any longer."

So he should have hated and feared Lion. It was in the fourth summer, the fourth time he had made one in the celebration of Major de Spain's and General Compson's birthday. In the early spring Major de Spain's mare had foaled a horse colt. One evening when Sam brought the horses and mules up to stable them for the night, the colt was missing and it was all he could do to get the frantic mare into the lot.

He had thought at first to let the mare lead him back to where she had become separated from the foal. But she would not do it. She would not even feint toward any particular part of the woods or even in any particular direction. She merely ran, as if she couldn't see, still frantic with terror. She whirled and ran at Sam once, as if to attack him in some ultimate desperation, as if she could not for the moment realize that he was a man and a long-familiar one. He got her into the lot at last. It was too dark by that time to back-track her, to unravel the erratic course she had doubtless pursued.

He came to the house and told Major de Spain. It was an animal, of course, a big one, and the colt was dead now, wherever it was. They all knew that. "It's a panther," General Compson said at once. "The same one. That doe and fawn last March." Sam had sent Major de Spain word of it when Boon Hogganbeck came to the camp on a routine visit to see how the stock had wintered—the doe's throat torn out, and the beast had run down the helpless fawn and killed it too.

"Sam never did say that was a panther," Major de Spain said. Sam said nothing now, standing behind Major de Spain where they sat at supper, inscrutable, as if he were just waiting for them to stop talking so he could go home. He didn't even seem to be looking at anything. "A panther might jump a doe, and he wouldn't have much trouble catching the fawn afterward. But no panther would have jumped that colt with the dam right there with it. It was Old Ben," Major de Spain said. "I'm disappointed in him. He has broken the rules. I didn't think he would have done that. He has killed mine and McCaslin's dogs, but that was all right. We gambled the dogs against him; we gave each other warning. But now he has come into my house and destroyed my property, out of season too. He broke the rules. It was Old Ben, Sam." Still Sam said nothing, standing there until Major de Spain should stop talking. "We'll back-track her tomorrow and see," Major de Spain said.

Sam departed. He would not live in the camp; he had built himself a little hut something like Joe Baker's, only stouter, tighter, on the bayou a quarter-mile away, and a stout log crib where he stored a little corn for the shoat he raised each year. The next morning he was waiting when they waked. He had already found the colt. They did not even wait for breakfast. It was not far, not five hundred yards from the stable—the three-months' colt lying on its side, its throat torn out and the entrails and one ham partly eaten. It lay not as if it had been dropped but as if it had been struck and hurled, and no cat-mark, no claw-mark where a panther would have gripped it while finding its throat. They read the tracks where the frantic mare had circled and at last rushed in with that same ultimate desperation with which she had whirled on Sam Fathers yesterday evening, and the long tracks of dead and terrified running and those of the beast which had not even rushed at her when she advanced but had merely walked three or four paces toward her until she broke, and General Compson said, "Good God, what a wolf!"

Still Sam said nothing. The boy watched him while the men knelt, measuring the tracks. There was something in Sam's face now. It was neither exultation nor joy nor hope. Later, a man, the boy realized what it had been, and that Sam had known all the time what had made the tracks and what had torn the throat out of the doe in the spring and killed the fawn. It had been foreknowledge in Sam's face that morning. *And he was glad,* he told himself. *He was old. He had no children, no people, none of his blood anywhere above earth that he would ever meet again. And even if he were to, he could not have touched it, spoken to it, because for seventy years now he had had to be a Negro. It was almost over now and he was glad.*

They returned to camp and had breakfast and came back with guns and the hounds. Afterward the boy realized that they also should have known then what killed the colt as well as Sam Fathers did. But that was neither the first nor the last time he had seen men rationalize from and even act upon their misconceptions. After Boon, standing astride the colt, had whipped the dogs away from it with his belt, they snuffed at the tracks. One of them, a young dog hound without judgment yet, bayed once, and they ran for a few feet on what seemed to be a trail. Then they stopped, looking back at the men, eager enough, not baffled, merely questioning, as if they were asking "Now what?" Then they rushed back to the colt, where Boon, still astride it, slashed at them with the belt.

"I never knew a trail to get cold that quick," General Compson said.

"Maybe a single wolf big enough to kill a colt with the dam right there beside it don't leave scent," Major de Spain said.

"Maybe it was a hant,"[4] Walter Ewell said. He looked at Tennie's Jim. "Hah, Jim?"

Because the hounds would not run it, Major de Spain had Sam hunt out and find the tracks a hundred yards farther on and they put the dogs on it again and again the young one bayed and not one of them realized then that the hound was not baying like a dog striking game but was merely bellowing like a country dog whose yard has been invaded. General Compson spoke to the boy and Boon and Tennie's Jim: to the squirrel hunters. "You boys keep the dogs with you this morning. He's probably hanging around somewhere, waiting to get his breakfast off the colt. You might strike him."

But they did not. The boy remembered how Sam stood watching

4. "Haunt," i.e., a supernatural creature.

them as they went into the woods with the leashed hounds—the Indian face in which he had never seen anything until it smiled, except that faint arching of the nostrils on that first morning when the hounds had found Old Ben. They took the hounds with them on the next day, though when they reached the place where they hoped to strike a fresh trail, the carcass of the colt was gone. Then on the third morning Sam was waiting again, this time until they had finished breakfast. He said, "Come." He led them to his house, his little hut, to the corn-crib beyond it. He had removed the corn and had made a deadfall of the door, baiting it with the colt's carcass; peering between the logs, they saw an animal almost the color of a gun or pistol barrel, what little time they had to examine its color or shape. It was not crouched nor even standing. It was in motion, in the air, coming toward them—a heavy body crashing with tremendous force against the door so that the thick door jumped and clattered in its frame, the animal, whatever it was, hurling itself against the door again seemingly before it could have touched the floor and got a new purchase to spring from. "Come away," Sam said, "fore he break his neck." Even when they retreated the heavy and measured crashes continued, the stout door jumping and clattering each time, and still no sound from the beast itself—no snarl, no cry.

"What in hell's name is it?" Major de Spain said.

"It's a dog," Sam said, his nostrils arching and collapsing faintly and steadily and that faint, fierce milkiness in his eyes again as on that first morning when the hounds had struck the old bear. "It's the dog."

"*The dog?*" Major de Spain said.

"That's gonter hold Old Ben."

"Dog the devil," Major de Spain said. "I'd rather have Old Ben himself in my pack than that brute. Shoot him."

"No," Sam said.

"You'll never tame him. How do you ever expect to make an animal like that afraid of you?"

"I don't want him tame," Sam said; again the boy watched his nostrils and the fierce milky light in his eyes. "But I almost rather he be tame than scared, of me or any man or any thing. But he won't be neither, of nothing."

"Then what are you going to do with it?"

"You can watch," Sam said.

Each morning through the second week they would go to Sam's crib. He had removed a few shingles from the roof and had put a rope on the colt's carcass and had drawn it out when the trap fell. Each morning they would watch him lower a pail of water into the crib while the dog hurled itself tirelessly against the door and dropped back and leaped again. It never made any sound and there was nothing frenzied in the act but only a cold and grim indomitable determination. Toward the end of the week it stopped jumping at the door. Yet it had not weakened appreciably and it was not as if it had rationalized the fact that the door was not going to give. It was as if for that time it simply disdained to jump any longer. It was not down. None of them had ever seen it down. It stood, and they could see it now—part mastiff, something of Airedale and something of a dozen other strains probably, better than thirty inches at the shoulders and weighing as they guessed almost ninety pounds, with cold yellow eyes and a tremendous chest and over all that strange color like a blued gun-barrel.

Then the two weeks were up. They prepared to break camp. The boy begged to remain and his cousin let him. He moved into the little hut with Sam Fathers. Each morning he watched Sam lower the pail of water into the crib. By the end of that week the dog was down. It would rise and half stagger, half crawl to the water and drink and collapse again. One morning it could not even reach the water, could not raise its forequarters even from the floor. Sam took a short stick and prepared to enter the crib. "Wait," the boy said. "Let me get the gun——"

"No," Sam said. "He can't move now." Nor could it. It lay on its side while Sam touched it, its head and the gaunted body, the dog lying motionless, the yellow eyes open. They were not fierce and there was nothing of petty malevolence in them, but a cold and almost impersonal malignance like some natural force. It was not even looking at Sam nor at the boy peering at it between the logs.

Sam began to feed it again. The first time he had to raise its head so it could lap the broth. That night he left a bowl of broth containing lumps of meat where the dog could reach it. The next morning the bowl was empty and the dog was lying on its belly, its head up, the cold yellow eyes watching the door as Sam entered, no change whatever in the cold yellow eyes and still no sound from it even when it sprang, its aim and coordination still bad from weakness so that Sam had time to strike it down with the stick and leap from the crib and slam the door as the dog, still without having had time to get its feet under it to jump again seemingly, hurled itself against the door as if the two weeks of starving had never been.

At noon that day someone came whooping through the woods from the direction of the camp. It was Boon. He came and looked for a while between the logs, at the tremendous dog lying again on its belly, its head up, the yellow eyes blinking sleepily at nothing: the indomitable and unbroken spirit. "What we better do," Boon said, "is to let that sonofabitch go and catch Old Ben and run him on the dog." He turned to the boy his weather-reddened and beetling face. "Get your traps together. Cass says for you to come on home. You been in here fooling with that horse-eating varmint long enough."

Boon had a borrowed mule at the camp; the buggy was waiting at the edge of the bottom. He was at home that night. He told McCaslin about it. "Sam's going to starve him again until he can go in and touch him. Then he will feed him again. Then he will starve him again, if he has to."

"But why?" McCaslin said. "What for? Even Sam will never tame that brute."

"We don't want him tame. We want him like he is. We just want him to find out at last that the only way he can get out of that crib and stay out of it is to do what Sam or somebody tells him to do. He's the dog that's going to stop Old Ben and hold him. We've already named him. His name is Lion."

Then November came at last. They returned to the camp. With General Compson and Major de Spain and his cousin and Walter and Boon he stood in the yard among the guns and bedding and boxes of food and watched Sam Fathers and Lion come up the lane from the lot—the Indian, the old man in battered overalls and rubber boots and a worn sheepskin coat and a hat which had belonged to the boy's father; the tremendous dog pacing gravely beside him. The hounds rushed out to meet them and stopped, except the young one which still had but little of judgment. It ran up to Lion, fawning. Lion didn't snap at it. He didn't even pause. He struck it rolling and yelping for five or six feet with a blow of one paw as a bear would have done and came on into the yard and stood, blinking sleepily at nothing, looking at no one, while Boon said, "Jesus. Jesus.—Will he let me touch him?"

"You can touch him," Sam said. "He don't care. He don't care about nothing or nobody."

The boy watched that too. He watched it for the next two years from that moment when Boon touched Lion's head and then knelt beside him, feeling the bones and muscles, the power. It was as if Lion were a woman—or perhaps Boon was the woman. That was more like it—the big, grave, sleepy-seeming dog which, as Sam Fathers said, cared about no man and no thing; and the violent, insensitive, hard-faced man with his touch of remote Indian blood and the mind almost of a child. He watched Boon take over Lion's feeding from Sam and Uncle Ash both. He would see Boon squatting in the cold rain beside the kitchen while Lion ate. Because Lion neither slept nor ate with the other dogs though none of them knew where he did sleep until in the second November, thinking until then that Lion slept in his kennel beside Sam Fathers' hut, when the boy's cousin McCaslin said something about it to Sam by sheer chance and Sam told him. And that night the boy and Major de Spain and McCaslin with a lamp entered the back room where Boon slept—the little, tight, airless room rank with the smell of Boon's unwashed body and his wet hunting-clothes—where Boon, snoring on his back, choked and waked and Lion raised his head beside him and looked back at them from his cold, slumbrous yellow eyes.

"Damn it, Boon," McCaslin said. "Get that dog out of here. He's got to run Old Ben tomorrow morning. How in hell do you expect him to smell anything fainter than a skunk after breathing you all night?"

"The way I smell ain't hurt my nose none that I ever noticed," Boon said.

"It wouldn't matter if it had," Major de Spain said. "We're not depending on you to trail a bear. Put him outside. Put him under the house with the other dogs."

Boon began to get up. "He'll kill the first one that happens to yawn or sneeze in his face or touches him."

"I reckon not," Major de Spain said. "None of them are going to risk yawning in his face or touching him either, even asleep. Put him outside. I want his nose right tomorrow. Old Ben fooled him last year. I don't think he will do it again."

Boon put on his shoes without lacing them; in his long soiled underwear, his hair still tousled from sleep, he and Lion went out. The others returned to the front room and the poker game where McCaslin's and Major de Spain's hands waited for them on the table. After a while McCaslin said, "Do you want me to go back and look again?"

"No," Major de Spain said. "I call," he said to Walter Ewell. He spoke to McCaslin again. "If you do, don't tell me. I am beginning to see the first sign of my increasing age: I don't like to know that my orders have been disobeyed, even when I knew when I gave them that they would be.—A small pair," he said to Walter Ewell.

"How small?" Walter said.

"Very small," Major de Spain said.

And the boy, lying beneath his piled quilts and blankets waiting for sleep, knew likewise that Lion was already back in Boon's bed, for the rest of that night and the next one and during all the nights of the next November and the next one. He thought then: *I wonder what Sam thinks. He could have Lion with him, even if Boon is a white man. He could ask Major or McCaslin either. And more than that. It was Sam's hand that touched Lion first and Lion knows it.* Then he became a man and he knew that too. It had been all right. That was the way it should have been. Sam was the chief, the prince; Boon, the plebeian, was his huntsman. Boon should have nursed the dogs.

On the first morning that Lion led the pack after Old Ben, seven strangers appeared in the camp. They were swampers: gaunt, malaria-ridden men appearing from nowhere, who ran trap-lines for coons or perhaps farmed little patches of cotton and corn along the edge of the bottom, in clothes but little better than Sam Fathers' and nowhere near as good as Tennie's Jim's, with worn shotguns and rifles, already squatting patiently in the cold drizzle in the side yard when day broke. They had a spokesman; afterward Sam Fathers told Major de Spain how all during the past summer and fall they had drifted into the camp singly or in pairs and threes, to look quietly at Lion for a while and then go away: "Mawnin, Major. We heerd you was aimin to put that ere blue dawg on that old two-toed bear this mawnin. We figgered we'd come up and watch, if you don't mind. We won't do no shooting, lessen he runs over us."

"You are welcome," Major de Spain said. "You are welcome to shoot. He's more your bear than ours."

"I reckon that ain't no lie. I done fed him enough cawn to have a sheer in him. Not to mention a shoat three years ago."

"I reckon I got a sheer too," another said. "Only it ain't in the bear." Major de Spain looked at him. He was chewing tobacco. He spat. "Hit was a heifer calf. Nice un too. Last year. When I finally found her, I reckon she looked about like that colt of yourn looked last June."

"Oh," Major de Spain said. "Be welcome. If you see game in front of my dogs, shoot it."

Nobody shot Old Ben that day. No man saw him. The dogs jumped him within a hundred yards of the glade where the boy had seen him that day in the summer of his eleventh year. The boy was less than a quarter-mile away. He heard the jump but he could distinguish no voice among the dogs that he did not know and therefore would be Lion's, and he thought, believed, that Lion was not among them. Even the fact that they were going much faster than he had ever heard them run behind Old Ben before and that the high thin note of hysteria was missing now from their voices was not enough to disabuse him. He didn't comprehend until that night, when Sam told him that Lion would never cry on a trail. "He gonter growl when he catches Old Ben's throat," Sam said. "But he ain't gonter never holler, no more than he ever done when he was jumping at that two-inch door. It's that blue dog in him. What you call it?"

"Airedale," the boy said.

Lion was there; the jump was just too close to the river. When Boon returned with Lion about eleven that night, he swore that Lion had stopped Old Ben once but that the hounds would not go in and Old Ben broke away and took to the river and swam for miles down it and he and Lion went down one bank for about ten miles and crossed and came up the other but it had begun to get dark before they struck any trail where Old Ben had come up out of the water, unless he was still in the water when he passed the ford where they crossed. Then he fell to cursing the hounds and ate the supper Uncle Ash had saved for him and went off to bed and after a while the boy opened the door of the little stale room thunderous with snoring and the great grave dog raised its head from Boon's pillow and blinked at him for a moment and lowered its head again.

When the next November came and the last day, the day which it was now becoming traditional to save for Old Ben, there were more than a dozen strangers waiting. They were not all swampers this time. Some of them were townsmen, from other county seats like Jefferson, who had heard about Lion and Old Ben and had come to watch the great blue dog keep his yearly rendezvous with the old two-toed bear. Some of them didn't even have guns and the hunting-clothes and boots they wore had been on a store shelf yesterday.

This time Lion jumped Old Ben more than five miles from the river and bayed and held him and this time the hounds went in, in a sort of desperate emulation. The boy heard them; he was that near. He heard Boon whooping; he heard the two shots when General Compson delivered both barrels, one containing five buckshot, the other a single ball, into the bear from as close as he could force his almost unmanageable horse. He heard the dogs when the bear broke free again. He was running now; panting, stumbling, his lungs bursting, he reached the place where General Compson had fired and where Old Ben had killed two of the hounds. He saw the blood from General Compson's shots, but he could go no further. He stopped, leaning against a tree for his breathing to ease and his heart to slow, hearing the sound of the dogs as it faded on and died away.

In camp that night—they had as guests five of the still terrified strangers in new hunting coats and boots who had been lost all day until Sam Fathers went out and got them—he heard the rest of it: how Lion had stopped and held the bear again but only the one-eyed mule which did not mind the smell of wild blood would approach and Boon was riding the mule and Boon had never been known to hit anything. He shot at the bear five times with his pump gun,[5] touching nothing, and Old Ben killed another hound and broke free once more and reached the river and was gone. Again Boon and Lion hunted as far down one bank as they dared. Too far; they crossed in the first of dusk and dark overtook them within a mile. And this time Lion found the broken trail, the blood perhaps, in the darkness where Old Ben had come up out of the water, but Boon had him on a rope, luckily, and he got down from the mule and fought Lion hand-to-hand until he got him back to camp. This time Boon didn't even curse. He stood in the door, muddy, spent, his huge gargoyle's face tragic and still amazed. "I missed him,"

5. Repeating shotgun with a slide action.

he said. "I was in twenty-five feet of him and I missed him five times."

"But we have drawn blood," Major de Spain said. "General Compson drew blood. We have never done that before."

"But I missed him," Boon said. "I missed him five times. With Lion looking right at me."

"Never mind," Major de Spain said. "It was a damned fine race. And we drew blood. Next year we'll let General Compson or Walter ride Katie, and we'll get him."

Then McCaslin said, "Where is Lion, Boon?"

"I left him at Sam's," Boon said. He was already turning away. "I ain't fit to sleep with him."

So he should have hated and feared Lion. Yet he did not. It seemed to him that there was a fatality in it. It seemed to him that something, he didn't know what, was beginning; had already begun. It was like the last act on a set stage. It was the beginning of the end of something, he didn't know what except that he would not grieve. He would be humble and proud that he had been found worthy to be a part of it too or even just to see it too.

III

It was December. It was the coldest December he had ever remembered. They had been in camp four days over two weeks, waiting for the weather to soften so that Lion and Old Ben could run their yearly race. Then they would break camp and go home. Because of these unforeseen additional days which they had had to pass waiting on the weather, with nothing to do but play poker, the whiskey had given out and he and Boon were being sent to Memphis with a suitcase and a note from Major de Spain to Mr. Semmes, the distiller, to get more. That is, Major de Spain and McCaslin were sending Boon to get the whiskey and sending him to see that Boon got back with it or most of it or at least some of it.

Tennie's Jim waked him at three. He dressed rapidly, shivering, not so much from the cold because a fresh fire already boomed and roared on the hearth, but in that dead winter hour when the blood and the heart are slow and sleep is incomplete. He crossed the gap between house and kitchen, the gap of iron earth beneath the brilliant and rigid night where dawn would not begin for three hours yet, tasting, tongue, palate, and to the very bottom of his lungs, the searing dark, and entered the kitchen, the lamplit warmth where the stove glowed, fogging the windows, and where Boon already sat at the table at breakfast, hunched over his plate, almost in his plate, his working jaws blue with stubble and his face innocent of water and his coarse, horse-mane hair innocent of comb—the quarter Indian, grandson of a Chickasaw squaw, who on occasion resented with his hard and furious fists the intimation of one single drop of alien blood and on others, usually after whiskey, affirmed with the same fists and the same fury that his father had been the full-blood Chickasaw and even a chief and that even his mother had been only half white. He was four inches over six feet; he had the mind of a child, the heart of a horse, and little hard shoe-button eyes without depth or meanness or generosity or viciousness or gentleness or anything else, in the ugliest face the boy had ever seen. It looked like somebody had found a walnut a little larger than a football and with a machinist's hammer had shaped features into it and then painted it, mostly red; not Indian red but a fine bright ruddy color which whiskey might have had something to do with but which was most just happy and violent out-of-doors, the wrinkles in it not the residue of the forty years it had survived but from squinting into the sun or into the gloom of cane-brakes where game had run, baked into it by the camp fires before which he had lain trying to sleep on the cold November or December ground while waiting for daylight so he could rise and hunt again, as though time were merely something he walked through as he did through air, aging him no more than air did. He was brave, faithful, improvident and unreliable; he had neither profession job nor trade and owned one vice and one virtue: whiskey, and that absolute and unquestioning fidelity to Major de Spain and the boy's cousin McCaslin. "Sometimes I'd call them both virtues," Major de Spain said once. "Or both vices," McCaslin said.

He ate his breakfast, hearing the dogs under the kitchen, wakened by the smell of frying meat or perhaps by the feet overhead. He heard Lion once, short and peremptory, as the best hunter in any camp has only to speak once to all save the fools, and none other of Major de Spain's and McCaslin's dogs were Lion's equal in size and strength and perhaps even in courage, but they were not fools; Old Ben had killed the last fool among them last year.

Tennie's Jim came in as they finished. The wagon was outside. Ash decided he would drive them over to the log-line where they would flag the outbound log-train and let Tennie's Jim wash the dishes. The boy knew why. It would not be the first time he had listened to old Ash badgering Boon.

It was cold. The wagon wheels banged and clattered on the frozen ground; the sky was fixed and brilliant. He was not shivering, he was shaking, slow and steady and hard, the food he had just eaten still warm and solid inside him while his outside shook slow and steady around it as though his stomach floated loose. "They won't run this morning," he said. "No dog will have any nose today."

"Cep Lion," Ash said. "Lion don't need no nose. All he need is a bear." He had wrapped his feet in towsacks and he had a quilt from his pallet bed on the kitchen floor drawn over his head and wrapped around him until in the thin brilliant starlight he looked like nothing at all that the boy had ever seen before. "He run a bear through a thousand-acre ice-house. Catch him too. Them other dogs don't matter because they ain't going to keep up with Lion nohow, long as he got a bear in front of him."

"What's wrong with the other dogs?" Boon said. "What the hell do you know about it anyway? This is the first time you've had your tail out of that kitchen since we got here except to chop a little wood."

"Ain't nothing wrong with them," Ash said. "And long as it's up to them, ain't nothing going to be. I just wish I had knowed all my life how to take care of my health good as them hounds knows."

"Well, they ain't going to run this morning," Boon said. His voice was harsh and positive. "Major promised they wouldn't until me and Ike get back."

"Weather gonter break today. Gonter soft up. Rain by night." Then Ash laughed, chuckled, somewhere inside the quilt which concealed even his face. "Hum up here, mules!" he said, jerking the reins so that the mules leaped forward and snatched the lurching and banging wagon for several feet before they slowed again into their quick, short-paced, rapid plodding. "Sides, I like to know why Major need to wait on you. It's Lion he aiming to use. I ain't never heard tell of you bringing no bear nor no other kind of meat into this camp."

Now Boon's going to curse Ash or maybe even hit him, the boy thought. But Boon never did, never had; the boy knew he never would even though four years ago Boon had shot five times with a borrowed pistol at a Negro on the street in Jefferson, with the same result as when he had shot five times at Old Ben last fall. "By God," Boon said, "he ain't going to put Lion or no other dog on nothing until I get back tonight. Because he promised me. Whip up them mules and keep them whipped up. Do you want me to freeze to death?"

They reached the log-line and built a fire. After a while the log-train came up out of the woods under the paling east and Boon flagged it. Then in the warm caboose the boy slept again while Boon and the conductor and brakemen talked about Lion and Old Ben as people later would talk about Sullivan and Kilrain and, later still, about Dempsey and Tunney.[6] Dozing, swaying as the springless caboose lurched and clattered, he would hear them still talking, about the shoats and calves Old Ben had killed and the cribs he had rifled and the traps and deadfalls he had wrecked and the lead he probably carried under his hide—Old Ben, the two-toed bear in a land where bears with trap-ruined feet had been called Two-Toe or Three-Toe or Cripple-Foot for fifty years,

6. Prizefighters of the nineteenth and early twentieth centuries.

only Old Ben was an extra bear (the head bear, General Compson called him) and so had earned a name such as a human man could have worn and not been sorry.

They reached Hoke's at sunup. They emerged from the warm caboose in their hunting clothes, the muddy boots and stained khaki and Boon's blue unshaven jowls. But that was all right. Hoke's was a sawmill and commissary and two stores and a loading-chute on a side-track from the main line, and all the men in it wore boots and khaki too. Presently the Memphis train came. Boon bought three packages of popcorn-and-molasses and a bottle of beer from the news butch and the boy went to sleep again to the sound of his chewing.

But in Memphis it was not all right. It was as if the high buildings and the hard pavements, the fine carriages and the horse cars and the men in starched collars and neckties made their boots and khaki look a little rougher and a little muddier and made Boon's beard look worse and more unshaven and his face look more and more like he should never have brought it out of the woods at all or at least out of reach of Major de Spain or McCaslin or someone who knew it and could have said, "Don't be afraid. He won't hurt you." He walked through the station, on the slick floor, his face moving as he worked the popcorn out of his teeth with his tongue, his legs spraddled and stiff in the hips as if he were walking on buttered glass, and that blue stubble on his face like the filings from a new gun barrel. They passed the first saloon. Even through the closed doors the boy could seem to smell the sawdust and the reek of old drink. Boon began to cough. He coughed for something less than a minute. "Damn this cold," he said. "I'd sure like to know where I got it."

"Back there in the station," the boy said.

Boon had started to cough again. He stopped. He looked at the boy. "What?" he said.

"You never had it when we left camp nor on the train either." Boon looked at him, blinking. Then he stopped blinking. He didn't cough again. He said quietly:

"Lend me a dollar. Come on. You've got it. If you ever had one, you've still got it. I don't mean you are tight with your money because you ain't. You just don't never seem to ever think of nothing you want. When I was sixteen a dollar bill melted off of me before I ever had time to read the name of the bank that issued it." He said quietly: "Let me have a dollar, Ike."

"You promised Major. You promised McCaslin. Not till we get back to camp."

"All right," Boon said in that quiet and patient voice. "What can I do on just one dollar? You ain't going to lend me another."

"You're damn right I ain't," the boy said, his voice quiet too, cold with rage which was not at Boon, remembering: Boon snoring in a hard chair in the kitchen so he could watch the clock and wake him and McCaslin and drive them the seventeen miles in to Jefferson to catch the train to Memphis; the wild, never-bridled Texas paint pony[7] which he had persuaded McCaslin to let him buy and which he and Boon had bought at auction for four dollars and seventy-five cents and fetched home wired between two gentle old mares with pieces of barbed wire and which had never even seen shelled corn before and didn't even know what it was unless the grains were bugs maybe, and at last (he was ten and Boon had been ten all his life) Boon said the pony was gentled and with a towsack over its head and four Negroes to hold it they backed it into an old two-wheeled cart and hooked up the gear and he and Boon got up and Boon said, "All right, boys. Let him go" and one of the Negroes—it was Tennie's Jim—snatched the towsack off and leaped for his life and they lost the first wheel against a post of the open gate only at that moment Boon caught him by the scruff of the neck and flung him into the roadside ditch so he only saw the rest of it in fragments: the other wheel as it slammed through the side gate and crossed the back yard and leaped up onto the gallery and scraps of the cart here and there along the road and Boon vanishing rapidly on his stomach in the leaping and spurting dust and still holding the reins until they broke too and two days later they finally caught the pony seven miles away still wearing the hames and the headstall of the bridle around its neck like a duchess with two necklaces at one time. He gave Boon the dollar.

"All right," Boon said. "Come on in out of the cold."

"I ain't cold," he said.

"You can have some lemonade."

"I don't want any lemonade."

The door closed behind him. The sun was well up now. It was a brilliant day, though Ash had said it would rain before night. Already it was warmer; they could run tomorrow. He felt the old lift of the heart, as pristine as ever, as on the first day; he would never lose it, no matter how old the hunting and pursuit: the best, the best of all breathing, the humility and the pride. He must stop thinking about it. Already it seemed to him that he was running, back to the station, to the tracks themselves: the first train going south; he must stop thinking about it. The street was busy. He watched the big Norman draft horses, the Percherons; the trim carriages from which the men in the fine overcoats and the ladies rosy in furs descended and entered the station. (They were still next door to it but one.) Twenty years ago his father had ridden into Memphis as a member of Colonel Sartoris' horse

7. Spotted horse. "Paint" is a translation of the Spanish *pinto*.

in Forrest's[8] command, up Main street and (the tale told) into the lobby of the Gayoso Hotel where the Yankee officers sat in the leather chairs spitting into the tall bright cuspidors and then out again, scot-free—

The door opened behind him. Boon was wiping his mouth on the back of his hand. "All right," he said. "Let's go tend to it and get the hell out of here."

They went and had the suitcase packed. He never knew where or when Boon got the other bottle. Doubtless Mr. Semmes gave it to him. When they reached Hoke's again at sundown, it was empty. They could get a return train to Hoke's in two hours; they went straight back to the station as Major de Spain and then McCaslin had told Boon to do and then ordered him to do and had sent the boy along to see that he did. Boon took the first drink from his bottle in the washroom. A man in a uniform cap came to tell him he couldn't drink there and looked at Boon's face once and said nothing. The next time he was pouring into his water glass beneath the edge of a table in the restaurant when the manager (she was a woman) did tell him he couldn't drink there and he went back to the washroom. He had been telling the Negro waiter and all the other people in the restaurant who couldn't help but hear him and who had never heard of Lion and didn't want to, about Lion and Old Ben. Then he happened to think of the zoo. He had found out that there was another train to Hoke's at three o'clock and so they would spend the time at the zoo and take the three o'clock train until he came back from the washroom for the third time. Then they would take the first train back to camp, get Lion and come back to the zoo where, he said, the bears were fed on ice cream and lady fingers and he would match Lion against them all.

So they missed the first train, the one they were supposed to take, but he got Boon onto the three o'clock train and they were all right again, with Boon not even going to the washroom now but drinking in the aisle and talking about Lion and the men he buttonholed no more daring to tell Boon he couldn't drink there than the man in the station had dared.

When they reached Hoke's at sundown, Boon was asleep. The boy waked him at last and got him and the suitcase off the train and he even persuaded him to eat some supper at the sawmill commissary. So he was all right when they got in the caboose of the log-train to go back into the woods, with the sun going down red and the sky already overcast and the ground would not freeze tonight. It was the boy who slept now, sitting behind the ruby stove while the springless caboose jumped and clattered and Boon and the brakeman and the conductor talked about Lion and Old Ben because they knew what Boon was talking

8. Confederate general Nathan Bedford Forrest (1821–1877).

about because this was home. "Overcast and already thawing," Boon said. "Lion will get him tomorrow."

It would have to be Lion, or somebody. It would not be Boon. He had never hit anything bigger than a squirrel that anybody ever knew, except the Negro woman that day when he was shooting at the Negro man. He was a big Negro and not ten feet away but Boon shot five times with the pistol he had borrowed from Major de Spain's Negro coachman and the Negro he was shooting at outed with a dollar-and-a-half mail-order pistol and would have burned Boon down with it only it never went off, it just went snicksnicksnicksnicksnick five times and Boon still blasting away and he broke a plate-glass window that cost McCaslin forty-five dollars and hit a Negro woman who happened to be passing in the leg only Major de Spain paid for that; he and McCaslin cut cards, the plate-glass window against the Negro woman's leg. And the first day on stand this year, the first morning in camp, the buck ran right over Boon; he heard Boon's old pump gun go whow. whow. whow. whow. whow. and then his voice: "God damn, here he comes! Head him! Head him!" and when he got there the buck's tracks and the five exploded shells were not twenty paces apart.

There were five guests in camp that night from Jefferson: Mr. Bayard Sartoris and his son and General Compson's son and two others. And the next morning he looked out the window, into the gray thin drizzle of daybreak which Ash had predicted, and there they were, standing and squatting beneath the thin rain, almost two dozen of them who had fed Old Ben corn and shoats and even calves for ten years, in their worn hats and hunting coats and overalls which any town Negro would have thrown away or burned and only the rubber boots strong and sound, and the worn and blueless guns,[9] and some even without guns. While they ate breakfast a dozen more arrived, mounted and on foot: loggers from the camp thirteen miles below and sawmill men from Hoke's and the only gun among them that one which the long-train conductor carried: so that when they went into the woods this morning Major de Spain led a party almost as strong, excepting that some of them were not armed, as some he had led in the last darkening days of '64 and '65.[1] The little yard would not hold them. They overflowed it, into the lane where Major de Spain sat his mare while Ash in his dirty apron thrust the greasy cartridges into his carbine and passed it up to him and the great grave blue dog stood at his stirrup not as a dog stands but as a horse stands, blinking his sleepy topaz eyes at nothing, deaf even to the yelling of the hounds which Boon and Tennie's Jim held on leash.

9. Guns so worn with use that the dark blue finish has been rubbed off the metal. 1. Near the end of the Civil War, when Southern forces were numerically depleted.

"We'll put General Compson on Katie this morning," Major de Spain said. "He drew blood last year; if he'd had a mule then that would have stood, he would have—"

"No," General Compson said. "I'm too old to go helling through the woods on a mule or a horse or anything else any more. Besides, I had my chance last year and missed it. I'm going on a stand this morning. I'm going to let the boy ride Katie."

"No, wait," McCaslin said. "Ike's got the rest of his life to hunt bears in. Let somebody else—"

"No," General Compson said. "I want Ike to ride Katie. He's already a better woodsman than you or me either and in another ten years he'll be as good as Walter."

At first he couldn't believe it, not until Major de Spain spoke to him. Then he was up, on the one-eyed mule which would not spook at wild blood, looking down at the dog motionless at Major de Spain's stirrup, looking in the gray streaming light bigger than a calf, bigger than he knew it actually was—the big head, the chest almost as big as his own, the blue hide beneath which the muscles flinched or quivered to no touch since the heart which drove blood to them loved no man and no thing, standing as a horse stands yet different from a horse which infers only weight and speed while Lion inferred not only courage and all else that went to make up the will and desire to pursue and kill, but endurance, the will and desire to endure beyond all imaginable limits of flesh in order to overtake and slay. Then the dog looked at him. It moved its head and looked at him across the trivial uproar of the hounds, out of the yellow eyes as depthless as Boon's, as free as Boon's of meanness or generosity or gentleness or viciousness. They were just cold and sleepy. Then it blinked, and he knew it was not looking at him and never had been, without even bothering to turn its head away.

That morning he heard the first cry. Lion had already vanished while Sam and Tennie's Jim were putting saddles on the mule and horse which had drawn the wagon and he watched the hounds as they crossed and cast, snuffing and whimpering, until they too disappeared. Then he and Major de Spain and Sam and Tennie's Jim rode after them and heard the first cry out of the wet and thawing woods not two hundred yards ahead, high, with that abject, almost human quality he had come to know, and the other hounds joining in until the gloomed woods rang and clamored. They rode then. It seemed to him that he could actually see the big blue dog boring on, silent, and the bear too: the thick, locomotive-like shape which he had seen that day four years ago crossing the blow-down, crashing on ahead of the dogs faster than he had believed it could have moved, drawing away even from the running mules. He heard a shotgun, once. The woods had opened, they were going fast, the clamor faint and fading on ahead; they passed the man who had fired—a swamper, a pointing arm, a gaunt face, the small black orifice of his yelling studded with rotten teeth.

He heard the changed note in the hounds' uproar and two hundred yards ahead he saw them. The bear had turned. He saw Lion drive in without pausing and saw the bear strike him aside and lunge into the yelling hounds and kill one of them almost in its tracks and whirl and run again. Then they were in a streaming tide of dogs. He heard Major de Spain and Tennie's Jim shouting and the pistol sound of Tennie's Jim's leather thong as he tried to turn them. Then he and Sam Fathers were riding alone. One of the hounds had kept on with Lion though. He recognized its voice. It was the young hound which even a year ago had had no judgment and which, by the lights of the other hounds anyway, still had none. *Maybe that's what courage is,* he thought. "Right," Sam said behind him. "Right. We got to turn him from the river if we can."

Now they were in cane: a brake. He knew the path through it as well as Sam did. They came out of the undergrowth and struck the entrance almost exactly. It would traverse the brake and come out onto a high open ridge above the river. He heard the flat clap of Walter Ewell's rifle, then two more. "No," Sam said. "I can hear the hound. Go on."

They emerged from the narrow roofless tunnel of snapping and hissing cane, still galloping, onto the open ridge below which the thick yellow river, reflectionless in the gray and streaming light, seemed not to move. Now he could hear the hound too. It was not running. The cry was a high frantic yapping and Boon was running along the edge of the bluff, his old gun leaping and jouncing against his back on its sling made of a piece of cotton plowline. He whirled and ran up to them, wild-faced, and flung himself onto the mule behind the boy. "That damn boat!" he cried. "It's on the other side! He went straight across! Lion was too close to him! That little hound too! Lion was so close I couldn't shoot! Go on!" he cried, beating his heels into the mule's flanks. "Go on!"

They plunged down the bank, slipping and sliding in the thawed earth, crashing through the willows and into the water. He felt no shock, no cold, he on one side of the swimming mule, grasping the pommel with one hand and holding his gun above the water with the other, Boon opposite him. Sam was behind them somewhere, and then the river, the water about them, was full of dogs. They swam faster than the mules; they were scrabbling up the bank before the mules touched bottom. Major de Spain was whooping from the bank they had just left and, looking back, he saw Tennie's Jim and the horse as they went into the water.

Now the woods ahead of them and the rain-heavy air were one uproar. It rang and clamored; it echoed and broke against the bank behind them and reformed and clamored and rang until it seemed to the boy that all the hounds which had ever bayed game in this land were yelling down at him. He got his leg over the mule as it came up out of the water. Boon didn't try to mount again. He grasped one stirrup as they went up the bank and crashed through the undergrowth which fringed the bluff and saw the bear, on its hind feet, its back against a tree while the bellowing hounds swirled around it and once more Lion drove it, leaping clear of the ground.

This time the bear didn't strike him down. It caught the dog in both arms, almost loverlike, and they both went down. He was off the mule now. He drew back both hammers of the gun but he could see nothing but moiling spotted houndbodies until the bear surged up again. Boon was yelling something, he could not tell what; he could see Lion still clinging to the bear's throat and he saw the bear, half erect, strike one of the hounds with one paw and hurl it five or six feet and then, rising and rising as though it would never stop, stand erect again and begin to rake at Lion's belly with its forepaws. Then Boon was running. The boy saw the gleam of the blade in his hand and watched him leap among the hounds, hurling them, kicking them aside as he ran, and fling himself astride the bear as he had hurled himself onto the mule, his legs locked around the bear's belly, his left arm under the bear's throat where Lion clung, and the glint of the knife as it rose and fell.

It fell just once. For an instant they almost resembled a piece of statuary: the clinging dog, the bear, the man astride its back, working and probing the buried blade. Then they went down, pulled over backward by Boon's weight, Boon underneath. It was the bear's back which reappeared first but at once Boon was astride it again. He had never released the knife and again the boy saw the almost infinitesimal movement of his arm and shoulder as he probed and sought; then the bear surged erect, raising with it the man and the dog too, and turned and still carrying the man and the dog it took two or three steps toward the woods on its hind feet as a man would have walked and crashed down. It didn't collapse, crumple. It fell all of a piece, as a tree falls, so that all three of them, man dog and bear, seemed to bounce once.

He and Tennie's Jim ran forward. Boon was kneeling at the bear's head. His left ear was shredded, his left coat sleeve was completely gone, his right boot had been ripped from knee to instep; the bright blood thinned in the thin rain down his leg and hand and arm and down the side of his face which was no longer wild but was quite calm. Together they prized Lion's jaws from the bear's throat. "Easy, goddamn it," Boon said. "Can't you see his guts are all out of him?" He began to remove his coat. He spoke to Tennie's Jim in that calm voice:

"Bring the boat up. It's about a hundred yards down the bank there. I saw it." Tennie's Jim rose and went away. Then, and he could not remember if it had been a call or an exclamation from Tennie's Jim or if he had glanced up by chance, he saw Tennie's Jim stooping and saw Sam Fathers lying motionless on his face in the trampled mud.

The mule had not thrown him. He remembered that Sam was down too even before Boon began to run. There was no mark on him whatever and when he and Boon turned him over, his eyes were open and he said something in that tongue which he and Joe Baker had used to speak together. But he couldn't move. Tennie's Jim brought the skiff up; they could hear him shouting to Major de Spain across the river. Boon wrapped Lion in his hunting coat and carried him down to the skiff and they carried Sam down and returned and hitched the bear to the one-eyed mule's saddle-bow with Tennie's Jim's leash-thong and dragged him down to the skiff and got him into it and left Tennie's Jim to swim the horse and the two mules back across. Major de Spain caught the bow of the skiff as Boon jumped out and past him before it touched the bank. He looked at Old Ben and said quietly: "Well." Then he walked into the water and leaned down and touched Sam and Sam looked up at him and said something in that old tongue he and Joe Baker spoke. "You don't know what happened?" Major de Spain said.

"No, sir," the boy said. "It wasn't the mule. It wasn't anything. He was off the mule when Boon ran in on the bear. Then we looked up and he was lying on the ground." Boon was shouting at Tennie's Jim, still in the middle of the river.

"Come on, goddamn it!" he said. "Bring me that mule!"

"What do you want with a mule?" Major de Spain said.

Boon didn't even look at him. "I'm going to Hoke's to get the doctor," he said in that calm voice, his face quite calm beneath the steady thinning of the bright blood.

"You need a doctor yourself," Major de Spain said. "Tennie's Jim—"

"Damn that," Boon said. He turned on Major de Spain. His face was still calm, only his voice was a pitch higher. "Can't you see his goddamn guts are all out of him?"

"Boon!" Major de Spain said. They looked at one another. Boon was a good head taller than Major de Spain; even the boy was taller now than Major de Spain.

"I've got to get the doctor," Boon said. "His goddamn guts—"

"All right," Major de Spain said. Tennie's Jim came up out of the water. The horse and the sound mule had already scented Old Ben; they surged and plunged all the way up to the top of the bluff, dragging Tennie's Jim with them, before he could stop them and tie them and come back. Major de Spain unlooped the leather thong of his compass from his buttonhole and gave it to Tennie's Jim. "Go straight to Hoke's," he said. "Bring Doctor Crawford back with you. Tell him there are two men to be looked at. Take my mare. Can you find the road from here?"

"Yes, sir," Tennie's Jim said.

"All right," Major de Spain said. "Go on." He turned to the boy. "Take the mules and the horse and go back and get the wagon. We'll go on down the river in the boat to Coon bridge. Meet us there. Can you find it again?"

"Yes, sir," the boy said.

"All right. Get started."

He went back to the wagon. He realized then how far they had run. It was already afternoon when he put the mules into the traces and tied the horse's lead-rope to the tail-gate. He reached Coon bridge at dusk. The skiff was already there. Before he could see it and almost before he could see the water he had to leap from the tilting wagon, still holding the reins, and work around to where he could grasp the bit and then the ear of the plunging sound mule and dig his heels and hold it until Boon came up the bank. The rope of the lead horse had already snapped and it had already disappeared up the road toward camp. They turned the wagon around and took the mules out and he led the sound mule a hundred yards up the road and tied it. Boon had already brought Lion up to the wagon and Sam was sitting up in the skiff now and when they raised him he tried to walk, up the bank and to the wagon and he tried to climb into the wagon but Boon did not wait; he picked Sam up bodily and set him on the seat. Then they hitched Old Ben to the one-eyed mule's saddle again and dragged him up the bank and set two skid-poles into the open tail-gate and got him into the wagon and he went and got the sound mule and Boon fought it into the traces, striking it across its hard hollow-sounding face until it came into position and stood trembling. Then the rain came down, as though it had held off all day waiting on them.

They returned to camp through it, through the streaming and sightless dark, hearing long before they saw any light the horn and the spaced shots to guide them. When they came to Sam's dark little hut he tried to stand up. He spoke again in the tongue of the old fathers; then he said clearly: "Let me out. Let me out."

"He hasn't got any fire," Major said. "Go on!" he said sharply.

But Sam was struggling now, trying to stand up. "Let me out, master," he said. "Let me go home."

So he stopped the wagon and Boon got down and lifted Sam out. He did not wait to let Sam try to walk this time. He carried him into the hut and Major de Spain got light on a paper spill from the buried embers on the hearth and lit the lamp and Boon put Sam on his bunk and drew off his boots and Major de Spain covered him and the boy was not there, he was holding the mules, the sound one which was trying again to bolt since when the wagon stopped Old Ben's scent drifted forward again along the streaming blackness of air, but Sam's eyes were probably open again on that profound look which saw further than them or the hut, further than the death of a bear and the dying of a dog. Then they went on, toward the long wailing of the horn and the shots which seemed each to linger intact somewhere in the thick streaming air until the next spaced report joined and blended with it, to the lighted house, the bright streaming windows, the quiet faces as Boon entered, bloody and quite calm, carrying the bundled coat. He laid Lion, blood coat and all, on his stale sheetless pallet bed which not even Ash, as deft in the house as a woman, could ever make smooth.

The sawmill doctor from Hoke's was already there. Boon would not let the doctor touch him until he had seen to Lion. He wouldn't risk giving Lion chloroform. He put the entrails back and sewed him up without it while Major de Spain held his head and Boon his feet. But he never tried to move. He lay there, the yellow eyes open upon nothing while the quiet men in the new hunting clothes and in the old ones crowded into the little airless room rank with the smell of Boon's body and garments, and watched. Then the doctor cleaned and disinfected Boon's face and arm and leg and bandaged them and, the boy in front with a lantern and the doctor and McCaslin and Major de Spain and General Compson following, they went to Sam Fathers' hut. Tennie's Jim had built up the fire; he squatted before it, dozing. Sam had not moved since Boon had put him in the bunk and Major de Spain had covered him with the blankets, yet he opened his eyes and looked from one to another of the faces and when McCaslin touched his shoulder and said, "Sam. The doctor wants to look at you," he even drew his hands out of the blanket and began to fumble at his shirt buttons until McCaslin said, "Wait. We'll do it." They undressed him. He lay there—the copper-brown, almost hairless body, the old man's body, the old man, the wild man not even one generation from the woods, childless, kinless, peopleless—motionless, his eyes open but no longer looking at any of them, while the doctor examined him and drew the blankets up and put the stethoscope back into his bag and snapped the bag and only the boy knew that Sam too was going to die.

"Exhaustion," the doctor said. "Shock maybe. A man his age swimming rivers in December. He'll be all right. Just make him stay in bed for a day or two. Will there be somebody here with him?"

"There will be somebody here," Major de Spain said.

They went back to the house, to the rank little room where Boon still sat on the pallet bed with Lion's head under his hand while the men, the ones who had hunted behind Lion and the ones who had never seen him before today, came quietly in to look at him and went away. Then it was dawn and they all went out into the yard to look at Old Ben, with his eyes open too and his lips snarled back from his worn teeth and his mutilated foot and the little hard lumps under his skin which were the old bullets (there were fifty-two of them, buckshot rifle and ball) and the single almost invisible slit under his left shoulder where Boon's blade had finally found his life. Then Ash began to beat on the bottom of the dishpan to call them to breakfast and it was the first time he could remember hearing no sound from the dogs under the kitchen while they were eating. It was as if the old bear, even dead there in the yard, was a more potent terror still than they could face without Lion between them.

The rain had stopped during the night. By midmorning the thin sun appeared, rapidly burning away mist and cloud, warming the air and the earth; it would be one of those windless Mississippi December days which are a sort of Indian summer's Indian summer. They moved Lion out to the front gallery, into the sun. It was Boon's idea. "Goddamn it," he said, "he never did want to stay in the house until I made him. You know that." He took a crowbar and loosened the floor boards under his pallet bed so it could be raised, mattress and all, without disturbing Lion's position, and they carried him out to the gallery and put him down facing the woods.

Then he and the doctor and McCaslin and Major de Spain went to Sam's hut. This time Sam didn't open his eyes and his breathing was so quiet, so peaceful that they could hardly see that he breathed. The doctor didn't even take out his stethoscope nor even touch him. "He's all right," the doctor said. "He didn't even catch cold. He just quit."

"Quit?" McCaslin said.

"Yes. Old people do that sometimes. Then they get a good night's sleep or maybe it's just a drink of whiskey, and they change their minds."

They returned to the house. And then they began to arrive—the swamp-dwellers, the gaunt men who ran trap-lines and lived on quinine and coons and river water, the farmers of little corn and cotton-patches along the bottom's edge whose fields and cribs and pigpens the old bear had rifled, the loggers from the camp, and the sawmill men from Hoke's, and the town men from further away than that, whose hounds the old bear had slain and whose traps and deadfalls he had wrecked and whose lead he carried. They came up mounted and on foot and in wagons, to enter the yard and look at him and then go on to the front porch where Lion lay, filling the little yard and overflowing it until there were almost a hundred of them squatting and standing in the warm and drowsing sunlight, talking quietly of hunting, of the game and the dogs which ran it, of hounds and bear and deer and men of yesterday vanished from the earth, while from time to time the great blue dog would open his eyes, not as if he were listening to them but as though to look at the woods for a moment before closing his eyes again, to remember the woods or to see that they were still there. He died at sundown.

Major de Spain broke camp that night. They carried Lion into the woods, or Boon carried him that is, wrapped in a quilt from his bed, just as he had refused to let anyone else touch Lion yesterday until the doctor got there; Boon carrying Lion, and the boy and General Compson and Walter and still almost fifty of them following with lanterns and lighted pine-knots—men from Hoke's and even further, who would have to ride out of the bottom in the dark, and swampers and trappers who would have to walk even, scattering toward the little hidden huts where they lived. And Boon would let nobody else dig the grave either and lay Lion in it and cover him, and then General Compson stood at the head of it while the blaze and smoke of the pine-knots streamed away among the winter branches and spoke as he would have spoken over a man. Then they returned to camp. Major de Spain and McCaslin and Ash had rolled and tied all the bedding. The mules were hitched to the wagon and pointed out of the bottom and the wagon was already loaded and the stove in the kitchen was cold and the table was set with scraps of cold food and bread and only the coffee was hot when the boy ran into the kitchen where Major de Spain and McCaslin had already eaten. "What?" he cried. "What? I'm not going."

"Yes," McCaslin said, "we're going out tonight. Major wants to get on back home."

"No!" he said. "I'm going to stay."

"You've got to be back in school Monday. You've already missed a week more than I intended. It will take you from now until Monday to catch up. Sam's all right. You heard Doctor Crawford. I'm going to leave Boon and Tennie's Jim both to stay with him until he feels like getting up."

He was panting. The others had come in. He looked rapidly and almost frantically around at the other faces. Boon had a fresh bottle. He upended it and started the cork by striking the bottom of the bottle with the heel of his hand and drew the cork with his teeth and spat it out and drank. "You're damn right you're going back to school," Boon said. "Or I'll burn the tail off you myself if Cass don't, whether you are sixteen or sixty. Where in hell do you expect to get without education? Where would Cass be? Where in hell would I be if I hadn't never went to school?"

He looked at McCaslin again. He could feel his breath coming shorter and shorter and shallower and shallower, as if there were not enough air in the kitchen for that many to breathe. "This is just Thursday. I'll come home Sunday night on one of the horses. I'll come home Sunday, then. I'll make up time I lost studying Sunday night, McCaslin," he said, without even despair.

"No, I tell you," McCaslin said. "Sit down here and eat your supper. We're going out to—"

"Hold up, Cass," General Compson said. The boy did not know General Compson had moved until he put his hand on his shoulder. "What is it, bud?" he said.

"I've got to stay," he said. "I've got to."

"All right," General Compson said. "You can stay. If missing an extra week of school is going to throw you so far behind you'll have to sweat to find out what some hired pedagogue put between the covers of a book, you better quit altogether.—And you shut up, Cass," he said, though McCaslin had not spoken. "You've got one foot straddled into a farm and the other foot straddled into a bank; you ain't even got a good hand-hold where this boy was already an old man long before you damned Sartorises and Edmondses invented farms and banks to keep yourselves from having to find out what this boy was born knowing, and fearing too maybe, but without being afraid, that could go ten miles on a compass because he wanted to look at a bear none of us had ever got near enough to put a bullet in and looked at the bear and came the ten miles back on the compass in the dark; maybe by God that's the why and the wherefore of farms and banks.—I reckon you still ain't going to tell what it is?"

But still he could not. "I've got to stay," he said.

"All right," General Compson said. "There's plenty of grub left. And you'll come home Sunday, like you promised McCaslin? Not Sunday night: Sunday."

"Yes, sir," he said.

"All right," General Compson said. "Sit down and eat, boys," he said. "Let's get started. It's going to be cold before we get home."

They ate. The wagon was already loaded and ready to depart; all they had to do was to get into it. Boon would drive them out to the road, to the farmer's stable where the surrey had been left. He stood beside the wagon, in silhouette on the sky, turbaned like a Paythan[2] and taller than any there, the bottle tilted. Then he flung the bottle from his lips without even lowering it, spinning and glinting in the faint starlight, empty. "Them that's going," he said, "get in the goddamn wagon. Them that ain't, get out of the goddamn way." The others got in. Boon mounted to the seat beside General Compson and the wagon moved, on into the obscurity until the boy could no longer see it, even the moving density of it amid the greater night. But he could still hear

2. I.e., the bandages on his head resembled the turban headdress worn in India.

it, for a long while: the slow, deliberate banging of the wooden frame as it lurched from rut to rut. And he could hear Boon even when he could no longer hear the wagon. He was singing, harsh, tuneless, loud.

That was Thursday. On Saturday morning Tennie's Jim left on McCaslin's woods-horse which had not been out of the bottom one time now in six years, and late that afternoon rode through the gate on the spent horse and on to the commissary where McCaslin was rationing the tenants and the wage-hands for the coming week, and this time McCaslin forestalled any necessity or risk of having to wait while Major de Spain's surrey was being horsed and harnessed. He took their own, and with Tennie's Jim already asleep in the back seat he drove in to Jefferson and waited while Major de Spain changed to boots and put on his overcoat, and they drove the thirty miles in the dark of that night and at daybreak on Sunday morning they swapped to the waiting mare and mule and as the sun rose they rode out of the jungle and onto the low ridge where they had buried Lion: the low mound of unannealed earth where Boon's spade-marks still showed, and beyond the grave the platform of freshly cut saplings bound between four posts and the blanket-wrapped bundle upon the platform[3] and Boon and the boy squatting between the platform and the grave until Boon, the bandage removed, ripped from his head so that the long scoriations of Old Ben's claws resembled crusted tar in the sunlight, sprang up and threw down upon them[4] with the old gun with which he had never been known to hit anything although McCaslin was already off the mule, kicked both feet free of the irons and vaulted down before the mule had stopped, walking toward Boon.

"Stand back," Boon said. "By God, you won't touch him. Stand back, McCaslin." Still McCaslin came on, fast yet without haste.

"Cass!" Major de Spain said. Then he said, "Boon! You, Boon!" and he was down too and the boy rose too, quickly, and still McCaslin came on not fast but steady and walked up to the grave and reached his hand steadily out, quickly yet still not fast, and took hold the gun by the middle so that he and Boon faced one another across Lion's grave, both holding the gun, Boon's spent indomitable amazed and frantic face almost a head higher than McCaslin's beneath the black scoriations of beast's claws and then Boon's chest began to heave as though there were not enough air in all the woods, in all the wilderness, for all of them, for him and anyone else, even for him alone.

"Turn it loose, Boon," McCaslin said.

"You damn little spindling—" Boon said. "Don't you know I can take it away from you? Don't you know I can tie it around your neck like a damn cravat?"

3. An alternative to burying a dead person; generally practiced by Indian tribes of southeastern U.S. 4. I.e., pointed his gun at them.

"Yes," McCaslin said. "Turn it loose, Boon."

"This is the way he wanted it. He told us. He told us exactly how to do it. And by God you ain't going to move him. So we did it like he said, and I been sitting here ever since to keep the damn wildcats and varmits away from him and by God—" Then McCaslin had the gun, downslanted while he pumped the slide, the five shells snicking out of it so fast that the last one was almost out before the first one touched the ground and McCaslin dropped the gun behind him without once having taken his eyes from Boon's.

"Did you kill him, Boon?" he said. Then Boon moved. He turned, he moved like he was still drunk and then for a moment blind too, one hand out as he blundered toward the big tree and seemed to stop walking before he reached the tree so that he plunged, fell toward it, flinging up both hands and catching himself against the tree and turning until his back was against it, backing with the tree's trunk his wild spent scoriated face and the tremendous heave and collapse of his chest, McCaslin following, facing him again, never once having moved his eyes from Boon's eyes. "Did you kill him, Boon?"

"No!" Boon said. "No!"

"Tell the truth," McCaslin said. "I would have done it if he had asked me to." Then the boy moved. He was between them, facing McCaslin; the water felt as if it had burst and sprung not from his eyes alone but from his whole face, like sweat.

"Leave him alone!" he cried. "Goddamn it! Leave him alone!"

IV

then he was twenty-one. He could say it, himself and his cousin juxtaposed not against the wilderness but against the tamed land[5] which was to have been his heritage, the land which old Carothers McCaslin, his grandfather, had bought with white man's money from the wild men whose grandfathers without guns hunted it, and tamed and ordered, or believed he had tamed and ordered it, for the reason that the human beings he held in bondage and in the power of life and death had removed the forest from it and in their sweat scratched the surface of it to a depth of perhaps fourteen inches in order to grow something out of it which had not been there before, and which could be translated back into the money he who believed he had bought it had had to pay to get it and hold it, and a reasonable profit too: and for which reason

5. In this long and clouded section of the story Isaac and his cousin McCaslin Edmonds are "juxtaposed" against the problems of the "tamed land"—i.e., the land that has been taken from the wilderness by settlement and cultivation, claimed as property to be bought and sold, and passed along from one generation to another by legal inheritance. Since the legality of such transfer is complicated by changing patterns of race relations, and tainted by the past enslavement of black people, Isaac declines to accept any share of the land coming to him from his grandfather Lucius Quintus Carothers McCaslin.

old Carothers McCaslin, knowing better, could raise his children, his descendants and heirs, to believe the land was his to hold and bequeath, since the strong and ruthless man has a cynical foreknowledge of his own vanity and pride and strength and a contempt for all his get: just as, knowing better, Major de Spain had his fragment of that wilderness which was bigger and older than any recorded deed: just as, knowing better, old Thomas Sutpen, from whom Major de Spain had had his fragment for money: just as Ikkemotubbe, the Chickasaw chief, from whom Thomas Sutpen had had the fragment for money or rum or whatever it was, knew in his turn that not even a fragment of it had been his to relinquish or sell

not against the wilderness but against the land, not in pursuit and lust but in relinquishment; and in the commissary as it should have been, not the heart perhaps but certainly the solarplexus of the repudiated and relinquished: the square, galleried, wooden building squatting like a portent above the fields whose laborers it still held in thrall, '65[6] or no, and placarded over with advertisements for snuff and cures for chills and salves and potions manufactured and sold by white men to bleach the pigment and straighten the hair of Negroes that they might resemble the very race which for two hundred years had held them in bondage and from which for another hundred years not even a bloody civil war would have set them completely free

himself and his cousin amid the old smells of cheese and salt meat and kerosene and harness, the ranked shelves of tobacco and overalls and bottled medicine and thread and plow-bolts, the barrels and kegs of flour and meal and molasses and nails, the wall pegs dependant with plowlines and plow-collars and hames and trace-chains, and the desk and the shelf above it on which rested the ledgers in which McCaslin recorded the slow outward trickle of food and supplies and equipment which returned each fall as cotton made and ginned and sold (two threads frail as truth and impalpable as equators yet cable-strong to bind for life them who made the cotton to the land their sweat fell on), and the older ledgers, clumsy and archaic in size and shape, on the yellowed pages of which were recorded in the faded hand of his father Theophilus and his uncle Amodeus[7] during the two decades before the Civil War the manumission, in title at least, of Carothers McCaslin's slaves:

'Relinquish,' McCaslin said. 'Relinquish. You, the direct male descendant of him who saw the opportunity and took it, bought the land, took the land, got the land no matter how, held it to bequeath, no matter how, out of the old grant, the first patent, when it was a wilderness of wild beasts and wilder men, and cleared it, translated it

6. 1865, year when the South surrendered. End of the Civil War. 7. Twin brothers, also called Uncle Buck and Uncle Buddy in the story.

into something to bequeath to his children, worthy of bequeathment for his descendants' ease and security and pride, and to perpetuate his name and accomplishments. Not only the male descendant but the only and last descendant in the male line and in the third generation, while I am not only four generations from old Carothers, I derived through a woman and the very McCaslin in my name is mine only by sufferance and courtesy and my grandmother's pride in what that man accomplished, whose legacy and monument you think you can repudiate.' and he

'I can't repudiate it. It was never mine to repudiate. It was never Father's and Uncle Buddy's to bequeath me to repudiate, because it was never Grandfather's to bequeath them to bequeath me to repudiate, because it was never old Ikkemotubbe's to sell to Grandfather for bequeathment and repudiation. Because it was never Ikkemotubbe's fathers' fathers' to bequeath Ikkemotubbe to sell to Grandfather or any man because on the instant when Ikkemotubbe discovered, realized, that he could sell it for money, on that instant it ceased ever to have been his forever, father to father to father, and the man who bought it bought nothing.'

'Bought nothing?' and he

'Bought nothing. Because He told in the Book how He created the earth, made it and looked at it and said it was all right, and then He made man. He made the earth first and peopled it with dumb creatures, and then He created man to be His overseer on the earth and to hold suzerainty over the earth and the animals on it in His name, not to hold for himself and his descendants inviolable title forever, generation after generation, to the oblongs and squares of the earth, but to hold the earth mutual and intact in the communal anonymity of brotherhood, and all the fee He asked was pity and humility and sufferance and endurance and the sweat of his face for bread. And I know what you are going to say,' he said: 'That nevertheless Grandfather—' and McCaslin

'—did own it. And not the first. Not alone and not the first since, as your Authority states, man was dispossessed of Eden. Nor yet the second and still not alone, on down through the tedious and shabby chronicle of His chosen sprung from Abraham; and of the sons of them who dispossessed Abraham,[8] and of the five hundred years during which half the known world and all it contained was chattel to one city, as this plantation and all the life it contained was chattel and revokeless thrall to this commissary store and those ledgers yonder during your grandfather's life; and the next thousand years while men fought over the fragments of that collapse until at last even the fragments were

8. See Genesis 25:5–8.

exhausted and men snarled over the gnawed bones of the old world's worthless evening until an accidental egg[9] discovered to them a new hemisphere. So let me say it: That nevertheless and notwithstanding old Carothers did own it. Bought it, got it, no matter; kept it, held it, no matter; bequeathed it: else why do you stand here relinquishing and repudiating? Held it, kept it for fifty years until you could repudiate it, while He—this Arbiter, this Architect, this Umpire—condoned—or did He? looked down and saw—or did He? Or at least did nothing: saw, and could not, or did not see; saw, and would not, or perhaps He would not see—perverse, impotent, or blind: which?' and he

'Dispossessed.' and McCaslin

'What?' and he

'Dispossessed. Not impotent: He didn't condone; not blind, because He watched it. And let me say it. Dispossessed of Canaan, and those who dispossessed him dispossessed, and the five hundred years of absentee landlords in the Roman bagnios, and the thousand years of wild men from the northern woods who dispossessed them and devoured their ravished substance ravished in turn again and then snarled in what you call the old world's worthless twilight over the old world's gnawed bones, blasphemous in His name until He used a simple egg to discover to them a new world where a nation of people could be found in humility and pity and sufferance and pride of one to another. And Grandfather did own the land nevertheless and notwithstanding because He permitted it, not impotent and not condoning and not blind, because He ordered and watched it. He saw the land already accursed even as Ikkemotubbe and Ikkemotubbe's father old Issetibbeha and old Issetibbeha's fathers too held it, already tainted even before any white man owned it by what Grandfather and his kind, his fathers, had brought into the new land which He had vouchsafed them out of pity and sufferance, on condition, from that old world's corrupt and worthless twilight as though in the sailfuls of the old world's tainted wind which drove the ships—' and McCaslin

'Ah.'

'—and no hope for the land anywhere so long as Ikkemotubbe and Ikkemotubbe's descendants held it in unbroken succession. Maybe He saw that only by voiding the land for a time of Ikkemotubbe's blood and substituting for it another blood, could He accomplish His purpose. Maybe He knew already what that other blood would be, maybe it was more than justice that only the white man's blood was avail-

9. According to legend, Columbus demonstrated the mental tactics which led him to the discovery of the New World by making an egg stand on end. He accomplished this almost impossibly difficult trick by slightly crushing the end of the eggshell.

able and capable to raise the white man's curse, more than vengeance when—' and McCaslin

'Ah.'

'—when He used the blood which had brought in the evil to destroy the evil as doctors use fever to burn up fever, poison to slay poison. Maybe He chose Grandfather out of all of them He might have picked. Maybe He knew that Grandfather himself would not serve His purpose because Grandfather was born too soon too, but that Grandfather would have descendants, the right descendants; maybe He had foreseen already the descendants Grandfather would have, maybe He saw already in Grandfather the seed progenitive of the three generations He saw it would take to set at least some of His lowly people free—' and McCaslin

'The sons of Ham.[1] You who quote the Book: the sons of Ham.' and he

'There are some things He said in the Book, and some things reported of Him that He did not say. And I know what you will say now: That if truth is one thing to me and another thing to you, how will we choose which is truth? You don't need to choose. The heart already knows. He didn't have His Book written to be read by what must elect and choose, but by the heart, not by the wise of the earth because maybe they don't need it or maybe the wise no longer have any heart, but by the doomed and lowly of the earth who have nothing else to read with but the heart. Because the men who wrote His Book for Him were writing about truth and there is only one truth and it covers all things that touch the heart.' and McCaslin

'So these men who transcribed His Book for Him were sometimes liars.' and he

'Yes. Because they were human men. They were trying to write down the heart's truth out of the heart's driving complexity, for all the complex and troubled hearts which would beat after them. What they were trying to tell, what He wanted said, was too simple. Those for whom they transcribed His words could not have believed them. It had to be expounded in the everyday terms which they were familiar with and could comprehend, not only those who listened but those who told it too, because if they who were that near to Him as to have been elected from among all who breathed and spoke language to transcribe and relay His words, could comprehend truth only through the complexity of passion and lust and hate and fear which drives the heart, what distance back to truth must they traverse whom truth could only reach by word-of-mouth?' and McCaslin

1. See Genesis 9:25. The black race was said to be descended from Canaan (son of Ham) and relegated by Noah to be forever the servants of other men.

'I might answer that, since you have taken to proving your points and disproving mine by the same text, I don't know. But I don't say that, because you have answered yourself: No time at all if, as you say, the heart knows truth, the infallible and unerring heart. And perhaps you are right, since although you admitted three generations from old Carothers to you, there were not three. There were not even completely two. Uncle Buck and Uncle Buddy. And they not the first and not alone. A thousand other Bucks and Buddies in less than two generations and sometimes less than one in this land which so you claim God created and man himself cursed and tainted. Not to mention 1865.' and he

'Yes. More men than Father and Uncle Buddy,' not even glancing toward the shelf above the desk, nor did McCaslin. They did not need to. To him it was as though the ledgers in their scarred cracked leather bindings were being lifted down one by one in their fading sequence and spread open on the desk or perhaps upon some apocryphal Bench, or even Altar, or perhaps before the Throne Itself for a last perusal and contemplation and refreshment of the Allknowledgeable, before the yellowed pages and the brown thin ink in which was recorded the injustice and a little at least of its amelioration and restitution faded back forever into the anonymous communal original dust

the yellowed pages scrawled in fading ink by the hand first of his grandfather and then of his father and uncle, bachelors up to and past fifty and then sixty, the one who ran the plantation and the farming of it, and the other who did the housework and the cooking and continued to do it even after his twin married and the boy himself was born

the two brothers who as soon as their father was buried moved out of the tremendously-conceived, the almost barnlike edifice which he had not even completed, into a one-room log cabin which the two of them built themselves and added other rooms to while they lived in it, refusing to allow any slave to touch any timber of it other than the actual raising into place the logs which two men alone could not handle, and domiciled all the slaves in the big house some of the windows of which were still merely boarded up with odds and ends of plank or with the skins of bear and deer nailed over the empty frames: each sundown the brother who superintended the farming would parade the negroes as a first sergeant dismisses a company, and herd them willy-nilly, man woman and child, without question protest or recourse, into the tremendous abortive edifice scarcely yet out of embryo, as if even old Carothers McCaslin had paused aghast at the concrete indication of his own vanity's boundless conceiving: he would call his mental roll and herd them in and with a hand-wrought nail as long as a flenching-knife and suspended from a short deer-hide thong attached to the door-jamb for that purpose, he would nail to the door of that house which lacked half its windows and had no hinged back door at all, so that presently, and for fifty years afterward, when the boy himself was big to hear and remember it, there was in the land a sort of folk-tale: of the countryside all night long full of skulking McCaslin slaves dodging the moonlit roads and the Patrol-riders to visit other plantations, and of the unspoken gentlemen's agreement between the two white men and the two dozen black ones that, after the white man had counted them and driven the home-made nail into the front door at sundown, neither of the white men would go around behind the house and look at the back door, provided that all the negroes were behind the front one when the brother who drove it drew out the nail again at daybreak

the twins who were identical even in their handwriting, unless you had specimens side by side to compare, and even when both hands appeared on the same page (as often happened, as if, long since past any oral intercourse, they had used the diurnally advancing pages to conduct the unavoidable business of the compulsion which had traversed all the waste wilderness of North Mississippi in 1830 and '40 and singled them out to drive) they both looked as though they had been written by the same perfectly normal ten-year-old boy, even to the spelling, except that the spelling did not improve as one by one the slaves which Carothers McCaslin had inherited and purchased—Roscius and Phoebe and Thucydides and Eunice and their descendants, and Sam Fathers and his mother for both of whom he had swapped an underbred trotting gelding to old Ikkemotubbe, the Chickasaw chief, from whom he had likewise bought the land, and Tennie Beauchamp whom the twin Amodeus had won from a neighbor in a poker-game, and the anomaly calling itself Percival Brownlee which the twin Theophilus had purchased, neither he nor his brother ever knew why apparently, from Bedford Forrest while he was still only a slave-dealer and not yet a general (It was a single page, not long and covering less than a year, not seven months in fact, begun in the hand which the boy had learned to distinguish as that of his father:

Percavil Brownly 26yr Old. cleark @ Bookepper, bought from N.B.Forest at Cold Water 3 Mar 1856 $265. dolars

and beneath that, in the same hand:

5 mar 1856 No bookepper any way Cant read. Can write his Name but I already put that down My self Says he can Plough but dont look like it to Me. sent to Feild to day Mar 5 1856

and the same hand:

6 Mar 1856 Cant plough either Says he aims to be a Precher so may be he can lead live stock to Crick to Drink and this time it was the other, the hand which he now recognized as his uncle's when he could see them both on the same page:

Mar 23th 1856 Cant do that either Except one at a Time Get shut of him

then the first again:

24 Mar 1856 Who in hell would buy him

then the second:

19th of Apr 1856 Nobody You put yourself out of Market at Cold Water two months ago I never said sell him Free him

the first:

22 Apr 1856 Ill get it out of him

the second:

Jun 13th 1856 How $1 per yr 265$ 265 yrs Wholl sign his Free paper

then the first again:

1 Oct 1856 Mule josephine Broke Leg @ shot Wrong stall wrong niger everything $100. dolars

and the same:

2 Oct 1856 Freed Debit McCaslin @ McCaslin $265. dolars

then the second again:

Oct 3th Debit Theophilus McCaslin Niger 265$ Mule 100$ 365$ He hasnt gone yet Father should be here

then the first:

3 Oct 1856 Son of a bitch wont leave What would father done

the second:

29th of Oct 1856 Renamed him

the first:

31 Oct 1856 Renamed him what

the second:

Chrstms 1856 Spintrius

) took substance and even a sort of shadowy life with their passions and complexities too, as page followed page and year year; all there, not only the general and condoned injustice and its slow amortization by the specific tragedy which had not been condoned and could never be amortized; the new page and the new ledger, the hand which he could now recognize at first glance as his father's:

Father dide Lucius Quintus Carothers McCaslin, Callina 1772 Missippy 1837. Dide and burid 27 June 1837
Roskus. rased by Granfather in Callina Dont know how old. Freed 27 June 1837 Dont want to leave. Dide and Burid 12 Jan 1841
Fibby Roskus Wife. bought by granfather in Callina say Fifty Freed 27 June 1837 Dont want to leave. Dide and burd 1 Aug 1849
Thucydus Roskus @ Fibby Son born in Callina 1779. Refused 10acre peace fathers Will 28 Jun 1837 Refused Cash offer $200. dolars from A. @ T. McCaslin 28 Jun 1837 Wants to stay and work it out

and beneath this and covering the next five pages and almost that many years, the slow, day-by-day accrument of the wages allowed him and the food and clothing—the molasses and meat and meal, the cheap durable shirts and jeans and shoes, and now and then a coat against rain and cold—charged against the slowly yet steadily mounting sum of balance (and it would seem to the boy that he could actually see the black man, the slave whom his white owner had forever manumitted by the very act from which the black man could never be free so long as memory lasted, entering the commissary, asking permission perhaps of the white man's son to see the ledger-page which he could not even read, not even asking for the white man's word, which he would have had to accept for the reason that there was absolutely no way under the sun for him to test it, as to how the account stood, how much longer before he could go and never return, even if only as far as Jefferson seventeen miles away), on to the double pen-stroke closing the final entry:

3 Nov 1841 By Cash to Thucydus McCaslin $200. dolars Set Up blaksmith in J. Dec 1841 Dide and burid in J. 17 feb 1854
Eunice Bought by Father in New Orleans 1807 $650. dolars. Marrid to Thucydus 1809 Drownd in Crick Cristmas Day 1832[2]

and then the other hand appeared, the first time he had seen it in the ledger to distinguish it as his uncle's, the cook and housekeeper whom

2. This ledger entry introduces a special complication in the genealogy descending from the grandfather Lucius Quintus Carothers McCaslin, obscurely picked up by later allusions. Old McCaslin had an adulterous sexual relation with the slave Eunice. She bore him a daughter Tomasina, with whom he presently had an incestuous relation resulting in the birth of a son named Terrel (also called Tomey's Turl). Thus the partly black descendants of Terrel are blood relations of Isaac McCaslin.

even McCaslin, who had known him and the boy's father for sixteen years before the boy was born, remembered as sitting all day long in the rocking chair from which he cooked the food, before the kitchen fire on which he cooked it:

June 21th 1833 Drownd herself

and the first:

23 June 1833 Who in hell ever heard of a niger drownding him self

and the second, unhurried, with a complete finality; the two identical entries might have been made with a rubber stamp save for the date:

Aug 13th 1833 Drownd herself

and he thought *But why? But why?* He was sixteen then. It was neither the first time he had been alone in the commissary nor the first time he had taken down the old ledgers familiar on their shelf above the desk ever since he could remember. As a child and even after nine and ten and eleven, when he had learned to read, he would look up at the scarred and cracked backs and ends but with no particular desire to open them, and though he intended to examine them someday because he realized that they probably contained a chronological and much more comprehensive though doubtless tedious record than he would ever get from any other source, not alone of his own flesh and blood but of all his people, not only the whites but the black ones too, who were as much a part of his ancestry as his white progenitors, and of the land which they had all held and used in common and fed from and on and would continue to use in common without regard to color or titular ownership, it would only be on some idle day when he was old and perhaps even bored a little, since what the old books contained would be after all these years fixed immutably, finished, unalterable, harmless. Then he was sixteen. He knew what he was going to find before he found it. He got the commissary key from McCaslin's room after midnight while McCaslin was asleep and with the commissary door shut and locked behind him and the forgotten lantern stinking anew the rank dead icy air, he leaned above the yellowed page and thought not Why drowned herself, but thinking what he believed his father had thought when he found his brother's first comment: Why did Uncle Buddy think she had drowned herself? finding, beginning to find on the next succeeding page what he knew he would find, only this was still not it because he already knew this:

Tomasina called Tomy Daughter of Thucydus @ Eunice Born 1810 dide in Child bed June 1833 and Burd. Yr stars fell nor the next:

Turl Son of Thucydus @ Eunice Tomy born Jun 1833 yr stars fell Fathers will

and nothing more, no tedious recording filling this page of wages, day by day, and food and clothing charged against them, no entry of his death and burial because he had outlived his white half-brothers and the books which McCaslin kept did not include obituaries: just *Fathers will* and he had seen that too: old Carothers' bold cramped hand far less legible than his sons' even and not much better in spelling, who while capitalizing almost every noun and verb, made no effort to punctuate or construct whatever, just as he made no effort either to explain or obfuscate the thousand-dollar legacy to the son of an unmarried slave-girl, to be paid only at the child's coming-of-age, bearing the consequence of the act of which there was still no definite incontrovertible proof that he acknowledged, not out of his own substance, but penalizing his sons with it, charging them a cash forfeit on the accident of their own paternity; not even a bribe for silence toward his own fame since his fame would suffer only after he was no longer present to defend it, flinging almost contemptuously, as he might a cast-off hat or pair of shoes, the thousand dollars which could have had no more reality to him under those conditions than it would have to the Negro, the slave who would not even see it until he came of age, twenty-one years too late to begin to learn what money was. *So I reckon that was cheaper than saying My son to a nigger,* he thought. *Even if My son wasn't but just two words. But there must have been love,* he thought. *Some sort of love. Even what he would have called love: not just an afternoon's or a night's spittoon.* There was the old man, old, within five years of his life's end, long a widower and, since his sons were not only bachelors but were approaching middleage, lonely in the house and doubtless even bored, since his plantation was established now and functioning and there was enough money now, too much of it probably for a man whose vices even apparently remained below his means; there was the girl, husbandless and young, only twenty-three when the child was born: perhaps he had sent for her at first out of loneliness, to have a young voice and movement in the house, summoned her, bade her mother send her each morning to sweep the floors and make the beds and the mother acquiescing since that was probably already understood, already planned: the only child of a couple who were not field hands and who held themselves something above the other slaves, not alone for that reason but because the husband and his father and mother too had been inherited by the white man from his father, and the white man himself had travelled three hundred miles and better to New

Orleans in a day when men travelled by horseback or steamboat, and bought the girl's mother as a wife for him

and that was all. The old frail pages seemed to turn of their own accord even while he thought, *His own daughter His own daughter. No. No Not even him,* back to that one where the white man (not even a widower then) who never went anywhere, any more than his sons in their time ever did, and who did not need another slave, had gone all the way to New Orleans and bought one. And Tomey's Terrel was still alive when the boy was ten years old and he knew from his own observation and memory that there had already been some white in Tomey's Terrel's blood before his father gave him the rest of it; and looking down at the yellowed page spread beneath the yellow glow of the lantern smoking and stinking in that rank chill midnight room fifty years later, he seemed to see her actually walking into the icy creek on that Christmas day six months before her daughter's and her lover's *(Her first lover's,* he thought. *Her first)* child was born, solitary, inflexible, griefless, ceremonial, in formal and succinct repudiation of grief and despair, who had already had to repudiate belief and hope

that was all. He would never need look at the ledgers again nor did he; the yellowed pages in their fading and implacable succession were as much a part of his consciousness and would remain so forever, as the fact of his own nativity:

Tennie Beauchamp 21yrs Won by Amodeus McCaslin from Hubert Beauchamp Esqre Possible Strait against three Treys in sigt Not called 1859 Marrid to Tomys Turl 1859

and no date of freedom because her freedom, as well as that of her first surviving child, derived not from Buck and Buddy McCaslin in the commissary but from a stranger in Washington, and no date of death and burial, not only because McCaslin kept no obituaries in his books, but because in this year 1883 she was still alive and would remain so to see a grandson by her last surviving child:

Amodeus McCaslin Beauchamp Son of tomys Turl @ Tennie Beauchamp 1859 died 1859

then his uncle's hand entire, because his father was now a member of the cavalry command of that man whose name as a slave-dealer he could not even spell: and not even a page and not even a full line:

Dauter Tomes Turl and tenny 1862

and not even a line and not even a sex and no cause given though the boy could guess it because McCaslin was thirteen then and he remembered how there was always enough to eat in more places than Vicksburg:

Child of tomes Turl and Tenny 1863

and the same hand again and this one lived, as though Tennie's perseverance and the fading and diluted ghost of old Carothers' ruthlessness had at last conquered even starvation: and clear, fuller, more carefully written and spelled than the boy had yet seen it, as if the old man, who should have been a woman to begin with, trying to run what was left of the plantation in his brother's absence in the intervals of cooking and caring for himself and the fourteen-year-old orphan, had taken as an omen for renewed hope the fact that this nameless inheritor of slaves was at least remaining alive long enough to receive a name:

James Thucydus Beauchamp Son of Tomes Turl and Tenny Beauchamp Born 29th december 1864 and both Well Wanted to call him Theophilus but Tride Amodeus McCaslin and Callina McCaslin and both dide so Disswaded Them Born at Two clock A,m, both Well

but no more, nothing; it would be another two years yet before the boy, almost a man now, would return from the abortive trip into Tennessee with the still-intact third of old Carothers' legacy to his Negro son and his descendants, which as the three surviving children established at last one by one their apparent intention of surviving, their white half-uncles had increased to a thousand dollars each, conditions permitting, as they came of age, and completed the page himself as far as it would even be completed when that day was long passed beyond which a man born in 1864 (or 1867 either, when he himself saw light) could have expected or himself hoped or even wanted to be still alive; his own hand now, queerly enough resembling neither his father's nor his uncle's nor even McCaslin's, but like that of his grandfather's save for the spelling:

Vanished sometime on night of his twenty-first birthday Dec 29 1885. Traced by Isaac McCaslin to Jackson Tenn. and there lost. His third of legacy $1000.00 returned to McCaslin Edmonds Trustee this day Jan 12 1886

but not yet: that would be two years yet, and now his father's again, whose old commander was now quit of soldiering and slave-trading both; once more in the ledger and then not again, and more illegible than ever, almost indecipherable at all from the rheumatism which now crippled him, and almost completely innocent now even of any sort of spelling as well as punctuation, as if the four years during which he had followed the sword of the only man ever breathing who ever sold him a Negro, let alone beat him in a trade, had convinced him not only of the vanity of faith and hope, but of orthography too:

Miss sophonsiba b drt t t @ t 1869

but not of belief and will because it was there, written, as McCaslin had told him, with the left hand, but there in the ledger one time more and then not again, for the boy himself was a year old, and when Lucas was born six years later, his father and uncle had been dead inside the same twelve-months almost five years; his own hand again, who was there and saw it, 1886, she was just seventeen, two years younger than himself, and he was in the commissary when McCaslin entered out of the first of dusk and said, 'He wants to marry Fonsiba,' like that: and he looked past McCaslin and saw the man, the stranger, taller than McCaslin and wearing better clothes than McCaslin and most of the other white men the boy knew habitually wore, who entered the room like a white man and stood in it like a white man, as though he had let McCaslin precede him into it not because McCaslin's skin was white but simply because McCaslin lived there and knew the way, and who talked like a white man too, looking at him past McCaslin's shoulder rapidly and keenly once and then no more, without further interest, as a mature and contained white man not impatient but just pressed for time might have looked. 'Marry Fonsiba?' he cried. 'Marry Fonsiba?' and then no more either, just watching and listening while McCaslin and the Negro talked:

'To live in Arkansas, I believe you said.'

'Yes. I have property there. A farm.'

'Property? A farm? You own it?'

'Yes.'

'You don't say Sir, do you?'

'To my elders, yes.'

'I see. You are from the North.'

'Yes. Since a child.'

'Then your father was a slave.'

'Yes. Once.'

'Then how do you own a farm in Arkansas?'

'I have a grant. It was my father's. From the United States. For military service.'

'I see,' McCaslin said. 'The Yankee army.'

'The United States army,' the stranger said; and then himself again, crying it at McCaslin's back:

'Call aunt Tennie! I'll go get her! I'll—" But McCaslin was not even including him; the stranger did not even glance back toward his voice, the two of them speaking to one another again as if he were not even there:

'Since you seem to have it all settled,' McCaslin said, 'why have you bothered to consult my authority at all?'

'I don't,' the stranger said. 'I acknowledge your authority only so far as you admit your responsibility toward her as a female member of the family of which you are the head. I don't ask your permission. I—'

'That will do!' McCaslin said. But the stranger did not falter. It was neither as if he were ignoring McCaslin nor as if he had failed to hear him. It was as though he were making, not at all an excuse and not exactly a justification, but simply a statement which the situation absolutely required and demanded should be made in McCaslin's hearing whether McCaslin listened to it or not. It was as if he were talking to himself, for himself to hear the words spoken aloud. They faced one another, not close yet at slightly less than foils' distance, erect, their voices not raised, not impactive, just succinct:

'—I inform you, notify you in advance as chief of her family. No man of honor could do less. Besides, you have, in your way, according to your lights and upbringing——'

'That's enough, I said,' McCaslin said. 'Be off this place by full dark. Go.' But for another moment the other did not move, contemplating McCaslin with that detached and heatless look, as if he were watching reflected in McCaslin's pupils the tiny image of the figure he was sustaining.

'Yes,' he said. 'After all, this is your house. And in your fashion you have. . . . But no matter. You are right. This is enough.' He turned back toward the door; he paused again but only for a second, already moving while he spoke: 'Be easy. I will be good to her.' Then he was gone.

'But how did she ever know him?' the boy cried. 'I never even heard of him before! And Fonsiba, that's never been off this place except to go to church since she was born——'

'Ha,' McCaslin said. 'Even their parents don't know until too late how seventeen-year-old girls ever met the men who marry them too, if they are lucky.' And the next morning they were both gone, Fonsiba too. McCaslin never saw her again, nor did he, because the woman he found at last, five months later, was no one he had ever known. He carried a third of the three-thousand-dollar fund in gold in a money-belt, as when he had vainly traced Tennie's Jim into Tennessee a year ago. They—the man—had left an address of some sort with Tennie, and three months later a letter came, written by the man although McCaslin's wife, Alice, had taught Fonsiba to read and write too a little. But it bore a different postmark from the address the man had left with Tennie, and he travelled by rail as far as he could and then by contracted stage and then by a hired livery rig and then by rail again for a distance: an experienced traveller by now and an experienced bloodhound too, and a successful one this time because he would have to be; as the slow interminable empty muddy December miles crawled and crawled and night followed night in hotels, in roadside taverns of rough logs and containing little else but a bar, and in the cabins of strangers, and the hay of lonely barns, in none of which he dared undress because of his secret golden girdle like that of a disguised one of the Magi travelling incognito and not even hope to draw him, but only determination and desperation, he would tell himself: *I will have to find her. I will have to. We have already lost one of them. I will have to find her this time.* He did. Hunched in the slow and icy rain, on a spent hired horse splashed to the chest and higher, he saw it—a single log edifice with a clay chimney, which seemed in process of being flattened by the rain to a nameless and valueless rubble of dissolution in that roadless and even pathless waste of unfenced fallow and wilderness jungle—no barn, no stable, not so much as a hen-coop: just a log cabin built by hand and no clever hand either, a meagre pile of clumsily-cut firewood sufficient for about one day and not even a gaunt hound to come bellowing out from under the house when he rode up—a farm only in embryo, perhaps a good farm, maybe even a plantation someday, but not now, not for years yet and only then with labor, hard and enduring and unflagging work and sacrifice; he shoved open the crazy kitchen door in its awry frame and entered an icy gloom where not even a fire for cooking burned, and after another moment saw, crouched into the wall's angle behind a crude table, the coffee-colored face which he had known all his life but knew no more, the body which had been born within a hundred yards of the room that he was born in and in which some of his own blood ran, but which was now completely inheritor of generation after generation to whom an unannounced white man on a horse was a white man's hired Patroller wearing a pistol sometimes and a blacksnake whip always; he entered the next room, the only other room the cabin owned, and found, sitting in a rocking chair before the hearth, the man himself, reading—sitting there in the only chair in the house, before that miserable fire for which there was not wood sufficient to last twenty-four hours, in the same ministerial clothing in which he had entered the commissary five months ago and a pair of gold-framed spectacles which, when he looked up and then rose to his feet, the boy saw did not even contain lenses, reading a book in the midst of that desolation, that muddy waste, fenceless and even pathless and without even a walled shed for stock to stand beneath: and over all, permanent, clinging to the man's very clothing and exuding from his skin itself, that rank stink of baseless and imbecile delusion, that boundless rapacity and folly, of the carpet-bagger followers of victorious armies.

'Don't you see?' he cried. 'Don't you see? This whole land, the whole South, is cursed, and all of us who derive from it, whom it ever suckled, white and black both, lie under the curse? Granted that my people brought the curse onto the land: maybe for that reason their descendants alone can—not resist it, not combat it—maybe just endure and outlast it until the curse is lifted. Then your peoples' turn will come because we have forfeited ours. But not now. Not yet. Don't you see?'

The other side stood now, the unfrayed garments still ministerial even if not quite so fine, the book closed upon one finger to keep the place, the lenseless spectacles held like a music master's wand in the other workless hand while the owner of it spoke his measured and sonorous imbecility of the boundless folly and the baseless hope: 'You're wrong. The curse you whites brought into this land has been lifted. It has been voided and discharged. We are seeing a new era, an era dedicated, as our founders intended it, to freedom, liberty and equality for all, to which this country will be the new Canaan—'[3]

'Freedom from what? From work? Canaan?' He jerked his arm, comprehensive, almost violent: whereupon it all seemed to stand there about them, intact and complete and visible in the drafty, damp, heatless, Negro-stale Negro-rank sorry room—the empty fields without plow or seed to work them, fenceless against the stock which did not exist within or without the walled stable which likewise was not there. 'What corner of Canaan is this?'

'You are seeing it at a bad time. This is winter. No man farms this time of year.'

'I see. And of course her need for food and clothing will stand while the land lies fallow.'

'I have a pension,' the other said. He said it as a man might say *I have grace or I own a gold mine*. 'I have my father's pension too. It will arrive on the first of the month. What day is this?'

'The eleventh,' he said. 'Twenty days more. And until then?'

'I have a few groceries in the house from my credit account with the merchant in Midnight who banks my pension check for me. I have executed to him a power of attorney to handle it for me as a matter of mutual—'

'I see. And if the groceries don't last the twenty days?'

'I still have one more hog.'

'Where?'

'Outside,' the other said. 'It is customary in this country to allow stock to range free during the winter for food. It comes up from time to time. But no matter if it doesn't; I can probably trace its footprints when the need—'

'Yes!' he cried. 'Because no matter: you still have the pension check. And the man in Midnight will cash it and pay himself out of it

3. The Promised Land of the Israelites.

for what you have already eaten and if there is any left over, it is yours. And the hog will be eaten by then or you still can't catch it, and then what will you do?'

'It will be almost spring then,' the other said. 'I am planning in the spring—'

'It will be January,' he said. 'And then February. And then more than half of March—' and when he stopped again in the kitchen she had not moved, she did not even seem to breathe or to be alive except her eyes watching him; when he took a step toward her it was still not movement because she could have retreated no further: only the tremendous, fathomless, ink-colored eyes in the narrow, thin, coffee-colored face watching him without alarm, without recognition, without hope, 'Fonsiba,' he said. 'Fonsiba. Are you all right?'

'I'm free,' she said. Midnight was a tavern, a livery stable, a big store (that would be where the pension check banked itself as a matter of mutual elimination of bother and fret, he thought) and a little one, a saloon and a blacksmith shop. But there was a bank there too. The president (the owner, for all practical purposes) of it was a translated Mississippian who had been one of Forrest's men too: and his body lightened of the golden belt for the first time since he left home eight days ago, with pencil and paper he multiplied three dollars by twelve months and divided it into one thousand dollars; it would stretch that way over almost twenty-eight years and for twenty-eight years at least she would not starve, the banker promising to send the three dollars himself by a trusty messenger on the fifteenth of each month and put it into her actual hand, and he returned home and that was all because in 1874 his father and his uncle were both dead and the old ledgers never again came down from the shelf above the desk to which his father had returned them for the last time that day in 1869. But he could have completed it:

Lucas Quintus Carothers McCaslin Beauchamp. Last surviving son and child of Tomey's Terrel and Tennie Beauchamp. March 17, 1874

except that there was no need: not *Lucius Quintus* @c@c@c, but *Lucas Quintus*, not refusing to be called Lucius, because he simply eliminated that word from the name; not denying, declining the name itself, because he used three quarters of it; but simply taking the name and changing, altering it, making it no longer the white man's but his own, by himself composed, himself selfprogenitive and nominate, by himself ancestored, as, for all the old ledgers recorded to the contrary, old Carothers himself was

and that was all: 1874 the boy; 1888 the man, repudiated denied and free; 1895 and husband but no father, unwidowered but without a wife, and found long since that no man is ever free and probably could not bear it if he were; married then and living in Jefferson in the little jerrybuilt bungalow which his wife's father had given them: and one morning Lucas stood suddenly in the doorway of the room where he was reading the Memphis paper and he looked at the paper's dateline and thought *It's his birthday. He's twenty-one today* and Lucas said: 'Whar's the rest of that money old Carothers left? I wants it. All of it.'

that was all: and McCaslin

'More men than that one Buck and Buddy to fumble-heed that truth so mazed for them that spoke it and so confused for them that heard yet still there was 1865:' and he

'But not enough. Not enough of even Father and Uncle Buddy to fumble-heed in even three generations not even three generations fathered by Grandfather not even if there had been nowhere beneath His sight any but Grandfather and so He would not even have needed to elect and choose. But He tried and I know what you will say. That having Himself created them He could have known no more of hope than He could have pride and grief, but He didn't hope He just waited because He had made them: not just because He had set them alive and in motion but because He had already worried with them so long: worried with them so long because He had seen how in individual cases they were capable of anything, any height or depth remembered in mazed incomprehension out of heaven where hell was created too, and so He must admit them or else admit his equal somewhere and so be no longer God and therefore must accept responsibility for what He Himself had done in order to live with Himself in His lonely and paramount heaven. And He probably knew it was vain but He had created them and knew them capable of all things because He had shaped them out of the primal Absolute which contained all and had watched them since in their individual exaltation and baseness, and they themselves not knowing why nor how nor even when: until at last He saw that they were all Grandfather all of them and that even from them the elected and chosen the best the very best He could expect (not hope mind: not hope) would be Bucks and Buddies and not even enough of them and in the third generation not even Bucks and Buddies but—' and McCaslin

'Ah:' and he

'Yes. If He could see Father and Uncle Buddy in Grandfather He must have seen me too. —an Isaac born into a later life than Abraham's and repudiating immolation: fatherless and therefore safe declining the altar because maybe this time the exasperated Hand might not supply the kid—' and McCaslin

'Escape:' and he

'All right. Escape.—Until one day He said what you told Fonsiba's husband that afternoon here in this room: *This will do. This is enough:* not in exasperation or rage or even just sick to death as you were sick that day: just *This is enough* and looked about for one last time, for one time more since He had created them, upon this land this South for which He had done so much with woods for game and streams for fish and deep rich soil for seed and lush springs to sprout it and long summers to mature it and serene falls to harvest it and short mild winters for men and animals, and saw no hope anywhere and looked beyond it where hope should have been, where to East North and West lay illimitable that whole hopeful continent dedicated as a refuge and sanctuary of liberty and freedom from what you called the old world's worthless evening, and saw the rich descendants of slavers, females of both sexes, to whom the black they shrieked of was another specimen another example like the Brazilian macaw brought home in a cage by a traveller, passing resolutions about horror and outrage in warm and air-proof halls: and the thundering cannonade of politicians earning votes and the medicine-shows of pulpiteers earning Chatauqua fees, to whom the outrage and the injustice were as much abstractions as Tariff or Silver or Immortality and who employed the very shackles of its servitude and the sorry rags of its regalia as they did the other beer and banners and mottoes, redfire and brimstone and sleight-of-hand and musical handsaws: and the whirling wheels which manufactured for a profit the pristine replacements of the shackles and shoddy garments as they wore out, and spun the cotton and made the gins which ginned it and the cars and ships which hauled it, and the men who ran the wheels for that profit and established and collected the taxes it was taxed with and the rates for hauling it and the commissions for selling it: and He could have repudiated them since they were his creation now and forever more throughout all their generations, until not only that old world from which He had rescued them but this new one too which He had revealed and led them to as a sanctuary and refuge were become the same worthless tideless rock cooling in the last crimson evening, except that out of all that empty sound and bootless fury one silence, among that loud and moiling all of them just one simple enough to believe that horror and outrage were first and last simply horror and outrage and crude enough to act upon that, illiterate and had no words for talking or perhaps was just busy and had no time to, one out of them all who did not bother Him with cajolery and adjuration then pleading then threat, and had not even bothered to inform Him in advance what he was about so that a lesser than He might have even missed the simple act of lifting the long ancestral musket down from the deerhorns above the door, whereupon He said *My name is Brown too* and the other *So is mine* and He *Then mine or yours can't be because I am against it* and the other *So am I* and He triumphantly *Then where are you going with that gun?* and the other told him in one sentence one word and He: amazed: Who knew neither hope nor pride nor grief *But your Association, your Committee, your Officers. Where are your Minutes, your Motions, your Parliamentary Procedures?* and the other *I ain't against them. They are all right I reckon for them that have the time. I am just against the weak because they are niggers being held in bondage by the strong just because they are white.* So He turned once more to this land which He still intended to save because He had done so much for it—' and McCaslin

'What?' and he

'—to these people He was still committed to because they were his creations—' and McCaslin

'Turned back to us? His face to us?' and he

'—whose wives and daughters at least made soups and jellies for them when they were sick, and carried the trays through the mud and the winter too into the stinking cabins, and sat in the stinking cabins and kept fires going until crises came and passed, but that was not enough: and when they were very sick had them carried into the big house itself into the company room itself maybe and nursed them there, which the white man would have done too for any other of his cattle that was sick but at least the man who hired one from a livery wouldn't have, and still that was not enough: so that He said and not in grief either, Who had made them and so could know no more of grief than He could of pride or hope: *Apparently they can learn nothing save through suffering, remember nothing save when underlined in blood*—' and McCaslin

'Ashby[4] on an afternoon's ride, to call on some remote maiden cousins of his mother or maybe just acquaintances of hers, comes by chance upon a minor engagement of outposts and dismounts and with his crimson-lined cloak for target leads a handful of troops he never saw before against an entrenched position of backwoods-trained riflemen. Lee's[5] battle-order, wrapped maybe about a handful of cigars and doubtless thrown away when the last cigar was smoked, found by a Yankee Intelligence officer on the floor of a saloon behind the Yankee lines after Lee had already divided his forces before Sharpsburg.[6] Jackson on the Plank Road, already rolled up the flank which Hooker believed could not be turned and, waiting only for night to pass to continue the brutal and incessant slogging which would fling that whole wing back into Hooker's lap where he sat on a front gallery in Chancellorsville drinking rum toddies and telegraphing Lincoln that he had defeated Lee, is shot from among a whole covey of minor officers and in the

4. Colonel Turner Ashby (1828–1862), Confederate leader of guerrilla raiders. 5. Robert E. Lee (1807–1870), commander in chief of Confederate forces. 6. Name of a major battle, also called the Battle of Antietam (September 17, 1862).

blind night by one of his own patrols,[7] leaving as next by seniority Stuart,[8] that gallant man born apparently already horsed and sabred and already knowing all there was to know about war except the slogging and brutal stupidity of it: and that same Stuart off raiding Pennsylvania hen-roosts when Lee should have known of all of Meade just where Hancock was on Cemetery Ridge: and Longstreet too at Gettysburg[9] and that same Longstreet shot out of saddle by his own men in the dark by mistake just as Jackson was. His face to us? His face to us?' and he

'How else have made them fight? Who else but Jacksons and Stuarts and Ashbys and Morgans and Forrests?—the farmers of the central and middle-west, holding land by the acre instead of the tens or maybe even the hundreds, farming it themselves and to no single crop of cotton or tobacco or cane, owning no slaves and needing and wanting none, and already looking toward the Pacific coast, not always as long as two generations there and having stopped where they did stop only through the fortuitous mischance that an ox died or a wagon-axle broke. And the New England mechanics who didn't even own land and measured all things by the weight of water and the cost of turning wheels, and the narrow fringe of traders and shipowners still looking backward across the Atlantic and attached to the continent only by their counting-houses. And those who should have had the alertness to see: the wildcat manipulators of mythical wilderness townsites; and the astuteness to rationalize: the bankers who held the mortgages on the land which the first were only waiting to abandon, and on the railroads and steamboats to carry them still further west, and on the factories and the wheels and the rented tenements those who ran them lived in; and the leisure and scope to comprehend and fear in time and even anticipate: the Boston-bred (even when not born in Boston) spinster, descendants of long lines of similarly-bred and likewise spinster aunts and uncles whose hands knew no callus except that of the indicting pen, to whom the wilderness itself began at the top of tide and who looked, if at anything other than Beacon Hill, only toward heaven—not to mention all the loud rabble of the camp-followers of pioneers: the bellowing of politicians, the mellifluous choiring of self-styled men of God, the—' and McCaslin

7. Events and personalities involved in the Battle of Chancellorsville (May 1–5, 1863). Union general Joseph Hooker (1814–1879) was opposed by Thomas Jonathan (Stonewall) Jackson (1824–1863), who had insured a Confederate victory before he was shot by his own men. 8. Confederate general J. E. B. (Jeb) Stuart (1833–1864). 9. Battle of Gettysburg (July 1–3, 1863). Union general George Gordon Meade (1815–1872) was in overall command of Northern forces. His subordinate General Winfield Scott Hancock (1824–1886) distinguished himself in the battle by holding the line along Cemetery Ridge against the main thrust of the Confederate attack. Confederate general James Longstreet (1821–1904) was sometimes blamed in the South for delay in executing Lee's orders. Longstreet was later wounded in the Battle of the Wilderness (May 5–6, 1864). *Morgan* (below): Confederate general John Hunt Morgan (1826–1864).

'Here, here. Wait a minute:' And he

'Let me talk now. I'm trying to explain to the head of my family something which I have got to do which I don't quite understand myself, not in justification of it but to explain it if I can. I could say I don't know why I must do it but that I do know I have got to because I have got myself to have to live with for the rest of my life and all I want is peace to do it in. But you are the head of my family. More. I knew a long time ago that I would never have to miss my father, even if you are just finding out that you have missed your son—the drawers of bills and the shavers of notes and the schoolmasters and the self-ordained to teach and lead and all that horde of the semi-literate with a white shirt but no change for it, with one eye on themselves and watching each other with the other one. Who else could have made them fight: could have struck them so aghast with fear and dread as to turn shoulder to shoulder and face one way and even stop talking for a while and even after two years of it keep them still so wrung with terror that some among them would seriously propose moving their very capital into a foreign country lest it be ravaged and pillaged by a people whose entire white male population would have little more than filled any one of their larger cities: except Jackson in the Valley[1] and three separate armies trying to catch him and none of them ever knowing whether they were just retreating from a battle or just running into one, and Stuart riding his whole command entirely around the biggest single armed force this continent[2] ever saw in order to see what it looked like from behind, and Morgan leading a cavalry charge against a stranded man-of-war. Who else could have declared a war against a power with ten times the area and a hundred times the men and a thousand times the resources, except men who could believe that all necessary to conduct a successful war was not acumen nor shrewdness nor politics nor diplomacy nor money nor even integrity and simple arithmetic, but just love of land and courage—'

'And an unblemished and gallant ancestry and the ability to ride a horse,' McCaslin said. 'Don't leave that out.' It was evening now, the tranquil sunset of October mazy with windless woodsmoke. The cotton was long since picked and ginned, and all day now the wagons loaded with gathered corn moved between field and crib, processional across the enduring land. 'Well, maybe that's what He wanted. At least, that's what He got.' This time there was no yellowed procession of fading and harmless ledger-pages. This was chronicled in a harsher book, and McCaslin, fourteen and fifteen and sixteen, had seen it and the boy himself had inherited it as Noah's grandchildren had inherited the Flood

1. Shenandoah Valley in Virginia. 2. Before the Seven Days' Battle (June 26–July 2, 1862), Stuart led his cavalry all the way around the Union Army commanded by General George McClellan (1826–1885).

although they had not been there to see the deluge: that dark corrupt and bloody time while three separate peoples had tried to adjust not only to another but to the new land which they had created and inherited too and must live in for the reason that those who had lost it were no less free to quit it than those who had gained it were:—those upon whom freedom and equality had been dumped overnight and without warning or preparation or any training in how to employ it or even just endure it and who misused it, not as children would nor yet because they had been so long in bondage and then so suddenly freed, but misused it as human beings always misuse freedom, so that he thought *Apparently there is a wisdom beyond even that learned through suffering necessary for a man to distinguish between liberty and license;* those who had fought for four years and lost to preserve a condition under which that franchisement was anomaly and paradox, not because they were opposed to freedom as freedom but for the old reasons for which man (not the generals and politicians but man) has always fought and died in wars: to preserve a status quo or to establish a better future one to endure for his children; and lastly, as if that were not enough for bitterness and hatred and fear, that third race even more alien to the people whom they resembled in pigment and in whom even the same blood ran, than to the people whom they did not,—that race threefold in one and alien even among themselves save for a single fierce will for rapine and pillage, composed of the sons of middleaged Quartermaster lieutenants and Army sutlers and contractors in military blankets and shoes and transport mules, who followed the battles they themselves had not fought and inherited the conquest they themselves had not helped to gain, sanctioned and protected even if not blessed, and left their bones and in another generation would be engaged in a fierce economic competition of small sloven farms with the black men they were supposed to have freed and the white descendants of fathers who had owned no slaves anyway whom they were supposed to have disinherited, and in the third generation would be back once more in the little lost county seats as barbers and garage mechanics and deputy sheriffs and mill- and gin-hands and power-plant firemen, leading, first in mufti then later in an actual formalized regalia of hooded sheets and passwords and fiery Christian symbols, lynching mobs against the race their ancestors had come to save: and of all that other nameless horde of speculators in human misery, manipulators of money and politics and land, who follow catastrophe and are their own protection as grasshoppers are and need no blessing and sweat no plow or axe-helve and batten and vanish and leave no bones, just as they derived apparently from no ancestry, no mortal flesh, no act even of passion or even of lust: and the Jew who came without protection too, since after two thousand years he had got out of the habit of being or needing it, and solitary, without even the solidarity of the locusts, and in this a sort of courage since he had come thinking not in terms of simple pillage but in terms of his great-grandchildren, seeking yet some place to establish them to endure even though forever alien: and unblessed: a pariah about the face of the Western earth which twenty centuries later was still taking revenge on him for the fairy tale with which he had conquered it. McCaslin had actually seen it, and the boy even at almost eighty would never be able to distinguish certainly between what he had seen and what had been told him: a lightless and gutted and empty land where women crouched with the huddled children behind locked doors and men armed in sheets and masks rode the silent roads and the bodies of white and black both, victims not so much of hate as of desperation and despair, swung from lonely limbs: and men shot dead in polling-booths with the still wet pen in one hand and the unblotted ballot in the other: and a United States marshal in Jefferson who signed his official papers with a crude cross, an ex-slave called Sickymo, not at all because his ex-owner was a doctor and apothecary but because, still a slave, he would steal his master's grain alcohol and dilute it with water and peddle it in pint bottles from a cache beneath the roots of a big sycamore tree behind the drug store, who had attained his high office because his half-white sister was the concubine of the Federal A.P.M.:[3] and this time McCaslin did not even say Look but merely lifted one hand, not even pointing, not even specifically toward the shelf of ledgers but toward the desk, toward the corner where it sat beside the scuffed patch on the floor where two decades of heavy shoes had stood while the white man at the desk added and multiplied and subtracted. And again he did not need to look because he had seen this himself and, twenty-three years after the Surrender and twenty-four after the Proclamation,[4] was still watching it: the ledgers, new ones now and filled rapidly, succeeding one another rapidly and containing more names than old Carothers or even his father and Uncle Buddy had ever dreamed of; new names and new faces to go with them, among which the old names and faces that even his father and uncle would have recognized, were lost, vanished—Tomey's Terrel dead, and even the tragic and miscast Percival Brownlee, who couldn't keep books and couldn't farm either, found his true niche at last, reappeared in 1862 during the boy's father's absence and had apparently been living on the plantation for at least a month before his uncle found out about it, conducting impromptu revival meetings among Negroes, preaching and leading the singing also in his high sweet true soprano voice and disappeared again on foot and at top speed, not

3. Federal Army Provost Marshal. 4. General Lee surrendered the Confederate armies at Appomattox Court House on April 9, 1865. The Emancipation Proclamation had been issued by President Abraham Lincoln (1809–1865) in 1862.

behind but ahead of a body of raiding Federal horse and reappeared for the third and last time in the entourage of a travelling Army paymaster, the two of them passing through Jefferson in a surrey at the exact moment when the boy's father (it was 1866) also happened to be crossing the Square, the surrey and its occupants traversing rapidly that quiet and bucolic scene and even in that fleeting moment, and to others beside the boy's father, giving an illusion of flight and illicit holiday like a man on an excursion during his wife's absence with his wife's personal maid, until Brownlee glanced up and saw his late co-master and gave him one defiant female glance and then broke again, leaped from the surrey and disappeared this time for good, and it was only by chance that McCaslin, twenty years later, heard of him again, an old man now and quite fat, as the well-to-do proprietor of a select New Orleans brothel; and Tennie's Jim gone, nobody knew where, and Fonsiba in Arkansas with her three dollars each month and the scholar-husband with his lenseless spectacles and frock coat and his plans for the spring; and only Lucas was left, the baby, the last save himself of old Carothers' doomed and fatal blood which in the male derivation seemed to destroy all it touched, and even he was repudiating and at least hoping to escape it;—Lucas, the boy of fourteen whose name would not even appear for six years yet among those rapid pages in the bindings new and dustless too since McCaslin lifted them down daily now to write into them the continuation of that record which two hundred years had not been enough to complete, and another hundred would not be enough to discharge; that chronicle which was a whole land in miniature, which multiplied and compounded was the entire South, twenty-three years after surrender and twenty-four from emancipation—that slow trickle of molasses and meal and meat, of shoes and straw hats and overalls, of plowlines and collars and heel-bolts and buckheads and clevises, which returned each fall as cotton—the two threads frail as truth and impalpable as equators yet cable-strong to bind for life them who made the cotton to the land their sweat fell on: and he

'Yes. Binding them for a while yet, a little while yet. Through and beyond that life and maybe through and beyond the life of that life's sons and maybe even through and beyond that of the sons of those sons. But not always, because they will endure. They will outlast us because they are—' it was not a pause, barely a falter even, possibly appreciable only to himself, as if he couldn't speak even to McCaslin, even to explain his repudiation, that which to him too, even in the act of escaping (and maybe this was the reality and the truth of his need to escape), was heresy: so that even in escaping he was taking with him more of that evil and unregenerate old man who could summon, because she was his property, a human being because she was old enough and female, to his widower's house and get a child on her and then dismiss her because she was of an inferior race, and then bequeath a thousand dollars to the infant because he would be dead then and wouldn't have to pay it, than even he had feared. 'Yes. He didn't want to. He had to. Because they will endure. They are better than we are. Stronger than we are. Their vices are vices aped from white men or that white men and bondage have taught them: improvidence and intemperance and evasion—not laziness: evasion: of what white men had set them to, not for their aggrandizement or even comfort but his own—' and McCaslin

'All right. Go on: Promiscuity. Violence. Instability and lack of control. Inability to distinguish between mine and thine—' and he

'How distinguish, when for two hundred years mine did not even exist for them?' and McCaslin.

'All right. Go on. And their virtues—' and he

'Yes. Their own. Endurance—' and McCaslin

'So have dogs:' and he

'—and pity and tolerance and forbearance and fidelity and love of children—' and McCaslin

'So have dogs:' and he

'—whether their own or not or black or not. And more: what they got not only not from white people but not even despite white people because they had it already from the old free fathers a longer time free than us because we have never been free—' and it was in McCaslin's eyes too, he had only to look at McCaslin's eyes and it was there, that summer twilight seven years ago, almost a week after they had returned from the camp before he discovered that Sam Fathers had told McCaslin: an old bear, fierce and ruthless not just to stay alive but ruthless with the fierce pride of liberty and freedom, jealous and proud enough of liberty and freedom to see it threatened not with fear nor even alarm but almost with joy, seeming deliberately to put it into jeopardy in order to savor it and keep his old strong bones and flesh supple and quick to defend and preserve it; an old man, son of a Negro slave and an Indian king, inheritor on the one hand of the long chronicle of a people who had learned humility through suffering and learned pride through the endurance which survived the suffering, and on the other side the chronicle of a people even longer in the land than the first, yet who now existed there only in the solitary brotherhood of an old and childless Negro's alien blood and the wild and invincible spirit of an old bear; a boy who wished to learn humility and pride in order to become skillful and worthy in the woods but found himself becoming so skillful so fast that he feared he would never become worthy, because he had not learned humility and pride though he had tried, until one day an old man, who could not have defined either, led him as though by the hand to where an old bear and a little mongrel dog showed him that, by possessing one thing other, he would possess them both; and a little dog, nameless and mongrel and many-feathered, grown yet weighing less than six pounds, who couldn't be dangerous because there was nothing anywhere much smaller, not fierce because that would have been called just noise, not humble because it was already too near the ground to genuflect, and not proud because it would not have been close enough for anyone to discern what was casting that shadow, and which didn't even know it was not going to heaven since they had already decided it had no immortal soul, so that all it could be was brave, even though they would probably call that too just noise. *'And you didn't shoot,' McCaslin said. 'How close were you?'*

'I don't know,' he said. 'There was a big wood tick just inside his off hind leg. I saw that. But I didn't have the gun then.'

'But you didn't shoot when you had the gun,' McCaslin said. 'Why?' But McCaslin didn't wait, rising and crossing the room, across the pelt of the bear he had killed two years ago and the bigger one McCaslin had killed before he was born, to the bookcase beneath the mounted head of his first buck, and returned with the book and sat down again and opened it. 'Listen,' he said. He read the five stanzas aloud and closed the book on his finger and looked up. 'All right,' he said. 'Listen,' and read again, but only one stanza this time and closed the book and laid it on the table. 'She cannot fade, though thou hast not thy bliss,' McCaslin said: 'Forever wilt thou love, and she be fair.'[5]

'He's talking about a girl,' he said.

'He had to talk about something,' McCaslin said. Then he said, 'He was talking about truth. Truth is one. It doesn't change. It covers all things which touch the heart—honor and pride and pity and justice and courage and love. Do you see now?' He didn't know. Somehow it had seemed simpler than that, simpler than somebody talking in a book about a young man and a girl he would never need to grieve over because he could never approach any nearer and would never have to get any further away. He had heard about an old bear and finally got big enough to hunt it and he hunted it four years and at last met it with a gun in his hands and he didn't shoot. Because a little dog—But he could have shot long before the fyce covered the twenty yards to where the bear waited, and Sam Fathers could have shot at any time during the interminable minute while Old Ben stood on his hind legs over them. . . . He ceased. McCaslin watched him, still speaking, the voice, the words as quiet as the twilight itself was: 'Courage and honor and pride, and pity and love of justice and of liberty. They all touch the heart, and what the heart holds to becomes truth, as far as we know truth. Do you see now?'

5. From "Ode on a Grecian Urn" by English poet John Keats (1795–1821).

and he could still hear them, intact in this twilight as in that one seven years ago, no louder still because they did not need to be because they would endure: and he had only to look at McCaslin's eyes beyond the thin and bitter smiling, the faint lip-lift which would have had to be called smiling;—his kinsman, his father almost, who had been born too late into the old time and too soon for the new, the two of them juxtaposed and alien now to each other against their ravaged patrimony, the dark and ravaged fatherland still prone and panting from its etherless operation:

'Habet[6] then.—So this land is, indubitably, of and by itself cursed:' and he

'Cursed:' and again McCaslin merely lifted one hand, not even speaking and not even toward the ledgers: so that, as the stereopticon condenses into one instantaneous field the myriad minutiae of its scope, so did that slight and rapid gesture establish in the small cramped and cluttered twilit room not only the ledgers but the whole plantation in its mazed and intricate entirety—the land, the fields and what they represented in terms of cotton ginned and sold, the men and women whom they fed and clothed and even paid a little cash money at Christmas-time in return for the labor which planted and raised and picked and ginned the cotton, the machinery and mules and gear with which they raised it and their cost and upkeep and replacement—that whole edifice intricate and complex and founded upon injustice and erected by ruthless rapacity and carried on even yet with at times downright savagery not only to the human beings but the valuable animals too, yet solvent and efficient and, more than that: not only still intact but enlarged, increased; brought still intact by McCaslin, himself little more than a child then, through and out of the debacle and chaos of twenty years ago where hardly one in ten survived, and enlarged and increased and would continue so, solvent and efficient and intact and still increasing so long as McCaslin and his McCaslin successors lasted, even though their surnames might not even be Edmonds then: and he

'Habet too. Because that's it: not the land, but us. Not only the blood, but the name too; not only its color but its designation: Edmonds, white, but, a female line, could have no other but the name his father bore; Beauchamp, the elder line and the male one, but black, could have had any name his father bore who had no name—' and McCaslin

'And since I know too what you know I will say now, once more let me say it: And one other, and in the third generation too, and the male, the eldest, the direct and sole and white and still McCaslin even, father to son to son—' and he

'I am free:' and this time McCaslin did not even gesture, no infer-

6. Consider. Or take into account.

ence of fading pages, no postulation of the stereoptic whole, but the frail and iron thread strong as truth and impervious as evil and longer than life itself and reaching beyond record and patrimony both to join him with the lusts and passions, the hopes and dreams and griefs, of bones whose names while still fleshed and capable even old Carothers' grandfather had never heard: and he:

'And of that too:' and McCaslin

'Chosen, I suppose (I will concede it) out of all your time by Him, as you say Buck and Buddy were from theirs. And it took Him a bear and an old man and four years just for you. And it took you fourteen years to reach that point and about that many, maybe more, for Old Ben, and more than seventy for Sam Fathers. And you are just one. How long then? How long?' and he

'It will be long. I have never said otherwise. But it will be all right because they will endure—' and McCaslin

'And anyway, you will be free.—No, not now nor ever, we from them nor they from us. So I repudiate too. I would deny even if I knew it were true. I would have to. Even you can see that I could do no else. I am what I am; I will be always what I was born and have always been. And more than me. More than me, just as there were more than Buck and Buddy in what you called His first plan which failed:' and he,

'And more than me:' and McCaslin

'No. Not even you. Because mark. You said how on that instant when Ikkemotubbe realized that he could sell the land to Grandfather, it ceased forever to have been his. All right; go on: Then it belonged to Sam Fathers, old Ikkemotubbe's son. And who inherited from Sam Fathers, if not you? co-heir perhaps with Boon, if not of his life maybe, at least of his quitting it?" and he

'Yes. Sam Fathers set me free.'

and Isaac McCaslin, not yet Uncle Ike, a long time yet before he would be uncle to half a county and still father to none, living in one small cramped fireless rented room in a Jefferson boardinghouse where petit juries were domiciled during court terms and itinerant horse- and mule-traders stayed, with his kit of brand-new carpenter's tools and the shotgun McCaslin had given him with his name engraved in silver and old General Compson's compass (and, when the General died, his silver-mounted horn too) and the iron cot and mattress and the blankets which he would take each fall into the woods for more than sixty years and the bright tin coffee-pot

there had been a legacy, from his Uncle Hubert Beauchamp, his godfather, that bluff burly roaring childlike man from whom Uncle Buddy had won Tomey's Terrel's wife Tennie in the poker-game in 1859—'posible strait against three Treys in sigt Not called'—; no pale sentence or paragraph scrawled in cringing fear of death by a weak and trembling hand as a last desperate sop flung backward at retribution, but a Legacy, a Thing, possessing weight to the hand and bulk to the eye and even audible: a silver cup filled with gold pieces and wrapped in burlap and sealed with his godfather's ring in the hot wax, which (intact still) even before his Uncle Hubert's death and long before his own majority, when it would be his, had become not only a legend but one of the family lares.[7] After his father's and his Uncle Hubert's sister's marriage they moved back into the big house, the tremendous cavern which old Carothers had started and never finished, cleared the remaining Negroes out of it and with his mother's dowry completed it, at least the rest of the windows and doors and moved into it, all of them save Uncle Buddy who declined to leave the cabin he and his twin had built, the move being the bride's notion and more than just a notion, and none ever to know if she really wanted to live in the big house or if she knew beforehand that Uncle Buddy would refuse to move: and two weeks after his birth in 1867, the first time he and his mother came down stairs one night, and the silver cup sitting on the cleared dining-room table beneath the bright lamp, and while his mother and his father and McCaslin and Tennie (his nurse: carrying him)—all of them again but Uncle Buddy—watched, his Uncle Hubert rang one by one into the cup the bright and glinting mintage and wrapped it into the burlap envelope and heated the wax and sealed it and carried it back home with him where he lived alone now without even his sister either to hold him down as McCaslin said or to try to raise him up as Uncle Buddy said, and (dark times then in Mississippi) Uncle Buddy said most of the niggers gone and the ones that didn't go even Hub Beauchamp could not have wanted: but the dogs remained and Uncle Buddy said Beauchamp fiddled while Nero fox-hunted.[8]

they would go and see it there; at last his mother would prevail and they would depart in the surrey, once more all save Uncle Buddy and McCaslin to keep Uncle Buddy company, until one winter Uncle Buddy began to fail and from then on it was himself, beginning to remember now, and his mother and Tennie and Tomey's Terrel to drive: the twenty-two miles into the next county, the twin gateposts on one of which McCaslin could remember the half-grown boy blowing a fox-horn at breakfast, dinner, and suppertime and jumping down to open to any passer who happened to hear it, but where there were no gates at all now, the shabby and overgrown entrance to what his mother still insisted that people call Warwick because her brother was, if truth but triumphed and justice but prevailed, the rightful earl of it, the paintless house which outwardly did not change but which on the inside

7. Spirits watching over a house.

8. A scrambled allusion to the legend that Roman emperor Nero fiddled while Rome burned.

seemed each time larger because he was too little to realize then that there was less and less of it of the fine furnishings, the rosewood and mahogany and walnut, which for him had never existed anywhere anyway save in his mother's tearful lamentations, and the occasional piece small enough to be roped somehow onto the rear or the top of the carriage on their return (And he remembered this, he had seen it: an instant, a flash, his mother's soprano 'Even my dress! Even my dress!' loud and outraged in the barren unswept hall; a face young and female and even lighter in color than Tomey's Terrel's for an instant in a closing door; a swirl, a glimpse of the silk gown and the flick and glint of an ear-ring: an apparition rapid and tawdry and illicit, yet somehow even to the child, the infant still almost, breathless and exciting and evocative: as though, like two limpid and pellucid streams meeting, the child which he still was had made serene and absolute and perfect rapport and contact through that glimpsed nameless illicit hybrid female flesh with the boy which had existed at that stage of inviolable and immortal adolescence in his uncle for almost sixty years; the dress, the face, the earrings gone in that same aghast flash and his uncle's voice: 'She's my cook! She's my new cook! I had to have a cook, didn't I?' then the uncle himself, the face alarmed and aghast too yet still innocently and somehow even indomitably of a boy, they retreating in their turn now, back to the front gallery, and his uncle again, pained and still amazed, in a sort of desperate resurgence if not of courage at least of self-assertion: 'They're free now; They're folks too just like we are!' and his mother: 'That's why! That's why! My mother's house! Defiled! Defiled!' and his uncle: 'Damn it, Sibbey, at least give her time to pack her grip:' then over, finished, the loud uproar and all, himself and Tennie and he remembered Tennie's inscrutable face at the broken shutterless window of the bare room which had once been the parlor while they watched, hurrying down the lane at a stumbling trot, the routed compounder of his uncle's uxory: the back, the nameless face which he had seen only for a moment, the once-hooped dress ballooning and flapping below a man's overcoat, the worn heavy carpet-bag jouncing and banging against her knee, routed and in retreat true enough and in the empty lane, solitary, young-looking, and forlorn, yet withal still exciting and evocative and wearing still the silken banner captured inside the very citadel of respectability, and unforgettable.)

the cup, the sealed inscrutable burlap, sitting on the shelf in the locked closet, Uncle Hubert unlocking the door and lifting it down and passing it from hand to hand: his mother, his father, McCaslin and even Tennie, insisting that each take it in turn and heft it for weight and shake it again to prove the sound, Uncle Hubert himself standing spraddled before the cold unswept hearth in which the very bricks themselves were crumbling into a litter of soot and dust and mortar and the droppings of chimney-sweeps, still roaring and still innocent and still indomitable: and for a long time he believed nobody but himself had noticed that his uncle now put the cup only into his hands, unlocked the door and lifted it down and put it into his hands and stood over him until he had shaken it obediently until it sounded then took it from him and locked it back into the closet before anyone else could have offered to touch it, and even later, when competent not only to remember but to rationalize, he could not say what it was or even if it had been anything because the parcel was still heavy and still rattled, not even when, Uncle Buddy dead and his father, at last and after almost seventy-five years in bed after the sun rose, said: 'Go get that damn cup. Bring that damn Hub Beauchamp too if you have to:' because it still rattled though his uncle no longer put it even into his hands now but carried it himself from one to the other, his mother, McCaslin, Tennie, shaking it before each in turn, saying: 'Hear it? Hear it?' his face still innocent, not quite baffled but only amazed and not very amazed and still indomitable:

and, his father and Uncle Buddy both gone now, one day without reason or any warning the almost completely empty house in which his uncle and Tennie's ancient and quarrelsome great-grandfather (who claimed to have seen Lafayette and McCaslin said in another ten years would be remembering God) lived, cooked and slept in one single room, burst into peaceful conflagration, a tranquil instantaneous sourceless unanimity of combustion, walls floors and roof: at sunup it stood where his uncle's father had built it sixty years ago, at sundown the four blackened and smokeless chimneys rose from a light white powder of ashes and a few charred ends of planks which did not even appear to have been very hot: and out of the last of evening, the last one of the twenty-two miles, on the old white mare which was the last of that stable which McCaslin remembered, the two old men riding double up to the sister's door, the one wearing his fox-horn on its braided deerhide thong and the other carrying the burlap parcel wrapped in a shirt, the tawny wax-daubed shapeless lump sitting again and on an almost identical shelf and his uncle holding the half-opened door now, his hand not only on the knob but one foot against it and the key waiting in the other hand, the face urgent and still not baffled but still and even indomitably not very amazed and himself standing in the half-opened door looking quietly up at the burlap shape, become almost three times its original height and a good half less than its original thickness, and turning away, and he would remember not his mother's look this time nor yet Tennie's inscrutable expression but McCaslin's dark and aquiline face grave insufferable and bemused:

then one night they waked him and fetched him still half-asleep into the lamp light, the smell of medicine which was familiar by now in that room and the smell of something else which he had not smelled before and knew at once and would never forget, the pillow, the worn and ravaged face from which looked out still the boy innocent and immortal and amazed and urgent, looking at him and trying to tell him until McCaslin moved and leaned over the bed and drew from the top of the night shirt the big iron key on the greasy cord which suspended it, the eyes saying Yes Yes Yes now, and cut the cord and unlocked the closet and brought the parcel to the bed, the eyes still trying to tell him even when he took the parcel so that was still not it, the hands still clinging to the parcel even while relinquishing it, the eyes more urgent than ever trying to tell him but they never did; and he was ten and his mother was dead too and McCaslin said, 'You are almost half-way now. You might as well open it:' and he: 'No. He said twenty-one:' and he was twenty-one and McCaslin shifted the bright lamp to the center of the cleared dining-room table and set the parcel beside it and laid his open knife beside the parcel and stood back with that expression of old grave intolerant and repudiating and he lifted it, the burlap lump which fifteen years ago had changed its shape completely overnight, which shaken gave forth a thin weightless not-quite-musical curiously muffled clatter, the bright knife-blade hunting amid the mazed intricacy of string, the knobby gouts of wax bearing his uncle's Beauchamp seal rattling onto the table's polished top and, standing amid the collapse of burlap folds, the unstained tin coffee-pot still brand new, the handful of copper coins and now he knew what had given them the muffled sound: a collection of minutely folded scraps of paper sufficient almost for a rat's nest, of good linen bond, of the crude ruled paper such as Negroes use, of raggedly-torn ledger-pages and the margins of newspapers and once the paper label from a new pair of overalls all dated and all signed, beginning with the first one not six months after they had watched him seal the silver cup into the burlap on this same table in this same room by the light even of this same lamp almost twenty-one years ago:

I owe my Nephew Isaac Beauchamp McCaslin five (5) pieces Gold which, I,O.U constitutes My note of hand with Interest at 5 percent.

Hubert Fitz-Hubert Beauchamp

at Warwick 27 Nov 1867

and he: 'Anyway he called it Warwick:' once at least, even if no more. But there was more:

Isaac 24 Dec 1867 I.O.U. 2 pieces Gold H.Fh.B.
I.O.U. Isaac 1 piece Gold 1 Jan 1868 H.Fh.B.

then five again then three then one then one then a long time and what dream, what dreamed splendid recoup, not of any injury or betrayal of trust because it had been merely a loan: nay, a partnership:

I.O.U. Beauchamp McCaslin or his heirs twenty-five (25) pieces Gold This & All preceeding constituting My notes of hand at twenty (20) percentum compounded annually. This date of 19th January 1873

Beauchamp

no location save that in time and signed by the single not name but word as the old proud earl himself might have scrawled Nevile:[9] and that made forty-three and he could not remember himself of course but the legend had it at fifty, which balanced: one: then one: then one: then one and then the last three and then the last chit, dated after he came to live in the house with them and written in the shaky hand not of a beaten old man because he had never been beaten to know it but of a tired old man maybe and even at that tired only on the outside and still indomitable, the simplicity of the last one the simplicity not of resignation but merely of amazement, like a simple comment or remark, and not very much of that:

One silver cup. Hubert Beauchamp

and McCaslin: 'So you have plenty of coppers anyway. But they are still not old enough yet to be either rarities or heirlooms. So you will have to take the money:' except that he didn't hear McCaslin, standing quietly beside the table and looking peacefully at the coffee-pot and the pot sitting one night later on the mantel above what was not even a fireplace in the little cramped ice-like room in Jefferson as McCaslin tossed the folded banknotes onto the bed and, still standing (there was nowhere to sit save on the bed) did not even remove his hat and overcoat: and he

'As a loan. From you. This one:' and McCaslin

'You can't. I have no money that I can lend to you. And you will have to go to the bank and get it next month because I won't bring it to you:' and he could not hear McCaslin now either, looking peacefully at McCaslin, his kinsman, his father almost yet no kin now as, at the last, even fathers and sons are no kin: and he

'It's seventeen miles, horseback and in the cold. We could both sleep here:' and McCaslin

'Why should I sleep here in my house when you won't sleep

9. Richard Neville, earl of Warwick (1428–1471), who inherited the earldom through marriage to Anne de Beauchamp.

yonder in yours?' and gone, and he looking at the bright rustless unstained tin and thinking, and not for the first time, how much it takes to compound a man (Isaac McCaslin for instance) and of the devious intricate choosing yet unerring path that man's (Isaac McCaslin's for instance) spirit takes among all that mass to make him at last what he is to be, not only to the astonishment of them (the ones who sired the McCaslin who sired his father and Uncle Buddy and their sister, and the ones who sired the Beauchamp who sired his Uncle Hubert and his Uncle Hubert's sister) who believed they had shaped him, but to Isaac McCaslin too

as a loan and used it though he would not have had to: Major de Spain offered him a room in his house as long as he wanted it and asked nor would ever ask any question, and his old General Compson more than that, to take him into his own room, to sleep in half of his own bed and more than Major de Spain because he told him baldly why: 'You sleep with me and before this winter is out, I'll know the reason. You'll tell me. Because I don't believe you just quit. It looks like you just quit but I have watched you in the woods too much and I don't believe you just quit even if it does look damn like it:' using it as a loan, paid his board and rent for a month and bought the tools, not simply because he was good with his hands because he had intended to use his hands and it could have been with horses, and not in mere static and hopeful emulation of the Nazarene,[1] as the young gambler buys a spotted shirt because the old gambler won in one yesterday, but (without the arrogance of false humility and without the false humbleness of pride, who intended to earn his bread, didn't especially want to earn it but had to earn it and for more than just bread) because if the Nazarene had found carpentering good for the life and ends He had assumed and elected to serve, it would be all right too for Isaac McCaslin even though Isaac McCaslin's ends, although simple enough in their apparent motivation, were and would be always incomprehensible to him, and his life, invincible enough in its needs, if he could have helped himself, not being the Nazarene, he would not have chosen it: and paid it back. He had forgotten the thirty dollars which McCaslin put into the bank in his name each month, fetched it in to him and flung it onto the bed that first one time but no more; he had a partner now or rather he was the partner: a blasphemous profane clever old dipsomaniac who had built blockade-runners in Charleston in '62 and '63 and had been a ship's carpenter since and appeared in Jefferson two years ago, nobody knew from where nor why, and spent a good part of his time since recovering from delirium tremens in the jail; they had put a new roof on the stable of the bank's president and (the old man in jail again still

1. Jesus of Nazareth.

celebrating that job) he went to the bank to collect for it and the president said, 'I should borrow from you instead of paying you:' and it had been seven months now and he remembered for the first time, two-hundred-and-ten dollars, and this was the first job of any size and when he left the bank the account stood at two-twenty, two-forty to balance, only twenty dollars more to go, then it did balance though by then the total had increased to three hundred and thirty and he said, 'I will transfer it now:' and the president said, 'I can't do that. McCaslin told me not to. Haven't you got another initial you could use and open another account?' but that was all right, the coins the silver and the bills as they accumulated knotted into a handkerchief and the coffee-pot wrapped in an old shirt as when Tennie's great-grandfather had fetched it from Warwick eighteen years ago, in the bottom of the iron-bound trunk which old Carothers had brought from Carolina and his landlady said, 'Not even a lock! And you don't even lock your door, not even when you leave!' and himself looking at her as peacefully as he had looked at McCaslin that first night in this same room, no kin to him at all yet more than kin as those who serve you even for pay are your kin and those who injure you are more than brother or wife

and he had the wife now; got the old man out of jail and fetched him to the rented room and sobered him by superior strength, did not even remove his own shoes for twenty-four hours, got him up and got food into him and they built the barn this time from the ground up and he married her: an only child, a small girl yet curiously bigger than she seemed at first, solider perhaps, with dark eyes and a passionate heart-shaped face, who had time even on that farm to watch most of the day while he sawed timbers to the old man's measurements: and she: 'Papa told me about you. That farm is really yours, isn't it?' and he

'And McCaslin's:' and she

'Was there a will leaving half of it to him?' and he

'There didn't need to be a will. His grandmother was my father's sister. We were the same as brothers:' and she

'You are the same as second cousins and that's all you ever will be. But I don't suppose it matters:' and they were married, they were married and it was the new country, his heritage too as it was the heritage of all, out of the earth, beyond the earth yet of the earth because his too was of the earth's long chronicle, his too because each must share with another in order to come into it, and in the sharing they become one: for that while, one: for that while at least, one: indivisible, that while at least irrevocable and unrecoverable, living in a rented room still but for just a little while and that room wall-less and topless and floorless in glory for him to leave each morning and return to at night; her father already owned the lot in town and furnished the material and he and his partner would build it, her dowry from one:

her wedding-present from three, she not to know it until the bungalow was finished and ready to be moved into and he never know who told her, not her father and not his partner and not even in drink though for a while he believed that, himself coming home from work and just time to wash and rest a moment before going down to supper, entering no rented cubicle since it would still partake of glory even after they would have grown old and lost it: and he saw her face then, just before she spoke: 'Sit down:' the two of them sitting on the bed's edge, not even touching yet, her face strained and terrible, her voice a passionate and expiring whisper of immeasurable promise: 'I love you. You know I love you. When are we going to move?' and he

'I didn't—I didn't know—Who told you—' the hot fierce palm clapped over his mouth, crushing his lips into his teeth, the fierce curve of fingers digging into his cheek and only the palm slacked off enough for him to answer:

'The farm. Our farm. Your farm:' and he

'I——' then the hand again, finger and palm, the whole enveloping weight of her although she still was not touching him save the hand, the voice: 'No! No!' and the fingers themselves seeming to follow through the cheek the impulse to speech as it died in his mouth, then the whisper, the breath again, of love and of incredible promise, the palm slackening again to let him answer:

'When?' and he

'——' then she was gone, the hand too, standing, her back to him and her head bent, the voice so calm now that for an instant it seemed no voice of hers that he ever remembered: 'Stand up and turn your back and shut your eyes:' and repeated before he understood and stood himself with his eyes shut and heard the bell ring for supper below stairs, and the calm voice again: 'Lock the door:' and he did so and leaned his forehead against the cold wood, his eyes closed, hearing his heart and the sound he had begun to hear before he moved until it ceased and the bell rang again below stairs and he knew it was time for them this time, and he heard the bed and turned and he had never seen her naked before, he had asked her to once, and why: that he wanted to see her naked because he loved her and he wanted to see her looking at him naked because he loved her, but after that he never mentioned it again, even turning his face when she put the nightgown on over her dress to undress at night and putting the dress on over the gown to remove it in the morning, and she would not let him get into bed beside her until the lamp was out and even in the heat of summer she would draw the sheet up over them both before she would let him turn to her: and the landlady came up the stairs up the hall and rapped on the door and then called their names but she didn't move, lying still on the bed outside the covers, her face turned away on the pillow, listening to nothing, thinking of nothing, not of him anyway he thought: then the landlady went away and she said, "Take off your clothes:' her head still turned away, looking at nothing, thinking of nothing, waiting for nothing, not even him, her hand moving as though with volition and vision of its own, catching his wrist at the exact moment when he paused beside the bed so that he never paused but merely changed the direction of moving, downward now, the hand drawing him and she moved at last, shifted, a movement one single complete inherent not practiced and one time older than man, looking at him now, drawing him still downward with the one hand down and down and he neither saw nor felt it shift, palm flat against his chest now and holding him away with the same apparent lack of any effort or any need for strength, and not looking at him now, she didn't need to, the chaste woman, the wife, already looked upon all the men who ever rutted and now her whole body had changed, altered, he had never seen it but once and now it was not even the one he had seen but composite of all woman-flesh since man that ever of its own will reclined on its back and opened, and out of it somewhere, without any movement of lips even, the dying and invincible whisper: 'Promise:' and he

'Promise?'

'The farm.' He moved. He had moved, the hand shifting from his chest once more to his wrist, grasping it, the arm still lax and only the light increasing pressure of the fingers as though arm and hand were a piece of wire cable with one looped end, only the hand tightening as he pulled against it. 'No,' he said. 'No:' and she was not looking at him still but not like the other, but still the hand: "No, I tell you. I won't. I can't. Never:' and still the hand and he said, for the last time, he tried to speak clearly and he knew it was still gently and he thought, *She already knows more than I with all the man-listening in camps where there was nothing to read ever even heard of. They are born already bored with what a boy approaches only at fourteen and fifteen with blundering and aghast trembling:* 'I can't. Not ever. Remember:' and still the steady and invincible hand and he said 'Yes' and he thought, *She is lost. She was born lost. We were all born lost* then he stopped thinking and even saying Yes, it was like nothing he had ever dreamed, let alone heard in mere man-talking until after a no-time he returned and lay spent on the insatiate immemorial beach and again with a movement one time more older than man she turned and freed herself and on their wedding night she had cried and he thought she was crying now at first, into the tossed and wadded pillow, the voice coming from somewhere between the pillow and the cachinnation: 'And that's all. That's all from me. If this don't get you that son you talk about, it won't be mine:' lying on her side, her back to the empty rented room, laughing and laughing

V

He went back to the camp one more time before the lumber company moved in and began to cut the timber. Major de Spain himself never saw it again. But he made them welcome to use the house and hunt the land whenever they liked, and in the winter following the last hunt when Sam Fathers and Lion died, General Compson and Walter Ewell invented a plan to corporate themselves, the old group, into a club and lease the camp and the hunting privileges of the woods—an invention doubtless of the somewhat childish old General but actually worthy of Boon Hogganbeck himself. Even the boy, listening, recognizing it for the subterfuge it was: to change the leopard's spots when they could not alter the leopard, a baseless and illusory hope to which even McCaslin seemed to subscribe for a while, that once they had persuaded Major de Spain to return to the camp he might revoke himself, which even the boy knew he would not do. And he did not. The boy never knew what occurred when Major de Spain declined. He was not present when the subject was broached and McCaslin never told him. But when June came and the time for the double birthday celebration there was no mention of it and when November came no one spoke of using Major de Spain's house and he never knew whether or not Major de Spain knew they were going on the hunt though without doubt old Ash probably told him: he and McCaslin and General Compson (and that one was the General's last hunt too) and Walter and Boon and Tennie's Jim and old Ash loaded two wagons and drove two days and almost forty miles beyond any country the boy had ever seen before and lived in tents for the two weeks. And the next spring they heard (not from Major de Spain) that he had sold the timber-rights to a Memphis lumber company and in June the boy came to town with McCaslin one Saturday and went to Major de Spain's office—the big, airy, book-lined, second-storey room with windows at one end opening upon the shabby hinder purlieus of stores and at the other a door giving onto the railed balcony above the Square, with its curtained alcove where sat a cedar water-bucket and a sugar-bowl and spoon and tumbler and a wicker-covered demijohn of whiskey, and the bamboo-and-paper punkah[2] swinging back and forth above the desk while old Ash in a tilted chair beside the entrance pulled the cord.

"Of course," Major de Spain said. "Ash will probably like to get off in the woods himself for a while, where he won't have to eat Daisy's cooking. Complain about it, anyway. Are you going to take anybody with you?"

"No sir," he said. "I thought that maybe Boon—" For six months

2. Fan suspended from the ceiling, operated by tugging on an attached rope. *Demijohn:* Large, wicker-covered bottle.

now Boon had been town-marshal at Hoke's; Major de Spain had compounded with the lumber company—or perhaps compromised was closer, since it was the lumber company who had decided that Boon might be better as a town-marshal than head of a logging gang.

"Yes," Major de Spain said. "I'll wire him today. He can meet you at Hoke's. I'll send Ash on by the train and they can take some food in and all you will have to do will be to mount your horse and ride over."

"Yes sir," he said. "Thank you." And he heard his voice again. He didn't know he was going to say it yet he did know, he had known it all the time: "Maybe if you . . ." His voice died. It was stopped, he never knew how because Major de Spain did not speak and it was not until his voice ceased that Major de Spain moved, turned back to the desk and the papers spread on it and even that without moving because he was sitting at the desk with a paper in his hand when the boy entered, the boy standing there looking down at the short plumpish gray-haired man in sober fine broadcloth and an immaculate glazed shirt whom he was used to seeing in boots and muddy corduroy, unshaven, sitting the shaggy powerful long-hocked mare with the worn Winchester carbine across the saddlebow and the great blue dog standing motionless as bronze at the stirrup, the two of them in that last year and to the boy anyway coming to resemble one another somehow as two people competent for love or for business who have been in love or in business together for a long time sometimes do. Major de Spain did not look up again.

"No. I will be too busy. But good luck to you. If you have it, you might bring me a young squirrel."

"Yes sir," he said. "I will."

He rode his mare, the three-year-old filly he had bred and raised and broken himself. He left home a little after midnight and six hours later, without even having sweated her, he rode into Hoke's, the tiny log-line junction which he had always thought of as Major de Spain's property too although Major de Spain had merely sold the company (and that many years ago) the land on which the sidetracks and loading-platforms and the commissary store stood, and looked about in shocked and grieved amazement even though he had had forewarning and had believed himself prepared: a new planing-mill already half completed which would cover two or three acres and what looked like miles and miles of stacked steel rails red with the light bright rust of newness and of piled crossties sharp with creosote, and wire corrals and feeding-troughs for two hundred mules at least and the tents for the men who drove them; so that he arranged for the care and stabling of his mare as rapidly as he could and did not look any more, mounted into the log-train caboose with his gun and climbed into the cupola and looked no more save toward the wall of wilderness ahead within which he would be able to hide himself from it once more anyway.

Then the little locomotive shrieked and began to move: a rapid churning of exhaust, a lethargic deliberate clashing of slack couplings travelling backward along the train, the exhaust changing to the deep slow clapping bites of power as the caboose too began to move and from the cupola he watched the train's head complete the first and only curve in the entire line's length and vanish into the wilderness, dragging its length of train behind it so that it resembled a small dingy harmless snake vanishing into weeds, drawing him with it too until soon it ran once more at its maximum clattering speed between the twin walls of unaxed wilderness as of old. It had been harmless once. Not five years ago Walter Ewell had shot a six-point buck from this same moving caboose, and there was the story of the half-grown bear: the train's first trip in to the cutting thirty miles away, the bear between the rails, its rear end elevated like that of a playing puppy while it dug to see what sort of ants or bugs they might contain or perhaps just to examine the curious symmetrical squared barkless logs which had appeared apparently from nowhere in one endless mathematical line overnight, still digging until the driver on the braked engine not fifty feet away blew the whistle at it, whereupon it broke frantically and took the first tree it came to: an ash sapling not much bigger than a man's thigh and climbed as high as it could and clung there, its head ducked between its arms as a man (a woman perhaps) might have done while the brakeman threw chunks of ballast at it, and when the engine returned three hours later with the first load of outbound logs the bear was halfway down the tree and once more scrambled back up as high as it could and clung again while the train passed and was still there when the engine went in again in the afternoon and still there when it came back out at dusk; and Boon had been in Hoke's with the wagon after a barrel of flour that noon when the train-crew told about it and Boon and Ash, both twenty years younger then, sat under the tree all that night to keep anybody from shooting it and the next morning Major de Spain had the log-train held at Hoke's and just before sundown on the second day, with not only Boon and Ash but Major de Spain and General Compson and Walter and McCaslin, twelve then, watching, it came down the tree after almost thirty-six hours without even water and McCaslin told him how for a minute they thought it was going to stop right there at the barrow-pit where they were standing and drink, how it looked at the water and paused and looked at them and at the water again, but did not, gone, running, as bears run, the two sets of feet, front and back, tracking two separate though parallel courses.

It had been harmless then. They would hear the passing log-train sometimes from the camp; sometimes, because nobody bothered to listen for it or not. They would hear it going in, running light and fast, the light clatter of the trucks, the exhaust of the diminutive locomotive and its shrill peanut-parcher whistle flung for one petty moment and absorbed by the brooding and inattentive wilderness without even an echo. They would hear it going out, loaded, not quite so fast now yet giving its frantic and toylike illusion of crawling speed, not whistling now to conserve steam, flinging its bitten laboring miniature puffing into the immemorial woodsface with frantic and bootless vainglory, empty and noisy and puerile, carrying to no destination or purpose sticks which left nowhere any scar or stump, as the child's toy loads and transports and unloads its dead sand and rushes back for more, tireless and unceasing and rapid yet never quite so fast as the hand which plays with it moves the toy burden back to load the toy again. But it was different now. It was the same train, engine cars and caboose, even the same enginemen brakeman and conductor to whom Boon, drunk then sober then drunk again then fairly sober once more all in the space of fourteen hours, had bragged that day two years ago about what they were going to do to Old Ben tomorrow, running with its same illusion of frantic rapidity between the same twin walls of impenetrable and impervious woods, passing the old landmarks, the old game crossings over which he had trailed bucks wounded and not wounded and more than once seen them, anything but wounded, bolt out of the woods and up and across the embankment which bore the rails and ties then down and into the woods again as the earth-bound supposedly move but crossing as arrows travel, groundless, elongated, three times its actual length and even paler, different in color, as if there were a point between immobility and absolute motion where even mass chemically altered, changing without pain or agony not only in bulk and shape but in color too, approaching the color of wind, yet this time it was as though the train (and not only the train but himself, not only his vision which had seen it and his memory which remembered it but his clothes too, as garments carry back into the clean edgeless blowing of air the lingering effluvium of a sick-room or of death) had brought with it into the doomed wilderness, even before the actual axe, the shadow and portent of the new mill not even finished yet and the rails and ties which were not even laid; and he knew now what he had known as soon as he saw Hoke's this morning but had not yet thought into words: why Major de Spain had not come back, and that after this time he himself, who had had to see it one time other, would return no more.

Now they were near. He knew it before the engine-driver whistled to warn him. Then he saw Ash and the wagon, the reins without doubt wrapped once more about the brake-lever as within the boy's own memory Major de Spain had been forbidding him for eight years to do, the train slowing, the slackened couplings jolting and clashing again from car to car, the caboose slowing past the wagon as he swung down with his gun, the conductor leaning out above him to signal the engine, the caboose still slowing, creeping, although the engine's exhaust was already slatting in mounting tempo against the unechoing wilderness, the crashing of drawbars once more travelling backward along the train, the caboose picking up speed at last. Then it was gone. It had not been. He could no longer hear it. The wilderness soared, musing, inattentive, myriad, eternal, green; older than any mill-shed, longer than any spur-line. "Mr. Boon here yet?" he said.

"He beat me in," Ash said. "Had the wagon loaded and ready for me at Hoke's yistiddy when I got there and setting on the front steps at camp last night when I got in. He already been in the woods since fo daylight this morning. Said he gwine up to the Gum tree and for you to hunt up that way and meet him." He knew where that was: a single big sweet-gum just outside the woods, in an old clearing; if you crept up to it very quietly this time of year and then ran suddenly into the clearing, sometimes you caught as many as a dozen squirrels in it, trapped, since there was no other tree near they could jump to. So he didn't get into the wagon at all.

"I will," he said.

"I figured you would," Ash said. "I fotch you a box of shells." He passed the shells down and began to unwrap the lines from the brake-pole.

"How many times up to now do you reckon Major has told you not to do that?" the boy said.

"Do which?" Ash said. Then he said: "And tell Boon Hogganbeck dinner gonter be on the table in a hour and if yawl want any to come on and eat it."

"In an hour?" he said. "It ain't nine o'clock yet." He drew out his watch and extended it face-toward Ash. "Look." Ash didn't even look at the watch.

"That's town time. You ain't in town now. You in the woods."

"Look at the sun then."

"Nemmine the sun too," Ash said. "If you and Boon Hogganbeck want any dinner, you better come on in and get it when I tole you. I aim to get done in that kitchen because I got my wood to chop. And watch your feet. They're crawling."[3]

"I will," he said.

Then he was in the woods, not alone but solitary; the solitude closed about him, green with summer. They did not change, and, timeless, would not, any more than would the green of summer and

3. I.e., there are many snakes in the woods.

the fire and rain of fall and the iron cold and sometimes even snow

the day, the morning when he killed the buck and Sam marked his face with its hot blood, they returned to camp and he remembered old Ash's blinking and disgruntled and even outraged disbelief until at last McCaslin had had to affirm the fact that he had really killed it: and that night Ash sat snarling and unapproachable behind the stove so that Tennie's Jim had to serve the supper and waked them with breakfast already on the table the next morning and it was only half-past one o'clock and at last out of Major de Spain's angry cursing and Ash's snarling and sullen rejoinders the fact emerged that Ash not only wanted to go into the woods and shoot a deer also but he intended to and Major de Spain said, 'By God, if we don't let him we will probably have to do the cooking from now on: and Walter Ewell said, 'Or get up at midnight to eat what Ash cooks:' and since he had already killed his buck for this hunt and was not to shoot again unless they needed meat, he offered his gun to Ash until Major de Spain took command and allotted that gun to Boon for the day and gave Boon's unpredictable pump gun to Ash, with two buckshot shells but Ash said, 'I got shells:' and showed them, four: one buck, one of number three shot for rabbits, two of bird-shot and told one by one their history and their origin and he remembered not Ash's face alone but Major de Spain's and Walter's and General Compson's too, and Ash's voice: 'Shoot? In course they'll shoot! Genl Cawmpson guv me this un'—the buckshot—'right outen the same gun he kilt that big buck with eight years ago. And this un'—it was the rabbit shell: triumphantly—'is oldern thisyer boy!' And that morning he loaded the gun himself, reversing the order: the bird-shot, the rabbit, then the buck so that the buck-shot would feed first into the chamber, and himself without a gun, he and Ash walked beside Major de Spain's and Tennie's Jim's horses and the dogs (that was the snow) until they cast and struck, the sweet strong cries ringing away into the muffled falling air and gone almost immediately, as if the constant and unmurmuring flakes had already buried even the unformed echoes beneath their myriad and weightless falling, Major de Spain and Tennie's Jim gone too, whooping on into the woods; and then it was all right, he knew as plainly as if Ash had told him that Ash had now hunted his deer and that even his tender years had been forgiven for having killed one, and they turned back toward home through the falling snow—that is, Ash said, 'Now whut?' and he said. 'This way'—himself in front because, although they were less than a mile from camp, he knew that Ash, who had spent two weeks of his life in the camp each year for the last twenty, had no idea whatever where they were, until quite soon the manner in which Ash carried Boon's gun was making him a good deal more than just nervous and he made Ash walk in front, striding on, talking now, an old man's garrulous mono-

logue beginning with where he was at the moment then of the woods and of camping in the woods and of eating in camps then of eating then of cooking it and of his wife's cooking then briefly of his old wife and almost at once and at length of a new light-colored woman who nursed next door to Major de Spain's and if she didn't watch out who she was switching her tail at he would show her how old was an old man or not if his wife just didn't watch him all the time, the two of them in a game trail through a dense brake of cane and brier which would bring them out within a quarter-mile of camp, approaching a big fallen tree-trunk lying athwart the path and just as Ash, still talking, was about to step over it the bear, the yearling, rose suddenly beyond the log, sitting up, its forearms against its chest and its wrists limply arrested as if it had been surprised in the act of covering its face to pray: and after a certain time Ash's gun yawed jerkily up and he said, 'You haven't got a shell in the barrel yet. Pump it:' but the gun already snicked and he said, 'Pump it. You haven't got a shell in the barrel yet:' and Ash pumped the action[4] and in a certain time the gun steadied again and snicked and he said, 'Pump it:' and watched the buckshot shell jerk, spinning heavily, into the cane. This is the rabbit shot: he thought and the gun snicked and he thought: The next is bird-shot: and he didn't have to say Pump it; he cried, 'Don't shoot! Don't shoot!' but that was already too late too, the light dry vicious snick! before he could speak and the bear turned and dropped to all-fours and then was gone and there was only the log, the cane, the velvet and constant snow and Ash said, 'Now whut?' and he said, 'This way. Come on:' and began to back away down the path and Ash said, 'I got to find my shells:' and he said, 'Goddamn it, goddamn it, come on:' but Ash leaned the gun against the log and returned and stooped and fumbled among the cane roots until he came back and stooped and found the shells and they rose and at that moment the gun, untouched, leaning against the log six feet away and for that while even forgotten by both of them, roared, bellowed and flamed, and ceased: and he carried it now, pumped out the last mummified shell and gave that one also to Ash and, the action still open, himself carried the gun until he stood it in the corner behind Boon's bed at the camp

—; summer, and fall, and snow, and wet and sap-rife spring in their ordered immortal sequence, the deathless and immemorial phases of the mother who had shaped him if any had toward the man he almost was, mother and father both to the old man born of a Negro slave and a Chickasaw chief who had been his spirit's father if any had, whom he had revered and harkened to and loved and lost and grieved; and he would marry someday and they too would own for their brief while

4. The part of the gun that locks the shell in the barrel.

that brief unsubstanced glory which inherently of itself cannot last and hence why glory: and they would, might, carry even the remembrance of it into the time when flesh no longer talks to flesh because memory at least does last: but still the woods would be his mistress and his wife.

He was not going toward the Gum Tree. Actually he was getting farther from it. Time was and not so long ago either when he would not have been allowed here without someone with him, and a little later, when he had begun to learn how much he did not know, he would not have dared be here without someone with him, and later still, beginning to ascertain, even if only dimly, the limits of what he did not know, he could have attempted and carried it through with a compass, not because of any increased belief in himself but because McCaslin and Major de Spain and Walter and General Compson too had taught him at last to believe the compass regardless of what it seemed to state. Now he did not even use the compass but merely the sun and that only subconsciously, yet he could have taken a scaled map and plotted at any time to within a hundred feet of where he actually was; and sure enough, at almost the exact moment when he expected it, the earth began to rise faintly, he passed one of the four concrete markers set down by the lumber company's surveyor to establish the four corners of the plot which Major de Spain had reserved out of the sale, then he stood on the crest of the knoll itself, the four corner-markers all visible now, blanched still even beneath the winter's weathering, lifeless and shockingly alien in that place where dissolution itself was a seething turmoil of ejaculation tumescence conception and birth, and death did not even exist. After two winters' blanketings of leaves and the flood-waters of two springs, there was no trace of the two graves any more at all. But those who would have come this far to find them would not need headstones but would have found them as Sam Fathers himself had taught him to find such: by bearings on trees: and did, almost the first thrust of the hunting knife finding (but only to see if it was still there) the round tin box manufactured for axle-grease and containing now Old Ben's dried mutilated paw, resting above Lion's bones.

He didn't disturb it. He didn't even look for the other grave where he and McCaslin and Major de Spain and Boon had laid Sam's body, along with his hunting horn and his knife and his tobacco-pipe, that Sunday morning two years ago; he didn't have to. He had stepped over it, perhaps on it. But that was all right. *He probably knew I was in the woods this morning long before I got here,* he thought, going on to the tree which had supported one end of the platform where Sam lay when McCaslin and Major de Spain found them—the tree, the other axle-grease tin nailed to the trunk, but weathered, rusted, alien too yet healed already into the wilderness' concordant generality, raising no tuneless note, and empty, long since empty of the food and tobacco he had put into it that day, as empty of that as it would presently be of this which he drew from his pocket—the twist of tobacco, the new bandanna handkerchief, the small paper sack of the peppermint candy which Sam had used to love; that gone too, almost before he had turned his back, not vanished but merely translated into the myriad life which printed the dark mold of these secret and sunless places with delicate fairy tracks; which, breathing and biding and immobile, watched him from beyond every twig and leaf until he moved, moving again, walking on; he had not stopped, he had only paused, quitting the knoll which was no abode of the dead because there was no death, not Lion and not Sam: not held fast in earth but free in earth and not in earth but of earth, myriad yet undiffused of every myriad part, leaf and twig and particle, air and sun and rain and dew and night, acorn oak and leaf and acorn again, dark and dawn and dark and dawn again in their immutable progression, and, being myriad, one: and Old Ben too. Old Ben too; they would give him his paw back even, certainly they would give him his paw back: then the long challenge and the long chase, no heart to be driven and outraged, no flesh to be mauled and bled—Even as he froze himself, he seemed to hear Ash's parting admonition. He could even hear the voice as he froze, immobile, one foot just taking his weight, the toe of the other just lifted behind him, not breathing, feeling again and as always the sharp shocking inrush from when Isaac McCaslin long yet was not, and so it was fear all right but not fright as he looked down at it. It had not coiled yet and the buzzer had not sounded either, only one thick rapid contraction, one loop cast sideways as though merely for purchase from which the raised head might start slightly backward, not in fright either, not in threat quite yet, more than six feet of it, the head raised higher than his knee and less than his knee's length away, and old, the once-bright markings of its youth dulled now to a monotone concordant too with the wilderness it crawled and lurked: the old one, the ancient and accursed about the earth, fatal and solitary and he could smell it now: the thin sick smell of rotting cucumbers and something else which had no name, evocative of all knowledge and an old weariness and of pariah-hood and of death. At last it moved. Not the head. The elevation of the head did not change as it began to glide away from him, moving erect yet off the perpendicular as if the head and that elevated third were complete and all: an entity walking on two feet and free of all laws of mass and balance, and should have been because even now he could not quite believe that all that shift and flow of shadow behind that walking head could have been one snake: going and then gone; he put the other foot down at last and didn't know it, standing with one hand raised as Sam had stood that afternoon six years ago when Sam led him into the wilderness and showed him and he ceased to be a child, speaking the old tongue which Sam had spoken that day without premeditation either: "Chief," he said: "Grandfather."

He couldn't tell when he first began to hear the sound, because when he became aware of it, it seemed to him that he had been already hearing it for several seconds—a sound as though someone were hammering a gun-barrel against a piece of railroad iron, a sound loud and heavy and not rapid yet with something frenzied about it, as if the hammerer were not only a strong man and an earnest one but a little hysterical too. Yet it couldn't be on the log-line because, although the track lay in that direction, it was at least two miles from him and this sound was not three hundred yards away. But even as he thought that, he realized where the sound must be coming from: whoever the man was and whatever he was doing, he was somewhere near the edge of the clearing where the Gum Tree was and where he was to meet Boon. So far, he had been hunting as he advanced, moving slowly and quietly and watching the ground and the trees both. Now he went on, his gun unloaded and the barrel slanted up and back to facilitate its passage through brier and undergrowth, approaching as it grew louder and louder that steady savage somehow queerly hysterical beating of metal on metal, emerging from the woods, into the old clearing, with the solitary gum tree directly before him. At first glance the tree seemed to be alive with frantic squirrels. There appeared to be forty or fifty of them leaping and darting from branch to branch until the whole tree had become one green maelstrom of mad leaves, while from time to time, singly or in twos and threes, squirrels would dart down the trunk then whirl without stopping and rush back up again as though sucked violently back by the vacuum of their fellows' frenzied vortex. Then he saw Boon, sitting, his back against the trunk, his head bent, hammering furiously at something on his lap. What he hammered with was the barrel of his dismembered gun, what he hammered at was the breech of it. The rest of the gun lay scattered about him in a half-dozen pieces while he bent over the piece on his lap his scarlet and streaming walnut face, hammering the disjointed barrel against the gun-breech with the frantic abandon of a madman. He didn't even look up to see who it was. Still hammering, he merely shouted back at the boy in a hoarse strangled voice:

"Get out of here! Don't touch them! Don't touch a one of them! They're mine!"

---

1. What virtues are developed in Isaac McCaslin by his apprenticeship as a hunter?

2. Why can he not get even a glimpse of Old Ben until he has put aside his gun, compass, and watch?
3. What forms the bond between Boon Hogganbeck and the dog Lion?
4. What is the difference between Isaac McCaslin's devotion to the wilderness and that of the older white men who love it?
5. Why is it Boon, who is so inept with firearms, who kills Old Ben?
6. What is signified by the time and circumstances of Sam Fathers' death?
7. What basic qualities in each put Isaac and his cousin McCaslin at odds in their argument about the ownership of land?
8. Is Isaac successful in his attempt to renounce what he considers to be the curse on his heritage? How is his marriage affected by his determination to seek justice?
9. What does Boon mean when he says of the squirrels in the Gum Tree, "They're mine"?
10. Discuss the relation between Section IV and the rest of the story.
11. What is gained or lost by the lack of clarity and the obscure allusions in some passages?
12. What is the relative importance of changes brought about by the outcome of the Civil War? Is it the prime historical event the characters must deal with?

F. Scott Fitzgerald

Fitzgerald (1896–1940) was born in St. Paul, Minnesota. After a glamorous undergraduate career at Princeton, he entered the Army as a second lieutenant and while he was in training camp met the beautiful girl who was to become his wife. He married Zelda Sayre as his literary career got off to a meteoric start in 1920. Through the 1920's when money seemed plentiful and postwar morality encouraged a reckless pursuit of happiness, he and Zelda traveled with a well-heeled crowd in Europe and New York, acting out the glamorous life-style he wrote of in his most popular magazine fiction. He was a spokesman for the so-called Jazz Age, setting a personal as well as literary example for a generation whose first commandment was: Do what you will. The tempo of his life slackened as his marriage was shredded by Zelda's insanity and his own self-destructive alcoholism. He fell from favor as a writer when the indulgent decade of his triumph went down under the impact of a worldwide Depression. Through years of emotional and physical collapse he struggled to repair his life by writing for Hollywood—producing at the same time a series of stories that exposed his humiliations there. His last three novels, The Great Gatsby *(1925),* Tender Is the Night *(1934), and* The Last Tycoon *(1941), amplify the melancholy he discovered beneath the glitter of American-style success. In his pathetically candid book* The Crack-up *(1945) Fitzgerald documents the shattering of his personal ambitions. His stories were collected in* Flappers and Philosophers *(1921),* Tales of the Jazz Age *(1922),* All the Sad Young Men *(1926), and* Taps at Reveille *(1935).*

Babylon Revisited[1]

"And where's Mr. Campbell?" Charlie asked.

"Gone to Switzerland. Mr. Campbell's a pretty sick man, Mr. Wales."

"I'm sorry to hear that. And George Hardt?" Charlie inquired.

"Back in America, gone to work."

"And where is the Snow Bird?"

"He was in here last week. Anyway, his friend, Mr. Schaeffer, is in Paris."

1. The ancient city of Babylon is a symbol of orgiastic decadence.

Two familiar names from the long list of a year and a half ago. Charlie scribbled an address in his notebook and tore out the page.

"If you see Mr. Schaeffer, give him this," he said. "It's my brother-in-law's address. I haven't settled on a hotel yet."

He was not really disappointed to find Paris was so empty. But the stillness in the Ritz bar[2] was strange and portentous. It was not an American bar any more—he felt polite in it, and not as if he owned it. It had gone back into France. He felt the stillness from the moment he got out of the taxi and saw the doorman, usually in a frenzy of activity at this hour, gossiping with a *chasseur*[3] by the servants' entrance.

Passing through the corridor, he heard only a single, bored voice in the once-clamorous women's room. When he turned into the bar he traveled the twenty feet of green carpet with his eyes fixed straight ahead by old habit; and then, with his foot firmly on the rail, he turned and surveyed the room, encountering only a single pair of eyes that fluttered up from a newspaper in the corner. Charlie asked for the head barman, Paul, who in the latter days of the bull market[4] had come to work in his own custom-built car—disembarking, however, with due nicety at the nearest corner. But Paul was at his country house today and Alix giving him information.

"No, no more," Charlie said, "I'm going slow these days."

Alix congratulated him: "You were going pretty strong a couple of years ago."

"I'll stick to it all right," Charlie assured him. "I've stuck to it for over a year and a half now."

"How do you find conditions in America?"

"I haven't been to America for months. I'm in business in Prague, representing a couple of concerns there. They don't know about me down there."

Alix smiled.

"Remember the night of George Hardt's bachelor dinner here?" said Charlie. "By the way, what's become of Claude Fessenden?"

Alix lowered his voice confidentially: "He's in Paris, but he doesn't come here any more. Paul doesn't allow it. He ran up a bill of thirty thousand francs, charging all his drinks and his lunches, and usually his dinner, for more than a year. And when Paul finally told him he had to pay, he gave him a bad check."

Alix shook his head sadly.

"I don't understand it, such a dandy fellow. Now he's all bloated up—" He made a plump apple of his hands.

2. Hangout for wealthy and glamorous Americans. 3. Hotel servant who runs various errands.
4. The period of prosperity for players of the stock market that immediately preceded the crash of 1929 and beginning of the Great Depression.

Charlie watched a group of strident queens installing themselves in a corner.

"Nothing affects them," he thought. "Stocks rise and fall, people loaf or work, but they go on forever." The place oppressed him. He called for the dice and shook with Alix for the drink.

"Here for long, Mr. Wales?"

"I'm here for four or five days to see my little girl."

"Oh-h! You have a little girl?"

Outside, the fire-red, gas-blue, ghost-green signs shone smokily through the tranquil rain. It was late afternoon and the streets were in movement; the *bistros*[5] gleamed. At the corner of the Boulevard des Capucines he took a taxi. The Place de la Concorde moved by in pink majesty; they crossed the logical Seine, and Charlie felt the sudden provincial quality of the Left Bank.[6]

Charlie directed his taxi to the Avenue de l'Opera, which was out of his way. But he wanted to see the blue hour spread over the magnificent façade, and imagine that the cab horns, playing endlessly the first few bars of *Le Plus que Lent*,[7] were the trumpets of the Second Empire.[8] They were closing the iron grill in front of Brentano's Bookstore, and people were already at dinner behind the trim little bourgeois hedge of Duval's. He had never eaten at a really cheap restaurant in Paris. Five-course dinner, four francs fifty, eighteen cents, wine included. For some odd reason he wished that he had.

As they rolled on to the Left Bank and he felt its sudden provincialism, he thought, "I spoiled this city for myself. I didn't realize it, but the days came along one after another, and then two years were gone, and everything was gone, and I was gone."

He was thirty-five, and good to look at. The Irish mobility of his face was sobered by a deep wrinkle between his eyes. As he rang his brother-in-law's bell in the Rue Palatine, the wrinkle deepened till it pulled down his brows; he felt a cramping sensation in his belly. From behind the maid who opened the door darted a lovely little girl of nine who shrieked "Daddy!" and flew up, struggling like a fish, into his arms. She pulled his head around by one ear and set her cheek against his.

"My old pie," he said.

"Oh, daddy, daddy, daddy, daddy, dads, dads, dads!"

She drew him into the salon, where the family waited, a boy and a girl his daughter's age, his sister-in-law and her husband. He greeted Marion with his voice pitched carefully to avoid either feigned enthu-

5. Small cafés. 6. South side of the Seine River; site of the student quarter and in recent tradition the Bohemian part of Paris. 7. "Slower than Slow": refers to "La Plus que Lente," parodistic piano composition by Claude Debussy (1862–1918). 8. The Empire of Louis Napoleon of France, 1852–70. A period of bourgeois ostentation that seemed, in retrospect, glamorous.

siasm or dislike, but her response was more frankly tepid, though she minimized her expression of unalterable distrust by directing her regard toward his child. The two men clasped hands in a friendly way and Lincoln Peters rested his for a moment on Charlie's shoulder.

The room was warm and comfortably American. The three children moved intimately about, playing through the yellow oblongs that led to other rooms; the cheer of six o'clock spoke in the eager smacks of the fire and the sounds of French activity in the kitchen. But Charlie did not relax; his heart sat up rigidly in his body and he drew confidence from his daughter, who from time to time came close to him, holding in her arms the doll he had brought.

"Really extremely well," he declared in answer to Lincoln's question. "There's a lot of business there that isn't moving at all, but we're doing even better than ever. In fact, damn well. I'm bringing my sister over from America next month to keep house for me. My income last year was bigger than it was when I had money. You see, the Czechs——"

His boasting was for a specific purpose; but after a moment, seeing a faint restiveness in Lincoln's eye, he changed the subject:

"Those are fine children of yours, well brought up, good manners."

"We think Honoria's a great little girl too."

Marion Peters came back from the kitchen. She was a tall woman with worried eyes, who had once possessed a fresh American loveliness. Charlie had never been sensitive to it and was always surprised when people spoke of how pretty she had been. From the first there had been an instinctive antipathy between them.

"Well, how do you find Honoria?" she asked.

"Wonderful. I was astonished how much she's grown in ten months. All the children are looking well."

"We haven't had a doctor for a year. How do you like being back in Paris?"

"It seems very funny to see so few Americans around."

"I'm delighted," Marion said vehemently. "Now at least you can go into a store without their assuming you're a millionaire. We've suffered like everybody, but on the whole it's a good deal pleasanter."

"But it was nice while it lasted," Charlie said. "We were a sort of royalty, almost infallible, with a sort of magic around us. In the bar this afternoon"—he stumbled, seeing his mistake—"there wasn't a man I knew."

She looked at him keenly. "I should think you'd have had enough of bars."

"I only stayed a minute. I take one drink every afternoon, and no more."

"Don't you want a cocktail before dinner?" Lincoln asked.

"I take only one drink every afternoon, and I've had that."

"I hope you keep to it," said Marion.

Her dislike was evident in the coldness with which she spoke, but Charlie only smiled; he had larger plans. Her very aggressiveness gave him an advantage, and he knew enough to wait. He wanted them to initiate the discussion of what they knew had brought him to Paris.

At dinner he couldn't decide whether Honoria was most like him or her mother. Fortunate if she didn't combine the traits of both that had brought them to disaster. A great wave of protectiveness went over him. He thought he knew what to do for her. He believed in character; he wanted to jump back a whole generation and trust in character again as the eternally valuable element. Everything else wore out.

He left soon after dinner, but not to go home. He was curious to see Paris by night with clearer and more judicious eyes than those of other days. He bought a *strapontin*[9] for the Casino and watched Josephine Baker go through her chocolate arabesques.

After an hour he left and strolled toward Montmartre,[1] up the Rue Pigalle into the Place Blanche. The rain had stopped and there were a few people in evening clothes disembarking from taxis in front of cabarets, and *cocottes* prowling singly or in pairs, and many Negroes. He passed a lighted door from which issued music, and stopped with the sense of familiarity; it was Bricktop's, where he had parted with so many hours and so much money. A few doors farther on he found another ancient rendezvous and incautiously put his head inside. Immediately an eager orchestra burst into sound, a pair of professional dancers leaped to their feet and a maître d'hôtel swooped toward him, crying, "Crowd just arriving, sir!" But he withdrew quickly.

"You have to be damn drunk," he thought.

Zelli's was closed, the bleak and sinister cheap hotels surrounding it were dark; up in the Rue Blanche there was more light and a local, colloquial French crowd. The Poet's Cave had disappeared, but the two great mouths of the Café of Heaven and the Café of Hell still yawned—even devoured, as he watched, the meager contents of a tourist bus—a German, a Japanese, and an American couple who glanced at him with frightened eyes.

So much for the effort and ingenuity of Montmartre. All the catering to vice and waste was on an utterly childish scale, and he suddenly realized the meaning of the word "dissipate"—to dissipate into thin air; to make nothing out of something. In the little hours of

9. Bracket seat in the aisle—cheaper than regular seats. Baker was a celebrated black dancer of the epoch. 1. District in northern Paris. Prostitutes *(cocottes)* flourished on the Boulevard Clichy between Pigalle and Place Blanche.

the night every move from place to place was an enormous human jump, an increase of paying for the privilege of slower and slower motion.

He remembered thousand-franc notes given to an orchestra for playing a single number, hundred-franc notes tossed to a doorman for calling a cab.

But it hadn't been given for nothing.

It had been given, even the most wildly squandered sum, as an offering to destiny that he might not remember the things most worth remembering, the things that now he would always remember—his child taken from his control, his wife escaped to a grave in Vermont.

In the glare of a *brasserie*[2] a woman spoke to him. He bought her some eggs and coffee, and then, eluding her encouraging stare, gave her a twenty-franc note and took a taxi to his hotel.

II

He woke upon a fine fall day—football weather. The depression of yesterday was gone and he liked the people on the streets. At noon he sat opposite Honoria at Le Grand Vatel, the only restaurant he could think of not reminiscent of champagne dinners and long luncheons that began at two and ended in a blurred and vague twilight.

"Now, how about vegetables? Oughtn't you to have some vegetables?"

"Well, yes."

"Here's *épinards* and *chou-fleur* and carrots and *haricots*."[3]

"I'd like *chou-fleur*."

"Wouldn't you like to have two vegetables?"

"I usually only have one at lunch."

The waiter was pretending to be inordinately fond of children. "*Qu'elle est mignonne la petite! Elle parle exactement comme une Française.*"[4]

"How about dessert? Shall we wait and see?"

The waiter disappeared. Honoria looked at her father expectantly.

"What are we going to do?"

"First, we're going to that toy store in the Rue Saint-Honoré and buy you anything you like. And then we're going to the vaudeville at the Empire."

She hesitated. "I like it about the vaudeville, but not the toy store."

"Why not?"

2. Small restaurant that also serves drinks. 3. "Spinach . . . cauliflower . . . beans." 4. "What a darling little girl! She speaks exactly like a French girl."

"Well, you brought me this doll." She had it with her. "And I've got lots of things. And we're not rich any more, are we?"

"We never were. But today you are to have anything you want."

"All right," she agreed resignedly.

When there had been her mother and a French nurse he had been inclined to be strict; now he extended himself, reached out for a new tolerance; he must be both parents to her and not shut any of her out of communication.

"I want to get to know you," he said gravely. "First let me introduce myself. My name is Charles J. Wales, of Prague."

"Oh, daddy!" her voice cracked with laughter.

"And who are you, please?" he persisted, and she accepted a rôle immediately: "Honoria Wales, Rue Palatine, Paris."

"Married or single?"

"No, not married. Single."

He indicated the doll. "But I see you have a child, madame."

Unwilling to disinherit it, she took it to her heart and thought quickly: "Yes, I've been married, but I'm not married now. My husband is dead."

He went on quickly, "And the child's name?"

"Simone. That's after my best friend at school."

"I'm very pleased that you're doing so well at school."

"I'm third this month," she boasted. "Elsie"—that was her cousin—"is only about eighteenth, and Richard is about at the bottom."

"You like Richard and Elsie, don't you?"

"Oh, yes. I like Richard quite well and I like her all right."

Cautiously and casually he asked: "And Aunt Marion and Uncle Lincoln—which do you like best?"

"Oh, Uncle Lincoln, I guess."

He was increasingly aware of her presence. As they came in, a murmur of ". . . adorable" followed them, and now the people at the next table bent all their silences upon her, staring as if she were something no more conscious than a flower.

"Why don't I live with you?" she asked suddenly. "Because mamma's dead?"

"You must stay here and learn more French. It would have been hard for daddy to take care of you so well."

"I don't really need much taking care of any more. I do everything for myself."

Going out of the restaurant, a man and a woman unexpectedly hailed him.

"Well, the old Wales!"

"Hello there, Lorraine. . . . Dunc."

Sudden ghosts out of the past: Duncan Schaeffer, a friend from college. Lorraine Quarrles, a lovely, pale blonde of thirty; one of a crowd who had helped them make months into days in the lavish times of three years ago.

"My husband couldn't come this year," she said, in answer to his question. "We're poor as hell. So he gave me two hundred a month and told me I could do my worst on that. . . . This your little girl?"

"What about coming back and sitting down?" Duncan asked.

"Can't do it." He was glad for an excuse. As always, he felt Lorraine's passionate, provocative attraction, but his own rhythm was different now.

"Well, how about dinner?" she asked.

"I'm not free. Give me your address and let me call you."

"Charlie, I believe you're sober," she said judicially. "I honestly believe he's sober, Dunc. Pinch him and see if he's sober."

Charlie indicated Honoria with his head. They both laughed.

"What's your address?" said Duncan skeptically.

He hesitated, unwilling to give the name of his hotel.

"I'm not settled yet. I'd better call you. We're going to see the vaudeville at the Empire."

"There! That's what I want to do," Lorraine said. "I want to see some clowns and acrobats and jugglers. That's just what we'll do, Dunc."

"We've got to do an errand first," said Charlie. "Perhaps we'll see you there."

"All right, you snot. . . . Good-by, beautiful little girl."

"Good-by."

Honoria bobbed politely.

Somehow, an unwelcome encounter. They liked him because he was functioning, because he was serious; they wanted to see him, because he was stronger than they were now, because they wanted to draw a certain sustenance from his strength.

At the Empire, Honoria proudly refused to sit upon her father's folded coat. She was already an individual with a code of her own, and Charlie was more and more absorbed by the desire of putting a little of himself into her before she crystallized utterly. It was hopeless to try to know her in so short a time.

Between the acts they came upon Duncan and Lorraine in the lobby where the band was playing.

"Have a drink?"

"All right, but not up at the bar. We'll take a table."

"The perfect father."

Listening abstractedly to Lorraine, Charlie watched Honoria's eyes leave their table, and he followed them wistfully about the room, wondering what they saw. He met her glance and she smiled.

"I liked that lemonade," she said.

What had she said? What had he expected? Going home in a taxi afterward, he pulled her over until her head rested against his chest.

"Darling, do you ever think about your mother?"

"Yes, sometimes," she answered vaguely.

"I don't want you to forget her. Have you got a picture of her?"

"Yes, I think so. Anyhow, Aunt Marion has. Why don't you want me to forget her?"

"She loved you very much."

"I loved her too."

They were silent for a moment.

"Daddy, I want to come and live with you," she said suddenly.

His heart leaped; he had wanted it to come like this.

"Aren't you perfectly happy?"

"Yes, but I love you better than anybody. And you love me better than anybody, don't you, now that mummy's dead?"

"Of course I do. But you won't always like me best, honey. You'll grow up and meet somebody your own age and go marry him and forget you ever had a daddy."

"Yes, that's true," she agreed tranquilly.

He didn't go in. He was coming back at nine o'clock and he wanted to keep himself fresh and new for the thing he must say then.

"When you're safe inside, just show yourself in that window."

"All right. Good-by, dads, dads, dads, dads."

He waited in the dark street until she appeared, all warm and glowing, in the window above and kissed her fingers out into the night.

III

They were waiting. Marion sat behind the coffee service in a dignified black dinner dress that just faintly suggested mourning. Lincoln was walking up and down with the animation of one who had already been talking. They were as anxious as he was to get into the question. He opened it almost immediately:

"I suppose you know what I want to see you about—why I really came to Paris."

Marion played with the black stars on her necklace and frowned.

"I'm awfully anxious to have a home," he continued. "And I'm awfully anxious to have Honoria in it. I appreciate your taking in Honoria for her mother's sake, but things have changed now"—he hesitated and then continued more forcibly—"changed radically with me, and I want to ask you to reconsider the matter. It would be silly for me to deny that about three years ago I was acting badly——"

Marion looked up at him with hard eyes.

"—but all that's over. As I told you, I haven't had more than a drink a day for over a year, and I take that drink deliberately, so that the idea of alcohol won't get too big in my imagination. You see the idea?"

"No," said Marion succinctly.

"It's a sort of stunt I set myself. It keeps the matter in proportion."

"I get you," said Lincoln. "You don't want to admit it's got any attraction for you."

"Something like that. Sometimes I forget and don't take it. But I try to take it. Anyhow, I couldn't afford to drink in my position. The people I represent are more than satisfied with what I've done, and I'm bringing my sister over from Burlington to keep house for me, and I want awfully to have Honoria too. You know that even when her mother and I weren't getting along well we never let anything that happened touch Honoria. I know she's fond of me and I know I'm able to take care of her and—well, there you are. How do you feel about it?"

He knew that now he would have to take a beating. It would last an hour or two hours, and it would be difficult, but if he modulated his inevitable resentment to the chastened attitude of the reformed sinner, he might win his point in the end.

Keep your temper, he told himself. You don't want to be justified. You want Honoria.

Lincoln spoke first: "We've been talking it over ever since we got your letter last month. We're happy to have Honoria here. She's a dear little thing, and we're glad to be able to help her, but of course that isn't the question——"

Marion interrupted suddenly. "How long are you going to stay sober, Charlie?" she asked.

"Permanently, I hope."

"How can anybody count on that?"

"You know I never did drink heavily until I gave up business and came over here with nothing to do. Then Helen and I began to run around with——"

"Please leave Helen out of it. I can't bear to hear you talk about her like that."

He stared at her grimly; he had never been certain how fond of each other the sisters were in life.

"My drinking only lasted about a year and a half—from the time we came over until I—collapsed."

"It was time enough."

"It was time enough," he agreed.

"My duty is entirely to Helen," she said. "I try to think what she would have wanted me to do. Frankly, from the night you did that terrible thing you haven't really existed for me. I can't help that. She was my sister."

"Yes."

"When she was dying she asked me to look out for Honoria. If you hadn't been in a sanitarium then, it might have helped matters."

He had no answer.

"I'll never in my life be able to forget the morning when Helen knocked at my door, soaked to the skin and shivering, and said you'd locked her out."

Charlie gripped the sides of the chair. This was more difficult than he expected; he wanted to launch out into a long expostulation and explanation, but he only said: "The night I locked her out—" and she interrupted, "I don't feel up to going over that again."

After a moment's silence Lincoln said: "We're getting off the subject. You want Marion to set aside her legal guardianship and give you Honoria. I think the main point for her is whether she has confidence in you or not.

"I don't blame Marion," Charlie said slowly, "but I think she can have entire confidence in me. I had a good record up to three years ago. Of course, it's within human possibilities I might go wrong any time. But if we wait much longer I'll lose Honoria's childhood and my chance for a home." He shook his head, "I'll simply lose her, don't you see?"

"Yes, I see," said Lincoln.

"Why didn't you think of all this before?" Marion asked.

"I suppose I did, from time to time, but Helen and I were getting along badly. When I consented to the guardianship, I was flat on my back in a sanitarium and the market had cleaned me out. I knew I'd acted badly, and I thought if it would bring any peace to Helen, I'd agree to anything. But now it's different. I'm functioning, I'm behaving damn well, so far as——"

"Please don't swear at me," Marion said.

He looked at her, startled. With each remark the force of her dislike became more and more apparent. She had built up all her fear of life into one wall and faced it toward him. This trivial reproof was possibly the result of some trouble with the cook several hours before. Charlie became increasingly alarmed at leaving Honoria in this atmosphere of hostility against himself; sooner or later it would come out, in a word here, a shake of the head there, and some of that distrust would be irrevocably implanted in Honoria. But he pulled his temper down out of his face and shut it up inside him; he had won a point, for Lincoln realized the absurdity of Marion's remark and asked her lightly since when she had objected to the word "damn."

"Another thing," Charlie said: "I'm able to give her certain advantages now. I'm going to take a French governess to Prague with me. I've got a lease on a new apartment——"

He stopped, realizing that he was blundering. They couldn't be expected to accept with equanimity the fact that his income was again twice as large as their own.

"I suppose you can give her more luxuries than we can," said Marion. "When you were throwing away money we were living along watching every ten francs. . . . I suppose you'll start doing it again."

"Oh, no," he said. "I've learned. I worked hard for ten years, you know—until I got lucky in the market, like so many people. Terribly lucky. It won't happen again."

There was a long silence. All of them felt their nerves straining, and for the first time in a year Charlie wanted a drink. He was sure now that Lincoln Peters wanted him to have his child.

Marion shuddered suddenly; part of her saw that Charlie's feet were planted on the earth now, and her own maternal feeling recognized the naturalness of his desire; but she had lived for a long time with a prejudice—a prejudice founded on a curious disbelief in her sister's happiness, and which, in the shock of one terrible night, had turned to hatred for him. It had all happened at a point in her life where the discouragement of ill health and adverse circumstances made it necessary for her to believe in tangible villainy and a tangible villain.

"I can't help what I think!" she cried out suddenly. "How much you were responsible for Helen's death, I don't know. It's something you'll have to square with your own conscience."

An electric current of agony surged through him; for a moment he was almost on his feet, an unuttered sound echoing in his throat. He hung on to himself for a moment, another moment.

"Hold on there," said Lincoln uncomfortably. "I never thought you were responsible for that."

"Helen died of heart trouble," Charlie said dully.

"Yes, heart trouble." Marion spoke as if the phrase had another meaning for her.

Then, in the flatness that followed her outburst, she saw him plainly and she knew he had somehow arrived at control over the situation. Glancing at her husband, she found no help from him, and as abruptly as if it were a matter of no importance, she threw up the sponge.

"Do what you like!" she cried, springing up from her chair. "She's your child. I'm not the person to stand in your way. I think if it were my child I'd rather see her—" She managed to check herself. "You two decide it. I can't stand this. I'm sick. I'm going to bed."

She hurried from the room; after a moment Lincoln said:

"This has been a hard day for her. You know how strongly she feels—" His voice was almost apologetic: "When a woman gets an idea in her head."

"Of course."

"It's going to be all right. I think she sees now that you—can provide for the child, and so we can't very well stand in your way or Honoria's way."

"Thank you, Lincoln."

"I'd better go along and see how she is."

"I'm going."

He was still trembling when he reached the street, but a walk down the Rue Bonaparte to the *quais*[5] set him up, and as he crossed the Seine, fresh and new by the *quai* lamps, he felt exultant. But back in his room he couldn't sleep. The image of Helen haunted him. Helen whom he had loved so until they had senselessly begun to abuse each other's love, tear it into shreds. On that terrible February night that Marion remembered so vividly, a slow quarrel had gone on for hours. There was a scene at the Florida, and then he attempted to take her home, and then she kissed young Webb at a table; after that there was what she had hysterically said. When he arrived home alone he turned the key in the lock in wild anger. How could he know she would arrive an hour later alone, that there would be a snowstorm in which she wandered about in slippers, too confused to find a taxi? Then the aftermath, her escaping pneumonia by a miracle, and all the attendant horror. They were "reconciled," but that was the beginning of the end, and Marion, who had seen with her own eyes and who imagined it to be one of many scenes from her sister's martyrdom, never forgot.

Going over it again brought Helen nearer, and in the white, soft light that steals upon half sleep near morning he found himself talking to her again. She said that he was perfectly right about Honoria and that she wanted Honoria to be with him. She said she was glad he was being good and doing better. She said a lot of other things—very friendly things—but she was in a swing in a white dress, and swinging faster and faster all the time, so that at the end he could not hear clearly all that she said.

IV

He woke up feeling happy. The door of the world was open again. He made plans, vistas, futures for Honoria and himself, but suddenly he grew sad, remembering all the plans he and Helen had made. She had not planned to die. The present was the thing—work to do and someone to love. But not to love too much, for he knew the injury that a

5. Paved river banks.

father can do to a daughter or a mother to a son by attaching them too closely: afterward, out in the world, the child would seek in the marriage partner the same blind tenderness and, failing probably to find it, turn against love and life.

It was another bright, crisp day. He called Lincoln Peters at the bank where he worked and asked if he could count on taking Honoria when he left for Prague. Lincoln agreed that there was no reason for delay. One thing—the legal guardianship. Marion wanted to retain that a while longer. She was upset by the whole matter, and it would oil things if she felt that the situation was still in her control for another year. Charlie agreed, wanting only the tangible, visible child.

Then the question of a governess. Charles sat in a gloomy agency and talked to a cross Béarnaise and to a buxom Breton peasant, neither of whom he could have endured. There were others whom he would see tomorrow.

He lunched with Lincoln Peters at Griffons, trying to keep down his exultation.

"There's nothing quite like your own child," Lincoln said. "But you understand how Marion feels too."

"She's forgotten how hard I worked for seven years there," Charlie said. "She just remembers one night."

"There's another thing." Lincoln hesitated. "While you and Helen were tearing around Europe throwing money away, we were just getting along. I didn't touch any of the prosperity because I never got ahead enough to carry anything but my insurance. I think Marion felt there was some kind of injustice in it—you not even working toward the end, and getting richer and richer."

"It went just as quick as it came," said Charlie.

"Yes, a lot of it stayed in the hands of *chasseurs* and saxophone players and maîtres d'hôtel—well, the big party's over now. I just said that to explain Marion's feeling about those crazy years. If you drop in about six o'clock tonight before Marion's too tired, we'll settle the details on the spot."

Back at his hotel, Charlie found a *pneumatique*[6] that had been redirected from the Ritz bar where Charlie had left his address for the purpose of finding a certain man.

> DEAR CHARLIE: You were so strange when we saw you the other day that I wondered if I did something to offend you. If so, I'm not conscious of it. In fact, I have thought about you too much for the last year, and it's always been in the back of my mind that I might see you if I came over here. We *did* have such good times that crazy spring, like

6. Message delivered speedily by special Parisian system.

> the night you and I stole the butcher's tricycle, and the time we tried to call on the president and you had the old derby rim and the wire cane. Everybody seems so old lately, but I don't feel old a bit. Couldn't we get together some time today for old time's sake? I've got a vile hangover for the moment, but will be feeling better this afternoon and will look for you about five in the sweatshop at the Ritz.
>
> Always devotedly,
> Lorraine

His first feeling was one of awe that he had actually, in his mature years, stolen a tricycle and pedaled Lorraine all over the Étoile between the small hours and dawn. In retrospect it was a nightmare. Locking out Helen didn't fit in with any other act of his life, but the tricycle incident did—it was one of many. How many weeks or months of dissipation to arrive at that condition of utter irresponsibility?

He tried to picture how Lorraine had appeared to him then—very attractive; Helen was unhappy about it, though she said nothing. Yesterday, in the restaurant, Lorraine had seemed trite, blurred, worn away. He emphatically did not want to see her, and he was glad Alix had not given away his hotel address. It was a relief to think, instead, of Honoria, to think of Sundays spent with her and of saying good morning to her and of knowing she was there in his house at night, drawing her breath in the darkness.

At five he took a taxi and bought presents for all the Peters—a piquant cloth doll, a box of Roman soldiers, flowers for Marion, big linen handkerchiefs for Lincoln.

He saw, when he arrived in the apartment, that Marion had accepted the inevitable. She greeted him now as though he were a recalcitrant member of the family, rather than a menacing outsider. Honoria had been told she was going; Charlie was glad to see that her tact made her conceal her excessive happiness. Only on his lap did she whisper her delight and the question "When?" before she slipped away with the other children.

He and Marion were alone for a minute in the room, and on an impulse he spoke out boldly:

"Family quarrels are bitter things. They don't go according to any rules. They're not like aches or wounds; they're more like splits in the skin that won't heal because there's not enough material. I wish you and I could be on better terms."

"Some things are hard to forget," she answered. "It's a question of confidence." There was no answer to this and presently she asked, "When do you propose to take her?"

"As soon as I can get a governess. I hoped the day after tomorrow."

"That's impossible. I've got to get her things in shape. Not before Saturday."

He yielded. Coming back into the room, Lincoln offered him a drink.

"I'll take my daily whisky," he said.

It was warm here, it was a home, people together by a fire. The children felt very safe and important; the mother and father were serious, watchful. They had things to do for the children more important than his visit here. A spoonful of medicine was, after all, more important than the strained relations between Marion and himself. They were not dull people, but they were very much in the grip of life and circumstances. He wondered if he couldn't do something to get Lincoln out of his rut at the bank.

A long peal at the door-bell; the *bonne à tout faire*[7] passed through and went down the corridor. The door opened upon another long ring, and then voices, and the three in the salon looked up expectantly; Richard moved to bring the corridor within his range of vision, and Marion rose. Then the maid came back along the corridor, closely followed by the voices, which developed under the light into Duncan Schaeffer and Lorraine Quarrles.

They were gay, they were hilarious, they were roaring with laughter. For a moment Charlie was astounded; unable to understand how they ferreted out the Peters' address.

"Ah-h-h!" Duncan wagged his finger roguishly at Charlie. "Ah-h-h!"

They both slid down another cascade of laughter. Anxious and at a loss, Charlie shook hands with them quickly and presented them to Lincoln and Marion. Marion nodded, scarcely speaking. She had drawn back a step toward the fire; her little girl stood beside her, and Marion put an arm about her shoulder.

With growing annoyance at the intrusion, Charlie waited for them to explain themselves. After some concentration Duncan said:

"We came to invite you out to dinner. Lorraine and I insist that all this shishi, cagy business 'bout your address got to stop."

Charlie came closer to them, as if to force them backward down the corridor.

"Sorry, but I can't. Tell me where you'll be and I'll phone you in half an hour."

This made no impression. Lorraine sat down suddenly on the side of a chair, and focusing her eyes on Richard, cried, "Oh, what a nice little boy! Come here, little boy." Richard glanced at his mother,

7. Maid of all work.

but did not move. With a perceptible shrug of her shoulders, Lorraine turned back to Charlie:

"Come and dine. Sure your cousins won' mine. See you so sel'om. Or solemn."

"I can't," said Charlie sharply. "You two have dinner and I'll phone you."

Her voice became suddenly unpleasant. "All right, we'll go. But I remember once when you hammered on my door at four A.M. I was enough of a good sport to give you a drink. Come on, Dunc."

Still in slow motion, with blurred, angry faces, with uncertain feet, they retired along the corridor.

"Good night," Charlie said.

"Good night!" responded Lorraine emphatically.

When he went back into the salon Marion had not moved, only now her son was standing in the circle of her other arm. Lincoln was still swinging Honoria back and forth like a pendulum from side to side.

"What an outrage!" Charlie broke out. "What an absolute outrage!"

Neither of them answered. Charlie dropped into an armchair, picked up his drink, set it down again and said:

"People I haven't seen for two years having the colossal nerve——"

He broke off. Marion had made the sound "Oh!" in one swift, furious breath, turned her body from him with a jerk and left the room.

Lincoln set down Honoria carefully.

"You children go in and start your soup," he said, and when they obeyed, he said to Charlie:

"Marion's not well and she can't stand shocks. That kind of people make her really physically sick."

"I didn't tell them to come here. They wormed your name out of somebody. They deliberately——"

"Well, it's too bad. It doesn't help matters. Excuse me a minute."

Left alone, Charlie sat tense in his chair. In the next room he could hear the children eating, talking in monosyllables, already oblivious to the scene between their elders. He heard a murmur of conversation from a farther room and then the ticking bell of a telephone receiver picked up, and in a panic he moved to the other side of the room and out of earshot.

In a minute Lincoln came back. "Look here, Charlie. I think we'd better call off dinner for tonight. Marion's in bad shape."

"Is she angry with me?"

"Sort of," he said, almost roughly. "She's not strong and——"

"You mean she's changed her mind about Honoria?"

"She's pretty bitter right now. I don't know. You phone me at the bank tomorrow."

"I wish you'd explain to her I never dreamed these people would come here. I'm just as sore as you are."

"I couldn't explain anything to her now."

Charlie got up. He took his coat and hat and started down the corridor. Then he opened the door of the dining room and said in a strange voice, "Good night, children."

Honoria rose and ran around the table to hug him.

"Good night, sweetheart," he said vaguely, and then trying to make his voice more tender, trying to conciliate something, "Good night, dear children."

V

Charlie went directly to the Ritz bar with the furious idea of finding Lorraine and Duncan, but they were not there, and he realized that in any case there was nothing he could do. He had not touched his drink at the Peters', and now he ordered a whisky-and-soda. Paul came over to say hello.

"It's a great change," he said sadly. "We do about half the business we did. So many fellows I hear about back in the States lost everything, maybe not in the first crash, but then in the second. Your friend George Hardt lost every cent, I hear. Are you back in the States?"

"No, I'm in business in Prague."

"I heard that you lost a lot in the crash."

"I did," and he added grimly, "but I lost everything I wanted in the boom."

"Selling short."

"Something like that."

Again the memory of those days swept over him like a nightmare—the people they had met travelling; then people who couldn't add a row of figures or speak a coherent sentence. The little man Helen had consented to dance with at the ship's party, who had insulted her ten feet from the table; the women and girls carried screaming with drink or drugs out of public places——

—The men who locked their wives out in the snow, because the snow of twenty-nine wasn't real snow. If you didn't want it to be snow, you just paid some money.

He went to the phone and called the Peters' apartment; Lincoln answered.

"I called up because this thing is on my mind. Has Marion said anything definite?"

"Marion's sick," Lincoln answered shortly. "I know this thing isn't altogether your fault, but I can't have her go to pieces about it. I'm afraid we'll have to let it slide for six months; I can't take the chance of working her up to this state again."

"I see."

"I'm sorry, Charlie."

He went back to his table. His whisky glass was empty, but he shook his head when Alix looked at it questioningly. There wasn't much he could do now except send Honoria some things; he would send her a lot of things tomorrow. He thought rather angrily that this was just money—he had given so many people money. . . .

"No, no more," he said to another waiter. "What do I owe you?"

He would come back some day; they couldn't make him pay forever. But he wanted his child, and nothing was much good now, beside that fact. He wasn't young any more, with a lot of nice thoughts and dreams to have by himself. He was absolutely sure Helen wouldn't have wanted him to be so alone.

---

1. Considered thematically, what does the story have to say about the relation between the Past, Present, and Future? Can Charlie Wales ever achieve the happiness he looks forward to? Did he ever have a chance of reaching it?
2. Near the beginning of Section IV Charlie agrees not to press for legal guardianship of his daughter—"wanting only the tangible, visible child." What does this language indicate about his conception of fatherhood?
3. An old axiom tells us that "character is fate." What are the fatal flaws in Charlie's character?
4. Define the roles of Duncan Schaeffer and Lorraine Quarrles in the past and present action. How do you interpret the statement that "they wanted to draw a certain sustenance from Charlie's strength." What sort of sustenance can he give them?
5. Discuss Charlie's self-criticism. Is it adequate? Is Marion's mistrust of him ill-founded? Is she clinging to narrow resentments or sizing him up well?

Gustave Flaubert

Flaubert (1821–1880) was born in Rouen, France, where his father was a leading doctor. For a time he studied law in Paris, but his romantic inclinations and a nervous malady akin to epilepsy brought him home to Rouen and the devoted practice of the literary art. Though he despised the banality of nineteenth-century provincial life, he spent seven years in the composition of Madame Bovary *(1856), a novel that depicts such life with a realism seldom matched. The supposed indecency of this book subjected Flaubert to prosecution, but its poignance and consummate craftsmanship mark a turning point in the development of modern fiction. In* Salammbô *(1862) Flaubert indulged the romantic side of his imagination by setting his tale in ancient Carthage. Aside from a few trips made in search of romantic settings and the color of heroic epochs, Flaubert's outward life was unadventurous. His one great love affair was with the poet Louise Colet (1810–1876), and their passions and arguments were often of literary origin. Because of his scrupulous dedication to the demands of his art, Flaubert stands as a sort of patron saint to many modern writers. His shorter works were published in* Three Tales *(1877). His other major novels are* The Sentimental Education *(1869) and* Bouvard and Pécuchet *(1881).*

The Legend of Saint Julian the Hospitaller[1]

I

Julian's father and mother dwelt in a castle built on the slope of a hill, in the heart of the woods.

The towers at its four corners had pointed roofs covered with leaden tiles, and the foundation rested upon solid rocks, which descended abruptly to the bottom of the moat.

In the courtyard, the stone flagging was as immaculate as the floor of a church. Long rain-spouts, representing dragons with yawning jaws, directed the water towards the cistern, and on each window-sill

1. Patron saint of travelers, hotelkeepers, and circus people; called "Hospitaller" because of his ministration to travelers.

of the castle a basil or a heliotrope bush bloomed, in painted flower-pots.

A second enclosure, surrounded by a fence, comprised a fruit-orchard, a garden decorated with figures wrought in bright-hued flowers, an arbour with several bowers, and a mall for the diversion of the pages. On the other side were the kennel, the stables, the bakery, the winepress and the barns. Around these spread a pasture, also enclosed by a strong hedge.

Peace had reigned so long that the portcullis was never lowered; the moats were filled with water; swallows built their nests in the cracks of the battlements, and as soon as the sun shone too strongly, the archer who all day long paced to and fro on the curtain,[2] withdrew to the watchtower and slept soundly.

Inside the castle, the locks on the doors shone brightly; costly tapestries hung in the apartments to keep out the cold; the closets overflowed with linen, the cellar was filled with casks of wine, and the oak chests fairly groaned under the weight of money-bags.

In the armoury could be seen, between banners and the heads of wild beasts, weapons of all nations and of all ages, from the sling of the Amalekites[3] and the javelins of the Garamantes, to the broadswords of the Saracens and the coats of mail of the Normans.[4]

The largest spit in the kitchen could hold an ox; the chapel was as gorgeous as a king's oratory. There was even a Roman bath in a secluded part of the castle, though the good lord of the manor refrained from using it, as he deemed it a heathenish practice.

Wrapped always in a cape made of foxskins, he wandered about the castle, rendered justice among his vassals and settled his neighbours' quarrels. In the winter, he gazed dreamily at the falling snow, or had stories read aloud to him. But as soon as the fine weather returned, he would mount his mule and sally forth into the country roads, edged with ripening wheat, to talk with the peasants, to whom he distributed advice. After a number of adventures he took unto himself a wife of high lineage.

She was pale and serious, and a trifle haughty. The horns of her head-dress touched the top of the doors and the hem of her gown trailed far behind her. She conducted her household like a cloister. Every morning she distributed work to the maids, supervised the making of preserves and unguents, and afterwards passed her time in spinning, or in embroidering altar-cloths. In response to her fervent prayers, God granted her a son!

Then there was great rejoicing; and they gave a feast which lasted

2. Wall between two towers of a castle. 3. Mideastern tribe descended from Esau.
4. Scandinavians who conquered part of France and all of Britain. *Garamantes:* ancient French noble family; *Saracens:* Muslims who opposed the Crusaders.

three days and four nights, with illuminations and soft music. Chickens as large as sheep, and the rarest spices were served; for the entertainment of the guests, a dwarf crept out of a pie; and when the bowls were too few, for the crowd swelled continuously, the wine was drunk from helmets and hunting-horns.

The young mother did not appear at the feast. She was quietly resting in bed. One night she awoke, and beheld in a moonbeam that crept through the window something that looked like a moving shadow. It was an old man clad in sackcloth, who resembled a hermit. A rosary dangled at his side and he carried a beggar's sack on his shoulder. He approached the foot of the bed, and without opening his lips said: "Rejoice, O mother! Thy son shall be a saint."

She would have cried out, but the old man, gliding along the moonbeam, rose through the air and disappeared. The songs of the banqueters grew louder. She could hear angels' voices, and her head sank back on the pillow, which was surmounted by the bone of a martyr, framed in precious stones.

The following day, the servants, upon being questioned, declared, to a man, that they had seen no hermit. Then, whether dream or fact this must certainly have been a communication from heaven; but she took care not to speak of it, lest she should be accused of presumption.

The guests departed at daybreak, and Julian's father stood at the castle gate, where he had just bidden farewell to the last one, when a beggar suddenly emerged from the mist and confronted him. He was a gipsy—for he had a braided beard and wore silver bracelets on each arm. His eyes burned and, in an inspired way, he muttered some disconnected words: "Ah! Ah! thy son!—great bloodshed—great glory—happy always—an emperor's family."

Then he stooped to pick up the alms thrown to him, and disappeared in the tall grass.

The lord of the manor looked up and down the road and called as loudly as he could. But no one answered him! The wind only howled and the morning mists were fast dissolving.

He attributed his vision to a dullness of the brain resulting from too much sleep. "If I should speak of it," quoth he, "people would laugh at me." Still, the glory that was to be his son's dazzled him, albeit the meaning of the prophecy was not clear to him, and he even doubted that he had heard it.

The parents kept their secret from each other. But both cherished the child with equal devotion, and as they considered him marked by God, they had great regard for his person. His cradle was lined with the softest feathers, and a lamp representing a dove burned continually over it; three nurses rocked him night and day, and with his pink cheeks and blue eyes, brocaded cloak and embroidered cap, he looked like a little Jesus. He cut all his teeth without even a whimper.

When he was seven years old his mother taught him to sing, and his father lifted him upon a tall horse, to inspire him with courage. The child smiled with delight, and soon became familiar with everything pertaining to chargers. An old and very learned monk taught him the Gospel, the Arabic numerals, the Latin letters, and the art of painting delicate designs on vellum. They worked in the top of a tower, away from all noise and disturbance.

When the lesson was over, they would go down into the garden and study the flowers.

Sometimes a herd of cattle passed through the valley below, in charge of a man in Oriental dress. The lord of the manor, recognising him as a merchant, would despatch a servant after him. The stranger, becoming confident, would stop on his way and after being ushered into the castle-hall, would display pieces of velvet and silk, trinkets and strange objects whose use was unknown in those parts. Then, in due time, he would take leave, without having been molested and with a handsome profit.

At other times, a band of pilgrims would knock at the door. Their wet garments would be hung in front of the hearth and after they had been refreshed by food they would relate their travels, and discuss the uncertainty of vessels on the high seas, their long journeys across burning sands, the ferocity of the infidels, the caves of Syria, the Manger and the Holy Sepulchre.[5] They made presents to the young heir of beautiful shells, which they carried in their cloaks.

The lord of the manor very often feasted his brothers-at-arms, and over the wine the old warriors would talk of battles and attacks, of war-machines and of the frightful wounds they had received, so that Julian, who was a listener, would scream with excitement; then his father felt convinced that some day he would be a conqueror. But in the evening, after the Angelus,[6] when he passed through the crowd of beggars who clustered about the church-door, he distributed his alms with so much modesty and nobility that his mother fully expected to see him become an archbishop in time.

His seat in the chapel was next to his parents, and no matter how long the services lasted, he remained kneeling on his *prie-dieu*,[7] with folded hands and his velvet cap lying close beside him on the floor.

One day, during mass, he raised his head and beheld a little white mouse crawling out of a hole in the wall. It scrambled to the first

5. Christ was born in a manger; the Holy Sepulchre was his tomb. 6. Bell tolled to signal the beginning of devotions in memory of the Annunciation. 7. Bench on which to kneel for prayers.

altar-step and then, after a few gambols, ran back in the same direction. On the following Sunday, the idea of seeing the mouse again worried him. It returned; and every Sunday after that he watched for it; and it annoyed him so much that he grew to hate it and resolved to do away with it.

So, having closed the door and strewn some crumbs on the steps of the altar, he placed himself in front of the hole with a stick. After a long while a pink snout appeared, and then the whole mouse crept out. He struck it lightly with his stick and stood stunned at the sight of the little, lifeless body. A drop of blood stained the floor. He wiped it away hastily with his sleeve, and picking up the mouse, threw it away, without saying a word about it to anyone.

All sorts of birds pecked at the seeds in the garden. He put some peas in a hollow reed, and when he heard birds chirping in a tree, he would approach cautiously, lift the tube and swell his cheeks; then, when the little creatures dropped about him in multitudes, he could not refrain from laughing and being delighted with his own cleverness.

One morning, as he was returning by way of the curtain, he beheld a fat pigeon sunning itself on the top of the wall. He paused to gaze at it; where he stood the rampart was cracked and a piece of stone was near at hand; he gave his arm a jerk and the well-aimed missile struck the bird squarely, sending it straight into the moat below.

He sprang after it, unmindful of the brambles, and ferreted around the bushes with the litheness of a young dog.

The pigeon hung with broken wings in the branches of a privet hedge.

The persistence of its life irritated the boy. He began to strangle it, and its convulsions made his heart beat quicker, and filled him with a wild tumultuous voluptuousness, the last throb of its heart making him feel like fainting.

At supper that night, his father declared that at his age a boy should begin to hunt; and he arose and brought forth an old writing-book which contained, in questions and answers, everything pertaining to the pastime. In it, a master showed a supposed pupil how to train dogs and falcons, lay traps, recognise a stag by its fumets,[8] and a fox or a wolf by footprints. He also taught the best way of discovering their tracks, how to start them, where their refuges are usually to be found, what winds are the most favourable, and further enumerated the various cries, and the rules of the quarry.

When Julian was able to recite all these things by heart, his father made up a pack of hounds for him. There were twenty-four greyhounds of Barbary,[9] speedier than gazelles, but liable to get out of temper;

8. Dung of a deer. 9. A region in North Africa.

seventeen couples of Breton[1] dogs, great barkers, with broad chests and russet coats flecked with white. For wild-boar hunting and perilous doublings, there were forty boarhounds as hairy as bears.

The red mastiffs of Tartary,[2] almost as large as donkeys, with broad backs and straight legs, were destined for the pursuit of the wild bull. The black coats of the spaniels shone like satin; the barking of the setters equalled that of the beagles. In a special enclosure were eight growling bloodhounds that tugged at their chains and rolled their eyes, and these dogs leaped at men's throats and were not afraid even of lions.

All ate wheat bread, drank from marble troughs, and had high-sounding names.

Perhaps the falconry surpassed the pack; for the master of the castle, by paying great sums of money, had secured Caucasian hawks, Babylonian sakers, German gerfalcons, and pilgrim falcons captured on the cliffs edging the cold seas, in distant lands. They were housed in a thatched shed and were chained to the perch in the order of size. In front of them was a little grass-plot where, from time to time, they were allowed to disport themselves.

Bag-nets, baits, traps and all sorts of snares were manufactured.

Often they would take out pointers who would set almost immediately; then the whippers-in, advancing step by step, would cautiously spread a huge net over their motionless bodies. At the command, the dogs would bark and arouse the quails; and the ladies of the neighbourhood, with their husbands, children and handmaids, would fall upon them and capture them with ease.

At other times they used a drum to start hares; and frequently foxes fell into the ditches prepared for them, while wolves caught their paws in the traps.

But Julian scorned these convenient contrivances; he preferred to hunt away from the crowd, alone with his steed and his falcon. It was almost always a large, snow-white, Scythian[3] bird. His leather hood was ornamented with a plume, and on his blue feet were bells; and he perched firmly on his master's arm while they galloped across the plains. Then Julian would suddenly untie his tether and let him fly, and the bold bird would dart through the air like an arrow. One might perceive two spots circle around, unite, and then disappear in the blue heights. Presently the falcon would return with a mutilated bird, and perch again on his master's gauntlet with trembling wings.

Julian loved to sound his trumpet and follow his dogs over hills and streams, into the woods; and when the stag began to moan under

1. Brittany. 2. Historical name of a vaguely defined region in east Europe and Asia. 3. Region in southeast Europe and western Asia.

their teeth, he would kill it deftly, and delight in the fury of the brutes, which would devour the pieces spread out on the warm hide.

On foggy days, he would hide in the marshes to watch for wild geese, otters and wild ducks.

At daybreak, three equerries[4] waited for him at the foot of the steps; and though the old monk leaned out of the dormer-window and made signs to him to return, Julian would not look around.

He heeded neither the broiling sun, the rain nor the storm; he drank spring water and ate wild berries, and when he was tired, he lay down under a tree; and he would come home at night covered with earth and blood, with thistles in his hair and smelling of wild beasts. He grew to be like them. And when his mother kissed him, he responded coldly to her caress and seemed to be thinking of deep and serious things.

He killed bears with a knife, bulls with a hatchet, and wild boars with a spear; and once, with nothing but a stick, he defended himself against some wolves, which were gnawing corpses at the foot of a gibbet.

One winter morning he set out before daybreak, with a bow slung across his shoulder and a quiver of arrows attached to the pommel of his saddle. The hoofs of his steed beat the ground with regularity and his two beagles trotted close behind. The wind was blowing hard and icicles clung to his cloak. A part of the horizon cleared, and he beheld some rabbits playing around their burrows. In an instant, the two dogs were upon them, and seizing as many as they could, they broke their backs in the twinkling of an eye.

Soon he came to a forest. A woodcock, paralysed by the cold, perched on a branch, with its head hidden under its wing. Julian, with a lunge of his sword, cut off its feet, and without stopping to pick it up, rode away.

Three hours later he found himself on the top of a mountain so high that the sky seemed almost black. In front of him, a long, flat rock hung over a precipice, and at the end, two wild goats stood gazing down into the abyss. As he had no arrows (for he had left his steed behind), he thought he would climb down to where they stood; and with bare feet and bent back he at last reached the first goat and thrust his dagger below its ribs. But the second animal, in its terror, leaped into the precipice. Julian threw himself forward to strike it, but his right foot slipped, and he fell, face downward and with outstretched arms, over the body of the first goat.

4. Servants in charge of horses.

After he returned to the plains, he followed a stream bordered by willows. From time to time, some cranes, flying low, passed over his head. He killed them with his whip, never missing a bird. He beheld in the distance the gleam of a lake which appeared to be of lead, and in the middle of it was an animal he had never seen before, a beaver with a black muzzle. Notwithstanding the distance that separated them, an arrow ended its life and Julian only regretted that he was not able to carry the skin home with him.

Then he entered an avenue of tall trees, the tops of which formed a triumphal arch to the entrance of a forest. A deer sprang out of the thicket and a badger crawled out of its hole, a stag appeared in the road, and a peacock spread its fan-shaped tail on the grass—and after he had slain them all, other deer, other stags, other badgers, other peacocks, and jays, blackbirds, foxes, porcupines, polecats, and lynxes, appeared; in fact, a host of beasts that grew more and more numerous with every step he took. Trembling, and with a look of appeal in their eyes, they gathered around Julian, but he did not stop slaying them; and so intent was he on stretching his bow, drawing his sword and whipping out his knife, that he had little thought for aught else. He knew that he was hunting in some country since an indefinite time, through the very fact of his existence, as everything seemed to occur with the ease one experiences in dreams. But presently an extraordinary sight made him pause.

He beheld a valley shaped like a circus[5] and filled with stags which, huddled together, were warming one another with the vapour of their breaths that mingled with the early mist.

For a few minutes, he almost choked with pleasure at the prospect of so great a carnage. Then he sprang from his horse, rolled up his sleeves, and began to aim.

When the first arrow whizzed through the air, the stags turned their heads simultaneously. They huddled closer, uttered plaintive cries, and a great agitation seized the whole herd. The edge of the valley was too high to admit of flight; and the animals ran around the enclosure in their efforts to escape. Julian aimed, stretched his bow and his arrows fell as fast and thick as raindrops in a shower.

Maddened with terror, the stags fought and reared and climbed on top of one another; their antlers and bodies formed a moving mountain which tumbled to pieces whenever it displaced itself.

Finally the last one expired. Their bodies lay stretched out on the sand with foam gushing from the nostrils and the bowels protruding. The heaving of their bellies grew less and less noticeable, and presently all was still.

5. Arena surrounded by sloping tiers of seats.

Night came, and behind the trees, through the branches, the sky appeared like a sheet of blood.

Julian leaned against a tree and gazed with dilated eyes at the enormous slaughter. He was now unable to comprehend how he had accomplished it.

On the opposite side of the valley, he suddenly beheld a large stag, with a doe and their fawn. The buck was black and of enormous size; he had a white beard and carried sixteen antlers. His mate was the color of dead leaves, and she browsed upon the grass, while the fawn, clinging to her udder, followed her step by step.

Again the bow was stretched, and instantly the fawn dropped dead, and seeing this, its mother raised her head and uttered a poignant, almost human wail of agony. Exasperated, Julian thrust his knife into her chest, and felled her to the ground.

The great stag had watched everything and suddenly he sprang forward. Julian aimed his last arrow at the beast. It struck him between his antlers and stuck there.

The stag did not appear to notice it; leaping over the bodies, he was coming nearer and nearer with the intention, Julian thought, of charging at him and ripping him open, and he recoiled with inexpressible horror. But presently the huge animal halted, and, with eyes aflame and the solemn air of a patriarch and a judge, repeated thrice, while a bell tolled in the distance:

"Accursed! Accursed! Accursed! some day, ferocious soul, thou wilt murder thy father and thy mother!"

Then he sank on his knees, gently closed his lids and expired.

At first Julian was stunned, and then a sudden lassitude and an immense sadness came over him. Holding his head between his hands, he wept for a long time.

His steed had wandered away; his dogs had forsaken him; the solitude seemed to threaten him with unknown perils. Impelled by a sense of sickening terror, he ran across the fields, and choosing a path at random, found himself almost immediately at the gates of the castle.

That night he could not rest, for, by the flickering light of the hanging lamp, he beheld again the huge black stag. He fought against the obsession of the prediction and kept repeating: "No! No! No! I cannot slay them!" and then he thought: "Still, supposing I desired to?—" and he feared that the devil might inspire him with this desire.

During three months, his distracted mother prayed at his bedside, and his father paced the halls of the castle in anguish. He consulted the most celebrated physicians, who prescribed quantities of medicine. Julian's illness, they declared, was due to some injurious wind or to amorous desire. But in reply to their questions, the young man only shook his head. After a time, his strength returned, and he was able to take a walk in the courtyard, supported by his father and the old monk.

But after he had completely recovered, he refused to hunt.

His father, hoping to please him, presented him with a large Saracen sabre.

It was placed on a panoply that hung on a pillar, and a ladder was required to reach it. Julian climbed up to it one day, but the heavy weapon slipped from his grasp, and in falling grazed his father and tore his cloak. Julian, believing he had killed him, fell in a swoon.

After that, he carefully avoided weapons. The sight of a naked sword made him grow pale, and this weakness caused great distress to his family.

In the end, the old monk ordered him in the name of God, and of his forefathers, once more to indulge in the sports of a nobleman.

The equerries diverted themselves every day with javelins and Julian soon excelled in the practice.

He was able to send a javelin into bottles, to break the teeth of the weather-cocks on the castle and to strike door-nails at a distance of one hundred feet.

One summer evening, at the hour when dusk renders objects indistinct, he was in the arbour in the garden, and thought he saw two white wings in the background hovering around the espalier.[6] Not for a moment did he doubt that it was a stork, and so he threw his javelin at it.

A heart-rending scream pierced the air.

He had struck his mother, whose cap and long streamers remained nailed to the wall.

Julian fled from home and never returned.

II

He joined a horde of adventurers who were passing through the place.

He learned what it was to suffer hunger, thirst, sickness and filth. He grew accustomed to the din of battles and to the sight of dying men. The wind tanned his skin. His limbs became hardened through contact with armour, and as he was very strong and brave, temperate and of good counsel, he easily obtained command of a company.

At the outset of a battle, he would electrify his soldiers by a motion of his sword. He would climb the walls of a citadel with a knotted rope, at night, rocked by the storm, while sparks of fire clung to his cuirass, and molten lead and boiling tar poured from the battlements.

Often a stone would break his shield. Bridges crowded with men

6. Plant trained to grow flat against a wall.

gave way under him. Once, by turning his mace, he rid himself of fourteen horsemen. He defeated all those who came forward to fight him on the field of honour, and more than a score of times it was believed that he had been killed.

However, thanks to Divine protection, he always escaped, for he shielded orphans, widows, and aged men. When he caught sight of one of the latter walking ahead of him, he would call to him to show his face, as if he feared that he might kill him by mistake.

All sorts of intrepid men gathered under his leadership, fugitive slaves, peasant rebels, and penniless bastards; he then organized an army which increased so much that he became famous and was in great demand.

He succoured in turn the Dauphin of France, the King of England, the Templars of Jerusalem, the General of the Parths, the Negus of Abyssinia and the Emperor of Calicut.[7] He fought against Scandinavians covered with fish-scales, against negroes mounted on red asses and armed with shields made of hippopotamus hide, against gold-coloured Indians who wielded great, shining swords above their heads. He conquered the Troglodytes and the cannibals. He travelled through regions so torrid that the heat of the sun would set fire to the hair on one's head; he journeyed through countries so glacial that one's arms would fall from the body; and he passed through places where the fogs were so dense that it seemed like being surrounded by phantoms.

Republics in trouble consulted him; when he conferred with ambassadors, he always obtained unexpected concessions. Also, if a monarch behaved badly, he would arrive on the scene and rebuke him. He freed nations. He rescued queens sequestered in towers. It was he and no other that killed the serpent of Milan and the dragon of Oberbirbach.

Now, the Emperor of Occitania, having triumphed over the Spanish Mussulmans, had taken the sister of the Caliph of Cordova as a concubine, and had had one daughter by her, whom he brought up in the teachings of Christ. But the Caliph, feigning that he wished to become converted, made him a visit, and brought with him a numerous escort. He slaughtered the entire garrison and threw the Emperor into a dungeon, and treated him with great cruelty in order to obtain possession of his treasures.

Julian went to his assistance, destroyed the army of infidels, laid siege to the city, slew the Caliph, chopped off his head and threw it over the fortifications like a cannon-ball.

As a reward for so great a service, the Emperor presented him

7. Exotic rulers of exotic countries.

with a large sum of money in baskets; but Julian declined it. Then the Emperor, thinking that the amount was not sufficiently large, offered him three quarters of his fortune, and on meeting a second refusal, proposed to share his kingdom with his benefactor. But Julian only thanked him for it, and the Emperor felt like weeping with vexation at not being able to show his gratitude, when he suddenly tapped his forehead and whispered a few words in the ear of one of his courtiers; the tapestry curtains parted and a young girl appeared.

Her large black eyes shone like two soft lights. A charming smile parted her lips. Her curls were caught in the jewels of her half-opened bodice, and the grace of her youthful body could be divined under the transparency of her tunic.

She was small and quite plump, but her waist was slender.

Julian was absolutely dazzled, all the more since he had always led a chaste life.

So he married the Emperor's daughter, and received at the same time a castle she had inherited from her mother; and when the rejoicings were over, he departed with his bride, after many courtesies had been exchanged on both sides.

The castle was of Moorish design, in white marble, erected on a promontory and surrounded by orange-trees.

Terraces of flowers extended to the shell-strewn shores of a beautiful bay. Behind the castle spread a fan-shaped forest. The sky was always blue, and the trees were swayed in turn by the ocean-breeze and by the winds that blew from the mountains that closed the horizon.

Light entered the apartments through the incrustations of the walls. High, reed-like columns supported the ceiling of the cupolas, decorated in imitation of stalactites.

Fountains played in the spacious halls; the courts were inlaid with mosaic; there were festooned partitions and a great profusion of architectural fancies; and everywhere reigned a silence so deep that the swish of a sash or the echo of a sigh could be distinctly heard.

Julian now had renounced war. Surrounded by a peaceful people, he remained idle, receiving every day a throng of subjects who came and knelt before him and kissed his hand in Oriental fashion.

Clad in sumptuous garments, he would gaze out of the window and think of his past exploits; and wish that he might again run in the desert in pursuit of ostriches and gazelles, hide among the bamboos to watch for leopards, ride through forests filled with rhinoceroses, climb the most inaccessible peaks in order to have a better aim at the eagles, and fight the polar bears on the icebergs of the northern sea.

Sometimes, in his dreams, he fancied himself like Adam in the midst of Paradise, surrounded by all the beasts; by merely extending his arm, he was able to kill them; or else they filed past him, in pairs, by order of size, from the lions and the elephants to the ermines and the ducks, as on the day they entered Noah's Ark.

Hidden in the shadow of a cave, he aimed unerring arrows at them; then came others and still others, until he awoke, wild-eyed.

Princes, friends of his, invited him to their meets, but he always refused their invitations, because he thought that by this kind of penance he might possibly avert the threatened misfortune; it seemed to him that the fate of his parents depended on his refusal to slaughter animals. But he suffered because he could not see them, and his other desire was growing well-nigh unbearable.

In order to divert his mind, his wife had dancers and jugglers come to the castle.

She went abroad with him in an open litter; at other times, stretched out on the edge of a boat, they watched for hours the fish disport themselves in the water, which was as clear as the sky. Often she playfully threw flowers at him or nestling at his feet she played melodies on an old mandolin; then, clasping her hands on his shoulder, she would inquire tremulously: "What troubles thee, my dear lord?"

He would not reply, or else he would burst into tears; but at last, one day, he confessed his fearful dread.

His wife scorned the idea and reasoned wisely with him: probably his father and mother were dead; and even if he should ever see them again, through what chance, to what end, would he arrive at this abomination? Therefore, his fears were groundless, and he should hunt again.

Julian listened to her and smiled, but he could not bring himself to yield to his desire.

One August evening when they were in their bed-chamber, she having just retired and he being about to kneel in prayer, he heard the yelping of a fox and light footsteps under the window; and he thought he saw things in the dark that looked like animals. The temptation was too strong. He seized his quiver.

His wife appeared astonished.

"I am obeying you," quoth he, "and I shall be back at sunrise."

However, she feared that some calamity would happen. But he reassured her and departed, surprised at her illogical moods.

A short time afterwards, a page came to announce that two strangers desired, in the absence of the lord of the castle, to see its mistress at once.

Soon a stooping old man and an aged woman entered the room; their coarse garments were covered with dust and each leaned on a stick.

They grew bold enough to say that they brought Julian news of his parents. She leaned out of the bed to listen to them. But after glancing at each other, the old people asked her whether he ever referred to them and if he still loved them.

"Oh! yes!" she said.

Then they exclaimed:

"We are his parents!" and they sat themselves down, for they were very tired.

But there was nothing to show the young wife that her husband was their son.

They proved it by describing to her the birthmarks he had on his body. Then she jumped out of bed, called a page, and ordered that a repast be served to them.

But although they were very hungry, they could scarcely eat, and she observed surreptitiously how their lean fingers trembled whenever they lifted their cups.

They asked a hundred questions about their son, and she answered each one of them, but she was careful not to refer to the terrible idea that concerned them.

When he failed to return, they had left their château; and had wandered for several years, following vague indications but without losing hope.

So much money had been spent at the tolls of the rivers and in inns, to satisfy the rights of princes and the demands of highwaymen, that now their purse was quite empty and they were obliged to beg. But what did it matter, since they were about to clasp again their son in their arms? They lauded his happiness in having such a beautiful wife, and did not tire of looking at her and kissing her.

The luxuriousness of the apartment astonished them; and the old man, after examining the wall, inquired why they bore the coat-of-arms of the Emperor of Occitania.

"He is my father," she replied.

And he marvelled and remembered the prediction of the gipsy, while his wife meditated upon the words the hermit had spoken to her. The glory of their son was undoubtedly only the dawn of eternal splendours, and the old people remained awed while the light from the candelabra on the table fell on them.

In the heyday of youth, both had been extremely handsome. The mother had not lost her hair, and bands of snowy whiteness framed her cheeks; and the father, with his stalwart figure and long beard, looked like a carved image.

Julian's wife prevailed upon them not to wait for him. She put them in her bed and closed the curtains; and they both fell asleep. The day broke and outdoors the little birds began to chirp.

Meanwhile, Julian had left the castle grounds and walked nervously through the forest, enjoying the velvety softness of the grass and the balminess of the air.

The shadow of the trees fell on the earth. Here and there, the moonlight flecked the glades and Julian feared to advance, because he mistook the silvery light for water and the tranquil surface of the pools for grass. A great stillness reigned everywhere, and he failed to see any of the beasts that only a moment ago were prowling around the castle. As he walked on, the woods grew thicker, and the darkness more impenetrable. Warm winds, filled with enervating perfumes, caressed him; he sank into masses of dead leaves, and after a while he leaned against on oak-tree to rest and catch his breath.

Suddenly a body blacker than the surrounding darkness sprang from behind the tree. It was a wild boar. Julian did not have time to stretch his bow, and he bewailed the fact as if it were some great misfortune. Presently, having left the woods, he beheld a wolf slinking along a hedge.

He aimed an arrow at him. The wolf paused, turned his head and quietly continued on his way. He trotted along, always keeping at the same distance, pausing now and then to look around and resuming his flight as soon as an arrow was aimed in his direction.

In this way Julian traversed an apparently endless plain, then sand-hills,and at last found himself on a plateau that dominated a great stretch of land. Large flat stones were interspersed among crumbling vaults; bones and skeletons covered the ground, and here and there some mouldy crosses stood desolate. But presently, shapes moved in the darkness of the tombs, and from them came panting, wild-eyed hyenas. They approached him and smelled him, grinning hideously and disclosing their gums. He whipped out his sword, but they scattered in every direction and continuing their swift, limping gallop, disappeared in a cloud of dust.

Some time afterwards, in a ravine, he encountered a wild bull, with threatening horns, pawing the sand with his hoofs. Julian thrust his lance between his dewlaps. But his weapon snapped as if the beast were made of bronze; then he closed his eyes in anticipation of his death. When he opened them again, the bull had vanished.

Then his soul collapsed with shame. Some supernatural power destroyed his strength, and he set out for home through the forest. The woods were a tangle of creeping plants that he had to cut with his sword, and while he was thus engaged, a weasel slid between his feet, a panther jumped over his shoulder, and a serpent wound itself around an ash-tree.

Among its leaves was a monstrous jackdaw that watched Julian intently, and here and there, between the branches, appeared great, fiery sparks as if the sky were raining all its stars upon the forest. But the sparks were the eyes of wild-cats, owls, squirrels, monkeys, and parrots.

Julian aimed his arrows at them, but the feathered weapons lighted on the leaves of the trees and looked like white butterflies. He threw stones at them; but the missiles did not strike, and fell to the ground. Then he cursed himself, and howled imprecations, and in his rage he could have struck himself.

Then all the beasts he had pursued appeared, and formed a narrow circle around him. Some sat on their hindquarters, while others stood at full height. And Julian remained among them, transfixed with terror and absolutely unable to move. By a supreme effort of his will-power, he took a step forward; those that perched in the trees opened their wings, those that trod the earth moved their limbs, and all accompanied him.

The hyenas strode in front of him, the wolf and the wild boar brought up the rear. On his right, the bull swung its head and on his left the serpent crawled through the grass while the panther, arching its back, advanced with velvety footfalls and long strides. Julian walked as slowly as possible, so as not to irritate them, while in the depth of the bushes he could distinguish porcupines, foxes, vipers, jackals, and bears.

He began to run; the brutes followed him. The serpent hissed, the malodorous beasts frothed at the mouth, the wild boar rubbed his tusks against his heels, and the wolf scratched the palms of his hands with the hairs of his snout. The monkeys pinched him and made faces, the weasel rolled over his feet. A bear knocked his cap off with its huge paw, and the panther disdainfully dropped an arrow it was about to put in its mouth.

Irony seemed to incite their sly actions. As they watched him out of the corners of their eyes, they seemed to meditate a plan of revenge, and Julian, who was deafened by the buzzing of the insects, bruised by the wings and tails of the birds, choked by the stench of animal breaths, walked with outstretched arms and closed lids, like a blind man, without even the strength to beg for mercy.

The crowing of a cock vibrated in the air. Other cocks responded; it was day; and Julian recognised the top of his palace rising above the orange-trees.

Then, on the edge of a field, he beheld some red partridges fluttering around a stubble-field. He unfastened his cloak and threw it over them like a net. When he lifted it, he found only a bird that had been dead a long time and was decaying.

This disappointment irritated him more than all the others. The thirst for carnage stirred afresh within him; animals failing him, he desired to slaughter men.

He climbed the three terraces and opened the door with a blow of his fist; but at the foot of the staircase, the memory of his beloved wife softened his heart. No doubt she was asleep, and he would go up and surprise her. Having removed his sandals, he unlocked the door softly and entered.

The stained windows dimmed the pale light of dawn. Julian stumbled over some garments lying on the floor and a little further on, he knocked against a table covered with dishes. "She must have eaten," he thought; so he advanced cautiously towards the bed which was concealed by the darkness in the back of the room. When he reached the edge, he leaned over the pillow where the two heads were resting close together and stooped to kiss his wife. His mouth encountered a man's beard.

He fell back, thinking he had become crazed; then he approached the bed again and his searching fingers discovered some hair which seemed to be very long. In order to convince himself that he was mistaken, he once more passed his hand slowly over the pillow. But this time he was sure that it was a beard and that a man was there! a man lying beside his wife!

Flying into an ingovernable passion, he sprang upon them with his drawn dagger, foaming, stamping, and howling like a wild beast. After a while he stopped.

The corpses, pierced through the heart, had not even moved. He listened attentively to the two death-rattles, they were almost alike, as they grew fainter, another voice, coming from far away, seemed to continue them. Uncertain at first, this plaintive voice came nearer and nearer, grew louder and louder and presently he recognised, with a feeling of abject terror, the bellowing of the great black stag.

And as he turned around, he thought he saw the spectre of his wife standing at the threshold with a light in her hand.

The sound of the murder had aroused her. In one glance she understood what had happened and fled in horror, letting the candle drop from her hand. Julian picked it up.

His father and mother lay before him, stretched on their backs, with gaping wounds in their breasts; and their faces, the expression of which was full of tender dignity, seemed to hide what might be an eternal secret.

Splashes and blotches of blood were on their white skin, on the bed-clothes, on the floor, and on an ivory Christ which hung in the alcove. The scarlet reflection of the stained window, which just then was struck by the sun, lighted up the bloody spots and appeared to scatter them around the whole room. Julian walked toward the corpses, repeating to himself and trying to believe that he was mistaken, that it was not possible, that there are often inexplicable likenesses.

At last he bent over to look closely at the old man and he saw, between the half-closed lids, a dead pupil that scorched him like fire. Then he went over to the other side of the bed, where the other corpse lay, but the face was partly hidden by bands of white hair. Julian slipped his finger beneath them and raised the head, holding it at arm's length to study its features, while, with his other hand he lifted the torch. Drops of blood oozed from the mattress and fell one by one upon the floor.

At the close of the day, he appeared before his wife, and in a changed voice commanded her first not to answer him, not to approach him, not even to look at him, and to obey, under the penalty of eternal damnation, every one of his orders, which were irrevocable.

The funeral was to be held in accordance with the written instructions he had left on a chair in the death-chamber.

He left her his castle, his vassals, all his worldly goods, without keeping even his clothes or his sandals, which would be found at the top of the stairs.

She had obeyed the will of God in bringing about his crime, and accordingly she must pray for his soul, since henceforth he should cease to exist.

The dead were buried sumptuously in the chapel of a monastery which it took three days to reach from the castle. A monk wearing a hood that covered his head followed the procession alone, for nobody dared to speak to him. And during the mass, he lay flat on the floor with his face downward and his arms stretched out at his sides.

After the burial, he was seen to take the road leading into the mountains. He looked back several times, and finally passed out of sight.

III

He left the country and begged his daily bread on his way.

He stretched out his hand to the horsemen he met in the roads, and humbly approached the harvesters in the fields; or else remained motionless in front of the gates of castles; and his face was so sad that he was never turned away.

Obeying a spirit of humility, he related his history to all men, and they would flee from him and cross themselves. In villages through which he had passed before, the good people bolted the doors, threatened him, and threw stones at him as soon as they recognised him. The more charitable ones placed a bowl on the window-sill and closed the shutters in order to avoid seeing him.

Repelled and shunned by everyone, he avoided his fellow men and nourished himself with roots and plants, stray fruits and shells which he gathered along the shores.

Often, at the bend of a hill, he could perceive a mass of crowded roofs, stone spires, bridges, towers and narrow streets, from which arose a continual murmur of activity.

The desire to mingle with men impelled him to enter the city. But the gross and beastly expression of their faces, the noise of their industries and the indifference of their remarks, chilled his very heart. On holidays, when the cathedral bells rang out at daybreak and filled the people's hearts with gladness, he watched the inhabitants coming out of their dwellings, the dancers in the public squares, the fountains of ale, the damask hangings spread before the houses of princes; and then, when night came, he would peer through the windows at the long tables where families gathered and where grandparents held little children on their knees; then sobs would rise in his throat and he would turn away and go back to his haunts.

He gazed with yearning at the colts in the pastures, the birds in their nests, the insects on the flowers; but they all fled from him at his approach and hid or flew away. So he sought solitude. But the wind brought to his ears sounds resembling death-rattles; the tears of the dew reminded him of heavier drops, and every evening, the sun would spread blood in the sky, and every night, in his dreams, he lived over his parricide.

He made himself a hair-cloth lined with iron spikes.[8] On his knees, he ascended every hill that was crowned with a chapel. But the unrelenting thought spoiled the splendour of the tabernacles and tortured him in the midst of his penances.

He did not rebel against God, who had inflicted his action, but he despaired at the thought that he had committed it.

He had such a horror of himself that he took all sorts of risks. He rescued paralytics from fire and children from the waves. But the ocean scorned him and the flames spared him. Time did not allay his torment, which became so intolerable that he resolved to die.

One day, while he was stooping over a fountain to judge of its depth, an old man appeared on the other side. He wore a white beard and his appearance was so lamentable that Julian could not keep back his tears. The old man also was weeping. Without recognising him, Julian remembered confusedly a face that resembled his. He uttered a cry; for it was his father who stood before him; and he gave up all thought of taking his own life.

Thus weighted down by his recollections, he travelled through

8. I.e., an intentionally uncomfortable garment.

many countries and arrived at a river which was dangerous, because of its violence and the slime that covered its shore. Since a long time nobody had ventured to cross it.

The bow of an old boat, whose stern was buried in the mud, showed among the reeds. Julian, on examining it closely found a pair of oars and hit upon the idea of devoting his life to the service of his fellow-men.

He began by establishing on the bank of the river a sort of road which would enable people to approach the edge of the stream; he broke his nails in his efforts to lift enormous stones which he pressed against the pit of his stomach in order to transport them from one point to another; he slipped in the mud, he sank into it, and several times was on the very brink of death.

Then he took to repairing the boat with débris of vessels, and afterwards built himself a hut with putty and trunks of trees.

When it became known that a ferry had been established, passengers flocked to it. They hailed him from the opposite side by waving flags, and Julian would jump into the boat and row over. The craft was very heavy, and the people loaded it with all sorts of baggage, and beasts of burden, who reared with fright, thereby adding greatly to the confusion. He asked nothing for his trouble; some gave him left-over victuals which they took from their sacks or worn-out garments which they could no longer use.

The brutal ones hurled curses at him, and when he rebuked them gently they replied with insults, and he was content to bless them.

A little table, a stool, a bed made of dead leaves and three earthen bowls were all he possessed. Two holes in the wall served as windows. On one side, as far as the eye could see, stretched barren wastes studded here and there with pools of water; and in front of him flowed the greenish waters of the wide river. In the spring, a putrid odor arose from the damp sod. Then fierce gales lifted clouds of dust that blew everywhere, even settling in the water and in one's mouth. A little later swarms of mosquitoes appeared, whose buzzing and stinging continued night and day. After that, came frightful frosts which communicated a stone-like rigidity to everything and inspired one with an insane desire for meat. Months passed when Julian never saw a human being. He often closed his lids and endeavored to recall his youth;—he beheld the courtyard of a castle, with greyhounds stretched out on a terrace, an armoury filled with valets, and under a bower of vines a youth with blond curls, sitting between an old man wrapped in furs and a lady with a high cap; presently the corpses rose before him, and then he would throw himself face downward on his cot and sob:

"Oh! poor father! poor mother! poor mother!" and would drop

into a fitful slumber in which the terrible visions recurred.

One night he thought that some one was calling to him in his sleep. He listened intently, but could hear nothing save the roaring of the waters.

But the same voice repeated: "Julian!"

It proceeded from the opposite shore, a fact which appeared extraordinary to him, considering the breadth of the river.

The voice called a third time: "Julian!"

And the high-pitched tones sounded like the ringing of a church-bell.

Having lighted his lantern, he stepped out of his cabin. A frightful storm raged. The darkness was complete and was illuminated here and there only by the white waves leaping and tumbling.

After a moment's hesitation, he untied the rope. The water presently grew smooth and the boat glided easily to the opposite shore, where a man was waiting.

He was wrapped in a torn piece of linen; his face was like a chalk mask, and his eyes were redder than glowing coals. When Julian held up his lantern he noticed that the stranger was covered with hideous sores; but notwithstanding this, there was in his attitude something like the majesty of a king.

As soon as he stepped into the boat, it sank deep into the water, borne downward by his weight; then it rose again and Julian began to row.

With each stroke of the oars, the force of the waves raised the bow of the boat. The water, which was blacker than ink, ran furiously along the sides. It formed abysses and then mountains, over which the boat glided, then it fell into yawning depths where, buffeted by the wind, it whirled around and around.

Julian leaned far forward and, bracing himself with his feet, bent backwards so as to bring his whole strength into play. Hail-stones cut his hands, the rain ran down his back, the velocity of the wind suffocated him. He stopped rowing and let the boat drift with the tide. But realising that an important matter was at stake, a command which could not be disregarded, he picked up the oars again; and the rattling of the tholes mingled with the clamourings of the storm.

The little lantern burned in front of him. Sometimes birds fluttered past it and obscured the light. But he could distinguish the eyes of the leper who stood at the stern, as motionless as a column.

And the trip lasted a long, long time.

When they reached the hut, Julian closed the door and saw the man sit down on the stool. The species of shroud that was wrapped around him had fallen below his loins, and his shoulders and chest and lean arms were hidden under blotches of scaly pustules. Enormous wrinkles crossed his forehead. Like a skeleton, he had a hole instead of a nose, and from his bluish lips came breath which was fetid and as thick as mist.

"I am hungry," he said.

Julian set before him what he had, a piece of pork and some crusts of coarse bread.

After he had devoured them, the table, the bowl, and the handle of the knife bore the same scales that covered his body.

Then he said: "I thirst!"

Julian fetched his jug of water and when he lifted it, he smelled an aroma that dilated his nostrils and filled his heart with gladness. It was wine; what a boon! but the leper stretched out his arm and emptied the jug at one draught.

Then he said: "I am cold!"

Julian ignited a bundle of ferns that lay in the middle of the hut. The leper approached the fire and, resting on his heels, began to warm himself; his whole frame shook and he was failing visibly; his eyes grew dull, his sores began to break, and in a faint voice he whispered:

"Thy bed!"

Julian helped him gently to it, and even laid the sail of his boat over him to keep him warm.

The leper tossed and moaned. The corners of his mouth were drawn up over his teeth; an accelerated death-rattle shook his chest and with each one of his aspirations, his stomach touched his spine. At last, he closed his eyes.

"I feel as if ice were in my bones! Lay thyself beside me!" he commanded. Julian took off his garments; and then, as naked as on the day he was born, he got into the bed; against his thigh he could feel the skin of the leper, and it was colder than a serpent and as rough as a file.

He tried to encourage the leper, but he only whispered:

"Oh! I am about to die! Come closer to me and warm me! Not with thy hands! No! with thy whole body."

So Julian stretched himself out upon the leper, lay on him, lips to lips, chest to chest.

Then the leper clasped him close and presently his eyes shone like stars; his hair lengthened into sunbeams; the breath of his nostrils had the scent of roses; a cloud of incense rose from the hearth, and the waters began to murmur harmoniously; an abundance of bliss, a superhuman joy, filled the soul of the swooning Julian, while he who clasped him to his breast grew and grew until his head and his feet touched the opposite walls of the cabin. The roof flew up in the air, disclosing the heavens, and Julian ascended into infinity face to face with our Lord Jesus Christ, who bore him straight to heaven.

And this is the story of Saint Julian the Hospitaller, as it is given on the stained-glass window of a church in my birthplace.

---

1. How many times does Julian's life change direction? Are all the courses he follows necessary to bring him to sainthood?
2. If you leave the supernatural out of account, does the remainder of the story seem psychologically true? Explain Julian's psychological motivations at the main stages of his life.
3. Can the three major prophecies about Julian be explained as wishes? How might the wishes influence the development of his character?
4. What major paradoxes do you find in the action and its outcome?
5. In the last paragraph the author tells us his story was "given" by a stained-glass window. What special qualities of description and narration seem to reflect this pictorial source?
6. How has the author shaped the tone of the story to fit his legendary subject matter?

E. M. Forster

Forster (1879–1970) was born in London. After completing his education at Cambridge, he traveled in Italy and Greece, forming impressions that were often to recur in the settings and themes of his fiction. While still a very young man, he began in 1905 to publish a group of novels that appeared in quick succession until 1910. These early novels are structured on conflicts between the stifling pettiness of conventional English life and the impulses of youth toward a larger and freer manner of living. After his first burst of productivity Forster published no more novels until 1924, when A Passage to India *appeared, and thereafter produced no more major fiction. (A novel,* Maurice, *which had evidently been withheld by its author because of its homosexual subject matter, was published posthumously in 1971.) During the latter decades of his life Forster remained quietly at home in Cambridge, reading happily at his own pace, refraining from literary or political controversies, and occasionally publishing criticism and essays which reflect his skeptical, good-natured humanism. The rich common sense of* Aspects of the Novel *(1927) makes it an invaluable primer for the critic of fiction.* Abinger Harvest *(1927) and* Two Cheers for Democracy *(1951) range widely over the culture of our times. Forster's novels include* The Longest Journey *(1907),* A Room with a View *(1908), and* Howards End *(1910). His short stories can be found in* The Collected Tales of E. M. Forster *(1947) and* The Life to Come and Other Stories *(1972).*

The Road from Colonus[1]

I

For no very intelligible reason, Mr. Lucas had hurried ahead of his party. He was perhaps reaching the age at which independence becomes valuable, because it is so soon to be lost. Tired of attention and consideration, he liked breaking away from the younger members, to ride by himself, and to dismount unassisted. Perhaps he also relished that more subtle pleasure of being kept waiting for lunch, and of telling the others on their arrival that it was of no consequence.

1. After blinding himself and fleeing Thebes when he learned he had killed his father and married his mother, Oedipus wandered with his daughters until he came to Colonus. There in a sacred grove he sat down and refused to leave. Presently, amid rumblings of the earth, the gods carried him off to his rest. See Sophocles' play *Oedipus at Colonus*.

So, with childish impatience, he battered the animal's sides with his heels, and made the muleteer bang it with a thick stick and prick it with a sharp one, and jolted down the hillsides through clumps of flowering shrubs and stretches of anemones and asphodel, till he heard the sound of running water, and came in sight of the group of plane trees where they were to have their meal.

Even in England those trees would have been remarkable, so huge were they, so interlaced, so magnificently clothed in quivering green. And here in Greece they were unique, the one cool spot in that hard brilliant landscape, already scorched by the heat of an April sun. In their midst was hidden a tiny Khan or country inn, a frail mud building with a broad wooden balcony in which sat an old woman spinning, while a small brown pig, eating orange peel, stood beside her. On the wet earth below squatted two children, playing some primeval game with their fingers; and their mother, none too clean either, was messing with some rice inside. As Mrs. Forman would have said, it was all very Greek, and the fastidious Mr. Lucas felt thankful that they were bringing their own food with them, and should eat it in the open air.

Still, he was glad to be there—the muleteer had helped him off—and glad that Mrs. Forman was not there to forestall his opinions—glad even that he should not see Ethel for quite half an hour. Ethel was his youngest daughter, still unmarried. She was unselfish and affectionate, and it was generally understood that she was to devote her life to her father, and be the comfort of his old age. Mrs. Forman always referred to her as Antigone,[2] and Mr. Lucas tried to settle down to the role of Oedipus, which seemed the only one that public opinion allowed him.

He had this in common with Oedipus, that he was growing old. Even to himself it had become obvious. He had lost interest in other people's affairs, and seldom attended when they spoke to him. He was fond of talking himself but often forgot what he was going to say, and even when he succeeded, it seldom seemed worth the effort. His phrases and gestures had become stiff and set, his anecdotes, once so successful, fell flat, his silence was as meaningless as his speech. Yet he had led a healthy, active life, had worked steadily, made money, educated his children. There was nothing and no one to blame: he was simply growing old.

At the present moment, here he was in Greece, and one of the dreams of his life was realized. Forty years ago he had caught the fever of Hellenism,[3] and all his life he had felt that could he but visit that land, he would not have lived in vain. But Athens had been dusty,

2. Daughter of Oedipus. 3. Spirit and culture of Greece.

Delphi[4] wet, Thermopylae[5] flat, and he had listened with amazement and cynicism to the rapturous exclamations of his companions. Greece was like England: it was a man who was growing old, and it made no difference whether that man looked at the Thames or the Eurotas.[6] It was his last hope of contradicting that logic of experience, and it was failing.

Yet Greece had done something for him, though he did not know it. It had made him discontented, and there are stirrings of life in discontent. He knew that he was not the victim of continual ill-luck. Something great was wrong, and he was pitted against no mediocre or accidental enemy. For the last month a strange desire had possessed him to die fighting.

"Greece is the land for young people," he said to himself as he stood under the plane trees, "but I will enter into it, I will possess it. Leaves shall be green again, water shall be sweet, the sky shall be blue. They were so forty years ago, and I will win them back. I do mind being old, and I will pretend no longer."

He took two steps forward, and immediately cold waters were gurgling over his ankle.

"Where does the water come from?" he asked himself. "I do not even know that." He remembered that all the hillsides were dry; yet here the road was suddenly covered with flowing streams.

He stopped still in amazement, saying: "Water out of a tree—out of a hollow tree? I never saw nor thought of that before."

For the enormous plane that leant towards the Khan was hollow—it had been burnt out for charcoal—and from its living trunk there gushed an impetuous spring, coating the bark with fern and moss, and flowing over the mule track to create fertile meadows beyond. The simple country folk had paid to beauty and mystery such tribute as they could, for in the rind of the tree a shrine was cut, holding a lamp and a little picture of the Virgin, inheritor of the Naiad's and Dryad's[7] joint abode.

"I never saw anything so marvellous before," said Mr. Lucas. "I could even step inside the trunk and see where the water comes from."

For a moment he hesitated to violate the shrine. Then he remembered with a smile his own thought—"the place shall be mine; I will enter it and possess it"—and leapt almost aggressively onto a stone within.

The water pressed up steadily and noiselessly from the hollow roots and hidden crevices of the plane, forming a wonderful amber pool ere it spilt over the lip of bark on to the earth outside. Mr. Lucas

4. Ancient Greek city famous for its oracle. 5. Pass in Eastern Greece where Persians defeated Spartans in 480 B.C. 6. Rivers in England and Greece. 7. Wood nymph; *naiad:* a water nymph.

tasted it and it was sweet, and when he looked up the black funnel of the trunk he saw sky which was blue, and some leaves which were green; and he remembered, without smiling, another of his thoughts.

Others had been before him—indeed he had a curious sense of companionship. Little votive offerings to the presiding Power were fastened on to the bark—tiny arms and legs and eyes in tin, grotesque models of the brain or the heart—all tokens of some recovery of strength or wisdom or love. There was no such thing as the solitude of nature, for the sorrows and joys of humanity had pressed even into the bosom of a tree. He spread out his arms and steadied himself against the soft charred wood, and then slowly leant back, till his body was resting on the trunk behind. His eyes closed, and he had the strange feeling of one who is moving, yet at peace—the feeling of the swimmer, who, after long struggling with chopping seas, finds that after all the tide will sweep him to his goal.

So he lay motionless, conscious only of the stream below his feet, and that all things were a stream, in which he was moving.

He was aroused at last by a shock—the shock of an arrival perhaps, for when he opened his eyes, something unimagined, indefinable, had passed over all things, and made them intelligible and good.

There was meaning in the stoop of the old woman over her work, and in the quick motions of the little pig, and in her diminishing globe of wool. A young man came singing over the streams on a mule, and there was beauty in his pose and sincerity in his greeting. The sun made no accidental patterns upon the spreading roots of the trees, and there was intention in the nodding clumps of asphodel, and in the music of the water. To Mr. Lucas, who, in a brief space of time, had discovered not only Greece, but England and all the world and life, there seemed nothing ludicrous in the desire to hang within the tree another votive offering—a little model of an entire man.

"Why, here's papa, playing at being Merlin."[8]

All unnoticed they had arrived—Ethel, Mrs. Forman, Mr. Graham, and the English-speaking dragoman.[9] Mr. Lucas peered out at them suspiciously. They had suddenly become unfamiliar, and all that they did seemed strained and coarse.

"Allow me to give you a hand," said Mr. Graham, a young man who was always polite to his elders.

Mr. Lucas felt annoyed. "Thank you, I can manage perfectly well by myself," he replied. His foot slipped as he stepped out of the tree, and went into the spring.

8. Legendary English magician associated with King Arthur's Court. 9. Interpreter.

"Oh papa, my papa!" said Ethel, "what are you doing? Thank goodness I have got a change for you on the mule."

She tended him carefully, giving him clean socks and dry boots, and then sat him down on the rug beside the lunch basket, while she went with the others to explore the grove.

They came back in ecstasies, in which Mr. Lucas tried to join. But he found them intolerable. Their enthusiasm was superficial, commonplace, and spasmodic. They had no perception of the coherent beauty that was flowering around them. He tried at least to explain his feelings, and what he said was:

"I am altogether pleased with the appearance of this place. It impresses me very favourably. The trees are fine, remarkably fine for Greece, and there is something very poetic in the spring of clear running water. The people too seem kindly and civil. It is decidedly an attractive place."

Mrs. Forman upbraided him for his tepid praise.

"Oh, it is a place in a thousand!" she cried, "I could live and die here! I really would stop if I had not to be back at Athens! It reminds me of the Colonus of Sophocles."

"Well, *I* must stop," said Ethel. "I positively must."

"Yes, do! You and your father! Antigone and Oedipus. Of course you must stop at Colonus!"

Mr. Lucas was almost breathless with excitement. When he stood within the tree, he had believed that his happiness would be independent of locality. But these few minutes' conversation had undeceived him. He no longer trusted himself to journey through the world, for old thoughts, old wearinesses might be waiting to rejoin him as soon as he left the shade of the planes, and the music of the virgin water. To sleep in the Khan with the gracious, kind-eyed country people, to watch the bats flit about within the globe of shade, and see the moon turn the golden patterns into silver—one such night would place him beyond relapse, and confirm him forever in the kingdom he had regained. But all his lips could say was: "I should be willing to put in a night here."

"You mean a week, papa! It would be sacrilege to put in less."

"A week then, a week," said his lips, irritated at being corrected, while his heart was leaping with joy. All through lunch he spoke to them no more, but watched the place he should know so well, and the people who would so soon be his companions and friends. The inmates of the Khan only consisted of an old woman, a middle-aged woman, a young man and two children, and to none of them had he spoken, yet he loved them as he loved everything that moved or breathed or existed beneath the benedictory shade of the planes.

"En route!"[1] said the shrill voice of Mrs. Forman. "Ethel! Mr. Graham! The best of things must end."

"Tonight," thought Mr. Lucas, "they will light the little lamp by the shrine. And when we all sit together on the balcony, perhaps they will tell me which offerings they put up."

"I beg your pardon, Mr. Lucas," said Graham, "but they want to fold up the rug you are sitting on."

Mr. Lucas got up, saying to himself: "Ethel shall go to bed first, and then I will try to tell them about my offering too—for it is a thing I must do. I think they will understand if I am left with them alone."

Ethel touched him on the cheek. "Papa! I've called you three times. All the mules are here."

"Mules? What mules?"

"Our mules. We're all waiting. Oh, Mr. Graham, do help my father on."

"I don't know what you're talking about, Ethel."

"My dearest papa, we must start. You know we have to get to Olympia tonight."

Mr. Lucas in pompous, confident tones replied: "I always did wish, Ethel, that you had a better head for plans. You know perfectly well that we are putting in a week here. It is your own suggestion."

Ethel was startled into impoliteness. "What a perfectly ridiculous idea. You must have known I was joking. Of course I meant I wished we could."

"Ah! if we could only do what we wished!" sighed Mrs. Forman, already seated on her mule.

"Surely," Ethel continued in calmer tones, "you didn't think I meant it."

"Most certainly I did. I have made all my plans on the supposition that we are stopping here, and it will be extremely inconvenient, indeed, impossible for me to start."

He delivered this remark with an air of great conviction, and Mrs. Forman and Mr. Graham had to turn away to hide their smiles.

"I am sorry I spoke so carelessly; it was wrong of me. But, you know, we can't break up our party, and even one night here would make us miss the boat at Patras."

Mrs. Forman, in an aside, called Mr. Graham's attention to the excellent way in which Ethel managed her father.

"I don't mind about the Patras boat. You said that we should stop here, and we are stopping."

It seemed as if the inhabitants of the Khan had divined in some mysterious way that the altercation touched them. The old woman

1. "On our way!"

stopped her spinning, while the young man and the two children stood behind Mr. Lucas, as if supporting him.

Neither arguments nor entreaties moved him. He said little, but he was absolutely determined, because for the first time he saw his daily life aright. What need had he to return to England? Who would miss him? His friends were dead or cold. Ethel loved him in a way, but, as was right, she had other interests. His other children he seldom saw. He had only one other relative, his sister Julia, whom he both feared and hated. It was no effort to struggle. He would be a fool as well as a coward if he stirred from the place which brought him happiness and peace.

At last Ethel, to humour him, and not disinclined to air her modern Greek, went into the Khan with the astonished dragoman to look at the rooms. The woman inside received them with loud welcomes, and the young man, when no one was looking, began to lead Mr. Lucas' mule to the stable.

"Drop it, you brigand!" shouted Graham, who always declared that foreigners could understand English if they chose. He was right, for the man obeyed, and they all stood waiting for Ethel's return.

She emerged at last, with close-gathered skirts, followed by the dragoman bearing the little pig, which he had bought at a bargain.

"My dear papa, I will do all I can for you, but stop in that Khan—no."

"Are there—fleas?" asked Mrs. Forman.

Ethel intimated that "fleas" was not the word.

"Well, I am afraid that settles it," said Mrs. Forman, "I know how particular Mr. Lucas is."

"It does not settle it," said Mr. Lucas. "Ethel, you go on. I do not want you. I don't know why I ever consulted you. I shall stop here alone."

"That is absolute nonsense," said Ethel, losing her temper. "How can you be left alone at your age? How would you get your meals or your bath? All your letters are waiting for you at Patras. You'll miss the boat. That means missing the London operas, and upsetting all your engagements for the month. And as if you could travel by yourself!"

"They might knife you," was Mr. Graham's contribution.

The Greeks said nothing; but whenever Mr. Lucas looked their way, they beckoned him towards the Khan. The children would even have drawn him by the coat, and the old woman on the balcony stopped her almost completed spinning, and fixed him with mysterious appealing eyes. As he fought, the issue assumed gigantic proportions, and he believed that he was not merely stopping because he had regained youth or seen beauty or found happiness, but because in that place and with those people a supreme event was awaiting him which would transfigure the face of the world. The moment was so tremendous that he abandoned words and arguments as useless, and rested on the strength of his mighty unrevealed allies: silent men, murmuring water, and whispering trees. For the whole place called with one voice, articulate to him, and his garrulous opponents became every minute more meaningless and absurd. Soon they would be tired and go chattering away into the sun, leaving him to the cool grove and the moonlight and the destiny he foresaw.

Mrs. Forman and the dragoman had indeed already started, amid the piercing screams of the little pig, and the struggle might have gone on indefinitely if Ethel had not called in Mr. Graham.

"Can you help me?" she whispered. "He is absolutely unmanageable."

"I'm no good at arguing—but if I could help you in any other way—" and he looked down complacently at his well-made figure.

Ethel hesitated. Then she said: "Help me in any way you can. After all, it is for his good that we do it."

"Then have his mule led up behind him."

So when Mr. Lucas thought he had gained the day, he suddenly felt himself lifted off the ground, and set sideways on the saddle, and at the same time the mule started off at a trot. He said nothing, for he had nothing to say, and even his face showed little emotion as he felt the shade pass and heard the sound of the water cease. Mr. Graham was running at his side, hat in hand, apologizing.

"I know I had no business to do it, and I do beg your pardon awfully. But I do hope that some day you too will feel that I was—damn!"

A stone had caught him in the middle of the back. It was thrown by the little boy, who was pursuing them along the mule track. He was followed by his sister, also throwing stones.

Ethel screamed to the dragoman, who was some way ahead with Mrs. Forman, but before he could rejoin them, another adversary appeared. It was the young Greek, who had cut them off in front, and now dashed down at Mr. Lucas' bridle. Fortunately Graham was an expert boxer, and it did not take him a moment to beat down the youth's feeble defense, and to send him sprawling with a bleeding mouth into the asphodel. By this time the dragoman had arrived, the children, alarmed at the fate of their brother, had desisted, and the rescue party, if such it is to be considered, retired in disorder to the trees.

"Little devils!" said Graham, laughing with triumph. "That's the modern Greek all over. Your father meant money if he stopped, and they consider we were taking it out of their pocket."

"Oh, they are terrible—simple savages! I don't know how I shall ever thank you. You've saved my father."

"I only hope you didn't think me brutal."

"No," replied Ethel with a little sigh. "I admire strength."

Meanwhile the cavalcade reformed, and Mr. Lucas, who, as Mrs. Forman said, bore his disappointment wonderfully well, was put comfortably on to his mule. They hurried up the opposite hillside, fearful of another attack, and it was not until they had left the eventful place far behind that Ethel found an opportunity to speak to her father and ask his pardon for the way she had treated him.

"You seemed so different, dear father, and you quite frightened me. Now I feel that you are your old self again."

He did not answer, and she concluded that he was not unnaturally offended at her behaviour.

By one of those curious tricks of mountain scenery, the place they had left an hour before suddenly reappeared far below them. The Khan was hidden under the green dome, but in the open there still stood three figures, and through the pure air rose up a faint cry of defiance or farewell.

Mr. Lucas stopped irresolutely, and let the reins fall from his hand.

"Come, father dear," said Ethel gently.

He obeyed, and in another moment a spur of the hill hid the dangerous scene forever.

II

It was breakfast time, but the gas was alight, owing to the fog. Mr. Lucas was in the middle of an account of a bad night he had spent. Ethel, who was to be married in a few weeks, had her arms on the table, listening.

"First the door bell rang, then you came back from the theater. Then the dog started, and after the dog the cat. And at three in the morning a young hooligan passed by singing. Oh yes: then there was the water gurgling in the pipe above my head."

"I think that was only the bath water running away," said Ethel, looking rather worn.

"Well, there's nothing I dislike more than running water. It's perfectly impossible to sleep in the house. I shall give it up. I shall give notice next quarter. I shall tell the landlord plainly, 'The reason I am giving up the house is this: it is perfectly impossible to sleep in it.' If he says—says—well, what has he got to say?"

"Some more toast, father?"

"Thank you, my dear." He took it, and there was an interval of peace.

But he soon recommenced. "I'm not going to submit to the practicing next door as tamely as they think. I wrote and told them so—didn't I?"

"Yes," said Ethel, who had taken care that the letter should not reach. "I have seen the governess, and she has promised to arrange it differently. And Aunt Julia hates noise. It will be sure to be all right."

Her aunt, being the only unattached member of the family, was coming to keep house for her father when she left him. The reference was not a happy one, and Mr. Lucas commenced a series of half articulate sighs, which was only stopped by the arrival of the post.

"Oh, what a parcel!" cried Ethel. "For me! What can it be! Greek stamps. This is most exciting!"

It proved to be some asphodel bulbs, sent by Mrs. Forman from Athens for planting in the conservatory.

"Doesn't it bring it all back! You remember the asphodels, father. And all wrapped up in Greek newspapers. I wonder if I can read them still. I used to be able to, you know."

She rattled on, hoping to conceal the laughter of the children next door—a favorite source of querulousness at breakfast time.

"Listen to me! 'A rural disaster.' Oh, I've hit on something sad. But never mind. 'Last Tuesday at Plataniste, in the province of Messenia, a shocking tragedy occurred. A large tree'—aren't I getting on well?—'blew down in the night and'—wait a minute—oh, dear! 'crushed to death the five occupants of the little Khan there, who had apparently been sitting in the balcony. The bodies of Maria Rhomaides, the aged proprietress, and of her daughter, aged forty-six, were easily recognizable, whereas that of her grandson'—oh, the rest is really too horrid; I wish I had never tried it, and what's more I feel to have heard the name Plataniste before. We didn't stop there, did we, in the spring?"

"We had lunch," said Mr. Lucas, with a faint expression of trouble on his vacant face. "Perhaps it was where the dragoman bought the pig."

"Of course," said Ethel in a nervous voice. "Where the dragoman bought the little pig. How terrible!"

"Very terrible!" said her father, whose attention was wandering to the noisy children next door. Ethel suddenly started to her feet with genuine interest.

"Good gracious!" she exclaimed. "This is an old paper. It happened not lately but in April—the night of Tuesday the eighteenth—and we—we must have been there in the afternoon."

"So we were," said Mr. Lucas. She put her hand to her heart, scarcely able to speak.

"Father, dear father, I must say it: you wanted to stop there. All those people, those poor half savage people, tried to keep you, they're dead. The whole place, it says, is in ruins, and even the stream has changed its course. Father, dear, if it had not been for me, and if Arthur had not helped me, you must have been killed."

Mr. Lucas waved his hand irritably. "It is not a bit of good speaking to the governess, I shall write to the landlord and say, 'The reason I am giving up the house is this: the dog barks, the children next door are intolerable, and I cannot stand the noise of running water.' "

Ethel did not check his babbling. She was aghast at the narrowness of the escape, and for a long time kept silence. At last she said: "Such a marvelous deliverance does make one believe in Providence."

Mr. Lucas, who was still composing his letter to the landlord, did not reply.

---

1. What is the importance of the setting? Of the references to mythology and antiquity?
2. The myth of Oedipus tells us that he blinded himself. What does this circumstance have to do with Mr. Lucas? Why does he try to "settle down" to the role of Oedipus?
3. What contrasts does Forster make between modern life and the life or spirit of antiquity?
4. Is Mr. Lucas lucky or unlucky to have escaped the fall of the tree?
5. Briefly state the theme of the story and relate it to the tone.

Mary E. Wilkins Freeman

Freeman (1852–1930) was born in Randolph, Massachusetts. As a child she was too frail to lead a normal life, and her schooling was irregular. When her immediate family died, she began to write in the hope of supporting herself and an aunt, publishing children's stories first before she found a more lucrative market with fiction for adults. For a time she was secretary to Oliver Wendell Holmes, Sr., father of the celebrated writer, and it was through this position that she made the acquaintance of established writers of her time. She left New England in 1902 when she married a doctor from New Jersey, but the majority of her two hundred and thirty stories and twelve novels dealt with characters in New England villages and the remnants of the Puritan culture. Among her novels are Jane Field *(1893),* Pembroke *(1894),* The Portion of Labor *(1901), and* The Shoulders of Atlas *(1908). Her books of short stories include* A New England Nun and Other Stories *(1891),* Young Lucretia *(1892), and* The Green Door *(1910).*

A New England Nun

It was late in the afternoon, and the light was waning. There was a difference in the look of the tree shadows out in the yard. Somewhere in the distance cows were lowing and a little bell was tinkling; now and then a farm-wagon tilted by, and the dust flew; some blue-shirted laborers with shovels over their shoulders plodded past; little swarms of flies were dancing up and down before the people's faces in the soft air. There seemed to be a gentle stir arising over everything for the mere sake of subsidence—a very premonition of rest and hush and night.

This soft diurnal commotion was over Louisa Ellis also. She had been peacefully sewing at her sitting-room window all the afternoon. Now she quilted her needle carefully into her work, which she folded precisely, and laid in a basket with her thimble and thread and scissors. Louisa Ellis could not remember that ever in her life she had mislaid one of these little feminine appurtenances, which had become, from long use and constant association, a very part of her personality.

Louisa tied a green apron round her waist, and got out a flat straw hat with a green ribbon. Then she went into the garden with a little blue crockery bowl, to pick some currants for her tea. After the currants were picked she sat on the back door-step and stemmed them, collecting the stems carefully in her apron, and afterwards throwing them into the hen-coop. She looked sharply at the grass beside the step to see if any had fallen there.

Louisa was slow and still in her movements; it took her a long time to prepare her tea; but when ready it was set forth with as much grace as if she had been a veritable guest to her own self. The little square table stood exactly in the centre of the kitchen, and was covered with a starched linen cloth whose border pattern of flowers glistened. Louisa had a damask napkin on her tea-tray, where were arranged a cut-glass tumbler full of teaspoons, a silver cream-pitcher, a china sugar-bowl, and one pink china cup and saucer. Louisa used china every day—something which none of her neighbors did. They whispered about it among themselves. Their daily tables were laid with common crockery, their sets of best china stayed in the parlor closet, and Louisa Ellis was no richer nor better bred than they. Still she would use the china. She had for her supper a glass dish full of sugared currants, a plate of little cakes, and one of light white biscuits. Also a leaf or two of lettuce, which she cut up daintily. Louisa was very fond of lettuce, which she raised to perfection in her little garden. She ate quite heartily, though in a delicate, pecking way; it seemed almost surprising that any considerable bulk of the food should vanish.

After tea she filled a plate with nicely baked thin corn-cakes, and carried them out into the back-yard.

"Caesar!" she called. "Caesar! Caesar!"

There was a little rush, and the clank of a chain, and a large yellow-and-white dog appeared at the door of his tiny hut, which was half hidden among the tall grasses and flowers. Louisa patted him and gave him the corn-cakes. Then she returned to the house and washed the tea-things, polishing the china carefully. The twilight had deepened; the chorus of the frogs floated in at the open window wonderfully loud and shrill, and once in a while a long sharp drone from a tree-toad pierced it. Louisa took off her green gingham apron, disclosing a shorter one of pink and white print. She lighted her lamp, and sat down again with her sewing.

In about half an hour Joe Dagget came. She heard his heavy step on the walk, and rose and took off her pink-and-white apron. Under that was still another—white linen with a little cambric edging on the bottom; that was Louisa's company apron. She never wore it without her calico sewing apron over it unless she had a guest. She had barely folded the pink and white one with methodical haste and laid it in a table-drawer when the door opened and Joe Dagget entered.

He seemed to fill up the whole room. A little yellow canary that had been asleep in his green cage at the south window woke up and fluttered wildly, beating his little yellow wings against the wires. He always did so when Joe Dagget came into the room.

"Good-evening," said Louisa. She extended her hand with a kind of solemn cordiality.

"Good-evening, Louisa," returned the man, in a loud voice.

She placed a chair for him, and they sat facing each other, with the table between them. He sat bolt-upright, toeing out his heavy feet squarely, glancing with a good-humored uneasiness around the room. She sat gently erect, folding her slender hands in her white-linen lap.

"Been a pleasant day," remarked Dagget.

"Real pleasant," Louisa assented, softly. "Have you been haying?" she asked, after a little while.

"Yes, I've been haying all day, down in the ten-acre lot. Pretty hot work."

"It must be."

"Yes, it's pretty hot work in the sun."

"Is your mother well to-day?"

"Yes, mother's pretty well."

"I suppose Lily Dyer's with her now?"

Dagget colored. "Yes, she's with her," he answered, slowly.

He was not very young, but there was a boyish look about his large face. Louisa was not quite as old as he, her face was fairer and smoother, but she gave people the impression of being older.

"I suppose she's a good deal of help to your mother," she said, further.

"I guess she is; I don't know how mother'd get along without her," said Dagget, with a sort of embarrassed warmth.

"She looks like a real capable girl. She's pretty-looking too," remarked Louisa.

"Yes, she is pretty fair looking."

Presently Dagget began fingering the books on the table. There was a square red autograph album, and a Young Lady's Gift-Book which had belonged to Louisa's mother. He took them up one after the other and opened them; then laid them down again, the album on the Gift-Book.

Louisa kept eying them with mild uneasiness. Finally she rose and changed the position of the books, putting the album underneath. That was the way they had been arranged in the first place.

Dagget gave an awkward little laugh. "Now what difference did it make which book was on top?" said he.

Louisa looked at him with a deprecating smile. "I always keep them that way," murmured she.

"You do beat everything," said Dagget, trying to laugh again. His large face was flushed.

He remained about an hour longer, then rose to take leave. Going out, he stumbled over a rug, and trying to recover himself, hit Louisa's work-basket on the table, and knocked it on the floor.

He looked at Louisa, then at the rolling spools; he ducked himself awkwardly toward them, but she stopped him. "Never mind," said she; "I'll pick them up after you're gone."

She spoke with a mild stiffness. Either she was a little disturbed, or his nervousness affected her, and made her seem constrained in her effort to reassure him.

When Joe Dagget was outside he drew in the sweet evening air with a sigh, and felt much as an innocent and perfectly well-intentioned bear might after his exit from a china shop.

Louisa, on her part, felt much as the kind-hearted, long-suffering owner of the china shop might have done after the exit of the bear.

She tied on the pink, then the green apron, picked up all the scattered treasures and replaced them in her work-basket, and straightened the rug. Then she set the lamp on the floor, and began sharply examining the carpet. She even rubbed her fingers over it, and looked at them.

"He's tracked in a good deal of dust," she murmured. "I thought he must have."

Louisa got a dust-pan and brush, and swept Joe Dagget's track carefully.

If he could have known it, it would have increased his perplexity and uneasiness, although it would not have disturbed his loyalty in the least. He came twice a week to see Louisa Ellis, and every time, sitting there in her delicately sweet room, he felt as if surrounded by a hedge of lace. He was afraid to stir lest he should put a clumsy foot or hand through the fairy web, and he had always the consciousness that Louisa was watching fearfully lest he should.

Still the lace and Louisa commanded perforce his perfect respect and patience and loyalty. They were to be married in a month, after a singular courtship which had lasted for a matter of fifteen years. For fourteen out of the fifteen years the two had not once seen each other, and they had seldom exchanged letters. Joe had been all those years in Australia, where he had gone to make his fortune, and where he had stayed until he made it. He would have stayed fifty years if it had taken so long, and come home feeble and tottering, or never come home at all, to marry Louisa.

But the fortune had been made in the fourteen years, and he had come home now to marry the woman who had been patiently and unquestioningly waiting for him all that time.

Shortly after they were engaged he had announced to Louisa his determination to strike out into new fields, and secure a competency before they should be married. She had listened and assented with the sweet serenity which never failed her, not even when her lover set forth on that long and uncertain journey. Joe, buoyed up as he was by his sturdy determination, broke down a little at the last, but Louisa kissed him with a mild blush, and said good-by.

"It won't be for long," poor Joe had said, huskily; but it was for fourteen years.

In that length of time much had happened. Louisa's mother and brother had died, and she was all alone in the world. But greatest happening of all—a subtle happening which both were too simple to understand—Louisa's feet had turned into a path, smooth maybe under a calm, serene sky, but so straight and unswerving that it could only meet a check at her grave, and so narrow that there was no room for any one at her side.

Louisa's first emotion when Joe Dagget came home (he had not apprised her of his coming) was consternation, although she would not admit it to herself, and he never dreamed of it. Fifteen years ago she had been in love with him—at least she considered herself to be. Just at that time, gently acquiescing with and falling into the natural drift of girlhood, she had seen marriage ahead as a reasonable feature and a probable desirability of life. She had listened with calm docility to her mother's views upon the subject. Her mother was remarkable for her cool sense and sweet, even temperament. She talked wisely to her daughter when Joe Dagget presented himself, and Louisa accepted him with no hesitation. He was the first lover she had ever had.

She had been faithful to him all these years. She had never dreamed of the possibility of marrying any one else. Her life, especially for the last seven years, had been full of a pleasant peace, she had never felt discontented nor impatient over her lover's absence; still she had always looked forward to his return and their marriage as the inevitable conclusion of things. However, she had fallen into a way of placing it so far in the future that it was almost equal to placing it over the boundaries of another life.

When Joe came she had been expecting him, and expecting to be married for fourteen years, but she was as much surprised and taken aback as if she had never thought of it.

Joe's consternation came later. He eyed Louisa with an instant confirmation of his old admiration. She had changed but little. She still kept her pretty manner and soft grace, and was, he considered, every whit as attractive as ever. As for himself, his stent was done; he had turned his face away from fortune-seeking, and the old winds of romance whistled as loud and sweet as ever through his ears. All the song which he had been wont to hear in them was Louisa; he had for a long time a loyal belief that he heard it still, but finally it seemed to him that although the winds sang always that one song, it had another name. But for Louisa the wind had never more than murmured; now it had gone down, and everything was still. She listened for a little while with half-wistful attention; then she turned quietly away and went to work on her wedding clothes.

Joe had made some extensive and quite magnificent alterations in his house. It was the old homestead; the newly-married couple would live there, for Joe could not desert his mother, who refused to leave her old home. So Louisa must leave hers. Every morning, rising and going about among her neat maidenly possessions, she felt as one looking her last upon the faces of dear friends. It was true that in a measure she could take them with her, but, robbed of their old environments, they would appear in such new guises that they would almost cease to be themselves. Then there were some peculiar features of her happy solitary life which she would probably be obliged to relinquish altogether. Sterner tasks than these graceful but half-needless ones would probably devolve upon her. There would be a large house to care for; there would be company to entertain; there would be Joe's rigorous and feeble old mother to wait upon; and it would be contrary to all thrifty village traditions for her to keep more than one servant. Louisa had a little still, and she used to occupy herself pleasantly in summer weather with distilling the sweet and aromatic essences from roses and peppermint and spearmint. By-and-by her still must be laid away. Her store of essences was already considerable, and there would be no time for her to distil for the mere pleasure of it. Then Joe's mother would think it foolishness; she had already hinted her opinion in the matter. Louisa dearly loved to sew a linen seam, not always for use, but for the simple, mild pleasure which she took in it. She would have been loath to confess how more than once she had ripped a seam for the mere delight of sewing it together again. Sitting at her window during long sweet afternoons, drawing her needle gently through the dainty fabric, she was peace itself. But there was small chance of such foolish comfort in the future. Joe's mother, domineering, shrewd old matron that she was even in her old age, and very likely even Joe himself, with his honest masculine rudeness, would laugh and frown down all these pretty but senseless old maiden ways.

Louisa had almost the enthusiasm of an artist over the mere order and cleanliness of her solitary home. She had throbs of genuine triumph at the sight of the window-panes which she had polished until they shone like jewels. She gloated gently over her orderly bureau-drawers, with their exquisitely folded contents redolent with lavender and sweet clover and very purity. Could she be sure of the endurance of even this? She had visions, so startling that she half repudiated them as indelicate, of coarse masculine belongings strewn about in endless litter; of dust and disorder arising necessarily from a coarse masculine presence in the midst of all this delicate harmony.

Among her forebodings of disturbance, not the least was with regard to Caesar. Caesar was a veritable hermit of a dog. For the greater part of his life he had dwelt in his secluded hut, shut out from the society of his kind and all innocent canine joys. Never had Caesar since his early youth watched at a woodchuck's hole; never had he known the delights of a stray bone at a neighbor's kitchen door. And it was all on account of a sin committed when hardly out of his puppyhood. No one knew the possible depth of remorse of which this mild-visaged, altogether innocent-looking old dog might be capable; but whether or not he had encountered remorse, he had encountered a full measure of righteous retribution. Old Caesar seldom lifted up his voice in a growl or a bark; he was fat and sleepy; there were yellow rings which looked like spectacles around his dim old eyes; but there was a neighbor who bore on his hand the imprint of several of Caesar's sharp white youthful teeth, and for that he had lived at the end of a chain, all alone in a little hut, for fourteen years. The neighbor, who was choleric and smarting with the pain of his wound, had demanded either Caesar's death or complete ostracism. So Louisa's brother, to whom the dog had belonged, had built him his little kennel and tied him up. It was now fourteen years since, in a flood of youthful spirits, he had inflicted that memorable bite, and with the exception of short excursions, always at the end of the chain, under the strict guardianship of his master or Louisa, the old dog had remained a close prisoner. It is doubtful if, with his limited ambition, he took much pride in the fact, but it is certain that he was possessed of considerable cheap fame. He was regarded by all the children in the village and by many adults as a very monster of ferocity. St. George's dragon could hardly have surpassed in evil repute Louisa Ellis's old yellow dog. Mothers charged their children with solemn emphasis not to go too near him, and the children listened and believed greedily, with a fascinated appetite for terror, and ran by Louisa's house stealthily, with many sidelong and backward glances at the terrible dog. If perchance he sounded a hoarse bark, there was a panic. Wayfarers chancing into Louisa's yard eyed him with respect, and inquired if the chain were stout. Caesar at large might have seemed a very ordinary dog, and excited no comment whatever; chained, his reputation overshadowed him, so that he lost his own proper outlines and looked darkly vague and enormous. Joe Dagget, however, with his good-humored sense and shrewdness, saw him as he was. He strode valiantly up to him and patted him on the head, in spite of Louisa's soft clamor of warning, and even attempted to set him loose. Louisa grew so alarmed that he desisted, but kept announcing his opinion in the matter quite forcibly at intervals. "There ain't a better-natured dog in town," he would say, "and it's downright cruel to keep him tied up there. Some day I'm going to take him out."

Louisa had very little hope that he would not, one of these days, when their interests and possessions should be more completely fused in one. She pictured to herself Caesar on the rampage through the quiet and unguarded village. She saw innocent children bleeding in his path. She was herself very fond of the old dog, because he had belonged to her dead brother, and he was always very gentle with her; still she had great faith in his ferocity. She always warned people not to go too near him. She fed him on ascetic fare of corn-mush and cakes, and never fired his dangerous temper with heating and sanguinary diet of flesh and bones. Louisa looked at the old dog munching his simple fare, and thought of her approaching marriage and trembled. Still no anticipation of disorder and confusion in lieu of sweet peace and harmony, no forebodings of Caesar on the rampage, no wild fluttering of her little yellow canary, were sufficient to turn her a hair's-breadth. Joe Dagget had been fond of her and working for her all these years. It was not for her, whatever came to pass, to prove untrue and break his heart. She put the exquisite little stitches into her wedding-garments, and the time went on until it was only a week before her wedding-day. It was a Tuesday evening, and the wedding was to be a week from Wednesday.

There was a full moon that night. About nine o'clock Louisa strolled down the road a little way. There were harvest-fields on either hand, bordered by low stone walls. Luxuriant clumps of bushes grew beside the wall, and trees—wild cherry and old apple-trees—at intervals. Presently Louisa sat down on the wall and looked about her with mildly sorrowful reflectiveness. Tall shrubs of blueberry and meadow-sweet, all woven together and tangled with blackberry vines and horsebriers, shut her in on either side. She had a little clear space between them. Opposite her, on the other side of the road, was a spreading tree; the moon shone between its boughs, and the leaves twinkled like silver. The road was bespread with a beautiful shifting dapple of silver and shadow; the air was full of a mysterious sweetness. "I wonder if it's wild grapes?" murmured Louisa. She sat there some time. She was just thinking of rising, when she heard footsteps and low voices, and remained quiet. It was a lonely place, and she felt a little timid. She thought she would keep still in the shadow and let the persons, whoever they might be, pass her.

But just before they reached her the voices ceased, and the footsteps. She understood that their owners had also found seats upon the stone wall. She was wondering if she could not steal away unobserved, when the voice broke the stillness. It was Joe Dagget's. She sat still and listened.

The voice was announced by a loud sigh, which was as familiar as itself. "Well," said Dagget, "you've made up your mind, then, I suppose?"

"Yes," returned another voice; "I'm going day after to-morrow."

"That's Lily Dyer," thought Louisa to herself. The voice embodied itself in her mind. She saw a girl tall and full-figured, with a firm, fair face, looking fairer and firmer in the moonlight, her strong yellow hair braided in a close knot. A girl full of a calm rustic strength and bloom, with a masterful way which might have beseemed a princess. Lily Dyer was a favorite with the village folk; she had just the qualities to arouse the admiration. She was good and handsome and smart. Louisa had often heard her praises sounded.

"Well," said Joe Dagget, "I ain't got a word to say."

"I don't know what you could say," returned Lily Dyer.

"Not a word to say," repeated Joe, drawing out the words heavily. Then there was silence. "I ain't sorry," he began at last, "that that happened yesterday—that we kind of let on how we felt to each other. I guess it's just as well we knew. Of course I can't do anything any different. I'm going right on an' get married next week. I ain't going back on a woman that's waited for me fourteen years, an' break her heart."

"If you should jilt her to-morrow, I wouldn't have you," spoke up the girl, with sudden vehemence.

"Well, I ain't going to give you the chance," said he; "but I don't believe you would, either."

"You'd see I wouldn't. Honor's honor, an' right's right. An' I'd never think anything of any man that went against 'em for me or any other girl; you'd find that out, Joe Dagget."

"Well, you'll find out fast enough that I ain't going against 'em for you or any other girl," returned he. Their voices sounded almost as if they were angry with each other. Louisa was listening eagerly.

"I'm sorry you feel as if you must go away," said Joe, "but I don't know but it's best."

"Of course it's best. I hope you and I have got common-sense."

"Well, I suppose you're right." Suddenly Joe's voice got an undertone of tenderness. "Say, Lily," said he, "I'll get along well enough myself, but I can't bear to think—You don't suppose you're going to fret much over it?"

"I guess you'll find out I sha'n't fret much over a married man."

"Well, I hope you won't—I hope you won't, Lily. God knows I

do. And—I hope—one of these days—you'll—come across somebody else—"

"I don't see any reason why I shouldn't." Suddenly her tone changed. She spoke in a sweet, clear voice, so loud that she could have been heard across the street. "No, Joe Dagget," said she, "I'll never marry any other man as long as I live. I've got good sense, an' I ain't going to break my heart nor make a fool of myself; but I'm never going to be married, you can be sure of that. I ain't that sort of a girl to feel this way twice."

Louisa heard an exclamation and a soft commotion behind the bushes; then Lily spoke again—the voice sounded as if she had risen. "This must be put a stop to," said she. "We've stayed here long enough. I'm going home."

Louisa sat there in a daze, listening to their retreating steps. After a while she got up and slunk softly home herself. The next day she did her housework methodically; that was as much a matter of course as breathing; but she did not sew on her wedding-clothes. She sat at her window and meditated. In the evening Joe came. Louisa Ellis had never known that she had any diplomacy in her, but when she came to look for it that night she found it, although meek of its kind, among her little feminine weapons. Even now she could hardly believe that she had heard aright, and that she would not do Joe a terrible injury should she break her troth-plight. She wanted to sound him without betraying too soon her own inclinations in the matter. She did it successfully, and they finally came to an understanding; but it was a difficult thing, for he was as afraid of betraying himself as she.

She never mentioned Lily Dyer. She simply said that while she had no cause of complaint against him, she had lived so long in one way that she shrank from making a change.

"Well, I never shrank, Louisa," said Dagget. "I'm going to be honest enough to say that I think maybe it's better this way; but if you'd wanted to keep on, I'd have stuck to you till my dying day. I hope you know that."

"Yes, I do," said she.

That night she and Joe parted more tenderly than they had done for a long time. Standing in the door, holding each other's hands, a last great wave of regretful memory swept over them.

"Well, this ain't the way we've thought it was all going to end, is it, Louisa?" said Joe.

She shook her head. There was a little quiver on her placid face.

"You let me know if there's ever anything I can do for you," said he. "I ain't ever going to forget you, Louisa." Then he kissed her, and went down the path.

Louisa, all alone by herself that night, wept a little, she hardly knew why; but the next morning, on waking, she felt like a queen who, after fearing lest her domain be wrested away from her, sees it firmly insured in her possession.

Now the tall weeds and grasses might cluster around Caesar's little hermit hut, the snow might fall on its roof year in and year out, but he never would go on a rampage through the unguarded village. Now the little canary might turn itself into a peaceful yellow ball night after night, and have no need to wake and flutter with wild terror against its bars. Louisa could sew linen seams, and distil roses, and dust and polish and fold away in lavender, as long as she listed. That afternoon she sat with her needle-work at the window, and felt fairly steeped in peace. Lily Dyer, tall and erect and blooming, went past; but she felt no qualm. If Louisa Ellis had sold her birthright she did not know it, the taste of the pottage[1] was so delicious, and had been her sole satisfaction for so long. Serenity and placid narrowness had become to her as the birthright itself. She gazed ahead through a long reach of future days strung together like pearls in a rosary, every one like the others, and all smooth and flawless and innocent, and her heart went up in thankfulness. Outside was the fervid summer afternoon; the air was filled with the sounds of the busy harvest of men and birds and bees; there were halloos, metallic clatterings, sweet calls, and long hummings. Louisa sat, prayerfully numbering her days, like an uncloistered nun.

---

1. Has Louisa been transformed by Joe's long absence, or has she been confirmed in her natural inclinations?
2. Do you suppose the marriage would have been disastrous if it had taken place? What might have been the form of the disaster?
3. Are Joe and Lily Dyer victims of their own sense of honor? Is Louisa a victim of circumstances?
4. What does Louisa lack that makes a true nun's vocation meaningful?

1. See Genesis 25:30–34. Esau sold his birthright to his brother for a mess of pottage.

Mavis Gallant

Gallant (1922–) was born in Montreal, Canada, and by virtue of her early contacts with the French-speaking people of Quebec has been bilingual from childhood. This early virtuosity is reflected in much of her later work, which explores the tangled customs, sensibilities, and expectations of characters from diverse origins meeting in a European setting. She began to write poems at five, and attendance at a strictly disciplined French convent school sharpened her eye for ironies of character and circumstance. From France, where she has spent many of her adult years, she has contributed a long string of stories to The New Yorker. *Her novels are* Green Water, Green Sky *(1959) and* A Fairly Good Time *(1970). Her stories have been collected in* The Other Paris *(1956),* My Heart Is Broken *(1964),* The Pegnitz Junction *(1973),* From the Fifteenth District *(1979),* Home Truths *(1985), and* Overhead in a Balloon *(1987).*

My Heart Is Broken

"When that Jean Harlow[1] died," Mrs. Thompson said to Jeannie, "I was on the 83 streetcar with a big, heavy paper parcel in my arms. I hadn't been married for very long, and when I used to visit my mother she'd give me a lot of canned stuff and preserves. I was standing up in the streetcar because nobody'd given me a seat. All the men were unemployed in those days, and they just sat down wherever they happened to be. You wouldn't remember what Montreal was like then. *You* weren't even on earth. To resume what I was saying to you, one of these men sitting down had an American paper—the *Daily News*, I guess it was—and I was sort of leaning over him, and I saw in big print 'JEAN HARLOW DEAD.' You can believe me or not, just as you want to, but that was the most terrible shock I ever had in my life. I never got over it."

Jeannie had nothing to say to that. She lay flat on her back across the bed, with her head toward Mrs. Thompson and her heels just touching the crate that did as a bedside table. Balanced on her flat stomach was an open bottle of coral-pink Cutex nail polish. She held

1. U.S. movie star (1911–1937) who died of uremic poisoning brought on by sunburn.

her hands up over her head and with some difficulty applied the brush to the nails of her right hand. Her legs were brown and thin. She wore nothing but shorts and one of her husband's shirts. Her feet were bare.

Mrs. Thompson was the wife of the paymaster in a road-construction camp in northern Quebec. Jeannie's husband was an engineer working on the same project. The road was being pushed through country where nothing had existed until now except rocks and lakes and muskeg.[2] The camp was established between a wild lake and the line of raw dirt that was the road. There were no towns between the camp and the railway spur, sixty miles distant.

Mrs. Thompson, a good deal older than Jeannie, had become her best friend. She was a nice, plain, fat, consoling sort of person, with varicosed legs, shoes unlaced and slit for comfort, blue flannel dressing gown worn at all hours, pudding-bowl haircut, and coarse gray hair. She might have been Jeannie's own mother, or her Auntie Pearl. She rocked her fat self in the rocking chair and went on with what she had to say: "What I was starting off to tell you is you remind me of her, of Jean Harlow. You've got the same teeny mouth, Jeannie, and I think your hair was a whole lot prettier before you started fooling around with it. That peroxide's no good. It splits the ends. I know you're going to tell me it isn't peroxide but something more modern, but the result is the same."

Vern's shirt was spotted with coral-pink that had dropped off the brush. Vern wouldn't mind; at least, he wouldn't say that he minded. If he hadn't objected to anything Jeannie did until now, he wouldn't start off by complaining about a shirt. The campsite outside the uncurtained window was silent and dark. The waning moon would not appear until dawn. A passage of thought made Mrs. Thompson say, "Winter soon."

Jeannie moved sharply and caught the bottle of polish before it spilled. Mrs. Thompson was crazy; it wasn't even September.

"Pretty soon," Mrs. Thompson admitted. "Pretty soon. That's a long season up here, but I'm one person doesn't complain. I've been up here or around here every winter of my married life, except for that one winter Pops was occupying Germany."

"I've been up here seventy-two days," said Jeannie, in her soft voice. "Tomorrow makes seventy-three."

"Is that right?" said Mrs. Thompson, jerking the rocker forward, suddenly snappish. "Is that a fact? Well, who asked you to come up here? Who asked you to come and start counting days like you was in some kind of jail? When you got married to Vern, you must of known

2. A bog of moss, sedge, and stunted trees.

where he'd be taking you. He told you, didn't he, that he liked road jobs, construction jobs, and that? Did he tell you, or didn't he?"

"Oh, he told me," said Jeannie.

"You know what, Jeannie?" said Mrs. Thompson. "If you'd of just listened to me, none of this would have happened. I told you that first day, the day you arrived here in your high-heeled shoes, I said, 'I know this cabin doesn't look much, but all the married men have the same sort of place.' You remember I said that? I said, 'You just get some curtains up and some carpets down and it'll be home.' I took you over and showed you my place, and you said you'd never seen anything so lovely."

"I meant it," said Jeannie. "Your cabin is just lovely. I don't know why, but I never managed to make this place look like yours."

Mrs. Thompson said, "That's plain enough." She looked at the cold grease spattered behind the stove, and the rag of towel over by the sink. "It's partly the experience," she said kindly. She and her husband knew exactly what to take with them when they went on a job, they had been doing it for so many years. They brought boxes for artificial flowers, a brass door knocker, a portable bar decorated with sea shells, a cardboard fireplace that looked real, and an electric fire that sent waves of light rippling over the ceiling and walls. A concealed gramophone played the records they loved and cherished—the good old tunes. They had comic records that dated back to the year 1, and sad soprano records about shipwrecks and broken promises and babies' graves. The first time Jeannie heard one of the funny records, she was scared to death. She was paying a formal call, sitting straight in her chair, with her skirt pulled around her knees. Vern and Pops Thompson were talking about the Army.

"I wish to God I was back," said old Pops.

"Don't I?" said Vern. He was fifteen years older than Jeannie and had been through a lot.

At first there were only scratching and whispering noises, and then a mosquito orchestra started to play, and a dwarf's voice came into the room. "Little Johnnie Green, Little Sallie Brown," squealed the dwarf, higher and faster than any human ever could. "Spooning in the park with the grass all around."

"Where is he?" Jeannie cried, while the Thompsons screamed with laughter and Vern smiled. The dwarf sang on: "And each little bird in the treetop high/Sang 'Oh you kid!' and winked his eye."

It was a record that had belonged to Pops Thompson's mother. He had been laughing at it all his life. The Thompsons loved living up north and didn't miss cities or company. Their cabin smelled of cocoa and toast. Over their beds were oval photographs of each other as children, and they had some Teddy bears and about a dozen dolls.

Jeannie capped the bottle of polish, taking care not to press it against her wet nails. She sat up with a single movement and set the bottle down on the bedside crate. Then she turned to face Mrs. Thompson. She sat cross-legged, with her hands outspread before her. Her face was serene.

"Not an ounce of fat on you," said Mrs. Thompson. "You know something? I'm sorry you're going. I really am. Tomorrow you'll be gone. You know that, don't you? You've been counting days, but you won't have to any more. I guess Vern'll take you back to Montreal. What do you think?"

Jeannie dropped her gaze, and began smoothing wrinkles on the bedspread. She muttered something Mrs. Thompson could not understand.

"Tomorrow you'll be gone," Mrs. Thompson continued. "I know it for a fact. Vern is at this moment getting his pay, and borrowing a jeep from Mr. Sherman, and a Polack driver to take you to the train. He sure is loyal to *you*. You know what I heard Mr. Sherman say? He said to Vern, 'If you want to send her off, Vern, you can always stay,' and Vern said, 'I can't very well do that, Mr. Sherman.' And Mr. Sherman said, 'This is the second time you've had to leave a job on account of her, isn't it?,' and then Mr. Sherman said, 'In my opinion, no man by his own self can rape a girl, so there were either two men or else she's invented the whole story.' Then he said, 'Vern, you're either a saint or a damn fool.' That was all I heard. I came straight over here, Jeannie, because I thought you might be needing me." Mrs. Thompson waited to hear she was needed. She stopped rocking and sat with her feet flat and wide apart. She struck her knees with her open palms and cried, "I *told* you to keep away from the men. I told you it would make trouble, all that being cute and dancing around. I said to you, I remember saying it, I said nothing makes trouble faster in a place like this than a grown woman behaving like a little girl. Don't you remember?"

"I only went out for a walk," said Jeannie. "Nobody'll believe me, but that's all. I went down the road for a walk."

"In high heels?" said Mrs. Thompson. "With a purse on your arm, and a hat on your head? You don't go taking a walk in the bush that way. There's no place to walk *to*. Where'd you think you were going? I could smell Evening in Paris a quarter mile away."

"There's no place to go," said Jeannie, "but what else is there to do? I just felt like dressing up and going out."

"You could have cleaned up your home a bit," said Mrs. Thompson. "There was always that to do. Just look at that sink. That basket of ironing's been under the bed since July. I know it gets boring around here, but you had the best of it. You had the summer. In winter it gets dark around three o'clock. Then the wives have a right to go crazy. I knew one used to sleep the clock around. When her Nembutal ran out, she took about a hundred aspirin. I knew another learned to distill her own liquor, just to kill time. Sometimes the men get so's they don't like the life, and that's death for the wives. But here you had a nice summer, and Vern liked the life."

"He likes it better than anything," said Jeannie. "He liked the Army, but this was his favorite life after that."

"There," said Mrs. Thompson. "You had every reason to be happy. What'd you do if he sent you off alone, now, like Mr. Sherman advised? You'd be alone and you'd have to work. Women don't know when they're well off. Here you've got a good, sensible husband working for you and you don't appreciate it. You have to go and do a terrible thing."

"I only went for a walk," said Jeannie. "That's all I did."

"It's possible," said Mrs. Thompson, "but it's a terrible thing. It's about the worst thing that's ever happened around here. I don't know why you let it happen. A woman can always defend what's precious, even if she's attacked. I hope you remembered to think about bacteria."

"What d'you mean?"

"I mean Javel,[3] or something."

Jeannie looked uncomprehending and then shook her head.

"I wonder what it must be like," said Mrs. Thompson after a time, looking at the dark window. "I mean, think of Berlin and them Russians and all. Think of some disgusting fellow you don't know. Never said hello to, even. Some girls ask for it, though. You can't always blame the man. The man loses his job, his wife if he's got one, everything, all because of a silly girl."

Jeannie frowned, absently. She pressed her nails together, testing the polish. She licked her lips and said, "I was more beaten up, Mrs. Thompson. It wasn't exactly what you think. It was only afterwards I thought to myself, Why, I was raped and everything."

Mrs. Thompson gasped, hearing the word from Jeannie. She said, "Have you got any marks?"

"On my arms. That's why I'm wearing this shirt. The first thing I did was change my clothes."

Mrs. Thompson thought this over, and went on to another thing: "Do you ever think about your mother?"

"Sure."

"Do you pray? If this goes on at nineteen—"

3. Antiseptic bleach that can be used for a disinfectant. Sodium hypochlorite.

"I'm twenty."

"—what'll you be by the time you're thirty? You've already got a terrible, terrible memory to haunt you all your life."

"I already can't remember it," said Jeannie. "Afterwards I started walking back to camp, but I was walking the wrong way. I met Mr. Sherman. The back of his car was full of coffee, flour, all that. I guess he'd been picking up supplies. He said, 'Well, get in.' He didn't ask any questions at first. I couldn't talk anyway."

"Shock," said Mrs. Thompson wisely.

"You know, I'd have to see it happening to know what happened. All I remember is that first we were only talking . . ."

"You and Mr. Sherman?"

"No, no, before. When I was taking my walk."

"Don't say who it was," said Mrs. Thompson. "We don't any of us need to know."

"We were just talking, and he got sore all of a sudden and grabbed my arm."

"Don't say the name!" Mrs. Thompson cried.

"Like when I was little, there was this Lana Turner[4] movie. She had two twins. She was just there and then a nurse brought her in the two twins. I hadn't been married or anything, and I didn't know anything, and I used to think if I just kept on seeing the movie I'd know how she got the two twins, you know, and I went, oh, I must have seen it six times, the movie, but in the end I never knew any more. They just brought her the two twins."

Mrs. Thompson sat quite still, trying to make sense of this. "Taking advantage of a woman is a criminal offense," she observed. "I heard Mr. Sherman say another thing, Jeannie. He said, 'If your wife wants to press a charge and talk to some lawyer, let me tell you,' he said, 'you'll never work again anywhere,' he said. Vern said, 'I know that, Mr. Sherman.' And Mr. Sherman said, 'Let me tell you, if any reporters or any investigators start coming around here, they'll get their . . . they'll never . . .' Oh, he was mad. And Vern said, 'I came over to tell you I was quitting, Mr. Sherman.' " Mrs. Thompson had been acting this with spirit, using a quiet voice when she spoke for Vern and a blustering tone for Mr. Sherman. In her own voice, she said, "If you're wondering how I came to hear all this, I was strolling by Mr. Sherman's office window—his bungalow, that is. I had Maureen out in her pram." Maureen was the Thompsons' youngest doll.

Jeannie might not have been listening. She started to tell something else. "You know, where we were before, on Vern's last job, we weren't in a camp. He was away a lot, and he left me in Amos, in a

4. U.S. film star (1920–).

hotel. I liked it. Amos isn't all that big, but it's better than here. There was this German in the hotel. He was selling cars. He'd drive me around if I wanted to go to a movie or anything. Vern didn't like him, so we left. It wasn't anybody's fault."

"So he's given up two jobs," said Mrs. Thompson. "One because he couldn't leave you alone, and now this one. Two jobs, and you haven't been married five months. Why should another man be thrown out of work? We don't need to know a thing. I'll be sorry if it was Jimmy Quinn," she went on slowly. "I like that boy. Don't say the name, dear. There's Evans. Susini. Palmer. But it might have been anybody, because you had them all on the boil. So it might have been Jimmy Quinn—let's say—and it could have been anyone else, too. Well, now let's hope they can get their minds back on the job."

"I thought they all liked me," said Jeannie sadly. "I get along with people. Vern never fights with me."

"Vern never fights with anyone. But he ought to have thrashed *you*."

"If he . . . you know. I won't say the name. If he'd liked me, I wouldn't have minded. If he'd been friendly. I really mean that. I wouldn't have gone wandering up the road, making all this fuss."

"Jeannie," said Mrs. Thompson, "you don't even know what you're saying."

"He could at least have liked me," said Jeannie. "He wasn't even friendly. It's the first time in my life somebody hasn't liked me. My heart is broken, Mrs. Thompson. My heart is just broken."

She has to cry, Mrs. Thompson thought. She has to have it out. She rocked slowly, tapping her foot, trying to remember how she'd felt about things when she was twenty, wondering if her heart had ever been broken, too.

---

1. How are details of the physical appearance of the two women and of the interiors of their residences used as indexes of character?
2. What means has the author used to convince us that Mrs. Thompson has really become Jeannie's "best friend"? What ironies lie in this term?
3. How does the response of the men Vern and Mr. Sherman to the rape qualify the significance of what has happened?
4. Granting that Jeannie is the victim of a serious crime, on whom does the guilt lie? To what extent is she her own victim?
5. How do you interpret Jeannie's assertion that her "heart is broken"?

Gabriel García Márquez

García Márquez (1928–) was born in Aracataca, Colombia, moved to Mexico in 1954, and in 1967 took up permanent residence in Barcelona, Spain. His first novel La hojarasca *was written when he was nineteen but was not published until eight years later in 1955 (translated as* Leaf Storm, *1972). Many of his short stories as well as his most ambitious novel* One Hundred Years of Solitude *(1967, trans. 1970) are drawn from the fictional town of Macondo, which some critics have seen as a counterpart of Faulkner's Yoknapatawpha County. This renowned novel presents six generations of one family, fusing magic, reality, fable, and fantasy in a fashion that expands the family saga into a panorama of civilization. His other novels include* In Evil Hour *(1962, trans. 1979),* The Autumn of the Patriarch *(1975, trans. 1976),* Chronicle of a Death Foretold *(1981, trans. 1982), and* Love in the Time of Cholera *(1987, trans. 1988). His stories are most easily found in* Collected Stories *(1984). In 1982 he was awarded the Nobel Prize for literature.*

The Handsomest Drowned Man in the World[1]

A *Tale for Children*

The first children who saw the dark and slinky bulge approaching through the sea let themselves think it was an empty ship. Then they saw it had no flags or masts and they thought it was a whale. But when it washed up on the beach, they removed the clumps of seaweed, the jellyfish tentacles, and the remains of fish and flotsam, and only then did they see that it was a drowned man.

They had been playing with him all afternoon, burying him in the sand and digging him up again, when someone chanced to see them and spread the alarm in the village. The men who carried him to the nearest house noticed that he weighed more than any dead man they had ever known, almost as much as a horse, and they said to each other that maybe he'd been floating too long and the water had got into his bones. When they laid him on the floor they said he'd been taller

1. Translated by Gregory Rabassa.

than all other men because there was barely enough room for him in the house, but they thought that maybe the ability to keep on growing after death was part of the nature of certain drowned men. He had the smell of the sea about him and only his shape gave one to suppose that it was the corpse of a human being, because the skin was covered with a crust of mud and scales.

They did not even have to clean off his face to know that the dead man was a stranger. The village was made up of only twenty-odd wooden houses that had stone courtyards with no flowers and which were spread about on the end of a desertlike cape. There was so little land that mothers always went about with the fear that the wind would carry off their children and the few dead that the years had caused among them had to be thrown off the cliffs. But the sea was calm and bountiful and all the men fit into seven boats. So when they found the drowned man they simply had to look at one another to see that they were all there. That night they did not go out to work at sea. While the men went to find out if anyone was missing in neighboring villages, the women stayed behind to care for the drowned man. They took the mud off with grass swabs, they removed the underwater stones entangled in his hair, and they scraped the crust off with tools used for scaling fish. As they were doing that they noticed that the vegetation on him came from faraway oceans and deep water and that his clothes were in tatters, as if he had sailed through labyrinths of coral. They noticed too that he bore his death with pride, for he did not have the lonely look of other drowned men who came out of the sea or that haggard, needy look of men who drowned in rivers. But only when they finished cleaning him off did they become aware of the kind of man he was and it left them breathless. Not only was he the tallest, strongest, most virile, and best built man they had ever seen, but even though they were looking at him there was no room for him in their imagination.

They could not find a bed in the village large enough to lay him on nor was there a table solid enough to use for his wake. The tallest men's holiday pants would not fit him, nor the fattest ones' Sunday shirts, nor the shoes of the one with the biggest feet. Fascinated by his huge size and his beauty, the women then decided to make him some pants from a large piece of sail and a shirt from some bridal brabant linen so that he could continue through his death with dignity. As they sewed, sitting in a circle and gazing at the corpse between stitches, it seemed to them that the wind had never been so steady nor the sea so restless as on that night and they supposed that the change had something to do with the dead man. They thought that if that magnificent man had lived in the village, his house would have had the widest doors, the highest ceiling, and the strongest floor, his bedstead would have been made from a midship frame held together by iron bolts, and his wife would have been the happiest woman. They thought that he would have had so much authority that he could have drawn fish out of the sea simply by calling their names and that he would have put so much work into his land that springs would have burst forth from among the rocks so that he would have been able to plant flowers on the cliffs. They secretly compared him to their own men, thinking that for all their lives theirs were incapable of doing what he could do in one night, and they ended up dismissing them deep in their hearts as the weakest, meanest, and most useless creatures on earth. They were wandering through that maze of fantasy when the oldest woman, who as the oldest had looked upon the drowned man with more compassion than passion, sighed:

"He has the face of someone called Esteban."

It was true. Most of them had only to take another look at him to see that he could not have any other name. The more stubborn among them, who were the youngest, still lived for a few hours with the illusion that when they put his clothes on and he lay among the flowers in patent leather shoes his name might be Lautaro. But it was a vain illusion. There had not been enough canvas, the poorly cut and worse sewn pants were too tight, and the hidden strength of his heart popped the buttons on his shirt. After midnight the whistling of the wind died down and the sea fell into its Wednesday drowsiness. The silence put an end to any last doubts: he was Esteban. The women who had dressed him, who had combed his hair, had cut his nails and shaved him were unable to hold back a shudder of pity when they had to resign themselves to his being dragged along the ground. It was then that they understood how unhappy he must have been with that huge body since it bothered him even after death. They could see him in life, condemned to going through doors sideways, cracking his head on crossbeams, remaining on his feet during visits, not knowing what to do with his soft, pink, sea lion hands while the lady of the house looked for her most resistant chair and begged him, frightened to death, sit here, Esteban, please, and he, leaning against the wall, smiling, don't bother, ma'am, I'm fine where I am, his heels raw and his back roasted from having done the same thing so many times whenever he paid a visit, don't bother, ma'am, I'm fine where I am, just to avoid the embarrassment of breaking up the chair, and never knowing perhaps that the ones who said don't go, Esteban, at least wait till the coffee's ready, were the ones who later on would whisper the big boob finally left, how nice, the handsome fool has gone. That was what the women were thinking beside the body a little before dawn. Later, when they covered his face with a handkerchief so that the light would not bother him, he looked so forever dead, so defenseless, so much like their men that the first furrows of tears opened in their hearts. It was one of the younger ones who began the weeping. The others, coming to, went from sighs to wails, and the more they sobbed the more they felt like weeping, because the drowned man was becoming all the more Esteban for them, and so they wept so much, for he was the most destitute, most peaceful, and most obliging man on earth, poor Esteban. So when the men returned with the news that the drowned man was not from the neighboring villages either, the women felt an opening of jubilation in the midst of their tears.

"Praise the Lord," they sighed, "he's ours!"

The men thought the fuss was only womanish frivolity. Fatigued because of the difficult nighttime inquiries, all they wanted was to get rid of the bother of the newcomer once and for all before the sun grew strong on that arid, windless day. They improvised a litter with the remains of foremasts and gaffs, tying it together with rigging so that it would bear the weight of the body until they reached the cliffs. They wanted to tie the anchor from a cargo ship to him so that he would sink easily into the deepest waves, where fish are blind and divers die of nostalgia, and bad currents would not bring him back to shore, as had happened with other bodies. But the more they hurried, the more the women thought of ways to waste time. They walked about like startled hens, pecking with the sea charms on their breasts, some interfering on one side to put a scapular of the good wind on the drowned man, some on the other side to put a wrist compass on him, and after a great deal of *get away from there, woman, stay out of the way, look, you almost made me fall on top of the dead man,* the men began to feel mistrust in their livers and started grumbling about why so many main-altar decorations for a stranger, because no matter how many nails and holy-water jars he had on him, the sharks would chew him all the same, but the women kept piling on their junk relics, running back and forth, stumbling, while they released in sighs what they did not in tears, so that the men finally exploded with *since when has there ever been such a fuss over a drifting corpse, a drowned nobody, a piece of cold Wednesday meat.* One of the women, mortified by so much lack of care, then removed the handkerchief from the dead man's face and the men were left breathless too.

He was Esteban. It was not necessary to repeat it for them to recognize him. If they had been told Sir Walter Raleigh,[2] even they might have been impressed with his gringo accent, the macaw on his shoulder, his cannibal-killing blunderbuss, but there could be only one Esteban in the world and there he was, stretched out like a sperm whale, shoeless, wearing the pants of an undersized child, and with those stony nails that had to be cut with a knife. They only had to take

2. English navigator, statesman, courtier, and author (1552–1618).

the handkerchief off his face to see that he was ashamed, that it was not his fault that he was so big or so heavy or so handsome, and if he had known that this was going to happen, he would have looked for a more discreet place to drown in, seriously, I even would have tied the anchor off a galleon around my neck and staggered off a cliff like someone who doesn't like things in order not to be upsetting people now with this Wednesday dead body, as you people say, in order not to be bothering anyone with this filthy piece of cold meat that doesn't have anything to do with me. There was so much truth in his manner that even the most mistrustful men, the ones who felt the bitterness of endless nights at sea fearing that their women would tire of dreaming about them and begin to dream of drowned men, even they and others who were harder still shuddered in the marrow of their bones at Esteban's sincerity.

That was how they came to hold the most splendid funeral they could conceive of for an abandoned drowned man. Some women who had gone to get flowers in the neighboring villages returned with other women who could not believe what they had been told, and those women went back for more flowers when they saw the dead man, and they brought more and more until there were so many flowers and so many people that it was hard to walk about. At the final moment it pained them to return him to the waters as an orphan and they chose a father and mother from among the best people, and aunts and uncles and cousins, so that through him all the inhabitants of the village became kinsmen. Some sailors who heard weeping from a distance went off course and people heard of one who had himself tied to the mainmast, remembering ancient fables about sirens.[3] While they fought for the privilege of carrying him on their shoulders along the steep escarpment by the cliffs, men and women became aware for the first time of the desolation of their streets, the dryness of their courtyards, the narrowness of their dreams as they faced the splendor and beauty of their drowned man. They let him go without an anchor so that he could come back if he wished and whenever he wished, and they all held their breath for the fraction of centuries the body took to fall into the abyss. They did not need to look at one another to realize that they were no longer all present, that they would never be. But they also knew that everything would be different from then on, that their houses would have wider doors, higher ceilings, and stronger floors so that Esteban's memory could go everywhere without bumping into beams and so that no one in the future would dare whisper the big boob finally died, too bad, the handsome fool has finally died, because they were going to paint their house fronts gay colors to make Esteban's memory

3. In Greek and Roman mythology sirens were sea nymphs who lured mariners to their destruction.

eternal and they were going to break their backs digging for springs among the stones and planting flowers on the cliffs so that in future years at dawn the passengers on great liners would awaken, suffocated by the smell of gardens on the high seas, and the captain would have to come down from the bridge in his dress uniform, with his astrolabe, his pole star, and his row of war medals and, pointing to the promontory of roses on the horizon, he would say in fourteen languages, look there, where the wind is so peaceful now that it's gone to sleep beneath the beds, over there, where the sun's so bright that the sunflowers don't know which way to turn, yes, that's Esteban's village.

---

1. What changes are made in the appearance of the village and in the lives of the villagers by Esteban's presence among them?
2. How do the villagers "know" the drowned man's name is Esteban?
3. Why are the women quicker than the men to respond to Esteban's presence?
4. What is indicated by the interest that passing ships take in the "promontory of roses on the horizon"?
5. What does the story say about the way myths originate?
6. How are we supposed to understand the subtitle?

Ellen Gilchrist

Gilchrist (1935–) was born in Vicksburg, Mississippi, and has developed a career that includes writing poetry, fiction, and journalism. Her first book of short stories was a notable success without the advertising and promotion usually required to launch a new writer. Her natural popularity springs from the wry depiction of children and adolescents—and of women "out on a limb trying to think of a way down." Her books of fiction are In the Land of Dreamy Dreams *(1981),* The Annunciation *(1983),* Victory over Japan *(1984),* Drunk with Love *(1987), and* The Anna Papers *(1988).* Victory over Japan *won the American Book Award.*

Traveler

It was June in southern Indiana. I was locked in the upstairs bathroom studying the directions on a box of Tampax when the invitation came.

"LeLe," my father called, coming up the stairs with the letter in his hand. "Come out of there. Come hear the news. You're going to the Delta."

It seems my cousin Baby Gwen Barksdale's mother had died of a weak liver, and rather than leave the poor girl alone in a house with a grieving widower the family had invited me to Mississippi to spend the summer as her companion. There was even a suggestion that I might stay and go to school there in the fall.

What luck that the invitation came just as my own mother, giving in to a fit of jealous rage, left my father and fled to New Orleans to have a nervous breakdown.

"You'll love it in Clarksville," my father assured me. "Baby Gwen is just your age and just your speed. She'll be so glad to see you." And he pressed several more twenty-dollar bills into my hand and helped me pack my summer clothes.

"You try it for the summer, LeLe," he said. "We'll decide about school later on."

He might need to decide later on, but my mind was made up. I couldn't wait to leave Franklin, Indiana, where the students at Franklin Junior High had made the mistake of failing to elect me cheerleader. I wasn't unpopular or anything like that, just a little on the plump side.

Baby Gwen Barksdale, I whispered to myself as I arranged my things on the Pullman seat. I was sweating heavily in a pink linen suit, and my straw hat was making my head itch, but I sat up straight, trying to look like a lady. I had the latest edition of *Hit Parade Magazine* on my lap, and I was determined to learn every word of the Top Ten on the train ride.

Baby Gwen Barksdale, I said to myself, remembering the stories my father had told me. Baby Gwen, queen of the Delta subdeb dances, daughter of the famous Gwendolyn Montgomery Paine of Shaw, granddaughter of my grandmother's sainted sister, Frances Paine of Natchez. Baby Gwen Barksdale, daughter of Britain Barksdale who played halfback on the Ole Miss Sugar Bowl team.

It was all too good to be true. I marched myself down to the diner and ate several desserts to calm myself down.

By the time the Illinois Central made it all the way to Clarksville, Mississippi, my linen dress was helplessly wrinkled, my third pair of white gloves was damp and stained from the dye of the magazine, and my teeth were worn out from being brushed.

But there on the platform she waited, Baby Gwen Barksdale herself, five feet two inches of sultry dark-skinned, dark-eyed beauty. (The Barksdales have French blood.) She looked exactly like Ida Lupino. She was wearing a navy blue dotted Swiss sun dress and high-heeled shoes and her slip was showing, a thin line of ecru lace. Her dark pink lipstick exactly matched her fingernail polish, and she smelled divinely of Aprodisia perfume.

She was accompanied by a strong boy who smiled a lot and turned out to be the sheriff's son. He had come along to carry the luggage.

"I'm so glad you could come," she said, hugging me for the fourth time. "I can't believe you came all the way on the train by yourself."

"No one in Franklin believed I'd do it either," I said. "I just got elected cheerleader and practically the whole football team came to tell me goodbye. They didn't believe I was leaving. Of course, they all knew about Bob Aaron. That's the college boy I love. He's got cancer of the thyroid gland. My parents won't let me go out with him because he's Jewish. He's already had about five operations. He's having one right now in St. Louis. So I might as well be down here."

"Oh, LeLe, that's terrible. It's like my mother. I know just how you feel."

"Well, anyway, I'm here now and we can stick together," I said, taking a deep breath of the Aprodisia. "I love your perfume. It's wonderful."

"It's my signature," she said. "I wear Aprodisia in the summer and Tigress in the winter. There's a bottle in my purse. You can put some on if you want to."

We walked over to the Oldsmobile and Baby Gwen got behind the wheel. She was so short she had to sit on straw pillows to see over the dash, but she turned out to be a superb driver. The sheriff's son climbed into the back seat with my bags, and the three of us drove off down the streets of the town, past the gin and the post office, and the Pontiac place, and on down the river road to a white frame house at the end of a street that dead-ended at the levee.

So I arrived in Clarksville, chattering away to a spellbound audience, spraying my neck and arms with Aprodisia perfume, happier than I had ever been in my life.

After her mother's funeral Baby Gwen had moved into the master bedroom as her father was too brokenhearted to ever enter that part of the house again.

I was led up the stairs and into a large sunny room with bay windows and a pale blue chaise lounge. There was a dressing room with a private bath and walk-in closets. Everything was just as Big Gwen had left it.

The closets were filled with unbelievable clothes. Navy blue and green and black silk dresses, gray and beige and brown gabardine suits, pastel evening dresses, house dresses, sun dresses, wool coats, skirts, jackets. There were twenty or thirty pairs of high-heeled shoes and a dozen hatboxes. There were drawers full of handmade underwear. There was a fur stole and several negligees and a real Japanese kimono.

It was all ours.

"You can wear anything you want to," Baby Gwen said. "Most of them are too long for me."

Best of all was the dressing table. It was three feet long with a padded stool and a large mirror surrounded by light bulbs.

On its surface, in a sea of spilled powder, were dozens of bottles and jars. Every product ever manufactured by Charles of the Ritz must have been there. There was foundation cream, astringent, eye shadow, rouge, clarifier, moisturizer, cleanser, refining oil, facial mask, night cream, hand cream, wrinkle cream, all pervaded by the unforgettable smell of Revenescence, Charles of the Ritz's secret formula moisturizer.

There were hairpins, hand mirrors, tweezers, eyelash curlers, combs, hair rollers, mascara wands, cuticle sticks, nail polish, emery boards. There were numerous bottles of perfume and cologne and a cut-glass bowl filled with lipsticks.

I had never seen anything like it. I could hardly wait to sit down on the little padded stool and get started.

"You want a Coca-Cola?" Baby Gwen asked, growing bored with my inspection of her riches. "Some boys I know are coming over later this afternoon to meet you."

"Can we smoke?" I asked, pulling my Pall Malls out of my purse.

"We can do anything we want to do," she said, picking a Ronson lighter off the dressing table and handing it to me. She was smiling the famous Barksdale slow smile.

That night we lay awake until two or three in the morning telling each other our life stories. I told her about Bob Aaron's lymph node cancer, and she told me about her cousin Maurice, who taught French and hated Clarksville and was married to an unpleasant woman who sang in the choir. Maurice was secretly in love with Baby Gwen. He couldn't help himself. He had confessed his love at a spring wedding reception. Now they were waiting for Baby Gwen to grow up so they could run away together. In the meantime Baby Gwen was playing the field so no one would suspect.

Finally, exhausted by our passions, we fell asleep in each other's arms, with the night breezes blowing in the windows off the river, in our ironed sheets and our silk pajamas and our night cream, with the radio playing an all-night station from New Orleans. Oh, Bob, Bob, I whispered into Baby Gwen's soft black hair. Oh, Maurice, Maurice, she sighed into my hair rollers.

In the morning I woke early and wandered downstairs. I went into the kitchen, opened the freezer, found a carton of vanilla ice cream, and began to eat it with my fingers, standing with the freezer door open, letting the cool air blow on my face.

After a while I heard the back door slam and Sirena came in. She was the middle-aged black woman who turned out to be the only person in charge of us in any way. Baby Gwen's father disappeared before dawn to carry the mail and came home in the evenings and sank into his chair with his bourbon and his memories. Occasionally he would put in an appearance at the noon meal and ask us if we wanted anything.

I barely managed to close the freezer door before Sirena caught me. "You want me to make you some breakfast?" she said.

"No, thank you," I said. "I don't eat in the daytime. I'm on a diet."

I have always believed Sirena found my fingerprints in that ice cream. One way or the other I wasn't fooling her, she knew a Yankee when she saw one, even if I was Mr. Leland's daughter.

I wandered into the living room and read a *Coronet* for a while.

Then I decided to go back upstairs and see if Baby Gwen was awake.

I found her in the bathroom sitting upright in a tub of soapy water while Sirena knelt beside it slowly and intently bathing her. I had never seen a grown person being bathed before.

Sirena was running her great black hand up and down Baby Gwen's white leg, soaping her with a terry-cloth washrag. The artesian well water was the color of urine and smelled of sulphur and sandalwood soap, and Sirena's dark hand was thick and strong moving along Baby Gwen's flawless skin. I sat down on the toilet and began to make conversation.

"You want to take a sunbath after a while," I said. "I'm afraid I'll lose my tan."

"Sure," she said. "We can do whatever you want to. Someone called a while ago and asked us to play bridge this afternoon. Do you like to play bridge?"

"I love it," I said. "That's practically all we do in Indiana. We play all the time. My mother plays duplicate. She's got about fifty silver ashtrays she won at tournaments."

"I bet you're really good," she said. She was squirming around while Sirena took her time finishing the other leg.

I lit a cigarette, trying not to look at Baby Gwen's black pubic hair. I had never seen anyone's pubic hair but my own, which was red. It had not occurred to me that there were different colors. "Want a drag?" I asked, handing her the cigarette. She nodded, wiped her hand on her terry-cloth turban, took a long luxurious drag, and French inhaled.

The smoke left her mouth in two little rivers, curled deliciously up over the dark hairs above her lips, and into her nostrils. She held it for a long moment, then exhaled slowly through her lips. The smoke mingled with the sunlight, and the steam coming from the bathwater rose in ragged circles and moved toward the open window.

Baby Gwen rose from the water, her flat body festooned with blossoms of sandalwood soap, and Sirena began to dry her with a towel.

So our life together took shape. In the mornings we sunbathed from 11:00 to 12:00. Thirty minutes on one side and thirty minutes on the other. There were two schools of thought concerning sunbathing. One, that it gave you wrinkles. The other, that it was worth it to look good while you were young.

Baby Gwen and I subscribed to the second theory. Still, we were careful to keep our faces oiled so we wouldn't ruin our complexions. There is no way you could believe how serious we were about such matters. The impenetrable mystery of physical beauty held us like a spell.

In the mornings we spread our blankets in the backyard where a patch of sunlight shone in through the high branches of the elm trees. We covered the blankets with white sheets and set out our supplies, bottles of baby oil, bottles of iodine, alarm clock, eye pads, sunglasses, magazines. We carefully mixed seven drops of iodine with seven ounces of baby oil, shook it for three minutes, then rubbed in on the uncovered parts of each other's bodies. How I loved the feel of Baby Gwen's rib cage under my fingers, the smoothness of her shaved legs. How I dreaded it when her fingers touched the baby fat on my own ribs.

When we were covered with oil we would lie back and continue our discussion of our romances. I talked of nothing but the ill-fated Bob Aaron, of the songs I would write and dedicate to his memory, of the trip I would take to his deathbed, of the night he drove me home from a football game and let me wear his gloves, of the child I would have by another man and name for him, Robert or Roberta, Bob or Bobbie.

The other thing that fascinated me was the development of my "reputation." I was intensely interested in what people thought of me, in what was being said about me. I set about to develop a reputation in Clarksville as a "madcap," a "wild child," a girl who would do anything. A summer visitor from Washington, D.C., said in my hearing that I reminded him of a young Zelda Fitzgerald[1] and, although I didn't know exactly who Zelda Fitzgerald was, I knew that she had married a writer and drank like a fish and once danced naked in a fountain in Rome. It seemed like a wonderful thing to have said about myself, and I resolved to try to live up to it.

How wonderful it was to be "home," where people knew "who I was," where people thought I was "hilarious" and "crazy" and "just like Leland." I did everything I could think of to feed my new image, becoming very outspoken, saying *damn* and *hell* at every opportunity, wearing dark glasses all the time, even to church. I must have been the first person of normal vision ever to attend the Clarksville Episcopal Church wearing dark glasses.

Baby Gwen's grandmother called every few days to see how we were getting along and once, in a burst of responsibility, came over bringing a dozen pairs of new cotton underpants she had bought for us at the Chinaman's store.

We never could figure out where she got the idea that we were in need of cotton underpants, unless Sirena had mentioned it to her. Perhaps Sirena had tired of hand washing the French lingerie we had taken to wearing every day.

The grandmother had outlived both her daughters and existed in a sort of dreamy half-world with her servants and her religion.

1. Wife of F. Scott Fitzgerald, notorious for her flamboyant pranks.

Mostly we kept her satisfied by glowing telephone reports of our popularity and by stopping by occasionally to sit on her porch and have a Coca-Cola.

I fell in love nearly every day with one or the other of the seemingly endless supply of boys who came to call from Drew and Cleveland and Itta Bena and Tutweiler and Rosedale and Leland. Baby Gwen drew boys like honey, and there were always plenty left over to sit around the living room listening to my nonstop conversation.

Boys came by in the evenings, boys called on the telephone, boys invaded our daily bridge games, boys showed up after church, boys took us swimming at the Clarksville Country Club, boys drove us around the cotton fields and down to the river and out to the bootlegger's shack.

The boy I liked best was a good-natured football player named Fielding Reid. Fielding had eyes so blue and hair so blonde and shoulders so wide and teased me so unmercifully about my accent that I completely forgot he was the steady boyfriend of Clarice Fitzhugh, who was off on a trip to Mexico with her family. Fielding had taken to hanging around Baby Gwen and me while he waited for Clarice's return.

He loved to kibitz on our bridge games, eating all the mints and pecans from the little dishes and leaning over my shoulder cheering me on. In the afternoons we played endless polite bridge games, so different from the bitter hard-fought bridge I had played in the forgotten state of Indiana.

Although I was an erratic and unpredictable bidder, I was a sought-after partner for I held good cards and nearly always won.

There was a girl from Drew named Sarah who came over several afternoons a week to play with us. She was Fielding's cousin and she had a wooden arm painted the color of her skin. It was not a particularly well made arm, and the paint was peeling in several places on the hand. She was pleasant enough looking otherwise and had nice clothes with loose sleeves that hid the place where the false arm joined the real one.

I made a great show of being nice to Sarah, lighting her cigarettes, asking her opinion about things, letting her be my bridge partner. She was delighted with the attention I gave her and was always telling someone how "wonderful" I was and how much it meant to her to have me in Clarksville.

The wrist and fingers of Sarah's false arm were hinged and she could move the joints with her good hand and lock them in place. She was in the habit of holding the wooden arm in front of her when she was seated at the bridge table. Then she would place her bridge hand in the wooden fingers and play out of it with her good hand.

Of course, anyone sitting on either side of her could see her cards by the slightest movement of their eyes. It took a lot of pressure off me when she was my partner.

Fielding thought I was "wonderful" too. He went around saying I was his "partner" and took me into his confidence, even telling me his fears that the absent Clarice Fitzhugh was being unfaithful to him in Mexico. That she might be "using" him.

Don't worry, I assured him. Clarice was a great girl. She wouldn't use anyone. He must trust her and not listen to idle gossip. Everything would be fine when she got home, and so forth. Part of my new reputation was that "LeLe never says a bad word about anyone," "LeLe always looks on the bright side," "everyone feels like they've known LeLe all their lives," "you can tell LeLe *anything*."

I was beginning to believe my own publicity, that I was someone very special, that there might be some special destiny in store for me.

Several times that summer I was filled with an elation so powerful and overwhelming that it felt as though my body were leaving the earth. This always happened at night, when I was alone in the yard, caught in the shadow of the Nandina bushes which covered the side of the house like bright dark clouds. I remember standing in the starlight filled with some inexpressible joy. It would become very intense, like music. I was terribly excited by these feelings and could not bring myself to speak of them, even to Baby Gwen.

Often that summer I was given to seizures of abrupt excitement while I was dressing. I would catch a glimpse of myself in a mirror and burst into laughter, or, deciding for a moment that I was pretty, begin to tremble and jump up and go dancing around the room.

I had a recurrent dream that summer. I dreamed that I was walking through our old house in Indiana and I would notice that the dining room opened up into rooms and rooms I had not known existed, strange and oddly shaped rooms full of heavy furniture, expensive dusty dressers with drawers full of treasures, old gowns and sweaters and capes, jewels and letters and old documents, wills and deeds and diaries. These rooms opened onto patios and sun porches and solariums, and I saw that we were wealthy people. I wanted to run back and find my parents and tell them what I had found, but my curiosity drove me forward. I had to keep opening doors until I knew the extent of our riches, so I kept on moving through the strange rooms until I woke.

One morning Fielding came by unexpectedly and asked me to go with him to see about some repairs for his car. We left it with a mechanic at the filling station and walked to the Mayflower Café, a place on the square where farmers and merchants gathered in the mornings for coffee and gossip. I had never been alone in a restaurant with a boy, and I was excited and began talking very fast to cover my excitement. I ordered doughnuts and began turning my turquoise ring around on my finger so the waitress would think it was a wedding band.

"I've been wanting to talk to you alone," Fielding said.

"Sure," I said, choking on a powdered doughnut. It was all too wonderful, sitting in a booth so early in the morning with a really good-looking boy.

"LeLe," he said, smiling at me and reaching across the table to hold my hand. There was his garnet class ring, blazing at me from the tabletop. At any moment it might be mine. I could scarcely breathe. "LeLe," he repeated, "I don't want you to get me wrong when I say this. I don't want to hurt your feelings or anything, but, well, I really want to tell you something." He squeezed my hand tighter. "LeLe, you would be a really beautiful girl if you lost ten pounds, do you know that? Because you have a beautiful face. I'm only saying this because we've gotten to be such good friends and I thought I ought . . ."

I was stunned. But I recovered. "I'm not really this fat," I said. "At home I'm a cheerleader and I'm on the swimming team and I'm very thin. But last year the boy I love got cancer and I've been having a lot of trouble with my thyroid since then. The doctors think there may be something wrong with my thyroid or my metabolism. I may have to have an operation pretty soon."

"Oh, LeLe," he said. "I didn't know it was anything like that. I thought maybe you ate too much or something." He reached out and took my hand. I was still holding part of a doughnut.

"Don't worry about it, Fielding. How could you know. You didn't hurt my feelings. Besides, I don't mind. The operation may not be so bad. It isn't like having polio or something they can't fix. At least I have something they can fix."

"Oh, LeLe."

"Don't worry about it. And don't tell anyone about it, even Baby Gwen. I don't want people feeling sorry for me. So it's a secret."

"Don't worry, LeLe. I'll never tell anyone. Are you sure it'll be all right? About the operation I mean?"

"Oh, sure. I might not even have to have it. My thyroid might get better all by itself."

After that Fielding and I were closer than ever. I began to half-way believe the part about the thyroid trouble. My mother was always talking about her thyroid and taking some sort of little white pill for it.

Late one afternoon Baby Gwen and I were sitting on the porch swing talking to Fielding. It was one of those days in August when you can smell autumn in the air, a feeling of change coming over the world. I had won at bridge that afternoon. I had made seven hearts doubled and redoubled with Fielding looking over my shoulder, and I was filled with a sense of power.

"Let's all go swimming tomorrow," I said. "They'll be closing the pool soon and I need to practice my strokes."

"Let's go to the lake," Fielding said. "I haven't made my summer swim across the lake. I was waiting for Russell to get home, but I don't guess he'll be back in time so I might as well go on and swim it myself."

"I'll swim it with you," I heard myself saying. "I'm a Junior Red Cross Lifesaver. I can swim forever,"

"You couldn't swim this," he said. "It's five miles."

"I can swim a lot further than that," I said. "I practically taught swimming at camp. I never get tired."

"What about your . . . you know . . . your condition?"

"That's all right," I said. "Exercise is good for me. I'm supposed to go swimming all I can. The doctors said it was the best thing I could do."

Baby Gwen looked puzzled. "You can't swim all the way across the lake without a boat," she said. "Girls don't ever swim across the lake."

"I can swim it," I said. "I've been further than that at camp lots of times. What time you want to go, Fielding?"

By the time he came to pick us up the next morning I had calmed Baby Gwen down and convinced her there was nothing to worry about. I really was a good swimmer. Swimming was of no importance to me one way or the other. What mattered to me was that a boy of my own choosing, a first-rate boy, was coming to take me somewhere. Not coming for Baby Gwen and taking me along to be nice, but *coming for me.*

I had been awake since dawn deciding what to wear. I finally settled on my old green Jantzen and a white blouse from Big Gwen's wardrobe. The blouse had little shoulder pads and big chunky buttons and fell across my shoulders and arms in soft pleats. I wasn't worried at all about swimming the lake. The only thing that worried me was whether the blouse was long enough to cover my stomach.

Baby Gwen went with us. As soon as we left the shore she was supposed to drive around to the other side and watch for us. All the way out to the lake she sat beside me looking worried.

"You ought to have a boat going along beside you," she said.

"We don't need a boat," I said. "I'm a Junior Red Cross Lifesaver. I can swim all day if I want."

"It's O.K.," Fielding said. "Russell and I do it every summer."

By the time we got to the lake I felt like I could swim the Atlantic Ocean. The sun was brilliant on the blue water, and as soon as Fielding stopped the car I jumped out and ran down to the shore and looked out across the water to the pine trees on the far shore. It didn't look so far away, only very blue and deep and mysterious. I took off my blouse and shoes and waded out into the water. How clean it felt, how cool. I put my face down and touched my cheek to the water. I felt the water across my legs and stomach. My body felt wonderful and light in the water. I rose up on my toes and my legs felt strong and tall. I pulled in my stomach until my ribs stuck out. I was beautiful. I was perfect. I began to throw handfuls of water up into the air. The water caught in the sunlight and fell back all around me, I threw more into the air and it fell all around me, falling in pieces of steel and glass and diamonds, diamonds falling all around me. I called out, "Come on, Fielding. Either we're swimming across this lake or we aren't."

"Wait," he called back. "Wait up." Then he was beside me in the water and I felt his hands around my waist and the pressure of his knee against my thigh. "Let's go then," he said in a low sweet voice. "Let's do this together."

Then we began to swim out, headed for the stand of pine and oak and cypress on the far shore.

The time passed as if in a dream. My arms moved easily, taking turns pulling the soft yielding water alongside my body. I was counting out the strokes, one, two, three, four, five, six, seven, eight, one, two, three, four, five, six, seven, eight . . . over and over in the good old-fashioned Australian crawl. Every now and then Fielding would touch my arm and we would roll over on our backs and rest for a few minutes, checking our position. Then we would swim for a while on our sides, resting. There were long banks of clouds on the horizon and far overhead a great hawk circling like a black planet. Everytime I looked up he was there.

We swam for what seemed to be a long, long time, but whenever I looked ahead the trees on the shore never seemed to come any closer.

"Are you sure we're going in a straight line," I said, when we turned over to rest for a moment.

"I think so," Fielding said. "The current might be pulling us a little to the left. There's nothing we can do about it now anyway."

"Why," I said. "Why can't we do anything about it?"

"Well, we can't go back," he said. "We're past the point of no return."

The point of no return, I said to myself. Maybe we would die out here and they would change the name of the lake in honor of us. Lake LeLe, Lake Leland Louise Arnold, Lover's Lake. "Don't worry about it then," I said. "Just keep on swimming."

Perhaps an hour went by, perhaps two. The sun was hot on the water, and every now and then a breeze blew up. Once a barge carrying logs to the sawmill passed us without noticing us. We treaded water while it passed and then rocked in the wake for several minutes. They had passed us as though we didn't exist. After the barge went by we began to swim with more determination. I was beginning to feel cold, but it didn't seem to really matter. Nothing mattered but this boy and the sun and the clouds and the great hawk circling and the water touching me everywhere. I put down my head and began to count with renewed vigor, one, two, three, four, five, six, seven, eight, one, two, three, four, . . .

"LeLe," Fielding called out. "LeLe, put your feet down. Put your feet down, LeLe." I looked up and he was standing a few feet away holding his hands up in the air. I let my feet drop and my toes touched the cool flat sand. We were on the sandbar. Then we were laughing and hugging and holding on to each other and moving toward the shore where Baby Gwen stood calling and calling to us. It was wonderful, wonderful, wonderful, wonderful. I was wonderful. I was dazzling. I was LeLe Arnold, the wildest girl in the Mississippi Delta, the girl who swam Lake Jefferson without a boat or a life vest. I was LeLe, the girl who would do anything.

All the way home in the car Fielding kept his arm around me while he drove and Baby Gwen fed me little pieces of the picnic lunch and I was happier than I had ever been in my life and I might have stayed that way forever but when we got home there was a message saying that my parents were on their way to Clarksville to take me home.

My parents. I had forgotten they existed. My father had gotten lonely and driven to New Orleans and talked my mother into coming home.

Later that afternoon they arrived. It seemed strange to see our Buick pulling up in Baby Gwen's driveway. My father got out looking very young and my mother was holding on to his arm. She looked like a stranger, thin and beautiful in a black cotton peasant dress with rows of colored rickrack around the hem and sleeves. Her hair was cut short and curled around her face in ringlets. I was almost afraid to touch her. Then she ran from my father's side and grabbed me in her arms and whirled me around and around and I smelled the delicate perfume on her skin and it made me feel like crying.

When she put me down I turned to my father. "I'm not going home," I said, putting my hands on my hips.

"Oh, yes you are," he said, so I went upstairs and began to pack my clothes.

Baby Gwen followed me up the stairs. "You can have the kimono," she said. "I want you to have it." She folded it carefully and packed it with tissue paper in a box from Nell's and Blum's and put it beside my suitcase.

"Come sit by me, Baby Gwen, and tell me the news," my mother said, and Baby Gwen went over and sat by her on the chaise. My mother put her arms around her and began to talk in a bright voice inviting her to spend Christmas with us in Indiana.

"It will snow for sure," my mother said. "And LeLe can show you the snow."

We left Clarksville early the next morning. Baby Gwen stood in the doorway waving goodbye. She was wearing a pink satin robe stained in places from where she had sweated in it during the hot nights of July, and her little nipples stuck out beneath the soft material.

I kept hoping maybe Fielding had gotten up early to come and tell me goodbye, but he didn't make it.

"I'll fix those hems when she comes to visit," my mother said, "and do something about that perfume."

I was too tired to argue. All the way to Indiana I slumped in the back seat eating potato chips and sneaking smokes in filling-station restrooms when we stopped for gas.

Then it was another morning and I woke up in my old room and put on my shorts and rode my bicycle over to Cynthia Carver's house. She was in the basement doing her Saturday morning ironing. Cynthia hated to iron. How many mornings had I sat on those basement steps watching the forlorn look on her face while she finished her seven blouses.

"So I might as well be dead," I said, taking a bite of a cookie. "So, anyway, I wish I was dead," I repeated, as Cynthia hung a blouse on a hanger and started on a dirndl skirt. "Here I am, practically engaged to this rich plantation owner's son . . . Fielding. Fielding Reid, LeLe Reid . . . so, anyway, my mother and father come and drag me home practically the same day we fell in love. I don't know how they got wind of it unless that damn Sirena called and told them. She was always watching everything I did. Anyway, they drag me home and I bet they won't even let him write to me."

"What's that perfume?" Cynthia said, lifting her eyes from the waistband of the skirt.

"That's my signature," I said. "That's what I wear now. Tigress in the winter and Aprodisia in the summer. That's what this writer's wife always wore. She got pneumonia or something from swimming in the winter and died when she was real young. Everyone in Clarksville thinks I'm just like her. She was from Mississippi or something. I think she's sort of my father's cousin."

Cynthia pulled the dirndl off the ironing board and began on a pair of pedal pushers. I leaned back on the stairs, watching the steam from the pedal pushers light up the space over Cynthia Carter's disgruntled Yankee head. I was dreaming of the lake, trying to remember how the water turned into diamonds in my hands.

---

1. Are LeLe's lies chiefly a means of satisfying herself, or do they enhance her relationships with others? Is there a consistent pattern to them?
2. Is being overweight a trait consistent with her general unreliability and disregard for the truth?
3. Has LeLe managed to loot Baby Gwen's personality and carry off what she wants?
4. Does LeLe's ability to swim the lake show a promise that she will make good someday on her presently frivolous boasts? Are her bravery and skill in the swim inconsistent with the rest of her behavior?

Nathaniel Hawthorne

Hawthorne (1804–1864) was born in Salem, Massachusetts, where he lived in quiet seclusion before and after his four years of attendance at Bowdoin College. Seldom leaving his room by daylight, he read, meditated, and wrote the stories and sketches that first appeared in 1837 in Twice-Told Tales. *They brought him neither renown nor money, so in 1839 he took a job in the Boston Custom House and, when he lost it, spent some time at Brook Farm, an experiment in communal living that provided him with background for his novel* The Blithedale Romance *(1852). At the time of his marriage in 1842 he took his wife to live in a historic house called the Old Manse in Concord, publishing more short pieces in 1846 in a volume called* Mosses from an Old Manse. The Scarlet Letter, *his greatest novel, published in 1850, brought him recognition as a major literary figure. In 1853 he was appointed consul to Liverpool by his college friend Franklin Pierce, who had become President of the United States. After four years of service in his post, Hawthorne traveled in England and Italy until his return to America in 1860. Much of his work is colored by romanticism, while the weight of his Puritan heritage, with its ethical biases and emphasis on sin, radically shaped his themes. The allegorical strain in much of his imaginative work is compensated by the clear and realistic picture of daily experience in his notebooks and in many travel sketches. His novels include* The House of Seven Gables *(1851) and* The Marble Faun *(1860). His books of short stories are two volumes of* Twice-Told Tales *(1837 and 1842) and* Mosses from an Old Manse *(1846).*

Young Goodman Brown

Young Goodman[1] Brown came forth at sunset into the street of Salem village; but put his head back, after crossing the threshold, to exchange a parting kiss with his young wife. And Faith, as the wife was aptly named, thrust her own pretty head into the street, letting the wind play with the pink ribbons of her cap while she called to Goodman Brown.

"Dearest heart," whispered she, softly and rather sadly, when her lips were close to his ear, "prithee put off your journey until sunrise and sleep in your own bed to-night. A lone woman is troubled

1. Title of respect for those below the rank of gentleman.

with such dreams and such thoughts that she's afeard of herself sometimes. Pray tarry with me this night, dear husband, of all nights in the year!"

"My love and my Faith," replied young Goodman Brown, "of all nights in the year, this one night must I tarry away from thee. My journey, as thou callest it, forth and back again, must needs be done 'twixt now and sunrise. What, my sweet, pretty wife, dost thou doubt me already, and we but three months married?"

"Then God bless you!" said Faith, with the pink ribbons; "and may you find all well when you come back."

"Amen!" cried Goodman Brown. "Say thy prayers, dear Faith, and go to bed at dusk, and no harm will come to thee."

So they parted; and the young man pursued his way until, being about to turn the corner by the meeting-house, he looked back and saw the head of Faith still peeping after him with a melancholy air, in spite of her pink ribbons.

"Poor little Faith!" thought he, for his heart smote him. "What a wretch am I to leave her on such an errand! She talks of dreams, too. Methought as she spoke there was trouble in her face, as if a dream had warned her what work is to be done to-night. But no, no; 't would kill her to think it. Well, she's a blessed angel on earth; and after this one night I'll cling to her skirts and follow her to heaven."

With this excellent resolve for the future, Goodman Brown felt himself justified in making more haste on his present evil purpose. He had taken a dreary road, darkened by all the gloomiest trees of the forest, which barely stood aside to let the narrow path creep through, and closed immediately behind. It was all as lonely as could be; and there is this peculiarity in such a solitude, that the traveler knows not who may be concealed by the innumerable trunks and the thick boughs overhead; so that with lonely footsteps he may yet be passing through an unseen multitude.

"There may be a devilish Indian behind every tree," said Goodman Brown to himself; and he glanced fearfully behind him as he added, "What if the devil himself should be at my very elbow!"

His head being turned back, he passed a crook of the road, and, looking forward again, beheld the figure of a man, in grave and decent attire, seated at the foot of an old tree. He arose at Goodman Brown's approach and walked onward side by side with him.

"You are late, Goodman Brown," said he. "The clock of the Old South was striking as I came through Boston,[2] and that is full fifteen minutes agone."

2. Boston is some fifteen miles from Salem—perhaps an indication of the supernatural speed of the speaker's travel.

"Faith kept me back a while," replied the young man, with a tremor in his voice, caused by the sudden appearance of his companion, though not wholly unexpected.

It was now deep dusk in the forest, and deepest in that part of it where these two were journeying. As nearly as could be discerned, the second traveller was about fifty years old, apparently in the same rank of life as Goodman Brown, and bearing a considerable resemblance to him, though perhaps more in expression than features. Still they might have been taken for father and son. And yet, though the elder person was as simply clad as the younger, and as simple in manner too, he had an indescribable air of one who knew the world, and would not have felt abashed at the governor's dinner table or in King William's[3] court, were it possible that his affairs should call him thither. But the only thing about him that could be fixed upon as remarkable was his staff, which bore the likeness of a great black snake, so curiously wrought that it might almost be seen to twist and wriggle itself like a living serpent. This, of course, must have been an ocular deception, assisted by the uncertain light.

"Come, Goodman Brown!" cried his fellow-traveller, "this is a dull pace for the beginning of a journey. Take my staff, if you are so soon weary."

"Friend," said the other, exchanging his slow pace for a full stop, "having kept covenant by meeting thee here, it is my purpose now to return whence I came. I have scruples touching the matter thou wot'st of."

"Sayest thou so?" replied he of the serpent, smiling apart. "Let us walk on, nevertheless, reasoning as we go; and if I convince thee not thou shalt turn back. We are but a little way in the forest yet."

"Too far, too far!" exclaimed the goodman, unconsciously resuming his walk. "My father never went into the woods on such an errand, nor his father before him. We have been a race of honest men and good Christians since the days of the martyrs; and shall I be the first of the name of Brown that ever took this path and kept—"

"Such company, thou wouldst say," observed the elder person, interpreting his pause. "Well said, Goodman Brown! I have been as well acquainted with your family as with ever a one among the Puritans; and that's no trifle to say. I helped your grandfather, the constable, when he lashed the Quaker woman so smartly through the streets of Salem; and it was I that brought your father a pitch-pine knot, kindled at my own hearth, to set fire to an Indian village, in King Philip's war.[4] They were my good friends, both; and many a pleasant walk have

3. King William III of England (ruled from 1689 to 1702).

4. Rebellion by Indians against white settlers, 1675–76.

we had along this path, and returned merrily after midnight. I would fain be friends with you for their sake."

"If it be as thou sayest," replied Goodman Brown, "I marvel they never spoke of these matters; or, verily, I marvel not, seeing that the least rumor of the sort would have driven them from New England. We are a people of prayer, and good works to boot, and abide no such wickedness."

"Wickedness or not," said the traveler with the twisted staff, "I have a very general acquaintance here in New England. The deacons of many a church have drunk the communion wine with me; the selectmen of divers towns make me their chairman; and a majority of the Great and General Court are firm supporters of my interest. The governor and I, too— But these are state secrets."

"Can this be so?" cried Goodman Brown, with a stare of amazement at his undisturbed companion. "Howbeit, I have nothing to do with the governor and council; they have their own ways, and are no rule for a simple husbandman like me. But, were I to go on with thee, how should I meet the eye of that good old man, our minister, at Salem village? Oh, his voice would make me tremble both Sabbath day and lecture day."

Thus far the elder traveller had listened with due gravity; but now burst into a fit of irrepressible mirth, shaking himself so violently that his snake-like staff actually seemed to wriggle in sympathy.

"Ha! ha! ha!" shouted he again and again; then composing himself, "Well, go on, Goodman Brown, go on; but, prithee, don't kill me with laughing."

"Well, then, to end the matter at once," said Goodman Brown, considerably nettled, "there is my wife, Faith. It would break her dear little heart; and I'd rather break my own."

"Nay, if that be the case," answered the other, "e'en go thy ways, Goodman Brown. I would not for twenty old women like the one hobbling before us that Faith should come to any harm."

As he spoke he pointed his staff at a female figure on the path, in whom Goodman Brown recognized a very pious and exemplary dame, who had taught him his catechism in youth, and was still his moral and spiritual adviser, jointly with the minister and Deacon Gookin.

"A marvel, truly, that Goody Cloyse should be so far in the wilderness at nightfall," said he. "But with your leave, friend, I shall take a cut through the woods until we have left this Christian woman behind. Being a stranger to you, she might ask whom I was consorting with and whither I was going."

"Be it so," said his fellow-traveller. "Betake you to the woods, and let me keep the path."

Accordingly the young man turned aside, but took care to watch his companion, who advanced softly along the road until he had come within a staff's length of the old dame. She, meanwhile, was making the best of her way, with singular speed for so aged a woman, and mumbling some indistinct words—a prayer, doubtless—as she went. The traveller put forth his staff and touched her withered neck with what seemed the serpent's tail.

"The devil!" screamed the pious old lady.

"Then Goody Cloyse knows her old friend?" observed the traveller, confronting her and leaning on his writhing stick.

"Ah, forsooth, and is it your worship indeed?" cried the good dame. "Yea, truly is it, and in the very image of my old gossip,[5] Goodman Brown, the grandfather of the silly fellow that now is. But—would your worship believe it?—my broomstick hath strangely disappeared, stolen, as I suspect, by that unhanged witch, Goody Cory, and that, too, when I was all anointed with the juice of smallage, and cinquefoil, and wolf's-bane—"[6]

"Mingled with fine wheat and the fat of a new-born babe," said the shape of old Goodman Brown.

"Ah, your worship knows the recipe," cried the old lady, cackling aloud. "So, as I was saying, being all ready for the meeting, and no horse to ride on, I made up my mind to foot it; for they tell me there is a nice young man to be taken into communion to-night. But now your good worship will lend me your arm, and we shall be there in a twinkling."

"That can hardly be," answered her friend. "I may not spare you my arm, Goody Cloyse; but here is my staff, if you will."

So saying, he threw it down at her feet, where, perhaps, it assumed life, being one of the rods which its owner had formerly lent to the Egyptian magi. Of this fact, however, Goodman Brown could not take cognizance. He had cast up his eyes in astonishment, and, looking down again, beheld neither Goody Cloyse nor the serpentine staff, but this fellow-traveller alone, who waited for him as calmly as if nothing had happened.

"That old woman taught me my catechism," said the young man; and there was a world of meaning in this simple comment.

They continued to walk onward, while the elder traveller exhorted his companion to make good speed and persevere in the path, discoursing so aptly that his arguments seemed rather to spring up in the bosom of his auditor than to be suggested by himself. As they went, he plucked a branch of maple, to serve for a walking stick, and began to strip it of the twigs and little boughs, which were wet with evening dew. The moment his fingers touched them they became strangely

5. Friend. 6. Plants used in witchcraft.

withered and dried up as with a week's sunshine. Thus the pair proceeded, at a good free pace, until suddenly, in a gloomy hollow of the road, Goodman Brown sat himself down on the stump of a tree and refused to go any farther.

"Friend," said he, stubbornly, "my mind is made up. Not another step will I budge on this errand. What if a wretched old woman do choose to go to the devil when I thought she was going to heaven: is that any reason why I should quit my dear Faith and go after her?"

"You will think better of this by and by," said his acquaintance, composedly. "Sit here and rest yourself a while; and when you feel like moving again, there is my staff to help you along."

Without more words, he threw his companion the maple stick, and was as speedily out of sight as if he had vanished into the deepening gloom. The young man sat a few moments by the roadside, applauding himself greatly, and thinking with how clear a conscience he should meet the minister in his morning walk, nor shrink from the eye of good old Deacon Gookin. And what calm sleep would be his that very night, which was to have been spent so wickedly, but so purely and sweetly now, in the arms of Faith! Amidst these pleasant and praiseworthy meditations, Goodman Brown heard the tramp of horses along the road, and deemed it advisable to conceal himself within the verge of the forest, conscious of the guilty purpose that had brought him thither, though now so happily turned from it.

On came the hoof tramps and the voices of the riders, two grave old voices, conversing soberly as they drew near. These mingled sounds appeared to pass along the road, within a few yards of the young man's hiding-place; but, owing doubtless to the depth of the gloom at that particular spot, neither the travellers nor their steeds were visible. Though their figures brushed the small boughs by the wayside, it could not be seen that they intercepted, even for a moment, the faint gleam from the strip of bright sky athwart which they must have passed. Goodman Brown alternately crouched and stood on tiptoe, pulling aside the branches and thrusting forth his head as far as he durst without discerning so much as a shadow. It vexed him the more, because he could have sworn, were such a thing possible, that he recognized the voices of the minister and Deacon Gookin, jogging along quietly, as they were wont to do, when bound to some ordination or ecclesiastical council. While yet within hearing, one of the riders stopped to pluck a switch.

"Of the two, reverend sir," said the voice like the deacon's, "I had rather miss an ordination dinner than to-night's meeting. They tell me that some of our community are to be here from Falmouth and beyond, and others from Connecticut and Rhode Island, besides several of the Indian powwows, who, after their fashion, know almost as much deviltry as the best of us. Moreover, there is a goodly young woman to be taken into communion."

"Mighty well, Deacon Gookin!" replied the solemn old tones of the minister. "Spur up, or we shall be late. Nothing can be done, you know, until I get on the ground."

The hoofs clattered again; and the voices, talking so strangely in the empty air, passed on through the forest, where no church had ever been gathered or solitary Christian prayed. Whither, then, could these holy men be journeying so deep into the heathen wilderness? Young Goodman Brown caught hold of a tree for support, being ready to sink down on the ground, faint and overburdened with the heavy sickness of his heart. He looked up to the sky, doubting whether there really was a heaven above him. Yet there was the blue arch, and the stars brightening in it.

"With heaven above and Faith below, I will yet stand firm against the devil!" cried Goodman Brown.

While he still gazed upward into the deep arch of the firmament and had lifted his hands to pray, a cloud, though no wind was stirring, hurried across the zenith and hid the brightening stars. The blue sky was still visible, except directly overhead, where this black mass of cloud was sweeping swiftly northward. Aloft in the air, as if from the depths of the cloud, came a confused and doubtful sound of voices. Once the listener fancied that he could distinguish the accents of townspeople of his own, men and women, both pious and ungodly, many of whom he had met at the communion table, and had seen others rioting at the tavern. The next moment, so indistinct were the sounds, he doubted whether he had heard aught but the murmur of the old forest, whispering without a wind. Then came a stronger swell of those familiar tones, heard daily in the sunshine at Salem village, but never until now from a cloud of night. There was one voice, of a young woman, uttering lamentations, yet with an uncertain sorrow, and entreating for some favor, which, perhaps, it would grieve her to obtain; and all the unseen multitude, both saints and sinners, seemed to encourage her onward.

"Faith!" shouted Goodman Brown, in a voice of agony and desperation; and the echoes of the forest mocked him, crying, "Faith! Faith!" as if bewildered wretches were seeking her all through the wilderness.

The cry of grief, rage, and terror was yet piercing the night, when the unhappy husband held his breath for a response. There was a scream, drowned immediately in a louder murmur of voices, fading into far-off laughter, as the dark cloud swept away, leaving the clear and silent sky above Goodman Brown. But something fluttered lightly down through the air and caught on the branch of a tree. The young man seized it, and beheld a pink ribbon.

"My Faith is gone!" cried he, after one stupefied moment. "There is no good on earth; and sin is but a name. Come, devil; for to thee is this world given."

And, maddened with despair, so that he laughed loud and long, did Goodman Brown grasp his staff and set forth again, at such a rate that he seemed to fly along the forest path rather than to walk or run. The road grew wilder and drearier and more faintly traced, and vanished at length, leaving him in the heart of the dark wilderness, still rushing onward with the instinct that guides mortal man to evil. The whole forest was peopled with frightful sounds—the creaking of the trees, the howling of wild beasts, and the yell of Indians; while sometimes the wind tolled like a distant church bell, and sometimes gave a broad roar around the traveller, as if all Nature were laughing him to scorn. But he was himself the chief horror of the scene, and shrank not from its other horrors.

"Ha! ha! ha!" roared Goodman Brown when the wind laughed at him. "Let us hear which will laugh loudest. Think not to frighten me with your deviltry. Come witch, come wizard, come Indian powwow, come devil himself, and here comes Goodman Brown. You may as well fear him as he fear you."

In truth, all through the haunted forest, there could be nothing more frightful than the figure of Goodman Brown. On he flew among the black pines, brandishing his staff with frenzied gestures, now giving vent to an inspiration of horrid blasphemy, and now shouting forth such laughter as set all the echoes of the forest laughing like demons around him. The fiend in his own shape is less hideous than when he rages in the breast of man. Thus sped the demoniac on his course, until, quivering among the trees, he saw a red light before him, as when the felled trunks and branches of a clearing have been set on fire, and throw up their lurid blaze against the sky, at the hour of midnight. He paused, in a lull of the tempest that had driven him onward, and heard the swell of what seemed a hymn, rolling solemnly from a distance with the weight of many voices. He knew the tune; it was a familiar one in the choir of the village meeting-house. The verse died heavily away, and was lengthened by a chorus, not of human voices, but of all the sounds of the benighted wilderness pealing in awful harmony together. Goodman Brown cried out, and his cry was lost to his own ear, by its unison with the cry of the desert.

In the interval of silence he stole forward until the light glared full upon his eyes. At one extremity of an open space, hemmed in by the dark wall of the forest, arose a rock, bearing some rude, natural resemblance either to an altar or a pulpit, and surrounded by four blazing pines, their tops aflame, their stems untouched, like candles at an evening meeting. The mass of foliage that had overgrown the summit of the rock was all on fire, blazing high into the night and fitfully illuminating the whole field. Each pendent twig and leafy festoon was in a blaze. As the red light arose and fell, a numerous congregation alternately shone forth, then disappeared in shadow, and again grew, as it were, out of the darkness, peopling the heart of the solitary woods at once.

"A grave and dark-clad company," quoth Goodman Brown.

In truth they were such. Among them, quivering to and fro between gloom and splendor, appeared faces that would be seen next day at the council board of the province, and others which, Sabbath after Sabbath, looked devoutly heavenward, and benignantly over the crowded pews, from the holiest pulpits in the land. Some affirm that the lady of the governor was there. At least there were high dames well known to her, and wives of honored husbands, and widows, a great multitude, and ancient maidens, all of excellent repute, and fair young girls, who trembled lest their mothers should espy them. Either the sudden gleams of light flashing over the obscure field bedazzled Goodman Brown, or he recognized a score of the church members of Salem village famous for their especial sanctity. Good old Deacon Gookin had arrived, and waited at the skirts of that venerable saint, his revered pastor. But, irreverently consorting with these grave, reputable, and pious people, these elders of the church, these chaste dames and dewy virgins, there were men of dissolute lives and women of spotted fame, wretches given over to all mean and filthy vice, and suspected even of horrid crimes. It was strange to see that the good shrank not from the wicked, nor were the sinners abashed by the saints. Scattered also among their pale-faced enemies were the Indian priests, or powwows, who had often scared their native forest with more hideous incantations than any known to English witchcraft.

"But where is Faith?" thought Goodman Brown; and, as hope came into his heart, he trembled.

Another verse of the hymn arose, a slow and mournful strain, such as the pious love, but joined to words which expressed all that our nature can conceive of sin, and darkly hinted at far more. Unfathomable to mere mortals is the lore of fiends. Verse after verse was sung, and still the chorus of the desert swelled between like the deepest tone of a mighty organ; and with the final peal of that dreadful anthem there came a sound, as if the roaring wind, the rushing streams, the howling beasts, and every other voice of the unconverted wilderness were mingling and according with the voice of guilty man in homage to the prince of all. The four blazing pines threw up a loftier flame, and obscurely discovered shapes and visages of horror on the smoke wreaths above the impious assembly. At the same moment the fire on the rock shot redly forth and formed a glowing arch above its base, where now appeared a figure. With reverence be it spoken, the apparition bore no slight similitude, both in garb and manner, to some grave divine of the New England churches.

"Bring forth the converts!" cried a voice that echoed through the field and rolled into the forest.

At the word, Goodman Brown stepped forth from the shadow of the trees and approached the congregation, with whom he felt a loathful brotherhood by the sympathy of all that was wicked in his heart. He could have well-nigh sworn that the shape of his own dead father beckoned him to advance, looking downward from a smoke wreath, while a woman, with dim features of despair, threw out her hand to warn him back. Was it his mother? But he had no power to retreat one step, nor to resist, even in thought, when the minister and good old Deacon Gookin seized his arms and led him to the blazing rock. Thither came also the slender form of a veiled female, led between Goody Cloyse, that pious teacher of the catechism, and Martha Carrier, who had received the devil's promise to be queen of hell. A rampant hag was she. And there stood the proselytes beneath the canopy of fire.

"Welcome, my children," said the dark figure, "to the communion of your race. Ye have found thus young your nature and your destiny. My children, look behind you!"

They turned; and flashing forth, as it were, in a sheet of flame, the fiend worshippers were seen; the smile of welcome gleamed darkly on every visage.

"There," resumed the sable form, "are all whom ye have reverenced from youth. Ye deemed them holier than yourselves, and shrank from your own sin, contrasting it with their lives of righteousness and prayerful aspirations heavenward. Yet here are they all in my worshipping assembly. This night it shall be granted you to know their secret deeds: how hoary-bearded elders of the church have whispered wanton words to the young maids of their households; how many a woman, eager for widows' weeds, has given her husband a drink at bedtime and let him sleep his last sleep in her bosom; how beardless youths have made haste to inherit their fathers' wealth; and how fair damsels—blush not, sweet ones—have dug little graves in the garden, and bidden me, the sole guest, to an infant's funeral. By the sympathy of your human hearts for sin ye shall scent out all the places—whether in church, bed-chamber, street, field, or forest—where crime has been committed, and shall exult to behold the whole earth one stain of guilt, one mighty blood spot. Far more than this. It shall be yours to penetrate, in every bosom, the deep mystery of sin, the fountain of all wicked arts, and which inexhaustibly supplies more evil impulses than human power—than my power at its utmost—can make manifest in deeds. And now, my children, look upon each other."

They did so; and, by the blaze of the hell-kindled torches, the wretched man beheld his Faith, and the wife her husband, trembling before that unhallowed altar.

"Lo, there ye stand, my children," said the figure, in a deep and solemn tone, almost sad with its despairing awfulness, as if his once angelic nature could yet mourn for our miserable race. "Depending upon one another's hearts, ye had still hoped that virtue were not all a dream. Now are ye undeceived. Evil is the nature of mankind. Evil must be your only happiness. Welcome again, my children, to the communion of your race."

"Welcome," repeated the fiend worshippers, in one cry of despair and triumph.

And there they stood, the only pair, as it seemed, who were yet hesitating on the verge of wickedness in this dark world. A basin was hollowed, naturally, in the rock. Did it contain water, reddened by the lurid light? or was it blood? or, perchance, a liquid flame? Herein did the shape of evil dip his hand and prepare to lay the mark of baptism upon their foreheads, that they might be partakers of the mystery of sin, more conscious of the secret guilt of others, both in deed and thought, than they could now be of their own. The husband cast one look at his pale wife, and Faith at him. What polluted wretches would the next glance show them to each other, shuddering alike at what they disclosed and what they saw!

"Faith! Faith!" cried the husband, "look up to Heaven, and resist the wicked one."

Whether Faith obeyed he knew not. Hardly had he spoken when he found himself amid calm night and solitude, listening to a roar of the wind which died heavily away through the forest. He staggered against the rock and felt it chill and damp, while a hanging twig, that had been all on fire, besprinkled his cheek with the coldest dew.

The next morning young Goodman Brown came slowly into the street of Salem village, staring around him like a bewildered man. The good old minister was taking a walk along the graveyard, to get an appetite for breakfast and meditate his sermon, and bestowed a blessing, as he passed, on Goodman Brown. He shrank from the venerable saint as if to avoid an anathema. Old Deacon Gookin was at domestic worship, and the holy words of his prayer were heard through the open window. "What God doth the wizard pray to?" quoth Goodman Brown. Goody Cloyse, that excellent old Christian, stood in the early sunshine, at her own lattice, catechizing a little girl who had brought her a pint of morning's milk. Goodman Brown snatched away the child as from the grasp of the fiend himself. Turning the corner by the meeting-house, he spied the head of Faith, with the pink ribbons, gazing anxiously forth, and bursting into such joy at sight of him that she skipped along the street and almost kissed her husband before the whole village. But Goodman Brown looked sternly and sadly into her face, and passed on without a greeting.

Had Goodman Brown fallen asleep in the forest, and only dreamed a wild dream of a witch-meeting?

Be it so if you will; but, alas! it was a dream of evil omen for young Goodman Brown. A stern, a sad, a darkly meditative, a distrustful, if not a desperate man did he become from the night of that fearful dream. On the Sabbath day, when the congregation were singing a holy psalm, he could not listen because an anthem of sin rushed loudly upon his ear and drowned all the blessed strain. When the minister spoke from the pulpit with power and fervid eloquence, and, with his hand on the open Bible, of the sacred truths of our religion, and of saint-like lives and triumphant deaths, and of future bliss or misery unutterable, then did Goodman Brown turn pale, dreading lest the roof should thunder down upon the gray blasphemer and his hearers. Often, awaking suddenly at midnight, he shrank from the bosom of Faith; and at morning or eventide, when the family knelt down at prayer, he scowled and muttered to himself, and gazed sternly at his wife, and turned away. And when he had lived long, and was borne to his grave a hoary corpse, followed by Faith, an aged woman, and children and grandchildren, a goodly procession, besides neighbors not a few, they carved no hopeful verse upon his tombstone, for his dying hour was gloom.

---

1. How are elements of the supernatural related to the psychology of Brown and other characters? Does it matter whether or not Brown merely dreamed the witch-meeting?
2. What was Brown's initial motive for going into the forest? Is this motive consistent with his reluctance to go along with the devil after they have met?
3. How do you interpret Brown's refusal to accept his wife's joyful welcome on his return?
4. How does the last paragraph relate to the action and theme of the story? What comment does it make on the workings of the devil?

The Birthmark

In the latter part of the last century there lived a man of science, an eminent proficient in every branch of natural philosophy, who not long before our story opens had made experience of a spiritual affinity more attractive than any chemical one. He had left his laboratory to the care of an assistant, cleared his fine countenance from the furnace smoke, washed the stain of acids from his fingers, and persuaded a beautiful woman to become his wife. In those days when the comparatively recent discovery of electricity and other kindred mysteries of Nature seemed to open paths into the region of miracle, it was not unusual for the love of science to rival the love of woman in its depth and absorbing energy. The higher intellect, the imagination, the spirit, and even the heart might all find their congenial aliment in pursuits which, as some of their ardent votaries believed, would ascend from one step of powerful intelligence to another, until the philosopher should lay his hand on the secret of creative force and perhaps make new worlds for himself. We know not whether Aylmer possessed this degree of faith in man's ultimate control over Nature. He had devoted himself, however, too unreservedly to scientific studies ever to be weaned from them by any second passion. His love for his young wife might prove the stronger of the two; but it could only be by intertwining itself with his love of science, and uniting the strength of the latter to his own.

Such a union accordingly took place, and was attended with truly remarkable consequences and a deeply impressive moral. One day, very soon after their marriage, Aylmer sat gazing at his wife with a trouble in his countenance that grew stronger until he spoke.

"Georgiana," said he, "has it never occurred to you that the mark upon your cheek might be removed?"

"No, indeed," said she, smiling; but perceiving the seriousness of his manner, she blushed deeply. "To tell the truth it has been so often called a charm that I was simple enough to imagine it might be so."

"Ah, upon another face perhaps it might," replied her husband; "but never on yours. No, dearest Georgiana, you came so nearly perfect from the hand of Nature that this slightest possible defect, which we hesitate whether to term a defect or a beauty, shocks me, as being the visible mark of earthly imperfection."

"Shocks you, my husband!" cried Georgiana, deeply hurt; at first reddening with momentary anger, but then bursting into tears. "Then why did you take me from my mother's side? You cannot love what shocks you!"

To explain this conversation it must be mentioned that in the centre of Georgiana's left cheek there was a singular mark, deeply interwoven, as it were, with the texture and substance of her face. In the usual state of her complexion—a healthy though delicate bloom—the mark wore a tint of deeper crimson, which imperfectly defined its shape amid the surrounding rosiness. When she blushed it gradually became more indistinct, and finally vanished amid the triumphant rush of blood that bathed the whole cheek with its brilliant glow. But if any shifting motion caused her to turn pale there was the mark again, a crimson stain upon the snow, in what Aylmer sometimes deemed an almost fearful distinctness. Its shape bore not a little similarity to the human hand, though of the smallest pygmy size. Georgiana's lovers were wont to say that some fairy at her birth hour had laid her tiny hand upon the infant's cheek, and left this impress there in token of the magic endowments that were to give her such sway over all hearts. Many a desperate swain would have risked life for the privilege of pressing his lips to the mysterious hand. It must not be concealed, however, that the impression wrought by this fairy sign manual varied exceedingly, according to the difference of temperament in the beholders. Some fastidious persons—but they were exclusively of her own sex—affirmed that the bloody hand, as they chose to call it, quite destroyed the effect of Georgiana's beauty, and rendered her countenance even hideous. But it would be as reasonable to say that one of those small blue stains which sometimes occur in the purest statuary marble would convert the Eve of Powers[1] to a monster. Masculine observers, if the birthmark did not heighten their admiration, contented themselves with wishing it away, that the world might possess one living specimen of ideal loveliness without the semblance of a flaw. After his marriage,—for he thought little or nothing of the matter before,—Aylmer discovered that this was the case with himself.

Had she been less beautiful,—if Envy's self could have found aught else to sneer at,—he might have felt his affection heightened by the prettiness of this mimic hand, now vaguely portrayed, now lost, now stealing forth again and glimmering to and fro with every pulse of emotion that throbbed within her heart; but seeing her otherwise so perfect, he found this one defect grow more and more intolerable with every moment of their united lives. It was the fatal flaw of humanity which Nature, in one shape or another, stamps ineffaceably on all her productions, either to imply that they are temporary and finite, or that their perfection must be wrought by toil and pain. The crimson hand expressed the ineludible gripe[2] in which mortality clutches the highest and purest of earthly mould, degrading them into kindred with the

1. Hiram Powers, American sculptor (1805–1873). 2. Grip.

lowest, and even with the very brutes, like whom their visible frames return to dust. In this manner, selecting it as the symbol of his wife's liability to sin, sorrow, decay, and death, Aylmer's sombre imagination was not long in rendering the birthmark a frightful object, causing him more trouble and horror than ever Georgiana's beauty, whether of soul or sense, had given him delight.

At all the seasons which should have been their happiest, he invariably and without intending it, nay, in spite of a purpose to the contrary, reverted to this one disastrous topic. Trifling as it at first appeared, it so connected itself with innumerable trains of thought and modes of feeling that it became the central point of all. With the morning twilight Aylmer opened his eyes upon his wife's face and recognized the symbol of imperfection; and when they sat together at the evening hearth his eyes wandered stealthily to her cheek, and beheld, flickering with the blaze of the wood fire, the spectral hand that wrote mortality where he would fain have worshipped. Georgiana soon learned to shudder at his gaze. It needed but a glance with the peculiar expression that his face often wore to change the roses of her cheek into a deathlike paleness, amid which the crimson hand was brought strongly out, like a bas-relief of ruby on the whitest marble.

Late one night when the lights were growing dim, so as hardly to betray the stain on the poor wife's cheek, she herself, for the first time, voluntarily took up the subject.

"Do you remember, my dear Aylmer," said she, with a feeble attempt at a smile, "have you any recollection of a dream last night about this odious hand?"

"None! none whatever!" replied Aylmer, starting; but then he added, in a dry, cold tone, affected for the sake of concealing the real depth of his emotion, "I might well dream of it; for before I fell asleep it had taken a pretty firm hold of my fancy."

"And you did dream of it?" continued Georgiana, hastily; for she dreaded lest a gush of tears should interrupt what she had to say. "A terrible dream! I wonder that you forget it. Is it possible to forget this one expression?—'It is in her heart now; we must have it out!' Reflect, my husband; for by all means I would have you recall that dream."

The mind is in a sad state when Sleep, the all-involving, cannot confine her spectres within the dim region of her sway, but suffers them to break forth, affrighting this actual life with secrets that perchance belong to a deeper one. Aylmer now remembered his dream. He had fancied himself with his servant Aminadab, attempting an operation for the removal of the birthmark; but the deeper went the knife, the deeper sank the hand, until at length its tiny grasp appeared to have caught hold of Georgiana's heart; whence, however, her husband was inexorably resolved to cut or wrench it away.

When the dream had shaped itself perfectly in his memory, Aylmer sat in his wife's presence with a guilty feeling. Truth often finds its way to the mind close muffled in robes of sleep, and then speaks with uncompromising directness of matters in regard to which we practise an unconscious self-deception during our waking moments. Until now he had not been aware of the tyrannizing influence acquired by one idea over his mind, and of the lengths which he might find in his heart to go for the sake of giving himself peace.

"Aylmer," resumed Georgiana, solemnly, "I know not what may be the cost to both of us to rid me of this fatal birthmark. Perhaps its removal may cause cureless deformity; or it may be the stain goes as deep as life itself. Again: do we know that there is a possibility, on any terms, of unclasping the firm gripe of this little hand which was laid upon me before I came into the world?"

"Dearest Georgiana, I have spent much thought upon the subject," hastily interrupted Aylmer. "I am convinced of the perfect practicability of its removal."

"If there be the remotest possibility of it," continued Georgiana, "let the attempt be made at whatever risk. Danger is nothing to me; for life, while this hateful mark makes me the object of your horror and disgust,—life is a burden which I would fling down with joy. Either remove this dreadful hand, or take my wretched life! You have deep science. All the world bears witness of it. You have achieved great wonders. Cannot you remove this little, little mark, which I cover with the tips of two small fingers? Is this beyond your power, for the sake of your own peace, and to save your poor wife from madness?"

"Noblest, dearest, tenderest wife," cried Aylmer, rapturously, "doubt not my power. I have already given this matter the deepest thought—thought which might almost have enlightened me to create a being less perfect than yourself. Georgiana, you have led me deeper than ever into the heart of science. I feel myself fully competent to render this dear cheek as faultless as its fellow; and then, most beloved, what will be my triumph when I shall have corrected what Nature left imperfect in her fairest work! Even Pygmalion,[3] when his sculptured woman assumed life, felt not greater ecstasy than mine will be."

"It is resolved, then," said Georgiana, faintly smiling. "And, Aylmer, spare me not, though you should find the birthmark take refuge in my heart at last."

Her husband tenderly kissed her cheek—her right cheek—not that which bore the impress of the crimson hand.

The next day Aylmer apprised his wife of a plan that he had formed whereby he might have opportunity for the intense thought and con-

3. King of Cyprus who fell in love with a female statue he had made. Aphrodite, goddess of love, made the statue live.

stant watchfulness which the proposed operation would require; while Georgiana, likewise, would enjoy the perfect repose essential to its success. They were to seclude themselves in the extensive apartments occupied by Aylmer as a laboratory, and where, during his toilsome youth, he had made discoveries in the elemental powers of Nature that had roused the admiration of all the learned societies in Europe. Seated calmly in this laboratory, the pale philosopher had investigated the secrets of the highest cloud region and of the profoundest mines; he had satisfied himself of the causes that kindled and kept alive the fires of the volcano; and had explained the mystery of fountains, and how it is that they gush forth, some so bright and pure, and others with such rich medicinal virtues, from the dark bosom of the earth. Here, too, at an earlier period, he had studied the wonders of the human frame, and attempted to fathom the very process by which Nature assimilates all her precious influences from earth and air, and from the spiritual world, to create and foster man, her masterpiece. The latter pursuit, however, Aylmer had long laid aside in unwilling recognition of the truth—against which all seekers sooner or later stumble—that our great creative Mother, while she amuses us with apparently working in the broadest sunshine, is yet severely careful to keep her own secrets, and, in spite of her pretended openness, shows us nothing but results. She permits us, indeed, to mar, but seldom to mend, and, like a jealous patentee, on no account to make. Now, however, Aylmer resumed these half-forgotten investigations; not, of course, with such hopes or wishes as first suggest them; but because they involved much physiological truth and lay in the path of his proposed scheme for the treatment of Georgiana.

As he led her over the threshold of the laboratory, Georgiana was cold and tremulous. Aylmer looked cheerfully into her face, with intent to reassure her, but was so startled with the intense glow of the birthmark upon the whiteness of her cheek that he could not restrain a strong convulsive shudder. His wife fainted.

"Aminadab! Aminadab!" shouted Aylmer, stamping violently on the floor.

Forthwith there issued from an inner apartment a man of low stature, but bulky frame, with shaggy hair hanging about his visage, which was grimed with the vapors of the furnace. This personage had been Aylmer's underworker during his whole scientific career, and was admirably fitted for that office by his great mechanical readiness, and the skill with which, while incapable of comprehending a single principle, he executed all the details of his master's experiments. With his vast strength, his shaggy hair, his smoky aspect, and the indescribable earthiness that incrusted him, he seemed to represent man's physical nature; while Aylmer's slender figure, and pale, intellectual face, were no less apt a type of the spiritual element.

"Throw open the door of the boudoir, Aminadab," said Aylmer, "and burn a pastil."[4]

"Yes, master," answered Aminadab, looking intently at the lifeless form of Georgiana; and then he muttered to himself, "If she were my wife, I'd never part with that birthmark."

When Georgiana recovered consciousness she found herself breathing an atmosphere of penetrating fragrance, the gentle potency of which had recalled her from her deathlike faintness. The scene around her looked like enchantment. Aylmer had converted those smoky, dingy, sombre rooms, where he had spent his brightest years in recondite pursuits, into a series of beautiful apartments not unfit to be the secluded abode of a lovely woman. The walls were hung with gorgeous curtains, which imparted the combination of grandeur and grace that no other species of adornment can achieve; and as they fell from the ceiling to the floor, their rich and ponderous folds, concealing all angles and straight lines, appeared to shut in the scene from infinite space. For aught Georgiana knew, it might be a pavilion among the clouds. And Aylmer, excluding the sunshine, which would have interfered with his chemical processes, had supplied its place with perfumed lamps, emitting flames of various hue, but all uniting in a soft, impurpled radiance. He now knelt by his wife's side, watching her earnestly, but without alarm; for he was confident in his science, and felt that he could draw a magic circle round her within which no evil might intrude.

"Where am I? Ah, I remember," said Georgiana, faintly; and she placed her hand over her cheek to hide the terrible mark from her husband's eyes.

"Fear not, dearest!" exclaimed he. "Do not shrink from me! Believe me, Georgiana, I even rejoice in this single imperfection, since it will be such a rapture to remove it."

"Oh, spare me!" sadly replied his wife. "Pray do not look at it again. I never can forget that convulsive shudder."

In order to soothe Georgiana, and, as it were, to release her mind from the burden of actual things, Aylmer now put in practice some of the light and playful secrets which science had taught him among its profounder lore. Airy figures, absolutely bodiless ideas, and forms of unsubstantial beauty came and danced before her, imprinting their momentary footsteps on beams of light. Though she had some indistinct idea of the method of these optical phenomena, still the illusion was almost perfect enough to warrant the belief that her husband pos-

4. Aromatic paste used in fumigation.

sessed sway over the spiritual world. Then again, when she felt a wish to look forth from her seclusion, immediately, as if her thoughts were answered, the procession of external existence flitted across a screen. The scenery and the figures of actual life were perfectly represented, but with that bewitching, yet indescribable difference which always makes a picture, an image, or a shadow so much more attractive than the original. When wearied of this, Aylmer bade her cast her eyes upon a vessel containing a quantity of earth. She did so, with little interest at first; but was soon startled to perceive the germ of a plant shooting upward from the soil. Then came the slender stalk; the leaves gradually unfolded themselves; and amid them was a perfect and lovely flower.

"It is magical!" cried Georgiana. "I dare not touch it."

"Nay, pluck it," answered Aylmer,—"pluck it, and inhale its brief perfume while you may. The flower will wither in a few moments and leave nothing save its brown seed vessels; but thence may be perpetuated a race as ephemeral as itself."

But Georgiana had no sooner touched the flower than the whole plant suffered a blight, its leaves turning coal-black as if by the agency of fire.

"There was too powerful a stimulus," said Aylmer, thoughtfully.

To make up for this abortive experiment, he proposed to take her portrait by a scientific process of his own invention. It was to be effected by rays of light striking upon a polished plate of metal. Georgiana assented; but, on looking at the result, was affrighted to find the features of the portrait blurred and indefinable; while the minute figure of a hand appeared where the cheek should have been. Aylmer snatched the metallic plate and threw it into a jar of corrosive acid.

Soon, however, he forgot these mortifying failures. In the intervals of study and chemical experiment he came to her flushed and exhausted, but seemed invigorated by her presence, and spoke in glowing language of the resources of his art. He gave a history of the long dynasty of the alchemists, who spent so many ages in quest of the universal solvent by which the golden principle might be elicited from all things vile and base. Aylmer appeared to believe that, by the plainest scientific logic, it was altogether within the limits of possibility to discover this long-sought medium; "but," he added, "a philosopher who should go deep enough to acquire the power would attain too lofty a wisdom to stoop to the exercise of it." Not less singular were his opinions in regard to the elixir vitae.[5] He more than intimated that it was at his option to concoct a liquid that should prolong life for years, perhaps interminably; but that it would produce a discord in Nature

5. Substance supposed capable of prolonging life.

which all the world, and chiefly the quaffer of the immortal nostrum, would find cause to curse.

"Aylmer, are you in earnest?" asked Georgiana, looking at him with amazement and fear. "It is terrible to possess such power, or even dream of possessing it."

"Oh, do not tremble, my love," said her husband. "I would not wrong either you or myself by working such inharmonious effects upon our lives; but I would have you consider how trifling, in comparison, is the skill requisite to remove this little hand."

At the mention of the birthmark, Georgiana, as usual, shrank as if a redhot iron had touched her cheek.

Again Aylmer applied himself to his labors. She could hear his voice in the distant furnace room giving directions to Aminadab, whose harsh, uncouth, misshapen tones were audible in response, more like the grunt or growl of a brute than human speech. After hours of absence, Aylmer reappeared and proposed that she should now examine his cabinet of chemical products and natural treasures of the earth. Among the former he showed her a small vial, in which, he remarked, was contained a gentle yet most powerful fragrance, capable of impregnating all the breezes that blow across a kingdom. They were of inestimable value, the contents of that little vial; and, as he said so, he threw some of the perfume into the air and filled the room with piercing and invigorating delight.

"And what is this?" asked Georgiana, pointing to a small crystal globe containing a gold-colored liquid. "It is so beautiful to the eye that I could imagine it the elixir of life."

"In one sense it is," replied Aylmer; "or, rather, the elixir of immortality. It is the most precious poison that ever was concocted in this world. By its aid I could apportion the lifetime of any mortal at whom you might point your finger. The strength of the dose would determine whether he were to linger out years, or drop dead in the midst of a breath. No king on his guarded throne could keep his life if I, in my private station, should deem that the welfare of millions justified me in depriving him of it."

"Why do you keep such a terrific drug?" inquired Georgiana in horror.

"Do not mistrust me, dearest," said her husband, smiling; "its virtuous potency is yet greater than its harmful one. But see! here is a powerful cosmetic. With a few drops of this in a vase of water, freckles may be washed away as easily as the hands are cleansed. A stronger infusion would take the blood out of the cheek, and leave the rosiest beauty a pale ghost."

"Is it with this lotion that you intend to bathe my cheek?" asked Georgiana, anxiously.

"Oh, no," hastily replied her husband; "this is merely superficial. Your case demands a remedy that shall go deeper."

In his interviews with Georgiana, Aylmer generally made minute inquiries as to her sensations and whether the confinement of the rooms and the temperature of the atmosphere agreed with her. These questions had such a particular drift that Georgiana began to conjecture that she was already subjected to certain physical influences, either breathed in with the fragrant air or taken with her food. She fancied likewise, but it might be altogether fancy, that there was a stirring up of her system—a strange, indefinite sensation creeping through her veins, and tingling, half painfully, half pleasurably, at her heart. Still, whenever she dared to look into the mirror, there she beheld herself pale as a white rose and with the crimson birthmark stamped upon her cheek. Not even Aylmer now hated it so much as she.

To dispel the tedium of the hours which her husband found it necessary to devote to the processes of combination and analysis, Georgiana turned over the volumes of his scientific library. In many dark old tomes she met with chapters full of romance and poetry. They were the works of the philosophers of the middle ages, such as Albertus Magnus, Cornelius Agrippa, Paracelsus, and the famous friar who created the prophetic Brazen Head.[6] All these antique naturalists stood in advance of their centuries, yet were imbued with some of their credulity, and therefore were believed, and perhaps imagined themselves to have acquired from the investigation of Nature a power above Nature, and from physics a sway over the spiritual world. Hardly less curious and imaginative were the early volumes of the Transactions of the Royal Society, in which the members, knowing little of the limits of natural possibility, were continually recording wonders or proposing methods whereby wonders might be wrought.

But to Georgiana the most engrossing volume was a large folio from her husband's own hand, in which he had recorded every experiment of his scientific career, its original aim, the methods adopted for its development, and its final success or failure, with the circumstances to which either event was attributable. The book, in truth, was both the history and emblem of his ardent, ambitious, imaginative, yet practical and laborious life. He handled physical details as if there were nothing beyond them; yet spiritualized them all, and redeemed himself from materialism by his strong and eager aspiration towards the infinite. In his grasp the veriest clod of earth assumed a soul. Georgiana, as she read, reverenced Aylmer and loved him more profoundly than ever, but with a less entire dependence on his judgment than heretofore. Much as he had accomplished, she could not but observe

6. All alchemists and philosophers who prepared the way for modern science.

that his most splendid successes were almost invariably failures, if compared with the ideal at which he aimed. His brightest diamonds were the merest pebbles, and felt to be so by himself, in comparison with the inestimable gems which lay hidden beyond his reach. The volume, rich with achievements that had won renown for its author, was yet as melancholy a record as ever mortal hand had penned. It was the sad confession and continual exemplification of the shortcomings of the composite man, the spirit burdened with clay and working in matter, and of the despair that assails the higher nature at finding itself so miserably thwarted by the earthly part. Perhaps every man of genius in whatever sphere might recognize the image of his own experience in Aylmer's journal.

So deeply did these reflections affect Georgiana that she laid her face upon the open volume and burst into tears. In this situation she was found by her husband.

"It is dangerous to read in a sorcerer's books," said he, with a smile, though his countenance was uneasy and displeased. "Georgiana, there are pages in that volume which I can scarcely glance over and keep my senses. Take heed lest it prove as detrimental to you."

"It has made me worship you more than ever," said she.

"Ah, wait for this one success," rejoined he, "then worship me if you will. I shall deem myself hardly unworthy of it. But come, I have sought you for the luxury of your voice. Sing to me, dearest."

So she poured out the liquid music of her voice to quench the thirst of his spirit. He then took his leave with a boyish exuberance of gayety, assuring her that her seclusion would endure but a little longer, and that the result was already certain. Scarcely had he departed when Georgiana felt irresistibly impelled to follow him. She had forgotten to inform Aylmer of a symptom which for two or three hours past had begun to excite her attention. It was a sensation in the fatal birthmark, not painful, but which induced a restlessness throughout her system. Hastening after her husband, she intruded for the first time into the laboratory.

The first thing that struck her eye was the furnace, that hot and feverish worker, with the intense glow of its fire, which by the quantities of soot clustered above it seemed to have been burning for ages. There was a distilling apparatus in full operation. Around the room were retorts, tubes, cylinders, crucibles, and other apparatus of chemical research. An electrical machine stood ready for immediate use. The atmosphere felt oppressively close, and was tainted with gaseous odors which had been tormented forth by the processes of science. The severe and homely simplicity of the apartment, with its naked walls and brick pavement, looked strange, accustomed as Georgiana had become to the fantastic elegance of her boudoir. But what chiefly, indeed almost solely, drew her attention, was the aspect of Aylmer himself.

He was pale as death, anxious and absorbed, and hung over the furnace as if it depended upon his utmost watchfulness whether the liquid which it was distilling should be the draught of immortal happiness or misery. How different from the sanguine and joyous mien that he had assumed for Georgiana's encouragement!

"Carefully now, Aminadab; carefully, thou human machine; carefully, thou man of clay!" muttered Aylmer, more to himself than his assistant. "Now, if there be a thought too much or too little, it is all over."

"Ho! ho!" mumbled Aminadab. "Look, master! look!"

Aylmer raised his eyes hastily, and at first reddened, then grew paler than ever, on beholding Georgiana. He rushed towards her and seized her arm with a gripe that left the print of his fingers upon it.

"Why do you come hither? Have you no trust in your husband?" cried he, impetuously. "Would you throw the blight of that fatal birthmark over my labors? It is not well done. Go, prying woman, go!"

"Nay, Aylmer," said Georgiana with the firmness of which she possessed no stinted endowment, "it is not you that have a right to complain. You mistrust your wife; you have concealed the anxiety with which you watch the development of this experiment. Think not so unworthily of me, my husband. Tell me all the risk we run, and fear not that I shall shrink; for my share in it is far less than your own."

"No, no, Georgiana!" said Aylmer, impatiently; "it must not be."

"I submit," replied she calmly. "And Aylmer, I shall quaff whatever draught you bring me; but it will be on the same principle that would induce me to take a dose of poison if offered by your hand."

"My noble wife," said Aylmer, deeply moved, "I knew not the height and depth of your nature until now. Nothing shall be concealed. Know, then, that this crimson hand, superficial as it seems, has clutched its grasp into your being with a strength of which I had no previous conception. I have already administered agents powerful enough to do aught except to change your entire physical system. Only one thing remains to be tried. If that fail us we are ruined."

"Why did you hesitate to tell me this?" asked she.

"Because, Georgiana," said Aylmer, in a low voice, "there is danger."

"Danger? There is but one danger—that this horrible stigma shall be left upon my cheek!" cried Georgiana. "Remove it, remove it, whatever be the cost, or we shall both go mad!"

"Heaven knows your words are too true," said Aylmer, sadly. "And now, dearest, return to your boudoir. In a little while all will be tested."

He conducted her back and took leave of her with a solemn tenderness which spoke far more than his words how much was now at stake. After his departure Georgiana became rapt in musings. She considered the character of Aylmer, and did it completer justice than at any previous moment. Her heart exulted, while it trembled, at his honorable love—so pure and lofty that it would accept nothing less than perfection nor miserably make itself contented with an earthlier nature than he had dreamed of. She felt how much more precious was such a sentiment than that meaner kind which would have borne with the imperfection for her sake, and have been guilty of treason to holy love by degrading its perfect idea to the level of the actual; and with her whole spirit she prayed that, for a single moment, she might satisfy his highest and deepest conception. Longer than one moment she well knew it could not be; for his spirit was ever on the march, ever ascending, and each instant required something that was beyond the scope of the instant before.

The sound of her husband's footsteps aroused her. He bore a crystal goblet containing a liquor colorless as water, but bright enough to be the draught of immortality. Aylmer was pale; but it seemed rather the consequence of a highly-wrought state of mind and tension of spirit than of fear or doubt.

"The concoction of the draught has been perfect," said he, in answer to Georgiana's look. "Unless all my science have deceived me, it cannot fail."

"Save on your account, my dearest Aylmer," observed his wife, "I might wish to put off this birthmark of mortality by relinquishing mortality itself in preference to any other mode. Life is but a sad possession to those who have attained precisely the degree of moral advancement at which I stand. Were I weaker and blinder it might be happiness. Were I stronger, it might be endured hopefully. But, being what I find myself, methinks I am of all mortals the most fit to die."

"You are fit for heaven without tasting death!" replied her husband. "But why do we speak of dying? The draught cannot fail. Behold its effect upon this plant."

On the window seat there stood a geranium diseased with yellow blotches, which had overspread all its leaves. Aylmer poured a small quantity of the liquid upon the soil in which it grew. In a little time, when the roots of the plant had taken up the moisture, the unsightly blotches began to be extinguished in a living verdure.

"There needed no proof," said Georgiana, quietly. "Give me the goblet. I joyfully stake all upon your word."

"Drink, then, thou lofty creature!" exclaimed Aylmer, with fervid admiration. "There is no taint of imperfection on thy spirit. Thy sensible frame, too, shall soon be all perfect."

She quaffed the liquid and returned the goblet to his hand.

"It is grateful," said she with a placid smile. "Methinks it is like water from a heavenly fountain; for it contains I know not what of unobtrusive fragrance and deliciousness. It allays a feverish thirst that had parched me for many days. Now, dearest, let me sleep. My earthly senses are closing over my spirit like the leaves around the heart of a rose at sunset."

She spoke the last words with a gentle reluctance, as if it required almost more energy than she could command to pronounce the faint and lingering syllables. Scarcely had they loitered through her lips ere she was lost in slumber. Aylmer sat by her side, watching her aspect with the emotions proper to a man the whole value of whose existence was involved in the process now to be tested. Mingled with this mood, however, was the philosophic investigation characteristic of the man of science. Not the minutest symptom escaped him. A heightened flush of the cheek, a slight irregularity of breath, a quiver of the eyelid, a hardly perceptible tremor through the frame,—such were the details which, as the moments passed, he wrote down in his folio volume. Intense thought had set its stamp upon every previous page of that volume, but the thoughts of years were all concentrated upon the last.

While thus employed, he failed not to gaze often at the fatal hand, and not without a shudder. Yet once, by a strange and unaccountable impulse, he pressed it with his lips. His spirit recoiled, however, in the very act; and Georgiana, out of the midst of her deep sleep, moved uneasily and murmured as if in remonstrance. Again Aylmer resumed his watch. Nor was it without avail. The crimson hand, which at first had been strongly visible upon the marble paleness of Georgiana's cheek, now grew more faintly outlined. She remained not less pale than ever; but the birthmark, with every breath that came and went, lost somewhat of its former distinctness. Its presence had been awful; its departure was more awful still. Watch the stain of the rainbow fading out of the sky, and you will know how that mysterious symbol passed away.

"By Heaven! it is well-nigh gone!" said Aylmer to himself, in almost irrepressible ecstasy. "I can scarcely trace it now. Success! success! And now it is like the faintest rose color. The lightest flush of blood across her cheek would overcome it. But she is so pale!"

He drew aside the window curtain and suffered the light of natural day to fall into the room and rest upon her cheek. At the same time he heard a gross, hoarse chuckle, which he had long known as his servant Aminadab's expression of delight.

"Ah, clod! ah, earthly mass!" cried Aylmer, laughing in a sort of frenzy, "you have served me well! Matter and spirit—earth and heaven—have both done their part in this! Laugh, thing of the senses! You have earned the right to laugh."

These exclamations broke Georgiana's sleep. She slowly unclosed her eyes and gazed into the mirror which her husband had arranged for that purpose. A faint smile flitted over her lips when she recognized how barely perceptible was now that crimson hand which had once blazed forth with such disastrous brilliancy as to scare away all their happiness. But then her eyes sought Aylmer's face with a trouble and anxiety that he could by no means account for.

"My poor Aylmer!" murmured she.

"Poor? Nay, richest, happiest, most favored!" exclaimed he. "My peerless bride, it is successful! You are perfect!"

"My poor Aylmer," she repeated, with a more than human tenderness, "you have aimed loftily; you have done nobly. Do not repent that with so high and pure a feeling, you have rejected the best the earth could offer. Aylmer, dearest Aylmer, I am dying!"

Alas! it was too true! The fatal hand had grappled with the mystery of life, and was the bond by which an angelic spirit kept itself in union with a mortal frame. As the last crimson tint of the birthmark—that sole token of human imperfection—faded from her cheek, the parting breath of the now perfect woman passed into the atmosphere, and her soul, lingering a moment near her husband, took its heavenward flight. Then a hoarse, chuckling laugh was heard again! Thus ever does the gross fatality of earth exult in its invariable triumph over the immortal essence which, in this dim sphere of half development, demands the completeness of a higher state. Yet, had Aylmer reached a profounder wisdom, he need not thus have flung away the happiness which would have woven his mortal life of the selfsame texture with the celestial. The momentary circumstance was too strong for him; he failed to look beyond the shadowy scope of time, and, living once for all in eternity, to find the perfect future in the present.

---

1. What is the significance of the mark on Georgiana's cheek? What does each of the three main characters represent?
2. What does this story say about the secrets of nature? About our attempts to learn them? Is Hawthorne's attitude toward science valid in light of modern scientific knowledge and practice?
3. What is the relation between Aylmer's love for science and his love of Georgiana?
4. Why do Aylmer's experiments with a plant and with photography turn into mortifying failures when he tries to demonstrate them to his wife?
5. The moral attached to the end of the story is plainly stated. Is it contradicted to any degree by the story itself?

Ernest Hemingway

Hemingway (1899–1961) was born in Oak Park, Illinois, the son of a doctor, who gave him an enduring enthusiasm for the outdoor life. As a boy Hemingway spent summer vacations in the woods of upper Michigan that became the setting for some of his best-known stories. He volunteered for service as an ambulance driver with the Italian Army and was seriously wounded in the fighting on the Austrian front toward the end of World War I. Recovering from his wounds, he went to Paris as a correspondent for the Toronto Star *and there met, among other writers, Ezra Pound and Gertrude Stein. They encouraged him in the invention of his own style, and by twenty-five he was well on his way to mastery of the craft of fiction. From the publication of his first books he was acclaimed as a spokesman for the "Lost Generation"—the young who had been disillusioned and cast adrift by the murderous blunders of those who had plunged the world into war. The Hemingway hero and his code of conduct—living with "grace under pressure"—were as widely emulated and admired as the style of his short stories and novels. He was an enthusiastic and discriminating bullfight fan, big-game hunter, and fisherman whose personal exploits kept him often in the limelight. During the Spanish Civil War he went to Spain as a war correspondent and wrote one of his best novels,* For Whom the Bell Tolls *(1940), about that conflict. Later he followed the American Army in Europe as a correspondent before returning to peacetime life at his home in Cuba. He was awarded the Nobel Prize in 1954. At a time when he seemed to be falling out of fashion and his old vigor was waning, he killed himself with a shotgun. His novels include* The Sun Also Rises *(1926),* A Farewell to Arms *(1929),* To Have and Have Not *(1937), and* The Old Man and the Sea *(1952). In* A Moveable Feast *(1964) he recreates the Paris of his earlier years. His story collections include* In Our Time *(1925),* Men without Women *(1927), and* Winner Take Nothing *(1933).*

Hills Like White Elephants

THE hills across the valley of the Ebro[1] were long and white. On this side there was no shade and no trees and the station was between two lines of rails in the sun. Close against the side of the station there was the warm shadow of the building and a curtain, made

1. River in northern Spain.

of strings of bamboo beads, hung across the open door into the bar, to keep out flies. The American and the girl with him sat at a table in the shade, outside the building. It was very hot and the express from Barcelona would come in forty minutes. It stopped at this junction for two minutes and went on to Madrid.

"What should we drink?" the girl asked. She had taken off her hat and put it on the table.

"It's pretty hot," the man said.

"Let's drink beer."

"Dos cervezas," the man said into the curtain.

"Big ones?" a woman asked from the doorway.

"Yes. Two big ones."

The woman brought two glasses of beer and two felt pads. She put the felt pads and the beer glasses on the table and looked at the man and the girl. The girl was looking off at the line of hills. They were white in the sun and the country was brown and dry.

"They look like white elephants," she said.

"I've never seen one," the man drank his beer.

"No, you wouldn't have."

"I might have," the man said. "Just because you say I wouldn't have doesn't prove anything."

The girl looked at the bead curtain. "They've painted something on it," she said. "What does it say?"

"Anis del Toro. It's a drink."

"Could we try it?"

The man called "Listen" through the curtain. The woman came out from the bar.

"Four reales."[2]

"We want two Anis del Toro."

"With water?"

"Do you want it with water?"

"I don't know," the girl said. "Is it good with water?"

"It's all right."

"You want them with water?" asked the woman.

"Yes, with water."

"It tastes like licorice," the girl said and put the glass down.

"That's the way with everything."

"Yes," said the girl. "Everything tastes of licorice. Especially all the things you've waited so long for, like absinthe."

"Oh, cut it out."

"You started it," the girl said. "I was being amused. I was having a fine time."

2. Spanish coins.

"Well, let's try and have a fine time."

"All right. I was trying. I said the mountains looked like white elephants. Wasn't that bright?"

"That was bright."

"I wanted to try this new drink. That's all we do, isn't it—look at things and try new drinks?"

"I guess so."

The girl looked across at the hills.

"They're lovely hills," she said. "They don't really look like white elephants. I just meant the coloring of their skin through the trees."

"Should we have another drink?"

"All right."

The warm wind blew the bead curtain against the table.

"The beer's nice and cool," the man said.

"It's lovely," the girl said.

"It's really an awfully simple operation, Jig," the man said. "It's not really an operation at all."

The girl looked at the ground the table legs rested on.

"I know you wouldn't mind it, Jig. It's really not anything. It's just to let the air in."

The girl did not say anything.

"I'll go with you and I'll stay with you all the time. They just let the air in and then it's all perfectly natural."

"Then what will we do afterward?"

"We'll be fine afterward. Just like we were before."

"What makes you think so?"

"That's the only thing that bothers us. It's the only thing that's made us unhappy."

The girl looked at the bead curtain, put her hand out and took hold of two of the strings of beads.

"And you think then we'll be all right and be happy."

"I know we will. You don't have to be afraid. I've known lots of people that have done it."

"So have I," said the girl. "And afterward they were all so happy."

"Well," the man said, "if you don't want to you don't have to. I wouldn't have you do it if you didn't want to. But I know it's perfectly simple."

"And you really want to?"

"I think it's the best thing to do. But I don't want you to do it if you don't really want to."

"And if I do it you'll be happy and things will be like they were and you'll love me?"

"I love you now. You know I love you."

"I know. But if I do it, then it will be nice again if I say things are like white elephants, and you'll like it?"

"I'll love it. I love it now but I just can't think about it. You know how I get when I worry."

"If I do it you won't ever worry?"

"I won't worry about that because it's perfectly simple."

"Then I'll do it. Because I don't care about me."

"What do you mean?"

"I don't care about me."

"Well, I care about you."

"Oh, yes. But I don't care about me. And I'll do it and then everything will be fine."

"I don't want you to do it if you feel that way."

The girl stood up and walked to the end of the station. Across, on the other side, were fields of grain and trees along the banks of the Ebro. Far away, beyond the river, were mountains. The shadow of a cloud moved across the field of grain and she saw the river through the trees.

"And we could have all this," she said. "And we could have everything and every day we make it more impossible."

"What did you say?"

"I said we could have everything."

"We can have everything."

"No, we can't."

"We can have the whole world."

"No, we can't."

"We can go everywhere."

"No, we can't. It isn't ours any more."

"It's ours."

"No, it isn't. And once they take it away, you never get it back."

"But they haven't taken it away."

"We'll wait and see."

"Come on back in the shade," he said. "You mustn't feel that way."

"I don't feel any way," the girl said. "I just know things."

"I don't want you to do anything that you don't want to do—"

"Nor that isn't good for me," she said. "I know. Could we have another beer?"

"All right. But you've got to realize—"

"I realize," the girl said. "Can't we maybe stop talking?"

They sat down at the table and the girl looked across at the hills on the dry side of the valley and the man looked at her and at the table.

"You've got to realize," he said, "that I don't want you to do it if you don't want to. I'm perfectly willing to go through with it if it means anything to you."

"Doesn't it mean anything to you? We could get along."

"Of course it does. But I don't want anybody but you. I don't want any one else. And I know it's perfectly simple."

"Yes, you know it's perfectly simple."

"It's all right for you to say that, but I do know it."

"Would you do something for me now?"

"I'd do anything for you."

"Would you please please please please please please please stop talking?"

He did not say anything but looked at the bags against the wall of the station. There were labels on them from all the hotels where they had spent nights.

"But I don't want you to," he said, "I don't care anything about it."

"I'll scream," the girl said.

The woman came out through the curtains with two glasses of beer and put them down on the damp felt pads. "The train comes in five minutes," she said.

"What did she say?" asked the girl.

"That the train is coming in five minutes."

The girl smiled brightly at the woman, to thank her.

"I'd better take the bags over to the other side of the station," the man said. She smiled at him.

"All right. Then come back and we'll finish the beer."

He picked up the two heavy bags and carried them around the station to the other tracks. He looked up the tracks but could not see the train. Coming back, he walked through the barroom, where people waiting for the train were drinking. He drank an Anis at the bar and looked at the people. They were all waiting reasonably for the train. He went out through the bead curtain. She was sitting at the table and smiled at him.

"Do you feel better?" he asked.

"I feel fine," she said. "There's nothing wrong with me. I feel fine."

---

1. Why has Hemingway provided so little information about the past lives and circumstances of the characters? What qualities of the dialogue make up for the lack of descriptions of gestures, appearance, and other identifying signs?
2. The girl seems to make a slip of the tongue when she says, "They don't

really look like white elephants. I just meant the coloring of their skin through the trees." As stated this means that hills have skins. What is expressed by this confusion in her speech?

3. Does the man seriously try to understand the girl's feeling about an abortion? Does she misunderstand his concern?
4. What is the significance of the setting?
5. Has the quarrel been resolved when the story ends?

Amy Hempel

Hempel (1951–) was born in Chicago and educated in California, with further study at Columbia University. Several of her short stories are collected in Reasons to Live *(1985).*

In the Cemetery Where Al Jolson Is Buried

for Jessica

TELL me things I won't mind forgetting," she said. "Make it useless stuff or skip it."

I began. I told her insects fly through rain, missing every drop, never getting wet. I told her no one in America owned a tape recorder before Bing Crosby did. I told her the shape of the moon is like a banana—you see it looking full, you're seeing it end-on.

The camera made me self-conscious and I stopped. It was trained on us from a ceiling mount—the kind of camera banks use to photograph robbers. It played our image to the nurses down the hall in Intensive Care.

"Go on, girl," she said, "you get used to it."

I had my audience. I went on. Did she know that Tammy Wynette had changed her tune? Really. That now she sings "Stand By Your *Friends*"? Paul Anka did it too, I said. Does "You're Having *Our* Baby." He got sick of all that feminist bitching.

"What else?" she said. "Have you got something else?"

Oh yes. For her I would always have something else.

"Did you know when they taught the first chimp to talk, it lied? When they asked her who did it on the desk, she signed back Max, the janitor. And when they pressed her, she said she was sorry, that it was really the project director. But she was a mother, so I guess she had her reasons."

"Oh, that's good," she said. "A parable."

"There's more about the chimp," I said. "But it will break your heart."

"No thanks," she says, and scratches at her mask.

We look like good-guy outlaws. Good or bad, I am not used to the mask yet. I keep touching the warm spot where my breath, thank God, comes out. She is used to hers. She only ties the strings on top. The other ones—a pro by now—she lets hang loose.

We call this place the Marcus Welby Hospital. It's the white one with the palm trees under the opening credits of all those shows. A Hollywood hospital, though in fact it is several miles west. Off camera, there is a beach across the street.

She introduces me to a nurse as "the Best Friend." The impersonal article is more intimate. It tells me that *they* are intimate, my friend and her nurse.

"I was telling her we used to drink Canada Dry Ginger Ale and pretend we were in Canada."

"That's how dumb *we* were," I say.

"You could be sisters," the nurse says.

So how come, I'll bet they are wondering, it took me so long to get to such a glamorous place? But do they ask?

They do not ask.

Two months, and how long is the drive?

The best I can explain it is this—I have a friend who worked one summer in a mortuary. He used to tell me stories. The one that really got to me was not the grisliest, but it's the one that did. A man wrecked his car on 101 going south. He did not lose consciousness. But his arm was taken down to the wet bone—and when he looked at it—it scared him to death. I mean, he died.

So I didn't dare look any closer. But now I'm doing it—and hoping I won't be scared to death.

She shakes out a summer-weight blanket, showing a leg you did not want to see. Except for that, you look at her and understand the law that requires *two* people to be with the body at all times.

"I thought of something," she says. "I thought of it last night. I think there is a real and present need here. You know," she says, "like for someone to do it for you when you can't do it yourself. You call them up whenever you want—like when push comes to shove."

She grabs the bedside phone and loops the cord around her neck.

"Hey," she says, "the End o' the Line."

She keeps on, giddy with something. But I don't know with what.

"The giveaway was the solarium," she says. "That's where Marcus Welby broke the news to his patients. Then here's the real doctor suggesting we talk in the solarium. So I knew I was going to die.

"I can't remember," she says, "what does Kübler-Ross[1] say comes after Denial?"

It seems to me Anger must be next. Then Bargaining, Depression, and so on and so forth. But I keep my guesses to myself.

"The only thing is," she says, "is where's Resurrection? God knows I want to do it by the book. But she left out Resurrection."

She laughs, and I cling to the sound the way someone dangling above a ravine holds fast to the thrown rope.

We could have cried then, but when we didn't, we couldn't.

"Tell me," she says, "about that chimp with the talking hands. What do they do when the thing ends and the chimp says, 'I don't want to go back to the zoo'?"

When I don't say anything, she says, "O.K.—then tell me another animal story. I like animal stories. But not a sick one—I don't want to know about all the Seeing Eye dogs going blind."

No, I would not tell her a sick one.

"How about the hearing-ear dogs?" I say. "They're not going deaf, but they are getting very judgmental. For instance, there's this golden retriever in Jersey, he wakes up the deaf mother and drags her into the daughter's room because the kid has got a flashlight and is reading under the covers."

"Oh, you're killing me," she says. "Yes, you're definitely killing me."

"They say the smart dog obeys, but the smarter dog knows when to *dis*obey."

"Yes," she says, "the smarter *anything* knows when to disobey. Now, for example."

She is flirting with the Good Doctor, who has just appeared. Unlike the Bad Doctor, who checks the I.V. drip before saying good morning, the Good Doctor says things like "God didn't give epileptics a fair shake." He awards himself points for the cripples he could have hit in the parking lot. Because the Good Doctor is a little in love with her he says maybe a year. He pulls a chair up to her bed and suggests I might like to spend an hour on the beach.

"Bring me something back," she says. "Anything from the beach. Or the gift shop. Taste is no object."

The doctor slowly draws the curtain around her bed.

"Wait!" she cries.

I look in at her.

1. Elisabeth Kübler-Ross (1926–), author of popular books on death and dying.

"Anything," she says, "except a magazine subscription."

The doctor turns away.

I watch her mouth laugh.

What seems dangerous often is not—black snakes, for example, or clear-air turbulence. While things that just lie there, like this beach, are loaded with jeopardy. A yellow dust rising from the ground, the heat that ripens melons overnight—this is earthquake weather. You can sit here braiding the fringe on your towel and the sand will all of a sudden suck down like an hourglass. The air roars. In the cheap apartments onshore, bathtubs fill themselves and gardens roll up and over like green waves. If nothing happens, the dust will drift and the heat deepen till fear turns to desire. Nerves like that are only bought off by catastrophe.

"It never happens when you're thinking about it," she observed once.

"Earthquake, earthquake, earthquake," she said.

"Earthquake, earthquake, earthquake," I said.

Like the aviaphobe who keeps the plane aloft with prayer, we kept it up till an aftershock cracked the ceiling.

That was after the big one in '72. We were in college; our dormitory was five miles from the epicenter. When the ride was over and my jabbering pulse began to slow, she served five parts champagne to one part orange juice and joked about living in Ocean View, Kansas. I offered to drive her to Hawaii on the new world psychics predicted would surface the next time, or the next.

I could not say that now—next. *Whose* next? she could ask.

Was I the only one who noticed that the experts had stopped saying *if* and now spoke of *when*? Of course not; the fearful ran to thousands. We watched the traffic of Japanese beetles for deviation. Deviation might mean more natural violence.

I wanted her to be afraid with me, but she said, "I don't know. I'm just not."

She was afraid of nothing, not even of flying.

I have this dream before a flight where we buckle in and the plane moves down the runway. It takes off at thirty-five miles an hour, and then we're airborne, skimming on tree tops. Still, we arrive in New York on time. It is so pleasant. One night I flew to Moscow this way.

She flew with me once. That time she flew with me she ate macadamia nuts while the wings bounced. She knows the wing tips can bend thirty feet up and thirty feet down without coming off. She believes it. She trusts the laws of aerodynamics. My mind stampedes. I can almost accept that a battleship floats, and everybody knows steel sinks.

I see fear in her now and am not going to try to talk her out of it. She is right to be afraid.

After a quake, the six o'clock news airs a film clip of first-graders yelling at the broken playground per their teacher's instructions.

"*Bad* earth!" they shout, because anger is stronger than fear.

But the beach is standing still today. Everyone on it is tranquilized, numb or asleep. Teenaged girls rub coconut oil on each other's hard-to-reach places. They smell like macaroons. They pry open compacts like clamshells; mirrors catch the sun and throw a spray of white rays across glazed shoulders. The girls arrange their wet hair with silk flowers the way they learned in *Seventeen*. They pose.

A formation of low-riders[2] pulls over to watch with a six-pack. They get vocal when the girls check their tan lines. When the beer is gone, so are they—flexing their cars on up the boulevard.

Above this aggressive health are the twin wrought-iron terraces, painted flamingo pink, of the Palm Royale. Someone dies there every time the sheets are changed. There's an ambulance in the driveway, so the remaining residents line the balconies, rocking and not talking, one-upped.

The ocean they stare at is dangerous, and not just the undertow. You can almost see the slapping tails of sand sharks keeping cruising bodies alive.

If she looked, she could see this, some of it, from her window. She would be the first to say how little it takes to make a thing all wrong.

There was a second bed in the room when I returned. For two beats I didn't get it. Then it hit me like an open coffin.

She wants every minute, I thought. She wants my life.

"You missed Gussie," she said.

Gussie is her parents' 300-pound narcoleptic maid. Her attacks often come at the ironing board. The pillowcases in that family are all bordered with scorch.

"It's a hard trip for her," I said. "How is she?"

"Well, she didn't fall asleep, if that's what you mean. Gussie's great—you know what she said? She said, 'Darlin' just keep prayin', down on your knees.' "

She shrugged, "See anybody good?"

"No," I said, "just the new Charlie's Angel. And I saw Cher's car down near the Arcade."

2. Drivers of rebuilt, underslung cars.

"Cher's car is worth *three* Charlie's Angels," she said. "What else am I missing?"

"It's earthquake weather," I told her.

"The best thing to do about earthquakes," she said, "is not to live in California."

"That's useful," I said. "You sound like Reverend Ike: 'The best thing to do for the poor is not be one of them.'"

We're crazy about Reverend Ike.

I noticed her face was bloated.

"You know," she said, "I feel like hell. I'm about to stop having fun."

"The ancients have a saying," I said. "'There are times when the wolves are silent; there are times when the moon howls.'"

"What's that, Navajo?"

"Palm Royale lobby graffiti," I said. "I bought a paper there. I'll read to you."

"Even though I care about nothing?" she said.

I turned to page three, to a UPI filler datelined Mexico City. I read her "Man Robs Bank with Chicken," about a man who bought a barbecued chicken at a stand down the block from a bank. Passing the bank, he got the idea. He walked in and approached a teller. He pointed the brown paper bag at her and she handed over the day's receipts. It was the smell of barbecue sauce that eventually led to his capture.

The story made her hungry, she said, so I took the elevator down six floors to the cafeteria and brought back all the ice cream she wanted. We lay side by side, adjustable beds cranked up for optimal TV viewing, littering the sheets with Good Humor wrappers, picking toasted almonds out of the gauze. We were Lucy and Ethel, Mary and Rhoda in extremis. The blinds were closed to keep light off the screen.

We watched a movie starring men we used to think we wanted to sleep with. Hers was a tough cop out to stop mine, a vicious rapist who went after cocktail waitresses.

"This is a good movie," she said, when snipers felled them both.

I missed her already; my straight man, my diary.

A Filipino nurse tiptoed in and gave her an injection. She removed the pile of Popsicle sticks from the nightstand—enough to splint a small animal.

The injection made us sleepy—me in the way I picked up her inflection till her mother couldn't tell us apart on the phone. We slept.

I dreamed she was a decorator, come to furnish my house. She worked in secret, singing to herself. When she finished, she guided me proudly to the door. "How do you like it?" she asked, easing me inside.

Every beam and sill and shelf and knob was draped in black bunting, with streamers and black crepe looped around darkened mirrors.

"I have to go home," I said when she woke up.

She thought I meant home to her house in the Canyon, and I had to say, No, *home* home. I twisted my hands in the hackneyed fashion of people in pain. I was supposed to offer something. The Best Friend. I could not even offer to come back.

I felt weak and small and failed. Also exhilarated. I had a convertible in the parking lot. Once out of that room, I would drive it too fast down the coast highway through the crab-smelling air. A stop in Malibu for sangria. The music in the place would be sexy and loud. They would serve papaya and shrimp and watermelon ice. After dinner I would pick up beach boys. I would shimmer with life, buzz with heat, vibrate with health, stay up all night with one and then the other.

Without a word, she yanked off her mask and threw it on the floor. She kicked at the blankets and moved to the door. She must have hated having to pause for breath and balance before slamming out of Isolation, and out of the second room, the one where you scrub and tie on the white masks.

A voice shouted her name in alarm, and people ran down the corridor. The Good Doctor was paged over the intercom. I opened the door and the nurses at the station stared hard, as if this flight had been my idea.

"Where is she?" I asked, and they nodded to the supply closet.

I looked in. Two nurses were kneeling beside her on the floor, talking to her in low voices. One held a mask over her nose and mouth, the other rubbed her back in slow circles. The nurses glanced up to see if I was the doctor, and when they saw I wasn't, they went back to what they were doing.

"There, there, honey," they cooed.

On the morning she was moved to the cemetery, the one where Al Jolson is buried, I enrolled in a Fear of Flying class. "What is your worst fear?" the instructor asked, and I answered, "That I will finish this course and still be afraid."

I sleep with a glass of water on the nightstand so I can see by its level if the coastal earth is trembling or if the shaking is still me.

What do I remember? I remember only the useless things I hear—that Bob Dylan's mother invented Wite-out, that twenty-three people must be in a room before there is a fifty-fifty chance two will have the same birthdate. Who cares whether or not it's true? In my head there are bath towels swaddling this stuff. Nothing else seeps through.

I review those things that will figure in the retelling: a kiss through surgical gauze, the pale hand correcting the position of the wig. I noted these gestures as they happened, not in any retrospect. Though I don't know why looking *back* should show us more than looking *at*. It is just possible I will say I stayed the night. And who is there that can say I did not?

Nothing else gets through until I think of the chimp, the one with the talking hands.

In the course of the experiment, that chimp had a baby. Imagine how her trainers must have thrilled when the mother, without prompting, began to sign to the newborn. Baby, drink milk. Baby, play ball. And when the baby died, the mother stood over the body, her wrinkled hands moving with animal grace, forming again and again the words, Baby, come hug, Baby, come hug, fluent now in the language of grief.

---

1. What is the relation between the trivia in the dialogue and the grim circumstances of the situation? In answering, consider the tone and theme of the story, the psychology of the characters, and the contemporary California setting.
2. Why does the narrator refuse to stay with her dying friend? Frame your answer with reference to motivation and plot.
3. How does the detail about earthquakes and fear of earthquakes relate to the central concern of the story?
4. What does the story say about the relative powers of fear and sympathy?
5. How is the figure of the chimpanzee exploited to emphasize the limits of language?

Shirley Jackson

Jackson (1919–1965) was born in San Francisco. Shortly after completing her undergraduate education at Syracuse University she married the literary critic Stanley Edgar Hyman, and when he became a teacher at Bennington College, they settled permanently there. She is a master of the gothic horror tale refurbished in the modern manner, rousing terror from situations that initially appear normal and even dull. Her novels include Hangsaman *(1951),* The Bird's Nest *(1954), and* We Have Always Lived in the Castle *(1962). Her short stories are collected in* The Lottery *(1944) and* The Magic of Shirley Jackson *(1966).*

The Lottery

The morning of June 27th was clear and sunny, with the fresh warmth of a full-summer day; the flowers were blossoming profusely and the grass was richly green. The people of the village began to gather in the square, between the post office and the bank, around ten o'clock; in some towns there were so many people that the lottery took two days and had to be started on June 26th, but in this village, where there were only about three hundred people, the whole lottery took less than two hours, so it could begin at ten o'clock in the morning and still be through in time to allow the villagers to get home for noon dinner.

The children assembled first, of course. School was recently over for the summer, and the feeling of liberty sat uneasily on most of them; they tended to gather together quietly for a while before they broke into boisterous play, and their talk was still of the classroom and the teacher, of books and reprimands. Bobby Martin had already stuffed his pockets full of stones, and the other boys soon followed his example, selecting the smoothest and roundest stones; Bobby and Harry Jones and Dickie Delacroix—the villagers pronounced this name "Dellacroy"—eventually made a great pile of stones in one corner of the square and guarded it against the raids of the other boys. The girls stood aside, talking among themselves, looking over their shoulders at the boys, and the very small children rolled in the dust or clung to the hands of their older brothers or sisters.

Soon the men began to gather, surveying their own children, speaking of planting and rain, tractors and taxes. They stood together, away from the pile of stones in the corner, and their jokes were quiet and they smiled rather than laughed. The women, wearing faded house dresses and sweaters, came shortly after their menfolk. They greeted one another and exchanged bits of gossip as they went to join their husbands. Soon the women, standing by their husbands, began to call to their children, and the children came reluctantly, having to be called four or five times. Bobby Martin ducked under his mother's grasping hand and ran, laughing, back to the pile of stones. His father spoke up sharply, and Bobby came quickly and took his place between his father and his oldest brother.

The lottery was conducted—as were the square dances, the teen-age club, the Halloween program—by Mr. Summers, who had time and energy to devote to civic activities. He was a round-faced, jovial man and he ran the coal business, and people were sorry for him, because he had no children and his wife was a scold. When he arrived in the square, carrying the black wooden box, there was a murmur of conversation among the villagers, and he waved and called, "Little late today, folks." The postmaster, Mr. Graves, followed him, carrying a three-legged stool, and the stool was put in the center of the square and Mr. Summers set the black box down on it. The villagers kept their distance, leaving a space between themselves and the stool, and when Mr. Summers said, "Some of you fellows want to give me a hand?" there was a hesitation before two men, Mr. Martin and his oldest son, Baxter, came forward to hold the box steady on the stool while Mr. Summers stirred up the papers inside it.

The original paraphernalia for the lottery had been lost long ago, and the black box now resting on the stool had been put into use even before Old Man Warner, the oldest man in town, was born. Mr. Summers spoke frequently to the villagers about making a new box, but no one liked to upset even as much tradition as was represented by the black box. There was a story that the present box had been made with some pieces of the box that had preceded it, the one that had been constructed when the first people settled down to make a village here. Every year, after the lottery, Mr. Summers began talking again about a new box, but every year the subject was allowed to fade off without anything's being done. The black box grew shabbier each year; by now it was no longer completely black but splintered badly along one side to show the original wood color, and in some places faded or stained.

Mr. Martin and his oldest son, Baxter, held the black box securely on the stool until Mr. Summers had stirred the papers thoroughly with his hand. Because so much of the ritual had been forgotten or discarded, Mr. Summers had been successful in having slips of paper substituted for the chips of wood that had been used for generations. Chips of wood, Mr. Summers had argued, had been all very well when the village was tiny, but now that the population was more than three hundred and likely to keep on growing, it was necessary to use something that would fit more easily into the black box. The night before the lottery, Mr. Summers and Mr. Graves made up the slips of paper and put them in the box, and it was then taken to the safe of Mr. Summers' coal company and locked up until Mr. Summers was ready to take it to the square next morning. The rest of the year, the box was put away, sometimes one place, sometimes another; it had spent one year in Mr. Graves's barn and another year underfoot in the post office, and sometimes it was set on a shelf in the Martin grocery and left there.

There was a great deal of fussing to be done before Mr. Summers declared the lottery open. There were the lists to make up—of heads of families, heads of households in each family, members of each household in each family. There was the proper swearing-in of Mr. Summers by the postmaster, as the official of the lottery; at one time, some people remembered, there had been a recital of some sort, performed by the official of the lottery, a perfunctory, tuneless chant that had been rattled off duly each year; some people believed that the official of the lottery used to stand just so when he said or sang it, others believed that he was supposed to walk among the people, but years and years ago this part of the ritual had been allowed to lapse. There had been, also, a ritual salute, which the official of the lottery had had to use in addressing each person who came up to draw from the box, but this also had changed with time, until now it was felt necessary only for the official to speak to each person approaching. Mr. Summers was very good at all this; in his clean white shirt and blue jeans, with one hand resting carelessly on the black box, he seemed very proper and important as he talked interminably to Mr. Graves and the Martins.

Just as Mr. Summers finally left off talking and turned to the assembled villagers, Mrs. Hutchinson came hurriedly along the path to the square, her sweater thrown over her shoulders, and slid into place in the back of the crowd. "Clean forgot what day it was," she said to Mrs. Delacroix, who stood next to her, and they both laughed softly. "Thought my old man was out back stacking wood," Mrs. Hutchinson went on, "and then I looked out the window and the kids was gone, and then I remembered it was the twenty-seventh and came a-running." She dried her hands on her apron, and Mrs. Delacroix said, "You're in time, though. They're still talking away up there."

Mrs. Hutchinson craned her neck to see through the crowd and found her husband and children standing near the front. She tapped

Mrs. Delacroix on the arm as a farewell and began to make her way through the crowd. The people separated good-humoredly to let her through; two or three people said, in voices just loud enough to be heard across the crowd, "Here comes your Missus, Hutchinson," and "Bill, she made it after all." Mrs. Hutchinson reached her husband, and Mr. Summers, who had been waiting, said cheerfully, "Thought we were going to have to get on without you, Tessie." Mrs. Hutchinson said, grinning, "Wouldn't have me leave m'dishes in the sink, now, would you, Joe?," and soft laughter ran through the crowd as the people stirred back into position after Mrs. Hutchinson's arrival.

"Well, now," Mr. Summers said soberly, "guess we better get started, get this over with, so's we can go back to work. Anybody ain't here?"

"Dunbar," several people said, "Dunbar, Dunbar."

Mr. Summers consulted his list. "Clyde Dunbar," he said. "That's right . He's broke his leg, hasn't he? Who's drawing for him?"

"Me, I guess," a woman said, and Mr. Summers turned to look at her. "Wife draws for her husband," Mr. Summers said. "Don't you have a grown boy to do it for you, Janey?" Although Mr. Summers and everyone else in the village knew the answer perfectly well, it was the business of the official of the lottery to ask such questions formally. Mr. Summers waited with an expression of polite interest while Mrs. Dunbar answered.

"Horace's not but sixteen yet," Mrs. Dunbar said regretfully. "Guess I gotta fill in for the old man this year."

"Right," Mr. Summers said. He made a note on the list he was holding. Then he asked, "Watson boy drawing this year?"

A tall boy in the crowd raised his hand. "Here," he said. "I'm drawing for m'mother and me." He blinked his eyes nervously and ducked his head as several voices in the crowd said things like "Good fellow, Jack," and "Glad to see your mother's got a man to do it."

"Well," Mr. Summers said, "guess that's everyone. Old Man Warner make it?"

"Here," a voice said, and Mr. Summers nodded.

A sudden hush fell on the crowd as Mr. Summers cleared his throat and looked at the list. "All ready?" he called. "Now, I'll read the names—heads of families first—and the men come up and take a paper out of the box. Keep the paper folded in your hand without looking at it until everyone has had a turn. Everything clear?"

The people had done it so many times that they only half listened to the directions; most of them were quiet, wetting their lips, not looking around. Then Mr. Summers raised one hand high and said, "Adams." A man disengaged himself from the crowd and came forward. "Hi, Steve," Mr. Summers said, and Mr. Adams said, "Hi, Joe." They grinned at one another humorlessly and nervously. Then Mr. Adams reached into the black box and took out a folded paper. He held it firmly by one corner as he turned and went hastily back to his place in the crowd, where he stood a little apart from his family, not looking down at his hand.

"Allen," Mr. Summers said. "Anderson. . . . Bentham."

"Seems like there's no time at all between lotteries any more," Mrs. Delacroix said to Mrs. Graves in the back row. "Seems like we got through with the last one only last week."

"Times sure goes fast," Mrs. Graves said.

"Clark. . . . Delacroix."

"There goes my old man," Mrs. Delacroix said. She held her breath while her husband went forward.

"Dunbar," Mr. Summers said, and Mrs. Dunbar went steadily to the box while one of the women said, "Go on, Janey," and another said, "There she goes."

"We're next," Mrs. Graves said. She watched while Mr. Graves came around from the side of the box, greeted Mr. Summers gravely, and selected a slip of paper from the box. By now, all through the crowd there were men holding the small folded papers in their large hands, turning them over and over nervously. Mrs. Dunbar and her two sons stood together, Mrs. Dunbar holding the slip of paper.

"Harburt. . . . Hutchinson."

"Get up there, Bill," Mrs. Hutchinson said, and the people near her laughed.

"Jones."

"They do say," Mr. Adams said to Old Man Warner, who stood next to him, "that over in the north village they're talking of giving up the lottery."

Old Man Warner snorted. "Pack of crazy fools," he said. "Listening to the young folks, nothing's good enough for *them.* Next thing you know, they'll be wanted to go back to living in caves, nobody work any more, live *that* way for a while. Used to be a saying about 'Lottery in June, corn be heavy soon.' First thing you know, we'd all be eating stewed chickweed and acorns. There's *always* been a lottery," he added petulantly. "Bad enough to see young Joe Summers up there joking with everybody."

"Some places have already quit lotteries," Mrs. Adams said.

"Nothing but trouble in *that,*" Old Man Warner said stoutly. "Pack of young fools."

"Martin." And Bobby Martin watched his father go forward. "Overdyke. . . . Percy."

"I wish they'd hurry," Mrs. Dunbar said to her older son. "I wish they'd hurry."

"They're almost through," her son said.

"You get ready to run tell Dad," Mrs. Dunbar said.

Mr. Summers called his own name and then stepped forward precisely and selected a slip from the box. Then he called, "Warner."

"Seventy-seventh year I been in the lottery," Old Man Warner said as he went through the crowd. "Seventy-seventh time."

"Watson." The tall boy came awkwardly through the crowd. Someone said, "Don't be nervous, Jack," and Mr. Summers said, "Take your time, son."

"Zanini."

After that, there was a long pause, a breathless pause, until Mr. Summers, holding his slip of paper in the air, said, "All right, fellows." For a minute, no one moved, and then all the slips of paper were opened. Suddenly, all the women began to speak at once, saying, "Who is it?," "Who's got it?," "Is it the Dunbars?," "Is it the Watsons?" Then the voices began to say, "It's Hutchinson. It's Bill," "Bill Hutchinson's got it."

"Go tell your father," Mrs. Dunbar said to her older son.

People began to look around to see the Hutchinsons. Bill Hutchinson was standing quiet staring down at the paper in his hand. Suddenly, Tessie Hutchinson shouted to Mr. Summers, "You didn't give him time enough to take any paper he wanted. I saw you. It wasn't fair."

"Be a good sport, Tessie," Mrs. Delacroix called, and Mrs. Graves said, "All of us took the same chance."

"Shut up, Tessie," Bill Hutchinson said.

"Well, everyone," Mr. Summers said, "that was done pretty fast, and now we've got to be hurrying a little more to get done in time." He consulted his next list. "Bill," he said, "you draw for the Hutchinson family. You got any other households in the Hutchinsons?"

"There's Don and Eva," Mrs. Hutchinson yelled. "Make *them* take their chance!"

"Daughters draw for their husbands' families, Tessie," Mr. Summers said gently. "You know that as well as anyone else."

"It wasn't *fair*," Tessie said.

"I guess not, Joe," Bill Hutchinson said regretfully. "My daughter draws with her husband's family, that's only fair. And I've got no other family except the kids."

"Then, as far as drawing for families is concerned, it's you," Mr. Summers said in explanation, "and as far as drawing for households is concerned, that's you, too. Right?"

"Right," Bill Hutchinson said.

"How many kids, Bill?" Mr. Summers asked formally.

"Three," Bill Hutchinson said. "There's Bill, Jr., and Nancy, and little Dave. And Tessie and me."

"All right, then," Mr. Summers said. "Harry, you got their tickets back?"

Mr. Graves nodded and held up the slips of paper. "Put them in the box, then," Mr. Summers directed. "Take Bill's and put it in."

"I think we ought to start over," Mrs. Hutchinson said, as quietly as she could, "I tell you it wasn't *fair*. You didn't give him time enough to choose. *Every*body saw that."

Mr. Graves had selected the five slips and put them in the box, and he dropped all the papers but those onto the ground, where the breeze caught them and lifted them off.

"Listen, everybody," Mrs. Hutchinson was saying to the people around her.

"Ready, Bill?" Mr. Summers asked, and Bill Hutchinson, with one quick glance around at his wife and children, nodded.

"Remember," Mr. Summers said, "take the slips and keep them folded until each person has taken one. Harry, you help little Dave." Mr. Graves took the hand of the little boy, who came willingly with him up to the box. "Take a paper out of the box, Davy," Mr. Summers said. Davy put his hand into the box and laughed. "Take just *one* paper," Mr. Summers said. "Harry, you hold it for him." Mr. Graves took the child's hand and removed the folded paper from the tight fist and held it while little Dave stood next to him and looked up at him wonderingly.

"Nancy next," Mr. Summers said. Nancy was twelve, and her school friends breathed heavily as she went forward, switching her skirt, and took a slip daintily from the box. "Bill, Jr.," Mr. Summers said, and Billy, his face red and his feet over-large, nearly knocked the box over as he got a paper out. "Tessie," Mr. Summers said. She hesitated for a minute, looking around defiantly, and then set her lips and went up to the box. She snatchd a paper out and held it behind her.

"Bill," Mr. Summers said, and Bill Hutchinson reached into the box and felt around, bringing his hand out at last with the slip of paper in it.

The crowd was quiet. A girl whispered, "I hope it's not Nancy," and the sound of the whisper reached the edges of the crowd.

"It's not the way it used to be," Old Man Warner said clearly. "People ain't the way they used to be."

"All right," Mr. Summers said. "Open the papers. Harry, you open little Dave's."

Mr. Graves opened the slip of paper and there was a general sigh through the crowd as he held it up and everyone could see that it was blank. Nancy and Bill, Jr. opened theirs at the same time, and both beamed and laughed, turning around to the crowd and holding their slips of paper above their heads.

"Tessie," Mr. Summers said. There was a pause, and then Mr. Summers looked at Bill Hutchinson, and Bill unfolded his paper and showed it. It was blank.

"It's Tessie," Mr. Summers said, and his voice was hushed. "Show us her paper, Bill."

Bill Hutchinson went over to his wife and forced the slip of paper out of her hand. It had a black spot on it, the black spot Mr. Summers had made the night before with the heavy pencil in the coal-company office. Bill Hutchinson held it up, and there was a stir in the crowd.

"All right, folks," Mr. Summers said. "Let's finish quickly."

Although the villagers had forgotten the ritual and lost the original black box, they still remembered to use stones. The pile of stones the boys had made earlier was ready; there were stones on the ground with the blowing scraps of paper that had come out of the box. Mrs. Delacroix selected a stone so large she had to pick it up with both hands and turned to Mrs. Dunbar. "Come on," she said. "Hurry up."

Mrs. Dunbar had small stones in both hands, and she said, gasping for breath, "I can't run at all. You'll have to go ahead and I'll catch up with you."

The children had stones already, and someone gave little Davy Hutchinson a few pebbles.

Tessie Hutchinson was in the center of a cleared space by now, and she held her hands out desperately as the villagers moved in on her. "It isn't fair," she said. A stone hit her on the side of the head.

Old Man Warner was saying, "Come on, come on, everyone." Steve Adams was in the front of the crowd of villagers, with Mrs. Graves beside him.

"It isn't fair, it isn't right," Mrs. Hutchinson screamed, and then they were upon her.

---

1. What are the first signs that something odd is taking place? The first signs of something sinister? The conclusive signs that the outcome will be dreadful?
2. What does the author accomplish by showing how familiar the proceedings are to the villagers? What does she show about mass psychology?
3. What is the theme of the story? Is it consistent with the tone?
4. Why do you suppose the author chose not to use the point of view of any of the characters?
5. What ironies are involved in the villagers' ideas of fairness?
6. What social rituals similar to the lottery do you participate in?

Henry James

James (1843–1916) was born in New York City. His father was a writer and religious philosopher; his brother was William James, the philosopher and psychologist. James's father chose to have him educated chiefly in Europe by tutors in several countries, and his foreign education was culminated by his acquaintance with several European writers, among them Turgenev, Flaubert, and de Maupassant. James's familiarity with life on both sides of the Atlantic led him, in much of his writing, to contrast European and American cultures and, above all, to show the effects of their mingling. In 1875 he took up permanent residence in England, becoming a naturalized citizen of that country in 1915 in protest against the initial neutrality of the United States in World War I. Throughout his later life James was the model of the professional writer, experimenting with ways of making his writing more pictorial, developing refinements in the handling of point of view, and commenting in many essays on these practices so that his theories of the art have been instructive to many later writers. He wrote several rather unsuccessful plays and more than seventy stories, which are most readily found in collected editions of his work or in paperback selections. Among his novels are The American *(1877),* The Portrait of a Lady *(1881),* The Ambassadors *(1903), and* The Golden Bowl *(1904).*

The Tree of Knowledge

I

It was one of the secret opinions, such as we all have, of Peter Brench that his main success in life would have consisted in his never having committed himself about the work, as it was called, of his friend Morgan Mallow. This was a subject on which it was, to the best of his belief, impossible with veracity to quote him, and it was nowhere on record that he had, in the connexion, on any occasion and in any embarrassment, either lied or spoken the truth. Such a triumph had its honour even for a man of other triumphs—a man who had reached fifty, who had escaped marriage, who had lived within his means, who had been in love with Mrs. Mallow for years without breathing it, and who, last but not least, had judged himself once for all. He had so judged himself in fact that he felt an extreme and general humility to be his proper portion; yet there was nothing that made him think so well of his parts as the course he had steered so often through the shallows just mentioned. It became thus a real wonder that the friends in whom he had most confidence were just those with whom he had most reserves. He couldn't tell Mrs. Mallow—or at least he supposed, excellent man, he couldn't—that she was the one beautiful reason he had never married; any more than he could tell her husband that the sight of the multiplied marbles in that gentleman's studio was an affliction of which even time had never blunted the edge. His victory, however, as I have intimated, in regard to these productions, was not simply in his not having let it out that he deplored them; it was, remarkably, in his not having kept it in by anything else.

The whole situation, among these good people, was verily a marvel, and there was probably not such another for a long way from the spot that engages us—the point at which the soft declivity of Hampstead began at that time to confess in broken accents to Saint John's Wood.[1] He despised Mallow's statues and adored Mallow's wife, and yet was distinctly fond of Mallow, to whom, in turn, he was equally dear. Mrs. Mallow rejoiced in the statues—though she preferred, when pressed, the busts; and if she was visibly attached to Peter Brench it was because of his affection for Morgan. Each loved the other moreover for the love borne in each case to Lancelot, whom the Mallows respectively cherished as their only child and whom the friend of their fireside identified as the third—but decidedly the handsomest—of his godsons. Already in the old years it had come to that—that no one, for such a relation, could possibly have occurred to any of them, even to the baby itself, but Peter. There was luckily a certain independence, of the pecuniary sort, all round: the Master could never otherwise have spent his solemn *Wanderjahre*[2] in Florence and Rome, and continued by the Thames as well as by the Arno and the Tiber[3] to add unpurchased group to group and model, for what was too apt to prove in the event mere love, fancy-heads of celebrities either too busy or too buried—too much of the age or too little of it—to sit. Neither could Peter, lounging in almost daily, have found time to keep the whole complicated tradition so alive by his presence. He was massive but mild, the depositary of these mysteries—large and loose and ruddy and curly, with deep tones, deep eyes, deep pockets, to say nothing of the habit of long pipes, soft hats and brownish greyish weather-faded clothes, apparently always the same.

He had "written," it was known, but had never spoken, never spoken in particular of that; and he had the air (since, as was believed,

1. Wooded area beyond Hampstead, a district in northwest London. 2. Years of travel by an apprentice learning his craft. 3. Rivers flowing through London, Florence, and Rome.

he continued to write) of keeping it up in order to have something more—as if he hadn't at the worst enough—to be silent about. Whatever his air, at any rate, Peter's occasional unmentioned prose and verse were quite truly the result of an impulse to maintain the purity of his taste by establishing still more firmly the right relation of fame to feebleness. The little green door of his domain was in a garden-wall on which the discoloured stucco made patches, and in the small detached villa behind it everything was old, the furniture, the servants, the books, the prints, the immemorial habits and the new improvements. The Mallows, at Carrara Lodge,[4] were within ten minutes, and the studio there was on their little land, to which they had added, in their happy faith, for building it. This was the good fortune, if it was not the ill, of her having brought him in marriage a portion that put them in a manner at their ease and enabled them thus, on their side, to keep it up. And they did keep it up—they always had—the infatuated sculptor and his wife, for whom nature had refined on the impossible by relieving them of the sense of the difficult. Morgan had at all events everything of the sculptor but the spirit of Phidias—the brown velvet, the becoming *beretto,* the "plastic" presence, the fine fingers, the beautiful accent in Italian and the old Italian factotum.[5] He seemed to make up for everything when he addressed Egidio with the "tu"[6] and waved him to turn one of the rotary pedestals of which the place was full. They were tremendous Italians at Carrara Lodge, and the secret of the part played by this fact in Peter's life was in a large degree that it gave him, sturdy Briton as he was, just the amount of "going abroad" he could bear. The Mallows were all his Italy, but it was in a measure for Italy he liked them. His one worry was that Lance—to which they had shortened his godson—was, in spite of a public school,[7] perhaps a shade too Italian. Morgan meanwhile looked like somebody's flattering idea of somebody's own person as expressed in the great room provided at the Uffizi Museum[8] for the general illustration of that idea by eminent hands. The Master's sole regret that he hadn't been born rather to the brush than to the chisel[9] sprang from his wish that he might have contributed to that collection.

It appeared with time at any rate to be to the brush that Lance had been born; for Mrs. Mallow, one day when the boy was turning twenty, broke it to their friend, who shared, to the last delicate morsel, their problems and pains, that it seemed as if nothing would really do but that he should embrace the career. It had been impossible longer

4. Named for Carrara, Italy, site of famous marble quarries. 5. I.e., Morgan affected the outward appearance of an artist but lacked the genius of Phidias, the most famous sculptor of classical Greece. A beret *(beretto)* served as part of the costume of the artist; his studio assistant (factotum), being Italian, completed the superficial picture. 6. I.e., using the Italian familiar second person pronoun to servants. 7. English private school. 8. World-famous art museum in Florence.
9. I.e., to have had a vocation as painter rather than as sculptor.

to remain blind to the fact that he was gaining no glory at Cambridge, where Brench's own college had for a year tempered its tone to him as for Brench's own sake. Therefore why renew the vain form of preparing him for the impossible? The impossible—it had become clear—was that he should be anything but an artist.

"Oh, dear, dear!" said poor Peter.

"Don't you believe in it?" asked Mrs. Mallow, who still, at more than forty, had her violet velvet eyes, her creamy satin skin and her silken chestnut hair.

"Believe in what?"

"Why in Lance's passion."

"I don't know what you mean by 'believing in it.' I've never been unaware, certainly, of his disposition, from his earliest time, to daub and draw; but I confess I've hoped it would burn out."

"But why should it," she sweetly smiled, "with his wonderful heredity? Passion is passion—though of course indeed *you*, dear Peter, know nothing of that. Has the Master's ever burned out?"

Peter looked off a little and, in his familiar formless way, kept up for a moment, a sound between a smothered whistle and a subdued hum. "Do you think he's going to be another Master?"

She seemed scarce prepared to go that length, yet she had on the whole a marvellous trust. "I know what you mean by that. Will it be a career to incur the jealousies and provoke the machinations that have been at times almost too much for his father? Well—say it may be, since nothing but clap-trap, in these dreadful days, *can*, it would seem, make its way, and since, with the curse of refinement and distinction, one may easily find one's self begging one's bread. Put it at the worst—say he *has* the misfortune to wing his flight further than the vulgar taste of his stupid countrymen can follow. Think, all the same, of the happiness—the same the Master has had. He'll *know*."

Peter looked rueful. "Ah but *what* will he know?"

"Quiet joy!" cried Mrs. Mallow, quite impatient and turning away.

II

He had of course before long to meet the boy himself on it and to hear that practically everything was settled. Lance was not to go up again,[1] but to go instead to Paris where, since the die was cast, he would find the best advantages. Peter had always felt that he must be taken as he was, but had never perhaps found him so much of that pattern as on this occasion. "You chuck Cambridge then altogether? Doesn't that seem rather a pity?"

1. I.e., not to return to school at Cambridge.

Lance would have been like his father, to his friend's sense, had he had less humour, and like his mother had he had more beauty. Yet it was a good middle way for Peter that, in the modern manner, he was, to the eye, rather the young stockbroker than the young artist. The youth reasoned that it was a question of time—there was such a mill to go through, such an awful lot to learn. He had talked with fellows and had judged. "One has got, today," he said, "don't you see? to know."

His interlocutor, at this, gave a groan. "Oh hang it, *don't* know!"

Lance wondered. " 'Don't'? Then what's the use—?"

"The use of what?"

"Why of anything. Don't you think I've talent?"

Peter smoked away for a little in silence; then went on: "It isn't knowledge, it's ignorance that—as we've been beautifully told—is bliss."

"Don't you think I've talent?" Lance repeated.

Peter, with his trick of queer kind demonstration, passed his arm round his godson and held him a moment. "How do I know?"

"Oh," said the boy, "if it's your own ignorance you're defending—!"

Again, for a pause, on the sofa, his godfather smoked. "It isn't. I've the misfortune to be omniscient."

"Oh well," Lance laughed again, "if you know *too* much—!"

"That's what I do, and it's why I'm so wretched."

Lance's gaiety grew. "Wretched? Come, I say!"

"But I forgot," his companion went on—"you're not to know about that. It would indeed for you to make the too much. Only I'll tell you what I'll do." And Peter got up from the sofa. "If you'll go up again I'll pay your way at Cambridge."

Lance stared, a little rueful in spite of being still more amused. "Oh, Peter! You disapprove so of Paris?"

"Well, I'm afraid of it."

"Ah I see!"

"No, you don't see—yet. But you will—that is you would. And you mustn't."

The young man thought more gravely. "But one's innocence, already—!"

"Is considerably damaged? Ah that won't matter," Peter persisted—"we'll patch it up here."

"Here? Then you want me to stay at home?"

Peter almost confessed it. "Well, we're so right—we four together—just as we are. We're so safe. Come, don't spoil it."

The boy, who had turned to gravity, turned from this, on the real pressure in his friend's tone, to consternation. "Then what's a fellow to be?"

"My particular care. Come, old man"—and Peter now fairly pleaded—"*I'll* look out for you."

Lance, who had remained on the sofa with his legs out and his hands in his pockets, watched him with eyes that showed suspicion. Then he got up. "You think there's something the matter with me—that I can't make a success."

"Well, what do you call a success?"

Lance thought again. "Why, the best sort, I suppose, is to please one's self. Isn't that the sort that, in spite of cabals and things, is—in his own peculiar line—the Master's?"

There were so much too many things in this question to be answered at once that they practically checked the discussion, which became particularly difficult in the light of such renewed proof that, though the young man's innocence might, in the course of his studies, as he contended, somewhat have shrunken, the finer essence of it still remained. That was indeed exactly what Peter had assumed and what above all he desired; yet perversely enough it gave him a chill. The boy believed in the cabals and things, believed in the peculiar line, believed, to be brief, in the Master. What happened a month or two later wasn't that he went up again at the expense of his godfather, but that a fortnight after he had got settled in Paris this personage sent him fifty pounds.

He had meanwhile at home, this personage, made up his mind to the worst; and what that might be had never yet grown quite so vivid to him as when, on his presenting himself one Sunday night, as he never failed to do, for supper, the mistress of Carrara Lodge met him with an appeal as to—of all things in the world—the wealth of the Canadians. She was earnest, she was even excited. "Are many of them *really* rich?"

He had to confess he knew nothing about them, but he often thought afterwards of that evening. The room in which they sat was adorned with sundry specimens of the Master's genius, which had the merit of being, as Mrs. Mallow herself frequently suggested, of an unusually convenient size. They were indeed of dimensions not customary in the products of the chisel, and they had the singularity that, if the objects and features intended to be small looked too large, the objects and features intended to be large looked too small. The Master's idea, either in respect to this matter or to any other, had in almost any case, even after years, remained undiscoverable to Peter Brench. The creations that so failed to reveal it stood about on pedestals and brackets, on tables and shelves, a little staring white population, heroic, idyllic, allegoric, mythic, symbolic, in which "scale" had so strayed and lost itself that the public square and the chimney-piece seemed to have changed places, the monumental being all diminutive and the diminutive all monumental; branches at any rate, markedly, of a family in which stature was rather oddly irrespective of function, age, and sex. They formed, like the Mallows themselves, poor Brench's own family—having at least to such a degree the note of familiarity. The occasion was one of those he had long ago learnt to know and to name—short flickers of the faint flame, soft gusts of a kinder air. Twice a year regularly the Master believed in his fortune, in addition to believing all the year round in his genius. This time it was to be made by a bereaved couple from Toronto, who had given him the handsomest order for a tomb to three lost children, each of whom they desired to see, in the composition, emblematically and characteristically represented.

Such was naturally the moral of Mrs. Mallow's question: if their wealth was to be assumed, it was clear, from the nature of their admiration, as well as from mysterious hints thrown out (they were a little odd!) as to other possibilities of the same mortuary sort, that their further patronage might be; and not less evident that should the Master become at all known in those climes nothing would be more inevitable than a run of Canadian custom. Peter had been present before at runs of custom, colonial and domestic—present at each of those of which the aggregation had left so few gaps in the marble company round him; but it was his habit never at these junctures to prick the bubble in advance. The fond illusion, while it lasted, eased the wound of elections never won, the long ache of medals and diplomas carried off, on every chance, by every one but the Master; it moreover lighted the lamp that would glimmer through the next eclipse. They lived, however, after all—as it was always beautiful to see—at a height scarce susceptible of ups and downs. They strained a point at times charmingly, strained it to admit that the public was here and there not too bad to buy; but they would have been nowhere without their attitude that the Master was always too good to sell. They were at all events deliciously formed, Peter often said to himself, for their fate; the Master had a vanity, his wife had a loyalty, of which success, depriving these things of innocence, would have diminished the merit and the grace. Any one could be charming under a charm, and as he looked about him at a world of prosperity more void of proportion even than the Master's museum he wondered if he knew another pair that so completely escaped vulgarity.

"What a pity Lance isn't with us to rejoice!" Mrs. Mallow on this occasion sighed at supper.

"We'll drink to the health of the absent," her husband replied, filling his friend's glass and his own and giving a drop to their companion; "but we must hope he's preparing himself for a happiness much less like this of ours this evening—excusable as I grant it to be!—than like the comfort we have always (whatever has happened or has not happened) been able to trust ourselves to enjoy. The comfort," the Master explained, leaning back in the pleasant lamplight and firelight, holding up his glass and looking round at his marble family, quartered more or less, a monstrous brood, in every room—"the comfort of art in itself!"

Peter looked a little shyly at his wine. "Well—I don't care what you may call it when a fellow doesn't—but Lance must learn to *sell*, you know. I drink to his acquisition of the secret of a base popularity!"

"Oh, yes, *he* must sell," the boy's mother, who was still more, however, this seemed to give out, the Master's wife, rather artlessly allowed.

"Ah," the sculptor after a moment confidently pronounced, "Lance *will*. Don't be afraid. He'll have learnt."

"Which is exactly what Peter," Mrs. Mallow gaily returned—"why in the world were you so perverse, Peter?—wouldn't when he told him hear of."

Peter, when this lady looked at him with accusatory affection—a grace on her part not infrequent—could never find a word; but the Master, who was always all amenity and tact, helped him out now as he had often helped him before. "That's his old idea, you know—on which we've so often differed: his theory that the artist should be all impulse and instinct. *I* go in of course for a certain amount of school. Not too much—but a due proportion. There's where his protest came in," he continued to explain to his wife, "as against what *might*, don't you see? be in question for Lance."

"Ah, well!"—and Mrs. Mallow turned the violet eyes across the table at the subject of this discourse—"he's sure to have meant of course nothing but good. Only that wouldn't have prevented him, if Lance *had* taken his advice, from being in effect horribly cruel."

They had a sociable way of talking of him to his face as if he had been in the clay or—at most—in the plaster, and the Master was unfailingly generous. He might have been waving Egidio to make him revolve. "Ah but poor Peter wasn't so wrong as to what it may after all come to that he *will* learn."

"Oh but nothing artistically bad," she urged—still, for poor Peter, arch and dewy.

"Why just the little French tricks," said the Master: on which their friend had to pretend to admit, when pressed by Mrs. Mallow, that these aesthetic vices had been the objects of his dread.

III

"I know now," Lance said to him the next year, "why you were so much against it." He had come back supposedly for a mere interval and was looking about him at Carrara Lodge, where indeed he had already on two or three occasions since his expatriation briefly reappeared. This had the air of a longer holiday. "Something rather awful has happened to me. It *isn't* so very good to know."

"I'm bound to say high spirits don't show in your face," Peter was rather ruefully forced to confess. "Still, are you very sure you do know?"

"Well, I at least know about as much as I can bear." These remarks were exchanged in Peter's den, and the young man, smoking cigarettes, stood before the fire with his back against the mantel. Something of his bloom seemed really to have left him.

Poor Peter wondered. "You're clear then as to what in particular I wanted you not to go for?"

"In particular?" Lance thought. "It seems to me that in particular there can have been only one thing."

They stood for a little sounding each other. "Are you quite sure?"

"Quite sure I'm a beastly duffer? Quite—by this time."

"Oh!"—and Peter turned away as if almost with relief.

"It's *that* that isn't pleasant to find out."

"Oh I don't care for 'that,' " said Peter, presently coming round again. "I mean I personally don't."

"Yet I hope you can understand a little that I myself should!"

"Well, what do you mean by it?" Peter sceptically asked.

And on this Lance had to explain—how the upshot of his studies in Paris had inexorably proved a mere deep doubt of his means. These studies had so waked him up that a new light was in his eyes; but what the new light did was really to show him too much. "Do you know what's the matter with me? I'm too horribly intelligent. Paris was really the last place for me. I've learnt what I can't do."

Poor Peter stared—it was a staggerer; but even after they had had, on the subject, a longish talk in which the boy brought out to the full the hard truth of his lesson, his friend betrayed less pleasure than usually breaks into a face to the happy tune of "I told you so!" Poor Peter himself made now indeed so little a point of having told him so that Lance broke ground in a different place a day or two after. "What was it then that—before I went—you were afraid I should find out?" This, however, Peter refused to tell him—on the ground that if he hadn't yet guessed perhaps he never would, and that in any case nothing at all for either of them was to be gained by giving the thing a name. Lance eyed him on this an instant with the bold curiosity of youth—with the air indeed of having in his mind two or three names, of which one or other would be right. Peter nevertheless, turning his back again, offered no encouragement, and when they parted afresh it was with some show of impatience on the side of the boy. Accordingly on their next encounter Peter saw at a glance that he had now, in the interval, divined and that, to sound his note, he was only waiting till they should find themselves alone. This he had soon arranged and he then broke straight out. "Do you know your conundrum has been keeping me awake? But in the watches of the night the answer came over me—so that, upon my honour, I quite laughed out. Had you been supposing I had to go to Paris to learn *that?*" Even now, to see him still so sublimely on his guard, Peter's young friend had to laugh afresh. "You won't give a sign till you're sure? Beautiful old Peter!" But Lance at last produced it. "Why, hang it, the truth about the Master."

It made between them for some minutes a lively passage, full of wonder for each at the wonder of the other. "Then how long have you understood—"

"The true value of his work? I understood it," Lance recalled, "as soon as I began to understand anything. But I didn't begin fully to do that, I admit, till I got *là-bas.*"[2]

"Dear, dear!"—Peter gasped with retrospective dread.

"But for what have you taken me? I'm a hopeless muff—that I *had* to have rubbed in. But I'm not such a muff as the Master!" Lance declared.

"Then why did you never tell me—?"

"That I hadn't after all"—the boy took him up—"remained such an idiot? Just because I never dreamed *you* knew. But I beg your pardon. I only wanted to spare you. And what I don't now understand is how the deuce then for so long you've managed to keep bottled."

Peter produced his explanation, but only after some delay and with a gravity not void of embarrassment. "It was for your mother."

"Oh!" said Lance.

"And that's the great thing now—since the murder *is* out. I want a promise from you. I mean"—and Peter almost feverishly followed it up—"a vow from you, solemn and such as you owe me here on the spot, that you'll sacrifice anything rather than let her ever guess—"

"That *I've* guessed?"—Lance took it in. "I see." He evidently after a moment had taken in much. "But what is it you've in mind that I may have a chance to sacrifice?"

"Oh one has always something."

Lance looked at him hard. "Do you mean that *you've* had—?"

2. Over there.

The look he received back, however, so put the question by that he found soon enough another. "Are you really sure my mother doesn't know?"

Peter, after renewed reflexion, was really sure. "If she does she's too wonderful."

"But aren't we all too wonderful?"

"Yes," Peter granted—"but in different ways. The thing's so desperately important because your father's little public consists only, as you know then," Peter developed—"well, of how many?"

"First of all," the Master's son risked, "of himself. And last of all too. I don't quite see of whom else."

Peter had an approach to impatience. "Of your mother, I say—*always*."

Lance cast it all up. "You absolutely feel that?"

"Absolutely."

"Well then with yourself that makes three."

"Oh *me!*"—and Peter, with a wag of his kind old head, modestly excused himself. "The number's at any rate small enough for any individual dropping out to be too dreadfully missed. Therefore, to put it in a nutshell, take care, my boy—that's all—that *you're* not!"

"I've got to keep on humbugging?" Lance wailed.

"It's just to warn you of the danger of your failing of that that I've seized this opportunity."

"And what do you regard in particular," the young man asked, "as the danger?"

"Why this certainty: that the moment your mother, who feels so strongly, should suspect your secret—well," said Peter desperately, "the fat would be on the fire."

Lance for a moment seemed to stare at the blaze. "She'd throw me over?"

"She'd throw *him* over."

"And come round to us?"

Peter, before he answered, turned away. "Come round to *you*." But he had said enough to indicate—and, as he evidently trusted, to avert—the horrid contingency.

IV

Within six months again, none the less, his fear was on more occasions than one all before him. Lance had returned to Paris for another trial; then had reappeared at home and had had, with his father, for the first time in his life, one of the scenes that strike sparks. He described it with much expression to Peter, touching whom (since they had never done so before) it was the sign of a new reserve on the part of the pair at Carrara Lodge that they at present failed, on a matter of intimate interest, to open themselves—if not in joy then in sorrow—to their good friend. This produced perhaps practically between the parties a shade of alienation and a slight intermission of commerce—marked mainly indeed by the fact that to talk at his ease with his old playmate Lance had in general to come to see him. The closest if not quite the gayest relation they had yet known together was thus ushered in. The difficulty for poor Lance was a tension at home—begotten by the fact that his father wished him to be at least the sort of success he himself had been. He hadn't "chucked" Paris—though nothing appeared more vivid to him than that Paris had chucked him: he would go back again because of the fascination in trying, in seeing, in sounding the depths—in learning one's lesson, briefly, even if the lesson were simply that of one's impotence in the presence of one's larger vision. But what did the Master, all aloft in his senseless fluency, know of impotence, and what vision—to be called such—had he in all his blind life ever had? Lance, heated and indignant, frankly appealed to his godparent on this score.

His father, it appeared, had come down on him for having, after so long, nothing to show, and hoped that on his next return this deficiency would be repaired. *The* thing, the Master complacently set forth was—for any artist, however inferior to himself—at least to "do" something. "What can you do? That's all I ask!" *He* had certainly done enough, and there was no mistake about what he had to show. Lance had tears in his eyes when it came thus to letting his old friend know how great the strain might be on the "sacrifice" asked of him. It wasn't so easy to continue humbugging—as from son to parent—after feeling one's self despised for not grovelling in mediocrity. Yet a noble duplicity was what, as they intimately faced the situation, Peter went on requiring; and it was still for a time what his young friend, bitter and sore, managed loyally to comfort him with. Fifty pounds more than once again, it was true, rewarded both in London and in Paris the young friend's loyalty; none the less sensibly, doubtless, at the moment, that the money was a direct advance on a decent sum for which Peter had long since privately prearranged an ultimate function. Whether by these arts or others, at all events, Lance's just resentment was kept for a season—but only for a season—at bay. The day arrived when he warned his companion that he could hold out—or hold in—no longer. Carrara Lodge had had to listen to another lecture delivered from a great height—an infliction really heavier at last than, without striking back or in some way letting the Master have the truth, flesh and blood could bear.

"And what I don't see is," Lance observed with a certain irritated eye for what was after all, if it came to that, owing to himself too; "what

I don't see is, upon my honour, how *you*, as things are going, can keep the game up."

"Oh the game for me is only to hold my tongue," said placid Peter. "And I have my reason."

"Still my mother?"

Peter showed a queer face as he had often shown it before—that is by turning it straight away. "What will you have? I haven't ceased to like her."

"She's beautiful—she's a dear of course," Lance allowed; "but what is she to you, after all, and what is it to you that, as to anything whatever, she should or she shouldn't?"

Peter, who had turned red, hung fire a little. "Well—it's simply what I make of it."

There was now, however, in his young friend a strange, an adopted insistence. "What are you after all to *her?*"

"Oh nothing. But that's another matter."

"She cares only for my father," said Lance the Parisian.

"Naturally—and that's just why."

"Why you've wished to spare her?"

"Because she cares so tremendously much."

Lance took a turn about the room, but with his eyes still on his host. "How awfully—always—you must have liked her!"

"Awfully. Always," said Peter Brench.

The young man continued for a moment to muse—then stopped again in front of him. "Do you know how much she cares?" Their eyes met on it, but Peter, as if his own found something new in Lance's, appeared to hesitate, for the first time in an age, to say he did know. "*I've* only just found out," said Lance. "She came to my room last night, after being present, in silence and only with her eyes on me, at what I had had to take from him; she came—and she was with me an extraordinary hour."

He had paused again and they had again for a while sounded each other. Then something—and it made him suddenly turn pale—came to Peter. "She *does* know?"

"She does know. She let it all out to me—so as to demand of me no more than 'that,' as she said, of which she herself had been capable. She has always, always known," said Lance without pity.

Peter was silent a long time; during which his companion might have heard him gently breathe, and on touching him might have felt within him the vibration of a long low sound suppressed. By the time he spoke at last he had taken everything in. "Then I do see how tremendously much."

"Isn't it wonderful?" Lance asked.

"Wonderful," Peter mused.

"So that if your original effort to keep me from Paris was to keep me from knowledge!—" Lance exclaimed as if with a sufficient indication of this futility.

It might have been at the futility Peter appeared for a little to gaze. "I think it must have been—without my quite at the time knowing it—to keep *me!*" he replied at last as he turned away.

---

1. What meanings do you find in the title and how are these related to the story?
2. Why doesn't Peter Brench want Lance to go to Paris? Is Brench justifiably proud of preserving the Mallows' illusions? Has he made unwarranted assumptions?
3. Is Brench finally the victim of his own illusions? Is he more severely damaged by the coming of knowledge than Lance is?
4. How seriously should we take Brench's love for Mrs. Mallow? How does he demonstrate it?
5. How many of the four main characters are truly concerned with sparing the feelings of others?
6. Discuss the author's use of figurative language. In what ways is it appropriate to the subject matter?
7. How would you characterize the kind of language used throughout the story? How do its qualities relate to the chosen point of view?

The Jolly Corner

I

Every one asks me what I 'think' of everything," said Spencer Brydon; "and I make answer as I can—begging or dodging the question, putting them off with any nonsense. It wouldn't matter to any of them really," he went on, "for, even were it possible to meet in that stand-and-deliver way so silly a demand on so big a subject, my 'thoughts' would still be almost altogether about something that concerns only myself." He was talking to Miss Staverton, with whom for a couple of months now he had availed himself of every possible occasion to talk; this disposition and this resource, this comfort and support, as the situation in fact presented itself, having promptly enough taken the first place in the considerable array of rather unattenuated surprises attending his so strangely belated return to America. Everything was somehow a surprise; and that might be natural when one had so long and so consistently neglected everything, taken pains to give surprises so much margin for play. He had given them more than thirty years—thirty-three, to be exact; and they now seemed to him to have organised their performance quite on the scale of that licence. He had been twenty-three on leaving New York—he was fifty-six today: unless indeed he were to reckon as he had sometimes, since his repatriation, found himself feeling; in which case he would have lived longer than is often allotted to man. It would have taken a century, he repeatedly said to himself, and said also to Alice Staverton, it would have taken a longer absence and a more averted mind than those even of which he had been guilty, to pile up the differences, the newnesses, the queernesses, above all the bignesses, for the better or the worse, that at present assaulted his vision wherever he looked.

The great fact all the while however had been the incalculability; since he *had* supposed himself, from decade to decade, to be allowing, and in the most liberal and intelligent manner, for brilliancy of change. He actually saw that he had allowed for nothing; he missed what he would have been sure of finding, he found what he would never have imagined. Proportions and values were upside-down; the ugly things he had expected, the ugly things of his far-away youth, when he had too promptly waked up to a sense of the ugly—these uncanny phenomena placed him rather, as it happened, under the charm; whereas the "swagger" things, the modern, the monstrous, the famous things, those he had more particularly, like thousands of ingenuous enquirers every year, come over to see, were exactly his sources of dismay. They were as so many set traps for displeasure, above all for reaction, of which his restless tread was constantly pressing the spring. It was interesting, doubtless, the whole show, but it would have been too disconcerting hadn't a certain finer truth saved the situation. He had distinctly not, in this steadier light, come over *all* for the monstrosities; he had come, not only in the last analysis but quite on the face of the act, under an impulse with which they had nothing to do. He had come—putting the thing pompously—to look at his "property," which he had thus for a third of a century not been within four thousand miles of; or, expressing it less sordidly, he had yielded to the humour of seeing again his house on the jolly corner, as he usually, and quite fondly, described it—the one in which he had first seen the light, in which various members of his family had lived and had died, in which the holidays of his overschooled boyhood had been passed and the few social flowers of his chilled adolescence gathered, and which, alienated then for so long a period, had, through the successive deaths of his two brothers and the termination of old arrangements, come wholly into his hands. He was the owner of another, not quite so "good"—the jolly corner having been, from far back, superlatively extended and consecrated; and the value of the pair represented his main capital, with an income consisting, in these later years, of their respective rents which (thanks precisely to their original excellent type) had never been depressingly low. He could live in "Europe," as he had been in the habit of living, on the product of these flourishing New York leases, and all the better since, that of the second structure, the mere number in its long row, having within a twelvemonth fallen in, renovation at a high advance had proved beautifully possible.

These were items of property indeed, but he had found himself since his arrival distinguishing more than ever between them. The house within the street, two bristling blocks westward, was already in course of reconstruction as a tall mass of flats; he had acceded, some time before, to overtures for this conversion—in which, now that it was going forward, it had been not the least of his astonishments to find himself able, on the spot, and though without a previous ounce of such experience, to participate with a certain intelligence, almost with a certain authority. He had lived his life with his back so turned to such concerns and his face addressed to those of so different an order that he scarce knew what to make of this lively stir, in a compartment of his mind never yet penetrated, of a capacity for business and a sense for construction. These virtues, so common all round him now, had been dormant in his own organism—where it might be said of them perhaps that they had slept the sleep of the just. At present, in the splendid autumn weather—the autumn at least was a pure boon in the terrible place—he loafed about his "work" undeterred, secretly agitated; not in the least "minding" that the whole proposition, as they said, was vulgar and sordid, and ready to climb ladders, to walk the plank, to handle materials and look wise about them, to ask questions, in fine, and challenge explanations and really "go into" figures.

It amused, it verily quite charmed him; and, by the same stroke, it amused, and even more, Alice Staverton, though perhaps charming her perceptibly less. She wasn't however going to be better off for it, as *he* was—and so astonishingly much: nothing was now likely, he knew, ever to make her better off than she found herself, in the afternoon of life, as the delicately frugal possessor and tenant of the small house in Irving Place[1] to which she had subtly managed to cling through her almost unbroken New York career. If he knew the way to it now better than to any other address among the dreadful multiplied numberings which seemed to him to reduce the whole place to some vast ledger-page, overgrown, fantastic, of ruled and criss-crossed lines and figures—if he had formed, for his consolation, that habit, it was really not a little because of the charm of his having encountered and recognized, in the vast wildness of the wholesale, breaking through the mere gross generalisation of wealth and force and success, a small still scene where

1. Formerly fashionable area in Manhattan north of Washington Square.

items and shades, all delicate things, kept the sharpness of the notes of a high voice perfectly trained, and where economy hung about like the scent of a garden. His old friend lived with one maid and herself dusted her relics and trimmed her lamps and polished her silver; she stood off, in the awful modern crush, when she could, but she sallied forth and did battle when the challenge was really to "spirit," the spirit she after all confessed to, proudly and a little shyly, as to that of the better time, that of *their* common, their quite far-away and antediluvian social period and order. She made use of the street-cars when need be, the terrible things that people scrambled for as the panic-stricken at sea scramble for the boats; she affronted, inscrutably, under stress, all the public concussions and ordeals; and yet, with that slim mystifying grace of her appearance, which defied you to say if she were a fair young woman who looked older through trouble, or a fine smooth older one who looked young through successful indifference; with her precious reference, above all, to memories and histories into which he could enter, she was as exquisite for him as some pale pressed flower (a rarity to begin with), and, failing other sweetnesses, she was a sufficient reward of his effort. They had communities of knowledge, "their" knowledge (this discriminating possessive was always on her lips) of presences of the other age, presences all overlaid, in his case, by the experience of a man and the freedom of a wanderer, overlaid by pleasure, by infidelity, by passages of life that were strange and dim to her, just by "Europe" in short, but still unobscured, still exposed and cherished, under that pious visitation of the spirit from which she had never been diverted.

She had come with him one day to see how his "apartment-house" was rising; he had helped her over gaps and explained to her plans, and while they were there had happened to have, before her, a brief but lively discussion with the man in charge, the representative of the building-firm that had undertaken his work. He had found himself quite "standing-up" to this personage over a failure on the latter's part to observe some detail of one of their noted conditions, and had so lucidly argued his case that, besides ever so prettily flushing, at the time, for sympathy in his triumph, she had afterwards said to him (though to a slightly greater effect of irony) that he had clearly for too many years neglected a real gift. If he had but stayed at home he would have anticipated the inventor of the skyscraper. If he had but stayed at home he would have discovered his genius in time really to start some new variety of awful architectural hare and run it till it burrowed in a gold-mine. He was to remember these words, while the weeks elapsed, for the small silver ring they had sounded over the queerest and deepest of his own lately most disguised and most muffled vibrations.

It had begun to be present to him after the first fortnight, it had broken out with the oddest abruptness, this particular wanton wonderment: it met him there—and this was the image under which he himself judged the matter, or at least, not a little, thrilled and flushed with it—very much as he might have been met by some strange figure, some unexpected occupant, at a turn of one of the dim passages of an empty house. The quaint analogy quite hauntingly remained with him, when he didn't indeed rather improve it by a still intenser form: that of his opening a door behind which he would have made sure of finding nothing, a door into a room shuttered and void, and yet so coming, with a great suppressed start, on some quite erect confronting presence, something planted in the middle of the place and facing him through the dusk. After that visit to the house in construction he walked with his companion to see the other and always so much the better one, which in the eastward direction formed one of the corners, the "jolly" one precisely, of the street now so generally dishonoured and disfigured in its westward reaches, and of the comparatively conservative Avenue.[2] The Avenue still had pretensions, as Miss Staverton said, to decency; the old people had mostly gone, the old names were unknown, and here and there an old association seemed to stray, all vaguely, like some very aged person, out too late, whom you might meet and feel the impulse to watch or follow, in kindness, for safe restoration to shelter.

They went in together, our friends; he admitted himself with his key, as he kept no one there, he explained, preferring, for his reasons, to leave the place empty, under a simple arrangement with a good woman living in the neighbourhood and who came for a daily hour to open windows and dust and sweep. Spencer Brydon had his reasons and was growingly aware of them; they seemed to him better each time he was there, though he didn't name them all to his companion, any more than he told her as yet how often, how quite absurdly often, he himself came. He only let her see for the present, while they walked through the great blank rooms, that absolute vacancy reigned and that, from top to bottom, there was nothing but Mrs. Muldoon's broomstick, in a corner, to tempt the burglar. Mrs. Muldoon was then on the premises, and she loquaciously attended the visitors, preceding them from room to room and pushing back shutters, and throwing up sashes—all to show them, as she remarked, how little there was to see. There was little indeed to see in the great gaunt shell where the main dispositions and the general apportionment of space, the style of an age of ampler allowances, had nevertheless for its master their honest pleading message, affecting him as some good old servant's, some lifelong retainer's appeal for a character, or even for a retiring-pension; yet it

2. I.e., Fifth Avenue; the street is Fourteenth Street.

was also a remark of Mrs. Muldoon's that, glad as she was to oblige him by her noonday round, there was a request she greatly hoped he would never make of her. If he should wish her for any reason to come in after dark she would just tell him, if he "plased," that he must ask it of somebody else.

The fact that there was nothing to see didn't militate for the worthy woman against what one *might* see, and she put it frankly to Miss Staverton that no lady could be expected to like, could she? "craping up to thim top storeys in the ayvil hours." The gas and electric light were off the house, and she fairly evoked a gruesome vision of her march through the great grey rooms—so many of them as there were too!—with her glimmering taper. Miss Staverton met her honest glare with a smile and the profession that she herself certainly would recoil from such an adventure. Spencer Brydon meanwhile held his peace—for the moment; the question of the "evil" hours in his old home had already become too grave for him. He had begun some time since to "crape," and he knew just why a packet of candles addressed to that pursuit had been stowed by his own hand, three weeks before, at the back of a drawer of the fine old sideboard that occupied, as a "fixture," the deep recess in the dining-room. Just now he laughed at his companions—quickly however changing the subject; for the reason that, in the first place, his laugh struck him even at that moment as starting the odd echo, the conscious human resonance (he scarce knew how to qualify it) that sounds made while he was there alone sent back to his ear or his fancy; and that, in the second, he imagined Alice Staverton for the instant on the point of asking him, with a divination, if he ever so prowled. There were divinations he was unprepared for, and he had at all events averted enquiry by the time Mrs. Muldoon had left them, passing on to other parts.

There was happily enough to say, on so consecrated a spot, that could be said freely and fairly; so that a whole train of declarations was precipitated by his friend's having herself broken out, after a yearning look around: "But I hope you don't mean they want you to pull *this* to pieces!" His answer came, promptly, with his reawakened wrath: it was of course exactly what they wanted, and what they were "at" him for, daily, with the iteration of people who couldn't for their life understand a man's liability to decent feelings. He had found the place, just as it stood and beyond what he could express, an interest and a joy. There were values other than the beastly rent-values, and in short, in short—! But it was thus Miss Staverton took him up. "In short you're to make so good a thing of your sky-scaper that, living in luxury on *those* ill-gotten gains, you can afford for a while to be sentimental here!" Her smile had for him, with the words, the particular mild irony with which he found half her talk suffused; an irony without bitterness and that came, exactly, from her having so much imagination—not, like the cheap sarcasms with which one heard most people, about the world of "society," bid for the reputation of cleverness, from nobody's really having any. It was agreeable to him at this very moment to be sure that when he had answered, after a brief demur, "Well yes: so, precisely, you may put it!" her imagination would still do him justice. He explained that even if never a dollar were to come to him from the other house he would nevertheless cherish this one; and he dwelt, further, while they lingered and wandered, on the fact of the stupefaction he was already exciting, the positive mystification he felt himself create.

He spoke of the value of all he read into it, into the mere sight of the walls, mere shapes of the rooms, mere sound of the floors, mere feel, in his hand, of the old silver-plated knobs of the several mahogany doors, which suggested the pressure of the palms of the dead; the seventy years of the past in fine that these things represented, the annals of nearly three generations, counting his grandfather's, the one that had ended there, and the impalpable ashes of his long-extinct youth, afloat in the very air like microscopic motes. She listened to everything; she was a woman who answered intimately but who utterly didn't chatter. She scattered abroad therefore no cloud of words; she could assent, she could agree, above all she could encourage, without doing that. Only at the last she went a little further than he had done himself. "And then how do you know? You may still, after all, want to live here." It rather indeed pulled him up, for it wasn't what he had been thinking, at least in her sense of the words. "You mean I may decide to stay on for the sake of it?"

"Well, *with* such a home—!" But, quite beautifully, she had too much tact to dot so monstrous an *i*, and it was precisely an illustration of the way she didn't rattle. How could any one—of any wit—insist on any one else's "wanting" to live in New York?

"Oh," he said, "I *might* have lived here (since I had my opportunity early in life); I might have put in here all these years. Then everything would have been different enough—and, I dare say, 'funny' enough. But that's another matter. And then the beauty of it—I mean of my perversity, of my refusal to agree to a 'deal'—is just in the total absence of a reason. Don't you see that if I had a reason about the matter at all it would *have* to be the other way, and would then be inevitably a reason of dollars? There are no reasons here *but* of dollars. Let us therefore have none whatever—not the ghost of one."

They were back in the hall then for departure, but from where they stood the vista was large, through an open door, into the great square main saloon,[3] with its almost antique felicity of brave spaces between windows. Her eyes came back from that reach and met his own a moment. "Are you very sure the 'ghost' of one doesn't, much rather, serve—?"

He had a positive sense of turning pale. But it was as near as they were then to come. For he made answer, he believed, between a glare and a grin: "Oh ghosts—of course the place must swarm with them! I should be ashamed of it if it didn't. Poor Mrs. Muldoon's right, and it's why I haven't asked her to do more than look in."

Miss Staverton's gaze again lost itself, and things she didn't utter, it was clear, came and went in her mind. She might even for the minute, off there in the fine room, have imagined some element dimly gathering. Simplified like the death-mask of a handsome face, it perhaps produced for her just then an effect akin to the stir of an expression in the "set" commemorative plaster. Yet whatever her impression may have been she produced instead a vague platitutde. "Well, if it were only furnished and lived in—!"

She appeared to imply that in case of its being still furnished he might have been a little less opposed to the idea of a return. But she passed straight into the vestibule, as if to leave her words behind her, and the next moment he had opened the house-door and was standing with her on the steps. He closed the door and, while he repocketed his key, looking up and down, they took in the comparatively harsh actuality of the Avenue, which reminded him of the assault of the outer light of the Desert on the traveller emerging from an Egyptian tomb. But he risked before they stepped into the street his gathered answer to her speech. "For me it *is* lived in. For me it *is* furnished." At which it was easy for her to sigh "Ah yes—!" all vaguely and discreetly; since his parents and his favourite sister, to say nothing of other kin, in numbers, had run their course and met their end there. That represented, within the walls, ineffaceable life.

It was a few days after this that, during an hour passed with her again, he had expressed his impatience of the too flattering curiosity—among the people he met—about his appreciation of New York. He had arrived at none at all that was socially producible, and as for that matter of his "thinking" (thinking the better or the worse of anything there) he was wholly taken up with one subject of thought. It was mere vain egoism, and it was moreover, if she liked, a morbid obsession. He found all things come back to the question of what he personally might have been, how he might have led his life and "turned out," if he had not so, at the outset, given it up. And confessing for the first time to

3. Salon—an elegant living room.

the intensity within him of this absurd speculation—which but proved also, no doubt, the habit of too selfishly thinking—he affirmed the impotence there of any other source of interest, any other native appeal. "What would it have made of me, what would it have made of me? I keep for ever wondering, all idiotically; as if I could possibly know! I see what it has made of dozens of others, those I meet, and it positively aches within me, to the point of exasperation, that it would have made something of me as well. Only I can't make out *what*, and the worry of it, the small rage of curiosity never to be satisfied, brings back what I remember to have felt, once or twice, after judging best, for reasons, to burn some important letter unopened. I've been sorry, I've hated it—I've never known what was in the letter. You may of course say it's a trifle—!"

"I don't say it's a trifle," Miss Staverton gravely interrupted.

She was seated by her fire, and before her, on his feet and restless, he turned to and fro between this intensity of his idea and a fitful and unseeing inspection, through his single eyeglass, of the dear little old objects on her chimney-piece. Her interruption made him for an instant look at her harder. "I shouldn't care if you did!" he laughed, however; "and it's only a figure, at any rate, for the way I now feel. *Not* to have followed my perverse young course—and almost in the teeth of my father's curse, as I may say; not to have kept it up, so, 'over there,' from that day to this, without a doubt or a pang; not, above all, to have liked it, to have loved it, so much, loved it, no doubt, with such an abysmal conceit of my own preference: some variation from *that*, I say, must have produced some different effect for my life and for my 'form.' I should have stuck here—if it had been possible; and I was too young, at twenty-three, to judge, *pour deux sous*,[4] whether it *were* possible. If I had waited I might have seen it was, and then I might have been, by staying here, something nearer to one of these types who have been hammered so hard and made so keen by their conditions. It isn't that I admire them so much—the question of any charm in them, or of any charm, beyond that of the rank money-passion, exerted by their conditions *for* them, has nothing to do with the matter: it's only a question of what fantastic, yet perfectly possible, development of my own nature I mayn't have missed. It comes over me that I had then a strange *alter ego* deep down somewhere within me, as the full-blown flower is in the small tight bud, and that I just took the course, I just transferred him to the climate, that blighted him for once and for ever."

"And you wonder about the flower," Miss Staverton said. "So do

4. For two cents, i.e., without real interest in the matter.

I, if you want to know; and so I've been wondering these several weeks. I believe in the flower," she continued, "I feel it would have been quite splendid, quite huge and monstrous."

"Monstrous above all!" her visitor echoed; "and I imagine, by the same stroke, quite hideous and offensive."

"You don't believe that," she returned; "if you did you wouldn't wonder. You'd know, and that would be enough for you. What you feel—and what I feel *for* you—is that you'd have had power."

"You'd have liked me that way?" he asked.

She barely hung fire. "How should I not have liked you?"

"I see. You'd have liked me, have preferred me, a billionaire!"

"How should I not have liked you?" she simply again asked.

He stood before her still—her question kept him motionless. He took it in, so much there was of it; and indeed his not otherwise meeting it testified to that. "I know at least what I am," he simply went on; "the other side of the medal's clear enough. I've not been edifying—I believe I'm thought in a hundred quarters to have been barely decent. I've followed strange paths and worshipped strange gods; it must have come to you again and again—in fact you've admitted to me as much—that I was leading, at any time these thirty years, a selfish frivolous scandalous life. And you see what it has made of me."

She just waited, smiling at him. "You see what it has made of *me*."

"Oh you're a person whom nothing can have altered. You were born to be what you are, anywhere, anyway: you've the perfection nothing else could have blighted. And don't you see how, without my exile, I shouldn't have been waiting till now?—" But he pulled up for the strange pang.

"The great thing to see," she presently said, "seems to me to be that it has spoiled nothing. It hasn't spoiled your being here at last. It hasn't spoiled this. It hasn't spoiled your speaking—" She also however faltered.

He wondered at everything her controlled emotion might mean. "Do you believe then—too dreadfully!—that I *am* as good as I might ever have been?"

"Oh no! Far from it!" With which she got up from her chair and was nearer to him. "But I don't care," she smiled.

"You mean I'm good enough?"

She considered a little. "Will you believe it if I say so? I mean will you let that settle your question for you?" And then as if making out in his face that he drew back from this, that he had some idea which, however absurd, he couldn't yet bargain away: "Oh you don't care either—but very differently: you don't care for anything but yourself."

Spencer Brydon recognised it—it was in fact what he had absolutely professed. Yet he importantly qualified. "*He* isn't myself. He's the just so totally other person. But I do want to see him," he added. "And I can. And I shall."

Their eyes met for a minute while he guessed from something in hers that she divined his strange sense. But neither of them otherwise expressed it, and her apparent understanding, with no protesting shock, no easy derision, touched him more deeply than anything yet, constituting for his stifled perversity, on the spot, an element that was like breathable air. What she said however was unexpected. "Well, *I've* seen him."

"You?—"

"I've seen him in a dream."

"Oh a 'dream'—!" It let him down.

"But twice over," she continued. "I saw him as I see you now."

"You've dreamed the same dream—?"

"Twice over," she repeated. "The very same."

This did somehow a little speak to him, as it also gratified him. "You dream about me at that rate?"

"Ah about *him!*" she smiled.

His eyes again sounded her. "Then you know all about him." And as she said nothing more: "What's the wretch like?"

She hesitated, and it was as if he were pressing her so hard that, resisting for reasons of her own, she had to turn away. "I'll tell you some other time!"

II

It was after this that there was most of a virtue for him, most of a cultivated charm, most of a preposterous secret thrill, in the particular form of surrender to his obsession and of address to what he more and more believed to be his privilege. It was what in these weeks he was living for—since he really felt life to begin but after Mrs. Muldoon had retired from the scene and, visiting the ample house from attic to cellar, making sure he was alone, he knew himself in safe possession and, as he tacitly expressed it, let himself go. He sometimes came twice in the twenty-four hours; the moments he liked best were those of gathering dusk, of the short autumn twilight; this was the time of which, again and again, he found himself hoping most. Then he could, as seemed to him, most intimately wander and wait, linger and listen, feel his fine attention, never in his life before so fine, on the pulse of the great vague place: he preferred the lampless hour and only wished he might have prolonged each day the deep crepuscular spell. Later—rarely much before midnight, but then for a considerable vigil—he watched with his glimmering light; moving slowly, holding it high, playing it far, rejoicing above all, as much as he might, in open vistas, reaches of communication between rooms and by passages; the long straight chance or show, as he would have called it, for the revelation he pretended to invite. It was a practice he found he could perfectly "work" without exciting remark; no one was in the least the wiser for it; even Alice Staverton, who was moreover a well of discretion, didn't quite fully imagine.

He let himself in and let himself out with the assurance of calm proprietorship; and accident so far favoured him that, if a fat Avenue "officer" had happened on occasion to see him entering at eleven-thirty, he had never yet, to the best of his belief, been noticed as emerging at two. He walked there on the crisp November nights, arrived regularly at the evening's end; it was as easy to do this after dining out as to take his way to a club or to his hotel. When he left his club, if he hadn't been dining out, it was ostensibly to go to his hotel; and when he left his hotel, if he had spent a part of the evening there, it was ostensibly to go to his club. Everything was easy in fine; everything conspired and promoted: there was truly even in the strain of his experience something that glossed over, something that salved and simplified, all the rest of consciousness. He circulated, talked, renewed, loosely and pleasantly, old relations—met indeed, so far as he could, new expectations and seemed to make out on the whole that in spite of the career, of such different contacts, which he had spoken of to Miss Staverton as ministering so little, for those who might have watched it, to edification, he was positively rather liked than not. He was a dim secondary social success—and all with people who had truly not an idea of him. It was all mere surface sound, this murmur of their welcome, this popping of their corks—just as his gestures of response were the extravagant shadows, emphatic in proportion as they meant little, of some game of *ombres chinoises*.[5] He projected himself all day, in thought, straight over the bristling line of hard unconscious heads and into the other, the real, the waiting life; the life that, as soon as he had heard behind him the click of his great housedoor, began for him, on the jolly corner, as beguilingly as the slow opening bars of some rich music follows the tap of the conductor's wand.

He always caught the first effect of the steel point of his stick on the old marble of the hall pavement, large black-and-white squares that he remembered as the admiration of his childhood and that had then made in him, as he now saw, for the growth of an early conception of style. This effect was the dim reverberating tinkle as of some far-off bell hung who should say where?—in the depths of the house, of the

5. Shadow play, literally Chinese shadows.

past, of that mystical other world that might have flourished for him had he not, for weal or woe, abandoned it. On this impression he did ever the same thing; he put his stick noiselessly away in a corner—feeling the place once more in the likeness of some great glass bowl, all precious concave crystal, set delicately humming by the play of a moist finger round its edge. The concave crystal held, as it were, this mystical other world, and the indescribably fine murmur of its rim was the sigh there, the scarce audible pathetic wail to his strained ear, of all the old baffled forsworn possibilities. What he did therefore by this appeal of his hushed presence was to wake them into such measure of ghostly life as they might still enjoy. They were shy, all but unappeasably shy, but they weren't really sinister; at least they weren't as he had hitherto felt them—before they had taken the Form he so yearned to make them take, the Form he at moments saw himself in the light of fairly hunting on tiptoe, the points of his evening-shoes, from room to room and from storey to storey.

That was the essence of his vision—which was all rank folly, if one would, while he was out of the house and otherwise occupied, but which took on the last verisimilitude as soon as he was placed and posted. He knew what he meant and what he wanted; it was as clear as the figure on a cheque presented in demand for cash. His *alter ego* "walked"—that was the note of his image of him, while his image of his motive for his own odd pastime was the desire to waylay him and meet him. He roamed, slowly, warily, but all restlessly, he himself did—Mrs. Muldoon had been right, absolutely, with her figure of their "craping"; and the presence he watched for would roam restlessly too. But it would be as cautious and as shifty; the conviction of its probable, in fact its already quite sensible, quite audible evasion of pursuit grew for him from night to night, laying on him finally a rigour to which nothing in his life had been comparable. It had been the theory of many superficially-judging persons, he knew, that he was wasting that life in a surrender to sensations, but he had tasted of no pleasure so fine as his actual tension, had been introduced to no sport that demanded at once the patience and the nerve of his stalking of a creature more subtle, yet at bay perhaps more formidable, than any beast of the forest. The terms, the comparisons, the very practices of the chase positively came again into play; there were even moments when passages of his occasional experience as a sportsman, stirred memories, from his younger time, of moor and mountain and desert, revived for him—and to the increase of his keenness—by the tremendous force of analogy. He found himself at moments—once he had placed his single light on some mantel-shelf or in some recess—stepping back into shelter or shade, effacing himself behind a door or in an embrasure, as he had sought of old the vantage of rock and tree; he found himself holding his breath and living in the joy of the instant, the supreme suspense created by big game alone.

He wasn't afraid (though putting himself the question as he believed gentlemen on Bengal tiger-shoots or in close quarters with the great bear of the Rockies had been known to confess to having put it); and this indeed—since here at least he might be frank!—because of the impression, so intimate and so strange, that he himself produced as yet a dread, produced certainly a strain, beyond the liveliest he was likely to feel. They fell for him into categories, they fairly became familiar, the signs, for his own perception, of the alarm his presence and his vigilance created; though leaving him always to remark, portentously, on his probably having formed a relation, his probably enjoying a consciousness, unique in the experience of man. People enough, first and last, had been in terror of apparitions, but who had ever before so turned the tables and become himself, in the apparitional world, an incalculable terror? He might have found this sublime had he quite dared to think of it; but he didn't too much insist, truly, on that side of his privilege. With habit and repetition he gained to an extraordinary degree the power to penetrate the dusk of distances and the darkness of corners, to resolve back into their innocence treacheries of uncertain light, the evil-looking forms taken in the gloom by mere shadows, by accidents of the air, by shifting effects of perspective; putting down his dim luminary he could still wander on without it, pass into other rooms and, only knowing it was there behind him in case of need, see his way about, visually project for his purpose a comparative clearness. It made him feel, this acquired faculty, like some monstrous stealthy cat; he wondered if he would have glared at these moments with large shining yellow eyes, and what it mightn't verily be, for the poor hard-pressed *alter ego*, to be confronted with such a type.

He liked however the open shutters; he opened everywhere those Mrs. Muldoon had closed, closing them as carefully afterwards, so that she shouldn't notice: he liked—oh this he did like, and above all in the upper rooms!—the sense of the hard silver of the autumn stars through the window-panes, and scarcely less the glare of the street-lamps below, the white electric lustre which it would have taken curtains to keep out. This was human actual social; this was of the world he had lived in, and he was more at his ease certainly for the countenance, coldly general and impersonal, that all the while and in spite of his detachment it seemed to give him. He had support of course mostly in the rooms at the wide front and the prolonged side; it failed him considerably in the central shades and the parts at the back. But if he sometimes, on his rounds, was glad of his optical reach, so none the less often the rear of the house affected him as the very jungle of his prey. The place was there more subdivided; a large "extension" in particular, where small rooms for servants had been multiplied, abounded in nooks and corners, in closets and passages, in the ramifications especially of an ample back staircase over which he leaned, many a time, to look far down—not deterred from his gravity even while aware that he might, for a spectator, have figured some solemn simpleton playing at hide-and-seek. Outside in fact he might himself make that ironic *rapprochement;*[6] but within the walls, and in spite of the clear windows, his consistency was proof against the cynical light of New York.

It had belonged to that idea of the exasperated consciousness of his victim to become a real test for him; since he had quite put it to himself from the first that, oh distinctly! he could "cultivate" his whole perception. He had felt it as above all open to cultivation—which indeed was but another name for his manner of spending his time. He was bringing it on, bringing it to perfection, by practice; in consequence of which it had grown so fine that he was now aware of impressions, attestations of his general postulate, that couldn't have broken upon him at once. This was the case more specifically with a phenomenon at last quite frequent for him in the upper rooms, the recognition—absolutely unmistakable, and by a turn dating from a particular hour, his resumption of his campaign after a diplomatic drop, a calculated absence of three nights—of his being definitely followed, tracked at a distance carefully taken and to the express end that he should the less confidently, less arrogantly, appear to himself merely to pursue. It worried, it finally quite broke him up, for it proved, of all the conceivable impressions, the one least suited to his book. He was kept in sight while remaining himself—as regards the essence of his position—sightless, and his only recourse then was in abrupt turns, rapid recoveries of ground. He wheeled about, retracing his steps, as if he might so catch in his face at least the stirred air of some other quick revolution. It was indeed true that his fully dislocalised thought of these manoeuvres recalled to him Pantaloon, at the Christmas farce, buffeted and tricked from behind by ubiquitous Harlequin;[7] but it left intact the influence of the conditions themselves each time he was re-exposed to them, so that in fact this association, had he suffered it to become constant, would on a certain side have but ministered to his intenser gravity. He had made, as I have said, to create on the premises the baseless sense of a reprieve, his three absences; and the result of the third was to confirm the after-effect of the second.

On his return, that night—the night succeeding his last intermission—he stood in the hall and looked up the staircase with a certainty more intimate than any he had yet known. "He's *there,* at the top, and waiting—not, as in general, falling back for disappearance. He's hold-

6. I.e., conclusion (literally "coming together"). 7. A character in Italian comedy, who plays tricks on slow-witted Pantaloon.

ing his ground, and it's the first time—which is a proof, isn't it? that something has happened for him." So Brydon argued with his hand on the banister and his foot on the lowest stair; in which position he felt as never before the air chilled by his logic. He himself turned cold in it, for he seemed of a sudden to know what now was involved. "Harder pressed?—yes, he takes it in, with its thus making clear to him that I've come, as they say, 'to stay.' He finally doesn't like and can't bear it, in the sense, I mean, that his wrath, his menaced interest, now balances with his dread. I've hunted him till he has 'turned': that, up there, is what has happened—he's the fanged or the antlered animal brought at last to bay." There came to him as I say—but determined by an influence beyond my notation!—the acuteness of this certainty; under which however the next moment he had broken into a sweat that he would as little have consented to attribute to fear as he would have dared immediately to act upon it for enterprise. It marked none the less a prodigious thrill, a thrill that represented sudden dismay, no doubt, but also represented, and with the selfsame throb, the strangest, the most joyous, possibly the next minute almost the proudest, duplication of consciousness.

"He has been dodging, retreating, hiding, but now, worked up to anger, he'll fight!"—this intense impression made a single mouthful, as it were, of terror and applause. But what was wondrous was that the applause, for the felt fact, was so eager, since, if it was his other self he was running to earth, this ineffable identity was thus in the last resort not unworthy of him. It bristled there—somewhere near at hand, however unseen still—as the hunted thing, even as the trodden worm of the adage *must* at last bristle; and Brydon at this instant tasted probably of a sensation more complex than had ever before found itself consistent with sanity. It was as if it would have shamed him that a character so associated with his own should triumphantly succeed in just skulking, should to the end not risk the open, so that the drop of this danger was, on the spot, a great lift of the whole situation. Yet with another rare shift of the same subtlety he was already trying to measure by how much more he himself might now be in peril of fear; so rejoicing that he could, in another form, actively inspire that fear, and simultaneously quaking for the form in which he might passively know it.

The apprehension of knowing it must after a little have grown in him, and the strangest moment of his adventure perhaps, the most memorable or really most interesting, afterwards, of his crisis, was the lapse of certain instants of concentrated conscious *combat*, the sense of a need to hold on to something, even after the manner of a man slipping and slipping on some awful incline; the vivid impulse, above all, to move, to act, to charge, somehow and upon something—to show himself, in a word, that he wasn't afraid. The state of "holding-on" was thus the state to which he was momentarily reduced; if there had been anything, in the great vacancy, to seize, he would presently have been aware of having clutched it as he might under a shock at home have clutched the nearest chair-back. He had been surprised at any rate—of this he *was* aware—into something unprecedented since his original appropriation of the place; he had closed his eyes, held them tight, for a long minute, as with that instinct of dismay and that terror of vision. When he opened them the room, the other contiguous rooms, extraordinarily, seemed lighter—so light, almost, that at first he took the change for day. He stood firm, however that might be, just where he had paused; his resistance had helped him—it was as if there were something he had tided over. He knew after a little what this was—it had been in the imminent danger of flight. He had stiffened his will against going; without this he would have made for the stairs, and it seemed to him that, still with his eyes closed, he would have descended them, would have known how, straight and swiftly, to the bottom.

Well, as he had held out, here he was—still at the top, among the more intricate upper rooms and with the gauntlet of the others, of all the rest of the house, still to run when it should be his time to go. He would go at his time—only at his time: didn't he go every night very much at the same hour? He took out his watch—there was light for that; it was scarcely a quarter past one, and he had never withdrawn so soon. He reached his lodgings for the most part at two—with his walk of a quarter of an hour. He would wait for the last quarter—he wouldn't stir till then; and he kept his watch there with his eye on it, reflecting while he held it that this deliberate wait, a wait with an effort, which he recognised, would serve perfectly for the attestation he desired to make. It would prove his courage—unless indeed the latter might most be proved by his budging at last from his place. What he mainly felt now was that, since he hadn't originally scuttled, he had his dignities—which had never in his life seemed so many—all to preserve and to carry aloft. This was before him in truth as a physical image, an image almost worthy of an age of greater romance. That remark indeed glimmered for him only to glow the next instant with a finer light; since what age of romance, after all, could have matched either the state of his mind or, "objectively," as they said, the wonder of his situation? The only difference would have been that, brandishing his dignities over his head as in a parchment scroll, he might then—that is in the heroic time—have proceeded downstairs with a drawn sword in his other grasp.

At present, really, the light he had set down on the mantel of the next room would have to figure his sword; which utensil, in the course of a minute, he had taken the requisite number of steps to possess himself of. The door between the rooms was open, and from the second another door opened to a third. These rooms, as he remembered, gave all three upon a common corridor as well, but there was a fourth, beyond them, without issue save through the preceding. To have moved, to have heard his step again, was appreciably a help; though even in recognising this he lingered once more a little by the chimney-piece on which his light had rested. When he next moved, just hesitating where to turn, he found himself considering a circumstance that, after his first and comparatively vague apprehension of it, produced in him the start that often attends some pang of recollection, the violent shock of having ceased happily to forget. He had come into sight of the door in which the brief chain of communication ended and which he now surveyed from the nearer threshold, the one not directly facing it. Placed at some distance to the left of this point, it would have admitted him to the last room of the four, the room without other approach or egress, had it not, to his intimate conviction, been closed *since* his former visitation, the matter probably of a quarter of an hour before. He stared with all his eyes at the wonder of the fact, arrested again where he stood and again holding his breath while he sounded its sense. Surely it had been *subsequently* closed—that is it had been on his previous passage indubitably open!

He took it full in the face that something had happened between—that he couldn't not have noticed before (by which he meant on his original tour of all the rooms that evening) that such a barrier had exceptionally presented itself. He had indeed since that moment undergone an agitation so extraordinary that it might have muddled for him any earlier view; and he tried to convince himself that he might perhaps then have gone into the room and, inadvertently, automatically, on coming out, have drawn the door after him. The difficulty was that this exactly was what he never did; it was against his whole policy, as he might have said, the essence of which was to keep vistas clear. He had them from the first, as he was well aware, quite on the brain: the strange apparition, at the far end of one of them, of his baffled "prey" (which had become by so sharp an irony so little the term now to apply!) was the form of success his imagination had most cherished, projecting into it always a refinement of beauty. He had known fifty times the start of perception that had afterwards dropped; had fifty times gasped to himself "There!" under some fond brief hallucination. The house, as the case stood, admirably lent itself; he might wonder at the taste, the native architecture of the particular time, which could rejoice so in the multiplication of doors—the opposite extreme to the modern, the actual almost complete proscription of them; but it had fairly contributed to provoke this obsession of the presence encountered telescopically, as he might say, focussed and studied in diminishing perspective and as by a rest for the elbow.

It was with these considerations that his present attention was charged—they perfectly availed to make what he saw portentous. He *couldn't*, by any lapse, have blocked that aperture; and if he hadn't, if it was unthinkable, why what else was clear but that there had been another agent? Another agent?—he had been catching, as he felt, a moment back, the very breath of him; but when had he been so close as in this simple, this logical, this completely personal act? It was so logical, that is, that one might have *taken* it for personal; yet for what did Brydon take it, he asked himself, while, softly panting, he felt his eyes almost leave their sockets. Ah this time at last they *were*, the two, the opposed projections of him, in presence; and this time, as much as one would, the question of danger loomed. With it rose, as not before, the question of courage—for what he knew the blank face of the door to say to him was "Show us how much you have!" It stared, it glared back at him with that challenge; it put to him the two alternatives: should he just push it open or not? Oh to have this consciousness was to *think*—and to think, Brydon knew, as he stood there, was, with the lapsing moments, not to have acted! Not to have acted—that was the misery and the pang—was even still not to act; was in fact *all* to feel the thing in another, in a new and terrible way. How long did he pause and how long did he debate? There was presently nothing to measure it; for his vibration had already changed—as just by the effect of its intensity. Shut up there, at bay, defiant, and with the prodigy of the thing palpably proveably *done*, thus giving notice like some stark signboard—under that accession of accent the situation itself had turned; and Brydon at last remarkably made up his mind on what it had turned to.

It had turned altogether to a different admonition; to a supreme hint, for him, of the value of Discretion! This slowly dawned, no doubt—for it could take its time; so perfectly, on his threshold, had he been stayed, so little as yet had he either advanced or retreated. It was the strangest of all things that now when, by his taking ten steps and applying his hand to a latch, or even his shoulder and his knee, if necessary, to a panel, all the hunger of his prime need might have been met, his high curiosity crowned, his unrest assuaged—it was amazing, but it was also exquisite and rare, that insistence should have, at a touch, quite dropped from him. Discretion—he jumped at that; and yet not, verily, at such a pitch, because it saved his nerves or his skin, but because, much more valuably, it saved the situation. When I say he "jumped" at it I feel the consonance of this term with the fact that—at the end indeed of I know not how long—he did move again, he crossed straight to the door. He wouldn't touch it—it seemed now that he might *if* he would: he would only just wait there a little, to show, to prove, that he wouldn't. He had thus another station, close to the thin partition by which revelation was denied him; but with his eyes bent and his hands held off in a mere intensity of stillness. He listened as if there had been something to hear, but this attitude, while it lasted, was his own communication. "If you won't then—good: I spare you and I give up. You affect me as by the appeal positively for pity: you convince me that for reasons rigid and sublime—what do I know?—we both of us should have suffered. I respect them then, and, though moved and privileged as, I believe, it has never been given to man, I retire, I renounce—never, on my honour, to try again. So rest for ever—and let *me!*"

That, for Brydon was the deep sense of this last demonstration—solemn, measured, directed, as he felt it to be. He brought it to a close, he turned away; and now verily he knew how deeply he had been stirred. He retraced his steps, taking up his candle, burnt, he observed, well-nigh to the socket, and marking again, lighten it as he would, the distinctness of his footfall; after which, in a moment, he knew himself at the other side of the house. He did here what he had not yet done at these hours—he opened half a casement, one of those in the front, and let in the air of the night; a thing he would have taken at any time previous for a sharp rupture of his spell. His spell was broken now, and it didn't matter—broken by his concession and his surrender, which made it idle henceforth that he should ever come back. The empty street—its other life so marked even by the great lamplit vacancy—was within call, within touch; he stayed there as to be in it again, high above it though he was still perched; he watched as for some comforting common fact, some vulgar human note, the passage of a scavenger or a thief, some night-bird however base. He would have blessed that sign of life; he would have welcomed positively the slow approach of his friend the policeman, whom he had hitherto only sought to avoid, and was not sure that if the patrol had come into sight he mightn't have felt the impulse to get into relation with it, to hail it, on some pretext, from his fourth floor.

The pretext that wouldn't have been too silly or too compromising, the explanation that would have saved his dignity and kept his name, in such a case, out of the papers, was not definite to him: he was so occupied with the thought of recording his Discretion—as an effect of the vow he had just uttered to his intimate adversary—that the importance of this loomed large and something had overtaken all ironically his sense of proportion. If there had been a ladder applied to the front of the house, even one of the vertiginous perpendiculars employed by painters and roofers and sometimes left standing overnight, he would have managed somehow, astride of the window-sill, to compass by outstretched leg and arm that mode of descent. If there had been some such uncanny thing as he had found in his room at hotels, a workable fire-escape in the form of notched cable or a canvas chute, he would have availed himself of it as a proof—well, of his present delicacy. He nursed that sentiment, as the question stood, a little in vain, and even—at the end of he scarce knew, once more, how long—found it, as by the action on his mind of the failure of response of the outer world, sinking back to vague anguish. It seemed to him he had waited an age for some stir of the great grim hush; the life of the town was itself under a spell—so unnaturally, up and down the whole prospect of known and rather ugly objects, the blankness and the silence lasted. Had they ever, he asked himself, the hardfaced houses, which had begun to look livid in the dim dawn, had they ever spoken so little to any need of his spirit? Great builded voids, great crowded stillnesses put on, often, in the heart of cities, for the small hours, a sort of sinister mask, and it was of this large collective negation that Brydon presently became conscious—all the more that the break of the day was, almost incredibly, now at hand, proving to him what a night he had made of it.

He looked again at his watch, saw what had become of his time-values (he had taken hours for minutes—not, as in other tense situations, minutes for hours) and the strange air of the streets was but the weak, the sullen flush of a dawn in which everything was still locked up. His choked appeal from his own open window had been the sole note of life, and he could but break off at last as for a worse despair. Yet while so deeply demoralised he was capable again of an impulse denoting—at least by his present measure—extraordinary resolution; of retracing his steps to the spot where he had turned cold with the extinction of his last pulse of doubt as to there being in the place another presence than his own. This required an effort strong enough to sicken him; but he had his reason, which over-mastered for the moment everything else. There was the whole of the rest of the house to traverse, and how should he screw himself to that if the door he had seen closed were at present open? He could hold to the idea that the closing had practically been for him an act of mercy, a chance offered him to descend, depart, get off the ground and never again profane it. This conception held together, it worked; but what it meant for him depended now clearly on the amount of forbearance his recent action, or rather his recent inaction, had engendered. The image of the "presence," whatever it was, waiting there for him to go—this image had not yet been so concrete for his nerves as when he stopped short of the point at which certainty would have come to him. For, with all his resolution, or more exactly with all his dread, he did stop short—he hung back from really seeing. The risk was too great and his fear too definite; it took at this moment an awful specific form.

He knew—yes, as he had never known anything—that, *should*

he see the door open, it would all too abjectly be the end of him. It would mean that the agent of his shame—for his shame was the deep abjection—was once more at large and in general possession; and what glared him thus in the face was the act that this would determine for him. It would send him straight about to the window he had left open, and by that window, be long ladder and dangling rope as absent as they would, he saw himself uncontrollably insanely fatally take his way to the street. The hideous chance of this he at least could avert; but he could only avert it by recoiling in time from assurance. He had the whole house to deal with, this fact was still there; only he now knew that uncertainty alone could start him. He stole back from where he had checked himself—merely to do so was suddenly like safety—and, making blindly for the greater staircase, left gaping rooms and sounding passages behind. Here was the top of the stairs, with a fine large dim descent and three spacious landings to mark off. His instinct was all for mildness, but his feet were harsh on the floors, and, strangely, when he had in a couple of minutes become aware of this, it counted somehow for help. He couldn't have spoken, the tone of his voice would have scared him, and the common conceit or resource of "whistling in the dark" (whether literally or figuratively) have appeared basely vulgar; yet he liked none the less to hear himself go, and when he had reached his first landing—taking it all with no rush, but quite steadily—that stage of success drew from him a gasp of relief.

The house, withal, seemed immense, the scale of space again inordinate; the open rooms, to no one of which his eyes deflected, gloomed in their shuttered state like mouths of caverns; only the high skylight that formed the crown of the deep well created for him a medium in which he could advance, but which might have been, for queerness of colour, some watery under-world. He tried to think of something noble, as that his property was really grand, a splendid possession; but this nobleness took the form too of the clear delight with which he was finally to sacrifice it. They might come in now, the builders, the destroyers—they might come as soon as they would. At the end of two flights he had dropped to another zone, and from the middle of the third, with only one more left, he recognised the influence of the lower windows, of half-drawn blinds, of the occasional gleam of streetlamps, of the glazed spaces of the vestibule. This was the bottom of the sea, which showed an illumination of its own and which he even saw paved—when at a given moment he drew up to sink a long look over the banisters—with the marble squares of his childhood. By that time indubitably he felt, as he might have said in a commoner cause, better; it had allowed him to stop and draw breath, and the ease increased with the sight of the old black-and-white slabs. But what he most felt was that now surely, with the element of impunity pulling him as by hard firm hands, the case was settled for what he might have seen above had he dared that last look. The closed door, blessedly remote now, was still closed—and he had only in short to reach that of the house.

He came down further, he crossed the passage forming the access to the last flight; and if here again he stopped an instant it was almost for the sharpness of the thrill of assured escape. It made him shut his eyes—which opened again to the straight slope of the remainder of the stairs. Here was impunity still, but impunity almost excessive; inasmuch as the side-lights and the high fan-tracery of the entrance were glimmering straight into the hall; an appearance produced, he the next instant saw, by the fact that the vestibule gaped wide, that the hinged halves of the inner door had been thrown far back. Out of that again the *question* sprang at him, making his eyes, as he felt, half-start from his head, as they had done, at the top of the house, before the sign of the other door. If he had left that one open, hadn't he left this one closed, and wasn't he now in *most* immediate presence of some inconceivable occult activity? It was as sharp, the question, as a knife in his side, but the answer hung fire still and seemed to lose itself in the vague darkness to which the thin admitted dawn, glimmering archwise over the whole outer door, made a semicircular margin, a cold silvery nimbus that seemed to play a little as he looked—to shift and expand and contract.

It was as if there had been something within it, protected by indistinctness and corresponding in extent with the opaque surface behind, the painted panels of the last barrier to his escape, of which the key was in his pocket. The indistinctness mocked him even while he stared, affected him as somehow shrouding or challenging certitude, so that after faltering an instant on his step he let himself go with the sense that here *was* at last something to meet, to touch, to take, to know—something all unnatural and dreadful, but to advance upon which was the conditon for him either of liberation or of supreme defeat. The penumbra, dense and dark, was the virtual screen of a figure which stood in it as still as some image erect in a niche or as some black-vizored sentinel guarding a treasure. Brydon was to know afterwards, was to recall and make out, the particular thing he had believed during the rest of his descent. He saw, in its great grey glimmering margin, the central vagueness diminish, and he felt it to be taking the very form toward which, for so many days, the passion of his curiosity had yearned. It gloomed, it loomed, it was something, it was somebody, the prodigy of a personal presence.

Rigid and conscious, spectral yet human, a man of his own substance and stature waited there to measure himself with his power to dismay. This only could it be—this only till he recognised, with his advance, that what made the face dim was the pair of raised hands that covered it and in which, so far from being offered in defiance, it was buried as for dark deprecation. So Brydon, before him, took him in; with every fact of him now, in the higher light, hard and acute—his planted stillness, his vivid truth, his grizzled bent head and white masking hands, his queer actuality of evening-dress, of dangling double eye-glass, of gleaming silk lappet and white linen, of pearl button and gold watch-guard and polished shoe. No portrait by a great modern master could have presented him with more intensity, thrust him out of his frame with more art, as if there had been "treatment," of the consummate sort, in his every shade and salience. The revulsion, for our friend, had become, before he knew it, immense—this drop, in the act of apprehension, to the sense of his adversary's inscrutable manoeuvre. That meaning at least, while he gaped, it offered him; for he could but gape at his other self in this other anguish, gape as a proof that *he*, standing there for the achieved, the enjoyed, the triumphant life, couldn't be faced in his triumph. Wasn't the proof in the splendid covering hands, strong and completely spread?—so spread and so intentional that, in spite of a special verity that surpassed every other, the fact that one of these hands had lost two fingers, which were reduced to stumps, as if accidentally shot away, the face was effectually guarded and saved.

"Saved," though, *would* it be?—Brydon breathed his wonder till the very impunity of his attitude and the very insistence of his eyes produced, as he felt, a sudden stir which showed the next instant as a deeper portent, while the head raised itself, the betrayal of a braver purpose. The hands, as he looked, began to move, to open; then, as if deciding in a flash, dropped from the face and left it uncovered and presented. Horror, with the sight, had leaped into Brydon's throat, gasping there in a sound he couldn't utter; for the bared identity was too hideous as *his*, and his glare was the passion of his protest. The face, *that* face, Spencer Brydon's?—he searched it still, but looking away from it in dismay and denial, falling straight from his height of sublimity. It was unknown, inconceivable, awful, disconnected from any possibility—! He had been "sold," he inwardly moaned, stalking such game as this: the presence before him was a presence, the horror within him a horror, but the waste of his nights had been only grotesque and the success of his adventure an irony. Such an identity fitted his at *no* point, made its alternative monstrous. A thousand times yes, as it came upon him nearer now—the face was the face of a stranger. It came upon him nearer now, quite as one of those expanding fantastic images projected by the magic lantern of childhood; for the stranger, whoever he might be, evil, odious, blatant, vulgar, had advanced as for aggression, and he knew himself give ground. Then harder pressed still, sick with the force of his shock, and falling back as under the hot breath and the roused passion of a life larger than his own, a rage of personality before which his own collapsed, he felt the whole vision turn to darkness and his very feet give way. His head went round; he was going; he had gone.

III

What had next brought him back, clearly—though after how long?—was Mrs. Muldoon's voice, coming to him from quite near, from so near that he seemed presently to see her as kneeling on the ground before him while he lay looking up at her; himself not wholly on the ground, but half-raised and upheld—conscious, yes, of tenderness of support and, more particularly, of a head pillowed in extraordinary softness and faintly refreshing fragrance. He considered, he wondered, his wit but half at his service; then another face intervened, bending more directly over him, and he finally knew that Alice Staverton had made her lap an ample and perfect cushion to him, and that she had to this end seated herself on the lowest degree of the staircase, the rest of his long person remaining stretched on his old black-and-white slabs. They were cold, these marble squares of his youth; but *he* somehow was not, in this rich return of consciousness—the most wonderful hour, little by little, that he had ever known, leaving him, as it did, so gratefully, so abysmally passive, and yet as with a treasure of intelligence waiting all around him for quiet appropriation; dissolved, he might call it, in the air of the place and producing the golden glow of a late autumn afternoon. He had come back, yes—come back from further away than any man but himself had ever travelled; but it was strange how with this sense what he had come back *to* seemed really the great thing, and as if his prodigious journey had been all for the sake of it. Slowly but surely his consciousness grew, his vision of his state thus completing itself: he had been miraculously *carried* back—lifted and carefully borne as from where he had been picked up, the uttermost end of an interminable grey passage. Even with this he was suffered to rest, and what had now brought him to knowledge was the break in the long mild motion.

It had brought him to knowledge, to knowledge—yes, this was the beauty of his state; which came to resemble more and more that of a man who has gone to sleep on some news of a great inheritance, and then, after dreaming it away, after profaning it with matters strange to it, has waked up again to serenity of certitude and has only to lie and watch it grow. This was the drift of his patience—that he had only to let it shine on him. He must moreover, with intermissions, still have been lifted and borne; since why and how else should he have known himself, later on, with the afternoon glow intenser, no longer at the foot of his stairs—situated as these now seemed at that dark other end of his tunnel—but on a deep window-bench of his high saloon, over which had been spread, couch-fashion, a mantle of soft stuff lined with grey fur that was familiar to his eyes and that one of his hands kept fondly feeling as for its pledge of truth. Mrs. Muldoon's face had gone, but the other, the second he had recognised, hung over him in a way that showed how he was still propped and pillowed. He took it all in, and the more he took it the more it seemed to suffice: he was as much at peace as if he had had food and drink. It was the two women who had found him, on Mrs. Muldoon's having plied, at her usual hour, her latch-key—and on her having above all arrived while Miss Staverton still lingered near the house. She had been turning away, all anxiety, from worrying the vain bell-handle—her calculation having been of the hour of the good woman's visit; but the latter, blessedly, had come up while she was still there, and they had entered together. He had then lain, beyond the vestibule, very much as he was lying now—quite, that is, as he appeared to have fallen, but all so wondrously without bruise or gash; only in a depth of stupor. What he most took in, however, at present, with the steadier clearance, was that Alice Staverton had for a long unspeakable moment not doubted he was dead.

"It must have been that I *was*." He made it out as she held him. "Yes—I can only have died. You brought me literally to life. Only," he wondered, his eyes rising to her, "only, in the name of all the benedictions, how?"

It took her but an instant to bend her face and kiss him, and something in the manner of it, and in the way her hands clasped and locked his head while he felt the cool charity and virtue of her lips, something in all this beatitude somehow answered everything. "And now I keep you," she said.

"Oh keep me, keep me!" he pleaded while her face still hung over him: in response to which it dropped again and stayed close, clingingly close. It was the seal of their situation—of which he tasted the impress for a long blissful moment in silence. But he came back. "Yet how did you know—?"

"I was uneasy. You were to have come, you remember—and you had sent no word."

"Yes, I remember—I was to have gone to you at one today." It caught on to their "old" life and relation—which were so near and so far. "I was still out there in my strange darkness—where was it, what was it? I must have stayed there so long." He could but wonder at the depth and the duration of his swoon.

"Since last night?" she asked with a shade of fear for her possible indiscretion.

"Since this morning—it must have been: the cold dim dawn of

today. Where have I been," he vaguely wailed, "where have I been?" He felt her hold him close, and it was as if this helped him now to make in all security his mild moan. "What a long dark day!"

All in her tenderness she had waited a moment. "In the cold dim dawn?" she quavered.

But he had already gone on piecing together the parts of the whole prodigy. "As I didn't turn up you came straight—?"

She barely cast about. "I went first to your hotel—where they told me of your absence. You had dined out last evening and hadn't been back since. But they appeared to know you had been at your club."

"So you had the idea of *this*—?"

"Of what?" she asked in a moment.

"Well—of what has happened."

"I believed at least you'd have been here. I've known, all along," she said, "that you've been coming."

" 'Known' it—?"

"Well, I've believed it. I said nothing to you after that talk we had a month ago—but I felt sure. I knew you *would*," she declared.

"That I'd persist, you mean?"

"That you'd see him."

"Ah but I didn't!" cried Brydon with his long wail. "There's somebody—an awful beast; whom I brought, too horribly, to bay. But it's not me."

At this she bent over him again, and her eyes were in his eyes. "No—it's not you." And it was as if, while her face hovered, he might have made out in it, hadn't it been so near, some particular meaning blurred by a smile. "No, thank heaven," she repeated—"it's not you! Of course it wasn't to have been."

"Ah but it *was*," he gently insisted. And he stared before him now as he had been staring for so many weeks. "I was to have known myself."

"You couldn't!" she returned consolingly. And then reverting, and as if to account further for what she had herself done, "But it wasn't only *that*, that you hadn't been at home," she went on. "I waited till the hour at which we had found Mrs. Muldoon that day of my going with you; and she arrived, as I've told you, while, failing to bring any one to the door, I lingered in my despair on the steps. After a little, if she hadn't come, by such a mercy, I should have found means to hunt her up. But it wasn't," said Alice Staverton, as if once more with her fine intention—"it wasn't only that."

His eyes, as he lay, turned back to her. "What more then?"

She met it, the wonder she had stirred. "In the cold dim dawn, you say? Well, in the cold dim dawn of this morning I too saw you."

"Saw *me*—?"

"Saw *him*," said Alice Staverton. "It must have been at the same moment."

He lay an instant taking it in—as if he wished to be quite reasonable. "At the same moment?"

"Yes—in my dream again, the same one I've named to you. He came back to me. Then I knew it for a sign. He had come to you."

At this Brydon raised himself; he had to see her better. She helped him when she understood his movement, and he sat up, steadying himself beside her there on the window-bench and with his right hand grasping her left. "*He* didn't come to me."

"You came to yourself," she beautifully smiled.

"Ah I've come to myself now—thanks to you, dearest. But this brute, with his awful face—this brute's a black stranger. He's none of *me*, even as I *might* have been," Brydon sturdily declared.

But she kept the clearness that was like the breath of infallibility. "Isn't the whold point that you'd have been different?"

He almost scowled for it. "As different as *that*—?"

Her look again was more beautiful to him than the things of this world. "Haven't you exactly wanted to know *how* different? So this morning," she said, "you appeared to me."

"Like *him*?"

"The black stranger!"

"Then how did you know it was I?"

"Because, as I told you weeks ago, my mind, my imagination, had worked so over what you might, what you mightn't have been—to show you, you see, how I've thought of you. In the midst of that you came to me—that my wonder might be answered. So I knew," she went on; "and believed that, since the question held you too so fast, as you told me that day, you too would see for yourself. And when this morning I again saw I knew it would be because you had—and also then, from the first moment, because you somehow wanted me. *He* seemed to tell me of that. So why," she strangely smiled, "shouldn't I like him?"

It brought Spencer Brydon to his feet. "You 'like' that horror—?"

"I *could* have liked him. And to me," she said, "he was no horror. I had accepted him."

" 'Accepted'—?" Brydon oddly sounded.

"Before, for the interest of his difference—yes. And as *I* didn't disown him, as *I* knew him—which you at last, confronted with him in his difference, so cruelly didn't, my dear—well, he must have been, you see, less dreadful to me. And it may have pleased him that I pitied him."

She was beside him on her feet, but still holding his hand—still with her arm supporting him. But though it all brought for him thus a dim light, "You 'pitied' him?" he grudgingly, resentfully asked.

"He has been unhappy; he has been ravaged," she said.

"And haven't I been unhappy? Am not I—you've only to look at me!—ravaged?"

"Ah I don't say I like him *better*," she granted after a thought. "But he's grim, he's worn—and things have happened to him. He doesn't make shift, for sight, with your charming monocle."

"No"—it struck Brydon: "I couldn't have sported mine 'down-town.' They'd have guyed[8] me there."

"His great convex pince-nez—I saw it, I recognised the kind—is for his poor ruined sight. And his poor right hand—!"

"Ah!" Brydon winced—whether for his proved identity or for his lost fingers. Then, "He has a million a year," he lucidly added. "But he hadn't you."

"And he isn't—no, he isn't—*you!*" she murmured as he drew her to his breast.

---

1. What is Brydon's response to the changes he finds when he returns to New York?
2. How does Miss Staverton whet his curiosity about what he would have been if he had not gone to live abroad?
3. Does the identity of the ghost set this apart from most ghost stories?
4. What is the best explanation you can give for the fact that Brydon's ghost finally turns at bay to confront him?
5. What is the final relationship between Brydon and his "other self"—the man he might have been? How does Miss Staverton help resolve the conflict?

8. Made fun of.

James Joyce

Joyce (1882–1941) was born in Dublin, and though he fled the narrowness of Catholic Ireland for the broader cultural horizons of Europe, the Dublin of his experience and imagination was the setting for all his major work. In 1904 he went to live permanently on the Continent, supporting himself—badly—by teaching in language schools in Trieste and Zurich. The fear of censorship, coupled with the timidity of his publisher, delayed until 1914 the publication of his short stories in Dubliners. *Soon after this, however, Joyce came to the attention of the energetic American poet Ezra Pound, who arranged for the first publication of* A Portrait of the Artist as a Young Man *(1916), Joyce's semiautobiographical novel. Pound's support continued through the following years while Joyce was writing what is generally acknowledged as his masterpiece, the novel* Ulysses *(1922). When parts of it began to appear in a literary magazine, it touched off a storm of controversy that brought him both notoriety and lasting fame. On the one hand, this work experimented more boldly with language and devices of narration, including use of the stream of consciousness, than any work in English which preceded it. On the other, some of the sexual passages were so candid that censors banned it from the United States until 1933. Joyce continued to explore the resources of language in his years of fame, these experiments reaching their height in* Finnegans Wake *(1939).*

Araby

North Richmond Street, being blind, was a quiet street except at the hour when the Christian Brothers' School set the boys free. An uninhabited house of two storeys stood at the blind end, detached from its neighbours in a square ground. The other houses of the street, conscious of decent lives within them, gazed at one another with brown imperturbable faces.

The former tenant of our house, a priest, had died in the back drawing-room. Air, musty from having been long enclosed, hung in all the rooms, and the waste room behind the kitchen was littered with old useless papers. Among these I found a few paper-covered books, the pages of which were curled and damp: *The Abbot*, by Walter Scott,

The Devout Communicant and *The Memoirs of Vidocq*.[1] I liked the last best because its leaves were yellow. The wild garden behind the house contained a central apple tree and a few straggling bushes, under one of which I found the late tenant's rusty bicycle-pump. He had been a very charitable priest; in his will he had left all his money to institutions and the furniture of his house to his sister.

When the short days of winter came, dusk fell before we had well eaten our dinners. When we met in the street the houses had grown sombre. The space of sky above us was the colour of ever-changing violet and towards it the lamps of the street lifted their feeble lanterns. The cold air stung us and we played till our bodies glowed. Our shouts echoed in the silent street. The career of our play brought us through the dark muddy lanes behind the houses, where we ran the gauntlet of the rough tribes from the cottages, to the back doors of the dark dripping gardens where odours arose from the ashpits, to the dark odorous stables where a coachman smoothed and combed the horse or shook music from the buckled harness. When we returned to the street, light from the kitchen windows had filled the areas. If my uncle was seen turning the corner, we hid in the shadow until we had seen him safely housed. Or if Mangan's sister came out on the doorstep to call her brother in to his tea, we watched her from our shadow peer up and down the street. We waited to see whether she would remain or go in and, if she remained, we left our shadow and walked up to Mangan's steps resignedly. She was waiting for us, her figure defined by the light from the half-opened door. Her brother always teased her before he obeyed, and I stood by the railings looking at her. Her dress swung as she moved her body, and the soft rope of her hair tossed from side to side.

Every morning I lay on the floor in the front parlour watching her door. The blind was pulled down to within an inch of the sash so that I could not be seen. When she came out on the doorstep my heart leaped. I ran to the hall, seized my books and followed her. I kept her brown figure always in my eye and, when we came near the point at which our ways diverged, I quickened my pace and passed her. This happened morning after morning. I had never spoken to her, except for a few casual words, and yet her name was like a summons to all my foolish blood.

Her image accompanied me even in places the most hostile to romance. On Saturday evenings when my aunt went marketing I had to go to carry some of the parcels. We walked through the flaring streets,

1. French police agent, soldier of fortune, and writer (1775–1857); Scott (1771–1832) was an English Romantic novelist; *The Devout Communicant* is a variant title for *Pious Meditations* (pub. 1813), a straightforward religious tract written by the Franciscan friar Pacificus Baker.

jostled by drunken men and bargaining women, amid the curses of labourers, the shrill litanies of shop-boys who stood on guard by the barrels of pigs' cheeks, the nasal chanting of street-singers, who sang a *come-all-you*[2] about O'Donovan Rossa, or a ballad about the troubles in our native land. These noises converged in a single sensation of life for me: I imagined that I bore my chalice safely through a throng of foes. Her name sprang to my lips at moments in strange prayers and praises which I myself did not understand. My eyes were often full of tears (I could not tell why) and at times a flood from my heart seemed to pour itself out into my bosom. I thought little of the future. I did not know whether I would ever speak to her or not or, if I spoke to her, how I would tell her of my confused adoration. But my body was like a harp and her words and gestures were like fingers running upon the wires.

One evening I went into the back drawing-room in which the priest had died. It was a dark rainy evening and there was no sound in the house. Through one of the broken panes I heard the rain impinge upon the earth, the fine incessant needles of water playing in the sodden beds. Some distant lamp or lighted window gleamed below me. I was thankful that I could see so little. All my senses seemed to desire to veil themselves and, feeling that I was about to slip from them, I presed the palms of my hands together until they trembled, murmuring: *"O love! O love!"* many times.

At last she spoke to me. When she addressed the first words to me I was so confused that I did not know what to answer. She asked me was I going to *Araby*.[3] I forgot whether I answered yes or no. It would be a splendid bazaar, she said she would love to go.

"And why can't you?" I asked.

While she spoke she turned a silver bracelet round and round her wrist. She could not go, she said, because there would be a retreat that week in her convent.[4] Her brother and two other boys were fighting for their caps and I was alone at the railings. She held one of the spikes, bowing her head towards me. The light from the lamp opposite our door caught the white curve of her neck, lit up her hair that rested there and, falling, lit up the hand upon the railing. It fell over one side of her dress and caught the white border of a petticoat, just visible as she stood at ease.

"It's well for you," she said.

2. Any popular song beginning "Come all you Irishmen . . ."; O'Donovan Rossa ("Dynamite Rossa") was Jeremiah O'Donovan (1831–1915), an Irish nationalist banished to the United States in 1870 for revolutionary activities. 3. A billboard sign of the time actually reads: "ARABY in DUBLIN Official Catalogue GRAND ORIENTAL FÊTE May 14th to 19th in aid of Jervis St. Hospital. Admission one shilling." 4. I.e., a gathering for prayer and meditation in her convent school.

"If I go," I said. "I will bring you something."

What innumerable follies laid waste my waking and sleeping thoughts after that evening! I wished to annihilate the tedious intervening days. I chafed against the work of school. At night in my bedroom and by day in the classroom her image came between me and the page I strove to read. The syllables of the word *Araby* were called to me through the silence in which my soul luxuriated and cast an Eastern enchantment over me. I asked for leave to go to the bazaar on Saturday night. My aunt was surprised and hoped it was not some Freemason affair.[5] I answered few questions in class. I watched my master's face pass from amiability to sternness; he hoped I was not beginning to idle. I could not call my wandering thoughts together. I had hardly any patience with the serious work of life which, now that it stood between me and my desire, seemed to me child's play, ugly monotonous child's play.

On Saturday morning I reminded my uncle that I wished to go to the bazaar in the evening. He was fussing at the hallstand, looking for the hat-brush, and answered me curtly:

"Yes, boy, I know."

As he was in the hall I could not go into the front parlour and lie at the window. I left the house in bad humour and walked slowly towards the school. The air was pitilessly raw and already my heart misgave me.

When I came home to dinner my uncle had not yet been home. Still it was early. I sat staring at the clock for some time and, when its ticking began to irritate me, I left the room. I mounted the staircase and gained the upper part of the house. The high, cold, empty, gloomy rooms liberated me and I went from room to room singing. From the front window I saw my companions playing below in the street. Their cries reached me weakened and indistinct and, leaning my forehead against the cool glass, I looked over at the dark house where she lived. I may have stood there for an hour, seeing nothing but a brown-clad figure cast by my imagination, touched discreetly by the lamplight at the curved neck, at the hand upon the railings and at the border below the dress.

When I came downstairs again I found Mrs Mercer sitting at the fire. She was an old, garrulous woman, a pawnbroker's widow, who collected used stamps for some pious purpose. I had to endure the gossip of the tea-table. The meal was prolonged beyond an hour and still my uncle did not come. Mrs Mercer stood up to go: she was sorry she couldn't wait any longer, but it was after eight o'clock and she did

5. The Masonic Order was felt by Catholics to be an enemy of the Church.

not like to be out late, as the night air was bad for her. When she had gone I began to walk up and down the room, clenching my fists. My aunt said:

"I'm afraid you may put off your bazaar for this night of Our Lord."

At nine o'clock I heard my uncle's latchkey in the hall door. I heard him talking to himself and heard the hallstand rocking when it had received the weight of his overcoat. I could interpret these signs. When he was midway through his dinner I asked him to give me the money to go to the bazaar. He had forgotten.

"The people are in bed and after their first sleep now," he said.

I did not smile. My aunt said to him energetically:

"Can't you give him the money and let him go? You've kept him late enough as it is."

My uncle said he was very sorry he had forgotten. He said he believed in the old saying: "All work and no play makes Jack a dull boy." He asked me where I was going and, when I had told him a second time, he asked me did I know *The Arab's Farewell to his Steed.*[6] When I left the kitchen he was about to recite the opening lines of the piece to my aunt.

I held a florin tightly in my hand as I strode down Buckingham Street towards the station. The sight of the streets thronged with buyers and glaring with gas recalled to me the purpose of my journey. I took my seat in a third-class carriage of a deserted train. After an intolerable delay the train moved out of the station slowly. It crept onward among ruinous houses and over the twinkling river. At Westland Row Station a crowd of people pressed to the carriage doors; but the porters moved them back, saying that it was a special train for the bazaar. I remained alone in the bare carriage. In a few minutes the train drew up beside an improvised wooden platform. I passed out on to the road and saw by the lighted dial of a clock that it was ten minutes to ten. In front of me was a large building which displayed the magical name.

I could not find any sixpenny entrance and, fearing that the bazaar would be closed, I passed in quickly through a turnstile, handing a shilling to a weary-looking man. I found myself in a big hall girdled at half its height by a gallery. Nearly all the stalls were closed and the greater part of the hall was in darkness. I recognized a silence like that which pervades a church after a service. I walked into the centre of the bazaar timidly. A few people were gathered about the stalls which were still open. Before a curtain, over which the words *Café Chantant*[7] were written in coloured lamps, two men were counting money on a salver. I listened to the fall of the coins.

6. Sentimental poem by Caroline Norton (1808–1877). The Arab imagines his heartbreak after selling his favorite horse. 7. Café offering musical entertainment.

Remembering with difficulty why I had come I went over to one of the stalls and examined porcelain vases and flowered tea-sets. At the door of the stall a young lady was talking and laughing with two young gentlemen. I remarked their English accents and listened vaguely to their conversation.

"O, I never said such a thing?"

"O, but you did!"

"O, but I didn't!"

"Didn't she say that?"

"Yes. I heard her."

"O, there's a . . . fib!"

Observing me, the young lady came over and asked me did I wish to buy anything. The tone of her voice was not encouraging; she seemed to have spoken to me out of a sense of duty. I looked humbly at the great jars that stood like eastern guards at either side of the dark entrance to the stall and murmured:

"No, thank you."

The young lady changed the position of one of the vases and went back to the two young men. They began to talk of the same subject. Once or twice the young lady glanced at me over her shoulder.

I lingered before her stall, though I knew my stay was useless, to make my interest in her wares seem the more real. Then I turned away slowly and walked down the middle of the bazaar. I allowed the two pennies to fall against the sixpence in my pocket. I heard a voice call from one end of the gallery that the light was out. The upper part of the hall was now completely dark.

Gazing up into the darkness I saw myself as a creature driven and derided by vanity; and my eyes burned with anguish and anger.

---

1. What are the chief qualities of the narrator's character? How are these emphasized by the feelings and behavior directed toward Mangan's sister?
2. What is the tone of the story and how is it affected by the narrator's language?
3. Discuss the importance of the setting.
4. Interpret the clause "I imagined that I bore my chalice safely through a throng of foes."
5. What is the character of the uncle, and how does he affect the boy's wishes and feelings?
6. Is anything gained by the narrator through his frustration and humiliation?

A Little Cloud

Eight years before he had seen his friend off at the North Wall[1] and wished him God-speed. Gallaher had got on. You could tell that at once by his travelled air, his well-cut tweed suit, and fearless accent. Few fellows had talents like his, and fewer still could remain unspoiled by such success. Gallaher's heart was in the right place and he had deserved to win. It was something to have a friend like that.

Little Chandler's thoughts ever since lunch-time had been of his meeting with Gallaher, of Gallaher's invitation, and of the great city London where Gallaher lived. He was called Little Chandler because, though he was but slightly under the average stature, he gave one the idea of being a little man. His hands were white and small, his frame was fragile, his voice was quiet and his manners were refined. He took the greatest care of his fair silken hair and moustache, and used perfume discreetly on his handkerchief. The half-moons of his nails were perfect, and when he smiled you caught a glimpse of a row of childish white teeth.

As he sat at his desk in the King's Inns[2] he thought what changes those eight years had brought. The friend whom he had known under a shabby and necessitous guise had become a brilliant figure on the London Press. He turned often from his tiresome writing to gaze out of the office window. The glow of a late autumn sunset covered the grass plots and walks. It cast a shower of kindly golden dust on the untidy nurses and decrepit old men who drowsed on the benches; it flickered upon all the moving figures—on the children who ran screaming along the gravel paths and on everyone who passed through the gardens. He watched the scene and thought of life; and (as always happened when he thought of life) he became sad. A gentle melancholy took possession of him. He felt how useless it was to struggle against fortune, this being the burden of wisdom which the ages had bequeathed to him.

He remembered the books of poetry upon his shelves at home. He had bought them in his bachelor days and many an evening, as he sat in the little room off the hall, he had been tempted to take one down from the bookshelf and read out something to his wife. But shyness had always held him back; and so the books had remained on their shelves. At times he repeated lines to himself and this consoled him.

1. Cluster of docks and railway stations in Dublin.
2. Offices and residences for lawyers comparable to London's Inns of Court.

When his hour had struck he stood up and took leave of his desk and of his fellow-clerks punctiliously. He emerged from under the feudal arch of the King's Inns, a neat modest figure, and walked swiftly down Henrietta Street. The golden sunset was waning and the air had grown sharp. A horde of grimy children populated the street. They stood or ran in the roadway, or crawled up the steps before the gaping doors, or squatted like mice upon the thresholds. Little Chandler gave them no thought. He picked his way deftly through all that minute vermin-like life and under the shadow of the gaunt spectral mansions in which the old nobility of Dublin had roystered. No memory of the past touched him, for his mind was full of a present joy.

He had never been in Corless's, but he knew the value of the name. He knew that people went there after the theatre to eat oysters and drink liqueurs; and he had heard that the waiters there spoke French and German. Walking swiftly by at night he had seen cabs drawn up before the door and richly-dressed ladies, escorted by cavaliers, alight and enter quickly. They wore noisy dresses and many wraps. Their faces were powdered and they caught up their dresses, when they touched earth, like alarmed Atalantas.[3] He had always passed without turning his head to look. It was his habit to walk swiftly in the street even by day, and whenever he found himself in the city late at night he hurried on his way apprehensively and excitedly. Sometimes, however, he courted the causes of his fear. He chose the darkest and narrowest streets and, as he walked boldly forward, the silence that was spread about his footsteps troubled him, the wandering, silent figures troubled him; and at times a sound of low fugitive laughter made him tremble like a leaf.

He turned to the right towards Capel Street. Ignatius Gallaher on the London Press! Who would have thought it possible eight years before? Still, now that he reviewed the past, Little Chandler could remember many signs of future greatness in his friend. People used to say that Ignatius Gallaher was wild. Of course, he did mix with a rakish set of fellows at that time; drank freely and borrowed money on all sides. In the end he had got mixed up in some shady affair, some money transaction: at least, that was one version of his flight. But nobody denied him talent. There was always a certain . . . something in Ignatius Gallaher that impressed you in spite of yourself. Even when he was out at elbows and at his wits' end for money he kept up a bold face. Little Chandler remembered (and the remembrance brought a slight flush of pride to his cheek) one of Ignatius Gallaher's sayings when he was in a tight corner:

3. Atalanta was a virgin huntress of classic mythology, who promised to marry the first man who could beat her in a foot race.

"Half-time now, boys," he used to say light-heartedly. "Where's my considering cap?"

That was Ignatius Gallaher all out; and, damn it, you couldn't but admire him for it.

Little Chandler quickened his pace. For the first time in his life he felt himself superior to the people he passed. For the first time his soul revolted against the dull inelegance of Capel Street. There was no doubt about it: if you wanted to succeed you had to go away. You could do nothing in Dublin. As he crossed Grattan Bridge he looked down the river towards the lower quays and pitied the poor stunted houses. They seemed to him a band of tramps, huddled together along the river-banks, their old coats covered with dust and soot, stupefied by the panorama of sunset and waiting for the first chill of night to bid them arise, shake themselves and begone. He wondered whether he could write a poem to express his idea. Perhaps Gallaher might be able to get it into some London paper for him. Could he write something original? He was not sure what idea he wished to express, but the thought that a poetic moment had touched him took life within him like an infant hope. He stepped onwards bravely.

Every step brought him nearer to London, further from his own sober inartistic life. A light began to tremble on the horizon of his mind. He was not so old—thirty-two. His temperament might be said to be just at the point of maturity. There were so many different moods and impressions that he wished to express in verse. He felt them within him. He tried to weigh his soul to see if it was a poet's soul. Melancholy was the dominant note of his temperament, he thought, but it was a melancholy tempered by recurrences of faith and resignation and simple joy. If he could give expression to it in a book of poems perhaps men would listen. He would never be popular: he saw that. He could not sway the crowd, but he might appeal to a little circle of kindred minds. The English critics, perhaps, would recognize him as one of the Celtic school[4] by reason of the melancholy tone of his poems; besides that, he would put in allusions. He began to invent sentences and phrases from the notice which his book would get. "*Mr Chandler has the gift of easy and graceful verse*" . . . "*A wistful sadness pervades these poems*" . . . "*The Celtic note.*" It was a pity his name was not more Irish-looking. Perhaps it would be better to insert his mother's name before the surname: Thomas Malone Chandler, or better still: T. Malone Chandler. He would speak to Gallaher about it.

He pursued his reverie so ardently that he passed his street and had to turn back. As he came near Corless's his former agitation began

4. Term applied by critics to Irish poets of the turn of the century who drew on Irish legend for their subject matter.

to overmaster him and he halted before the door in indecision. Finally he opened the door and entered.

The light and noise of the bar held him at the doorways for a few moments. He looked about him, but his sight was confused by the shining of many red and green wine-glasses. The bar seemed to him to be full of people and he felt that the people were observing him curiously. He glanced quickly to right and left (frowning slightly to make his errand appear serious), but when his sight cleared a little he saw that nobody had turned to look at him: and there, sure enough, was Ignatius Gallaher leaning with his back against the counter and his feet planted far apart.

"Hallo, Tommy, old hero, here you are! What is it to be! What will you have? I'm taking whisky: better stuff than we get across the water. Soda? Lithia?[5] No mineral? I'm the same. Spoils the flavour . . . Here, *garçon*,[6] bring us two halves of malt whisky, like a good fellow . . . Well, and how have you been pulling along since I saw you last? Dear God, how old we're getting! Do you see any signs of ageing in me—eh, what? A little grey and thin on the top—what?"

Ignatius Gallaher took off his hat and displayed a large closely cropped head. His face was heavy, pale and clean-shaven. His eyes, which were of bluish slate-colour, relieved his unhealthy pallor and shone out plainly above the vivid orange tie[7] he wore. Between these rival features the lips appeared very long and shapeless and colourless. He bent his head and felt with two sympathetic fingers the thin hair at the crown. Little Chandler shook his head as a denial. Ignatius Gallaher put on his hat again.

"It pulls you down," he said. "Press life. Always hurry and scurry, looking for copy and sometimes not finding it: and then, always to have something new in your stuff. Damn proofs and printers, I say, for a few days. I'm deuced glad, I can tell you, to get back to the old country. Does a fellow good, a bit of a holiday. I feel a ton better since I landed again in dear, dirty Dublin . . . Here you are, Tommy. Water? Say when."

Little Chandler allowed his whisky to be very much diluted.

"You don't know what's good for you, my boy," said Ignatius Gallaher. "I drink mine neat."

"I drink very little as a rule," said Little Chandler modestly. "An odd half-one or so when I meet any of the old crowd: that's all."

"Ah, well," said Ignatius Gallaher, cheerfully, "here's to us and to old times and old acquaintance."

They clinked glasses and drank the toast.

5. Mineral water. 6. Waiter. 7. Wearing an orange tie, Gallagher seems to be flaunting his allegiance to England. Orangemen (called after William of Orange, last British conqueror of Ireland) were supporters of Anglo-Irish Protestantism.

"I met some of the old gang today," said Ignatius Gallaher. "O'Hara seems to be in a bad way. What's he doing?"

"Nothing," said Little Chandler. "He's gone to the dogs."

"But Hogan has a good sit,[8] hasn't he?"

"Yes; he's in the Land Commission."

"I met him one night in London and he seemed to be very flush . . . . Poor O'Hara! Booze, I suppose?"

"Other things, too," said Little Chandler shortly.

Ignatius Gallaher laughed.

"Tommy," he said, "I see you haven't changed an atom. You're the very same serious person that used to lecture me on Sunday mornings when I had a sore head and a fur on my tongue. You'd want to knock about a bit in the world. Have you never been anywhere even for a trip?"

"I've been to the Isle of Man,"[9] said Little Chandler.

Ignatius Gallaher laughed.

"The Isle of Man!" he said. "Go to London or Paris: Paris, for choice. That'd do you good."

"Have you seen Paris?"

"I should think I have! I've knocked about there a little."

"And is it really so beautiful as they say?" asked Little Chandler.

He sipped a little of his drink while Ignatius Gallaher finished his boldly.

"Beautiful?" said Ignatius Gallaher, pausing on the word and on the flavour of his drink. "It's not so beautiful, you know. Of course, it is beautiful . . . But it's the life of Paris; that's the thing. Ah, there's no city like Paris for gaiety, movement, excitement . . ."

Little Chandler finished his whisky and, after some trouble, succeeded in catching the barman's eye. He ordered the same again.

I've been to the Moulin Rouge,"[1] Ignatius Gallaher continued when the barman had removed their glasses, "and I've been to all the Bohemian cafés. Hot stuff! Not for a pious chap like you, Tommy."

Little Chandler said nothing until the barman returned with two glasses: then he touched his friend's glass lightly and reciprocated the former toast. He was beginning to feel somewhat disillusioned. Gallaher's accent and way of expressing himself did not please him. There was something vulgar in his friend which he had not observed before. But perhaps it was only the result of living in London amid the bustle and competition of the Press. The old personal charm was still there under this new gaudy manner. And, after all, Gallaher had lived, he had seen the world. Little Chandler looked at his friend enviously.

8. Situation. 9. In the Irish Sea, not far from Dublin. 1. Red Mill—a famous Parisian dance hall.

"Everything in Paris is gay," said Ignatius Gallaher. "They believe in enjoying life—and don't you think they're right? If you want to enjoy yourself properly you must go to Paris. And, mind you, they've a great feeling for the Irish there. When they heard I was from Ireland they were ready to eat me, man."

Little Chandler took four or five sips from his glass.

"Tell me," he said, "is it true that Paris is so . . . immoral as they say?"

Ignatius Gallaher made a catholic gesture with his right arm.

"Every place is immoral," he said. "Of course you do find spicy bits in Paris. Go to one of the students' balls, for instance. That's lively, if you like, when the *cocottes*[2] begin to let themselves loose. You know what they are, I suppose?"

"I've heard of them," said Little Chandler.

Ignatius Gallaher drank off his whisky and shook his head.

"Ah," he said, "you may say what you like. There's no woman like the Parisienne—for style, for go."

"Then it is an immoral city," said Little Chandler, with timid insistence—"I mean, compared with London or Dublin?"

"London!" said Ignatius Gallaher. "It's six of one and half a dozen of the other. You ask Hogan, my boy. I showed him a bit about London when he was over there. He'd open your eye . . . I say, Tommy, don't make punch of that whisky: liquor up."

"No, really . . ."

"O come on, another one won't do you any harm. What is it? The same again, I suppose?"

"Well . . . all right."

"*François*, the same again . . . Will you smoke, Tommy?"

Ignatius Gallaher produced his cigar-case. The two friends lit their cigars and puffed at them in silence until their drinks were served.

"I'll tell you my opinion," said Ignatius Gallaher, emerging after some time from the clouds of smoke in which he had taken refuge, "it's a rum world. Talk of immorality! I've heard of cases—what am I saying?—I've know them: cases of . . . immorality . . ."

Ignatius Gallaher puffed thoughtfully at his cigar and then, in a calm historian's tone, he proceeded to sketch for his friend some pictures of the corruption which was rife abroad. He summarized the vices of many capitals and seemed inclined to award the palm to Berlin. Some things he could not vouch for (his friends had told him), but of others he had had personal experience. He spared neither rank nor caste. He revealed many of the secrets of religious houses on the Continent and described some of the practices which were fashionable in

2. Prostitutes.

high society, and ended by telling, with details, a story about an English duchess—a story which he knew to be true. Little Chandler was astonished.

"Ah, well," said Ignatius Gallaher, "here we are in old jog-along Dublin where nothing is known of such things."

"How dull you must find it," said Little Chandler, "after all the other places you've seen!"

"Well," said Ignatius Gallaher, "it's a relaxation to come over here, you know. And, after all, it's the old country, as they say, isn't it? You can't help having a certain feeling for it. That's human nature . . . But tell me something about yourself. Hogan told me you had . . . tasted the joys of connubial bliss. Two years ago, wasn't it?"

Little Chandler blushed and smiled.

"Yes," he said. "I was married last May twelve months."

"I hope it's not too late in the day to offer my best wishes," said Ignatius Gallaher. "I didn't know your address or I'd have done so at the time."

He extended his hand, which Little Chandler took.

"Well, Tommy," he said, "I wish you and yours every joy in life, old chap, and tons of money, and may you never die till I shoot you. And that's the wish of a sincere friend, an old friend. You know that?"

"I know that," said Little Chandler.

"Any youngsters?" said Ignatius Gallaher.

Little Chandler blushed again.

"We have one child," he said.

"Son or daughter?"

"A little boy."

Ignatius Gallaher slapped his friend sonorously on the back.

"Bravo," he said, "I wouldn't doubt you, Tommy."

Little Chandler smiled, looked confusedly at his glass and bit his lower lip with three childishly white front teeth.

"I hope you'll spend an evening with us," he said, "before you go back. My wife will be delighted to meet you. We can have a little music and . . ."

"Thanks awfully, old chap," said Ignatius Gallaher, "I'm sorry we didn't meet earlier. But I must leave tomorrow night."

"Tonight, perhaps . . . ?"

"I'm awfully sorry, old man. You see I'm over here with another fellow, clever young chap he is too, and we arranged to go to a little card-party. Only for that . . ."

"O, in that case . . ."

"But who knows?" said Ignatius Gallaher considerately. "Next year I may take a little skip over here now that I've broken the ice. It's only a pleasure deferred."

"Very well," said Little Chandler, "the next time you come we must have an evening together. That's agreed now, isn't it?"

"Yes, that's agreed," said Ignatius Gallaher. "Next year if I come, *parole d'honneur*."[3]

"And to clinch the bargain," said Little Chandler, "we'll just have one more now."

Ignatius Gallaher took out a large gold watch and looked at it.

"Is it to be the last?" he said. "Because you know, I have an a.p."[4]

"O, yes, positively," said Little Chandler.

"Very well, then," said Ignatius Gallaher, "let us have another one as a *deoc an doruis*[5]—that's good vernacular for a small whisky, I believe."

Little Chandler ordered the drinks. The blush which had risen to his face a few moments before was establishing itself. A trifle made him blush at any time: and now he felt warm and excited. Three small whiskies had gone to his head and Gallaher's strong cigar had confused his mind, for he was a delicate and abstinent person. The adventure of meeting Gallaher after eight years, of finding himself with Gallaher in Corless's surrounded by lights and noise, of listening to Gallaher's stories and of sharing for a brief space Gallaher's vagrant and triumphant life, upset the equipoise of his sensitive nature. He felt acutely the contrast between his own life and his friend's, and it seemed to him unjust. Gallaher was his inferior in birth and education. He was sure that he could do something better than his friend had ever done, or could ever do, something higher than mere tawdry journalism if he only got the chance. What was it that stood in his way? His unfortunate timidity! He wished to vindicate himself in some way, to assert his manhood. He saw behind Gallaher's refusal of his invitation. Gallaher was only patronizing him by his friendliness just as he was patronizing Ireland by his visit.

The barman brought their drinks. Little Chandler pushed one glass towards his friend and took up the other boldly.

"Who knows?" he said, as they lifted their glasses. "When you come next year I may have the pleasure of wishing long life and happiness to Mr and Mrs Ignatius Gallaher."

Ignatius Gallaher in the act of drinking closed one eye expressively over the rim of his glass. When he had drunk, he smacked his lips decisively, set down his glass and said:

"No blooming fear of that, my boy. I'm going to have my fling first and see a bit of life and the world before I put my head in the sack—if I ever do."

"Some day you will," said Little Chandler calmly.

3. My word of honor. 4. Author's proof, i.e., trial printing which Gallaher as journalist would have to correct before sending it to press. 5. Literally "a door-drink," a drink as one departs.

Ignatius Gallaher turned his orange tie and slate-blue eyes full upon his friend.

"You think so?" he said.

"You'll put your head in the sack," repeated Little Chandler stoutly, "like everyone else if you can find the girl."

He had slightly emphasized his tone, and he was aware that he had betrayed himself; but, though the colour had heightened in his cheek, he did not flinch from his friend's gaze. Ignatius Gallaher watched him for a few moments and then said:

"If ever it occurs, you may bet your bottom dollar there'll be no mooning and spooning about it. I mean to marry money. She'll have a good fat account at the bank or she won't do for me."

Little Chandler shook his head.

"Why, man alive," said Ignatius Gallaher, vehemently, "do you know what it is? I've only to say the word and tomorrow I can have the woman and the cash. You don't believe it? Well, I know it. There are hundreds—what am I saying?—thousands of rich Germans and Jews, rotten with money, that'd only be too glad . . . You wait a while, my boy. See if I don't play my cards properly. When I go about a thing I mean business, I tell you. You just wait."

He tossed his glass to his mouth, finished his drink and laughed loudly. Then he looked thoughtfully before him and said in a calmer tone:

"But I'm in no hurry. They can wait. I don't fancy tying myself up to one woman, you know."

He imitated with his mouth the act of tasting and made a wry face.

"Must get a bit stale, I should think," he said.

Little Chandler sat in the room off the hall, holding a child in his arms. To save money they kept no servant, but Annie's young sister Monica came for an hour or so in the morning and an hour or so in the evening to help. But Monica had gone home long ago. It was a quarter to nine. Little Chandler had come home late for tea and, moreover, he had forgotten to bring Annie home the parcel of coffee from Bewley's. Of course she was in a bad humour and gave him short answers. She said she would do without any tea, but when it came near the time at which the shop at the corner closed she decided to go out herself for a quarter of a pound of tea and two pounds of sugar. She put the sleeping child deftly in his arms and said:

"Here. Don't waken him."

A little lamp with a white china shade stood upon the table and its light fell over a photograph which was enclosed in a frame of crumpled horn. It was Annie's photograph. Little Chandler looked at it, pausing at the thin tight lips. She wore the pale blue summer blouse which he had brought her home as a present one Saturday. It had cost him ten and elevenpence; but what an agony of nervousness it had cost him! How he had suffered that day, waiting at the shop door until the shop was empty, standing at the counter and trying to appear at his ease while the girl piled ladies' blouses before him, paying at the desk and forgetting to take up the odd penny of his change, being called back by the cashier, and finally, striving to hide his blushes as he left the shop by examining the parcel to see if it was securely tied. When he brought the blouse home Annie kissed him and said it was very pretty and stylish; but when she heard the price she threw the blouse on the table and said it was a regular swindle to charge ten and elevenpence for it. At first she wanted to take it back, but when she tried it on she was delighted with it, especially with the make of the sleeves, and kissed him and said he was very good to think of her.

Hm! . . .

He looked coldly into the eyes of the photograph and they answered coldly. Certainly they were pretty and the face itself was pretty. But he found something mean in it. Why was it so unconscious and ladylike? The composure of the eyes irritated him. They repelled him and defied him: there was no passion in them, no rapture. He thought of what Gallaher had said about rich Jewesses. Those dark Oriental eyes, he thought, how full they are of passion, of voluptuous longing! . . . Why had he married the eyes in the photograph?

He caught himself up at the question and glanced nervously round the room. He found something mean in the pretty furniture which he had bought for his house on the hire system.[6] Annie had chosen it herself and it reminded him of her. It too was prim and pretty. A dull resentment against his life awoke within him. Could he not escape from his little house? Was it too late for him to try to live bravely like Gallaher? Could he go to London? There was the furniture still to be paid for. If he could only write a book and get it published, that might open the way for him.

A volume of Byron's[7] poems lay before him on the table. He opened it cautiously with his left hand lest he should waken the child and began to read the first poem in the book:

> Hushed are the winds and still the evening gloom,
>   Not e'en a Zephyr wanders through the grove,
> Whilst I return to view my Margaret's tomb
>   And scatter flowers on the dust I love.

6. The installment plan. 7. George Gordon, Lord Byron (1788–1824), English Romantic poet. The stanza is from Byron's *On the Death of a Young Lady*.

He paused. He felt the rhythm of the verse about him in the room. How melancholy it was! Could he, too, write like that, express the melancholy of his soul in verse? There were so many things he wanted to describe: his sensation of a few hours before on Grattan Bridge, for example. If he could get back again into that mood . . .

The child awoke and began to cry. He turned from the page and tried to hush it: but it would not be hushed. He began to rock it to and fro in his arms, but its wailing cry grew keener. He rocked it faster while his eyes began to read the second stanza:

> Within this narrow cell reclines her clay,
> That clay where once . . .

It was useless. He couldn't read. He couldn't do anything. The wailing of the child pierced the drum of his ear. It was useless, useless! He was a prisoner for life. His arms trembled with anger and suddenly bending to the child's face he shouted:

"Stop!"

The child stopped for an instant, had a spasm of fright, and began to scream. He jumped up from his chair and walked hastily up and down the room with the child in his arms. It began to sob piteously, losing its breath for four or five seconds, and then bursting out anew. The thin walls of the room echoed the sound. He tried to soothe it, but it sobbed more convulsively. He looked at the contracted and quivering face of the child and began to be alarmed. He counted seven sobs without a break between them and caught the child to his breast in fright. If it died! . . .

The door was burst open and a young woman ran in, panting.

"What is it? What is it?" she cried.

The child, hearing its mother's voice, broke out into a paroxysm of sobbing.

"It's nothing, Annie . . . it's nothing . . . He began to cry . . ."

She flung her parcels on the floor and snatched the child from him.

"What have you done to him?" she cried, glaring into his face.

Little Chandler sustained for one moment the gaze of her eyes and his heart closed together as he met the hatred in them. He began to stammer:

"It's nothing . . . He . . . he began to cry . . . I couldn't . . . I didn't do anything . . . What?"

Giving no heed to him she began to walk up and down the room, clasping the child tightly in her arms and murmuring:

"My little man! My little mannie! Was 'ou frightened, love? . . .

There now, love! There now! . . . Lambabaun! Mamma's little lamb of the world! . . . There now!"

Little Chandler felt his cheeks suffused with shame and he stood back out of the lamplight. He listened while the paroxysm of the child's sobbing grew less and less; and tears of remorse started to his eyes.

---

1. What makes Little Chandler unable to use the fine potentials he feels within himself? Is he truly a better man than his friend Gallaher? How are Chandler's "poetic" sentiments related to his character and his predicament?
2. Do Chandler and Gallaher have the same attitude toward the "immorality" of English and European capitals? Why does Chandler raise the question of their immorality?
3. What does the story say about the provincialism of Dublin?
4. How does the episode with the baby shape the meaning of the story as a whole?
5. In the last paragraph Chandler feels "shame." For what? Has he fallen from his general state of melancholy into something worse?

The Dead

Lily, the caretaker's daughter, was literally run off her feet. Hardly had she brought one gentleman into the little pantry behind the office on the ground floor and helped him off with his overcoat, than the wheezy hall-door bell clanged again and she had to scamper along the bare hallway to let in another guest. It was well for her she had not to attend to the ladies also. But Miss Kate and Miss Julia had thought of that and had converted the bathroom upstairs into a ladies' dressing-room. Miss Kate and Miss Julia were there, gossiping and laughing and fussing, walking after each other to the head of the stairs, peering down over the banisters and calling down to Lily to ask her who had come.

It was always a great affair, the Misses Morkan's annual dance. Everybody who knew them came to it, members of the family, old friends of the family, the members of Julia's choir, any of Kate's pupils that were grown up enough, and even some of Mary Jane's pupils too. Never once had it fallen flat. For years and years it had gone off in splendid style, as long as anyone could remember; ever since Kate and Julia, after the death of their brother, Pat, had left the house in Stoney Batter and taken Mary Jane, their only niece, to live with them in the dark, gaunt house on Usher's Island, the upper part of which they had rented from Mr Fulham, the corn-factor[1] on the ground floor. That was a good thirty years ago if it was a day. Mary Jane, who was then a little girl in short clothes, was now the main prop of the household, for she had the organ in Haddington Road. She had been through the Academy[2] and gave a pupils' concert every year in the upper room of the Antient Concert Rooms. Many of her pupils belonged to the better-class families on the Kingstown and Dalkey line. Old as they were, her aunts also did their share. Julia, though she was quite grey, was still the leading soprano in Adam and Eve's,[3] and Kate, being too feeble to go about much, gave music lessons to beginners on the old square piano in the back room. Lily, the caretaker's daughter, did housemaid's work for them. Though their life was modest, they believed in eating well; the best of everything: diamond-bone sirloins, three-shilling tea and the best bottled stout. But Lily seldom made a mistake in the orders, so that she got on well with her three mistresses. They were fussy, that was all. But the only thing they would not stand was back answers.

Of course, they had good reason to be fussy on such a night. And then it was long after ten o'clock and yet there was no sign of Gabriel and his wife. Besides they were dreadfully afraid that Freddy Malins might turn up screwed.[4] They would not wish for worlds that any of Mary Jane's pupils should see him under the influence; and when he was like that it was sometimes very hard to manage him. Freddy Malins always came late, but they wondered what could be keeping Gabriel: and that was what brought them every two minutes to the banisters to ask Lily had Gabriel or Freddy come.

"O, Mr Conroy," said Lily to Gabriel when she opened the door for him, "Miss Kate and Miss Julia thought you were never coming. Good night, Mrs Conroy."

"I'll engage they did," said Gabriel, "but they forgot that my wife here takes three mortal hours to dress herself."

He stood on the mat, scraping the snow from his goloshes, while Lily led his wife to the foot of the stairs and called out:

"Miss Kate, here's Mrs Conroy."

Kate and Julia came toddling down the dark stairs at once. Both of them kissed Gabriel's wife, said she must be perished alive, and asked was Gabriel with her.

"Here I am as right as the mail, Aunt Kate! Go on up. I'll follow," called out Gabriel from the dark.

He continued scraping his feet vigorously while the three women went upstairs, laughing, to the ladies' dressing-room. A light fringe of

1. Agent or broker dealing in grain. 2. The Royal Academy of Music; the Antient Concert Rooms was a building in which rooms could be rented for musical or dramatic productions. 3. A Dublin church. 4. Drunk.

snow lay like a cape on the shoulders of his overcoat and like toecaps on the toes of his goloshes; and, as the buttons of his overcoat slipped with a squeaking noise through the snow-stiffened frieze, a cold, fragrant air from out-of-doors escaped from crevices and folds.

"Is it snowing again, Mr Conroy?" asked Lily.

She had preceded him into the pantry to help him off with his overcoat. Gabriel smiled at the three syllables she had given his surname and glanced at her. She was a slim, growing girl, pale in complexion and with hay-coloured hair. The gas in the pantry made her look still paler. Gabriel had known her when she was a child and used to sit on the lowest step nursing a rag doll.

"Yes, Lily," he answered, "and I think we're in for a night of it."

He looked up at the pantry ceiling, which was shaking with the stamping and shuffling of feet on the floor above, listened for a moment to the piano and then glanced at the girl, who was folding his overcoat carefully at the end of a shelf.

"Tell me, Lily," he said in a friendly tone, "do you still go to school?"

"O no, sir," she answered. "I'm done schooling this year and more."

"O, then," said Gabriel gaily, "I suppose we'll be going to your wedding one of these fine days with your young man, eh?"

The girl glanced back at him over her shoulder and said with great bitterness:

"The men that is now is only all palaver and what they can get out of you."

Gabriel coloured, as if he felt he had made a mistake and, without looking at her, kicked off his goloshes and flicked actively with his muffler at his patent-leather shoes.

He was a stout, tallish young man. The high colour of his cheeks pushed upwards even to his forehead, where it scattered itself in a few formless patches of pale red; and on his hairless face there scintillated restlessly the polished lenses and the bright gilt rims of the glasses which screened his delicate and restless eyes. His glossy black hair was parted in the middle and brushed in a long curve behind his ears where it curled slightly beneath the groove left by his hat.

When he had flicked lustre into his shoes he stood up and pulled his waistcoat down more tightly on his plump body. Then he took a coin rapidly from his pocket.

"O Lily," he said, thrusting it into her hands, "it's Christmastime, isn't it? Just . . . here's a little . . ."

He walked rapidly towards the door.

"Oh no, sir!" cried the girl, following him. "Really, sir, I wouldn't take it."

"Christmas-time! Christmas-time!" said Gabriel, almost trotting to the stairs and waving his hand to her in deprecation.

The girl, seeing that he had gained the stairs, called out after him:

"Well, thank you, sir."

He waited outside the drawing-room door until the waltz should finish, listening to the skirts that swept against it and to the shuffling of feet. He was still discomposed by the girl's bitter and sudden retort. It had cast a gloom over him which he tried to dispel by arranging his cuffs and the bows of his tie. He then took from his waistcoat pocket a little paper and glanced at the headings he had made for his speech. He was undecided about the lines from Robert Browning,[5] for he feared they would be above the heads of his hearers. Some quotation that they would recognize from Shakespeare or from the Melodies[6] would be better. The indelicate clacking of the men's heels and the shuffling of their soles reminded him that their grade of culture differed from his. He would only make himself ridiculous by quoting poetry to them which they could not understand. They would think that he was airing his superior education. He would fail with them just as he had failed with the girl in the pantry. He had taken up a wrong tone. His whole speech was a mistake from the first to last, an utter failure.

Just then his aunts and his wife came out of the ladies' dressing-room. His aunts were two small, plainly dressed old women. Aunt Julia was an inch or so the taller. Her hair, drawn low over the tops of her ears, was grey; and grey also, with darker shadows, was her large flaccid face. Though she was stout in build and stood erect, her slow eyes and parted lips gave her the appearance of a woman who did not know where she was or where she was going. Aunt Kate was more vivacious. Her face, healthier than her sister's, was all puckers and creases, like a shrivelled red apple, and her hair, braided in the same old-fashioned way, had not lost its ripe nut colour.

They both kissed Gabriel frankly. He was their favourite nephew, the son of their dead elder sister, Ellen, who had married T. J. Conroy of the Port and Docks.[7]

"Gretta tells me you're not going to take a cab back to Monkstown tonight, Gabriel," said Aunt Kate.

"No," said Gabriel, turning to his wife, "we had quite enough of that last year, hadn't we? Don't you remember, Aunt Kate, what a cold Gretta got out of it? Cab windows rattling all the way, and the east wind blowing in after we passed Merrion. Very jolly it was. Gretta caught a dreadful cold."

5. English poet (1812–1889). 6. The "Irish Melodies" by Thomas Moore, Irish poet (1779–1852). 7. Government bureau.

Aunt Kate frowned severely and nodded her head at every word.

"Quite right, Gabriel, quite right," she said. "You can't be too careful."

"But as for Gretta there," said Gabriel, "she'd walk home in the snow if she were let."

Mrs Conroy laughed.

"Don't mind him, Aunt Kate," she said. "He's really an awful bother, what with green shades for Tom's eyes at night and making him do the dumb-bells, and forcing Eva to eat the stirabout.[8] The poor child! And she simply hates the sight of it! . . . O, but you'll never guess what he makes me wear now!"

She broke out into a peal of laughter and glanced at her husband, whose admiring and happy eyes had been wandering from her dress to her face and hair. The two aunts laughed heartily, too, for Gabriel's solicitude was a standing joke with them.

"Goloshes!" said Mrs Conroy. "That's the latest. Whenever it's wet underfoot I must put on my goloshes. Tonight even, he wanted me to put them on, but I wouldn't. The next thing he'll buy me will be a diving-suit."

Gabriel laughed nervously and patted his tie reassuringly, while Aunt Kate nearly doubled herself, so heartily did she enjoy the joke. The smile soon faded from Aunt Julia's face and her mirthless eyes were directed towards her nephew's face. After a pause she asked:

"And what are goloshes, Gabriel?"

"Goloshes, Julia!" exclaimed her sister. "Goodness me, don't you know what goloshes are! You wear them over your . . . over your boots, Gretta, isn't it?"

"Yes," said Mrs Conroy. "Gutta-percha things.[9] We both have a pair now. Gabriel says everyone wears them on the Continent."

"O, on the Continent," murmured Aunt Julia, nodding her head slowly.

Gabriel knitted his brows and said, as if he were slightly angered:

"It's nothing very wonderful, but Gretta thinks it very funny because she says the word reminds her of Christy Minstrels."[1]

"But tell me, Gabriel," said Aunt Kate, with brisk tact. "Of course, you've seen about the room. Gretta was saying . . ."

"O, the room is all right," replied Gabriel. "I've taken one in the Gresham."

"To be sure," said Aunt Kate, "by far the best thing to do. And the children, Gretta, you're not anxious about them?"

"O, for one night," said Mrs Conroy. "Besides, Bessie will look after them."

8. Porridge. 9. Similar to rubber. 1. Well-known 19th-century minstrel show organized by Edwin T. Christy.

"To be sure," said Aunt Kate again. "What a comfort it is to have a girl like that, one you can depend on! There's that Lily, I'm sure I don't know what has come over her lately. She's not the girl she was at all."

Gabriel was about to ask his aunt some questions on this point, but she broke off suddenly to gaze after her sister, who had wandered down the stairs and was craning her neck over the banisters.

"Now, I ask you," she said almost testily, "where is Julia going? Julia! Julia! Where are you going?"

Julia, who had gone half-way down one flight, came back and announced blandly: "Here's Freddy."

At the same moment a clapping of hands and a final flourish of the pianist told that the waltz had ended. The drawing-room door was opened from within and some couples came out. Aunt Kate drew Gabriel aside hurriedly and whispered into his ear:

"Slip down, Gabriel, like a good fellow, and see if he's all right, and don't let him up if he's screwed. I'm sure he's screwed. I'm sure he is."

Gabriel went to the stairs and listened over the banisters. He could hear two persons talking in the pantry. Then he recognized Freddy Malins's laugh. He went down the stairs noisily.

"It's such a relief," said Aunt Kate to Mrs Conroy, "that Gabriel is here. I always feel easier in my mind when he's here . . . Julia, there's Miss Daly and Miss Power will take some refreshment. Thanks for your beautiful waltz, Miss Daly. It made lovely time."

A tall wizen-faced man, with a stiff grizzled moustache and swarthy skin, who was passing out with his partner, said:

"And may we have some refreshment, too, Miss Morkan?"

"Julia," said Aunt Kate summarily, "and here's Mr Browne and Miss Furlong. Take them in, Julia, with Miss Daly and Miss Power."

"I'm the man for the ladies," said Mr Browne, pursing his lips until his moustache bristled and smiling in all his wrinkles. "You know, Miss Morkan, the reason they are so fond of me is . . ."

He did not finish his sentence, but, seeing that Aunt Kate was out of earshot, at once led the three young ladies into the back room. The middle of the room was occupied by two square tables placed end to end, and on these Aunt Julia and the caretaker were straightening and smoothing a large cloth. On the sideboard were arrayed dishes and plates, and glasses and bundles of knives and forks and spoons. The top of the closed square piano served also as a sideboard for viands and sweets. At a smaller sideboard in one corner two young men were standing, drinking hop-bitters.

Mr Browne led his charges thither and invited them all, in jest, to some ladies' punch, hot, strong and sweet. As they said they never took anything strong, he opened three bottles of lemonade for them. Then he asked one of the young men to move aside, and, taking hold of the decanter, filled out for himself a goodly measure of whisky. The young men eyed him respectfully while he took a trial sip.

"God help me," he said, smiling. "It's the doctor's orders."

His wizened face broke into a broader smile, and the three young ladies laughed in musical echo to his pleasantry, swaying their bodies to and fro, with nervous jerks of their shoulders. The boldest said:

"O, now, Mr Browne, I'm sure the doctor never ordered anything of the kind."

Mr Browne took another sip of his whisky and said, with sidling mimicry:

"Well, you see, I'm like the famous Mrs Cassidy, who is reported to have said: 'Now, Mary Grimes, if I don't take it, make me take it, for I feel I want it.' "

His hot face had leaned forward a little too confidentially and he had assumed a very low Dublin accent so that the young ladies, with one instinct, received his speech in silence. Miss Furlong, who was one of Mary Jane's pupils, asked Miss Daly what was the name of the pretty waltz she had played; and Mr Browne, seeing that he was ignored, turned promptly to the two young men who were more appreciative.

A red-faced young woman, dressed in pansy, came into the room, excitedly clapping her hands and crying:

"Quadrilles! Quadrilles!"[2]

Close on her heels came Aunt Kate, crying:

"Two gentlemen and three ladies, Mary Jane!"

"O, here's Mr Bergin and Mr Kerrigan," said Mary Jane. "Mr Kerrigan, will you take Miss Power? Miss Furlong, may I get you a partner, Mr Bergin. O, that'll just do now."

"Three ladies, Mary Jane," said Aunt Kate.

The two young gentlemen asked the ladies if they might have the pleasure, and Mary Jane turned to Miss Daly.

"O, Miss Daly, you're really awfully good, after playing for the last two dances, but really we're so short of ladies tonight."

"I don't mind in the least, Miss Morkan."

"But I've a nice partner for you, Mr Bartell D'Arcy, the tenor. I'll get him to sing later on. All Dublin is raving about him."

"Lovely voice, lovely voice!" said Aunt Kate.

As the piano had twice begun the prelude to the first figure Mary Jane led her recruits quickly from the room. They had hardly gone when Aunt Julia wandered slowly into the room, looking behind her at something.

2. A square dance.

"What is the matter, Julia?" asked Aunt Kate anxiously. "Who is it?"

Julia, who was carrying in a column of table-napkins, turned to her sister and said, simply, as if the question had surprised her:

"It's only Freddy, Kate, and Gabriel with him."

In fact right behind her Gabriel could be seen piloting Freddy Malins across the landing. The latter, a young man of about forty, was of Gabriel's size and build, with very round shoulders. His face was fleshy and pallid, touched with colour only at the thick hanging lobes of his ears and at the wide wings of his nose. He had coarse features, a blunt nose, a convex and receding brow, tumid and protruded lips. His heavy-lidded eyes and the disorder of his scanty hair made him look sleepy. He was laughing heartily in a high key at a story which he had been telling Gabriel on the stairs and at the same time rubbing the knuckles of his left fist backwards and forwards into his left eye.

"Good evening, Freddy," said Aunt Julia.

Freddy Malins bade the Misses Morkan good evening in what seemed an offhand fashion by reason of the habitual catch in his voice and then, seeing that Mr Browne was grinning at him from the sideboard, crossed the room on rather shaky legs and began to repeat in an undertone the story he had just told to Gabriel.

"He's not so bad, is he?" said Aunt Kate to Gabriel.

Gabriel's brows were dark, but he raised them quickly and answered:

"Oh, no, hardly noticeable."

"Now, isn't he a terrible fellow!" she said. "And his poor mother made him take the pledge[3] on New Year's Eve. But come on, Gabriel, into the drawing-room."

Before leaving the room with Gabriel she signalled to Mr Browne by frowning and shaking her forefinger in warning to and fro. Mr Browne nodded in answer and, when she had gone, said to Freddy Malins:

"Now, then, Teddy, I'm going to fill you out a good glass of lemonade just to buck you up."

Freddy Malins, who was nearing the climax of his story, waved the offer aside impatiently, but Mr Browne, having first called Freddy Malins's attention to a disarray in his dress, filled out and handed him a full glass of lemonade. Freddy Malins's left hand accepted the glass mechanically, his right hand being engaged in the mechanical readjustment of his dress. Mr Browne, whose face was once more wrinkling with mirth, poured out for himself a glass of whisky while Freddy Malins exploded, before he had well reached the climax of his story, in a kink of high-pitched bronchitic laughter and, setting down his untasted

3. A formal pledge not to drink.

and overflowing glass, began to rub the knuckles of his left fist backwards and forwards into his left eye, repeating words of his last phrase as well as his fit of laughter would allow him.

Gabriel could not listen while Mary Jane was playing her Academy piece, full of runs and difficult passages, to the hushed drawing-room. He liked music, but the piece she was playing had no melody for him and he doubted whether it had any melody for the other listeners, though they had begged Mary Jane to play something. Four young men, who had come from the refreshment-room to stand in the doorway at the sound of the piano, had gone away quietly in couples after a few minutes. The only persons who seemed to follow the music were Mary Jane herself, her hands racing along the keyboard or lifted from it at the pauses like those of a priestess in momentary imprecation, and Aunt Kate standing at her elbow to turn the page.

Gabriel's eyes, irritated by the floor, which glittered with beeswax under the heavy chandelier, wandered to the wall above the piano. A picture of the balcony scene in *Romeo and Juliet* hung there and beside it was a picture of the two murdered princes in the Tower[4] which Aunt Julia had worked in red, blue and brown wools when she was a girl. Probably in the school they had gone to as girls that kind of work had been taught for one year. His mother had worked for him as a birthday present a waistcoat of purple tabinet, with little foxes' heads upon it, lined with brown satin and having round mulberry buttons. It was strange that his mother had had no musical talent, though Aunt Kate used to call her the brains carrier of the Morkan family. Both she and Julia had always seemed a little proud of their serious and matronly sister. Her photograph stood before the pier-glass.[5] She held an open book on her knees and was pointing out something in it to Constantine who, dressed in a man-o'-war suit,[6] lay at her feet. It was she who had chosen the names of her sons, for she was very sensible of the dignity of family life. Thanks to her, Constantine was now senior curate in Balbriggan and, thanks to her, Gabriel himself had taken his degree in the Royal University. A shadow passed over his face as he remembered her sullen opposition to his marriage. Some slighting phrases she had used still rankled in his memory; she had once spoken of Gretta as being country cute and that was not true of Gretta at all. It was Gretta who had nursed her during all her last long illness in their house at Monkstown.

He knew that Mary Jane must be near the end of her piece, for she was playing again the opening melody with runs of scales after

4. Edward and Richard, sons of King Edward IV of England. The two princes were murdered by order of King Richard III. 5. A tall mirror. 6. Sailor suit.

every bar, and while he waited for the end the resentment died down in his heart. The piece ended with a trill of octaves in the treble and a final deep octave in the bass. Great applause greeted Mary Jane as, blushing and rolling up her music nervously, she escaped from the room. The most vigorous clapping came from the four young men in the doorway who had gone away to the refreshment-room at the beginning of the piece but had come back when the piano had stopped.

Lancers[7] were arranged. Gabriel found himself partnered with Miss Ivors. She was a frank-mannered talkative young lady, with a freckled face and prominent brown eyes. She did not wear a low-cut bodice, and the large brooch which was fixed in the front of her collar bore on it an Irish device and motto.

When they had taken their places she said abruptly:

"I have a crow to pluck with you."[8]

"With me?" said Gabriel.

She nodded her head gravely.

"What is it?" asked Gabriel, smiling at her solemn manner.

"Who is G. C.?" answered Miss Ivors, turning her eyes upon him.

Gabriel coloured and was about to knit his brows, as if he did not understand, when she said bluntly:

"O, innocent Amy! I have found out that you write for the *Daily Express.*[9] Now, aren't you ashamed of yourself?"

"Why should I be ashamed of myself?" asked Gabriel, blinking his eyes and trying to smile.

"Well, I'm ashamed of you," said Miss Ivors frankly. "To say you'd write for a paper like that. I didn't think you were a West Briton."[1]

A look of perplexity appeared on Gabriel's face. It was true that he wrote a literary column every Wednesday in the *Daily Express*, for which he was paid fifteen shillings. But that did not make him a West Briton surely. The books he received for review were almost more welcome than the paltry cheque. He loved to feel the covers and turn over the pages of newly printed books. Nearly every day when his teaching in the college was ended he used to wander down the quays to the second-hand booksellers, to Hickey's on Bachelor's Walk, to Webb's or Massey's on Aston's Quay, or to O'Clohissey's in the bystreet. He did not know how to meet her charge. He wanted to say that literature was above politics. But they were friends of many years' standing and their careers had been parallel, first at the University and then as teachers: he could not risk a grandiose phrase with her. He

7. A set of quadrilles, danced in sequence. 8. Equivalent of "I have a bone to pick . . ." 9. A newspaper opposed to Irish liberation. 1. In context this means he considers himself British rather than Irish.

continued blinking his eyes and trying to smile and murmured lamely that he saw nothing political in writing reviews of books.

When their turn to cross had come he was still perplexed and inattentive. Miss Ivors promptly took his hand in a warm grasp and said in a soft friendly tone:

"Of course, I was only joking. Come, we cross now."

When they were together again she spoke of the University question[2] and Gabriel felt more at ease. A friend of hers had shown her his review of Browning's poems. That was how she had found out the secret: but she liked the review immensely. Then she said suddenly:

"O, Mr Conroy, will you come for an excursion to the Aran Isles[3] this summer? We're going to stay there a whole month. It will be splendid out in the Atlantic. You ought to come. Mr Clancy is coming, and Mr Kilkelly and Kathleen Kearney. It would be splendid for Gretta too if she'd come. She's from Connacht,[4] isn't she?"

"Her people are," said Gabriel shortly.

"But you will come, won't you?" said Miss Ivors, laying her warm hand eagerly on his arm.

"The fact is," said Gabriel, "I have just arranged to go . . ."

"Go where?" asked Miss Ivors.

"Well, you know, every year I go for a cycling tour with some fellows and so . . ."

"But where?" asked Miss Ivors.

"Well, we usually go to France or Belgium or perhaps Germany," said Gabriel awkwardly.

"And why do you go to France and Belgium," said Miss Ivors, "instead of visiting your own land?"

"Well," said Gabriel, "it's partly to keep in touch with the languages and partly for a change."

"And haven't you your own language to keep in touch with—Irish?" asked Miss Ivors.

"Well," said Gabriel, "if it comes to that, you know, Irish is not my language."

Their neighbours had turned to listen to the cross-examination. Gabriel glanced right and left nervously and tried to keep his good humour under the ordeal, which was making a blush invade his forehead.

"And haven't you your own land to visit," continued Miss Ivors,

2. The issue was whether to provide equal educational opportunities for Roman Catholic students at the overwhelmingly Protestant Trinity College in Dublin. 3. Off the west coast of Ireland. Irish traditions were preserved by their Gaelic-speaking natives. 4. Province in northwest Ireland. Probably considered backwoods by Dubliners.

"that you know nothing of, your own people, and your own country?"

"O, to tell you the truth," retorted Gabriel suddenly, "I'm sick of my own country, sick of it!"

"Why?" asked Miss Ivors.

Gabriel did not answer for his retort had heated him.

"Why?" repeated Miss Ivors.

They had to go visiting together and, as he had not answered her, Miss Ivors said warmly:

"Of course, you've no answer."

Gabriel tried to cover his agitation by taking part in the dance with great energy. He avoided her eyes for he had seen a sour expression on her face. But when they met in the long chain he was surprised to feel his hand firmly pressed. She looked at him from under her brows for a moment quizzically until he smiled. Then, just as the chain was about to start again, she stood on tiptoe and whispered into his ear:

"West Briton!"

When the lancers were over Gabriel went away to a remote corner of the room where Freddy Malins's mother was sitting. She was a stout, feeble old woman with white hair. Her voice had a catch in it like her son's and she stuttered slightly. She had been told that Freddy had come and that he was nearly all right. Gabriel asked her whether she had had a good crossing. She lived with her married daughter in Glasgow and came to Dublin on a visit once a year. She answered placidly that she had had a beautiful crossing and that the captain had been most attentive to her. She spoke also of the beautiful house her daughter kept in Glasgow, and of all the friends they had there. While her tongue rambled on Gabriel tried to banish from his mind all memory of the unpleasant incident with Miss Ivors. Of course the girl, or woman, or whatever she was, was an enthusiast, but there was a time for all things. Perhaps he ought not to have answered her like that. But she had no right to call him a West Briton before people, even in joke. She had tried to make him ridiculous before people, heckling him and staring at him with her rabbit's eyes.

He saw his wife making her way towards him through the waltzing couples. When she reached him she said into his ear:

"Gabriel, Aunt Kate wants to know won't you carve the goose as usual. Miss Daly will carve the ham and I'll do the pudding."

"All right," said Gabriel.

"She's sending in the younger ones first as soon as this waltz is over so that we'll have the table to ourselves."

"Were you dancing?" asked Gabriel.

"Of course I was. Didn't you see me? What row had you with Molly Ivors?"

"No row. Why? Did she say so?"

"Something like that. I'm trying to get that Mr D'Arcy to sing. He's full of conceit, I think."

"There was no row," said Gabriel moodily, "only she wanted me to go for a trip to the west of Ireland and I said I wouldn't."

His wife clasped her hands excitedly and gave a little jump.

"O, do go, Gabriel," she cried. "I'd love to see Galway[5] again."

"You can go if you like," said Gabriel coldly.

She looked at him for a moment, then turned to Mrs Malins and said:

"There's a nice husband for you, Mrs Malins."

While she was threading her way back across the room Mrs Malins, without adverting to the interruption, went on to tell Gabriel what beautiful places there were in Scotland and beautiful scenery. Her son-in-law brought them every year to the lakes and they used to go fishing. Her son-in-law was a splendid fisher. One day he caught a beautiful big fish and the man in the hotel cooked it for dinner.

Gabriel hardly heard what she said. Now that supper was coming near he began to think again about his speech and about the quotation. When he saw Freddy Malins coming across the room to visit his mother Gabriel left the chair free for him and retired into the embrasure of the window. The room had already cleared and from the back room came the clatter of plates and knives. Those who still remained in the drawing-room seemed tired of dancing and were conversing quietly in little groups. Gabriel's warm trembling fingers tapped the cold pane of the window. How cool it must be outside! How pleasant it would be to walk out alone, first along by the river and then through the park! The snow would be lying on the branches of the trees and forming a bright cap on the top of the Wellington Monument.[6] How much more pleasant it would be there than at the supper-table!

He ran over the headings of his speech: Irish hospitality, sad memories, the Three Graces, Paris,[7] the quotation from Browning. He repeated to himself a phrase he had written in his review: "One feels that one is listening to a thought-tormented music." Miss Ivors had praised the review. Was she sincere? Had she really any life of her own behind all her propagandism? There had never been any ill-feeling between them until that night. It unnerved him to think that she would be at the supper-table, looking up at him while he spoke with her critical quizzing eyes. Perhaps she would not be sorry to see him

5. Capital of Connacht. 6. Monument to the Duke of Wellington (1769–1852), Irish-born hero of the Napoleonic Wars. 7. Goddesses representing aspects of beauty—Aglaia (Brilliance), Euphrosyne (Joy), and Thalia (Bloom); Paris was the Trojan prince who was obliged to choose among the goddesses Hera, Athena, and Aphrodite. He awarded the prize (the apple of discord) to Aphrodite who then helped him carry off Helen.

fail in his speech. An idea came into his mind and gave him courage. He would say, alluding to Aunt Kate and Aunt Julia: "Ladies and Gentlemen, the generation which is now on the wane among us may have had its faults, but for my part I think it had certain qualities of hospitality, of humour, of humanity, which the new and very serious and hypereducated generation that is growing up around us seems to me to lack." Very good: that was one for Miss Ivors. What did he care that his aunts were only two ignorant old women?

A murmur in the room attracted his attention. Mr Browne was advancing from the door, gallantly escorting Aunt Julia, who leaned upon his arm, smiling and hanging her head. An irregular musketry of applause escorted her also as far as the piano and then, as Mary Jane seated herself on the stool, and Aunt Julia, no longer smiling, half turned so as to pitch her voice fairly into the room, gradually ceased. Gabriel recognized the prelude. It was that of an old song of Aunt Julia's—*Arrayed for the Bridal.* Her voice, strong and clear in tone, attacked with great spirit the runs which embellish the air and though she sang very rapidly she did not miss even the smallest of the grace notes. To follow the voice, without looking at the singer's face, was to feel and share the excitement of swift and secure flight. Gabriel applauded loudly with all the others at the close of the song and loud applause was borne in from the invisible supper-table. It sounded so genuine that a little colour struggled into Aunt Julia's face as she bent to replace in the music-stand the old leather-bound song-book that had her initials on the cover. Freddy Malins, who had listened with his head perched sideways to hear her better, was still applauding when everyone else had ceased and talking animatedly to his mother, who nodded her head gravely and slowly in acquiescence. At last, when he could clap no more, he stood up suddenly and hurried across the room to Aunt Julia whose hand he seized and held in both his hands, shaking it when words failed him or the catch in his voice proved too much for him.

"I was just telling my mother," he said, "I never heard you sing so well, never. No, I never heard your voice so good as it is tonight. Now! Would you believe that now? That's the truth. Upon my word and honour that's the truth. I never heard your voice sound so fresh and so . . . so clear and fresh, never."

Aunt Julia smiled broadly and murmured something about compliments as she released her hand from his grasp. Mr Browne extended his open hand towards her and said to those who were near him in the manner of a showman introducing a prodigy to an audience:

"Miss Julia Morkan, my latest discovery!"

He was laughing very heartily at this himself when Freddy Malins turned to him and said:

"Well, Browne, if you're serious you might make a worse discovery. All I can say is I never heard her sing half so well as long as I am coming here. And that's the honest truth."

"Neither did I," said Mr Browne. "I think her voice has greatly improved."

Aunt Julia shrugged her shoulders and said with meek pride:

"Thirty years ago I hadn't a bad voice as voices go."

"I often told Julia," said Aunt Kate emphatically, "that she was simply thrown away in that choir. But she never would be said by me."

She turned as if to appeal to the good sense of the others against a refractory child while Aunt Julia gazed in front of her, a vague smile of reminiscence playing on her face.

"No," continued Aunt Kate, "she wouldn't be said or led by anyone, slaving there in that choir night and day, night and day. Six o'clock on Christmas morning! And all for what?"

"Well, isn't it for the honour of God, Aunt Kate?" asked Mary Jane, twisting round on the piano-stool and smiling.

Aunt Kate turned fiercely on her niece and said:

"I know all about the honour of God, Mary Jane, but I think it's not at all honourable for the Pope to turn out the women out of the choirs that have slaved there all their lives and put little whipper-snappers of boys over their heads. I suppose it is for the good of the Church if the Pope does it. But it's not just, Mary Jane, and it's not right."

She had worked herself into a passion and would have continued in defence of her sister, for it was a sore subject with her, but Mary Jane, seeing that all the dancers had come back, intervened pacifically:

"Now, Aunt Kate, you're giving scandal to Mr Browne who is of the other persuasion."

Aunt Kate turned to Mr Browne, who was grinning at this allusion to his religion, and said hastily:

"O, I don't question the Pope's being right. I'm only a stupid old woman and I wouldn't presume to do such a thing. But there's such a thing as common everyday politeness and gratitude. And if I were in Julia's place I'd tell that Father Healey straight up to his face. . . ."

"And besides, Aunt Kate," said Mary Jane, "we really are all hungry and when we are hungry we are all very quarrelsome."

"And when we are thirsty we are also quarrelsome," added Mr Browne.

"So that we had better go to supper," said Mary Jane, "and finish the discussion afterwards."

On the landing outside the drawing-room Gabriel found his wife and Mary Jane trying to persuade Miss Ivors to stay for supper. But Miss Ivors, who had put on her hat and was buttoning her cloak, would not stay. She did not feel in the least hungry and she had already overstayed her time.

"But only for ten minutes, Molly," said Mrs Conroy. "That won't delay you."

"To take a pick itself," said Mary Jane, "after all your dancing."

"I really couldn't," said Miss Ivors.

"I am afraid you didn't enjoy yourself at all," said Mary Jane hopelessly.

"Ever so much, I assure you," said Miss Ivors, "but you really must let me run off now."

"But how can you get home?" asked Mrs Conroy.

"O, it's only two steps up the quay."

Gabriel hesitated a moment and said:

"If you will allow me, Miss Ivors, I'll see you home if you are really obliged to go."

But Miss Ivors broke away from them.

"I won't hear of it," she cried. "For goodness' sake go in to your suppers and don't mind me. I'm quite well able to take care of myself."

"Well, you're the comical girl, Molly," said Mrs Conroy frankly.

"*Beannacht libh,*"[8] cried Miss Ivors, with a laugh, as she ran down the staircase.

Mary Jane gazed after her, a moodily puzzled expression on her face, while Mrs Conroy leaned over the banisters to listen for the hall door. Gabriel asked himself was he the cause of her abrupt departure. But she did not seem to be in ill humour: she had gone away laughing. He stared blankly down the staircase.

At the moment, Aunt Kate came toddling out of the supper-room, almost wringing her hands in despair.

"Where is Gabriel?" she cried. "Where on earth is Gabriel? There's everyone waiting in there, stage to let, and nobody to carve the goose!"

"Here I am, Aunt Kate!" cried Gabriel, with sudden animation, "ready to carve a flock of geese, if necessary."

A fat brown goose lay at one end of the table and at the other end, on a bed of creased paper strewn with sprigs of parsley, lay a great ham, stripped of its outer skin and peppered over with crust crumbs, a neat paper frill round its shin, and beside this was a round of spiced beef. Between these rival ends ran parallel lines of side-dishes: two little minsters of jelly, red and yellow; a shallow dish full of blocks of blancmange and red jam, a large green leaf-shaped dish with a stalk-shaped handle, on which lay bunches of purple raisins and peeled almonds, a companion dish on which lay a solid rectangle of Smyrna figs, a dish of custard topped with grated nutmeg, a small bowl full of

8. "Blessings on you" (Gaelic).

chocolates and sweets wrapped in gold and silver papers and a glass vase in which stood some tall celery stalks. In the centre of the table there stood, as sentries to a fruit-stand which upheld a pyramid of oranges and American apples, two squat old-fashioned decanters of cut glass, one containing port and the other dark sherry. On the closed square piano a pudding in a huge yellow dish lay in waiting and behind it were three squads of bottles of stout and ale and minerals, drawn up according to the colours of their uniforms, the first two black, with brown and red labels, the third and smallest squad white, with transverse green sashes.

Gabriel took his seat boldly at the head of the table and, having looked to the edge of the carver, plunged his fork firmly into the goose. He felt quite at ease now for he was an expert carver and liked nothing better than to find himself at the head of a well-laden table.

"Miss Furlong, what shall I send you?" he asked. "A wing or a slice of the breast?"

"Just a small slice of the breast."

"Miss Higgins, what for you?"

"O, anything at all, Mr Conroy."

While Gabriel and Miss Daly exchanged plates of goose and plates of ham and spiced beef, Lily went from guest to guest with a dish of hot floury potatoes wrapped in a white napkin. This was Mary Jane's idea and she had also suggested apple sauce for the goose, but Aunt Kate had said that plain roast goose without any apple sauce had always been good enough for her and she hoped she might never eat worse. Mary Jane waited on her pupils and saw that they got the best slices, and Aunt Kate and Aunt Julia opened and carried across from the piano bottles of stout and ale for the gentlemen and bottles of minerals for the ladies. There was a great deal of confusion and laughter and noise, the noise of orders and counter-orders, of knives and forks, of corks and glass-stoppers. Gabriel began to carve second helpings as soon as he had finished the first round without serving himself. Everyone protested loudly so that he compromised by taking a long draught of stout, for he had found the carving hot work. Mary Jane settled down quietly to her supper, but Aunt Kate and Aunt Julia were still toddling round the table, walking on each other's heels, getting in each other's way and giving each other unheeded orders. Mr Browne begged of them to sit down and eat their suppers and so did Gabriel, but they said there was time enough, so that, at last, Freddy Malins stood up and, capturing Aunt Kate, plumped her down on her chair amid general laughter.

When everyone had been well served Gabriel said, smiling:

"Now, if anyone wants a little more of what vulgar people call stuffing let him or her speak."

A chorus of voices invited him to begin his own supper, and Lily came forward with three potatoes which she had reserved for him.

"Very well," said Gabriel amiably, as he took another preparatory draught, "kindly forget my existence, ladies and gentlemen, for a few minutes."

He set to his supper and took no part in the conversation with which the table covered Lily's removal of the plates. The subject of talk was the opera company which was then at the Theatre Royal. Mr Bartell D'Arcy, the tenor, a dark-complexioned young man with a smart moustache, praised very highly the leading contralto of the company, but Miss Furlong thought she had a rather vulgar style of production. Freddy Malins said there was a Negro chieftain singing in the second part of the Gaiety pantomime who had one of the finest tenor voices he had ever heard.

"Have you heard him?" he asked Mr Bartell D'Arcy across the table.

"No," answered Mr Bartell D'Arcy carelessly.

"Because," Freddy Malins explained, "now I'd be curious to hear your opinion of him. I think he has a grand voice."

"It takes Teddy to find out the really good things," said Mr Browne familiarly to the table.

"And why couldn't he have a voice too?" asked Freddy Malins sharply. "Is it because he's only a black?"

Nobody answered this question and Mary Jane led the table back to the legitimate opera. One of her pupils had given her a pass for *Mignon*.[9] Of course it was very fine, she said, but it made her think of poor Georgina Burns. Mr Browne could go back further still, to the old Italian companies that used to come to Dublin—Tietjens, Ilma de Murzka, Campanini, the great Trebelli, Giuglini, Ravelli, Aramburo.[1] Those were the days, he said, when there was something like singing to be heard in Dublin. He told too of how the top gallery of the old Royal used to be packed night after night, of how one night an Italian tenor had sung five encores to *Let me like a Soldier fall*,[2] introducing a high C every time, and of how the gallery boys would sometimes in their enthusiasm unyoke the horses from the carriage of some great *prima donna* and pull her themselves through the streets to her hotel. Why did they never play the grand old operas now, he asked, *Dinorah, Lucrezia Borgia*?[3] Because they could not get the voices to sing them: that was why.

9. Opera by Ambroise Thomas, French composer (1811–1896). 1. Some 19th-century singing stars. Therese Tietjens (1831–1877), Ilma di Murzka (1836–1889), Italo Campanini (1845–1896), Zelia Trebelli (1838–1892), Antonio Giuglini (1827–1865). Others not identified. 2. From *Maritana* by Brunn, Fitzball, and Wallace. 3. Operas by Giacomo Meyerbeer, German composer (1791–1864); and by Gaetano Donizetti, Italian composer (1797–1848).

"O, well," said Mr Bartell D'Arcy, "I presume there are as good singers today as there were then."

"Where are they?" asked Mr Browne defiantly.

"In London, Paris, Milan," said Mr Bartell D'Arcy warmly. "I suppose Caruso,[4] for example, is quite as good, if not better than any of the men you have mentioned."

"Maybe so," said Mr Browne. "But I may tell you I doubt it strongly."

"O, I'd give anything to hear Caruso sing," said Mary Jane.

"For me," said Aunt Kate, who had been picking a bone, "there was only one tenor. To please me, I mean. But I suppose none of you ever heard of him."

"Who was he, Miss Morkan?" asked Mr Bartell D'Arcy politely.

"His name," said Aunt Kate, "was Parkinson.[5] I heard him when he was in his prime and I think he had then the purest tenor voice that was ever put into a man's throat."

"Strange," said Mr Bartell D'Arcy. "I never even heard of him."

"Yes, yes, Miss Morkan is right," said Mr Browne. "I remember hearing of old Parkinson, but he's too far back for me."

"A beautiful, pure, sweet mellow English tenor," said Aunt Kate with enthusiasm.

Gabriel having finished, the huge pudding was transferred to the table. The clatter of forks and spoons began again. Gabriel's wife served out spoonfuls of the pudding and passed the plates down the table. Midway down they were held up by Mary Jane, who replenished them with raspberry or orange jelly or with blancmange and jam. The pudding was of Aunt Julia's making, and she received praises for it from all quarters. She herself said that it was not quite brown enough.

"Well, I hope, Miss Morkan," said Mr Browne, "that I'm brown enough for you because, you know, I'm all brown."

All the gentlemen, except Gabriel, ate some of the pudding out of compliment to Aunt Julia. As Gabriel never ate sweets the celery had been left for him. Freddy Malins also took a stalk of celery and ate it with his pudding. He had been told that celery was a capital thing for the blood and he was just then under doctor's care. Mrs Malins, who had been silent all through the supper, said that her son was going down to Mount Melleray[6] in a week or so. The table then spoke of Mount Melleray, how bracing the air was down there, how hospitable the monks were and how they never asked for a penny-piece from their guests.

"And do you mean to say," asked Mr Browne incredulously, "that

4. Enrico Caruso, operatic tenor (1873–1921). 5. Not identified; perhaps fictional. 6. Trappist monastery in the south of Ireland.

a chap can go down there and put up there as if it were a hotel and live on the fat of the land and then come away without paying anything?"

"O, most people give some donation to the monastery when they leave," said Mary Jane.

"I wish we had an institution like that in our Church," said Mr Browne candidly.

He was astonished to hear that the monks never spoke, got up at two in the morning and slept in their coffins. He asked what they did it for.

"That's the rule of the order," said Aunt Kate firmly.

"Yes, but why?" asked Mr Browne.

Aunt Kate repeated that it was the rule, that was all. Mr Browne still seemed not to understand. Freddy Malins explained to him, as best he could, that the monks were trying to make up for the sins committed by all the sinners in the outside world. The explanation was not very clear for Mr Browne grinned and said:

"I like that idea very much, but wouldn't a comfortable spring bed do them as well as a coffin?"

"The coffin," said Mary Jane, "is to remind them of their last end."

As the subject had grown lugubrious it was buried in a silence of the table, during which Mrs Malins could be heard saying to her neighbour in an indistinct undertone:

"They are very good men, the monks, very pious men."

The raisins and almonds and figs and apples and oranges and chocolates and sweets were now passed about the table and Aunt Julia invited all the guests to have either port or sherry. At first Mr Bartell D'Arcy refused to take either, but one of his neighbours nudged him and whispered something to him, upon which he allowed his glass to be filled. Gradually as the last glasses were being filled the conversation ceased. A pause followed, broken only by the noise of the wine and by unsettlings of chairs. The Misses Morkan, all three, looked down at the tablecloth. Someone coughed once or twice and then a few gentlemen patted the table gently as a signal for silence. The silence came and Gabriel pushed back his chair and stood up.

The patting at once grew louder in encouragement and then ceased altogether. Gabriel leaned his ten trembling fingers on the tablecloth and smiled nervously at the company. Meeting a row of upturned faces he raised his eyes to the chandelier. The piano was playing a waltz tune and he could hear the skirts sweeping against the drawing-room door. People, perhaps, were standing in the snow on the quay outside, gazing up at the lighted windows and listening to the waltz music. The air was pure there. In the distance lay the park where the trees were weighted with snow. The Wellington Monument wore a gleaming cap of snow that flashed westwards over the white field of Fifteen Acres.[7]

He began:

"Ladies and Gentlemen,

"It has fallen to my lot this evening, as in years past, to perform a very pleasing task, but a task for which I am afraid my poor powers as a speaker are all too inadequate."

"No, no!" said Mr Browne.

"But, however that may be, I can only ask you tonight to take the will for the deed, and to lend me your attention for a few moments while I endeavour to express to you in words what my feelings are on this occasion.

"Ladies and Gentlemen, it is not the first time that we have gathered together under this hospitable roof, around this hospitable board. It is not the first time that we have been the recipients—or perhaps, I had better say, the victims—of the hospitality of certain good ladies."

He made a circle in the air with his arm and paused. Everyone laughed or smiled at Aunt Kate and Aunt Julia and Mary Jane who all turned crimson with pleasure. Gabriel went on more boldly:

"I feel more strongly with every recurring year that our country has no tradition which does it so much honour and which it should guard so jealously as that of its hospitality. It is a tradition that is unique as far as my experience goes (and I have visited not a few places abroad) among the modern nations. Some would say, perhaps, that with us it is rather a failing than anything to be boasted of. But granted even that, it is, to my mind, a princely failing, and one that I trust will long be cultivated among us. Of one thing, at least, I am sure. As long as this one roof shelters the good ladies aforesaid—and I wish from my heart it may do so for many and many a long year to come—the tradition of genuine warm-hearted courteous Irish hospitality, which our forefathers have handed down to us and which we in turn must hand down to our descendants, is still alive among us."

A hearty murmur of assent ran round the table. It shot through Gabriel's mind that Miss Ivors was not there and that she had gone away discourteously: and he said with confidence in himself:

"Ladies and Gentlemen,

"A new generation is growing up in our midst, a generation actuated by new ideas and new principles. It is serious and enthusiastic for these new ideas and its enthusiasm, even when it is misdirected, is, I believe, in the main sincere. But we are living in a sceptical and, if I may use the phrase, a thought-tormented age: and sometimes I fear that this new generation, educated or hypereducated as it is, will lack those qualities of humanity, of hospitality, of kindly humour which

7. Section of Phoenix Park in which the Wellington Monument stands.

belonged to an older day. Listening tonight to the names of all those great singers of the past it seemed to me, I must confess, that we were living in a less spacious age. Those days might, without exaggeration, be called spacious days: and if they are gone beyond recall let us hope, at least, that in gatherings such as this we shall still speak of them with pride and affection, still cherish in our hearts the memory of those dead and gone great ones whose fame the world will not willingly let die."

"Hear, hear!" said Mr Browne loudly.

"But yet," continued Gabriel, his voice falling into a softer inflection, "there are always in gatherings such as this sadder thoughts that will recur to our minds: thoughts of the past, of youth, of changes, of absent faces that we miss here tonight. Our path through life is strewn with many such sad memories: and were we to brood upon them always we could not find the heart to go on bravely with our work among the living. We have all of us living duties and living affections which claim, and rightly claim, our strenuous endeavours.

"Therefore, I will not linger on the past. I will not let any gloomy moralizing intrude upon us here tonight. Here we are gathered together for a brief moment from the bustle and rush of our everyday routine. We are met here as friends, in the spirit of good-fellowship, as colleagues, also to a certain extent, in the true spirit of *camaraderie*, and as the guests of—what shall I call them?—the Three Graces of the Dublin musical world."

The table burst into applause and laughter at this allusion. Aunt Julia vainly asked each of her neighbours in turn to tell her what Gabriel had said.

"He says we are the Three Graces, Aunt Julia," said Mary Jane.

Aunt Julia did not understand, but she looked up, smiling, at Gabriel, who continued in the same vein:

"Ladies and Gentlemen,

"I will not attempt to play tonight the part that Paris played on another occasion. I will not attempt to choose between them. The task would be an invidious one and one beyond my poor powers. For when I view them in turn, whether it be our chief hostess herself, whose good heart, whose too good heart, has become a byword with all who know her; or her sister, who seems to be gifted with perennial youth and whose singing must have been a surprise and a revelation to us all tonight; or, last but not least, when I consider our youngest hostess, talented, cheerful, hard-working and the best of nieces, I confess, Ladies and Gentlemen, that I do not know to which of them I should award the prize."

Gabriel glanced down at his aunts and, seeing the large smile on

Aunt Julia's face and the tears which had risen to Aunt Kate's eyes, hastened to his close. He raised his glass of port gallantly, while every member of the company fingered a glass expectantly, and said loudly:

"Let us toast them all three together. Let us drink to their health, wealth, long life, happiness and prosperity, and may they long continue to hold the proud and self-won position which they hold in their profession and the position of honour and affection which they hold in our hearts."

All the guests stood up, glass in hand, and turning towards the three seated ladies, sang in unison, with Mr Browne as leader:

"For they are jolly gay fellows,
For they are jolly gay fellows,
For they are jolly gay fellows,
Which nobody can deny."

Aunt Kate was making frank use of her handkerchief and even Aunt Julia seemed moved. Freddy Malins beat time with his pudding-fork and the singers turned towards one another, as if in melodious conference, while they sang with emphasis:

"Unless he tells a lie,
Unless he tells a lie."

Then, turning once more towards their hostess, they sang:

"For they are jolly gay fellows,
For they are jolly gay fellows,
For they are jolly gay fellows,
Which nobody can deny."

The acclamation which followed was taken up beyond the door of the supper-room by many of the other guests and renewed time after time, Freddy Malins acting as officer with his fork on high.

The piercing morning air came into the hall where they were standing so that Aunt Kate said:

"Close the door, somebody. Mrs Malins will get her death of cold."

"Browne is out there, Aunt Kate," said Mary Jane.

"Browne is everywhere," said Aunt Kate, lowering her voice.

Mary Jane laughed at her tone.

"Really," she said archly, "he is very attentive."

"He has been laid on[8] here like the gas," said Aunt Kate in the same tone, "all during the Christmas."

She laughed herself this time good-humouredly and then added quickly:

"But tell him to come in, Mary Jane, and close the door. I hope to goodness he didn't hear me."

At that moment the hall door was opened and Mr Browne came in from the doorstep, laughing as if his heart would break. He was dressed in a long green overcoat with mock astrakhan cuffs and collar and wore on his head an oval fur cap. He pointed down the snow-covered quay from where the sound of shrill prolonged whistling was borne in.

"Teddy will have all the cabs in Dublin out," he said.

Gabriel advanced from the little pantry behind the office, struggling into his overcoat and, looking round the hall, said:

"Gretta not down yet?"

"She's getting on her things, Gabriel," said Aunt Kate.

"Who's playing up there?" asked Gabriel.

"Nobody. They're all gone."

"O no, Aunt Kate," said Mary Jane. "Bartell D'Arcy and Miss O'Callaghan aren't gone yet."

"Someone is fooling at the piano anyhow," said Gabriel.

Mary Jane glanced at Gabriel and Mr Browne and said with a shiver:

"It makes me feel cold to look at you two gentlemen muffled up like that. I wouldn't like to face your journey home at this hour."

"I'd like nothing better this minute," said Mr Browne stoutly, "than a rattling fine walk in the country or a fast drive with a good spanking goer between the shafts."

"We used to have a very good horse and trap[9] at home," said Aunt Julia sadly.

"The never-to-be-forgotten Johnny," said Mary Jane, laughing.

Aunt Kate and Gabriel laughed too.

"Why, what was wonderful about Johnny?" asked Mr Browne.

"The late lamented Patrick Morkan, our grandfather, that is," explained Gabriel, "commonly known in his later years as the old gentleman, was a glue-boiler."

"O, now, Gabriel," said Aunt Kate, laughing, "he had a starch mill."

"Well, glue or starch," said Gabriel, "the old gentleman had a horse by the name of Johnny. And Johnny used to work in the old gentleman's mill, walking round and round in order to drive the mill.

8. Supplied. 9. One-horse carriage.

That was all very well; but now comes the tragic part about Johnny. One fine day the old gentleman thought he'd like to drive out with the quality[1] to a military review in the park."

"The Lord have mercy on his soul," said Aunt Kate compassionately.

"Amen," said Gabriel. "So the old gentleman, as I said, harnessed Johnny and put on his very best tall hat and his very best stock collar and drove out in grand style from his ancestral mansion somewhere near Back Lane, I think."

Everyone laughed, even Mrs Malins, at Gabriel's manner, and Aunt Kate said:

"O, now, Gabriel, he didn't live in Back Lane really. Only the mill was there."

"Out from the mansion of his forefathers," continued Gabriel, "he drove with Johnny. And everything went on beautifully until Johnny came in sight of King Billy's[2] statue: and whether he fell in love with the horse King Billy sits on or whether he thought he was back again in the mill, anyhow he began to walk round the statue."

Gabriel paced in a circle round the hall in his goloshes amid the laughter of the others.

"Round and round he went," said Gabriel, "and the old gentleman, who was a very pompous old gentleman, was highly indignant. 'Go on, sir! What do you mean, sir? Johnny! Johnny! Most extraordinary conduct! Can't understand the horse!' "

The peals of laughter which followed Gabriel's imitation of the incident was interrupted by a resounding knock at the hall door. Mary Jane ran to open it and let in Freddy Malins. Freddy Malins, with his hat well back on his head and his shoulders humped with cold, was puffing and steaming after his exertions.

"I could only get one cab," he said.

"O, we'll find another along the quay," said Gabriel.

"Yes," said Aunt Kate. "Better not keep Mrs Malins standing in the draught."

Mrs Malins was helped down the front steps by her son and Mr Browne, and, after many manoeuvres, hoisted into the cab. Freddy Malins clambered in after her and spent a long time settling her on the seat, Mr Browne helping him with advice. At last she was settled comfortably and Freddy Malins invited Mr Browne into the cab. There was a good deal of confused talk, and then Mr Browne got into the cab. The cabman settled his rug over his knees, and bent down for the address. The confusion grew greater and the cabman was directed dif-

1. Upper classes. 2. Equestrian statue of King William III of England, last military conquerer of Ireland (in 1690).

ferently by Freddy Malins and Mr Browne, each of whom had his head out through a window of the cab. The difficulty was to know where to drop Mr Browne along the route, and Aunt Kate, Aunt Julia and Mary Jane helped the discussion from the doorstep with cross-directions and contradictions and abundance of laughter. As for Freddy Malins he was speechless with laughter. He popped his head in and out of the window every moment to the great danger of his hat, and told his mother how the discussion was progressing, till at last Mr Browne shouted to the bewildered cabman above the din of everybody's laughter:

"Do you know Trinity College?"

"Yes, sir," said the cabman.

"Well, drive bang up against Trinity College gates," said Mr Browne, "and then we'll tell you where to go. You understand now?"

"Yes, sir," said the cabman.

"Make like a bird for Trinity College."

"Right, sir," said the cabman.

The horse was whipped up and the cab rattled off along the quay amid a chorus of laughter and adieus.

Gabriel had not gone to the door with the others. He was in a dark part of the hall gazing up the staircase. A woman was standing near the top of the first flight, in the shadow also. He could not see her face but he could see the terra-cotta and salmon-pink panels of her skirt which the shadow made appear black and white. It was his wife. She was leaning on the banisters, listening to something. Gabriel was surprised at her stillness and strained his ear to listen also. But he could hear little save the noise of laughter and dispute on the front steps, a few chords struck on the piano and a few notes of a man's voice singing.

He stood still in the gloom of the hall, trying to catch the air that the voice was singing and gazing up at his wife. There was grace and mystery in her attitude as if she were a symbol of something. He asked himself what is a woman standing on the stairs in the shadow, listening to distant music, a symbol of. If he were a painter he would paint her in that attitude. Her blue felt hat would show off the bronze of her hair against the darkness and the dark panels of her skirt would show off the light ones. *Distant Music* he would call the picture if he were a painter.

The hall door was closed; and Aunt Kate, Aunt Julia and Mary Jane came down the hall, still laughing.

"Well, isn't Freddy terrible?" said Mary Jane. "He's really terrible."

Gabriel said nothing, but pointed up the stairs towards where his wife was standing. Now that the hall door was closed the voice and the piano could be heard more clearly. Gabriel held up his hand for them to be silent. The song seemed to be in the old Irish tonality and the singer seemed uncertain both of his words and of his voice. The voice, made plaintive by distance and by the singer's hoarseness, faintly illuminated the cadence of the air with words expressing grief:

"O, the rain falls on my heavy locks
And the dew wets my skin,
My babe lies cold . . ."

"O," exclaimed Mary Jane. "It's Bartell D'Arcy singing and he wouldn't sing all the night. O, I'll get him to sing a song before he goes."

"O, do, Mary Jane," said Aunt Kate.

Mary Jane brushed past the others and ran to the staircase, but before she reached it the singing stopped and the piano was closed abruptly.

"O, what a pity!" she cried. "Is he coming down, Gretta?"

Gabriel heard his wife answer yes and saw her come down towards them. A few steps behind her were Mr Bartell D'Arcy and Miss O'Callaghan.

"O, Mr D'Arcy," cried Mary Jane, "it's downright mean of you to break off like that when we were all in raptures listening to you."

"I have been at him all the evening," said Miss O'Callaghan, "and Mrs Conroy, too, and he told us he had a dreadful cold and couldn't sing."

"O, Mr D'Arcy," said Aunt Kate, "now that was a great fib to tell."

"Can't you see that I'm as hoarse as a crow?" said Mr D'Arcy roughly.

He went into the pantry hastily and put on his overcoat. The others, taken aback by his rude speech, could find nothing to say. Aunt Kate wrinkled her brows and made signs to the others to drop the subject. Mr D'Arcy stood swathing his neck carefully and frowning.

"It's the weather," said Aunt Julia, after a pause.

"Yes, everybody has colds," said Aunt Kate readily, "everybody."

"They say," said Mary Jane, "we haven't had snow like it for thirty years; and I read this morning in the newspapers that the snow is general all over Ireland."

"I love the look of snow," said Aunt Julia sadly.

"So do I," said Miss O'Callaghan. "I think Christmas is never really Christmas unless we have the snow on the ground."

"But poor Mr D'Arcy doesn't like the snow," said Aunt Kate, smiling.

Mr D'Arcy came from the pantry, fully swathed and buttoned,

and in a repentant tone told them the history of his cold. Every one gave him advice and said it was a great pity and urged him to be very careful of his throat in the night air. Gabriel watched his wife, who did not join in the conversation. She was standing right under the dusty fanlight and the flame of the gas lit up the rich bronze of her hair, which he had seen her drying at the fire a few days before. She was in the same attitude and seemed unaware of the talk about her. At last she turned towards them and Gabriel saw that there was colour on her cheeks and that her eyes were shining. A sudden tide of joy went leaping out of his heart.

"Mr D'Arcy," she said, "what is the name of that song you were singing?"

"It's called *The Lass of Aughrim,*"[3] said Mr D'Arcy, "but I couldn't remember it properly. Why? Do you know it?"

"*The Lass of Aughrim,*" she repeated. "I couldn't think of the name."

"It's a very nice air," said Mary Jane. "I'm sorry you were not in voice tonight."

"Now, Mary Jane," said Aunt Kate, "don't annoy Mr D'Arcy. I won't have him annoyed."

Seeing that all were ready to start she shepherded them to the door, where good night was said:

"Well, good night, Aunt Kate, and thanks for the pleasant evening."

"Good night, Gabriel. Good night, Gretta!"

"Good night, Aunt Kate, and thanks ever so much. Good night, Aunt Julia."

"O, good night, Gretta, I didn't see you."

"Good night, Mr D'Arcy. Good night, Miss O'Callaghan."

"Good night, Miss Morkan."

"Good night, again."

"Good night, all. Safe home."

"Good night. Good night."

The morning was still dark. A dull, yellow light brooded over the houses and the river; and the sky seemed to be descending. It was slushy underfoot; and only streaks and patches of snow lay on the roofs, on the parapets of the quay and on the area railings. The lamps were still burning redly in the murky air and, across the river, the palace of the Four Courts stood out menacingly against the heavy sky.

She was walking on before him with Mr Bartell D'Arcy, her shoes in a brown parcel tucked under one arm and her hands holding her

3. Variant of *The Lass of Loch Royal*, Child's ballad No. 76. It tells of a girl seduced and abandoned. She stands in the rain outside the house of her seducer with her baby in her arms.

skirt up from the slush. She had no longer any grace of attitude, but Gabriel's eyes were still bright with happiness. The blood went bounding along his veins; and the thoughts went rioting through his brain, proud, joyful, tender, valorous.

She was walking on before him so lightly and so erect that he longed to run after her noiselessly, catch her by the shoulders and say something foolish and affectionate into her ear. She seemed to him so frail that he longed to defend her against something and then to be alone with her. Moments of their secret life together burst like stars upon his memory. A heliotrope envelope was lying beside his breakfast-cup and he was caressing it with his hand. Birds were twittering in the ivy and the sunny web of the curtain was shimmering along the floor: he could not eat for happiness. They were standing on the crowded platform and he was placing a ticket inside the warm palm of her glove. He was standing with her in the cold, looking in through a grated window at a man making bottles in a roaring furnace. It was very cold. Her face, fragrant in the cold air, was quite close to his; and suddenly he called out to the man at the furnace:

"Is the fire hot, sir?"

But the man could not hear with the noise of the furnace. It was just as well. He might have answered rudely.

A wave of yet more tender joy escaped from his heart and went coursing in warm flood along his arteries. Like the tender fire of stars moments of their life together, that no one knew of or would ever know of, broke upon and illumined his memory. He longed to recall to her those moments, to make her forget the years of their dull existence together and remember only their moments of ecstasy. For the years, he felt, had not quenched his soul or hers. Their children, his writing, her household cares had not quenched all their souls' tender fire. In one letter that he had written to her then he had said: "Why is it that words like these seem to me so dull and cold? Is it because there is no word tender enough to be your name?"

Like distant music these words that he had written years before were borne towards him from the past. He longed to be alone with her. When the others had gone away, when he and she were in the room in the hotel, then they would be alone together. He would call her softly:

"Gretta!"

Perhaps she would not hear at once: she would be undressing. Then something in his voice would strike her. She would turn and look at him . . .

At the corner of Winetavern Street they met a cab. He was glad of its rattling noise as it saved him from conversation. She was looking out of the window and seemed tired. The others spoke only few words, pointing out some building or street. The horse galloped along wearily under the murky morning sky, dragging his old rattling box after his heels, and Gabriel was again in a cab with her, galloping to catch the boat, galloping to their honeymoon.

As the cab drove across O'Connell Bridge Miss O'Callaghan said:

"They say you never cross O'Connell Bridge without seeing a white horse."

"I see a white man this time," said Gabriel.

"Where?" asked Mr Bartell D'Arcy.

Gabriel pointed to the statue, on which lay patches of snow. Then he nodded familiarly to it and waved his hand.

"Good night, Dan,"[4] he said gaily.

When the cab drew up before the hotel, Gabriel jumped out and, in spite of Mr Bartell D'Arcy's protest, paid the driver. He gave the man a shilling over his fare. The man saluted and said:

"A prosperous New Year to you, sir."

"The same to you," said Gabriel cordially.

She leaned for a moment on his arm in getting out of the cab and while standing at the kerbstone, bidding the others good night. She leaned lightly on his arm, as lightly as when she had danced with him a few hours before. He had felt proud and happy then, happy that she was his, proud of her grace and wifely carriage. But now, after the kindling again of so many memories, the first touch of her body, musical and strange and perfumed, sent through him a keen pang of lust. Under cover of her silence he pressed her arm closely to his side; and, as they stood at the hotel door, he felt that they had escaped from their lives and duties, escaped from home and friends and run away together with wild and radiant hearts to a new adventure.

An old man was dozing in a great hooded chair in the hall. He lit a candle in the office and went before them to the stairs. They followed him in silence, their feet falling in soft thuds on the thickly carpeted stairs. She mounted the stairs behind the porter, her head bowed in the ascent, her frail shoulders curved as with a burden, her skirt girt tightly about her. He could have flung his arms about her hips and held her still, for his arms were trembling with desire to seize her and only the stress of his nails against the palms of his hands held the wild impulse of his body in check. The porter halted on the stairs to settle his guttering candle. They halted, too, on the steps below him. In the silence Gabriel could hear the falling of the molten wax into the tray and the thumping of his own heart against his ribs.

The porter led them along a corridor and opened a door. Then

4. The statue is of Daniel O'Connell (1775–1847), Irish patriot for whom the bridge is named.

he set his unstable candle down on a toilet-table and asked at what hour they were to be called in the morning.

"Eight," said Gabriel.

The porter pointed to the tap of the electric-light and began a muttered apology, but Gabriel cut him short.

"We don't want any light. We have light enough from the street. And I say," he added, pointing to the candle, "you might remove that handsome article, like a good man."

The porter took up his candle again, but slowly, for he was surprised by such a novel idea. Then he mumbled good night and went out. Gabriel shot the lock to.

A ghastly light from the street lamp lay in a long shaft from one window to the door. Gabriel threw his overcoat and hat on a couch and crossed the room towards the window. He looked down into the street in order that his emotion might calm a little. Then he turned and leaned against a chest of drawers with his back to the light. She had taken off her hat and cloak and was standing before a large swinging mirror, unhooking her waist. Gabriel paused for a few moments, watching her, and then said: "Gretta!"

She turned away from the mirror slowly and walked along the shaft of light towards him. Her face looked so serious and weary that the words would not pass Gabriel's lips. No, it was not the moment yet.

"You looked tired," he said.

"I am a little," she answered.

"You don't feel ill or weak?"

"No, tired: that's all."

She went on to the window and stood there, looking out. Gabriel waited again and then, fearing that diffidence was about to conquer him, he said abruptly:

"By the way, Gretta!"

"What is it?"

"You know that poor fellow Malins?" he said quickly.

"Yes. What about him?"

"Well, poor fellow, he's a decent sort of chap, after all," continued Gabriel in a false voice. "He gave me back that sovereign[5] I lent him, and I didn't expect it, really. It's a pity he wouldn't keep away from that Browne, because he's not a bad fellow, really."

He was trembling now with annoyance. Why did she seem so abstracted? He did not know how he could begin. Was she annoyed, too, about something? If she would only turn to him or come to him of

5. Gold coin worth one pound.

her own accord! To take her as she was would be brutal. No, he must see some ardour in her eyes first. He longed to be master of her strange mood.

"When did you lend him the pound?" she asked, after a pause.

Gabriel strove to restrain himself from breaking out into brutal language about the sottish Malins and his pound. He longed to cry to her from his soul, to crush her body against his, to overmaster her. But he said:

"O, at Christmas, when he opened that little Christmas-card shop in Henry Street."

He was in such a fever of rage and desire that he did not hear her come from the window. She stood before him for an instant, looking at him strangely. Then, suddenly raising herself on tiptoe and resting her hands lightly on his shoulders, she kissed him.

"You are a very generous person, Gabriel," she said.

Gabriel, trembling with delight at her sudden kiss and at the quaintness of her phrase, put his hands on her hair and began smoothing it back, scarcely touching it with his fingers. The washing had made it fine and brilliant. His heart was brimming over with happiness. Just when he was wishing for it she had come to him of her own accord. Perhaps her thoughts had been running with his. Perhaps she had felt the impetuous desire that was in him, and then the yielding mood had come upon her. Now that she had fallen to him so easily, he wondered why he had been so diffident.

He stood, holding her head between his hands. Then, slipping one arm swiftly about her body and drawing her towards him, he said softly:

"Gretta, dear, what are you thinking about?"

She did not answer nor yield wholly to his arm. He said again, softly:

"Tell me what it is, Gretta. I think I know what is the matter. Do I know?"

She did not answer at once. Then she said in an outburst of tears:

"O, I am thinking about that song, *The Lass of Aughrim.*"

She broke loose from him and ran to the bed and, throwing her arms across the bed-rail, hid her face. Gabriel stood stock-still for a moment in astonishment and then followed her. As he passed in the way of the cheval-glass he caught sight of himself in full length, his broad, well-fitted shirt-front, the face whose expression always puzzled him when he saw it in a mirror, and his glimmering gilt-rimmed eyeglasses. He halted a few paces from her and said:

"What about the song? Why does that make you cry?"

She raised her head from her arms and dried her eyes with the back of her hand like a child. A kinder note than he had intended went into his voice.

"Why, Gretta?" he asked.

"I am thinking about a person long ago who used to sing that song."

"And who was the person long ago?" asked Gabriel, smiling.

"It was a person I used to know in Galway when I was living with my grandmother," she said.

The smile passed away from Gabriel's face. A dull anger began to gather again at the back of his mind and the dull fires of his lust began to glow angrily in his veins.

"Someone you were in love with?" he asked ironically.

"It was a young boy I used to know," she answered, "named Michael Furey. He used to sing that song, *The Lass of Aughrim*. He was very delicate."

Gabriel was silent. He did not wish her to think that he was interested in this delicate boy.

"I can see him so plainly," she said, after a moment. "Such eyes as he had: big, dark eyes! And such an expression in them—an expression!"

"O, then, you are in love with him?" said Gabriel.

"I used to go out walking with him," she said, "when I was in Galway."

A thought flew across Gabriel's mind.

"Perhaps that was why you wanted to go to Galway with that Ivors girl?" he said coldly.

She looked at him and asked in surprise:

"What for?"

Her eyes made Gabriel feel awkward. He shrugged his shoulders and said:

"How do I know? To see him, perhaps."

She looked away from him along the shaft of light towards the window in silence.

"He is dead," she said at length. "He died when he was only seventeen. Isn't it a terrible thing to die so young as that?"

"What was he?" asked Gabriel, still ironically.

"He was in the gasworks," she said.

Gabriel felt humiliated by the failure of his irony and by the evocation of this figure from the dead, a boy in the gasworks. While he had been full of memories of their secret life together, full of tenderness and joy and desire, she had been comparing him in her mind with another. A shameful consciousness of his own person assailed him. He saw himself as a ludicrous figure, acting as a pennyboy[6] for his aunts, a nervous, well-meaning sentimentalist, orating to vulgarians and idealizing his own clownish lusts, the pitiable fatuous fellow he had caught a glimpse of in the mirror. Instinctively he turned his back more to the light lest she might see the shame that burned upon his forehead.

He tried to keep up his tone of cold interrogation, but his voice when he spoke was humble and indifferent.

"I suppose you were in love with this Michael Furey, Gretta," he said.

"I was great with him at that time," she said.

Her voice was veiled and sad. Gabriel, feeling now how vain it would be to try to lead her whither he had purposed, caressed one of her hands and said, also sadly:

"And what did he die of so young, Gretta? Consumption, was it?"

"I think he died for me," she answered.

A vague terror seized Gabriel at this answer, as if, at that hour when he had hoped to triumph, some impalpable and vindictive being was coming against him, gathering forces against him in its vague world. But he shook himself free of it with an effort of reason and continued to caress her hand. He did not question her again, for he felt that she would tell him of herself. Her hand was warm and moist: it did not respond to his touch, but he continued to caress it just as he had caressed her first letter to him that spring morning.

"It was in the winter," she said, "about the beginning of the winter when I was going to leave my grandmother's and come up here to the convent. And he was ill at the time in his lodgings in Galway and wouldn't be let out, and his people in Oughterard[7] were written to. He was in decline, they said, or something like that. I never knew rightly."

She paused for a moment and sighed.

"Poor fellow," she said. "He was very fond of me and he was such a gentle boy. We used to go out together, walking, you know, Gabriel, like the way they do in the country. He was going to study singing only for his health. He had a very good voice, poor Michael Furey."

"Well; and then?" asked Gabriel.

"And then when it came to the time for me to leave Galway and come up to the convent he was much worse and I wouldn't be let see him so I wrote him a letter saying I was going up to Dublin and would be back in the summer, and hoping he would be better then."

She paused for a moment to get her voice under control, and then went on:

6. Errand boy. 7. Town in Connacht, 20 miles north of Galway.

"Then the night before I left, I was in my grandmother's house in Nuns' Island, packing up, and I heard gravel thrown up against the window. The window was so wet I couldn't see, so I ran downstairs as I was and slipped out the back into the garden and there was the poor fellow at the end of the garden, shivering."

"And did you not tell him to go back?" asked Gabriel.

"I implored of him to go home at once and told him he would get his death in the rain. But he said he did not want to live. I can see his eyes as well as well! He was standing at the end of the wall where there was a tree."

"And did he go home?" asked Gabriel.

"Yes, he went home. And when I was only a week in the convent he died and he was buried in Oughterard, where his people came from. O, the day I heard that, that he was dead!"

She stopped, choking with sobs, and, overcome by emotion, flung herself face downwards on the bed, sobbing in the quilt. Gabriel held her hand for a moment longer, irresolutely, and then, shy of intruding on her grief, let it fall gently and walked quietly to the window.

She was fast asleep.

Gabriel, leaning on his elbow, looked for a few moments unresentfully on her tangled hair and half-open mouth, listening to her deep-drawn breath. So she had had that romance in her life: a man had died for her sake. It hardly pained him now to think how poor a part he, her husband, had played in her life. He watched her while she slept, as though he and she had never lived together as man and wife. His curious eyes rested long upon her face and on her hair: and, as he thought of what she must have been then, in that time of her first girlish beauty, a strange, friendly pity for her entered his soul. He did not like to say even to himself that her face was no longer beautiful, but he knew that it was no longer the face for which Michael Furey had braved death.

Perhaps she had not told him all the story. His eyes moved to the chair over which she had thrown some of her clothes. A petticoat string dangled to the floor. One boot stood upright, its limp upper fallen down: the fellow of it lay upon its side. He wondered at his riot of emotions of an hour before. From what had it proceeded? From his aunt's supper, from his own foolish speech, from the wine and dancing, the merry-making when saying good night in the hall, the pleasure of the walk along the river in the snow. Poor Aunt Julia! She, too, would soon be a shade with the shade of Patrick Morkan and his horse. He had caught that haggard look upon her face for a moment when she was singing *Arrayed for the Bridal*. Soon, perhaps, he would be sitting in that same drawing-room, dressed in black, his silk hat on his knees.

The blinds would be drawn down and Aunt Kate would be sitting beside him, crying and blowing her nose and telling him how Julia had died. He would cast about in his mind for some words that might console her, and would find only lame and useless ones. Yes, yes: that would happen very soon.

The air of the room chilled his shoulders. He stretched himself cautiously along under the sheets and lay down beside his wife. One by one, they were all becoming shades. Better pass boldly into that other world, in the full glory of some passion, than fade and wither dismally with age. He thought of how she who lay beside him had locked in her heart for so many years that image of her lover's eyes when he had told her that he did not wish to live.

Generous tears filled Gabriel's eyes. He had never felt that himself towards any woman, but he knew that such a feeling must be love. The tears gathered more thickly in his eyes and in the partial darkness he imagined he saw the form of a young man standing under a dripping tree. Other forms were near. His soul had approached that region where dwell the vast hosts of the dead. He was conscious of, but could not apprehend, their wayward and flickering existence. His own identity was fading out into a grey impalpable world: the solid world itself, which these dead had one time reared and lived in, was dissolving and dwindling.

A few light taps upon the pane made him turn to the window. It had begun to snow again. He watched sleepily the flakes, silver and dark, falling obliquely against the lamplight. The time had come for him to set out on his journey westwards. Yes, the newspapers were right: snow was general all over Ireland. It was falling on every part of the dark central plain, on the treeless hills, falling softly upon the Bog of Allen[8] and, further westwards, softly falling into the dark mutinous Shannon waves. It was falling, too, upon every part of the lonely churchyard on the hill where Michael Furey lay buried. It lay thickly drifted on the crooked crosses and headstones, on the spears of the little gate, on the barren thorns. His soul swooned slowly as he heard the snow falling faintly through the universe and faintly falling, like the descent of their last end, upon all the living and the dead.

---

1. What is the central conflict of the story? Among the numerous minor characters, which contribute most to the development of the conflict?
2. What is the significance of the song sung by Bartell D'Arcy? Is it significant that he has a bad cold and sings it hoarsely?
3. What ideological conflicts enter the story? How are they related to personal conflicts?

8. Southwest of Dublin; Shannon is a river flowing westward through Ireland.

4. What is the prevailing tone of the party? Is it in conformity with the tone of the whole story?
5. Why do you suppose Joyce gave so complete an itemization of the food on the supper table? Why give Gabriel's speech in full?
6. How does the party prepare the "riot of emotions" in Gabriel's psyche?
7. What suggestions of discord and incompatibility between Gabriel and his wife appear before they go to their hotel room?
8. Gretta tells Gabriel that he is a "very generous person." To what extent is this praise supported by what we learn of him? Has his generosity been modified or lessened by what Gretta tells him of Michael Furey?
9. Since most of the story is told from Gabriel's point of view, what is gained by opening the story before he comes on the scene?
10. The structure may suggest that of a play in two scenes. What would be omitted if the material were presented as a play rather than as fiction? Would the omissions radically alter its meaning or effectiveness?

Franz Kafka

*Kafka (1883–1924) was born in Prague, the son of a middle-class Jewish family. After obtaining a law degree at the German University in Prague, he held an inconspicuous position in the civil service for many years. His few intimates remembered him as a warmly humorous man; however, his deep sense of inferiority to his father, the frailty of his health, his indecisive and prolonged engagement that never led to marriage, his preoccupation with suicide, and his last years of struggle against the tuberculosis that killed him suggest some origins of the great anxiety that pervades his literary production. He was not altogether a pessimist but was tormented by the conviction that goodness is very remote and nearly impossible to attain. Though he considered his writing the major task of his life, he had completed very few of his projects at the time of his death and published even fewer. He directed his friend Max Brod to burn his remaining manuscripts when he died. Brod ignored the command and saw that many of them were published. Three unfinished novels—*The Trial *(1925),* The Castle *(1926), and* Amerika *(1927)—brought Kafka his first posthumous fame, but the fairly large body of stories published under Brod's sponsorship show the complexity of the author's imagination and metaphysical irony perhaps more comprehensively than the novels that earned him his place as a major spokesman for the Age of Anxiety. His stories in English translation can be found in* The Great Wall of China *(1933),* The Penal Colony *(1948), and* The Complete Stories *(1976).*

The Metamorphosis[1]

I

As Gregor Samsa awoke one morning from uneasy dreams he found himself transformed in his bed into a gigantic insect. He was lying on his hard, as it were armor-plated, back and when he lifted his head a little he could see his dome-like brown belly divided into stiff arched segments on top of which the bed quilt could hardly keep in position and was about to slide off completely. His numerous legs, which were pitifully thin compared to the rest of his bulk, waved helplessly before his eyes.

1. Translated by Edwin and Willa Muir.

What has happened to me? he thought. It was no dream. His room, a regular human bedroom, only rather too small, lay quiet between the four familiar walls. Above the table on which a collection of cloth samples was unpacked and spread out—Samsa was a commercial traveler—hung the picture which he had recently cut out of an illustrated magazine and put into a pretty gilt frame. It showed a lady, with a fur cap on and a fur stole, sitting upright and holding out to the spectator a huge fur muff into which the whole of her forearm had vanished!

Gregor's eyes turned next to the window, and the overcast sky—one could hear rain drops beating on the window gutter—made him quite melancholy. What about sleeping a little longer and forgetting all this nonsense, he thought, but it could not be done, for he was accustomed to sleep on his right side and in his present condition he could not turn himself over. However violently he forced himself towards his right side he always rolled on to his back again. He tried it at least a hundred times, shutting his eyes to keep from seeing his struggling legs, and only desisted when he began to feel in his side a faint dull ache he had never experienced before.

Oh God, he thought, what an exhausting job I've picked on! Traveling about day in, day out. It's much more irritating work than doing the actual business in the office, and on top of that there's the trouble of constant traveling, of worrying about train connections, the bed and irregular meals, casual acquaintances that are always new and never become intimate friends. The devil take it all! He felt a slight itching up on his belly; slowly pushed himself on his back nearer to the top of the bed so that he could lift his head more easily; identified the itching place which was surrounded by many small white spots the nature of which he could not understand and made to touch it with a leg, but drew the leg back immediately, for the contact made a cold shiver run through him.

He slid down again into his former position. This getting up early, he thought, makes one quite stupid. A man needs his sleep. Other commercials live like harem women. For instance, when I come back to the hotel of a morning to write up the orders I've got, these others are only sitting down to breakfast. Let me just try that with my chief; I'd be sacked on the spot. Anyhow, that might be quite a good thing for me, who can tell? If I didn't have to hold my hand because of my parents I'd have given notice long ago, I'd have gone to the chief and told him exactly what I think of him. That would knock him endways from his desk! It's a queer way of doing, too, this sitting on high at a desk and talking down to employees, especially when they have to come quite near because the chief is hard of hearing. Well, there's still hope; once I've saved enough money to pay back my parents' debts to him—that should take another five or six years—I'll do it without fail.

I'll cut myself completely loose then. For the moment, though, I'd better get up, since my train goes at five.

He looked at the alarm clock ticking on the chest. Heavenly Father! he thought. It was half-past six o'clock and the hands were quietly moving on, it was even past the half-hour, it was getting on toward a quarter to seven. Had the alarm clock not gone off? From the bed one could see that it had been properly set for four o'clock; of course it must have gone off. Yes, but was it possible to sleep quietly through that ear-splitting noise? Well, he had not slept quietly, yet apparently all the more soundly for that. But what was he to do now? The next train went at seven o'clock; to catch that he would need to hurry like mad and his samples weren't even packed up, and he himself wasn't feeling particularly fresh and active. And even if he did catch the train he wouldn't avoid a row with the chief, since the firm's porter would have been waiting for the five o'clock train and would have long since reported his failure to turn up. The porter was a creature of the chief's, spineless and stupid. Well, supposing he were to say he was sick? But that would be most unpleasant and would look suspicious, since during his five years' employment he had not been ill once. The chief himself would be sure to come with the sick-insurance doctor, would reproach his parents with their son's laziness and would cut all excuses short by referring to the insurance doctor, who of course regarded all mankind as perfectly healthy malingerers. And would he be so far wrong on this occasion? Gregor really felt quite well, apart from a drowsiness that was utterly superfluous after such a long sleep, and he was even unusually hungry.

As all this was running through his mind at top speed without his being able to decide to leave his bed—the alarm clock had just struck a quarter to seven—there came a cautious tap at the door behind the head of his bed. "Gregor," said a voice—it was his mother's—"it's a quarter to seven. Hadn't you a train to catch?" That gentle voice! Gregor had a shock as he heard his own voice answering hers, unmistakably his own voice, it was true, but with a persistent horrible twittering squeak behind it like an undertone, that left the words in their clear shape only for the first moment and then rose up reverberating round them to destroy their sense, so that one could not be sure one had heard them rightly. Gregor wanted to answer at length and explain everything, but in the circumstances he confined himself to saying: "Yes, yes, thank you, Mother, I'm getting up now." The wooden door between them must have kept the change in his voice from being noticeable outside, for his mother contented herself with this statement and shuffled away. Yet this brief exchange of words had made the other members of the family aware that Gregor was still in the house, as they had not expected, and at one of the side doors his father was already knocking, gently, yet with his fist. "Gregor, Gregor," he called, "what's the matter with you?" And after a little while he called again in a deeper voice: "Gregor! Gregor!" At the other side door his sister was saying in a low, plaintive tone: "Gregor? Aren't you well? Are you needing anything?" He answered them both at once: "I'm just ready," and did his best to make his voice sound as normal as possible by enunciating the words very clearly and leaving long pauses between them. So his father went back to his breakfast, but his sister whispered: "Gregor, open the door, do." However, he was not thinking of opening the door, and felt thankful for the prudent habit he had acquired in traveling of locking all doors during the night, even at home.

His immediate intention was to get up quietly without being disturbed, to put on his clothes and above all eat his breakfast, and only then to consider what else was to be done, since in bed, he was well aware, his meditations would come to no sensible conclusion. He remembered that often enough in bed he had felt small aches and pains, probably caused by awkward postures, which had proved purely imaginary once he got up, and he looked forward eagerly to seeing this morning's delusions gradually fall away. That the change in his voice was nothing but the precursor of a severe chill, a standing ailment of commercial travelers, he had not the least possible doubt.

To get rid of the quilt was quite easy; he had only to inflate himself a little and it fell off by itself. But the next move was difficult, especially because he was so uncommonly broad. He would have needed arms and hands to hoist himself up; instead he had only the numerous little legs which never stopped waving in all directions and which he could not control in the least. When he tried to bend one of them it was the first to stretch itself straight; and did he succeed at last in making it do what he wanted, all the other legs meanwhile waved the more wildly in a high degree of unpleasant agitation. "But what's the use of lying idle in bed," said Gregor to himself.

He thought that he might get out of bed with the lower part of his body first, but this lower part, which he had not yet seen and of which he could form no clear conception, proved too difficult to move; it shifted so slowly; and when finally, almost wild with annoyance, he gathered his forces together and thrust out recklessly, he had miscalculated the direction and bumped heavily against the lower end of the bed, and the stinging pain he felt informed him that precisely this lower part of his body was at the moment probably the most sensitive.

So he tried to get the top part of himself out first, and cautiously moved his head towards the edge of the bed. That proved easy enough, and despite its breadth and mass the bulk of his body at last slowly followed the movement of his head. Still, when he finally got his head free over the edge of the bed he felt too scared to go on advancing, for after all if he let himself fall in this way it would take a miracle to keep his head from being injured. And at all costs he must not lose consciousness now, precisely now; he would rather stay in bed.

But when after a repetition of the same efforts he lay in his former position again, sighing, and watched his little legs struggling against each other more wildly than ever, if that were possible, and saw no way of bringing any order into this arbitrary confusion, he told himself again that it was impossible to stay in bed and that the most sensible course was to risk everything for the smallest hope of getting away from it. At the same time he did not forget meanwhile to remind himself that cool reflection, the coolest possible, was much better than desperate resolves. In such moments he focused his eyes as sharply as possible on the window, but, unfortunately, the prospect of the morning fog, which muffled even the other side of the narrow street, brought him little encouragement and comfort. "Seven o'clock already," he said to himself when the alarm clock chimed again, "seven o'clock already and still such a thick fog." And for a little while he lay quiet, breathing lightly, as if perhaps expecting such complete repose to restore all things to their real and normal condition.

But then he said to himself: "Before it strikes a quarter past seven I must be quite out of this bed, without fail. Anyhow, by that time someone will have come from the office to ask for me, since it opens before seven." And he set himself to rocking his whole body at once in a regular rhythm, with the idea of swinging it out of the bed. If he tipped himself out in that way he could keep his head from injury by lifting it at an acute angle when he fell. His back seemed to be hard and was not likely to suffer from a fall on the carpet. His biggest worry was the loud crash he would not be able to help making, which would probably cause anxiety, if not terror, behind all the doors. Still, he must take the risk.

When he was already half out of the bed—the new method was more a game than an effort, for he needed only to hitch himself across by rocking to and fro—it struck him how simple it would be if he could get help. Two strong people—he thought of his father and the servant girl—would be amply sufficient; they would only have to thrust their arms under his convex back, lever him out of the bed, bend down with their burden and then be patient enough to let him turn himself right over on to the floor, where it was to be hoped his legs would then find their proper function. Well, ignoring the fact that the doors were all locked, ought he really to call for help? In spite of his misery he could not suppress a smile at the very idea of it.

He had got so far that he could barely keep his equilibrium when he rocked himself strongly, and he would have to nerve himself very soon for the final decision since in five minutes' time it would be a quarter past seven—when the front door bell rang. "That's someone from the office," he said to himself, and grew almost rigid, while his little legs only jigged about all the faster. For a moment everything stayed quiet. "They're not going to open the door," said Gregor to himself, catching at some kind of irrational hope. But then of course the servant girl went as usual to the door with her heavy tread and opened it. Gregor needed only to hear the first good morning of the visitor to know immediately who it was—the chief clerk himself. What a fate, to be condemned to work for a firm where the smallest omission at once gave rise to the gravest suspicion! Were all employees in a body nothing but scoundrels, was there not among them one single loyal devoted man who, had he wasted only an hour or so of the firm's time in a morning, was so tormented by conscience as to be driven out of his mind and actually incapable of leaving his bed? Wouldn't it really have been sufficient to send an apprentice to inquire—if any inquiry were necessary at all—did the chief clerk himself have to come and thus indicate to the entire family, an innocent family, that this suspicious circumstance could be investigated by no one less versed in affairs then himself? And more through the agitation caused by these reflections than through any act of will Gregor swung himself out of bed with all his strength. There was a loud thump, but it was not really a crash. His fall was broken to some extent by the carpet, his back, too, was less stiff than he thought, and so there was merely a dull thud, not so very startling. Only he had not lifted his head carefully enough and had hit it; he turned it and rubbed it on the carpet in pain and irritation.

"That was something falling down in there," said the chief clerk in the next room to the left. Gregor tried to suppose to himself that something like what had happened to him today might some day happen to the chief clerk; one really could not deny that it was possible. But as if in brusque reply to this supposition the chief clerk took a couple of firm steps in the next-door room and his patent leather boots creaked. From the right-hand room his sister was whispering to inform him of the situation: "Gregor, the chief clerk's here." "I know," muttered Gregor to himself; but he didn't dare to make his voice loud enough for his sister to hear it.

"Gregor," said his father now from the left-hand room, "the chief clerk has come and wants to know why you didn't catch the early train. We don't know what to say to him. Besides, he wants to talk to you in person. So open the door, please. He will be good enough to excuse the untidiness of your room." "Good morning, Mr. Samsa," the chief clerk was calling amiably meanwhile. "He's not well," said his mother to the visitor, while his father was still speaking through the door, "he's not well, sir, believe me. What else would make him miss a train! The boy thinks about nothing but his work. It makes me almost cross the way he never goes out in the evenings; he's been here the last eight days and has stayed at home every single evening. He just sits there quietly at the table reading a newspaper or looking through railway timetables. The only amusement he gets is doing fretwork. For instance, he spent two or three evenings cutting out a little picture frame; you would be surprised to see how pretty it is; it's hanging in his room; you'll see it in a minute when Gregor opens the door. I must say I'm glad you've come, sir; we should never have got him to unlock the door by ourselves; he's so obstinate; and I'm sure he's unwell, though he wouldn't have it to be so this morning." "I'm just coming," said Gregor slowly and carefully, not moving an inch for fear of losing one word of the conversation. "I can't think of any other explanation, madam," said the chief clerk, "I hope it's nothing serious. Although on the other hand I must say that we men of business—fortunately or unfortunately—very often simply have to ignore any slight indisposition, since business must be attended to." "Well, can the chief clerk come in now?" asked Gregor's father impatiently, again knocking on the door. "No," said Gregor. In the left-hand room a painful silence followed this refusal, in the right-hand room his sister began to sob.

Why didn't his sister join the others? She was probably newly out of bed and hadn't even begun to put on her clothes yet. Well, why was she crying? Because he wouldn't get up and let the chief clerk in, because he was in danger of losing his job, and because the chief would begin dunning his parents again for the old debts? Surely these were things one didn't need to worry about for the present. Gregor was still at home and not in the least thinking of deserting the family. At the moment, true, he was lying on the carpet and no one who knew the condition he was in could seriously expect him to admit the chief clerk. But for such a small discourtesy, which could plausibly be explained away somehow later on, Gregor could hardly be dismissed on the spot. And it seemed to Gregor that it would be much more sensible to leave him in peace for the present than to trouble him with tears and entreaties. Still, of course, their uncertainty bewildered them all and excused their behavior.

"Mr. Samsa," the chief clerk called now in a louder voice, "what's the matter with you? Here you are, barricading yourself in your room, giving only 'yes' and 'no' for answers, causing your parents a lot of unnecessary trouble and neglecting—I mention this only in passing—neglecting your business duties in an incredible fashion. I am speaking here in the name of your parents and of your chief, and I beg you quite seriously to give me an immediate and precise explanation. You amaze me, you amaze me. I thought you were a quiet, dependable person, and now all at once you seem bent on making a disgraceful exhibition of yourself. The chief did hint to me early this morning a possible explanation for your disappearance—with reference to the cash payments that were entrusted to you recently—but I almost pledged my solemn word of honor that this could not be so. But now that I see how incredibly obstinate you are, I no longer have the slightest desire to take your part at all. And your position in the firm is not so unassailable. I came with the intention of telling you all this in private, but since you are wasting my time so needlessly I don't see why your parents shouldn't hear it too. For some time past your work has been most unsatisfactory; this is not the season of the year for a business boom, of course, we admit that, but a season of the year for doing no business at all, that does not exist, Mr. Samsa, must not exist."

"But, sir," cried Gregor, beside himself and in his agitation forgetting everything else, "I'm just going to open the door this very minute. A slight illness, an attack of giddiness, has kept me from getting up. I'm still lying in bed. But I feel all right again. I'm getting out of bed now. Just give me a moment or two longer! I'm not quite so well as I thought. But I'm all right, really. How a thing like that can suddenly strike one down! Only last night I was quite well, my parents can tell you, or rather I did have a slight presentiment. I must have showed some sign of it. Why didn't I report it at the office! But one always thinks that an indisposition can be got over without staying in the house. Oh sir, do spare my parents! All that you're reproaching me with now has no foundation; no one has ever said a word to me about it. Perhaps you haven't looked at the last orders I sent in. Anyhow, I can still catch the eight o'clock train, I'm much the better for my few hours' rest. Don't let me detain you here, sir; I'll be attending to business very soon, and do be good enough to tell the chief so and to make my excuses to him!"

And while all this was tumbling out pell-mell and Gregor hardly knew what he was saying, he had reached the chest quite easily, perhaps because of the practice he had had in bed, and was now trying to lever himself upright by means of it. He meant actually to open the door, actually to show himself and speak to the chief clerk; he was eager to find out what the others, after all their insistence, would say at the sight of him. If they were horrified then the responsibility was no longer his and he could stay quiet. But if they took it calmly, then he had no reason either to be upset, and could really get to the station for the eight o'clock train if he hurried. At first he slipped down a few times from the polished surface of the chest, but at length with a last heave he stood upright; he paid no more attention to the pains in the lower part of his body, however they smarted. Then he let himself fall against the back of a near-by chair, and clung with his little legs to the edges of it. That brought him into control of himself again and he stopped speaking, for now he could listen to what the chief clerk was saying.

"Did you understand a word of it?" the chief clerk was asking; "surely he can't be trying to make fools of us?" "Oh dear," cried his mother, in tears, "perhaps he's terribly ill and we're tormenting him. Grete! Grete!" she called out then. "Yes Mother?" called his sister from the other side. They were calling to each other across Gregor's room. "You must go this minute for the doctor. Gregor is ill. Go for the doctor, quick. Did you hear how he was speaking?" "That was no human voice," said the chief clerk in a voice noticeably low beside the shrillness of the mother's. "Anna! Anna!" his father was calling through the hall to the kitchen, clapping his hands, "get a locksmith at once!" And the two girls were already running through the hall with a swish of skirts—how could his sister have got dressed so quickly?—and were tearing the front door open. There was no sound of its closing again; they had evidently left it open, as one does in houses where some great misfortune has happened.

But Gregor was now much calmer. The words he uttered were no longer understandable, apparently, although they seemed clear enough to him, even clearer than before, perhaps because his ear had grown accustomed to the sound of them. Yet at any rate people now believed that something was wrong with him, and were ready to help him. The positive certainty with which these first measures had been taken comforted him. He felt himself drawn once more into the human circle and hoped for great and remarkable results from both the doctor and the locksmith, without really distinguishing precisely between them. To make his voice as clear as possible for the decisive conversation that was now imminent he coughed a little, as quietly as he could, of course, since this noise too might not sound like a human cough for all he was able to judge. In the next room meanwhile there was complete silence. Perhaps his parents were sitting at the table with the chief clerk, whispering, perhaps they were all leaning against the door and listening.

Slowly Gregor pushed the chair towards the door, then let go of it, caught hold of the door for support—the soles at the end of his little legs were somewhat sticky—and rested against it for a moment after his efforts. Then he set himself to turning the key in the lock with his mouth. It seemed, unhappily, that he hadn't really any teeth—what could he grip the key with?—but on the other hand his jaws were certainly very strong; with their help he did manage to set the key in motion, heedless of the fact that he was undoubtedly damaging them somewhere, since a brown fluid issued from his mouth, flowed over the key and dripped on the floor. "Just listen to that," said the chief clerk next door; "he's turning the key." That was a great encouragement to Gregor; but they should all have shouted encouragement to him, his father and mother too: "Go on, Gregor," they should have called out, "keep going, hold on to that key!" And in the belief that they were all following his efforts intently, he clenched his jaws recklessly on the key with all the force at his command. As the turning of the key progressed he circled round the lock, holding on now only with his mouth, pushing on the key, as required, or pulling it down again with all the weight of his body. The louder click of the finally yielding lock literally quickened Gregor. With a deep breath of relief he said to himself: "So I didn't need the locksmith," and laid his head on the handle to open the door wide.

Since he had to pull the door towards him, he was still invisible when it was really wide open. He had to edge himself slowly round the near half of the double door, and to do it very carefully if he was not to fall plump upon his back just on the threshold. He was still carrying out this difficult manoeuvre, with no time to observe anything else, when he heard the chief clerk utter a loud "Oh!"—it sounded like a gust of wind—and now he could see the man, standing as he was nearest to the door, clapping one hand before his open mouth and slowly backing away as if driven by some invisible steady pressure. His mother—in spite of the chief clerk's being there her hair was still undone and sticking up in all directions—first clasped her hands and looked at his father, then took two steps towards Gregor and fell on the floor among her outspread skirts, her face quite hidden on her breast. His father knotted his fist with a fierce expression on his face as if he meant to knock Gregor back into his room, then looked uncertainly round the living room, covered his eyes with his hands and wept till his great chest heaved.

Gregor did not go now into the living room, but leaned against the inside of the firmly shut wing of the door, so that only half his body was visible and his head above it bending sideways to look at the others. The light had meanwhile strengthened; on the other side of the street one could see clearly a section of the endlessly long, dark gray building opposite—it was a hospital—abruptly punctuated by its row of regular windows; the rain was still falling, but only in large singly discernible and literally singly splashing drops. The breakfast dishes were set out on the table lavishly, for breakfast was the most important meal of the day to Gregor's father, who lingered it out for hours over various newspapers. Right opposite Gregor on the wall hung a photograph of himself on military service, as a lieutenant, hand on sword, a carefree smile on his face, inviting one to respect his uniform and military bearing. The door leading to the hall was open, and one could see that the front door stood open too, showing the landing beyond and the beginning of the stairs going down.

"Well," said Gregor, knowing perfectly that he was the only one who had retained any composure, "I'll put my clothes on at once, pack up my samples and start off. Will you only let me go? You see, sir, I'm not obstinate, and I'm willing to work; traveling is a hard life, but I couldn't live without it. Where are you going, sir? To the office? Yes? Will you give a true account of all this? One can be temporarily incapacitated, but that's just the moment for remembering former services and bearing in mind that later on, when the incapacity has been got over, one will certainly work with all the more industry and concentration. I'm loyally bound to serve the chief, you know that very well. Besides, I have to provide for my parents and my sister. I'm in great difficulties, but I'll get out of them again. Don't make things any worse for me than they are. Stand up for me in the firm. Travelers are not popular there, I know. People think they earn sacks of money and just have a good time. A prejudice there's no particular reason for revising. But you, sir, have a more comprehensive view of affairs than the rest of the staff, yes, let me tell you in confidence, a more comprehensive view than the chief himself, who, being the owner, lets his judgment easily be swayed against one of his employees. And you know very well that the traveler, who is never seen in the office almost the whole year round, can so easily fall a victim to gossip and ill luck and unfounded complaints, which he mostly knows nothing about, except when he comes back exhausted from his rounds, and only then suffers in person from their evil consequences, which he can no longer trace back to the original causes. Sir, sir, don't go away without a word to me to show that you think me in the right at least to some extent!"

But at Gregor's very first words the chief clerk had already backed away and only stared at him with parted lips over one twitching shoulder. And while Gregor was speaking he did not stand still one moment but stole away towards the door, without taking his eyes off Gregor, yet only an inch at a time, as if obeying some secret injunction to leave the room. He was already at the hall, and the suddenness with which he took his last step out of the living room would have made one believe he had burned the sole of his foot. Once in the hall he stretched his right arm before him towards the staircase, as if some supernatural power were waiting there to deliver him.

Gregor perceived that the chief clerk must on no account be allowed to go away in this frame of mind if his position in the firm were not to be endangered to the utmost. His parents did not undersand this so well; they had convinced themselves in the course of years that Gregor was settled for life in this firm, and besides they were so occupied with their immediate troubles that all foresight had forsaken them. Yet Gregor had this foresight. The chief clerk must be detained, soothed, persuaded and finally won over; the whole future of Gregor and his family depended on it! If only his sister had been there! She was intelligent; she had begun to cry while Gregor was still lying quietly on his back. And no doubt the chief clerk, so partial to ladies, would have been guided by her; she would have shut the door of the flat and in the hall talked him out of his horror. But she was not there, and Gregor would have to handle the situation himself. And without remembering that he was still unaware what powers of movement he possessed, without even remembering that his words in all possibility, indeed in all likelihood, would again be unintelligible, he let go the wing of the door, pushed himself through the opening, started to walk towards the chief clerk, who was already ridiculously clinging with both hands to the railing on the landing; but immediately, as he was feeling for a support, he fell down with a little cry upon all his numerous legs. Hardly was he down when he experienced for the first time this morning a sense of physical comfort; his legs had firm ground under them; they were completely obedient, as he noted with joy; they even strove to carry him forward in whatever direction he chose; and he was inclined to believe that a final relief from all his sufferings was at hand. But in the same moment as he found himself on the floor, rocking with suppressed eagerness to move, not far from his mother, indeed just in front of her, she, who had seemed so completely crushed, sprang all at once to her feet, her arms and fingers outspread, cried: "Help, for God's sake, help!" bent her head down as if to see Gregor better, yet on the contrary kept backing senselessly away; had quite forgotten that the laden table stood behind her; sat upon it hastily, as if in absence of mind, when she bumped into it; and seemed altogether unaware that the big coffee pot beside her was upset and pouring coffee in a flood over the carpet.

"Mother, Mother," said Gregor in a low voice, and looked up at her. The chief clerk, for the moment, had quite slipped from his mind; instead, he could not resist snapping his jaws together at the sight of the streaming coffee. That made his mother scream again, she fled from the table and fell into the arms of his father, who hastened to catch her. But Gregor had now no time to spare for his parents; the chief clerk was already on the stairs; with his chin on the banisters he was taking one last backward look. Gregor made a spring, to be as sure as possible of overtaking him; the chief clerk must have divined his intention, for he leaped down several steps and vanished; he was still yelling "Ugh!" and it echoed through the whole staircase.

Unfortunately, the flight of the chief clerk seemed completely to upset Gregor's father, who had remained relatively calm until now, for instead of running after the man himself, or at least not hindering Gregor in his pursuit, he seized in his right hand the walking stick which the chief clerk had left behind on a chair, together with a hat and greatcoat, snatched in his left hand a large newspaper from the table and began stamping his feet and flourishing the stick and the newspaper to drive Gregor back into his room. No entreaty of Gregor's availed, indeed no entreaty was even understood; however humbly he bent his head his father only stamped on the floor the more loudly. Behind his father his mother had torn open a window, despite the cold weather, and was leaning far out of it with her face in her hands. A strong draught set in from the street to the staircase, the window curtains blew in, the newspapers on the table fluttered, stray pages whisked over the floor. Pitilessly Gregor's father drove him back, hissing and crying "Shoo!" like a savage. But Gregor was quite unpracticed in walking backwards, it really was a slow business. If he only had a chance to turn round he could get back to his room at once, but he was afraid of exasperating his father by the slowness of such a rotation and at any moment the stick in his father's hand might hit him a fatal blow on the back or on the head. In the end, however, nothing else was left for him to do since to his horror he observed that in moving backwards he could not even control the direction he took; and so, keeping an anxious eye on his father all the time over his shoulder, he began to turn round as quickly as he could, which was in reality very slowly. Perhaps his father noted his good intentions, for he did not interfere except every now and then to help him in the manoeuvre from a distance with the point of the stick. If only he would have stopped making that unbearable hissing noise! It made Gregor quite lose his head. He had turned almost completely round when the hissing noise so distracted him that he even turned a little the wrong way again. But when at last his head was fortunately right in front of the doorway, it appeared that his body was too broad simply to get through the opening. His father, of course, in his present mood was far from thinking of such a thing as opening the other half of the door, to let Gregor have enough space. He had merely the fixed idea of driving Gregor back into his room as quickly as possible. He would never have suffered Gregor to make the circumstantial preparations for standing up on end and perhaps slipping his way through the door. Maybe he was now making more noise than ever to urge Gregor forward, as if no obstacle impeded him; to Gregor, anyhow, the noise in his rear sounded no longer like the voice of one single father; this was really no joke, and Gregor thrust himself—come what might—into the doorway. One side of his body rose up, he was tilted at an angle in the doorway, his flank was quite bruised, horrid blotches stained the white door, soon he was stuck fast and, left to himelf, could not have moved at all, his legs on one side fluttered trembling in the air, those on the other were crushed painfully to the floor—when from behind his father gave him a strong push which was literally a deliverance and he flew far into the room, bleeding freely. The door was slammed behind him with the stick, and then at last there was silence.

II

Not until it was twilight did Gregor awake out of a deep sleep, more like a swoon than a sleep. He would certainly have waked up of his own accord not much later, for he felt himself sufficiently rested and well-slept, but it seemed to him as if a fleeting step and a cautious shutting of the door leading into the hall had aroused him. The electric lights in the street cast a pale sheen here and there on the ceiling and the upper surfaces of the furniture, but down below, where he lay, it was dark. Slowly, awkwardly trying out his feelers, which he now first learned to appreciate, he pushed his way to the door to see what had been happening there. His left side felt like one single long, unpleasantly tense scar, and he had actually to limp on his two rows of legs. One little leg, moreover, had been severely damaged in the course of that morning's events—it was almost a miracle that only one had been damaged—and trailed uselessly behind him.

He had reached the door before he discovered what had really drawn him to it: the smell of food. For there stood a basin filled with fresh milk in which floated little sops of white bread. He could almost have laughed with joy, since he was now still hungrier than in the morning, and he dipped his head almost over the eyes straight into the milk. But soon in disappointment he withdrew it again; not only did he find it difficult to feed because of his tender left side—and he could only feed with the palpitating collaboration of his whole body—he did not like the milk either, although milk had been his favorite drink and that was certainly why his sister had set it there for him, indeed it was almost with repulsion that he turned away from the basin and crawled back to the middle of the room.

He could see through the crack of the door that the gas was turned on in the living room, but while usually at this time his father made a habit of reading the afternoon newspaper in a loud voice to his mother and occasionally to his sister as well, not a sound was now to be heard. Well, perhaps his father had recently given up this habit of reading aloud, which his sister had mentioned so often in conversation and in her letters. But there was the same silence all around, although the flat was certainly not empty of occupants. "What a quiet life our family has been leading," said Gregor to himself, and as he sat there motionless staring into the darkness he felt great pride in the fact that he had been able to provide such a life for his parents and sister in such a fine flat. But what if all the quiet, the comfort, the contentment were now to end in horror? To keep himself from being lost in such thoughts Gregor took refuge in movement and crawled up and down the room.

Once during the long evening one of the side doors was opened a little and quickly shut again, later the other side door too; someone had apparently wanted to come in and then thought better of it. Gregor now stationed himself immediately before the living room door, determined to persuade any hesitating visitor to come in or at least to discover who it might be; but the door was not opened again and he waited in vain. In the early morning, when the doors were locked, they had all wanted to come in, now that he had opened one door and the other had apparently been opened during the day, no one came in and even the keys were on the other side of the doors.

It was late at night before the gas went out in the living room, and Gregor could easily tell that his parents and his sister had all stayed awake until then, for he could clearly hear the three of them stealing away on tiptoe. No one was likely to visit him, not until the morning, that was certain; so he had plenty of time to meditate at his leisure on how he was to arrange his life afresh. But the lofty, empty room in which he had to lie flat on the floor filled him with an apprehension he could not account for, since it had been his very own room for the past five years—and with a half-unconscious action, not without a slight feeling of shame, he scuttled under the sofa, where he felt comfortable at once, although his back was a little cramped and he could not lift his head up, and his only regret was that his body was too broad to get the whole of it under the sofa.

He stayed there all night, spending the time partly in a light slumber, from which his hunger kept waking him up with a start, and partly in worrying and sketching vague hopes, which all led to the same conclusion, that he must lie low for the present and, by exercising patience and the utmost consideration, help the family to bear the inconvenience he was bound to cause them in his present condition.

Very early in the morning, it was still almost night, Gregor had the chance to test the strength of his new resolutions, for his sister, nearly fully dressed, opened the door from the hall and peered in. She did not see him at once, yet when she caught sight of him under the sofa—well, he had to be somewhere, he couldn't have flown away, could he?—she was so startled that without being able to help it she slammed the door shut again. But as if regretting her behavior she opened the door again immediately and came in on tiptoe, as if she were visiting an invalid or even a stranger. Gregor had pushed his head forward to the very edge of the sofa and watched her. Would she notice that he had left the milk standing, and not for lack of hunger, and would she bring in some other kind of food more to his taste? If she did not do it of her own accord, he would rather starve than draw her attention to the fact, although he felt a wild impulse to dart out from under the sofa, throw himself at her feet and beg her for something to eat. But his sister at once noticed, with surprise, that the basin was still full, except for a little milk that had been spilt all around it, she lifted it immediately, not with her bare hands, true, but with a cloth and carried it away. Gregor was wildly curious to know what she would bring instead, and made various speculations about it. Yet what she actually did next, in the goodness of her heart, he could never have guessed at. To find out what he liked she brought him a whole selection of food, all set out on an old newspaper. There were old, half-decayed vegetables, bones from last night's supper covered with a white sauce that had thickened; some raisins and almonds; a piece of cheese that Gregor would have called uneatable two days ago; a dry roll of bread, a buttered roll, and a roll both buttered and salted. Besides all that, she set down again the same basin, into which she had poured some water, and which was apparently to be reserved for his exclusive use. And with fine tact, knowing that Gregor would not eat in her presence, she withdrew quickly and even turned the key, to let him understand that he could take his ease as much as he liked. Gregor's legs all whizzed towards the food. His wounds must have healed completely, moreover, for he felt no disability, which amazed him and made him reflect how more than a month ago he had cut one finger a little with a knife and had still suffered pain from the wound only the day before yesterday. Am I less sensitive now? he thought, and sucked greedily at the cheese, which above all the other edibles attracted him at once and strongly. One after another and with tears of satisfaction in his eyes he quickly devoured the cheese, the vegetables and the sauce; the fresh food, on the other hand, had no charms for him, he could not even stand the smell of it and actually dragged away to some little distance the things he could eat. He had long finished his meal and was only lying lazily on the same spot when his sister turned the key slowly as a sign for him to retreat. That roused him at once, although he was nearly asleep, and he hurried under the sofa again. But it took considerable self-control for him to stay under the sofa, even for the short time his sister was in the room, since the large meal had swollen his body somewhat and he was so cramped he could hardly breathe. Slight attacks of breathlessness afflicted him and his eyes were starting a little out of his head as he watched his unsuspecting sister sweeping together with a broom not only the remains of what he had eaten but even the things he had not touched, as if these were now of no use to anyone, and hastily shoveling it all into a bucket, which she covered with a wooden lid and carried away. Hardly had she turned her back when Gregor came from under the sofa and stretched and puffed himself out.

In this manner Gregor was fed, once in the early morning while his parents and the servant girl were still asleep, and a second time after they had all had their midday dinner, for then his parents took a short nap and the servant girl could be sent out on some errand or other by his sister. Not that they would have wanted him to starve, of course, but perhaps they could not have borne to know more about his feeding than from hearsay, perhaps too his sister wanted to spare them such little anxieties wherever possible, since they had quite enough to bear as it was.

Under what pretext the doctor and the locksmith had been got rid of on that first morning Gregor could not discover, for since what he said was not understood by the others it never struck any of them, not even his sister, that he could understand what they said, and so whenever his sister came into his room he had to content himself with hearing her utter only a sigh now and then and an occasional appeal to the saints. Later on, when she had got a little used to the situation—of course she could never get completely used to it—she sometimes threw out a remark which was kindly meant or could be so interpreted. "Well, he liked his dinner today," she would say when Gregor had made a good clearance of his food; and when he had not eaten, which gradually happened more and more often, she would say almost sadly: "Everything's been left standing again."

But although Gregor could get no news directly, he overheard a lot from the neighboring rooms, and as soon as voices were audible, he would run to the door of the room concerned and press his whole body against it. In the first few days especially there was no conversation that did not refer to him somehow, even if only indirectly. For two whole days there were family consultations at every mealtime about what should be done; but also between meals the same subject was discussed, for there were always at least two members of the family at home, since no one wanted to be alone in the flat and to leave it quite empty was unthinkable. And on the very first of these days the household cook—it was not quite clear what and how much she knew of the situation—went down on her knees to his mother and begged leave to go, and when she departed, a quarter of an hour later, gave thanks for her dismissal with tears in her eyes as if for the greatest benefit that could have been conferred on her, and without any prompting swore a solemn oath that she would never say a single word to anyone about what had happened.

Now Gregor's sister had to cook too, helping her mother; true, the cooking did not amount to much, for they ate scarcely anything. Gregor was always hearing one of the family vainly urging another to eat and getting no answer but: "Thanks, I've had all I want," or something similar. Perhaps they drank nothing either. Time and again his sister kept asking his father if he wouldn't like some beer and offered kindly to go and fetch it herself, and when he made no answer suggested that she could ask the concierge to fetch it, so that he need feel no sense of obligation, but then a round "No" came from his father and no more was said about it.

In the course of that very first day Gregor's father explained the family's financial position and prospects to both his mother and his sister. Now and then he rose from the table to get some voucher or memorandum out of the small safe he had rescued from the collapse of his business five years earlier. One could hear him opening the complicated lock and rustling papers out and shutting it again. This statement made by his father was the first cheerful information Gregor had heard since his imprisonment. He had been of the opinion that nothing at all was left over from his father's business, at least his father had never said anything to the contrary, and of course he had not asked him directly. At that time Gregor's sole desire was to do his utmost to help the family to forget as soon as possible the catastrophe which had overwhelmed the business and thrown them all into a state of complete despair. And so he had set to work with unusual ardor and almost overnight had become a commercial traveler instead of a little clerk, with of course much greater chances of earning money, and his success was immediately translated into good round coin which he could lay on the table for his amazed and happy family. These had been fine times, and they had never recurred, at least not with the same sense of glory, although later on Gregor had earned so much money that he was able to meet the expenses of the whole household and did so. They had simply got used to it, both the family and Gregor; the money was gratefully accepted and gladly given, but there was no special uprush of warm feeling. With his sister alone had he remained intimate, and it was a secret plan of his that she, who loved music, unlike himself, and could play movingly on the violin, should be sent next year to study at the Conservatorium, despite the great expense that would entail, which must be made up in some other way. During his brief visits home the Conservatorium was often mentioned in the talks he had with his sister, but always merely as a beautiful dream which could never come true, and his parents discouraged even these innocent references to it; yet Gregor had made up his mind firmly about it and meant to announce the fact with due solemnity on Christmas Day.

Such were the thoughts, completely futile in his present condition, that went through his head as he stood clinging upright to the door and listening. Sometimes out of sheer weariness he had to give up listening and let his head fall negligently against the door, but he always had to pull himself together again at once, for even the slight sound his head made was audible next door and brought all conversation to a stop. "What can he be doing now?" his father would say after a while, obviously turning towards the door, and only then would the interrupted conversation gradually be set going again.

Gregor was now informed as amply as he could wish—for his father tended to repeat himself in his explanations, partly because it was a long time since he had handled such matters and partly because his mother could not always grasp things at once—that a certain amount of investments, a very small amount it was true, had survived the wreck of their fortunes and had even increased a little because the dividends had not been touched meanwhile. And besides that, the money Gregor brought home every month—he had kept only a few dollars for himself—had never been quite used up and now amounted to a small capital sum. Behind the door Gregor nodded his head eagerly, rejoiced at this evidence of unexpected thrift and foresight. True, he could really have paid off some more of his father's debts to the chief with his extra money, and so brought much nearer the day on which he could quit his job, but doubtless it was better the way his father had arranged it.

Yet this capital was by no means sufficient to let the family live on the interest of it; for one year, perhaps, or at the most two, they could live on the principal, that was all. It was simply a sum that ought not to be touched and should be kept for a rainy day; money for living expenses would have to be earned. Now his father was still hale enough but an old man, and he had done no work for the past five years and could not be expected to do much; during these five years, the first years of leisure in his laborious though unsuccessful life, he had grown rather fat and become sluggish. And Gregor's old mother, how was she to earn a living with her asthma, which troubled her even when she walked through the flat and kept her lying on a sofa every other day panting for breath beside an open window? And was his sister to earn her bread, she who was still a child of seventeen and whose life hitherto had been so pleasant, consisting as it did in dressing herself nicely, sleeping long, helping in the housekeeping, going out to a few modest entertainments and above all playing the violin? At first whenever the need for earning money was mentioned Gregor let go his hold on the door and threw himself down on the cool leather sofa beside it, he felt so hot with shame and grief.

Often he just lay there the long nights through without sleeping at all, scrabbling for hours on the leather. Or he nerved himself to the great effort of pushing an armchair to the window, then crawled up over the window sill and, braced against the chair, leaned against the window panes, obviously in some recollection of the sense of freedom that looking out of a window always used to give him. For in reality day by day things that were even a little way off were growing dimmer to his sight; the hospital across the street, which he used to execrate for being all too often before his eyes, was now quite beyond his range of vision, and if he had not known that he lived in Charlotte Street, a quiet street but still a city street, he might have believed that his window gave on a desert waste where gray sky and gray land blended indistinguishably into each other. His quick-witted sister only needed to observe twice that the armchair stood by the window; after that whenever she had tidied the room she always pushed the chair back to the same place at the window and even left the inner casements open.

If he could have spoken to her and thanked her for all she had to do for him, he could have borne her ministrations better; as it was, they oppressed him. She certainly tried to make as light as possible of whatever was disagreeable in her task, and as time went on she succeeded, of course, more and more, but time brought more enlightenment to Gregor too. The very way she came in distressed him. Hardly was she in the room when she rushed to the window, without even taking time to shut the door, careful as she was usually to shield the sight of Gregor's room from the others, and as if she were almost suffocating tore the casements open with hasty fingers, standing then in the open draught for a while even in the bitterest cold and drawing deep breaths. This noisy scurry of hers upset Gregor twice a day; he would crouch trembling under the sofa all the time, knowing quite well that she would certainly have spared him such a disturbance had she found it at all possible to stay in his presence without opening a window.

On one occasion, about month after Gregor's metamorphosis, when there was surely no reason for her to be still startled at his appearance, she came a little earlier than usual and found him gazing out of the window, quite motionless, and thus well placed to look like a bogey. Gregor would not have been surprised had she not come in at all, for she could not immediately open the window while he was there, but not only did she retreat, she jumped back as if in alarm and banged the door shut; a stranger might well have thought that he had been lying in wait for her there meaning to bite her. Of course he hid himself under the sofa at once, but he had to wait until midday before she came again, and she seemed more ill at ease than usual. This made him realize how repulsive the sight of him still was to her, and that it was bound to go on being repulsive, and what an effort it must cost her not to run away even from the sight of the small portion of his body that stuck out from under the sofa. In order to spare her that, therefore, one day he carried a sheet on his back to the sofa—it cost him four hours' labor—and arranged it there in such a way as to hide him completely, so that even if she were to bend down she could not see him. Had she considered the sheet unnecessary, she would certainly have stripped it off the sofa again, for it was clear enough that this curtaining and confining of himself was not likely to conduce Gregor's comfort, but she left it where it was, and Gregor even fancied that he caught a thankful glance from her eye when he lifted the sheet carefully a very little with his head to see how she was taking the new arrangement.

For the first fortnight his parents could not bring themselves to the point of entering his room, and he often heard them expressing their appreciation of his sister's activities, whereas formerly they had frequently scolded her for being as they thought a somewhat useless daughter. But now, both of them often waited outside the door, his father and his mother, while his sister tidied his room, and as soon as she came out she had to tell them exactly how things were in the room, what Gregor had eaten, how he had conducted himself this time and whether there was not perhaps some slight improvement in his condition. His mother, moreover, began relatively soon to want to visit him, but his father and sister dissuaded her at first with arguments which Gregor listened to very attentively and altogether approved. Later, however, she had to be held back by main force, and when she cried out: "Do let me in to Gregor, he is my unfortunate son! Can't you understand that I must go to him?" Gregor thought that it might be well to have her come in, not every day, of course, but perhaps once a week; she understood things, after all, much better than his sister, who was only a child despite the efforts she was making and had perhaps taken on so difficult a task merely out of childish thoughtlessness.

Gregor's desire to see his mother was soon fulfilled. During the daytime he did not want to show himself at the window, out of consideration for his parents, but he could not crawl very far around the few square yards of floor space he had, nor could he bear lying quietly at rest all during the night, while he was fast losing any interest he had ever taken in food, so that for mere recreation he had formed the habit of crawling crisscross over the walls and ceiling. He especially enjoyed hanging suspended from the ceiling; it was much better than lying on the floor; one could breathe more freely; one's body swung and rocked lightly; and in the almost blissful absorption induced by this suspension it could happen to his own surprise that he let go and fell plump on the floor. Yet he now had his body much better under control than formerly, and even such a big fall did him no harm. His sister at once remarked the new distraction Gregor had found for himself—he left traces behind him of the sticky stuff on his soles wherever he crawled—and she got the idea in her head of giving him as wide a field as possible to crawl in and of removing the pieces of furniture that hindered him, above all the chest of drawers and the writing desk. But that was more than she could manage all by herself; she did not dare ask her father to help her; and as for the servant girl, a young creature of sixteen who had had the courage to stay on after the cook's departure, she could not be asked to help, for she had begged as an especial favor that she might keep the kitchen door locked and open it only on a definite summons; so there was nothing left but to apply to her mother at an hour when her father was out. And the old lady did come, with exclamations of joyful eagerness, which, however, died away at the door of Gregor's room. Gregor's sister, of course, went in first, to see that everything was in order before letting his mother enter. In great haste Gregor pulled the sheet lower and rucked it more in folds so that it really looked as if it had been thrown accidentally over the sofa. And this time he did not peer out from under it; he renounced the pleasure of seeing his mother on this occasion and was only glad that she had come at all. "Come in, he's out of sight," said his sister, obviously leading her mother in by the hand. Gregor could now hear the two women struggling to shift the heavy old chest from its place, and his sister claiming the greater part of the labor for herself, without listening to the admonitions of her mother who feared she might overstrain herself. It took a long time. After at least a quarter of an hour's tugging his mother objected that the chest had better be left where it was, for in the first place it was too heavy and could never be got out before his father came home, and standing in the middle of the room like that it would only hamper Gregor's movements, while in the second place it was not at all certain that removing the furniture would be doing a service to Gregor. She was inclined to think to the contrary; the sight of the naked walls made her own heart heavy, and why shouldn't Gregor have the same feeling, considering that he had been used to his furniture for so long and might feel forlorn without it. "And doesn't it look," she concluded in a low voice—in fact she had been almost whispering all the time as if to avoid letting Gregor, whose exact whereabouts she did not know, hear even the tones of her voice, for she was convinced that he could not understand her words—"doesn't it look as if we were showing him, by taking away his furniture, that we have given up hope of his ever getting better and are just leaving him coldly to himself? I think it would be best to keep his room exactly as it has always been, so that when he comes back to us he will find everything unchanged and be able all the more easily to forget what has happened in between."

On hearing these words from his mother Gregor realized that the lack of all direct human speech for the past two months together with the monotony of family life must have confused his mind, otherwise he could not account for the fact that he had quite earnestly looked forward to having his room emptied of furnishing. Did he really want his warm room, so comfortably fitted with old family furniture, to be turned into a naked den in which he would certainly be able to crawl unhampered in all directions but at the price of shedding simultaneously all recollection of his human background? He had indeed been so near the brink of forgetfulness that only the voice of his mother, which he had not heard for so long, had drawn him back from it. Nothing should be taken out of his room; everything must stay as it was; he could not dispense with the good influence of the furniture on his state of mind; and even if the furniture did hamper him in his senseless crawling round and round, that was no drawback but a great advantage.

Unfortunately his sister was of the contrary opinion; she had grown accustomed, and not without reason, to consider herself an expert in Gregor's affairs as against her parents, and so her mother's advice was now enough to make her determined on the removal not only of the chest and the writing desk, which had been her first intention, but of all the furniture except the indispensable sofa. This determination was not, of course, merely the outcome of childish recalcitrance and of the self-confidence she had recently developed so unexpectedly and at such cost; she had in fact perceived that Gregor needed a lot of space to crawl about in, while on the other hand he never used the furniture at all, so far as could be seen. Another factor might have been also the enthusiastic temperament of an adolescent girl, which seeks to indulge itself on ever opportunity and which now tempted Grete to exaggerate the horror of her brother's circumstances in order that she might do all the more for him. In a room where Gregor lorded it all alone over empty walls no one save herself was likely ever to set foot.

And so she was not to be moved from her resolve by her mother who seemed moreover to be ill at ease in Gregor's room and therefore unsure of herself, was soon reduced to silence and helped her daughter as best she could to push the chest outside. Now, Gregor could do without the chest, if need be, but the writing desk he must retain. As soon as the two women had got the chest out of his room, groaning as they pushed it, Gregor stuck his head out from under the sofa to see how he might intervene as kindly and cautiously as possible. But as bad luck would have it, his mother was the first to return, leaving Grete clasping the chest in the room next door where she was trying to shift it all by herself, without of course moving it from the spot. His mother however was not accustomed to the sight of him, it might sicken her and so in alarm Gregor backed quickly to the other end of the sofa, yet could not prevent the sheet from swaying a little in front. That was enough to put her on the alert. She paused, stood still for a moment and then went back to Grete.

Although Gregor kept reassuring himself that nothing out of the way was happening, but only a few bits of furniture were being changed round, he soon had to admit that all this trotting to and fro of the two women, their little ejaculations and the scraping of furniture along the floor affected him like a vast disturbance coming from all sides at once, and however much he tucked in his head and legs and cowered to the very floor he was bound to confess that he would not be able to stand it for long. They were clearing his room out; taking away everything he loved; the chest in which he kept his fret saw and other tools was already dragged off; they were now loosening the writing desk which had almost sunk into the floor, the desk at which he had done all his homework when he was at the commercial academy, at the grammar school before that, and, yes, even at the primary school—he had no more time to waste in weighing the good intentions of the two women, whose existence he had by now almost forgotten, for they were so exhausted that they were laboring in silence and nothing could be heard but the heavy scuffling of their feet.

And so he rushed out—the women were just leaning against the writing desk in the next room to give themselves a breather—and four times changed his direction, since he really did not know what to rescue first, then on the wall opposite, which was already otherwise cleared, he was struck by the picture of the lady muffled in so much fur and quickly crawled up to it and pressed himself to the glass, which was a good surface to hold on to and comforted his hot belly. This picture at least, which was entirely hidden beneath him, was going to be removed by nobody. He turned his head towards the door of the living room so as to observe the women when they came back.

They had not allowed themselves much of a rest and were already coming; Grete had twined her arm round her mother and was almost supporting her. "Well, what shall we take now?" said Grete, looking round. Her eyes met Gregor's from the wall. She kept her composure, presumably because of her mother, bent her head down to her mother, to keep her from looking up, and said, although in a fluttering, unpremeditated voice: "Come, hadn't we better go back to the living room for a moment?" Her intentions were clear enough to Gregor, she wanted to bestow her mother in safety and then chase him down from the wall. Well, just let her try it! He clung to his picture and would not give it up. He would rather fly in Grete's face.

But Grete's words had succeeded in disquieting her mother, who took a step to one side, caught sight of the huge brown mass on the flowered wallpaper, and before she was really conscious that what she saw was Gregor screamed in a loud, hoarse voice: "Oh God, oh God!" fell with outspread arms over the sofa as if giving up and did not move. "Gregor!" cried his sister, shaking her fist and glaring at him. This was the first time she had directly addressed him since his metamorphosis. She ran into the next room for some aromatic essence with which to rouse her mother from her fainting fit. Gregor wanted to help too—

there was still time to rescue the picture—but he was stuck fast to the glass and had to tear himself loose; he then ran after his sister into the next room as if he could advise her, as he used to do; but then had to stand helplessly behind her; she meanwhile searched among various small bottles and when she turned round started in alarm at the sight of him; one bottle fell on the floor and broke; a splinter of glass cut Gregor's face and some kind of corrosive medicine splashed him; without pausing a moment longer Grete gathered up all the bottles she could carry and ran to her mother with them; she banged the door shut with her foot. Gregor was not cut off from his mother, who was perhaps nearly dying because of him; he dared not open the door for fear of frightening away his sister, who had to stay with her mother; there was nothing he could do but wait; and harassed by self-reproach and worry he began now to crawl to and fro, over everything, walls, furniture and ceiling, and finally in his despair, when the whole room seemed to be reeling round him, fell down on to the middle of the big table.

A little while elapsed, Gregor was still lying there feebly and all around was quiet, perhaps that was a good omen. Then the doorbell rang. The servant girl was of course locked in her kitchen, and Grete would have to open the door. It was his father. "What's been happening?" were his first words; Grete's face must have told him everything. Grete answered in a muffled voice, apparently hiding her head on his breast: "Mother has been fainting, but she's better now. Gregor's broken loose." "Just what I expected," said his father, "just what I've been telling you, but you women would never listen." It was clear to Gregor that his father had taken the worst interpretation of Grete's all too brief statement and was assuming that Gregor had been guilty of some violent act. Therefore Gregor must now try to propitiate his father, since he had neither time nor means for an explanation. And so he fled to the door of his own rom and crouched against it, to let his father see as soon as he came in from the hall that his son had the good intention of getting back into his room immediately and that it was not necessary to drive him there, but that if only the door were opened he would disappear at once.

Yet his father was not in the mood to perceive such fine distinctions. "Ah!" he cried as soon as he appeared, in a tone which sounded at once angry and exultant. Gregor drew his head back from the door and lifted it to look at his father. Truly, this was not the father he had imagined to himself; admittedly he had been too absorbed of late in his new recreation of crawling over the ceiling to take the same interest as before in what was happening elsewhere in the flat, and he ought really to be prepared for some changes. And yet, and yet, could that be his father? The man who used to lie wearily sunk in bed whenever Gregor set out on a business journey; who welcomed him back of an evening lying in a long chair in a dressing gown; who could not really rise to his feet but only lifted his arms in greeting, and on the rare occasions when he did go out with his family, on one or two Sundays a year and on high holidays, walked between Gregor and his mother, who were slow walkers anyhow, even more slowly than they did, muffled in his old greatcoat, shuffling laboriously forward with the help of his crook-handled stick which he set down most cautiously at every step and, whenever he wanted to say anything, nearly always came to a full stop and gathered his escort around him? Now he was standing there in fine shape; dressed in a smart blue uniform with gold buttons, such as bank messengers wear; his strong double chin bulged over the stiff high collar of his jacket; from under his bushy eyebrows his black eyes darted fresh and penetrating glances; his onetime tangled white hair had been combed flat on either side of a shining and carefully exact parting. He pitched his cap, which bore a gold monogram, probably the badge of some bank, in a wide sweep across the whole room on to a sofa and with the tail-ends of his jacket thrown back, his hands in his trouser pockets, advanced with a grim visage towards Gregor. Likely enough he did not himself know what he meant to do; at any rate he lifted his feet uncommonly high, and Gregor was dumbfounded at the enormous size of his shoe soles. But Gregor could not risk standing up to him, aware as he had been from the very first day of his new life that his father believed only the severest measures suitable for dealing with him. And so he ran before his father, stopping when he stopped and scuttling forward again when his father made any kind of move. In this way they circled the room several times without anything decisive happening; indeed the whole operation did not even look like a pursuit because it was carried out so slowly. And so Gregor did not leave the floor, for he feared that his father might take as a piece of peculiar wickedness any excursion of his over the walls or the ceiling. All the same, he could not stay this course much longer, for while his father took one step he had to carry out a whole series of movements. He was already beginning to feel breathless, just as in his former life his lungs had not been very dependable. As he was staggering along, trying to concentrate his energy on running, hardly keeping his eyes open; in his dazed state never even thinking of any other escape than simply going forward; and having almost forgotten that the walls were free to him, which in this room were well provided with finely carved pieces of furniture full of knobs and crevices—suddenly something lightly flung landed close behind him and rolled before him. It was an apple; a second apple followed immediately; Gregor came to a stop in alarm; there was no point in running on, for his father was determined to bombard him. He had filled his pockets with fruit from the dish on the sideboard and was now shying apple after apple, without taking particularly good aim for the moment. The small red apples rolled about the floor as if magnetized and cannoned into each other. An apple thrown without much force grazed Gregor's back and glanced off harmlessly. But another following immediately landed right on his back and sank in; Gregor wanted to drag himself forward, as if this startling, incredible pain could be left behind him; but he felt as if nailed to the spot and flattened himself out in a complete derangement of all his senses. With his last conscious look he saw the door of his room being torn open and his mother rushing out ahead of his screaming sister, in her underbodice, for her daughter had loosened her clothing to let her breathe more freely and recover from her swoon, he saw his mother rushing towards his father, leaving one after another behind her on the floor her loosened petticoats, stumbling over her petticoats straight to his father and embracing him, in complete union with him—but here Gregor's sight began to fail—with her hands clasped round his father's neck as she begged for her son's life.

III

The serious injury done to Gregor, which disabled him for more than a month—the apple went on sticking in his body as a visible reminder, since no one ventured to remove it—seemed to have made even his father recollect that Gregor was a member of the family, despite his present unfortunate and repulsive shape, and ought not to be treated as an enemy, that, on the contrary, family duty required the suppression of disgust and the exercise of patience, nothing but patience.

And although his injury had impaired, probably forever, his power of movement, and for the time being it took him long, long minutes to creep across his room like an old invalid—there was no question now of crawling up the wall—yet in his own opinion he was sufficiently compensated for this worsening of his condition by the fact that towards evening the living-room door, which he used to watch intently for an hour or two beforehand, was always thrown open, so that lying in the darkness of his room, invisible to the family, he could see them all at the lamp-lit table and listen to their talk, by general consent as it were, very different from his earlier eavesdropping.

True, their intercourse lacked the lively character of former times, which he had always called to mind with a certain wistfulness in the small hotel bedrooms where he had been wont to throw himself down, tired out, on damp bedding. They were now mostly very silent. Soon after supper his father would fall asleep in his armchair; his mother and sister would admonish each other to be silent; his mother, bending low over the lamp, stitched at fine sewing for an underwear firm; his sister, who had taken a job as a salesgirl, was learning shorthand and French in the evenings on the chance of bettering herself. Sometimes his father woke up, and as if quite unaware that he had been sleeping said to his mother: "What a lot of sewing you're doing today!" and at once fell asleep again, while the two women exchanged a tired smile.

With a kind of mulishness his father persisted in keeping his uniform on even in the house; his dressing gown hung uselessly on its peg and he slept fully dressed where he sat, as if he were ready for service at any moment and even here only at the beck and call of his superior. As a result, his uniform, which was not brand-new to start with, began to look dirty, despite all the loving care of the mother and sister to keep it clean, and Gregor often spent whole evenings gazing at the many greasy spots on the garment, gleaming with gold buttons always in a high state of polish, in which the old man sat sleeping in extreme discomfort and yet quite peacefully.

As soon as the clock struck ten his mother tried to rouse his father with gentle words and to persuade him after that to get into bed, for sitting there he could not have a proper sleep and that was what he needed most, since he had to go on duty at six. But with the mulishness that had obsessed him since he became a bank messenger he always insisted on staying longer at the table, although he regularly fell asleep again and in the end only with the greatest trouble could be got out of his armchair and into his bed. However insistently Gregor's mother and sister kept urging him with gentle reminders, he would go on slowly shaking his head for a quarter of an hour, keeping his eyes shut, and refuse to get to his feet. The mother plucked at his sleeve, whispering endearments in his ear, the sister left her lessons to come to her mother's help, but Gregor's father was not to be caught. He would only sink down deeper in his chair. Not until the two women hoisted him up by the armpits did he open his eyes and look at them both, one after the other, usually with the remark: "This is a life. This is the peace and quiet of my old age." And leaning on the two of them he would heave himself up, with difficulty, as if he were a great burden to himself, suffer them to lead him as far as the door and then wave them off and go on alone, while the mother abandoned her needlework and the sister her pen in order to run after him and help him farther.

Who could find time, in this overworked and tired-out family, to bother about Gregor more than was absolutely needful? The household was reduced more and more; the servant girl was turned off; a gigantic bony charwoman with white hair flying round her head came in morning and evening to do the rough work; everything else was done by Gregor's mother, as well as great piles of sewing. Even various family ornaments, which his mother and sister used to wear with pride at parties and celebrations, had to be sold, as Gregor discovered of an evening from hearing them all discuss the prices obtained. But what they lamented most was the fact that they could not leave the flat which was much too big for their present circumstances, because they could not think of any way to shift Gregor. Yet Gregor saw well enough that consideration for him was not the main difficulty preventing the removal, for they could have easily shifted him in some suitable box with a few air holes in it; what really kept them from moving into another flat was rather their own complete hopelessness and the belief that they had been singled out for a misfortune such as had never happened to any of their relations or acquaintances. They fulfilled to the uttermost all that the world demands of poor people, the father fetched breakfast for the small clerks in the bank, the mother devoted her energy to making underwear for strangers, the sister trotted to and fro behind the counter at the behest of customers, but more than this they had not the strength to do. And the wound in Gregor's back began to nag at him afresh when his mother and sister, after getting his father into bed, came back again, left their work lying, drew close to each other and sat cheek by cheek; when his mother, pointing towards his room, said: "Shut that door now, Grete," and he was left again in darkness, while next door the women mingled their tears or perhaps sat dry-eyed staring at the table.

Gregor hardly slept at all by night or by day. He was often haunted by the idea that next time the door opened he would take the family's affairs in hand again just as he used to do; once more, after this long interval, there appeared in his thoughts the figures of the chief and the chief clerk, the commercial travelers and the apprentices, the porter who was so dull-witted, two or three friends in other firms, a chambermaid in one of the rural hotels, a sweet and fleeting memory, a cashier in a milliner's shop, whom he had wooed earnestly but too slowly—they all appeared, together with strangers or people he had quite forgotten, but instead of helping him and his family they were one and all unapproachable and he was glad when they vanished. At other times he would not be in the mood to bother about his family, he was only filled with rage at the way they were neglecting him, and although he had no clear idea of what he might care to eat he would make plans for getting into the larder to take the food that was after all his due, even if he were not hungry. His sister no longer took thought to bring him what might especially please him, but in the morning and at noon before she went to business hurriedly pushed into his room with her foot any food that was available, and in the evening cleared it out again with one sweep of the broom, heedless of whether it had been merely tasted, or—as most frequently happened—left untouched. The cleaning of his room, which she now did always in the evenings, could not have been more hastily done. Streaks of dirt stretched along the walls, here and there lay balls of dust and filth. At first Gregor used to station himself in some particularly filthy corner when his sister arrived, in order to reproach her with it, so to speak. But he could have sat there for weeks without getting her to make any improvements; she could see the dirt as well as he did, but she had simply made up her mind to leave it alone. And yet, with a touchiness that was new to her, which seemed anyhow to have infected the whole family, she jealously guarded her claim to be the sole caretaker of Gregor's room. His mother once subjected his room to a thorough cleaning, which was achieved only by means of several buckets of water—all this dampness of course upset Gregor too and he lay widespread, sulky and motionless on the sofa—but she was well punished for it. Hardly had his sister noticed the changed aspect of his room that evening than she rushed in high dudgeon into the living room and, despite the imploringly raised hands of her mother, burst into a storm of weeping, while her parents—her father had of course been startled out of his chair—looked on at first in helpless amazement; then they too began to go into action; the father reproached the mother on his right for not having left the cleaning of Gregor's room to his sister; shrieked at the sister on his left that never again was she to be allowed to clean Gregor's room; while the mother tried to pull the father into his bedroom, since he was beyond himself with agitation; the sister, shaken with sobs, then beat upon the table with her small fists; and Gregor hissed loudly with rage because not one of them thought of shutting the door to spare him such a spectacle and so much noise.

Still, even if the sister, exhausted by her daily work, had grown tired of looking after Gregor as she did formerly, there was no need for his mother's intervention or for Gregor's being neglected at all. The charwoman was there. This old widow, whose strong bony frame had enabled her to survive the worst a long life could offer, by no means recoiled from Gregor. Without being in the least curious she had once by chance opened the door of his room and at the sight of Gregor, who, taken by surprise, began to rush to and fro although no one was chasing him, merely stood there with her arms folded. From that time she never failed to open his door a little for a moment, morning and evening, to have a look at him. At first she even used to call him to her, with words which apparently she took to be friendly, such as: "Come along, then, you old dung beetle!" or "Look at the old dung beetle, then!" To such allocutions Gregor made no answer, but stayed motionless where he was, as if the door had never been opened. Instead of being allowed to disturb him so senselessly whenever the whim took her, she should rather have been ordered to clean out his room daily, that charwoman! Once, early in the morning—heavy rain was lashing on the windowpanes, perhaps a sign that spring was on the way—Gregor was so exasperated when she began addressing him again that he ran at her, as if to attack her, although slowly and feebly enough. But the charwoman instead of showing fright merely lifted high a chair that happened to be beside the door, and as she stood there with her mouth wide open it was clear that she meant to shut it only when she brought the chair down on Gregor's back. "So you're not coming any nearer?" she asked, as Gregor turned away again, and quietly put the chair back into the corner.

Gregor was now eating hardly anything. Only when he happened to pass the food laid out for him did he take a bit of something in his mouth as a pastime, kept it there for an hour at a time and usually spat it out again. At first he thought it was chagrin over the state of his room that prevented him from eating, yet he soon got used to the various changes in his room. It had become a habit in the family to push into his room things there was no room for elsewhere, and there were plenty of these now, since one of the rooms had been let to three lodgers. These serious gentlemen—all three of them with full beards, as Gregor once observed through a crack in the door—had a passion for order, not only in their own room but, since they were now members of the household, in all its arrangements, especially in the kitchen. Superfluous, not to say dirty, objects they could not bear. Besides, they had brought with them most of the furnishings they needed. For this reason many things could be dispensed with that it was no use trying to sell but that should not be thrown away either. All of them found their way into Gregor's room. The ash can likewise and the kitchen garbage can. Anything that was not needed for the moment was simply flung into Gregor's room by the charwoman, who did everything in a hurry; fortunately Gregor usually saw only the object, whatever it was, and the hand that held it. Perhaps she intended to take the things away again as time and opportunity offered, or to collect them until she could throw them all out in a heap, but in fact they just lay wherever she happened to throw them, except when Gregor pushed his way through the junk heap and shifted it somewhat, at first out of necessity, because he had not room enough to crawl, but later with increasing enjoyment, although after such excursions, being sad and weary to death, he would lie motionless for hours. And since the lodgers often ate their supper at home in the common living room, the living-room door stayed shut many an evening, yet Gregor reconciled himself quite easily to the shutting of the door, for often enough on evenings when it was opened he had disregarded it entirely and lain in the darkest corner of his room, quite unnoticed by the family. But on one occasion the charwoman left the door open a little and it stayed ajar even when the lodgers came in for supper and the lamp was lit. They set themselves at the top end of the table where formerly Gregor and his father and mother had eaten their meals, unfolded their napkins and took knife and fork in hand. At once his mother appeared in the other doorway with a dish of meat and close behind her his sister with a dish of potatoes piled high. The food steamed with a thick vapor. The lodgers bent over the food set before them as if to scrutinize it before eating, in fact the man in the middle, who seemed to pass for an authority with the other two, cut a piece of meat as it lay on the dish, obviously to discover if it were tender or should be sent back to the kitchen. He showed satifaction, and Gregor's mother and sister, who had been watching anxiously, breathed freely and began to smile.

The family itself took its meals in the kitchen. Nonetheless, Gregor's father came into the living room before going into the kitchen and with one prolonged bow, cap in hand, made a round of the table. The lodgers all stood up and murmured something in their beards. When they were alone again they ate their food in almost complete silence. It seemed remarkable to Gregor that among the various noises coming from the table he could always distinguish the sound of their masticating teeth, as if this were a sign to Gregor that one needed teeth in order to eat, and that with toothless jaws even of the finest make one could do nothing. "I'm hungry enough," said Gregor sadly to himself, "But not for that kind of food. How these lodgers are stuffing themselves, and here am I dying of starvation!"

On that very evening—during the whole of his time there Gregor could not remember ever having heard the violin—the sound of violin-playing came from the kitchen. The lodgers had already finished their supper, the one in the middle had brought out a newspaper and given the other two a page apiece, and now they were leaning back at ease reading and smoking. When the violin began to play they pricked up their ears, got to their feet, and went on tiptoe to the hall door where they stood huddled together. Their movements must have been heard in the kitchen, for Gregor's father called out: "Is the violin-playing disturbing you, gentlemen? It can be stopped at once." "On the contrary," said the middle lodger, "could not Fräulein Samsa come and play in this room, beside us, where it is much more convenient and comfortable?" "Oh certainly," cried Gregor's father, as if he were the violin-player. The lodgers came back into the living room and waited. Presently Gregor's father arrived with the music stand, his mother carrying the music and his sister with the violin. His sister quietly made everything ready to start playing; his parents, who had never let rooms before and so had an exaggerated idea of the courtesy due to lodgers, did not venture to sit down on their own chairs; his father leaned against the door, the right hand thrust between two buttons of his livery coat, which was formally buttoned up; but his mother was offered a chair by one of the lodgers and, since she left the chair just where he had happened to put it, sat down in a corner to one side.

Gregor's sister began to play; the father and mother, from either side, intently watched the movements of her hands. Gregor, attracted by the playing, ventured to move forward a little until his head was actually inside the living room. He felt hardly any surprise at his growing lack of consideration for the others; there had been a time when he prided himself on being considerate. And yet just on this occasion he had more reason than ever to hide himself, since owing to the amount of dust which lay thick in his room and rose into the air at the slightest movement, he too was covered with dust; fluff and hair and remnants of food trailed with him, caught on his back and along his sides; his indifference to everything was much too great for him to turn on his back and scrape himself clean on the carpet, as once he had done several times a day. And in spite of his condition, no shame deterred him from advancing a little over the spotless floor of the living room.

To be sure, no one was aware of him. The family was entirely absorbed in the violin-playing; the lodgers, however, who first of all had stationed themselves, hands in pockets, much too close behind the music stand so that they could all have read the music, which must have bothered his sister, had soon retreated to the window, half-whispering with downbent heads, and stayed there while his father turned an anxious eye on them. Indeed, they were making it more than obvious that they had been disappointed in their expectation of hearing good or enjoyable violin-playing, that they had had more than enough of the performance and only out of courtesy suffered a continued disturbance of their peace. From the way they all kept blowing the smoke of their cigars high in the air through nose and mouth one could divine their irritation. And yet Gregor's sister was playing so beautifully. Her face leaned sideways, intently and sadly her eyes followed the notes of music. Gregor crawled a little farther forward and lowered his head to the ground so that it might be possible for his eyes to meet hers. Was he an animal, that music had such an effect upon him? He felt as if the way were opening before him to the unknown nourishment he craved. He was determined to push forward till he reached his sister, to pull at her skirt and so let her know that she was to come into his room with her violin, for no one here appreciated her playing as he would appreciate it. He would never let her out of his room, at least, not so long as he lived; his frightful appearance would become, for the first time, useful to him; he would watch all the doors of his room at once and spit at intruders; but his sister should need no constraint, she should stay with him of her own free will; she should sit beside him on the sofa, bend down her ear to him and hear him confide that he had had the firm intention of sending her to the Conservatorium, and that, but for his mishap, last Christmas—surely Christmas was long past?—he would have announced it to everybody without allowing a single objection. After this confession his sister would be so touched that she would burst into tears, and Gregor would then raise himself to her shoulder and kiss her on the neck, which, now that she went to business, she kept free of any ribbon or collar.

"Mr. Samsa!" cried the middle lodger, to Gregor's father, and pointed, without wasting any more words, at Gregor, now working himself slowly forwards. The violin fell silent, the middle lodger first smiled to his friends with a shake of the head and then looked at Gregor again. Instead of driving Gregor out, his father seemed to think it more needful to begin by soothing down the lodgers, although they were not at all agitated and apparently found Gregor more entertaining than the violin-playing. He hurried toward them and, spreading out his arms, tried to urge then back into their own room and at the same time to block their view of Gregor. They now began to be really a little angry, one could not tell whether because of the old man's behavior or because it had just dawned on them that all unwittingly they had such a neighbor as Gregor next door. They demanded explanations of his father, they waved their arms like him, tugged uneasily at their beards, and only with reluctance backed towards their room. Meanwhile Gregor's sister, who stood there as if lost when her playing was so abruptly broken off, came to life again, pulled herself together all at once after standing for a while holding violin and bow in nervelessly hanging hands and staring at her music, pushed her violin into the lap of her mother, who was still sitting in her chair fighting asthmatically for breath, and ran into the lodgers' room to which they were now being shepherded by her father rather more quickly than before. One could see the pillows and blankets on the beds flying under her accustomed fingers and being laid in order. Before the lodgers had actually reached their room she had finished making the beds and slipped out.

The old man seemed once more to be so possessed by his mulish self-assertiveness that he was forgetting all the respect he should show to his lodgers. He kept driving them on and driving them on until in the very door of the bedroom the middle lodger stamped his foot loudly on the floor and so brought him to a halt. "I beg to announce," said the lodger, lifting one hand and looking also at Gregor's mother and sister, "that because of the disgusting conditions prevailing in this household and family"—here he spat on the floor with emphatic brevity—"I give you notice on the spot. Naturally I won't pay you a penny for the days I have lived here, on the contrary I shall consider bringing an action for damages against you, based on claims—believe me—that will be easily susceptible of proof." He ceased and stared straight in front of him, as if he expected something. In fact his two friends at once rushed into the breach with these words: "And we too give notice on the spot." On that he seized the door-handle and shut the door with a slam.

Gregor's father, groping with his hands, staggered forward and fell into his chair; it looked as if he were stretching himself there for his ordinary evening nap, but the marked jerkings of his head, which was as if uncontrollable, showed that he was far from asleep. Gregor had simply stayed quietly all the time on the spot where the lodgers had espied him. Disappointment at the failure of his plan, perhaps also the weakness arising from extreme hunger, made it impossible for him to move. He feared, with a fair degree of certainty, that at any moment the general tension would discharge itself in a combined attack upon him, and he lay waiting. He did not react even to the noise made by the violin as it fell off his mother's lap from under her trembling fingers and gave out a resonant note.

"My dear parents," said his sister, slapping her hand on the table by way of introduction, "things can't go on like this. Perhaps you don't realize that, but I do. I won't utter my brother's name in the presence of this creature, and so all I say is: we must try to get rid of it. We've tried to look after it and to put up with it as far as is humanly possible, and I don't think anyone could reproach us in the slightest."

"She is more than right," said Gregor's father to himself. His mother, who was still choking for lack of breath, began to cough hollowly into her hand with a wild look in her eyes.

His sister rushed over to her and held her forehead. His father's thoughts seemed to have lost their vagueness at Grete's words, he sat more upright, fingering his service cap that lay among the plates still lying on the table from the lodgers' supper, and from time to time looked at the still form of Gregor.

"We must try to get rid of it," his sister now said explicitly to her father, since her mother was coughing too much to hear a word, "it will be the death of both of you, I can see that coming. When one has to work as hard as we do, all of us, one can't stand this continual torment at home on top of it. At least I can't stand it any longer." And she burst into such a passion of sobbing that her tears dropped on her mother's face, where she wiped them off mechanically.

"My dear," said the old man sympathetically, and with evident understanding, "but what can we do?"

Gregor's sister merely shrugged her shoulders to indicate the feeling of helplessness that had now overmastered her during her weeping fit, in contrast to her former confidence.

"If he could understand us," said her father, half questioningly; Grete, still sobbing, vehemently waved a hand to show how unthinkable that was.

"If he could understand us," repeated the old man, shutting his eyes to consider his daughter's conviction that understanding was impossible, "then perhaps we might come to some agreement with him. But as it is—"

"He must go," cried Gregor's sister, "that's the only solution, Father. You must just try to get rid of the idea that this is Gregor. The fact that we've believed it for so long is the root of all our trouble. But how can it be Gregor? If this were Gregor, he would have realized long ago that human beings can't live with such a creature, and he'd have gone away on his own accord. Then we wouldn't have any brother, but we'd be able to go on living and keep his memory in honor. As it is, this creature persecutes us, drives away our lodgers, obviously wants the whole apartment to himself and would have us all sleep in the gutter. Just look, Father," she shrieked all at once, "he's at it again!" and in an access of panic that was quite incomprehensible to Gregor she even quitted her mother, literally thrusting the chair from her as if she would rather sacrifice her mother than stay so near to Gregor, and rushed behind her father, who also rose up, being simply upset by her agitation, and half-spread his arms out as if to protect her.

Yet Gregor had not the slightest intention of frightening anyone, far less his sister. He had only begun to turn round in order to crawl back to his room, but it was certainly a startling operation to watch, since because of his disabled condition he could not execute the difficult turning movements except by lifting his head and then bracing it against the floor over and over again. He paused and looked round. His good intentions seemed to have been recognized; the alarm had only been momentary. Now they were all watching him in melancholy silence. His mother lay in her chair, her legs stiffly outstretched and pressed together, her eyes almost closing for sheer weariness; his father and his sister were sitting beside each other, his sister's arm around the old man's neck.

Perhaps I can go on turning round now, thought Gregor, and began his labors again. He could not stop himself from panting with the effort, and had to pause now and then to take breath. Nor did anyone harass him, he was left entirely to himself. When he had completed the turn-round he began at once to crawl straight back. He was amazed at the distance separating him from his room and could not understand how in his weak state he had managed to accomplish the same journey so recently, almost without remarking it. Intent on crawling as fast as possible, he barely noticed that not a single word, not an ejaculation from his family, interfered with his progress. Only when he was already in the doorway did he turn his head round, not completely, for his neck muscles were getting stiff, but enough to see that nothing had changed behind him except that his sister had risen to her feet. His last glance fell on his mother, who was not quite overcome by sleep.

Hardly was he well inside his room when the door was hastily pushed shut, bolted and locked. The sudden noise in his rear startled him so much that his little legs gave beneath him. It was his sister who had shown such haste. She had been standing ready waiting and had made a light spring forward, Gregor had not even heard her coming, and she cried "At last!" to her parents as she turned the key in the lock.

"And what now?" said Gregor to himself, looking round in the darkness. Soon he made the discovery that he was now unable to stir a limb. This did not surprise him, rather it seemed unnatural that he should ever actually have been able to move on these feeble little legs. Otherwise he felt relatively comfortable. True, his whole body was aching, but it seemed that the pain was gradually growing less and would finally pass away. The rotting apple in his back and the inflamed area around it, all covered with soft dust, already hardly troubled him. He thought of his family with tenderness and love. The decision that he must disappear was one that he held to even more strongly than his sister, if that were possible. In this state of vacant and peaceful meditation he remained until the tower clock struck three in the morning. The first broadening of light in the world outside the window entered his consciousness once more. Then his head sank to the floor of its own accord and from his nostrils came the last faint flicker of his breath.

When the charwoman arrived early in the morning—what between her strength and her impatience she slammed all the doors so loudly, never mind how often she had been begged not to do so, that no one in the whole apartment could enjoy any quiet sleep after her arrival—she noticed nothing unusual as she took her customary peep into Gregor's room. She thought he was lying motionless on purpose, pretending to be in the sulks; she credited him with every kind of intelligence. Since she happened to have the long-handled broom in her hand she tried to tickle him up with it from the doorway. When that too produced no reaction she felt provoked and poked at him a little harder, and only when she had pushed him along the floor without meeting any resistance was her attention aroused. It did not take her long to establish the truth of the matter, and her eyes widened, she let out a whistle, yet did not waste much time over it but tore open the door of the Samsas' bedroom and yelled into the darkness at the top of her voice: "Just look at this, it's dead; it's lying here dead and done for!"

Mr. and Mrs. Samsa started up in their double bed and before they realized the nature of the charwoman's announcement had some difficulty in overcoming the shock of it. But then they got out of bed quickly, one on either side, Mr. Samsa throwing a blanket over his shoulders, Mrs. Samsa in nothing but her nightgown; in this array they entered Gregor's room. Meanwhile the door of the living room opened, too, where Grete had been sleeping since the advent of the lodgers; she was completely dressed as if she had not been to bed, which seemed to be confirmed also by the paleness of her face. "Dead?" said Mrs. Samsa, looking questioningly at the charwoman, although she could have investigated for herself, and the fact was obvious enough without investigation. "I should say so," said the charwoman, proving her words by pushing Gregor's corpse a long way to one side with her broomstick. Mrs. Samsa made a movement as if to stop her, but checked it. "Well," said Mr. Samsa, "now thanks be to God." He crossed himself, and the three women followed his example. Grete, whose eyes never left the corpse, said: "Just see how thin he was. It's such a long time since he's eaten anything. The food came out again just as it went in." Indeed, Gregor's body was completely flat and dry, as could only now be seen when it was no longer supported by the legs and nothing prevented one from looking closely at it.

"Come in beside us, Grete, for a little while," said Mrs. Samsa with a tremulous smile, and Grete, not without looking back at the corpse, followed her parents into their bedroom. The charwoman shut the door and opened the window wide. Although it was so early in the morning a certain softness was perceptible in the fresh air. After all, it was already the end of March.

The three lodgers emerged from their room and were surprised to see no breakfast; they had been forgotten. "Where's our breakfast?" said the middle lodger peevishly to the charwoman. But she put her finger to her lips and hastily, without a word, indicated by gestures that they should go into Gregor's room. They did so and stood, their hands in the pockets of their somewhat shabby coats, around Gregor's corpse in the room where it was now fully light.

At that the door of the Samsas' bedroom opened and Mr. Samsa appeared in his uniform, his wife on one arm, his daughter on the other. They all looked a little as if they had been crying; from time to time Grete hid her face on her father's arm.

"Leave my house at once!" said Mr. Samsa, and pointed to the door without disengaging himself from the women. "What do you mean by that?" said the middle lodger, taken somewhat aback, with a feeble smile. The two others put their hands behind them and kept rubbing them together, as if in gleeful expectation of a fine set-to in which they were bound to come off the winners. "I mean just what I say," answered Mr. Samsa, and advanced in a straight line with his two companions towards the lodger. He stood his ground at first quietly, looking at the floor as if his thoughts were taking a new pattern in his head. "Then let us go, by all means," he said, and looked up at Mr. Samsa as if in a sudden access of humility he were expecting some renewed sanction for this decision. Mr. Samsa merely nodded briefly once or twice with meaning eyes. Upon that the lodger really did go with long strides into the hall, his two friends had been listening and had quite stopped rubbing their hands for some moments and now went scuttling after him as if afraid that Mr. Samsa might get into the hall before them and cut them off from their leader. In the hall they all three took their hats from the rack, their sticks from the umbrella stand, bowed in silence and quitted the apartment. With a suspiciousness which proved quite unfounded Mr. Samsa and the two women followed them out to the landing; leaning over the banister they watched the three figures slowly but surely going down the long stairs, vanishing from sight at a certain turn of the staircase on every floor and coming into view again after a moment or so; the more they dwindled, the more the Samsa family's interest in them dwindled, and when a butcher's boy met them and passed them on the stairs coming up proudly with a tray on his head, Mr. Samsa and the two women soon left the landing and as if a burden had been lifted from them went back into their apartment.

They decided to spend this day in resting and going for a stroll; they had not only deserved such a respite from work, but absolutely needed it. And so they sat down at the table and wrote three notes of excuse, Mr. Samsa to his board of management, Mrs. Samsa to her employer and Grete to the head of her firm. While they were writing, the charwoman came in to say that she was going now, since her morning's work was finished. At first they only nodded without looking up, but as she kept hovering there they eyed her irritably. "Well?" said Mr. Samsa. The charwoman stood grinning in the doorway as if she had good news to impart to the family but meant not to say a word unless properly questioned. The small ostrich feather standing upright on her hat, which had annoyed Mr. Samsa ever since she was engaged, was waving gaily in all directions. "Well, what is it then?" asked Mrs. Samsa, who obtained more respect from the charwoman than the others. "Oh," said the charwoman, giggling so amiably thathat she could not at once continue, "just this, you don't need to bother about how to get rid of the thing next door. It's been seen to already." Mrs. Samsa and Grete bent over their letters again, as if preoccupied; Mr. Samsa, who perceived that she was eager to begin describing it all in detail, stopped her with a decisive hand. But since she was not allowed to tell her story, she remembered the great hurry she was in, being obviously deeply huffed: "Bye, everybody," she said, whirling off violently, and departed with a frightful slamming of doors.

"She'll be given notice tonight," said Mr. Samsa, but neither from his wife nor his daughter did he get any answer, for the charwoman seemed to have shattered again the composure they had barely achieved. They rose, went to the window and stayed there, clasping each other tight. Mr. Samsa turned in his chair to look at them and quietly observed them for a little. Then he called out: "Come along, now, do. Let bygones be bygones. And you might have some consideration for me." The two of them complied at once, hastened to him, caressed him and quickly finished their letters.

Then they all three left the apartment together, which was more than they had done for months, and went by tram into the open country outside the town. The tram, in which they were the only passengers, was filled with warm sunshine. Leaning comfortably back in their seats they canvassed their prospects for the future, and it appeared on closer inspection that these were not at all bad, for the jobs they had got, which so far they had never really discussed with each other, were all three admirable and likely to lead to better things later on. The greatest immediate improvement in their condition would of course arise from moving to another house; they wanted to take a smaller and cheaper but also better situated and more easily run apartment than the one they had, which Gregor had selected. While they were thus conversing, it struck both Mr. and Mrs. Samsa, almost at the same moment, as they became aware of their daughter's increasing vivacity, that in spite of all the sorrow of recent times, which had made her cheeks pale, she had bloomed into a pretty girl with a good figure. They grew quieter and half unconsciously exchanged glances of complete agreement, having come to the conclusion that it would soon be time to find a good husband for her. And it was like a confirmation of their new dreams and excellent intentions that at the end of their journey their daughter sprang to her feet first and stretched her young body.

---

1. Is there any real surprise in this novella after the first sentence? What does the author accomplish by accounting at such length for the consequences of Gregor's transformation?
2. Is Gregor increasingly aware of the significance of intrafamily relationships after his transformation?
3. What is the general tone of the story? How is this affected by telling it mostly from Gregor's point of view?
4. In what ways does the character of Gregor's sister change? How do the changes in her attitude toward Gregor contribute to the progress and meaning of the story?
5. In what ways could Gregor's misfortune be compared to a severe or crippling illness in a family situation? Is the focus of the whole story more on the family than on Gregor as an individual? Explain.

6. If you take Gregor's transformation as a metaphorical symbol of guilt, from what does the guilt arise?
7. What roles do the lodgers, the charwoman, and the chief clerk play in the action?
8. What is the meaning of the picture of the woman in furs?

A Hunger Artist[1]

During these last decades the interest in professional fasting has markedly diminished. It used to pay very well to stage such great performances under one's own management, but today that is quite impossible. We live in a different world now. At one time the whole town took a lively interest in the hunger artist; from day to day of his fast the excitement mounted; everybody wanted to see him at least once a day; there were people who bought season tickets for the last few days and sat from morning till night in front of his small barred cage; even in the nighttime there were visiting hours, when the whole effect was heightened by torch flares; on fine days the cage was set out in the open air, and then it was the children's special treat to see the hunger artist; for their elders he was often just a joke that happened to be in fashion, but the children stood open-mouthed, holding each other's hands for greater security, marveling at him as he sat there pallid in black tights, with his ribs sticking out so prominently, not even on a seat but down among straw on the ground, sometimes giving a courteous nod, answering questions with a constrained smile, or perhaps stretching an arm through the bars so that one might feel how thin it was, and then again withdrawing deep into himself, paying no attention to anyone or anything, not even to the all-important striking of the clock that was the only piece of furniture in his cage, but merely staring into vacancy with half shut eyes, now and then taking a sip from a tiny glass of water to moisten his lips.

Besides casual onlookers there were also relays of permanent watchers selected by the public, usually butchers, strangely enough, and it was their task to watch the hunger artist day and night, three of them at a time, in case he should have some secret recourse to nourishment. This was nothing but a formality, instituted to reassure the masses, for the initiates knew well enough that during his fast the artist would never in any circumstances, not even under forcible compulsion, swallow the smallest morsel of food: the honor of his profession forbade it. Not every watcher, of course, was capable of understanding

1. Translated by Edwin and Willa Muir.

this, there were often groups of night watchers who were very lax in carrying out their duties and deliberately huddled together in a retired corner to play cards with great absorption, obviously intending to give the hunger artist the chance of a little refreshment, which they supposed he could draw from some private hoard. Nothing annoyed the artist more than such watchers; they made him miserable; they made his fast seem unendurable; sometimes he mastered his feebleness sufficiently to sing during their watch for as long as he could keep going, to show them how unjust their suspicions were. But that was of little use; they only wondered at his cleverness in being able to fill his mouth even while singing. Much more to his taste were the watchers who sat close up to the bars, who were not content with the dim night lighting of the hall but focused him in the full glare of the electric pocket torch given them by the impresario. The harsh light did not trouble him at all, in any case he could never sleep properly, and he could always drowse a little, whatever the light, at any hour, even when the hall was thronged with noisy onlookers. He was quite happy at the prospect of spending a sleepless night with such watchers; he was ready to exchange jokes with them, to tell them stories out of his nomadic life, anything at all to keep them awake and demonstrate to them again that he had no eatables in his cage and that he was fasting as not one of them could fast. But his happiest moment was when the morning came and an enormous breakfast was brought them, at his expense, on which they flung themselves with the keen appetite of healthy men after a weary night of wakefulness. Of course there were people who argued that this breakfast was an unfair attempt to bribe the watchers, but that was going rather too far, and when they were invited to take on a night's vigil without a breakfast, merely for the sake of the cause, they made themselves scarce, although they stuck stubbornly to their suspicions.

Such suspicions, anyhow, were a necessary accompaniment to the profession of fasting. No one could possibly watch the hunger artist continuously, day and night, and so no one could produce first-hand evidence that the fast had really been rigorous and continuous; only the artist himself could know that, he was therefore bound to be the sole completely satisfied spectator of his own fast. Yet for other reasons he was never satisfied; it was not perhaps mere fasting that had brought him to such skeleton thinness that many people had regretfully to keep away from his exhibitions, because the sight of him was too much for them, perhaps it was dissatisfaction with himself that had worn him down. For he alone knew, what no other initiate knew, how easy it was to fast. It was the easiest thing in the world. He made no secret of this, yet people did not believe him, at the best they set him down as modest, most of them, however, thought he was out for publicity or else was some kind of cheat who found it easy to fast because he had discovered a way of making it easy, and then had the impudence to admit the fact, more or less. He had to put up with all that, and in the course of time had got used to it, but his inner dissatisfaction always rankled, and never yet, after any term of fasting—this must be granted to his credit—had he left the cage of his own free will. The longest period of fasting was fixed by his impresario at forty days, beyond that term he was not allowed to go, not even in great cities, and there was good reason for it, too. Experience had proved that for about forty days the interest of the public could be stimulated by a steadily increasing pressure of advertisement, but after that the town began to lose interest, sympathetic support began notably to fall off; there were of course local variations as between one town and another or one country and another, but as a general rule forty days marked the limit. So on the fortieth day the flower-bedecked cage was opened, enthusiastic spectators filled the hall, a military band played, two doctors entered the cage to measure the results of the fast, which were announced through a megaphone, and finally two young ladies appeared, blissful at having been selected for the honor, to help the hunger artist down the few steps leading to a small table on which was spread a carefully chosen invalid repast. And at this very moment the artist always turned stubborn. True, he would entrust his bony arms to the outstretched helping hands of the ladies bending over him, but stand up he would not. Why stop fasting at this particular moment, after forty days of it? He had held out for a long time, an illimitably long time; why stop now, when he was in his best fasting form, or rather, not yet quite in his best fasting form? Why should he be cheated of the fame he would get for fasting longer, for being not only the record hunger artist of all time, which presumably he was already, but for beating his own record by a performance beyond human imagination, since he felt that there were no limits to his capacity for fasting? His public pretended to admire him so much, why should it have so little patience with him; if he could endure fasting longer, why shouldn't the public endure it? Besides, he was tired, he was comfortable sitting in the straw, and now he was supposed to lift himself to his full height and go down to a meal the very thought of which gave him a nausea that only the presence of the ladies kept him from betraying, and even that with an effort. And he looked up into the eyes of the ladies who were apparently so friendly and in reality so cruel, and shook his head, which felt too heavy on its strengthless neck. But then there happened yet again what always happened. The impresario came forward, without a word—for the band made speech impossible—lifted his arms in the air above the artist, as if inviting Heaven to look down upon its creature here in the straw, this suffering martyr, which indeed he was, although in quite another sense; grasped him round the emaciated waist, with exaggerated caution, so that the frail condition he was in might be appreciated; and committed him to the care of the blenching ladies, not without secretly giving him a shaking so that his legs and body tottered and swayed. The artist now submitted completely; his head lolled on his breast as if it had landed there by chance; his body was hollowed out; his legs in a spasm of self-preservation clung close to each other at the knees, yet scraped on the ground as if it were not really solid ground, as if they were only trying to find solid ground; and the whole weight of his body, a feather-weight after all, relapsed onto one of the ladies, who, looking round for help and panting a little—this post of honor was not at all what she had expected it to be—first stretched her neck as far as she could to keep her face at least free from contact with the artist, when finding this impossible, and her more fortunate companion not coming to her aid but merely holding extended on her own trembling hand the little bunch of knucklebones that was the artist's, to the great delight of the spectators burst into tears and had to be replaced by an attendant who had long been stationed in readiness. Then came the food, a little of which the impresario managed to get between the artist's lips, while he sat in a kind of half-fainting trance, to the accompaniment of cheerful patter designed to distract the public's attention from the artist's condition; after that, a toast was drunk to the public, supposedly prompted by a whisper from the artist in the impresario's ear; the band confirmed it with a mighty flourish, the spectators melted away, and no one had any cause to be dissatisfied with the proceedings, no one except the hunger artist himself, he only, as always.

So he lived for many years, with small regular intervals of recuperation, in visible glory, honored by the world, yet in spite of that troubled in spirit, and all the more troubled because no one would take his trouble seriously. What comfort could he possibly need? What more could he possibly wish for? And if some good-natured person, feeling sorry for him, tried to console him by pointing out that his melancholy was probably caused by fasting, it could happen, especially when he had been fasting for some time, that he reacted with an outburst of fury and to the general alarm began to shake the bars of his cage like a wild animal. Yet the impresario had a way of punishing these outbreaks which he rather enjoyed putting into operation. He would apologize publicly for the artist's behavior, which was only to be excused, he admitted, because of the irritability caused by fasting; a condition hardly to be understood by well-fed people; then by natural transition he went on to mention the artist's equally incomprehensible boast that he could fast for much longer than he was doing; he praised the high ambition, the good will, the great self-denial undoubtedly implicit in such a statement; and then quite simply countered it by bringing out photographs, which were also on sale to the public, showing the artist on the fortieth day of a fast lying in bed almost dead from exhaustion. This perversion of the truth, familiar to the artist though it was, always unnerved him afresh and proved too much for him. What was a consequence of the premature ending of his fast was here presented as the cause of it! To fight against this lack of understanding, against a whole world of non-understanding, was impossible. Time and again in good faith he stood by the bars listening to the impresario, but as soon as the photographs appeared he always let go and sank with a groan back on to his straw, and the reassured public could once more come close and gaze at him.

A few years later when the witnesses of such scenes called them to mind, they often failed to understand themselves at all. For meanwhile the aforementioned change in public interest had set in; it seemed to happen almost overnight; there may have been profound causes for it, but who was going to bother about that; at any rate the pampered hunger artist suddenly found himself deserted one fine day by the amusement seekers, who went streaming past him to other more favored attractions. For the last time the impresario hurried him over half Europe to discover whether the old interest might still survive here and there; all in vain; everywhere, as if by secret agreement, a positive revulsion from professional fasting was in evidence. Of course it could not really have sprung up so suddenly as all that, and many premonitory symptoms which had not been sufficiently remarked or suppressed during the rush and glitter of success now came retrospectively to mind, but it was now too late to take any countermeasures. Fasting would surely come into fashion again at some future date, yet that was no comfort for those living in the present. What, then, was the hunger artist to do? He had been applauded by thousands in his time and could hardly come down to showing himself in a street booth at village fairs, and as for adopting another profession, he was not only too old for that but too fanatically devoted to fasting. So he took leave of the impresario, his partner in an unparalleled career, and hired himself to a large circus; in order to spare his own feelings he avoided reading the conditions of his contract.

A large circus with its enormous traffic in replacing and recruiting men, animals and apparatus can always find a use for people at any time, even for a hunger artist, provided of course that he does not ask too much, and in this particular case anyhow it was not only the artist who was taken on but his famous and long-known name as well, indeed considering the peculiar nature of his performance, which was not impaired by advancing age, it could not be objected that here was an artist past his prime, no longer at the height of his professional skill, seeking a refuge in some quiet corner of a circus; on the contrary, the hunger artist averred that he could fast as well as ever, which was entirely credible, he even alleged that if he were allowed to fast as he liked, and this was at once promised him without more ado, he could astound the world by establishing a record never yet achieved, a statement which certainly provoked a smile among the other professionals, since it left out of account the change in public opinion, which the hunger artist in his zeal conveniently forgot.

He had not, however, actually lost his sense of the real situation and took it as a matter of course that he and his cage should be stationed, not in the middle of the ring as a main attraction, but outside, near the animal cages, on a site that was after all easily accessible. Large and gaily painted placards made a frame for the cage and announced what was to be seen inside it. When the public came thronging out in the intervals to see the animals, they could hardly avoid passing the hunger artist's cage and stopping there for a moment, perhaps they might even have stayed longer had not those pressing behind them in the narrow gangway, who did not understand why they should be held up on their way toward the excitements of the menagerie, made it impossible for anyone to stand gazing quietly for any length of time. And that was the reason why the hunger artist, who had of course been looking forward to these visiting hours as the main achievement of his life, began instead to shrink from them. At first he could hardly wait for the intervals; it was exhilarating to watch the crowds come streaming his way, until only too soon—not even the most obstinate self-deception, clung to almost consciously, could hold out against the fact—the conviction was borne in upon him that these people, most of them, to judge from their actions, again and again, without exception, were all on their way to the menagerie. And the first sight of them from the distance remained the best. For when they reached his cage he was at once deafened by the storm of shouting and abuse that arose from the two contending factions, which renewed themselves continuously, of those who wanted to stop and stare at him—he soon began to dislike them more than the others—not out of real interest but only out of obstinate self-assertiveness, and those who wanted to go straight on to the animals. When the first great rush was past, the stragglers came along, and these, whom nothing could have prevented from stopping to look at him as long as they had breath, raced past with long strides, hardly even glancing at him, in their haste to get to the menagerie in time. And all too rarely did it happen that he had a stroke of luck, when some father of a family fetched up before him with his children, pointed a finger at the hunger artist and explained at length what the phenomenon meant, telling stories of earlier years when he himself had watched similar but much more thrilling performances, and the children, still rather uncomprehending, since neither inside nor outside school had they been sufficiently prepared for this lesson—what did they care about fasting?—yet showed by the brightness of their intent eyes that new and better times might be coming. Perhaps, said the hunger artist to himself many a time, things would be a little better if his cage were set not quite so near the menagerie. That made it too easy for people to make their choice, to say nothing of what he suffered from the stench of the menagerie, the animals' restlessness by night, the carrying past of raw lumps of flesh for the beasts of prey, the roaring at feeding times, which depressed him continually. But he did not dare to lodge a complaint with the management; after all, he had the animals to thank for the troops of people who passed his cage, among whom there might always be one here and there to take an interest in him, and who could tell where they might seclude him if he called attention to his existence and thereby to the fact that, strictly speaking, he was only an impediment on the way to the menagerie.

A small impediment, to be sure, one that grew steadily less. People grew familiar with the strange idea that they could be expected, in times like these, to take an interest in a hunger artist, and with this familiarity the verdict went out against him. He might fast as much as he could, and he did so; but nothing could save him now, people passed him by. Just try to explain to anyone the art of fasting! Anyone who has no feeling for it cannot be made to understand it. The fine placards grew dirty and illegible, they were torn down; the little notice board telling the number of fast days achieved, which at first was changed carefully every day, had long stayed at the same figure, for after the first few weeks even this small task seemed pointless to the staff; and so the artist simply fasted on and on, as he had once dreamed of doing, and it was no trouble to him, just as he had always foretold, but no one counted the days, no one, not even the artist himself, knew what records he was already breaking, and his heart grew heavy. And when once in a time some leisurely passer-by stopped, made merry over the old figure on the board and spoke of swindling, that was in its way the stupidest lie ever invented by indifference and inborn malice, since it was not the hunger artist who was cheating; he was working honestly, but the world was cheating him of his reward.

Many more days went by, however, and that too came to an end. An overseer's eye fell on the cage one day and he asked the attendants why this perfectly good cage should be left standing there unused with dirty straw inside it; nobody knew, until one man, helped out by the notice board, remembered about the hunger artist. They poked into the straw with sticks and found him in it. "Are you still fasting?" asked the overseer. "When on earth do you mean to stop?" "Forgive me, everybody," whispered the hunger artist; only the overseer, who had his ear to the bars, understood him. "Of course," said the overseer, and tapped his forehead with a finger to let the attendants know what state the man was in, "we forgive you." "I always wanted you to admire my fasting," said the hunger artist. "We do admire it," said the overseer, affably. "But you shouldn't admire it," said the hunger artist. "Well, then we don't admire it," said the overseer, "but why shouldn't we admire it?" "Because I have to fast, I can't help it," said the hunger artist. "What a fellow you are," said the overseer, "and why can't you help it?" "Because," said the hunger artist, lifting his head a little and speaking, with his lips pursed, as if for a kiss, right into the overseer's ear, so that no syllable might be lost, "because I couldn't find the food I liked. If I had found it, believe me, I should have made no fuss and stuffed myself like you or anyone else." These were his last words, but in his dimming eyes remained the firm though no longer proud persuasion that he was still continuing to fast.

"Well, clear this out now!" said the overseer, and they buried the hunger artist, straw and all. Into the cage they put a young panther. Even the most insensitive felt it refreshing to see this wild creature leaping around the cage that had so long been dreary. The panther was all right. The food he liked was brought him without hesitation by the attendants; he seemed not even to miss his freedom; his noble body, furnished almost to the bursting point with all that it needed, seemed to carry freedom around with it too; somewhere in his jaws it seemed to lurk; and the joy of life streamed with such ardent passion from his throat that for the onlookers it was not easy to stand the shock of it. But they braced themselves, crowded round the cage, and did not want ever to move away.

---

1. What are the usual motives for fasting? Do any of these apply in the case of the protagonist? What allegorical or symbolical meanings can be attached to his fasting?
2. What does he mean when we are told that fasting for him "was the easiest thing in the world"? What does "easy" mean in this context?
3. Does the protagonist fit your usual ideas of (1) an artist, (2) a naturally gifted athlete, or (3) a sideshow freak? How does the story change or develop your identification of him as any of the above?
4. Is it significant that the protagonist's impresario misrepresents him to the public? Why does the hunger artist submit to the dictates of the impresario?
5. Does the fasting man deserve admiration? Does his act represent a human perversity from which animals—like the panther that replaces him—are free?
6. What is the tone of the narration? What is accomplished by the omission of allusions to particular real places, historical events, and persons? Where and when do you imagine the events of the story to have taken place?

Rudyard Kipling

Kipling (1865–1936) was born in Bombay, India, and after spending his youth in England returned to Bombay at seventeen to work as a reporter and editor. Struck by the color, variety, and exoticism of Indian and military life, he soon began to write poems and short stories that expressed the vividness of what went on before his eyes. His first books of poems were Departmental Ditties *(1886) and* Barrack Room Ballads *(1892), and the stories of that epoch were collected in* Plain Tales from the Hills *(1888) and* Soldiers Three *(1888). From the first, these spirited tales and poems were extremely popular; the meteoric energy of his mind elicited worldwide admiration. His romanticizing of British imperialism fitted the spirit of an age of expansion. His rendition of soldier slang struck many readers as a charming novelty.*

Kipling returned to London in 1889 and there published a novel, The Light That Failed *(1889), which fell somewhat short of the popularity of his first works. Subsequently he migrated to the United States and lived here for four years while he wrote overwhelmingly successful children's books:* The Jungle Book *(1894),* The Second Jungle Book *(1895),* Kim *(1901),* Just So Stories *(1902), and* Captains Courageous *(1904). In the long life remaining to him Kipling's productivity waned, and with the disasters of imperialism before and during World War I, his popularity dimmed. Nevertheless, while it was still at its peak he became in 1907 the first Englishman to win the Nobel Prize.*

The Man Who Would Be King

"Brother to a Prince and Fellow to a Beggar if He Be Found Worthy."

The law, as quoted, lays down a fair conduct of life, and one not easy to follow. I have been fellow to a beggar again and again under circumstances which prevented either of us finding out whether the other was worthy. I have still to be brother to a Prince, though I once came near to kinship with what might have been a veritable King and was promised the reversion of a Kingdom—army, law courts, revenue and policy all complete. But, today, I greatly fear that my King is dead, and if I want a crown I must go and hunt it for myself.

The beginning of everything was in a railway train upon the road to Mhow from Ajmir.[1] There had been a Deficit in the Budget, which necessitated traveling, not Second-class, which is only half as dear as First-class, but by Intermediate, which is very awful indeed. There are no cushions in the Intermediate-class, and the population are either Intermediate, which is Eurasian, or native, which for a long night journey is nasty, or Loafer, which is amusing though intoxicated. Intermediates do not patronize refreshment rooms. They carry their food in bundles and pots, and buy sweets from the native sweetmeat-sellers, and drink the roadside water. That is why in the hot weather Intermediates are taken out of the carriages dead, and in all weathers are most properly looked down upon.

My particular Intermediate happened to be empty till I reached Nasirabad, when a huge gentleman in shirt sleeves entered, and, following the custom of Intermediates, passed the time of day. He was a wanderer and a vagabond like myself, but with an educated taste for whisky. He told tales of things he had seen and done, of out-of-the-way corners of the Empire into which he had penetrated, and of adventures in which he risked his life for a few days' food. "If India was filled with men like you and me, not knowing more than the crows where they'd get their next day's rations, it isn't seventy millions of revenue the land would be paying—it's seven hundred millions," said he; and as I looked at his mouth and chin I was disposed to agree with him. We talked politics—the politics of Loaferdom that sees things from the underside where the lath and plaster is not smoothed off—and we talked postal arrangements because my friend wanted to send a telegram back from the next station to Ajmir, which is the turning-off place from the Bombay to the Mhow line as you travel westward. My friend had no money beyond eight annas which he wanted for dinner, and I had no money at all, owing to the hitch in the Budget before-mentioned. Further, I was going into a wilderness where, though I should resume touch with the Treasury, there were no telegraph offices. I was, therefore, unable to help him in any way.

"We might threaten a Stationmaster, and make him send a wire on tick," said my friend, "but that'd mean inquiries for you and for me, and I've got my hands full these days. Did you say you are traveling back along this line within any days?"

"Within ten," I said.

"Can't you make it eight?" said he. "Mine is rather urgent business."

"I can send your telegram within ten days if that will serve you," I said.

1. Cities in northwestern India.

"I couldn't trust the wire to fetch him now I think of it. It's this way. He leaves Delhi on the twenty-third for Bombay. That means he'll be running through Ajmir about the night of the twenty-third."

"But I'm going into the Indian Desert," I explained.

"Well *and* good," said he. "You'll be changing at Marwar Junction to get into Jodhpore territory—you must do that—and he'll be coming through Marwar Junction in the early morning of the twenty-fourth by the Bombay Mail. Can you be at Marwar Junction on that time? 'Twon't be inconveniencing you because I know that there's precious few pickings to be got out of these Central India States—even though you pretend to be correspondent of the *Backwoodsman*."

"Have you ever tried that trick?" I asked.

"Again and again, but the Residents find you out, and then you get escorted to the Border before you've time to get your knife into them. But about my friend here. I *must* give him a word o' mouth to tell him what's come to me or else he won't know where to go. I would take it more than kind of you if you was to come out of Central India in time to catch him at Marwar Junction, and say to him, 'He has gone South for the week.' He'll know what that means. He's a big man with a red beard, and a great swell he is. You'll find him sleeping like a gentleman with all his luggage round him in a Second-class compartment. But don't you be afraid. Slip down the window, and say, 'He has gone South for the week,' and he'll tumble. It's only cutting your time of stay in those parts by two days. I ask you as a stranger—going to the West," he said, with emphasis.

"Where have *you* come from?" said I.

"From the East," said he, "and I am hoping that you will give him the message on the Square—for the sake of my Mother as well as your own."

Englishmen are not usually softened by appeals to the memory of their mothers, but for certain reasons, which will be fully apparent, I saw fit to agree.

"It's more than a little matter," said he, "and that's why I ask you to do it—and now I know that I can depend on you doing it. A Second-class carriage at Marwar Junction, and a red-haired man asleep in it. You'll be sure to remember. I get out at the next station, and I must hold on there till he comes or sends me what I want."

"I'll give the message if I catch him," I said, "and for the sake of your Mother as well as mine I'll give you a word of advice. Don't try to run the Central India States just now as the correspondent of the *Backwoodsman*. There's a real one knocking about here, and it might lead to trouble."

"Thank you," said he, simply, "and when will the swine be gone?

I can't starve because he's ruining my work. I wanted to get hold of the Degumber Rajah down here about his father's widow, and give him a jump."

"What did he do to his father's widow, then?"

"Filled her up with red pepper and slippered her to death as she hung from a beam. I found that out myself, and I'm the only man that would dare going into the State to get hush money for it. They'll try to poison me, same as they did in Chortumna when I went on the loot there. But you'll give the man at Marwar Junction my message?"

He got out at a little roadside station, and I reflected. I had heard, more than once, of men personating correspondents of newspapers and bleeding small Native States with threats of exposure, but I had never met any of the caste before. They lead a hard life, and generally die with great suddenness. The Native States have a wholesome horror of English newspapers, which may throw light on their peculiar methods of government, and do their best to choke correspondents with champagne, or drive them out of their mind with four-in-hand barouches. They do not understand that nobody cares a straw for the internal administration of Native States so long as oppression and crime are kept within decent limits, and the ruler is not drugged, drunk, or diseased from one end of the year to the other. Native States were created by Providence in order to supply picturesque scenery, tigers, and tall writing. They are the dark places of the earth, full of unimaginable cruelty, touching the Railway and the Telegraph on one side, and, on the other, the days of Harun-al-Raschid.[2] When I left the train I did business with divers Kings, and in eight days passed through many changes of life. Sometimes I wore dress clothes and consorted with Princes and Politicals, drinking from crystal and eating from silver. Sometimes I lay out upon the ground and devoured what I could get, from a plate made of a flapjack, and drank the running water, and slept under the same rug as my servant. It was all in the day's work.

Then I headed for the Great Indian Desert upon the proper date, as I had promised, and the night Mail set me down at Marwar Junction, where a funny little, happy-go-lucky, native-managed railway runs to Jodhpore. The Bombay Mail from Delhi makes a short halt at Marwar. She arrived as I got in, and I had just time to hurry to her platform and go down the carriages. There was only one Second-class on the train. I slipped the window, and looked down upon a flaming red beard, half covered by a railway rug. That was my man, fast asleep, and I dug him gently in the ribs. He woke with a grunt, and I saw his face in the light of the lamps. It was a great and shining face.

2. (C. 764–809), great caliph of Baghdad.

"Tickets again?" said he.

"No," said I. "I am to tell you that he is gone South for the week. He is gone South for the week!"

The train had begun to move out. The red man rubbed his eyes. "He has gone South for the week," he repeated. "Now that's just like his impidence. Did he say that I was to give you anything?—'Cause I won't."

"He didn't," I said, and dropped away, and watched the red lights die out in the dark. It was horribly cold, because the wind was blowing off the sands. I climbed into my own train—not an Intermediate Carriage this time—and went to sleep.

If the man with the beard had given me a rupee I should have kept it as a memento of a rather curious affair. But the consciousness of having done my duty was my only reward.

Later on I reflected that two gentlemen like my friends could not do any good if they foregathered and personated correspondents of newspapers, and might, if they "stuck up" one of the little rat-trap states of Central India or Southern Rajputana, get themselves into serious difficulties. I therefore took some trouble to describe them as accurately as I could remember to people who would be interested in deporting them; and succeeded, so I was later informed, in having them headed back from Degumber borders.

Then I became respectable, and returned to an Office where there were no Kings and no incidents except the daily manufacture of a newspaper. A newspaper office seems to attract every conceivable sort of person, to the prejudice of discipline. Zenana-mission ladies arrive, and beg that the Editor will instantly abandon all his duties to describe a Christian prize-giving in a back-slum of a perfectly inaccessible village; Colonels who have been overpassed for commands sit down and sketch the outline of a series of ten, twelve, or twenty-four leading articles on Seniority *versus* Selection; missionaries wish to know why they have not been permitted to escape from their regular vehicles of abuse and swear at a brother missionary under special patronage of the editorial We; stranded theatrical companies troop up to explain that they cannot pay for their advertisements, but on their return from New Zealand or Tahiti will do so with interest; inventors of patent punkah-pulling machines, carriage couplings, and unbreakable swords and axletrees call with specifications in their pockets and hours at their disposal; tea companies enter and elaborate their prospectuses with the office pens; secretaries of ball committees clamor to have the glories of their last dance more fully expounded; strange ladies rustle in and say, "I want a hundred lady's cards printed *at once*, please," which is manifestly part of an Editor's duty; and every dissolute ruffian that ever tramped the Grand Trunk Road makes it his business to ask for employment as a proofreader. And, all the time, the telephone bell is ringing madly, and Kings are being killed on the Continent, and Empires are saying—"You're another," and Mister Gladstone[3] is calling down brimstone upon the British Dominions, and the little black copy boys are whining, "*kaa-pi chay-ha-yeh*" (copy wanted) like tired bees, and most of the paper is as blank as Modred's shield.[4]

But that is the amusing part of the year. There are other six months wherein none ever come to call, and the thermometer walks inch by inch up to the top of the glass, and the office is darkened to just above reading light, and the press machines are red-hot of touch, and nobody writes anything but accounts of amusements in the Hill stations or obituary notices. Then the telephone becomes a tinkling terror, because it tells you of the sudden deaths of men and women that you knew intimately, and the prickly heat covers you as with a garment, and you sit down and write: "A slight increase of sickness is reported from the Khuda Janta Khan District. The outbreak is purely sporadic in its nature, and, thanks to the energetic efforts of the District authorities, is now almost at an end. It is, however, with deep regret we record the death, etc."

Then the sickness really breaks out, and the less recording and reporting the better for the peace of the subscribers. But the Empires and the Kings continue to divert themselves as selfishly as before, and the Foreman thinks that a daily paper really ought to come out once in twenty-four hours, and all the people at the Hill stations in the middle of their amusements say, "Good gracious! Why can't the paper be sparkling? I'm sure there's plenty going on up here."

That is the dark half of the moon, and, as the advertisements say, "must be experienced to be appreciated."

It was in that season, and a remarkably evil season, that the paper began running the last issue of the week on Saturday night, which is to say, Sunday morning, after the custom of a London paper. This was a great convenience, for immediately after the paper was put to bed, the dawn would lower the thermometer from 96° to almost 84° for half an hour, and in that chill—you have no idea how cold is 84° on the grass until you begin to pray for it—a very tired man could set off to sleep ere the heat roused him.

One Saturday night it was my pleasant duty to put the paper to bed alone. A King or courtier or a courtesan or a community was going to die or get a new Constitution, or do something that was important on the other side of the world, and the paper was to be held open till the latest possible minute in order to catch the telegram. It was a pitchy

3. William Ewart Gladstone (1809–1898), four times prime minister of England. 4. In Arthurian legend, Modred was son, nephew, and betrayer of King Arthur.

black night, as stifling as a June night can be, and the *loo*, the red-hot wind from the westward, was booming among the tinder-dry trees and pretending that the rain was on its heels. Now and again a spot of almost boiling water would fall on the dust with the flop of a frog, but all our weary world knew that was only pretense. It was a shade cooler in the press room than the office, so I sat there, while the type clicked and clicked and the nightjars hooted at the windows, and the all but naked compositors wiped the sweat from their foreheads and called for water. The thing that was keeping us back, whatever it was, would not come off, though the *loo* dropped and the last type was set, and the whole round earth stood still in the choking heat, with its finger on its lip, to wait the event. I drowsed, and wondered whether the telegraph was a blessing, and whether this dying man, or struggling people, was aware of the inconvenience the delay was causing. There was no special reason beyond the heat and worry to make tension, but, as the clock hands crept up to three o'clock and the machines spun their fly-wheels two or three times to see that all was in order, before I said the word that would set them off, I could have shrieked aloud.

Then the roar and rattle of the wheels shivered the quiet into little bits. I rose to go away, but two men in white clothes stood in front of me. The first one said, "It's him!" The second said, "So it is!" And they both laughed almost as loudly as the machinery roared, and mopped their foreheads. "We see there was a light burning across the road and we were sleeping in that ditch there for coolness, and I said to my friend here, 'The office is open. Let's come along and speak to him as turned us back from the Degumber State,' " said the smaller of the two. He was the man I had met in the Mhow train, and his fellow was the red-bearded man of Marwar Junction. There was no mistaking the eyebrows of the one or the beard of the other.

I was not pleased, because I wished to go to sleep, not to squabble with Loafers. "What do you want?" I asked.

"Half an hour's talk with you cool and comfortable, in the office," said the red-bearded man. "We'd *like* some drink—the Contrack doesn't begin yet, Peachey, so you needn't look—but what we really want is advice. We don't want money. We ask you as a favor, because you did us a bad turn about Degumber."

I led from the press room to the stifling office with the maps on the walls, and the red-haired man rubbed his hands. "That's something like," said he. "This was the proper shop to come to. Now, Sir, let me introduce to you Brother Peachey Carnehan, that's him, and Brother Daniel Dravot, that is *me*, and the less said about our professions the better, for we have been most things in our time. Soldier, sailor, compositor, photographer, proofreader, street preacher, and correspondents of the *Backwoodsman* when we thought the paper wanted one. Carnehan is sober, and so am I. Look at us first and see that's sure. It will save you cutting into my talk. We'll take one of your cigars apiece, and you shall see us light."

I watched the test. The men were absolutely sober, so I gave them each a tepid peg.

"Well *and* good," said Carnehan of the eyebrows, wiping the froth from his mustache. "Let me talk now, Dan. We have been all over India, mostly on foot. We have been boiler-fitters, engine-drivers, petty contractors, and all that, and we have decided that India isn't big enough for such as us."

They certainly were too big for the office. Dravot's beard seemed to fill half the room and Carnehan's shoulders the other half, as they sat on the big table. Carnehan continued: "The country isn't half worked out because they that governs it won't let you touch it. They spend all their blessed time in governing it, and you can't lift a spade, nor chip a rock, nor look for oil, nor anything like that without all the Government saying, 'Leave it alone and let us govern.' Therefore, such as it is, we will let it alone, and go away to some other place where a man isn't crowded and can come to his own. We are not little men, and there is nothing that we are afraid of except Drink, and we have signed a Contrack on that. *Therefore*, we are going away to be Kings."

"Kings in our own right," muttered Dravot.

"Yes, of course," I said. "You've been tramping in the sun, and it's a very warm night, and hadn't you better sleep over the notion? Come tomorrow."

"Neither drunk nor sunstruck," said Dravot. "We have slept over the notion half a year, and require to see Books and Atlases, and we have decided that there is only one place now in the world that two strong men can Sar-a-*whack*.[5] They call it Kafiristan. By my reckoning it's the top right-hand corner of Afghanistan, not more than three hundred miles from Peshawur. They have two and thirty heathen idols there, and we'll be the thirty-third. It's a mountainous country, and the women of those parts are very beautiful."

"But that is provided against in the Contrack," said Carnehan. "Neither Women nor Liqu-or, Daniel."

"And that's all we know, except that no one has gone there, and they fight, and in any place where they fight, a man who knows how to drill men can always be a King. We shall go to those parts and say to any King we find, 'D'you want to vanquish your foes?' and we will

5. The sultan of Sarawak, on the island of Borneo, had named an adventuring Englishman raja of the country.

show him how to drill men; for that we know better than anything else. Then we will subvert that King and seize his Throne and establish a Dy-nasty."

"You'll be cut to pieces before you're fifty miles across the Border," I said. "You have to travel through Afghanistan to get to that country. It's one mass of mountains and peaks and glaciers, and no Englishman has been through it. The people are utter brutes, and even if you reached them you couldn't do anything."

"That's more like," said Carnehan. "If you could think us a little more mad we would be more pleased. We have come to you to know about this country, to read a book about it, and be shown maps. We want you to tell us that we are fools and to show us your books." He turned to the bookcases.

"Are you at all in earnest?" I said.

"A little," said Dravot, sweetly. "As big a map as you have got, even if it's all blank where Kafiristan is, and any books you've got. We can read, though we aren't very educated."

I uncased the big thirty-two-miles-to-the-inch map of India, and two smaller Frontier maps, hauled down volume INF-KAN of the *Encyclopaedia Britannica*, and the men consulted them.

"See here!" said Dravot, his thumb on the map. "Up to Jagdallak, Peachey and me know the road. We was there with Robert's Army. We'll have to turn off to the right at Jagdallak through Laghmann territory. Then we get among the hills—fourteen thousand feet—fifteen thousand—it will be cold work there, but it don't look very far on the map."

I handed him Wood on the *Sources of the Oxus*. Carnehan was deep in the *Encyclopaedia*.

"They're a mixed lot," said Dravot, reflectively; "and it won't help us to know the names of their tribes. The more tribes the more they'll fight, and the better for us. From Jagdallak to Ashang. H'mm!"

"But all the information about the country is as sketchy and inaccurate as can be," I protested. "No one knows anything about it really. Here's the file of the *United Services' Institute*. Read what Bellew says."

"Blow Bellew!" said Carnehan. "Dan, they're an all-fired lot of heathens, but this book here says they think they're related to us English."

I smoked while the men pored over *Raverty*, *Wood*, the maps, and the *Encyclopaedia*.

"There is no use of your waiting," said Dravot, politely. "It's about four o'clock now. We'll go before six o'clock if you want to sleep, and we won't steal any of the papers. Don't you sit up. We're two harmless lunatics and if you come, tomorrow evening, down to the Serai we'll say good-by to you."

"You *are* two fools," I answered. "You'll be turned back at the Frontier or cut up the minute you set foot in Afghanistan. Do you want any money or a recommendation down-country? I can help you to the chance of work next week."

"Next week we shall be hard at work ourselves, thank you," said Dravot. "It isn't so easy being a King as it looks. When we've got our Kingdom in going order we'll let you know, and you can come up and help us to govern it."

"Would two lunatics make a Contrack like that?" said Carnehan, with subdued pride, showing me a greasy half sheet of note paper on which was written the following. I copied it, then and there, as a curiosity:

This Contract between me and you pursuing witnesseth in the name of God—Amen and so forth.

(ONE) *That me and you will settle this matter together:* i.e., *to be Kings of Kafiristan.*

(TWO) *That you and me will not, while this matter is being settled, look at any Liquor, nor any Woman, black, white or brown, so as to get mixed up with one or the other harmful.*

(THREE) *That we conduct ourselves with dignity and discretion and if one of us gets into trouble the other will stay by him.*

Signed by you and me this day.

PEACHEY TALIAFERRO CARNEHAN.
DANIEL DRAVOT.
Both Gentlemen at Large.

"There was no need for the last article," said Carnehan, blushing modestly; "but it looks regular. Now you know the sort of men that Loafers are—we *are* Loafers, Dan, until we get out of India—and *do* you think that we would sign a Contrack like that unless we was in earnest? We have kept away from the two things that make life worth having."

"You won't enjoy your lives much longer if you are going to try this idiotic adventure. Don't set the office on fire," I said, "and go away before nine o'clock."

I left them still poring over the maps and making notes on the back of the "Contrack." "Be sure to come down to the Serai tomorrow," were their parting words.

The Kumharsen Serai is the great four-square sink of humanity where the strings of camels and horses from the North load and unload. All the nationalities of Central Asia may be found there, and most of the folk of India proper. Balkh and Bokhara there meet Bengal and Bombay, and try to draw eyeteeth. You can buy ponies, turquoises, Persian pussy cats, saddlebags, fat-tailed sheep, and musk in the Kumharsen Serai, and get many strange things for nothing. In the afternoon

I went down there to see whether my friends intended to keep their word or were lying about drunk.

A priest attired in fragments of ribbons and rags stalked up to me, gravely twisting a child's paper whirligig. Behind was his servant bending under the load of a crate of mud toys. The two were loading up two camels, and the inhabitants of the Serai watched them with shrieks of laughter.

"The priest is mad," said a horse-dealer to me. "He is going up to Kabul to sell toys to the Amir. He will either be raised to honor or have his head cut off. He came in here this morning and has been behaving madly ever since."

"The witless are under the protection of God," stammered a flat-cheeked Usbeg in broken Hindi. "They foretell future events."

"Would they could have foretold that my caravan would have been cut up by the Shinwaris almost within shadow of the Pass!" grunted the Eusufzai agent of a Rajputana trading house whose goods had been feloniously diverted into the hands of other robbers just across the Border, and whose misfortunes were the laughingstock of the bazaar. "Ohé, priest, whence come you and whither do you go?"

"From Roum have I come," shouted the priest, waving his whirligig; "from Roum, blown by the breath of a hundred devils across the sea! O thieves, robbers, liars, the blessing of Pir Khan on pigs, dogs, and perjurers! Who will take the Protected of God to the North to sell charms that are never still to the Amir? The camels shall not gall, the sons shall not fall sick, and the wives shall remain faithful while they are away, of the men who give me place in their caravan. Who will assist me to slipper the King of the Roos with a golden slipper with a silver heel? The protection of Pir Khan be upon his labors!" He spread out the skirts of his garberdine and pirouetted between the lines of tethered horses.

"There starts a caravan from Peshawur to Kabul in twenty days, *Huzrut*," said the Eusufzai trader. "My camels go therewith. Do thou also go and bring us good luck."

"I will go even now!" shouted the priest. "I will depart upon my winged camels, and be at Peshawur in a day! Ho! Hazar Mir Khan," he yelled to his servant, "drive out the camels, but let me first mount my own."

He leaped on the back of his beast as it knelt, and, turning round to me, cried, "Come thou also, Sahib, a little along the road, and I will sell thee a charm—an amulet that shall make thee King of Kafiristan."

Then the light broke upon me, and I followed the two camels out of the Serai till we reached open road and the priest halted.

"What d'you think o' that?" said he in English. "Carnehan can't talk their patter, so I've made him my servant. He makes a handsome servant. 'Tisn't for nothing that I've been knocking about the country for fourteen years. Didn't I do that talk neat? We'll hitch on to a caravan at Peshawur till we get to Jagdallak, and then we'll see if we can get donkeys for our camels, and strike into Kafiristan. Whirligigs for the Amir, O Lor'! Put your hand under the camel bags and tell me what you feel."

I felt the butt of a Martini,[6] and another and another.

"Twenty of 'em," said Dravot, placidly. "Twenty of 'em, and ammunition to correspond, under the whirligigs and the mud dolls."

"Heaven help you if you are caught with those things!" I said. "A Martini is worth her weight in silver among the Pathans."

"Fifteen hundred rupees of capital—every rupee we could beg, borrow, or steal—are invested on these two camels," said Dravot. "We won't get caught. We're going through the Khyber with a regular caravan. Who'd touch a poor mad priest?"

"Have you got everything you want?" I asked, overcome with astonishment.

"Not yet, but we shall soon. Give us a memento of your kindness, *Brother*. You did me a service yesterday, and that time in Marwar. Half my Kingdom shall you have, as the saying is." I slipped a small charm compass from my watch chain and handed it up to the priest.

"Good-bye," said Dravot, giving me hand cautiously. "It's the last time we'll shake hands with an Englishman these many days. Shake hands with him, Carnehan," he cried, as the second camel passed me.

Carnehan leaned down and shook hands. Then the camels passed away along the dusty road, and I was left alone to wonder. My eye could detect no failure in the disguises. The scene in Serai attested that they were complete to the native mind. There was just the chance, therefore, that Carnehan and Dravot would be able to wander through Afghanistan without detection. But, beyond, they would find death, certain and awful death.

Ten days later a native friend of mine, giving me the news of the day from Peshawur, wound up his letter with:—"There has been much laughter here on account of a certain mad priest who is going in his estimation to sell petty gauds and insignificant trinkets which he ascribes as great charms to H. H. the Amir of Bokhara. He passed through Peshawur and associated himself to the Second Summer caravan that goes to Kabul. The merchants are pleased, because through superstition they imagine that such mad fellows bring good fortune."

The two, then, were beyond the Border. I would have prayed for them, but, that night, a real King died in Europe, and demanded an obituary notice.

6. Military rifle.

The wheel of the world swings through the same phases again and again. Summer passed and winter thereafter, and came and passed again. The daily paper continued and I with it, and upon the third summer there fell a hot night, a night issue, and a strained waiting for something to be telegraphed from the other side of the world, exactly as had happened before. A few great men had died in the past two years, the machines worked with more clatter, and some of the trees in the Office garden were a few feet taller. But that was all the difference.

I passed over to the press room, and went through just such a scene as I have already described. The nervous tension was stronger than it had been two years before, and I felt the heat more acutely. At three o'clock I cried, "Print off," and turned to go, when there crept to my chair what was left of a man. He was bent into a circle, his head was sunk between his shoulders, and he moved his feet one over the other like a bear. I could hardly see whether he walked or crawled—this rag-wrapped, whining cripple who addressed me by name, crying that he was come back. "Can you give me a drink?" he whimpered. "For the Lord's sake, give me a drink!"

I went back to the office, the man followed with groans of pain, and I turned up the lamp.

"Don't you know me?" he gasped, dropping into a chair, and he turned his drawn face, surmounted by a shock of gray hair, to the light.

I looked at him intently. Once before had I seen eyebrows that met over the nose in an inch-broad black band, but for the life of me I could not tell where.

"I don't know you," I said, handing him the whisky. "What can I do for you?"

He took a gulp of the spirit raw, and shivered in spite of the suffocating heat.

"I've come back," he repeated; "and I was the King of Kafiristan—me and Dravot—crowned Kings we was! In this office we settled it—you setting there and giving us the books. I am Peachey—Peachey Taliaferro Carnehan, and you've been setting here ever since—O Lord!"

I was more than a little astonished, and expressed my feelings accordingly.

"It's true," said Carnehan, with a dry cackle, nursing his feet, which were wrapped in rags. "True as gospel. Kings we were, with crowns upon our heads—me and Dravot—poor Dan—oh, poor, poor Dan, that would never take advice, not though I begged of him!"

"Take the whisky," I said, "and take your own time. Tell me all you can recollect of everything from beginning to end. You got across the border on your camels, Dravot dressed as a mad priest and you his servant. Do you remember that?"

"I ain't mad—yet, but I shall be that way soon. Of course I remember. Keep looking at me, or maybe my words will go all to pieces. Keep looking at me in my eyes and don't say anything."

I leaned forward and looked into his face as steadily as I could. He dropped one hand upon the table and I grasped it by the wrist. It was twisted like a bird's claw, and upon the back was a ragged, red, diamond-shaped scar.

"No, don't look there. Look at *me*," said Carnehan. "That comes afterward, but for the Lord's sake don't distrack me. We left with that caravan, me and Dravot playing all sorts of antics to amuse the people we were with. Dravot used to make us laugh in the evenings when all the people was cooking their dinners—cooking their dinners, and . . . what did they do then? They lit little fires with sparks that went into Dravot's beard, and we all laughed—fit to die. Little red fires they was, going into Dravot's big red beard—so funny." His eyes left mine and he smiled foolishly.

"You went as far as Jagdallak with that caravan," I said, at a venture, "after you had lit those fires. To Jagdallak, where you turned off to try to get into Kafiristan."

"No, we didn't neither. What are you talking about? We turned off before Jagdallak, because we heard the roads was good. But they wasn't good enough for our two camels—mine and Dravot's. When we left the caravan, Dravot took off all his clothes and mine too, and said we would be heathen, because the Kafirs didn't allow Mohammedans to talk to them. So we dressed betwixt and between, and such a sight as Daniel Dravot I never saw yet nor expect to see again. He burned half his beard, and slung a sheepskin over his shoulder, and shaved his head into patterns. He shaved mine, too, and made me wear outrageous things to look like a heathen. That was in a most mountaineous country, and our camels couldn't go along any more because of the mountains. They were tall and black, and coming home I saw them fight like wild goats—there are lots of goats in Kafiristan. And these mountains, they never keep still, no more than goats. Always fighting they are, and don't let you sleep at night."

"Take some more whisky," I said, very slowly. "What did you and Daniel Dravot do when the camels could go no further because of the rough roads that led into Kafiristan?"

"What did which do? There was a party called Peachey Taliaferro Carnehan that was with Dravot. Shall I tell you about him? He died out there in the cold. Slap from the bridge fell old Peachey, turning and twisting in the air like a penny whirligig that you can sell to the Amir— No; they was two for three ha'pence, those whirligigs, or I am much mistaken and woeful sore. And then these camels were no use, and Peachey said to Dravot—'For the Lord's sake, let's get out of this before our heads are chopped off,' and with that they killed the camels all among the mountains, not having anything in particular to eat, but first they took off the boxes with the guns and the ammunition, till two men came along driving four mules. Dravot up and dances in front of them, singing,—'Sell me four mules.' Says the first man,—'If you are rich enough to buy, you are rich enough to rob'; but before ever he could put his hand to his knife, Dravot breaks his neck over his knee, and the other party runs away. So Carnehan loaded the mules with the rifles that was taken off the camels, and together we starts forward into those bitter cold mountaineous parts, and never a road broader than the back of your hand."

He paused for a moment, while I asked him if he could remember the nature of the country through which he had journeyed.

"I am telling you as straight as I can, but my head isn't as good as it might be. They drove nails through it to make me hear better how Dravot died. The country was mountaineous and the mules were most contrary, and the inhabitants was dispersed and solitary. They went up and up, and down and down, and that other party, Carnehan, was imploring of Dravot not to sing and whistle so loud, for fear of bringing down the tremenjus avalanches. But Dravot says that if a King couldn't sing it wasn't worth being King, and whacked the mules over the rump, and never took no heed for ten cold days. We came to a big level valley all among the mountains, and the mules were near dead, so we killed them, not having anything in special for them or us to eat. We sat upon the boxes, and played odd and even with the cartridges that was jolted out.

"Then ten men with bows and arrows ran down that valley, chasing twenty men with bows and arrows, and the row was tremenjus. They was fair men—fairer than you or more—with yellow hair and remarkable well built. Says Dravot, unpacking the guns—'This is the beginning of the business. We'll fight for the ten men,' and with that he fires two rifles at the twenty men, and drops one of them at two hundred yards from the rock where we was sitting. The other men began to run, but Carnehan and Dravot sits on the boxes picking them off at all ranges, up and down the valley. Then we goes up to the ten men that had run across the snow too, and they fires a footy little arrow at us. Dravot he shoots above their heads and they all falls down flat. Then he walks over and kicks them, and then he lifts them up and shakes hands all around to make them friendly like. He calls them and gives them the boxes to carry, and waves his hand for all the world as though he was King already. They takes the boxes and him across the valley and up the hill into a pine wood on the top, where there was half a dozen big stone idols. Dravot he goes to the biggest—a fellow they call Imbra—and lays a rifle and a cartridge at his feet, rubbing his nose respectful with his own nose, patting him on the head, and saluting in front of it. He turns round to the men and nods his head, and says, 'That's all right. I'm in the know too, and all these old jim-jams are my friends.' Then he opens his mouth and points down it, and when the first man brings him food, he says 'No'; and when the second man brings him food, he says 'No'; but when one of the old priests and the boss of the village brings him food, he says 'Yes'; very haughty, and eats it slow. That was how we came to our first village, without any trouble, just as though we had tumbled from the skies. But we tumbled from one of those damned rope bridges, you see, and you couldn't expect a man to laugh much after that."

"Take some more whisky and go on," I said. "That was the first village you came into. How did you get to be King?"

"I wasn't King," said Carnehan. "Dravot he was the King, and a handsome man he looked with the gold crown on his head and all. Him and the other party stayed in that village, and every morning Dravot sat by the side of old Imbra, and the people came and worshiped. That was Dravot's order. Then a lot of men came into the valley, and Carnehan and Dravot picks them off with the rifles before they knew where they was, and runs down into the valley and up again the other side, and finds another village, same as the first one, and the people all falls down flat on their faces, and Dravot says, 'Now what is the trouble between you two villages?' and the people points to a woman, as fair as you or me, that was carried off, and Dravot takes her back to the first village and counts up the dead—eight there was. For each dead man Dravot pours a little milk on the ground and waves his arms like a whirligig and 'That's all right,' says he. Then he and Carnehan takes the big boss of each village by the arm and walks them down into the valley, and shows them how to scratch a line with a spear right down the valley, and gives each a sod of turf from both sides o' the line. Then all the people comes down and shouts like the devil and all, and Dravot says, 'Go and dig the land, and be fruitful and multiply,' which they did, though they didn't understand. Then we asks the names of things in their lingo—bread and water and fire and idols and such, and Dravot leads the priest of each village up to the idol, and says he must sit there and judge the people, and if anything goes wrong he is to be shot.

"Next week they was all turning up the land in the valley as quiet as bees and much prettier, and the priests heard all the complaints and told Dravot in dumb show what it was about. 'That's just the beginning,' says Dravot. 'They think we're Gods.' He and Carnehan picks out twenty good men and shows them how to click off a rifle, and form fours, and advance in line, and they was very pleased to do so, and clever to see the hang of it. Then he takes out his pipe and his 'baccy pouch and leaves one at one village and one at the other, and off we two goes to see what was to be done in the next valley. That was all rock, and there was a little village there, and Carnehan says, 'Send 'em to the old valley to plant,' and takes 'em there and gives 'em some land that wasn't took before. They were a poor lot, and we blooded 'em with a kid before letting 'em into the new Kingdom. That was to impress the people, and then they settled down quiet, and Carnehan went back to Dravot, who had got into another valley, all snow and ice and most mountaineous. There was no people there, and the Army got afraid, so Dravot shoots one of them, and goes on till he finds some people in a village, and the Army explains that unless the people wants to be killed they had better not shoot their little matchlocks; for they had matchlocks. We makes friends with the priest and I stays there alone with two of the Army, teaching the men how to drill, and a thundering big Chief comes across the snow with kettledrums and horns twanging, because he heard there was a new God kicking about. Carnehan sights for the brown of the men half a mile across the snow and wings one of them. Then he sends a message to the Chief that, unless he wished to be killed, he must come and shake hands with me and leave his arms behind. The Chief comes alone first, and Carnehan shakes hands with him and whirls his arms about, same as Dravot used, and very much surprised that Chief was, and strokes my eyebrows. Then Carnehan goes alone to the Chief, and asks him in dumb show if he had an enemy he hated. 'I have,' says the Chief. So Carnehan weeds out the pick of his men, and sets the two of the Army to show them drill, and at the end of two weeks the men can maneuver about as well as Volunteers. So he marches with the Chief to a great big plain on the top of a mountain, and the Chief's men rushes into a village and takes it; we three Martinis firing into the brown of the enemy. So we took that village too, and I gives the Chief a rag from my coat and says, 'Occupy till I come'; which was scriptural. By way of a reminder, when me and the Army was eighteen hundred yards away, I drops a bullet near him standing on the snow, and all the people falls flat on their faces. Then I sends a letter to Dravot, wherever he be by land or by sea."

At the risk of throwing the creature out of train I interrupted, "How could you write a letter up yonder?"

"The letter?—Oh!—The letter! Keep looking at me between the eyes, please. It was a string-talk letter, that we'd learned the way of it from a blind beggar in the Punjab."

I remember that there had once come to the office a blind man with a knotted twig and a piece of string which he wound round the twig according to some cipher of his own. He could, after the lapse of days or hours, repeat the sentence which he had reeled up. He had reduced the alphabet to eleven primitive sounds; and tried to teach me his method, but failed.

"I sent that letter to Dravot," said Carnehan; "and told him to come back because this Kingdom was growing too big for me to handle, and then I struck for the first valley, to see how the priests were working. They called the village we took along with the Chief, Bashkai, and the first village we took, Er-Heb. The priests at Er-Heb was doing all right, but they had a lot of pending cases about land to show me, and some men from another village had been firing arrows at night. I went out and looked for that village and fired four rounds at it from a thousand yards. That used all the cartridges I cared to spend, and I waited for Dravot, who had been away two or three months, and I kept my people quiet.

"One morning I heard the devil's own noise of drums and horns, and Dan Dravot marches down the hill with his Army and a tail of hundreds of men, and, which was the most amazing—a great gold crown on his head. 'My Gord, Carnehan,' says Daniel, 'this is a tremenjus business, and we've got the whole country as far as it's worth having. I am the son of Alexander by Queen Semiramis, and you're my younger brother and a God too! It's the biggest thing we've ever seen. I've been marching and fighting for six weeks with the Army, and every footy little village for fifty miles has come in rejoiceful; and more than that, I've got the key of the whole show, as you'll see, and I've got a crown for you! I told 'em to make two of 'em at a place called Shu, where the gold lies in the rock like suet in mutton. Gold I've seen, and turquoise I've kicked out of the cliffs, and there's garnets in the sands of the river, and here's a chunk of amber that a man brought me. Call up all the priests and, here, take your crown.'

"One of the men opens a black hair bag and I slips the crown on. It was too small and too heavy, but I wore it for the glory. Hammered gold it was—five pound weight, like a hoop of a barrel.

" 'Peachey,' says Dravot, 'we don't want to fight no more. The Craft's[7] the trick, so help me!' and he brings forward that same Chief that I left at Bashkai—Billy Fish we called him afterward, because he was so like Billy Fish that drove the big tank engine at Mach on the Bolan in the old days. 'Shake hands with him,' says Dravot, and I shook hands and nearly dropped, for Billy Fish gave me the Grip. I said nothing, but tried him with the Fellow Craft Grip. He answers, all right, and I tried the Master's Grip, but that was a slip. 'A Fellow Craft he is!' I says to Dan. 'Does he know the word?' 'He does,' says Dan, 'and all the priests know. It's a miracle! The Chiefs and the priests can work a Fellow Craft Lodge in a way that's very like ours, and they've cut the marks on the rocks, but they don't know the Third Degree, and they've come to find out. It's Gord's Truth. I've known these long

7. Masonic rituals and emblems.

years that the Afghans knew up to the Fellow Craft Degree, but this is a miracle. A God and a Grand Master of the Craft am I, and a Lodge in the Third Degree I will open, and we'll raise the head priests and the Chiefs of the villages.'

" 'It's against all the law,' I says, 'holding a Lodge without warrant from anyone; and we never held office in any Lodge.'

" 'It's a master stroke of policy,' says Dravot. 'It means running the country as easy as a four-wheeled bogy on a down grade. We can't stop to inquire now, or they'll turn against us. I've forty Chiefs at my heel, and passed and raised according to their merit they shall be. Billet these men on the villages and see that we run up a Lodge of some kind. The temple of Imbra will do for the Lodge room. The women must make aprons as you show them. I'll hold a levee of Chiefs tonight and Lodge tomorrow.'

"I was fair run off my legs, but I wasn't such a fool as not to see what a pull this Craft business gave us. I showed the priests' families how to make aprons of the degrees, but for Dravot's apron the blue border and marks was made of turquoise lumps on white hide, not cloth. We took a great square stone in the temple for the Master's chair, and little stones for the officers' chairs, and painted the black pavement with white squares, and did what we could to make things regular.

"At the levee which was held that night on the hillside with big bonfires, Dravot gives out that him and me were Gods and sons of Alexander, and Past Grand Masters in the Craft, and was come to make Kafiristan a country where every man should eat in peace and drink in quiet, and specially obey us. Then the Chiefs come round to shake hands, and they was so hairy and white and fair it was just shaking hands with old friends. We gave them names according as they was like men we had known in India—Billy Fish, Holly Wilworth, Pikky Kergan that was Bazaar-master when I was at Mhow, and so on and so on.

"*The* most amazing miracle was at Lodge next night. One of the old priests was watching us continuous, and I felt uneasy, for I knew we'd have to fudge the Ritual, and I didn't know what the men knew. The old priest was a stranger come in from beyond the village of Bashkai. The minute Dravot puts on the Master's apron that the girls had made for him, the priest fetches a whoop and a howl, and tried to overturn the stone that Dravot was sitting on. 'It's all up now,' I says. 'That comes of meddling with the Craft without warrant!' Dravot never winked an eye, not when ten priests took and tilted over the Grand Master's chair—which was to say the stone of Imbra. The priest begins rubbing the bottom end of it to clear away the black dirt, and presently he shows all the other priests the Master's Mark, same as was on Dravot's apron, cut into the stone. Not even the priests of the temple of Imbra knew it was there. The old chap falls flat on his face at Dravot's feet and kisses 'em. 'Luck again,' says Dravot, across the Lodge to me, 'they say it's the missing Mark that no one could understand the why of. We're more than safe now.' Then he bangs the butt of his gun for a gavel and says, 'By virtue of the authority vested in me by my own right hand and the help of Peachey, I declare myself Grand Master of all Freemasonry in Kafiristan in this the Mother Lodge o' the country, and King of Kafiristan equally with Peachey!' At that he puts on his crown and I puts on mine—I was doing Senior Warden—and we opens the Lodge in most ample form. It was a amazing miracle! The priests moved in Lodge through the first two degrees almost without telling, as if the memory was coming back to them. After that, Peachey and Dravot raised such as was worthy—high priests and Chiefs of far-off villages. Billy Fish was the first, and I can tell you we scared the soul out of him. It was not in any way according to Ritual, but it served our turn. We didn't raise more than ten of the biggest men, because we didn't want to make the Degree common. And they was clamoring to be raised.

" 'In another six months,' says Dravot, 'we'll hold another Communication and see how you are working.' Then he asks them about their villages, and learns that they was fighting one against the other and were fair sick and tired of it. And when they wasn't doing that they was fighting with the Mohammedans. 'You can fight those when they come into our country,' says Dravot. 'Tell off every tenth man of your tribes for a Frontier guard, and send two hundred at a time to this valley to be drilled. Nobody is going to be shot or speared any more so long as he does well, and I know that you won't cheat me because you're white people—sons of Alexander—and not like common, black Mohammedans. You are *my* people and by God,' says he, running off into English at the end—'I'll make a damned fine Nation of you, or I'll die in the making!'

"I can't tell all we did for the next six months because Dravot did a lot I couldn't see the hang of, and he learned their lingo in a way I never could. My work was to help the people plow, and now and again go out with some of the Army and see what the other villages were doing, and make 'em throw rope bridges across the ravines which cut up the country horrid. Dravot was very kind to me, but when he walked up and down in the pine wood pulling that bloody red beard of his with both fists I knew he was thinking plans I could not advise him about, and I just waited for orders.

"But Dravot never showed me disrespect before the people. They were afraid of me and the Army, but they loved Dan. He was the best of friends with the priests and the Chiefs; but anyone could come across the hills with a complaint and Dravot would hear him out fair, and call four priests together and say what was to be done. He used to call in Billy Fish from Bashkai, and Pikky Kergan from Shu, and an old Chief we called Kafuzelum—it was like enough to his real name—and hold councils with 'em when there was any fighting to be done in small villages. That was his Council of War, and the four priests of Bashkai, Shu, Khawak, and Madora was his Privy Council. Between the lot of 'em they sent me, with forty men and twenty rifles, and sixty men carrying turquoises, into the Ghorband country to buy those hand-made Martini rifles, that come out of the Amir's workshops at Kabul, from one of the Amir's Herati regiments that would have sold the very teeth out of their mouths for turquoises.

"I stayed in Ghorband a month, and gave the Governor there the pick of my baskets for hush money, and bribed the Colonel of the regiment some more, and, between the two and the tribespeople, we got more than a hundred hand-made Martinis, a hundred good Kohat Jezails that'll throw to six hundred yards, and forty manloads of very bad ammunition for the rifles. I came back with what I had, and distributed 'em among the men that the Chiefs sent to me to drill. Dravot was too busy to attend to those things, but the old Army that we first made helped me, and we turned out five hundred men that could drill, and two hundred that knew how to hold arms pretty straight. Even those corkscrewed, hand-made guns was a miracle to them. Dravot talked big about powder shops and factories, walking up and down in the pine wood when the winter was coming on.

" 'I won't make a Nation,' says he. 'I'll make an Empire! These men aren't niggers; they're English! Look at their eyes—look at their mouths. Look at the way they stand up. They sit on chairs in their own houses. They're the Lost Tribes, or something like it, and they've grown to be English. I'll take a census in the spring if the priests don't get frightened. There must be a fair two million of 'em in these hills. The villages are full o' little children. Two million people—two hundred and fifty thousand fighting men—and all English! They only want the rifles and a little drilling. Two hundred and fifty thousand men, ready to cut in on Russia's right flank when she tries for India! Peachey, man,' he says, chewing his beard in great hunks, 'we shall be Emperors—Emperors of the Earth! Rajah Brooke[8] will be a suckling to us. I'll treat with the Vice-roy on equal terms. I'll ask him to send me twelve picked English—twelve that I know of—to help us govern a bit. There's Mackray, Sergeant-pensioner at Segowli—many's the good dinner he's given me, and his wife a pair of trousers. There's Donkin, the Warder

8. Sir Charles Brooke (1829–1917), one of three members of the family who governed Sarawak from 1841 to 1942.

of Tounghoo Jail; there's hundreds that I could lay my hand on if I was in India. The Vice-roy shall do it for me. I'll send a man through in the spring for those men, and I'll write for a dispensation from the Grand Lodge for what I've done as Grand Master. That—and all the Sniders[9] that'll be thrown out when the native troops in India take up the Martini. They'll be worn smooth, but they'll do for fighting in these hills. Twelve English, a hundred thousand Sniders run through the Amir's country in driblets—I'd be content with twenty thousand in one year—and we'd be an Empire. When everything was shipshape, I'd hand over the crown—this crown I'm wearing now—to Queen Victoria on my knees, and she'd say: "Rise up, Sir Daniel Dravot." Oh, it's big! It's big, I tell you! But there's so much to be done in every place—Bashkai, Khawak, Shu, and everywhere else.'

" 'What is it?' I says. 'There are no more men coming in to be drilled this autumn. Look at those fat, black clouds. They're bringing the snow.'

" 'It isn't that,' says Daniel, putting his hand very hard on my shoulder; 'and I don't wish to say anything that's against you, for no other living man would have followed me and made me what I am as you have done. You're a first-class Commander-in-Chief, and the people know you; but—it's a big country, and somehow you can't help me, Peachey, in the way I want to be helped.'

" 'Go to your blasted priests, then!' I said, and I was sorry when I made that remark, but it did hurt me sore to find Daniel talking so superior when I'd drilled all the men, and done all he told me.

" 'Don't let's quarrel, Peachey,' says Daniel, without cursing. 'You're a King, too, and the half of this Kingdom is yours; but can't you see, Peachey, we want cleverer men than us now—three or four of 'em, that we can scatter about for our Deputies. It's a hugeous great State, and I can't always tell the right thing to do, and I haven't time for all I want to do, and here's the winter coming on and all.' He put half his beard into his mouth, and it was as red as the gold of his crown.

" 'I'm sorry, Daniel,' says I. 'I've done all I could. I've drilled the men and shown the people how to stack their oats better; and I've brought in those tinware rifles from Ghorband—but I know what you're driving at. I take it Kings always feel oppressed that way.'

" 'There's another thing too,' says Dravot, walking up and down. 'The winter's coming and these people won't be giving much trouble and if they do we can't move about. I want a wife.'

" 'For Gord's sake leave the women alone!' I says. 'We've both got all the work we can, though I *am* a fool. Remember the Contrack, and keep clear o' women.'

9. Obsolete military rifles.

" 'The Contrack only lasted till such time as we was Kings; and Kings we have been these months past,' says Dravot, weighing his crown in his hand. 'You go get a wife too, Peachey—a nice, strappin', plump girl that'll keep you warm in the winter. They're prettier than English girls, and we can take the pick of 'em. Boil 'em once or twice in hot water, and they'll come as fair as chicken and ham.'

" 'Don't tempt me!' I says. 'I will not have any dealings with a woman not till we are a dam' side more settled than we are now. I've been doing the work o' two men, and you've been doing the work o' three. Let's lie off a bit, and see if we can get some better tobacco from Afghan country and run in some good liquor; but no women.'

" 'Who's talking o' *women?*' says Dravot. 'I said *wife*—a Queen to breed a King's son for the King. A Queen out of the strongest tribe, that'll make them your blood brothers, and that'll lie by your side and tell you all the people thinks about you and their own affairs. That's what I want.'

" 'Do you remember that Bengali woman I kept at Mogul Serai when I was a plate layer?' says I. 'A fat lot o' good she was to me. She taught me the lingo and one or two other things; but what happened? She ran away with the Stationmaster's servant and half my month's pay. Then she turned up at Dadur Junction in tow of a half-caste, and had the impidence to say I was her husband—all among the drivers in the running shed!'

" 'We've done with that,' says Dravot. 'These women are whiter than you or me, and a Queen I will have for the winter months.'

" 'For the last time o' asking, Dan, do *not,*' I says. 'It'll only bring us harm. The Bible says that Kings ain't to waste their strength on women, 'specially when they've got a new raw Kingdom to work over.'

" 'For the last time of answering, I will,' said Dravot, and he went away through the pine trees looking like a big red devil. The low sun hit his crown and beard on one side and the two blazed like hot coals.

"But getting a wife was not as easy as Dan thought. He put it before the Council, and there was no answer till Billy Fish said that he'd better ask the girls. Dravot damned them all around. 'What's wrong with me?' he shouts, standing by the idol Imbra. 'Am I a dog or am I not enough of a man for your wenches? Haven't I put the shadow of my hand over this country? Who stopped the last Afghan raid?' It was me really, but Dravot was too angry to remember. 'Who brought your guns? Who repaired the bridges? Who's the Grand Master of the sign cut in the stone?' and he thumped his hand on the block that he used to sit on in Lodge, and at Council, which opened like Lodge always. Billy Fish said nothing, and no more did the others. 'Keep your hair on, Dan,' said I; 'and ask the girls. That's how it's done at Home, and these people are quite English.'

" 'The marriage of the King is a matter of State,' says Dan, in a white-hot rage, for he could feel, I hope, that he was going against his better mind. He walked out of the Council room, and the others sat still, looking at the ground.

" 'Billy Fish,' says I to the Chief of Bashkai, 'what's the difficulty here? A straight answer to a true friend.' 'You know,' says Billy Fish. 'How should a man tell you who know everything? How can daughters of men marry Gods or Devils? It's not proper.'

"I remembered something like that in the Bible; but if, after seeing us as long as they had, they still believed we were Gods, it wasn't for me to undeceive them.

" 'A God can do anything,' says I. 'If the King is fond of a girl he'll not let her die.' 'She'll have to,' said Billy Fish. 'There are all sorts of Gods and Devils in these mountains, and now and again a girl marries one of them and isn't seen any more. Besides, you two know the Mark cut in the stone. Only the Gods know that. We thought you were men till you showed the sign of the Master.'

"I wished then that we had explained about the loss of the genuine secrets of a Master Mason at the first go-off; but I said nothing. All that night there was a blowing of horns in a little dark temple halfway down the hill, and I heard a girl crying fit to die. One of the priests told us that she was being prepared to marry the King.

" 'I'll have no nonsense of that kind,' says Dan. 'I don't want to interfere with your customs, but I'll take my own wife.' 'The girl's a little bit afraid,' says the priest. 'She thinks she's going to die, and they are a-heartening of her up down in the temple.'

" 'Hearten her very tender, then,' says Dravot, 'or I'll hearten you with the butt of a gun so that you'll never want to be heartened again.' He licked his lips, did Dan, and stayed up walking about more than half the night, thinking of the wife that he was going to get in the morning. I wasn't any means comfortable, for I knew that dealings with a woman in foreign parts, though you was a crowned King twenty times over, could not but be risky. I got up very early in the morning while Dravot was asleep, and I saw the priests talking together in whispers, and the Chiefs talking together too, and they looked at me out of the corners of their eyes.

" 'What is up, Fish?' I says to the Bashkai man, who was wrapped up in his furs and looking splendid to behold.

" 'I can't rightly say,' says he; 'but if you can induce the King to drop all this nonsense about marriage, you'll be doing him and me and yourself a great service.'

" 'That I do believe,' says I. 'But sure, you know, Billy, as well as me, having fought against and for us, that the King and me are nothing more than two of the finest men that God Almighty ever made. Nothing more, I do assure you.'

" 'That may be,' says Billy Fish, 'and yet I should be sorry if it was.' He sinks his head upon his great fur cloak for a minute and thinks. 'King,' says he, 'be you man or God or Devil, I'll stick by you today. I have twenty of my men with me, and they will follow me. We'll go to Bashkai until the storm blows over.'

"A little snow had fallen in the night, and everything was white except the greasy fat clouds that blew down and down from the north. Dravot came out with his crown on his head, swinging his arms and stamping his feet, and looking more pleased than Punch.

" 'For the last time, drop it, Dan,' says I, in a whisper. 'Billy Fish here says that there will be a row.'

" 'A row among my people!' says Dravot. 'Not much. Peachey, you're a fool not to get a wife too. Where's the girl?' says he, with a voice as loud as the braying of a jackass. 'Call up all the Chiefs and priests, and let the Emperor see if his wife suits him.'

"There was no need to call anyone. They were all there leaning on their guns and spears round the clearing in the center of the pine wood. A deputation of priests went down to the little temple to bring up the girl, and the horns blew up fit to wake the dead. Billy Fish saunters round and gets as close to Daniel as he could, and behind him stood his twenty men with matchlocks. Not a man of them under six feet. I was next to Dravot, and behind me was twenty men of the regular Army. Up comes the girl, and a strapping wench she was, covered with silver and turquoises, but white as death, and looking back every minute at the priests.

" 'She'll do,' said Dan, looking her over. 'What's to be afraid of, lass? Come and kiss me.' He puts his arm round her. She shuts her eyes, gives a bit of a squeak, and down goes her face in the side of Dan's flaming red beard.

" 'The slut's bitten me!' says he, clapping his hand to his neck, and, sure enough, his hand was red with blood. Billy Fish and two of his matchlock men catches hold of Dan by his shoulders and drags him into the Bashkai lot, while the priests howl in their lingo, 'Neither God nor Devil, but a man!' I was all taken aback, for a priest cut at me in front, and the Army behind began firing into the Bashkai men.

" 'God A-mighty!' says Dan. 'What is the meaning o' this?'

" 'Come back! Come away!' says Billy Fish, 'Ruin and Mutiny is the matter. We'll break for Bashkai if we can.'

"I tried to give some sort of orders to my men—the men o' the regular Army—but it was no use, so I fired into the brown of 'em with an English Martini and drilled three beggars in a line. The valley was full of shouting, howling creatures, and every soul was shrieking, 'Not a God not a Devil, but only a man!' The Bashkai troops stuck to Billy Fish all they were worth, but their matchlocks wasn't half as good as the Kabul breechloaders, and four of them dropped. Dan was bellowing like a bull, for he was very wrathy; and Billy Fish had a hard job to prevent him running out at the crowd.

" 'We can't stand,' says Billy Fish. 'Make a run for it down the valley! The whole place is against us.' The matchlock men ran, and we went down the valley in spite of Dravot's protestations. He was swearing horribly and crying out that he was a King. The priests rolled great stones on us, and the regular Army fired hard, and there wasn't more than six men, not counting Dan, Billy Fish, and Me, that came down to the bottom of the valley alive.

"Then they stopped firing and the horns in the temple blew again. 'Come away—for Gord's sake come away!' says Billy Fish. 'They'll send runners out to all the villages before ever we get to Bashkai. I can protect you there, but I can't do anything now.'

"My own notion is that Dan began to go mad in his head from that hour. He stared up and down like a stuck pig. Then he was all for walking back alone and killing the priests with his bare hands; which he could have done. 'An Emperor am I,' says Daniel, 'and next year I shall be a Knight of the Queen.'

" 'All right, Dan,' says I; 'but come along now while there's time.'

" 'It's your fault,' says he, 'for not looking after your Army better. There was mutiny in the midst and you didn't know—you damned engine-driving, plate-laying, missionary's-pass-hunting hound!' He sat upon a rock and called me every foul name he could lay tongue to. I was too heartsick to care, though it was all his foolishness that brought the smash.

" 'I'm sorry, Dan,' says I, 'but there's no accounting for natives. This business is our Fifty-Seven.[1] Maybe we'll make something out of it yet, when we've got to Bashkai.'

" 'Let's get to Bashkai, then,' says Dan, 'and, by God, when I come back here again I'll sweep the valley so there isn't a bug in a blanket left!'

"We walked all that day, and all that night Dan was stumping up and down on the snow, chewing his beard and muttering to himself.

" 'There's no hope o' getting clear,' said Billy Fish. 'The priests will have sent runners to the villages to say that you are only men. Why didn't you stick on as Gods till things was more settled? I'm a

1. The Indian Mutiny of 1857–1858, in which a revolt of Indian soldiers serving the British led to a widespread uprising against British rule.

dead man,' says Billy Fish, and he throws himself down on the snow and begins to pray to his Gods.

"Next morning we was in a cruel bad country—all up and down, no level ground at all, and no food either. The six Bashkai men looked at Billy Fish hungrywise as if they wanted to ask something, but they said never a word. At noon we came to the top of a flat mountain all covered with snow, and when we climbed up into it, behold, there was an Army in position waiting in the middle!

" 'The runners have been very quick,' says Billy Fish, with a little bit of a laugh. 'They are waiting for us.'

"Three or four men began to fire from the enemy's side, and a chance shot took Daniel in the calf of the leg. That brought him to his senses. He looks across the snow at the Army, and sees the rifles that we had brought into the country.

" 'We're done for,' says he. 'They are Englishmen, these people—and it's my blasted nonsense that has brought you to this. Get back, Billy Fish, and take your men away; you've done what you could, and now cut for it. Carnehan,' says he, 'shake hands with me and go along with Billy. Maybe they won't kill you. I'll go and meet 'em alone. It's me that did it. Me, the King!'

" 'Go!' says I. 'Go to Hell, Dan. I'm with you here. Billy Fish, you clear out, and we two will meet those folk.'

" 'I'm a Chief,'' says Billy Fish, quite quiet. 'I stay with you. My men can go.'

"The Bashkai fellows didn't wait for a second word, but ran off, and Dan and Me and Billy Fish walked across to where the drums were drumming and the horns were horning. It was cold—awful cold. I've got that cold in the back of my head now. There's a lump of it there."

The punkah coolies had gone to sleep. Two kerosene lamps were blazing in the office, and the perspiration poured down my face and splashed on the blotter as I leaned forward. Carnehan was shivering, and I feared that his mind might go. I wiped my face, took a fresh grip of the piteously mangled hands, and said, "What happened after that?"

The momentary shift of my eyes had broken the clear current.

"What was you pleased to say?" whined Carnehan. "They took them without any sound. Not a little whisper all along the snow, not though the King knocked down the first man that set hand on him—not though old Peachey fired his last cartridge into the brown of 'em. Not a single solitary sound did those swines make. They just closed up tight, and I tell you their furs stunk. There was a man called Billy Fish, a good friend of us all, and they cut his throat, Sir, then and there, like a jig; and the King kicks up the bloody snow and says, 'We've had a dashed fine run for our money. What's coming next?' But Peachey, Peachey Taliaferro, I tell you, Sir, in confidence as betwixt two friends, he lost his head, Sir. No, he didn't neither. The King lost his head, so he did, all along o' one of those cunning rope bridges. Kindly let me have the paper cutter, Sir. It tilted this way. They marched him a mile across that snow to a rope bridge over a ravine with a river at the bottom. You may have seen such. They prodded him behind like an ox. 'Damn your eyes!' says the King. 'D'you suppose I can't die like a gentleman?' He turns to Peachey—Peachey that was crying like a child. 'I've brought you to this, Peachey,' says he. 'Brought you out of your happy life to be killed in Kafiristan, where you was late Commander-in-Chief of the Emperor's forces. Say you forgive me, Peachey.' 'I do,' says Peachey. 'Fully and freely do I forgive you, Dan.' 'Shake hands, Peachey,' says he. 'I'm going now.' Out he goes, looking neither right nor left, and when he was plumb in the middle of those dizzy dancing ropes, 'Cut, you beggars,' he shouts; and they cut, and old Dan fell, turning round and round and round twenty thousand miles, for he took half an hour to fall till he struck the water, and I could see his body caught on a rock with the gold crown close beside.

"But do you know what they did to Peachey between two pine trees? They crucified him, Sir, as Peachey's hand will show. They used wooden pegs for his hands and his feet; and he didn't die. He hung there and screamed, and they took him down next day, and said it was a miracle that he wasn't dead. They took him down—poor old Peachey that hadn't done them any harm—that hadn't done them any . . ."

He rocked to and fro and wept bitterly, wiping his eyes with the back of his scarred hands and moaning like a child for some ten minutes.

"They was cruel enough to feed him up in the temple, because they said he was more of a God than old Daniel that was a man. Then they turned him out on the snow, and told him to go home, and Peachey came home in about a year, begging along the roads quite safe; for Daniel Dravot he walked before and said, 'Come along, Peachey. It's a big thing we're doing.' The mountains they danced at night, and the mountains they tried to fall on Peachey's head, but Dan he held up his hand, and Peachey came along bent double. He never let go of Dan's hand, and he never let go of Dan's head. They gave it to him as a present in the temple, to remind him not to come again, and though the crown was pure gold, and Peachey was starving, never would Peachey sell the same. You knew Dravot, Sir! You knew Right Worshipful Brother Dravot! Look at him now!"

He fumbled in the mass of rags round his bent waist; brought out a black horsehair bag embroidered with silver thread; and shook therefrom on to my table—the dried, withered head of Daniel Dravot! The morning sun that had long been paling the lamps struck the red beard and blind sunken eyes; struck, too, a heavy circlet of gold studded with raw turquoises, that Carnehan placed tenderly on the battered temples.

"You behold now," said Carnehan, "the Emperor in his habit as he lived—the King of Kafiristan with his crown upon his head. Poor old Daniel that was a monarch once!"

I shuddered, for, in spite of defacements manifold, I recognized the head of the man of Marwar Junction. Carnehan rose to go. I attempted to stop him. He was not fit to walk abroad. "Let me take away the whisky, and give me a little money," he gasped. "I was a King once. I'll go to the Deputy Commissioner and ask to set in the Poorhouse till I get my health. No, thank you, I can't wait till you get a carriage for me. I've urgent private affairs—in the South—at Marwar."

He shambled out of the office and departed in the direction of the Deputy Commissioner's house. That day at noon I had occasion to go down the blinding hot Mall, and I saw a crooked man crawling along the white dust of the roadside, his hat in his hand, quavering dolorously after the fashion of street-singers at Home. There was not a soul in sight, and he was out of all possible earshot of the houses. And he sang through his nose, turning his head from right to left:

The Son of Man goes forth to war,
  A golden crown to gain;
His blood-red banner streams afar—
  Who follows in his train?

I waited to hear no more, but put the poor wretch into my carriage and drove him off to the nearest missionary for eventual transfer to the Asylum. He repeated the hymn twice while he was with me, whom he did not in the least recognize, and I left him singing it to the missionary.

Two days later I inquired after his welfare of the Superintendent of the Asylum.

"He was admitted suffering from sunstroke. He died early yesterday morning," said the Superintendent. "Is it true that he was half an hour bareheaded in the sun at midday?"

"Yes," said I, "but do you happen to know if he had anything upon him by any chance when he died?"

"Not to my knowledge," said the Superintendent.

And there the matter rests.

---

1. What significant differences do you find in the characters of Dravot and Carnehan?

2. What evolution is to be noted in Dravot's ambition once he is established as king? Does his downfall come from a nobler vision?
3. What devices of suspense are used by the author to increase the excitement of the tale?
4. Is the narrator as emotionally detached as he seems to be? Does he efface his emotions in order to let the action speak for itself?
5. What does the story say about varieties of loyalty?
6. How does the setting enhance the emotional power of the story?

Margaret Laurence

Laurence (1926–) was born in Neepawa, Manitoba. She wrote from childhood on, devoting herself seriously to her art when she went with her husband to live in Somaliland and Ghana in Africa. In 1954 the Somali government published A Tree of Poverty, *her translation of Somali folktales and poetry, the first such collection ever published in English. Her novels are* This Side Jordan *(1960),* The Stone Angel *(1964),* A Jest of God *(1966),* The Fire-Dwellers *(1969), and* The Diviners *(1974). Her account of the life of Somali nomads was published in 1964 as* New Wind in a Dry Land. *Some of her stories were collected in* The Tomorrow-Tamer *(1964) and* A Bird in the House *(1970).*

The Loons

Just below Manawaka, where the Wachakwa River ran brown and noisy over the pebbles, the scrub oak and grey-green willow and chokecherry bushes grew in a dense thicket. In a clearing at the centre of the thicket stood the Tonnerre family's shack. The basis of this dwelling was a small square cabin made of poplar poles and chinked with mud, which had been built by Jules Tonnerre some fifty years before, when he came back from Batoche with a bullet in his thigh, the year that Riel was hung and the voices of the Metis entered their long silence.[1] Jules had only intended to stay the winter in the Wachakwa Valley, but the family was still there in the thirties, when I was a child. As the Tonnerres had increased, their settlement had been added to, until the clearing at the foot of the town hill was a chaos of lean-tos, wooden packing cases, warped lumber, discarded car tyres, ramshackle chicken coops, tangled strands of barbed wire and rusty tin cans.

The Tonnerres were French halfbreeds, and among themselves they spoke a *patois*[2] that was neither Cree nor French. Their English was broken and full of obscenities. They did not belong among the Cree of the Galloping Mountain reservation, further north, and they

1. Louis Riel (1844–85) led two rebellions of Indians and Métis (people of mixed French and Indian blood) in 1869–70 and 1884–85. The latter rebellion was crushed in the battle of Batoche, Manitoba, and Riel was executed. 2. Dialect.

did not belong among the Scots-Irish and Ukrainians of Manawaka, either. They were, as my Grandmother MacLeod would have put it, neither flesh, fowl, nor good salt herring. When their men were not working at odd jobs or as section hands on the C.P.R.[3] they lived on relief. In the summers, one of the Tonnerre youngsters, with a face that seemed totally unfamiliar with laughter, would knock at the doors of the town's brick houses and offer for sale a lard-pail full of bruised wild strawberries, and if he got as much as a quarter he would grab the coin and run before the customer had time to change her mind. Sometimes old Jules, or his son Lazarus, would get mixed up in a Saturday-night brawl, and would hit out at whoever was nearest or howl drunkenly among the offended shoppers on Main Street, and then the Mountie would put them for the night in the barred cell underneath the Court House, and the next morning they would be quiet again.

Piquette Tonnerre, the daughter of Lazarus, was in my class at school. She was older than I, but she had failed several grades, perhaps because her attendance had always been sporadic and her interest in schoolwork negligible. Part of the reason she had missed a lot of school was that she had had tuberculosis of the bone, and had once spent many months in hospital. I knew this because my father was the doctor who had looked after her. Her sickness was almost the only thing I knew about her, however. Otherwise, she existed for me only as a vaguely embarrassed presence, with her hoarse voice and her clumsy limping walk and her grimy cotton dresses that were always miles too long. I was neither friendly nor unfriendly towards her. She dwelt and moved somewhere within my scope of vision, but I did not actually notice her very much until that peculiar summer when I was eleven.

"I don't know what to do about that kid," my father said at dinner one evening. "Piquette Tonnerre, I mean. The damn bone's flared up again. I've had her in hospital for quite a while now, and it's under control all right, but I hate like the dickens to send her home again."

"Couldn't you explain to her mother that she has to rest a lot?" my mother said.

"The mother's not there," my father replied. "She took off a few years back. Can't say I blame her. Piquette cooks for them, and she says Lazarus would never do anything for himself as long as she's there. Anyway, I don't think she'd take much care of herself, once she got back. She's only thirteen, after all. Beth, I was thinking—what about taking her up to Diamond Lake with us this summer? A couple of months rest would give that bone a much better chance."

My mother looked stunned.

"But Ewen—what about Roddie and Vanessa?"

3. Canadian Pacific Railroad.

"She's not contagious," my father said. "And it would be company for Vanessa."

"Oh dear," my mother said in distress, "I'll bet anything she has nits in her hair."

"For Pete's sake," my father said crossly, "do you think Matron would let her stay in the hospital for all this time like that? Don't be silly, Beth."

Grandmother MacLeod, her delicately featured face as rigid as a cameo, now brought her mauve-veined hands together as though she were about to begin prayer.

"Ewen, if that halfbreed youngster comes along to Diamond Lake, I'm not going," she announced. "I'll go to Morag's for the summer."

I had trouble in stifling my urge to laugh, for my mother brightened visibly and quickly tried to hide it. If it came to a choice between Grandmother MacLeod and Piquette, Piquette would win hands down, nits or not.

"It might be quite nice for you, at that," she mused. "You haven't seen Morag for over a year, and you might enjoy being in the city for a while. Well, Ewen dear, you do what you think best. If you think it would do Piquette some good, then we'll be glad to have her, as long as she behaves herself."

So it happened that several weeks later, when we all piled into my father's old Nash,[4] surrounded by suitcases and boxes of provisions and toys for my ten-month-old brother, Piquette was with us and Grandmother MacLeod, miraculously, was not. My father would only be staying at the cottage for a couple of weeks, for he had to get back to his practice, but the rest of us would stay at Diamond Lake until the end of August.

Our cottage was not named, as many were, "Dew Drop Inn" or "Bide-a-Wee," or "Bonnie Doon". The sign on the roadway bore in austere letters only our name, MacLeod. It was not a large cottage, but it was on the lakefront. You could look out the windows and see, through the filigree of the spruce trees, the water glistening greenly as the sun caught it. All around the cottage were ferns, and sharp-branched raspberry bushes, and moss that had grown over fallen tree trunks. If you looked carefully among the weeds and grass, you could find wild strawberry plants which were in white flower now and in another month would bear fruit, the fragrant globes hanging like miniature scarlet lanterns on the thin hairy stems. The two grey squirrels were still there, gossiping at us from the tall spruce beside the cottage, and by the end of the summer they would again be tame enough to take pieces of crust from my hands. The broad moose antlers that hung above the back

4. Former make of automobiles.

door were a little more bleached and fissured after the winter, but otherwise everything was the same. I raced joyfully around my kingdom, greeting all the places I had not seen for a year. My brother, Roderick, who had not been born when we were here last summer, sat on the car rug in the sunshine and examined a brown spruce cone, meticulously turning it round and round in his small and curious hands. My mother and father toted the luggage from car to cottage, exclaiming over how well the place had wintered, no broken windows, thank goodness, no apparent damage from storm-felled branches or snow.

Only after I had finished looking around did I notice Piquette. She was sitting on the swing, her lame leg held stiffly out, and her other foot scuffing the ground as she swung slowly back and forth. Her long hair hung black and straight around her shoulders, and her broad coarse-featured face bore no expression—it was blank, as though she no longer dwelt within her own skull, as though she had gone elsewhere. I approached her very hesitantly.

"Want to come and play?"

Piquette looked at me with a sudden flash of scorn.

"I ain't a kid," she said.

Wounded, I stamped angrily away, swearing I would not speak to her for the rest of the summer. In the days that followed, however, Piquette began to interest me, and I began to want to interest her. My reasons did not appear bizarre to me. Unlikely as it may seem, I had only just realised that the Tonnerre family, whom I had always heard called halfbreeds, were actually Indians, or as near as made no difference. My acquaintance with Indians was not extensive. I did not remember ever having seen a real Indian, and my new awareness that Piquette sprang from the people of Big Bear and Poundmaker, of Tecumseh, of the Iroquois who had eaten Father Brébeuf's heart[5]—all this gave her an instant attraction in my eyes. I was devoted reader of Pauline Johnson at this age, and sometimes would orate aloud and in an exalted voice, *West Wind, blow from your prairie nest; Blow from the mountains, blow from the west*[6]—and so on. It seemed to me that Piquette must be in some way a daughter of the forest, a kind of junior prophetess of the wilds, who might impart to me, if I took the right approach, some of the secrets which she undoubtedly knew—where the whippoorwill made her nest, how the coyote reared her young, or whatever it was that it said in Hiawatha.[7]

I set about gaining Piquette's trust. She was not allowed to go

5. Jean de Brébeuf (1593–1649), Jesuit missionary to the Hurons; Tecumseh (1768?–1813), chief of the Shawnee; Big Bear and Poundmaker (1842–1886), leaders of the Cree. 6. The first two lines from "The Song My Paddle Sings" by Pauline Johnson (1861–1913), Canadian poet who was the daughter of an English woman and a Mohawk chief. 7. Romantic poem about Indians by Henry Wadsworth Longfellow (1807–1882).

swimming, with her bad leg, but I managed to lure her down to the beach—or rather, she came because there was nothing else to do. The water was always icy, for the lake was fed by springs, but I swam like a dog, thrashing my arms and legs around at such speed and with such an output of energy that I never grew cold. Finally, when I had enough, I came out and sat beside Piquette on the sand. When she saw me approaching, her hand squashed flat the sand castle she had been building, and she looked at me sullenly, without speaking.

"Do you like this place?" I asked, after a while, intending to lead on from there into the question of forest lore.

Piquette shrugged. "It's okay. Good as anywhere."

"I love it," I said. "We come here every summer."

"So what?" Her voice was distant, and I glanced at her uncertainly, wondering what I could have said wrong.

"Do you want to come for a walk?" I asked her. "We wouldn't need to go far. If you walk just around the point there, you come to a bay where great big reeds grow in the water, and all kinds of fish hang around there. Want to? Come on."

She shook her head.

"Your dad said I ain't supposed to do no more walking than I got to." I tried another line.

"I bet you know a lot about the woods and all that, eh?" I began respectfully.

Piquette looked at me from her large dark unsmiling eyes.

"I don't know what in hell you're talkin' about," she replied. "You nuts or somethin'? If you mean where my old man, and me, and all them live, you better shut up, by Jesus, you hear?"

I was startled and my feelings were hurt, but I had a kind of dogged perseverance. I ignored her rebuff.

"You know something, Piquette? There's loons here, on this lake. You can see their nests just up the shore there, behind those logs. At night, you can hear them even from the cottage, but it's better to listen from the beach. My dad says we should listen and try to remember how they sound, because in a few years when more cottages are built at Diamond Lake and more people come in, the loons will go away."

Piquette was picking up stones and snail shells and then dropping them again.

"Who gives a good goddamn?" she said.

It became increasingly obvious that, as an Indian, Piquette was a dead loss. That evening I went out by myself, scrambling through the bushes that overhung the steep path, my feet slipping on the fallen spruce needles that covered the ground. When I reached the shore, I walked along the firm damp sand to the small pier that my father had built, and sat down there. I heard someone else crashing through the undergrowth and the bracken, and for a moment I thought Piquette had changed her mind, but it turned out to be my father. He sat beside me on the pier and we waited, without speaking.

At night the lake was like black glass with a streak of amber which was the path of the moon. All around, the spruce trees grew tall and close-set, branches blackly sharp against the sky, which was lightened by a cold flickering of stars. Then the loons began their calling. They rose like phantom birds from the nests on the shore, and flew out onto the dark still surface of the water.

No one can ever describe that ululating sound, the crying of the loons, and no one who has heard it can ever forget it. Plaintive, and yet with a quality of chilling mockery, those voices belonged to a world separated by aeons from our neat world of summer cottages and the lighted lamps of home.

"They must have sounded just like that," my father remarked, "before any person ever set foot here."

Then he laughed. "You could say the same, of course, about sparrows, or chipmunks, but somehow it only strikes you that way with the loons."

"I know," I said.

Neither of us suspected that this would be the last time we would ever sit here together on the shore, listening. We stayed for perhaps half an hour, and then we went back to the cottage. My mother was reading beside the fireplace. Piquette was looking at the burning birch log, and not doing anything.

"You should have come along," I said, although in fact I was glad she had not.

"Not me," Piquette said. "You wouldn' catch me walkin' way down there jus' for a bunch of squawkin' birds."

Piquette and I remained ill at ease with one another. I felt I had somehow failed my father, but I did not know what was the matter, nor why she would not or could not respond when I suggested exploring the woods or playing house. I thought it was probably her slow and difficult walking that held her back. She stayed most of the time in the cottage with my mother, helping her with the dishes or with Roddie, but hardly ever talking. Then the Duncans arrived at their cottage, and I spent my days with Mavis, who was my best friend. I could not reach Piquette at all, and I soon lost interest in trying. But all that summer she remained as both a reproach and a mystery to me.

That winter my father died of pneumonia, after less than a week's illness. For some time I saw nothing around me, being completely immersed in my own pain and my mother's. When I looked outward once more, I scarcely noticed that Piquette Tonnerre was no longer at school. I do not remember seeing her at all until four years later, one

Saturday night when Mavis and I were having Cokes in the Regal Café. The jukebox was booming like tuneful thunder, and beside it, leaning lightly on its chrome and its rainbow glass, was a girl.

Piquette must have been seventeen then, although she looked about twenty. I stared at her, astounded that anyone could have changed so much. Her face, so stolid and expressionless before, was animated now with a gaiety that was almost violent. She laughed and talked very loudly with the boys around her. Her lipstick was bright carmine, and her hair was cut short and frizzily permed. She had not been pretty as a child, and she was not pretty now, for her features were still heavy and blunt. But her dark and slightly slanted eyes were beautiful, and her skin-tight skirt and orange sweater displayed to enviable advantage a soft and slender body.

She saw me, and walked over. She teetered a little, but it was not due to her once-tubercular leg, for her limp was almost gone.

"Hi, Vanessa." Her voice had the same hoarseness. "Long time no see, eh?"

"Hi," I said. "Where've you been keeping yourself, Piquette?"

"Oh, I been around," she said. "I been away almost two years now. Been all over the place—Winnipeg, Regina, Saskatoon. Jesus, what I could tell you! I come back this summer, but I ain't stayin'. You kids goin' to the dance?"

"No," I said abruptly, for this was a sore point with me. I was fifteen, and thought I was old enough to go to the Saturday-night dances at the Flamingo. My mother, however, thought otherwise.

"Y'oughta come," Piquette said. "I never miss one. It's just about the on'y thing in this jerkwater town that's any fun. Boy, you couldn' catch me stayin' here. I don' give a shit about this place. It stinks."

She sat down beside me, and I caught the harsh over-sweetness of her perfume.

"Listen, you wanna know something, Vanessa?" she confided, her voice only slightly blurred. "Your dad was the only person in Manawaka that ever done anything good to me."

I nodded speechlessly. I was certain she was speaking the truth. I knew a little more than I had that summer at Diamond Lake, but I could not reach her now any more than I had then. I was ashamed, ashamed of my own timidity, the frightened tendency to look the other way. Yet I felt no real warmth towards her—I only felt that I ought to, because of that distant summer and because my father had hoped she would be company for me, or perhaps that I would be for her, but it had not happened that way. At this moment, meeting her again, I had to admit that she repelled and embarrassed me, and I could not help despising the self-pity in her voice. I wished she would go away. I did not want to see her. I did not know what to say to her. It seemed that we had nothing to say to one another.

"I'll tell you something else," Piquette went on. "All the old bitches an' biddies in this town will sure be surprised. I'm gettin' married this fall—my boyfriend, he's an English fella, works in the stockyards in the city there, a very tall guy, got blond wavy hair. Gee, is he ever handsome. Got this real classy name. Alvin Gerald Cummings—some handle, eh? They call him Al."

For the merest instant, then, I saw her. I really did see her, for the first and only time in all the years we had both lived in the same town. Her defiant face, momentarily, became unguarded and unmasked, and in her eyes there was a terrifying hope.

"Gee, Piquette—" I burst out awkwardly, "that's swell. That's really wonderful. Congratulations—good luck—I hope you'll be happy—"

As I mouthed the conventional phrases, I could only guess how great her need must have been, that she had been forced to seek the very things she so bitterly rejected.

When I was eighteen, I left Manawaka and went away to college. At the end of my first year, I came back home for the summer. I spent the first few days in talking non-stop with my mother, as we exchanged all the news that somehow had not found its way into letters—what had happened in my life and what had happened here in Manawaka while I was away. My mother searched her memory for events that concerned people I knew.

"Did I ever write you about Piquette Tonnerre, Vanessa?" she asked one morning.

"No, I don't think so," I replied. "Last I heard of her, she was going to marry some guy in the city. Is she still there?"

My mother looked perturbed, and it was a moment before she spoke, as though she did not know how to express what she had to tell and wished she did not need to try.

"She's dead," she said at last. Then, as I stared at her, "Oh, Vanessa, when it happened, I couldn't help thinking of her as she was that summer—so sullen and gauche and badly dressed. I couldn't help wondering if we could have done something more at that time—but what could we do? She used to be around in the cottage there with me all day, and honestly it was all I could do to get a word out of her. She didn't even talk to your father very much, although I think she liked him in her way."

"What happened?" I asked.

"Either her husband left her, or she left him," my mother said. "I don't know which. Anyway, she came back here with two youngsters, both only babies—they must have been born very close together. She kept house, I guess, for Lazarus and her brothers, down in the valley there, in the old Tonnerre place. I used to see her on the street sometimes, but she never spoke to me. She'd put on an awful lot of weight, and she looked a mess, to tell you the truth, a real slattern, dressed any old how. She was up in court a couple of times—drunk and disorderly, of course. One Saturday night last winter, during the coldest weather, Piquette was alone in the shack with the children. The Tonnerres made home brew all the time, so I've heard, and Lazarus said later she'd been drinking most of the day when he and the boys went out that evening. They had an old woodstove there—you know the kind, with exposed pipes. The shack caught fire. Piquette didn't get out, and neither did the children."

I did not say anything. As so often with Piquette, there did not seem to be anything to say. There was a kind of silence around the image in my mind of the fire and the snow, and I wished I could put from my memory the look that I had seen once in Piquette's eyes.

I went up to Diamond Lake for a few days that summer, with Mavis and her family. The MacLeod cottage had been sold after my father's death, and I did not even go to look at it, not wanting to witness my long-ago kingdom possessed now by strangers. But one evening I went down to the shore by myself.

The small pier which my father had built was gone, and in its place there was a large and solid pier built by the government, for Galloping Mountain was now a national park, and Diamond Lake had been re-named Lake Wapakata, for it was felt that an Indian name would have a greater appeal to tourists. The one store had become several dozen, and the settlement had all the attributes of a flourishing resort—hotels, dance-hall, cafés with neon signs, the penetrating odours of potato chips and hot dogs.

I sat on the government pier and looked out across the water. At night the lake at least was the same as it had always been, darkly shining and bearing within its black glass the streak of amber that was the path of the moon. There was no wind that evening, and everything was quiet all around me. It seemed too quiet, and then I realized that the loons were no longer here. I listened for some time, to make sure, but never once did I hear that long-drawn call, half mocking and half plaintive, spearing through the stillness across the lake.

I did not know what had happened to the birds. Perhaps they had gone away to some far place of belonging. Perhaps they had been unable to find such a place, and had simply died out, having ceased to care any longer whether they lived or not.

I remembered how Piquette had scorned to come along, when my father and I sat there and listened to the lake birds. It seemed to me now that in some unconscious and totally unrecognized way, Piquette might have been the only one, after all, who had heard the crying of the loons.

---

1. How is the disappearance of the loons related to the theme of this story?
2. What is the role of the father in developing the narrator's understanding of Piquette?
3. Can you put into words what the narrator has heard in the "half mocking and half plaintive" call of the loons?
4. What is the relation between the narrator and Piquette and how does it change?
5. Why does the narrator surmise that Piquette might be the only one who heard the crying of the loons?

D. H. Lawrence

Lawrence (1885–1930) was born in Eastwood, Nottinghamshire, England. His father was a coal miner, his mother a former schoolteacher whose thwarted life and fierce ambition for her son pushed him to struggle up into the world of culture. The anguish of this effort amid family tensions is the subject of the novel Sons and Lovers *(1913), which established him as a major literary figure. Before World War I he eloped to the Continent with the wife of a Nottingham professor, but spent the war years miserably in England, suspected of disloyalty because his wife was of German origin and oppressed by disgust at what was happening to his country. Through all the years of his maturity he was harassed by efforts to censor his books and paintings. His distaste for the industrialization and commercialism of English life in his time sent him wandering to Italy, Australia, Mexico, and the mountains of New Mexico in search of an alternative. As he continued to outrage the guardians of public morals—and to reply to them in many of his works with polemic attacks and warnings of the disasters they were brewing—he attracted passionate disciples. His stature as prophet and critic of modern culture has always been a matter of controversy; his explorations of the dark strata of the unconsciousness, his shrewdly intuitive revisions of conventional notions of human motivation, and the vital energy of his style place him unarguably among the great poets and novelists of his age. His life has inspired a flood of biographies; his remarkable marriage and his death by tuberculosis in the south of France seem hardly distinguishable from his creations in prose and verse. Some of his best known novels are* The Rainbow *(1915),* Women in Love *(1920), and* Lady Chatterley's Lover *(1928). His shorter works and poems are most easily found in* The Complete Stories *(1961),* Four Short Novels *(1965), and* Complete Poems *(1964).*

The Blind Man

Isabel Pervin[1] was listening for two sounds—for the sound of wheels on the drive outside and for the noise of her husband's footsteps in the hall. Her dearest and oldest friend, a man who seemed almost indispensable to her living, would drive up in the rainy dusk of the

1. Though the family name Pervin also occurs in "The Horse Dealer's Daughter," it should not be assumed Lawrence intended any family relationship between the characters of the two stories. Each is a separate conception.

closing November day. The trap[2] had gone to fetch him from the station. And her husband, who had been blinded in Flanders,[3] and who had a disfiguring mark on his brow, would be coming in from the outhouses.

He had been home for a year now. He was totally blind. Yet they had been very happy. The Grange was Maurice's own place. The back was a farmstead, and the Wernhams, who occupied the rear premises, acted as farmers. Isabel lived with her husband in the handsome rooms in front. She and he had been almost entirely alone together since he was wounded. They talked and sang and read together in a wonderful and unspeakable intimacy. Then she reviewed books for a Scottish newspaper, carrying on her old interest, and he occupied himself a good deal with the farm. Sightless, he could still discuss everything with Wernham, and he could also do a good deal of work about the place—menial work, it is true, but it gave him satisfaction. He milked the cows, carried in the pails, turned the separator, attended to the pigs and horses. Life was still very full and strangely serene for the blind man, peaceful with the almost incomprehensible peace of immediate contact in darkness. With his wife he had a whole world, rich and real and invisible.

They were newly and remotely happy. He did not even regret the loss of his sight in these times of dark, palpable joy. A certain exultance swelled his soul.

But as time wore on, sometimes the rich glamour would leave them. Sometimes, after months of this intensity, a sense of burden overcame Isabel, a weariness, a terrible ennui, in that silent house approached between a colonnade of tall-shafted pines. Then she felt she would go mad, for she could not bear it. And sometimes he had devastating fits of depression, which seemed to lay waste his whole being. It was worse than depression—a black misery, when his own life was a torture to him, and when his presence was unbearable to his wife. The dread went down to the roots of her soul as these black days recurred. In a kind of panic she tried to wrap herself up still further in her husband. She forced the old spontaneous cheerfulness and joy to continue. But the effort it cost her was almost too much. She knew she could not keep it up. She felt she would scream with the strain, and would give anything, anything, to escape. She longed to possess her husband utterly; it gave her inordinate joy to have him entirely to herself. And yet, when again he was gone in a black and massive misery, she could not bear him, she could not bear herself; she wished she could be snatched away off the earth altogether, anything rather than live at this cost.

2. A light, one-horse carriage. 3. A deadly battleground of World War I.

Dazed, she schemed for a way out. She invited friends, she tried to give him some further connection with the outer world. But it was no good. After all their joy and suffering, after their dark, great year of blindness and solitude and unspeakable nearness, other people seemed to them both shallow, prattling, rather impertinent. Shallow prattle seemed presumptuous. He became impatient and irritated, she was wearied. And so they lapsed into their solitude again. For they preferred it.

But now, in a few weeks' time, her second baby would be born. The first had died, an infant, when her husband first went out to France. She looked with joy and relief to the coming of the second. It would be her salvation. But also she felt some anxiety. She was thirty years old, her husband was a year younger. They both wanted the child very much. Yet she could not help feeling afraid. She had her husband on her hands, a terrible joy to her, and a terrifying burden. The child would occupy her love and attention. And then, what of Maurice? What would he do? If only she could feel that he, too, would be at peace and happy when the child came! She did so want to luxuriate in a rich, physical satisfaction of maternity. But the man, what would he do? How could she provide for him, how avert those shattering black moods of his, which destroyed them both?

She sighed with fear. But at this time Bertie Reid wrote to Isabel. He was her old friend, a second or third cousin, a Scotsman, as she was a Scotswoman. They had been brought up near to one another, and all her life he had been her friend, like a brother, but better than her own brothers. She loved him—though not in the marrying sense. There was a sort of kinship between them, an affinity. They understood one another instinctively. But Isabel would never have thought of marrying Bertie. It would have seemed like marrying in her own family.

Bertie was a barrister and a man of letters, a Scotsman of the intellectual type, quick, ironical, sentimental, and on his knees before the women he adored but did not want to marry. Maurice Pervin was different. He came of a good old country family—the Grange was not a very great distance from Oxford. He was passionate, sensitive, perhaps over-sensitive, wincing—a big fellow with heavy limbs and a forehead that flushed painfully. For his mind was slow, as if drugged by the strong provincial blood that beat in his veins. He was very sensitive to his own mental slowness, his feelings being quick and acute. So that he was just the opposite to Bertie, whose mind was much quicker than his emotions, which were not so very fine.

From the first the two men did not like each other. Isabel felt that they *ought* to get on together. But they did not. She felt that if only each could have the clue to the other there would be such a rare understanding between them. It did not come off, however. Bertie adopted a slightly ironical attitude, very offensive to Maurice, who returned the Scotch irony with English resentment, a resentment which deepened sometimes into stupid hatred.

This was a little puzzling to Isabel. However, she accepted it in the course of things. Men were made freakish and unreasonable. Therefore, when Maurice was going out to France for the second time, she felt that, for her husband's sake, she must discontinue her friendship with Bertie. She wrote to the barrister to this effect. Bertram Reid simply replied that in this, as in all other matters, he must obey her wishes, if these were indeed her wishes.

For nearly two years nothing had passed between the two friends. Isabel rather gloried in the fact; she had no compunction. She had one great article of faith, which was, that husband and wife should be so important to one another, that the rest of the world simply did not count. She and Maurice were husband and wife. They loved one another. They would have children. Then let everybody and everything else fade into insignificance outside this connubial felicity. She professed herself quite happy and ready to receive Maurice's friends. She was happy and ready: the happy wife, the ready woman in possession. Without knowing why, the friends retired abashed, and came no more. Maurice, of course, took as much satisfaction in this connubial absorption as Isabel did.

He shared in Isabel's literary activities, she cultivated a real interest in agriculture and cattle-raising. For she, being at heart perhaps an emotional enthusiast, always cultivated the practical side of life, and prided herself on her mastery of practical affairs. Thus the husband and wife had spent the five years of their married life. The last had been one of blindness and unspeakable intimacy. And now Isabel felt a great indifference coming over her, a sort of lethargy. She wanted to be allowed to bear her child in peace, to nod by the fire and drift vaguely, physically, from day to day. Maurice was like an ominous thunder-cloud. She had to keep waking up to remember him.

When a little note came from Bertie, asking if he were to put up a tombstone to their dead friendship, and speaking of the real pain he felt on account of her husband's loss of sight, she felt a pang, a fluttering agitation of re-awakening. And she read the letter to Maurice.

"Ask him to come down," he said.

"Ask Bertie to come here!" she re-echoed.

"Yes—if he wants to."

Isabel paused for a few moments.

"I know he wants to—he'd only be too glad," she replied. "But what about you, Maurice? How would you like it?"

"I should like it."

"Well—in that case—— But I thought you didn't care for him——"

"Oh, I don't know. I might think differently of him now," the blind man replied. It was rather abstruse to Isabel.

"Well, dear," she said, "if you're quite sure——"

"I'm sure enough. Let him come," said Maurice.

So Bertie was coming, coming this evening, in the November rain and darkness. Isabel was agitated, racked with her old restlessness and indecision. She had always suffered from this pain of doubt, just an agonising sense of uncertainty. It had begun to pass off, in the lethargy of maternity. Now it returned, and she resented it. She struggled as usual to maintain her calm, composed, friendly bearing, a sort of mask she wore over all her body.

A woman had lighted a tall lamp beside the table, and spread the cloth. The long dining-room was dim, with its elegant but rather severe pieces of old furniture. Only the round table glowed softly under the light. It had a rich, beautiful effect. The white cloth glistened and dropped its heavy, pointed lace corners almost to the carpet, the china was old and handsome, creamy-yellow, with a blotched pattern of harsh red and deep blue, the cups large and bell-shaped, the teapot gallant. Isabel looked at it with superficial appreciation.

Her nerves were hurting her. She looked automatically again at the high, uncurtained windows. In the last dusk she could just perceive outside a huge fir tree swaying its boughs: it was as if she thought it rather than saw it. The rain came flying on the window panes. Ah, why had she no peace? These two men, why did they tear at her? Why did they not come—why was there this suspense?

She sat in a lassitude that was really suspense and irritation. Maurice, at least, might come in—there was nothing to keep him out. She rose to her feet. Catching sight of her reflection in a mirror, she glanced at herself with a slight smile of recognition, as if she were an old friend to herself. Her face was oval and calm, her nose a little arched. Her neck made a beautiful line down to her shoulder. With hair knotted loosely behind, she had something of a warm, maternal look. Thinking this of herself, she arched her eyebrows and her rather heavy eyelids, with a little flicker of a smile, and for a moment her grey eyes looked amused and wicked, a little sardonic, out of her transfigured Madonna face.

Then, resuming her air of womanly patience—she was really fatally self-determined—she went with a little jerk towards the door. Her eyes were slightly reddened.

She passed down the wide hall, and through a door at the end. Then she was in the farm premises. The scent of dairy, and of farm-kitchen, and of farmyard and of leather almost overcame her: but particularly the scent of dairy. They had been scalding out the pans. The flagged passage in front of her was dark, puddled and wet. Light came out from the open kitchen door. She went forward and stood in the doorway. The farm-people were at tea, seated at a little distance from her, round a long, narrow table, in the centre of which stood a white lamp. Ruddy faces, ruddy hands holding food, red mouths working, heads bent over the tea-cups: men, land-girls[4] boys: it was tea-time, feeding-time. Some faces caught sight of her. Mrs. Wernham, going round behind the chairs with a large black teapot, halting slightly in her walk, was not aware of her for a moment. Then she turned suddenly.

"Oh, is it Madame!" she exclaimed. "Come in, then, come in! We're at tea." And she dragged forward a chair.

"No, I won't come in," said Isabel. "I'm afraid I interrupt your meal."

"No—no—not likely, Madame, not likely."

"Hasn't Mr. Pervin come in, do you know?"

"I'm sure I couldn't say! Missed him, have you, Madame?"

"No, I only wanted him to come in," laughed Isabel, as if shyly.

"Wanted him, did ye? Get up, boy—get up, now——"

Mrs. Wernham knocked one of the boys on the shoulder. He began to scrape to his feet, chewing largely.

"I believe he's in top stable," said another face from the table.

"Ah! No, don't get up. I'm going myself," said Isabel.

"Don't you go out of a dirty night like this. Let the lad go. Get along wi' ye, boy," said Mrs. Wernham.

"No, no," said Isabel, with a decision that was always obeyed. "Go on with your tea, Tom. I'd like to go across to the stable, Mrs. Wernham."

"Did ever you hear tell!" exclaimed the woman.

"Isn't the trap late?" asked Isabel.

"Why, no," said Mrs. Wernham, peering into the distance at the tall, dim clock. "No, Madame—we can give it another quarter or twenty minutes yet, good—yes, every bit of a quarter."

"Ah! It seems late when darkness falls so early," said Isabel.

"It do, that it do. Bother the days, that they draw in so," answered Mrs. Wernham. "Proper miserable!"

"They are," said Isabel, withdrawing.

She pulled on her over-shoes, wrapped a large tartan shawl around her, put on a man's felt hat, and ventured out along the causeways of the first yard. It was very dark. The wind was roaring in the great elms

4. Girls hired for farm work.

behind the out-houses. When she came to the second yard the darkness seemed deeper. She was unsure of her footing. She wished she had brought a lantern. Rain blew against her. Half she liked it, half she felt unwilling to battle.

She reached at last the just visible door of the stable. There was no sign of a light anywhere. Opening the upper half, she looked in: Into a simple well of darkness. The smell of horses, ammonia, and of warmth was startling to her, in that full night. She listened with all her ears, but could hear nothing save the night, and the stirring of a horse.

"Maurice!" she called, softly and musically, though she was afraid. "Maurice—are you there?"

Nothing came from the darkness. She knew the rain and wind blew in upon the horses, the hot animal life. Feeling it wrong, she entered the stable, and drew the lower half of the door shut, holding the upper part close. She did not stir, because she was aware of the presence of the dark hind-quarters of the horses, though she could not see them, and she was afraid. Something wild stirred in her heart.

She listened intensely. Then she heard a small noise in the distance—far away, it seemed—the chink of a pan, and a man's voice speaking a brief word. It would be Maurice, in the other part of the stable. She stood motionless, waiting for him to come through the partition door. The horses were so terrifyingly near to her, in the invisible.

The loud jarring of the inner door-latch made her start; the door was opened. She could hear and feel her husband entering and invisibly passing among the horses near to her, in darkness as they were, actively intermingled. The rather low sound of his voice as he spoke to the horses came velvety to her nerves. How near he was, and how invisible! The darkness seemed to be in a strange swirl of violent life, just upon her. She turned giddy.

Her presence of mind made her call, quietly and musically:

"Maurice! Maurice—dea-ar!"

"Yes," he answered. "Isabel?"

She saw nothing, and the sound of his voice seemed to touch her.

"Hello!" she answered cheerfully, straining her eyes to see him. He was still busy, attending to the horses near her, but she saw only darkness. It made her almost desperate.

"Won't you come in, dear?" she said.

"Yes, I'm coming. Just half a minute. *Stand over—now!* Trap's not come, has it?"

"Not yet," said Isabel.

His voice was pleasant and ordinary, but it had a slight suggestion of the stable to her. She wished he would come away. While he was so utterly invisible she was afraid of him.

"How's the time?" he asked.

"Not yet six," she replied. She disliked to answer into the dark. Presently he came very near to her, and she retreated out of doors.

"The weather blows in here," he said, coming steadily forward, feeling for the doors. She shrank away. At last she could dimly see him.

"Bertie won't have much of a drive," he said, as he closed the doors.

"He won't indeed!" said Isabel calmly, watching the dark shape at the door.

"Give me your arm, dear," she said.

She pressed his arm closer to her, as she went. But she longed to see him, to look at him. She was nervous. He walked erect, with face rather lifted, but with a curious tentative movement of his powerful, muscular legs. She could feel the clever, careful, strong contact of his feet with the earth, as she balanced against him. For a moment he was a tower of darkness to her, as if he rose out of the earth.

In the house-passage he wavered, and went cautiously, with a curious look of silence about him as he felt for the bench. Then he sat down heavily. He was a man with rather sloping shoulders, but with heavy limbs, powerful legs that seemed to know the earth. His head was small, usually carried high and light. As he bent down to unfasten his gaiters and boots he did not look blind. His hair was brown and crisp, his hands were large, reddish, intelligent, the veins stood out in the wrists; and his thighs and knees seemed massive. When he stood up his face and neck were surcharged with blood, the veins stood out on his temples. She did not look at his blindness.

Isabel was always glad when they had passed through the dividing door into their own regions of repose and beauty. She was a little afraid of him, out there in the animal grossness of the back. His bearing also changed, as he smelt the familiar, indefinable odour that pervaded his wife's surroundings, a delicate, refined scent, very faintly spicy. Perhaps it came from the pot-pourri bowls.

He stood at the foot of the stairs, arrested, listening. She watched him, and her heart sickened. He seemed to be listening to fate.

"He's not here yet," he said. "I'll go up and change."

"Maurice," she said, "you're not wishing he wouldn't come, are you?"

"I couldn't quite say," he answered. "I feel myself rather on the *qui vive*."

"I can see you are," she answered. And she reached up and kissed his cheek. She saw his mouth relax into a slow smile.

"What are you laughing at?" she said roguishly.

"You consoling me," he answered.

"Nay," she answered. "Why should I console you? You know we

love each other—you know *how* married we are! What does anything else matter?"

"Nothing at all, my dear."

He felt for her face, and touched it, smiling.

"*You're* all right, aren't you?" he asked, anxiously.

"I'm wonderfully all right, love," she answered. "It's you I am a little troubled about, at times."

"Why me?" he said, touching her cheeks delicately with the tips of his fingers. The touch had an almost hypnotising effect on her.

He went away upstairs. She saw him mount into the darkness, unseeing and unchanging. He did not know that the lamps on the upper corridor were unlighted. He went on into the darkness with unchanging step. She heard him in the bathroom.

Pervin moved about almost unconsciously in his familiar surroundings, dark though everything was. He seemed to know the presence of objects before he touched them. It was a pleasure to him to rock thus through a world of things, carried on the flood in a sort of blood-prescience. He did not think much or trouble much. So long as he kept this sheer immediacy of blood-contact with the substantial world he was happy, he wanted no intervention of visual consciousness. In this state there was a certain rich positivity, bordering sometimes on rapture. Life seemed to move in him like a tide lapping, lapping, and advancing, enveloping all things darkly. It was a pleasure to stretch forth the hand and meet the unseen object, clasp it, and possess it in pure contact. He did not try to remember, to visualise. He did not want to. The new way of consciousness substituted itself in him.

The rich suffusion of this state generally kept him happy, reaching its culmination in the consuming passion for his wife. But at times the flow would seem to be checked and thrown back. Then it would beat inside him like a tangled sea, and he was tortured in the shattered chaos of his own blood. He grew to dread this arrest, this throw-back, this chaos inside himself, when he seemed merely at the mercy of his own powerful and conflicting elements. How to get some measure of control or surety, this was the question. And when the question rose maddening in him, he would clench his fists as if he would *compel* the whole universe to submit to him. But it was in vain. He could not even compel himself.

To-night, however, he was still serene, though little tremors of unreasonable exasperation ran through him. He had to handle the razor very carefully, as he shaved, for it was not at one with him, he was afraid of it. His hearing also was too much sharpened. He heard the woman lighting the lamps on the corridor, and attending to the fire in the visitor's room. And then, as he went to his room he heard the trap arrive. Then came Isabel's voice, lifted and calling, like a bell ringing:

"Is it you, Bertie? Have you come?"

And a man's voice answered out of the wind:

"Hello, Isabel! There you are."

"Have you had a miserable drive? I'm so sorry we couldn't send a closed carriage. I can't see you at all, you know."

"I'm coming. No, I liked the drive—it was like Perthshire. Well, how are you? You're looking fit as ever, as far as I can see."

"Oh, yes," said Isabel. "I'm wonderfully well. How are you? Rather thin, I think——"

"Worked to death—everybody's old cry. But I'm all right, Ciss. How's Pervin?—isn't he here?"

"Oh, yes, he's upstairs changing. Yes, he's awfully well. Take off your wet things; I'll send them to be dried."

"And how are you both, in spirits? He doesn't fret?"

"No—no, not at all. No, on the contrary, really. We've been wonderfully happy, incredibly. It's more than I can understand—so wonderful: the nearness, and the peace——"

"Ah! Well, that's awfully good news——"

They moved away. Pervin heard no more. But a childish sense of desolation had come over him, as he heard their brisk voices. He seemed shut out—like a child that is left out. He was aimless and excluded, he did not know what to do with himself. The helpless desolation came over him. He fumbled nervously as he dressed himself, in a state almost of childishness. He disliked the Scotch accent in Bertie's speech, and the slight response it found on Isabel's tongue. He disliked the slight purr of complacency in the Scottish speech. He disliked intensely the glib way in which Isabel spoke of their happiness and nearness. It made him recoil. He was fretful and beside himself like a child, he had almost a childish nostalgia to be included in the life circle. And at the same time he was a man, dark and powerful and infuriated by his own weakness. By some fatal flaw, he could not be by himself, he had to depend on the support of another. And this very dependence enraged him. He hated Bertie Reid, and at the same time he knew the hatred was nonsense, he knew it was the outcome of his own weakness.

He went downstairs. Isabel was alone in the dining-room. She watched him enter, head erect, his feet tentative. He looked so strong-blooded and healthy, and, at the same time, cancelled. Cancelled—that was the word that flew across her mind. Perhaps it was his scars suggested it.

"You heard Bertie come, Maurice?" she said.

"Yes—isn't he here?"

"He's in his room. He looks very thin and worn."

"I suppose he works himself to death."

A woman came in with a tray—and after a few minutes Bertie

came down. He was a little dark man, with a very big forehead, thin, wispy hair, and sad, large eyes. His expression was inordinately sad—almost funny. He had odd, short legs.

Isabel watched him hesitate under the door, and glance nervously at her husband. Pervin heard him and turned.

"Here you are, now," said Isabel. "Come, let us eat."

Bertie went across to Maurice.

"How are you, Pervin?" he said, as he advanced.

The blind man stuck his hand out into space, and Bertie took it.

"Very fit. Glad you've come," said Maurice.

Isabel glanced at them, and glanced away, as if she could not bear to see them.

"Come," she said. "Come to table. Aren't you both awfully hungry? I am, tremendously."

"I'm afraid you waited for me," said Bertie, as they sat down.

Maurice had a curious monolithic way of sitting in a chair, erect and distant. Isabel's heart always beat when she caught sight of him thus.

"No," she replied to Bertie. "We're very little later than usual. We're having a sort of high tea, not dinner. Do you mind? It gives us such a nice long evening uninterrupted."

"I like it," said Bertie.

Maurice was feeling, with curious little movements, almost like a cat kneading her bed, for his place, his knife and fork, his napkin. He was getting the whole geography of his cover into his consciousness. He sat erect and inscrutable, remote-seeming. Bertie watched the static figure of the blind man, the delicate tactile discernment of the large, ruddy hands, and the curious mindless silence of the brow, above the scar. With difficulty he looked away, and without knowing what he did, picked up a little crystal bowl of violets from the table, and held them to his nose.

"They are sweet-scented," he said. "Where do they come from?"

"From the garden—under the windows," said Isabel.

"So late in the year—and so fragrant! Do you remember the violets under Aunt Bell's south wall?"

The two friends looked at each other and exchanged a smile, Isabel's eyes lighting up.

"Don't I?" she replied. "*Wasn't* she queer!"

"A curious old girl," laughed Bertie. "There's a streak of freakishness in the family, Isabel."

"Ah—but not in you and me, Bertie," said Isabel. "Give them to Maurice, will you?" she added, as Bertie was putting down the flowers. "Have you smelled the violets, dear? Do!—they are so scented."

Maurice held out his hand, and Bertie placed the tiny bowl against his large, warm-looking fingers. Maurice's hand closed over the thin white fingers of the barrister. Bertie carefully extricated himself. Then the two watched the blind man smelling the violets. He bent his head and seemed to be thinking. Isabel waited.

"Aren't they sweet, Maurice?" she said at last, anxiously.

"Very," he said. And he held out the bowl. Bertie took it. Both he and Isabel were a little afraid, and deeply disturbed.

The meal continued. Isabel and Bertie chatted spasmodically. The blind man was silent. He touched his food repeatedly, with quick, delicate touches of his knife-point, then cut irregular bits. He could not bear to be helped. Both Isabel and Bertie suffered: Isabel wondered why. She did not suffer when she was alone with Maurice. Bertie made her conscious of a strangeness.

After the meal the three drew their chairs to the fire, and sat down to talk. The decanters were put on a table near at hand. Isabel knocked the logs on the fire, and clouds of brilliant sparks went up the chimney. Bertie noticed a slight weariness in her bearing.

"You will be glad when your child comes now, Isabel?" he said.

She looked up to him with a quick wan smile.

"Yes, I shall be glad," she answered. "It begins to seem long. Yes, I shall be very glad. So will you, Maurice, won't you?" she added.

"Yes, I shall," replied her husband.

"We are both looking forward so much to having it," she said.

"Yes, of course," said Bertie.

He was a bachelor, three or four years older than Isabel. He lived in beautiful rooms overlooking the river, guarded by a faithful Scottish manservant. And he had his friends among the fair sex—not lovers, friends. So long as he could avoid any danger of courtship or marriage, he adored a few good women with constant and unfailing homage, and he was chivalrously fond of quite a number. But if they seemed to encroach on him, he withdrew and detested them.

Isabel knew him very well, knew his beautiful constancy, and kindness, also his incurable weakness, which made him unable ever to enter into close contact of any sort. He was ashamed of himself, because he could not marry, could not approach women physically. He wanted to do so. But he could not. At the centre of him he was afraid, helplessly and even brutally afraid. He had given up hope, had ceased to expect any more that he could escape his own weakness. Hence he was a brilliant and successful barrister, also *littérateur*[5] of high repute, a rich man, and a great social success. At the centre he felt himself neuter, nothing.

Isabel knew him well. She despised him even while she admired

5. Writer.

him. She looked at his sad face, his little short legs, and felt contempt of him. She looked at his dark grey eyes, with uncanny, almost child-like intuition, and she loved him. He understood amazingly—but she had no fear of his understanding. As a man she patronised him.

And she turned to the impassive, silent figure of her husband. He sat leaning back, with folded arms, and face a little up-tilted. His knees were straight and massive. She sighed, picked up the poker, and again began to prod the fire, to rouse the clouds of soft, brilliant sparks.

"Isabel tells me," Bertie began suddenly, "that you have not suffered unbearably from the loss of sight."

Maurice straightened himself to attend, but kept his arms folded.

"No," he said, "not unbearably. Now and again one struggles against it, you know. But there are compensations."

"They say it is much worse to be stone deaf," said Isabel.

"I believe it is," said Bertie. "Are there compensations?" he added, to Maurice.

"Yes. You cease to bother about a great many things." Again Maurice stretched his figure, stretched the strong muscles of his back, and leaned backwards, with uplifted face.

"And that is a relief," said Bertie. "But what is there in place of the bothering? What replaces the activity?"

There was a pause. At length the blind man replied, as out of a negligent, unattentive thinking:

"Oh, I don't know. There's a good deal when you're not active."

"Is there?" said Bertie. "What, exactly? It always seems to me that when there is no thought and no action, there is nothing."

Again Maurice was slow in replying.

"There is something," he replied. "I couldn't tell you what it is."

And the talk lapsed once more, Isabel and Bertie chatting gossip and reminiscence, the blind man silent.

At length Maurice rose restlessly, a big, obtrusive figure. He felt tight and hampered. He wanted to go away.

"Do you mind," he said, "if I go and speak to Wernham?"

"No—go along, dear," said Isabel.

And he went out. A silence came over the two friends. At length Bertie said:

"Nevertheless, it is a great deprivation, Cissie."

"It is, Bertie. I know it is."

"Something lacking all the time," said Bertie.

"Yes, I know. And yet—and yet—Maurice is right. There is something else, something *there*, which you never knew was there, and which you can't express."

"What is there?" asked Bertie.

"I don't know—it's awfully hard to define it—but something strong and immediate. There's something strange in Maurice's presence—indefinable—but I couldn't do without it. I agree that it seems to put one's mind to sleep. But when we're alone I miss nothing; it seems awfully rich, almost splendid, you know."

"I'm afraid I don't follow," said Bertie.

They talked desultorily. The wind blew loudly outside, rain chattered on the window-panes, making a sharp drum-sound, because of the closed, mellow-golden shutters inside. The logs burned slowly, with hot, almost invisible small flames. Bertie seemed uneasy, there were dark circles round his eyes. Isabel, rich with her approaching maternity, leaned looking into the fire. Her hair curled in odd, loose strands, very pleasing to the man. But she had a curious feeling of old woe in her heart, old, timeless night-woe.

"I suppose we're all deficient somewhere," said Bertie.

"I suppose so," said Isabel wearily.

"Damned, sooner or later."

"I don't know," she said, rousing herself. "I feel quite all right, you know. The child coming seems to make me indifferent to everything, just placid. I can't feel that there's anything to trouble about, you know."

"A good thing, I should say," he replied slowly.

"Well, there it is. I suppose it's just Nature. If only I felt I needn't trouble about Maurice, I should be perfectly content——"

"But you feel you must trouble about him?"

"Well—I don't know——" She even resented this much effort.

The evening passed slowly. Isabel looked at the clock. "I say," she said. "It's nearly ten o'clock. Where can Maurice be? I'm sure they're all in bed at the back. Excuse me a moment."

She went out, returning almost immediately.

"It's all shut up and in darkness," she said. "I wonder where he is. He must have gone out to the farm——"

Bertie looked at her.

"I suppose he'll come in," he said.

"I suppose so," she said. "But it's unusual for him to be out now."

"Would you like me to go out and see?"

"Well—if you wouldn't mind. I'd go, but——" She did not want to make the physical effort.

Bertie put on an old overcoat and took a lantern. He went out from the side door. He shrank from the wet and roaring night. Such weather had a nervous effect on him: too much moisture everywhere made him feel almost imbecile. Unwilling, he went through it all. A dog barked violently at him. He peered in all the buildings. At last, as he opened the upper door of a sort of intermediate barn, he heard a grinding noise, and looking in, holding up his lantern, saw Maurice, in his shirt-sleeves, standing listening, holding the handle of a turnip-pulper. He had been pulping sweet roots, a pile of which lay dimly heaped in a corner behind him.

"That you, Wernham?" said Maurice, listening.

"No, it's me," said Bertie.

A large, half-wild grey cat was rubbing at Maurice's leg. The blind man stooped to rub its sides. Bertie watched the scene, then unconsciously entered and shut the door behind him. He was in a high sort of barn-place, from which, right and left, ran off the corridors in front of the stalled cattle. He watched the slow, stooping motion of the other man, as he caressed the great cat.

Maurice straightened himself.

"You came to look for me?" he said.

"Isabel was a little uneasy," said Bertie.

"I'll come in. I like messing about doing these jobs."

The cat had reared her sinister, feline length against his leg, clawing at his thigh affectionately. He lifted her claws out of his flesh.

"I hope I'm not in your way at all at the Grange here," said Bertie, rather shy and stiff.

"My way? No, not a bit. I'm glad Isabel has somebody to talk to. I'm afraid it's I who am in the way. I know I'm not very lively company. Isabel's all right, don't you think? She's not unhappy, is she?"

"I don't think so."

"What does she say?"

"She says she's very content—only a little troubled about you."

"Why me?"

"Perhaps afraid that you might brood," said Bertie cautiously.

"She needn't be afraid of that." He continued to caress the flattened grey head of the cat with his fingers. "What I am a bit afraid of," he resumed, "is that she'll find me a dead weight, always alone with me down here."

"I don't think you need think that," said Bertie, though this was what he feared himself.

"I don't know," said Maurice. "Sometimes I feel it isn't fair that she's saddled with me." Then he dropped his voice curiously. "I say," he asked, secretly struggling, "is my face much disfigured? Do you mind telling me?"

"There is the scar," said Bertie, wondering. "Yes, it is a disfigurement. But more pitiable than shocking."

"A pretty bad scar, though," said Maurice.

"Oh yes."

There was a pause.

"Sometimes I feel I am horrible," said Maurice, in a low voice, talking as if to himself. And Bertie actually felt a quiver of horror.

"That's nonsense," he said.

Maurice again straightened himself, leaving the cat.

"There's no telling," he said. Then again, in an odd tone, he added: "I don't really know you, do I?"

"Probably not," said Bertie.

"Do you mind if I touch you?"

The lawyer shrank away instinctively. And yet, out of very philanthropy, he said, in a small voice: "Not at all."

But he suffered as the blind man stretched out a strong, naked hand to him. Maurice accidentally knocked off Bertie's hat.

"I thought you were taller," he said, starting. Then he laid his hand on Bertie Reid's head, closing the dome of the skull in a soft, firm grasp, gathering it, as it were; then, shifting his grasp and softly closing again, with a fine, close pressure, till he had covered the skull and the face of the smaller man, tracing the brows, and touching the full, closed eyes, touching the small nose and the nostrils, the rough, short moustache, the mouth, the rather strong chin. The hand of the blind man grasped the shoulder, the arm, the hand of the other man. He seemed to take him, in the soft, travelling grasp.

"You seem young," he said quietly, at last.

The lawyer stood almost annihilated, unable to answer.

"Your head seems tender, as if you were young," Maurice repeated. "So do your hands. Touch my eyes, will you?—touch my scar."

Now Bertie quivered with revulsion. Yet he was under the power of the blind man, as if hypnotised. He lifted his hand, and laid the fingers on the scar, on the scarred eyes. Maurice suddenly covered them with his own hand, pressed the fingers of the other man upon his disfigured eye-sockets, trembling in every fibre, and rocking slightly, slowly, from side to side. He remained thus for a minute or more, whilst Bertie stood as if in a swoon, unconscious, imprisoned.

Then suddenly Maurice removed the hand of the other man from his brow, and stood holding it in his own.

"Oh, my God," he said, "we shall know each other now, shan't we? We shall know each other now."

Bertie could not answer. He gazed mute and terror-struck, overcome by his own weakness. He knew he could not answer. He had an unreasonable fear, lest the other man should suddenly destroy him. Whereas Maurice was actually filled with hot, poignant love, the passion of friendship. Perhaps it was this very passion of friendship which Bertie shrank from most.

"We're all right together now, aren't we?" said Maurice. "It's all right now, as long as we live, so far as we're concerned."

"Yes," said Bertie, trying by any means to escape.

Maurice stood with head lifted, as if listening. The new delicate fulfilment of mortal friendship had come as a revelation and surprise to him, something exquisite and unhoped-for. He seemed to be listening to hear if it were real.

Then he turned for his coat.

"Come," he said, "we'll go to Isabel."

Bertie took the lantern and opened the door. The cat disappeared. The two men went in silence along the causeways. Isabel, as they came, thought their footsteps sounded strange. She looked up pathetically and anxiously for their entrance. There seemed a curious elation about Maurice. Bertie was haggard, with sunken eyes.

"What is it?" she asked.

"We've become friends," said Maurice, standing with his feet apart, like a strange colossus.

"Friends!" re-echoed Isabel. And she looked again at Bertie. He met her eyes with a furtive, haggard look; his eyes were as if glazed with misery.

"I'm so glad," she said, in sheer perplexity.

"Yes," said Maurice.

He was indeed so glad. Isabel took his hand with both hers, and held it fast.

"You'll be happier now, dear," she said.

But she was watching Bertie. She knew that he had one desire—to escape from this intimacy, this friendship, which had been thrust upon him. He could not bear it that he had been touched by the blind man, his insane reserve broken in. He was like a mollusc whose shell is broken.

---

1. What emotions and qualities of character have been enhanced in Isabel by living with a blind husband?
2. Does the distinction between the farm buildings and the living quarters of the Pervins represent a division important to the meaning of the story as a whole?
3. We are told that "while he was so utterly invisible" in the darkness of the barn, Isabel was afraid of her husband. Does she identify him with the darkness?
4. How is Bertie transformed by Maurice's touch? Has the touch been a blessing? If so, why is he so frightened by it and eager to escape its effect?
5. How do setting and weather complement the expression of the story?

The Horse Dealer's Daughter

"Well, Mabel, and what are you going to do with yourself?" asked Joe, with foolish flippancy. He felt quite safe himself. Without listening for an answer, he turned aside, worked a grain of tobacco to the tip of his tongue, and spat it out. He did not care about anything, since he felt safe himself.

The three brothers and the sister sat round the desolate breakfast-table, attempting some sort of desultory consultation. The morning's post had given the final tap to the family fortunes, and all was over. The dreary dining-room itself, with its heavy mahogany furniture, looked as if it were waiting to be done away with.

But the consultation amounted to nothing. There was a strange air of ineffectuality about the three men, as they sprawled at table, smoking and reflecting vaguely on their own condition. The girl was alone, a rather short, sullen-looking young woman of twenty-seven. She did not share the same life as her brothers. She would have been good-looking, save for the impressive fixity of her face, "bull-dog," as her brothers called it.

There was a confused tramping of horses' feet outside. The three men all sprawled round in their chairs to watch. Beyond the dark holly bushes that separated the strip of lawn from the high-road, they could see a cavalcade of shire horses swinging out of their own yard, being taken for exercise. This was the last time. These were the last horses that would go through their hands. The young men watched with critical, callous look. They were all frightened at the collapse of their lives, and the sense of disaster in which they were involved left them no inner freedom.

Yet they were three fine, well-set fellows enough. Joe, the eldest, was a man of thirty-three, broad and handsome in a hot, flushed way. His face was red, he twisted his black moustache over a thick finger, his eyes were shallow and restless. He had a sensual way of uncovering his teeth when he laughed, and his bearing was stupid. Now he watched the horses with a glazed look of helplessness in his eyes, a certain stupor of downfall.

The great draught-horses swung past. They were tied head to tail, four of them, and they heaved along to where a lane branched off from the high-road, planting their great hoofs floutingly in the fine black mud, swinging their great rounded haunches sumptuously, and trotting a few sudden steps as they were led into the lane, round the corner. Every movement showed a massive, slumbrous strength, and a stupidity which held them in subjection. The groom at the head looked back, jerking the leading rope. And the cavalcade moved out of sight up the lane, the tail of the last horse, bobbed up tight and stiff, held out taut from the swinging great haunches as they rocked behind the hedges in a motion-like sleep.

Joe watched with glazed hopeless eyes. The horses were almost like his own body to him. He felt he was done for now. Luckily he was engaged to a woman as old as himself, and therefore her father, who was steward of a neighbouring estate, would provide him with a job. He would marry and go into harness. His life was over, he would be a subject animal now.

He turned uneasily aside, the retreating steps of the horses echoing in his ears. Then, with foolish restlessness, he reached for the scraps of bacon-rind from the plates, and making a faint whistling sound, flung them to the terrier that lay against the fender. He watched the dog swallow them, and waited till the creature looked into his eyes. Then a faint grin came on his face, and in a high, foolish voice he said:

"You won't get much more bacon, shall you, you little b——?"

The dog faintly and dismally wagged its tail, then lowered its haunches, circled round, and lay down again.

There was another helpless silence at the table. Joe sprawled uneasily in his seat, not willing to go till the family conclave was dissolved. Fred Henry, the second brother, was erect, clean-limbed, alert. He had watched the passing of the horses with more *sang-froid*.[1] If he was an animal, like Joe, he was an animal which controls, not one which is controlled. He was master of any horse, and he carried himself with a well-tempered air of mastery. But he was not master of the situations of life. He pushed his coarse brown moustache upwards, off his lip, and glanced irritably at his sister, who sat impassive and inscrutable.

"You'll go and stop with Lucy for a bit, shan't you?" he asked. The girl did not answer.

"I don't see what else you can do," persisted Fred Henry.

"Go as a skivvy,"[2] Joe interpolated laconically.

The girl did not move a muscle.

"If I was her, I should go in for training for a nurse," said Malcolm, the youngest of them all. He was the baby of the family, a young man of twenty-two, with a fresh, jaunty *museau*.[3]

But Mabel did not take any notice of him. They had talked at her and round her for so many years, that she hardly heard them at all.

The marble clock on the mantelpiece softly chimed the half-hour, the dog rose uneasily from the hearth-rug and looked at the party at the breakfast-table. But still they sat in an ineffectual conclave.

1. Coolness. 2. Menial worker. 3. Face.

"Oh, all right," said Joe suddenly, apropos of nothing. "I'll get a move on."

He pushed back his chair, straddled his knees with a downward jerk, to get them free, in horsey fashion, and went to the fire. Still he did not go out of the room; he was curious to know what the others would do or say. He began to charge his pipe, looking down at the dog and saying in a high, affected voice:

"Going wi' me? Going wi' me are ter? Tha'rt goin' further than tha counts on just now, dost hear?"

The dog faintly wagged his tail, the man stuck out his jaw and covered his pipe with his hands, and puffed intently, losing himself in the tobacco, looking down all the while at the dog with an absent brown eye. The dog looked up at him in mournful distrust. Joe stood with his knees stuck out, in real horsey fashion.

"Have you had a letter from Lucy?" Fred Henry asked of his sister.

"Last week," came the neutral reply.

"And what does she say?"

There was no answer.

"Does she *ask* you to go and stop there?" persisted Fred Henry.

"She says I can if I like."

"Well, then, you'd better. Tell her you'll come on Monday."

This was received in silence.

"That's what you'll do then, is it?" said Fred Henry, in some exasperation.

But she made no answer. There was a silence of futility and irritation in the room. Malcolm grinned fatuously.

"You'll have to make up your mind between now and next Wednesday," said Joe loudly, "or else find yourself lodgings on the kerbstone."

The face of the young woman darkened, but she sat on immutable.

"Here's Jack Ferguson!" exclaimed Malcolm, who was looking aimlessly out of the window.

"Where?" exclaimed Joe loudly.

"Just gone past."

"Coming in?"

Malcolm craned his neck to see the gate.

"Yes," he said.

There was a silence. Mabel sat on like one condemned, at the head of the table. Then a whistle was heard from the kitchen. The dog got up and barked sharply. Joe opened the door and shouted:

"Come on."

After a moment a young man entered. He was muffled up in

overcoat and a purple woollen scarf, and his tweed cap, which he did not remove, was pulled down on his head. He was of medium height, his face was rather long and pale, his eyes looked tired.

"Hello, Jack! Well, Jack!" exclaimed Malcolm and Joe. Fred Henry merely said: "Jack."

"What's doing?" asked the newcomer, evidently addressing Fred Henry.

"Same. We've got to be out by Wednesday. Got a cold?"

"I have—got it bad, too."

"Why don't you stop in?"

"*Me* stop in? When I can't stand on my legs, perhaps I shall have a chance." The young man spoke huskily. He had a slight Scotch accent.

"It's a knock-out, isn't it," said Joe, boisterously, "if a doctor goes round croaking with a cold. Looks bad for the patients, doesn't it?"

The young doctor looked at him slowly.

"Anything the matter with *you*, then?" he asked sarcastically.

"Not as I know of. Damn your eyes, I hope not. Why?"

"I thought you were very concerned about the patients, wondered if you might be one yourself."

"Damn it, no, I've never been patient to no flaming doctor, and hope I never shall be," returned Joe.

At this point Mabel rose from the table, and they all seemed to become aware of her existence. She began putting the dishes together. The young doctor looked at her, but did not address her. He had not greeted her. She went out of the room with the tray, her face impassive and unchanged.

"When are you off then, all of you?" asked the doctor.

"I'm catching the eleven-forty," replied Malcolm. "Are you goin' down wi' th' trap, Joe?"

"Yes, I've told you I'm going down wi' th' trap, haven't I?"

"We'd better be getting her in then. So long Jack, if I don't see you before I go," said Malcolm, shaking hands.

He went out, followed by Joe, who seemed to have his tail between his legs.

"Well, this is the devil's own," exclaimed the doctor, when he was left alone with Fred Henry. "Going before Wednesday, are you?"

"That's the orders," replied the other.

"Where, to Northampton?"

"That's it."

"The devil!" exclaimed Ferguson, with quiet chagrin.

And there was silence between the two.

"All settled up, are you?" asked Ferguson.

"About."

There was another pause.

"Well, I shall miss yer, Freddy, boy," said the young doctor.

"And I shall miss thee, Jack," returned the other.

"Miss you like hell," mused the doctor.

Fred Henry turned aside. There was nothing to say. Mabel came in again, to finish clearing the table.

"What are *you* going to do, then, Miss Pervin?" asked Ferguson. "Going to your sister's, are you?"

Mabel looked at him with her steady, dangerous eyes, that always made him uncomfortable, unsettling his superficial ease.

"No," she said.

"Well, what in the name of fortune *are* you going to do? Say what you mean to do," cried Fred Henry, with futile intensity.

But she only averted her head, and continued her work. She folded the white table-cloth, and put on the chenille cloth.

"The sulkiest bitch that ever trod!" muttered her brother.

But she finished her task with perfectly impassive face, the young doctor watching her interestedly all the while. Then she went out.

Fred Henry stared after her, clenching his lips, his blue eyes fixing in sharp antagonism, as he made a grimace of sour exasperation.

"You could bray her into bits, and that's all you'd get out of her," he said, in a small, narrowed tone.

The doctor smiled faintly.

"What's she *going* to do, then?" he asked.

"Strike me if *I* know!" returned the other.

There was a pause. Then the doctor stirred.

"I'll be seeing you tonight, shall I?" he said to his friend.

"Ay—where's it to be? Are we going over to Jessdale?"

"I don't know. I've got such a cold on me. I'll come round to the 'Moon and Stars', anyway."

"Let Lizzie and May miss their night for once, eh?"

"That's it—if I feel as I do now."

"All's one——"

The two young men went through the passage and down to the back door together. The house was large, but it was servantless now, and desolate. At the back was a small brick house-yard and beyond that a big square, graveled fine and red, and having stables on two sides. Sloping, dank, winter-dark fields stretched away on the open sides.

But the stables were empty. Joseph Pervin, the father of the family, had been a man of no education, who had become a fairly large horse dealer. The stables had been full of horses, there was a great turmoil and come-and-go of horses and of dealers and grooms. Then the kitchen was full of servants. But of late things had declined. The old man had married a second time, to retrieve his fortunes. Now he was dead and everything was gone to the dogs, there was nothing but debt and threatening.

For months, Mabel had been servantless in the big house, keeping the home together in penury for her ineffectual brothers. She had kept house for ten years. But previously it was with unstinted means. Then, however brutal and coarse everything was, the sense of money had kept her proud, confident. The men might be foul-mouthed, the women in the kitchen might have bad reputations, her brothers might have illegitimate children. But so long as there was money, the girl felt herself established, and brutally proud, reserved.

No company came to the house, save dealers and coarse men. Mabel had no associates of her own sex, after her sister went away. But she did not mind. She went regularly to church, she attended to her father. And she lived in the memory of her mother, who had died when she was fourteen, and whom she had loved. She had loved her father, too, in a different way, depending upon him, and feeling secure in him, until at the age of fifty-four he married again. And then she had set hard against him. Now he had died and left them all hopelessly in debt.

She had suffered badly during the period of poverty. Nothing, however, could shake the curious, sullen, animal pride that dominated each member of the family. Now, for Mabel, the end had come. Still she would not cast about her. She would follow her own way just the same. She would always hold the keys of her own situation. Mindless and persistent, she endured from day to day. Why should she think? Why should she answer anybody? It was enough that this was the end, and there was no way out. She need not pass any more darkly along the main street of the small town, avoiding every eye. She need not demean herself any more, going into the shops and buying the cheapest food. This was at an end. She thought of nobody, not even of herself. Mindless and persistent, she seemed in a sort of ecstasy to be coming nearer to her fulfilment, her own glorification, approaching her dead mother, who was glorified.

In the afternoon, she took a little bag, with shears and sponge and a small scrubbing-brush, and went out. It was a grey, wintry day, with saddened, dark green fields and an atmosphere blackened by the smoke of foundries not far off. She went quickly, darkly along the causeway, heeding nobody, through the town to the churchyard.

There she always felt secure, as if no one could see her, although as a matter of fact she was exposed to the stare of everyone who passed along under the churchyard wall. Nevertheless, once under the shadow of the great looming church, among the graves, she felt immune from the world, reserved within the thick churchyard wall as in another country.

Carefully she clipped the grass from the grave, and arranged the pinky white, small chrysanthemums in the tin cross. When this was done, she took an empty jar from a neighbouring grave, brought water, and carefully, most scrupulously sponged the marble headstone and the coping-stone.

It gave her sincere satisfaction to do this. She felt in immediate contact with the world of her mother. She took minute pains, went through the park in a state bordering on pure happiness, as if in performing this task she came into a subtle, intimate connection with her mother. For the life she followed here in the world was far less real than the world of death she inherited from her mother.

The doctor's house was just by the church. Ferguson, being a mere hired assistant, was slave to the country-side. As he hurried now to attend to the out-patients in the surgery, glancing across the graveyard with his quick eye, he saw the girl at her task at the grave. She seemed so intent and remote, it was like looking into another world. Some mystical element was touched in him. He slowed down as he walked, watching her as if spellbound.

She lifted her eyes, feeling him looking. Their eyes met. And each looked away again at once, each feeling, in some way, found out by the other. He lifted his cap and passed on down the road. There remained distinct in his consciousness, like a vision, the memory of her face, lifted from the tombstone in the churchyard, and looking at him with slow, large, portentous eyes. It *was* portentous, her face. It seemed to mesmerize him. There was a heavy power in her eyes which laid hold of his whole being, as if he had drunk some powerful drug. He had been feeling weak and done before. Now the life came back into him, he felt delivered from his own fretted, daily self.

He finished his duties at the surgery as quickly as might be, hastily filling up the bottles of the waiting people with cheap drugs. Then, in perpetual haste, he set off again to visit several cases in another part of his round, before tea-time. At all times he preferred to walk if he could, but particularly when he was not well. He fancied the motion restored him.

The afternoon was falling. It was grey, deadened, and wintry, with a slow, moist, heavy coldness sinking in and deadening all the faculties. But why should he think or notice? He hastily climbed the hill and turned across the dark green fields, following the black cinder-track. In the distance, across a shallow dip in the country, the small town was clustered like smouldering ash, a tower, a spire, a heap of low, raw, extinct houses. And on the nearest fringe of the town, sloping into the dip, was Oldmeadow, the Pervins' house. He could see the stables and the outbuildings distinctly, as they lay towards him on the slope. Well, he would not go there many more times! Another resource would be lost to him, another place gone: the only company he cared for in the alien, ugly little town he was losing. Nothing but work, drudgery, constant hastening from dwelling to dwelling among the colliers and the iron-workers. It wore him out, but at the same time he had a craving for it. It was a stimulant to him to be in the homes of the working people, moving, as it were, through the innermost body of their life. His nerves were excited and gratified. He could come so near, into the very lives of the rough, inarticulate, powerfully emotional men and women. He grumbled, he said he hated the hellish hole. But as a matter of fact it excited him, the contact with the rough, strongly-feeling people was a stimultant applied direct to his nerves.

Below Oldmeadow, in the green, shallow, soddened hollow of fields, lay a square, deep pond. Roving across the landscape, the doctor's quick eye detected a figure in black passing through the gate of the field, down towards the pond. He looked again. It would be Mabel Pervin. His mind suddenly became alive and attentive.

Why was she going down there? He pulled up on the path on the slope above, and stood staring. He could just make sure of the small black figure moving in the hollow of the failing day. He seemed to see her in the midst of such obscurity, that he was like a clairvoyant, seeing rather with the mind's eye than with ordinary sight. Yet he could see her positively enough, whilst he kept his eye attentive. He felt, if he looked away from her, in the thick, ugly falling dusk, he would lose her altogether.

He followed her minutely as she moved, direct and intent, like something transmitted rather than stirring in voluntary activity, straight down the field towards the pond. There she stood on the bank for a moment. She never raised her head. Then she waded slowly into the water.

He stood motionless as the small black figure walked slowly and deliberately towards the center of the pond, very slowly, gradually moving deeper into the motionless water, and still moving forward as the water got up to her breast. Then he could see her no more in the dusk of the dead afternoon.

"There!" he exclaimed. "Would you believe it?"

And he hastened straight down, running over the wet, soddened fields, pushing through the hedges, down into the depression of callous wintry obscurity. It took him several minutes to come to the pond. He stood on the bank, breathing heavily. He could see nothing. His eyes seemed to penetrate the dead water. Yes, perhaps that was the dark shadow of her black clothing beneath the surface of the water.

He slowly ventured into the pond. The bottom was deep, soft clay, he sank in, and the water clasped dead cold round his legs. As he stirred he could smell the cold, rotten clay that fouled up into the water. It was objectionable in his lungs. Still, repelled and yet not heeding, he moved deeper into the pond. The cold water rose over his thighs, over his loins, upon his abdomen. The lower part of his body was all sunk in the hideous cold element. And the bottom was so deeply soft and uncertain, he was afraid of pitching with his mouth underneath. He could not swim, and was afraid.

He crouched a little, spreading his hands under the water and moving them round, trying to feel for her. The dead cold pond swayed upon his chest. He moved again, a little deeper, and again, with his hands underneath, he felt all around under the water. And he touched her clothing. But it evaded his fingers. He made a desperate effort to grasp it.

And so doing he lost his balance and went under, horribly, suffocating in the foul earthy water, struggling madly for a few moments. At last, after what seemed an eternity, he got his footing, rose again into the air and looked around. He gasped, and knew he was in the world. Then he looked at the water. She had risen near him. He grasped her clothing, and drawing her nearer, turned to take his way to land again.

He went very slowly, carefully, absorbed in the slow progress. He rose higher, climbing out of the pond. The water was now only about his legs; he was thankful, full of relief to be out of the clutches of the pond. He lifted her and staggered onto the bank, out of the horror of wet, grey clay.

He laid her down on the bank. She was quite unconscious and running with water. He made the water come from her mouth, he worked to restore her. He did not have to work very long before he could feel the breathing begin again in her; she was breathing naturally. He worked a little longer. He could feel her live beneath his hands; she was coming back. He wiped her face, wrapped her in his overcoat, looked round into the dim, dark grey world, then lifted her and staggered down the bank and across the fields.

It seemed an unthinkably long way, and his burden so heavy he felt he would never get to the house. But at last he was in the stable-yard, and then in the house-yard. He opened the door and went into the house. In the kitchen he laid her down on the hearth-rug and called. The house was empty. But the fire was burning in the grate.

Then again he kneeled to attend to her. She was breathing regularly, her eyes were wide open and as if conscious, but there seemed something missing in her look. She was conscious in herself, but unconscious of her surroundings.

He ran upstairs, took blankets from a bed, and put them before the fire to warm. Then he removed her saturated, earthy-smelling clothing, rubbed her dry with a towel, and wrapped her naked in the blankets. Then he went into the dining-room, to look for spirits. There was a little whisky. He drank a gulp himself, and put some into her mouth.

The effect was instantaneous. She looked full into his face, as if she had been seeing him for some time, and yet had only just become conscious of him.

"Dr. Ferguson?" she said.

"What?" he answered.

He was divesting himself of his coat, intending to find some dry clothing upstairs. He could not bear the smell of the dead, clayey water, and he was mortally afraid for his own health.

"What did I do?" she asked.

"Walked into the pond," he replied. He had begun to shudder like one sick, and could hardly attend to her. Her eyes remained full on him, he seemed to be going dark in his mind, looking back at her helplessly. The shuddering became quieter in him, his life came back to him, dark and unknowing, but strong again.

"Was I out of my mind?" she asked, while her eyes were fixed on him all the time.

"Maybe, for the moment," he replied. He felt quiet, because his strength had come back. The strange fretful strain had left him.

"Am I out of my mind now?" she asked.

"Are you?" he reflected a moment. "No," he answered truthfully. "I don't see that you are." He turned his face aside. He was afraid now, because he felt dazed, and felt dimly that her power was stronger than his, in this issue. And she continued to look at him fixedly all the time. "Can you tell me where I shall find some dry things to put on?" he asked.

"Did you dive into the pond for me?" she asked.

"No," he answered. "I walked in. But I went in over head as well."

There was silence for a moment. He hesitated. He very much wanted to go upstairs to get into dry clothing. But there was another desire in him. And she seemed to hold him. His will seemed to have gone to sleep, and left him, standing there slack before her. But he felt warm inside himself. He did not shudder at all, though his clothes were sodden on him.

"Why did you?" she asked.

"Because I didn't want you to do such a foolish thing," he said.

"It wasn't foolish," she said, still gazing at him as she lay on the floor, with a sofa cushion under her head. "It was the right thing to do. *I* knew best, then."

"I'll go and shift these wet things," he said. But still he had not the power to move out of her presence, until she sent him. It was as if she had the life of his body in her hands, and he could not extricate himself. Or perhaps he did not want to.

Suddenly she sat up. Then she became aware of her own immediate condition. She felt the blankets about her, she knew her own limbs. For a moment it seemed as if her reason were going. She looked round, with wild eye, as if seeking something. He stood still with fear. She saw her clothing lying scattered.

"Who undressed me?" she asked, her eyes resting full and inevitable on his face.

"I did," he replied, "to bring you round."

For some moments she sat and gazed at him awfully, her lips parted.

"Do you love me, then?" she asked.

He only stood and stared at her, fascinated. His soul seemed to melt.

She shuffled forward on her knees, and put her arms round him, round his legs, as he stood there, pressing her breasts against his knees and thighs, clutching him with strange, convulsive certainty, pressing his thighs against her, drawing him to her face, her throat, as she looked up at him with flaring, humble eyes of transfiguration, triumphant in first possession.

"You love me," she murmured, in strange transport, yearning and triumphant and confident. "You love me. I know you love me, I know."

And she was passionately kissing his knees, through the wet clothing, passionately and indiscriminately kissing his knees, his legs, as if unaware of everything.

He looked down at the tangled wet hair, the wild, bare, animal shoulders. He was amazed, bewildered, and afraid. He had never thought of loving her. He had never wanted to love her. When he rescued her and restored her, he was a doctor, and she was a patient. He had had no single personal thought of her. Nay, this introduction of the personal element was very distasteful to him, a violation of his professional honour. It was horrible to have her there embracing his knees. It was horrible. He revolted from it, violently. And yet—and yet—he had not the power to break away.

She looked at him again, with the same supplication of powerful love, and that same transcendent, frightening light of triumph. In view of the delicate flame which seemed to come from her face like a light, he was powerless. And yet he had never intended to love her. He had never intended. And something stubborn in him could not give way.

"You love me," she repeated, in a murmur of deep, rhapsodic assurance. "You love me."

Her hands were drawing him, drawing him down to her. He was

afraid, even a little horrified. For he had, really, no intention of loving her. Yet her hands were drawing him towards her. He put out his hand quickly to steady himself, and grasped her bare shoulder. A flame seemed to burn the hand that grasped her soft shoulder. He had no intention of loving her: his whole will was against his yielding. It was horrible. And yet wonderful was the touch of her shoulders, beautiful the shining of her face. Was she perhaps mad? He had a horror of yielding to her. Yet something in him ached also.

He had been staring away at the door, away from her. But his hand remained on her shoulder. She had gone suddenly very still. He looked down at her. Her eyes were now wide with fear, with doubt, the light was dying from her face, a shadow of terrible greyness was returning. He could not bear the touch of her eyes' question upon him, and the look of death behind the question.

With an inward groan he gave way, and let his heart yield towards her. A sudden gentle smile came on his face. And her eyes, which never left his face, slowly, slowly filled with tears. He watched the strange water rise in her eyes, like some slow fountain coming up. And his heart seemed to burn and melt away in his breast.

He could not bear to look at her any more. He dropped on his knees and caught her head with his arms and pressed her face against his throat. She was very still. His heart, which seemed to have broken, was burning with a kind of agony in his breast. And he felt her slow, hot tears wetting his throat. But he could not move.

He felt the hot tears wet his neck and the hollows of his neck, and he remained motionless, suspended through one of man's eternities. Only now it had become indispensable to him to have her face pressed close to him; he could never let her go again. He could never let her head go away from the close clutch of his arm. He wanted to remain like that for ever, with his heart hurting him in a pain that was also life to him. Without knowing, he was looking down on her damp, soft brown hair.

Then, as it were suddenly, he smelt the horrid stagnant smell of that water. And at the same moment she drew away from him and looked at him. Her eyes were wistful and unfathomable. He was afraid of them, and he fell to kissing her, not knowing what he was doing. He wanted her eyes not to have that terrible, wistful, unfathomable look.

When she turned her face to him again, a faint delicate flush was glowing, and there was again dawning that terrible shining of joy in her eyes, which really terrified him, and yet which he now wanted to see, because he feared the look of doubt still more.

"You love me?" she said, rather faltering.

"Yes." The word cost him a painful effort. Not because it wasn't true. But because it was too newly true, the *saying* seemed to tear open again his newly-torn heart. And he hardly wanted it to be true, even now.

She lifted her face to him, and he bent forward and kissed her on the mouth, gently, with the one kiss that is an eternal pledge. And as he kissed her his heart strained again in his breast. He never intended to love her. But now it was over. He had crossed over the gulf to her, and all that he had left behind had shrivelled and become void.

After the kiss, her eyes again slowly filled with tears. She sat still, away from him, with her face drooped aside, and her hands folded in her lap. The tears fell very slowly. There was complete silence. He too sat there motionless and silent on the hearth-rug. The strange pain of his heart that was broken seemed to consume him. That he should love her? That this was love! That he should be ripped open in this way! Him, a doctor! How they would all jeer if they knew! It was agony to him to think they might know.

In the curious naked pain of the thought he looked again to her. She was sitting there drooped into a muse. He saw a tear fall, and his heart flared hot. He saw for the first time that one of her shoulders was quite uncovered, one arm bare, he could see one of her small breasts; dimly, because it had become almost dark in the room.

"Why are you crying?" he asked, in an altered voice.

She looked up at him, and behind her tears the consciousness of her situation for the first time brought a dark look of shame to her eyes.

"I'm not crying, really," she said, watching him, half frightened.

He reached his hand, and softly closed it on her bare arm.

"I love you! I love you!" he said in a soft, low vibrating voice, unlike himself.

She shrank, and dropped her head. The soft, penetrating grip of his hand on her arm distressed her. She looked up at him.

"I want to go," she said. "I want to go and get you some dry things."

"Why?" he said. "I'm all right."

"But I want to go," she said. "And I want you to change your things."

He released her arm, and she wrapped herself in the blanket, looking at him rather frightened. And still she did not rise.

"Kiss me," she said wistfully.

He kissed her, but briefly, half in anger.

Then, after a second, she rose nervously, all mixed up in the blanket. He watched her in her confusion as she tried to extricate herself and wrap herself up so that she could walk. He watched her relentlessly, as she knew. And as she went, the blanket trailing, and as he saw a glimpse of her feet and her white leg, he tried to remember her as she was when he had wrapped her in the blanket. But then he didn't want to remember, because she had been nothing to him then, and his nature revolted from remembering her as she was when she was nothing to him.

A tumbling, muffled noise from within the dark house startled him. Then he heard her voice: "There are clothes." He rose and went to the foot of the stairs, and gathered up the garments she had thrown down. Then he came back to the fire, to rub himself down and dress. He grinned at his own appearance when he had finished.

The fire was sinking, so he put on coal. The house was now quite dark, save for the light of a street-lamp that shone in faintly from beyond the holly trees. He lit the gas with matches he found on the mantelpiece. Then he emptied the pockets of his own clothes, and threw all his wet things in a heap into the scullery. After which he gathered up her sodden clothes, gently, and put them in a separate heap on the copper-top in the scullery.

It was six o'clock on the clock. His own watch had stopped. He ought to go back to the surgery. He waited, and still she did not come down. So he went to the foot of the stairs and called:

"I shall have to go."

Almost immediately he heard her coming down. She had on her best dress of black voile, and her hair was tidy, but still damp. She looked at him—and in spite of herself, smiled.

"I don't like you in those clothes," she said.

"Do I look a sight?" he answered.

They were shy of one another.

"I'll make you some tea," she said.

"No, I must go."

"Must you?" And she looked at him again with the wide, strained, doubtful eyes. And again, from the pain of his breast, he knew how he loved her. He went and bent to kiss her, gently, passionately, with his heart's painful kiss.

"And my hair smells so horrible," she murmured in distraction. "And I'm so awful, I'm so awful! Oh no, I'm too awful." And she broke into bitter, heart-broken sobbing. "You can't want to love me, I'm horrible."

"Don't be silly, don't be silly," he said, trying to comfort her, kissing her, holding her in his arms. "I want you, I want to marry you, we're going to be married, quickly, quickly—to-morrow if I can."

But she only sobbed terribly, and cried:

"I feel awful. I feel awful. I feel I'm horrible to you."

"No, I want you, I want you," was all he answered, blindly, with that terrible intonation which frightened her almost more than her horror lest he should *not* want her.

---

1. What values does Lawrence seem to place on personality, rational intentions, and civilized ideas of duty?
2. How has the point of view been adapted to the requirements of the material? Couldn't everything essential have been told from Ferguson's point of view?
3. What is the prevailing mood of the story? How much of this is contributed by the language and the descriptive passages?
4. Does Mabel purposely misconstrue Ferguson's motives in undressing her? Does she understand them better than he does? If you think she does, what gives her this ability?
5. Is Lawrence trying to picture eccentric characters and a freakish turn of events, or is he trying to say something that is universally true about men, women, and love?
6. Does the story struggle against our common-sense views of reality? In what parts or details?

The Rocking-Horse Winner

There was a woman who was beautiful, who started with all the advantages, yet she had no luck. She married for love, and the love turned to dust. She had bonny children, yet she felt they had been thrust upon her, and she could not love them. They looked at her coldly, as if they were finding fault with her. And hurriedly she felt she must cover up some fault in herself. Yet what it was that she must cover up she never knew. Nevertheless, when her children were present, she always felt the centre of her heart go hard. This troubled her, and in her manner she was all the more gentle and anxious for her children, as if she loved them very much. Only she herself knew that at the centre of her heart was a hard little place that could not feel love, no, not for anybody. Everybody else said of her: "She is such a good mother. She adores her children." Only she herself, and her children themselves, knew it was not so. They read it in each other's eyes.

There were a boy and two little girls. They lived in a pleasant house, with a garden, and they had discreet servants, and felt themselves superior to anyone in the neighbourhood.

Although they lived in style, they felt always an anxiety in the house. There was never enough money. The mother had a small income, and the father had a small income, but not nearly enough for the social position which they had to keep up. The father went in to town to some office. But though he had good prospects, these prospects never materialized. There was always the grinding sense of the shortage of money, though the style was always kept up.

At last the mother said: "I will see if *I* can't make something." But she did not know where to begin. She racked her brains, and tried this thing and the other, but could not find anything successful. The failure made deep lines come into her face. Her children were growing up, they would have to go to school. There must be more money, there must be more money. The father, who was always very handsome and expensive in his tastes, seemed as if he never *would* be able to do anything worth doing. And the mother, who had a great belief in herself, did not succeed any better, and her tastes were just as expensive.

And so the house came to be haunted by the unspoken phrase: *There must be more money! There must be more money!* The children could hear it all the time, though nobody said it aloud. They heard it at Christmas, when the expensive and splendid toys filled the nursery. Behind the shining modern rocking-horse, behind the smart doll's-house, a voice would start whispering: "There *must* be more money! There *must* be more money!" And the children would stop playing, to listen for a moment. They would look into each other's eyes, to see if they had all heard. And each one saw in the eyes of the other two that they too had heard. "There *must* be more money! There *must* be more money!"

It came whispering from the springs of the still-swaying rocking-horse, and even the horse, bending his wooden, champing head, heard it. The big doll, sitting so pink and smirking in her new pram,[1] could hear it quite plainly, and seemed to be smirking all the more self-consciously because of it. The foolish puppy, too, that took the place of the teddy-bear, he was looking so extraordinarily foolish for no other reason but that he heard the secret whisper all over the house: "There *must* be more money!"

Yet nobody ever said it aloud. The whisper was everywhere, and therefore no one spoke it. Just as no one ever says: "We are breathing!" in spite of the fact that breath is coming and going all the time.

"Mother," said the boy Paul one day, "why don't we keep a car of our own? Why do we always use uncle's, or else a taxi?"

"Because we're the poor members of the family," said the mother.

"But why *are* we, mother?"

"Well—I suppose," she said slowly and bitterly, "it's because your father has no luck."

The boy was silent for some time.

"Is luck money, mother?" he asked rather timidly.

"No, Paul. Not quite. It's what causes you to have money."

1. Baby buggy.

"Oh!" said Paul vaguely. "I thought when Uncle Oscar said *filthy lucker*, it meant money."

"*Filthy lucre* does mean money," said the mother. "But it's lucre, not luck."

"Oh!" said the boy. "Then what *is* luck, mother?"

"It's what causes you to have money. If you're lucky you have money. That's why it's better to be born lucky than rich. If you're rich, you may lose your money. But if you're lucky, you will always get more money."

"Oh! Will you? And is father not lucky?"

"Very unlucky, I should say," she said bitterly.

The boy watched her with unsure eyes.

"Why?" he asked.

"I don't know. Nobody ever knows why one person is lucky and another unlucky."

"Don't they? Nobody at all? Does *nobody* know?"

"Perhaps God. But He never tells."

"He ought to, then. And aren't you lucky either, mother?"

"I can't be, if I married an unlucky husband."

"But by yourself, aren't you?"

"I used to think I was, before I married. Now I think I am very unlucky indeed."

"Why?"

"Well—never mind! Perhaps I'm not really," she said.

The child looked at her, to see if she meant it. But he saw, by the lines of her mouth, that she was only trying to hide something from him.

"Well, anyhow," he said stoutly, "I'm a lucky person."

"Why?" said his mother, with a sudden laugh.

He stared at her. He didn't even know why he had said it.

"God told me," he asserted, brazening it out.

"I hope He did, dear!" she said, again with a laugh, but rather bitter.

"He did, mother!"

"Excellent!" said the mother, using one of her husband's exclamations.

The boy saw she did not believe him; or, rather, that she paid no attention to his assertion. This angered him somewhat, and made him want to compel her attention.

He went off by himself, vaguely, in a childish way, seeking for the clue to "luck." Absorbed, taking no heed of other people, he went about with a sort of stealth, seeking inwardly for luck. He wanted luck, he wanted it, he wanted it. When the two girls were playing dolls in the nursery, he would sit on his big rocking-horse, charging madly into space, with a frenzy that made the little girls peer at him uneasily. Wildly the horse careered, the waving dark hair of the boy tossed, his eyes had a strange glare in them. The little girls dared not speak to him.

When he had ridden to the end of his mad little journey, he climbed down and stood in front of his rocking-horse, staring fixedly into its lowered face. Its red mouth was slightly open, its big eye was wide and glassy-bright.

"Now!" he would silently command the snorting steed. "Now, take me to where there is luck! Now take me!"

And he would slash the horse on the neck with the little whip he had asked Uncle Oscar for. He *knew* the horse could take him to where there was luck, if only he forced it. So he would mount again, and start on his furious ride, hoping at last to get there. He knew he could get there.

"You'll break your horse, Paul!" said the nurse.

"He's always riding like that! I wish he'd leave off!" said his elder sister Joan.

But he only glared down on them in silence. Nurse gave him up. She could make nothing of him. Anyhow he was growing beyond her.

One day his mother and his Uncle Oscar came in when he was on one of his furious rides. He did not speak to them.

"Hallo, you young jockey! Riding a winner?" said his uncle.

"Aren't you growing too big for a rocking-horse? You're not a very little boy any longer, you know," said his mother.

But Paul only gave a blue glare from his big, rather close-set eyes. He would speak to nobody when he was in full tilt. His mother watched him with an anxious expression on her face.

At last he suddenly stopped forcing his horse into the mechanical gallop, and slid down.

"Well, I got there!" he announced fiercely, his blue eyes still flaring, and his sturdy long legs straddling apart.

"Where did you get to?" asked his mother.

"Where I wanted to go," he flared back at her.

"That's right, son!" said Uncle Oscar. "Don't you stop till you get there. What's the horse's name?"

"He doesn't have a name," said the boy.

"Gets on without all right?" asked the uncle.

"Well, he has different names. He was called Sansovino last week."

"Sansovino, eh? Won the Ascot.[2] How did you know his name?"

"He always talks about horse-races with Bassett," said Joan.

2. Major annual horse race, as are the Lincoln, Grand National, Derby, and Lincolnshire, mentioned later.

The uncle was delighted to find that his small nephew was posted with all the racing news. Bassett, the young gardener, who had been wounded in the left foot in the war and had got his present job through Oscar Cresswell, whose batman[3] he had been, was a perfect blade of the "turf."[4] He lived in the racing events, and the small boy lived with him.

Oscar Cresswell got it all from Bassett.

"Master Paul comes and asks me, so I can't do more than tell him, sir," said Bassett, his face terribly serious, as if he were speaking of religious matters.

"And does he ever put anything on a horse he fancies?"

"Well—I don't want to give him away—he's a young sport, a fine sport, sir. Would you mind asking him himself? He sort of takes a pleasure in it, and perhaps he'd feel I was giving him away, sir, if you don't mind."

Bassett was serious as a church.

The uncle went back to his nephew and took him off for a ride in the car.

"Say, Paul, old man, do you ever put anything on a horse?" the uncle asked.

The boy watched the handsome man closely.

"Why, do you think I oughtn't to?" he parried.

"Not a bit of it! I thought perhaps you might give me a tip for the Lincoln."

The car sped on into the country, going down to Uncle Oscar's place in Hampshire.[5]

"Honour bright?" said the nephew.

"Honour bright, son!" said the uncle.

"Well, then, Daffodil."

"Daffodil! I doubt it, sonny. What about Mirza?"

"I only know the winner," said the boy. "That's Daffodil."

"Daffodil, eh?"

There was a pause. Daffodil was an obscure horse comparatively.

"Uncle!"

"Yes, son?"

"You won't let it go any further, will you? I promised Bassett."

"Bassett be damned, old man! What's he got to do with it?"

"We're partners. We've been partners from the first. Uncle, he lent me my first five shillings, which I lost. I promised him, honour bright, it was only between me and him; only you gave me that ten-shilling note I started winning with, so I thought you were lucky. You won't let it go any further, will you?"

3. Orderly. 4. I.e., horse-racing fan. 5. County in southern England.

The boy gazed at his uncle from those big, hot, blue eyes, set rather close together. The uncle stirred and laughed uneasily.

"Right you are, son! I'll keep your tip private. Daffodil, eh? How much are you putting on him?"

"All except twenty pounds," said the boy. "I keep that in reserve."

The uncle thought it a good joke.

"You keep twenty pounds in reserve, do you, you young romancer? What are you betting, then?"

"I'm betting three hundred," said the boy, gravely. "But it's between you and me, Uncle Oscar! Honour bright?"

The uncle burst into a roar of laughter.

"It's between you and me all right, you young Nat Gould,"[6] he said, laughing. "But where's your three hundred?"

"Bassett keeps it for me. We're partners."

"You are, are you! And what is Bassett putting on Daffodil?"

"He won't go quite as high as I do, I expect. Perhaps he'll go a hundred and fifty."

"What, pennies?" laughed the uncle.

"Pounds," said the child, with a surprised look at his uncle. "Bassett keeps a bigger reserve than I do."

Between wonder and amusement Uncle Oscar was silent. He pursued the matter no further, but he determined to take his nephew with him to the Lincoln races.

"Now, son," he said, "I'm putting twenty on Mirza, and I'll put five for you on any horse you fancy. What's your pick?"

"Daffodil, uncle."

"No, not the fiver on Daffodil!"

"I should if it was my own fiver," said the child.

"Good! Good! Right you are! A fiver for me and a fiver for you on Daffodil."

The child had never been to a race-meeting before, and his eyes were blue fire. He pursed his mouth tight, and watched. A Frenchman just in front had put his money on Lancelot. Wild with excitement, he flayed his arms up and down, yelling *"Lancelot! Lancelot!"* in his French accent.

Daffodil came in first, Lancelot second, Mirza third. The child, flushed and with eyes blazing, was curiously serene. His uncle brought him four five-pound notes, four to one.

"What am I to do with these?" he cried, waving them before the boy's eyes.

"I suppose we'll talk to Bassett," said the boy. "I expect I have

6. English writer and journalist (1857–1919), the author of more than a hundred popular novels about horse-racing.

fifteen hundred now; and twenty in reserve; and this twenty."

His uncle studied him for some moments.

"Look here, son!" he said. "You're not serious about Bassett and that fifteen hundred, are you?"

"Yes, I am. But it's between you and me, uncle. Honour bright!"

"Honour bright all right, son! But I must talk to Bassett."

"If you'd like to be a partner, uncle, with Bassett and me, we could all be partners. Only, you'd have to promise, honour bright, uncle, not to let it go beyond us three. Bassett and I are lucky, and you must be lucky, because it was your ten shillings I started winning with. . . ."

Uncle Oscar took both Bassett and Paul into Richmond Park for an afternoon, and there they talked.

"It's like this, you see, sir," Bassett said. "Master Paul would get me talking about racing events, spinning yarns, you know, sir. And he was always keen on knowing if I'd made or if I'd lost. It's about a year since, now, that I put five shillings on Blush of Dawn for him—and we lost. Then the luck turned, with the ten shillings he had from you, that we put on Singhalese. And since that time, it's been pretty steady, all things considering. What do you say, Master Paul?"

"We're all right when we're sure," said Paul. "It's when we're not quite sure that we go down."

"Oh, but we're careful then," said Bassett.

"But when are you *sure?*" smiled Uncle Oscar.

"It's Master Paul, sir," said Bassett, in a secret, religious voice. "It's as if he had it from heaven. Like Daffodil, now, for the Lincoln. That was as sure as eggs."

"Did you put anything on Daffodil?" asked Oscar Cresswell.

"Yes, sir. I made my bit."

"And my nephew?"

Bassett was obstinately silent, looking at Paul.

"I made twelve hundred, didn't I, Bassett? I told uncle I was putting three hundred on Daffodil."

"That's right," said Bassett, nodding.

"But where's the money?" asked the uncle.

"I keep it safe locked up, sir. Master Paul he can have it any minute he likes to ask for it."

"What, fifteen hundred pounds?"

"And twenty! And *forty*, that is, with the twenty he made on the course."

"It's amazing!" said the uncle.

"If Master Paul offers you to be partners, sir, I would, if I were you; if you'll excuse me," said Bassett.

Oscar Cresswell thought about it.

"I'll see the money," he said.

They drove home again, and sure enough, Bassett came round to the garden-house with fifteen hundred pounds in notes. The twenty pounds reserve was left with Joe Glee, in the Turf Commission deposit.

"You see, it's all right, uncle, when I'm *sure!* Then we go strong, for all we're worth. Don't we, Bassett?"

"We do that, Master Paul"

"And when are you sure?" said the uncle, laughing.

"Oh, well, sometimes I'm *absolutely* sure, like about Daffodil," said the boy; "and sometimes I have an idea; and sometimes I haven't even an idea, have I, Bassett? Then we're careful, because we mostly go down."

"You do, do you! And when you're sure, like about Daffodil, what makes you sure, sonny?"

"Oh, well, I don't know," said the boy uneasily. "I'm sure, you know, uncle; that's all."

"It's as if he had it from heaven, sir," Bassett reiterated.

"I should say so!" said the uncle.

But he became a partner. And when the Leger was coming on, Paul was "sure" about Lively Spark, which was a quite inconsiderable horse. The boy insisted on putting a thousand on the horse, Bassett went for five hundred, and Oscar Cresswell two hundred. Lively Spark came in first, and the betting had been ten to one against him. Paul had made ten thousand.

"You see," he said, "I was absolutely sure of him."

Even Oscar Cresswell had cleared two thousand.

"Look here, son," he said, "this sort of thing makes me nervous."

"It needn't, uncle! Perhaps I shan't be sure again for a long time."

"But what are you going to do with your money?" asked the uncle.

"Of course," said the boy, "I started it for mother. She said she had no luck, because father is unlucky, so I thought if *I* was lucky, it might stop whispering."

"What might stop whispering?"

"Our house. I *hate* our house for whispering."

"What does it whisper?"

"Why—why"—the boy fidgeted—"why, I don't know. But it's always short of money, you know, uncle."

"I know it, son, I know it."

"You know people send mother writs,[7] don't you, uncle?"

"I'm afraid I do," said the uncle.

"And then the house whispers, like people laughing at you behind your back. It's awful, that is! I thought if I was lucky . . ."

7. Legal threats.

"You might stop it," added the uncle.

The boy watched him with big blue eyes, that had an uncanny cold fire in them, and he said never a word.

"Well, then!" said the uncle. "What are we doing?"

"I shouldn't like mother to know I was lucky," said the boy.

"Why not, son?"

"She'd stop me."

"I don't think she would."

"Oh!"—and the boy writhed in an odd way—"I *don't* want her to know, uncle."

"All right, son! We'll manage it without her knowing."

They managed it very easily. Paul, at the other's suggestion, handed over five thousand pounds to his uncle, who deposited it with the family lawyer, who was then to inform Paul's mother that a relative had put five thousand pounds into his hands, which sum was to be paid out a thousand pounds at a time, on the mother's birthday, for the next five years.

"So she'll have a birthday present of a thousand pounds for five successive years," said Uncle Oscar. "I hope it won't make it all the harder for her later."

Paul's mother had her birthday in November. The house had been "whispering" worse than ever lately, and, even in spite of his luck, Paul could not bear up against it. He was very anxious to see the effect of the birthday letter, telling his mother about the thousand pounds.

When there were no visitors, Paul now took his meals with his parents, as he was beyond the nursery control. His mother went into town nearly every day. She had discovered that she had an odd knack of sketching furs and dress materials, so she worked secretly in the studio of a friend who was the chief "artist" for the leading drapers. She drew the figures of ladies in furs and ladies in silk and sequins for the newspaper advertisements. This young woman artist earned several thousand pounds a year, but Paul's mother only made several hundreds, and she was again dissatisfied. She so wanted to be first in something, and she did not succeed, even in making sketches for drapery advertisements.

She was down to breakfast on the morning of her birthday. Paul watched her face as she read her letters. He knew the lawyer's letter. As his mother read it, her face hardened and became more expressionless. Than a cold, determined look came on her mouth. She hid the letter under the pile of others, and said not a word about it.

"Didn't you have anything nice in the post for your birthday, mother?" said Paul.

"Quite moderately nice," she said, her voice cold and absent.

She went away to town without saying more.

But in the afternoon Uncle Oscar appeared. He said Paul's mother had had a long interview with the lawyer, asking if the whole five thousand could not be advanced at once, as she was in debt.

"What do you think, uncle?" said the boy.

"I leave it to you, son."

"Oh, let her have it, then! We can get some more with the other," said the boy.

"A bird in the hand is worth two in the bush, laddie!" said Uncle Oscar.

"But I'm sure to *know* for the Grand National; or the Lincolnshire; or else the Derby. I'm sure to know for *one* of them," said Paul.

So Uncle Oscar signed the agreement, and Paul's mother touched the whole five thousand. Then something very curious happened. The voices in the house suddenly went mad, like a chorus of frogs on a spring evening. There were certain new furnishings, and Paul had a tutor. He was *really* going to Eton,[8] his father's school, in the following autumn. There were flowers in the winter, and a blossoming of the luxury Paul's mother had been used to. And yet the voices in the house, behind the sprays of mimosa and almond blossom, and from under the piles of iridescent cushions, simply trilled and screamed in a sort of ecstasy: "There *must* be more money! Oh-h-h; there *must* be more money Oh, now, now-w! Now-w-w—there *must* be more money!—more than ever! More than ever!"

It frightened Paul terribly. He studied away at his Latin and Greek with his tutors. But his intense hours were spent with Bassett. The Grand National had gone by: he had not "known," and had lost a hundred pounds. Summer was at hand. He was in agony for the Lincoln. But even for the Lincoln he didn't "know," and he lost fifty pounds. He became wild-eyed and strange, as if something were going to explode in him.

"Let it alone, son! Don't you bother about it!" urged Uncle Oscar. But it was as if the boy couldn't really hear what his uncle was saying.

"I've got to know for the Derby! I've got to know for the Derby!" the child reiterated, his big blue eyes blazing with a sort of madness.

His mother noticed how overwrought he was.

"You'd better go to the seaside. Wouldn't you like to go now to the seaside, instead of waiting? I think you'd better," she said, looking down at him anxiously, her heart curiously heavy because of him.

But the child lifted his uncanny blue eyes.

8. Famous "public" (i.e., private) school where the sons of upper-class families are prepared for a university—usually Oxford or Cambridge.

"I couldn't possibly go before the Derby, mother!" he said. "I couldn't possibly!"

"Why not?" she said, her voice becoming heavy when she was opposed. "Why not? You can still go from the seaside to see the Derby with your Uncle Oscar, if that's what you wish. No need for you to wait here. Besides, I think you care too much about these races. It's a bad sign. My family has been a gambling family, and you won't know till you grow up how much damage it has done. But it has done damage. I shall have to send Bassett away, and ask Uncle Oscar not to talk racing to you, unless you promise to be reasonable about it; go away to the seaside and forget it. You're all nerves!"

"I'll do what you like, mother, so long as you don't send me away till after the Derby," the boy said.

"Send you away from where? Just from this house?"

"Yes," he said, gazing at her.

"Why, you curious child, what makes you care about this house so much, suddenly? I never knew you loved it."

He gazed at her without speaking. He had a secret within a secret, something he had not divulged, even to Bassett or to his Uncle Oscar.

But his mother, after standing undecided and a little bit sullen for some moments, said:

"Very well, then! Don't go to the seaside till after the Derby, if you don't wish it. But promise me you won't let your nerves go to pieces. Promise you won't think so much about horse-racing and events, as you call them!"

"Oh, no," said the boy casually. "I won't think much about them, mother. You needn't worry. I wouldn't worry, mother, if I were you."

"If you were me and I were you," said his mother, "I wonder what we *should* do!"

"But you know you needn't worry, mother, don't you?" the boy repeated.

"I should be awfully glad to know it," she said wearily.

"Oh, well, you *can*, you know. I mean, you *ought* to know you needn't worry," he insisted.

"Ought I? Then I'll see about it," she said.

Paul's secret of secrets was his wooden horse, that which had no name. Since he was emancipated from a nurse and a nursery-governess, he had had his rocking-horse removed to his own bedroom at the top of the house.

"Surely, you're too big for a rocking-horse!" his mother had remonstrated.

"Well, you see, mother, till I can have a *real* horse, I like to have *some* sort of animal about," had been his quaint answer.

"Do you feel he keeps you company?" she laughed.

"Oh, yes! He's very good, he always keeps me company, when I'm there," said Paul.

So the horse, rather shabby, stood in an arrested prance in the boy's bedroom.

The Derby was drawing near, and the boy grew more and more tense. He hardly heard what was spoken to him, he was very frail, and his eyes were really uncanny. His mother had sudden strange seizures of uneasiness about him. Sometimes, for half-an-hour, she would feel a sudden anxiety about him that was almost anguish. She wanted to rush to him at once, and know he was safe.

Two nights before the Derby, she was at a big party in town, when one of her rushes of anxiety about her boy, her first-born, gripped her heart till she could hardly speak. She fought with the feeling, might and main, for she believed in common-sense. But it was too strong. She had to leave the dance and go downstairs to telephone to the country. The children's nursery-governess was terribly surprised and startled at being rung up in the night.

"Are the children all right, Miss Wilmot?"

"Oh, yes, they are quite all right."

"Master Paul? Is he all right?"

"He went to bed as right as a trivet. Shall I run up and look at him?"

"No," said Paul's mother reluctantly. "No! Don't trouble. It's all right. Don't sit up. We shall be home fairly soon." She did not want her son's privacy intruded upon.

"Very good," said the governess.

It was about one o'clock when Paul's mother and father drove up to their house. All was still. Paul's mother went to her room and slipped off her white fur cloak. She had told her maid not to wait up for her. She heard her husband downstairs, mixing a whisky-and-soda.

And then, because of the strange anxiety at her heart, she stole upstairs to her son's room. Noiselessly she went along the upper corridor. Was there a faint noise? What was it?

She stood, with arrested muscles, outside his door, listening. There was a strange, heavy, and yet not loud noise. Her heart stood still. It was a soundless noise, yet rushing and powerful. Something huge, in violent, hushed motion. What was it? What in God's name was it? She ought to know. She felt that she knew the noise. She knew what it was.

Yet she could not place it. She couldn't say what it was. And on and on it went, like a madness.

Softly, frozen with anxiety and fear, she turned the door-handle.

The room was dark. Yet in the space near the window, she heard and saw something plunging to and fro. She gazed in fear and amazement.

Then suddenly she switched on the light, and saw her son, in his green pyjamas, madly surging on the rocking-horse. The blaze of light suddenly lit him up, as he urged the wooden horse, and lit her up, as she stood, blonde, in her dress of pale green and crystal, in the doorway.

"Paul!" she cried. "Whatever are you doing?"

"It's Malabar!" he screamed, in a powerful, strange voice. "It's Malabar!"

His eyes blazed at her for one strange and senseless second, as he ceased urging his wooden horse. Then he fell with a crash to the ground, and she, all her tormented motherhood flooding upon her, rushed to gather him up.

But he was unconscious, and unconscious he remained, with some brain-fever. He talked and tossed, and his mother sat stonily by his side.

"Malabar! It's Malabar! Bassett, Bassett, I *know!* It's Malabar!"

So the child cried, trying to get up and urge the rocking-horse that gave him his inspiration.

"What does he mean by Malabar?" asked the heart-frozen mother.

"I don't know," said the father stonily.

"What does he mean by Malabar?" she asked her brother Oscar.

"It's one of the horses running for the Derby," was the answer.

And, in spite of himself, Oscar Cresswell spoke to Bassett, and himself put a thousand on Malabar: at fourteen to one.

The third day of the illness was critical: they were waiting for a change. The boy, with his rather long, curly hair, was tossing ceaselessly on the pillow. He neither slept nor regained consciousness, and his eyes were like blue stones. His mother sat, feeling her heart had gone, turned actually into a stone.

In the evening, Oscar Cresswell did not come, but Bassett sent a message, saying could he come up for one moment, just one moment? Paul's mother was very angry at the intrusion, but on second thought she agreed. The boy was the same. Perhaps Bassett might bring him to consciousness.

The gardener, a shortish fellow with a little brown moustache, and sharp little brown eyes, tip-toed into the room, touched his imaginary cap to Paul's mother, and stole to the bedside, staring with glittering, smallish eyes, at the tossing, dying child.

"Master Paul!" he whispered. "Master Paul! Malabar came in first all right, a clean win. I did as you told me. You've made over seventy thousand pounds, you have; you've got over eighty thousand. Malabar came in all right, Master Paul."

"Malabar! Malabar! Did I say Malabar, mother? Did I say Malabar? Do you think I'm lucky, mother? I knew Malabar, didn't I? Over eighty thousand pounds! I call that lucky, don't you, mother? Over eighty thousand pounds! I knew, didn't I know I knew! Malabar came in all right. If I ride my horse till I'm sure, then I tell you, Bassett, you can go as high as you like. Did you go for all you were worth, Bassett?"

"I went a thousand on it, Master Paul."

"I never told you, mother, that if I can ride my horse, and *get there*, then I'm absolutely sure—oh absolutely! Mother, did I ever tell you? I *am* lucky!"

"No, you never did," said the mother.

But the boy died in the night.

And even as he lay dead, his mother heard her brother's voice saying to her: "My God, Hester, you're eighty-odd thousand to the good, and a poor devil of a son to the bad. But, poor devil, poor devil, he's best gone out of a life where he rides his rocking-horse to find a winner."

---

1. What does the rocking horse represent? Is it significant that at one point it is called a "shining modern" rocking horse?
2. Why isn't the mother pleased by her birthday present? Discuss her character and her relation to her son.
3. What is Uncle Oscar's role in the story? Is his last comment cynical?
4. How do you interpret the "whispering" of the house? Is this a reference to something supernatural?
5. The story brings into conflict different meanings of *luck*. Discuss.
6. What is the moral of the story? Is the moral more prominent and important than in other stories you have read in this text?

Ursula K. Le Guin

Le Guin (1929–) was born in Berkeley, California. She was educated at Radcliffe College and Columbia University and spent a year as a Fulbright student in Paris, where she married the historian Charles Le Guin. She has won an extraordinary number of science fiction prizes, and her thematically charged use of the medium has caught the mood of concerned readers of the Seventies and Eighties. Some of her novels are A Wizard of Earthsea *(1968),* The Tombs of Atuan *(1971),* The Farthest Shore *(1972) (which comprise the* Earthsea Trilogy*),* The Left Hand of Darkness *(1969),* The Dispossessed *(1974),* The Beginning Place *(1980), and* Always Coming Home *(1985). Some of her shorter works have been collected in* The Wind's Twelve Quarters *(1975) and* Orsinian Tales *(1976).*

The Ones Who Walk Away from Omelas

(Variations on a Theme by William James)[1]

With a clamor of bells that set the swallows soaring, the Festival of Summer came to the city Omelas, bright-towered by the sea. The rigging of the boats in harbor sparkled with flags. In the streets between houses with red roofs and painted walls, between old moss-grown gardens and under avenues of trees, past great parks and public buildings, processions moved. Some were decorous: old people in long stiff robes of mauve and grey, grave master workmen, quiet, merry women carrying their babies and chatting as they walked. In other streets the music beat faster, a shimmering of gong and tambourine, and the people went dancing, the procession was a dance. Children dodged in and out, their high calls rising like the swallows' crossing flights over the music and the singing. All the processions wound towards the north side of the city, where on the great water-meadow called the Green Fields boys and girls, naked in the bright air, with mud-stained feet and ankles and long, lithe arms, exercised their restive horses before the race. The horses wore no gear at all but a halter without bit.

1. American philosopher and experimental psychologist (1842–1910).

Their manes were braided with streamers of silver, gold, and green. They flared their nostrils and pranced and boasted to one another; they were vastly excited, the horse being the only animal who has adopted our ceremonies as his own. Far off to the north and west the mountains stood up half encircling Omelas on her bay. The air of morning was so clear that the snow still crowning the Eighteen Peaks burned with white-gold fire across the miles of sunlit air, under the dark blue of the sky. There was just enough wind to make the banners that marked the racecourse snap and flutter now and then. In the silence of the broad green meadows one could hear the music winding through the city streets, farther and nearer and ever approaching, a cheerful faint sweetness of the air that from time to time trembled and gathered together and broke out into the great joyous clanging of the bells.

Joyous! How is one to tell about joy? How describe the citizens of Omelas?

They were not simple folk, you see, though they were happy. But we do not say the words of cheer much any more. All smiles have become archaic. Given a description such as this one tends to make certain assumptions. Given a description such as this one tends to look next for the King, mounted on a splendid stallion and surrounded by his noble knights, or perhaps in a golden litter borne by great-muscled slaves. But there was no king. They did ot use swords, or keep slaves. They were not barbarians. I do not know the rules and laws of their society, but I suspect that they were singularly few. As they did without monarchy and slavery, so they also got on without the stock exchange, the advertisement, the secret police, and the bomb. Yet I repeat that these were not simple folk, not dulcet shepherds, noble savages, bland utopians. They were not less complex than us. The trouble is that we have a bad habit, encouraged by pedants and sophisticates, of considering happiness as something rather stupid. Only pain is intellectual, only evil interesting. This is the treason of the artist: a refusal to admit the banality of evil and the terrible boredom of pain. If you can't lick 'em, join 'em. If it hurts, repeat it. But to praise despair is to condemn delight, to embrace violence is to lose hold of everything else. We have almost lost hold, we can no longer describe a happy man, nor make any celebration of joy. How can I tell you about the people of Omelas? They were not naïve and happy children—though their children were, in fact, happy. They were mature, intelligent, passionate adults whose lives were not wretched. O miracle! but I wish I could describe it better. I wish I could convince you. Omelas sounds in my words like a city in a fairy tale, long ago and far away, once upon a time. Perhaps it would be best if you imagined it as your own fancy bids, assuming it will rise to the occasion, for certainly I cannot suit you all. For instance, how about technology? I think that there would be no cars or helicopters in and above the streets; this follows from the fact that the people of Omelas are happy people. Happiness is based on a just discrimination of what is necessary, what is neither necessary nor destructive, and what is destructive. In the middle category, however—that of the unnecessary but undestructive, that of comfort, luxury, exuberance, etc.—they could perfectly well have central heating, subway trains, washing machines, and all kinds of marvelous devices not yet invented here, floating light-sources, fuelless power, a cure for the common cold. Or they could have none of that: it doesn't matter. As you like it. I incline to think that people from towns up and down the coast have been coming in to Omelas during the last days before the Festival on very fast little trains and double-decked trams, and that the train station of Omelas is actually the handsomest building in town, though plainer than the magnificent Farmers' Market. But even granted trains, I fear that Omelas so far strikes some of you as goody-goody. Smiles, bells, parades, horses, bleh. If so, please add an orgy. If an orgy would help, don't hesitate. Let us not, however, have temples from which issue beautiful nude priests and priestesses already half in ecstasy and ready to copulate with any man or woman, lover or stranger, who desires union with the deep godhead of the blood, although that was my first idea. But really it would be better not to have any temples in Omelas—at least, not manned temples. Religion yes, clergy no. Surely the beautiful nudes can just wander about, offering themselves like divine soufflés to the hunger of the needy and the rapture of the flesh. Let them join the processions. Let tambourines be struck above the copulations, and the glory of desire be proclaimed upon the gongs, and (a not unimportant point) let the offspring of these delightful rituals be beloved and looked after by all. One thing I know there is none of in Omelas is guilt. But what else should there be? I thought at first there were no drugs, but that is puritanical. For those who like it, the faint insistent sweetness of *drooz* may perfume the ways of the city, *drooz* which first brings a great lightness and brilliance to the mind and limbs, and then after some hours a dreamy languor, and wonderful visions at last of the very arcana and inmost secrets of the Universe, as well as exciting the pleasure of sex beyond all belief; and it is not habit-forming. For more modest tastes I think there ought to be beer. What else, what else belongs in the joyous city? The sense of victory, surely, the celebration of courage. But as we did without clergy, let us do without soldiers. The joy built upon successful slaughter is not the right kind of joy; it will not do; it is fearful and it is trivial. A boundless and generous contentment, a magnanimous triumph felt not against some outer enemy but in communion with the finest and fairest in the souls of all men everywhere and the splendor of the world's summer: this is what swells the hearts of the people of Omelas, and the victory they celebrate is that of life. I really don't think many of them need to take *drooz*.

Most of the procession have reached the Green Fields by now. A marvelous smell of cooking goes forth from the red and blue tents of the provisioners. The faces of small children are amiably sticky; in the benign grey beard of a man a couple of crumbs of rich pastry are entangled. The youths and girls have mounted their horses and are beginning to group around the starting line of the course. An old woman, small, fat, and laughing, is passing out flowers from a basket, and tall young men wear her flowers in their shining hair. A child of nine or ten sits at the edge of the crowd, alone, playing on a wooden flute. People pause to listen, and they smile, but they do not speak to him, for he never ceases playing and never sees them, his dark eyes wholly rapt in the sweet, thin magic of the tune.

He finishes, and slowly lowers his hands holding the wooden flute.

As if that little private silence were the signal, all at once a trumpet sounds from the pavilion near the starting line: imperious, melancholy, piercing. The horses rear on their slender legs, and some of them neigh in answer. Sober-faced, the young riders stroke the horses' necks and soothe them, whispering, "Quiet, quiet, there my beauty, my hope. . . ." They begin to form in rank along the starting line. The crowds along the racecourse are like a field of grass and flowers in the wind. The Festival of Summer has begun.

Do you believe? Do you accept the festival, the city, the joy? No? Then let me describe one more thing.

In a basement under one of the beautiful public buildings of Omelas, or perhaps in the cellar of one of its more spacious private homes, there is a room. It has one locked door, and no window. A little light seeps in dustily between cracks in the boards, secondhand from a cobwebbed window somewhere across the cellar. In one corner of the little room a couple of mops, with stiff, clotted, foul-smelling heads, stand near a rusty bucket. The floor is dirt, a little damp to the touch, as cellar dirt usually is. The room is about three paces long and two wide: a mere broom closet or disused tool room. In the room a child is sitting. It could be a boy or a girl. It looks about six, but actually is nearly ten. It is feeble-minded. Perhaps it was born defective, or perhaps it has become imbecile through fear, malnutrition, and neglect. It picks its nose and occasionally fumbles vaguely with its toes or genitals, as it sits hunched in the corner farthest from the bucket and the two mops. It is afraid of the mops. It finds them horrible. It shuts its eyes, but it knows the mops are still standing there; and the door is locked; and nobody will come. The door is always locked; and nobody ever comes, except that sometimes—the child has no understanding of time or interval—sometimes the door rattles terribly and opens, and a person, or several people, are there. One of them may come in and kick the child to make it stand up. The others never come close, but peer in at it with frightened, disgusted eyes. The food bowl and the water jug are hastily filled, the door is locked, the eyes disappear. The people at the door never say anything, but the child, who has not always lived in the tool room, and can remember sunlight and its mother's voice, sometimes speaks. "I will be good," it says. "Please let me out. I will be good!" They never answer. The child used to scream for help at night, and cry a good deal, but now it only makes a kind of whining, "eh-haa, eh-haa," and it speaks less and less often. It is so thin there are no calves to its legs; its belly protrudes; it lives on a half-bowl of corn meal and grease a day. It is naked. Its buttocks and thighs are a mass of festered sores, as it sits in its own excrement continually.

They all know it is there, all the people of Omelas. Some of them have come to see it, others are content merely to know it is there. They all know that it has to be there. Some of them understand why, and some do not, but they all understand that their happiness, the beauty of their city, the tenderness of their friendships, the health of their children, the wisdom of their scholars, the skill of their makers, even the abundance of their harvest and the kindly weathers of their skies, depend wholly on this child's abominable misery.

This is usually explained to children when they are between eight and twelve, whenever they seem capable of understanding; and most of those who come to see the child are young people, though often enough an adult comes, or comes back, to see the child. No matter how well the matter has been explained to them, these young spectators are always shocked and sickened at the sight. They feel disgust, which they had thought themselves superior to. They feel anger, outrage, impotence, despite all the explanations. They would like to do something for the child. But there is nothing they can do. If the child were brought up into the sunlight out of the vile place, if it were cleaned and fed and comforted, that would be a good thing, indeed; but if it were done, in that day and hour all the prosperity and beauty and delight of Omelas would wither and be destroyed. Those are the terms. To exchange all the goodness and grace of every life in Omelas for that single, small improvement: to throw away the happiness of thousands for the chance of the happiness of one: that would be to let guilt within the walls indeed.

The terms are strict and absolute; there may not even be a kind word spoken to the child.

Often the young people go home in tears, or in a tearless rage, when they have seen the child and faced this terrible paradox. They may brood over it for weeks or years. But as time goes on they begin to realize that even if the child could be released, it would not get much good of its freedom: a little vague pleasure of warmth and food, no doubt, but little more. It is too degraded and imbecile to know any real joy. It has been afraid too long ever to be free of fear. Its habits are too uncouth for it to respond to humane treatment. Indeed, after so long it would probably be wretched without walls about it to protect it, and darkness for its eyes, and its own excrement to sit in. Their tears at the bitter injustice dry when they begin to perceive the terrible justice of reality, and to accept it. Yet it is their tears and anger, the trying of their generosity and the acceptance of their helplessness, which are perhaps the true source of the splendor of their lives. Theirs is no vapid, irresponsible happiness. They know that they, like the child, are not free. They know compassion. It is the existence of the child, and their knowledge of its existence, that makes possible the nobility of their architecture, the poignancy of their music, the profundity of their science. It is because of the child that they are so gentle with children. They know that if the wretched one were not there snivelling in the dark, the other one, the flute-player, could make no joyful music as the young riders line up in their beauty for the race in the sunlight of the first morning of summer.

Now do you believe in them? Are they not more credible? But there is one more thing to tell, and this is quite incredible.

At times one of the adolescent girls or boys who go to see the child does not go home to weep or rage, does not, in fact, go home at all. Sometimes also a man or woman much older falls silent for a day or two, and then leaves home. These people go out into the street, and walk down the street alone. They keep walking, and walk straight out of the city of Omelas, through the beautiful gates. They keep walking across the farmlands of Omelas. Each one goes alone, youth or girl, man or woman. Night falls; the traveler must pass down village streets, between the houses with yellow-lit windows, and on out into the darkness of the fields. Each alone, they go west or north, towards the mountains. They go on. They leave Omelas, they walk ahead into the darkness, and they do not come back. The place they go towards is a place even less imaginable to most of us than the city of happiness. I cannot describe it at all. It is possible that it does not exist. But they seem to know where they are going, the ones who walk away from Omelas.

---

1. Comment on the narrator's assertion that happiness "is based on a just discrimination of what is necessary."
2. Why is the narrator so uncertain about what Omelas looks like and the kind of technology it depends on? Why so tentative about describing the qualities of a happy community life?

3. Why does the presence of the tormented child and the attitude of the citizens toward it make the imaginary picture of Omelas more believable?
4. Is the narrator correct in saying "we have a bad habit . . . of considering happiness as something rather stupid"?
5. Why is the destination of those who reject Omelas and walk away "even less imaginable than the city of happiness"? Can you give a name to this other place?

Ella Leffland

Leffland (1931–) was born in Martinez, California, grew up there, and attended San Jose State College. Her stories appeared in a wide variety of periodicals before being collected in Last Courtesies *(1980). She is the author of three novels,* Mrs. Munck *(1970),* Love Out of Season *(1974), and* Rumors of Peace *(1985).*

The Linden Tree

In the early years there had been passion, but now they were just a couple who had grown old together. The last twenty years they had owned a rooming house, where they lived contentedly on the ground floor with their cat, Baby.

Giulio was a great putterer. You could always see him sweeping the front steps or polishing the doorknobs, stopping to gossip with the neighbors. He was a slight, pruny man of sixty-eight, perfectly bald, dressed in heavy trousers, a bright sports shirt with a necktie, and an old man's sweater-jacket, liver-colored and hanging straight to the knees. He had a thick Italian accent and gesticulated wildly when he was excited.

George was quite different. Everything about him was slow and solid, touched by grandeur. Though he was a Negro from the Midwest, he spoke with an accent that sounded British, yet not exactly. He was seventy-four, but looked much younger, with a hard body and a hard face with only a few deep fissures in it. Giulio was a neat dresser, but George was attired. His perfectly creased trousers, his crisp white shirt, smoothly knotted tie, and gray sleeveless sweater seemed out of place in the stuffy little flat.

A home is usually the wife's creation, and so it was in their case. The doilies, the vases with their wax flowers, the prints of saints hanging among gaudy floral calendars—all these were Giulio's. George's contribution was less concrete but more important. He made their life possible, dealing with the rents and taxes, attending to the heavy chores, ousting tenants who drank or brawled. If Giulio were to run the building he would soon come to grief, for he had no real sense of work, and as for the rents, it was all he could do to add two digits together. In addition, he was fussy and fault-finding, so that he often took a dislike to perfectly good tenants, yet countenanced glib bullies.

They were a nicely balanced couple, and for years had been happy. When they were young they had had their troubles—living quarters had been hard to find not only because of George's color, but because of their relationship. In those days Giulio had had fetching ways, too obvious to be ignored. But gradually he passed into a fussy dotage, and now people thought of the pair merely as two lonely old men who lived together. George's color no longer presented problems now that he had proved what was not necessarily demanded of those who asked for proof: that he was a responsible man, an asset to the neighborhood. His building was the best kept on the block, his rents reasonable, his tenants, for the most part, permanent. He would not rent to the fly-by-night element that was slowly invading the district.

The tenants consisted of a pair of raddled, gadabout sisters, a World War I veteran with one leg, and a few clerks and students. Giulio regaled George with facts about these people he gleaned by snooping through their rooms in their absence, and George put him down for this, even threatened him, but it did no good. And in any case, the tenants did not seem to care; there was something so simple about Giulio that his spying was like that of a mouse or a bird. They called him Aunty Nellie (his last name being Antonelli), and the younger ones sometimes invited him into their rooms so that his teeth might be enjoyed. These were ill-fitting, too large for his mouth, and clicked through his speech. When he grew excited, they slipped out of place, at which he would pause in a natural, businesslike way to jam them back in before going on.

Giulio was forever dragging the carpet sweeper up and down the halls, looking for an ear to gossip in. George, on the other hand, talked very little. Only tenants who had lived there a long time got to know him at all, when, once in a great while, he would invite them in for a glass of sherry when they came to pay the rent.

In his flat, the tenants found George to be a different man, less aloof and forbidding. Sitting there with Giulio and Baby, the cat, he had something patient, indulgent, altogether loving in his face. Giulio looked with pride at him, glancing now and then at the guest, as though to say: Isn't he wonderful? Sometimes he would go so far as to confess, "I no good at the paper work, but George, George, he *smart*." Or, "We live together fifty years, never a yell, always happy." And George would give him a look to show him that he was saying too much, and then Giulio would sulk and refuse to rejoin the conversation. But the next day he would be the same as ever, whirling creakily around the steps with his broom, or around his garden with a green visor clamped to his head.

He had a shrine in the garden, with statues of the saints standing in sun-blanched profusion. He was an ardent Catholic, and there was no one with a greater collection of religious objects—rosaries and crosses and vestments, which he kept in his bureau drawer and brought out to enjoy their varied glass, wooden, and satin richness. But religious as he was, he would not divest his beloved garden of one fresh bloom for his saints. It was a skimpy garden, heavily bolstered with potted geraniums, and he was so proud of each green shoot that struggled through the hard ground, and attended its subsequent flowering with such worried care, that it was only when a flower had finally begun to wither on the stem that he would pluck it as an offering to his statues.

George understood this attitude and was properly grateful when once a year on his birthday he received a sacrifice of fresh daisies and marigolds. He was amused by Giulio's niggardliness toward the saints. He himself did not care about them. He, too, was a Catholic, but had become one only so that he and Giulio might be buried together. Two fully paid-for plots, side by side, awaited them under a linden tree in Our Lady of Mercy Cemetery just outside town. Whoever was the first to go, George because he was older, Giulio because he was frailer, the other would join him in due time. Giulio had vague visions of an afterlife. The older man did not. He had had a good life, everything considered, and he would be content to die and be done with when the time came, and have his bones rest by his friend's forever. Sometimes he thought of the linden tree and gave a satisfied nod.

But lately George had noticed something strange about Giulio. His large red ears seemed to have grown less red.

"Giulio," he said one day, "your ears don't seem to be as red as they used to be."

Giulio touched his ear. When he was young he had been sensitive about their largeness. "Nothing wrong with my ears," he said defensively.

"I'm not criticizing you, Giulio. I think it's just strange." And now he realized that some definite change had been taking place in his friend, but he could not put his finger on it. It was as though he were a little smaller. The jacket seemed to hang lower than it had.

Ah, well, he thought, we're both getting old.

A few days later, as Giulio was raking the leaves in the garden, he complained to George of shortness of breath, and there was the faintest touch of blue in his lips.

"Why don't you go to the doctor for a checkup?" Goerge asked as casually as he could.

Giulio shook his head and continued his raking.

That night, as Giulio was turning on the television set, he suddenly stepped back and dropped into a chair with his hand spread across his chest. "Help!" he shouted into the air. "Help!" and when his friend ran to his side, he gasped, "I gotta pain. Here! Here!" And his hand clutched at his heart so hard that the knuckles were white.

The next day George took him to the doctor, and sat by his side through all the tests. Giulio was terrified, but when it was all over and they came out of the doctor's office he seemed restored.

"See," he said, "I'm okay. The doctor he say no worry."

George's face did not reflect Giulio's good spirits. "I know he says not to worry, but . . ."

"He say no worry," Giulio repeated cheerfully.

But from then on Giulio was visited frequently by the paralyzing pains. He would stop what he was doing and crouch over, his eyes darting frenziedly in their sockets. If George was there he would hurry to his friend's side, but at these moments Giulio seemed totally alone even though his hand grasped George's arm. When it was over he would be stripped of his little ways; he would wander slowly around the room or stand for long moments looking at nothing. Patiently George would wait, and eventually the old Giulio returned. Uneasily, fretfully, he would say, "I no understand. Looka me, I never hurt a fly in all my life, and this pain, he come and scare me. It's not right."

"Well," George would venture soothingly, "if you'd just eat fewer starches and stop worrying, these pains would go away. You've got plenty of years ahead of you . . ."

"Plenty years?" Giulio would break in sharply. "I *know*, I *know* I got plenty years ahead. This pain, he no *important*, he just *scare* me."

In an effort to distract him, George broke a lifelong precedent and invited Myrna and Alice Heppleworth, the two aging sisters who lived on the third floor, down to the flat for the evening. He himself did not like women, but Giulio did, in a way that George could not understand. Giulio loved to gossip with them, and afterward delighted in describing their clothes and manners, which he usually found distressing. He was more interested in the Heppleworth sisters than in anyone else in the building, and always pursed his lips when he saw them going out with their rheumy escorts, and could never forget that he had once found a bottle of gin in a dresser drawer ostensibly given over to scarves and stockings.

The Heppleworth sisters came, drank all their wine, and turned the television set up as high as it would go. George grew rigid; Giulio went to bed. The sisters were not asked again.

It seemed to George that Giulio failed daily. His ears were as pale as his face, and this seemed particularly significant to George. He found himself suddenly looking at his friend to check his ears, and each time they looked whiter. He never discussed this with Giulio, because

Giulio refused to speak about his fears, as though not daring to give them authority by acknowledging them.

And then one morning Giulio gave up this pretense. As he was getting out of bed he had an attack, and when he recovered this time he let out a piercing wail and began to weep, banging his head from side to side. The rest of the day he spent immobile, wrapped from head to foot in a patchwork quilt.

Toward evening George made him get up and walk in the garden with him. George pointed to the flowers, praising them, and gently turned his friend's face to the shrine. The white plaster faces looked peaceful. Even he, George, felt it, and he realized that for weeks he had been in need of some comfort, something outside himself.

"Look," he said, and that was all, fearing to sound presumptuous, because the statues belonged to Giulio and the Church—he himself understood nothing of them.

Giulio looked without interest, and then, forgetting them, he took George's arm and his eyes swam with tears. "What can I do?" he asked. "What will happen?"

As they walked slowly back to the house he drew his lips back from his big false teeth and whispered, "I'm gonna die."

"No, no, don't think that way," George soothed, but he felt helpless, and resentful that his friend must go through this terror. And now that Giulio had said the words, his terror would grow, just as the pain of a bad tooth grows when you finally acknowledge the decay and are plunged into a constant probing of it with your tongue.

When they came back inside Giulio went straight to bed. George stood in the kitchen and looked at his face in the little mirror that hung on the wall. He feared Giulio would die this very minute in the bedroom as he was removing his carpet slippers, and he wanted with every muscle to run to him. But it would not do to become as hysterical as Giulio, and he stood still. Presently the sound of the bedsprings released a sigh from his throat. The flat was silent. He looked again at his face in the mirror. It was as though he were one person and the reflection another, and he was uneasy and embarrassed, and yet could not look away. He felt deeply aware of himself standing there, staring, and it seemed he was out of place, lost. He whirled around, catching his breath. He had felt entirely alone for the first time in fifty years.

The next day he decided to call for Father Salmon, the young priest from the neighborhood church Giulio attended. Father Salmon dropped in for friendly chats now and then, and Giulio liked him very much, so much, in fact, that the priest often had to silence him when he got carried away with intimate gossip.

A few days later the priest knocked on the door. He was horse-faced, with thinning hair and rimless glasses, and he was quiet and pleasant.

Giulio was wrapped up in his quilt in the armchair. He did not greet the priest with his usual beam of pleasure; he did not even smile.

"Well, Giulio," the priest said, "how are you feeling? I haven't seen you at church lately."

Giulio said at once, "Father, I'm dying."

"What is the trouble?" the priest asked gently.

"It's my heart," Giulio shot back, his hand scrounging around his shirtfront and fumbling with the buttons until it was clutching his bare chest. He looked as though he were prepared to pull the heart out for inspection. His eyes pleaded with the priest to set it right. The priest sat down next to him.

"What does your doctor say?" he asked.

"Oh, Father," Giulio moaned, "the doctor is a stupid. He never tell me one real thing. In and out and all around, around the bush. He no understand, but *I* understand—this heart, he gonna kill me. You think so, Father? What do you think? You think so?"

"Surely, Giulio," the priest replied, "you must accept the doctor's word. If he says there's no reason to fear . . ."

Giulio looked away, black with melancholy.

The priest sat silently for a moment, then began again. "Giulio, death is as natural as birth. Think of your flowers out there in the garden, how they grow from little seeds and then fade and fall—what could be more natural? God has been with you all your life, and He will not forsake you now . . ."

But Giulio, his eyes shutting tighter and tighter as the priest spoke, got up from his chair and crept into the bedroom, dragging his quilt behind him.

Afterward he said to George, "I no wanna see Father Salmon again."

"Father Salmon is trying to help," George told him.

Giulio shook his head, his fingers rubbing the area of his heart.

What a strange person he is, George thought, looking at him closely. All these years he has been immersed in the church, and now, suddenly, the church means nothing to him. He recalled a conversation he had overheard a few days ago as he was fixing a faulty burner in the second floor kitchen. Two of the students were going down the hall, talking. One had commented on Giulio's bad health. The other had replied, "Don't worry, Aunty Nellie could never do anything so profound as to die."

George had bristled, as he always did whenever anyone made fun of his friend—but it was true that Giulio was not profound. He liked pretty things, and the church gave him its rich symbols; he liked intimate conversation, and the church gave him patient Father Salmon; he liked the idea of an afterlife, and the church gave him that, too. He loved the church, but when you came right down to it, he believed only what he could see with his two eyes, and he could see only his blue lips and wasted face in the mirror. This oddly realistic attitude explained his stinginess toward the saints; they were, after all, only plaster. And yet when Baby had once jumped up on the shrine and relieved himself on St. Francis's foot, Giulio had screamed at the animal until the neighbors hung from the windows.

All these amiable contradictions in Giulio had been known to George for fifty years, and he had always believed that they would sustain his friend through everything. Now the contradictions were gone. All that was left in Giulio was the certainty of death. It made George feel forlorn, on the outside. He sensed that nothing could be set right, that Giulio would live consumed by fear until he died consumed by fear, and the linden tree would not mark two intertwined lives, but forever cast its shadow between two strangers.

They had met for the first time in front of the Minneapolis train station in the first decade of the century. George sat in the driver's seat of a Daimler, in his duster and goggles. His employer had gone inside to meet one Giulio Antonelli, just arrived from Calabria, nephew of the head gardener. When he emerged he had in tow a thin boy of eighteen dressed in a shabby suit and carrying a suitcase that looked like a wicker basket. He wore cherry-colored cigar bands on his fingers, and had a shoot of wilted wild flowers stuck through the buttonhole of his jacket. His eyes were red-rimmed; apparently he had been crying all the way from Calabria. Delicate and terrified, his cigar bands glittering hectically in the sunlight, he crawled into the Daimler and collapsed in a corner.

George had worked as a chauffeur and handyman on his employer's estate for five years, but was originally from an isolated Finnish farming community where God knows what fates had conspired to bring his parents, a bitter, quarreling, aloof, and extremely poor black couple. George became friends with only one thing native to that cold country, the stones that littered the fields. He could not say what attracted him to them, but he felt a great bond with them. When he was ten he built a wall of the stones. It was only a foot high and not very long, and there was nothing in the world for it to guard there in the middle of the empty field, but he knew he had discovered the proper use of the stones, and all his life he had the feeling he was that wall.

In Minneapolis, on the estate, he kept to himself. He liked the

Daimler, which he drove with authority, and the appearance of which on the streets caused people to gawk with admiration. He picked up his employer's speech habits, and this, combined with the Finnish accent he had absorbed, gave a peculiar, unplaceable ring to his words, which he relished, because it was his alone.

The Calabrian boy turned out to be a poor gardener, not because he was listless with homesickness, for that soon passed, but because he made favorites of certain flowers and would have nothing to do with the others. The tulips, for instance, he apparently considered stout and silly-looking, and he made disparaging faces at them. He liked the wild flowers that cropped up in odd corners.

George was fascinated by Giulio, although he did not like him. He reminded him of a woman. Women had never respected George's wall, at least a certain type of woman had not—the bold Finnish farm girls, some of the hired women here on the estate. He was well favored, and maybe there was something in his coloring, too, that attracted women, something tawny, reminiscent of the sun, here, where everyone else looked like a peeled banana. In any case, they were always after him. He was not flattered. He felt they were not interested in him as he knew himself, proud and valuable, but in some small part of him that they wanted for their own use, quickly, in a dark corner.

But Giulio, though girlish, had no boldness in him. He would leave the garden and lean against the garage door where George was polishing the Daimler. "*Bella, bella,*" he would murmur, and his face shone with a kind of radiant simplemindedness. There was no calculation in him—sometimes you could see him cocking his head and singing before the wild flowers in the garden. Watching George, the boy spoke foreign words rich in their tones of admiration, and his quick, glittering fingers—he had bought flashy rings with his pay—seemed anxious to catch the sun and make a present of it to the tall, mute figure in the gloom of the garage.

Two months after his arrival Giulio was fired. George, filled with fear for himself, feeling a great chasm opening before him, quit his job, and the two of them, with hardly a word between them, took the train to San Francisco, where Giulio had another uncle. All during the trip George asked himself: "Why am I doing this? Why am I going with him? I don't even like him. He's a silly, ridiculous person; there's something the matter with him."

They got off at the San Francisco depot, and before George was even introduced to the uncle, who stood waiting, he picked up his baggage and, without a word of farewell to Giulio, walked quickly away from him.

First he found odd jobs, and finally he wound up on Rincon Hill with another Daimler. On his half day off each week he would wander around the city, looking at the sights. Whenever he saw a quick, thin figure that reminded him of Giulio his heart would pound, and he would say to himself, "Thank God it's not Giulio, I don't want to see him again." And then he found that what had begun as a casual walk around the city was turning into a passionate weekly search. The day he caught sight of Giulio sadly and ineffectively constructing a pyramid of cabbages in a vegetable market, he had to restrain himself from throwing his arms around him.

Giulio's face had blanched with surprise when he looked up, and then his eyes had filled with a dazzling welcome, and he had extended his hand to his returned friend with a tenderness George never forgot.

They were together from then on. In time they bought a vegetable stand, and as a result of George's frugality and common sense he was able to save in spite of Giulio's extravagances. They worked and invested, and in thirty years they were able to buy, for cash, the old apartment building they now lived in. Life had always been strangely easy for them. They had been incapable of acknowledging affronts, even when they were refused lodgings or openly stared at on the street, and the last twenty years in the security of their own flat had been free from problems, satisfying in all ways.

Now Giulio moaned, "Oh, I gotta pain, I gotta pain."

George would take his hand and say, "I'm here, Giulio, I'm here."

But Giulio would look through him, as though he did not exist.

"Don't we *know* each other?" George finally exploded one day, causing Baby to speed under a table with his ears laid back. "Are we strangers after all these years?"

Giulio closed his eyes, involved with his fear.

George sighed, stroking his friend's hand, thin and waxy as a sliver of soap. "What are you thinking about now, this very minute, Giulio? You must tell me."

"I'm thinking of my dog," Giulio said, after a silence.

"What dog was that?" George asked softly.

"I had him in Nocera."

"And what about him?"

"He died, and my father he dug a hole and put him in." His lips turned down. "I dug him up later, I was lonely for him."

"What a foolish thing to do, my poor Giulio."

"His own mother wouldn'a wanted him. Bones and worms . . ."

"Hush, Giulio."

"Gonna happen to me."

"But your soul . . ."

"What's my soul look like?" Giulio asked quickly.

"Like you, Giulio . . . it's true . . ."

Giulio cast him a look of contempt George would not have thought him capable of.

"The little hole, the bones and worms," Giulio moaned.

"But you've *had* a life!" George suddenly cried with exasperation. "Do you want to live forever?"

"Yes," Giulio said simply.

From then on George felt a fury. In the past all Giulio's little fears had been bearable because he, George, could exorcise them, like a stevedore bearing a small load away. But this final cowardice excluded him. And there was nothing, no one he could turn to. He went halfheartedly to church, but got nothing from it. He began making small overtures to his tenants, but his sociability was stiff with rust. He looked with curiosity at the black people on the street, and thought there were more of them than there used to be. When a young black couple stopped him on a corner one day he listened attentively as they talked of civil rights. He accepted a pamphlet from them and read it thoroughly. But afterward he threw it out. He felt no connection with the problems it presented.

He cursed Giulio as he had cursed him fifty years ago when he had walked away from him at the train depot, and he wished for the oneness with himself that he had known in the empty fields of his youth.

In the daytime he was angrily helpful, like a disapproving orderly, but at night, as they sat in the small living room with Baby flicking his tail back and forth across the blank television screen, he went to Giulio and mutely pleaded with him. Giulio sighed abstractedly; he seemed far away, deep inside himself, listening to every heartbeat, counting every twinge, with a deep frown line between his eyes.

George moved the twin beds together, and Giulio allowed his hand to be held through the night. From then on they slept that way, hand in hand. George slept lightly, waking often. It was almost as if he wished to be awake, to enjoy the only hours of closeness he had with his friend as he held his hand. And also, in the back of his mind was the fear that if he drifted off, Giulio would be released into the arms of death. And so he lay quietly, listening to Giulio's breathing, to the wind in the trees.

Then gradually the bedroom window would turn from black to gray, and the breeze that ruffled the curtain carried in the scent of early morning. Dawn brought him sleep; the rising sun gave him a sense of security. Bad things never happened in the daytime—at least one felt that way. And so his fingers grew lax in Giulio's hand as he trusted his friend to the kindness of the dawning day.

But when he awoke later it would be with a sharp sense of foreboding. Quickly he would turn to look at Giulio, his eyes narrowed against the possible shock. But Giulio would be breathing evenly, his bluish lips parted over his gums, his teeth grinning from a water glass on the bureau. Giulio's clothes were neatly laid out, his liver-colored jacket hung over the back of a chair. How lifeless the jacket looked. George would shut his eyes, knowing that the sight of that empty jacket would be unbearable when Giulio was gone. He shook the thought from his head, wondering if life could be more painful than this. Then Giulio's eyes would open, George's face take on a formal nonchalance. And so another night had passed. Their hands parted.

"How do you feel!" George would ask shortly.

Giulio would sigh.

They took their breakfast. The sun shone through the kitchen window with a taunting golden light. George snapped at Giulio. Giulio was unmoved.

One summer morning George persuaded Giulio to sit outside in the backyard. He hoped that watching him work in the garden, Giulio might be persuaded to putter around again. He settled his friend into a chair and picked up the rake, but as the minutes wore on and he moved around the garden in the hot sun, raking the leaves together, Giulio showed no sign of interest. George stopped and put the rake down. Not knowing if he wished to please Giulio or anger him, he suddenly broke off the largest marigold in the garden and held it out.

Giulio shaded his watering eyes with his hand; then his eyes drifted away from the flower like two soap bubbles in the air. George flung the flower to the ground, staring at Giulio, then strode to the shrine and stood there with his hands in fists, blindly determined to do something that would shake his friend open, break him in two if need be. He grabbed the arm of the Virgin Mary and lifted the statue high, and heard Giulio's voice.

"George."

"That's right," George growled, replacing the statue and breathing threateningly through his nostrils, "I would have smashed it to bits!"

"Smash what?" Giulio asked indifferently, and George saw that under the awning of his thin hand his eyes were closed.

"Were your eyes closed?" George thundered. "Didn't you *see* me?"

"You no care that I can't open my eyes—this sun, he hurt them. You *mean*, George, make me sit out here. Too hot. Make me feel sick. I wanna go inside."

"I was going to smash your Virgin Mary!" George cried.

Giulio shrugged. "I wanna go inside."

And then George's shoulders hunched, his face twisted up, and he broke into a storm of tears. Turning his head aside with shame, he made for the back door; then he turned around and hurried back, glancing up at the windows, where he hoped no one stood watching him cry. He put his arm around Giulio and helped him up from his chair, and the two old men haltingly crossed the garden out of the sun.

"Humiliating," George whispered when they were inside, shaking his head and pressing his eyes with a handkerchief. He slowly folded the handkerchief into a square and replaced it in his pocket. He gave a loud sniff and squared his shoulders, and looked with resignation at his distant friend.

Giulio was settling himself into the armchair, plucking the patchwork quilt around him. "Time for pills," he muttered, reaching next to him, and he poured a glass of water from a decanter and took two capsules, smacking his lips mechanically, like a goldfish. Sitting back, he looked around the room in his usual blank, uninterested way. Then a puzzled expression came into his eyes.

"Why you cry then, George?"

George shook his head silently.

"I do something you no like?"

"You never talk. It's as though we're strangers." And he broke off with a sigh. "I've told you all that before—what's the use?"

"I got big worry, George. No time to talk."

"It would be better than to think and think. What do you think about all day?"

Giulio slowly raised his eyebrows, as though gazing down upon a scene. "Bones and worms."

"Giulio, Giulio."

"Big worry, George."

"You'll drive yourself mad that way."

"I no mad at you. Just him." He laid one thin finger on his heart, lightly, as though afraid of rousing it.

"I don't mean angry . . ."

But Giulio was already tired of talking, and was plucking at the quilt again, ill, annoyed, retreating into sleep.

"Giulio, please, you've talked a little. Talk a little more—stay."

With an effort, his eyes sick and distant, Giulio stayed.

But now that he had his attention, George did not know where to begin, what to say. His mind spun; his tongue formed a few tentative words; then, clubbed by an immense fatigue, he sank into a chair with his head in his hands.

"I'm a sick man," Giulio explained tonelessly, closing his eyes. After a silence he opened them and looked over at George, painfully, as though from under a crushing weight. "Tonight I hold your hand in bed again, like always. Hold your hand every night, you know that."

"You hold *my* hand?" George asked softly, lifting his head.

"In daytime," Giulio said slowly, his eyes laboriously fixed on George's attentive face, "in daytime only the bones and worms. But in the night . . . in the night, I see other things, too . . ." He was silent for a moment until a twinge had passed, then spoke again. "See you, George. And I hold your hand. Make you feel better . . ." His eyes still fixed on George's face, he gave an apologetic twitch of the lip as his lids closed, and slowly he nodded off to sleep.

---

1. What is the significance of the wall George built when he was a child?
2. There is scarcely any allusion to the sexual relationship in their early days as a couple. In what ways is its trace left in their long life together?
3. Why is it unthinkable for George to leave Giulio as he did once before?
4. Is it possible that Giulio really holds George's hand at night to keep George from being afraid?

Doris Lessing

Lessing (1919–) was born in Kermanshah, Persia (now Iran), the daughter of a bank manager, and was taken by her family to Rhodesia (now Zimbabwe) in 1924. Fleeing the loneliness of an unhappy childhood, she went to the capital of Salisbury (Harare) at eighteen and there involved herself in politics and the intellectual life. She became a Communist and retained her party affiliation until she had moved to London, where disillusion led her to break with the Party. She was twice married and twice divorced before her departure from Africa. She published a well-made, conventional novel, The Grass Is Singing, *in 1950 and soon thereafter began to experiment more freely with work that combines autobiography and fiction in an unorthodox attempt to come at the dilemmas of the modern woman struggling for emancipation. Following this vein she published five novels between 1952 and 1969 under the general title* Children of Violence. The Golden Notebook *(1962) has the form of several overlapping notebooks prepared by a writer simultaneously preparing and postponing the composition of a novel. In her despair of rational solutions to political and sexual disorders of our times Lessing has entertained the possibilities for reorientation that lie in extrasensory perception and in the visions of the insane. Among her novels are* Briefing for a Descent into Hell *(1971),* The Summer before the Dark *(1973), the tetralogy* Canopus in Argos: Archives *(1981), two novels collected under the title* The Diaries of Jane Somers *(1984),* The Good Terrorist *(1985), and* The Fifth Child *(1988). Many of her stories are collected in* African Stories *(1964) and* Stories *(1978).*

To Room Nineteen

This is a story, I suppose, about a failure in intelligence: the Rawlings' marriage was grounded in intelligence.

They were older when they married than most of their married friends: in their well-seasoned late twenties. Both had had a number of affairs, sweet rather than bitter; and when they fell in love—for they did fall in love—had known each other for some time. They joked that they had saved each other "for the real thing." That they had waited so long (but not too long) for this real thing was to them a proof of their sensible discrimination. A good many of their friends had married young, and now (they felt) probably regretted lost opportunities; while others, still unmarried, seemed to them arid, self-doubting, and likely to make desperate or romantic marriages.

Not only they, but others, felt they were well-matched: their friends' delight was an additional proof of their happiness. They had played the same roles, male and female, in this group or set, if such a wide, loosely connected, constantly changing constellation of people could be called a set. They had both become, by virtue of their moderation, their humour, and their abstinence from painful experience, people to whom others came for advice. They could be, and were, relied on. It was one of those cases of a man and a woman linking themselves whom no one else had ever thought of linking, probably because of their similarities. But then everyone exclaimed: Of course! How right! How was it we never thought of it before!

And so they married amid general rejoicing, and because of their foresight and their sense for what was probable, nothing was a surprise to them.

Both had well-paid jobs. Matthew was a subeditor on a large London newspaper, and Susan worked in an advertising firm. He was not the stuff of which editors or publicised journalists are made, but he was much more than "a subeditor," being one of the essential background people who in fact steady, inspire and make possible the people in the limelight. He was content with this position. Susan had a talent for commercial drawing. She was humorous about the advertisements she was responsible for, but she did not feel strongly about them one way or the other.

Both, before they married, had had pleasant flats, but they felt it unwise to base a marriage on either flat, because it might seem like a submission of personality on the part of the one whose flat it was not. They moved into a new flat in South Kensington[1] on the clear understanding that when their marriage had settled down (a process they knew would not take long, and was in fact more a humorous concession to popular wisdom than what was due to themselves) they would buy a house and start a family.

And this is what happened. They lived in their charming flat for two years, giving parties and going to them, being a popular young married couple, and then Susan became pregnant, she gave up her job, and they bought a house in Richmond.[2] It was typical of this couple that they had a son first, then a daughter, then twins, son and daughter. Everything right, appropriate, and what everyone would wish for, if they could choose. But people did feel these two had chosen; this balanced and sensible family was no more than what was due to them because of their infallible sense for *choosing* right.

1. Part of the fashionable West End of London. 2. One of the outer boroughs of Greater London.

And so they lived with their four children in their gardened house in Richmond and were happy. They had everything they had wanted and had planned for.

And yet . . .

Well, even this was expected, that there must be a certain flatness. . . .

Yes, yes, of course, it was natural they sometimes felt like this. Like what?

Their life seemed to be like a snake biting its tail. Matthew's job for the sake of Susan, children, house, and garden—which caravanserai needed a well-paid job to maintain it. And Susan's practical intelligence for the sake of Matthew, the children, the house and the garden—which unit would have collapsed in a week without her.

But there was no point about which either could say: "For the sake of *this* is all the rest." Children? But children can't be a centre of life and a reason for being. They can be a thousand things that are delightful, interesting, satisfying, but they can't be a wellspring to live from. Or they shouldn't be. Susan and Matthew knew that well enough.

Matthew's job? Ridiculous. It was an interesting job, but scarcely a reason for living. Matthew took pride in doing it well, but he could hardly be expected to be proud of the newspaper; the newspaper he read, *his* newspaper, was not the one he worked for.

Their love for each other? Well, that was nearest it. If this wasn't a centre, what was? Yes, it was around this point, their love, that the whole extraordinary structure revolved. For extraordinary it certainly was. Both Susan and Matthew had moments of thinking so, of looking in secret disbelief at this thing they had created: marriage, four children, big house, garden, charwomen, friends, cars . . . and this *thing*, this entity, all of it had come into existence, been blown into being out of nowhere, because Susan loved Matthew and Matthew loved Susan. Extraordinary. So that was the central point, the wellspring.

And if one felt that it simply was not strong enough, important enough, to support it all, well whose fault was that? Certainly neither Susan's nor Matthew's. It was in the nature of things. And they sensibly blamed neither themselves nor each other.

On the contrary, they used their intelligence to preserve what they had created from a painful and explosive world: they looked around them, and took lessons. All around them, marriages collapsing, or breaking, or rubbing along (even worse, they felt). They must not make the same mistakes, they must not.

They had avoided the pitfall so many of their friends had fallen into—of buying a house in the country *for the sake of the children*, so that the husband became a weekend husband, a weekend father, and the wife always careful not to ask what went on in the town flat which they called (in joke) a bachelor flat. No, Matthew was a full-time husband, a full-time father, and at night, in the big married bed in the big married bedroom (which had an attractive view of the river), they lay beside each other talking and he told her about his day, and what he had done, and whom he had met; and she told him about her day (not as interesting, but that was not her fault), for both knew of the hidden resentments and deprivations of the woman who has lived her own life—and above all, has earned her own living—and is now dependent on a husband for outside interests and money.

Nor did Susan make the mistake of taking a job for the sake of her independence, which she might very well have done, since her old firm, missing her qualities of humour, balance, and sense, invited her often to go back. Children needed their mother to a certain age, that both parents knew and agreed on; and when these four healthy wisely brought up children were of the right age, Susan would work again, because she knew, and so did he, what happened to women of fifty at the height of their energy and ability, with grownup children who no longer needed their full devotion.

So here was this couple, testing their marriage, looking after it, treating it like a small boat full of helpless people in a very stormy sea. Well, of course, so it was. . . . The storms of the world were bad, but not too close—which is not to say they were selfishly felt: Susan and Matthew were both well-informed and responsible people. And the inner storms and quicksands were understood and charted. So everything was all right. Everything was in order. Yes, things were under control.

So what did it matter if they felt dry, flat? People like themselves, fed on a hundred books (psychological, anthropological, sociological), could scarcely be unprepared for the dry, controlled wistfulness which is the distinguishing mark of the intelligent marriage. Two people, endowed with education, with discrimination, with judgement, linked together voluntarily from their will to be happy together and to be of use to others—one sees them everywhere, one knows them, one even is that thing oneself: sadness because so much is after all so little. These two, unsurprised, turned towards each other with even more courtesy and gentle love: this was life, that two people, no matter how carefully chosen, could not be everything to each other. In fact, even to say so, to think in such a way, was banal; they were ashamed to do it.

It was banal, too, when one night Matthew came home late and confessed he had been to a party, taken a girl home and slept with her. Susan forgave him, of course. Except that forgiveness is hardly the word. Understanding, yes. But if you understand something, you don't forgive it, you are the thing itself: forgiveness is for what you *don't* understand. Nor had he *confessed*—what sort of word is that?

The whole thing was not important. After all, years ago they had joked: Of course I'm not going to be faithful to you, no one can be faithful to one other person for a whole lifetime. (And there was the word "faithful"—stupid, all these words, stupid, belonging to a savage old world.) But the incident left both of them irritable. Strange, but they were both bad-tempered, annoyed. There was something unassimilable about it.

Making love splendidly after he had come home that night, both had felt that the idea that Myra Jenkins, a pretty girl met at a party, could be even relevant was ridiculous. They had loved each other for over a decade, would love each other for years more. Who, then, was Myra Jenkins?

Except, thought Susan, unaccountably bad-tempered, she was (is?) the first. In ten years. So either the ten years' fidelity was not important, or she isn't. (No, no, there is something wrong with this way of thinking, there must be.) But if she isn't important, presumably it wasn't important either when Matthew and I first went to bed with each other that afternoon whose delight even now (like a very long shadow at sundown) lays a long, wandlike finger over us. (Why did I say sundown?) Well, if what we felt that afternoon was not important, nothing is important, because if it hadn't been for what we felt, we wouldn't be Mr. and Mrs. Rawlings with four children, et cetera, et cetera. The whole thing is *absurd*—for him to have come home and told me was absurd. For him not to have told me was absurd. For me to care or, for that matter, not to care, is absurd . . . and who is Myra Jenkins? Why, no one at all.

There was only one thing to do, and of course these sensible people did it; they put the thing behind them, and consciously, knowing what they were doing, moved forward into a different phase of their marriage, giving thanks for past good fortune as they did so.

For it was inevitable that the handsome, blond, attractive, manly man, Matthew Rawlings, should be at times tempted (oh, what a word!) by the attractive girls at parties she could not attend because of the four children; and that sometimes he would succumb (a word even more repulsive, if possible) and that she, a goodlooking woman in the big well-tended garden at Richmond, would sometimes be pierced as by an arrow from the sky with bitterness. Except that bitterness was not in order, it was out of court. Did the casual girls touch the marriage? They did not. Rather it was they who knew defeat because of the handsome Matthew Rawlings' marriage body and soul to Susan Rawlings.

In that case why did Susan feel (though luckily not for longer than a few seconds at a time) as if life had become a desert, and that nothing mattered, and that her children were not her own?

Meanwhile her intelligence continued to assert that all was well. What if her Matthew did have an occasional sweet afternoon, the odd affair? For she knew quite well, except in her moments of aridity, that they were very happy, that the affairs were not important.

Perhaps that was the trouble? It was in the nature of things that the adventures and delights could no longer be hers, because of the four children and the big house that needed so much attention. But perhaps she was secretly wishing, and even knowing that she did, that the wildness and the beauty could be his. But he was married to her. She was married to him. They were married inextricably. And therefore the gods could not strike him with the real magic, not really. Well, was it Susan's fault that after he came home from an adventure he looked harassed rather than fulfilled? (In fact, that was how she knew he had been *unfaithful*, because of his sullen air, and his glances at her, similar to hers at him: What is it that I share with this person that shields all delight from me?) But none of it by anybody's fault. (But what did they feel ought to be somebody's fault?) Nobody's fault, nothing to be at fault, no one to blame, no one to offer or to take it . . . and nothing wrong, either, except that Matthew never was really struck, as he wanted to be, by joy; and that Susan was more and more often threatened by emptiness. (It was usually in the garden that she was invaded by this feeling: she was coming to avoid the garden, unless the children or Matthew were with her.) There was no need to use the dramatic words "unfaithful," "forgive," and the rest: intelligence forbade them. Intelligence barred, too, quarrelling, sulking, anger, silences of withdrawal, accusations and tears. Above all, intelligence forbids tears.

A high price has to be paid for the happy marriage with the four healthy children in the large white gardened house.

And they were paying it, willingly, knowing what they were doing. When they lay side by side or breast to breast in the big civilised bedroom overlooking the wild sullied river, they laughed, often, for no particular reason; but they knew it was really because of these two small people, Susan and Matthew, supporting such an edifice on their intelligent love. The laugh comforted them; it saved them both, though from what, they did not know.

They were now both fortyish. The older children, boy and girl, were ten and eight, at school. The twins, six, were still at home. Susan did not have nurses or girls to help her: childhood is short; and she did not regret the hard work. Often enough she was bored, since small children can be boring; she was often very tired; but she regretted nothing. In another decade, she would turn herself back into being a woman with a life of her own.

Soon the twins would go to school, and they would be away from home from nine until four. These hours, so Susan saw it, would be the preparation for her own slow emancipation away from the role of hub-of-the-family into woman-with-her-own-life. She was already planning for the hours of freedom when all the children would be "off her hands." That was the phrase used by Matthew and by Susan and by their friends, for the moment when the youngest child went off to school. "They'll be off your hands, darling Susan, and you'll have time to yourself." So said Matthew, the intelligent husband, who had often enough commended and consoled Susan, standing by her in spirit during the years when her soul was not her own, as she said, but her children's.

What it amounted to was that Susan saw herself as she had been at twenty-eight, unmarried; and then again somewhere about fifty, blossoming from the root of what she had been twenty years before. As if the essential Susan were in abeyance, as if she were in cold storage. Matthew said something like this to Susan one night: and she agreed that it was true—she did feel something like that. What, then, was this essential Susan? She did not know. Put like that it sounded ridiculous, and she did not really feel it. Anyway, they had a long discussion about the whole thing before going off to sleep in each other's arms.

So the twins went off to their school, two bright affectionate children who had no problems about it, since their older brother and sister had trodden this path so successfully before them. And now Susan was going to be alone in the big house, every day of the school term, except for the daily woman who came in to clean.

It was now, for the first time in this marriage, that something happened which neither of them had foreseen.

This is what happened. She returned, at nine-thirty, from taking the twins to the school by car, looking forward to seven blissful hours of freedom. On the first morning she was simply restless, worrying about the twins "naturally enough" since this was their first day away at school. She was hardly able to contain herself until they came back. Which they did happily, excited by the world of school, looking forward to the next day. And the next day Susan took them, dropped them, came back, and found herself reluctant to enter her big and beautiful home because it was as if something was waiting for her there that she did not wish to confront. Sensibly, however, she parked the car in the garage, entered the house, spoke to Mrs. Parkes, the daily woman, about her duties, and went up to her bedroom. She was possessed by a fever which drove her out again, downstairs, into the kitchen, where Mrs. Parkes was making cake and did not need her, and into the garden. There she sat on a bench and tried to calm herself looking at trees, at a brown glimpse of the river. But she was filled with tension, like a panic: as if an enemy was in the garden with her. She spoke to herself severely, thus: All this is quite natural. First, I spent twelve years of my adult life working, *living my own life*. Then I married, and from the moment I became pregnant for the first time I signed myself over, so to speak, to other people. To the children. Not for one moment in twelve years have I been alone, had time to myself. So now I have to learn to be myself again. That's all.

And she went indoors to help Mrs. Parkes cook and clean, and found some sewing to do for the children. She kept herself occupied every day. At the end of the first term she understood she felt two contrary emotions. First: secret astonishment and dismay that during those weeks when the house was empty of children she had in fact been more occupied (had been careful to keep herself occupied) than ever she had been when the children were around her needing her continual attention. Second: that now she knew the house would be full of them, and for five weeks, she resented the fact she would never be alone. She was already looking back at those hours of sewing, cooking (but by herself) as at a lost freedom which would not be hers for five long weeks. And the two months of term which would succeed the five weeks stretched alluringly open to her—freedom. But what freedom—when in fact she had been so careful *not* to be free of small duties during the last weeks? She looked at herself, Susan Rawlings, sitting in a big chair by the window in the bedroom, sewing shirts or dresses, which she might just as well have bought. She saw herself making cakes for hours at a time in the big family kitchen: yet usually she bought cakes. What she saw was a woman alone, that was true, but she had not felt alone. For instance, Mrs. Parkes was always somewhere in the house. And she did not like being in the garden at all, because of the closeness there of the enemy—irritation, restlessness, emptiness, whatever it was—which keeping her hands occupied made less dangerous for some reason.

Susan did not tell Matthew of these thoughts. They were not sensible. She did not recognize herself in them. What should she say to her dear friend and husband, Matthew? "When I go into the garden, that is, if the children are not there, I feel as if there is an enemy there waiting to invade me." "What enemy, Susan darling?" "Well I don't know, really. . . ." "Perhaps you should see a doctor?"

No, clearly this conversation should not take place. The holidays began and Susan welcomed them. Four children, lively, energetic, intelligent, demanding: she was never, not for a moment of her day, alone. If she was in a room, they would be in the next room, or waiting for her to do something for them; or it would soon be time for lunch or tea, or to take one of them to the dentist. Something to do: five weeks of it, thank goodness.

On the fourth day of these so welcome holidays, she found she was storming with anger at the twins; two shrinking beautiful children who (and this is what checked her) stood hand in hand looking at her with sheer dismayed disbelief. This was their calm mother, shouting at them. And for what? They had come to her with some game, some bit of nonsense. They looked at each other, moved closer for support, and went off hand in hand, leaving Susan holding on to the windowsill of the livingroom, breathing deep, feeling sick. She went to lie down, telling the older children she had a headache. She heard the boy Harry telling the little ones: "It's all right, Mother's got a headache." She heard that *It's all right* with pain.

That night she said to her husband: "Today I shouted at the twins, quite unfairly." She sounded miserable, and he said gently: "Well, what of it?"

"It's more of an adjustment than I thought, their going to school."

"But Susie, Susie darling. . . ." For she was crouched weeping on the bed. He comforted her: "Susan, what is all this about? You shouted at them? What of it? If you shouted at them fifty times a day it wouldn't be more than the little devils deserve." But she wouldn't laugh. She wept. Soon he comforted her with his body. She became calm. Calm, she wondered what was wrong with her, and why she should mind so much that she might, just once, have behaved unjustly with the children. What did it matter? They had forgotten it all long ago: Mother had a headache and everything was all right.

It was a long time later that Susan understood that that night, when she had wept and Matthew had driven the misery out of her with his big solid body, was the last time, ever in their married life, that they had been—to use their mutual language—with each other. And even that was a lie, because she had not told him of her real fears at all.

The five weeks passed, and Susan was in control of herself, and good and kind, and she looked forward to the end of the holidays with a mixture of fear and longing. She did not know what to expect. She took the twins off to school (the elder children took themselves to school) and she returned to the house determined to face the enemy wherever he was, in the house, or the garden or—where?

She was again restless, she was possessed by restlessness. She cooked and sewed and worked as before, day after day, while Mrs. Parkes remonstrated: "Mrs. Rawlings, what's the need for it? I can do that, it's what you pay me for."

And it was so irrational that she checked herself. She would put the car into the garage, go up to her bedroom, and sit, hands in her lap, forcing herself to be quiet. She listened to Mrs. Parkes moving around the house. She looked out into the garden and saw the branches shake the trees. She sat defeating the enemy, restlessness. Emptiness. She ought to be thinking about her life, about herself. But she did not. Or perhaps she could not. As soon as she forced her mind to think about Susan (for what else did she want to be alone for?), it skipped off to thoughts of butter or school clothes. Or it thought of Mrs. Parkes. She realised that she sat listening for the movements of the cleaning woman, following her every turn, bend, thought. She followed her in her mind from kitchen to bathroom, from table to oven, and it was as if the duster, the cleaning cloth, the saucepan, were in her own hand. She would hear herself saying: No, not like that, don't put that there. . . . Yet she did not give a damn what Mrs. Parkes did, or if she did it at all. Yet she could not prevent herself from being conscious of her, every minute. Yes, this was what was wrong with her: she needed, when she was alone, to be really alone, with no one near. She could not endure the knowledge that in ten minutes or in half an hour Mrs. Parkes would call up the stairs: "Mrs. Rawlings, there's no silver polish. Madam, we're out of flour."

So she left the house and went to sit in the garden where she was screened from the house by trees. She waited for the demon to appear and claim her, but he did not.

She was keeping him off, because she had not, after all, come to an end of arranging herself.

She was planning how to be somewhere where Mrs. Parkes would not come after her with a cup of tea, or a demand to be allowed to telephone (always irritating, since Susan did not care who she telephoned or how often), or just a nice talk about something. Yes, she needed a place, or a state of affairs, where it would not be necessary to keep reminding herself: In ten minutes I must telephone Matthew about . . . and at half past three I must leave early for the children because the car needs cleaning. And at ten o'clock tomorrow I must remember. . . . She was possessed with resentment that the seven hours of freedom in every day (during weekdays in the school term) were not free, that never, not for one second, ever, was she free from the pressure of time, from having to remember this or that. She could never forget herself; never really let herself go into forgetfulness.

Resentment. It was poisoning her. (She looked at this emotion and thought it was absurd. Yet she felt it.) She was a prisoner. (She looked at this thought too, and it was no good telling herself it was a ridiculous one.) She must tell Matthew—but what? She was filled with emotions that were utterly ridiculous, that she despised, yet that nevertheless she was feeling so strongly she could not shake them off.

The school holidays came round, and this time they were for

nearly two months, and she behaved with a conscious controlled decency that nearly drove her crazy. She would lock herself in the bathroom, and sit on the edge of the bath, breathing deep, trying to let go into some kind of calm. Or she went up into the spare room, usually empty, where no one would expect her to be. She heard the children calling "Mother, Mother," and kept silent, feeling guilty. Or she went to the very end of the garden, by herself, and looked at the slow-moving brown river; she looked at the river and closed her eyes and breathed slow and deep, taking it into her being, into her veins.

Then she returned to the family, wife and mother, smiling and responsible, feeling as if the pressure of these people—four lively children and her husband—were a painful pressure on the surface of her skin, a hand pressing on her brain. She did not once break down into irritation during these holidays, but it was like living out a prison sentence, and when the children went back to school, she sat on a white stone seat near the flowing river, and she thought: It is not even a year since the twins went to school, since *they were off my hands* (What on earth did I think I meant when I used that stupid phrase?), and yet I'm a different person. I'm simply not myself. I don't understand it.

Yet she had to understand it. For she knew that this structure—big white house, on which the mortgage still cost four hundred[3] a year, a husband, so good and kind and insightful; four children, all doing so nicely; and the garden where she sat; and Mrs. Parkes, the cleaning woman—all this depended on her, and yet she could not understand why, or even what it was she contributed to it.

She said to Matthew in their bedroom: "I think there must be something wrong with me."

And he said: "Surely not, Susan? You look marvellous—you're as lovely as ever."

She looked at the handsome blond man, with his clear, intelligent, blue-eyed face, and thought: Why is it I can't tell him? Why not? And she said: "I need to be alone more than I am."

At which he swung his slow blue gaze at her, and she saw what she had been dreading: Incredulity. Disbelief. And fear. An incredulous blue stare from a stranger who was her husband, as close to her as her own breath.

He said: "But the children are at school and off your hands."

She said to herself: I've got to force myself to say: Yes, but do you realize that I never feel free? There's never a moment I can say to myself: There's nothing I have to remind myself about, nothing I have to do in half an hour, or an hour, or two hours. . . .

But she said: "I don't feel well."

3. I.e., four hundred pounds.

He said: "Perhaps you need a holiday."

She said, appalled: "But not without you, surely?" For she could not imagine herself going off without him. Yet that was what he meant. Seeing her face, he laughed, and opened his arms, and she went into them, thinking: Yes, yes, but why can't I say it? And what is it I have to say?

She tried to tell him, about never being free. And he listened and said: "But Susan, what sort of freedom can you possibly want—short of being dead! Am I ever free? I go to the office, and I have to be there at ten—all right, half past ten, sometimes. And I have to do this or that, don't I? Then I've got to come home at a certain time—I don't mean it, you know I don't—but if I'm not going to be back home at six I telephone you. When can I ever say to myself: I have nothing to be responsible for in the next six hours?"

Susan, hearing this, was remorseful. Because it was true. The good marriage, the house, the children, depended just as much on his voluntary bondage as it did on hers. But why did he not feel bound? Why didn't he chafe and become restless? No, there was something really wrong with her and this proved it.

And that word "bondage"—why had she used it? She had never felt marriage, or the children, as bondage. Neither had he, or surely they wouldn't be together lying in each other's arms content after twelve years of marriage.

No, her state (whatever it was) was irrelevant, nothing to do with her real good life with her family. She had to accept the fact that, after all, she was an irrational person and to live with it. Some people had to live with crippled arms, or stammers, or being deaf. She would have to live knowing she was subject to a state of mind she could not own.

Nevertheless, as a result of this conversation with her husband, there was a new regime next holidays.

The spare room at the top of the house now had a cardboard sign saying: PRIVATE! DO NOT DISTURB! on it. (This sign had been drawn in coloured chalks by the children, after a discussion between the parents in which it was decided this was psychologically the right thing.) The family and Mrs. Parkes knew this was "Mother's Room" and that she was entitled to her privacy. Many serious conversations took place between Matthew and the children about not taking Mother for granted. Susan overheard the first, between father and Harry, the older boy, and was surprised at her irritation over it. Surely she could have a room somewhere in that big house and retire into it without such a fuss being made? Without it being so solemnly discussed? Why couldn't she simply have announced: "I'm going to fit out the little top room for myself, and when I'm in it I'm not to be disturbed for anything short of fire"? Just that, and finished; instead of long earnest discussions.

When she heard Harry and Matthew explaining it to the twins with Mrs. Parkes coming in—"Yes, well, a family sometimes gets on top of a woman"—she had to go right away to the bottom of the garden until the devils of exasperation had finished their dance in her blood.

But now there was a room, and she could go there when she liked, she used it seldom: she felt even more caged there than in her bedroom. One day she had gone up there after a lunch for ten children she had cooked and served because Mrs. Parkes was not there, and had sat alone for a while looking into the garden. She saw the children stream out from the kitchen and stand looking up at the window where she sat behind the curtains. They were all—her children and their friends—discussing Mother's Room. A few minutes later, the chase of children in some game came pounding up the stairs, but ended as abruptly as if they had fallen over a ravine, so sudden was the silence. They had remembered she was there, and had gone silent in a great gale of "Hush! Shhhhhh! Quiet, you'll disturb her. . . ." And they went tiptoeing downstairs like criminal conspirators. When she came down to make tea for them, they all apologised. The twins put their arms around her, from front and back, making a human cage of loving limbs, and promised it would never occur again. "We forgot, Mummy, we forgot all about it!"

What it amounted to was that Mother's Room, and her need for privacy, had become a valuable lesson in respect for other people's rights. Quite soon Susan was going up to the room only because it was a lesson it was a pity to drop. Then she took sewing up there, and the children and Mrs. Parkes came in and out: it had become another family room.

She sighed, and smiled, and resigned herself—she made jokes at her own expense with Matthew over the room. That is, she did from the self she liked, she respected. But at the same time, something inside her howled with impatience, with rage. . . . And she was frightened. One day she found herself kneeling by her bed and praying: "Dear God, keep it away from me, keep him away from me." She meant the devil, for she now thought of it, not caring if she was irrational, as some sort of demon. She imagined him, or it, as a youngish man, or perhaps a middleaged man pretending to be young. Or a man young-looking from immaturity? At any rate, she saw the young-looking face which, when she drew closer, had dry lines about mouth and eyes. He was thinnish, meagre in build. And he had a reddish complexion, and ginger hair. That was he—a gingery, energetic man, and he wore a reddish hairy jacket, unpleasant to the touch.

Well, one day she saw him. She was standing at the bottom of the garden, watching the river ebb past, when she raised her eyes and saw this person, or being, sitting on the white stone bench. He was looking at her, and grinning. In his hand was a long crooked stick, which he had picked off the ground, or broken off the tree above him. He was absent-mindedly, out of an absent-minded or freakish impulse of spite, using the stick to stir around in the coils of a blindworm or a grass snake (or some kind of snakelike creature: it was whitish and unhealthy to look at, unpleasant). The snake was twisting about, flinging its coils from side to side in a kind of dance of protest against the teasing prodding stick.

Susan looked at him thinking: Who is the stranger? What is he doing in our garden? Then she recognised the man around whom her terrors had crystallised. As she did so, he vanished. She made herself walk over to the bench. A shadow from a branch lay across thin emerald grass, moving jerkily over its roughness, and she could see why she had taken it for a snake, lashing and twisting. She went back to the house thinking: Right, then, so I've seen him with my own eyes, so I'm not crazy after all—there *is* a danger because I've seen him. He is lurking in the garden and sometimes even in the house, and he wants to *get into me and to take me over*.

She dreamed of having a room or a place, anywhere, where she could go and sit, by herself, no one knowing where she was.

Once, near Victoria,[4] she found herself outside a news agent that had Rooms to Let advertised. She decided to rent a room, telling no one. Sometimes she could take the train into Richmond and sit alone in it for an hour or two. Yet how could she? A room would cost three or four pounds a week, and she earned no money, and how could she explain to Matthew that she needed such a sum? What for? It did not occur to her that she was taking it for granted she wasn't going to tell him about the room.

Well, it was out of the question, having a room; yet she knew she must.

One day, when a school term was well established, and none of the children had measles or other ailments, and everything seemed in order, she did the shopping early, explained to Mrs. Parkes she was meeting an old school friend, took the train to Victoria, searched until she found a small quiet hotel, and asked for a room for the day. They did not let rooms by the day, the manageress said, looking doubtful, since Susan so obviously was not the kind of woman who needed a room for unrespectable reasons. Susan made a long explanation about not being well, being unable to shop without frequent rests for lying down. At last she was allowed to rent the room provided she paid a full night's price for it. She was taken up by the manageress and a maid, both concerned over the state of her health . . . which must be pretty

4. One of the main railway stations in central London.

bad if, living at Richmond (she had signed her name and address in the register), she needed a shelter at Victoria.

The room was ordinary and anonymous, and was just what Susan needed. She put a shilling in the gas fire, and sat, eyes shut, in a dingy armchair with her back to a dingy window. She was alone. She was alone. She was alone. She could feel pressures lifting off her. First the sounds of traffic came very loud; then they seemed to vanish; she might even have slept a little. A knock on the door: it was Miss Townsend, the manageress, bringing her a cup of tea with her own hands, so concerned was she over Susan's long silence and possible illness.

Miss Townsend was a lonely woman of fifty, running this hotel with all the rectitude expected of her, and she sensed in Susan the possibility of understanding companionship. She stayed to talk. Susan found herself in the middle of a fantastic story about her illness, which got more and more improbable as she tried to make it tally with the large house at Richmond, well-off husband, and four children. Suppose she said instead: Miss Townsend, I'm here in your hotel because I need to be alone for a few hours, above all *alone and with no one knowing where I am*. She said it mentally, and saw, mentally, the look that would inevitably come on Miss Townsend's elderly maiden's face. "Miss Townsend, my four children and my husband are driving me insane, do you understand that? Yes, I can see from the gleam of hysteria in your eyes that comes from loneliness controlled but only just contained that I've got everything in the world you've ever longed for. Well, Miss Townsend, I don't want any of it. You can have it, Miss Townsend. I wish I was absolutely alone in the world, like you. Miss Townsend, I'm besieged by seven devils, Miss Townsend, Miss Townsend, let me stay here in your hotel where the devils can't get me. . . ." Instead of saying all this, she described her anaemia, agreed to try Miss Townsend's remedy for it, which was raw liver, minced, between whole-meal bread, and said yes, perhaps it would be better if she stayed at home and let a friend do shopping for her. She paid her bill and left the hotel, defeated.

At home Mrs. Parkes said she didn't really like it, no, not really, when Mrs. Rawlings was away from nine in the morning until five. The teacher had telephoned from school to say Joan's teeth were paining her, and she hadn't known what to say; and what was she to make for the children's tea, Mrs. Rawlings hadn't said.

All this was nonsense, of course. Mrs. Parkes's complaint was that Susan had withdrawn herself spiritually, leaving the burden of the big house on her.

Susan looked back at her day of "freedom" which had resulted in her becoming a friend of the lonely Miss Townsend, and in Mrs. Parkes's remonstrances. Yet she remembered the short blissful hour of being alone, really alone. She was determined to arrange her life, no matter what it cost, so that she could have that solitude more often. An absolute solitude, where no one knew her or cared about her.

But how? She thought of saying to her old employer: I want you to back me up in a story with Matthew that I am doing part-time work for you. The truth is that . . . But she would have to tell him a lie too, and which lie? She could not say: I want to sit by myself three or four times a week in a rented room. And besides, he knew Matthew, and she could not really ask him to tell lies on her behalf, apart from being bound to think it meant a lover.

Suppose she really took a part-time job, which she could get through fast and efficiently, leaving time for herself. What job? Addressing envelopes? Canvassing?

And there was Mrs. Parkes, working widow, who knew exactly what she was prepared to give to the house, who knew by instinct when her mistress withdrew in spirit from her responsibilities. Mrs. Parkes was one of the servers of this world, but she needed someone to serve. She had to have Mrs. Rawlings, her madam, at the top of the house or in the garden, so that she could come and get support from her: "Yes, the bread's not what it was when I was a girl. . . . Yes, Harry's got a wonderful appetite, I wonder where he puts it all. . . . Yes, it's lucky the twins are so much of a size, they can wear each other's shoes, that's a saving in these hard times. . . . Yes, the cherry jam from Switzerland is not a patch on the jam from Poland, and three times the price . . ." And so on. That sort of talk Mrs. Parkes must have, every day, or she would leave, not knowing herself why she left.

Susan Rawlings, thinking these thoughts, found that she was prowling through the great thicketed garden like a wild cat: she was walking up the stairs, down the stairs, through the rooms into the garden, along the brown running river, back, up through the house, down again. . . . It was a wonder Mrs. Parkes did not think it strange. But, on the contrary, Mrs. Rawlings could do what she liked, she could stand on her head if she wanted, provided she was *there*. Susan Rawlings prowled and muttered through her house, hating Mrs. Parkes, hating poor Miss Townsend, dreaming of her hour of solitude in the dingy respectability of Miss Townsend's hotel bedroom, and she knew quite well she was mad. Yes, she was mad.

She said to Matthew that she must have a holiday. Matthew agreed with her. This was not as things had been once—how they had talked in each other's arms in the marriage bed. He had, she knew, diagnosed her finally as *unreasonable*. She had become someone outside himself that he had to manage. They were living side by side in this house like two tolerably friendly strangers.

Having told Mrs. Parkes—or rather, asked for her permission—

she went off on a walking holiday in Wales. She chose the remotest place she knew of. Every morning the children telephoned her before they went off to school, to encourage and support her, just as they had over Mother's Room. Every evening she telephoned them, spoke to each child in turn, and then to Matthew. Mrs. Parkes, given permission to telephone for instructions or advice, did so every day at lunchtime. When, as happened three times, Mrs. Rawlings was out on the mountainside, Mrs. Parkes asked that she should ring back at such-and-such a time, for she would not be happy in what she was doing without Mrs. Rawlings' blessing.

Susan prowled over wild country with the telephone wire holding her to her duty like a leash. The next time she must telephone, or wait to be telephoned, nailed her to her cross. The mountains themselves seemed trammelled by her unfreedom. Everywhere on the mountains, where she met no one at all, from breakfast time to dusk, excepting sheep, or a shepherd, she came face to face with her own craziness, which might attack her in the broadest valleys, so that they seemed too small, or on a mountaintop from which she could see a hundred other mountains and valleys, so that they seemed too low, too small, with the sky pressing down too close. She would stand gazing at a hillside brilliant with ferns and bracken, jewelled with running water, and see nothing but her devil, who lifted inhuman eyes at her from where he leaned negligently on a rock, switching at his ugly yellow boots with a leafy twig.

She returned to her home and family, with the Welsh emptiness at the back of her mind like a promise of freedom.

She told her husband she wanted to have an *au pair* girl.[5]

They were in their bedroom, it was late at night, the children slept. He sat, shirted and slippered, in a chair by the window, looking out. She sat brushing her hair and watching him in the mirror. A time-hallowed scene in the connubial bedroom. He said nothing, while she heard the arguments coming into his mind, only to be rejected because every one was *reasonable*.

"It seems strange to get one now; after all, the children are in school most of the day. Surely the time for you to have help was when you were stuck with them day and night. Why don't you ask Mrs. Parkes to cook for you? She's even offered to—I can understand if you are tired of cooking for six people. But you know that an *au pair* girl means all kinds of problems, it's not like having an ordinary char in during the day. . . ."

Finally he said carefully: "Are you thinking of going back to work?"

5. Young woman, usually foreign, who lives in with a family, doing housework and babysitting in exchange for room and board.

"No," she said, "no, not really," She made herself sound vague, rather stupid. She went on brushing her black hair and peering at herself so as to be oblivious of the short uneasy glances her Matthew kept giving her. "Do you think we can't afford it?" she went on vaguely, not at all the old efficient Susan who knew exactly what they could afford.

"It's not that," he said, looking out of the window at dark trees, so as not to look at her. Meanwhile she examined a round, candid, pleasant face with clear dark brows and clear grey eyes. A sensible face. She brushed thick healthy black hair and thought: Yet that's the reflection of a madwoman. How very strange! Much more to the point if what looked back at me was the gingery green-eyed demon with his dry meagre smile. . . . Why wasn't Matthew agreeing? After all, what else could he do? She was breaking her part of the bargain and there was no way of forcing her to keep it: that her spirit, her soul, should live in this house, so that the people in it could grow like plants in water, and Mrs. Parkes remain content in their service. In return for this, he would be a good loving husband, and responsible towards the children. Well, nothing like this had been true of either of them for a long time. He did his duty, perfunctorily; she did not even pretend to do hers. And he had become like other husbands, with his real life in his work and the people he met there, and very likely a serious affair. All this was her fault.

At last he drew heavy curtains, blotting out the trees, and turned to force her attention: "Susan, are you really sure we need a girl?" But she would not meet his appeal at all. She was running the brush over her hair again and again, lifting fine black clouds in a small hiss of electricity. She was peering in and smiling as if she were amused at the clinging hissing hair that followed the brush.

"Yes, I think it would be a good idea, on the whole," she said, with the cunning of a madwoman evading the real point.

In the mirror she could see her Matthew lying on his back, his hands behind his head, staring upwards, his face sad and hard. She felt her heart (the old heart of Susan Rawlings) soften and call out to him. But she set it to be indifferent.

He said: "Susan, the children?" It was an appeal that *almost* reached her. He opened his arms, lifting them palms up, empty. She had only to run across and fling herself into them, onto his hard, warm chest, and melt into herself, into Susan. But she could not. She would not see his lifted arms. She said vaguely: "Well, surely it'll be even better for them? We'll get a French or a German girl and they'll learn the language."

In the dark she lay beside him, feeling frozen, a stranger. She felt as if Susan had been spirited away. She disliked very much this woman who lay here, cold and indifferent beside a suffering man, but she could not change her.

Next morning she set about getting a girl, and very soon came Sophie Traub from Hamburg, a girl of twenty, laughing, healthy, blue-eyed, intending to learn English. Indeed, she already spoke a good deal. In return for a room—"Mother's Room"—and her food, she undertook to do some light cooking, and to be with the children when Mrs. Rawlings asked. She was an intelligent girl and understood perfectly what was needed. Susan said: "I go off sometimes, for the morning or for the day—well, sometimes the children run home from school, or they ring up, or a teacher rings up. I should be here, really. And there's the daily woman. . . ." And Sophie laughed her deep fruity *Fräulein*'s laugh, showed her fine white teeth and her dimples, and said: "You want some person to play mistress of the house sometimes, not so?"

"Yes, that is just so," said Susan, a bit dry, despite herself, thinking in secret fear how easy it was, how much nearer to the end she was than she thought. Healthy Fräulein Traub's instant understanding of their position proved this to be true.

The *au pair* girl, because of her own commonsense, or (as Susan said to herself, with her new inward shudder) because she had been *chosen* so well by Susan, was a success with everyone, the children liking her, Mrs. Parkes forgetting almost at once that she was German, and Matthew finding her "nice to have around the house." For he was now taking things as they came, from the surface of life, withdrawn both as a husband and a father from the household.

One day Susan saw how Sophie and Mrs. Parkes were talking and laughing in the kitchen, and she announced that she would be away until tea time. She knew exactly where to go and what she must look for. She took the District Line to South Kensington, changed to the Circle, got off at Paddington,[6] and walked around looking at the smaller hotels until she was satisfied with one which had FRED'S HOTEL painted on windowpanes that needed cleaning. The facade was a faded shiny yellow, like unhealthy skin. A door at the end of a passage said she must knock; she did, and Fred appeared. He was not at all attractive, not in any way, being fattish, and run-down, and wearing a tasteless striped suit. He had small sharp eyes in a white creased face, and was quite prepared to let Mrs. Jones (she chose the farcical name deliberately, staring him out) have a room three days a week from ten until six. Provided of course that she paid in advance each time she came? Susan produced fifteen shillings (no price had been set by him) and held it out, still fixing him with a bold unblinking challenge she

6. Railway and subway station in London. The Circle is the Circle Line of the subway.

had not known until then she could use at will. Looking at her still, he took up a ten-shilling note from her palm between thumb and forefinger, fingered it; then shuffled up two half-crowns,[7] held out his own palm with these bits of money displayed thereon, and let his gaze lower broodingly at them. They were standing in the passage, a red-shaded light above, bare boards beneath, and a strong smell of floor polish rising about them. He shot his gaze up at her over the still-extended palm, and smiled as if to say: What do you take me for? "I shan't," said Susan, "be using this room for the purposes of making money." He still waited. She added another five shillings, at which he nodded and said: "You pay, and I ask no questions." "Good," said Susan. He now went past her to the stairs, and there waited a moment: the light from the street door being in her eyes, she lost sight of him momentarily. Then she saw a sober-suited, white-faced, white-balding little man trotting up the stairs like a waiter, and she went after him. They proceeded in utter silence up the stairs of this house where no questions were asked—Fred's Hotel, which could afford the freedom for its visitors that poor Miss Townsend's hotel could not. The room was hideous. It had a single window, with thin green brocade curtains, a three-quarter bed that had a cheap green satin bedspread on it, a fireplace with a gas fire and a shilling meter by it, a chest of drawers, and a green wicker armchair.

"Thank you," said Susan, knowing that Fred (if this was Fred, and not George, or Herbert or Charlie) was looking at her, not so much with curiosity, an emotion he would not own to, for professional reasons, but with a philosophical sense of what was appropriate. Having taken her money and shown her up and agreed to everything, he was clearly disapproving of her for coming here. She did not belong here at all, so his look said. (But she knew, already, how very much she did belong: the room had been waiting for her to join it.) "Would you have me called at five o'clock, please?" and he nodded and went downstairs.

It was twelve in the morning. She was free. She sat in the armchair, she simply sat, she closed her eyes and sat and let herself be alone. She was alone and no one knew where she was. When a knock came on the door she was annoyed, and prepared to show it: but it was Fred himself, it was five o'clock and he was calling her as ordered. He flicked his sharp little eyes over the room—bed, first. It was undisturbed. She might never have been in the room at all. She thanked him, said she would be returning the day after tomorrow, and left. She was back home in time to cook supper, to put the children to bed, to cook a second supper for her husband and herself later. And to wel-

7. Coins worth 5 shillings each.

come Sophie back from the pictures where she had gone with a friend. All these things she did cheerfully, willingly. But she was thinking all the time of the hotel room; she was longing for it with her whole being.

Three times a week. She arrived promptly at ten, looked Fred in the eyes, gave him twenty shillings, followed him up the stairs, went into the room, and shut the door on him with gentle firmness. For Fred, disapproving of her being here at all, was quite ready to let friendship, or at least acquaintanceship, follow his disapproval, if only she would let him. But he was content to go off on her dismissing nod, with the twenty shillings in his hand.

She sat in the armchair and shut her eyes.

What did she *do* in the room? Why, nothing at all. From the chair, when it had rested her, she went to the window, stretching her arms, smiling, treasuring her anonymity, to look out. She was no longer Susan Rawlings, mother of four, wife of Matthew, employer of Mrs. Parkes and of Sophie Traub, with these and those relations with friends, school-teachers, tradesmen. She no longer was mistress of the big white house and garden, owning clothes suitable for this and that activity or occasion. She was Mrs. Jones, and she was alone, and she had no past and no future. Here I am, she thought, after all these years of being married and having children and playing those roles of responsibility—and I'm just the same. Yet there have been times I thought that nothing existed of me except the roles that went with being Mrs. Matthew Rawlings. Yes, here I am, and if I never saw any of my family again, here I would still be . . . how very strange that is! And she leaned on the sill, and looked into the street, loving the men and women who passed, because she did not know them. She looked at the downtrodden buildings over the street, and at the sky, wet and dingy, or sometimes blue, and she felt she had never seen buildings or sky before. And then she went back to the chair, empty, her mind a blank. Sometimes she talked aloud, saying nothing—an exclamation, meaningless, followed by a comment about the floral pattern on the thin rug, or a stain on the green satin coverlet. For the most part, she wool-gathered—what word is there for it?—brooded, wandered, simply went dark, feeling emptiness run deliciously through her veins like the movement of her blood.

This room had become more her own than the house she lived in. One morning she found Fred taking her a flight higher than usual. She stopped, refusing to go up, and demanded her usual room, Number 19. "Well, you'll have to wait half an hour, then," he said. Willingly she descended to the dark disinfectant-smelling hall, and sat waiting until the two, man and woman, came down the stairs, giving her swift indifferent glances before they hurried out into the street, separating at the door. She went up to the room, *her* room, which they had just vacated. It was no less hers, though the windows were set wide open, and a maid was straightening the bed as she came in.

After these days of solitude, it was both easy to play her part as mother and wife, and difficult—because it was so easy: she felt an impostor. She felt as if her shell moved here, with her family, answering to Mummy, Mother, Susan, Mrs. Rawlings. She was surprised no one saw through her, that she wasn't turned out of doors, as a fake. On the contrary, it seemed the children loved her more; Matthew and she "got on" pleasantly, and Mrs. Parkes was happy in her work under (for the most part, it must be confessed) Sophie Traub. At night she lay beside her husband, and they made love again, apparently just as they used to, when they were really married. But she, Susan, or the being who answered so readily and improbably to the name of Susan, was not there: she was in Fred's Hotel, in Paddington, waiting for the easing hours of solitude to begin.

Soon she made a new arrangement with Fred and with Sophie. It was for five days a week. As for the money, five pounds, she simply asked Matthew for it. She saw that she was not even frightened he might ask what for: he would give it to her, she knew that, and yet it was terrifying it could be so, for this close couple, these partners, had once known the destination of every shilling they must spend. He agreed to give her five pounds a week. She asked for just so much, not a penny more. He sounded indifferent about it. It was as if he were paying her, she thought: *paying her off*—yes, that was it. Terror came back for a moment when she understood this, but she stilled it: things had gone too far for that. Now, every week, on Sunday nights, he gave her five pounds, turning away from her before their eyes could meet on the transaction. As for Sophie Traub, she was to be somewhere in or near the house until six at night, after which she was free. She was not to cook, or to clean; she was simply to be there. So she gardened or sewed, and asked friends in, being a person who was bound to have a lot of friends. If the children were sick, she nursed them. If teachers telephoned, she answered them sensibly. For the five daytimes in the school week, she was altogether the mistress of the house.

One night in the bedroom, Matthew asked: "Susan, I don't want to interfere—don't think that, please—but are you sure you are well?"

She was brushing her hair at the mirror. She made two more strokes on either side of her head, before she replied: "Yes, dear, I am sure I am well."

He was again lying on his back, his blond head on his hands, his elbows angled up and part-concealing his face. He said: "Then Susan, I have to ask you this question, though you must understand, I'm not putting any sort of pressure on you." (Susan heard the word "pressure" with dismay, because this was inevitable; of course she could not go on like this.) "Are things going to go on like this?"

"Well," she said, going vague and bright and idiotic again, so as to escape: "Well, I don't see why not."

He was jerking his elbows up and down, in annoyance or in pain, and, looking at him, she saw he had got thin, even gaunt; and restless angry movements were not what she remembered of him. He said: "Do you want a divorce, is that it?"

At this, Susan only with the greatest difficulty stopped herself from laughing: she could hear the bright bubbling laughter she *would* have emitted, had she let herself. He could only mean one thing: she had a lover, and that was why she spent her days in London, as lost to him as if she had vanished to another continent.

Then the small panic set in again: she understood that he hoped she did have a lover, he was begging her to say so, because otherwise it would be too terrifying.

She thought this out as she brushed her hair, watching the fine black stuff fly up to make its little clouds of electricity, hiss, hiss, hiss. Behind her head, across the room, was a blue wall. She realised she was absorbed in watching the black hair making shapes against the blue. She should be answering him. "Do *you* want a divorce, Matthew?"

He said: "That surely isn't the point, is it?"

"You brought it up, I didn't," she said, brightly, suppressing meaningless tinkling laughter.

Next day she asked Fred: "Have enquiries been made for me?"

He hesitated, and she said: "I've been coming here a year now. I've made no trouble, and you've been paid every day. I have a right to be told."

"As a matter of fact, Mrs. Jones, a man did come asking."

"A man from a detective agency?"

"Well, he could have been, couldn't he?"

"I was asking you. . . . Well, what did you tell him?"

"I told him a Mrs. Jones came every weekday from ten until five or six and stayed in Number 19 by herself."

"Describing me?"

"Well, Mrs. Jones, I had no alternative. Put yourself in my place."

"By rights I should deduct what that man gave you for the information."

He raised shocked eyes: she was not the sort of person to make jokes like this! Then he chose to laugh: a pinkish wet slit appeared across his white crinkled face; his eyes positively begged her to laugh, otherwise he might lose some money. She remained grave, looking at him.

He stopped laughing and said: "You want to go up now?"—returning to the familiarity, the comradeship, of the country where no questions are asked, on which (and he knew it) she depended completely.

She went up to sit in her wicker chair. But it was not the same. Her husband had searched her out. (The world had searched her out.) The pressures were on her. She was here with his connivance. He might walk in at any moment, here, into Room 19. She imagined the report from the detective agency: "A woman calling herself Mrs. Jones, fitting the description of your wife (et cetera, et cetera, et cetera), stays alone all day in Room No. 19. She insists on this room, waits for it if it is engaged. As far as the proprietor knows, she receives no visitors there, male or female." A report something on these lines Matthew must have received.

Well, of course he was right: things couldn't go on like this. He had put an end to it all simply by sending the detective after her.

She tried to shrink herself back into the shelter of the room, a snail pecked out of its shell and trying to squirm back. But the peace of the room had gone. She was trying consciously to revive it, trying to let go into the dark creative trance (or whatever it was) that she had found there. It was no use, yet she craved for it, she was as ill as a suddenly deprived addict.

Several times she returned to the room, to look for herself there, but instead she found the unnamed spirit of restlessness, a pricking fevered hunger for movement, an irritable self-consciousness that made her brain feel as if it had coloured lights going on and off inside it. Instead of the soft dark that had been the room's air, were now waiting for her demons that made her dash blindly about, muttering words of hate; she was impelling herself from point to point like a moth dashing itself against a windowpane, sliding to the bottom, fluttering off on broken wings, then crashing into the invisible barrier again. And again and again. Soon she was exhausted, and she told Fred that for a while she would not be needing the room, she was going on holiday. Home she went, to the big white house by the river. The middle of a weekday, and she felt guilty at returning to her own home when not expected. She stood unseen, looking in at the kitchen window. Mrs. Parkes, wearing a discarded floral overall of Susan's, was stooping to slide something into the oven. Sophie, arms folded, was leaning her back against a cupboard and laughing at some joke made by a girl not seen before by Susan—a dark foreign girl, Sophie's visitor. In an armchair Molly, one of the twins, lay curled, sucking her thumb and watching the grownups. She must have some sickness, to be kept from school. The child's listless face, the dark circles under her eyes, hurt Susan:

Molly was looking at the three grownups working and talking in exactly the same way Susan looked at the four through the kitchen window: she was remote, shut off from them.

But then, just as Susan imagined herself going in, picking up the little girl, and sitting in an armchair with her, stroking her probably heated forehead, Sophie did just that: she had been standing on one leg, the other knee flexed, its foot set against the wall. Now she let her foot in its ribbon-tied red shoe slide down the wall, stood solid on two feet, clapping her hands before and behind her, and sang a couple of lines in German, so that the child lifted her heavy eyes at her and began to smile. Then she walked, or rather skipped, over to the child, swung her up, and let her fall into her lap at the same moment she sat herself. She said "Hopla! Hopla! Molly . . ." and began stroking the dark untidy young head that Molly laid on her shoulder for comfort.

Well. . . . Susan blinked the tears of farewell out of her eyes, and went quietly up through the house to her bedroom. There she sat looking at the river through the trees. She felt at peace, but in a way that was new to her. She had no desire to move, to talk, to do anything at all. The devils that had haunted the house, the garden, were not there; but she knew it was because her soul was in Room 19 in Fred's Hotel; she was not really here at all. It was a sensation that should have been frightening: to sit at her own bedroom window, listening to Sophie's rich young voice sing German nursery songs to her child, listening to Mrs. Parkes clatter and move below, and to know that all this had nothing to do with her: she was already out of it.

Later, she made herself go down and say she was home: it was unfair to be here unannounced. She took lunch with Mrs. Parkes, Sophie, Sophie's Italian friend Maria, and her daughter Molly, and felt like a visitor.

A few days later, at bedtime, Matthew said: "Here's your five pounds," and pushed them over at her. Yet he must have known she had not been leaving the house at all.

She shook her head, gave it back to him, and said, in explanation, not in accusation: "As soon as you knew where I was, there was no point."

He nodded, not looking at her. He was turned away from her: thinking, she knew, how best to handle this wife who terrified him.

He said: "I wasn't trying to . . . It's just that I was worried."

"Yes, I know."

"I must confess that I was beginning to wonder . . ."

"You thought I had a lover?"

"Yes, I am afraid I did."

She knew that he wished she had. She sat wondering how to say:

"For a year now I've been spending all my days in a very sordid hotel room. It's the place where I'm happy. In fact, without it I don't exist." She heard herself saying this, and understood how terrified he was that she might. So instead she said: "Well, perhaps you're not far wrong."

Probably Matthew would think the hotel proprietor lied: he would want to think so.

"Well," he said, and she could hear his voice spring up, so to speak, with relief, "in that case I must confess I've got a bit of an affair on myself."

She said, detached and interested: "Really? Who is she?" and saw Matthew's startled look because of this reaction.

"It's Phil. Phil Hunt."

She had known Phil Hunt well in the old unmarried days. She was thinking: No, she won't do, she's too neurotic and difficult. She's never been happy yet. Sophie's much better. Well, Matthew will see that himself, as sensible as he is.

This line of thought went on in silence, while she said aloud: "It's no point in telling you about mine, because you don't know him."

Quick, quick, invent, she thought. Remember how you invented all that nonsense for Miss Townsend.

She began slowly, careful not to contradict herself: "His name is Michael" *(Michael What?)*—"Michael Plant." (What a silly name!) "He's rather like you—in looks, I mean." And indeed, she could imagine herself being touched by no one but Matthew himself. "He's a publisher." (Really? Why?) "He's got a wife already and two children."

She brought out this fantasy, proud of herself.

Matthew said: "Are you two thinking of marrying?"

She said, before she could stop herself: "Good God, *no!*"

She realised, if Matthew wanted to marry Phil Hunt, that this was too emphatic, but apparently it was all right, for his voice sounded relieved as he said: "It is a bit impossible to imagine oneself married to anyone else, isn't it?" With which he pulled her to him, so that her head lay on his shoulder. She turned her face into the dark of his flesh, and listened to the blood pounding through her ears saying: I am alone, I am alone, I am alone.

In the morning Susan lay in bed while he dressed.

He had been thinking things out in the night, because now he said: "Susan, why don't we make a foursome?"

Of course, she said to herself, of course he would be bound to say that. If one is sensible, if one is reasonable, if one never allows oneself a base thought or an envious emotion, naturally one says: Let's make a foursome!

"Why not?" she said.

"We could all meet for lunch. I mean, it's ridiculous, you sneaking off to filthy hotels, and me staying late at the office, and all the lies everyone has to tell."

What on earth did I say his name was?—she panicked, then said: "I think it's a good idea, but Michael is away at the moment. When he comes back, though—and I'm sure you two would like each other."

"He's away, is he? So that's why you've been . . ." Her husband put his hand to the knot of his tie in a gesture of male coquetry she would not before have associated with him; and he bent to kiss her cheek with the expression that goes with the words: Oh you naughty little puss! And she felt its answering look, naughty and coy, come onto her face.

Inside she was dissolving in horror at them both, at how far they had both sunk from honesty of emotion.

So now she was saddled with a lover, and he had a mistress! How ordinary, how reassuring, how jolly! And now they would make a foursome of it, and go about to theatres and restaurants. After all, the Rawlings could well afford that sort of thing, and presumably the publisher Michael Plant could afford to do himself and his mistress quite well. No, there was nothing to stop the four of them developing the most intricate relationship of civilised tolerance, all enveloped in a charming afterglow of autumnal passion. Perhaps they would all go off on holidays together? She had known people who did. Or perhaps Matthew would draw the line there? Why should he, though, if he was capable of talking about "foursomes" at all?

She lay in the empty bedroom, listening to the car drive off with Matthew in it, off to work. Then she heard the children clattering off to school to the accompaniment of Sophie's cheerfully ringing voice. She slid down into the hollow of the bed, for shelter against her own irrelevance. And she stretched out her hand to the hollow where her husband's body had lain, but found no comfort there: he was not her husband. She curled herself up in a small tight ball under the clothes: she could stay here all day, all week, indeed, all her life.

But in a few days she must produce Michael Plant, and—but how? She must presumably find some agreeable man prepared to impersonate a publisher called Michael Plant. And in return for which she would—what? Well, for one thing they would make love. The idea made her want to cry with sheer exhaustion. Oh no, she had finished with all that—the proof of it was that the words "make love," or even imagining it, trying hard to revive no more than the pleasures of sensuality, let alone affection, or love, made her want to run away and hide from the sheer effort of the thing. . . . Good Lord, why make love at all? Why make love with anyone? Or if you are going to make love, what does it matter who with? Why shouldn't she simply walk into the street, pick up a man and have a roaring sexual affair with him? Why not? Or even with Fred? What difference did it make?

But she had let herself in for it—an interminable stretch of time with a lover, called Michael, as part of a gallant civilised foursome. Well, she could not, and she would not.

She got up, dressed, went down to find Mrs. Parkes, and asked her for the loan of a pound, since Matthew, she said, had forgotten to leave her money. She exchanged with Mrs. Parkes variations on the theme that husbands are all the same, they don't think, and without saying a word to Sophie, whose voice could be heard upstairs from the telephone, walked to the underground, travelled to South Kensington, changed to the Inner Circle, got out at Paddington, and walked to Fred's Hotel. There she told Fred that she wasn't going on holiday after all, she needed the room. She would have to wait an hour, Fred said. She went to a busy tearoom-cum-restaurant around the corner, and sat watching the people flow in and out the door that kept swinging open and shut, watched them mingle and merge, and separate, felt her being flow into them, into their movement. When the hour was up, she left a half-crown for her pot of tea, and left the place without looking back at it, just as she had left her house, the big, beautiful white house, without another look, but silently dedicating it to Sophie. She returned to Fred, received the key of Number 19, now free, and ascended the grimy stairs slowly, letting floor after floor fall away below her, keeping her eyes lifted, so that floor after floor descended jerkily to her level of vision, and fell away out of sight.

Number 19 was the same. She saw everything with an acute, narrow, checking glance: the cheap shine of the satin spread, which had been replaced carelessly after the two bodies had finished their convulsions under it; a trace of powder on the glass that topped the chest of drawers; an intense green shade in a fold of the curtain. She stood at the window, looking down, watching people pass and pass and pass until her mind went dark from the constant movement. Then she sat in the wicker chair, letting herself go slack. But she had to be careful, because she did not want, today, to be surprised by Fred's knock at five o'clock.

The demons were not here. They had gone forever, because she was buying her freedom from them. She was slipping already into the dark fructifying dream that seemed to caress her inwardly, like the movement of her blood . . . but she had to think about Matthew first. Should she write a letter for the coroner? But what should she say? She would like to leave him with the look on his face she had seen this morning—banal, admittedly, but at least confidently healthy. Well, that was impossible, one did not look like that with a wife dead from suicide. But how to leave him believing she was dying because of a man—because of the fascinating publisher Michael Plant? Oh, how ridiculous! How absurd! How humiliating! But she decided not to trouble about it, simply not to think about the living. If he wanted to believe she had a lover, he would believe it. And he *did* want to believe it. Even when he had found out that there was no publisher in London called Michael Plant, he would think: Oh poor Susan, she was afraid to give me his real name.

And what did it matter whether he married Phil Hunt or Sophie? Though it ought to be Sophie, who was already the mother of those children . . . and what hypocrisy to sit here worrying about the children, when she was going to leave them because she had not got the energy to stay.

She had about four hours. She spent them delightfully, darkly, sweetly, letting herself slide gently, gently, to the edge of the river. Then, with hardly a break in her consciousness, she got up, pushed the thin rug against the door, made sure the windows were tight shut, put two shillings in the meter, and turned on the gas. For the first time since she had been in the room she lay on the hard bed that smelled stale, that smelled of sweat and sex.

She lay on her back on the green satin cover, but her legs were chilly. She got up, found a blanket folded in the bottom of the chest of drawers, and carefully covered her legs with it. She was quite content lying there, listening to the faint soft hiss of the gas that poured into the room, into her lungs, into her brain, as she drifted off into the dark river.

---

1. Interpret the first sentence in the light of the story as a whole. What ambiguities lie in the words "a failure of intelligence"?
2. Is one partner more to blame than the other for the disappointments of married life? Explain.
3. Does the author seem to favor or oppose any person or social pattern depicted here?
4. Are the husband's adulteries truly decisive in determining the outcome? The timing of the adulteries or his explanation of them?
5. Is there any decisive event in Susan's life or flaw in her character which motivates her to commit suicide?

James Alan McPherson

McPherson (1943–) was born in Savannah, Georgia. He worked in a supermarket, delivered papers as a child, and worked as a dining car waiter during a summer when he was attending college. At Harvard, where he graduated from the Law School, he did part-time work as a janitor, community organizer, and research assistant. After taking his law degree, he spent some time as a reporter for a black newspaper in Roxbury, Massachusetts. His craftsmanship, compassion, and humor have distinguished him among the younger generation of black writers. His stories were collected in Hue and Cry *(1969) and* Elbow Room *(1977), which won a Pulitzer Prize.*

Gold Coast

I

That spring, when I had a great deal of potential and no money at all, I took a job as a janitor. That was when I was still very young and spent money very freely, and when, almost every night, I drifted off to sleep lulled by sweet anticipation of that time when my potential would suddenly be realized and there would be capsule biographies of my life on dust jackets of many books, all proclaiming: ". . . He knew life on many levels. From shoeshine boy, freelance waiter, 3rd cook, janitor, he rose to . . ." I had never been a janitor before and I did not really have to be one and that is why I did it. But now, much later, I think it might have been because it is possible to be a janitor without really becoming one, and at parties or at mixers when asked what it was I did for a living, it was pretty good to hook my thumbs in my vest pockets and say comfortably: "Why, I am an apprentice janitor." The hippies would think it degenerate and really dig me and it made me feel good that people in Philosophy and Law and Business would feel uncomfortable trying to make me feel better about my station while wondering how the hell I had managed to crash the party.

"What's an apprentice janitor?" they would ask.

"I haven't got my card yet," I would reply. "Right now I'm just taking lessons. There's lots of complicated stuff you have to learn before you get your card and your own building."

"What kind of stuff?"

"Human nature, for one thing. *Race* nature, for another."

"Why race?"

"Because," I would say in a low voice looking around lest someone else should overhear, "you have to be able to spot Jews and Negroes who are passing."[1]

"That's terrible," would surely be said then with a hint of indignation.

"It's an art," I would add masterfully.

After a good pause I would invariably be asked: "But you're a Negro yourself, how can you keep your own people out?"

At which point I would look terribly disappointed and say: "*I* don't keep them out. But if they get in it's my job to make their stay just as miserable as possible. Things are changing."

Now the speaker would just look at me in disbelief.

"It's Janitorial Objectivity," I would say to finish the thing as the speaker began to edge away. "Don't hate me," I would call after him to his considerable embarrassment. "Somebody has to do it."

It was an old building near Harvard Square. Conrad Aiken had once lived there and in the days of the Gold Coast,[2] before Harvard built its great Houses, it had been a very fine haven for the rich; but that was a world ago, and this building was one of the few monuments of that era which had survived. The lobby had a high ceiling with thick redwood beams and it was replete with marble floor, fancy ironwork, and an old-fashioned house telephone that no longer worked. Each apartment had a small fireplace, and even the large bathtubs and chain toilets, when I was having my touch of nature, made me wonder what prominent personage of the past had worn away all the newness. And, being there, I felt a certain affinity toward the rich.

It was a funny building: because the people who lived there made it old. Conveniently placed as it was between the Houses and Harvard Yard, I expected to find it occupied by a company of hippies, hopeful working girls, and assorted graduate students. Instead, there were a majority of old maids, dowagers, asexual middle-aged men, homosexual young men, a few married couples and a teacher. No one was shacking up there, and walking through the quiet halls in the early evening, I sometimes had the urge to knock on a door and expose myself just to hear someone breathe hard for once.

It was a Cambridge spring: down by the Charles[3] happy students were making love while sad-eyed middle-aged men watched them from the bridge. It was a time of activity: Law students were busy sublimating, Business School people were making records of the money they would make, the Harvard Houses were clearing out, and in the Square

1. I.e., who present themselves as being Christian and white. 2. A once fashionable block of expensive apartment houses south of Harvard Yard. Aiken (1889–1973) was an American poet, novelist, and critic. 3. The Charles River.

bearded pot-pushers were setting up their restaurant tables in anticipation of the Summer School faithfuls. There was a change of season in the air, and to comply with its urgings, James Sullivan, the old superintendent, passed his three beaten garbage cans on to me with the charge that I should take up his daily rounds of the six floors, and with unflinching humility, gather whatever scraps the old-maid tenants had refused to husband.

I then became very rich, with my own apartment, a sensitive girl, a stereo, two speakers, one tattered chair, one fork, a job, and the urge to acquire. Having all this and youth besides made me pity Sullivan: he had been in that building thirty years and had its whole history recorded in the little folds of his mind, as his own life was recorded in the wrinkles of his face. All he had to show for his time there was a berserk dog, a wife almost as mad as the dog, three cats, bursitis, acute myopia, and a drinking problem. He was well over seventy and could hardly walk, and his weekly check of twenty-two dollars from the company that managed the building would not support anything. So, out of compromise, he was retired to superintendent of my labor.

My first day as a janitor, while I skillfully lugged my three overflowing cans of garbage out of the building, he sat on his bench in the lobby, faded and old and smoking in patched, loose blue pants. He watched me. He was a chain smoker and I noticed right away that he very carefully dropped all of the ashes and butts on the floor and crushed them under his feet until there was a yellow and gray smear. Then he laboriously pushed the mess under the bench with his shoe, all the while eyeing me like a cat in silence as I hauled the many cans of muck out to the big disposal unit next to the building. When I had finished, he gave me two old plates to help stock my kitchen and his first piece of advice.

"Sit down, for Chrissake, and take a load off your feet," he told me.

I sat on the red bench next to him and accepted the wilted cigarette he offered me from the crushed package he kept in his sweater pocket.

"Now I'll tell you something to help you get along in the building," he said.

I listened attentively.

"If any of these sons-of-bitches ever ask you to do something extra, be sure to charge them for it."

I assured him that I absolutely would.

"If they can afford to live here, they can afford to pay. The bastards."

"Undoubtedly," I assured him again.

"And another thing," he added. "Don't let any of these girls shove any cat shit under your nose. That ain't your job. You tell them to put it in a bag and take it out themselves."

I reminded him that I knew very well my station in life, and that I was not about to haul cat shit or anything of that nature. He looked at me through his thick-lensed glasses. He looked like a cat himself. "That's right," he said at last. "And if they still try to sneak it in the trash be sure to make the bastards pay. They can afford it." He crushed his seventh butt on the floor and scattered the mess some more while he lit up another. "I never hauled out no cat shit in the thirty years I been here and you don't do it either."

"I'm going up to wash my hands," I said.

"Remember," he called after me, "don't take no shit from any of them."

I protested once more that, upon my life, I would never, never do it, not even for the prettiest girl in the building. Going up in the elevator, I felt comfortably resolved that I would never do it. There were no pretty girls in the building.

I never found out what he had done before he came there, but I do know that being a janitor in that building was as high as he ever got in life. He had watched two generations of the rich pass the building on their way to the Yard, and he had seen many governors ride white horses thirty times into that same Yard[4] to send sons and daughters of the rich out into life to produce, to acquire, to procreate and to send back sons and daughters so that the cycle would continue. He had watched the cycle from when he had been able to haul the cans out for himself, and now he could not, and he was bitter.

He was Irish, of course, and he took pride in Irish accomplishments when he could have none of his own. He had known Frank O'Connor[5] when that writer had been at Harvard. He told me on many occasions how O'Connor had stopped to talk every day on his way to the Yard. He had also known James Michael Curley,[6] and his most colorful memory of the man was a long ago day when he and James Curley sat in a Boston bar and one of Curley's runners had come in and said: "Hey Jim, Sol Bernstein the Jew wants to see you." And Curley, in his deep, memorial voice had said to James Sullivan: "Let us go forth and meet this Israelite Prince." These were his memories, and I would obediently put aside my garbage cans and laugh with him over the hundred or so colorful, insignificant little details which made up a whole lifetime of living in the basement of Harvard. And although they were of little value to me then, I knew that they were the reflections of a lifetime and the happiest moments he would ever have, being

4. The governor of Massachusetts is always one of the many dignitaries invited to be present at a Harvard commencement. 5. Pen name of Michael John O'Donovan (1903–1966), Irish short-story writer. 6. Four-time mayor of Boston (1874–1958).

sold to me cheap, as youthful time is cheap, for as little time and interest as I wanted to spend. It was a buyer's market.

II

In those days I believed myself gifted with a boundless perception and attacked my daily garbage route with a gusto superreinforced by the happy knowledge that behind each of the fifty or so doors in our building lived a story which could, if I chose to grace it with the magic of my pen, become immortal. I watched my tenants fanatically, noting their perversions, their visitors, and their eating habits. So intense was my search for material that I had to restrain myself from going through their refuse scrap by scrap; but at the topmost layers of muck, without too much hand-soiling in the process, I set my perceptions to work. By late June, however, I had discovered only enough to put together a skimpy, rather naïve Henry Miller[7] novel. The most colorful discoveries being:

(1) The lady in #24 was an alumna of Paducah College.
(2) The couple in #55 made love at least five hundred times a week and the wife had not yet discovered the pill.
(3) The old lady in #36 was still having monthly inconvenience.
(4) The two fatsos in #56 consumed nightly an extraordinary amount of chili.
(5) The fat man in #54 had two dogs that were married to each other, but he was not married to anyone at all.
(6) The middle-aged man in #63 threw out an awful lot of flowers.

Disturbed by the snail's progress I was making, I confessed my futility to James one day as he sat on his bench chain-smoking and smearing butts on my newly waxed lobby floor. "So you want to know about the tenants?" he said, his cat's eyes flickering over me.

I nodded.

"Well the first thing to notice is how many Jews there are."

"I haven't noticed many Jews," I said.

He eyed me in amazement.

"Well, a few," I said quickly to prevent my treasured perception from being dulled any further.

"A few, hell," he said. "There's more Jews here than anybody."

"How can you tell?"

He gave me that undecided look again. "Where do you think all that garbage comes from?" He nodded feebly toward my bulging cans. I looked just in time to prevent a stray noodle from slipping over the

7. American novelist (1891–1980), especially noted for his explicit handling of sexual themes.

brim. "That's right," he continued. "Jews are the biggest eaters in the world. They eat the best too."

I confessed then that I was of the chicken-soup generation and believed that Jews ate only enough to muster strength for their daily trips to the bank.

"Not so!" he replied emphatically. "You never heard the expression: 'Let's get to the restaurant before the Jews get there'?"

I shook my head sadly.

"You don't know that in certain restaurants they take the free onions and pickles off the tables when they see Jews coming?"

I held my head down in shame over the bounteous heap.

He trudged over to my can and began to turn back the leaves of noodles and crumpled tissues from #47 with his hand. After a few seconds of digging he unmucked an empty paté can. "Look at that," he said triumphantly. "Gourmet stuff, no less."

"That's from #44," I said.

"What else?" he said all-knowingly. "In 1946 a Swedish girl moved in up there and took a Jewish girl for her roommate. Then the Swedish girl moved out and there's been a Jewish Dynasty up there ever since."

I recalled that #44 was occupied by a couple that threw out a good number of S. S. Pierce cans, Chivas Regal bottles, assorted broken records, and back issues of *Evergreen* and the *Realist*.[8]

"You're right," I said.

"Of course," he replied as if there was never any doubt. "I can spot them anywhere, even when they think they're passing." He leaned closer and said in a you-and-me voice: "But don't ever say anything bad about them in public, the Anti-Defamation League[9] will get you."

Just then his wife screamed for him from the second floor, and the dog joined her and beat against the door. He got into the elevator painfully and said: "Don't ever talk about them in public. You don't know who they are and that Defamation League will take everything you got."

Sullivan did not really hate Jews. He was just bitter toward anyone better off than himself. He liked me because I seemed to like hauling garbage and because I listened to him and seemed to respect what he said and seemed to imply, by lingering on even when he repeated himself, that I was eager to take what wisdom he had for no other reason than that I needed it in order to get along.

He lived with his wife on the second floor and his apartment was dirty because both of them were sick and old, and neither could move very well. His wife swept dirt out into the hall, and two hours after I

8. Radical intellectual magazines; S. S. Pierce was a fashionable Boston gourmet store; Chivas Regal is an expensive brand of Scotch whisky.   9. Organization formed to combat anti-Semitism.

had mopped and waxed their section of the floor, there was sure to be a layer of dirt, grease, and crushed-scattered tobacco from their door to the end of the hall. There was a smell of dogs and cats and age and death about their door, and I did not ever want to have to go in there for any reason because I feared something about it I cannot name.

Mrs. Sullivan, I found out, was from South Africa. She loved animals much more than people and there was a great deal of pain in her face. She kept little pans of meat posted at strategic points about the building, and I often came across her in the early morning or late at night throwing scraps out of the second-floor window to stray cats. Once, when James was about to throttle a stray mouse in their apartment, she had screamed at him to give the mouse a sporting chance. Whenever she attempted to walk she had to balance herself against a wall or a rail, and she hated the building because it confined her. She also hated James and most of the tenants. On the other hand, she loved the *Johnny Carson Show*, she loved to sit outside on the front steps (because she could get no further unassisted), and she loved to talk to anyone who would stop to listen. She never spoke coherently except when she was cursing James, and then she had a vocabulary like a sailor. She had great, shrill lungs, and her screams, accompanied by the rabid barks of the dog, could be heard all over the building. She was never really clean, her teeth were bad, and the first most pathetic thing in the world was to see her sitting on the steps in the morning watching the world pass, in a stained smock and a fresh summer blue hat she kept just to wear downstairs, with no place in the world to go. James told me, on the many occasions of her screaming, that she was mentally disturbed and could not control herself. The admirable thing about him was that he never lost his temper with her, no matter how rough her curses became and no matter who heard them. And the second most pathetic thing in the world was to see them slowly making their way in Harvard Square, he supporting her, through the hurrying crowds of miniskirted summer girls, J-Pressed[1] Ivy Leaguers, beatniks, and bused Japanese tourists, decked in cameras, who would take pictures of every inch of Harvard Square except them. Once, he told me, a hippie had brushed past them and called back over his shoulder: "Don't break any track records, Mr. and Mrs. Speedy Molasses."

Also on the second floor lived Miss O'Hara, a spinster who hated Sullivan as only an old maid can hate an old man. Across from her lived a very nice, gentle, celibate named Murphy who had once served with Montgomery[2] in North Africa and who was now spending the rest of

1. Wearing men's attire from J. Press clothing store. 2. Bernard Law Montgomery (1887–1976), British field marshall and leading Allied commander of World War II.

his life cleaning his little apartment and gossiping with Miss O'Hara. It was an Irish Floor.

I never found out just why Miss O'Hara hated the Sullivans with such a passion. Perhaps it was because they were so unkempt and she was so superciliously clean. Perhaps it was because Miss O'Hara had a great deal of Irish pride and they were stereotyped Irish. Perhaps it was because she merely had no reason to like them. She was a fanatic about cleanliness and put out her little bit of garbage wrapped very neatly in yesterday's *Christian Science Monitor* and tied in a bow with a fresh piece of string. Collecting all those little neat packages, I would wonder where she got the string and imagined her at night picking meat-market locks with a hairpin and hobbling off with yards and yards of white cord concealed under the gray sweater she always wore. I could even imagine her back in her little apartment chuckling and rolling the cord into a great white ball by candlelight. Then she would stash it away in her breadbox. Miss O'Hara kept her door slightly open until late at night, and I suspected that she heard everything that went on in the building. I had the feeling that I should never dare to make love with gusto for fear that she would overhear and write down all my happy-time phrases, to be maliciously recounted to me if she were ever provoked.

She had been in the building longer than Sullivan, and I suppose that her greatest ambition in life was to outlive him and then attend his wake with a knitting ball and needles. She had been trying to get him fired for twenty-five years or so and did not know when to quit. On summer nights when I painfully mopped the second floor, she would offer me root beer, apples, or cupcakes while trying to pump me for evidence against him.

"He's just a filthy old man, Robert," she would declare in a little-old-lady whisper. "And don't think you have to clean up those dirty old butts of his. Just report him to the Company."

"Oh, I don't mind," I would tell her, gulping the root beer as fast as possible.

"Well, they're both a couple of lushes, if you ask me. They haven't been sober a day in twenty-five years."

"Well, she's sick too, you know."

"Ha!" She would throw up her hands in disgust. "She's only sick when he doesn't give her the booze."

I fought to keep down a burp. "How long have *you* been here?"

She motioned for me to step out of the hall and into her dark apartment. "Don't tell him,"—she nodded towards Sullivan's door—"but I've been here for thirty-four years." She waited for me to be taken aback. Then she added: "And it was a better building before those two lushes came."

She then offered me an apple, asked five times if the dog's barking bothered me, forced me to take a fudge brownie, said that the cats had wet the floor again last night, got me to dust the top of a large chest too high for her to reach, had me pick up the minute specks of dust which fell from my dustcloth, pressed another root beer on me, and then showed me her family album. As an afterthought, she had me take down a big old picture of her greatgrandfather, also too high for her to reach, so that I could dust that too. Then together we picked up the dust from it which might have fallen to the floor. "He's really a filthy old man, Robert," she said in closing, "and don't be afraid to report him to the property manager any time you want."

I assured her that I would do it at the slightest provocation from Sullivan, finally accepted an apple but refused the money she offered, and escaped back to my mopping. Even then she watched me, smiling, from her half-opened door.

"Why does Miss O'Hara hate you?" I asked James once.

He lifted his cigaretted hand and let the long ash fall elegantly to the floor. "That old bitch has been an albatross around my neck ever since I got here," he said. "Don't trust her, Robert. It was her kind that sat around singing hymns and watching them burn saints in this state."

There was never an adequate answer to my question. And even though the dog was noisy and would surely kill someone if it ever got loose, no one could really dislike the old man because of it. The dog was all they had. In his garbage each night, for every wine bottle, there would be an equally empty can of dog food. Some nights he took the brute out for a long walk, when he could barely walk himself, and both of them had to be led back to the building.

III

In those days I had forgotten that I was first of all a black and I had a very lovely girl who was not first of all a black. We were both young and optimistic then, and she believed with me in my potential and liked me partly because of it; and I was happy because she belonged to me and not to the race, which made her special. It made me special too because I did not have to wear a beard or hate or be especially hip or ultra-Ivy Leaguish. I did not have to smoke pot or supply her with it, or be for any other cause at all except myself. I only had to be myself, which pleased me; and I only had to produce, which pleased both of us. Like many of the artistically inclined rich, she wanted to own in someone else what she could not own in herself. But this I did not mind, and I forgave her for it because she forgave me moods and the constant smell of garbage and a great deal of latent hostility. She only minded James Sullivan and all the valuable time I was wasting listening to him rattle on and on. His conversations, she thought, were useless, repetitious, and promised nothing of value to me. She was accustomed to the old-rich whose conversations meandered around a leitmotiv of how well off they were and how much they would leave behind very soon. She was not at all cold, but she had been taught how to tolerate the old-poor and perhaps toss them a greeting in passing. But nothing more.

Sullivan did not like her when I first introduced them because he saw that she was not a hippie and could not be dismissed. It is in the nature of things that liberal people will tolerate two interracial hippies more than they will an intelligent, serious-minded mixed couple. The former liaison is easy to dismiss as the dregs of both races, deserving of each other and the contempt of both races; but the latter poses a threat because there is no immediacy or overpowering sensuality or "you-pick-my-fleas-I'll-pick-yours" apparent on the surface of things, and people, even the most publicly liberal, cannot dismiss it so easily.

"That girl is Irish, isn't she?" he had asked one day in my apartment soon after I had introduced them.

"No," I said definitely.

"What's her name again?"

"Judy Smith," I said, which was not her name at all.

"Well, I can spot it," he said. "She's got Irish blood, all right."

"Everybody's got a little Irish blood," I told him.

He looked at me cattily and craftily from behind his thick lenses. "Well, she's from a good family, I suppose."

"I suppose," I said.

He paused to let some ashes fall to the rug. "They say the Colonel's lady and Nelly O'Grady are sisters under the skin."[3] Then he added: "Rudyard Kipling."

"That's true," I said with equal innuendo, "that's why you have to maintain a distinction by marrying the Colonel's Lady."

An understanding passed between us then, and we never spoke more on the subject.

Almost every night the cats wet the second floor while Meg Sullivan watched the *Johnny Carson Show* and the dog howled and clawed the door. During commercials Meg would curse James to get out and stop dropping ashes on the floor or to take the dog out or something else, totally unintelligible to those of us on the fourth, fifth and sixth

3. From "The Ladies" by Rudyard Kipling (1865–1936): "For the Colonel's Lady an' Judy O'Grady/ Are sisters under their skins."

floors. Even after the *Carson Show* she would still curse him to get out, until finally he would go down to the basement and put away a bottle or two of wine. There was a steady stench of cat functions in the basement, and with all the grease and dirt, discarded trunks, beer bottles, chairs, old tools and the filthy sofa on which he sometimes slept, seeing him there made me want to cry. He drank the cheapest sherry, the wino kind, straight from the bottle; and on many nights that summer at 2:00 A.M. my phone would ring me out of bed.

"Rob? Jimmy Sullivan here. What are you doing?"

There was nothing suitable to say.

"Come on down to the basement for a drink."

"I have to be at work at eight-thirty," I would protest.

"Can't you have just one drink?" he would say pathetically.

I would carry down my own glass so that I would not have to drink out of the bottle. Looking at him on the sofa, I could not be mad because now I had many records for my stereo, a story that was going well, a girl who believed in me and belonged to me and not to the race, a new set of dishes, and a tomorrow morning with younger people.

"I don't want to burden you unduly," he would always preface.

I would force myself not to look at my watch and say: "Of course not."

"My Meg is not in the best health, you know," he would say, handing the bottle to me.

"She's just old."

"The doctors say she should be in an institution."

"That's no place to be."

"I'm a sick man myself, Rob. I can't take much more. She's crazy."

"Anybody who loves animals can't be crazy."

He took another long draw from the bottle. "I won't live another year. I'll be dead in a year."

"You don't know that."

He looked at me closely, without his glasses, so that I could see the desperation in his eyes. "I just hope Meg goes before I do. I don't want them to put her in an institution after I'm gone."

At 2:00 A.M. with the cat stench in my nose and a glass of bad sherry standing still in my hand because I refused in my mind to touch it, and when all my dreams of greatness were above him and the basement and the building itself, I did not know what to say. The only way I could keep from hating myself was to talk about the AMA[4] or the Medicare program or hippies. He was pure hell on all three. To him, the medical profession was "morally bankrupt," Medicare was a great

4. American Medical Association.

farce which deprived oldsters like himself of their "rainy-day dollars," and hippies were "dropouts from the human race." He could rage on and on in perfect phrases about all three of his major dislikes, and I had the feeling that because the sentences were so well constructed and well turned, he might have memorized them from something he had read. But then he was extremely well read and it did not matter if he had borrowed a phrase or two from someone else. The ideas were still his own.

It would be 3:00 A.M. before I knew it, and then 3:30, and still he would go on. He hated politicians in general and liked to recount, at these times, his private catalogue of political observations. By the time he got around to Civil Rights it would be 4:00 A.M., and I could not feel sorry or responsible for him at that hour. I would begin to yawn and at first he would just ignore it. Then I would start to edge toward the door, and he would see that he could hold me no longer, not even by declaring that he wanted to be an honorary Negro because he loved the race so much.

"I hope I haven't burdened you unduly," he would say again.

"Of course not," I would say, because it was over then and I could leave him and the smell of the cats there and sometimes I would go out in the cool night and walk around the Yard and be thankful that I was only an assistant janitor, and a transient one at that. Walking in the early dawn and seeing the Summer School fellows sneak out of the girls' dormitories in the Yard gave me a good feeling, and I thought that tomorrow night it would be good to make love myself so that I could be busy when he called.

IV

"Why don't you tell that old man your job doesn't include babysitting with him?" Jean told me many times when she came over to visit during the day and found me sleeping.

I would look at her and think to myself about social forces and the pressures massing and poised, waiting to attack us. It was still July then. It was hot and I was working good. "He's just an old man," I said. "Who else would listen to him?"

"You're too soft. As long as you do your work you don't have to be bothered with him."

"He could be a story if I listened long enough."

"There are too many stories about old people."

"No," I said, thinking about us again, "there are just too many people who have no stories."

Sometimes he would come up and she would be there, but I would let him come in anyway, and he would stand in the room looking dirty and uncomfortable, offering some invented reason for having intruded. At these times something silent would pass between them, something I cannot name, which would reduce him to exactly what he was: an old man, come out of his basement to intrude where he was not wanted. But all the time this was being communicated, there would be a surface, friendly conversation between them. And after five minutes or so of being unwelcome, he would apologize for having come, drop a few ashes on the rug and back out the door. Downstairs we could hear his wife screaming.

We endured and aged and August was almost over. Inside the building the cats were still wetting, Meg was still screaming, the dog was getting madder, and Sullivan began to drink during the day. Outside it was hot and lush and green, and the summer girls were wearing shorter miniskirts and no panties and the middle-aged men down by the Charles were going wild on their bridge. Everyone was restless for change, for August is the month when undone summer things must be finished or regretted all through the winter.

V

Being imaginative people, Jean and I played a number of original games. One of them we called "Social Forces," the object of which was to see which side could break us first. We played it with the unknown nightriders who screamed obscenities from passing cars. And because that was her side I would look at her expectantly, but she would laugh and say: "No." We played it at parties with unaware blacks who attempted to enchant her with skillful dances and hip vocabulary, believing her to be community property. She would be polite and aloof, and much later, it then being my turn, she would look at me expectantly. And I would force a smile and say: "No." The last round was played while taking her home in a subway car, on a hot August night, when one side of the car was black and tense and hating and the other side was white and of the same mind. There was not enough room on either side for the two of us to sit and we would not separate; and so we stood, holding on to a steel post through all the stops, feeling all the eyes, between the two sides of the car and the two sides of the world. We aged. And, getting off finally at the stop which was no longer ours, we looked at each other, again expectantly, and there was nothing left to say.

I began to avoid the old man, would not answer the door when I knew it was he who was knocking, and waited until very late at night, when he could not possibly be awake, to haul the trash down. I hated the building then; and I was really a janitor for the first time. I slept a lot and wrote very little. And I did not give a damn about Medicare, the AMA, the building, Meg or the crazy dog. I began to consider moving out.

In that same month, Miss O'Hara finally succeeded in badgering Murphy, the celibate Irishman, and a few other tenants into signing a complaint about the dog. No doubt Murphy signed because he was a nice fellow and women like Miss O'Hara had always dominated him. He did not really mind the dog: he did not really mind anything. She called him "Frank Dear," and I had the feeling that when he came to that place, fresh from Montgomery's Campaign, he must have had a will of his own; but she had drained it all away, year by year, so that now he would do anything just to be agreeable.

One day soon after the complaint, the Property Manager came around to tell Sullivan that the dog had to be taken away. Miss O'Hara told me the good news later, when she finally got around to my door.

"Well, that crazy dog is gone now, Robert. Those two are enough."

"Where is the dog?" I asked.

"I don't know, but Albert Rustin made them get him out. You should have seen the old drunk's face," she said. "That dirty useless old man."

"You should be at peace now," I said.

"Almost," was her reply. "The best thing would be to get rid of those two old boozers along with the dog."

I congratulated Miss O'Hara again and then went out. I knew that the old man would be drinking and would want to talk. I did not want to talk. But very late that evening he called on the telephone and caught me in.

"Rob?" he said. "James Sullivan here. Would you come down to my apartment like a good fellow? I want to ask you something important."

I had never been in his apartment before and did not want to go then. But I went down anyway.

They had three rooms, all grimy from corner to corner. There was a peculiar odor in that place I did not want to ever smell again, and his wife was dragging herself around the room talking in mumbles. When she saw me come in the door, she said: "I can't clean it up. I just can't. Look at that window. I can't reach it. I can't keep it clean." She threw up both her hands and held her head down and to the side. "The whole place is dirty and I can't clean it up."

"What do you want?" I said to Sullivan.

"Sit down." He motioned me to a kitchen chair. "Have you changed that bulb on the fifth floor?"

"It's done."

He was silent for a while, drinking from a bottle of sherry, and he offered me some and a dirty glass. "You're the first person who's been in here in years," he said. "We couldn't have company because of the dog."

Somewhere in my mind was a note that I should never go into his apartment. But the dog had not been the reason. "Well, he's gone now," I said, fingering the dirty glass of sherry.

He began to cry. "They took my dog away," he said. "It was all I had. How can they take a man's dog away from him?"

There was nothing I could say.

"I couldn't do nothing," he continued. After a while he added: "But I know who it was. It was that old bitch O'Hara. Don't ever trust her, Rob. She smiles in your face but it was her kind that laughed when they burned Joan of Arc in this state."

Seeing him there, crying and making me feel unmanly because I wanted to touch him or say something warm, also made me eager to be far away and running hard. "Everybody's got problems," I said. "I don't have a girl now."

He brightened immediately, and for a while he looked almost happy in his old cat's eyes. Then he staggered over to my chair and held out his hand. I did not touch it, and he finally pulled it back. "I know how you feel," he said. "I know just how you feel."

"Sure," I said.

"But you're a young man, you have a future. But not me. I'll be dead inside of a year."

Just then his wife dragged in to offer me a cigar. They were being hospitable and I forced myself to drink a little of the sherry.

"They took my dog away today," she mumbled. "That's all I had in the world, my dog."

I looked at the old man. He was drinking from the bottle.

VI

During the first week of September one of the middle-aged men down by the Charles got tired of looking and tried to take a necking girl away from her boyfriend. The police hauled him off to jail, and the girl pulled down her dress tearfully. A few days later another man exposed himself near the same spot. And that same week a dead body was found on the banks of the Charles.

The miniskirted brigade had moved out of the Yard and it was quiet and green and peaceful there. In our building another Jewish couple moved into #44. They did not eat gourmet stuff and, on occasion, threw out pork-and-beans cans. But I had lost interest in perception. I now had many records for my stereo, loads of S. S. Pierce stuff, and a small bottle of Chivas Regal which I never opened. I was working good again and did not miss other things as much; or at least I told myself that.

The old man was coming up steadily now, at least three times a day, and I had resigned myself to it. If I refused to let him in he would always come back later with a missing bulb on the fifth floor. We had taken to buying cases of beer together, and when he had finished his half, which was very frequently, he would come up to polish off mine. I began to enjoy talking about politics, the AMA, Medicare, and hippies, and listening to him recite from books he had read. I discovered that he was very well read in history, philosophy, literature and law. He was extraordinarily fond of saying: "I am really a cut above being a building superintendent. Circumstances made me what I am." And even though he was drunk and dirty and it was very late at night, I believed him and liked him anyway because having him there was much better than being alone. After he had gone I could sleep and I was not lonely in sleep; and it did not really matter how late I was at work the next morning, because when I really thought about it all, I discovered that nothing really matters except not being old and being alive and having potential to dream about, and not being alone.

Whenever I passed his wife on the steps she would say: "That no-good bastard let them take my dog away." And whenever her husband complained that he was sick she said: "That's good for him. He took my dog away."

Sullivan slept in the basement on the sofa almost every night because his wife would think about the dog after the *Carson Show* and blame him for letting it be taken away. He told her, and then me, that the dog was on a farm in New Hampshire; but that was unlikely because the dog had been near mad, and it did not appease her. It was nearing autumn and she was getting violent. Her screams could be heard for hours through the halls and I knew that beyond her quiet door Miss O'Hara was plotting again. Sullivan now had little cuts and bruises on his face and hands, and one day he said: "Meg is like an albatross around my neck. I wish she was dead. I'm sick myself and I can't take much more. She blames me for the dog and I couldn't help it."

"Why don't you take her out to see the dog?" I said.

"I couldn't help it Rob," he went on. "I'm old and I couldn't help it."

"You ought to just get her out of here for a while."

He looked at me, drunk as usual. "Where would we go? We can't even get past the Square."

There was nothing left to say.

"Honest to God, I couldn't help it," he said. He was not saying it to me.

That night I wrote a letter from a mythical New Hampshire farmer telling them that the dog was very fine and missed them a great deal because he kept trying to run off. I said that the children and all the other dogs liked him and that he was not vicious any more. I wrote that the open air was doing him a lot of good and added that they should feel absolutely free to come up to visit the dog at any time. That same night I gave him the letter.

One evening, some days later, I asked him about it.

"I tried to mail it, I really tried," he said.

"What happened?"

"I went down to the Square and looked for cars with New Hampshire license plates. But I never found anybody."

"That wasn't even necessary, was it?"

"It had to have a New Hampshire postmark. You don't know my Meg."

"Listen," I said. "I have a friend who goes up there. Give me the letter and I'll have him mail it."

He held his head down. "I'll tell you the truth. I carried that letter in my pocket so much it got ragged and dirty and I got tired of carrying it. I finally just tore it up."

Neither one of us said anything for a while.

"If I could have sent it off it would have helped some," he said at last. "I know it would have helped."

"Sure," I said.

"I wouldn't have to ask anybody if I had my strength."

"I know."

"If I had my strength I would have mailed it myself."

"I know," I said.

That night we both drank from his bottle of sherry and it did not matter at all that I did not provide my own glass.

VII

In late September the Cambridge police finally picked up the bearded pot-pusher in the Square. He had been in a restaurant all summer, at the same table, with the same customers flocking around him; but now that summer was over, they picked him up. The leaves were changing. In the early evening students passed the building and Meg, blue-hatted and waiting on the steps, carrying sofas and chairs and coffee tables to their suites in the Houses. Down by the Charles the middle-aged men were catching the last phases of summer sensuality before the grass grew cold and damp, and before the young would be forced indoors to play. I wondered what those hungry, spying men did in the winter or at night when it was too dark to see. Perhaps, I thought, they just stood there and listened.

In our building Miss O'Hara was still listening. She had never stopped. When Meg was outside on the steps it was very quiet and I felt good that Miss O'Hara had to wait a long, long time before she heard anything. The company gave the halls and ceilings a new coat of paint, but it was still old in the building. James Sullivan got his yearly two-week vacation and they went to the Boston Common[5] for six hours: two hours going, two hours sitting on the benches, and two hours coming back. Then they both sat on the steps, watching and waiting.

At first I wanted to be kind because he was old and dying in a special way and I was young and ambitious. But at night, in my apartment, when I heard his dragging feet in the hall outside and knew that he would be drunk and repetitious and imposing on my privacy, I did not want to be kind any more. There were girls outside and I knew that I could have one now because that desperate look had finally gone somewhere deep inside. I was young and now I did not want to be bothered.

"Did you read about the lousy twelve per cent Social Security increase those bastards in Washington gave us?"

"No."

He would force himself past me, trying to block the door with my body, and into the room. "When those old pricks tell me to count my blessings, I tell them, 'You're not one of them.' " He would seat himself at the table without meeting my eyes. "The cost of living's gone up more than twelve per cent in the last six months."

"I know."

"What unmitigated bastards."

I would try to be busy with something at my desk.

"But the Texas Oil Barons got another depletion allowance."

"They can afford to bribe politicians," I would mumble.

"They tax away our rainy-day dollars and give us a lousy twelve per cent."

"It's tough."

He would know that I did not want to hear any more and he would know that he was making a burden of himself. It made me feel bad that it was so obvious to him, but I could not help myself. It made me feel bad that I disliked him more every time I heard a girl laugh on the street far below my window. So I would nod occasionally and say half-phrases and smile slightly at something witty he was saying for the third time. If I did not offer him a drink he would go sooner and so I

5. Park in downtown Boston.

gave him Coke when he hinted at how dry he was. Then, when he had finally gone, saying, "I hope I haven't burdened you unduly," I went to bed and hated myself.

VIII

If I am a janitor it is either because I have to be a janitor or because I want to be a janitor. And if I do not have to do it, and if I no longer want to do it, the easiest thing in the world, for a young man, is to step up to something else. Any move away from it is a step up because there is no job more demeaning than that of a janitor. One day I made myself suddenly realize that the three dirty cans would never contain anything of value to me, unless, of course, I decided to gather material for Harold Robbins[6] or freelance for the *Realist*. Neither alternative appealed to me.

Toward dawn one day, during the first part of October, I rented a U-Haul truck and took away two loads of things I had accumulated. The records I packed very carefully, and the stereo I placed on the front seat of the truck beside me. I slipped the Chivas Regal and a picture of Jean under some clothes in a trunk I will not open for a long time. And I left the rug on the floor because it was dirty and too large for my new apartment. I also left the two plates given to me by James Sullivan, for no reason at all. Sometimes I want to go back to get them, but I do not know how to ask for them or explain why I left them in the first place. But sometimes at night, when there is a sleeping girl beside me, I think that I cannot have them again because I am still young and do not want to go back into that building.

I saw him once in the Square walking along very slowly with two shopping bags, and they seemed very heavy. As I came up behind him I saw him put them down and exercise his arms while the crowd moved in two streams around him. I had an instant impulse to offer help and I was close enough to touch him before I stopped. I will never know why I stopped. And after a few seconds of standing behind him and knowing that he was not aware of anything at all except the two heavy bags waiting to be lifted after his arms were sufficiently rested, I moved back into the stream of people which passed on the left of him. I never looked back.

---

1. What is the difference between Rob's state of mind at the beginning and end of the story?
2. What worth is there in Jean's warning to Rob to give less of himself to Sullivan?

6. Popular American novelist (1916–   ).

3. What does the story say about the wisdom acquired by aging?
4. How does Rob's loss of Jean fit into the general action and meaning of the story?
5. Why does Rob tend to ally himself more with Sullivan than with the tenants of the building?
6. What does the last paragraph say about Rob's adjustment after the summer in which the main action takes place?

Norman Mailer

Mailer (1923–) was born in Long Branch, New Jersey. He was attending Harvard University and already showing both interest and promise in writing fiction when he was drafted into the army in 1943. He fought in the South Pacific, and while he was campaigning in the Philippines he was gathering a rich store of experience that would presently make him one of the very best writers to come out of World War II and one of the most famous young men of his generation. The first fruits of his experience were gathered in an awesome novel, The Naked and the Dead *(1948). This fully mature work is still cited as among the best representations of men at war to appear in our century.*

The instant fame that burst upon Mailer was accompanied by his realization that henceforth he must work in different veins, and for four decades he has done just that, producing not only varicolored fiction but innovative and sometimes explosive essays, biography, drama, and reportage. He has ventured into filmmaking, political activism, and cultural reform. With his definitions of the hipster, he did much to draw a program for the social rebel of the fifties and sixties. On the public stage, Mailer once ran for office as mayor of New York City. In the vitality and showmanship of his pursuits he has, like Hemingway, indicated that writing is not necessarily a sedentary trade. The competition with Hemingway as a character of his own creation is not unself-conscious. Speaking in the vernacular of sports, Mailer has expressed the ambition of dethroning Hemingway as the "heavyweight champion." Among Mailer's best-known novels are Barbary Shore *(1951),* The Deer Park *(1955),* An American Dream *(1965),* Why Are We in Vietnam? *(1967), and* Tough Guys Don't Dance *(1984). Some of his most brilliant reportage is found in* Armies of the Night *(1968),* Miami and the Siege of Chicago *(1968), and* Of a Fire on the Moon *(1970). In* Marilyn: a Biography *(1987) he analyzed and celebrated one of the legendary women of the age.*

The Language of Men

In the beginning, Sanford Carter was ashamed of becoming an Army cook. This was not from snobbery, at least not from snobbery of the most direct sort. During the two and a half years Carter had been in the Army he had come to hate cooks more and more. They existed for him as a symbol of all that was corrupt, overbearing, stupid, and privileged in Army life. The image which came to mind was a fat cook with an enormous sandwich in one hand, and a bottle of beer in the other, sweat pouring down a porcine face, foot on a flour barrel, shouting at the K.P.'s, "Hurry up, you men, I ain't got all day." More than once in those two and a half years, driven to exasperation, Carter had been on the verge of throwing his food into a cook's face as he passed on the serving line. His anger often derived from nothing: the set of a pair of fat lips, the casual heavy thump of the serving spoon into his plate, or the resentful conviction that the cook was not serving him enough. Since life in the Army was in most aspects a marriage, this rage over apparently harmless details was not a sign of unbalance. Every soldier found some particular habit of the Army spouse impossible to support.

Yet Sanford Carter became a cook and, to elaborate the irony, did better as a cook than he had done as anything else. In a few months he rose from a Private to a first cook with the rank of Sergeant, Technician. After the fact, it was easy to understand. He had suffered through all his Army career from an excess of eagerness. He had cared too much, he had wanted to do well, and so he had often been tense at moments when he would better have been relaxed. He was very young, twenty-one, had lived the comparatively gentle life of a middle-class boy, and needed some success in the Army to prove to himself that he was not completely worthless.

In succession, he had failed as a surveyor in Field Artillery, a clerk in an Infantry headquarters, a telephone wireman, and finally a rifleman. When the war ended, and his regiment went to Japan, Carter was still a rifleman; he had been a rifleman for eight months. What was more to the point, he had been in the platoon as long as any of its members; the skilled hard-bitten nucleus of veterans who had run his squad had gone home one by one, and it seemed to him that through seniority he was entitled to at least a corporal's rating. Through seniority he was so entitled, but on no other ground. Whenever responsibility had been handed to him, he had discharged it miserably, tensely, overconscientiously. He had always asked too many questions, he had worried the task too severely, he had conveyed his nervousness to the men he was supposed to lead. Since he was also sensitive enough and proud enough never to curry favor with the noncoms in the platoons, he was in no position to sit in on their occasional discussions about who was to succeed them. In a vacuum of ignorance, he had allowed himself to dream that he would be given a squad to lead, and his hurt was sharp when the squad was given to a replacement who had joined the platoon months after him.

The war was over, Carter had a bride in the States (he had lived with her for only two months), he was lonely, he was obsessed with going home. As one week dragged into the next, and the regiment, the company, and his own platoon continued the same sort of training which they had been doing ever since he had entered the Army, he thought he would snap. There were months to wait until he would be discharged and meanwhile it was intolerable to him to be taught for the fifth time the nomenclature of the machine gun, to stand a retreat parade three evenings a week. He wanted some niche where he could lick his wounds, some Army job with so many hours of work and so many hours of complete freedom, where he could be alone by himself. He hated the Army, the huge Army which had proved to him that he was good at no work, and incapable of succeeding at anything. He wrote long, aching letters to his wife, he talked less and less to the men around him and he was close to violent attacks of anger during the most casual phases of training—during close-order drill or cleaning his rifle for inspection. He knew that if he did not find his niche it was possible that he would crack.

So he took an opening in the kitchen. It promised him nothing except a day of work, and a day of leisure which would be completely at his disposal. He found that he liked it. He was given at first the job of baking the bread for the company, and every other night he worked till early in the morning, kneading and shaping his fifty-pound mix of dough. At two or three he would be done, and for his work there would be the tangible reward of fifty loaves of bread, all fresh from the oven, all clean and smelling of fertile accomplished creativity. He had the rare and therefore intensely satisfying emotion of seeing at the end of an Army chore the product of his labor.

A month after he became cook the regiment was disbanded, and those men who did not have enough points to go home were sent to other outfits. Carter ended at an ordnance company in another Japanese city. He had by now given up all thought of getting a noncom's rating before he was discharged, and was merely content to work each alternate day. He took his work for granted and so he succeeded at it. He had begun as a baker in the new company kitchen; before long he was the first cook. It all happened quickly. One cook went home on points, another caught a skin disease, a third was transferred from the kitchen after contracting a venereal infection. On the shift which Carter worked there were left only himself and a man who was illiterate. Carter was put nominally in charge, and was soon actively in charge. He looked up each menu in an Army recipe book, collected the items, combined them in the order indicated, and after the proper time had elapsed, took them from the stove. His product tasted neither better nor worse than the product of all other Army cooks. But the mess sergeant was impressed. Carter had filled a gap. The next time ratings were given out Carter jumped at a bound from Private to Sergeant T/4.

On the surface he was happy; beneath the surface he was overjoyed. It took him several weeks to realize how grateful and delighted he felt. The promotion coincided with his assignment to a detachment working in a small seaport up the coast. Carter arrived there to discover that he was in charge of cooking for thirty men, and would act as mess sergeant. There was another cook, and there were four permanent Japanese K.P.'s, all of them good workers. He still cooked every day, but there was always time between meals to take a break of at least an hour and often two; he shared a room with the other cook and lived in comparative privacy for the first time in several years; the seaport was beautiful; there was only one officer, and he left the men alone; supplies were plentiful due to a clerical error which assigned rations for forty men rather than thirty; and in general everything was fine. The niche had become a sinecure.

This was the happiest period of Carter's life in the Army. He came to like his Japanese K.P.'s. He studied their language, he visited their homes, he gave them gifts of food from time to time. They worshiped him because he was kind to them and generous, because he never shouted, because his good humor bubbled over into games, and made the work of the kitchen seem pleasant. All the while he grew in confidence. He was not a big man, but his body filled out from the heavy work; he was likely to sing a great deal, he cracked jokes with the men on the chow line. The kitchen became his property, it became his domain, and since it was a warm room, filled with sunlight, he came to take pleasure in the very sight of it. Before long his good humor expanded into a series of efforts to improve the food. He began to take little pains and make little extra efforts which would have been impossible if he had been obliged to cook for more than thirty men. In the morning he would serve the men fresh eggs scrambled or fried to their desire in fresh butter. Instead of cooking sixty eggs in one large pot he cooked two eggs at a time in a frying pan, turning them to the taste of each soldier. He baked like a housewife satisfying her young husband; at lunch and dinner there was pie or cake, and often both. He went to great lengths. He taught the K.P.'s how to make the toast come out right. He traded excess food for spices in Japanese stores. He rubbed paprika and garlic on the chickens. He even made pastries to cover such staples as corn beef hash and meat and vegetable stew.

It all seemed to be wasted. In the beginning the men might have noticed these improvements, but after a period they took them for granted. It did not matter how he worked to satisfy them; they trudged through the chow line with their heads down, nodding coolly at him, and they ate without comment. He would hang around the tables after the meal, noticing how much they consumed, and what they discarded; he would wait for compliments, but the soldiers seemed indifferent. They seemed to eat without tasting the food. In their faces he saw mirrored the distaste with which he had once stared at cooks.

The honeymoon was ended. The pleasure he took in the kitchen and himself curdled. He became aware again of his painful desire to please people, to discharge responsibility, to be a man. When he had been a child, tears had come into his eyes at a cross word, and he had lived in an atmosphere where his smallest accomplishment was warmly praised. He was the sort of young man, he often thought bitterly, who was accustomed to the attention and the protection of women. He would have thrown away all he possessed—the love of his wife, the love of his mother, the benefits of his education, the assured financial security of entering his father's business—if he had been able just once to dig a ditch as well as the most ignorant farmer.

Instead, he was back in the painful unprotected days of his first entrance into the Army. Once again the most casual actions became the most painful, the events which were most to be taken for granted grew into the most significant, and the feeding of the men at each meal turned progressively more unbearable.

So Sanford Carter came full circle. If he had once hated the cooks, he now hated the troops. At mealtimes his face soured into the belligerent scowl with which he had once believed cooks to be born. And to himself he muttered the age-old laments of the housewife: how little they appreciated what he did.

Finally there was an explosion. He was approached one day by Corporal Taylor, and he had come to hate Taylor, because Taylor was the natural leader of the detachment and kept the other men endlessly amused with his jokes. Taylor had the ability to present himself as inefficient, shiftless, and incapable, in such a manner as to convey that really the opposite was true. He had the lightest touch, he had the greatest facility, he could charm a geisha in two minutes and obtain anything he wanted from a supply sergeant in five. Carter envied him, envied his grace, his charmed indifference; then grew to hate him.

Taylor teased Carter about the cooking, and he had the knack of knowing where to put the knife. "Hey, Carter," he would shout across the mess hall while breakfast was being served, "you turned my eggs twice, and I asked for them raw." The men would shout with laughter. Somehow Taylor had succeeded in conveying all of the situation, or so it seemed to Carter, insinuating everything, how Carter worked and how it meant nothing, how Carter labored to gain their affection and earned their contempt. Carter would scowl, Carter would answer in a rough voice, "Next time I'll crack them over your head." "You crack 'em, I'll eat 'em," Taylor would pipe back, "but just don't put your fingers in 'em." And there would be another laugh. He hated the sight of Taylor.

It was Taylor who came to him to get the salad oil. About twenty of the soldiers were going to have a fish fry at the geisha house; they had bought the fish at the local market, but they could not buy oil, so Taylor was sent as the deputy to Carter. He was charming to Carter, he complimented him on the meal, he clapped him on the back, he dissolved Carter to warmth, to private delight in the attention, and the thought that he had misjudged Taylor. Then Taylor asked for the oil.

Carter was sick with anger. Twenty men out of the thirty in the detachment were going on the fish fry. It meant only that Carter was considered one of the ten undesirables. It was something he had known, but the proof of knowledge is always more painful than the acquisition of it. If he had been alone his eyes would have clouded. And he was outraged at Taylor's deception. He could imagine Taylor saying ten minutes later, "You should have seen the grease job I gave to Carter. I'm dumb, but man, he's dumber."

Carter was close enough to giving him the oil. He had a sense of what it would mean to refuse Taylor, he was on the very edge of mild acquiescence. But he also had a sense of how he would despise himself afterward.

"No," he said abruptly, his teeth gritted, "you can't have it."

"What do you mean we can't have it?"

"I won't give it to you." Carter could almost feel the rage which Taylor generated at being refused.

"You won't give away a lousy five gallons of oil to a bunch of G.I.'s having a party?"

"I'm sick and tired," Carter began.

"So am I." Taylor walked away.

Carter knew he would pay for it. He left the K.P.'s and went to change his sweat-soaked work shirt, and as he passed the large dormitory in which most of the detachment slept he could hear Taylor's high-pitched voice. Carter did not bother to take off his shirt. He returned instead to the kitchen, and listened to the sound of men going back and forth through the hall and of a man shouting with rage. That was Hobbs, a Southerner, a big man with a big bellowing voice.

There was a formal knock on the kitchen door. Taylor came in. His face was pale and his eyes showed a cold satisfaction. "Carter," he said, "the men want to see you in the big room."

Carter heard his voice answer huskily. "If they want to see me, they can come into the kitchen."

He knew he would conduct himself with more courage in his own kitchen than anywhere else. "I'll be here for a while."

Taylor closed the door, and Carter picked up a writing board to which was clamped the menu for the following day. Then he made a pretense of examining the food supplies in the pantry closet. It was his habit to check the stocks before deciding what to serve the next day, but on this night his eyes ranged thoughtlessly over the canned goods. In a corner were seven five-gallon tins of salad oil, easily enough cooking oil to last a month. Carter came out of the pantry and shut the door behind him.

He kept his head down and pretended to be writing the menu when the soldiers came in. Somehow there were even more of them than he had expected. Out of the twenty men who were going to the party, all but two or three had crowded through the door.

Carter took his time, looked up slowly. "You men want to see me?" he asked flatly.

They were angry. For the first time in his life he faced the hostile expressions of many men. It was the most painful and anxious moment he had ever known.

"Taylor says you won't give us the oil," someone burst out.

"That's right, I won't," said Carter. He tapped his pencil against the scratchboard, tapping it slowly and, he hoped, with an appearance of calm.

"What a stink deal," said Porfirio, a little Cuban whom Carter had always considered his friend.

Hobbs, the big Southerner, stared down at Carter. "Would you mind telling the men why you've decided not to give us the oil?" he asked quietly.

" 'Cause I'm blowed if I'm going to cater to you men. I've catered enough," Carter said. His voice was close to cracking with the outrage he had suppressed for so long, and he knew that if he continued he might cry. "I'm the acting mess sergeant," he said as coldly as he could, "and I decide what goes out of this kitchen." He stared at each one in turn, trying to stare them down, feeling mired in the rut of his own failure. They would never have dared this approach to another mess sergeant.

"What crud," someone muttered.

"You won't give a lousy five-gallon can of oil for a G.I. party," Hobbs said more loudly.

"I won't. That's definite. You men can get out of here."

"Why, you lousy little snot," Hobbs burst out, "how many five-gallon cans of oil have you sold on the black market?"

"I've never sold any." Carter might have been slapped with the flat of a sword. He told himself bitterly, numbly, that this was the reward he received for being perhaps the single honest cook in the whole

United States Army. And he even had time to wonder at the obscure prejudice which had kept him from selling food for his own profit.

"Man, I've seen you take it out," Hobbs exclaimed. "I've seen you take it to the market."

"I took food to trade for spices," Carter said hotly.

There was an ugly snicker from the men.

"I don't mind if a cook sells," Hobbs said, "every man has his own deal in this Army. But a cook ought to give a little food to a G.I. if he wants it."

"Tell him," someone said.

"It's bull," Taylor screeched. "I've seen Carter take butter, eggs, every damn thing to the market."

Their faces were red, they circled him.

"I never sold a thing," Carter said doggedly.

"And I'm telling you," Hobbs said, "that you're a two-bit crook. You been raiding that kitchen, and that's why you don't give to us now."

Carter knew there was only one way he could possibly answer if he hoped to live among these men again. "That's a goddam lie," Carter said to Hobbs. He laid down the scratchboard, he flipped his pencil slowly and deliberately to one corner of the room, and with his heart aching he lunged toward Hobbs. He had no hope of beating him. He merely intended to fight until he was pounded unconscious, advancing the pain and bruises he would collect as collateral for his self-respect.

To his indescribable relief Porfirio darted between them, held them apart with the pleased ferocity of a small man breaking up a fight. "Now, stop this! Now, stop this!" he cried out.

Carter allowed himself to be pushed back, and he knew that he had gained a point. He even glimpsed a solution with some honor.

He shrugged violently to free himself from Porfirio. He was in a rage, and yet it was a rage he could have ended at any instant. "All right, you men," he swore, "I'll give you the oil, but now that we're at it, I'm going to tell you a thing or two." His face red, his body perspiring, he was in the pantry and out again with a five-gallon tin. "Here," he said, "you better have a good fish fry, 'cause it's the last good meal you're going to have for quite a while. I'm sick of trying to please you. You think I have to work—" he was about to say, my fingers to the bone—"well, I don't. From now on, you'll see what chow in the Army is supposed to be like." He was almost hysterical. "Take that oil. Have your fish fry." The fact that they wanted to cook for themselves was the greatest insult of all. "Tomorrow I'll give you real Army cooking."

His voice was so intense that they backed away from him. "Get out of this kitchen," he said. "None of you has any business here."

They filed out quietly, and they looked a little sheepish.

Carter felt weary, he felt ashamed of himself, he knew he had not meant what he said. But half an hour later, when he left the kitchen and passed the large dormitory, he heard shouts of raucous laughter, and he heard his name mentioned and then more laughter.

He slept badly that night, he was awake at four, he was in the kitchen by five, and stood there white-faced and nervous, waiting for the K.P.'s to arrive. Breakfast that morning landed on the men like a lead bomb. Carter rummaged in the back of the pantry and found a tin of dehydrated eggs covered with dust, memento of a time when fresh eggs were never on the ration list. The K.P.'s looked at him in amazement as he stirred the lumpy powder into a pan of water. While it was still half-dissolved he put it on the fire. While it was still wet, he took it off. The coffee was cold, the toast was burned, the oatmeal stuck to the pot. The men dipped forks into their food, took cautious sips of their coffee, and spoke in whispers. Sullenness drifted like vapors through the kitchen.

At noontime Carter opened cans of meat-and-vegetable stew. He dumped them into a pan and heated them slightly. He served the stew with burned string beans and dehydrated potatoes which tasted like straw. For dessert the men had a single luke-warm canned peach and cold coffee.

So the meals continued. For three days Carter cooked slop, and suffered even more than the men. When mealtime came he left the chow line to the K.P.'s and sat in his room, perspiring with shame, determined not to yield and sick with the determination.

Carter won. On the fourth day a delegation of men came to see him. They told him that indeed they had appreciated his cooking in the past, they told him that they were sorry they had hurt his feelings, they listened to his remonstrances, they listened to his grievances, and with delight Carter forgave them. That night, for supper, the detachment celebrated. There was roast chicken with stuffing, lemon meringue pie and chocolate cake. The coffee burned their lips. More than half the men made it a point to compliment Carter on the meal.

In the weeks which followed the compliments diminished, but they never stopped completely. Carter became ashamed at last. He realized the men were trying to humor him, and he wished to tell them it was no longer necessary.

Harmony settled over the kitchen. Carter even became friends with Hobbs, the big Southerner. Hobbs approached him one day, and in the manner of a farmer talked obliquely for an hour. He spoke about his father, he spoke about his girl friends, he alluded indirectly to the night they had almost fought, and finally with the courtesy of a Southerner he said to Carter, "You know, I'm sorry about shooting off my mouth. You were right to want to fight me, and if you're still mad I'll fight you to give you the satisfaction, although I just as soon would not."

"No, I don't want to fight with you now," Carter said warmly. They smiled at each other. They were friends.

Carter knew he had gained Hobbs' respect. Hobbs respected him because he had been willing to fight. That made sense to a man like Hobbs. Carter liked him so much at this moment that he wished the friendship to be more intimate.

"You know," he said to Hobbs, "it's a funny thing. You know I really never did sell anything on the black market. Not that I'm proud of it, but I just didn't."

Hobbs frowned. He seemed to be saying that Carter did not have to lie. "I don't hold it against a man," Hobbs said, "if he makes a little money in something that's his own proper work. Hell, I sell gas from the motor pool. It's just I also give gas if one of the G.I.'s wants to take the jeep out for a joy ride, kind of."

"No, but I never did sell anything." Carter had to explain. "If I ever had sold on the black market, I would have given the salad oil without question."

Hobbs frowned again, and Carter realized he still did not believe him. Carter did not want to lose the friendship which was forming. He thought he could save it only by some further admission. "You know," he said again, "remember when Porfirio broke up our fight? I was awful glad when I didn't have to fight you." Carter laughed, expecting Hobbs to laugh with him, but a shadow passed across Hobbs' face.

"Funny way of putting it," Hobbs said.

He was always friendly thereafter, but Carter knew that Hobbs would never consider him a friend. Carter thought about it often, and began to wonder about the things which made him different. He was no longer so worried about becoming a man; he felt that to an extent he had become one. But in his heart he wondered if he would ever learn the language of men.

---

1. Do Carter's virtues alone account for his estrangement from the other men? Examine any other aspects of his character that might account for it.
2. Why are his efforts to improve the food so little appreciated?
3. Is the focus of interest Carter's character or a study in group behavior?
4. Discuss the importance of the setting, including the postwar situation of the troops.

Bernard Malamud

Malamud (1914–1986) was born in Brooklyn, New York. He was educated at City College of New York and Columbia University before going to teach for several years at Oregon State University. He was, from 1961 until his death, a professor at Bennington College. From the 1950s on, he was recognized as one of the best of the writers who have portrayed Jewish life and sensibility in American fiction, affirming through his special subject matter the general human capacity to resist social and political afflictions. His numerous honors included two National Book Awards and the Pulitzer Price. His novels are The Natural *(1952),* The Assistant *(1957),* A New Life *(1961),* The Fixer *(1966),* Pictures of Fidelman: An Exhibition *(1969),* The Tenants *(1971), and* Dubin's Lives *(1979). His stories have been collected in* The Magic Barrel *(1958),* Idiots First *(1963), and* Rembrandt's Hat *(1973).*

Angel Levine

Manischevitz, a tailor, in his fifty-first year suffered many reverses and indignities. Previously a man of comfortable means, he overnight lost all he had, when his establishment caught fire and, after a metal container of cleaning fluid exploded, burned to the ground. Although Manischevitz was insured against fire, damage suits by two customers who had been hurt in the flames deprived him of every penny he had collected. At almost the same time, his son, of much promise, was killed in the war, and his daughter, without so much as a word of warning, married a lout and disappeared with him as off the face of the earth. Thereafter Manischevitz was victimized by excruciating backaches and found himself unable to work even as a presser—the only kind of work available to him—for more than an hour or two daily, because beyond that the pain from standing became maddening. His Fanny, a good wife and mother, who had taken in washing and sewing, began before his eyes to waste away. Suffering shortness of breath, she at last became seriously ill and took to her bed. The doctor, a former customer of Manischevitz, who out of pity treated them, at first had difficulty diagnosing her ailment but later put it down as hardening of the arteries at an advanced stage. He took Manischevitz aside, prescribed complete rest for her, and in whispers gave him to know there was little hope.

Throughout his trials Manischevitz had remained somewhat stoic, almost unbelieving that all this had descended upon his head, as if it were happening, let us say, to an acquaintance or some distant relative; it was in sheer quantity of woe incomprehensible. It was also ridiculous, unjust, and because he had always been a religious man, it was in a way an affront to God. Manischevitz believed this in all his suffering. When his burden had grown too crushingly heavy to be borne he prayed in his chair with shut hollow eyes: "My dear God, sweetheart, did I deserve that this should happen to me?" Then recognizing the worthlessness of it, he put aside the complaint and prayed humbly for assistance: "Give Fanny back her health, and to me for myself that I shouldn't feel pain in every step. Help now or tomorrow is too late. This I don't have to tell you." And Manischevitz wept.

Manischevitz's flat, which he had moved into after the disastrous fire, was a meager one, furnished with a few sticks of chairs, a table, and bed, in one of the poorer sections of the city. There were three rooms: a small, poorly-papered living room; an apology for a kitchen, with a wooden icebox; and the comparatively large bedroom where Fanny lay in a sagging secondhand bed, gasping for breath. The bedroom was the warmest room of the house and it was here, after his outburst to God, that Manischevitz, by the light of two small bulbs overhead, sat reading his Jewish newspaper. He was not truly reading, because his thoughts were everywhere; however the print offered a convenient resting place for his eyes, and a word or two, when he permitted himself to comprehend them, had the momentary effect of helping him forget his troubles. After a short while he discovered, to his surprise, that he was actively scanning the news, searching for an item of great interest to him. Exactly what he thought he would read he couldn't say—until he realized, with some astonishment, that he was expecting to discover something about himself. Manischevitz put his paper down and looked up with the distinct impression that someone had entered the apartment, though he could not remember having heard the sound of the door opening. He looked around: the room was very still, Fanny sleeping, for once, quietly. Half-frightened, he watched her until he was satisfied she wasn't dead; then, still disturbed by the thought of an unannounced visitor, he stumbled into the living room and there had the shock of his life, for at the table sat a Negro reading a newspaper he had folded up to fit into one hand.

"What do you want here?" Manischevitz asked in fright.

The Negro put down the paper and glanced up with a gentle expression. "Good evening." He seemed not to be sure of himself, as if he had got into the wrong house. He was a large man, bonily built, with a heavy head covered by a hard derby, which he made no attempt to remove. His eyes seemed sad, but his lips, above which he wore a slight mustache, sought to smile; he was not otherwise prepossessing. The cuffs of his sleeves, Manischevitz noted, were frayed to the lining and the dark suit was badly fitted. He had very large feet. Recovering from his fright, Manischevitz guessed he had left the door open and was being visited by a case worker from the Welfare Department—some came at night—for he had recently applied for relief. Therefore he lowered himself into a chair opposite the Negro, trying, before the man's uncertain smile, to feel comfortable. The former tailor sat stiffly but patiently at the table, waiting for the investigator to take out his pad and pencil and begin asking questions; but before long he became convinced the man intended to do nothing of the sort.

"Who are you?" Manischevitz at last asked uneasily.

"If I may, insofar as one is able to, identify myself, I bear the name of Alexander Levine."

In spite of all his troubles Manischevitz felt a smile growing on his lips. "You said Levine?" he politely inquired.

The Negro nodded. "That is exactly right."

Carrying the jest farther, Manischevitz asked, "You are maybe Jewish?"

"All my life I was, willingly."

The tailor hesitated. He had heard of black Jews but had never met one. It gave an unusual sensation.

Recognizing in afterthought something odd about the tense of Levine's remark, he said doubtfully, "You ain't Jewish anymore?"

Levine at this point removed his hat, revealing a very white part in his black hair, but quickly replaced it. He replied, "I have recently been disincarnated into an angel. As such, I offer you my humble assistance, if to offer is within my province and ability—in the best sense." He lowered his eyes in apology. "Which calls for added explanation: I am what I am granted to be, and at present the completion is in the future."

"What kind of angel is this?" Manischevitz gravely asked.

"A bona fide angel of God, within prescribed limitations," answered Levine, "not to be confused with the members of any particular sect, order, or organization here on earth operating under a similar name."

Manischevitz was thoroughly disturbed. He had been expecting something but not this. What sort of mockery was it—provided Levine was an angel—of a faithful servant who had from childhood lived in the synagogues, always concerned with the word of God?

To test Levine he asked, "Then where are your wings?"

The Negro blushed as well as he was able. Manischevitz understood this from his changed expression. "Under certain circumstances we lose privileges and prerogatives upon returning to earth, no matter for what purpose, or endeavoring to assist whosoever."

"So tell me," Manischevitz said triumphantly, "how did you get here?"

"I was transmitted."

Still troubled, the tailor said, "If you are a Jew, say the blessing for bread."

Levine recited it in sonorous Hebrew.

Although moved by the familiar words Manischevitz still felt doubt that he was dealing with an angel.

"If you are an angel," he demanded somewhat angrily, "give me the proof."

Levine wet his lips. "Frankly, I cannot perform either miracles or near miracles, due to the fact that I am in a condition of probation. How long that will persist or even consist, I admit, depends on the outcome."

Manischevitz racked his brains for some means of causing Levine positively to reveal his true identity, when the Negro spoke again:

"It was given me to understand that both your wife and you require assistance of a salubrious nature?"

The tailor could not rid himself of the feeling that he was the butt of a jokester. Is this what a Jewish angel looks like? he asked himself. This I am not convinced.

He asked a last question. "So if God sends to me an angel, why a black? Why not a white that there are so many of them?"

"It was my turn to go next," Levine explained.

Manischevitz could not be persuaded. "I think you are a faker."

Levine slowly rose. His eyes showed disappointment and worry. "Mr. Manischevitz," he said tonelessly, "if you should desire me to be of assistance to you any time in the near future, or possibly before, I can be found"—he glanced at his fingernails—"in Harlem."

He was by then gone.

The next day Manischevitz felt some relief from his backache and was able to work four hours at pressing. The day after, he put in six hours; and the third day four again. Fanny sat up a little and asked for some halvah to suck. But on the fourth day the stabbing, breaking ache afflicted his back, and Fanny again lay supine, breathing with blue-lipped difficulty.

Manischevitz was profoundly disappointed at the return of his active pain and suffering. He had hoped for a longer interval of easement, long enough to have some thought other than of himself and his troubles. Day by day, hour by hour, minute after minute, he lived in pain, pain his only memory, questioning the necessity of it, inveighing against it, also, though with affection, against God. Why *so much*, Gottenyu? If He wanted to teach His servant a lesson for some reason, some cause—the nature of His nature—to teach him, say, for reasons of his weakness, his pride, perhaps, during his years of prosperity, his frequent neglect of God—to give him a little lesson, why then any of the tragedies that had happened to him, any *one* would have sufficed to chasten him. But *all together*— the loss of both his children, his means of livelihood, Fanny's health and his—that was too much to ask one frail-boned man to endure. Who, after all, was Manischevitz that he had been given so much to suffer? A tailor. Certainly not a man of talent. Upon him suffering was largely wasted. It went nowhere, into nothing: into more suffering. His pain did not earn him bread, nor fill the cracks in the wall, nor lift, in the middle of the night, the kitchen table; only lay upon him, sleepless, so sharply, oppressively, that he could many times have cried out yet not heard himself through this thickness of misery.

In this mood he gave no thought to Mr. Alexander Levine, but at moments when the pain waivered, slightly diminishing, he sometimes wondered if he had been mistaken to dismiss him. A black Jew and angel to boot—very hard to believe, but suppose he *had* been sent to succor him, and he, Manischevitz, was in his blindness too blind to comprehend? It was this thought that put him on the knife-point of agony.

Therefore the tailor, after much self-questioning and continuing doubt, decided he would seek the self-styled angel in Harlem. Of course he had great difficulty, because he had not asked for specific directions, and movement was tedious to him. The subway took him to 116th Street, and from there he wandered in the dark world. It was vast and its lights lit nothing. Everywhere were shadows, often moving. Manischevitz hobbled along with the aid of a cane, and not knowing where to seek in the blackened tenement buildings, looked fruitlessly through store windows. In the stores he saw people and *everybody* was black. It was an amazing thing to observe. When he was too tired, too unhappy to go farther, Manischevitz stopped in front of a tailor's store. Out of familiarity with the appearance of it, with some sadness he entered. The tailor, an old skinny Negro with a mop of woolly gray hair, was sitting cross-legged on his workbench, sewing a pair of full-dress pants that had a razor slit all the way down the seat.

"You'll excuse me, please, gentleman," said Manischevitz, admiring the tailor's deft, thimbled fingerwork, "but you know maybe somebody by the name Alexander Levine?"

The tailor, who Manischevitz thought, seemed a little antagonistic to him, scratched his scalp.

"Cain't say I ever heared dat name."

"Alex-ander Lev-ine," Manischevitz repeated it.

The man shook his head. "Cain't say I heared."

About to depart, Manischevitz remembered to say: "He is an angel, maybe."

"Oh *him*," said the tailor clucking. "He hang out in dat honky tonk down here a ways." He pointed with his skinny finger and returned to the pants.

Manischevitz crossed the street against a red light and was almost run down by a taxi. On the block after the next, the sixth store from the corner was a cabaret, and the name in sparkling lights was Bella's. Ashamed to go in, Manischevitz gazed through the neon-lit window, and when the dancing couples had parted and drifted away, he discovered at a table on the side, towards the rear, Levine.

He was sitting alone, a cigarette butt hanging from the corner of his mouth, playing solitaire with a dirty pack of cards, and Manischevitz felt a touch of pity for him, for Levine had deteriorated in appearance. His derby was dented and had a gray smudge on the side. His ill-fitting suit was shabbier, as if he had been sleeping in it. His shoes and trouser cuffs were muddy, and his face was covered with an impenetrable stubble the color of licorice. Manischevitz, though deeply disappointed, was about to enter, when a big-breasted Negress in a purple evening gown appeared before Levine's table, and with much laughter through many white teeth, broke into a vigorous shimmy. Levine looked straight at Manischevitz with a haunted expression, but the tailor was too paralyzed to move or acknowledge it. As Bella's gyrations continued, Levine rose, his eyes lit in excitement. She embraced him with vigor, both his hands clasped around her big restless buttocks and they tangoed together across the floor, loudly applauded by the noisy customers. She seemed to have lifted Levine off his feet and his large shoes hung limp as they danced. They slid past the windows where Manischevitz, white-faced, stood staring in. Levine winked slyly and the tailor left for home.

Fanny lay at death's door. Through shrunken lips she muttered concerning her childhood, the sorrows of the marriage bed, the loss of her children, yet wept to live. Manischevitz tried not to listen, but even without ears he would have heard. It was not a gift. The doctor panted up the stairs, a broad but bland, unshaven man (it was Sunday), and soon shook his head. A day at most, or two. He left at once, not without pity, to spare himself Manischevitz's multiplied sorrow; the man who never stopped hurting. He would someday get him into a public home.

Manischevitz visited a synagogue and there spoke to God, but

God had absented himself. The tailor searched his heart and found no hope. When she died he would live dead. He considered taking his life although he knew he wouldn't. Yet it was something to consider. Considering, you existed. He railed against God—Can you love a rock, a broom, an emptiness? Baring his chest, he smote the naked bones, cursing himself for having believed.

Asleep in a chair that afternoon, he dreamed of Levine. He was standing before a faded mirror, preening small decaying opalescent wings. "This means," mumbled Manischevitz, as he broke out of sleep, "that it is possible he could be an angel." Begging a neighbor lady to look in on Fanny and occasionally wet her lips with a few drops of water, he drew on his thin coat, gripped his walking stick, exchanged some pennies for a subway token, and rode to Harlem. He knew this act was the last desperate one of his woe: to go without belief, seeking a black magician to restore his wife to invalidism. Yet if there was no choice, he did at least what was chosen.

He hobbled to Bella's but the place had changed hands. It was now, as he breathed, a synagogue in a store. In the front, towards him, were several rows of empty wooden benches. In the rear stood the Ark, its portals of rough wood covered with rainbows of sequins; under it a long table on which lay the sacred scroll unrolled, illuminated by the dim light from a bulb on a chain overhead. Around the table, as if frozen to it and the scroll, which they all touched with their fingers, sat four Negroes wearing skullcaps. Now as they read the Holy Word, Manischevitz could, through the plate glass window, hear the singsong chant of their voices. One of them was old, with a gray beard. One was bubble-eyed. One was humpbacked. The fourth was a boy, no older than thirteen. Their heads moved in rhythmic swaying. Touched by this sight from his childhood and youth, Manischevitz entered and stood silent in the rear.

"Neshoma," said bubble eyes, pointing to the word with a stubby finger. "Now what dat mean?"

"That's the word that means soul," said the boy. He wore glasses.

"Let's git on wid de commentary," said the old man.

"Ain't necessary," said the humpback. "Souls is immaterial substance. That's all. The soul is derived in that manner. The immateriality is derived from the substance, and they both, causally an' otherwise, derived from the soul. There can be no higher."

"That's the highest."

"Over de top."

"Wait a minute," said bubble eyes. "I don't see what is dat immaterial substance. How come de one gits hitched up to de odder?" He addressed the humpback.

"Ask me something hard. Because it is substanceless immateriality. It couldn't be closer together, like all the parts of the body under one skin—closer."

"Hear now," said the old man.

"All you done is switched de words."

"It's the primum mobile, the substanceless substance from which comes all things that were incepted in the idea—you, me and everything and body else."

"Now how did all dat happen? Make it sound simple."

"It de speerit," said the old man. "On de face of de water moved de speerit. An' dat was good. It say so in de Book. From de speerit ariz de man."

"But now listen here. How come it become substance if it all de time a spirit?"

"God alone done dat."

"Holy! Holy! Praise His Name."

"But has dis spirit got some kind of a shade or color?" asked bubble eyes, deadpan.

"Man, of course not. A spirit is a spirit."

"Then how come we is colored?" he said with a triumphant glare.

"Ain't got nothing to do wid dat."

"I still like to know."

"God put the spirit in all things," answered the boy. "He put it in the green leaves and the yellow flowers. He put it with the gold in the fishes and the blue in the sky. That's how come it came to us."

"Amen."

"Praise Lawd and utter loud His speechless name."

"Blow de bugle till it bust the sky."

They fell silent, intent upon the next word. Manischevitz approached them.

"You'll excuse me," he said. "I am looking for Alexander Levine. You know him maybe?"

"That's the angel," said the boy.

"Oh, *him,*" snuffed bubble eyes.

"You'll find him at Bella's. It's the establishment right across the street," the humpback said.

Manischevitz said he was sorry that he could not stay, thanked them, and limped across the street. It was already night. The city was dark and he could barely find his way.

But Bella's was bursting with the blues. Through the window Manischevitz recognized the dancing crowd and among them sought Levine. He was sitting loose-lipped at Bella's side table. They were tippling from an almost empty whiskey fifth. Levine had shed his old clothes, wore a shiny new checkered suit, pearl-gray derby, cigar, and big, two-tone button shoes. To the tailor's dismay, a drunken look had settled upon his formerly dignified face. He leaned toward Bella, tickled her ear lobe with his pinky, while whispering words that sent her into gales of raucous laughter. She fondled his knee.

Manischevitz, girding himself, pushed open the door and was not welcomed.

"This place reserved."

"Beat it, pale puss."

"Exit, Yankel, Semitic trash."

But he moved towards the table where Levine sat, the crowd breaking before him as he hobbled forward.

"Mr. Levine," he spoke in a trembly voice. "Is here Manischevitz."

Levine glared blearily. "Speak yo' piece, son."

Manischevitz shuddered. His back plagued him. Cold tremors tormented his crooked legs. He looked around, everybody was all ears.

"You'll excuse me. I would like to talk to you in a private place."

"Speak, Ah is a private pusson."

Bella laughed piercingly. "Stop it, boy, you killin' me."

Manischevitz, no end disturbed, considered fleeing but Levine addressed him:

"Kindly state the pu'pose of yo' communication with yo's truly."

The tailor wet cracked lips. "You are Jewish. This I am sure."

Levine rose, nostrils flaring. "Anythin' else yo' got to say?"

Manischevitz's tongue lay like stone.

"Speak now or fo'ever hold off."

Tears blinded the tailor's eyes. Was ever man so tried? Should he say he believed a half-drunken Negro to be an angel?

The silence slowly petrified.

Manischevitz was recalling scenes of his youth as a wheel in his mind whirred: believe, do not, yes, no, yes, no. The pointer pointed to yes, to between yes and no, to no, no it was yes. He sighed. It moved but one had still to make a choice.

"I think you are an angel from God." He said it in a broken voice, thinking. If you said it it was said. If you believed it you must say it. If you believed, you believed.

The hush broke. Everybody talked but the music began and they went on dancing. Bella, grown bored, picked up the cards and dealt herself a hand.

Levine burst into tears. "How you have humiliated me."

Manischevitz apologized.

"Wait'll I freshen up." Levine went to the men's room and returned in his old clothes.

No one said goodbye as they left.

They rode to the flat via subway. As they walked up the stairs Manischevitz pointed with his cane at his door.

"That's all been taken care of," Levine said. "You best go in while I take off."

Disappointed that it was so soon over but torn by curiosity, Manischevitz followed the angel up three flights to the roof. When he got there the door was already padlocked.

Luckily he could see through a small broken window. He heard an odd noise, as though of a whirring of wings, and when he strained for a wider view, could have sworn he saw a dark figure borne aloft on a pair of magnificent black wings.

A feather drifted down. Manischevitz gasped as it turned white, but it was only snowing.

He rushed downstairs. In the flat Fanny wielded a dust mop under the bed and then upon the cobwebs on the wall.

"A wonderful thing, Fanny," Manischevitz said. "Believe me, there are Jews everywhere."

---

1. Look for parallels between this story and the story of Job in the Bible.
2. What is said about the nature and requirements of faith?
3. What finally breaks Manischevitz's skepticism about the angel? Is there any outward manifestation to convince him?
4. What are Manischevitz's reservations about black people?

Thomas Mann

Mann (1875–1955) was born in Lübeck, Germany, the son of a distinguished merchant family. His brother Heinrich also became a well-known writer. In 1900 Mann told the story of several generations of this family in his first novel, Buddenbrooks, *which, upon its appearance, made the author immediately famous. For the remainder of his long life he was something of a literary statesman, whose task was to reconcile the distinctive qualities of the German temperament with the more general currents of European thought and culture. In* The Magic Mountain *(1924) he uses the setting of an isolated sanitarium to stage the encounter of an easygoing and naive young German with representatives of the nationalisms and ideologies competing in Europe on the eve of the First World War. Mann's vocal opposition to the Nazis led him to exile after they came to power in 1933. He spent most of the next twelve years in the United States, writing novels and political attacks against the Hitler Regime. He became an American citizen in 1944. After the defeat of the Axis powers, he returned to Europe, still painfully concerned about the political situation and the beginnings of the cold war. His novel* Doctor Faustus *(1947) is, among other things, an allegory of the fall of Germany and the cultural crisis manifested in that collapse. Some of his other novels are* The Beloved Returns *(translated in 1940),* Joseph and His Brethren *(1933–44), and* Confessions of Felix Krull, Confidence Man *(1954). His stories are collected in* Stories of Three Decades *(1936).*

Disorder and Early Sorrow[1]

The principal dish at dinner had been croquettes made of turnip greens. So there follows a trifle, concocted out of one of those dessert powders we use nowadays,[2] that taste like almond soap. Xaver, the youthful manservant, in his outgrown striped jacked, white woollen gloves, and yellow sandals, hands it round, and the "big folk" take this opportunity to remind their father, tactfully, that company is coming today.

The "big folk" are two, Ingrid and Bert. Ingrid is brown-eyed, eighteen, and perfectly delightful. She is on the eve of her exams, and

1. Translated by H. T. Lowe-Porter. 2. I.e., during the hard times of German inflation following World War I; a trifle is a dessert of sponge cake spread with jam or jelly.

will probably pass them, if only because she knows how to wind masters, and even headmasters, round her finger. She does not, however, mean to use her certificate once she gets it; having leanings towards the stage, on the ground of her ingratiating smile, her equally ingratiating voice, and a marked and irresistible talent for burlesque. Bert is blond and seventeen. He intends to get done with school somehow, anyhow, and fling himself into the arms of life. He will be a dancer, or a cabaret actor, possibly even a waiter—but not a waiter anywhere else save at the Cairo, the night-club, whither he has once already taken flight, at five in the morning, and been brought back crestfallen. Bert bears a strong resemblance to the youthful manservant Xaver Kleinsgutl, of about the same age as himself; not because he looks common—in features he is strikingly like his father, Professor Cornelius—but by reason of an approximation of types, due in its turn to far-reaching compromises in matters of dress and bearing generally. Both lads wear their heavy hair very long on top, with a cursory parting in the middle, and give their heads the same characteristic toss to throw it off the forehead. When one of them leaves the house, by the garden gate, bareheaded in all weathers, in a blouse rakishly girt with a leather strap, and sheers off bent well over with his head on one side; or else mounts his push-bike—Xaver makes free with his employers', of both sexes, or even, in acutely irresponsible mood, with the Professor's own—Dr. Cornelius from his bedroom window cannot, for the life of him, tell whether he is looking at his son or his servant. Both, he thinks, look like young moujiks.[3] And both are impassioned cigarette-smokers, though Bert has not the means to compete with Xaver, who smokes as many as thirty a day, of a brand named after a popular cinema star. The big folk call their father and mother the "old folk"—not behind their backs, but as a form of address and in all affection: "Hullo, old folks," they will say; though Cornelius is only forty-seven years old and his wife eight yours younger. And the Professor's parents, who lead in his household the humble and hesitant life of the really old, are on the big folk's lips the "ancients." As for the "little folk," Ellie and Snapper, who take their meals upstairs with blue-faced Ann—so-called because of her prevailing facial hue—Ellie and Snapper follow their mother's example and address their father by his first name, Abel. Unutterably comic it sounds, in its pert, confiding familiarity; particularly on the lips, in the sweet accents, of five-year-old Eleanor, who is the image of Frau Cornelius's baby pictures and whom the Professor loves above everything else in the world.

"Darling old thing," says Ingrid affably, laying her large but shapely hand on his, as he presides in proper middle-class style over the family

3. Russian peasants.

table, with her on his left and the mother opposite: "Parent mine, may I ever so gently jog your memory, for you have probably forgotten: this is the afternoon we were to have our little jollification, our turkey-trot with eats to match. You haven't a thing to do but just bear up and not funk it; everything will be over by nine o'clock."

"Oh—ah!" says Cornelius, his face falling. "Good!" he goes on, and nods his head to show himself in harmony with the inevitable. "I only meant—is this really the day? Thursday, yes. How time flies! Well, what time are they coming?"

"Half past four they'll be dropping in, I should say," answers Ingrid, to whom her brother leaves the major rôle in all dealings with the father. Upstairs, while he is resting, he will hear scarcely anything, and from seven to eight he takes his walk. He can slip out by the terrace if he likes.

"Tut!" says Cornelius deprecatingly, as who should say: "You exaggerate." But Bert puts in: "It's the one evening in the week Wanja doesn't have to play. Any other night he'd have to leave by half past six, which would be painful for all concerned."

Wanja is Ivan Herzl, the celebrated young leading man at the Stadttheater.[4] Bert and Ingrid are on intimate terms with him, they often visit him in his dressing-room and have tea. He is an artist of the modern school, who stands on the stage in strange and, to the Professor's mind, utterly affected dancing attitudes, and shrieks lamentably. To a professor of history, all highly repugnant; but Bert has entirely succumbed to Herzl's influence, blackens the lower rim of his eyelids—despite painful but fruitless scenes with the father—and with youthful carelessness of the ancestral anguish declares that not only will he take Herzl for his model if he becomes a dancer, in case he turns out to be a waiter at the Cairo he means to walk precisely thus.

Cornelius slightly raises his brows and makes his son a little bow—indicative of the unassumingness and self-abnegation that befits his age. You could not call it a mocking bow or suggestive in any special sense. Bert may refer it to himself or equally to his so talented friend.

"Who else is coming?" next inquires the master of the house. They mention various people, names all more or less familiar, from the city, from the suburban colony, from Ingrid's school. They still have some telephoning to do, they say. They have to phone Max. This is Max Hergesell, an engineering student; Ingrid utters his name in the nasal drawl which according to her is the traditional intonation of all the Hergesells. She goes on to parody it in the most abandonedly funny and lifelike way, and the parents laugh until they nearly choke over

4. Municipal theater.

the wretched trifle. For even in these times when something funny happens people have to laugh.

From time to time the telephone bell rings in the Professor's study, and the big folk run across, knowing it is their affair. Many people had to give up their telephones the last time the price rose, but so far the Corneliuses have been able to keep theirs, just as they have kept their villa, which was built before the war, by dint of the salary Cornelius draws as professor of history—a million marks,[5] and more or less adequate to the chances and changes of post-war life. The house is comfortable, even elegant, though sadly in need of repairs that cannot be made for lack of materials, and at present disfigured by iron stoves with long pipes. Even so, it is still the proper setting of the upper middle class, though they themselves look odd enough in it, with their worn and turned clothing and altered way of life. The children, of course, know nothing else; to them it is normal and regular, they belong by birth to the "villa proletariat." The problem of clothing troubles them not at all. They and their like have evolved a costume to fit the time, by poverty out of taste for innovation: in summer it consists of scarcely more than a belted linen smock and sandals. The middle-class parents find things rather more difficult.

The big folk's table-napkins hang over their chair-backs, they talk with their friends over the telephone. These friends are the invited guests who have rung up to accept or decline or arrange; and the conversation is carried on in the jargon of the clan, full of slang and high spirits, of which the old folk understand hardly a word. These consult together meantime about the hospitality to be offered to the impending guests. The Professor displays a middle-class ambitiousness: he wants to serve a sweet—or something that looks like a sweet—after the Italian salad and brown-bread sandwiches. But Frau Cornelius says that would be going too far. The guests would not expect it, she is sure—and the big folk, returning once more to their trifle, agree with her.

The mother of the family is of the same general type as Ingrid, though not so tall. She is languid; the fantastic difficulties of the housekeeping have broken and worn her. She really ought to go and take a cure, but feels incapable; the floor is always swaying under her feet, and everything seems upside down. She speaks of what is uppermost in her mind: the eggs, they simply must be bought today. Six thousand marks apiece they are, and just so many are to be had on this one day of the week at one single shop fifteen minutes' journey away. Whatever else they do, the big folk must go and fetch them immediately after luncheon, with Danny, their neighbour's son, who will soon be calling

5. His monthly salary. The high figure indicates the monetary inflation after World War I.

for them; and Xaver Kleinsgutl will don civilian garb and attend his young master and mistress. For no single household is allowed more than five eggs a week; therefore the young people will enter the shop singly, one after another, under assumed names, and thus wring twenty eggs from the shopkeeper for the Cornelius family. This enterprise is the sporting event of the week for all participants, not excepting the moujik Kleinsgutl, and most of all for Ingrid and Bert, who delight in misleading and mystifying their fellowmen and would revel in the performance even if it did not achieve one single egg. They adore impersonating fictitious characters; they love to sit in a bus and carry on long lifelike conversations in a dialect which they otherwise never speak, the most commonplace dialogue about politics and people and the price of food, while the whole bus listens open-mouthed to this incredibly ordinary prattle, though with a dark suspicion all the while that something is wrong somewhere. The conversation waxes ever more shameless, it enters into revolting detail about these people who do not exist. Ingrid can make her voice sound ever so common and twittering and shrill as she impersonates a shop-girl with an illegitimate child, said child being a son with sadistic tendencies, who lately out in the country treated a cow with such unnatural cruelty that no Christian could have borne to see it. Bert nearly explodes at her twittering, but restrains himself and displays a grisly sympathy; he and the unhappy shop-girl entering into a long, stupid, depraved, and shuddery conversation over the particular morbid cruelty involved; until an old gentleman opposite, sitting with his ticket folded between his index finger and his seal ring, can bear it no more and makes public protest against the nature of the themes these young folk are discussing with such particularity. He uses the Greek plural: "themata." Whereat Ingrid pretends to be dissolving in tears, and Bert behaves as though his wrath against the old gentleman was with difficulty being held in check and would probably burst out before long. He clenches his fists, he gnashes his teeth, he shakes from head to foot; and the unhappy old gentleman, whose intentions had been of the best, hastily leaves the bus at the next stop.

Such are the diversions of the big folk. The telephone plays a prominent part in them: they ring up any and everybody—members of government, opera singers, dignitaries of the Church—in the character of shop assistants, or perhaps as Lord or Lady Doolittle.[6] They are only with difficulty persuaded that they have the wrong number. Once they emptied their parents' card-tray[7] and distributed its contents among the neighbours' letter-boxes, wantonly, yet not without enough impish sense of the fitness of things to make it highly upset-

6. Fictitious comic characters. 7. For people of the professor's class it was customary to leave calling cards in a tray when one paid a call.

ting, God only knowing why certain people should have called where they did.

Xaver comes in to clear away, tossing the hair out of his eyes. Now that he has taken off his gloves you can see the yellow chain-ring on his left hand. And as the Professor finishes his watery eight-thousand-mark beer and lights a cigarette, the little folk can be heard scrambling down the stair, coming, by established custom, for their after-dinner call on Father and Mother. They storm the dining-room, after a struggle with the latch, clutched by both pairs of little hands at once; their clumsy small feet twinkle over the carpet, in red felt slippers with the socks falling down on them. With prattle and shoutings each makes for his own place: Snapper to Mother, to climb on her lap, boast of all he has eaten, and thump his fat little tum; Ellie to her Abel, so much hers because she is so very much his; because she consciously luxuriates in the deep tenderness—like all deep feeling, concealing a melancholy strain—with which he holds her small form embraced; in the love in his eyes as he kisses her little fairy hand or the sweet brow with its delicate tracery of tiny blue veins.

The little folk look like each other, with the strong undefined likeness of brother and sister. In clothing and hair-cut they are twins. Yet they are sharply distinguished after all, and quite on sex lines. It is a little Adam and a little Eve. Not only is Snapper the sturdier and more compact, he appears consciously to emphasize his four-year-old masculinity in speech, manner, and carriage, lifting his shoulders and letting the little arms hang down quite like a young American athlete, drawing down his mouth when he talks and seeking to give his voice a gruff and forthright ring. But all this masculinity is the result of effort rather than natively his. Born and brought up in these desolate, distracted times, he has been endowed by them with an unstable and hypersensitive nervous system and suffers greatly under life's disharmonies. He is prone to sudden anger and outbursts of bitter tears, stamping his feet at every trifle; for this reason he is his mother's special nursling and care. His round, round eyes are chestnut brown and already inclined to squint, so that he will need glasses in the near future. His little nose is long, the mouth small—the father's nose and mouth they are, more plainly than ever since the Professor shaved his pointed beard and goes smooth-faced. The pointed beard had become impossible—even professors must make some concession to the changing times.

But the little daughter sits on her father's knee, his Eleonorchen, his little Eve, so much more gracious a little being, so much sweeter-faced than her brother—and he holds his cigarette away from her while she fingers his glasses with her dainty wee hands. The lenses are divided for reading and distance, and each day they tease her curiosity afresh.

At bottom he suspects that his wife's partiality may have a firmer basis than his own: that Snapper's refractory masculinity perhaps is solider stuff than his own little girl's more explicit charm and grace. But the heart will not be commanded, that he knows; and once and for all his heart belongs to the little one, as it has since the day she came, since the first time he saw her. Almost always when he holds her in his arms he remembers that first time: remembers the sunny room in the Women's Hospital, where Ellie first saw the light, twelve years after Bert was born. He remembers how he drew near, the mother smiling the while, and cautiously put aside the canopy of the diminutive bed that stood beside the large one. There lay the little miracle among the pillows: so well formed, so encompassed, as it were, with the harmony of sweet proportions, with little hands that even then, though so much tinier, were beautiful as now; with wide-open eyes blue as the sky and brighter than the sunshine—and almost in that very second he felt himself captured and held fast. This was love at first sight, love everlasting: a feeling unknown, unhoped for, unexpected—in so far as it could be a matter of conscious awareness; it took entire possession of him, and he understood, with joyous amazement, that this was for life.

But he understood more. He knows, does Dr. Cornelius, that there is something not quite right about his feeling, so unaware, so undreamed of, so involuntary. He has a shrewd suspicion that it is not by accident it has so utterly mastered him and bound itself up with his existence; that he had—even subconsciously—been preparing for it, or, more precisely, been prepared for it. There is, in short, something in him which at a given moment was ready to issue in such a feeling; and this something, highly extraordinary to relate, is his essence and quality as a professor of history. Dr. Cornelius, however, does not actually say this, even to himself; he merely realizes it, at odd times, and smiles a private smile. He knows that history professors do not love history because it is something that comes to pass, but only because it is something that *has* come to pass; that they hate a revolution[8] like the present one because they feel it is lawless, incoherent, irrelevant—in a word, unhistoric; that their hearts belong to the coherent, disciplined, historic past. For the temper of timelessness, the temper of eternity—thus the scholar communes with himself when he takes his walk by the river before supper—that temper broods over the past; and it is a temper much better suited to the nervous system of a history professor than are the excesses of the present. The past is immortalized; that is to say, it is dead; and death is the root of all godliness and all abiding significance. Dr. Cornelius, walking alone in the dark, has a profound insight into this truth. It is this conservative instinct of his,

8. I.e., the worldwide revolution of society that followed World War I.

his sense of the eternal, that has found in his love for his little daughter a way to save itself from the wounding inflicted by the times. For father love, and a little child on its mother's breast—are not these timeless, and thus very, very holy and beautiful? Yet Cornelius, pondering there in the dark, descries something not perfectly right and good in his love. Theoretically, in the interests of science, he admits it to himself. There is something ulterior about it, in the nature of it; that something is hostility, hostility against the history of today, which is still in the making and thus not history at all, in behalf of the genuine history that has already happened—that is to say, death. Yes, passing strange though all this is, yet it is true; true in a sense, that is. His devotion to this priceless little morsel of life and new growth has something to do with death, it clings to death as against life; and that is neither right nor beautiful—in a sense. Though only the most fanatical asceticism could be capable, on no other ground than such casual scientific perception, of tearing this purest and most precious of feelings out of his heart.

He holds his darling on his lap and her slim rosy legs hang down. He raises his brows as he talks to her, tenderly, with a half-teasing note of respect, and listens enchanted to her high, sweet little voice calling him Abel. He exchanges a look with the mother, who is caressing her Snapper and reading him a gentle lecture. He must be more reasonable, he must learn self-control; today again, under the manifold exasperations of life, he has given way to rage and behaved like a howling dervish. Cornelius casts a mistrustful glance at the big folk now and then, too; he thinks it not unlikely they are not unaware of those scientific preoccupations of his evening walks. If such be the case they do not show it. They stand there leaning their arms on their chair-backs and with a benevolence not untinctured with irony look on at the parental happiness.

The children's frocks are of a heavy, brick-red stuff, embroidered in modern "arty" style. They once belonged to Ingrid and Bert and are precisely alike, save that little knickers come out beneath Snapper's smock. And both have their hair bobbed. Snapper's is a streaky blond, inclined to turn dark. It is bristly and sticky and looks for all the world like a droll, badly fitting wig. But Ellie's is chestnut brown, glossy and fine as silk, as pleasing as her whole little personality. It covers her ears—and these ears are not a pair, one of them being the right size, the other distinctly too large. Her father will sometimes uncover this little abnormality and exclaim over it as though he had never noticed it before, which both makes Ellie giggle and covers her with shame. Her eyes are now golden brown, set far apart and with sweet gleams in them—such a clear and lovely look! The brows above are blond; the nose still unformed, with thick nostrils and almost circular holes; the mouth large and expressive, with a beautifully arching and mobile upper lip. When she laughs, dimples come in her cheeks and she shows her teeth like loosely strung pearls. So far she has lost but one tooth, which her father gently twisted out with his handkerchief after it had grown very wobbling. During this small operation she had paled and trembled very much. Her cheeks have the softness proper to her years, but they are not chubby; indeed, they are rather concave, due to her facial structure, with its somewhat prominent jaw. On one, close to the soft fall of her fair, is a downy freckle.

Ellie is not too well pleased with her looks—a sign that already she troubles about such things. Sadly she thinks it is best to admit it once for all, her face is "homely"; though the rest of her, "on the other hand," is not bad at all. She loves expressions like "on the other hand"; they sound choice and grown-up to her, and she likes to string them together, one after the other: "very likely, " "probably," "after all." Snapper is self-critical too, though more in the moral sphere: he suffers from remorse for his attacks of rage and considers himself a tremendous sinner. He is quite certain that heaven is not for such as he; he is sure to go to "the bad place" when he dies, and no persuasions will convince him to the contrary—as that God sees the heart and gladly makes allowances. Obstinately he shakes his head, with a comic, crooked little peruke,[9] and vows there is no place for him in heaven. When he has a cold he is immediately quite choked with mucus; rattles and rumbles from top to toe if you even look at him; his temperature flies up at once and he simply puffs. Nursy is pessimistic on the score of his constitution: such fat-blooded children as he might get a stroke any minute. Once she even thought she saw the moment at hand: Snapper had been in one of his berserker rages, and in the ensuing fit of penitence stood himself in the corner with his back to the room. Suddenly Nursy noticed that his face had gone all blue, far bluer, even, than her own. She raised the alarm, crying out that the child's all too rich blood had at length brought him to his final hour; and Snapper, to his vast astonishment, found himself, so far from being rebuked for evil-doing, encompassed in tenderness and anxiety—until it turned out that his colour was not caused by apoplexy but by the distempering[1] on the nursery wall, which had come off on his tear-wet face.

Nursy has come downstairs too, and stands by the door, sleek-haired, owl-eyed, with her hands folded over her white apron, and a severely dignified manner born of her limited intelligence. She is very proud of the care and training she gives her nurslings and declares that they are "enveloping wonderfully." She has had seventeen suppurated teeth lately removed from her jaws and been measured for a set of symmetrical yellow ones in dark rubber gums; these now embellish

9. I.e., his hair looks like a wig. 1. Soluble paint.

her peasant face. She is obessed with the strange conviction that these teeth of hers are the subject of general conversation, that, as it were, the sparrows on the house-tops chatter of them. "Everybody knows I've had a false set put in," she will say; "there has been a great deal of foolish talk about them." She is much given to dark hints and veiled innuendo: speaks, for instance, of a certain Dr. Bleifuss,[2] whom every child knows, and "there are even some in the house who pretend to be him." All one can do with talk like this is charitably to pass it over in silence. But she teaches the children nursery rhymes: gems like:

Puff, puff, here comes the train!
Puff, puff, toot, toot,
Away it goes again.

Or that gastronomical jingle, so suited, in its sparseness, to the times, and yet seemingly with a blitheness of its own:

Monday we begin the week,
Tuesday there's a bone to pick.
Wednesday we're half way through,
Thursday what a great to-do!
Friday we eat what fish we're able,
Saturday we dance round the table.
Sunday brings us pork and greens—
Here's a feast for kings and queens!

Also a certain four-line stanza with a romantic appeal, unutterable and unuttered:

Open the gate, open the gate
And let the carriage drive in.
Who is it in the carriage sits:
A lordly sir with golden hair.

Or, finally that ballad about golden-haired Marianne who sat on a, sat on a, sat on a stone, and combed out her, combed out her, combed out her hair; and about bloodthirsty Rudolph, who pulled out a, pulled out a, pulled out a knife—and his ensuing direful end. Ellie enunciates all these ballads charmingly, with her mobile little lips, and sings them in her sweet little voice—much better than Snapper. She does everything better than he does, and he pays her honest admiration and homage and obeys her in all things except when visited by one of his attacks.

2. "Dr. Leadfoot," character in a nursery tale.

Sometimes she teaches him, instructs him upon the birds in the picture-book and tells him their proper names: "This is a chaffinch, Buddy, this is a bullfinch, this is a cowfinch." He has to repeat them after her. She gives him medical instruction too, teaches him the names of diseases, such as infammation of the lungs, infammation of the blood, infammation of the air. If he does not pay attention and cannot say the words after her, she stands him in the corner. Once she even boxed his ears, but was so ashamed that she stood herself in the corner for a long time. Yes, they are fast friends, two souls with but a single thought, and have all their adventures in common. They come home from a walk and relate as with one voice that they have seen two moollies and a teenty-weenty baby calf. They are on familiar terms with the kitchen, which consists of Xaver and the ladies Hinterhofer, two sisters once of the lower middle class who, in these evil days, are reduced to living "*au pair*"[3] as the phrase goes and officiating as cook and housemaid for their board and keep. The little ones have a feeling that Xaver and the Hinterhofers are on much the same footing with their father and mother as they are themselves. At least sometimes, when they have been scolded, they go downstairs and announce that the master and mistress are cross. But playing with the servants lacks charm compared with the joys of playing upstairs. The kitchen could never rise to the height of the games their father can invent. For instance, there is "four gentlemen taking a walk." When they play it Abel will crook his knees until he is the same height with themselves and go walking with them, hand in hand. They never get enough of this sport; they could walk round and round the dining-room a whole day on end, five gentlemen in all, counting the diminished Abel.

Then there is the thrilling cushion game. One of the children, usually Ellie, seats herself, unbeknownst to Abel, in his seat at table. Still as a mouse she awaits his coming. He draws near with his head in the air, descanting in loud, clear tones upon the surpassing comfort of his chair; and sits down on top of Ellie. "What's this, what's this?" says he. And bounces about, deaf to the smothered giggles exploding behind him. "Why have they put a cushion in my chair? And what a queer, hard, awkward-shaped cushion it is!" he goes on. "Frightfully uncomfortable to sit on!" And keeps pushing and bouncing about more and more on the astonishing cushion and clutching behind him into the rapturous giggling and squeaking, until at last he turns round, and the game ends with a magnificent climax of discovery and recognition. They might go through all this a hundred times without diminishing by an iota its power to thrill.

Today is no time for such joys. The imminent festivity disturbs

3. As household helpers.

the atmosphere, and besides there is work to be done, and, above all, the eggs to be got. Ellie has just time to recite "Puff, puff," and Cornelius to discover that her ears are not mates, when they are interrupted by the arrival of Danny, come to fetch Bert and Ingrid. Xaver, meantime, has exchanged his striped livery for an ordinary coat, in which he looks rather rough-and-ready, though as brisk and attractive as ever. So then Nursy and the children ascend to the upper regions, the Professor withdraws to his study to read, as always after dinner, and his wife bends her energies upon the sandwiches and salad that must be prepared. And she has another errand as well. Before the young people arrive she has to take her shopping-basket and dash into town on her bicycle, to turn into provisions a sum of money she has in hand, which she dares not keep lest it lose all value.

Cornelius reads, leaning back in his chair, with his cigar between his middle and index fingers. First he reads Macaulay[4] on the origin of the English public debt at the end of the seventeenth century; then an article in a French periodical on the rapid increase in the Spanish debt towards the end of the sixteenth. Both these for his lecture on the morrow. He intends to compare the astonishing prosperity which accompanied the phenomenon in England with its fatal effects a hundred years earlier in Spain, and to analyse the ethical and psychological grounds of the difference in results. For that will give him a chance to refer back from the England of William III,[5] which is the actual subject in hand, to the time of Philip II and the Counter-Reformation,[6] which is his own special field. He has already written a valuable work on this period; it is much cited and got him his professorship. While his cigar burns down and gets strong, he excogitates a few pensive sentences in a key of gentle melancholy, to be delivered before his class next day: about the practically hopeless struggle carried on by the belated Philip against the whole trend of history: against the new, the kingdom-disrupting power of the Germanic ideal of freedom and individual liberty.[7] And about the persistent, futile struggle of the aristocracy, condemned by God and rejected of man, against the forces of progress and change. He savours his sentences; keeps on polishing them while he puts back the books he has been using; then goes upstairs for the

4. Thomas Babington Macaulay (1800–1859), English historian and essayist. 5. William III of England (1658–1702) became king in 1689, ruling jointly with his wife Mary. Through him England advanced toward constitutional monarchy. 6. Catholic reforms of the 16th and 17th century, aimed at halting the Protestant Reformation and winning back the peoples and territories the Roman Church had lost. Philip II of Spain (1555–1598) was a leader of the Counter Reformation. Supremacy of the Catholic faith was his first priority, and for this end he persecuted Protestants and sent the Armada to punish Queen Elizabeth I of England. 7. A reference to the Reformation, the 16th-century movement to liberalize doctrines and institutions of the Catholic church. Led by Martin Luther (1483–1546), it brought about the separation of Protestants from Catholicism and rolled onward with profound political consequences for Europe.

usual pause in his day's work, the hour with drawn blinds and closed eyes, which he so imperatively needs. But today, he recalls, he will rest under disturbed conditions, amid the bustle of preparations for the feast. He smiles to find his heart giving a mild flutter at the thought. Disjointed phrases on the theme of black-clad Philip and his times mingle with a confused consciousness that they will soon be dancing down below. For five minutes or so he falls asleep.

As he lies and rests he can hear the sound of the garden gate and the repeated ringing at the bell. Each time a little pang goes through him, of excitement and suspense, at the thought that the young people have begun to fill the floor below. And each time he smiles at himself again—though even his smile is slightly nervous—is tinged with the pleasurable anticipations people always feel before a party. At half past four—it is already dark—he gets up and washes at the wash-stand. The basin has been out of repair for two years. It is supposed to tip, but has broken away from its socket on one side and cannot be mended because there is nobody to mend it; neither replaced because no shop can supply another. So it has to be hung up above the vent and emptied by lifting in both hands and pouring out the water. Cornelius shakes his head over this basin, as he does several times a day—whenever, in fact, he has occasion to use it. He finishes his toilet with care, standing under the ceiling light to polish his glasses till they shine. Then he goes downstairs.

On his way to the dining-room he hears the gramophone already going, and the sound of voices. He puts on a polite, society air; at his tongue's end is the phrase he means to utter: "Pray don't let me disturb you," as he passes directly into the dining-room for his tea. "Pray don't let me disturb you"—it seems to him precisely the *mot juste*;[8] towards the guests cordial and considerate, for himself a very bulwark.

The lower floor is lighted up, all the bulbs in the chandelier are burning save one that has burned out. Cornelius pauses on a lower step and surveys the entrance hall. It looks pleasant and cosy in the bright light, with its copy of Marée over the brick chimney-piece, its wainscoted walls—wainscoted in soft wood—and red-carpeted floor, where the guests stand in groups, chatting, each with his teacup and slice of bread-and-butter spread with anchovy paste. There is a festal haze, faint scents of hair and clothing and human breath come to him across the room, it is all characteristic and familiar and highly evocative. The door into the dressing-room is open, guests are still arriving.

A large group of people is rather bewildering at first sight. The Professor takes in only the general scene. He does not see Ingrid, who is standing just at the foot of the steps, in a dark silk frock with a

8. The exact word.

pleated collar falling softly over the shoulders, and bare arms. She smiles up at him, nodding and showing her lovely teeth.

"Rested?" she asks, for his private ear. With a quite unwarranted start he recognizes her, and she presents some of her friends.

"May I introduce Herr Zuber?" she says. "And this is Fräulein Plaichinger."

Herr Zuber is insignificant. But Fräulein Plaichinger is a perfect Germania, blond and voluptuous, arrayed in floating draperies. She has a snub nose, and answers the Professor's salutation in the high, shrill pipe so many stout women have.

"Delighted to meet you," he says. "How nice of you to come! A classmate of Ingrid's, I suppose?"

And Herr Zuber is a golfing partner of Ingrid's. He is in business; he works in his uncle's brewery. Cornelius makes a few jokes about the thinness of the beer and professes to believe that Herr Zuber could easily do something about the quality if he would. "But pray don't let me disturb you," he goes on, and turns towards the dining-room.

"There comes Max," says Ingrid. "Max, you sweep, what do you mean by rolling up at this time of day?" For such is the way they talk to each other, offensively to an older ear; of social forms, of hospitable warmth, there is no faintest trace. They all call each other by their first names.

A young man comes up to them out of the dressing-room and makes his bow; he has an expanse of white shirt-front and a little black string tie. He is as pretty as a picture, dark, with rosy cheeks, clean-shaven of course, but with just a sketch of side-whisker. Not a ridiculous or flashy beauty, not like a gypsy fiddler, but just charming to look at, in a winning, well-bred way, with kind dark eyes. He even wears his dinner-jacket a little awkwardly.

"Please don't scold me, Cornelia," he says; "it's the idiotic lectures." And Ingrid presents him to her father as Herr Hergesell.

Well, and so this is Herr Hergesell. He knows his manners, does Herr Hergesell, and thanks the master of the house quite ingratiatingly for his invitation as they shake hands. "I certainly seem to have missed the bus," says he jocosely. "Of course I have lectures today up to four o'clock; I would have; and after that I had to go home to change." Then he talks about his pumps, with which he has just been struggling in the dressing-room.

"I brought them with me in a bag," he goes on. "Mustn't tramp all over the carpet in our brogues—it's not done. Well, I was ass enough not to fetch along a shoe-horn, and I find I simply can't get in! What a sell! They are the tightest I've ever had, the numbers don't tell you a thing, and all the leather today is just cast iron. It's not leather at all. My poor finger"—he confidingly displays a reddened digit and once more characterizes the whole thing as a "sell," and a putrid sell into the bargain. He really does talk just as Ingrid said he did, with a peculiar nasal drawl, not affectedly in the least, but merely because that is the way of all the Hergesells.

Dr. Cornelius says it is very careless of them not to keep a shoehorn in the cloak-room and displays proper sympathy with the mangled finger. "But now you *really* must not let me disturb you any longer," he goes on. "*Auf wiedersehen!*"[9] And he crosses the hall into the dining-room.

There are guests there too, drinking tea; the family table is pulled out. But the Professor goes at once to his own little upholstered corner with the electric light bulb above it—the nook where he usually drinks his tea. His wife is sitting there talking with Bert and two other young men, one of them Herzl, whom Cornelius knows and greets; the other a typical "Wandervogel"[1] named Möller, a youth who obviously neither owns nor cares to own the correct evening dress of the middle classes (in fact, there is no such thing any more), nor to ape the manners of a gentleman (and, in fact, there is no such thing any more either). He has a wilderness of hair, horned spectacles, and a long neck, and wears golf stockings and a belted blouse. His regular occupation, the Professor learns, is banking, but he is by way of being an amateur folk-lorist and collects folk-songs from all localities and in all languages. He sings them, too, and at Ingrid's command has brought his guitar; it is hanging in the dressing-room in an oilcloth case. Herzl, the actor, is small and slight, but he has a strong growth of black beard, as you can tell by the thick coat of powder on his cheeks. His eyes are larger than life, with a deep and melancholy glow. He has put on rouge besides the powder—those dull carmine high-lights on the cheeks can be nothing but a cosmetic. "Queer," thinks the Professor. "You would think a man would be one thing or the other—not melancholic and use face paint at the same time. It's a psychological contradiction. How can a melancholy man rouge? But here we have a perfect illustration of the abnormality of the artist soul-form. It can make possible a contradiction like this—perhaps it even consists in the contradiction. All very interesting—and no reason whatever for not being polite to him. Politeness is a primitive convention—and legitimate. . . . Do take some lemon, Herr Hofschauspieler!"[2]

Court actors and court theatres—there are no such things any more, really. But Herzl relishes the sound of the title, notwithstanding he is a revolutionary artist. This must be another contradiction inherent in his soul-form; so, at least, the Professor assumes, and he is prob-

9. "Good-by." Literally, "till we see each other again." 1. A rootless, footloose person. 2. "Mr. Actor in the court theater."

ably right. The flattery he is guilty of is a sort of atonement for his previous hard thoughts about the rouge.

"Thank you so much—it's really too good of you, sir," says Herzl, quite embarrassed. He is so overcome that he almost stammers; only his perfect enunciation saves him. His whole bearing towards his hostess and the master of the house is exaggeratedly polite. It is almost as though he had a bad conscience in respect of his rouge; as though an inward compulsion had driven him to put it on, but now, seeing it through the Professor's eyes, he disapproves of it himself, and thinks, by an air of humility toward the whole of unrouged society, to mitigate its effect.

They drink their tea and chat: about Möller's folk-songs, about Basque[3] folk-songs and Spanish folk-songs; from which they pass to the new production of *Don Carlos*[4] at the Stadttheater, in which Herzl plays the title-rôle. He talks about his own rendering of the part and says he hopes his conception of the character has unity. They go on to criticize the rest of the cast, the setting, and the production as a whole; and Cornelius is struck, rather painfully, to find the conversation trending towards his own special province, back to Spain and the Counter-Reformation. He has done nothing at all to give it this turn, he is perfectly innocent, and hopes it does not look as though he has sought an occasion to play the professor. He wonders, and falls silent, feeling relieved when the little folk come up to the table. Ellie and Snapper have on their blue velvet Sunday frocks; they are permitted to partake in the festivities up to bedtime. They look shy and large-eyed as they say how-do-you-do to the strangers and, under pressure, repeat their names and ages. Herr Möller does nothing but gaze at them solemnly, but Herzl is simply ravished. He rolls his eyes up to heaven and puts his hands over his mouth; he positively blesses them. It all, no doubt, comes from his heart, but he is so addicted to theatrical methods of making an impression and getting an effect that both words and behaviour ring frightfully false. And even his enthusiasm for the little folk looks too much like part of his general craving to make up for the rouge on his cheeks.

The tea-table has meanwhile emptied of guests, and dancing is going on in the hall. The children run off, the Professor prepares to retire. "Go and enjoy yourselves," he says to Möller and Herzl, who have sprung from their chairs as he rises from his. They shake hands and he withdraws into his study, his peaceful kingdom, where he lets down the blinds, turns on the desk lamp, and sits down to his work.

It is work which can be done, if necessary, under disturbed con-

3. From a region in northern Spain and southern France. 4. Play by Friedrich Schiller (1759–1805), German playwright. It is set in the Spain of Philip II.

ditions: nothing but a few letters and a few notes. Of course, Cornelius's mind wanders. Vague impressions float through it: Herr Hergesell's refractory pumps, the high pipe in that plump body of the Plaichinger female. As he writes, or leans back in his chair and stares into space, his thoughts go back to Herr Möller's collection of Basque folk-songs, to Herzl's posings and humility, to "his" Carlos and the court of Philip II. There is something strange, he thinks, about conversations. They are so ductile, they will flow of their own accord in the direction of one's dominating interest. Often and often he has seen this happen. And while he is thinking, he is listening to the sounds next door—rather subdued, he finds them. He hears only voices, no sounds of footsteps. The dancers do not glide or circle round the room; they merely walk about over the carpet, which does not hamper their movements in the least. Their way of holding each other is quite different and strange, and they move to the strains of the gramophone, to the weird music of the new world. He concentrates on the music and makes out that it is a jazz-band record, with various percussion instruments and the clack and clatter of castanets, which, however, are not even faintly suggestive of Spain, but merely jazz like the rest. No, not Spain. . . . His thoughts are back at their old round.

Half an hour goes by. It occurs to him it would be no more than friendly to go and contribute a box of cigarettes to the festivities next door. Too bad to ask the young people to smoke their own—though they have probably never thought of it. He goes into the empty dining-room and takes a box from his supply in the cupboard: not the best ones, nor yet the brand he himself prefers, but a certain long, thin kind he is not averse to getting rid of—after all, they are nothing but youngsters. He takes the box into the hall, holds it up with a smile, and deposits it on the mantel-shelf. After which he gives a look round and returns to his own room.

There comes a lull in dance and music. The guests stand about the room in groups or round the table at the window or are seated in a circle by the fireplace. Even the built-in stairs, with their worn velvet carpet, are crowded with young folks as in an amphitheatre: Max Hergesell is there, leaning back with one elbow on the step above and gesticulating with his free hand as he talks to the shrill, voluptuous Plaichinger. The floor of the hall is nearly empty, save just in the centre: there, directly beneath the chandelier, the two little ones in their blue velvet frocks clutch each other in an awkward embrace and twirl silently round and round, oblivious of all else. Cornelius, as he passes, strokes their hair, with a friendly word; it does not distract them from their small solemn preoccupation. But at his own door he turns to glance round and sees young Hergesell push himself off the stair by his elbow—

probably because he noticed the Professor. He comes down into the arena, takes Ellie out of her brother's arms, and dances with her himself. It looks very comic, without the music, and he crouches down just as Cornelius does when he goes walking with the four gentlemen, holding the fluttered Ellie as though she were grown up and taking little "shimmying" steps. Everybody watches with huge enjoyment, the gramophone is put on again, dancing becomes general. The Professor stands and looks, with his hand on the door-knob. He nods and laughs; when he finally shuts himself into his study the mechanical smile still lingers on his lips.

Again he turns over pages by his desk lamp, takes notes, attends to a few simple matters. After a while he notices that the guests have forsaken the entrance hall for his wife's drawing-room, into which there is a door from his own study as well. He hears their voices and the sounds of a guitar being tuned. Herr Möller, it seems, is to sing—and does so. He twangs the strings of his instrument and sings in a powerful bass a ballad in a strange tongue, possibly Swedish. The Professor does not succeed in identifying it, though he listens attentively to the end, after which there is great applause. The sound is deadened by the portière that hangs over the dividing door. The young bank-clerk begins another song. Cornelius goes softly in.

It is half-dark in the drawing-room; the only light is from the shaded standard lamp, beneath which Möller sits, on the divan, with his legs crossed, picking his strings. His audience is grouped easily about; as there are not enough seats, some stand, and more, among them many young ladies, are simply sitting on the floor with their hands clasped round their knees or even with their legs stretched out before them. Hergesell sits thus, in his dinner jacket, next to the piano, with Fräulein Plaichinger beside him. Frau Cornelius is holding both children on her lap as she sits in her easy-chair opposite the singer. Snapper, the Boeotian,[5] begins to talk loud and clear in the middle of the song and has to be intimidated with hushings and finger-shakings. Never, never would Ellie allow herself to be guilty of such conduct. She sits there daintily erect and still on her mother's knee. The Professor tries to catch her eye and exchange a private signal with his little girl; but she does not see him. Neither does she seem to be looking at the singer. Her gaze is directed lower down.

Möller sings the "joli tambour":[6]

Sire, mon roi, donnez-moi votre fille—[7]

5. A dull person, a "Philistine." 6. Pretty drum. 7. "Lord, my king, give me your daughter—."

They are all enchanted. "How good!" Hergesell is heard to say, in the odd, nasally condescending Hergesell tone. The next one is a beggar ballad, to a tune composed by young Möller himself; it elicits a storm of applause:

Gypsy lassie a-goin' to the fair,
Huzza!
Gypsie laddie a-goin' to be there—
Huzza, diddlety umpty dido!

Laughter and high spirits, sheer reckless hilarity, reigns after this jovial ballad. "Frightfully good!" Hergesell comments again, as before. Follows another popular song, this time a Hungarian one; Möller sings it in its own outlandish tongue, and most effectively. The Professor applauds with ostentation. It warms his heart and does him good, this outcropping of artistic, historic, and cultural elements all amongst the shimmying. He goes up to young Möller and congratulates him, talks about the songs and their sources, and Möller promises to lend him a certain annotated book of folk songs. Cornelius is the more cordial because all the time, as fathers do, he has been comparing the parts and achievements of this young stranger with those of his own son, and being gnawed by envy and chagrin. This young Möller, he is thinking, is a capable bank-clerk (though about Möller's capacity he knows nothing whatever) and has this special gift besides, which must have taken talent and energy to cultivate. "And here is my poor Bert, who knows nothing and can do nothing and thinks of nothing except playing the clown, without even talent for that!" He tries to be just; he tells himself that, after all, Bert has innate refinement; that probably there is a good deal more to him than there is to the successful Möller; that perhaps he has even something of the poet in him, and his dancing and table-waiting are due to mere boyish folly and the distraught times. But paternal envy and pessimism win the upper hand; when Möller begins another song, Dr. Cornelius goes back to his room.

He works as before, with divided attention, at this and that, while it gets on for seven o'clock. Then he remembers a letter he may just as well write, a short letter and not very important, but letter-writing is wonderful for the way it takes up the time, and it is almost half past when he has finished. At half past eight the Italian salad will be served; so now is the prescribed moment for the Professor to go out into the wintry darkness to post his letters and take his daily quantum of fresh air and exercise. They are dancing again, and he will have to pass through the hall to get his hat and coat; but they are used to him now, he need not stop and beg them not to be disturbed. He lays away his papers, takes up the letters he has written, and goes out. But he sees his wife sitting near the door of his room and pauses a little by her easy-chair.

She is watching the dancing. Now and then the big folk or some of their guests stop to speak to her; the party is at its height, and there are more onlookers than these two: blue-faced Ann is standing at the bottom of the stairs, in all the dignity of her limitations. She is waiting for the children, who simply cannot get their fill of these unwonted festivities, and watching over Snapper, lest his all too rich blood be churned to the danger-point by too much twirling round. And not only the nursery but the kitchen takes an interest: Xaver and the two ladies Hinterhofer are standing by the pantry door looking on with relish. Fräulein Walburga, the elder of the two sunken sisters (the culinary section—she objects to being called a cook), is a whimsical, good-natured sort, brown-eyed, wearing glasses with thick circular lenses; the nose-piece is wound with a bit of rag to keep it from pressing on her nose. Fräulein Cecilia is younger, though not so precisely young either. Her bearing is as self-assertive as usual, this being her way of sustaining her dignity as a former member of the middle class. For Fräulein Cecilia feels acutely her descent into the ranks of domestic service. She positively declines to wear a cap or other badge of servitude, and her hardest trial is on the Wednesday evening when she has to serve the dinner while Xaver has his afternoon out. She hands the dishes with averted face and elevated nose—a fallen queen; and so distressing is it to behold her degradation that one evening when the little folk happened to be at table and saw her they both with one accord burst into tears. Such anguish is unknown to young Xaver. He enjoys serving and does it with an ease born of practice as well as talent, for he was once a "piccolo."[8] But otherwise he is a thorough-paced good-for-nothing and windbag—with quite distinct traits of character of his own, as his long-suffering employers are always ready to concede, but perfectly impossible and a bag of wind for all that. One must just take him as he is, they think, and not expect figs from thistles. He is the child and product of the disrupted times, a perfect specimen of his generation, follower of the revolution, Bolshevist[9] sympathizer. The Professor's name for him is the "minute-man," because he is always to be counted on in any sudden crisis, if only it address his sense of humour or love of novelty, and will display therein amazing readiness and resources. But he utterly lacks a sense of duty and can as little be trained to the performance of the daily round and common task as some kinds of dog can be taught to jump over a stick. It goes so plainly against the grain that criticism is disarmed. One becomes resigned. On grounds that appealed to him as unusual and amusing he would be ready to turn out of his bed at any hour of the night. But he simply cannot get up before eight

8. An apprentice waiter. 9. Communist.

in the morning, he cannot do it, he will not jump over the stick. Yet all day long the evidence of this free and untrammelled existence, the sound of his mouth-organ, his joyous whistle, or his raucous but expressive voice lifted in song, rises to the hearing of the world abovestairs; and the smoke of his cigarettes fills the pantry. While the Hinterhofer ladies work he stands and looks on. Of a morning while the Professor is breakfasting, he tears the leaf off the study calendar—but does not lift a finger to dust the room. Dr. Cornelius has often told him to leave the calendar alone, for he tends to tear off two leaves at a time and thus to add to the general confusion. But young Xaver appears to find joy in this activity, and will not be deprived of it.

Again, he is fond of children, a winning trait. He will throw himself into games with the little folk in the garden, make and mend their toys with great ingenuity, even read aloud from their books—and very droll it sounds in his thick-lipped pronounciation. With his whole soul he loves the cinema; after an evening spent there he inclines to melancholy and yearning and talking to himself. Vague hopes stir in him that some day he may make his fortune in that gay world and belong to it by rights—hopes based on his shock of hair and his physical agility and daring. He likes to climb the ash tree in the front garden, mounting branch by branch to the very top and frightening everybody to death who sees him. Once there he lights a cigarette and smokes it as he sways to and fro, keeping a look-out for a cinema director who might chance to come along and engage him.

If he changed his striped jacket for mufti,[1] he might easily dance with the others and no one would notice the difference. For the big folk's friends are rather anomalous in their clothing: evening dress is worn by a few, but it is by no means the rule. There is quite a sprinkling of guests, both male and female, in the same general style of Möller the ballad-singer. The Professor is familiar with the circumstances of most of this young generation he is watching as he stands beside his wife's chair; he has heard them spoken of by name. They are students at the high school or at the School of Applied Art; they lead, at least the masculine portion, that precarious and scrambling existence which is purely the product of the time. There is a tall, pale, spindling youth, the son of a dentist, who lives by speculation. From all the Professor hears, he is a perfect Aladdin. He keeps a car, treats his friends to champagne suppers, and showers presents upon them on every occasion, costly little trifles in mother-of-pearl and gold. So today he has brought gifts to the young givers of the feast: for Bert a gold lead-pencil, and for Ingrid a pair of ear-rings of barbaric size, great gold circlets that fortunately do not have to go through the little ear-

1. Ordinary civilian clothing (i.e., not a servant's uniform).

lobe, but are fastened over it by means of a clip. The big folk come laughing to their parents to display these trophies; and the parents shake their heads even while they admire—Aladdin bowing over and over from afar.

The young people appear to be absorbed in their dancing—if the performance they are carrying out with so much still concentration can be called dancing. They stride across the carpet, slowly, according to some unfathomable prescript, strangely embraced; in the newest attitude, tummy advanced and shoulders high, waggling the hips. They do not get tired, because nobody could. There is no such thing as heightened colour or heaving bosoms. Two girls may dance together or two young men—it is all the same. They move to the exotic strains of the gramophone, played with the loudest needles to procure the maximum of sound: shimmies, foxtrots, one-steps, double foxes, African shimmies, Java dances, and Creole polkas, the wild musky melodies follow one another, now furious, now languishing, a monotonous Negro programme in unfamiliar rhythm, to a clacking, clashing, and strumming orchestral accompaniment.

"What is that record?" Cornelius inquires of Ingrid, as she passes him by in the arms of the pale young speculator, with reference to the piece then playing, whose alternate languors and furies he finds comparatively pleasing and showing a certain resourcefulness in detail.

"*Prince of Pappenheim:* 'Console thee, dearest child,' " she answers, and smiles pleasantly back at him with her white teeth.

The cigarette smoke wreathes beneath the chandelier. The air is blue with a festal haze compact of sweet and thrilling ingredients that stir the blood with memories of green-sick pains and are particularly poignant to those whose youth—like the Professor's own—has been over-sensitive. . . . The little folk are still on the floor. They are allowed to stop up until eight, so great is their delight in the party. The guests have got used to their presence; in their own way, they have their place in the doings of the evening. They have separated, anyhow: Snapper revolves all alone in the middle of the carpet, in his little blue velvet smock, while Ellie is running after one of the dancing couples, trying to hold the man fast by his coat. It is Max Hergesell and Fräulein Plaichinger. They dance well, it is a pleasure to watch them. One has to admit that these mad modern dances, when the right people dance them, are not so bad after all—they have something quite taking. Young Hergesell is a capital leader, dances according to rule, yet with individuality. So it looks. With what aplomb can he walk backwards—when space permits! And he knows how to be graceful standing still in a crowd. And his partner supports him well, being unsuspectedly lithe and buoyant, as fat people often are. They look at each other, they are talking, paying no heed to Ellie, though others are smiling to see the child's persistence. Dr. Cornelius tries to catch up his little sweetheart as she passes and draw her to him. But Ellie eludes him, almost peevishly; her dear Abel is nothing to her now. She braces her little arms against his chest and turns her face away with a persecuted look. Then escapes to follow her fancy once more.

The Professor feels an involuntary twinge. Uppermost in his heart is hatred for this party, with its power to intoxicate and estrange his darling child. His love for her—that not quite disinterested, not quite unexceptionable love of his—is easily wounded. He wears a mechanical smile, but his eyes have clouded, and he stares fixedly at a point in the carpet, between the dancers' feet.

"The children ought to go to bed," he tells his wife. But she pleads for another quarter of an hour; she has promised already, and they do love it so! He smiles again and shakes his head, stands so a moment and then goes across to the cloak-room, which is full of coats and hats and scarves and overshoes. He has trouble in rummaging out his own coat, and Max Hergesell comes out of the hall, wiping his brow.

"Going out, sir?" he asks, in Hergesellian accents, dutifully helping the older man on with his coat. "Silly business this, with my pumps," he says. "They pinch like hell. The brutes are simply too tight for me, quite apart from the bad leather. They press just here on the ball of my great toe"—he stands on one foot and holds the other in his hand—"it's simply unbearable. There's nothing for it but to take them off; my brogues will have to do the business. . . . Oh, let me help you, sir."

"Thanks," says Cornelius. "Don't trouble. Get rid of your own tormentors. . . . Oh, thanks very much!" For Hergesell has gone on one knee to snap the fasteners of his snow-boots.

Once more the Professor expresses his gratitude; he is pleased and touched by so much sincere respect and youthful readiness to serve. "Go and enjoy yourself," he counsels. "Change your shoes and make up for what you have been suffering. Nobody can dance in shoes that pinch. Good-bye, I must be off to get a breath of fresh air."

"I'm going to dance with Ellie now," calls Hergesell after him. "She'll be a first-rate dancer when she grows up, and that I'll swear to."

"Think so?" Cornelius answers, already half out. "Well, you are a connoisseur, I'm sure. Don't get curvature of the spine with stooping."

He nods again and goes. "Fine lad," he thinks as he shuts the door. "Student of engineering. Knows what he's bound for, got a good clear head, and so well set up and pleasant too." And again paternal envy rises as he compares his poor Bert's status with this young man's, which he puts in the rosiest light that his son's may look the darker. Thus he sets out on his evening walk.

He goes up the avenue, crosses the bridge, and walks along the bank on the other side as far as the next bridge but one. The air is wet and cold, with a little snow now and then. He turns up his coat-collar and slips the crook of his cane over the arm behind his back. Now and then he ventilates his lungs with a long deep breath of the night air. As usual when he walks, his mind reverts to his professional preoccupations; he thinks about his lectures and the things he means to say tomorrow about Philip's struggle against the Germanic revolution, things steeped in melancholy and penetratingly just. Above all just, he thinks. For in one's dealings with the young it behooves one to display the scientific spirit, to exhibit the principles of enlightenment—not only for purposes of mental discipline, but on the human and individual side, in order not to wound them or indirectly offend their political sensibilities; particularly in these days, when there is so much tinder in the air, opinions are so frightfully split up and chaotic, and you may so easily incur attacks from one party or the other, or even give rise to scandal, by taking sides on a point of history. "And taking sides is unhistoric anyhow," so he muses. "Only justice, only impartiality is historic." And could not, properly considered, be otherwise. . . . For justice can have nothing of youthful fire and blithe, fresh, loyal conviction. It is by nature melancholy. And, being so, has secret affinity with the lost cause and the forlorn hope rather than with the fresh and blithe and loyal—perhaps this affinity is its very essence and without it it would not exist at all! . . . "And is there then no such thing as justice?" the Professor asks himself, and ponders the question so deeply that he absently posts his letters in the next box and turns round to go home. This thought of his is unsettling and disturbing to the scientific mind—but is it not after all itself scientific, psychological, conscientious, and therefore to be accepted without prejudice, no matter how upsetting? In the midst of which musings Dr. Cornelius finds himself back at his own door.

On the outer threshold stands Xaver, and seems to be looking for him.

"Herr Professor," says Xaver, tossing back his hair, "go upstairs to Ellie straight off. She's in a bad way."

"What's the matter?" asks Cornelius in alarm. "Is she ill?"

"No-o, not to say ill," answers Xaver. "She's just in a bad way and crying fit to burst her little heart. It's along o' that chap with the shirt-front that danced with her—Herr Hergesell. She couldn't be got to go upstairs peaceably, not at no price at all, and she's b'en crying bucketfuls."

"Nonsense," says the Professor, who has entered and is tossing off his things in the cloak-room. He says no more; opens the glass door and without a glance at the guests turns swiftly to the stairs. Takes them two at a time, crosses the upper hall and the small room leading into the nursery. Xaver follows at his heels, but stops at the nursery door.

A bright light still burns within, showing the gay frieze that runs all round the room, the large row of shelves heaped with a confusion of toys, the rocking-horse on his swaying platform, with red-varnished nostrils and raised hoofs. On the linoleum lie other toys—building blocks, railway trains, a little trumpet. The two white cribs stand not far apart, Ellie's in the window corner, Snapper's out in the room.

Snapper is asleep. He has said his prayers in loud, ringing tones, prompted by Nurse, and gone off at once into vehement, profound, and rosy slumber—from which a cannon-ball fired at close range could not rouse him. He lies with both fists flung back on the pillows on either side of the tousled head with its funny crooked little slumber-tossed wig.

A circle of females surrounds Ellie's bed: not only blue-faced Ann is there, but the Hinterhofer ladies too, talking to each other and to her. They make way as the Professor comes up and reveal the child sitting all pale among her pillows, sobbing and weeping more bitterly than he has ever seen her sob and weep in her life. Her lovely little hands lie on the coverlet in front of her, the nightgown with its narrow lace border has slipped down from her shoulder—such a thin, birdlike little shoulder—and the sweet head Cornelius loves so well, set on the neck like a flower on its stalk, her head is on one side, with the eyes rolled up to the corner between wall and ceiling above her head. For there she seems to envisage the anguish of her heart and even to nod to it—either on purpose or because her head wobbles as her body is shaken with the violence of her sobs. Her eyes rain down tears. The bow-shaped lips are parted, like a little *mater dolorosa's*,[2] and from them issue long, low wails that in nothing resemble the unnecessary and exasperating shrieks of a naughty child, but rise from the deep extremity of her heart and wake in the Professor's own a sympathy that is well-nigh intolerable. He has never seen his darling so before. His feelings find immediate vent in an attack on the ladies Hinterhofer.

"What about the supper?" he asks sharply. "There must be a great deal to do. Is my wife being left to do it alone?"

For the acute sensibilities of the former middle class this is quite enough. The ladies withdraw in righteous indignation, and Xaver Kleingutl jeers at them as they pass out. Having been born to low life

2. Allusion to the standard image in pictorial art of the grieving mother of Christ.

instead of achieving it, he never loses a chance to mock at their fallen state.

"Childie, childie," murmurs Cornelius, and sitting down by the crib enfolds the anguished Ellie in his arms. "What is the trouble with my darling?"

She bedews his face with her tears.

"Abel . . . Abel . . ." she stammers between sobs. "Why—isn't Max—my brother? Max ought to be—my brother!"

Alas, alas! What mischance is this? Is this what the party has wrought, with its fatal atmosphere? Cornelius glances helplessly up at blue-faced Ann standing there in all the dignity of her limitations with her hands before her on her apron. She purses up her mouth and makes a long face. "It's pretty young," she says, "for the female instincts to be showing up."

"Hold your tongue," snaps Cornelius, in his agony. He has this much to be thankful for, that Ellie does not turn from him now; she does not push him away as she did downstairs, but clings to him in her need, while she reiterates her absurd, bewildered prayer that Max might be her brother, or with a fresh burst of desire demands to be taken downstairs so that he can dance with her again. But Max, of course, is dancing with Fräulein Plaichinger, that behemoth who is his rightful partner and has every claim upon him; whereas Ellie—never, thinks the Professor, his heart torn with the violence of his pity, never has she looked so tiny and birdlike as now, when she nestles to him shaken with sobs and all unaware of what is happening to her little soul. No, she does not know. She does not comprehend that her suffering is on account of Fräulein Plaichinger, fat, overgrown, and utterly within her rights in dancing with Max Hergesell, whereas Ellie may only do it once, by way of a joke, although she is incomparably the more charming of the two. Yet it would be quite mad to reproach young Hergesell with the state of affairs or to make fantastic demands upon him. No, Ellie's suffering is without help or healing and must be covered up. Yet just as it is without understanding, so it is also without restraint—and that is what makes it so horribly painful. Xaver and blue-faced Ann do not feel this pain, it does not affect them—either because of native callousness or because they accept it as the way of nature. But the Professor's fatherly heart is quite torn by it, and by a distressful horror of this passion, so hopeless and so absurd.

Of no avail to hold forth to poor Ellie on the subject of the perfectly good little brother she already has. She only casts a distraught and scornful glance over at the other crib, where Snapper lies vehemently slumbering, and with fresh tears calls again for Max. Of no avail either the promise of a long, long walk tomorrow, all five gentlemen, round and round the dining-room table; or a dramatic description of the thrilling cushion games they will play. No, she will listen to none of all this, nor to lying down and going to sleep. She will not sleep, she will sit bolt upright and suffer. . . . But on a sudden they stop and listen, Abel and Ellie; listen to something miraculous that is coming to pass, that is approaching by strides, two strides, to the nursery door, that now overwhelmingly appears. . . .

It is Xaver's work, not a doubt of that. He has not remained by the door where he stood to gloat over the ejection of the Hinterhofers. No, he has bestirred himself, taken a notion; likewise steps to carry it out. Downstairs he has gone, twitched Herr Hergesell's sleeve, and made a thick-lipped request. So here they both are. Xaver, having done his part, remains by the door; but Max Hergesell comes up to Ellie's crib; in his dinner-jacket, with his sketchy side-whisker and charming black eyes; obviously quite pleased with his rôle of swan knight and fairy prince, as one who should say: "See, here am I, now all losses are restored and sorrows end."

Cornelius is almost as much overcome as Ellie herself.

"Just look," he says feebly, "look who's here. This is uncommonly good of you, Herr Hergesell."

"Not a bit of it," says Hergesell. "Why shouldn't I come to say good-night to my fair partner?"

And he approaches the bars of the crib, behind which Ellie sits struck mute. She smiles blissfully through her tears. A funny, high little note that is half a sigh of relief comes from her lips, then she looks dumbly up at her swan knight with her golden-brown eyes—tear-swollen though they are, so much more beautiful than the fat Plaichinger's. She does not put up her arms. Her joy, like her grief, is without understanding; but she does not do that. The lovely little hands lie quiet on the coverlet, and Max Hergesell stands with his arms leaning over the rail as on a balcony.

"And now," he says smartly, "she need not 'sit the livelong night and weep upon her bed'!" He looks at the Professor to make sure he is receiving due credit for the quotation. "Ha ha!" he laughs, "she's beginning young. 'Console thee, dearest child!' Never mind, you're all right! Just as you are you'll be wonderful! You've only got to grow up. . . . And you'll lie down and go to sleep like a good girl, now I've come to say good-night? And not cry any more, little Lorelei?"[3]

Ellie looks up at him, transfigured. One birdlike shoulder is bare; the Professor draws the lace-trimmed nighty over it. There comes into his mind a sentimental story he once read about a dying child who longs to see a clown he had once, with unforgettable ecstasy, beheld

3. Siren in German legend; her song lures sailors to destruction.

in a circus. And they bring the clown to the bedside marvellously arrayed, embroidered before and behind with silver butterflies; and the child dies happy. Max Hergesell is not embroidered, and Ellie, thank God, is not going to die, she has only "been in a bad way." But, after all, the effect is the same. Young Hergesell leans over the bars of the crib and rattles on, more for the father's ear than the child's, but Ellie does not know that—and the father's feelings towards him are a most singular mixture of thankfulness, embarrassment, and hatred.

"Good night, little Lorelei," says Hergesell, and gives her his hand through the bars. Her pretty, soft, white little hand is swallowed up in the grasp of his big, strong, red one. "Sleep well," he says, "and sweet dreams! But don't dream about me—God forbid! Not at your age—ha ha!" And then the fairy clown's visit is at an end. Cornelius accompanies him to the door. "No, no positively, no thanks called for, don't mention it," he large-heartedly protests; and Xaver goes downstairs with him, to help serve the Italian salad.

But Dr. Cornelius returns to Ellie, who is now lying down, with her cheek pressed into her flat little pillow.

"Well, wasn't that lovely?" he says as he smooths the covers. She nods, with one last little sob. For a quarter of an hour he sits beside her and watches while she falls asleep in her turn, beside the little brother who found the right way so much earlier than she. Her silky brown hair takes the enchanting fall it always does when she sleeps; deep, deep lie the lashes over the eyes that late so abundantly poured forth their sorrow; the angelic mouth with its bowed upper lip is peacefully relaxed and a little open. Only now and then comes a belated catch in her slow breathing.

And her small hands, like pink and white flowers, lie so quietly, one on the coverlet, the other on the pillow by her face—Dr. Cornelius, gazing, feels his heart melt with tenderness as with strong wine.

"How good," he thinks, "that she breathes in oblivion with every breath she draws! That in childhood each night is a deep, wide gulf between one day and the next. Tomorrow, beyond all doubt, young Hergesell will be a pale shadow, powerless to darken her little heart. Tomorrow, forgetful of all but present joy, she will walk with Abel and Snapper, all five gentlemen, round and round the table, will play the ever-thrilling cushion game."

Heaven be praised for that!

---

1. What special effect is achieved by telling this story in the present tense? Does this effect have anything to do with the subject and theme?
2. In what sense is there something "not quite right" about the professor's

feeling for his daughter Ellie? What is not quite right in his feeling about the subject he teaches? Does the author mean that he is a bad professor or a bad father?

3. How important to the developing action of the story are the symptoms of disorder caused by the postwar German inflation? Is the conflict symptomatic of a general modern crisis?
4. Does the professor over-interpret what is going on during the party? Does the trouble come simply from his over-interpretation of inconsequential frictions and disorders that in themselves are all within the limits of normality? Since Ellie is certainly not going to die from her heartbreak, does it make sense to say that "after all, the effect is the same" as if she were?
5. The atmosphere of the party is called "fatal." The word as it is used here probably means that fate is more than usually discernible in the character and events in the party. In what ways is the party, then, prophetic of things to come?

Katherine Mansfield

Mansfield (1888–1923) was born in Wellington, New Zealand. Though her intention in going to England at the end of her teens was to study music, there she made the acquaintance of literary people—among them D. H. Lawrence, who was for a while a close friend, and John Middleton Murry, whom she later married. Under their influence she began to write, first as a journalist and then as an innovative artist in the short story. The impressionism of many of her stories has led to some comparisons with Chekhov, who was, in any case, an example on whom she meant to model her working life. Her persisting ill health and the death of a beloved brother in World War I were among the circumstances that darkened her personal life more than they influenced the temper of her fiction, which remained eager and venturesome. Her keen satire was often directed at the self-righteousness of the upper classes and the intelligentsia, at the complacencies insulating them from the realities of existence as experienced by ordinary people. Her best-known collections of stories are Bliss and Other Stories *(1920),* The Garden Party and Other Stories *(1922), and* The Dove's Nest and Other Stories *(1923).*

Bliss

Although Bertha Young was thirty she still had moments like this when she wanted to run instead of walk, to take dancing steps on and off the pavement, to bowl a hoop, to throw something up in the air and catch it again, or to stand still and laugh at—nothing—at nothing, simply.

What can you do if you are thirty and, turning the corner of your own street, you are overcome, suddenly, by a feeling of bliss—absolute bliss!—as though you'd suddenly swallowed a bright piece of that late afternoon sun and it burned in your bosom, sending out a little shower of sparks into every particle, into every finger and toe . . . ?

Oh, is there no way you can express it without being "drunk and disorderly"? How idiotic civilization is! Why be given a body if you have to keep it shut up in a case like a rare, rare fiddle?

"No, that about the fiddle is not quite what I mean," she thought, running up the steps and feeling in her bag for the key—she'd forgotten it, as usual—and rattling the letter-box. "It's not what I mean, because—Thank you, Mary"—she went into the hall. "Is nurse back?"

"Yes, M'm."

"And has the fruit come?"

"Yes, M'm. Everything's come."

"Bring the fruit up to the dining-room, will you? I'll arrange it before I go upstairs."

It was dusky in the dining-room and quite chilly. But all the same Bertha threw off her coat; she could not bear the tight clasp of it another moment, and the cold air fell on her arms.

But in her bosom there was still that bright glowing place—that shower of little sparks coming from it. It was almost unbearable. She hardly dared to breath for fear of fanning it higher, and yet she breathed deeply, deeply. She hardly dared to look into the cold mirror—but she did look, and it gave her back a woman, radiant, with smiling, trembling lips, with big, dark eyes and an air of listening, waiting for something . . . divine to happen . . . that she knew must happen . . . infallibly.

Mary brought in the fruit on a tray and with it a glass bowl, and a blue dish, very lovely, with a strange sheen on it as though it had been dipped in milk.

"Shall I turn on the light, M'm?"

"No, thank you. I can see quite well."

There were tangerines and apples stained with strawberry pink. Some yellow pears, smooth as silk, some white grapes covered with a silver bloom and a big cluster of purple ones. These last she had bought to tone in with the new living-room carpet. Yes, that did sound rather far-fetched and absurd, but it was really why she had bought them. She had thought in the shop: "I must have some purple ones to bring the carpet up to the table." And it had seemed quite sense at the time.

When she had finished with them and had made two pyramids of these bright round shapes, she stood away from the table to get the effect—and it really was most curious. For the dark table seemed to melt into the dusky light and the glass dish and the blue bowl to float in the air. This, of course in her present mood, was so incredibly beautiful. . . . She began to laugh.

"No, no. I'm getting hysterical." And she seized her bag and coat and ran upstairs to the nursery.

Nurse sat at a low table giving Little B her supper after her bath. The baby had on a white flannel gown and a blue woollen jacket, and her dark, fine hair was brushed up into a funny little peak. She looked up when she saw her mother and began to jump.

"Now, my lovey, eat it up like a good girl," said Nurse, setting her lips in a way that Bertha knew, and that meant she had come into the nursery at another wrong moment.

"Has she been good, Nanny?"

"She's been a little sweet all the afternoon," whispered Nanny. "We went to the park and I sat down on a chair and took her out of the pram and a big dog came along and put its head on my knee and she clutched its ear, tugged it. Oh, you should have seen her."

Bertha wanted to ask if it wasn't rather dangerous to let her clutch at a strange dog's ear. But she did not dare to. She stood watching them, her hands by her side, like the poor little girl in front of the rich little girl with the doll.

The baby looked up at her again, stared, and then smiled so charmingly that Bertha couldn't help crying:

"Oh, Nanny, do let me finish giving her her supper while you put the bath things away."

"Well, M'm, she oughtn't to be changed hands while she's eating," said Nanny, still whispering. "It unsettles her; it's very likely to upset her."

How absurd it was. Why have a baby if it has to be kept—not in a case like a rare, rare fiddle—but in another woman's arms?

"Oh, I must!" said she.

Very offended, Nanny handed her over.

"Now, don't excite her after her supper. You know you do, M'm. And I have such a time with her after!"

Thank heaven! Nanny went out of the room with the bath towels.

"Now I've got you to myself, my little precious," said Bertha, as the baby leaned against her.

She ate delightfully, holding up her lips for the spoon and then waving her hands. Sometimes she wouldn't let the spoon go; and sometimes, just as Bertha had filled it, she waved it away to the four winds.

When the soup was finished Bertha turned round to the fire.

"You're nice—you're very nice!" said she, kissing her warm baby. "I'm fond of you. I like you."

And, indeed, she loved Little B so much—her neck as she bent forward, her exquisite toes as they shone transparent in the firelight—that all her feeling of bliss came back again, and again she didn't know how to express it—what to do with it.

"You're wanted on the telephone," said Nanny, coming back in triumph and seizing *her* Little B.

Down she flew. It was Harry.

"Oh, is that you, Ber? Look here. I'll be late. I'll take a taxi and come along as quickly as I can, but get dinner put back ten minutes—will you? All right?"

"Yes, perfectly. Oh, Harry!"

"Yes?"

What had she to say? She'd nothing to say. She only wanted to get in touch with him for a moment. She couldn't absurdly cry: "Hasn't it been a divine day!"

"What is it?" rapped out the little voice.

"Nothing. *Entendu,*"[1] said Bertha, and hung up the receiver, thinking how more than idiotic civilization was.

They had people coming to dinner. The Norman Knights—a very sound couple—he was about to start a theatre, and she was awfully keen on interior decoration, a young man, Eddie Warren, who had just published a little book of poems and whom everybody was asking to dine, and a "find" of Bertha's called Pearl Fulton. What Miss Fulton did, Bertha didn't know. They had met at the club and Bertha had fallen in love with her, as she always did fall in love with beautiful women who had something strange about them.

The provoking thing was that, though they had been about together and met a number of times and really talked, Bertha couldn't yet make her out. Up to a certain point Miss Fulton was rarely, wonderfully frank, but the certain point was there, and beyond that she would not go.

Was there anything beyond it? Harry said "No." Voted her dullish, and "cold like all blond women, with a touch, perhaps, of anæmia of the brain." But Bertha wouldn't agree with him; not yet, at any rate.

"No, the way she has of sitting with her head a little on one side, and smiling, has something behind it, Harry, and I must find out what that something is."

"Most likely it's a good stomach," answered Harry.

He made a point of catching Bertha's heels with replies of that kind . . . "liver frozen, my dear girl," or "pure flatulence," or "kidney disease," . . . and so on. For some strange reason Bertha liked this, and almost admired it in him very much.

She went into the drawing-room and lighted the fire; then, picking up the cushions, one by one, that Mary had disposed so carefully, she threw them back on to the chairs and the couches. That made all the difference; the room came alive at once. As she was about to throw the last one she surprised herself by suddenly hugging it to her, passionately, passionately. But it did not put out the fire in her bosom. Oh, on the contrary!

1. Understood.

The windows of the drawing-room opened on to a balcony overlooking the garden. At the far end, against the wall, there was a tall, slender pear tree in fullest, richest bloom; it stood perfect, as though becalmed against the jade-green sky. Bertha couldn't help feeling, even from this distance, that it had not a single bud or a faded petal. Down below, in the garden beds, the red and yellow tulips, heavy with flowers, seemed to lean upon the dusk. A grey cat, dragging its belly, crept across the lawn, and a black one, its shadow, trailed after. The sight of them, so intent and so quick, gave Bertha a curious shiver.

"What creepy things cats are!" she stammered, and she turned away from the window and began walking up and down. . . .

How strong the jonquils smelled in the warm room. Too strong? Oh, no. And yet, as though overcome, she flung down on a couch and pressed her hands to her eyes.

"I'm too happy—too happy!" she murmured.

And she seemed to see on her eyelids the lovely pear tree with its wide open blossoms as a symbol of her own life.

Really—really—she had everything. She was young. Harry and she were as much in love as ever, and they got on together splendidly and were really good pals. She had an adorable baby. They didn't have to worry about money. They had this absolutely satisfactory house and garden. And friends—modern, thrilling friends, writers and painters and poets or people keen on social questions—just the kind of friends they wanted. And then there were books, and there was music, and she had found a wonderful little dressmaker, and they were going abroad in the summer, and their new cook made the most superb omelettes. . . .

"I'm absurd. Absurd!" She sat up; but she felt quite dizzy, quite drunk. It must have been the spring.

Yes, it was the spring. Now she was so tired she could not drag herself upstairs to dress.

A white dress, a string of jade beads, green shoes and stockings. It wasn't intentional. She had thought of this scheme hours before she stood at the drawing-room window.

Her petals rustled softly into the hall, and she kissed Mrs. Norman Knight, who was taking off the most amusing orange coat with a procession of black monkeys round the hem and up the fronts.

". . . Why! Why! Why is the middle-class so stodgy—so utterly without a sense of humour! My dear, it's only by a fluke that I am here at all—Norman being the protective fluke. For my darling monkeys so upset the train that it rose to a man and simply ate me with its eyes. Didn't laugh—wasn't amused—that I should have loved. No, just stared—and bored me through and through."

"But the cream of it was," said Norman, pressing a large tortoise-shell-rimmed monocle into his eye, "you don't mind me telling this, Face, do you?" (In their home and among their friends they called each other Face and Mug.) "The cream of it was when she, being full fed, turned to the woman beside her and said: 'Haven't you ever seen a monkey before?' "

"Oh, yes!" Mrs. Norman Knight joined in the laughter. "Wasn't that too absolutely creamy?"

And a funnier thing still was that now her coat was off she did look like a very intelligent monkey—who had even made that yellow silk dress out of scraped banana skins. And her amber ear-rings; they were like little dangling nuts.

"This is a sad, sad fall!" said Mug, pausing in front of Little B's perambulator. "When the perambulator comes into the hall—" and he waved the rest of the quotation away.

The bell rang. It was lean, pale Eddie Warren (as usual) in a state of acute distress.

"It *is* the right house, *isn't* it?" he pleaded.

"Oh, I think so—I hope so," said Bertha brightly.

"I have had such a *dreadful* experience with a taxi-man; he was *most* sinister. I couldn't get him to *stop*. The *more* I knocked and called the *faster* he went. And *in* the moonlight this *bizarre* figure with the *flattened* head *crouching* over the *lit-tle* wheel. . . ."

He shuddered, taking off an immense white silk scarf. Bertha noticed that his socks were white, too—most charming.

"But how dreadful!" she cried.

"Yes, it really was," said Eddie, following her into the drawing-room. "I saw myself *driving* through Eternity in a *timeless* taxi."

He knew the Norman Knights. In fact, he was going to write a play for N. K. when the theatre scheme came off.

"Well, Warren, how's the play?" said Norman Knight, dropping his monocle and giving his eye a moment in which to rise to the surface before it was screwed down again.

And Mrs. Norman Knight: "Oh, Mr. Warren, what happy socks!"

"I *am* so glad you like them," said he, staring at his feet. "They seem to have got so *much* whiter since the moon rose." And he turned his lean sorrowful young face to Bertha. "There *is* a moon, you know."

She wanted to cry: "I am sure there is—often—often!"

He really was a most attractive person. But so was Face, crouched before the fire in her banana skins, and so was Mug, smoking a cigarette and saying as he flicked the ash: "Why doth the bridegroom tarry?"

"There he is, now."

Bang went the front door open and shut. Harry shouted: "Hullo, you people. Down in five minutes." And they heard him swarm up the stairs. Bertha couldn't help smiling; she knew how he loved doing things at high pressure. What, after all, did an extra five minutes matter? But he would pretend to himself that they mattered beyond measure. And then he would make a great point of coming into the drawing-room, extravagantly cool and collected.

Harry had such a zest for life. Oh, how she appreciated it in him. And his passion for fighting—for seeking in everything that came up against him another test of his power and of his courage—that, too, she understood. Even when it made him just occasionally, to other people, who didn't know him well, a little ridiculous perhaps. . . . For there were moments when he rushed into battle where no battle was. . . . She talked and laughed and positively forgot until he had come in (just as she had imagined) that Pearl Fulton had not turned up.

"I wonder if Miss Fulton has forgotten?"

"I expect so," said Harry. "Is she on the 'phone?"

"Ah! There's a taxi, now." And Bertha smiled with that little air of proprietorship that she always assumed while her women finds were new and mysterious. "She lives in taxis."

"She'll run to fat if she does," said Harry coolly, ringing the bell for dinner. "Frightful danger for blond women."

"Harry—don't," warned Bertha, laughing up at him.

Came another tiny moment, while they waited, laughing and talking, just a trifle too much at their ease, a trifle too unaware. And then Miss Fulton, all in silver, with a silver fillet binding her pale blond hair, came in smiling, her head a little on one side.

"Am I late?"

"No, not at all," said Bertha. "Come along." And she took her arm and they moved into the dining-room.

What was there in the touch of that cool arm that could fan—fan—start blazing—blazing—the fire of bliss that Bertha did not know what to do with?

Miss Fulton did not look at her; but then she seldom did look at people directly. Her heavy eyelids lay upon her eyes and the strange half smile came and went upon her lips as though she lived by listening rather than seeing. But Bertha knew, suddenly, as if the longest, most intimate look had passed between them—as if they had said to each other: "You, too?"—that Pearl Fulton, stirring the beautiful red soup in the grey plate, was feeling just what she was feeling.

And the others? Face and Mug, Eddie and Harry, their spoons rising and falling—dabbing their lips with their napkins, crumbling bread, fiddling with the forks and glasses and talking.

"I met her at the Alpha show—the weirdest little person. She'd not only cut off her hair, but she seemed to have taken a dreadfully good snip off her legs and arms and her neck and her poor little nose as well."

"Isn't she very *liée*[2] with Michael Oat?"

"The man who wrote *Love in False Teeth*?"

"He wants to write a play for me. One act. One man. Decides to commit suicide. Gives all the reasons why he should and why he shouldn't. And just as he has made up his mind either to do it or not to do it—curtain. Not half a bad idea."

"What's he going to call it—'Stomach Trouble'?"

"I *think* I've come across the *same* idea in a lit-tle French review, *quite* unknown in England."

No, they didn't share it. They were dears—dears—and she loved having them there, at her table, and giving them delicious food and wine. In fact, she longed to tell them how delightful they were, and what a decorative group they made, how they seemed to set one another off and how they reminded her of a play by Tchekof![3]

Harry was enjoying his dinner. It was part of his—well, not his nature, exactly, and certainly not his pose—his—something or other—to talk about food and to glory in his "shameless passion for the white flesh of the lobster" and "the green of pistachio ices—green and cold like the eyelids of Egyptian dancers."

When he looked up at her and said: "Bertha, this is a very admirable *soufflé*!" she almost could have wept with child-like pleasure.

Oh, why did she feel so tender towards the whole world tonight? Everything was good—was right. All that happened seemed to fill again her brimming cup of bliss.

And still, in the back of her mind, there was the pear tree. It would be silver now, in the light of poor dear Eddie's moon, silver as Miss Fulton, who sat there turning a tangerine in her slender fingers that were so pale a light seemed to come from them.

What she simply couldn't make out—what was miraculous—was how she should have guessed Miss Fulton's mood so exactly and so instantly. For she never doubted for a moment that she was right, and yet what had she to go on? Less than nothing.

"I believe this does happen very, very rarely between women. Never between men," thought Bertha. "But while I am making the coffee in the drawing-room perhaps she will 'give a sign.' "

What she meant by that she did not know, and what would happen after that she could not imagine.

While she thought like this she saw herself talking and laughing. She had to talk because of her desire to laugh.

"I must laugh or die."

But when she noticed Face's funny little habit of tucking some-

2. Involved. 3. Variant spelling for Chekhov, Russian playwright and short-story writer (1860–1904).

thing down the front of her bodice—as if she kept a tiny, secret hoard of nuts there, too—Bertha had to dig her nails into her hands—so as not to laugh too much.

It was over at last. And: "Come and see my new coffee machine," said Bertha.

"We only have a new coffee machine once a fortnight," said Harry. Face took her arm this time; Miss Fulton bent her head and followed after.

The fire had died down in the drawing-room to a red, flickering "nest of baby phœnixes," said Face.

"Don't turn up the light for a moment. It is so lovely." And down she crouched by the fire again. She was always cold . . . "without her little red flannel jacket, of course," thought Bertha.

At that moment Miss Fulton "gave the sign."

"Have you a garden?" said the cool, sleepy voice.

This was so exquisite on her part that all Bertha could do was to obey. She crossed the room, pulled the curtains apart, and opened those long windows.

"There!" she breathed.

And the two women stood side by side looking at the slender, flowering tree. Although it was so still it seemed, like the flame of a candle, to stretch up, to point, to quiver in the bright air, to grow taller and taller as they gazed—almost to touch the rim of the round, silver moon.

How long did they stand there? Both, as it were, caught in that circle of unearthly light, understanding each other perfectly, creatures of another world, and wondering what they were to do in this one with all this blissful treasure that burned in their bosoms and dropped, in silver flowers, from their hair and hands?

For ever—for a moment? And did Miss Fulton murmur: "Yes. Just *that*." Or did Bertha dream it?

Then the light was snapped on and Face made the coffee and Harry said: "My dear Mrs. Knight, don't ask me about my baby. I never see her. I shan't feel the slightest interest in her until she has a lover," and Mug took his eye out of the conservatory for a moment and then put it under glass again and Eddie Warren drank his coffee and set down the cup with a face of anguish as though he had drunk and seen the spider.

"What I want to do is to give the young men a show. I believe London is simply teeming with first-chop, unwritten plays. What I want to say to 'em is: 'Here's the theatre. Fire ahead.' "

"You know, my dear, I am going to decorate a room for the Jacob Nathans. Oh, I am so tempted to do a fried-fish scheme, with the backs of the chairs shaped like frying pans and lovely chip potatoes embroidered all over the curtains."

"The trouble with our young writing men is that they are still too romantic. You can't put out to sea without being seasick and wanting a basin. Well, why won't they have the courage of those basins?"

"A *dreadful* poem about a *girl* who was *violated* by a beggar *without* a nose in a lit-tle wood. . . ."

Miss Fulton sank into the lowest, deepest chair and Harry handed round the cigarettes.

From the way he stood in front of her shaking the silver box and saying abruptly: "Egyptian? Turkish? Virginian? They're all mixed up," Bertha realized that she not only bored him; he really disliked her. And she decided from the way Miss Fulton said: "No, thank you, I won't smoke," that she felt it, too, and was hurt.

"Oh, Harry, don't dislike her. You are quite wrong about her. She's wonderful, wonderful. And, besides, how can you feel so differently about someone who means so much to me. I shall try to tell you when we are in bed to-night what has been happening. What she and I have shared."

At those last words something strange and almost terrifying darted into Bertha's mind. And this something blind and smiling whispered to her: "Soon these people will go. The house will be quiet—quiet. The lights will be out. And you and he will be alone together in the dark room—the warm bed. . . ."

She jumped up from her chair and ran over to the piano.

"What a pity someone does not play!" she cried. "What a pity somebody does not play."

For the first time in her life Bertha Young desired her husband.

Oh, she'd loved him—she'd been in love with him, of course, in every other way, but just not in that way. And, equally, of course, she'd understood that he was different. They'd discussed it so often. It had worried her dreadfully at first to find that she was so cold, but after a time it had not seemed to matter. They were so frank with each other—such good pals. That was the best of being modern.

But now—ardently! ardently! The word ached in her ardent body! Was this what that feeling of bliss had been leading up to? But then, then—

"My dear," said Mrs. Norman Knight, "you know our shame. We are the victims of time and train. We live in Hampstead.[4] It's been so nice."

4. A suburb of London.

"I'll come with you into the hall," said Bertha. "I loved having you. But you must not miss the last train. That's so awful, isn't it?"

"Have a whisky, Knight, before you go?" called Harry.

"No, thanks, old chap."

Bertha squeezed his hand for that as she took it.

"Good night, good-bye," she cried from the top step, feeling that this self of hers was taking leave of them for ever.

When she got back into the drawing-room the others were on the move.

". . . Then you can come part of the way in my taxi."

"I shall be *so* thankful *not* to have to face *another* drive *alone* after my *dreadful* experience."

"You can get a taxi at the rank[5] just at the end of the street. You won't have to walk more than a few yards."

"That's a comfort. I'll go and put on my coat."

Miss Fulton moved towards the hall and Bertha was following when Harry almost pushed past.

"Let me help you."

Bertha knew that he was repenting his rudeness—she let him go. What a boy he was in some ways—so impulsive—so—simple.

And Eddie and she were left by the fire.

"I *wonder* if you have seen Bilks' *new* poem called *Table d'Hôte,*" said Eddie softly. "It's *so* wonderful. In the last Anthology. Have you got a copy? I'd *so* like to *show* it to you. It begins with an *incredibly* beautiful line: 'Why Must it Always be Tomato Soup?' "

"Yes," said Bertha. And she moved noiselessly to a table opposite the drawing-room door and Eddie glided noiselessly after her. She picked up the little book and gave it to him; they had not made a sound.

While he looked it up she turned her head towards the hall. And she saw . . . Harry with Miss Fulton's coat in his arms and Miss Fulton with her back turned to him and her head bent. He tossed the coat away, put his hands on her shoulders and turned her violently to him. His lips said: "I adore you," and Miss Fulton laid her moonbeam fingers on his cheeks and smiled her sleepy smile. Harry's nostrils quivered; his lips curled back in a hideous grin while he whispered. "Tomorrow," and with her eyelids Miss Fulton said: "Yes."

"Here it is," said Eddie. " 'Why Must it Always be Tomato Soup?' It's so *deeply* true, don't you feel? Tomato soup is so *dreadfully* eternal."

"If you prefer," said Harry's voice, very loud, from the hall. "I can phone you a cab to come to the door."

5. Stand.

"Oh, no. It's not necessary," said Miss Fulton, and she came up to Bertha and gave her the slender fingers to hold.

"Good-bye. Thank you so much."

"Good-bye," said Bertha.

Miss Fulton held her hand a moment longer.

"Your lovely pear tree!" she murmured.

And then she was gone, with Eddie following, like the black cat following the grey cat.

"I'll shut up shop," said Harry, extravagantly cool and collected.

"Your lovely pear tree—pear tree—pear tree!"

Bertha simply ran over to the long windows.

"Oh, what is going to happen now?" she cried.

But the pear tree was as lovely as ever and as full of flower and as still.

---

1. What is Bertha's relation to her husband and baby? Discuss this in terms of her maturity and life-style.
2. What qualifications are put on the marriage by the statement that Bertha and her husband are "really good pals"?
3. Does the management of point of view permit the reader any solid evidence of what is really going on? Discuss the relation between suggestiveness and the presentation of solid evidence.
4. What ironies lie in the fact that on this evening Bertha feels desire for her husband "for the first time in her life"?
5. What does the pear tree symbolize? How does the symbolism work in the consciousness of the chief character?

The Garden-Party

And after all the weather was ideal. They could not have had a more perfect day for a garden-party if they had ordered it. Windless, warm, the sky without a cloud. Only the blue was veiled with a haze of light gold, as it is sometimes in early summer. The gardener had been up since dawn, mowing the lawns and sweeping them, until the grass and the dark flat rosettes where the daisy plants had been seemed to shine. As for the roses, you could not help feeling they understood that roses are the only flowers that impress people at garden-parties; the only flowers that everybody is certain of knowing. Hundreds, yes, literally hundreds, had come out in a single night; the green bushes bowed down as though they had been visited by archangels.

Breakfast was not yet over before the men came to put up the marquee.[1]

"Where do you want the marquee put, mother?"

"My dear child, it's no use asking me. I'm determined to leave everything to you children this year. Forget I am your mother. Treat me as an honoured guest."

But Meg could not possibly go and supervise the men. She had washed her hair before breakfast, and she sat drinking her coffee in a green turban, with a dark wet curl stamped on each cheek. Jose, the butterfly, always came down in a silk petticoat and a kimono jacket.

"You'll have to go, Laura; you're the artistic one."

Away Laura flew, still holding her piece of bread-and-butter. It's so delicious to have an excuse for eating out of doors, and besides, she loved having to arrange things; she always felt she could do it so much better than anybody else.

Four men in their shirt-sleeves stood grouped together on the garden path. They carried staves covered with rolls of canvas, and they had big tool-bags slung on their backs. They looked impressive. Laura wished now that she had not got the bread-and-butter, but there was nowhere to put it, and she couldn't possibly throw it away. She blushed and tried to look severe and even a little bit short-sighted as she came up to them.

"Good morning," she said, copying her mother's voice. But that sounded so fearfully affected that she was ashamed, and stammered like a little girl, "Oh—er—have you come—is it about the marquee?"

"That's right, miss," said the tallest of the men, a lanky, freckled fellow, and he shifted his tool-bag, knocked back his straw hat and smiled down at her. "That's about it."

His smile was so easy, so friendly that Laura recovered. What nice eyes he had, small, but such a dark blue! And now she looked at the others, they were smiling too. "Cheer up, we won't bite," their smile seemed to say. How very nice workmen were! And what a beautiful morning! She musn't mention the morning; she must be business-like. The marquee.

"Well, what about the lily-lawn? Would that do?"

And she pointed to the lily-lawn with the hand that didn't hold the bread-and-butter. They turned, they stared in the direction. A little fat chap thrust out his under-lip, and the tall fellow frowned.

"I don't fancy it," said he. "Not conspicuous enough. You see, with a thing like a marquee," and he turned to Laura in his easy way, "you want to put it somewhere where it'll give you a bang slap in the eye, if you follow me."

1. Canvas shelter set up for outdoor parties.

Laura's upbringing made her wonder for a moment whether it was quite respectful of a workman to talk to her of bangs slap in the eye. But she did quite follow him.

"A corner of the tennis-court," she suggested. "But the band's going to be in one corner."

"H'm, going to have a band, are you?" said another of the workmen. He was pale. He had a haggard look as his dark eyes scanned the tennis-court. What was he thinking?

"Only a very small band," said Laura gently. Perhaps he wouldn't mind so much if the band was quite small. But the tall fellow interrupted.

"Look here, miss, that's the place. Against those trees. Over there. That'll do fine."

Against the karakas. Then the karaka trees would be hidden. And they were so lovely, with their broad, gleaming leaves, and their clusters of yellow fruit. They were like trees you imagined growing on a desert island, proud, solitary, lifting their leaves and fruits to the sun in a kind of silent splendour. Must they be hidden by a marquee?

They must. Already the men had shouldered their staves and were making for the place. Only the tall fellow was left. He bent down, pinched a sprig of lavender, put his thumb and forefinger to his nose and snuffed up the smell. When Laura saw that gesture she forgot all about the karakas in her wonder at him caring for things like that—caring for the smell of lavender. How many men that she knew would have done such a thing? Oh, how extraordinarily nice workmen were, she thought. Why couldn't she have workmen for friends rather than the silly boys she danced with and who came to Sunday night supper? She would get on much better with men like these.

It's all the fault, she decided, as the tall fellow drew something on the back of an envelope, something that was to be looped up or left to hang, of these absurd class distinctions. Well, for her part, she didn't feel them. Not a bit, not an atom. . . . And now there came the chock-chock of wooden hammers. Some one whistled, some one sang out, "Are you right there, matey?" "Matey!" The friendliness of it, the—the— Just to prove how happy she was, just to show the tall fellow how at home she felt, and how she despised stupid conventions, Laura took a big bite of her bread-and-butter as she stared at the little drawing. She felt just like a work-girl.

"Laura, Laura, where are you? Telephone, Laura!" a voice cried from the house.

"Coming!" Away she skimmed, over the lawn, up the path, up the steps, across the verandah, and into the porch. In the hall her father and Laurie were brushing their hats ready to go to the office.

"I say, Laura," said Laurie very fast, "you might just give a squiz at my coat before this afternoon. See if it wants pressing."

"I will," said she. Suddenly she couldn't stop herself. She ran at Laurie and gave him a small, quick squeeze. "Oh, I do love parties, don't you?" gasped Laura.

"Rather," said Laurie's warm, boyish voice, and he squeezed his sister too, and gave her a gentle push. "Dash off to the telephone, old girl."

The telephone. "Yes, yes; oh yes. Kitty? Good morning, dear. Come to lunch? Do, dear. Delighted of course. It will only be a very scratch meal—just the sandwich crusts and broken meringue-shells and what's left over. Yes, isn't it a perfect morning? Your white? Oh, I certainly should. One moment—hold the line. Mother's calling." And Laura sat back. "What, mother? Can't hear."

Mrs. Sheridan's voice floated down the stairs. "Tell her to wear that sweet hat she had on last Sunday."

"Mother says you're to wear that *sweet* hat you had on last Sunday. Good. One o'clock. Bye-bye."

Laura put back the receiver, flung her arms over her head, took a deep breath, stretched and let them fall. "Huh," she sighed, and the moment after the sigh she sat up quickly. She was still, listening. All the doors in the house seemed to open. The house was alive with soft, quick steps and running voices. The green baize door that led to the kitchen regions swung open and shut with a muffled thud. And now there came a long, chuckling absurd sound. It was the heavy piano being moved on its stiff castors. But the air! If you stopped to notice, was the air always like this? Little faint winds were playing chase, in at the tops of the windows, out at the doors. And there were two tiny spots of sun, one on the inkpot, one on a silver photograph frame, playing too. Darling little spots. Especially the one on the inkpot lid. It was quite warm. A warm little silver star. She could have kissed it.

The front door bell pealed, and there sounded the rustle of Sadie's print skirt on the stairs. A man's voice murmured; Sadie answered, careless, "I'm sure I don't know. Wait. I'll ask Mrs. Sheridan."

"What is it, Sadie?" Laura came into the hall.

"It's the florist, Miss Laura."

It was, indeed. There, just inside the door, stood a wide, shallow tray full of pots of pink lilies. No other kind. Nothing but lilies—canna lilies, big pink flowers, wide open, radiant, almost frighteningly alive on bright crimson stems.

"O-oh, Sadie!" said Laura, and the sound was like a little moan. She crouched down as if to warm herself at that blaze of lilies; she felt they were in her fingers, on her lips, growing in her breast.

"It's some mistake," she said faintly. "Nobody ever ordered so many. Sadie, go and find mother."

But at that moment Mrs. Sheridan joined them.

"It's quite right," she said calmly. "Yes, I ordered them. Aren't they lovely?" She pressed Laura's arm. "I was passing the shop yesterday, and I saw them in the window. And I suddenly thought for once in my life I shall have enough canna lilies. The garden-party will be a good excuse."

"But I thought you said you didn't mean to interfere," said Laura. Sadie had gone. The florist's man was still outside at his van. She put her arm round her mother's neck and gently, very gently, she bit her mother's ear.

"My darling child, you wouldn't like a logical mother, would you? Don't do that. Here's the man."

He carried more lilies still, another whole tray.

"Bank them up, just inside the door, on both sides of the porch, please," said Mrs. Sheridan. "Don't you agree, Laura?"

"Oh, I *do* mother."

In the drawing-room Meg, Jose and good little Hans had at last succeeded in moving the piano.

"Now, if we put this chesterfield against the wall and move everything out of the room except the chairs, don't you think?"

"Quite."

"Hans, move these tables into the smoking-room, and bring a sweeper to take these marks off the carpet and—one moment, Hans—" Jose loved giving orders to the servants, and they loved obeying her. She always made them feel they were taking part in some drama. "Tell mother and Miss Laura to come here at once."

"Very good, Miss Jose."

She turned to Meg. "I want to hear what the piano sounds like, just in case I'm asked to sing this afternoon. Let's try over 'This life is Weary.' "

Pom! Ta-ta-ta *Tee*-ta! The piano burst out so passionately that Jose's face changed. She clasped her hands. She looked mournfully and enigmatically at her mother and Laura as they came in.

This Life is *Wee*-ary,
A Tear—a Sigh.
A Love that *Chan*-ges,
    This life is *Wee*-ary,
A Tear—a Sigh.
A Love that *Chan*-ges,
And then . . . Good-bye!

But at the word "Good-bye," and although the piano sounded more desperate than ever, her face broke into a brilliant, dreadfully unsympathetic smile.

"Aren't I in good voice, mummy?" she beamed.

This Life is *Wee*-ary,
Hope comes to Die.
A Dream—a *Wa*-kening.

But now Sadie interrupted them. "What is it, Sadie?"

"If you please, m'm, cook says have you got the flags[2] for the sandwiches?"

"The flags for the sandwiches, Sadie?" echoed Mrs. Sheridan dreamily. And the children knew by her face that she hadn't got them. "Let me see." And she said to Sadie firmly, "Tell cook I'll let her have them in ten minutes."

Sadie went.

"Now, Laura," said her mother quickly. "Come with me into the smoking-room. I've got the names somewhere on the back of an envelope. You'll have to write them out for me. Meg, go upstairs this minute and take that wet thing off your head. Jose, run and finish dressing this instant. Do you hear me, children, or shall I have to tell your father when he comes home to-night? And—and, Jose, pacify cook if you do go into the kitchen, will you? I'm terrified of her this morning."

The envelope was found at last behind the dining-room clock, though how it had got there Mrs. Sheridan could not imagine.

"One of you children must have stolen it out of my bag, because I remember vividly—cream cheese and lemon-curd. Have you done that?"

"Yes."

"Egg and—" Mrs. Sheridan held the envelope away from her. "It looks like mice. It can't be mice, can it?"

"Olive, pet," said Laura, looking over her shoulder.

"Yes, of course, olive. What a horrible combination it sounds. Egg and olive."

They were finished at last, and Laura took them off to the kitchen. She found Jose there pacifying the cook, who did not look at all terrifying.

"I have never seen such exquisite sandwiches," said Jose's rapturous voice. "How many kinds did you say there were, cook? Fifteen?"

2. Toothpick and paper decorations.

"Fifteen, Miss Jose."

"Well, cook, I congratulate you."

Cook swept up crusts with the long sandwich knife, and smiled broadly.

"Godber's has come," announced Sadie, issuing out of the pantry. She had seen the man pass the window.

That meant the cream puffs had come. Godber's were famous for their cream puffs. Nobody ever thought of making them at home.

"Bring them in and put them on the table, my girl," ordered cook.

Sadie brought them in and went back to the door. Of course Laura and Jose were far too grown-up to really care about such things. All the same, they couldn't help agreeing that the puffs looked very attractive. Very. Cook began arranging them, shaking off the extra icing sugar.

"Don't they carry one back to all one's parties?" said Laura.

"I suppose they do," said practical Jose, who never liked to be carried back. "They look beautifully light and feathery, I must say."

"Have one each, my dears," said cook in her comfortable voice. "Yer ma won't know."

Oh, impossible. Fancy cream puffs so soon after breakfast. The very idea made one shudder. All the same, two minutes later Jose and Laura were licking their fingers with that absorbed inward look that only comes from whipped cream.

"Let's go into the garden, out by the back way," suggested Laura. "I want to see how the men are getting on with the marquee. They're such awfully nice men."

But the back door was blocked by cook, Sadie, Godber's man and Hans.

Something had happened.

"Tuk-tuk-tuk," clucked cook like an agitated hen. Sadie had her hand clapped to her cheek as though she had toothache. Han's face was screwed up in the effort to understand. Only Godber's man seemed to be enjoying himself; it was his story.

"What's the matter? What's happened?"

"There's been a horrible accident," said cook. "A man killed."

"A man killed! Where? How? When?"

But Godber's man wasn't going to have his story snatched from under his very nose.

"Know those little cottages just below here, miss?" Know them? Of couse, she knew them. "Well, there's a young chap living there, name of Scott, a carter. His horse shied at a traction-engine, corner of Hawke Street this morning, and he was thrown out on the back of his head. Killed."

"Dead!" Laura stared at Godber's man.

"Dead when they picked him up," said Godber's man with relish. "They were taking the body home as I come up here." And he said to the cook, "He's left a wife and five little ones."

"Jose, come here." Laura caught hold of her sister's sleeve and dragged her though the kitchen to the other side of the green baize door. There she paused and leaned against it. "Jose!" she said, horrified, "however, are we going to stop everything?"

"Stop everything, Laura!" cried Jose in astonishment. "What do you mean?"

"Stop the garden-party, of course." Why did Jose pretend?

But Jose was still more amazed. "Stop the garden-party? My dear Laura, don't be so absurd. Of course we can't do anything of the kind. Nobody expects us to. Don't be so extravagant."

"But we can't possibly have a garden-party with a man dead just outside the front gate."

That really was extravagant, for the little cottages were in a lane to themselves at the very bottom of a steep rise that led up to the house. A broad road ran between. True, they were far too near. They were the greatest possible eyesore, and they had no right to be in that neighbourhood at all. They were little mean dwellings painted a chocolate brown. In the garden patches there was nothing but cabbage stalks, sick hens and tomato cans. The very smoke coming out of their chimneys was poverty-stricken. Little rags and shreds of smoke, so unlike the great silvery plumes that uncurled from the Sheridans' chimneys. Washerwomen lived in the lane and sweeps and a cobbler, and a man whose house-front was studded all over with minute birdcages. Children swarmed. When the Sheridans were little they were forbidden to set foot there because of the revolting language and of what they might catch. But since they were grown up, Laura and Laurie on their prowls sometimes walked through. It was disgusting and sordid. They came out with a shudder. But still one must go everywhere; one must see everything. So through they went.

"And just think of what the band would sound like to that poor woman," said Laura.

"Oh, Laura!" Jose began to be seriously annoyed. "If you're going to stop a band playing every time some one has an accident, you'll lead a very strenuous life. I'm every bit as sorry about it as you. I feel just as sympathetic." Her eyes hardened. She looked at her sister just as she used to when they were little and fighting together. "You won't bring a drunken workman back to life by being sentimental," she said softly.

"Drunk! Who said he was drunk?" Laura turned furiously on Jose.

She said, just as they had used to say on those occasions, "I'm going straight up to tell mother."

"Do, dear," cooed Jose.

"Mother, can I come into your room?" Laura turned the big glass door-knob.

"Of course, child. Why, what's the matter? What's given you such a colour?" And Mrs. Sheridan turned round from her dressing table. She was trying on a new hat.

"Mother, a man's been killed," began Laura.

"*Not* in the garden?" interrupted her mother.

"No, no!"

"Oh, what a fright you gave me!" Mrs. Sheridan sighed with relief, and took off the big hat and held it on her knees.

"But listen, mother," said Laura. Breathless, half-choking, she told the dreadful story. "Of course, we can't have our party, can we?" she pleaded. "The band and everybody arriving. They'd hear us, mother; they're nearly neighbours!"

To Laura's astonishment her mother behaved just like Jose, it was harder to bear because she seemed amused. She refused to take Laura seriously.

"But, my dear child, use your common sense. It's only by accident we've heard of it. If some one had died there normally—and I can't understand how they keep alive in those poky little holes—we should still be having our party, shouldn't we?"

Laura had to say "yes" to that, but she felt it was all wrong. She sat down on her mother's sofa and pinched the cushion frill.

"Mother, isn't it really terribly heartless of us?" she asked.

"Darling!" Mrs. Sheridan got up and came over to her, carrying the hat. Before Laura could stop her she had popped it on. "My child!" said her mother, "the hat is yours. It's made for you. It's much too young for me. I have never seen you look such a picture. Look at yourself!" And she held up her hand-mirror.

"But, mother," Laura began again. She couldn't look at herself; she turned aside.

This time Mrs. Sheridan lost patience just as Jose had done.

"You are being very absurd, Laura," she said coldly. "People like that don't expect sacrifices from us. And it's not very sympathetic to spoil everybody's enjoyment as you're doing now."

"I don't understand," said Laura, and she walked quickly out of the room into her own bedroom. There, quite by chance, the first thing she saw was this charming girl in the mirror, in her black hat trimmed with gold daisies, and a long black velvet ribbon. Never had she imagined she could look like that. Is mother right? she thought. And now she hoped her mother was right. Am I being extravagant?

Perhaps it was extravagant. Just for a moment she had another glimpse of that poor woman and those little children, and the body being carried into the house. But it all seemed blurred, unreal, like a picture in the newspaper. I'll remember it again after the party's over, she decided. And somehow that seemed quite the best plan. . . .

Lunch was over by half past one. By half past two they were all ready for the fray. The green-coated band had arrived and was established in a corner of the tennis-court.

"My dear!" trilled Kitty Maitland, "aren't they too like frogs for words? You ought to have arranged them round the pond with the conductor in the middle on a leaf."

Laurie arrived and hailed them on his way to dress. At the sight of him Laura remembered the accident again. She wanted to tell him. If Laurie agreed with the others, then it was bound to be all right. And she followed him into the hall.

"Laurie!" "Hallo!" He was half-way upstairs, but when he turned round and saw Laura he suddenly puffed out his cheeks and goggled his eyes at her. "My word, Laura; you do look stunning," said Laurie. "What an absolutely topping hat!"

Laura said faintly "Is it?" and smiled up at Laurie, and didn't tell him after all.

Soon after that people began coming in streams. The band struck up; the hired waiters ran from the house to the marquee. Wherever you looked there were couples strolling, bending to the flowers, greeting, moving on over the lawn. They were like bright birds that had alighted in the Sheridans' garden for this one afternoon, on their way to—where? Ah, what happiness it is to be with people who all are happy, to press hands, press cheeks, smile into eyes.

"Darling Laura, how well you look!"

"What a becoming hat, child!"

"Laura, you look quite Spanish. I've never seen you look so striking."

And Laura, glowing, answered softly, "Have you had tea? Won't you have an ice? The passion-fruit ices really are rather special." She ran to her father and begged him. "Daddy darling, can't the band have something to drink?"

And the perfect afternoon slowly ripened, slowly faded, slowly its petals closed.

"Never a more delightful garden-party . . ." "The greatest success . . ." "Quite the most . . ."

Laura helped her mother with the good-byes. They stood side by side in the porch till it was all over.

"All over, all over, thank heaven," said Mrs. Sheridan. "Round up the others, Laura. Let's go and have some fresh coffee. I'm exhausted.

Yes, it's been very successful. But oh, these parties, these parties! Why will you children insist on giving parties!" And they all of them sat down in the deserted marquee.

"Have a sandwich, daddy dear. I wrote the flag."

"Thanks." Mr. Sheridan took a bite and the sandwich was gone. He took another. "I suppose you didn't hear of a beastly accident that happened to-day?" he said.

"My dear," said Mrs. Sheridan, holding up her hand, "we did. It nearly ruined the party. Laura insisted we should put it off."

"Oh, mother!" Laura didn't want to be teased about it.

"It was a horrible affair all the same," said Mr. Sheridan. "The chap was married too. Lived just below in the lane, and leaves a wife and half a dozen kiddies, so they say."

An awkward little silence fell. Mrs. Sheridan fidgeted with her cup. Really, it was very tactless of father . . .

Suddenly she looked up. There on the table were all those sandwiches, cakes, puffs, all uneaten, all going to be wasted. She had one of her brilliant ideas.

"I know," she said. "Let's make up a basket. Let's send that poor creature some of this perfectly good food. At any rate, it will be the greatest treat for the children. Don't you agree? And she's sure to have neighbours calling in and so on. What a point to have it all ready prepared. Laura!" She jumped up. "Get me the big basket out of the stairs cupboard."

"But, mother, do you really think it's a good idea?" said Laura.

Again, how curious, she seemed to be different from them all. To take scraps from their party. Would the poor woman really like that?

"Of course! What's the matter with you to-day? An hour or two ago you were insisting on us being sympathetic, and now—"

Oh, well! Laura ran for the basket. It was filled, it was heaped by her mother.

"Take it yourself, darling," said she. "Run down just as you are. No, wait, take the arum lilies too. People of that class are so impressed by arum lilies."

"The stems will ruin her lace frock," said practical Jose.

So they would. Just in time. "Only the basket, then. And, Laura!" —her mother followed her out of the marquee—"don't on any account—"

"What, mother?"

No, better not put such ideas into the child's head! "Nothing! Run along."

It was just growing dusky as Laura shut their garden gates. A big dog ran by like a shadow. The road gleamed white, and down below in the hollow the little cottages were in deep shade. How quiet it seemed after the afternoon. Here she was going down the hill to somewhere where a man lay dead, and she couldn't realize it. Why couldn't she? She stopped a minute. And it seemed to her that kisses, voices, tinkling spoons, laughter, the smell of crushed grass were somehow inside her. She had no room for anything else. How strange! She looked up at the pale sky, and all she thought was, "Yes, it was the most successful party."

Now the broad road was crossed. The lane began, smoky and dark. Women in shawls and men's tweed caps hurried by. Men hung over the palings; the children played in the doorways. A low hum came from the mean little cottages. In some of them there was a flicker of light, and a shadow, crab-like, moved across the window. Laura bent her head and hurried on. She wished now she had put on a coat. How her frock shone! And the big hat with the velvet streamer—if only it was another hat! Were the people looking at her? They must be. It was a mistake to have come; she knew all along it was a mistake. Should she go back even now?

No, too late. This was the house. It must be. A dark knot of people stood outside, Beside the gate an old, old woman with a crutch sat in a chair, watching. She had her feet on a newspaper. The voices stopped as Laura drew near. The group parted. It was as though she was expected, as though they had known she was coming here.

Laura was terribly nervous. Tossing the velvet ribbon over her shoulder, she said to a woman standing by, "Is this Mrs. Scott's house?" and the woman, smiling queerly, said, "It is, my lass."

Oh, to be away from this! She actually said, "Help me, God," as she walked up the tiny path and knocked. To be away from those staring eyes, or to be covered up in anything, one of those women's shawls even. I'll just leave the basket and go, she decided. I shan't even wait for it to be emptied.

Then the door opened. A little woman in black showed in the gloom.

Laura said, "Are you Mrs. Scott?" But to her horror the woman answered, "Walk in please, miss," and she was shut in the passage.

"No," said Laura, "I don't want to come in. I only want to leave this basket. Mother sent—"

The little woman in the gloomy passage seemed not to have heard her. "Step this way, please, miss," she said in an oily voice, and Laura followed her.

She found herself in a wretched little low kitchen, lighted by a smoky lamp. There was a woman sitting before the fire.

"Em," said the little creature who had let her in. "Em! It's a young lady." She turned to Laura. She said meaningly, "I'm 'er sister, miss. You'll excuse 'er, won't you?"

"Oh, but of course!" said Laura. "Please, don't disturb her. I—I only want to leave—"

But at that moment the woman at the fire turned round. Her face, puffed up, red, with swollen eyes and swollen lips, looked terrible. She seemed as though she couldn't understand why Laura was there. What did it mean? Why was this stranger standing in the kitchen with a basket? What was it all about? And the poor face puckered up again.

"All right, my dear," said the other. "I'll thank the young lady."

And again she began, "You'll excuse her, miss, I'm sure," and her face, swollen too, tried an oily smile.

Laura only wanted to get out, to get away. She was back in the passage. The door opened. She walked straight through into the bedroom, where the dead man was lying.

"You'd like a look at 'im, wouldn't you?" said Em's sister, and she brushed past Laura over to the bed. "Don't be afraid, my lass,—" and now her voice sounded fond and sly, and fondly she drew down the sheet—" 'e looks a picture. There's nothing to show. Come along, my dear."

Laura came.

There lay a young man, fast asleep—sleeping so soundly, so deeply, that he was far, far away from them both. Oh, so remote, so peaceful. He was dreaming. Never wake him up again. His head was sunk in the pillow, his eyes were closed; they were blind under the closed eyelids. He was given up to his dream. What did garden-parties and baskets and lace frocks matter to him? He was far from all those things. He was wonderful, beautiful. While they were laughing and while the band was playing, this marvel had come to the lane. Happy . . . happy. . . . All is well, said that sleeping face. This is just as it should be. I am content.

But all the same you had to cry, and she couldn't go out of the room without saying something to him. Laura gave a loud childish sob.

"Forgive my hat," she said.

And this time she didn't wait for Em's sister. She found her way out of the door, down the path, past all those dark people. At the corner of the lane she met Laurie.

He stepped out of the shadow. "Is that you, Laura?"

"Yes."

"Mother was getting anxious. Was it all right?"

"Yes, quite. Oh, Laurie!" She took his arm, she pressed up against him.

"I say, you're not crying, are you?" asked her brother.

Laura shook her head. She was.

Laurie put his arm round her shoulder. "Don't cry," he said in his warm, loving voice. "Was it awful?"

"No," sobbed Laura. "It was simply marvellous. But. Laurie—" She stopped, she looked at her brother. "Isn't life," she stammered, "Isn't life—" But what life was she couldn't explain. No matter. He quite understood.

"*Isn't* it, darling?" said Laurie.

---

1. How have the events of the day changed Laura? Would the same experience have affected her sisters in the same way?
2. Why is the point of view confined so closely to Laura's impressions?
3. How is the class structure used in the design of the story?
4. Examine the use of minor characters in the development of Laura's awareness. Are all of them useful in directing her attitudes? Are any of them in serious conflict with her?
5. How is Laura surprised by what she sees in the dead man's house? Can you definitely label the change that comes over her?

Bobbie Ann Mason

Mason (1940–   ) has written for Movie Stars, Movie Life, *and* T.V. Star Parade, *earned a doctorate, and taught English. She has been awarded a Guggenheim Foundation Fellowship, has had stories in* Best American Short Stories *in 1981 and 1983, and won the Pushcart Prize for fiction in 1983.* Shiloh and Other Stories *(1982) was her first collection and earned nominations for both the National Book Critics Circle Award and the American Book Award and won the Ernest Hemingway Foundation Award. She has also written a novel,* In Country *(1985), a short novel,* Spence and Lila *(1988), and a second collection of short stories,* Love Life *(1989).*

Shiloh

Leroy Moffitt's wife, Norma Jean, is working on her pectorals. She lifts three-pound dumbbells to warm up, then progresses to a twenty-pound barbell. Standing with her legs apart, she reminds Leroy of Wonder Woman.

"I'd give anything if I could just get these muscles to where they're real hard," says Norma Jean. "Feel this arm. It's not as hard as the other one."

"That's cause you're right-handed," says Leroy, dodging as she swings the barbell in an arc.

"Do you think so?"

"Sure."

Leroy is a truckdriver. He injured his leg in a highway accident four months ago, and his physical therapy, which involves weights and a pulley, prompted Norma Jean to try building herself up. Now she is attending a body-building class. Leroy has been collecting temporary disability since his tractor-trailer jackknifed in Missouri, badly twisting his left leg in its socket. He has a steel pin in his hip. He will probably not be able to drive his rig again. It sits in the backyard, like a gigantic bird that has flown home to roost. Leroy has been home in Kentucky for three months, and his leg is almost healed, but the accident frightened him and he does not want to drive any more long hauls. He is not sure what to do next. In the meantime, he makes things from craft kits. He started by building a miniature log cabin from notched Popsicle sticks. He varnished it and placed it on the TV set, where it remains. It reminds him of a rustic Nativity scene. Then he tried string art (sailing ships on black velvet), a macramé owl kit, a snap-together B-17 Flying Fortress, and a lamp made out of a model truck, with a light fixture screwed in the top of the cab. At first the kits were diversions, something to kill time, but now he is thinking about building a full-scale log house from a kit. It would be considerably cheaper than building a regular house, and besides, Leroy has grown to appreciate how things are put together. He has begun to realize that in all the years he was on the road he never took time to examine anything. He was always flying past scenery.

"They won't let you build a log cabin in any of the new subdivisions," Norma Jean tells him.

"They will if I tell them it's for you," he says, teasing her. Ever since they were married, he has promised Norma Jean he would build her a new home one day. They have always rented, and the house they live in is small and nondescript. It does not even feel like a home, Leroy realizes now.

Norma Jean works at the Rexall drugstore, and she has acquired an amazing amount of information about cosmetics. When she explains to Leroy the three stages of complexion care, involving creams, toners, and moisturizers, he thinks happily of other petroleum products—axle grease, diesel fuel. This is a connection between him and Norma Jean. Since he has been home, he has felt unusually tender about his wife and guilty over his long absences. But he can't tell what she feels about him. Norma Jean has never complained about his traveling; she has never made hurt remarks, like calling his truck a "widow-maker." He is reasonably certain she has been faithful to him, but he wishes she would celebrate his permanent homecoming more happily. Norma Jean is often startled to find Leroy at home, and he thinks she seems a little disappointed about it. Perhaps he reminds her too much of the early days of their marriage, before he went on the road. They had a child who died as an infant, years ago. They never speak about their memories of Randy, which have almost faded, but now that Leroy is home all the time, they sometimes feel awkward around each other, and Leroy wonders if one of them should mention the child. He has the feeling that they are waking up out of a dream together—that they must create a new marriage, start afresh. They are lucky they are still married. Leroy has read that for most people losing a child destroys the marriage—or else he heard this on *Donahue*. He can't always remember where he learns things anymore.

At Christmas, Leroy bought an electric organ for Norma Jean. She used to play the piano when she was in high school. "It don't leave you," she told him once. "It's like riding a bicycle."

The new instrument had so many keys and buttons that she was bewildered by it at first. She touched the keys tentatively, pushed some buttons, then pecked out "Chopsticks." It came out in an amplified fox-trot rhythm, with marimba sounds.

"It's an orchestra!" she cried.

The organ had a pecan-look finish and eighteen preset chords, with optional flute, violin, trumpet, clarinet, and banjo accompaniments. Norma Jean mastered the organ almost immediately. At first she played Christmas songs. Then she bought *The Sixties Songbook* and learned every tune in it, adding variations to each with the rows of brightly colored buttons.

"I didn't like these old songs back then," she said. "But I have this crazy feeling I missed something."

"You didn't miss a thing," said Leroy.

Leroy likes to lie on the couch and smoke a joint and listen to Norma Jean play "Can't Take My Eyes Off You" and "I'll Be Back." He is back again. After fifteen years on the road, he is finally settling down with the woman he loves. She is still pretty. Her skin is flawless. Her frosted curls resemble pencil trimmings.

Now that Leroy has come home to stay, he notices how much the town has changed. Subdivisions are spreading across western Kentucky like an oil slick. The sign at the edge of town says "Pop: 11,500"—only seven hundred more than it said twenty years before. Leroy can't figure out who is living in all the new houses. The farmers who used to gather around the courthouse square on Saturday afternoons to play checkers and spit tobacco juice have gone. It has been years since Leroy has thought about the farmers, and they have disappeared without his noticing.

Leroy meets a kid named Stevie Hamilton in the parking lot at the new shopping center. While they pretend to be strangers meeting over a stalled car, Stevie tosses an ounce of marijuana under the front seat of Leroy's car. Stevie is wearing orange jogging shoes and a T-shirt that says CHATTAHOOCHEE SUPER-RAT. His father is a prominent doctor who lives in one of the expensive subdivisons in a new white-columned brick house that looks like a funeral parlor. In the phone book under his name there is a separate number, with the listing "Teenagers."

"Where do you get this stuff?" asks Leroy. "From your pappy!"

"That's for me to know and you to find out," Stevie says. He is slit-eyed and skinny.

"What else you got?"

"What you interested in?'

"Nothing special. Just wondered."

Leroy used to take speed on the road. Now he has to go slowly. He needs to be mellow. He leans back against the car and says, "I'm aiming to build me a log house, soon as I get time. My wife, though, I don't think she likes the idea."

"Well, let me know when you want me again," Stevie says. He has a cigarette in his cupped palm, as though sheltering it from the wind. He takes a long drag, then stomps it on the asphalt and slouches away.

Stevie's father was two years ahead of Leroy in high school. Leroy is thirty-four. He married Norma Jean when they were both eighteen, and their child Randy was born a few months later, but he died at the age of four months and three days. He would be about Stevie's age now. Norma Jean and Leroy were at the drive-in, watching a double feature (*Dr. Strangelove* and *Lover Come Back*), and the baby was sleeping in the back seat. When the first movie ended, the baby was dead. It was the sudden infant death syndrome. Leroy remembers handing Randy to a nurse at the emergency room, as though he were offering her a large doll as a present. A dead baby feels like a sack of flour. "It just happens sometimes," said the doctor, in what Leroy always recalls as a nonchalant tone. Leroy can hardly remember the child anymore, but he still sees vividly a scene from *Dr. Strangelove* in which the President of the United States was talking in a folksy voice on the hot line to the Soviet premier about the bomber accidentally headed toward Russia. He was in the War Room, and the world map was lit up. Leroy remembers Norma Jean catatonically beside him in the hospital and himself thinking: Who is this strange girl? He had forgotten who she was. Now scientists are saying that crib death is caused by a virus. Nobody knows anything, Leroy thinks. The answers are always changing.

When Leroy gets home from the shopping center, Norma Jean's mother, Mabel Beasley, is there. Until this year, Leroy has not realized how much time she spends with Norma Jean. When she visits, she inspects the closets and then the plants, informing Norma Jean when a plant is droopy or yellow. Mabel calls the plants "flowers," although there are never any blooms. She always notices if Norma Jean's laundry is piling up. Mabel is a short, overweight woman whose tight, brown-dyed curls look more like a wig than the actual wig she sometimes wears. Today she has brought Norma Jean an off-white dust ruffle she made for the bed; Mabel works in a custom-upholstery shop.

"This is the tenth one I made this year," Mabel says. "I got started and couldn't stop."

"It's real pretty," says Norma Jean.

"Now we can hide things under the bed," says Leroy, who gets along with his mother-in-law primarily by joking with her. Mabel has never really forgiven him for disgracing her by getting Norma Jean pregnant. When the baby died, she said that fate was mocking her.

"What's that thing?" Mabel says to Leroy in a loud voice, pointing to a tangle of yarn on a piece of canvas.

Leroy holds it up for Mabel to see. "It's my needlepoint," he explains. "This is a *Star Trek* pillow cover."

"That's what a woman would do," says Mabel. "Great day in the morning!"

"All the big football players on TV do it," he says.

"Why, Leroy, you're always trying to fool me. I don't believe you for one minute. You don't know what to do with yourself—that's the whole trouble. Sewing!"

"I'm aiming to build us a log house," says Leroy. "Soon as my plans come."

"Like *heck* you are," says Norma Jean. She takes Leroy's needlepoint and shoves it into a drawer. "You have to find a job first. Nobody can afford to build now anyway."

Mabel straightens her girdle and says, "I still think before you get tied down y'all ought to take a little run to Shiloh."

"One of these days, Mama," Norma Jean says impatiently.

Mabel is talking about Shiloh, Tennessee. For the past few years, she has been urging Leroy and Norma Jean to visit the Civil War battleground there. Mabel went there on her honeymoon—the only real trip she ever took. Her husband died of a perforated ulcer when Norma Jean was ten, but Mabel, who was accepted into the United Daughters of the Confederacy in 1975, is still preoccupied with going back to Shiloh.

"I've been to kingdom come and back in that truck out yonder," Leroy says to Mabel, "but we never yet set foot in that battleground. Ain't that something? How did I miss it?"

"It's not even that far," Mabel says.

After Mabel leaves, Norma Jean reads to Leroy from a list she has made. "Thing you could do," she announces. "You could get a job as a guard at Union Carbide, where they'd let you set on a stool. You could get on at the lumberyard. You could do a little carpenter work, if you want to build so bad. You could—"

"I can't do something where I'd have to stand up all day."

"You ought to try standing up all day behind a cosmetics counter. It's amazing that I have strong feet, coming from two parents that never had strong feet at all." At the moment Norma Jean is holding on to the kitchen counter, raising her knees one at a time as she talks. She is wearing two-pound ankle weights.

"Don't worry," says Leroy. "I'll do something."

"You could truck calves to slaughter for somebody. You wouldn't have to drive any big old truck for that."

"I'm going to build you this house," says Leroy. "I want to make you a real home."

"I don't want to live in any log cabin."

"It's not a cabin. It's a house."

"I don't care. It looks like a cabin."

"You and me together could lift those logs. It's just like lifting weights."

Norma Jean doesn't answer. Under her breath, she is counting. Now she is marching through the kitchen. She is doing goose steps.

Before his accident, when Leroy came home he used to stay in the house with Norma Jean, watching TV in bed and playing cards. She would cook fried chicken, picnic ham, chocolate pie—all his favorites. Now he is home alone much of the time. In the mornings, Norma Jean disappears, leaving a cooling place in the bed. She eats a cereal called Body Buddies, and she leaves the bowl on the table, with soggy tan balls floating in a milk puddle. He sees things about Norma Jean that he never realized before. When she chops onions, she stares off into a corner, as if she can't bear to look. She puts on her house slippers almost precisely at nine o'clock every evening and nudges her jogging shoes under the couch. She saves bread heels for the birds. Leroy watches the birds at the feeder. He notices the peculiar way goldfinches fly past the window. They close their wings, then fall, then spread their wings to catch and lift themselves. He wonders if they close their eyes when they fall. Norma Jean closes her eyes when they are in bed. She wants the lights turned out. Even then, he is sure she closes her eyes.

He goes for long drives around town. He tends to drive a car rather carelessly. Power steering and an automatic shift make a car feel so small and inconsequential that his body is hardly involved in the driving process. His injured leg stretches out comfortably. Once or twice he has almost hit something, but even the prospect of an accident seems minor in a car. He cruises the new subdivisions, feeling like a criminal rehearsing for a robbery. Norma Jean is probably right about a log house being inappropriate here in the new subdivisions. All the houses look grand and complicated. They depress him.

One day when Leroy comes home from a drive he finds Norma Jean in tears. She is in the kitchen making a potato and mushroom-soup casserole, with grated-cheese topping. She is crying because her mother caught her smoking.

"I didn't hear her coming. I was standing here puffing away pretty as you please," Norma Jean says, wiping her eyes.

"I knew it would happen sooner or later," says Leroy, putting his arm around her.

"She don't know the meaning of the word 'knock,' " says Norma Jean. "It's a wonder she hadn't caught me years ago."

"Think of it this way," Leroy says. "What if she caught me with a joint?"

"You better not let her!" Norma Jean shrieks. "I'm warning you, Leroy Moffitt!"

"I'm just kidding. Here, play me a tune. That'll help you relax."

Norma Jean puts the casserole in the oven and sets the timer. Then she plays a ragtime tune, with horns and banjo, as Leroy lights up a joint and lies on the couch, laughing to himself about Mabel's catching him at it. He thinks of Stevie Hamilton—a doctor's son pushing grass. Everything is funny. The whole town seems crazy and small. He is reminded of Virgil Mathis, a boastful policeman Leroy used to shoot pool with. Virgil recently led a drug bust in a back room at a bowling alley, where he seized ten thousand dollars' worth of marijuana. The newspaper had a picture of him holding up the bags of grass and grinning widely. Right now, Leroy can imagine Virgil breaking down the door and arresting him with a lungful of smoke. Virgil would probably have been alerted to the scene because of all the racket Norma Jean is making. Now she sounds like a hard-rock band. Norma Jean is terrific. When she switches to a latin-rhythm version of "Sunshine Superman," Leroy hums along. Norma Jean's foot goes up and down, up and down.

"Well, what do you think?" Leroy says, when Norma Jean pauses to search through her music.

"What do I think about what?"

His mind has gone blank. Then he says, "I'll sell my rig and build us a house." That wasn't what he wanted to say. He wanted to know what she thought—what she *really* thought—about them.

"Don't start in on that again," says Norma Jean. She begins playing "Who'll Be the Next in Line?"

Leroy used to tell hitchhikers his whole life story—about his travels, his hometown, the baby. He would end with a question: "Well, what do you think?" It was just a rhetorical question. In time, he had the feeling that he'd been telling the same story over and over to the same hitchhikers. He quit talking to hitchhikers when he realized how his voice sounded—whining and self-pitying, like some teenage-tragedy song. Now Leroy has the sudden impulse to tell Norma Jean about himself, as if he had just met her. They have known each other so long they have forgotten a lot about each other. They could become reacquainted. But when the oven timer goes off and she runs to the kitchen, he forgets why he wants to do this.

The next day, Mabel drops by. It is Saturday and Norma Jean is cleaning. Leroy is studying the plans of his log house, which have finally come in the mail. He has them spread out on the table—big sheets of stiff blue paper, with diagrams and numbers printed in white. While Norma Jean runs the vacuum, Mabel drinks coffee. She sets her coffee cup on a blueprint.

"I'm just waiting for time to pass," she says to Leroy, drumming her fingers on the table.

As soon as Norma Jean switches off the vacuum, Mabel says in a loud voice, "Did you hear about the datsun dog that killed the baby?"

Norma Jean says, "The word is 'dachshund.' "

"They put the dog on trial. It chewed the baby's legs off. The mother was in the next room all the time." She raises her voice. "They thought it was neglect."

Norma Jean is holding her ears. Leroy manages to open the refrigerator and get some Diet Pepsi to offer Mabel. Mabel still has some coffee and she waves away the Pepsi.

"Datsuns are like that," Mabel says. "They're jealous dogs. They'll tear a place to pieces if you don't keep an eye on them."

"You better watch out what you're saying, Mabel," says Leroy.

"Well, facts is facts."

Leroy looks out the window at his rig. It is like a huge piece of furniture gathering dust in the backyard. Pretty soon it will be an antique. He hears the vacuum cleaner. Norma Jean seems to be cleaning the living room rug again.

Later, she says to Leroy, "She just said that about the baby because she caught me smoking. She's trying to pay me back."

"What are you talking about?" Leroy says, nervously shuffling blueprints.

"You know good and well," Norma Jean says. She is sitting in a kitchen chair with her feet up and her arms wrapped around her knees. She looks small and helpless. She says, "The very idea, her bringing up a subject like that! Saying it was neglect."

"She didn't mean that," Leroy says.

"She might not have *thought* she meant it. She always says things like that. You don't know how she goes on."

"But she didn't really mean it. She was just talking."

Leroy opens a king-sized bottle of beer and pours it into two glasses, dividing it carefully. He hands a glass to Norma Jean and she takes it from him mechanically. For a long time, they sit by the kitchen window watching the birds at the feeder.

Something is happening. Norma Jean is going to night school. She has graduated from her six-week body-building course and now she is taking an adult-education course in composition at Paducah Community College. She spends her evenings outlining paragraphs.

"First you have a topic sentence," she explains to Leroy. "Then you divide it up. Your secondary topic has to be connected to your primary topic."

To Leroy, this sounds intimidating. "I never was any good in English," he says.

"It makes a lot of sense."

"What are you doing this for, anyhow?"

She shrugs. "It's something to do." She stands up and lifts her dumbbells a few times.

"Driving a rig, nobody cared about my English."

"I'm not criticizing your English."

Norma Jean used to say, "If I lose ten minutes' sleep, I just drag all day." Now she stays up late, writing compositions. She got a B on her first paper—a how-to theme on soup-based casseroles. Recently Norma Jean has been cooking unusual foods—tacos, lasagna, Bombay chicken. She doesn't play the organ anymore, though her second paper was called "Why Music Is Important to Me." She sits at the kitchen table, concentrating on her outlines, while Leroy plays with his log house plans, practicing with a set of Lincoln Logs. The thought of getting a truckload of notched, numbered logs scares him, and he wants to be prepared. As he and Norma Jean work together at the kitchen table, Leroy has the hopeful thought that they are sharing something, but he knows he is a fool to think this. Norma Jean is miles away. He knows he is going to lose her. Like Mabel, he is just waiting for time to pass.

One day, Mabel is there before Norma Jean gets home from work, and Leroy finds himself confiding in her. Mabel, he realizes, must know Norma Jean better than he does.

"I don't know what's got into that girl," Mabel says. "She used to go to bed with the chickens. Now you say she's up all hours. Plus her a-smoking. I like to died."

"I want to make her this beautiful home," Leroy says, indicating the Lincoln Logs. "I don't think she even wants it. Maybe she was happier with me gone."

"She don't know what to make of you, coming home like this."

"Is that it?"

Mabel takes the roof off his Lincoln Log cabin. "You couldn't get *me* in a log cabin," she says. "I was raised in one. It's no picnic, let me tell you."

"They're different now," says Leroy.

"I tell you what," Mabel says, smiling oddly at Leroy.

"What?"

"Take her on down to Shiloh. Y'all need to get out together, stir a little. Her brain's all balled up over them books."

Leroy can see traces of Norma Jean's features in her mother's face. Mabel's face has the texture of crinkled cotton, but suddenly she looks pretty. It occurs to Leroy that Mabel has been hinting all along that she wants them to take her with them to Shiloh.

"Let's all go to Shiloh," he says. "You and me and her. Come Sunday."

Mabel throws up her hands in protest. "Oh, no, not me. Young folks want to be by theirselves."

When Norma Jean comes in with groceries, Leroy says excitedly, "Your mama here's been dying to go to Shiloh for thirty-five years. It's about time we went, don't you think?"

"I'm not going to butt in on anybody's second honeymoon," Mabel says.

"Who's going on a honeymoon, for Christ's sake?" Norma Jean says loudly.

"I never raised no daughter of mine to talk that-a-way," Mabel says.

"You ain't seen nothing yet," says Norma Jean. She starts putting away boxes and cans, slamming cabinet doors.

"There's a log cabin at Shiloh." Mabel says, "It was there during the battle. There's bullet holes in it."

"When are you going to *shut up* about Shiloh, Mama?" asks Norma Jean.

"I always thought Shiloh was the prettiest place, so full of history," Mabel goes on. "I just hoped y'all could see it once before I die, so you could tell me about it." Later, she whispers to Leroy, "You do what I said. A little change is what she needs."

"Your name means 'the king,'" Norma Jean says to Leroy that evening. He is trying to get her to go to Shiloh, and she is reading a book about another century.

"Well, I reckon I ought to be right proud."

"I guess so."

"Am I still king around here?"

Norma Jean flexes her biceps and feels them for hardness. "I'm not fooling around with anybody, if that's what you mean," she says.

"Would you tell me if you were?"

"I don't know."

"What does *your* name mean?"

"It was Marilyn Monroe's real name."

"No kidding!"

"Norma comes from the Normans. They were invaders," she says. She closes her book and looks hard at Leroy. "I'll go to Shiloh with you if you'll stop staring at me."

On Sunday, Norma Jean packs a picnic and they go to Shiloh. To Leroy's relief, Mabel says she does not want to come with them. Norma Jean drives, and Leroy, sitting beside her, feels like some boring hitchhiker she has picked up. He tries some conversation, but she answers him in monosyllables. At Shiloh, she drives aimlessly through the park, past bluffs and trails and steep ravines. Shiloh is an immense place, and Leroy cannot see it as a battleground. It is not what he expected. He thought it would look like a golf course. Monuments are everywhere, showing through the thick clusters of trees. Norma Jean passes the log cabin Mabel mentioned. It is surrounded by tourists looking for bullet holes.

"That's not the kind of log house I've got in mind," says Leroy apologetically.

"I know *that*."

"This is a pretty place. Your mama was right."

"It's O.K.," says Norma Jean. "Well, we've seen it. I hope she's satisfied."

They burst out laughing together.

At the park museum, a movie on Shiloh is shown every half hour, but they decide that they don't want to see it. They buy a souvenir Confederate flag for Mabel, and then they find a picnic spot near the cemetery. Norma Jean has brought a picnic cooler, with pimiento sandwiches, soft drinks, and Yodels. Leroy eats a sandwich and then smokes a joint, hiding it behind the picnic cooler. Norma Jean has quit smoking altogether. She is picking cake crumbs from the cellophane wrapper, like a fussy bird.

Leroy says, "So the boys in gray ended up in Corinth. The Union soldiers zapped 'em finally. April 7, 1862."

They both know that he doesn't know any history. He is just talking about some of the historical plaques they have read. He feels awkward, like a boy on a date with an older girl. They are still just making conversation.

"Corinth is where Mama eloped to," says Norma Jean.

They sit in silence and stare at the cemetery for the Union dead and, beyond, at a tall cluster of trees. Campers are parked nearby, bumper to bumper, and small children in bright clothing are cavorting and squealing. Norma Jean wads up the cake wrapper and squeezes it tightly in her hand. Without looking at Leroy, she says, "I want to leave you."

Leroy takes a bottle of Coke out of the cooler and flips off the cap. He holds the bottle poised near his mouth but cannot remember to take a drink. Finally he says, "No, you don't."

"Yes, I do."

"I won't let you."

"You can't stop me."

"Don't do me that way."

Leroy knows Norma Jean will have her own way. "Didn't I promise to be home from now on?" he says.

"In some ways, a woman prefers a man who wanders," says Norma Jean. "That sounds crazy, I know."

"You're not crazy."

Leroy remembers to drink from his Coke. Then he says, "Yes, you *are* crazy. You and me could start all over again. Right back at the beginning."

"We *have* started all over again," says Norma Jean. "And this is how it turned out."

"What did I do wrong?"

"Nothing."

"Is this one of those women's lib things?" Leroy asks.

"Don't be funny."

The cemetery, a green slope dotted with white markers, looks like a subdivision site. Leroy is trying to comprehend that his marriage is breaking up, but for some reason he is wondering about white slabs in a graveyard.

"Everything was fine till Mama caught me smoking," says Norma Jean, standing up. "That set something off."

"What are you talking about?"

"She won't leave me alone—*you* won't leave me alone." Norma Jean seems to be crying, but she is looking away from him. "I feel eighteen again. I can't face that all over again." She starts walking away. "No, it *wasn't* fine. I don't know what I'm saying. Forget it."

Leroy takes a lungful of smoke and closes his eyes as Norma Jean's words sink in. He tries to focus on the fact that thirty-five hundred soldiers died on the grounds around him. He can only think of that war as a board game with plastic soldiers. Leroy almost smiles, as he compares the Confederates' daring attack on the Union camps and Virgil Mathis's raid on the bowling alley. General Grant, drunk and furious, shoved the Southerners back to Corinth, where Mabel and Jet Beasley were married years later, when Mabel was still thin and good-looking. The next day, Mabel and Jet visited the battleground, and then Norma Jean was born, and then she married Leroy and they had a baby, which they lost, and now Leroy and Norma Jean are here at the same battleground. Leroy knows he is leaving out a lot. He is leaving out the insides of history. History was always just names and dates to him. It occurs to him that building a house out of logs is similarly empty—too simple. And the real inner workings of a marriage, like most of history, have escaped him. Now he sees that building a log house is the dumbest idea he could have had. It was clumsy of him to think Norma Jean would want a log house. It was a crazy idea. He'll have to think of something else, quickly. He will wad the blueprints into tight balls and fling them into the lake. Then he'll get moving again. He opens his eyes. Norma Jean has moved away and is walking through the cemetery, following a serpentine brick path.

Leroy gets up to follow his wife, but his good leg is asleep and his bad leg still hurts him. Norma Jean is far away, walking rapidly toward the bluff by the river, and he tries to hobble toward her. Some children run past him, screaming noisily. Norma Jean has reached the bluff, and she is looking out over the Tennessee River. Now she turns toward Leroy and waves her arms. Is she beckoning to him? She seems to be doing an exercise for her chest muscles. The sky is unusually pale—the color of the dust ruffle Mabel made for their bed.

---

1. How do the material details of the story—like Norma Jean's electric organ and Leroy's plans for the log cabin—define the magnitude of the problems facing them?
2. Are Norma Jean's hopes of escaping the marriage and changing her life fully or partly realistic?
3. What promise is there in Leroy's intention to "get moving again"?
4. Discuss the tension between the comic tone and the apparent grimness of the situation. Is the author making fun of doomed characters?

Guy de Maupassant

Maupassant (1850–1893) was born near Dieppe, France. His parents were friends of the novelist Gustave Flaubert, whose views on literature and the artistic life were influential with Maupassant even in his early years. Rebellious in school, he accepted Army discipline during the Franco-Prussian war of 1870–71 and then for nearly ten years apprenticed himself to Flaubert to learn the craft of fiction, discarding most of what he wrote. In 1880 he became famous with the publication of a single story, Boule de Suif *(Ball of Fat), which contrasts the patriotism of a young prostitute with the amorality of middle-class citizens. Maupassant published, during the next ten years, nearly three hundred short stories, half a dozen novels, some plays, verse, and travel books. The short stories, which appeared regularly in popular periodicals, sampled military and peasant life, the decadent world of politics and journalism, prostitution, perversion, the supernatural, and the hypocrisies of solid citizens. Maupassant's income from his prodigious literary output permitted him to indulge the appetites for women and luxury that had always been part of his character, but in his last years the syphilis which he apparently contracted before he was twenty began to unravel his capacity for concentrated work. He sought relief in drugs and travels on his yacht but became completely insane before he died of paresis. His novels include* Une Vie *(A Life) (1883),* Bel Ami *(Handsome Friend) (1885), and* Pierre et Jean *(1888). His short stories are most readily available in his collected works.*

The Necklace[1]

She was one of those pretty and charming girls who are sometimes, as if by a mistake of destiny, born in a family of clerks. She had no dowry, no expectations, no means of being known, understood, loved, wedded by any rich and distinguished man; and she let herself be married to a little clerk at the Ministry of Public Instruction.

She dressed plainly because she could not dress well, but she was as unhappy as though she had really fallen from her proper station, since with women there is neither caste nor rank: and beauty, grace and charm act instead of family and birth. Natural fineness, instinct

1. Translated by Marjorie Laurie.

for what is elegant, suppleness of wit, are the sole hierarchy, and make from women of the people the equals of the very greatest ladies.

She suffered ceaselessly, feeling herself born for all the delicacies and all the luxuries. She suffered from the poverty of her dwelling, from the wretched look of the walls, from the worn-out chairs, from the ugliness of the curtains. All those things, of which another woman of her rank would never even have been conscious, tortured her and made her angry. The sight of the little Breton peasant who did her humble housework aroused in her regrets which were despairing, and distracted dreams. She thought of the silent antechambers hung with Oriental tapestry, lit by tall bronze candelabra, and of the two great footmen in knee breeches who sleep in the big armchairs, made drowsy by the heavy warmth of the hot-air stove. She thought of the long *salons*[2] fitted up with ancient silk, of the delicate furniture carrying priceless curiosities, and of the coquettish perfumed boudoirs made for talks at five o'clock with intimate friends, with men famous and sought after, whom all women envy and whose attention they all desire.

When she sat down to dinner, before the round table covered with a tablecloth three days old, opposite her husband, who uncovered the soup tureen and declared with an enchanted air, "Ah, the good *pot-au-feu!*[3] I don't now anything better than that," she thought of dainty dinners, of shining silverware, of tapestry which peopled the walls with ancient personages and with strange birds flying in the midst of a fairy forest; and she thought of delicious dishes served on marvelous plates, and of the whispered gallantries which you listen to with a sphinxlike smile, while you are eating the pink flesh of a trout or the wings of a quail.

She had no dresses, no jewels, nothing. And she loved nothing but that; she felt made for that. She would so have liked to please, to be envied, to be charming, to be sought after.

She had a friend, a former schoolmate at the convent, who was rich, and whom she did not like to go and see any more, because she suffered so much when she came back.

But one evening, her husband returned home with a triumphant air, and holding a large envelope in his hand.

"There," said he. "Here is something for you."

She tore the paper sharply, and drew out a printed card which bore these words:

"The Minister of Public Instruction and Mme. Georges Ramponneau request the honor of M. and Mme. Loisel's company at the palace of the Ministry on Monday evening, January eighteenth."

2. Drawing rooms. 3. Stew.

Instead of being delighted, as her husband hoped, she threw the invitation on the table with disdain, murmuring:

"What do you want me to do with that?"

"But, my dear, I thought you would be glad. You never go out, and this is such a fine opportunity. I had awful trouble to get it. Everyone wants to go; it is very select, and they are not giving many invitations to clerks. The whole official world will be there."

She looked at him with an irritated glance, and said, impatiently:

"And what do you want me to put on my back?"

He had not thought of that; he stammered:

"Why, the dress you go to the theater in. It looks very well, to me."

He stopped, distracted, seeing his wife was crying. Two great tears descended slowly from the corners of her eyes toward the corners of her mouth. He stuttered:

"What's the matter? What's the matter?"

But, by violent effort, she had conquered her grief, and she replied, with a calm voice, while she wiped her wet cheeks:

"Nothing. Only I have no dress and therefore I can't go to this ball. Give your card to some colleague whose wife is better equipped than I."

He was in despair. He resumed:

"Come, let us see, Mathilde. How much would it cost, a suitable dress, which you could use on other occasions, something very simple?"

She reflected several seconds, making her calculations and wondering also what sum she could ask without drawing on herself an immediate refusal and a frightened exclamation from the economical clerk.

Finally, she replied, hesitatingly:

"I don't know exactly, but I think I could manage it with four hundred francs."

He had grown a little pale, because he was laying aside just that amount to buy a gun and treat himself to a little shooting next summer on the plain of Nanterre, with several friends who went to shoot larks down there, of a Sunday.

But he said:

"All right. I will give you four hundred francs. And try to have a pretty dress."

The day of the ball drew near, and Mme. Loisel seemed sad, uneasy, anxious. Her dress was ready, however. Her husband said to her one evening:

"What is the matter? Come, you've been so queer these last three days."

And she answered:

"It annoys me not to have a single jewel, not a single stone, nothing to put on. I shall look like distress. I should almost rather not go at all."

He resumed:

"You might wear natural flowers. It's very stylish at this time of the year. For ten francs you can get two or three magnificent roses."

She was not convinced.

"No; there's nothing more humiliating than to look poor among other women who are rich."

But her husband cried:

"How stupid you are! Go look up your friend Mme. Forestier, and ask her to lend you some jewels. You're quite thick enough with her to do that."

She uttered a cry of joy:

"It's true. I never thought of it."

The next day she went to her friend and told of her distress.

Mme. Forestier went to a wardrobe with a glass door, took out a large jewel-box, brought it back, opened it, and said to Mme. Loisel:

"Choose, my dear."

She saw first of all some bracelets, then a pearl necklace, then a Venetian cross, gold and precious stones of admirable workmanship. She tried on the ornaments before the glass, hesitated, could not make up her mind to part with them, to give them back. She kept asking:

"Haven't you any more?"

"Why, yes. Look. I don't know what you like."

All of a sudden she discovered, in a black satin box, a superb necklace of diamonds, and her heart began to beat with an immoderate desire. Her hands trembled as she took it. She fastened it around her throat, outside her high-necked dress, and remained lost in ecstasy at the sight of herself.

Then she asked, hesitating, filled with anguish:

"Can you lend me that, only that?"

"Why, yes, certainly."

She sprang upon the neck of her friend, kissed her passionately, then fled with her treasure.

The day of the ball arrived. Mme. Loisel made a great success. She was prettier than them all, elegant, gracious, smiling, and crazy with joy. All the men looked at her, asked her name, endeavored to be introduced. All the attachés of the Cabinet wanted to waltz with her. She was remarked by the minister himself.

She danced with intoxication, with passion, made drunk by pleasure, forgetting all, in the triumph of her beauty, in the glory of her success, in a sort of cloud of happiness composed of all this homage, of all this admiration, of all these awakened desires, and of that sense of complete victory which is so sweet to a woman's heart.

She went away about four o'clock in the morning. Her husband had been sleeping since midnight, in a little deserted anteroom, with three other gentlemen whose wives were having a very good time. He threw over her shoulders the wraps which he had brought, modest wraps of common life, whose poverty contrasted with the elegance of the ball dress. She felt this, and wanted to escape so as not to be remarked by the other women, who were enveloping themselves in costly furs.

Loisel held her back.

"Wait a bit. You will catch cold outside. I will go and call a cab."

But she did not listen to him, and rapidly descended the stairs. When they were in the street they did not find a carriage; and they began to look for one, shouting after the cabmen whom they saw passing by at a distance.

They went down toward the Seine, in despair, shivering with cold. At last they found on the quay one of those ancient noctambulant coupés which, exactly as if they were ashamed to show their misery during the day, are never seen round Paris until after nightfall.

It took them to their door in the Rue des Martyrs, and once more, sadly, they climbed up homeward. All was ended, for her. And as to him, he reflected that he must be at the Ministry at ten o'clock.

She removed the wraps which covered her shoulders, before the glass, so as once more to see herself in all her glory. But suddenly she uttered a cry. She no longer had the necklace around her neck!

Her husband, already half undressed, demanded:

"What is the matter with you?"

She turned madly towards him:

"I have—I have—I've lost Mme. Forestier's necklace."

He stood up, distracted.

"What!—how?—impossible!"

And they looked in the folds of her dress, in the folds of her cloak, in her pockets, everywhere. They did not find it.

He asked:

"You're sure you had it on when you left the ball?"

"Yes, I felt it in the vestibule of the palace."

"But if you had lost it in the street we should have heard it fall. It must be in the cab."

"Yes. Probably. Did you take his number?"

"No. And you, didn't you notice it?"

"No."

They looked, thunderstruck, at one another. At last Loisel put on his clothes.

"I shall go back on foot," said he, "over the whole route which we have taken to see if I can find it."

And he went out. She sat waiting on a chair in her ball dress, without strength to go to bed, overwhelmed, without fire, without a thought.

Her husband came back about seven o'clock. He had found nothing.

He went to Police Headquarters, to the newspaper offices, to offer a reward; he went to the cab companies—everywhere, in fact, whither he was urged by the least suspicion of hope.

She waited all day, in the same condition of mad fear before this terrible calamity.

Loisel returned at night with a hollow, pale face; he had discovered nothing.

"You must write to your friend," said he, "that you have broken the clasp of her necklace and that you are having it mended. That will give us time to turn round."

She wrote at his dictation.

At the end of a week they had lost all hope.

And Loisel, who had aged five years, declared:

"We must consider how to replace that ornament."

The next day they took the box which had contained it, and they went to the jeweler whose name was found within. He consulted his books.

"It was not I, madame, who sold that necklace; I must simply have furnished the case."

Then they went from jeweler to jeweler, searching for a necklace like the other, consulting their memories, sick both of them with chagrin and anguish.

They found, in a shop at the Palais Royal, a string of diamonds which seemed to them exactly like the one they looked for. It was worth forty thousand francs. They could have it for thirty-six.

So they begged the jeweler not to sell it for three days yet. And they made a bargain that he should buy it back for thirty-four thousand francs, in case they found the other one before the end of February.

Loisel possessed eighteen thousand francs which his father had left him. He would borrow the rest.

He did borrow, asking a thousand francs of one, five hundred of another, five louis[4] here, three louis there. He gave notes, took up ruinous obligations, dealt with usurers and all the race of lenders. He compromised all the rest of his life, risked his signature without even knowing if he could meet it; and, frightened by the pains yet to come,

4. A louis was worth 20 francs.

by the black misery which was about to fall upon him, by the prospect of all the physical privation and of all the moral tortures which he was to suffer, he went to get the new necklace, putting down upon the merchant's counter thirty-six thousand francs.

When Mme. Loisel took back the necklace, Mme. Forestier said to her, with a chilly manner:

"You should have returned it sooner; I might have needed it."

She did not open the case, as her friend had so much feared. If she had detected the substitution, what would she have thought, what would she have said? Would she not have taken Mme. Loisel for a thief?

Mme. Loisel now knew the horrible existence of the needy. She took her part, moreover, all of a sudden, with heroism. That dreadful debt must be paid. She would pay it. They dismissed their servant; they changed their lodgings; they rented a garret under the roof.

She came to know what heavy housework meant and the odious cares of the kitchen. She washed the dishes, using her rosy nails on the greasy pots and pans. She washed the dirty linen, the shirts, and the dishcloths, which she dried upon a line; she carried the slops down to the street every morning, and carried up the water, stopping for breath at every landing. And, dressed like a woman of the people, she went to the fruiterer, the grocer, the butcher, her basket on her arm, bargaining, insulted, defending her miserable money sou by sou.

Each month they had to meet some notes, renew others, obtain more time.

Her husband worked in the evening making a fair copy of some tradesman's accounts, and late at night he often copied manuscript for five sous a page.

And this life lasted for ten years.

At the end of ten years, they had paid everything, everything, with the rates of usury, and the accumulations of the compound interest.

Mme. Loisel looked old now. She had become the woman of impoverished households—strong and hard and rough. With frowsy hair, skirts askew, and red hands, she talked loud while washing the floor with great swishes of water. But sometimes, when her husband was at the office, she sat down near the window, and she thought of that gay evening of long ago, of the ball where she had been so beautiful and so fêted.

What would have happened if she had not lost that necklace? Who knows? Who knows? How life is strange and changeful! How little a thing is needed for us to be lost or to be saved!

But, one Sunday, having gone to take a walk in the Champs Elysées to refresh herself from the labor of the week, she suddenly perceived a woman who was leading a child. It was Mme. Forestier, still young, still beautiful, still charming.

Mme. Loisel felt moved. Was she going to speak to her? Yes, certainly. And now that she had paid, she was going to tell her all about it. Why not?

She went up.

"Good-day, Jeanne."

The other, astonished to be familiarly addressed by this plain goodwife, did not recognize her at all, and stammered:

"But—madam!—I do not know—You must be mistaken."

"No. I am Mathilde Loisel."

Her friend uttered a cry.

"Oh, my poor Mathilde! How you are changed!"

"Yes, I have had days hard enough, since I have seen you, days wretched enough—and that because of you!"

"Of me! How so?"

"Do you remember that diamond necklace which you lent me to wear at the ministerial ball?"

"Yes. Well?"

"Well, I lost it."

"What do you mean? You brought it back."

"I brought you back another just like it. And for this we have been ten years paying. You can understand that it was not easy for us, us who had nothing. At last it is ended, and I am very glad."

Mme. Forestier had stopped.

"You say that you bought a necklace of diamonds to replace mine?"

"Yes. You never noticed it, then! They were very like."

And she smiled with a joy which was proud and naïve at once.

Mme. Forestier, strongly moved, took her two hands.

"Oh, my poor Mathilde! Why, my necklace was paste. It was worth at most five hundred francs!"

---

1. What might have been the quality of Mme. Loisel's life if she had not lost the necklace?
2. What changes take place in her character during the ten years covered by the story? What irony is there in the kind of changes that take place?
3. To what extent is pride a consistent motive for the heroine?
4. What is the husband's character? Does he have much to do with the outcome of the story?
5. What effect do we expect from the revelation that the lost necklace was made of false stones? Does the story stop short of its natural ending?
6. What does the story tell us about the manners and values of the society in which it is set?

Herman Melville

Melville (1819–1891) was born in New York City, the son of a merchant from New England who died when Melville was still young. He took on jobs as clerk, farmhand, and schoolteacher before shipping to the South Seas on the whaler Acushnet. *In a helter-skelter period of adventure he deserted from his ship, lived among cannibals, took part in a mutiny on an Australian vessel, and then spent almost two years on an American man-of-war returning to his home country. Then he began successfully to romanticize these adventures in fiction. In six years he published seven novels, among them* Moby-Dick *(1851), which is generally regarded as one of the masterworks of American fiction. His popularity was already waning by the time he published this great novel, and it continued to decline until, at his death, he was virtually forgotten. The short stories in* Piazza Tales *(1856) did little to refurbish his reputation. In 1876 he published a long narrative poem,* Clarel, *that received hardly any notice, and his last fictional masterpiece,* Billy Budd, *was not published until 1924, long after his death. As his writing activities declined, Melville made another sea voyage around Cape Horn to San Francisco on a clipper ship commanded by his brother, and for nineteen quiet years he was a customs inspector in New York. It was not until the 1920's that critical interest in his work revived. Since then it has increased in fervor and scope, discovering the richly ambiguous thought structured into his most ambitious work. His novels include* Typee *(1846),* Omoo *(1847),* Mardi *(1849), and* Pierre *(1852).*

Bartleby the Scrivener

A Story of Wall Street

I am a rather elderly man. The nature of my avocations for the last thirty years has brought me into more than ordinary contact with what would seem an interesting and somewhat singular set of men, of whom as yet nothing that I know of has ever been written:—I mean the law-copyists or scriveners. I have known very many of them, professionally and privately, and if I pleased, could relate divers histories, at which good-natured gentlemen might smile, and sentimental souls might weep. But I waive the biographies of all other scriveners for a few passages in the life of Bartleby, who was a scrivener the strangest I ever saw or heard of. While of other law-copyists I might write the complete life, of Bartleby nothing of that sort can be done. I believe that no materials exist for a full and satisfactory biography of this man. It is an irreparable loss to literature. Bartleby was one of those beings of whom nothing is ascertainable, except from the original sources, and in his case those are very small. What my own astonished eyes saw of Bartleby, *that* is all I know of him, except, indeed, one vague report which will appear in the sequel.

Ere introducing the scrivener, as he first appeared to me, it is fit I make some mention of myself, my *employés*, my business, my chambers, and general surroundings; because some such description is indispensable to an adequate understanding of the chief character about to be presented.

Imprimis:[1] I am a man who, from his youth upward, has been filled with a profound conviction that the easiest way of life is the best. Hence, though I belong to a profession proverbially energetic and nervous, even to turbulence, at times, yet nothing of that sort have I ever suffered to invade my peace. I am one of those unambitious lawyers who never addresses a jury, or in any way draws down public applause; but in the cool tranquillity of a snug retreat, do a snug business among rich men's bonds and mortgages and title-deeds. All who know me, consider me an eminently *safe* man. The late John Jacob Astor,[2] a personage little given to poetic enthusiasm, had no hesitation in pronouncing my first grand point to be prudence; my next, method. I do not speak it in vanity, but simply record the fact, that I was not unemployed in my profession by the late John Jacob Astor; a name which, I admit, I love to repeat, for it hath a rounded and orbicular sound to it, and rings like unto bullion. I will freely add, that I was not insensible to the late John Jacob Astor's good opinion.

Some time prior to the period at which this little history begins, my avocations had been largely increased. The good old office, now extinct in the State of New-York, of a Master in Chancery,[3] had been conferred upon me. It was not a very arduous office, but very pleasantly remunerative. I seldom lose my temper; much more seldom indulge in dangerous indignation at wrongs and outrages; but I must be permitted to be rash here and declare, that I consider the sudden and violent abrogation of the office of Master in Chancery, by the new Constitution, as a —— premature act; inasmuch as I had counted upon a life-lease of the profits, whereas I only received those of a few short years. But this is by the way.

My chambers were upstairs at No. ——Wall-street. At one end they looked upon the white wall of the interior of a spacious skylight

1. In the first place. 2. American landowner, capitalist, and fur merchant (1763–1848). His name signified great wealth. 3. The duty of this office was to temper the rigidity of the law with "dictates of conscience."

shaft, penetrating the building from top to bottom. This view might have been considered rather tame than otherwise, deficient in what landscape painters call "life." But if so, the view from the other end of my chambers offered, at least, a contrast, if nothing more. In that direction my windows commanded an unobstructed view of a lofty brick wall, black by age and everlasting shade; which wall required no spy-glass to bring out its lurking beauties, but for the benefit of all near-sighted spectators, was pushed up to within ten feet of my window panes. Owing to the great height of the surrounding buildings, and my chambers being on the second floor, the interval between this wall and mine not a little resembled a huge square cistern.

At the period just preceding the advent of Bartleby, I had two persons as copyists in my employment, and a promising lad as an office-boy. First, Turkey; second, Nippers; third, Ginger Nut. These may seem names, the like of which are not usually found in the Directory.[4] In truth they were nicknames, mutually conferred upon each other by my three clerks, and were deemed expressive of their respective persons or characters. Turkey was a short, pursy Englishman of about my own age, that is, somewhere not far from sixty. In the morning, one might say, his face was of a fine florid hue, but after twelve o'clock, meridian—his dinner hour—it blazed like a grate full of Christmas coals; and continued blazing—but, as it were, with a gradual wane—till 6 o'clock P.M. or thereabouts, after which I saw no more of the proprietor of the face, which, gaining its meridian with the sun, seemed to set with it, to rise, culminate, and decline the following day, with the like regularity and undiminished glory. There are many singular coincidences I have known in the course of my life, not the least among which was the fact, that exactly when Turkey displayed his fullest beams from his red and radiant countenance, just then, too, at that critical moment, began the daily period when I considered his business capacities as seriously disturbed for the remainder of the twenty-four hours. Not that he was absolutely idle, or averse to business then; far from it. The difficulty was, he was apt to be altogether too energetic. There was a strange, inflamed, flurried, flighty recklessness of activity about him. He would be incautious in dipping his pen into his inkstand. All his blots upon my documents, were dropped there after twelve o'clock, meridian. Indeed, not only would he be reckless and sadly given to making blots in the afternoon, but some days he went further, and was rather noisy. At such times, too, his face flamed with augmented blazonry, as if cannel coal had been heaped on anthracite.[5] He made an unpleasant racket with his chair; spilled his sand-box;[6] in mending his

4. Post Office Directory. 5. Oily, quick-burning coal heaped on slower burning kind. 6. I.e., sand used to dry ink.

pens, impatiently split them all to pieces, and threw them on the floor in a sudden passion; stood up and leaned over his table, boxing his papers about in a most indecorous manner, very sad to behold in an elderly man like him. Nevertheless, as he was in many ways a most valuable person to me, and all the time before twelve o'clock, meridian, was the quickest, steadiest creature, too, accomplishing a great deal of work in a style not easy to be matched—for these reasons, I was willing to overlook his eccentricities, though indeed, occasionally, I remonstrated with him. I did this very gently, however, because, though the civilest, nay, the blandest and most reverential of men in the morning, yet in the afternoon he was disposed, upon provocation, to be slightly rash with his tongue, in fact, insolent. Now, valuing his morning services as I did, and resolved not to lose them—yet, at the same time made uncomfortable by his inflamed ways after twelve o'clock; and being a man of peace, unwilling by my admonitions to call forth unseemly retorts from him—I took upon me, one Saturday noon (he was always worse on Saturdays), to hint to him, very kindly, that perhaps now that he was growing old, it might be well to abridge his labors; in short, he need not come to my chambers after twelve o'clock, but, dinner over, had best go home to his lodgings and rest himself till tea-time. But no; he insisted upon his afternoon devotions. His countenance became intolerably fervid, as he oratorically assured me—gesticulating with a long ruler at the other end of the room—that if his services in the morning were useful, how indispensable, then, in the afternoon?

"With submission, sir," said Turkey on this occasion, "I consider myself your right-hand man. In the morning I but marshal and deploy my columns; but in the afternoon I put myself at their head, and gallantly charge the foe, thus!"—and he made a violent thrust with the ruler.

"But the blots, Turkey," intimated I.

"True,—but, with submission, sir, behold these hairs! I am getting old. Surely, sir, a blot or two of a warm afternoon is not to be severely urged against gray hairs. Old age—even if it blot the page—is honorable. With submission, sir, we *both* are getting old."

This appeal to my fellow-feeling was hardly to be resisted. At all events, I saw that go he would not. So I made up my mind to let him stay, resolving, nevertheless, to see to it, that during the afternoon he had to do with my less important papers.

Nippers, the second on my list, was a whiskered, sallow, and, upon the whole, rather piratical-looking young man of about five and twenty. I always deemed him the victim of two evil powers—ambition and indigestion. The ambition was evinced by a certain impatience of the duties of a mere copyist—an unwarrantable usurpation of strictly professional affairs, such as the original drawing up of legal documents. The indigestion seemed betokened in an occasional nervous testiness and grinning irritability, causing the teeth to audibly grind together over mistakes committed in copying; unnecessary maledictions, hissed, rather than spoken, in the heat of business; and especially by a continual discontent with the height of the table where he worked. Though of a very ingenious mechanical turn, Nippers could never get this table to suit him. He put chips under it, blocks of various sorts, bits of pasteboard, and at last went so far as to attempt an exquisite adjustment by final pieces of folded blotting-paper. But no invention would answer. If, for the sake of easing his back, he brought the table lid at a sharp angle well up towards his chin, and wrote there like a man using the steep roof of a Dutch house for his desk—then he declared that it stopped the circulation in his arms. If now he lowered the table to his waistbands, and stooped over it in writing, then there was a sore aching in his back. In short, the truth of the matter was, Nippers knew not what he wanted. Or, if he wanted anything, it was to be rid of a scrivener's table altogether. Among the manifestations of his diseased ambition was a fondness he had for receiving visits from certain ambiguous-looking fellows in seedy coats, whom he called his clients. Indeed I was aware that not only was he, at times, considerable of a ward-politician, but he occasionally did a little business at the Justices' courts, and was not unknown on the steps of the Tombs.[7] I have good reason to believe, however, that one individual who called upon him at my chambers, and who, with a grand air, he insisted was his client, was no other than a dun,[8] and the alleged title-deed, a bill. But with all his failings, and the annoyances he caused me, Nippers, like his compatriot Turkey, was a very useful man to me; wrote a neat, swift hand; and, when he chose, was not deficient in a gentlemanly sort of deportment. Added to this, he always dressed in a gentlemanly sort of way; and so, incidentally, reflected credit upon my chambers. Whereas with respect to Turkey, I had much ado to keep him from being a reproach to me. His clothes were apt to look oily and smell of eating-houses. He wore his pantaloons very loose and baggy in summer. His coats were execrable; his hat not to be handled. But while the hat was a thing of indifference to me, inasmuch as his natural civility and deference, as a dependent Englishman, always led him to doff it the moment he entered the room, yet his coat was another matter. Concerning his coats, I reasoned with him; but with no effect. The truth was, I suppose, that a man with so small an income, could not afford to sport such a lustrous face and a lustrous coat at one and the same time. As Nippers once

7. A prison in New York City; as "ward-politician" Nippers was a fixer who seems to have made extralegal arrangements for constituents of his district of the city when they had legal problems. 8. Bill-collector.

observed, Turkey's money went chiefly for red ink. One winter day I presented Turkey with a highly-respectable looking coat of my own, a padded gray coat, of a most comfortable warmth, and which buttoned straight up from the knee to the neck. I thought Turkey would appreciate the favour, and abate his rashness and obstreperousness of afternoons. But no. I verily believe that buttoning himself up in so downy and blanket-like a coat had a pernicious effect upon him; upon the same principle that too much oats are bad for horses. In fact, precisely as a rash, restive horse is said to feel his oats, so Turkey felt his coat. It made him insolent. He was a man whom prosperity harmed.

Though concerning the self-indulgent habits of Turkey I had my own private surmises, yet touching Nippers I was well persuaded that whatever might be his faults in other respects, he was, at least, a temperate young man. But, indeed, nature herself seemed to have been his vintner, and at his birth charged him so thoroughly with an irritable, brandy-like disposition, that all subsequent potations were needless. When I consider how, amid the stillness of my chambers, Nippers would sometimes impatiently rise from his seat, and stooping over his table, spread his arms wide apart, seize the whole desk, and move it, and jerk it, with a grim, grinding motion on the floor, as if the table were a perverse voluntary agent, intent on thwarting and vexing him; I plainly perceive that for Nippers, brandy and water were altogether superfluous.

It was fortunate for me that, owing to its peculiar cause—indigestion—the irritability and consequent nervousness of Nippers, were mainly observable in the morning, while in the afternoon he was comparatively mild. So that Turkey's paroxysms only coming on about twelve o'clock, I never had to do with their eccentricities at one time. Their fits relieved each other like guards. When Nippers' was on, Turkey's was off; and *vice versa*. This was a good natural arrangement under the circumstances.

Ginger Nut, the third on my list, was a lad some twelve years old. His father was a carman,[9] ambitious of seeing his son on the bench instead of a cart, before he died. So he sent him to my office as student at law, errand boy, and cleaner and sweeper, at the rate of one dollar a week. He had a little desk to himself, but he did not use it much. Upon inspection, the drawer exhibited a great array of the shells of various sorts of nuts. Indeed, to this quick-witted youth the whole noble science of the law was contained in a nut-shell. Not the least among the employments of Ginger Nut, as well as one which he discharged with the most alacrity, was his duty as cake and apple pur-

9. Driver of a cart.

veyor for Turkey and Nippers. Copying law papers being proverbially a dry, husky sort of business, my two scriveners were fain to moisten their mouths very often with Spitzenbergs[1] to be had at the numerous stalls nigh the Custom House and Post Office. Also, they sent Ginger Nut very frequently for that peculiar cake—small, flat, round, and very spicy—after which he had been named by them. Of a cold morning when business was but dull, Turkey would gobble up scores of these cakes, as if they were mere wafers—indeed they sell them at the rate of six or eight for a penny—the scrape of his pen blending with the crunching of the crisp particles in his mouth. Of all the fiery afternoon blunders and flurried rashnesses of Turkey, was his once moistening a ginger-cake between his lips, and clapping it on to a mortgage for a seal. I came within an ace of dismissing him then. But he mollified me by making an oriental bow, and saying—"With submission, sir, it was generous of me to find[2] you in stationery on my own account."

Now my original business—that of a conveyancer and title hunter,[3] and drawer-up of recondite documents of all sorts—was considerably increased by receiving the master's office. There was now great work for scriveners. Not only must I push the clerks already with me, but I must have additional help. In answer to my advertisement, a motionless young man one morning stood upon my office threshold, the door being open, for it was summer. I can see that figure now—pallidly neat, pitiably respectable, incurably forlorn! It was Bartleby.

After a few words touching his qualifications, I engaged him, glad to have among my corps of copyists a man of so singularly sedate an aspect, which I thought might operate beneficially upon the flighty temper of Turkey, and the fiery one of Nippers.

I should have stated before that ground glass folding-doors divided my premises into two parts, one of which was occupied by my scriveners, the other by myself. According to my humour I threw open these doors, or closed them. I resolved to assign Bartleby a corner by the folding-doors, but on my side of them, so as to have this quiet man within easy call, in case any trifling thing was to be done. I placed his desk close up to a small side-window in that part of the room, a window which originally had afforded a lateral view of certain grimy back-yards and bricks, but which, owing to subsequent erections, commanded at present no view at all, though it gave some light. Within three feet of the panes was a wall, and the light came down from far above, between two lofty buildings, as from a very small opening in a dome. Still further to a satisfactory arrangement, I procured a high green folding screen, which might entirely isolate Bartleby from my sight, though

1. Apples. 2. "To provide you with." 3. A conveyance is a legal paper for transferring property; title hunting is examining the abstract of property deeds.

not remove him from my voice. And thus, in a manner, privacy and society were conjoined.

At first Bartleby did an extraordinary quantity of writing. As if long famishing for something to copy, he seemed to gorge himself on my documents. There was no pause for digestion. He ran a day and night line, copying by sun-light and by candle-light. I should have been quite delighted with his application, had he been cheerfully industrious. But he wrote on silently, palely, mechanically.

It is, of course, an indispensable part of a scrivener's business to verify the accuracy of his copy, word by word. Where there are two or more scriveners in an office, they assist each other in this examination, one reading from the copy, the other holding the original. It is a very dull, wearisome, and lethargic affair. I can readily imagine that to some sanguine temperaments it would be altogether intolerable. For example, I cannot credit that the mettlesome poet Byron would have contentedly sat down with Bartleby to examine a law document of, say five hundred pages, closely written in a crimpy hand.

Now and then, in the haste of business, it had been my habit to assist in comparing some brief document myself, calling Turkey or Nippers for this purpose. One object I had in placing Bartleby so handy to me behind the screen, was to avail myself of his services on such trivial occasions. It was on the third day, I think, of his being with me, and before any necessity had arisen for having his own writing examined, that, being much hurried to complete a small affair I had in hand, I abruptly called to Bartleby. In my haste and natural expectancy of instant compliance, I sat with my head bent over the original on my desk, and my right hand sideways, and somewhat nervously extended with the copy, so that immediately upon emerging from his retreat, Bartleby might snatch it and proceed to business without the least delay.

In this very attitude did I sit when I called to him, rapidly stating what it was I wanted him to do—namely, to examine a small paper with me. Imagine my surprise, nay, my consternation, when without moving from his privacy, Bartleby in a singularly mild, firm voice, replied, "I would prefer not to."

I sat awhile in perfect silence, rallying my stunned faculties. Immediately it occurred to me that my ears had deceived me, or Bartleby had entirely misunderstood my meaning. I repeated my request in the clearest tone I could assume. But in quite as clear a one came the previous reply, "I would prefer not to."

"Prefer not to," echoed I, rising in high excitement, and crossing the room with a stride. "What do you mean? Are you moon-struck?[4] I

4. This popular synonym for "crazy" incorporates the old belief that the lunatic was affected by phases of the moon (Latin: *luna*).

want you to help me compare this sheet here—take it," and I thrust it toward him.

"I would prefer not to," said he.

I looked at him steadfastly. His face was leanly composed; his gray eye dimly calm. Not a wrinkle of agitation rippled him. Had there been the least uneasiness, anger, impatience or impertinence in his manner; in other words, had there been anything ordinarily human about him, doubtless I should have violently dismissed him from the premises. But as it was, I should have as soon thought of turning my pale plaster-of-paris bust of Cicero out of doors. I stood gazing at him awhile, as he went on with his own writing, and then reseated myself at my desk. This is very strange, thought I. What had one best do? But my business hurried me. I concluded to forget the matter for the present, reserving it for my future leisure. So calling Nippers from the other room, the paper was speedily examined.

A few days after this, Bartleby concluded four lengthy documents, being quadruplicates of a week's testimony taken before me in my High Court of Chancery. It became necessary to examine them. It was an important suit, and great accuracy was imperative. Having all things arranged, I called Turkey, Nippers and Ginger Nut from the next room, meaning to place the four copies in the hands of my four clerks, while I should read from the original. Accordingly Turkey, Nippers and Ginger Nut had taken their seats in a row, each with his document in hand, when I called to Bartleby to join this interesting group.

"Bartleby! quick, I am waiting."

I heard a slow scrape of his chair legs on the uncarpeted floor, and soon he appeared standing at the entrance of his hermitage.

"What is wanted?" said he mildly.

"The copies, the copies," said I hurriedly. "We are going to examine them. There"—and I held towards him the fourth quadruplicate.

"I would prefer not to," he said, and gently disappeared behind the screen.

For a few moments I was turned into a pillar of salt,[5] standing at the head of my seated column of clerks. Recovering myself, I advanced toward the screen, and demanded the reason for such extraordinary conduct.

"*Why* do you refuse?"

"I would prefer not to."

With any other man I should have flown outright into a dreadful passion, scorned all further words, and thrust him ignominiously from

5. I.e., was paralyzed. The allusion is to Genesis 19:26; Lot's wife is turned into a pillar of salt when she looks back at the destruction of Sodom.

my presence. But there was something about Bartleby that not only strangely disarmed me, but in a wonderful manner touched and disconcerted me. I began to reason with him.

"These are your own copies we are about to examine. It is labour saving to you, because one examination will answer for your four papers. It is common usage. Every copyist is bound to help examine his copy. Is it not so? Will you not speak? Answer!"

"I prefer not to," he replied in a flute-like tone. It seemed to me that while I had been addressing him, he carefully revolved every statement that I made; fully comprehended the meaning; could not gainsay the irresistible conclusion; but, at the same time, some paramount consideration prevailed with him to reply as he did.

"You are decided, then, not to comply with my request—a request made according to common usage and common sense?"

He briefly gave me to understand that on that point my judgment was sound. Yes: his decision was irreversible.

It is not seldom the case that when a man is browbeaten in some unprecedented and violently unreasonable way, he begins to stagger in his own plainest faith. He begins, as it were, vaguely to surmise that, wonderful as it may be, all the justice and all the reason are on the other side. Accordingly, if any disinterested persons are present, he turns to them for some reinforcement for his own faltering mind.

"Turkey," said I, "what do you think of this? Am I not right?"

"With submission, sir," said Turkey, with his blandest tone, "I think that you are."

"Nippers," said I, "what do *you* think of it?"

"I think I should kick him out of the office."

(The reader of nice perceptions will here perceive that, it being morning, Turkey's answer is couched in polite and tranquil terms, but Nippers's reply in ill-tempered ones. Or, to repeat a previous sentence, Nippers's ugly mood was on duty, and Turkey's off.)

"Ginger Nut," said I, willing to enlist the smallest suffrage in my behalf, "what do *you* think of it?"

"I think, sir, he's a little *luny*,"[6] replied Ginger Nut, with a grin.

"You hear what they say," said I, turning towards the screen, "come forth and do your duty."

But he vouchsafed no reply. I pondered a moment in sore perplexity. But once more business hurried me. I determined again to postpone the consideration of this dilemma to my future leisure. With a little trouble we made out to examine the papers without Bartleby, though at every page or two, Turkey deferentially dropped his opinion that this proceeding was quite out of the common; while Nippers,

6. Loony—here Melville's spelling recalls the word *lunatic*.

twitching in his chair with a dyspeptic nervousness, ground out between his set teeth occasional hissing maledictions against the stubborn oaf behind the screen. And for his (Nippers's) part, this was the first and the last time he would do another man's business without pay.

Meanwhile Bartleby sat in his hermitage, oblivious to everything but his own peculiar business there.

Some days passed, the scrivener being employed upon another lengthy work. His late remarkable conduct led me to regard his ways narrowly. I observed that he never went to dinner; indeed that he never went any where. As yet I had never of my personal knowledge known him to be outside of my office. He was a perpetual sentry in the corner. At about eleven o'clock though, in the morning, I noticed that Ginger Nut would advance toward the opening in Bartleby's screen, as if silently beckoned thither by a gesture invisible to me where I sat. The boy would then leave the office jingling a few pence, and reappear with a handful of ginger-nuts which he delivered in the hermitage, receiving two of the cakes for his trouble.

He lives, then, on ginger-nuts, thought I; never eats a dinner, properly speaking; he must be a vegetarian then; but no; he never eats even vegetables, he eats nothing but ginger-nuts. My mind then ran on in reveries concerning the probable effects upon the human constitution of living entirely on ginger-nuts. Ginger-nuts are so called because they contain ginger as one of their peculiar constituents, and the final flavoring one. Now what was ginger? A hot, spicy thing. Was Bartleby hot and spicy? Not at all. Ginger, then, had no effect upon Bartleby. Probably he preferred it should have none.

Nothing so aggravates an earnest person as a passive resistance. If the individual so resisted be of a not inhumane temper, and the resisting one perfectly harmless in his passivity; then, in the better moods of the former, he will endeavor charitably to construe to his imagination what proves impossible to be solved by his judgment. Even so, for the most part, I regarded Bartleby and his ways. Poor fellow! thought I, he means no mischief; it is plain he intends no insolence; his aspect sufficiently evinces that his eccentricities are involuntary. He is useful to me. I can get along with him. If I turn him away, the chances are he will fall in with some less indulgent employer, and then he will be rudely treated, and perhaps driven forth miserably to starve. Yes. Here I can cheaply purchase a delicious self-approval. To befriend Bartleby; to humour him in his strange wilfulness, will cost me little or nothing, while I lay up in my soul what will eventually prove a sweet morsel for my conscience. But this mood was not invariable with me. The passiveness of Bartleby sometimes irritated me. I felt strangely goaded on to encounter him in new opposition, to elicit some angry spark from him answerable to my own. But indeed I might as well have essayed to strike fire with my knuckles against a bit of Windsor soap. But one afternoon the evil impulse in me mastered me, and the following little scene ensued:

"Bartleby," said I, "when those papers are all copied, I will compare them with you."

"I would prefer not to."

"How? Surely you do not mean to persist in that mulish vagary?"

No answer.

I threw open the folding-doors near by, and turning upon Turkey and Nippers, exclaimed in an excited manner:

"He says, a second time, he won't examine his papers. What do you think of it, Turkey?"

It was afternoon, be it remembered. Turkey sat glowing like a brass boiler, his bald head steaming, his hands reeling among his blotted papers.

"Think of it?" roared Turkey; "I think I'll just step behind his screen, and black his eyes for him!"

So saying, Turkey rose to his feet and threw his arms into a pugilistic position. He was hurrying away to make good his promise, when I detained him, alarmed at the effect of incautiously rousing Turkey's combativeness after dinner.

"Sit down, Turkey," said I, "and hear what Nippers has to say. What do you think of it, Nippers? Would I not be justified in immediately dismissing Bartleby?"

"Excuse me, that is for you to decide, sir. I think his conduct quite unusual, and indeed unjust, as regards Turkey and myself. But it may only be a passing whim."

"Ah," exclaimed I, "You have strangely changed your mind then—you speak very gently of him now."

"All beer," cried Turkey; "gentleness is effects of beer—Nippers and I dined together to-day. You see how gentle *I* am, sir. Shall I go and black his eyes?"

"You refer to Bartleby, I suppose. No, not to-day, Turkey," I replied; "pray, put up your fists."

I closed the doors, and again advanced towards Bartleby. I felt additional incentives tempting me to my fate. I burned to be rebelled against again. I remembered that Bartleby never left the office.

"Bartleby," said I, "Ginger Nut is away; just step round to the Post Office, won't you? (it was but a three minutes' walk), and see if there is any thing for me."

"I would prefer not to."

"You *will* not?"

"I *prefer* not."

I staggered to my desk, and sat there in a deep study. My blind inveteracy returned. Was there any other thing in which I could procure myself to be ignominiously repulsed by this lean, penniless wight?—my hired clerk? What added thing is there, perfectly reasonable, that he will be sure to refuse to do?

"Bartleby!"

No answer.

"Bartleby," in a louder tone.

No answer.

"Bartleby," I roared.

Like a very ghost, agreeably to the laws of magical invocation, at the third summons, he appeared at the entrance of his hermitage.

"Go to the next room, and tell Nippers to come to me."

"I prefer not to," he respectfully and slowly said, and mildly disappeared.

"Very good, Bartleby," said I, in a quiet sort of serenely severe self-possessed tone, intimating the unalterable purpose of some terrible retribution very close at hand. At the moment I half intended something of the kind. But upon the whole, as it was drawing towards my dinner-hour, I thought it best to put on my hat and walk home for the day, suffering much from perplexity and distress of mind.

Shall I acknowledge it? The conclusion of this whole business was, that it soon became a fixed fact of my chambers, that a pale young scrivener, by the name of Bartleby, had a desk there; that he copied for me at the usual rate of four cents a folio (one hundred words); but he was permanently exempt from examining the work done by him, that duty being transferred to Turkey and Nippers, out of compliment doubtless to their superior acuteness; moreover, said Bartleby was never on any account to be despatched on the most trivial errand of any sort; and that even if entreated to take upon him such a matter, it was generally understood that he would prefer not to—in other words, that he would refuse point-blank.

As days passed on, I became considerably reconciled to Bartleby. His steadiness, his freedom from all dissipation, his incessant industry (except when he chose to throw himself into a standing revery behind his screen), his great stillness, his unalterableness of demeanor under all circumstances, made him a valuable acquisition. One prime thing was this,—*he was always there;*—first in the morning, continually through the day, and the last at night. I had a singular confidence in his honesty. I felt my most precious papers perfectly safe in his hands. Sometimes to be sure I could not, for the very soul of me, avoid falling into sudden spasmodic passions with him. For it was exceeding difficult to bear in mind all the time those strange peculiarities, privileges, and unheard of exemptions, forming the tacit stipulations on Bartleby's part under which he remained in my office. Now and then, in the eagerness of despatching pressing business, I would inadvertently summon Bartleby, in a short, rapid tone, to put his finger, say, on the incipient tie of a bit of red tape with which I was about compressing some papers. Of course, from behind the screen the usual answer, "I prefer not to," was sure to come; and then, how could a human creature with common infirmities of our nature, refrain from bitterly exclaiming upon such perverseness—such unreasonableness. However, every added repulse of this sort which I received only tended to lessen the probability of my repeating the inadvertence.

Here it must be said, that according to the customs of most legal gentlemen occupying chambers in densely-populated law buildings, there were several keys to my door. One was kept by a woman residing in the attic, which person weekly scrubbed and daily swept and dusted my apartments. Another was kept by Turkey for convenience sake. The third I sometimes carried in my own pocket. The fourth I knew not who had.

Now, one Sunday morning I happened to go to Trinity Church,[7] to hear a celebrated preacher, and finding myself rather early on the ground, I thought I would walk round to my chambers for awhile. Luckily I had my key with me; but upon applying it to the lock, I found it resisted by something inserted from the inside. Quite surprised, I called out; when to my consternation a key was turned from within; and thrusting his lean visage at me, and holding the door ajar, the apparition of Bartleby appeared, in his shirt sleeves, and otherwise in a strangely tattered dishabille, saying quietly that he was sorry, but he was deeply engaged just then, and—preferred not admitting me at present. In a brief word or two, he moreover added, that perhaps I had better walk round the block two or three times, and by that time he would probably have concluded his affairs.

Now, the utterly unsurmised appearance of Bartleby, tenanting my law-chambers of a Sunday morning, with his cadaverously gentlemanly *nonchalance*, yet withal firm and self-possessed, had such a strange effect upon me, that incontinently I slunk away from my own door, and did as desired. But not without sundry twinges of impotent rebellion against the mild effrontery of this unaccountable scrivener. Indeed, it was his wonderful mildness chiefly, which not only disarmed me, but unmanned me, as it were. For I consider that one, for the time, is in a way unmanned when he tranquilly permits his hired clerk to dictate to him, and order him away from his own premises. Furthermore, I was full of uneasiness as to what Bartleby could possibly be doing in my office in his shirt sleeves, and in an otherwise dismantled condition of a Sunday morning. Was any thing amiss going on? Nay, that was out

7. Venerable church in the Wall Street district.

of the question. It was not to be thought of for a moment that Bartleby was an immoral person. But what could he be doing there—copying? Nay again, whatever might be his eccentricities, Bartleby was an eminently decorous person. He would be the last man to sit down to his desk in any state approaching to nudity. Besides, it was Sunday; and there was something about Bartleby that forbade the supposition that he would by any secular occupation violate the proprieties of the day.

Nevertheless, my mind was not pacified; and full of a restless curiosity, at last I returned to the door. Without hindrance I inserted my key, opened it, and entered. Bartleby was not to be seen. I looked round anxiously, peeped behind his screen; but it was very plain that he was gone. Upon more closely examining the place, I surmised that for an indefinite period Bartleby must have ate, dressed, and slept in my office, and that too without plate, mirror, or bed. The cushioned seat of a ricketty old sofa in one corner bore the faint impress of a lean, reclining form. Rolled away under his desk, I found a blanket; under the empty grate, a blacking box[8] and brush; on a chair, a tin basin, with soap and a ragged towel; in a newspaper a few crumbs of ginger-nuts and a morsel of cheese. Yes, thought I, it is evident enough that Bartleby has been making his home here, keeping bachelor's hall all by himself. Immediately then the thought came sweeping across me, What miserable friendlessness and loneliness are here revealed! His poverty is great; but his solitude, how horrible! Think of it. Of a Sunday, Wall street is deserted as Petra;[9] and every night of every day it is an emptiness. This building too, which of week-days hums with industry and life, at nightfall echoes with sheer vacancy, and all through Sunday is forlorn. And here Bartleby makes his home; sole spectator of a solitude which he has seen all populous—a sort of innocent and transformed Marius brooding among the ruins of Carthage![1]

For the first time in my life a feeling of overpowering stinging melancholy seized me. Before, I had never experienced aught but a not-unpleasing sadness. The bond of a common humanity now drew me irresistibly to gloom. A fraternal melancholy! For both I and Bartleby were sons of Adam. I remembered the bright silks and sparkling faces I had seen that day, in gala trim, swan-like sailing down the Mississippi of Broadway; and I contrasted them with the pallid copyist, and thought to myself, Ah, happiness courts the light, so we deem the world is gay; but misery hides aloof, so we deem that misery there is none. These sad fancyings—chimeras, doubtless, of a sick and silly brain—led on to other and more special thoughts, concerning the eccentricities of Bartleby. Presentiments of strange discoveries hov-

8. Box of shoe polish. 9. Long-ruined and deserted Middle Eastern city. 1. Roman consul and general expelled from Rome and seeking sanctuary in the city Rome had destroyed; i.e., a ruined man in a ruined city.

ered round me. The scrivener's pale form appeared to me laid out, among uncaring strangers, in its shivering winding sheet.

Suddenly I was attracted by Bartleby's closed desk, the key in open sight left in the lock.

I mean no mischief, seek the gratification of no heartless curiosity, thought I; besides, the desk is mine, and its contents too, so I will make bold to look within. Everything was methodically arranged, the papers smoothly placed. The pigeon holes were deep, and, removing the files of documents, I groped into their recesses. Presently I felt something there, and dragged it out. It was an old bandanna handkerchief, heavy and knotted. I opened it, and saw it was a savings' bank.

I now recalled all the quiet mysteries which I had noted in the man. I remembered that he never spoke but to answer; that though at intervals he had considerable time to himself, yet I had never seen him reading—no, not even a newspaper; that for long periods he would stand looking out, at his pale window behind the screen, upon the dead brick wall; I was quite sure he never visited any refectory or eating-house; while his pale face clearly indicated that he never drank beer like Turkey, or tea and coffee even, like other men; that he never went anywhere in particular that I could learn; never went out for a walk, unless indeed that was the case at present; that he had declined telling who he was, or whence he came, or whether he had any relatives in the world; that though so thin and pale, he never complained of ill health. And more than all, I remembered a certain unconscious air of pallid—how shall I call it?—of pallid haughtiness, say, or rather an austere reserve about him, which had positively awed me into my tame compliance with his eccentricities, when I had feared to ask him to do the slightest incidental thing for me, even though I might know, from his long-continued motionlessness, that behind his screen he must be standing in one of those dead-wall reveries of his.

Revolving all these things, and coupling them with the recently discovered fact that he made my office his constant abiding place and home, and not forgetful of his morbid moodiness; revolving all these things, a prudential feeling began to steal over me. My first emotions had been those of pure melancholy and sincerest pity; but just in proportion as the forlornness of Bartleby grew and grew to my imagination, did that same melancholy merge into fear, that pity into repulsion. So true it is, and so terrible too, that up to a certain point the thought or sight of misery enlists our best affections; but, in certain special cases, beyond that point it does not. They err who would assert that invariably this is owing to the inherent selfishness of the human heart. It rather proceeds from a certain hopelessness of remedying excessive and organic ill. To a sensitive being, pity is not seldom pain. And when at last it is perceived that such pity cannot lead to effectual succor, common sense bids the soul be rid of it. What I saw that morning persuaded me that the scrivener was the victim of innate and incurable disorder. I might give alms to his body; but his body did not pain him; it was his soul that suffered, and his soul I could not reach.

I did not accomplish the purpose of going to Trinity Church that morning. Somehow, the things I had seen disqualified me for the time from church-going. I walked homeward, thinking what I would do with Bartleby. Finally, I resolved upon this:—I would put certain calm questions to him the next morning, touching his history, &c., and if he declined to answer them openly and unreservedly (and I supposed he would prefer not), then to give him a twenty dollar bill over and above whatever I might owe him, and tell him his services were no longer required; but that if in any other way I could assist him, I would be happy to do so, especially if he desired to return to his native place, wherever that might be, I would willingly help to defray the expenses. Moreover, if, after reaching home, he found himself at any time in want of aid, a letter from him would be sure of a reply.

The next morning came.

"Bartleby," said I, gently calling to him behind his screen.

No reply.

"Bartleby," said I, in a still gentler tone, "come here; I am not going to ask you to do anything you would prefer not to do—I simply wish to speak to you."

Upon this he noiselessly slid into view.

"Will you tell me, Bartleby, where you were born?"

"I would prefer not to."

"Will you tell me *anything* about yourself?"

"I would prefer not to."

"But what reasonable objection can you have to speak to me? I feel friendly towards you."

He did not look at me while I spoke, but kept his glance fixed upon my bust of Cicero, which, as I then sat, was directly behind me, some six inches above my head.

"What is your answer, Bartleby?" said I, after waiting a considerable time for a reply, during which his countenance remained immovable, only there was the faintest conceivable tremor of the white attenuated mouth.

"At present I prefer to give no answer," he said, and retired into his hermitage.

It was rather weak in me I confess, but his manner on this occasion nettled me. Not only did there seem to lurk in it a certain calm disdain, but his perverseness seemed ungrateful, considering the undeniable good usage and indulgence he had received from me.

Again I sat ruminating what I should do. Mortified as I was at his behavior, and resolved as I had been to dismiss him when I entered my office, nevertheless I strangely felt something superstitious knocking at my heart, and forbidding me to carry out my purpose, and denouncing me for a villain if I dared to breathe one bitter word against this forlornest of mankind. At last, familiarly drawing my chair behind his screen, I sat down and said: "Bartleby, never mind then about revealing your history; but let me entreat you, as a friend, to comply as far as may be with the usages of this office. Say now you will help to examine papers to-morrow or next day: in short, say now that in a day or two you will begin to be a little reasonable:—say so, Bartleby."

"At present I would prefer not to be a little reasonable," was his mildly cadaverous reply.

Just then the folding-doors opened, and Nippers approached. He seemed suffering from an unusually bad night's rest, induced by severer indigestion than common. He overheard those final words of Bartleby.

"*Prefer not*, eh?" gritted Nippers—"I'd *prefer* him, if I were you, sir," addressing me—"I'd *prefer* him; I'd give him preferences, the stubborn mule! What is it, sir, pray, that he *prefers* not to do now?"

Bartleby moved not a limb.

"Mr. Nippers," said I, "I'd prefer that you would withdraw for the present."

Somehow, of late I had got into the way of involuntarily using this word "prefer" upon all sorts of not exactly suitable occasions. And I trembled to think that my contact with the scrivener had already and seriously affected me in a mental way. And what further and deeper aberration might it not yet produce? This apprehension had not been without efficacy in determining me to summary means.

As Nippers, looking very sour and sulky, was departing, Turkey blandly and deferentially approached.

"With submission, sir," said he, "yesterday I was thinking about Bartleby here, and I think that if he would but prefer to take a quart of good ale every day, it would do much towards mending him, and enabling him to assist in examining his papers."

"So you have got the word too," said I, slightly excited.

"With submission, what word, sir," asked Turkey, respectfully crowding himself into the contracted space behind the screen, and by so doing, making me jostle the scrivener. "What word, sir?"

"I would prefer to be left alone here," said Bartleby, as if offended at being mobbed in his privacy.

"*That's* the word, Turkey," said I—"*that's* it."

"Oh, *prefer?* oh, yes—queer word. I never use it myself. But, sir, as I was saying, if he would but prefer—"

"Turkey," interrupted I, "you will please withdraw."

"Oh certainly, sir, if you prefer that I should."

As he opened the folding-door to retire, Nippers at his desk caught a glimpse of me, and asked whether I would prefer to have a certain paper copied on blue paper or white. He did not in the least roguishly accent the word prefer. It was plain that it involuntarily rolled from his tongue. I thought to myself, surely I must get rid of a demented man, who already has in some degree turned the tongues, if not the heads, of myself and clerks. But I thought it prudent not to break the dismission at once.

The next day I noticed that Bartleby did nothing but stand at his window in his dead-wall revery. Upon asking him why he did not write, he said that he had decided upon doing no more writing.

"Why, how now? what next?" exclaimed I, "do no more writing?"

"No more."

"And what is the reason?"

"Do you not see the reason for yourself," he indifferently replied.

I looked steadfastly at him, and perceived that his eyes looked dull and glazed. Instantly it occurred to me, that his unexampled diligence in copying by his dim window for the first few weeks of his stay with me might have temporarily impaired his vision.

I was touched. I said something in condolence with him. I hinted that of course he did wisely in abstaining from writing for a while, and urged him to embrace that opportunity of taking wholesome exercise in the open air. This, however, he did not do. A few days after this, my other clerks being absent, and being in a great hurry to dispatch certain letters by the mail, I thought that, having nothing else earthly to do, Bartleby would surely be less inflexible than usual, and carry these letters to the Post Office. But he blankly declined. So, much to my inconvenience, I went myself.

Still added days went by. Whether Bartleby's eyes improved or not, I could not say. To all appearance, I thought they did. But when I asked him if they did, he vouchsafed no answer. At all events, he would do no copying. At last, in reply to my urgings, he informed me that he had permanently given up copying.

"What!" exclaimed I; "suppose your eyes should get entirely well—better than ever before—would you not copy then?"

"I have given up copying," he answered and slid aside.

He remained as ever, a fixture in my chamber. Nay—if that were possible—he became still more of a fixture than before. What was to be done? He would do nothing in the office: why should he stay there? In plain fact, he had now become a millstone[2] to me, not only useless

2. Conventional image of a burden hung on someone. Matthew 18:6: "But whoso shall offend one of these little ones which believe in me, it were better for him that a millstone were hanged about his neck, and that he were drowned in the depths of the sea."

as a necklace, but afflictive to bear. Yet I was sorry for him. I speak less than truth when I say that, on his own account, he occasioned me uneasiness. If he would but have named a single relative or friend, I would instantly have written, and urged their taking the poor fellow away to some convenient retreat. But he seemed alone, absolutely alone in the universe. A bit of wreckage in the mid-Atlantic. At length, necessities connected with my business tyrannized over all other considerations. Decently as I could, I told Bartleby that in six days' time he must unconditionally leave the office. I warned him to take measures, in the interval, for procuring some other abode. I offered to assist him in this endeavor, if he himself would but take the first step towards a removal. "And when you finally quit me, Bartleby," added I, "I shall see that you go away not entirely unprovided. Six days from this hour, remember."

At the expiration of that period, I peeped behind the screen, and lo! Bartleby was there.

I buttoned up my coat, balanced myself; advanced slowly towards him, touched his shoulder, and said, "The time has come; you must quit this place; I am sorry for you; here is money; but you must go."

"I would prefer not," he replied, with his back still towards me.

"You *must*."

He remained silent.

Now I had an unbounded confidence in this man's common honesty. He had frequently restored to me sixpences and shillings carelessly dropped upon the floor, for I am apt to be very reckless in such shirt-button affairs. The proceeding then which followed will not be deemed extraordinary.

"Bartleby," said I, "I owe you twelve dollars on account; here are thirty-two; the odd twenty are yours.—Will you take it?" and I handed the bills towards him.

But he made no motion.

"I will leave them here then," putting them under a weight on the table. Then taking my hat and cane and going to the door, I tranquilly turned and added—"After you have removed your things from these offices, Bartleby, you will of course lock the door—since every one is now gone for the day but you—and if you please, slip your key underneath the mat, so that I may have it in the morning. I shall not see you again; so good-bye to you. If hereafter in your new place of abode I can be of any service to you, do not fail to advise me by letter. Good-bye, Bartleby, and fare you well."

But he answered not a word; like the last column of some ruined temple, he remained standing mute and solitary in the middle of the otherwise deserted room.

As I walked home in a pensive mood, my vanity got the better of my pity. I could not but highly plume myself on my masterly management in getting rid of Bartleby. Masterly I call it, and such it must appear to any dispassionate thinker. The beauty of my procedure seemed to consist in its perfect quietness. There was no vulgar bullying, no bravado of any sort, no choleric hectoring, no striding to and fro across the apartment, jerking out vehement commands for Bartleby to bundle himself off with his beggarly traps.[3] Nothing of the kind. Without loudly bidding Bartleby depart—as an inferior genius might have done—I *assumed* the ground that depart he must; and upon that assumption built all I had to say. The more I thought over my procedure, the more I was charmed with it. Nevertheless, next morning, upon awakening, I had my doubts,—I had somehow slept off the fumes of vanity. One of the coolest and wisest hours a man has, is just after he awakes in the morning. My procedure seemed as sagacious as ever,—but only in theory. How it would prove in practice—there was the rub. It was truly a beautiful thought to have assumed Bartleby's departure; but, after all, that assumption was simply my own, and none of Bartleby's. The great point was, not whether I had assumed that he would quit me, but whether he would prefer so to do. He was more a man of preferences than assumptions.

After breakfast, I walked down town, arguing the probabilities *pro* and *con*. One moment I thought it would prove a miserable failure, and Bartleby would be found all alive at my office as usual; the next moment it seemed certain that I should see his chair empty. And so I kept veering about. At the corner of Broadway and Canal Street, I saw quite an excited group of people standing in earnest conversation.

"I'll take odds he doesn't," said a voice as I passed.

"Doesn't go?—done!" said I, "put up your money."

I was instinctively putting my hand in my pocket to produce my own, when I remembered that this was an election day. The words I had overheard bore no reference to Bartleby, but to the success or non-success of some candidate for the mayoralty. In my intent frame of mind, I had, as it were, imagined that all Broadway shared in my excitement, and were debating the same question with me. I passed on, very thankful that the uproar of the street screened my momentary absent-mindedness.

As I had intended, I was earlier than usual at my office door. I stood listening for a moment. All was still. He must be gone. I tried the knob. The door was locked. Yes, my procedure had worked to a charm; he indeed must be vanished. Yet a certain melancholy mixed with this: I was almost sorry for my brilliant success. I was fumbling under the door mat for the key, which Bartleby was to have left there

3. Personal belongings.

for me, when accidentally my knee knocked against a panel, producing a summoning sound, and in response a voice came to me from within—"Not yet; I am occupied."

It was Bartleby.

I was thunderstruck. For an instant I stood like the man who, pipe in mouth, was killed one cloudless afternoon long ago in Virginia, by summer lightning; at his own warm open window he was killed, and remained leaning out there upon the dreamy afternoon, till some one touched him, and he fell.

"Not gone!" I murmured at last. But again obeying that wondrous ascendancy which the inscrutable scrivener had over me—and from which ascendancy, for all my chafing, I could not completely escape—I slowly went down stairs and out into the street, and while walking round the block, considered what I should next do in this unheard-of perplexity. Turn the man out by an actual thrusting I could not; to drive him away by calling him hard names would not do; calling in the police was an unpleasant idea; and yet, permit him to enjoy his cadaverous triumph over me,—this too I could not think of. What was to be done? or, if nothing could be done, was there anything further that I could *assume* in the matter? Yes, as before I had prospectively assumed that Bartleby would depart, so now I might retrospectively assume that departed he was. In the legitimate carrying out of this assumption, I might enter my office in a great hurry, and pretending not to see Bartleby at all, walk straight against him as if he were air. Such a proceeding would in a singular degree have the appearance of a home-thrust.[4] It was hardly possible that Bartleby could withstand such an application of the doctrine of assumptions. But, upon second thought, the success of the plan seemed rather dubious. I resolved to argue the matter over with him again.

"Bartleby," said I, entering the office, with a quietly severe expression, "I am seriously displeased. I am pained, Bartleby. I had thought better of you. I had imagined you of such a gentlemanly organization, that in any delicate dilemma a slight hint would suffice—in short, an assumption. But it appears I am deceived. Why," I added, unaffectedly starting, "you have not even touched that money yet," pointing to it, just where I had left it the evening previous.

He answered nothing.

"Will you, or will you not, quit me?" I now demanded in a sudden passion, advancing close to him.

"I would prefer *not* to quit you," he replied, gently emphasizing the *not*.

4. I.e., an action that accomplishes its purpose.

"What earthly right have you to stay here? Do you pay any rent? Do you pay my taxes? Or is this property yours?"

He answered nothing.

"Are you ready to go on and write now? Are your eyes recovered? Could you copy a small paper for me this morning? or help examine a few lines? or step round to the Post Office? In a word, will you do any thing at all, to give a colouring to your refusal to depart the premises?"

He silently retired into his hermitage.

I was now in such a state of nervous resentment that I thought it but prudent to check myself, at present, from further demonstrations. Bartleby and I were alone. I remembered the tragedy of the unfortunate Adams and the still more unfortunate Colt[5] in the solitary office of the latter; and how poor Colt, being dreadfully incensed by Adams, and imprudently permitting himself to get wildly excited, was at unawares hurried into his fatal act—an act which certainly no man could possibly deplore more than the actor himself. Often it had occurred to me in my ponderings upon the subject, that had that altercation taken place in the public street, or at a private residence, it would not have terminated as it did. It was the circumstance of being alone in a solitary office, upstairs, of a building entirely unhallowed by humanizing domestic associations—an uncarpeted office, doubtless, of a dusty, haggard sort of appearance;—this it must have been, which greatly helped to enhance the irritable desperation of the hapless Colt.

But when this old Adam[6] of resentment rose in me and tempted me concerning Bartleby, I grappled him and threw him. How? Why, simply by recalling the divine injunction: "A new commandment give I unto you, that ye love one another."[7] Yes, this it was that saved me. Aside from higher considerations, charity often operates as a vastly wise and prudent principle—a great safeguard to its possessor. Men have committed murder for jealousy's sake, and anger's sake, and hatred's sake, and selfishness' sake, and spiritual pride's sake; but no man that ever I heard of, ever committed a diabolical murder for sweet charity's sake. Mere self-interest, then, if no better motive can be enlisted, should, especially with high-tempered men, prompt all beings to charity and philanthropy. At any rate, upon the occasion in question, I strove to drown my exasperated feelings towards the scrivener by benevolently constructing his conduct. Poor fellow, poor fellow! thought I, he doesn't mean any thing; and besides, he has seen hard times, and ought to be indulged.

I endeavored also immediately to occupy myself, and at the same

5. In 1841 John C. Colt, brother of the famous gunmaker, killed Samuel Adams, a printer, when he hit him on the head during a fight. 6. The sinful element in man. 7. John 13:34 and John 15:17.

time to comfort my despondency. I tried to fancy that in the course of the morning, at such time as might prove agreeable to him, Bartleby, of his own free accord, would emerge from his hermitage, and take up some decided line of march in the direction of the door. But no. Half-past twelve o'clock came; Turkey began to glow in the face, overturn his inkstand, and become generally obstreperous; Nippers abated down into quietude and courtesy; Ginger Nut munched his noon apple; and Bartleby remained standing at his window in one of his profoundest dead-wall reveries. Will it be credited? Ought I to acknowledge it? That afternoon I left the office without saying one further word to him.

Some days now passed, during which, at leisure intervals I looked a little into "Edwards on the Will," and "Priestley on Necessity."[8] Under the circumstances, those books induced a salutary feeling. Gradually I slid into the persuasion that these troubles of mine, touching the scrivener, had been all predestinated from eternity, and Bartleby was billeted upon me for some mysterious purpose of an all-wise Providence, which it was not for a mere mortal like me to fathom. Yes, Bartleby, stay there behind your screen, thought I; I shall persecute you no more; you are harmless and noiseless as any of these old chairs; in short, I never feel so private as when I know you are here. At least I see it, I feel it; I penetrate to the predestinated purpose of my life. I am content. Others may have loftier parts to enact; but my mission in this world, Bartleby, is to furnish you with office-room for such period as you may see fit to remain.

I believe that this wise and blessed frame of mind would have continued with me, had it not been for the unsolicited and uncharitable remarks obtruded upon me by my professional friends who visited the rooms. But thus it often is, that the constant friction of illiberal minds wears out at last the best resolves of the more generous. Though to be sure, when I reflected upon it, it was not strange that people entering my office should be struck by the peculiar aspect of the unaccountable Bartleby, and so be tempted to throw out some sinister observations concerning him. Sometimes an attorney having business with me, and calling at my office, and finding no one but the scrivener there, would undertake to obtain some sort of precise information from him touching my whereabouts; but without heeding his idle talk, Bartleby would remain standing immovable in the middle of the room. So, after contemplating him in that position for a time, the attorney would depart, no wiser than he came.

Also, when a Reference[9] was going on, and the room full of law-

8. The reference is obscure because of the form Melville has given the titles, but the books indicated are probably *The Freedom of the Will* by Jonathan Edwards (1703–1758) and *The Doctrine of Philosophical Necessity* by Joseph Priestley (1733–1804). The theses of these two books conform to the "persuasion" Melville here describes. 9. Conference.

yers and witnesses and business was driving fast, some deeply occupied legal gentleman present, seeing Bartleby wholly unemployed, would request him to run round to his (the legal gentleman's) office and fetch some papers for him. Thereupon, Bartleby would tranquilly decline, and yet remain idle as before. Then the lawyer would give a great stare, and turn to me. And what could I say? At last I was made aware that all through the circle of my professional acquaintance, a whisper of wonder was running round, having reference to the strange creature I kept at my office. This worried me very much. And as the idea came upon me of his possibly turning out a long-lived man, and keep occupying my chambers, and denying my authority; and perplexing my visitors; and scandalizing my professional reputation; and casting a general gloom over the premises; keeping soul and body together to the last upon his savings (for doubtless he spent but half a dime a day), and in the end perhaps outlive me, and claim possession of my office by right of his perpetual occupancy: as all these dark anticipations crowded upon me more and more, and my friends continually intruded their relentless remarks upon the apparition in my room, a great change was wrought in me. I resolved to gather all my faculties together, and for ever rid me of this intolerable incubus.[1]

Ere revolving any complicated project, however, adapted to this end, I first simply suggested to Bartleby the propriety of his permanent departure. In a calm and serious tone, I commended the idea to his careful and mature consideration. But having taken three days to meditate upon it, he apprised me that his original determination remained the same; in short, that he still preferred to abide with me.

What shall I do? I now said to myself, buttoning up my coat to the last button. What shall I do? what ought I to do? what does conscience say I *should* do with this man, or rather ghost? Rid myself of him, I must; go, he shall. But how? You will not thrust him, the poor, pale, passive mortal,—you will not thrust such a helpless creature out of your door? you will not dishonour yourself by such cruelty? No, I will not, I cannot do that. Rather would I let him live and die here, and then mason up his remains in the wall. What then will you do? For all your coaxing, he will not budge. Bribes he leaves under your own paper-weight on your table; in short, it is quite plain that he prefers to cling to you.

Then something severe, something unusual must be done. What! surely you will not have him collared by a constable, and commit his innocent pallor to the common jail? And upon what ground could you procure such a thing to be done?—a vagrant, is he? What! he a vagrant, a wanderer, who refuses to budge? It is because he will *not* be a vagrant,

1. Imaginary demon supposed to descend on sleepers.

then, that you seek to count him *as* a vagrant. That is too absurd. No visible means of support: there I have him. Wrong again: for indubitably he *does* support himself, and that is the only unanswerable proof that any man can show of his possessing the means so to do. No more then. Since he will not quit me, I must quit him. I will change my offices; I will move elsewhere; and give him fair notice, that if I find him on my new premises I will then proceed against him as a common trespasser.

Acting accordingly, next day I thus addressed him: "I find these chambers too far from the City Hall; the air is unwholesome. In a word, I propose to remove my offices next week, and shall no longer require your services. I tell you this now, in order that you may seek another place."

He made no reply, and nothing more was said.

On the appointed day I engaged carts and men, proceeded to my chambers, and having but little furniture, every thing was removed in a few hours. Throughout all, the scrivener remained standing behind the screen, which I directed to be removed the last thing. It was withdrawn; and being folded up like a huge folio, left him the motionless occupant of a naked room. I stood in the entry watching him a moment, while something from within me upbraided me.

I re-entered, with my hand in my pocket—and—and my heart in my mouth.

"Good-bye, Bartleby; I am going—good-bye, and God some way bless you; and take that," slipping something in his hand. But it dropped upon the floor, and then—strange to say—I tore myself from him whom I had so longed to be rid of.

Established in my new quarters, for a day or two I kept the door locked, and started at every footfall in the passages. When I returned to my rooms after any little absence, I would pause at the threshold for an instant, and attentively listen, ere applying my key. But these fears were needless. Bartleby never came nigh me.

I thought all was going well, when a perturbed looking stranger visited me, inquiring whether I was the person who had recently occupied rooms at No. —— Wall-street.

Full of forebodings, I replied that I was.

"Then sir," said the stranger, who proved a lawyer, "you are responsible for the man you left there. He refuses to do any copying, he refuses to do any thing; he says he prefers not to; and he refuses to quit the premises."

"I am very sorry, sir," said I, with assumed tranquillity, but an inward tremor, "but, really, the man you allude to is nothing to me—he is no relation or apprentice of mine, that you should hold me responsible for him."

"In mercy's name, who is he?"

"I certainly cannot inform you. I know nothing about him. Formerly I employed him as a copyist; but he has done nothing for me now for some time past."

"I shall settle him then,—good morning, sir."

Several days passed, and I heard nothing more; and though I often felt a charitable prompting to call at the place and see poor Bartleby, yet a certain squeamishness of I know not what withheld me.

All is over with him, by this time, thought I at last, when through another week no further intelligence reached me. But coming to my room the day after, I found several persons waiting at my door in a high state of nervous excitement.

"That's the man—here he comes," cried the foremost one, whom I recognized as the lawyer who had previously called upon me alone.

"You must take him away, sir, at once," cried a portly person among them, advancing upon me, and whom I knew to be the landlord of No. ____ Wall-street. "These gentlemen, my tenants, cannot stand it any longer; Mr. B____," pointing to the lawyer, "has turned him out of his room, and he now persists in haunting the building generally, sitting upon the banisters of the stairs by day, and sleeping in the entry by night. Everybody is concerned; clients are leaving the offices; some fears are entertained of a mob; something you must do, and that without delay."

Aghast at this torrent, I fell back before it, and would fain have locked myself in my new quarters. In vain I persisted that Bartleby was nothing to me—no more than to any one else. In vain:—I was the last person known to have anything to do with him, and they held me to the terrible account. Fearful then of being exposed in the papers (as one person present obscurely threatened) I considered the matter, and at length said, that if the lawyer would give me a confidential interview with the scrivener, in his (the lawyer's) own room, I would that afternoon strive my best to rid them of the nuisance they complained of.

Going up stairs to my old haunt, there was Bartleby silently sitting upon the banister at the landing.

"What are you doing here, Bartleby?" said I.

"Sitting upon the banister," he mildly replied.

I motioned him into the lawyer's room, who then left us.

"Bartleby," said I, "are you aware that you are the cause of great tribulation to me, by persisting in occupying the entry after being dismissed from the office?"

No answer.

"Now one of two things must take place. Either you must do something, or something must be done to you. Now what sort of business would you like to engage in? Would you like to re-engage in copying for some one?"

"No; I would prefer not to make any change."

"Would you like a clerkship in a dry-goods store?"

"There is too much confinement about that. No, I would not like a clerkship; but I am not particular."

"Too much confinement," I cried, "why you keep yourself confined all the time!"

"I would prefer not to take a clerkship," he rejoined, as if to settle that little item at once.

"How would a bar tender's business suit you? There is no trying of the eyesight in that."

"I would not like it at all; though, as I said before, I am not particular."

His unwonted wordiness inspirited me. I returned to the charge.

"Well then, would you like to travel through the country collecting bills for the merchants? That would improve your health."

"No, I would prefer to be doing something else."

"How then would going as a companion to Europe to entertain some young gentleman with your conversation,—how would that suit you?"

"Not at all. It does not strike me that there is anything definite about that. I like to be stationary. But I am not particular."

"Stationary you shall be then," I cried, now losing all patience, and for the first time in all my exasperating connection with him fairly flying into a passion. "If you do not go away from these premises before night, I shall feel bound—indeed I *am* bound—to—to—to quit the premises myself!" I rather absurdly concluded, knowing not with what possible threat to try to frighten his immobility into compliance. Despairing of all further efforts, I was precipitately leaving him, when a final thought occurred to me—one which had not been wholly unindulged before.

"Bartleby," said I, in the kindest tone I could assume under such exciting circumstances, "will you go home with me now—not to my office, but my dwelling—and remain there till we can conclude upon some convenient arrangement for you at our leisure? Come, let us start now, right away."

"No: at present I would prefer not to make any change at all."

I answered nothing; but effectually dodging every one by the suddenness and rapidity of my flight, rushed from the building, ran up Wall street towards Broadway, and jumping into the first omnibus was soon removed from pursuit. As soon as tranquillity returned I distinctly perceived that I had now done all that I possibly could, both in respect to the demands of the landlord and his tenants, and with regard to my own desire and sense of duty, to benefit Bartleby, and shield him from rude persecution. I now strove to be entirely care-free and quiescent; and my conscience justified me in the attempt; though indeed it was not so successful as I could have wished. So fearful was I of being again hunted out by the incensed landlord and his exasperated tenants, that, surrendering my business to Nippers, for a few days I drove about the upper part of the town and through the suburbs, in my rockaway;[2] crossed over to Jersey City and Hoboken, and paid fugitive visits to Manhattanville and Astoria. In fact I almost lived in my rockaway for the time.

When again I entered my office, lo, a note from the landlord lay upon the desk. I opened it with trembling hands. It informed me that the writer had sent to the police, and had Bartleby removed to the Tombs[3] as a vagrant. Moreover, since I knew more about him than any one else, he wished me to appear at that place, and make a suitable statement of the facts. These tidings had a conflicting effect upon me. At first I was indignant; but at last almost approved. The landlord's energetic, summary disposition had led him to adopt a procedure which I do not think I would have decided upon myself; and yet as a last resort, under such peculiar circumstances, it seemed the only plan.

As I afterwards learned, the poor scrivener, when told that he must be conducted to the Tombs, offered not the slightest obstacle, but in his pale, unmoving way silently acquiesced.

Some of the compassionate and curious bystanders joined the party; and headed by one of the constables, arm in arm with Bartleby the silent procession filed its way through all the noise, and heat, and joy of the roaring thoroughfares at noon.

The same day I received the note I went to the Tombs, or, to speak more properly, the Halls of Justice. Seeking the right officer, I stated the purpose of my call, and was informed that the individual I described was indeed within. I then assured the functionary that Bartleby was a perfectly honest man, and greatly to be a compassionated, (however unaccountable) eccentric. I narrated all I knew, and closed by suggesting the idea of letting him remain in as indulgent confinement as possible till something less harsh might be done—though indeed I hardly knew what. At all events, if nothing else could be decided upon, the alms-house must receive him. I then begged to have an interview.

Being under no disgraceful charge, and quite serene and harmless in all his ways, they had permitted him freely to wander about the prison, and especially in the inclosed grass-platted yards thereof. And

2. Light, four-wheeled carriage. 3. The Manhattan House of Detention is often called "the Tombs" because of its distinctive Egyptian architecture.

so I found him there, standing all alone in the quietest of the yards, his face towards a high wall—while all around, from the narrow slits of the jail windows, I thought I saw peering out upon him the eyes of murderers and thieves.

"Bartleby!"

"I know you," he said, without looking round,—"and I want nothing to say to you."

"It was not I that brought you here, Bartleby," said I, keenly pained at his implied suspicion. "And to you, this should not be so vile a place. Nothing reproachful attaches to you by being here. And see, it is not so sad a place as one might think. Look, there is the sky and here is the grass."

"I know where I am," he replied, but would say nothing more, and so I left him.

As I entered the corridor again, a broad, meat-like man, in an apron, accosted me, and jerking his thumb over his shoulder said—"Is that your friend?"

"Yes."

"Does he want to starve? If he does, let him live on the prison fare, that's all."

"Who are you?" asked I, not knowing what to make of such an unofficially speaking person in such a place.

"I am the grub-man. Such gentlemen as have friends here, hire me to provide them with something good to eat."

"Is this so?" said I, turning to the turnkey.

He said it was.

"Well then," said I, slipping some silver into the grub-man's hands (for so they called him), "I want you to give particular attention to my friend there; let him have the best dinner you can get. And you must be as polite to him as possible."

"Introduce me, will you?" said the grub-man, looking at me with an expression which seemed to say he was all impatience for an opportunity to give a specimen of his breeding.

Thinking it would prove of benefit to the scrivener, I acquiesced; and asking the grub-man his name, went up with him to Bartleby.

"Bartleby, this is Mr. Cutlets; you will find him very useful to you."

"Your sarvant, sir, your sarvant," said the grub-man, making a low salutation behind his apron. "Hope you find it pleasant here, sir;—spacious grounds—cool apartments, sir—hope you'll stay with us some time—try to make it agreeable. May Mrs. Cutlets and I have the pleasure of your company to dinner, sir, in Mrs. Cutlets' private room?"

"I prefer not to dine to-day," said Bartleby, turning away. "It would disagree with me; I am unused to dinners." So saying, he slowly moved to the other side of the inclosure and took up a position fronting the dead-wall.

"How's this?" said the grub-man, addressing me with a stare of astonishment. "He's odd, aint he?"

"I think he is a little deranged," said I, sadly.

"Deranged? deranged is it? Well now, upon my word, I thought that friend of yourn was a gentleman forger; they are always pale and genteel-like, them forgers. I can't help pity 'em—can't help it, sir. Did you know Monroe Edwards?" he added touchingly, and paused. Then, laying his hand pityingly on my shoulder, sighed, "he died of consumption at Sing-Sing.[4] So you weren't acquainted with Monroe?"

"No, I was never socially acquainted with any forgers. But I cannot stop longer. Look to my friend yonder. You will not lose by it. I will see you again."

Some few days after this, I again obtained admission to the Tombs, and went through the corridors in quest of Bartleby; but without finding him.

"I saw him coming from his cell not long ago," said a turnkey, "maybe he's gone to loiter in the yards."

So I went in that direction.

"Are you looking for the silent man?" said another turnkey passing me. "Yonder he lies—sleeping in the yard there. 'Tis not twenty minutes since I saw him lie down."

The yard was entirely quiet. It was not accessible to the common prisoners. The surrounding walls, of amazing thickness, kept off all sounds behind them. The Egyptian character of the masonry weighed upon me with its gloom. But a soft imprisoned turf grew under foot. The heart of the eternal pyramids, it seemed, wherein, by some strange magic, through the clefts grass-seed, dropped by birds, had sprung.

Strangely huddled at the base of the wall—his knees drawn up, and lying on his side, his head touching the cold stones—I saw the wasted Bartleby. But nothing stirred. I paused; then went close up to him; stooped over, and saw that his dim eyes were open; otherwise he seemed profoundly sleeping. Something prompted me to touch him. I felt his hand, when a tingling shiver ran up my arm and down my spine to my feet.

The round face of the grub-man peered upon me now. "His dinner is ready. Won't he dine to-day, either? Or does he live without dining?"

"Lives without dining," said I, and closed the eyes.

4. State prison at Ossining, New York.

"Eh!—He's asleep, aint he?"

"With kings and counsellors,"[5] murmured I.

There would seem little need for proceeding further in this history. Imagination will readily supply the meagre recital of poor Bartleby's interment. But ere parting with the reader, let me say, that if this little narrative has sufficiently interested him, to awaken curiosity as to who Bartleby was, and what manner of life he led prior to the present narrator's making his acquaintance, I can only reply, that in such curiosity I fully share—but am wholly unable to gratify it. Yet here I hardly know whether I should divulge one little item of rumour, which came to my ear a few months after the scrivener's decease. Upon what basis it rested, I could never ascertain; and hence, how true it is I cannot now tell. But inasmuch as this vague report has not been without a certain strange suggestive interest to me, however sad, it may prove the same with some others; and so I will briefly mention it. The report was this: that Bartleby had been a subordinate clerk in the Dead Letter Office[6] at Washington, from which he had been suddenly removed by a change in the administration. When I think over this rumor I cannot adequately express the emotions which seize me. Dead letters! Does it not sound like dead men? Conceive a man by nature and misfortune prone to a pallid hopelessness: can any business seem more fitted to heighten it than that of continually handling these dead letters, and assorting them for the flames? For by the cart-load they are annually burned. Sometimes from out the folded paper the pale clerk takes a ring:—the finger it was meant for, perhaps, moulders in the grave; a bank-note sent in swiftest charity:—he whom it would relieve, nor eats nor hungers any more; pardon for those who died despairing; hope for those who died unhoping; good tidings for those who died stifled by unrelieved calamities. On errands of life, these letters speed to death.

Ah Bartleby! Ah humanity!

---

1. Discuss fully the meaning of Bartleby's "preference."
2. What is the character of the narrator? Is it changed by his association with Bartleby?
3. How does the tone of the narrator's language help to characterize him?
4. What use does Melville make of the setting to develop the theme of the story? What is the theme?
5. Are there any suggestions—either overt or implied—that Bartleby might have been fulfilled by a different occupation?
6. Is the story a satire on the business world? Or on the human condition in general? Explain.

5. Job 3:13–14: ". . . then had I been at rest, With kings and counsellors of the earth, which built desolate places for themselves." 6. Place for storage and disposition of undeliverable mail.

Yukio Mishima

Mishima is the pen name of Kimitake Hiraoka (1925–1970), who was born in Tokyo and educated at the Imperial University in that city. An extremely prolific writer, he was also known as an actor and established himself in the public eye as a spokesman for traditional Japanese virtues amid the cosmopolitanism that accompanied Japan's economic reconstruction after World War II. His public activities led to political organization: he founded the Shield Society, a band of young men who were to be the guardians of modern Japan as the samurai warriors had been in ancient times. Apparently as a gesture of protest against Japan's "spineless" military posture, he committed suicide in 1970—a public display of disemboweling and decapitation quite in keeping with the flamboyance of his entire career. His translated novels include The Temple of the Golden Pavilion *(1959),* After the Banquet *(1963),* The Sailor Who Fell from Grace with the Sea *(1965),* Sun and Steel *(1970), and the tetralogy,* Sea of Fertility *(1975). His translated stories can be found in* Death in Midsummer and Other Stories *(1966).*

Patriotism[1]

I

On the twenty-eighth of February, 1936 (on the third day, that is, of the February 26 incident),[2] Lieutenant Shinji Takeyama of the Konoe Transport Battalion—profoundly disturbed by the knowledge that his closest colleagues had been with the mutineers from the beginning, and indignant at the imminent prospect of Imperial troops attacking Imperial troops—took his officer's sword and ceremonially disemboweled himself in the eight-mat[3] room of his private residence in the sixth block of Aoba-chō, in Yotsuya Ward. His wife, Reiko, followed him, stabbing herself to death. The lieutenant's farewell note consisted of one sentence: "Long live the Imperial Forces." His wife's, after apologies for her unfilial conduct in thus preceding her parents to the grave, concluded: "The day which, for a soldier's wife, had to come, has come.

1. Translated by Geoffrey W. Sargent. 2. An important event in modern Japanese history. A number of young Japanese officers, protesting the corruption and complacency of the government, revolted and assassinated several moderate officials. The result was to intensify the militaristic spirit that led the country into World War II. 3. Japanese room sizes are measured by the number of standard three-by-six-foot straw mats required to cover the floor.

. . ." The last moments of this heroic and dedicated couple were such as to make the gods themselves weep. The lieutenant's age, it should be noted, was thirty-one, his wife's twenty-three; and it was not half a year since the celebration of their marriage.

II

Those who saw the bride and bridegroom in the commemorative photograph—perhaps no less than those actually present at the lieutenant's wedding—had exclaimed in wonder at the bearing of this handsome couple. The lieutenant, majestic in military uniform, stood protectively beside his bride, his right hand resting upon his sword, his officer's cap held at his left side. His expression was severe, and his dark brows and wide-gazing eyes well conveyed the clear integrity of youth. For the beauty of the bride in her white over-robe no comparisons were adequate. In the eyes, round beneath soft brows, in the slender, finely shaped nose, and in the full lips, there was both sensuousness and refinement. One hand, emerging shyly from a sleeve of the over-robe, held a fan, and the tips of the fingers, clustering delicately, were like the bud of a moonflower.

After the suicide, people would take out this photograph and examine it, and sadly reflect that too often there was a curse on these seemingly flawless unions. Perhaps it was no more than imagination, but looking at the picture after the tragedy it almost seemed as if the two young people before the gold-lacquered screen were gazing, each with equal clarity, at the deaths which lay before them.

Thanks to the good offices of their go-between, Lieutenant General Ozeki, they had been able to set themselves up in a new home at Aoba-chō in Yotsuya. "New home" is perhaps misleading. It was an old three-room rented house backing onto a small garden. As neither the six- nor the four-and-a-half-mat room downstairs was favored by the sun, they used the upstairs eight-mat room as both bedroom and guest room. There was no maid, so Reiko was left alone to guard the house in her husband's absence.

The honeymoon trip was dispensed with on the grounds that these were times of national emergency.[4] The two of them had spent the first night of their marriage at this house. Before going to bed, Shinji, sitting erect on the floor with his sword laid before him, had bestowed upon his wife a soldierly lecture. A woman who had become the wife of a soldier should know and resolutely accept that her husband's death might come at any moment. It could be tomorrow. It could be the day

4. Japan was at that time militarily engaged on the mainland of Asia.

after. But, no matter when it came—he asked—was she steadfast in her resolve to accept it? Reiko rose to her feet, pulled open a drawer of the cabinet, and took out what was the most prized of her new possessions, the dagger her mother had given her. Returning to her place, she laid the dagger without a word on the mat before her, just as her husband had laid his sword. A silent understanding was achieved at once, and the lieutenant never again sought to test his wife's resolve.

In the first few months of her marriage Reiko's beauty grew daily more radiant, shining serene like the moon after rain.

As both were possessed of young, vigorous bodies, their relationship was passionate. Nor was this merely a matter of the night. On more than one occasion, returning home straight from maneuvers, and begrudging even the time it took to remove his mud-splashed uniform, the lieutenant had pushed his wife to the floor almost as soon as he had entered the house. Reiko was equally ardent in her response. For a little more or a little less than a month, from the first night of their marriage Reiko knew happiness, and the lieutenant, seeing this, was happy too.

Reiko's body was white and pure, and her swelling breasts conveyed a firm and chaste refusal; but, upon consent, those breasts were lavish with their intimate, welcoming warmth. Even in bed these two were frighteningly and awesomely serious. In the very midst of wild, intoxicating passions, their hearts were sober and serious.

By day the lieutenant would think of his wife in the brief rest periods between training; and all day long, at home, Reiko would recall the image of her husband. Even when apart, however, they had only to look at the wedding photograph for their happiness to be once more confirmed. Reiko felt not the slightest surprise that a man who had been a complete stranger until a few months ago should now have become the sun about which her whole world revolved.

All these things had a moral basis, and were in accordance with the Education Rescript's[5] injunction that "husband and wife should be harmonious." Not once did Reiko contradict her husband, nor did the lieutenant ever find reason to scold his wife. On the god shelf below the stairway, alongside the tablet from the Great Ise Shrine,[6] were set photographs of their Imperial Majesties, and regularly every morning, before leaving for duty, the lieutenant would stand with his wife at this hallowed place and together they would bow their heads low. The offering water was renewed each morning, and the sacred sprig of *sasaki*[7]

5. Code of conduct promulgated by Imperial edict. 6. The shrine in the city of Ise at which the Imperial family was first established as rulers of Japan. *God shelf:* small shrine in the home for burning incense and making offerings to ancestors in Shinto ceremonies. 7. Traditional evergreen plant used in Shinto ceremony.

was always green and fresh. Their lives were lived beneath the solemn protection of the gods and were filled with an intense happiness which set every fiber in their bodies trembling.

III

Although Lord Privy Seal Saitō's[8] house was in their neighborhood, neither of them heard any noise of gunfire on the morning of February 26. It was a bugle, sounding muster in the dim, snowy dawn, when the ten-minute tragedy had already ended, which first disrupted the lieutenant's slumbers. Leaping at once from his bed, and without speaking a word, the lieutenant donned his uniform, buckled on the sword held ready for him by his wife, and hurried swiftly out into the snow-covered streets of the still darkened morning. He did not return until the evening of the twenty-eighth.

Later, from the radio news, Reiko learned the full extent of this sudden eruption of violence. Her life throughout the subsequent two days was lived alone, in complete tranquillity, and behind locked doors.

In the lieutenant's face, as he hurried silently out into the snowy morning, Reiko had read the determination to die. If her husband did not return, her own decision was made: she too would die. Quietly she attended to the disposition of her personal possessions. She chose her sets of visiting kimonos as keepsakes for friends of her schooldays, and she wrote a name and address on the stiff paper wrapping in which each was folded. Constantly admonished by her husband never to think of the morrow, Reiko had not even kept a diary and was now denied the pleasure of assiduously rereading her record of the happiness of the past few months and consigning each page to the fire as she did so. Ranged across the top of the radio were a small china dog, a rabbit, a squirrel, a bear, and a fox. There were also a small vase and a water pitcher. These comprised Reiko's one and only collection. But it would hardly do, she imagined, to give such things as keepsakes. Nor again would it be quite proper to ask specifically for them to be included in the coffin. It seemed to Reiko, as these thoughts passed through her mind, that the expressions on the small animals' faces grew even more lost and forlorn.

Reiko took the squirrel in her hand and looked at it. And then, her thoughts turning to a realm far beyond these child-like affections, she gazed up into the distance at the great sunlike principle which her husband embodied. She was ready, and happy, to be hurtled along to her destruction in that gleaming sun chariot—but now, for these few

8. Member of the Emperor's cabinet assassinated by the rebels.

moments of solitude, she allowed herself to luxuriate in this innocent attachment to trifles. The time when she had genuinely loved these things, however, was long past. Now she merely loved the memory of having once loved them, and their place in her heart had been filled by more intense passions, by a more frenzied happiness. . . . For Reiko had never, even to herself, thought of those soaring joys of the flesh as a mere pleasure. The February cold, and the icy touch of the china squirrel, had numbed Reiko's slender fingers; yet, even so, in her lower limbs, beneath the ordered repetition of the pattern which crossed the skirt of her trim *meisen* kimono,[9] she could feel now, as she thought of the lieutenant's powerful arms reaching out toward her, a hot moistness of the flesh which defied the snows.

She was not in the least afraid of the death hovering in her mind. Waiting alone at home, Reiko firmly believed that everything her husband was feeling or thinking now, his anguish and distress, was leading her—just as surely as the power in his flesh—to a welcome death. She felt as if her body could melt away with ease and be transformed to the merest fraction of her husband's thought.

Listening to the frequent announcements on the radio, she heard the names of several of her husband's colleagues mentioned among those of the insurgents. This was news of death. She followed the developments closely, wondering anxiously, as the situation became daily more irrevocable, why no Imperial ordinance was sent down, and watching what had at first been taken as a movement to restore the nation's honor come gradually to be branded with the infamous name of mutiny. There was no communication from the regiment. At any moment, it seemed, fighting might commence in the city streets, where the remains of the snow still lay.

Toward sundown on the twenty-eighth Reiko was startled by a furious pounding on the front door. She hurried downstairs. As she pulled with fumbling fingers at the bolt, the shape dimly outlined beyond the frosted-glass panel made no sound, but she knew it was her husband. Reiko had never known the bolt on the sliding door to be so stiff. Still it resisted. The door just would not open.

In a moment, almost before she knew she had succeeded, the lieutenant was standing before her on the cement floor inside the porch, muffled in a khaki greatcoat, his top boots heavy with slush from the street. Closing the door behind him, he returned the bolt once more to its socket. With what significance, Reiko did not understand.

"Welcome home."

Reiko bowed deeply, but her husband made no response. As he

9. An everyday garment, equivalent to a housedress.

had already unfastened his sword and was about to remove his greatcoat, Reiko moved around behind to assist. The coat, which was cold and damp and had lost the odor of horse dung it normally exuded when exposed to the sun, weighed heavily upon her arm. Draping it across a hanger, and cradling the sword and leather belt in her sleeves, she waited while her husband removed his top boots and then followed behind him into the "living room." This was the six-mat room downstairs.

Seen in the clear light from the lamp, her husband's face, covered with a heavy growth of bristle, was almost unrecognizably wasted and thin. The cheeks were hollow, their luster and resilience gone. In his normal good spirits he would have changed into old clothes as soon as he was home and have pressed her to get supper at once, but now he sat before the table still in his uniform, his head drooping dejectedly. Reiko refrained from asking whether she should prepare the supper.

After an interval the lieutenant spoke.

"I knew nothing. They hadn't asked me to join. Perhaps out of consideration, because I was newly married. Kanō, and Homma too, and Yamaguchi."

Reiko recalled momentarily the faces of high-spirited young officers, friends of her husband, who had come to the house occasionally as guests.

"There may be an Imperial ordinance sent down tomorrow. They'll be posted as rebels, I imagine. I shall be in command of a unit with orders to attack them. . . . I can't do it. It's impossible to do a thing like that."

He spoke again.

"They've taken me off guard duty, and I have permission to return home for one night. Tomorrow morning, without question, I must leave to join the attack. I can't do it, Reiko."

Reiko sat erect with lowered eyes. She understood clearly that her husband had spoken of his death. The lieutenant was resolved. Each word, being rooted in death, emerged sharply and with powerful significance against this dark, unmovable background. Although the lieutenant was speaking of his dilemma, already there was no room in his mind for vacillation.

However, there was a clarity, like the clarity of a stream fed from melting snows, in the silence which rested between them. Sitting in his own home after the long two-day ordeal, and looking across at the face of his beautiful wife, the lieutenant was for the first time experiencing true peace of mind. For he had at once known, though she said nothing, that his wife divined the resolve which lay beneath his words.

"Well, then . . ." The lieutenant's eyes opened wide. Despite his exhaustion they were strong and clear, and now for the first time they looked straight into the eyes of his wife. "Tonight I shall cut my stomach."

Reiko did not flinch.

Her round eyes showed tension, as taut as the clang of a bell.

"I am ready," she said. "I ask permission to accompany you."

The lieutenant felt almost mesmerized by the strength in those eyes. His words flowed swiftly and easily, like the utterances of a man in delirium, and it was beyond his understanding how permission in a matter of such weight could be expressed so casually.

"Good. We'll go together. But I want you as a witness, first, for my own suicide. Agreed?"

When this was said a sudden release of abundant happiness welled up in both their hearts. Reiko was deeply affected by the greatness of her husband's trust in her. It was vital for the lieutenant, whatever else might happen, that there should be no irregularity in his death. For that reason there had to be a witness. The fact that he had chosen his wife for this was the first mark of his trust. The second, and even greater mark, was that though he had pledged that they should die together he did not intend to kill his wife first—he had deferred her death to a time when he would no longer be there to verify it. If the lieutenant had been a suspicious husband, he would doubtless, as in the usual suicide pact, have chosen to kill his wife first.

When Reiko said, "I ask permission to accompany you," the lieutenant felt these words to be the final fruit of the education which he had himself given his wife, starting on the first night of their marriage, and which had schooled her, when the moment came, to say what had to be said without a shadow of hesitation. This flattered the lieutenant's opinion of himself as a self-reliant man. He was not so romantic or conceited as to imagine that the words were spoken spontaneously, out of love for her husband.

With happiness welling almost too abundantly in their hearts, they could not help smiling at each other. Reiko felt as if she had returned to her wedding night.

Before her eyes was neither pain nor death. She seemed to see only a free and limitless expanse opening out into vast distances.

"The water is hot. Will you take your bath now?"

"Ah yes, of course."

"And supper . . . ?"

The words were delivered in such level, domestic tones that the lieutenant came near to thinking, for the fraction of a second, that everything had been a hallucination.

"I don't think we'll need supper. But perhaps you could warm some Sake?"[1]

"As you wish."

As Reiko rose and took a *tanzen* gown[2] from the cabinet for after the bath, she purposely directed her husband's attention to the opened drawer. The lieutenant rose, crossed to the cabinet, and looked inside. From the ordered array of paper wrappings he read, one by one, the addresses of the keepsakes. There was no grief in the lieutenant's response to this demonstration of heroic resolve. His heart was filled with tenderness. Like a husband who is proudly shown the childish purchases of a young wife, the lieutenant, overhelmed by affection, lovingly embraced his wife from behind and implanted a kiss upon her neck.

Reiko felt the roughness of the lieutenant's unshaven skin against her neck. This sensation, more than being just a thing of this world, was for Reiko almost the world itself, but now—with the feeling that it was soon to be lost forever—it had freshness beyond all her experience. Each moment had its own vital strength, and the senses in every corner of her body were reawakened. Accepting her husband's caresses from behind, Reiko raised herself on the tips of her toes, letting the vitality seep through her entire body.

"First the bath, and then, after some Sake . . . lay out the bedding upstairs, will you?"

The lieutenant whispered the words into his wife's ear. Reiko silently nodded.

Flinging off his uniform, the lieutenant went to the bath. To faint background noises of slopping water Reiko tended the charcoal brazier in the living room and began the preparations for warming the sake.

Taking the *tanzen*, a sash, and some underclothes, she went to the bathroom to ask how the water was. In the midst of a coiling cloud of steam the lieutenant was sitting cross-legged on the floor, shaving, and she could dimly discern the rippling movements of the muscles on his damp, powerful back as they responded to the movement of his arms.

There was nothing to suggest a time of any special significance. Reiko, going busily about her tasks, was preparing side dishes from odds and ends in stock. Her hands did not tremble. If anything, she managed even more efficiently and smoothly than usual. From time to time, it is true, there was a strange throbbing deep within her breast. Like distant lightning, it had a moment of sharp intensity and then

1. Rice wine. 2. Long, thick kimono, padded for warmth.

vanished without trace. Apart from that, nothing was in any way out of the ordinary.

The lieutenant, shaving in the bathroom, felt his warmed body miraculously healed at last of the desperate tiredness of the days of indecision and filled—in spite of the death which lay ahead—with pleasurable anticipation. The sound of his wife going about her work came to him faintly. A healthy physical craving, submerged for two days, reasserted itself.

The lieutenant was confident there had been no impurity in that joy they had experienced when resolving upon death. They had both sensed at that moment—though not, of course, in any clear and conscious way—that those permissible pleasures which they shared in private were once more beneath the protection of Righteousness and Divine Power, and of a complete and unassailable morality. On looking into each other's eyes and discovering there an honorable death, they had felt themselves safe once more behind steel walls which none could destroy, encased in an impenetrable armor of Beauty and Truth. Thus, so far from seeing any inconsistency or conflict between the urges of his flesh and the sincerity of his patriotism, the lieutenant was even able to regard the two as parts of the same thing.

Thrusting his face close to the dark, cracked, misted wall mirror, the lieutenant shaved himself with great care. This would be his death face. There must be no unsightly blemishes. The clean-shaven face gleamed once more with a youthful luster, seeming to brighten the darkness of the mirror. There was a certain elegance, he even felt, in the association of death with this radiantly healthy face.

Just as it looked now, this would become his death face! Already, in fact, it had half departed from the lieutenant's personal possession and had become the bust above a dead soldier's memorial. As an experiment he closed his eyes tight. Everything was wrapped in blackness, and he was no longer a living, seeing creature.

Returning from the bath, the traces of the shave glowing faintly blue beneath his smooth cheeks, he seated himself beside the now well-kindled charcoal brazier. Busy though Reiko was, he noticed, she had found time lightly to touch up her face. Her cheeks were gay and her lips moist. There was no shadow of sadness to be seen. Truly, the lieutenant felt, as he saw this mark of his young wife's passionate nature, he had chosen the wife he ought to have chosen.

As soon as the lieutenant had drained his sake cup he offered it to Reiko. Reiko had never before tasted sake, but she accepted without hesitation and sipped timidly.

"Come here," the lieutenant said.

Reiko moved to her husband's side and was embraced as she leaned backward across his lap. Her breast was in violent commotion, as if sadness, joy, and the potent sake were mingling and reacting within her. The lieutenant looked down into his wife's face. It was the last face he would see in this world, the last face he would see of his wife. The lieutenant scrutinized the face minutely, with the eyes of a traveler bidding farewell to splendid vistas which he will never revisit. It was a face he could not tire of looking at—the features regular yet not cold, the lips lightly closed with a soft strength. The lieutenant kissed those lips, unthinkingly. And suddenly, though there was not the slightest distortion of the face into the unsightliness of sobbing, he noticed that tears were welling slowly from beneath the long lashes of the closed eyes and brimming over into a glistening stream.

When, a little later, the lieutenant urged that they should move to the upstairs bedroom, his wife replied that she would follow after taking a bath. Climbing the stairs alone to the bedroom, where the air was already warmed by the gas heater, the lieutenant lay down on the bedding with arms outstretched and legs apart. Even the time at which he lay waiting for his wife to join him was no later and no earlier than usual.

He folded his hands beneath his head and gazed at the dark boards of the ceiling in the dimness beyond the range of the standard lamp. Was it death he was now waiting for? Or a wild ecstasy of the senses? The two seemed to overlap, almost as if the object of this bodily desire was death itself. But, however that might be, it was certain that never before had the lieutenant tasted such total freedom.

There was the sound of a car outside the window. He could hear the screech of its tires skidding in the snow piled at the side of the street. The sound of its horn re-echoed from nearby walls. . . . Listening to these noises he had the feeling that this house rose like a solitary island in the ocean of a society going as restlessly about its business as ever. All around, vastly and untidily, stretched the country for which he grieved. He was to give his life for it. But would that great country, with which he was prepared to remonstrate to the extent of destroying himself, take the slightest heed of his death? He did not know; and it did not matter. His was a battlefield without glory, a battlefield where none could display deeds of valor: it was the front line of the spirit.

Reiko's footsteps sounded on the stairway. The steep stairs in this old house creaked badly. There were fond memories in that creaking, and many a time, while waiting in bed, the lieutenant had listened to its welcome sound. At the thought that he would hear it no more he listened with intense concentration, striving for every corner of every moment of this precious time to be filled with the sound of those soft footfalls on the creaking stairway. The moments seemed transformed to jewels, sparkling with inner light.

Reiko wore a Nagoya sash about the waist of her *yukata*,[3] but as the lieutenant reached toward it, its redness sobered by the dimness of the light, Reiko's hand moved to his assistance and the sash fell away, slithering swiftly to the floor. As she stood before him, still in her *yukata*, the lieutenant inserted his hands through the side slits beneath each sleeve, intending to embrace her as she was; but at the touch of his finger tips upon the warm naked flesh, and as the armpits closed gently about his hands, his whole body was suddenly aflame.

In a few moments the two lay naked before the glowing gas heater.

Neither spoke the thought, but their hearts, their bodies, and their pounding breasts blazed with the knowledge that this was the very last time. It was as if the words "The Last Time" were spelled out, in invisible brushstrokes, across every inch of their bodies.

The lieutenant drew his wife close and kissed her vehemently. As their tongues explored each other's mouths, reaching out into the smooth, moist interior, they felt as if the still-unknown agonies of death had tempered their senses to the keenness of red-hot steel. The agonies they could not yet feel, the distant pains of death, had refined their awareness of pleasure.

"This is the last time I shall see your body," said the lieutenant. "Let me look at it closely." And, tilting the shade on the lampstand to one side, he directed the rays along the full length of Reiko's outstretched form.

Reiko lay still with her eyes closed. The light from the low lamp clearly revealed the majestic sweep of her white flesh. The lieutenant, not without a touch of egocentricity, rejoiced that he would never see this beauty crumble in death.

At his leisure, the lieutenant allowed the unforgettable spectacle to engrave itself upon his mind. With one hand he fondled the hair, with the other he softly stroked the magnificent face, implanting kisses here and there where his eyes lingered. The quiet coldness of the high, tapering forehead, the closed eyes with their long lashes beneath faintly etched brows, the set of the finely shaped nose, the gleam of teeth glimpsed between full, regular lips, the soft cheeks and the small, wise chin . . . these things conjured up in the lieutenant's mind the vision of a truly radiant death face, and again and again he pressed his lips tight against the white throat—where Reiko's own hand was soon to strike—and the throat reddened faintly beneath his kisses. Returning to the mouth he laid his lips against it with the gentlest of pressures, and moved them rhythmically over Reiko's with the light rolling motion of a small boat. If he closed his eyes, the world became a rocking cradle.

3. Thin cotton kimono, worn in summer or in the house.

Wherever the lieutenant's eyes moved his lips faithfully followed. The high, swelling breasts, surmounted by nipples like the buds of a wild cherry, hardened as the lieutenant's lips closed about them. The arms flowed smoothly downward from each side of the breast, tapering toward the wrists, yet losing nothing of their roundness or symmetry, and at their tips were those delicate fingers which had held the fan at the wedding ceremony. One by one, as the lieutenant kissed them, the fingers withdrew behind their neighbor as if in shame. . . . The natural hollow curving between the bosom and the stomach carried in its lines a suggestion not only of softness but of resilient strength, and while it gave forewarning of the rich curves spreading outward from here to the hips it had, in itself, an appearance only of restraint and proper discipline. The whiteness and richness of the stomach and hips was like milk brimming in a great bowl, and the sharply shadowed dip of the navel could have been the fresh impress of a raindrop, fallen there that very moment. Where the shadows gathered more thickly, hair clustered, gentle and sensitive, and as the agitation mounted in the now no longer passive body there hung over this region a scent like the smoldering of fragrant blossoms, growing steadily more pervasive.

At length, in a tremulous voice, Reiko spoke.

"Show me. . . . Let me look too, for the last time."

Never before had he heard from his wife's lips so strong and unequivocal a request. It was as if something which her modesty had wished to keep hidden to the end had suddenly burst its bonds of constraint. The lieutenant obediently lay back and surrendered himself to his wife. Lithely she raised her white, trembling body, and—burning with an innocent desire to return to her husband what he had done for her—placed two white fingers on the lieutenant's eyes, which gazed fixedly up at her, and gently stroked them shut.

Suddenly overwhelmed by tenderness, her cheeks flushed by a dizzying uprush of emotion, Reiko threw her arms about the lieutenant's close-cropped head. The bristly hairs rubbed painfully against her breast, the prominent nose was cold as it dug into her flesh, and his breath was hot. Relaxing her embrace, she gazed down at her husband's masculine face. The severe brows, the closed eyes, the splendid bridge of the nose, the shapely lips drawn firmly together . . . the blue, clean-shaven cheeks reflecting the light and gleaming smoothly. Reiko kissed each of these. She kissed the broad nape of the neck, the strong, erect shoulders, the powerful chest with its twin circles like shields and its russet nipples. In the armpits, deeply shadowed by the ample flesh of the shoulders and chest, a sweet and melancholy odor emanated from the growth of hair, and in the sweetness of this odor was contained, somehow, the essence of young death. The lieutenant's naked skin glowed like a field of barley, and everywhere the muscles showed in sharp relief, converging on the lower abdomen about the small, unassuming navel. Gazing at the youthful, firm stomach, modestly covered by a vigorous growth of hair, Reiko thought of it as it was soon to be, cruelly cut by the sword, and she laid her head upon it, sobbing in pity, and bathed it with kisses.

At the touch of his wife's tears upon his stomach the lieutenant felt ready to endure with courage the cruelest agonies of his suicide.

What ecstasies they experienced after these tender exchanges may well be imagined. The lieutenant raised himself and enfolded his wife in a powerful embrace, her body now limp with exhaustion after her grief and tears. Passionately they held their faces close, rubbing cheek against cheek. Reiko's body was trembling. Their breasts, moist with sweat, were tightly joined, and every inch of the young and beautiful bodies had become so much one with the other that it seemed impossible there should ever again be a separation. Reiko cried out. From the heights they plunged into the abyss, and from the abyss they took wing and soared once more to dizzying heights. The lieutenant panted like the regimental standard-bearer on a route march. . . . As one cycle ended, almost immediately a new wave of passion would be generated, and together—with no trace of fatigue—they would climb again in a single breathless movement to the very summit.

IV

When the lieutenant at last turned away, it was not from weariness. For one thing, he was anxious not to undermine the considerable strength he would need in carrying out his suicide. For another, he would have been sorry to mar the sweetness of these last memories by overindulgence.

Since the lieutenant had clearly desisted, Reiko too, with her usual compliance, followed his example. The two lay naked on their backs, with fingers interlaced, staring fixedly at the dark ceiling. The room was warm from the heater, and even when the sweat had ceased to pour from their bodies they felt no cold. Outside, in the hushed night, the sounds of passing traffic had ceased. Even the noises of the trains and streetcars around Yotsuya station did not penetrate this far. After echoing through the region bounded by the moat, they were lost in the heavily wooded part fronting the broad driveway before Akasaka Palace.[4] It was hard to believe in the tension gripping this whole quarter, where the two factions of the bitterly divided Imperial Army now confronted each other, poised for battle.

4. Part of the Imperial Palace complex in Tokyo.

Savoring the warmth glowing within themselves, they lay still and recalled the ecstasies they had just known. Each moment of the experience was relived. They remembered the taste of kisses which had never wearied, the touch of naked flesh, episode after episode of dizzying bliss. But already, from the dark boards of the ceiling, the face of death was peering down. These joys had been final, and their bodies would never know them again. Not that joy of this intensity—and the same thought had occurred to them both—was ever likely to be reexperienced, even if they should live on to old age.

The feel of their fingers intertwined—this too would soon be lost. Even the wood-grain patterns they now gazed at on the dark ceiling boards would be taken from them. They could feel death edging in, nearer and nearer. There could be no hesitation now. They must have the courage to reach out to death themselves, and to seize it.

"Well, let's make our preparations," said the lieutenant. The note of determination in the words was unmistakable, but at the same time Reiko had never heard her husband's voice so warm and tender.

After they had risen, a variety of tasks awaited them.

The lieutenant, who had never once before helped with the bedding, now cheerfully slid back the door of the closet, lifted the mattress across the room by himself, and stowed it away inside.

Reiko turned off the gas heater and put away the lamp standard. During the lieutenant's absence she had arranged this room carefully, sweeping and dusting it to a fresh cleanness, and now—if one overlooked the rosewood table drawn into one corner—the eight-mat room gave all the appearance of a reception room ready to welcome an important guest.

"We've seen some drinking here, haven't we? With Kanō and Homma and Noguchi . . ."

"Yes, they were great drinkers, all of them."

"We'll be meeting them before long, in the other world. They'll tease us, I imagine, when they find I've brought you with me."

Descending the stairs, the lieutenant turned to look back into this calm, clean room, now brightly illuminated by the ceiling lamp. There floated across his mind the faces of the young officers who had drunk there, and laughed, and innocently bragged. He had never dreamed then that he would one day cut open his stomach in this room.

In the two rooms downstairs husband and wife busied themselves smoothly and serenely with their respective preparations. The lieutenant went to the toilet, and then to the bathroom to wash. Meanwhile Reiko folded away her husband's padded robe, placed his uniform tunic, his trousers, and a newly cut bleached loincloth in the bathroom, and set out sheets of paper on the living-room table for the farewell notes. Then she removed the lid from the writing box and began rubbing ink from the ink tablet. She had already decided upon the wording of her own note.

Reiko's fingers pressed hard upon the cold gilt letters of the ink tablet, and the water in the shallow well at once darkened, as if a black cloud had spread across it. She stopped thinking that this repeated action, this pressure from her fingers, this rise and fall of faint sound, was all and solely for death. It was a routine domestic task, a simple paring away of time until death should finally stand before her. But somehow, in the increasingly smooth motion of the tablet rubbing on the stone, and in the scent from the thickening ink, there was unspeakable darkness.

Neat in his uniform, which he now wore next to his skin, the lieutenant emerged from the bathroom. Without a word he seated himself at the table, bolt upright, took a brush in his hand, and stared undecidedly at the paper before him.

Reiko took a white silk kimono with her and entered the bathroom. When she reappeared in the living room, clad in the white kimono and with her face lightly made up, the farewell note lay completed on the table beneath the lamp. The thick black brushstrokes said simply:

"Long Live the Imperial Forces—Army Lieutenant Takeyama Shinji."

While Reiko sat opposite him writing her own note, the lieutenant gazed in silence, intensely serious, at the controlled movement of his wife's pale fingers as they manipulated the brush.

With their respective notes in their hands—the lieutenant's sword strapped to his side, Reiko's small dagger thrust into the sash of her white kimono—the two of them stood before the god shelf and silently prayed. Then they put out all the downstairs lights. As he mounted the stairs the lieutenant turned his head and gazed back at the striking, white-clad figure of his wife, climbing behind him, with lowered eyes, from the darkness beneath.

The farewell notes were laid side by side in the alcove of the upstairs room. They wondered whether they ought not to remove the hanging scroll, but since it had been written by their go-between, Lieutenant General Ozeki, and consisted, moreover, of two Chinese characters signifying "Sincerity," they left it where it was. Even if it were to become stained with splashes of blood, they felt that the lieutenant general would understand.

The lieutenant, sitting erect with his back to the alcove, laid his sword on the floor before him.

Reiko sat facing him, a mat's width away. With the rest of her so severely white the touch of rouge on her lips seemed remarkably seductive.

Across the dividing mat they gazed intently into each other's eyes. The lieutenant's sword lay before his knees. Seeing it, Reiko recalled their first night and was overwhelmed with sadness. The lieutenant spoke, in a hoarse voice:

"As I have no second to help me I shall cut deep. It may look unpleasant, but please do not panic. Death of any sort is a fearful thing to watch. You must not be discouraged by what you see. Is that all right?"

"Yes."

Reiko nodded deeply.

Looking at the slender white figure of his wife the lieutenant experienced a bizarre excitement. What he was about to perform was an act in his public capacity as a soldier, something he had never previously shown his wife. It called for a resolution equal to the courage to enter battle; it was a death of no less degree and quality than death in the front line. It was his conduct on the battlefield that he was now to display.

Momentarily the thought led the lieutenant to a strange fantasy. A lonely death on the battlefield, a death beneath the eyes of his beautiful wife . . . in the sensation that he was now to die in these two dimensions, realizing an impossible union of them both, there was sweetness beyond words. This must be the very pinnacle of good fortune, he thought. To have every moment of his death observed by those beautiful eyes—it was like being borne to death on a gentle, fragrant breeze. There was some special favor here. He did not understand precisely what it was, but it was a domain unknown to others: a dispensation granted to no one else had been permitted to himself. In the radiant, bridelike figure of his white-robed wife the lieutenant seemed to see a vision of all those things he had loved and for which he was to lay down his life—the Imperial Household, the Nation, the Army Flag. All these, no less than the wife who sat before him, were presences observing him closely with clear and never-faltering eyes.

Reiko too was gazing intently at her husband, so soon to die, and she thought that never in this world had she seen anything so beautiful. The lieutenant always looked well in uniform, but now, as he contemplated death with severe brows and firmly closed lips, he revealed what was perhaps masculine beauty at its most superb.

"It's time to go," the lieutenant said at last.

Reiko bent her body low to the mat in a deep bow. She could not raise her face. She did not wish to spoil her make-up with tears, but the tears could not be held back.

When at length she looked up she saw hazily through the tears that her husband had wound a white bandage around the blade of his now unsheathed sword, leaving five or six inches of naked steel showing at the point.

Resting the sword in its cloth wrapping on the mat before him, the lieutenant rose from his knees, resettled himself crosslegged, and unfastened the hooks of his uniform collar. His eyes no longer saw his wife. Slowly, one by one, he undid the flat brass buttons. The dusky brown chest was revealed, and then the stomach. He unclasped his belt and undid the buttons of his trousers. The pure whiteness of the thickly coiled loincloth showed itself. The lieutenant pushed the cloth down with both hands, further to ease his stomach, and then reached for the white-bandaged blade of his sword. With his left hand he massaged his abdomen, glancing downward as he did so.

To reassure himself on the sharpness of his sword's cutting edge the lieutenant folded back the left trouser flap, exposing a little of his thigh, and lightly drew the blade across the skin. Blood welled up in the wound at once, and several streaks of red trickled downward, glistening in the strong light.

It was the first time Reiko had ever seen her husband's blood, and she felt a violent throbbing in her chest. She looked at her husband's face. The lieutenant was looking at the blood with calm appraisal. For a moment—though thinking at the same time that it was hollow comfort—Reiko experienced a sense of relief.

The lieutenant's eyes fixed his wife with an intense, hawklike stare. Moving the sword around to his front, he raised himself slightly on his hips and let the upper half of his body lean over the sword point. That he was mustering his whole strength was apparent from the angry tension of the uniform at his shoulders. The lieutenant aimed to strike deep into the left of his stomach. His sharp cry pierced the silence of the room.

Despite the effort he had himself put into the blow, the lieutenant had the impression that someone else had struck the side of his stomach agonizingly with a thick rod of iron. For a second or so his head reeled and he had no idea what had happened. The five or six inches of naked point had vanished completely into his flesh, and the white bandage, gripped in his clenched fist, pressed directly against his stomach.

He returned to consciousness. The blade had certainly pierced the wall of the stomach, he thought. His breathing was difficult, his chest thumped violently, and in some far deep region, which he could hardly believe was a part of himself, a fearful and excruciating pain came welling up as if the ground had split open to disgorge a boiling stream of molten rock. The pain came suddenly nearer, with terrifying speed. The lieutenant bit his lower lip and stifled an instinctive moan.

Was this *seppuku?*[5]—he was thinking. It was a sensation of utter chaos, as if the sky had fallen on his head and the world was reeling drunkenly. His will power and courage, which had seemed so robust before he made the incision, had now dwindled to something like a single hairlike thread of steel, and he was assailed by the uneasy feeling that he must advance along this thread, clinging to it with desperation. His clenched fist had grown moist. Looking down, he saw that both his hand and the cloth about the blade were drenched in blood. His loin-cloth too was dyed a deep red. It struck him as incredible that, amidst this terrible agony, things which could be seen could still be seen, and existing things existed still.

The moment the lieutenant thrust the sword into his left side and she saw the deathly pallor fall across his face, like an abruptly lowered curtain, Reiko had to struggle to prevent herself from rushing to his side. Whatever happened, she must watch. She must be a witness. That was the duty her husband had laid upon her. Opposite her, a mat's space away, she could clearly see her husband biting his lip to stifle the pain. The pain was there, with absolute certainty, before her eyes. And Reiko had no means of rescuing him from it.

The sweat glistened on her husband's forehead. The lieutenant closed his eyes, and then opened them again, as if experimenting. The eyes had lost their luster, and seemed innocent and empty like the eyes of a small animal.

The agony before Reiko's eyes burned as strong as the summer sun, utterly remote from the grief which seemed to be tearing herself apart within. The pain grew steadily in stature, stretching upward. Reiko felt that her husband had already become a man in a separate world, a man whose whole being had been resolved into pain, a prisoner in a cage of pain where no hand could reach out to him. But Reiko felt no pain at all. Her grief was not pain. As she thought about this, Reiko began to feel as if someone had raised a cruel wall of glass high between herself and her husband.

Ever since her marriage her husband's existence had been her own existence, and every breath of his had been a breath drawn by herself. But now, while her husband's existence in pain was a vivid reality, Reiko could find in this grief of hers no certain proof at all of her own existence.

With only his right hand on the sword the lieutenant began to cut sideways across his stomach. But as the blade became entangled with the entrails it was pushed constantly outward by their soft resilience; and the lieutenant realized that it would be necessary, as he cut, to use both hands to keep the point pressed deep into his stomach. He

5. The traditional suicide of military men.

pulled the blade across. It did not cut as easily as he had expected. He directed the strength of his whole body into his right hand and pulled again. There was a cut of three or four inches.

The pain spread slowly outward from the inner depths until the whole stomach reverberated. It was like the wild clanging of a bell. Or like a thousand bells which jangled simultaneously at every breath he breathed and every throb of his pulse, rocking his whole being. The lieutenant could no longer stop himself from moaning. But by now the blade had cut its way through to below the navel, and when he noticed this he felt a sense of satisfaction, and a renewal of courage.

The volume of blood had steadily increased, and now it spurted from the wound as if propelled by the beat of the pulse. The mat before the lieutenant was drenched red with splattered blood, and more blood overflowed onto it from pools which gathered in the folds of the lieutenant's khaki trousers. A spot, like a bird, came flying across to Reiko and settled on the lap of her white silk kimono.

By the time the lieutenant had at last drawn the sword across to the right side of his stomach, the blade was already cutting shallow and had revealed its naked tip, slippery with blood and grease. But, suddenly stricken by a fit of vomiting, the lieutenant cried out hoarsely. The vomiting made the fierce pain fiercer still, and the stomach, which had thus far remained firm and compact, now abruptly heaved, opening wide its wound, and the entrails burst through, as if the wound too were vomiting. Seemingly ignorant of their master's suffering, the entrails gave an impression of robust health and almost disagreeable vitality as they slipped smoothly out and spilled over into the crotch. The lieutenant's head drooped, his shoulders heaved, his eyes opened to narrow slits, and a thin trickle of saliva dribbled from his mouth. The gold markings on his epaulettes caught the light and glinted.

Blood was scattered everywhere. The lieutenant was soaked in it to his knees, and he sat now in a crumpled and listless posture, one hand on the floor. A raw smell filled the room. The lieutenant, his head drooping, retched repeatedly, and the movement showed vividly in his shoulders. The blade of the sword, now pushed back by the entrails and exposed to its tip, was still in the lieutenant's right hand.

It would be difficult to imagine a more heroic sight than that of the lieutenant at this moment, as he mustered his strength and flung back his head. The movement was performed with sudden violence, and the back of his head struck with a sharp crack against the alcove pillar. Reiko had been sitting until now with her face lowered, gazing in fascination at the tide of blood advancing toward her knees, but the sound took her by surprise and she looked up.

The lieutenant's face was not the face of a living man. The eyes were hollow, the skin parched, the once so lustrous cheeks and lips the color of dried mud. The right hand alone was moving. Laboriously gripping the sword, it hovered shakily in the air like the hand of a marionette and strove to direct the point at the base of the lieutenant's throat. Reiko watched her husband make this last, most heart-rending, futile exertion. Glistening with blood and grease, the point was thrust at the throat again and again. And each time it missed its aim. The strength to guide it was no longer there. The straying point struck the collar and the collar badges. Although its hooks had been unfastened, the stiff military collar had closed together again and was protecting the throat.

Reiko could bear the sight no longer. She tried to go to her husband's help, but she could not stand. She moved through the blood on her knees, and her white skirts grew deep red. Moving to the rear of her husband, she helped no more than by loosening the collar. The quivering blade at last contacted the naked flesh of the throat. At that moment Reiko's impression was that she herself had propelled her husband forward; but that was not the case. It was a movement planned by the lieutenant himself, his last exertion of strength. Abruptly he threw his body at the blade, and the blade pierced his neck, emerging at the nape. There was a tremendous spurt of blood and the lieutenant lay still, cold blue-tinged steel protruding from his neck at the back.

V

Slowly, her socks slippery with blood, Reiko descended the stairway. The upstairs room was now completely still.

Switching on the ground-floor lights, she checked the gas jet and the main gas plug and poured water over the smoldering, half-buried charcoal in the brazier. She stood before the upright mirror in the four-and-a-half-mat room and held up her skirts. The bloodstains made it seem as if a bold, vivid pattern was printed across the lower half of her white kimono. When she sat down before the mirror, she was conscious of the dampness and coldness of her husband's blood in the region of her thighs, and she shivered. Then, for a long while, she lingered over her toilet preparations. She applied the rouge generously to her cheeks, and her lips too she painted heavily. This was no longer make-up to please her husband. It was make-up for the world which she would leave behind, and there was a touch of the magnificent and the spectacular in her brushwork. When she rose, the mat before the mirror was wet with blood. Reiko was not concerned about this.

Returning from the toilet, Reiko stood finally on the cement floor of the porchway. When her husband had bolted the door here last night it had been in preparation for death. For a while she stood immersed in the consideration of a simple problem. Should she now leave the bolt drawn? If she were to lock the door, it could be that the neighbors might not notice their suicide for several days. Reiko did not relish the thought of their two corpses putrifying before discovery. After all, it seemed, it would be best to leave it open. . . . She released the bolt, and also drew open the frosted-glass door a fraction. . . . At once a chill wind blew in. There was no sign of anyone in the midnight streets, and stars glittered ice-cold through the trees in the large house opposite.

Leaving the door as it was, Reiko mounted the stairs. She had walked here and there for some time and her socks were no longer slippery. About halfway up, her nostrils were already assailed by a peculiar smell.

The lieutenant was lying on his face in a sea of blood. The point protruding from his neck seemed to have grown even more prominent than before. Reiko walked heedlessly across the blood. Sitting beside the lieutenant's corpse, she stared intently at the face, which lay on one cheek on the mat. The eyes were opened wide, as if the lieutenant's attention had been attracted by something. She raised the head, folding it in her sleeve, wiped the blood from the lips, and bestowed a last kiss.

Then she rose and took from the closet a new white blanket and a waist cord. To prevent any derangement of her skirts, she wrapped the blanket about her waist and bound it there firmly with the cord.

Reiko sat herself on a spot about one foot distant from the lieutenant's body. Drawing the dagger from her sash, she examined its dully gleaming blade intently, and held it to her tongue. The taste of the polished steel was slightly sweet.

Reiko did not linger. When she thought how the pain which had previously opened such a gulf between herself and her dying husband was now to become a part of her own experience, she saw before her only the joy of herself entering a realm her husband had already made his own. In her husband's agonized face there had been something inexplicable which she was seeing for the first time. Now she would solve that riddle. Reiko sensed that at last she too would be able to taste the true bitterness and sweetness of that great moral principle in which her husband believed. What had until now been tasted only faintly through her husband's example she was about to savor directly with her own tongue.

Reiko rested the point of the blade against the base of her throat. She thrust hard. The wound was only shallow. Her head blazed, and her hands shook uncontrollably. She gave the blade a strong pull sideways. A warm substance flooded into her mouth, and everything before her eyes reddened, in a vision of spouting blood. She gathered her strength and plunged the point of the blade deep into her throat.

---

1. Which feelings and motivations of the lieutenant and his wife can you share? Do some remain foreign or incomprehensible? Which ones?
2. How is erotic passion related to the decision to commit suicide? Compare the language and amount of detail in the passages devoted to sex with those devoted to the suicides.
3. The author stresses the purity of motive on the part of his main characters. Does "purity" have anything to do with the value of these motives or the acts to which they lead?
4. Is there ever any doubt about the outcome of the story? If not, and if there is no suspense, what compensates for its absence?
5. Does the lieutenant expect to affect his country's policies by his sacrifice? Why does he feel he is "on the front line of the spirit"?
6. Does Reiko kill herself solely out of obedience to her husband's wishes? What does the story say about the proper relation of wives to husbands?

Alice Munro

Munro (1931–) was born in Wingham, Ontario, and was educated at the University of Western Ontario. Her first collection of stories, Dance of the Happy Shades *(1968), won the Governor General's literary award, and her novel* Lives of Girls and Women *(1971) won the Canadian Booksellers' award. In 1978 she once again won the Governor General's award with a book of stories published in Canada under the title* Who Do You Think You Are? *and published in the United States in 1979 as* The Beggar Maid. *Her other books are* A Place for Everything *(1970),* Something I've Been Meaning to Tell You *(1974),* The Moons of Jupiter *(1982), and* The Progress of Love *(1986).*

Royal Beatings

Royal beating. That was Flo's promise. You are going to get one Royal Beating.

The word Royal lolled on Flo's tongue, took on trappings. Rose had a need to picture things, to pursue absurdities, that was stronger than the need to stay out of trouble, and instead of taking this threat to heart she pondered: how is a beating royal? She came up with a tree-lined avenue, a crowd of formal spectators, some white horses and black slaves. Someone knelt, and the blood came leaping out like banners. An occasion both savage and splendid. In real life they didn't approach such dignity, and it was only Flo who tried to supply the event with some high air of necessity and regret. Rose and her father soon got beyond anything presentable.

Her father was king of the royal beatings. Those Flo gave never amounted to much; they were quick cuffs and slaps dashed off while her attention remained elsewhere. You get out of my road, she would say. You mind your own business. You take that look off your face.

They lived behind a store in Hanratty, Ontario. There were four of them: Rose, her father, Flo, Rose's young half brother Brian. The store was really a house, bought by Rose's father and mother when they married and set up here in the furniture and upholstery repair business. Her mother could do upholstery. From both parents Rose should have inherited clever hands, a quick sympathy with materials, an eye for the nicest turns of mending, but she hadn't. She was clumsy, and when something broke she couldn't wait to sweep it up and throw it away.

Her mother had died. She said to Rose's father during the afternoon, "I have a feeling that is so hard to describe. It's like a boiled egg in my chest, with the shell left on." She died before night, she had a blood clot on her lung. Rose was a baby in a basket at the time, so of course could not remember any of this. She heard it from Flo, who must have heard it from her father. Flo came along soon afterward, to take over Rose in the basket, marry her father, open up the front room to make a grocery store. Rose, who had known the house only as a store, who had known only Flo for a mother, looked back on the sixteen or so months her parents spent here as an orderly, far gentler and more ceremonious time, with little touches of affluence. She had nothing to go on but some egg cups her mother had bought, with a pattern of vines and birds on them, delicately drawn as if with red ink; the pattern was beginning to wear away. No books or clothes or pictures of her mother remained. Her father must have got rid of them, or else Flo would. Flo's only story about her mother, the one about her death, was oddly grudging. Flo liked the details of a death: the things people said, the way they protested or tried to get out of bed or swore or laughed (some did those things), but when she said that Rose's mother mentioned a hard-boiled egg in her chest she made the comparison sound slightly foolish, as if her mother really was the kind of person who might think you could swallow an egg whole.

Her father had a shed out behind the store, where he worked at his furniture repairing and restoring. He caned chair seats and backs, mended wickerwork, filled cracks, put legs back on, all most admirably and skillfully and cheaply. That was his pride: to startle people with such fine work, such moderate, even ridiculous charges. During the Depression people could not afford to pay more, perhaps, but he continued the practice through the war, through the years of prosperity after the war, until he died. He never discussed with Flo what he charged or what was owing. After he died she had to go out and unlock the shed and take all sorts of scraps of paper and torn envelopes from the big wicked-looking hooks that were his files. Many of these she found were not accounts or receipts at all but records of the weather, bits of information about the garden, things he had been moved to write down.

Ate new potatoes 25th June. Record.
Dark Day, 1880's, nothing supernatural. Clouds of ash from forest fires.
Aug 16, 1938. Giant thunderstorm in evng. Lightning str. Pres. Church, Turberry Twp. Will of God?

Scald strawberries to remove acid.
All things are alive. Spinoza.[1]

Flo thought Spinoza must be some new vegetable he planned to grow, like broccoli or eggplant. He would often try some new thing. She showed the scrap of paper to Rose and asked, did she know what Spinoza was? Rose did know, or had an idea—she was in her teens by that time—but she replied that she did not. She had reached an age where she thought she could not stand to know any more, about her father, or about Flo; she pushed any discovery aside with embarrassment and dread.

There was a stove in the shed, and many rough shelves covered with cans of paint and varnish, shellac and turpentine, jars of soaking brushes and also some dark sticky bottles of cough medicine. Why should a man who coughed constantly, whose lungs took in a whiff of gas in the War (called, in Rose's earliest childhood, not the First, but the Last,[2] War) spend all his days breathing fumes of paint and turpentine? At the time, such questions were not asked as often as they are now. On the bench outside Flo's store several old men from the neighborhood sat gossiping, drowsing, in the warm weather, and some of these old men coughed all the time too. The fact is they were dying, slowly and discreetly, of what was called, without any particular sense of grievance, "the foundry disease." They had worked all their lives at the foundry in town, and now they sat still, with their wasted yellow faces, coughing, chuckling, drifting into aimless obscenity on the subject of women walking by, or any young girl on a bicycle.

From the shed came not only coughing, but speech, a continual muttering, reproachful or encouraging, usually just below the level at which separate words could be made out. Slowing down when her father was at a tricky piece of work, taking on a cheerful speed when he was doing something less demanding, sandpapering or painting. Now and then some words would break through and hang clear and nonsensical on the air. When he realized they were out, there would be a quick bit of cover-up coughing, a swallowing, an alert, unusual silence.

"Macaroni, pepperoni, Botticelli,[3] beans—"

What could that mean? Rose used to repeat such things to herself. She could never ask him. The person who spoke these words and the person who spoke to her as her father were not the same, though they seemed to occupy the same space. It would be the worst sort of taste to acknowledge the person who was not supposed to be there; it would not be forgiven. Just the same, she loitered and listened.

1. Benedict Spinoza (1632–1677), Dutch philosopher. 2. World War I was euphemistically referred to as "the war to end all wars." 3. Sandro Botticelli (1444?–1510), Italian painter.

The cloud-capped towers, she heard him say once.

"The cloud-capped towers, the gorgeous palaces."[4]

That was like a hand clapped against Rose's chest, not to hurt, but astonish her, to take her breath away. She had to run then, she had to get away. She knew that was enough to hear, and besides, what if he caught her? It would be terrible.

This was something the same as bathroom noises. Flo had saved up, and had a bathroom put in, but there was no place to put it except in a corner of the kitchen. The door did not fit, the walls were only beaverboard. The result was that even the tearing of a piece of toilet paper, the shifting of a haunch, was audible to those working or talking or eating in the kitchen. They were all familiar with each other's nether voices, not only in their more explosive moments but in their intimate sighs and growls and pleas and statements. And they were all most prudish people. So no one ever seemed to hear, or be listening, and no reference was made. The person creating the noises in the bathroom was not connected with the person who walked out.

They lived in a poor part of town. There was Hanratty and West Hanratty, with the river flowing between them. This was West Hanratty. In Hanratty the social structure ran from doctors and dentists and lawyers down to foundry workers and factory workers and draymen; in West Hanratty it ran from factory workers and foundry workers down to large improvident families of casual bootleggers and prostitutes and unsuccessful thieves. Rose thought of her own family as straddling the river, belonging nowhere, but that was not true. West Hanratty was where the store was and they were, on the straggling tail end of the main street. Across the road from them was a blacksmith shop, boarded up about the time the war started, and a house that had been another store at one time. The Salada Tea sign had never been taken out of the front window; it remained as a proud and interesting decoration though there was no Salada Tea for sale inside. There was just a bit of sidewalk, too cracked and tilted for roller-skating, though Rose longed for roller skates and often pictured herself whizzing along in a plaid skirt, agile and fashionable. There was one street light, a tin flower; then the amenities gave up and there were dirt roads and boggy places, front-yard dumps and strange-looking houses. What made the houses strange-looking were the attempts to keep them from going completely to ruin. With some the attempt had never been made. These were gray and rotted and leaning over, falling into a landscape of scrub hollows, frog ponds, cattails and nettles. Most houses, however, had been patched up with tarpaper, a few fresh shingles, sheets

4. "The cloud-capped towers, the gorgeous palaces, / The solemn temples, the great globe itself. / Yea, all which it inherit, shall dissolve, / And, like this insubstantial pageant faded, / Leave not a wrack behind." Shakespeare's *Tempest*, IV. i.

of tin, hammered-out stovepipes, even cardboard. This was, of course, in the days before the war, days of what would later be legendary poverty, from which Rose would remember mostly low-down things—serious-looking anthills and wooden steps, and a cloudy, interesting, problematical light on the world.

There was a long truce between Flo and Rose in the beginning. Rose's nature was growing like a prickly pineapple, but slowly, and secretly, hard pride and skepticism overlapping, to make something surprising even to herself. Before she was old enough to go to school, and while Brian was still in the baby carriage, Rose stayed in the store with both of them—Flo sitting on the high stool behind the counter, Brian asleep by the window; Rose knelt or lay on the wide creaky floorboards working with crayons on pieces of brown paper too torn or irregular to be used for wrapping.

People who came to the store were mostly from the houses around. Some country people came too, on their way home from town, and a few people from Hanratty, who walked across the bridge. Some people were always on the main street, in and out of stores, as if it was their duty to be always on display and their right to be welcomed. For instance, Becky Tyde.

Becky Tyde climbed up on Flo's counter, made room for herself beside an open tin of crumbly jam-filled cookies.

"Are these any good?" she said to Flo, and boldly began to eat one. "When are you going to give us a job, Flo?"

"You could go and work in the butcher shop," said Flo innocently. "You could go and work for your brother."

"Roberta?" said Becky with a stagey sort of contempt. "You think I'd work for him?" Her brother who ran the butcher shop was named Robert but often called Roberta, because of his meek and nervous ways. Becky Tyde laughed. Her laugh was loud and noisy like an engine bearing down on you.

She was a big-headed loud-voiced dwarf, with a mascot's sexless swagger, a red velvet tam, a twisted neck that forced her to hold her head on one side, always looking up and sideways. She wore little polished high-heeled shoes, real lady's shoes. Rose watched her shoes, being scared of the rest of her, of her laugh and her neck. She knew from Flo that Becky Tyde had been sick with polio as a child, that was why her neck was twisted and why she had not grown any taller. It was hard to believe that she had started out differently, that she had ever been normal. Flo said she was not cracked, she had as much brains as anybody, but she knew she could get away with anything.

"You know I used to live out here?" Becky said, noticing Rose. "Hey! What's-your-name! Didn't I used to live out here, Flo?"

"If you did it was before my time," said Flo, as if she didn't know anything.

"That was before the neighborhood got so downhill. Excuse me saying so. My father built his house out here and he built his slaughterhouse and we had half an acre of orchard."

"Is that so?" said Flo, using her humoring voice, full of false geniality, humility even. "Then why did you ever move away?"

"I told you, it got to be such a downhill neighborhood," said Becky. She would put a whole cookie in her mouth if she felt like it, let her cheeks puff out like a frog's. She never told any more.

Flo knew anyway, and who didn't. Everyone knew the house, red brick with the veranda pulled off and the orchard, what was left of it, full of the usual outflow—car seats and washing machines and bedsprings and junk. The house would never look sinister, in spite of what had happened in it, because there was so much wreckage and confusion all around.

Becky's old father was a different kind of butcher from her brother according to Flo. A bad-tempered Englishman. And different from Becky in the matter of mouthiness. His was never open. A skinflint, a family tyrant. After Becky had polio he wouldn't let her go back to school. She was seldom seen outside the house, never outside the yard. He didn't want people gloating. That was what Becky said, at the trial. Her mother was dead by that time and her sisters married. Just Becky and Robert at home. People would stop Robert on the road and ask him, "How about your sister, Robert? Is she altogether better now?"

"Yes."

"Does she do the housework? Does she get your supper?"

"Yes."

"And is your father good to her, Robert?"

The story being that the father beat them, had beaten all his children and beaten his wife as well, beat Becky more now because of her deformity, which some people believed he had caused (they did not understand about polio). The stories persisted and got added to. The reason that Becky was kept out of sight was now supposed to be her pregnancy, and the father of the child was supposed to be her own father. Then people said it had been born, and disposed of.

"What?"

"Disposed of," Flo said. "They used to say go and get your lamb chops at Tyde's, get them nice and tender! It was all lies in all probability," she said regretfully.

Rose could be drawn back—from watching the wind shiver along the old torn awning, catch in the tear—by this tone of regret, caution, in Flo's voice. Flo telling a story—and this was not the only one, or even the most lurid one, she knew—would incline her head and let her face go soft and thoughtful, tantalizing, warning.

"I shouldn't even be telling you this stuff."

More was to follow.

Three useless young men, who hung around the livery stable, got together—or were got together, by more influential and respectable men in town—and prepared to give old man Tyde a horsewhipping, in the interests of public morality. They blacked their faces. They were provided with whips and a quart of whiskey apiece, for courage. They were: Jelly Smith, a horse-racer and a drinker; Bob Temple, a ballplayer and strongman; and Hat Nettleton, who worked on the town dray,[5] and had his nickname from a bowler hat he wore, out of vanity as much as for the comic effect. He still worked on the dray, in fact; he had kept the name if not the hat, and could often be seen in public almost as often as Becky Tyde—delivering sacks of coal, which blackened his face and arms. That should have brought to mind his story, but didn't. Present time and past, the shady melodramatic past of Flo's stories, were quite separate, at least for Rose. Present people could not be fitted into the past. Becky herself, town oddity and public pet, harmless and malicious, could never match the butcher's prisoner, the cripple daughter, a white streak at the window: mute, beaten, impregnated. As with the house, only a formal connection could be made.

The young men primed to do the horsewhipping showed up late, outside Tyde's house, after everybody had gone to bed. They had a gun, but they used up their ammunition firing it off in the yard. They yelled for the butcher and beat on the door; finally they broke it down. Tyde concluded they were after his money, so he put some bills in a handkerchief and sent Becky down with them, maybe thinking those men would be touched or scared by the sight of a little wry-necked girl, a dwarf. But that didn't content them. They came upstairs and dragged the butcher out from under his bed, in his nightgown. They dragged him outside and stood him in the snow. The temperature was four below zero, a fact noted later in court. They meant to hold a mock trial but they could not remember how it was done. So they began to beat him and kept beating him until he fell. They yelled at him, *Butcher's meat!* and continued beating him while his nightgown and the snow he was lying in turned red. His son Robert said in court that he had not watched the beating. Becky said that Robert had watched at first but had run away and hid. She herself had watched all the way through. She watched the men leave at last and her father make his delayed bloody progress through the snow and up the steps of the

5. Wagon used for carrying heavy loads for hire.

veranda. She did not go out to help him, or open the door until he got to it. Why not? she was asked in court, and she said she did not go out because she just had her nightgown on, and she did not open the door because she did not want to let the cold into the house.

Old man Tyde then appeared to have recovered his strength. He sent Robert to harness the horse, and made Becky heat water so that he could wash. He dressed and took all the money and with no explanation to his children got into the cutter and drove to Belgrave where he left the horse tied in the cold and took the early morning train to Toronto. On the train he behaved oddly, groaning and cursing as if he was drunk. He was picked up on the streets of Toronto a day later, out of his mind with fever, and was taken to a hospital, where he died. He still had all the money. The cause of death was given as pneumonia.

But the authorities got wind, Flo said. The case came to trial. The three men who did it all received long prison sentences. A farce, said Flo. Within a year they were all free, had all been pardoned, had jobs waiting for them. And why was that? It was because too many higher-ups were in on it. And it seemed as if Becky and Robert had no interest in seeing justice done. They were left well-off. They bought a house in Hanratty. Robert went into the store. Becky after her long seclusion started on a career of public sociability and display.

That was all. Flo put the lid down on the story as if she was sick of it. It reflected no good on anybody.

"Imagine," Flo said.

Flo at this time must have been in her early thirties. A young woman. She wore exactly the same clothes that a woman of fifty, or sixty, or seventy, might wear: print housedresses loose at the neck and sleeves as well as the waist; bib aprons, also of print, which she took off when she came from the kitchen into the store. This was a common costume at the time, for a poor though not absolutely poverty-stricken woman; it was also, in a way, a scornful deliberate choice. Flo scorned slacks, she scorned the outfits of people trying to be in style, she scorned lipstick and permanents. She wore her own black hair cut straight across, just long enough to push behind her ears. She was tall but fine-boned, with narrow wrists and shoulders, a small head, a pale, freckled, mobile, monkeyish face. If she had thought it worthwhile, and had the resources, she might have had a black-and-pale, fragile, nurtured sort of prettiness; Rose realized that later. But she would have to have been a different person altogether; she would have to have learned to resist making faces, at herself and others.

Rose's earliest memories of Flo were of extraordinary softness and hardness. The soft hair, the long, soft, pale cheeks, soft almost invisible fuzz in front of her ears and above her mouth. The sharpness of her knees, hardness of her lap, flatness of her front.

When Flo sang:

> Oh the buzzin' of the bees in the cigarette trees
> And the soda-*water* fountain . . .[6]

Rose thought of Flo's old life before she married her father, when she worked as a waitress in the coffee shop in Union Station, and went with her girl friends Mavis and Irene to Centre Island,[7] and was followed by men on dark streets and knew how pay phones and elevators worked. Rose heard in her voice the reckless dangerous life of cities, the gum-chewing sharp answers.

And when she sang:

> Then slowly, slowly, she got up
> And slowly she came nigh him
> And all she said, that she ever did say,
> Was young man I think, you're dyin'![8]

Rose thought of a life Flo seemed to have had beyond that, earlier than that, crowded and legendary, with Barbara Allen and Becky Tyde's father and all kinds of outrages and sorrows jumbled up together in it.

The royal beatings. What got them started?

Suppose a Saturday, in spring. Leaves not out yet but the doors open to the sunlight. Crows. Ditches full of running water. Hopeful weather. Often on Saturdays Flo left Rose in charge of the store—it's a few years now, these are the years when Rose was nine, ten, eleven, twelve—while she herself went across the bridge to Hanratty (going uptown they called it) to shop and see people, and listen to them. Among the people she listened to were Mrs. Lawyer Davies, Mrs. Anglican Rector Henley-Smith, and Mrs. Horse-Doctor McKay. She came home and imitated their flibberty voices. Monsters, she made them seem; of foolishness, and showiness, and self-approbation.

When she finished shopping she sent into the coffee shop of the Queen's Hotel and had a sundae. What kind? Rose and Brian wanted to know when she got home, and they would be disappointed if it was only pineapple or butterscotch, pleased if it was a Tin Roof, or Black and White. Then she smoked a cigarette. She had some ready-rolled, that she carried with her, so that she wouldn't have to roll one in public. Smoking was the one thing she did that she would have called showing off in anybody else. It was a habit left over from her working

6. From the ballad "The Big Rock Candy Mountain." 7. Park in Toronto Harbour. Union Station is the main railroad terminal in Toronto. 8. From the ballad "Barbara Allen."

days, from Toronto. She knew it was asking for trouble. Once the Catholic priest came over to her right in the Queen's Hotel, and flashed his lighter at her before she could get her matches out. She thanked him but did not enter into conversation, lest he should try to convert her.

Another time, on the way home, she saw at the town end of the bridge a boy in a blue jacket, apparently looking at the water. Eighteen, nineteen years old. Nobody she knew. Skinny, weakly looking, something the matter with him, she saw at once. Was he thinking of jumping? Just as she came up even with him, what does he do but turn and display himself, holding his jacket open, also his pants. What he must have suffered from the cold, on a day that had Flo holding her coat collar tight around her throat.

When she first saw what he had in his hand, Flo said, all she could think of was, what is he doing out here with a baloney sausage?

She could say that. It was offered as truth; no joke. She maintained that she despised dirty talk. She would go out and yell at the old men sitting in front of her store.

"If you want to stay where you are you better clean your mouths out!"

Saturday, then. For some reason Flo is not going uptown, has decided to stay home and scrub the kitchen floor. Perhaps this has put her in a bad mood. Perhaps she was in a bad mood anyway, due to people not paying their bills, or the stirring-up of feelings in spring. The wrangle with Rose has already commenced, has been going on forever, like a dream that goes back and back into other dreams, over hills and through doorways, maddeningly dim and populous and familiar and elusive. They are carting all the chairs out of the kitchen preparatory to the scrubbing, and they have also got to move some extra provisions for the store, some cartons of canned goods, tins of maple syrup, coal-oil cans, jars of vinegar. They take these things out to the woodshed. Brian who is five or six by this time is helping drag the tins.

"Yes," says Flo, carrying on from our lost starting point. "Yes, and that filth you taught to Brian."

"What filth?"

"And he doesn't know any better."

There is one step down from the kitchen to the woodshed, a bit of carpet on it so worn Rose can't even remember seeing the pattern. Brian loosens it, dragging a tin.

"Two Vancouvers," she says softly.

Flo is back in the kitchen. Brian looks from Flo to Rose and Rose says again in a slightly louder voice, an encouraging singsong, "Two Vancouvers—"

"Fried in snot!" finishes Brian, not able to control himself any longer.

"Two pickled arseholes—"

"—tied in a knot!"

There it is. The filth.

> Two Vancouvers fried in snot!
> Two pickled arseholes tied in a knot!

Rose has known that for years, learned it when she first went to school. She came home and asked Flo, what is a Vancouver?

"It's a city. It's a long ways away."

"What else besides a city?"

Flo said, what did she mean, what else? How could it be fried, Rose said, approaching the dangerous moment, the delightful moment, when she would have to come out with the whole thing.

"Two Vancouvers fried in snot! / Two pickled arseholes tied in a knot!"

"You're going to get it!" cried Flo in a predictable rage. "Say that again and you'll get a good clout!"

Rose couldn't stop herself. She hummed it tenderly, tried saying the innocent words aloud, humming through the others. It was not just the words snot and arsehole that gave her pleasure, though of course they did. It was the pickling and tying and the unimaginable Vancouvers. She saw them in her mind shaped rather like octopuses, twitching in the pan. The tumble of reason; the spark and spit of craziness.

Lately she has remembered it again and taught it to Brian, to see if it has the same effect on him, and of course it has.

"Oh, I heard you!" says Flo. "I heard that! And I'm warning you!"

So she is. Brian takes the warning. He runs away, out the woodshed door, to do as he likes. Being a boy, free to help or not, involve himself or not. Not committed to the household struggle. They don't need him anyway, except to use against each other, they hardly notice his going. They continue, can't help continuing, can't leave each other alone. When they seem to have given up they really are just waiting and building up steam.

Flo gets out the scrub pail and the brush and the rag and the pad for her knees, a dirty red rubber pad. She starts to work on the floor. Rose sits on the kitchen table, the only place left to sit, swinging her legs. She can feel the cool oilcloth, because she is wearing shorts, last summer's tight faded shorts dug out of the summer-clothes bag. They smell a bit moldy from winter storage.

Flo crawls underneath, scrubbing with the brush, wiping with the rag. Her legs are long, white and muscular, marked all over with blue veins as if somebody had been drawing rivers on them with an indelible pencil. An abnormal energy, a violent disgust, is expressed in the chewing of the brush at the linoleum, the swish of the rag.

What do they have to say to each other? It doesn't really matter. Flo speaks of Rose's smart-aleck behavior, rudeness and sloppiness and conceit. Her willingness to make work for others, her lack of gratitude. She mentions Brian's innocence, Rose's corruption. Oh, don't you think you're somebody, says Flo, and a moment later, Who do you think you are? Rose contradicts and objects with such poisonous reasonableness and mildness, displays theatrical unconcern. Flo goes beyond her ordinary scorn and self-possession and becomes amazingly theatrical herself, saying it was for Rose that she sacrificed her life. She saw her father saddled with a baby daughter and she thought, what is that man going to do? So she married him, and here she is, on her knees.

At that moment the bell rings, to announce a customer in the store. Because the fight is on, Rose is not permitted to go into the store and wait on whoever it is. Flo gets up and throws off her apron, groaning—but not communicatively, it is not a groan whose exasperation Rose is allowed to share—and goes in and serves. Rose hears her using her normal voice.

"About time! Sure is!"

She comes back and ties on her apron and is ready to resume.

"You never have a thought for anybody but your ownself! You never have a thought for what I'm doing."

"I never asked you to do anything. I wish you never had. I would have been a lot better off."

Rose says this smiling directly at Flo, who has not yet gone down on her knees. Flo sees the smile, grabs the scrub rag that is hanging on the side of the pail, and throws it at her. It may be meant to hit her in the face but instead it falls against Rose's leg and she raises her foot and catches it, swinging it negligently against her ankle.

"All right," says Flo. "You've done it this time. All right."

Rose watches her go to the woodshed door, hears her tramp through the woodshed, pause in the doorway, where the screen door hasn't yet been hung, and the storm door is standing open, propped with a brick. She calls Rose's father. She calls him in a warning, summoning voice, as if against her will preparing him for bad news. He will know what this is about.

The kitchen floor has five or six different patterns of linoleum on it. Ends, which Flo got for nothing and ingeniously trimmed and fitted together, bordering them with tin strips and tacks. While Rose sits on the table waiting, she looks at the floor, at this satisfying arrangement of rectangles, triangles, some other shape whose name she is trying to remember. She hears Flo coming back through the woodshed, on the creaky plank walk laid over the dirt floor. She is loitering, waiting, too. She and Rose can carry this no further, by themselves.

Rose hears her father come in. She stiffens, a tremor runs through her legs, she feels them shiver on the oilcloth. Called away from some peaceful, absorbing task, away from the words running in his head, called out of himself, her father has to say something. He says, "Well? What's wrong?"

Now comes another voice of Flo's. Enriched, hurt, apologetic, it seems to have been manufactured on the spot. She is sorry to have called him from his work. Would never have done it, if Rose was not driving her to distraction. How to distraction? With her back talk and impudence and her terrible tongue. The things Rose has said to Flo are such that, if Flo had said them to her mother, she knows her father would have thrashed her into the ground.

Rose tries to butt in, to say this isn't true.

What isn't true?

Her father raises a hand, doesn't look at her, says, "Be quiet."

When she says it isn't true, Rose means that she herself didn't start this, only responded, that she was goaded by Flo, who is now, she believes, telling the grossest sort of lies, twisting everything to suit herself. Rose puts aside her other knowledge that whatever Flo has said or done, whatever she herself has said or done, does not really matter at all. It is the struggle itself that counts, and that can't be stopped, can never be stopped, short of where it has got to, now.

Flo's knees are dirty, in spite of the pad. The scrub rag is still hanging over Rose's foot.

Her father wipes his hands, listening to Flo. He takes his time. He is slow at getting into the spirit of things, tired in advance, maybe, on the verge of rejecting the role he has to play. He won't look at Rose, but at any sound or stirring from Rose, he holds up his hand.

"Well we don't need the public in on this, that's for sure," Flo says, and she goes to lock the door of the store, putting in the store window the sign that says BACK SOON, a sign Rose made for her with a great deal of fancy curving and shading of letters in black and red crayon. When she comes back she shuts the door to the store, then the door to the stairs, then the door to the woodshed.

Her shoes have left marks on the clean wet part of the floor.

"Oh, I don't know," she says now, in a voice worn down from its emotional peak. "I don't know what to do about her." She looks down and sees her dirty knees (following Rose's eyes) and rubs at them viciously with her bare hands, smearing the dirt around.

"She humiliates me," she says, straightening up. There it is, the explanation. "She humiliates me," she repeats with satisfaction. "She has no respect."

"I do not!"

"Quiet, you!" says her father.

"If I hadn't called your father you'd still be sitting there with that grin on your face! What other way is there to manage you?"

Rose detects in her father some objections to Flo's rhetoric, some embarrassment and reluctance. She is wrong, and ought to know she is wrong, in thinking that she can count on this. The fact that she knows about it, and he knows she knows, will not make things any better. He is beginning to warm up. He gives her a look. This look is at first cold and challenging. It informs her of his judgment, of the hopelessness of her position. Then it clears, it begins to fill up with something else, the way a spring fills up when you clear the leaves away. It fills with hatred and pleasure. Rose sees that and knows it. Is that just a description of anger, should she see his eyes filling up with anger? No. Hatred is right. Pleasure is right. His face loosens and changes and grows younger, and he holds up his hand this time to silence Flo.

"All right," he says, meaning that's enough, more than enough, this part is over, things can proceed. He starts to loosen his belt.

Flo has stopped anyway. She has the same difficulty Rose does, a difficulty in believing that what you know must happen really will happen, that there comes a time when you can't draw back.

"Oh, I don't know, don't be too hard on her." She is moving around nervously as if she has thoughts of opening some escape route. "Oh, you don't have to use the belt on her. Do you have to use the belt?"

He doesn't answer. The belt is coming off, not hastily. It is being grasped at the necessary point. *All right you.* He is coming over to Rose. He pushes her off the table. His face, like his voice, is quite out of character. He is like a bad actor, who turns a part grotesque. As if he must savor and insist on just what is shameful and terrible about this. That is not to say he is pretending, that he is acting, and does not mean it. He is acting, and he means it. Rose knows that, she knows everything about him.

She has since wondered about murders, and murderers. Does the thing have to be carried through, in the end, partly for the effect, to prove to the audience of one—who won't be able to report, only register, the lesson—that such a thing can happen, that there is nothing that can't happen, that the most dreadful antic is justified, feelings can be found to match it?

She tries again looking at the kitchen floor, that clever and comforting geometrical arrangement, instead of looking at him or his belt. How can this go on in front of such daily witnesses—the linoleum, the calendar with the mill and creek and autumn trees, the old accommodating pots and pans?

Hold out your hand!

Those things aren't going to help her, none of them can rescue her. They turn bland and useless, even unfriendly. Pots can show malice, the patterns of linoleum can leer up at you, treachery is the other side of dailiness.

At the first, or maybe the second, crack of pain, she draws back. She will not accept it. She runs around the room, she tries to get to the doors. Her father blocks her off. Not an ounce of courage or of stoicism in her, it would seem. She runs, she screams, she implores. Her father is after her, cracking the belt at her when he can, then abandoning it and using his hands. Bang over the ear, then bang over the other ear. Back and forth, her head ringing. Bang in the face. Up against the wall and bang in the face again. He shakes her and hits her against the wall, he kicks her legs. She in incoherent, insane, shrieking. *Forgive me! Oh please, forgive me!*

Flo is shrieking too. *Stop, stop!*

Not yet. He throws Rose down. Or perhaps she throws herself down. He kicks her legs again. She has given up on words but is letting out a noise, the sort of noise that makes Flo cry, *Oh, what if people can hear her?* The very last-ditch willing sound of humiliation and defeat it is, for it seems Rose must play her part in this with the same grossness, the same exaggeration, that her father displays, playing his. She plays his victim with a self-indulgence that arouses, and maybe hopes to arouse, his final, sickened contempt.

They will give this anything that is necessary, it seems, they will go to any lengths.

Not quite. He has never managed really to injure her, though there are times, of course, when she prays that he will. He hits her with an open hand, there is some restraint in his kicks.

Now he stops, he is out of breath. He allows Flo to move in, he grabs Rose up and gives her a push in Flo's direction, making a sound of disgust. Flo retrieves her, opens the stair door, shoves her up the stairs.

"Go on up to your room now! Hurry!"

Rose goes up the stairs, stumbling, letting herself stumble, letting herself fall against the steps. She doesn't bang her door because a gesture like that could still bring him after her, and anyway, she is weak. She lies on the bed. She can hear through the stovepipe hole Flo snuffling and remonstrating, her father saying angrily that Flo should have kept quiet then, if she did not want Rose punished she should not have recommended it. Flo says she never recommended a hiding like that.

They argue back and forth on this. Flo's frightened voice is growing stronger, getting its confidence back. By stages, by arguing, they are being drawn back into themselves. Soon it's only Flo talking; he will not talk anymore. Rose has had to fight down her noisy sobbing, so as to listen to them, and when she loses interest in listening, and wants to sob some more, she finds she can't work herself up to it. She has passed into a state of calm, in which outrage is perceived as complete and final. In this state events and possibilities take on a lovely simplicity. Choices are mercifully clear. The words that come to mind are not the quibbling, seldom the conditional. Never is a word to which the right is suddenly established. She will never speak to them, she will never look at them with anything but loathing, she will never forgive them. She will punish them; she will finish them. Encased in these finalities, and in her bodily pain, she floats in curious comfort, beyond herself, beyond responsibility.

Suppose she dies now? Suppose she commits suicide? Suppose she runs away? Any of these things would be appropriate. It is only a matter of choosing, of figuring out the way. She floats in her pure superior state as if kindly drugged.

And just as there is a moment, when you are drugged, in which you feel perfectly safe, sure, unreachable, and then without warning and right next to it a moment in which you know the whole protection has fatally cracked, though it is still pretending to hold soundly together, so there is a moment now—the moment, in fact, when Rose hears Flo step on the stairs—that contains for her both present peace and freedom and a sure knowledge of the whole downspiraling course of events from now on.

Flo comes into the room without knocking, but with a hesitation that shows it might have occurred to her. She brings a jar of cold cream. Rose is hanging on to advantage as long as she can, lying face down on the bed, refusing to acknowledge or answer.

"Oh come on," Flo says uneasily. "You aren't so bad off, are you? You put some of this on and you'll feel better."

She is bluffing. She doesn't know for sure what damage has been done. She has the lid off the cold cream. Rose can smell it. The intimate, babyish, humiliating smell. She won't allow it near her. But in order to avoid it, the big ready clot of it in Flo's hand, she has to move. She scuffles, resists, loses dignity, and lets Flo see there is not really much the matter.

"All right," Flo says. "You win. I'll leave it here and you can put it on when you like."

Later still a tray will appear. Flo will put it down without a word and go away. A large glass of chocolate milk on it, made with Vita-Malt from the store. Some rich streaks of Vita-Malt around the bottom of the glass. Little sandwiches, neat and appetizing. Canned salmon of the first quality and reddest color, plenty of mayonnaise. A couple of butter tarts from a bakery package, chocolate biscuits with a peppermint filling. Rose's favorites, in the sandwich, tart and cookie line. She will turn away, refuse to look, but left alone with these eatables will be miserably tempted, roused and troubled and drawn back from thoughts of suicide or flight by the smell of salmon, the anticipation of crisp chocolate, she will reach out a finger, just to run it around the edge of one of the sandwiches (crusts cut off!) to get the overflow, get a taste. Then she will decide to eat one, for strength to refuse the rest. One will not be noticed. Soon, in helpless corruption, she will eat them all. She will drink the chocolate milk, eat the tarts, eat the cookies. She will get the malty syrup out of the bottom of the glass with her finger, though she sniffles with shame. Too late.

Flo will come up and get the tray. She may say, "I see you got your appetite still," or, "Did you like the chocolate milk, was it enough syrup in it?" depending on how chastened she is feeling, herself. At any rate, all advantage will be lost. Rose will understand that life has started up again, that they will all sit around the table eating again, listening to the radio news. Tomorrow morning, maybe even tonight. Unseemly and unlikely as that may be. They will be embarrassed, but rather less than you might expect considering how they have behaved. They will feel a queer lassitude, a convalescent indolence, not far off satisfaction.

One night after a scene like this they were all in the kitchen. It must have been summer, or at least warm weather, because her father spoke of the old men who sat on the bench in front of the store.

"Do you know what they're talking about now?" he said, and nodded his head toward the store to show who he meant, though of course they were not there now, they went home at dark.

"Those old coots," said Flo. "What?"

There was about them both a geniality not exactly false but a bit more emphatic than was normal, without company.

Rose's father told them then that the old men had picked up the idea somewhere that what looked like a star in the western sky, the first star that came out after sunset, the evening star, was in reality an airship hovering over Bay City, Michigan, on the other side of Lake Huron. An American invention, sent up to rival the heavenly bodies. They were all in agreement about this, the idea was congenial to them. They believed it to be lit by ten thousand electric light bulbs. Her father had ruthlessly disagreed with them, pointing out that it was the planet Venus they saw, which had appeared in the sky long before the invention of an electric light bulb. They had never heard of the planet Venus.

"Ignoramuses," said Flo. At which Rose knew, and knew her father knew, that Flo had never heard of the planet Venus either. To distract them from this, or even apologize for it, Flo put down her teacup, stretched out with her head resting on the chair she had been sitting on and her feet on another chair (somehow she managed to tuck her dress modestly between her legs at the same time), and lay stiff as a board, so that Brian cried out in delight, "Do that! Do that!"

Flo was double-jointed and very strong. In moments of celebration or emergency she would do tricks.

They were silent while she turned herself around, not using her arms at all but just her strong legs and feet. Then they all cried out in triumph, though they had seen it before.

Just as Flo turned herself Rose got a picture in her mind of that airship, an elongated transparent bubble, with its strings of diamond lights, floating in the miraculous American sky.

"The planet Venus!" her father said, applauding Flo. "Ten thousand electric lights!"

There was a feeling of permission, relaxation, even a current of happiness, in the room.

Years later, many years later, on a Sunday morning, Rose turned on the radio. This was when she was living by herself in Toronto.

Well Sir.

It was a different kind of place in our day. Yes it was.

It was all horses then. Horses and buggies. Buggy races up and down the main street on the Saturday nights.

"Just like the chariot races," says the announcer's, or interviewer's, smooth encouraging voice.

I never seen a one of them.

"No sir, that was the old Roman chariot races I was referring to. That was before your time."

Musta been before my time. I'm a hunerd and two years old.

"That's a wonderful age, sir."

It is so.

She left it on, as she went around the apartment kitchen, making coffee for herself. It seemed to her that this must be a staged interview, a scene from some play, and she wanted to find out what it was. The old man's voice was so vain and belligerent, the interviewer's quite hopeless and alarmed, under its practiced gentleness and ease. You were surely meant to see him holding the microphone up to some toothless, reckless, preening centenarian, wondering what in God's name he was doing here, and what would he say next?

"They must have been fairly dangerous."

What was dangerous?

"Those buggy races."

They was. Dangerous. Used to be the runaway horses. Used to be a-plenty of accidents. Fellows was dragged along on the gravel and cut their face open. Wouldna matter so much if they was dead. Heh.

Some of them horses was the high-steppers. Some, they had to have the mustard under their tail. Some wouldn step out for nothin. That's the thing it is with the horses. Some'll work and pull till they drop down dead and some wouldn pull your cock out of a pail of lard. Hehe.

It must be a real interview after all. Otherwise they wouldn't have put that in, wouldn't have risked it. It's all right if the old man says it. Local color. Anything rendered harmless and delightful by his hundred years.

Accidents all the time then. In the mill. Foundry. Wasn't the precautions.

"You didn't have so many strikes then, I don't suppose? You didn't have so many unions?"

Everybody taking it easy nowadays. We worked and we was glad to get it. Worked and was glad to get it.

"You didn't have television."

Didn't have no TV. Didn't have no radio. No picture show.

"You made your own entertainment."

That's the way we did.

"You had a lot of experiences young men growing up today will never have."

Experiences.

"Can you recall any of them for us?"

I eaten groundhog meat one time. One winter. You wouldna cared for it. Heh.

There was a pause, of appreciation, it would seem, then the announcer's voice saying that the foregoing had been an interview with Mr. Wilfred Nettleton of Hanratty, Ontario, made on his hundred and second birthday, two weeks before his death, last spring. A living link with our past. Mr. Nettleton had been interviewed in the Wawanash County Home for the aged.

Hat Nettleton.

Horsewhipper into centenarian. Photographed on his birthday, fussed over by nurses, kissed no doubt by a girl reporter. Flash bulbs popping at him. Tape recorder drinking in the sound of his voice. Oldest resident. Oldest horsewhipper. Living link with our past.

Looking out from her kitchen window at the cold lake, Rose was longing to tell somebody. It was Flo who would enjoy hearing. She thought of her saying *Imagine!* in a way that meant she was having her worst suspicions gorgeously confirmed. But Flo was in the same place

Hat Nettleton had died in, and there wasn't any way Rose could reach her. She had been there even when that interview was recorded, though she would not have heard it, would not have known about it. After Rose put her in the Home, a couple of years earlier, she had stopped talking. She had removed herself, and spent most of her time sitting in a corner of her crib, looking crafty and disagreeable, not answering anybody, though she occasionally showed her feelings by biting a nurse.

---

1. What is Rose's fundamental feeling toward Flo? How does it change over the years and what is it at the end?
2. What is Flo's character and how is it revealed in her actions with Rose?
3. What are the fathers's motives in administering the beatings to Rose? In what ways can he also be considered a victim?
4. What is the tone of the story and is it consistent with the grimness of the subject matter?
5. What does the story of the Tyde family and Hat Nettleton have to do with the main story of Rose and her family?

Prue

Prue used to live with Gordon. This was after Gordon left his wife and before he went back to her—a year and four months in all. Some time later, he and his wife were divorced. After that came a period of indecision, of living together off and on; then the wife went away to New Zealand, most likely for good.

Prue did not go back to Vancouver Island, where Gordon had met her when she was working as a dining-room hostess in a resort hotel. She got a job in Toronto, working in a plant shop. She had many friends in Toronto by that time, most of them Gordon's friends and his wife's friends. They liked Prue and were ready to feel sorry for her, but she laughed them out of it. She is very likable. She has what eastern Canadians call an English accent, though she was born in Canada—in Duncan, on Vancouver Island. This accent helps her to say the most cynical things in a winning and light-hearted way. She presents her life in anecdotes, and though it is the point of most of her anecdotes that hopes are dashed, dreams ridiculed, things never turn out as expected, everything is altered in a bizarre way and there is no explanation ever, people always feel cheered up after listening to her; they say of her that it is a relief to meet somebody who doesn't take herself too seriously, who is so unintense, and civilized, and never makes any real demands or complaints.

The only thing she complains about readily is her name. Prue is a schoolgirl, she says, and Prudence is an old virgin; the parents who gave her that name must have been too shortsighted even to take account of puberty. What if she had grown a great bosom, she says, or developed a sultry look? Or was the name itself a guarantee that she wouldn't? In her late forties now, slight and fair, attending to customers with a dutiful vivacity, giving pleasure to dinner guests, she might not be far from what those parents had in mind: bright and thoughtful, a cheerful spectator. It is hard to grant her maturity, maternity, real troubles.

Her grownup children, the products of an early Vancouver Island marriage she calls a cosmic disaster, come to see her, and instead of wanting money, like other people's children, they bring presents, try to do her accounts, arrange to have her house insulated. She is delighted with their presents, listens to their advice, and, like a flighty daughter, neglects to answer their letters.

Her children hope she is not staying on in Toronto because of Gordon. Everybody hopes that. She would laugh at the idea. She gives parties and goes to parties; she goes out sometimes with other men. Her attitude toward sex is very comforting to those of her friends who get into terrible states of passion and jealousy, and feel cut loose from their moorings. She seems to regard sex as a wholesome, slightly silly indulgence, like dancing and nice dinners—something that shouldn't interfere with people's being kind and cheerful to each other.

Now that his wife is gone for good, Gordon comes to see Prue occasionally, and sometimes asks her out for dinner. They may not go to a restaurant; they may go to his house. Gordon is a good cook. When Prue or his wife lived with him he couldn't cook at all, but as soon as he put his mind to it he became—he says truthfully—better than either of them.

Recently he and Prue were having dinner at his house. He had made chicken Kiev, and crème brûlée for dessert. Like most new, serious cooks, he talked about food.

Gordon is rich, by Prue's—and most people's—standards. He is a neurologist. His house is new, built on a hillside north of the city, where there used to be picturesque, unprofitable farms. Now there are one-of-a-kind, architect-designed, very expensive houses on half-acre lots. Prue, describing Gordon's house, will say, "Do you know there are four bathrooms? So that if four people want to have baths at the same time there's no problem. It seems a bit much, but it's very nice, really, and you'd never have to go through the hall."

Gordon's house has a raised dining area—a sort of platform, surrounded by a conversation pit, a music pit, and a bank of heavy greenery under sloping glass. You can't see the entrance area from the dining area, but there are no intervening walls, so that from one area you can hear something of what is going on in the other.

During dinner the doorbell rang. Gordon excused himself and went down the steps. Prue heard a female voice. The person it belonged to was still outside, so she could not hear the words. She heard Gordon's voice, pitched low, cautioning. The door didn't close—it seemed the person had not been invited in—but the voices went on, muted and angry. Suddenly there was a cry from Gordon, and he appeared halfway up the steps, waving his arms.

"The crême brûlée," he said. "Could you?" He ran back down as Prue got up and went into the kitchen to save the dessert. When she returned he was climbing the stairs more slowly, looking both agitated and tired.

"A friend," he said gloomily. "Was it all right?"

Prue realized he was speaking of the crême brûlée, and she said yes, it was perfect, she had got it just in time. He thanked her but did not cheer up. It seemed it was not the dessert he was troubled over but whatever had happened at the door. To take his mind off it, Prue started asking him professional questions about the plants.

"I don't know a thing about them," he said. "You know that."

"I thought you might have picked it up. Like the cooking."

"She takes care of them."

"Mrs. Carr?" said Prue, naming his housekeeper.

"Who did you think?"

Prue blushed. She hated to be thought suspicious.

"The problem is that I think I would like to marry you," said Gordon, with no noticeable lightening of his spirits. Gordon is a large man, with heavy features. He likes to wear thick clothing, bulky sweaters. His blue eyes are often bloodshot, and their expression indicates that there is a helpless, baffled soul squirming around inside this doughty fortress.

"What a problem," said Prue lightly, though she knew Gordon well enough to know that it was.

The doorbell rang again, rang twice, three times, before Gordon could get to it. This time there was a crash, as of something flung and landing hard. The door slammed and Gordon was immediately back in view. He staggered on the steps and held his hand to his head, meanwhile making a gesture with the other hand to signify that nothing serious had happened, Prue was to sit down.

"Bloody overnight bag," he said. "She threw it at me."

"Did it hit you?"

"Glancing."

"It made a hard sound for an overnight bag. Were there rocks in it?"

"Oh."

Prue watched him pour himself a drink. "I'd like some coffee, if I might," she said. She went to the kitchen to put the water on, and Gordon followed her.

"I think I'm in love with this person," he said.

"Who is she?"

"You don't know her. She's quite young."

"Oh."

"But I do think I want to marry you, in a few years' time."

"After you get over being in love?"

"Yes."

"Well. I guess nobody knows what can happen in a few years' time."

When Prue tells about this, she says, "I think he was afraid I was going to laugh. He doesn't know why people laugh or throw their overnight bags at him, but he's noticed they do. He's such a proper person, really. The lovely dinner. Then she comes and throws her overnight bag. And it's quite reasonable to think of marrying me in a few years' time, when he gets over being in love. I think he first thought of telling me to sort of put my mind at rest."

She doesn't mention that the next morning she picked up one of Gordon's cufflinks from his dresser. The cufflinks are made of amber and he bought them in Russia, on the holiday he and wife took when they got back together again. They look like squares of candy, golden, translucent, and this one warms quickly in her hand. She drops it into the pocket of her jacket. Taking one is not a real theft. It could be a reminder, an intimate prank, a piece of nonsense.

She is alone in Gordon's house; he has gone off early, as he always does. The housekeeper does not come till nine. Prue doesn't have to be at the shop until ten; she could make herself breakfast, stay and have coffee with the housekeeper, who is her friend from olden times. But once she has the cufflink in her pocket she doesn't linger. The house seems too bleak a place to spend an extra moment in. It was Prue, actually, who helped choose the building lot. But she's not responsible for approving the plans—the wife was back by that time.

When she gets home she puts the cufflink in an old tobacco tin. The children bought this tobacco tin in a junk shop years ago, and gave it to her for a present. She used to smoke, in those days, and the children were worried about her, so they gave her this tin full off toffees, jelly beans, and gumdrops, with a note saying, "Please get fat instead." That was for her birthday. Now the tin has in it several things besides the cufflink—all small things, not of great value but not worthless, either. A little enamelled dish, a sterling-silver spoon for salt, a crystal fish. These are not sentimental keepsakes. She never looks at them, and often forgets what she has there. They are not booty, they don't have ritualistic significance. She does not take something every time she goes to Gordon's house, or every time she stays over, or to mark what she might call memorable visits. She doesn't do it in a daze and she doesn't seem to be under a compulsion. She just takes something, every now and then, and puts it away in the dark of the old tobacco tin, and more or less forgets about it.

---

1. How does the name of the central character (in its regular and diminutive forms) condition her or shape her role?
2. How is Gordon characterized by his new house?
3. On what terms is the marriage of Gordon and Prue conceivable?
4. Discuss the tone of the story and the way tone influences the reader's view of the main characters.
5. What is represented by the objects Prue gathers in her tobacco can? By the tobacco can itself?

Vladimir Nabokov

Nabokov (1899–1977) was born in St. Petersburg—now Leningrad—Russia, of rich and cultured parents. At the time of the Communist Revolution, he fled with his family into Western Europe. He attended Cambridge University in England and took a degree in modern languages there in 1922. Thereafter he spent years in Berlin and Paris, supporting himself by coaching tennis and making up chess problems—and all the while writing novels in Russian, German, French, and English. Living in France when it was overrun by the Nazis, he escaped with his family to the United States, where he became a citizen and—by a remarkable imaginative transformation—an American writer. He taught Russian literature at Cornell University until Lolita, *a bestseller in 1955, and subsequent novels gave him enough money to allow him a fulltime commitment to writing. He then lived in Montreux, Switzerland. His complete works in all languages would run to thirty or forty volumes, exemplifying the complexity of his life and his interests in language and experience. In most of his fiction memories of a dissolving past mingle with an ironic sense of the precariousness of the present. Among his novels are* Laughter in the Dark *(translated in 1938),* Lolita *(1955),* Pnin *(1957),* Pale Fire *(1962), and* Ada; Or, Ardor: A Family Chronicle *(1969). Books of stories include* Nabokov's Dozen *(1958) and* Nabokov's Quartet *(1967).*

Signs and Symbols

I

For the fourth time in as many years they were confronted with the problem of what birthday present to bring a young man who was incurably deranged in his mind. He had no desires. Man-made objects were to him either hives of evil, vibrant with a malignant activity that he alone could perceive, or gross comforts for which no use could be found in his abstract world. After eliminating a number of articles that might offend him or frighten him (anything in the gadget line for instance was taboo), his parents chose a dainty and innocent trifle: a basket with ten different fruit jellies in ten little jars.

At the time of his birth they had been married already for a long time; a score of years had elapsed, and now they were quite old. Her drab gray hair was done anyhow. She wore cheap black dresses. Unlike other women of her age (such as Mrs. Sol, their next-door neighbor, whose face was all pink and mauve with paint and whose hat was a cluster of brookside flowers), she presented a naked white countenance to the fault-finding light of spring days. Her husband, who in the old country had been a fairly successful businessman, was now wholly dependent on his brother Isaac, a real American of almost forty years standing. They seldom saw him and had nicknamed him "the Prince."

That Friday everything went wrong. The underground train lost its life current between two stations, and for a quarter of an hour one could hear nothing but the dutiful beating of one's heart and the rustling of newspapers. The bus they had to take next kept them waiting for ages; and when it did come, it was crammed with garrulous high-school children. It was raining hard as they walked up the brown path leading to the sanitarium. There they waited again; and instead of their boy shuffling into the room as he usually did (his poor face blotched with acne, ill-shaven, sullen, and confused), a nurse they knew, and did not care for, appeared at last and brightly explained that he had again attempted to take his life. He was all right, she said, but a visit might disturb him. The place was so miserably understaffed, and things got mislaid or mixed up so easily, that they decided not to leave their present in the office but to bring it to him next time they came.

She waited for her husband to open his umbrella and then took his arm. He kept clearing his throat in a special resonant way he had when he was upset. They reached the bus-stop shelter on the other side of the street and he closed his umbrella. A few feet away, under a swaying and dripping tree, a tiny half-dead unfledged bird was helplessly twitching in a puddle.

During the long ride to the subway station, she and her husband did not exchange a word; and every time she glanced at his old hands (swollen veins, brown-spotted skin), clasped and twitching upon the handle of his umbrella, she felt the mounting pressure of tears. As she looked around trying to hook her mind onto something, it gave her a kind of soft shock, a mixture of compassion and wonder, to notice that one of the passengers, a girl with dark hair and grubby red toenails, was weeping on the shoulder of an older woman. Whom did that woman resemble? She resembled Rebecca Borisovna, whose daughter had married one of the Soloveichiks—in Minsk,[1] years ago.

The last time he had tried to do it, his method had been, in the doctor's words, a masterpiece of inventiveness; he would have succeeded, had not an envious fellow patient thought he was learning to fly—and stopped him. What he really wanted to do was to tear a hole in his world and escape.

1. A city in western Russia.

The system of his delusions had been the subject of an elaborate paper in a scientific monthly, but long before that she and her husband had puzzled it out for themselves. "Referential mania," Herman Brink had called it. In these very rare cases the patient imagines that everything happening around him is a veiled reference to his personality and existence. He excludes real people from the conspiracy—because he considers himself to be so much more intelligent than other men. Phenomenal nature shadows him wherever he goes. Clouds in the staring sky transmit to one another, by means of slow signs, incredibly detailed information regarding him. His inmost thoughts are discussed at nightfall, in manual alphabet,[2] by darkly gesticulating trees. Pebbles or stains or sun flecks form patterns representing in some awful way messages which he must intercept. Everything is a cipher and of everything he is the theme. Some of the spies are detached observers, such as glass surfaces and still pools; others, such as coats in store windows, are prejudiced witnesses, lynchers at heart; others again (running water, storms) are hysterical to the point of insanity, have a distorted opinion of him and grotesquely misinterpret his actions. He must be always on his guard and devote every minute and module of life to the decoding of the undulation of things. The very air he exhales is indexed and filed away. If only the interest he provokes were limited to his immediate surroundings—but alas it is not! With distance the torrents of wild scandal increase in volume and volubility. The silhouettes of his blood corpuscles, magnified a million times, flit over vast plains; and still farther, great mountains of unbearable solidity and height sum up in terms of granite and groaning firs the ultimate truth of his being.

II

When they emerged from the thunder and foul air of the subway, the last dregs of the day were mixed with the street lights. She wanted to buy some fish for supper, so she handed him the basket of jelly jars, telling him to go home. He walked up to the third landing and then remembered he had given her his keys earlier in the day.

In silence he sat down on the steps and in silence rose when some ten minutes later she came, heavily trudging upstairs, wanly smiling, shaking her head in deprecation of her silliness. They entered their two-room flat and he at once went to the mirror. Straining the corners of his mouth apart by means of his thumbs, with a horrible masklike grimace, he removed his new hopelessly uncomfortable dental plate and severed the long tusks of saliva connecting him to it. He

2. Sign language used by the deaf.

read his Russian-language newspaper while she laid the table. Still reading, he ate the pale victuals that needed no teeth. She knew his moods and was also silent.

When he had gone to bed, she remained in the living room with her pack of soiled cards and her old albums. Across the narrow yard where the rain tinkled in the dark against some battered ash cans, windows were blandly alight and in one of them a black-trousered man with his bare elbows raised could be seen lying supine on an untidy bed. She pulled the blind down and examined the photographs. As a baby he looked more surprised than most babies. From a fold in the album, a German maid they had had in Leipzig and her fat-faced fiancé fell out. Minsk, the Revolution,[3] Leipzig, Berlin, Leipzig, a slanting house front badly out of focus. Four years old, in a park: moodily, shyly, with puckered forehead, looking away from an eager squirrel as he would from any other stranger. Aunt Rose, a fussy, angular, wild-eyed old lady, who had lived in a tremulous world of bad news, bankruptcies, train accidents, cancerous growths—until the Germans put her to death, together with all the people she had worried about. Age six—that was when he drew wonderful birds with human hands and feet, and suffered from insomnia like a grown-up man. His cousin, now a famous chess player. He again, aged about eight, already difficult to understand, afraid of the wallpaper in the passage, afraid of a certain picture in a book which merely showed an idyllic landscape with rocks on a hillside and an old cart wheel hanging from the branch of a leafless tree. Aged ten: the year they left Europe. The shame, the pity, the humiliating difficulties, the ugly, vicious, backward children he was with in that special school. And then came a time in his life, coinciding with a long convalescence after pneumonia, when those little phobias of his which his parents had stubbornly regarded as the eccentricities of a prodigiously gifted child hardened as it were into a dense tangle of logically interacting illusions, making him totally inaccessible to normal minds.

This, and much more, she accepted—for after all living did mean accepting the loss of one joy after another, not even joys in her case—mere possibilities of improvement. She thought of the endless waves of pain that for some reason or other she and her husband had to endure; of the invisible giants hurting her boy in some unimaginable fashion; of the incalculable amount of tenderness contained in the world; of the fate of this tenderness, which is either crushed, or wasted, or transformed into madness; of neglected children humming to themselves in unswept corners; of beautiful weeds that cannot hide from the farmer

3. Leipzig is a city in Germany; the Revolution is the Russian Revolution of 1917–22.

and helplessly have to watch the shadow of his simian stoop leave mangled flowers in its wake, as the monstrous darkness approaches.

III

It was past midnight when from the living room she heard her husband moan; and presently he staggered in, wearing over his nightgown the old overcoat with astrakhan[4] collar which he much preferred to the nice blue bathrobe he had.

"I can't sleep," he cried.

"Why," she asked, "why can't you sleep? You were so tired."

"I can't sleep because I am dying," he said and lay down on the couch.

"Is it your stomach? Do you want me to call Dr. Solov?"

"No doctors, no doctors," he moaned. "To the devil with doctors! We must get him out of there quick. Otherwise we'll be responsible. Responsible!" he repeated and hurled himself into a sitting position, both feet on the floor, thumping his forehead with his clenched fist.

"All right," she said quietly, "we shall bring him home tomorrow morning."

"I would like some tea," said her husband and retired to the bathroom.

Bending with difficulty, she retrieved some playing cards and a photograph or two that had slipped from the couch to the floor: knave of hearts, nine of spades, ace of spades, Elsa and her bestial beau.

He returned in high spirits, saying in a loud voice:

"I have it all figured out. We will give him the bedroom. Each of us will spend part of the night near him and the other part on this couch. By turns. We will have the doctor see him at least twice a week. It does not matter what the Prince says. He won't have to say much anyway because it will come out cheaper."

The telephone rang. It was an unusual hour for their telephone to ring. His left slipper had come off and he groped for it with his heel and toe as he stood in the middle of the room, and childishly, toothlessly, gaped at his wife. Having more English than he did, it was she who attended to calls.

"Can I speak to Charlie," said a girl's dull little voice.

"What number you want? No. That is not the right number."

The receiver was gently cradled. Her hand went to her old tired heart.

"It frightened me," she said.

He smiled a quick smile and immediately resumed his excited

4. Lustrous, closely curled wool (from Astrakhan, a city in southeast Soviet Union).

monologue. They would fetch him as soon as it was day. Knives would have too be kept in a locked drawer. Even at his worst he presented no danger to other people.

The telephone rang a second time. The same toneless anxious young voice asked for Charlie.

"You have the incorrect number. I will tell you what you are doing: you are turning the letter O instead of zero."

They sat down to their unexpected festive midnight tea. The birthday present stood on the table. He sipped noisily; his face was flushed; every now and then he imparted a circular motion to his raised glass so as to make the sugar dissolve more thoroughly. The vein on the side of his bald head where there was a large birthmark stood out conspicuously and, although he had shaved that morning, a silvery bristle showed on his chin. While she poured him another glass of tea, he put on his spectacles and re-examined with pleasure the luminous yellow, green, red little jars. His clumsy moist lips spelled out their eloquent labels: apricot, grape, beech plum, quince. He had got to crab apple, when the telephone rang again.

---

1. Is there any logical explanation for the ringing of the telephone at the end of the story? Suppose that someone is merely calling a wrong number. Is that a meaningful or a meaningless coincidence?
2. Does the story suggest that everything we see has a message for us . . . or that to believe so is a form of insanity?
3. If we take this to be a sort of mystery story, can we find enough clues to decipher and explain the mystery? Or has the author deliberately stopped short of providing the clues we would need? Is a story satisfactory if it presents a riddle and then withholds the means of solving it?
4. Does the story in any way challenge your ideas of what reality is? Discuss.
5. Are language and imagery uniform throughout? Discuss the effect of any shifts you may note.

Gloria Naylor

Naylor (1950–) was born in New York City. She attended Brooklyn College and later studied in the program of Afro-American studies at Yale. Her first book, which she calls "a novel in seven stories," was The Women of Brewster Place *(1982). In these interrelated stories she surveys the black female experience in America, portraying women with different dreams and aspirations that in various ways fail them and precipitate them into the common travail of our times. She has subsequently published* Linden Hills *(1985) and* Mama Day *(1988).*

Lucielia Louise Turner

The sunlight was still watery as Ben trudged into Brewster Place, and the street had just begun to yawn and stretch itself. He eased himself onto his garbage can, which was pushed against the sagging brick wall that turned Brewster into a dead-end street. The metallic cold of the can's lid seeped into the bottom of his thin trousers. Sucking on a piece of breakfast sausage caught in his back teeth, he began to muse. Mighty cold, these spring mornings. The old days you could build a good trash fire in one of them barrels to keep warm. Well, don't want no summons now, and can't freeze to death. Yup, can't freeze to death.

His daily soliloquy completed, he reached into his coat pocket and pulled out a crumpled brown bag that contained his morning sun. The cheap red liquid moved slowly down his throat, providing immediate justification as the blood began to warm in his body. In the hazy light a lean dark figure began to make its way slowly up the block. It hesitated in front of the stoop at 316, but looking around and seeing Ben, it hurried over.

"Yo, Ben."

"Hey, Eugene, I thought that was you. Ain't seen ya round for a coupla days."

"Yeah." The young man put his hands in his pockets, frowned into the ground, and kicked the edge of Ben's can. "The funeral's today, ya know."

"Yeah."

"You going?" He looked up into Ben's face.

"Naw, I ain't got no clothes for them things. Can't abide 'em no way—too sad—it being a baby and all."

"Yeah. I was going myself, people expect it, ya know?"

"Yeah."

"But, man, the way Ciel's friends look at me and all—like I was filth or something. Hey, I even tried to go see Ciel in the hospital, heard she was freaked out and all."

"Yeah, she took it real bad."

"Yeah, well, damn, I took it bad. It was my kid, too, ya know. But Mattie, that fat, black bitch, just standin' in the hospital hall sayin' to me—to me, now, 'Whatcha want?' Like I was a fuckin' germ or something. Man, I just turned and left. You gotta be treated with respect, ya know?"

"Yeah."

"I mean, I should be there today with my woman in the limo and all, sittin' up there, doin' it right. But how you gonna be a man with them ball-busters tellin' everybody it was my fault and I should be the one dead? Damn!"

"Yeah, a man's gotta be a man." Ben felt the need to wet his reply with another sip. "Have some?"

"Naw, I'm gonna be heading on—Ciel don't need me today. I bet that frig, Mattie, rides in the head limo, wearing the pants. Shit—let 'em." He looked up again. "Ya know?"

"Yup."

"Take it easy, Ben." He turned to go.

"You too, Eugene."

"Hey, you going?"

"Naw."

"Me neither. Later."

"Later, Eugene."

Funny, Ben thought, Eugene ain't stopped to chat like that for a long time—near on a year, yup, a good year. He took another swallow to help him bring back the year-old conversation, but it didn't work; the second and third one didn't either. But he did remember that it had been an early spring morning like this one, and Eugene had been wearing those same tight jeans. He had hesitated outside of 316 then, too. But that time he went in . . .

Lucielia had just run water into the tea kettle and was putting it on the burner when she heard the cylinder turn. He didn't have to knock on the door; his key still fit the lock. Her thin knuckles gripped the handle of the kettle, but she didn't turn around. She knew. The last eleven months of her life hung compressed in the air between the click of the lock and his "Yo, baby."

The vibrations from those words rode like parasites on the air waves and came rushing into her kitchen, smashing the compression into indistinguishable days and hours that swirled dizzily before her. It was all there: the frustration of being left alone, sick, with a month-old baby; her humiliation reflected in the caseworker's blue eyes for the unanswerable "you can find him to have it, but can't find him to take care of it" smile; the raw urges that crept, uninvited, between her thighs on countless nights; the eternal whys all meshed with the explainable hate and unexplainable love. They kept circling in such a confusing pattern before her that she couldn't seem to grab even one to answer him with. So there was nothing in Lucielia's face when she turned it toward Eugene, standing in her kitchen door holding a ridiculously pink Easter bunny, nothing but sheer relief. . . .

"So he's back." Mattie sat at Lucielia's kitchen table, playing with Serena. It was rare that Mattie ever spoke more than two sentences to anybody about anything. She didn't have to. She chose her words with the grinding precision of a diamond cutter's drill.

"You think I'm a fool, don't you?"

"I ain't said that."

"You didn't have to," Ciel snapped.

"Why you mad at me, Ciel? It's your life, honey."

"Oh, Mattie, you don't understand. He's really straightened up this time. He's got a new job on the docks that pays real good, and he was just so depressed before with the new baby and no work. You'll see. He's even gone out now to buy paint and stuff to fix up the apartment. And, and Serena needs a daddy."

"You ain't gotta convince me, Ciel."

No, she wasn't talking to Mattie, she was talking to herself. She was convincing herself it was the new job and the paint and Serena that let him back into her life. Yet, the real truth went beyond her scope of understanding. When she laid her head in the hollow of his neck there was a deep musky scent to his body that brought back the ghosts of the Tennessee soil of her childhood. It reached up and lined the inside of her nostrils so that she inhaled his presence almost every minute of her life. The feel of his sooty flesh penetrated the skin of her fingers and coursed through her blood and became one, somewhere, wherever it was, with her actual being. But how do you tell yourself, let alone this practical old woman who loves you, that he was back because of that. So you don't.

You get up and fix you both another cup of coffee, calm the fretting baby on your lap with her pacifier, and you pray silently—very silently—behind veiled eyes that the man will stay.

Ciel was trying to remember exactly when it had started to go wrong again. Her mind sought for the slender threads of a clue that she could trace back to—perhaps—something she had said or done. Her brow was set tightly in concentration as she folded towels and smoothed the wrinkles over and over, as if the answer lay concealed in the stubborn creases of the terry cloth.

The months since Eugene's return began to tick off slowly before her, and she examined each one to pinpoint when the nagging whispers of trouble had begun in her brain. The friction on the towels increased when she came to the month that she had gotten pregnant again, but it couldn't be that. Things were different now. She wasn't sick as she had been with Serena, he was still working—no it wasn't the baby. It's not the baby, it's not the baby—the rhythm of those words sped up the motion of her hands, and she had almost yanked and folded and pressed them into a reality when, bewildered, she realized that she had run out of towels.

Ciel jumped when the front door slammed shut. She waited tensely for the metallic bang of his keys on the coffee table and the blast of the stereo. Lately that was how Eugene announced his presence home. Ciel walked into the living room with the motion of a swimmer entering a cold lake.

"Eugene, you're home early, huh?"

"You see anybody else sittin' here?" He spoke without looking at her and rose to turn up the stereo.

He wants to pick a fight, she thought, confused and hurt. He knows Serena's taking her nap, and now I'm supposed to say, Eugene, the baby's asleep, please cut the music down. Then he's going to say, you mean a man can't even relax in his own home without being picked on? I'm not picking on you, but you're going to wake up the baby. Which is always supposed to lead to: You don't give a damn about me. Everybody's more important than me—that kid, your friends, everybody. I'm just chickenshit around here, huh?

All this went through Ciel's head as she watched him leave the stereo and drop defiantly back down on the couch. Without saying a word, she turned and went into the bedroom. She looked down on the peaceful face of her daughter and softly caressed her small cheek. Her heart became full as she realized, this is the only thing I have ever loved without pain. She pulled the sheet gently over the tiny shoulders and firmly closed the door, protecting her from the music. She then went into the kitchen and began washing the rice for their dinner.

Eugene, seeing that he had been left alone, turned off the stereo and came and stood in the kitchen door.

"I lost my job today," he shot at her, as if she had been the cause.

The water was turning cloudy in the rice pot, and the force of the stream from the faucet caused scummy bubbles to rise to the surface. These broke and sprayed tiny starchy particles onto the dirty surface. Each bubble that broke seemed to increase the volume of the dogged whispers she had been ignoring for the last few months. She poured the dirty water off the rice to destroy and silence them, then watched with a malicious joy as they disappeared down the drain.

"So now, how in the hell I'm gonna make it with no money, huh? And another brat comin' here, huh?"

The second change of the water was slightly clearer, but the starch-speckled bubbles were still there, and this time there was no way to pretend deafness to their message. She had stood at that sink countless times before, washing rice, and she knew the water was never going to be totally clear. She couldn't stand there forever—her fingers were getting cold, and the rest of the dinner had to be fixed, and Serena would be waking up soon and wanting attention. Feverishly she poured the water off and tried again.

"I'm fuckin' sick of never getting ahead. Babies and bills, that's all you good for."

The bubbles were almost transparent now, but when they broke they left light trails of starch on top of the water that curled around her fingers. She knew it would be useless to try again. Defeated, Ciel placed the wet pot on the burner, and the flames leaped up bright red and orange, turning the water droplets clinging on the outside into steam.

Turning to him, she silently acquiesced. "All right, Eugene, what do you want me to do?"

He wasn't going to let her off so easily. "Hey, baby, look, I don't care what you do. I just can't have all these hassles on me right now, ya know?"

"I'll get a job. I don't mind, but I've got no one to keep Serena, and you don't want Mattie watching her."

"Mattie—no way. That fat bitch'll turn the kid against me. She hates my ass, and you know it."

"No, she doesn't, Eugene." Ciel remembered throwing that at Mattie once. "You hate him, don't you?" "Naw, honey," and she had cupped both hands on Ciel's face. "Maybe I just loves you too much."

"I don't give a damn what you say—she ain't minding my kid."

"Well, look, after the baby comes, they can tie my tubes—I don't care." She swallowed hard to keep down the lie.

"And what the hell we gonna feed it when it gets here, huh—air? With two kids and you on my back, I ain't never gonna have nothin'." He came and grabbed her by the shoulders and was shouting into her face. "Nothin', do you hear me, nothin'!"

"Nothing to it, Mrs. Turner." The face over hers was as calm and antiseptic as the room she lay in. "Please, relax. I'm going to give you a local anesthetic and then perform a simple D&C, or what you'd call a scraping to clean out the uterus. Then you'll rest here for about an hour and be on your way. There won't even be much bleeding." The voice droned on in its practiced monologue, peppered with sterile kindness.

Ciel was not listening. It was important that she keep herself completely isolated from these surroundings. All the activities of the past week of her life were balled up and jammed on the right side of her brain, as if belonging to some other woman. And when she had endured this one last thing for her, she would push it up there, too, and then one day give it all to her—Ciel wanted no part of it.

The next few days Ciel found it difficult to connect herself up again with her own world. Everything seemed to have taken on new textures and colors. When she washed the dishes, the plates felt peculiar in her hands, and she was more conscious of their smoothness and the heat of the water. There was a disturbing split second between someone talking to her and the words penetrating sufficiently to elicit a response. Her neighbors left her presence with slight frowns of puzzlement, and Eugene could be heard mumbling, "Moody bitch."

She became terribly possessive of Serena. She refused to leave her alone, even with Eugene. The little girl went everywhere with Ciel, toddling along on plump uncertain legs. When someone asked to hold or play with her, Ciel sat nearby, watching every move. She found herself walking into the bedroom several times when the child napped to see if she was still breathing. Each time she chided herself for this unreasonable foolishness, but within the next few minutes some strange force still drove her back.

Spring was slowly beginning to announce itself at Brewster Place. The arthritic cold was seeping out of the worn gray bricks, and the tenants with apartment windows facing the street were awakened by six o'clock sunlight. The music no longer blasted inside of 3C, and Ciel grew strong with the peacefulness of her household. The playful laughter of her daughter, heard more often now, brought a sort of redemption with it.

"Isn't she marvelous, Mattie? You know she's even trying to make whole sentences. Come on, baby, talk for Auntie Mattie."

Serena, totally uninterested in living up to her mother's proud claims, was trying to tear a gold-toned button off the bosom of Mattie's dress.

"It's so cute. She even knows her father's name. She says, my da da is Gene."

"Better teach her your name," Mattie said, while playing with the baby's hand. "She'll be using it more."

Ciel's mouth flew open to ask her what she meant by that, but she checked herself. It was useless to argue with Mattie. You could take her words however you wanted. The burden of their truth lay with you, not her.

Eugene came through the front door and stopped short when he saw Mattie. He avoided being around her as much as possible. She was always polite to him, but he sensed a silent condemnation behind even her most innocent words. He constantly felt the need to prove himself in front of her. These frustrations often took the form of unwarranted rudeness on his part.

Serena struggled out of Mattie's lap and went toward her father and tugged on his legs to be picked up. Ignoring the child and cutting short the greetings of the two women, he said coldly, "Ciel, I wanna talk to you."

Sensing trouble, Mattie rose to go. "Ciel, why don't you let me take Serena downstairs for a while. I got some ice cream for her."

"She can stay right here," Eugene broke in. "If she needs ice cream, I can buy it for her."

Hastening to soften his abruptness, Ciel said, "That's okay, Mattie, it's almost time for her nap. I'll bring her later—after dinner."

"All right. Now you all keep good." Her voice was warm. "You too, Eugene," she called back from the front door.

The click of the lock restored his balance to him. "Why in the hell is she always up here?"

"You just had your chance—why didn't you ask her yourself? If you don't want her here, tell her to stay out," Ciel snapped back confidently, knowing he never would.

"Look, I ain't got time to argue with you about that old hag. I got big doings in the making, and I need you to help me pack." Without waiting for a response, he hurried into the bedroom and pulled his old leather suitcase from under the bed.

A tight, icy knot formed in the center of Ciel's stomach and began to melt rapidly, watering the blood in her legs so that they almost refused to support her weight. She pulled Serena back from following Eugene and sat her in the middle of the living room floor.

"Here, honey, play with the blocks for Mommy—she has to talk to Daddy." She piled a few plastic alphabet blocks in front of the child, and on her way out of the room, she glanced around quickly and removed the glass ashtrays off the coffee table and put them on a shelf over the stereo.

Then, taking a deep breath to calm her racing heart, she started toward the bedroom.

Serena loved the light colorful cubes and would sometimes sit for an entire half-hour, repeatedly stacking them up and kicking them over with her feet. The hollow sound of their falling fascinated her, and she would often bang two of them together to re-create the magical noise. She was sitting, contentedly engaged in this particular activity, when a slow dark movement along the baseboard caught her eye.

A round black roach was making its way from behind the couch toward the kitchen. Serena threw one of her blocks at the insect, and, feeling the vibrations of the wall above it, the roach sped around the door into the kitchen. Finding a totally new game to amuse herself, Serena took off behind the insect with a block in each hand. Seeing her moving toy trying to bury itself under the linoleum by the garbage pail she threw another block, and the frantic roach now raced along the wall and found security in the electric wall socket under the kitchen table.

Angry at losing her plaything, she banged the block against the socket, attempting to get it to come back out. When that failed, she unsuccessfully tried to poke her chubby finger into the thin horizontal slit. Frustrated, tiring of the game, she sat under the table and realized she had found an entirely new place in the house to play. The shiny chrome of the table and chair legs drew her attention, and she experimented with the sound of the block against their smooth surfaces.

This would have entertained her until Ciel came, but the roach, thinking itself safe, ventured outside of the socket. Serena gave a cry of delight and attempted to catch her lost playmate, but it was too quick and darted back into the wall. She tried once again to poke her finger into the slit. Then a bright slender object, lying dropped and forgotten, came into her view. Picking up the fork, Serena finally managed to fit the thin flattened prongs into the electric socket.

Eugene was avoiding Ciel's eyes as he packed. "You know, baby, this is really a good deal after me bein' out of work for so long." He moved around her still figure to open the drawer that held his T-shirts and shorts. "And hell, Maine ain't far. Once I get settled on the docks up there, I'll be able to come home all the time."

"Why can't you take us with you?" She followed each of his movements with her eyes and saw herself being buried in the case under the growing pile of clothes.

" 'Cause I gotta check out what's happening before I drag you and the kid up there."

"I don't mind. We'll make do. I've learned to live on very little."

"No, it just won't work right now. I gotta see my way clear first."

"Eugene, please." She listened with growing horror to herself quietly begging.

"No, and that's it!" He flung his shoes into the suitcase.

"Well, how far is it? Where did you say you were going?" She moved toward the suitcase.

"I told ya—the docks in Newport."

"That's not in Maine. You said you were going to Maine."

"Well, I made a mistake."

"How could you know about a place so far up? Who got you the job?"

"A friend."

"Who?"

"None of your damned business!" His eyes were flashing with the anger of a caged animal. He slammed down the top of the suitcase and yanked it off the bed.

"You're lying, aren't you? You don't have a job, do you? Do you?"

"Look, Ciel, believe whatever the fuck you want to. I gotta go." He tried to push past her.

She grabbed the handle of the case. "No, you can't go."

"Why?"

Her eyes widened slowly. She realized that to answer that would require that she uncurl that week of her life, pushed safely up into her head, when she had done all those terrible things for that other woman who had wanted an abortion. She and she alone would have to take responsibility for them now. He must understand what those actions had meant to her, but somehow, he had meant even more. She sought desperately for the right words, but it all came out as—

"Because I love you."

"Well, that ain't good enough."

Ciel had let the suitcase go before he jerked it away. She looked at Eugene, and the poison of reality began to spread through her body like gangrene. It drew his scent out of her nostrils and scraped the veil from her eyes, and he stood before her just as he really was—a tall, skinny black man with arrogance and selfishness twisting his mouth into a strange shape. And, she thought, I don't feel anything now. But soon, very soon, I will start to hate you. I promise—I will hate you. And I'll never forgive myself for not having done it sooner—soon enough to have saved my baby. Oh, dear God, my baby.

Eugene thought the tears that began to crowd into her eyes were for him. But she was allowing herself this one last luxury of brief mourning for the loss of something denied to her. It troubled her that she wasn't sure exactly what that something was, or which one of them was to blame for taking it away. Ciel began to feel the overpowering need to be near someone who loved her. I'll get Serena and we'll go visit Mattie now, she thought in a daze.

Then they heard the scream from the kitchen.

The church was small and dark. The air hung about them like a stale blanket. Ciel looked straight ahead, oblivious to the seats filling up behind her. She didn't feel the damp pressure of Mattie's heavy arm or the doubt that invaded the air over Eugene's absence. The plaintive Merciful Jesuses, lightly sprinkled with sobs, were lost on her ears. Her dry eyes were locked on the tiny pearl-gray casket, flanked with oversized arrangements of red-carnationed bleeding hearts and white-lilied eternal circles. The sagging chords that came loping out of the huge organ and mixed with the droning voice of the black-robed old man behind the coffin were also unable to penetrate her.

Ciel's whole universe existed in the seven feet of space between herself and her child's narrow coffin. There was not even room for this comforting God whose melodious virtues floated around her sphere, attempting to get in. Obviously, He had deserted or damned her, it didn't matter which. All Ciel knew was that her prayers had gone unheeded—that afternoon she had lifted her daughter's body off the kitchen floor, those blank days in the hospital, and now. So she was left to do what God had chosen not to.

People had mistaken it for shock when she refused to cry. They thought it some special sort of grief when she stopped eating and even drinking water unless forced to; her hair went uncombed and her body unbathed. But Ciel was not grieving for Serena. She was simply tired of hurting. And she was forced to slowly give up the life that God had refused to take from her.

After the funeral the well-meaning came to console and offer their dog-eared faith in the form of coconut cakes, potato pies, fried chicken, and tears. Ciel sat in the bed with her back resting against the headboard; her long thin fingers, still as midnight frost on a frozen pond, lay on the covers. She acknowledged their kindnesses with nods of her head and slight lip movements, but no sound. It was as if her voice was too tired to make the journey from the diaphragm through the larynx to the mouth.

Her visitors' impotent words flew against the steel edge of her pain, bled slowly, and returned to die in the senders' throats. No one came too near. They stood around the door and the dressing table, or sat on the edges of the two worn chairs that needed upholstering, but they unconsciously pushed themselves back against the wall as if her hurt was contagious.

A neighbor woman entered in studied certainty and stood in the middle of the room. "Child, I know how you feel, but don't do this to yourself. I lost one, too. The Lord will . . ." And she choked, because the words were jammed down into her throat by the naked force of Ciel's eyes. Ciel had opened them fully now to look at the woman, but raw fires had eaten them worse than lifeless—worse than death. The woman saw in that mute appeal for silence the ragings of a personal hell flowing through Ciel's eyes. And just as she went to reach for the girl's hand, she stopped as if a muscle spasm had overtaken her body and, cowardly, shrank back. Reminiscences of old, dried-over pains were no consolation in the face of this. They had the effect of cold beads of water on a hot iron—they danced and fizzled up while the room stank from their steam.

Mattie stood in the doorway, and an involuntary shudder went through her when she saw Ciel's eyes. Dear God, she thought, she's dying, and right in front of our faces.

"Merciful Father, no!" she bellowed. There was no prayer, no bended knee or sackcloth supplication in those words, but a blasphemous fireball that shot forth and went smashing against the gates of heaven, raging and kicking, demanding to be heard.

"No! No! No!" Like a black Brahman cow, desperate to protect her young, she surged into the room, pushing the neighbor woman and the others out of her way. She approached the bed with her lips clamped shut in such force that the muscles in her jaw and the back of her neck began to ache.

She sat on the edge of the bed and enfolded the tissue-thin body in her huge ebony arms. And she rocked. Ciel's body was so hot it burned Mattie when she first touched her, but she held on and rocked. Back and forth, back and forth—she had Ciel so tightly she could feel her young breasts flatten against the buttons of her dress. The black mammoth gripped so firmly that the slightest increase of pressure would have cracked the girl's spine. But she rocked.

And somewhere from the bowels of her being came a moan from Ciel, so high at first it couldn't be heard by anyone there, but the yard dogs began an unholy howling. And Mattie rocked. And then, agonizingly slow, it broke its way through the parched lips in a spaghetti-thin column of air that could be faintly heard in the frozen room.

Ciel moaned. Mattie rocked. Propelled by the sound, Mattie rocked her out of that bed, out of that room, into a blue vastness just underneath the sun and above time. She rocked her over Aegean seas so clean they shone like crystal, so clear the fresh blood of sacrificed babies torn from their mothers' arms and given to Neptune could be seen like pink froth on the water. She rocked her on and on, past Dachau, where soul-gutted Jewish mothers swept their children's entrails off laboratory floors. They flew past the spilled brains of Senegalese infants whose mothers had dashed them on the wooden sides of slave ships. And she rocked on.

She rocked her into her childhood and let her see murdered dreams. And she rocked her back, back into the womb, to the nadir of her hurt, and they found it—a slight silver splinter, embedded just below the surface of the skin. And Mattie rocked and pulled—and the splinter gave way, but its roots were deep, gigantic, ragged, and they tore up flesh with bits of fat and muscle tissue clinging to them. They left a huge hole, which was already starting to pus over, but Mattie was satisfied. It would heal.

The bile that had formed a tight knot in Ciel's stomach began to rise and gagged her just as it passed her throat. Mattie put her hand over the girl's mouth and rushed her out the now-empty room to the toilet. Ciel retched yellowish-green phlegm, and she brought up white lumps of slime that hit the seat of the toilet and rolled off, splattering onto the tiles. After a while she heaved only air, but the body did not seem to want to stop. It was exorcising the evilness of pain.

Mattie cupped her hands under the faucet and motioned for Ciel to drink and clean her mouth. When the water left Ciel's mouth, it tasted as if she had been rinsing with a mild acid. Mattie drew a tub of hot water and undressed Ciel. She let the nightgown fall off the narrow shoulders, over the pitifully thin breasts and jutting hipbones. She slowly helped her into the water, and it was like a dried brown autumn leaf hitting the surface of a puddle.

And slowly she bathed her. She took the soap, and, using only her hands, she washed Ciel's hair and the back of her neck. She raised her arms and cleaned the armpits, soaping well the downy brown hair there. She let the soap slip between the girl's breasts, and she washed each one separately, cupping it in her hands. She took each leg and even cleaned under the toenails. Making Ciel rise and kneel in the tub, she cleaned the crack in her behind, soaped her pubic hair, and gently washed the creases in her vagina—slowly, reverently, as if handling a newborn.

She took her from the tub and toweled her in the same manner she had been bathed—as if too much friction would break the skin tissue. All of this had been done without either woman saying a word. Ciel stood there, naked, and felt the cool air play against the clean surface of her skin. She had the sensation of fresh mint coursing through her pores. She closed her eyes and the fire was gone. Her tears no longer fried within her, killing her internal organs with their steam. So Ciel began to cry—there, naked, in the center of the bathroom floor.

Mattie emptied the tub and rinsed it. She led the still-naked Ciel to a chair in the bedroom. The tears were flowing so freely now Ciel couldn't see, and she allowed herself to be led as if blind. She sat on the chair and cried—head erect. Since she made no effort to wipe them away, the tears dripped down her chin and landed on her chest and rolled down to her stomach and onto her dark pubic hair. Ignoring Ciel, Mattie took away the crumpled linen and made the bed, stretching the sheets tight and fresh. She beat the pillows into a virgin plumpness and dressed them in white cases.

And Ciel sat. And cried. The unmolested tears had rolled down her parted thighs and were beginning to wet the chair. But they were cold and good. She put out her tongue and began to drink in their saltiness, feeding on them. The first tears were gone. Her thin shoulders began to quiver, and spasms circled her body as new tears came—this time, hot and stinging. And she sobbed, the first sound she'd made since the moaning.

Mattie took the edges of the dirty sheet she'd pulled off the bed and wiped the mucus that had been running out of Ciel's nose. She then led her freshly wet, glistening body, baptized now, to the bed. She covered her with one sheet and laid a towel across the pillow—it would help for a while.

And Ciel lay down and cried. But Mattie knew the tears would end. And she would sleep. And morning would come.

---

1. What is fundamentally to blame for Ciel's troubles?
2. Why is the conventional sympathy of friends and family unable to reach her?
3. How important are the environment and life-style in giving point to the story?
4. Is the bathing scene a baptism? If you consider it to be that, explain how it fits with the religious implications of the story. How does it recreate hope?

Joyce Carol Oates

Oates (1938–) was born in Lockport, New York. She received degrees from Syracuse University and the University of Wisconsin before launching one of the more spectacular careers among contemporary writers. Poet and critic as well as fiction writer, she continues to astonish readers with the ingenuity of her formal innovations as with the sheer volume of her production. Violence, madness, and social disorder are frequently her subject matter. The mysteries of psychological and sociological motivation fascinate her; she constructs ingenious theories to explain them and to focus their moral significance. Her novels include A Garden of Earthly Delights *(1967),* Expensive People *(1968),* Them *(1969),* Childwold *(1976),* Bellefleur *(1980),* Marya: A Life *(1986),* You Must Remember This *(1987), and* American Appetites *(1989). Her short stories are collected in* By the North Gate *(1963),* Upon the Sweeping Flood and Other Stories *(1966),* The Wheel of Love and Other Stories *(1970),* Marriages and Infidelities *(1972),* The Seduction and Other Stories *(1976),* Night-Side *(1977),* A Sentimental Education *(1981),* Last Days: Stories *(1984), and* The Assignation *(1988).*

How I Contemplated the World from the Detroit House of Correction and Began My Life Over Again

Notes for an Essay for an English Class at Baldwin Country Day School; Poking Around in Debris; Disgust and Curiosity; A Revelation of the Meaning of Life; A Happy Ending . . .

I. Events

The girl (myself) is walking through Branden's, that excellent store. Suburb of a large famous city that is a symbol for large famous American cities. The event sneaks up on the girl, who believes she is herding it along with a small fixed smile, a girl of fifteen, innocently experienced. She dawdles in a certain style by a counter of costume jewelry. Rings, earrings, necklaces. Prices from $5 to $50, all within reach. All ugly. She eases over to the glove counter, where everything is ugly too. In her close-fitted coat with its black fur collar she contemplates the luxury of Branden's, which she has known for many years: its many mild pale lights, easy on the eye and the soul, its elaborate tinkly decorations, its women shoppers with their excellent shoes and coats and hairdos, all dawdling gracefully, in no hurry.

Who was ever in a hurry here?

2. The girl seated at home. A small library, paneled walls of oak. Some one is talking to me. An earnest, husky, female voice drives itself against my ears, nervous, frightened, groping around my heart, saying, "If you wanted gloves, why didn't you say so? Why didn't you ask for them?" That store, Branden's, is owned by Raymond Forrest who lives on Du Maurier Drive. We live on Sioux Drive. Raymond Forrest. A handsome man? An ugly man? A man of fifty or sixty, with gray hair, or a man of forty with earnest, courteous eyes, a good golf game; who is Raymond Forrest, this man who is my salvation? Father has been talking to him. Father is not his physician; Dr. Berg is his physician. Father and Dr. Berg refer patients to each other. There is a connection. Mother plays bridge with . . . On Mondays and Wednesdays our maid Billie works at . . . The strings draw together in a cat's cradle, making a net to save you when you fall. . . .

3. *Harriet Arnold's.* A small shop, better than Branden's. Mother in her black coat, I in my close-fitted blue coat. Shopping. Now look at this, isn't this cute, do you want this, why don't you want this, try this on, take this with you to the fitting room, take this also, what's wrong with you, what can I do for you, why are you so strange . . . ? "I wanted to steal but not to buy," I don't tell her. The girl droops along in her coat and gloves and leather boots, her eyes scan the horizon, which is pastel pink and decorated like Branden's, tasteful walls and modern ceilings with graceful glimmering lights.

4. Weeks later, the girl at a bus stop. Two o'clock in the afternoon, a Tuesday; obviously she has walked out of school.

5. The girl stepping down from a bus. Afternoon, weather changing to colder. Detroit. Pavement and closed-up stores; grillwork over the windows of a pawnshop. What is a pawnshop, exactly?

II. Characters

1. The girl stands five feet five inches tall. An ordinary height. Baldwin Country Day School draws them up to that height. She dreams along the corridors and presses her face against the Thermoplex glass. No frost or steam can ever form on that glass. A smudge of grease from

her forehead . . . could she be boiled down to grease? She wears her hair loose and long and straight in suburban teen-age style, 1968. Eyes smudged with pencil, dark brown. Brown hair. Vague green eyes. A pretty girl? An ugly girl? She sings to herself under her breath, idling in the corridor, thinking of her many secrets (the thirty dollars she once took from the purse of a friend's mother, just for fun, the basement window she smashed in her own house just for fun) and thinking of her brother who is at Susquehanna Boys' Academy, an excellent preparatory school in Maine, remembering him unclearly . . . he has long manic hair and a squeaking voice and he looks like one of the popular teen-age singers of 1968, one of those in a group, *The Certain Forces, The Way Out, The Maniacs Responsible*. The girl in her turn looks like one of those fieldsful of girls who listen to the boys' singing, dreaming and mooning restlessly, breaking into high sullen laughter, innocently experienced.

2. The mother. A Midwestern woman of Detroit and suburbs. Belongs to the Detroit Athletic Club. Also the Detroit Golf Club. Also the Bloomfield Hills Country Club. The Village Women's Club at which lectures are given each winter on Genet and Sartre and James Baldwin,[1] by the Director of the Adult Education Program at Wayne State University. . . . The Bloomfield Art Association. Also the Founders Society of the Detroit Institute of Arts. Also . . . Oh, she is in perpetual motion, this lady, hair like blown-up gold and finer than gold, hair and fingers and body of inestimable grace. Heavy weighs the gold on the back of her hairbrush and hand mirror. Heavy heavy the candlesticks in the dining room. Very heavy is the big car, a Lincoln, long and black, that on one cool autumn day split a squirrel's body in two unequal parts.

3. The father. Dr. ______. He belongs to the same clubs as #2. A player of squash and golf; he has a golfer's umbrella of stripes. Candy stripes. In his mouth nothing turns to sugar, however; saliva works no miracles here. His doctoring is of the slightly sick. The sick are sent elsewhere (to Dr. Berg?), the deathly sick are sent back for more tests and their bills are sent to their homes, the unsick are sent to Dr. Coronet (Isabel, a lady), an excellent psychiatrist for unsick people who angrily believe they are sick and want to do something about it. If they demand a male psychiatrist, the unsick are sent by Dr. ______(my father) to Dr. Lowenstein, a male psychiatrist, excellent and expensive, with a limited practice.

1. Jean Genet (1910–1986), French novelist and playwright; Jean Paul Sartre (1905–1980), French novelist, dramatist, and philosopher; James Baldwin (1924–1987), American novelist and essayist.

4. Clarita. She is twenty, twenty-five, she is thirty or more? Pretty, ugly, what? She is a woman lounging by the side of a road, in jeans and a sweater, hitchhiking, or she is slouched on a stool at a counter in some roadside diner. A hard line of jaw. Curious eyes. Amused eyes. Behind her eyes processions move, funeral pageants, cartoons. She says, "I never can figure out why girls like you bum around down here. What are you looking for anyway?" An odor of tobacco about her. Unwashed underclothes, or no underclothes, unwashed skin, gritty toes, hair long and falling into strands, not recently washed.

5. Simon. In this city the weather changes abruptly, so Simon's weather changes abruptly. He sleeps through the afternoon. He sleeps through the morning. Rising, he gropes around for something to get him going, for a cigarette or a pill to drive him out to the street, where the temperature is hovering around 35°. Why doesn't it drop? Why, why doesn't the cold clean air come down from Canada; will he have to go up into Canada to get it? will he have to leave the Country of his Birth and sink into Canada's frosty fields . . . ? Will the F.B.I. (which he dreams about constantly) chase him over the Canadian border on foot, hounded out in a blizzard of broken glass and horns . . . ?

"Once I was Huckleberry Finn," Simon says, "but now I am Roderick Usher."[2] Beset by frenzies and fears, this man who makes my spine go cold, he takes green pills, yellow pills, pills of white and capsules of dark blue and green . . . he takes other things I may not mention, for what if Simon seeks me out and climbs into my girl's bedroom here in Bloomfield Hills and strangles me, what then . . . ? (As I write this I begin to shiver. Why do I shiver? I am now sixteen and sixteen is not an age for shivering.) It comes from Simon, who is always cold.

III. World Events

Nothing.

IV. People and Circumstances Contributing to This Delinquency

Nothing.

V. Sioux Drive

George, Clyde G. 240 Sioux. A manufacturer's representative; children, a dog, a wife. Georgian with the usual columns. You think of the White House, then of Thomas Jefferson, then your mind goes blank

2. I.e., he has changed from a wholesome American boy into a morbid neurotic. Usher is the chief character in Edgar Allan Poe's *Fall of the House of Usher*. Huck Finn is the young hero of Mark Twain's novel *Adventures of Huckleberry Finn*.

on the white pillars and you think of nothing. Norris, Ralph W. 246 Sioux. Public relations. Colonial. Bay window, brick, stone, concrete, wood, green shutters, sidewalk, lantern, grass, trees, blacktop drive, two children, one of them my classmate Esther (Esther Norris) at Baldwin. Wife, cars. Ramsey, Michael D. 250 Sioux. Colonial. Big living room, thirty by twenty-five, fireplaces in living room, library, recreation room, paneled walls wet bar five bathrooms five bedrooms two lavatories central air conditioning automatic sprinkler automatic garage door three children one wife two cars a breakfast room a patio a large fenced lot fourteen trees a front door with a brass knocker never knocked. Next is our house. Classic contemporary. Traditional modern. Attached garage, attached Florida room, attached patio, attached pool and cabana, attached roof. A front door mail slot through which pour *Time Magazine, Fortune, Life, Business Week,* the *Wall Street Journal,* the *New York Times,* the *New Yorker,* the *Saturday Review, M.D., Modern Medicine, Disease of the Month* . . . and also. . . . And in addition to all this, a quiet sealed letter from Baldwin saying: *Your daughter is not doing work compatible with her performance on the Stanford-Binet.*[3] . . . And your son is not doing well, not well at all, very sad. Where is your son anyway? Once he stole trick-and-treat candy from some six-year-old kids, he himself being a robust ten. The beginning. Now your daughter steals. In the Village Pharmacy she made off with, yes she did, don't deny it, she made off with a copy of *Pageant Magazine* for no reason, she swiped a roll of Life Savers in a green wrapper and was in no need of saving her life or even in need of sucking candy; when she was no more than eight years old she stole, don't blush, she stole a package of Tums only because it was out on the counter and available, and the nice lady behind the counter (now dead) said nothing. . . . Sioux Drive. Maples, oaks, elms. Diseased elms cut down. Sioux Drive runs into Roosevelt Drive. Slow, turning lanes, not streets, all drives and lanes and ways and passes. A private police force. Quiet private police, in unmarked cars. Cruising on Saturday evenings with paternal smiles for the residents who are streaming in and out of houses, going to and from parties, a thousand parties, slightly staggering, the women in their furs alighting from automobiles bought of Ford and General Motors and Chrysler, very heavy automobiles. No foreign cars. Detroit. In 275 Sioux, down the block in that magnificent French-Normandy mansion, lives ______ himself, who has the C______ account itself, imagine that! Look at where he lives and look at the enormous trees and chimneys, imagine his many fireplaces, imagine his wife and children, imagine his wife's hair, imagine her fingernails, imagine her bathtub of smooth clean glowing pink, imagine their embraces, his

3. An intelligence test.

trouser pockets filled with odd coins and keys and dust and peanuts, imagine their ecstasy on Sioux Drive, imagine their income tax returns, imagine their little boy's pride in his experimental car, a scaled down C______, as he roars round the neighborhood on the sidewalks frightening dogs and Negro maids, oh imagine all these things, imagine everything, let your mind roar out all over Sioux Drive and Du Maurier Drive and Roosevelt Drive and Ticonderoga Pass and Burning Bush Way and Lincolnshire Pass and Lois Lane.

When spring comes, its winds blow nothing to Sioux Drive, no odors of hollyhocks or forsythia, nothing Sioux Drive doesn't already possess, everything is planted and performing. The weather vanes, had they weather vanes, don't have to turn with the wind, don't have to contend with the weather. There is no weather.

VI. Detroit

There is always weather in Detroit. Detroit's temperature is always 32°. Fast-falling temperatures. Slow-rising temperatures. Wind from the north-northeast four to forty miles an hour, small-craft warnings, partly cloudy today and Wednesday changing to partly sunny through Thursday . . . small warnings of frost, soot warnings, traffic warnings, hazardous lake conditions for small craft and swimmers, restless Negro gangs, restless cloud formations, restless temperatures aching to fall out the very bottom of the thermometer or shoot up over the top and boil everything over in red mercury.

Detroit's temperature is 32°. Fast-falling temperatures. Slow-rising temperatures. Wind from the north-northeast four to forty miles an hour. . . .

VII. Events

1. The girl's heart is pounding. In her pocket is a pair of gloves! In a plastic bag! Airproof breathproof plastic bag, gloves selling for twenty-five dollars on Branden's counter! In her pocket! Shoplifted! . . . In her purse is a blue comb, not very clean. In her purse is a leather billfold (a birthday present from her grandmother in Philadelphia) with snapshots of the family in clean plastic windows, in the billfold are bills, she doesn't know how many bills. . . . In her purse is an ominous note from her friend Tykie *What's this about Joe H. and the kids hanging around at Louise's Sat. night? You heard anything?* . . . passed in French class. In her purse is a lot of dirty yellow Kleenex, her mother's heart would break to see such very dirty Kleenex, and at the bottom of her purse are brown hairpins and safety pins and a broken pencil and a ballpoint pen (blue) stolen from somewhere forgotten and a purse-

size compact of Cover Girl Make-Up, Ivory Rose. . . . Her lipstick is Broken Heart, a corrupt pink; her fingers are trembling like crazy; her teeth are beginning to chatter; her insides are alive; her eyes glow in her head; she is saying to her mother's astonished face *I want to steal but not to buy.*

2. At Clarita's. Day or night? What room is this? A bed, a regular bed, and a mattress on the floor nearby. Wallpaper hanging in strips. Clarita says she tore it like that with her teeth. She was fighting a barbaric tribe that night, high from some pills; she was battling for her life with men wearing helmets of heavy iron and their faces no more than Christian crosses to breathe through, every one of those bastards looking like her lover Simon, who seems to breathe with great difficulty through the slits of mouth and nostrils in his face. Clarita has never heard of Sioux Drive. Raymond Forrest cuts no ice with her, nor does the C______ account and its millions; Harvard Business School could be at the corner of Vernor and 12th Street for all she cares, and Vietnam might have sunk by now into the Dead Sea under its tons of debris, for all the amazement she could show . . . her face is overworked, overwrought, at the age of twenty (thirty?) it is already exhausted but fanciful and ready for a laugh. Clarita says mournfully to me *Honey somebody is going to turn you out let me give you warning.* In a movie shown on late television Clarita is not a mess like this but a nurse, with short neat hair and a dedicated look, in love with her doctor and her doctor's patients and their diseases, enamored of needles and sponges and rubbing alcohol. . . . Or no: she is a private secretary. Robert Cummings is her boss. She helps him with fantastic plots, the canned audience laughs, no, the audience doesn't laugh because nothing is funny, instead her boss is Robert Taylor and they are not boss and secretary but husband and wife, she is threatened by a young starlet, she is grim, handsome, wifely, a good companion for a good man. . . . She is Claudette Colbert. Her sister too is Claudette Colbert. They are twins, identical. Her husband Charles Boyer[4] is a very rich handsome man and her sister, Claudette Colbert, is plotting her death in order to take her place as the rich man's wife, no one will know because they are *twins*. . . . All these marvelous lives Clarita might have lived, but she fell out the bottom at the age of thirteen. At the age when I was packing my overnight case for a slumber party at Toni Deshield's she was tearing filthy sheets off a bed and scratching up a rash on her arms. . . . Thirteen is uncommonly young for a white girl in Detroit, Miss Brock of the Detroit House of Correction said in a sad newspaper interview for the *Detroit News;* fifteen and sixteen are more likely.

4. Boyer, Colbert, Taylor, and Cummings are romantic film stars of the 1930's, '40's, and '50's.

Eleven, twelve, thirteen are not surprising in colored . . . they are more precocious. What can we do? Taxes are rising and the tax base is falling. The temperature rises slowly but falls rapidly. Everything is falling out the bottom, Woodward Avenue is filthy, Livernois Avenue is filthy! Scraps of paper flutter in the air like pigeons, dirt flies up and hits you right in the eye, oh Detroit is breaking up into dangerous bits of newspaper and dirt, watch out. . . .

Clarita's apartment is over a restaurant. Simon her lover emerges from the cracks at dark. Mrs. Olesko, a neighbor of Clarita's, an aged white wisp of a woman, doesn't complain but sniffs with contentment at Clarita's noisy life and doesn't tell the cops, hating cops, when the cops arrive. I should give more fake names, more blanks, instead of telling all these secrets. I myself am a secret; I am a minor.

3. My father reads a paper at a medical convention in Los Angeles. There he is, on the edge of the North American continent, when the unmarked detective put his hand so gently on my arm in the aisle of Branden's and said, "Miss, would you like to step over here for a minute?"

And where was he when Clarita put her hand on my arm, that wintry dark sulphurous aching day in Detroit, in the company of closed-down barber shops, closed-down diners, closed-down movie houses, homes, windows, basements, faces . . . she put her hand on my arm and said, "Honey, are you looking for somebody down here?"

And was he home worrying about me, gone for two weeks solid, when they carried me off . . . ? It took three of them to get me in the police cruiser, so they said, and they put more than their hands on my arm.

4. I work on this lesson. My English teacher is Mr. Forest, who is from Michigan State. Not handsome, Mr. Forest, and his name is plain, unlike Raymond Forrest's, but he is sweet and rodentlike, he has conferred with the principal and my parents, and everything is fixed . . . treat her as if nothing has happened, a new start, begin again, only sixteen years old, what a shame, how did it happen?—nothing happened, nothing could have happened, a slight physiological modification known only to a gynecologist or to Dr. Coronet. I work on my lesson. I sit in my pink room. I look around the room with my sad pink eyes. I sigh, I dawdle, I pause. I eat up time. I am limp and happy to be home, I am sixteen years old suddenly, my head hangs heavy as a pumpkin on my shoulders, and my hair has just been cut by Mr. Faye at the Crystal Salon and is said to be very becoming.

(Simon too put his hand on my arm and said, "Honey, you have got to come with me," and in his six-by-six room we got to know each other. Would I go back to Simon again? Would I lie down with him in all that filth and craziness? Over and over again.

a Clarita is being betrayed as in front of a Cunningham Drug Store she is nervously eying a colored man who may or may not have money, or a nervous white boy of twenty with sideburns and an Appalachian look, who may or may not have a knife hidden in his jacket pocket, or a husky red-faced man of friendly countenance who may or may not be a member of the Vice Squad out for an early twilight walk.)

I work on my lesson for Mr. Forest. I have filled up eleven pages. Words pour out of me and won't stop. I want to tell everything . . . what was the song Simon was always humming, and who was Simon's friend in a very new trench coat with an old high school graduation ring on his finger . . . ? Simon's bearded friend? When I was down too low for him, Simon kicked me out and gave me to him for three days, I think, on Fourteenth Street in Detroit, an airy room of cold cruel drafts with newspapers on the floor. . . . Do I really remember that or am I piercing it together from what they told me? Did they tell the truth? Did they know much of the truth?

VIII. Characters

1. Wednesdays after school, at four; Saturday mornings at ten. Mother drives me to Dr. Coronet. Ferns in the office, plastic or real, they look the same. Dr. Coronet is queenly, an elegant nicotine-stained lady who would have studied with Freud had circumstances not prevented it, a bit of a Catholic, ready to offer you some mystery if your teeth will ache too much without it. Highly recommended by Father! Forty dollars an hour, Father's forty dollars! Progress! Looking up! Looking better! That new haircut is so becoming, says Dr. Coronet herself, showing how normal she is for a woman with an I.Q. of 180 and many advanced degrees.

2. Mother. A lady in a brown suede coat. Boots of shiny black material, black gloves, a black fur hat. She would be humiliated could she know that of all the people in the world it is my ex-lover Simon who walks most like her . . . self-conscious and unreal, listening to distant music, a little bowlegged with craftiness. . . .

3. Father. Tying a necktie. In a hurry. On my first evening home he put his hand on my arm and said, "Honey, we're going to forget all about this."

4. Simon. Outside, a plane is crossing the sky, in here we're in a hurry. Morning. It must be morning. The girl is half out of her mind, whimpering and vague; Simon her dear friend is wretched this morning . . . he is wretched with morning itself . . . he forces her to give him an injection with that needle she knows is filthy, she had a dread of needles and surgical instruments and the odor of things that are to be sent into the blood, thinking somehow of her father. . . . This is a bad morning, Simon says that his mind is being twisted out of shape, and so he submits to the needle that he usually scorns and bites his lip with his yellowish teeth, his face going very pale. *Ah baby!* he says in his soft mocking voice, which with all women is a mockery of love, *do it like this—Slowly*—And the girl, terrified, almost drops the precious needle but manages to turn it up to the light from the window . . . is it an extension of herself then? She can give him this gift then? I *wish you wouldn't do this to me,* she says, wise in her terror, because it seems to her that Simon's danger—in a few minutes he may be dead—is a way of pressing her against him that is more powerful than any other embrace. She has to work over his arm, the knotted corded veins of his am, her forehead wet with perspiration as she pushes and releases the needle, staring at that mixture of liquid now stained with Simon's bright blood. . . . When the drug hits him she can feel it herself, she feels that magic that is more than any woman can give him, striking the back of his head and making his face stretch as if with the impact of a terrible sun. . . . She tries to embrace him but he pushes her aside and stumbles to his feet. *Jesus Christ,* he says. . . .

5. Princess, a Negro girl of eighteen. What is her charge? She is closed-mouthed about it, shrewd and silent, you know that no one had to wrestle her to the sidewalk to get her in here; she came with dignity. In the recreation room she sits reading *Nancy Drew and the Jewel Box Mystery,*[5] which inspires in her face tiny wrinkles of alarm and interest: what a face! Light brown skin, heavy shaded eyes, heavy eyelashes, a serious sinister dark brow, graceful fingers, graceful wristbones, graceful legs, lips, tongue, a sugar-sweet voice, a leggy stride more masculine than Simon's and my mother's, decked out in a dirty white blouse and dirty white slacks; vaguely nautical is Princess' style. . . . At breakfast she is in charge of clearing the table and leans over me, saying, *Honey you sure you ate enough?*

6. The girl lies sleepless, wondering. Why here, why not there? Why Bloomfield Hills and not jail? Why jail and not her pink room?

5. Mystery story for juveniles.

Why downtown Detroit and not Sioux Drive? What is the difference? Is Simon all the difference? The girl's head is a parade of wonders. She is nearly sixteen, her breath is marvelous with wonders, not long ago she was coloring with crayons and now she is smearing the landscape with paints that won't come off and won't come off her fingers either. She says to the matron *I am not talking about anything*, not because everyone has warned her not to talk but because, because she will not talk; because she won't say anything about Simon, who is her secret. And she says to the matron, *I won't go home*, up until that night in the lavatory when everything was changed. . . . "No, I won't go home I want to stay here," she says, listening to her own words with amazement, thinking that weeds might climb everywhere over that marvelous $180,000 house and dinosaurs might return to muddy the beige carpeting, but never never will she reconcile four o'clock in the morning in Detroit with eight o'clock breakfasts in Bloomfield Hills. . . . oh, she aches still for Simon's hands and his caressing breath, though he gave her little pleasure, he took everything from her (five-dollar bills, ten-dollar bills, passed into her numb hands by men and taken out of her hands by Simon) until she herself was passed into the hands of other men, police, when Simon evidently got tired of her and her hysteria. . . . *No, I won't go home, I don't want to be bailed out.* The girl thinks as a *Stubborn and Wayward Child* (one of several charges lodged against her), and the matron understands her crazy white-rimmed eyes that are seeking out some new violence that will keep her in jail, should someone threaten to let her out. Such children try to strangle the matrons, the attendants, or one another . . . they want the locks locked forever, the doors nailed shut . . . and this girl is no different up until that night her mind is changed for her. . . .

IX. That Night

Princess and Dolly, a little white girl of maybe fifteen, hardy however as a sergeant and in the House of Correction for armed robbery, corner her in the lavatory at the farthest sink and the other girls look away and file out to bed, leaving her. God, how she is beaten up! Why is she beaten up? Why do they pound her, why such hatred? Princess vents all the hatred of a thousand silent Detroit winters on her body, this girl whose body belongs to me, fiercely she rides across the Midwestern plains on this girl's tender bruised body . . . revenge on the oppressed minorities of America! revenge on the slaughtered Indians! revenge on the female sex, on the male sex, revenge on Bloomfield Hills, revenge revenge. . . .

X. Detroit

In Detroit, weather weighs heavily upon everyone. The sky looms large. The horizon shimmers in smoke. Downtown the buildings are imprecise in the haze. Perpetual haze. Perpetual motion inside the haze. Across the choppy river is the city of Windsor, in Canada. Part of the continent has bunched up here and is bulging outward, at the tip of Detroit; a cold hard rain is forever falling on the expressways. . . . Shoppers shop grimly, their cars are not parked in safe places, their windshields may be smashed and graceful ebony hands may drag them out through their shatterproof smashed windshields, crying, *Revenge of the Indians!* Ah, they all fear leaving Hudson's and being dragged to the very tip of the city and thrown off the parking roof of Cobo Hall, that expensive tomb, into the river. . . .

XI. Characters We Are Forever Entwined With

1. Simon drew me into his tender rotting arms and breathed gravity into me. Then I came to earth, weighed down. He said, *You are such a little girl,* and he weighed me down with his delight. In the palms of his hands were teeth marks from his previous life experiences. He was thirty-five, they said. Imagine Simon in this room, in my pink room: he is about six feet tall and stoops slightly, in a feline cautious way, always thinking, always on guard, with his scuffed light suede shoes and his clothes that are anyone's clothes, slightly rumpled ordinary clothes that ordinary men might wear to not-bad jobs. Simon has fair long hair, curly hair, spent languid curls that are like . . . exactly like the curls of wood shavings to the touch, I am trying to be exact . . . and he smells of unheated mornings and coffee and too many pills coating his tongue with a faint green-white scum. . . . Dear Simon, who would be panicked in this room and in this house (right now Billie is vacuuming next door in my parents' room; a vacuum cleaner's roar is a sign of all good things), Simon who is said to have come from a home not much different from this, years ago, fleeing all the carpeting and the polished banisters . . . Simon has a deathly face, only desperate people fall in love with it. His face is bony and cautious, the bones of his cheeks prominent as if with the rigidity of his ceaseless thinking, plotting, for he has to make money out of girls to whom money means nothing, they're so far gone they can hardly count it, and in a sense money means nothing to him either except as a way of keeping on with his life. *Each Day's Proud Struggle,* the title of a novel we could read at jail. . . . Each day he needs a certain amount of money. He devours it. It wasn't love he uncoiled in me with his hollowed-out eyes and his courteous smile, that remnant of a prosperous past, but a dark terror

that needed to press itself flat against him, or against another man . . . but he was the first, he came over to me and took my arm, a claim. We struggled on the stairs and I said, *Let me loose, you're hurting my neck, my face,* it was such a surprise that my skin hurt where he rubbed it, and afterward we lay face to face and he breathed everything into me. In the end I think he turned me in.

2. Raymond Forrest. I just read this morning that Raymond Forrest's father, the chairman of the board at ______, died of a heart attack on a plane bound for London. I would like to write Raymond Forrest a note of sympathy. I would like to thank him for not pressing charges against me one hundred years ago, saving me, being so generous . . . well, men like Raymond Forrest are generous men, not like Simon. I would like to write him a letter telling of my love, or of some other emotion that is positive and healthy. Not like Simon and his poetry, which he scrawled down when he was high and never changed a word . . . but when I try to think of something to say, it is Simon's language that comes back to me, caught in my head like a bad song, it is always Simon's language:

> There is no reality only dreams
> Your neck may get snapped when you wake
> My love is drawn to some violent end
> She keeps wanting to get away
> My love is heading downward
> And I am heading upward
> She is going to crash on the sidewalk
> And I am going to dissolve into the clouds

XII. Events

1. Out of the hospital, bruised and saddened and converted, with Princess' grunts still tangled in my hair . . . and Father in his overcoat, looking like a prince himself, come to carry me off. Up the expressway and out north to home. Jesus Christ, but the air is thinner and cleaner here. Monumental houses. Heartbreaking sidewalks, so clean.

2. Weeping in the living room. The ceiling is two stories high and two chandeliers hang from it. Weeping, weeping, though Billie the maid is *probably listening*. I will never leave home again. Never. Never leave home. Never leave this home again, never.

3. Sugar doughnuts for breakfast. The toaster is very shiny and my face is distorted in it. Is that my face?

4. The car is turning in the driveway. Father brings me home. Mother embraces me. Sunlight breaks in movieland patches on the roof of our traditional-contemporary home, which was designed for the famous automotive stylist whose identity, if I told you the name of the famous car he designed, you would all know, so I can't tell you because my teeth chatter at the thought of being sued . . . or having someone climb into my bedroom window with a rope to strangle me. . . . The car turns up the blacktop drive. The house opens to me like a doll's house, so lovely in the sunlight, the big living room beckons to me with its walls falling away in a delirium of joy at my return, Billie the maid is *no doubt* listening from the kitchen as I burst into tears and the hysteria Simon got so sick of. Convulsed in Father's arms, I say I will never leave again, never, why did I leave, where did I go, what happened, my mind is gone wrong, my body is one big bruise, my backbone was sucked dry, it wasn't the men who hurt me and Simon never hurt me but only those girls . . . my God, how they hurt me . . . I will never leave home again. . . . The car is perpetually turning up the drive and I am perpetually breaking down in the living room and we are perpetually taking the right exit from the expressway (Lahser Road) and the wall of the rest room is perpetually banging against my head and perpetually are Simon's hands moving across my body and adding everything up and so too are Father's hands on my shaking bruised back, far from the surface of my skin on the surface of my good blue cashmere coat (dry-cleaned for my release). . . . I weep for all the money here, for God in gold and beige carpeting, for the beauty of chandeliers and the miracle of a clean polished gleaming toaster and faucets that run both hot and cold water, and I tell them, *I will never leave home, this is my home, I love everything here, I am in love with everything here. . . .*

I am home.

---

1. How has the author used the apparent incoherence of preparatory notes to fashion a complete and coherent story? (Identify the basic elements of fiction used here—plot, character, exposition, complication, for example.)
2. Why is the girl submissive to Simon and Clarita? Is there a personal pathology involved? A social pathology?
3. What comment does the story make on the phenomenon of "dropping out"?
4. Does the story suggest that corporal punishment—beatings, etc.—are a better remedy for the problems of youth than psychiatry? Support your answer.
5. Is the story, as the subtitle suggests, "a revelation of the meaning of life"? In what ways? What is the theme?
6. Which characters are "generous," which are not? Is generosity an important value in the story? What has it to do with the "meaning of life"?

Tim O'Brien

O'Brien (1946–) was born in Austin, Minnesota, and educated at Macalester College. He served in the U.S. Army in Vietnam and emerged as one of the most brilliant chroniclers of that carnage. Though there is a solid vein of realism in his work, it also has something in common with the "magic realism" of contemporary South American novelists, and fantasy is entwined with his reliable reportage. He is the author of If I Die in a Combat Zone, Box Me Up and Ship Me Home *(1973),* Northern Lights *(1974),* Going after Cacciato *(1978), and* The Nuclear Age *(1985).*

The Things They Carried

First Lieutenant Jimmy Cross carried letters from a girl named Martha, a junior at Mount Sebastian College in New Jersey. They were not love letters, but Lieutenant Cross was hoping, so he kept them folded in plastic at the bottom of his rucksack. In the late afternoon, after a day's march, he would dig his foxhole, wash his hands under a canteen, unwrap the letters, hold them with the tips of his fingers, and spend the last hour of light pretending. He would imagine romantic camping trips into the White Mountains in New Hampshire. He would sometimes taste the envelope flaps, knowing her tongue had been there. More than anything, he wanted Martha to love him as he loved her, but the letters were mostly chatty, elusive on the matter of love. She was a virgin, he was almost sure. She was an English major at Mount Sebastian, and she wrote beautifully about her professors and roommates and midterm exams, about her respect for Chaucer and her great affection for Virginia Woolf. She often quoted lines of poetry; she never mentioned the war, except to say, Jimmy, take care of yourself. The letters weighed ten ounces. They were signed "Love, Martha," but Lieutenant Cross understood that "Love" was only a way of signing and did not mean what he sometimes pretended it meant. At dusk, he would carefully return the letters to his rucksack. Slowly, a bit distracted, he would get up and move among his men, checking the perimeter, then at full dark he would return to his hole and watch the night and wonder if Martha was a virgin.

The things they carried were largely determined by necessity. Among the necessities or near necessities were P-38 can openers, pocket knives, heat tabs, wrist watches, dog tags, mosquito repellent, chewing gum, candy, cigarettes, salt tablets, packets of Kool-Aid, lighters, matches, sewing kits, Military Payment Certificates, C rations, and two or three canteens of water. Together, these items weighed between fifteen and twenty pounds, depending upon a man's habits or rate of metabolism. Henry Dobbins, who was a big man, carried extra rations; he was especially fond of canned peaches in heavy syrup over pound cake. Dave Jensen, who practiced field hygiene, carried a toothbrush, dental floss, and several hotel-size bars of soap he'd stolen on R&R[1] in Sydney, Australia. Ted Lavender, who was scared, carried tranquilizers until he was shot in the head outside the village of Than Khe in mid-April. By necessity, and because it was SOP,[2] they all carried steel helmets that weighed five pounds including the liner and camouflage cover. They carried the standard fatigue jackets and trousers. Very few carried underwear. On their feet they carried jungle boots—2.1 pounds—and Dave Jensen carried three pairs of socks and a can of Dr. Scholl's foot powder as a precaution against trench foot. Until he was shot, Ted Lavender carried six or seven ounces of premium dope, which for him was a necessity. Mitchell Sanders, the RTO,[3] carried condoms. Norman Bowker carried a diary. Rat Kiley carried comic books. Kiowa, a devout Baptist, carried an illustrated New Testament that had been presented to him by his father, who taught Sunday school in Oklahoma City, Oklahoma. As a hedge against bad times, however, Kiowa also carried his grandmother's distrust of the white man, his grandfather's old hunting hatchet. Necessity dictated. Because the land was mined and booby-trapped, it was SOP for each man to carry a steel-centered, nylon-covered flak jacket, which weighed 6.7 pounds, but which on hot days seemed much heavier. Because you could die so quickly, each man carried at least one large compress bandage, usually in the helmet band for easy access. Because the nights were cold, and because the monsoons were wet, each carried a green plastic poncho that could be used as a raincoat or ground sheet or makeshift tent. With its quilted liner, the poncho weighed almost two pounds, but it was worth every ounce. In April, for instance, when Ted Lavender was shot, they used his poncho to wrap him up, then to carry him across the paddy, then to lift him into the chopper that took him away.

They were called legs or grunts.

To carry something was to "hump" it, as when Lieutenant Jimmy

1. Rest and rehabilitation leave. 2. Standard operating procedure. 3. Radio and telephone operator.

Cross humped his love for Martha up the hills and through the swamps. In its intransitive form, "to hump" meant "to walk," or "to march," but it implied burdens far beyond the intransitive.

Almost everyone humped photographs. In his wallet, Lieutenant Cross carried two photographs of Martha. The first was a Kodachrome snapshot signed "Love," though he knew better. She stood against a brick wall. Her eyes were gray and neutral, her lips slightly open as she stared straight-on at the camera. At night, sometimes, Lieutenant Cross wondered who had taken the picture, because he knew she had boyfriends, because he loved her so much, and because he could see the shadow of the picture taker spreading out against the brick wall. The second photograph had been clipped from the 1968 Mount Sebastian yearbook. It was an action shot—women's volleyball—and Martha was bent horizontal to the floor, reaching, the palms of her hands in sharp focus, the tongue taut, the expression frank and competitive. There was no visible sweat. She wore white gym shorts. Her legs, he thought, were almost certainly the legs of a virgin, dry and without hair, the left knee cocked and carrying her entire weight, which was just over one hundred pounds. Lieutenant Cross remembered touching that left knee. A dark theater, he remembered, and the movie was *Bonnie and Clyde*, and Martha wore a tweed skirt, and during the final scene, when he touched her knee, she turned and looked at him in a sad, sober way that made him pull his hand back, but he would always remember the feel of the tweed skirt and the knee beneath it and the sound of the gunfire that killed Bonnie and Clyde, how embarrassing it was, how slow and oppressive. He remembered kissing her good night at the dorm door. Right then, he thought, he should've done something brave. He should've carried her up the stairs to her room and tied her to the bed and touched that left knee all night long. He should've risked it. Whenever he looked at the photographs, he thought of new things he should've done.

What they carried was partly a function of rank, partly of field specialty.

As a first lieutenant and platoon leader, Jimmy Cross carried a compass, maps, code books, binoculars, and a .45-caliber pistol that weighed 2.9 pounds fully loaded. He carried a strobe light and the responsibility for the lives of his men.

As an RTO, Mitchell Sanders carried the PRC-25 radio, a killer, twenty-six pounds with its battery.

As a medic, Rat Kiley carried a canvas satchel filled with morphine and plasma and malaria tablets and surgical tape and comic books and all the things a medic must carry, including M&M's[4] for especially bad wounds, for a total weight of nearly twenty pounds.

As a big man, therefore a machine gunner, Henry Dobbins carried the M-60, which weighed twenty-three pounds unloaded, but which was almost always loaded. In addition, Dobbins carried between ten and fifteen pounds of ammunition draped in belts across his chest and shoulders.

As PCFs or Spec 4s, most of them were common grunts and carried the standard M-16 gas-operated assault rifle. The weapon weighed 7.5 pounds unloaded, 8.2 pounds with its full twenty-round magazine. Depending on numerous factors, such as topography and psychology, the riflemen carried anywhere from twelve to twenty magazines, usually in cloth bandoliers, adding on another 8.4 pounds at minimum, fourteen pounds at maximum. When it was available, they also carried M-16 maintenance gear—rods and steel brushes and swabs and tubes of LSA oil—all of which weighed about a pound. Among the grunts, some carried the M-79 grenade launcher, 5.9 pounds unloaded, a reasonably light weapon except for the ammunition, which was heavy. A single round weighed ten ounces. The typical load was twenty-five rounds. But Ted Lavender, who was scared, carried thirty-four rounds when he was shot and killed outside Than Khe, and he went down under an exceptional burden, more than twenty pounds of ammunition, plus the flak jacket and helmet and rations and water and toilet paper and tranquilizers and all the rest, plus the unweighed fear. He was dead weight. There was no twitching or flopping. Kiowa, who saw it happen, said it was like watching a rock fall, or a big sandbag or something—just boom, then down—not like the movies where the dead guy rolls around and does fancy spins and goes ass over teakettle—not like that, Kiowa said, the poor bastard just flat-fuck fell. Boom. Down. Nothing else. It was a bright morning in mid-April. Lieutenant Cross felt the pain. He blamed himself. They stripped off Lavender's canteens and ammo, all the heavy things, and Rat Kiley said the obvious, the guy's dead, and Mitchell Sanders used his radio to report one U.S. KIA[5] and to request a chopper. Then they wrapped Lavender in his poncho. They carried him out to a dry paddy, established security, and sat smoking the dead man's dope until the chopper came. Lieutenant Cross kept to himself. He pictured Martha's smooth young face, thinking he loved her more than anything, more than his men, and now Ted Lavender was dead because he loved her so much and could not stop thinking about her. When the dust-off[6] arrived, they carried Lavender aboard. Afterward they burned Than Khe. They marched until dusk,

4. Slang for medications of various types. 5. Killed in action. 6. Helicopter.

then dug their holes, and that night Kiowa kept explaining how you had to be there, how fast it was, how the poor guy just dropped like so much concrete. Boom-down, he said. Like cement.

In addition to the three standard weapons—the M-60, M-16, and M-79—they carried whatever presented itself, or whatever seemed appropriate as a means of killing or staying alive. They carried catch-as-catch-can. At various times, in various situations, they carried M-14s and CAR-15s and Swedish Ks and grease guns and captured AK-47s and Chi-Coms and RPGs and Simonov carbines and black-market Uzis and .38-caliber Smith & Wesson handguns and 66 mm LAWs and shotguns and silencers and blackjacks and bayonets and C-4 plastic explosives. Lee Strunk carried a slingshot; a weapon of last resort, he called it. Mitchell Sanders carried brass knuckles. Kiowa carried his grandfather's feathered hatchet. Every third or fourth man carried a Claymore antipersonnel mine—3.5 pounds with its firing device. They all carried fragmentation grenades—fourteen ounces each. They all carried at least one M-18 colored smoke grenade—twenty-four ounces. Some carried CS or tear-gas grenades. Some carried white-phosphorus grenades. They carried all they could bear, and then some, including a silent awe for the terrible power of the things they carried.

In the first week of April, before Lavender died, Lieutenant Jimmy Cross received a good-luck charm from Martha. It was a simple pebble, an ounce at most. Smooth to the touch, it was a milky-white color with flecks of orange and violet, oval-shaped, like a miniature egg. In the accompanying letter, Martha wrote that she had found the pebble on the Jersey shoreline, precisely where the land touched water at high tide, where things came together but also separated. It was this separate-but-together quality, she wrote, that had inspired her to pick up the pebble and to carry it in her breast pocket for several days, where it seemed weightless, and then to send it through the mail, by air, as a token of her truest feelings for him. Lieutenant Cross found this romantic. But he wondered what her truest feelings were, exactly, and what she meant by separate-but-together. He wondered how the tides and waves had come into play on that afternoon along the Jersey shoreline when Martha saw the pebble and bent down to rescue it from geology. He imagined bare feet. Martha was a poet, with the poet's sensibilities, and her feet would be brown and bare, the toenails unpainted, the eyes chilly and somber like the ocean in March, and though it was painful, he wondered who had been with her that afternoon. He imagined a pair of shadows moving along the strip of sand where things came together but also separated. It was phantom jealousy, he knew, but he couldn't help himself. He loved her so much. On the march, through the hot days of early April, he carried the pebble in his mouth, turning it with his tongue, tasting sea salts and moisture. His mind wandered. He had difficulty keeping his attention on the war. On occasion he would yell at his men to spread out the column, to keep their eyes open, but then he would slip away into daydreams, just pretending, walking barefoot along the Jersey shore, with Martha, carrying nothing. He would feel himself rising. Sun and waves and gentle winds, all love and lightness.

What they carried varied by mission.

When a mission took them to the mountains, they carried mosquito netting, machetes, canvas tarps, and extra bug juice.

If a mission seemed especially hazardous, or if it involved a place they knew to be bad, they carried everything they could. In certain heavily mined AOs,[7] where the land was dense with Toe Poppers and Bouncing Betties, they took turns humping a twenty-eight-pound mine detector. With its headphones and big sensing plate, the equipment was a stress on the lower back and shoulders, awkward to handle, often useless because of the shrapnel in the earth, but they carried it anyway, partly for safety, partly for the illusion of safety.

On ambush, or other night missions, they carried peculiar little odds and ends. Kiowa always took along his New Testament and a pair of moccasins for silence. Dave Jensen carried night-sight vitamins high in carotin. Lee Strunk carried his slingshot; ammo, he claimed, would never be a problem. Rat Kiley carried brandy and M&M's. Until he was shot, Ted Lavender carried the starlight scope, which weighed 6.3 pounds with its aluminum carrying case. Henry Dobbins carried his girlfriend's pantyhose wrapped around his neck as a comforter. They all carried ghosts. When dark came, they would move out single file across the meadows and paddies to their ambush coordinates, where they would quietly set up the Claymores and lie down and spend the night waiting.

Other missions were more complicated and required special equipment. In mid-April, it was their mission to search out and destroy the elaborate tunnel complexes in the Than Khe area south of Chu Lai. To blow the tunnels, they carried one-pound blocks of pentrite high explosives, four blocks to a man, sixty-eight pounds in all. They carried wiring, detonators, and battery-powered clackers. Dave Jensen carried earplugs. Most often, before blowing the tunnels, they were ordered by higher command to search them, which was considered bad news, but by and large they just shrugged and carried out orders. Because he was a big man, Henry Dobbins was excused from tunnel duty. The others would draw numbers. Before Lavender died there were sev-

7. Areas of operations.

enteen men in the platoon, and whoever drew the number seventeen would strip off his gear and crawl in head first with a flashlight and Lieutenant Cross's .45-caliber pistol. The rest of them would fan out as security. They would sit down or kneel, not facing the hole, listening to the ground beneath them, imagining cobwebs and ghosts, whatever was down there—the tunnel walls squeezing in—how the flashlight seemed impossibly heavy in the hand and how it was tunnel vision in the very strictest sense, compression in all ways, even time, and how you had to wiggle in—ass and elbows—a swallowed-up feeling—and how you found yourself worrying about odd things—will your flashlight go dead? Do rats carry rabies? If you screamed, how far would the sound carry? Would your buddies hear it? Would they have the courage to drag you out? In some respects, though not many, the waiting was worse than the tunnel itself. Imagination was a killer.

On April 16, when Lee Strunk drew the number seventeen, he laughed and muttered something and went down quickly. The morning was hot and very still. Not good, Kiowa said. He looked at the tunnel opening, then out across a dry paddy toward the village of Than Khe. Nothing moved. No clouds or birds or people. As they waited, the men smoked and drank Kool-Aid, not talking much, feeling sympathy for Lee Strunk but also feeling the luck of the draw. You win some, you lose some, said Mitchell Sanders, and sometimes you settle for a rain check. It was a tired line and no one laughed.

Henry Dobbins ate a tropical chocolate bar. Ted Lavender popped a tranquilizer and went off to pee.

After five minutes, Lieutenant Jimmy Cross moved to the tunnel, leaned down, and examined the darkness. Trouble, he thought—a cave-in maybe. And then suddenly, without willing it, he was thinking about Martha. The stresses and fractures, the quick collapse, the two of them buried alive under all that weight. Dense, crushing love. Kneeling, watching the hole, he tried to concentrate on Lee Strunk and the war, all the dangers, but his love was too much for him, he felt paralyzed, he wanted to sleep inside her lungs and breathe her blood and be smothered. He wanted her to be a virgin and not a virgin, all at once. He wanted to know her. Intimate secrets—why poetry? Why so sad? Why that grayness in her eyes? Why so alone? Not lonely, just alone—riding her bike across campus or sitting off by herself in the cafeteria. Even dancing, she danced alone—and it was the aloneness that filled him with love. He remembered telling her that one evening. How she nodded and looked away. And how, later, when he kissed her, she received the kiss without returning it, her eyes wide open, not afraid, not a virgin's eyes, just flat and uninvolved.

Lieutenant Cross gazed at the tunnel. But he was not there. He was buried with Martha under the white sand at the Jersey shore. They were pressed together, and the pebble in his mouth was her tongue. He was smiling. Vaguely, he was aware of how quiet the day was, the sullen paddies, yet he could not bring himself to worry about matters of security. He was beyond that. He was just a kid at war, in love. He was twenty-two years old. He couldn't help it.

A few moments later Lee Strunk crawled out of the tunnel. He came up grinning, filthy but alive. Lieutenant Cross nodded and closed his eyes while the others clapped Strunk on the back and made jokes about rising from the dead.

Worms, Rat Kiley said. Right out of the grave. Fuckin' zombie.

The men laughed. They all felt great relief.

Spook City, said Mitchell Sanders.

Lee Strunk made a funny ghost sound, a kind of moaning, yet very happy, and right then, when Strunk made that high happy moaning sound, when he went *Ahhooooo*, right then Ted Lavender was shot in the head on his way back from peeing. He lay with his mouth open. The teeth were broken. There was a swollen black bruise under his left eye. The cheekbone was gone. Oh shit, Rat Kiley said, the guy's dead. The guy's dead, he kept saying, which seemed profound—the guy's dead. I mean really.

The things they carried were determined to some extent by superstition. Lieutenant Cross carried his good-luck pebble. Dave Jensen carried a rabbit's foot. Norman Bowker, otherwise a very gentle person, carried a thumb that had been presented to him as a gift by Mitchell Sanders. The thumb was dark brown, rubbery to the touch, and weighed four ounces at most. It had been cut from a VC corpse, a boy of fifteen or sixteen. They'd found him at the bottom of an irrigation ditch, badly burned, flies in his mouth and eyes. The boy wore black shorts and sandals. At the time of his death he had been carrying a pouch of rice, rifle, and three magazines of ammunition.

You want my opinion, Mitchell Sanders said, there's a definite moral here.

He put his hand on the dead boy's wrist. He was quiet for a time, as if counting a pulse, then he patted the stomach, almost affectionately, and used Kiowa's hunting hatchet to remove the thumb.

Henry Dobbins asked what the moral was.

Moral?

You know. *Moral*.

Sanders wrapped the thumb in toilet paper and handed it across to Norman Bowker. There was no blood. Smiling, he kicked the boy's head, watched the flies scatter, and said, It's like with that old TV show—Paladin. Have gun, will travel.

Henry Dobbins thought about it.

Yeah, well, he finally said. I don't see no moral.
There it *is*, man.
Fuck off.

They carried USO stationery and pencils and pens. They carried Sterno, safety pins, trip flares, signal flares, spools of wire, razor blades, chewing tobacco, liberated joss sticks and statuettes of the smiling Buddha, candles, grease pencils, *The Stars and Stripes*, fingernail clippers, Psy Ops[8] leaflets, bush hats, bolos, and much more. Twice a week, when the resupply choppers came in, they carried hot chow in green Mermite cans and large canvas bags filled with iced beer and soda pop. They carried plastic water containers, each with a two-gallon capacity. Mitchell Sanders carried a set of starched tiger fatigues for special occasions. Henry Dobbins carried Black Flag insecticide. Dave Jensen carried empty sandbags that could be filled at night for added protection. Lee Strunk carried tanning lotion. Some things they carried in common. Taking turns, they carried the big PRC-77 scrambler radio, which weighed thirty pounds with its battery. They shared the weight of memory. They took up what others could no longer bear. Often, they carried each other, the wounded or weak. They carried infections. They carried chess sets, basketballs, Vietnamese-English dictionaries, insignia of rank, Bronze Stars and Purple Hearts, plastic cards imprinted with the Code of Conduct. They carried diseases, among them malaria and dysentery. They carried lice and ringworm and leeches and paddy algae and various rots and molds. They carried the land itself—Vietnam, the place, the soil—a powdery orange-red dust that covered their boots and fatigues and faces. They carried the sky. The whole atmosphere, they carried it, the humidity, the monsoons, the stink of fungus and decay, all of it, they carried gravity. They moved like mules. By daylight they took sniper fire, at night they were mortared, but it was not battle, it was just the endless march, village to village, without purpose, nothing won or lost. They marched for the sake of the march. They plodded along slowly, dumbly, leaning forward against the heat, unthinking, all blood and bone, simple grunts, soldiering with their legs, toiling up the hills and down into the paddies and across the rivers and up again and down, just humping, one step and then the next and then another, but no volition, no will, because it was automatic, it was anatomy, and the war was entirely a matter of posture and carriage, the hump was everything, a kind of inertia, a kind of emptiness, a dullness of desire and intellect and conscience and hope and human sensibility. Their principles were in their feet.

8. Psychological Operations.

Their calculations were biological. They had no sense of strategy or mission. They searched the villages without knowing what to look for, not caring, kicking over jars of rice, frisking children and old men, blowing tunnels, sometimes setting fires and sometimes not, then forming up and moving on to the next village, then other villages, where it would always be the same. They carried their own lives. The pressures were enormous. In the heat of early afternoon, they would remove their helmets and flak jackets, walking bare, which was dangerous but which helped ease the strain. They would often discard things along the route of march. Purely for comfort, they would throw away rations, blow their Claymores and grenades, no matter, because by nightfall the resupply choppers would arrive with more of the same, then a day or two later still more, fresh watermelons and crates of ammunition and sunglasses and woolen sweaters—the resources were stunning—sparklers for the Fourth of July, colored eggs for Easter. It was the great American war chest—the fruits of science, the smokestacks, the canneries, the arsenals at Hartford, the Minnesota forests, the machine shops, the vast fields of corn and wheat—they carried like freight trains; they carried it on their backs and shoulders—and for all the ambiguities of Vietnam, all the mysteries and unknowns, there was at least the single abiding certainty that they would never be at a loss for things to carry.

After the chopper took Lavender away, Lieutenant Jimmy Cross led his men into the village of Than Khe. They burned everything. They shot chickens and dogs, they trashed the village well, they called in artillery and watched the wreckage, then they marched for several hours through the hot afternoon, and then at dusk, while Kiowa explained how Lavender died, Lieutenant Cross found himself trembling.

He tried not to cry. With his entrenching tool, which weighed five pounds, he began digging a hole in the earth.

He felt shame. He hated himself. He had loved Martha more than his men, and as a consequence Lavender was now dead, and this was something he would have to carry like a stone in his stomach for the rest of the war.

All he could do was dig. He used his entrenching tool like an ax, slashing, feeling both love and hate, and then later, when it was full dark, he sat at the bottom of his foxhole and wept. It went on for a long while. In part, he was grieving for Ted Lavender, but mostly it was for Martha, and for himself, because she belonged to another world, which was not quite real, and because she was a junior at Mount Sebastian College in New Jersey, a poet and a virgin and uninvolved, and because he realized she did not love him and never would.

Like cement, Kiowa whispered in the dark. I swear to God—boom-down. Not a word.

I've heard this, said Norman Bowker.

A pisser, you know? Still zipping himself up. Zapped while zipping.

All right, fine. That's enough.

Yeah, but you had to see it, the guy just—

I *heard*, man. Cement. So why not shut the fuck *up*?

Kiowa shook his head sadly and glanced over at the hole where Lieutenant Jimmy Cross sat watching the night. The air was thick and wet. A warm, dense fog had settled over the paddies and there was the stillness that precedes rain.

After a time Kiowa sighed.

One thing for sure, he said. The Lieutenant's in some deep hurt. I mean that crying jag—the way he was carrying on—it wasn't fake or anything, it was real heavy-duty hurt. The man cares.

Sure, Norman Bowker said.

Say what you want, the man does care.

We all got problems.

Not Lavender.

No, I guess not. Bowker said. Do me a favor, though.

Shut up?

That's a smart Indian. Shut up.

Shrugging, Kiowa pulled off his boots. He wanted to say more, just to lighten up his sleep, but instead he opened his New Testament and arranged it beneath his head as a pillow. The fog made things seem hollow and unattached. He tried not to think about Ted Lavender, but then he was thinking how fast it was, no drama, down and dead, and how it was hard to feel anything except surprise. It seemed un-Christian. He wished he could find some great sadness, or even anger, but the emotion wasn't there and he couldn't make it happen. Mostly he felt pleased to be alive. He liked the smell of the New Testament under his cheek, the leather and ink and paper and glue, whatever the chemicals were. He liked hearing the sounds of night. Even his fatigue, it felt fine, the stiff muscles and the prickly awareness of his own body, a floating feeling. He enjoyed not being dead. Lying there, Kiowa admired Lieutenant Jimmy Cross's capacity for grief. He wanted to share the man's pain, he wanted to care as Jimmy Cross cared. And yet when he closed his eyes, all he could think was Boom-down, and all he could feel was the pleasure of having his boots off and the fog curling in around him and the damp soil and the Bible smells and the plush comfort of night.

After a moment Norman Bowker sat up in the dark.

What the hell, he said. You want to talk, *talk*. Tell it to me.

Forget it.

No, man, go on. One thing I hate, it's a silent Indian.

For the most part they carried themselves with poise, a kind of dignity. Now and then, however, there were times of panic, when they squealed or wanted to squeal but couldn't, when they twitched and made moaning sounds and covered their heads and said Dear Jesus and flopped around on the earth and fired their weapons blindly and cringed and sobbed and begged for the noise to stop and went wild and made stupid promises to themselves and to God and to their mothers and fathers, hoping not to die. In different ways, it happened to all of them. Afterward, when the firing ended, they would blink and peek up. They would touch their bodies, feeling shame, then quickly hiding it. They would force themselves to stand. As if in slow motion, frame by frame, the world would take on the old logic—absolute silence, then the wind, then sunlight, then voices. It was the burden of being alive. Awkwardly, the men would reassemble themselves, first in private, then in groups, becoming soldiers again. They would repair the leaks in their eyes. They would check for casualties, call in dust-offs, light cigarettes, try to smile, clear their throats and spit and begin cleaning their weapons. After a time someone would shake his head and say, No lie, I almost shit my pants, and someone else would laugh, which meant it was bad, yes, but the guy had obviously not shit his pants, it wasn't that bad, and in any case nobody would ever do such a thing and then go ahead and talk about it. They would squint into the dense, oppressive sunlight. For a few moments, perhaps, they would fall silent, lighting a joint and tracking its passage from man to man, inhaling, holding in the humiliation. Scary stuff, one of them might say. But then someone else would grin or flick his eyebrows and say, Roger-dodger, almost cut me a new asshole, *almost*.

There were numerous such poses. Some carried themselves with a sort of wistful resignation, others with pride or stiff soldierly discipline or good humor or macho zeal. They were afraid of dying but they were even more afraid to show it.

They found jokes to tell.

They used a hard vocabulary to contain the terrible softness. *Greased*, they'd say. *Offed, lit up, zapped while zipping*. It wasn't cruelty, just stage presence. They were actors and the war came at them in 3-D. When someone died, it wasn't quite dying, because in a curious way it seemed scripted, and because they had their lines mostly memorized, irony mixed with tragedy, and because they called it by other names, as if to encyst and destroy the reality of death itself. They kicked corpses. They cut off thumbs. They talked grunt lingo. They told stories about Ted Lavender's supply of tranquilizers, how the poor guy didn't feel a thing, how incredibly tranquil he was.

There's a moral here, said Mitchell Sanders.

They were waiting for Lavender's chopper, smoking the dead man's dope.

The moral's pretty obvious, Sanders said, and winked. Stay away from drugs. No joke, they'll ruin your day every time.

Cute, said Henry Dobbins.

Mind-blower, get it? Talk about wiggy—nothing left, just blood and brains.

They made themselves laugh.

There it is, they'd say, over and over, as if the repetition itself were an act of poise, a balance between crazy and almost crazy, knowing without going. There it is, which meant be cool, let it ride, because oh yeah, man, you can't change what can't be changed, there it is, there it absolutely and positively and fucking well *is*.

They were tough.

They carried all the emotional baggage of men who might die. Grief, terror, love, longing—these were intangibles, but the intangibles had their own mass and specific gravity, they had tangible weight. They carried shameful memories. They carried the common secret of cowardice barely restrained, the instinct to run or freeze or hide, and in many respects this was the heaviest burden of all, for it could never be put down, it required perfect balance and perfect posture. They carried their reputations. They carried the soldier's greatest fear, which was the fear of blushing. Men killed, and died, because they were embarrassed not to. It was what had brought them to the war in the first place, nothing positive, no dreams of glory or honor, just to avoid the blush of dishonor. They died so as not to die of embarrassment. They crawled into tunnels and walked point and advanced under fire. Each morning, despite the unknowns, they made their legs move. They endured. They kept humping. They did not submit to the obvious alternative, which was simply to close the eyes and fall. So easy, really. Go limp and tumble to the ground and let the muscles unwind and not speak and not budge until your buddies picked you up and lifted you into the chopper that would roar and dip its nose and carry you off to the world. A mere matter of falling, yet no one ever fell. It was not courage, exactly; the object was not valor. Rather, they were too frightened to be cowards.

By and large they carried these things inside, maintaining the masks of composure. They sneered at sick call. They spoke bitterly about guys who had found release by shooting off their own toes or fingers. Pussies, they'd say. Candyasses. It was fierce, mocking talk, with only a trace of envy or awe, but even so, the image played itself out behind their eyes.

They imagined the muzzle against flesh. They imagined the quick, sweet pain, then the evacuation to Japan, then a hospital with warm beds and cute geisha nurses.

They dreamed of freedom birds.

At night, on guard, staring into the dark, they were carried away by jumbo jets. They felt the rush of takeoff. *Gone*! they yelled. And then velocity, wings and engines, a smiling stewardess—but it was more than a plane, it was a real bird, a big sleek silver bird with feathers and talons and high screeching. They were flying. The weights fell off, there was nothing to bear. They laughed and held on tight, feeling the cold slap of wind and altitude, soaring, thinking *It's over, I'm gone*!—they were naked, they were light and free—it was all lightness, bright and fast and buoyant, light as light, a helium buzz in the brain, a giddy bubbling in the lungs as they were taken up over the clouds and the war, beyond duty, beyond gravity and mortification and global entanglements—*Sin loi*![9] they yelled, *I'm sorry, motherfuckers, but I'm out of it, I'm goofed, I'm on a space cruise, I'm gone*!—and it was a restful, disencumbered sensation, just riding the light waves, sailing that big silver freedom bird over the mountains and oceans, over America, over the farms and great sleeping cities and cemeteries and highways and the golden arches of McDonald's. It was flight, a kind of fleeing, a kind of falling, falling higher and higher, spinning off the edge of the earth and beyond the sun and through the vast, silent vacuum where there were no burdens and were everything weighed exactly nothing. *Gone*! they screamed, *I'm sorry but I'm gone*! And so at night, not quite dreaming, they gave themselves over to lightness, they were carried, they were purely borne.

On the morning after Ted Lavender died, First Lieutenant Jimmy Cross crouched at the bottom of his foxhole and burned Martha's letters. Then he burned the two photographs. There was a steady rain falling, which made it difficult, but he used heat tabs and Sterno to build a small fire, screening it with his body, holding the photographs over the tight blue flame with the tips of his fingers.

He realized it was only a gesture. Stupid, he thought. Sentimental, too, but mostly just stupid.

Lavender was dead. You couldn't burn the blame.

Besides, the letters were in his head. And even now, without photographs, Lieutenant Cross could see Martha playing volleyball in

9. "Sorry about that."

her white gym shorts and yellow T-shirt. He could see her moving in the rain.

When the fire died out, Lieutenant Cross pulled his poncho over his shoulders and ate breakfast from a can.

There was no great mystery, he decided.

In those burned letters Martha had never mentioned the war, except to say, Jimmy, take care of yourself. She wasn't involved. She signed the letters "Love," but it wasn't love, and all the fine lines and technicalities did not matter.

The morning came up wet and blurry. Everything seemed part of everything else, the fog and Martha and the deepening rain.

It was a war, after all.

Half smiling, Lieutenant Jimmy Cross took out his maps. He shook his head hard, as if to clear it, then bent forward and began planning the day's march. In ten minutes, or maybe twenty, he would rouse the men and they would pack up and head west, where the maps showed the country to be green and inviting. They would do what they had always done. The rain might add some weight, but otherwise it would be one more day layered upon all the other days.

He was realistic about it. There was that new hardness in his stomach.

No more fantasies, he told himself.

Henceforth, when he thought about Martha, it would be only to think that she belonged elsewhere. He would shut down the day-dreams. This was not Mount Sebastian, it was another world, where there were no pretty poems or midterm exams, a place where men died because of carelessness and gross stupidity. Kiowa was right. Boom-down, and you were dead, never partly dead.

Briefly, in the rain, Lieutenant Cross saw Martha's gray eyes gazing back at him.

He understood.

It was very sad, he thought. The things men carried inside. The things men did or felt they had to do.

He almost nodded at her, but didn't.

Instead he went back to his maps. He was now determined to perform his duties firmly and without negligence. It wouldn't help Lavender, he knew that, but from this point on he would comport himself as a soldier. He would dispose of his good-luck pebble. Swallow it, maybe, or use Lee Strunk's slingshot, or just drop it along the trail. On the march he would impose strict field discipline. He would be careful to send out flank security, to prevent straggling or bunching up, to keep his troops moving at the proper pace and at the proper interval. He would insist on clean weapons. He would confiscate the remainder of Lavender's dope. Later in the day, perhaps, he would call the men together and speak to them plainly. He would accept the blame for what had happened to Ted Lavender. He would be a man about it. He would look them in the eyes, keeping his chin level, and he would issue the new SOPs in a calm, impersonal tone of voice, an officer's voice, leaving no room for argument or discussion. Commencing immediately, he'd tell them, they would no longer abandon equipment along the route of march. They would police up their acts. They would get their shit together, and keep it together, and maintain it neatly and in good working order.

He would not tolerate laxity. He would show strength, distancing himself.

Among the men there would be grumbling, of course, and maybe worse, because their days would seem longer and their loads heavier, but Lieutenant Cross reminded himself that his obligation was not to be loved but to lead. He would dispense with love; it was not now a factor. And if anyone quarreled or complained, he would simply tighten his lips and arrange his shoulders in the correct command posture. He might give a curt little nod. Or he might not. He might just shrug and say Carry on, then they would saddle up and form into a column and move out toward the villages of Than Khe.

---

1. What means does the author use to show that these men are, in a profound sense, a unit? Is Lieutenant Cross more an individual than a member of the unit?
2. What baffles the men about Lavender's death?
3. What is signified by the profusion of things carried by these men?
4. What relation does the figure of Martha have to the situation in Vietnam?
5. Why does Lieutenant Cross burn Martha's letters and her picture? What change has been made in him by Lavender's death?

Flannery O'Connor

O'Connor (1925–1964) was born in Savannah, Georgia. Her undergraduate writing at the Georgia State College for Women won her a fellowship to the Writers' Workshop of the University of Iowa, where she received an MFA degree. She began her professional career with two years in New York, but serious illness forced her to return to Georgia, where she lived with her mother on a farm near Milledgeville, raising peafowls, writing, and painting. For the rest of her life disease restricted her activities, though she traveled occasionally to give lectures and read from her work. She was a devout and uncompromising Christian; the extraordinary violences of her fiction are designed to expose the precarious conditions of the spirit in a temporal world, as the startling comedy disintegrates the pretenses of a facile civilization. During her lifetime she won a number of honors, including three O. Henry first prizes and (posthumously) the National Book Award for The Complete Stories *(1971). Her novels are* Wise Blood *(1952) and* The Violent Bear It Away *(1960). Her other books of short stories are* A Good Man Is Hard to Find *(1955) and* Everything That Rises Must Converge *(1965). A selection of her letters was edited by Sally Fitzgerald and published in 1979 under the title* The Habit of Being.

A Good Man Is Hard to Find

The grandmother didn't want to go to Florida. She wanted to visit some of her connections in east Tennessee and she was seizing every chance to change Bailey's mind. Bailey was the son she lived with, her only boy. He was sitting on the edge of his chair at the table, bent over the orange sports section of the *Journal*. "Now look here, Bailey," she said, "see here, read this," and she stood with one hand on her thin hip and the other rattling the newspaper at his bald head. "Here this fellow that calls himself The Misfit is aloose from the Federal Pen and headed toward Florida and you read here what it says he did to these people. Just you read it. I wouldn't take my children in any direction with a criminal like that aloose in it. I couldn't answer to my conscience if I did."

Bailey didn't look up from his reading so she wheeled around then and faced the children's mother; a young woman in slacks, whose face was as broad and innocent as a cabbage and was tied around with a green headkerchief that had two points on the top like rabbit's ears. She was sitting on the sofa, feeding the baby his apricots out of a jar. "The children have been to Florida before," the old lady said. "You all ought to take them somewhere else for a change so they would see different parts of the world and be broad. They never have been to east Tennessee."

The children's mother didn't seem to hear her, but the eight-year-old boy, John Wesley, a stocky child with glasses, said, "If you don't want to go to Florida, why dontcha stay at home?" He and the little girl, June Star, were reading the funny papers on the floor.

"She wouldn't stay at home to be queen for a day," June Star said without raising her yellow head.

"Yes, and what would you do if this fellow, The Misfit, caught you?" the grandmother asked.

"I'd smack his face," John Wesley said.

"She wouldn't stay at home for a million bucks," June Star said. "Afraid she'd miss something. She has to go everywhere we go."

"All right, Miss," the grandmother said. "Just remember that the next time you want me to curl your hair."

June Star said her hair was naturally curly.

The next morning the grandmother was the first one in the car, ready to go. She had her big black valise that looked like the head of a hippopotamus in one corner, and underneath it she was hiding a basket with Pitty Sing,[1] the cat, in it. She didn't intend for the cat to be left alone in the house for three days because he would miss her too much and she was afraid he might brush against one of the gas burners and accidentally asphyxiate himself. Her son, Bailey, didn't like to arrive at a motel with a cat.

She sat in the middle of the back seat with John Wesley and June Star on either side of her. Bailey and the children's mother and the baby sat in the front and they left Atlanta at eight forty-five with the mileage on the car at 55890. The grandmother wrote this down because she thought it would be interesting to say how many miles they had been when they got back. It took them twenty minutes to reach the outskirts of the city.

The old lady settled herself comfortably, removing her white cotton gloves and putting them up with her purse on the shelf in front of the back window. The children's mother still had on slacks and still had her head tied up in a green kerchief, but the grandmother had on a navy blue straw sailor hat with a bunch of white violets on the brim and a navy blue dress with a small white dot in the print. Her collar

1. Also the name of a character in *The Mikado*, an operetta (1885) by Gilbert and Sullivan.

and cuffs were white organdy trimmed with lace and at her neckline she had pinned a purple spray of cloth violets containing a sachet. In case of an accident, anyone seeing her dead on the highway would know at once that she was a lady.

She said she thought it was going to be a good day for driving, neither too hot nor too cold, and she cautioned Bailey that the speed limit was fifty-five miles an hour and that the patrolmen hid themselves behind billboards and small clumps of trees and sped out after you before you had a chance to slow down. She pointed out interesting details of the scenery: Stone Mountain; the blue granite that in some places came up to both sides of the highway; the brilliant red clay banks slightly streaked with purple; and the various crops that made rows of green lace-work on the ground. The trees were full of silver-white sunlights and the meanest of them sparkled. The children were reading comic magazines and their mother had gone back to sleep.

"Let's go through Georgia fast so we won't have to look at it much," John Wesley said.

"If I were a little boy," said the grandmother, "I wouldn't talk about my native state that way. Tennessee has the mountains and Georgia has the hills."

"Tennessee is just a hillbilly dumping ground," John Wesley said, "and Georgia is a lousy state too."

"You said it," June Star said.

"In my time," said the grandmother, folding her thin veined fingers, "children were more respectful of their native states and their parents and everything else. People did right then. Oh look at the cute little pickaninny!" she said and pointed to a Negro child standing in the door of a shack. "Wouldn't that make a picture, now?" she asked and they all turned and looked at the little Negro out of the back window. He waved.

"He didn't have any britches on," June Star said.

"He probably didn't have any," the grandmother explained. "Little niggers in the country don't have things like we do. If I could paint, I'd paint that picture," she said.

The children exchanged comic books.

The grandmother offered to hold the baby and the children's mother passed him over the front seat to her. She set him on her knee and bounced him and told him about the things they were passing. She rolled her eyes and screwed up her mouth and stuck her leathery thin face into his smooth bland one. Occasionally he gave her a faraway smile. They passed a large cotton field with five or six graves fenced in the middle of it, like a small island. "Look at the graveyard!" the grandmother said, pointing it out. "That was the old family burying ground. That belonged to the plantation."

"Where's the plantation?" John Wesley asked.

"Gone With the Wind,"[2] said the grandmother. "Ha. Ha."

When the children finished all the comic books they had brought, they opened the lunch and ate it. The grandmother ate a peanut butter sandwich and an olive and would not let the children throw the box and the paper napkins out the window. When there was nothing else to do they played a game by choosing a cloud and making the other two guess what shape it suggested. John Wesley took one the shape of a cow and June Star guessed a cow and John Wesley said, no, an automobile, and June Star said he didn't play fair, and they began to slap each other over the grandmother.

The grandmother said she would tell them a story if they would keep quiet. When she told a story, she rolled her eyes and waved her head and was very dramatic. She said once when she was a maiden lady she had been courted by a Mr. Edgar Atkins Teagarden from Jasper, Georgia. She said he was a very good-looking man and a gentleman and that he brought her a watermelon every Saturday afternoon with his initials cut in it, E.A.T. Well, one Saturday, she said, Mr. Teagarden brought the watermelon and there was nobody at home and he left it on the front porch and returned in his buggy to Jasper, but she never got the watermelon, she said, because a nigger boy ate it when he saw the initials, E.A.T.! This story tickled John Wesley's funny bone and he giggled and giggled but June Star didn't think it was any good. She said she wouldn't marry a man that just brought her a watermelon on Saturday. The grandmother said she would have done well to marry Mr. Teagarden because he was a gentleman and had bought Coca-Cola stock when it first came out and that he had died only a few years ago, a very wealthy man.

They stopped at The Tower for barbecued sandwiches. The Tower was a part-stucco and part-wood filling station and dance hall set in a clearing outside of Timothy. A fat man named Red Sammy Butts ran it and there were signs stuck here and there on the building and for miles up and down the highway saying, TRY RED SAMMY'S FAMOUS BARBECUE. NONE LIKE FAMOUS RED SAMMY'S! RED SAM! THE FAT BOY WITH THE HAPPY LAUGH. A VETERAN! RED SAMMY'S YOUR MAN!

Red Sammy was lying on the bare ground outside The Tower with his head under a truck while a gray monkey about a foot high, chained to a small chinaberry tree, chattered nearby. The monkey sprang back into the tree and got on the highest limb as soon as he saw the children jump out of the car and run toward him.

Inside, The Tower was a long dark room with a counter at one

2. Title of the best-selling novel by Margaret Mitchell about the passing of the old South; published in 1936 and made into a very popular movie in 1939.

end and tables at the other and dancing space in the middle. They all sat down at a broad table next to the nickelodeon and Red Sam's wife, a tall burnt-brown woman with hair and eyes lighter than her skin, came and took their order. The children's mother put a dime in the machine and played "The Tennessee Waltz," and the grandmother said that tune always made her want to dance. She asked Bailey if he would like to dance but he only glared at her. He didn't have a naturally sunny disposition like she did and trips made him nervous. The grandmother's brown eyes were very bright. She swayed her head from side to side and pretended she was dancing in her chair. June Star said play something she could tap to so the children's mother put in another dime and played a fast number and June Star stepped out onto the dance floor and did her tap routine.

"Ain't she cute?" Red Sam's wife said, leaning over the counter. "Would you like to come be my little girl?"

"No, I certainly wouldn't," June Star said. "I wouldn't live in a broken-down place like this for a million bucks!" and she ran back to the table.

"Ain't she cute?" the woman repeated, stretching her mouth politely.

"Aren't you ashamed?" hissed the grandmother.

Red Sam came in and told his wife to quit lounging on the counter and hurry up with these people's order. His khaki trousers reached just to his hip bones and his stomach hung over them like a sack of meal swaying under his shirt. He came over and sat down at a table nearby and let out a combination sigh and yodel. "You can't win," he said. "You can't win," and he wiped his sweating red face off with a gray handkerchief. "These days you don't know who to trust," he said. "Ain't that the truth?"

"People are certainly not nice like they used to be," said the grandmother.

"Two fellers come in here last week," Red Sammy said, "driving a Chrysler. It was an old beat-up car but it was a good one and these boys looked all right to me. Said they worked at the mill and you know I let them fellers charge the gas they bought? Now why did I do that?"

"Because you're a good man!" the grandmother said at once.

"Yes'm, I suppose so," Red Sam said as if he were struck with this answer.

His wife brought the orders, carrying the five plates all at once without a tray, two in each hand and one balanced on her arm. "It isn't a soul in this green world of God's that you can trust," she said. "And I don't count nobody out of that, not nobody," she repeated, looking at Red Sammy.

"Did you read about that criminal, The Misfit, that's escaped?" asked the grandmother.

"I wouldn't be a bit surprised if he didn't attack this place right here," said the woman. "If he hears about it being here, I wouldn't be none surprised to see him. If he hears it's two cent in the cash register, I wouldn't be a tall surprised if he . . ."

"That'll do," Red Sam said. "Go bring these people their Co'-Colas," and the woman went off to get the rest of the order.

"A good man is hard to find," Red Sammy said. "Everything is getting terrible. I remember the day you could go off and leave your screen door unlatched. Not no more."

He and the grandmother discussed better times. The old lady said that in her opinion Europe was entirely to blame for the way things were now. She said the way Europe acted you would think we were made of money and Red Sam said it was no use talking about it, she was exactly right. The children ran outside into the white sunlight and looked at the monkey in the lacy chinaberry tree. He was busy catching fleas on himself and biting each one carefully between his teeth as if it were a delicacy.

They drove off again into the hot afternoon. The grandmother took cat naps and woke up every few minutes with her own snoring. Outside of Toombsboro she woke up and recalled an old plantation that she had visited in this neighborhood once when she was a young lady. She said the house had six white columns across the front and that there was an avenue of oaks leading up to it and two little wooden trellis arbors on either side in front where you sat down with your suitor after a stroll in the garden. She recalled exactly which road to turn off to get to it. She knew that Bailey would not be willing to lose any time looking at an old house, but the more she talked about it, the more she wanted to see it once again and find out if the little twin arbors were still standing. "There was a secret panel in this house," she said craftily, not telling the truth but wishing that she were, "and the story went that all the family silver was hidden in it when Sherman[3] came through but it was never found . . ."

"Hey!" John Wesley said. "Let's go see it! We'll find it! We'll poke all the woodwork and find it! Who lives there? Where do you turn off at? Hey Pop, can't we turn off there?"

"We never have seen a house with a secret panel!" June Star shrieked. "Let's go to the house with the secret panel! Hey, Pop, can't we go see the house with the secret panel!"

3. In November and December 1864 the Union General William Tecumseh Sherman marched his army from Atlanta to the Atlantic coast, plundering and burning as they went.

"It's not far from here, I know," the grandmother said. "It wouldn't take over twenty minutes."

Bailey was looking straight ahead. His jaw was as rigid as a horseshoe. "No," he said.

The children began to yell and scream that they wanted to see the house with the secret panel. John Wesley kicked the back of the front seat and June Star hung over her mother's shoulder and whined desperately into her ear that they never had any fun even on their vacation, that they could never do what THEY wanted to do. The baby began to scream and John Wesley kicked the back of the seat so hard that his father could feel the blows in his kidney.

"All right!" he shouted and drew the car to a stop at the side of the road. "Will you all shut up? Will you all just shut up for one second? If you don't shut up, we won't go anywhere."

"It would be very educational for them," the grandmother murmured.

"All right," Bailey said, "but get this. This is the only time we're going to stop for anything like this. This is the one and only time."

"The dirt road that you have to turn down is about a mile back," the grandmother directed. "I marked it when we passed."

"A dirt road," Bailey groaned.

After they had turned around and were headed toward the dirt road, the grandmother recalled other points about the house, the beautiful glass over the front doorway and the candle lamp in the hall. John Wesley said that the secret panel was probably in the fireplace.

"You can't go inside this house," Bailey said. "You don't know who lives there."

"While you all talk to the people in front, I'll run around behind and get in a window," John Wesley suggested.

"We'll all stay in the car," his mother said.

They turned onto the dirt road and the car raced roughly along in a swirl of pink dust. The grandmother recalled the times when there were no paved roads and thirty miles was a day's journey. The dirt road was hilly and there were sudden washes in it and sharp curves on dangerous embankments. All at once they would be on a hill, looking down over the blue tops of trees for miles around, then the next minute, they would be in a red depression with the dust-coated trees looking down on them.

"This place had better turn up in a minute," Bailey said, "or I'm going to turn around."

The road looked as if no one had traveled on it in months.

"It's not much farther," the grandmother said and just as she said it, a horrible thought came to her. The thought was so embarrassing that she turned red in the face and her eyes dilated and her feet jumped up, upsetting her valise in the corner. The instant the valise moved, the newspaper top she had over the basket under it rose with a snarl and Pitty Sing, the cat, sprang onto Bailey's shoulder.

The children were thrown to the floor and their mother, clutching the baby, was thrown out the door onto the ground; the old lady was thrown into the front seat. The car turned over once and landed right-side-up in a gulch on the side of the road. Bailey remained in the driver's seat with the cat—gray-striped with a broad white face and an orange nose—clinging to his neck like a caterpillar.

As soon as the children saw they could move their arms and legs, they scrambled out of the car, shouting, "We've had an ACCIDENT!" The grandmother was curled up under the dashboard, hoping she was injured so that Bailey's wrath would not come down on her all at once. The horrible thought she had had before the accident was that the house she had remembered so vividly was not in Georgia but in Tennessee.

Bailey removed the cat from his neck with both hands and flung it out the window against the side of a pine tree. Then he got out of the car and started looking for the children's mother. She was sitting against the side of the red gutted ditch, holding the screaming baby, but she only had a cut down her face and a broken shoulder. "We've had an ACCIDENT!" the children screamed in a frenzy of delight.

"But nobody's killed," June Star said with disappointment as the grandmother limped out of the car, her hat still pinned to her head but the broken front brim standing up at a jaunty angle and the violet spray hanging off the side. They all sat down in the ditch, except the children, to recover from the shock. They were all shaking.

"Maybe a car will come along," said the children's mother hoarsely.

"I believe I have injured an organ," said the grandmother, pressing her side, but no one answered her. Bailey's teeth were clattering. He had on a yellow sport shirt with bright blue parrots designed in it and his face was as yellow as the shirt. The grandmother decided that she would not mention that the house was in Tennessee.

The road was about ten feet above and they could see only the tops of the trees on the other side of it. Behind the ditch they were sitting in there were more woods, tall and dark and deep. In a few minutes they saw a car some distance away on top of a hill, coming slowly as if the occupants were watching them. The grandmother stood up and waved both arms dramatically to attract their attention. The car continued to come on slowly, disappeared around a bend and appeared again, moving even slower, on top of the hill they had gone over. It was a big black battered hearselike automobile. There were three men in it.

It came to a stop over them and for some minutes, the driver looked down with a steady expressionless gaze to where they were sitting, and didn't speak. Then he turned his head and muttered something to the other two and they got out. One was a fat boy in black trousers and a red sweat shirt with a silver stallion embossed on the front of it. He moved around on the right side of them and stood staring, his mouth partly open in a kind of loose grin. The other had on khaki pants and a blue striped coat and a gray hat pulled down very low, hiding most of his face. He came around slowly on the left side. Neither spoke.

The driver got out of the car and stood by the side of it, looking down at them. He was an older man than the other two. His hair was just beginning to gray and he wore silver-rimmed spectacles that gave him a scholarly look. He had a long creased face and didn't have on any shirt or undershirt. He had on blue jeans that were too tight for him and was holding a black hat and a gun. The two boys also had guns.

"We've had an ACCIDENT!" the children screamed.

The grandmother had the peculiar feeling that the bespectacled man was someone she knew. His face was as familiar to her as if she had known him all her life but she could not recall who he was. He moved away from the car and began to come down the embankment, placing his feet carefully so that he wouldn't slip. He had on tan and white shoes and no socks, and his ankles were red and thin. "Good afternoon," he said. "I see you all had you a little spill."

"We turned over twice!" said the grandmother.

"Oncet," he corrected. "We seen it happen. Try their car and see will it run, Hiram," he said quietly to the boy with the gray hat.

"What you got that gun for?" John Wesley asked. "Whatcha gonna do with that gun?"

"Lady," the man said to the children's mother, "would you mind calling them children to sit down by you? Children make me nervous. I want all you all to sit down right together there were you're at."

"What are you telling us what to do for?" June Star asked.

Behind them the line of woods gaped like a dark open mouth. "Come here," said their mother.

"Look here now," Bailey began suddenly, "we're in a predicament! We're in . . ."

The grandmother shrieked. She scrambled to her feet and stood staring.

"You're The Misfit!" she said. "I recognized you at once!"

"Yes'm," the man said, smiling slightly as if he were pleased in spite of himself to be known, "but it would have been better for all of you, lady, if you hadn't of reckernized me."

Bailey turned his head sharply and said something to his mother that shocked even the children. The old lady began to cry and The Misfit reddened.

"Lady," he said, "don't you get upset. Sometimes a man says things he don't mean. I don't reckon he meant to talk to you thataway."

"You wouldn't shoot a lady, would you?" the grandmother said and removed a clean handkerchief from her cuff and began to slap at her eyes with it.

The Misfit pointed the toe of his shoe into the ground and made a little hole and then covered it up again. "I would hate to have to," he said.

"Listen," the grandmother almost screamed, "I know you're a good man. You don't look a bit like you have common blood. I know you must come from nice people!"

"Yes mam," he said, "finest people in the world." When he smiled he showed a row of strong white teeth. "God never made a finer woman than my mother and my daddy's heart was pure gold," he said. The boy with the red sweat shirt had come around behind them and was standing with his gun at his hip. The Misfit squatted down on the ground. "Watch them children, Bobby Lee," he said. "You know they make me nervous." He looked at the six of them huddled together in front of him and he seemed to be embarrassed as if he couldn't think of anything to say. "Ain't a cloud in the sky," he remarked, looking up at it. "Don't see no sun but don't see no cloud neither."

"Yes, it's a beautiful day," said the grandmother. "Listen," she said, "you shouldn't call yourself The Misfit because I know you're a good man at heart. I can just look at you and tell."

"Hush!" Bailey yelled. "Hush! Everybody shut up and let me handle this!" He was squatting in the position of a runner about to spring forward but he didn't move.

"I pre-chate that, lady," The Misfit said and drew a little circle in the ground with the butt of his gun.

"It'll take a half a hour to fix this here car," Hiram called, looking over the raised hood of it.

"Well, first you and Bobby Lee get him and that little boy to step over yonder with you," The Misfit said, pointing to Bailey and John Wesley. "The boys want to ask you something," he said to Bailey. "Would you mind stepping back in them woods there with them?"

"Listen," Bailey began, "we're in a terrible predicament! Nobody realizes what this is," and his voice cracked. His eyes were as blue and intense as the parrots in his shirt and he remained perfectly still.

The grandmother reached up to adjust her hat brim as if she were going to the woods with him but it came off in her hand. She stood staring at it and after a second she let it fall on the ground. Hiram pulled Bailey up by the arm as if he were assisting an old man. John

Wesley caught hold of his father's hand and Bobby Lee followed. They went off toward the woods and just as they reached the dark edge, Bailey turned and supporting himself against a gray naked pine trunk, he shouted, "I'll be back in a minute, Mamma, wait on me!"

"Come back this instant!" his mother shrilled but they all disappeared into the woods.

"Bailey Boy!" the grandmother called in a tragic voice but she found she was looking at The Misfit squatting on the ground in front of her. "I just know you're a good man," she said desperately. "You're not a bit common!"

"Nome, I ain't a good man," The Misfit said after a second as if he had considered her statement carefully, "but I ain't the worst in the world neither. My daddy said I was a different breed of dog from my brothers and sisters. 'You know,' Daddy said, 'it's some that can live their whole life out without asking about it and it's others has to know why it is, and this boy is one of the latters. He's going to be into everything!' " He put on his black hat and looked up suddenly and then away deep into the woods as if he were embarrassed again. "I'm sorry I don't have on a shirt before you ladies," he said, hunching his shoulders slightly. "We buried our clothes that we had on when we escaped and we're just making do until we can get better. We borrowed these from some folks we met," he explained.

"That's perfectly all right," the grandmother said. "Maybe Bailey has an extra shirt in his suitcase."

"I'll look and see terrectly," The Misfit said.

"Where are they taking him?" the children's mother screamed.

"Daddy was a card himself," The Misfit said. "You couldn't put anything over on him. He never got in trouble with the Authorities though. Just had the knack of handling them."

"You could be honest too if you'd only try," said the grandmother. "Think how wonderful it would be to settle down and live a comfortable life and not have to think about somebody chasing you all the time."

The Misfit kept scratching in the ground with the butt of his gun as if he were thinking about it. "Yes'm, somebody is always after you," he murmured.

The grandmother noticed how thin his shoulder blades were just behind his hat because she was standing up looking down on him. "Do you ever pray?" she asked.

He shook his head. All she saw was the black hat wiggle between his shoulder blades. "Nome," he said.

There was a pistol shot from the woods, followed closely by another. Then silence. The old lady's head jerked around. She could hear the wind move through the tree tops like a long satisfied insuck of breath. "Bailey Boy!" she called.

"I was a gospel singer for a while," The Misfit said. "I been most everything. Been in the arm service, both land and sea, at home and abroad, been twict married, been an undertaker, been with the railroads, plowed Mother Earth, been in a tornado, seen a man burnt alive oncet," and he looked up at the children's mother and the little girl who were sitting close together, their faces white and their eyes glassy; "I even seen a woman flogged," he said.

"Pray, pray," the grandmother began, "pray, pray . . ."

"I never was a bad boy that I remember of," The Misfit said in an almost dreamy voice, "but somewheres along the line I done something wrong and got sent to the penitentiary. I was buried alive," and he looked up and held her attention to him by a steady stare.

"That's when you should have started to pray," she said. "What did you do to get sent to the penitentiary that first time?"

"Turn to the right, it was a wall," The Misfit said, looking up again at the cloudless sky. "Turn to the left, it was a wall. Look up it was a ceiling, look down it was a floor. I forget what I done, lady. I set there and set there, trying to remember what it was I done and I ain't recalled it to this day. Oncet in a while, I would think it was coming to me, but it never come."

"Maybe they put you in by mistake," the old lady said vaguely.

"Nome," he said. "It wasn't no mistake. They had the papers on me."

"You must have stolen something," she said.

The Misfit sneered slightly. "Nobody had nothing I wanted," he said. "It was a head-doctor at the penitentiary said what I had done was kill my daddy but I known that for a lie. My daddy died in nineteen ought nineteen of the epidemic flu[4] and I never had a thing to do with it. He was buried in the Mount Hopewell Baptist churchyard and you can go there and see for yourself."

"If you would pray," the old lady said, "Jesus would help you."

"That's right," The Misfit said.

"Well then, why don't you pray?" she asked trembling with delight suddenly.

"I don't want no hep," he said. "I'm doing all right by myself."

Bobby Lee and Hiram came ambling back from the woods. Bobby Lee was dragging a yellow shirt with bright blue parrots in it.

"Throw me that shirt, Bobby Lee," The Misfit said. The shirt came flying at him and landed on his shoulder and he put it on. The

4. There was a devastating, worldwide epidemic of flu in 1919, an aftermath of World War I.

grandmother couldn't name what the shirt reminded her of. "No, lady," The Misfit said while he was buttoning up, "I found out the crime don't matter. You can do one thing or you can do another, kill a man or take a tire off his car, because sooner or later you're going to forget what it was you done and just be punished for it."

The children's mother had begun to make heaving noises as if she couldn't get her breath. "Lady," he asked, "would you and that little girl like to step off yonder with Bobby Lee and Hiram and join your husband?"

"Yes, thank you," the mother said faintly. Her left arm dangled helplessly and she was holding the baby, who had gone to sleep, in the other. "Hep that lady up, Hiram," The Misfit said as she struggled to climb out of the ditch, "and Bobby Lee, you hold onto that little girl's hand."

"I don't want to hold hands with him," June Star said. "He reminds me of a pig."

The fat boy blushed and laughed and caught her by the arm and pulled her off into the woods after Hiram and her mother.

Alone with The Misfit, the grandmother found that she had lost her voice. There was not a cloud in the sky nor any sun. There was nothing around her but woods. She wanted to tell him that he must pray. She opened and closed her mouth several times before anything came out. Finally she found herself saying, "Jesus, Jesus," meaning, Jesus will help you, but the way she was saying it, it sounded as if she might be cursing.

"Yes'm," The Misfit said as if he agreed. "Jesus thrown everything off balance. It was the same case with Him as with me except He hadn't committed any crime and they could prove I had committed one because they had the papers on me. Of course," he said, "they never shown me my papers. That's why I sign myself now. I said long ago, you get you a signature and sign everything you do and keep a copy of it. Then you'll know what you done and you can hold up the crime to the punishment and see do they match and in the end you'll have something to prove you ain't been treated right. I call myself The Misfit," he said, "because I can't make what all I done wrong fit what all I gone through in punishment."

There was a piercing scream from the woods, followed closely by a pistol report. "Does it seem right to you, lady, that one is punished a heap and another ain't punished at all?"

"Jesus!" the old lady cried. "You've got good blood! I know you wouldn't shoot a lady! I know you come from nice people! Pray! Jesus, you ought not to shoot a lady. I'll give you all the money I've got!"

"Lady," The Misfit said, looking beyond her far into the woods, "there never was a body that give the undertaker a tip."

There were two more pistol reports and the grandmother raised her head like a parched old turkey hen crying for water and called, "Bailey Boy, Bailey Boy!" as if her heart would break.

"Jesus was the only One that ever raised the dead," The Misfit continued, "and He shouldn't have done it. He thrown everything off balance. If He did what He said, then it's nothing for you to do but throw away everything and follow Him, and if He didn't then it's nothing for you to do but enjoy the few minutes you got left the best way you can—by killing somebody or burning down his house or doing some other meanness to him. No pleasure but meanness," he said and his voice had become almost a snarl.

"Maybe He didn't raise the dead," the old lady mumbled, not knowing what she was saying and feeling so dizzy that she sank down in the ditch with her legs twisted under her.

"I wasn't there so I can't say He didn't," The Misfit said. "I wisht I had of been there," he said, hitting the ground with his fist. "It ain't right I wasn't there because if I had of been there I would of known. Listen lady," he said in a high voice, "if I had of been there I would of known and I wouldn't be like I am now." His voice seemed about to crack and the grandmother's head cleared for an instant. She saw the man's face twisted close to her own as if he were going to cry and she murmured, "Why, you're one of my babies. You're one of my own children!" She reached out and touched him on the shoulder. The Misfit sprang back as if a snake had bitten him and shot her three times through the chest. Then he put his gun down on the ground and took off his glasses and began to clean them.

Hiram and Bobby Lee returned from the woods and stood over the ditch, looking down at the grandmother who half sat and half lay in a puddle of blood with her legs crossed under her like a child's and her face smiling up at the cloudless sky.

Without his glasses, The Misfit's eyes were red-rimmed and pale and defenseless-looking. "Take her off and throw her where you thrown the others," he said, picking up the cat that was rubbing itself against his leg.

"She was a talker, wasn't she?" Bobby Lee said, sliding down the ditch with a yodel.

"She would of been a good woman," The Misfit said, "if it had been somebody there to shoot her every minute of her life."

"Some fun!" Bobby Lee said.

"Shut up, Bobby Lee," The Misfit said. "It's no real pleasure in life."

1. Which parts of the story are convincingly realistic and which parts are exaggerated, fanciful, or improbable? What is accomplished by the mixture of realistic and unrealistic elements?
2. Do the various weaknesses and shortcomings of the traveling family have any bearing on their fate? Would the outcome have been the same if they had acted differently?
3. What is the significance of their being on the wrong road at the time of the automobile accident?
4. To what extent does the comedy of the story depend on shock?
5. Explain The Misfit's statement that Jesus "thrown everything off balance." Is The Misfit a philosopher or a psychopath?
6. What is the significance of the title?

Everything That Rises Must Converge

Her doctor had told Julian's mother that she must lose twenty pounds on account of her blood pressure, so on Wednesday nights Julian had to take her downtown on the bus for a reducing class at the Y. The reducing class was designed for working girls over fifty, who weighed from 165 to 200 pounds. His mother was one of the slimmer ones, but she said ladies did not tell their age or weight. She would not ride the buses by herself at night since they had been integrated, and because the reducing class was one of her few pleasures, necessary for her health, and *free*, she said Julian could at least put himself out to take her, considering all she did for him. Julian did not like to consider all she did for him, but every Wednesday night he braced himself and took her.

She was almost ready to go, standing before the hall mirror, putting on her hat, while he, his hands behind him, appeared pinned to the door frame, waiting like Saint Sebastian[1] for the arrows to begin piercing him. The hat was new and had cost her seven dollars and a half. She kept saying, "Maybe I shouldn't have paid that for it. No, I shouldn't have. I'll take it off and return it tomorrow. I shouldn't have bought it."

Julian raised his eyes to heaven. "Yes, you should have bought it," he said. "Put it on and let's go." It was a hideous hat. A purple velvet flap came down on one side of it and stood up on the other; the rest of it was green and looked like a cushion with the stuffing out. He

1. Roman martyr, symbol of calm indifference to suffering.

decided it was less comical than jaunty and pathetic. Everything that gave her pleasure was small and depressed him.

She lifted the hat one more time and set it down slowly on top of her head. Two wings of gray hair protruded on either side of her florid face, but her eyes, sky-blue, were as innocent and untouched by experience as they must have been when she was ten. Were it not that she was a widow who had struggled fiercely to feed and clothe and put him through school and who was supporting him still, "until he got on his feet," she might have been a little girl that he had to take to town.

"It's all right, it's all right," he said. "Let's go." He opened the door himself and started down the walk to get her going. The sky was a dying violet and the houses stood out darkly against it, bulbous liver-colored monstrosities of a uniform ugliness though no two were alike. Since this had been a fashionable neighborhood forty years ago, his mother persisted in thinking they did well to have an apartment in it. Each house had a narrow collar of dirt around it in which sat, usually, a grubby child. Julian walked with his hands in his pockets, his head down and thrust forward and his eyes glazed with the determination to make himself completely numb during the time he would be sacrificed to her pleasure.

The door closed and he turned to find the dumpy figure, surmounted by the atrocious hat, coming toward him. "Well," she said, "you only live once and paying a little more for it, I at least won't meet myself coming and going."

"Some day I'll start making money," Julian said gloomily—he knew he never would—"and you can have one of those jokes whenever you take the fit." But first they would move. He visualized a place where the nearest neighbors would be three miles away on either side.

"I think you're doing fine," she said, drawing on her gloves. "You've only been out of school a year. Rome wasn't built in a day."

She was one of the few members of the Y reducing class who arrived in hat and gloves and who had a son who had been to college. "It takes time," she said, "and the world is in such a mess. This hat looked better on me than any of the others, though when she brought it out I said, 'Take that thing back. I wouldn't have it on my head,' and she said, 'Now wait till you see it on,' and when she put it on me, I said, 'We-ull,' and she said, 'If you ask me, that hat does something for you and you do something for the hat, and besides,' she said, 'with that hat, you won't meet yourself coming and going.' "

Julian thought he could have stood his lot better if she had been selfish, if she had been an old hag who drank and screamed at him. He walked along, saturated in depression, as if in the midst of his martyrdom he had lost his faith. Catching sight of his long, hopeless, irritated face, she stopped suddenly with a grief-stricken look, and pulled back on his arm. "Wait on me," she said. "I'm going back to the house and take this thing off and tomorrow I'm going to return it. I was out of my head. I can pay the gas bill with that seven-fifty."

He caught her arm in a vicious grip. "You are not going to take it back," he said. "I like it."

"Well," she said, "I don't think I ought . . ."

"Shut up and enjoy it," he muttered, more depressed than ever.

"With the world in the mess it's in," she said, "it's a wonder we can enjoy anything. I tell you, the bottom rail is on the top."

Julian sighed.

"Of course," she said, "if you know who are you, you can go anywhere." She said this every time he took her to the reducing class. "Most of them in it are not our kind of people," she said, "but I can be gracious to anybody. I know who I am."

"They don't give a damn for your graciousness," Julian said savagely. "Knowing who you are is good for one generation only. You haven't the foggiest idea where you stand now or who you are."

She stopped and allowed her eyes to flash at him. "I most certainly do know who I am," she said, "and if you don't know who you are, I'm ashamed of you."

"Oh hell," Julian said.

"Your great-grandfather was a former governor of this state," she said. "Your grandfather was a prosperous land-owner. Your grandmother was a Godhigh."

"Will you look around you," he said tensely, "and see where you are now?" and he swept his arm jerkily out to indicate the neighborhood, which the growing darkness at least made less dingy.

"You remain what you are," she said. "Your great-grandfather had a plantation and two hundred slaves."

"There are no more slaves," he said irritably.

"They were better off when they were," she said. He groaned to see that she was off on that topic. She rolled onto it every few days like a train on an open track. He knew every stop, every junction, every swamp along the way, and knew the exact point at which her conclusion would roll majestically into the station: "It's ridiculous. It's simply not realistic. They should rise, yes, but on their own side of the fence."

"Let's skip it," Julian said.

"The ones I feel sorry for," she said, "are the ones that are half white. They're tragic."

"Will you skip it?"

"Suppose we were half white. We would certainly have mixed feelings."

"I have mixed feelings now," he groaned.

"Well let's talk about something pleasant," she said. "I remember going to Grandpa's when I was a little girl. Then the house had double stairways that went up to what was really the second floor—all the cooking was done on the first. I used to like to stay down in the kitchen on account of the way the walls smelled. I would sit with my nose pressed against the plaster and take deep breaths. Actually the place belonged to the Godhighs but your grandfather Chestny paid the mortgage and saved it for them. They were in reduced circumstances," she said, "but reduced or not, they never forgot who they were."

"Doubtless that decayed mansion reminded them," Julian muttered. He never spoke of it without contempt or thought of it without longing. He had seen it once when he was a child before it had been sold. The double stairways had rotted and been torn down. Negroes were living in it. But it remained in his mind as his mother had known it. It appeared in his dreams regularly. He would stand on the wide porch, listening to the rustle of oak leaves, then wander through the high-ceilinged hall into the parlor that opened onto it and gaze at the worn rugs and faded draperies. It occurred to him that it was he, not she, who could have appreciated it. He preferred its threadbare elegance to anything he could name and it was because of it that all the neighborhoods they had lived in had been a torment to him—whereas she had hardly known the difference. She called her insensitivity "being adjustable."

"And I remember the old darky who was my nurse, Caroline. There was no better person in the world. I've always had a great respect for my colored friends," she said. "I'd do anything in the world for them and they'd . . ."

"Will you for God's sake get off that subject?" Julian said. When he got on a bus by himself, he made it a point to sit down beside a Negro, in reparation as it were for his mother's sins.

"You're mighty touchy tonight," she said. "Do you feel all right?"

"Yes I feel all right," he said. "Now lay off."

She pursed her lips. "Well, you certainly are in a vile humor," she observed. "I just won't speak to you at all."

They had reached the bus stop. There was no bus in sight and Julian, his hands still jammed in his pockets and his head thrust forward, scowled down the empty street. The frustration of having to wait on the bus as well as ride on it began to creep up his neck like a hot hand. The presence of his mother was borne in upon him as she gave a pained sigh. He looked at her bleakly. She was holding herself very erect under the preposterous hat, wearing it like a banner of her imaginary dignity. There was in him an evil urge to break her spirit. He suddenly unloosened his tie and pulled it off and put it in his pocket.

She stiffened. "Why must you look like *that* when you take me to town?" she said. "Why must you deliberately embarrass me?"

"If you'll never learn where you are," he said, "you can at least learn where I am."

"You look like a—thug," she said.

"Then I must be one," he murmured.

"I'll just go home," she said. "I will not bother you. If you can't do a little thing like that for me . . ."

Rolling his eyes upward, he put his tie back on. "Restored to my class," he muttered. He thrust his face toward her and hissed, "True culture is in the mind, the *mind*," he said, and tapped his head, "the mind."

"It's in the heart," she said, "and in how you do things and how you do things is because of who you *are*."

"Nobody in the damn bus cares who you are."

"I care who I am," she said icily.

The lighted bus appeared on top of the next hill and as it approached, they moved out into the street to meet it. He put his hand under her elbow and hoisted her up on the creaking step. She entered with a little smile, as if she were going into a drawing room where everyone had been waiting for her. While he put in the tokens, she sat down on one of the broad front seats for three which faced the aisle. A thin woman with protruding teeth and long yellow hair was sitting on the end of it. His mother moved up beside her and left room for Julian beside herself. He sat down and looked at the floor across the aisle where a pair of thin feet in red and white canvas sandals were planted.

His mother immediately began a general conversation meant to attract anyone who felt like talking. "Can it get any hotter?" she said and removed from her purse a folding fan, black with a Japanese scene on it, which she began to flutter before her.

"I reckon it might could," the woman with the protruding teeth said, "but I know for a fact my apartment couldn't get no hotter."

"It must get the afternoon sun," his mother said. She sat forward and looked up and down the bus. It was half filled. Everybody was white. "I see we have the bus to ourselves," she said. Julian cringed.

"For a change," said the woman across the aisle, the owner of the red and white canvas sandals. "I come on one the other day and they were thick as fleas—up front and all through."

"The world is in a mess everywhere," his mother said. "I don't know how we've let it get in this fix."

"What gets my goat is all those boys from good families stealing automobile tires," the woman with the protruding teeth said. "I told my boy, I said you may not be rich but you been raised right and if I ever catch you in any such mess, they can send you on to the reformatory. Be exactly where you belong."

"Training tells," his mother said. "Is your boy in high school?"

"Ninth grade," the woman said.

"My son just finished college last year. He wants to write but he's selling typewriters until he gets started," his mother said.

The woman leaned forward and peered at Julian. He threw her such a malevolent look that she subsided against the seat. On the floor across the aisle there was an abandoned newspaper. He got up and got it and opened it out in front of him. His mother discreetly continued the conversation in a lower tone but the woman across the aisle said in a loud voice, "Well that's nice. Selling typewriters is close to writing. He can go right from one to the other."

"I tell him," his mother said, "that Rome wasn't built in a day."

Behind the newspaper Julian was withdrawing into the inner compartment of his mind where he spent most of his time. This was a kind of mental bubble in which he established himself when he could not bear to be a part of what was going on around him. From it he could see out and judge but in it he was safe from any kind of penetration from without. It was the only place where he felt free of the general idiocy of his fellows. His mother had never entered it but from it he could see her with absolute clarity.

The old lady was clever enough and he thought that if she had started from any of the right premises, more might have been expected of her. She lived according to the laws of her own fantasy world, outside of which he had never seen her set foot. The law of it was to sacrifice herself for him after she had first created the necessity to do so by making a mess of things. If he had permitted her sacrifices, it was only because her lack of foresight had made them necessary. All of her life had been a struggle to act like a Chestny without the Chestny goods, and to give him everything she thought a Chestny ought to have; but since, said she, it was fun to struggle, why complain? And when you had won, as she had won, what fun to look back on the hard times! He could not forgive her that she had enjoyed the struggle and that she thought *she* had won.

What she meant when she said she had won was that she had brought him up successfully and had sent him to college and that he had turned out so well—good looking (her teeth had gone unfilled so that his could be straightened), intelligent (he realized he was too intelligent to be a success), and with a future ahead of him (there was of course no future ahead of him). She excused his gloominess on the grounds that he was still growing up and his radical ideas on his lack of practical experience. She said he didn't yet know a thing about "life," that he hadn't even entered the real world—when already he was as disenchanted with it as a man of fifty.

The further irony of all this was that in spite of her, he had turned out so well. In spite of going to only a third-rate college, he had, on his own initiative, come out with a first-rate education; in spite of growing up dominated by a small mind, he had ended up with a large one; in spite of all her foolish views, he was free of prejudice and unafraid to face facts. Most miraculous of all, instead of being blinded by love for her as she was for him, he had cut himself emotionally free of her and could see her with complete objectivity. He was not dominated by his mother.

The bus stopped with a sudden jerk and shook him from his meditation. A woman from the back lurched forward with little steps and barely escaped falling in his newspaper as she righted herself. She got off and a large Negro got on. Julian kept his paper lowered to watch. It gave him a certain satisfaction to see injustice in daily operation. It confirmed his view that with a few exceptions there was no one worth knowing within a radius of three hundred miles. The Negro was well dressed and carried a briefcase. He looked around and then sat down on the other end of the seat where the woman with the red and white canvas sandals was sitting. He immediately unfolded a newspaper and obscured himself behind it. Julian's mother's elbow at once prodded insistently into his ribs. "Now you see why I won't ride on these buses by myself," she whispered.

The woman with the red and white canvas sandals had risen at the same time the Negro sat down and had gone further back in the bus and taken the seat of the woman who had got off. His mother leaned forward and cast her an approving look.

Julian rose, crossed the aisle, and sat down in the place of the woman with the canvas sandals. From this position, he looked serenely across at his mother. Her face had turned an angry red. He stared at her, making his eyes the eyes of a stranger. He felt his tension suddenly lift as if he had openly declared war on her.

He would have liked to get in conversation with the Negro and to talk with him about art or politics or any subject that would be above the comprehension of those around them, but the man remained entrenched behind his paper. He was either ignoring the change of seating or had never noticed it. There was no way for Julian to convey his sympathy.

His mother kept her eyes fixed reproachfully on his face. The woman with the protruding teeth was looking at him avidly as if he were a type of monster new to her.

"Do you have a light?" he asked the Negro.

Without looking away from his paper, the man reached in his pocket and handed him a packet of matches.

"Thanks," Julian said. For a moment he held the matches foolishly. A NO SMOKING sign looked down upon him from over the door. This alone would not have deterred him; he had no cigarettes. He had quit smoking some months before because he could not afford it. "Sorry," he muttered and handed back the matches. The Negro lowered the paper and gave him an annoyed look. He took the matches and raised the paper again.

His mother continued to gaze at him but she did not take advantage of his momentary discomfort. Her eyes retained their battered look. Her face seemed to be unnaturally red, as if her blood pressure had risen. Julian allowed no glimmer of sympathy to show on his face. Having got the advantage, he wanted desperately to keep it and carry it through. He would have liked to teach her a lesson that would last her a while, but there seemed no way to continue the point. The Negro refused to come out from behind his paper.

Julian folded his arms and looked stolidly before him, facing her but as if he did not see her, as if he had ceased to recognize her existence. He visualized a scene in which, the bus having reached their stop, he would remain in his seat and when she said, "Aren't you going to get off?" he would look at her as a stranger who had rashly addressed him. The corner they got off on was usually deserted, but it was well lighted and it would not hurt her to walk by herself the four blocks to the Y. He decided to wait until the time came and then decide whether or not he would let her get off by herself. He would have to be at the Y at ten to bring her back, but he could leave her wondering if he was going to show up. There was no reason for her to think she could always depend on him.

He retired again into the high-ceilinged room sparsely settled with large pieces of antique furniture. His soul expanded momentarily but then he became aware of his mother across from him and the vision shriveled. He studied her coldly. Her feet in little pumps dangled like a child's and did not quite reach the floor. She was training on him an exaggerated look of reproach. He felt completely detached from her. At that moment he could with pleasure have slapped her as he would have slapped a particularly obnoxious child in his charge.

He began to imagine various unlikely ways by which he could teach her a lesson. He might make friends with some distinguished Negro professor or lawyer and bring him home to spend the evening. He would be entirely justified but her blood pressure would rise to 300. He could not push her to the extent of making her have a stroke, and moreover, he had never been successful at making any Negro friends. He had tried to strike up an acquaintance on the bus with some of the better types, with ones that looked like professors or ministers or lawyers. One morning he had sat down next to a distinguished-looking dark brown man who had answered his questions with a sonorous solemnity but who had turned out to be an undertaker. Another day he had sat down beside a cigar-smoking Negro with a diamond ring on his finger, but after a few stilted pleasantries, the Negro had rung the buzzer and risen, slipping two lottery tickets into Julian's hand as he climbed over him to leave.

He imagined his mother lying desperately ill and his being able to secure only a Negro doctor for her. He toyed with that idea for a few minutes and then dropped it for a momentary vision of himself participating as a sympathizer in a sit-in demonstration. This was possible but he did not linger with it. Instead, he approached the ultimate horror. He brought home a beautiful suspiciously Negroid woman. Prepare yourself, he said. There is nothing you can do about it. This is the woman I've chosen. She's intelligent, dignified, even good, and she's suffered and she hasn't thought it *fun*. Now persecute us, go ahead and persecute us. Drive her out of here, but remember, you're driving me too. His eyes were narrowed and through the indignation he had generated, he saw his mother across the aisle, purple-faced, shrunken to the dwarf-like proportions of her moral nature, sitting like a mummy beneath the ridiculous banner of her hat.

He was tilted out of his fantasy again as the bus stopped. The door opened with a sucking hiss and out of the dark a large, gaily dressed, sullen-looking colored woman got on with a little boy. The child, who might have been four, had on a short plaid suit and a Tyrolean hat with a blue feather in it. Julian hoped that he would sit down beside him and that the woman would push in beside his mother. He could think of no better arrangement.

As she waited for her tokens, the woman was surveying the seating possibilities—he hoped with the idea of sitting where she was least wanted. There was something familiar-looking about her but Julian could not place what it was. She was a giant of a woman. Her face was set not only to meet opposition but to seek it out. The downward tilt of her large lower lip was like a warning sign: DON'T TAMPER WITH ME. Her bulging figure was encased in a green crepe dress and her feet overflowed in red shoes. She had on a hideous hat. A purple velvet flap came down on one side of it and stood up on the other; the rest of it was green and looked like a cushion with the stuffing out. She carried a mammoth red pocketbook that bulged throughout as if it were stuffed with rocks.

To Julian's disappointment, the little boy climbed up on the empty seat beside his mother. His mother lumped all children, black and white, into the common category, "cute," and she thought little Negroes were on the whole cuter than little white children. She smiled at the little boy as he climbed on the seat.

Meanwhile the woman was bearing down upon the empty seat beside Julian. To his annoyance, she squeezed herself into it. He saw his mother's face change as the woman settled herself next to him and he realized with satisfaction that this was more objectionable to her than it was to him. Her face seemed almost gray and there was a look of dull recognition in her eyes, as if suddenly she had sickened at some awful confrontation. Julian saw that it was because she and the woman had, in a sense, swapped sons. Though his mother would not realize the symbolic significance of this, she would feel it. His amusement showed plainly on his face.

The woman next to him muttered something unintelligible to herself. He was conscious of a kind of bristling next to him, a muted growling like that of an angry cat. He could not see anything but the red pocketbook upright on the bulging green thighs. He visualized the woman as she had stood waiting for her tokens—the ponderous figure, rising from the red shoes upward over the solid hips, the mammoth bosom, the haughty face, to the green and purple hat.

His eyes widened.

The vision of the two hats, identical, broke upon him with the radiance of a brilliant sunrise. His face was suddenly lit with joy. He could not believe that Fate had thrust upon his mother such a lesson. He gave a loud chuckle so that she would look at him and see that he saw. She turned her eyes on him slowly. The blue in them seemed to have turned a bruised purple. For a moment he had an uncomfortable sense of her innocence, but it lasted only a second before principle rescued him. Justice entitled him to laugh. His grin hardened until it said to her as plainly as if he were saying aloud: Your punishment exactly fits your pettiness. This should teach you a permanent lesson.

Her eyes shifted to the woman. She seemed unable to bear looking at him and to find the woman preferable. He became conscious again of the bristling presence at his side. The woman was rumbling like a volcano about to become active. His mother's mouth began to twitch slightly at one corner. With a sinking heart, he saw incipient signs of recovery on her face and realized that this was going to strike her suddenly as funny and was going to be no lesson at all. She kept her eyes on the woman and an amused smile came over her face as if the woman were a monkey that had stolen her hat. The little Negro was looking up at her with large fascinated eyes. He had been trying to attract her attention for some time.

"Carver!" the woman said suddenly. "Come heah!"

When he saw that the spotlight was on him at last, Carver drew his feet up and turned himself toward Julian's mother and giggled.

"Carver!" the woman said. "You heah me? Come heah!"

Carver slid down from the seat but remained squatting with his back against the base of it, his head turned slyly around toward Julian's mother, who was smiling at him. The woman reached a hand across the aisle and snatched him to her. He righted himself and hung backwards on her knees, grinning at Julian's mother. "Isn't he cute?" Julian's mother said to the woman with the protruding teeth.

"I reckon he is," the woman said without conviction.

The Negress yanked him upright but he eased out of her grip and shot across the aisle and scrambled, giggling wildly, onto the seat beside his love.

"I think he likes me," Julian's mother said, and smiled at the woman. It was the smile she used when she was being particularly gracious to an inferior. Julian saw everything was lost. The lesson had rolled off her like rain on a roof.

The woman stood up and yanked the little boy off the seat as if she were snatching him from contagion. Julian could feel the rage in her at having no weapon like his mother's smile. She gave the child a sharp slap across his leg. He howled once and then thrust his head into her stomach and kicked his feet against her shins. "Behave," she said vehemently.

The bus stopped and the Negro who had been reading the newspaper got off. The woman moved over and set the little boy down with a thump between herself and Julian. She held him firmly by the knee. In a moment he put his hands in front of his face and peeped at Julian's mother through his fingers.

"I see yoooooooo!" she said and put her hand in front of her face and peeped at him.

The woman slapped his hand down. "Quit yo' foolishness," she said, "before I knock the living Jesus out of you!"

Julian was thankful that the next stop was theirs. He reached up and pulled the cord. The woman reached up and pulled it at the same time. Oh my God, he thought. He had the terrible intuition that when they got off the bus together, his mother would open her purse and give the little boy a nickel. The gesture would be as natural to her as breathing. The bus stopped and the woman got up and lunged to the front, dragging the child, who wished to stay on, after her. Julian and his mother got up and followed. As they neared the door, Julian tried to relieve her of her pocketbook.

"No," she murmured, "I want to give the little boy a nickel."

"No!" Julian hissed. "No!"

She smiled down at the child and opened her bag. The bus door opened and the woman picked him up by the arm and descended with him, hanging at her hip. Once in the street she set him down and shook him.

Julian's mother had to close her purse while she got down the bus step but as soon as her feet were on the ground, she opened it again and began to rummage inside. "I can't find but a penny," she whispered, "but it looks like a new one."

"Don't do it!" Julian said fiercely between his teeth. There was a streetlight on the corner and she hurried to get under it so that she could better see into her pocketbook. The woman was heading off rapidly down the street with the child still hanging backward on her hand.

"Oh little boy!" Julian's mother called and took a few quick steps and caught up with them just beyond the lamppost. "Here's a bright new penny for you," and she held out the coin, which shone bronze in the dim light.

The huge woman turned and for a moment stood, her shoulders lifted and her face frozen with frustrated rage, and stared at Julian's mother. Then all at once she seemed to explode like a piece of machinery that had been given one ounce of pressure too much. Julian saw the black fist swing out with the red pocketbook. He shut his eyes and cringed as he heard the woman shout, "He don't take nobody's pennies!" When he opened his eyes, the woman was disappearing down the street with the little boy staring wide-eyed over her shoulder. Julian's mother was sitting on the sidewalk.

"I told you not to do that," Julian said angrily. "I told you not to do that!"

He stood over her for a minute, gritting his teeth. Her legs were stretched out in front of her and her hat was on her lap. He squatted down and looked her in the face. It was totally expressionless. "You got exactly what you deserved," he said. "Now get up."

He picked up her pocketbook and put what had fallen out back in it. He picked the hat up off her lap. The penny caught his eye on the sidewalk and he picked that up and let it drop before her eyes into the purse. Then he stood up and leaned over and held his hands out to pull her up. She remained immobile. He sighed. Rising above them on either side were black apartment buildings, marked with irregular rectangles of light. At the end of the block a man came out of a door and walked off in the opposite direction. "All right," he said, "suppose somebody happens by and wants to know why you're sitting on the sidewalk?"

She took the hand and, breathing hard, pulled heavily up on it and then stood for a moment, swaying slightly as if the spots of light in the darkness were circling around her. Her eyes, shadowed and confused, finally settled on his face. He did not try to conceal his irritation. "I hope this teaches you a lesson," he said. She leaned forward and her eyes raked his face. She seemed trying to determine his identity. Then, as if she found nothing familiar about him, she started off with a headlong movement in the wrong direction.

"Aren't you going on to the Y?" he asked.

"Home," she muttered.

"Well, are we walking?"

For answer she kept going. Julian followed along, his hands behind him. He saw no reason to let the lesson she had had go without backing it up with an explanation of its meaning. She might as well be made to understand what had happened to her. "Don't think that was just an uppity Negro woman," he said. "That was the whole colored race which will no longer take your condescending pennies. That was your black double. She can wear the same hat as you, and to be sure," he added gratuitously (because he thought it was funny), "it looked better on her than it did on you. What all this means," he said, "is that the old world is gone. The old manners are obsolete and your graciousness is not worth a damn." He thought bitterly of the house that had been lost for him. "You aren't who you think you are," he said.

She continued to plow ahead, paying no attention to him. Her hair had come undone on one side. She dropped her pocketbook and took no notice. He stooped and picked it up and handed it to her but she did not take it.

"You needn't act as if the world had come to an end," he said, "because it hasn't. From now on you've got to live in a new world and face a few realities for a change. Buck up," he said, "it won't kill you."

She was breathing fast.

"Let's wait on the bus," he said.

"Home," she said thickly.

"I hate to see you behave like this," he said. "Just like a child. I should be able to expect more of you." He decided to stop where he was and make her stop and wait for a bus. "I'm not going any farther," he said stopping. "We're going on the bus."

She continued to go on as if she had not heard him. He took a few steps and caught her arm and stopped her. He looked into her face and caught his breath. He was looking into a face he had never seen before. "Tell Grandpa to come get me," she said.

He stared, stricken.

"Tell Caroline to come get me," she said.

Stunned, he let her go and she lurched forward again, walking as if one leg were shorter than the other. A tide of darkness seemed to be sweeping her from him. "Mother!" he cried. "Darling, sweetheart, wait!" Crumpling, she fell to the pavement. He dashed forward and fell at her side, crying, "Mamma, Mamma!" He turned her over. Her face was fiercely distorted. One eye, large and staring, moved slightly to the left as if it had become unmoored. The other remained fixed on him, raked his face again, found nothing and closed.

"Wait here, wait here!" he cried and jumped up and began to run for help toward a cluster of lights he saw in the distance ahead of him. "Help, help!" he shouted, but his voice was thin, scarcely a thread of sound. The lights drifted farther away the faster he ran and his feet moved numbly as if they carried him nowhere. The tide of darkness seemed to sweep him back to her, postponing from moment to moment his entry into the world of guilt and sorrow.

---

1. List the things that Julian believes in and the things his mother believes in. Are the lists totally dissimilar?
2. Is Julian right when he tells his mother "the old world is gone"? Does that statement mean what he thinks it means? Is it merely a statement of Julian's prejudices?
3. Why is Julian angry with his mother after she has been knocked down?
4. Interpret the words spoken by Julian's mother after the attack. What has happened to her?
5. Can this story be interpreted without bringing moral judgments into play? Is it possible to decide who is guilty and who is innocent?

Parker's Back

Parker's wife was sitting on the front porch floor, snapping beans. Parker was sitting on the step, some distance away, watching her sullenly. She was plain, plain. The skin on her face was thin and drawn as tight as the skin on an onion and her eyes were gray and sharp like the points of two icepicks. Parker understood why he had married her—he couldn't have got her any other way—but he couldn't understand why he stayed with her now. She was pregnant and pregnant women were not his favorite kind. Nevertheless, he stayed as if she had him conjured. He was puzzled and ashamed of himself.

The house they rented sat alone save for a single tall pecan tree on a high embankment overlooking a highway. At intervals a car would shoot past below and his wife's eyes would swerve suspiciously after the sound of it and then come back to rest on the newspaper full of beans in her lap. One of the things she did not approve of was automobiles. In addition to her other bad qualities, she was forever sniffing up sin. She did not smoke or dip,[1] drink whiskey, use bad language or paint her face, and God knew some paint would have improved it, Parker thought. Her being against color, it was the more remarkable she married him. Sometimes he supposed that she had married him because she meant to save him. At other times he had a suspicion that

1. I.e., dip snuff.

she actually liked everything she said she didn't. He could account for her one way or another; it was himself he could not understand.

She turned her head in his direction and said, "It's no reason you can't work for a man. It don't have to be a woman."

"Aw shut your mouth for a change," Parker muttered.

If he had been certain she was jealous of the woman he worked for he would have been pleased but more likely she was concerned with the sin that would result if he and the woman took a liking to each other. He had told her that the woman was a hefty young blonde; in fact she was nearly seventy years old and too dried up to have an interest in anything except getting as much work out of him as she could. Not that an old woman didn't sometimes get an interest in a young man, particularly if he was as attractive as Parker felt he was, but this old woman looked at him the same way she looked at her old tractor—as if she had to put up with it because it was all she had. The tractor had broken down the second day Parker was on it and she had set him at once to cutting bushes, saying out of the side of her mouth to the nigger, "Everything he touches, he breaks." She also asked him to wear his shirt when he worked; Parker had removed it even though the day was not sultry; he put it back on reluctantly.

This ugly woman Parker married was his first wife. He had had other women but he had planned never to get himself tied up legally. He had first seen her one morning when his truck broke down on the highway. He had managed to pull it off the road into a neatly swept yard on which sat a peeling two-room house. He got out and opened the hood of the truck and began to study the motor. Parker had an extra sense that told him when there was a woman nearby watching him. After he had leaned over the motor a few minutes, his neck began to prickle. He cast his eye over the empty yard and porch of the house. A woman he could not see was either nearby beyond a clump of honeysuckle or in the house, watching him out the window.

Suddenly Parker began to jump up and down and fling his hand about as if he had mashed it in the machinery. He doubled over and held his hand close to his chest. "God dammit!" he hollered, "Jesus Christ in hell! Jesus God Almighty damm! God dammit to hell!" he went on, flinging out the same few oaths over and over as loud as he could.

Without warning a terrible bristly claw slammed the side of his face and he fell backwards on the hood of the truck. "You don't talk no filth here!" a voice close to him shrilled.

Parker's vision was so blurred that for an instant he thought he had been attacked by some creature from above, a giant hawk-eyed angel wielding a hoary weapon. As his sight cleared, he saw before him a tall raw-boned girl with a broom.

"I hurt my hand," he said. "I HURT my hand." He was so incensed that he forgot he hadn't hurt his hand. "My hand may be broke," he growled although his voice was still unsteady.

"Lemme see it," the girl demanded.

Parker stuck out his hand and she came closer and looked at it. There was no mark on the palm and she took the hand and turned it over. Her own hand was dry and hot and rough and Parker felt himself jolted back to life by her touch. He looked more closely at her. I don't want nothing to do with this one, he thought.

The girl's sharp eyes peered at the back of the stubby reddish hand she held. There emblazoned in red and blue was a tattooed eagle perched on a cannon. Parker's sleeve was rolled to the elbow. Above the eagle a serpent was coiled about a shield and in the spaces between the eagle and the serpent there were hearts, some with arrows through them. Above the serpent there was a spread hand of cards. Every space on the skin of Parker's arm, from wrist to elbow, was covered in some loud design. The girl gazed at this with an almost stupefied smile of shock, as if she had accidentally grasped a poisonous snake; she dropped the hand.

"I got most of my other ones in foreign parts," Parker said. "These here I mostly got in the United States. I got my first one when I was only fifteen year old."

"Don't tell me," the girl said, "I don't like it. I ain't got any use for it."

"You ought to see the ones you can't see," Parker said and winked.

Two circles of red appeared like apples on the girl's cheeks and softened her appearance. Parker was intrigued. He did not for a minute think that she didn't like the tattoos. He had never yet met a woman who was not attracted to them.

Parker was fourteen when he saw a man in a fair, tattooed from head to foot. Except for his loins which were girded with a panther hide, the man's skin was patterned in what seemed from Parker's distance—he was near the back of the tent, standing on a bench—a single intricate design of brilliant color. The man, who was small and sturdy, moved about on the platform, flexing his muscles so that the arabesque of men and beasts and flowers on his skin appeared to have a subtle motion of its own. Parker was filled with emotion, lifted up as some people are when the flag passes. He was a boy whose mouth habitually hung open. He was heavy and earnest, as ordinary as a loaf of bread. When the show was over, he had remained standing on the bench, staring where the tattooed man had been, until the tent was almost empty.

Parker had never before felt the least motion of wonder in himself. Until he saw the man at the fair, it did not enter his head that there was anything out of the ordinary about the fact that he existed. Even then it did not enter his head, but a peculiar unease settled in him. It was as if a blind boy had been turned so gently in a different direction that he did not know his destination had been changed.

He had his first tattoo some time after—the eagle perched on the cannon. It was done by a local artist. It hurt very little, just enough to make it appear to Parker to be worth doing. This was peculiar too for before he had thought that only what did not hurt was worth doing. The next year he quit school because he was sixteen and could. He went to the trade school for a while, then he quit the trade school and worked for six months in a garage. The only reason he worked at all was to pay for more tattoos. His mother worked in a laundry and could support him, but she would not pay for any tattoo except her name on a heart, which he had put on, grumbling. However, her name was Betty Jean and nobody had to know it was his mother. He found out that the tattoos were attractive to the kind of girls he liked but who had never liked him before. He began to drink beer and get in fights. His mother wept over what was becoming of him. One night she dragged him off to a revival with her, not telling him where they were going. When he saw the big lighted church, he jerked out of her grasp and ran. The next day he lied about his age and joined the navy.

Parker was large for the tight sailor's pants but the silly white cap, sitting low on his forehead, made his face by contrast look thoughtful and almost intense. After a month or two in the navy, his mouth ceased to hang open. His features hardened into the features of a man. He stayed in the navy five years and seemed a natural part of the gray mechanical ship, except for his eyes, which were the same pale slate-color as the ocean and reflected the immense spaces around him as if they were a microcosm of the mysterious sea. In port Parker wandered about comparing the run-down places he was in to Birmingham, Alabama. Everywhere he went he picked up more tattoos.

He had stopped having lifeless ones like anchors and crossed rifles. He had a tiger and a panther on each shoulder, a cobra coiled about a torch on his chest, hawks on his thighs, Elizabeth II and Philip[2] over where his stomach and liver were respectively. He did not much care what the subject was so long as it was colorful; on his abdomen he had a few obscenities but only because that seemed the proper place for them. Parker would be satisfied with each tattoo about a month, then something about it that had attracted him would wear off. Whenever a decent-sized mirror was available, he would get in front of it and study his overall look. The effect was not of one intricate arabesque of colors but of something haphazard and botched. A huge dissatisfaction would

2. Elizabeth II, Queen of England, and Prince Philip, her husband.

come over him and he would go off and find another tattooist and have another space filled up. The front of Parker was almost completely covered but there were no tattoos on his back. He had no desire for one anywhere he could not readily see it himself. As the space on the front of him for tattoos decreased, his dissatisfaction grew and became general.

After one of his furloughs, he didn't go back to the navy but remained away without official leave, drunk, in a rooming house in a city he did not know. His dissatisfaction, from being chronic and latent, had suddenly become acute and raged in him. It was as if the panther and the lion and the serpents and the eagles and the hawks had penetrated his skin and lived inside him in a raging warfare. The navy caught up with him, put him in the brig for nine months and then gave him a dishonorable discharge.

After that Parker decided that country air was the only kind fit to breathe. He rented the shack on the embankment and bought the old truck and took various jobs which he kept as long as it suited him. At the time he met his future wife, he was buying apples by the bushel and selling them for the same price by the pound to isolated homesteaders on back country roads.

"All that there," the woman said, pointing to his arm, "is no better than what a fool Indian would do. It's a heap of vanity." She seemed to have found the word she wanted. "Vanity of vanities,"[3] she said.

Well what the hell do I care what she thinks of it? Parker asked himself, but he was plainly bewildered. "I reckon you like one of these better than another anyway," he said, dallying until he thought of something that would impress her. He thrust the arm back at her. "Which you like best?"

"None of them," she said, "but the chicken is not as bad as the rest."

"What chicken?" Parker almost yelled.

She pointed to the eagle.

"That's an eagle," Parker said. "What fool would waste their time having a chicken put on themself?"

"What fool would have any of it?" the girl said and turned away. She went slowly back to the house and left him there to get going. Parker remained for almost five minutes, looking agape at the dark door she had entered.

The next day he returned with a bushel of apples. He was not one to be outdone by anything that looked like her. He liked women with meat on them, so you didn't feel their muscles, much less their bones. When he arrived, she was sitting on the top step and the yard

3. Ecclesiastes 1:2.

was full of children, all as thin and poor as herself; Parker remembered it was Saturday. He hated to be making up to a woman when there were children around, but it was fortunate he had brought the bushel of apples off the truck. As the children approached him to see what he carried, he gave each child an apple and told it to get lost; in that way he cleared out the whole crowd.

The girl did nothing to acknowledge his presence. He might have been a stray pig or goat that had wandered into the yard and she too tired to take up the broom and send it off. He set the bushel of apples down next to her on the step. He sat down a lower step.

"Hep yourself," he said, nodding at the basket; then he lapsed into silence.

She took an apple quickly as if the basket might disappear if she didn't make haste. Hungry people made Parker nervous. He had always had plenty to eat himself. He grew very uncomfortable. He reasoned he had nothing to say so why should he say it? He could not think now why he had come or why he didn't go before he wasted another bushel of apples on the crowd of children. He supposed they were her brothers and sisters.

She chewed the apple slowly but with a kind of relish of concentration, bent slightly but looking out ahead. The view from the porch stretched off across a long incline studded with iron weed and across the highway to a vast vista of hills and one small mountain. Long views depressed Parker. You look out into space like that and you begin to feel as if someone were after you, the navy or the government or religion.

"Who them children belong to, you?" he said at length.

"I ain't married yet," she said. "They belong to momma." She said it as if it were only a matter of time before she would be married.

Who in God's name would marry her? Parker thought.

A large barefooted woman with a wide gap-toothed face appeared in the door behind Parker. She had apparently been there for several minutes.

"Good evening," Parker said.

The woman crossed the porch and picked up what was left of the bushel of apples. "We thank you," she said and returned with it into the house.

"That your old woman?" Parker muttered.

The girl nodded. Parker knew a lot of sharp things he could have said like "You got my sympathy," but he was gloomily silent. He just sat there, looking at the view. He thought he must be coming down with something.

"If I pick up some peaches tomorrow I'll bring you some," he said.

"I'll be much obliged to you," the girl said.

Parker had no intention of taking any basket of peaches back there but the next day he found himself doing it. He and the girl had almost nothing to say to each other. One thing he did say was, "I ain't got any tattoo on my back."

"What you got on it?" the girl said.

"My shirt," Parker said. "Haw."

"Haw, haw," the girl said politely.

Parker thought he was losing his mind. He could not believe for a minute that he was attracted to a woman like this. She showed not the least interest in anything but what he brought until he appeared the third time with two cantaloups. "What's your name?" she asked.

"O. E. Parker," he said.

"What does the O.E. stand for?"

"You can just call me O.E.," Parker said. "Or Parker. Don't nobody call me by my name."

"What's it stand for?" she persisted.

"Never mind," Parker said. "What's yours?"

"I'll tell you when you tell me what them letters are the short of," she said. There was just a hint of flirtatiousness in her tone and it went rapidly to Parker's head. He had never revealed the name to any man or woman, only to the files of the navy and the government, and it was on his baptismal record which he got at the age of a month; his mother was a Methodist. When the name leaked out of the navy files, Parker narrowly missed killing the man who used it.

"You'll go blab it around," he said.

"I'll swear I'll never tell nobody," she said. "On God's holy word I swear it."

Parker sat for a few minutes in silence. Then he reached for the girl's neck, drew her ear close to his mouth and revealed the name in a low voice.

"Obadiah," she whispered. Her face slowly brightened as if the name came as a sign to her. "Obadiah," she said.

The name still stank in Parker's estimation.

"Obadiah Elihue,"[4] she said in a reverent voice.

"If you call me that aloud, I'll bust your head open," Parker said. "What's yours?"

"Sarah Ruth Cates," she said.

"Glad to meet you, Sarah Ruth," Parker said.

Sarah Ruth's father was a Straight Gospel preacher but he was away, spreading it in Florida. Her mother did not seem to mind his

4. Both are biblical names (Obadiah is a minor prophet, and Elihue figures in Job 32-37), as are Sarah and Ruth (below).

attention to the girl so long as he brought a basket of something with him when he came. As for Sarah Ruth herself, it was plain to Parker after he had visited three times that she was crazy about him. She liked him even though she insisted that pictures on the skin were vanity of vanities and even after hearing him curse, and even after she had asked him if he was saved and he had replied that he didn't see it was anything in particular to save him from. After that, inspired, Parker had said, "I'd be saved enough if you was to kiss me."

She scowled. "That ain't being saved," she said.

Not long after that she agreed to take a ride in his truck. Parker parked it on a deserted road and suggested to her that they lie down together in the back of it.

"Not until after we're married," she said—just like that.

"Oh that ain't necessary," Parker said and as he reached for her, she thrust him away with such force that the door of the truck came off and he found himself flat on his back on the ground. He made up his mind then and there to have nothing further to do with her.

They were married in the County Ordinary's[5] office because Sarah Ruth thought churches were idolatrous. Parker had no opinion about that one way or the other. The Ordinary's office was lined with cardboard file boxes and record books with dusty yellow slips of paper hanging on out of them. The Ordinary was an old woman with red hair who had held office for forty years and looked as dusty as her books. She married them from behind the iron-grill of a stand-up desk and when she finished, she said with a flourish, "Three dollars and fifty cents and till death do you part!" and yanked some forms out of a machine.

Marriage did not change Sarah Ruth a jot and it made Parker gloomier than ever. Every morning he decided he had had enough and would not return that night; every night he returned. Whenever Parker couldn't stand the way he felt, he would have another tattoo, but the only surface left on him now was his back. To see a tattoo on his own back he would have to get two mirrors and stand between them in just the correct position and this seemed to Parker a good way to make an idiot of himself. Sarah Ruth who, if she had had better sense, could have enjoyed a tattoo on his back, would not even look at the ones he had elsewhere. When he attempted to point out especial details of them, she would shut her eyes tight and turn her back as well. Except in total darkness, she preferred Parker dressed and with his sleeves rolled down.

"At the judgement seat of God, Jesus is going to say to you, 'What you been doing all your life besides have pictures drawn all over you?' " she said.

5. A justice of the peace.

"You don't fool me none," Parker said, "you're just afraid that hefty girl I work for'll like me so much she'll say, 'Come on, Mr. Parker, let's you and me . . .' "

"You're tempting sin," she said, "and at the judgement seat of God you'll have to answer for that too. You ought to go back to selling the fruits of the earth."

Parker did nothing much when he was at home but listen to what the judgement seat of God would be like for him if he didn't change his ways. When he could, he broke in with tales of the hefty girl he worked for. " 'Mr. Parker,' " he said she said, " 'I hired you for your brains.' " (She had added, "So why don't you use them?")

"And you should have seen her face the first time she saw me without my shirt," he said. " 'Mr. Parker,' she said, 'you're a walking panner-rammer!' " This had, in fact, been her remark but it had been delivered out of one side of her mouth.

Dissatisfaction began to grow so great in Parker that there was no containing it outside of a tattoo. It had to be his back. There was no help for it. A dim half-formed inspiration began to work in his mind. He visualized having a tattoo put there that Sarah Ruth would not be able to resist—a religious subject. He thought of an open book with HOLY BIBLE tattooed under it and an actual verse printed on the page. This seemed just the thing for a while; then he began to hear her say, "Ain't I already got a real Bible? What you think I want to read the same verse over and over for when I can read it all?" He needed something better even than the Bible! He thought about it so much that he began to lose sleep. He was already losing flesh—Sarah Ruth just threw food in the pot and let it boil. Not knowing for certain why he continued to stay with a woman who was both ugly and pregnant and no cook made him generally nervous and irritable, and he developed a little tic in the side of his face.

Once or twice he found himself turning around abruptly as if someone were trailing him. He had had a granddaddy who had ended in the state mental hospital, although not until he was seventy-five, but as urgent as it might be for him to get a tattoo, it was just as urgent that he get exactly the right one to bring Sarah Ruth to heel. As he continued to worry over it, his eyes took on a hollow preoccupied expression. The old woman he worked for told him that if he couldn't keep his mind on what he was doing, she knew where she could find a fourteen-year-old colored boy who could. Parker was too preoccupied even to be offended. At any time previous, he would have left her then and there, saying drily, "Well, you go ahead on and get him then."

Two or three mornings later he was baling hay with the old woman's sorry baler and her broken down tractor in a large field, cleared save for one enormous old tree standing in the middle of it. The old woman was the kind who would not cut down a large old tree because it was a large old tree. She had pointed it out to Parker as if he didn't have eyes and told him to be careful not to hit it as the machine picked up hay near it. Parker began at the outside of the field and made circles inward toward it. He had to get off the tractor every now and then and untangle the baling cord or kick a rock out of the way. The old woman had told him to carry the rocks to the edge of the field, which he did when she was there watching. When he thought he could make it, he ran over them. As he circled the field his mind was on a suitable design for his back. The sun, the size of a golf ball, began to switch regularly from in front to behind him, but he appeared to see it both places as if he had eyes in the back of his head. All at once he saw the tree reaching out to grasp him. A ferocious thud propelled him into the air, and he heard himself yelling in an unbelievably loud voice, "GOD ABOVE!"

He landed on his back while the tractor crashed upside-down into the tree and burst into flame. The first thing Parker saw were his shoes, quickly being eaten by the fire; one was caught under the tractor, the other was some distance away, burning by itself. He was not in them. He could feel the hot breath of the burning tree on his face. He scrambled backwards, still sitting, his eyes cavernous, and if he had known how to cross himself he would have done it.

His truck was on a dirt road at the edge of the field. He moved toward it, still sitting, still backwards, but faster and faster; halfway to it he got up and began a kind of forward-bent run from which he collapsed on his knees twice. His legs felt like two old rusted rain gutters. He reached the truck finally and took off in it, zigzagging up the road. He drove past his house on the embankment and straight for the city, fifty miles distant.

Parker did not allow himself to think on the way to the city. He only knew that there had been a great change in his life, a leap forward into a worse unknown, and that there was nothing he could do about it. It was for all intents accomplished.

The artist had two large cluttered rooms over a chiropodist's office on a back street. Parker, still barefooted, burst silently in on him at a little after three in the afternoon. The artist, who was about Parker's own age—twenty-eight—but thin and bald, was behind a small drawing table, tracing a design in green ink. He looked up with an annoyed glance and did not seem to recognize Parker in the hollow-eyed creature before him.

"Let me see the book you got with all the pictures of God in it," Parker said breathlessly. "The religious one."

The artist continued to look at him with his intellectual, superior stare. "I don't put tattoos on drunks," he said.

"You know me!" Parker cried indignantly. "I'm O. E. Parker!

You done work for me before and I always paid!"

The artist looked at him another moment as if he were not altogether sure. "You've fallen off some," he said. "You must have been in jail."

"Married," Parker said.

"Oh," said the artist. With the aid of mirrors the artist had tattooed on the top of his head a miniature owl, perfect in every detail. It was about the size of a half-dollar and served him as a show piece. There were cheaper artists in town but Parker had never wanted anything but the best. The artist went over to a cabinet at the back of the room and began to look over some art books. "Who are you interested in?" he said, "saints, angels, Christs or what?"

"God," Parker said.

"Father, Son or Spirit?"

"Just God," Parker said impatiently. "Christ, I don't care. Just so it's God."

The artist returned with a book. He moved some papers off another table and put the book down on it and told Parker to sit down and see what he liked. "The up-t-date ones are in the back," he said.

Parker sat down with the book and wet his thumb. He began to go through it, beginning at the back where the up-to-date pictures were. Some of them he recognized—The Good Shepherd, Forbid Them Not, The Smiling Jesus, Jesus the Physician's Friend, but he kept turning rapidly backwards and the pictures became less and less reassuring. One showed a gaunt green dead face streaked with blood. One was yellow with sagging purple eyes. Parker's heart began to beat faster and faster until it appeared to be roaring inside him like a great generator. He flipped the pages quickly, feeling that when he reached the one ordained, a sign would come. He continued to flip through until he had almost reached the front of the book. On one of the pages a pair of eyes glanced at him swiftly. Parker sped on, then stopped. His heart too appeared to cut off; there was absolute silence. It said as plainly as if silence were a language itself, GO BACK.

Parker returned to the picture—the haloed head of a flat stern Byzantine[6] Christ with all-demanding eyes. He sat there trembling; his heart began slowly to beat again as if it were being brought to life by a subtle power.

"You found what you want?" the artist asked.

Parker's throat was too dry to speak. He got up and thrust the book at the artist, opened at the picture.

"That'll cost you plenty," the artist said. "You don't want all those little blocks though, just the outline and some better features."

6. Highly formalized, and in this case, a mosaic picture—little blocks of colored tile composed to represent a face. The art of the Byzantine Empire flourished from the fifth to the eighth century A.D.

"Just like it is," Parker said, "just like it is or nothing."

"It's your funeral," the artist said, "but I don't do that kind of work for nothing."

"How much?" Parker asked.

"It'll take maybe two days work."

"How much?" Parker said.

"On time or cash?" the artist asked. Parker's other jobs had been on time, but he had paid.

"Ten down and ten for every day it takes," the artist said.

Parker drew ten dollar bills out of his wallet; he had three left in.

"You come back in the morning," the artist said, putting the money in his own pocket. "First I'll have to trace that out of the book."

"No no!" Parker said. "Trace it now or gimme my money back," and his eyes blared as if he were ready for a fight.

The artist agreed. Any one stupid enough to want a Christ on his back, he reasoned, would be just as likely as not to change his mind the next minute, but once the work was begun he could hardly do so.

While he worked on the tracing, he told Parker to go wash his back at the sink with the special soap he used there. Parker did it and returned to pace back and forth across the room, nervously flexing his shoulders. He wanted to go look at the picture again but at the same time he did not want to. The artist got up finally and had Parker lie down on the table. He swabbed his back with ethyl chloride and then began to outline the head on it with his iodine pencil. Another hour passed before he took up his electric instrument. Parker felt no particular pain. In Japan he had had a tattoo of the Buddha done on his upper arm with ivory needles; in Burma, a little brown root of a man had made a peacock on each of his knees using thin pointed sticks, two feet long; amateurs had worked on him with pins and soot. Parker was usually so relaxed and easy under the hand of the artist that he often went to sleep, but this time he remained awake, every muscle taut.

At midnight the artist said he was ready to quit. He propped one mirror, four feet square, on a table by the wall and took a smaller mirror off the lavatory wall and put it in Parker's hands. Parker stood with his back to the one on the table and moved the other until he saw a flashing burst of color reflected from his back. It was almost completely covered with little red and blue and ivory and saffron squares; from them he made out the lineaments of the face—a mouth, the beginning of heavy brows, a straight nose, but the face was empty; the eyes had not yet been put in. The impression for the moment was almost as if the artist had tricked him and done the Physician's Friend.

"It don't have eyes," Parker cried out.

"That'll come," the artist said, "in due time. We have another day to go on it yet."

Parker spent the night on a cot at the Haven of Light Christian Mission. He found these the best places to stay in the city because they were free and included a meal of sorts. He got the last available cot and because he was still barefooted, he accepted a pair of second-hand shoes which, in his confusion, he put on to go to bed; he was still shocked from all that had happened to him. All night he lay awake in the long dormitory of cots with lumpy figures on them. The only light was from a phosphorescent cross glowing at the end of the room. The tree reached out to grasp him again, then burst into flame; the shoe burned quietly by itself; the eyes in the book said to him distinctly GO BACK and at the same time did not utter a sound. He wished that he were not in this city, not in this Haven of Light Mission, not in a bed by himself. He longed miserably for Sarah Ruth. Her sharp tongue and icepick eyes were the only comfort he could bring to mind. He decided he was losing it. Her eyes appeared soft and dilatory compared with the eyes in the book, for even though he could not summon up the exact look of those eyes, he could still feel their penetration. He felt as though, under their gaze, he was as transparent as the wing of a fly.

The tattooist had told him not to come until ten in the morning, but when he arrived at that hour, Parker was sitting in the dark hallway on the floor, waiting for him. He had decided upon getting up that, once the tattoo was on him, he would not look at it, that all his sensations of the day and night before were those of a crazy man and that he would return to doing things according to his own sound judgement.

The artist began where he left off. "One thing I want to know," he said presently as he worked over Parker's back, "why do you want this on you? Have you gone and got religion? Are you saved?" he asked in a mocking voice.

Parker's throat felt salty and dry. "Naw," he said, "I ain't got no use for none of that. A man can't save his self from whatever it is he don't deserve none of my sympathy." These words seemed to leave his mouth like wraiths and to evaporate at once as if he had never uttered them.

"Then why . . ."

"I married this woman that's saved," Parker said. "I never should have done it. I ought to leave her. She's done gone and got pregnant."

"That's too bad," the artist said. "Then it's her making you have this tattoo."

"Naw," Parker said, "she don't know anything about it. It's a surprise for her."

"You think she'll like it and lay off you for a while?"

"She can't hep herself," Parker said. "She can't say she don't like the looks of God." He decided he had told the artist enough of his business. Artists were all right in their place but he didn't like them poking their noses into the affairs of regular people. "I didn't get no sleep last night," he said. "I think I'll get some now."

That closed the mouth of the artist but it did not bring him any sleep. He lay there, imagining how Sarah Ruth would be struck speechless by the face on his back and every now and then this would be interrupted by a vision of the tree of fire and his empty shoe burning beneath it.

The artist worked steadily until nearly four o'clock, not stopping to have lunch, hardly pausing with the electric instrument except to wipe the dripping dye off Parker's back as he went along. Finally he finished. "You can get up and look at it now," he said.

Parker sat up but he remained on the edge of the table.

The artist was pleased with his work and wanted Parker to look at it at once. Instead Parker continued to sit on the edge of the table, bent forward slightly but with a vacant look. "What ails you?" the artist said. "Go look at it."

"Ain't nothing ail me," Parker said in a sudden belligerent voice. "That tattoo ain't going nowhere. It'll be there when I get there." He reached for his shirt and began gingerly to put it on.

The artist took him roughly by the arm and propelled him between the two mirrors. "Now *look*," he said, angry at having his work ignored.

Parker looked, turned white and moved away. The eyes in the reflected face continued to look at him—still, straight, all-demanding, enclosed in silence.

"It was your idea, remember," the artist said. "I would have advised something else."

Parker said nothing. He put on his shirt and went out the door while the artist shouted. "I'll expect all of my money!"

Parker headed toward a package shop on the corner. He bought a pint of whiskey and took it into a nearby alley and drank it all in five minutes. Then he moved on to a pool hall nearby which he frequented when he came to the city. It was a well-lighted barn-like place with a bar up one side and gambling machines on the other and pool tables in the back. As soon as Parker entered, a large man in a red and black checkered shirt hailed him by slapping him on the back and yelling, "Yeyyyyyy boy! O. E. Parker!"

Parker was not yet ready to be struck on the back. "Lay off," he said, "I got a fresh tattoo there."

"What you got this time?" the man asked and then yelled to a few at the machines. "O.E.'s got him another tattoo."

"Nothing special this time," Parker said and slunk over to a machine that was not being used.

"Come on," the big man said, "let's have a look at O.E.'s tattoo," and while Parker squirmed in their hands, they pulled up his shirt. Parker felt all the hands drop away instantly and his shirt fell again like a veil over his face. There was a silence in the pool room which seemed to Parker to grow from the circle around him until it extended to the foundations under the building and upward through the beams in the roof.

Finally some one said, "Christ!" Then they all broke into noise at once. Parker turned around, an uncertain grin on his face.

"Leave it to O.E.!" the man in the checkered shirt said. "That boy's a real card!"

"Maybe he's gone and got religion," some one yelled.

"Not on your life," Parker said.

"O.E.'s got religion and is witnessing for Jesus, ain't you, O.E.?" a little man with a piece of cigar in his mouth said wryly. "An original way to do it if I ever saw one."

"Leave it to Parker to think of a new one!" the fat man said.

"Yyeeeeeeyyyyyy boy!" someone yelled and they all began to whistle and curse in compliment until Parker said, "Aaa shut up."

"What'd you do it for?" somebody asked.

"For laughs," Parker said. "What's it to you?"

"Why ain't you laughing then?" somebody yelled. Parker lunged into the midst of them and like a whirlwind on a summer's day there began a fight that raged and overturned tables and swinging fists until two of them grabbed him and ran to the door with him and threw him out. Then a calm descended on the pool hall as nerve shattering as if the long barn-like room were the ship from which Jonah had been cast into the sea.

Parker sat for a long time on the ground in the alley behind the pool hall, examining his soul. He saw it as a spider web of facts and lies that was not at all important to him but which appeared to be necessary in spite of his opinion. The eyes that were now forever on his back were eyes to be obeyed. He was as certain of it as he had ever been of anything. Throughout his life, grumbling and sometimes cursing, often afraid, once in rapture, Parker had obeyed whatever instinct of this kind had come to him—in rapture when his spirit had lifted at the sight of the tattooed man at the fair, afraid when he had joined the navy, grumbling when he had married Sarah Ruth.

The thought of her brought him slowly to his feet. She would know what he had to do. She would clear up the rest of it, and she would at least be pleased. It seemed to him that, all along, that was what he wanted, to please her. His truck was still parked in front of the building where the artist had his place, but it was not far away. He got in it and drove out of the city and into the country night. His head was almost clear of liquor and he observed that his dissatisfaction was gone, but he felt not quite like himself. It was as if he were himself but a stranger to himself, driving into a new country though everything he saw was familiar to him, even at night.

He arrived finally at the house on the embankment, pulled the truck under the pecan tree and got out. He made as much noise as possible to assert that he was still in charge here, that his leaving her for a night without word meant nothing except it was the way he did things. He slammed the car door, stamped up the two steps and across the porch and rattled the door knob. It did not respond to his touch. "Sarah Ruth!" he yelled, "let me in."

There was no lock on the door and she had evidently placed the back of a chair against the knob. He began to beat on the door and rattle the knob at the same time.

He heard the bed springs screak and bent down and put his head to the keyhole, but it was stopped up with paper. "Let me in!" he hollered, bamming on the door again. "What you got me locked out for?"

A sharp voice close to the door said, "Who's there?"

"Me," Parker said, "O.E."

He waited a moment.

"Me," he said impatiently, "O.E."

Still no sound from inside.

He tried once more. "O.E.," he said, bamming the door two or three more times. "O. E. Parker. You know me."

There was a silence. Then the voice said slowly, "I don't know no O.E."

"Quit fooling," Parker pleaded. "You ain't got any business doing me this way. It's me, old O.E., I'm back. You ain't afraid of me."

"Who's there?" the same unfeeling voice said.

Parker turned his head as if he expected someone behind him to give him the answer. The sky had lightened slightly and there were two or three streaks of yellow floating above the horizon. Then as he stood there, a tree of light burst over the skyline.

Parker fell back against the door as if he had been pinned there by a lance.

"Who's there?" the voice from inside said and there was a quality about it now that seemed final. The knob rattled and the voice said peremptorily, "Who's there, I ast you?"

Parker bent down and put his mouth near the stuffed keyhole. "Obadiah," he whispered and all at once he felt the light pouring through him, turning his spider web soul into a perfect arabesque of colors, a garden of trees and birds and beasts.

"Obadiah Elihue!" he whispered.

The door opened and he stumbled in. Sarah Ruth loomed there, hands on her hips. She began at once, "That was no hefty blonde woman you was working for and you'll have to pay her every penny on her tractor you busted up. She don't keep insurance on it. She came here and her and me had us a long talk and I . . . "

Trembling, Parker set about lighting the kerosene lamp.

"What's the matter with you, wasting the kerosene this near daylight?" she demanded. "I ain't got to look at you."

A yellow glow enveloped them. Parker put the match down and began to unbutton his shirt.

"And you ain't going to have none of me this near morning," she said.

"Shut your mouth," he said quietly. "Look at this and then I don't want to hear no more out of you." He removed the shirt and turned his back to her.

"Another picture," Sarah Ruth growled. "I might have known you was off after putting some more trash on yourself."

Parker's knees went hollow under him. He wheeled around and cried, "Look at it! Don't just say that! *Look* at it!"

"I done looked," she said.

"Don't you know who it is?" he cried in anguish.

"No, who is it?" Sarah Ruth said. "It ain't anybody I know."

"It's him," Parker said.

"Him who?"

"God!" Parker cried.

"God? God don't look like that!"

"What do you know how he looks?" Parker moaned. "You ain't seen him."

"He don't *look*," Sarah Ruth said. "He's a spirit. No man shall see his face."

"Aw listen," Parker groaned, "this is just a picture of him."

"Idolatry!" Sarah Ruth screamed. "Idolatry! Enflaming yourself with idols under every green tree! I can put up with lies and vanity but I don't want no idolator in this house!" and she grabbed up the broom and began to thrash him across the shoulder with it.

Parker was too stunned to resist. He sat there and let her beat him until she had nearly knocked him senseless and large welts had formed on the face of the tattooed Christ. Then he staggered up and made for the door.

She stamped the broom two or three times on the floor and went to the window and shook it out to get the taint of him off it. Still gripping it, she looked toward the pecan tree and her eyes hardened still more. There he was—who called himself Obadiah Elihue—leaning against the tree, crying like a baby.

1. What accounts for the ferocity of the struggle between Parker and his wife? Does the author express any attitude toward women by her representation of Sarah Ruth?
2. Discuss Parker's character, paying particular attention to his motives for marrying a woman who gives him so much trouble.
3. What is the symbolism of the burning tractor? How does it serve to motivate Parker?
4. What does it mean that Sarah Ruth raises welts on the image of Christ on Parker's back?
5. Discuss the handling of chronology. What is added to the story by including glimpses of Parker's life before he met Sarah Ruth?
6. What serious comments does the story make about idolatry and true religion?

Frank O'Connor

O'Connor is the pen name of Michael O'Donovan (1903–1966), who was born in Cork, Ireland, of a family too poor to give him a university education. During Ireland's struggle for independence he was briefly a member of the Irish Republican Army. Then he worked as a librarian in Cork and Dublin and for a time was director of the Abbey Theatre before he was established as a writer of short stories. From 1931 on he published regularly in American magazines and taught for some years at Harvard and Northwestern Universities. His declared objective was to find the natural rhythms and stresses of the storyteller's voice in shaping his material. He rewrote many of his stories—often after first publication—ten, twenty, or thirty times. The subsequent publication of these revisions makes it hard to pin down the exact scale of his life's work since some of his books contain pieces that appeared in different form in previous volumes. He was in any event a prolific historian of Irish manners and the Irish character. His titles include Guests of the Nation *(1931),* Crab Apple Jelly *(1944),* The Stories of Frank O'Connor *(1956), and* A Set of Variations *(1971).*

Guests of the Nation

I

At dusk the big Englishman, Belcher, would shift his long legs out of the ashes and say "Well, chums, what about it?" and Noble or me would say "All right, chum" (for we had picked up some of their curious expressions), and the little Englishman, Hawkins, would light the lamp and bring out the cards. Sometimes Jeremiah Donovan would come up and supervise the game and get excited over Hawkins's cards, which he always played badly, and shout at him as if he was one of our own "Ah, you divil, you, why didn't you play the tray?"

But ordinarily Jeremiah was a sober and contented poor devil like the big Englishman, Belcher, and was looked up to only because he was a fair hand at documents, though he was slow enough even with them. He wore a small cloth hat and big gaiters over his long pants, and you seldom saw him with his hands out of his pockets. He reddened when you talked to him, tilting from toe to heel and back, and looking down all the time at his big farmer's feet. Noble and me used to make fun of his broad accent, because we were from the town.

I couldn't at the time see the point of me and Noble guarding Belcher and Hawkins at all, for it was my belief that you could have planted that pair down anywhere from this to Claregalway and they'd have taken root there like a native weed. I never in my short experience seen two men to take to the country as they did.

They were handed on to us by the Second Battalion when the search[1] for them became too hot, and Noble and myself, being young, took over with a natural feeling of responsibility, but Hawkins made us look like fools when he showed that he knew the country better than we did.

"You're the bloke they calls Bonaparte," he says to me. "Mary Brigid O'Connell told me to ask you what you done with the pair of her brother's socks you borrowed."

For it seemed, as they explained it, that the Second used to have little evenings, and some of the girls of the neighbourhood turned in, and, seeing they were such decent chaps, our fellows couldn't leave the two Englishmen out of them. Hawkins learned to dance "The Walls of Limerick," "The Siege of Ennis," and "The Waves of Tory"[2] as well as any of them, though naturally, he couldn't return the compliment, because our lads at that time did not dance foreign dances on principle.

So whatever privileges Belcher and Hawkins had with the Second they just naturally took with us, and after the first day or two we gave up all pretence of keeping a close eye on them. Not that they could have got far, for they had accents you could cut with a knife and wore khaki tunics and overcoats with civilian pants and boots. But it's my belief that they never had any idea of escaping and were quite content to be where they were.

It was a treat to see how Belcher got off with the old woman of the house where we were staying. She was a great warrant to scold, and cranky even with us, but before ever she had a chance to giving our guests, as I may call them, a lick of her tongue, Belcher had made her his friend for life. She was breaking sticks, and Belcher, who hadn't been more than ten minutes in the house, jumped up from his seat and went over to her.

"Allow me, madam," he says, smiling his queer little smile, "please allow me"; and he takes the bloody hatchet. She was struck too paralytic to speak, and after that, Belcher would be at her heels, carrying a bucket, a basket, or a load of turf, as the case might be. As Noble said, he got into looking before she leapt, and hot water, or any little thing she wanted, Belcher would have it ready for her. For such a huge man (and though I am five foot ten myself I had to look up at him) he

1. Belcher and Hawkins are English soldiers, captured during the Irish battle for independence of 1922. The British Army and its collaborators are searching for them. 2. Native Irish dances.

had an uncommon shortness—or should I say lack?—of speech. It took us some time to get used to him, walking in and out, like a ghost, without a word. Especially because Hawkins talked enough for a platoon, it was strange to hear big Belcher with his toes in the ashes come out with a solitary "Excuse me, chum," or "That's right, chum." His one and only passion was cards, and I will say for him that he was a good card-player. He could have fleeced myself and Noble, but whatever we lost to him Hawkins lost to us, and Hawkins played with the money Belcher gave him.

Hawkins lost to us because he had too much old gab, and we probably lost to Belcher for the same reason. Hawkins and Noble would spit at one another about religion into the early hours of the morning, and Hawkins worried the soul out of Noble, whose brother was a priest, with a string of questions that would puzzle a cardinal. To make it worse even in treating of holy subjects, Hawkins had a deplorable tongue. I never in all my career met a man who could mix such a variety of cursing and bad language into an argument. He was a terrible man, and a fright to argue. He never did a stroke of work, and when he had no one else to talk to, he got stuck in the old woman.

He met his match in her, for one day when he tried to get her to complain profanely of the drought, she gave him a great comedown by blaming it entirely on Jupiter Pluvius (a deity neither Hawkins nor I had ever heard of, though Noble said that among the pagans it was believed that he had something to do with the rain).[3] Another day he was swearing at the capitalists for starting the German war[4] when the old lady laid down her iron, puckered up her little crab's mouth, and said: "Mr. Hawkins, you can say what you like about the war, and think you'll deceive me because I'm only a simple poor countrywoman, but I know what started the war. It was the Italian Count that stole the heathen divinity out of the temple in Japan. Believe me, Mr. Hawkins, nothing but sorrow and want can follow the people that disturb the hidden powers."

A queer old girl, all right.

II

We had our tea one evening, and Hawkins lit the lamp and we all sat into cards. Jeremiah Donovan came in too, and sat down and watched us for a while, and it suddenly struck me that he had no great love for the two Englishmen. It came as a great surprise to me, because I hadn't noticed anything about him before.

Late in the evening a really terrible argument blew up between

3. In fact the Roman god Jupiter had many functions, among them bringing rain for the crops, hence Pluvius—"Rainy." 4. World War I, in which England was at war with Germany.

Hawkins and Noble, about capitalists and priests and love of your country.

"The capitalists," says Hawkins with an angry gulp, "pays the priests to tell you about the next world so as you won't notice what the bastards are up to in this."

"Nonsense, man!" says Noble, losing his temper. "Before ever a capitalist was thought of, people believed in the next world."

Hawkins stood up as though he was preaching a sermon.

"Oh, they did, did they?" he says with a sneer. "They believed all the things you believe, isn't that what you mean? And you believe that God created Adam, and Adam created Shem, and Shem created Jehoshophat.[5] You believe all that silly old fairytale about Eve and Eden and the apple. Well, listen to me, chum. If you're entitled to hold a silly belief like that, I'm entitled to hold my silly belief—which is that the first thing your God created was a bleeding capitalist, with morality and Rolls-Royce complete. Am I right, chum?" he says to Belcher.

"You're right, chum," says Belcher with his amused smile, and got up from the table to stretch his long legs into the fire and stroke his moustache. So, seeing that Jeremiah Donovan was going, and that there was no knowing when the argument about religion would be over, I went out with him. We strolled down to the village together, and then he stopped and started blushing and mumbling and saying I ought to be behind, keeping guard on the prisoners. I didn't like the tone he took with me, and anyway I was bored with life in the cottage, so I replied by asking him what the hell we wanted guarding them at all for. I told him I'd talked it over with Noble, and that we'd both rather be out with a fighting column.

"What use are those fellows to us?" says I.

He looked at me in surprise and said: "I thought you knew we were keeping them as hostages."

"Hostages?" I said.

"The enemy have prisoners belonging to us," he says, "and now they're talking of shooting them. If they shoot our prisoners, we'll shoot theirs."

"Shoot them?" I said.

"What else did you think we were keeping them for?" he says.

"Wasn't it very unforeseen of you not to warn Noble and myself of that in the beginning?" I said.

"How was it?" says he. "You might have known it."

"We couldn't know it, Jeremiah Donovan," says I. "How could we when they were on our hands so long?"

5. Hawkins' scrambled version of Old Testament lore.

"The enemy have our prisoners as long and longer," says he.

"That's not the same thing at all," says I.

"What difference is there?" says he.

I couldn't tell him, because I knew he wouldn't understand. If it was only an old dog that was going to the vet's, you'd try and not get too fond of him, but Jeremiah Donovan wasn't a man that would ever be in danger of that.

"And when is this thing going to be decided?" says I.

"We might hear tonight," he says. "Or tomorrow or the next day at latest. So if it's only hanging round here that's a trouble to you, you'll be free soon enough."

It wasn't the hanging round that was a trouble to me at all by this time. I had worse things to worry about. When I got back to the cottage the argument was still on. Hawkins was holding forth in his best style, maintaining that there was no next world, and Noble was maintaining that there was; but I could see that Hawkins had had the best of it.

"Do you know what, chum?" he was saying with a saucy smile. "I think you're just as big a bleeding unbeliever as I am. You say you believe in the next world, and you know just as much about the next world as I do, which is sweet damn-all. What's heaven? You don't know. Where's heaven? You don't know. You know sweet damn-all! I ask you again, do they wear wings?"

"Very well, then," says Noble, "they do. Is that enough for you? They do wear wings."

"Where do they get them, then? Who makes them? Have they a factory for wings? Have they a sort of store where you hands in your chit and takes your bleeding wings?"

"You're an impossible man to argue with," says Noble. "Now, listen to me—" And they were off again.

It was long after midnight when we locked up and went to bed. As I blew out the candle I told Noble what Jeremiah Donovan was after telling me. Noble took it very quietly. When we'd been in bed about an hour he asked me did I think we ought to tell the Englishmen. I didn't think we should, because it was more than likely that the English wouldn't shoot our men, and even if they did, the brigade officers, who were always up and down with the Second Battalion and knew the Englishmen well, wouldn't be likely to want them plugged. "I think so too," says Noble. "It would be great cruelty to put the wind to them now."

"It was very unforeseen of Jeremiah Donovan anyhow," says I.

It was next morning that we found it so hard to face Belcher and Hawkins. We went about the house all day scarcely saying a word. Belcher didn't seem to notice; he was stretched into the ashes as usual, with his look unusual of waiting in quietness for something unforeseen to happen, but Hawkins noticed and put it down to Noble's being beaten in the argument of the night before.

"Why can't you take a discussion in the proper spirit?" he says severely. "You and your Adam and Eve! I'm a Communist, that's what I am. Communist or anarchist, it all comes to much the same thing." And for hours he went round the house, muttering when the fit took him. "Adam and Eve! Adam and Eve! Nothing better to do with their time than picking bleeding apples!"

III

I don't know how we got through that day, but I was very glad when it was over, the tea things were cleared away, and Belcher said in his peaceable way: "Well, chums, what about it?" We sat round the table and Hawkins took out the cards, and just then I heard Jeremiah Donovan's footstep on the path and a dark presentiment crossed my mind. I rose from the table and caught him before he reached the door.

"What do you want?" I asked.

"I want those two soldier friends of yours," he says, getting red.

"Is that the way, Jeremiah Donovan?" I asked.

"That's the way. There were four of our lads shot this morning, one of them a boy of sixteen."

"That's bad," I said.

At that moment Noble followed me out, and the three of us walked down the path together, talking in whispers. Feeney, the local intelligence officer, was standing by the gate.

"What are you going to do about it?" I asked Jeremiah Donovan.

"I want you and Noble to get them out; tell them they're being shifted again; that'll be the quietest way."

"Leave me out of that," says Noble under his breath.

Jeremiah Donovan looks at him hard.

"All right," he says. "You and Feeney get a few tools from the shed and dig a hole by the far end of the bog. Bonaparte and myself will be after you. Don't let anyone see you with the tools. I wouldn't like it to go beyond ourselves."

We saw Feeney and Noble go round to the shed and went in ourselves. I left Jeremiah Donovan to do the explanations. He told them that he had orders to send them back to the Second Battalion. Hawkins let out a mouthful of curses, and you could see that though Belcher didn't say anything, he was a bit upset too. The old woman was for having them stay in spite of us, and she didn't stop advising them until Jeremiah Donovan lost his temper and turned on her. He had a nasty temper, I noticed. It was pitch-dark in the cottage by this time, but no one thought of lighting the lamp, and in the darkness the two Englishmen fetched their topcoats and said good-bye to the old woman.

"Just as a man makes a home of a bleeding place, some bastard at headquarters thinks you're too cushy and shunts you off," says Hawkins, shaking her hand.

"A thousand thanks, madam," says Belcher. "A thousand thanks for everything"—as though he'd made it up.

We went round to the back of the house and down towards the bog. It was only then that Jeremiah Donovan told them. He was shaking with excitement.

"There were four of our fellows shot in Cork this morning and now you're to be shot as a reprisal."

"What are you talking about?" snaps Hawkins. "It's bad enough being mucked about as we are without having to put up with your funny jokes."

"It isn't a joke," says Donovan. "I'm sorry, Hawkins, but it's true," and begins on the usual rigmarole about duty and how unpleasant it is.

I never noticed that people who talk a lot about duty find it much of a trouble to them.

"Oh, cut it out!" says Hawkins.

"Ask Bonaparte," says Donovan, seeing that Hawkins isn't taking him seriously. "Isn't it true, Bonaparte?"

"It is," I say, and Hawkins stops.

"Ah, for Christ's sake, chum!"

"You don't sound as if you meant it."

"If he doesn't mean it, I do," says Donovan, working himself up.

"What have you against me, Jeremiah Donovan?"

"I never said I had anything against you. But why did your people take out four of our prisoners and shoot them in cold blood?"

He took Hawkins by the arm and dragged him on, but it was impossible to make him understand that we were in earnest. I had the Smith and Wesson[6] in my pocket and I kept fingering it and wondering what I'd do if they put up a fight for it or ran, and wishing to God they'd do one or the other. I knew if they did run for it, that I'd never fire on them. Hawkins wanted to know was Noble in it, and when we said yes, he asked us why Noble wanted to plug him. Why did any of us want to plug him? What had he done to us? Weren't we all chums? Didn't we understand him and didn't he understand us? Did we imagine for an instant that he'd shoot us for all the so-and-so officers in the so-and-so British Army?

By this time we'd reached the bog, and I was so sick I couldn't

6. Revolver, as is the Webley, below.

even answer him. We walked along the edge of it in the darkness, and every now and then Hawkins would call a halt and begin all over again, as if he was wound up, about our being chums, and I knew that nothing but the sight of the grave would convince him that we had to do it. And all the time I was hoping that something would happen; that they'd run for it or that Noble would take over the responsibility from me. I had the feeling that it was worse on Noble than on me.

IV

At last we saw the lantern in the distance and made towards it. Noble was carrying it, and Feeney was standing somewhere in the darkness behind him, and the picture of them so still and silent in the bogland brought it home to me that we were in earnest, and banished the last bit of hope I had.

Belcher, on recognizing Noble, said: "Hallo, chum," in his quiet way, but Hawkins flew at him at once, and the argument began all over again, only this time Noble had nothing to say for himself and stood with his head down, holding the lantern between his legs.

It was Jeremiah Donovan who did the answering. For the twentieth time, as though it was haunting his mind, Hawkins asked if anybody thought he'd shoot Noble.

"Yes, you would," says Jeremiah Donovan.

"No, I wouldn't, damn you!"

"You would, because you'd know you'd be shot for not doing it."

"I wouldn't, not if I was to be shot twenty times over. I wouldn't shoot a pal. And Belcher wouldn't—isn't that right, Belcher?"

"That's right, chum," Belcher said, but more by way of answering the question than of joining in the argument. Belcher sounded as though whatever unforeseen thing he'd always been waiting for had come at last.

"Anyway, who says Noble would be shot if I wasn't? What do you think I'd do if I was in his place, out in the middle of a blasted bog?"

"What would you do?" asks Donovan.

"I'd go with him wherever he was going, of course. Share my last bob with him and stick by him through thick and thin. No one can ever say of me that I let down a pal."

"We had enough of this," says Jeremiah Donovan, cocking his revolver. "Is there any message you want to send?"

"No, there isn't."

"Do you want to say your prayers?"

Hawkins came out with a cold-blooded remark that even shocked me and turned on Noble again.

"Listen to me, Noble," he says. "You and me are chums. You

can't come over to my side, so I'll come over to your side. That show you I mean what I say? Give me a rifle and I'll go along with you and the other lads."

Nobody answered him. We knew that was no way out.

"Hear what I'm saying?" he says. "I'm through with it. I'm a deserter or anything else you like. I don't believe in your stuff, but it's no worse than mine. That satisfy you?"

Noble raised his head, but Donovan began to speak and he lowered it again without replying.

"For the last time, have you any messages to send?" says Donovan in a cold excited sort of voice.

"Shut up, Donovan! You don't understand me, but these lads do. They're not the sort to make a pal and kill a pal. They're not the tools of any capitalist."

I alone of the crowd saw Donovan raise his Webley to the back of Hawkins's neck, and as he did so I shut my eyes and tried to pray. Hawkins had begun to say something else when Donovan fired, and as I opened my eyes at the bang, I saw Hawkins stagger at the knees and lie out flat at Noble's feet, slowly and as quiet as a kid falling asleep, with the lantern-light on his lean legs and bright farmer's boots. We all stood very still, watching him settle out in the last agony.

Then Belcher took out a handkerchief and began to tie it about his own eyes (in our excitement we'd forgotten to do the same for Hawkins), and, seeing it wasn't big enough, turned and asked for the loan of mine. I gave it to him and he knotted the two together and pointed with his foot at Hawkins.

"He's not quite dead," he says. "Better give him another."

Sure enough, Hawkins's left knee is beginning to rise. I bend down and put my gun to his head; then, recollecting myself, I get up again. Belcher understands what's in my mind.

"Give him his first," he says. "I don't mind. Poor bastard, we don't know what's happening to him now."

I knelt and fired. By this time I didn't seem to know what I was doing. Belcher, who was fumbling a bit awkwardly with the handkerchiefs, came out with a laugh as he heard the shot. It was the first time I heard him laugh and it sent a shudder down my back; it sounded so unnatural.

"Poor bugger!" he said quietly. "And last night he was so curious about it all. It's very queer, chums, I always think. Now he knows as much about it as they'll ever let him know, and last night he was all in the dark."

Donovan helped him to tie the handkerchiefs about his eyes. "Thanks, chum," he said. Donovan asked if there were any messages he wanted sent.

"No, chum," he says. "Not for me. If any of you would like to write to Hawkins's mother, you'll find a letter from her in his pocket. He and his mother were great chums. But my missus left me eight years ago. Went away with another fellow and took the kid with her. I like the feeling of a home, as you may have noticed, but I couldn't start again after that."

It was an extraordinary thing, but in those few minutes Belcher said more than in all the weeks before. It was just as if the sound of the shot had started a flood of talk in him and he could go on the whole night like that, quite happily, talking about himself. We stood round like fools now that he couldn't see us any longer. Donovan looked at Noble, and Noble shook his head. Then Donovan raised his Webley, and at that moment Belcher gives his queer laugh again. He may have thought we were talking about him, or perhaps he noticed the same thing I'd noticed and couldn't understand it.

"Excuse me, chums," he says. "I feel I'm talking the hell of a lot, and so silly, about my being so handy about a house and things like that. But this thing came on me suddenly. You'll forgive me, I'm sure."

"You don't want to say a prayer?" asks Donovan.

"No, chum," he says. "I don't think it would help. I'm ready, and you boys want to get it over."

"You understand that we're only doing our duty?" says Donovan.

Belcher's head was raised like a blind man's so that you could only see his chin and the tip of his nose in the lantern-light.

"I never could make out what duty was myself," he said. "I think you're all good lads, if that's what you mean. I'm not complaining."

Noble, just as if he couldn't bear any more of it, raised his fist at Donovan, and in a flash Donovan raised his gun and fired. The big man went over like a sack of meal, and this time there was no need for a second shot.

I don't remember much about the burying, but that it was worse than all the rest because we had to carry them to the grave. It was all mad lonely with nothing but a patch of lantern-light between ourselves and the dark, and birds hooting and screeching all round, disturbed by the guns. Noble went through Hawkins's belongings to find the letter from his mother, and then joined his hands together. He did the same with Belcher. Then, when we'd filled in the grave, we separated from Jeremiah Donovan and Feeney and took our tools back to the shed. All the way we didn't speak a word. The kitchen was dark and cold as we'd left it, and the old woman was sitting over the hearth, saying her beads. We walked past her into the room, and Noble struck a match to light the lamp. She rose quietly and came to the doorway with all her cantankerousness gone.

"What did ye do with them?" she asked in a whisper, and Noble started so that the match went out in his hand.

"What's that?" he asked without turning round.

"I heard ye," she said.

"What did you hear?" asked Noble.

"I heard ye. Do ye think I didn't hear ye, putting the spade back in the houseen?"[7]

Noble struck another match and this time the lamp lit for him.

"Was that what ye did to them?" she asked.

Then, by God, in the very doorway, she fell on her knees and began praying, and after looking at her for a minute or two Noble did the same by the fireplace. I pushed my way out past her and left them at it. I stood at the door, watching the stars and listening to the shrieking of the birds dying out over the bogs. It is so strange what you feel at times like that that you can't describe it. Noble says he saw everything ten times the size, as though there were nothing in the whole world but that little patch of bog with the two Englishmen stiffening into it, but with me it was as if the patch of bog where the Englishmen were was a million miles away, and even Noble and the old woman, mumbling behind me, and the birds and the bloody stars were all far away, and I was somehow very small and very lost and lonely like a child astray in the snow. And anything that happened me afterwards, I never felt the same about again.

---

1. List some of the reasons why their friends kill Hawkins and Belcher. Is there any one of these reasons so important that, if you took it away, the others would not have brought matters to such a conclusion?
2. Are the arguments about religion conducted in terms that make them merely ridiculous? Why are they included instead of—say—arguments about women or sports?
3. Discuss Donovan's character and his role in the action.
4. How are we to take the old woman's explanation of what started the war?
5. How has the author handled the flow of time in each of the numbered sections?
6. Is it out of character for Belcher to become talkative in the last section?
7. How does the use of first person narrative contribute to the effect of the whole?

7. Shed.

My Oedipus Complex[1]

Father was in the army all through the war—the first war,[2] I mean—so, up to the age of five, I never saw much of him, and what I saw did not worry me. Sometimes I woke and there was a big figure in khaki peering down at me in the candlelight. Sometimes in the early morning I heard the slamming of the front door and the clatter of nailed boots down the cobbles of the lane. These were Father's entrances and exits. Like Santa Claus he came and went mysteriously.

In fact, I rather liked his visits, though it was an uncomfortable squeeze between Mother and him when I got into the big bed in the early morning. He smoked, which gave him a pleasant musty smell, and shaved, an operation of astounding interest. Each time he left a trail of souvenirs—model tanks and Gurkha knives[3] with handles made of bullet cases, and German helmets and cap badges and button-sticks, and all sorts of military equipment—carefully stowed away in a long box on top of the wardrobe, in case they ever came in handy. There was a bit of the magpie about Father; he expected everything to come in handy. When his back was turned, Mother let me get a chair and rummage through his treasures. She didn't seem to think so highly of them as he did.

The war was the most peaceful period of my life. The window of my attic faced southeast. My mother had curtained it, but that had small effect. I always woke with the first light and, with all the responsibilities of the previous day melted, feeling myself rather like the sun, ready to illumine and rejoice. Life never seemed so simple and clear and full of possibilities as then. I put my feet out from under the clothes—I called them Mrs. Left and Mrs. Right—and invented dramatic situations for them in which they discussed the problems of the day. At least Mrs. Right did; she was very demonstrative, but I hadn't the same control of Mrs. Left, so she mostly contented herself with nodding agreement.

They discussed what Mother and I should do during the day, what Santa Claus should give a fellow for Christmas, and what steps should be taken to brighten the home. There was that little matter of the baby, for instance. Mother and I could never agree about that. Ours was the only house in the terrace without a new baby, and Mother said we couldn't afford one till Father came back from the war because

1. Term in Freudian psychology for the condition in which a male child develops an excessive love for his mother, which is usually accompanied by hatred for the father; from the Greek legend of Oedipus, king of Thebes, who killed his father and married his mother.
2. I.e., World War I.
3. Short swords with broad blades used by Indian soldiers; "button-sticks" were sticks made to protect the cloth of a military tunic while polishing the buttons.

they cost seventeen and six.[4] That showed how simple she was. The Geneys up the road had a baby, and everyone knew they couldn't afford seventeen and six. It was probably a cheap baby, and Mother wanted something really good, but I felt she was too exclusive. The Geneys' baby would have done us fine.

Having settled my plans for the day, I got up, put a chair under the attic window, and lifted the frame high enough to stick out my head. The window overlooked the front gardens of the terrace behind ours, and beyond these it looked over a deep valley to the tall, red-brick houses terraced up the opposite hillside, which were all still in shadow, while those at our side of the valley were all lit up, though with long strange shadows that made them seem unfamiliar; rigid and painted.

After that I went into Mother's room and climbed into the big bed. She woke and I began to tell her of my schemes. By this time, though I never seem to have noticed it, I was petrified in my night-shirt, and I thawed as I talked until, the last frost melted, I fell asleep beside her and woke again only when I heard her below in the kitchen, making the breakfast.

After breakfast we went into town, heard Mass at St. Augustine's and said a prayer for Father, and did the shopping. If the afternoon was fine we either went for a walk in the country or a visit to Mother's great friend in the convent, Mother St. Dominic. Mother had them all praying for Father, and every night, going to bed, I asked God to send him back safe from the war to us. Little, indeed, did I know what I was praying for!

One morning, I got into the big bed, and there, sure enough, was Father in his usual Santa Claus manner, but later, instead of uniform, he put on his best blue suit, and Mother was as pleased as anything. I saw nothing to be pleased about, because, out of uniform, Father was altogether less interesting, but she only beamed, and explained that our prayers had been answered, and off we went to Mass to thank God for having brought Father safely home.

The irony of it! That very day when he came in to dinner he took off his boots and put on his slippers, donned the dirty old cap he wore about the house to save him from colds, crossed his legs, and began to talk gravely to Mother, who looked anxious. Naturally, I disliked her looking anxious, because it destroyed her good looks, so I interrupted him.

"Just a moment, Larry!" she said gently.

This was only what she said when we had boring visitors, so I attached no importance to it and went on talking.

4. Seventeen shillings and six pence.

"Do be quiet, Larry!" she said impatiently. "Don't you hear me talking to Daddy?"

This was the first time I had heard those ominous words, "talking to Daddy," and I couldn't help feeling that if this was how God answered prayers, he couldn't listen to them very attentively.

"Why are you talking to Daddy?" I asked with as great a show of indifference as I could muster.

"Because Daddy and I have business to discuss. Now, don't interrupt again!"

In the afternoon, at Mother's request, Father took me for a walk. This time we went into town instead of out to the country, and I thought at first, in my usual optimistic way, that it might be an improvement. It was nothing of the sort. Father and I had quite different notions of a walk in town. He had no proper interest in trams, ships, and horses, and the only thing that seemed to divert him was talking to fellows as old as himself. When I wanted to stop he simply went on, dragging me behind him by the hand; when he wanted to stop I had no alternative but to do the same. I noticed that it seemed to be a sign that he wanted to stop for a long time whenever he leaned against a wall. The second time I saw him do it I got wild. He seemed to be settling himself forever. I pulled him by the coat and trousers, but, unlike Mother who, if you were too persistent, got into a wax and said: "Larry, if you don't behave yourself, I'll give you a good slap," Father had an extraordinary capacity for amiable inattention. I sized him up and wondered would I cry, but he seemed to be too remote to be annoyed even by that. Really, it was like going for a walk with a mountain! He either ignored the wrenching and pummeling entirely, or else glanced down with a grin of amusement from his peak. I had never met anyone so absorbed in himself as he seemed.

At teatime, "talking to Daddy" began again, complicated this time by the fact that he had an evening paper, and every few minutes he put it down and told Mother something new out of it. I felt this was foul play. Man for man, I was prepared to compete with him any time for Mother's attention, but when he had it all made up for him by other people it left me no chance. Several times I tried to change the subject without success.

"You must be quiet while Daddy is reading, Larry," Mother said impatiently.

It was clear that she either genuinely liked talking to Father better than talking to me, or else that he had some terrible hold on her which made her afraid to admit the truth.

"Mummy," I said that night when she was tucking me up, "do you think if I prayed hard God would send Daddy back to the war?"

She seemed to think about that for a moment.

"No, dear," she said with a smile. "I don't think he would."

"Why wouldn't he, Mummy?"

"Because there isn't a war any longer, dear."

"But, Mummy, couldn't God make another war, if He liked?"

"He wouldn't like to, dear. It's not God who makes wars, but bad people."

"Oh!" I said.

I was disappointed about that. I began to think that God wasn't quite what he was cracked up to be.

Next morning I woke at my usual hour, feeling like a bottle of champagne. I put out my feet and invented a long conversation in which Mrs. Right talked of the trouble she had with her own father till she put him in the Home. I didn't quite know what the Home was but it sounded the right place for Father. Then I got my chair and stuck my head out of the attic window. Dawn was just breaking, with a guilty air that made me feel I had caught it in the act. My head bursting with stories and schemes, I stumbled in next door, and in the half-darkness scrambled into the big bed. There was no room at Mother's side so I had to get between her and Father. For the time being I had forgotten about him, and for several minutes I sat bolt upright, racking my brains to know what I could do with him. He was taking up more than his fair share of the bed, and I couldn't get comfortable, so I gave him several kicks that made him grunt and stretch. He made room all right, though. Mother waked and felt for me. I settled back comfortably in the warmth of the bed with my thumb in my mouth.

"Mummy!" I hummed, loudly and contentedly.

"Sssh! dear," she whispered. "Don't wake Daddy!"

This was a new development, which threatened to be even more serious than "talking to Daddy." Life without my early-morning conferences was unthinkable.

"Why?" I asked severely.

"Because poor Daddy is tired."

This seemed to me a quite inadequate reason, and I was sickened by the sentimentality of her "poor Daddy." I never liked that sort of gush; it always struck me as insincere.

"Oh!" I said lightly. Then in my most winning tone: "Do you know where I want to go with you today, Mummy?"

"No, dear," she sighed.

"I want to go down the Glen and fish for thornybacks with my new net, and then I want to go out to the Fox and Hounds, and—"

"Don't-wake-Daddy!" she hissed angrily, clapping her hand across my mouth.

But it was too late. He was awake, or nearly so. He grunted and reached for the matches. Then he stared incredulously at his watch.

"Like a cup of tea, dear?" asked Mother in a meek, hushed voice I had never heard her use before. It sounded almost as though she were afraid.

"Tea?" he exclaimed indignantly. "Do you know what the time is?"

"And after that I want to go up the Rathcooney Road," I said loudly, afraid I'd forget something in all those interruptions.

"Go to sleep at once, Larry!" she said sharply.

I began to snivel. I couldn't concentrate, the way that pair went on, and smothering my early-morning schemes was like burying a family from the cradle.

Father said nothing, but lit his pipe and sucked it, looking out into the shadows without minding Mother or me. I knew he was mad. Every time I made a remark Mother hushed me irritably. I was mortified. I felt it wasn't fair; there was even something sinister in it. Every time I had pointed out to her the waste of making two beds when we could both sleep in one, she had told me it was healthier like that, and now here was this man, this stranger, sleeping with her without the least regard for her health!

He got up early and made tea, but though he brought Mother a cup he brought none for me.

"Mummy," I shouted, "I want a cup of tea, too."

"Yes, dear," she said patiently. "You can drink from Mummy's saucer."

That settled it. Either Father or I would have to leave the house. I didn't want to drink from Mother's saucer; I wanted to be treated as an equal in my own home, so, just to spite her, I drank it all and left none for her. She took that quietly, too.

But that night when she was putting me to bed she said gently:

"Larry, I want you to promise me something."

"What is it?" I asked.

"Not to come in and disturb poor Daddy in the morning. Promise?"

"Poor Daddy" again! I was becoming suspicious of everything involving that quite impossible man.

"Why?" I asked.

"Because poor Daddy is worried and tired and he doesn't sleep well."

"Why doesn't he, Mummy?"

"Well, you know, don't you, that while he was at the war Mummy got the pennies from the Post Office!"

"From Miss MacCarthy?"

"That's right. But now, you see, Miss MacCarthy hasn't any more pennies, so Daddy must go out and find us some. You know what would happen if he couldn't?"

"No," I said, "tell us."

"Well, I think we might have to go out and beg for them like the poor old woman on Fridays. We wouldn't like that, would we?"

"No," I agreed. "We wouldn't."

"So you'll promise not to come in and wake him?"

"Promise."

Mind you, I meant that. I knew pennies were a serious matter, and I was all against having to go out and beg like the old woman on Fridays. Mother laid out all my toys in a complete ring around the bed so that, whatever way I got out, I was bound to fall over one of them.

When I woke I remembered my promise all right. I got up and sat on the floor and played—for hours, it seemed to me. Then I got my chair and looked out the attic window for more hours. I wished it was time for Father to wake; I wished someone would make me a cup of tea. I didn't feel in the least like the sun; instead, I was bored and so very, very cold! I simply longed for the warmth and depth of the big featherbed.

At last I could stand it no longer. I went into the next room. As there was still no room at Mother's side I climbed over her and she woke with a start.

"Larry," she whispered, gripping my arm very tightly, "what did you promise?"

"But I did, Mummy," I wailed, caught in the very act. "I was quiet for ever so long."

"Oh, dear, and you're perished!" she said sadly, feeling me all over. "Now, if I let you stay will you promise not to talk?"

"But I want to talk, Mummy," I wailed.

"That has nothing to do with it," she said with a firmness that was new to me. "Daddy wants to sleep. Now, do you understand that?"

I understood it only too well. I wanted to talk, he wanted to sleep—whose house was it, anyway?

"Mummy," I said with equal firmness, "I think it would be healthier for Daddy to sleep in his own bed."

That seemed to stagger her, because she said nothing for a while.

"Now, once and for all," she went on, "you're to be perfectly quiet or go back to your own bed. Which is it to be?"

The injustice of it got me down. I had convicted her out of her own mouth of inconsistency and unreasonableness, and she hadn't even attempted to reply. Full of spite, I gave Father a kick, which she didn't notice but which made him grunt and open his eyes in alarm.

"What time is it?" he asked in a panic-stricken voice, not looking at Mother but at the door, as if he saw someone there.

"It's early yet," she replied soothingly. "It's only the child. Go to sleep again. . . . Now, Larry," she added, getting out of bed, "you've wakened Daddy and you must go back."

This time, for all her quiet air, I knew she meant it, and knew that my principal rights and privileges were as good as lost unless I asserted them at once. As she lifted me, I gave a screech, enough to wake the dead, not to mind Father. He groaned.

"That damn child! Doesn't he ever sleep?"

"It's only a habit, dear," she said quietly, though I could see she was vexed.

"Well, it's time he got out of it," shouted Father, beginning to heave in the bed. He suddenly gathered all the bedclothes about him, turned to the wall, and then looked back over his shoulder with nothing showing only two small, spiteful, dark eyes. The man looked very wicked.

To open the bedroom door, Mother had to let me down, and I broke free and dashed for the farthest corner, screeching. Father sat bolt upright in bed.

"Shut up, you little puppy!" he said in a choking voice.

I was so astonished that I stopped screeching. Never, never had anyone spoken to me in that tone before. I looked at him incredulously and saw his face convulsed with rage. It was only then that I fully realized how God had codded[5] me, listening to my prayers for the safe return of this monster.

"Shut up, you!" I bawled, beside myself.

"What's that you said?" shouted Father, making a wild leap out of the bed.

"Mick, Mick!" cried Mother. "Don't you see the child isn't used to you?"

"I see he's better fed than taught," snarled Father, waving his arms wildly. "He wants his bottom smacked."

All his previous shouting was as nothing to these obscene words referring to my person. They really made my blood boil.

"Smack your own!" I screamed hysterically. "Smack your own! Shut up! Shut up!"

At this he lost his patience and let fly at me. He did it with the lack of conviction you'd expect of a man under Mother's horrified eyes, and it ended up as a mere tap, but the sheer indignity of being struck at all by a stranger, a total stranger who had cajoled his way back from the war into our big bed as a result of my innocent intercession, made me completely dotty. I shrieked and shrieked, and danced in my bare

5. Fooled, deceived.

feet, and Father, looking awkward and hairy in nothing but a short grey army shirt, glared down at me like a mountain out for murder. I think it must have been then that I realized he was jealous too. And there stood Mother in her nightdress, looking as if her heart was broken between us. I hoped she felt as she looked. It seemed to me that she deserved it all.

From that morning out my life was hell. Father and I were enemies, open and avowed. We conducted a series of skirmishes against one another, he trying to steal my time with Mother and I his. When she was sitting on my bed, telling me a story, he took to looking for some pair of old boots which he alleged he had left behind him at the beginning of the war. While he talked to Mother I played loudly with my toys to show my total lack of concern. He created a terrible scene one evening when he came in from work and found me at his box, playing with his regimental badges, Gurkha knives and button-sticks. Mother got up and took the box from me.

"You mustn't play with Daddy's toys unless he lets you, Larry," she said severely. "Daddy doesn't play with yours."

For some reason Father looked at her as if she had struck him and then turned away with a scowl.

"Those are not toys," he growled, taking down the box again to see had I lifted anything. "Some of those curios are very rare and valuable."

But as time went on I saw more and more how he managed to alienate Mother and me. What made it worse was that I couldn't grasp his method or see what attraction he had for Mother. In every possible way he was less winning than I. He had a common accent and made noises at his tea. I thought for a while that it might be the newspapers she was interested in, so I made up bits of news of my own to read to her. Then I thought it might be the smoking, which I personally thought attractive, and took his pipes and went round the house dribbling into them till he caught me. I even made noises at my tea, but Mother only told me I was disgusting. It all seemed to hinge round that unhealthy habit of sleeping together, so I made a point of dropping into their bedroom and nosing round, talking to myself, so that they wouldn't know I was watching them, but they were never up to anything that I could see. In the end it beat me. It seemed to depend on being grown-up and giving people rings, and I realized I'd have to wait.

But at the same time I wanted him to see that I was only waiting, not giving up the fight. One evening when he was being particularly obnoxious, chattering away well above my head, I let him have it.

"Mummy," I said, "do you know what I'm going to do when I grow up?"

"No dear," she replied. "What?"

"I'm going to marry you," I said quietly.

Father gave a great guffaw out of him, but he didn't take me in. I knew it must only be pretence. And Mother, in spite of everything, was pleased. I felt she was probably relieved to know that one day Father's hold on her would be broken.

"Won't that be nice!" she said with a smile.

"It'll be very nice," I said confidently. "Because we're going to have lots and lots of babies."

"That's right, dear," she said placidly. "I think we'll have one soon, and then you'll have plenty of company."

I was no end pleased about that because it showed that in spite of the way she gave in to Father she still considered my wishes. Besides, it would put the Geneys in their place.

It didn't turn out like that, though. To begin with, she was very preoccupied—I suppose about where she would get the seventeen and six—and though Father took to staying out late in the evenings it did me no particular good. She stopped taking me for walks, became as touchy as blazes, and smacked me for nothing at all. Sometimes I wished I'd never mentioned the confounded baby—I seemed to have a genius for bringing calamity on myself.

And calamity it was! Sonny arrived in the most appalling hullabaloo—even that much he couldn't do without a fuss—and from the first moment I disliked him. He was a difficult child—so far as I was concerned he was always difficult—and demanded far too much attention. Mother was simply silly about him, and couldn't see when he was only showing off. As company he was worse than useless. He slept all day, and I had to go round the house on tiptoe to avoid waking him. It wasn't any longer a question of not waking Father. The slogan now was "Don't-wake-Sonny!" I couldn't understand why the child wouldn't sleep at the proper time, so whenever Mother's back was turned I woke him. Sometimes to keep him awake I pinched him as well. Mother caught me at it one day and gave me a most unmerciful flaking.

One evening, when Father was coming in from work, I was playing trains in the front garden. I let on not to notice him; instead, I pretended to be talking to myself, and said in a loud voice: "If another bloody baby comes into this house, I'm going out."

Father stopped dead and looked at me over his shoulder.

"What's that you said?" he asked sternly.

"I was only talking to myself," I replied, trying to conceal my panic. "It's private."

He turned and went in without a word. Mind you, I intended it as a solemn warning, but its effect was quite different. Father started being quite nice to me. I could understand that, of course. Mother was quite sickening about Sonny. Even at mealtimes she'd get up and gawk at him in the cradle with an idiotic smile, and tell Father to do the same. He was always polite about it, but he looked so puzzled you could see he didn't know what she was talking about. He complained of the way Sonny cried at night, but she only got cross and said that Sonny never cried except when there was something up with him—which was a flaming lie, because Sonny never had anything up with him, and only cried for attention. It was really painful to see how simple-minded she was. Father wasn't attractive, but he had a fine intelligence. He saw through Sonny, and now he knew that I saw through him as well.

One night I woke with a start. There was someone beside me in the bed. For one wild moment I felt sure it must be Mother, having come to her senses and left Father for good, but then I heard Sonny in convulsions in the next room, and Mother saying: "There! There! There!" and I knew it wasn't she. It was Father. He was lying beside me, wide awake, breathing hard and apparently as mad as hell.

After a while it came to me what he was mad about. It was his turn now. After turning me out of the big bed, he had been turned out himself. Mother had no consideration now for anyone but that poisonous pup, Sonny. I couldn't help feeling sorry for Father. I had been through it all myself, and even at that age I was magnanimous. I began to stroke him down and say: "There! There!" He wasn't exactly responsive.

"Aren't you asleep either?" he snarled.

"Ah, come on and put your arm around us, can't you?" I said, and he did, in a sort of way. Gingerly, I suppose, is how you'd describe it. He was very bony but better than nothing.

At Christmas he went out of his way to buy me a really nice model railway.

---

1. Does the boy seem to be undergoing a major psychological crisis? Relate your answer to the title. Is it seriously intended or facetious?
2. What devices are used to characterize the mother and father?
3. Does the action provide any signs that the boy is maturing? Is there a decisive point at which he changes?
4. Are there significant changes in the character of the narrator from childhood to the time at which he recollects these childhood events?
5. What is the narrator's attitude toward his behavior as a child? How does this attitude affect the tone of the story?

Tillie Olsen

Olsen (1913–   ) was born in Omaha, Nebraska. She began to write during the 1930's, but most of her life has been committed to working in industry and raising her children. When her rare stories began to appear in the 1950's, she attracted a small group of enthusiastic readers, who loyally acclaimed her talents until she gained a wider recognition. Her stories are collected in Tell Me a Riddle *(1961).* Silences *(1978) is a collection of essays and meditations. Her novel* Yonnondio *was published in 1974.*

Tell Me a Riddle

"*These Things Shall Be*"

I

For forty-seven years they had been married. How deep back the stubborn, gnarled roots of the quarrel reached, no one could say—but only now, when tending to the needs of others no longer shackled them together, the roots swelled up visible, split the earth between them, and the tearing shook even to the children, long since grown.

Why now, why now? wailed Hannah.

As if when we grew up weren't enough, said Paul.

Poor Ma. Poor Dad. It hurts so for both of them, said Vivi. They never had very much; at least in old age they should be happy.

Knock their heads together, insisted Sammy; tell 'em: you're too old for this kind of thing; no reason not to get along now.

Lennie wrote to Clara: They've lived over so much together; what could possibly tear them apart?

Something tangible enough.

Arthritic hands, and such work as he got, occasional. Poverty all his life, and there was little breath left for running. He could not, could not turn away from this desire: to have the troubling of responsibility, the fretting with money, over and done with; to be free, to be *care*free where success was not measured by accumulation, and there was use for the vitality still in him.

There was a way. They could sell the house, and with the money join his lodge's Haven, co-operative for the aged. Happy communal life, and was he not already an official; had he not helped organize it, raise funds, served as a trustee?

But she—would not consider it.

"What do we need all this for?" he would ask loudly, for her hearing aid was turned down and the vacuum was shrilling. "Five rooms" (pushing the sofa so she could get into the corner) "furniture" (smoothing down the rug) "floors and surfaces to make work. Tell me, why do we need it?" And he was glad he could ask in a scream.

"Because I'm use't."

"Because you're use't. This is a reason, Mrs. Word Miser? Used to can get unused!"

"Enough unused I have to get used to already. . . . Not enough words?" turning off the vacuum a moment to hear herself answer. "Because soon enough we'll need only a little closet, no windows, no furniture, nothing to make work, but for worms. Because now I want room . . . Screech and blow like you're doing, you'll need that closet even sooner. . . . Ha, again!" for the vacuum bag wailed, puffed half up, hung stubbornly limp. "This time fix it so it stays; quick before the phone rings and you get too important-busy."

But while he struggled with the motor, it seethed in him. Why fix it? Why have to bother? And if it can't be fixed, have to wring the mind with how to pay the repair? At the Haven they come in with their own machines to clean your room or your cottage; you fish, or play cards, or make jokes in the sun, not with knotty fingers fight to mend vacuums.

Over the dishes, coaxingly: "For once in your life, to be free, to have everything done for you, like a queen."

"I never liked queens."

"No dishes, no garbage, no towel to sop, no worry what to buy, what to eat."

"And what else would I do with my empty hands? Better to eat at my own table when I want, and to cook and eat how I want."

"In the cottages they buy what you ask, and cook it how you like. *You* are the one who always used to say: better mankind born without mouths and stomachs than always to worry for money to buy, to shop, to fix, to cook, to wash, to clean."

"How cleverly you hid that you heard. I said it then because eighteen hours a day I ran. And you never scraped a carrot or knew a dish towel sops. Now—for you and me—who cares? A herring out of a jar is enough. But when *I* want, and nobody to bother." And she turned off her ear button, so she would not have to hear.

But as *he* had no peace, juggling and rejuggling the money to figure: how will I pay for this now?; prying out the storm windows (there they take care of this); jolting in the streetcar on errands (there I would not have to ride to take care of this or that); fending the patronizing relatives just back from Florida (there it matters what one is, not what one can afford), he gave *her* no peace.

"Look! In their bulletin. A reading circle. Twice a week it meets."

"Haumm," her answer of not listening.

"A reading circle. Chekhov they read that you like, and Peretz.[1] Cultured people at the Haven that you would enjoy."

"Enjoy!" She tasted the word. "Now, when it pleases you, you find a reading circle for me. And forty years ago when the children were morsels and there was a Circle, did you stay home with them once so I could go? Even once? You trained me well. I do not need others to enjoy. Others!" Her voice trembled. "Because you want to be there with others. Already it makes me sick to think of you always around others. Clown, grimacer, floormat, yesman, entertainer, whatever they want of you."

And now it was he who turned on the television loud so he need not hear.

Old scar tissue ruptured and the wounds festered anew. Chekhov indeed. She thought without softness of that young wife, who in the deep night hours while she nursed the current baby, and perhaps held another in her lap, would try to stay awake for the only time there was to read. She would feel again the weather of the outside on his cheek when, coming late from a meeting, he would find her so, and stimulated and ardent, sniffing her skin, coax: "I'll put the baby to bed, and you—put the book away, don't read, don't read."

That had been the most beguiling of all the "don't read, put your book away" her life had been. Chekhov indeed!

"Money?" She shrugged him off. "Could we get poorer than once we were? And in America, who starves?"

But as still he pressed:

"Let me alone about money. Was there ever enough? Seven little ones—for every penny I had to ask—and sometimes, remember, there was nothing. But always *I* had to manage. Now *you* manage. Rub your nose in it good."

But from those years she had had to manage, old humiliations and terrors rose up, lived again, and forced her to relive them. The children's needings; that grocer's face or this merchant's wife she had had to beg credit from when credit was a disgrace; the scenery of the long blocks walked around when she could not pay; school coming, and the desperate going over the old to see what could yet be remade;

1. I. L. Peretz (1852–1915), Russian author of poems, plays, and stories in Yiddish, "the Jewish Chekhov"; Anton Chekhov, Russian writer (1860–1904).

the soups of meat bones begged "for-the-dog" one winter. . . .

Enough. Now they had no children. Let *him* wrack his head for how they would live. She would not exchange her solitude for anything. *Never again to be forced to move to the rhythms of others.*

For in this solitude she had won to a reconciled peace.

Tranquillity from having the empty house no longer an enemy, for it stayed clean—not as in the days when it was her family, the life in it, that had seemed the enemy: tracking, smudging, littering , dirtying, engaging her in endless defeating battle—and on whom her endless defeat had been spewed.

The few old books, memorized from rereading; the pictures to ponder (the magnifying glass superimposed on her heavy eyeglasses). Or if she wishes, when he is gone, the phonograph, that if she turns up very loud and strains, she can hear: the ordered sounds and the struggling.

Out in the garden, growing things to nurture. Birds to be kept out of the pear tree, and when the pears are heavy and ripe, the old fury of work, for all must be canned, nothing wasted.

And her one social duty (for she will not go to luncheons or meetings) the boxes of old clothes left with her, as with a life-practised eye for finding what is still wearable within the worn (again the magnifying glass superimposed on the heavy glasses) she scans and sorts—this for rag or rummage, that for mending and cleaning, and this for sending away.

Being able at last to live within, and not move to the rhythms of others, as life had forced her to: denying; removing; isolating; taking the children one by one; then deafening, half-blinding—and at last, presenting her solitude.

And in it she had won to a reconciled peace.

Now he was violating it with his constant campaigning: *Sell the house and move to the Haven.* (You sit, you sit—there too you could sit like a stone.) He was making of her a battleground where old grievances tore. (Turn on your ear button—I am talking.) And stubbornly she resisted—so that from wheedling, reasoning, manipulation, it was bitterness he now started with.

And it came to where every happening lashed up a quarrel.

"I will sell the house anyway," he flung at her one night. "I am putting it up for sale. There will be a way to make you sign."

The television blared, as always it did on the evenings he stayed home, and as always it reached her only as noise. She did not know if the tumult was in her or outside. Snap! she turned the sound off. "Shadows," she whispered to him, pointing to the screen, "look, it is only shadows." And in a scream: "Did you say that you will sell the house? Look at me, not at that. I am no shadow. You cannot sell without me."

"Leave on the television. I am watching."

"Like Paulie, like Jenny, a four-year-old. Staring at shadows. *You cannot sell the house.*"

"I will. We are going to the Haven. There you would not hear the television when you do not want it. I could sit in the social room and watch. You could lock yourself up to smell your unpleasantness in a room by yourself—for who would want to come near you?"

"No, no selling." A whisper now.

"The television is shadows. Mrs. Enlightened! Mrs. Cultured! A world comes into your house—and it is shadows. People you would never meet in a thousand lifetimes. Wonders. When you were four years old, yes, like Paulie, like Jenny, did you know of Indian dances, alligators, how they use bamboo in Malaya? No, you scratched in your dirt with the chickens and thought Olshana[2] was the world. Yes, Mrs. Unpleasant, I will sell the house, for there better can we be rid of each other than here."

She did not know if the tumult was outside, or in her. Always a ravening inside, a pull to the bed, to lie down, to succumb.

"Have you thought maybe Ma should let a doctor have a look at her?" asked their son Paul after Sunday dinner, regarding his mother crumpled on the couch, instead of, as was her custom, busying herself in Nancy's kitchen.

"Why not the President too?"

"Seriously, Dad. This is the third Sunday she's lain down like that after dinner. Is she that way at home?"

"A regular love affair with the bed. Every time I start to talk to her."

Good protective reaction, observed Nancy to herself. The workings of hos-til-ity.

"Nancy could take her. I just don't like how she looks. Let's have Nancy arrange an appointment."

"You think she'll go?" regarding his wife gloomily. "All right, we have to have doctor bills, we have to have doctor bills." Loudly: "Something hurts you?"

She startled, looked to his lips. He repeated: "Mrs. Take It Easy, something hurts?"

"Nothing. . . . Only you."

"A woman of honey. That's why you're lying down?"

"Soon I'll get up to do the dishes, Nancy."

2. Village in Russia.

"Leave them, Mother, I like it better this way."

"Mrs. Take It Easy, Paul says you should start ballet. You should go to see a doctor and ask: how soon can you start ballet?"

"A doctor?" she begged. "Ballet?"

"We were talking, Ma," explained Paul, "you don't seem any too well. It would be a good idea for you to see a doctor for a checkup."

"I get up now to do the kitchen. Doctors are bills and foolishness, my son. I need no doctors."

"At the Haven," he could not resist pointing out, "a doctor is *not* bills. He lives beside you. You start to sneeze, he is there before you open up a Kleenex. You can be sick there for free, all you want."

"Diarrhea of the mouth, is there a doctor to make you dumb?"

"Ma. Promise me you'll go. Nancy will arrange it."

"It's all of a piece when you think of it," said Nancy, "the way she attacks my kitchen, scrubbing under every cup hook, doing the inside of the oven so I can't enjoy Sunday dinner, knowing that half-blind or not, she's going to find every speck of dirt. . . ."

"Don't Nancy, I've told you—it's the only way she knows to be useful. What did the *doctor* say?"

"A real fatherly lecture. Sixty-nine is young these days. Go out, enjoy life, find interests. Get a new hearing aid, this one is antiquated. Old age is sickness only if one makes it so. Geriatrics, Inc."

"So there was nothing physical."

"Of course there was. How can you live to yourself like she does without there being? Evidence of a kidney disorder, and her blood count is low. He gave her a diet, and she's to come back for follow-up and lab work. . . . But he was clear enough: Number One prescription—start living like a human being. When I think of your dad, who could really play the invalid with that arthritis of his, as active as a teenager, and twice as much fun. . . ."

"You didn't tell me the doctor says your sickness is in you, how you live." He pushed his advantage. "Life and enjoyments you need better than medicine. And this diet, how can you keep it? To weigh each morsel and scrape away each bit of fat, to make this soup, that pudding. There, at the Haven, they have a dietician, they would do it for you."

She is silent.

"You would feel better there, I know it," he says gently. "There there is life and enjoyments all around."

"What is the matter, Mr. Importantbusy, you have no card game or meeting you can go to?"—turning her face to the pillow.

For a while he cut his meetings and going out, fussed over her diet, tried to wheedle her into leaving the house, brought in visitors:

> "I should come to a fashion tea. I should sit and look at pretty babies in clothes I cannot buy. This is pleasure?"
> "Always you are better than everyone else. The doctor said you should go out. Mrs. Brem comes to you with goodness and you turn her away."
> "Because *you* asked her to, she asked me."
>
> "They won't come back. People you need, the doctor said. Your own cousins I asked; they were willing to come and make peace as if nothing had happened. . . ."
> "No more crushers of people, pushers, hypocrites, around me. No more in *my* house. You go to them if you like."
>
> "Kind he is to visit. And you, like ice."
> "A babbler. All my life around babblers. Enough!"

"She's even worse, Dad? Then let her stew a while," advised Nancy. "You can't let it destroy you; it's a psychological thing, maybe too far gone for any of us to help."

So he let her stew. More and more she lay silent in bed, and sometimes did not even get up to make the meals. No longer was the tongue-lashing inevitable if he left the coffee cup where it did not belong, or forgot to take out the garbage or mislaid the broom. The birds grew bold that summer and for once pocked the pears, undisturbed.

A bellyful of bitterness and every day the same quarrel in a new way and a different old grievance the quarrel forced her to enter and relive. And the new torment: I am not really sick, the doctor said it, then why do I feel so sick?

One night she asked him: "You have a meeting tonight? Do not go. Stay . . . with me."

He had planned to watch "This Is Your Life," but half sick himself from the heavy heat, and sickening therefore the more after the brooks and woods of the Haven, with satisfaction he grated:

"Hah, Mrs. Live Alone And Like It wants company all of a sudden. It doesn't seem so good the time of solitary when she was a girl exile in Siberia. 'Do not go. Stay with me.' A new song for Mrs. Free As A Bird. Yes, I am going out, and while I am gone chew this aloneness good, and think how you keep us both from where if you want people you do not need to be alone."

"Go, go. All your life you have gone without me."

After him she sobbed curses he had not heard in years, old-country curses from their childhood: Grow, oh shall you grow like an onion, with your head in the ground. Like the hide of a drum shall you be, beaten in life, beaten in death. Oh shall you be like a chandelier, to hang, and to burn. . . .

She was not in their bed when he came back. She lay on the cot on the sun-porch. All week she did not speak or come near him; nor did he try to make peace or care for her.

He slept badly, so used to her next to him. After all the years, old harmonies and dependencies deep in their bodies; she curled to him, or he coiled to her, each warmed, warming, turning as the other turned, the nights a long embrace.

It was not the empty bed or the storm that woke him, but a faint singing. *She* was singing. Shaking off the drops of rain, the lightning riving her lifted face, he saw her so; the cot covers on the floor.

"This is a private concert?" he asked. "Come in, you are wet."

"I can breathe now," she answered; "my lungs are rich." Though indeed the sound was hardly a breath.

"Come in, come in." Loosing the bamboo shades. "Look how wet you are." Half helping, half carrying her, still faint-breathing her song.

A Russian love song of fifty years ago.

He had found a buyer, but before he told her, he called together those children who were close enough to come. Paul, of course, Sammy from New Jersey, Hannah from Connecticut, Vivi from Ohio.

With a kindling of energy for her beloved visitors, she arrayed the house, cooked and baked. She was not prepared for the solemn after-dinner conclave, they too probing in and tearing. Her frightened eyes watched from mouth to mouth as each spoke.

His stories were eloquent and funny of her refusal to go back to the doctor; of the scorned invitations; of her stubborn silence or the bile "like a Niagara"; of her contrariness: "If I clean it's no good how I cleaned; if I don't clean, I'm still a master who thinks he has a slave."

(Vinegar he poured on me all his life; I am well marinated; how can I be honey now?)

Deftly he marched in the rightness for moving to the Haven; their money from social security free for visiting the children, not sucked into daily needs and into the house; the activities in the Haven for him; but mostly the Haven for *her:* her health, her need of care, distraction, amusement, friends who shared her interests.

"This does offer an outlet for Dad," said Paul; "he's always been an active person. And economic peace of mind isn't to be sneezed at, either. I could use a little of that myself."

But when they asked: "And you, Ma, how do you feel about it?" could only whisper:

"For him it is good. It is not for me. I can no longer live between people."

"You lived all your life *for* people," Vivi cried.

"Not with." Suffering doubly for the unhappiness on her children's faces.

"You have to find some compromise," Sammy insisted. "Maybe sell the house and buy a trailer. After forty-seven years there's surely some way you can find to live in peace."

"There is no help, my children. Different things we need."

"Then live alone!" He could control himself no longer. "I have a buyer for the house. Half the money for you, half for me. Either alone or with me to the Haven. You think I can live any longer as we are doing now?"

"Ma doesn't have to make a decision this minute, however you feel, Dad," Paul said quickly, "and you wouldn't want her to. Let's let it lay a few months, and then talk some more."

"I think I can work it out to take Mother home with me for a while," Hannah said. "You both look terrible, but especially you, Mother. I'm going to ask Phil to have a look at you."

"Sure," cracked Sammy. "What's the use of a doctor husband if you can't get free service out of him once in a while for the family? And absence might make the heart . . . you know."

"There was something after all," Paul told Nancy in a colorless voice. "That was Hannah's Phil calling. Her gall bladder. . . . Surgery."

"Her *gall* bladder. If that isn't classic. 'Bitter as gall'—talk of psychosom——"

He stepped closer, put his hand over her mouth, and said in the same colorless, plodding voice. "We have to get Dad. They operated at once. The cancer was everywhere, surrounding the liver, everywhere. They did what they could . . . at best she has a year. Dad . . . we have to tell him."

II

Honest in his weakness when they told him, and that she was not to know. "I'm not an actor. She'll know right away by how I am. Oh that poor woman. I am old too, it will break me into pieces. Oh that poor woman. She will spit on me: 'So my sickness was how I live.' Oh Paulie, how she will be, that poor woman. Only she should not suffer. . . .

I can't stand sickness, Paulie, I can't go with you."

But went. And play-acted.

"A grand opening and you did not even wait for me. . . . A good thing Hannah took you with her."

"Fashion teas I needed. They cut out what tore in me; just in my throat something hurts yet. . . . Look! so many flowers, like a funeral. Vivi called, did Hannah tell you? And Lennie from San Francisco, and Clara; and Sammy is coming." Her gnome's face pressed happily into the flowers.

> It is impossible to predict in these cases, but once over the immediate effects of the operation, she should have several months of comparative well-being.
>
> *The money, where will come the money?*
>
> Travel with her, Dad. Don't take her home to the old associations. The other children will want to see her.
>
> *The money, where will I wring the money?*
>
> Whatever happens, she is not to know. No, you can't ask her to sign papers to sell the house; nothing to upset her. Borrow instead, then after. . . .
>
> *I had wanted to leave you each a few dollars to make life easier, as other fathers do. There will be nothing left now. (Failure! you and your "business is exploitation." Why didn't you make it when it could be made?—Is that what you're thinking, Sammy?)*
>
> Sure she's unreasonable, Dad—but you have to stay with her. If there's to be any happiness in what's left of her life, it depends on you.
>
> *Prop me up, children, think of me, too. Shuffled, chained with her, bitter woman. No Haven, and the little money going. . . . How happy she looks, poor creature.*

The look of excitement. The straining to hear everything (the new hearing aid turned full). Why are you so happy, dying woman?

How the petals are, fold on fold, and the gladioli color. The autumn air.

Stranger grandsons, tall above the little gnome grandmother, the little spry grandfather. Paul in a frenzy of picture-taking before going.

She, wandering the great house. Feeling the books; laughing at the maple shoemaker's bench of a hundred years ago used as a table. The ear turned to music.

"Let us go home. See how good I walk now." "One step from the hospital," he answers, "and she wants to fly. Wait till Doctor Phil says."

"Look—the birds too are flying home. Very good Phil is and will not show it, but he is sick of sickness by the time he comes home."

"Mrs. Telepathy, to read minds," he answers; "read mine what it says: when the trunks of medicines become a suitcase, then we will go."

The grandboys, they do not know what to say to us. . . . Hannah, she runs around here, there, when is there time for herself?

Let us go home. Let us go home.

Musing; gentleness—*but for the incidents of the rabbi in the hospital, and of the candles of benediction.*

Of the rabbi in the hospital:

Now tell me what happened, Mother.

From the sleep I awoke, Hannah's Phil, and he stands there like a devil in a dream and calls me by name. I cannot hear. I think he prays. Go away, please, I tell him, I am not a believer. Still he stands, while my heart knocks with fright.

You scared *him*, Mother. He thought you were delirious.

Who sent him? Why did he come to *me*?

It is a custom. The men of God come to visit those of their religion they might help. The hospital makes up the list for them—race, religion—and you are on the Jewish list.

Not for rabbis. At once go and make them change. Tell them to write: Race, human; Religion, none.

And of the candles of benediction:

Look, how you have upset yourself, Mrs. Excited Over Nothing. Pleasant memories you should leave.

Go in, go back to Hannah and the lights. Two weeks I saw candles and said nothing. But she asked me.

So what was so terrible? She forgets you never did, she asks you to light the Friday candles and say the benediction like Phil's mother when she visits. If the candles give her pleasure, why shouldn't she have the pleasure?

Not for pleasure she does it. For emptiness. Because his family does. Because all around her do.

That is not a good reason too? But you did not hear her. For heritage, she told you. For the boys, from the past they should have tradition.

Superstition! From our ancestors, savages, afraid of the dark, of themselves: mumbo words and magic lights to scare away ghosts.

She told you: how it started does not take away the goodness. For centuries, peace in the house it means.

Swindler! does she look back on the dark centuries? Candles bought instead of bread and stuck into a potato for a candlestick? Religion that stifled and said: in Paradise, woman, you will be the footstool of your husband, and in life—poor chosen Jew—ground under, despised, trembling in cellars. And cremated. And cremated.

This is religion's fault? You think you are still an orator of the 1905 revolution?[3] Where are the pills for quieting? Which are they?

Heritage. How have we come from our savage past, how no longer to be savages—this to teach. To look back and learn what humanizes—this to teach. To smash all ghettos that divide us—not to go back, not to go back—this to teach. Learned books in the house, will humankind live or die, and she gives to her boys—superstition.

Hannah that is so good to you. Take your pill, Mrs. Excited For Nothing, swallow.

Heritage! But when did I have time to teach? Of Hannah I asked only hands to help.

Swallow.

Otherwise—musing; gentleness.

Not to travel. To go home.

The children want to see you. We have to show them you are as thorny a flower as ever.

Not to travel.

Vivi wants you should see her new baby. She sent the tickets—airplane tickets—a Mrs. Roosevelt[4] she wants to make of you. To Vivi's we have to go.

A new baby. How many warm, seductive babies. She holds him stiffly, *away* from her, so that he wails. And a long shudder begins, and the sweat beads on her forehead.

"Hush, shush," croons the grandfather, lifting him back. "You should forgive your grandmamma, little prince, she has never held a baby before, only seen them in glass cases. Hush, shush."

"You're tired, Ma," says Vivi. "The travel and the noisy dinner. I'll take you to lie down."

(A long travel from, to, what the feel of a baby evokes.)

In the airplane, cunningly designed to encase from motion (no wind, no feel of flight), she had sat severely and still, her face turned to the sky through which they cleaved and left no scar.

So this was how it looked, the determining, the crucial sky, and

3. Attempt to establish a democracy in czarist Russia. It was crushed by totalitarian terror.
4. Eleanor Roosevelt (1844–1962), wife of President Franklin D. Roosevelt, was famous for extensive, frequent travels.

this was how man moved through it, remote above the dwindled earth, the concealed human life. Vulnerable life, that could scar.

There was a steerage ship[5] of memory that shook across a great, circular sea: clustered, ill human beings; and through the thick-stained air, tiny fretting waters in a window round like the airplane's—sun round, moon round. (The round thatched roofs of Olshana.) Eye round—like the smaller window that framed distance the solitary year of exile when only her eyes could travel, and no voice spoke. And the polar winds hurled themselves across snows trackless and endless and white—like the clouds which had closed together below and hidden the earth.

Now they put a baby in her lap. Do not ask me, she would have liked to beg. Enough the worn face of Vivi, the remembered grandchildren, I cannot, cannot. . . .

Cannot what? Unnatural grandmother, not able to make herself embrace a baby.

She lay there in the bed of the two little girls, her new hearing aid turned full, listening to the sound of the children going to sleep, the baby's fretful crying and hushing, the clatter of dishes being washed and put away. They thought she slept. Still she rode on.

It was not that she had not loved her babies, her children. The love—the passion of tending—had risen with the need like a torrent; and like a torrent drowned and immolated all else. But when the need was done—oh the power that was lost in the painful damming back and drying up of what still surged, but had nowhere to go. Only the thin pulsing left that could not quiet, suffering over lives one felt, but could no longer hold nor help.

On that torrent she had borne them to their own lives, and the riverbed was desert long years now. Not there would she dwell, a memoried wraith. Surely that was not all, surely there was more. Still the springs, the springs were in her seeking. Somewhere an older power that beat for life. Somewhere coherence, transport, meaning. If they would but leave her in the air now stilled of clamor, in the reconciled solitude, to journey on.

And they put a baby in her lap. Immediacy to embrace, and the breath of *that* past: warm flesh like this that had claims and nuzzled away all else and with lovely mouths devoured; hot-living like an animal—intensely and now; the turning maze; the long drunkenness; the drowning into needing and being needed. Severely she looked back—and the shudder seized her again, and the sweat. Not that way. Not there, not now could she, not yet. . . .

And all that visit, she could not touch the baby.

5. I.e., a ship having only the lowest class of accommodations.

"Daddy, is it the . . . sickness she's like that?" asked Vivi. "I was so glad to be having the baby—for her. I told Tim, it'll give her more happiness than anything, being around a baby again. And she hasn't played with him once."

He was not listening. "Aahh little seed of life, little charmer," he crooned, "Hollywood should see you. A heart of ice you would melt. Kick, kick. The future you'll have for a ball. In 2050 still kick. Kick for your grandaddy then."

Attentive with the older children; sat through their performances (command performance; we command you to be the audience); helped Ann sort autumn leaves to find the best for a school program; listened gravely to Richard tell about his rock collection, while her lips mutely formed the words to remember: *igneous, sedimentary, metamorphic;*[6] looked for missing socks, books and bus tickets; watched the children whoop after their grandfather who knew how to tickle, chuck, lift, toss, do tricks, tell secrets, make jokes, match riddle for riddle. (Tell me a riddle, Grammy. I know no riddles, child.) Scrubbed sills and woodwork and furniture in every room; folded the laundry; straightened drawers; emptied the heaped baskets waiting for ironing (while he or Vivi or Tim nagged: You're supposed to rest here, you've been sick) but to none tended or gave food—and could not touch the baby.

After a week she said: "Let us go home. Today call about the tickets."

"You have important business, Mrs. Inahurry? The President waits to consult with you?" He shouted, for the fear of the future raced in him. "The clothes are still warm from the suitcase, your children cannot show enough how glad they are to see you, and you want home. There is plenty of time for home. We cannot be with the children at home."

"Blind to around you as always: the little ones sleep four in a room because we take their bed. We are two more people in a house with a new baby, and no help."

"Vivi is happy so. The children should have their grandparents a while, she told to me. I should have my mommy and daddy. . . ."

"Babbler and blind. Do you look at her so tired? How she starts to talk and she cries? I am not strong enough yet to help. Let us go home."

(To reconciled solitude.)

For it seemed to her the crowded noisy house was listening to her, listening for *her. She could feel it like a great ear pressed under*

6. Basic types of rocks.

her heart. And everything knocked: quick constant raps: let me in, let me in.

How was it that soft reaching tendrils also became blows that knocked?

C'mon, Grandma, I want to show you. . . .
Tell me a riddle, Grandma. *(I know no riddles.)*
Look, Grammy, he's so dumb he can't even find his hands. (Dody and the baby on a blanket over the fermenting autumn mould.)
I made them—for you. (Ann) (Flat paper dolls with aprons that lifted on scalloped skirts that lifted on flowered pants; hair of yarn and great ringed questioning eyes.)
Watch me, Grandma. (Richard snaking up the tree, hanging exultant, free, with one hand at the top. Below Dody hunching over in pretend-cooking.) *(Climb too, Dody, climb and look.)*
Be my nap bed, Grammy. (The "No!" too late.) Morty's abandoned heaviness, while his fingers ladder up and down her hearing-aid cord to his drowsy chant: eentsiebeentsiespider. *(Children trust.)*
It's to start off your own rock collection, Grandma. That's a trilobite fossil, 200 million years old (millions of years on a boy's mouth) and that one's obsidian, black glass.

Knocked and knocked.

Mother, I *told* you the teacher said we had to bring it back all filled out this morning. Didn't you even ask Daddy? Then tell *me* which plan and I'll check it: evacuate or stay in the city or wait for you to come and take me away. (Seeing the look of straining to hear.) It's for Disaster, Grandma.[7] *(Children trust.)*

Vivi in the maze of the long, the lovely drunkenness. The old old noises: baby sounds; screaming of a mother flayed to exasperation; children quarreling; children playing; singing; laughter.

And Vivi's tears and memories, spilling so fast, half the words not understood.

She had started remembering out loud deliberately, so her mother would know the past was cherished, still lived in her.

Nursing the baby: My friends marvel, and I tell them, oh it's easy to be such a cow. I remember how beautiful my mother seemed nursing my brother, and the milk just flows. . . . Was that Davy? It must have been Davy. . . .

7. During the 1950's, with the encouragement of the federal government, a number of American communities built fallout shelters and drew up evacuation ("Disaster") plans to be used in a nuclear attack.

Lowering a hem: How did you ever . . . when I think how you made everything we wore . . . Tim, just think, seven kids and Mommy sewed everything . . . do I remember you sang while you sewed? That white dress with the red apples on the skirt you fixed over for me, was it Hannah's or Clara's before it was mine?

Washing sweaters: Ma, I'll never forget, one of those days so nice you washed clothes outside; one of the first spring days it must have been. The bubbles just danced up and down while you scrubbed, and we chased after, and you stopped to show us how to blow our own bubbles with green onion stalks . . . you always. always. . . .

"Strong onion, to still make you cry after so many years," her father said, to turn the tears into laughter.

While Richard bent over his homework: Where is it now, do we still have it, the Book of the Martyrs? It always seemed so, well—exalted, when you'd put it on the round table and we'd all look at it together; there was even a halo from the lamp. The lamp with the beaded fringe you could move up and down; they're in style again, pulley lamps like that, but without the fringe. You know the book I'm talking about, Daddy, the Book of the Martyrs, the first picture was a bust of Spartacus? . . . Socrates? I wish there was something like that for the children, Mommy, to give them what you. . . . (And the tears splashed again.)

(What I intended and did not? Stop it, daughter, stop it, leave that time. And he, the hypocrite, sitting there with tears in his eyes—it was nothing to you then, nothing.)

. . . The time you came to school and I almost died of shame because of your accent and because I knew you knew I was ashamed; how could I? . . . Sammy's harmonica and you danced to it once, yes you did, you and Davy squealing in your arms. . . . That time you bundled us up and walked us down to the railway station to stay the night 'cause it was heated and we didn't have any coal, that winter of the strike, you didn't think I remembered that, did you, Mommy? . . . How you'd call us out to see the sunsets. . . .

Day after day, the spilling memories. Worse now, questions, too. Even the grandchildren: Grandma, in the olden days, when you were little. . . .

It was the afternoons that saved.

While they thought she napped, she would leave the mosaic on the wall (of children's drawings, maps, calendars, pictures, Ann's cardboard dolls with their great ringed questioning eyes) and hunch in the girls' closet, on the low shelf where the shoes stood, and the girls' dresses covered.

For that while she would painfully sheathe against the listening house, the tendrils and noises that knocked, and Vivi's spilling memories. Sometimes it helped to braid and unbraid the sashes that dangled, or to trace the pattern on the hoop slips.

Today she had jacks and children under jet trails to forget. Last night, Ann and Dody silhouetted in the window against a sunset of flaming man-made clouds of jet trail, their jacks ball accenting the peaceful noise of dinner being made. Had she told them, yes she had told them of how they played jacks in her village though there was no ball, no jacks. Six stones, round and flat, toss them out, the seventh on the back of the hand, toss, catch and swoop up as many as possible, toss again. . . .

Of stones (repeating Richard) there are three kinds: earth's fire jetting; rock of layered centuries; crucibled new out of the old (*igneous, sedimentary, metamorphic*). But there was that other—frozen to black glass, never to transform or hold the fossil memory . . . (let not my seed fall on stone). There was an ancient one who fought to heights a great rock that crashed back down eternally—eternal labor, freedom, labor . . . (stone will perish, but the word remain).[8] And you, David, who with a stone slew, screaming: Lord, take my heart of stone and give me flesh.

Who was screaming? Why was she back in the common room of the prison, the sun motes dancing in the shafts of light, and the informer being brought in, a prisoner now, like themselves. And Lisa leaping, yes, Lisa, the gentle and tender, biting at the betrayer's jugular. Screaming and screaming.

No, it is the children screaming. Another of Paul and Sammy's terrible fights?

In Vivi's house. Severely: you are in Vivi's house.

Blows, screams, a call: "Grandma!" For her? Oh please not for her. Hide, hunch behind the dresses deeper. But a trembling little body hurls itself beside her—surprised, smothered laughter, arms surround her neck, tears rub dry on her cheek, and words too soft to understand whisper into her ear (Is this where you hide too, Grammy? It's my secret place, we have a secret now).

And the sweat beads, and the long shudder seizes.

It seemed the great ear pressed inside now, and the knocking. "We have to go home," she told him, "I grow ill here."

"It is your own fault, Mrs. Bodybusy, you do not rest, you do too much." He raged, but the fear was in his eyes. "It was a serious operation, they told you to take care. . . . All right, we will go to where you can rest."

8. An allusion to the myth of Sisyphus, who was punished in Tartarus (below Hades) by having to roll a huge stone uphill; each time he approached the top, the stone would roll back.

But where? Not home to death, not yet. He had thought to Lennie's, to Clara's; beautiful visits with each of the children. She would have to rest first, be stronger. If they could but go to Florida—it glittered before him, the never-realized promise of Florida. California: of course. (The money, the money, dwindling!) Los Angeles first for sun and rest, then to Lennie's in San Francisco.

He told her the next day, "You saw what Nancy wrote: snow and wind back home, a terrible winter. And look at you—all bones and a swollen belly. I called Phil: he said: 'A prescription, Los Angeles sun and rest.' "

She watched the words on his lips. "You have sold the house," she cried, "that is why we do not go home. That is why you talk no more of the Haven, why there is money for travel. After the children you will drag me to the Haven."

"The Haven! Who thinks of the Haven any more? Tell her, Vivi, tell Mrs. Suspicious: a prescription, sun and rest, to make you healthy. . . . And how could I sell the house without *you*?"

At the place of farewells and greetings, of winds of coming and winds of going, they say their good-byes.

They look back at her with the eyes of others before them: Richard with her own blue blaze; Ann with the Nordic eyes of Tim; Morty's dreaming brown of a great-grandmother he will never know; Dody with the laughing eyes of him who had been her springtide love (who stands beside her now); Vivi's, all tears.

The baby's eyes are closed in sleep.

Good-bye, my children.

III

It is to the back of the great city he brought her, to the dwelling places of the cast-off old. Bounded by two lines of amusement piers to the north and to the south, and between a long straight paving rimmed with black benches facing the sand—sands so wide the ocean is only a far fluting.

In the brief vacation season, some of the boarded stores fronting the sands open, and families, young people and children, may be seen. A little tasselled tram shuttles between the piers, and the lights of roller coasters prink and tweak over those who come to have sensation made in them.

The rest of the year it is abandoned to the old, all else boarded up and still; seemingly empty, except the occasional days and hours when the sun, like a tide, sucks them out of the low rooming houses, casts them on to the benches and sandy rim of the walk—and sweeps them into decaying enclosures back again.

A few newer apartments glint among the low bleached squares. It is in one of these Lennie's Jeannie has arranged their rooms. "Only a few miles north and south people pay hundreds of dollars a month for just this gorgeous air, Grandaddy, just this ocean closeness."

She had been ill on the plane, lay ill for days in the unfamiliar room. Several times the doctor came by—left medicine she would not take. Several times Jeannie drove in the twenty miles from work, still in her Visiting Nurse uniform, the lightness and brightness of her like a healing.

"Who can believe it is winter?" he asked one morning. "Beautiful it is outside like an ad. Come, Mrs. Invalid, come to taste it. You are well enough to sit in here, you are well enough to sit outside. The doctor said it too."

But the benches were encrusted with people, and the sands at the sidewalk's edge. Besides, she had seen the far ruffle of the sea: "there take me," and though she leaned against him, it was she who led.

Plodding and plodding, sitting often to rest, he grumbling. Patting the sand so warm. Once she scooped up a handful, cradling it close to her better eye; peered, and flung it back. And as they came almost to the brink and she could see the glistening wet, she sat down, pulled off her shoes and stockings, left him and began to run. "You'll catch cold," he screamed, but the sand in his shoes weighed him down—he who had always been the agile one—and already the white spray creamed her feet.

He pulled her back, took a handkerchief to wipe off the wet and the sand. "Oh no," she said, "the sun will dry," seized the square and smoothed it flat, dropped on it a mound of sand, knotted the kerchief corners and tied it to a bag—"to look at with the strong glass" (for the first time in years explaining an action of hers)—and lay down with the little bag against her cheek, looking toward the shore that nurtured life as it first crawled toward consciousness the millions of years ago.

He took her one Sunday in the evil-smelling bus, past flat miles of blister houses, to the home of relatives. Oh what is this? she cried as the light began to smoke and the houses to dim and recede. Smog, he said, everyone knows but you. . . . Outside he kept his arms about her, but she walked with hands pushing the heavy air as if to open it, whispered: who has done this? sat down suddenly to vomit at the curb and for a long while refused to rise.

One's age as seen on the altered face of those known in youth. Is this they he has come to visit? This Max and Rose, smooth and pleasant, introducing them to polite children, disinterested grandchildren, "the whole family, once a month on Sundays. And why not? We have the room, the help, the food."

Talk of cars, of houses, of success: this son that, that daughter this. And *your* children? Hastily skimped over, the intermarriages, the obscure work—"my doctor son-in-law, Phil"—all he has to offer. She silent in a corner. (Car-sick like a baby, he explains.) Years since he has taken her to visit anyone but the children, and old apprehensions prickle: "no incidents," he silently begs, "no incidents." He itched to tell them. "A very sick woman," significantly, indicating her with his eyes, "a very sick women." Their restricted faces did not react. "Have you thought maybe she'd do better at Palm Springs?" Rose asked. "Or at least a nicer section of the beach, nicer people, a pool." Not to have to say "money" he said instead: "would she have sand to look at through a magnifying glass?" and went on, detail after detail, the old habit betraying of parading the queerness of her for laughter.

After dinner—the others into the living-room in men- or women-clusters, or into the den to watch TV—the four of them alone. She sat close to him, and did not speak. Jokes, stories, people they had known, beginning of reminiscence, Russia fifty-sixty years ago. Strange words across the Duncan Phyfe table: *hunger; secret meetings; human rights; spies; betrayals; prison; escape*—interrupted by one of the grandchildren: "Commercial's on; any Coke left? Gee, you're missing a real hair-raiser." And then a granddaughter (Max proudly: "look at her, an American queen") drove them home on her way back to U.C.L.A. No incident—except that there had been no incidents.

The first few mornings she had taken with her the magnifying glass, but he would sit only on the benches, so she rested at the foot, where slatted bench shadows fell, and unless she turned her hearing aid down, other voices invaded.

Now on the days when the sun shone and she felt well enough, he took her on the tram to where the benches ranged in oblongs, some with tables for draughts or cards. Again the blanket on the sand in the striped shadows, but she no longer brought the magnifying glass. He played cards, and she lay in the sun and looked towards the waters; or they walked—two blocks down to the scaling hotel, two blocks back—past chili-hamburger stands, open-doored bars, Next to New and Perpetual Rummage Sale stores.

Once, out of the aimless walkers, slow and shuffling like themselves, someone ran unevenly towards them, embraced, kissed, wept: "dear friends, old friends." A friend of *hers*, not his: Mrs. Mays who had lived next door to them in Denver when the children were small.

Thirty years are compressed into a dozen sentences; and the present, not even in three. All is told: the children scattered; the husband dead; she lives in a room two blocks up from the sing hall—and points to the domed auditorium jutting before the pier. The leg? phlebitis; the heavy breathing? that, one does not ask. She, too, comes to the benches each day to sit. And tomorrow, tomorrow, are they going to the community sing? Of course he would have heard of it, everybody goes—the big doings they wait for all week. They have never been? She will come for them to dinner tomorrow and they will all go together.

So it is that she sits in the wind of the singing, among the thousand various faces of age.

She had turned off her hearing aid at once they came into the auditorium—as she would have wished to turn off sight.

One by one they streamed by and imprinted on her—and though the savage zest of their singing came voicelessly soft and distant, the faces still roared—the faces densened the air—chorded into

children-chants, mother-croons, singing of the chained
love serenades, Beethoven storms, mad Lucia's scream
drunken joy-songs, keens for the dead, work-singing

> *while from floor to balcony to dome a bare-footed sore-covered little girl threaded the sound-thronged tumult, danced her ecstasy of grimace to flutes that scratched at a cross-roads village wedding*

Yes, faces became sound, and the sound became faces; and faces and sound became weight—pushed, pressed

"Air"—her hands claw his.

"Whenever I enjoy myself. . . ." Then he saw the grey sweat on her face. "Here. Up. Help me, Mrs. Mays," and they support her out to where she can gulp the air in sob after sob.

"A doctor, we should get for her a doctor."

"Tch, it's nothing," says Ellen Mays, "I get it all the time. You've missed the tram; come to my place. Fix your hearing aid, honey . . . close . . . tea. My view. See, she *wants* to come. Steady now, that's how." Adding mysteriously: "Remember your advice, easy to keep your head above water, empty things float. Float."

The singing a fading march for them, tall woman with a swollen leg, weaving little man, and the swollen thinness they help between.

The stench in the hall: mildew? decay? "We sit and rest then climb My gorgeous view. We help each other and here we are."

The stench along into the slab of room. A wash stand for a sink, a box with oilcloth tacked around for a cupboard, a three-burner gas plate. Artificial flowers, colorless with dust. Everywhere pictures foaming: wedding, baby, party, vacation, graduation, family pictures. From the narrow couch under a slit of window, sure enough the view: lurching rooftops and a scallop of ocean heaving, preening, twitching under the moon.

"While the water heats. Excuse me . . . down the hall." Ellen Mays has gone.

"You'll live?" he asks mechanically, sat down to feel his fright; tried to pull her alongside.

She pushed him away. "For air," she said; stood clinging to the dresser. Then, in a terrible voice:

After a lifetime of room. Of many rooms.

Shhh.

You remember how she lived. Eight children. And now one room   like a coffin.

She pays rent!

Shrinking the life of her   into one room   like a coffin Rooms and rooms like this   I lie on the quilt and hear them talk

Please, Mrs. Orator-without-Breath.

Once you went for coffee   I walked   I saw   A Balzac[9]   a Chekhov to write it   Rummage   Alone   On scraps

Better old here than in the old country!

On scraps   Yet they sang like   like   Wondrous! *Humankind one has to believe*   So strong   for what?   To rot not grow?

Your poor lungs beg you. They sob between each word.

Singing.   Unused   the life in them.   She   in this poor room with her pictures   Max   You   The children   Everywhere unused the life   And who has meaning?   Century after century still all in us   not   to grow?

Coffins, rummage, plants: sick woman. Oh lay down. We will get for you the doctor.

"And when will it end. Oh, *the end.*" *That* nightmare thought, and this time she writhed, crumpled against him, seized his hand (for a moment again the weight, the soft distant roaring of humanity) and on the strangled-for breath, begged: "Man . . . we'll destroy ourselves?"

And looking for answer—in the helpless pity and fear for her (for *her*) that distorted his face—she understood the last months, and knew that she was dying.

9. Honoré de Balzac, French writer (1799–1850).

IV

"Let us go home," she said after several days.

"You are in training for a cross-country run? That is why you do not even walk across the room? Here, like a prescription Phil said, till you are stronger from the operation. You want to break doctor's orders?"

She saw the fiction was necessary to him, was silent; then: "At home I will get better. If the doctor here says?"

"And winter? And the visits to Lennie and to Clara? All right," for he saw the tears in her eyes, "I will write Phil, and talk to the doctor."

Days passed. He reported nothing. Jeannie came and took her out for air, past the boarded concessions, the hooded and tented amusement rides, to the end of the pier. They watched the spent waves feeding the new, the gulls in the clouded sky; even up where they sat, the wind-blown sand stung.

She did not ask to go down the crooked steps to the sea.

Back in her bed, while he was gone to the store, she said: "Jeannie, this doctor, he is not one I can ask questions. Ask him for me, can I go home?"

Jeannie looked at her, said quickly: "Of course, poor Granny. You want your own things around you, don't you? I'll call him tonight. . . . Look, I've something to show you," and from her purse unwrapped a large cookie, intricately shaped like a little girl. "Look at the curls—can you hear me well, Granny?—and the darling eyelashes. I just came from a house where they were baking them."

"The dimples, there in the knees," she marvelled, holding it to the better light, turning, studying, "like art. Each singly they cut, or a mold?"

"Singly," said Jeannie, "and if it is a child only the mother can make them. Oh Granny, it's the likeness of a real little girl who died yesterday—Rosita. She was three years old. *Pan del Muerto*, the Bread of the Dead. It was the custom in the part of Mexico they came from."

Still she turned and inspected. "Look, the hollow in the throat, the little cross necklace. . . . I think for the mother it is a good thing to be busy with such bread. You know the family?"

Jeannie nodded. "On my rounds. I nursed. . . . Oh Granny, it is like a party; they play songs she liked to dance to. The coffin is lined with pink velvet and she wears a white dress. There are candles. . . ."

"In the house?" Surprised, "They keep her in the house?"

"Yes," said Jeannie, "and it *is* against the health law. The father said it will be sad to bury her in this country; in Oaxaca they have a feast night with candles each year; everyone picnics on the graves of those they loved until dawn."

"Yes, Jeannie, the living must comfort themselves." And closed her eyes.

"You want to sleep, Granny?"

"Yes, tired from the pleasure of you. I may keep the Rosita? There stand it, on the dresser, where I can see; something of my own around me."

In the kitchenette, helping her grandfather unpack the groceries, Jeannie said in her light voice:

"I'm resigning my job, Grandaddy."

"Ah, the lucky young man. Which one is he?"

"Too late. You're spoken for." She made a pyramid of cans, unstacked, and built again.

"Something is wrong with the job?"

"With me. I can't be"—she searched for the word—"What they call professional enough. I let myself feel things. And tomorrow I have to report a family. . . ." The cans clicked again. "It's not that, either. I just don't know what I want to do, maybe go back to school, maybe go to art school. I thought if you went to San Francisco I'd come along and talk it over with Momma and Daddy. But I don't see how you can go. She wants to go home. She asked me to ask the doctor."

The doctor told her himself. "Next week you may travel, when you are a little stronger." But next week there was the fever of an infection, and by the time that was over, she could not leave the bed—a rented hospital bed that stood beside the double bed he slept in alone now.

Outwardly the days repeated themselves. Every other afternoon and evening he went out to his newfound cronies, to talk and play cards. Twice a week, Mrs. Mays came. And the rest of the time, Jeannie was there.

By the sickbed stood Jeannie's FM radio. Often into the room the shapes of music came. She would lie curled on her side, her knees drawn up, intense in listening (Jeannie sketched her so, coiled, convoluted like an ear), then thresh her hand out and abruptly snap the radio mute—still to lie in her attitude of listening, concealing tears.

Once Jeannie brought in a young Marine to visit, a friend from high-school days she had found wandering near the empty pier. Because Jeannie asked him to, gravely, without self-consciousness, he sat himself cross-legged on the floor and performed for them a dance of his native Samoa.

Long after they left, a tiny thrumming sound could be heard where, in her bed, she strove to repeat the beckon, flight, surrender of his hands, the fluttering footbeats, and his low plaintive calls.

Hannah and Phil sent flowers. To deepen her pleasure, he placed one in her hair. "Like a girl," he said, and brought the hand mirror so she could see. She looked at the pulsing red flower, the yellow skull face; a desolate, excited laugh shuddered from her, and she pushed the mirror away—but let the flower burn.

The week Lennie and Helen came, the fever returned. With it the excited laugh, and incessant words. She, who in her life had spoken but seldom and then only when necessary (never having learned the easy, social uses of words), now in dying, spoke incessantly.

In a half-whisper: "Like Lisa she is, your Jeannie. Have I told you of Lisa who taught me to read? Of the highborn she was, but noble in herself. I was sixteen; they beat me; my father beat me so I would not go to her. It was forbidden, she was a Tolstoyan.[1] At night, past dogs that howled, terrible dogs, my son, in the snows of winter to the road, I to ride in her carriage like a lady, to books. To her, life was holy, knowledge was holy, and she taught me to read. They hung her. Everything that happens one must try to understand why. She killed one who betrayed many. Because of betrayal, betrayed all she lived and believed. In one minute she killed, before my eyes (there is so much blood in a human being, my son), in prison with me. All that happens, one must try to understand.

"The name?" Her lips would work. "The name that was their pole star; the doors of the death houses fixed to open on it; I read of it my year of penal servitude. Thuban!" very excited, "Thuban, in ancient Egypt the pole star. Can you see, look out to see it, Jeannie, if it swings around *our* pole star that seems to *us* not to move.

"Yes, Jeannie, at your age my mother and grandmother had already buried children . . . yes, Jeannie, it is more than oceans between Olshana and you . . . yes, Jeannie, they danced, and for all the bodies they had they might as well be chickens, and indeed, they scratched and flapped their arms and hopped.

"And Andrei Yefimitch, who was twenty years had never known of it and never wanted to know, said as if he wanted to cry: but why my dear friend this malicious laughter?" Telling to herself half-memorized phrases from her few books. "Pain I answer with tears and cries, baseness with indignation, meanness with repulsion . . . for life may be hated or wearied of, but never despised."

Delirious: "Tell me, my neighbor, Mrs. Mays, the pictures never lived, but what of the flowers? Tell them who ask: no rabbis, no ministers, no priests, no speeches, no ceremonies: ah, false—let the living comfort themselves. Tell Sammy's boy, he who flies, tell him to go to

1. I.e., a follower of Leo Tolstoy (1828–1910), Russian novelist, social reformer, and teacher of nonviolence.

Stuttgart[2] and see where Davy has no grave. And what? . . . And what? where millions have no graves—save air."

In delirium or not, wanting the radio on; not seeming to listen, the words still jetting, wanting the music on. Once, silencing it abruptly as of old, she began to cry, unconcealed tears this time. "You have pain, Granny?" Jeannie asked.

"The music," she said, "still it is there and we do not hear; knocks, and our poor human ears too weak. What else, what else we do not hear?"

Once she knocked his hand aside as he gave her a pill, swept the bottles from her bedside table: "no pills, let me feel what I feel," and laughed as on his hands and knees he groped to pick them up.

Nighttimes her hand reached across the bed to hold his.

A constant retching began. Her breath was too faint for sustained speech now, but still the lips moved:

When no longer necessary   to injure others
Pick   pick pick   Blind chicken
As a human being   responsibility

"David!" imperious, "Basin!" and she would vomit, rinse her mouth, the wasted throat working to swallow, and begin the chant again.

She will be better off in the hospital now, the doctor said.

He sent the telegrams to the children, was packing her suitcase, when her hoarse voice startled. She had roused, was pulling herself to sitting.

"Where now?" she asked. "Where now do you drag me?"

"You do not even have to have a baby to go this time," he soothed, looking for the brush to pack. "Remember, after Davy you told me—worthy to have a baby for the pleasure of the ten-day rest in the hospital?"

"Where now? Not home yet?" Her voice mourned. "Where *is* my home?"

He rose to ease her back. "The doctor, the hospital," he started to explain, but deftly, like a snake, she had slithered out of bed and stood swaying, propped behind the night table.

"Coward," she hissed, "runner."

"You stand," he said senselessly.

"To take me there and run. Afraid of a little vomit."

2. City in Germany, figuring in World War II.

He reached her as she fell. She struggled against him, half slipped from his arms, pulled herself up again.

"Weakling," she taunted, "to leave me there and run. Betrayer. All your life you have run."

He sobbed, telling Jeannie. "A Marilyn Monroe to run for her virtue. Fifty-nine pounds she weighs, the doctor said, and she beats at me like a Dempsey.[3] Betrayer, she cries, and I running like a dog when she calls; day and night, running to her, her vomit, the bedpan. . . ."

"She needs you, Grandaddy," said Jeannie. "Isn't that what they call love? I'll see if she sleeps, and if she does, poor worn-out darling, we'll have a party, you and I; I brought us rum babas."

They did not move her. By her bed now stood the tall hooked pillar that held the solutions—blood and dextrose—to feed her veins. Jeannie moved down the hall to take over the sickroom, her face so radiant, her grandfather asked her once: "you are in love?" (Shameful the joy, the pure overwhelming joy from being with her grandmother; the peace, the serenity that breathed.) "My darling escape," she answered incoherently, "my darling Granny"—as if that explained.

Now one by one the children came, those that were able. Hannah, Paul, Sammy. Too late to ask: and what did you learn with your living, Mother, and what do we need to know?

Clara, the eldest, clenched:

Pay me back, Mother, pay me back for all you took from me. Those others you crowded into your heart. The hands I needed to be for you, the heaviness, the responsibility.

Is this she? Noises the dying make, the crablike hands crawling over the covers. The ethereal singing.

She hears that music, that singing from childhood; forgotten sound—not heard since, since. . . . And the hardness breaks like a cry: Where did we lose each other, first mother, singing mother?

Annulled: the quarrels, the gibing, the harshness between; the fall into silence and the withdrawal.

I do not know you, Mother. Mother, I never knew you.

Lennie, suffering not alone for her who was dying, but for that in her which never lived (for that which in him might never come to live).

3. Jack Dempsey, world heavyweight champion boxer in the 1920's.

From him too, unspoken words: *good-bye Mother who taught me to mother myself.*

Not Vivi, who must stay with her children; not Davy, but he is already here, having to die again with *her* this time, for the living take their dead with them when they die.

Light she grew, like a bird, and, like a bird, sound bubbled in her throat while the body fluttered in agony. Night and day, asleep or awake (though indeed there was no difference now) the songs and the phrases leaping.

And he, who had once dreaded a long dying (from fear of himself, from horror of the dwindling money) now desired her quick death profoundly, for *her* sake. He no longer went out, except when Jeannie forced him; no longer laughed, except when, in the bright kitchenette, Jeannie coaxed his laughter (and she, who seemed to hear nothing else, would laugh too, conspiratorial wisps of laughter).

Light, like a bird, the fluttering body, the little claw hands, the beaked shadow on her face; and the throat, bubbling, straining.

He tried not to listen, as he tried not to look on the face in which only the forehead remained familiar, but trapped with her the long nights in that little room, the sounds worked themselves into his consciousness, with their punctuation of death swallows, whimpers, gurglings.

Even in reality (swallow) *life's lack of it*
Slaveships   deathtrains   clubs   eeenough
The bell   summon what enables

78,000[4] *in one minute* (whisper of a scream) *78,000 human beings we'll destroy ourselves?*

"Aah, Mrs. Miserable," he said, as if she could hear, "all your life working, and now in bed you lie, servants to tend, you do not even need to call to be tended, and still you work. Such hard work it is to die? Such hard work?"

The body threshed, her hand clung in his. A melody, ghost-thin, hovered on her lips, and like a guilty ghost, the vision of her bent in listening to it, silencing the record instantly he was near. Now, heedless of his presence, she floated the melody on and on.

"Hid it from me," he complained, "how many times you listened to remember it so?" And tried to think when she had first played it, or first begun to silence her few records when he came near—but could reconstruct nothing. There was only this room with its tall hooked pillar and its swarm of sounds.

4. The number killed in Hiroshima by the first atomic bomb.

No man one except through others
Strong with the not yet in the now
Dogma dead war dead one country

"It helps, Mrs. Philosopher, words from books? It helps?" And it seemed to him that for seventy years she had hidden a tape recorder, infinitely microscopic, within her, that it had coiled infinite mile on mile, trapping every song, every melody, every word read, heard, and spoken—and that maliciously she was playing back only what said nothing of him, of the children, of their intimate life together.

"Left us indeed, Mrs. Babbler," he reproached, "you who called others babbler and cunningly saved your words. A lifetime you tended and loved, and now not a word of us, for us. Left us indeed? Left me."

And he took out his solitaire deck, shuffled the cards loudly, slapped them down.

Lift high banner of reason (tatter of an orator's voice) *justice freedom light*
Humankind life worthy capacities
Seeks (blur of shudder) *belong human being*

"Words, words," he accused, "and what human beings did *you* seek around you, Mrs. Live Alone, and what mankind think worthy?"

Though even as he spoke, he remembered she had not always been isolated, had not always to be alone (as he knew there had been a voice before this gossamer one; before the hoarse voice that broke from silence to lash, make incidents, shame him—a girl's voice of eloquence that spoke their holiest dreams). But again he could reconstruct, image, nothing of what had been before, or when, or how, it had changed.

Ace, queen, jack. The pillar shadow fell, so, in two tracks; in the mirror depths glistened a moonlike blob, the empty solution bottle. And it worked in him: *of reason and justice and freedom . . . Dogma dead:* he remembered the full quotation, laughed bitterly. "Hah, good you do not know what you say; good Victor Hugo[5] died and did not see it, his twentieth century."

Deuce, ten, five. Dauntlessly she began a song of their youth of belief:

These things shall be,[6] a loftier race
than e'er the world hath known shall rise
with flame of freedom in their souls
and light of knowledge in their eyes

5. Victor Hugo (1802–1885), French writer and champion of liberty; he prophesied the triumph of peace and liberty in the twentieth century.

6. Century-old socialist song, for a United Nations hymn. The first line is a translation of the French Revolutionary slogan "Ça ira."

King, four, jack. "In the twentieth century, hah!"

They shall be gentle, brave and strong
to spill no drop of blood, but dare
all . . .

on earth and fire and sea and air

"To spill no drop of blood, hah! So, cadaver, and you too, cadaver Hugo, 'in the twentieth century ignorance will be dead, dogma will be dead, war will be dead, and for all mankind one country—of fulfilment?' Hah!"

And every life (long strangling cough) *shall be a song*

The cards fell from his fingers. Without warning, the bereavement and betrayal he had sheltered—compounded through the years—hidden even from himself—revealed itself,
uncoiled,
released,
sprung

and with it the monstrous shapes of what had actually happened in the century.

A ravening hunger or thirst seized him. He groped into the kitchenette, switched on all three lights, piled a tray—"you have finished your night snack, Mrs. Cadaver, now I will have mine." And he was shocked at the tears that splashed on the tray.

"Salt tears. For free. I forgot to shake on salt?"

Whispered: "Lost, how much I lost."

Escaped to the grandchildren whose childhoods were childish, who had never hungered, who lived unravaged by disease in warm houses of many rooms, had all the school for which they cared, could walk on any street, stood a head taller than their grandparents, towered above—beautiful skins, straight backs, clear straightforward eyes. "Yes, you in Olshana," he said to the town of sixty years ago, "they would look nobility to you."

And was this not the dream then, come true in ways undreamed? he asked.

And are there no other children in the world? he answered, as if in her harsh voice.

And the flame of freedom, the light of knowledge?

And the drop, to spill no drop of blood?

And he thought that at six Jeannie would get up and it would be his turn to go to her room and sleep, that he could press the buzzer and she would come now; that in the afternoon Ellen Mays was coming, and this time they would play cards and he could marvel at how rouge can stand half an inch on the cheek; that in the evening the doctor would come, and he could beg him to be merciful, to stop the feeding solutions, to let her die.

To let her die, and with her their youth of belief out of which her bright, betrayed words foamed; stained words, that on her working lips came stainless.

Hours yet before Jeannie's turn. He could press the buzzer and wake her to come now; he could take a pill, and with it sleep; he could pour more brandy into his milk glass, though what he had poured was not yet touched.

Instead he went back, checked her pulse, gently tended with his knotty fingers as Jeannie had taught.

She was whimpering; her hand crawled across the covers for his. Compassionately he enfolded it, and with his free hand gathered up the cards again. Still was there thirst or hunger ravening in him.

That world of their youth—dark, ignorant, terrible with hate and disease—how was it that living in it, in the midst of corruption, filth, treachery, degradation, they had not mistrusted man nor themselves; had believed so beautifully, so . . . falsely?

"Aaah, children," he said out loud, "how we believed, how we belonged." And he yearned to package for each of the children, the grandchildren, for everyone, *that joyous certainty, that sense of mattering, of moving and being moved, of being one and indivisible with the great of the past, with all that freed, ennobled.* Package it, stand on corners, in front of stadiums and on crowded beaches, knock on doors, give it as a fabled gift.

"And why not in cereal boxes, in soap packages?" he mocked himself. "Aah. You have taken my senses, cadaver."

Words foamed, died unsounded. Her body writhed; she made kissing motions with her mouth. (Her lips moving as she read, poring over the Book of the Martyrs, the magnifying glass superimposed over the heavy eyeglasses.) *Still she believed?* "Eva!" he whispered. "Still you believed? You lived by it? These Things Shall Be?"

"One pound soup meat," she answered distinctly, "one soup bone."

"My ears heard you. Ellen Mays was witness: 'Humankind . . . one has to believe.' " Imploringly: "Eva!"

"Bread, day-old." She was mumbling. "Please, in a wooden box . . . for kindling. The thread, hah, the thread breaks. Cheap thread"—and a gurgling, enormously loud, began in her throat.

"I ask for stone; she gives me bread—day-old." He pulled his hand away, shouted: "Who wanted questions? Everything you have to wake?" Then dully, "Ah, let me help you turn, poor creature."

Words jumbled, cleared. In a voice of crowded terror:

"Paul, Sammy, don't fight.

"Hannah, have I ten hands?

"How can I give it, Clara, how can I give it if I don't have?"

"You lie," he said sturdily, "there was joy too." Bitterly: "Ah how cheap you speak of us at the last."

As if to rebuke him, as if her voice had no relationship with her flailing body, she sang clearly, beautifully, a school song the children had taught her when they were little; begged:

"Not look   my hair   when they cut. . . ."

(The crown of braids shorn.) And instantly he left the mute old woman poring over the Book of the Martyrs; went past the mother treadling at the sewing machine, singing with the children; past the girl in her wrinkled prison dress, hiding her hair with scarred hands, lifting to him her awkward, shamed, imploring eyes of love; and took her in his arms, dear, personal, fleshed, in all the heavy passion he had loved to rouse from her.

"Eva!"

Her little claw hand beat the covers. How much, how much can a man stand? He took up the cards, put them down, circled the beds, walked to the dresser, opened, shut drawers, brushed his hair, moved his hand bit by bit over the mirror to see what of the reflection he could blot out with each move, and felt that at any moment he would die of what was endurable. Went to press the buzzer to wake Jeannie, looked down, saw on Jeannie's sketch pad the hospital bed, with *her;* the double bed alongside, with him; the tall pillar feeding into her veins, and their hands, his and hers, clasped, feeding each other. And as if he had been instructed he went to his bed, lay down, holding the sketch (as if it could shield against the monstrous shapes of loss, of betrayal, of death) and with his free hand took hers back into his.

So Jeannie found them in the morning.

That last day the agony was perpetual. Time after time it lifted her almost off the bed, so they had to fight to hold her down. He could not endure and left the room; wept as if there never would be tears enough.

Jeannie came to comfort him. In her light voice she said: Grandaddy, Grandaddy don't cry. She is not there, she promised me. On the last day, she said she would go back to when she first heard music, a little girl on the road of the village where she was born. She promised me. It is a wedding and they dance, while the flutes so joyous and vibrant tremble in the air. Leave her there, Grandaddy, it is all right. She promised me. Come back, come back and help her poor body to die.

For my mother, my father,
and
Two of that generation
Seevya and Genya
Infinite, dauntless, incorruptible

Death deepens the wonder

---

1. What is contributed to the effect and meaning by the use of stream-of-consciousness passages?
2. Why doesn't the approaching death of the wife put a stop to the quarreling? How does the nature of the quarreling change as the story progresses?
3. Of what importance are the revolutionary sentiments of the dying woman in the whole context of the story? What has the fate of the revolutionary Lisa to do with the meaning of present events?
4. Are there any clear notes of optimism? From what do they come?
5. Is Jeannie's interpretation of the situation adequate to the riddle it presents? In the last paragraph she says "it is all right." Is it?
6. What, in the view of the dying woman, is the worst thing about death?

Grace Paley

Paley (1922–) was born in New York City. She attended Hunter College and later was a teacher at Syracuse University. Presently she teaches at Sarah Lawrence College and gives frequent readings from her work. During the Vietnam War she was active in the antiwar movement but refuses to blame such commitments for her relatively small production. Though few, her stories have been admired for their stylistic liveliness and for their fusion of sardonic observation with spare, expressive form. Her books of stories are The Little Disturbances of Man *(1959),* Enormous Changes at the Last Minute *(1974), and* Later the Same Day *(1985).*

The Used-Boy Raisers

There were two husbands disappointed by eggs.

I don't like them that way either, I said. Make your own eggs. They sighed in unison. One man was livid; one was pallid.

There isn't a drink around here, is there? asked Livid.

Never find one here, said Pallid. Don't look; driest damn house. Pallid pushed the eggs away, pain and disgust his escutcheon.

Livid said, Now really, isn't there a drink? Beer? he hoped.

Nothing, said Pallid, who'd been through the pantries, closets, and refrigerators looking for a white shirt.

You're damn right, I said. I buttoned the high button of my powder-blue duster. I reached under the kitchen table for a brown paper bag full of an embroidery which asked God to Bless Our Home.

I was completing this motto for the protection of my sons, who were also Livid's. It is true that some months earlier, from a far place—the British plains in Africa—he had written hospitably to Pallid: I do think they're fine boys, you understand. I love them too, but Faith is their mother and now Faith is your wife. I'm so much away. If you want to think of them as yours, old man, go ahead.

Why, thank you, Pallid had replied, airmail, overwhelmed. Then he implored the boys, when not in use, to play in their own room. He made all efforts to be kind.

Now as we talked of time past and upon us, I pierced the ranch house that nestles in the shade of a cloud and a Norway maple, just under the golden script.

Ha-ha, said Livid, dripping coffee on his pajama pants, you'll never guess whom I met up with, Faith.

Who? I asked.

Saw your old boy friend Clifford at the Green Coq. He looks well. One thing must be said, he addressed Pallid, she takes good care of her men.

True, said Pallid.

How is he? I asked coolly. What's he doing? I haven't seen him in two years.

Oh, you'll never guess. He's marrying. A darling girl. She was with him. Little tootsies, little round bottom, little tummy—she must be twenty-two, but she looks seventeen. One long yellow braid down her back. A darling girl. Stubby nose, fat little underlip. Her eyes put on in pencil. Shoulders down like a dancer . . . slender neck. Oh, darling, darling.

You certainly observed her, said Pallid.

I have a functioning retina, said Livid. Then he went on. Better watch out, Faith. You'd be surprised, the dear little chicks are hatching out all over the place. All the sunny schoolgirls rolling their big black eyes. I hope you're really settled this time. To me, whatever is under the dam is in another county; however, in my life you remain an important person historically, he said. And that's why I feel justified in warning you. I must warn you. Watch out, sweetheart! he said, leaning forward to whisper harshly and give me a terrible bellyache.

What's all this about? asked Pallid innocently. In the first place, she's settled . . . and then she's still an attractive woman. Look at her.

Oh yes, said Livid, looking. An attractive woman. Magnificent, sometimes.

We were silent for several seconds in honor of that generous remark.

Then Livid said, Yes, magnificent, but I just wanted to warn you, Faith.

He pushed his eggs aside finally and remembered Clifford. A mystery wrapped in an enigma . . . I wonder why he wants to marry.

I don't know, it just ties a man down, I said.

And yet, said Pallid seriously, what would I be without marriage? In luminous recollection—a gay dog, he replied.

At this moment, the boys entered: Richard the horse thief and Tonto the crack shot.

Daddy! they shouted. They touched Livid, tickled him, unbuttoned his pajama top, whistled at the several gray hairs coloring his chest. They tweaked his ear and rubbed his beard the wrong way.

Well, well, he cautioned. How are you boys, have you been well? You look fine. Sturdy. How are your grades? he inquired. He dreamed that they were just up from Eton[1] for the holidays.

I don't go to school, said Tonto. I go to the park.

I'd like to hear the child read, said Livid.

Me. I can read, Daddy, said Richard. I have a book with a hundred pages.

Well, well, said Livid. Get it.

I kindled a fresh pot of coffee. I scrubbed cups and harassed Pallid into opening a sticky jar of damson-plum jam. Very shortly, what could be read, had been, and Livid, knotting the tie strings of his pants vigorously, approached me at the stove. Faith, he admonished, that boy can't read a tinker's damn. Seven years old.

Eight years old, I said.

Yes, said Pallid, who had just remembered the soap cabinet and was rummaging in it for a pint. If they were my sons in actuality as they are in everyday life, I would send them to one of the good parochial schools in the neighborhood where reading is taught. Reading. St. Bartholomew's, St. Bernard's, St. Joseph's.

Livid became deep purple and gasped. Over my dead body, *Merde*,[2] he said in deference to the children. I've said, yes, you may think of the boys as your own, but if I ever hear they've come within an inch of that church, I'll run you through, you bastard. I was fourteen years old when in my own good sense I walked out of that grotto of deception, head up. You sonofabitch, I don't give a damn how *au courant*[3] it is these days, how gracious to be seen under a dome on Sunday. . . . Shit! Hypocrisy. Corruption. Cave dwellers. Idiots. Morons.

Recalling childhood and home, poor Livid writhed in his seat. Pallid listened, head to one side, his brows gathering the onsets of grief.

You know, he said slowly, we iconoclasts . . . we free-thinkers . . . we latter-day masons . . . we idealists . . . we dreamers . . . we are never far from our nervous old mother, the Church. She is never far from us.

Wherever we are, we can hear, no matter how faint, her hourly bells, tolling the countryside, reverberating in the cities, bringing to our civilized minds the passionate deed of Mary. Every hour on the hour we are startled with remembrance of what was done for us. FOR US.

Livid muttered in great pain. Those bastards, oh oh oh, those contemptible, goddamnable bastards. Do we have to do the nine-

1. Eton College, the "toniest" of England's public (i.e., private) schools. 2. Shit. 3. Up to date.

teenth century all over again? All right, he bellowed, facing us all, I'm ready. That Newman![4]

He turned to me for approval.

You know, I said, this subject has never especially interested me. It's your little dish of lava.

Pallid spoke softly, staring past the arched purple windows of his soul. I myself, although I lost God a long time ago, have never lost faith.

What the hell are you talking about, you moron? roared Livid. I have never lost my love for the wisdom of the Church of the World. When I go to sleep at night, I inadvertently pray. I also do so when I rise. It is not to God, it is to that unifying memory out of childhood. The first words I ever wrote were: What are the sacraments? Faith, can you ever forget your old grandfather intoning Kaddish?[5] It will sound in your ears forever.

Are you kidding? I was furious to be drawn into their conflict. Kaddish? What do I know about Kaddish. Who's dead? You know my opinions perfectly well. I believe in the Diaspora,[6] not only as a fact but a tenet. I'm against Israel on technical grounds. I'm very disappointed that they decided to become a nation in my lifetime. I believe in the Diaspora. After all, they *are* the chosen people. Don't laugh. They really are. But once they're huddled in one little corner of a desert, they're like anyone else: Frenchies, Italians, temporal nationalities. Jews have one hope only—to remain a remnant in the basement of world affairs—no, I mean something else—a splinter in the toe of civilizations, a victim to aggravate the conscience.

Livid and Pallid were astonished at my outburst, since I rarely express my opinion on any serious matter but only live out my destiny, which is to be, until my expiration date, laughingly the servant of man.

I continued. I hear they don't even look like Jews any more. A bunch of dirt farmers with no time to read.

They're your own people, Pallid accused, dilating in the nostril, clenching his jaw. And they're under the severest attack. This is not the time to revile them.

I had resumed my embroidery. I sighed. My needle was now deep in the clouds which were pearl gray and late afternoon. I am only trying to say that they aren't meant for geographies but for history. They are not supposed to take up space but to continue in time.

They looked at me with such grief that I decided to consider all sides of the matter. I said, Christ probably had all that trouble—now

4. John Henry Cardinal Newman (1801–1890), an English convert to Catholicism who became an influential Catholic writer. 5. Jewish prayer, recited at regular services and in mourning for relatives. 6. Dispersion of Jews from their homeland.

that you mention it—because he knew he was going to gain the whole world but he forgot Jerusalem.

When you married us, said Pallid, and accused me, didn't you forget Jerusalem?

I never forget a thing, I said. Anyway, guess what, I just read somewhere that England is bankrupt. The country is wadded with installment paper.[7]

Livid's hand trembled as he offered Pallid a light. Nonsense, he said. That's not true. Nonsense. The great British Island is the tight little fist of the punching arm of the Commonwealth.

What's true is true, I said, smiling.

Well, I said, since no one stirred, do you think you'll ever get to work today. Either of you?

Oh, my dear, I haven't even seen you and the boys in over a year. It's quite pleasant and cozy here this morning, said Livid.

Yes, isn't it? said Pallid, the surprised host. Besides, it's Saturday.

How do you find the boys? I asked Livid, the progenitor.

American, American, rowdy, uncontrolled. But you look well, Faith. Plumper, but womanly and well.

Very well, said Pallid, pleased.

But the boys, Faith. Shouldn't they be started on something? Just lining up little plastic cowboys. It's silly, really.

They're so young, apologized Pallid, the used-boy raiser.

You'd both better go to work, I suggested, knotting the pearl-gray late-afternoon thread. Please put the dishes in the sink first. Please. I'm sorry about the eggs.

Livid yawned, stretched, peeked at the clock, sighed. Saturday or no, alas, my time is not my own. I've got an appointment downtown in about forty-five minutes, he said.

I do too, said Pallid. I'll join you on the subway.

I'm taking a cab, said Livid.

I'll split it with you, said Pallid.

They left for the bathroom, where they shared things nicely—shaving equipment, washstand, shower, and so forth.

I made the beds and put the aluminum cot away. Livid would find a hotel room by nightfall. I did the dishes and organized the greedy day; dinosaurs in the morning, park in the afternoon, peanut butter in between, and at the end of it all, to reward us for a week of beans endured, a noble rib roast with little onions, dumplings, and pink applesauce.

7. Unpaid credit balances.

Faith, I'm going now, Livid called from the hall. I put my shopping list aside and went to collect the boys, who were wandering among the rooms looking for Robin Hood. Go say goodbye to your father, I whispered.

Which one? they asked.

The real father, I said. Richard ran to Livid. They shook hands manfully. Pallid embraced Tonto and was kissed eleven times for his affection.

Goodbye now, Faith, said Livid. Call me if you want anything at all. Anything at all, my dear. Warmly with sweet propriety he kissed my cheek. Ascendant, Pallid kissed me with considerable business behind the ear.

Goodbye, I said to them.

I must admit that they were at last clean and neat, rather attractive, shiny men in their thirties, with the grand affairs of the day ahead of them. Dark night, the search for pleasure and oblivion were well ahead. Goodbye, I said, have a nice day. Goodbye, they said once more, and set off in pride on paths which are not my concern.

---

1. Is Faith better matched with her present husband than with her former one? If not, what does this seem to say about the source of her marital problems?
2. Is either man the "real" father of the boys? What does the story say about the role of fathers or the nature of fatherhood?
3. What is the narrator's fundamental attitude toward both husbands?
4. Do the boys play any decisive part in this encounter between their parents?
5. If you conclude that the story is, in whole or part, satiric, what is being satirized?
6. What does the story say about the forces that shape personality and destiny?

Jayne Anne Phillips

Phillips (1952–) was born in Buckhannon, West Virginia, and educated at West Virginia University and the University of Iowa. Some of her stories and short prose pieces were collected in Sweethearts *(1976) and* Counting *(1978), published by small presses. Her first full-scale collection was* Black Tickets *(1979); her novel* Machine Dreams *was published in 1984.*

Souvenir

Kate always sent her mother a card on Valentine's Day. She timed the mails from wherever she was so that the cards arrived on February 14th. Her parents had celebrated the day in some small fashion, and since her father's death six years before, Kate made a gesture of compensatory remembrance. At first, she made the cards herself: collage and pressed grass on construction paper sewn in fabric. Now she settled for art reproductions, glossy cards with blank insides. Kate wrote in them with colored inks, "You have always been my Valentine," or simply "Hey, take care of yourself." She might enclose a present as well, something small enough to fit into an envelope; a sachet, a perfumed soap, a funny tintype of a prune-faced man in a bowler hat.

This time, she forgot. Despite the garish displays of paper cupids and heart-shaped boxes in drugstore windows, she let the day nearly approach before remembering. It was too late to send anything in the mail. She called her mother long-distance at night when the rates were low.

"Mom? How are you?"

"It's you! How are *you?*" Her mother's voice grew suddenly brighter; Kate recognized a tone reserved for welcome company. Sometimes it took a while to warm up.

"I'm fine," answered Kate. "What have you been doing?"

"Well, actually I was trying to sleep."

"Sleep? You should be out setting the old hometown on fire."

"The old hometown can burn up without me tonight."

"Really? What's going on?"

"I'm running in-service training sessions for the primary teachers." Kate's mother was a school superintendent. "They're driving me batty. You'd think their brains were rubber."

"They are," Kate said. "Or you wouldn't have to train them. Think of them as a salvation, they create a need for your job."

"Some salvation. Besides, your logic is ridiculous. Just because someone needs training doesn't mean they're stupid."

"I'm just kidding. But *I'm* stupid. I forgot to send you a Valentine's card."

"You did? That's bad. I'm trained to receive one. They bring me luck."

"You're receiving a phone call instead," Kate said. "Won't that do?"

"Of course," said her mother, "but this is costing you money. Tell me quick, how are you?"

"Oh, you know. Doctoral pursuits. Doing my student trip, grooving with the professors."

"The professors? You'd better watch yourself."

"It's a joke, Mom, a joke. But what about you? Any men on the horizon?"

"No, not really. A married salesman or two asking me to dinner when they come through the office. Thank heavens I never let those things get started."

"You should do what you want to," Kate said.

"Sure," said her mother. "And where would I be then?"

"I don't know. Maybe Venezuela."

"They don't even have plumbing in Venezuela."

"Yes, but their sunsets are perfect, and the villages are full of dark passionate men in blousy shirts."

"That's your department, not mine."

"Ha," Kate said, "I wish it were my department. Sounds a lot more exciting than teaching undergraduates."

Her mother laughed. "Be careful," she said. "You'll get what you want. End up sweeping a dirt floor with a squawling baby around your neck."

"A dark baby," Kate said, "to stir up the family blood."

"Nothing would surprise me," her mother said as the line went fuzzy. Her voice was submerged in static, then surfaced. "Listen," she was saying. "Write to me. You seem so far away."

They hung up and Kate sat watching the windows of the neighboring house. The curtains were transparent and flowered and none of them matched. Silhouettes of the window frames spread across them like single dark bars. Her mother's curtains were all the same, white cotton hemmed with a ruffle, tiebacks blousing the cloth into identical shapes. From the street it looked as if the house was always in order.

Kate made a cup of strong Chinese tea, turned the lights off, and sat holding the warm cup in the dark. Her mother kept no real tea in the house, just packets of instant diabetic mixture which tasted of chemical sweetener and had a bitter aftertaste. The packets sat on the shelf next to her mother's miniature scales. The scales were white. Kate saw clearly the face of the metal dial on the front, its markings and trembling needle. Her mother weighed portions of food for meals: frozen broccoli, slices of plastic-wrapped Kraft cheese, careful chunks of roast beef. A dog-eared copy of *The Diabetic Diet* had remained propped against the salt shaker for the last two years.

Kate rubbed her forehead. Often at night she had headaches. Sometimes she wondered if there were an agent in her body, a secret in her blood making ready to work against her.

The phone blared repeatedly, careening into her sleep. Kate scrambled out of bed, naked and cold, stumbling, before she recognized the striped wallpaper of her bedroom and realized the phone was right there on the bedside table, as always. She picked up the receiver.

"Kate?" said her brother's voice. "It's Robert. Mom is in the hospital. They don't know what's wrong but she's in for tests."

"Tests? What's happened? I just talked to her last night."

"I'm not sure. She called the neighbors and they took her to the emergency room around dawn." Robert's voice still had that slight twang Kate knew was disappearing from her own. He would be calling from his insurance office, nine o'clock their time, in his thick glasses and wide, perfectly knotted tie. He was a member of the million-dollar club[1] and his picture, tiny, the size of a postage stamp, appeared in the Mutual of Omaha magazine. His voice seemed small too over the distance. Kate felt heavy and dull. She would never make much money, and recently she had begun wearing make-up again, waking in smeared mascara as she had in high school.

"Is Mom all right?" she managed now. "How serious is it?"

"They're not sure," Robert said. "Her doctor thinks it could have been any of several things, but they're doing X rays."

"Her doctor *thinks*? Doesn't he know? Get her to someone else. There aren't any doctors in that one-horse town."

"I don't know about that," Robert said defensively. "Anyway, I can't force her. You know how she is about money."

"Money? She could have a stroke and drop dead while her doctor wonders what's wrong."

"Doesn't matter. You know you can't tell her what to do."

1. I.e., has been honored by his employees for selling more than a million dollars worth of insurance.

"Could I call her somehow?"

"No, not yet. And don't get her all worried. She's been scared enough as it is. I'll tell her what you said about getting another opinion, and I'll call you back in a few hours when I have some news. Meanwhile, she's all right, do you hear?"

The line went dead with a click and Kate walked to the bathroom to wash her face. She splashed her eyes and felt guilty about the Valentine's card. Slogans danced in her head like reprimands. *For a Special One. Dearest Mother. My Best Friend.* Despite Robert, after breakfast she would call the hospital.

She sat a long time with her coffee, waiting for minutes to pass, considering how many meals she and her mother ate alone. Similar times of day, hundreds of miles apart. Women by themselves. The last person Kate had eaten breakfast with had been someone she'd met in a bar. He was passing through town. He liked his fried eggs gelatinized in the center, only slightly runny, and Kate had studiously looked away as he ate. The night before he'd looked down from above her as he finished and she still moved under him. "You're still wanting," he'd said. "That's nice." Mornings now, Kate saw her own face in the mirror and was glad she'd forgotten his name. When she looked at her reflection from the side, she saw a faint etching of lines beside her mouth. She hadn't slept with anyone for five weeks, and the skin beneath her eyes had taken on a creamy darkness.

She reached for the phone but drew back. It seemed bad luck to ask for news, to push toward whatever was coming as though she had no respect for it.

Standing in the kitchen last summer, her mother had stirred gravy and argued with her.

"I'm thinking of your own good, not mine," she'd said. "Thinking of what you put yourself through. And how can you feel right about it? You were born here. I don't care what you say." Her voice broke and she looked, perplexed, at the broth in the pan.

"But, hypothetically," Kate continued, her own voice unaccountably shaking, "if I'm willing to endure whatever I have to, do you have a right to object? You're my mother. You're supposed to defend my choices."

"You'll have enough trouble without choosing more for yourself. Using birth control that'll ruin your insides, moving from one place to another. I can't defend your choices. I can't even defend myself against you." She wiped her eyes on a napkin.

"Why do you have to make me feel so guilty?" Kate said, fighting tears of frustration. "I'm not attacking you."

"You're not? Then who are you talking to?"

"Oh Mom, give me a break."

"I've tried to give you more than that," her mother said. "I know what your choices are saying to me." She set the steaming gravy off the stove. "You may feel differently later on. It's just a shame I won't be around to see it."

"Oh? Where will you be?"

"Floating around on a fleecy cloud."

Kate got up to set the table before she realized her mother had already done it.

The days went by. They'd gone shopping before Kate left. Standing at the cash register in an antique shop on Main Street, they bought each other pewter candle holders. "A souvenir," her mother said. "A reminder to always be nice to yourself. If you live alone you should eat by candlelight."

"Listen," Kate said, "I eat in a heart-shaped tub with bubbles to my chin. I sleep on satin sheets and my mattress has a built-in massage engine. My overnight guests are impressed. You don't have to tell me about solitary pleasures."

They laughed and touched hands.

"Well," her mother said. "If you like yourself, I must have done something right."

Robert didn't phone until evening. His voice was fatigued and thin. "I've moved her to the university hospital," he said. "They can't deal with it at home."

Kate waited, saying nothing. She concentrated on the toes of her shoes. They needed shining. *You never take care of anything*, her mother would say.

"She has a tumor in her head." He said it firmly, as though Kate might challenge him.

"I'll take a plane tomorrow morning," Kate answered, "I'll be there by noon."

Robert exhaled. "Look," he said, "don't even come back here unless you can keep your mouth shut and do it my way."

"Get to the point."

"The point is they believe she has a malignancy and we're not going to tell her. I almost didn't tell you." His voice faltered. "They're going to operate but if they find what they're expecting, they don't think they can stop it."

For a moment there was no sound except an oceanic vibration of distance on the wire. Even that sound grew still. Robert breathed. Kate could almost see him, in a booth at the hospital, staring straight ahead at the plastic instructions screwed to the narrow rectangular body of the telephone. It seemed to her that she was hurtling toward him.

"I'll do it your way," she said.

The hospital cafeteria was a large room full of orange Formica tables. Its southern wall was glass. Across the highway, Kate saw a small park modestly dotted with amusement rides and bordered by a narrow band of river. How odd, to build a children's park across from a medical center. The sight was pleasant in a cruel way. The rolling lawn of the little park was perfectly, relentlessly green.

Robert sat down. Their mother was to have surgery in two days. "After it's over," he said, "they're not certain what will happen. The tumor is in a bad place. There may be some paralysis."

"What kind of paralysis?" Kate said. She watched him twist the green-edged coffee cup around and around on its saucer.

"Facial. And maybe worse."

"You've told her this?"

He didn't answer.

"Robert, what is she going to think if she wakes up and—"

He leaned forward, grasping the cup and speaking through clenched teeth. "Don't you think I thought of that?" He gripped the sides of the table and the cup rolled onto the carpeted floor with a dull thud. He seemed ready to throw the table after it, then grabbed Kate's wrists and squeezed them hard.

"You didn't drive her here," he said. "She was so scared she couldn't talk. How much do you want to hand her at once?"

Kate watched the cup sitting solidly on the nubby carpet.

"We've told her it's benign," Robert said, "that the surgery will cause complications, but she can learn back whatever is lost."

Kate looked at him. "Is that true?"

"They hope so."

"We're lying to her, all of us, more and more." Kate pulled her hands away and Robert touched her shoulder.

"What do *you* want to tell her, Kate? 'You're fifty-five and you're done for'?"

She stiffened. "Why put her through the operation at all?"

He sat back and droppped his arms, lowering his head. "Because without it she'd be in bad pain. Soon." They were silent, then he looked up. "And anyway," he said softly, "we don't *know*, do we? She may have a better chance than they think."

Kate put her hands on her face. Behind her closed eyes she saw a succession of blocks tumbling over.

They took the elevator up to the hospital room. They were alone and they stood close together. Above the door red numerals lit up, flashing. Behind the illuminated shapes droned an impersonal hum of machinery.

Then the doors opened with a sucking sound. Three nurses stood waiting with a lunch cart, identical covered trays stacked in tiers. There was a hot bland smell, like warm cardboard. One of the women caught the thick steel door with her arm and smiled. Kate looked quickly at their rubber-soled shoes. White polish, the kind that rubs off. And their legs seemed only white shapes, boneless and two-dimensional, stepping silently into the metal cage.

She looked smaller in the white bed. The chrome side rails were pulled up and she seemed powerless behind them, her dark hair pushed back from her face and her forearms delicate in the baggy hospital gown. Her eyes were different in some nearly imperceptible way; she held them wider, they were shiny with a veiled wetness. For a moment the room seemed empty of all else; there were only her eyes and the dark blossoms of the flowers on the table beside her. Red roses with pine. Everyone had sent the same thing.

Robert walked close to the bed with his hands clasped behind his back, as though afraid to touch. "Where did all the flowers come from?" he asked.

"From school, and the neighbors. And Katie." She smiled.

"FTD," Kate said. "Before I left home. I felt so bad for not being here all along."

"That's silly," said their mother. "You can hardly sit at home and wait for some problem to arise."

"Speaking of problems," Robert said, "the doctor tells me you're not eating. Do I have to urge you a little?" He sat down on the edge of the bed and shook the silverware from its paper sleeve.

Kate touched the plastic tray. "Jell-O and canned cream of chicken soup. Looks great. We should have brought you something."

"They don't *want* us to bring her anything," Robert said. "This is a hospital. And I'm sure your comments make her lunch seem even more appetizing."

"I'll eat it!" said their mother in mock dismay. "Admit they sent you in here to stage a battle until I gave in."

"I'm sorry," Kate said. "He's right."

Robert grinned. "Did you hear that? She says I'm right. I don't believe it." He pushed the tray closer to his mother's chest and made a show of tucking a napkin under her chin.

"Of course you're right, dear." She smiled and gave Kate an obvious wink.

"Yeah," Robert said, "I know you two. But seriously, you eat this. I have to go make some business calls from the motel room."

Their mother frowned. "That motel must be costing you a fortune."

"No, it's reasonable," he said. "Kate can stay for a week or two and I'll drive back and forth from home. If you think this food is bad, you should see the meals in that motel restaurant." He got up to go, flashing Kate a glance of collusion. "I'll be back after supper."

His footsteps echoed down the hallway. Kate and her mother looked wordlessly at each other, relieved. Kate looked away guiltily. Then her mother spoke, apologetic. "He's so tired," she said. "He's been with me since yesterday."

She looked at Kate, then into the air of the room. "I'm in a fix," she said. "Except for when the pain comes, it's all a show that goes on without me. I'm like an invalid, or a lunatic."

Kate moved close and touched her mother's arms. "That's all right, we're going to get you through it. Someone's covering for you at work?"

"I had to take a leave of absence. It's going to take a while afterward—"

"I know. But it's the last thing to worry about, it can't be helped."

"Like spilt milk. Isn't that what they say?"

"I don't know what they say. But why didn't you tell me? Didn't you know something was wrong?"

"Yes . . . bad headaches. Migraines, I thought, or the diabetes getting worse. I was afraid they'd start me on insulin." She tightened the corner of her mouth. "Little did I know . . ."

They heard the shuffle of slippers. An old woman stood at the open door of the room, looking in confusedly. She seemed about to speak, then moved on.

"Oh," said Kate's mother in exasperation, "shut that door, please? They let these old women wander around like refugees." She sat up, reaching for a robe. "And let's get me out of this bed."

They sat near the window while she finished eating. Bars of moted yellow banded the floor of the room. The light held a tinge of spring which seemed painful because it might vanish. They heard the rattle of the meal cart outside the closed door, and the clunk-slide of patients with aluminum walkers. Kate's mother sighed and pushed away the half-empty soup bowl.

"They'll be here after me any minute. More tests. I just want to stay with you." Her face was warm and smooth in the slanted light, lines in her skin delicate, unreal; as though a face behind her face was now apparent after many years. She sat looking at Kate and smiled.

"One day when you were about four you were dragging a broom around the kitchen. I asked what you were doing and you told me that when you got old you were going to be an angel and sweep the rotten rain off the clouds."

"What did you say to that?"

"I said that when you were old I was sure God would see to it." Her mother laughed. "I'm glad you weren't such a smart aleck then," she said. "You would have told me my view of God was paternalistic."

"Ah yes," sighed Kate. "God, that famous dude. Here I am, getting old, facing unemployment, alone, and where is He?"

"You're not alone," her mother said, "I'm right here."

Kate didn't answer. She sat motionless and felt her heart begin to open like a box with a hinged lid. The fullness had no edges.

Her mother stood. She rubbed her hands slowly, twisting her wedding rings. "My hands are so dry in the winter," she said softly, "I brought some hand cream with me but I can't find it anywhere, my suitcase is so jumbled. Thank heavens spring is early this year. . . . They told me that little park over there doesn't usually open till the end of March . . ."

She's helping me, thought Kate, I'm not supposed to let her down.

". . . but they're already running it on weekends. Even past dusk. We'll see the lights tonight. You can't see the shapes this far away, just the motion . . ."

A nurse came in with a wheelchair. Kate's mother pulled a wry face. "This wheelchair is a bit much," she said.

"We don't want to tire you out," said the nurse.

The chair took her weight quietly. At the door she put out her hand to stop, turned, and said anxiously, "Kate, see if you can find that hand cream?"

It was the blue suitcase from years ago, still almost new. She's brought things she never used for everyday; a cashmere sweater, lace slips, silk underpants wrapped in tissue. Folded beneath was a stack of postmarked envelopes, slightly ragged, tied with twine. Kate opened one and realized that all the cards were there, beginning with the first of the marriage. There were a few photographs of her and Robert, baby pictures almost indistinguishable from each other, and then Kate's homemade Valentines, fastened together with rubber bands. Kate stared. *What will I do with these things?* She wanted air; she needed to breathe. She walked to the window and put the bundled papers on the sill. She'd raised the glass and pushed back the screen when suddenly, her mother's clock radio went off with a flat buzz. Kate moved to switch it off and brushed the cards with her arm. Envelopes shifted and slid, scattering on the floor of the room. A few snapshots wafted silently out the window. They dipped and turned, twirling. Kate didn't try to reach them. They seemed only scraps, buoyant and yellowed, blown away, the faces small as pennies. Somewhere far-off there were sirens, almost musical, drawn out and carefully approaching.

The nurse came in with evening medication. Kate's mother lay in bed. "I hope this is strong enough," she said. "Last night I couldn't sleep at all. So many sounds in a hospital . . ."

"You'll sleep tonight," the nurse assured her.

Kate winked at her mother. "That's right," she said, "I'll help you out if I have to."

They stayed up for an hour, watching the moving lights outside and the stationary glows of houses across the distant river. The halls grew darker, were lit with night lights, and the hospital dimmed. Kate waited. Her mother's eyes fluttered and finally she slept. Her breathing was low and regular.

Kate didn't move. Robert had said he'd be back; where was he? She felt a sunken anger and shook her head. She'd been on the point of telling her mother everything. The secrets were a travesty. What if there were things her mother wanted done, people she needed to see? Kate wanted to wake her before these hours passed in the dark and confess that she had lied. Between them, through the tension, there had always been a trusted clarity. Now it was twisted. Kate sat leaning forward, nearly touching the hospital bed.

Suddenly her mother sat bolt upright, her eyes open and her face transfixed. She looked blindly toward Kate but seemed to see nothing. "Who are you?" she whispered. Kate stood, at first unable to move. The woman in the bed opened and closed her mouth several times, as though she were gasping. Then she said loudly, "Stop moving the table. Stop it this instant!" Her eyes were wide with fright and her body was vibrating.

Kate reached her. "Mama, wake up, you're dreaming." Her mother jerked, flinging her arms out. Kate held her tightly.

"I can hear the wheels," she moaned.

"No, no," Kate said. "You're here with me."

"It's not so?"

"No," Kate said. "It's not so."

She went limp. Kate felt for her pulse and found it rapid, then regular. She sat rocking her mother. In a few minutes she lay her back on the pillows and smoothed the damp hair at her temples, smoothed the sheets of the bed. Later she slept fitfully in a chair, waking repeatedly to assure herself that her mother was breathing.

Near dawn she got up, exhausted, and left the room to walk in the corridor. In front of the window at the end of the hallway she saw a man slumped on a couch; the man slowly stood and wavered before her like a specter. It was Robert.

"Kate?" he said.

Years ago he had flunked out of a small junior college and their mother sat in her bedroom rocker, crying hard for over an hour while Kate tried in vain to comfort her. Kate went to the university the next fall, so anxious that she studied frantically, outlining whole textbooks in yellow ink. She sat in the front rows of large classrooms to take voluminous notes, writing quickly in her thick notebook. Robert had gone home, held a job in a plant that manufactured business forms and worked his way through the hometown college. By that time their father was dead, and Robert became, always and forever, the man of the house.

"Robert," Kate said, "I'll stay. Go home."

After breakfast they sat waiting for Robert, who had called and said he'd arrive soon. Kate's fatigue had given way to an intense awareness of every sound, every gesture. How would they get through the day? Her mother had awakened from the drugged sleep still groggy, unable to eat. The meal was sent away untouched and she watched the window as though she feared the walls of the room.

"I'm glad your father isn't here to see this," she said. There was a silence and Kate opened her mouth to speak. "I mean," said her mother quickly, "I'm going to look horrible for a few weeks, with my head all shaved." She pulled an afghan up around her lap and straightened the magazines on the table beside her chair.

"Mom," Kate said, "your hair will grow back."

Her mother pulled the afghan closer. "I've been thinking of your father," she said. "It's not that I'd have wanted him to suffer. But if he had to die, sometimes I wish he'd done it more gently. That heart attack, so finished; never a warning. I wish I'd had some time to nurse him. In a way, it's a chance to settle things."

"Did things need settling?"

"They always do, don't they?" She sat looking out the window, then said softly, "I wonder where I'm headed."

"You're not headed anywhere." Kate said. "I want you right here to see me settle down into normal American womanhood."

Her mother smiled reassuringly. "Where are my grandchildren?" she said. "That's what I'd like to know."

"You stick around," said Kate, "and I promise to start working on it." She moved her chair closer, so that their knees were touching and they could both see out the window. Below them cars moved on the highway and the Ferris wheel in the little park was turning.

"I remember when you were one of the little girls in the parade at the county fair. You weren't even in school yet; you were beautiful in that white organdy dress and pinafore. You wore those shiny black patent shoes and a crown of real apple blossoms. Do you remember?"

"Yes," Kate said. "That long parade. They told me not to move and I sat so still my legs went to sleep. When they lifted me off the float I couldn't stand up. They put me under a tree to wait for you, and you came, in a full white skirt and white sandals, your hair tied back in a red scarf. I can see you yet."

Her mother laughed. "Sounds like a pretty exaggerated picture."

Kate nodded. "I was little. You were big."

"You loved the county fair. You were wild about the carnivals." They looked down at the little park. "Magic, isn't it?" her mother said.

"Maybe we could go see it," said Kate. "I'll ask the doctor."

They walked across a pedestrian footbridge spanning the highway. Kate had bundled her mother into a winter coat and gloves despite the sunny weather. The day was sharp, nearly still, holding its bright air like illusion. Kate tasted the brittle water of her breath, felt for the cool handrail and thin steel of the webbed fencing. Cars moved steadily under the bridge. Beyond a muted roar of motors the park spread green and wooded, its limits clearly visible.

Kate's mother had combed her hair and put on lipstick. Her mouth was defined and brilliant; she linked arms with Kate like an escort. "I was afraid they'd tell us no," she said. "I was ready to run away!"

"I promised I wouldn't let you. And we only have ten minutes, long enough for the Ferris wheel." Kate grinned.

"I haven't ridden one in years. I wonder if I still know how."

"Of course you do. Ferris wheels are genetic knowledge."

"All right, whatever you say." She smiled. "We'll just hold on."

They drew closer and walked quickly through the sounds of the highway. When they reached the grass it was ankle-high and thick, longer and more ragged than it appeared from a distance. The Ferris wheel sat squarely near a grove of swaying elms, squat and laboring, taller than trees. Its neon lights still burned, pale in the sun, spiraling from inside like an imagined bloom. The naked elms surrounded it, their topmost branches tapping. Steel ribs of the machine were graceful and slightly rusted, squeaking faintly above a tinkling music. Only a few people were riding.

"Looks a little rickety," Kate said.

"Oh, don't worry," said her mother.

Kate tried to buy tickets but the ride was free. The old man running the motor wore an engineer's cap and patched overalls. He stopped the wheel and led them on a short ramp to an open car. It dipped gently, padded with black cushions. An orderly and his children rode in the car above. Kate saw their dangling feet, the girls' dusty sandals and gray socks beside their father's shoes and the hem of his white pants. The youngest one swung her feet absently, so it seemed the breeze blew her legs like fabric hung on a line.

Kate looked at her mother. "Are you ready for the big sky?" They laughed. Beyond them the river moved lazily. Houses on the opposite bank seemed empty, but a few rowboats bobbed at the docks. The surface of the water lapped and reflected clouds, and as Kate watched, searching for a definition of line, the Ferris wheel jerked into motion. The car rocked. They looked into the distance and Kate caught her mother's hand as they ascended.

Far away the hospital rose up white and glistening, its windows catching the glint of the sun. Directly below, the park was nearly deserted. There were a few cars in the parking lot and several dogs chasing each other across the grass. Two or three lone women held children on the teeter-totters and a wind was coming up. The forlorn swings moved on their chains. Kate had a vision of the park at night, totally empty, wind weaving heavily through the trees and children's playthings like a great black fish about to surface. She felt a chill on her arms. The light had gone darker, quietly, like a minor chord.

"Mom," Kate said, "it's going to storm." Her own voice seemed distant, the sound strained through layers of screen or gauze.

"No," said her mother, "it's going to pass over." She moved her hand to Kate's knee and touched the cloth of her daughter's skirt.

Kate gripped the metal bar at their waists and looked straight ahead. They were rising again and she felt she would scream. She tried to breathe rhythmically, steadily. She felt the immense weight of the air as they moved through it.

They came almost to the top and stopped. The little car swayed back and forth.

"You're sick, aren't you," her mother said.

Kate shook her head. Below them the grass seemed to glitter coldly, like a sea. Kate sat wordless, feeling the touch of her mother's hand. The hand moved away and Kate felt the absence of the warmth.

They looked at each other levelly.

"I know all about it," her mother said, "I know what you haven't told me."

The sky circled around them, a sure gray movement. Kate swallowed calmly and let their gaze grow endless. She saw herself in her mother's wide brown eyes and felt she was falling slowly into them.

---

1. What does the information about the Valentine cards tell us about Kate's evolving relation with her mother?

2. What is Robert's character and the significance of his behavior?
3. How satisfying to Kate are her attempts to establish an independent life?
4. How does the present crisis clarify Kate's role in the family?
5. Does the story end without a real resolution? What do you still want to know?

Luigi Pirandello

Pirandello (1867–1936) was born in Girgenti, Sicily. As a young man he studied at the University of Rome and in Bonn, Germany. Subsequently he became a professor of literature but was chiefly famous for his prodigious output as a playwright and as the author of novels and short stories. In all, he wrote forty-three plays, the bulk of them elaborating the conflict between illusion and reality. The best known and most typical of his imaginative constructions is "Six Characters in Search of an Author," in which the characters of an unfinished play assert their claims to be more real than the drab existences from which they emerge. Pirandello's inversions of reality and make-believe had a strong influence on modern drama; his practices were often imitated. His extraordinary scrambling of normal expectations led to many charges that he perpetrated hoaxes. Nevertheless, he was awarded the Nobel Prize in 1934.

War

The passengers who had left Rome by the night express had had to stop until dawn at the small station of Fabriano in order to continue their journey by the small old-fashioned local joining the main line with Sulmona.

At dawn, in a stuffy and smoky second-class carriage in which five people had already spent the night, a bulky woman in deep mourning was hoisted in—almost like a shapeless bundle. Behind her, puffing and moaning, followed her husband—a tiny man, thin and weakly, his face death-white, his eyes small and bright and looking shy and uneasy.

Having at last taken a seat he politely thanked the passengers who had helped his wife and who had made room for her; then he turned round to the woman trying to pull down the collar of her coat, and politely inquired:

"Are you all right, dear?"

The wife, instead of answering, pulled up her collar again to her eyes, so as to hide her face.

"Nasty world," muttered the husband with a sad smile.

And he felt it his duty to explain to his traveling companions that the poor woman was to be pitied, for the war was taking away from her

her only son, a boy of twenty to whom both had devoted their entire life, even breaking up their home at Sulmona to follow him to Rome, where he had to go as a student, then allowing him to volunteer for war with an assurance, however, that at least for six months he would not be sent to the front and now, all of a sudden, receiving a wire saying that he was due to leave in three days' time and asking them to go and see him off.

The woman under the big coat was twisting and wriggling, at times growling like a wild animal, feeling certain that all those explanations would not have aroused even a shadow of sympathy from those people who—most likely—were in the same plight as herself. One of them, who had been listening with particular attention, said:

"You should thank God that your son is only leaving now for the front. Mine has been sent there the first day of the war. He has already come back twice wounded and been sent back again to the front."

"What about me? I have two sons and three nephews at the front," said another passenger.

"Maybe, but in our case it is our *only* son," ventured the husband.

"What difference can it make? You may spoil your only son with excessive attentions, but you cannot love him more than you would all your other children if you had any. Paternal love is not like bread that can be broken into pieces and split amongst the children in equal shares. A father gives *all* his love to each one of his children without discrimination, whether it be one or ten, and if I am suffering now for my two sons, I am not suffering half for each of them but double . . ."

"True . . . true . . ." sighed the embarrassed husband, "but suppose (of course we all hope it will never be your case) a father has two sons at the front and he loses one of them, there is still one left to console him . . . while . . ."

"Yes," answered the other, getting cross, "a son left to console him but also a son left for whom he must survive, while in the case of the father of an only son if the son dies the father can die too and put an end to his distress. Which of the two positions is the worse? Don't you see how my case would be worse than yours?"

"Nonsense," interrupted another traveler, a fat, red-faced man with bloodshot eyes of the palest gray.

He was panting. From his bulging eyes seemed to spurt inner violence of an uncontrolled vitality which his weakened body could hardly contain.

"Nonsense," he repeated, trying to cover his mouth with his hand so as to hide the two missing front teeth. "Nonsense. Do we give life to our children for our own benefit?"

The other travelers stared at him in distress. The one who had

had his son at the front since the first day of the war sighed: "You are right. Our children do not belong to us, they belong to the Country. . . ."

"Bosh," retorted the fat traveler. "Do we think of the Country when we give life to our children? Our sons are born because . . . well, because they must be born and when they come to life they take our own life with them. This is the truth. We belong to them but they never belong to us. And when they reach twenty they are exactly what we were at their age. We too had a father and mother, but there were so many other things as well . . . girls, cigarettes, illusions, new ties . . . and the Country, of course, whose call we would have answered—when we were twenty—even if father and mother had said no. Now at our age, the love of our Country is still great, of course, but stronger than it is the love for our children. Is they any one of us here who wouldn't gladly take his son's place at the front if he could?"

There was a silence all round, everybody nodding as to approve.

"Why then," continued the fat man, "shouldn't we consider the feelings of our children when they are twenty? Isn't it natural that at their age they should consider the love for their Country (I am speaking of decent boys, of course) even greater than the love for us? Isn't it natural that it should be so, as after all they must look upon us as upon old boys who cannot move any more and must stay at home? If Country exists, if Country is a natural necessity, like bread, of which each of us must eat in order not to die of hunger, somebody must go to defend it. And our sons go, when they are twenty, and they don't want tears, because if they die, they die inflamed and happy (I am speaking, of course, of decent boys). Now, if one dies young and happy, without having the ugly sides of life, the boredom of it, the pettiness, the bitterness of disillusion . . . what more can we ask for him? Everyone should stop crying; everyone should laugh, as I do . . . or at least thank God—as I do—because my son, before dying, sent me a message saying that he was dying satisfied at having ended his life in the best way he could have wished. That is why, as you see, I do not even wear mourning. . . ."

He shook his light fawn coat as to show it; his livid lip over his missing teeth was trembling, his eyes were watery and motionless, and soon after he ended with a shrill laugh which might well have been a sob.

"Quite so . . . quite so . . ." agreed the others.

The woman who, bundled in a corner under her coat, had been sitting and listening had—for the last three months—tried to find in the words of her husband and her friends something to console her in her deep sorrow, something that might show her how a mother should resign herself to send her son not even to death but to a probably dangerous life. Yet not a word had she found amongst the many which had been said . . . and her grief had been greater in seeing that nobody—as she thought—could share her feelings.

But now the words of the traveler amazed and almost stunned her. She suddenly realized that it wasn't the others who were wrong and could not understand her but herself who could not rise up to the same height of those fathers and mothers willing to resign themselves, without crying, not only to the departure of their sons but even to their death.

She lifted her head, she bent over from her corner trying to listen with great attention to the details which the fat man was giving to his companions about the way his son had fallen as a hero, for his King and his Country, happy and without regrets. It seemed to her that she had stumbled into a world she had never dreamt of, a world so far unknown to her and she was so pleased to hear everyone joining in congratulating that brave father who could so stoically speak of his child's death.

Then suddenly, just as if she had heard nothing of what had been said and almost as if waking up from a dream, she turned to the old man, asking him:

"Then . . . is your son really dead?"

Everybody stared at her. The old man, too, turned to look at her, fixing his great, bulging, horribly watery light gray eyes, deep in her face. For some little time he tried to answer, but words failed him. He looked and looked at her, almost as if only then—at that silly, incongruous question—he had suddenly realized at last that his son was really dead—gone for ever—for ever. His face contracted, became horribly distorted, then he snatched in haste a handkerchief from his pocket and, to the amazement of everyone, broke into harrowing, heart-rending, uncontrollable sobs.

---

1. The conflict of this story is presented almost in the form of a debate. Characterize the conflicting positions of the speakers.
2. How do the unattractive appearance and behavior of the fat mother prepare for the resolution of the story?
3. What is the force of the word "really" in her question "is your son really dead?" How much of the force of this story depends on this single word?
4. What do we learn about the ability of the fat man to accept the death of his son? Is our insight deepened by what he has said?

Edgar Allan Poe

Poe (1809–1849) was born in Boston, the son of itinerant actors who died before he was three years old. He became the ward of a Virginia couple, the Allans, whose name he added to his own. His student days at the University of Virginia were brought to a quick end by his drinking and gambling, but then, enlisting in the Army, he served soberly and well from 1827 to 1829. Accepted into West Point in 1830, he quickly ruined his prospects for a military career by more carousing, and that established a pattern he never again escaped. In 1836 he married his cousin Virginia Clemm, then a girl of thirteen, and tried to support her by writing and editing. He was an editor of the Richmond Southern Literary Messenger, *among other publications, and for a time had his own magazine* The Stylus. *He won a number of literary prizes early in his writing career, but his earnings remained meager and alcoholic excesses repeatedly cost him his jobs in journalism. After his wife died in 1847, he became engaged to a wealthy widow; there was hope of relief from his long run of misfortune and poverty. Traveling to meet the widow in 1849, he met some acquaintances and with them set out to celebrate the change in his luck. After this binge he was found unconscious in a Baltimore street and died a few days later. His short fiction, with its effects of terror and its supernatural trappings, made him a household name for American readers, though in fact there are few traces of American experience in his work. Gothic devices and the mood of German romanticism were his specialty. He has been called the inventor of the detective story. His critical writings have deeply influenced literary taste and practice—for example, his insistence on unity of effect in the short story. His poetry has been admired more greatly and persistently abroad, particularly in France, than at home. He is remembered, as well, for the picturesqueness of his career, for his striking personal appearance, his fine manners, his debauchery, and his poverty—the stuff of a romantic legend. His work is most readily available in numerous anthologies and in collected editions.*

The Fall of the House of Usher

Son cœur est un luth suspendu;
Sitôt qu'on le touche il résonne.
—De Béranger[1]

During the whole of a dull, dark, and soundless day in the autumn of the year, when the clouds hung oppressively low in the heavens, I had been passing alone, on horseback, through a singularly dreary tract of country; and at length found myself, as the shades of the evening drew on, within view of the melancholy House of Usher. I know not how it was—but, with the first glimpse of the building, a sense of insufferable gloom pervaded my spirit. I say insufferable; for the feeling was unrelieved by any of that half-pleasurable, because poetic, sentiment, with which the mind usually receives even the sternest natural images of the desolate or terrible. I looked upon the scene before me—upon the mere house, and the simple landscape features of the domain, upon the bleak walls, upon the vacant eye-like windows, upon a few rank sedges, and upon a few white trunks of decayed trees—with an utter depression of soul which I can compare to no earthly sensation more properly than to the after-dream of the reveller upon opium: the bitter lapse into everyday life, the hideous dropping off of the veil. There was an iciness, a sinking, a sickening of the heart, an unredeemed dreariness of thought which no goading of the imagination could torture into aught of the sublime. What was it—I paused to think—what was it that so unnerved me in the contemplation of the House of Usher? It was a mystery all insoluble; nor could I grapple with the shadowy fancies that crowded upon me as I pondered. I was forced to fall back upon the unsatisfactory conclusion, that while, beyond doubt, there *are* combinations of very simple natural objects which have the power of thus affecting us, still the analysis of this power lies among considerations beyond our depth. It was possible, I reflected, that a mere different arrangement of the particulars of the scene, of the details of the picture, would be sufficient to modify, or perhaps to annihilate its capacity for sorrowful impression; and, acting upon this idea, I reined my horse to the precipitous brink of a black and lurid tarn that lay in unruffled lustre by the dwelling, and gazed down—but with a shudder even more thrilling than before—upon the remodelled and inverted images of the gray sedge, and the ghastly tree-stems, and the vacant and eye-like windows.

Nevertheless, in this mansion of gloom I now proposed to myself a sojourn of some weeks. Its proprietor, Roderick Usher, had been one

1. "His heart is a ready lute / As soon as it is touched it resounds"; "Le Refus" (lines 41–42), by Pierre Jean Beranger, French poet (1780–1857).

of my boon companions in boyhood; but many years had elapsed since our last meeting. A letter, however, had lately reached me in a distant part of the country—a letter from him—which, in its wildly importunate nature, had admitted of no other than a personal reply. The MS. gave evidence of nervous agitation. The writer spoke of acute bodily illness, of a mental disorder, which oppressed him, and of an earnest desire to see me, as his best, and indeed his only personal friend, with a view of attempting, by the cheerfulness of my society, some alleviation of his malady. It was the manner in which all this, and much more, was said—it was the apparent *heart* that went with his request—which allowed me no room for hesitation; and I accordingly obeyed forthwith what I still considered a very singular summons.

Although, as boys, we had been even intimate associates, yet I really knew little of my friend. His reserve had been always excessive and habitual. I was aware, however, that his very ancient family had been noted, time out of mind, for a peculiar sensibility of temperament, displaying itself, through long ages, in many works of exalted art, and manifested, of late, in repeated deeds of munificent yet unobtrusive charity, as well as in a passionate devotion to the intricacies, perhaps even more than to the orthodox and easily recognizable beauties, of musical science. I had learned, too, the very remarkable fact, that the stem of the Usher race, all time-honored as it was, had put forth, at no period, any enduring branch; in other words, that the entire family lay in the direct line of descent, and had always, with very trifling and very temporary variation, so lain. It was this deficiency, I considered, while running over in thought the perfect keeping of the character of the premises with the accredited character of the people, and while speculating upon the possible influence which the one, in the long lapse of centuries, might have exercised upon the other—it was this deficiency, perhaps, of collateral issue, and the consequent undeviating transmission, from sire to son, of the patrimony with the name, which had, at length, so identified the two as to merge the original title of the estate in the quaint and equivocal appellation of the "House of Usher"—an appellation which seemed to include, in the minds of the peasantry who used it, both the family and the family mansion.

I have said that the sole effect of my somewhat childish experiment, that of looking down within the tarn, had been to deepen the first singular impression. There can be no doubt that the consciousness of the rapid increase of my superstition—for why should I not so term it?—served mainly to accelerate the increase itself. Such, I have long known, is the paradoxical law of all sentiments having terror as a basis. And it might have been for this reason only, that, when I again uplifted my eyes to the house itself, from its image in the pool, there grew in my mind a strange fancy—a fancy so ridiculous, indeed, that I but mention it to show the vivid force of the sensations which oppressed me. I had so worked upon my imagination as really to believe that about the whole mansion and domain there hung an atmosphere peculiar to themselves and their immediate vicinity: an atmosphere which had no affinity with the air of heaven, but which had reeked up from the decayed trees, and the gray wall, and the silent tarn: a pestilent and mystic vapor, dull, sluggish, faintly discernible, and leaden-hued.

Shaking off from my spirit what *must* have been a dream, I scanned more narrowly the real aspect of the building. Its principal feature seemed to be that of an excessive antiquity. The discoloration of ages had been great. Minute fungi overspread the whole exterior, hanging in a fine tangled web-work from the eaves. Yet all this was apart from any extraordinary dilapidation. No portion of the masonry had fallen; and there appeared to be a wild inconsistency between its still perfect adaptation of parts, and the crumbling condition of the individual stones. In this there was much that reminded me of the specious totality of old wood-work which has rotted for long years in some neglected vault, with no disturbance from the breath of the external air. Beyond this indication of extensive decay, however, the fabric gave little token of instability. Perhaps the eye of a scrutinizing observer might have discovered a barely perceptible fissure, which, extending from the roof of the building in front, made its way down the wall in a zigzag direction, until it became lost in the sullen waters of the tarn.

Noticing these things, I rode over a short causeway to the house. A servant in waiting took my horse, and I entered the Gothic archway of the hall. A valet, of stealthy step, thence conducted me, in silence, through many dark and intricate passages in my progress to the *studio* of his master. Much that I encountered on the way contributed, I know not how, to heighten the vague sentiments of which I have already spoken. While the objects around me—while the carvings of the ceilings, the sombre tapestries of the walls, the ebon blackness of the floors, and the phantasmagoric armorial trophies which rattled as I strode, were but matters to which, or to such as which, I had been accustomed from my infancy—while I hesitated not to acknowledge how familiar was all this—I still wondered to find how unfamiliar were the fancies which ordinary images were stirring up. On one of the staircases, I met the physician of the family. His countenance, I thought, wore a mingled expression of low cunning and perplexity. He accosted me with trepidation and passed on. The valet now threw open a door and ushered me into the presence of his master.

The room in which I found myself was very large and lofty. The windows were long, narrow, and pointed, and at so vast a distance from the black oaken floor as to be altogether inaccessible from within. Feeble gleams of encrimsoned light made their way through the trellised panes, and served to render sufficiently distinct the more prominent objects around; the eye, however, struggled in vain to reach the remoter angles of the chamber, or the recesses of the vaulted and fretted ceiling. Dark draperies hung upon the walls. The general furniture was profuse, comfortless, antique, and tattered. Many books and musical instruments lay scattered about, but failed to give any vitality to the scene. I felt that I breathed an atmosphere of sorrow. An air of stern, deep, and irredeemable gloom hung over and pervaded all.

Upon my entrance, Usher arose from a sofa upon which he had been lying at full length, and greeted me with a vivacious warmth which had much in it, I at first thought of an overdone cordiality—of the constrained effort of the *ennuyé*[2] man of the world. A glance, however, at his countenance convinced me of his perfect sincerity. We sat down; and for some moments, while he spoke not, I gazed upon him with a feeling half of pity, half of awe. Surely, man had never before so terribly altered, in so brief a period, as had Roderick Usher! It was with difficulty that I could bring myself to admit the identity of the wan being before me with the companion of my early boyhood. Yet the character of his face had been at all times remarkable. A cadaverousness of complexion; an eye large, liquid, and luminous beyond comparison, lips somewhat thin and very pallid, but of a surpassingly beautiful curve; a nose of a delicate Hebrew model, but with a breadth of nostril unusual in similar formations; a finely moulded chin, speaking, in its want of prominence, of a want of moral energy; hair of a more than web-like softness and tenuity; these features, with an inordinate expansion above the regions of the temple, made up altogether a countenance not easily to be forgotten. And now in the mere exaggeration of the prevailing character of these features, and of the expression they were wont to convey, lay so much of change that I doubted to whom I spoke. The now ghastly pallor of the skin, and the now miraculous lustre of the eye, above all things startled and even awed me. The silken hair, too, had been suffered to grow all unheeded, and as, in its wild gossamer texture, it floated rather than fell about the face, I could not, even with effort, connect its Arabesque[3] expression with any idea of simple humanity.

In the manner of my friend I was at once struck with an incoherence—an inconsistency; and I soon found this to arise from a series of feeble and futile struggles to overcome an habitual trepidancy, an excessive nervous agitation. For something of this nature I had indeed been prepared, no less by his letter, than by reminiscences of certain boyish traits, and by conclusions deduced from his peculiar physical

2. Bored, jaded. 3. Curving, in the manner of Arab decorations.

conformation and temperament. His action was alternately vivacious and sullen. His voice varied rapidly from a tremulous indecision (when the animal spirits seemed utterly in abeyance) to that species of energetic concision—that abrupt, weighty, unhurried, and hollow-sounding enunciation—that leaden, self-balanced and perfectly modulated gutteral utterance, which may be observed in the lost drunkard, or the irreclaimable eater of opium, during the periods of his most intense excitement.

It was thus that he spoke of the object of my visit, of his earnest desire to see me, and of the solace he expected me to afford him. He entered, at some length, into what he conceived to be the nature of his malady. It was, he said, a constitutional and a family evil, and one for which he despaired to find a remedy—a mere nervous affection, he immediately added, which would undoubtedly soon pass off. It displayed itself in a host of unnatural sensations. Some of these, as he detailed them, interested and bewildered me; although, perhaps, the terms, and the general manner of the narration had their weight. He suffered much from a morbid acuteness of the senses; the most insipid food was alone endurable; he could wear only garments of certain texture; the odors of all flowers were oppressive; his eyes were tortured by even a faint light; and there were but peculiar sounds, and these from stringed instruments, which did not inspire him with horror.

To an anomalous species of terror I found him a bounden slave. "I shall perish," said he, "I *must* perish in this deplorable folly. Thus, thus, and not otherwise, shall I be lost. I dread the events of the future, not in themselves, but in their results. I shudder at the thought of any, even the most trivial, incident, which may operate upon this intolerable agitation of soul. I have, indeed, no abhorrence of danger, except in its absolute effect—in terror. In this unnerved—in this pitiable condition, I feel that I must inevitably abandon life and reason together, in some struggle with the grim phantasm, FEAR."

I learned, moreover, at intervals, and through broken and equivocal hints, another singular feature of his mental condition. He was enchained by certain superstitious impressions in regard to the dwelling which he tenanted, and from whence, for many years, he had never ventured forth—in regard to an influence whose suppositious force was conveyed in terms too shadowy here to be re-stated—an influence which some peculiarities in the mere form and substance of his family mansion, had, by dint of long sufferance, he said, obtained over his spirit—an effect which the *physique* of the gray walls and turrets, and of the dim tarn into which they all looked down, had, at length, brought about upon the *morale* of his existence.

He admitted, however, although with hesitation, that much of the peculiar gloom which thus afflicted him could be traced to a more natural and far more palpable origin—to the severe and long-continued illness, indeed to the evidently approaching dissolution, of a tenderly beloved sister—his sole companion for long years, his last and only relative on earth. "Her decease," he said, with a bitterness which I can never forget, "would leave him (him the hopeless and the frail) the last of the ancient race of the Ushers." While he spoke, the lady Madeline (for so was she called) passed slowly through a remote portion of the apartment, and, without having noticed my presence, disappeared. I regarded her with an utter astonishment not unmingled with dread, and yet I found it impossible to account for such feelings. A sensation of stupor oppressed me, as my eyes followed her retreating steps. When a door, at length, closed upon her, my glance sought instinctively and eagerly the countenance of the brother; but he had buried his face in his hands, and I could only perceive that a far more than ordinary wanness had overspread the emaciated fingers through which trickled many passionate tears.

The disease of the lady Madeline had long baffled the skill of her physicians. A settled apathy, a gradual wasting away of the person, and frequent although transient affections of a partially cataleptical character, were the unusual diagnosis. Hitherto she had steadily borne up against the pressure of her malady, and had not betaken herself finally to bed; but, on the closing in of the evening of my arrival at the house, she succumbed (as her brother told me at night with inexpressible agitation) to the prostrating power of the destroyer; and I learned that the glimpse I had obtained of her person would thus probably be the last I should obtain—that the lady, at least while living, would be seen by me no more.

For several days ensuing, her name was unmentioned by either Usher or myself: and, during this period, I was busied in earnest endeavors to alleviate the melancholy of my friend. We painted and read together; or I listened, as if in a dream, to the wild improvisations of his speaking guitar. And thus, as a closer and still closer intimacy admitted me more unreservedly into the recesses of his spirit, the more bitterly did I perceive the futility of all attempt at cheering a mind from which darkness, as if an inherent positive quality, poured forth upon all objects of the moral and physical universe, in one unceasing radiation of gloom.

I shall ever bear about me a memory of the many solemn hours I thus spent alone with the master of the House of Usher. Yet I should fail in any attempt to convey an idea of the exact character of the studies, or of the occupations, in which he involved me, or led me the way. An excited and highly distempered ideality threw a sulphureous lustre over all. His long improvised dirges will ring for ever in my ears. Among other things, I hold painfully in mind a certain singular perversion and amplification of the wild air of the last waltz of Von Weber.[4] From the paintings over which his elaborate fancy brooded, and which grew, touch by touch, into vaguenesses at which I shuddered the more thrillingly, because I shuddered knowing not why;—from these paintings (vivid as their images now are before me) I would in vain endeavor to educe more than a small portion which should lie within the compass of merely written words. By the utter simplicity, by the nakedness of his designs, he arrested and over-awed attention. If ever mortal painted an idea, that mortal was Roderick Usher. For me at least—in the circumstances then surrounding me, there arose out of the pure abstractions which the hypochondriac contrived to throw upon his canvas, an intensity of intolerable awe, no shadow of which felt I ever yet in the contemplation of the certainly glowing yet too concrete reveries of Fuseli.[5]

One of the phantasmagoric conceptions of my friend, partaking not so rigidly of the spirit of abstraction, may be shadowed forth, although feebly, in words. A small picture presented the interior of an immensely long and rectangular vault or tunnel, with low walls, smooth, white, and without interruption or device. Certain accessory points of the design served well to convey the idea that this excavation lay at an exceeding depth below the surface of the earth. No outlet was observed in any portion of its vast extent, and no torch, or other artificial source of light was discernible; yet a flood of intense rays rolled throughout, and bathed the whole in a ghastly and inappropriate splendor.

I have just spoken of that morbid condition of the auditory nerve which rendered all music intolerable to the sufferer, with the exception of certain effects of stringed instruments. It was, perhaps, the narrow limits to which he thus confined himself upon the guitar, which gave birth, in great measure, to the fantastic character of his performances. But the fervid *facility* of his impromptus could not be so accounted for. They must have been, and were, in the notes, as well as in the words of his wild fantasias (for he not unfrequently accompanied himself with rhymed verbal improvisations), the result of that intense mental collectedness and concentration to which I have previously alluded as observable only in particular moments of the highest artificial excitement. The words of one of these rhapsodies I have easily remembered. I was, perhaps, the more forcibly impressed with it, as he gave it, because, in the under or mystic current of its meaning, I fancied that I perceived, and for the first time, a full consciousness on the part of Usher, of the tottering of his lofty reason upon her throne.

4. Carl Maria von Weber, German composer (1786–1826). Karl Gottlieb Reissiger succeeded Weber as conductor of the German Opera at Dresden. A nondramatic work by Reissiger contains a piece misleadingly known as *Weber's Last Waltz* or, literally, *Weber's Last Thought*. 5. Henry Fuseli (Johann Heinrich Füssli; 1741–1825), Swiss painter.

The verses, which were entitled "The Haunted Palace," ran very nearly, if not accurately, thus:

In the greenest of our valleys,
By good angels tenanted,
Once a fair and stately palace—
Radiant palace—reared its head.
In the monarch Thought's dominion,
It stood there!
Never seraph spread a pinion
Over fabric half so fair.

Banners yellow, glorious, golden,
On its roof did float and flow,
(This—all this—was in the olden
Time long ago)
And every gentle air that dallied,
In that sweet day,
Along the ramparts plumed and pallid,
A wingèd odor went away.

Wanderers in that happy valley
Through two luminous windows, saw
Spirits moving musically
To a lute's well-tunèd law,
Round about a throne where, sitting
Porphyrogene![6]
In state his glory well befitting,
The ruler of the realm was seen.

And all with pearl and ruby glowing
Was the fair palace door,
Through which came flowing, flowing, flowing,
And sparkling evermore,
A troop of Echoes, whose sweet duty
Was but to sing,
In voices of surpassing beauty,
The wit and wisdom of their king.

But evil things, in robes of sorrow,
Assailed the monarch's high estate;
(Ah, let us mourn!—for never morrow
Shall dawn upon him, desolate!)

6. One born to the purple—i.e., of royal blood.

And, round about his home, the glory
    That blushed and bloomed
Is but a dim-remembered story
    Of the old time entombed.

And travellers now, within that valley,
    Through the red-litten[7] windows see
Vast forms that move fantastically
    To a discordant melody;
While, like a ghastly rapid river,
    Through the pale door
A hideous throng rush out forever,
    And laugh—but smile no more.

I well remember that suggestions arising from this ballad led us into a train of thought wherein there became manifest an opinion of Usher's which I mention not so much on account of its novelty, (for other men have thought thus), as on account of the pertinacity with which he maintained it. This opinion, in its general form, was that of the sentience of all vegetable things. But, in his disordered fancy, the idea had assumed a more daring character, and trespassed, under certain conditions, upon the kingdom of inorganization. I lack words to express the full extent, or the earnest *abandon* of his persuasion. The belief, however, was connected (as I have previously hinted) with the gray stones of the home of his forefathers. The condition of the sentience had been here, he imagined, fulfilled in the method of collocation of these stones—in the order of their arrangement, as well as in that of the many *fungi* which overspread them, and of the decayed trees which stood around—above all, in the long undisturbed endurance of this arrangement, and in its reduplication in the still waters of the tarn. Its evidence—the evidence of the sentience—was to be seen, he said, (and I here started as he spoke), in the gradual yet certain condensation of an atmosphere of their own about the waters and the walls. The result was discoverable, he added, in that silent, yet importunate and terrible influence which for centuries had moulded the destinies of his family, and which made *him* what I now saw him—what he was. Such opinions need no comment, and I will make none.

Our books—the books which, for years, had formed no small portion of the mental existence of the invalid—were, as might be supposed, in strict keeping with this character of phantasm. We pored together over such works as the *Ververt et Chartreuse* of Gresset; the *Belphegor* of Machiavelli; the *Heaven and Hell* of Swedenborg; the

7. Lit with red.

Subterranean Voyage of Nicholas Klimm by Holberg; the *Chiromancy* of Robert Flud, of Jean d'Indaginé, and of De la Chambre; the *Journey into the Blue Distance* of Tieck; and the *City of the Sun* of Campanella. One favorite volume was a small octavo edition of the *Directorium Inquisitorium*, by the Dominican Eymeric de Gironne; and there were passages in Pomponius Mela, about the old African Satyrs and Aegipans, over which Usher would sit dreaming for hours.[8] His chief delight, however, was found in the perusal of an exceedingly rare and curious book in quarto Gothic—the manual of a forgotten church—the *Vigilae Mortuorum Secundum Chorum Ecclesiæ Maguntinæn.*[9]

I could not help thinking of the wild ritual of this work, and of its probable influence upon the hypochondriac, when, one evening, having informed me abruptly that the lady Madeline was no more, he stated his intention of preserving her corpse for a fortnight, (previously to its final interment), in one of the numerous vaults within the main walls of the building. The wordly reason, however, assigned for this singular proceeding, was one which I did not feel at liberty to dispute. The brother had been led to his resolution (so he told me) by considerations of the unusual character of the malady of the deceased, of certain obtrusive and eager inquiries on the part of her medical men,[1] and of the remote and exposed situation of the burial-ground of the family, I will not deny that when I called to mind the sinister countenance of the person whom I met upon the staircase, on the day of my arrival at the house, I had no desire to oppose what I regarded as at best but a harmless, and by no means an unnatural, precaution.

At the request of Usher, I personally aided him in the arrangements for the temporary entombment. The body having been encoffined, we two alone bore it to its rest. The vault in which we placed it (and which had been so long unopened that our torches, half smothered in its oppressive atmosphere, gave us little opportunity for investigation) was small, damp, and entirely without means of admission for light; lying, at great depth, immediately beneath that portion of the

8. Exotic and romantic literary works. *Ververt* and *Chartreuse* are anticlerical satires by French poet and dramatist Jean Baptiste Louis Gresset (1709–1777); the novel of Niccolò Machiavelli (1469–1527) concerns a demon come to earth to prove that the damnation of man is woman; Emmanuel Swedenborg (1688–1772), a Swedish scientist and theologian, offers in *Heaven and Hell* (1758) an argument concerning the continuity of spiritual identity; the book of Ludwig Holberg (1684–1754), a German dramatist, concerns a round-trip voyage to the world of the dead; chiromancy, the art of palmreading, is the concern of Robert Flud (1574–1637), British alchemist, of Jean D'Indaginé (*Chiromantia*, 1522), and of Marin Cureau de la Chambre (*Principes de la Chiromancie*, 1653); the next two titles by the German novelist Johann Ludwig Tieck (1773–1853) and the Italian scientist and philosopher Tommasso Campanella (1568–1639) respectively, are concerned with voyages to other worlds; the Spanish historian Nicolas Eymeric de Girone (1320–1399) in *Inquisitorium Directorium* gives an outline of tortures and appropriate procedures; Pomponius Mela, a Roman of the first century A.D., gives an account of "Aegipans," supposedly goatmen of Africa, in his work *Geography;* satyrs were goatmen of Greek mythology. 9. Vigil for the Dead, Second Chorus, Church of Maguntinae.
1. Usher appers to be afraid the doctors will dig up her corpse to satisfy their professional curiosity about her ailment.

building in which was my own sleeping apartment. It had been used, apparently, in remote feudal times, for the worst purposes of a donjon-keep, and, in later days, as a place of deposit for powder, or other highly combustible substance, as a portion of its floor, and the whole interior of a long archway through which we reached it, were carefully sheathed with copper. The door, of massive iron, had been, also, similarly protected. Its immense weight caused an unusually sharp grating sound, as it moved upon its hinges.

Having deposited our mournful burden upon tressels within this region of horror, we partially turned aside the yet unscrewed lid of the coffin, and looked upon the face of the tenant. The exact similitude between the brother and sister now first arrested my attention; and Usher, divining, perhaps, my thoughts, murmured out some few words from which I learned that the deceased and himself had been twins, and that sympathies of a scarcely intelligible nature had always existed between them. Our glances, however, rested not long upon the dead—for we could not regard her unawed. The disease which had thus entombed the lady in the maturity of youth, had left, as usual in all maladies of a strictly cataleptical character, the mockery of a faint blush upon the bosom and the face, and that suspiciously lingering smile upon the lip which is so terrible in death. We replaced and screwed down the lid, and, having secured the door of iron, made our way, with toil, into the scarcely less gloomy apartments of the upper portion of the house.

And now, some days of bitter grief having elapsed, an observable change came over the features of the mental disorder of my friend. His ordinary manner had vanished. His ordinary occupations were neglected or forgotten. He roamed from chamber to chamber with hurried, unequal, and objectless step. The pallor of his countenance had assumed, if possible, a more ghastly hue—but the luminousness of his eye had utterly gone out. The once occasional huskiness of his tone was heard no more; and a tremulous quaver, as if of extreme terror, habitually characterized his utterance. There were times, indeed, when I thought his unceasingly agitated mind was laboring with an oppressive secret, to divulge which he struggled for the necessary courage. At times, again, I was obliged to resolve all into the mere inexplicable vagaries of madness, as I beheld him gazing upon vacancy for long hours, in an attitude of the profoundest attention, as if listening to some imaginary sound. It was no wonder that his condition terrified—that it infected me. I felt creeping upon me, by slow yet certain degrees, the wild influences of his own fantastic yet impressive superstitions.

It was, especially, upon retiring to bed late in the night of the seventh or eighth day after the placing of the lady Madeline within the donjon, that I experienced the full power of such feelings. Sleep came not near my couch—while the hours waned and waned away. I struggled to reason off the nervousness which had dominion over me. I endeavored to believe that much, if not all of what I felt, was due to the bewildering influence of the gloomy furniture of the room—of the dark and tattered draperies, which, tortured into motion by the breath of a rising tempest, swayed fitfully to and fro upon the walls, and rustled uneasily about the decorations of the bed. But my efforts were fruitless. An irrepressible tremor gradually pervaded my frame; and, at length, there sat upon my very heart an incubus of utterly causeless alarm. Shaking this off with a gasp and a struggle, I uplifted myself upon the pillows, and, peering earnestly within the intense darkness of the chamber, harkened—I know not why, except that an instinctive spirit prompted me—to certain low and indefinite sounds which came, through the pauses of the storm, at long intervals I knew not whence. Overpowered by an intense sentiment of horror, unaccountable yet unendurable, I threw on my clothes with haste (for I felt that I should sleep no more during the night), and endeavored to arouse myself from the pitiable condition into which I had fallen, by pacing rapidly to and fro through the apartment.

I had taken but few turns in this manner, when a light step on an adjoining staircase arrested my attention. I presently recognized it as that of Usher. In an instant afterward he rapped, with a gentle touch, at my door, and entered, bearing a lamp. His countenance was, as usually, cadaverously wan—but there was a species of mad hilarity in his eyes—an evidently restrained *hysteria* in his whole demeanor. His air appalled me—but anything was preferable to the solitude which I had so long endured, and I even welcomed his presence as a relief.

"And you have not seen it?" he said abruptly, after having stared about him for some moments in silence—"you have not then seen it?—but, stay! you shall." Thus speaking, and having carefully shaded his lamp, he hurried to one of the casements, and threw it freely open to the storm.

The impetuous fury of the entering gust nearly lifted us from our feet. It was, indeed, a tempestuous yet sternly beautiful night, and one wildly singular in its terror and its beauty. A whirlwind had apparently collected its force in our vicinity; for there were frequent and violent alterations in the direction of the wind; and the exceeding density of the clouds (which hung so low as to press upon the turrets of the house) did not prevent our perceiving the life-like velocity with which they flew careering from all points against each other, without passing away into the distance. I say that even their exceeding density did not prevent our perceiving this; yet we had no glimpse of the moon or stars, nor was there any flashing forth of the lightning. But the under surfaces of the huge masses of agitated vapor, as well as all terrestrial objects immediately around us, were glowing in the unnatural light of a faintly luminous and distinctly visible gaseous exhalation which hung about and enshrouded the mansion.

"You must not—you shall not behold this!" said I, shudderingly, to Usher, as I led him, with a gentle violence, from the window to a seat. "These appearances, which bewilder you, are merely electrical phenomena not uncommon—or it may be that they have their ghastly origin in the rank miasma of the tarn. Let us close this casement; the air is chilling and dangerous to your frame. Here is one of your favorite romances. I will read, and you shall listen; and so we will pass away this terrible night together."

The antique volume which I had taken up was the *Mad Trist* of Sir Launcelot Canning; but I had called it a favorite of Usher's more in sad jest than in earnest; for, in truth, there is little in its uncouth and unimaginative prolixity which could have had interest for the lofty and spiritual ideality of my friend. It was, however, the only book immediately at hand; and I indulged a vague hope that the excitement which now agitated the hypochondriac might find relief (for the history of mental disorder is full of similar anomalies) even in the extremeness of the folly which I should read. Could I have judged, indeed, by the wild, overstrained air of vivacity with which he hearkened, or apparently hearkened, to the words of the tale, I might have well congratulated myself upon the success of my design.

I had arrived at that well-known portion of the story where Ethelred, the hero of the *Trist*, having sought in vain for peaceable admission into the dwelling of the hermit, proceeds to make good an entrance by force. Here, it will be remembered, the words of the narrative run thus:

> And Ethelred, who was by nature of a doughty heart, and who was now mighty withal, on account of the powerfulness of the wine which he had drunken, waited no longer to hold parley with the hermit, who, in sooth, was of an obstinate and maliceful turn, but, feeling the rain upon his shoulders, and fearing the rising of the tempest, uplifted his mace outright, and, with blows, made quickly room in the plankings of the door for his gauntleted hand; and now pulling therewith sturdily, he so cracked, and ripped, and tore all asunder, that the noise of the dry and hollow-sounding wood alarumed and reverberated throughout the forest.

At the termination of this sentence I started, and, for a moment, paused; for it appeared to me (although I at once concluded that my excited fancy had deceived me)—it appeared to me that, from some very remote portion of the mansion, there came, indistinctly, to my ears, what might have been, in its exact similarity of character, the echo (but a stifled and dull one certainly) of the very cracking and ripping sound which Sir Launcelot had so particularly described. It was, beyond doubt, the coincidence alone which had arrested my attention; for, amid the rattling of the sashes of the casements, and the ordinary commingled noises of the still increasing storm, the sound, in itself, had nothing, surely, which should have interested or disturbed me. I continued the story:

> But the good champion Ethelred, now entering within the door, was sore enraged and amazed to perceive no signal of the maliceful hermit; but, in the stead thereof, a dragon of scaly and prodigious demeanor, and of a fiery tongue, which sate in guard before a palace of gold, with a floor of silver; and upon the wall there hung a shield of shining brass with this legend enwritten—
>
> *Who entereth herein, a conqueror hath bin,*
> *Who slayeth the dragon, the shield he shall win.*
>
> And Ethelred uplifted his mace, and struck upon the head of the dragon, which fell before him, and gave up his pesty breath, with a shriek so horrid and harsh, and withal so piercing, that Ethelred had fain to close his ears with his hands against the dreadful noise of it, the like whereof was never before heard.

Here again I paused abruptly, and now with a feeling of wild amazement—for there could be no doubt whatever that, in this instance, I did actually hear (although from what direction it proceeded I found it impossible to say) a low and apparently distant, but harsh, protracted, and most unusual screaming or grating sound—the exact counterpart of what my fancy had already conjured up as the sound of the dragon's unnatural shriek as described by the romancer.

Oppressed, as I certainly was, upon the occurrence of this second and most extraordinary coincidence, by a thousand conflicting sensations, in which wonder and extreme terror were predominant, I still retained sufficient presence of mind to avoid exciting, by any observation, the sensitive nervousness of my companion. I was by no means certain that he had noticed the sounds in question; although, assuredly, a strange alteration had, during the last few minutes, taken place in his demeanor. From a position fronting my own, he had gradually brought round his chair, so as to sit with his face to the door of the chamber; and thus I could but partially perceive his features, although I saw that his lips trembled as if he were murmuring inaudibly. His head had dropped upon his breast—yet I knew that he was not asleep, from the wide and rigid opening of the eye, as I caught a glance of it in profile. The motion of his body, too, was at variance with this idea—for he rocked from side to side with a gentle yet constant and uniform sway. Having rapidly taken notice of all this, I resumed the narrative of Sir Launcelot, which thus proceeded:

> And now, the champion, having escaped from the terrible fury of the dragon, bethinking himself of the brazen shield, and of the breaking up of the enchantment which was upon it, removed the carcass from out of the way before him, and approached valorously over the silver pavement of the castle to where the shield was upon the wall; which in sooth tarried not for his full coming, but fell down at his feet upon the silver floor, with a mighty great and terrible ringing sound.

No sooner had these syllables passed my lips, than—as if a shield of brass had indeed, at the moment, fallen heavily upon a floor of silver—I became aware of a distinct, hollow, metallic and clangorous yet apparently muffled reverberation. Completely unnerved, I leaped to my feet; but the measured rocking movement of Usher was undisturbed. I rushed to the chair in which he sat. His eyes were bent fixedly before him, and throughout his whole countenance there reigned a more than stony rigidity. But as I laid my hand upon his shoulder, there came a strong shudder over his whole person; a sickly smile quivered about his lips; and I saw that he spoke in a low, hurried, and gibbering murmur, as if unconscious of my presence. Bending closely over him, I at length drank in the hideous import of his words.

"Not hear it?—yes, I hear it, and *have* heard it. Long—long—long—many minutes, many hours, many days, have I heard it—yet I dared not—oh, pity me; miserable wretch that I am!—I dared not—I *dared* not speak! *We have put her living in the tomb!* Said I not that my senses were acute?—I *now* tell you that I heard her first feeble movements in the hollow coffin. I heard them—many, many days ago—yet I dared not—*I dared not speak!* And now—to-night—Ethelred—ha! ha!—the breaking of the hermit's door, and the death-cry of the dragon, and the clangor of the shield!—say, rather, the rending of her coffin, and the grating of the iron hinges of her prison, and her struggles within the coppered archway of the vault! Oh whither shall I fly? Will she not be here anon? Is she not hurrying to upbraid me for my haste? Have I not heard her footstep on the stair? Do I not distinguish that heavy and horrible beating of her heart? MADMAN!" here he sprang violently to his feet, and shrieked out his syllables, as if in the effort he were giving up his soul—"*Madman! I tell you that she now stands without the door!*"

As if in the superhuman energy of his utterance there had been found the potency of a spell, the huge antique panels to which the speaker pointed, threw slowly back, upon the instant, their ponderous and ebony jaws. It was the work of the rushing gust—but then without those doors there DID stand the lofty and enshrouded figure of the lady Madeline of Usher. There was blood upon her white robes, and the evidence of some bitter struggle upon every portion of her emaciated frame. For a moment she remained trembling and reeling to and fro upon the threshold—then, with a low moaning cry, fell heavily inward upon the person of her brother, and in her violent and now final death-agonies, bore him to the floor a corpse, and a victim to the terrors he had anticipated.

From that chamber, and from that mansion, I fled aghast. The storm was still abroad in all its wrath as I found myself crossing the old causeway. Suddenly there shot along the path a wild light, and I turned to see whence a gleam so unusual could have issued; for the vast house and its shadows were alone behind me. The radiance was that of the full, setting, and blood-red moon, which now shone vividly through that once barely-discernible fissure of which I have before spoken as extending from the roof of the building, in a zigzag direction, to the base. While I gazed, this fissure rapidly widened—there came a fierce breath of the whirlwind—the entire orb of the satellite burst at once upon my sight—my brain reeled as I saw the mighty walls rushing asunder—there was a long tumultuous shouting sound like the voice of a thousand waters—and the deep and dank tarn at my feet closed sullenly and silently over the fragments of the HOUSE OF USHER.

---

1. Identify some of the means used by Poe to achieve the mood of this story.
2. In what ways is Roderick Usher a picture of the artistic personality? A psychotic?
3. How is Usher's ballad related to the story as a whole?
4. In what ways is his sister a mirror image of Usher and his afflictions? What evidence is there that she has an independent existence?
5. What suggestions are there that Poe considers the imagination, in itself, to be a disease?
6. In what ways does the story conform to modern psychological ideas? Is psychological analysis of Usher possible on the basis of evidence given in the story?

The Purloined Letter

Nil sapientae odiosius acumine nimio.
—Seneca[1]

At Paris, just after dark one gusty evening in the autumn of 18—, I was enjoying the twofold luxury of meditation and a meerschaum, in company with my friend C. Auguste Dupin, in his little back library, or book-closet, *au troisième, No. 33, Rue Dunôt, Faubourg St. Germain.*[2] For one hour at least we had maintained a profound silence; while each, to any casual observer, might have seemed intently and exclusively occupied with the curling eddies of smoke that oppressed the atmosphere of the chamber. For myself, however, I was mentally discussing certain topics which had formed matter for conversation between us at an earlier period of the evening; I mean the affair of the Rue Morgue, and the mystery attending the murder of Marie Rogêt.[3] I looked upon it, therefore, as something of coincidence, when the door of our apartment was thrown open and admitted our old acquaintance, Monsieur G——, the Prefect of the Parisian police.

We gave him a hearty welcome; for there was nearly half as much of the entertaining as of the contemptible about the man, and we had not seen him for several years. We had been sitting in the dark, and Dupin now arose for the purpose of lighting a lamp, but sat down again, without doing so, upon G.'s saying that he had called to consult us, or rather to ask the opinion of my friend, about some official business which had occasioned a great deal of trouble.

"If it is any point requiring reflection," observed Dupin, as he forebore to enkindle the wick, "we shall examine it to better purpose in the dark."

"That is another of your odd notions," said the Prefect, who had a fashion of calling every thing "odd" that was beyond his comprehension, and thus lived amid an absolute legion of "oddities."

"Very true," said Dupin, as he supplied his visitor with a pipe, and rolled towards him a very comfortable chair.

"And what is the difficulty now?" I asked. "Nothing more in the assassination way, I hope?"

"Oh no; nothing of that nature. The fact is, the business is *very* simple indeed, and I make no doubt that we can manage it sufficiently well ourselves; but then I thought Dupin would like to hear the details of it, because it is so excessively *odd.*"

1. "Nothing is more distasteful to good sense than too much cunning"; Lucius Annaeus Seneca (4 B.C.–65 A.D.), Roman poet and philosopher. 2. Fashionable quarter of Paris. The "troisième" is literally the third floor, but is equivalent to the fourth floor in North America. 3. "The Mystery of Marie Rogêt" and "The Murders in the Rue Morgue" are titles of earlier Dupin tales by Poe.

"Simple and odd," said Dupin.

"Why, yes; and not exactly that, either. The fact is, we have all been a good deal puzzled because the affair *is* so simple, and yet baffles us altogether."

"Perhaps it is the very simplicity of the thing which puts you at fault," said my friend.

"What nonsense you *do* talk!" replied the Prefect, laughing heartily.

"Perhaps the mystery is a little *too* plain," said Dupin.

"Oh, good heavens! who ever heard of such an idea?"

"A little *too* self-evident."

"Ha! ha! ha!—ha! ha! ha!—ho! ho! ho!" roared out our visitor, profoundly amused, "oh, Dupin, you will be the death of me yet!"

"And what, after all, *is* the matter on hand?" I asked.

"Why, I will tell you," replied the Prefect, as he gave a long, steady, and contemplative puff, and settled himself in his chair. "I will tell you in a few words; but, before I begin, let me caution you that this is an affair demanding the greatest secrecy, and that I should most probably lose the position I now hold, were it known that I confided it to any one."

"Proceed," said I.

"Or not," said Dupin.

"Well, then; I have received personal information, from a very high quarter, that a certain document of the last importance, has been purloined from the royal apartments. The individual who purloined it is known; this beyond a doubt; he was seen to take it. It is known, also, that it still remains in his possession."

"How is this known?" asked Dupin.

"It is clearly inferred," replied the Prefect, "from the nature of the document, and from the non-appearance of certain results which would at once arise from its passing *out* of the robber's possession;—that is to say, from his employing it as he must design in the end to employ it."

"Be a little more explicit," I said.

"Well, I may venture so far as to say that the paper gives its holder a certain power in a certain quarter where such power is immensely valuable." The Prefect was fond of the cant of diplomacy.

"Still I do not quite understand," said Dupin.

"No? Well; the disclosure of the document to a third person, who shall be nameless, would bring in question the honour of a personage of most exalted station; and this fact gives the holder of the document an ascendancy over the illustrious personage whose honour and peace are so jeopardized."

"But this ascendancy," I interposed, "would depend upon the

robber's knowledge of the loser's knowledge of the robber. Who would dare—"

"The thief," said G, "is the Minister D——, who dares all things, those unbecoming as well as those becoming a man. The method of the theft was not less ingenious than bold. The document in question—a letter, to be frank—had been received by the personage robbed while alone in the royal *boudoir*. During its perusal she was suddenly interrupted by the entrance of the other exalted personage from whom especially it was her wish to conceal it. After a hurried and vain endeavour to thrust it in a drawer, she was forced to place it, open as it was, upon a table. The address, however, was uppermost, and the contents thus unexposed, the letter escaped notice. At this juncture enters the Minister D——. His lynx eye immediately perceives the paper, recognises the handwriting of the address, observes the confusion of the personage addressed, and fathoms her secret. After some business transactions, hurried through in his ordinary manner, he produces a letter somewhat similar to the one in question, opens it, pretends to read it, and then places it in close juxtaposition to the other. Again he converses, for some fifteen minutes, upon the public affairs. At length, in taking leave, he takes also from the table the letter to which he had no claim. Its rightful owner saw, but, of course, dared not call attention to the act, in the presence of the third personage who stood at her elbow. The minister decamped; leaving his own letter—one of no importance—upon the table."

"Here, then," said Dupin to me, "you have precisely what you demand to make the ascendancy complete—the robber's knowledge of the loser's knowledge of the robber."

"Yes," replied the Prefect; "and the power thus attained has, for some months past, been wielded, for political purposes, to a very dangerous extent. The personage robbed is more thoroughly convinced, every day, of the necessity of reclaiming her letter. But this, of course, cannot be done openly. In fine, driven to despair, she has committed the matter to me."

"Than whom," said Dupin, amid a perfect whirlwind of smoke, "no more sagacious agent could, I suppose, be desired, or even imagined."

"You flatter me," replied the Prefect; "but it is possible that some such opinion may have been entertained."

"It is clear," said I, "as you observe, that the letter is still in possession of the minister; since it is this possession, and not any employment of the letter, which bestows the power. With the employment the power departs."

"True," said G.; "and upon this conviction I proceeded. My first care was to make thorough search of the minister's hotel;[4] and here my chief embarrassment lay in the necessity of searching without his knowledge. Beyond all things, I have been warned of the danger which would result from giving him reason to suspect our design."

"But," said I, "you are quite *au fait*[5] in these investigations. The Parisian police have done this thing often before."

"O yes; and for this reason I did not despair. The habits of the minister gave me, too, a great advantage. He is frequently absent from home all night. His servants are by no means numerous. They sleep at a distance from their master's apartment, and, being chiefly Neapolitans, are readily made drunk. I have keys, as you know, with which I can open any chamber or cabinet in Paris. For three months a night has not passed, during the greater part of which I have not been engaged, personally, in ransacking the D—— Hôtel. My honour is interested, and, to mention a great secret, the reward is enormous. So I did not abandon the search until I had become fully satisfied that the thief is a more astute man than myself. I fancy that I have investigated every nook and corner of the premises in which it is possible that the paper can be concealed."

"But is it not possible," I suggested, "that although the letter may be in possession of the minister, as it unquestionably is, he may have concealed it elsewhere than upon his own premises?"

"This is barely possible," said Dupin. "The present peculiar condition of affairs at court, and especially of those intrigues in which D—— is known to be involved, would render the instant availability of the document—its susceptibility of being produced at a moment's notice—a point of nearly equal importance with its possession."

"Its susceptibility of being produced?" said I.

"That is to say, of being *destroyed*," said Dupin.

"True," I observed; "the paper is clearly then upon the premises. As for its being upon the person of the minister, we may consider that as out of the question."

"Entirely," said the Prefect. "He has been twice waylaid, as if by footpads, and his person rigorously searched under my own inspection."

"You might have spared yourself this trouble," said Dupin. "D——, I presume, is not altogether a fool, and, if not, must have anticipated these waylayings, as a matter of course."

"Not *altogether* a fool," said G., "but then he's a poet, which I take to be only one remove from a fool."

"True," said Dupin, after a long and thoughtful whiff from his

4. I.e., town house. 5. Adept.

meerschaum, "although I have been guilty of certain doggerel myself."

"Suppose you detail," said I, "the particulars of your search."

"Why the fact is, we took our time, and we searched *every where*. I have had long experience in these affairs. I took the entire building, room by room; devoting the nights of a whole week to each. We examined, first, the furniture of each apartment. We opened every possible drawer; and I presume you know that, to a properly trained police agent, such a thing as a *secret* drawer is impossible. Any man is a dolt who permits a 'secret' drawer to escape him in a search of this kind. The thing is *so* plain. There is a certain amount of bulk—of space—to be accounted for in every cabinet. Then we have accurate rules.[6] The fiftieth part of a line could not escape us. After the cabinets we took the chairs. The cushions we probed with the fine long needles you have seen me employ. From the tables we removed the tops."

"Why so?"

"Sometimes the top of a table, or other similarly arranged piece of furniture, is removed by the person wishing to conceal an article; then the leg is excavated, the article deposited within the cavity, and the top replaced. The bottoms and tops of bedposts are employed in the same way."

"But could not the cavity be detected by sounding?" I asked.

"By no means, if, when the article is deposited, a sufficient wadding of cotton be placed around it. Besides, in our case, we were obliged to proceed without noise."

"But you could not have removed—you could not have taken to pieces *all* articles of furniture in which it would have been possible to make a deposit in the manner you mention. A letter may be compressed into a thin spiral roll, not differing much in shape or bulk from a large knitting-needle, and in this form it might be inserted into the rung of a chair, for example. You did not take to pieces all the chairs?"

"Certainly not; but we did better—we examined the rungs of every chair in the hotel, and, indeed, the jointings of every description of furniture, by the aid of a most powerful microscope.[7] Had there been any traces of recent disturbance we should not have failed to detect it instantly. A single grain of gimlet-dust, for example, would have been as obvious as an apple. Any disorder in the glueing—any unusual gaping in the joints—would have sufficed to insure detection."

"I presume you looked to the mirrors, between the boards and the plates, and you probed the beds and the bed-clothes, as well as the curtains and carpets."

"That of course; and when we had absolutely completed every

6. Rulers. 7. Magnifying glass.

particle of the furniture in this way, then we examined the house itself. We divided its entire surface into compartments, which we numbered, so that none might be missed; then we scrutinized each individual square inch throughout the premises, including the two houses immediately adjoining, with the microscope, as before."

"The two houses adjoining!" I exclaimed; "you must have had a great deal of trouble."

"We had; but the reward offered is prodigious."

"You include the *grounds* about the houses?"

"All the grounds are paved with brick. They gave us comparatively little trouble. We examined the moss between the bricks, and found it undisturbed."

"You looked among D——'s papers, of course, and into the books of the library?"

"Certainly; we opened every package and parcel; we not only opened every book, but we turned over every leaf in each volume, not contenting ourselves with a mere shake, according to the fashion of some of our police officers. We also measured the thickness of every book-*cover*, with the most accurate admeasurement, and applied to each the most jealous scrutiny of the microscope. Had any of the bindings been recently meddled with, it would have been utterly impossible that the fact should have escaped observation. Some five or six volumes, just from the hands of the binder, we carefully probed, longitudinally, with the needles."

"You explored the floors beneath the carpets?"

"Beyond doubt. We removed every carpet, and examined the boards with the microscope."

"And the paper on the walls?"

"Yes."

"You looked into the cellars?"

"We did.

"Then," I said, "you have been making a miscalculation, and the letter is *not* upon the premises, as you suppose."

"I fear you are right there," said the Prefect. "And now, Dupin, what would you advise me to do?"

"To make a thorough re-search of the premises."

"That is absolutely needless," replied G——. "I am not more sure that I breathe than I am that the letter is not at the Hôtel."

"I have no better advice to give you," said Dupin. "You have, of course, an accurate description of the letter?"

"Oh yes!"—And here the Prefect, producing a memorandum-book, proceeded to read aloud a minute account of the internal, and especially of the external, appearance of the missing document. Soon after finishing the perusal of this description, he took his departure, more entirely depressed in spirits than I had ever known the good gentleman before.

In about a month afterwards he paid us another visit, and found us occupied very nearly as before. He took a pipe and a chair and entered into some ordinary conversation. At length I said;—

"Well, but G——, what of the purloined letter? I presume you have at last made up your mind that there is no such thing as over-reaching the Minister?"

"Confound him, say I—yes; I made the re-examination, however, as Dupin suggested—but it was all labour lost, as I knew it would be."

"How much was the reward offered, did you say?" asked Dupin.

"Why, a very great deal—a *very* liberal reward—I don't like to say how much, precisely; but one thing I *will* say, that I wouldn't mind giving my individual check for fifty thousand francs to any one who could obtain me that letter. The fact is, it is becoming of more and more importance every day; and the reward has been lately doubled. If it were trebled, however, I could do no more than I have done."

"Why, yes," said Dupin, drawlingly, between the whiffs of his meerschaum, "I really—think, G——, you have not exerted yourself—to the utmost in this matter. You might—do a little more, I think, eh?"

"How?—in what way?"

"Why—puff, puff—you might—puff, puff—employ counsel in the matter, eh?—puff, puff, puff. Do you remember the story they tell of Abernethy?"

"No; hang Abernethy!"

"To be sure! hang him and welcome. But, once upon a time, a certain rich miser conceived the design of spunging upon this Abernethy for a medical opinion. Getting up, for this purpose, an ordinary conversation in a private company, he insinuated his case to the physician, as that of an imaginary individual.

" 'We will suppose,' said the miser, 'that his symptoms are such and such; now, doctor, what would *you* have directed him to take?'

" 'Take!' said Abernethy, 'why, take *advice*, to be sure.' "

"But," said the Prefect, a little discomposed, "I am *perfectly* willing to take advice, and to pay for it. I would *really* give fifty thousand francs to any one who would aid me in the matter."

"In that case," replied Dupin, opening a drawer, and producing a check-book, "you may as well fill me up a check for the amount mentioned. When you have signed it, I will hand you the letter."

I was astounded. The Prefect appeared absolutely thunder-stricken. For some minutes he remained speechless and motionless, looking incredulously at my friend with open mouth, and eyes that seemed starting from their sockets; then, apparently recovering himself in some measure, he seized a pen, and after several pauses and vacant stares, finally filled up and signed a check for fifty thousand francs, and handed it across the table to Dupin. The latter examined it carefully and deposited it in his pocket-book; then, unlocking an *escritoire*,[8] took thence a letter and gave it to the Prefect. This functionary grasped it in a perfect agony of joy, opened it with a trembling hand, cast a rapid glance at its contents, and then, scrambling and struggling to the door, rushed at length unceremoniously from the room and from the house, without having uttered a syllable since Dupin had requested him to fill up the check.

When he had gone, my friend entered into some explanations.

"The Parisian police," he said, "are exceedingly able in their way. They are persevering, ingenious, cunning, and thoroughly versed in the knowledge which their duties seem chiefly to demand. Thus, when G—— detailed to us his mode of searching the premises at the Hôtel D——, I felt the entire confidence in his having made a satisfactory investigation—so far as his labours extended."

"So far as his labours extended?" said I.

"Yes," said Dupin. "The measures adopted were not only the best of their kind, but carried out to absolute perfection. Had the letter been deposited within the range of their search, these fellows would, beyond a question, have found it."

I merely laughed—but he seemed quite serious in all that he said.

"The measures, then," he continued, "were good in their kind, and well executed; their defect lay in their being inapplicable to the case, and to the man. A certain set of highly ingenious resources are, with the Prefect, a sort of Procrustean bed,[9] to which he forcibly adapts his designs. But he perpetually errs by being too deep or too shallow, for the matter in hand; and many a schoolboy is a better reasoner than he. I knew one about eight years of age, whose success at guessing in the game of 'even and odd' attracted universal admiration. This game is simple, and is played with marbles. One player holds in his hand a number of these toys, and demands of another whether that number is even or odd. If the guess is right, the guesser wins one; if wrong, he loses one. The boy to whom I allude won all the marbles of the school. Of course he had some principle of guessing; and this lay in mere observation and admeasurement of the astuteness of his opponents. For example, an arrant simpleton is his opponent, and, holding up his closed hand, asks: 'Are they even or odd?' Our schoolboy replies 'Odd,' and loses; but upon the second trial he wins, for he then says to him-

8. A writing table. 9. In Greek mythology the giant Procrustes tied travelers to an iron bed and made them fit it by either stretching or amputating their limbs.

self, 'The simpleton had them even upon the first trial, and his amount of cunning is just sufficient to make him have them odd upon the second; I will therefore guess odd;'—he guesses odd, and wins. Now, with a simpleton a degree above the first, he would have reasoned thus: 'This fellow finds that in the first instance I guessed odd, and, in the second, he will propose to himself, upon the first impulse, a simple variation from even to odd, as did the first simpleton; but then a second thought will suggest that this is too simple a variation, and finally he will decide upon putting it even as before. I will therefore guess even;'—he guesses even, and wins. Now this mode of reasoning in the schoolboy, whom his fellows termed 'lucky,'—what, in its last analysis, is it?"

"It is merely," I said, "an identification of the reasoner's intellect with that of his opponent."

"It is," said Dupin; "and, upon inquiring of the boy by what means he effected the *thorough* identification in which his success consisted, I received answer as follows: 'When I wish to find out how wise, or how stupid, or how good, or how wicked is any one, or what are his thoughts at the moment, I fashion the expression on my face, as accurately as possible, in accordance with the expression of his, and then wait to see what thoughts or sentiments arise in my mind or heart, as if to match or correspond with the expression.' This response of the schoolboy lies at the bottom of all the spurious profundity which has been attributed to Rochefoucault, to La Bougive, to Machiavelli, and to Campanella."[1]

"And the identification," I said, "of the reasoner's intellect with that of his opponent, depends, if I understand you aright, upon the accuracy with which the opponent's intellect is admeasured."

"For its practical value it depends upon this," replied Dupin; "and the Prefect and his cohort fail so frequently, first, by default of this identification, and, secondly, by ill-admeasurement, or rather through non-admeasurement, of the intellect with which they are engaged. They consider only their *own* ideas of ingenuity; and, in searching for anything hidden, advert only to the modes in which *they* would have hidden it. They are right in this much—that their own ingenuity is a faithful representative of that of *the mass;* but when the cunning of the individual felon is diverse in character from their own, the felon foils them, of course. This always happens when it is above their own, and very usually when it is below. They have no variation of principle in their investigations; at best, when urged by some unusual emergency—by some extraordinary reward—they extend or exaggerate their old modes of *practice*, without touching their principles. What,

1. François, Duc de la Rochefoucauld (1613–1680), French moralist and courtier; La Bougive is probably Jean de la Bruyere (1645–1696); Niccolò Machiavelli (1469–1527), Italian statesman and writer; Tommaso Campanella (1568–1639), Italian philosopher and Dominican monk.

for example, in this case of D——, has been done to vary the principle of action? What is all this boring, and probing, and sounding, and scrutinizing with the microscope, and dividing the surface of the building into registered square inches—what is it all but an exaggeration *of the application* of the one principle or set of principles of search, which are based upon the one set of notions regarding human ingenuity, to which the Prefect, in the long routine of his duty, has been accustomed? Do you not see he has taken it for granted that *all* men proceed to conceal a letter,—not exactly in a gimlet-hole bored in a chair-leg—but, at least in *some* out-of-the-way hole or corner suggested by the same tenor of thought which would urge a man to secrete a letter in a gimlet-hole bored in a chair-leg? And do you not see also, that such *recherchés*[2] nooks for concealment are adapted only for ordinary occasions, and would be adopted only by ordinary intellects; for, in all cases of concealment, a disposal of the article concealed—a disposal of it in this *recherché* manner—is, in the very first instance, presumable and presumed; and thus its discovery depends, not at all upon the acumen, but altogether upon the mere care, patience, and determination of the seekers; and where the case is of importance—or, what amounts to the same thing in the political eyes, when the reward is of magnitude,—the qualities in question have *never* been known to fail. You will now understand what I meant in suggesting that, had the purloined letter been hidden anywhere within the limits of the Prefect's examination—in other words, had the principle of its concealment been comprehended within the principles of the Prefect—its discovery would have been a matter altogether beyond question. This functionary, however, has been thoroughly mystified; and the remote source of his defeat lies in the supposition that the Minister is a fool, because he has acquired renown as a poet. All fools are poets; this the Prefect *feels;* and he is merely guilty of a *non distributio medii*[3] in thence inferring that all poets are fools."

"But is this really the poet?" I asked. "There are two brothers, I know; and both have attained reputation in letters. The Minister I believe has written learnedly on the Differential Calculus. He is a mathematician, and no poet."

"You are mistaken; I know him well; he is both. As poet *and* mathematician, he would reason well; as mere mathematician, he could not have reasoned at all, and thus would have been at the mercy of the Prefect."

"You surprise me," I said, "by these opinions, which have been contradicted by the voice of the world. You do not mean to set at naught the well-digested idea of centuries. The mathematical reason

2. I.e., excessively cunning. 3. The undistributed middle, an error in logic.

has long been regarded as *the* reason *par excellence*."

" '*Il y a à parier*,' " replied Dupin, quoting from Chamfort, " '*que toute idée publique, toute convention reçue, est une sottise, car elle a convenue au plus grand nombre*.'[4] The mathematicians, I grant you, have done their best to promulgate the popular error to which you allude, and which is none the less an error for its promulgation as truth. With an art worthy a better cause, for example, they have insinuated the term 'analysis' into application to algebra. The French are the originators of this particular deception; but if a term is of any importance—if words derive any value from applicability—then 'analysis' conveys 'algebra' about as much as, in Latin, '*ambitus*' implies 'ambition,' '*religio*' 'religion,' or '*homines honesti*,' a set of *honourable* men."

"You have a quarrel on hand, I see," said I, "with some of the algebraists of Paris; but proceed."

"I dispute the availability, and thus the value, of that reason which is cultivated in any especial form other than the abstractly logical. I dispute, in particular, the reason educed by mathematical study. The mathematics are the science of form and quantity; mathematical reasoning is merely logic applied to observation upon form and quantity. The great error lies in supposing that even the truths of what is called *pure* algebra, are abstract or general truths. And this error is so egregious that I am confounded at the universality with which it has been received. Mathematical axioms are *not* axioms of general truth. What is true of *relation*—of form and quantity—is often grossly false in regard to morals, for example. In this latter science it is very usually *un*true that the aggregated parts are equal to the whole. In chemistry also the axiom fails. In the consideration of motive it fails; for two motives, each of a given value, have not, necessarily, a value when united, equal to the sum of their values apart. There are numerous other mathematical truths which are only truths within the limits of *relation*. But the mathematician argues, from his *finite truths*, through habit, as if they were of absolutely general applicability—as the world indeed imagines them to be. Bryant, in his very learned 'Mythology,'[5] mentions an analogous source of error, when he says that 'although the Pagan fables are not believed, yet we forget ourselves continually, and make inferences from them as existing realities.' With the algebraists, however, who are Pagans themselves, the 'Pagan fables' *are* believed, and the inferences are made, not so much through lapse of memory, as through an unaccountable addling of the brains. In short, I never yet encountered the mere mathematician who could be trusted out of equal roots, or one who did

4. "The odds are that every popular idea, every accepted convention is nonsense, because it has suited itself to the majority"; from *Maximes et Pensées* by Sébastian Chamfort (1741–1794). 5. *A New System, or an Analysis of Antient Mythology*, by Jacob Bryant (1715–1804), an English scholar.

not clandestinely hold it as a point of his faith x^2+px was absolutely and unconditionally equal to q. Say to one of these gentlemen, by way of experiment, if you please, that you believe occasions may occur where x^2+px is *not* altogether equal to q, and, having made him understand what you mean, get out of his reach as speedily as convenient, for, beyond doubt, he will endeavour to knock you down.

"I mean to say," continued Dupin, while I merely laughed at his last observations, "that if the Minister had been no more than a mathematician, the Prefect would have been under no necessity of giving me this check. I knew him, however, as both mathematician and poet, and my measures were adapted to his capacity, with reference to the circumstances by which he was surrounded. I knew him as a courtier, too, and as a bold *intriguant*.[6] Such a man, I considered, could not fail to be aware of the ordinary political modes of action. He could not have failed to anticipate—and events have proved that he did not fail to anticipate—the waylayings to which he was subjected. He must have foreseen, I reflected, the secret investigations of his premises. His frequent absences from home at night, which were hailed by the Prefect as certain aids to his success, I regarded only as *ruses*, to afford opportunity for thorough search to the police, and thus the sooner to impress them with the conviction to which G——, in fact, did finally arrive—the conviction that the letter was not upon the premises. I felt, also, that the whole train of thought, which I was at some pains in detailing to you just now, concerning the invariable principle of political action in searches for articles concealed—I felt that this whole train of thought would necessarily pass through the mind of the Minister. It would imperatively lead him to despise all the ordinary *nooks* of concealment. *He* could not, I reflected, be so weak as not to see that the most intricate and remote recess of his hotel would be as open as his commonest closets to the eyes, to the probes, to the gimlets, and to the microscopes of the Prefect. I saw, in fine, that he would be driven, as a matter of course, to simplicity, if not deliberately induced to it as a matter of choice. You will remember, perhaps how desperately the Prefect laughed when I suggested, upon our first interview, that it was just possible this mystery troubled him so much on account of its being so *very* self-evident."

"Yes," said I, "I remember his merriment well. I really thought he would have fallen into convulsions."

"The material world," continued Dupin, "abounds with very strict analogies to the immaterial; and thus some color of truth has been given to the rhetorical dogma, that metaphor, or simile, may be made to strengthen an argument as well as to embellish a description. The

6. Intriguer.

principle of *vis inertiae*,[7] for example, seems to be identical in physics and metaphysics. It is not more true in the former, that a large body is with more difficulty set in motion than a smaller one, and that its subsequent *momentum* is commensurate with this difficulty, than it is, in the latter, that intellects of the vaster capacity, while more forcible, more constant, and more eventful in their movements than those of inferior grade, are yet the less readily moved, and more embarrassed and full of hesitation in the first few steps of their progress. Again: have you ever noticed which of the street signs, over the shop doors, are the most attractive of attention?"

"I have never given the matter a thought," I said.

"There is a game of puzzles," he resumed, "which is played upon a map. One party playing requires another to find a given word—the name of town, river, state, or empire—any word, in short, upon the motley and perplexed surface of the chart. A novice in the game generally seeks to embarrass his opponents by giving them the most minutely lettered names; but the adept selects such words as stretch, in large characters, from one end of the chart to the other. These, like the over-largely lettered signs and placards of the street, escape observation by dint of being excessively obvious; and here the physical oversight is precisely analogous with the moral inapprehension by which the intellect suffers to pass unnoticed those considerations which are too obtrusively and too palpably self-evident. But this is a point, it appears, somewhat above or beneath the understanding of the Prefect. He never once thought it probable, or possible, that the Minister had deposited the letter immediately beneath the nose of the whole world, by way of best preventing any portion of that world from perceiving it.

"But the more I reflected upon the daring, dashing, and discriminating ingenuity of D——; upon the fact that the document must always have been *at hand*, if he intended to use it to good purpose; and upon the decisive evidence, obtained by the Prefect, that it was not hidden within the limits of that dignitary's ordinary search—the more satisfied I became that, to conceal this letter, the Minister had resorted to the comprehensive and sagacious expedient of not attempting to conceal it at all.

"Full of these ideas, I prepared myself with a pair of green spectacles, and called one fine morning, quite by accident, at the Ministerial hotel. I found D—— at home, yawning, lounging, and dawdling as usual, and pretending to be in the last extremity of *ennui*. He is, perhaps, the most really energetic human being now alive—but that is only when nobody sees him.

"To be even with him, I complained of my weak eyes, and

7. The power of inertia.

lamented the necessity of the spectacles, under cover of which I cautiously and thoroughly surveyed the whole apartment, while seemingly intent only upon the conversation of my host.

"I paid especial attention to a large writing-table near which he sat, and upon which lay confusedly, some miscellanous letters and other papers, with one or two musical instruments and a few books. Here, however, after a long and very deliberate scrutiny, I saw nothing to excite particular suspicion.

"At length my eyes, in going the circuit of the room, fell upon a trumpery filigree card-rack of pasteboard, that hung dangling by a dirty blue ribbon, from a little brass knob just beneath the middle of the mantel-piece. In this rack, which had three or four compartments, were five or six visiting cards, and a solitary letter. This last was much soiled and crumpled. It was torn nearly in two, across the middle—as if a design, in the first instance, to tear it entirely up as worthless, had been altered, or stayed, in the second. It had a large black seal, bearing the D—— cipher *very* conspicuously, and was addressed, in a diminutive female hand, to D——, the minister, himself. It was thrust carelessly, and even, as it seemed, contemptuously, into one of the uppermost divisions of the rack.

"No sooner had I glanced at this letter than I concluded it to be that of which I was in search. To be sure, it was, to all appearance, radically different from the one of which the Prefect had read us so minute a description. Here the seal was large and black, with the D—— cipher; there, it was small and red, with the ducal arms of the S—— family. Here, the address, to the minister, was diminutive and feminine; there, the superscription, to a certain royal personage, was markedly bold and decided; the size alone formed a point of correspondence. But, then, the *radicalness* of these differences, which was excessive; the dirt; the soiled and torn condition of the paper, so inconsistent with the *true* methodical habits of D——, and so suggestive of a design to delude the beholder into an idea of the worthlessness of the document; these things, together with the hyperobtrusive situation of this document, full in the view of every visitor, and thus exactly in accordance with the conclusions to which I had previously arrived; these things, I say, were strongly corroborative of suspicion, in one who came with the intention to suspect.

"I protracted my visit as long as possible, and, while I maintained a most animated discussion with the minister, upon a topic which I knew well had never failed to interest and excite him, I kept my attention really riveted upon the letter. In this examination, I committed to memory its external appearance and arrangement in the rack; and also fell, at length, upon a discovery which set at rest whatever trivial doubt I might have entertained. In scrutinizing the edges of the paper, I observed them to be more *chafed* than seemed necessary. They presented the *broken* appearance which is manifested when a stiff paper, having been once folded and pressed with a folder, is refolded in a reversed direction, in the same creases or edges which had formed the original fold. This discovery was sufficient. It was clear to me that the letter had been turned, as a glove, inside out, re-directed, and re-sealed. I bade the Minister good morning and took my departure at once, leaving a gold snuff-box upon the table.

"The next morning I called for the snuff-box, when we resumed, quite eagerly, the conversation of the preceding day. While thus engaged, however, a loud report, as if of a pistol, was heard immediately beneath the windows of the hotel, and was succeeded by a series of fearful screams, and the shoutings of a mob. D—— rushed to a casement, threw it open, and looked out. In the meantime, I stepped to the card-rack, took the letter, put it in my pocket, and replaced it by a *fac-simile,* (so far as regards externals) which I had carefully prepared at my lodgings; imitating the D—— cipher, very readily, by means of a seal formed of bread.

"The disturbance in the street had been occasioned by the frantic behaviour of a man with a musket. He had fired it among a crowd of women and children. It proved, however, to have been without ball, and the fellow was suffered to go his way as a lunatic or a drunkard. When he had gone, D—— came from the window, whither I had followed him immediately upon securing the object in view. Soon afterward I bade him farewell. The pretended lunatic was a man in my own pay."

"But what purpose had you," I asked, "in replacing the letter by a *fac-simile?* Would it not have been better, at the first visit, to have seized it openly, and departed?"

"D——," replied Dupin, "is a desperate man, and a man of nerve. His hotel, too, is not without attendants devoted to his interests. Had I made the wild attempt you suggest, I should never have left the ministerial presence alive. The good people of Paris would have heard of me no more. But I had an object apart from these considerations. You know my political prepossessions. In this matter, I act as a partisan of the lady concerned. For eighteen months the minister has had her in his power. She has now him in hers; since, being unaware that the letter is not in his possession, he will proceed with his exactions as if it was. Thus will he inevitably commit himself, at once, to his political destruction. His downfall, too, will not be more precipitate than awkward. It is all very well to talk about the *facilis descensus Averni;*[8] but

8. "Easy is the descent into hell . . . but to recall thy steps and issue to upper air, this is the task, this the burden"; *Aeneid* 6.126, by Virgil (70–19 B.C.), Roman poet.

in all kinds of climbing, as Catalini[9] said of singing, it is far more easy to get up than to come down. In the present instance I have no sympathy—at least no pity for him who descends. He is that *monstrum horrendum*,[1] an unprincipled man of genius. I confess, however, that I should like very well to know the precise character of his thoughts, when, being defied by her whom the Prefect terms 'a certain personage,' he is reduced to opening the letter which I left for him in the card-rack."

"How? did you put any thing particular in it?"

"Why—it did not seem altogether right to leave the interior blank—that would have been insulting. To be sure, D——, at Vienna once, did me an evil turn, which I told him, quite good-humouredly, that I should remember. So, as I knew he would feel some curiosity in regard to the identity of the person who had outwitted him, I thought it a pity not to give him a clue. He is well acquainted with my MS., and I just copied into the middle of the blank sheet the words—

> '*—Un dessein si funeste,*
> *S'il n'est digne d'Atrée, est digne de Thyeste.*'

They are to be found in Crébillon's 'Atrée.' "[2]

---

1. What is the relationship between the narrator and Dupin? What aspects in the character of each is it based on?
2. Since the rightful owner of the letter knows who stole it, why can't she simply demand its return?
3. How does Dupin define and take advantage of the blind spots in the best of institutional methods? What does he say about the importance of the individual intellect?
4. How has Dupin assured the punishment of the thief? Was there any other option for insuring punishment?
5. What does the story say about the role of games in the management of human affairs?

9. Angelica Catalini (1780–1844), Italian singer. 1. The description of Polyphemus the Cyclops after his one eye had been put out by Ulysses; *Aeneid* 3.658. 2. "So baneful a plot, if not worthy of Atreus, is worthy of Thyestes"; from *Atrée et Thyeste* by Prosper Jolyot de Crébillon (1674–1762).

Katherine Anne Porter

Porter (1890–1980) was born in Indian Creek, Texas, and brought up in that state and in Louisiana. She was educated at home, in private schools, and in an Ursuline convent. Though she began to write stories as soon as she could form letters on paper, she made no attempt to publish until she was past thirty, and she associated with no literary people until she had become something of a celebrity with the publication of her first book of stories, Flowering Judas *(1930). Before and after that date she earned a meager living by journalism, traveling from city to city with little baggage except her manuscripts—trunkfuls of which were destroyed, bit by bit, as she found them inadequate to meet her exacting standards. She lived for a time in Mexico, which provided material for some of her most famous stories. Her novel* Ship of Fools *was begun during the 1930's but not finished for more than two decades. It was at last published in 1962. Her nomadic career took her to Europe to live some of her later years. Her shorter works have been collected also in* Hacienda: A Story of Mexico *(1934),* Pale Horse, Pale Rider *(1939), and* The Leaning Tower and Other Stories *(1944).* The Collected Stories of Katherine Anne Porter *appeared in 1965, winning the Pulitzer Prize and the National Book Award.*

Theft

She had the purse in her hand when she came in. Standing in the middle of the floor, holding her bathrobe around her and trailing a damp towel in one hand, she surveyed the immediate past and remembered everything clearly. Yes, she had opened the flap and spread it out on the bench after she had dried the purse with her handkerchief.

She had intended to take the Elevated,[1] and naturally she looked in her purse to make certain she had the fare, and was pleased to find forty cents in the coin envelope. She was going to pay her own fare, too, even if Camilo did have the habit of seeing her up the steps and dropping a nickel in the machine before he gave the turnstile a little push and sent her through it with a bow. Camilo by a series of compromises had managed to make effective a fairly complete set of smaller

1. The elevated railway in New York City.

courtesies, ignoring the larger and more troublesome ones. She had walked with him to the station in a pouring rain, because she knew he was almost as poor as she was, and when he insisted on a taxi, she was firm and said, "You know it simply will not do." He was wearing a new hat of a pretty biscuit shade, for it never occurred to him to buy anything of a practical color; he had put it on for the first time and the rain was spoiling it. She kept thinking, "But this is dreadful, where will he get another?" She compared it with Eddie's hats that always seemed to be precisely seven years old and as if they had been quite purposely left out in the rain, and yet they sat with a careless and incidental rightness on Eddie. But Camilo was far different; if he wore a shabby hat it would be merely shabby on him, and he would lose his spirits over it. If she had not feared Camilo would take it badly, for he insisted on the practice of his little ceremonies up to the point he had fixed for them, she would have said to him as they left Thora's house, "Do go home. I can surely reach the station by myself."

"It is written that we must be rained upon tonight," said Camilo, "so let it be together."

At the foot of the platform stairway she staggered slightly—they were both nicely set up on Thora's cocktails—and said: "At least Camilo, do me the favor not to climb these stairs in your present state, since for you it is only a matter of coming down again at once, and you'll certainly break your neck."

He made three quick bows, he was Spanish, and leaped off through the rainy darkness. She stood watching him, for he was a very graceful young man, thinking that tomorrow morning he would gaze soberly at his spoiled hat and soggy shoes and possibly associate her with his misery. As she watched, he stopped at the far corner and took off his hat and hid it under his overcoat. She felt she had betrayed him by seeing, because he would have been humiliated if he thought she even suspected him of trying to save his hat.

Roger's voice sounded over her shoulder above the clang of the rain falling on the stairway shed, wanting to know what she was doing out in the rain at this time of night, and did she take herself for a duck? His long, imperturbable face was streaming with water, and he tapped a bulging spot on the breast of his buttoned-up overcoat: "Hat," he said. "Come on, let's take a taxi."

She settled back against Roger's arm which he laid around her shoulders, and with the gesture they exchanged a glance full of long amiable associations, then she looked through the window at the rain changing the shapes of everything, and the colors. The taxi dodged in and out between the pillars of the Elevated, skidding slightly on every curve, and she said: "The more it skids the calmer I feel, so I really must be drunk."

"You must be," said Roger. "This bird is a homicidal maniac, and I could do with a cocktail myself this minute."

They waited on the traffic at Fortieth Street and Sixth Avenue, and three boys walked before the nose of the taxi. Under the globes of light they were cheerful scarecrows, all very thin and all wearing very seedy snappy-cut suits and gay neckties. They were not very sober either, and they stood for a moment wobbling in front of the car, and there was an argument going on among them. They leaned toward each other as if they were getting ready to sing, and the first one said: "When I get married it won't be jus' for getting married, I'm gonna marry for *love, see?*" and the second one said, "Aw, gwan and tell that stuff to *her*, why n't yuh?" and the third one gave a kind of hoot, and said, "Hell, dis guy? Wot the hell's he got?" and the first one said: "Aaah, shurrup yuh mush, I got plenty." Then they all squealed and scrambled across the street beating the first one on the back and pushing him around.

"Nuts," commented Roger, "pure nuts."

Two girls were skittering by in short transparent raincoats, one green, one red, their heads tucked against the drive of the rain. One of them was saying to the other, "Yes, I know all about *that*. But what about me? You're always so sorry for *him* . . ." and they ran on with their little pelican legs flashing back and forth.

The taxi cab backed up suddenly and leaped forward again, and after a while Roger said: "I had a letter from Stella today, and she'll be home on the twenty-sixth, so I suppose she's made up her mind and it's all settled."

"I had a sort of letter today too," she said, "making up my mind for me. I think it is time for you and Stella to do something definite."

When the taxi stopped on the corner of West Fifty-third Street, Roger said, "I've just enough if you'll add ten cents," so she opened her purse and gave him a dime, and he said, "That's beautiful, that purse."

"It's a birthday present," she told him, "and I like it. How's your show coming?"

"Oh, still hanging on, I guess. I don't go near the place. Nothing sold yet. I mean to keep right on the way I'm going and they can take it or leave it. I'm through with the argument."

"It's absolutely a matter of holding out, isn't it?"

"Holding out's the tough part."

"Good night, Roger."

"Good night, you should take aspirin and push yourself into a tub of hot water, you look as though you're catching cold."

"I will."

With the purse under her arm she went upstairs, and on the first landing Bill heard her step and poked his head out with his hair tumbled and his eyes red, and he said: "For Christ's sake, come in and have a drink with me. I've had some bad news.

"You're perfectly sopping," said Bill, looking at her drenched feet. They had two drinks, while Bill told how the director had thrown his play out after the cast had been picked over twice, and had gone through three rehearsals. "I said to him, 'I didn't say it was a masterpiece, I said it would make a good show.' And he said, 'It just doesn't *play*, do you see? It needs a doctor.' So I'm stuck, absolutely stuck," said Bill, on the edge of weeping again. "I've been crying," he told her, "in my cups." And he went on to ask her if she realized his wife was ruining him with her extravagance. "I send her ten dollars every week of my unhappy life, and I don't really have to. She threatens to jail me if I don't, but she can't do it. God, let her try it after the way she treated me! She's no right to alimony and she knows it. She keeps on saying she's got to have it for the baby and I keep on sending it because I can't bear to see anybody suffer. So I'm way behind on the piano and the victrola, both—"

"Well, this is a pretty rug, anyhow," she said.

Bill stared at it and blew his nose. "I got it at Ricci's for ninety-five dollars," he said. "Ricci told me it once belonged to Marie Dressler,[2] and cost fifteen hundred dollars, but there's a burnt place on it, under the divan. Can you beat that?"

"No," she said. She was thinking about her empty purse and that she could not possibly expect a check for her latest review for another three days, and her arrangement with the basement restaurant could not last much longer if she did not pay something on account. "It's no time to speak of it," she said, "but I've been hoping you would have by now that fifty dollars you promised for my scene in the third act. Even if it doesn't play. You were to pay me for the work anyhow out of your advance."

"Weeping Jesus," said Bill, "you, too?" He gave a loud sob, or hiccough, in his moist handkerchief. "Your stuff was no better than mine, after all. Think of that."

"But you got something for it," she said. "Seven hundred dollars."

Bill said, "Do me a favor, will you? Have another drink and forget about it. I can't, you know I can't, I would if I could, but you know the fix I'm in."

"Let it go, then," she found herself saying almost in spite of herself. She had meant to be quite firm about it. They drank again without speaking, and she went to her apartment on the floor above.

2. American actress (1873–1934).

There, she now remembered distinctly, she had taken the letter out of the purse before she spread the purse out to dry.

She had sat down and read the letter over again: but there were phrases that insisted on being read many times, they had a life of their own separate from the others, and when she tried to read past and around them, they moved with the movement of her eyes, and she could not escape them . . . "thinking about you more than I mean to . . . yes, I even talk about you . . . why were you so anxious to destroy . . . even if I could see you now I would not . . . not worth all this abominable . . . the end . . ."

Carefully she tore the letter into narrow strips and touched a lighted match to them in the coal grate.

Early the next morning she was in the bathtub when the janitress knocked and then came in, calling out that she wished to examine the radiators before she started the furnace going for the winter. After moving about the room for a few minutes, the janitress went out, closing the door very sharply.

She came out of the bathroom to get a cigarette from the package in the purse. The purse was gone. She dressed and made coffee, and sat by the window while she drank it. Certainly the janitress had taken the purse, and certainly it would be impossible to get it back without a great deal of ridiculous excitement. Then let it go. With this decision of her mind, there rose coincidentally in her blood a deep almost murderous anger. She set the cup carefully in the center of the table, and walked steadily downstairs, three long flights and a short hall and a steep short flight into the basement, where the janitress, her face streaked with coal dust, was shaking up the furnace. "Will you please give me back my purse? There isn't any money in it. It was a present, and I don't want to lose it."

The janitress turned without straightening up and peered at her with hot flickering eyes, a red light from the furnace reflected in them. "What do you mean, your purse?"

"The gold cloth purse you took from the wooden bench in my room," she said. "I must have it back."

"Before God I never laid eyes on your purse, and that's the holy truth," said the janitress.

"Oh, well then, keep it," she said, but in a very bitter voice; "keep it if you want it so much." And she walked away.

She remembered how she had never locked a door in her life, on some principle of rejection in her that made her uncomfortable in the ownership of things, and her paradoxical boast before the warnings of her friends, that she had never lost a penny by theft; and she had been pleased with the bleak humility of this concrete example designed to illustrate and justify a certain fixed, otherwise baseless and general faith which ordered the movements of her life without regard to her will in the matter.

In this moment she felt that she had been robbed of an enormous number of valuable things, whether material or intangible: things lost or broken by her own fault, things she had forgotten and left in houses when she moved: books borrowed from her and not returned, journeys she had planned and had not made, words she had waited to hear spoken to her and had not heard, and the words she had meant to answer with; bitter alternatives and intolerable substitutes worse than nothing, and yet inescapable: the long patient suffering of dying friendships and the dark inexplicable death of love—all that she had had, and all that she had missed, were lost together, and were twice lost in this landslide of remembered losses.

The janitress was following her upstairs with the purse in her hand and the same deep red fire flickering in her eyes. The janitress thrust the purse towards her while they were still a half dozen steps apart, and said: "Don't never tell on me. I musta been crazy. I get crazy in the head sometimes, I swear I do. My son can tell you."

She took the purse after a moment, and the janitress went on: "I got a niece who is going on seventeen, and she's a nice girl and I thought I'd give it to her. She needs a pretty purse. I musta been crazy; I thought maybe you wouldn't mind, you leave things around and don't seem to notice much."

She said: "I missed this because it was a present to me from someone . . ."

The janitress said: "He'd get you another if you lost this one. My niece is young and needs pretty things, we oughta give the young ones a chance. She's got young men after her maybe will want to marry her. She oughta have nice things. She needs them bad right now. You're a grown woman, you've had your chance, you ought to know how it is!"

She held the purse out to the janitress saying: "You don't know what you're talking about. Here, take it, I've changed my mind. I really don't want it."

The janitress looked up at her with hatred and said: "I don't want it either now. My niece is young and pretty, she don't need fixin' up to be pretty, she's young and pretty anyhow! I guess you need it worse than she does!"

"It wasn't really yours in the first place," she said, turning away. "You mustn't talk as if I had stolen it from you."

"It's not from me, it's from her you're stealing it," said the janitress, and went back downstairs.

She laid the purse on the table and sat down with the cup of chilled coffee, and thought: I was right not to be afraid of any thief but myself, who will end by leaving me nothing.

---

1. Enumerate the kinds of theft (or cheating) touched on by the story.
2. How are the shortcomings of Camilo and Bill related to the theme?
3. By what details do we learn about the kind of life led by the central character? Why is her name never given?
4. To what extent and in what ways does she bring her troubles on herself?
5. Comment on the thematic relation between material possessions and the integrity of the self.

Flowering Judas

Braggioni sits heaped upon the edge of a straight-backed chair much too small for him, and sings to Laura in a furry, mournful voice. Laura has begun to find reasons for avoiding her own house until the latest possible moment, for Braggioni is there almost every night. No matter how late she is, he will be sitting there with a surly, waiting expression, pulling at his kinky yellow hair, thumbing the strings of his guitar, snarling a tune under his breath. Lupe the Indian maid meets Laura at the door, and says with a flicker of a glance towards the upper room, "He waits."

Laura wishes to lie down, she is tired of her hairpins and the feel of her long tight sleeves, but she says to him, "Have you a new song for me this evening?" If he says yes, she asks him to sing it. If he says no, she remembers his favorite one, and asks him to sing it again. Lupe brings her a cup of chocolate and a plate of rice, and Laura eats at the small table under the lamp, first inviting Braggioni, whose answer is always the same: "I have eaten, and besides, chocolate thickens the voice."

Laura says, "Sing, then," and Braggioni heaves himself into song. He scratches the guitar familiarly as though it were a pet animal, and sings passionately off key, taking the high notes in a prolonged painful squeal. Laura, who haunts the markets listening to the ballad singers, and stops every day to hear the blind boy playing his reed-flute in Sixteenth of September Street,[1] listens to Braggioni with pitiless courtesy, because she dares not smile at his miserable performance. Nobody dares to smile at him. Braggioni is cruel to everyone, with a kind of

1. Street in Mexico City named to commemorate the date of the enactment of a new Mexican constitution in 1857.

specialized insolence, but he is so vain of his talents, and so sensitive to slights, it would require a cruelty and vanity greater than his own to lay a finger on the vast cureless wound of his self-esteem. It would require courage, too, for it is dangerous to offend him, and nobody has this courage.

Braggioni loves himself with such tenderness and amplitude and eternal charity that his followers—for he is a leader of men, a skilled revolutionist, and his skin has been punctured in honorable warfare—warm themselves in the reflected glow, and say to each other: "He has a real nobility, a love of humanity raised above mere personal affections." The excess of this self-love has flowed out, inconveniently for her, over Laura, who, with so many others, owes her comfortable situation and her salary to him. When he is in a very good humor, he tells her, "I am tempted to forgive you for being a *gringa, gringita!*"[2] and Laura, burning, imagines herself leaning forward suddenly, and with a sound back-handed slap wiping the suety smile from his face. If he notices her eyes at these moments he gives no sign.

She knows what Braggioni would offer her, and she must resist tenaciously without appearing to resist, and if she could avoid it she would not admit even to herself the slow drift of his intention. During these long evenings which have spoiled a long month for her, she sits in her deep chair with an open book on her knees, resting her eyes on the consoling rigidity of the printed page when the sight and sound of Braggioni singing threaten to identify themselves with all her remembered afflictions and to add their weight to her uneasy premonitions of the future. The gluttonous bulk of Braggioni has become a symbol of her many disillusions, for a revolutionist should be lean, animated by heroic faith, a vessel of abstract virtues. This is nonsense, she knows it now and is ashamed of it. Revolution must have leaders, and leadership is a career for energetic men. She is, her comrades tell her, full of romantic error, for what she defines as cynicism in them is merely "a developed sense of reality." She is almost too willing to say, "I am wrong, I suppose I don't really understand the principles," and afterward she makes a secret truce with herself, determined not to surrender her will to such expedient logic. But she cannot help feeling that she has been betrayed irreparably by the disunion between her way of living and her feeling of what life should be, and at times she is almost contented to rest in this sense of grievance as a private store of consolation. Sometimes she wishes to run away, but she stays. Now she longs to fly out of this room, down the narrow stairs, and into the street where the houses lean together like conspirators under a single mottled lamp, and leave Braggioni singing to himself.

2. Diminutive form of *gringa*, a somewhat derogatory term for a fair-haired woman, especially an American.

Instead she looks at Braggioni, frankly and clearly, like a good child who understands the rules of behavior. Her knees cling together under sound blue serge, and her round white collar is not purposely nun-like. She wears the uniform of an idea, and has renounced vanities. She was born Roman Catholic, and in spite of her fear of being seen by someone who might make a scandal of it, she slips now and again into some crumbling little church, kneels on the chilly stone, and says a Hail Mary on the gold rosary she bought in Tehuantepec.[3] It is no good and she ends by examining the altar with its tinsel flowers and ragged brocades, and feels tender about the battered doll-shape of some male saint whose white, lace-trimmed drawers hang limply around his ankles below the hieratic dignity of his velvet robe. She has encased herself in a set of principles derived from her early training, leaving no detail of gesture or of personal taste untouched, and for this reason she will not wear lace made on machines. This is her private heresy, for in her special group the machine is sacred, and will be the salvation of the workers. She loves fine lace, and there is a tiny edge of fluted cobweb on this collar, which is one of twenty precisely alike, folded in blue tissue paper in the upper drawer of her clothes chest.

Braggioni catches her glance solidly as if he had been waiting for it, leans forward, balancing his paunch between his spread knees, and sings with tremendous emphasis, weighing his words. He has, the song relates, no father and no mother, nor even a friend to console him; lonely as a wave of the sea he comes and goes, lonely as a wave. His mouth opens round and yearns sideways, his balloon cheeks grow oily with the labor of song. He bulges marvelously in his expensive garments. Over his lavender collar, crushed upon a purple necktie, held by a diamond hoop: over his ammunition belt of tooled leather worked in silver, buckled cruelly around his gasping middle: over the tops of his glossy yellow shoes Braggioni swells with ominous ripeness, his mauve silk hose stretched taut, his ankles bound with the stout leather thongs of his shoes.

When he stretches his eyelids at Laura she notes again that his eyes are the true tawny yellow cat's eyes. He is rich, not in money, he tells her, but in power, and this power brings with it the blameless ownership of things, and the right to indulge his love of small luxuries. "I have a taste for the elegant refinements," he said once, flourishing a yellow silk handkerchief before her nose. "Smell that? It is Jockey Club, imported from New York." Nonetheless he is wounded by life. He will say so presently. "It is true everything turns to dust in the hand, to gall on the tongue." He sighs and his leather belt creaks like a saddle girth. "I am disappointed in everything as it comes. Every-

3. City in southern Mexico.

thing." He shakes his head. "You, poor thing, you will be disappointed too. You are born for it. We are more alike than you realize in some things. Wait and see. Some day you will remember what I have told you, you will know that Braggioni was your friend."

Laura feels a slow chill, a purely physical sense of danger, a warning in her blood that violence, mutilation, a shocking death, wait for her with lessening patience. She has translated this fear into something homely, immediate, and sometimes hesitates before crossing the street. "My personal fate is nothing, except as the testimony of a mental attitude," she reminds herself, quoting from some forgotten philosophic primer, and is sensible enough to add, "Anyhow, I shall not be killed by an automobile if I can help it."

"It may be true I am as corrupt, in another way, as Braggioni," she thinks in spite of herself, "as callous, as incomplete," and if this is so, any kind of death seems preferable. Still she sits quietly, she does not run. Where could she go? Uninvited she has promised herself to this place; she can no longer imagine herself as living in another country, and there is no pleasure in remembering her life before she came here.

Precisely what is the nature of this devotion, its true motives, and what are its obligations? Laura cannot say. She spends part of her days in Xochimilco, near by, teaching Indian children to say in English, "The cat is on the mat." When she appears in the classroom they crowd about her with smiles on their wise, innocent, clay-colored faces, crying, "Good morning, my titcher!" in immaculate voices, and they make of her desk a fresh garden of flowers every day.

During her leisure she goes to union meetings and listens to busy important voices quarreling over tactics, methods, internal politics. She visits the prisoners of her own political faith in their cells, where they entertain themselves with counting cockroaches, repenting of their indiscretions, composing their memoirs, writing out manifestoes and plans for their comrades who are still walking about free, hands in pockets, sniffing fresh air. Laura brings them food and cigarettes and a little money, and she brings messages disguised in equivocal phrases from the men outside who dare not set foot in the prison for fear of disappearing into the cells kept empty for them. If the prisoners confuse night and day, and complain, "Dear little Laura, time doesn't pass in this infernal hole, and I won't know when it is time to sleep unless I have a reminder," she brings them their favorite narcotics, and says in a tone that does not wound them with pity, "Tonight will really be night for you," and though her Spanish amuses them, they find her comforting, useful. If they lose patience and all faith, and curse the slowness of their friends in coming to their rescue with money and influence, they trust her not to repeat everything, and if she inquires,

"Where do you think we can find money, or influence?" they are certain to answer, "Well, there is Braggioni, why doesn't he do something?"

She smuggles letters from headquarters to men hiding from firing squads in back streets in mildewed houses, where they sit in tumbled beds and talk bitterly as if all Mexico were at their heels, when Laura knows positively they might appear at the band concert in the Alameda[4] on Sunday morning, and no one would notice them. But Braggioni says, "Let them sweat a little. The next time they may be careful. It is very restful to have them out of the way for a while." She is not afraid to knock on any door in any street after midnight, and enter in the darkness, and say to one of these men who is really in danger: "They will be looking for you—seriously—tomorrow morning after six. Here is some money from Vicente. Go to Vera Cruz and wait."

She borrows money from the Roumanian agitator to give to his bitter enemy the Polish agitator. The favor of Braggioni is their disputed territory, and Braggioni holds the balance nicely, for he can use them both. The Polish agitator talks love to her over café tables, hoping to exploit what he believes is her secret sentimental preference for him, and he gives her misinformation which he begs her to repeat as the solemn truth to certain persons. The Roumanian is more adroit. He is generous with his money in all good causes, and lies to her with an air of ingenuous candor, as if he were her good friend and confidant. She never repeats anything they may say. Braggioni never asks questions. He has other ways to discover all that he wishes to know about them.

Nobody touches her, but all praise her gray eyes, and the soft, round under lip which promises gayety, yet is always grave, nearly always firmly closed: and they cannot understand why she is in Mexico. She walks back and forth on her errands, with puzzled eyebrows, carrying her little folder of drawings and music and school papers. No dancer dances more beautifully than Laura walks, and she inspires some amusing, unexpected ardors, which cause little gossip, because nothing comes of them. A young captain who had been a soldier in Zapata's[5] army attempted, during a horseback ride near Cuernavaca, to express his desire for her with the noble simplicity befitting a rude folk-hero: but gently, because he was gentle. This gentleness was his defeat, for when he alighted, and removed her foot from the stirrup, and essayed to draw her down into his arms, her horse, ordinarily a tame one, shied fiercely, reared and plunged away. The young hero's horse careened blindly after his stable-mate, and the hero did not return to the hotel

4. Public square in Mexico City. 5. Emiliano Zapata (1883–1919), Mexican revolutionary general and agrarian reformer.

until rather late that evening. At breakfast he came to her table in full charro dress,[6] gray buckskin jacket and trousers with strings of silver buttons down the leg, and he was in a humorous, careless mood. "May I sit with you?" and "You are a wonderful rider. I was terrified that you might be thrown and dragged. I should never have forgiven myself. But I cannot admire you enough for your riding."

"I learned to ride in Arizona," said Laura.

"If you will ride with me again this morning, I promise you a horse that will not shy with you," he said. But Laura remembered that she must return to Mexico City at noon.

Next morning the children made a celebration and spent their playtime writing on the blackboard, "We lov ar ticher," and with tinted chalks they drew wreaths of flowers around the words. The young hero wrote her a letter: "I am a very foolish, wasteful, impulsive man. I should have first said I love you, and then you would not have run away. But you shall see me again." Laura thought, "I must send him a book of colored crayons," but she was trying to forgive herself for having spurred her horse at the wrong moment.

A brown, shock-haired youth came and stood in her patio one night and sang like a lost soul for two hours, but Laura could think of nothing to do about it. The moonlight spread a wash of gauzy silver over the clear spaces of the garden, and the shadows were cobalt blue. The scarlet blossoms of the Judas tree[7] were dull purple, and the names of the colors repeated themselves automatically in her mind, while she watched not the boy, but his shadow, fallen like a dark garment across the fountain rim, trailing in the water. Lupe came silently and whispered expert counsel in her ear: "If you will throw him one little flower, he will sing another song or two and go away." Laura threw the flower, and he sang a last song and went away with the flower tucked in the band of his hat. Lupe said, "He is one of the organizers of the Typographers Union, and before that he sold corridos[8] in the Merced market, and before that, he came from Guanajuato, where I was born. I would not trust any man, but I trust least those from Guanajuato."

She did not tell Laura that he would be back again the next night, and the next, nor that he would follow her at a certain fixed distance around the Merced market, through the Zócolo, up Francisco I. Madero Avenue, and so along the Paseo de la Reforma to Chapultepec Park, and into the Philosopher's Footpath,[9] still with that flower withering in his hat, and an indivisible attention in his eyes.

Now Laura is accustomed to him, it means nothing except that he is nineteen years old and is observing a convention with all propri-

6. Cowboy dress. 7. So called because Judas is said to have hanged himself on a tree of this kind. 8. Bullfight tickets. 9. Streets and parks in Mexico City. Francisco I. Madero (1873–1913) led the revolution against the dictator Porfirio Diaz (1830–1915).

ety, as though it were founded on a law of nature, which in the end it might well prove to be. He is beginning to write poems which he prints on a wooden press, and he leaves them stuck like handbills in her door. She is pleasantly disturbed by the abstract, unhurried watchfulness of his black eyes which will in time turn easily towards another object. She tells herself that throwing the flower was a mistake, for she is twenty-two years old and knows better; but she refuses to regret it, and persuades herself that her negation of all external events as they occur is a sign that she is gradually perfecting herself in the stoicism she strives to cultivate against that disaster she fears, though she cannot name it.

She is not at home in the world. Every day she teaches children who remain strangers to her, though she loves their tender round hands and their charming opportunist savagery. She knocks at unfamiliar doors not knowing whether a friend or a stranger shall answer, and even if a known face emerges from the sour gloom of that unknown interior, still it is the face of a stranger. No matter what this stranger says to her, nor what her message to him, the very cells of her flesh reject knowledge and kinship in one monotonous word. No. No. No. She draws her strength from this one holy talismanic word which does not suffer her to be led into evil. Denying everything, she may walk anywhere in safety, she looks at everything without amazement.

No, repeats this firm unchanging voice of her blood; and she looks at Braggioni without amazement. He is a great man, he wishes to impress this simple girl who covers her great round breasts with thick dark cloth, and who hides long, invaluably beautiful legs under a heavy skirt. She is almost thin except for the incomprehensible fullness of her breasts, like a nursing mother's, and Braggioni, who considers himself a judge of women, speculates again on the puzzle of her notorious virginity, and takes the liberty of speech which she permits without a sign of modesty, indeed, without any sort of sign, which is disconcerting.

"You think you are so cold, *gringita!* Wait and see. You will surprise yourself some day! May I be there to advise you!" He stretches his eyelids at her, and his ill-humored cat's eyes waver in a separate glance for the two points of light marking the opposite ends of a smoothly drawn path between the swollen curve of her breasts. He is not put off by that blue serge, nor by her resolutely fixed gaze. There is all the time in the world. His cheeks are bellying with the wind of song. "O girl with the dark eyes," he sings, and reconsiders. "But yours are not dark. I can change all that. O girl with the green eyes, you have stolen my heart away!" Then his mind wanders to the song, and Laura feels the weight of his attention being shifted elsewhere. Singing thus, he seems harmless, he is quite harmless, there is nothing to do but sit patiently and say "No," when the moment comes. She draws a full breath, and her mind wanders also, but not far. She dares not wander too far.

Not for nothing has Braggioni taken pains to be a good revolutionist and a professional lover of humanity. He will never die of it. He has the malice, the cleverness, the wickedness, the sharpness of wit, the hardness of heart, stipulated for loving the world profitably. *He will never die of it.* He will live to see himself kicked out from his feeding trough by other hungry world-saviors. Traditionally he must sing in spite of his life which drives him to bloodshed, he tells Laura, for his father was a Tuscany peasant who drifted to Yucatan and married a Maya woman:[1] a woman of race, an aristocrat. They gave him the love and knowledge of music, thus: and under the rip of his thumbnail, the strings of the instrument complain like exposed nerves.

Once he was called Delgadito by all the girls and married women who ran after him; he was so scrawny all his bones showed under his thin cotton clothing, and he could squeeze his emptiness to the very backbone with his two hands. He was a poet and the revolution was only a dream then; too many women loved him and sapped away his youth, and he could never find enough to eat anywhere, anywhere! Now he is a leader of men, crafty men who whisper in his ear, hungry men who wait for hours outside his office for a word with him, emaciated men with wild faces who waylay him at the street gate with a timid, "Comrade, let me tell you . . ." and they blow the foul breath from their empty stomachs in his face.

He is always sympathetic. He gives them handfuls of small coins from his own pockets, he promises them work, there will be demonstrations, they must join the unions and attend the meetings, above all they must be on the watch for spies. They are closer to him than his own brothers, without them he can do nothing—until tomorrow, comrade!

Until tomorrow. "They are stupid, they are lazy, they are treacherous, they would cut my throat for nothing," he says to Laura. He has good food and abundant drink, he hires an automobile and drives in the Paseo on Sunday morning, and enjoys plenty of sleep in a soft bed beside a wife who dares not disturb him; and he sits pampering his bones in easy billows of fat, singing to Laura, who knows and thinks these things about him. When he was fifteen, he tried to drown himself because he loved a girl, his first love, and she laughed at him. "A thousand women have paid for that," and his tight little mouth turns

1. I.e., an Indian woman. Tuscany is a region in west central Italy.

down at the corners. Now he perfumes his hair with Jockey Club, and confides to Laura: "One woman is really as good as another for me, in the dark. I prefer them all."

His wife organizes unions among the girls in the cigarette factories, and walks in picket lines, and even speaks at meetings in the evening. But she cannot be brought to acknowledge the benefits of true liberty. "I tell her I must have my freedom, net. She does not understand my point of view." Laura has heard this many times. Braggioni scratches the guitar and meditates. "She is an instinctively virtuous woman, pure gold, no doubt of that. If she were not, I should lock her up, and she knows it."

His wife, who works so hard for the good of the factory girls, employs part of her leisure lying on the floor weeping because there are so many women in the world, and only one husband for her, and she never knows where nor when to look for him. He told her: "Unless you can learn to cry when I am not here, I must go away for good." That day he went away and took a room at the Hotel Madrid.

It is this month of separation for the sake of higher principles that has been spoiled not only for Mrs. Braggioni, whose sense of reality is beyond criticism, but for Laura, who feels herself bogged in a nightmare. Tonight Laura envies Mrs. Braggioni, who is alone, and free to weep as much as she pleases about a concrete wrong. Laura has just come from a visit to the prison, and she is waiting for tomorrow with a bitter anxiety as if tomorrow may not come, but time may be caught immovably in this hour, with herself transfixed, Braggioni singing on forever, and Eugenio's body not yet discovered by the guard.

Braggioni says: "Are you going to sleep?" Almost before she can shake her head, he begins telling her about the May-day disturbances coming on in Morelia, for the Catholics hold a festival in honor of the Blessed Virgin, and the Socialists celebrate their martyrs on that day. "There will be two independent processions, starting from either end of town, and they will march until they meet, and the rest depends . . ." He asks her to oil and load his pistols. Standing up, he unbuckles his ammunition belt, and spreads it laden across her knees. Laura sits with the shells slipping through the cleaning cloth dipped in oil, and he says again he cannot understand why she works so hard for the revolutionary idea unless she loves some man who is in it. "Are you not in love with someone?" "No," says Laura. "And no one is in love with you?" "No." "Then it is your own fault. No woman need go begging. Why, what is the matter with you? The legless beggar woman in the Alameda has a perfectly faithful lover. Did you know that?"

Laura peers down the pistol barrel and says nothing, but a long, slow faintness rises and subsides in her; Braggioni curves his swollen fingers around the throat of the guitar and softly smothers the music out of it, and when she hears him again he seems to have forgotten her, and is speaking in the hypnotic voice he uses when talking in small rooms to a listening, close-gathered crowd. Some day this world, now seemingly so composed and eternal, to the edges of every sea shall be merely a tangle of gaping trenches, of crashing walls and broken bodies. Everything must be torn from its accustomed place where it has rotted for centuries, hurled skyward and distributed, cast down again clean as rain, without separate identity. Nothing shall survive that the stiffened hands of poverty have created for the rich and no one shall be left alive except the elect spirits destined to procreate a new world cleansed of cruelty and injustice, ruled by benevolent anarchy: "Pistols are good, I love them, cannon are even better, but in the end I pin my faith to good dynamite," he concludes, and strokes the pistol lying in her hands. "Once I dreamed of destroying this city, in case it offered resistance to General Ortiz,[2] but it fell into his hands like an over-ripe pear."

He is made restless by his own words, rises and stands waiting. Laura holds up the belt to him: "Put that on, and go kill somebody in Morelia, and you will be happier," she says softly. The presence of death in the room makes her bold. "Today, I found Eugenio going into a stupor. He refused to allow me to call the prison doctor. He had taken all the tablets I brought him yesterday. He said he took them because he was bored."

"He is a fool, and his death is his own business," says Braggioni, fastening his belt carefully.

"I told him if he had waited only a little while longer, you would have got him set free," says Laura. "He said he did not want to wait."

"He is a fool and we are well rid of him," says Braggioni, reaching for his hat.

He goes away. Laura knows his mood has changed, she will not see him any more for a while. He will send word when he needs her to go on errands into strange streets, to speak to the strange faces that will appear, like clay masks with the power of human speech, to mutter their thanks to Braggioni for his help. Now she is free, and she thinks, I must run while there is time. But she does not go.

Braggioni enters his own house where for a month his wife has spent many hours every night weeping and tangling her hair upon her pillow. She is weeping now, and she weeps more at the sight of him, the cause of all her sorrows. He looks about the room. Nothing is changed, the smells are good and familiar, he is well acquainted with the woman who comes toward him with no reproach except grief on her face. He says to her tenderly: "You are so good, please don't cry

2. Pascual Ortiz Rubio (1877–1963) was a revolutionary who became president of Mexico.

any more, you dear good creature." She says, "Are you tired, my angel? Sit here and I will wash your feet." She brings a bowl of water, and kneeling, unlaces his shoes, and when from her knees she raises her sad eyes under her blackened lids, he is sorry for everything, and bursts into tears. "Ah, yes, I am hungry, I am tired, let us eat something together," he says, between sobs. His wife leans her head on his arm and says, "Forgive me!" and this time he is refreshed by the solemn, endless rain of her tears.

Laura takes off her serge dress and puts on a white linen nightgown and goes to bed. She turns her head a little to one side, and lying still, reminds herself that it is time to sleep. Numbers tick in her brain like little clocks, soundless doors close of themselves around her. If you would sleep, you must not remember anything, the children will say tomorrow, good morning, my teacher, the poor prisoners who come every day bringing flowers to their jailor. 1-2-3-4-5—it is monstrous to confuse love with revolution, night with day, life with death—ah, Eugenio!

The tolling of the midnight bell is a signal, but what does it mean? Get up, Laura, and follow me: come out of your sleep, out of your bed, out of this strange house. What are you doing in this house? Without a word, without fear she rose and reached for Eugenio's hand, but he eluded her with a sharp, sly smile and drifted away. This is not all, you shall see—Murderer, he said, follow me, I will show you a new country, but it is far away and we must hurry. No, said Laura, not unless you take my hand, no; and she clung first to the stair rail, and then to the topmost branch of the Judas tree that bent down slowly and set her upon the earth, and then to the rocky ledge of a cliff, and then to the jagged wave of a sea that was not water but a desert of crumbling stone. Where are you taking me, she asked in wonder but without fear. To death, and it is a long way off, and we must hurry, said Eugenio. No, said Laura, not unless you take my hand. Then eat these flowers, poor prisoner, said Eugenio in a voice of pity, take and eat: and from the Judas tree he stripped the warm bleeding flowers, and held them to her lips. She saw that his hand was fleshless, a cluster of small white petrified branches, and his eye sockets were without light, but she ate the flowers greedily for they satisfied both hunger and thirst. Murderer! said Eugenio, and Cannibal! This is my body and my blood.[3] Laura cried No! and at the sound of her own voice, she awoke trembling, and was afraid to sleep again.

---

1. What advantages and disadvantages does Laura get from her friendship with Braggioni?

3. Allusion to Christ's words at the Last Supper. Luke 22:19–20.

2. What sets Laura apart from all the people she habitually deals with?
3. How has the author related past times and events to the present action of a single evening?
4. In what ways has Laura's Catholic background prepared her present attitudes as a revolutionary?
5. In what ways is the dream at the end a resolution of the conflicts of the story? Can there be a resolution for a person like Laura?

J. F. Powers

Powers (1917–) was born in Jacksonville, Illinois. After attending Northwestern University he was working in a Chicago bookstore when he wrote the first of the stories that brought him to prominence. Some of his best early stories deal with racial conflict in and around Chicago, but for the most part he has written about the moral and practical quandaries of Catholic life, particularly as these are manifested in the priesthood. He has published two novels, Morte D'Urban *(1962) and* Wheat That Springeth Green *(1988). His short stories have been collected in* Prince of Darkness and Other Stories *(1947),* The Presence of Grace *(1956), and* Look How the Fish Live *(1975).*

The Valiant Woman

They had come to the dessert in a dinner that was a shambles.

"Well, John," Father Nulty said, turning away from Mrs. Stoner and to Father Firman, long gone silent at his own table. "You've got the bishop coming for confirmations next week."

"Yes," Mrs. Stoner cut in, "and for dinner. And if he don't eat any more than he did last year—"

Father Firman, in a rare moment, faced it. "Mrs. Stoner, the bishop is not well. You know that."

"And after I fixed that fine dinner and all." Mrs. Stoner pouted in Father Nulty's direction.

"I wouldn't feel bad about it, Mrs. Stoner," Father Nulty said. "He never eats much anywhere."

"It's funny. And that new Mrs. Allers said he ate just fine when he was there," Mrs. Stoner argued, and then spit out, "but she's a damned liar!"

Father Nulty, unsettled but trying not to show it, said, "Who's Mrs. Allers?"

"She's at Holy Cross," Mrs. Stoner said.

"She's the housekeeper," Father Firman added, thinking Mrs. Stoner made it sound as though Mrs. Allers were the pastor there.

"I swear I don't know what to do about the dinner this year," Mrs. Stoner said.

Father Firman moaned. "Just do as you've always done, Mrs. Stoner."

"Huh! And have it all to throw out! Is that any way to do?"

"Is there any dessert?" Father Firman asked coldly.

Mrs. Stoner leaped up from the table and bolted into the kitchen, mumbling. She came back with a birthday cake. She plunged it in the center of the table. She found a big wooden match in her apron pocket and thrust it at Father Firman.

"I don't like this bishop," she said. "I never did. And the way he went and cut poor Ellen Kennedy out of Father Doolin's will!"

She went back into the kitchen.

"Didn't they talk a lot of filth about Doolin and the housekeeper?" Father Nulty asked.

"I should think they did," Father Firman said. "All because he took her to the movies on Sunday night. After he died and the bishop cut her out of the will, though I hear he gives her a pension privately, they talked about the bishop."

"I don't like this bishop at all," Mrs. Stoner said, appearing with a cake knife. "Bishop Doran—there was the man!"

"We know," Father Firman said. "All man and all priest."

"He did know real estate," Father Nulty said.

Father Firman struck the match.

"Not on the chair!" Mrs. Stoner cried, too late.

Father Firman set the candle burning—it was suspiciously large and yellow, like a blessed one, but he could not be sure. They watched the fluttering flame.

"I'm forgetting the lights!" Mrs. Stoner said, and got up to turn them off. She went into the kitchen again.

The priests had a moment of silence in the candle-light.

"Happy birthday, John," Father Nulty said softly. "Is it fifty-nine you are?"

"As if you didn't know, Frank," Father Firman said, "and you the same but one."

Father Nulty smiled, the old gold of his incisors shining in the flickering light, his collar whiter in the dark, and raised his glass of water, which would have been wine or better in the bygone days, and toasted Father Firman.

"Many of 'em, John."

"Blow it out," Mrs. Stoner said, returning to the room. She waited by the light switch for Father Firman to blow out the candle.

Mrs. Stoner, who ate no desserts, began to clear the dishes into the kitchen, and the priests, finishing their cake and coffee in a hurry, went to sit in the study.

Father Nulty offered a cigar.

"John?"

"My ulcers, Frank."

"Ah, well, you're better off." Father Nulty lit the cigar and crossed his long black legs. "Fish Frawley has got him a Filipino, John. Did you hear?"

Father Firman leaned forward, interested. "He got rid of the woman he had?"

"He did. It seems she snooped."

"Snooped, eh?"

"She did. And gossiped. Fish introduced two town boys to her, said, 'Would you think these boys were my nephews?' That's all, and the next week the paper had it that his two nephews were visiting him from Erie. After that, he let her believe he was going East to see his parents, though both are dead. The paper carried the story. Fish returned and made a sermon out of it. Then he got the Filipino."

Father Firman squirmed with pleasure in his chair. "That's like Fish, Frank. He can do that." He stared at the tips of his fingers bleakly. "You could never get a Filipino to come to a place like this."

"Probably not," Father Nulty said. "Fish is pretty close to Minneapolis. Ah, say, do you remember the trick he played on us all in Marmion Hall!"

"That I'll never forget!" Father Firman's eyes remembered. "Getting up New Year's morning and finding the toilet seats all painted!"

"*Happy Circumcision!* Hah!" Father Nulty had a coughing fit.

When he had got himself together again, a mosquito came and sat on his wrist. He watched it a moment before bringing his heavy hand down. He raised his hand slowly, viewed the dead mosquito, and sent it spinning with a plunk of his middle finger.

"Only the female bites," he said.

"I didn't know that," Father Firman said.

"Ah, yes . . ."

Mrs. Stoner entered the study and sat down with some sewing—Father Firman's black socks.

She smiled pleasantly at Father Nulty. "And what do you think of the atom bomb, Father?"

"Not much," Father Nulty said.

Mrs. Stoner had stopped smiling. Father Firman yawned.

Mrs. Stoner served up another: "Did you read about this communist convert, Father?"

"He's been in the Church before," Father Nulty said, "and so it's not a conversion, Mrs. Stoner."

"No? Well, I already got him down on my list of Monsignor's[1] converts."

"It's better than a conversion, Mrs. Stoner, for there is more

1. Monsignor Fulton Sheen (1895–1979), famous for converting celebrities to Catholicism.

rejoicing in heaven over the return of . . . uh, he that was lost, Mrs. Stoner, is found."

"And that congresswoman, Father?"

"Yes. A convert—she."

"And Henry Ford's grandson, Father. I got him down."

"Yes, to be sure."

Father Firman yawned, this time audibly, and held his jaw.

"But he's one only by marriage, Father," Mrs. Stoner said. "I always say you got to watch those kind."

"Indeed you do, but a convert nonetheless, Mrs. Stoner. Remember, Cardinal Newman[2] himself was one."

Mrs. Stoner was unimpressed. "I see where Henry Ford's making steering wheels out of soybeans, Father."

"I didn't see that."

"I read it in the *Reader's Digest* or some place."

"Yes, well . . ." Father Nulty rose and held his hand out to Father Firman. "John," he said. "It's been good."

"I heard Hirohito's[3] next," Mrs. Stoner said, returning to converts.

"Let's wait and see, Mrs. Stoner," Father Nulty said.

The priests walked to the door.

"You know where I live, John."

"Yes. Come again, Frank. Good night."

Father Firman watched Father Nulty go down the walk to his car at the curb. He hooked the screen door and turned off the porch light. He hesitated at the foot of the stairs, suddenly moved to go to bed. But he went back into the study.

"Phew!" Mrs. Stoner said. "I thought he'd never go. Here it is after eight o'clock."

Father Firman sat down in his rocking chair. "I don't see him often," he said.

"I give up!" Mrs. Stoner exclaimed, flinging the holey socks upon the horsehair sofa. "I'd swear you had a nail in your shoe."

"I told you I looked."

"Well, you ought to look again. And cut your toenails, why don't you? Haven't I got enough to do?"

Father Firman scratched in his coat pocket for a pill, found one, swallowed it. He let his head sink back against the chair and closed his eyes. He could hear her moving about the room, making the preparations; and how he knew them—the fumbling in the drawer for a pencil with a point, the rip of the page from his daily calendar, and finally the leg of the card table sliding up against his leg.

2. Henry Cardinal Newman (1801–1890), an English convert to Catholicism who became an influential Catholic writer. 3. (1901–1989), emperor of Japan from 1926 to his death.

He opened his eyes. She yanked the floor lamp alongside the table, setting the bead fringe tinkling on the shade, and pulled up her chair on the other side. She sat down and smiled at him for the first time that day. Now she was happy.

She swept up the cards and began to shuffle with the abandoned virtuosity of an old riverboat gambler, standing them on end, fanning them out, whirling them through her fingers, dancing them halfway up her arm, cracking the whip over them. At last they lay before him tamed into a neat deck.

"Cut?"

"Go ahead," he said. She liked to go first.

She gave him her faint, avenging smile and drew a card, cast it aside for another which he thought must be an ace from the way she clutched it face down.

She was getting all the cards, as usual, and would have been invincible if she had possessed his restraint and if her cunning had been of a higher order. He knew a few things about leading and lying back that she would never learn. Her strategy was attack, forever attack, with one baffling departure: she might sacrifice certain tricks as expendable if only she could have the last ones, the heartbreaking ones, if she could slap them down one after another, shatteringly.

She played for blood, no bones about it, but for her there was no other way; it was her nature, as it was the lion's, and for this reason he found her ferocity pardonable, more a defect of the flesh, venial, while his own trouble was all in the will, mortal.[4] He did not sweat and pray over each card as she must, but he did keep an eye out for reneging and demanded a cut now and then just to aggravate her, and he was always secretly hoping for aces.

With one card left in her hand, the telltale trick coming next, she delayed playing it, showing him first the smile, the preview of defeat. She laid it on the table—so! She held one more trump than he had reasoned possible. Had she palmed it from somewhere? No, she would not go that far; that would not be fair, was worse than reneging, which so easily and often happened accidentally, and she believed in being fair. Besides he had been watching her.

God smote the vines with hail, the sycamore trees with frost, and offered up the flocks to the lightning—but Mrs. Stoner! What a cross Father Firman had from God in Mrs. Stoner! There were other housekeepers as bad, no doubt, walking the rectories of the world, yes, but . . . yes. He could name one and maybe two priests who were worse off. One, maybe two. Cronin. His scraggly blonde of sixty—take her,

4. "Venial": describing a sin committed in a minor matter without reflection and hence pardonable; "mortal": a sin committed with awareness of guilt and full consent, held in Roman Catholicism to bring death to the soul.

with her everlasting banging on the grand piano, the gift of the pastor; her proud talk about the goiter operation at the Mayo Brothers',[5] also a gift; her honking the parish Buick at passing strange priests because they were all in the game together. She was worse. She was something to keep the home fires burning. Yes sir. And Cronin said she was not a bad person really, but what was he? He was quite a freak himself.

For that matter, could anyone say that Mrs. Stoner was a bad person? No. He could not say it himself, and he was no freak. She had her points, Mrs. Stoner. She was clean. And though she cooked poorly, could not play the organ, would not take up the collection in an emergency, and went to card parties, and told all—even so, she was clean. She washed everything. Sometimes her underwear hung down beneath her dress like a paratrooper's pants, but it and everything she touched was clean. She washed constantly. She was clean.

She had her other points, to be sure—her faults, you might say. She snooped—no mistake about it—but it was not snooping for snooping's sake; she had a reason. She did other things, always with a reason. She overcharged on rosaries and prayer books, but that was for the sake of the poor. She censored the pamphlet rack, but that was to prevent scandal. She pried into the baptismal and matrimonial records, but there was no other way if Father was out, and in this way she had once uncovered a bastard and flushed him out of the rectory, but that was the perverted decency of the times. She held her nose over bad marriages in the presence of the victims, but that was her sorrow and came from having her husband buried in a mine. And he had caught her telling a bewildered young couple that there was only one good reason for their wanting to enter into a mixed marriage—the child had to have a name, and that—that was what?

She hid his books, kept him from smoking, picked his friends (usually the pastors of her colleagues), bawled out people for calling after dark, had no humor, except at cards, and then it was grim, very grim, and she sat hatchet-faced every morning at Mass. But she went to Mass, which was all that kept the church from being empty some mornings. She did annoying things all day long. She said annoying things into the night. She said she had given him the best years of her life. Had she? Perhaps—for the miner had her only a year. It was too bad, sinfully bad, when he thought of it like that. But all talk of best years and life was nonsense. He had to consider the heart of the matter, the essence. The essence was that housekeepers were hard to get, harder to get than ushers, than willing workers, than organists, than secretaries—yes, harder to get than assistants or vocations.[6]

And she was a *saver*—saved money, saved electricity, saved string,

5. The Mayo Clinic in Rochester, Minnesota.

6. An authentic call from God to the priesthood.

bags, sugar, saved—him. That's what she did. That's what she said she did, and she was right, in a way. In a way, she was usually right. In fact, she was always right—in a way. And you could never get a Filipino to come way out here and live. Not a young one anyway, and he had never seen an old one. Not a Filipino. They liked to dress up and live.

Should he let it drop about Fish having one, just to throw a scare into her, let her know he was doing some thinking? No. It would be a perfect cue for the one about a man needing a woman to look after him. He was not up to that again, not tonight.

Now she was doing what she liked most of all. She was making a grand slam, playing it out card for card, though it was in the bag, prolonging what would have been cut short out of mercy in gentle company. Father Firman knew the agony of losing.

She slashed down the last card, a miserable deuce trump, and did in the hapless king of hearts he had been saving.

"Skunked you!"

She was awful in victory. Here was the bitter end of their long day together, the final murderous hour in which all they wanted to say—all he wouldn't and all she couldn't—came out in the cards. Whoever won at honeymoon[7] won the day, slept on the other's scalp, and God alone had to help the loser.

"We've been at it long enough, Mrs. Stoner," he said, seeing her assembling the cards for another round.

"Had enough, huh!"

Father Firman grumbled something.

"No?"

"Yes."

She pulled the table away and left it against the wall for the next time. She went out of the study carrying the socks, content and clucking. He closed his eyes after her and began to get under way in the rocking chair, the nightly trip to nowhere. He could hear her brewing a cup of tea in the kitchen and conversing with the cat. She made her way up the stairs, carrying the tea, followed by the cat, purring.

He waited, rocking out to sea, until she would be sure to be through in the bathroom. Then he got up and locked the front door (she looked after the back door) and loosened his collar going upstairs.

In the bathroom he mixed a glass of antiseptic, always afraid of pyorrhea, and gargled to ward off pharyngitis.

When he turned on the light in his room, the moths and beetles began to batter against the screens, the lighter insects humming. . . .

Yes, and she had the guest room. How did she come to get that?

7. Honeymoon bridge, a two-player version of a normally four-player game.

Why wasn't she in the back room, in her proper place? He knew, if he cared to remember. The screen in the back room—it let in mosquitoes, and if it didn't do that she'd love to sleep back there, Father, looking out at the steeple and the blessed cross on top, Father, if it just weren't for the screen, Father. Very well, Mrs. Stoner, I'll get it fixed or fix it myself. Oh, could you now, Father? I could, Mrs. Stoner, and I will. In the meantime you take the guest room. Yes, Father, and thank you, Father, the house ringing with amenities then. Years ago, all that. She was a pie-faced girl then, not really a girl perhaps, but not too old to marry again. But she never had. In fact, he could not remember that she had even tried for a husband since coming to the rectory, but, of course, he could be wrong, not knowing how they went about it. God! God save us! Had she got her wires crossed and mistaken him all these years for *that? That!* Him! Suffering God! No. That was going too far. That was getting morbid. No. He must not think of that again, ever. No.

But just the same she had got the guest room and she had it yet. Well, did it matter? Nobody ever came to see him any more, nobody to stay overnight anyway, nobody to stay very long . . . not any more. He knew how they laughed at him. He had heard Frank humming all right—before he saw how serious and sad the situation was and took pity—humming, "Wedding Bells Are Breaking Up That Old Gang of Mine." But then they'd always laughed at him for something—for not being an athlete, for wearing glasses, for having kidney trouble . . . and mail coming addressed to Rev. and Mrs. Stoner.

Removing his shirt, he bent over the table to read the volume left open from last night. He read, translating easily, "Eisdem licet cum illis . . . Clerics are allowed to reside only with women about whom there can be no suspicion, either because of a natural bond (as mother, sister, aunt) or of advanced age, combined in both cases with good repute."

Last night he had read it, and many nights before, each time as though this time to find what was missing, to find what obviously was not in the paragraph, his problem considered, a way out. She was not mother, not sister, not aunt, and *advanced age* was a relative term (why, she was younger than he was) and so, eureka, she did not meet the letter of the law—but, alas, how she fulfilled the spirit! And besides it would be a slimy way of handling it after all her years of service. He could not afford to pension her off, either.

He slammed the book shut. He slapped himself fiercely on the back, missing the wily mosquito, and whirled to find it. He took a magazine and folded it into a swatter. Then he saw it—oh, the preternatural cunning of it!—poised in the beard of St. Joseph on the bookcase. He could not hit it there. He teased it away, wanting it to light on the wall, but it knew his thoughts and flew high away. He swung wildly, hoping to stun it, missed, swung back, catching St. Joseph across the neck. The statue fell to the floor and broke.

Mrs. Stoner was panting in the hall outside his door.

"What is it!"

"Mosquitoes!"

"What is it, Father? Are you hurt?"

"Mosquitoes—damn it! And only the female bites!"

Mrs. Stoner, after a moment, said, "Shame on you, Father. She needs the blood for her eggs."

He dropped the magazine and lunged at the mosquito with his bare hand.

She went back to her room, saying, "Pshaw, I thought it was burglars murdering you in your bed."

He lunged again.

---

1. How much of Father Firman's life is summed up in the short span of the evening's action?
2. Is Mrs. Stoner alone responsible for having made his life a "shambles"?
3. Is Mrs. Stoner aware of how she has distorted her position in the household? Is her relative ignorance the same as relative innocence? Does the story suggest that intelligence may be a handicap in dealing with stupid people?
4. Why, precisely, can't Father Firman get rid of Mrs. Stoner? What has this to do with his inability to swat the mosquito that is tormenting him?
5. What does Father Firman mean by "the perverted decency of the times"?

Mary Robison

Robison (1949–) was born in Washington, D.C., and was educated at Ohio State University and Johns Hopkins. She has subsequently taught writing at Harvard and other universities. Her novel Oh! *was published in 1981. Many of her stories are collected in* Days *(1979),* An Amateur's Guide to the Night *(1983), and* Believe Them *(1988).*

Coach

I

The August two-a-day practice sessions were sixty-seven days away, Coach calculated. He was drying breakfast dishes. He swabbed a coffee cup and made himself listen to his wife, who was across the kitchen, sponging the stove's burner coils.

"I know I'm no Rembrandt," Sherry said, "but I have so damn much fun trying, and this little studio—this room—we can afford. I could get out of your way by going there and get you and Daphne out of my way. No offense."

"I'm thinking," Coach said.

His wife coasted from appliance to appliance. She swiped the face of the oven clock with her sponge. "You're thinking too slow. Your reporter's coming at nine and it's way after eight now. Should I give them a deposit on the studio or not? Yes or no?"

Coach was staring at the sink, at a thread of water that came from one of the taps. He thought of the lake place where they used to go in North Carolina. He saw green water being thickly sliced by a power boat; the boat towing Sherry, who was blonde and laughing on her skis, her rounded back strong, her suit shining red.

"Of course, of course, give them the money," he said.

Their daughter, Daphne, wandered into the kitchen. She was dark-haired, lazy-looking, fifteen. Her eyes were lost behind bangs. She drew open the enormous door of the refrigerator.

"Don't hang, Daphne, you'll unhinge things," her mother said. "What are you after?"

"Food mainly," Daphne said.

Sherry went away, to the little sun patio off the kitchen. Coach pushed the glass door sideways after her and it smacked shut.

"Eat and run," he said to Daphne. "I've got a reporter coming in short order. Get dressed." He spoke firmly but in the smaller voice he always used for his child.

"Yes, sir," Daphne said. She broke into the freezer compartment and ducked to let its gate pass over her head. "Looks bad. Nothing in here but Eggos."

"I ate Eggos. Just hustle up," Coach said.

"Can I be here for this guy?" Daphne asked.

"Who guy? The reporter? Nuh-uh. He's just from the college, Daph. Coming to see if the new freshman coach has three heads or just two."

Daphne was nodding at the food jars racked on the wide refrigerator door. "Hey, lookit," she said. She blew a breath in front of the freezer compartment and made a short jet of mist.

Coach remembered a fall night, a Friday-game night, long ago, when he had put Daphne on the playing field. It was during the ceremonies before his unbeaten squad had taken on Ignatius South High School. Parents' Night. He had laced shoulder pads on Daphne and draped the trainer's gag jersey—number 1/2—over her, and balanced Tim-somebody's helmet on her eight-year-old head. She was lost in the getup, a small pile of equipment out on the fifty-yard line. She had applauded when the loudspeaker announced her name, when the p.a. voice, garbled by amplification and echo, had rung out, "Daughter of our coach, Harry Noonan, and his wife—number one-half, Daphne Noonan!" She had stood in the bath of floodlights, shaking as the players and their folks strolled by—the players grim in their war gear, the parents tiny and apologetic-seeming in civilian clothes. The co-captain of the team, awesome in his pads and cleats and steaming from warm-up running, had palmed Daphne's big helmet and twisted it sideways. From behind, from the home stands, Coach had heard, "Haaa!" as Daphne turned circles of happy confusion, trying to right the helmet. Through the ear hole her left eye had twinkled, Coach remembered. He had heard, "God, that's funny," and "Coach's kid."

On the sun porch now, his wife was doing a set of tennis exercises. She was between Coach and the morning sun, framed by the glass doors. He could see through the careless weave of her caftan, enough to make out the white flesh left by her swimsuit.

"I knew you wouldn't let me," Daphne said. She had poured a glass of chocolate milk. She pulled open a chilled banana. "I bet Mom gets to be here."

"Daph, this isn't a big deal. We've been through it all before," Coach said.

"Not for a college paper," Daphne said. "Wait a minute, I'll be right back." She left the kitchen.

"I'll hold my breath and count the heartbeats," Coach said to the space she had left behind.

They were new to the little town, new to Pennsylvania. Coach was assuming charge of the freshman squad, in a league where freshmen weren't eligible for the varsity. He had taken the job, not sure if it was a step up for him or a serious misstep. The money was so-so. But he wanted the college setting for his family—especially for Daphne. She had been seeming to lose interest in the small celebrity they achieved in high-school towns. She had acted bored at the Noonans' Sunday spaghetti dinners for standout players. She had stopped fetching plates of food for the boys, who were too game-sore to get their own. She had even stopped wearing the charm bracelet her parents had put together for her—a silver bracelet with a tiny megaphone, the numerals 68—a league championship year—and, of course, a miniature football.

Coach took a seat at the kitchen table. He ate grapes from a bowl. He spilled bottled wheat germ into his palm. On the table were four chunky ring binders, their black leatherette covers printed with the college seal—which still looked strange to him. These were his playbooks, and he was having trouble getting the play tactics into his head.

"Will you turn off the radio?" he yelled.

The bleat from Daphne's upstairs bedroom ceased. A minute later she came down and into the kitchen. She had a cardboard folder and some textbooks with her. "Later on, would you look at this stuff and help me? Can you do these?" she asked Coach.

He glanced over one of her papers. It was penciled with algebra equations, smutty with erasures and scribbled-out parts. "I'd have to see the book, but no. Not now, not later. I don't want to and I don't have time."

"That's just great," Daphne said.

"Your mother and I got our Algebra homework done already, Daph. We turned ours in," Coach said. "This was in nineteen fifty-six."

"Mom!" Daphne said, pushing aside the glass door.

"Forget it," Sherry said.

II

Toby, the boy sent from *The Rooter* to interview Coach, was unshaven and bleary-eyed. He wore a rumpled cerise polo shirt and faded Levi's. He asked few questions, dragging his words. Now and then he grumbled of a hangover and no sleep. He yawned during Coach's answers. He took no notes.

"You're getting this now?" Coach said.

"Oh, yeah, it's writing itself, I'm such a pro," Toby said, and Coach wasn't certain if the boy was kidding.

"So, you've been here just a little while. Lucky you," Toby said. "Less than a month?"

"Is that like a question? It seems less than less than a month—less than week—a day and a half," Coach said.

For the interview, he had put on white sports slacks and a maroon pullover with a gold collar—the college's colors. The pullover he had bought at Campus World. The clothes had a snug fit that flattered Coach and showed off his flat stomach and heavy biceps.

He and Toby were on either end of the sofa in the living room of the house, a wooden two-story Coach had found and would be paying off for decades, he was sure.

Toby said, "Well, believe it or not, I've got enough for a couple sticks, which is shoptalk among we press men for two columns. If you're going to be home tomorrow, there's a girl who'll come and take your picture—Marcia. She's a drag, I warn you."

"One thing about this town, there aren't any damn sidewalks, and the cars don't give you much room if you're jogging," Coach said, standing up.

"Hell, tell me about it. When I'm hitching, I wear an orange poncho and carry a red flat and paint a big X on my back. Of course, I'm probably just making a better target," the reporter said.

"I jog down at the track now. It's a great facility, comparable to a Big Ten's. I like the layout," Coach said.

"Okay, but the interview's over," Toby said.

"Well, I came from high schools, remember. In Indiana and Ohio—good schools with good budgets, mind you, but high schools, nonetheless."

"Yeah, I got where you're coming from," Toby said.

"Did you need to know what courses I'll be handling? Fall quarter, they've got me lined up for two things: The Atlantic World is the first one, and Colloquium on European Industrial Development, I think it is. Before, I always taught World History. P.O.D.,[1] once or twice."

"That three-eighty-one you're going to teach is a tit course, in case nobody's informed you. It's what we call lunch," Toby said.

"It's, in nature, a refresher class," Coach said.

"Yeah, or out of nature," Toby said.

1. Problems of Democracy.

Daphne came from the long hall steps into the living room. Her dark hair was brushed and lifting with static. Her eyes seemed to Coach larger than usual, and a little sooty around the lashes.

"You're just leaving, aren't you, buster?" Coach said to her.

"Retrieving a pencil," Daphne said.

"Is your name really Buster?" Toby asked.

"Get your pencil and scoot. This is Toby here. Toby, this is my daughter, Daphne," Coach said.

"Nice to meet you," Daphne said. She slipped into a deep chair at the far corner of the long living room.

"Can she hear us over in that country?" Toby said. "Do you read me?" he shouted.

Daphne smiled. Coach saw bangs and her very white teeth.

"Come on, Daph, hit the trail," he said.

"I've got a joke for her first," Toby said. "What's green and moves very fast?"

"Frog in a blender," Daphne said. "Dad? Some friends invited me to go swimming with them at the Natatorium. May I?"

"You've got to see the Nat. It's the best thing," Toby said.

"What about your class, though? She's in makeup school here, Toby, catching up on some algebra that didn't take the first time around."

Toby wrinkled his nose at Daphne. "At first, I thought you meant *makeup* school, like lipstick and rouge."

"I wish," Daphne said.

She slipped her foot from her leather sandal and casually stroked the toes.

"She's a nut for swimming," Coach said.

"You'll be so bored here. Most nights, your options are either ordering a pizza or slashing your wrists," Toby told Daphne.

"Oh," she said, rolling her chin on her shoulder in a rather seductive way.

"Take it from Toby," he said.

Coach let Toby through the front door, and watched until he was down the street.

"He was nice," Daphne said.

"Aw, Daph. That's what you say about everybody. There's a lot better things you could say—more on-the-beam things."

"I guess you're mad," she said.

Coach went to the kitchen, to sit down with his playbooks again. Daphne came after him.

"Aren't you?" she said.

"I guess you thought he was cute," Coach said. He flapped through some mimeographed pages, turning them on the notebook's silver rings.

"I don't mean to shock you about it, but you'd be wasting your time there, Daph. You'd be trying to start a fire with a wet match."

Daphne stared at her father. "That's sick!" she said.

"I'm not criticizing him for it. I'm just telling you," Coach said.

III

"This is completely wrong," Coach said sadly. He read further. "Oh, no," he said. He drowned the newspaper in his bath water and slogged the pages over into a corner by the commode.

His wife handed him a dry edition, one of the ten or twelve *Rooters* Daphne had brought home.

Sherry was parallel to Coach on the edge of the tub, sitting with her back braced against the wall. "Oh, cheer up," she said. "Nobody reads a free newspaper."

Coach quartered the dry *Rooter* into a package around Toby's article. "Well, I wasn't head coach at Elmgrove, and I sure wasn't Phi Beta Kappa. And look at this picture," Coach said.

"What's wrong with it?" Sherry said.

"Where did he get that you were at Mt. Holyoke? And I didn't bitch about the sidewalks this much."

"You didn't?" Sherry said. "That's almost too bad. I thought that was the best part of the article."

Coach slunk farther into the warm water until it crowded his chin. He kept the newspaper aloft. "Oh, come on, give me some credit here! Don't they have any supervision over in Journalism? I don't see how he could get away with this shit. It's an unbelievably sloppy job."

"It's just a dinky article in a handout paper, Coach. What do you care? It wouldn't matter if he said we were a bright-green family with scales," Sherry said.

"He didn't think of that or he would have. This breaks my heart," Coach said.

"Daph liked it," Sherry said.

Coach wearily chopped bath water with the side of his hand and threw a splash at the soap recess in the tiled wall. "I tell you, I'm going to be spending my whole first year here explaining how none of it's true."

"What difference does true make?" Sherry said.

IV

Coach was seated awkwardly on an iron stool at a white table on the patio of the Dairy Frost. Daphne was across from him, fighting the early evening heat for her mocha-fudge cone. She tilted her head at the cone, lapping at it.

"You aren't saying anything," Coach said.

"Wait," Daphne said.

She worked on the cone.

"I've been waiting."

"If you two want to separate, it's none of my business," she said.

They were facing the busy parking lot when a new Pontiac turned in off the highway, glided easily onto the gravel, took a parking slot close by. In the driver's seat was a boy with built-up shoulders—a boy who looked very familiar to Coach. In the back was a couple in their fifties—the boy's parents, Coach thought—both talking at once.

"Have I been spilling all this breath for nothing? *Not* a separation," Coach said. "Not anything like it."

"All right, not," Daphne said. She stopped in her attack on the cone long enough to watch the Pontiac boy step out. Dark brown ice cream streamed between her knuckles and down the inside of her wrist.

"You're losing it, honey," Coach said.

Daphne dabbed around the cone and her hand, making repairs.

"Hell, *real* trouble your father wouldn't tell you about at a *Dairy* Frost. This apartment your mom found is like an office or something. A studio for her to go to and get away every now and then. That kid's in my backfield. What the *hell's* his name?"

They watched as the young man took orders from his parents, then went inside the Dairy Frost. He looked both wider and taller than the other patrons, out of their scale. His rump and haunches were thick with muscle. His neck was fat but tight.

"Bobby Stark!" Coach said, and smiled very quickly at the parents in the Pontiac. He turned back to his daughter.

"She wants to get away from us," Daphne said.

"Definitely not. She gave me a list, is how this whole thing started. She's got stuff she wants to do, and you with your school problems and me with the team—we're too much for her, see? She could spend her entire day on us, if you think about it, and never have one second for herself. If you think about it fairly, Daphne, you'll agree."

Daphne seemed to consider. She was focused on the inside of the Dairy Frost building, and for a while she kept still.

"That guy looks dumb. One of the truly dumb," she said.

"My halfback? He's not. He was his class salutatorian," Coach said.

"He doesn't know *you*."

"Just embarrassed," Coach said. "Can we stick to the point, Daph? And quit rocking the boat. Look what you're doing?" Daphne's arm was on the table and she was violently swinging her legs under her chair.

She made a sigh and marched over to a trash can to deposit her slumping cone. Then she washed up at the children's drinking fountain and rejoined Coach, who had finished his Brown Cow but had kept the plastic spoon in his mouth.

"What was on this list of Mom's?" Daphne asked.

"Adult stuff," Coach said.

"Just give me an example."

Coach removed the plastic spoon and cracked it in half.

"Your mother's list is for five years. In that time, she wants to be speaking French regularly. She wants to follow up on her printmaking."

"This is adult stuff?" Daphne said.

Coach raised a hand to Bobby Stark. Stark had three malt cups in a cardboard carrier and he was moving toward the parking lot.

"Hey, those all for you?" Coach called out.

"I got a month to get fat, Coach. You'll have five months to beat it off me," the boy called back.

The people at some of the tables around Coach's lit up with grins. Bobby Stark's parents were grinning.

"Every hit of that junk takes a second off your time in the forty—just remember that!" Coach shouted.

Stark wagged his head ruefully, his cheeks blushing. He pretended to hide the malts behind his arm.

"Duh," Daphne said in a hoarse voice. "Which way to the door, Coach?"

"He can hear you," Coach said.

"Duh, kin I have a candy bar, Coach?" she rasped.

They faced Stark, who smiled a little crookedly at Daphne, and threw her a wink so dazzling, she went silent.

V

Coach was in the basement laundry room, both arms busy hugging a bundle of jogging clothes. He was waiting on the washer, waiting for Sherry to unload her clothes.

"The Cowboys are soaking their players in a sense-deprivation tub of warm saltwater," she said.

"We know," Coach said.

"If Dallas is doing it, I just thought you might want to consider it."

"We have. Hustle up a little with your stuff, will you?" Coach said.

"It's like my apartment," Sherry said. "A place apart."

Coach cut her off. "Don't go on about how much you love your apartment."

"I wasn't going to," Sherry said. She slung her wet slacks and blouses into the dryer.

Coach had just two weeks before the start of the heavy practices. His team would have him then, he knew, almost straight through the Christmas holidays.

"I like that," Coach said. "A place apart."

A half hour later, Coach and his wife were on the side patio. They could hear the tick of the clothes dryer downstairs. Sherry had changed into a halter top. She was taking sun on her back, adding to her tan.

"You know what's odd?" she said. "Daphne's popularity here. I don't mean it's odd."

"She's always done terrific with people, always gone over well," Coach said.

"*Your* people, though. These are hers," Sherry said. "Like that reporter."

"Yeah, they're like sisters," Coach said.

VI

It was a week before the two-a-day practice sessions would begin. The sky was colorless and glazed, like milk glass. When Coach looked at the sun, his eyes ached, his head screamed.

He had run some wind sprints on the stadium field, and now he was doing an easy lap. A stopwatch on a noose of ribbon swung against his chest. He cut through the goalposts and trotted for the sidelines, for the twenty, where he had dumped his clipboard and a towel.

Someone called to him.

Blond Bobby Stark came out from under the stands. His football shoes were laced together and draped around his neck. He wore a midriff-cut T-shirt and shorts. He walked gingerly in white wool socks.

"Did everybody go? Or am I the first one here?" he called to Coach.

"'Bout a half hour," Coach said, heaving.

Stark sat down to untangle his shoes, and Coach, sweating, stood over him.

Coach spat. He folded his arms in a way that pushed out his muscles. He sniffed, twisting his whole nose and mouth to the left. He said, "You know Stark, you were salutatorian for your class."

"High school," the boy said. He grinned up at Coach, an eye pinched against the glare.

"That counts, believe me. Maybe we can use you to help some of our slower players along—some of the linemen, maybe I'm thinking."

"What do you mean—tutor?" Stark said.

"Naw. Teach them to eat without biting off their fingers. How to tie a necktie. Some of your style," Coach said, and Stark bobbed his head.

Stark settled the fit of his right shoe. He said, "But there aren't any really dumb ones on our squad, because they'd just get flunked out. Recruiters won't touch them in this league. There wouldn't be any percentage in it."

"Then I'm greatly relieved," Coach said.

He planted his foot along a furrow of lime-eaten grass. He faced the open end of the stadium, where the enormous library building stood shimmering and uncertain behind sheets of heat that rose from the parking area.

Stark stood up and studied his shoes as he began jogging in place. He danced twenty yards down the field; loped back.

Other players were arriving for the informal session. Coach meant to time them in the mile, and in some dashes.

Stark looked jittery. He walked in semicircles, crowding Coach.

"What're you worried about?" Coach asked him. "Girl problems you got? You pull a muscle already?"

Stark glanced quickly around them. He said, "I live all my life two doors down from Coach Burton's house. My mom and Burton's wife are best friends, so I always know what's going on."

Burton had been the head coach of the varsity team for over a decade.

"You probably know about it already, anyway," Stark said. "Do you?"

"What the hell are you talking about, Stark?"

"You don't know? Typical. Burton's leaving, see? Like at the end of this year. His wife wants him out real bad, and the alumni want him out because they're tired of losing seasons. So what I heard was you were brought in because of it. And if we do okay this season, like you'll be varsity coach next year."

"That's conjecture," Coach said. But he was excited.

It was three o'clock, still hot. Coach was moving along a sidewalk with Bobby Stark, who was balanced on a racing bicycle, moving just enough to keep the machine upright.

"Three things," Coach said, "I've seen all the game films from last year, and I came here personally and witnessed the Tech game. No one lost because of the coaching. A coach can work miracles with a good team, but he is *helpless* if his personnel don't want it bad enough. That's the worst part about running a team—you can't climb down into your people's hearts and change them."

Some college girls in a large expensive car went past. They shrieked and whistled at Bobby Stark.

"Lifeguards at the pool," he explained.

"I don't know if Burton's leaving or not," Coach continued. "But if his wife wants him to go, he probably will. If you're ever thinking about a career in coaching someday, Bob, think about that. Your family's either with you or you've had it. And remember, whether you stay someplace or not depends completely on a bunch of *kids*. I swear, I'd give up a leg for a chance to get in a game myself—just one play, with what I know now."

Stark nodded. They went on a block, and he said, "I turn off here. You going to tell your daughter about the job?"

"My daughter?" Coach said, and smiled.

VII

No one was home. A magnet under a plastic ladybug held a note to the face of the refrigerator. The note read:

> *Harry, I'm at my place. Daph's with Toby K. somewhere, fooling around. Be good now, Sherry Baby.*

"Dope," Coach said.

He felt very good.

He took a beer upstairs and drank it while he showered. He cinched on a pair of sweat pants and, wearing only these, went back down and fetched another beer.

He watched some of a baseball game on cable. He thought over his conversation with Bobby Stark. "Boy, is that true!" Coach said, and then was not at all sure why he had said it.

He frowned, remembering that in his second year of college, the only year he had been on the varsity team, he had proved an indifferent player.

"Not now," he whispered. "Not anymore."

He squashed the shape out of his beer can and stood it on top of the television.

There was a thump over his head. The ceiling creaked.

"Someone came home while I was in the shower," he said to himself, and ran his hand over his belly, feeling for signs of bloat from the beer.

He took the stairs in three leaps, strode into the master bedroom, calling, "Sherry?"

The dark figure in the room surprised Coach.

He yelled, "Hey!"

Daphne was dancing in front of the full-length mirror. She had improvised a look—sweeping her hair over her right ear, and stretching the neck of her shirt until her right shoulder was bared. A thing by the Commodores shrieked from her transistor.

"Nothing," she said.

"You're not home. Aren't you with whoosis? You're supposed to be out. You are *beet* red," Coach said.

Daphne lowered her head and squared her shirt, which bagged around her small torso. "Okay, Dad," she said.

"No, but how did your audience like the show? I bet they loved it," Coach said. He smiled at himself in the mirror. "I'm just kidding you, Daph. You looked great."

"Come *on*, Dad," she said, and tried to pass.

Coach chimed in with the radio. He shuffled his feet. "Hey, Daph, you know what time it is?" he said.

"Let me out, please," Daphne said.

"It's monkey time." Coach did a jerky turn, keeping in the way of the exit door. "Do the shing-a-ling. Do the Daphne." He rolled his shoulder vampishly. He kissed his own hand. He sang along.

"Thanks a lot," Daphne said. She gave up on trying to get around him. She leaned over and snapped off her radio. "You've got to use a mirror so you don't look stupid," she said. "Everybody does."

"I was only kidding. Seriously. I know dancing is important," Coach said.

"May I go now? I've got algebra." Daphne brought her hair from behind her ear.

"Before that, you have to hear the news. Here's a news bulletin, flash extra."

"You're drunk. You and Mom are going to live in different cities," Daphne said. "Somebody shot somebody."

"No, this is good news. I'm going to be coach here of the varsity. Me." Coach pointed to his chest.

"Now let me out, please," Daphne said.

Coach let her pass. He followed her down the narrow hallway to her bedroom.

"More money," he said. "I'll even be on TV. I'll have my own show on Sundays. And I'll get written up in the press all the time. By *real* reporters. Hey! Why am I yelling at wood, here?"

VIII

Coach was drunk at the kitchen table. He was enjoying the largeness of the room, and he was making out a roster for his dream team. He had put the best kids from his fifteen years of coaching in the positions they had played for him. He was puzzling over the tight-end spot. "Jim Wyckoff or Jerry Kinney?" he said aloud. He penciled "Kinney" into his diagram.

He heard Daphne on the stairs. It occurred to him to clear the beer cans from the table. Instead, he snapped open a fresh can. "Daphne?" he called.

"Wait a second. What?" she said from the living room.

"Just wondered who else was alive besides me," Coach said. "Your mom's still not home."

Daphne entered the kitchen.

"You're sorry you were rude before? That's perfectly okay, honey, just forget it. All right, Father, but I really am ashamed of myself anyway," Coach said.

"You guzzled all those?" Daphne said.

"Hold still. What've you got on?" Coach asked her. He hauled his chair around so that he could see his daughter.

"Two, four, five," Daphne said, counting the cans.

She was wearing one of the fan shirts that Coach had seen on a few summer coeds. On the front, against a maroon field, in gold, was GO. Across the back was GRIFFINS.

"Now you're talking," Coach said.

"It was free. This guy I met—well, these two guys, really—who work at Campus World, they gave it to me. It's dumb, but I want you to see I care. I do care. Not just for you, but because I want to stay here. Do you think we can maybe? Do your people look any good this year?"'

"Winners," Coach said.

"Yeah," Daphne said.

Coach skidded his chair forward. "Have a beer," he said. "Sit down here and let me show you on paper the material they've given me to work with. Then maybe you'll be a believer. Now these guys are fast and big for once. I'm not overestimating them, either. I've seen what I've seen," Coach said.

A car crept into the drive, and then its engine noise filled the garage. Coach and Daphne were quiet until Sherry bustled down the short hall that connected the garage to the kitchen.

"Really late. Sorry, sorry," she said.

"It's a party in here, I warn you," Coach said.

"So I noticed." Sherry had a grocery sack, but it was almost empty. There were bright streaks of paint on her brown arms.

Daphne plucked a bag of Oreo cookies from the groceries.

"Shoot me one of those," Coach said.

"Is there any beer left for me?" Sherry said. "I want to drown my disappointment. I can't paint!"

"You *can* paint," Coach said.

"Let's face it," Sherry said. "An artist? The wife of a coach?"

---

1. Discuss the pattern of selfishness and generosity running through the story. Are Coach's ambitions primarily selfish or generous?
2. What means are used to reveal Coach's feelings? In examining their adequacy, try to define what he is feeling as the story ends.
3. What chance has Coach of reconciling the demands of his family, his job, and his own wishes?
4. To what extent does the story mirror normal family tensions? What exaggerates or minimizes these?
5. What is revealed about the characters of Coach and his wife by their reactions to the story in the student newspaper?

Philip Roth

Roth (1933–) was born in Newark, New Jersey, and was educated at Bucknell University and the University of Chicago. He attracted serious critical attention from the time his first stories began to appear in magazines, and his first book, Goodbye, Columbus *(1959), a novella and collection of stories, was a prizewinner that established him as a major writer. Since then he has demonstrated his mastery of form in the well-made novel* When She Was Good *(1967) and his gift for ribald, acid comedy in* Portnoy's Complaint *(1969). Roth has collected many awards and has taught intermittently at a number of universities. His other books include* The Breast *(1972),* My Life as a Man *(1974),* The Professor of Desire *(1977),* The Ghost Writer *(1979),* Zuckerman Unbound *(1981), and* The Anatomy Lesson *(1983). His collection* Zuckerman Bound *(1985) includes the previous three novels plus the novella* The Prague Orgy.

The Conversion of the Jews

"You're a real one for opening your mouth in the first place," Itzie said. "What do you open your mouth all the time for?"

"I didn't bring it up, Itz, I didn't," Ozzie said.

"What do you care about Jesus Christ for anyway?"

"I didn't bring up Jesus Christ. He did. I didn't even know what he was talking about. Jesus is historical, he kept saying. Jesus is historical." Ozzie mimicked the monumental voice of Rabbi Binder.

"Jesus was a person that lived like you and me," Ozzie continued. "That's what Binder said—"

"Yeah? . . . So what! What do I give two cents whether he lived or not. And what do you gotta open your mouth!" Itzie Lieberman favored closed-mouthedness, especially when it came to Ozzie Freedman's questions. Mrs. Freedman had to see Rabbi Binder twice before about Ozzie's questions and this Wednesday at four-thirty would be the third time. Itzie preferred to keep *his* mother in the kitchen; he settled for behind-the-back subtleties such as gestures, faces, snarls and other less delicate barnyard noises.

"He was a real person, Jesus, but he wasn't like God, and we don't believe he is God." Slowly, Ozzie was explaining Rabbi Binder's position to Itzie, who had been absent from Hebrew School the previous afternoon.

"The Catholics," Itzie said helpfully, "they believe in Jesus Christ, that he's God." Itzie Lieberman used "the Catholics" in its broadest sense—to include the Protestants.

Ozzie received Itzie's remark with a tiny head bob, as though it were a footnote, and went on. "His mother was Mary, and his father probably was Joseph," Ozzie said. "But the New Testament says his real father was God."

"His *real* father?"

"Yeah," Ozzie said, "that's the big thing, his father's supposed to be God."

"Bull."

"That's what Rabbi Binder says, that it's impossible—"

"Sure it's impossible. That stuff's all bull. To have a baby you gotta get laid," Itzie theologized. "Mary hadda get laid."

"That's what Binder says: 'The only way a woman can have a baby is to have intercourse with a man.' "

"He said *that*, Ozz?" For a moment it appeared that Itzie had put the theological question aside. "He said that, intercourse?" A little curled smile shaped itself in the lower half of Itzie's face like a pink mustache. "What you guys do, Ozz, you laugh or something?"

"I raised my hand."

"Yeah? Whatja say?"

"That's when I asked the question."

Itzie's face lit up. "Whatja ask about—intercourse?"

"No, I asked the question about God, how if He could create the heaven and earth in six days, and make all the animals and the fish and the light in six days—the light especially, that's what always gets me, that He could make the light. Making fish and animals, that's pretty good—"

"That's damn good." Itzie's appreciation was honest but unimaginative: it was as though God had just pitched a one-hitter.

"But making light . . . I mean when you think about it, it's really something," Ozzie said. "Anyway, I asked Binder if He could make all that in six days, and He could *pick* the six days he wanted right out of nowhere, why couldn't He let a woman have a baby without having intercourse."

"You said intercourse, Ozz, to Binder?"

"Yeah."

"Right in class?"

"Yeah."

Itzie smacked the side of his head.

"I mean, no kidding around," Ozzie said, "that'd really be nothing. After all that other stuff, that'd practically be nothing."

Itzie considered a moment. "What'd Binder say?"

"He started all over again explaining how Jesus was historical and how he lived like you and me but he wasn't God. So I said I under*stood* that. What I wanted to know was different."

What Ozzie wanted to know was always different. The first time he had wanted to know how Rabbi Binder could call the Jews "The Chosen People" if the Declaration of Independence claimed all men to be created equal. Rabbi Binder tried to distinguish for him between political equality and spiritual legitimacy, but what Ozzie wanted to know, he insisted vehemently, was different. That was the first time his mother had to come.

Then there was the plane crash. Fifty-eight people had been killed in a plane crash at La Guardia.[1] In studying a casualty list in the newspaper his mother had discovered among the list of those dead eight Jewish names (his grandmother had nine but she counted Miller as a Jewish name); because of the eight she said the plane crash was "a tragedy." During free-discussion time on Wednesday Ozzie had brought to Rabbi Binder's attention this matter of "some of his relations" always picking out the Jewish names. Rabbi Binder had begun to explain cultural unity and some other things when Ozzie stood up at his seat and said that what he wanted to know was different. Rabbi Binder insisted that he sit down and it was then that Ozzie shouted that he wished all fifty-eight were Jews. That was the second time his mother came.

"And he kept explaining about Jesus being historical, and so I kept asking him. No kidding, Itz, he was trying to make me look stupid."

"So what he finally do?"

"Finally he starts screaming that I was deliberately simple-minded and a wise guy, and that my mother had to come, and this was the last time. And that I'd never get bar-mitzvahed[2] if he could help it. Then, Itz, then he starts talking in that voice like a statue, real slow and deep, and he says that I better think over what I said about the Lord. He told me to go to his office and think it over." Ozzie leaned his body towards Itzie. "Itz, I thought it over for a solid hour, and now I'm convinced God could do it."

Ozzie had planned to confess his latest transgression to his mother as soon as she came home from work. But it was a Friday night in November and already dark, and when Mrs. Freedman came through the door she tossed off her coat, kissed Ozzie quickly on the face, and went to the kitchen table to light the three yellow

1. Airport in New York City. 2. The bar mitzvah is the Jewish initiatory ceremony performed on a boy's thirteenth birthday, recognizing his acceptance of religious responsibility and duties.

candles, two for the Sabbath and one for Ozzie's father.

When his mother lit the candles she would move her two arms slowly towards her, dragging them through the air, as though persuading people whose minds were half made up. And her eyes would get glassy with tears. Even when his father was alive Ozzie remembered that her eyes had gotten glassy, so it didn't have anything to do with his dying. It had something to do with lighting the candles.

As she touched the flaming match to the unlit wick of a Sabbath candle, the phone rang, and Ozzie, standing only a foot from it, plucked it off the receiver and held it muffled to his chest. When his mother lit candles Ozzie felt there should be no noise; even breathing, if you could manage it, should be softened. Ozzie pressed the phone to his breast and watched his mother dragging whatever she was dragging, and he felt his own eyes get glassy. His mother was a round, tired, gray-haired penguin of a woman whose gray skin had begun to feel the tug of gravity and the weight of her own history. Even when she was dressed up she didn't look like a chosen person. But when she lit candles she looked like something better; like a woman who knew momentarily that God could do anything.

After a few mysterious minutes she was finished. Ozzie hung up the phone and walked to the kitchen table where she was beginning to lay the two places for the four-course Sabbath meal. He told her that she would have to see Rabbi Binder next Wednesday at four-thirty, and then he told her why. For the first time in their life together she hit Ozzie across the face with her hand.

All through the chopped liver and chicken soup part of the dinner Ozzie cried; he didn't have any appetite for the rest.

On Wednesday, in the largest of the three basement classrooms of the synagogue, Rabbi Marvin Binder, a tall, handsome, broad-shouldered man of thirty with thick strong-fibered black hair, removed his watch from his pocket and saw that it was four o'clock. At the rear of the room Yakov Blotnik, the seventy-one-year-old custodian, slowly polished the large window, mumbling to himself, unaware that it was four o'clock or six o'clock, Monday or Wednesday. To most of the students Yakov Blotnik's mumbling, along with his brown curly beard, scythe nose, and two heel-trailing black cats, made of him an object of wonder, a foreigner, a relic, towards whom they were alternately fearful and disrespectful. To Ozzie the mumbling had always seemed a monotonous, curious prayer; what made it curious was the old Blotnik had been mumbling so steadily for so many years, Ozzie suspected he had memorized the prayers and forgotten all about God.

"It is now free-discussion time," Rabbi Binder said. "Feel free to talk about any Jewish matter at all—religion, family, politics, sports—"

There was silence. It was a gusty, clouded November afternoon and it did not seem as though there ever was or could be a thing called baseball. So nobody this week said a word about that hero from the past, Hank Greenberg[3]—which limited free discussion considerably.

And the soul-battering Ozzie Freedman had just received from Rabbi Binder had imposed its limitation. When it was Ozzie's turn to read aloud from the Hebrew book the rabbi had asked him petulantly why he didn't read more rapidly. He was showing no progress. Ozzie said he could read faster but that if he did he was sure not to understand what he was reading. Nevertheless, at the rabbi's repeated suggestion Ozzie tried, and showed a great talent, but in the midst of a long passage he stopped short and said he didn't understand a word he was reading, and started in again at a drag-footed pace. Then came the soul-battering.

Consequently when free-discussion time rolled around none of the students felt too free. The rabbi's invitation was answered only by the mumbling of feeble old Blotnik.

"Isn't there anything at all you would like to discuss?" Rabbi Binder asked again, looking at his watch. "No questions or comments?"

There was a small grumble from the third row. The rabbi requested that Ozzie rise and give the rest of the class the advantage of his thought.

Ozzie rose. "I forget it now," he said, and sat down in his place.

Rabbi Binder advanced a seat towards Ozzie and poised himself on the edge of the desk. It was Itzie's desk and the rabbi's frame only a dagger's-length away from his face snapped him to sitting attention.

"Stand up again, Oscar," Rabbi Binder said calmly, "and try to assemble your thoughts."

Ozzie stood up. All his classmates turned in their seats and watched as he gave an unconvincing scratch to his forehead.

"I can't assemble any," he announced, and plunked himself down.

"Stand up!" Rabbi Binder advanced from Itzie's desk to the one directly in front of Ozzie; when the rabbinical back was turned Itzie gave it five-fingers off the tip of his nose, causing a small titter in the room. Rabbi Binder was too absorbed in squelching Ozzie's nonsense once and for all to bother with titters. "Stand up, Oscar. What's your question about?"

Ozzie pulled a word out of the air. It was the handiest word. "Religion."

"Oh, now you remember?"

"Yes."

"What is it?"

Trapped, Ozzie blurted the first thing that came to him.

3. Jewish baseball star, with the Detroit Tigers, 1934–45.

"Why can't He make anything He wants to make!"

As Rabbi Binder prepared an answer, a final answer, Itzie, ten feet behind him, raised one finger on his left hand, gestured it meaningfully towards the rabbi's back, and brought the house down.

Binder twisted quickly to see what had happened and in the midst of the commotion Ozzie shouted into the rabbi's back what he couldn't have shouted to his face. It was a loud, toneless sound that had the timbre of something stored inside for about six days.

"You don't know! You don't know anything about God!"

The rabbi spun back towards Ozzie. "What?"

"You don't know—you don't—"

"Apologize, Oscar, apologize!" It was a threat.

"You don't—"

Rabbi Binder's hand flicked out at Ozzie's cheek. Perhaps it had only been meant to clamp the boy's mouth shut, but Ozzie ducked and the palm caught him squarely on the nose.

The blood came in a short, red spurt on to Ozzie's shirt front.

The next moment was all confusion. Ozzie screamed, "You bastard, you bastard!" and broke for the classroom door. Rabbi Binder lurched a step backwards, as though his own blood had started flowing violently in the opposite direction, then gave a clumsy lurch forward and bolted out the door after Ozzie. The class followed after the rabbi's huge blue-suited back, and before old Blotnik could turn from his window, the room was empty and everyone was headed full speed up the three flights leading to the roof.

If one should compare the light of day to the life of man: sunrise to birth; sunset—the dropping down over the edge—to death; then as Ozzie Freedman wiggled through the trapdoor of the synagogue roof, his feet kicking backwards bronco-style at Rabbi Binder's outstretched arms—at that moment the day was fifty years old. As a rule, fifty or fifty-five reflects accurately the age of late afternoons in November, for it is in that month, during those hours, that one's awareness of light seems no longer a matter of seeing, but of hearing: light begins clicking away. In fact, as Ozzie locked shut the trapdoor in the rabbi's face, the sharp click of the bolt into the lock might momentarily have been mistaken for the sound of the heavier gray that had just throbbed through the sky.

With all his weight Ozzie kneeled on the locked door; any instant he was certain that Rabbi Binder's shoulder would fling it open, splintering the wood into shrapnel and catapulting his body into the sky. But the door did not move and below him he heard only the rumble of feet, first loud then dim, like thunder rolling away.

A question shot through his brain. "Can this be *me?*" For a thirteen-year-old who had just labeled his religious leader a bastard, twice, it was not an improper question. Louder and louder the question came to him—"Is it me? Is it me?"—until he discovered himself no longer kneeling, but racing crazily towards the edge of the roof, his eyes crying, his throat screaming, and his arms flying everywhichway as though not his own.

"Is it me? Is it me ME ME ME ME! It has to be me—but is it!"

It is the question a thief must ask himself the night he jimmies open his first window, and it is said to be the question with which bridegrooms quiz themselves before the altar.

In the few wild seconds it took Ozzie's body to propel him to the edge of the roof, his self-examination began to grow fuzzy. Gazing down at the street, he became confused as to the problem beneath the question: was it, is-it-me-who-called-Binder-a-bastard? or, is-it-me-prancing-around-on-the-roof? However, the scene below settled all, for there is an instant in any action when whether it is you or somebody else is academic. The thief crams the money in his pockets and scoots out the window. The bridegroom signs the hotel register for two. And the boy on the roof finds a streetful of people gaping at him, necks stretched backwards, faces up, as though he were the ceiling of the Hayden Planetarium.[4] Suddenly you know it's you.

"Oscar! Oscar Freedman!" A voice rose from the center of the crowd, a voice that, could it have been seen, would have looked like the writing on a scroll. "Oscar Freedman, get down from there. Immediately!" Rabbi Binder was pointing one arm stiffly up at him; and at the end of that arm, one finger aimed menacingly. It was the attitude of a dictator, but one—the eyes confessed all—whose personal valet had spit neatly in his face.

Ozzie didn't answer. Only for a blink's length did he look towards Rabbi Binder. Instead his eyes began to fit together the world beneath him, to sort out people from places, friends from enemies, participants from spectators. In little jagged starlike clusters his friends stood around Rabbi Binder, who was still pointing. The topmost point on a star compounded not of angels but of five adolescent boys with Itzie. What a world it was, with those stars below, Rabbi Binder below . . . Ozzie, who a moment earlier hadn't been able to control his own body, started to feel the meaning of the word control: he felt Peace and he felt Power.

"Oscar Freedman, I'll give you three to come down."

Few dictators give their subjects three to do anything; but, as always, Rabbi Binder only looked dictatorial.

"Are you ready, Oscar?"

Ozzie nodded his head yes, although he had no intention in the

4. An auditorium with a domed ceiling on which movements of stars and constellations are projected with spots of light, in New York City.

world—the lower one or the celestial one he'd just entered—of coming down even if Rabbi Binder should give him a million.

"All right then," said Rabbi Binder. He ran a hand through his black Samson hair as though it were the gesture prescribed for uttering the first digit. Then, with his other hand cutting a circle out of the small piece of sky around him, he spoke. "One!"

There was no thunder. On the contrary, at that moment, as though "one" was the cue for which he had been waiting, the world's least thunderous person appeared on the synagogue steps. He did not so much come out the synagogue door as lean out, onto the darkening air. He clutched at the doorknob with one hand and looked up at the roof.

"Oy!"

Yakov Blotnik's old mind hobbled slowly, as if on crutches, and though he couldn't decide precisely what the boy was doing on the roof, he knew it wasn't good—that is, it wasn't-good-for-the-Jews. For Yokov Blotnik life had fractionated itself simply: things were either good-for-the-Jews or no-good-for-the-Jews.

He smacked his free hand to his in-sucked cheek, gently. "Oy, Gut!"[5] And then quickly as he was able, he jacked down his head and surveyed the street. There was Rabbi Binder (like a man at an auction with only three dollars in his pocket, he had just delivered a shaky "Two!"); there were the students, and that was all. So far it-wasn't-so-bad-for-the-Jews. But the boy had to come down immediately, before anybody saw. The problem: how to get the boy off the roof?

Anybody who has ever had a cat on the roof knows how to get him down. You call the fire department. Or first you call the operator and you ask her for the fire department. And the next thing there is great jamming of brakes and clanging of bells and shouting of instructions. And then the cat is off the roof. You do the same thing to get a boy off the roof.

That is, you do the same thing if you are Yakov Blotnik and you once had a cat on the roof.

When the engines, all four of them, arrived, Rabbi Binder had four times given Ozzie the count of three. The big hook-and-ladder swung around the corner and one of the firemen leaped from it, plunging headlong towards the yellow fire hydrant in front of the synagogue. With a huge wrench he began to unscrew the top nozzle. Rabbi Binder raced over to him and pulled at his shoulder.

"There's no fire . . ."

5. "Oh, good!"

The fireman mumbled back over his shoulder and, heatedly, continued working at the nozzle.

"But there's no fire, there's no fire . . ." Binder shouted. When the fireman mumbled again, the rabbi grasped his face with both his hands and pointed it up at the roof.

To Ozzie it looked as though Rabbi Binder was trying to tug the fireman's head out of his body, like a cork from a bottle. He had to giggle at the picture they made: it was a family portrait—rabbi in black skullcap, fireman in red fire hat, and the little yellow hydrant squatting beside like a kid brother, bareheaded. From the edge of the roof Ozzie waved at the portrait, a one-handed, flapping, mocking wave; in doing it his right foot slipped from under him. Rabbi Binder covered his eyes with his hands.

Firemen work fast. Before Ozzie had even regained his balance, a big, round, yellowed net was being held on the synagogue lawn. The firemen who held it looked up at Ozzie with stern, feelingless faces.

One of the firemen turned his head towards Rabbi Binder. "What, is the kid nuts or something?"

Rabbi Binder unpeeled his hands from his eyes, slowly, painfully, as if they were tape. Then he checked: nothing on the sidewalk, no dents in the net.

"Is he gonna jump, or what?" the fireman shouted.

In a voice not at all like a statue, Rabbi Binder finally answered. "Yes, yes, I think so . . . He's been threatening to . . ."

Threatening to? Why, the reason he was on the roof, Ozzie remembered, was to get away; he hadn't even thought about jumping. He had just run to get away, and the truth was that he hadn't really headed for the roof as much as he'd been chased there.

"What's his name, the kid?"

"Freedman," Rabbi Binder answered. "Oscar Freedman."

The fireman looked up at Ozzie. "What is it with you, Oscar? You gonna jump, or what?"

Ozzie did not answer. Frankly, the question had just arisen.

"Look, Oscar, if you're gonna jump, jump—and if you're not gonna jump, don't jump. But don't waste our time, willya?"

Ozzie looked at the fireman and then at Rabbi Binder. He wanted to see Rabbi Binder cover his eyes one more time.

"I'm going to jump."

And then he scampered around the edge of the roof to the corner, where there was no net below, and he flapped his arms at his sides, swishing the air and smacking his palms to his trousers on the downbeat. He began screaming like some kind of engine, "Wheeeee . . . wheeeeee," and leaning way out over the edge with the upper half of his body. The firemen whipped around to cover the ground with the net. Rabbi Binder mumbled a few words to Somebody and covered his eyes. Everything happened quickly, jerkily, as in a silent movie. The crowd, which had arrived with the fire engines, gave out a long, Fourth-of-July fireworks oooh-aahhh. In the excitement no one had paid the crowd much heed, except, of course, Yakov Blotnik, who swung from the doorknob counting heads. "Fier und tsvansik . . . finf und tsvantsik[6] . . . Oy, Gut!" It wasn't like this with the cat.

Rabbi Binder peeked through his fingers, checked the sidewalk and net. Empty. But there was Ozzie racing to the other corner. The firemen raced with him but were unable to keep up. Whenever Ozzie wanted to he might jump and splatter himself upon the sidewalk, and by the time the firemen scooted to the spot all they could do with their net would be to cover the mess.

"Wheeeee . . . wheeeee . . ."

"Hey, Oscar," the winded fireman yelled, "What the hell is this, a game or something?"

"Wheeeee . . . wheeeee . . ."

"Hey, Oscar—"

But he was off now to the other corner, flapping his wings fiercely. Rabbi Binder couldn't take it any longer—the fire engines from nowhere, the screaming suicidal boy, the net. He fell to his knees, exhausted, and with his hands curled together in front of his chest, like a little dome, he pleaded, "Oscar, stop it, Oscar. Don't jump, Oscar. Please come down . . . Please don't jump."

And further back in the crowd a single voice, a single young voice, shouted a lone word to the boy on the roof.

"Jump!"

It was Itzie. Ozzie momentarily stopped flapping.

"Go ahead, Ozz—jump!"

Itzie broke off his point of the star and courageously, with the inspiration not of a wise-guy but of a disciple, stood alone. "Jump, Ozz, jump!"

Still on his knees, his hands still curled, Rabbi Binder twisted his body back. He looked at Itzie, then, agonizingly, back to Ozzie.

"OSCAR, DON'T JUMP! PLEASE, DON'T JUMP . . . please please . . ."

"Jump!" This time it wasn't Itzie but another point of the star. By the time Mrs. Freedman arrived to keep her four-thirty appointment with Rabbi Binder, the whole little upside down heaven was shouting and pleading for Ozzie to jump, and Rabbi Binder no longer

6. "Twenty-four . . . twenty-five . . ."

was pleading with him not to jump, but was crying into the dome of his hands.

Understandably Mrs. Freedman couldn't figure out what her son was doing on the roof. So she asked.

"Ozzie, my Ozzie, what are you doing? My Ozzie, what is it?"

Ozzie stopped wheeeeeing and slowed his arms down to a cruising flap, the kind birds use in soft winds, but he did not answer. He stood against the low, clouded, darkening sky—light clicked down swiftly now, as on a small gear—flapping softly and gazing down at the small bundle of a woman who was his mother.

"What are you doing, Ozzie?" She turned towards the kneeling Rabbi Binder and rushed so close that only a paper-thickness of dusk lay between her stomach and his shoulders.

"What is my baby doing?"

Rabbi Binder gaped up at her but he too was mute. All that moved was the dome of his hands; it shook back and forth like a weak pulse.

"Rabbi, get him down! He'll kill himself. Get him down, my only baby . . ."

"I can't," Rabbi Binder said, "I can't . . ." and he turned his handsome head towards the crowd of boys behind him. "It's them. Listen to them."

And for the first time Mrs. Freedman saw the crowd of boys, and she heard what they were yelling.

"He's doing it for them. He won't listen to me. It's them." Rabbi Binder spoke like one in a trance.

"For them?"

"Yes."

"Why for them?"

"They want him to . . ."

Mrs. Freedman raised her two arms upward as though she were conducting the sky. "For them he's doing it!" And then in a gesture older than pyramids, older than prophets and floods, her arms came slapping down to her sides. "A martyr I have. Look!" She tilted her head to the roof. Ozzie was still flapping softly. "My martyr."

"Oscar, come down, *please*," Rabbi Binder groaned.

In a startlingly even voice Mrs. Freedman called to the boy on the roof. "Ozzie, come down, Ozzie. Don't be a martyr, my baby."

As though it were a litany, Rabbi Binder repeated her words. "Don't be martyr, my baby. Don't be a martyr."

"Gawhead, Ozz—*be* a Martin!" It was Itzie. "Be a Martin, be a Martin," and all the voices joined in singing for Martindom, whatever *it* was. "Be a Martin, be a Martin . . ."

Somehow when you're on a roof the darker it gets the less you can hear. All Ozzie knew was that two groups wanted two new things: his friends were spirited and musical about what they wanted; his mother and the rabbi were even-toned, chanting, about what they didn't want. The rabbi's voice was without tears now and so was his mother's.

The big net stared up at Ozzie like a sightless eye. The big, clouded sky pushed down. From beneath it looked like a gray corrugated board. Suddenly, looking up into that unsympathetic sky, Ozzie realized all the strangeness of what these people, his friends, were asking: they wanted him to jump, to kill himself; they were singing about it now—it made them that happy. And there was an even greater strangeness: Rabbi Binder was on his knees, trembling. If there was a question to be asked now it was not "Is it me?" but rather "Is it us? . . . Is it us?"

Being on the roof, it turned out, was a serious thing. If he jumped would the singing become dancing? Would it? What would jumping stop? Yearningly, Ozzie wished he could rip open the sky, plunge his hands through, and pull out the sun; and on the sun, like a coin, would be stamped JUMP or DON'T JUMP.

Ozzie's knees rocked and sagged a little under him as though they were setting him for a dive. His arms tightened, stiffened, froze, from shoulders to fingernails. He felt as if each part of his body were going to vote as to whether he should kill himself or not—and each part as though it were independent of *him*.

The light took an unexpected click down and the new darkness, like a gag, hushed the friends singing for this and the mother and rabbi chanting for that.

Ozzie stopped counting votes, and in a curiously high voice, like one who wasn't prepared for speech, he spoke.

"Mamma?"

"Yes, Oscar."

"Mamma, get down on your knees, like Rabbi Binder."

"Oscar—"

"Get down on your knees," he said, "or I'll jump."

Ozzie heard a whimper, then a quick rustling, and when he looked down where his mother had stood he saw the top of a head and beneath that a circle of dress. She was kneeling beside Rabbi Binder.

He spoke again. "Everybody kneel." There was the sound of everybody kneeling.

Ozzie looked around. With one hand he pointed towards the synagogue entrance. "Make *him* kneel."

There was a noise, not of kneeling, but of body-and-cloth stretching. Ozzie could hear Rabbi Binder saying in a gruff whisper, ". . . or he'll *kill* himself," and when next he looked there was Yakov Blotnik off the doorknob and for the first time in his life upon his knees in the Gentile posture of prayer.

As for the firemen—it was not as difficult as one might imagine to hold a net taut while you are kneeling.

Ozzie looked around again; and then he called to Rabbi Binder.

"Rabbi?"

"Yes, Oscar."

"Rabbi Binder, do you believe in God?"

"Yes."

"Do you believe God can do Anything?" Ozzie leaned his head out into the darkness. "Anything?"

"Oscar, I think—"

"Tell me you believe God can do Anything."

There was a second's hesitation. Then: "God can do Anything."

"Tell me you believe God can make a child without intercourse."

"He can."

"Tell me!"

"God," Rabbi Binder admitted, "can make a child without intercourse."

"Mamma, you tell me."

"God can make a child without intercourse," his mother said.

"Make *him* tell me." There was no doubt who *him* was.

In a few moments Ozzie heard an old comical voice say something to the increasing darkness about God.

Next, Ozzie made everybody say it. And then he made them all say they believed in Jesus Christ—first one at a time, then all together.

When the catechizing was through it was the beginning of evening. From the street it sounded as if the boy on the roof might have sighed.

"Ozzie?" A woman's voice dared to speak. "You'll come down now?"

There was no answer, but the woman waited, and when a voice finally did speak it was thin and crying, and exhausted as that of an old man who has just finished pulling the bells.

"Mamma, don't you see—you shouldn't hit me. He shouldn't hit me. You shouldn't hit me about God, Mamma. You should never hit anybody about God—"

"Ozzie, please come down now."

"Promise me, promise me you'll never hit anybody about God."

He had asked only his mother, but for some reason everyone kneeling in the street promised he would never hit anybody about God.

Once again there was silence.

"I can come down now, Mamma," the boy on the roof finally said. He turned his head both ways as though checking the traffic lights. "Now I can come down . . ."

And he did, right into the center of the yellow net that glowed in the evening's edge like an overgrown halo.

---

1. What distinguishes this story from a mere anecdote? How has the author revealed the truly important issues built into the conflict?
2. What is Yakov Blotnik's role? Why is Ozzie insistent on converting him?
3. What brings on Ozzie's uncertainty about who he is?
4. Is there any implication that a real and irreversible conversion has taken place? Or are all the statements of belief in Christ made to deceive Ozzie until he is safe on the ground?
5. Why does Ozzie jump from the roof when he could have gone back down the stairs? Does he safely reach the ground? How do you know?

Isaac Bashevis Singer

Singer (1904–) was born in Radzymin, Poland. His father, a rabbi, was an author, as was his brother, the novelist I. J. Singer. Before he emigrated to the United States in 1935, Singer worked as a journalist in Warsaw, and in New York he resumed similar work with the Jewish Daily Forward. *As a master of Yiddish, he continues to write in that language. His fiction is characteristically in the tradition of the spoken tale, mingling forthright literalness about the visible world with an equally literal rendition of fantastic and supernatural forms. Flavored with the colorful residue of folk tales, his explorations of Jewish life, past and present, are haunted allegories of the irrationality of history. He has written a number of books for children. His stories are most easily found in* The Collected Stories of Isaac Bashevis Singer *(1982). Among his novels are* The Family Moskat *(1950),* The Slave *(1962),* The Manor *(1967),* The Estate *(1970),* Enemies: A Love Story *(1972), and* Shosha *(1978). He was awarded the Nobel Prize in 1978.*

Gimpel the Fool[1]

I

I am Gimpel the fool. I don't think myself a fool. On the contrary. But that's what folks call me. They gave me the name while I was still in school. I had seven names in all: imbecile, donkey, flax-head, dope, glump, ninny, and fool. The last name stuck. What did my foolishness consist of? I was easy to take in. They said, "Gimpel, you know the rabbi's wife has been brought to childbed?" So I skipped school. Well, it turned out to be a lie. How was I supposed to know? She hadn't had a big belly. But I never looked at her belly. Was that really so foolish? The gang laughed and hee-hawed, stomped and danced and chanted a good-night prayer. And instead of the raisins they give when a woman's lying in, they stuffed my hand full of goat turds. I was no weakling. If I slapped someone he'd see all the way to Cracow. But I'm really not a slugger by nature. I think to myself: Let it pass. So they take advantage of me.

I was coming home from school and heard a dog barking. I'm not

1. Translated by Saul Bellow.

afraid of dogs, but of course I never want to start up with them. One of them may be mad, and if he bites there's not a Tartar[2] in the world who can help you. So I made tracks. Then I looked around and saw the whole market place wild with laughter. It was no dog at all but Wolf-Leib the thief. How was I supposed to know it was he? It sounded like a howling bitch.

When the pranksters and leg-pullers found that I was easy to fool, every one of them tried his luck with me. "Gimpel, the czar is coming to Frampol; Gimpel, the moon fell down in Turbeen; Gimpel, little Hodel Furpiece found a treasure behind the bathhouse." And I like a golem[3] believed everyone. In the first place, everything is possible, as it is written in *The Wisdom of the Fathers*. I've forgotten just how. Second, I had to believe when the whole town came down on me! If I ever dared to say, "Ah, you're kidding!" there was trouble. People got angry. "What do you mean! You want to call everyone a liar?" What was I to do? I believed them, and I hope at least that did them some good.

I was an orphan. My grandfather who brought me up was already bent toward the grave. So they turned me over to a baker, and what a time they gave me there! Every woman or girl who came to bake a batch of noodles had to fool me at least once. "Gimpel, there's a fair in Heaven; Gimpel, the rabbi gave birth to a calf in the seventh month; Gimpel, a cow flew over the roof and laid brass eggs." A student from the yeshiva came once to buy a roll, and he said, "You, Gimpel, while you stand here scraping with your baker's shovel the Messiah has come. The dead have risen." "What do you mean?" I said. "I heard no one blowing the ram's horn!" He said, "Are you deaf?" And all began to cry, "We heard it, we heard!" Then in came Rietze the candle-dipper and called out in her hoarse voice, "Gimpel, your father and mother have stood up from the grave. They're looking for you."

To tell the truth, I knew very well that nothing of the sort had happened, but all the same, as folks were talking, I threw on my wool vest and went out. Maybe something had happened. What did I stand to lose by looking? Well, what a cat music went up! And then I took a vow to believe nothing more. But that was no go either. They confused me so that I didn't know the big end from the small.

I went to the rabbi to get some advice. He said, "It is written, better to be a fool all your days than for one hour to be evil. You are not a fool. They are the fools. For he who causes his neighbor to feel shame loses Paradise himself." Nevertheless, the rabbi's daughter took me in. As I left the rabbinical court she said, "Have you kissed the wall yet?" I said, "No; what for?" She answered, "It's the law; you've got to

2. A people with a reputation for fighting. 3. An artificial human being.

do it after every visit." Well, there didn't seem to be any harm in it. And she burst out laughing. It was a fine trick. She put one over on me, all right.

I wanted to go off to another town, but then everyone got busy matchmaking, and they were after me so they nearly tore my coat tails off. They talked at me and talked until I got water on the ear. She was no chaste maiden, but they told me she was virgin pure. She had a limp, and they said it was deliberate, from coyness. She had a bastard, and they told me the child was her little brother. I cried, "You're wasting your time. I'll never marry that whore." But they said indignantly, "What a way to talk! Aren't you ashamed of yourself? We can take you to the rabbi and have you fined for giving her a bad name." I saw then that I wouldn't escape them so easily and I thought: They're set on making me their butt. But when you're married the husband's the master, and if that's all right with her it's agreeable to me too. Besides, you can't pass through life unscathed, nor expect to.

I went to her clay house, which was built on the sand, and the whole gang, hollering and chorusing, came after me. They acted like bearbaiters. When we came to the well they stopped all the same. They were afraid to start anything with Elka. Her mouth would open as if it were on a hinge, and she had a fierce tongue. I entered the house. Lines were strung from wall to wall and clothes were drying. Barefoot she stood by the tub, doing the wash. She was dressed in a warn hand-me-down gown of plush. She had her hair put up in braids and pinned across her head. It took my breath away, almost, the reek of it all.

Evidently she knew who I was. She took a look at me and said, "Look who's here! He's come, the drip. Grab a seat."

I told her all; I denied nothing. "Tell me the truth," I said, "are you really a virgin, and is that mischievous Yechiel actually your little brother? Don't be deceitful with me, for I'm an orphan."

"I'm an orphan myself," she answered, "and whoever tries to twist you up, may the end of his nose take a twist. But don't let them think they can take advantage of me. I want a dowry of fifty guilders, and let them take up a collection besides. Otherwise they can kiss my you-know-what." She was very plainspoken. I said, "It's the bride and not the groom who gives a dowry." Then she said, "Don't bargain with me. Either a flat yes or a flat no. Go back where you came from."

I thought: No bread will ever be baked from *this* dough. But ours is not a poor town. They consented to everything and proceeded with the wedding. It so happened that there was a dysentery epidemic at the time. The ceremony was held at the cemetery gates, near the little corpse-washing hut. The fellows got drunk. While the marriage contract was being drawn up I heard the most pious high rabbi ask, "Is the bride a widow or a divorced woman?" And the sexton's wife answered for her, "Both a widow and divorced." It was a black moment for me. But what was I to do, run away from under the marriage canopy?

There was singing and dancing. An old granny danced opposite me, hugging a braided white hallah.[4] The master of revels made a "God 'a mercy" in memory of the bride's parents. The schoolboys threw burrs, as on Tishe b'Av fast day. There were a lot of gifts after the sermon: a noodle board, a kneading trough, a bucket, brooms, ladles, household articles galore. Then I took a look and saw two strapping young men carrying a crib. "What do we need this for?" I asked. So they said, "Don't rack your brains about it. It's all right, it'll come in handy." I realized I was going to be rooked. Take it another way though, what did I stand to lose? I reflected: I'll see what comes of it. A whole town can't go altogether crazy.

II

At night I came where my wife lay, but she wouldn't let me in. "Say, look here, is this what they married us for?" I said. And she said, "My monthly has come." "But yesterday they took you to the ritual bath, and that's afterwards, isn't it supposed to be?" "Today isn't yesterday," said she, "and yesterday's not today. You can beat it if you don't like it." In short, I waited.

Not four months later, she was in childbed. The townsfolk hid their laughter with their knuckles. But what could I do? She suffered intolerable pains and clawed at the walls. "Gimpel," she cried, "I'm going. Forgive me!" The house filled with women. They were boiling pans of water. The screams rose to the welkin.

The thing to do was to go to the house of prayer to repeat psalms, and that was what I did.

The townsfolk liked that, all right. I stood in a corner saying psalms and prayers, and they shook their heads at me. "Pray, pray!" they told me. "Prayer never made any woman pregnant." One of the congregation put a straw to my mouth and said, "Hay for the cows." There was something to that too, by God!

She gave birth to a boy. Friday at the synagogue the sexton stood up before the Ark, pounded on the reading table, and announced, "The wealthy Reb Gimpel invites the congregation to a feast in honor of the birth of a son." The whole house of prayer rang with laughter. My face was flaming. But there was nothing I could do. After all, I *was* the one responsible for the circumcision honors and rituals.

Half the town came running. You couldn't wedge another soul in. Women brought peppered chick-peas, and there was a keg of beer

4. Or "challah," a kind of bread.

from the tavern. I ate and drank as much as anyone, and they all congratulated me. Then there was a circumcision, and I named the boy after my father, may he rest in peace. When all were gone and I was left with my wife alone, she thrust her head through the bed-curtain and called me to her.

"Gimpel," said she, "why are you silent? Has your ship gone and sunk?"

"What shall I say?" I answered. "A fine thing you've done to me! If my mother had known of it she'd have died a second time."

She said, "Are you crazy, or what?"

"How can you make such a fool," I said, "of one who should be the lord and master?"

"What's the matter with you?" she said. "What have you taken it into your head to imagine?"

I saw that I must speak bluntly and openly. "Do you think this is the way to use an orphan?" I said. "You have borne a bastard."

She answered, "Drive this foolishness out of your head. The child is yours."

"How can he be mine?" I argued. "He was born seventeen weeks after the wedding."

She told me then that he was premature. I said, "Isn't he a little too premature?" She said, she had had a grandmother who carried just as short a time and she resembled this grandmother of hers as one drop of water does another. She swore to it with such oaths that you would have believed a peasant at the fair if he had used them. To tell the plain truth, I didn't believe her; but when I talked it over the next day with the schoolmaster, he told me that the very same thing had happened to Adam and Eve. Two they went up to bed, and four they descended.

"There isn't a woman in the world who is not the granddaughter of Eve," he said.

That was how it was; they argued me dumb. But then, who really knows how such things are?

I began to forget my sorrow. I loved the child madly, and he loved me too. As soon as he saw me he'd wave his little hands and want me to pick him up, and when he was colicky I was the only one who could pacify him. I bought him a little bone teething ring and a little gilded cap. He was forever catching the evil eye from someone, and then I had to run to get one of those abracadabras for him that would get him out of it. I worked like an ox. You know how expenses go up when there's an infant in the house. I don't want to lie about it; I didn't dislike Elka either, for that matter. She swore at me and cursed, and I couldn't get enough of her. What strength she had! One of her looks could rob you of the power of speech. And her orations! Pitch and sulphur, that's what they were full of, and yet somehow also full of charm. I adored her every word. She gave me bloody wounds though.

In the evening I brought her a white loaf as well as a dark one, and also poppyseed rolls I baked myself. I thieved because of her and swiped everything I could lay hands on: macaroons, raisins, almonds, cakes. I hoped I may be forgiven for stealing from the Saturday pots the women left to warm in the baker's oven. I would take out scraps of meat, a chunk of pudding, a chicken leg or head, a piece of tripe, whatever I could nip quickly. She ate and became fat and handsome.

I had to sleep away from home all during the week, at the bakery. On Friday nights when I got home she always made an excuse of some sort. Either she had heartburn, or a stitch in the side, or hiccups, or headaches. You know what women's excuses are. I had a bitter time of it. It was rough. To add to it, this little brother of hers, the bastard, was growing bigger. He'd put lumps on me, and when I wanted to hit back she'd open her mouth and curse so powerfully I saw a green haze floating before my eyes. Ten times a day she threatened to divorce me. Another man in my place would have taken French leave and disappeared. But I'm the type that bears it and says nothing. What's one to do? Shoulders are from God, and burdens too.

One night there was a calamity at the bakery; the oven burst, and we almost had a fire. There was nothing to do but go home, so I went home. Let me, I thought, also taste the joy of sleeping in bed in midweek. I didn't want to wake the sleeping mite and tiptoed into the house. Coming in, it seemed to me that I heard not the snoring of one but, as it were, a double snore, one a thin enough snore and the other like the snoring of a slaughtered ox. Oh, I didn't like that! I didn't like it at all. I went up to the bed, and things suddenly turned black. Next to Elka lay a man's form. Another in my place would have made an uproar, and enough noise to rouse the whole town, but the thought occurred to me that I might wake the child. A little thing like that—why frighten a little swallow, I thought. All right then, I went back to the bakery and stretched out on a sack of flour and till morning I never shut an eye. I shivered as if I had had malaria. "Enough of being a donkey," I said to myself. "Gimpel isn't going to be a sucker all his life. There's a limit even to the foolishness of a fool like Gimpel."

In the morning I went to the rabbi to get advice, and it made a great commotion in the town. They sent the beadle for Elka right away. She came, carrying the child. And what do you think she did? She denied it, denied everything, bone and stone! "He's out of his head," she said. "I know nothing of dreams of divinations." They yelled at her, warned her, hammered on the table, but she stuck to her guns: it was a false accusation, she said.

The butchers and the horse-traders took her part. One of the lads from the slaughterhouse came by and said to me, "We've got our eye on you, you're a marked man." Meanwhile, the child started to bear down and soiled itself. In the rabbinical court there was an Ark of the Covenant, and they couldn't allow that, so they sent Elka away.

I said to the rabbi, "What shall I do?"

"You must divorce her at once," said he.

"And what if she refuses?" I asked.

He said, "You must serve the divorce. That's all you'll have to do."

I said, "Well, all right, Rabbi. Let me think about it."

"There's nothing to think about," said he. "You mustn't remain under the same roof with her."

"And if I want to see the child?" I asked.

"Let her go, the harlot," said he, "and her brood of bastards with her."

The verdict he gave was that I mustn't even cross her threshold—never again, as long as I should live.

During the day it didn't bother me so much. I thought: It was bound to happen, the abscess had to burst. But at night when I stretched out upon the sacks I felt it all very bitterly. A longing took me, for her and for the child. I wanted to be angry, but that's my misfortune exactly, I don't have it in me to be really angry. In the first place—this was how my thoughts went—there's bound to be a slip sometimes. You can't live without errors. Probably that lad who was with her led her on and gave her presents and what not, and women are often long on hair and short on sense, and so he got around her. And then since she denies it so, maybe I was only seeing things? Hallucinations do happen. You see a figure or a mannikin or something, but when you come up closer it's nothing, there's not a thing there. And if that's so, I'm doing her an injustice. And when I got so far in my thoughts I started to weep. I sobbed so that I wet the flour where I lay. In the morning I went to the rabbi and told him that I had made a mistake. The rabbi wrote on with his quill, and he said that if that were so he would have to reconsider the whole case. Until he had finished I wasn't to go near my wife, but I might send her bread and money by messenger.

III

Nine months passed before all the rabbis could come to an agreement. Letters went back and forth. I hadn't realized that there could be so much erudition about a matter like this.

Meanwhile, Elka gave birth to still another child, a girl this time. On the Sabbath I went to the synagogue and invoked a blessing on her. They called me up to the Torah, and I named the child for my mother-in-law—may she rest in peace. The louts and loudmouths of the town who came into the bakery gave me a going over. All Frampol refreshed its spirits because of my trouble and grief. However, I resolved that I would always believe what I was told. What's the good of *not* believing? Today it's your wife you don't believe; tomorrow it's God Himself you won't take stock in.

By an apprentice who was her neighbor I sent her daily a corn or a wheat loaf, or a piece of pastry, rolls or bagels, or, when I got the chance, a slab of pudding, a slice of honeycake, or wedding strudel—whatever came my way. The apprentice was a goodhearted lad, and more than once he added something on his own. He had formerly annoyed me a lot, plucking my nose and digging me in the ribs, but when he started to be a visitor to my house he became kind and friendly. "Hey, you, Gimpel," he said to me, "you have a very decent little wife and two find kids. You don't deserve them."

"But the things people say about her," I said.

"Well, they have long tongues," he said, "and nothing to do with them but babble. Ignore it as you ignore the cold of last winter."

One day the rabbi sent for me and said, "Are you certain, Gimpel, that you were wrong about your wife?"

I said, "I'm certain."

"Why, but look here! You yourself saw it."

"It must have been a shadow," I said.

"The shadow of what?"

"Just of one of the beams, I think."

"You can go home then. You owe thanks to the Yanover rabbi. He found an obscure reference in Maimonides[5] that favored you."

I seized the rabbi's hand and kissed it.

I wanted to run home immediately. It's no small thing to be separated for so long a time from wife and child. Then I reflected: I'd better go back to work now, and go home in the evening. I said nothing to anyone, although as far as my heart was concerned it was like one of the Holy Days. The women teased and twitted me as they did every day, but my thought was: Go on, with your loose talk. The truth is out, like the oil upon the water. Maimonides says it's right, and therefore it is right!

At night, when I had covered the dough to let it rise, I took my share of bread and a little sack of flour and started homeward. The moon was full and the stars were glistening, something to terrify the soul. I hurried onward, and before me darted a long shadow. It was winter, and a fresh snow had fallen. I had a mind to sing, but it was growing late and I didn't want to wake the householders. Then I felt

5. Jewish scholastic philosopher (1135–1204).

like whistling, but I remembered that you don't whistle at night because it brings the demons out. So I was silent and walked as fast as I could.

Dogs in the Christian yards barked at me when I passed, but I thought: Bark your teeth out! What are you but mere dogs? Whereas I am a man, the husband of a fine wife, the father of promising children.

As I approached the house my heart started to pound as though it were the heart of a criminal. I felt no fear, but my heart went thump! thump! Well, no drawing back. I quietly lifted the latch and went in. Elka was asleep. I looked at the infant's cradle. The shutter was closed, but the moon forced its way through the cracks. I saw the newborn child's face and loved it as soon as I saw it—immediately—each tiny bone.

Then I came near to the bed. And what did I see but the apprentice lying there beside Elka. The moon went out all at once. It was utterly black, and I trembled. My teeth chattered. The bread fell from my hands, and my wife waked and said, "Who is that, ah?"

I muttered, "It's me."

"Gimpel?" she asked. "How come you're here? I thought it was forbidden."

"The rabbi said," I answered and shook as with a fever.

"Listen to me, Gimpel," she said, "go out to the shed and see if the goat's all right. It seems she's been sick." I have forgotten to say that we had a goat. When I heard she was unwell I went into the yard. The nannygoat was a good little creature. I had nearly human feeling for her.

With hesitant steps I went up to the shed and opened the door. The goat stood there on her four feet. I felt her everywhere, drew her by the horns, examined her udders, and found nothing wrong. She had probably eaten too much bark. "Good night, little goat," I said. "Keep well." And the little beast answered with a "Maa" as though to thank me for the good will.

I went back. The apprentice had vanished.

"Where," I asked, "is the lad?"

"What lad?" my wife answered.

"What do you mean?" I said. "The apprentice. You were sleeping with him."

"The things I have dreamed this night and the night before," she said, "may they come true and lay you low, body and soul! An evil spirit has taken root in you and dazzles your sight." She screamed out, "You hateful creature! You moon calf! You spook! You uncouth man! Get out, or I'll scream all Frampol out of bed!"

Before I could move, her brother sprang out from behind the oven and struck me a blow on the back of the head. I thought he had broken my neck. I felt that something about me was deeply wrong, and I said, "Don't make a scandal. All that's needed now is that people should accuse me of raising spooks and dybbuks."[6] For that was what she had meant. "No one will touch bread of my baking."

In short, I somehow calmed her.

"Well," she said, "that's enough. Lie down, and be shattered by wheels."

Next morning I called the apprentice aside. "Listen here, brother!" I said. And so on and so forth. "What do you say?" He stared at me as though I had dropped from the roof or something.

"I swear," he said, "you'd better go to an herb doctor or some healer. I'm afraid you have a screw loose, but I'll hush it up for you." And that's how the thing stood.

To make a long story short, I lived twenty years with my wife. She bore me six children, four daughters and two sons. All kinds of things happened, but I neither saw nor heard. I believed, and that's all. The rabbi recently said to me, "Belief in itself is beneficial. It is written that a good man lives by his faith."

Suddenly my wife took sick. It began with a trifle, a little growth upon the breast. But she evidently was not destined to live long; she had no years. I spent a fortune on her. I have forgotten to say that by this time I had a bakery of my own and in Frampol was considered to be something of a rich man. Daily the healer came, and every witch doctor in the neighborhood was brought. They decided to use leeches, and after that to try cupping. They even called a doctor from Lublin, but it was too late. Before she died she called me to her bed and said, "Forgive me, Gimpel."

I said, "What is there to forgive? You have been a good and faithful wife."

"Woe, Gimpel!" she said. "It was ugly how I deceived you all these years. I want to go clean to my Maker, and so I have to tell you that the children are not yours."

If I had been clouted on the head with a piece of wood it couldn't have bewildered me more.

"Whose are they?" I asked.

"I don't know," she said. "There were a lot . . . but they're not yours." And as she spoke she tossed her head to the side, her eyes turned glassy, and it was all up to Elka. On her whitened lips there remained a smile.

I imagined that, dead as she was, she was saying, "I deceived Gimpel. That was the meaning of my brief life."

6. Ghosts and wandering souls.

IV

One night, when the period of mourning was done, as I lay dreaming on the flour sacks, there came the Spirit of Evil himself and said to me, "Gimpel, why do you sleep?"

I said, "What should I be doing? Eating kreplech?"

"The whole world deceives you," he said, "and you ought to deceive the world in your turn."

"How can I deceive all the world?" I asked him.

He answered, "You might accumulate a bucket of urine every day and at night pour it into the dough. Let the sages of Frampol eat filth."

"What about the judgment in the world to come?" I said.

"There is no world to come," he said. "They've sold you a bill of goods and talked you into believing you carried a cat in your belly. What nonsense!"

"Well then," I said, "and is there a God?"

He answered, "There is no God either."

"What," I said, "*is* there, then?"

"A thick mire."

He stood before my eyes with a goatish beard and horn, long-toothed, and with a tail. Hearing such words, I wanted to snatch him by the tail, but I tumbled from the flour sacks and nearly broke a rib. Then it happened that I had to answer the call of nature, and, passing, I saw the risen dough, which seemed to say to me, "Do it!" In brief, I let myself be persuaded.

At dawn the apprentice came. We kneaded the bread, scattered caraway seeds on it, and set it to bake. Then the apprentice went away, and I was left sitting in the little trench by the oven, on a pile of rags. Well, Gimpel, I thought, you've revenged yourself on them for all the shame they've put on you. Outside the frost glittered, but it was warm beside the oven. The flames heated my face. I bent my head and fell into a doze.

I saw in a dream, at once, Elka in her shroud. She called to me, "What have you done, Gimpel?"

I said to her, "It's all your fault," and started to cry.

"You fool!" she said. "You fool! Because I was false is everything false too? I never deceived anyone but myself. I'm paying for it all, Gimpel. They spare you nothing here."

I looked at her face. It was black; I was startled and waked, and remained sitting dumb. I sensed that everything hung in the balance. I seized the long shovel and took out the loaves, carried them into the yard, and started to dig a hole in the frozen earth.

My apprentice came back as I was doing it. "What are you doing boss?" he said, and grew pale as a corpse.

"I know what I'm doing," I said, and I buried it all before his very eyes.

Then I went home, took my hoard from its hiding place, and divided it among the children. "I saw your mother tonight," I said. "She's turning black, poor thing."

They were so astounded they couldn't speak a word.

"Be well," I said, "and forget that such a one as Gimpel ever existed." I put on my short coat, a pair of boots, took the bag that held my prayer shawl in one hand, my stock in the other, and kissed the mezuzah. When people saw me in the street they were greatly surprised.

"Where are you going?" they said.

I answered, "Into the world." And so I departed from Frampol.

I wandered over the land, and good people did not neglect me. After many years I became old and white; I heard a great deal, many lies and falsehoods, but the longer I lived the more I understood that there were really no lies. Whatever doesn't really happen is dreamed at night. It happens to one if it doesn't happen to another, tomorrow if not today, or a century hence if not next year. What difference can it make? Often I heard tales of which I said, "Now this is a thing that cannot happen." But before a year had elapsed I heard that it actually had come to pass somewhere.

Going from place to place, eating at strange tables, it often happens that I spin yarns—improbable things that could never have happened—about devils, magicians, windmills, and the like. The children run after me, calling, "Grandfather, tell us a story." Sometimes they ask for particular stories, and I try to please them. A fat young boy once said to me, "Grandfather, it's the same story you told us before." The little rogue, he was right.

So it is with dreams too. It is many years since I left Frampol, but as soon as I shut my eyes I am there again. And whom do you think I see? Elka. She is standing by the washtub, as at our first encounter, but her face is shining and her eyes are as radiant as the eyes of a saint, and she speaks outlandish words to me, strange things. When I wake I have forgotten it all. But while the dream lasts I am comforted. She answers all my queries, and what comes out is that all is right. I weep and implore, "Let me be with you." And she consoles me and tells me to be patient. The time is nearer than it is far. Sometimes she strokes and kisses me and weeps upon my face. When I awaken I feel her lips and taste the salt of her tears.

No doubt the world is entirely an imaginary world, but it is only once removed from the true world. At the door of the hovel where I lie, there stands the plank on which the dead are taken away. The grave-digger Jew has his spade ready. The grave waits and the worms are hungry; the shrouds are prepared—I carry them in my beggar's sack. Another *shnorrer*[7] is waiting to inherit my bed of straw. When the time comes I will go joyfully. Whatever may be there, it will be real, without complication, without ridicule, without deception. God be praised: there even Gimpel cannot be deceived.

---

1. Is Gimpel's gullibility self-chosen—or is it in some way a gift of God?
2. How is his wife's infidelity transformed into a true marriage bond?
3. What does Gimpel pay for and give up for his choice to believe?
4. Does the story deliver a moral, or is its chief point entertainment?
5. Can you assign motives to Gimpel's wife? to any of the subordinate characters?

7. Beggar, sponger.

Jean Stafford

Stafford (1915–1979) was born in Covina, California, the daughter of a writer. She was educated at the University of Colorado and Heidelberg University. Though she has written of cosmopolitan scenes, at the heart of many stories is a self-conscious, vulnerable child, viewing the promises of the world with an aching mistrust. Her novels include Boston Adventure *(1944) and* The Mountain Lion *(1947). Her stories have been brought together in* Children Are Bored on Sunday *(1953),* Bad Characters *(1964), and* The Collected Stories *(1969).*

In the Zoo

Keening harshly in his senility, the blind polar bear slowly and ceaselessly shakes his head in the stark heat of the July and mountain noon. His open eyes are blue. No one stops to look at him; an old farmer, in passing, sums up the old bear's situation by observing, with a ruthless chuckle, that he is a "back number." Patient and despairing, he sits on his yellowed haunches on the central rock of his pool, his huge toy paws wearing short boots of mud.

The grizzlies to the right of him, a conventional family of father and mother and two spring cubs, alternately play the clown and sleep. There is a blustery, scoundrelly, half-likable bravado in the manner of the black bear on the polar's left; his name, according to the legend on his cage, is Clancy, and he is a rough-and-tumble, brawling blowhard, thundering continually as he paces back and forth, or pauses to face his audience of children and mothers and release from his great, gray-tongued mouth a perfectly Vesuvian roar. If he were to be reincarnated in human form, he would be a man of action, possibly a football coach, probably a politician. One expects to see his black hat hanging from a branch of one of his trees; at any moment he will light a cigar.

The polar bear's next-door neighbors are not the only ones who offer so sharp and sad a contrast to him. Across a reach of scrappy grass and litter is the convocation of conceited monkeys, burrowing into each other's necks and chests for fleas, picking their noses with their long, black, finicky fingers, swinging by their gifted tails on the flying trapeze, screaming bloody murder. Even when they mourn—one would think the male orangutan was on the very brink of suicide—they are comedians; they only fake depression, for they are firmly secure in their rambunctious tribalism and in their appalling insight and contempt. Their flibbertigibbet gamboling is a sham, and, stealthily and shiftily, they are really watching the pitiful polar bear ("Back number," they quote the farmer. "That's *his* number all right," they snigger), and the windy black bear ("Life of the party. Gasbag. Low I.Q.," they note scornfully on his dossier), and the stupid, bourgeois grizzlies ("It's feed the face and hit the sack for them," the monkeys say). And they are watching my sister and me, two middle-aged women, as we sit on a bench between the exhibits, eating popcorn, growing thirsty. We are thoughtful.

A chance remark of Daisy's a few minutes before has turned us to memory and meditation. "I don't know why," she said, "but that poor blind bear reminds me of Mr. Murphy." The name "Mr. Murphy" at once returned us both to childhood, and we were floated far and fast, our later lives diminished. So now we eat our popcorn in silence with the ritualistic appetite of childhood, which has little to do with hunger; it is not so much food as a sacrament, and in tribute to our sisterliness and our friendliness I break the silence to say that this is the best popcorn I have ever eaten in my life. The extravagance of my statement instantly makes me feel self-indulgent, and for some time I uneasily avoid looking at the blind bear. My sister does not agree or disagree; she simply says that popcorn is the only food she has ever really liked. For a long time, then, we eat without a word, but I know, because I know her well and know her similarity to me, that Daisy is thinking what I am thinking; both of us are mournfully remembering Mr. Murphy, who, at one time in our lives, was our only friend.

This zoo is in Denver, a city that means nothing to my sister and me except as a place to take or meet trains. Daisy lives two hundred miles farther west, and it is her custom, when my every-other-year visit with her is over, to come across the mountains to see me off on my eastbound train. We know almost no one here, and because our stays are short, we have never bothered to learn the town in more than the most desultory way. We know the Burlington[1] uptown office and the respectable hotels, a restaurant or two, the Union Station, and, beginning today, the zoo in the city park.

But since the moment that Daisy named Mr. Murphy by name our situation in Denver has been only corporeal; our minds and our hearts are in Adams, fifty miles north, and we are seeing, under the white sun at its pitiless meridian, the streets of that ugly town, its parks

1. Burlington Railway.

and trees and bridges, the bandstand in its dreary park, the roads that lead away from it, west to the mountains and east to the plains, its mongrel and multitudinous churches, its high school shaped like a loaf of bread, the campus of its college, an oasis of which we had no experience except to walk through it now and then, eyeing the woodbine on the impressive buildings. These things are engraved forever on our minds with a legibility so insistent that you have only to say the name of the town aloud to us to rip the rinds from our nerves and leave us exposed in terror and humiliation.

We have supposed in later years that Adams was not so bad as all that, and we know that we magnified its ugliness because we looked upon it as the extension of the possessive, unloving, scornful, complacent foster mother, Mrs. Placer, to whom, at the death of our parents within a month of each other, we were sent like Dickensian grotesqueries[2]—cowardly, weak-stomached, given to tears, backward in school. Daisy was ten and I was eight when, unaccompanied, we made the long trip from Marblehead to our benefactress, whom we had never seen and, indeed, never heard of until the pastor of our church came to tell us of the arrangement our father had made on his deathbed, seconded by our mother on hers. This man, whose name and face I have forgotten and whose parting speeches to us I have not forgiven, tried to dry our tears with talk of Indians and of buffaloes; he spoke, however, at much greater length, and in preaching cadences, of the Christian goodness of Mrs. Placer. She was, he said, childless and fond of children, and for many years she had been a widow, after the lingering demise of her tubercular husband, for whose sake she had moved to the Rocky Mountains. For his support and costly medical care, she had run a boarding house, and after his death, since he had left her nothing, she was obliged to continue running it. She had been a girlhood friend of our paternal grandmother, and our father, in the absence of responsible relatives, had made her the beneficiary of his life insurance on the condition that she lodge and rear us. The pastor, with a frankness remarkable considering that he was talking to children, explained to us that our father had left little more than a drop in the bucket for our care, and he enjoined us to give Mrs. Placer, in return for her hospitality and sacrifice, courteous help and eternal thanks. "Sacrifice" was a word we were never allowed to forget.

And thus it was, in grief for our parents, that we came cringing to the dry Western town and to the house where Mrs. Placer lived, a house in which the square, uncushioned furniture was cruel and the pictures on the walls were either dour or dire and the lodgers, who lived in the upper floors among shadowy wardrobes and chiffoniers,

2. Like the caricaturish characters in Charles Dickens's novels.

had come through the years to resemble their landlady in appearance as well as in deportment.

After their ugly-colored evening meal, Gran—as she bade us call her—and her paying guests would sit, rangy and aquiline, rocking on the front porch on spring and summer and autumn nights, tasting their delicious grievances: those slights delivered by ungrateful sons and daughters, those impudences committed by trolley-car conductors and uppity salesgirls in the ready-to-wear, all those slurs and calculated elbow-jostlings that were their daily crucifixion and their staff of life. We little girls, washing the dishes in the cavernous kitchen, listened to their even, martyred voices, fixed like leeches to their solitary subject and their solitary creed—that life was essentially a matter of being done in, let down, and swindled.

At regular intervals, Mrs. Placer, chairwoman of the victims, would say, "Of course, I don't care; I just have to laugh," and then would tell a shocking tale of an intricate piece of skulduggery perpetrated against her by someone she did not even know. Sometimes, with her avid, partial jury sitting there on the porch behind the bitter hopvines in the heady mountain air, the cases she tried involved Daisy and me, and, listening, we travailed, hugging each other, whispering, "I wish she wouldn't! Oh, how did she find out?" How *did* she? Certainly we never told her when we were snubbed or chosen last on teams, never admitted to a teacher's scolding or to the hoots of laughter that greeted us when we bit on silly, unfair jokes. But she knew. She knew about the slumber parties we were not invited to, the beefsteak fries at which we were pointedly left out; she knew that the singing teacher had said in so many words that I could not carry a tune in a basket and that the sewing superintendent had said that Daisy's fingers were all thumbs. With our teeth chattering in the cold of our isolation, we would hear her protestant, litigious voice defending our right to be orphans, paupers, wholly dependent on her—except for the really ridiculous pittance from our father's life insurance—when it was all she could do to make ends meet. She did not care, but she had to laugh that people in general were so small-minded that they looked down on fatherless, motherless waifs like us and, by association, looked down on her. It seemed funny to her that people gave her no credit for taking on these sickly youngsters who were not even kin but only the grandchildren of a friend.

If a child with braces on her teeth came to play with us, she was, according to Gran, slyly lording it over us because our teeth were crooked but there was no money to have them straightened. And what could be the meaning of our being asked to come for supper at the doctor's house? Were the doctor and his la-di-da New York wife and those pert girls with their sold-gold barrettes and their Shetland pony going to shame her poor darlings? Or shame their poor Gran by making them sorry to come home to the plain but honest life that was all she could provide for them?

There was no stratum of society not reeking with the effluvium of fraud and pettifoggery. And the school system was almost the worst of all: if we could not understand fractions, was that not our teacher's fault? And therefore what right had she to give us F? It was as plain as a pikestaff[3] to Gran that the teacher was only covering up her own inability to teach. It was unlikely, too—highly unlikely—that it was by accident that time and time again the free medical clinic was closed for the day just as our names were about to be called out, so that nothing was done about our bad tonsils, which meant that we were repeatedly sick in the winter, with Gran fetching and carrying for us, climbing those stairs a jillion times a day with her game leg and her heart that was none too strong.

Steeped in these mists of accusation and hidden plots and double meanings, Daisy and I grew up like worms. I think no one could have withstood the atmosphere in that house where everyone trod on eggs that a little bird had told them were bad. They spied on one another, whispered behind doors, conjectured, drew parallels beginning "With all due respect . . ." or "It is a matter of indifference to *me* but . . ." The vigilantes patrolled our town by day, and by night returned to lay their goodies at their priestess's feet and wait for her oracular interpretation of the innards of the butcher, the baker, the candlestick maker, the soda jerk's girl, and the barber's unnatural deaf white cat.

Consequently, Daisy and I also became suspicious. But it was suspicion of ourselves that made us mope and weep and grimace with self-judgment. Why were we not happy when Gran had sacrificed herself to the bone for us? Why did we not cut dead the paper boy who had called her a filthy name? Why did we persist in our willful friendliness with the grocer who had tried, unsuccessfully, to overcharge her on a case of pork and beans?

Our friendships were nervous and surreptitious; we sneaked and lied, and as our hungers sharpened, our debasement deepened; we were pitied; we were shifty-eyed, always on the lookout for Mrs. Placer or one of her tattletale lodgers; we were hypocrites.

Nevertheless, one thin filament of instinct survived, and Daisy and I in time found asylum in a small menagerie down by the railroad tracks. It belonged to a gentle alcoholic ne'er-do-well, who did nothing all day long but drink bathtub gin in rickeys and play solitaire and smile to himself and talk to his animals. He had a little, stunted red vixen

3. "Plain as day."

and a deodorized skunk, a parrot from Tahiti that spoke Parisian French, a woebegone coyote, and two capuchin monkeys, so serious and humanized, so small and sad and sweet, and so religious-looking with their tonsured heads that it was impossible not to think their gibberish was really an ordered language with the grammar that some day some philologist would understand.

Gram knew about our visits to Mr. Murphy and she did not object, for it gave her keen pleasure to excoriate him when we came home. His vice was not a matter of guesswork; it was an established fact that he was half-seas over from dawn till midnight. "With the black Irish," said Gran, "the taste for drink is taken in with the mother's milk and is never mastered. Oh, I know all about those promises to join the temperance movement and not to touch another drop. The way to hell is paved with good intentions."

We were still little girls when we discovered Mr. Murphy, before the shattering disease of adolescence was to make our bones and brains ache even more painfully than before, and we loved him and we hoped to marry him when we grew up. We loved him, and we loved his monkeys to exactly the same degree and in exactly the same way; they were husbands and fathers and brothers, these three little, ugly, dark, secret men who minded their own business and let us mind ours. If we stuck our fingers through the bars of the cage, the monkeys would sometimes take them in their tight, tiny hands and look into our faces with a tentative, somehow absent-minded sorrow, as if they terribly regretted that they could not place us but were glad to see us all the same. Mr. Murphy, playing a solitaire game of cards called "once in a blue moon" on a kitchen table in his back yard beside the pens, would occasionally look up and blink his beautiful blue eyes and say, "You're peaches to make over my wee friends. I love you for it." There was nothing demanding in his voice, and nothing sticky; on his lips the word "love" was jocose and forthright, it had no strings attached. We would sit on either side of him and watch him regiment his ranks of cards and stop to drink as deeply as if he were dying of thirst and wave to his animals and say to them, "Yes, lads, you're dandies."

Because Mr. Murphy was as reserved with us as the capuchins were, as courteously noncommittal, we were surprised one spring day when he told us that he had a present for us, which he hoped Mrs. Placer would let us keep; it was a puppy, for whom the owner had asked him to find a home—half collie and half Labrador retriever, blue-blooded on both sides.

"You might tell Mrs. Placer—" he said, smiling at the name, for Gran was famous in the town. "You might tell Mrs. Placer," said Mr. Murphy, "that this lad will make a fine watchdog. She'll never have to fear for her spoons again. Or her honor." The last he said to himself, not laughing but tucking his chin into his collar; lines sprang to the corners of his eyes. He would not let us see the dog, whom we could hear yipping and squealing inside his shanty, for he said that our disappointment would weigh on his conscience if we lost our hearts to the fellow and then could not have him for our own.

That evening at supper, we told Gran about Mr. Murphy's present. A dog? In the first place, why a dog? Was it possible that the news had reached Mr. Murphy's ears that Gran had just this very day finished planting her spring garden, the very thing that a rampageous dog would have in his mind to destroy? What sex was it? A male! Females, she had heard, were more trustworthy; males roved and came home smelling of skunk; such a consideration as this, of course, would not have crossed Mr. Murphy's fuddled mind. Was this young male dog housebroken? We had not asked? That was the limit!

Gran appealed to her followers, too raptly fascinated by Mr. Murphy's machinations to eat their Harvard beets. "Am I being far-fetched or does it strike you as decidedly queer that Mr. Murphy is trying to fob off on my little girls a young cur that has not been trained?" she asked them. "If it were housebroken, he would have said so, so I feel it is safe to assume that it is not. Perhaps cannot *be* housebroken. I've heard of such cases."

The fantasy spun on, richly and rapidly, with all the skilled helping hands at work at once. The dog was tangibly in the room with us, shedding his hair, scratching his fleas, shaking rain off himself to splatter the walls, dragging some dreadful carcass across the floor, chewing up slippers, knocking over chairs with his tail, gobbling the chops from the platter, barking, biting, fathering, fighting, smelling to high heaven of carrion, staining the rug with his muddy feet, scratching the floor with his claws. He developed rabies; he bit a child, two children! Three! Everyone in town! And Gran and her poor darlings went to jail for harboring this murderous, odoriferous, drunk, Roman Catholic dog.

And yet, astoundingly enough, she came around to agreeing to let us have the dog. It was, as Mr. Murphy had predicted, the word "watchdog" that deflected the course of the trial. The moment Daisy uttered it, Gran halted, marshaling her reverse march; while she rallied and tacked and reconnoitered, she sent us to the kitchen for the dessert. And by the time this couse was under way, the uses of a dog, the enormous potentialities for investigation and law enforcement in a dog trained by Mrs. Placer, were being minutely and passionately scrutinized by the eight upright bloodhounds sitting at the table wolfing their brown Betty as if it were fresh-killed rabbit. The dog now sat at attention beside his mistress, fiercely alert, ears cocked, nose aquiver, the protector of widows, of orphans, of lonely people who had no homes. He made short shrift of burglars, homicidal maniacs, Peeping Toms, gypsies, bogus missionaries, Fuller Brush men with a risqué spiel. He went to the store and brought back groceries, retrieved the evening paper from the awkward place the boy had meanly thrown it, rescued cripples from burning houses, saved children from drowning, heeled at command, begged, lay down, stood up, sat, jumped through a hoop, ratted.

Both times—when he was a ruffian of the blackest delinquency and then a pillar of society—he was full-grown in his prefiguration, and when Laddy appeared on the following day, small, unsteady, and whimpering lonesomely, Gran and her lodgers were taken aback; his infant, clumsy paws embarrassed them, his melting eyes were unapropos. But it could never be said of Mrs. Placer, as Mrs. Placer her own self said, that she was a women who went back on her word, and her darlings were going to have their dog, softheaded and feckless as he might be. All the first night, in his carton in the kitchen, he wailed for his mother, and in the morning, it was true, he had made a shambles of the room—fouled the floor, and pulled off the tablecloth together with a ketchup bottle, so that thick gore lay everywhere. At breakfast, the lodgers confessed they had had a most amusing night, for it had actually been funny the way the dog had been determined not to let anyone get a wink of sleep. After that first night, Laddy slept in our room, receiving from us, all through our delighted, sleepless nights, pats and embraces and kisses and whispers. He was our baby, our best friend, the smartest, prettiest, nicest dog in the entire wide world. Our soft and rapid blandishments excited him to yelp at us in pleased bewilderment, and then we would playfully grasp his muzzle, so that he would snarl, deep in this throat like an adult dog, and shake his head violently, and, when we freed him, nip us smartly with great good will.

He was an intelligent and genial dog and we trained him quickly. He steered clear of Gran's radishes and lettuce after she had several times given him a brisk comeuppance with a strap across the rump, and he soon left off chewing shoes and the laundry on the line, and he outgrew his babyish whining. He grew like a weed; he lost his spherical softness, and his coat, which had been sooty fluff, came in stiff and rusty black; his nose grew aristocratically long, and his clever, pointed ears stood at attention. He was all bronzy, lustrous black except for an Elizabethan ruff[4] of white and a tip of white at the end of his perky tail. No one could deny that he was exceptionally handsome and that he had, as well, great personal charm and style. He escorted Daisy and me to school in the morning, laughing interiorly out of the enormous pleasure of his life as he gracefully cantered ahead of us, distracted

4. I.e., a collar of thick, marked hair accentuating the head, looking like the collar worn by Elizabethan gentlemen.

occasionally by his private interest in smells or unfamiliar beings in the grass but, on the whole, engrossed in his role of chaperone. He made friends easily with other dogs, and sometimes he went for a long hunting weekend into the mountains with a huge and bossy old red hound named Mess, who had been on the county[5] most of his life and had made a good thing of it, particularly at the fire station.

It was after one of these three-day excursions into the high country that Gran took Laddy in hand. He had come back spent and filthy, his coat a mass of cockleburs and ticks, his eyes bloodshot, loud *râles*[6] in his chest; for half a day he lay motionless before the front door like someone in a hangover, his groaning eyes explicitly saying "Oh, for God's sake, leave me be" when we offered him food or bowls of water. Gran was disapproving, then affronted, and finally furious. Not, of course, with Laddy, since all inmates of her house enjoyed immunity, but with Mess, whose caddish character, together with that of his nominal masters, the firemen, she examined closely under a strong light, with an air of detachment, with her not caring but her having, all the same, to laugh. A lodger who occupied the back west room had something to say about the fire chief and his nocturnal visits to a certain house occupied by a certain group of young women, too near the same age to be sisters and too old to be the daughters of the woman who claimed to be their mother. What a story! The exophthalmic librarian—she lived in one of the front rooms—had some interesting insinuations to make about the deputy marshal, who had borrowed, significantly, she thought, a book on hypnotism. She also knew—she was, of course, in a most useful position in the town, and from her authoritative pen in the middle of the library her mammiform and azure eyes and her eager ears missed nothing—that the fire chief's wife was not as scrupulous as she might be when she was keeping score on bridge night at the Sorosis.

There was little at the moment that Mrs. Placer and her disciples could do to save the souls of the Fire Department and their families, and therefore save the town from holocaust (a very timid boarder—a Mr. Beaver, a newcomer who was not to linger long—had sniffed throughout this recitative as if he were smelling burning flesh), but at least the unwholesome bond between Mess and Laddy could and would be severed once and for all. Gran looked across the porch at Laddy, who lay stretched at full length in the darkest corner, shuddering and baying abortively in his throat as he chased jack rabbits in his dreams, and she said, "A dog can have morals like a human." With this declaration Laddy's randy, manly holidays were finished. It may have been telepathy that woke him; he lifted his heavy head from his paws, laboriously got up, hesitated for a moment, and then padded languidly

5. On welfare. 6. Abnormal sounds accompanying the normal respiratory murmur, as in pulmonary diseases.

across the porch to Gran. He stood docilely beside her chair, head down, tail drooping as if to say, "O.K., Mrs. Placer, show me how and I'll walk the straight and narrow."

The very next day, Gran changed Laddy's name to Caesar, as being more dignified, and a joke was made at the supper table that he had come, seen, and conquered Mrs. Placer's heart—for within her circle, where the magnanimity she lavished upon her orphans was daily demonstrated, Mrs. Placer's heart was highly thought of. On that day also, although we did not know it yet, Laddy ceased to be our dog. Before many weeks passed, indeed, he ceased to be anyone we had ever known. A week or so after he became Caesar, he took up residence in her room, sleeping alongside her bed. She broke him of the habit of taking us to school (temptation to low living was rife along those streets; there was a chow—well, never mind) by the simple expedient of chaining him to a tree as soon as she got up in the morning. This discipline, together with the stamina building cuffs she gave his sensitive ears from time to time, gradually but certainly remade his character. From a sanguine, affectionate, easygoing Gael (with the fits of melancholy that alternated with the larkiness), he turned into an overbearing, military, efficient, loud-voiced Teuton.[7] His bark, once wide of range, narrowed to one dark, glottal tone.

Soon the paper boy flatly refused to serve our house after Caesar efficiently removed the bicycle clip from his pants leg; the skin was not broken, or even bruised, but it was a matter of principle with the boy. The milkman approached the back door in a seizure of shakes like St. Vitus's dance. The metermen, the coal men, and the garbage collector crossed themselves if they were Catholics and, if they were not, tried whistling in the dark. "Good boy, good Caesar," they caroled, and, unctuously lying, they said they knew his bark was worse than his bite, knowing full well that it was not, considering the very nasty nip, requiring stitches, he had given a representative of the Olson Rug Company, who had had the folly to pat him on the head. Caesar did not molest the lodgers, but he disdained them and he did not brook being personally addressed by anyone except Gran. One night, he wandered into the dining room, appearing to be in search of something he had mislaid, and, for some reason that no one was ever able to divine, suddenly stood stock-still and gave the easily upset Mr. Beaver a long and penetrating look. Mr. Beaver, trembling from head to toe, stammered, "Why—er, hello there, Caesar, old boy, old boy," and Caesar charged. For a moment, it was touch and go, but Gran saved Mr. Beaver, only to lose him an hour later when he departed, bag and baggage, for the Y.M.C.A. This rout and the consequent loss of revenue would more

7. The terms Gael and Teuton are here used to refer to different kinds of temperament. The author is invoking popularized stereotypes to represent this difference.

than likely have meant Caesar's downfall and his deportation to the pound if it had not been that a newly widowed druggist, very irascible and very much Gran's style, had applied for a room in her house a week or so before, and now he moved in delightedly, as if he were coming home.

Finally, the police demanded that Caesar be muzzled and they warned that if he committed any major crime again—they cited the case of the Olson man—he would be shot on sight. Mrs. Placer, although she had no respect for the law, knowing as much as she did about its agents, obeyed. She obeyed, that is, in part; she put the muzzle on Caesar for a few hours a day, usually early in the morning when the traffic was light and before the deliveries had started, but the rest of the time his powerful jaws and dazzling white saber teeth were free and snapping. There was between these two such preternatural rapport, such an impressive conjugation of suspicion, that he, sensing the approach of a policeman, could convey instantly to her the immediate necessity of clapping his nose cage on. And the policeman, sent out on the complaint of a terrorized neighbor, would be greeted by this law-abiding pair at the door.

Daisy and I wished we were dead. We were divided between hating Caesar and loving Laddy, and we could not give up the hope that something, some day, would change him back into the loving animal he had been before he was appointed vice-president of the Placerites. Now at the meetings after supper on the porch he took an active part, standing rigidly at Gran's side except when she sent him on an errand. He carried out these assignments not with an air of a servant but with that of an accomplice. "Get me the paper, Caesar," she would say to him, and he, dismayingly intelligent and a shade smart-alecky, would open the screen door by himself and in a minute come back with the *Bulletin,* from which Mrs. Placer would then read an item, like the Gospel of the day, and then read between the lines of it, scandalized.

In the deepening of our woe and our bereavement and humiliation, we mutely appealed to Mr. Murphy. We did not speak outright to him, for Mr. Murphy lived in a state of indirection, and often when he used the pronoun "I," he seemed to be speaking of someone standing a little to the left of him, but we went to see him and his animals each day during the sad summer, taking what comfort we could from the cozy, quiet indolence of his back yard, where small black eyes encountered ours politely and everyone was half asleep. When Mr. Murphy inquired about Laddy in his bland, inattentive way, looking for a stratagem whereby to shift the queen of hearts into position by the king, we would say, "Oh, he's fine," or "Laddy is a nifty dog." And Mr. Murphy, reverently slaking the thirst that was his talent and his concubine, would murmur, "I'm glad."

We wanted to tell him, we wanted his help, or at least his sympathy, but how could we cloud his sunny world? It was awful to see Mr. Murphy ruffled. Up in the calm clouds as he generally was, he could occasionally be brought to earth with a thud, as we had seen and heard one day. Not far from his house, there lived a bad, troublemaking boy of twelve, who was forever hanging over the fence trying to teach the parrot obscene words. He got nowhere, for she spoke no English and she would flabbergast him with her cold eye and sneer, "*Tant pis.*"[8] One day, this boorish fellow went too far; he suddenly shot his head over the fence like a jack-in-the-box and aimed a water pistol at the skunk's face. Mr. Murphy leaped to his feet in a scarlet rage; he picked up a stone and threw it accurately, hitting the boy square in the back, so hard that he fell right down in a mud puddle and lay there kicking and squalling and, as it turned out, quite badly hurt. "If you ever come back here again, I'll kill you!" roared Mr. Murphy. I think he meant it, for I have seldom seen an anger so resolute, so brilliant, and so voluble. "How dared he!" he cried, scambling into Mallow's cage to hug and pet and soothe her. "He must be absolutely mad! He must be the Devil!" He did not go back to his game after that but paced the yard, swearing a blue streak and only pausing to croon to his animals, now as frightened by him as they had been by the intruder, and to drink straight from the bottle, not bothering with fixings. We were fascinated by this unfamiliar side of Mr. Murphy, but we did not want to see it ever again, for his face had grown so dangerously purple and the veins of his forehead seemed ready to burst and his eyes looked scorched. He was the closest thing to a maniac we had ever seen. So we did not tell him about Laddy; what he did not know would not hurt him, although it was hurting us, throbbing in us like a great, bleating wound.

But eventually Mr. Murphy heard about our dog's conversion, one night at the pool hall, which he visited from time to time when he was seized with a rare but compelling garrulity, and the next afternoon when he asked us how Laddy was and we replied that he was fine, he tranquilly told us, as he deliberated whether to move the jack of clubs now or to bide his time, that we were sweet girls but we were lying in our teeth. He did not seem at all angry but only interested, and all the while he questioned us, he went on about his business with the gin and the hearts and spades and diamonds and clubs. It rarely happened that he won the particular game he was playing, but that day he did, and when he saw all the cards laid out in their ideal pattern, he leaned back, looking disappointed, and he said, "I'm damned." He then scooped

8. "Too bad."

up the cards, in a gesture unusually quick and tidy for him, stacked them together, and bound them with a rubber band. Then he began to tell us what he thought of Gran. He grew as loud and apoplectic as he had been that other time, and though he kept repeating that he knew *we* were innocent and he put not a shred of the blame on us, we were afraid he might suddenly change his mind, and, speechless, we cowered against the monkeys' cage. In dread, the monkeys clutched the fingers we offered to them and made soft, protesting noises, as if to say, "Oh, stop it, Murphy! Our nerves!"

As quickly as it had started, the tantrum ended. Mr. Murphy paled to his normal complexion and said calmly that the only practical thing was to go and have it out with Mrs. Placer. "At once," he added, although he said he bitterly feared that it was too late and there would be no exorcising the fiend from Laddy's misused spirit. And because he had given the dog to us and not to her, he required that we go along with him, stick up for our rights, stand on our own mettle, get up our Irish, and give the old bitch something to put in her pipe and smoke.

Oh, it was hot that day! We walked in a kind of delirium through the summer, where only the grasshoppers had the energy to move, and I remember wondering if ether smelled like the gin on Mr. Murphy's breath. Daisy and I, in one way or another, were going to have our gizzards cut out along with our hearts and our souls and our pride, and I wished I were as drunk as Mr. Murphy, who swam effortlessly through the heat, his lips parted comfortably, his eyes half closed. When we turned into the path at Gran's house, my blood began to scald my veins. It was futile and so dangerous and so absurd. Here we were on a high moral mission, two draggletailed, gumptionless little girls and a toper whom no one could take seriously, partly because he was little more than a gurgling bottle of booze and partly because of the clothes he wore. He was a sight, as he always was when he was out of his own yard. There, somehow, in the carefree disorder, his clothes did not look especially strange, but on the streets of the town, in the barbershop or the post office or on Gran's path, they were fantastic. He wore a pair of hound's-tooth pants, old but maintaining a vehement pattern, and with them he wore a collarless blue flannelette shirt. His hat was the silliest of all, because it was a derby three sizes too big. And as if Shannon, too, was a part of his funny-paper costume, the elder capuchin rode on his shoulder, tightly embracing his thin red neck.

Gran and Caesar were standing side by side behind the screen door, looking as if they had been expecting us all along. For a moment, Gran and Mr. Murphy faced each other across the length of weedy brick between the gate and the front porch, and no one spoke. Gran took no notice at all of Daisy and me. She adjusted her eyeglasses, using both hands, and then looked down at Caesar and matter-of-factly asked, "Do you want out?"

Caesar flung himself full-length upon the screen and it sprang open like a jaw. I ran to meet him and head him off, and Daisy threw a library book at his head, but he was on Mr. Murphy in one split second and had his monkey off his shoulder and had broken Shannon's neck in two shakes. He would have gone on nuzzling and mauling and growling over the corpse for hours if Gran had not marched out of the house and down the path and slapped him lightly on the flank and said, in a voice that could not have deceived an idiot, "Why, Caesar, you scamp! You've hurt Mr. Murphy's monkey! Aren't you ashamed!"

Hurt the monkey! In one final, apologetic shudder, the life was extinguished from the little fellow. Bloody and covered with slather, Shannon lay with his arms suppliantly stretched over his head, his leather fingers curled into loose, helpless fists. His hind legs and his tail lay limp and helter-skelter on the path. And Mr. Murphy, all of a sudden reeling drunk, burst into the kind of tears that Daisy and I knew well—the kind that time alone could stop. We stood aghast in the dark-red sunset, killed by our horror and our grief for Shannon and our unforgivable disgrace. We stood upright in a dead faint, and an eon passed before Mr. Murphy picked up Shannon's body and wove away, sobbing, "I don't believe it! I don't *believe* it!"

The very next day, again at morbid, heavy sunset, Caesar died in violent convulsions, knocking down two tall hollyhocks in his throes. Long after his heart had stopped, his right hind leg continued to jerk in aimless reflex. Madly methodical, Mr. Murphy had poisoned some meat for him, had thoroughly envenomed a whole pound of hamburger, and early in the morning, before sunup, when he must have been near collapse with his hangover, he had stolen up to Mrs. Placer's house and put it by the kitchen door. He was so stealthy that Caesar never stirred in his fool's paradise there on the floor by Gran. We knew these to be the facts, for Mr. Murphy made no bones about them. Afterward, he had gone home and said a solemn Requiem for Shannon in so loud a voice that someone sent for the police, and they took him away in the Black Maria to sober him up on strong green tea. By the time he was in the lockup and had confessed what he had done, it was far too late, for Caesar had already gulped down the meat. He suffered an undreamed-of agony in Gran's flower garden, and Daisy and I, unable to bear the sight of it, hiked up to the red rocks and shook there, wretchedly ripping to shreds the sand lilies that grew in the cracks. Flight was the only thing we could think of, but where could we go? We stared west at the mountains and quailed at the look of the stern white glacier; we wildly scanned the prairies for escape. "If only we were something besides kids! Besides girls!" mourned Daisy. I could not speak at all; I huddled in a niche of the rocks and cried.

No one in town, except, of course, her lodgers, had the slightest sympathy for Gran. The townsfolk allowed that Mr. Murphy was a drunk and was fighting Irish, but he had a heart and this was something that could never be said of Mrs. Placer. The neighbor who had called the police when he was chanting the *Dies Irae*[9] before breakfast in that deafening monotone had said, "The poor guy is having some kind of a spell, so don't be rough on him, hear?" Mr. Murphy became, in fact, a kind of hero; some people, stretching a point, said he was a saint for the way that every day and twice on Sunday he sang a memorial Mass over Shannon's grave, now marked with a chipped, cheap plaster figure of Saint Francis. He withdrew from the world more and more, seldom venturing into the streets at all, except when he went to the bootlegger to get a new bottle to snuggle into. All summer, all fall, we saw him as we passed by his yard, sitting at his dilapidated table, enfeebled with gin, graying, withering, turning his head ever and ever more slowly as he maneuvered the protocol of the kings and the queens and the knaves. Daisy and I could never stop to visit him again.

It went on like this, year after year. Daisy and I lived in a mesh of lies and evasions, baffled and mean, like rats in a maze. When we were old enough for beaux, we connived like sluts to see them, but we would never admit to their existence until Gran caught us out by some trick. Like this one, for example: Once, at the end of a long interrogation, she said to me, "I'm more relieved than I can tell you that you *don't* have anything to do with Jimmy Gilmore, because I happen to know that he is after only one thing in a girl," and then, off guard in the loving memory of sitting in the movies the night before with Jimmy, not even holding hands, I defended him and defeated myself, and Gran, smiling with success, said, "I *thought* you knew him. It's a pretty safe rule of thumb that where there's smoke there's fire." That finished Jimmy and me, for afterward I was nervous with him and I confounded and alarmed and finally bored him by trying to convince him, although the subject had not come up, that I did not doubt his good intentions.

Daisy and I would come home from school, or, later, from our jobs, with a small triumph or an interesting piece of news, and if we forgot ourselves and, in our exuberance, told Gran, we were hustled into court at once for cross-examination. Once, I remember, while I was still in high school, I told her about getting a part in a play. How very nice for me, she said, if that kind of make-believe seemed to me worth while. But what was my role? An old woman! A widow woman believed to be a witch? She did not care a red cent, but she did have

9. Latin hymn, *The Day of Wrath* or *The Day of Judgment*.

to laugh in view of the fact that Miss Eccles, in charge of dramatics, had almost run her down in her car. And I would forgive her, would I not, if she did not come to see the play, and would not think her eccentric for not wanting to see herself ridiculed in public?

My pleasure strangled, I crawled, joy-killed, to our third-floor room. The room was small and its monstrous furniture was too big and the rag rugs were repulsive, but it was bright. We would not hang a blind at the window, and in this day I stood there staring into the mountains that burned with the sun. I feared the mountains, but at times like this their massiveness consoled me; they, at least, could not be gossiped about.

Why did we stay until we were grown? Daisy and I ask ourselves this question as we sit here on the bench in the municipal zoo, reminded of Mr. Murphy by the polar bear, reminded by the monkeys not of Shannon but of Mrs. Placer's insatiable gossips at their post-prandial feast.

"But how could we have left?" says Daisy, wringing her buttery hands. "It was the depression. We had no money. We had nowhere to go."

"All the same, we could have gone," I say, resentful still of the waste of all those years. "We could have come here and got jobs as waitresses. Or prostitutes, for that matter."

"I wouldn't have wanted to be a prostitute," says Daisy.

We agree that under the circumstances it would have been impossible for us to run away. The physical act would have been simple, for the city was not far and we could have stolen the bus fare or hitched a ride. Later, when we began to work as salesgirls in Kress's,[1] it would have been no trick at all to vanish one Saturday afternoon with our week's pay, without so much as going home to say goodbye. But it had been infinitely harder than that, for Gran, as we now see, held us trapped by our sense of guilt. We were vitiated, and we had no choice but to wait, flaccidly, for her to die.

You may be sure we did not unlearn those years as soon as we put her out of sight in the cemetery and sold her house for a song to the first boob who would buy it. Nor did we forget when we left the town for another one, where we had jobs at a dude camp—the town where Daisy now lives with a happy husband and two happy sons. The succubus did not relent for years, and I can still remember, in the beginning of our days at the Lazy S 3, overhearing an edgy millionaire say to his wife, naming my name, "That girl gives me the cold shivers. One would think she had just seen a murder." Well, I had. For years,

1. Chain of dime stores.

whenever I woke in the night in fear or pain or loneliness, I would increase my suffering by the memory of Shannon, and my tears were as bitter as poor Mr. Murphy's.

We have never been back to Adams. But we see that house plainly, with the hopvines straggling over the porch. The windows are hung with the cheapest grade of marquisette, dipped into coffee to impart to it an unwilling color, neither white nor tan but individual and spitefully unattractive. We see the wicker rockers and the swing, and through the screen door we dimly make out the slightly veering corridor, along one wall of which stands a glass-doored bookcase; when we were children, it had contained not books but stale old cardboard boxes filled with such things as W.C.T.U.[2] tracts and anti-cigarette literature and newspaper clippings relating to sexual sin in the Christianized islands of the Pacific.

Even if we were able to close our minds' eyes to the past, Mr. Murphy would still be before us in the apotheosis of the polar bear. My pain become intolerable, and I am relieved when Daisy rescues us. "We've got to go," she says in a sudden panic. "I've got asthma coming on." We rush to the nearest exit of the city park and hail a cab, and, once inside it, Daisy gives herself an injection of adrenalin and then leans back. We are heartbroken and infuriated, and we cannot speak.

Two hours later, beside my train, we clutch each other as if we were drowning. We ought to go out to the nearest policeman and say, "We are not responsible women. You will have to take care of us because we cannot take care of ourselves." But gradually the storm begins to lull.

"You're sure you've got your ticket?" says Daisy. "You'll surely be able to get a roomette once you're on."

"I don't know about that," I say. "If there are any V.I.P.s on board, I won't have a chance. 'Spinsters and Orphans Last' is the motto of this line."

Daisy smiles. "I didn't care," she says, "but I had to laugh when I saw that woman nab the redcap[3] you had signaled to. I had a good notion to give her a piece of my mind."

"It will be a miracle if I ever see my bags again," I say, mounting the steps of the train. "Do you suppose that blackguardly porter knows about the twenty-dollar gold piece in my little suitcase?"

"Anything's possible!" cries Daisy, and begins to laugh. She is so pretty, standing there in her bright-red linen suit and her black velvet

2. Woman's Christian Temperance Union, an association of women formed in the United States in 1874 for the advancement of total abstinence and prohibition, by organizing educational, evangelistic, and legal work. 3. Train station porter.

hat. A solitary ray of sunshine comes through a broken pane in the domed vault of the train shed and lies on her shoulder like a silver arrow.

"So long, Daisy!" I call as the train begins to move.

She walks quickly along beside the train. "Watch out for pick-pockets!" she calls.

"You, too!" My voice is thin and lost in the increasing noise of the speeding train wheels. "Goodbye, old dear!"

I go at once to the club car and I appropriate the writing table, to the vexation of a harried priest, who snatches up the telegraph pad and gives me a sharp look. I write Daisy approximately the same letter I always write her under this particular set of circumstances, the burden of which is that nothing for either of us can ever be as bad as the past before Gran mercifully died. In a postscript I add: "There is a Roman Catholic priest (that is to say, he is *dressed* like one) sitting behind me although all the chairs on the opposite side of the car are empty. I can only conclude that he is looking over my shoulder, and while I do not want to cause you any alarm, I think you would be advised to be on the lookout for any appearance of miraculous medals, scapulars, papist booklets, etc., in the shops of your town. It really makes me laugh to see the way he is pretending that all he wants is for me to finish this letter so that he can have the table."

I sign my name and address the envelope, and I give up my place to the priest, who smiles nicely at me, and then I move across the car to watch the fields as they slip by. They are alfalfa fields, but you can bet your bottom dollar that they are chockablock with marijuana.

I begin to laugh. The fit is silent but it is devastating; it surges and rattles in my rib cage, and I turn my face to the window to avoid the narrow gaze of the Filipino bar boy. I must think of something sad to stop this unholy giggle, and I think of the polar bear. But even his bleak tragedy does not sober me. Wildly I fling open the newspaper I have brought and I pretend to be reading something screamingly funny. The words I see are in a Hollywood gossip column: "How a well-known starlet can get a divorce in Nevada without her crooner husband's consent, nobody knows. It won't be worth a plugged nickel here."

---

1. What ways of life are represented by Gran and by Mr. Murphy? To what extent is the story a conflict between them for the souls of the children? Who wins the conflict?
2. How are human problems worked out or clarified by the actions and destinies of various animals?
3. How do style and point of view contribute to the meaning of the action?

4. How is the present meeting between the sisters a suitable occasion for sorting out events of the fairly remote past? What would be lost if there were no perspective of time on those events?
5. What does the story say about the cooperation of victims with the oppressor?

John Steinbeck

Steinbeck (1902–1968) was born in Salinas, California. His mother was a former schoolteacher, who encouraged him to read widely as a child, but his formal schooling made little impression on him. He attended Stanford intermittently, leaving in 1926 to drift through an array of odd jobs that educated him in the life of working people. His first, rather romantic novel, Cup of Gold, *appeared in 1929. By 1936 his involvement with the struggles of migrant workers resulted in his militantly political novel* In Dubious Battle. *In 1937 his short novel* Of Mice and Men *proved immensely popular and provided the base for an equally popular film, as did* The Grapes of Wrath *in 1939. He served as a war correspondent during World War II. In 1962 he was awarded the Nobel Prize. His postwar novels include* East of Eden *(1952) and* The Winter of Our Discontent *(1961). Several of his stories are collected in* The Long Valley *(1938).*

The Chrysanthemums

The high grey-flannel fog of winter closed off the Salinas Valley from the sky and from all the rest of the world. On every side it sat like a lid on the mountains and made of the great valley a closed pot. On the broad, level land floor the gang ploughs bit deep and left the black earth shining like metal where the shares had cut. On the foot-hill ranches across the Salinas River, the yellow stubble fields seemed to be bathed in pale cold sunshine, but there was no sunshine in the valley now in December. The thick willow scrub along the river flamed with sharp and positive yellow leaves.

It was a time of quiet and of waiting. The air was cold and tender. A light wind blew up from the southwest so that the farmers were mildly hopeful of a good rain before long; but fog and rain do not go together.

Across the river, on Henry Allen's foot-hill ranch there was little work to be done, for the hay was cut and stored and the orchards were ploughed up to receive the rain deeply when it should come. The cattle on the higher slopes were becoming shaggy and rough-coated.

Elisa Allen, working in her flower garden, looked down across the yard and saw Henry, her husband, talking to two men in business suits. The three of them stood by the tractor-shed, each man with one foot on the side of the little Fordson. They smoked cigarettes and studied the machine as they talked.

Elisa watched them for a moment and then went back to her work. She was thirty-five. Her face was lean and strong and her eyes were as clear as water. Her figure looked blocked and heavy in her gardening costume, a man's black hat pulled low down over her eyes, clod-hopper shoes, a figured print dress almost completely covered by a big corduroy apron with four big pockets to hold the snips, the trowel and scratcher, the seeds and the knife she worked with. She wore heavy leather gloves to protect her hands while she worked.

She was cutting down the old year's chrysanthemum stalks with a pair of short and powerful scissors. She looked down toward the men by the tractor-shed now and then. Her face was eager and mature and handsome; even her work with the scissors was overeager, over-powerful. The chrysanthemum stems seemed too small and easy for her energy.

She brushed a cloud of hair out of her eyes with the back of her glove, and left a smudge of earth on her cheek in doing it. Behind her stood the neat white farmhouse with red geraniums close-banked around it as high as the windows. It was a hard-swept-looking little house, with hard-polished windows, and a clean mud-mat on the front steps.

Elisa cast another glance toward the tractor-shed. The strangers were getting into their Ford coupé. She took off a glove and put her strong fingers down into the forest of new green chrysanthemum sprouts that were growing around the old roots. She spread the leaves and looked down among the close-growing stems. No aphids were there, no sow bugs or snails or cutworms. Her terrier fingers destroyed such pests before they could get started.

Elisa started at the sound of her husband's voice. He had come near quietly, and he leaned over the wire fence that protected her flower garden from cattle and dogs and chickens.

"At it again," he said. "You've got a strong new crop coming."

Elisa straightened her back and pulled on the gardening glove again. "Yes. They'll be strong this coming year." In her tone and on her face there was a little smugness.

"You've got a gift with things," Henry observed. "Some of those yellow chrysanthemums you had this year were ten inches across. I wish you'd work out in the orchard and raise some apples that big."

Her eyes sharpened. "Maybe I could do it, too. I've a gift with things, all right. My mother had it. She could stick anything in the ground and make it grow. She said it was having planters' hands that knew how to do it."

"Well, it sure works with flowers," he said.

"Henry, who were those men you were talking to?"

"Why, sure, that's what I came to tell you. They were from the Western Meat Company. I sold those thirty head of three-year-old steers. Got nearly my own price, too."

"Good," she said. "Good for you."

"And I thought," he continued, "I thought how it's Saturday afternoon, and we might go into Salinas for dinner at a restaurant, and then to a picture show—to celebrate, you see."

"Good," she repeated. "Oh, yes. That will be good."

Henry put on his joking tone. "There's fights tonight. How'd you like to go to the fights?"

"Oh, no," she said breathlessly. "No, I wouldn't like fights."

"Just fooling, Elisa. We'll go to a movie. Let's see. It's two now. I'm going to take Scotty and bring down those steers from the hill. It'll take us maybe two hours. We'll go in town about five and have dinner at the Cominos Hotel. Like that?"

"Of course I'll like it. It's good to eat away from home."

"All right, then. I'll go get up a couple of horses."

She said: "I'll have plenty of time to transplant some of these sets, I guess."

She heard her husband calling Scotty down by the barn. And a little later she saw the two men ride up the pale yellow hillside in search of the steers.

There was a little square sandy bed kept for rooting the chrysanthemums. With her trowel she turned the soil over and over, and smoothed it and patted it firm. Then she dug ten parallel trenches to receive the sets. Back at the chrysanthemum bed she pulled out the little crisp shoots, trimmed off the leaves of each one with her scissors and laid it on a small orderly pile.

A squeak of wheels and plod of hoofs came from the road. Elisa looked up. The country road ran along the dense bank of willows and cottonwoods that bordered the river, and up this road came a curious vehicle, curiously drawn. It was an old spring-wagon, with a round canvas top on it like the cover of a prairie schooner. It was drawn by an old bay horse and a little grey-and-white burro. A big stubble-bearded man sat between the cover flaps and drove the crawling team. Underneath the wagon, between the hind wheels, a lean and rangy mongrel dog walked sedately. Words were painted on the canvas, in clumsy, crooked letters. "Pots, pans, knives, sisors, lawn mores, Fixed." Two rows of articles, and the triumphantly definitive "Fixed" below. The black paint had run down in little sharp points beneath each letter.

Elisa, squatting on the ground, watched to see the crazy, loose-jointed wagon pass by. But it didn't pass. It turned into the farm road in front of her house, crooked old wheels skirling and squeaking. The rangy dog darted from between the wheels and ran ahead. Instantly the two ranch shepherds flew out at him. Then all three stopped, and with stiff and quivering tails, with taut straight legs, with ambassadorial dignity, they slowly circled, sniffing daintily. The caravan pulled up to Elisa's wire fence and stopped. Now the newcomer dog, feeling outnumbered, lowered his tail and retired under the wagon with raised hackles and bared teeth.

The man on the wagon seat called out: "That's a bad dog in a fight when he gets started."

Elisa laughed. "I see he is. How soon does he generally get started?"

The man caught up her laughter and echoed it heartily. "Sometimes not for weeks and weeks," he said. He climbed stiffly down, over the wheel. The horse and the donkey drooped like unwatered flowers.

Elisa saw that he was a very big man. Although his hair and beard were greying, he did not look old. His worn black suit was wrinkled and spotted with grease. The laughter had disappeared from his face and eyes the moment his laughing voice ceased. His eyes were dark, and they were full of the brooding that gets in the eyes of teamsters and of sailors. The calloused hands he rested on the wire fence were cracked, and every crack was a black line. He took off his battered hat.

"I'm off my general road, ma'am," he said. "Does this dirt road cut over across the river to the Los Angeles highway?"

Elisa stood up and shoved the thick scissors in her apron pocket. "Well, yes, it does, but it winds around and then fords the river. I don't think your team could pull through the sand."

He replied with some asperity: "It might surprise you what them beasts can pull through."

"When they get started?" she asked.

He smiled for a second. "Yes. When they get started."

"Well,'" said Elisa, "I think you'll save time if you go back to the Salinas road and pick up the highway there."

He drew a big finger down the chicken wire and made it sing. "I ain't in any hurry, ma'am. I go from Seattle to San Diego and back every year. Takes all my time. About six months each way. I aim to follow nice weather."

Elisa took off her gloves and stuffed them in the apron pocket with the scissors. She touched the under edge of her man's hat, searching for fugitive hairs. "That sounds like a nice kind of way to live," she said.

He leaned confidentially over the fence. "Maybe you noticed the writing on my wagon. I mend pots and sharpen knives and scissors. You got any of them things to do?"

"Oh, no," she said quickly. "Nothing like that." Her eyes hardened with resistance.

"Scissors is the worst thing," he explained. "Most people just ruin scissors trying to sharpen 'em, but I know how. I got a special tool. It's a little bobbit kind of thing, and patented. But it sure does the trick."

"No. My scissors are all sharp."

"All right, then. Take a pot," he continued earnestly, "a bent pot, or a pot with a hole. I can make it like new so you don't have to buy no new ones. That's a saving for you.

"No," she said shortly. "I tell you I have nothing like that for you to do."

His face fell to an exaggerated sadness. His voice took on a whining undertone. "I ain't had a thing to do today. Maybe I won't have no supper tonight. You see I'm off my regular road. I know folks on the highway clear from Seattle to San Diego. They save their things for me to sharpen up because they know I do it so good and save them money."

"I'm sorry," Elisa said irritably. "I haven't anything for you to do."

His eyes left her face and fell to searching the ground. They roamed about until they came to the chrysanthemum bed where she had been working. "What's them plants, ma'am?"

The irritation and resistance melted from Elisa's face. "Oh, those are chrysanthemums, giant whites and yellows. I raise them every year, bigger than anybody around here."

"Kind of a long-stemmed flower? Looks like a quick puff of colored smoke?" he asked.

"That's it. What a nice way to describe them."

"They smell kind of nasty till you get used to them," he said.

"It's a good bitter smell," she retorted, "not nasty at all."

He changed his tone quickly. "I like the smell myself."

"I had ten-inch blooms this year," she said.

The man leaned farther over the fence. "Look. I know a lady down the road a piece, has got the nicest garden you ever seen. Got nearly every kind of flower but no chrysanthemums. Last time I was mending a copper-bottom washtub for her (that's a hard job but I do it good), she said to me: 'If you ever run acrost some nice chrysanthemums I wish you'd try to get me a few seeds.' That's what she told me."

Elisa's eyes grew alert and eager. "She couldn't have known much about chrysanthemums. You *can* raise them from seed, but it's much easier to root the little sprouts you see here."

"Oh," he said. "I s'pose I can't take none to her, then."

"Why yes you can," Elisa cried. "I can put some in damp sand, and you can carry them right along with you. They'll take root in the pot if you keep them damp. And then she can transplant them."

"She'd sure like to have some, ma'am. You say they're nice ones?"

"Beautiful," she said. "Oh, beautiful." Her eyes shone. She tore off the battered hat and shook out her dark pretty hair. "I'll put them in a flowerpot, and you can take them right with you. Come into the yard."

While the man came through the picket gate Elisa ran excitedly along the geranium-bordered path to the back of the house. And she returned carrying a big red flower-pot. The gloves were forgotten now. She kneeled on the ground by the starting bed and dug up the sandy soil with her fingers and scooped it into the bright new flower-pot. Then she picked up the little pile of shoots she had prepared. With her strong fingers she pressed them into the sand and tamped around them with her knuckles. The man stood over her. "I'll tell you what to do," she said. "You remember so you can tell the lady."

"Yes, I'll try to remember."

"Well, look. These will take root in about a month. Then she must set them out, about a foot apart in good rich earth like this, see?" She lifted a handful of dark soil for him to look at. "They'll grow fast and tall. Now remember this: In July tell her to cut them down, about eight inches from the ground.

"Before they bloom?" he asked.

"Yes, before they bloom." Her face was tight with eagerness. "They'll grow right up again. About the last of September the buds will start."

She stopped and seemed perplexed. "It's the budding that takes the most care," she said hesitantly. "I don't know how to tell you." She looked deep into his eyes, searchingly. Her mouth opened a little, and she seemed to be listening. "I'll try to tell you," she said. "Did you ever hear of planting hands?"

"Can't say I have, ma'am."

"Well, I can only tell you what it feels like. It's when you're picking off the buds you don't want. Everything goes right down into your fingertips. You watch your fingers work. They do it themselves. You can feel how it is. They pick and pick the buds. They never make a mistake. They're with the plant. Do you see? Your fingers and the plant. You can feel that, right up your arm. They know. They never make a mistake. You can feel it. When you're like that you can't do anything wrong. Do you see that? Can you understand that?"

She was kneeling on the ground looking up at him. Her breast swelled passionately.

The man's eyes narrowed. He looked away self-consciously.

"Maybe I know," he said. "Sometimes in the night in the wagon there——"

Elisa's voice grew husky. She broke in on him: "I've never lived as you do, but I know what you mean. When the night is dark—why, the stars are sharp-pointed, and there's quiet. Why, you rise up and up! Every pointed star gets driven into your body. It's like that. Hot and sharp and—lovely."

Kneeling there, her hand went out toward his legs in the greasy black trousers. Her hesitant fingers almost touch the cloth. Then her hand dropped to the ground. She crouched low like a fawning dog.

He said: "It's nice, just like you say. Only when you don't have no dinner, it ain't."

She stood up then, very straight, and her face was ashamed. She held the flower-pot out to him and placed it gently in his arms. "Here. Put it in your wagon, on the seat, where you can watch it. Maybe I can find something for you to do."

At the back of the house she dug in the can pile and found two old and battered aluminum saucepans. She carried them back and gave them to him. "Here, maybe you can fix these."

His manner changed. He became professional. "Good as new I can fix them." At the back of his wagon he set a little anvil, and out of an oily tool-box dug a small machine hammer. Elisa came through the gate to watch him while he pounded out the dents in the kettles. His mouth grew sure and knowing. At a difficult part of the work he sucked his underlip.

"You sleep right in the wagon?" Elisa asked.

"Right in the wagon, ma'am. Rain or shine I'm dry as a cow in there."

"It must be nice," she said. "It must be very nice. I wish women could do such things."

"It ain't the right kind of a life for a woman."

Her upper lip raised a little, showing her teeth. "How do you know? How can you tell?" she said.

"I don't know, ma'am," he protested. "Of course I don't know. Now here's your kettles, done. You don't have to buy no new ones."

"How much?"

"Oh, fifty cents'll do. I keep my prices down and my work good. That's why I have all them satisfied customers up and down the highway."

Elisa brought him a fifty-cent piece from the house and dropped it in his hand. "You might be surprised to have a rival some time. I can sharpen scissors, too. And I can beat the dents out of little pots. I could show you what a woman might do."

He put his hammer back in the oily box and shoved the little anvil out of sight. "It would be a lonely life for a woman, ma'am, and a scarey life, too, with animals creeping under the wagon all night." He climbed over the single-tree, steadying himself with a hand on the burro's white rump. He settled himself in the seat, picked up the lines. "Thank you kindly ma'am," he said. "I'll do like you told me; I'll go back and catch the Salinas road."

"Mind," she called, "if you're long in getting there, keep the sand damp."

"Sand, ma'am? . . . Sand? Oh, sure. You mean around the chrysanthemums. Sure I will." He clucked his tongue. The beasts leaned luxuriously into their collars. The mongrel dog took his place between the back wheels. The wagon turned and crawled out the entrance road and back the way it had come, along the river.

Elisa stood in front of her wire fence watching the slow progress of the caravan. Her shoulders were straight, her head thrown back, her eyes half-closed, so that the scene came vaguely into them. Her lips moved silently, forming the words "Good-bye—good-bye." Then she whispered: "That's a bright direction. There's a glowing there." The sound of her whisper startled her. She shook herself free and looked about to see whether anyone had been listening. Only the dogs had heard. They lifted their heads toward her from their sleeping in the dust, and then stretched out their chins and settled asleep again. Elisa turned and ran hurriedly into the house.

In the kitchen she reached behind the stove and felt the water tank. It was full of hot water from the noonday cooking. In the bathroom she tore off her soiled clothes and flung them into the corner. And then she scrubbed herself with a little block of pumice, legs and thighs, loins and chest and arms, until her skin was scratched and red. When she had dried herself she stood in front of a mirror in her bedroom and looked at her body. She tightened her stomach and threw out her chest. She turned and looked over her shoulders at her back.

After a while she began to dress, slowly. She put on her newest underclothing and her nicest stockings and the dress which was the symbol of her prettiness. She worked carefully on her hair, pencilled her eyebrows and rouged her lips.

Before she was finished she heard the little thunder of hoofs and the shouts of Henry and his helper as they drove the red steers into the corral. She heard the gate bang shut and set herself for Henry's arrival.

His step sounded on the porch. He entered the house calling: "Elisa, where are you?"

"In my room, dressing. I'm not ready. There's hot water for your bath. Hurry up. It's getting late."

When she heard him splashing in the tub, Elisa laid his dark suit on the bed, and shirt and socks and tie beside it. She stood his polished shoes on the floor beside the bed. Then she went to the porch and sat primly and stiffly down. She looked toward the river road where the willow-line was still yellow with frosted leaves so that under the high grey fog they seemed a thin band of sunshine. This was the only color in the grey afternoon. She sat unmoving for a long time. Her eyes blinked rarely.

Henry came banging out of the door, shoving his tie inside his vest as he came. Elisa stiffened and her face grew tight. Henry stopped short and looked at her. "Why—why, Elisa. You look so nice!"

"Nice? You think I look nice? What do you mean by 'nice'?"

Henry blundered on. "I don't know. I mean you look different, strong and happy."

"I am strong? Yes, strong. What do you mean 'strong'?"

He looked bewildered. "You're playing some kind of a game," he said helplessly. "It's a kind of a play. You look strong enough to break a calf over your knee, happy enough to eat it like a watermelon."

For a second she lost her rigidity. "Henry! Don't talk like that. You didn't know what you said." She grew complete again. "I'm strong," she boasted. "I never knew before how strong."

Henry looked down toward the tractor-shed, and when he brought his eyes back to her, they were his own again. "I'll get out the car. You can put on your coat while I'm starting."

Elisa went into the house. She heard him drive to the gate and idle down his motor, and then she took a long time to put on her hat. She pulled it here and pressed it there. When Henry turned the motor off she slipped into her coat and went out.

The little roadster bounced along on the dirt road by the river, raising the birds and driving the rabbits into the brush. Two cranes flapped heavily over the willow-line and dropped into the river-bed.

Far ahead on the road Elisa saw a dark speck. She knew.

She tried not to look as they passed it, but her eyes would not obey. She whispered to herself sadly: "He might have thrown them off the road. That wouldn't have been much trouble, not very much. But he kept the pot," she explained. "He had to keep the pot. That's why he couldn't get them off the road."

The roadster turned a bend and she saw the caravan ahead. She swung full around toward her husband so she could not see the little covered wagon and the mis-matched team as the car passed them.

In a moment it was over. The thing was done. She did not look back.

She said loudly, to be heard above the motor: "It will be good, tonight, a good dinner."

"Now you've changed again," Henry complained. He took one

hand from the wheel and patted her knee. "I ought to take you in to dinner oftener. It would be good for both of us. We get so heavy out on the ranch."

"Henry," she asked, "could we have wine at dinner?"

"Sure we could. Say! That will be fine."

She was silent for a while; then she said: "Henry, at those prize-fights, do the men hurt each other very much?"

"Sometimes a little, not often. Why?"

"Well, I've read how they break noses, and blood runs down their chests. I've read how the fighting gloves get heavy and soggy with blood."

He looked around at her. "What's the matter, Elisa? I didn't know you read things like that." He brought the car to a stop, then turned to the right over the Salinas River bridge.

"Do any women ever go to the fights?" she asked.

"Oh, sure, some. What's the matter, Elisa? Do you want to go? I don't think you'd like it, but I'll take you if you really want to go."

She relaxed limply in the seat. "Oh, no. No. I don't want to go. I'm sure I don't." Her face was turned away from him. "It will be enough if we can have wine. It will be plenty." She turned up her coat collar so he could not see that she was crying weakly—like an old woman.

---

1. What details of imagery and physical description serve as evidence of Elisa's frustration in her role as housewife? Of what importance is it that she and the stranger share laughter at the beginning of their conversation?
2. What ironies are contained in the frequent but contradictory uses of the word "nice"? How do these ironies fit with the ironies of Elisa's situation?
3. Explain the significance of the scene in which Elisa bathes.
4. Why does Elisa finally imagine the prize fights to be so gory? Why does she decide against going after her husband offers to take her?
5. Who or what is ultimately responsible for Elisa's troubles?

Robert Stone

Stone (1937–) was born in Brooklyn and has in recent years been associated with Amherst College. He was given the William Faulkner Award for his first novel, Hall of Mirrors *(1968), and the National Book Award for his second,* Dog Soldiers *(1974). His critics have been particularly impressed by the way he shows the grip of the underworld on its inhabitants. His work is colored by the dark glamour of drugs and alcohol, and a somber tone shadows his view of contemporary destinies.* Children of Light *(1986) continues his distinguished publications.*

Helping

One gray November day, Elliot went to Boston for the afternoon. The wet streets seemed cold and lonely. He sensed a broken promise in the city's elegance and verve. Old hopes tormented him like phantom limbs, but he did not drink. He had joined Alcoholics Anonymous fifteen months before.

Christmas came, childless, a festival of regret. His wife went to Mass and cooked a turkey. Sober, Elliot walked in the woods.

In January, blizzards swept down from the Arctic until the weather became too cold for snow. The Shawmut Valley grew quiet and crystalline. In the white silences, Elliot could hear the boards of his house contract and feel a shrinking in his bones. Each dusk, starveling deer came out of the wooded swamp behind the house to graze his orchard for whatever raccoons had uncovered and left behind. At night he lay beside his sleeping wife listening to the baying of dog packs running them down in the deep moon-shadowed snow.

Day in, day out, he was sober. At times it was almost stimulating. But he could not shake off the sensations he had felt in Boston. In his mind's eye he could see dead leaves rattling along brick gutters and savor that day's desperation. The brief outing had undermined him.

Sober, however, he remained, until the day a man named Blankenship came into his office at the state hospital for counseling. Blankenship had red hair, a brutal face, and a sneaking manner. He was a sponger and petty thief whom Elliot had seen a number of times before.

"I been having this dream," Blankenship announced loudly. His voice was not pleasant. His skin was unwholesome. Every time he got arrested the court sent him to the psychiatrists and the psychiatrists, who spoke little English, sent him to Elliot.

Blankenship had joined the Army after his first burglary but had never served east of the Rhine. After a few months in Wiesbaden, he had been discharged for reasons of unsuitability, but he told everyone he was a veteran of the Vietnam War. He went about in a tiger suit. Elliot had had enough of him.

"Dreams are boring," Elliot told him.

Blankenship was outraged. "Whaddaya mean?" he demanded.

During counseling sessions Elliot usually moved his chair into the middle of the room in order to seem accessible to his clients. Now he stayed securely behind his desk. He did not care to seem accessible to Blankenship. "What I said, Mr. Blankenship. Other people's dreams are boring. Didn't you ever hear that?"

"Boring?" Blankenship frowned. He seemed unable to imagine a meaning for the word.

Elliot picked up a pencil and set its point quivering on his desktop blotter. He gazed into his client's slack-jawed face. The Blankenship family made their way through life as strolling litigants, and young Blankenship's specialty was slipping on ice cubes. Hauled off the pavement, he would hassle the doctors in Emergency for pain pills and hurry to a law clinic. The Blankenships had threatened suit against half the property owners in the southern part of the state. What they could not extort at law they stole. But even the Blankenship family had abandoned Blankenship. His last visit to the hospital had been subsequent to an arrest for lifting a case of hot-dog rolls from Woolworth's. He lived in a Goodwill depository bin in Wyndham.

"Now I suppose you want to tell me your dream? Is that right, Mr. Blankenship?"

Blankenship looked left and right like a dog surrendering eye contact. "Don't you want to hear it?" he asked humbly.

Elliot was unmoved. "Tell me something, Blankenship. Was your dream about Vietnam?"

At the mention of the word "Vietnam," Blankenship customarily broke into a broad smile. Now he looked guilty and guarded. He shrugged. "Ya."

"How come you have dreams about that place, Blankenship? You were never there."

"Whaddaya mean?" Blankenship began to say, but Elliot cut him off.

"You were never there, my man. You never saw the goddam

place. You have no business dreaming about it! You better cut it out!"

He had raised his voice to the extent that the secretary outside his open door paused at her word processor.

"Lemme alone," Blankenship said fearfully. "Some doctor you are."

"It's all right," Elliot assured him. "I'm not a doctor."

"Everybody's on my case," Blankenship said. His moods were volatile. He began to weep.

Elliot watched the tears roll down Blankenship's chapped, pitted cheeks. He cleared his throat. "Look, fella . . ." he began. He felt at a loss. He felt like telling Blankenship that things were tough all over.

Blankenship sniffed and telescoped his neck and after a moment looked at Elliot. His look was disconcertingly trustful; he was used to being counselled.

"Really, you know, it's ridiculous for you to tell me your problems have to do with Nam. You were never over there. It was me over there, Blankenship. Not you."

Blankenship leaned forward and put his forehead on his knees.

"Your troubles have to do with here and now," Elliot told his client. "Fantasies aren't helpful."

His voice sounded overripe and hypocritical in his own ears. What a dreadful business, he thought. What an awful job this is. Anger was driving him crazy.

Blankenship straightened up and spoke through his tears. "This dream . . ." he said. "I'm scared."

Elliot felt ready to endure a great deal in order not to hear Blankenship's dream.

"I'm not the one you see about that," he said. In the end he knew his duty. He sighed. "O.K. All right. Tell me about it."

"Yeah?" Blankenship asked with leaden sarcasm. "Yeah? You think dreams are friggin' boring!"

"No, no," Elliot said. He offered Blankenship a tissue and Blankenship took one. "That was sort of off the top of my head. I didn't really mean it."

Blankenship fixed his eyes on dreaming distance. "There's a feeling that goes with it. With the dream." Then he shook his head in revulsion and looked at Elliot as though he had only just awakened. "So what do you think? You think it's boring?"

"Of course not," Elliot said. "A physical feeling?"

"Ya. It's like I'm floating in rubber."

He watched Elliot stealthily, aware of quickened attention. Elliot had caught dengue in Vietnam and during his weeks of delirium had felt vaguely as though he were floating in rubber.

"What are you seeing in this dream?"

Blankenship only shook his head. Elliot suffered a brief but intense attack of rage.

"Hey, Blankenship," he said equably, "here I am, man. You can see I'm listening."

"What I saw was black," Blankenship said. He spoke in an odd tremolo. His behavior was quite different from anything Elliot had come to expect from him.

"Black? What was it?"

"Smoke. The sky maybe."

"The sky?" Elliot asked.

"It was all black. I was scared."

In a waking dream of his own, Elliot felt the muscles on his neck distend. He was looking up at a sky that was black, filled with smoke-swollen clouds, lit with fires, damped with blood and rain.

"What were you scared of?" he asked Blankenship.

"I don't know," Blankenship said.

Elliot could not drive the black sky from his inward eye. It was as though Blankenship's dream had infected his own mind.

"You don't know? You don't know what you were scared of?"

Blankenship's posture was rigid. Elliot, who knew the aspect of true fear, recognized it there in front of him.

"The Nam," Blankenship said.

"You're not even old enough," Elliot told him.

Blankenship sat trembling with joined palms between his thighs. His face was flushed and not in the least ennobled by pain. He had trouble with alcohol and drugs. He had trouble with everything.

"So wherever your black sky is, it isn't Vietnam."

Things were so unfair, Elliot thought. It was unfair of Blankenship to appropriate the condition of a Vietnam veteran. The trauma inducing his post-traumatic stress had been nothing more serious than his own birth, a routine procedure. Now, in addition to the poverty, anxiety, and confusion that would always be his life's lot, he had been visited with irony. It was all arbitrary and some people simply got elected. Everyone knew that who had been where Blankenship had not.

"Because, I assure you, Mr. Blankenship, you were never there."

"Whaddaya mean?" Blankenship asked.

When Blankenship was gone, Elliot leafed through his file and saw that the psychiatrists had passed him upstairs without recording a diagnosis. Disproportionately angry, he went out to the secretary's desk.

"Nobody wrote up that last patient," he said. "I'm not supposed to see people without a diagnosis. The shrinks are just passing the buck."

The secretary was a tall, solemn redhead with prominent front teeth and a slight speech disorder. "Dr. Sayyid will have kittens if he hears you call him a shrink, Chas. He's already complained. He hates being called a shrink."

"Then he came to the wrong country," Elliot said. "He can go back to his own."

The woman giggled. "He *is* the doctor, Chas."

"Hates being called a shrink!" He threw the file on the secretary's table and stormed back toward his office. "That fucking little zip couldn't give you a decent haircut. He's a prescription clerk."

The secretary looked about her guiltily and shook her head. She was used to him.

Elliot succeeded in calming himself down after a while, but the image of black sky remained with him. At first he thought he would be able to simply shrug the whole thing off. After a few minutes, he picked up his phone and dialed Blankenship's probation officer.

"The Vietnam thing is all he has," the probation officer explained. "I guess he picked it up around."

"His descriptions are vivid," Elliot said.

"You mean they sound authentic?"

"I mean he had me going today. He was ringing my bells."

"Good for Blanky. Think he believes it himself?"

"Yes," Elliot said. "He believes it himself now."

Elliot told the probation officer about Blankenship's current arrest, which was for showering illegally at midnight in the Wyndham Regional High School. He asked what Probation knew about Blankenship's present relationship with his family.

"You kiddin'?" the P.O. asked. "They're all locked down. The whole family's inside. The old man's in Bridgewater. Little Donny's in San Quentin or somewhere. Their dog's in the pound."

Elliot had lunch alone in the hospital staff cafeteria. On the far side of the double-glazed windows, the day was darkening as an expected snowstorm gathered. Along Route 7, ancient elms stood frozen against the gray sky. When he had finished his sandwich and coffee, he sat staring out at the winter afternoon. His anger had given way to an insistent anxiety.

On the way back to his office, he stopped at the hospital gift shop for a copy of *Sports Illustrated* and a candy bar. When he was inside again, he closed the door and put his feet up. It was Friday and he had no appointments for the remainder of the day, nothing to do but write a few letters and read the office mail.

Elliot's cubicle in the social-services department was windowless and lined with bookshelves. When he found himself unable to concentrate on the magazine and without any heart for his paperwork, he ran his eye over the row of books beside his chair. There were volumes by Heinrich Muller and Carlos Casteneda, Jones' life of Freud, and *The Golden Bough*. The books aroused a revulsion in Elliot. Their present uselessness repelled him.

Over and over again, detail by detail, he tried to recall his conversation with Blankenship.

"You were never there," he heard himself explaining. He was trying to get the whole incident straightened out after the fact. Something was wrong. Dread crept over him like a paralysis. He ate his candy bar without tasting it. He knew that the craving for sweets was itself a bad sign.

Blankenship had misappropriated someone else's dream and made it his own. It made no difference whether you had been there, after all. The dreams had crossed the ocean. They were in the air.

He took his glasses off and put them on his desk and sat with his arms folded, looking into the well of light from his desk lamp. There seemed to be nothing but whirl inside him. Unwelcome things came and went in his mind's eye. His heart beat faster. He could not control the headlong promiscuity of his thoughts.

It was possible to imagine larval dreams traveling in suspended animation undetectable in a host brain. They could be divided and regenerate like flatworms, hide in seams and bedding, in war stories, laughter, snapshots. They could rot your socks and turn your memory into a black-and-green blister. Green for the hills, black for the sky above. At daybreak they hung themselves up in rows like bats. At dusk they went out to look for dreamers.

Elliot put his jacket on and went into the outer office, where the secretary sat frowning into the measured sound and light of her machine. She must enjoy its sleekness and order, he thought. She was divorced. Four redheaded kids between ten and seventeen lived with her in an unpainted house across from Stop & Shop. Elliot liked her and had come to find her attractive. He managed a smile for her.

"Ethel, I think I'm going to pack it in," he declared. It seemed awkward to be leaving early without a reason.

"Jack wants to talk to you before you go, Chas."

Elliot looked at her blankly.

Then his colleague, Jack Sprague, having heard his voice, called from the adjoining cubicle. "Chas, what about Sunday's games? Shall I call you with the spread?"

"I don't know," Elliot said. "I'll phone you tomorrow."

"This is a big decision for him," Jack Sprague told the secretary. "He might lose twenty-five bucks."

At present, Elliot drew a slightly higher salary than Jack Sprague, although Jack had a Ph.D. and Elliot was simply an M.S.W.[1] Different branches of the state government employed them.

"Twenty-five bucks," said the woman. "If you guys have no better use for twenty-five bucks, give it to me."

"Where are you off to, by the way?" Sprague asked.

Elliot began to answer, but for a moment no reply occurred to him. He shrugged. "I have to get back," he finally stammered. "I promised Grace."

"Was that Blankenship I saw leaving?"

Elliot nodded.

"It's February," Jack said. "How come he's not in Florida?"

"I don't know," Elliot said. He put on his coat and walked to the door. "I'll see you."

"Have a nice weekend," the secretary said. She and Sprague looked after him indulgently as he walked toward the main corridor.

"Are Chas and Grace going out on the town?" she said to Sprague. "What do you think?"

"That would be the day," Sprague said. "Tomorrow he'll come back over here and read all day. He spends every weekend holed up in this goddam office while she does something or other at the church." He shook his head. "Every night he's at A.A. and she's home alone."

Ethel savored her overbite. "Jack," she said teasingly, "are you thinking what I think you're thinking? Shame on you."

"I'm thinking I'm glad I'm not him, that's what I'm thinking. That's as much as I'll say."

"Yeah, well, I don't care," Ethel said. "Two salaries and no kids, that's the way to go, boy."

Elliot went out through the automatic doors of the emergency bay and the cold closed over him. He walked across the hospital parking lot with his eyes on the pavement, his hands thrust deep in his overcoat pockets, skirting patches of shattered ice. There was no wind, but the motionless air stung; the metal frames of his glasses burned his skin. Curlicues of mud-brown ice coated the soiled snowbanks along the street. Although it was still afternoon, the street lights had come on.

The lock on his car door had frozen and he had to breathe on the keyhole to fit the key. When the engine turned over, Jussi Björling's

1. Master of Social Work, an academic degree.

recording of the Handel Largo[2] filled the car interior. He snapped it off at once.

Halted at the first stoplight, he began to feel the want of a destination. The fear and impulse to flight that had got him out of the office faded, and he had no desire to go home. He was troubled by a peculiar impatience that might have been with time itself. It was as though he were waiting for something. The sensation made him feel anxious; it was unfamiliar but not altogether unpleasant. When the light changed he drove on, past the Gulf station and the firehouse and between the greens of Ilford Common. At the far end of the common he swung into the parking lot of the Packard Conway Library and stopped with the engine running. What he was experiencing, he thought, was the principle of possibility.

He turned off the engine and went out again into the cold. Behind the leaded library windows he could see the librarian pouring coffee in her tiny private office. The librarian was a Quaker of socialist principles named Candace Music, who was Elliot's cousin.

The Conway Library was all dark wood and etched mirrors, a Gothic saloon. Years before, out of work and booze-whipped, Elliot had gone to hide there. Because Candace was a classicist's widow and knew some Greek, she was one of the few people in the valley with whom Elliot had cared to speak in those days. Eventually, it had seemed to him that all their conversations tended toward Vietnam, so he had gone less and less often. Elliot was the only Vietnam veteran Candace knew well enough to chat with, and he had come to suspect that he was being probed for the edification of the East Ilford Friends Meeting. At that time he had still pretended to talk easily about his war and had prepared little discourses and picaresque anecdotes to recite on demand. Earnest seekers like Candace had caused him great secret distress.

Candace came out of her office to find him at the checkout desk. He watched her brow furrow with concern as she composed a smile. "Chas, what a surprise. You haven't been in for an age."

"Sure I have, Candace. I went to all the Wednesday films last fall. I work just across the road."

"I know, dear," Candace said. "I always seem to miss you."

A cozy fire burned in the hearth, an antique brass clock ticked along on the marble mantel above it. On a couch near the fireplace an old man sat upright, his mouth open, asleep among half a dozen soiled plastic bags. Two teen-age girls whispered over their homework at a table under the largest window.

2. Stately aria from the opera *Serse (Xerxes)* by George Frideric Handel (1685–1759), German-born English composer. Björling (1911–1960) was a famous Swedish tenor.

"Now that I'm here," he said, laughing, "I can't remember what I came to get."

"Stay and get warm," Candace told him. "Got a minute? Have a cup of coffee."

Elliot had nothing but time, but he quickly realized that he did not want to stay and pass it with Candace. He had no clear idea of why he had come to the library. Standing at the checkout desk, he accepted coffee. She attended him with an air of benign supervision, as though he were a Chinese peasant and she a medical missionary, like her father. Candace was tall and plain, more handsome in her middle sixties than she had ever been.

"Why don't we sit down?"

He allowed her to gentle him into a chair by the fire. They made a threesome with the sleeping old man.

"Have you given up translating, Chas? I hope not."

"Not at all," he said. Together they had once rendered a few fragments of Sophocles[3] into verse. She was good at clever rhymes.

"You come in so rarely, Chas. Ted's books go to waste."

After her husband's death, Candace had donated his books to the Conway, where they reposed in a reading room inscribed to his memory, untouched among foreign-language volumes, local genealogies, and books in large type for the elderly.

"I have a study in the barn," he told Candace. "I work there. When I have time." The lie was absurd, but he felt the need of it.

"And you're working with Vietnam veterans," Candace declared.

"Supposedly," Elliot said. He was growing impatient with her nodding solicitude.

"Actually," he said, "I came in for the new Oxford 'Classical World.' I thought you'd get it for the library and I could have a look before I spent my hard-earned cash."

Candace beamed. "You've come to the right place, Chas, I'm happy to say." He thought she looked disproportionately happy. "I have it."

"Good," Elliot said, standing. "I'll just take it, then. I can't really stay."

Candace took his cup and saucer and stood as he did. When the library telephone rang, she ignored it, reluctant to let him go. "How's Grace?" she asked.

"Fine," Elliot said. "Grace is well."

At the third ring she went to the desk. When her back was turned, he hesitated for a moment and then went outside.

The gray afternoon had softened into night, and it was snowing.

3. Greek dramatist (496–406 B.C.).

The falling snow whirled like a furious mist in the headlight beams on Route 7 and settled implacably on Elliot's cheeks and eyelids. His heart, for no good reason, leaped up in childlike expectation. He had run away from a dream and encountered possibility. He felt in possession of a promise. He began to walk toward the roadside lights.

Only gradually did he begin to understand what had brought him there and what the happy anticipation was that fluttered in his breast. Drinking, he had started his evenings from the Conway Library. He would arrive hung over in the early afternoon to browse and read. When the old pain rolled in with dusk, he would walk down to the Midway Tavern for a remedy. Standing in the snow outside the library, he realized that he had contrived to promise himself a drink.

Ahead, through the storm, he could see the beer signs in the Midway's window warm and welcoming. Snowflakes spun around his head like an excitement.

Outside the Midway's package store, he paused with his hand on the doorknob. There was an old man behind the counter whom Elliot remembered from his drinking days. When he was inside, he realized that the old man neither knew nor cared who he was. The package store was thick with dust; it was on the counter, the shelves, the bottles themselves. The old counterman looked dusty. Elliot bought a bottle of King William Scotch and put it in the inside pocket of his overcoat.

Passing the windows of the Midway Tavern, Elliot could see the ranks of bottles aglow behind the bar. The place was crowded with men leaving the afternoon shifts at the shoe and felt factories. No one turned to note him when he passed inside. There was a single stool vacant at the bar and he took it. His heart beat faster. Bruce Springsteen was on the jukebox.

The bartender was a club fighter from Pittsfield called Jackie G., with whom Elliot had often gossiped. Jackie G. greeted him as though he had been in the previous evening. "Say, babe?"

"How do," Elliot said.

A couple of the men at the bar eyed his shirt and tie. Confronted with the bartender, he felt impelled to explain his presence. "Just thought I'd stop by," he told Jackie G. "Just thought I'd have one. Saw the light. The snow . . ." He chuckled expansively.

"Good move," the bartender said. "Scotch?"

"Double," Elliot said.

When he shoved two dollars forward along the bar, Jackie G. pushed one of the bills back to him. "Happy hour, babe."

"Ah," Elliot said. He watched Jackie pour the double. "Not a moment too soon."

For five minutes or so, Elliot sat in his car in the barn with the engine running and his Handel tape on full volume. He had driven over from East Ilford in a Baroque ecstasy, swinging and swaying and singing along. When the tape ended, he turned off the engine and poured some Scotch into an apple-juice container to store providentially beneath the car seat. Then he took the tape and the Scotch into the house with him. He was lying on the sofa in the dark living room, listening to the Largo, when he heard his wife's car in the driveway. By the time Grace had made her way up the icy back-porch steps, he was able to hide the Scotch and rinse his glass clean in the kitchen sink. The drinking life, he thought, was lived moment by moment.

Soon she was in the tiny cloakroom struggling off with her overcoat. In the process she knocked over a cross-country ski, which stood propped against the cloakroom wall. It had been more than a year since Elliot had used the skis.

She came into the kitchen and sat down at the table to take off her boots. Her lean, freckled face was flushed with the cold, but her eyes looked weary. "I wish you'd put those skis down in the barn," she told him. "You never use them."

"I always like to think," Elliot said, "that I'll start the morning off skiing."

"Well, you never do," she said. "How long have you been home?"

"Practically just walked in," he said. Her pointing out that he no longer skied in the morning enraged him. "I stopped at the Conway Library to get the new Oxford 'Classical World.' Candace ordered it."

Her look grew troubled. She had caught something in his voice. With dread and bitter satisfaction, Elliot watched his wife detect the smell of whiskey.

"Oh God," she said. "I don't believe it."

Let's get it over with, he thought. Let's have the song and dance.

She sat up straight in her chair and looked at him in fear.

"Oh, Chas," she said, "how could you?"

For a moment he was tempted to try to explain it all.

"The fact is," Elliot told his wife, "I hate people who start the day cross-country skiing."

She shook her head in denial and leaned her forehead on her palm and cried.

He looked into the kitchen window and saw his own distorted image. "The fact is I think I'll start tomorrow morning by stringing head-high razor wire across Anderson's trail."

The Andersons were the Elliots' nearest neighbors. Loyall Anderson was a full professor of government at the state university, thirty miles away. Anderson and his wife were blond and both of them were over six feet tall. They had two blond children, who qualified for the gifted class in the local school but attended regular classes in token of the Andersons' opposition to élitism.

"Sure," Elliot said. "Stringing wire's good exercise. It's life-affirming in its own way."

The Andersons started each and every day with a brisk morning glide along a trail that they partly maintained. They skied well and presented a pleasing, wholesome sight. If, in the course of their adventure, they encountered a snowmobile, Darlene Anderson would affect to choke and cough, indicating her displeasure. If the snowmobile approached them from behind and the trail was narrow, the Andersons would decline to let it pass, asserting their statutory right-of-way.

"I don't want to hear your violent fantasies," Grace said.

Elliot was picturing razor wire, the Army kind. He was picturing the decapitated Andersons, their blood and jaunty ski caps bright on the white trail. He was picturing their severed heads, their earnest blue eyes and large white teeth reflecting the virginal morning snow. Although Elliot hated snowmobiles, he hated the Andersons far more.

He looked at his wife and saw that she had stopped crying. Her long, elegant face was rigid and lipless.

"Know what I mean? One string at Mommy and Daddy level for Loyall and Darlene. And a bitty wee string at kiddie level for Skippy and Samantha, those cunning little whizzes."

"Stop it," she said to him.

"Sorry," Elliott told her.

Stiff with shame, he went and took his bottle out of the cabinet into which he had thrust it and poured a drink. He was aware of her eyes on him. As he drank, a fragment from old Music's translation of "Medea"[4] came into his mind. "Old friend, I have to weep. The gods and I went mad together and made things as they are." It was such a waste; eighteen months of struggle thrown away. But there was no way to get the stuff back in the bottle.

"I'm very sorry," he said. "You know I'm very sorry, don't you, Grace?"

The delectable Handel arias spun on in the next room.

"You must stop," she said. "You must make yourself stop before it takes over."

"It's out of my hands," Elliot said. He showed her his empty hands. "It's beyond me."

"You'll lose your job, Chas." She stood at the table and leaned on it, staring wide-eyed at him. Drunk as he was, the panic in her voice frightened him. "You'll end up in jail again."

4. Play by Greek dramatist Euripides (480?–406? B.C.).

"One engages," Elliot said, "and then one sees."

"How can you have done it?" she demanded. "You promised me."

"First the promises," Elliot said, "and then the rest."

"Last time was supposed to be the last time," she said.

"Yes," he said, "I remember."

"I can't stand it," she said. "You reduce me to hysterics." She wrung her hands for him to see. "See? Here I am, I'm in hysterics."

"What can I say?" Elliot asked. He went to the bottle and refilled his glass. "Maybe you shouldn't watch."

"You want me to be forbearing, Chas? I'm not going to be."

"The last thing I want," Elliot said, "is an argument."

"I'll give you a fucking argument. You didn't have to drink. All you had to do was come home."

"That must have been the problem," he said.

Then he ducked, alert at the last possible second to the missile that came for him at hairline level. Covering up, he heard the shattering of glass, and a fine rain of crystals enveloped him. She had sailed the sugar bowl at him; it had smashed against the wall above his head and there was sugar and glass in his hair.

"You bastard!" she screamed. "You are undermining me!"

"You ought not to throw things at me," Elliot said. "I don't throw things at you."

He left her frozen into her follow-through and went into the living room to turn the music off. When he returned she was leaning back against the wall, rubbing her right elbow with her left hand. Her eyes were bright. She had picked up one of her boots from the middle of the kitchen floor and stood holding it.

"What the hell do you mean, that must have been the problem?"

He set his glass on the edge of the sink with an unsteady hand and turned to her. "What do I mean? I mean that most of the time I'm putting one foot in front of the other like a good soldier and I'm out of it from the neck up. But there are times when I don't think I will ever be dead enough—or dead long enough—to get the taste of this life off my teeth. That's what I mean!"

She looked at him dry-eyed. "Poor fella," she said.

"What you have to understand, Grace, is that this drink I'm having"—he raised the glass toward her in a gesture of salute—"is the only worthwhile thing I've done in the last year and a half. It's the only thing in my life that means jack shit, the closest thing to satisfaction I've had. Now how can you begrudge me that? It's the best I'm capable of."

"You'll go too far," she said to him. "You'll see."

"What's that, Grace? A threat to walk?" He was grinding his teeth. "Don't make me laugh. You, walk? You, the friend of the unfortunate?"

"Don't you hit me," she said when she looked at his face. "Don't you dare."

"You, the Christian Queen of Calvary, walk? Why, I don't believe that for a minute."

She ran a hand through her hair and bit her lip. "No, we stay," she said. Anger and distraction made her look young. Her cheeks blazed rosy against the general pallor of her skin. "In my family we stay until the fella dies. That's the tradition. We stay and pour it for them and they die."

He put his drink down and shook his head.

"I thought we'd come through," Grace said. "I was sure."

"No," Elliot said. "Not altogether."

They stood in silence for a minute. Elliot sat down at the oilcloth-covered table. Grace walked around it and poured herself a whiskey.

"You are undermining me, Chas. You are making things impossible for me and I just don't know." She drank and winced. "I'm not going to stay through another drunk. I'm telling you right now. I haven't got it in me. I'll die."

He did not want to look at her. He watched the flakes settle against the glass of the kitchen door. "Do what you feel the need of," he said.

"I just can't take it," she said. Her voice was not scolding but measured and reasonable. "It's February. And I went to court this morning and lost Vopotik."

Once again, he thought, my troubles are going to be obviated by those of the deserving poor. He said, "Which one was that?"

"Don't you remember them? The three-year-old with the broken fingers?"

He shrugged. Grace sipped her whiskey.

"I told you. I said I had a three-year-old with broken fingers, and you said, 'Maybe he owed somebody money.' "

"Yes," he said, "I remember now."

"You ought to see the Vopotiks, Chas. The woman is young and obese. She's so young that for a while I thought I could get to her as a juvenile. The guy is a biker. They believe the kid came from another planet to control their lives. They believe this literally, both of them."

"You shouldn't get involved that way," Elliot said. "You should leave it to the caseworkers."

"They scared their first caseworker all the way to California. They were following me to work."

"You didn't tell me."

"Are you kidding?" she asked. "Of course I didn't." To Elliot's surprise, his wife poured herself a second whiskey. "You know how they address the child? As 'dude.' She says to it, 'Hey, dude.' " Grace shuddered with loathing. "You can't imagine! The woman munching Twinkies. The kid smelling of shit. They're high morning, noon, and night, but you can't get anybody for that these days."

"People must really hate it," Elliot said, "when somebody tells them they're not treating their kids right."

"They definitely don't want to hear it," Grace said. "You're right." She sat stirring her drink, frowning into the glass. "The Vopotik child will die, I think."

"Surely not," Elliot said.

"This one I think will die." Grace said. She took a deep breath and puffed out her cheeks and looked at him forlornly. "The situation's extreme. Of course, sometimes you wonder whether it makes any difference. That's the big question, isn't it?"

"I would think," Elliot said, "that would be the one question you didn't ask."

"But you do," she said. "You wonder: Ought they to live at all? To continue the cycle?" She put a hand to her hair and shook her head as if in confusion. "Some of these folks, my God, the poor things cannot put Wednesday on top of Tuesday to save their lives."

"It's a trick," Elliot agreed, " a lot of them can't manage."

"And kids are small, they're handy and underfoot. They make noise. They can't hurt you back."

"I suppose child abuse is something people can do together," Elliot said.

"Some kids are obnoxious. No question about it."

"I wouldn't know," Elliot said.

"Maybe you should stop complaining. Maybe you're better off. Maybe your kids are better off unborn."

"Better off or not," Elliot said, "it looks like they'll stay that way."

"I mean our kids, of course," Grace said. "I'm not blaming you, understand? It's just that here we are with you drunk again and me losing Vopotik, so I thought why not get into the big unaskable questions." She got up and folded her arms and began to pace up and down the kitchen. "Oh," she said when her eye fell upon the bottle, "that's good stuff, Chas. You won't mind if I have another? I'll leave you enough to get loaded on."

Elliot watched her pour. So much pain, he thought; such anger and confusion. He was tired of pain, anger, and confusion; they were what had got him in trouble that very morning.

The liquor seemed to be giving him a perverse lucidity when all he now required was oblivion. His rage, especially, was intact in its salting of alcohol. Its contours were palpable and bleeding at the borders. Booze was good for rage. Booze could keep it burning through the darkest night.

"What happened in court?" he asked his wife.

She was leaning on one arm against the wall, her long, strong body flexed at the hip. Holding her glass, she stared angrily toward the invisible fields outside. "I lost the child," she said.

Elliot thought that a peculiar way of putting it. He said nothing.

"The court convened in an atmosphere of high hilarity. It may be Hate Month around here but it was buddy-buddy over at Ilford Courthouse. The room was full of bikers and bikers' lawyers. A colorful crowd. There was a lot of bonding." She drank and shivered. "They didn't think too well of me. They don't think too well of broads as lawyers. Neither does the judge. The judge has the common touch. He's one of the boys."

"Which judge?" Elliot asked.

"Buckley. A man of about sixty. Know him? Lots of veins on his nose?"

Elliot shrugged.

"I thought I had done my homework," Grace told him. "But suddenly I had nothing but paper. No witnesses. It was Margolis at Valley Hospital who spotted the radiator burns. He called us in the first place. Suddenly he's got to keep his reservation for a campsite in St. John. So Buckley threw his deposition out." She began to chew on a fingernail. "The caseworkers have vanished—one's in L.A., the other's in Nepal. I went in there and got run over. I lost the child."

"It happens all the time," Elliot said. "Doesn't it?"

"This one shouldn't have been lost, Chas. These people aren't simply confused. They're weird. They stink."

"You go messing into anybody's life," Elliot said, "that's what you'll find."

"If the child stays in that house," she said, "he's going to die."

"You did your best," he told his wife. "Forget it."

She pushed the bottle away. She was holding a water glass that was almost a third full of whiskey.

"That's what the commissioner said."

Elliot was thinking of how she must have looked in court to the cherry-faced judge and the bikers and their lawyers. Like the schoolteachers who had tormented their childhoods, earnest and tight-assed, humorless and self-righteous. It was not surprising that things had gone against her.

He walked over to the window and faced his reflection again. "Your optimism always surprises me."

"My optimism? Where I grew up our principal cultural expression was the funeral. Whatever keeps me going, it isn't optimism."

"No?" he asked. "What is it?"

"I forget," she said.

"Maybe it's your religious perspective. Your sense of the divine plan."

She sighed in exasperation. "Look, I don't think I want to fight anymore. I'm sorry I threw the sugar at you. I'm not your keeper. Pick on someone your own size."

"Sometimes," Elliot said, "I try to imagine what it's like to believe that the sky is full of care and concern."

"You want to take everything from me, do you?" She stood leaning against the back of her chair. "That you can't take. It's the only part of my life you can't mess up."

He was thinking that if it had not been for her he might not have survived. There could be no forgiveness for that. "Your life? You've got all this piety strung out between Monadnock and Central America. And look at yourself. Look at your life."

"Yes," she said, "look at it."

"You should have been a nun. You don't know how to live."

"I know that," she said. "That's why I stopped doing counseling. Because I'd rather talk the law than life." She turned to him. "You got everything I had, Chas. What's left I absolutely require."

"I swear I would rather be a drunk," Elliot said, "than force myself to believe such trivial horseshit."

"Well, you're going to have to do it without a straight man," she said, "because this time I'm not going to be here for you. Believe it or not."

"I don't believe it," Elliot said. "Not my Grace."

"You're really good at this," she told him. "You make me feel ashamed of my own name."

"I love your name," he said.

The telephone rang. They let it ring three times, and then Elliot went over and answered it.

"Hey, who's that?" a good-humored voice on the phone demanded.

Elliot recited their phone number.

"Hey, I want to talk to your woman, man. Put her on."

"I'll give her a message," Elliot said.

"You put your woman on, man. Run and get her."

Elliot looked at the receiver. He shook his head. "Mr. Vopotik?"

"Never you fuckin' mind, man. I don't want to talk to you. I want to talk to the skinny bitch."

Elliot hung up.

"Is it him?" she asked.

"I guess so."

They waited for the phone to ring again and it shortly did.

"I'll talk to him," Grace said. But Elliot already had the phone.

"Who are you, asshole?" the voice inquired. "What's your fuckin' name, man?"

"Elliot," Elliot said.

"Hey, don't hang up on me, Elliot. I won't put up with that. I told you go get that skinny bitch, man. You go do it."

There were sounds of festivity in the background on the other end of the line—a stereo and drunken voices.

"Hey," the voice declared, "Hey, don't keep me waiting, man."

"What do you want to say to her?" Elliot asked.

"That's none of your fucking business, fool. Do what I told you."

"My wife is resting," Elliot said. "I'm taking her calls."

He was answered by a shout of rage. He put the phone aside for a moment and finished his glass of whiskey. When he picked it up again the man on the line was screaming at him. "That bitch tried to break up my family, man! She almost got away with it. You know what kind of pain my wife went through?"

"What kind?" Elliot asked.

For a few seconds he heard only the noise of the party. "Hey, you're not drunk, are you, fella?"

"Certainly not," Elliot insisted.

"You tell that skinny bitch she's gonna pay for what she did to my family, man. You tell her she can run but she can't hide. I don't care where you go—California, anywhere—I'll get to you."

"Now that I have you on the phone," Elliot said. "I'd like to ask you a couple of questions. Promise you won't get mad?"

"Stop it!" Grace said to him. She tried to wrench the phone from his grasp, but he clutched it to his chest.

"Do you keep a journal?" Elliot asked the man on the phone. "What's your hat size?"

"Maybe you think I can't get to you," the man said. "But I can get to you, man. I don't care who you are, I'll get to you. The brothers will get to you.

"Well, there's no need to go to California. You know where we live."

"For God's sake," Grace said.

"Fuckin' right," the man on the telephone said. "Fuckin' right I know."

"Come on over," Elliot said.

"How's that?" the man on the phone asked.

"I said come on over. We'll talk about space travel. Comets and stuff. We'll talk astral projection. The moons of Jupiter."

"You're making a mistake, fucker."

"Come on over," Elliot insisted. "Bring your fat wife and your beat-up kid. Don't be embarrassed if your head's a little small."

The telephone was full of music and shouting. Elliot held it away from his ear.

"Good work," Grace said to him when he had replaced the receiver.

"I hope he comes," Elliot said. "I'll pop him."

He went carefully down the cellar stairs, switched on the overhead light, and began searching among the spiderwebbed shadows and fouled fishing line for his shotgun. It took him fifteen minutes to find it and his cleaning case. While he was still downstairs, he heard the telephone ring again and his wife answer it. He came upstairs and spread his shooting gear across the kitchen table. "Was that him?"

She nodded wearily. "He called back to play us the chain saw."

"I've heard that melody before," Elliot said.

He assembled his cleaning rod and swabbed out the shotgun barrel. Grace watched him, a hand to her forehead. "God," she said. "What have I done? I'm so drunk."

"Most of the time," Elliot said, sighting down the barrel, "I'm helpless in the face of human misery. Tonight I'm ready to reach out."

"I'm finished," Grace said. "I'm through, Chas. I mean it."

Elliot rammed three red shells into the shotgun and pumped one forward into the breech with a satisfying report. "Me, I'm ready for some radical problem-solving. I'm going to spray that no-neck Slovak all over the yard."

"He isn't a Slovak," Grace said. She stood in the middle of the kitchen with her eyes closed. Her face was chalk white.

"What do you mean?" Elliot demanded. "Certainly he's a Slovak."

"No he's not," Grace said.

"Fuck him anyway. I don't care what he is. I'll grease his ass."

He took a handful of deer shells from the box and stuffed them in his jacket pockets.

"I'm not going to stay with you, Chas. Do you understand me?"

Elliot walked to the window and peered out at his driveway. "He won't be alone. They travel in packs."

"For God's sake!" Grace cried, and in the next instant bolted for the downstairs bathroom. Elliot went out, turned off the porch light and switched on a spotlight over the barn door. Back inside, he could hear Grace in the toilet being sick. He turned off the light in the kitchen.

He was still standing by the window when she came up behind him. It seemed strange and fateful to be standing in the dark near her, holding the shotgun. He felt ready for anything.

"I can't leave you alone down here drunk with a loaded shotgun," she said. "How can I?"

"Go upstairs," he said.

"If I went upstairs it would mean I didn't care what happened. Do you understand? If I go it means I don't care anymore. Understand?"

"Stop asking me if I understand," Elliot said. "I understand fine."

"I can't think," she said in a sick voice. "Maybe I don't care. I don't know. I'm going upstairs."

"Good," Elliot said.

When she was upstairs, Elliot took his shotgun and the whiskey into the dark living room and sat down in an armchair beside one of the lace-curtained windows. The powerful barn light illuminated the length of his driveway and the whole of the back yard. From the window at which he sat, he commanded a view of several miles in the direction of East Ilford. The two-lane blacktop road that ran there was the only one along which an enemy could pass.

He drank and watched the snow, toying with the safety of his 12-gauge Remington. He felt neither anxious nor angry now but only impatient to be done with whatever the night would bring. Drunkenness and the silent rhythm of the falling snow combined to make him feel outside of time and syntax.

Sitting in the dark room, he found himself confronting Blankenship's dream. He saw the bunkers and wire of some long-lost perimeter.[5] The rank smell of night came back to him, the dread evening and quick dusk, the mysteries of outer darkness: fear, combat, and death. Enervated by liquor, he began to cry. Elliot was sympathetic with other people's tears but ashamed of his own. He thought of his own tears as childish and excremental. He stifled whatever it was that had started them.

Now his whiskey tasted thin as water. Beyond the lightly frosted glass, illuminated snowflakes spun and settled sleepily on weighted pine boughs. He had found a life beyond the war after all, but in it he was still sitting in darkness, armed, enraged, waiting.

His eyes grew heavy as the snow came down. He felt as though he could be drawn up into the storm and he began to imagine that. He imagined his life with all its artifacts and appetites easing up the spout into white oblivion, everything obviated and foreclosed. He thought maybe he could go for that.

When he awakened, his left hand had gone numb against the trigger guard of his shotgun. The living room was pull of pale, delicate light. He looked outside and saw that the storm was done with and the

5. Outer ring of a military defense.

sky radiant and cloudless. The sun was still below the horizon.

Slowly Elliot got to his feet. The throbbing poison in his limbs served to remind him of the state of things. He finished the glass of whiskey on the windowsill beside his easy chair. Then he went to the hall closet to get a ski jacket, shouldered his shotgun, and went outside.

There were two cleared acres behind his house; beyond them a trail descended into a hollow of pine forest and frozen swamp. Across the hollow, white pastures stretched to the ridge-line, lambent under the lightening sky. A line of skeletal elms weighted with snow marked the course of frozen Shawmut Brook.

He found a pair of ski goggles in a jacket pocket and put them on and set out toward the tree line, gripping the shotgun, step by careful step in the knee-deep snow. Two raucous crows wheeled high overhead, their cries exploding the morning's silence. When the sun came over the ridge, he stood where he was and took in a deep breath. The risen sun warmed his face and he closed his eyes. It was windless and very cold.

Only after he had stood there for a while did he realize how tired he had become. The weight of the gun taxed him. It seemed infinitely wearying to contemplate another single step in the snow. He opened his eyes and closed them again. With sunup the world had gone blazing blue and white, and even with his tinted goggles its whiteness dazzled him and made his head ache. Behind his eyes, the hypnagogic patterns formed a monsoon-heavy tropical sky. He yawned. More than anything, he wanted to lie down in the soft, pure snow. If he could do that, he was certain he could go to sleep at once.

He stood in the middle of the field and listened to the crows. Fear, anger, and sleep were the three primary conditions of life. He had learned that over there. Once he had thought fear the worst, but he had learned that the worst was anger. Nothing could fix it; neither alcohol nor medicine. It was a worm. It left him no peace. Sleep was the best.

He opened his eyes and pushed on until he came to the brow that overlooked the swamp. Just below, gliding along among the frozen cattails and bare scrub maple, was a man on skis. Elliot stopped to watch the man approach.

The skier's face was concealed by a red-and-blue ski mask. He wore snow goggles, a blue jumpsuit, and a red woolen Norwegian hat. As he came, he leaned into the turns of the trail, moving silently and gracefully along. At the foot of the slope on which Elliot stood, the man looked up, saw him, and slid to a halt. The man stood staring at him for a moment and then began to herringbone up the slope. In no time at all the skier stood no more than ten feet away, removing his goggles, and inside the woolen mask Elliot recognized the clear blue eyes of his neighbor, Professor Loyall Anderson. The shotgun Elliot was carrying seemed to grow heavier. He yawned and shook his head, trying unsuccessfully to clear it. The sight of Anderson's eyes gave him a thrill of revulsion.

"What are you after?" the young professor asked him, nodding toward the shotgun Elliot was cradling.

"Whatever there is," Elliot said.

Anderson took a quick look at the distant pasture behind him and then turned back to Elliot. The mouth hole of the professor's mask filled with teeth. Elliot thought that Anderson's teeth were quite as he had imagined them earlier. "Well, Polonski's cows are locked up," the professor said. "So they at least are safe."

Elliot realized that the professor had made a joke and was smiling. "Yes," he agreed.

Professor Anderson and his wife had been the moving force behind an initiative to outlaw the discharge of firearms within the boundaries of East Ilford Township. The initiative had been defeated, because East Ilford was not that kind of town.

"I think I'll go over by the river," Elliot said. He said it only to have something to say, to fill the silence before Anderson spoke again. He was afraid of what Anderson might say to him and of what might happen.

"You know," Anderson said, "that's all bird sanctuary over there now."

"Sure," Elliot agreed.

Outfitted as he was, the professor attracted Elliot's anger in an elemental manner. The mask made him appear a kind of doll, a kachina figure or a marionette. His eyes and mouth, all on their own, were disagreeable.

Elliot began to wonder if Anderson could smell the whiskey on his breath. He pushed the little red bull's-eye safety button on his gun to Off.

"Seriously," Anderson said, "I'm always having to run hunters out of there. Some people don't understand the word 'posted.' "

"I would never do that," Elliot said. "I would be afraid."

Anderson nodded his head. He seemed to be laughing. "Would you?" he asked Elliot merrily.

In imagination, Elliot rested the tip of his shotgun barrel against Anderson's smiling teeth. If he fired a load of deer shot into them, he thought, they might make a noise like broken china. "Yes," Elliot said. "I wouldn't know who they were or where they'd been. They might resent my being alive. Telling them where they could shoot and where not."

Anderson's teeth remained in place. "That's pretty strange," he said. "I mean, to talk about resenting someone for being alive."

"It's all relative," Elliot said. "They might think, 'Why should he be alive when some brother of mine isn't?' Or they might think, 'Why should he be alive when I'm not?' "

"Oh," Anderson said.

"You see?" Elliot said. Facing Anderson, he took a long step backward. "All relative."

"Yes," Anderson said.

"That's so often true, isn't it?" Elliot asked. "Values are often relative."

"Yes," Anderson said. Elliot was relieved to see that he had stopped smiling.

"I've hardly slept, you know," Elliot told Professor Anderson. "Hardly at all. All night. I've been drinking."

"Oh," Anderson said. He licked his lips in the mouth of the mask. "You should get some rest."

"You're right," Elliot said.

"Well,"Anderson said, "got to go now."

Elliot thought he sounded a little thick in the tongue. A little slow in the jaw.

"It's a nice day," Elliot said, wanting now to be agreeable.

"It's great," Anderson said, shuffling on his skis.

"Have a nice day," Elliot said.

"Yes," Anderson said, and pushed off.

Elliot rested the shotgun across his shoulders and watched Anderson withdraw through the frozen swamp. It was in fact a nice day, but Elliot took no comfort in the weather. He missed night and the falling snow.

As he walked back toward his house, he realized that now there would be whole days to get through, running before the antic energy of whiskey. The whiskey would drive him until he dropped. He shook his head in regret. "It's a revolution," he said aloud. He imagined himself talking to his wife.

Getting drunk was an insurrection, a revolution—a bad one. There would be outsize bogus emotions. There would be petty moral blackmail and cheap remorse. He had said dreadful things to his wife. He had bullied Anderson with his violence and unhappiness, and Anderson would not forgive him. There would be damn little justice and no mercy.

Nearly to the house, he was startled by the desperate feathered drumming of a pheasant's rush. He froze, and out of instinct brought the gun up in the direction of the sound. When he saw the bird break from its cover and take wing, he tracked it, took a breath, and fired once. The bird was a little flash of opulent color against the bright-blue sky. Elliot felt himself flying for a moment. The shot missed.

Lowering the gun, he remembered the deer shells he had loaded. A hit with the concentrated shot would have pulverized the bird, and he was glad he had missed. He wished no harm to any creature. Then he thought of himself wishing no harm to any creature and began to feel fond and sorry for himself. As soon as he grew aware of the emotion he was indulging, he suppressed it. Pissing and moaning, mourning and weeping, that was the nature of the drug.

The shot echoed from the distant hills. Smoke hung in the air. He turned and looked behind him and saw, far away cross the pasture, the tiny blue-and-red figure of Professor Anderson motionless against the snow. Then Elliot turned again toward his house and took a few labored steps and looked up to see his wife at the bedroom window. She stood perfectly still, and the morning sun lit her nakedness. He stopped where he was. She had heard the shot and run to the window. What had she thought to see? Burnt rags and blood on the snow. How relieved was she now? How disappointed?

Elliot thought he could feel his wife trembling at the window. She was hugging herself. Her hands clasped her shoulders. Elliot took his snow goggles off and shaded his eyes with his hand. He stood in the field staring.

The length of the gun was between them, he thought. Somehow she had got out in front of it, to the wrong side of the wire. If he looked long enough he would find everything out there. He would find himself down the sight.

How beautiful she is, he thought. The effect was striking. The window was so clear because he had washed it himself, with vinegar. At the best of times he was a difficult, fussy man.

Elliot began to hope for forgiveness. He leaned the shotgun on his forearm and raised his left hand and waved to her. Show a hand, he thought. Please just show a hand.

He was cold, but it had got light. He wanted no more than the gesture. It seemed to him that he could build another day on it. Another day was all you needed. He raised his hand higher and waited.

---

1. What are Elliot's apparent deficiencies as a counselor? Do they correspond with his fragilities as a person?
2. How do the setting and the weather fuel Elliot's emotions? Does the author hint at a conspiracy between inward and outward malevolences shaping Elliot's life?
3. What are the positive and negative aspects of Elliot's marriage? Does his wife believe he can be saved?

4. Is his hatred for the Anderson family in any way justified? Is his imaginary killing of Anderson an index of a general rage against life?
5. Is the end of the story tinged with hope? Can we detect the beginning of a change that may bring Elliot out of his troubles?

Peter Taylor

Taylor (1917–   ) was born in Trenton, Tennessee. He was educated at Vanderbilt University and Kenyon College, where he became a lifelong friend of the poet Robert Lowell. Through most of his adult life he has taught writing at a number of American colleges and universities and is now at the University of Virginia. Unlike many Southern writers of his period he has written, in elegantly unobstrusive style, of the bewilderments and aspirations of genteel, resourceful people, who weave the strands of tradition into the tensions of new times with grace and persistent responsibility. He has published two novels, A Woman of Means *(1950) and* A Summons to Memphis *(1986). His books of stories include* A Long Fourth and Other Stories *(1948),* Miss Leonora When Last Seen and Fifteen Other Stories *(1963),* The Collected Stories of Peter Taylor *(1969), and* In the Miro District and Other Stories *(1977).*

Miss Leonora When Last Seen

I

HERE in Thomasville we are all concerned over the whereabouts of Miss Leonora Logan. She has been missing for two weeks, and though a half dozen postcards have been received from her, stating that she is in good health and that no anxiety should be felt for her safety, still the whole town can talk of nothing else. She was last seen in Thomasville heading south on Logan Lane, which is the narrow little street that runs alongside her family property. At four-thirty on Wednesday afternoon—Wednesday before last, that is to say—she turned out of the dirt driveway that comes down from her house and drove south on the lane toward its intersection with the bypass of the Memphis-Chattanooga highway. She has not been seen since. Officially, she is away from home on a little trip. Unofficially, in the minds of the townspeople, she is a missing person, and because of events leading up to her departure none of us will rest easy until we know that the old lady is safe at home again.

Miss Leonora's half dozen postcards have come to us from points in as many states: Alabama, Georgia, North Carolina, West Virginia, Kentucky—in that order. It is considered a fair guess that her next card will come from Missouri or Arkansas, and that the one after that will be from Mississippi or Louisiana. She seems to be orbiting her native state of Tennessee. But, on the other hand, there is no proof that she has not crossed the state, back and forth, a number of times during the past two weeks. She is quite an old lady, and is driving a 1942 Dodge convertible. Anyone traveling in the region indicated should watch out for two characteristics of her driving. First, she hates to be overtaken and passed by other vehicles—especially by trucks. The threat of such is apt to make her bear down on the accelerator and try to outdistance the would-be passer. Or, if passed, she can be counted on to try to overtake and pass the offender at first chance. The second characteristic is: when driving after dark, she invariably refuses to dim her lights unless an approaching car has dimmed its own while at least five hundred feet away. She is a good judge of distances, and she is not herself blinded by bright lights on the highway. And one ought to add that, out of long habit and for reasons best known to herself, Miss Leonora nearly always drives by night.

Some description will be due, presently, of this lady's person and of how she will be dressed while traveling. But that had better wait a while. It might seem prejudicial and even misleading with reference to her soundness of mind. And any question of that sort, no matter what the rest of the world may think, has no bearing upon the general consternation that her going away has created here.

Wherever Miss Leonora Logan is today, she knows in her heart that in the legal action recently taken against her in Thomasville there was no malice directed toward her personally. She knows this, and would say so. At this very moment she may be telling some new-found friend the history of the case—because I happen to know that when she is away from home she talks to people about herself and her forebears as she would never do to anyone here. And chances are she is giving a completely unbiased version of what has happened, since that is her way.

The cause of all our present tribulation is this: The Logan property, which Miss Leonora inherited from one of her paternal great-uncles and which normally upon her death would have gone to distant relatives of hers in Chicago, has been chosen as the site for our county's new consolidated high school. A year and a half ago, Miss Leonora was offered a fair price for the three-acre tract and the old house, and she refused it. This summer, condemnation proceedings were begun, and two weeks ago the county court granted the writ. This will seem to you a bad thing for the town to have done, especially in view of the fact that Miss Lenora has given long years of service to our school system. She retired ten years ago after teaching for twenty-five years in the old high school. To be sure, four of us who are known hereabouts as Miss

Leonora Logan's favorites among the male citizenry refused to have any part in the action. Two of us even preferred to resign from the school board. But still, times do change, and the interests of one individual cannot be allowed to hinder the progress of a whole community. Miss Leonora understands that. And she knows that her going away can only delay matters for a few weeks at most. Nevertheless, she is making it look very bad for Thomasville, and we want Miss Leonora to come home.

The kind of jaunt that she has gone off on isn't anything new for the old lady. During the ten years since her retirement she has been setting out on similar excursions rather consistently every month or so, and never, I believe, with a specific itinerary or destination in mind. Until she went away this time, people had ceased to bother themselves with the question of her whereabouts while she was gone or to be concerned about any harm that might come to her. We have been more inclined to think of the practical value her trips have for us. In the past, you see, she was never away for more than a week or ten days, and on her return she would gladly give anyone a full and accurate account of places visited and the condition of roads traveled. It has, in fact, become the custom when you are planning an automobile trip to address yourself to Miss Leonora on the public square one day and ask her advice on the best route to take. She is our authority not only on the main highways north, south, east, and west of here, in a radius of six or eight hundred miles, but even on the secondary and unimproved roads in places as remote as Brown County, Indiana, and the Outer Banks of North Carolina. Her advice is often very detailed, and will include warnings against "single-lane bridges" or "soft shoulders" or even "cops patrolling in unmarked cars."

It is only the facts she gives you, though. She doesn't express appreciation for the beauty of the countryside or her opinion of the character of towns she passes through. The most she is likely to say is that such-and-such a road is "regarded" as the scenic route, or that a certain town has a "well-worked-out traffic system." No one can doubt that, while driving, Miss Leonora keeps her eyes and mind on the road. And that may be the reason why we have never worried about her. But one asks oneself, What pleasure can she ever have derived from these excursions? She declares that she hates the actual driving. And when giving advice on the roads somewhere she will always say that it is a dull and tedious trip and that the traveler will wish himself home in Thomasville a thousand times before he gets to wherever he is going.

Miss Leonora's motivation for taking these trips was always, until the present instance, something that it seemed pointless even to speculate on. It just seemed that the mood came on her and she was off and away. But if anything happens to her now, all the world will blame *us* and say we *sent* her on this journey, sent her out alone and possibly in a dangerous frame of mind. In particular, the blame will fall on the four timid male citizens who were the last to see her in Thomasville (for I do not honestly believe we will ever see her alive here again) and who, as old friends and former pupils of hers at the high school, ought to have prevented her going away. As a matter of fact, I am the one who opened the car door for the old lady that afternoon and politely assisted her into the driver's seat—and without even saying I thought it unwise of her to go. I *thought* it unwise, but at the moment it was as if I were still her favorite pupil twenty years before, and as if I feared she might reprove me for any small failure of courtesy like not opening the car door.

That's how the old lady is—or was. Whatever your first relation to her might have been, she would never allow it to change, and some people even say that that is why she discourages us so about the trips we plan. She cannot bear to think of us away from Thomasville. She thinks this is where all of us belong. I remember one day at school when some boy said to her that he wished he lived in a place like Memphis or Chattanooga. She gave him the look she usually reserved for the people she caught cheating. I was seated in the first row of the class that day, and I saw the angry patches of red appear on her broad, flat cheeks and on her forehead. She paused a moment to rearrange the combs in her hair and to give the stern yank to her corset that was a sure sign she was awfully mad. (We used to say that, with her spare figure, she only wore a corset for the sake of that expressive gesture.) The class was silent, waiting. Miss Leonora looked out the window for a moment, squinting up her eyes as if she could actually make out the Memphis or even the Chattanooga skyline on the horizon. Then, turning back to the unfortunate boy, she said, grinding out her words to him through clenched teeth, "I wish I could *throw* you there!"

But it is ten years now since Miss Leonora retired, and, strange as it may sound, the fact of her having once taught in our school system was never introduced into the deliberations of the school board last spring—their deliberations upon whether or not they ought to sue for condemnation of the Logan home place. No doubt it was right that they didn't let this influence their decision. But what really seems to have happened is that nobody even recalled that the old lady had once been a teacher—or nobody but a very few, who did not want to remind the others.

What they remembered, to the exclusion of everything else, and what they always remember is that Miss Leonora is the last of the Logan family in Thomasville, a family that for a hundred years and more did all it could to impede the growth and progress of our town.

It was a Logan, for instance, who kept the railroad from coming through town; it was another Logan who prevented the cotton mill and the snuff factory from locating here. They even kept us from getting the county seat moved here, until after the Civil War, when finally it became clear that nobody was ever going to buy lots up at Logan City, where they had put the first courthouse. Their one idea was always to keep the town unspoiled, unspoiled by railroads or factories or even county politics. Perhaps they should not be blamed for wanting to keep the town unspoiled. Yet I am not quite sure about that. It is a question that even Miss Leonora doesn't feel sure about. Otherwise, why does she always go into that question with the people she meets away from home?

I must tell you about the kind of lodging Miss Leonora takes when she stops for rest, and about the kind of people she finds to talk to. She wouldn't talk to you or me, and she wouldn't put up at a hotel like mine, here on the square, or even at a first-class motel like one of those out on the Memphis-Chattanooga bypass. I have asked her very direct questions about this, pleading a professional interest, and I have filled in with other material furnished by her friends of the road who have from time to time stopped in here at my place.

On a pretty autumn day like today, she will have picked a farmhouse that has one of those little home-lettered signs out by the mailbox saying "Clean Rooms for Tourists—Modern Conveniences." (She will, that is, unless she has changed her ways and taken to a different life, which is the possibility that I do not like to think of.) She stops only at places that are more or less in that category—old-fashioned tourist homes run by retired farm couples or, if the place is in town, by two old-maid sisters. Such an establishment usually takes its name from whatever kind of trees happen to grow in the yard—Maple Lawn or Elmwood or The Oaks. Or when there is a boxwood plant, it will be called Boxwood Manor. If the place is in the country, like the one today, it may be called Oak Crest.

You can just imagine how modern the modern conveniences at Oak Crest are. But it is cheap, which is a consideration for Miss Leonora. And the proprietors are probably good listeners, which is another consideration. She generally stops in the daytime, but since even in the daytime she can't sleep for long, she is apt to be found helping out with the chores. Underneath the Oak Crest "Clean Rooms for Tourists" sign there may be one that says "Sterile Day-Old Eggs" or, during the present season, "Delicious Apples and Ripe Tomatoes." It wouldn't surprise me if you found Miss Leonora today out by the roadside assisting with the sale of Oak Crest's garden produce. And if that's the case she is happy in the knowledge that any passer-by will mistake her for the proprietress's mother or old-maid sister, and never suppose she is a paying guest. In her carefully got-up costume she sits there talking to her new friend. Or else she is in the house or in the chicken yard, talking away while she helps out with the chores . . . It is Miss Leonora's way of killing time—killing time until night falls and she can take to the road again.

Miss Leonora is an intellectual woman, and at the same time she is an extremely practical and simple kind of person. This makes it hard for any two people to agree on what she is really like. It is hard even for those of us who were her favorites when we went to school to her. For, in the end, we didn't really know her any better than anybody else did. Sometimes she would have one of us up to her house for coffee and cookies on a winter afternoon, but it was hardly a social occasion. We went up there strictly as her students. We never saw any of the house except the little front room that she called her "office" and that was furnished with a roll-top desk, oak bookcases, and three or four of the hardest chairs you ever sat in. It looked more like a schoolroom than her own classroom did, over at the high school. While you sat drinking coffee with her, she was still your English teacher or your history teacher or your Latin teacher, whichever she happened to be at the time, and you were supposed to make conversation with her about *Silas Marner* or Tom Paine or Cicero.[1] If it was a good session and you had shown a little enthusiasm, then she would talk to you some about your future and say you ought to begin thinking about college—because she was always going to turn her favorites into professional men. That was how she was going to populate the town with the sort of people she thought it ought to have. She never got but one of us to college, however, and he came back home as a certified druggist instead of the doctor she had wanted him to be. (Our doctors are always men who have moved in here from somewhere else, and our lawyers are people Miss Leonora wouldn't pay any attention to when they were in school.) . . . I used to love to hear Miss Leonora talk, and I went along with her and did pretty well till toward the end of my last year, when I decided that college wasn't for me. I ought to have gone to college, and I had no better reason for deciding against it than any of the others did. It was just that during all the years when Miss Leonora was talking to you about making something of yourself and making Thomasville a more civilized place to live in, you were hearing at home and everywhere else about what the Logans had done to the town and how they held themselves above everybody else. I got to feeling ashamed of being known as her protégé.

As I said, Miss Leonora is an intellectual woman. She seldom

1. Roman statesman (106–43 B.C.), orator, and writer; *Silas Marner:* novel by George Eliot (1819–1880), English writer; Thomas Paine (1737–1809), American patriot and writer on government.

comes out of the post office without a book under her arm that she has specially ordered or that has come to her from one of the national book clubs she belongs to; and she also reads all the cheapest kind of trash that's to be had at the drugstore. She is just a natural-born reader, and enjoys reading the way other people enjoy eating or sleeping. It used to be that she would bedevil all the preachers we got here, trying to talk theology with them, and worry the life out of the lawyers with talk about Hamilton and Jefferson[2] and her theories about men like Henry Clay and John Marshall.[3] But about the time she quit teaching she gave up all that, too.

Aside from the drugstore trash, nobody knows what she reads any more, though probably it is the same as always. We sometimes doubt that she knows herself what she reads nowadays. Her reading seems to mean no more to her than her driving about the country does, and one wonders why she goes on with it, and what she gets out of it. Every night, the light in her office burns almost all night, and when she comes out of the post office with a new book, she has the wrappings off before she is halfway across the square and is turning the pages and reading away—a mile a minute, so it seems—as she strolls through the square and then heads up High Street toward Logana, which is what the Logans have always called their old house. If someone speaks to her, she pretends not to hear the first time. If it is important, if you want some information about the roads somewhere, you have to call her name a second time. The first sign that she is going to give you her attention comes when she begins moving her lips, hurriedly finishing off a page or a paragraph. Then she slams the book closed, as though she is through with it for all time, and before you can phrase your question she begins asking you how you and all your family are. Nobody can give a warmer greeting and make you feel he is gladder to see you than she can. She stands there beating the new book against her thigh, as though the book were some worthless object that she would just as soon throw away, and when she has asked you about yourself and your family she is ready then to talk about any subject under the sun—anything, I ought to add, except herself. If she makes a reference to the book in her hand, it is only to comment on the binding or the print or the quality of the paper. Or she may say that the price of books has gotten all out of bounds and that the postal rate for books is too high. It's always something that any field hand could understand and is a far cry from the way she used to talk about books when we were in school.

I am reminded of one day six or eight years ago when I saw Miss Leonora stopped on the square by an old colored man named Hominy

2. Alexander Hamilton (1757–1804), first U.S. Secretary of the Treasury; Thomas Jefferson (1743–1826), third president of the U.S. 3. Clay (1777–1852) was a U.S. statesman and orator. Marshall (1755–1852) was chief justice of the U.S.

Atkinson. Or his name may really be Harmony Atkinson. I once asked him which it was, and at first he merely grinned and shrugged his shoulders. But then he said thoughtfully, as though it hadn't ever occurred to him before, "Some does call me the one, I s'pose, and some the other." He is a dirty old ignoramous, and the other Negroes say that in the summertime he has his own private swarm of flies that follows him around. His flies were with him that day when he stopped Miss Leonora. He was in his wagon, the way you always see him, and he managed to block the old lady's path when she stepped down off the curb and began to cross the street in front of the post office and had cut diagonally across the courthouse lawn. It was the street over there on the other side of the square that she was about to cross. I was standing nearby with a group of men, under the willow oak trees beside the goldfish pool. Twice before Miss Leonora looked up, Hominy Atkinson lifted a knobby hand to shoo the flies away from his head. In the wagon he was seated on a squat split-bottom chair; and on another chair beside him was his little son Albert. Albert was eight or nine years old at the time, a plump little fellow dressed up in an old-fashioned Buster Brown outfit[4] as tidy and clean as his daddy's rags were dirty.

This Albert is the son of Hominy and the young wife that Hominy took after he was already an old man. The three of them live on a worn-out piece of land three or four miles from town. Albert is a half-grown boy now, and there is nothing very remarkable about him except that they say he still goes to school more regularly than some of the other colored children do. But when he was a little fellow his daddy and mama spoiled and pampered him till, sitting up there in the wagon that day, he had the look of a fat little priss. The fact is, from the time he could sit up in a chair Hominy used never to go anywhere without him—he was so proud of the little pickaninny, and he was so mortally afraid something might happen to him when he was out of his sight. Somebody once asked Hominy why he didn't leave the child home with his mama, and Hominy replied that her hands were kept busy just washing and ironing and sewing for the boy. "It's no easy matter to raise up a clean child," he pronounced. Somebody else asked Hominy one time if he thought it right to take the boy to the square on First Monday,[5] where he would be exposed to some pretty rough talk, or to the fairgrounds during Fair Week. Hominy replied, "What ain't fittin' for him to hear ain't fittin' for me." And it was true that you seldom saw Hominy on that corner of the square where the Negro men congregated or in the stable yard at the fairgrounds.

Before Miss Leonora looked up at Hominy that morning, he sat

4. Clothing typified by a wide, starched collar. 5. First Monday of each month, when all the country people come to town for shopping and socializing.

with his old rag of a hat in his lap, smiling down at her. Finally, she slammed her book shut and lifted her eyes. But Hominy didn't try to ask his question until she had satisfied herself that he, his young wife, and Albert there beside him were in good health, and several other of his relatives whose names she knew. Then he asked it.

"What does you need today, Miss Leonora?" he said. "Me, *I* needs a dollar bill."

She replied without hesitating. "I don't need anything I'd pay *you* a dollar for, Hominy." Hominy didn't bat an eye, only sat there gazing down at her while she spoke. "I have a full herd of your kind up at Logana, Hominy, who'll fetch and go for me without any dollar bill. You know that."

She was referring to the Negro families who live in the outbuildings up at her place. People say that some of them live right in the house with her, but when I used to go up there as a boy she kept them all out of sight. There was not even a sound of them on the place. She didn't even let her cook bring in the coffee things, and it gave you the queer feeling that either she was protecting you from them or them from you.

"What do you think you need a dollar for, Hominy?" she asked presently.

"I needs to buy the boy a book," he said.

"What book?" It was summertime, and she knew the boy wouldn't be in school.

"Why, most any book," said Hominy. "I jist can't seem to keep him in reading."

Miss Leonora peered around Hominy at Albert, who sat looking down at his own fat little washed-up hands, as if he might be ashamed of his daddy's begging. Then Miss Leonora glanced down at the book she had got in the mail. "Here, give him this," she said, handing the brand-new book up to that old tatterdemalion. It was as if she agreed with the old ignoramous that it didn't matter what kind of book the boy got so long as it was a book.

And now Albert himself couldn't resist raising his eyes to see the book that was coming his way. He gave Miss Leonora a big smile, showing a mouthful of teeth as white as his starched shirt collar. "Miss Leonora, you oughtn't to do—" he began in an airy little voice.

But his daddy put a stop to it. "Hush your mouth, honey. Miss Leonora knows what she's doing. Don't worry about that none." He handed the book over to Albert, hardly looking at it himself. Those of us over by the goldfish pool were never able to make out what the book was.

"I certainly thank you, Miss Leonora," Albert piped.

And Hominy said solemnly, "Yes'm, we are much obliged to you."

"Then move this conveyance of yours and let me pass," said Miss Leonora.

Hominy flipped the reins sharply on the rump of his mule and said, "Giddap, Bridesmaid." The old mule flattened its ears back on its head and pulled away with an angry jerk.

But even when the wagon was out of her way Miss Leonora continued to stand there for a minute or so, watching the receding figure of Albert perched on his chair in the wagon bed and bent over his book examining it the way any ordinary child would have examined a new toy. As long as she stood there the old lady kept her eyes on the little black boy. And before she finally set out across the street, we heard her say aloud and almost as if for our benefit. "It may be . . . It may be . . . I suppose, yes, it may be."

II

School integration is not yet a burning issue in Thomasville. But some men in town were at first opposed to consolidation of our county high schools until it could be seen what kind of pressures are going to be put on us. In the past eighteen months, however, those men have more or less reversed their position. And they do not deny that their change of mind was influenced by the possibility that Logana might be acquired for the site of the new school. Nor do they pretend that it is because they think Logana such an ideal location. They have agreed to go along with the plan, so they say, because it is the only way of getting rid of the little colony of Negroes who have always lived up there and who would make a serious problem for us if it became a question of zoning the town, in some way, as a last barrier against integration. What they say sounds very logical, and any stranger would be apt to accept the explanation at face value. But the truth of the matter is that there are people here who dislike the memory of the Logans even more than they do the prospect of integration. They are willing to risk integration in order to see that last Logan dispossessed of his last piece of real estate in Thomasville. With them it is a matter of superstition almost that until this happens Thomasville will not begin to realize its immemorial aspirations to grow and become a citified place.

So that you will better understand this dislike of the Logan name, I will give you a few more details of their history here. In the beginning, and for a long while, the Logan family didn't seem to want to spoil Thomasville with their own presence even. General Logan laid out the town in 1816, naming it after a little son of his who died in infancy. But during the first generation the Logan wives stayed mostly over in Middle Tennessee, where they felt there were more people of their own kind. And the men came and went only as their interest in the cotton crops required. In those years, Logana was occupied by a succession of slave-driving overseers, as was also the Logans' other, Suzannehouse, which used to stand five miles below here at Logan's Landing.

Now, we might have done without the Logan women and without the county seat, which the women didn't want here, but when the Logans kept the railroad out everybody saw the handwriting on the wall. The general's grandson did that. He was Harwell Logan, for many years chief justice of the state, and a man so powerful that in one breath, so to speak, he could deny the railroad company a right of way through town and demand that it give the name Logan Station to our nearest flag stop . . . And what was it the chief justice's son did? Why, it was he who prevented the cotton mill and snuff factory from locating here. The snuff factory would have polluted the air. And the cotton mill would have drawn in the riffraff from all over the county . . . Along about the turn of the century it looked as though we were going to get the insane aslyum for West Tennessee, but one of the Logans was governor of the state; he arranged for it to go to Bolivar instead. Even by then, none of the Logan men was coming back here very much except to hunt birds in the fall. They had already scattered out and were living in the big cities where there was plenty of industry and railroads for them to invest their money in; and they had already sold off most of their land to get the money to invest. But they didn't forget Thomasville. No matter how far up in the world a Logan may advance, he seems to go on having sweet dreams about Thomasville. Even though he has never actually lived here himself, Thomasville is the one place he doesn't want spoiled.

Just after the First World War, there was talk of our getting the new veterans' hospital. During the Depression, we heard about a CCC[6] camp. At the beginning of the Second World War, people came down from Washington and took option on big tracts of land for "Camp Logan." Very mysteriously all of those projects failed to materialize. Like everything else, they would have spoiled the town. But what else is there, I ask you, for a town to have except the things that tend to spoil it? What else is there to give it life? We used to have a boys' academy here, and a girls' institute, which is where Miss Leonora did her first teaching. They were boarding schools, and boys and girls came here from everywhere, and spent their money on the public square. It wasn't much, but it was *something*.

The boys' academy closed down before I was born even, and there isn't a trace left of it. The Thomasville Female Institute burned in 1922, and nothing is left of it, either, except the crumbing shells of

6. Civilian Conservation Corps, an agency of the U.S. government operated from 1933–1943 to provide employment and work to conserve natural resources.

the old brick buildings. All we have now that you don't see on the square is the cotton gin and the flour mill and the ice plant. We claim a population of eighteen hundred, counting white and colored, which is about five hundred short of what we claimed in the year 1880. It has been suggested that in the next census we count the trees in Thomasville instead of the people. They outnumber us considerably and they have more influence, too. It was to save the willow oaks on the public square and the giant sycamores along High Street that someone arranged to have the Memphis-Chattanooga bypass built in 1952 instead of bringing the new highway through town. It was some Logan who arranged that, you may be sure, and no doubt it gladdens his heart to see the new motels that have gone up out there and to know that the old hotel on the square is never overcrowded by a lot of silly tourists.

To my mind, Miss Leonora Logan is a very beautiful woman. But to think she is beautiful nowadays perhaps you would have to have first seen her as I did when I was not yet five years old. And perhaps you would have to have seen her under the same circumstances exactly.

I don't remember what the occasion was. We were on a picnic of some kind at Bennett's Wood, and it seems to me that half the town was there. Probably it was the Fourth of July, though I don't remember any flags or speeches. A band was playing in the bandstand, and as I walked along between my mother and father I noticed that the trunks of the walnut trees had been freshly white-washed. The bare earth at the roots of the trees was still dappled with the droppings from the lime buckets. My father pointed out a row of beehives on the far edge of the grove and said he hoped to God nobody would stir the bees up today as some bad boys had once done when there was an outing at Bennett's Wood. My father smiled at Mother when he said this, and my guess is that he had been amongst the boys who did it. My mother smiled, too, and we continued our walk.

It was just before dusk. My impression is that the actual picnicking and the main events of the day were already over. I was holding my mother's hand as we came out from under the trees and into the clearing where Bennett's Pond is. Several groups were out on the pond in rowboats, drifting about among the lily pads. One boat had just drawn up to the grassy bank on the side where we were. My mother leaned toward my father and said in a quiet voice, "Look at Miss Leonora Logan. Isn't she beautiful!"

She was dressed all in white. She had stood up in the boat the moment it touched shore, and it seemed to me that she had risen out of the water itself and were about to step from one of the lily pads onto the bank. I was aware of her being taller than most women whose beauty I had heard admired, and I knew that she was already spoken of as an old maid—that she was older than my mother even; but when she placed the pointed toe of her white shoe on the green sod beside the pond, it was as if that lovely white point had pierced my soul and awakened me to a beauty I had not dreamed of. Her every movement was all lightness and grace, and her head of yellow hair dazzled.

The last rays of the sun were at that moment coming directly toward me across the pond, and presently I had to turn my face away from its glare. But I had the feeling that it was Miss Leonora's eyes and the burning beauty of her countenance that had suddenly blinded me, and when my mother asked me fretfully what was the matter and why I hung back so, I was ashamed. I imagined that Mother could read the thoughts in my head. I imagined also that my mother, who was a plain woman and who as the wife of the hotelkeeper made no pretension to elegance—I imagined that she was now jealous of my admiration for Miss Leonora. With my face still averted, I silently reproached her for having herself suggested the thoughts to me by her remark to my father. I was very angry, and my anger and shame must have brought a deep blush to my whole face and neck. I felt my mother's two fingers thrust under the collar of my middy, and then I was soothed by her sympathetic voice saying "Why, child, you're feverish. We'd better get you home."

I must have had many a glimpse of Miss Leonora when I was a small boy playing on the hotel porch. But the next profound impression she made on me was when I was nine years old. One of the boarding students at the Institute had been stealing the other girls' things. It fell to Miss Leonora to apprehend the thief, who proved to be none other than a member of the Logan clan itself—a sad-faced, unattractive girl, according to all reports, but from a very rich branch of the family. She had been sent back to Thomasville to school all the way from Omaha, Nebraska.

Several hours after Miss Leonora had obtained unmistakable evidence of the girl's guilt and had told her she was to be sent home, it was discovered that the girl had disappeared. Word got out in the town that they were dragging the moat around the old windmill on the Institute grounds for the girl's body. Soon a crowd of townspeople gathered on the lawn before the Institute, near to where the windmill stood. This windmill was no longer used to pump the school's water—the school had town water by then—and there was not even a shaft or any vanes in evidence. But the old brick tower had been left standing. With its moat of stagnant, mossy water around it, it was thought to be picturesque.

The crowd assembled on the lawn some fifty or sixty feet away from the tower, and from there we watched the two Negro men at their work in the moat. The moat was fed by a sluggish wet-weather spring. It was about twenty feet wide and was estimated to be from ten to fifteen feet deep. And so the two men had had to bring in a boat to do their work from. On the very edge of the moat stood Miss Leonora, alongside Dr. Perkins, the chancellor of the Institute, and with them were several other teachers in their dark-blue uniforms. They all kept staring up at the windows of the old brick residence hall, as if to make sure that none of the girls was peering out at the distressing scene.

Presently we heard one of the Negro men say something to the other and heard the other mumble something in reply. We couldn't make out what they said, but we knew that they had found the girl's body. In a matter of two or three minutes they were hauling it up, and all the women teachers except Miss Leonora buried their faces in their hands. From where we were, the slimy object was hardly recognizable as anything human, but despite this, or because of it, the crowd sent up a chorus of gasps and groans.

Hearing our chorus, Miss Leonora whirled about. She glared at us across the stretch of lawn for a moment, and then she came striding toward us, waving both hands in the air and ordering us to leave. "Go away! Go away!" she called out. "What business have you coming here with your wailing and moaning? A lot you care about that dead girl!" As she drew nearer, I could see her glancing at the ground now and then as if looking for a stick to drive us away with. "Go away!" she cried. "Take your curious eyes away. What right have you to be curious about *our* dead?"

A general retreat began, down the lawn and through the open gateway in the spiked iron fence. I hurried along with the others, but I kept looking back at Miss Leonora, who now stood on the brow of the terraced lawn, watching the retreat with a proud, bemused expression, seeming for the moment to have forgotten the dead young woman in the moat.

How handsome she was standing there, with her high color and her thick yellow hair that seemed about to come loose on her head and fall down on the shoulders of her blue shirtwaist.

Beyond her I had glimpses of the two Negro men lifting the dead body out of the water. They moved slowly and cautiously, but after they had got the girl into the boat and were trying to move her out of the boat onto the lawn, I saw the girl's head fall back. Her wet hair hung down like Spanish moss beneath her, and when the winter sunlight struck it, all at once it looked as green as seaweed. It was very beautiful, and yet, of course, I didn't feel right in thinking it was. It is something I have never been able to forget.

One day when we were in high school, a girl in the class asked Miss Leonora to tell us about "the Institute girl who did away with herself"—because Miss Leonora did sometimes tell us about the old days at the Institute. She stood looking out the classroom window, and seemed to be going over the incident in her mind and trying to decide whether or not it was something we ought to know more about. Finally she said, "No, we'll go on with the lesson now."

But the class, having observed her moment of indecision, began to beg. "Please tell us, Miss Leonora. Please." I don't know how many of the others had been in the crowd that day when they pulled the girl out of the moat. I was not the only one, I'm sure. I think that everybody knew most of the details and only wanted to see if she would refer to the way it ended with her driving the crowd away. But Miss Leonora wouldn't have cared at all, even if she had thought that was our motive. She would have given us her version if she had wanted to.

"Open your books," she said.

But still we persisted, and I was bold enough to ask, "Why not?"

"I'll just tell you why not," she said, suddenly blazing out at me. "Because there is nothing instructive in the story for you."

After that day, I realized, as never before, that though she often seemed to wander from the subject in class, it was never really so. She was eternally instructing us. If only once she had let up on the instruction, we might have learned something—or I might have. I used to watch her for a sign—any sign—of her caring about what we thought of her, or of her *not* caring about her mission among us, if that's what it was. More and more it came to seem incredible to me that she was the same woman I had gone feverish over at Bennett's Wood that time, which was probably before Miss Leonora had perceived her mission. And yet I have the feeling she was the same woman still. Looking back on those high-school days, I know that all along she was watching me and others like me for some kind of sign from us—any sign—that would make us seem worthy of knowing what we wanted to know about her.

I suppose that what we wanted to know, beyond any doubt, was that the old lady had suffered for being just what she was—for being born with her cold, rigid, intellectual nature, and for being born to represent something that had never taken root in Thomasville and that would surely die with her. But not knowing that that was what we wanted to know, we looked for other, smaller things. She didn't, for instance, have lunch in the lunchroom with the other teachers, and she didn't go home for lunch. She had a Negro woman bring her lunch to her on a tray all the way from Logana, on the other side of town. Generally she ate alone in her classroom. Sometimes we made excuses to go back to the room during lunch hour, and when we came out we pretended to the others that we had had a great revelation—that we had caught Miss Leonora Logan eating peas with her knife or sopping her plate with a biscuit. We never caught her doing anything so improper, of course, but it gave us a wonderful pleasure to imagine it.

It was while I was in high school that Miss Leonora inherited

Logana. She had already been living in the house most of her life—all of it except for the years when she taught and lived at the Institute—but the house had really belonged to her grandfather's brother in St. Louis. The morning we heard she had inherited the place, we thought surely she would be in high spirits about her good fortune, and before she came into the room that morning one of the girls said she was going to ask her how it felt to be an heiress. It was a question that never got asked, however, because when our teacher finally appeared before us she was dressed in black. She had inherited the house where she had lived most of her life as a poor relation, but she was also in mourning for the dead great-uncle away in St. Louis. For us it was impossible to detect either the joy over the one event or grief over the other. Perhaps she felt neither, or perhaps she had to hide her feelings because she felt that it was really the great-uncle's death in St. Louis she had inherited and the house in Thomasville she had lost. Our lessons went on that day as though nothing at all had happened.

But before I ever started going to the high school, and before Miss Leonora went there to teach, I had seen her on yet another memorable occasion up at the Institute—the most memorable and dramatic of all, because it was the night that the place burned down. I remember the events of that night very clearly. It was a February night in 1922. The temperature was in the low twenties, and no doubt they had thrown open the drafts in every one of the coal-burning heaters up at the Institute.

The fire broke out in the refectory and spread very rapidly to the residence hall and the classrooms building. Like any big fire, it quickly drew the whole town to the scene. Before most of us got there it was already out of hand. All over town the sky looked like Judgment Day. On the way to the fire, we could hear the floors of the old buildings caving in, one after the other; and so from the beginning there was not much anybody could do. The town water-works couldn't get enough pressure up there to be of any real use, and after that girl drowned herself they had filled in the old moat around the windmill.

The first thing that happened after I got in sight of the place was that the gingerbread porches,[7] which were already on fire, began to fall away from the buildings. There were porches on the second and third floors of the residence hall, and suddenly they fell away like flaming ladders that somebody had given a kick to. The banisters and posts and rafters fell out into the evergreen shrubbery, and pretty soon the smell of burning hemlock and cedar filled the air . . . The teachers had got all the girls out safely, and the first men to arrive even saved some of the furniture and the books, but beyond that there was nothing to

7. Wooden porches characterized by elaborate scrollwork.

be done except to stand and watch the flames devour the innards of the buildings. This was very fascinating to everybody, and the crowd shifted from one point to another, always trying to get a better view and to see into which room or down which corridor the flames would move next.

Miss Leonora was as fascinated as any of the rest of us, and it was this about her that impressed me that night. It was not till later that I heard about how she behaved during the first phase of the fire. She had dashed about from building to building screaming orders to everyone, even to the fire brigade when it arrived. She would not believe it when the firemen told her that the water pressure could not be increased. She threw a bucket of water in one man's face when he refused to take that bucket and climb up a second-story porch with it.

I didn't see any of that. When I arrived, Miss Leonora was already resigned to the total loss that was inevitable. On a little knob of earth on the north side of the lawn, which people used to call the Indian Mound, she had taken her position all alone and isolated from the general crowd. The other teachers had been sent off with the Institute girls to the hotel, where my mother was waiting to receive them. But wrapped in a black fur cape—it was bearskin, I think, and must have been a hand-me-down from some relative—Miss Leonora was seated on one of the iron benches that were grouped over there on the mound. Her only companions were two iron deer that stood nearby, one with its head lowered as if grazing, the other with its iron antlers lifted and its blank iron eyes fixed on the burning buildings.

She sat there very erect, looking straight ahead. It was hard to tell whether she was watching the flames or watching the people watch the flames. Perhaps she was fascinated equally by both. It was all over for her. She knew that practically nothing was going to be saved, but still she wanted to see how it would go. Now and then a shaft of flame would shoot up into the overcast sky, lighting up the mixture of cloud and smoke above us, and also lighting up the figure of Miss Leonora over on the mound. Some of the women whispered amongst themselves, "Poor Miss Leonora! The school was her life." But if you caught a glimpse of her in one of those moments when the brightest light was on her, it wasn't self-pity or despair you saw written on her face. You saw her awareness of what was going on around her, and a kind of curiosity about it all that seemed almost inhuman and that even a child was bound to resent somewhat. She looked dead herself, but at the same time very much alive to what was going on around her.

III

When Miss Leonora's house was condemned two weeks ago, *somebody* had to break the news to her. They couldn't just send the clerk up there with the notice, or, worse still, let her read it in the newspaper. The old lady had to be warned of how matters had gone . . . We left the courthouse at four o'clock that afternoon, and set out for the Logan place on foot. None of us wanted to go, but who else would go if we didn't? That was how Judge Potter had put it to us. I suppose we elected to go on foot merely because it would take longer to get up there that way.

It was while we walked along under the sycamores on High Street that I let the others talk me into doing the job alone. They said that I had, after all, been her very favorite—by which they meant only that I was her first favorite—and that if we went in a group she might take it as a sign of cowardice, might even tell us it was that to our faces. It was a funny business, and we laughed about it a little amongst ourselves, though not much. Finally, I agreed that the other three men should wait behind the sumac and elderberry down in the lane, while I went up to see Miss Leonora alone.

Once this was settled, the other three men turned to reminiscing about their experiences with Miss Leonora when they were in high school. But I couldn't concentrate on what they said. It may have been because I knew their stories so well. Or maybe it wasn't that. At any rate, when we had walked two blocks up High Street I realized that I was out of cigarettes, and I told the others to wait a minute while I stepped into the filling station, on the corner there, to buy a package. When I paid for the cigarettes, Buck Wallace, who operates the station, looked at me and said, "Well, how did it go? Do we condemn?"

I nodded and said, "We're on the way up there to tell her, Buck."

"I guessed you were," he said. He glanced out the windows at the others, and I looked out at them, too. For a second it seemed that I was seeing them through Buck Wallace's eyes—them and myself. And the next second it seemed, for some reason, that I was seeing them through Miss Leonora's eyes—them and myself. We all had on our business suits, our lightweight topcoats, our gray fedoras; we were the innkeeper, the druggist, a bank clerk, and the rewrite man from the weekly paper. Our ages range from thirty to fifty—with me at the top—but we were every one of us decked out to look like the same kind of thing. We might have just that minute walked out of the Friday-noon meeting of the Exchange Club. In Buck Wallace's eyes, however, we were certainly not the cream of the Exchange Club crop—*not* the men who were going to get Thomasville its due. And in Miss Leonora's eyes we were a cut above the Exchange Club's ringleaders, though not enough above them to matter very much. To both her and Buck we were merely the go-betweens. It just happened that we were the last people left in town that the old lady would speak to, and so now we—or, rather, I—was going up to Logana and tell her she would have to accept the town's terms of unconditional surrender.

"You may be too late," Buck added as I was turning away. I looked back at him with lifted eyebrows. "She was in here a while ago," he went on to report, "getting her car gassed up. She said how she was about to take off on one of her trips. She said she might wait till she heard from the courthouse this afternoon and again she might not . . . She was got up kind of peculiar."

When I rejoined the other men outside, I didn't tell them what Buck had said. Suddenly I mistrusted them, and I didn't trust myself. Or rather I knew I *could* trust myself to let *them* have their way if they thought Miss Leonora was about to leave town. I was pretty sure she wouldn't leave without hearing from us, and I was pretty sure they would want to head us back to the courthouse immediately and send official word up there before she could get away. It would have been the wise thing to do, but I didn't let it happen.

In the filling station Buck Wallace had said to me that she was "got up kind of peculiar," and that meant, to my understanding, that Miss Leonora was dressed in one of two ways. Neither was a way that I had ever seen her dressed, and I wanted to see for myself. It meant either that she was got up in a lot of outmoded finery or she was wearing her dungarees! Because that is how, for ten years now, the old lady has been turning up at the tourist homes where she stops, and that is how, if you wanted to recognize her on the road, you would have to watch out for her. Either she would be in her finery—with the fox fur piece, and the diamond earrings, and the high-crowned velvet hat, and the kind of lace choker that even old ladies don't generally go in for any more and that Miss Leonora has never been seen to wear in Thomasville except by a very few—or she would be in her dungarees! The dungarees are the hardest to imagine, of course. With them she wears a home-knit, knee-length cardigan sweater. And for headgear she pulls on a big poke bonnet she has resurrected from somewhere, or sometimes she stuffs her long hair up under a man's hunting cap or an old broad-brimmed straw hat. A queer sight she must present riding about the countryside these autumn nights; and if she rides with the top of her convertible put back, as I've heard of her doing in the dead of winter even, why, it's enough to scare any children who may see her and some grown people, too . . . Here in Thomasville, only Buck Wallace and a few others have seen her so garbed, and they only rarely, only sometimes when she was setting out on a trip. They say she looks like some inmate who has broken out of the asylum over at Bolivar.

But that's how she turns up at the tourist homes. If she is with the two old maids at Boxwood Manor or Maple Lawn, she affects the choker and the diamond earrings. She sits down in their parlor and removes the high-crowned velvet, and she talks about how the traditions and institutions of our country have been corrupted and says that soon not one stone will be left upon another. And, still using such terms and phrases, she will at last get round to telling them the story of her life and the history of the Logan family in Thomasville. She tells it all in the third person, pretending it is some friend of hers she has in mind, and the family of that friend. But the old maids know right along that it is herself she is speaking of, and they say she seems to know they know it and seems not to care . . . And if she is with the farm couple at Oak Crest, then she's in her dungarees. She at once sets about helping with the chores, if they will let her. She talks religion to them and says there is no religion left amongst the people in the towns, says that they have forsaken the fountain of living waters and hewed them out broken cisterns that can hold no water—or something like that. And finally she gets round to telling *them* her story, again pretending that it is some friend of hers she is speaking of, and again with her listeners knowing it is herself. The farm couple won't like seeing an old woman wearing dungarees, but they will catch the spirit of her get-up, and they understand what it means. For they have known other old women there in the country who, thrown entirely on their own, living alone and in desperate circumstances, have gotten so they dress in some such outrageous way. And the two old maids probably still have some eye for fashion and they find Miss Leonora pretty ridiculous. But they remember other old ladies who did once dress like that, and it seems somehow credible that there might still be one somewhere.

When Miss Leonora is at home in Thomasville, it is hard to believe she ever dresses herself up so. Here we are used to seeing her always in the most schoolteacherish, ready-made-looking clothes. After the Institute burned, she changed from the uniform that the Institute teachers wore to what amounts to a uniform for our high-school teachers—the drab kind of street dresses that can be got through the mail-order catalogues. Right up till two weeks ago, that's how we were still seeing the old lady dressed. It was hard to realize that in her old age she had had a change of heart and was wishing that either she had played the role of the spinster great lady the way it is usually played or that she had married some dirt farmer and spent her life working alongside him in the fields.

I even used to think that perhaps Miss Leonora didn't really want to go off masquerading around the country—that it was a kind of madness and meant something that would be much more difficult to explain, and that all the time she was at home she was dreading her next seizure. Recently, however, I've come to realize that that wasn't the case. For years, her only satisfaction in life has been her periodic escapes into a reality that is scattered in bits and pieces along the highways and back roads of the country she travels. And what I hope above all else is that Miss Leonora *is* stopping today at Oak Crest or Boxwood Manor and *does* have on her dungarees or lace choker.

But now I must tell what makes me doubt that she is, after all, staying at one of those tourist homes she likes, and what makes me afraid that we may never see her here again.

I left the other men down at the corner of the lane and went up the dirt driveway to Logana alone. Her car was parked at the foot of the porch steps, and so there was no question about her being there. I saw her first through one of the sidelights at the front door and wasn't sure it was she. Then she opened the door, saying, "Dear boy, come in." I laughed, it was so unlike her to call me that. That was not her line at all. She laughed, too, but it was a kind of laugh that was supposed to put me at my ease rather than to criticize or commend me, which would have been very much more in her line . . . I saw at a glance that this wasn't the Miss Leonora I had known, and wasn't one that I had heard about from her tourist-home friends, either.

She had done an awful thing to her hair. Her splendid white mane, with its faded yellow streaks and its look of being kept up on her head only by the two tortoise-shell combs at the back, was no more. She had cut it off, thinned it, and set it in little waves close to her head, and, worse still, she must have washed it in a solution of indigo bluing. She had powdered the shine off her nose, seemed almost to have powered its sharpness and longness away. She may have applied a little rouge and lipstick, though hardly enough to be noticeable, only enough to make you realize it wasn't the natural coloring of an old lady and enough to make you *think* how old she was. And the dress she had on was exactly right with the hair and the face, though at first I couldn't tell why.

As I walked beside her from the center hall into her "office," her skirt made an unpleasant swishing sound that seemed out of place in Miss Leonora's house and that made me observe more closely what the dress was really like. It was of a dark silk stuff, very stiff, with a sort of middy-blouse collar, and sleeves that stopped a couple of inches above the wrists, and a little piece of belt in back, fastened on with two big buttons—very stylish, I think. For a minute I couldn't remember where it was I had seen this very woman before. Then it came to me. All that was lacking was a pair of pixie glasses with rhinestone rims, and a half dozen bracelets on her wrists. She was one of those old women who come out here from Memphis looking for antiques and country hams and who tell you how delighted they are to find a Southern town that is truly unchanged.

Even so, I half expected Miss Leonora to begin by asking me about my family and then about what kind of summer I had had. "Now, I know you have had a fine summer—all summers are fine to a boy your age," she would say. "So don't tell me what you have been doing. Tell me what you have been *thinking*, what you have been *reading*." It was the room that made me imagine she would still go on that way. Because the room was the same as it used to be. Even the same coffee cups and blue china coffeepot were set out on the little octagonal oak table, beside the plate of butter cookies. And for a moment I had the same guilty feeling I used always to have; because, of course, I hadn't been reading anything and hadn't been thinking anything she would want to hear about.

What she actually said was much kinder and was what anybody might have said under the circumstances. "I've felt so bad about your having to come here like this. I knew they would put it off on you. Even you must have dreaded coming, and you must hate me for putting you in such a position."

"Why, no. I wanted to come, Miss Leonora," I lied. "And I hope you have understood that I had no part in the proceedings." It was what, for months, I had known I would say, and it came out very easily.

"I do understand that," she said. "And we don't even need to talk about any of it."

But I said, "The county court has granted the writ condemning your property. They will send a notice up to you tomorrow morning. You ought to have had a lawyer represent you, and you ought to have come yourself."

I had said what I had promised Judge Potter I would say; she had her warning. And now I was on my own. She motioned me to sit down in a chair near the table where the coffee things were. When she poured out the coffee into our two cups, it was steaming hot. It smelled the way it used to smell in that room on winter afternoons, as fresh as if it were still brewing on the stove. I knew she hadn't made it herself, but, as in the old days, too, the Negro woman who had made it didn't appear or make a sound in the kitchen. You wouldn't have thought there was one of them on the place. There didn't seem to be another soul in the house but just herself and me. But *I* knew that the house was full of them, really. And there was still the feeling that either she was protecting me from them or them from me. I experienced the old uneasiness in addition to something new. And as for Miss Leonora, she seemed to sense from the start that the other three men were waiting down the lane—the three who had been even less willing than I to come, and who were that much nearer to the rest of the town in their feelings.

Several times she referred to them, giving a little nod of her head in the directions of the very spot where I had left them waiting.

"When I think of the old days, the days when I used to have you up here—you and the others, too—I realize I was too hard on you. I asked too much of my pupils. I know that now."

It was nothing like the things the real Miss Leonora used to say. It was something anybody might have said.

And a little later: "I was unrealistic. I tried to be to you children what I thought you needed to have somebody be. That's a mistake, always. One has to try to be with people what they want one to be. Each of *you* tried to be that for me, to an admirable degree. Tim Hadley tried hardest—he went to college—but he didn't have your natural endowments." Then she took pains to say something good and something forgiving about each of the four. And, unless I imagined it, for each of those that hadn't come up with me she gave another nod in the direction of the elderberry and sumac thicket down at the corner.

"We were a dumb bunch, all along the line," I said, not meaning it—or not meaning it about myself.

"Nonsense. You were all fine boys, and *you* were my brightest hope," she said, with an empty cheerfulness.

"But you can't make a silk purse out of—" I began.

"Nonsense," she said again. "It was neither you nor I that failed." But she didn't care enough to make any further denial or explanation. She set her cup down on the table and rose from her chair. "It's been like old times, hasn't it," she said with a vague smile.

I looked away from her and sat gazing about the office, still holding my empty cup in my hand. It hadn't been like old times at all, of course. The room and the silence of the house were the same, but Miss Leonora was already gone, and without her the house was nothing but a heap of junk. I thought to myself that the best thing that could happen would be for them to begin moving out the furniture and moving out the Negroes and tearing the place down as soon as possible. Suddenly, I spied her black leather traveling bag over beside the doorway, and she must have seen my eyes light upon it. "I'm about to get off on a little trip," she said.

I set my cup down on the table and looked up at her. I could see she was expecting me to protest. "Will it be long?" I asked, not protesting.

"I don't know, dear boy. You know how I am."

I glanced at the traveling bag again, and this time I noticed her new cloth coat lying on the straight chair beside the bag. I got up and went over and picked up the coat and held it for her.

On the way out to the car, I kept reminding myself that this was really Miss Leonora Logan and that she was going away before receiving any official notice of the jury's verdict. Finally, when we were standing beside her car and she was waiting for me to put the bag, which I was carrying, inside the car, I looked squarely into her eyes. And there is no denying it; the eyes were still the same as always, not just their hazel color but their expression, their look of awareness—awareness of you, the individual before her, a very flattering awareness until presently you realized it was merely of you as an individual in her scheme of things for Thomasville. She was still looking at me as though I were one of the village children that she would like so much to make something of. I opened the car door. I tossed the bag into the space behind the driver's seat. I even made sure I did the thing to her satisfaction by putting one hand out to her elbow as she slipped stiffly in under the steering wheel.

Neither of us made any pretense of saying goodbye. I stood there and watched the car as it bumped along down the driveway, raising a little cloud of dust in the autumn air. The last I saw of her was a glimpse of her bluinged head through the rear window of her convertible. When she turned out into the lane and headed away from town toward the bypass, I knew that the other three men would be watching. But they wouldn't be able to see how she was got up, and I knew they would hardly believe me when I told them.

I have told nearly everybody in town about it, and I think nobody really believes me. I have almost come to doubt it myself. And, anyway, I like to think that in her traveling bag she had the lace-choker outfit that she could change into along the way, and the dungarees, too; and that she is stopping at her usual kind of place today and is talking to the proprietors about Thomasville. Otherwise, there is no use in anyone's keeping an eye out for her. She will look too much like a thousand others, and no doubt will be driving on the highway the way everybody else does, letting other people pass her, dimming her lights for everyone. Maybe she even drives in the daytime, and maybe when she stops for the night it is at a big, modern motel with air conditioning and television in every room. The postcards she sends us indicate nothing about how she is dressed, of course, or about where and in what kind of places she is stopping. She says only that she is in good health, that it is wonderful weather for driving about the country, and that the roads have been improved everywhere. She says nothing about when we can expect her to come home.

---

1. What opposing views of "progress" are in conflict here? Who represents each of these views? Does the narrator espouse any of them?
2. Since the question of Miss Leonora's sanity is raised, discuss the evidence for considering her to be mentally ill.

3. Discuss the narrator's question: "What else is there . . . for a town to have except the things that tend to spoil it?"
4. Part of the town's tradition involves the relation of black and white people. What does the story say about progress or change in this relationship?
5. Has Miss Leonora at last conceded that her lifetime struggle was useless? If so, who or what is to blame for her defeat?
6. What is the meaning of her clothing and hairstyle when she is last seen by the narrator? How has the author used these details to round out the theme of the story?

James Thurber

Thurber (1894–1961) was born in Columbus, Ohio. The loss of an eye in boyhood kept him from military service in World War I, but he served in Europe as a code clerk and after some time as a reporter for the Columbus Dispatch, *he returned to Paris in 1924 to sample the world of the expatriate. He was back in New York by 1926, submitting his humorous pieces to* The New Yorker *in its early days, working briefly as its managing editor and then contributing regularly to its "Talk of the Town" department. Thurber had drawn before he began to write, and* The New Yorker *printed several series of his cartoons as well as fables, essays, comment, and short stories through the many years of his association with the magazine. With his friend Elliott Nugent he wrote a successful play,* The Male Animal *(1940). His zany humor—with its occasional bite of terror and dismay—follows no formula. His carefully wrought style faithfully embodies the richness of the American vernacular. Most of his books contain mixed offerings of stories, essays, fables, and cartoons. Among them are* Fables for Our Time *(1940),* My World—and Welcome to It *(1942),* The Thurber Carnival *(1945), and* Thurber Country *(1953).*

The Secret Life of Walter Mitty

"We're going through!" The Commander's voice was like thin ice breaking. He wore his full-dress uniform, with the heavily braided white cap pulled down rakishly over one cold gray eye. "We can't make it, sir. It's spoiling for a hurricane, if you ask me." "I'm not asking you, Lieutenant Berg," said the Commander. "Throw on the power lights! Rev her up to 8,500! We're going through!" The pounding of the cylinders increased: ta-pocketa-pocketa-pocketa-*pocketa-pocketa*. The Commander stared at the ice forming on the pilot window. He walked over and twisted a row of complicated dials. "Switch on No. 8 auxiliary!" he shouted. "Switch on No. 8 auxiliary!" repeated Lieutenant Berg. "Full strength in No. 3 turret!" shouted the Commander. "Full strength in No. 3 turret!" The crew, bending to their various tasks in the huge, hurtling eight-engined Navy hydroplane, looked at each other and grinned. "The Old Man'll get us through," they said to one another. "The Old Man ain't afraid of Hell!" . . .

"Not so fast! You're driving too fast!" said Mrs. Mitty. "What are you driving so fast for?"

"Hmm?" said Walter Mitty. He looked at his wife, in the seat beside him, with shocked astonishment. She seemed grossly unfamiliar, like a strange woman who had yelled at him in a crowd. "You were up to fifty-five," she said. "You know I don't like to go more than forty. You were up to fifty-five." Walter Mitty drove on toward Waterbury in silence, the roaring of the SN202 through the worst storm in twenty years of Navy flying fading in the remote, intimate airways of his mind. "You're tensed up again," said Mrs. Mitty. "It's one of your days. I wish you'd let Dr. Renshaw look you over."

Walter Mitty stopped the car in front of the building where his wife went to have her hair done. "Remember to get those overshoes while I'm having my hair done," she said. "I don't need overshoes," said Mitty. She put her mirror back into her bag. "We've been all through that," she said, getting out of the car. "You're not a young man any longer." He raced the engine a little. "Why don't you wear your gloves? Have you lost your gloves?" Walter Mitty reached in a pocket and brought out the gloves. He put them on, but after she had turned and gone into the building and he had driven on to a red light, he took them off again. "Pick it up, brother!" snapped a cop as the light changed, and Mitty hastily pulled on his gloves and lurched ahead. He drove around the streets aimlessly for a time, and then he drove past the hospital on his way to the parking lot.

. . . "It's the millionaire banker, Wellington McMillan," said the pretty nurse. "Yes?" said Walter Mitty, removing his gloves slowly. "Who has the case?" "Dr. Renshaw and Dr. Benbow, but there are two specialists here, Dr. Remington from New York and Mr. Pritchard-Mitford from London. He flew over." A door opened down a long, cool corridor and Dr. Renshaw came out. He looked distraught and haggard. "Hello, Mitty," he said. "We're having the devil's own time with McMillan, the millionaire banker and close personal friend of Roosevelt. Obstreosis of the ductal tract. Tertiary.[1] Wish you'd take a look at him." "Glad to," said Mitty.

In the operating room there were whispered introductions: "Dr. Remington, Dr. Mitty. Mr. Pritchard-Mitford, Dr. Mitty." "I've read your book on streptothricosis," said Pritchard-Mitford, shaking hands. "A brilliant performance, sir." "Thank you," said Walter Mitty. "Didn't know you were in the States, Mitty," grumbled Remington. "Coals to Newcastle, bringing Mitford and me up here for a tertiary." "You are very kind," said Mitty. A huge, complicated machine, connected to

1. I.e., at the third—advanced—stage of the disease. "Obstreosis" and "streptothricosis" (below) are nonsense words for imaginary diseases.

the operating table, with many tubes and wires, began at this moment to go pocketa-pocketa-pocketa. "The new anesthetizer is giving way!" shouted an interne. "There is no one in the East who knows how to fix it!" "Quiet, man!" said Mitty, in a low, cool voice. He sprang to the machine, which was now going pocketa-pocketa-queep-pocketa-queep. He began fingering delicately a row of glistening dials: "Give me a fountain pen!" he snapped. Someone handed him a fountain pen. He pulled a faulty piston out of the machine and inserted the pen in its place. "That will hold for ten minutes," he said. "Get on with the operation." A nurse hurried over and whispered to Renshaw, and Mitty saw the man turn pale. "Coreopsis[2] has set in," said Renshaw nervously. "If you would take over, Mitty?" Mitty looked at him and at the craven figure of Benbow, who drank, and at the grave uncertain faces of the two great specialists. "If you wish," he said. They slipped a white gown on him; he adjusted a mask and drew on thin gloves; nurses handed him shining . . .

"Back it up, Mac! Look out for that Buick!" Walter Mitty jammed on the brakes. "Wrong lane, Mac," said the parking-lot attendant, looking at Mitty closely. "Gee. Yeh," muttered Mitty. He began cautiously to back out of the lane marked "Exit Only." "Leave her sit there," said the attendant: "I'll put her away." Mitty got out of the car. "Hey, better leave the key." "Oh," said Mitty, handing the man the ignition key. The attendant vaulted into the car, backed it up with insolent skill, and put it where it belonged.

They're so damn cocky, thought Walter Mitty, walking along Main Street; they think they know everything. Once he had tried to take his chains off, outside New Milford, and he had got them wound around the axles. A man had had to come out in a wrecking car and unwind them, a young, grinning garageman. Since then Mrs. Mitty always made him drive to a garage to have the chains taken off. The next time, he thought, I'll wear my right arm in a sling; they won't grin at me then. I'll have my right arm in a sling and they'll see I couldn't possibly take the chains off myself. He kicked at the slush on the sidewalk. "Overshoes," he said to himself, and he began looking for a shoe store.

When he came out into the street again, with the overshoes in a box under his arm, Walter Mitty began to wonder what the other thing was his wife had told him to get. She had told him, twice, before they set out from their house for Waterbury. In a way he hated these weekly trips to town—he was always getting something wrong. Kleenex, he thought, Squibb's, razor blades? No. Toothpaste, toothbrush, bicarbonate, carborundum, initiative and referendum? He gave it up. But she would remember it. "Where's the what's-its-name?" she would

2. A genus of herb, not a medical condition.

ask. "Don't tell me you forgot the what's-its-name." A newsboy went by shouting something about the Waterbury trial.

. . . "Perhaps this will refresh your memory." The District Attorney suddenly thrust a heavy automatic at the quiet figure on the witness stand. "Have you ever seen this before?" Walter Mitty took the gun and examined it expertly. "This is my Webley-Vickers 50.80," he said calmly. An excited buzz ran around the courtroom. The Judge rapped for order. "You are a crack shot with any sort of firearms, I believe?" said the District Attorney, insinuatingly. "Objection!" shouted Mitty's attorney. "We have shown that the defendant could not have fired the shot. We have shown that he wore his right arm in a sling on the night of the fourteenth of July." Walter Mitty raised his hand briefly and the bickering attorneys were stilled. "With any known make of gun," he said evenly, "I could have killed Gregory Fitzhurst at three hundred feet *with my left hand*." Pandemonium broke loose in the courtroom. A woman's scream rose above the bedlam and suddenly a lovely, dark-haired girl was in Walter Mitty's arms. The District Attorney struck at her savagely. Without rising from his chair, Mitty let the man have it on the point of the chin. "You miserable cur!" . . .

"Puppy biscuit," said Walter Mitty. He stopped walking and the buildings of Waterbury rose up out of the misty courtroom and surrounded him again. A woman who was passing laughed. "He said 'Puppy biscuit,' " she said to her companion. "That man said 'Puppy biscuit' to himself." Walter Mitty hurried on. He went into an A & P, not the first one he came to but a smaller one farther up the street. "I want some biscuit for small, young dogs," he said to the clerk. Any special brand, sir?" The greatest pistol shot in the world thought a moment. "It says 'Puppies Bark for It' on the box," said Walter Mitty.

His wife would be through at the hairdresser's in fifteen minutes, Mitty saw in looking at his watch, unless they had trouble drying it; sometimes they had trouble drying it. She didn't like to get to the hotel first; she would want him to be there waiting for her as usual. He found a big leather chair in the lobby, facing a window, and he put the overshoes and the puppy biscuit on the floor beside it. He picked up an old copy of *Liberty*[3] and sank down into the chair. "Can Germany Conquer the World Through the Air?" Walter Mitty looked at the pictures of bombing planes and of ruined streets.

. . . "The cannonading has got the wind up in young Raleigh, sir," said the sergeant. Captain Mitty looked up at him through tousled hair. "Get him to bed," he said wearily. "With the others. I'll fly alone."

3. Popular weekly magazine (1924–1951).

"But you can't sir," said the sergeant anxiously. "It takes two men to handle that bomber and the Archies[4] are pounding hell out of the air. Von Richtman's circus[5] is between here and Saulier." "Somebody's got to get that ammunition dump," said Mitty. "I'm going over. Spot of brandy?" He poured a drink for the sergeant and one for himself. War thundered and whined around the dugout[6] and battered at the door. There was a rending of wood and splinters flew through the room. "A bit of a near thing," said Captain Mitty carelessly. "The box barrage[7] is closing in," said the sergeant. "We only live once, Sergeant," said Mitty, with his faint, fleeting smile. "Or do we?" He poured another brandy and tossed it off. "I never see a man could hold his brandy like you, sir," said the sergeant. "Begging your pardon, sir." Captain Mitty stood up and strapped on his huge Webley-Vickers automatic. "It's forty kilometers through hell, sir," said the sergeant. Mitty finished one last brandy. "After all," he said softly, "what isn't?" The pounding of the cannon increased; there was the rat-tat-tatting of machine guns, and from somewhere came the menacing pocketa-pocketa-pocketa of the new flame-throwers. Walter Mitty walked to the door of the dugout humming "Auprès de Ma Blonde."[8] He turned and waved to the sergeant. "Cheerio!" he said. . . .

Something struck his shoulder. "I've been looking all over this hotel for you," said Mrs. Mitty. "Why do you have to hide in this old chair? How did you expect me to find you?" "Things close in," said Walter Mitty vaguely. "What?" Mrs. Mitty said. "Did you get the what's-its-name? The puppy biscuit? What's in that box?" "Overshoes," said Mitty. "Couldn't you have put them on in the store?" "I was thinking," said Walter Mitty. "Does it ever occur to you that I am sometimes thinking?" She looked at him. "I'm going to take your temperature when I get you home," she said.

They went out through the revolving doors that made a faintly derisive whistling sound when you pushed them. It was two blocks to the parking lot. At the drugstore on the corner she said, "Wait here for me. I forgot something. I won't be a minute." She was more than a minute. Walter Mitty lighted a cigarette. It began to rain, rain with sleet in it. He stood up against the wall of the drugstore, smoking. . . . He put his shoulders back and his heels together. "To hell with the handkerchief," said Walter Mitty scornfully. He took one last drag on his cigarette and snapped it away. Then, with that faint, fleeting smile

4. Slang for antiaircraft guns. 5. In World War I the battle groups of fighter squadrons were known as "flying circuses"; the group commanded by Baron Manfred von Richthofen (1892–1918) was the most deadly German flying circus. 6. Sheltered area dug out of the side of a trench. 7. An artillery barrage from all four sides. 8. "Close to My Blonde," French song popular during World War I.

playing about his lips, he faced the firing squad; erect and motionless, proud and disdainful, Walter Mitty the Undefeated, inscrutable to the last.

---

1. For what circumstances in his real life do Mitty's fantasies compensate?
2. Enumerate the details that link the fantasies with what is really happening.
3. In what sense may it be said that Mitty's fantasies reveal his character more truly than his behavior?
4. From what sources are the fantasies drawn?
5. What is the relationship between the last fantasy and all that has gone before? How does this fantasy shape the theme of the story?

Leo Tolstoy

Tolstoy (1828–1910)—generally considered the greatest of nineteenth-century novelists—was born at Yasnaya Polyana, Russia, into the Russian nobility. His youth was restless and without direction. He was vain, dissolute, and immoderate, a poor student and a reckless gambler. It was only after he entered military service that he became interested in writing—autobiographical stories first, then sketches of military life as he knew it during the Crimean War. Leaving the Army in 1857, he traveled in Western Europe, but his disdain for the vanities of cultured life was merely deepened by what he saw in Paris. On his return to Russia he started an experimental school for children, structuring it on generally anarchic principles. At the same time he was making the major effort that produced War and Peace *(1869) and* Anna Karenina *(1877), the novels that assure him his place in world literature. The former is an account of Russia in the years of Napoleon's conquests and his attempt to consolidate his empire by the conquest of Russia. The second is the story of a woman caught in the immemorial conflict of personal, biological, and social demands, whirled down to destruction by her inability to reconcile them. In spite of his triumph with these novels, Tolstoy, as he grew older, was painfully dissatisfied with them and considered them flawed by the earthly preoccupations he was trying to escape. He tried to appease his self-doubt by adopting a primitive version of Christianity that often put him at odds with the established church. For nearly twenty years he wrote chiefly on moral and spiritual matters, and these later moralistic writings, including the novel* The Resurrection *(1899), gave him enormous influence throughout the world as a guide to conscience. His home at Yasnaya Polyana became a mecca for pilgrims who sought his advice on the right way to live. Inside Russia his followers were persecuted by the government, though he himself remained immune from outward pressure. But he never found the inner peace for which he struggled; the turbulence of his mental conflicts moved him several times to leave his home and his wife, and on one of these tormented flights he died in a railway station.*

The Death of Ivan Ilych[1]

I

DURING an interval in the Melvinski trial in the large building of the Law Courts, the members and public prosecutor met in Ivan Egorovich Shebek's private room, where the conversation turned on the celebrated Krasovski case. Fëdor Vasilievich warmly maintained that it was not subject to their jurisdiction, Ivan Egorovich maintained the contrary, while Peter Ivanovich, not having entered into the discussion at the start, took no part in it but looked through the *Gazette* which had just been handed in.

"Gentlemen," he said, "Ivan Ilych has died!"

"You don't say so!"

"Here, read it yourself," replied Peter Ivanovich, handing Fëdor Vasilievich the paper still damp from the press. Surrounded by a black border were the words: "Praskovya Fëdorovna Golovina, with profound sorrow, informs relatives and friends of the demise of her beloved husband Ivan Ilych Golovin, Member of the Court of Justice, which occurred on February the 4th of this year 1882. The funeral will take place on Friday at one o'clock in the afternoon."

Ivan Ilych had been a colleague of the gentlemen present and was liked by them all. He had been ill for some weeks with an illness said to be incurable. His post had been kept open for him, but there had been conjectures that in case of his death Alexeev might receive his appointment, and that either Vinnikov or Shtabel would succeed Alexeev. So on receiving the news of Ivan Ilych's death the first thought of each of the gentlemen in that private room was of the changes and promotions it might occasion among themselves or their acquaintances.

"I shall be sure to get Shtabel's place or Vinnikov's," thought Fëdor Vasilievich. "I was promised that long ago, and the promotion means an extra eight hundred rubles a year for me besides the allowance."

"Now I must apply for my brother-in-law's transfer from Kaluga," thought Peter Ivanovich. "My wife will be very glad, and then she won't be able to say that I never do anything for her relations."

"I thought he would never leave his bed again," said Peter Ivanovich aloud. "It's very sad."

"But what really was the matter with him?"

1. Translated by Louise and Aylmer Maude.

"The doctors couldn't say—at least they could, but each of them said something different. When last I saw him I thought he was getting better."

"And I haven't been to see him since the holidays. I always meant to go."

"Had he any property?"

"I think his wife had a little—but something quite trifling."

"We shall have to go to see her, but they live so terribly far away."

"Far away from you, you mean. Everything's far away from your place."

"You see, he never can forgive my living on the other side of the river," said Peter Ivanovich, smiling at Shebek. Then, still talking of the distances between different parts of the city, they returned to the Court.

Besides considerations as to the possible transfers and promotions likely to result from Ivan Ilych's death, the mere fact of the death of a near acquaintance aroused, as usual, in all who heard of it the complacent feeling that, "it is he who is dead and not I."

Each one thought or felt, "Well, he's dead but I'm alive!" But the more intimate of Ivan Ilych's acquaintances, his so-called friends, could not help thinking also that they would now have to fulfil the very tiresome demands of propriety by attending the funeral service and paying a visit of condolence to the window.

Fëdor Vasilievich and Peter Ivanovich had been his nearest acquaintances. Peter Ivanovich had studied law with Ivan Ilych and had considered himself to be under obligations to him.

Having told his wife at dinner-time of Ivan Ilych's death and of his conjecture that it might be possible to get her brother transferred to their circuit,[2] Peter Ivanovich sacrificed his usual nap, put on his evening clothes, and drove to Ivan Ilych's house.

At the entrance stood a carriage and two cabs. Leaning against the wall in the hall downstairs near the cloak-stand was a coffin-lid covered with cloth of gold, ornamented with gold cord and tassels, that had been polished up with metal powder. Two ladies in black were taking off their fur cloaks. Peter Ivanovich recognized one of them as Ivan Ilych's sister, but the other was a stranger to him. His colleague Schwartz was just coming downstairs, but on seeing Peter Ivanovich enter he stopped and winked at him, as if to say: "Ivan Ilych has made a mess of things—not like you and me."

Schwartz's face with his Piccadilly whiskers and his slim figure in

2. District to which a judge is assigned.

evening dress, had as usual an air of elegant solemnity which contrasted with the playfulness of his character and had a special piquancy here, or so it seemed to Peter Ivanovich.

Peter Ivanovich allowed the ladies to precede him and slowly followed them upstairs. Schwartz did not come down but remained where he was, and Peter Ivanovich understood that he wanted to arrange where they should play bridge that evening. The ladies went upstairs to the widow's room, and Schwartz with seriously compressed lips but a playful look in his eyes, indicated by a twist of his eyebrows the room to the right where the body lay.

Peter Ivanovich, like everyone else on such occasions, entered feeling uncertain what he would have to do. All he knew was that at such times it is always safe to cross oneself. But he was not quite sure whether one should make obeisances while doing so. He therefore adopted a middle course. On entering the room he began crossing himself and made a slight movement resembling a bow. At the same time, as far as the motion of his head and arm allowed, he surveyed the room. Two young men—apparently nephews, one of whom was a high-school pupil—were leaving the room, crossing themselves as they did so. An old woman was standing motionless, and a lady with strangely arched eyebrows was saying something to her in a whisper. A vigorous, resolute Church Reader, in a frock-coat, was reading something in a loud voice with an expression that precluded any contradiction. The butler's assistant, Gerasim, stepping lightly in front of Peter Ivanovich, was strewing something on the floor. Noticing this, Peter Ivanovich was immediately aware of a faint odour of a decomposing body.

The last time he had called on Ivan Ilych, Peter Ivanovich had seen Gerasim in the study. Ivan Ilych had been particularly fond of him and he was performing the duty of a sick nurse.

Peter Ivanovich continued to make the sign of the cross slightly inclining his head in an intermediate direction between the coffin, the Reader, and the icons on the table in a corner of the room. Afterwards, when it seemed to him that this movement of his arm in crossing himself had gone on too long, he stopped and began to look at the corpse.

The dead man lay, as dead men always lie, in a specially heavy way, his rigid limbs sunk in the soft cushions of the coffin, with the head forever bowed on the pillow. His yellow waxen brow with bald patches over his sunken temples was thrust up in the way peculiar to the dead, the protruding nose seeming to press on the upper lip. He was much changed and had grown even thinner since Peter Ivanovich had last seen him, but, as is always the case with the dead, his face was handsomer and above all more dignified than when he was alive. The expression on the face said that what was necessary had been accomplished, and accomplished rightly. Besides this there was in that expression a reproach and a warning to the living. This warning seemed to Peter Ivanovich out of place, or at least not applicable to him. He felt a certain discomfort and so he hurriedly crossed himself once more and turned and went out the door—too hurriedly and too regardless of propriety, as he himself was aware.

Schwartz was waiting for him in the adjoining room with legs spread wide apart and both hands toying with his top-hat behind his back. The mere sight of that playful, well-groomed, and elegant figure refreshed Peter Ivanovich. He felt that Schwartz was above all these happenings and would not surrender to any depressing influences. His very look said that this incident of a church service for Ivan Ilych could not be a sufficient reason for infringing the order of the session—in other words, that it would certainly not prevent his unwrapping a new pack of cards and shuffling them that evening while a footman placed four fresh candles on the table: in fact, that there was no reason for supposing that this incident would hinder their spending the evening agreeably. Indeed he said this in a whisper as Peter Ivanovich passed him, proposing that they should meet for a game at Fëdor Vasilievich's. But apparently Peter Ivanovich was not destined to play bridge that evening. Praskovya Fëdorovna (a short, fat woman who despite all efforts to the contrary had continued to broaden steadily from her shoulders downwards and who had the same extraordinarily arched eyebrows as the lady who had been standing by the coffin), dressed all in black, her head covered with lace, came out of her own room with some other ladies, conducted them to the room where the dead body lay, and said: "The service will begin immediately. Please go in."

Schwartz, making an indefinite bow, stood still, evidently neither accepting nor declining this invitation. Praskovya Fëdorovna, recognizing Peter Ivanovich, sighed, went close up to him, took his hand, and said: "I know you were a true friend to Ivan Ilych . . ." and looked at him awaiting some suitable response. And Peter Ivanovich knew that, just as it had been the right thing to cross himself in that room, so what he had to do here was to press her hand, sigh, and say, "Believe me. . . ." So he did all this and as he did it felt that the desired result had been achieved: that both he and she were touched.

"Come with me. I want to speak to you before it begins," said the widow. "Give me your arm."

Peter Ivanovich gave her his arm and they went to the inner rooms, passing Schwartz, who winked at Peter Ivanovich compassionately.

"That does for our bridge! Don't object if we find another player. Perhaps you can cut in when you do escape," said his playful look.

Peter Ivanovich sighed still more deeply and despondently, and Praskovya Fëdorovna pressed his arm gratefully. When they reached the drawing-room, upholstered in pink cretonne and lighted by a dim lamp, they sat down at the table—she on a sofa and Peter Ivanovich on a low pouffe, the springs of which yielded spasmodically under his weight. Praskovya Fëdorovna had been on the point of warning him to take another seat, but felt that such a warning was out of keeping with her present condition and so changed her mind. As he sat down on the pouffe Peter Ivanovich recalled how Ivan Ilych had arranged this room and had consulted him regarding the pink cretonne with green leaves. The whole room was full of furniture and knick-knacks, and on her way to the sofa the lace of the widow's black shawl caught on the carved edge of the table. Peter Ivanovich rose to detach it, and the springs of the pouffe, relieved of his weight, rose also and gave him a push. The widow began detaching her shawl herself, and Peter Ivanovich again sat down, suppressing the rebellious springs of the pouffe under him. But the widow had not quite freed herself and Peter Ivanovich got up again, and again the pouffe rebelled and even creaked. When this was all over she took out a clean cambric handkerchief and began to weep. The episode with the shawl and the struggle with the pouffe had cooled Peter Ivanovich's emotions and he sat there with a sullen look on his face. This awkward situation was interrupted by Sokolov, Ivan Ilych's butler, who came to report that the plot in the cemetery that Praskovya Fëdorovna had chosen would cost two hundred rubles. She stopped weeping and, looking at Peter Ivanovich with the air of a victim, remarked in French that it was very hard for her. Peter Ivanovich made a silent gesture signifying his full conviction that it must indeed be so.

"Please smoke," she said in a magnanimous yet crushed voice, and turned to discuss with Sokolov the price of the plot for the grave.

Peter Ivanovich while lighting his cigarette heard her inquiring very circumstantially into the prices of different plots in the cemetery and finally decided which she would take. When that was done she gave instructions about engaging the choir. Sokolov then left the room.

"I look after everything myself," she told Peter Ivanovich, shifting the albums that lay on the table; and noticing that the table was endangered by his cigarette-ash, she immediately passed him an ash-tray, saying as she did so: "I consider it an affectation to say that my grief prevents my attending to practical affairs. On the contrary, if anything can—I won't say console me, but—distract me, it is seeing to everything concerning him." She again took out her handkerchief as if preparing to cry, but suddenly, as if mastering her feeling, she shook herself and began to speak calmly. "But there is something I want to talk to you about."

Peter Ivanovich bowed, keeping control of the springs of the pouffe, which immediately began quivering under him.

"He suffered terribly the last few days."

"Did he?" said Peter Ivanovich.

"Oh, terribly! He screamed unceasingly, not for minutes but for hours. For the last three days he screamed incessantly. It was unendurable. I cannot understand how I bore it; you could hear him three rooms off. Oh, what I have suffered!"

"Is it possible that he was conscious all that time?" asked Peter Ivanovich.

"Yes," she whispered. "To the last moment. He took leave of us a quarter of an hour before he died, and asked us to take Vasya[3] away."

The thought of the sufferings of this man he had known so intimately, first as a merry little boy, then as a school-mate, and later as a grown-up colleague, suddenly struck Peter Ivanovich with horror, despite an unpleasant consciousness of his own and this woman's dissimulation. He again saw that brow, and that nose pressing down on the lip, and felt afraid for himself.

"Three days of frightful suffering and then death! Why, that might suddenly, at any time, happen to me," he thought, and for a moment felt terrified. But—he did not himself know how—the customary reflection at once occurred to him that this had happened to Ivan Ilych and not to him, and that it should not and could not happen to him, and that to think that it could would be yielding to depression which he ought not to do, as Schwartz's expression plainly showed. After which reflection Peter Ivanovich felt reassured, and began to ask with interest about the details of Ivan Ilych's death, as though death was an accident natural to Ivan Ilych but certainly not to himself.

After many details of the really dreadful physical sufferings Ivan Ilych had endured (which details he learnt only from the effect those sufferings had produced on Praskovya Fëdorovna's nerves) the widow apparently found it necessary to get to business.

"Oh, Peter Ivanovich, how hard as it! How terribly, terribly hard!" and she again began to weep.

Peter Ivanovich sighed and waited for her to finish blowing her nose. When she had done so he said, "Believe me . . ." and she again began talking and brought out what was evidently her chief concern with him—namely, to question him as to how she could obtain a grant of money from the government on the occasion of her husband's death. She made it appear that she was asking Peter Ivanovich's advice about her pension, but he soon saw that she already knew about that to the minutest detail, more even than he did himself. She knew how much could be got out of the government in consequence of her husband's death, but wanted to find out whether she could not possibly extract

3. Diminutive of Vasily, Ivan Ilych's son.

something more. Peter Ivanovich tried to think of some means of doing so, but after reflecting for a while and, out of propriety, condemning the government for its niggardliness, he said he thought that nothing more could be got. Then she sighed and evidently began to devise means of getting rid of her visitor. Noticing this, he put out his cigarette, rose, pressed her hand, and went out into the anteroom.

In the dining-room where the clock stood that Ivan Ilych had liked so much and had bought at an antique shop, Peter Ivanovich met a priest and a few acquaintances who had come to attend the service, and he recognized Ivan Ilych's daughter, a handsome young woman. She was in black and her slim figure appeared slimmer than ever. She had a gloomy, determined, almost angry expression, and bowed to Peter Ivanovich as though he were in some way to blame. Behind her, with the same offended look, stood a wealthy young man, an examining magistrate, whom Peter Ivanovich also knew and who was her fiancé, as he had heard. He bowed mournfully to them and was about to pass into the death-chamber, when from under the stairs appeared the figure of Ivan Ilych's schoolboy son, who was extremely like his father. He seemed a little Ivan Ilych, such as Peter Ivanovich remembered when they studied law together. His tear-stained eyes had in them the look that is seen in the eyes of boys of thirteen or fourteen who are not pure-minded. When he saw Peter Ivanovich he scowled morosely and shamefacedly. Peter Ivanovich nodded to him and entered the death-chamber. The service began: candles, groans, incense, tears, and sobs. Peter Ivanovich stood looking gloomily down at his feet. He did not look once at the dead man, did not yield to any depressing influence, and was one of the first to leave the room. There was no one in the anteroom, but Gerasim darted out of the dead man's room, rummaged with his strong hands among the fur coats to find Peter Ivanovich's and helped him on with it.

"Well, friend Gerasim," said Peter Ivanovich, so as to say something. "It's a sad affair, isn't it?"

"It's God's will. We shall all come to it some day," said Gerasim, displaying his teeth—the even, white teeth of a healthy peasant—and, like a man in the thick of urgent work, he briskly opened the front door, called the coachman, helped Peter Ivanovich into the sledge, and sprang back to the porch as if in readiness for what he had to do next.

Peter Ivanovich found the fresh air particularly pleasant after the smell of incense, the dead body, and carbolic acid.

"Where to, sir?" asked the coachman.

"It's not too late even now. . . . I'll call round on Fëdor Vasilievich."

He accordingly drove there and found them just finishing the first rubber,[4] so that it was quite convenient for him to cut in.

II

Ivan Ilych's life had been most simple and most ordinary and therefore most terrible.

He had been a member of the Court of Justice, and died at the age of forty-five. His father had been an official who after serving in various ministries and departments in Petersburg had made the sort of career which brings men to positions from which by reason of their long service they cannot be dismissed, though they were obviously unfit to hold any responsible position, and for whom therefore posts are specially created, which though fictitious carry salaries of from six to ten thousand rubles that are not fictitious, and in receipt of which they live on to a great age.

Such was the Privy Councillor and superfluous member of various superfluous institutions, Ilya Epimovich Golovin.

He had three sons, of whom Ivan Ilych was the second. The eldest son was following in his father's footsteps only in another department, and was already approaching that stage in the service at which a similar sinecure would be reached. The third son was a failure. He had ruined his prospects in a number of positions and was now serving in the railway department. His father and brothers, and still more their wives, not merely disliked meeting him, but avoided remembering his existence unless compelled to do so. His sister had married Baron Greff, a Petersburg official of her father's type. Ivan Ilych was *le phénix de la famille*[5] as people said. He was neither as cold and formal as his elder brother nor as wild as the younger, but was a happy mean between them—an intelligent, polished, lively and agreeable man. He had studied with his younger brother at the School of Law, but the latter had failed to complete the course and was expelled when he was in the fifth class. Ivan Ilych finished the course well. Even when he was at the School of Law he was just what he remained for the rest of his life: a capable, cheerful, good-natured, and sociable man, though strict in the fulfillment of what he considered to be his duty: and he considered his duty to be what was so considered by those in authority. Neither as a boy nor as a man was he a toady, but from early youth was by nature attracted to people of high station as a fly is drawn to the light, assimilating their ways and view of life and establishing friendly relations with them. All the enthusiasms of childhood and youth passed without leaving much

4. Round of hands in bridge. 5. The paragon of the family.

trace on him; he succumbed to sensuality, to vanity, and latterly among the highest classes to liberalism, but always within limits which his instinct unfailingly indicated to him as correct.

At school he had done things which had formerly seemed to him very horrid and made him feel disgusted with himself when he did them; but when later on he saw that such actions were done by people of good position and that they did not regard them as wrong, he was able not exactly to regard them as right, but to forget about them entirely or not be at all troubled at remembering them.

Having graduated from the School of Law and qualified for the tenth rank of the civil service, and having received money from his father for his equipment, Ivan Ilych ordered himself clothes at Scharmer's, the fashionable tailor, hung a medallion inscribed *respice finem*[6] on his watch-chain, took leave of his professor and the prince who was patron of the school, had a farewell dinner with his comrades at Donon's first-class restaurant, and with his new and fashionable portmanteau, linen, clothes, shaving and other toilet appliances, and a traveling rug, all purchased at the best shops, he set off for one of the provinces where, through his father's influence, he had been attached to the Governor as an official for special service.

In the province Ivan Ilych soon arranged as easy and agreeable a position for himself as he had had at the School of Law. He performed his official tasks, made his career, and at the same time amused himself pleasantly and decorously. Occasionally he paid official visits to country districts, where he behaved with dignity both to his superiors and inferiors, and performed the duties entrusted to him, which related chiefly to the sectarians,[7] with an exactness and incorruptible honesty of which he could not but feel proud.

In official matters, despite his youth and taste for frivolous gaiety, he was exceedingly reserved, punctilious, and even severe; but in society he was often amusing and witty, and always good-natured, correct in his manner, and *bon enfant*,[8] as the governor and his wife—with whom he was like one of the family—used to say of him.

In the province he had an affair with a lady who made advances to the elegant young lawyer, and there was also a milliner; and there were carousals with aides-de-camp who visited the district, and after-supper visits to a certain outlying street of doubtful reputation; and there was too some obsequiousness to his chief and even to his chief's wife, but all this was done with such a tone of good breeding that no hard names could be applied to it. It all came under the heading of the

6. I.e., "look before you leap." 7. The Old Believers (so called because they rejected various church reforms) had broken with the Orthodox Church in the 1600's; they were subject to many legal restrictions. 8. Good old boy.

French saying: "*Il faut que jeunesse se passe.*"[9] It was all done with clean hands, in clean linen, with French phrases, and above all among people of the best society and consequently with the approval of people of rank.

So Ivan Ilych served for five years and then came a change in his official life. The new and reformed judicial institutions were introduced, and new men were needed. Ivan Ilych became such a new man. He was offered the post of examining magistrate, and he accepted it though the post was in another province and obliged him to give up the connexions he had formed and to make new ones. His friends met to give him a send-off; they had a group-photograph taken and presented him with a silver cigarette-case, and he set off to his new post.

As examining magistrate Ivan Ilych was just as *comme il faut*[1] and decorous a man, inspiring general respect and capable of separating his official duties from his private life, as he had been when acting as an official on special service. His duties now as examining magistrate were far more interesting and attractive than before. In his former position it had been pleasant to wear an undress uniform made by Scharmer, and to pass through the crowd of petitioners and officials who were timorously awaiting an audience with the governor, and who envied him as with free and easy gait he went straight into his chief's private room to have a cup of tea and a cigarette with him. But not many people had then been directly dependent on him—only police officials and the sectarians when he went on special missions—and he liked to treat them politely, almost as comrades, as if he were letting them feel that he who had the power to crush them was treating them in this simple, friendly way. There were then but few such people. But now, as an examining magistrate, Ivan Ilych felt that everyone without exception, even the most important and self-satisfied, was in his power, and that he need only write a few words on a sheet of paper with a certain heading, and this or that important, self-satisfied person would be brought before him in the role of an accused person or a witness, and if he did not choose to allow him to sit down, would have to stand before him and answer his questions. Ivan Ilych never abused his power; he tried on the contrary to soften its expression, but the consciousness of it and of the possibility of softening its effect, supplied the chief interest and attraction of his office. In his work itself, especially in his examinations, he very soon acquired a method of eliminating all considerations irrelevant to the legal aspect of the case, and reducing even the most complicated case to a form in which it would be presented on paper only in its externals, completely excluding his personal opinion

9. "Youth must have its fling." 1. In good taste.

of the matter, while above all observing every prescribed formality. The work was new and Ivan Ilych was one of the first men to apply the new Code of 1864.[2]

On taking up the post of examining magistrate in a new town, he made new acquaintances and connexions, placed himself on a new footing, and assumed a somewhat different tone. He took up an attitude of rather dignified aloofness towards the provincial authorities, but picked out the best circle of legal gentlemen and wealthy gentry living in the town and assumed a tone of slight dissatisfaction with the government, of moderate liberalism, and of enlightened citizenship. At the same time, without at all altering the elegance of his toilet, he ceased shaving his chin and allowed his beard to grow as it pleased.

Ivan Ilych settled down very pleasantly in this new town. The society there, which inclined towards opposition to the Governor, was friendly, his salary was larger, and he began to play *vint*,[3] which he found added not a little to the pleasure of life, for he had a capacity for cards, played good-humouredly, and calculated rapidly and astutely, so that he usually won.

After living there for two years he met his future wife, Praskovya Fëdorovna Mikhel, who was the most attractive, clever, and brilliant girl of the set in which he moved, and among other amusements and relaxations from his labours as examining magistrate, Ivan Ilych established light and playful relations with her.

While he had been an official on special service he had been accustomed to dance, but now as an examining magistrate it was exceptional for him to do so. If he danced now, he did it as if to show that though he served under the reformed order of things, and had reached the fifth official rank, yet when it came to dancing he could do it better than most people. So at the end of an evening he sometimes danced with Praskovya Fëdorovna, and it was chiefly during these dances that he captivated her. She fell in love with him. Ivan Ilych had at first no definite intention of marrying, but when the girl fell in love with him he said to himself: "Really, why shouldn't I marry?"

Praskovya Fëdorovna came of a good family, was not bad looking, and had some little property. Ivan Ilych might have aspired to a more brilliant match, but even this was good. He had his salary, and she, he hoped, would have an equal income. She was well connected, and was a sweet, pretty, and thoroughly correct young woman. To say that Ivan Ilych married because he fell in love with Praskovya Fëdorovna and found that she sympathized with his views of life would be as incorrect as to say that he married because his social circle approved of the match.

2. A thorough reform of judicial proceedings in Russia, which followed the freeing of the serfs in 1861. 3. A form of bridge.

He was swayed by both these considerations: the marriage gave him personal satisfaction, and at the same time it was considered the right thing by the most highly placed of his associates.

So Ivan Ilych got married.

The preparations for marriage and the beginning of married life, with its conjugal caresses, the new furniture, new crockery, and new linen, were very pleasant until his wife became pregnant—so that Ivan Ilych had begun to think that marriage would not impair the easy, agreeable, gay and always decorous character of his life, approved of by society and regarded by himself as natural, but would even improve it. But from the first months of his wife's pregnancy, something new, unpleasant, depressing, and unseemly, and from which there was no way of escape, unexpectedly showed itself.

His wife, without any reason—*de gaieté de coeur*[4] as Ivan Ilych expressed it to himself—began to disturb the pleasure and propriety of their life. She began to be jealous without any cause, expected him to devote his whole attention to her, found fault with everything, and made coarse and ill-mannered scenes.

At first Ivan Ilych hoped to escape from the unpleasantness of this state of affairs by the same easy and decorous relation to life that had served him heretofore: he tried to ignore his wife's disagreeable moods, continued to live in his usual easy and pleasant way, invited friends to his house for a game of cards, and also tried going out to his club or spending his evenings with friends. But one day his wife began upbraiding him so vigorously, using such coarse words, and continued to abuse him every time he did not fulfil her demands, so resolutely and with such evident determination not to give way till he submitted—that is, till he stayed at home and was bored just as she was—that he became alarmed. He now realized that matrimony—at any rate with Praskovya Fëdorovna—was not always conducive to the pleasures and amenities of life, but on the contrary often infringed both comfort and propriety, and that he must therefore entrench himself against such infringement. And Ivan Ilych began to seek for means of doing so. His official duties were the one thing that imposed upon Praskovya Fëdorovna, and by means of his official work and the duties attached to it he began struggling with his wife to secure his own independence.

With the birth of their child, the attempts to feed it and the various failures in doing so, and with the real and imaginary illnesses of mother and child, in which Ivan Ilych's sympathy was demanded but about which he understood nothing, the need of securing for himself an existence outside his family life became still more imperative.

As his wife grew more irritable and exacting and Ivan Ilych trans-

4. From sheer animal spirits.

ferred the centre of gravity of his life more and more to his official work, so did he grow to like his work better and became more ambitious than before.

Very soon, within a year of his wedding, Ivan Ilych had realized that marriage, though it may add some comforts to life, is in fact a very intricate and difficult affair towards which in order to perform one's duty, that is, to lead a decorous life approved of by society, one must adopt a definite attitude just as towards one's official duties.

And Ivan Ilych evolved such an attitude towards married life. He only required of it those conveniences—dinner at home, housewife, and bed—which it could give him, and above all that propriety of external forms required by public opinion. For the rest he looked for light-hearted pleasure and propriety, and was very thankful when he found them, but if he met with antagonism and querulousness he at once retired into his separate fenced-off world of official duties, where he found satisfaction.

Ivan Ilych was esteemed a good official, and after three years was made Assistant Public Prosecutor. His new duties, their importance, the possibility of indicting and imprisoning anyone he chose, the publicity his speeches received, and the success he had in all these things, made his work still more attractive.

More children came. His wife became more and more querulous and ill-tempered, but the attitude Ivan Ilych had adopted towards his home life rendered him almost impervious to her grumbling.

After seven years' service in that town he was transferred to another province as Public Prosecutor. They moved, but were short of money and his wife did not like the place they moved to. Though the salary was higher the cost of living was greater, besides which two of their children died and family life became still more unpleasant for him.

Praskovya Fëdorovna blamed her husband for every inconvenience they encountered in their new home. Most of the conversations between husband and wife, especially as to the children's education, led to topics which recalled former disputes, and those disputes were apt to flare up again at any moment. There remained only those rare periods of amorousness which still came to them at times but did not last long. These were islets at which they anchored for a while and then again set out upon that ocean of veiled hostility which showed itself in their aloofness from one another. This aloofness might have grieved Ivan Ilych had he considered that it ought not to exist, but he now regarded the position as normal, and even made it the goal at which he aimed in family life. His aim was to free himself more and more from those unpleasantnesses and to give them a semblance of harmlessness and propriety. He attained this by spending less and less time with his family, and when obliged to be at home he tried to safeguard his position by the presence of outsiders. The chief thing however was that he had his official duties. The whole interest of his life now centred in the official world and that interest absorbed him. The consciousness of his power, being able to ruin anybody he wished to ruin, the importance, even the external dignity of his entry into court, or meetings with his subordinates, his success with superiors and inferiors, and above all his masterly handling of cases, of which he was conscious—all this gave him pleasure and filled his life, together with chats with his colleagues, dinners, and bridge. So that on the whole Ivan Ilych's life continued to flow as he considered it should do—pleasantly and properly.

So things continued for another seven years. His eldest daughter was already sixteen, another child had died, and only one son was left, a schoolboy and a subject of dissension. Ivan Ilych wanted to put him in the School of Law, but to spite him Praskovya Fëdorovna entered him at the High School.[5] The daughter had been educated at home and had turned out well: the boy did not learn badly either.

III

So Ivan Ilych lived for seventeen years after his marriage. He was already a Public Prosecutor of long standing, and had declined several proposed transfers while awaiting a more desirable post, when an unanticipated and unpleasant occurrence quite upset the peaceful course of his life. He was expecting to be offered the post of presiding judge in a University town, but Happe somehow came to the front and obtained the appointment instead. Ivan Ilych became irritable, reproached Happe, and quarreled both with him and with his immediate superiors—who became colder to him and again passed him over when other appointments were made.

This was in 1880, the hardest year of Ivan Ilych's life. It was then that it became evident on the one hand that his salary was insufficient for them to live on, and on the other that he had been forgotten, and not only this, but that what was for him the greatest and most cruel injustice appeared to others a quite ordinary occurrence. Even his father did not consider it his duty to help him. Ivan Ilych felt himself abandoned by everyone, and that they regarded his position with a salary of 3,500 rubles as quite normal and even fortunate. He alone knew that with the consciousness of the injustices done him, with his wife's incessant nagging, and with the debts he had contracted by living beyond his means, his position was far from normal.

In order to save money that summer he obtained leave of absence

5. Schools of equal level in this period.

and went with his wife to live in the country at her brother's place.

In the country, without his work, he experienced *ennui* for the first time in his life, and not only *ennui* but intolerable depression, and he decided that it was impossible to go on living like that, and that it was necessary to take energetic measures.

Having passed a sleepless night pacing up and down the veranda, he decided to go to Petersburg and bestir himself, in order to punish those who had failed to appreciate him and to get transferred to another ministry.

Next day, despite many protests from his wife and her brother, he started for Petersburg with the sole object of obtaining a post with a salary of five thousand rubles a year. He was no longer bent on any particular department, or tendency, or kind of activity. All he now wanted was an appointment to another post with a salary of five thousand rubles, either in the administration, in the banks, with the railways, in one of the Empress Marya's Institutions,[6] or even in the customs—but it had to carry with it a salary of five thousand rubles and be in a ministry other than that in which they had failed to appreciate him.

And this quest of Ivan Ilych's was crowned with remarkable and unexpected success. At Kursk an acquaintance of his, F. I. Ilyin, got into the first-class carriage, sat down beside Ivan Ilych, and told him of a telegram just received by the Governor of Kursk announcing that a change was about to take place in the ministry: Peter Ivanovich was to be superseded by Ivan Semënovich.

The proposed change, apart from its significance for Russia, had a special significance for Ivan Ilych, because by bringing forward a new man, Peter Petrovich, and consequently his friend Zachar Ivanovich, it was highly favourable for Ivan Ilych, since Zachar Ivanovich was a friend and colleague of his.

In Moscow this news was confirmed, and on reaching Petersburg Ivan Ilych found Zachar Ivanovich and received a definite promise of an appointment in his former department of Justice.

A week later he telegraphed to his wife: "Zachar in Miller's place. I shall receive appointment on presentation of report."

Thanks to this change of personnel, Ivan Ilych had unexpectedly obtained an appointment in his former ministry which placed him two stages above his former colleagues besides giving him five thousand rubles salary and three thousand five hundred rubles for expenses connected with his removal. All his ill humour towards his former enemies and the whole department vanished, and Ivan Ilych was completely happy.

6. Charitable organizations founded by the wife of Tsar Paul I (1754–1801).

He returned to the country more cheerful and contented than he had been for a long time. Praskovya Fëdorovna also cheered up and a truce was arranged between them. Ivan Ilych told of how he had been fêted by everybody in Petersburg, how all those who had been his enemies were put to shame and now fawned on him, how envious they were of his appointment, and how much everybody in Petersburg had liked him.

Praskovya Fëdorovna listened to all this and appeared to believe it. She did not contradict anything, but only made plans for their life in the town to which they were going. Ivan Ilych saw with delight that these plans were his plans, that he and his wife agreed, and that, after a stumble, his life was regaining its due and natural character of pleasant lightheartedness and decorum.

Ivan Ilych had come back for a short time only, for he had to take up his new duties on the 10th of September. Moreover, he needed time to settle into the new place, to move all his belongings from the province, and to buy and order many additional things: in a word, to make such arrangements as he had resolved on, which were almost exactly what Praskovya Fëdorovna too had decided on.

Now that everything had happened so fortunately, and that he and his wife were at one in their aims and moreover saw so little of one another, they got on together better than they had done since the first years of marriage. Ivan Ilych had thought of taking his family away with him at once, but the insistence of his wife's brother and her sister-in-law, who had suddenly become particularly amiable and friendly to him and his family, induced him to depart alone.

So he departed, and the cheerful state of mind induced by his success and by the harmony between his wife and himself, the one intensifying the other, did not leave him. He found a delightful house, just the thing both he and his wife had dreamt of. Spacious, lofty reception rooms in the old style, a convenient and dignified study, rooms for his wife and daughter, a study for his son—it might have been specially built for them. Ivan Ilych himself superintended the arrangements, chose the wallpapers, supplemented the furniture (preferably with antiques which he considered particularly *comme il faut*), and supervised the upholstering. Everything progressed and progressed and approached the ideal he had set himself: even when things were only half completed they exceeded his expectations. He saw what a refined and elegant character, free from vulgarity, it would all have when it was ready. On falling asleep he pictured to himself how the reception-room would look. Looking at the yet unfinished drawing-room he could see the fireplace, the screen, the what-not, the little chairs dotted here and there, the dishes and plates on the walls, and the bronzes, as they would be when everything was in place. He was pleased by the thought of how his wife and daughter, who shared his taste in this matter, would be impressed by it. They were certainly not expecting as much. He had been particularly successful in finding, and buying cheaply, antiques which gave a particularly aristocratic character to the whole place. But in his letters he intentionally understated everything in order to be able to surprise them. All this so absorbed him that his new duties—though he liked his official work—interested him less than he had expected. Sometimes he even had moments of absent-mindedness during the Court Sessions, and would consider whether he should have straight or curved cornices for his curtains. He was so interested in it all that he often did things himself, rearranging the furniture, or rehanging the curtains. Once when mounting a step-ladder to show the upholsterer, who did not understand, how he wanted the hangings draped, he made a false step and slipped, but being a strong and agile man he clung on and only knocked his side against the knob of the window frame. The bruised place was painful but the pain soon passed, and he felt particularly bright and well just then. He wrote: "I feel fifteen years younger." He thought he would have everything ready by September, but it dragged on till mid-October. But the result was charming not only in his eyes but to everyone who saw it.

In reality it was just what is usually seen in the houses of people of moderate means who want to appear rich, and therefore succeed only in resembling others like themselves: there were damasks, dark wood, plants, rugs, and dull and polished bronzes—all the things people of a certain class have in order to resemble other people of that class. His house was so like the others that it would never have been noticed, but to him it all seemed to be quite exceptional. He was very happy when he met his family at the station and brought them to the newly furnished house all lit up, where a footman in a white tie opened the door into the hall decorated with plants, and when they went on into the drawing-room and the study uttering exclamations of delight. He conducted them everywhere, drank in their praises eagerly, and beamed with pleasure. At tea that evening, when Praskovya Fëdorovna among other things asked him about his fall, he laughed and showed them how he had gone flying and had frightened the upholsterer.

"It's a good thing I'm a bit of an athlete. Another man might have been killed, but I merely knocked myself, just here; it hurts when it's touched, but it's passing off already—it's only a bruise."

So they began living in their new home—in which, as always happens, when they got thoroughly settled in they found they were just one room short—and with the increased income, which as always was just a little (some five hundred rubles) too little, but it was all very nice.

Things went particularly well at first, before everything was finally arranged and while something had still to be done: this thing bought, that thing ordered, another thing moved, and something else adjusted. Though there were some disputes between husband and wife, they were both so well satisfied and had so much to do that it all passed off without any serious quarrels. When nothing was left to arrange it became rather dull and something seemed to be lacking, but they were then making acquaintances, forming habits, and life was growing fuller.

Ivan Ilych spent his mornings at the law court and came home to dinner, and at first he was generally in a good humour, though he occasionally became irritable just on account of his house. (Every spot on the tablecloth or the upholstery, and every broken window-blind string, irritated him. He had devoted so much trouble to arranging it all that every disturbance of it distressed him.) But on the whole his life ran its course as he believed life should do: easily, pleasantly, and decorously.

He got up at nine, drank his coffee, read the paper, and then put on his undress uniform and went to the law courts. There the harness in which he worked had already been stretched to fit him and he donned it without a hitch: petitioners, inquiries at the chancery, the chancery itself, and the sittings public and administrative. In all this the thing was to exclude everything fresh and vital, which always disturbs the regular course of official business, and to admit only official relations with people, and then only on official grounds. A man would come, for instance, wanting some information. Ivan Ilych, as one in whose sphere the matter did not lie, would have nothing to do with him: but if the man had some business with him in his official capacity, something that could be expressed on officially stamped paper, he would do everything, positively everything he could within the limits of such relations, and in doing so would maintain the semblance of friendly human relations, that is, would observe the courtesies of life. As soon as the official relations ended, so did everything else. Ivan Ilych possessed this capacity to separate his real life from the official side of affairs and not mix the two, in the highest degree, and by long practice and natural aptitude had brought it to such a pitch that sometimes, in the manner of a virtuoso, he would even allow himself to let the human and official relations mingle. He let himself do this just because he felt that he could at any time he chose resume the strictly official attitude again and drop the human relation. And he did it all easily, pleasantly, correctly, and even artistically. In the intervals between the sessions he smoked, drank tea, chatted a little about politics, a little about general topics, a little about cards, but most of all about official appointments. Tired, but with the feelings of a virtuoso—one of the first violins who has played his part in an orchestra with precision—he would return home to find that his wife and daughter had been out paying calls, or had a visitor, and that his son had been to school, had done his homework with his tutor, and was duly learning what is taught at High Schools. Everything was as it should be. After dinner, if they had no visitors, Ivan Ilych sometimes read a book that was being much discussed at the time, and in the evening settled down to work, that is, read official papers, compared the depositions of witnesses, and noted paragraphs of the Code applying to them. This was neither dull nor amusing. It was dull when he might have been playing bridge, but if no bridge was available it was at any rate better than doing nothing or sitting with his wife. Ivan Ilych's chief pleasure was giving little dinners to which he invited men and women of good social position, and just as his drawing-room resembled all other drawing-rooms so did his enjoyable little parties resemble all other such parties.

Once they even gave a dance. Ivan Ilych enjoyed it and everything went off well, except that it led to a violent quarrel with his wife about the cakes and sweets. Praskovya Fëdorovna had made her own plans, but Ivan Ilych insisted on getting everything from an expensive confectioner and ordered too many cakes, and the quarrel occurred because some of those cakes were left over and the confectioner's bill came to forty-five rubles. It was a great and disagreeable quarrel. Praskovya Fëdorovna called him "a fool and an imbecile," and he clutched at his head and made angry allusions to divorce.

But the dance itself had been enjoyable. The best people were there, and Ivan Ilych had danced with Princess Trufonova, a sister of the distinguished founder of the Society "Bear My Burden."

The pleasures connected with his work were pleasures of ambition; his social pleasures were those of vanity; but Ivan Ilych's greatest pleasure was playing bridge. He acknowledged that whatever disagreeable incident happened in his life, the pleasure that beamed like a ray of light above everything else was to sit down to bridge with good players, not noisy partners, and of course to four-handed bridge (with five players it was annoying to have to stand out, though one pretended not to mind), to play a clever and serious game (when the cards allowed it) and then to have supper and drink a glass of wine. After a game of bridge, especially if he had won a little (to win a large sum was unpleasant), Ivan Ilych went to bed in specially good humour.

So they lived. They formed a circle of acquaintances among the best people and were visited by people of importance and by young folk. In their views as to their acquaintances, husband, wife and daughter were entirely agreed, and tacitly and unanimously kept at arm's length and shook off the various shabby friends and relations who, with much show of affection, gushed into the drawing-room with its Japanese plates on the walls. Soon these shabby friends ceased to obtrude themselves and only the best people remained in the Golovins' set.

Young men made up to Lisa, and Petrishchev, an examining magistrate and Dmitri Ivanovich Petrishchev's son and sole heir, began to be so attentive to her that Ivan Ilych had already spoken to Praskovya Fëdorovna about it, and considered whether they should not arrange a party for them, or get up some private theatricals.

So they lived, and all went well, without change, and life flowed pleasantly.

IV

They were all in good health. It could not be called ill health if Ivan Ilych sometimes said that he had a queer taste in his mouth and felt some discomfort in his left side.

But this discomfort increased and, though not exactly painful, grew into a sense of pressure in his side accompanied by ill humour. And his irritability became worse and worse and began to mar the agreeable, easy, and correct life that had established itself in the Golovin family. Quarrels between husband and wife became more and more frequent, and soon the ease and amenity disappeared and even the decorum was barely maintained. Scenes again became frequent, and very few of those islets remained on which husband and wife could meet without an explosion. Praskovya Fëdorovna now had good reason to say that her husband's temper was trying. With characteristic exaggeration she said he had always had a dreadful temper, and that it had needed all her good nature to put up with it for twenty years. It was true that now the quarrels were started by him. His bursts of temper always came just before dinner, often just as he began to eat his soup. Sometimes he noticed that a plate or dish was chipped, or the food was not right, or his son put his elbow on the table, or his daughter's hair was not done as he liked it, and for all this he blamed Praskovya Fëdorovna. At first she retorted and said disagreeable things to him, but once or twice he fell into such a rage at the beginning of dinner that she realized it was due to some physical derangement brought on by taking food, and so she restrained herself and did not answer, but only hurried to get the dinner over. She regarded this self-restraint as highly praiseworthy. Having come to the conclusion that her husband had a dreadful temper and made her life miserable, she began to feel sorry for herself, and the more she pitied herself the more she hated her husband. She began to wish he would die; yet she did not want him to die because then his salary would cease. And this irritated her against him still more. She considered herself dreadfully unhappy just because not even his death could save her, and though she concealed her exasperation, that hidden exasperation of hers increased his irritation also.

After one scene in which Ivan Ilych had been particularly unfair and after which he had said in explanation that he certainly was irritable but that it was due to his not being well, she said that if he was ill it should be attended to, and insisted on his going to see a celebrated doctor.

He went. Everything took place as he had expected and as it always does. There was the usual waiting and the important air assumed by the doctor, with which he was so familiar (resembling that which he himself assumed in court), and the surrounding and listening, and the questions which called for answers that were foregone conclusions and were evidently unnecessary, and the look of importance which implied that "if only you put yourself in our hands we will arrange everything—we know indubitably how it has to be done, always in the same way for everybody alike." It was all just as it was in the law courts. The doctor put on just the same air towards him as he himself put on towards an accused person.

The doctor said that so-and-so indicated that there was so-and-so inside the patient, but if the investigation of so-and-so did not confirm this, then he must assume that and that. If he assumed that and that, then . . . and so on. To Ivan Ilych only one question was important: was his case serious or not? But the doctor ignored that inappropriate question. From his point of view it was not the one under consideration, the real question was to decide between a floating kidney, chronic catarrh, or appendicitis. It was not a question of Ivan Ilych's life or death, but one between a floating kidney and appendicitis. And that question the doctor solved brilliantly, as it seemed to Ivan Ilych, in favour of the appendix, with the reservation that should an examination of the urine give fresh indications the matter would be reconsidered. All this was just what Ivan Ilych had himself brilliantly accomplished a thousand times in dealing with men on trial. The doctor summed up just as brilliantly, looking over his spectacles triumphantly and even gaily at the accused. From the doctor's summing up Ivan Ilych concluded that things were bad, but that for the doctor, and perhaps for everybody else, it was a matter of indifference, though for him it was bad. And this conclusion struck him painfully, arousing in him a great feeling of pity for himself and of bitterness towards the doctor's indifference to a matter of such importance.

He said nothing of this, but rose, placed the doctor's fee on the table, and remarked with a sigh: "We sick people probably often put inappropriate questions. But tell me, in general, in this complaint dangerous, or not? . . ."

The doctor looked at him sternly over his spectacles with one eye, as if to say: "Prisoner, if you will not keep to the questions put to you, I shall be obliged to have you removed from the court."

"I have already told you what I consider necessary and proper. The analysis may show something more." And the doctor bowed.

Ivan Ilych went out slowly, seated himself disconsolately in his sledge, and drove home. All the way home he was going over what the doctor had said, trying to translate those complicated, obscure, scientific phrases into plain language and find in them an answer to the question: "Is my condition bad? Is it very bad? Or is there as yet nothing much wrong?" And it seemed to him that the meaning of what the doctor had said was that it was very bad. Everything in the streets seemed depressing. The cabmen, the houses, the passers-by, and the shops, were dismal. His ache, this dull gnawing ache that never ceased for a moment, seemed to have acquired a new and more serious significance from the doctor's dubious remarks. Ivan Ilych now watched it with a new and oppressive feeling.

He reached home and began to tell his wife about it. She listened, but in the middle of his account his daughter came in with her hat on, ready to go out with her mother. She sat down reluctantly to listen to this tedious story, but could not stand it long, and her mother too did not hear him to the end.

"Well, I am very glad," she said. "Mind now to take your medicine regularly. Give me the prescription and I'll send Gerasim to the chemist's." And she went to get ready to go out.

While she was in the room Ivan Ilych had hardly taken time to breathe, but he sighed deeply when she left it.

"Well," he thought, "perhaps it isn't so bad after all."

He began taking his medicine and following the doctor's directions, which had been altered after the examination of the urine. But then it happened that there was a contradiction between the indications drawn from the examination of the urine and the symptoms that showed themselves. It turned out that what was happening differed from what the doctor had told him, and that he had either forgotten, or blundered, or hidden something from him. He could not, however, be blamed for that, and Ivan Ilych still obeyed his orders implicitly and at first derived some comfort from doing so.

From the time of his visit to the doctor, Ivan Ilych's chief occupation was the exact fulfilment of the doctor's instructions regarding hygiene and the taking of medicine, and the observation of his pain and his excretions. His chief interests came to be people's ailments and people's health. When sickness, deaths, or recoveries were mentioned in his presence, especially when the illness resembled his own, he listened with agitation which he tried to hide, asked questions, and applied what he heard to his own case.

The pain did not grow less, but Ivan Ilych made efforts to force himself to think that he was better. And he could do this so long as nothing agitated him. But as soon as he had any unpleasantness with his wife, any lack of success in his official work, or held bad cards at bridge, he was at once acutely sensible of his disease. He had formerly borne such mischances, hoping soon to adjust what was wrong, to master it and attain success, or make a grand slam. But now every mischance upset him and plunged him into despair. He would say to himself: "There now, just as I was beginning to get better and the medicine had begun to take effect, comes this accursed misfortune, or unpleasantness. . . ." And he was furious with the mishap, or with the people who were causing the unpleasantness and killing him, for he felt that this fury was killing him but could not restrain it. One would have thought that it should have been clear to him that this exasperation with circumstances and people aggravated his illness, and that he ought therefore to ignore unpleasant occurrences. But he drew the very opposite conclusion: he said that he needed peace, and he watched for everything that might disturb it and became irritable at the slightest infringement of it. His condition was rendered worse by the fact that he read medical books and consulted doctors. The progress of his disease was so gradual that he could deceive himself when comparing one day with another—the difference was so slight. But when he consulted the doctors it seemed to him that he was getting worse, and even very rapidly. Yet despite this he was continually consulting them.

That month he went to see another celebrity, who told him almost the same as the first had done but put his questions rather differently, and the interview with this celebrity only increased Ivan Ilych's doubts and fears. A friend of a friend of his, a very good doctor, diagnosed his illness again quite differently from the others, and though he predicted recovery, his questions and suppositions bewildered Ivan Ilych still more and increased his doubts. A homeopathist diagnosed the disease in yet another way, and prescribed medicine which Ivan Ilych took secretly for a week. But after a week, not feeling any improvement and having lost confidence both in the former doctor's treatment and in this one's, he became still more despondent. One day a lady acquaintance mentioned a cure effected by a wonder-working icon. Ivan Ilych caught himself listening attentively and beginning to believe that it had occurred. This incident alarmed him. "Has my mind really weakened to such an extent?" he asked himself. "Nonsense! It's all rubbish. I mustn't give way to nervous fears but having chosen a doctor must keep strictly to his treatment. That is what I will do. Now it's all settled. I won't think about it, but will follow the treatment seriously till summer, and then we shall see. From now there must be no more of this wavering!" This was easy to say but impossible to carry out. The pain in his side oppressed him and seemed to grow worse and more incessant, while the taste in his mouth grew stranger and stranger. It seemed to him that his breath had a disgusting smell, and he was conscious of a loss of appetite and strength. There was no deceiving himself: something terrible, new, and more important than anything before in his life, was taking place within him of which he alone was aware. Those about him did not understand or would not understand it, but thought everything in the world was going on as usual. That tormented Ivan Ilych more than anything. He saw that his household, especially his wife and daughter who were in a perfect whirl of visiting, did not understand anything of it and were annoyed that he was so depressed and so exacting, as if he were to blame for it. Though they tried to disguise it he saw that he was an obstacle in their path, and that his wife had adopted a definite line in regard to his illness and kept to it regardless of anything he said or did. Her attitude was this: "You know," she would say to her friends, "Ivan Ilych can't do as other people do, and keep to the treatment prescribed for him. One day he'll take his drops and keep strictly to his diet and go to bed in good time, but the next day unless I watch him he'll suddenly forget his medicine, eat sturgeon—which is forbidden—and sit up playing cards till one o'clock in the morning."

"Oh, come, when was that?" Ivan Ilych would ask in vexation. "Only once at Peter Ivanovich's."

"And yesterday with Shebek."

"Well, even if I hadn't stayed up, the pain would have kept me awake."

"Be that as it may you'll never get well like that, but will always make us wretched."

Praskovya Fëdorovna's attitude to Ivan Ilych's illness, as she expressed it both to others and to him, was that it was his own fault and was another of the annoyances he caused her. Ivan Ilych felt that this opinion escaped her involuntarily—but that did not make it easier for him.

At the law courts too, Ivan Ilych noticed, or thought he noticed, a strange attitude towards himself. It sometimes seemed to him that people were watching him inquisitively as a man whose place might soon be vacant. Then again, his friends would suddenly begin to chaff him in a friendly way about his low spirits, as if the awful, horrible, and unheard-of thing that was going on within him, incessantly gnawing at him and irresistibly drawing him away, was a very agreeable subject for jests. Schwartz in particular irritated him by his jocularity, vivacity, and *savoir-faire*,[7] which reminded him of what he himself had been ten years ago.

Friends came to make up a set and they sat down to cards. They dealt, bending the new cards to soften them, and he sorted the diamonds in his hand and found he had seven. His partner said "No trumps" and supported him with two diamonds. What more could be wished for? It ought to be jolly and lively. They would make a grand slam. But suddenly Ivan Ilych was conscious of that gnawing pain, that taste in his mouth, and it seemed ridiculous that in such circumstances he should be pleased to make a grand slam.

He looked at his partner Mikhail Mikhaylovich, who rapped the table with his strong hand and instead of snatching up the tricks pushed the cards courteously and indulgently towards Ivan Ilych that he might have the pleasure of gathering them up without the trouble of stretching out his hand for them. "Does he think I am too weak to stretch out my arm?" thought Ivan Ilych, and forgetting what he was doing he over-trumped his partner, missing the grand slam by three tricks. And what was most awful of all was that he saw how upset Mikhail Mikhaylovich was about it but did not himself care. And it was dreadful to realize why he did not care.

They all saw that he was suffering, and said: "We can stop if you are tired. Take a rest." Lie down? No, he was not at all tired, and he finished the rubber. All were gloomy and silent. Ivan Ilych felt that he had diffused this gloom over them and could not dispel it. They had supper and went away, and Ivan Ilych was left alone with the consciousness that his life was poisoned and was poisoning the lives of others, and that this poison did not weaken but penetrated more and more deeply into his whole being.

With this consciousness, and with physical pain besides the terror, he must go to bed, often to lie awake the greater part of the night. Next morning he had to get up again, dress, go to the law courts, speak, and write; or if he did not go out, spend at home those twenty-four hours a day each of which was a torture. And he had to live thus all alone on the brink of an abyss, with no one who understood or pitied him.

V

So one month passed and then another. Just before the New Year his brother-in-law came to town and stayed at their house. Ivan Ilych was at the law courts and Praskovya Fëdorovna had gone shopping. When

7. Tact, knowing the proper action.

Ivan Ilych came home and entered his study he found his brother-in-law there—a healthy, florid man—unpacking his portmanteau himself. He raised his head on hearing Ivan Ilych's footsteps and looked up at him for a moment without a word. That stare told Ivan Ilych everything. His brother-in-law opened his mouth to utter an exclamation of surprise but checked himself, and that action confirmed it all.

"I have changed, eh?"

"Yes, there is a change."

And after that, try as he would to get his brother-in-law to return to the subject of his looks, the latter would say nothing about it. Praskovya Fëdorovna came home and her brother went out to her. Ivan Ilych locked the door and began to examine himself in the glass, first full face, then in profile. He took up a portrait of himself taken with his wife, and compared it with what he saw in the glass. The change in him was immense. Then he bared his arms to the elbow, looked at them, drew the sleeves down again, sat down on an ottoman, and grew blacker than night.

"No, no, this won't do!" he said to himself, and jumped up, went to the table, took up some law papers and began to read them, but could not continue. He unlocked the door and went into the reception-room. The door leading to the drawing-room was shut. He approached it on tiptoe and listened.

"No, you are exaggerating!" Praskovya Fëdorovna was saying.

"Exaggerating! Don't you see it? Why, he's a dead man! Look at his eyes—there's no light in them. But what is it that is wrong with him?"

"No one knows. Nikolaevich [that was another doctor] said something, but I don't know what. And Leshchetitsky [this was the celebrated specialist] said quite the contrary . . ."

Ivan Ilych walked away, went to his own room, lay down, and began musing: "The kidney, a floating kidney." He recalled all the doctors had told him of how it detached itself and swayed about. And by an effort of imagination he tried to catch that kidney and arrest it and support it. So little was needed for this, it seemed to him. "No, I'll go to see Peter Ivanovich again." [That was the friend whose friend was a doctor.] He rang, ordered the carriage, and got ready to go.

"Where are you going, Jean?"[8] asked his wife, with a specially sad and exceptionally kind look.

This exceptionally kind look irritated him. He looked morosely at her.

"I must go to see Peter Ivanovich."

8. The French equivalent for Ivan. Russians of the upper classes frequently spoke French to each other in the nineteenth century.

He went to see Peter Ivanovich, and together they went to see his friend, the doctor. He was in, and Ivan Ilych had a long talk with him.

Reviewing the anatomical and physiological details of what in the doctor's opinion was going on inside him, he understood it all.

There was something, a small thing, in the vermiform appendix. It might all come right. Only stimulate the energy of one organ and check the activity of another, then absorption would take place and everything would come right. He got home rather late for dinner, ate his dinner, and conversed cheerfully, but could not for a long time bring himself to go back to work in his room. At last, however, he went to his study and did what was necessary, but the consciousness that he had put something aside—an important, intimate matter which he would revert to when his work was done—never left him. When he had finished his work he remembered that this intimate matter was the thought of his vermiform appendix. But he did not give himself up to it, and went to the drawing-room for tea. There were callers there, including the examining magistrate who was a desirable match for his daughter, and they were conversing, playing the piano, and singing. Ivan Ilych, as Praskovya Fëdorovna remarked, spent that evening more cheerfully than usual, but he never for a moment forgot that he had postponed the important matter of the appendix. At eleven o'clock he said good-night and went to his bedroom. Since his illness he had slept alone in a small room next to his study. He undressed and took up a novel by Zola,[9] but instead of reading it he fell into thought, and in his imagination that desired improvement in the vermiform appendix occurred. There was the absorption and evacuation and the re-establishment of normal activity. "Yes, that's it!" he said to himself. "One need only assist nature, that's all." He remembered his medicine, rose, took it, and lay down on his back watching for the beneficient action of the medicine and for it to lessen the pain. "I need only take it regularly and avoid all injurious influences. I am already feeling better, much better." He began touching his side: it was not painful to the touch. "There, I really don't feel it. It's much better already." He put out the light and turned on his side. . . . "The appendix is getting better, absorption is occurring." Suddenly he felt the old, familiar, dull, gnawing pain, stubborn and serious. There was the same familiar loathsome taste in his mouth. His heart sank and he felt dazed. "My God! My God!" he muttered. "Again, again! and it will never cease." And suddenly the matter presented itself in a quite different aspect. "Vermiform appendix! Kidney!" he said to himself. "It's not a question of

9. Émile Zola (1840–1902), French novelist.

appendix or kidney, but of life and . . . death. Yes, life was there and now it is going, going and I cannot stop it. Yes. Why deceive myself? Isn't it obvious to everyone but me that I'm dying, and that it's only a question of weeks, days . . . it may happen this moment. There was light and now there is darkness. I was here and now I'm going there! Where?" A chill came over him, his breathing ceased, and he felt only the throbbing of his heart.

"When I am not, what will there be? There will be nothing. Then where shall I be when I am no more? Can this be dying? No, I don't want to!" He jumped up and tried to light the candle, felt for it with trembling hands, dropped candle and candlestick on the floor, and fell back on his pillow.

"What's the use? It makes no difference," he said to himself, staring with wide-open eyes into the darkness. "Death. Yes, death. And none of them know or wish to know it, and they have no pity for me. Now they are playing." (He heard through the door the distant sound of a song and its accompaniment.) "It's all the same to them, but they will die too! Fools! I first, and they later, but it will be the same for them. And now they are merry . . . the beasts!"

Anger choked him and he was agonizingly, unbearably miserable. "It is impossible that all men have been doomed to suffer this awful horror!" He raised himself.

"Something must be wrong. I must calm myself—must think it all over from the beginning." And he again began thinking. "Yes, the beginning of my illness: I knocked my side, but I was still quite well that day and the next. It hurt a little, then rather more. I saw the doctors, then followed despondency and anguish, more doctors, and I drew nearer to the abyss. My strength grew less and I kept coming nearer and nearer, and now I have wasted away and there is no light in my eyes. I think of the appendix—but this is death! I think of mending the appendix, and all the while here is death! Can it really be death?" Again terror seized him and he gasped for breath. He leant down and began feeling for the matches, pressing with his elbow on the stand beside the bed. It was in his way and hurt him, he grew furious with it, pressed on it still harder, and upset it. Breathless and in despair he fell on his back, expecting death to come immediately.

Meanwhile the visitors were leaving. Praskovya Fëdorovna was seeing them off. She heard something fall and came in.

"What has happened?"

"Nothing. I knocked it over accidentally."

She went out and returned with a candle. He lay there panting heavily, like a man who has run a thousand yards, and stared upwards at her with a fixed look.

"What is it, Jean?"

"No . . . no . . . thing. I upset it." ("Why speak of it? She won't understand," he thought.)

And in truth she did not understand. She picked up the stand, lit his candle, and hurried away to see another visitor off. When she came back he still lay on his back, looking upwards.

"What is it? Do you feel worse?"

"Yes."

She shook her head and sat down.

"Do you know, Jean, I think we must ask Leshchetitsky to come and see you here."

This meant calling in the famous specialist, regardless of expense. He smiled malignantly and said "No." She remained a little longer and then went up to him and kissed his forehead.

While she was kissing him he hated her from the bottom of his soul and with difficulty refrained from pushing her away.

"Good-night. Please God you'll sleep."

"Yes."

VI

Ivan Ilych saw that he was dying, and he was in continual despair.

In the depth of his heart he knew he was dying, but not only was he not accustomed to the thought, he simply did not and could not grasp it.

The syllogism he had learnt from Kiezewetter's Logic:[1] "Caius is a man, men are mortal, therefore Caius is mortal," had always seemed to him correct as applied to Caius, but certainly not as applied to himself. That Caius—man in the abstract—was mortal, was perfectly correct, but he was not Caius, not an abstract man, but a creature quite, quite separate from all others. He had been little Vanya, with a mamma and a papa, with Mitya and Volodya, with the toys, a coachman and a nurse, afterwards with Katenka and with all the joys, griefs, and delights of childhood, boyhood, and youth. What did Caius know of the smell of that striped leather ball Vanya had been so fond of? Had Caius kissed his mother's hand like that, and did the silk of her dress rustle so for Caius? Had he rioted like that at school when the pastry was bad? Had Caius been in love like that? Could Caius preside at a session as he did? "Caius really was mortal, and it was right for him to die; but for me, little Vanya, Ivan Ilych, with all my thoughts and emotions, it's

1. The *Outline of Logic According to Kantian Principles* by Klaus Kiezewetter (1766–1819) was widely used as a Russian textbook.

altogether a different matter. It cannot be that I ought to die. That would be too terrible."

Such was his feeling.

"If I had to die like Caius I should have known it was so. An inner voice would have told me so, but there was nothing of the sort in me and I and all my friends felt that our case was quite different from that of Caius. And now here it is!" he said to himself. "It can't be. It's impossible! But here it is. How is this? How is one to understand it?"

He could not understand it, and tried to drive this false, incorrect, morbid thought away and to replace it by other proper and healthy thoughts. But that thought, and not the thought only but the reality itself, seemed to come and confront him.

And to replace that thought he called up a succession of others, hoping to find in them some support. He tried to get back into the former current of thoughts that had once screened the thought of death from him. But strange to say, all that had formerly shut off, hidden, and destroyed, his consciousness of death, no longer had that effect. Ivan Ilych now spent most of his time in attempting to re-establish that old current. He would say to himself: "I will take up my duties again—after all I used to live by them." And banishing all doubts he would go to the law courts, enter into conversation with his colleagues, and sit carelessly as was his wont, scanning the crowd with a thoughtful look and leaning both his emaciated arms on the arms of his oak chair; bending over as usual to a colleague and drawing his papers nearer he would interchange whispers with him, and then suddenly raising his eyes and sitting erect would pronounce certain words and open the proceedings. But suddenly in the midst of those proceedings the pain in his side, regardless of the stage the proceedings had reached, would begin its own gnawing work. Ivan Ilych would turn his attention to it and try to drive the thought of it away, but without success. *It* would come and stand before him and look at him, and he would be petrified and the light would die out of his eyes, and he would again begin asking himself whether *It* alone was true. And his colleagues and subordinates would see with surprise and distress that he, the brilliant and subtle judge, was becoming confused and making mistakes. He would shake himself, try to pull himself together, manage somehow to bring the sitting to a close, and return home with the sorrowful consciousness that his judicial labours could not as formerly hide from him what he wanted them to hide, and could not deliver him from *It*. And what was worst of all was that *It* drew his attention to itself not in order to make him take some action but only that he should look at *It*, look it straight in the face: look at it and without doing anything, suffer inexpressibly.

And to save himself from this condition Ivan Ilych looked for consolations—new screens—and new screens were found and for a while seemed to save him, but then they immediately fell to pieces or rather became transparent, as if *It* penetrated them and nothing could veil *It*.

In these latter days he would go into the drawing-room he had arranged—that drawing-room where he had fallen and for the sake of which (how bitterly ridiculous it seemed) he had sacrificed his life—for he knew that his illness originated with that knock. He would enter and see that something had scratched the polished table. He would look for the cause of this and find that it was the bronze ornamentation of an album, that had got bent. He would take up the expensive album which he had lovingly arranged, and feel vexed with his daughter and her friends for their untidiness—for the album was torn here and there and some of the photographs turned upside down. He would put it carefully in order and bend the ornamentation back into position. Then it would occur to him to place all those things in another corner of the room, near the plants. He could call the footman, but his daughter or wife would come to help him. They would not agree, and his wife would contradict him, and he would dispute and grow angry. But that was all right, for then he did not think about *It*. *It* was invisible.

But then, when he was moving something himself, his wife would say: "Let the servants do it. You will hurt yourself again." And suddenly *It* would flash through the screen and he would see it. It was just a flash, and he hoped it would disappear, but he would involuntarily pay attention to his side. "It sits there as before, gnawing just the same!" And he could no longer forget *It*, but could distinctly see it looking at him from behind the flowers. "What is it all for?"

"It really is so! I lost my life over that curtain as I might have done when storming a fort. Is that possible? How terrible and how stupid. It can't be true! It can't, but it is."

He would go to his study, lie down, and again be alone with *It*: face to face with *It*. And nothing could be done with *It* except to look at it and shudder.

VII

How it happened it is impossible to say because it came about step by step, unnoticed, but in the third month of Ivan Ilych's illness, his wife, his daughter, his son, his acquaintances, the doctors, the servants, and above all he himself, were aware that the whole interest he had for other people was whether he would soon vacate his place, and at last release the living from the discomfort caused by his presence and be himself released from his sufferings.

He slept less and less. He was given opium and hypodermic injections of morphine, but this did not relieve him. The dull depression he experienced in a somnolent condition at first gave him a little relief, but only as something new, afterwards it became as distressing as the pain itself or even more so.

Special foods were prepared for him by the doctors' orders, but all those foods became increasingly distasteful and disgusting to him.

For his excretions also special arrangements had to be made, and this was a torment to him every time—a torment from the uncleanliness, the unseemliness, and the smell, and from knowing that another person had to take part in it.

But just through this most unpleasant matter, Ivan Ilych obtained comfort. Gerasim, the butler's young assistant, always came in to carry the things out. Gerasim was a clean, fresh peasant lad, grown stout on town food and always cheerful and bright. At first the sight of him, in his clean Russian peasant costume, engaged on that disgusting task embarrassed Ivan Ilych.

Once when he got up from the commode too weak to draw up his trousers, he dropped into a soft armchair and looked with horror at his bare, enfeebled thighs with the muscles so sharply marked on them.

Gerasim with a firm light tread, his heavy boots emitting a pleasant smell of tar and fresh winter air, came in wearing a clean Hessian apron, the sleeves of his print shirt tucked up over his strong bare young arms; and refraining from looking at his sick master out of consideration for his feelings, and restraining the joy of life that beamed from his face, he went up to the commode.

"Gerasim!" said Ivan Ilych in a weak voice.

Gerasim started, evidently afraid he might have committed some blunder, and with a rapid movement turned his fresh, kind, simple young face which just showed the first downy signs of a beard.

"Yes, sir?"

"That must be very unpleasant for you. You must forgive me. I am helpless."

"Oh, why, sir," and Gerasim's eyes beamed and he showed his glistening white teeth, "what's a little trouble? It's a case of illness with you, sir."

And his deft strong hands did their accustomed task, and he went out of the room stepping lightly. Five minutes later he as lightly returned.

Ivan Ilych was still sitting in the same position in the armchair.

"Gerasim," he said when the latter had replaced the freshly-washed utensil. "Please come here and help me." Gerasim went up to him. "Lift me up. It is hard for me to get up, and I have sent Dmitri away."

Gerasim went up to him, grasped his master with his strong arms deftly but gently, in the same way that he stepped—lifted him, supported him with one hand, and with the other drew up his trousers and would have set him down again, but Ivan Ilych asked to be led to the sofa. Gerasim, without an effort and without apparent pressure, led him, almost lifting him, to the sofa and placed him on it.

"Thank you. How easily and well you do it all!"

Gerasim smiled again and turned to leave the room. But Ivan Ilych felt his presence such a comfort that he did not want to let him go.

"One thing more, please move up that chair. No, the other one—under my feet. It is easier for me when my feet are raised."

Gerasim brought the chair, set it down gently in place, and raised Ivan Ilych's legs on to it. It seemed to Ivan Ilych that he felt better while Gerasim was holding up his legs.

"It's better when my legs are higher," he said. "Place that cushion under them."

Gerasim did so. He again lifted the legs and placed them, and again Ivan Ilych felt better while Gerasim held his legs. When he set them down Ivan Ilych fancied he felt worse.

"Gerasim," he said. "Are you busy now?"

"Not at all, sir," said Gerasim, who had learnt from the townsfolk how to speak to gentlefolk.

"What have you still to do?"

"What have I to do? I've done everything except chopping the logs for tomorrow."

"Then hold my legs up a bit higher, can you?"

"Of course I can. Why not?" And Gerasim raised his master's legs higher and Ivan Ilych thought that in that position he did not feel any pain at all.

"And how about the logs?"

"Don't trouble about that, sir. There's plenty of time."

Ivan Ilych told Gerasim to sit down and hold his legs, and began to talk to him. And strange to say it seemed to him that he felt better while Gerasim held his legs up.

After that Ivan Ilych would sometimes call Gerasim and get him to hold his legs on his shoulders, and he liked talking to him. Gerasim did it all easily, willingly, simply, and with a good nature that touched Ivan Ilych. Health, strength, and vitality in other people were offensive to him, but Gerasim's strength and vitality did not mortify but soothed him.

What tormented Ivan Ilych most was the deception, the lie, which for some reason they all accepted, that he was not dying but was simply ill, and that he only need keep quiet and undergo a treatment and then something very good would result. He however knew that do what they would nothing would come of it, only still more agonizing suffering and death. This deception tortured him—their not wishing to admit what they all knew and what he knew, but wanting to lie to him concerning his terrible condition, and wishing and forcing him to participate in that lie. Those lies—lies enacted over him on the eve of his death and destined to degrade this awful, solemn act to the level of their visitings, their curtains, their sturgeon for dinner—were a terrible agony for Ivan Ilych. And strangely enough, many times when they were going through their antics over him he had been within a hairbreadth of calling out to them: "Stop lying! You know and I know that I am dying. Then at least stop lying about it!" But he had never had the spirit to do it. The awful, terrible act of his dying was, he could see, reduced by those about him to the level of a casual, unpleasant, and almost indecorous incident (as if someone entered a drawing-room diffusing an unpleasant odour) and this was done by that very decorum which he had served all his life long. He saw that no one felt for him, because no one even wished to grasp his position. Only Gerasim recognized it and pitied him. And so Ivan Ilych felt at ease only with him. He felt comforted when Gerasim supported his legs (sometimes all night long) and refused to go to bed, saying: "Don't you worry, Ivan Ilych. I'll get sleep enough later on," or when he suddenly became familiar and exclaimed: "If you weren't sick it would be another matter, but as it is, why should I grudge a little trouble?" Gerasim alone did not lie; everything showed that he alone understood the facts of the case and did not consider it necessary to disguise them, but simply felt sorry for his emaciated and enfeebled master. Once when Ivan Ilych was sending him away he even said straight out: "We shall all of us die, so why should I grudge a little trouble?"—expressing the fact that he did not think his work burdensome, because he was doing it for a dying man and hoped someone would do the same for him when his time came.

Apart from this lying, or because of it, what most tormented Ivan Ilych was that no one pitied him as he wished to be pitied. At certain moments after prolonged suffering he wished most of all (though he would have been ashamed to confess it) for someone to pity him as a sick child is pitied. He longed to be petted and comforted. He knew he was an important functionary, that he had a beard turning grey, and that therefore what he longed for was impossible, but still he longed for it. And in Gerasim's attitude towards him there was something akin to what he wished for, and so that attitude comforted him. Ivan Ilych wanted to weep, wanted to be petted and cried over, and then his colleague Shebek would come, and instead of weeping and being petted, Ivan Ilych would assume a serious, severe, and profound air, and by force of habit would express his opinion on a decision of the Court of Cassation[2] and would stubbornly insist on that view. This falsity around him and within him did more than anything else to poison his last days.

VIII

It was morning. He knew it was morning because Gerasim had gone, and Peter the footman had come and put out the candles, drawn back one of the curtains, and begun quietly to tidy up. Whether it was morning or evening, Friday or Sunday, made no difference, it was all just the same: the gnawing, unmitigated, agonizing pain, never ceasing for an instant, the consciousness of life inexorably waning but not yet extinguished, the approach of that ever dreaded and hateful Death which was the only reality, and always the same falsity. What were days, weeks, hours, in such a case?

"Will you have some tea, sir?"

"He wants things to be regular, and wishes the gentlefolk to drink tea in the morning," thought Ivan Ilych, and only said "No."

"Wouldn't you like to move onto the sofa, sir?"

"He wants to tidy up the room, and I'm in the way. I am uncleanliness and disorder," he thought, and said only:

"No, leave me alone."

The man went on bustling about. Ivan Ilych stretched out his hand. Peter came up, ready to help.

"What is it, sir?"

"My watch."

Peter took the watch which was close at hand and gave it to his master.

"Half-past eight. Are they up?"

"No, sir, except Vasily Ivanich" (the son) "who has gone to school. Praskovya Fëdorovna ordered me to wake her if you asked for her. Shall I do so?"

"No, there's no need to." "Perhaps I'd better have some tea," he thought, and added aloud: "Yes, bring me some tea."

Peter went to the door, but Ivan Ilych dreaded being left alone. "How can I keep him here? Oh yes, my medicine." "Peter, give me my medicine." "Why not? Perhaps it may still do me some good." He took a spoonful and swallowed it. "No, it won't help. It's all tomfoolery, all deception," he decided as soon as he became aware of the familiar, sickly, hopeless taste. "No, I can't believe in it any longer. But the pain, why this pain? If it would only cease just for a moment!" And he

2. The highest court of appeal constituted by the council of state.

moaned. Peter turned towards him. "It's all right. Go and fetch me some tea."

Peter went out. Left alone Ivan Ilych groaned not so much with pain, terrible though that was, as from mental anguish. Always and for ever the same, always these endless days and nights. If only it would come quicker! If only *what* would come quicker? Death, darkness? . . . No, no! Anything rather than death!

When Peter returned with the tea on a tray, Ivan Ilych stared at him for a time in perplexity, not realizing who and what he was. Peter was disconcerted by that look and his embarrassment brought Ivan Ilych to himself.

"Oh, tea! All right, put it down. Only help me to wash and put on a clean shirt."

And Ivan Ilych began to wash. With pauses for rest, he washed his hands and then his face, cleaned his teeth, brushed his hair, and looked in the glass. He was terrified by what he saw, especially by the limp way in which his hair clung to his pallid forehead.

While his shirt was being changed he knew that he would be still more frightened at the sight of his body, so he avoided looking at it. Finally he was ready. He drew on a dressing-gown, wrapped himself in a plaid, and sat down in the armchair to take his tea. For a moment he felt refreshed, but as soon as he began to drink the tea he was again aware of the same taste, and the pain also returned. He finished it with an effort, and then lay down stretching out his legs, and dismissed Peter.

Always the same. Now a spark of hope flashes up, then a sea of despair rages, and always pain; always pain, always despair, and always the same. When alone he had a dreadful and distressing desire to call someone, but he knew beforehand that with others present it would be still worse. "Another dose of morphine—to lose consciousness. I will tell him, the doctor, that he must think of something else. It's impossible, impossible, to go on like this."

An hour and another pass like that. But now there is a ring at the door bell. Perhaps it's the doctor? It is. He comes in fresh, hearty, plump, and cheerful, with that look on his face that seems to say: "There now, you're in a panic about something, but we'll arrange it all for you directly!" The doctor knows this expression is out of place here, but he has put it on once for all and can't take it off—like a man who has put on a frock-coat in the morning to pay a round of calls.

The doctor rubs his hands vigorously and reassuringly.

"Brr! How cold it is! There's such a sharp frost; just let me warm myself!" he says, as if it were only a matter of waiting till he was warm, and then he would put everything right.

"Well now, how are you?"

Ivan Ilych feels that the doctor would like to say: "Well, how are our affairs?" but that even he feels that this would not do, and says instead: "What sort of a night have you had?"

Ivan Ilych looks at him as much as to say: "Are you really never ashamed of lying?" But the doctor does not wish to understand this question, and Ivan Ilych says: "Just as terrible as ever. The pain never leaves me and never subsides. If only something . . ."

"Yes, you sick people are always like that. . . . There, now I think I am warm enough. Even Praskovya Fëdorovna, who is so particular, could find no fault with my temperature. Well, now I can say good-morning," and the doctor presses his patient's hand.

Then, dropping his former playfulness, he begins with a most serious face to examine the patient, feeling his pulse and taking his temperature, and then begins the sounding and auscultation.

Ivan Ilych knows quite well and definitely that all this is nonsense and pure deception, but when the doctor, getting down on his knee, leans over him, putting his ear first higher then lower, and performs various gymnastic movements over him with a significant expression on his face, Ivan Ilych submits to it all as he used to submit to the speeches of the lawyers, though he knew very well that they were all lying and why they were lying.

The doctor, kneeling on the sofa, is still sounding him when Praskovya Fëdorovna's silk dress rustles at the door and she is heard scolding Peter for not having let her know of the doctor's arrival.

She comes in, kisses her husband, and at once proceeds to prove that she has been up a long time already, and only owing to a misunderstanding failed to be there when the doctor arrived.

Ivan Ilych looks at her, scans her all over, sets against her the whiteness and plumpness and cleanness of her hands and neck, the gloss of her hair, and the sparkle of her vivacious eyes. He hates her with his whole soul. And the thrill of hatred he feels for her makes him suffer from her touch.

Her attitude towards him and his disease is still the same. Just as the doctor had adopted a certain relation to his patient which he could not abandon, so had she formed one towards him—that he was not doing something he ought to do and was himself to blame, and that she reproached him lovingly for this—and she could not now change that attitude.

"You see he doesn't listen to me and doesn't take his medicine at the proper time. And above all he lies in a position that is no doubt bad for him—with his legs up."

She described how he made Gerasim hold his legs up.

The doctor smiled with a contemptuous affability that said: "What's to be done? These sick people do have foolish fancies of that kind, but we must forgive them."

When the examination was over the doctor looked at his watch, and then Praskovya Fëdorovna announced to Ivan Ilych that it was of course as he pleased, but she had sent today for a celebrated specialist who would examine him and have a consultation with Michael Danilovich (their regular doctor).

"Please don't raise any objections. I am doing this for my own sake," she said ironically, letting it be felt that she was doing it all for his sake and only said this to leave him no right to refuse. He remained silent, knitting his brows. He felt that he was so surrounded and involved in a mesh of falsity that it was hard to unravel anything.

Everything she did for him was entirely for her own sake, and she told him she was doing for herself what she actually was doing for herself, as if that was so incredible that he must understand the opposite.

At half-past eleven the celebrated specialist arrived. Again the sounding began and the significant conversations in his presence and in another room, about the kidneys and the appendix, and the questions and answers, with such an air of importance that again, instead of the real question of life and death which now alone confronted him, the question arose of the kidney and appendix which were not behaving as they ought to and would now be attacked by Michael Danilovich and the specialist and forced to amend their ways.

The celebrated specialist took leave of him with a serious though not hopeless look, and in reply to the timid question Ivan Ilych, with eyes glistening with fear and hope, put to him as to whether there was a chance of recovery, said that he could not vouch for it but there was a possibility. The look of hope with which Ivan Ilych watched the doctor out was so pathetic that Praskovya Fëdorovna, seeing it, even wept as she left the room to hand the doctor his fee.

The gleam of hope kindled by the doctor's encouragement did not last long. The same room, the same pictures, curtains, wall-paper, medicine bottles, were all there, and the same aching suffering body, and Ivan Ilych began to moan. They gave him a subcutaneous injection and he sank into oblivion.

It was twilight when he came to. They brought him his dinner and he swallowed some beef tea with difficulty, and then everything was the same again and night was coming on.

After dinner, at seven o'clock, Praskovya Fëdorovna came into the room in evening dress, her full bosom pushed by her corset, and with traces of powder on her face. She had reminded him in the morning that they were going to the theatre. Sarah Bernhardt[3] was visiting the town and they had a box, which he had insisted on their taking. Now he had forgotten about it and her toilet offended him, but he concealed his vexation when he remembered that he had himself insisted on their securing a box and going because it would be an instructive and aesthetic pleasure for the children.

Praskovya Fëdorovna came in, self-satisfied but yet with a rather guilty air. She sat down and asked how he was, but, as he saw, only for the sake of asking and not in order to learn about it, knowing that there was nothing to learn—and then went on to what she really wanted to say: that she would not on any account have gone but that the box had been taken and Helen and their daughter were going, as well as Petrishchev (the examining magistrate, their daughter's fiancé) and that it was out of the question to let them go alone; but that she would have much preferred to sit with him for a while; and he must be sure to follow the doctor's orders while she was away.

"Oh, and Fëdor Petrovich" (the fiancé) "would like to come in. May he? And Lisa?"

"All right."

Their daughter came in in full evening dress, her fresh young flesh exposed (making a show of that very flesh which in his own case caused so much suffering), strong, healthy, evidently in love, and impatient with illness, suffering, and death, because they interfered with her happiness.

Fëdor Petrovich came in too, in evening dress, his hair curled *à la Capoul*,[4] a tight stiff collar round his long sinewy neck, an enormous white shirt-front and narrow black trousers tightly stretched over his strong thighs. He had one white glove tightly drawn on, and was holding his opera hat in his hand.

Following him the schoolboy crept in unnoticed, in a new uniform, poor little fellow, and wearing gloves. Terribly dark shadows showed under his eyes, the meaning of which Ivan Ilych knew well.

His son had always seemed pathetic to him, and now it was dreadful to see the boy's frightened look of pity. It seemed to Ivan Ilych that Vasya was the only one besides Gerasim who understood and pitied him.

They all sat down and again asked how he was. A silence followed. Lisa asked her mother about the opera-glasses, and there was an altercation between mother and daughter as to who had taken them and where they had been put. This occasioned some unpleasantness.

Fëdor Petrovich inquired of Ivan Ilych whether he had ever seen

3. French actress (1844–1923), who had a great popular following.

4. An ornate and elaborate form of man's hair style.

Sarah Bernhardt. Ivan Ilych did not at first catch the question, but then replied: "No, have you seen her before?"

"Yes, in *Adrienne Lecouvreur*."[5]

Praskovya Fëdorovna mentioned some rôles in which Sarah Bernhardt was particularly good. Her daughter disagreed. Conversation sprang up as to the elegance and realism of her acting—the sort of conversation that is always repeated and is always the same.

In the midst of the conversation Fëdor Petrovich glanced at Ivan Ilych and became silent. The others also looked at him and grew silent. Ivan Ilych was staring with glittering eyes straight before him, evidently indignant with them. This had to be rectified, but it was impossible to do so. The silence had to be broken, but for a time no one dared to break it and they all became afraid that the conventional deception would suddenly become obvious and the truth become plain to all. Lisa was the first to pluck up courage and break that silence, but by trying to hide what everybody was feeling, she betrayed it.

"Well, if we are going it's time to start," she said, looking at her watch, a present from her father, and with a faint and significant smile at Fëdor Petrovich relating to something known only to them. She got up with a rustle of her dress.

They all rose, said good-night, and went away.

When they had gone it seemed to Ivan Ilych that he felt better; the falsity had gone with them. But the pain remained—that same pain and that same fear that made everything monotonously alike, nothing harder and nothing easier. Everything was worse.

Again minute followed minute and hour followed hour. Everything remained the same and there was no cessation. And the inevitable end of it all became more and more terrible.

"Yes, send Gerasim here," he replied to a question Peter asked.

IX

His wife returned late at night. She came in on tiptoe, but he heard her, opened his eyes, and made haste to close them again. She wished to send Gerasim away and to sit with him herself, but he opened his eyes and said: "No, go away."

"Are you in great pain?"

"Always the same."

"Take some opium."

He agreed and took some. She went away.

Till about three in the morning he was in a state of stupefied misery. It seemed to him that he and his pain were being thrust into a

5. A comedy by Eugène Scribe (1791–1861) and Ernest Legouvé (1807–1903), written in 1849.

narrow, deep black sack, but though they were pushed further and further in they could not be pushed to the bottom. And this, terrible enough in itself, was accompanied by suffering. He was frightened yet wanted to fall through the sack, he struggled but yet co-operated. And suddenly he broke through, fell, and regained consciousness. Gerasim was sitting at the foot of the bed dozing quietly and patiently, while he himself lay with his emaciated stockinged legs resting on Gerasim's shoulders; the same shaded candle was there and the same unceasing pain.

"Go away, Gerasim," he whispered.

"It's all right, sir. I'll stay a while."

"No. Go away."

He removed his legs from Gerasim's shoulders, turned sideways onto his arm, and felt sorry for himself. He only waited till Gerasim had gone into the next room and then restrained himself no longer but wept like a child. He wept on account of his helplessness, his terrible loneliness, the cruelty of man, the cruelty of God, and the absence of God.

"Why hast Thou done all this? Why hast Thou brought me here? Why, why dost Thou torment me so terribly?"

He did not expect an answer and yet wept because there was no answer and could be none. The pain again grew more acute, but he did not stir and did not call. He said to himself: "Go on! Strike me! But what is it for? What have I done to Thee? What is it for?"

Then he grew quiet and not only ceased weeping but even held his breath and became all attention. It was as though he were listening not to an audible voice but to the voice of his soul, to the current of thoughts arising within him.

"What is it you want?" was the first clear conception capable of expression in words, that he heard.

"What do you want? What do you want?" he repeated to himself.

"What do I want? To live and not to suffer," he answered.

And again he listened with such concentrated attention that even his pain did not distract him.

"To live? How?" asked his inner voice.

"Why, to live as I used to—well and pleasantly."

"As you lived before, well and pleasantly?" the voice repeated.

And in imagination he began to recall the best moments of his pleasant life. But strange to say none of those best moments of his pleasant life now seemed at all what they had then seemed—none of them except the first recollections of childhood. There, in childhood, there had been something really pleasant with which it would be possible to live if it could return. But the child who had experienced that happiness existed no longer, it was like a reminiscence of somebody else.

As soon as the period began which had produced the present Ivan Ilych, all that had then seemed joys now melted before his sight and turned into something trivial and often nasty.

And the further he departed from childhood and the nearer he came to the present the more worthless and doubtful were the joys. This began with the School of Law. A little that was really good was still found there—there was light-heartedness, friendship, and hope. But in the upper classes there had already been fewer of such good moments. Then during the first years of his official career, when he was in the service of the Governor, some pleasant moments again occurred: they were the memories of love for a woman. Then all became confused and there was still less of what was good; later on again there was still less that was good, and the further he went the less there was. His marriage, a mere accident, then the disenchantment that followed it, his wife's bad breath and the sensuality and hypocrisy: then the deadly official life and those preoccupations about money, a year of it, and two, and ten, and twenty, and always the same thing. And the longer it lasted the more deadly it became. "It is as if I had been going downhill while I imagined I was going up. And that is really what it was. I was going up in public opinion, but to the same extent life was ebbing away from me. And now it is all done and there is only death."

"Then what does it mean? Why? It can't be that life is so senseless and horrible. But if it really has been so horrible and senseless, why must I die and die in agony? There is something wrong!"

"Maybe I did not live as I ought to have done," it suddenly occurred to him. "But how could that be, when I did everything properly?" he replied, and immediately dismissed from his mind this, the sole solution of all the riddles of life and death, as something quite impossible.

"Then what do you want now? To live? Live how? Live as you lived in the law courts when the usher proclaimed 'The judge is coming!' The judge is coming, the judge!" he repeated to himself. "Here he is, the judge. But I am not guilty!" he exclaimed angrily. "What is it for?" And he ceased crying, but turning his face to the wall continued to ponder on the same question: Why, and for what purpose, is there all this horror? But however much he pondered he found no answer. And whenever the thought occurred to him, as it often did, that it all resulted from his not having lived as he ought to have done, he at once recalled the correctness of his whole life and dismissed so strange an idea.

X

Another fortnight passed. Ivan Ilych now no longer left his sofa. He would not lie in bed but lay on the sofa, facing the wall nearly all the time. He suffered ever the same unceasing agonies and in his loneliness pondered always on the same insoluble question: "What is this? Can it be that it is Death?" And the inner voice answered: "Yes, it is Death."

"Why these sufferings?" And the voice answered, "For no reason—they just are so." Beyond and besides this there was nothing.

From the very beginning of his illness, ever since he had first been to see the doctor, Ivan Ilych's life had been divided between two contrary and alternating moods: now it was despair and the expectation of this uncomprehended and terrible death, and now hope and an intently interested observation of the functioning of his organs. Now before his eyes there was only a kidney or an intestine that temporarily evaded its duty, and now only that incomprehensible and dreadful death from which it was impossible to escape.

These two states of mind had alternated from the very beginning of his illness, but the further it progressed the more doubtful and fantastic became the conception of the kidney, and the more real the sense of impending death.

He had but to call to mind what he had been three months before and what he was now, to call to mind with what regularity he had been going downhill, for every possibility of hope to be shattered.

Latterly during that loneliness in which he found himself as he lay facing the back of the sofa, a loneliness in the midst of a populous town and surrounded by numerous acquaintances and relations but that yet could not have been more complete anywhere—either at the bottom of the sea or under the earth—during that terrible loneliness Ivan Ilych had lived only in memories of the past. Pictures of his past rose before him one after another. They always began with what was nearest in time and then went back to what was most remote—to his childhood—and rested there. If he thought of the stewed prunes that had been offered him that day, his mind went back to the raw shrivelled French plums of his childhood, their peculiar flavour and the flow of saliva when he sucked their stones, and along with the memory of that taste came a whole series of memories of those days: his nurse, his brother, and their toys. "No, I mustn't think of that. . . . It is too painful," Ivan Ilych said to himself, and brought himself back to the present—to the button on the back of the sofa and the creases in its morocco. "Morocco is expensive, but it does not wear well: there had been a quarrel about it. It was a different kind of quarrel and a different kind of morocco that time when we tore father's portfolio and were punished, and mama brought us some tarts. . . ." And again his thoughts dwelt on his childhood, and again it was painful and he tried to banish them and fix his mind on something else.

Then again together with that chain of memories another series passed through his mind—of how his illness had progressed and grown worse. There also the further back he looked the more life there had been. There had been more of what was good in life and more of life itself. The two merged together. "Just as the pain went on getting worse and worse, so my life grew worse and worse," he thought. "There is one bright spot there at the back, at the beginning of life, and afterwards all becomes blacker and blacker and proceeds more and more rapidly—in inverse ratio to the square of the distance from death," thought Ivan Ilych. And the example of a stone falling downwards with increasing velocity entered his mind. Life, a series of increasing sufferings, flies further and further towards its end—the most terrible suffering. "I am flying. . . ." He shuddered, shifted himself, and tried to resist, but was already aware that resistance was impossible, and again with eyes weary of gazing but unable to cease seeing what was before them, he stared at the back of the sofa and waited—awaiting that dreadful fall and shock and destruction.

"Resistance is impossible!" he said to himself. "If I could only understand what it is all for! But that too is impossible. An explanation would be possible if it could be said that I have not lived as I ought to. But it is impossible to say that," and he remembered all the legality, correctitude, and propriety of his life. "That at any rate can certainly not be admitted," he thought, and his lips smiled ironically as if someone could see that smile and be taken in by it. "There is no explanation! Agony, death . . . What for?"

XI

Another two weeks went by in this way and during that fortnight an event occurred that Ivan Ilych and his wife had desired. Petrishchev formally proposed. It happened in the evening. The next day Praskovya Fëdorovna came into her husband's room considering how best to inform him of it, but that very night there had been a fresh change for the worse in his condition. She found him still lying on the sofa but in a different position. He lay on his back, groaning and staring fixedly straight in front of him.

She began to remind him of his medicines, but he turned his eyes towards her with such a look that she did not finish what she was saying; so great an animosity, to her in particular, did that look express.

"For Christ's sake let me die in peace!" he said.

She would have gone away, but just then their daughter came in and went up to say good morning. He looked at her as he had done at his wife, and in reply to her inquiry about his health said dryly that he would soon free them all of himself. They were both silent and after sitting with him for a while went away.

"Is it our fault?" Lisa said to her mother. "It's as if we were to blame! I am sorry for papa, but why should we be tortured?"

The doctor came at his usual time. Ivan Ilych answered "Yes" and "No," never taking his angry eyes from him, and at last said: "You know you can do nothing for me, so leave me alone."

"We can ease your sufferings."

"You can't even do that. Let me be."

The doctor went into the drawing-room and told Praskovya Fëdorovna that the case was very serious and that the only resource left was opium to allay her husband's sufferings, which must be terrible.

It was true, as the doctor said, that Ivan Ilych's physical sufferings were terrible, but worse than the physical sufferings were his mental sufferings, which were his chief torture.

His mental sufferings were due to the fact that that night, as he looked at Gerasim's sleepy, good-natured face with its prominent cheekbones, the question suddenly occurred to him: "What if my whole life has really been wrong?"

It occurred to him that what had appeared perfectly impossible before, namely that he had not spent his life as he should have done, might after all be true. It occurred to him that his scarcely perceptible attempts to struggle against what was considered good by the most highly placed people, those scarcely noticeable impulses which he had immediately suppressed, might have been the real thing, and all the rest false. And his professional duties and the whole arrangement of his life and of his family, and all his social and official interests, might all have been false. He tried to defend all those things to himself and suddenly felt the weakness of what he was defending. There was nothing to defend.

"But if that is so," he said to himself, "and I am leaving this life with the consciousness that I have lost all that was given me and it is impossible to rectify it—what then?"

He lay on his back and began to pass his life in review in quite a new way. In the morning when he saw first his footman, then his wife, then his daughter, and then the doctor, their every word and movement confirmed to him the awful truth that had been revealed to him during the night. In them he saw himself—all that for which he had lived—and saw clearly that it was not real at all, but a terrible and huge deception which had hidden both life and death. This consciousness intensified his physical suffering tenfold. He groaned and tossed about, and pulled at his clothing which choked and stifled him. And he hated them on that account.

He was given a large dose of opium and became unconscious, but at noon his sufferings began again. He drove everybody away and tossed from side to side.

His wife came to him and said:

"Jean, my dear, do this for me. It can't do any harm and often helps. Healthy people often do it."

He opened his eyes wide.

"What? Take communion? Why? It's unnecessary! However . . ."

She began to cry.

"Yes, do, my dear. I'll send for our priest. He is such a nice man."

"All right. Very well," he muttered.

When the priest came and heard his confession, Ivan Ilych was softened and seemed to feel a relief from his doubts and consequently from his sufferings, and for a moment there came a ray of hope. He again began to think of the vermiform appendix and the possibility of correcting it. He received the sacrament with tears in his eyes.

When they laid him down again afterwards he felt a moment's ease, and the hope that he might live awoke in him again. He began to think of the operation that had been suggested to him. "To live! I want to live!" he said to himself.

His wife came in to congratulate him after his communion, and when uttering the usual conventional words she added:

"You feel better, don't you?"

Without looking at her he said "Yes."

Her dress, her figure, the expression of her face, the tone of her voice, all revealed the same thing. "This is wrong, it is not as it should be. All you have lived for and still live for is falsehood and deception, hiding life and death from you." And as soon as he admitted that thought, his hatred and his agonizing physical suffering again sprang up, and with that suffering a consciousness of the unavoidable, approaching end. And to this was added a new sensation of grinding shooting pain and a feeling of suffocation.

The expression of his face when he uttered that "yes" was dreadful. Having uttered it, he looked her straight in the eyes, turned on his face with a rapidity extraordinary in his weak state and shouted:

"Go away! Go away and leave me alone!"

XII

From that moment the screaming began that continued for three days, and was so terrible that one could not hear it through two closed doors without horror. At the moment he answered his wife he realized that he was lost, that there was no return, that the end had come, the very end, and his doubts were still unsolved and remained doubts.

"Oh! Oh! Oh!" he cried in various intonations. He had begun by screaming "I won't!" and continued screaming on the letter O.

For three whole days, during which time did not exist for him, he struggled in that black sack into which he was being thrust by an invisible, resistless force. He struggled as a man condemned to death struggles in the hands of the executioner, knowing that he cannot save himself. And every moment he felt that despite all his efforts he was drawing nearer and nearer to what terrified him. He felt that his agony was due to his being thrust into that black hole and still more to his not being able to get right into it. He was hindered from getting into it by his conviction that his life had been a good one. That very justification of his life held him fast and prevented his moving forward, and it caused him most torment of all.

Suddenly some force struck him in the chest and side, making it still harder to breathe, and he fell through the hole and there at the bottom was a light. What had happened to him was like the sensation one sometimes experiences in a railway carriage when one thinks one is going backwards while one is really going forwards and suddenly becomes aware of the real direction.

"Yes, it was all not the right thing," he said to himself, "but that's no matter. It can be done. But what *is* the right thing?" he asked himself, and suddenly grew quiet.

This occurred at the end of the third day, two hours before his death. Just then his schoolboy son had crept softly in and gone up to the bedside. The dying man was still screaming desperately and waving his arms. His hand fell on the boy's head, and the boy caught it, pressed it to his lips, and began to cry.

At that very moment Ivan Ilych fell through and caught sight of the light, and it was revealed to him that though his life had not been what it should have been, this could still be rectified. He asked himself, "What *is* the right thing?" and grew still, listening. Then he felt that someone was kissing his hand. He opened his eyes, looked at his son, and felt sorry for him. His wife came up to him and he glanced at her. She was gazing at him open-mouthed, with undried tears on her nose and cheek and a despairing look on her face. He felt sorry for her too.

"Yes, I am making them wretched," he thought. "They are sorry, but it will be better for them when I die." He wished to say this but had not the strength to utter it. "Besides, why speak? I must act," he thought. With a look at his wife he indicated his son and said: "Take him away . . . sorry for him . . . sorry for you too. . . ." He tried to add, "forgive me," but said "forgo" and waved his hand, knowing that He whose understanding mattered would understand.

And suddenly it grew clear to him that what had been oppressing him and would not leave him was all dropping away at once from two sides, from ten sides, and from all sides. He was sorry for them, he must act so as not to hurt them: release them and free himself from these sufferings. "How good and how simple!" he thought. "And the pain?" he asked himself. "What has become of it? Where are you, pain?"

He turned his attention to it.

"Yes, here it is. Well, what of it? Let the pain be."

"And death . . . where is it?"

He sought his former accustomed fear of death and did not find it. "Where is it? What death?" There was no fear because there was no death.

In place of death there was light.

"So that's what it is!" he suddenly exclaimed aloud. "What joy!"

To him all this happened in a single instant, and the meaning of that instant did not change. For those present his agony continued for another two hours. Something rattled in his throat, his emaciated body twitched, then the gasping and rattle became less and less frequent.

"It is finished!" said someone near him.

He heard these words and repeated them in his soul.

"Death is finished," he said to himself. "It is no more!"

He drew in a breath, stopped in the midst of a sigh, stretched out, and died.

---

1. How do his colleagues, friends, and family respond to Ivan Ilych's death? How does the presentation of their response set the stage for an account of his life?
2. What guided him in choosing the course his life would follow? What options did he neglect?
3. How does he deal with the difficulties of marriage and fatherhood?
4. Is there significance in the timing of the accident that leads to his death?
5. What are his feelings about the power given him as a magistrate?
6. What does the author suggest about the value of doctors?
7. Why does Ivan Ilych find no consolation in philosophizing about death?
8. Discuss the role of Gerasim in the last phases of Ivan Ilych's suffering. Is there a particular lesson in the young man's attitude, behavior, or character?
9. Interpret the sentence: "Ivan Ilych's life had been most simple, most ordinary, and therefore most terrible." Why "therefore"?
10. What is his final attitude toward what his life has been? Does this attitude reconcile him to dying?

John Updike

Updike (1932–) was born in Shillington, Pennsylvania, an only child. His mother—a writer—gave him the idea that being a painter or writer would lead him to a happy life, so he launched himself as a cartoonist for the Harvard Lampoon *during his college years and for a year after graduation studied drawing in England. Soon after this he joined the staff of* The New Yorker *and served the magazine in a number of capacities until 1957; he continues to contribute verse, reviews, and fiction to its pages. His fiction is often topical—people trapped in American fads and prejudices figure often in his most characteristic writing. His novels include* Rabbit, Run *(1960),* Couples *(1968),* Rabbit Redux *(1971),* Rabbit Is Rich *(1982),* The Witches of Eastwick *(1984),* Roger's Version *(1986),* Trust Me *(1987), and* S *(1988). His stories have been collected in* Pigeon Feathers and Other Stories *(1962),* The Music School *(1966),* Bech: A Book *(1970),* Museums and Women and Other Stories *(1972), and* Problems and Other Stories *(1979).*

A & P

In walks these three girls in nothing but bathing suits. I'm in the third checkout slot, with my back to the door, so I don't see them until they're over by the bread. The one that caught my eye first was the one in the plaid green two-piece. She was a chunky kid, with a good tan and a sweet broad soft-looking can with those two crescents of white just under it, where the sun never seems to hit, at the top of the backs of her legs. I stood there with my hand on a box of HiHo crackers trying to remember if I rang it up or not. I ring it up again and the customer starts giving me hell. She's one of these cash-register-watchers, a witch about fifty with rouge on her cheekbones and no eyebrows, and I know it made her day to trip me up. She'd been watching cash registers for fifty years and probably never seen a mistake before.

By the time I got her feathers smoothed and her goodies into a bag—she gives me a little snort in passing, if she'd been born at the right time they would have burned her over in Salem[1]—by the time I

1. A seaport in Massachusetts, famous for the execution of "witches" in 1692.

get her on her way the girls had circled around the bread and were coming back, without a pushcart, back my way along the counters, in the aisle between the checkouts and the Special bins. They didn't even have shoes on. There was this chunky one, with the two-piece—it was bright green and the seams on the bra were still sharp and her belly was still pretty pale so I guessed she just got it (the suit)—there was this one, with one of those chubby berry-faces, the lips all bunched together under her nose, this one, and a tall one, with black hair that hadn't quite frizzed right, and one of these sunburns right across under the eyes, and a chin that was too long—you know, the kind of girl other girls think is very "striking" and "attractive" but never quite makes it, as they very well know, which is why they like her so much—and then the third one, that wasn't quite so tall. She was the queen. She kind of led them, the other two peeking around and making their shoulders round. She didn't look around, not this queen, she just walked straight on slowly, on these long white primadonna legs. She came down a little hard on her heels, as if she didn't walk in bare feet that much, putting down her heels and then letting the weight move along to her toes as if she was testing the floor with every step, putting a little deliberate extra action into it. You never know for sure how girls' minds work (do you really think it's a mind in there or just a little buzz like a bee in a glass jar?) but you got the idea she had talked the other two into coming here with her, and now she was showing them how to do it, walk slow and hold yourself straight.

She had on a kind of dirty-pink—beige maybe, I don't know—bathing suit with a little nubble all over it and, what got me, the straps were down. They were off her shoulders looped loose around the cool tops of her arms, and I guess as a result the suit had slipped a little on her, so all around the top of the cloth there was this shining rim. If it hadn't been there you wouldn't have known there could have been anything whiter than those shoulders. With the straps pushed off, there was nothing between the top of the suit and the top of her head except just *her*, this clean bare plane of the top of her chest down from the shoulder bones like a dented sheet of metal tilted in the light. I mean, it was more than pretty.

She had a sort of oaky hair that the sun and salt had bleached, done up in a bun that was unravelling, and a kind of prim face. Walking into the A & P with your straps down, I suppose it's the only kind of face you *can* have. She held her head so high her neck, coming up out of those white shoulders, looked kind of stretched, but I didn't mind. The longer her neck was, the more of her there was.

She must have felt in the corner of her eye me and over my shoulder Stokesie in the second slot watching, but she didn't tip. Not this queen. She kept her eyes moving across the racks, and stopped, and turned so slow it made my stomach rub the inside of my apron, and buzzed to the other two, who kind of huddled against her for relief, and then they all three of them went up the cat-and-dog-food-breakfast-cereal-macaroni-rice-raisins-seasonings-spreads-spaghetti-soft-drinks-crackers-and-cookies aisle. From the third slot I look straight up this aisle to the meat counter, and I watched them all the way. The fat one with the tan sort of fumbled with the cookies, but on second thought she put the package back. The sheep pushing their carts down the aisle—the girls were walking against the usual traffic (not that we have one-way signs or anything)—were pretty hilarious. You could see them, when Queenie's white shoulders dawned on them, kind of jerk, or hop, or hiccup, but their eyes snapped back to their own baskets and on they pushed. I bet you could set off dynamite in an A & P and the people would by and large keep reaching and checking oatmeal off their lists and muttering "Let me see, there was a third thing, began with A, asparagus, no, ah, yes, applesauce!" or whatever it is they do mutter. But there was no doubt, this jiggled them. A few houseslaves in pin curlers even looked around after pushing their carts past to make sure what they had seen was correct.

You know, it's one thing to have a girl in a bathing suit down on the beach, where what with the glare nobody can look at each other much anyway, and another thing in the cool of the A & P, under the fluorescent lights, against all those stacked packages, with her feet paddling along naked over our checker-board green-and-cream rubber-tile floor.

"Oh Daddy," Stokesie said beside me. "I feel so faint."

"Darling," I said. "Hold me tight." Stokesie's married, with two babies chalked up on his fuselage already, but as far as I can tell that's the only difference. He's twenty-two, and I was nineteen this April.

"Is it done?" he asks, the responsible married man finding his voice. I forgot to say he thinks he's going to be manager some sunny day, maybe in 1990 when it's called the Great Alexandrov and Petrooshki Tea Company or something.

What he meant was, our town is five miles from a beach, with a big summer colony out on the Point, but we're right in the middle of town, and the women generally put on a shirt or shorts or something before they get out of the car into the street. And anyway these are usually women with six children and varicose veins mapping their legs and nobody, including them, could care less. As I say, we're right in the middle of town, and if you stand at our front doors you can see two banks and the Congregational church and the newspaper store and three real-estate offices and about twenty-seven old freeloaders tearing up Central Street because the sewer broke again. It's not as if we're on the Cape;[2] we're north of Boston and there's people in this town haven't seen the ocean for twenty years.

The girls had reached the meat counter and were asking McMahon something. He pointed, they pointed, and they shuffled out of sight behind a pyramid of Diet Delight peaches. All that was left for us to see was old McMahon patting his mouth and looking after them sizing up their joints. Poor kids, I began to feel sorry for them, they couldn't help it.

Now here comes the sad part of the story, at least my family says it's sad, but I don't think it's so sad myself. The store's pretty empty, it being Thursday afternoon, so there was nothing much to do except lean on the register and wait for the girls to show up again. The whole store was like a pinball machine and I din't know which tunnel they'd come out of. After a while they come around out of the far aisle, around the light bulbs, records at discount of the Caribbean Six or Tony Martin Sings or some such gunk you wonder they waste the wax on, six-packs of candy bars, and plastic toys done up in cellophane that fall apart when a kid looks at them anyway. Around they come, Queenie still leading the way, and holding a little gray jar in her hand. Slots Three through Seven are unmanned and I could see her wondering between Stokes and me, but Stokesie with his usual luck draws an old party in baggy gray pants who stumbles up with four giant cans of pineapple juice (what do these bums *do* with all that pineapple juice? I've often asked myself) so the girls come to me. Queenie puts down the jar and I take it into my fingers icy cold. Kingfish Fancy Herring Snacks in Pure Sour Cream: 49¢. Now her hands are empty, not a ring or a bracelet, bare as God made them, and I wonder where the money's coming from. Still with that prim look she lifts a folded dollar bill out of the hollow at the center of her nubbled pink top. The jar went heavy in my hand. Really, I thought that was so cute.

Then everybody's luck begins to run out. Lengel comes in from haggling with a truck full of cabbages on the lot and is about to scuttle into that door marked MANAGER behind which he hides all day when the girls touch his eye. Lengel's pretty dreary, teaches Sunday school and the rest, but he doesn't miss that much. He comes over and says, "Girls, this isn't the beach."

Queenie blushes, though maybe it's just a brush of sunburn I was noticing for the first time, now that she was so close. "My mother asked me to pick up a jar of herring snacks." Her voice kind of startled me, the way voices do when you see the people first, coming out so flat and

2. Cape Cod, Massachusetts, a resort area where fashions of dress are usually informal.

dumb yet kind of tony, too, the way it ticked over "pick up" and "snacks." All of a sudden I slid right down her voice into her living room. Her father and the other men were standing around in ice-cream coats and bow ties and the women were in sandals picking up herring snacks on toothpicks off a big glass plate and they were all holding drinks the color of water with olives and sprigs of mint in them. When my parents have somebody over they get lemonade and if it's a real racy affair Schlitz in tall glasses with "They'll Do It Every Time" cartoons stencilled on.

"That's all right," Lengel said. "But this isn't the beach." His repeating this struck me as funny, as if it had just occurred to him, and he had been thinking all these years the A & P was a great big dune and he was the head lifeguard. He didn't like my smiling—as I say he doesn't miss much—but he concentrates on giving the girls that sad Sunday-school-superintendent stare.

Queenie's blush is no sunburn now, and the plump one in plaid, that I liked better from the back—a really sweet can—pipes up, "We weren't doing any shopping. We just came in for the one thing."

"That makes no difference," Lengel tells her, and I could see from the way his eyes went that he hadn't noticed she was wearing a two-piece before. "We want you decently dressed when you come in here."

"We *are* decent," Queenie says suddenly, her lower lip pushing, getting sore now that she remembers her place, a place from which the crowd that runs the A & P must look pretty crummy. Fancy Herring Snacks flashed in her very blue eyes.

"Girls, I don't want to argue with you. After this come in here with your shoulders covered. It's our policy." He turns his back. That's policy for you. Policy is what the kingpins want. What the others want is juvenile delinquency.

All this while, the customers had been showing up with their carts but, you know, sheep, seeing a scene, they had all bunched up on Stokesie, who shook open a paper bag as gently as peeling a peach, not wanting to miss a word. I could feel in the silence everybody getting nervous, most of all Lengel, who asks me, "Sammy, have you rung up their purchase?"

I thought and said "No" but it wasn't about that I was thinking. I go through the punches, 4, 9, GROC, TOT—it's more complicated than you think, and after you do it often enough, it begins to make a little song, that you hear words to, in my case "Hello *(bing)* there, you *(gung)* hap-py *pee*-pul *(splat)!*"—the *splat* being the drawer flying out. I uncrease the bill, tenderly as you may imagine, it just having come from between the two smoothest scoops of vanilla I had ever known there were, and pass a half and a penny into her narrow pink palm, and nestle the herrings in a bag and twist its neck and hand it over, all the time thinking.

The girls, and who'd blame them, are in a hurry to get out, so I say "I quit" to Lengel quick enough for them to hear, hoping they'll stop and watch me, their unsuspected hero. They keep right on going, into the electric eye; the door flies open and they flicker across the lot to their car, Queenie and Plaid and Big Tall Goony-Goony (not that as raw material she was so bad), leaving me with Lengel and a kink in his eyebrow.

"Did you say something, Sammy?"

"I said I quit."

"I thought you did."

"You didn't have to embarrass them."

"It was they who were embarrassing us."

I started to say something that came out "Fiddle-de-do." It's a saying of my grandmother's, and I know she would have been pleased.

"I don't think you know what you're saying," Lengel said.

"I know you don't," I said. "But I do." I pull the bow at the back of my apron and start shrugging it off my shoulders. A couple of customers that had been heading for my slot begin to knock against each other, liked scared pigs in a chute.

Lengel sighs and begins to look very patient and old and gray. He's been a friend of my parents for years. "Sammy, you don't want to do this to your Mom and Dad," he tells me. It's true, I don't. But it seems to me that once you begin a gesture it's fatal not to go through with it. I fold the apron, "Sammy" stitched in red on the pocket, and put it on the counter, and drop the bow tie on top of it. The bow tie is theirs, if you've ever wondered. "You'll feel this for the rest of your life," Lengel says, and I know that's true, too, but remembering how he made that pretty girl blush makes me so scrunchy inside I punch the No Sale tab and the machine whirs "pee-pul" and the drawer splats out. One advantage to this scene taking place in summer, I can follow this up with a clean exit, there's no fumbling around getting your coat and galoshes, I just saunter into the electric eye in my white shirt that my mother ironed the night before, and the door heaves itself open, and outside the sunshine is skating around on the asphalt.

I look around for my girls, but they're gone, of course. There wasn't anybody but some young married screaming with her children about some candy they didn't get by the door of a powder-blue Falcon station wagon. Looking back in the big windows, over the bags of peat moss and aluminum lawn furniture stacked on the pavement, I could see Lengel in my place in the slot, checking the sheep through. His face was dark gray and his back stiff, as if he's just had an injection of iron, and my stomach kind of fell as I felt how hard the world was going to be to me hereafter.

---

1. Does Sammy understand why he sticks by his decision to quit? Is it "in character" for him to quit? What does the reader know about Sammy that he doesn't realize himself? Has something new emerged out of the ingredients of his character?
2. What is the importance of the fact that the girls are wearing bathing suits? Of calling one of the girls "Queenie"? Of the fact that there are three girls together?
3. To what extent does the conflict depend on different interpretations of such concepts as decency and policy?
4. Do you think the girls meant to cause trouble by coming to the store in bathing suits? If so, what has this to do with the theme of the story and any mythic allusions called up by the situation itself?
5. Is Sammy right in thinking the world will be a harder place for him hereafter? If it is, will this be a gain or a loss for him?

Alice Walker

Walker (1944–) was born in Eatonton, Georgia, and graduated from Sarah Lawrence College. After experience in the civil-rights movement and as a case worker for the New York City welfare department, she became a teacher of creative writing and black literature at Jackson State College, Tougaloo College, Wellesley, and Yale. Her short stories are collected in In Love and Trouble: Stories of Black Women *(1973) and* You Can't Keep a Good Woman Down *(1982). Her novels include* The Third Life of Grange Copeland *(1970),* Meridian *(1976),* The Color Purple *(1982), for which she won the Pulitzer Prize, and* The Temple of My Familiar *(1989).*

Everyday Use

for your grandmamma

I will wait for her in the yard that Maggie and I made so clean and wavy yesterday afternoon. A yard like this is more comfortable than most people know. It is not just a yard. It is like an extended living room. When the hard clay is swept clean as a floor and the fine sand around the edges lined with tiny, irregular grooves, anyone can come and sit and look up into the elm tree and wait for the breezes that never come inside the house.

Maggie will be nervous until after her sister goes: she will stand hopelessly in corners, homely and ashamed of the burn scars down her arms and legs, eying her sister with a mixture of envy and awe. She thinks her sister has held life always in the palm of one hand, that "no" is a word the world never learned to say to her.

You've no doubt seen those TV shows where the child who has "made it" is confronted, as a surprise, by her own mother and father, tottering in weakly from backstage. (A pleasant surprise, of course: What would they do if parent and child came on the show only to curse out and insult each other?) On TV mother and child embrace and smile into each other's faces. Sometimes the mother and father weep, the child wraps them in her arms and leans across the table to tell how she would not have made it without their help. I have seen these programs.

Sometimes I dream a dream in which Dee and I are suddenly brought together on a TV program of this sort. Out of a dark and soft-seated limousine I am ushered into a bright room filled with many people. There I meet a smiling, gray, sporty man like Johnny Carson who shakes my hand and tells me what a fine girl I have. Then we are on the stage and Dee is embracing me with tears in her eyes. She pins on my dress a large orchid, even though she has told me once that she thinks orchids are tacky flowers.

In real life I am a large, big-boned woman with rough, man-working hands. In the winter I wear flannel nightgowns to bed and overalls during the day. I can kill and clean a hog as mercilessly as a man. My fat keeps me hot in zero weather. I can work outside all day, breaking ice to get water for washing; I can eat pork liver cooked over the open fire minutes after it comes steaming from the hog. One winter I knocked a bull calf straight in the brain between the eyes with a sledge hammer and had the meat hung up to chill before nightfall. But of course all this does not show on television. I am the way my daughter would want me to be: a hundred pounds lighter, my skin like an uncooked barley pancake. My hair glistens in the hot bright lights. Johnny Carson has much to do to keep up with my quick and witty tongue.

But that is a mistake. I know even before I wake up. Who ever knew a Johnson with a quick tongue? Who can even imagine me looking a strange white man in the eye? It seems to me I have talked to them always with one foot raised in flight, with my head turned in whichever way is farthest from them. Dee, though. She would always look anyone in the eye. Hesitation was no part of her nature.

"How do I look, Mama?" Maggie says, showing just enough of her thin body enveloped in pink skirt and red blouse for me to know she's there, almost hidden by the door.

"Come out into the yard," I say.

Have you ever seen a lame animal, perhaps a dog run over by some careless person rich enough to own a car, sidle up to someone who is ignorant enough to be kind to them? That is the way my Maggie walks. She has been like this, chin on chest, eyes on ground, feet in shuffle, ever since the fire that burned the other house to the ground.

Dee is lighter than Maggie, with nicer hair and a fuller figure. She's a woman now, though sometimes I forget. How long ago was it that the other house burned? Ten, twelve years? Sometimes I can still hear the flames and feel Maggie's arms sticking to me, her hair smoking and her dress falling off her in little black papery flakes. Her eyes seemed stretched open, blazed open by the flames reflected in them. And Dee. I see her standing off under the sweet gum tree she used to dig gum out of; a look of concentration on her face as she watched the last dingy gray board of the house fall in toward the red-hot brick chimney. Why don't you do a dance around the ashes? I'd wanted to ask her. She had hated the house that much.

I used to think she hated Maggie, too. But that was before we raised the money, the church and me, to send her to Augusta to school. She used to read to us without pity; forcing words, lies, other folks' habits, whole lives upon us two, sitting trapped and ignorant underneath her voice. She washed us in a river of make-believe, burned us with a lot of knowledge we didn't necessarily need to know. Pressed us to her with the serious way she read, to shove us away at just the moment, like dimwits, we seemed about to understand.

Dee wanted nice things. A yellow organdy dress to wear to her graduation from high school; black pumps to match a green suit she'd made from an old suit somebody gave me. She was determnined to stare down any disaster in her efforts. Her eyelids would not flicker for minutes at a time. Often I fought off the temptation to shake her. At sixteen she had a style of her own: and knew what style was.

I never had an education myself. After second grade the school was closed down. Don't ask me why: in 1927 colored asked fewer questions than they do now. Sometimes Maggie reads to me. She stumbles along good naturedly but can't see well. She knows she is not bright. Like good looks and money, quickness passed her by. She will marry John Thomas (who has mossy teeth in an earnest face) and then I'll be free to sit here and I guess just sing church songs to myself. Although I never was a good singer. Never could carry a tune. I was always better at a man's job. I used to love to milk till I was hooked[1] in the side in '49. Cows are soothing and slow and don't bother you, unless you try to milk them the wrong way.

I have deliberately turned my back on the house. It is three rooms, just like the one that burned, except the roof is tin; they don't make shingle roofs any more. There are no real windows, just some holes cut in the sides, like the portholes in a ship, but not round and not square, with rawhide holding the shutters up on the outside. This house is in a pasture, too, like the other one. No doubt when Dee sees it she will want to tear it down. She wrote me once that no matter where we "choose" to live, she will manage to come see us. But she will never bring her friends. Maggie and I thought about this and Maggie asked me, "Mama, when did Dee ever *have* any friends?"

1. I.e., by the horn of the cow being milked.

She had a few. Furtive boys in pink shirts hanging about on washday after school. Nervous girls who never laughed. Impressed with her they worshiped the well-turned phrase, the cute shape, the scalding humor that erupted like bubbles in lye. She read to them.

When she was courting Jimmy T she didn't have much time to pay to us, but turned all her faultfinding power on him. He *flew* to marry a cheap city girl from a family of ignorant flashy people. She hardly had time to recompose herself.

When she comes I will meet—but there they are!

Maggie attempts to make a dash for the house, in her shuffling way, but I stay her with my hand. "Come back here," I say. And she stops and tries to dig a well in the sand with her toe.

It is hard to see them clearly through the strong sun. But even the first glimpse of leg out of the car tells me it is Dee. Her feet were always neat-looking, as if God himself had shaped them with a certain style. From the other side of the car comes a short, stocky man. Hair is all over his head a foot long and hanging from his chin like a kinky mule tail. I hear Maggie suck in her breath. "Uhnnnh," is what it sounds like. Like when you see the wriggling end of a snake just in front of your foot on the road. "Uhnnnh."

Dee next. A dress down to the ground, in this hot weather. A dress so loud it hurts my eyes. There are yellows and oranges enough to throw back the light of the sun. I feel my whole face warming from the heat waves it throws out. Earrings gold, too, and hanging down to her shoulders. Bracelets dangling and making noises when she moves her arm up to shake the folds of the dress out of her armpits. The dress is loose and flows, and as she walks closer, I like it. I hear Maggie go "Uhnnnh" again. It is her sister's hair. It stands straight up like the wool on a sheep. It is black as night and around the edges are two long pigtails that rope about like small lizards disappearing behind her ears.

"Wa-su-zo-Tean-o!" she says, coming on in that gliding way the dress makes her move. The short stocky fellow with the hair to his navel is all grinning and he follows up with "Asalamalakim,[2] my mother and sister!" He moves to hug Maggie but she falls back, right up against the back of my chair. I feel her trembling there and when I look up I see the perspiration falling off her chin.

"Don't get up," says Dee. Since I am stout it takes something of a push. You can see me trying to move a second or two before I make it. She turns, showing white heels through her sandals, and goes back

2. Phonetic rendering of a Muslim greeting. "Wa-su-zo-Tean-o" is a similar rendering of an African dialect salutation.

to the car. Out she peeks next with a Polaroid. She stoops down quickly and lines up picture after picture of me sitting there in front of the house with Maggie cowering behind me. She never takes a shot without making sure the house is included. When a cow comes nibbling around the edge of the yard she snaps it and me and Maggie *and* the house. Then she puts the Polaroid in the back seat of the car, and comes up and kisses me on the forehead.

Meanwhile Asalamalakim is going through motions with Maggie's hand. Maggie's hand is as limp as a fish, and probably as cold, despite the sweat, and she keeps trying to pull it back. It looks like Asalamalakim wants to shake hands but wants to do it fancy. Or maybe he don't know how people shake hands. Anyhow, he soon gives up on Maggie.

"Well," I say. "Dee."

"No, Mama," she says. "Not 'Dee,' Wangero Leewanika Kemanjo!"

"What happened to 'Dee'?" I wanted to know.

"She's dead," Wangero said. "I couldn't bear it any longer, being named after the people who oppress me."

"You know as well as me you was named after your aunt Dicie," I said. Dicie is my sister. She named Dee. We called her "Big Dee" after Dee was born.

"But who was *she* named after?" asked Wangero.

"I guess after Grandma Dee," I said.

"And who was she named after?" asked Wangero.

"Her mother," I said, and saw Wangero was getting tired. "That's about as far back as I can trace it," I said. Though, in fact, I probably could have carried it back beyond the Civil War through the branches.

"Well," said Asalamalakim, "there you are."

"Uhnnnh," I heard Maggie say.

"There I was not," I said, "before 'Dicie' cropped up in our family, so why should I try to trace it that far back?"

He just stood there grinning, looking down on me like somebody inspecting a Model A car. Every once in a while he and Wangero sent eye signals over my head.

"How do you pronounce this name?" I asked.

"You don't have to call me by it if you don't want to," said Wangero.

"Why shouldn't I?" I asked. "If that's what you want us to call you, we'll call you."

"I know it might sound awkward at first," said Wangero.

"I'll get used to it," I said. "Ream it out again."

Well, soon we got the name out of the way. Asalamalakim had a name twice as long and three times as hard. After I tripped over it two or three times he told me to just call him Hakim-a-barber. I wanted to ask him was he a barber, but I didn't really think he was, so I didn't ask.

"You must belong to those beef-cattle peoples down the road," I said. They said "Asalamalakim" when they met you, too, but they didn't shake hands. Always too busy: feeding the cattle, fixing the fences, putting up salt-lick shelters, throwing down hay. When the white folks poisoned some of the herd the men stayed up all night with rifles in their hands. I walked a mile and a half just to see the sight.

Hakim-a-barber said, "I accept some of their doctrines, but farming and raising cattle is not my style." (They didn't tell me, and I didn't ask, whether Wangero (Dee) had really gone and married him.)

We sat down to eat and right away he said he didn't eat collards and pork was unclean. Wangero, though, went on through the chitlins and corn bread, the greens and everything else. She talked a blue streak over the sweet potatoes. Everything delighted her. Even the fact that we still used the benches her daddy made for the table when we couldn't afford to buy chairs.

"Oh, Mama!" she cried. Then turned to Hakim-a-barber. "I never knew how lovely these benches are. You can feel the rump prints," she said, running her hands underneath her and along the bench. Then she gave a sigh and her hand closed over Grandma Dee's butter dish. "That's it!" she said. "I knew there was something I wanted to ask you if I could have." She jumped up from the table and went over in the corner where the churn stood, the milk in it clabber by now. She looked at the churn and looked at it.

"This churn top is what I need," she said. "Didn't Uncle Buddy whittle it out of a tree you all used to have?"

"Yes," I said.

"Uh huh," she said happily. "And I want the dasher, too."

"Uncle Buddy whittle that, too?" asked the barber.

Dee (Wangero) looked up at me.

"Aunt Dee's first husband whittled the dash," said Maggie so low you almost couldn't hear her. "His name was Henry, but they called him Stash."

"Maggie's brain is like an elephant's," Wangero said, laughing. "I can use the churn top as a centerpiece for the alcove table," she said, sliding a plate over the churn, "and I'll think of something artistic to do with the dasher."

When she finished wrapping the dasher the handle stuck out. I took it for a moment in my hands. You didn't even have to look close to see where hands pushing the dasher up and down to make butter had left a kind of sink in the wood. In fact, there were a lot of small sinks; you could see where thumbs and fingers had sunk into the wood.

It was beautiful light yellow wood, from a tree that grew in the yard where Big Dee and Stash had lived.

After dinner Dee (Wangero) went to the trunk at the foot of my bed and started rifling through it. Maggie hung back in the kitchen over the dishpan. Out came Wangero with two quilts. They had been pieced by Grandma Dee and then Big Dee and me had hung them on the quilt frames on the front porch and quilted them. One was in the Lone Star pattern. The other was Walk Around the Mountain. In both of them were scraps of dresses Grandma Dee had worn fifty and more years ago. Bits and pieces of Grandpa Jarrell's Paisley shirts. And one teeny faded blue piece, about the size of a penny matchbox, that was from Great Grandpa Ezra's uniform that he wore in the Civil War.

"Mama," Wangero said sweet as a bird. "Can I have these old quilts?"

I heard something fall in the kitchen, and a minute later the kitchen door slammed.

"Why don't you take one or two of the others?" I asked. "These old things was just done by me and Big Dee from some tops your grandma pieced before she died."

"No," said Wangero. "I don't want those. They are stitched around the borders by machine."

"That'll make them last better," I said.

"That's not the point," said Wangero. "These are all pieces of dresses Grandma used to wear. She did all this stitching by hand. Imagine!" She held the quilts securely in her arms, stroking them.

"Some of the pieces, like those lavender ones, come from old clothes her mother handed down to her," I said, moving up to touch the quilts. Dee (Wangero) moved back just enough so that I couldn't reach the quilts. They already belonged to her.

"Imagine!" she breathed again, clutching them closely to her bosom.

"The truth is," I said, "I promised to give them quilts to Maggie, for when she marries John Thomas."

She gasped like a bee had stung her.

"Maggie can't appreciate these quilts!" she said. "She'd probably be backward enough to put them to everyday use."

"I reckon she would," I said. "God knows I been saving 'em for long enough with nobody using 'em. I hope she will!" I didn't want to bring up how I had offered Dee (Wangero) a quilt when she went away to college. Then she had told me they were old-fashioned, out of style.

"But they're *priceless!*" she was saying now, furiously; for she has a temper. "Maggie would put them on the bed and in five years they'd be in rags. Less than that!"

"She can always make some more," I said. "Maggie knows how to quilt."

Dee (Wangero) looked at me with hatred. "You just will not understand. The point is these quilts, *these* quilts!"

"Well," I said, stumped. "What would *you* do with them?"

"Hang them," she said. As if that was the only thing you *could* do with quilts.

Maggie by now was standing in the door. I could almost hear the sound her feet made as they scraped over each other.

"She can have them, Mama," she said, like somebody used to never winning anything, or having anything reserved for her. "I can 'member Grandma Dee without the quilts."

I looked at her hard. She had filled her bottom lip with checkerberry snuff and it gave her a face a kind of dopey, hangdog look. It was Grandma Dee and Big Dee who taught her how to quilt herself. She stood there with her scarred hands hidden in the folds of her skirt. She looked at her sister with something like fear but she wasn't mad at her. This was Maggie's portion. This was the way she knew God to work.

When I looked at her like that something hit me in the top of my head and ran down to the soles of my feet. Just like when I'm in church and the spirit of God touches me and I get happy and shout. I did something I never had done before: hugged Maggie to me, then dragged her on into the room, snatched the quilts out of Miss Wangero's hands and dumped them into Maggie's lap. Maggie just sat there on my bed with her mouth open.

"Take one or two of the others," I said to Dee.

But she turned without a word and went out to Hakim-a-barber.

"You just don't understand," she said, as Maggie and I came out to the car.

"What don't I understand?" I wanted to know.

"Your heritage," she said. And then she turned to Maggie, kissed her, and said, "You ought to try to make something of yourself, too, Maggie. It's really a new day for us. But from the way you and Mama still live you'd never know it."

She put on some sunglasses that hid everything above the tip of her nose and her chin.

Maggie smiled; maybe at the sunglasses. But a real smile, not scared. After we watched the car dust settle I asked Maggie to bring me a dip of snuff. And then the two of us sat there just enjoying, until it was time to go in the house and go to bed.

---

1. What is the mother's feeling toward Dee? How is it changed in the course of the story?

2. Why has Dee rarely had friends? Does she want friends or expect to have them?
3. How does Maggie feel in the presence of her sister?
4. What does Dee's attitude toward the quilts say about her sense of her family and her roots?
5. Is the conflict of the story between two equally justifiable views of life? Can these views be reconciled?
6. What is implied by the subtitle in the form of a dedication?

Eudora Welty

Welty (1909–) was born in Jackson, Mississippi, where she has lived for most of her productive life. She received her formal education at the Mississippi State College for Women and the University of Wisconsin, studying advertising at Columbia University for a brief period. Her early ambitions to be a painter were subordinated by the success of her first book of stories, A Curtain of Green and Other Stories *(1941). Readers recognized in this and following works a writer who gives full value to the quality and spectacle of her home region and the people she knows best while at the same time she displays a cosmopolitan awareness and technical sophistication. Other books of short stories are* The Wide Net and Other Stories *(1943),* The Golden Apples *(1949),* The Bride of the Innisfallen and Other Stories *(1955),* Thirteen Stories *(1965), and the* Collected Stories of Eudora Welty *(1980). Her novels include* Delta Wedding *(1946),* The Ponder Heart *(1954), and* The Optimist's Daughter *(1972).* One Writer's Beginnings *(1983), based on three lectures Welty delivered at Harvard, is autobiographical.*

Powerhouse

Powerhouse is playing!

He's here on tour from the city—"Powerhouse and His Keyboard"—"Powerhouse and His Tasmanians"—think of the things he calls himself! There's no one in the world like him. You can't tell what he is. "Nigger man"?—he looks more Asiatic, monkey, Jewish, Babylonian, Peruvian, fanatic, devil. He has pale gray eyes, heavy lids, maybe horny like a lizard's, but big glowing eyes when they're open. He has African feet of the greatest size, stomping, both together, on each side of the pedals. He's not coal black—beverage colored—looks like a preacher when his mouth is shut, but then it opens—vast and obscene. And his mouth is going every minute: like a monkey's when it looks for something. Improvising, coming on a light and childish melody—*smooch*—he loves it with his mouth.

Is it possible that he could be this! When you have him there performing for you, that's what you feel. You know people on a stage—and people of a darker race—so likely to be marvelous, frightening.

This is a white dance. Powerhouse is not a show-off like the Harlem boys, not drunk, not crazy—he's in a trance; he's a person of joy, a fanatic. He listens as much as he performs, a look of hideous, powerful rapture on his face. Big arched eyebrows that never stop traveling, like a Jew's—wandering-Jew eyebrows. When he plays he beats down piano and seat and wears them away. He is in motion every moment—what could be more obscene? There he is with his great head, fat stomach, and little round piston legs, and long yellow-sectioned strong big fingers, at rest about the size of bananas. Of course you know how he sounds—you've heard him on records—but still you need to see him. He's going all the time, like skating around the skating rink or rowing a boat. It makes everybody crowd around, here in this shadowless steel-trussed hall with the rose-like posters of Nelson Eddy[1] and the testimonial for the mind-reading horse in handwriting magnified five hundred times. Then all quietly he lays his finger on a key with the promise and serenity of a sibyl touching the book.

Powerhouse is so monstrous he sends everybody into oblivion. When any group, any performers, come to town, don't people always come out and hover near, leaning inward about them, to learn what it is? What is it? Listen. Remember how it was with the acrobats. Watch them carefully, hear the least word, especially what they say to one another, in another language—don't let them escape you; it's the only time for hallucination, the last time. They can't stay. They'll be somewhere else this time tomorrow.

Powerhouse has as much as possible done by signals. Everybody, laughing as if to hide a weakness, will sooner or later hand him up a written request. Powerhouse reads each one, studying with a secret face: that is the face which looks like a mask—anybody's; there is a moment when he makes a decision. Then a light slides under his eyelids, and he says, "92!" or some combination of figures—never a name. Before a number the band is all frantic, misbehaving, pushing, like children in a classroom, and he is the teacher getting silence. His hands over the keys, he says sternly. "You-all ready? You-all ready to do some serious walking?"—waits—then, STAMP. Quiet. STAMP, for the second time. This is absolute. Then a set of rhythmic kicks against the floor to communicate the tempo. Then, O Lord! say the distended eyes from beyond the boundary of the trumpets, Hello and good-bye, and they are all down the first note like a waterfall.

This note marks the end of any known discipline. Powerhouse seems to abandon them all—he himself seems lost—down in the song, yelling up like somebody in a whirlpool—not guiding them—hailing them only. But he knows, really. He cries out, but he must know

1. Popular and sentimental American baritone, singing star of musical films (1901–1967).

exactly. "Mercy! . . . What I say! . . . Yeah!" And then drifting, listening—"Where that skin beater?"—wanting drums, and starting up and pouring it out in the greatest delight and brutality. On the sweet pieces such a leer for everybody! He looks down so benevolently upon all our faces and whispers the lyrics to us. And if you could hear him at this moment on "Marie, the Dawn is Breaking"! He's going up the keyboard with a few fingers in some very derogatory triplet-routine, he gets higher and higher, and then he looks over the end of the piano, as if over a cliff. But not in a show-off way—the song makes him do it.

He loves the way they all play, too—all those next to him. The far section of the band is all studious, wearing glasses, every one—they don't count. Only those playing around Powerhouse are the real ones. He has a bass fiddler from Vicksburg, black as pitch, named Valentine, who plays with his eyes shut and talking to himself, very young: Powerhouse has to keep encouraging him. "Go on, go on, give it up, bring it on out there!" When you heard him like that on records, did you know he was really pleading?

He calls Valentine out to take a solo.

"What you going to play?" Powerhouse looks out kindly from behind the piano; he opens his mouth and shows his tongue, listening.

Valentine looks down, drawing against his instrument, and says without a lip movement, " 'Honeysuckle Rose.' "

He has a clarinet player named Little Brother, and loves to listen to anything he does. He'll smile and say, "Beautiful!" Little Brother takes a step forward when he plays and stands at the very front, with the whites of his eyes like fishes swimming. Once when he played a low note, Powerhouse muttered a dirty praise. "He went clear downstairs to get that one!"

After a long time, he holds up the number of fingers to tell the band how many choruses still to go—usually five. He keeps his directions down to signals.

It's a bad night outside. It's a white dance, and nobody dances, except a few straggling jitterbugs and two elderly couples. Everybody just stands around the band and watches Powerhouse. Sometimes they steal glances at one another, as if to say, Of course, you know how it is with *them*—Negroes—band leaders—they would play the same way, giving all they've got, for an audience of one. . . . When somebody, no matter who, gives everything, it makes people feel ashamed for him.

Late at night they play the one waltz they will ever consent to play—by request, "Pagan Love Song." Powerhouse's head rolls and sinks like a weight between his waving shoulders. He groans, and his fingers drag into the keys heavily, holding on to the notes, retrieving. It is a sad song.

"You know what happened to me?" says Powerhouse.

Valentine hums a response, dreaming at the base.

"I got a telegram my wife is dead," says Powerhouse, with wandering fingers.

"Uh-uh?"

His mouth gathers and forms a barbarous O while his fingers walk up straight, unwillingly, three octaves.

"Gypsy? Why how come her to die, didn't you just phone her up in the night last night long distance?"

"Telegram say—here the words: Your wife is dead." He puts 4/4 over the 3/4.

"Not but four words?" This is the drummer, an unpopular boy named Scoot, a disbelieving maniac.

Powerhouse is shaking his vast cheeks. "What the hell was she trying to do? What was she up to?"

"What name has it got signed, if you got a telegram?" Scoot is spitting away with those wire brushes.

Little Brother, the clarinet player, who cannot now speak, glares and tilts back.

"Uranus Knockwood is the name signed." Powerhouse lifts his eyes open. "Ever hear of him?" A bubble shoots out on his lip like a plate on a counter.

Valentine is beating slowly on with his palm and scratching the strings with his long blue nails. He is fond of a waltz. Powerhouse interrupts him.

"I don't know him. Don't know who he is." Valentine shakes his head with the closed eyes.

"Say it again."

"Uranus Knockwood."

"That ain't Lenox Avenue."[2]

"It ain't Broadway."

"Ain't ever seen it wrote out in any print, even for horse racing."

"Hell, that's on a star, boy, ain't it?" Crash of the cymbals.

"What the hell was she up to?" Powerhouse shudders. "Tell me, tell me, tell me." He makes triplets, and begins a new chorus. He holds three fingers up.

"You say you got a telegram." This is Valentine, patient and sleepy, beginning again.

Powerhouse is elaborate. "Yas, the time I go out, go way down-

2. Street in Harlem, well known for night spots.

stairs along a long cor-ri-dor to where they puts us: coming back along the cor-ri-dor: steps out and hands me a telegram: Your wife is dead."

"Gypsy?" The drummer like a spider over his drums.

"Aaaaaaaaa!" shouts Powerhouse, flinging out both powerful arms for three whole beats to flex his muscles, then kneading a dough of bass notes. His eyes glitter. He plays the piano like a drum sometimes—why not?

"Gypsy? Such a dancer?"

"Why you don't hear it straight from your agent? Why it ain't come from headquarters? What you been doing, getting telegrams in the *corridor*, signed nobody?"

They all laugh. End of that chorus.

"What time is it?" Powerhouse calls. "What the hell place is this? Where is my watch and chain?"

"I hang it on you," whimpers Valentine. "It still there."

There it rides on Powerhouse's great stomach, down where he can never see it.

"Sure did hear some clock striking twelve while ago. Must be *midnight*.

"It going to be intermission," Powerhouse declares, lifting up his finger with the signet ring.

He draws the chorus to an end. He pulls a big Northern hotel towel out of the deep pocket in his vast, special-cut tux pants and pushes his forehead into it.

"If she went and killed herself!" he says with a hidden face. "If she up and jumped out that window!" He gets to his feet, turning vaguely, wearing the towel on his head.

"Ha, ha!"

"Sheik, sheik!"

"She wouldn't do that." Little Brother sets down his clarinet like a precious vase, and speaks. He still looks like an East Indian queen, implacable, divine, and full of snakes. "You ain't going to expect people doing what they says over long distance."

"Come on!" roars Powerhouse. He is already at the back door, he has pulled it wide open, and with a wild, gathered-up face is smelling the terrible night.

Powerhouse, Valentine, Scoot and Little Brother step outside into the drenching rain.

"Well, they emptying buckets," says Powerhouse in a modified voice. On the street he holds his hands out and turns up the blanched palms like sieves.

A hundred dark, ragged, silent, delighted Negroes have come around from under the eaves of the hall, and follow wherever they go.

"Watch out Little Brother don't shrink," says Powerhouse. "You just the right size now, clarinet don't suck you in. You got a dry throat, Little Brother, you in the desert?" He reaches into the pocket and pulls out a paper of mints. "Now hold 'em in your mouth—don't chew 'em. I don't carry around nothing without limit."

"Go in that joint and have beer," says Scoot, who walks ahead.

"Beer? Beer? You know what beer is? What do they say is beer? What's beer? Where I been?"

"Down yonder where it say World Café—that do?" They are in Negrotown now.

Valentine patters over and holds open a screen door warped like a sea shell, bitter in the wet, and they walk in, stained darker with the rain and leaving footprints. Inside, sheltered dry smells stand like screens around a table covered with red-checkered cloth, in the center of which flies hang onto an obelisk-shaped ketchup bottle. The midnight walls are checkered again with admonishing "Not Responsible" signs and black-figured, smoky calendars. It is a waiting, silent, limp room. There is a burned-out-looking nickelodeon and right beside it a long-necked wall instrument labeled "Business Phone, Don't Keep Talking." Circled phone numbers are written up everywhere. There is a worn-out peacock feather hanging by a thread to an old, thin, pink, exposed light bulb, where it slowly turns around and around, whoever breathes.

A waitress watches.

"Come here, living statue, and get all this big order of beer we fixing to give."

"Never seen you before anywhere." The waitress moves and comes forward and slowly shows little gold leaves and tendrils over her teeth. She shoves up her shoulders and breasts. "How I going to know who you might be? Robbers? Coming in out of the black of night right at midnight, setting down so big at my table?"

"Boogers,"[3] says Powerhouse, his eyes opening lazily as in a cave.

The girls screams delicately with pleasure. O Lord, she likes talk and scares.

"Where you going to find enough beer to put out on this here table?"

She runs to the kitchen with bent elbows and sliding steps.

"Here's a million nickels," says Powerhouse, pulling his hand out of his pocket and sprinkling coins out, all but the last one, which he makes vanish like a magician.

Valentine and Scoot take the money over to the nickelodeon, which looks as battered as a slot machine, and read all the names of the records out loud.

"Whose 'Tuxedo Junction'?" asks Powerhouse.

3. Bogey men.

"You know whose."

"Nickelodeon, I request you please to play 'Empty Bed Blues' and let Bessie Smith[4] sing."

Silence: they hold it like a measure.

"Bring me all those nickels on back here," says Powerhouse. "Look at that! What you tell me the name of this place?"

"White dance, week night, raining, Alligator, Mississippi, long ways from home."

"Uh-huh."

"Sent for You Yesterday and Here You Come Today" plays.

The waitress, setting the tray of beer down on a back table, comes up taut and apprehensive as a hen. "Says in the kitchen, back there putting their eyes to little hole peeping out, that you is Mr. Powerhouse. . . . They knows from a picture they seen."

"They seeing right tonight, that is him," says Little Brother.

"You him?"

"That is him in the flesh," says Scoot.

"Does you wish to touch him?" asks Valentine. "Because he don't bite."

"You passing through?"

"Now you got everything right."

She waits like a drop, hands languishing together in front.

"Little-Bit, ain't you going to bring the beer?"

She brings it, and goes behind the cash register and smiles, turning different ways. The little fillet of gold in her mouth is gleaming.

"The Mississippi River's here," she says once.

Now all the watching Negroes press in gently and bright-eyed through the door, as many as can get in. One is a little boy in a straw sombrero which has been coated with aluminum paint all over.

Powerhouse, Valentine, Scoot and Little Brother drink beer, and their eyelids come together like curtains. The wall and the rain and the humble beautiful waitress waiting on them and the other Negroes watching enclose them.

"Listen!" whispers Powerhouse, looking into the ketchup bottle and slowly spreading his performer's hands over the damp, wrinkling cloth with the red squares. "Listen how it is. My wife gets missing me. Gypsy. She goes to the window. She looks out and sees you know what. Street. Sign saying Hotel. People walking. Somebody looks up. Old man. She looks down, out the window. Well? . . . *Ssssst! Plooey!* What she do? Jump out and burst her brains all over the world."

He opens his eyes.

"That's it," agrees Valentine. "You gets a telegram."

4. Greatest of female blues singers (1895–1930).

"Sure she misses you," Little Brother adds.

"No, it's night time." How softly he tells them! "Sure. It's the night time. She say, What do I hear? Footsteps walking up the hall? That him? Footsteps go on off. It's not me. I'm in Alligator, Mississippi, she's crazy. Shaking all over. Listen till her ears and all grow out like old music-box horns but still she can't hear a thing. She says, All right! I'll jump out the window then. Got on her nightgown. I know that nightgown, and her thinking there. Says, Ho hum, all right, and jumps out the window. Is she mad at me! Is she crazy! She don't leave *nothing* behind her!"

"Ya! Ha!"

"Brains and insides everywhere, Lord, Lord."

All the watching Negroes stir in their delight, and to their higher delight he says affectionately, "Listen! Rats in here."

"That must be the way, boss."

"Only, naw, Powerhouse, that ain't true. That sound too *bad*."

"Does I even know who finds her," cries Powerhouse. "That no-good pussy-footed crooning creeper, that creeper that follow around after me, coming up like weeds behind me, following around after me everything I do and messing around on the trail I leave. Bets my numbers, sings my songs, gets close to my agent like a Betsy-bug; when I going out he just coming in. I got him now! I got my eye on him."

"Know who he is?"

"Why, it's that old Uranus Knockwood!"

"Ya! Ha!"

"Yeah, and he coming now, he going to find Gypsy. There he is, coming around that corner, and Gypsy kadoodling down, oh-oh, watch out! *Ssssst! Plooey!* See, there she is in her little old nightgown, and her insides and brains all scattered round."

A sigh fills the room.

"Hush about her brains. Hush about her insides."

"Ya! Ha! You talking about her brains and insides—old Uranus Knockwood," says Powerhouse, "look down and say Jesus! He say, Look here what I'm walking round in!"

They all burst into halloos of laughter. Powerhouse's face looks like a big hot iron stove.

"Why, he picks her up and carries her off!" he says.

"Ya! Ha!"

"Carries her *back* around the corner. . . ."

"Oh, Powerhouse!"

"You know him."

"Uranus Knockwood!"

"Yeahhh!"

"He takes our wives when we gone!"

"He come in when we goes out!"

"Uh-huh!"

"He go out when we comes in!"

"Yeahhh!"

"He standing behind the door!"

"Old Uranus Knockwood."

"You know him."

"Middle-size man."

"Wears a hat."

"That's him."

Everybody in the room moans with pleasure. The little boy in the fine silver hat opens a paper and divides out a jelly roll among his followers.

And out of the breathless ring somebody moves forward like a slave, leading a great logy Negro with bursting eyes, and says, "This here is Sugar-Stick Thompson, that dove down to the bottom of July Creek and pulled up all those drownded white people fall out of a boat. Last summer, pulled up fourteen."

"Hello," says Powerhouse, turning and looking around at them all with his great daring face until they nearly suffocate.

Sugar-Stick, their instrument, cannot speak; he can only look back at the others.

"Can't even swim. Done it by holding his breath," says the fellow with the hero.

Powerhouse looks at him seekingly.

"I his half brother," the fellow puts in.

They step back.

"Gypsy say," Powerhouse rumbles gently again, looking at *them*, " 'What is the use? I'm gonna jump out so far—so far. . . .' *Ssssst—!*"

"Don't, boss, don't do it again," says Little Brother.

"It's awful," says the waitress. "I hates that Mr. Knockwoods. All that the truth?"

"Want to see the telegram I got from him?" Powerhouse's hands goes to the vast pocket.

"Now wait, now wait, boss." They all watch him.

"It must be the real truth," says the waitress, sucking in her lower lip, her luminous eyes turning sadly, seeking the windows.

"No, babe, it ain't the truth." His eyebrows fly up, and he begins to whisper to her out of his vast oven mouth. His hand stays in his pocket. "Truth is something worse, I ain't said what, yet. It's something hasn't come to me, but I ain't saying it won't. And when it does, then want me to tell you?" He sniffs all at once, his eyes come open and turn up, almost too far. He is dreamily smiling.

"Don't, boss, don't, Powerhouse!"

"Oh!" the waitress screams.

"Go on get out of here!" bellows Powerhouse, taking his hand out of his pocket and clapping after her red dress.

The ring of watchers breaks and falls away.

"*Look* at that! Intermission is up," says Powerhouse.

He folds money under a glass, and after they go out, Valentine leans back in and drops a nickel in the nickelodeon behind them, and it lights up and begins to play "The Goona Goo." The feather dangles still.

"Take a telegram!" Powerhouse shouts suddenly up into the rain over the street. "Take a answer. Now what was the name?"

They get a little tired.

"Uranus Knockwood."

"You ought to know."

"Yas? Spell it to me."

They spell it all the ways it could be spelled. It puts them in a wonderful humor.

"Here's the answer. I got it right here. 'What in the hell you talking about? Don't make any difference: I gotcha.' Name signed: Powerhouse."

"That going to reach him, Powerhouse?" Valentine speaks in a maternal voice.

"Yas, yas."

All hushing, following him up the dark street at a distance, like old rained-on black ghosts, the Negroes are afraid they will die laughing.

Powerhouse throws back his vast head into the streaming rain, and a look of hopeful desire seems to blow somehow like a vapor from his own dilated nostrils over his face and bring a mist to his eyes.

"Reach him and come out the other side."

"That's it, Powerhouse, that's it. You got him now."

Powerhouse lets out a long sigh.

"But ain't you going back there to call up Gypsy long distance, the way you did last night in that other place? I seen a telephone. . . . Just to see if she there at home?"

There is a measure of silence. That is one crazy drummer that's going to get his neck broken some day.

"No," growls Powerhouse. "No! How many thousand times tonight I got to say No?"

He holds up his arm in the rain.

"You sure-enough unroll your voice some night, it about reach up yonder to her," says Little Brother, dismayed.

They go on up the street, shaking the rain off and on them like birds.

Back in the dance hall, they play "San" (99). The jitterbugs start up like windmills stationed over the floor, and in their orbits—one circle, another, a long stretch and a zigzag—dance the elderly couples with old smoothness, undisturbed and stately.

When Powerhouse first came back from intermission, no doubt full of beer, they said, he got the band tuned up again in his own way. He didn't strike the piano keys for pitch—he simply opened his mouth and gave falsetto howls—in A, D and so on—they tuned by him. Then he took hold of the piano, as if he saw it for the first time in his life, and tested it for strength, hit it down in the bass, played an octave with his elbow, lifted the top, looked inside and leaned against it with all his might. He sat down and played it for a few minutes with outrageous force and got it under his power—a bass deep and coarse as a sea net—then produced something glimmering and fragile, and smiled. And who could ever remember any of the things he says? They are just inspired remarks that roll out of his mouth like smoke.

They've requested "Somebody Loves Me," and he's already done twelve or fourteen choruses, piling them up nobody knows how, and it will be a wonder if he ever gets through. Now and then he calls and shouts. " 'Somebody loves me! Somebody loves me, I wonder who!' " His mouth gets to be nothing but a volcano. "I wonder who!"

"Maybe . . ." He uses all his right hand on a trill.

"Maybe . . ." He pulls back his spread fingers and looks out upon the place where he is. A vast, impersonal and yet furious grimace transfigures his wet face.

". . . Maybe it's you!"

---

1. What is the relation between his music and the story Powerhouse tells about his wife and Uranus Knockwood? What does Knockwood represent?
2. What leads the waitress to believe Powerhouse's story is true? Why does he deny that it is? What might be "worse" than the story he has told?
3. What does the story say about charisma and its sources? Why do all the listeners in the bar "moan with pleasure" while listening to Powerhouse's tales?
4. How are point of view and the use of the present tense suited to the material of the story?

A Worn Path

It was December—a bright frozen day in the early morning. Far out in the country there was an old Negro woman with her head tied in a red rag, coming along a path through the pinewoods. Her name was Phoenix Jackson. She was very old and small and she walked slowly in the dark pine shadows, moving a little from side to side in her steps, with the balanced heaviness and lightness of a pendulum in a grandfather clock. She carried a thin, small cane made from an umbrella, and with this she kept tapping the frozen earth in front of her. This made a grave and persistent noise in the still air, that seemed meditative like the chirping of a solitary little bird.

She wore a dark striped dress reaching down to her shoe tops, and an equally long apron of bleached sugar sacks, with a full pocket: all neat and tidy, but every time she took a step she might have fallen over her shoelaces, which dragged from her unlaced shoes. She looked straight ahead. Her eyes were blue with age. Her skin had a pattern all its own of numberless branching wrinkles and as though a whole little tree stood in the middle of her forehead, but a golden color ran underneath, and the two knobs of her cheeks were illumined by a yellow burning under the dark. Under the red rag her hair came down on her neck in the frailest of ringlets, still black, and with an odor like copper.

Now and then there was a quivering in the thicket. Old Phoenix said, "Out of my way, all you foxes, owls, beetles, jack rabbits, coons and wild animals! . . . Keep out from under these feet, little bob-whites. . . . Keep the big wild hogs out of my path. Don't let none of those come running my direction. I got a long way." Under her small black-freckled hand her cane, limber as a buggy whip, would switch at the brush as if to rouse up any hiding things.

On she went. The woods were deep and still. The sun made the pine needles almost too bright to look at, up where the wind rocked. The cones dropped as light as feathers. Down in the hollow was the mourning dove—it was not too late for him.

The path ran up a hill. "Seem like there is chains about my feet, time I get this far," she said, in the voice of argument old people keep to use with themselves. "Something always take a hold of me on this hill—pleads I should stay."

After she got to the top she turned and gave a full, severe look behind her where she had come. "Up through pines," she said at length. "Now down through oaks."

Her eyes opened their widest, and she started down gently. But before she got to the bottom of the hill a bush caught her dress.

Her fingers were busy and intent, but her skirts were full and long, so that before she could pull them free in one place they were caught in another. It was not possible to allow the dress to tear. "I in the thorny bush," she said. "Thorns, you doing your appointed work. Never want to let folks pass, no sir. Old eyes thought you was a pretty little *green* bush."

Finally, trembling all over, she stood free, and after a moment dared to stoop for her cane.

"Sun so high!" she cried, leaning back and looking, while the thick tears went over her eyes. "The time getting all gone here."

At the foot of this hill was a place where a log was laid across the creek.

"Now comes the trial," said Phoenix.

Putting her right foot out, she mounted the log and shut her eyes. Lifting her skirt, leveling her cane fiercely before her, like a festival figure in some parade, she began to march across. Then she opened her eyes and she was safe on the other side.

"I wasn't as old as I thought," she said.

But she sat down to rest. She spread her skirts on the bank around her and folded her hands over her knees. Up above her was a tree in a pearly cloud of mistletoe. She did not dare to close her eyes, and when a little boy brought her a plate with a slice of marble-cake on it she spoke to him. "That would be acceptable," she said. But when she went to take it there was just her own hand in the air.

So she left that tree, and had to go through a barbed-wire fence. There she had to creep and crawl, spreading her knees and stretching her fingers like a baby trying to climb the steps. But she talked loudly to herself: she could not let her dress be torn now, so late in the day, and she could not pay for having her arm or her leg sawed off if she got caught fast where she was.

At last she was safe through the fence and risen up out in the clearing. Big dead trees, like black men with one arm, were standing in the purple stalks of the withered cotton field. There sat a buzzard.

"Who you watching?"

In the furrow she made her way along.

"Glad this not the season for bulls," she said, looking sideways, "and the good Lord made his snakes to curl up and sleep in the winter. A pleasure I don't see no two-headed snake coming around that tree, where it come once. It took a while to get by him, back in the summer."

She passed through the old cotton and went into a field of dead corn. It whispered and shook and was taller than her head. "Through the maze now," she said, for there was no path.

Then there was something tall, black, and skinny there, moving before her.

At first she took it for a man. It could have been a man dancing in the field. But she stood still and listened, and it did not make a sound. It was as silent as a ghost.

"Ghost," she said sharply, "who be you the ghost of? For I have heard of nary death close by."

But there was no answer—only the ragged dancing in the wind.

She shut her eyes, reached out her hand, and touched a sleeve. She found a coat and inside that an emptiness, cold as ice.

"You scarecrow," she said. Her face lighted. "I ought to be shut up for good," she said with laughter. "My senses is gone. I too old. I the oldest people I ever know. Dance, old scarecrow," she said, "while I dancing with you."

She kicked her foot over the furrow, and with mouth drawn down, shook her head once or twice in a little strutting way. Some husks blew down and whirled in streamers about her skirts.

Then she went on, parting her way from side to side with the cane, through the whispering field. At last she came to the end, to a wagon track where the silver grass blew between the red ruts. The quail were walking around like pullets, seeming all dainty and unseen.

"Walk pretty," she said. "This the easy place. This the easy going."

She followed the track, swaying through the quiet bare fields, through the little strings of trees silver in their dead leaves, past cabins silver from weather, with the doors and windows boarded shut, all like old women under a spell sitting there. "I walking in their sleep," she said, nodding her head vigorously.

In a ravine she went where a spring was silently flowing through a hollow log. Old Phoenix bent and drank. "Sweet-gum makes the water sweet," she said, and drank more. "Nobody know who made this well, for it was here when I was born."

The track crossed a swampy part where the moss hung as white as lace from every limb. "Sleep on, alligators, and blow your bubbles." Then the track went into the road.

Deep, deep the road went down between the high green-colored banks. Overhead the live-oaks met, and it was as dark as a cave.

A black dog with a lolling tongue came up out of the weeds by the ditch. She was meditating, and not ready, and when he came at her she only hit him a little with her cane. Over she went in the ditch, like a little puff of milkweed.

Down there, her senses drifted away. A dream visited her, and she reached her hand up, but nothing reached down and gave her a pull. So she lay there and presently went to talking. "Old woman," she said to herself, "that black dog come up out of the weeds to stall you off, and now there he sitting on his fine tail, smiling at you."

A white man finally came along and found her—a hunter, a young man, with his dog on a chain.

"Well, Granny!" he laughed. "What are you doing there?"

"Lying on my back like a June-bug waiting to be turned over, mister," she said, reaching up her hand.

He lifted her up, gave her a swing in the air, and set her down. "Anything broken, Granny?"

"No sir, them old dead weeds is springy enough," said Phoenix, when she had got her breath. "I thank you for your trouble."

"Where do you live, Granny?" he asked, while the two dogs were growling at each other.

"Away back yonder, sir, behind the ridge. You can't even see it from here."

"On your way home?"

"No sir, I going to town."

"Why, that's too far! That's as far as I walk when I come out myself, and I get something for my trouble." He patted the stuffed bag he carried, and there hung down a little closed claw. It was one of the bob-whites, with its beak hooked bitterly to show it was dead. "Now you go on home, Granny!"

"I bound to go to town, mister," said Phoenix. "The time come around."

He gave another laugh, filling the whole landscape. "I know you old colored people! Wouldn't miss going to town to see Santa Claus!"

But something held old Phoenix very still. The deep lines in her face went into a fierce and different radiation. Without warning, she had seen with her own eyes a flashing nickel fall out of the man's pocket onto the ground.

"How old are you, Granny?" he was saying.

"There's no telling, mister," she said, "no telling."

Then she gave a little cry and clapped her hands and said, "Git on away from here, dog! Look! Look at that dog!" She laughed as if in admiration. "He ain't scared of nobody. He a big black dog." She whispered, "Sic him!"

"Watch me get rid of that cur," said the man. "Sic him, Pete! Sic him!"

Phoenix heard the dogs fighting, and heard the man running and throwing sticks. She even heard a gunshot. But she was slowly bending forward by that time, further and further forward, the lid stretched down over her eyes, as if she were doing this in her sleep. Her chin was lowered almost to her knees. The yellow palm of her hand came out from the fold of her apron. Her fingers slid down and along the ground under the piece of money with the grace and care they would have in lifting an egg from under a setting hen. Then she slowly straightened up, she stood erect, and the nickel was in her apron pocket. A bird flew by. Her lips moved. "God watching me the whole time. I come to stealing."

The man came back, and his own dog panted about them. "Well, I scared him off that time," he said, and then he laughed and lifted his gun and pointed it at Phoenix.

She stood straight and faced him.

"Doesn't the gun scare you?" he said, still pointing it.

"No, sir, I seen plenty go off closer by, in my day, and for less than what I done," she said, holding utterly still.

He smiled, and shouldered the gun. "Well, Granny," he said, "you must be a hundred years old, and scared of nothing. I'd give you a dime if I had any money with me. But you take my advice and stay home, and nothing will happen to you."

"I bound to go on my way, mister," said Phoenix. She inclined her head in the red rag. Then they went in different directions, but she could hear the gun shooting again and again over the hill.

She walked on. The shadows hung from the oak trees to the road like curtains. Then she smelled wood-smoke, and smelled the river, and she saw a steeple and the cabins on their steep steps. Dozens of little black children whirled around her. There ahead was Natchez shining. Bells were ringing. She walked on.

In the paved city it was Christmas time. There were red and green electric lights strung and crisscrossed everywhere, and all turned on in the daytime. Old Phoenix would have been lost if she had not distrusted her eyesight and depended on her feet to know where to take her.

She paused quietly on the sidewalk where people were passing by. A lady came along in the crowd, carrying an armful of red-, green- and silver-wrapped presents; she gave off perfume like the red roses in hot summer, and Phoenix stopped her.

"Please, missy, will you lace up my shoe?" She held up her foot.

"What do you want, Grandma?"

"See my shoe," said Phoenix. "Do all right for out in the country, but wouldn't look right to go in a big building."

"Stand still then, Grandma," said the lady. She put her packages down on the sidewalk beside her and laced and tied both shoes tightly.

"Can't lace 'em with a cane," said Phoenix. "Thank you, missy. I doesn't mind asking a nice lady to tie up my shoe, when I gets out on the street."

Moving slowly and from side to side, she went into the big building, and into the tower of steps, where she walked up and around and around until her feet knew to stop.

She entered a door, and there she saw nailed up on the wall the document that had been stamped with the gold seal and framed in the gold frame, which matched the dream that was hung up in her head.

"Here I be," she said. There was a fixed and ceremonial stiffness over her body.

"A charity case, I suppose," said an attendant who sat at the desk before her.

But Phoenix only looked above her head. There was sweat on her face, the wrinkles in her skin shone like a bright net.

"Speak up, Grandma," the woman said. "What's your name? We must have your history, you know. Have you been here before? What seems to be the trouble with you?"

Old Phoenix only gave a twitch to her face as if a fly were bothering her.

"Are you deaf?" cried the attendant.

But then the nurse came in.

"Oh, that's just old Aunt Phoenix," she said. "She doesn't come for herself—she has a little grandson. She makes these trips just as regular as clockwork. She lives away back off the Old Natchez Trace." She bent down. "Well, Aunt Phoenix, why don't you just take a seat? We won't keep you standing after your long trip." She pointed.

The old woman sat down, bolt upright in the chair.

"Now, how is the boy?" asked the nurse.

Old Phoenix did not speak.

"I said, how is the boy?"

But Phoenix only waited and stared straight ahead, her face very solemn and withdrawn into rigidity.

"Is his throat any better?" asked the nurse. "Aunt Phoenix, don't you hear me? Is your grandson's throat any better since the last time you came for the medicine?"

With her hands on her knees, the old woman waited, silent, erect and motionless, just as if she were in armor.

"You mustn't take up our time this way, Aunt Phoenix," the nurse said. "Tell us quickly about your grandson, and get it over. He isn't dead, is he?"

At last there came a flicker and then a flame of comprehension across her face, and she spoke.

"My grandson. It was my memory had left me. There I sat and forgot why I made my long trip."

"Forgot?" The nurse frowned. "After you came so far?"

Then Phoenix was like an old woman begging a dignified forgiveness for waking up frightened in the night. "I never did go to school, I was too old at the Surrender,"[1] she said in a soft voice. "I'm an old woman without an education. It was my memory fail me. My little grandson, he is just the same, and I forgot it in the coming."

"Throat never heals, does it?" said the nurse, speaking in a loud, sure voice to old Phoenix. By now she had a card with something written on it, a little list. "Yes. Swallowed lye. When was it?—January—two-three years ago—"

Phoenix spoke unmasked now. "No, missy, he not dead, he just the same. Every little while his throat begin to close up again, and he not able to swallow. He not get his breath. He not able to help himself. So the time come around, and I go on another trip for the soothing medicine."

"All right. The doctor said as long as you came to get it, you could have it," said the nurse. "But it's an obstinate case."

"My little grandson, he sit up there in the house all wrapped up, waiting by himself," Phoenix went on. "We is the only two left in the world. He suffer and it don't seem to put him back at all. He got a sweet look. He going to last. He wear a little patch quilt and peep out holding his mouth open like a little bird. I remembers so plain now. I not going to forget him again, no, the whole enduring time. I could tell him from all the others in creation."

"All right." The nurse was trying to hush her now. She brought her a bottle of medicine. "Charity," she said, making a check mark in a book.

Old Phoenix held the bottle close to her eyes, and then carefully put it into her pocket.

"I thank you," she said.

"It's Christmas time, Grandma," said the attendant. "Could I give you a few pennies out of my purse?"

"Five pennies is a nickel," said Phoenix stiffly.

"Here's a nickel," said the attendant.

Phoenix rose carefully and held out her hand. She received the nickel and then fished the other nickel out of her pocket and laid it beside the new one. She stared at her palm closely, with her head on one side.

Then she gave a tap with her cane on the floor.

"This is what come to me to do," she said. "I going to the store and buy my child a little windmill they sells, made out of paper. He going to find it hard to believe there such a thing in the world. I'll march myself back where he waiting, holding it straight up in this hand."

1. The surrender of General Robert E. Lee (1807–1870) of the Confederacy on April 9, 1865, to General Ulysses S. Grant (1822–1885) of the Union, thus ending the Civil War.

She lifted her free hand, gave a little nod, turned around, and walked out of the doctor's office. Then her slow step began on the stairs, going down.

---

1. How does the point of view help in characterizing Phoenix? Cite examples showing how point of view is managed.
2. What is the significance of the title? Of Phoenix's name?
3. Why does the hunter point his gun at Phoenix?
4. What does the story say about human dignity and what is required to maintain it? Does it in any way protest against the conditions in which Phoenix lives?

Edith Wharton

Wharton (1862–1937) was born into a wealthy and socially prominent family in New York City. Moved by the loneliness of her childhood, she began to write early in life and after 1890 published regularly in Scribner's Magazine *and as the author of books. She and her husband spent much of their time in Europe until his prolonged mental illness led to their divorce in 1913. She was a close friend of Henry James in his last twelve years, a period of significant development in her thought and her creative work. Her essays on the art she practiced may be found in* The Writing of Fiction *(1925). Among her novels are* The House of Mirth *(1905),* Ethan Frome *(1911),* The Age of Innocence *(1920), and* Hudson River Bracketed *(1929). Her numerous collections of short stories include* The Greater Inclination *(1899),* Crucial Instances *(1901), and* Tales of Men and Ghosts *(1910).*

The Muse's Tragedy

I

Danyers afterwards liked to fancy that he had recognized Mrs. Anerton at once; but that, of course, was absurd, since he had seen no portrait of her—she affected a strict anonymity refusing even her photograph to the most privileged—and from Mrs. Memorall, whom he revered and cultivated as her friend, he had extracted but the one impressionist phrase: "Oh, well, she's like one of those old prints where the lines have the value of color."

He was almost certain, at all events, that he had been thinking of Mrs. Anerton as he sat over his breakfast in the empty hotel restaurant, and that, looking up on the approach of the lady who seated herself at the table near the window, he had said to himself, *"That might be she."*

Ever since his Harvard days—he was still young enough to think of them as immensely remote—Danyers had dreamed of Mrs. Anerton, the Silvia of Vincent Rendle's immortal sonnet-cycle, the Mrs. A. of the *Life and Letters.* Her name was enshrined in some of the noblest English verse of the nineteenth century—and of all past or future centuries, as Danyers, from the stand-point of a maturer judgment, still believed. The first reading of certain poems—of the *Antinous,* the *Pia Tolomei,* the *Sonnets to Silvia,*—had been epochs in Danyers's growth, and the verse seemed to gain in mellowness, in amplitude, in meaning as one brought to its interpretation more experience of life, a finer emotional sense. Where, in his boyhood, he had felt only the perfect, the almost austere beauty of form, the subtle interplay of vowel-sounds, the rush and fulness of lyric emotion, he now thrilled to the close-packed significance of each line, the allusiveness of each word—his imagination lured hither and thither on fresh trails of thought, and perpetually spurred by the sense that, beyond what he had already discovered, more marvellous regions lay waiting to be explored. Danyers had written, at college, the prize essay on Rendle's poetry (it chanced to be the moment of the great man's death); he had fashioned the fugitive verse of his own storm-and-stress period on the forms which Rendle had first given to English metre; and when two years later the *Life and Letters* appeared, and the Silvia of the sonnets took substance as Mrs. A., he had included in his worship of Rendle the woman who had inspired not only such divine verse but such playful, tender, incomparable prose.

Danyers never forgot the day when Mrs. Memorall happened to mention that she knew Mrs. Anerton. He had known Mrs. Memorall for a year or more, and had somewhat contemptuously classified her as the kind of woman who runs cheap excursions to celebrities; when one afternoon she remarked, as she put a second lump of sugar in his tea:

"Is it right this time? You're almost as particular as Mary Anerton."

"Mary Anerton?"

"Yes, I never *can* remember how she likes her tea. Either it's lemon *with* sugar, or lemon without sugar, or cream without either, and whichever it is must be put into the cup before the tea is poured in; and if one hasn't remembered, one must begin all over again. I suppose it was Vincent Rendle's way of taking his tea and has become a sacred rite."

"Do you *know* Mrs. Anerton?" cried Danyers, disturbed by this careless familiarity with the habits of his divinity.

" 'And did I once see Shelley plain?'[1] Mercy, yes! She and I were at school together—she's an American, you know. We were at a *pension* near Tours[2] for nearly a year; then she went back to New York, and I didn't see her again till after her marriage. She and Anerton spent a winter in Rome while my husband was attached to our Legation there, and she used to be with us a great deal." Mrs. Memorall smiled reminiscently. "It was *the* winter."

"The winter they first met?"

"Precisely—but unluckily I left Rome just before the meeting

1. "Ah, did you once see Shelley plain/And did he stop and speak to you. . . ?" are the opening lines of Robert Browning's "Memorabilia." 2. City in west central France.

took place. Wasn't it too bad? I might have been in the *Life and Letters.* You know he mentions that stupid Madame Vodki, at whose house he first saw her."

"And did you see much of her after that?"

"Not during Rendle's life. You know she has lived in Europe almost entirely, and though I used to see her off and on when I went abroad, she was always so engrossed, so preoccupied, that one felt one wasn't wanted. The fact is, she cared only about his friends—she separated herself gradually from all her own people. Now, of course, it's different; she's desperately lonely; she's taken to writing to me now and then; and last year, when she heard I was going abroad, she asked me to meet her in Venice, and I spent a week with her there."

"And Rendle?"

Mrs. Memorall smiled and shook her head. "Oh, I never was allowed a peep at *him;* none of her old friends met him, except by accident. Ill-natured people say that was the reason she kept him so long. If one happened in while he was there, he was hustled into Anerton's study, and the husband mounted guard till the inopportune visitor had departed. Anerton, you know, was really much more ridiculous about it than his wife. Mary was too clever to lose her head, or at least to show she'd lost it—but Anerton couldn't conceal his pride in the conquest. I've seen Mary shiver when he spoke of Rendle as *our poet.* Rendle always had to have a certain seat at the dinner-table, away from the draught and not too near the fire, and a box of cigars that no one else was allowed to touch, and a writing-table of his own in Mary's sitting-room—and Anerton was always telling one of the great man's idiosyncrasies: how he never would cut the ends of his cigars, though Anerton himself had given him a gold cutter set with a star-sapphire, and how untidy his writing-table was, and how the house-maid had orders always to bring the wastepaper basket to her mistress before emptying it, lest some immortal verse should be thrown into the dust-bin."

"The Anertons never separated, did they?"

"Separated? Bless you, no. He never would have left Rendle! And besides, he was very fond of his wife."

"And she?"

"Oh, she saw he was the kind of man who was fated to make himself ridiculous, and she never interfered with his natural tendencies."

From Mrs. Memorall, Danyers further learned that Mrs. Anerton, whose husband had died some years before her poet, now divided her life between Rome, where she had a small apartment, and England, where she occasionally went to stay with those of her friends who had been Rendle's. She had been engaged, for some time after his death, in editing some juvenilia which he had bequeathed to her care; but that task being accomplished, she had been left without definite occupation, and Mrs. Memorall, on the occasion of their last meeting, had found her listless and out of spirits.

"She misses him too much—her life is too empty. I told her so—I told her she ought to marry."

"Oh!"

"Why not, pray? She's a young woman still—what many people would call young," Mrs. Memorall interjected, with a parenthetic glance at the mirror. "Why not accept the inevitable and begin over again? All the King's horses and all the King's men won't bring Rendle to life—and besides, she didn't marry *him* when she had the chance."

Danyers winced slightly at this rude fingering of his idol. Was it possible that Mrs. Memorall did not see what an anti-climax such a marriage would have been? Fancy Rendle "making an honest woman" of Silvia; for so society would have viewed it! How such a reparation would have vulgarized their past—it would have been like "restoring" a masterpiece; and how exquisite must have been the perceptions of the woman who, in defiance of appearances, and perhaps of her own secret inclination, chose to go down to posterity as Silvia rather than as Mrs. Vincent Rendle!

Mrs. Memorall, from this day forth, acquired an interest in Danyers' eyes. She was like a volume of unindexed and discursive memoirs, through which he patiently plodded in the hope of finding embedded amid layers of dusty twaddle some precious allusion to the subject of his thought. When, some months later, he brought out his first slim volume, in which the remodelled college essay on Rendle figured among a dozen somewhat overstudied "appreciations," he offered a copy to Mrs. Memorall; who surprised him, the next time they met, with the announcement that she had sent the book to Mrs. Anerton.

Mrs. Anerton in due time wrote to thank her friend. Danyers was privileged to read the few lines in which, in terms that suggested the habit of "acknowledging" similar tributes, she spoke of the author's "feeling and insight," and was "so glad of the opportunity," etc. He went away disappointed, without clearly knowing what else he had expected.

The following spring, when he went abroad, Mrs. Memorall offered him letters to everybody, from the Archbishop of Canterbury to Louise Michel.[3] She did not include Mrs. Anerton, however, and Danyers knew, from a previous conversation, that Silvia objected to people who "brought letters." He knew also that she travelled during the summer, and was unlikely to return to Rome before the term of his holiday

3. French historian (1830–1905).

should be reached, and the hope of meeting her was not included among his anticipations.

The lady whose entrance broke upon his solitary repast in the restaurant of the Hotel Villa d'Este[4] had seated herself in such a way that her profile was detached against the window; and thus viewed, her domed forehead, small arched nose, and fastidious lip suggested a silhouette of Marie Antoinette.[5] In the lady's dress and movements—in the very turn of her wrist as she poured out her coffee—Danyers thought he detected the same fastidiousness, the same air of tacitly excluding the obvious and unexceptional. Here was a woman who had been much bored and keenly interested. The waiter brought her a *Secolo*,[6] and as she bent above it Danyers noticed that the hair rolled back from her forehead was turning gray; but her figure was straight and slender, and she had the invaluable gift of a girlish back.

The rush of Anglo-Saxon travel had not set toward the lakes, and with the exception of an Italian family or two, and a hump-backed youth with an *abbé*,[7] Danyers and the lady had the marble halls of the Villa d'Este to themselves.

When he returned from his morning ramble among the hills he saw her sitting at one of the little tables at the edge of the lake. She was writing, and a heap of books and newspapers lay on the table at her side. That evening they met again in the garden. He had strolled out to smoke a last cigarette before dinner, and under the black vaulting of ilexes, near the steps leading down to the boat-landing, he found her leaning on the parapet above the lake. At the sound of his approach she turned and looked at him. She had thrown a black lace scarf over her head, and in this sombre setting her face seemed thin and unhappy. He remembered afterwards that her eyes, as they met his, expressed not so much sorrow as profound discontent.

To his surprise she stepped toward him with a detaining gesture.

"Mr. Lewis Danyers, I believe?"

He bowed.

"I am Mrs. Anerton. I saw your name on the visitors' list and wished to thank you for an essay on Mr. Rendle's poetry—or rather to tell you how much I appreciated it. The book was sent to me last winter by Mrs. Memorall."

She spoke in even melancholy tones, as though the habit of perfunctory utterance had robbed her voice of more spontaneous accents; but her smile was charming.

They sat down on a stone bench under the ilexes, and she told him how much pleasure his essay had given her. She thought it the

4. Celebrated hotel on Lake Como in northern Italy. 5. Wife of Louis XVI of France (1755–1793). Executed during the French Revolution. 6. Aperitif wine. 7. Member of the French Catholic clergy.

best in the book—she was sure he had put more of himself into it than into any other; was she not right in conjecturing that he had been very deeply influenced by Mr. Rendle's poetry? *Pour comprendre il faut aimer*,[8] and it seemed to her that, in some ways, he had penetrated the poet's inner meaning more completely than any other critic. There were certain problems, of course, that he had left untouched; certain aspects of that many-sided mind that he had perhaps failed to seize—

"But then you are young," she concluded gently, "and one could not wish you, as yet, the experience that a fuller understanding would imply."

II

She stayed a month at Villa d'Este, and Danyers was with her daily. She showed an unaffected pleasure in his society; a pleasure so obviously founded in their common veneration of Rendle, that the young man could enjoy it without fear of fatuity. At first he was merely one more grain of frankincense on the altar of her insatiable divinity; but gradually a more personal note crept into their intercourse. If she still liked him only because he appreciated Rendle, she had least perceptibly distinguished him from the herd of Rendle's appreciators.

Her attitude toward the great man's memory struck Danyers as perfect. She neither proclaimed nor disavowed her identity. She was frankly Silvia to those who knew and cared; but there was no trace of the Egeria[9] in her pose. She spoke often of Rendle's books, but seldom of himself; there was no posthumous conjugality, no use of the possessive tense, in her abounding reminiscences. Of the master's intellectual life, of his habits of thought and work, she never wearied of talking. She knew the history of each poem; by what scene or episode each image had been evoked; how many times the words in a certain line had been transposed; how long a certain adjective had been sought, and what had at last suggested it; she could even explain that one impenetrable line, the torment of critics, the joy of detractors, the last line of *The Old Odysseus*.

Danyers felt that in talking of these things she was no mere echo of Rendle's thought. If her identity had appeared to be merged in his it was because they thought alike, not because he had thought for her. Posterity is apt to regard the women whom poets have sung as chance pegs on which they hung their garlands; but Mrs. Anerton's mind was like some fertile garden wherein, inevitably, Rendle's imagination had rooted itself and flowered. Danyers began to see how many threads of his complex mental tissue the poet had owed to the blending of her

8. "In order to understand it is necessary to love." 9. I.e., a female advisor. In Roman mythology a fountain nymph who advised the second king of Rome, Numa Pompilius.

temperament with his; in a certain sense Silvia had herself created the *Sonnets to Silvia*.

To the custodian of Rendle's inner self, the door, as it were, to the sanctuary, had at first seemed to Danyers so comprehensive a privilege that he had the sense, as his friendship with Mrs. Anerton advanced, of forcing his way into a life already crowded. What room was there, among such towering memories, for so small an actuality as his? Quite suddenly, after this, he discovered that Mrs. Memorall knew better: his fortunate friend was bored as well as lonely.

"You have had more than any other woman!" he had exclaimed to her one day; and her smile flashed a derisive light on his blunder. Fool that he was, not to have seen that she had not had enough! That she was young still—do years count?—tender, human, a woman; that the living have need of the living.

After that, when they climbed the alleys of the hanging park, resting in one of the little ruined temples, or watching, through a ripple of foliage, the remote blue flash of the lake, they did not always talk of Rendle or of literature. She encouraged Danyers to speak of himself; to confide his ambitions to her; she asked him the questions which are the wise woman's substitute for advice.

"You must write," she said, administering the most exquisite flattery that human lips could give.

Of course he meant to write—why not to do something great in his turn? His best, at least; with the resolve, at the outset, that his best should be *the* best. Nothing less seemed possible with that mandate in his ears. How she had divined him; lifted and disentangled his groping ambitions; laid the awakening touch on his spirit with her creative *Let there be light!*[1]

It was his last day with her, and he was feeling very hopeless and happy.

"You ought to write a book about *him*," she went on gently.

Danyers started; he was beginning to dislike Rendle's way of walking in unannounced.

"You ought to do it," she insisted. "A complete interpretation—a summing-up of his style, his purpose, his theory of life and art. No one else could do it as well."

He sat looking at her perplexedly. Suddenly—dared he guess?

"I couldn't do it without you," he faltered.

"I could help you—I would help you, of course."

They sat silent, both looking at the lake.

It was agreed, when they parted, that he should rejoin her six weeks later in Venice. There they were to talk about the book.

1. Genesis 1:3: "And God said, Let there be light."

III

Lago d'Iseo, August 14th.

When I said good-by to you yesterday I promised to come back to Venice in a week: I was to give you your answer then. I was not honest in saying that; I didn't mean to go back to Venice or to see you again. I was running away from you—and I mean to keep on running! If *you* won't, *I* must. Somebody must save you from marrying a disappointed woman of—well, you say years don't count, and why should they, after all, since you are not to marry me?

That is what I dare not go back to say. *You are not to marry me.* We have had our month together in Venice (such a good month, was it not?) and now you are to go home and write a book—any book but the one we—didn't talk of!—and I am to stay here, attitudinizing among my memories like a sort of female Tithonus.[2] The dreariness of this enforced immortality!

But you shall know the truth. I care for you, or at least for your love, enough to owe you that.

You thought it was because Vincent Rendle had loved me that there was so little hope for you. I had had what I wanted to the full; wasn't that what you said? It is just when a man begins to think he understands a woman that he may be sure he doesn't! It is because Vincent Rendle *didn't love me* that there is no hope for you. I never had what I wanted, and never, never, never will I stoop to wanting anything else.

Do you begin to understand? It was all a sham then, you say? No, it was all real as far as it went. You are young—you haven't learned, as you will later, the thousand imperceptible signs by which one gropes one's way through the labyrinth of human nature; but didn't it strike you, sometimes, that I never told you any foolish little anecdotes about him? His trick, for instance, of twirling a paper-knife round and round between his thumb and forefinger while he talked; his mania for saving the backs of notes; his greediness for wild strawberries, the little pungent Alpine ones; his childish delight in acrobats and jugglers; his way of always calling me *you—dear you*, every letter began—I never told you a word of all that, did I? Do you suppose I could have helped telling you, if he had loved me? These little things would have been mine, then, a part of my life—of our life—they would have slipped out in spite of me (It's only your unhappy woman who is always reticent and dignified). But there never was any "our life"; it was always "our lives" to the end. . . .

If you knew what a relief it is to tell some one at last, you would

2. In Greek mythology Tithonus prevailed on the gods to grant him immortality but forgot to ask for eternal youth.

bear with me, you would let me hurt you! I shall never be quite so lonely again, now that some one knows.

Let me begin at the beginning. When I first met Vincent Rendle I was not twenty-five. That was twenty years ago. From that time until his death, five years ago, we were fast friends. He gave me fifteen years, perhaps the best fifteen years, of his life. The world, as you know, thinks that his greatest poems were written during those years; I am supposed to have "inspired" them, and in a sense I did. From the first, the intellectual sympathy between us was almost complete; my mind must have been to him (I fancy) like some perfectly tuned instrument on which he was never tired of playing. Someone told me of his once saying of me that I "always understood;" it is the only praise I ever heard of his giving me. I don't even know if he thought me pretty, though I hardly think my appearance could have been disagreeable to him, for he hated to be with ugly people. At all events he fell into the way of spending more and more of his time with me. He liked our house; our ways suited him. He was nervous, irritable; people bored him and yet he disliked solitude. He took sanctuary with us. When we travelled he went with us; in the winter he took rooms near us in Rome. In England or on the continent he was always with us for a good part of the year. In small ways I was able to help him in his work; he grew dependent on me. When we were apart he wrote to me continually—he liked to have me share in all he was doing or thinking; he was impatient for my criticism of every new book that interested him; I was a part of his intellectual life. The pity of it was that I wanted to be something more. I was a young woman and I was in love with him—not because he was Vincent Rendle, but just because he was himself!

People began to talk, of course—I was Vincent Rendle's Mrs. Anerton; when the *Sonnets of Silvia* appeared, it was whispered that I was Sylvia. Wherever he went, I was invited; people made up to me in the hope of getting to know him; when I was in London my doorbell never stopped ringing. Elderly peeresses, aspiring hostesses, love-sick girls and struggling authors overwhelmed me with their assiduities. I hugged my success, for I knew what it meant—they thought that Rendle was in love with me! Do you know, at times, they almost made me think so too? Oh, there was no phase of folly I didn't go through. You can't imagine the excuses a woman will invent for a man's not telling her that he loves her—pitiable arguments that she would see through at a glance if any other woman used them! But all the while, deep down, I knew he had never cared. I should have known it if he had made love to me every day of his life. I could never guess whether he knew what people said about us—he listened so little to what people said; and cared still less, when he heard. He was always quite honest and straightforward with me; he treated me as one man treats another;

and yet at times I felt he *must* see that with me it was different. If he did see, he made no sign. Perhaps he never noticed—I am sure he never meant to be cruel. He had never made love to me; it was no fault of his if I wanted more than he could give me. The *Sonnets to Sylvia*, you say? But what are they? A cosmic philosophy, not a love-poem; addressed to Woman, not to a woman!

But then, the letters? Ah, the letters! Well, I'll make a clean breast of it. You have noticed the breaks in the letters here and there, just as they seem to be on the point of growing a little—warmer? The critics, you may remember, praised the editor for his commendable delicacy and good taste (so rare in these days!) in omitting from the correspondence all personal allusions, all those *détails intimes*[3] which should be kept sacred from the public gaze. They referred, of course, to the asterisks in the letters to Mrs. A. Those letters I myself prepared for publication; that is to say, I copied them out for the editor, and every now and then I put in a line of asterisks to make it appear that something had been left out. You understand? The asterisks were a sham—*there was nothing to leave out.*

No one but a woman could understand what I went through during those years—the moments of revolt, when I felt I must break away from it all, fling the truth in his face and never see him again; the inevitable reaction, when not to see him seemed the one unendurable thing, and I trembled lest a look or word of mine should disturb the poise of our friendship; the silly days when I hugged the delusion that he *must* love me, since everybody thought he did; the long periods of numbness, when I didn't seem to care whether he loved me or not. Between these wretched days came others when our intellectual accord was so perfect that I forgot everything else in the joy of feeling myself lifted up on the wings of his thought. Sometimes, then, the heavens seemed to be opened. . . .

All this time he was so dear a friend! He had the genius of friendship, and he spent it all on me. Yes, you were right when you said that I have had more than any other woman. *Il faut de l'adresse pour aimer*, Pascal says;[4] and I was so quiet, so cheerful, so frankly affectionate with him, that in all those years I am almost sure I never bored him. Could I have hoped as much if he had loved me?

You mustn't think of him, though, as having been tied to my skirts. He came and went as he pleased, and so did his fancies. There was a girl once (I am telling you everything), a lovely being who called his poetry "deep" and gave him *Lucile*[5] on his birthday. He followed

3. Intimate details. 4. "It takes an intention to love"—or, "one falls in love only from an intent to do so"; Blaise Pascal (1623–1662), French philosopher. 5. Slick novel by Edward Robert Bulwer-Lytton (1831–1891), published under the pseudonym Owen Meredith.

her to Switzerland one summer, and all the time that he was dangling after her (a little too conspicuously, I always thought, for a Great Man), he was writing to *me* about his theory of vowel-combinations—or was it his experiments in English hexameter? The letters were dated from the very places where I knew they went and sat by waterfalls together and he thought out adjectives for her hair. He talked to me about it quite frankly afterwards. She was perfectly beautiful and it *had* been a pure delight to watch her; but she *would* talk, and her mind, he said, was "all elbows." And yet, the next year, when her marriage was announced, he went away alone, quite suddenly . . . and it was just afterwards that he published *Love's Viaticum.*[6] Men are queer!

After my husband died—I am putting things crudely, you see—I had a return of hope. It was because he loved me, I argued, that he had never spoken; because he had always hoped some day to make me his wife; because he wanted to spare me the "reproach." Rubbish! I knew well enough, in my heart of hearts, that my one chance lay in the force of habit. He had grown used to me; he was no longer young; he dreaded new people and new ways; *il avait pris son pli.*[7] Would it not be easier to marry me?

I don't believe he ever thought of it. He wrote me what people call "a beautiful letter;" he was kind, considerate, decently commiserating; then, after a few weeks, he slipped into his old way of coming in every afternoon, and our interminable talks began again just where they had left off. I heard later that people thought I had shown "such good taste" in not marrying him.

So we jogged on for five years longer. Perhaps they were the best years, for I had given up hoping. Then he died.

After this death—this is curious—there came to me a kind of mirage of love. All the books and articles written about him, all the reviews of the "Life," were full of discreet allusions to Silvia. I became again the Mrs. Anerton of the glorious days. Sentimental girls and dear lads like you turned pink when somebody whispered, "that was Silvia you were talking to." Idiots begged for my autograph—publishers urged me to write my reminiscences of him—critics consulted me about the reading of doubtful lines. And I knew that, to all these people, I was the woman Vincent Rendle had loved.

After a while that fire went out too and I was left alone with my past. Alone—quite alone; for he had never really been with me. The intellectual union counted for nothing now. It had been soul to soul, but never hand in hand, and there were no little things to remember him by.

Then there set in a kind of Arctic winter. I crawled into myself

6. *Viaticum* (Latin), provisions for a journey. 7. "He had become set in his ways."

as into a snow-hut. I hated my solitude and yet dreaded any one who disturbed it. That phase, of course, passed like the others. I took up life again, and began to read the papers and consider the cut of my gowns. But there was one question that I could not be rid of, that haunted me night and day. Why had he never loved me? Why had I been so much to him, and no more? Was I so ugly, so essentially unlovable, that though a man might cherish me as his mind's comrade, he could not care for me as a woman? I can't tell you how that question tortured me. It became an obsession.

My poor friend, do you begin to see? I had to find out what some other man thought of me. Don't be too hard on me! Listen first—consider. When I first met Vincent Rendle I was a young woman, who had married early and led the quietest kind of life; I had had no "experiences." From the hour of our first meeting to the day of his death I never looked at any other man, and never noticed whether any other man looked at me. When he died, five years ago, I knew the extent of my powers no more than a baby. Was it too late to find out? Should I never know *why*?

Forgive me—forgive me. You are so young; it will be an episode, a mere "document," to you so soon! And, besides, it wasn't as deliberate, as cold-blooded as these disjointed lines have made it appear. I didn't plan it, like a woman in a book. Life is so much more complex than any rendering of it can be. I liked you from the first—I was drawn to you (you must have seen that)—I wanted you to like me; it was not a mere psychological experiment. And yet in a sense it was that, too—I must be honest. I had to have an answer to that question; it was a ghost that had to be laid.

At first I was afraid—oh, so much afraid—that you cared for me only because I was Silvia, that you loved me because you thought Rendle had loved me. I began to think there was no escaping my destiny.

How happy I was when I discovered that you were growing jealous of my past; that you actually hated Rendle! My heart beat like a girl's when you told me you meant to follow me to Venice.

After our parting at Villa d'Este my old doubts reasserted themselves. What did I know of your feeling for me, after all? Were you capable of analyzing it yourself? Was it not likely to be two-thirds vanity and curiosity, and one-third literary sentimentality? You might easily fancy that you cared for Mary Anerton when you were really in love with Silvia—the heart is such a hypocrite! Or you might be more calculating than I had supposed. Perhaps it was you who had been flattering *my* vanity in the hope (the pardonable hope!) of turning me, after a decent interval, into a pretty little essay with a margin.

When you arrived in Venice and we met again—do you remember the music on the lagoon, that evening, from my balcony?—I was so afraid you would begin to talk about the book—the book, you remember, was your ostensible reason for coming. You never spoke of it, and I soon saw your one fear was *I* might do so—might remind you of your object in being with me. Then I knew you cared for me! Yes, at that moment really cared! We never mentioned the book once, did we, during that month in Venice?

I have read my letter over; and now I wish that I had said this to you instead of writing it. I could have felt my way then, watching your face and seeing if you understood. But, no, I could not go back to Venice; and I could not tell you (though I tried) while we were there together. I couldn't spoil that month—my one month. It was so good, for once in my life, to get away from literature. . . .

You will be angry with me at first—but, alas! not for long. What I have done would have been cruel if I had been a younger woman; as it is, the experiment will hurt no one but myself. And it will hurt me horribly (as much as, in your first anger, you may perhaps wish), because it has shown me, for the first time, all that I have missed. . . .

---

1. Is Mrs. Anerton being selfishly cruel in rejecting Danyers? Is he also a victim of Rendle's eccentricities?
2. Is her separation from Danyers a second tragedy or the culmination of a single tragic pattern?
3. What does the story say about the entanglement of public images with private lives?
4. What do you suppose Danyers' feelings to be when he gets Mrs. Anerton's letter?
5. Do you understand Rendle's treatment of Mrs. Anerton? What further kinds of information would make his character and motivation more comprehensible?

William Carlos Williams

Williams (1883–1963) was born in Rutherford, New Jersey. He took a medical degree at the University of Pennsylvania and practiced as a pediatrician through the long years of his literary career. Defining himself as utterly American in taste and spirit, he became the friend, supporter, and colleague of several of the leaders of the avant-garde in American literature. His work as a poet culminated in the massive chronicle Paterson *(1946–58), and the imagination that shaped his verse informed his speculations on our history and its character in his book of essays* In the American Grain *(1925). In his fiction as in his several plays he achieves an illuminated mirror image of the flat banality of ordinary lives. His novels include* White Mule *(1937) and* In the Money *(1940). His short stories are collected in* The Knife of the Times *(1932),* Make Light of It *(1950), and* The Doctor Stories *(1984).*

The Use of Force

They were new patients to me, all I had was the name, Olson. Please come down as soon as you can, my daughter is very sick. When I arrived I was met by the mother, a big startled looking woman, very clean and apologetic who merely said, Is this the doctor? and let me in. In the back, she added. You must excuse us, doctor, we have her in the kitchen where it is warm. It is very damp here sometimes.

The child was fully dressed and sitting on her father's lap near the kitchen table. He tried to get up, but I motioned for him not to bother, took off my overcoat and started to look things over. I could see that they were all very nervous, eyeing me up and down distrustfully. As often, in such cases, they weren't telling me more than they had to, it was up to me to tell them; that's why they were spending three dollars on me.

The child was fairly eating me up with her cold, steady eyes, and no expression to her face whatever. She did not move and seemed, inwardly, quiet; an unusually attractive little thing, and as strong as a heifer in appearance. But her face was flushed, she was breathing rapidly, and I realized that she had a high fever. She had magnificent blonde hair, in profusion. One of those picture children often reproduced in advertising leaflets and the photogravure sections of the Sunday papers.

She's had a fever for three days, began the father and we don't know what it comes from. My wife has given her things, you know, like people do, but it don't do no good. And there's been a lot of sickness around. So we tho't you'd better look her over and tell us what is the matter.

As doctors often do I took a trial shot at it as a point of departure. Has she had a sore throat?

Both parents answered me together, No . . . No, she says her throat don't hurt her.

Does your throat hurt you? added the mother to the child. But the little girl's expression didn't change nor did she move her eyes from my face.

Have you looked?

I tried to, said the mother, but I couldn't see.

As it happens we had been having a number of cases of diphtheria in the school to which this child went during that month and we were all, quite apparently, thinking of that, though no one had as yet spoken of the thing.

Well, I said, suppose we take a look at the throat first. I smiled in my best professional manner and asking for the child's first name I said, come on, Mathilda, open your mouth and let's take a look at your throat.

Nothing doing.

Aw, come on, I coaxed, just open your mouth wide and let me take a look. Look, I said opening both hands wide, I haven't anything in my hands. Just open up and let me see.

Such a nice man, put in the mother. Look how kind he is to you. Come on, do what he tells you to. He won't hurt you.

At that I ground my teeth in disgust. If only they wouldn't use the word "hurt" I might be able to get somewhere. But I did not allow myself to be hurried or disturbed but speaking quietly and slowly I approached the child again.

As I moved my chair a little nearer suddenly with one catlike movement both her hands clawed instinctively for my eyes and she almost reached them too. In fact she knocked my glasses flying and they fell, though unbroken, several feet away from me on the kitchen floor.

Both the mother and father almost turned themselves inside out in embarrassment and apology. You bad girl, said the mother, taking her and shaking her by one arm. Look what you've done. The nice man . . .

For heaven's sake, I broke in. Don't call me a nice man to her.

I'm here to look at her throat on the chance that she might have diphtheria and possibly die of it. But that's nothing to her. Look here, I said to the child, we're going to look at your throat. You're old enough to understand what I'm saying. Will you open it now by yourself or shall we have to open it for you?

Not a move. Even her expression hadn't changed. Her breaths however were coming faster and faster. Then the battle began. I had to do it. I had to have a throat culture for her own protection. But first I told the parents that it was entirely up to them. I explained the danger but said that I would not insist on a throat examination so long as they would take the responsibility.

If you don't do what the doctor says you'll have to go to the hospital, the mother admonished her severely.

Oh yeah? I had to smile to myself. After all, I had already fallen in love with the savage brat, the parents were contemptible to me. In the ensuing struggle they grew more and more abject, crushed, exhausted while she surely rose to magnificent heights of insane fury of effort bred of her terror of me.

The father tried his best, and he was a big man but the fact that she was his daughter, his shame at her behavior and his dread of hurting her made him release her just at the critical times when I had almost achieved success, till I wanted to kill him. But his dread also that she might have diphtheria made him tell me to go on, go on though he himself was almost fainting, while the mother moved back and forth behind us raising and lowering her hands in an agony of apprehension.

Put her in front of you on your lap, I ordered, and hold both her wrists.

But as soon as he did the child let out a scream. Don't, you're hurting me. Let go of my hands. Let them go I tell you. Then she shrieked terrifyingly, hysterically. Stop it! Stop it! You're killing me!

Do you think she can stand it, doctor! said the mother.

You get out, said the husband to his wife. Do you want her to die of diphtheria?

Come on now, hold her, I said.

Then I grasped the child's head with my left hand and tried to get the wooden tongue depressor between her teeth. She fought, with clenched teeth, desperately! But now I also had grown furious—at a child. I tried to hold myself down but I couldn't. I know how to expose a throat for inspection. And I did my best. When finally I got the wooden spatula behind the last teeth and just the point of it into the mouth cavity, she opened up for an instant but before I could see anything she came down again and gripped the wooden blade between her molars she reduced it to splinters before I could get it out again.

Aren't you ashamed, the mother yelled at her. Aren't you ashamed to act like that in front of the doctor?

Get me a smooth-handled spoon of some sort, I told the mother. We're going through with this. The child's mouth was already bleeding. Her tongue was cut and she was screaming in wild hysterical shrieks. Perhaps I should have desisted and come back in an hour or more. No doubt it would have been better. But I have seen at least two children lying dead in bed of neglect in such cases, and feeling that I must get a diagnosis now or never I went at it again. But the worst of it was that I too had got beyond reason. I could have torn the child apart in my own fury and enjoyed it. It was a pleasure to attack her. My face was burning with it.

The damned little brat must be protected against her own idiocy, one says to one's self at such times. Others must be protected against her. It is a social necessity. And all these things are true. But a blind fury, a feeling of adult shame, bred of a longing for muscular release are the operatives. One goes on to the end.

In the final unreasoning assault I overpowered the child's neck and jaws. I forced the heavy silver spoon back of her teeth and down her throat till she gagged. And there it was—both tonsils covered with membrane. She had fought valiantly to keep me from knowing her secret. She had been hiding that sore throat for three days at least and lying to her parents in order to escape just such an outcome as this.

Now truly she was furious. She had been on the defensive before but now she attacked. Tried to get off her father's lap and fly at me while tears of defeat blinded her eyes.

---

1. Since we know nothing of the past history of these characters, what means does the author rely on to make us understand them?
2. Does the sick girl's physical beauty have anything to do with the outcome and the meaning of this encounter?
3. Can you find any fault with the doctor's behavior? Has he done something that is simultaneously good and evil? Was the component of evil avoidable?
4. Since the use of force seems a necessity in preserving orderly civilization, what does the story say about civilized life in general?
5. What has the straightforward simplicity of the narration to do with the emotional effect of the story?

Tobias Wolff

Wolff (1945–) was born in Alabama and grew up in Washington State. Since his education at Oxford and Stanford Universities he has taught at Syracuse University and Indiana University. Many of his stories are collected in In the Garden of the North American Martyrs *(1981). His short novel* The Barracks Thief *was published in 1984 and his memoir* This Boy's Life *in 1989.*

In the Garden of the North American Martyrs

When she was young, Mary saw a brilliant and original man lose his job because he had expressed ideas that were offensive to the trustees of the college where they both taught. She shared his views, but did not sign the protest petition. She was, after all, on trial herself—as a teacher, as a woman, as an interpreter of history.

Mary watched herself. Before giving a lecture she wrote it out in full, using the arguments and often the words of other, approved writers, so that she would not by chance say something scandalous. Her own thoughts she kept to herself, and the words for them grew faint as time went on; without quite disappearing they shrank to remote, nervous points, like birds flying away.

When the department turned into a hive of cliques, Mary went about her business and pretended not to know that people hated each other. To avoid seeming bland she let herself become eccentric in harmless ways. She took up bowling, which she learned to love, and founded the Brandon College chapter of a society dedicated to restoring the good name of Richard III.[1] She memorized comedy routines from records and jokes from books; people groaned when she rattled them off, but she did not let that stop her, and after a time the groans became the point of the jokes. They were a kind of tribute to Mary's willingness to expose herself.

In fact no one at the college was safer than Mary, for she was

1. English king (1452–1485) generally regarded as ruthless and brutal.

making herself into something institutional, like a custom, or a mascot—part of the college's idea of itself.

Now and then she wondered whether she had been too careful. The things she said and wrote seemed flat to her, pulpy, as though someone else had squeezed the juice out of them. And once, while talking with a senior professor, Mary saw herself reflected in a window: she was leaning toward him and had her head turned so that her ear was right in front of his moving mouth. The sight disgusted her. Years later, when she had to get a hearing aid, Mary suspected that her deafness was a result of always trying to catch everything everyone said.

In the second half of Mary's fifteenth year at Brandon the provost called a meeting of all faculty and students to announce that the college was bankrupt and would not open its gates again. He was every bit as much surprised as they; the report from the trustees had reached his desk only that morning. It seemed that Brandon's financial manager had speculated in some kind of futures and lost everything. The provost wanted to deliver the news in person before it reached the papers. He wept openly and so did the students and teachers, with only a few exceptions—some cynical upperclassmen who claimed to despise the education they had received.

Mary could not rid her mind of the word "speculate." It meant to guess, in terms of money to gamble. How could a man gamble a college? Why would he want to do that, and how could it be that no one stopped him? To Mary, it seemed to belong to another time; she thought of a drunken plantation owner gaming away his slaves.

She applied for jobs and got an offer from a new experimental college in Oregon. It was her only offer so she took it.

The college was in one building. Bells rang all the time, lockers lined the hallways, and at every corner stood a buzzing water fountain. The student newspaper came out twice a month on mimeograph paper which felt wet. The library, which was next to the band room, had no librarian and no books.

The countryside was beautiful, though, and Mary might have enjoyed it if the rain had not caused her so much trouble. There was something wrong with her lungs that the doctors couldn't agree on, and couldn't cure; whatever it was, the dampness made it worse. On rainy days condensation formed in Mary's hearing aid and shorted it out. She began to dread talking with people, never knowing when she would have to take out her control box and slap it against her leg.

It rained nearly every day. When it was not raining it was getting ready to rain, or clearing. The ground glinted under the grass, and the light had a yellow undertone that flared up during storms.

There was water in Mary's basement. Her walls sweated, and she had found toadstools growing behind the refrigerator. She felt as though she were rusting out, like one of those old cars people thereabouts kept in their front yards, on pieces of wood. Mary knew that everyone was dying, but it did seem to her that she was dying faster than most.

She continued to look for another job, without success. Then, in the fall of her third year in Oregon, she got a letter from a woman named Louise who'd once taught in Brandon. Louise had scored a great success with a book on Benedict Arnold[2] and was now on the faculty of a famous college in upstate New York. She said that one of her colleagues would be retiring at the end of the year and asked whether Mary would be interested in the position.

The letter surprised Mary. Louise thought of herself as a great historian and of almost everyone else as useless; Mary had not known that she felt differently about her. Moreover, enthusiasm for other people's causes did not come easily to Louise, who had a way of sucking in her breath when familiar names were mentioned, as though she knew things that friendship kept her from disclosing.

Mary expected nothing, but sent a résumé and copies of her two books. Shortly after that Louise called to say that the search committee, of which she was chairwoman, had decided to grant Mary an interview in early November. "Now don't get your hopes too high," Louise said.

"Oh, no," Mary said, but thought: Why shouldn't I hope? They would not go to the bother and expense of bringing her to the college if they weren't serious. And she was certain that the interview would go well. She would make them like her, or at least give them no cause to dislike her.

She read about the area with a strange sense of familiarity, as if the land and its history were already known to her. And when her plane left Portland and climbed easily into the clouds, Mary felt like she was going home. The feeling stayed with her, growing stronger when they landed. She tried to describe it to Louise as they left the airport at Syracuse and drove toward the college, an hour or so away. "It's like *déjà vu,*" she said.

"*Déjà vu* is a hoax," Louise said. "It's just a chemical imbalance of some kind."

"Maybe so," Mary said, "but I still have this sensation."

"Don't get serious on me," Louise said. "That's not your long suit. Just be your funny, wisecracking old self. Tell me now—honestly—how do I look?"

It was night, too dark to see Louise's face well, but in the airport she had seemed gaunt and pale and intense. She reminded Mary of a

2. U.S. general (1741–1801) in Revolutionary War, who became a traitor.

description in the book she'd been reading, of how Iroquois[3] warriors gave themselves visions by fasting. She had that kind of look about her. But she wouldn't want to hear that. "You look wonderful," Mary said.

"There's a reason," Louise said. "I've taken a lover. My concentration has improved, my energy level is up, and I've lost ten pounds. I'm also getting some color in my cheeks, though that could be the weather. I recommend the experience highly. But you probably disapprove."

Mary didn't know what to say. She said that she was sure Louise knew best, but that didn't seem to be enough. "Marriage is a great institution," she added, "but who wants to live in an institution?"

Louise groaned. "I know you," she said, "and I know that right now you're thinking 'But what about Ted? What about the children?' The fact is, Mary, they aren't taking it well at all. Ted has become a nag." She handed Mary her purse. "Be a good girl and light me a cigarette, will you? I know I told you I quit, but this whole thing has been very hard on me, very hard, and I'm afraid I've started again."

They were in the hills now, heading north on a narrow road. Tall trees arched above them. As they topped a rise Mary saw the forest all around, deep black under the plum-colored sky. There were a few lights and these made the darkness seem even greater.

"Ted has succeeded in completely alienating the children from me," Louise was saying. "There is no reasoning with any of them. In fact, they refuse to discuss the matter at all, which is very ironical because over the years I have tried to instill in them a willingness to see things from the other person's point of view. If they could just *meet* Jonathan I know they would feel differently. But they won't hear of it. Jonathan," she said, "is my lover."

"I see," Mary said, and nodded.

Coming around a curve they caught two deer in the headlights. Their eyes lit up and their hindquarters tensed; Mary could see them trembling as the car went by. "Deer," she said.

"I don't know," Louise said, "I just don't know. I do my best and it never seems to be enough. But that's enough about me—let's talk about you. What did you think of my latest book?" She squawked and beat her palms on the steering wheel. "God, I love that joke," she said. "Seriously, though, what about you? It must have been a real shockeroo when good old Brandon folded."

"It was hard. Things haven't been good but they'll be a lot better if I get this job."

"At least you have work," Louise said. "You should look at it from the bright side."

3. A tribe native to the lower Great Lakes region. War-loving by reputation.

"I try."

"You seem so gloomy. I hope you're not worrying about the interview, or the class. Worrying won't do you a bit of good. Be happy."

"Class? What class?"

"The class you're supposed to give tomorrow, after the interview. Didn't I tell you? *Mea culpa*, hon, *mea maxima culpa*. I've been uncharacteristically forgetful lately."

"But what will I do?"

"Relax," Louise said. "Just pick a subject and wing it."

"Wing it?"

"You know, open your mouth and see what comes out. Extemporize."

"But I always work from a prepared lecture."

Louise sighed. "All right. I'll tell you what. Last year I wrote an article on the Marshall Plan[4] that I got bored with and never published. You can read that."

Parroting what Louise had written seemed wrong to Mary, at first; then it occurred to her that she had been doing the same kind of things for many years, and that this was not the time to get scruples. "Thanks," she said. "I appreciate it."

"Here we are," Louise said, and pulled into a circular drive with several cabins grouped around it. In two of the cabins lights were on; smoke drifted straight up from the chimneys. "This is the visitors' center. The college is another two miles thataway." Louise pointed down the road. "I'd invite you to stay at my house, but I'm spending the night with Jonathan and Ted is not good company these days. You would hardly recognize him."

She took Mary's bags from the trunk and carried them up the steps of a darkened cabin. "Look," she said, "they've laid a fire for you. All you have to do is light it." She stood in the middle of the room with her arms crossed and watched as Mary held a match under the kindling. "There," she said. "You'll be snugaroo in no time. I'd love to stay and chew the fat but I can't. You just get a good night's sleep and I'll see you in the morning."

Mary stood in the doorway and waved as Louise pulled out of the drive, spraying gravel. She filled her lungs, to taste the air: it was tart and clear. She could see the stars in their figurations, and the vague streams of light that ran among the stars.

She still felt uneasy about reading Louise's work as her own. It would be her first complete act of plagiarism. It would change her. It would make her less—how much less, she did not know. But what else

4. Plan for rehabilitating European economies devastated by WW II, formulated by George Catlett Marshall (1880–1959), U.S. chief of staff.

could she do? She certainly wouldn't "wing it." Words might fail her, and then what? Mary had a dread of silence. When she thought of silence she thought of drowning, as if it were a kind of water she could not swim in.

"I want this job," she said, and settled deep into her coat. It was cashmere and Mary had not worn it since moving to Oregon, because people there thought you were pretentious if you had on anything but a Pendleton shirt or, of course, raingear. She rubbed her cheek against the upturned collar and thought of a silver moon shining through bare black branches, a white house with green shutters, red leaves falling in a hard blue sky.

Louise woke her a few hours later. She was sitting on the edge of the bed, pushing at Mary's shoulder and snuffling loudly. When Mary asked her what was wrong she said, "I want your opinion on something. It's very important. Do you think I'm womanly?"

Mary sat up. "Louise, can this wait?"

"No."

"Womanly?"

Louise nodded.

"You are very beautiful," Mary said, "and you know how to present yourself."

Louise stood and paced the room. "That son of a bitch," she said. She came back and stood over Mary. "Let's suppose someone said I have no sense of humor. Would you agree or disagree?"

"In some things you do. I mean, yes, you have a good sense of humor."

"What do you mean, 'in some things?' What kind of things?"

"Well, if you heard that someone had been killed in an unusual way, like by an exploding cigar, you would think that was funny."

Louise laughed.

"That's what I mean," Mary said.

Louise went on laughing. "Oh, Lordy," she said. "Now it's my turn to say something about you." She sat down beside Mary.

"Please," Mary said.

"Just one thing," Louise said.

Mary waited.

"You're trembling," Louise said. "I was just going to say—oh, forget it. Listen, do you mind if I sleep on the couch? I'm all in."

"Go ahead."

"Sure it's okay? You've got a big day tomorrow." She fell back on the sofa and kicked off her shoes. "I was just going to say, you should use some liner on those eyebrows of yours. They sort of disappear and the effect is disconcerting."

Neither of them slept. Louise chain-smoked cigarettes and Mary watched the coals burn down. When it was light enough that they could see each other Louise got up. "I'll send a student for you," she said. "Good luck."

The college looked the way colleges are supposed to look. Roger, the student assigned to show Mary around, explained that it was an exact copy of a college in England, right down to the gargoyles and stained-glass windows. It looked so much like a college that moviemakers sometimes used it as a set. *Andy Hardy Goes to College*[5] had been filmed there, and every fall they had an Andy Hardy Goes to College Day, with raccoon coats and goldfish-swallowing contests.

Above the door of the Founder's Building was a Latin motto which, roughly translated, meant "God helps those who help themselves." As Roger recited the names of illustrious graduates Mary was struck by the extent to which they had taken this precept to heart. They had helped themselves to railroads, mines, armies, states; to empires of finance with outposts all over the world.

Roger took Mary to the chapel and showed her a plaque bearing the names of alumni who had been killed in various wars, all the way back to the Civil War. There were not many names. Here too, apparently, the graduates had helped themselves. "Oh yes," Roger said as they were leaving, "I forgot to tell you. The communion rail comes from some church in Europe where Charlemagne[6] used to go."

They went to the gymnasium, and the three hockey rinks, and the library, where Mary inspected the card catalogue, as though she would turn down the job if they didn't have the right books. "We have a little more time," Roger said as they went outside. "Would you like to see the power plant?"

Mary wanted to keep busy until the last minute, so she agreed.

Roger led her into the depths of the service building, explaining things about the machine, which was the most advanced in the country. "People think the college is really old-fashioned," he said, "but it isn't. They let girls come here now, and some of the teachers are women. In fact, there's a statute that says they have to interview at least one woman for each opening. There it is."

They were standing on an iron catwalk above the biggest machine Mary had ever beheld. Roger, who was majoring in Earth Sciences, said that it had been built from a design pioneered by a professor in his department. Where before he had been gabby Roger now became

5. Before and during WW II the series of Hardy Family films was extremely popular in the U.S. Andy Hardy was played by film star Mickey Rooney. 6. King of the Franks (742–814) and emperor of the Holy Roman Empire.

reverent. It was clear that for him this machine was the soul of the college, that the purpose of the college was to provide outlets for the machine. Together they leaned against the railing and watched it hum.

Mary arrived at the committee room exactly on time for her interview, but the room was empty. Her two books were on the table, along with a water pitcher and some glasses. She sat down and picked up one of the books. The binding cracked as she opened it. The pages were smooth, clean, unread. Mary turned to the first chapter, which began, "It is generally believed that . . ." How dull, she thought.

Nearly twenty minutes later Louise came in with several men. "Sorry we're late," she said. "We don't have much time so we'd better get started." She introduced Mary to the men, but with one exception the names and faces did not stay together. The exception was Dr. Howells, the department chairman, who had a porous blue nose and terrible teeth.

A shiny-faced man to Dr. Howells's right spoke first. "So," he said, "I understand you once taught at Brandon College."

"It was a shame that Brandon had to close," said a young man with a pipe in his mouth. "There is a place for schools like Brandon." As he talked the pipe wagged up and down.

"Now you're in Oregon," Dr. Howells said. "I've never been there. How do you like it?"

"Not very much," Mary said.

"Is that right?" Dr. Howells leaned toward her. "I thought everyone liked Oregon. I heard it's very green."

"That's true," Mary said.

"I suppose it rains a lot," he said.

"Nearly every day."

"I wouldn't like that," he said, shaking his head. "I like it dry. Of course it snows here, and you have your rain now and then, but it's a *dry* rain. Have you ever been to Utah? There's a state for you. Bryce Canyon. The Mormon Tabernacle Choir."

"Dr. Howells was brought up in Utah," said the young man with the pipe.

"It was a different place altogether in those days," Dr. Howells said. "Mrs. Howells and I have always talked about going back when I retire, but now I'm not so sure."

"We're a little short on time," Louise said.

"And here I've been going on and on," Dr. Howells said. "Before we wind things up, is there anything you want to tell us?"

"Yes. I think you should give me the job." Mary laughed when she said this, but no one laughed back, or even looked at her. They all looked away. Mary understood then that they were not really considering her for the position. She had been brought here to satisfy a rule. She had no hope.

The men gathered their papers and shook hands with Mary and told her how much they were looking forward to her class. "I can't get enough of the Marshall Plan," Dr. Howells said.

"Sorry about that," Louise said when they were alone. "I didn't think it would be so bad. That was a real bitcheroo."

"Tell me something," Mary said. "You already know who you're going to hire, don't you?"

Louise nodded.

"Then why did you bring me here?"

Louise began to explain about the statute and Mary interrupted. "I know all that. But why me? Why did you pick *me?*"

Louise walked to the window. She spoke with her back to Mary. "Things haven't been going very well for old Louise," she said. "I've been unhappy and I thought you might cheer me up. You used to be so funny, and I was sure you would enjoy the trip—it didn't cost you anything, and it's pretty this time of year with the leaves and everything. Mary, you don't know the things my parents did to me. And Ted is no barrel of laughs either. Or Jonathan, the son of a bitch. I deserve some love and friendship but I don't get any." She turned and looked at her watch. "It's almost time for your class. We'd better go."

"I would rather not give it. After all, there's not much point, is there?"

"But you *have* to give it. That's part of the interview." Louise handed Mary a folder. "All you have to do is read this. It isn't much, considering all the money we've laid out to get you here."

Mary followed Louise down the hall to the lecture room. The professors were sitting in the front row with their legs crossed. They smiled and nodded at Mary. Behind them the room was full of students, some of whom had spilled over into the aisles. One of the professors adjusted the microphone to Mary's height, crouching down as he went to the podium and back as though he would prefer not to be seen.

Louise called the room to order. She introduced Mary and gave the subject of the lecture. But Mary had decided to wing it after all. Mary came to the podium unsure of what she would say; sure only that she would rather die than read Louise's article. The sun poured through the stained glass onto the people around her, painting their faces. Thick streams of smoke from the young professor's pipe drifted through a circle of red light at Mary's feet, turning crimson and twisting like flames.

"I wonder how many of you know," she began, "that we are in the Long House,[7] the ancient domain of the Five Nations of the Iroquois."

Two professors looked at each other.

"The Iroquois were without pity," Mary said. "They hunted people down with clubs and arrows and spears and nets, and blowguns made from elder stalks. They tortured their captives, sparing no one, not even the little children. They took scalps and practiced cannibalism and slavery. Because they had no pity they became powerful, so powerful that no other tribe dared to oppose them. They made the other tribes pay tribute, and when they had nothing more to pay the Iroquois attacked them."

Several of the professors began to whisper. Dr. Howells was saying something to Louise, and Louise was shaking her head.

"In one of their raids," Mary said, "they captured two Jesuit priests, Jean de Brébeuf and Gabriel Lalement.[8] They covered Lalement with pitch and set him on fire in front of Brébeuf. When Brébeuf rebuked them they cut off his lips and put a burning iron down his throat. They hung a collar of red-hot hatchets around his neck, and poured boiling water over his head. When he continued to preach to them they cut strips of flesh from his body and ate them before his eyes. While he was still alive, they scalped him and cut open his breast and drank his blood. Later, their chief tore out Brébeuf's heart and ate it, but just before he did this Brébeuf spoke to them one last time. He said—"

"That's enough!" yelled Dr. Howells, jumping to his feet.

Louise stopped shaking her head. Her eyes were perfectly round.

Mary had come to the end of her facts. She did not know what Brébeuf had said. Silence rose up around her; just when she thought she would go under and be lost in it she heard someone whistling in the hallway outside, trilling the notes like a bird, like many birds.

"Mend your lives," she said. "You have deceived yourselves in the pride of your hearts, and the strength of your arms. Though you soar aloft like the eagle, though your nest is set among the stars, thence I will bring you down, says the Lord.[9] Turn from power to love. Be kind. Do justice. Walk humbly."

Louise was waving her arms. "Mary!" she shouted.

But Mary had more to say, much more; she waved back at Louise, then turned off her hearing aid so that she would not be distracted again.

7. Communal Indian dwelling, in actuality a wooden frame covered with bark. 8. The two most famous martyrs among the Jesuit missionaries in North America. Tortured and killed by the Iroquois in 1649. 9. Obadiah 1:4.

1. Trace the thematic conflict between rationalization and truth through the developments of the plot.
2. What is the relation between the savage past of the Indians and the present situation?
3. How has Mary's history of compromise and capitulation prepared her for her ultimate rebellion?
4. What is the relation between the general tone of the story and the tone of the sermon at the end? What has the author expressed by the shift in tone?
5. What does Mary's hearing aid symbolize? What do you make of the fact that she has belatedly turned it off?

Virginia Woolf

Woolf (1882–1941) was born in London, the daughter of a distinguished man of letters, Sir Leslie Stephen. At her father's death in 1904 she moved with her sister and two brothers to Bloomsbury, the fashionably bohemian section of London, and when she began to publish she was firmly associated with the "Bloomsbury Group" of writers and intellectuals. In 1912 she married the journalist and political philosopher Leonard Woolf and with him established the Hogarth Press that published so many of her works. By the example of her first novels and in essays she made a case against the heavy objective realism of such then popular practitioners as Arnold Bennett. Her preference was for lyric adaptations of the stream-of-consciousness, best exemplified by To the Lighthouse *(1927) and* The Waves *(1931). In her popular* Mrs. Dalloway *(1925) she had shown the possibilities of her methods in developing the nondramatic, contrapuntal presentation of a sensitive, deranged war veteran and an unfulfilled woman committed to the maintenance of her social position—perhaps a fictional transformation of two major aspects of Woolf's own personality. In 1916 she suffered a terrifying mental breakdown and killed herself in 1941 in fear of its recurrence.* A Room of One's Own *(1929) is a feminist tract of enduring influence, and the essays on literature collected in the two volumes of* The Common Reader *(1925–32) did much to shape modern taste with their easy, keen suggestiveness. Her stories were collected in* A Haunted House and Other Stories *(1943).*

Kew Gardens[1]

From the oval-shaped flower-bed there rose perhaps a hundred stalks spreading into heart-shaped or tongue-shaped leaves half-way up and unfurling at the tip red or blue or yellow petals marked with spots of colour raised upon the surface; and from the red, blue or yellow gloom of the throat emerged a straight bar, rough with gold dust and slightly clubbed at the end. The petals were voluminous enough to be stirred by the summer breeze, and when they moved, the red, blue and yellow lights passed one over the other, staining an inch of the brown earth beneath with a spot of the most intricate colour. The light

1. Established as a state institution in 1841, Kew Gardens is the home of the Royal Botanic Gardens; it is in the London suburb of Kew, Surrey, England.

fell either upon the smooth, grey back of a pebble, or the shell of a snail with its brown, circular veins, or falling into a raindrop, it expanded with such intensity of red, blue and yellow the thin walls of water that one expected them to burst and disappear. Instead, the drop was left in a second silver grey once more, and the light now settled upon the flesh of a leaf, revealing the branching thread of fibre beneath the surface, and again it moved on and spread its illumination in the vast green spaces beneath the dome of the heart-shaped and tongue-shaped leaves. Then the breeze stirred rather more briskly overhead and the colour was flashed into the air above, into the eyes of the men and women who walk in Kew Gardens in July.

The figures of these men and women straggled past the flower-bed with a curiously irregular movement not unlike that of the white and blue butterflies who crossed the turf in zig-zag flights from bed to bed. The man was about six inches in front of the woman, strolling carelessly, while she bore on with greater purpose, only turning her head now and then to see that the children were not too far behind. The man kept this distance in front of the woman purposely, though perhaps unconsciously, for he wished to go on with his thoughts.

"Fifteen years ago I came here with Lily," he thought. "We sat somewhere over there by a lake and I begged her to marry me all through the hot afternoon. How the dragonfly kept circling round us: how clearly I see the dragonfly and her shoe with the square silver buckle at the toe. All the time I spoke I saw her shoe and when it moved impatiently I knew without looking up what she was going to say: the whole of her seemed to be in her shoe. And my love, my desire, were in the dragonfly; for some reason I thought that if it settled there, on that leaf, the broad one with the red flower in the middle of it, if the dragonfly settled on the leaf she would say 'Yes' at once. But the dragonfly went round and round: it never settled anywhere—of course not, happily not, or I shouldn't be walking here with Eleanor and the children. Tell me, Eleanor. D'you ever think of the past?"

"Why do you ask, Simon?"

"Because I've been thinking of the past. I've been thinking of Lily, the woman I might have married. . . . Well, why are you silent? Do you mind my thinking of the past?"

"Why should I mind, Simon? Doesn't one always think of the past, in a garden with men and women lying under the trees. Aren't they one's past, all that remains of it, those men and women, those ghosts lying under the trees, . . . one's happiness, one's reality?"

"For me, a square silver shoe buckle and a dragonfly—"

"For me, a kiss. Imagine six little girls sitting before their easels twenty years ago, down by the side of a lake, painting the water-lilies, the first red water-lilies I'd ever seen. And suddenly a kiss, there on the back of my neck. And my hand shook all the afternoon so that I couldn't paint. I took out my watch and marked the hour when I would allow myself to think of the kiss for five minutes only—it was so precious—the kiss of an old grey-haired woman with a wart on her nose, the mother of all my kisses all my life. Come, Caroline, come, Hubert."

They walked on past the flower-bed, now walking four abreast, and soon diminished in size among the trees and looked half transparent as the sunlight and shade swam over their backs in large trembling irregular patches.

In the oval flower-bed the snail, whose shell had been stained red, blue and yellow for the space of two minutes or so, now appeared to be moving very slightly in its shell, and next began to labour over the crumbs of loose earth which broke away and rolled down as it passed over them. It appeared to have a definite goal in front of it, differing in this respect from the singular high stepping angular green insect who attempted to cross in front of it, and waited for a second with its antennae trembling as if in deliberation, and then stepped off as rapidly and strangely in the opposite direction. Brown cliffs with deep green lakes in the hollows, flat, blade-like trees that waved from root to tip, round boulders of grey stone, vast crumpled surfaces of a thin crackling texture—all these objects lay across the snail's progress between one stalk and another to his goal. Before he had decided whether to circumvent the arched tent of a dead leaf or to breast it there came past the bed the feet of other human beings.

This time they were both men. The younger of the two wore an expression of perhaps unnatural calm; he raised his eyes and fixed them very steadily in front of him while his companion spoke, and directly his companion had done speaking he looked on the ground again and sometimes opened his lips only after a long pause and sometimes did not open them at all. The elder man had a curiously uneven and shaky method of walking, jerking his hand forward and throwing up his head abruptly, rather in the manner of an impatient carriage horse tired of waiting outside a house; but in the man these gestures were irresolute and pointless. He talked almost incessantly; he smiled to himself and again began to talk, as if the smile had been an answer. He was talking about spirits—the spirits of the dead, who, according to him, were even now telling him all sorts of odd things about their experiences in Heaven.

"Heaven was known to the ancients as Thessaly, William, and now, with this war, the spirit matter[2] is rolling between the hills like thunder." He paused, seemed to listen, smiled, jerked his head and continued:

2. "Spirit matter": spiritualism; "this war": World War I; Thessaly: a region in Greece.

"You have a small electric battery and a piece of rubber to insulate the wire—isolate?—insulate?—well, we'll skip the details, no good going into details that wouldn't be understood—and in short the little machine stands in any convenient position by the head of the bed, we will say, on a neat mahogany stand. All arrangements being properly fixed by workmen under my direction, the widow applies her ear and summons the spirit by sign as agreed. Women! Widows! Women in black—"

Here he seemed to have caught sight of a woman's dress in the distance, which in the shade looked a purple black. He took off his hat, placed his hand upon his heart, and hurried towards her muttering and gesticulating feverishly. But William caught him by the sleeve and touched a flower with the tip of his walking-stick in order to divert the old man's attention. After looking at it for a moment in some confusion the old man bent his ear to it and seemed to answer a voice speaking from it, for he began talking about the forests of Uruguay which he had visited hundreds of years ago in company with the most beautiful young woman in Europe. He could be heard murmuring about forests of Uruguay blanketed with the wax petals of tropical roses, nightingales, sea beaches, mermaids, and women drowned at sea, as he suffered himself to be moved on by William, upon whose face the look of stoical patience grew slowly deeper and deeper.

Following his steps so closely as to be slightly puzzled by his gestures came two elderly women of the lower middle class, one stout and ponderous, the other rosy cheeked and nimble. Like most people of their station they were frankly fascinated by other signs of eccentricity betokening a disordered brain, especially in the well-to-do; but they were too far off to be certain whether the gestures were merely eccentric or genuinely mad. After they had scrutinized the old man's back in silence for a moment and given each other a queer, sly look, they went on energetically piecing together their very complicated dialogue:

"Nell, Bert, Lot, Cess, Phil, Pa, he says, I says, she says, I says, I says—"

"My Bert, Sis, Bill, Grandad, the old man, sugar,

> Sugar, flour, kippers, greens,
> Sugar, sugar, sugar."

The ponderous woman looked through the pattern of falling words at the flowers standing cool, firm, and upright in the earth, with a curious expression. She saw them as a sleeper waking from a heavy sleep sees a brass candlestick reflecting the light in an unfamiliar way, and closes his eyes and opens them, and seeing the brass candlestick again, finally starts broad awake and stares at the candlestick with all his powers. So the heavy woman came to a standstill opposite the oval-shaped flower-bed, and ceased even to pretend to listen to what the other woman was saying. She stood there letting the words fall over her, swaying the top part of her body slowly backwards and forwards, looking at the flowers. Then she suggested that they should find a seat and have their tea.

The snail had now considered every possible method of reaching his goal without going round the dead leaf or climbing over it. Let alone the effort needed for climbing a leaf, he was doubtful whether the thin texture which vibrated with such an alarming crackle when touched even by the tips of his horns would bear his weight; and this determined him finally to creep beneath it, for there was a point where the leaf curved high enough from the ground to admit him. He had just inserted his head in the opening and was taking stock of the high brown roof and was getting used to the cool brown light when two other people came past outside on the turf. This time they were both young, a young man and a young woman. They were both in the prime of youth, the season before the smooth pink folds of the flower have burst their gummy case, when the wings of the butterfly, though fully grown, are motionless in the sun.

"Lucky it isn't Friday," he observed.

"Why? D'you believe in luck?"

"They make you pay sixpence on Friday."

"What's a sixpence anyway? Isn't it worth sixpence?"

"What's 'it'—what do you mean by 'it'?"

"O, anything—I mean—you know what I mean."

Long pauses came between each of these remarks; they were uttered in toneless and monotonous voices. The couple stood still on the edge of the flower-bed, and together pressed the end of her parasol deep down into the soft earth. The action and the fact that his hand rested on the top of hers expressed their feelings in a strange way, as these short insignificant words also expressed something, words with short wings for their heavy body of meaning, inadequate to carry them far and thus alighting awkwardly upon the very common objects that surrounded them, and were to their inexperienced touch so massive; but who knows (so they thought as they pressed the parasol into the earth) what precipices aren't concealed in them, or what slopes of ice don't shine in the sun on the other side? Who knows? Who has ever seen this before? Even when she wondered what sort of tea they gave you at Kew, he felt that something loomed up behind her words, and stood vast and solid behind them; and the mist very slowly rose and uncovered—O, Heavens, what were those shapes?—little white tables, and waitresses who looked first at her and then at him; and there was a bill that he would pay with a real two-shilling piece, and it was real, all real, he assured himself, fingering the coin in his pocket, real to everyone except to him and to her; even to him it began to seem real; and then—but it was too exciting to stand and think any longer, and he pulled the parasol out of the earth with a jerk and was impatient to find the place where one had tea with other people, like other people.

"Come along, Trissie; it's time we had our tea."

"Wherever *does* one have one's tea?" she asked with the oddest thrill of excitement in her voice, looking vaguely round and letting herself be drawn down the grass path, trailing her parasol; turning her head this way and that way forgetting her tea, wishing to go down there and then down there, remembering orchids and cranes among wild flowers, a Chinese pagoda and a crimson crested bird; but he bore her on.

Thus one couple after another with much the same irregular and aimless movement passed the flower-bed and were enveloped in layer after layer of green-blue vapour, in which at first their bodies had substance and a dash of colour, but later both substance and colour dissolved in the green-blue atmosphere. How hot it was! So hot that even the thrush chose to hop, like a mechanical bird, in the shadow of the flowers, with long pauses between one movement and the next; instead of rambling vaguely the white butterflies dance one above another, making with their white shifting flakes the outline of a shattered, marble column above the tallest flowers; the glass roofs of the palm house shone as if a whole market full of shiny green umbrellas had opened in the sun; and in the drone of the aeroplane the voice of the summer sky murmured its fierce soul. Yellow and black, pink and snow white, shapes of all these colours, men, women, and children were spotted for a second upon the horizon, and then, seeing the breadth of yellow that lay upon the grass, they wavered and sought shade beneath the trees, dissolving like drops of water in the yellow and green atmosphere, staining it faintly with red and blue. It seemed as if all gross and heavy bodies had sunk down in the heat motionless and lay huddled upon the ground, but their voices went wavering from them as if they were flames lolling from the thick waxen bodies of candles. Voices. Yes, voices. Wordless voices, breaking the silence suddenly with such depth of contentment, such passion of desire, or, in the voices of children, such freshness of surprise; breaking the silence? But there was no silence; all the time the motor omnibuses were turning their wheels and changing their gear; like a vast nest of Chinese boxes all of wrought steel turning ceaselessly one within another the city murmured; on the top of which the voices cried aloud and the petals of myriads of flowers flashed their colours into the air.

1. Why is there little more information about the people in the story than about the flowers and insects? What happens to point of view in such a treatment as this? What happens to human values?
2. What, if anything, relates the various passersby to each other?
3. Discuss the importance of style and imagery in establishing the tone and meaning of the story. Is there a theme?
4. Can you locate any devices of personification? What do they contribute to the meaning of the whole?
5. Is the personality of the author rendered or implied by the manner in which the story is told?'

Richard Wright

Wright (1908–1960) was born on a plantation near Natchez, Mississippi, the son of a mill worker and a schoolteacher. Deserted by his father at an early age, he lived intermittently in orphan asylums or wandered with his mother from city to city in an erratic pattern that continued for him after her death. In 1927 he turned up in Chicago, where he joined the Communist party and began to write. A growing reputation as a short story writer was solidified with the publication in 1940 of his first novel, Native Son, *a pathetic and gory narrative of a young black man hurled blindly into crime.* Black Boy, *a vivid personal narrative, was published in 1945, followed in 1953 by the novel* The Outsider *and in 1954 by* Black Power, *an extensive report on the Africa Gold Coast countries. Several of his stories are collected in* Uncle Tom's Children *(1938) and* Eight Men *(1961).*

The Man Who Was Almost a Man

Dave struck out across the fields, looking homeward through paling light. Whuts the usa talkin wid em niggers in the field? Anyhow, his mother was putting supper on the table. Them niggers can't understand *nothing*. One of these days he was going to get a gun and practice shooting, then they can't talk to him as though he were a little boy. He slowed, looking at the ground. Shucks, Ah ain scareda them even ef they are biggern me! Aw, Ah know whut Ahma do. . . . Ahm going by ol Joe's sto n git that Sears Roebuck catlog n look at them guns. Mabbe Ma will lemme buy one when she gits mah pay from ol man Hawkins. Ahma beg her t gimme some money. Ahm ol ernough to hava gun. Ahm seventeen. Almos a man. He strode, feeling his long, loose-jointed limbs. Shucks, a man oughta hava little gun aftah he done worked hard all day. . . .

He came in sight of Joe's store. A yellow lantern glowed on the front porch. He mounted steps and went through the screen door, hearing it bang behind him. There was a strong smell of coal oil and mackerel fish. He felt very confident until he saw fat Joe walk in through the rear door, then his courage began to ooze.

"Howdy, Dave! Whutcha want?"

"How yuh, Mistah Joe? Aw, Ah don wanna buy nothing. Ah jus wanted t see ef yuhd lemme look at tha ol catlog erwhile."

"Sure! You wanna see it here?"

"Nawsuh. Ah wans t take it home wid me. Ahll bring it back termorrow when Ah come in from the fiels."

"You plannin on buyin something?"

"Yessuh."

"Your ma letting you have your own money now?"

"Shucks. Mistah Joe, Ahm gittin t be a man like anybody else!"

Joe laughed and wiped his greasy white face with a red bandanna.

"Whut you plannin on buyin?"

Dave looked at the floor, scratched his head, scratched his thigh, and smiled. Then he looked up shyly.

"Ahll tell yuh, Mistah Joe, ef yuh promise yuh won't tell."

"I promise."

"Waal, Ahma buy a gun."

"A gun? Whut you want with a gun?"

"Ah wanna keep it."

"You ain't nothing but a boy. You don't need a gun."

"Aw, lemme have the catlog, Mistah Joe. Ahll bring it back."

Joe walked through the rear door. Dave was elated. He looked around at barrels of sugar and flour. He heard Joe coming back. He craned his neck to see if he were bringing the book. Yeah, he's got it! Gawddog, he's got it!

"Here; but be sure you bring it back. It's the only one I got."

"Sho, Mistah Joe."

"Say, if you wanna buy a gun, why don't you buy one from me. I gotta gun to sell."

"Will it shoot?"

"Sure it'll shoot."

"Whut kind is it?"

"Oh, it's kinda old. . . . A Lefthand Wheeler. A pistol. A big one."

"Is it got bullets in it?"

"It's loaded."

"Kin Ah see it?"

"Where's your money?"

"Whu yuh wan fer it?"

"I'll let you have it for two dollars."

"Just *two* dollahs? Shucks, Ah could buy tha when Ah git mah pay."

"I'll have it here when you want it."

"Awright, suh. Ah be in fer it."

He went through the door, hearing it slam again behind him. Ahma git some money from Ma n buy me a gun! Only *two* dollahs! He tucked the thick catalogue under his arm and hurried.

"Where yuh been, boy?" His mother held a steaming dish of black-eyed peas.

"Aw, Ma, Ah jus stopped down the road t talk wid th boys."

"Yuh know bettah than t keep suppah waitin."

He sat down, resting the catalogue on the edge of the table.

"Yuh git up from there and git to the well n wash yosef! Ah ain feedin no hogs in mah house!"

She grabbed his shoulder and pushed him. He stumbled out of the room, then came back to get the catalogue.

"Whut this?"

"Aw, Ma, it's jusa catlog."

"Who yuh git it from?"

"From Joe, down at the sto."

"Waal, thas good. We kin use it around the house."

"Naw, Ma." He grabbed for it. "Gimme mah catlog, Ma."

She held onto it and glared at him.

"Quit hollerin at me! Whuts wrong wid yuh? Yuh crazy?"

"But ma, please. It ain mine! It's Joe's! He tol me t bring it back t im termorrow."

She gave up the book. He stumbled down the back steps, hugging the thick book under his arm. When he had splashed water on his face and hands, he groped back to the kitchen and fumbled in a corner for the towel. He bumped into a chair; it clattered to the floor. The catalogue sprawled at his feet. When he had dried his eyes he snatched up the book and held it again under his arm. His mother stood watching him.

"Now, ef yuh gonna acka fool over that ol book, Ahll take it n burn it up."

"Naw, Ma, please."

"Waal, set down n be still!"

He sat and drew the oil lamp close. He thumbed page after page, unaware of the food his mother set on the table. His father came in. Then his small brother.

"Whutcha got there, Dave?" his father asked.

"Jusa catlog," he answered, not looking up.

"Ywah, here they is!" His eyes glowed at blue and black revolvers. He glanced up, feeling sudden guilt. His father was watching him. He eased the book under the table and rested it on his knees. After the blessing was asked, he ate. He scooped up peas and swallowed fat meat without chewing. Buttermilk helped to wash it down. He did not want to mention money before his father. He would do much better by cornering his mother when she was alone. He looked at his father uneasily out of the edge of his eye.

"Boy, how come yuh don quit foolin wid tha book n eat yo suppah?"

"Yessuh."

"How yuh n ol man Hawkins gittin erlong?"

"Suh?"

"Can't yuh hear? Why don yuh lissen? Ah ast yuh how wuz yuh n ol man Hawkins gittin erlong?"

"Oh, swell, Pa. Ah plows mo lan than anybody over there."

"Waal, yuh oughta keep yo min on whut yuh doin."

"Yessuh."

He poured his plate full of molasses and sopped at it slowly with a chunk of cornbread. When all but his mother had left the kitchen, he still sat and looked again at the guns in the catalogue. Lawd, ef Ah only had the pretty one! He could almost feel the slickness of the weapon with his fingers. If he had a gun like that he would polish it and keep it shining so it would never rust. N Ahd keep it loaded, by Gawd!

"Ma?"

"Hunh?"

"Ol man Hawkins give yuh mah money yit?"

"Yeah, but ain no usa yuh thinkin bout thowin nona it erway. Ahm keepin tha money sos yuh kin have cloes t go to school this winter."

He rose and went to her side with the open catalogue in his palms. She was washing dishes, her head bent low over a pan. Shyly he raised the open book. When he spoke his voice was husky, faint.

"Ma, Gawd knows Ah wans one of these."

"One of whut?" she asked, not raising her eyes.

"One of *these*," he said again, not daring even to point. She glanced up at the page, then at him with wide eyes.

"Nigger is yuh gone plum crazy?"

"Ah, Ma——"

"Git outta here! Don yuh talk t me bout no gun! Yuh a fool!"

"Ma, Ah kin buy one fer *two* dollahs."

"Not ef Ah knows it yuh ain!"

"But yuh promised me one——"

"Ah don care whut Ah promised! Yuh ain nothing but a boy yit!"

"Ma, ef yuh lemme buy one Ahll *never* ast yuh fer nothing no mo."

"Ah tol yuh t git outta here! Yuh ain gonna toucha penny of tha money fer no gun! Thas how come Ah has Mistah Hawkins t pay yo wages to me, cause Ah knows yuh ain got no sense."

"But Ma, we needa gun. Pa ain got no gun. We needa gun in the house. Yuh kin never tell whut might happen."

"Now don yuh try to maka fool outta me, boy! Ef we did hava gun yuh wouldn't have it!"

He laid the catalogue down and slipped his arm around her waist.

"Aw, Ma, Ah done worked hard alla summer n ain ast yuh fer nothin, is Ah, now?"

"Thas whut yuh spose to do!"

"But Ma, Ah wans a gun. Yuh kin lemme have two dollahs outta mah money. Please, Ma. I kin give it to Pa . . . Please, Ma! Ah loves yuh, Ma."

When she spoke her voice came soft and low.

"Whut yuh wan wida gun, Dave? Yun don need no gun. Yuhll git in trouble. N ef yo Pa jus *thought* Ah let yuh have money t buy a gun he'd hava fit."

"Ahll hide it, Ma, it ain but two dollahs."

"Lawd, chil, whuts wrong wid yuh?"

"Ain nothing wrong, Ma. Ahm almos a man now. Ah wants a gun."

"Who gonna sell yuh a gun?"

"Ol Joe at the sto."

"N it don cos but two dollahs?"

"Thas all, Ma. Just two dollahs. Please, Ma."

She was stacking the plates away; her hands moved slowly, reflectively. Dave kept an anxious silence. Finally, she turned to him.

"Ahll let yuh git tha gun ef yuh promise me one thing."

"Whuts that, Ma?"

"Yuh bring it straight back to *me,* yuh hear? Itll be fer Pa."

"Yessum! Lemme go now, Ma."

She stooped, turned slightly to one side, raised the hem of her dress, rolled down the top of her stocking, and came up with a slender wad of bills.

"Here," she said, "Lawd knows yuh don need no gun. But yer Pa does. Yuh bring it right back to *me,* yuh hear? Ahma put it up. Now ef yuh don, Ahma have yuh Pa lick yuh so hard yuh won ferget it."

"Yessum."

He took the money, ran down the steps, and across the yard.

"Dave! Yuuuuuh Daaaaave!"

He heard, but he was not going to stop now. "Naw, Lawd!"

The first movement he made the following morning was to reach under his pillow for the gun. In the gray light of dawn he held it loosely, feeling a sense of power. Could killa man wida gun like this. Kill anybody, black er white. And if he were holding his gun in his hand nobody could run over him; they would have to respect him. It was a big gun, with a long barrel and a heavy handle. He raised and lowered it in his hand, marveling at its weight.

He had not come straight home with it as his mother had asked; instead he had stayed out in the fields, holding the weapon in his hand, aiming it now and then at some imaginary foe. But he had not fired it; he had been afraid that his father might hear. Also he was not sure he knew how to fire it.

To avoid surrendering the pistol he had not come into the house until he knew that all were asleep. When his mother had tiptoed to his bedside late that night and demanded the gun, he had first played 'possum; then he had told her that the gun was hidden outdoors, that he would bring it to her in the morning. Now he lay turning it slowly in his hands. He broke it, took out the cartridges, felt them, and then put them back.

He slid out of bed, got a long strip of old flannel from a trunk, wrapped the gun in it, and tied it to his naked thigh while it was still loaded. He did not go in to breakfast. Even though it was not yet daylight, he started for Jim Hawkins' plantation. Just as the sun was rising he reached the barns where the mules and plows were kept.

"Hey! That you, Dave?"

He turned. Jim Hawkins stood eying him suspiciously.

"Whatre yuh doing here so early?"

"Ah didn't know Ah wuz gittin up so early, Mistah Hawkins. Ah wuz fixin t hitch up ol Jenny n take her t the fiels."

"Good. Since you're here so early, how about plowing that stretch down by the woods?"

"Suits me, Mistah Hawkins."

"O.K. Go to it!"

He hitched Jenny to a plow and started across the fields. Hot dog! This was just what he wanted. If he could get down by the woods, he could shoot his gun and nobody would hear. He walked behind the plow, hearing the traces creaking, feeling the gun tied tight to his thigh.

When he reached the woods, he plowed two whole rows before he decided to take out the gun. Finally, he stopped, looked in all directions, then untied the gun and held it in his hand. He turned to the mule and smiled.

"Know whut this is, Jenny? Naw, yuh wouldn't know! Yuhs jusa ol mule! Anyhow, this is a gun, n it kin shoot, by Gawd!"

He held the gun at arm's length. Whut t hell, Ahma shoot this thing! He looked at Jenny again.

"Lissen here, Jenny! When Ah pull this ol trigger Ah don wan yuh t run n acka fool now."

Jenny stood with head down, her short ears pricked straight. Dave walked off about twenty feet, held the gun far out from him, at arm's length, and turned his head. Hell, he told himself, Ah ain afraid. The gun felt loose in his fingers; he waved it wildly for a moment. Then he shut his eyes and tightened his forefinger. *Blooom!* A report half-deafened him and he thought his right hand was torn from his arm. He heard Jenny whinnying and galloping over the field, and he found himself on his knees, squeezing his fingers hard between his legs. His hand was numb; he jammed it into his mouth, trying to warm it, trying to stop the pain. The gun lay at his feet. He did not quite know what had happened. He stood up and stared at the gun as though it were a live thing. He gritted his teeth and kicked the gun. Yuh almos broke mah arm! He turned to look for Jenny; she was far over the fields, tossing her head and kicking wildly.

"Hol on ther, ol mule!"

When he caught up with her she stood trembling, walling her big white eyes at him. The plow was far away; the traces had broken. Then Dave stopped short, looking, not believing. Jenny was bleeding. Her left side was red and wet with blood. He went closer. Lawd have mercy! Wondah did Ah shoot this mule? He grabbed for Jenny's mane. She flinched, snorted, whirled, tossing her head.

"Hol on now! Hol on."

Then he saw the hole in Jenny's side, right between the ribs. It was round, wet, red. A crimson stream streaked down the front leg, flowing fast. Good Gawd! Ah wuznt shootin at tha mule. . . . He felt panic. He knew he had to stop that blood, or Jenny would bleed to death. He had never seen so much blood in all his life. He ran the mule for half a mile, trying to catch her. Finally, she stopped, breathing hard, stumpy tail half arched. He caught her mane and led her back to where the plow and gun lay. Then he stopped and grabbed handfuls of damp black earth and tried to plug the bullet hole. Jenny shuddered, whinnied, and broke from him.

"Hol on! Hol on now!"

He tried to plug it again, but blood came anyhow. His fingers were hot and sticky. He rubbed dirt hard into his palms, trying to dry them. Then again he attempted to plug the bullet hole, but Jenny shied away, kicking her heels high. He stood helpless. He had to do something. He ran at Jenny; she dodged him. He watched a red stream of blood flow down Jenny's leg and form a bright pool at her feet.

"Jenny . . . Jenny . . ." he called weakly.

His lips trembled. She's bleeding t death! He looked in the direction of home, wanting to go back, wanting to get help. But he saw the pistol lying in the damp black clay. He had a queer feeling that if he only did something, this would not be; Jenny would not be there bleeding to death.

When he went to her this time, she did not move. She stood with sleepy, dreamy eyes; and when he touched her she gave a low-pitched whinny and knelt to the ground, her front knees slopping in blood.

"Jenny . . . Jenny . . ." he whispered.

For a long time she held her neck erect; then her head sank, slowly. Her ribs swelled with a mighty heave and she went over.

Dave's stomach felt empty, very empty. He picked up the gun and held it gingerly between his thumb and forefinger. He buried it at the foot of a tree. He took a stick and tried to cover the pool of blood with dirt—but what was the use? There was Jenny lying with her mouth open and her eyes walled and glassy. He could not tell Jim Hawkins he had shot his mule. But he had to tell something. Yeah, Ahll tell em Jenny started gittin wil n fell on the joint of the plow. . . . But that would hardly happen to a mule. He walked across the field slowly, head down.

It was sunset. Two of Jim Hawkins' men were over near the edge of the woods digging a hole in which to bury Jenny. Dave was surrounded by a knot of people; all of them were looking down at the dead mule.

"I don't see how in the world it happened," said Jim Hawkins for the tenth time.

The crowd parted and Dave's mother, father, and small brother pushed into the center.

"Where Dave?" his mother called.

"There he is," said Jim Hawkins.

His mother grabbed him.

"Whut happened, Dave? Whut yuh done?"

"Nothing."

"C'mon, boy, talk," his father said.

Dave took a deep breath and told the story he knew nobody believed.

"Waal," he drawled. "Ah brung ol Jenny down here sos Ah could do mah plowin. Ah plowed bout two rows, just like yuh see." He stopped and pointed at the long rows of upturned earth. "Then something musta been wrong wid ol Jenny. She wouldn't ack right atall. She started snortin n kickin her heels. Ah tried to hol her, but she pulled erway, rearin n goin on. Then when the point of the plow was stickin up in the air, she swung erroun n twisted hersef back on it. . . . She stuck hersef n started t bleed. N fo Ah could do anything, she wuz dead."

"Did you ever hear of anything like that in all your life?" asked Jim Hawkins.

There were white and black standing in the crowd. They murmured. Dave's mother came close to him and looked hard into his face.

"Tell the truth, Dave," she said.

"Looks like a bullet hole ter me," said one man.

"Dave, whut yuh do wid tha gun?" his mother asked.

The crowd surged in, looking at him. He jammed his hands into his pockets, shook his head slowly from left to right, and backed away. His eyes were wide and painful.

"Did he hava gun?" asked Jim Hawkins.

"By Gawd, Ah tol yuh tha wuz a *gun* wound," said a man, slapping his thigh.

His father caught his shoulders and shook him till his teeth rattled.

"Tell whut happened, yuh rascal! Tell whut . . ."

Dave looked at Jenny's stiff legs and began to cry.

"Whut yuh do wid tha gun?" his mother asked.

"Whut wuz he doin wida gun?" his father asked.

"Come on and tell the truth," said Hawkins. "Ain't nobody going to hurt you . . ."

His mother crowded close to him.

"Did yuh shoot that mule, Dave?"

Dave cried, seeing blurred white and black faces.

"Ahh ddinnt gggo tt sshoooot hher. . . . Ah ssswear ffo Gawd Ahh ddint. . . . Ah wuz a-tryin t sssee ef the ol gggun would sshoot——"

"Where yuh git the gun from?" his father asked.

"Ah got it from Joe, at the sto."

"Where yuh git the money?"

"Ma give it t me."

"He kept worryin me, Bob. . . . Ah had t. . . . Ah tol im t bring the gun right back t me. . . . It was fer yuh, the gun."

"But how yuh happen to shoot that mule?" asked Jim Hawkins.

"Ah wuznt shootin at the mule, Mistah Hawkins. The gun jumped when Ah pulled the trigger . . . N fo Ah knowed anything Jenny wuz there a-bleedin."

Somebody in the crowd laughed. Jim Hawkins walked close to Dave and looked into his face.

"Well, looks like you have bought you a mule, Dave."

"Ah swear fo Gawd, Ah didn't go t kill the mule, Mistah Hawkins!"

"But you killed her!"

All the crowd was laughing now. They stood on tiptoe and poked heads over one another's shoulders.

"Well, boy, looks like yuh done bought a dead mule! Hahaha!"

"Ain tha ershame."

"Hohohohoho."

Dave stood head down, twisting his feet in the dirt.

"Well, you needn't worry about it, Bob," said Jim Hawkins to Dave's father. "Just let the boy keep on working and pay me two dollars a month."

"Whut yuh wan fer yo mule, Mistah Hawkins?"

Jim Hawkins screwed up his eyes.

"Fifty dollars."

"Whut yuh do wid tha gun?" Dave's father demanded.

Dave said nothing.

"Yuh wan me t take a tree lim n beat yuh till yuh talk!"

"Nawsuh!"

"Whut yuh do wid it?"

"Ah thowed it erway."

"Where?"

"Ah . . . Ah thowed it in the creek."

"Waal, c mon home. N firs thing in the mawnin git to tha creek n fin tha gun."

"Yessuh."

"Whut yuh pay fer it?"

"Two dollahs."

"Take tha gun n git yo money back n carry it t Mistah Hawkins, yuh hear? N don fergit Ahma lam yo black bottom good fer this! Now march yosef on home, suh!"

Dave turned and walked slowly. He heard people laughing. Dave glared, his eyes welling with tears. Hot anger bubbled in him. Then he swallowed and stumbled on.

That night Dave did not sleep. He was glad that he had gotten out of killing the mule so easily, but he was hurt. Something hot seemed to turn over inside him each time he remembered how they had laughed. He tossed on his bed, feeling his hard pillow. N Pa says he's gonna beat me. . . . He remembered other beatings, and his back quivered. Naw, naw, Ah sho don wan im t beat me tha way no mo. . . . Dam em *all!* Nobody ever gave him anything. All he did was work. They treat me lika mule. . . . N then they beat me. . . . He gritted his teeth. N Ma had t tell on me.

Well, if he had to, he would take old man Hawkins that two dollars. But that meant selling the gun. And he wanted to keep that gun. Fifty dollahs for a dead mule.

He turned over, thinking of how he had fired the gun. He had an itch to fire it again. Ef other men kin shoota gun, by Gawd, Ah kin! He was still listening. Mebbe they all sleepin now. . . . The house was still. He heard the soft breathing of his brother. Yes, now! He would go down and get that gun and see if he could fire it! He eased out of bed and slipped into overalls.

The moon was bright. He ran almost all the way to the edge of the woods. He stumbled over the ground, looking for the spot where he had buried the gun. Yeah, here it is. Like a hungry dog scratching for a bone he pawed it up. He puffed his black cheeks and blew dirt from the trigger and barrel. He broke it and found four cartridges unshot. He looked around; the fields were filled with silence and moonlight. He clutched the gun stiff and hard in his fingers. But as soon as he wanted to pull the trigger, he shut his eyes and turned his head. Naw, Ah can't shoot wid mah eyes closed n mah head turned. With effort he held his eyes open; then he squeezed. *Blooooom!* He was stiff, not breathing. The gun was still in his hands. Dammit, he'd done it! He fired again. *Bloooom!* He smiled. *Bloooom! Bloooom! Click, click.* There! It was empty. If anybody could shoot a gun, he could. He put the gun into his hip pocket and started across the fields.

When he reached the top of a ridge he stood straight and proud in the moonlight, looking at Jim Hawkins' big white house, feeling the gun sagging in his pocket. Lawd, ef Ah had jus one mo bullet Ahd taka shot at tha house. Ahd like t scare ol man Hawkins jusa little. . . . Jusa enough t let im know Dave Sanders is a man.

To his left the road curved, running to the tracks of the Illinois Central. He jerked his head, listening. From far off came a faint *hoooof-hoooof; hoooof-hoooof; hoooof-hoooof* . . . Tha's number eight. He took a swift look at Jim Hawkins' white house; he thought of pa, of ma, of his little brother, and the boys. He thought of the dead mule and heard *hoooof-hoooof; hoooof-hoooof; hoooof-hoooof* . . . He stood rigid. Two dollahs a mont. Les see now. . . . Tha means itll take bout two years. Shucks! Ahll be dam!

He started down the road, toward the tracks. Yeah, here she comes! He stood beside the track and held himself stiffly. Here she comes, erroun the ben. . . . C mon, yuh slow poke! C mon! He had his hand on his gun; something quivered in his stomach. Then the train thundered past, the gray and brown box cars rumbling and clinking. He gripped the gun tightly; then he jerked his hand out of his pocket. Ah betcha Bill wouldn't do it! Ah betcha. . . . The cars slid past, steel grinding upon steel. Ahm riding yuh ternight so hep me Gawd! He was hot all over. He hesitated just a moment; then he grabbed, pulled atop of a car, and lay flat. He felt his pocket; the gun was still there.

Ahead the long rails were glinting in the moonlight, stretching away, away to somewhere, somewhere where he could be a man. . . .

---

1. What is the importance of the social setting in shaping Dave's motives and course of action?
2. How do the dialogue and limited point of view help reveal the meaning of local social pressures?
3. To what extent is the accidental shooting of the mule crucial to Dave's departure from home? Does it merely hasten him on a course he would in any case have followed?
4. What sort of future for Dave is implied by the last paragraphs?
5. Discuss the role of the minor characters in shaping Dave's character and in determining his actions.

Writing about Fiction

To write a paper about some story that has taken hold of your imagination gives you the chance to organize your thoughts and account for the emotions stirred while you were reading. There are several inviting ways to seize the material and give a solid shape to your impressions. Some possible approaches are suggested by the questions following each story. Every question touches on a topic that might be developed into an essay of some length. Class discussions also may have begun a train of thought that you want to push further. Encountering ideas, characters, behavior, or unfamiliar attitudes in a story can move you to challenge what you have read and reassess your values by writing a response.

For convenience in making a start on your paper, note that most of your options will fall in one of three general categories. First—you might want to assume that you are introducing a story to someone who has not yet read it. This can be thought of as the approach of a book reviewer, who must give a brief but comprehensive overview of the work under consideration while enumerating some of the components that give it flavor and significance.

A second mode of approach would be to suppose you are writing for someone who is quite familiar with the story but who may not have fully weighed some aspects of it which seem to you worth reconsideration. For simplicity's sake we can categorize this as the tactic of the critic, who never concedes that the last word has been said on his or her subject—who, in fact, often debates prior interpretations as a means of focusing attention on points that may have been slighted.

Broadest and most open of all is the category of personal response, in which your experience in reading, your values, your surprise, dismay, or delight, and your image of yourself are made a mirror for whatever a story has to offer. Here the virtues of detachment and objectivity are deliberately set aside or postponed in favor of concentrating on your adventure as an impassioned, impressionable partner in a dialogue with the author.

None of these approaches is inherently better than the others. The sky is the limit in each. Failure and muddle lurk as possibilities—less likely, of course, for the student whose imagination and understanding have been heated in advance of the commitment to writing. Surely reading well is half the battle of writing good papers. Just as certainly, writing well about fiction stabilizes and extends your skill as a reader.

Reviewing a Story

A good reviewer will not simply aim at reducing the story to capsule form nor be content to point out the interest of the subject matter. True, enough of the story line should be sketched to show the essential conflict the author has exploited. But beyond this, the reviewer wants to illustrate the flavor of the work, its dependence on the language of perceptive narration and of dialogue. Even the briefest review can be enhanced by quotes from the work being introduced. It is with a preliminary selection of usable quotations that you might well begin your preparation for writing.

In "A Rose for Emily" one can hardly help being struck by memorable words, phrases, or lines. Miss Emily is characterized at one point with these adjectives—"dear, inescapable, impervious, tranquil, and perverse." The bafflement of the town in dealing with her is represented by the outraged question of Judge Stevens: "Dammit, sir . . . will you accuse a lady to her face of smelling bad?" "She carried her head high—even when we believed she was fallen." And the statement at the end of section II: ". . . we knew that with nothing left, she would have to cling to that which robbed her, as people will."

If such samplings of Faulknerian language will be useful in showing the flavor of his work, you would do well to make sure they can be handily retrieved when the time comes to put them in your paper. A simple way of doing this is to underline them while reading, or mark them with a highlighting pen. Or jot them in a notebook. The point is that composition is a growth process. The first steps of writing are taken while you are still reading.

The lines which conclude section II could well serve as introduction and topic sentence for a paper about "A Rose for Emily," for the declaration implicitly raises questions that need to be answered with some amplitude:

Why does Miss Emily have nothing left?
Who or what has robbed her of what she had?
How does she cling to the first and second robbers?
What is the referent of the pronoun "we"?
What is the relation between "we" and the "people" who will cling to what robbed them, just as the central character will?

To set down in outline form the declarative answers to these questions might be the second step in preparing to write the paper. There is a natural progression from the quoted topic sentence to an explanation of why, at the death of her father, Miss Emily appeared to have nothing left, and how she clings to the man Homer Barron, who has robbed her of honor and the hope of marriage. What ought to be added to this, certainly, is some accounting for the use of the first person plural in the narration, since this peculiarity distinguishes Faulkner's story from most others.

In expanding your account you will show that there are good reasons for this use of the plural pronoun. The narrator immerses his singular identity in the common plurality of townspeople to emphasize the preeminence of community opinion in this situation. While Miss Emily lives out her long life bereft of ties to other individuals, yet she has a profound, tenacious bond with the community at large, with those numerous townsfolk who think of themselves as "we." Recognizing this, we also note that Faulkner has told us about a town undergoing transitions over a period of decades, so the ambiguities of common perceptions of the woman are echoed in their bonds to a whole set of outmoded values. Commenting on this for your hypothetical readers will round out your paper and indicate what they should be prepared for when they go to Faulkner's text. It is almost always unnecessary and usually ill-advised to tell your readers flatly whether you liked the story, or how much. The tone of your paper, if it be honestly and thoroughly done, will sufficiently indicate the value you give the story. Salting in some of the other quotes I noted above will give clues to your readers about what particularly engaged your sympathies.

Let me recommend, then—without overstressing—the advantage of borrowing quotes to liven the prose of your writing about fiction. Some of the best student papers I have graded in my time have been distinguished by the integration of well chosen quotes with the writer's expository passages. Others have done without. Yet, even in the latter cases, I inferred that somewhere, at some stage of preparation, the writer had gathered them as notes or underlinings, still using them as guidance in reconstructing the spirit of the original.

So you must develop the habit of seeking out such key words, phrases, or lines as will serve to lure your readers into sharing your reading experience. If the option of using direct quotes doesn't suit your intent, then some salient detail of character or action can be chosen to serve in much the same way for topic sentence or lead.

For example: "At the end of 'The Open Boat' one of the four shipwrecked men is dead."

Or: "Slaying his mother and father is the unavoidable

threshold of Julian's progress to sainthood." ("The Legend of St. Julian the Hospitaller")

Or: "A doctor's professional motives are sometimes at glaring odds with his emotional impulses." ("The Use of Force")

Or: "Following one's preference in this world is a quick way to exit from it." ("Bartleby the Scrivener")

Each of these declarations raises a series of questions like those I set down as rising from the Faulkner quotation. Answering those questions and linking the answers is the way to compose a paper that fits the requirements of a review.

Critical Concentration

Probing into a piece of fiction already known to your readers usually requires narrowing your subject matter in some ways, deepening and reinforcing attention paid to some aspect of it. When this is your intent, it is probably wasteful to recap the story line or central conflict—though, to be sure, there may be a need to refer to these. It may be necessary to reach out for comparisons to the work of other writers. Your progress in understanding has been consolidated by comparisons. Comparisons incorporated in your paper can weight the evidence you need to substantiate the interpretation you are arguing for. The trick is to subordinate everything irrelevant to the point you want to make.

Here again you might get valuable prompting from the questions in the text, for most of them are designed to focus one or another critical approach, emphasizing some singular aspect of a story. For instance, question 5 following "The Rocking-Horse Winner" asks you to discuss the meanings of *luck* that Lawrence exploited.

The interesting thing here is that luck is about as commonly understood as any topic we can quickly think of, and yet the kind of reconsideration that is the specialty of criticism quickly meshes with the mysteries and contradictions Lawrence has drawn on. A "review" of his story might, in passing, note that luck is often mentioned by the author and his characters but still leaves the big riddle inadequately examined.

The common-sense way to start a critical examination of luck in the story would be to reread it, marking those instances where the word is used. Next examine the context of these various repetitions of the word and the shifts in meaning given to it as the story progresses.

The term appears earliest, of course, in the first sentence. It is followed immediately by mention of the apparently fortunate marriage and the "bonny children" born to the woman—major bits of good luck, both somehow utterly spoiled by something not yet named. The writer of criticism would point out that her marital and parental unhappiness could be called bad luck, a souring of good luck, or (as the woman herself chooses to think of it) a lack of luck, since she seems to recognize luck only in its positive and benevolent manifestations. At any rate (the critical writer would note and point out), for her, luck is something for which she has no responsibility. She knows herself as a superior person, tending to define luck as her due.

She also makes a close association between luck and having money. (Enough for what? Her failure to answer, or even address, that question, qualifies the validity of any definition she might give to *luck*.) Consciously she will not equate luck and money. When her son Paul asks if they are the same thing, she answers, "Not quite." But then she poisons him by retreating only far enough to say that luck is "what causes you to have money." Perhaps it is really the mother's voice the children hear when the house whispers, "There *must* be more money!"

Troubled by his mother's unhappiness the (unlucky?) boy seeks "for the clue to 'luck.' " He seeks "inwardly" for it. (Something strange is going on here. If luck is money, one cannot seek "inwardly" for money—not without generally endangering oneself, at any rate.) Some sense of the fatal misidentification of luck with money pops out when the boy tells his uncle, "I shouldn't like mother to know I was lucky. . . . She'd stop me."

Skipping on to the end of the story—as you would not do if you were writing a thorough critical paper—you come upon an ironic use of a synonym for luck when the uncle says Paul is "best gone out of a life where he rides his rocking-horse to find a winner." That translates almost automatically into "he's lucky to have escaped by dying." And leaves a further question—escaped what? A cruel world? Or the malevolence of his mother's dissatisfaction? Was she, after all, responsible for the bad luck that tormented her and has now been compounded by the loss of her son?

I have—intentionally—merely scratched at the many instances calling for critical scrutiny of this all-important term and concept in a rich story that you might, if you chose, approach from quite a different angle. One further tip—as you assay the meanings Lawrence gave to the word, you ought to bring into play all you have learned about luck, from reading, from experience, and you ought to be very alert to ambiguities that deserve your comment. For instance, Paul's father is referred to as an "unlucky husband." Remember that *unlucky* is sometimes a euphemism for *bad*, as when we say of an ugly person that he has an "unlucky" face or figure.

I have merely meant to go far enough to illustrate how the questions in the text may be used as points of departure for critical analysis. If none of those printed here quite suits your interests, revamp them, or take them as models for a question of your own that would serve you better as you bore into language and structure of any story that fascinates you.

As you see, many of the questions have to do with one part or another of the technique the author has employed. For a critical paper, an option much to be recommended is for you to examine a single aspect of technique as this is exemplified in a number of stories. You could begin with the choice of a single item from the *Glossary of Critical Terms* (p. 1734).

Were you to start, say, with "point of view," you would need to select a group of stories illustrating the range of possibilities in stories told in the third person. (In first-person narration, the point of view is more narrowly restricted to that of the narrator.) In "Babylon Revisited" and "The Garden-Party" you will see that the point of view is closely limited to the thoughts and experience of the central character. Also there is such a close connection between the language of this character and that used by the author you should categorize these as examples of an "effaced narrator" (see glossary). In "The Rocking-Horse Winner," on the other hand, not only does the point of view shift from one character to another, one is constantly aware of a clear distinction between the voice telling the story and that of any of the characters it includes. The point of view in "Hills Like White Elephants" is completely detached and impersonal, as if it were that of a disinterested third person present on the scene, eavesdropping as he watches a pair of strangers. The detachment of the early part of "Flowering Judas" is by no means as impersonal or unemotional, and it is shifted in the last passages to a very intense identification with Laura's interior monologue.

In these cases—or in others you might choose—you should acknowledge that the material and focus of interest (see glossary again) have influenced the handling of the point of view. To indicate the probable reasons for the author's choice in each case will help you display your working knowledge of the critical term you are illustrating. Matters of tone, use of flashback and imagery, pace, immediacy, omniscience or objectivity—in fact, all or any of the aspects of fiction—can best be treated by assembling a number of examples from different story sources.

Analysis of character and motivation is not precisely a consideration of an author's technique. It draws, as well, on your knowledge of human nature and behavior and on the way one is revealed by the other. Yet it is a prime mistake ever to write about a character or action as if these existed in the actual world rather than in your reading. After all, what we may know of a fictional character is what the author has developed by means of his or her choosing and by a selection of evidence or by some form of special pleading to engage the reader's sympathies. Since, in matters of literature, we are concerned with life as it is exposed by arrangements of written words, a truly critical approach obliges us to examine the means used to represent actuality. If you choose to limit your examination of "The Chrysanthemums" to the character and motivations of Elisa Allen, probably you would show how Steinbeck set up a sequence of revelations that altogether add up to what we can know of her. There is, first of all, her appearance as she works among her flowers. We are told her age and that her attire seems to masculinize her. Her husband's comment about her "gift" adds another touch to the picture. Her speech and behavior in the scene with the vagabond tinker shows us the turbulence of her suppressed yearnings. In the aftermath of his visit we see evidence of its effect in her husband's exclamation, "You look so nice!" Then, after she has been hurt by the rejection of the gift, she flares up to wish she could see men bloody each other. Her quickly suppressed resentment rounds out our sympathy with her predicament. The art of arranging such evidence in the meaningful sequence of a story line is what you ought to account for in writing about character. If you can *show* how meaning has been developed by the writer, you have gone an important step beyond a mere statement of that meaning.

While it remains very much worth critical scrutiny, "The Chrysanthemums" is one of the most conventional and straightforward stories in this collection. As such it could be used as a norm against which you could measure the peculiarities of some that are deliberately unconventional—"experimental" as we say. "A Hunger Artist" and "How I Contemplated the World from the Detroit House of Correction and Began My Life Over Again" are striking examples of unconventional subject matter and unconventional presentation. They offer special challenges and opportunities to the writer of a critical paper.

The subheads of Oates's story indicate that within the unconventional sequence the fundamental elements of fiction are somehow given their due: "Characters," "Events" (for action and plot), and "Sioux Drive" (for setting). But where Steinbeck wove these elements into a continuous narrative following a simple chronology, Oates segregates them in categories to imitate notes made in preparation for writing a coherent account. Reading about the adolescent girl and her adventures among some desperate characters in the seamy side of Detroit may seem very much like solving a jigsaw puzzle. We find a few bits and pieces that fit together. Once they are assembled in our mind the patterns revealed indicate whether other details have to fit in. When we reflect on the story after reading it all, we can remember that there is a chronological sequence of events no more at odds with our common experience of time than that of Steinbeck's straightforward presentation.

It should occur to us that if we were really reading notes compiled by a disturbed girl, the chances are very great that we could not retrieve such a chronology or be nearly as certain of when, where, and how the details spewed forth could be fitted in. In a word, the author has taken pains to select details that can be linked together by normal association, and then to plant clues of time and place that assist the reader in following the patterns of sequence. Your detective work in writing analytically would involve locating, sorting out, and illustrating the types of clues used to make this, in fact, a polished story rather than the jumble of notes it pretends to be. For example, you would note that "weeks later" is a perfectly conventional indication of the time involved between the theft of the gloves and the girl's running away from home. "In the end I think he turned me in" marks her move from Simon's room to the House of Correction. The newspaper account of Raymond Forrest's death and the "new haircut" noticed by the psychiatrist also serve as time markers, as do numerous other physical details correlated with phases of the girl's flight and return. For purposes of a critical paper, you might think it enough to show how the author has achieved unity and coherence under the pretense of incoherence. Or you could go beyond this to speculate about what may have been gained or lost by the indirections of the imitative form. What you learn from your writing evidently depends on how far you want to push it. And on how much effort and insight you will pay to get what you want.

The Hand-to-Hand Engagement

Great critics long ago taught us that unless both the head and the heart are involved, understanding will be lopsided. Perceptions, even of the physical world, will be distorted unless we "attend and value" as Coleridge put it. While we need not argue the relevance of this in scientific studies, it is overwhelmingly important in literary education. Detachment and cool objectivity are great virtues—in their proper place. But surely the experience of reading fiction would be barren if it were not colored by passion, sympathy, and the engagement of irrational (and sometimes precious) prejudices. By the same token, writing about fiction can be a shallow exercise when it is stripped of the force of sympathy, outrage, disappointment, fear, and delight that began in reading a story.

You want—as you should—to write responsibly and truly. But from fear of falsifying we can be trapped in falsification. A perfectly legitimate distrust of sentimentality—reinforced often enough by what you have been taught in many classrooms—can choke up the emotional recognition of truths conveyed in imaginative literature. A hard heart is not a mental asset, nor is an artificial posture of impersonality a persuasive ingredient in your writing. Some of the best illuminations of literature can come from candid exposure of how, in fact, one story or another worked on the imagination of the person you know yourself to be.

Were you to note—with the greatest conceivable objectivity—that the last paragraph of "Flowering Judas" is more highly charged with dread than any that have preceded it and that this transition into undiluted terror is important evidence of Laura's character, you would still fall short of expressing what you know about the nature of such terror—and therefore fall short of expressing what you know intuitively of the person in the story. The external threats around her are in no way magnified at the story's end. Perhaps they are even ebbing when Braggioni relents in his courtship. At last she is terrified of what she is, of what she has become, and each one of us knows the magnitude of such dread, for we have all felt it at moments—though not in circumstances that match Laura's. It is by the recognition of our personal memory that we identify with her and recognize her story as part of our own confessional.

I risk the word *confession* with some trepidation, since I don't want to encourage a notion that writing about fiction should be an excuse for flights into autobiography merely triggered by something mentioned in a story. What is important is to find how the pattern of the story extends and clarifies the dilemmas in which we have groped as the characters do.

The right starting point is the admission that we laugh, grow anxious, indignant, or appalled, we grieve, scorn, and clutch after comfort among platitudes until we are swept by convictions generated by our reading. Then your paper must explain why the fictive evidence worked as it did on you, of all people.

Why were you amused and perhaps distressed as you read "Royal Beatings"? Here is a story about the politics of family life. Probably the setting and the members of the family are quite different from those you grew up with. Yet here is a prototype of the twists and turns by which members of every family play the others off against each other in a kind of blind ritual without reasonable objectives. However painful her beatings, Rose seems to invite them compulsively, and however shabby or distressed her memories of the family may be, in the end they are transfigured into a bond she cannot reject, does not wish to deny. By relating this prototypical formation of family bonds to what you have seen in your own family—exploring with honesty and candor—you simultaneously bring the story to life and find in life a pattern in the chaos of stressful relationships.

Falling in love, trying to manage sexual love once it has us by the throat, is a prototypical human experience of another sort. Stories like "The Horse Dealer's Daughter" and "The Muse's Tragedy" offer variations of the bafflement nearly every one must go through. You need not have reached Mrs. Anerton's age to learn the tragedy of being needed but unloved by a person whom you love dearly—nor to incorporate some additional insights with what Edith Wharton has to say on the subject. You need not have rescued a girl from a pond in the dead of winter to know that a rescued party has some profound claim on the rescuer—nor to write a paper drawing on your own experience which would touch some complications Lawrence left out of his tale.

For all its marvelous variety, the greater part of fiction draws on the major prototypes of love, war, sex, death, families, religion, and politics. And at the level of the prototype you will find in both your reading and writing the links between your own time and place and things that happened long ago and far away. The relation of children and parents is the subject of multitudinous stories—for the very good reason that though certain typical patterns occur generation after generation there are novelties we can always find to make individual experience seem painfully unique. Parents seem always to be an embarrassment to their children, by virtue of their traits, ideas, appearance, or whatever. In "Everything That Rises Must Converge" a young man named Julian hopes to reform his mother by pushing her into humiliation. That is, he tries to reeducate her without any clear idea, or much concern, about the cost to either of them if he gets his wish. Surely any but the most nonchalant reading of this story will call up the problems you have with your own parents. And just as your life situation has conditioned the way you interpret the story on a first reading, the story will influence your assessment of the situation in real life when you try to connect reality and fiction by writing a personal response. It would be vainglorious to expect either the story itself or your paper to *solve* what you feel as a personal problem. Literature is not therapy nor social engineering. Yet something has been saved from the darkness when you write full tilt about the way a story has played on your judgments and attitudes toward people close to you.

"Everything That Rises Must Converge" surely engages your opinions about race and class, as well as those about families. What will you make of the moral ambiguity at the story's end? Julian's "good," "tolerant," and "unbiased" attitudes have certainly not triumphed in the test of action. Their inadequacy is exposed; they have been redefined as prejudices no better than those his mother clung to. Now, if Julian's positions happen to be those you cherish, how will you respond when you find them downgraded by the resolution of the story conflict? Will you evade the challenge by dismissing the story as "mere fiction"? Or will you risk the comfort of your convictions by setting them among contrary claims of the sort the story sets forth as part of the whole moral equation?

It is far from my purpose to suggest what response you should make—only to underline the fact that literature offers something like test cases, fictive situations in which you can make choices about where you would hope to stand. What you write may, if it is seriously done, force you to a readjustment of values—or perhaps to an altered view of who you are and how you came to hold the opinions you do.

Emerson advises: "Put more range in your scale." Stories that go beyond the moral boundaries of your life thus far can provide that range. In writing a personal response to a difficult story, you can make choices life has not yet given you the chance to make. At the simplest level such response may be only, "I would (or wouldn't) have done (or judged) as the character did." You can create something considerably more sophisticated and satisfying if you take into account the conditioning motives the author built into the story and your own susceptibility to such motives. By playing the game according to the full set of rules required by sympathetic reading, you can keep your paper from straying into personal manifesto or autobiography.

For this kind of paper turn to those questions in the text that bear on the meaning and nature of human affairs rather than those having to do with technique. For example, one of the questions following "The Dead" asks about Gabriel's "generosity." It is not conceivable that the term should mean exactly the same for all of us. Furthermore, for most of us, our idea of generosity fluctuates a good deal. When we come to write about Gabriel's generosity, we can't help noting that it has variable significances in Joyce's treatment. Yes, it is genuine, but of small worth to Gabriel in grappling with the demands life puts on him. By expounding on this qualification, you should not aim at making yourself either more or less generous, but rather at refining a key term in your vocabulary of personal values.

While in most papers intended as a personal response to a story, theme and author's attitude will take precedence over a consideration of technique, it is well never to forget that all the ingredients woven into fiction condition the thematic statements emerging from it. So it follows that in this approach to writing about fiction you must not leave any of them out of account.

We find that some stories which begin with quiet objectivity move to an emotional crescendo where feeling and intuition take over. Think of these stories as good models for the paper you are writing. Borrow their devices. Imitate the tension they are built from. Wax hot, wax cold. Be lyrical, be matter-of-fact. Make a pattern of lights and shadows, risks and certainties, as fiction writers do, even though you are not writing fiction at this point. Don't neglect the tone of your paper. It is one resource for shaping what it means.

Finally, acceptance or challenge of an author's thematic statement will make you realize that in the human realm there is no such thing as a "value-free" occurrence. Stephen Crane in "The Open Boat" seems to postulate a purely indifferent universe confronting the shipwrecked men. But yet, from the magic of his art we perceive that the impassioned men are part of that universe; their concerns for their plight, their lives, and their souls transform the environing indifference. The concern you generate in a written response to Crane's work extends the passionate conflict and its circles of implication. This is how literature moves in concentric waves through the substance of life—continuous far beyond the point at which an author sends the finished manuscript to be published. The prime requirement for you is to keep it moving by an exercise of candor and intelligence worthy of what you believe literature to be.

Writing Fiction

One of the very good ways to learn more about the art of fiction is to practice it—to take the plunge and write stories of your own. It is also a very natural outgrowth of the emotional and intellectual excitement that reading the top-flight work collected here has generated. Whether or not you have written any fiction before, like most people you have been *telling* stories for most of your life. The next step is to make the more complex effort of giving them a written form of the sort your story has taught you to respect. Often teachers offer the option of writing a story as an alternative to preparing at least one of the papers required in a course where the main emphasis is on improving skills in reading. The relation between reading and writing is so important—and so intimate—that more than one form of written work can help you read with keener enthusiasm and a constantly expanded understanding of what can be communicated in fiction.

Courses specifically devoted to fiction writing are enhanced by the guidance offered in masterful variety by the authors whose finest efforts are assembled in this text. In years to come great work will be done by some of you in writing classes who are now beginning a serious apprenticeship, learning your craft by a devoted scrutiny of what has been accomplished by remote and recent generations of fiction writers.

Thus, whatever the nature of the class—and whatever your long- or short-range expectations may be when you set out to write your first, or fifth, or twentieth short story—it must be obvious as a general principle that models of short fiction can discipline and accelerate your progress. To be sure, everything will depend eventually on the quality of your personal and unique imagination, your judgment, your dexterity with language fit for your subject, and the excellence of your observation of life. The happy truth is that drawing on models will not impede your personal talents—it will release them by sparing you the waste and frustration of striking blind.

Surely the writer you hope to become must be an observer and a listener, sharp-eyed and attentive to experience, and with the ability to retain or recall things seen and heard: the shape of a child's mouth when his birthday balloon pops in his hands; the words your sister used to describe a new boyfriend to your parents; the atmosphere in a forest clearing on a summer day. And if you are already very good at such observation, the chances are that your reading of stories has been an essential part of your preparation as an observer.

The genius of fiction is to train readers in what it is *important* to take note of among the incredible profusion of details and events crowding everyday existence—to train us to select what counts, what signifies, what fits with other details of observation to give a sum of meaning to patterns emerging from the superficial chaos of life. In a word, readers of fiction are continuously modeling their habits of observation on that of writers who, in their turn, no doubt, modeled theirs on a continuous narrative tradition still evolving.

But when we have conceded the inevitable role of models in the formation of skill and craft in writing fiction, we may still bog down on a widespread prejudice which, I will guess, is stirring in your mind as you read this. You may have a vaguely reasoned, but stubborn, resistance to the very idea of following models. To do so smacks of imitation, and the cardinal motive for creative writing is to be *original,* is it not? You want to write stories in order to free yourself from the formulas and limitations that inhibit your other kinds of writing.

Seriously, I know you want to—and should—turn out something original when you are ready to do so. Seriously I believe you haven't a very good chance of doing so until you have learned more ways of observing and shaping your material as the masters of the art have done. When students in creative-writing classes don't or won't accept good models for their development, all too often they begin half-consciously to model their stories on each other's. The blind follow the blind, and standards are much lower than they should be for all the investment of labor and good intention.

Having gone thus far in trying to persuade you to use what is freely offered by excellent models of fiction in our text, I had better come down to specifics about the ways you can effectively go about it. Actually using these stories as models, in all the ways they can be used, requires more than devout appreciation. It requires putting words on paper, whether as exercises, as notes, or as part of a story of your own.

Imitation and Comparison

To begin with a bedrock, basic form of exercise, let me note that some writers have found it useful to copy passages word for word from an admired example. Such "slavish" copying (let's face the term at once and have done with it) may have the merit of training you in habits of syntax and verbal rhythm that worked well for writers from whom you intend to learn. Word for word copying might be good for a daily—or occasional—warm-up exercise to get the juices of your imagination flowing. As an icebreaker it can coordinate the sheer mechanics of writing with word processor or typewriter or pen or pencil with a flow of idea and emotion into words on paper. (Though I won't take time to go into this now, please believe that a writer should never, never, never consider the physical means of composition to be a matter of indifference.)

Better than this, a bit of literal copying may be a specially rigorous way of *reading*, which forces you to pay some attention to each word without skimming. And if you have the devotion to make it so, it may be the occasion for pondering the function of each word and each syntactical element as these build into sentences and paragraphs.

Please don't just nod over my suggestion and pass on. Far better to grab your portable and type out the first paragraph of Frank O'Connor's "Guests of the Nation." Had you noticed before how this first person narration is identified as such by the three pronouns "me," "we," and "our"? How the time of day (dusk) is made more concrete by the lighting of the lamp? How the crucial word "chum" (a synonym for *friend*) is emphasized by repetition and set in opposition to the word "divil" (a synonym for *enemy* or *hated adversary*)? Yes, of course you can understand the meaning of the paragraph without dwelling on such trivial indicators of the situation and the conflict to come. But *by* dwelling on them—as you are privileged and perhaps enticed to do in the exercise of copying—you may learn something almighty precious about a potent and economical way of getting a story started. Your task will only be slavish if you let it be so. And as much can be said for any other assignment, even if self-assigned.

Yet, your verbal imagination will no doubt be more constructively engaged if you base another sort of exercise on O'Connor's paragraph (or a passage from some other story you admire). It is this: following his sentence pattern closely, substitute language and subject matter of your own. Your subject might be the relation of two antagonistic groups in your school or community. As you know, the narrator need not be yourself, but can be an imagined character. Whichever way your imagination veers, the result might be something like this:

> At lunchtime the pockmarked Nicaraguan boy Manuel would jingle his change and ask, "Amigos, you up for it today?" and Scott would say, "Why not, amigo?" (since we pretended we also spoke Spanish) and the smaller Nicaraguan Greniero would brush off a table and roll out his own set of dice. As often as not Martin Stark would join us to watch and get angry at Greniero's style, which was pretty gaudy, and read him out the way he did us "Come on you clown, why are you wobbling the table?"

As you see, we have made a transition from outright copying to parody. And though this example of parody (or the one you will now write) may be only a warm-up for truly original composition, pause to reflect that parody *can* be pushed to the level of the highest art, as readers of Joyce's *Ulysses* know so well.

Most of the time when we are developing our own material with the guidance of models, we aren't so committed to a single text or author as in the case of parodistic exercises. While we continue to learn by a sort of imitation and constant comparison, our comparisons usually range freely over three distinct items: (1) our own manuscript, in whatever state of development it may have reached, (2) the segment of reality we mean to represent, and (3) the story-telling tactics and styles of several writers who have dealt similarly with similar subjects.

Particularly in matters of diction and dialogue we continue this simultaneous three-layered scrutiny as a natural part of the writing process. We go on observing and listening to tangible things around us—in fact observation is now intensified because we have given it focus by beginning to write about some segment of observable behavior, and we listen more intently to test whether people like our fictional characters really do speak as we are saying in our story that they do. We want to add more beads to the string, so we listen for characterizing utterances we have not been able to imagine or remember. And—while we are verifying our writing in progress by what might be called field work—we are turning back to the text of this book to see how Bellow or Powers, Hemingway or Faulkner, Oates or Munro have handled confrontations like those we are writing about. We reassess Hemingway's exploitation of understatement, Faulkner's probing with highly charged rhetoric—and are encouraged to remember that either tactic is available to us if we can fit it to the material we are now developing. We turn to the pages of our predecessors for promptings, and when we are lucky we bring away something which sharpens what we have begun.

What we are searching for in such repeated comparative surveys is probably not something we can directly parody, but a principle or an approach suitable to many fine stories. Thus, if we turn to Carver's "Where I'm Calling From" while we are at work on a story in which the voice of the first-person narrator is a necessary component, it is not at all with the aim of imitating the particular voice Carver has created, but to see as sharply as we can how small modifications of flat and rather impersonal language can further individualize the character beginning to emerge on our own pages. And to see how this author has fused the idiosyncrasies of speech with the flavor of the situation being recounted. It is very important to remember that Carver's effects are not and could not be achieved merely by inventive manipulation on his part. Clearly he has listened—in actuality and over and over again in memory—to voices that bumble and blunder and strain until their sheer awkwardness becomes supremely expressive. One of the most valuable things you can learn from choosing his story as a model is that you must go into the corners of your world and back in to the dark labyrinth of your own memory listening for the timbre of such voices.

Dialogue passages in such stories as "Hills Like White Elephants," "The Valiant Woman," and the climactic last scene from "The Dead" can teach you, first of all, what to listen for in actual conversation and, second, how to structure the patterns of ordinary speech into revealing and dramatic sequences. As you become a keener listener, you will note that dialogue is not usually a matter of question and answer or direct responses to purely rational propositions.

The man in Hemingway's story says: ". . . But you've got to realize—." Without waiting for him to finish the sentence the young woman responds, "I realize. Can't we maybe stop talking?" Her impatient breaking in reveals better than any explanation that could be provided by the author how weary she is of the persistent argument. Yet, just a moment later her despair of reaching agreement is modulated when she catches at something he says and echoes it back. ". . . if it means anything to you," he says, and she answers, "Doesn't it mean anything to you? We could get along." Even in despair she is still fighting to make him really hear something besides his own voice, his own wish. If you read such a passage aloud—instead of copying it on your typewriter—you will see how skillfully the author has implied the tones of voice of the two speakers. In some comparable scene in one of your own stories you can use the same effect.

In "The Dead" Gabriel Conroy asks his wife, " 'And what did he die of so young, Gretta? Consumption, was it?' 'I think he died for me,' she answered." At first glance this may appear to be a direct response on the wife's part. But look again at the context of the question and answer. The powerful shock in her reply comes from the fact that the two are speaking in quite distinct levels of discourse—his mundane, hers mystic and profound. It is from this revelation of incompatible modes of adjusting to reality that the resolution of the story emerges.

" 'Mother, isn't it terribly heartless of us?' " asks Laura in "The Garden Party." " 'Darling!' Mrs. Sheridan got up and came over to her, carrying the hat. Before Laura could stop her she had popped it on. 'My child!' said her mother, 'that hat is yours. It's made for you. It's much too young for me. I have never seen you look such a picture. Look at yourself!' And she held up her hand-mirror." The mother is not directly answering Laura's question, but by changing the subject she is making a significant reply.

These examples illustrate the principle that what we call dialogue is often, in truth, two or more monologues rather loosely fitted together by the circumstances of the scene.

Even when you are not intentionally searching for model fragments of written dialogue, you will come across one sort or another of striking examples that you will want to collect for later reference. It is a fairly simple matter to photocopy such passages and keep them handy in a notebook or file—a very good practice for the writer commencing a serious career.

Story-Generating Models

As the Canterbury pilgrims went on their way, a story told by one of them prompted a story from another. So it goes with all of us. When we hear or read a story, we are reminded of something we have to tell. Like the spreading wake of a boat, waves of memory veer out, stirring flotsam that has lain dormant on the beach, activating inert material we have not yet quite imagined might be the stuff for a story of our own. It will be like—and yet fascinatingly different from—the example that stirred the waves of imagination.

Consider Sherwood Anderson's "I Want to Know Why," which deals with a boy's disillusionment following a moment of triumph. Surely very many of its readers will be reminded of similar shocks in their own lives. It would not be surprising if a lot of them toyed with the possibility of writing about how such a common disappointment seemed very particular and very personal to them—nor that most of them felt balked by uncertainty about how to come at their material, which is plentiful enough but unmanageably formless in the rag bag of memory.

Well, a story not only stimulates a reader's memory, its form gives bold hints about the way you might shape up what you are moved to write about. Anderson opens his story with the *arrival* of the narrator and some other boys, at Saratoga, where the climactic race will be run. Then, in an apparently rambling fashion, the boy's feelings about horses and racing are spilled out. In fact these clumsy declarations are put forth as a preparation before the horse Sunstreak is named—before they are all summed up and focused on the actual drama of the race and the disillusioning aftermath when Jerry Tillford brags in the company of prostitutes.

A decision to follow Anderson's example would, first of all, oblige you to concentrate on the end, the dramatic resolution of your fictional situation, and then to measure out the necessary preparation of material, feelings, and circumstances required to give full force to this resolution. In a word, the model shows you how to construct your story backward, starting to work from the end and adding the material required for the opening. What feelings and what qualities will your central character have? I haven't the faintest notion. But you have not only a faint notion—the more you review your material and cull the possibilities, something approaching certainty will be established, for memory works that way once we guide it by fictional craft. Of course in your reminiscence you will be directed by the need to choose a character who has the potential for jolting the protagonist as Jerry Tillford jolts the narrator. That is, you may have to invent, or change, the personages when those you remember do not quite fit the requirements of the story.

Almost as universal as Anderson's basic story of the loss of innocence is the situation in Walker's "Everyday Use." Much of the tension in the American experience generally is the conflict between those who have clung to the places where they have their roots and those who have "gone to the city"—migrated in search of a broader or more fulfilling life. Most students returning home during their college years find themselves caught in a cross fire between old values and new ones. Walker built her story around a number of physical details of setting—the grassless yard, the churn, and the quilts—which have different values and potentials for the stay-at-homes and for the daughter who has briefly returned.

In preparing to write a story about the return of an offspring to the original home you might well begin by (1) listing a number of such specific things in the setting you know or imagine, (2) by noting after each one of the potentially different values they might have for those with conflicting life-styles, and (3) imagining or simply remembering the characters who would be most likely to clash in their perception of the cardinal values in such possessions.

Making lists of the sort here called for is not at all the cut-and-dried matter you might suppose before you try it. Selection of sights and sounds, names and voices, thunderstorms and carnivals, the furniture in church basements, things stored in attics or garages—picking over such things, mentally following streams of association, and then building complete sentences around the things named in your list is creative work of the richest kind. It is a preliminary shaping of the substance that will give life to your finished story. There is no rule for choosing which of the concrete details you assemble will function most effectively in the development of plot, characterization, or theme. But, rather than trying to select details to fit some predetermined idea or outline, you ought to be always eager to follow the significance suggested by the details themselves. Thus an imitation of Walker's approach can be transformed into something uniquely and unpredictably original.

Many of the same suggestions can be made if Joyce's "Araby" is chosen as a model. Again the basic experience is close to being universal—humiliation in an encounter between romantic expectation and banal actuality. (None of you could convince me you haven't pushed some childish desire until it burst in a shattering embarrassment, that you haven't found yourself "driven and derided by vanity." Conversely, I am sure that the meaning and circumstances of what happened to you were different enough from those in Joyce's story that they are worth telling. So this model will serve, as it probably has already served, for hundreds of excellent new efforts.)

We note that "Araby," like "I Want to Know Why" and "Everyday Use," is told in the first person. We may concede there were ample reasons why this mode was chosen by the three authors. Yet, just because you may be modeling your work on theirs, this does not mean your story will or should be told in the first person, however close to your actual experience it may be. The decision whether to use first- or third-person narration ought to be based on some trials and some sketch work in both methods. You might learn something useful by recasting the final scene of "Araby" as a third person account with a somewhat altered point of view (probably one more detached from the consciousness of the main character). You will find that much more is required than a simple change of pronouns from first to third person if either the emotion of the story or the significance of its resolution is to be retained.

Suppose you were to rewrite "Everyday Use" from the point of view of the daughter Dee, in either first or third person. What modifications would have to be made to reveal the same significance in the circumstances? Some useful answers to such a question will occur to you from purely passive analysis. Better answers—and ones much more useful to you as a committed student of the craft of fiction—can only come from your putting on paper at least a partial rewrite of your model. However much you respect that model in its published form, you must realize it came to that form through a series of authorial choices of the kind you are forced to make in your reconstruction.

Probably most of the stories in this text could be used as pathfinding models as you develop conceptions of your own. But, as a matter of practical fact, no one has time to follow so many leads systematically. You will be served best by choosing those that are written in a more or less contemporary idiom. Great as they may be, Poe, Hawthorne, and Melville wrote in an epoch when both diction and conceptions of man in society were different from those you have grown up with. Some of the practices of earlier masters could be downright misleading to you in this latter part of the twentieth century.

Yet, even as I put down this common-sense warning, I am teased with a hankering to see someone write a totally up-to-date "Bartleby."

Wouldn't it be worthwhile to take something marvelous, old, and outmoded and make it new?

Models for Revision

Today there is a good deal of talk about electronic word processors. By technological wizardry they are supposed to take the curse off revision—the implication being that revision is always unpleasant, though necessary, and that use of a labor-saving device is the best way to have done with it.

My own experience has always been that revision is simply a continuation of the imaginative act of writing, and for me it has been the most pleasant part. It is in revision that the nice touches can be laid on, the tones and colors harmonized, and clarifications made to show the precise meaning of what was often cloudy or indistinct in some phases of the compositional process.

To go even further, let us admit that revision is not merely the final phase of the process. It has been going on since the concept first began to take shape. Very few of us write as much as a sentence on paper without some juggling and readjustment of an idea and the words that seem fit to express it. We change the nouns and verbs that first entered our minds; we add or drop some adjectives or move them around in the process of inscribing a sentence on a page. As the sentences follow each other, we keep shifting our thoughts by reviewing what has already been put down and what is now required to keep the story flowing and to prepare for what is still to come. At the end of a page or the end of a draft of the whole story, our minds are still teeming with reasons for the choice of wording we have made and the possibilities that have been rejected. Or, if this still-bubbling mental activity *isn't* continuing, then no state-of-the-art electronic aid is going to be of any help.

The only absolute requirement for revision is that there must be something to revise. This means that in your initial surge you have got something on paper. Something that won't shift and fade and drift away as a purely mental construct often does. Something that can be examined and reconsidered on the morning after, marked for change, or cut apart and repasted. A writer is not a daydreamer, but is a worker with paper, and the joy of the craft can only be experienced by the trials and revisions made on paper. You have finished a story only when nothing remains to be done to improve it.

This is worth repeating for emphasis: Just because you have written a story through from beginning to end, this does not mean you have finished it. If it is good in the form you have first given it—even if it is published or publishable—it may be bettered by revisions. It may be brought closer to what you have to say; it may be modified to fit the editorial requirements of one publication or another. This text contains a major work by William Faulkner, "The Bear," which can be found in two other published versions, both very interesting as examples of revision—particularly interesting in their relation to what has come to be regarded as the definitive version included here. In 1925 Faulkner published "Lion: A Story" which contains not only episodes leading to the death of the great dog and mythic bear but a great deal of the language you will find on the pages of this text. Yet (among other significant differences and omissions) "Uncle Ike" McCaslin is only a peripheral character in that first version, narrated by a boy far less personally involved with or conditioned by the bear's fate than Ike will be in the definitive text. Though the other magazine version (published almost simultaneously with the appearance of the present text in book form) is narrated in the third person, the character of the boy is held to about the same dimensions as in "Lion: A Story." In this intermediary version, the climactic episode is the attack the little fyce dog makes on the bear, with the lessons about courage to be learned from that. But the revision which shows the great range of Faulkner's maturing conception moves Ike McCaslin to the center of the action in the forest and focuses in his life the major themes and conceptual conflicts.

You need not be already a successfully published author to take to heart the example of Faulkner as he coaxed greater and wider significance into his material by his revisions. When you have a "finished" draft of a story in hand, you have come to a point where it is natural to pause, take a long hard look, and weigh the possibilities still to be wrung from material you have successfully coaxed this far along. Such points offer a natural occasion for comparing what you have done with examples from the text that may prod your imagination with suggestions for improvement.

Suppose that, for reasons that seemed sufficient, you began your story with a striking line of dialogue and moved directly into a scene beginning the central action. Now you will reflect that the risk of such a brisk leap into the action is that the characters are more shallowly drawn than they must be to bring out the significance of what they are doing or saying to each other. While it is certainly not necessary to explain characters before you let them move, background information, histories, and individual idiosyncrasies must be incorporated somewhere and somehow without impeding the movements of events.

When your work is fresh and hot—and unfinished—on the desk in front of you, the time is favorable for comparing your opening presentation with Lawrence's in "The Horse Dealer's Daughter" and

Powers's in "The Valiant Woman." Each of these stories (like several others you might also want to scan) begins with dialogue that is part of an extended scene. Yet the scenes are managed quite differently. Powers has confined his *almost* exclusively to dialogue. Lawrence has stretched the intervals between the utterances of his characters to make some explanatory observations about them, clearly not from the point of view of any one of them. Has Powers, then, shaped his dialogue so such explanation becomes irrelevant and unnecessary? Not really. Rather, he has placed the exposition elsewhere in the story, postponing it until the relatively low-keyed game of cards played by the priest and his housekeeper offers a natural opportunity for recollection of the past from the priest's point of view.

To note even this much about the tactics of the two authors might suggest to you a better way to place and weave in the background information required to give fuller dimensions to your characters.

Pause a little longer. Before you decide where to insert such information, review "Hills Like White Elephants." There Hemingway has dispensed with such information almost entirely. Perhaps you could modify the dramatic scenes you have written, sharpening and loading the dialogue itself, intensifying the conflict it carries as he has done so that background information becomes less necessary.

In any event, such midway pauses for comparison with relevant models will light up the options for maneuvering your material to best advantage. The value of analytic comparison can here, also, be enhanced by written experiments, made not only on your own manuscript (which remains your ultimate concern, to be sure) but on the text of the models consulted. First you might try interspersing the informational passages of the Powers story with the dialogue of its opening pages, until it more nearly resembles Lawrence's method. Or take the Lawrence story and clean all the general family information out of the opening dialogue, designing a way to insert it at some lull in the action farther along.

It should go without saying that you cannot move material around in this fashion without rewriting it somewhat to make it fit together. A practical way to begin such experimental revision is to photocopy the text, cut it up with scissors or a razor blade, and paste together a rough version of the new sequences before you begin writing in or revising the connectives that are now required to make it readable.

Before undertaking a second draft of your story, it is worth reconsidering and making comparisons of all the elements of fiction you have learned by reading and discussion to identify. Consult examples of descriptive passages, narrative passages in which long stretches of time are compressed, and scenes. Note that the lush and detailed description which opens "Kew Gardens" functions in a certain way to serve the peculiar demands of that story, while the descriptions of Parisian street scenes accomplish something distinctly different in "Babylon Revisited." In "The Open Boat" an insistent series of sensory descriptions of the ocean and the shoreline runs as an accompaniment to the adventure of the shipwrecked men, vivifying their experience and contributing much to the reader's inferences about what it all means. "The horizon narrowed and widened, and dipped and rose, and at all times its edge was jagged with waves that seemed thrust up in points like rocks." ". . . the color of the sea changed from slate to emerald green streaked with amber lights, and the foam was like tumbling snow." "On the distant dunes were set many little black cottages, and a tall white windmill reared above them. No man, nor dog, nor bicycle appeared on the beach." Surely such a series of pictorial renditions is worth imitating if your story requires its characters to be immersed in conflict with their environment—just as surely it would be inappropriate if the conflict were more confined to personal oppositions.

In "The Veldt" Bradbury plays a very nifty trick in his description of the images projected on the nursery walls. That is, instead of describing them as if they were, indeed, *pictures*, he slants the descriptions forcibly to make them seem as if he were talking about direct encounters with the dangerous African habitat itself—as in the twist of his fantasy, they turn out to be. Descriptions of the barbecue stand in "A Good Man Is Hard to Find" intensify the atmosphere of grotesque contemporary reality. The coming of dawn at the end of "Barn Burning" serves as an indirect revelation of the emotional state of the boy who has—for good reasons—betrayed his own father. You can and should continue your list of examples, make a collection for convenient reference, *and* remember that no one descriptive device is suitable for all kinds of story objectives.

How long a period of time is covered by the action of your story? If it is several years, months, days, or even hours, the chances are that you will need to account for the longer stretches with what I am here calling *narrative passages*—those in which the language is specifically adapted to show persisting as distinct from immediate action. Time is compressed by statements on the order of "during July he exercised daily in the college gym." There is a tendency for such passages to become thin, flat, and lacking in concrete detail. In the example just given, no picture is drawn of the person at his exercise, the weather or the mood of the summer, nor the sounds, sights, and smells of a gym during this season.

In a fully finished story this will not be the case—as you can see by taking the example of, say, de Maupassant in "The Necklace" when he tells us about the ten years in which Mme. Loisel is doing her part to help pay off the debt:

> She came to know what heavy housework meant and the odious cares of the kitchen. She washed the dishes, using her rosy nails on the greasy pots and pans. . . . She carried the slops down to the street every morning, and carried up the water, stopping for breath at every landing. And, dressed like a woman of the people, she went to the fruiterer, the grocer, the butcher, her basket on her arm, bargaining, insulted, defending her miserable money sou by sou.

Part of "Everyday Use" compresses time just as effectively—without losing richness of concrete detail—in the reminiscence of the narrator. "I used to think she hated Maggie, too. But that was before we raised the money, the church and me, to send her to Augusta to school. She used to read to us without pity. . . . She washed us in a river of make-believe, burned us with a lot of knowledge we didn't necessarily need to know. . . . Often I fought off the temptation to shake her. At sixteen she had a style of her own; and knew what style was."

These are brief examples, and you will want to collect more. As you accumulate them from other stories that reach over too much time to be presented in continuous scenes, pay particular attention to the time-modifiers that indicate the action is an extended one—"she would often," "by the time he graduated he had," etc. These mechanical connectives can, and should, be given the function of keeping your story vivid and convincing, just as the detail and dialogue of a scene will do.

Perhaps for the beginning writer scenes are the easiest part of writing fiction. At least, the most fun. In such writing you are more likely to have ready-made models from life as you observe it. A conversation begins, and the exchange back and forth between characters builds naturally, because the response of the second speaker is roughly governed by what the first one has said. You follow the example of movies, in which essentially everything is revealed by a succession of related scenes, requiring no authorial account of what has ripened or changed in the interim between them. But the more demanding a craftsman you become—coming up hard against the difficulties of fitting one item with another to make a fictional pattern—the more you'll perceive the need for specific models.

A number of stories in this text consist of a single scene, and we turn naturally to something like Updike's "A & P" for a precise examination of the way in which the characters are brought into the reader's view, how their encounter is progressively complicated, and how the concluding action gives point and meaning to the dramatized spectacle. The mere presence of the three girls in the store and the narrator's appraisal of them would have made a fictional scene, in the bare technical meaning of the word, but it is the intervention of the store manager in the midst of the scene that makes it, all by itself, a story in which no follow-up material is needed to round it out.

Compare "A & P" with "Everyday Use"—another story that contains only a single scene. In the latter the design is significantly different. The author sets up her characters and their traits with an extended expository passage before the main action starts. What is then required of the scene is that it dramatize the traits already enumerated and show what they amount to when brought to the test. The correspondence between the mother's analysis and what Dee (Wangero) reveals by her spoken lines should be closly analyzed as a model for what can be intensified in a scene you have written that may have been perfect in its versimilitude but lacking in point.

With material requiring a number of scenes for its full development one needs not only the aptitude for getting the most out of each scene—there must be a suitable design for the sequence in which the scenes will be laid out, and a series of connectives to move economically from one scene to another. There is also an ever-present question of proportion—which of the scenes can be treated summarily and briefly, which must be given some amplitude. Fitzgerald's example in "Babylon Revisited" can be useful for a start in learning such management. Mark the beginnings and ends of all the scenes in this story, and then ask of each one: What is accomplished to advance the story by this scene? How have we been brought into it from the preceding one?

The first, between Charlie and Alix in the bar, is what may be called an "establishing" scene. It presents the main character on his return to a once-familiar environment and ticks off some changes in him, in the places he is taking another look at, and in his judgment and perception.

The next full scene takes place in the home of Charlie's in-laws. But how has he come there from scene one? He has taxied across Paris (a bit of drab and routine transportation that *should* have been omitted—except that the author uses it to give another glimpse of the Parisian setting and to record Charlie's regret at having "spoiled" this good place for himself). The second scene serves to demonstrate the bond of affection between father and daughter—and to signal the potential for opposition, hostility, and dislike between Charlie and the woman who will be his chief antagonist in the principal conflict of the story.

The third scene gives us Charlie alone in the city which once proved an irresistible temptation for his dissipations. It is a test intended to demonstrate (to the reader as well as to the character himself) how far he has recovered from the previous crackup. It climaxes in his rejection of the woman who encourages him to plunge into vice once more. He has not failed the test. As the section ends, his hopes are bright for showing that he is now fit to reclaim his daughter.

What occurs in the first scene of Section II is crucial preparation for the outcome of the story. Not only does Charlie have a pleasant, promising lunch with Honoria, he seems to have once again side-stepped formerly destructive temptations by his coolness to Duncan and Lorraine. But what the author has, in fact, accomplished here is to plant a superficially successful evasion as the time bomb that will presently blast Charlie's prospects and hopes.

I will not take space here to complete the map of scenes that round out the design of this story. Having indicated how you *can* block out the elements of design in a story with several scenes, I'll only say, *Do it*, and do it conscientiously with the intent of making use of what you learn from it in revising the design of whatever similar project you are engaged in. If the scene pattern in "Babylon Revisited" only partially resolves your problem, take another story, or several, and bear down until you get what you need.

Though I cut short my analysis of this story—and of others herein mentioned—I would like you to believe that in a long career as a writer and teacher I have knuckled down on repeated occasions in which I trained myself with exercises and analyses of examples of craft. I tried early and late to take over as much as I could from admired writers who went ahead of me. Much earlier in my comments you may have been jolted by the suspicion that what I was actually recommending could not be finished within the limits of any given semester or year of work.

Quite so. I did not truly intend to lay out a program limited by the duration of a class, but to offer an approach to getting good use from your reading of fiction, taking it as a guide to a craft that none of us will ever completely master. We are on an endless quest. Semester by semester and year by year we do our best with such native abilities as we have and with the skills we are acquiring for the sake of what can be done next year. The better you work along lines I have indicated here, the better you will work along lines I have not mentioned or maybe haven't imagined yet.

With that hopeful qualification, I turn you back to your own reading and writing and to other teachers—those who meet with you regularly in the classroom and those you will only know through their published works.

Glossary of Critical Terms

Action Most simply, what happens to, or what is done by, the characters in a story. A somewhat more technical usage—in which "**action**" is nearly synonymous with "**plot**" (below)—makes the term signify a unified sequence of events with a beginning, middle, and end.

Allegory A literary work in which the characters and their situations clearly represent general qualities and types—as, in an animal fable, each animal may represent a type of human personality. Often the characters of allegory represent abstract vices or virtues such as avarice, charity, innocence, or prudery. See **symbol.**

Ambiguity Any story or element in a story that can be interpreted in different ways is said to be ambiguous. Ambiguity can be a fault that obstructs clear communication, but it can also provide enrichment by clustering associated and complementary meanings. See **irony** and **paradox.**

Atmosphere The enveloping spirit or mood of a story. Used in the same sense as in actual life, it might describe the feeling that prevails at a family reunion, a funeral, or the beginning of a vacation. See also **mood, tone.**

Author intrusion Explanations or statements that go beyond a rendering of the situation to make an interpretive comment about it. The author seems to address the reader directly, abandoning the illusion of his or her tale in order to deliver an opinion.

Character 1. One of the people who has a part in the story. 2. The quality or the sum of the qualities of such a person. In most stories we can easily distinguish between central characters—on whom most of the author's attention is focused—and the minor characters—who play some part in the development of the situation. **Round characters** are those presented as having the complex or contradictory qualities that we note in most human beings. **Flat characters** are those who display only a small fraction of normal human complexity. Most good stories will show examples of both flat and round characters according to the requirements of the **focus of interest.**

Chronology The clock or calendar of events presented in a story. Chronology may be straightforward—with the narrative beginning at the earliest and running uninterruptedly to the latest point in time—or complicated—with the narrative opening somewhere in the middle and leapfrogging backward or forward. Faulkner's "The Bear" provides an excellent example for study of complicated chronology. See **flashback.**

Climax The outcome of the main action of a story. That point at which the reader can see what the complications were leading to. Often the climax is a decisive encounter between characters who have been in conflict.

Coherence The consistency of various parts of a story. We expect a character's speech and actions to be consistent with his nature. We expect certain consequences to follow from a particular act, certain feelings to rise from disappointments or rewards. Certain kinds of language will be in keeping with the material described. See **unity, style.**

Complication The emergence of a problem out of the interaction between characters and the situation that prevails as the story begins. See **exposition** and **resolution.**

Concreteness Joseph Conrad wrote: "All art . . . appeals primarily to the senses. . . . My task . . . is, by the power of the written word, to make you hear, to make you feel—it is, before all, to make you *see.*" Fiction renders those concrete details of sensuous experience from which moral and emotional interpretations can be made. Fiction *shows* an action in progress. See **credibility, illusion, setting.**

Conflict The active opposition of characters, ideas, ways of life. A dynamic test of the capacities of one thing or person to overcome whatever competes with or frustrates it or him. Conflict is often considered the soul of fiction, since it gives rise to suspense, drama, and the emotional tension that sharpens our intuitions about characters and the values they are contending for.

Convention Any aspect of the literary art that has been established by earlier and repeated usage as part of the way in which language represents experience. Punctuation, syntax, and the alphabet itself are conventions. So are such things as the use of a narrator, the freedom of the author to substitute his or her language for that of the characters, the use of paragraphs in dialogue passages, etc.

Conventional This term frequently has a pejorative meaning—though it derives directly from *convention,* without which no communication would be possible. When used disparagingly, *conventional* means that the writer has tried to find approval by clinging to familiar narrative types and procedures, and noncontroversial values.

Credibility Is the author telling you something that is unbelievable because it is impossible? If it is possible, is it probable? There are degrees of credibility in all reports of human events, and we measure what we read in fiction much as we measure history or the daily news. Just because a report is credible it need not be interesting, emotionally convincing, or intuitively comprehensible. See **concreteness, illusion.**

Denouement A synonym for **resolution.** See **resolution.**

Description Those passages devoted to a presentation of the appearance of characters or the setting. Descriptions may appear in passages of dialogue, but they are usually provided by the author or narrator.

Dialogue The actual speech of characters in a story, usually punctuated with quotation marks. See **illusion, immediacy.**

Diction The choice and arrangement of words. By disciplining their vocabulary to a degree of conformity with the passions and actions of the story, writers enhance their power to convince. See **illusion, unity.**

Didactic A story is said to be didactic if it deliberately teaches some lesson about the way people should behave. The use of fiction for such teaching was one of its traditional justifications. Most modern fiction tends to show humanity as it is rather than as it should be, but even such stories point to general values and distinguish between admirable and contemptible behavior. See **moral, parable.**

Distance Like many other valuable terms that are now conventionally used to discuss fiction, this one is both metaphorical and ambiguous. It may mean the distinction authors preserve between themselves and their central characters (also called **objectivity**). It may refer to a use of language that separates the adventure described from the experience of the reader. It may mean a lack of **immediacy.** The author may choose to let crucial events take place offstage. In such a case they seem to be taking place at a greater distance than events presented directly to our eyes.

Dramatic This term is most useful in fictional criticism when it is taken to mean "like something presented on the stage of a theater." The modern writer of fiction tries, most of the time, to *show* us an action rather than simply to *tell* us about it. The writer sets a stage and peoples it. However, the term *dramatic* is also quite properly used in a different sense as a synonym for *exciting* or *suspenseful*. **See concreteness, objectivity.**

Effaced narrator In third-person narration we frequently find that part of the description and narrative is given in a language attributable to the character whose point of view has been assumed by the author, while other parts are in a language that must be attributed to the author's own understanding and observations. This latter is said to come from the effaced narrator, the speaker standing hidden behind his or her character.

Episode A single part of the continuing action of a story.

Episodic Usually signifies a loosely constructed or incoherent series of actions. See **coherence.**

Exposition That part of a story—frequently at the beginning or near it—which gives information about the characters and their situation before the action begins to change them.

First- and third-person narration In first-person narration the story is told by a character who habitually refers to himself or herself with the pronoun "I." In third-person all characters are referred to by third-person pronouns and the story is told directly by the author.

Flashback A break in the chronological sequence of a story made to deal with earlier events. See **chronology.**

Focus of interest Whatever the author tries to make most prominent in his or her narration. May be plot, setting, characters, situation, a social problem, or a moral enigma.

Foreshadowing Hints of things to come. A foolish, impulsive judgment on a small matter hints that a character may be similarly susceptible in the great crises of life. Sometimes *foreshadowing* is accomplished by a prophetic episode, sometimes by author's language or by the dialogue.

Form A term so broad that it sums up all the others in this glossary. The totality of conventions exploited and modified by an author in his or her creative act. See **convention.**

Illusion No story provides optical illusions. Sensory experiences can only be evoked by language; they cannot be duplicated. Nevertheless, in varying degrees, stories can provide the sense that one is morally and emotionally involved in a situation shared with fictional characters. *They* smell the roses and feel the pain of a stab wound, but the reader envies the former experience and sympathizes with the latter, much as he or she would if the experiences were real. See **credibility.**

Imagery 1. Figures of speech. Similes. Metaphors. 2. More generally, all descriptions that prompt the reader to visualize characters in their setting. These visualizations, in turn, set off imaginative analogies that extend the implications of the story beyond its literal limits.

Immediacy The effect or illusion of sharing the experience that the characters in a story are undergoing. An author may gear all the devices of language, including dialogue and a use of the present tense, to promote this effect. It may be enhanced by a deliberate choice of subject matter that will play on the reader's enthusiasms or apprehensions. See **illusion.**

Interior monologue Sometimes—more popularly—called **stream of consciousness.**

Irony A discrepancy between what is expected and what is revealed. It may be found either in language usage or in the working out of the action of a story. Surprise endings always depend on some sort of irony, often crude. Irony may appear in the difference between a character's understanding of his or her situation and the reader's estimate of it. See **paradox.**

Milieu The political, social, cultural, economic, and intellectual aspects of the setting. Milieu is to setting as Greek culture is to Greek geography. See **setting.**

Mood The prevailing feeling of a story, generated by language, setting, and the quality of the action. The term is naturally analogous to the moods of our experience—grim, gay, solemn, remorseful, angry, ecstatic, melancholy, anxious, etc. See **atmosphere.**

Moral The instructive point of a story. (See **didactic.**) The lesson drawn or to be drawn from the outcome of the action. While modern taste inclines away from the pat and clear morals that once adorned a lot of stories, a shrewd and important moral in fiction will have the same worth as a shrewd and important axiom delivered without fictional illustration. Handsome is as handsome does.

Motivation The internal and external forces which compel a character to take action. Sometimes these forces may be chiefly psychological, sometimes sociological, and sometimes a matter of hostility or opportunity in the physical environment. For credibility, motivation should be consistent with character.

Narration 1. A synonym for story-telling, whether the story is told by literary means, by the cinema, or in pantomime. 2. In fiction, narrative passages are to be distinguished from *descriptions* and *scenes*. In narrative passages the chronology is condensed so that relatively few words will encompass the events of an extended period of time. Most writers of short stories use narrative passages to fill in the links between events given a scenic treatment.

Narrator In first-person narration, the character who tells the story in his or her own words. It is not uncommon in third-person narration for one of the characters to tell an extended story. In such a case it is quite proper to refer to him or her as a narrator.

Objectivity Telling a story without bias; telling a story without the interpretive comment to be expected from a partisan or sympathetic observer.

Omniscience A convention in which the author speaks directly to the reader about events that will come in the future and other matters beyond the knowledge of the central character or of all the characters. This contrasts with the discipline of adhering to the point of view of a single character and is little used in modern practice. See **point of view.**

Pace The speed at which writers develop any given part of a story. Usually they will hasten over unimportant things, slow to give a detailed view of what is essential.

Parable A story told to point a moral or teach a lesson.

Paradox A statement that appears to be contradictory or inconsistent with common sense—though it may be quite true.

Parody Mimicry of a work or a style of expression. Sometimes the mimicry is undertaken to make fun of what is parodied; sometimes it is done in a sincere effort to gain the understanding that comes from painstaking imitation. Parody is akin to paraphrase, the translation of a work into your own language to make sure you have grasped it.

Pathos The pity roused by the situation or the misfortunes of the characters in a story.

Pattern Another metaphorical and ambiguous term. It is generally taken to refer to changes in the relative position of the characters—as if they were pieces on a game board, shifted, developed, and sometimes sacrificed by the progress of the action. Thus if Character A is happy and prosperous in the beginning and becomes poor and wretched while Character B moves out of poverty and achieves happiness, there is said to be a "crossing pattern." The term may also refer to the way the author lays out blocks of material. If the author provides a number of small episodes not linked with transitional passages, he or she has made a "mosaic pattern."

Point of view The events of a story may be told as they appear to one or more participants or observers. In first-person narration the point of view is automatically that of the narrator. More variation is possible in third-person narration, where the author may choose to limit his or her report to what could have been observed or known by one of the characters at any given point in the action—or may choose to report the observations and thoughts of several characters. The author might also choose to intrude his or her own point of view. See **omniscience.**

Plot Consists of the phases of action in a story which are linked together by a chain of causal relationships. Event A causes or provides motivation for event B. B causes C, etc. Where this chain of causality is not apparent, the story is said to be **episodic.** A well-made plot leads from the potentialities revealed in the **exposition** directly to the situation left in the wake of the **resolution.** Plot may be subordinated to some other **focus of interest** in many stories, but it is one of the most important aspects of fiction, for we understand things best when we are shown what caused them to be as they are.

Protagonist Chief character.

Realism An interest in and emphasis on life as it is. In literature this does not mean that writers copy what they see and hear. (Perhaps that is impossible, anyhow.) It means that they will select from their observations the material suitable for constructing a story that faithfully represents what they have understood.

Resolution The point in a story at which the conflict is decided one way or another and the struggle concluded. The expectations of the reader and of the characters have, at this point, been confirmed or refuted.

Satire The satirist aims to correct, by an exposure to ridicule, deviations from normal conduct or reasonable opinion. The chief tool of satire is to exaggerate deformities to the point at which their absurdity is unmistakably apparent.

Sentimentality An author's attempt to produce an emotional response greater than is warranted by what he or she has to tell. While the student should not be fooled by sentimentality, it is well to remember that the symmetrical and equal fault is hardheartedness, a cold insensitivity to the trouble and joys of the human condition.

Setting The physical and cultural environment within which an action takes place. The stage that serves to demonstrate the qualities of a protagonist. An arena suitable for the conflict. Weather moods, urban uproar, the majesty and menace of the ocean can signal moods of human characters. See **concreteness, milieu.**

Stream of consciousness A fictional device or convention in which the author undertakes an imitation of a mind responding to exterior experiences. Frequently it involves a free association of ideas in which normal syntax and logical coherence are suspended. It is usually intended to shortcut the processes of reflection and reconsideration that stand between raw experience and logical statement. See **convention, immediacy, interior monologue.**

Style A writer's habitual way of expressing himself or herself is his or her style. Examination of it requires consideration of vocabulary, sentence patterns, and other compositional elements. More generally, the appreciation of an author's style comes with a recognition of the way his or her mind plays with experience and literary form.

Symbol An act, a person, a thing, or a spectacle that stands for something else, usually something less palpable than the named symbol. The relationship between the symbol and its referent is not often one of simple equivalence. Allegorical symbols usually express a neater equivalence with what they stand for than the symbols found in modern realistic fiction. See **allegory.**

Tension The emotional and intellectual force generated by disparate potentials within a literary work. In every ambiguity there is a tension between the primary meaning and the secondary meanings of a word, phrase, or larger unit of expression. There may be tension between a comic tone and pathetic subject matter. See **ambiguity, tone.**

Theme The unifying point or meaning of a story. Often the theme is implicit in the outcome of the action. It is rarely directly stated, though often it is closely paraphrased by an author's observation or by a statement made by one of the characters.

Tone A wide-ranging, metaphorical term that usually invites analogy to the tone of voice in which a speaker relates an episode. The speaker might be trying to make light of something that frightened him or her. If we conclude he or she is doing so, the fear will seem magnified by the attempt to disguise it. Tone reveals a storyteller's attitude toward the material.

Understatement The technique of playing down or underemphasizing a statement. It is a rhetorical trick intended to bring the imagination of the reader into play with a resulting magnification of emotional response. The style of Ernest Hemingway offers some of the best modern examples of this device.

Unity The shape and consistency of a story. When all the elements and devices of storytelling have been harmonized and nothing extraneous has been included in the text, we speak of it as unified. See **action, coherence, diction, point of view.**

Voice May be the characteristic mode of expression of a first-person narrator. (See **diction.**) Sometimes the term refers to the total, individualistic effect of all the devices a writer habitually employs, the combination of tactics that distinguishes his or her work from other fiction.

PERMISSIONS ACKNOWLEDGMENTS

SHERWOOD ANDERSON: "I Want to Know Why," from *The Triumph of the Egg*. Reprinted by permission of Harold Ober Associates Incorporated. Copyright © 1921 by B. W. Huebsch, Inc. Copyright renewed 1948 by Eleanor Anderson.

MARGARET ATWOOD: "Rape Fantasies," from *Bluebeard's Egg* by Margaret Atwood. Reprinted by permission of Margaret Atwood and the Canadian publishers, McClelland and Steward, Toronto. Copyright © 1977.

ISAAC BABEL: "My First Goose." Reprinted by permission of S. G. Phillips, Inc., from *The Collected Stories of Isaac Babel*. Copyright © 1955 by S. G. Phillips, Inc.

JAMES BALDWIN: "Sonny's Blues," from *Going to Meet the Man*. Copyright © 1948, 1951, 1957, 1958, 1960, 1965 by James Baldwin. Reprinted by permission of Doubleday, a division of Bantam, Doubleday, Dell Publishing Group, Inc.

ANN BEATTIE: "Janus," copyright © 1986 by Irony and Pity, Inc. Reprinted by permission of Linden Press, a division of Simon & Schuster, Inc.

SAUL BELLOW: "Leaving the Yellow House," from *Mosbie's Memoirs and Other Stories* by Saul Bellow. Copyright © 1957, renewed © 1985 by Saul Bellow. Reprinted by permission of Viking Penguin, Inc.

JORGE LUIS BORGES: "Pierre Menard, Author of the Quixote." Reprinted by permission of Grove Press, a division of Wheatland Corporation. Copyright © 1962 by Grove Press, Inc. Translated from the Spanish copyright © 1956 by Emecee Editores, S. A., Buenos Aires.

KAY BOYLE: "Art Colony," from *Life Being the Best and Other Stories*. Copyright © 1935 by Kay Boyle. Reprinted by permission of New Directions Publishing Corporation.

RAY BRADBURY: "The Veldt," reprinted by permission of Don Congdon Associates, Inc. Copyright © 1950 by Ray Bradbury; renewed 1978 by Ray Bradbury.

MORLEY CALLAGHAN: "Now That April's Here," reprinted by permission of Don Congdon Associates, Inc. Copyright © 1936 by Morley Callaghan, renewed 1964.

ITALO CALVINO: "The Distance of the Moon," from *Cosmicomics* by Italo Calvino, copyright © 1965 by Giulio Einaudi Editore, Torino, and English translation copyright © 1968 by Harcourt Brace Jovanovich, Inc., and Jonathan Cape Limited, reprinted by permission of Harcourt Brace Jovanovich, Inc., and Jonathan Cape Limited.

RAYMOND CARVER: "Where I'm Calling From," from *Cathedral* by Raymond Carver. Copyright © 1981, 1982, 1983 by Raymond Carver. Reprinted by permission of Alfred A. Knopf, Inc.

R. V. CASSILL: "The Father," from *The Father and Other Stories* by R. V. Cassill, published by Simon & Schuster, Inc. Copyright © 1950, 1962, by R. V. Cassill. Copyright © 1965 by Simon & Schuster, Inc. Reprinted by permission of the author.

JOHN CHEEVER: "The Enormous Radio," copyright © 1947 by John Cheever. "The Five-Forty-Eight," copyright © 1945 by John Cheever. Both stories from *The Stories of John Cheever*. Reprinted by permission of Alfred A. Knopf, Inc.

ANTON CHEKHOV: "The Lady with the Dog," from *Short Novels and Stories* by A. P. Chekhov, translated by Ivy Litvinov (Moscow: Foreign Languages, n. d.). "A Visit to Friends," from *The Unknown Chekhov*, translated by Avrahm Yarmolinsky. Copyright 1954 by Avrahm Yarmolinsky. Copyright renewed © 1982 by Babette Deutsch Yarmolinsky. Reprinted by permission of Farrar, Straus & Giroux, Inc. "Dushechka," from *Best Russian Short Stories*, translated by Rosa Graham (New York: Boni & Liveright, 1917).

ARTHUR C. CLARKE: "The Star," from *The Other Side of the Sky* by Arthur C. Clarke, copyright © 1955 by Royal Publications, reprinted by permission of Harcourt Brace Jovanovich, Inc.

FRANZ KAFKA: "The Metamorphosis" and "A Hunger Artist," from *The Metamorphosis, The Penal Colony, and Other Stories* by Franz Kafka, translated by Willa and Edwin Muir. Copyright 1948 by Schocken Books, Inc. Copyright renewed 1975 by Schocken Books, Inc. Reprinted by permission of Schocken Books, published by Pantheon Books, a division of Random House, Inc.

MARGARET LAURENCE: "The Loons," from *A Bird in the House* by Margaret Laurence. Reprinted by permission of the estate of Margaret Laurence. Copyright © 1970 by Margaret Laurence.

D. H. LAWRENCE: "The Blind Man," "The Horse-Dealer's Daughter," and "The Rocking-Horse Winner," from *The Complete Short Stories of D. H. Lawrence,* vol. 2. Copyright © 1922 by Thomas Seltzer, Inc. Copyright renewed 1950 by Frieda Lawrence. Copyright renewed 1961 by Angelo Ravagli and C. M. Weekley, executors of the estate of Frieda Lawrence Ravagli. All rights reserved. Reprinted by permission of Viking Penguin, a division of Penguin Books USA, Inc.

URSULA K. LE GUIN: "The Ones Who Walk Away from Omelas," copyright © 1973, 1975 by Ursula K. Le Guin; reprinted by permission of the author and the author's agent, Virginia Kidd.

ELLA LEFFLAND: "The Linden Tree," from *Last Courtesies* by Ella Leffland. Copyright © 1980 by Ella Leffland. Reprinted by permission of Harper & Row, Publishers, Inc.

DORIS LESSING: "To Room Nineteen," copyright © 1958, 1962, 1963 by Doris Lessing. Reprinted by permission of Simon & Schuster, Inc., and Jonathan Clowes, Limited, on behalf of Doris Lessing.

JAMES ALAN MCPHERSON: "Gold Coast," from *Hue and Cry* by James Alan McPherson. Copyright © 1968 by James Alan McPherson. By permission of Little, Brown & Company.

NORMAN MAILER: "The Language of Men," reprinted by permission of the author and the author's agents, Scott Meredith Literary Agency, Inc., 845 Third Avenue, New York, NY 10022.

BERNARD MALAMUD: "Angel Levine," from *The Magic Barrel* by Bernard Malamud. Copyright © 1955 by Bernard Malamud. Copyright renewal © 1983 by Bernard Malamud. Reprinted by permission of Farrar, Straus & Giroux, Inc.

THOMAS MANN: "Disorder and Early Sorrow," copyright 1936 and renewed 1964 by Alfred A. Knopf, Inc. Reprinted from *Stories of Three Decades* by Thomas Mann, translated by H. T. Lowe-Porter, by permission of Alfred A. Knopf, Inc.

KATHERINE MANSFIELD: "Bliss" and "The Garden-Party," copyright 1920, 1922 by Alfred A. Knopf, Inc., and renewed 1948, 1950 by John Middleton Murry. Reprinted from *The Short Stories of Katherine Mansfield* by permission of the publisher.

BOBBIE ANN MASON: "Shiloh," from *Shiloh and Others Stories* by Bobbie Ann Mason. Originally appeared in *The New Yorker.* Copyright © 1982 by Bobbie Ann Mason. Reprinted by permission of Harper & Row, Publishers, Inc.

YUKIO MISHIMA: "Patriotism," from *Death in Midsummer.* Copyright © 1966 by New Directions Publishing Corporation. Reprinted by permission of New Directions Publishing Corporation.

ALICE MUNRO: "Prue," from *The Moons of Jupiter and Other Stories* by Alice Munro. Copyright © 1982 by Alice Munro. Reprinted by permission of Alfred A. Knopf, Inc., and Macmillan of Canada, a division of Canada Publishing Corporation. "Royal Beatings," from *The Beggar Maid* by Alice Munro. Copyright © 1977, 1978 by Alice Munro. Originally published in *The New Yorker.* Published in Canada under the title *Who Do You Think You Are?* by Macmillan Canada. Reprinted by permission of Alfred A. Knopf, Inc., and Virginia Barber Literary Agency, Inc.

VLADIMIR NABOKOV: "Signs and Symbols" by Vladimir Nabokov. Copyright 1948 by Vladimir Nabokov. Reprinted by permission of Doubleday & Company, Inc.

GLORIA NAYLOR: "Lucielia Louise Turner," from *The Women of Brewster Place* by Gloria Naylor. Copyright © 1980, 1982 by Gloria Naylor. All rights reserved. Reprinted by permission of Viking Penguin, Inc.

Index of Titles